Printed in the United States of America

First Hardcover Edition, May 2024
10 9 8 7 6 5 4 3 2 1

FAC-004510-24099

Design by Winnie Ho
Composition and layout by Susan Gerber

Library of Congress Control Number: 2023951369

ISBN 978-1-368-10022-9

Visit disneybooks.com

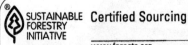

SUSTAINABLE FORESTRY INITIATIVE

Certified Sourcing

www.forests.org
SFI-01681

Logo Applies to Text Stock Only

INSIDE OUT 2

ALL IN THE MIND

By **Meredith Rusu**

DISNEP PRESS

Los Angeles • New York

Chapter 1

"Whoa!"

Twelve-year-old Riley leapt out of the way of a tall student just in time. He'd nearly crashed into her. Riley's backpack slipped from her arm, spilling papers, pencils, and eraser tops onto the floor. Her hockey puck keychain fell off its chain (for the hundredth time) and rolled along the hall.

"Sorry, kid!" the student shouted back before zipping around a corner.

Riley pulled a face. He could have helped her. She began stuffing her spilled school supplies into her backpack. The polished concrete floors of her middle school still looked strange to her: cold and harsh and weirdly institutional. The floors at her old school in Minnesota had been tile; she remembered that specifically because she'd always counted the number of tiles between each deep magenta runner proudly displaying the school mascot. (Go, Reindeer!)

But this wasn't her old school. Or Minnesota. This was fall in San Francisco, where she was still relatively new and no one really remembered her name yet, and there were so many kids that she couldn't even make her way through the hall without a near collision.

The familiar ache of homesickness welled up in her chest. Although Riley's life had slowly gotten easier over the past few months, this school and San Francisco still didn't feel like *home*. Would things ever feel normal again?

The warning bell rang. She was going to be late.

"Ahhh! What do we do? What do we do?"

Fear flailed his wobbly purple arms. Beside him, all Riley's other Emotions—Joy, Sadness, Anger, and Disgust—watched a screen showing Riley's perspective as she struggled to gather her stuff.

A console stretched before them. It was dotted with colorful buttons and levers that connected the Emotions to Riley. Smooth metal tracks looped around the room, carrying glowing spheres of various colors—mostly happy golden—which represented Riley's memories. The spheres whizzed and whirled into tubes that led to the depths of Riley's mind, fueling the beautiful Islands of Personality, which stood proud and tall beyond the grand windows of the command center.

This was Riley's Headquarters, fondly referred to as HQ by her Emotions, all of whom shared a common goal: to keep their girl safe and happy.

That was the *opposite* of what was happening right now.

"We're going to be late!" Fear cried. "The teacher will kick us out!"

"Riley's not going to get kicked out," Joy, glowing with golden self-assurance, told him. Joy prided herself on staying calm when things spun out of control. After all, there wasn't any sticky situation that couldn't be turned around with a positive spin. They just had to look on the bright side.

"Has this floor ever been *cleaned*?" Disgust said, dramatically brushing a green strand of hair from her face as Riley picked up a dusty, slightly chewed pencil. "Eww!" Disgust gagged. "This isn't even our pencil! Gross!" Riley chucked the pencil away.

"I know who I'd clean the floor with," Anger said, pounding a fist into his opposite palm. "That punk who knocked into us!"

"He didn't even see us," Sadness moaned. "No one ever sees us. It was never like this back in Minnesota."

Sadness instinctively touched a glowing white button on the console, turning it a watery blue. Riley shed a tear.

Joy gently grasped Sadness's hand. "I know she needs you," Joy said with a comforting smile. "But right now we need to help her get to class. There will be time to let her feel the sadness—at home, with Mom and Dad."

"Okay," Sadness agreed. She removed her hand, and the button turned white once more.

Joy couldn't help thinking that it still felt a little strange to be working in tandem with Sadness and allowing Riley's good and not-so-good feelings to flow freely. Not long before, Joy would have tried to stop Sadness from overtaking Riley's feelings and memories. But doing that had proven disastrous.

When Riley and her parents had first moved to San Francisco, everything had changed drastically and all at once. For all eleven years of her life, Riley had been a bubbly, goofy, and perpetually positive girl. Sure, she'd had her moments of frustration. But Mom and Dad liked to say that Riley was their spot of sunshine in the thickest of clouds—their sweet, silly little monkey.

But in San Francisco, Riley had turned sullen. Her best memories had faded from their normal golden glow to blue. And at first, Joy had thought that there was something wrong—that she, Joy, needed to work overtime to keep all Riley's memories glowing gold with happiness. She'd tried to stop Sadness from touching any of Riley's memories. In doing so, she had accidentally gotten both herself and Sadness swept away to the depths of Riley's mind. It had been a long, perilous journey to make it back to Headquarters.

Meanwhile, without Joy and Sadness in HQ, Riley hadn't acted like herself at all. She'd been extra nervous (thanks to Fear), extra moody (thanks to Disgust), and extra, *extra* angry (thanks to Anger). She'd even made the terrible decision to try to run away from home to go back to Minnesota. Luckily, Joy and Sadness had made it back to HQ just in time to stop her—but it had been up to Sadness to change Riley's mind.

Along their journey, Joy had realized that Riley needed to feel *all* her emotions—even sadness—to be her true self. With Sadness at the wheel, Riley was finally able to express how homesick she was to her parents so that they could help her feel better. And the help of others was one of the most powerful, positive forces in Riley's life.

Joy would never again make the mistake of holding back a fellow Emotion.

"We'll be able to let all the tears flow back at home," Joy assured Sadness. "Riley's even keeping a journal now. That will—"

"Is this yours?"

The Emotions jumped at the new voice. It was coming from what was on-screen.

Through Riley's eyes, they saw a girl standing in front of her, holding out the hockey puck keychain.

"Who is *that*?" asked Fear. "Why is she talking to us?"

"She's in some of our classes!" Disgust said. "I always thought her braids were so pretty. Why did our hair have to be stringy today?"

"What should we do?" Sadness asked uncertainly.

Riley accepted the keychain. "Yeah, thanks."

The girl bent down to help Riley pick up her stuff.

"Thanks for your help," said Riley.

"No problem!" the girl replied, handing Riley books and papers from the floor. "I'll see you in Mrs. Wilken's class. Good luck on the quiz today!"

"See you." Riley smiled as she watched the girl walk down the hall.

Later that night, the Emotions were settling in for some much-needed shut-eye. Sadness stretched and yawned as she snuggled under her soft blue bedspread. Anger adjusted his little nightcap. (Why didn't it ever seem big enough for his head?) Disgust and Fear, meanwhile, were already snoring away.

That was when . . .

"You guys, something incredible is happening!" Joy burst into the bedroom, her energy glowing as bright as the morning sunrise.

Fear jerked out of his slumber. "Red alert! Abandon ship!"

"Could you keep it down?" Disgust raised her sleep mask. "You do *not* want to see me if I don't get a full night's beauty sleep."

"Yeah, what are you so percolator peppy about?" Anger asked huffily. "It's after hours. Time to simmer things down, not boil them up."

"Okay, you guys are *not* going to believe this," Joy

bubbled on. "I was doing some final checks before bed, and I found this platform on the floor I'd never seen before, and I thought, 'That's weird, why is this here? Where did it come from?' So I pushed a bunch of buttons—maybe I shouldn't have done that, but I had to see what would happen—and these doors popped up and . . . you guys just have to come and see!"

Yawning, the Emotions stumbled after Joy to a platform in HQ that now held a narrow cylinder with a set of doors.

"What is *that*?" Fear asked, suddenly nervous.

"It looks like an elevator," Disgust said.

"It is! And you'll never guess where it leads!" said Joy, bouncing with excitement.

"Do we—do we go down?" Sadness asked uncertainly.

"I am *not* getting in there," Fear said, trembling. "Nothing good comes from going down creepy elevators after ten p.m."

"But I already did!" said Joy. "It's totally safe and totally cool, I promise. Come on!"

Curious, Anger and Disgust stepped in first. The elevator descended and returned empty a few moments later. Fear hesitantly entered next.

Joy reached out to Sadness. "Sadness, you can squeeze in with Fear and me."

"I—I don't know if I should," Sadness said. "Something tells me . . . I don't know. I just don't want to mess anything up."

"You won't!" Joy insisted. "I promise!"

"No—you guys go first," Sadness said. "I'll stay here and keep an eye on things."

"Are you sure?" Joy asked, a little deflated.

Fear moved to leave. "Well, if Sadness isn't going, then I certainly don't have—"

But before he could finish, the doors closed, and instantly, the elevator plummeted through the depths of Riley's mind.

"I don't like this!" Fear clenched his eyes shut. "We shouldn't be riding this thing!"

"Just trust me!" Joy exclaimed. "You'll see!"

The ride lasted only moments, but to everyone except Joy, it felt like a roller coaster into the unknown. Finally, the elevator slowed to a halt, and the double doors whooshed open.

Fear's eyes grew wide. "What is this place?"

Before them stretched a cavernous hall with a babbling brook filled with what looked like memory spheres. Echoes of Riley's past adventures swirled in the stream. Up from the floor, glowing tendrils were growing like vines. They stretched, reaching far above, toward the place where the Emotions had just come from—HQ.

Joy and Fear joined Disgust and Anger, who stood outside the elevator, too uncertain to move farther into the cavern. They stared in awe.

"What are those?" Disgust asked. "I've never seen anything *growing* in Riley's mind before."

"They must be something new!" Joy exclaimed. "I think they grow from her memories. See how there are memories in the water?" She stepped forward and reached out to touch one of the tendrils.

"Are you crazy?" Anger protested. "Don't touch that thing!"

"What if it bites you?" Fear urged.

"I've already touched it!" Joy insisted. "Listen!"

She gently strummed the string and it vibrated with a soothing hum.

I'm a good student, the string echoed in Riley's voice.

"Is that Riley?" asked Disgust.

"Why would she be talking down here?" Anger asked, confused.

"I don't know." Joy gazed up at the growing tendrils. "I think this is a deeper part of her. Something that's just forming. Maybe because she's twelve now."

She reached out to strum a few more delicate strings.

I'm smart.

I'm funny.

"What do they all mean?" Anger asked, confused.

"And where are they going?" Disgust looked up.

"You mean where are they *growing*?" Fear corrected her.

Joy's gaze never left the empty reaches above. "I guess we'll just have to wait and see."

Chapter 2

The next week, as Riley entered her social studies class, she noticed a lack of the usual pre-bell chatter. Everyone sat at their desks, reviewing note cards, chewing their nails, or staring off into space. And that meant one thing: presentation day.

"Woo! Presentation day!" Joy cheered.

"How can you be excited at a time like this?" cried Fear. "On the list of Most Terrifying Things, public speaking is definitely top three!"

"It'll be great!" Joy insisted. "Riley has been practicing for weeks." She recalled a memory of Riley rehearsing in her room and even in front of her parents. "She's got this in the bag."

The teacher had asked all the students to present an idea that they believed could change the world.

"I still think our presentation should have been about hockey," Anger grumbled.

"That's not even on topic," said Disgust. "How would *hockey* change the world?"

"It could change the world if more people watched it!" Anger argued. "They don't know what they're missing!"

Finally, class was underway, and the presentations began. The first presenter was a girl named Grace Hsieh. Her hands were shaking as she carried a large jar full of coins up to the front of the room. She stood behind a lectern and placed the jar on top.

"Hi, I'm Grace," she started with a tremble in her voice. "And this is my presentation on how the change in your couch could *change* the world." She picked up the jar by its lid. "Did you know—"

CRASH!

The jar fell to the ground, scattering coins around the classroom.

"Oh, no!" Grace cried. She dropped to the floor to pick up the coins. But in her haste, she bumped into the lectern, which knocked into the teacher's desk and tipped over a computer monitor . . . and then spilled a cup of coffee. The class erupted in laughter.

But there was one person who wasn't laughing: Riley.

"Oh, no," said Joy. "We should do something."

"No," said Disgust firmly. "Just back away. That girl is a social death sentence."

A tinkling sound suddenly echoed throughout Headquarters. The Emotions turned to see a pedestal rising from the floor. Bright wisps of light spiraled and intertwined together on top.

"Are those Riley's beliefs?" Disgust asked. "From her Belief System?"

That was what the Emotions had come to call the new space deep below Headquarters: the Belief System. The beautiful glowing strings grew from Riley's memories and echoed different things she believed in: *I'm great at hockey. I'm strong. I'm smart.* But the Emotions hadn't known exactly what the belief strings were growing toward until then.

"Are they forming *into* something?" Fear gasped.

"But why? What are they doing?" Sadness asked.

The light stabilized, revealing a perfectly twisted knot of belief strings. It looked like a radiant flower.

"Whoa," breathed Joy, in awe of the new addition to Headquarters. She approached the object and strummed it like a belief string.

I'm a good person, it said in Riley's voice.

At that moment, Riley got out of her seat and began picking up coins with Grace.

"It's okay," Riley whispered. "I drop things all the time. I'm Riley."

Another girl joined them.

Disgust gasped. "It's the girl from before! The one who helped us pick up our stuff!"

"Hello again," said the girl. "I'm Bree."

The three girls smiled at each other.

The bell rang, and Riley headed to her locker, relieved that that nightmare was finally over. After Grace's mishap, the other presentations moved along smoothly. Even Riley got through hers without too much drama. But she felt for Grace. She knew exactly what it was like to have a whole class staring and laughing at you. She wouldn't wish it on her worst enemy.

"Hey, Riley," said someone behind her.

Riley turned around. Grace and Bree were there.

"Thank you for your help earlier," said Grace. "I thought I was going to die up there all alone."

"Presentations should be illegal," said Riley. "Whoever thought those were a good idea?"

Grace giggled. Riley was happy to have cheered her up a little.

"I'm glad we ran into each other again," Bree said. "We should hang out sometime!"

"I'd love that!" Riley answered without hesitation. She knew she was being too enthusiastic, but this could be her chance to finally make some real friends at this school. She realized there was one complication.

"The only thing is that my hockey league is starting soon, so I'll have to work around practices and games and stuff. But I definitely want to hang out," Riley said.

Grace gasped. "Wait, you play hockey? *We* play hockey!"

"Seriously?" cried Riley. "That's amazing!"

"Which team are you playing for?" asked Bree.

"The Foghorns," replied Riley. "I played in Minnesota, so this will be my first team in San Francisco."

Grace's and Bree's jaws dropped.

"*We* play for the Foghorns!" exclaimed Grace, whipping out her phone to show Riley a team photo. "This is, like, fate. It's a little creepy, but I'm not mad about it."

Riley couldn't believe her luck. What were the odds of meeting two girls who played hockey *and* played for the same team as she did?

"Welcome to the team!" Bree cheered. "Now we can hang out all the time!"

"Definitely!" added Grace. "We'll introduce you to everyone during our next practice. How long have you been playing? What position are you? What was it like playing hockey in Minnesota? Am I asking too many questions?"

Riley laughed and closed her locker. As she walked side by side with her new friends, she thought, *Maybe this place could feel like home after all.*

Chapter 3

"Come on, Riley! You got this!"

Inside Headquarters, the Emotions were in a flurry as they watched Riley zoom toward the goal. It was the fall opener game for the Foghorns against the Polar Bears. And Riley wasn't just cleaning up on the ice—she was looking *good* doing it.

"She's going too fast!" Fear squeaked, covering his eyes. "She's going to crash into the wall!"

"Then the wall had better get out of our way." Anger cracked his knuckles. "Nothing's slowing down Riley today!"

"Are you even listening to yourself?" Disgust scoffed. "We are *not* face-planting against the wall."

"Of course we aren't." Joy mirrored Riley's skating expertise, gliding across HQ's floor in a fluid motion. "Because Riley is the best—"

BAM!

Fear shrieked. Riley had slammed into the wall! It wasn't a face-plant, but it was enough to knock her down to her butt on the ice.

"Ooooh," the Emotions all said, cringing. Butt ice wasn't a good look.

"How come the wall didn't get out of our way?" Disgust said, goading Anger.

"Don't . . . even . . ." Anger fumed. He hit a button on the console, sending a streak of red running across it.

Riley clenched her fist, upset with herself for not paying closer attention.

"Are you okay?" Bree, who was the Foghorns' goalie, shouted from across the ice. "Anything hurt?"

"Only my pride," Riley called back, recalling the phrase from a teen movie she'd seen recently.

Grace helped her up. "We've got a game to win. Let's do Thread the Needle!" she said eagerly. "I've been dying to try it!"

"Oh, no—not Thread the Needle!" Fear quavered. "It's not ready yet!"

Riley, Bree, and Grace had been inseparable for nearly a year both at school and at the ice rink. They had been practicing a new hockey maneuver in secret.

Joy smiled knowingly. "It's ready."

In a flash, Riley gained control of the puck from the opposing team. (*She's just* that *good!* Joy thought.) She passed it to Bree, who ricocheted it off the wall back to Riley, confusing their opponents. Riley looked across the ice at Grace, who was keeping pace with her near the left wall of the rink. Grace nodded and fell back.

"Do you think she can do it?" Sadness asked. "What if we miss?"

"We won't!" Joy insisted. She pressed a button on the console, and Riley shot forward toward the middle.

"Outta the way!" Anger pushed a lever. Riley careened between two players, narrowly missing them.

"Watch it!" Disgust chastised him. "We almost checked them."

"Fortune favors the brave," Anger retorted.

"Have you been reading Dad's motivational calendar again?" Disgust asked.

Anger arched an eyebrow. "Maybe."

Meanwhile, two opposing players were hot on Riley's trail. The taller of the two scowled and put on a burst of speed, shooting in front of Riley and blocking her shot toward the goal. The second opponent charged at Riley, trying to steal the puck.

"We're clear!" Joy exclaimed. "Ready . . . steady . . . now!"

Riley unexpectedly snapped the puck back through the second opponent's legs to Grace, who was waiting behind them—in the center of the ice, with a completely clear shot of the goal. Grace slapped the puck forward at lightning speed.

"Goooooaallllll!" the Emotions cheered in Headquarters.

Riley's team formed a circle around her and Grace, cheering and hugging. Thread the Needle had worked! Not only that, but it had gotten them their first big win of the season.

"Joy, look at Riley's Sense of Self," Sadness whispered. "It's shining so bright."

Joy nodded. "That's our girl."

Ever since it appeared on Riley's presentation day, the Sense of Self had become Riley's guiding light, helping her make good choices. To Joy and the other Emotions, it was their masterpiece: a symbol of their hard work, patience, and endless love for Riley.

I'm a good person.

This single certainty, housed in a beautifully twisted knot of brilliant glowing strings, was what made Riley, well, Riley.

Joy took control of the console. "Oh, yeah, it's celebration time! And that means only one thing—the *Celly
Dance!*"

Joy smashed down a flashing rainbow button on the
console, and a disco ball lowered in Headquarters. Riley,
Bree, and Grace began a wiggly, arm-flailing dance on
the ice, complete with an imitation of a foghorn.

"Ahhh-woooga! Ahhh-woooga!" the three of them
chanted together as the rest of the team laughed and
clapped a thumping beat.

Joy still remembered when Riley, Bree, and Grace had
come up with the Celly Dance. It had all started when
they passed one of those inflatable arm-flailing guys at a
car dealership as Riley's mom drove them to practice. The
girls had taken turns mimicking its silly movements, and
although no one could fully agree who had suggested it
first, the Celly Dance became a staple of the Foghorns'
victory celebrations.

"Oh, man, that dance gets me every time!" Joy
cracked up.

"I like these friends," Sadness said.

"Me too," Joy said, wiping a happy tear from her eye.
"Just look at how much Friendship Island has grown!"

The Emotions turned to gaze out at the Islands of

Personality beyond the windows. The core islands were still there, like always, although ever since Joy and Sadness's adventure, they had become intertwined, and they even sported a large Golden Gate Bridge connecting all of them. There was Family Island, featuring a statue of Riley's mom and dad with their arms circled around their daughter. And there was Hockey Island, complete with a Foghorns logo painted on a giant billboard. Honesty Island had its hall of justice high atop a mountain peak. And Joy's personal favorite, Goofball Island, was loaded with Ferris wheels and carnival games and a very weird-looking clown.

There were even a few smaller one-off islands that popped up and crumbled every now and then. In the past year alone, there had been several. Retro Island had appeared, then vanished. (Fanny packs had made a comeback *hard* at Bridgeview Middle School for about three months.) And then Royalty Island came and went just as quickly. (Thank goodness that had passed. Riley couldn't do a British accent to save her life.) Boy Band Island appeared and disappeared in a flash of pyro-technics, much to Disgust's relief.

But the island that had grown and expanded the

most was Friendship Island. It was bursting with framed snapshots of Riley's best times with Bree and Grace, all cascading like a waterfall of happy memories into a pool of stars and sparkles.

"It's like they're bringing out the best in Riley," Sadness said with a rare smile crossing her face.

"They sure are," said Joy.

Later that night, when HQ was darkened and Riley had long since fallen asleep, all the Emotions were snoring.

All except Joy.

She sat at the console, turning over in her hands the red memory sphere of Riley accidentally slamming into the ice rink wall. Riley had recalled it all afternoon long. Even in sleep, she was still thinking about it, because Dream Productions was sending up weird versions of the accident for Riley to dream about. In one dream, the wall crumbled with the impact. In another, Riley got ejected from the game for destroying the rink. Joy could feel Riley tossing and turning uneasily in her sleep.

Joy winced. *Of all the memories from today, why is Riley*

fixating on that one? she wondered. There had been so much to celebrate! The ice-butt moment was just a blip.

I wish these sorts of memories wouldn't weigh Riley down, Joy thought. *Everything is going so great. Riley's at her best when she remembers her best—not her worst.*

Now Dream Productions was sending up a warped image of a Zamboni crashing through the broken rink wall and chasing Riley on the ice, blasting a police siren.

"If only there was a tube that was a one-way ticket to the Back of the Mind," Joy mused, "where the bad memories that Riley doesn't need never got recalled . . ."

Joy furrowed her brow and looked down at the red memory sphere. She instinctively yanked on a cord, interrupting the feed from Dream Productions and turning the dream dark.

"Ever . . ." she said quietly.

She had an idea.

Chapter 4

The candles on the HQ screen twinkled. This was it—the biggest day of all days: Riley's birthday! And it was not just any birthday. Riley was . . .

"Turning thirteen!" Joy clasped the other Emotions in a massive hug. "Our girl is officially a teenager!"

"I know," Fear said, his mouth squished under Joy's embrace so that his words came out muffled. "Just think of all the new things to be afraid of."

"Aw," said Sadness, "it's Riley's last year of middle school. That's sad."

They watched Riley's birthday candles on-screen as she blew them out.

"Happy Birthday, monkey!" her mom and dad cheered. Then Riley's dad picked up a cake server to cut Riley the first piece.

"Ew," Disgust said, eyeing the monitor. "Did Dad think we wouldn't see him lick frosting off his finger?"

"You guys, stop focusing on the negative!" Joy spun around the room. "Our girl is growing up! There are so many incredible things to look forward to as a teenager. Like high school!"

"Let's just get through eighth grade first." Fear shuddered.

"And school dances!" Joy twirled.

"Does Riley know how to dance?" Fear quavered.

"And driving!" Joy cried.

"Driving?" Fear exclaimed. "Who said anything about driving?"

"Well, in a few years, anyway." Joy brushed Fear's worry aside. "But being a teenager is when the action happens! When Riley becomes her best self! Alongside her best friends!"

As if on cue, the doorbell rang at Riley's house. Bree and Grace, holding balloons and a box with a bow, were at the door.

"Ahhh!" screamed Riley.

"Ahhhhhh!" screamed Bree and Grace. "Happy birthday!"

"What's with all the screaming?" Anger asked. "Are we looking to start something?"

"The only thing that's starting is the party!" Joy slapped the rainbow button on the console, lowering the HQ disco ball.

Riley started the Celly Dance. *"Ahhh-woooga! Ahhh-woooga!"*

Bree and Grace joined in. Joy thought she might burst from happiness.

The girls bustled into the living room.

"Open your present!" Grace exclaimed.

The Emotions watched with curiosity as Riley tore open the gift.

"Oh my gosh!" Joy gasped. "Ohmygoshohmygoshohmygosh."

"I love it!" Riley squealed as she held up a colorful jacket inscribed with the signatures of her all-time favorite girl band, Get Up and Glow. "This is the limited-edition jacket! It's been sold out for months! How did you get it? How?"

"We have our ways," Bree said, winking at Grace.

"Bree means her dad works with a guy who knows a guy who—"

"Put it on!" Bree exclaimed. "Put it on!"

"Put it on!" Joy echoed in HQ.

Riley put the jacket on over her favorite T-shirt (which was getting a little too tight, even though Riley refused to admit it).

"It's *so* Glow Glamorous!" the girls all shrieked together.

Anger rubbed his temples. "Someone, please make it stop."

"I can't believe it," Joy said with her eyes shining. "Bree and Grace know Riley better than anyone. They love her so much."

Riley flung her arms around her friends. "You guys are the best! I love you so much!"

"We love you, too, Riley!" Bree and Grace smooshed their faces against Riley's cheeks.

Later that spring, the big event Riley thought would never get there finally arrived.

It wasn't middle school graduation. (That was the next week.)

It wasn't the Foghorns' hockey championship playoffs. (Those were the next month.)

And it wasn't getting her braces off. (That wouldn't be for a while. Riley had only just gotten them on.)

No, this event was bigger than all three of those combined.

Because that night, Riley, Bree, and Grace were attending their Very. First. Get Up and Glow concert.

Riley could scarcely tell if the vibrations in her chest were from the hum of the crowd or her own excited jitters. They were surrounded by a massive number of fans in a cavernous arena Riley knew well because it was where the professional hockey teams played their games during the season. The rink usually sported a freshly smoothed sheet of ice, and the stadium was normally so cold that your breath would form little puffs even in the nosebleed section. But that night, the floor was covered by a huge stage plastered with Get Up and Glow logos.

Grace's mom had gotten them tickets to see the band on tour as a middle school graduation gift—and now they were about to watch them perform in person.

"I can't believe we're here!" Riley couldn't stop smiling.

"Where's your mom's seat?" Bree asked Grace.

"Oh, she's somewhere up there." Grace pointed to the nosebleed section at the top of the arena. Her mom had generously given the girls better seats so they would have a great first-concert experience. "I think she's just as excited as we are."

"Your mom is so cool," Riley said.

"Speaking of cool, check this out." Grace took a huge slurp of her slushy and then stuck out her tongue. The center had been dyed neon blue by the frosty drink. "Lizard tongue!"

"Haha! Your tongue matches your nails!" Riley laughed, pointing to Grace's electric-blue nails.

"It's my new look!" Grace said, sticking out her tongue and wiggling her fingers. "Here—try some slushy! I swear, it makes your brain freeze blue!"

Riley took a huge gulp (from the opposite side of the cup Grace had been drinking from, because germs weirded her out). Then she immediately squeezed her eyes shut and shook her head. "Ack! Brain freeze!"

Just then, a huge roar went up from the crowd as the arena lights dimmed and several strobe lights began pulsing onstage.

"They're starting!" Bree shouted.

The three best friends jumped and screamed as the Get Up and Glow band members stepped into the spotlight. And as the first pounding beats of Riley's favorite song echoed throughout the arena, and as she fist-pumped and cheered in time along with Bree and Grace amid the sea of fans, Riley couldn't help thinking that for this one brief moment in time, she was right where she belonged.

Chapter 5

"This is Joy, coming to you live from inside Riley's mind!" Joy pretended to be an announcer. "And we're expecting a great championship today with the Foghorns!"

It was late June, exactly three weeks since middle school graduation. And now it was the final game of the hockey playoffs, against the Foghorns' rivals, the Sea Lions. Riley's team was in it to win it!

"Foghorns on three!" Riley was telling her team. "One, two, three, Foghorns!"

"Let me at 'em!" Anger cracked his knuckles and strode up to the console. With an expert smack of his fist, he pounded a glowing red "pump it up" button.

Riley powered past two opposing team members and slapped the puck into the goal.

"Goal!" Joy shouted. Riley's perspective shifted to the

stands, where her parents were dressed head to toe in white and teal to support her team.

"Go, Riley!" her mom and dad shouted.

Joy flushed with pride.

"Can you believe how strong and beautiful our girl is?" Joy asked the others. "Isn't she the best?"

"Sorry, what was that?" Fear looked up from his clipboard. "I was just finishing up the championship safety checklist. Gloves . . . kneepads . . . mouth guard—"

"No, no, no—not *that* mouth guard!" Disgust urgently hit a button on the console. Riley had almost picked up a teammate's mouth guard to put in *her* mouth!

Joy smiled and shook her head. Riley wouldn't be Riley without her team of Emotions there to support her. But right then, Joy was gosh-darned proud of their girl out there on the ice, leading *her* team to victory, with the love and support of her parents and friends.

"Oh, no, Joy. Look." Sadness interrupted Joy's thoughts and pointed to the screen.

The game was tied. Riley was just getting out of the penalty box for accidentally tripping another player. And there was only a minute left.

"How are we going to score in time?" Disgust asked.

"We need an idea!" Joy said, pulling a box of light bulbs from beneath the console.

Anger and Fear grabbed two different ideas and placed them in the console.

"We use our slap shot!" said Fear.

"We charge the goalie!" Anger asserted.

"But Grace hasn't scored yet!" Sadness noted.

Joy pulled out an idea and placed it in the console. "Riley will make the right choice."

The Sense of Self glowed as Riley decided on the third idea. She smiled and nodded to Bree and Grace.

"C'mon, Riley," Joy whispered. Their girl was about to execute the play she'd perfected with her besties—the play they could do in their sleep because they worked so well together. Because that was what best friends did.

Bree ricocheted the puck off the wall to Riley.

Riley shot forward with a burst of speed. But three opponents were hot on her trail.

Ten seconds left. Nine . . . eight . . .

The goalie tensed, prepared to block the shot.

Riley's Sense of Self sparkled.

She snapped the puck back between the legs of the

opponent beside her. Grace was ready and waiting with a clear shot of the goal.

Three . . . two . . .

Grace took the shot.

"Goooooal!" cheered all the Emotions in HQ.

All Riley's teammates dogpiled her, Grace, and Bree on the ice. It was a collision of smiles and high fives and cheers of *"We won! We won the championship!"*

The entire team began the famous Celly Dance, and in HQ, Riley's Sense of Self cast a prismatic light that twinkled like diamonds.

The league president presented the championship trophy to the Foghorns. Riley, Grace, and Bree hoisted it in the air for their teammates to see.

"We did it!" Riley led them in a cheer. "Champions!"

Joy watched as a yellow memory sphere rolled into Headquarters. There was no better ending to a season— and an era! This was Riley, Bree, and Grace's final game on the Foghorns. High schoolers weren't allowed to play on the club team. With luck they'd all do well in the high school team tryouts that fall. But as for their time on the Foghorns, they had quite a victory to go out on.

As the team exited the ice, Grace hopped up on the

bench and raised her arms in triumph. "Funnel cake for all!" she yelled.

"Yeah!" everyone cheered.

"Aw, the postgame funnel cake tradition is my favorite," said Joy.

"I hope we still get to do this in high school," said Sadness.

"Of course!" Joy insisted. "Grace, Bree, and funnel cake aren't going anywhere!"

"Hey, girls!" someone suddenly called out behind Riley.

Riley and her friends turned to see a tall woman smiling at them. "Congratulations on your win!"

"That's the high school coach!" Joy gasped. And it wasn't just any high school coach. This was the *varsity* hockey coach, Coach Roberts. And she was congratulating *them* on their win!

Bree nudged Riley in the side. Her friends were as excited as she was.

"What a game!" Coach Roberts continued. "That last play, woo! The three of you were impressive."

"Thanks, Coach Roberts!" Riley said in a voice a little higher pitched than she intended.

"Look, it's last minute," the coach said, "but every year

I do a three-day skills camp. I invite all the best players in the area. It starts tomorrow. If you want, I'd love for you girls to come."

In Headquarters, the Emotions were as stunned as Riley was.

"Are we in a dream right now?" Fear said. "Please, can somebody pinch me?"

Anger punched him instead.

"Ow!" Fear exclaimed. "Definitely awake."

"If we impress Coach," Joy said, "she'll put the three of us on the team next year!"

"Oooh, the Fire Hawks!" Anger exclaimed as he put on a Fire Hawks cap. "Finally! A team I can get behind."

"What do you say?" Coach Roberts asked the girls.

Riley, Bree, and Grace answered in the affirmative.

"Yes!"

"Thank you so much!"

"We'll so be there!"

Coach Roberts nodded. "Great! We'll see ya tomorrow."

As she walked away, Riley huddled with her friends.

"Did that seriously just happen?" she asked. "Did the high school coach ask *us* to come to her skills camp?"

"This is big!" Bree agreed. "Bigger than big—wicked warped big!"

"We have to find our parents!" Grace exclaimed.

Together, the girls thundered up the bleachers to where their parents were talking.

"There are our champions!" Riley's mom exclaimed. "We were wondering where you were! We need some commemorative photographs!"

"For when our monkey is going to be a professional player someday!" Riley's dad said, scooping her up in a hug.

"Dad!" Riley laughed.

"You'll never believe what just happened!" Bree urgently told her mom and dad. "Coach Roberts just asked the three of us to go to her skills camp!"

"Coach Roberts?" Bree's dad gave her an odd look. "Wait—isn't that the other high school co—"

"That doesn't matter!" Bree said quickly. "Dad, she's a *varsity* coach. It's a huge deal for her to invite us. And the camp starts tomorrow!"

"Tomorrow?" Riley's mom asked, surprised.

"Tomorrow!" Riley's dad echoed. "That's great!"

"Is it?" Riley's mom gave him a pointed look. "That's kind of short notice."

"Can I go, Mom? Please?" Riley begged.

"I'm not sure . . ." Riley's mom said slowly. "Is this the overnight camp I've heard about? At the college campus?"

41

"Please, Mrs. Andersen, can Riley come with us?" Bree and Grace said.

"Hang on, girls," Bree's mom said. "We didn't say you could go yet, either."

"Pleeeeeease?" the three girls begged. "We can't say no to Coach Roberts!"

"Exactly! There's no saying no to the varsity coach!" Riley's dad insisted.

"You're not helping, honey." Riley's mom gave him an even more pointed look.

"Listen to Dad!" Anger shouted from HQ. "He gets us."

"Oh, no," Sadness said. "What do we do if Mom says no?"

For a gut-wrenching moment, Riley and the Emotions held their breath. But then Mom's face softened.

"Okay," Riley's mom said. "You three did just win the state championship. If anyone deserves to go, it's you."

"Oh, thank you!" Riley said. "Thank you, thank you, thank you!"

"Thank you!" Riley's dad squeezed her mom and jumped up and down.

"And us?" Bree and Grace turned hopefully to their parents.

Bree's mom and Grace's mom looked at each other, then at their husbands. "I guess we can't say no. . . ."

"Ahhh!" Riley hugged her friends. "We're going to the skills camp!"

"Let's shove down some funnel cake and get packing!" Grace said with a fist pump.

The trio was starting to race off when suddenly Bree's and Grace's parents each put a hand on their daughters' shoulders.

"You all go ahead," Bree's dad said to Riley and her parents. "We'll be right there. We just need to talk with the girls for a sec."

"Oh, okay," Riley said.

"Are Grace and Bree in trouble?" asked Disgust. "They seem worried."

"Who could be worried at a time like this?" said Joy. "We just won the championship and now we're going to camp with our best friends!"

Dad put his arm around Riley's shoulders and started chanting, "Champions! Champions!" As Riley joined in, all worries faded from her mind.

Chapter 6

Later that night, Riley sat on her bed, taping her hockey stick in preparation for the hockey camp. She couldn't stop smiling. First they'd won the championship, and now she and her besties were invited to a skills camp—hosted by the varsity coach! Would it be hard? she wondered. Would she know anyone else there? Probably not, since it was mostly high schoolers. But she'd have Bree and Grace with her. Just wait until everyone saw what the three of them could do!

Her parents knocked on her half-open door.

"What a big day!" her mom said.

"Ha-ha! You're such an all-star!" Riley's dad picked her up in a huge hug and began rocking her back and forth. "You're going to knock that coach's skates off!"

"Dad, stop," Riley said, laughing. "It's just her hockey camp. Who knows what will happen?"

A sudden thought struck Riley: what if she *didn't* do well? What if she messed up so badly that Coach Roberts thought inviting Riley to the camp had been a mistake? The memory of getting a penalty for tripping another player during the championship game flashed through her mind.

"My penalty almost lost us the game today," Riley, downcast, told her parents. "What if I get to camp and screw it up?"

"Hey, don't talk like that," her dad said reassuringly. "You did great today, honey. Those Fire Hawks will be lucky to have you!"

"Yeah, I guess," Riley said, giving her dad a half smile.

"We're so proud of you." Riley's mom kissed the top of her head. That made her feel better.

"Night, monkey," said her dad.

Riley smiled, already feeling sleepy. "Night, Dad. Night, Mom."

"Oh, Riley's so hard on herself," said Sadness. Riley had fallen asleep, and the Emotions were discussing what had just happened. They hated seeing Riley happy one moment and then deflated by a painful memory the next.

Joy observed her fellow Emotions' expressions and took a deep breath. She hadn't been sure when she was going to be ready to show them the big idea she'd been working on. But now seemed like the perfect time.

"What if . . ." Joy started slowly, "what if we can make everything easier?"

"What do you mean, Joy?" asked Sadness.

"Behold!" Joy grabbed a long hook to open a panel in the ceiling. A tube was released, and it lowered to the floor. Joy had been adapting it—and secretly using it—for months. Anytime Riley had a memory roll through that made her feel less than her best self, Joy would send it straight to the back of Riley's mind, where it couldn't hurt her. "This is my super-high-tech Riley protection system!"

A piece of metal fell off the tube and clanged to the floor.

"Heh, heh." Joy scrambled to place it back on. "Don't look at that. It's fine."

"It's a high-tech-a-ma-whatsit?" Fear asked uncertainly.

"This is for all those memories that belong in the Back of the Mind!" Joy explained. She held up the blue memory sphere replaying Riley's penalty from the game. "Like this penalty one. It's weighing on her, so let's lighten the load!"

Joy placed the blue penalty sphere into the tube opening. She pulled back and released a plunger, springing the memory like a pinball up into the tube and out of sight. "This tube is a one-way expressway to 'we're not going to think about that right now'!"

Joy beamed as the other Emotions reacted, clearly impressed.

"Not bad, Joy." Anger nodded.

"You take such good care of Riley," Sadness concurred.

"Thanks." Joy mock polished her nails on her shoulder. "I try. Okay, let's do a sweep!"

The Emotions collected spheres from the memory wall that were negative, unfortunate, or just cringeworthy.

"Here's one where she waved at a guy who was actually waving at a girl behind her," said Disgust.

"Ohhh, that was so bad." Joy nodded. "Good choice."

"And here's when she forgot that girl's name," Anger said.

"That was super awkward," Joy agreed.

"What *was* her name?" Disgust asked.

Joy shrugged. "I don't know. Janet or something? Whatever, let's just get rid of it."

Together they loaded armfuls of unpleasant memories into Joy's jerry-rigged Back of the Mind tube. Joy closed the seal and pulled back on the plunger.

"We keep the best and toss the rest!" Joy proclaimed before shooting all the memory spheres to the depths of Riley's mind. Mission accomplished. What good were memories if they weren't the best ones to help their girl shine?

After one more quick sweep, the Emotions sent the remaining day's memories down to Long Term, then stretched and yawned.

"Good work, everybody," Joy said, selecting one final golden sphere from the memory wall. Inside played the memory of Riley, Bree, and Grace hoisting the championship trophy. She had special plans for that one. "You guys go get some shut-eye. Big day tomorrow. I'm just going to finish cleaning up a bit."

As Anger, Disgust, and Fear traipsed off to bed, Sadness lingered behind. "Joy?" she asked. "Are you taking that where I think you're taking that?"

Joy smiled. "You want to come this time?"

"Yes . . ." Sadness said hesitantly. "I mean, no. Oh, no, I really shouldn't."

Joy put an arm around Sadness's shoulders. "You know, you're the only one who hasn't been to the Belief System."

"Yeah," Sadness admitted. "It's just that it's new, and I know how important it is, and I don't want to mess it up or break it or burn it to the ground or anything."

"Sadness, you won't hurt it," Joy assured her. "I promise. Have I ever steered you wrong before?"

"Many times."

"Come on." Joy pressed a sequence of buttons on the platform to summon the elevator. "Where I go, you go." She held Sadness's hand as they stepped inside.

The depths of Riley's Belief System were unlike anything Sadness had ever seen before. She had heard the other Emotions talking about it for months. But seeing it for the first time took her breath away.

What stood before Joy and Sadness was a rich forest of glowing strings fed by a constant stream of memories from throughout Riley's mind.

"Whoa," Sadness breathed, her face bathed in the forest's glow.

"Pretty impressive, huh?" Joy beamed. She stepped forward and lightly strummed one of the strings.

Mom and Dad are proud of me.

Sadness timidly plucked a strand.

I'm kind.

"Aw, that's nice," Sadness said.

Joy and Sadness took turns strumming the different beliefs one by one.

Homework should be illegal. Get Up and Glow is the best band in the world. I make great friends.

Then, gently, Joy placed the golden memory sphere of Riley's championship victory into the stream. A brilliant rainbow glow rippled throughout the water as the memory fed a new belief string that stretched up and attached itself to the rest of the system.

I'm a winner.

"Riley's the best," Sadness said, overwhelmed with love for their girl.

Joy nodded. "And it's only going to get better."

Chapter 7

Beep. *Beep. Beep.*

Joy stirred in her sleep. Something was making a strange beeping sound. *Did Anger leave one of his burritos in the microwave again?* she wondered, half in a dream.

Beep. Beep. Beep.

She lifted her head groggily and listened. For a moment, the beeping stopped. *Hmmm.* Maybe she had imagined it? Joy rested her head back on her pillow.

Beep. Beep. Beep.

Now all the Emotions shot up in their beds, alarmed.

"What the heck is that?" Sadness asked.

They anxiously crept down the stairs from their bedroom and into central HQ. Anger held a bat just in case. The beeping was steady now and seemed to be coming from the console.

Joy walked over and scanned all the buttons. Everything looked normal—except for a tiny flashing red light.

Sadness leaned closer. "It's the Pooberty Alarm."

"Oh, yeah. I forgot about that thing," Joy said. The red button labeled PUBERTY ALARM had been a part of the console since the Mind Workers had modified it when Riley was twelve. So far, it hadn't done anything. The Emotions had figured it was there for decoration.

But now it blinked red and continued its incessant beeping.

Beep. Beep. Beep.

"What's it doing?" Fear asked nervously as they huddled closer.

BEEEEEEEEEEEEEEEP!

The Puberty Alarm blared a high-pitched siren.

"This is the end, people!" Fear freaked out. "It's the apocalypse!"

"Joy, make it stop!" Disgust plugged her ears with her fingers.

Joy frantically tried to smother the alarm with her hands, but it was no use. The siren was deafening. They had to get this thing out of HQ! Thinking fast, she wriggled the alarm loose and chucked it into her homemade Back of the Mind tube.

BEEEEeeeeeeeeep . . .

The siren faded and the Emotions breathed a sigh of relief.

"Whew. Problem solved," Joy said, feeling rather pleased with herself.

That was when . . .

CRASH!

The Emotions jumped and screamed once again. A massive wrecking ball had smashed into one of the windows in Headquarters! Shards of glass flew everywhere as the entire frame collapsed.

"What is going on?" Joy shouted.

They watched, horrified, as a construction lift rose outside the demolished window. It carried dozens of Mind Workers wearing hard hats and holding sledgehammers.

"Okay, let's clear it all out!" the foreman ordered, hopping down from the lift, with glass crunching under his steel-toed boots. "It's *demo day!*"

The Emotions gasped as Mind Workers poured into HQ. The Mind Workers cheerfully chatted even as they began demolishing walls and jackhammering the floor.

"What's going on? *Ahhh!*" Anger flared angrily—right next to a box of dynamite the Mind Workers had just set down.

"No, no, no!" Joy rushed over to settle him down before he blew Headquarters to smithereens.

Fear noticed the box of dynamite inches from Anger's flame and ran away screaming.

"Who *are* you people?" Disgust demanded as a worker smashed a hammer into the wall behind her. But the worker ignored her.

"Excuse me!" Joy ran to the foreman, who was holding a clipboard. "Are you in charge here? Could you do me a favor and *stop* tearing Headquarters apart?"

"No can do." The foreman clicked his pen. "Didn't ya hear? Permits just came through."

"Permits?" Joy asked, confused. "For what?"

The foreman dropped a stack of permits into Joy's hands. "Expanding the place! You know, for the others."

"Others? What others?" Joy cringed as something exploded across the room, billowing dust everywhere.

"They're not here yet?" the foreman asked. He put his pen in his pocket and called out, "Hey, Margie! You got that console?"

A Mind Worker opened a panel in the console and fiddled with some wiring. "Yup! She's all set!" She slammed the lid shut and locked it.

"Set with what?" Joy gripped her hair, distraught at the

chaos around her. What was happening to their beautiful Headquarters?

Suddenly, all the lights kicked on.

Riley was awake.

The foreman blew a whistle. "Lunch break!" he called to the workers.

"Wait—you can't leave it like this!" Joy wailed.

But it was no use. The workers filed out, crunching debris under their boots, just as the Emotions heard Riley's dad's voice on-screen.

"Come on, Riley! We're going to be late! Grace is waiting."

This wasn't good.

Riley groggily lifted her head off her pillow. She had a horrible taste in her mouth. It must have been from all that garlic pizza she'd celebrated with the night before. But worse than that, Riley simply felt . . . gross. Her face was oily. She ran a hand through her hair. *Ugh.* It was tangled and knotted. And her pajamas were sweaty, even though she'd kicked off the blankets in the middle of the night.

"Riley?" her mom asked, walking into the room. "Grace is waiting downstairs." She eyed Riley's empty suitcase and frowned. "You're not packed yet?"

"*Ugh!*" Riley shouted, inexplicably annoyed. "*You're always on me! Can't you lay off for, like, one second?*"

Her mom's eyes widened. "Riley, what's wrong?"

"Overreact much?" Disgust said, shooting Anger a look. Inside HQ, Anger had just pushed the button that had sent Riley into the tirade.

"I barely touched it!" Anger insisted. "Those morons broke the console!"

On-screen, Riley's mom was looking at her with concern. "Are you okay?"

"Oh, Mom looks sad." Sadness gently touched one of her watery blue buttons. Normally her pushing that button would make Riley sigh deeply. But not that day. . . .

"*I'm the worst!*" Riley burst into tears.

Sadness held up her hands. "I barely touched it!"

"That's what I said!" Anger replied.

Disgust cracked her knuckles and approached the console. "Let the professional handle this."

Riley suddenly stopped crying and sniffed her armpit. *"I'm too gross to go to camp or anywhere ever again!"*

"Oh yeah, this thing is totally broken," Disgust agreed.

"But what do we do?" Fear panicked. "We can't help Riley without the controls!"

"Here, let's try this!" Joy rushed up with a long stick. "We'll tap the buttons from a distance."

On-screen, Riley's mom was talking. "You're not gross, honey. You're just changing. Remember that beautiful butterfly we saw in the park last week? It started as a caterpillar, and just like that caterpillar, you're about to get wings. Not literal wings . . ."

"What is she *talking* about?" Disgust asked as the whole group reached out with the stick from a distance.

"Easy," Joy cautioned them. "We'll just barely tap the button. . . ."

The stick made contact.

"Oh my gosh, Mom! Just go away! Ugh!" Riley stormed out of the room.

The Emotions collapsed in a pile. Thanks to whatever those Mind Workers had done, it was going to be a long day.

Chapter 8

The Andersen family car rumbled along the road, and Riley and her Emotions soaked up the sights of their first visit to a college campus. San Francisco's busy city streets had fallen away a short while before, but here, on the wooded approach to the skills camp, it felt almost like a different world. Pathways meandered from the main road, leading up hills to modern academic buildings boasting wooden beams and entire walls of windows. A few summer college students, reading or listening to music, reclined on blankets stretched wide on the pristine grass. A backdrop of tall redwoods surrounded the entire campus, giving the impression that the car was entering a secret emerald-green forest retreat, with the trees' canopy forming a secure border perfectly outlined against a vivid blue sky.

Joy tried to take in the scenery, but she was still worried about the console. If they were careful, everything would be fine, she told herself. Plus being around Grace and Bree always gave Riley a mood boost.

"You guys, I'm *so* psyched!" Grace exclaimed.

"Me too!" Bree replied.

Riley beamed. "How great is next year gonna be? Coach Roberts's team has been state champs, like, every year!" She scrolled through her phone for a moment and then showed Bree and Grace a picture of a tall, confident girl with wavy hair that had a streak of iconic Fire Hawk red running through it. "And Val Ortiz is the captain now!"

"This Valentina Ortiz obsession is out of control," Anger said, rolling his eyes.

But regardless of Anger's opinion, Valentina Ortiz (Val for short) was Riley's hero. Riley didn't know Val. But Val's hockey prowess was the stuff of legend at Bridgeview Middle School. Valentina Ortiz had made the varsity team as a freshman. Her moves on the ice were unparalleled, and her slap shots were rumored to go one hundred miles per hour. But above all that, Val exuded *cool*. Real Fire Hawks material.

"All we have to do is be super awesome at camp," Riley

said. "Coach will put us on the team, and we'll all be Fire Hawks!"

At that, Bree and Grace shared a look.

Disgust's eyes narrowed. "Wait. What was that?"

"What was what?" asked Joy.

"We got a look," said Disgust. "I don't like this."

"What? You're paranoid," Joy said dismissively.

"I never miss a look," Disgust asserted.

She hit a button, prompting a miniature workstation to rise from the floor. She recalled the memory and paused on Bree's face. "Enhance fifteen to thirty-three," she commanded. "Track forty-five right. Zoom in." The computer zoomed in on Bree's eyebrow.

"See? Right there!" Disgust exclaimed, pointing at the image. Bree's eyebrow had raised a tenth of an inch.

"So?" Anger asked, confused.

Disgust didn't take her eyes off the screen. "She's hiding something! But what?" After a moment, she nodded. "Only one way to find out."

Disgust tapped a button, causing Riley to make the tiniest expression change.

Bree stared at Riley, the two in a silent standoff. Grace's eyes darted back and forth between her two friends. Finally, she couldn't take it anymore.

"Coach Roberts isn't going to be our coach next year!" Grace blurted out.

Bree smacked Grace on the shoulder and gave her an admonishing look.

"We . . . got assigned to a different high school," Bree finally admitted.

"Aha!" Disgust exclaimed. Then it sunk in. "Oh. Oh, no . . ."

"This is a *huge* deal!" Fear exclaimed.

"We can't go to high school without Bree and Grace!" said Anger.

"We won't know anybody," Sadness whimpered.

"Oh, okay," Riley began, trying to hide the chaos of her Emotions. "No big deal."

"We'll still get to hang out," Bree said.

"And we'll have this weekend?" Grace's voice was more questioning than reassuring. "Which means we'll get one last time playing on the same team?"

"Friends are forever, right?" Bree held out her hand to fist-bump Riley.

Not knowing how else to respond, Riley fist-bumped Bree and Grace, like she always did. "Yeah, of course."

"Oh, this is *so sad*!" Sadness lunged for the console.

"Wait, Sadness!" All the Emotions rushed to block her.

"Touchy console!"

"Don't do it!"

"You can't!"

"Just hold on until they're out of the car!" Disgust pleaded. They couldn't let Bree and Grace see Riley turn into a blubbering pile of tears. Then they really *wouldn't* want to be best friends anymore.

The Emotions watched, with Sadness still straining and sobbing, as the family car pulled up to the drop-off area.

"Here we are!" Dad said. "Wow, it looks pretty cool. You sure you don't need an assistant coach? I'm available."

Disgust rolled her eyes.

"Bill," Riley's mom chided him.

"Okay, okay. We'll see you in a few days," Riley's dad said.

"Thanks for the ride!" Bree and Grace hopped out of the car.

Sadness welled up with a fresh wave of anguish. It took everything the Emotions had to restrain her.

Riley hesitated for a moment but then started to follow her friends.

"Honey, hold on," Riley's mom said. "Are you sure you have everything? Stick?"

"Yes," Riley replied.

"Gloves?"

"Yes," Riley repeated, more annoyed now.

"What's with the interrogation?" Anger complained.

"They're worried," Sadness said, still trying to push her way to the console. "We can cry in front of them."

"No! Then they may not let Riley stay at camp," said Joy. "Just give it a few more seconds, until Riley is alone."

"You have your phone?" Riley's dad asked.

"Yes, of course," Riley replied.

"Okay, call us if you need us," Riley's dad said. "I love you. Go get 'em."

"Okay, love you guys," Riley said as she hopped out of the car.

"Don't forget your deodorant!" her mom called.

"Mom!" Riley exclaimed. She looked around to make sure no one had heard.

"Bye, monkey!" her dad added.

Riley closed the door and watched as they drove away.

Finally, the Emotions released their grip on Sadness, and she collapsed against the console, turning it a rippling blue. Riley burst into tears.

Joy put a hand on Sadness's shoulder. "It's okay. We need this."

Still crying, Riley turned around only to realize that some girls were standing right in front of her.

Sadness gasped and stepped away from the console.

"We can't cry in front of our peers!" Disgust exclaimed in horror.

Fear trembled. "There are so many people to make a bad first impression on!"

Joy couldn't let their negativity continue. "It's okay. We'll have plenty of time to think about this after camp. We just need to find Bree and Grace."

She turned to the console.

"We get one last hurrah with our besties," Joy said, more to herself than the others. "And we're going to make the most of it."

Chapter 9

Riley quickly wiped away her tears as she scanned the group of teenagers filtering into the camp. She didn't recognize anyone; all these girls were high schoolers. The way they chatted and strode into the camp like they knew exactly where to go made Riley feel small and alone. Had Bree and Grace gone inside already?

I guess they have each other, she thought bitterly. *Why would they need me?* Riley knew she was being harsh. Part of her understood it wasn't Bree and Grace's fault they got assigned to a different high school. But they could have at least given her a heads-up. Now here she was standing in a crowd of strangers and wondering what she was going to do as a high school freshman with no friends. Meanwhile, Bree and Grace were wherever they were—*not* worrying about that.

Finally, she spotted them in the distance. She began to rush over when . . .

BAM!

She collided with another person and fell on her butt.

"Gah!" Riley exclaimed, rubbing her tailbone.

"Whoa—are you okay?"

Riley looked up at the person she'd whacked into—and she gasped.

She couldn't believe it.

It was Valentina Ortiz.

She had smacked into Valentina Ortiz—and landed on her butt. Riley stared agape, with no words coming out.

Valentina took Riley's hand to help her up. "Hey, hi. My name's Valentina."

"I know!" Riley's voice squeaked with a higher pitch than usual. "You're the varsity captain. You set the all-time goal record as a junior. Your favorite color is red, and your skate size is nine and a half—just like me!"

O.M.G. *What* was she saying?

Luckily, Val didn't seem weirded out. Instead, she smiled. "Oh! You're the one Coach told us about. Riley from Michigan, right?"

Riley could barely keep her thoughts straight. This

was Valentina Ortiz—*the* Valentina Ortiz. Talking to her! And Val had *heard* of her! Sure, Val had gotten the state wrong, but Riley wasn't sure she was supposed to correct her. What if she embarrassed Val? Or sounded like a know-it-all? No, no, no—she couldn't do that.

"Yeah," Riley said, laughing nervously. "That's me. Riley from good old Michigan."

"What are we saying?" Disgust smacked her head, still gagging from Riley's stalker-level list of random Valentina Ortiz facts.

"We are so uncool," Sadness said, shaking her head.

"Why are we still holding her hand?" Fear flailed in a panic.

"And why didn't Riley tell her the truth?" Joy's brow furrowed. "We're not from Michigan."

Suddenly, the console glowed bright orange.

"Orange?" Joy asked. "Who made the console orange?"

She looked at the others one by one. They all shook their heads.

"Do I look orange?" Anger asked, irked.

"I didn't touch it!" Fear insisted.

"Orange is *not* my color," Disgust said.

"Not me," Sadness added.

"But then, who . . ." Joy turned to look back at the console—and came face to face with a bizarre-looking creature she had never seen before.

"Hello, everybody!" the creature exclaimed.

"Ahhhh!" the Emotions all screamed at once. Fear, Sadness, Disgust, and Anger ran and hid behind Joy.

The orange creature scooted closer, with a bounce in her step so peppy she was borderline vibrating. She was short and wiry, with bugged-out eyes and a shock of hair that stuck straight up atop her head. She tugged nervously at the striped turtleneck rolled beneath her wide chin and mouth.

"Oh my gosh, I am just such a *huge* fan of yours! And now here I am meeting you face to face! Okay, how can I help?" she said.

"Uhhh . . ." Joy and the others were very, *very* unsettled. What was going on? Since when were there visitors to HQ? Mind Workers came and went occasionally. But this was no Mind Worker.

"I can take notes," the newcomer said as she whipped out a pen and pad from her deep-pocketed brown pants.

"Multitask? Follow you around? Carry your things? Watch you sleep?"

"Wow!" Joy said uncertainly. "You . . . have a lot of energy. Maybe you could just stay where I can see you."

"Anything!" the creature exclaimed. "Just call my name, and I am here for you."

"And . . . what was your name again?" Joy asked.

"Oh! I'm sorry. I can get ahead of myself. I'm Anxiety. I'm one of Riley's new Emotions!" She puffed out her chest proudly, though she was still vibrating a little. Joy could tell because her stringy stalk of hair was quavering. "And we are just super jazzed to be here."

"Wait, what do you mean 'we'?" Disgust asked.

Suddenly, a tiny blue-green hand crept up, trying to reach the buttons on the console. "I wish I was as tall as all of you," the owner of the hand whined.

"Ahh!" Joy and the others jumped back. There were more weird Emotions invading HQ!

This one was pint-sized, with big puppy dog eyes and a head too large for her body. Her wavy teal hair stuck out in messy poofs like a preschooler's.

"Who the heck are *you*?" Anger asked.

"I'm Envy," the new Emotion said. She gave each of

them an unsettlingly sweet grin before spotting Disgust's sleek green hair. "Oooh." She reached out to touch it. "Look at your hair. . . ."

Disgust whacked her little hand away. "Not happening."

Envy turned her attention to the screen, where Val was still talking with Riley. Envy's wide eyes grew even wider. "Oooh—look at *her* hair." She admired Val's wavy brown locks with a streak of red running through them. "We need hair like that!"

Before anyone could stop her, Envy pressed a button on the console. On-screen, Riley reached out toward Val's hair. "Oh my gosh, I love the red in your hair!"

"Oh, I—" Val pulled back awkwardly from Riley's attempt to touch her hair.

"What are you doing?" Disgust cried, horrified. She snatched Envy away from the console. "We don't just *touch* people!"

Riley shuffled, realizing she'd messed up. "Hey, maybe when I make the team, I can join Team Red Head, too! Yeah, yeah!" She gave a weak fist pump.

Joy and the other core Emotions cringed. This wasn't like their girl at all!

Suddenly, the console lit up with a pink glow.

"Now what?" Anger fumed, turning to see yet another

new Emotion standing in HQ. Unlike Envy, this one was massive. He had a squishy pink body stuffed into a mauve fleece hoodie. His nose was so big and round it looked like a marshmallow stuck to his face. And his oversized sweaty palms were all over the console, turning it pink.

Riley's cheeks flushed as she fumbled for words. "Sorry, that was a totally dorky thing to say."

"Okay, who's this guy?" Anger demanded.

The looming pink Emotion pulled the drawstrings of his hoodie tighter, closing the hood around his face so that only his eyes peeked out.

"What's your name, big fella?" Sadness asked.

"That's Embarrassment!" Anxiety popped up out of nowhere—again. "He's not big on eye contact or, uh, like, talking. But he's a really sweet guy."

"Well, welcome to Headquarters, Embarrassment!" Joy tried to shake hands with him, but Embarrassment went for a fist bump instead. He blushed a deeper pink.

Meanwhile, Val was offering to show Riley the way into camp. "Hey, do you want to come with me, actually?" she said. "You can meet some of the other Fire Hawks."

Anxiety started vibrating with eager energy. "Oooh! This is exciting! But we can't let her know we're excited."

The console suddenly glowed deep purple, and Riley

pretended to be nonchalant about Val's offer. "Yeah, sounds good."

"What Emotion was that?" Anger asked, more confused than ever.

"That's Ennui," Anxiety said.

"Enn-what?" Joy raised an eyebrow.

The Emotions all turned to where a long droopy purple Emotion was lying on the couch, scrolling on her phone. She gave a deeply annoyed sigh.

"It's pronounced *ON-WEE*," Ennui corrected Joy in her French accent. "It's what you would call the 'boredom.'"

Joy looked at the others and shrugged. This Emotion had a chip on her shoulder.

"Well, come on up here, Ennn-wuuur? Am I saying it right? En-waa. No," Joy said.

Ennui did not respond.

"Oh, nicknames!" Joy tried to salvage the situation. "I'm going to call you Wee-wee!"

Ennui didn't look up from her phone. *"Non."*

The console glowed purple once more even though Ennui wasn't touching it.

"How are you driving?" Fear asked.

Ennui held up her phone, displaying a picture of the console. "Console app."

Anger couldn't hold back any longer. "Hey! Stop it! That's enough!"

"Now, now," said Joy, "if there's one thing I've learned, it's that all Emotions deserve to be here, even the ones you want to—*grrr* . . ." She put her arm around Sadness a little too tightly. "You know? But it's important. To work together. To grow and change."

Even though Joy didn't fully trust these new Emotions, she didn't want to repeat the mistakes she had made with Sadness.

Anger shrugged. "If you say so."

With Ennui driving the console once more, Riley picked up her bag and tossed it over her shoulder. "Lead the way," she told Val.

"Oh, but what about our friends?" Sadness said.

The Emotions could see Bree and Grace nearby on-screen. Bree and Grace didn't see Riley, though. Riley paused as she decided what to do.

"Val is our future," Envy said simply.

Anxiety nodded vigorously. "Yes, I agree completely. We need new friends, or we'll be totally alone in high school! Right, Joy?"

"Well, um, actually . . ." Joy started.

"Great!" Anxiety exclaimed. She began driving.

Riley hurried after Val. "Wait up! Thanks for showing me around!"

Joy gasped. "Why did you do that?"

"Oh, no, sorry!" Anxiety whipped her hands away from the buttons like a kid who had been caught doing something naughty. "What did I do?"

Joy gave her a perturbed look. What did she mean? She knew exactly what she'd done. "We just left our best friends behind."

"But what about the new ones that we're about to meet?" Anxiety asked, confused.

Behind her, Envy, Embarrassment, and Ennui nodded.

Joy stared at them. Bree and Grace were Riley's best friends for life. They brought out the best in Riley. Anxiety couldn't toss that all away for people they barely knew.

"What? No!" Joy said incredulously. "These next three days need to be about Bree and Grace."

Anxiety's expression changed. "Joy," she said in a serious tone, "the next three days could determine the next *four years* of our lives."

"I think that's overstating things a bit," Joy said.

To Joy's surprise, the new Emotions snickered.

"Ooh la la. Joy is so old-school," Ennui said mockingly.

"What?" Joy said, rather offended, though she wasn't sure what Ennui even meant.

"Look, Joy," Anxiety said, "we all have a job to do. You make Riley happy. Sadness makes her sad. Fear protects her from the scary stuff she can see. And *my* job is to protect her from the scary stuff she *can't* see. I plan for the future. Here, let me show you."

Anxiety touched an indentation in the console, causing a screen to pop up through it.

"Oh, that's what that does," Sadness said, surprised.

"I was using that as a cup holder," Joy added under her breath.

"Okay, so my team has run all the data, and we're looking at the following likely scenarios." Anxiety began tapping the screen, showing projections of things that could happen to Riley in the future. "First, we don't take this camp seriously and we goof off with Bree and Grace." An image of Riley, Grace, and Bree acting silly appeared. "Riley looks really uncool in front of Val. She fails to impress Coach." The image switched to Coach kicking Riley out of camp while all the older girls laughed at her. "She does *not* become a Fire Hawk and finally arrives at high school with no one. She eats alone, and only the teachers know her name." A final image popped up of Riley, sad and alone, sitting at a high school cafeteria table.

"Ew." Disgust recoiled.

"Okay, you and I are going to be friends," Fear said, impressed.

"Oh, this is a sad story," Sadness said, getting teary-eyed.

"It's a *ridiculous* story," Joy said. Who did this newbie think she was, projecting all these horrible thoughts into Riley's head? It was time to get things back under control.

"Again, I love the energy," Joy said authoritatively, pulling rank, "but you're being silly. *None* of this will actually happen."

Joy's tone must have worked, because Anxiety began fidgeting like a student who had been told they were out of line. "Right, right." She switched off the projection screen. "Whatever you say. You're the boss."

Chapter 10

Riley followed Val closely down the winding halls and into the locker room of the ice rink. She tried to take some deep, calming breaths, but she couldn't stop shaking. Why was she so nervous?

It's just hockey practice like normal, Riley thought, trying to convince herself.

But obviously it wasn't. This was Coach Roberts's varsity skills camp. And though the locker room was pungent with the familiar musty smell of skates, sweat, and bleach, as soon as Riley stepped through the red double doors and saw all the self-assured high school students unpacking their gear, talking and laughing like they'd been there their whole lives, she felt a pang of longing for *her* familiar locker room and *her* familiar faces at the Foghorns' training sessions. Maybe she should have waited for Bree and Grace after all. Things didn't feel the same without them.

Luckily, Val didn't seem to notice how nervous Riley was. "Come on!" Val said cheerfully. "I want you to meet the other Fire Hawks."

She led Riley to a group of girls lacing up their skates. Each had a streak of red in her hair, like Val.

"Hey, what's up?" the girls said, nodding in Riley's direction.

"Hey." Riley waved meekly. These girls were *so* cool. She tried to picture herself sitting there by that time next year, lacing up her skates and confidently shooting passing teammates a "what's up?" nod, with a streak of red running through her own sandy-blond hair.

"Riley is from Michigan," Val told the other girls.

Gah! Riley *really* couldn't correct Val now—not in front of the other Fire Hawks. She guessed Michigan was her new, unofficial home state.

"Oh, cool." A Fire Hawk with cropped brown hair and an eyebrow piercing snapped her gum. "Where in Michigan are you from?"

"Uh . . ." Riley gulped. *Think fast—think fast!* "I'm from . . . all over."

"Nice," the girl said. "I've got a cousin in Minneapolis."

"Cool." Riley nodded, knowing full well that Minneapolis was in Minnesota, not Michigan—because *she* was from Minnesota, not Michigan.

"Dani, that's *Minnesota*," another Fire Hawk said, correcting her. "Two completely different states."

Riley felt sweat pooling under her arms.

"Hey, you want to sit with us?" Val motioned to an empty space on the bench.

"She wants to sit with us! Everything is beautiful!" Anxiety cheered. She pushed Joy toward the console.

Joy shot her a look. "There's not enough room for Bree and Grace." She saw an empty bench nearby. "Oh! We should go sit over there."

"Oh, sorry . . ." Riley said to Val. "I was going to go save seats for my friends."

Val shrugged. "Oh, okay. It's cool."

Riley headed to the empty bench and put her bag down.

"See? Was that so hard?" Joy said.

Beside her, the little orange Emotion vibrated vigorously, and Anxiety's left eye twitched. "No, that was super great."

Riley saw Bree and Grace hurrying into the locker room. "Bree! Grace!" She waved, motioning them to the bench.

"There you are!" Grace said. "We lost sight of you!"

Riley hugged her friends, and the three of them laughed happily.

"Time to celebrate!" Joy exclaimed, hitting a button on the console.

"Say 'ahhh-woooga'!" Riley exclaimed, doing the Celly Dance with her friends.

"AHHH-WOOOGA!" the three girls cheered, snapping silly selfies with their phones.

There was a murmur in the locker room as a heavy door closed somewhere.

"Okay, ladies, let's all settle in." Coach Roberts's voice came from off-screen. She didn't sound very celebratory.

"Uh . . . Joy?" Anxiety warned her.

But Joy was too busy driving the console and keeping the party going to notice. "Aw, yeah!" she said, laughing.

"Skills camp selfies!" Riley made a peace sign with her fingers, snapping another photo of her, Bree, and Grace.

"Ladies, 'settle in' means settle down." Coach's voice

was sterner. "I need your focus." She came into view on the screen in front of Riley and looked with distaste at her phone, the source of the distraction. "Which means now I'm going to need your cell phones. All of them."

The players groaned.

"*What?*"

"Thanks, new girl."

"Are you serious?"

They shut their mouths when Coach Roberts glanced their way.

"You're here to work. Not to goof around." Coach Roberts turned to Riley. "Got that, Andersen?"

Inside HQ, Embarrassment lumbered forward and leaned heavily on the console.

"Yes, Coach." Riley turned beet red.

Coach Roberts collected everyone's phones in a basket while several players continued muttering under their breath.

Next to Riley, Grace whispered, "Wow. Coach is so serious."

"Aw, see?" Joy smiled. "Grace gets us. Besties always understand."

Joy nudged Embarrassment's squishy arm over a bit, mingling a hint of yellow with the pink on the console.

"Uh, Joy, maybe I could help a little. . . ." Anxiety tugged at her turtleneck.

"Thank you, not now," Joy replied.

The gold spread, and they heard Riley whisper to Grace, "I know, right?"

The two of them giggled, catching Coach's attention again.

"Oh, you think this is funny?" Coach shot them a withering look. "Well, you know what else is funny? Skating lines. Now hit the ice, ladies!"

Once again, everyone in the locker room groaned.

"Ugh!"

"Come on!"

"Thanks a lot, Michigan!"

Dani, the Fire Hawk with the eyebrow piercing, bumped into Riley on her way to the ice. "Nice, Andersen," she said, her tone now much less civil.

Ennui walked up beside Joy, who had finally removed her hands from the console, her expression stricken.

"Bravo, Joy," Ennui said. "Riley's *totally* fitting in now."

"Oh, thanks so much, Wee-wee," Joy snapped sarcastically.

Chapter 11

Riley had never skated so hard in her life. She was no stranger to skating lines. But seeing as she was the one who had gotten the whole team into trouble, she figured it was up to her to show Coach that she *was* taking camp seriously. No more messing around for Riley Andersen. Somehow she had to turn this around.

The whole time, she heard the other high school players grumbling, "This is the worst," and "What a way to start camp." Riley began to wonder if she had already completely messed up camp—perhaps even her entire high school existence. But she pushed the thought away and instead skated harder.

At least Bree and Grace didn't hate her for making them skate lines. *They* knew it wasn't Riley's fault.

But then again, Bree and Grace wouldn't be there to back her up in high school the next year, would they?

Coach Roberts finally blew her whistle. "All right, ladies. Take a breather! Then we'll divide into teams."

Exhausted, Riley exited the rink, then caught her breath beside the stadium seats.

That was when she heard it: "Oof. That Michigan girl is off to a rough start."

Riley gasped. She peeked through the stair railing, careful to stay out of sight. Some of the Fire Hawks were sitting together, drinking from water bottles.

"I'd heard good things about her. But now I don't know what to think."

The girls shrugged, and Riley, flushing crimson, felt heat in her cheeks.

Were they talking about *her*?

"Oh, no . . ." Anxiety looked like she was about to throw up. "Are they talking about *us*?"

The Emotions watched, stunned, from Riley's vantage point behind the railing.

"Coach isn't going to put her on the team if she can't get it together," Dani said, chuckling, and popped a fresh piece of gum in her mouth.

"What's that hotshot think is so funny?" Anger fumed.

"Oh, right, Dani." Val rolled her eyes. "Like you had it all together when you were a freshman?"

"Come on," Dani protested. "I wasn't *that* immature."

Inside HQ, Embarrassment let out a strangled gasp. He collapsed spectacularly across the console, practically melting into the board and hitting with his massive marshmallow body every button possible—except one.

"Oh, I got you, big guy," Sadness offered. She pressed the last button.

Hot tears of humiliation burned Riley's eyes. Her chest heaved.

"I always wanted people to talk about us, but not like this!" Envy whined.

"Oh, Joy, what do we do now?" Sadness asked.

Everyone turned to Joy, who could feel the heat of uncertainty creeping up inside her as well.

"Um . . . we can just—We're fine. . . ."

"Fine?" Ennui huffed. "This is a disaster."

"I have an idea!" Anxiety popped up beside Joy, startling her for what seemed like the umpteenth time. "If we can get Val on our side, everything will be okay!"

Out of nowhere, Anxiety held up an idea light bulb and slotted it into the console. Instantly, it lit up.

Wiping her eyes, Riley took a deep breath. All the Fire Hawks had headed to the locker room except for Val, who sat on the bleachers, adjusting her skates.

"Uh, Val . . ." Riley started nervously.

Val looked up. "Oh, hey, Riley." She sounded awkward.

"I'm just—" Riley was so embarrassed and miserable she felt like she was falling apart. She just wanted Val to like her again. "I'm so sorry. I didn't mean to get the whole team skating lines. I feel terrible. I respect you so much. And I would never do anything to mess it up. You're a great hockey player, and you lead the team so amazingly, and I really look up to you and—"

"Okay, okay." Val let out a small laugh and held up her hand to stop Riley's effusive praise. "Thanks. Listen, Coach was hard on you today. But that's not a bad thing. It means you're on her radar."

A glimmer of hope rose in Riley.

"Really?" she asked.

Val stood. "Hey, I'm glad you came to talk with me. Let's try to be on the same team later, okay?"

Riley nodded, feeling a tiny bit better. "Oh, yeah! Cool."

She took a shaky breath. Maybe she could turn things around after all.

Inside HQ, the new Emotions clapped.

"Good job. Wow." Ennui looked pleased despite herself.

"Now that was . . . yes, wow," Fear agreed. "How did you do that?"

Envy reached up to touch the edge of Anxiety's sweater. "I wish I could do that!"

"Aw, you guys," Anxiety said sheepishly. "I mean, it really wasn't anything. I'm just trying to help."

Joy watched as the new Emotions nodded in agreement and even the core Emotions seemed to be considering Anxiety's strategy. She didn't like this. It didn't feel right. It didn't feel like it was best for Riley.

"I agree. Great job, Anxiety," Joy said, ushering the vibrating orange Emotion away from the console. "I stepped back, you stepped in, you got Riley back on track, now I'm ready to step back in—"

"Oh, uh, but that was just part one of my plan," Anxiety said, interrupting her.

"There's a part two?" Joy asked. She was getting a bad feeling about this.

"A good plan has many parts, Joy," Anxiety said.

Chapter 12

"Okay, ladies!" Coach Roberts blew her whistle as everyone filtered back onto the ice. "We're going to form your teams for the rest of camp. Split yourselves down the middle—Team One on the right, Team Two on the left."

Riley stood off to the side, cold sweat making her uniform damp and uncomfortably sticky under her protective padding. *Everything will be okay,* she kept telling herself. *Val wants me on her team. So that's a win. I'll be with the Fire Hawks and show them that I'm serious, and then they'll know I'm cool and not a loser—*

"Hey, Riley!" Bree and Grace skated up behind her.

Gah! Riley mentally smacked herself. She'd been so focused on Val she'd completely forgotten she had promised to be on the same team as Bree and Grace.

"Oh, hey . . ." she started.

"Let's do this!" Bree energetically held out her knuckles for a fist bump.

"One more time on the same team, right?" Grace grinned.

"Right . . ." Riley said hesitantly. She turned to look at Val, who was lining up with the other Fire Hawks. "Hey, let's join Team One," she said hopefully.

"Nah, they're full." Grace nodded to the other group of girls, gathering on the left. "Let's go over on this side."

Riley's heart started to beat faster as she did a quick mental count of Team One. *Ugh, hockey sticks!* Grace was right. They had room for only one more player if the teams were going to be even.

"Come on!" Bree said, leading the way toward Team Two.

Riley looked longingly at Team One. Val was motioning for her to join them.

Riley stood, paralyzed, in the center of the ice.

She had to choose.

What was she going to do?

"Val wants us!" Envy whined, jumping up and down beside the console like a toddler who couldn't reach the countertop.

"But we promised Bree and Grace!" Joy insisted.

Anxiety's left eye twitched. "Joy, we have to let go of the past." Before Joy could stop her, Anxiety quickly tapped on the console. But something strange happened: the console didn't respond.

"Come on, Riley. Move!" Anxiety's voice shook. "Move those feet! Val's on Team One. You want to be on Team One. Let's go!"

When the console still didn't respond, Anxiety changed tactics and tapped the projection screen, bringing up an image of Riley playing with the Fire Hawks. A streak of red ran through her perfectly pulled-back hair. "Look! If we can use this camp to befriend the Fire Hawks, high school will be amazing!"

Still, Riley didn't move. She remained frozen in the center of the ice. The teams were fully formed except for an open spot remaining on Team One. Bree and Grace were waving for Riley to join them. Another player on Team Two noticed and began to shift toward Team One, making space for Riley so the teams would be even. Val gave Riley a confused look, one that said, *Are you coming or not?* It was now or never.

"She made a promise to her friends," Joy said confidently. This newbie might know a few nifty tricks, but she clearly didn't know their girl the way Joy did. "She's not going to break it."

Anxiety's hands stopped tapping the console. She stood very still.

"You're so right, Joy," she said.

Without another word, Anxiety walked over to the Sense of Self, grasped it, and yanked it off the base.

Everyone gasped as the light emanating from Headquarters dimmed and receded.

"What are you doing?" Joy cried, beside herself.

Riley, now with a blank and indifferent expression, turned to skate toward Val.

Joy sprinted at Anxiety and grabbed the Sense of Self. "No! You can't have that! Put that back!"

The two Emotions struggled over the Sense of Self until Joy pried it out of Anxiety's hands and placed it back on the pedestal. *"This* is Riley."

Riley's expression changed to concern as she turned to skate toward Bree and Grace instead.

Joy sighed in relief. Their girl was back.

"No, Joy!" Anxiety exclaimed. "You just don't understand! Please let me do this. I promise it's for the best!"

Before Joy could stop her, Anxiety zipped past and pulled the Sense of Self off the pedestal again. She pulled down the Back of the Mind tube and loaded the Sense of Self inside.

"Stop!" Joy shouted, desperately scrambling to reach her. "No! Don't!"

But it was too late. Anxiety pulled back the plunger and launched Riley's Sense of Self into the farthest reaches of her mind.

Joy sank to her knees. Sadness, Anger, Disgust, and Fear were too shocked and horrified to know what to say or do.

"No . . ." Joy whimpered.

Anxiety turned back to the console. "I know change is scary, but—but watch!"

Riley finally skated to Team One and stood in their ranks.

"Riley?" Bree and Grace, clearly hurt, stared at her.

"Teams all formed?" Coach Roberts called. "All right, let's get going."

Val smiled and put an arm around Riley's shoulders in a genuinely kind way, almost like she was taking her under her wing. "Welcome to our team, Michigan."

"That is *not* Riley!" Joy shouted, practically shaking with rage. For once she understood how Anger felt all the time.

"I know! It's a better Riley!" Anxiety's tone was elated, like she had just figured out the solution to all their problems. "We build her a new Sense of Self. A brand-new her!"

"A Riley who won't be alone next year!" Envy added. She scurried to the elevator platform and pressed the buttons to call the Belief System elevator to HQ. The double doors slid open.

Meanwhile, Anxiety walked over to the wall where fresh memory spheres were rolling in. She selected an orange one and replayed the memory of Val telling Riley she should join her team. She moved toward the elevator with the memory sphere in her hands.

"Whoa, whoa, whoa," Joy said. "Put that back! You can't go down there with that!"

She and the other core Emotions blocked Anxiety's path to the elevator.

"Over my dead flaming body!" Anger added for good measure.

Anxiety studied each of them. Her expression had gone strangely grim.

"I am truly sorry," she said at last. "I was so looking forward to working with you guys." She nodded to Embarrassment, and the hulking pink Emotion walked over and scooped up Joy and her friends in one fell swoop.

"Hey!" Joy struggled against Embarrassment's squishy yet strong arms. "What do you think you're doing?"

"Riley's life is more complex now," Anxiety continued matter-of-factly. "It requires more sophisticated Emotions than all of you. You just aren't what she needs anymore, Joy."

Joy felt as though she'd been hit in the stomach.

"How dare you, madam!" Fear exclaimed, sounding angrier than he had, well, ever.

"You can't just bottle us up!" Joy countered.

At that, Anxiety smiled. "Oh! That's a great idea!"

Anxiety called the Mind Police, and minutes later, several officers brought in a gigantic glass jar. Joy's stomach plummeted with a sickening feeling. Anxiety was going to bottle them up—literally.

"Wait!" Joy exclaimed, distraught. "No! You can't do this!"

"Where did those guys come from?" Anger fumed.

"Where did they even *find* that?" Disgust asked.

But Anxiety offered no explanations. She simply motioned for Embarrassment to do her bidding. The lumbering Emotion tossed Joy and her friends inside the jar, closed the lid, and poked a few air holes in the top. The Mind cops pushed the jar to the construction lift outside the windows of HQ.

"It's not forever," said Anxiety. "It's just until Riley makes varsity or until she turns eighteen. Or—or maybe forever. I don't know! We'll see!"

"She's all set," one of the cops said into a walkie-talkie. "Lower her down."

On command, the construction lift began lowering the jar to the ground.

The Emotions shouted in protest.

"Stop!"

"Let us out!"

"We don't belong here!"

"You can't do this, Anxiety!"

But within moments, they were gone.

Envy, Embarrassment, and Ennui looked at each other

nervously. HQ suddenly seemed large and empty with just the four new Emotions left.

"Let Operation: New Riley begin," Anxiety announced. She cradled the orange memory sphere. "Don't worry, Riley," she said reassuringly, watching the memory with Val replaying over and over. "You're in good hands." She stepped toward the elevator.

Ding!

The elevator doors whooshed open. The four new Emotions pushed and jostled their way out of the tight space into the cavernous Belief System.

"Okay, next time we take two trips," Ennui said, stretching and massaging her long arms.

Embarrassment stared in awe at the expanse of beautiful belief strings and memories. He plucked one of the strings.

I'm kind.

Embarrassment smiled. He was certain that was one of his favorite beliefs.

Envy wanted to know more about Anxiety's plan. "How

do we build a new Riley if it took the other Emotions thirteen years to build the old one?"

"Well, the good news is we're not starting from scratch," Anxiety said, gesturing to the existing belief strings. She didn't want to change Riley completely. Many of these beliefs made Riley the special person she was. But to Anxiety, there was always room for improvement. "And the better news is that Joy taught us how to cheat the system."

She held the orange memory sphere and knelt next to the pool.

"One belief at a time," she murmured.

"I wanna plant one," Envy whined.

"Next time," Anxiety said, placing the memory into the water. An orange belief string sprouted from the memory sphere and attached to the larger system.

"By the time we're done with this place, you won't even recognize it," Anxiety said. She plucked the new belief.

If I'm a Fire Hawk, I won't be alone.

Orange light pulsed from the Belief System up to the base of Headquarters. The other belief strings flickered. Anxiety knew if they had enough beliefs, the orange light would eventually envelop all of Headquarters. It would then lead to a new Sense of Self and a new Riley, who would be prepared for high school.

Anxiety couldn't wait to get started.

Chapter 13

Every muscle in Riley's body ached. There were muscles she'd never known she had that ached, thanks to one of the hardest training sessions she had ever been through in her life. Her misguided giggle in the locker room was a distant memory after the intense drills Coach Roberts had put them through. There was no doubt skills camp meant business, and those high school girls were *tough*. Every single Fire Hawk seemed to know how to perform complex maneuvers like they'd been born with skates on their feet.

And yet . . . Riley had done okay, she thought. She'd run every single drill they had, and she'd even helped set up a goal for Dani once. It had been hard, but at least she hadn't caused the players to have to skate lines anymore. Coach Roberts had even nodded approvingly in her direction at one point. That had to count for something, right?

The locker room was mostly empty now, except for a few players from Team Two who were finishing packing up their stuff. Bree and Grace were nowhere in sight. Riley breathed a small sigh of relief. She felt terrible remembering the looks of disappointment on their faces when she'd chosen Val's team instead of theirs. They hadn't said a word to her for the rest of practice.

Riley slung her bag over her shoulder and pushed through the red double doors.

"Hey! Riley!"

Uh-oh. Grace was standing there, with her arms crossed over her chest. Bree was next to her. They both looked upset, and Riley was pretty sure they'd been talking about her.

"Oh, hey, guys," Riley said.

Grace frowned. "Why did you do that?"

"Hmmm. They do not sound *très* happy," Ennui commented as she collapsed onto the couch.

The Emotions had returned to Headquarters from their quick field trip to the Belief System just in time.

Anxiety took a deep breath. Bree's and Grace's looks of confusion, disappointment, and betrayal were hard to ignore. She didn't want to hurt them—really, she didn't. Was this too harsh? Would they hate Riley forever?

Envy scurried to the console with a little step stool she'd made out of construction debris and used it to hop up so she could see. "What should we do?"

Anxiety tapped on the projection screen, bringing up the image of Riley skating with the Fire Hawks in high school. A streak of red ran through her hair. She looked happy and proud. More importantly, she looked like she *belonged*.

The one and only *Valentina Ortiz* had invited them to be on her team. How were they supposed to say no to that? It wasn't like they would have anyone else looking out for them at their new high school. This was their only option.

"We stay focused. We have bigger and better plans now," Anxiety said.

"Oooh." Envy watched the projection hungrily. "I like that."

On-screen, Bree had her arms crossed. "We all agreed to play on the same team. We fist-bumped. You never go back on a fist bump."

"I know," Riley replied. "It's just . . . Val asked me to join her team—"

"'Val'?" Grace raised an eyebrow. "What, are you guys on a nickname basis now?"

"Yeah, kind of." Riley bristled. "She's actually really nice."

"But this was supposed to be our last chance to play together," Bree insisted.

"You really left us hanging there." Grace was clearly bitter.

"I just . . . I figured . . ." Riley was struggling to find the words.

Anxiety brought up the projection of Riley as a Fire Hawk once more, reminding Riley of their true goal.

"I just figured I should get some time in with the team I'll be playing with next year," Riley said finally.

"But, Riley, it's nearly impossible to get on varsity as a freshman," Bree said, her tone matter of fact.

Grace nodded. "I know you want to be a Fire Hawk. But let's be real. Valentina Ortiz is the exception, not the rule."

"Are they making fun of us?" Anxiety exclaimed. "How

can they call themselves our best friends if they don't even believe in us?"

"You think I can't?" Riley snapped.

Bree looked at Grace. "I think we wanted to all play together one last time."

"Let me handle this," Ennui said. Her fingers tapped away in a rapid-fire sequence on her phone.

"Whatever. I'm going to go get something to eat," Riley said. She started walking off toward the cafeteria, which was open late especially for the skills camp.

"Wait, Riley! Don't be like that. We'll come with you." Bree hurried to match Riley's pace, and Grace followed, though she shuffled her feet in doing so.

"Forget about the teams." Bree clearly wanted to smooth things over. "At least we're still here together, right?"

Riley looked straight ahead. "I guess."

"Hey, maybe there will be funnel cake in the cafeteria," said Bree. "Or blue slushy?" She nudged Grace. "You never know when Lizard Tongue will strike."

Riley recalled a memory from the Get Up and Glow concert, of Grace slurping up her slushy and sticking out her electric-blue tongue. For the past month, she'd burst into a fit of giggles every time she thought about it.

But right then, she couldn't even bring herself to smile.

Chapter 14

"**Where** are you putting us?" Fear wailed as two Mind cops pushed the glass jar containing all the core Emotions down a long darkened hallway. They passed door after door sealed with heavy metal padlocks, keeping whatever was inside from escaping.

"The same place we keep all of Riley's secrets," one of the cops said matter-of-factly. "The Vault."

"We're *not* secrets!" Fear protested.

"Oh, yeah, yeah, yeah. 'We're not secrets. You're making a big mistake,'" the other cop said, making air quotes with his fingers.

His partner chuckled. "Never heard that before."

They finally came to an open safe door deep within the Vault, and the Mind cops shoved the jar inside. They sealed the door shut with a resounding thunk.

And just like that, the Emotions were trapped in a

pitch-black room, locked away in the depths of Riley's mind with no escape.

"We are suppressed emotions!" Fear wailed, turning on his emergency flashlight.

All at once, the Emotions began to panic.

"Let us out right now!" Anger flared.

"We don't belong in a jar!" Disgust cried.

"Poor Riley!" Sadness wailed.

Joy, pushing aside the panic she, too, felt rising in her chest, motioned for everyone to calm down. "No, no, no! Riley's going to be fine! Totally fine!" *She has to be,* Joy thought desperately. *She has to be. She's our girl!*

"Hey there!" A singsongy voice echoed in the darkness. "Do you know what we call that? Denial! Can you say 'denial'?"

All the Emotions whipped around. Using his flash-light, Fear illuminated a bucktoothed purple cartoon dog wearing a ball cap and a fanny pack.

"Ahhhh!" the Emotions screamed.

"Hi, friends!" the cartoon dog said, giving them a big rainbow wave. "Welcome! It's so good to have you here with us today!"

"Wait. . . ." Joy took a cautious step closer, squinting.

The dog looked familiar, like from a long-ago memory—
one Riley hadn't recalled since she was in . . .

"It's Bloofy!" Joy realized with a laugh.

"From that preschool show Riley used to like?" Disgust
asked.

Bloofy's bucktoothed grin grew wider. "That's *right*!
And here's a little secret. . . ." He leaned in closer to the
jar. "Riley *still* likes the show."

The Emotions watched, dumbfounded, as Bloofy broke
into a silly song and dance. *"Stomp like an elephant. Scurry
like a mouse. Make your way down to Bloofy's house!"*

"Please kill me," Anger said.

"Bloofy!" Joy begged with renewed urgency. "We're in
a real pickle! Could you help us get out of here?"

Bloofy turned to the blank safe wall and addressed it
like it was an audience. "Uh-oh! We're going to need *your*
help! Can *you* find a way out?"

"Who are you talking to?" Anger raised an eyebrow.

"My friends!" Bloofy gleefully gestured to the wall.
He turned his attention back to his make-believe studio
audience. "Do *you* see a key?" He paused for a long
moment. "Hmm. I don't, either."

"Okay. We're doomed," said Fear.

Someone else spoke through the darkness. "Indeed. Welcome to your eternal fate."

Fear turned the flashlight onto a towering man with flowing dark magenta hair and piercing green eyes. He wore a warrior's tunic and gleaming shoulder armor, like an anime hero.

Disgust gasped. "Lance Slashblade?"

"But he's a video game character," Sadness pointed out. "Why is he here?"

Lance Slashblade wielded his massive hero's sword and struck a pose. His long hair billowed out behind him though there was no wind.

"Yeah, I always thought Riley had a secret crush on him," Disgust explained.

Joy shook her head. "I never saw the appeal."

Lance Slashblade clenched an anguished fist against his chest. "I long to be a hero," he proclaimed, his voice filled with unfathomable angst. "But darkness haunts my past."

"Oh, I get it." Anger nodded appreciatively.

"I'm in a hundred percent," Fear agreed.

"I just want to brush his hair," Disgust said with a sigh.

Without warning, a third voice emanated from

somewhere within the safe. But this was no ordinary voice. Instead of words, it rumbled a deep, unsettling growl.

"Uh . . ." Fear quavered. "Who's that?"

"Oh!" Bloofy did a happy little tap dance. "That's Riley's Deep Dark Secret."

The outline of an enormous hooded creature with glowing eyes appeared behind Lance Slashblade.

Fear whimpered. "What—what is the secret?"

Lance Slashblade shook his head. "You don't want to know."

"Riley's secrets!" Joy suddenly announced, trying to take back control. "A rogue Emotion has taken over Headquarters. Now, if you could just open the jar—"

Bloofy cut her off with a wag of his finger. "Hey, kids! Let's learn some Latin! Do you know 'quid pro quo'?" He chuckled. "We get you out of that jar. Then *you* get *us* out of this safe!"

"No, Bloofy." Lance Slashblade's voice held the weight of a thousand sorrows. "Their destiny is not ours to change. We were all banished here—deemed unfit. Worthless."

"Don't you dare say that!" Disgust pressed her hands against the glass jar and gazed at him. "You do not deserve to be thrown away!"

"Uh, one second, Lance," Joy said, pulling Disgust aside. "Don't you remember his power move?" she whispered.

"Well, yeah," Disgust admitted, recalling that Lance Slashblade's special video game move was rolling along the ground like a little balled-up hedgehog. Whenever Riley had used it, she had lost. "But it's not his fault!" Disgust insisted. "The Curse of the Wretched Roll was placed on him because the High Spirits were jealous that the underworld princess had entrusted the Immortal Slashblade to him!"

Disgust wheeled back to Lance Slashblade with her hands against her heart. "You listen to me, Lance Slashblade! No one is totally worthless!"

"But I am a warrior cursed with a feeble attack." Lance buried his perfectly angular face in his hands. His hair billowed out again in a nonexistent breeze.

"Then you must make your curse your gift!" Disgust implored him.

Lance looked up at her. Their eyes connected. A renewed determination lit his expression. He sheathed his sword and took an attack stance. "Shield yourselves, my friends. For I . . . shall set you all *free*!" he declared.

Everyone watched with bated breath as the legendary

hero dropped to the floor and a purple halo illuminated him. He was preparing to do his special attack!

And then . . .

Lance Slashblade curled up into a tight little ball and rolled at the jar, feebly tapping into it again and again like a helpless hedgehog.

"Ugh!" he grunted pathetically with each tap. "Ugh!"

"Oh, boy," Anger said.

"Psst," Joy whispered to Riley's Deep Dark Secret. "A little help?"

Deep Dark Secret grumbled and struck the jar with a massive hand. The glass shattered in one blow.

"Great job, Dark Secret!" Bloofy praised him as the Emotions stepped out, free. "Now it's your turn to help us! My fanny pack has just the thing to get us out of here. Everybody say, 'Oh, Pouchy!'"

The Emotions looked at one another and shrugged. "Oh, Pouchy!"

In a burst of green sparkles, the fanny pack around Bloofy's waist unbuckled and spiraled into the air, revealing two round cartoon eyes and a huge zipper grin.

"Hi, everybody!" the fanny pack said in a squeaky voice. "I'm Pouchy!"

"Pouchy, we need to escape," Bloofy explained. "Do you have anything that can help us?"

"I have lots of items!" Pouchy chirped. "Which one do you think will work the best?"

Items magically began appearing beside Pouchy in the air.

"A tomato?" Pouchy squeaked as a red tomato popped into existence. "A frog? Or exploding dynamite?"

"Oh, for crying out loud." Anger grabbed the dynamite, lit the top with his flaming head, and threw it toward the safe door.

KA-BOOM!

The safe blasted open, freeing the Emotions and Riley's secrets.

"We did it, everyone!" Bloofy cheered. "Let's all sing the 'We Did It' song!" Bloofy took a deep breath.

"No time!" Joy said, stopping him. They needed to save Riley.

"Thank you, friends." Lance Slashblade swept into a deep, dramatic bow. "I must be leaving you."

"What about Dark Secret?" Sadness looked over Lance's shoulder at Riley's Deep Dark Secret, who lingered inside the busted safe.

Deep Dark Secret picked up the safe door from the

ground. "Not yeeeeeeeet." His voice faded as he slowly fit the door back into place, sealing himself inside.

"Yeah, that's probably best for everybody," Joy said.

Suddenly, a police whistle shrieked behind them.

"Hey!" shouted one of the Mind cops they'd seen before. He was now holding a steaming cup of coffee and a donut. "Who let you out? Get back in there!"

The Emotions gasped as a line of Mind cops sprinted around the corner and headed straight toward them.

"Oh, no!" Fear exclaimed.

"What are we going to do?" Disgust groaned.

Beside her, Lance Slashblade looked down at the small green Emotion, and his eyes burned with determination. He knelt in front of her.

"Oh, Disgusted One, as you once believed in me, I will now believe in myself."

Dropping his sword to the ground, Lance Slashblade curled into a ball once more.

The Mind cops stopped, weirded out.

"What—what's he doing?" one asked nervously.

Lance began a slow roll toward the cops. He missed them all, but he knocked into a mop as he passed by. It hit a cop on the head. That cop bumped into a second cop, who caused a third cop to spill his coffee, which made a fourth slip and fall into an open safe door. All the while, Lance continued rolling forward, not hitting a single Mind cop, but somehow causing each and every one to incapacitate themselves until they all accidentally locked themselves in a vault.

"Whaaa?" Sadness said in disbelief.

"Heh, heh, yeah!" Anger fist-pumped approvingly. "I love a good slapstick routine!"

"Oh, Lance." Disgust swooned.

Lance Slashblade rolled to the end of the hall. "Goodbye, friends!" His voice echoed as he rolled around a corner, vanishing from sight. "Hello, destiny!"

"Well, there's a lid for every pot," Joy said. Then she turned to the others. "Come on! We have to save Riley!"

Chapter 15

Headquarters was dark. Ennui lay snoring on the couch, her long purple arms draped lazily over the armrest, while Envy was curled up at her feet, snuggled under a blanket. Anxiety slept awkwardly in an office-style rolling chair, her head repeatedly lolling to one side before she straightened it up in her sleep, only for it to loll to the side once again in her restless slumber. Even in sleep, Anxiety vibrated.

Eventually the new Emotions would have their own beds, just like the core Emotions did. But Headquarters was still undergoing its overhaul, and in all the commotion, things like beds had taken a back burner. For now, sofas and rolling chairs would have to do.

At least it was peaceful. Riley was a sound sleeper, and thanks to her exhaustion from Coach Roberts's intense training session, she was deep in a dreamless sleep cycle.

Occasionally, Ennui's phone would buzz with a console update alert. But otherwise, Headquarters was quiet.

That is, it was until the emergency phone rang. Anxiety jerked awake, the pupils of her buggy eyes dilated in the darkness. She shook the cobwebs of sleep away. Ennui and Envy must have been sound asleep, because they didn't even stir. Anxiety picked up the phone.

"Uh, Headquarters," a Mind cop nervously said, "we have a situation."

"What is it?" Anxiety asked, her voice croaky.

"The, uh—the prisoners," the Mind cop said. "They, uh—they escaped."

All traces of grogginess drained from Anxiety as adrenaline kicked in. She vibrated with annoyance.

"I see," she said before hanging up. Then she turned her attention to the imageless projection screen, situated above the gently pulsing lights of the control console.

She had work to do.

"What do we do?" Fear exclaimed as the core Emotions raced down the stairs of the Vault. Even though they had busted out, it was only a matter of time before swarms of Mind cops would be on them again. How were they going to make it back?

"Those new Emotions have control of Riley!" Disgust gazed at Headquarters, which was slowly filling with orange light.

"Well, what are we waiting for?" Anger pounded a fist into his palm. "Let's go!"

"Whoa," Joy said, blocking Anger's path. "Where are you going?"

Anger was confused. "Back to Headquarters! To help Riley!"

"Riley's not up there," Joy said. "She's out *there*." She pointed toward the Back of the Mind, where they could see the tiny glowing dot of the Sense of Self on the horizon.

They'd been in tough spots before. They could do this. They just needed a plan, and plans started with first steps, and the first step was to get back their girl—the one Anxiety had banished to the Back of the Mind.

"We can't go back without her Sense of Self," Joy explained.

"You want us to go to the Back of the Mind?" Fear looked like his eyes were going to pop out. "Are you out of *your* mind?"

"But, Joy," said Sadness, "how will we get back if no one goes up to Headquarters?"

Just then, an alarm from the Vault went off, its blaring siren slicing through the moment of quiet. Their time was up. Joy began running in the opposite direction of Headquarters. Even though they still didn't understand the plan, the other Emotions followed.

"We need to get our Riley back before Anxiety makes a new one," Joy said.

"But how do we get there?" asked Disgust. "Do you even have a plan, Joy?"

"I bet Anxiety would have a really good plan," Fear said.

"A plan? Sure! Of course I do," Joy said, trying not to be offended by Disgust's and Fear's comments. "Anxiety's not the only one who can project the future. How hard could it be?"

The other Emotions looked at her doubtfully, but Joy pushed on. "First, all we have to do is . . . umm . . . follow the Stream of Consciousness!"

The Emotions nodded, picturing the river that flowed through Riley's mind, carrying all sorts of random memories and thoughts and objects.

"Then we take a nice, easy float all the way to the Back of the Mind!" Joy added.

"Oh! Where all the bad memories are!" Fear interjected. He remembered the few bad memories they had sent to the Back of the Mind using the tube.

"Exactly! And Riley's true Sense of Self!" Joy said. "We put her Sense of Self back. Then Riley will be Riley again." She imagined herself kneeling next to a crying Anxiety. "And then I tell Anxiety, 'Hey, don't worry so much anymore.' And she'll say, 'Wow, Joy, I never thought of that before! Thank you!' And then we hug and become best friends."

"And then I punt her into the dump," Anger added.

"What? No! Anger!" Joy admonished him.

"Okay, fine. No punting," Anger agreed.

"That's all great, Joy," said Sadness. "But how are we going to—"

"Get to the stream?" Joy interrupted. "Great question, Sadness! It's right over there!"

She led everyone to an area of Riley's mind called Long Term Memory, where long stacks of shelves, stretching as far as the eye could see, held countless memory spheres. Joy sprinted around the corner of a tall stack of memories, leading the Emotions . . . right into a dead end.

"Huh?" Joy said, confused. That hadn't been there the last time she and Sadness had been in Long Term Memory—at least not that Joy remembered. *Oh, no.*

"Uh, Joy? This is a dead end," Disgust pointed out super helpfully.

"Those are the worst kinds of ends!" Fear fretted.

"Everything is changing so fast." Sadness melted to the floor in an immovable pool of woe.

"So we're lost." Anger's flame smoldered.

"No!" Joy protested. "You're never lost if you're having . . . fun!"

Disgust gave her a condescending look as the police siren blared closer. "No one is having fun, Joy."

"Oh, come on." Joy gestured to Sadness, who was face down on the ground. "Look at Sadness! She's having a great time!"

"I thought you knew where you were going," Anger said.

"I do! I did—I just—*Ugh!*" Joy huffed in exasperation. Could these guys seriously be any more negative? It felt like she was the only one trying to keep things together. Didn't they get how hard she was trying? "I just need a moment. . . ."

But Disgust rolled her eyes. "She doesn't know."

"We're stuck here!" Fear wailed.

Anger shook his fist in the air. "Curse you, puberty!"

Joy was about to say something—she didn't know

what, but something very, very authoritative to refute the Emotions' attitudes, because they were most definitely *not* stuck if only they could all look on the bright side for one single time in their lives—when, suddenly, the world lit up.

"Oh! Riley's awake!" Sadness picked up her head from the ground, where she was still collapsed in a puddle.

"Something's not right," Joy said. She had a bad feeling in the pit of her stomach. What was Anxiety doing to their girl? They couldn't afford more delays. "Come on! We'll find another way!"

As the Emotions dashed toward the glowing speck of the Sense of Self in the distance, Joy hoped with everything she had that their girl would hang on for just a while longer.

"Don't worry, Riley," Joy murmured. "We're coming."

Chapter 16

The chill air stung Riley's cheeks as she skated around the empty rink. The sun hadn't even risen yet, and the sound of her skates slicing across the ice was the only noise in the deserted arena. Her muscles were still sore from the previous day's training, and they ached in protest as she warmed up, but this was the only way, she thought. She needed extra time on the ice. She needed to get better. Normally Riley was a sound sleeper, but that morning she'd woken up at four in her dorm room, thinking about what Grace and Bree had said, and she hadn't been able to stop their words from rattling around in her head.

It's nearly impossible to get on varsity as a freshman. Let's be real.

Riley *was* being real. Two days earlier it hadn't mattered as much if she made varsity in her freshman year. But now it did, because she wanted—no, needed—this chance to turn things around. To make them right. To go into high school knowing that a whole team of friends would have her back—that she wouldn't be alone.

I need to play better than ever, Riley thought, gathering a cart of hockey pucks and preparing to run an Iron Cross drill. *I need to prove I can do it. I need to make the team. Or else . . .*

She didn't want to think about the alternative.

Ennui groaned as she sat up from the couch, her lanky body stiff and awkwardly twisted. She stretched and blinked. Envy was no longer curled up at her feet. Instead, the little teal Emotion's blanket was discarded in a heap on the floor and she was standing across the room beside Anxiety, who was scribbling furiously at her whiteboard. The screen was on, and it was bright in HQ despite Ennui's phone saying it was still five in the morning.

"Okay, team. Let's get going," said Anxiety.

"Why did we wake up Riley so early?" Ennui groaned.

"Joy got out," Anxiety said shortly. "So we need to

speed things up." She turned and flashed Ennui a twitchy smile. "Pop quiz! We're here so Riley has what next year?"

Envy raised her hand like an eager student. "What everyone else has!"

"Close," Anxiety said, pointing her dry-erase marker at Envy.

"Detached discontent?" Ennui quipped.

"No!" Anxiety said.

Embarrassment lumbered over to them. There hadn't been a couch or a chair big enough for him to sleep on the previous night, so he'd slept on the floor. The large pink Emotion whispered something in Anxiety's ear.

"That's right!" Anxiety said. "Friends!" She flipped her whiteboard over and wrote the word in huge capital letters. "We *need* her to be a Fire Hawk so she has *friends*. That means we hit the ice early and we practice like we've never practiced before!"

Everyone turned to watch Riley running an Iron Cross drill on the ice. Her skates moved in perfect rhythm as she expertly swiveled the puck back and forth with her hockey stick.

"Aren't we already good at hockey?" Envy asked.

"We are, but we need to be great!" Anxiety insisted.

Riley shot the puck at the goal and missed.

"Every time we miss, we skate a lap around the rink." Anxiety pressed a button on the console.

Disappointed in herself, Riley grunted in frustration and skated a lap. Then she repeated the drill and lined up another shot. She missed.

"Hockey is not a game. It's a sport!" Anxiety proclaimed as Riley skated another lap.

Riley took shot after shot and skated lap after lap until, finally, she scored a goal.

"Wow! That was amazing!" Envy breathed.

"But we could be better!" Anxiety's face glowed in the light of the screen. "Let's run it again!"

On the ice, Riley reveled in her perfect shot for the briefest of moments before thinking about the previous thirty she'd missed.

Come on, Andersen, she thought bitterly. *Step it up. You should be making every single one of these shots. You're better than this.*

Grace's words floated through her head.

Let's be real.

"Oh, I'm real," Riley said to herself. "And I'm good. I just need to make sure that they see it every single time." She took a deep breath. She was going to practice this drill all morning if she had to. What time was it, anyway?

Riley turned to see if there was a clock on the arena wall, and she gasped.

She wasn't alone. Val was standing at the entrance to the rink.

"Aye!" Val waved and smiled. "I see I'm not the only one who likes to start early."

"You guys!" Anxiety smacked the other Emotions' shoulders enthusiastically. "It's Val! We had the same idea!"

"We're basically the same person!" Envy squealed. "We're going to be best friends!"

As Val skated up to Riley on the rink, she glanced at the net and noticed the number of pucks piled up around it. "Uh . . . how long have you been here?"

Embarrassment gently touched a button on the console, and Riley rubbed the back of her neck, her cheeks flushing pink. "I don't know," she said. "Maybe an hour? I just wanted to get in some extra ice time."

Luckily, Val didn't seem to think Riley's answer was weird. In fact, she smiled. "I'm the same way."

"Oh my gosh, she gets us!" Anxiety exclaimed.

Val put an arm around Riley's shoulder like a big sister. "See? I told the other girls you'd figure it out. You get what it takes to be the best."

In HQ, a tinkling sound emanated as a new orange memory sphere rolled out. Anxiety hummed with excitement as she rushed to collect it. Inside the shimmering sphere was an image of Val saying "what it takes to be the best."

"This is going great!" Envy cheered.

"Yup!" Anxiety agreed. "But we need Val to really like us."

"We should ask Val lots of questions!" Envy suggested. "People love talking about themselves!"

"So, what was freshman year on the Fire Hawks like?" Riley asked, shooting another puck into the goal.

"I mean, it was a lot of work," Val admitted. "But it's also how I met my best friends."

Anxiety could scarcely believe how well this was going. "Val is *sharing* things with us!"

"Hey." Val stopped on the ice like an idea had struck

her. "A few of us are just going to hang out tonight, order some food. You should come."

"Ooh," Envy cooed. "An exclusive invitation. We're going!"

"Really?" Riley asked Val, her voice filled with hope.

"Definitely." Val nodded. "It'll be fun."

Just then, all the remaining hockey players arrived, chatting and ready to hit the ice for practice. Some held half-eaten bagels in their hands, while others were still stretching and yawning. Val noticed Bree and Grace as they waved at Riley.

"You should bring your friends," Val said.

"Sure." Riley smiled, though her voice was a little tight.

"We are *not* sharing Val with them!" Envy's eyes flashed.

"And think about what you want to eat!" Val added.

"What do cool people eat?" Envy panicked.

Anxiety hurried to the memory wall and gathered an armful of orange spheres. "Envy, you're in the zone. Take the wheel. I'll be back."

Envy looked like she might launch into the air as she bounced up and down with excitement. "She picked me!" Envy squeaked. "Did you see that, Ennui? She picked me!"

Ennui rolled her eyes. "You care too much about things."

While Envy managed the console, Anxiety scurried to the Belief System elevator doors with her armful of orange memories. She took the long ride down.

After exiting the elevator, Anxiety strode to the stream and dropped the pile of orange memories into it, causing the water to ripple and radiate with an orange glow. New belief strings began to grow, stretching up, tall and strong.

Anxiety plucked a string, and Riley's voice echoed.

If I'm good at hockey, I'll have friends.

Anxiety exhaled in relief. "If we just stick to my plan, everything will be all right."

Chapter 17

"See! I told you I'd find it! The Stream of Consciousness!"

Joy panted as she and the other core Emotions came upon a wide river flowing with objects inspired by Riley's thoughts. Because Riley was thinking about what she wanted to eat at Val's hangout, the stream was full of Riley's favorite food. Joy followed its path with her gaze, watching as it flowed steadily deeper into Riley's mind. This waterway was their ticket to the Back of the Mind, where, they hoped, Riley's true Sense of Self was still intact. Joy cringed when she remembered the way Anxiety had ripped it from its pedestal. And now Anxiety's beliefs were growing like weeds, overtaking and weakening every belief strand Joy and the other core Emotions had worked so hard to help Riley build. Joy had to keep reminding herself that their girl was strong; Riley wouldn't let her old Sense of Self die away—not that easily.

Fear noticed all the food in the stream. "Whoa! Our girl is hungry!"

"Come on! Hop on something delicious!" Joy said. She noticed a slice of pizza floating past and grabbed it.

Disgust, Fear, and Anger took a seat on the pillowy crust.

"Ooh, deep dish," said Disgust. "That's nice."

"And it's still warm!" Fear added, settling into the bubbly cheese.

"First class all the way!" Joy cheered.

Before Joy hopped onto the pizza boat, Sadness stopped her. "But I've been trying to tell you. We can't take the tube back. Someone has to be at the console to recall us."

"She's right, Joy," said Disgust. "We'd be stranded."

Fear shook his head. "I bet Anxiety would've thought of that."

Disgust, Fear, and Anger jumped off the pizza back to shore.

Joy sighed, frustrated that there was a massive flaw in her plan. She watched the pizza slice float downstream. Then she noticed a recall tube nearby. She pointed at it. "Well . . . then someone's gonna have to crawl up that tube and go back to Headquarters and, at the right moment, recall us!"

Anger mashed his fists together. "Oh, I'll do it. I'll pound that orange—"

"I don't think so, punty," said Joy. Anger might mean business, but he might also forget his business of bringing them back while taking care of "punting" business.

"Then who?" Anger quietly smoldered.

They all looked at Fear.

"Ah . . . well, here's the thing . . ." Fear started nervously.

"You were never an option." Joy shook her head.

Fear sighed in relief. "Oh, good."

Next they looked at Disgust.

"Me, crawl through a tube?" Disgust pointed to herself indignantly. "In this? I don't think so."

Finally, they all stared at Sadness.

"Oh, no! Not me!" Sadness protested.

"Yes, Sadness! You could do it!" Joy insisted. "You know the console better than anybody! You've read the manuals cover to cover."

"I mean, you say that, but I know a lot less about Manual 28, Chapter 7, 'How to Recall Non-Memory Objects,' than most folks realize," Sadness pointed out.

Joy smiled. "See, all I heard there was 'Blah, blah, blah. I'm in, Joy!'"

She grabbed two walkie-talkies from a nearby pile of construction debris. They crackled to life when she hit the "on" switch. "We'll signal you when we've got Riley's Sense of Self. And then you bring us back!"

But Sadness trembled as Joy opened the hatch to the recall tube. The Mind cops' sirens grew louder.

"Ohhh . . ." Sadness groaned, looking like she would rather be anywhere in the world than there.

"Sadness, it's the fastest way back to Headquarters," Joy told her.

"Joy, I can't do it." Sadness shook her head vehemently. "I'm not strong like you."

Joy locked eyes with her friend. "I know you, Sadness. You *are* strong. I can't give you specific examples right now, but you got this!" With effort, Joy heaved Sadness up inside the tube.

Reluctantly, Sadness wiggled into the tube and began the long climb back to Headquarters. "Oh, yeah, I can do it . . ." she said, sobbing, as Joy closed the hatch.

"She'll be okay, right?" Joy asked Anger.

"Eh, fifty-fifty," Anger replied.

After more intense drills with the team, Riley took a water break with Val. Riley's stomach emitted a loud gurgle. Her eyes darted to Val.

"What was *that*?" Anxiety exclaimed.

"All that thinking about food made us hungry!" said Envy.

Val offered her protein bar to Riley. "Want a bite?"

Anxiety gasped. "We can't say no to Val!"

"But we hate those things," Envy whined. "They taste like sawdust!"

"We don't have a choice!" Anxiety gulped.

"Uh, sure," Riley said hesitantly. She took a bite, trying to hide a grimace.

Val smiled. "Tastes great, right?"

Joy, Anger, Fear, and Disgust returned to the Stream of Consciousness.

"Okay, everyone. Jump on the next cheesy, melt-in-your-mouth slice of pizza you see," Joy said.

But instead of Riley's favorite food drifting in the peaceful stream, Riley's most hated food swirled and crashed through raging rapids.

Joy gasped. "Tomatoes? Cauliflower? Asparagus? Riley hates this food! What are they doing to her up there?" She tried to pull the gross things out of the stream.

Anger grabbed a giant broccoli floret. "I don't know, but we have to go."

"No! No way am I stepping one foot on that," Disgust insisted.

"We have to!" Anger exclaimed. "Riley needs us!"

Disgust groaned. Reluctantly, she stepped onto the squishy broccoli. "Ew! Ew! Ew!"

Fear followed, but Joy was still busy plucking objects out of the stream.

"Joy! Come on!" Anger shouted.

Joy knew she had to let it go. She jumped onto the broccoli, and it tossed and turned in the swirling rapids.

"To the Back of the Mind!" Anger exclaimed.

Disgust gagged. "I think I'm going to be sick!"

Joy hadn't imagined sailing down the Stream of Consciousness on a broccoli floret. But as it swept them away to destinations unknown, she hoped it was taking them to the Riley they desperately needed to save.

Chapter 18

Riley breathed hard, her skates practically moving on their own as she powered forward on the ice, all her attention laser-focused on Val, who was maneuvering the puck along the left side of the rink. Riley was dead center, facing off against Bree, who stood goalie for Team Two.

Val snapped the puck to Riley, who lifted her hockey stick and walloped the puck straight past Bree's out-stretched goalie glove and into the net.

"Okay, Miss Riley!" Val cheered.

"Nice one, Michigan!" Dani called from across the ice.

Riley lifted her face mask and grinned at them both. From the corner of her eye, she saw Bree shaking her head, frustrated that she'd let the puck get by.

"All right, ladies!" Coach Roberts blew her whistle. She

jotted something down in a red notebook she'd been holding throughout camp and then nodded approvingly at the players. "Great day today. Take it easy tonight."

Riley exhaled, relaxing her aching shoulder muscles. She'd made it through day two. And more important, she'd made it to that night—her first time hanging out with the Fire Hawks! It was her chance to show them the true Riley—the Riley they could joke around with and have fun with and maybe one day even take selfies with, the same way she used to take selfies with . . .

She glanced at Bree and Grace, who were exiting the rink. She hadn't invited them to hang out, like Val had offered. But it wasn't Riley's job to make sure Bree and Grace knew *every* single detail about what was going on at camp, right? They could figure things out on their own, like Riley had been doing.

After changing back into her normal clothes, Riley joined the Fire Hawks outside the locker room.

"Hey, Michigan, how you holding up?" one of the girls asked as they all started walking.

"Oh, uh, pretty good, I guess," Riley said, suddenly aware that everyone's eyes had shifted to her. "I'm a little sore." Why was just talking making her heart pound?

"Yeah, Coach can be tough," another girl chimed in. "But you get used to it."

"Speaking of . . ." Dani pointed toward Coach Roberts's office, which was a small room she'd been borrowing from the main college coach during the skills camp. Coach Roberts wasn't inside. She must have already left for the evening. However, her red notebook lay in the center of the desk.

"There it is," Dani said in an ominous tone to Riley. "The red notebook."

Val rolled her eyes. "Don't say it like that. You'll freak her out."

Confused, Riley looked at them. "Why would it freak me out?" Lots of coaches had notebooks, didn't they? To write down plays and stuff?

"Everything Coach thinks about you is in there," Dani said. "The good *and* the bad. Whether she wants you on the team . . ."

"Or not," another Fire Hawk, named Sofia, added in a serious tone right beside Riley, causing her to shiver.

Some of the girls chuckled in good fun, but Val huffed. "You guys! Too much."

"What?" Sofia shrugged. "It's the truth. She's going to find out sooner or later."

"Come on. I'm starving." Val moved them along. "Whatever Coach Roberts has written in there, we'll never know anyway, right?"

The Fire Hawks continued down the hall, but Riley stayed back for a moment, staring at the notebook.

Coach had written something in there after Riley had scored the goal on Bree.

Could everything Riley needed to know really be sitting right there in one little red notebook?

"What do you think she's written about us?" Envy's eyes were wide as she studied the notebook on the screen inside Headquarters.

"I don't know!" Anxiety exclaimed. "Do you think it's bad?"

"What if she's made a list of all her favorite players and we're not on it?" Envy wondered.

"Or a list of all the worst players and we're at the top," Anxiety added.

"Or worse," said Envy, "we're not on either list, and we fade into obscurity!"

Anxiety felt her panic rising. "What if she wrote down flaws in our game that we didn't even know existed?"

Envy gasped. "What if she drew a caricature of our face just because she can?"

"Um, they are walking away," Ennui interrupted.

Riley pushed away her worries and caught up to the Fire Hawks. She walked with them through the tall redwoods on the way to the dormitory common area. Everyone was chatting and enjoying themselves, but Riley couldn't figure out what to say. Never mind that: she couldn't even figure out how to walk normally.

"Uh, why do our arms swing like this when we walk?" Anxiety vibrated as she noted that not a single other girl's arms were swinging the way Riley's were.

"Try to keep them still," Envy suggested.

Anxiety pressed a button on the console, and Riley's arms went stiff at her sides.

"That's *more* weird!" Anxiety cried.

"What do we do?" Envy fretted.

From her lounging position on the couch, Ennui sighed heavily. "What did you think pockets were for?" She tapped an icon on her console app, and Riley immediately shoved her hands into her pockets.

"Ah, nice one!" Anxiety said appreciatively.

Someone told a joke up ahead, and everyone laughed—except Riley.

"What are they laughing about?" Envy asked urgently. "Does anyone know what cool people laugh about?"

"I don't know." Anxiety shook. "We were too focused on the arms thing. Just pretend like we got the joke!"

A bit too forcefully, Anxiety pushed a console lever forward, and Riley let out an awkwardly loud laugh. Some of the Fire Hawks turned to give her an odd look.

Embarrassment face-palmed and hit the console, flooding it with pink.

Riley's cheeks flushed, and her laugh petered out as the Fire Hawks turned away.

Frustrated, Anxiety vibrated and tugged at her hair.

They just needed to play it cool. How hard was it to play it cool?

Chapter 19

In the depths of Riley's mind, the core Emotions continued their journey along the Stream of Consciousness. The river stretched on endlessly, and the Emotions struggled to balance on their very unstable broccoli boat. It didn't help that random objects bonked into them, threatening to topple them over. Anger, Fear, and Disgust bickered endlessly.

"Quit moving around!"

"You're making it worse!"

"I'm not moving. *You're* moving!"

"No, move left!"

"Get off me!"

"You're going to tip us!"

"I don't like this vessel," Fear whined.

"Well, that's all we have," Joy, unfazed, told him.

"How much longer until we get there?" Anger asked.

"We'll get there when we get there," Joy answered, remembering a phrase Riley's dad said often on long car trips.

"I bet Anxiety would know how long," said Fear. "Down to the minute."

Joy gritted her teeth, refusing to take the bait. "Well, she just knows everything, doesn't she?"

"Look, I don't like her words," Fear clarified. "I don't like her actions. I just—I think I could change her."

"You know what?" Joy said, her frustration uncharacteristically threatening to bubble over. Then she looked at each one of them before taking a deep breath and pushing her frustration down even deeper than before.

"*We are so close!*" she exclaimed with a forced smile. "Let's just be quiet until we get there!"

The dormitory common area reminded Riley of a large but cozy ski lodge as the Fire Hawks spread out on the various couches and armchairs. The ceiling's wooden beams were hewn from richly stained redwood, and there was even a stone fireplace. A few study tables were nestled along the walls with little reading lamps, and a vending machine by the exit to the dorm rooms offered the promise of soda and candy (though, unfortunately, the only item in stock was water). In the center of the room was a foosball table, where some of the Fire Hawks were playing a game.

Riley was glad that the Fire Hawks had ordered pizza for dinner. She'd even managed to nab a garlic breadstick before they were all gone. But her first big hang with the group was proving awkward. Riley wished she had something to contribute to their conversations, but it seemed almost like they were speaking a different language, with their talk of driver's permits and social media scandals and advanced course selections. Every now and again someone mentioned one of the skills camp drills, and Riley nodded enthusiastically, ready to chime in. But just as swiftly, the topic shifted, and Riley swallowed the breath she'd taken to speak. She couldn't help feeling like a third wheel.

Then someone turned on a song that Riley had never heard before.

"Aw, heck yes!" Val exclaimed. "I love this song."

"Yeah, this is going on my birthday playlist," Dani replied.

"Oh, will you share that with me?" Val asked. "I still listen to the one you made last year."

A girl named Ally turned to Riley. "Who's your favorite band, Michigan?"

Riley exhaled in relief. This was an easy question. "Oh, Get Up and Glow!" she answered confidently. "They're awesome!"

"Get Up and Glow!" Val exclaimed. "I was all over them in middle school."

Dani scoffed. "Are you serious?"

"Yeah, I was a Glow Girlie," Val said with a laugh.

Riley gasped. What had she done?

"In middle school?" Anxiety said. "As in, when Val was a little kid? Does Val think *we're* a little kid? Do they *all* think we're a little kid?"

Embarrassment went to drive, but it was too much. He fainted.

"We need a band they think is cool. Not one we actually like!" said Anxiety.

"We need to recall everything we know about music!" Envy added.

Anxiety urgently hit a flashing recall button on the console.

Unbeknownst to Anxiety, deep within the recall tube, Sadness continued her long crawl back to Headquarters. Her sobs had dried out, mainly because she had to maintain her energy for the trek. If only there were a way to speed things along. But there wasn't a magical propulsion system within the tube unless someone recalled a memory from that specific passageway. And that was a one-in-a-million chance. So along Sadness crept, alone with her thoughts in the cramped, empty tube. . . .

Suddenly, a rumbling sounded somewhere behind her. Sadness turned just in time to see a slew of memory spheres hurtling toward her as the recall tube suction sprang to life.

"Uh-oh . . ." she said.

In Headquarters, Anxiety watched impatiently as a massive pile of memory spheres burst out onto the floor. There must have been some punk rock in there somewhere, because she could have sworn she heard a scream as the spheres arrived. One memory dropped into Riley's recall projector. Anxiety hoped it was a good band. They all listened closely to hear what Riley had recalled.

TripleDent Gum will make you smile! The jingle echoed throughout HQ.

"Ugh! Get that out of there!" Anxiety cried.

Embarrassment (who had woken up from fainting) and Envy turned back to the pile and hurried to search for a better song. Embarrassment seemed a little distracted for some reason, probably because he was still discombobulated. But Envy was on the case, tossing sphere after sphere to the side.

"Keep searching!" Anxiety demanded. "Our future depends on a better answer!"

"That's the best we have!" Envy groaned. "These are mostly jingles and Dad's yacht rock."

Dani's voice emanated from the screen. "You don't still like them, do you?" She was looking right at Riley.

"What do we do?" Anxiety panicked. "If we don't like their music, we have nothing to offer these girls. We'll be outed as the imposter we so obviously are."

With a deep, dramatic sigh, Ennui finally stirred from her lounging position on the couch. She stretched and cracked her knuckles. "Pardon. *Excusez-moi.* I've been waiting my whole life for this very moment."

Anxiety, vibrating with terrified nerves, watched as Ennui sauntered over and pressed a single console button.

"Oh, yeah, I *loooooove* Get Up and Glow," Riley said, her voice dripping with sarcasm. She wasn't sure how the idea had come to her; it was almost like she was being sarcastic by instinct. But miraculously, a couple of the Fire Hawks chuckled, and Riley grinned. It had worked! She'd covered up her mistake.

"Oh, yeah, Get Up and Glow is *soooo* awesome," she said, overly dramatic again.

The Fire Hawks laughed now, enjoying the joke. Even Val seemed to get that Riley had just been messing around about liking Get Up and Glow, even though, well, Riley *did* like them. But there was no way she would ever admit to that again. No way, nohow.

"Riley, what are you talking about?"

Bree's voice startled Riley from across the room. Riley turned to see Bree and Grace arriving, carrying sandwiches from the college cafeteria.

Bree stared at Riley in surprise. "You love Get Up and Glow."

"My mom literally just took us to their concert," Grace added. She sounded more annoyed than surprised.

Riley felt her heart race again. She was caught in a lie. *Hockey sticks!* Why had Bree and Grace come in right then?

"Well, yeah. I mean, sure, but—"

"But what?" Grace pressed her. "We had a great time."

Riley eyed the Fire Hawks. They were all watching her. Every single one of them was watching her.

So she did the only thing she could think of to save face.

"Yeah, we had a *greaaat* time." Riley dramatically slipped back into her sarcastic tone.

The Fire Hawks laughed again at Riley's performance. And Riley leaned into the moment.

"Yeah, best night of my *liiiiife.*"

Now some of the Fire Hawks had tears from laughing so hard. *This is working,* Riley thought. *They like my jokes!*

But Bree and Grace didn't look amused. Not at all.

"Well, this has been hilarious," Grace said curtly.

"But we're gonna go," Bree finished.

They each shot Riley an icy look before turning to leave.

"Ennui, that was inspired!" Anxiety bubbled in Headquarters. "Masterwork!"

Ennui polished her phone on her shirt and returned to the couch. "I know."

A memory sphere rolled out, replaying the memory of the Fire Hawks laughing at Riley's jokes. "See?" Anxiety chirped. "As long as we like what they like, we've got all the friends we need!"

Bree's and Grace's annoyed expressions hadn't escaped Anxiety's notice. She had never before seen them give Riley that look, almost as if they didn't even like her. Maybe the Emotions had overdone the sarcasm. Anxiety hadn't meant to make Bree and Grace so mad. Should Riley apologize?

Anxiety eyed the Fire Hawks on the screen. She couldn't lose focus.

"They're our future," she murmured. "As long as we do everything we need to do to make them like us, we'll be okay."

Chapter 20

Anxiety and the other new Emotions had no idea that Riley's sarcasm had reverberated across the Mind World.

"I think we're almost there," Joy promised the others. The Stream of Consciousness current was moving faster now, and Joy watched as they passed half-constructed structures on either bank of the river. The Mind Workers were busy back in that part of Riley's mind, though what they were building wasn't exactly clear. Everything looked rather abstract and unfinished—like half-formed thoughts.

Joy wasn't actually sure how much farther they needed to go, but she needed to be a leader right then for Riley's sake, and that meant keeping everyone's spirits up. "I can almost see the Back of the Mind!"

Suddenly, Riley's voice echoed around them. It seemed to come from high above.

"Oh, yeah, I loooooove Get Up and Glow."

"Riley?" Joy whispered. What was going on?

The water rippled around them, and a low rumble shook their boat. Ahead, the ground split into a giant chasm, and water from the Stream of Consciousness spilled right through. They were headed straight for it!

"Ahhh!" screamed the Emotions.

"Abandon ship!" Joy shouted.

Everyone leapt for the nearest riverbank and grabbed hold of anything to keep themselves from floating over the colossal waterfall. Anger and Disgust held tight to Fear and made it to dry ground, but Joy was the last to jump, and she just missed the bank. With a cry, she grabbed the edge of the chasm and barely kept herself from dropping into the abyss.

"Joy!" Disgust shouted.

Joy watched as their broccoli boat plummeted over the edge, splashing down into the depths below. Even amid the chaos, Joy recognized that the multicolored splash pattern looked like the one in Riley's Belief System.

"Give us your hand!" Anger yelled as he, Disgust, and

Fear formed a chain to reach her. With adrenaline-fueled effort, they hoisted Joy to safety.

"Are you okay?" Disgust asked.

Joy nodded, barely able to speak because she was breathing so hard.

"What *is* that?" screamed Fear.

A nearby Mind Worker ran up to them. "That's a Sar-chasm. Riley's a teenager. This could open for miles! Run for your lives!" Then he dashed away.

"Sar-chasm?" Disgust repeated, confused.

Above, Riley's voice echoed again. *"Oh yeah, Get Up and Glow is my faaaaavorite band."*

"But she loves Get Up and Glow," Joy said, worried. "She has all their albums!"

"What's next, Anxiety?" Anger shouted toward Headquarters. "First our birth state, now our music! Is anything good enough for you?"

Fear began pacing in circles. "What now? If we can't follow the stream, we don't know where we're going! If we don't know where we're going, we can't follow the stream! It's an endless loop of tragedy and consequence!"

"Or we could just go ask those guys." Joy pointed to two Mind Workers operating a crane on the opposite side of the massive canyon.

"Oh, yeah, or that," Fear said.

Together, the Emotions waved wildly to get the Mind Workers' attention.

"Boy, are we lucky we ran into you guys!" Joy shouted.

"Please, we really need your help!" Fear cried.

"I bet you're the best crane crew in the world!" Disgust added, trying to butter them up.

On the other side of the Sar-chasm, the Mind Workers paused their crane when they heard the Emotions' shouts.

"Boy, are we *luckyyyyyy* we ran into you guys!" Joy's voice echoed, but because of the Sar-chasm, its tone sounded super snarky.

"Huh?" One of the Mind Workers raised an eyebrow.

"We *reaaallllly* need your *helllp*," Fear called.

The Mind Worker looked at his companion. "What's their problem?"

Then came Disgust's voice. *"I bet you're the bessssst crane crew in the worrrrld."*

The Mind Workers frowned. "Wow. Those guys are jerks."

"They're not even going to answer us?" Anger huffed, perturbed. "Wow. Those guys are jerks."

Riley's voice echoed again. *"Yeah, we had a greeeeeeat time."*

Another rumble erupted and the chasm widened.

"How are we going to get across if it keeps getting bigger?" Disgust asked.

"What would Anxiety do?" Anger wondered.

Fear nodded. "I think she'd probably build a bridge of some sort using found objects. She's so resourceful."

Joy took a breath and surveyed the situation. The truth was she didn't really have a clue how they were going to get to the Back of the Mind now. But the absolute worst thing they could do was stop, and if the others didn't have faith in her to lead them, that was exactly what was going to happen. Joy had to be the beacon of hope for everyone. She had to be the one to keep them going, for Riley's sake.

"Well, I can't do that," she admitted. "So we're just gonna have to walk around it! The long way—which is the best way!" When they all looked at her dubiously, she added, "A little exercise never hurt anyone."

"Are you sure about this?" Anger asked.

"Yep!" Joy said with a forced smile. "Stretch those hammies! Let's go!"

"Well, I'm gonna go to bed." Val stood up from her armchair in the common area and stretched.

"Oh, really?" Riley asked, a little bummed. Some of the Fire Hawks were starting another round of foosball, but Riley wasn't sure she should stick around if Val wasn't there.

"Yeah, it's late," Val said. "Plus you'll want to get some sleep before tomorrow's scrimmage."

Riley blinked. "What scrimmage?"

"It's just something Coach always does on the last day," Val explained.

"It's how Val made the team as a freshman," Dani added, spinning her foosball players to knock the ball into her opponent's goal.

"What? Don't tell her that," Val said, shooting Dani a look.

"Val scored two goals," Dani continued, scoring a foosball goal of her own for emphasis. "No freshman had ever done that."

"Dani, stop," Val warned her. Riley couldn't tell if Val was embarrassed by the accolades or if the scrimmage the next day was actually a really big deal.

"Technically, it's not your tryout for next year," Ally chimed in, grabbing a cold slice of pizza from one of the boxes. "But it basically is."

Yikes! There was no doubt now. The scrimmage *was* a big deal. Riley's mind started to race with a thousand questions.

Val must have seen that Riley was a little freaked out, because she put a hand on Riley's shoulder. "You'll do great. Just be yourself." Then she offered a fist bump.

"Did you hear that?" Anxiety hummed with nervous energy. "We could become a Fire Hawk tomorrow!"

Anxiety and the other Emotions in HQ couldn't believe it. They had less than twelve hours to transform Riley into the newer, better version of herself to impress Coach *and* the Fire Hawks.

"But how do we be ourself if our new self isn't ready yet?" Envy wondered. She glanced toward the empty pedestal.

Anxiety turned to the wall of orange memories that had rolled into HQ. "Then let's move these babies downstairs."

Together, Anxiety and Envy scooped up armfuls of

the orange memory spheres to carry down to the Belief System. Unseen by either of them, Sadness, who had toppled in with the overload of music memories earlier, spied them from her spot in a hidden corner.

"Poor Riley," Sadness whispered.

And unseen by Sadness, Embarrassment was watching *her*, his hood drawn so tightly it nearly covered his whole face. He'd spotted the little blue Emotion when she'd first come in with the recalled memories, but he hadn't said anything. He commiserated with Sadness; even though they'd met for only a short bit before, she seemed to get him. He had a feeling she really wanted what was best for Riley. He knew keeping her presence a secret would get him in trouble with Anxiety. And yet he had a feeling he should—at least for now.

Chapter 21

Days. It felt to the core Emotions like they had been traveling for days, trekking along the unending precipice of the Sar-chasm. In reality, it had been only a few hours. But their legs burned, their heads pounded, and each one of them was pretty sure they now knew how physically drained Riley felt after a week's worth of hockey practice. Yet finally, they reached the end of the Sar-chasm and were able to walk around to the other side.

"There! We did it!" Joy panted.

"My quads burn with the heat of a thousand suns," Fear said, collapsing dramatically.

"See? Exercise!" Joy said brightly even as her own muscles screamed in protest.

"I can't see Riley's Sense of Self anywhere!" Anger shouted.

Joy gazed at the reverse trek before them on the opposite side of the chasm. "Don't worry. We'll just double back the same distance we just walked."

"*Uggghhh*," the other Emotions groaned. But they followed Joy. They followed her straight into . . .

Bonk.

A wall. On the other side of the Sar-chasm was a wall blocking their return path.

"Oh! Good news!" Joy laughed a little hysterically. "There's a wall! But you know what they say: so what!"

Exhausted and without any other options, the Emotions followed Joy along the wall leading even deeper into Long Term Memory. Neither Joy nor Sadness had been that far into the depths of Riley's mind.

"We're getting deeper and deeper in, Joy," Anger said.

"Great observation!" Joy said cheerily. "Who wants to sing a song?"

"I know a song," Disgust replied. "It's called 'I Give Up.'"

Joy forced a smile so wide she looked like a bizarre mannequin. None of them got it, did they? None of them understood *how hard* she was working to simply keep it together and lead them to the Back of the Mind in a desperate attempt to save their girl.

"Or . . . let's play the quiet game!" Joy said a little too loudly. "One, two, three, *hush*."

Anger ignored her. "I haven't seen Riley's Sense of Self since we passed that new Procrastination Land."

"That place was weird," Disgust said. "The sign said 'Coming Soon,' but no one seemed to be working on it."

"What's 'procrastination' mean?" Fear asked.

Anger shrugged. "We'll look it up later."

As they reached another set of shelves, Joy spotted two Forgetters. They were Mind Workers who vacuumed up old memories that Riley didn't need to remember anymore.

"Excuse me," Joy said to the Forgetters. "Can you help us? We're—" She stopped as she noticed the memories they were vacuuming. "Wait, are you—Is that Bree and Grace? We can't forget about them."

One of the Forgetters, named Paula, barely even looked at Joy and the Emotions. "Sorry, the job's the job."

"And our job is to follow orders from Headquarters," said the other Forgetter, named Bobby.

"But those are Riley's best friends," said Joy.

"That's not what we heard," said Paula. She held up a paper called *The Rumor Mill* with the headline BREE AND GRACE GET UP AND GO . . . AWAY!

Joy was horrified.

"Now if you'll excuse us," said Bobby, "we've got a job to do." He aimed the vacuum at the shelf, but he and Paula suddenly stopped.

"Wait, what were we doing?" asked Paula.

"I don't remember," said Bobby.

Paula and Bobby eventually moved on to another shelf, completely forgetting their interaction with the Emotions.

Disgust sighed. "This is useless. Real Riley might be out there somewhere, but we're never going to find her!"

"No, I can find her," Joy insisted. "I just need to get a better view."

Just then, she spotted a ray of hope—the one thing that could get them out of their impossible situation. It was a freestanding construction lift meant for carrying Mind Workers to the top of the tall Long Term stacks. And it was unattended, meaning anyone could ride it, like four rogue Emotions. . . .

Desperately, she pressed the control buttons to bring

it to life. Aside from a few creaks and groans, nothing happened.

"Okay, well, this isn't working." Joy could feel one of her eyes twitching, like Anxiety's had the other day. Before they'd been kicked out of their home. Before everything had gone wrong. She swallowed hard, her mouth dry. "And that's fine," she said. "Everything's fine."

"Joy, face it," Anger said. "You don't know what you're doing."

"I know it seems like that now," Joy countered. "And also earlier. And also back in Headquarters, but—"

Disgust shook her head. "I say we cut our losses and walk back. This is hopeless."

"This whole trip is just a series of deader and deader ends," Fear agreed.

"Ever since that Puberty Alarm went off, nothing around here works the way it's supposed to," Anger added.

"I don't even recognize this place anymore." Disgust sighed. "It's light outside at one in the morning!"

"I have *never* been inside so many jars in my life!" cried Fear.

Joy could feel herself losing it. *Keep it together,* she mentally urged herself. *Keep. It. Together.*

"Riley's Sense of Self is lost," Disgust said. "We are never getting back to Headquarters."

"And if Joy can't see that," Anger said, "well, then, she's *delusional.*"

That was the end of Joy's patience. One too many jabs, one too many protests, one too many moans and groans and whines and cries and *why was she the only one trying here?*

"Of course I'm delusional!" Joy exploded. "Do you know how *hard* it is to stay positive all the time? When all you folks do is complain, complain, complain? Jiminy mother-lovin' toaster strudel! Do you think I have all the answers? Of course I don't!"

Anger, Fear, and Disgust stared at her, taken aback. Joy was never that out of control.

"I know we're not getting out of this!" Joy shouted, flooding with regret at the reality of those words. "Anxiety is right: we're not sophisticated Emotions. We can't even find the back of our own mind!"

Exhausted, Joy collapsed beside the defunct lift. In a weird way, it was a relief to finally express her pent-up desperation. But on the other hand, it made it that much more definite: this was a hopeless cause. The chances of finding Riley's old Sense of Self and getting it back to HQ in time were one in a million. Their poor, poor girl. What would happen to her?

"The truth is Riley doesn't need us as much as she needs them," Joy said sadly. "And that hurts. It really hurts."

Silence fell over the friends for a moment, with just the distant hammers of Mind Workers building something somewhere echoing around them.

"Joy," Anger began, "you've made a lot of mistakes. *A lot*. And you'll make a whole lot more in the future. But if you let that stop you, we might as well lie down and give up now."

Joy looked up at him.

"Well, actually, that does sound kind of nice," Fear mused.

Disgust flicked him on the nose.

"Ow! What?"

Joy smiled. Anger smiled in return and held out his hand. "Come on."

The reassurance in his voice made Joy feel like she was about to cry. She took his hand.

Anger nodded and then approached the Forgetters.

"Excuse us," he said with authority. In one quick motion, he snatched the vacuum from their hands.

"Hey! You can't use that!" Paula exclaimed.

"Sure we can," said Anger.

"Yeah, you told us we could use this whenever we wanted," added Disgust.

"We did?" asked Bobby.

Disgust nodded. "You must have forgotten."

"Oh. Oh yeah," said Paula.

"That does sound like us," Bobby agreed.

Anger, Fear, and Disgust mounted the hose.

Anger turned to Joy. "Hop on."

Joy climbed aboard just before Anger flipped the vacuum switch to reverse.

Ploom! Dozens of memory spheres shot out, propelling the team into the air.

"Ahhhh!" shouted the Emotions.

With a thud, they landed on top of the Long Term stacks. They were a bit rattled but not much worse for wear.

"There it is!" Fear cried.

It was the Sense of Self!

Seeing the glowing beacon filled Joy with hope. She

looked at her friends and felt a rush of gratitude as they each nodded in turn.

"Go ahead," Anger told her confidently. "We're right behind you."

Riley sat on the bed in her dorm room, holding the Get Up and Glow limited edition jacket Bree and Grace had gotten her for her birthday. She didn't know why she'd even brought it to camp, since it was summer. But in the rush to shove everything into her suitcase the other morning, she'd rolled it up and stuffed it in, thinking maybe she might be chilly if they had downtime on the ice.

Riley cringed, remembering the way Bree and Grace had looked at her earlier. She really hadn't meant for them to overhear her making fun of Get Up and Glow. It wasn't anything against them at all, but she could tell from the looks on their faces that they had taken it that way. What a mess. Maybe she should go talk to them.

And . . . tell them what? That she was pretending to like the stuff the Fire Hawks liked so they would like her? That sounded pathetic, even though Riley knew it was *exactly* what she was doing. But it wasn't like she had time to get to know them the way she'd gotten to know Bree and Grace over the past year. Things were complicated now. Riley had to build a new team around herself, and for what it was worth, the Fire Hawks seemed really nice. That Ally girl had even mentioned Riley could be playing with them the next year, which meant they believed in her! More than Bree and Grace did, anyway.

She thought about the pizza party they'd just had and how she'd cheered on Dani in her final foosball match and how the girls had all waved good night before heading off to their dorms, like . . . friends.

Bree and Grace knew Riley better than anyone else in the world. They knew what her favorite soda was and that she had a fear of snakes, and they knew about that one time when she laughed so hard that her sports drink spewed out of her nose. But Riley liked being with the Fire Hawks, too. Hanging out with them made her feel like a winner. Her dad said she would knock the coach's skates off. With the Fire Hawks, she could do that.

"Ugh." Riley balled up the jacket and tossed it back into her suitcase. She didn't want to think about all that stuff right then. It was too confusing. Instead, she leaned back on her pillow and closed her eyes, images of laughing

with the Fire Hawks over pizza replaying in her mind. That was a good memory—one worth dreaming about.

"This is great." Anxiety rubbed her hands together. "The Fire Hawks have accepted us. *But* if Coach doesn't put us on the team, none of that matters." She looked at the screen—Riley was just beginning to drift off—and she began pressing buttons on the console.

"Tomorrow is everything," Envy agreed.

"Which is why we're going to need more help!" Anxiety declared. She glanced at Ennui, who lazily tapped away at her phone.

"Ennui, are you paying attention?" Anxiety snapped.

"Non," Ennui replied without looking up.

Anxiety rolled her eyes and turned to Embarrassment. "Embarrassment? How about you?"

Embarrassment didn't respond. He was preoccupied with watching some memory from the memory wall.

"Embarrassment? Hello?" Anxiety said. Then she let out a disgruntled sigh. "Ugh, never mind."

Embarrassment had heard Anxiety talking to him. But he couldn't pull his eyes away from the memory sphere he held in his hands. It showed the moment Bree and Grace had given Riley the icy look and walked away.

"Well, this has been hilarious."

"But we're gonna go."

Embarrassment hugged his hoodie a little tighter around himself. He wasn't sure how to feel about the memory. Riley had saved herself from being embarrassed in front of the Fire Hawks. But meanwhile, she'd done something worse. She'd felt ashamed in front of Bree and Grace. Anxiety might not see it that way. But he did.

He was about to walk over to the console when he heard a soft clunk in the construction debris behind him. Curious, he peeked under a demolished I beam. He gasped.

Sadness was hiding right there! She crouched, frozen, realizing she'd been caught.

Embarrassment looked at the other Emotions and then back at Sadness. None of them had spotted her.

Sadness gazed up at him with wide, watery eyes. "Shhh," she whispered.

She was trusting him. Why was she trusting him? Perhaps for the same reason he hadn't sounded the alarm when he saw her sneak in. He couldn't help feeling like he and Sadness understood each other.

Embarrassment reached out, and Sadness shrank back, probably thinking he was going to nab her. Then he shifted a pile of books in front of her so she was fully hidden. Sadness peeked out and smiled before ducking down behind the books. And under his hoodie, Embarrassment smiled, too.

Meanwhile, Anxiety was furiously at work over the console. She popped up her projection laptop, and it glowed to life. "All right, guys, it's going to be a long night." She chugged an energy drink and crushed the can. "Let's get the team ready."

Chapter 22

The Sense of Self glowed in the distance, its light growing closer even though the core Emotions still had a long way to go. They had finally reached the end of the Long Term stacks, and they came upon a colorful entrance to what looked like a theme park.

"Imagination Land!" Joy exclaimed. She and Sadness had been there once before, when they'd been lost during their first adventure together, but unlike at the Vault or the Stream of Consciousness, there was nothing scary here. Imagination Land was a wonderful place filled with whimsy and color and fun. "Oh, you guys are going to love it." Joy led the way. "There's French Fry Forest and Cloud Town and—"

She stopped short, taking in her surroundings. Imagination Land might have still been there, but it was *not* the same.

"Whoa, this place has changed," Joy said. Gone were the balloon animals riding sparkling waterslides and the gummy bear parades. Instead, there were fashion boutiques and movie star posters and even a mountain with the faces of four boys, one of which looked like Lance Slashblade, carved into it.

"That must be . . . 'Mount Crushmore'?" Joy said, reading a plaque at the base of the monument.

"*Those* are her top four?" Fear asked doubtfully.

"The only one that matters is Lance," Disgust said dreamily.

"Well, at least they got his good side," muttered Joy.

"*Every* side is his good side," Disgust said with a sigh.

A series of tabloid leaflets drifted down around them, scattered by the turbines of an old-timey windmill nearby. It was the Rumor Mill, which Joy remembered from Forgetter Paula's article about Bree and Grace.

Some Mind Newsies were distributing more pages nearby. "Extra! Extra! Read all about it! Piping hot rumors right off the Mill!"

Disgust grabbed one of the pages. "Abbie R.'s been texting Mike T., but Mike T.'s been flexing for Sarah M."

"I knew it!" said Fear with a gasp.

"Where's the journalistic integrity?" Anger grumbled.

Joy picked up another paper. "'Val laughs at Riley's jokes. But did she mean it?' Ugh! Why is Riley worrying about that?" She crumpled up the paper and tossed it aside.

Then she noticed a large building in the distance. "Oh! Fort Pillowton's still here! This is a really good place to jump around. And it even got bigger!"

"And . . . orange," Disgust said. She then noticed some Mind Workers pushing a cart of office supplies inside the fort.

"What is it?" asked Joy.

"Everything else here has changed," said Disgust. "Why is that still here?"

Curiosity and concern getting the better of them, the Emotions pushed through the poofy orange pillow wall. Joy gasped. Inside was a massive room of cubicles, each one occupied by Mind Workers furiously drawing pictures and scanning them into machines that projected the images onto screens around the room. And in the center was the biggest screen of all, showing none other than Anxiety.

"We need to help Riley prepare!" she commanded the workers. "Now's the time to send up every possible thing that could go wrong."

The workers scribbled furiously, sending their projections up to the screens.

"We're looking to the future," Anxiety continued. "Every possible mistake she could make." She noticed a blank screen. "Come on, Seventeen! I'm not seeing anything from you!"

A stressed Mind Worker scrambled to complete the projection.

"Riley misses an open goal. Coach writes about it in her notebook," said Anxiety. "Yes, great! I love the aggressive underlining. I need more like that!"

The core Emotions watched in dismay as projection after projection popped up on the screens. Anxiety sent the best ones to Riley, overwhelming her with a cascade of terrible images. Riley falling on the ice. Bree and Grace's team winning, making Riley look like a loser. Val laughing at her, saying she was such a little girl for thinking she could make the team.

"They're using Riley's imagination against her!" Disgust said with a gasp.

From her giant screen, Anxiety shouted down to the workers. "Val and her friends like us now! But if we don't make the team, will they like us tomorrow?"

"We can't let her do this to Riley!" Joy said, knowing

that their girl was tossing and turning in her bed. "We have to shut this down."

"But what can we do?" Disgust asked. "There are four of us and like three hundred of them!"

Instinctively, Joy rushed to an empty cubicle and started drawing.

"Why are you drawing a hippo?" Anger asked.

"That's Riley!" Joy said, a bit offended.

"Joy, you forgot her ponytail," Disgust pointed out.

"Oh, good idea!" Joy scribbled the rest of her drawing and scanned it into the projector, sending the image up to Screen 81.

Anxiety saw the image pop up, and she frowned. "Riley scores and everyone hugs her? Eighty-one, that's not helping!"

The other Emotions got in on the projection action, too.

"Riley paints her nails to match her jersey. Everyone copies her! She is so cool!" Disgust sent her image up to the screen.

"Riley wears kneepads!" Fear's drawing was a little jittery but not half bad.

"We buy flowers for the losing team!" Anger drew furiously. He looked up when he realized the others were staring at him. "What? I can't always be the rage guy."

Meanwhile, Anxiety was not pleased with the incoming positive projections. "Nail polish? Kneepads? Do you all understand the assignment?"

At that moment, Embarrassment threw an empty energy drink can across the room. Anxiety looked toward the noise, allowing Embarrassment to hit a button on the console. Anger's projection of Riley buying flowers went to Riley. She stopped tossing and turning and instead had a slight smile on her face.

Embarrassment quickly took his hand off the console as Anxiety whirled around. "Who sent that projection to Riley?"

"Why would I know that?" said Ennui.

"How should I know?" added Envy.

Embarrassment looked back at Sadness in her hiding spot. She gave him a smile and a thumbs-up.

"What is going on?" said Anxiety. "Who's sending up all this positive—" She stopped, her eyes narrowing. "Joy." She moved closer on the screen, giving the sense that she was looming over all the Mind Workers and was ready to pounce. "I know you're in there."

"Whoa, is she really here? Joy from Headquarters?" The Mind Workers began to murmur.

"Well, you're cut off!" Anxiety cut the feed from Joy's projector. "The Mind Police are on their way."

That only made Joy more determined. She stood up on her desk and addressed the Mind Workers. "Don't listen to Anxiety! She's using these horrible projections to change Riley! But we know who Riley is!"

"Joy, I'm doing this for *you*!" Anxiety retorted. "This is so Riley can be happier."

"If you wanted her to be happy, then you'd stop hurting her!" Joy held her arms out wide to the Mind Workers. "Who's with me?"

The workers looked at her skeptically, remaining silent. Someone coughed.

"Really? Nothing?" Joy slumped a little.

"Sorry, Joy," Anxiety said.

But then a fresh image popped up on a projection screen. Number 87 had drawn Riley with a cat.

"Yeah! I see you, Eighty-seven!" Joy cheered. "A cat! A little off topic, but I'll take it! Who else? Come on!"

"What if Riley is better than Val, and so Val hates her?" Anxiety jumped in to grab everyone's attention.

"*Or* . . . what if Riley is better than Val, and Val *respects* her!" Joy countered.

Anxiety and Joy shouted ideas back and forth, each vying for the workers' loyalty.

"What if Riley is so bad she has to give up hockey forever?"

"What if Riley does so well that the coach cries! And the Olympics call, and she rallies a weary nation to victory!"

More and more positive projections began popping up on the screens, infuriating Anxiety.

"Ugh—noooo!" she cried.

Anger leapt up to join Joy on the desk. "Anxiety has got you all chained to desks, drawing nightmares! But you don't have to take it anymore!"

"Pencils down, projections off!" Joy shouted.

"Yeah!" the workers cheered. Some of them began pushing their projectors off their desks, smashing them on the ground.

"Enough is enough!" some started shouting. They grabbed pillows and hurled them across the room. Feathers flew everywhere. It was a full-on pillow fort riot!

"Ahh! My projections!" Anxiety wailed as the screens all went blank. "Curse that sunny-side up vigilante—"

Anxiety's voice cut off as her own screen blacked out and everything dimmed in Fort Pillowton. Riley had finally fallen asleep.

Joy was relieved, but the chaos was still in full swing. Projectors went flying, along with plumes of pillow fluff.

"Okay, it's time to go," Fear said.

"Yeah, I think so," Joy agreed.

Just then, the Mind Police stormed the fort. Mind Workers linked arms, refusing to let them cross the picket line, but the cops had spotted Joy and were heading straight for the Emotions.

Anger grinned and raised his fists. "Bring it on, coppers!"

"Oh, no, no, no," Joy said, lowering his fists. "We need to get out of here!"

The Emotions sprinted after Joy.

"We got Riley to sleep!" Disgust cheered.

"Good call on going in there!" Anger said. "Thank goodness we listened to you."

"What now?" asked Fear, looking over his shoulder at the dozens of Mind cops headed their way.

"Quick! To the Parade of Future Careers!" Joy shouted.

She led them to a section just outside Fort Pillowton where a long line of oversized parade balloons floated, tethered to the ground. Each one was shaped like Riley in a different future career.

"Grab a balloon!" Joy instructed them.

"The pastry chef one!" Disgust pointed to a balloon shaped like baker Riley.

"Underpaid!" Joy said.

"Art teacher!" Fear pointed to a balloon depicting Riley with an art palette.

"Underappreciated!" Joy said.

"Ethnomusicologist!" Anger grabbed hold of a balloon showing Riley holding a pair of hand drums and a sheet of music.

"Don't know what that is!" Joy said. Then she spotted the biggest balloon of all, which was clearly the winner. "Ooh! Supreme Court justice! Grab on!"

Together, the Emotions untethered the balloon and ran through the streets of Imagination Land, their feet lifting off the ground as the balloon began to soar.

"Stop right there!" The Mind cops blew their whistles. But they were too late. Joy and the Emotions were sailing higher and higher to safety.

"Here we go!" Joy cried, pointing the way to the Sense of Self beacon. "Just don't look down!"

Fear looked down. "*Ahhh!* I miss the jar!"

Chapter 23

In the darkened Headquarters, Anxiety fumed. "Joy doesn't get it. Without our projections, we won't be prepared. Tomorrow's game is everything!"

Envy nodded. "Coach will either make us a Fire Hawk or doom us to a friendless future."

"I wish we knew what Coach thought of us," Anxiety said quietly. "That would help us impress her."

Envy's eyes grew wide. "Her notebook!"

"Yes!" Anxiety smiled. She quickly recalled the memory of the Fire Hawks telling Riley the importance of the notebook.

Everything Coach thinks about you is in there. Whether she wants you on the team . . . or not.

The memory did exactly what Anxiety hoped it would: it jolted Riley awake. With a flicker, the lights brightened inside HQ.

Anxiety's hands flew over the console controls. "All we've got to do is sneak into Coach's office and read it."

But Riley didn't move. She stayed in bed, only shifting to glance at the time: 3:00 a.m.

"Come on, Riley, move those feet!" Anxiety urged her.

"She doesn't want to," Envy said. "Her beliefs won't let her."

Anxiety looked at the empty Sense of Self pedestal. She frowned. Riley's beliefs still had sway over her, but forcing Riley down this path didn't seem like the best solution.

"Are we pushing her too far?" Anxiety said, hesitating.

"We gotta see what's in the notebook!" Envy insisted. "Riley's future depends on it!"

"Well, then," Anxiety said with a sigh, "there's only one thing to do."

She picked up a pair of scissors from a nearby table and walked over to the Belief System's elevator doors. "I'll be right back."

Unseen by either Envy or Anxiety, Sadness witnessed the whole exchange. She gasped.

"Oh, no," she moaned. "Anxiety is going to change Riley so much she'll do something really, really bad. I have to do something!"

Over the deserted wasteland leading to the very back of Riley's mind, Joy, Fear, Disgust, and Anger clung to the ropes of their Supreme Court justice Riley balloon. Daylight had returned to the Mind World, indicating that Riley was awake again.

What is happening to our girl? Joy worried to herself.

Suddenly, her walkie-talkie crackled to life. "Joy, come in, Joy."

Joy pulled the walkie-talkie out of her pocket. "Sadness? Is that you? What's wrong? Why is Riley awake again?"

For a moment, there was static on the other end.

"You're breaking up!" Joy shouted.

"Anxiety is making Riley break into the coach's office!" Sadness cried.

"What?" Joy exclaimed.

"She knows better than that!" Anger interjected.

"Remember when she stole Mom's credit card?" said Disgust.

Joy didn't like thinking about that memory—when Riley had completely shut out the Emotions, stolen Mom's credit card, and tried to leave San Francisco.

"She felt guilty for a month!" Disgust continued. "She swore she'd never do anything like that again."

"So why is she acting so weird?" Fear asked.

"Yeah, I dunno," Joy admitted. Her imagination went into overdrive and she thought of all the terrible things Anxiety could have done to Riley. Joy held the walkie-talkie to her mouth. "Sadness, you have to stop her! Just don't get caught."

The elevator doors whooshed open in Riley's Belief System. Anxiety's face was somber as she strode forward, scissors in hand, carefully plucking the belief strings one by one.

Everything happens for a reason. Aw, that was sweet.

I'm a nice person. Mm-hmm.

Follow the rules. Bingo. That was the one.

She started to snip the string, but her hand hesitated just as she was about to close the scissors. For a second time, she wondered if this was the right move. Riley wasn't someone who broke rules and snuck around. But her beliefs weren't helping her if they were holding her back, were they?

Furrowing her brow, Anxiety reached over and plucked an orange belief string growing up from the pool of swirling water.

If I'm a Fire Hawk, I won't be alone, the belief string echoed.

See? Anxiety thought. Riley knew what she had to do. And it wasn't like they'd be stealing; they just wanted to read the notebook to be better prepared.

Follow the rules.

Anxiety cut the string.

The empty halls of the hockey arena seemed eerie in the dead of night. Riley shivered as she entered through a fortuitously unlocked door. The latch echoed a little too loudly as it closed. *This is really dangerous,* she thought. What if someone spotted her? What if Coach caught her? She could get kicked out of the skills camp—or worse.

But she hadn't been able to get rid of the idea that if she just *knew* what Coach was thinking about her, everything would be all right. If Coach had written that she was doing a good job, she would just keep doing what she was doing. If Coach had written that she needed to focus on her footwork, Riley would do that in the next day's game. (Actually, *that* day's game, seeing as it was almost four o'clock in the morning.)

She tiptoed up to Coach Roberts's office door and tried the handle. *Yes!* It was unlocked.

But then she heard footsteps echoing somewhere down the hall. Her heartbeat quickened. Someone else was there!

A flashlight skimmed the wall, and she realized with a sickening feeling that a security guard was about to come around the corner.

Gah! She couldn't get caught! Holy cow—would the guard call the police?

As quick as she could, Riley slipped inside Coach's office and locked the door behind her. Then she crouched down low, making herself as small as possible so she wouldn't be spotted through the door's window.

Scarcely breathing, she listened as the guard's footsteps approached the door. She could see his flashlight shine through the window above her, and she shrank down farther in the shadows. The guard tried the door handle and found it locked. For an agonizingly long moment, he remained by the door, shining his flashlight inside.

Then, finally, he moved off down the hall.

Riley exhaled, her entire body shaking violently.

This was a mistake. This was a mistake this was a mistake this was a mistake.

But she was there now, and the notebook was on Coach's desk just an arm's length away.

Riley crept over and picked up the book. She held it in her hands and stared at Coach's firm handwriting on the cover, each letter so official.

Everything she needed to know was in there. And yet . . .

Riley's chest felt heavy, and tears formed in the corners of her eyes.

What was she doing? Who *was* she anymore? She felt like she didn't even know herself. Riley looked at a mirror and saw her reflection. Her blond hair was ashy in the office security lights, and her skin was sallow. Was this who she really was?

"What happened?" Anxiety asked. She went to push some buttons on the console and saw that the entire thing was glowing watery blue.

"Sadness?" Anxiety said, confused. She looked up and

around the console, but there was no one there except her, Envy, Embarrassment, and Ennui, whose eyes were uncharacteristically riveted to the screen.

"Ennui, where's your phone?" Anxiety asked slowly.

With a gasp, Ennui checked her pockets.

"Ooh la la, my phone," she said, panicking. "Where is my phone? Seriously! This is not happening!"

Anxiety put two and two together. Somehow, Sadness was in HQ, and she was driving the console with Ennui's phone app.

"She's here somewhere," Anxiety said. "Find her!"

Anxiety, Envy, and Ennui began scouring Headquarters while Embarrassment attempted to hang back, not wanting to reveal Sadness's hiding spot. But it didn't matter, because within moments, Anxiety spotted a soft light coming from the Emotions' bedroom. The glow of Ennui's phone emanating through the bedcovers had given away the little blue Emotion.

"Sadness?" Anxiety said softly.

"Um, no?" Sadness squeaked.

Anxiety yanked the covers off Sadness and took the phone away.

"I know Riley sneaking around feels wrong," Anxiety

said, sitting next to Sadness. "But it's the only way to help her."

"This isn't who Riley is," Sadness pleaded.

"It's not about who Riley is. It's about who she needs to be."

"No, I won't let you do this," Sadness said, trying to keep the tremble out of her voice.

Anxiety sighed. There was only one option.

A couple minutes later, Sadness sat in a bucket. Using a pulley and rope, Anxiety raised the bucket to the ceiling of Headquarters, trapping Sadness midair.

"Sorry, Sadness," Anxiety said as she tied off the rope. "I don't want to do this, either. But desperate times call for desperate measures."

Then Anxiety returned to the console.

In Coach's office, Riley finally stopped crying. She looked down again at the notebook. *This may not feel right, but it is the only way,* she told herself. Just this one time, she would do something a little wrong so that she could make sure things went a lot right.

Before she could second-guess herself again, Riley flipped through the pages, scanning Coach Roberts's scribbled notes until—

She let out a strangled cry.

The words were right there, plain as day. She couldn't unsee them now.

ANDERSEN: NOT READY YET

Riley's hand flew to her mouth.

She had wanted to know, and now she did.

But she had never imagined that her chances of being a Fire Hawk were already gone.

Chapter 24

"This. Can't. Be. Happening," Envy said, distraught.

Anxiety was so shocked she couldn't even vibrate like normal. "How could Coach have decided already?"

"What do we do?" Envy started to panic. "What do we do!"

"Okay, okay, okay," Anxiety said, gripping her hair. "We're gonna have to change Coach's mind. Which means we're gonna need ideas. *Lots* of them."

Anxiety cranked levers and spun wheels on the console, sending a tremor through the whole of Headquarters. In the distance, there was a rumbling sound, and the recall tubes leading into HQ rattled ominously.

"Look! We're so close, you guys!" Joy shouted to the Emotions.

Seeing the glow from the Sense of Self in the distance reminded them that the old Riley—*their* Riley—was still alive. And that meant hope was alive, too.

Somewhere behind them, there was a sound like thunder, and dark storm clouds started rolling in.

"Uhhhh . . ." Fear said nervously.

Idea bulbs began pouring from the sky, hitting the Emotions on their heads and bouncing precariously off the balloon.

"Oh, no, it's a brainstorm!" warned Anger.

Lightning crackled across the sky as more and more ideas rained down. Joy grabbed a few as the balloon floated past.

"Trip the ref. Eat the puck," she said, analyzing each one. "We can't let these bad ideas get to Riley!"

Ideas were pouring into Headquarters, and Embarrassment raced between the tubes, collecting them in large buckets.

Anxiety sifted through the piles, growing more annoyed as she did so. "No, no, no! We need more! More, more, get more!"

Joy grabbed the wooden stake that was tied to the bottom of her rope. She started using it to shatter all the bad ideas that flew past her.

In the meantime, the balloon moved closer and closer to the center of the fierce brainstorm.

"We need to steer around it!" Disgust cried. She pointed out a path that would lead them away from the storm and back toward the Sense of Self.

"Everybody, get on this side!" Anger shouted.

Disgust and Fear moved over to Anger's rope. Their combined weight tilted the balloon slightly to the right. But it wasn't enough. They needed more weight.

"Joy!" Anger called.

But Joy was single-minded in her goal. She ignored him and continued to smash the bad ideas.

"Joy!" Anger shouted more urgently.

It was too late. The wind pulled them into the storm and spun the balloon around and around. The Emotions clung to the ropes.

"Get on the balloon!" Disgust exclaimed.

The group climbed to the top of the balloon as lightning flashed and ideas rained down.

"I'm gonna be sick," Disgust groaned, somehow looking even greener than usual.

Anger shut his eyes. "I hate this so much."

"We're gonna die!" Fear shrieked.

"What are we gonna do?" Disgust cried.

Fear looked up and noticed the ideas leaving the storm through tubes bound for Headquarters.

"The only way out is up!" he shouted. "Quick, grab on to an idea!"

Disgust caught a medium-sized idea and held it aloft. It lifted her for a moment but quickly sank back down to the balloon.

Anger shook his head. "These ideas are too small. We need something bigger!"

They turned to look at Joy, who was holding a massive idea. She was preparing to smash it.

"Wait!" Fear exclaimed. "We need that idea!"

"But this is a terrible idea!" Joy insisted.

"Sometimes bad ideas can lead to something good," Fear replied. "Like getting us out of this brainstorm!"

"If Riley takes one of these ideas, it could be a disaster!" Joy insisted.

"Joy, worst case, she'll live," said Fear. "I can't say the same for us!"

Although she was still hesitant, Joy couldn't argue with Fear's logic. She nodded.

The Emotions held on to the big idea. It rose in the air, zoomed out of the storm, and headed toward a tube. The Emotions had no choice but to jump off.

"Ahhh!" they all screamed.

The giant idea bulb squeezed into Headquarters, distending the recall tube with its girth. It was so big it crushed Embarrassment's collection bucket, spilling smaller, shattered idea bulbs everywhere.

Anxiety and Envy rushed over to the colossal idea. It reflected their eyes as they watched the images playing inside, which suggested a course of action for Riley.

"Haha! Yeah!" Anxiety cheered.

"Big," Envy agreed.

No one had ever before done anything as big as this idea at skills camp.

This idea would change everything.

Most important, it was guaranteed to change Coach's mind.

Anxiety was certain.

The Emotions plummeted to the ground.

"Hold me!" Fear shrieked. Then, more insistently, he repeated, *"Hold me!"*

Everyone grabbed on to Fear when suddenly . . .

POOF!

A parachute deployed, gliding them gently through the air.

"Fear!" Joy exclaimed in surprise.

Disgust was equally stunned. She looked up at him. "You have a parachute?"

"Uh, yeah," Fear said as though it was a silly question. "The real question is, why don't any of you?"

The Emotions landed softly on the ground and brushed themselves off.

"Stuck the landing!" Fear exclaimed.

"We did it!" Anger cheered.

Disgust sighed in relief. "We made it!"

Anger turned toward the Sense of Self in the distance. "We'd better make up for lost time. Come on."

As Anger, Fear, and Disgust headed toward the Back of the Mind, Joy stood quietly by herself. She was full of guilt and embarrassment over endangering her friends and nearly jeopardizing their mission. But she couldn't dwell on it for too long. She gathered her remaining strength and followed the other Emotions.

Chapter 25

The moment had finally arrived: it was game time. Anxiety picked up the big idea and lugged it to the console.

"We have to be flawless in today's scrimmage," Anxiety said. "And this is the way we're going to do it." She plugged the idea into the console. "Be like Val, only better."

In the locker room, Riley began her preparations—starting with her hair. All it had taken was some conditioner and an entire packet of Cherry Quencher powder to add the signature streak of fiery red to Riley's sandy-blond locks. Riley flipped her hair, showing off her handiwork.

Anxiety beamed. She then lowered Sadness and the bucket. "What do you think, Sadness?"

"Well, I—"

"Awesome!" Anxiety cut her off and raised the bucket again.

"We look amazing!" Envy cheered.

At that moment, Grace and Bree made their way into the locker room.

"Hey, Riley," Grace said.

"Hey . . ." Riley replied.

Bree looked confused. "What did you do to your hair?"

Before Riley could answer, Bree and Grace looked down at Riley's hands, which were stained red from the hair dye.

"It looks like you killed someone," said Grace.

"Whatever," Riley scoffed.

"In a way, you kinda did," Bree said softly. She and Grace exchanged looks and walked away.

Sadness and Embarrassment were shocked to see this version of Riley. She had never treated her friends that way before. Envy and Ennui were not as concerned.

"What do they know?" Envy said dismissively.

Ennui rolled her eyes. "They wouldn't know cool if it hit them in the face."

Val and some of the Fire Hawks arrived next. Val raised an eyebrow at Riley's new look. "Hey, Michigan. Rockin' the red, huh?"

"I hope it's okay," Riley said. "I know I'm not officially a

Fire Hawk yet, but I figured since we're on the same team today, we should match, right?"

"Uh . . ." Val noticed the dark circles under Riley's eyes. "Did you sleep last night?"

"No!" Riley said brightly. "How could I? Big game today!"

"You mean the camp scrimmage?" another Fire Hawk said, glancing up at her.

"Leave her alone. She's in her zone," Val said. She gave Riley a thumbs-up. "Get ready to score some goals!"

"See?" Anxiety exclaimed. "Val is the only one who understands!"

Envy climbed up to the console. "So what's the plan for the game?"

"Val scored two goals in this scrimmage to become a Fire Hawk," Anxiety stated.

Envy nodded. "So we need to score two goals to be just like her!"

"Actually, Envy," said Anxiety, "you know what's better than two? Three!"

"Whoa! A hat trick?" Envy exclaimed. "I wish I'd thought of that."

In her spot on the couch, Ennui deigned to glance up. "And how are we going to score three goals?"

Anxiety stretched her arms and twisted from side to side. She needed to be warmed up, too. "Simple. We do whatever it takes."

Joy and the Emotions climbed a steep hill in the Back of the Mind.

"Are we there yet?" Fear gasped in exhaustion.

"How much farther?" Anger panted.

"Almost there, guys!" Joy said, urging them on. "I can feel it. Look!" She could see the hill's peak. She turned to the others. "C'mon, grab my hand. You got it!"

Joy helped the Emotions reach the top, which would give them a full view of the Back of the Mind.

"We're so close!" Joy said encouragingly. "The tube is just on top of that—" She turned around to see the landscape. "Mountain," Joy finished quietly.

But this was no mountain. It was a massive pile of discarded memory spheres. There were hundreds—perhaps thousands—of them, each one replaying a memory Joy had deemed hurtful to Riley.

"Whaaat?" Fear said in shock.

"How many memories did you *send* back here?" Disgust asked. "This is way more than you told us about."

Joy processed the enormity of the pile. Sure, she'd been doing a little mind-scaping every night. A cringeworthy memory here, an "oof, that's hurtful" recollection there. She honestly hadn't realized how many she'd placed into the tube, but they must have added up over time.

"I may have tossed some when you guys weren't around," she admitted. "But Riley doesn't need to remember any of these!" She noticed a memory nearby. "When she failed that math quiz..." She picked up another one. "That time the librarian shushed her... When she caught Dad cheating on family game night..."

"Riley called Dad out!" Anger argued.

"Riley *yelled* at Dad," Joy pointed out. "She lost screen time for a week!"

"Riley stood up for herself!" Anger countered.

Joy huffed, getting a little annoyed by the others' judgment. They were finally at the finish line, and they were choosing *now* to second-guess her past actions? "Are we here to nitpick, or are we here to save our girl?" She pointed to the top of the mountain impatiently. "Now, come on!"

Out on the ice, Riley was in the thick of the game, scoring goals and looking good doing it. She'd already made a fast and easy slap shot right past Bree's goalie glove. The Fire Hawks had been super impressed. Now it was time to zone in on goal number two.

Riley spotted Dani with the puck. With Anxiety driving hard, Riley tried to steal the puck from her own teammate.

"Get the puck!" Anxiety demanded. "Get the puck!"

"Michigan, what are you doing?" Dani said in confusion.

Riley shoved her, took the puck, and sped toward the goal. She smacked the puck past Bree, straight into the net. Coach Roberts wrote something in her notebook.

"That's right, Coach," Envy said smugly. "R-I-L-E-Y! Future Fire Hawk superstar!"

Everything was going according to plan. Riley *would* be a Fire Hawk. Coach couldn't deny her a spot on the team if she scored more goals than any other player ever had in the history of the skills camp.

"We're so close!" Anxiety's eyes glowed. "Just one more goal. *Just one more.*"

But Riley didn't make the next shot, or the next or the next. Time ticked down as the scrimmage entered its second half, and play after play, Riley continuously missed the shot. At one point, she even tripped and fell. It was as if that third goal was just out of reach.

With the puck again, Riley plowed toward the goal. But someone was in her way.

"Outta the way!" Anxiety shouted.

Riley shoved the player with her shoulder, causing the person to slide into the boards. But her sole focus was reaching that goal—

WHACK!

She smashed the puck toward the net, but Bree stopped it again.

"Arrrgghhh!" Anxiety groaned.

Coach blew her whistle. "Andersen!" she shouted. "Penalty box! Two minutes!"

As Riley skated to the penalty box, she noticed the other girls helping Grace off the ice.

"Grace! Are you okay?" Bree called.

Sadness, Ennui, Envy, and Embarrassment gasped.

"We hurt Grace!" Envy exclaimed in horror.

But Anxiety couldn't worry about that. There were only a few minutes left in the game, and Riley would be spending two of those minutes in the penalty box.

"Riley's just—she just—" Anxiety looked at the Sense of

Self pedestal, which, despite all her efforts—everything she'd done to make Riley the best—still sat empty. "She just needs her new Sense of Self."

Anxiety walked over to the memory wall and selected the memories of Riley's two goals. "This will put us over the top." She then moved to the Belief System elevator. "I'll be back . . . with a new Sense of Self!"

The core Emotions struggled up the mountain. Joy dug through the endless pile of memories as they went. She knew the Sense of Self had to be there somewhere.

Finally, she unearthed a glowing flower-like object.

I'm a good person.

"I found her!" Joy cried, picking it up.

All at once, Joy felt an overwhelming rush of feelings. It was Riley—their Riley. They had found her old Sense of Self.

"Thank goodness!" Fear said.

"Yes! Riley's back, baby!" Disgust cheered.

There was one more thing left to do.

"We gotta get to the tube," said Joy.

Chapter 26

Orange luminescence from the new belief strings radiated throughout the Belief System. Anxiety tossed the memories of Riley's two goals into the water and returned to the elevator. An enormous pulse of energy surged from the swirling water.

Anxiety arrived back in HQ just as the entire room filled with orange light. She watched in triumph as the once-empty pedestal glowed and revealed a new, brilliant, perfect, better-than-ever-before Sense of Self.

It hummed with energy before echoing in Riley's voice: *I'M NOT GOOD ENOUGH.*

"W-what?" Anxiety said in surprise and confusion.

"Oh, why does it say that?" Sadness asked from her spot in the bucket.

"Uh, um—" Anxiety stammered, "because she knows she can always be better! You'll see. This is good. We're *good*. We can work with this."

The other Emotions shared uncertain glances as Anxiety walked back to the console and cracked her knuckles.

Suddenly, Sadness heard Joy's voice from the walkie-talkie. "Sadness, we have the Sense of Self. Recall us!"

Anxiety was too preoccupied at the console to hear Joy's command, but Embarrassment heard every word. Sadness looked down at him, silently begging for help. Embarrassment glanced from her to Anxiety.

Finally, he untied the rope and lowered Sadness's bucket to the ground. Sadness smiled at him in gratitude. She then signaled him to the Back of the Mind tube. Embarrassment nodded in understanding.

Sadness snuck toward the console while Embarrassment moved to the tube. They watched Anxiety closely, waiting for the right moment. As Anxiety got distracted by something on-screen, Embarrassment lowered the tube and Sadness pushed the recall button.

At the peak of the mountain of memory spheres, Joy waited for a sign from Sadness. *What if Sadness got caught?* she wondered. *What if she didn't hear my message?*

Joy heard a whoosh of air overhead from the Back of the Mind tube. It was turned on!

"She did it!" Joy cheered. "Good ol' Sadness!"

She held the Sense of Self above her head. Up it went into the tube!

"Now us!" Anger exclaimed.

But before the Emotions could move to the tube, some of the surrounding memory spheres were sucked into it.

"No, stop!" Joy shouted. "Riley doesn't need these!"

At that moment in Headquarters, Anxiety realized Sadness was at the console. Then, to her horror, she saw Embarrassment standing next to the Back of the Mind tube.

"Sadness!" she exclaimed. She grabbed a long hook. "Don't you understand? I know what's best for Riley!"

"No! Please!" Sadness wailed.

But it was no use. Anxiety walked over to the Back of the Mind tube and used the hook to rip the entire contraption right out of the ceiling. The tube clattered to the floor, destroyed, and Sadness could hear the remainder of the tube crumbling with a ripple effect way out beyond Headquarters.

It was over. There was no way to bring back her friends now.

Joy struggled to hold down the memory spheres. She couldn't let all those bad memories and mistakes get back to Riley.

Fear pointed at Headquarters with a trembling hand. "Oh, no . . ."

Joy and the others watched as the Back of the Mind tube dropped from the sky in the distance. They could see the glow of the Sense of Self as it plummeted from the tube and smashed into a million pieces. Finally, the last remnants of the tube crashed beside them. The Mind World settled into silence.

"It . . . it can't be," Anger said in disbelief. "That was our only way back."

Disgust looked out at Headquarters, with its orange light radiating across the landscape.

"But . . . we came so far. We were so close."

"Oh, Riley," Joy whispered, devastated.

Chapter 27

They were too late. They had failed their girl. How would they ever get their Riley back now?

Joy's knees buckled. She dropped to the ground, and her eyes blurred with tears. Colors from the discarded memories were striated in her misty vision, making the memories playing inside look like images in a kaleidoscope. She gazed at the one closest to her: the memory of Riley stealing her mom's credit card the day she ran away from home.

Joy gazed at memory after memory of times Riley had made mistakes and had fallen short. She had insisted these memories were hurting Riley and that was the reason they needed to be sent far away. Joy lowered her head in shame.

Behind her, the other Emotions blamed themselves.

"Anxiety is right. We are unsophisticated Emotions," Fear said.

Anger nodded. "This is our fault."

"We failed Riley," Disgust agreed. "We got what we deserve."

Joy couldn't help herself: she let out an involuntary sob. "No. You guys didn't fail her. I did."

Disgust, Anger, and Fear looked at Joy in surprise and confusion.

"I thought I was helping her by throwing these back here. But this is why she's been acting so wrong: breaking into Coach's office, insulting her friends. She knows better—she *should* know better! If she remembered these, she wouldn't have done those things! But I made her forget."

Joy looked at all the memories around her. "I thought mistakes were something to avoid. But these could've made her stronger. More compassionate. A better person! And we'll never get to see that—the Riley she could have been. Because of me." She curled into a ball, making herself as small as possible. "I did this to her. I'm no good for Riley."

Anger, Fear, and Disgust had never seen Joy so low. They knelt beside her.

"Joy, we could have stopped you," Anger said.

"We let it happen," Disgust added. "This is our mistake, too."

"But let's fix this," Anger said, determined. "It doesn't have to be too late. It was just a mistake, right? Let's get all these back to her."

Joy looked up. "But . . . how?"

Fear perked up with a sudden idea. "I got it!"

The other Emotions watched as Fear dropped a memory sphere into the canyon below. It headed toward Headquarters and eventually fell into the Sar-chasm. The orange light from Headquarters dimmed almost imperceptibly.

"Look!" said Fear. "That Sar-chasm leads to the Stream of Consciousness, which connects to the Belief System! We just gotta get all these memories into that canyon!"

Joy thought back to the beautiful rainbow water in Riley's Belief System that had fed all her belief strings. She had noticed the rainbow splash the broccoli floret made at the bottom of the Sar-chasm. They were one and the same, she had realized. If they could get all these memories into that chasm, they would flow back into Riley's Belief System and into her Sense of Self. But how would they get all these memories into the Sar-chasm?

As though reading her mind, Fear said, "I checked out the cliff as we climbed up. It's not very stable. There's a weak spot underneath. All we have to do is break it off!"

"Break the cliff?" Disgust asked, confused. "How would we do that?"

"I . . . didn't get that far," Fear admitted.

Anger sighed. "I have an idea, but I really don't like it." He took a deep breath. "Oh, Pouchy!"

Nothing happened.

"Well, what are you waiting for?" Anger exclaimed. "Say the words!"

The Emotions shouted at the top of their lungs: *"Oh, Pouchy!"*

A faint glimmer appeared in the sky like a distant star. Then it drew closer and closer to the Emotions, swooping toward them in a stream of sparkles, until the unmistakable cartoon fanny pack was hovering right in front of them.

"Hi, everybody! I'm Pouchy!"

"We know," Anger grumbled.

"Pouchy, we need to get these memories to the Belief System," Joy explained. "Do you have anything that could help us?"

"I have lots of items!" Pouchy said cheerfully. "Which one do you think will work best? A roll of tape? A rubber ducky? Or—"

"No time!" Anger shouted.

With a lunge, he tackled Pouchy to the ground and shoved his hand right inside Pouchy's zipper mouth. He reached around, feeling for the right item, amid Pouchy's protests. He pulled out a giant crowbar, some rope, and a mallet, but he still wasn't satisfied.

"Where's the exploding dynamite?" he demanded.

Pouchy's words were muffled because of Anger's arm. He spit it out. "You already used that!" he exclaimed. "What? Do you think I have everything in here?"

Sitting in the penalty box, Riley had never felt so stressed before. It was as though everything she'd ever worked for in her entire life was coming down to this one game, and she wasn't sure if she could succeed anymore. Why couldn't she just play better? Why couldn't she just finish this? She had missed so many shots. She was playing like such a loser. Was she even good enough to do the hat trick? She'd been so certain earlier, but minute by minute, her chance at proving herself was slipping away. She began to hyperventilate.

In Headquarters, Anxiety gripped the edges of the console, her knuckles white with tension. "No, no, no. We're running out of time!"

The other Emotions exchanged looks of doubt as Anxiety began spiraling out of control. "Stupid, stupid, stupid!" she muttered to herself.

"Stupid, stupid, stupid! You can't do anything right!" Riley said, smacking her head in frustration.

Anxiety spun around the console, driving hard and pressing buttons and pulling levers. She moved so quickly that she nearly formed a tornado around the console.

"Stop!" Envy demanded. "You're putting too much pressure on her."

Envy tried to reach the console but was flung backward by the power of Anxiety's spiral. Embarrassment tried next, but he couldn't break through, either.

Riley couldn't catch her breath. She took off her helmet as her penalty time—and the time left in the game—wound down.

An overwhelmed Anxiety continued spinning around the console, causing Headquarters to shake.

"Either we score the goal, or our life is over," Anxiety said to Riley. "We got this! *You and me!*"

In the Back of the Mind, the Emotions improvised with the items Pouchy provided. Anger and Fear had noticed a crack in the cliff overhang that held the mountain of memory spheres in place. Using the mallet and crowbar, they widened the fissure as much as possible.

Beneath the overhang was the weak spot that Fear had found: a narrow rock pillar that hardly seemed sturdy enough to support the cliff overhang and the memory spheres. Joy tied Pouchy's rope around it.

If Fear's plan worked, the Emotions would pull and topple the pillar, the overhang would collapse, and the entire load of memory spheres would cascade straight into the canyon leading to the Belief System.

"This would have been so much easier with some dynamite," Anger grumbled.

"Well, it's the best plan we have," said Joy. "Everyone get in position!"

The Emotions stood beneath the cliff overhang, holding on to the rope.

"Okay, when I say 'three,' everyone pull!" Joy directed. "That should send everything crashing . . . right down . . . on top of us. Wait! Wait!"

"What?" Anger said impatiently.

"If this works," said Joy, "we may not survive. You guys move aside. I'll do this." This was her mistake to fix.

"No, Joy. We're not afraid," said Fear in the calmest voice Joy had ever heard from him.

Disgust shrugged. "This outfit is already ruined."

"And anyway, there's only one reason we do anything," added Anger.

Joy looked at him.

"For Riley."

Joy smiled. "Yes. For Riley."

Through all the uncertainty of the past few days, that was the one thing Joy knew to be true: they would do anything for Riley.

"Can we get on with this already?" Anger exclaimed. "I've got some smashing to do!"

"Let's do this!" Joy shouted. "One . . . two . . . three!"

The Emotions pulled the rope with all their might. As the pillar fell, the overhang collapsed. Memory spheres surged toward the Emotions like a tidal wave.

There was no escape. But they were ready.

The memories thundered into the canyon. The Emotions tried to stay afloat, but the weight and speed of the avalanche pulled them under. The memories cascaded into the Sar-chasm, creating a rainbow waterfall that plunged into the Stream of Consciousness.

Joy swam to the surface of the water. She pushed against the memory spheres that had become like a ceiling above her. But there were too many. They wouldn't budge.

As her eyes began to lose focus, Joy's only thought was of her girl.

Chapter 28

Joy sank deeper and deeper into the darkness. Then in front of her floated a glowing figure. It was a young Riley! Joy smiled. She didn't know how this was possible, but she didn't care. Her Riley was there. They held hands, swirling around in a dance.

"Riley," said Joy, "I've made so many mistakes. I'm so sorry."

The smiling young Riley released Joy, silently drifting away.

"Wait, don't leave," Joy begged. "Please."

Riley beckoned Joy to follow.

"Riley!" Joy called.

Suddenly, Joy burst through the water's surface. She gasped for air as she made her way to the shore.

"Riley," Joy panted. *What was that?* she wondered. She doubted the Mind Manuals had anything to say about the apparition she had just seen. But regardless, Riley had saved her.

Joy then realized where she was: in the Belief System.

The discarded memories flooded in, swirling through the water and sending streaks of multicolored light shooting up as hundreds of new belief strings started to grow. One by one, they shimmered prismatically, shifting from orange to gold to red, blue, purple, and green.

Joy gasped. "We did it! We did it, guys! They're all here! Back in the system!" She looked around. "Fear? Anger? Disgust?"

No one answered.

"Guys?" Joy cried, her panic rising.

Finally, Fear, Anger, and Disgust emerged from the water, coughing and sputtering.

"Let's do that again!" Fear cheered.

Anger laughed in relief. "I thought I was a goner!"

"We did it!" Disgust exclaimed.

Joy and the other Emotions watched, mesmerized by the new belief strings. Joy saw the memory of Riley's tripping penalty slide in next to the championship memory; they nestled side by side, the good and the bad. The two beliefs then intertwined, creating a shimmering spiral. The innermost part of the Belief System began to glow with an ethereal light.

The penalty timer went off, allowing Riley to return to the game. But Riley, still hyperventilating, couldn't move from her spot.

"What are you doing?" Anxiety screeched. "Put your helmet on!"

Coach Roberts noticed Riley sitting in the box. "Andersen! Come on!"

The other Emotions watched with horror and helplessness as Anxiety's spiral worsened. Headquarters continued to shake, sending piles of construction material toppling over. Sparks flew off the console as it went into overdrive.

"You have to score that goal, Riley!" Anxiety pleaded.

But Riley could only curl up into a ball on the ground and clutch her chest. *I can't do it,* she thought. *I'm not good enough. I'm not good enough. I'm not good enough.*

At that moment, Joy and the other Emotions

emerged from the elevator. They were stunned to see the chaos unfolding in Headquarters. Sadness, Envy, Embarrassment, and Ennui were pinned to the walls by the force of Anxiety's storm.

"Sadness?" Joy called.

"Joy, you've got to help her!" Sadness shouted.

Joy looked around, unsure of what Sadness was talking about.

"There!" Sadness pointed toward the console, which was enveloped by the storm.

Joy tried to move but continued to get pushed into the wall. The wind was too powerful.

Suddenly, she realized she was moving forward. All the Emotions—core and new—worked together to push her toward Anxiety.

"Push! Push!" Fear chanted. "Put your shoulders into it! For Riley!"

Inch by inch, Joy moved closer to the console until she reached the center of the vortex. It was silent. Anxiety stood at the console, tense and still.

Joy leaned back toward the other Emotions, who were holding each other up outside the vortex. "When I give the signal, grab me and pull!"

She took a couple deep breaths and wrapped her arms around Anxiety.

But Joy's arms went straight through her! Seven clones of Anxiety materialized, each standing at the console in a different position. As quickly as she had multiplied, Anxiety combined into a single figure once more.

"What's happening, Joy?" Fear shouted.

Joy analyzed Anxiety more closely. She could see her twitching and glitching like an image on an old television. Anxiety seemed to be paralyzed, unable to release the controls.

"Anxiety," Joy said gently, "you can let go now. I'm here for you."

Anxiety's hands seemed to grasp the controls even tighter.

"You know you need to let her go," Joy continued. "And when you do, I'll be right here, okay? Give me a sign that you understand."

A single tear fell from one of Anxiety's eyes.

"Okay, I'm right here," Joy said reassuringly. "Anytime. I'm ready."

Finally, Anxiety released the controls.

Joy grabbed her. "Now! Pull!"

The Emotions yanked Joy and Anxiety out of the vortex and tumbled to the other side of the room.

Joy cradled Anxiety in her arms. "I got you. It's okay. I got you."

Anxiety took deep breaths. "Thank you, Joy."

Joy smiled.

"I was trying to help," Anxiety explained. "I only wanted what's best for Riley."

"I know," replied Joy. "But sometimes we don't know what's best for her. She needs to make her own choices."

Anxiety took in Joy's words for a moment before passing out in exhaustion.

The swirling vortex slowed and dissipated, allowing Riley to catch her breath.

Suddenly, the light from the Belief System burst forth. All of Headquarters glowed, and the entire Mind World illuminated.

The light from Riley's beliefs washed over Joy, warming her heart and calming her mind. She had Riley's strength within her, shared from every single piece that made their girl who she was.

They hadn't lost Riley. They just needed to let her shine.

A new Sense of Self formed on the pedestal. Joy

approached it, noticing how it continued to morph and shift, never staying in one state.

I'm kind.

I'm selfish.

I'm not good enough.

I'm a good person.

I'm capable.

I'm not good at anything.

I'm brave, but I get scared.

I'm strong, but I need help sometimes.

"What does it mean?" Envy asked. "Did we do something wrong?"

Joy admired the Sense of Self, every form more beautiful than the last. "I think . . . it's exactly what she needs to be," she murmured.

Meanwhile, Riley took a deep breath. She felt as though she had emerged from the depths of the ocean. She heard the other players on the ice.

"Okay! I see your moves!" Val exclaimed.

Riley touched her hockey stick as though seeing it for the first time.

Then a memory began to play in Headquarters. It was of a young Riley skating and gliding across a lake in Minnesota. She skated with pure happiness and abandon.

"Who recalled that?" Fear asked.

"Riley did," said Envy.

Just then, glowing golden particles pulled from Joy and floated to the console. Joy watched in wonder as, eventually, a stream of sparkles led from her to the controls.

"Joy," said Sadness, "Riley wants you."

Joy was terrified of disturbing this moment. After everything she had done and all the mistakes she had made, she wondered if her connection to Riley had been severed completely. But like the apparition of young Riley in the water, Riley seemed to be calling to Joy.

The Emotions parted to make a path for Joy. She cautiously walked to the console. When she touched the controls, it emitted a yellow glow.

Riley smiled. She still felt shaky but managed to leave the penalty box and skate onto the ice. A player passed the puck to her. Riley paused for a moment. Instead of charging at the goal before time ran out, she tossed the puck around on her stick like a hacky sack.

Suddenly, she passed it to Grace, who caught it with her stick in surprise. Riley smiled, skating a circle around Grace, and the joy she felt must have been contagious, because despite clearly still being sore from the penalty, Grace couldn't help giggling and passing the puck to

Bree. Bree smiled wholeheartedly as the three of them continued to skate and pass, three best friends having fun on the ice, the way they had wanted to from the start.

One by one, the Fire Hawks joined them, unable to resist a moment of levity after such an intense game.

Riley looped around, enjoying the feel of the ice under her skates; the smooth, secure motion of her hockey stick strokes; and the crisp, cool scent of the arena she'd grown to love. Joy matched Riley's movements, and they glided and skated together almost as one. Joy had never felt such overwhelming pride and love for her girl.

The final buzzer went off. The game was over, and Riley hadn't finished the hat trick. And yet she was still okay. She heard Grace, Bree, Val, and Dani congratulating each other.

Riley skated over to her friends. She wrapped Grace and Bree in a fierce hug.

"I really messed up," she admitted. "When you guys told me you were going to a different school, I freaked out, and I just—I couldn't—" She sighed. "I was such a jerk to you guys. I'm so sorry."

Grace and Bree exchanged looks of surprise as Riley turned to Val and Dani.

"And I look up to you guys so much . . . and I want to play on varsity, and I'm terrified to play on varsity, and I want to be with my friends, and I want new friends, and I want for things to never change, but they are and . . . I don't know." She took a shaky breath. "I'm a mess, and everything just looks so easy for everyone else."

The whole time at camp, Riley had felt like she hadn't known who she was anymore, like she needed to be a different Riley or a better Riley. Something had nearly snapped in her during that last drive for the goal. She'd almost let the stress get the best of her. Perhaps that was the push she needed to experience a moment of clarity, seeing beyond the game and the goal and the need to be perfect.

Because the Riley who cared only about being the best and who was willing to power through anyone and anything to achieve it wasn't the Riley she wanted to be. She didn't want or need to be *the* best. She just wanted to be the best Riley. What more could anyone ask of her? What more could she ask of herself?

"I mess up all the time," Val assured Riley.

"You do?" Riley asked in surprise.

"Yeah, I'm—I'm just really good at hiding it."

"I have no idea what I'm doing ever!" Dani blurted out.

"Oh my gosh, me either!" Grace laughed in relief.

The girls all began talking at once.

"I had no idea you felt that way!"

"I'm totally a mess!"

"It feels so good to say that out loud!"

When Riley had approached her friends, she wasn't sure how the conversation would go. But she never would have anticipated this. Riley's honesty allowed everyone else to admit their own insecurities and weaknesses. She was proud of her friends—and herself.

Bree turned to Riley. "We should have told you sooner about the school thing."

"Sorry, Riley," Grace added. "We didn't know how to tell you, so I just screamed it in your face."

"It's okay," said Riley, feeling lighter than she had all during camp. But there was one last admission to make to the Fire Hawks. Riley took a deep breath. "I'm not from Michigan. I'm from Minnesota."

The Fire Hawks stared at her, and then everyone burst into giggles as Coach Roberts skated over.

"All right, ladies. That's camp! Great work this weekend!" She turned to Riley. "Hey, Andersen."

"Yes, Coach?" Riley replied nervously.

"You know, when you got goin' out there today, I wasn't sure what to think," Coach said. "But something changed in those last few minutes. I want you to bring that to tryouts in the fall. Okay?"

Riley beamed. "You bet!"

Chapter 29

As Riley headed off with her teammates to the locker room, all the Emotions gathered around the new Sense of Self on its pedestal. Even the weakened but relieved Anxiety joined in.

The Sense of Self looked different, stretching and morphing into various shapes and fading from one color to the next, like an alien object in constant flux.

Joy gingerly reached out to the new Sense of Self, feeling its warmth on her hand. She knew it would probably continue to change for a while.

Anxiety wringed her hands nervously. "I'm—I'm sorry," she told everyone. "About everything. I didn't mean to cause such a mess."

The Emotions glanced around Headquarters, which looked like one of Pouchy's dynamite bundles had gone off inside—several times.

"'Mess' is one way to describe it," Disgust said, pulling a face.

"You all must hate me!" Anxiety tugged at her hair.

"There was talk of punting . . ." Anger said under his breath.

"I was just trying to help Riley," Anxiety insisted. "I was just trying—"

"We know." Joy put a hand on Anxiety's shoulder. "We're all trying to help Riley in our own way. None of us are perfect."

She smiled at the screen. Riley was finally together with Bree and Grace, laughing. They'd even found some funnel cake in the college cafeteria.

"Neither is our girl. Because she's not supposed to be. She's just supposed to be Riley."

The Emotions all nodded in agreement, watching as the new Sense of Self stretched into an amorphous bundle.

"Always changing, always growing," Joy whispered. "And we'll be here for her every step of the way."

"Wait, you guys seriously have a half day because of the heat?" Riley propped up her phone on her bed so Bree and Grace could still see her on their three-way video call as she stuffed papers and her school tablet into her backpack. It was several months after camp, and their freshman year of high school was in full swing. The girls had promised one another that they would video chat in the mornings to hold them over until they could meet up in the afternoon. "How is that even possible?" Riley said, searching for her math textbook.

"Dude, have you been outside?" Grace asked. "There's, like, a bizarre heat wave going on."

"Not all high schools in the Bay Area are fancy and have air-conditioning," Bree quipped.

"Only the best ones," Riley said teasingly.

"Hey!" Grace snorted. "At least *our* school has a fall dance! You have whatever that collaborative harvest festival thing is."

"Yeah, it's super weird," Riley agreed. "I don't even know if I'm going to go."

"Aw, you should," Bree said. "It sounds kind of fun."

"And you don't have to worry about finding a date," Grace said, laughing.

Riley smiled to herself, daydreaming for a moment about being at Bree and Grace's high school and taking Lance Slashblade to the fall dance as her date.

"I think the Fire Hawks are going to wear their jerseys to the festival," Riley commented. "Does your school hockey team wear their jerseys to the dance?"

"I'm not sure," Bree said. "Our tryouts aren't until next week."

"Wait—isn't today the day you find out if you made the team?" Grace asked, suddenly remembering.

Riley gulped. It *was* the big day. Her tryout had been the previous week with Coach Roberts. She thought it had gone well. There hadn't been any hat trick, but it had been nice that Val, Dani, and the others had all wished her luck beforehand.

"Yeah," Riley said, her voice a little tight with nerves. "Coach is going to email the list out this afternoon."

"I'm sure you made it," Bree said. "I mean, how could you not?"

"Seriously, you crushed it at the skills camp," Grace said. "You crushed it so hard that you literally crushed some of the other players."

"I've apologized for knocking you over like a million times!" Riley protested, though all three friends were smiling. "Will you ever forgive me?"

"Depends how much victory funnel cake you buy me," Grace said.

"When you get the news that you made the team," Bree added, grinning.

Riley laughed, shook her head, and zipped up her backpack. "I've gotta go, or I'm going to be late for school." She paused. "I miss you both."

Bree and Grace waved. "We miss you, too. See you after school?"

"You know it," Riley said.

Anxiety could hardly stand the pressure. She tugged at her turtleneck and chewed on her fingernails as she watched the minutes pass by on Riley's phone, which rested on the table beside their girl.

"Six minutes!" She vibrated nervously. "Six minutes!"

All the Emotions had their eyes fixed on the screen as Riley sat in the cafeteria. She was surrounded by the Fire Hawks. Her (maybe) future teammates had gathered with her to wait for the tryout results.

"Hey, Minnesota"—Val passed Riley a bag of pretzels— "how long are you going to stare at your phone?"

Riley chewed her lip. "Coach said she'd email the list of who made the team by two p.m."

"What happens if we don't become a Fire Hawk?" Anxiety fretted.

"Anxiety," Joy cautioned her gently.

But Anxiety was worked up. "Thanks for asking, Joy. I'll tell you!" She popped up her projection screen and frantically began scrolling.

"First, Mom and Dad are very disappointed." The projection board flashed an image of Riley's parents shaking their heads. "We don't go pro, and we find work as an ethnomusicologist, even though we don't know what that is, and"—the screen showed Riley standing beside a xylophone and holding a clipboard before that morphed into an image of a gravestone—"we have no friends, and we die alone. *Ahhh!*"

Joy smiled, shook her head, and soothingly placed a hand on the orange Emotion's shoulder. As soon as she did, Anxiety untensed—for the most part.

"Okay, well, none of that is happening right now. Is it, Anxiety?"

"No . . ."

"So why don't we take a seat in our special chair?" Joy suggested, guiding Anxiety to a plushy massage chair.

"Yeah, that's a great idea," Anxiety said.

As Joy turned on the chair, Anxiety sighed. "Oh yeah, that's the stuff."

"Plus we followed our new varsity-caliber training program," Joy said.

"Oh, I wish I thought of that," Envy whined.

"You did," Joy said in confusion.

"Wait, you're right!" Envy exclaimed. "I'm jealous of myself. Ah! That is hard to process, but I'm enjoying it."

"We can't control whether Riley makes the team," Joy reminded everyone. "But what can we control?"

"Well, um . . ." Anxiety thought. "Oh! We have a Spanish test tomorrow. We need to study!"

"You're right!" Joy gasped. "We totally—"

"Olvidamos," Anxiety finished for her.

Joy raised an eyebrow. "What's that mean?"

" 'Forgot.' "

"Nice job, Anxiety!" Disgust and Envy said together.

"Thanks for the reminder," Fear and Sadness told her.

"We're learning Spanish?" Ennui asked from the couch.

Anxiety blushed a deeper shade of orange. "Thanks, guys."

"You're welcome!" a high-pitched cartoon voice called from somewhere inside Headquarters.

"Who said that?" Joy asked, startled.

"It's my new buddy," Anger told her. He turned around to reveal none other than Pouchy fastened around his waist.

"Hi, everybody!" Pouchy cried.

"Confetti if we make the team!" Anger declared as Pouchy spit out a plume of colorful confetti all over Fear.

"Gah!" Fear yelped.

"That's great," Joy said. "But either way, we love our girl."

"Confetti if we don't!" Anger cheered. Pouchy spit even more confetti at Fear, causing him to run off with his arms flailing.

Just then, Riley's phone beeped on the cafeteria table. The Emotions gasped.

"Is it Coach's email?" Val asked Riley.

But as Riley picked up her phone, she realized it was something even sweeter: a photo from Grace and Bree with the message "Good luck today!"

"Oh, I miss those girls," Joy said.

"Me too," agreed Disgust.

The school bell chimed, signaling that it was three minutes before class began.

"It's three minutes to two," Anxiety breathed. "You got this, Riley."

Joy nodded. "She's got this . . ."

"'Cause she's got us!" Embarrassment finished with his fist up. He got shy as everyone turned to look at him. "Right? Maybe?"

"All right, Embarrassment!" Joy cheered. "Everybody, look at Embarrassment!" She gave him a high five.

Sadness patted Embarrassment on the arm. "Nice job, big guy."

In the cafeteria, Riley began gathering her phone and books. Coach's email still hadn't come through, but she needed to get to her next class.

Val must have understood how much making the team meant to Riley, because before she left, she offered her a fist bump. "If you don't make it this year, there's always next year."

Riley smiled. "I know."

And all the Emotions swelled with pride.

"I love our girl," Anxiety sighed.

"How could you not?" Joy agreed. She gazed at the shimmering, shifting Sense of Self and thought back on all the perfectly imperfect moments that had made Riley who she was right then.

In front of her locker mirror, Riley put up her hair in a scraggly bun and blew a strand out of her face just as her phone beeped with a new email. She looked down at it and read the message, and a small smile spread across her lips.

Joy nodded proudly. No matter what happened now or in the future, Joy and the Emotions loved *all* of their girl—every messy, beautiful piece of her.

Stephen J. Pyne is a Regents Professor in the School of Life Sciences, Arizona State University. An award-winning environmental historian, he is the author of *Year of the Fires*, *The Ice*, and *How the Canyon Became Grand*. He is a recipient of the Robert Kirsch Award from the *Los Angeles Times*.

Praise for *Voyager*

"*Voyager*, a meditation on the nature and meaning of exploration itself, disguised as a chronicle of the life and times of a space mission."
—*The New York Times Book Review*

"For space geeks, it's a sweet read; for everyone else, it's an eye-opener."
—*Time*

"Even the most passionate aficionado, who devoured every digital bit sent back by the Voyagers, will find this overview enriching."
—*The Washington Post*

"The Voyager spacecraft have not only clocked up a far better understanding of the outer planets, they also illustrate mankind's third great age of discovery, according to Stephen Pyne in a fascinating new book."
—*The Economist*

"The Voyager story itself is an amazing one, and Mr. Pyne tells it skillfully. . . . Mr. Pyne deftly shows how the development of rocketry, of orbital science, and of computer technology all came together just in time to take advantage of a once-every-176-years planetary alignment that would allow a spacecraft to make close passes of outer planets— Jupiter, Saturn, Uranus, and Neptune—all in one long trip." —*The Wall Street Journal*

"Pyne's book isn't just an overview of the Voyager program; it's a sweeping history of what Pyne calls the 'third age of discovery,' beginning with the first sputterings of Sputnik and reaching all the way to our recent space shuttle disasters. Along the way, we're treated to a dense but intriguing sweep of the eras of exploration past." —Salon.com

"Today both Voyagers are still in operation and are passing beyond the edge of the solar system, serving as distant ambassadors for humankind. In this book, Pyne puts that quest in grand perspective." —*Science News*

"A challenging but immensely rewarding read."
—*Kirkus Reviews* (starred review)

"Pyne manages to set alight the story of the Voyagers as few space writers have ever done. In a marvelous twist on the usually self-important chronicles of space missions, he places the Voyagers in their historical and sociological context." —*The Dallas Morning News*

"This is not just a history of the remarkable Voyager program. Instead, it is an attempt to analyze it as part of the broad sweep of exploration stretching back to the likes of Christopher Columbus, focusing more on the politics and culture behind these ventures than on their scientific returns." —*New Scientist*

"Pyne captures the Western passion for exploration and the lure of the unknown, while relating the fascinating story of two fragile spacecraft continuing after three decades their brave quest across space and time." —*Publishers Weekly* (starred review)

"If NASA's historic achievement in manned spaceflight is a source of wonder and pride for all Americans, the agency's epic triumphs with satellites should be just as widely known and celebrated. Stephen Pyne's masterful *Voyager* shows us just how the United States continues to command the forefront of a third age of discovery in exploring our beautiful and astonishing universe." —Craig Nelson, author of *Rocket Men: The Epic Story of the First Men on the Moon*

"Stephen Pyne's *Voyager* is perhaps the greatest of his many books, much as the Voyager voyages are perhaps the greatest achievement of what Pyne terms 'A Third Great Age of Discovery.' Pyne chronicles these space expeditions in brilliant and detailed prose that is almost a new and poetic scientific language. It is a must-read for every intelligent human." —William H. Goetzmann, Jack Blanton Professor of American Studies and History

"There is an argument that what Americans do best is send extraordinary missions into space. Stephen Pyne, with a swift eye to the history of great exploration, positions the Voyager probe perfectly as it exits our solar system, beyond which are regions that exceed our imagination." —George Butler, producer and director of the documentary films *The Endurance: Shackleton's Legendary Antarctic Expedition* and *Roving Mars*

"Like the phenomenal missions it evokes, *Voyager* is destined for enduring eminence. A mind-boggling synthesis of science, history, and poetry." —Laurence Bergreen, author of *Marco Polo: From Venice to Xanadu* and *Over the Edge of the World: Magellan's Terrifying Circumnavigation of the Globe*

Voyager

**EXPLORATION, SPACE, AND THE
THIRD GREAT AGE OF DISCOVERY**

Stephen J. Pyne

PENGUIN BOOKS

PENGUIN BOOKS

Published by the Penguin Group

Penguin Group (USA) Inc., 375 Hudson Street, New York, New York 10014, U.S.A. • Penguin Group (Canada), 90 Eglinton Avenue East, Suite 700, Toronto, Ontario, Canada M4P 2Y3 (a division of Pearson Penguin Canada Inc.) • Penguin Books Ltd, 80 Strand, London WC2R 0RL, England • Penguin Ireland, 25 St. Stephen's Green, Dublin 2, Ireland (a division of Penguin Books Ltd) • Penguin Books Australia Ltd, 250 Camberwell Road, Camberwell, Victoria 3124, Australia (a division of Pearson Australia Group Pty Ltd) • Penguin Books India Pvt Ltd, 11 Community Centre, Panchsheel Park, New Delhi – 110 017, India • Penguin Group (NZ), 67 Apollo Drive, Rosedale, Auckland, 0632, New Zealand (a division of Pearson New Zealand Ltd) • Penguin Books (South Africa) (Pty) Ltd, 24 Sturdee Avenue, Rosebank, Johannesburg 2196, South Africa

Penguin Books Ltd, Registered Offices:
80 Strand, London WC2R 0RL, England

First published in the United States of America by Viking Penguin,
a member of Penguin Group (USA) Inc. 2010
Published in Penguin Books 2011

1   3   5   7   9   10   8   6   4   2

THE LIBRARY OF CONGRESS HAS CATALOGED THE HARDCOVER EDITION AS FOLLOWS:
Pyne, Stephen J., 1949–
Voyager : seeking newer worlds in the third great age of discovery / Stephen J. Pyne.
p.   cm.
Includes bibliographical references and index.
ISBN 978-0-670-02183-3 (hc.)
ISBN 978-0-14-311959-3 (pbk.)
1. Voyager Project.   2. Astronautics—United States—History.
3. Aeronautics—United States—History.   4. Planets—Exploration.   I. Title.
TL789.8.U6V5275 2010
919.9′204—dc22   2009046305

Printed in the United States of America
Set in ITC Legacy
Designed by Daniel Lagin

To Sonja
a polestar, as always
and Lydia, Molly, Karlie, Ashley, Lindsey, Colten, Julie, and Ivy
a new constellation in the heavens

An age will come after many years when the Ocean will loose the chains of things, and a huge land lie revealed; when Tethys will disclose new worlds and Thule no more be the ultimate.

—Seneca, *Medea* (ca. AD 40)

Throw back the portals which have been closed since the world's beginning at the dawn of time. There yet remain for you new lands, ample realms, unknown peoples; they wait yet, I say, to be discovered.

—Richard Hakluyt, *The Principal Navigations,*
Voyages, Traffiques, and Discoveries of the English
Nation (1587)

Come, my friends,
'Tis not too late to seek a newer world.

—Alfred Tennyson, "Ulysses" (1842)

There are no more unknown lands; the new frontiers for adventure are the ocean floors and limitless space.

—J. Tuzo Wilson, *I.G.Y.: The Year of the New*
Moons (1961)

Contents

Illustrations

Mission Statement:
Voyager of Discovery

On August 20 and September 5, 1977, two spacecraft, Voyager 2 and Voyager 1, respectively, lifted off atop Titan/Centaur rockets from Cape Canaveral, Florida, to begin a Grand Tour of the outer planets. Some 33 years and 21 billion kilometers later, having surveyed Jupiter, Saturn, Uranus, Neptune, their moons, and the interplanetary medium, and sent back enough digital information to fill a Library of Congress, they find themselves within the diaphanous heliosheath that divides the Sun from the stars. They have sufficient power for another ten years of operation, and racing at 440 million kilometers a year, that should grant them enough stamina to sail beyond the reach of the solar gases altogether and enter the interstellar winds before they expire.

The Voyager mission culminated what many of its contemporaries have come to regard as a golden age of American planetary exploration and what the future may well identify as the grand gesture of a Third Great Age of Discovery, the most recent revival of geographic journeying and questing in a chronicle that, for Western civilization, traces back to the fifteenth century. Yet what it has done for geography, the Voyager mission also does for history: the saga of the Voyagers' trek is carrying the inherited narrative of exploration to its outer limits, and perhaps beyond.

The countdown for the Grand Tour began twenty years earlier when, within the context of the International Geophysical Year (IGY), the Soviet Union lofted Sputnik 1 into orbit on October 4, 1957. The feat caused a sensation. Orbiting every ninety minutes, it sent out a beep that broadcast both triumph and taunt. The United States failed in its counter-launch of Vanguard 1 before succeeding with Explorer 1, on January 31, 1958. Thereafter, the two rival superpowers of the cold war began a long volley of launches that extended their geopolitical rivalry beyond the confines of scientific competition and the gravitational reach of Earth, and that, whether they intended the outcome or not, helped birth a new epoch of geographic exploration. Modern rockets had breached an ancient barrier to beyond.

From 1962 to 1978 America launched a flotilla of spacecraft—Pioneer, Mariner, Viking, and Voyager—to orbit the inner planets and survey the outer ones. In an outburst comparable to that of the sixteenth-century Portuguese *marinheiros* into and across the Indian Ocean or the eruption of eighteenth-century circumnavigators into the Pacific, American spacecraft would visit all the major bodies of the solar system save Pluto. But even as Voyager was wending through the asteroid belt, the institutional apparatus that launched it was collapsing. Less than a year after Voyager 1 launched, the Pioneer Venus Orbiter fired off, and then, for eleven years, no other American spacecraft trekked beyond the bonds of Earth. Throughout those years the Voyagers defined the American planetary program.

For some participants, those years bracket the acme of American space exploration. For others, the borders of a golden age are more elastic, reaching back to Explorer 1 or even to the lonely experiments of Robert Goddard and extending onward to the recent journey of Cassini to Saturn and the brave sojourn of New Horizons to extraplanetary Pluto and the Kuiper Belt. Others scorn so American an emphasis and insist that the circle include such visionaries as Hermann Oberth and Konstantin Tsiolkovsky, the relentless outpouring of Soviet spacecraft, the proliferating efforts of the European Space Agency, and the satellites of Japan, India, and China, all of which expand the scope of the undertaking. For a few observers—the most visionary or fanciful—the epic begins in evolutionary mists, when marine life first crawled onto land, or when early *Homo* of an unquenchable curiosity acquired fire; and for such prophets, the tale can end only when humanity, perhaps genetically self-engineered beyond recognition, wanders outside the solar system altogether.[1]

But all seem to agree that what lifted off from launchpads at Tyuratam and Cape Canaveral was something both novel and inevitable, and that it portended a fabulous new era of discovery, a journey beyond anything humanity had known before. In the past, geopolitics had repeatedly projected rivalries internal to Europe outward onto a wider world. With the launches of Sputnik and Explorer the cold war prepared to do the same, and this time the competition would transcend Earth itself. It would reach beyond sordid politics and the blinkered ambitions of its originating time and place. Those who meditated on the launches believed they were witnessing a transit of history that would define the dimensions of human time, like the transit of a planet across the Sun that demarked the dimensions of space. They did not know what lay beyond, or how they might reach it, only that they were determined to go.

After the launch of Explorer 1 in 1958, a press conference led to one of the canonical images of the ensuing space age, as three men—Wernher von Braun, James Van Allen, and William Pickering—hefted a mock-up of Explorer 1 over their heads. That tableau made visible the competition that drove the launches, a cold war that refused to be bound by Earth and carried its geopolitical jousting into space. But there, too, in the personality of each man and the cultural ambitions he represented, were the internal rivalries, both institutional and intellectual, behind the launch. Each man stood for a competing vision of what space might represent.

Wernher von Braun was in the tableau because he had overseen the development of the rocket that launched Explorer 1, and was the most prominent advocate for space as an arena for extraterrestrial colonization. He represented a tradition that identified far journeying with human settlement; he promised, in particular, to project the American experience outward to the Moon, then to Mars, and ultimately beyond. The von Braun narrative was one in which explorers were simply the vanguard of colonizers. It built on a heritage of European expansion since the Crusades.

James Van Allen was there because he had developed the instrument package for the satellite, and he became a public voice for space as a new laboratory for science. He stood for a tradition of systematic inquiry that had happily looked beyond Earth since the pre-Socratics, one that Galileo had refurbished and bonded to modern science with his invention of the telescope and, through that instrument, his questioning of the Ptolemaic model of the solar system. Rockets promised to take proxies of scientists—robots with instruments—beyond the limits of earthbound telescopes. The Van Allen narrative was one of an ever-searching science, always pushing against the limits of what was possible to know, an inquiry that had easily allied itself with geographic exploration.

The third man was William Pickering, then director of the Jet Propulsion Laboratory, the institution responsible for getting rocket and satellite together and on trajectory, and he would argue that Explorer 1, as its name indicated, was a vehicle for interplanetary discovery. Its larger purpose was to continue an erstwhile legacy of exploration—one certainly outfitted with the instruments of modern science, and one that would likely lead someday to outposts staffed with humans, if not to outright colonization. But sending robotic spacecraft was in and of itself a worthy exercise in an honored tradition of exploring. Of course that sentiment was never alone sufficient to justify such costly enterprises, which had to acquire other ends as well; but ultimately America should explore because that is what America had always done and what made America what it is. The Pickering narrative was one organized around half a millennium of geographic discovery by Western civilization and its rambunctious offspring, not least the United States.

All three visions shaped the evolving American space program, although each sought to point it in a different direction. Von Braun looked to the Moon and Mars, both potential sites for settlement. Van Allen sought to place instruments beyond the obscuring atmosphere, whether in wide Earth orbit or through interplanetary space.

Pickering (JPL) wished to send spacecraft to other planetary worlds; the journey itself was a medium for the message; the enterprise was, literally, a voyage of discovery. When money was flush, all three ambitions could claim more or less what they wanted. But when money became tight, the program had to choose among them; and while some tasks could overlap—the visions were not mutually exclusive—not every project or launch could satisfy each ambition equally, and consensus could fray and unravel.

This internal competition, separate from any geopolitical rivalry, was not solely about money. It was also about meaning; it was about what the Voyagers might do, what they signified, and why we should care. Explorer 1 could hold the space clans together, for each party could project into future launches what it hoped would happen. But that was possible because Explorer 1 first raised the curtain; twenty years later it was not possible to stage from a collective script. The forced unity among contestants could no longer heft a common project. In reality, one purpose or another would tend to dominate.

Voyager chose the journey; or rather, it passed through all of the purposes, as it did regions of the solar system. It began as part of cold war saber rattling little distinguishable from geopolitics, or at least the squabbling for spheres of influence if not outright imperialism that had so shaped the history of both the United States and the USSR. But in bypassing the Moon and Mars, Voyager left that purpose behind. It then became more purely science as its Grand Tour subjected the miniature systems of the outer planets to instrumented scans, one stunning encounter after another. Still, it continued, and as it has persisted it has become more and more the expression of an earlier genre of exploration, the quest, for which the narrative itself is a purpose and product. As the Voyager twins pass outside the solar system, pushing well beyond their engineered limits, they have seemingly transcended their origins and the received story by which to explain their mission.

The Voyagers are among exploration's purest expressions, and among both its strangest and its most revelatory. For more than five hundred years the West has relied on exploration to shape its encounter with a wider world, and to seek newer ones. That process has alloyed with adventure, curiosity and colonization, wanderlust, greed, war, pilgrimage, slavery, trade and missionizing, technological innovation, sheer animal instincts for survival, and moral imperatives, a vast historical cavalcade that has morphed and trod across, below, and beyond Earth, yet has organized itself in ways that align with the ambitions, the understandings, and the hopes of its sustaining society.

That chronicle has been neither random nor unbroken. It tacks and veers with changes in the technologies of travel and in modes of inquiry, with the opening of previously unknown lands, with the onset of fresh competitors and aspirations—in brief, with the core values and understandings of the culture that propels it. There are periods of quickening and of slackening; times when enthusiasm flames, and times when it smolders; eras when aggressive expansion seems irresistible, and eras when it appears to intellectuals as quaint, repugnant, or laughable. Twice in the past, geographic discovery as a project had been so reorganized in its fundamentals as to constitute an identifiable phase; call it a Great Age. This happened with the Great Voyages of the Renaissance, and it happened again as the Enlightenment dispatched Corps of Discovery to resurvey the old lands and to inventory whole continents with the sharpened eyes of science. Such eras rise from the general chronicle like mountain ranges, between which lie valleys of exhaustion or indifference. Beginning with the International Geophysical Year, another such Great Age has come into definition, drawn to new domains of geographic discovery, equipped with robots and remote sensors, and outfitted with a very different cultural syndrome, what might be termed a Greater Modernism. The Voyager mission nests within this narrative, and it may serve for this latest phase as a defining gesture of what it is about.

Yet a certain uneasiness hovers over this latest phase. It's dehumanized in sometimes unsettling ways. It has dispatched expeditions to new worlds, yes, but worlds inoculated against life, where no natives can guide and enlighten explorers, where no explorer can possibly live off the land, and where colonization is a fantasy. And perhaps most fundamentally the Voyager mission and its kind do not rely on human discoverers. The mantle of explorer rests on robots. How is this exploration? In what respects is this age continuous with and distinct from those that went before? In what ways does this new era of discovery recapitulate old ones, and in what ways does it exhibit new conceptions as well as technologies? How might its own enterprise be a novelty as spectacular as anything its journeys have unveiled? What has the era meant to the half-millennial saga of geographic exploration by Europe and its cognate civilizations? And why might that matter?

All this, Voyager has gathered from history, as its instruments have collected cosmic rays from deep space. The Voyager mission amassed the pieces of this new era, miniaturized and assembled them into working machines, and dispatched them on an immense journey. Those two spacecraft look back across five centuries of looking outward. Their trek is a complex fugue of past and future, of tradition and novelty, a narrative that pushes onward to newer worlds by constantly realigning with a legacy of exploration to older ones. The Voyagers' journey is an apt symbol for what might be considered a Third Great Age of Discovery, which is our own.

part 1

THE BEGINNING OF BEYOND:
JOURNEY OF AN IDEA

I cannot rest from travel; I will drink
Life to the lees . . .
There lies the port; the vessel puffs her sail;
There gloom the dark, broad seas.

—Alfred Tennyson, "Ulysses"

1. Escape Velocity

A Great Age of Discovery, like the epic voyages it encompasses, requires places to visit, the means to get there, and the will to go. For decades, after sledging over Antarctica and suffering through world wars and a global depression, exploration had sunk into a deep trough. But by the late 1950s all those errant requirements, separately evolving, had come into auspicious alignment. With Sputnik, a new era of planetary exploration achieved escape velocity.

There now existed technologies to carry instruments and people into places implacably hostile to life, and once there, to measure, map, and inventory by remote sensing. Some were mechanical devices such as rockets and submersibles; some, intellectual inventions such as maneuvers to boost spacecraft through gravitational assists. Together, machines and minds made possible forays over the ice fields of Antarctica and Greenland, across and down into the oceans' abysses, and through the solar system, the primary geographic arenas for new discovery. And there were motives aplenty from science, ever competitive, always pushy; from communities of believers and enthusiasts, explorers and space cultists, eager to exploit a congealing alloy of interests; from cultural longings, especially traditions of adventuring and questing, however projected afar; from businesses keen to supply the products of desire, particularly when refracted through governments; military ambitions, either for defense or forward strategies to forestall moves by antagonists.

This bundle of new motives, means, and opportunities made the exploration of the solar system possible, beginning with planet Earth. By themselves, however, they could not guarantee a new great age. Left to its own momentum, scientific inquiry and technological inventiveness would have slowly opened more of Antarctica, here and there, as coastal bases appeared and sledging parties converted from dogs to Sno-Cats and Bell 212 helicopters. Instrumented vessels would have probed the continental shelves and the occasional abyssal plain. Rockets would have supplanted balloons for sampling the upper atmosphere and the fringes of interplanetary space. Geographic adventuring would have merged with extreme sports and exotic tourism. The process would likely have been slow and sporadic, not unlike the Portuguese coasting that mapped the shores of Africa in fits and starts over the course of the fifteenth century or that slowly seeped across South America during the sixteenth.

The cold war, however, whipped those long swells into the whitecaps of a cultural storm. Golden ages involve concentrated outbursts, contained frenzies of discovery, typically within a single generation or two. The dynamics of the latter twentieth century offered a close paraphrase of those that powered previous outbursts such as the Iberian reconnaissance of the late fifteenth and early sixteenth centuries, the Russian leap across Eurasia in the mid-seventeenth century, the British and French circumnavigations of the late eighteenth, the North American blitz from the Appalachians to the Pacific in the early nineteenth century, the three-decade scramble across Africa that commenced in the late nineteenth, and the twentieth century's spectacular if brief heroic age in Antarctica. Now, as another fever of discovery spread, new expeditions looked to their predecessors not only for navigational aid but for models by which to define their character.

THE COLDEST WAR

In 1599 Vargas Machuca asserted the valence between geopolitics and exploration by declaring simply, *"a la espada y el compas, mas y mas y mas y mas."* By the sword and compass, more and more and more and more.

Some 350 years later the cold war reconfirmed that alliance. Rockets and remote sensing owed their rapid development to military sponsorship and the perceived need to control the new high ground of near-Earth space. Submersibles plumbed the oceans to map the terrain for nuclear-armed submarines. Both kinds of vehicles, moreover, whether beyond the atmosphere or beneath the seas, required secure communications, always an incentive to investigate new media and the paths of technology. The bonding of science with a national security state, begun during World War II, stabilized amid the early cold war and was then bolstered by the political panic that followed Sputnik. The primary institutions of contemporary exploration, even those nominally civilian, as often as not had Defense Department funding or acted as civilian surrogates to the same geopolitical ends—NASA doing for the space program, for example, what it was hoped the Peace Corps might do to forestall insurgencies. The superpower rivalry played out amid gestures of cultural superiority, from counting Olympic medals to technological triumphalism in rocketry, and it played out on the coldest of terrains from Antarctic ice to deep-ocean abyss to interplanetary space.

The prime mover of exploration remained what it had historically always been: the competition not between Europe and others but among the Europeans themselves, or among their former colonies and empires. However removed from overt confrontation, however benign compared to hot-war battlefields, space launches were a form of saber rattling. Whatever they had to say about distant planets, they spoke first to and about Earth. Just as Europe's internal competitions had pushed it into colonial conflicts, so the cold war projected Earth's dominant rivalry into the heavens. This appeal to exploration for geopolitical ambitions had a long pedigree. The monarchy that England could not assault in Madrid it could hobble on the Spanish Main. What France failed to achieve in Alsace, it could relocate to the Atlas Mountains. What Holland could not seize in North America, it might claim in the Spice Islands. The containment of communism that the United States was unable to achieve in the Mekong Delta it might overcome on the Sea of Tranquility. If it trailed the USSR in rockets, it could best its rival in satellites and science. "Space exploration," conceded Bruce Murray, co-founder of the Planetary Society and director of JPL during Voyager's passage through Saturn, "burst forth amid open belligerence and armed confrontation between the United States and the Soviet Union."[1]

Curiosity, a passion to explore, economic spinoffs, intellectual sparks cast from the whetstone of political necessity, cultural rejuvenation, government investment as a fiscal stimulant, renewed frontiers—whatever reason *could* be associated with the enterprise likely *would* be. After World War II, American oceanographers, for example, seemingly appealed to any and every cause that might fill their coffers and advance their standing as scientists. If the U.S. Navy had technical needs, then it could meet them. If foreign policy required international "cooperation," then that became the sustaining rationale. If assistance in "development" for emerging nations drove national interest, then that served. But in the postwar era, all these jostled under the covering umbrella of the cold war. National defense, broadly defined, was the overarching conceit, both unanswerable and sufficiently elastic to justify and disguise whatever real purpose a proponent intended.[2]

Yet those selfish pursuits emanated from a common culture, and it is precisely such amalgams—the sloppier and less precise, the better—that allow scattered acts of discovery and exploring expeditions to congeal into a Great Age of Discovery. The power of exploration derives from the power it shares with its sustaining society. The more deeply it can draft from that culture, the more interests it can tap, the more robust will be its support and the richer its impact. Still, something has to hold those oft-disparate pieces together to reach a goal: a colossal rivalry does just that, as internal dissensions shrink in comparison with the distance to a common foe. That was the catalytic effect of the cold war. Paradoxically, while they emanated from very different societies, the two superpowers displayed vital commonalities. Both identified themselves as expansionist nations founded on an ethos of exploration. Both committed themselves to similar state-sponsored technologies and came to mirror each other in their exploring styles; even civilian institutions morphed into looking-glass versions of their military cognates.[3]

The core issue for those interested in transforming stunning gestures into a program of space exploration and colonization was not whether the cold war could spark a golden age—it clearly did. The issue was whether such an era could sustain itself once that catalytic competition was gone.

EXPLORATION'S NATION

What this era of discovery means—why it happened when it did, what precedents it taps, even whether it constitutes a special age at all—depends on how those framing issues are placed and to what purposes. It configures one way within the cold war; another within sagas of imperial expansion, folk wanderlust, or colonization; still others within chronicles of technological innovation and scientific inquiry. Most advocates are eager to seize whatever justifications can be mustered, gathering any and all auxiliaries under the banner of their master purpose.[4]

But every proponent of a space program has instinctively appealed to exploration as a cause and consequence. Whatever else planetary spacecraft do, they explore, and whatever else they might mean, they belong necessarily in that illustrious pantheon of humans and societies that have pushed beyond frontiers to reveal a wider world. Against such motives, boosters assert, there can be no appeal. Exploration is politically deserving, culturally enriching, and genetically obligatory. It just is, and it must be.

In July 1969 William Pickering, director of JPL, responded to a request from Thomas O. Paine, head of NASA, for thoughts about the future direction of agency programs. Over the previous decade, Pickering noted, "the contest with the Soviet Union" provided the "necessary incentive" for Apollo. After Apollo 11 that external stimulus no longer existed, and Pickering, perhaps surprisingly, argued against an explicit replacement such as "a scheduled goal to land men on Mars." But how otherwise to "describe and justify the NASA purpose" remained tricky.[5]

He ticked through the usual roster. The advancement of scientific knowledge was "not worth $4 billion for a relatively narrow area of knowledge having no obvious relevance to everyday problems." The spinoffs from new technologies were "not good enough." (The public had already waited in vain for ten years for some "dramatic application of space technology" and had gotten Tang and the DustBuster.) The sense of "human adventure" was "interesting" but awkward to justify at these expenditures. National security was important, but it was hard to see how the present array of programs contributed. No single factor was, in truth, sufficient.[6]

Rather, the answer lay in "combining the several factors." That required an "integrating factor," which in Pickering's mind should be "exploration." Exploration could rally public sentiment. The country had always celebrated its "explorers and pioneers who tamed a continent." Now that the entire Earth had been "thoroughly explored from pole to pole, from mountain top to ocean depth," it fell to NASA to project that saga across the solar system. This, he concluded, was "a fitting task for the U.S."[7]

Exploration was, in brief, the final frontier of justification that potentially absorbed all the others and whose claims, in some respects, seemed unanswerable. Yet the appeal the space community made to the actual history of exploration was often both banal and irrelevant. That chronicle existed in the minds of many proponents only to motivate. The worst offenders were the colonizers, who saw themselves as true cosmopolites—literally citizens of the cosmos, who were willing to tap any nationalist chauvinism that would advance their cause. In particular, they became adept at phrasing the arguments for space travel in ways that would make critics seem to question the significance of the New World and especially the success of the American experiment.

In writing a history of space travel, with the help of two associates, Wernher von Braun concluded with a panegyric:

During the Renaissance, Prince Henry the Navigator of Portugal established in his seaside castle of Sagres the closest precedent to what the space community is trying to accomplish in our time. He systematically collected maps, ship designs, and navigational instruments from all over the world. He attracted Portugal's most experienced mariners. He laid out a step-by-step program aimed at the exploration of Africa's Atlantic coast as well as the discovery of the continent's southernmost tip, which he knew had to be circumnavigated if India were to be reached by the sea. With equal determination he pushed for the possibly shorter westbound route to the Far East. Prince Henry trained the astronauts of his time—men such as Bartolomeu Diaz, Ferdinand Magellan, and Vasco de Gama, and he created the exploratory environment that launched Christopher Columbus from neighboring Spain on his historic voyage.[8]

Not a word of that valedictory screed is true. This is an engineer's history, redesigned as one might rework a faulty engine to make it run better. It is a prophet's history, selectively culled and shaped to anticipate a premonitory future. And it is a rationalizer's history, gliding over the character of early rocketeers—the freelance pilots of the twentieth century—who offered their services to whatever power might advance their millennial ends. It is, too, a manifesto that justifies exploration as a scouting party for colonization. Discovery nests within a narrative of Western imperialism. It does not exist within a narrative of exploration as an act and institution in its own right.

To the believers, historical distortions mattered less than the value of historical appeal. "Henry the Navigator," von Braun continued, "would have been hard put had he been requested to justify his actions on a rational basis, or to predict the payoff or cost-effectiveness of his program of exploration. He committed an act of faith and the world became richer for it. Exploration of space is the challenge of our day. If we continue to put our faith in it and pursue it, it will reward us handsomely." Again, not a word rings true, save the appeal to faith, that history might justify what reason could not. What matters to the prophet is motive: if old faiths could move mountains, new ones could move to Mars.[9]

Still, whatever else it was, the space program *was* at least partly exploration, and its historical position remains a triangulation between past and future. If there is a new great age of discovery aborning, it will help to know its parentage, for like all progeny, the offspring will share some traits with its forebears and show new ones. The Voyagers tapped into that heritage and took it in directions never before attempted, so much so that they displayed the ideal expression not only for a new era of exploration but also for what might be considered a new species of explorer.

2. Grand Tour

In its origins, Voyager was both a mission in search of an opportunity and an opportunity in search of a mission.

Although the means to send spacecraft beyond Earth's gravity had become possible, and the rivalry with the USSR, rekindled by hysteria over Sputnik, made some undertaking obligatory, it was not obvious where such vehicles should go. The "new ocean" of space—a Black Sea of Darkness, as it were—beckoned powerfully, if vaguely. Beyond the Moon, an obvious first port of call, destinations depended on personalities, institutional preferences, ideas in the wind, real or anticipated moves by rivals, and that element of chance that is both randomness and opportunity.

FROM THE EARTH TO THE MOON, AND BEYOND

The clamor of voices after Sputnik was furious. Whatever the gloss of science applied to Sputnik, journalists and the public saw the satellite as a surrogate for nuclear-armed intercontinental ballistic missiles (ICBMs). Congress immediately commenced inquiries to restore American prestige, principally under the Preparedness Investigating Subcommittee of the Senate Armed Services Committee, which for its

Texan chair, Lyndon Johnson, meant being first and biggest. The Pentagon made its own claims early and loudly, offering compelling reasons why space belonged under its aegis, particularly the near-Earth environs of orbiting satellites for weather, communication, and espionage, and of course the powerful rockets necessary to launch payloads for any purpose; each service had its own claims, and collectively the Department of Defense funded an Advanced Research Projects Agency. The Rocket and Satellite Research Panel, a scientific advisory group under the Naval Research Laboratory, issued proposals within six weeks after Sputnik. The National Academy of Sciences evolved a Space Science Board out of its International Geophysical Year panel. The President's Science Advisory Committee staked a claim. The National Advisory Committee for Aeronautics (NACA) insisted that space best belonged within its bailiwick. And of course there were professional societies, commercial vendors, and citizen prophets. Each proposed programs tailored to its own purposes.[10]

What emerged was a consensus that the United States needed to demonstrate political will by besting the Soviet technological triumphs, that this might be achieved most blatantly by a high-visibility mission, and that however powerful the military substrate, the program ought to be ostensibly civilian. The institutional compromise, urged by a cautious President Eisenhower, was to recharter the National Advisory Committee for Aeronautics, originally established in 1915 to coordinate among academia, industry, and government, into a National Aeronautics and Space Administration (NASA) on July 29, 1958. The technological compromise was to have the civilians adapt military rockets to nominally scientific goals. And the political compromise was to leave NASA's founding purposes ambiguous, allowing each competing group to see in the NASA charter the realization of its own ambitions. Beyond an understood imperative to produce a publicity event equivalent to Sputnik, everyone could project onto NASA what they wished to see. The agency thus had a difficult birth that led to a troubled adolescence.

As long as money sloshed through the system and a clearly defined space race was on, the fissures within NASA were small and easily spanned. But the conflicts were present at the creation: military control versus civilian purposes, the need to ensure engineering success versus the desire to expand the frontiers of science, the preference for many small vehicles versus a few opulent ones, the desire—as the Rocket and Satellite Research Panel proposed in November 1958—to conduct "scientific exploration" and, at the same time, to carry out "the eventual habitation of outer space." One group envisioned a specific political reply to the Soviet challenge; another, an agenda for scientific discovery through prosthetic vehicles that could carry soundings from Earth's upper atmosphere to those of the other planets; still others, an implied mandate to colonize the solar system for which robotic spacecraft had meaning only as reconnaissance parties for subsequent human settlers; and most, perhaps all, hoped that such ambitions complemented rather than competed. The quarrels over means and ends, they wanted to believe, were merely squabbles over timing.[11]

NASA's charter did not prescribe particular programs, only an institution and a process. Conflicting interests would meet where a democracy best handled them, in open politics. Significantly, NASA's first administrator, T. Keith Glennan, was at once an academic (Case Institute of Technology), a military researcher (Navy's New London Underwater Sound Laboratory), and a member of a government agency (Atomic Energy Commission). NASA simply consolidated existing programs, which basically meant continuing NACA research and extending projects begun under the International Geophysical Year, discipline by discipline. At its organization meeting in June 1958, the National Academy of Sciences' Space Science Board concluded that "the immediate program would integrate results" of the IGY Committee's study, "which is now or has recently been completed." In brief, the emerging space establishment rounded up the usual suspects and prepared to give them money and rockets to go "beyond the atmosphere."

From the outset planetary exploration was deemed an essential part of a space program. The inspiration and prototype came from the International Geophysical Year (1957–58). As with so much of the

Third Age, IGY was catalyst, announcement, and model. It first melded science, exploration, new technologies, and geographies of discovery into a style that was recognizably different from earlier epochs of exploration, and so helped kindle a Third Age, much as the eighteenth century's endeavors to survey the transits of Venus had galvanized a Second Age. This was evident not only in its themes but in how it had morphed beyond them. IGY had begun more modestly, as a Third International Polar Year that intended to focus on Antarctica. But the opportunities seemed too fabulous not to scale up into a full-body scan of planet Earth, including its upper atmosphere; and it was within this context that Sputnik and Explorer launched. It seemed unavoidable, then, that IGY's successor institutions such as NASA would likewise leap beyond their founding conceptions, in this case to push beyond Earth to the solar system overall. The real questions were not whether to go but when, where, and how.

The Moon was an obvious first target, and as soon as the early Sputniks had racked up their orbital triumphs, the Soviets sent Lunik I past the Moon and Lunik II to its surface (both while the IGY was still in progress); and Lunik II sent gasps around the world when it broadcast a photo of the Moon's dark side. So even before NASA was founded, America planned to launch counter-probes to the Moon under the auspices of the Defense Department's Advanced Research Projects Agency—three Pioneer spacecraft by the air force and two through a collaboration between the army and the Jet Propulsion Laboratory.

JPL, in particular, was already imagining a future of planetary exploration far beyond the Moon. It had long ties with the army, not only with the "Propulsion" of its moniker, but more significantly for interplanetary travel, with guidance systems, telemetry, and communications—an early recognition that hardware was only as good as its accompanying software. A mere seventeen days after Sputnik I, the Lab urged that America "regain its stature in the eyes of the world by producing a significant technological advance over the Soviet Union." Director William Pickering recommended going to the Moon "instead of just going into orbit." But the institution aspired to much more. In January 1959 NASA accepted JPL's concept for a deep-space communication network, and in March it approved Project VEGA, an upper-stage rocket and spacecraft, thus partially substantiating JPL's bid to become the prime center for extra-lunar space flights. Ideas swelled like a supernova.[12]

Still, when congressional hearings in March reviewed "The Next Ten Years in Space, 1959–1969," the focus was on near-Earth sites that were achievable with expected engineering (and likely military) payoffs: orbital settings, the Moon, the neighboring Earth-like planets. Exploration for its own sake had little standing. What was done not only had to be doable. It also had to satisfy a political purpose.

Meanwhile, the Soviets had essentially claimed the Moon. A true triumph to counter the endless string of Soviet firsts required a still untouched target. That pointed to Venus and Mars. In February 1961 the Soviet Union made two attempts at Venus. Sputnik IV failed on launch, and Venera I missed its rendezvous with the planet. The opportunity for an American coup remained open. In November JPL engineer Allan Hazard submitted "A Plan for Manned Lunar and Planetary Exploration" that would place astronauts permanently on the Moon by the early 1970s, on Mars by mid-decade, and on Mercury, Venus, and "the outer Planets and their satellites" at some unspecified time thereafter. Though officially disavowed, the scheme showed where Lab thinking was headed. Then NASA pulled the plug in December 1959 by reversing itself and canceling Project VEGA.[13]

The Moon was far closer and more essential. Whatever might go to the planets would be field-tested on the Moon. NASA's founding interplanetary mission, in fact, began as a Moon shot before being diverted into orbit between Earth and Venus. While a first for America, Pioneer 5, jointly assembled by the air force, the Space Technology Laboratories, and Goddard Space Flight Center, had the appearance of a consolation prize after the Soviet spectaculars on both sides of the Moon. There seemed little more possible. The United States lacked a rocket capable of launching interplanetary spacecraft, and there was little incentive to push to the planets when the Moon still proved elusive. Nonetheless, Pioneer 5 sparked a need for an administrative structure—what became NASA's Office of Lunar and

Planetary Programs, which included an Office of Space Science and Applications.[14]

An office, however, needs missions, and missions need both a vehicle and a purpose. What emerged was Ranger, a program for lunar exploration based on a prototype for a true interplanetary spacecraft, one that was not simply an instrumented hunk of metal but an automated system. A JPL team sketched the basics in February 1960 with a study, "Spacecraft Design Criteria and Considerations; General Concepts, Spacecraft S-1." This established the foundational framework for JPL vehicles: a hexagonal frame, modular electronics and subsystem compartments, and a "bus-and-passenger" design that could accommodate a variety of payloads in what became a "hallmark of lunar and planetary missions." Ranger was its prototype, the progenitor for what became Mariner and through Mariner, Voyager.[15]

Yet Ranger's record was ghastly—six failures, finally followed by three redemptive successes. Its successor, the soft-landing Surveyor, hit the Moon five times out of seven. With the announcement by President Kennedy that the United States would seek to put a man on the Moon and return him safely by the end of the decade, the gravitational pull of Earth became less than the political attraction of the Moon.

Still, the planets beckoned. With a new upper-stage rocket, the Centaur, under development, the idea was floated to use some of its developmental test flights to send a spacecraft to Venus or Mars. The launch would occur anyway; the planetary probe would free-ride. Although the needs of Centaur determined the launch window, here was an opportunity to go beyond the Moon, and with NASA's acquiescence, JPL projected a new class of spacecraft, Mariner. The hope was that Mariner A would go to Venus, and Mariner B to Mars, probably in 1962, when planners projected a happy coincidence of developmental timetables and favorable trajectories. Planetary exploration was officially on the books.

Then Centaur encountered troubles, and scrambling for an alternative, JPL proposed in August 1961 that instead of a Titan/Centaur rocket, the launch could rely on an Atlas/Agena, and instead of a new spacecraft, they could construct one out of Ranger, what became Mariner R. So, despite having gone no farther than orbits around Earth, NASA approved two launches to Venus for July–August 1962. With barely a year to prepare, "not knowing that the proposed mission was almost impossible," as Oran Nicks recalled, "we laid out a plan, reprogrammed funding and hardware, and went ahead and did it." Mariner 1 failed on launch; Mariner 2 made the first planetary flyby, coming within 34,400 kilometers of Venus on December 14, 1962. A month before closest approach, NASA approved two Mariner-class spacecraft to go to Mars in 1964.[16]

Going to other planets carried the rivalries advertised in Explorer 1 farther out. Escaping Earth did not, for one, mean escaping the cold war, whose rivals soon sought allies among the planets. Mars and Venus were the prizes, and while both superpowers sent probes to each, the United States held a particular fascination with Mars, while the USSR came to regard Venus as its sphere of influence. But neither did leaving Earth dissolve the rivalries within the American space community. In particular, scientists, colonizers, and explorers could squabble over where and when to go.

Early on, a consensus emerged for Mars. After the success of Mariner 4's flyby in 1964, proposals for further unmanned probes flashed like meteor showers. The American Astronomical Society sponsored a symposium in 1965 on "Unmanned Exploration of the Solar System." The NAS Space Science Board declared that Martian exploration, in particular, including a search for life, should be a "National Goal in Space," a planetary counterpart to the Apollo enterprise. At the same time JPL constituted a Mars Study Committee. Headed by Bruce Murray, the committee stimulated a furious discussion that led to proposals for a dazzling full-bore program of exploration that would include flybys, orbiters, and landers. The last would involve a new state-of-the-art spacecraft called Voyager.[17]

But going to Mars in a colossal way was less politically compelling than getting out of Vietnam, and being tied neither to military necessity nor to Great Society programs, the ballooning costs made the project both visible and vulnerable. In August 1967 Congress canceled funding. By various juggling, and by reverting to a plain vanilla Mariner spacecraft, NASA salvaged enough money to keep the planetary program flying. There were two Venus flights scheduled for 1967 and two Mars flights for 1971. The grandiose Voyager program, once killed, was subsequently resurrected as Viking, a mission to Mars timed for (and justified by) the American bicentennial.[18]

Much as the planetary program had to insinuate itself, almost by accident, into the dominant Moon agenda, so a scheme to visit the outer planets had to finesse its way past Mars.

THE GRAND TOUR CONCEIVED

All the parts came together. Motive: a surrogate cold war played out in space. Means: the rapidly revolving technologies of rockets, spacecraft, communications, and guidance systems. These were trickier, because in the mid-1960s the capabilities for travel beyond the inner planets did not exist. Opportunity: a Grand Tour to the outer planets so compelling it could move the fantastic into the realm of the hypothetical. Although projects were only as good as the capability to encode them into metal and missions, a fabulous idea could—just might—impose a reality of its own.[19]

The practical range of space travel remained limited to the combustion that engineers could ram through thrusters, and Mariner 2 was already pushing those limits. While bigger rockets, with bigger payloads, were on the drawing boards, travel beyond the Earth-like inner planets demanded a far greater propellant. Even the most powerful rocket, the Saturn V, would require thirty years to send a probe to Neptune solely on its own impulse. Such propulsion alone could never make the trek quickly enough. The payload spacecraft would expire from natural causes before it reached the farthest planets, and politics would never commit to projects that imposed immediate costs for such remote payback. For scientists, too, the horizons were dim; and for public politics, they were as invisible to the naked eye as Uranus.

When a solution was found, it came from software rather than hardware. It appeared in the form of a suggestion that it was possible to outflank the superpower sparring around the inner planets and go directly to the outer ones, and that the propulsion to do so was latent within the very purpose of the mission. Robert Frost once explained that a poem, like a block of ice, should "ride on its own melt." Far planetary exploration needed a mission that could likewise ride on the melt of its design.

The two vital insights emerged not from machine shops or government offices but from densely mathematical studies of hypothetical trajectories. One involved finding a way to get spacecraft to the outer planets, and the other, a time and reason to do so.

The first took shape in 1961, from work by a mathematics graduate student, Michael Minovitch, hired for the summer by JPL's mission-design program to explore trajectories to carry spacecraft from Earth to Venus and back again. Over the next couple of years Minovitch went further and came to realize that a spacecraft behaved like a small planetary body, subject to the same gravitational accelerations and decelerations as asteroids and comets. By approaching a larger body in the same direction as its orbital motion, a spacecraft would accelerate, and thereby achieve additional momentum—a "slingshot" effect. Relative to the planet, it would lose what it gained as it sped away, but relative to the Sun, it would have gained overall, and where the planet producing acceleration was massive, the spacecraft would acquire far more propulsion than it ever could from prospective launch vehicles on Earth, which were soon to approach their upper limits. Moreover, the gravity-assist maneuver could be used more than once in a single mission.[20]

Minovitch organized his thoughts in a 1963 technical report to JPL's trajectory group. His insight did not instantly galvanize his colleagues, however, and they continued to experiment with mixes of propulsion systems, trajectories, and potential projects. Whatever its mathematical elegance, the concept had little engineering relevance until it got coded into a machine and a mission. The defining event came the next year, when Gary Flandro, a postdoc at JPL, distilled the "gravitational perturbation technique" to its essential equations and applied the results to a select suite of trajectories for the outer planets. The "great challenge," Flandro appreciated, was "to try to make exploration of the outer planets practical."[21]

His research took him to Walter Hohmann, and then to Gaetano Arturo Crocco, an Italian who in 1956 had published a scheme for repeated close flybys of Earth, Mars, and Venus in what he termed a "grand tour." Mostly Flandro fixed on Krafft Ehricke's *Space Flight*, which expressed in general language what might be interpreted as gravity assistance. Then Joe Cutting, the group's supervisor, recommended Minovitch's work, particularly that which targeted Jupiter. Here, Flandro thought, was "the key to the outer solar system." To his mind, however, the work done so far had been "elementary" and abstract. What was needed were calculations for "realistic mission profiles so that estimates of actual flight times, payloads, and planetary approach distances and speeds could be made." Especially critical was an identification of "launch windows."[22]

What emerged by the spring of 1965 was a stunning recognition that a once-in-176-years alignment of planets meant that a single spacecraft could fling itself from one to another within a period comparable to the life of a probe. The required conjunction would occur in the early 1980s, which meant that a spacecraft launched in the late 1970s could reach Jupiter, the critical accelerant, just in time to ride a gravitational wave train to Saturn, Uranus, and Neptune. It was, Flandro recalled, "a rare moment of great exhilaration." But as always the inspiration was only as good as its expression. He found that the "trajectory computer programs" crafted by Minovitch were "not truly adequate," and he replaced them with a "hand method using tabulations and graphs." Since Minovitch worked at night, he and Flandro did not meet. It mattered little, since it was not Minovitch's general solution that made Voyager possible, or his computational methods, but the providential alignment of the outer planets that tipped the scale of possibilities. Flandro circulated his results internally in 1965, even as the American Astronomical Society sponsored a symposium on "Unmanned Exploration of the Solar System." The next year, he published the scheme for the space community in *Acta Astronautica*, identifying ideal launch dates and sketching prospective trajectories.[23]

Initially, there was ample skepticism, even at JPL. At issue were engineering concerns: guidance, communications, and particularly the durability of spacecraft, for even an accelerated journey to Uranus would take ten years, while existing mechanical and electronic devices could barely survive a nine-month trip to Mars. But the idea itself soon accelerated, flung from one study to another much as the hypothetical spacecraft it imagined might career from planet to planet. In December 1966 Homer Joe Stewart, director of JPL's Advanced Studies Office, instantly saw the significance of the idea and published a prospectus in *Astronautics and Aeronautics*, and it was he who proposed to transfer Crocco's term "grand tour" from the inner planets to the outer. Meanwhile, Bruce Murray, who had previously headed the Mars Study Committee, was busy outlining the particulars—what seemed to most partisans to be veritable axioms—for the mission, or rather a suite of missions. The scientific harvest was stupendous, the engineering challenge magnificent, the potential cultural impact "great and enduring," and its value as cold war propaganda immeasurable. Here was a space spectacular that America was especially equipped to win. The Grand Tour was a noble complement to Apollo.[24]

By early 1969 JPL had sketched the practical requirements of spacecraft design and launch trajectories for variants of an outer-planet survey, and was even using its dazzling vision as a recruiting device. James Long summarized the options for a multiple-year, multiple-mission reconnaissance, concluding that such a scheme was feasible as well as "a timely—virtually unique—opportunity for exploration." Within the year William Pickering was promoting the Grand Tour through *American Scientist*. Throughout, there were two selling points: one, that the cost of going to the outer planets was essentially the same as going to Jupiter alone, since the critical added velocities came from Jupiter's gravitational assist; and two, that the alignment of the planets was, from a programmatic perspective, providential. There was every incentive not only to seize the "super-window" offered but to make as complex a mission as possible in order to magnify that opportunity, perhaps including orbiters and landers. What the Viking mission would do on Mars, the Grand Tour could do across the solar system.[25]

In this, the first of its journeys, Voyager had achieved a break-through by means of a shift in reference frames, and that is exactly what Voyager has continued to do throughout its long trek. The process started at its conception, by seeing a hypothetical spacecraft differently, and it will end by forcing us to see ourselves differently. But as William James once put it, "truth *happens* to an idea." Gravity assist happened when Mariner 10, launched in 1973, swung around Venus and Mercury exactly as predicted. The scheme worked, shaving rocket fuel loads as much as 70 percent. A spacecraft could reach the outer planets and still be sentient, if not fully ambulatory.

The primary propulsion system for Voyager was, in the end, intellec-tual. It was the idea of the Grand Tour.

It seemed irresistible. Both the scientific community and the American media seized on the scheme. By 1971 the Space Science Board had endorsed the proposal; NASA lent approval for further studies, and JPL had plunged into a flurry of inquiries. Here was the scotched Mars Voyager resurrected. Here was a dazzling prospect for technological challenge and first-order exploration. Here was prom-ised a marker in the centuries-long saga of exploration. The last time this planetary conjunction had appeared, Alexander von Humboldt was halfway through his monumental trek across South America; before that, Jan Carstensz had just navigated around Australia's Gulf of Carpentaria, finding nothing of worth, and Plymouth Plantation had settled in New England, still looking eastward, and more intent on the reformation of the Old World than westward to the coloni-zation of a New; and before that, Portugal had barely passed Cape Verde, still stutter-stepping toward the Renaissance's Great Voyages. By the next conjunction, 2153, the planets would have been explored singly. The exploration of the solar system for the first time could happen only once. A Grand Tour could do that.

Enthusiasm was keen: opportunity seemed like inevitability. How could anyone oppose such a fabulous conception? By 1977, when the ideal launch window would appear, the technology, the managerial skills, the instrumentation, and the hands-on experience of navigat-ing probes through interplanetary space would be sufficient. Were the launch window to come five years earlier, those means would not have existed, and had they arrived five years later, the opportunity might have been lost. It was inconceivable that anyone might deny the Grand Tour its call to destiny.

Studies boomed, not least because the options for surveying the outer planets, especially if two spacecraft were launched, were surprisingly rich. Three combinations particularly intrigued planners. One was a three-planet mission to Jupiter, Uranus, and Neptune. Another three-planet mission targeted Jupiter, Saturn, and Pluto. The last version was a four-planet mission to Jupiter, Saturn, Uranus, and Neptune. Each mission would involve multiple launches. It was even possible, if barely, to imagine a flotilla of missions that would collectively sample all of the outer planets with reasonable completeness.[26]

Meanwhile, on July 31, 1969, only fifteen days after Apollo 11 landed on the Moon, Mariner 6 entered orbit around Mars, followed five days later by Mariner 7, offering for the first time an effort to synchronize two simultaneously exploring spacecraft. To observers it seemed that a Grand Tour had to follow. Nothing else could claim anything like its cachet. It remained only to select the most savory of the potential offerings and then render it into a machine to cross the solar system, even though neither the technology nor launch vehicle for such an enterprise existed, nor the political determination to go. JPL's preference was for a program built around a new vehicle, a spacecraft more durable, expansive, and autonomous than the Mariner series, and one that could survive a hostile decade in space. This required, among many features, a computer that could undertake on its own some routine testing and repairs, and an energy system not dependent on sunlight. The new vehicle, called Thermoelectric Outer Planet Spacecraft (TOPS), promised to be as expensive as it was daring. The Grand Tour deserved nothing less.

By 1970 NASA had formally assigned an Outer Planets Grand Tours program to JPL, which endowed a Grand Tour Project Office, which commenced to sort through the preliminary studies and announced a call for proposals for the scientific package. Estimated costs ranged from $750 million to $900 million, a prince's ransom at the time. Still, the Office of Management and Budget (OMB) liked it as an expression of national prestige, and approved some funding for planning. On March 7 President Nixon declared unequivocally for a Grand Tour, with preparations to begin in 1972. By summer some five hundred scientists had submitted proposals for what would be a dozen experimental slots. But in some respects, the winnowing hardly mattered. Where so little was known, everything was there to be learned. JPL petitioned NASA headquarters for a formal authorization, and NASA approved, contingent on congressional funding.[27]

THE GRAND TOUR OPPOSED

Yet what excites some can cause in others an allergic reaction. The Grand Tour unexpectedly rallied a grand alliance to oppose it. The usual motives came into play, from squabbling over money to disciplinary jealousies, some reasons honorable, some petty. The bottom line was, what the cold war gave, it could also take away, by proposing competitors eager for the same government funds and stature. Nor was the space community united. What seemed to true believers a juggernaut providentially aligned with the stars appeared to others more like Oliver Wendell Holmes's rickety "one-hoss shay."

The most universal concern was cost, which was serious and might go ballistic despite close attention. Even before Apollo 11, NASA's budget was fast ebbing, and the commitment to the space shuttle threatened to become (and did become) a fathomless fiscal sinkhole. Apollo 16 and 17 were canceled. President Nixon decided, along with NASA strategists, that the future belonged with the space shuttle, an American Concorde, which could also quell industry unrest over the cancellation of a supersonic transport (SST). There was not enough in the Treasury to support both robotic Grand Tours and human-steered SSTs, much less fight foreign wars and finance a Great Society. Besides, the political calculations were overwhelming. The shuttle meant thousands of jobs; an outer-planets spacecraft, prime work for a thousandth as many voters. The reality was what Harris "Bud" Schurmeier, a key JPL manager and prime mover behind the embryonic Voyager mission, blandly said it was, that "planetary exploration has inevitably been insignificant on a national scale, low on the agenda, small in the budget." Start-up funds for the Grand Tour were slashed to $10 million from a requested $30 million.[28]

The funding might be finessed. A single mission, even if expensive, might be easier to sell than five, each of which offered tempting political targets. But what threatened to fatally compromise the Grand Tour was intramural fighting among space scientists. A Grand Tour was big science that risked alienating academic little science, and it was a big-budget item that competed directly with a big-budget item craved by astronomers: a space telescope. Those groups whose research did not extend to the outer planets or who were not slated to join the eleven science teams on the spacecraft offered tepid support, or became hostile, viewing the funds lavished on the Grand Tour as siphoning precious monies that might go to their own projects. There was already a big-science mission on the boards, the reincarnation of Mars Voyager into Viking; and the search for life on Mars seemed likely to muster broader enthusiasm from both the scientific community and public than mapping the magnetosphere of Uranus.

Even enthusiasts for outer-planet exploration could legitimately doubt whether now was the proper time, or a Grand Tour the proper means. The NAS Space Science Board had conducted a major study in 1965. While urging NASA to think beyond the Moon, the board had concluded that an intensive study of Jupiter was a better bet than far-ranging flybys; and that if missions to the other gaseous planets were feasible, single shots were a more conservative hedge than a romantic Grand Tour. NASA then constituted an Outer Planets Working Group, with representatives from all its field centers that had an interest in the scheme, and again the consensus favored parsing the Grand Tour into more manageable excursions or crafting a compromise in which two missions would each tour three of the outer planets—all this on the grounds that the engineering was more likely to succeed and the richer returns would be more widely distributed among planetary scientists (a narrower version of the jobs argument).[29]

In June 1969 NASA invited the Space Science Board to reconsider.

The Board reconfirmed its belief that "study of the outer solar system" was a "major objective of space science" and that the community was "eager and excited." It urged that NASA increase the fraction of its budget devoted to planetary exploration, that Pioneer-class spacecraft lead the endeavor, and that Jupiter be the first object of outer-planet missions, with a mix of Grand Tour projects to follow if funding proved adequate. But it also reasserted its original position that the Grand Tour should be not one but several missions. Specifically, it argued for five, all of which would either target Jupiter or use it for gravity propulsion. The JPL scheme was deemed at or beyond the limits of engineering expertise. It was risky, its success uncertain, and its costs extreme.[30]

The Grand Tour's promised payoff, while glamorous, seemed meager compared to what might be done by other means, and worse, its unstanched costs threatened to bleed space science dry. (By now Voyager had become a surrogate for criticism of Viking, which was further along in its development and much more costly.) The SSB nearly recommended outright termination. After discussions with the OMB, NASA returned to what was becoming the default setting: two missions launched over two or three years to reach two or three planets. Had the Grand Tour been a launched missile, with its wobbly path so badly out of trajectory, it would have been blown up. It was kept, although its woes seemed an unsavory augury for what became Voyager. Meanwhile, the SSB, while sanctioning planetary exploration as a "major objective," recommended halving the funding level, thus taking away with one hand what it gave with the other. The SSB urged more near-Earth activity and, led by astronomers, wanted an orbiting telescope. If robotic spacecraft could do science that humans couldn't, then a telescope could do much of that science without the robots. The proposal in effect sought to sever science from exploration.[31]

Other critics, led most visibly by James Van Allen of the University of Iowa, protested the magnitude of the NASA investment in crewed programs to the detriment of robotic missions; the former did no science worth mentioning, and given a fixed (or inflation-ablated) budget, a sharp tilt toward manned space flights, in a kind of bureaucratic sheet erosion, would drain funds away from all the rest. (With no specific appropriation for the shuttle, NASA had to absorb internally its development costs, which escalated from $12.5 million in 1970 to $78.5 million the next year.) This promised to scrap everything that could not fit into the shuttle's bay. The opposition to crewed programs spurred a counter-protest against robots, and gave NASA critics overall additional arguments against both programs.[32]

The deeper concern, though only implied, was to question whether science needed spacecraft at all. For the present it did, as the SSB observed. Several fields of interest—the kind that the International Geophysical Year had pursued in the upper atmosphere of Earth—had "no known alternative to the techniques of direct observation near, or within, the object of investigation." The only way to put an instrument in such proximity was with a spacecraft. But if other means became available, they might well, from the perspective of science, be superior. One could dispense with spacecraft as robotic spacecraft did with astronauts.[33]

Even within NASA, competition was keen. The agency was a forced merger of institutions that had their own traditions, goals, and styles, and that were avid to contest against one another. So long as money had been ample, every research group and every facility could get something that it wanted; but when choices had to be made among them, a competitive scramble resulted among institutions, among projects, among personalities, among ideas, among visions of what "space," "science," and "exploration" meant. This held even as NASA's head, James Fletcher, insisted that no such internal trade-offs existed (no one believed him) and that the space science community had to unite behind all programs. "Science" by itself had "very little political support," he noted, but "space" meant "technology, applications, and political prestige" (all of which was marginally more acceptable). Regardless, the space science community fissured, and that chasm split the larger space lobby.[34]

The crunch came in 1971. The NAS Space Science Board met for an intensive study seminar in early August, argued again to bolster NASA's planetary program, reaffirmed a 1970 study that established priorities for space research, and concluded that regular or even intermediate funding was not sufficient for Grand Tour missions "without jeopardizing the Planetary Explorers [Pioneer] and key programs of the other scientific disciplines." The 1971 session also folded in recommendations from the President's Science Advisory Committee. For the outer planets, it urged as a priority a Jupiter study by "Pioneer-level technology." The JPL ambition for a Grand Tour with a new spacecraft found support only if NASA received its "HIGHER budget program"—an improbable outcome. Still, the SSB supported development of TOPS-class spacecraft and an enhanced Titan rocket to launch it; and it introduced the prospects for "satellite imaging," which it thought might "constitute the most solid justification for [a] Grand Tour." The intellectual returns from remote moons, however, could not outflank the staggering expenses and the aroused alliance of rivals within NASA and the space-science community.[35]

A body in shock pools blood from its outer limbs to its vital organs; so, too, with bureaucracies. Congress had not backed Nixon's rhetoric with real money. NASA redirected the flow of funds from the outer planets to near-Earth activities and to that most Earth-like planet, Mars. Like the tall poppy that gets cut down, the high-visibility Grand Tour was a tempting target—something almost everyone liked in principle but few were willing to sacrifice for. NASA decided that its institutional future lay with humans in space. In December 1971 Administrator James Fletcher wrote the Office of Management and Budget that NASA would cancel the Grand Tour. In January 1972 that announcement became public.[36]

THE GRAND TOUR REVIVED

The Grand Tour was dead. Its spirit, however, proved harder to kill, and it quickly transmigrated into another avatar.

Within ten days, JPL proposed an alternative. It would scale back the full-bore Grand Tour into paired visits to Jupiter and Saturn. It would adapt the proven Mariner spacecraft rather than, Viking-like, invent a new one from scratch such as TOPS. It would pare costs from $900 million to $360 million. It would co-opt critics from the start, particularly enlisting support from the SSB and OMB. And it would, with sly ambiguity, allow for the option of tweaking the second flight to swing past Saturn and rendezvous with Uranus and perhaps Neptune. The metempsychosis was complete. The Grand Tour had become Mariner Jupiter/Saturn 1977 (MJS 77).[37]

NASA accepted the proposal in June and signed a formal project agreement in December, assigning Bud Schurmeier as project manager and assembling a Science Steering Group. JPL began reorganizing immediately. Even this furled-sail mission went far beyond anything attempted to date, not only geographically but technologically and administratively. (Pickering insisted that "something more than 'organized arm waving'" was needed to ensure confidence that a spacecraft could even survive to a "far planet encounter.") Just getting to Saturn was tricky enough: the projected three-and-a-half-year voyage was six times longer than any that had flown. The most advanced power source would last only a year; sensitive equipment had to endure the hazards of interplanetary and near-planetary space, ranging from micrometeorite bombardment to saturated radiation; and navigating a spacecraft through rings, radiation belts, and moons while adjusting sensor platforms demanded an unprecedented choreography of commands. Communications could barely handle a trek to Venus or Mars, and while improvements were expected, the distances were too great to rely on human judgment during crises, which meant a spacecraft would have to analyze and repair itself. Some technology had to be new, not simply adapted. Some could be expected to need correction based on the Pioneer 10's encounter with Jupiter in 1973 and Pioneer 11's encounters with Jupiter and Saturn in 1974 and 1979, respectively. The whole science selection process had to be renewed, which was certain to revive ill feelings. And while everything had to be done on schedule and on budget, nothing done should inherently prevent a reincarnated full-bore Grand Tour.[38]

The pressures, both internal and external, got worse with each year. The internal pressures were many: to reengineer the Mariner spacecraft to accommodate the best features of TOPS; to create sufficient reservoirs of power and propulsion for the vehicle; to upgrade the means of communication through the Deep Space Network with its receivers in

Spain, Australia, and California; to harden electronics after Pioneer 10 had its circuits fried by the gargantuan radiation around Jupiter; to create an onboard computer at a time when even simple personal computers did not exist; to absorb administrative regime changes as Bruce Murray replaced William Pickering and John Casani succeeded Bud Schurmeier; and to affix some kind of permanent message to the spacecraft beyond the plaques created for Pioneers 10 and 11. In October 1974 some 116 "concerns" remained before the Final Spacecraft System Design Review scheduled for March 1975 could determine if the spacecraft could meet launch dates.[39]

The external pressures were no less daunting: the constant downsizing of a post-Apollo NASA determined to retain Skylab, Apollo-Soyuz, and the shuttle, all major tributaries to the budget drain; the cost-accounting for work done by other NASA labs and the Defense Department; the need for contractors, though overseen by JPL; the awkward siting of JPL within the NASA bureaucracy as both an agency branch and a part of Caltech; and not least, the potential crisis over a launch vehicle. Planners had assumed from the onset that it would launch with a Titan IV (of which NASA still had two); but NASA's subservience to the shuttle had decreed that it be the agency's primary launcher, a decision that threatened to eliminate any prospects for outer-planet exploration. Yet throughout, the hope for a resuscitated Grand Tour remained embedded in the design. As John Casani remarked, "We knew what the strategy was; we knew what we were going to do; we knew what the decision points were."[40]

In February 1976 NASA granted final approval for "Mariner Jupiter/Saturn 1977 Planetary Exploration (Outer Planets Missions)." The mission called for two spacecraft that would journey for a scientific reconnaissance of the nearest of the outer planets and their moons. Launch would occur in 1977. But the enabling authorization included two prospects for an extended mission, provided the designated goals at Jupiter and Saturn were satisfied and the spacecraft were still performing well beyond their warranty ("a miracle," as Casani himself put it). One allowed for "retargeting" the second spacecraft to go to Uranus. The other imagined the trek of the spacecraft to the edge of the solar system, to the shores of interstellar space, the Third Age's Sea of Darkness.[41]

By month's end NASA had accepted in principle an extended mission, first to Uranus and, ultimately, beyond the solar system. The official Voyager Project Plan allotted one spacecraft, "as long as it continues to function," to break through the heliopause and into the interstellar medium. It allotted the other, if it, too, was still working, to "permit an encounter with Uranus," with objectives similar to those for Jupiter and Saturn. And implied, but left unsaid, was the prospect for an encounter with Neptune.[42]

Again, software—the dominance of guidance over hardwiring, the power of ideas and culture, the self-capacity to adapt—had proved critical. The will had found a way.

As the parts assembled, the official name, Mariner Jupiter/Saturn 1977 Planetary Exploration (Outer Planets Mission), or, in shorthand, MJS 77, seemed inadequate to the reality of the spacecraft and the half-submerged ambitions of the mission. Or at least it did to John Casani, who announced a competition for a new name. He had recently come on board as project manager, thought the label lame, awkward, and overly bureaucratic, and despite the fact that a contest had recently settled on an MJS 77 logo, he reopened the issue, with a case of champagne promised to the winner. It appeared that names no less than visions might be reborn.[43]

Candidates bubbled up: Nomad, Pilgrim, Pioneer, Antares, and a name that had surfaced for missions twice before but had never stuck, Voyager. It had most recently attached to the ambitious Mars mission that got scrapped before being resurrected as Viking. After a superstitious hesitation—the previous project had, after all, been canceled—a counter-consensus emerged. Voyager Mars had failed because of costs, not because it was a doomed idea, and it had spawned a marvelous replacement. "Voyager" thus seems to have careened around the bureaucracy and the imaginations of JPL designers in a kind of noumenal Grand Tour of its own. A general vote approved it. In March 1977, five months before liftoff, NASA agreed.[44]

There were three spacecraft constructed. The first (VGR 77-1) was trucked to Florida in March, feeling its way over highways and through the perils of overland traffic. The others arrived on April 21 and May 19.

There they underwent rigorous prelaunch checks. When the second (VGR 77-2) revealed fatal flaws, it was left behind as a bed for spares and as a model on which engineers could test reported glitches. It could make explicable in a lab what signals from the others might indicate were problems in space. VGR 77-3 took its place. The differences between the two launched spacecraft were minor. Voyager 2 included, for example, a slightly greater power source and several more robust sensors (and camera), since it might, just might, pivot around Saturn and go to Uranus. The Voyager triplets had become twins, and the greatest tag team in planetary discovery.

EXPLORING POLITICS

The Voyagers' journey from vision to launch—through the vacuum and hazards of mind, institutions, engineering, and politics to the materialization of ideas and ambitions—was itself a daunting, extraordinary trek. It took as long to move from Flandro's 1965 insights to the actual launch in 1977 as it took the Voyagers to travel from Florida to Neptune. Political hazards could be as fatal as radiation, and Congress as dangerous as asteroid belts. But it had always been so.

Few private entities could afford the cost of exploring over the Ocean Sea or across new worlds, and as soon as they appealed for public support, they became subject to public control. When private companies dispatched exploring parties, they did so under the political cover of letters patent or charters, and even private persons could not evade the political context of their travels and required letters of transit or risk charges that they were spies. John Ledyard's daffy ambition to walk from Europe to America ended in 1788 when the Russian empress Catherine had him arrested and deported. Alexander von Humboldt had to seek permission from Carlos IV in 1798 before he could tour New Spain.

To fanatics aflame with their vision quest, the goal is so self-evident, so tantalizingly palpable, so urgent, that they can imagine any question or impediment only as crude harassment. To those less addled by such schemes, the expenditure of public money must satisfy public interest, and having foreign nationals wandering about the world can loose political conflicts that others will have to clean up. A traveler seized or killed becomes a traveler politicized, a hostage that demands rescue, a national honor besmirched and crying out for retribution, a cause célèbre. Voyager's long, troubled gestation is more norm than exception.

Conviction is not knowledge, resolve not rightness; and vision is only as good as the times it lives in. Five centuries before Voyager, Portugal waited ten years after the return of Bartolomeu Dias before it sent Vasco da Gama to India; yet the route was there, needing only the will to send vessels; and no other prize so dominated the imagination of the Great Voyages as the passage to India. Still, Portugal procrastinated, obsessed with more immediate crises and opportunities, not least a change in monarch and court. Exploration existed to promote Portugal, not Portugal exploration.

Today's partisans for the colonization of space had their counterpart in proponents for the development of the spice trade. The latter were loud, pesky, persistent, and they enjoyed an alliance of convenience with a claimant to the throne, Manuel I, who finally assumed the crown in 1495. All this makes reasonable the suggestion that da Gama's first voyage was a political bone tossed to appease a noisy distraction while the court attended to the important affairs of state, notably its enduring tensions with Castile and endless wars with Morocco. "The low priority given to this expedition, the appointment of a minor fidalgo to the command, and the fact that the mission carried with it so little in the way of diplomatic gifts or trade goods," suggests Malyn Newitt, indicate it was a "minimal gesture" to "silence" a marginal cabal, while providing the young monarch with a symbolic means of maintaining what had become a nearly century-long tradition.[45]

The politics could go both ways. While the obvious might lie rotting at anchor, the idiotic might set sail. Captain Thomas James found sponsors in his quest to discern a route to the South Seas through Hudson Bay. John Cleves Symmes inspired a republic skeptical of intellectuals to outfit ships to explore a "hole at the pole" that he argued was a mathematical certainty and would lead to the center of the Earth. Christopher Columbus and his brother hawked his ideas for a western voyage to the Indies—flawed, as it turns out, but lucky— for years. In the 1830s the United States could find no senior officer willing to command its great Exploring Expedition to the South Seas and around the world. It all depended on tide and time.

To those enthralled by the Grand Tour, the politics of authorization was tedious, perverse, and needless, an encumbrance and an embarrassment, a monarch-in-waiting begging alms in the sordid corridors of Washington. But over the centuries, while politics has erred in both omission and commission, it has remained the preferred medium for discourse. Occasionally it has financed the foolish, and not infrequently it has dismissed the savvy, but whatever else exploration was or aspired to be, it could not divorce itself from the politics of court and congress and especially not from the geopolitics of competing empires. The quirky trek of Voyager through NASA bureaucracy, scientific commissions, congressional committees, partisan critics, and prophetic seers places the mission squarely within a tradition harking back to the very origins of exploration as a systematic enterprise.

Because of politics, the expedition almost didn't happen, and because of politics, it finally did.

3. Great Ages of Discovery

The Voyagers left Earth atop Titan/Centaur rockets. The Titan had two stages, to which the Centaur, with its own propulsion system, added a third. Titan put Centaur into rough orbit; then the Centaur's rocket fired twice to bring it into cruise orbit. Finally the Voyagers' own propulsion modules sent them on their prescribed trajectories.

As they moved beyond the limits of Earth-orbiting satellites, the Voyagers also moved beyond the limits of earthbound exploration. Yet that past lifted them as surely as their Titan/Centaur rockets, whose stages of propellants might well stand for the three great ages of discovery of which the Voyagers were a culminating payload.

EXPLORATION, LUMPED AND SPLIT

Why three ages? There are those who see many more, and those who see none at all, for exploration history, too, has its lumpers and splitters.

The lumpers view the long saga of geographic exploration by Western civilization as continuous and thematically indivisible. The Viking landers on Mars are but an iteration of the longships that colonized Greenland. The Eagle, the Command Module orbiter, and the

Saturn V rocket that propelled the Apollo 11 mission to the Moon are avatars of Columbus's *Niña, Pinta,* and *Santa Maria.* The "new ocean" of interplanetary space is simply extending the bounds of the old. The *ur*-lumpers would go further. The origins of all exploration, including Europe's, reside in the genetic code of humanity's inextinguishable curiosity. Even more, space exploration, they insist, shares an evolutionary impulse. Through humanity, life will clamber out of its home planet much as pioneering species crawled out of the salty seas and onto land. The impulse to explore is providential; the chain of discovery, unbroken; the drivers behind it, as full of evolutionary inevitability as the linkage between DNA and proteins. The urge, the motivating imperative, resides indelibly within our character as *Homo sapiens sapiens.*[46]

The splitters see it differently. Exploration pulses, expanding and contracting. Ming China launched seven dazzling voyages of discovery, and then outlawed all foreign travel and prohibited the construction of multimasted boats. Medieval Islam sponsored great travelers before shrinking into the ritual pilgrimage of the haj. The Norse spanned the Atlantic, then withered on the fjords of Greenland. Plenty of peoples have stayed where they were: they lacked the technological means, the fiery incentives and desperate insecurities, or the compelling circumstances to push themselves to explore beyond their homeland. Like Australia's Aborigines, they were content to cycle through their ancestral Dreamtime, and felt little urgency to search beyond the daunting seas or looming peaks. A walkabout was world enough.

To the splitters, what determines the cadences of exploration are the cultural particulars—the social conditions that prompt and sustain discovery. What is commonly called "geographic exploration" has been, in truth, a highly ethnocentric enterprise. It will thrive or shrivel as particular peoples choose. There is nothing predestined about geographic discovery, any more than there is about a Renaissance, a tradition of Gothic cathedrals, or the invention of the electric lightbulb. From such a perspective, the European era of exploration that has dominated the past five centuries is simply another in a constellation of cultural inventions that have shaped how peoples have encountered a world beyond themselves. It is an institution, and it derives much of its power because it bonds geographic travel to cultural movements, because it taps into deep rivalries, and because its narrative conveys a moral message. It can accordingly be parsed into historical eras.

For Western civilization, these fall most easily into three grand eras. Each had its primary geographic domain, each bonded with its prevailing intellectual syndrome, each tapped a moral energy. Each had its own peculiar dynamic of geopolitical rivals and cultural enthusiasms. Each found a gesture that came to express its character. And each stage had to be rekindled. A successful launch only appears continuous in broad-brush retrospect; on closer inspection, it shows a rhythm of spark and extinction.

GREAT VOYAGES: THE RENAISSANCE EXPLORES

The Great Ages of Discovery opened with centuries of false dawns. Part of the difficulty is disentangling exploration from other forms of travel—from migration, walkabout, exile, wars of conquest, enslavement, trading expeditions, reconnaissance, long hunts, great treks, missionizing, pilgrimage, tourism, and just plan wanderlust. Roman merchants had contact with the Canaries and Cathay. European pilgrims trekked from Hibernia to the Holy Land. Franciscan scholars trudged to the court of the Great Khan. Each age of expansion, every expansionist people, experienced a burst of discovery about a larger world.[47]

What made events of the fifteenth century special was that these exploring contacts did not end in a rapid contraction. They became welded to a revived expansion of Europe that would stretch over half a millennium; they bonded with revolutionary epochs of learning and political reform. Exploring became institutionalized. Exploration became the outward projection of internal unrest that would not let the momentum long languish.

That Portugal pioneered the Great Voyages should alert us to the process's uncertain origins and its often desperate character. There was little in Portuguese history from which someone might predict, in 1450, that the nation would leap across whole seas and over unknown continents, establish the world's first global empire, and create the raw template for European expansion, whose outposts would survive until the twenty-first century. Yet that is precisely what happened. For several hundred years, exploring nations sought to emulate the Portuguese paradigm. Within a generation, it came to be said that it was the fate of a Portuguese to be born in a small country but to have the whole world to die in.

Why Portugal led remains an exercise in historical alchemy. One can find reasons for its ingredients, but not a simple explanation for why they mixed as they did. There is a certain logic embedded in Portugal's geographic setting. Here, at Europe's land's end, the two major traditions of boat construction converged, the Mediterranean with the Baltic. It was a place on the edge. Its isolation forced it to take to the sea; its smallness compelled it to find nimble ways to outflank rivals and enemies; its precarious politics surrounded it with competitors. In particular, it waged a ceaseless dynastic war with Castile that left those two states as the drivers of European expansionism during the late Renaissance; and it fought endlessly with Morocco. Under Henry the Navigator it had discovered and colonized Atlantic isles from 1420, a cameo of what it would attempt with its passage to India. Yet if the causes seem feeble, the outcome was unmistakable. More than anyone, Portuguese sailed the Great Voyages, whether as sponsors or pilots in the service of others, and they plotted out the terms of European imperialism. Columbus learned his trade on the Portuguese circuit. Magellan sailed for Spain only after his native Portugal had rejected his scheme.

Exploration became—directly, or indirectly through charters—an organ of the state, and because no single state dominated Europe, many joined the rush. Geographical exploration became a means of knowing, of creating commercial empires, of outmaneuvering political, economic, religious, and military competitors—it was war, diplomacy, proselytizing, scholarship, and trade by other means. For this reason, it could not cease. For every champion, there existed a handful of challengers. This competitive dynamic—embedded in a squabbling Europe's very fabric—helps explain why European exploration did not crumble as quickly as it congealed.

On the contrary, many Europeans absorbed discovery into their understanding of who they were, even in some cases writing explorers into a founding mythology, a cultural creation story. In short, where exploring became a force, something beyond buccaneering, it interbred with the rest of its sustaining society. The broader those cultural kinship ties, the deeper the commitment. Societies dispatched explorers; explorers reshaped society. Exploration became an institution. The explorer became a role.

The fabled Great Voyages announced a First Age of Discovery. Its particular domain was the exploration of the world ocean: it ultimately proved that all the world's seas were one, that it was possible to sail from any shore and reach any other. Of course there were some grand entradas in the Americas, and missionaries, Jesuits especially, penetrated into the vast interiors of the Americas, Africa, and Asia. But as J. H. Parry observes, it was the world sea that defined the scope and achievements of the First Age. Mapping its littoral was the era's finest intellectual achievement.[48]

The map reminds us that the First Age coincided with a Renaissance. The era unveiled two new worlds, one of geography, another of learning. Francis Bacon conveyed this sense perfectly when he used as a frontispiece to his *Instauratio Magna* the image of a sailing ship pushing beyond the Pillars of Hercules. The voyage of discovery became a metaphor for an age of inquiry that would venture far beyond the dominion of the Mediterranean and the inherited wisdom of the ancients. The discoveries overwhelmed a text-based scholarship. Scholasticism, that arid discourse that resulted from too many scholars and not enough texts, collapsed as new information poured into Europe like New World bullion into Spain, and like it, caused an inflationary spiral of knowledge.

The nature of learning differed, too. It came not from recovered texts but from newly discovered lands and peoples, and not from the ancients but from encountered living cultures. Very little of the terrestrial world Europe discovered was uninhabited, which is to say, unknown to humanity. It was unknown to Europe, and Europe learned about it through its indigenes. Interpreters, guides, cultural brokers—all assisted in the transfer of learning from various enclaves to Europe, which proceeded to sew them together into a global quilt. Voyages were the stitches; seas, straits, and societies, the patches. Over and again, explorers succeeded by relying upon (or seizing) local pilots, and by learning the language of, and emulating the dress and mores of, the native peoples. This meant that the central act of discovery, the encounter, was almost always an encounter between peoples.

An age of discovery thus demands more than curiosity and craft and yields more than data points or lore hoarded like bullion. Acquired knowledge has to be minted into useful currency; and exploring has to speak to deeper longings and fears and folk identities than science and scholarship. An expedition voyages into a moral universe that explains who a people are and how they should behave, that criticizes and justifies both the sustaining society and those it encounters. The Great Voyages provided that moral shock: they forced Europe to confront beliefs and mores far beyond the common understanding of Western civilization. The Renaissance expansion of Europe profoundly altered Europe's understanding of itself and its place in the world. There was plenty of hollow triumphalism, of course, but those contacts also inspired Montaigne's celebrated preference for the cannibalism of Brazil's noble savages to that of Versailles's courtiers, and Las Casas's excoriating denunciation of the conquistadors. The contacts also compelled a reexamination of the political and ethical principles underlying Christendom and its secular principalities.

While all peoples are ethnocentric, Europe was distinctive in that its *mappa mundi* placed the cartographic center of creation in the Holy Land, leaving Europe to the margins. In the early fifteenth century that displacement accurately depicted Europe's standing in the world. A century later, however, Europe could relocate itself to the center.

CORPS OF DISCOVERY:
THE ENLIGHTENMENT EXPLORES

By the early eighteenth century, exploration had found itself becalmed, even moribund. Discovery had achieved its purpose. It had found serviceable routes—the only ones, really—to the wealth of the East. Its sponsors felt little need to search for more, or to probe remote regions of the globe without prospects for commerce or plunder. Mariners did more poaching and piracy than original questing; the explorer blurred into the fantasist and the fraud, a promoter of Mississippi and South Seas bubbles. Expeditions of adventurers persisted largely because interlopers tried to outflank established competitors.

By almost any index, exploration sagged. Although missionaries and *bandeirantes* had worked through the rivers of South America, and fur traders had done likewise for the main lakes and rivers of northern Asia and North America, few new islands were unveiled, and nothing of the interiors of Africa, and nothing of the outlines of Australia and Antarctica; and what was learned was often hoarded. They had not, of course, surveyed the Earth in its fullness; until the late eighteenth century, even the world's coastlines still had unmapped gaps. But the implacable will (or the internal furies) that had driven explorers now flagged. Exploration seemed destined to be left marooned on the shore of a fast-ebbing historical tide. As with a Titan/Centaur launch, the saga of exploration also had its coasting periods.

Then the historical dynamics changed. A period of coasting and consolidating ceased. The elements for a revival of exploration positioned themselves. Cultural engines again burned and boosted a new stage of exploration upward.

The long rivalry between Britain and France, the penetration of high culture by the Enlightenment, and a hunger for new markets, all combined to move Europe again out of dry dock and onto the high seas of commerce and conquest. The grand tour became a global excursion around the Earth. Perhaps most extraordinarily, the missionary emerged out of a secularizing chrysalis as the naturalist. Increasingly, scientists replaced priests as the chroniclers and observers of expeditions—Linnaeus's apostles supplanted Saint Francis Xavier's Jesuits—and scientific inquiry substituted for and justified the proselytizing that had helped sanctify an often violent and tragic collision of cultures.

The era's annunciatory events were two sets of expeditions. The first was a paired undertaking sponsored by the Paris Academy of Sciences in 1735 to measure an arc of the meridian. One expedition went to Lapland under Pierre Maupertuis and one to Ecuador under Charles-Marie de la Condamine. For the first time abstruse questions of natural philosophy, in this case involving the shape of Earth and competing theories of gravity, drove expeditions. The second cluster proved significantly more impressive as it mounted an international campaign to measure the transit of Venus, first in 1761 and again in 1769.

Here was a scientific campaign urged by scientists, to be conducted by scientists, aimed at simultaneous global surveys that would measure a critical value needed to understand models of the solar system, whose calculated working had become the exemplar of Enlightenment science. It was, to advocates, a unique opportunity, a passage of astronomical alignments across a suitable civilizational setting. In its request for funding, the Royal Society of London appealed to two principal "Motives": the "Improvement of Astronomy and the Honour of this Nation." There was national glory to be gained from success, and national shame to be endured from failure, and of course one could necessarily expect economic spinoffs from the inevitable improvements in scientific knowledge that would result. The 1761 transit featured 120 observations, of which 106 were in Europe; the 1769 transit, 150 from European outposts around the Earth.[49]

The swarm of expeditions helped rouse geographic discovery from its long slumber; they defined the terms by which exploration, empire, and Enlightenment might find common causes; they midwifed a transition from an exploring science welded to natural philosophy to one bonded to natural history. The expeditions of Baptiste Chappe d'Auteroche to Tobolsk and then to Baja California, of Legentil de la Galaissière to the Indies and Alexandre-Guy

Pingrè to Rodrigues and Haiti, and especially the voyage of the HMS *Endeavour* under Captain James Cook to the Pacific galvanized public opinion and helped spark a revolution in scientific discovery—a model less for measuring the distance of Earth from the Sun than for inventorying the splendor of Earth. Here in cameo was demonstrated the ambition and means to inspire a new age of discovery.

Over the next century every aspiring great power dispatched fleets to seek out new wealth and knowledge, to loudly go where others had not yet staked claims. Once again, the rivalries among the Europeans were as great as anything between Europeans and other peoples. In 1769 James Bruce reached Lake Tana, the traditional source of the Blue Nile, while James Cook arrived at Tahiti to measure the transit of Venus. One journey represented rediscovery, a reconnection by a new sensibility with classical lore; the other, a new discovery, a barely known place subject to vision.

Circumnavigation revived, but ships proved mostly a means to reposition explorers, who promptly moved inland. The world's continents replaced the world sea as a primary arena for discovery, and the cross-continental traverse substituted for circumnavigation as its boldest expression. The voyaging conquistador metamorphosed into the Romantic naturalist. The transition matters because as the nineteenth century ripened, Europe was no longer content to remain as a trafficker on the beaches of the world sea. Like its exploring emissaries, it shoved and swarmed inland. Trading ventures became imperial institutions, coastal colonies evolved into continental nations, and the politics of commerce gave way to outright conquest. Exploration as a reconnaissance for trade segued into surveys for settlement; imperialism moved from founding coastal trading factories to establishing states over which they would rule, some of which they would populate with émigré Europeans.

The outcome was a fabulous era for exploring scientists. New intellectual disciplines bubbled up out of the slush of specimens shipped home. The returns from the earliest explorers to a particular place were often phenomenal—the scholarly equivalent to placer mining or, in the First Age, to the sacking of Tenochtitlán or Malacca. A revolution in geographic discovery again accompanied a revolution in learning, aptly symbolized by the simultaneous recognition by two exploring naturalists, Charles Darwin and Alfred Wallace, of evolution by natural selection.

The moral drama changed accordingly. Secularization and science translated Vasco da Gama's famous declaration that he had come to the Indies for "Christians and spices" into a cry for civilization and commerce. The deeper drama concerned that fraction of Europe's imperium colonized by European emigrants. These settler societies tended to look upon discovery as part of a national epic, and to honor explorers as vital protagonists—a Moses, an Aeneas—of those founding events. Their subsequent folk expansions proceeded hand in glove with formal exploration, such that Daniel Boone, not George Washington, became America's folk-epic hero. These were new worlds, premised on the prospects for a new order of society. America truly was, in William Goetzmann's words, "exploration's nation"; but so were Russia, Australia, Canada, and others.[50]

Discovery metastasized. As measured by the number of exploring expeditions, a slight increase appears in the latter eighteenth century and then erupts into a supernova of discovery that spans the globe. In 1859 the last unknown Pacific island, Midway, was discovered; by the 1870s, explorers had managed comprehensive traverses—cross sections of natural history—for every continent save Antarctica. With the partition of Africa, expeditions proliferated to assess what the lines drawn on maps in Berlin libraries actually meant on the ground. Exploration had become an index of national prestige and power. The first International Polar Year (1882) had turned attention to the Arctic. An announcement by the Sixth International Geographical Congress in 1896 that Antarctica remained the last continent for untrammeled geographic discovery inspired a swarm of explorers to head to its icy shores; even Belgium and Japan sponsored expeditions. (America's attention remained fixated on the North Pole and that other stampede to the Klondike.) Ernest Shackleton's celebrated 1914 Imperial Trans-Antarctic Expedition was, after all, an attempt to complete for that continent the grand gesture that had crowned every other.[51]

But Antarctica was the last. There were no more unvisited lands to traverse, other than such backwaters as the Red Centre of Australia, the crenulated valleys and highlands of New Guinea, and the wind-swept Gobi. The enthusiasm for boundary surveys and natural history excursions—for imperialism itself—waned with the slaughter of the Great War. Plotting the number of exploring expeditions reveals the Second Age as a kind of historical monadnock, rising like a chronological volcano above a level terrain. The peak crests in the last decades of the nineteenth century, as exploration crossed the summit of the Second Age. Then it began a descent down the other side.

Like a cycle of economic boom and bust, what had ramped up now ramped down. The process went into reverse—exploration's equivalent of deleveraging. The reasons are many. One is simply that Europe completed its swarm over the (to it) unknown surfaces of the planet. There was nowhere else for the Humboldtian explorer to go, and there were no more lands to meaningfully settle. Antarctica, the deep oceans, interplanetary space—these arenas for geographic discovery might be claimed, but they would not be colonized.

No less important, the dynamic behind exploration changed. The Second Age had kindled with a rivalry between Britain and France, much as the contest between Portugal and Spain had powered the First Age. Thereafter virtually every competition featured Britain, which is why its explorers so dominate the age. Britain and France clashed in India, the Pacific, and Africa; Britain and the United States in North America; Britain and Russia, the Great Game, across central Asia; Britain and all comers in Antarctica. But after the Great War, Britain and France could no longer afford the enterprise. Russia turned inward with revolution. The United States had few places other than Antarctica in which discovery had geopolitical meaning. The Second Great Age of Discovery, like the First before it, deflated. Moreover, the old rivalries, once projected outward, now turned inward, and Europe brought its colonial wars home in what ended with near self-immolation.

By the middle twentieth century, after two world wars, a global depression, and the sudden shedding of colonies, Kipling's "Recessional" had become prophetic. The Great Powers were exhausted, Europe sought to quench its internecine wars by severing its colonial ties, and the resulting decolonization accompanied an implosion of exploration. Europe turned inward, quelling the ancient quarrels that had restlessly and violently propelled it around the globe, pulling itself together rather than projecting itself outward.

And as in the past, there were cultural factors also at work. The Second Age had served as the exploring instrument of the Enlightenment. Geographic discovery had bonded with modern science such that no serious expedition could claim public interest without a complement of naturalists, while some of the most robust new sciences, such as geology and biology, relied on exploration to cart back the data that fueled them. Science, particularly natural history, had shown itself as implacably aggressive as politics, full of national rivalries and conceptual competitions, and through exploration, it appeared to answer, or at least could address, questions of keen interest to the culture. It could exhume the age of the Earth, reveal the evolution of life, celebrate scenic monuments to nationalism and Nature's God. Artists such as Thomas Baines and Thomas Moran joined expeditions, or as John James Audubon did, mounted their own surveys. General intellectuals eagerly studied narratives of discovery. Exploring accounts and traveler narratives became best sellers; explorers were cultural heroes; exploration was part and parcel of national epics; exploration was a means to fame and sometimes fortune. The Second Age, in brief, braided together many of the dominant cultural strands of its time.

By the early twentieth century, however, this splendid tapestry was unraveling. A Greater Enlightenment found itself challenged by a Greater Modernism. One consequence was that, in field after field, intellectuals turned to subjects that no longer lent themselves to explication by exploration. Natural scientists looked to the very large and the very small, to redshifting nebulae and subatomic particles or molecular genes. Artists turned inward, probing themselves and the foundations of art, not outward to representational landscapes. High culture was more inclined to follow Sigmund Freud into the symbol-laden depths of the unconscious, or Joseph Conrad into a heart of imperial darkness, than to ascend Chimborazo with Humboldt or to paddle with John Wesley Powell through the gorges of the Grand Canyon. The Second Age sagged not simply from the exhaustion of closed frontiers but from a more profound weariness and ironic dismay with the entire enterprise of Enlightenment and empire.

Once more Western exploration began to coast. In the early nineteenth century an intellectual could claim international acclaim by exploring new lands. By the early twentieth he could not, if he could even find suitable lands. There were a few spectacular exceptions. The gold-prospecting Leahy brothers trooped into the unknown highlands of New Guinea. Richard Byrd wistfully erected Little America on the Ross Ice Shelf. Roy Chapman Andrews, with carbine and Model T, whisked across the Gobi in search of dinosaur eggs, the very model of a Hollywood action hero (and inspiration for Indiana Jones). But there was overall a rueful, forlorn quality to the striving, aptly expressed when the American Museum of Natural History, with Andrews in command, dispatched an expedition to Shiva Temple, an isolated mesa within the Grand Canyon, to look for exotic creatures, as though it stood somewhere between the Galapagos and Shangri-La. Sixty years before, the Canyon had claimed center stage not only for geographical discovery but also for the answers it offered to fundamental questions about the Earth's age and organic evolution. Now the press boosted a minor foray into a journey to Arthur Conan Doyle's *Lost World*. Lost world, indeed.

INTO THE ABYSS: MODERNISM EXPLORES

Then it happened again. New lands became available; new technologies and ideas made them enticing; and rivalries between institutions, companies, nations, and personalities mixed combustibly.

Of a sudden, unexpected realms had appeared. Places previously off-limits because of hostile environs, rivals of comparable power, technological feebleness, or ignorance or timidity had opened up. These were the ice sheets (and sub-ice terrains) of Greenland and especially Antarctica, the deep oceans with their abyssal plains and immense trenches, and of course a solar system, full of worlds that beckoned beyond the vision of earthbound observatories. As powerful instruments and remote-sensing technologies emerged, as manned vehicles and unmanned probes plummeted to the depths and beyond the atmosphere, the prospects for a revival of exploration became possible. Suddenly, a Pacific Ocean that had seemingly yielded its last island to discovery a century before revealed hundreds of new islands in the form of submerged seamounts.

Antarctica was the transition. It was an abiotic landscape not much accessible to Enlightenment art and science, with no prospects for colonizing settlement, the last of the continental frontiers and the one where the Second Age exhausted itself. Twice before—in 1882 and 1932—a global science had rallied for "polar years." The earlier versions had focused heavily on the Arctic; this time, after a half century of world wars, proponents hoped to concentrate on the Antarctic.

The scheme soon snowballed into a call for a more general eighteen-month scientific scan of the Earth, what became known as the International Geophysical Year (1957-1958). The roster of participants was a veritable United Nations of science—some sixty-eight nations in all. It was here, for the first time, that the contours of a new age of discovery came together. IGY's explorers would visit places inimical not only to humans but to life itself. They would rely on remote-sensing instruments, tracked vehicles, rockets, and robots. They would inventory a planet whole, of which Earth would be the prototype: the home planet became, intellectually, a new world, the first of a dawning age of discovery that would propagate to the fringe of the solar winds. The voyages that followed to planets such as Venus, Jupiter, and Neptune would carry essentially the same instruments and ask the same questions of them as IGY did for Earth.

Through the infrastructure provided by IGY, noted J. Tuzo Wilson, the "science of the solid earth" was "absorbed into the broader framework of a new planetary science." Yet Earth's fluids interested the founders as much as its solids. They peered with special fascination into the upper atmosphere—geophysics, after all, was embedded in the project's very name. Auroras in particular had pointed to Antarctica as an insufficiently exploited platform for earthly observation, which was where a third polar year had been headed. But the fast-morphing capabilities of rocketry made it possible to send instruments directly into the auroral belts. Both the United States and the Soviet Union had long-extant, if semi-dormant, plans to launch instrumented missiles beyond the realm of high-altitude balloons, leaving rockets as a new means to ask inherited questions.[52]

IGY escalated those scientific yearnings into a political probability. It did for the Third Age what the voyages of Columbus and da Gama did for the First, and the transits of Venus did for the Second. But where the successors to the transits belonged with Enlightenment and empire, the successors to IGY looked, however uneasily, to a Greater Modernism and a postcolonial age. The character of exploration morphed, for IGY did not simply revive the Second Age but assembled the pieces for a Third. The International Geophysical Year was barely three months along when, under its auspices, the Soviet Union launched Sputnik 1. Twenty years after Sputnik leaped into earthly orbit, the Voyagers were flying toward a rendezvous with the moons of Neptune.

Still, dazzling technologies and an invigorated curiosity are not enough to spontaneously combust into an era of exploration: cultural engagement also demands a sharp rivalry. Those competitive energies flourished with the cold war.

In retrospect, the great game between the United States and the Soviet Union lasted far less than those between Spain and Portugal, or Britain and France, but the era is young, and if it does in fact mark a Third Age, some other competitors, keen to secure national advantage or prestige through sponsored discovery, may emerge. Without the cold war, however, there would have been scant incentive to erect bases on the Antarctic ice, scour the oceans for submerged mountain ranges and trenches, or launch spacecraft. Two geopolitical rivals, both with active exploring traditions, chose to divert some of their contest away from battlefields and onto untrodden landscapes. The cold war was the final propulsion module that boosted planetary exploration out of Earth orbit.

Most observers assumed that technology drove discovery. Surely without rockets and remote-sensing devices, the age could not have unfurled. But inventions followed ideas. The pioneering rocketeers had envisioned migrations off Earth and experimented with rocketry as a technological means to move their enthusiasm into space. Nor was the apparatus of the Enlightenment designed to cope with the realms of the Third Age. It broke down on ice, abyss, and space as it did with atoms, relativistic quasars, and self-referential logic. The Second Age had neither the technology nor the software to plunge into those uninhabitable domains; but the intellectual revolution that we might lump together as Modernism could. The most successful explorers of the Third Age would be modernists, whether they willed it or not.

Yet there was a paradox in its pith. Modernism could deal with such realms, but most modernists lacked the incentive to do so. Outside the sciences they were more inclined to look inward than outward. The culture's software lagged behind its hardware. The ability to voyage anew appeared before the capacity arose among elites to wish to do it. Pragmatism was a philosophy suited for pioneering; existentialism was not. Those sciences that were most moribund were precisely those most closely bound with the Second Age. Geology was seemingly done more in libraries than in the field; certainly personalities such as Wilson, so despairing of earth science, hoped IGY would spark a reformation. A new era of exploration might ignite, as it had in the eighteenth century, a paradigm shift. (Interestingly, the anticipated revolution occurred exactly between the dates of the two editions of Thomas Kuhn's *The Structure of Scientific Revolutions*, 1962 and 1970, which introduced the concept of scientific paradigms, and thus furnished a kind of manifesto.)[53]

What bridged the gap, meanwhile, was popular culture. Exploration did not wither away, because the culture had not only institutionalized but also internalized discovery. This was a civilization that could hardly imagine itself as other than exploring. Accordingly, it forged new institutions, of which the International Geophysical Year is an apt annunciation; and with spacecraft dispatched across the solar system, it recapitulated the entire half-millennium saga of Western exploration. Those vessels crossed what enthusiasts were

pleased to call "this new ocean," and in the outer planets they discovered new worlds, miniature solar systems, full of unknown seas
and isles. Out of that encounter came a reformed earth science and a
comparative planetary science.

In the Voyager mission, the Third Age stripped exploration down
to its essentials. The twin spacecraft went into Earth orbit atop a
long heritage of experience and expectation, but they had their own
boosters as well, and they used them to point outward and fire into
a distinctive trajectory that traced what may well be the age's most
spectacular and defining gesture. If the Voyagers departed Earth full
of inertia from the past, they also added a momentum of their own
that sent them into the future. They looked back even as they looked
beyond. Their trajectory was a constant triangulation of both.

4. Voyager

Exploration has always been something done by explorers. Of course they used the technology of their times. They traveled by ships, wagons, rail, balloons, and bathyspheres; they relied on astrolabes, compasses, barometers, and sextants. But it was the person of the explorer, or of an exploring corps, that propelled the expedition, did the necessary tasks, and embodied its purpose. To invoke the name of the explorer was to evoke the mission overall.

The Voyagers challenged this traditional formulation. They were robots: the technology *was* the exploring agent. They were something more than dumb machines, because they had a degree of autonomy and had to act, within limits, independently of their handlers. They were more than simple ganglia of instruments, because they carried their own motive power, which granted them the means to journey. Like any artifact of human contrivance, they exhibited a style that embodied the imagination and values of their creators, which granted them a simulacrum of personality. They could be anthropomorphized in ways that the *Santa Maria* or the HMS *Resolution* could not, yet they were far from human, or even alive. In sailing beyond the realm of previous exploration, they also journeyed beyond the realm of expectation about how discovery might be done and what constituted an explorer.

VOYAGER AS SPACECRAFT

Like its mission, the Voyager spacecraft was an alloy of ambition and practice, a compromise between the high-end hopes of TOPS and the low-end practicality of the Pioneers that in the end left them as a modified Mariner. The Voyagers were large for their time, built around a hexagonal bus that could be modified to suit particular packets of instrumentation and propulsion. With their ultimate dimensions set by Titan/Centaur, they nonetheless boosted the Mariner frame into another weight class, like a caravel reworked into a small carrack.

Each spacecraft weighed 1,817 pounds, of which 232 pounds were its scientific payload. There were eleven instruments in all: cosmic ray and plasma detectors, narrow- and wide-angle imaging cameras, ultraviolet and infrared spectrometers, a photopolarimeter, a radiometer, high- and low-field magnetometers, a low-energy charged-particle detector, and antennas for planetary radio astronomy and plasma waves. Bolted against the bus frame was the vessel's most distinctive visual feature, a high-gain dish antenna. Bristling outward were booms to hold assorted instruments, two antennas, the low-field magnetometer, and the spacecraft's nuclear power source, a radioisotope thermoelectric generator. (The RTG meant Voyager lacked perhaps the most distinctive visual feature of Mariner: its fan of solar panels.) Adding to its weight were sixteen hydrazine thrusters, a suite of onboard computers, and a propulsion module. Reflective blankets wrapped those portions that required some temperature regulation. The core spacecraft was twelve feet high (the diameter of the high-gain dish antenna), but with its booms fully extended, its width swelled to fifty-seven feet, to its which the propulsion module added another nine. With its reach spanning three dimensions, Voyager claimed an impressive volume.[54]

They were larger than most American spacecraft and smaller than Soviet counterparts. Pioneers 10 and 11, which also had to fit into Centaur, were more compact, with a 9-foot main antenna, booms that reached out 10 feet, and a total weight of 570 pounds. They had shed weight by eliminating the onboard computer; by shrinking the size of the antennas, since communication would not have to extend to the outer planets; and by having the spacecraft spin, making it a gyroscope, rather than stabilizing it by multiple thrusters, as Voyager did. Soviet spacecraft were larger and more ponderous, since heavy-lift rockets were the norm and, from the onset, the Soviet space community intended to send people. At least at JPL, Americans were content with robots, and could miniaturize electronic prostheses, and in any event, granted the reality of their lighter-lift launch vehicles, they had to accept the smaller machines.[55]

The Voyager spacecraft was within the range of smaller exploring vessels. A nineteenth-century keelboat of the type used by Lewis and Clark and later by exploring fur trappers on the Missouri River, had a length of fifteen feet and a width of ten, comparable to Voyager in its Centaur shroud. Columbus's *Niña*, his favorite, which he used on his second voyage as well, was a caravel approximately fifty-five to sixty-seven feet long and twenty-one feet wide. The unfurled Voyager, including masts and booms, might claim a rudely comparable volume. For his imaging during the Great Surveys of the American West, relying on glass-plate photography, Timothy O'Sullivan required a small boat on the river and a mule-drawn covered wagon overland. Both vehicles were smaller than the cocooned Voyager.[56]

More interesting is the comparative scientific punch. The Great Voyages had almost none, save the captain's log and charts, and the overland entradas such as Coronado's or De Soto's left nothing more than letters and the occasional journal. The Second Age had science as a prominent purpose, but still could allocate only a fraction of space to its practice. Captain Cook's HMS *Endeavour* was exceptional in its commitment to the "scientifics" (not least because Joseph Banks paid for them), but they were five out of a crew of ninety-seven, and commanded a similar fraction of the working vessel, even allowing for use of the "great cabin." Charles Darwin shared a small room aft on the HMS *Beagle,* in which hammock, table, instruments, chest of drawers, and shelves constituted his residence, laboratory, and library; probably less than 2 percent of the available floor space of the ship. Where the science ratio was high, it was because the treks were short and did not require transport and sustenance over long distances. John Wesley Powell took three specially constructed dories and a pilot boat, nine men (none of them scientists), and a handful of instruments (sextant, compass, barometer) on his descent through the gorges of the Colorado River; science weighed literally less than his ration of beans. G. K. Gilbert took four men (one of them an assistant) and a complement of mules to the Henry Mountains, the last mountain range to be explored in the United States. Of the 138 species of goods carried, from machine oil and postcards to salt and rice, 41 (30 percent) had some direct bearing on doing science, though they composed probably less than 5 percent by weight; to this, one should add the mules, packs, blankets, and saddles, all of which reduced the scientific load to little more than a backpack. Even a dedicated vessel like the converted steam corvette HMS Challenger, surveying the world's oceans for over four years and 127,500 kilometers, with 15 of its 17 guns and spare spars removed, had only a scintilla of its space allotted to laboratories. Of three decks and the hold, scientific work claimed perhaps 2 percent, with an equivalent amount devoted to quarters for its practitioners. The reason of course is that most of the enterprise went to caring for the crew, and the larger the crew, the larger the proportion of space and time committed to their sustenance.[57]

The space program has investments both greater and lesser. For crewed vessels, the fraction is minimal. Apollo 11 carried small tools and returned 21.7 kilograms of moon rock. Of the twelve astronauts the Apollo program put on the Moon, only one, Harrison Schmitt, was a formal scientist. The reason for the consistently low proportion devoted to inquiry, not only in space but over the long arc of exploration, is of course that the transporting vessel must support not only itself but people, and can do so only by establishing an artificial habitat. It's as though Mariner 4 or Pioneer 11 had to launch encased in the assembly labs at JPL or Ames.

Robotic spacecraft could manage a far higher ratio of science to bulk. Of Voyager's total weight, 1,817 pounds, some 232 (almost 13 percent) came directly from scientific instruments, and a goodly fraction of the rest came from the thrusters and antennas required to position those instruments, not to transport or sustain the spacecraft overall. It was a powered high-tech lab. It needed to carry no flour or salt, no water, no rum, no saddles or pack frames; it housed no mess, no kitchen, no bunks, no dispensary; it held neither library nor ballast. And not least, the spacecraft carried no weapons. It had no armaments: no cannon, shot, or powder. It had shields to protect against micrometeorites and radiation and reflective wrapping to ward off sunlight, but no thick-beamed oaken sides to slow shot. Vacuum had its own peculiar hazards, but they were not such that an onboard arquebus or a guard of marines were needed to repel them.[58]

The chief check on Voyager's size was the properties of the launch vehicle—the thrust of the Titan rocket and the dimensions of the Centaur shroud. Once in space it would be weightless, in need only of internal power for electricity and thrusters. It was exploration stripped to its essences.

Actual fabrication started in 1975. Since each spacecraft was custom-built, testing was continual, and since not all hazards were known, engineers had to work without the prospects for repairs. That required close attention, constant testing, and redundancy.

Each NASA lab had its own protocols to validate design and parts. For JPL, since the early days of Ranger, this had meant running individual components through trials before assembly, then constructing a mock-up model to test the system's mechanical features, a thermal control model to verify its ability to withstand interplanetary space, notably heat and vacuum, and finally a proof test model that replicated the spacecraft as fully as possible. The standards were severe, not only because of the known hazards but also because of the uncertainties. Whether or not Voyager went on to Uranus, it was expected that a subsequent vehicle based on its pattern would, so the spacecraft had to survive the equivalent of several mechanical lifetimes beyond what had been attempted.[59]

The remaining hazards resided within the spacecraft and were inherent to long treks through interplanetary space. Even robots needed protection, and space-sensing instruments, a habitat. Their demands might command far less space and shielding than those for humans, but they required shelter surrogates nonetheless. To survive extremes of heating and cooling, the spacecraft needed some shielding; and to survive the gusts of Jovian (and other) radiation, it needed hardened electronics, just as vessels in tropical seas were sheathed with copper, or oaken vessels in polar seas strengthened against ice. For the rest it would have to depend on high-reliability components and redundancy. It could not return to have a faulty boom replaced or a hydrazine-powered thruster cleaned, as the vessels of the Great Voyages could replace a broken rudder or a torn sail. It could not replace scurvied or dead crew with new recruits.[60]

Over the course of construction the validation procedures racked up 3,500 reports of problems or failures—this out of a machine that had 65,000 individual parts, and complicated interactions among all of them, guided by first-time software. Some of those "parts," moreover, were themselves electronic composites. (Each Voyager was estimated to have the "electronic circuit complexity" of 2,000 color TV sets.) As launch approached, the pace of testing quickened—provisioning at port has always seemed a frenzy. Program manager John Casani recalled a "lot of crisis activity" during those last few months—"changing radio systems and switching things around," many of these difficulties "unexpected" and "quite challenging." In that final rush a major loss of detectors occurred, because the building in which the spacecraft was being tested got painted, and spray ("some hydrocarbons") was sucked inside the assembly room through the air handler and contaminated the sensors.[61]

Not all the testing failures resulted from instruments. Engineers had not fully appreciated the actual stresses from launch, and had not tested Voyager for them, and at one point during launch thought they "might have lost the spacecraft." What had actually happened was that Voyager's own self-protection systems had kicked in, confusing controllers, who thought they were witnessing outright failure instead of fail-safe software working as it should. The breakdown lay in not devising the right tests. Before Voyager 1 launched, some minor mechanical adaptations were made to dampen the effects the second time around. The reliance on software, however, suggested an alternative to simple redundancy: Voyager's onboard computers could be reprogrammed. That meant that not every task had to be replicated in metal, or potential failure anticipated; adjustments could be improvised as needed. Voyager could substitute flexibility and redundancy for size.[62]

Raymond Heacock observed that the level of redundancy was such that each Voyager contained "almost two spacecrafts within a single structure." In truth, the issue went well beyond that, since the Voyagers were triplets, and each did work. The proof test model proved critical when, during final assembly, problems cropped up in VGR-2, and the nominally spare spacecraft had to launch in its place. The on-ground model subsequently helped engineers understand glitches and breakdowns when Voyager 1 had its scan platform stick and then had a capacitor short out, and again when Voyager 2 lost its primary receiver. By experimenting with the grounded spacecraft, it was possible to replicate in the lab what telemetry was reporting from space.[63]

Despite breakdowns in some critical components and problems with "scientific instruments," Heacock noted that there was "essentially no mission loss due to failures." The prime objectives were met—and more. Redundancy once again proved an almost indispensable index of successful exploration.[64]

For that reason as well there were two spacecraft. Launch windows were unforgiving, interplanetary space hostile, and distances impossibly remote. If something went wrong, there was no opportunity to return, or to sail to a nearby port or to temporarily beach on a remote moon for careening or repairs. The simplest solution was to send multiple vessels.

Almost all the Great Voyages were fleets. Columbus sailed with three vessels, then seventeen (a hapless experiment in colonizing), six, and four; da Gama, Cabral, and Magellan each launched with five. John Davis sailed first with two, then four, and then three. James Cook had only the *Endeavour* on his first voyage (and nearly foundered on the Great Barrier Reef), then sailed with two vessels on his subsequent circumnavigations. There were of course solitary ships, mostly to the better known North Atlantic. On his first voyage, John Cabot discovered "New Found Land" in the *Matthew*, and returned to tell the tale. That reconnaissance inspired plans to establish a trading colony and a five-ship voyage, of which one ship crept back to Bristol while the other four were lost at sea.

Even major expeditions had to accept whatever ships they could claim, very few of which were new or prime. (Da Gama's voyage mattered sufficiently to warrant the construction of two new ships, but that was an anomaly.) While Magellan was assembling his fleet, the Portuguese consul in Seville reported gleefully that his ships were "very old and patched up," and that he personally "would not care to sail to the Canaries in such old crates; their ribs are soft as butter." In the end only one patched-up ship and eighteen men survived (although one, the *San Antonio*, had deserted earlier). That was far from exceptional. Even repairs required extra materiél, and unlike with Voyager, no spare vessel would be left at port to edify engineers. The Great Voyages went in groups.[65]

On the continents, save in extreme environments such as Antarctica, the Sahara, and Greenland, it was possible to live off the land or trade with indigenes, so the demands for redundancy could be reduced. That gain was frequently offset by the need in hostile or truly unknown lands for a military escort; the same was true for fleets. A sensible fraction of exploring armadas was devoted to firepower. The more a mission sought to go beyond simple reconnaissance, the more complex its arrangements, the greater the tendency to replace lone travelers with a corps. The Long Expedition of 1819–21 (the first of five by Stephen Long) took nineteen men up the Platte to the Rocky Mountains, beginning with the first steamboat, the *Western Explorer*, on the Missouri River. It was, one observer exalted, a veritable cavalcade of the era. "Botanists, mineralogists, chemists, artisans, cultivators, scholars, soldiers; the love of peace, the capacity for war: philosophical apparatus and military supplies; telescopes and cannon, garden seeds and gunpowder; the arts of civil life and the force to defend them—all are seen aboard."[66]

That was the norm. The magnitude of the investment, the uncertainties of the hazards, and the expectations of losses, all trended toward small numbers of costly expeditions rather than swarms of inexpensive ones. There were plenty of exceptions, especially by first-voyaging nations. John Cabot sailed to the New World in the *Matthew*, a navicula about the size of Columbus's *Niña*. Some single ships even ventured around the world, as Francis Drake did in the *Golden Hind* and William Dampier in the *Cygnet*, but they were privateers, and many of the famous scientific expeditions during the Second Age involved single vessels—think Thomas Huxley in the *Rattlesnake* and Charles Darwin in the *Beagle*. But the latter had well-established ports of call at which to provision, and they were surveying points of navigational interest such as the Strait of Magellan or the Torres Strait rather than blue-water voyaging into the unknown.

The geography of launch windows also argued for multiple or paired launches. Since the ideal Hohmann trajectories to Mars came every twenty-six months, it became the norm wherever possible to launch two spacecraft at each cycle. Some failed on launch; some failed at Mars; but few cycles passed altogether without some contact. Moreover, even paired spacecraft on the same mission might have incommensurable objectives: it was not possible, for example, to fully survey both Titan and Saturn's rings in one traverse. In this respect, as in many others, planetary exploration more resembles the voyages of the First Age than it does the Second. Voyager, however, was the last of the paired missions. Double-launching spacecraft had become, in John Casani's words, "an insurance policy that now we can't afford to take." In this, too, it resembles its Iberian predecessors who over time risked more and more with less and less.[67]

So there were two Voyagers, as there were two captains in the Corps of Discovery, and two ships on Cook's second and third voyages. But unlike those others, they would not communicate between themselves. They had separate tasks, and once separated, they would not rejoin.

VOYAGER AS EXPLORER

Voyager was an autonomous spacecraft; by most standards, the first. "Autonomous," however, is a relative concept, and its operational meaning is specific to particular tasks.

There were things the Voyager spacecraft could do—had to

do—that previous spacecraft could not. It had to self-regulate. It had to monitor its machinery, take remedial steps in case of sudden ruptures or emergencies, restart, and from time to time accept new orders. Those needs increased over time. So great was the distance that even at the speed of light, messages to Earth and back would take too long, and so extended was the journey that constant text-messaging with, and micro-managing by, JPL would exhaust the spacecraft's reserves of energy. Voyager had to tend to itself—identify problems, shut down troubled parts, restart anew. It had to assist ground controllers with adjusting trajectories and transmitting scientific data. It had to execute the split-second maneuvers of close encounters through pre-programmed codes, each rewritten based on past experiences. It had to recognize when its onboard machinery for overseeing such tasks had itself failed or become corrupt. It had, within limits, to exercise self-control.

The technology that made this possible was the digital computer, which coevolved with the space program. Gordon Moore announced his eponymous law in 1965, the same year that Gary Flandro outlined the prospects for a Grand Tour. The second would depend on the first. Moore's Law states that the number of transistors that can be placed inexpensively on an integrated circuit increases exponentially—specifically, it doubles roughly every eighteen to twenty-four months. From this derives nearly every metric of computing power. By the time Voyager launched, twelve years after those dual announcements, six doubling periods had passed, or a sixty-four-fold increase in computing capabilities. Voyager was on the cutting edge of working computers, and particularly miniature ones. By the time it encountered Saturn, another doubling period had come and gone, and the personal computer was arriving. Voyager seemed vaguely archaic. When it encountered Neptune ten years later, another five doubling periods had so pumped up computing power that Voyager stood to an average cell phone as a caravel to a Centaur rocket.

Onboard computers evolved out of sequencers, or preprogrammed counters that triggered a series of operations. Once started, a sequencer performed a series of activities that allowed a spacecraft to disengage from rockets, unfurl, and fly past a planet while recording data and images and transmitting them back. Earth controllers initiated the sequence and uploaded new ones for each phase of the mission. A central computer could oversee several such sequencers. For longer flights, such redundancy was mandatory, and as computing power swelled, programmable computers could replace simple sequencers. Voyager had three such computer systems, each with a backup. During its cruise phases, a "sequence load" was uplinked to the spacecraft every four weeks. The uplinked sequences quickened during encounters.[68]

The Attitude and Articulation Control Subsystem computers assisted with navigation. No ground controller could hope to maintain the constant monitoring that told Voyager where it was in the solar system and how to stabilize its three axes. The AACS computer could, and it kept the spacecraft's antenna directed to Earth. The Flight Data Subsystem computers performed analogous tasks for the scientific instruments and the transmission of data. Overseeing both subsystems, along with the programmable sequencers that monitored the spacecraft and piloted its encounters, was the Computer Command Subsystem. The CCS was virtually identical to the computer used for the Viking mission. The FDS had to be constructed uniquely. To conserve power, the FDS and AACS computers could go into sleep mode.[69]

Command was distributed, redundant, and capable of hibernation. While it ultimately rested with NASA (through JPL), it routinely resided within Voyager. If Voyager went awry, its Earth-based human controllers would have to reclaim and recharter the spacecraft. If within Voyager one computer failed, its backup would step forward, and if one system failed, another might be able to compensate. The ability to upload new software meant that fresh orders could be rewritten as the mission evolved, particularly if Voyager 1's success meant a Grand Tour was possible. The capacity to power down when not in use meant the RTG power packs could sustain the long journey.

Yet autonomy, while necessary, could introduce instabilities of its own. Voyager's understanding was literal and did not always coincide with that of its human controllers. There were occasions when the nominal controllers were confused and onboard computers had to intervene to correct them. (This happened, for example, during Voyager 1's launch.) There were also events in which the people forgot to perform tasks or did them incorrectly, and the spacecraft went into backup or safe modes. And there were incidents in which "the computers on board displayed certain traits that seemed almost humanly perverse—and perhaps a little psychotic," as one staffer observed. The programming was too tight, the instructions too sensitive, the tolerance for the quotidian of flight, even cruising, too fine to accommodate the realities of interplanetary travel. The computers overreacted, a kind of automaton hysteria. Some software therapy in the form of new programming sedated the machine and allowed it to regain equilibrium.[70]

Even mutiny was possible. There could be internal arguments among the onboard computers, perhaps temporarily paralyzing decisions. But most spectacularly it could happen as it did to Voyager while en route to Saturn, in which new commands were uploaded, only to be refused on the grounds that they contradicted more fundamental instructions and would result in catastrophe. Such insubordination could not be flogged away or strung up on an instrument boom yardarm. The source of the confusion had to be found, and corrected. In this case Voyager—which made the proper decision—was able to defend itself without a court-martial conducted through the Deep Space Network.[71]

How much autonomy was technically possible? Some, with increasing degrees of self-control possible as physics improved computing. How much was desirable? That question edged into metaphysics. No explorer has been fully autonomous. All have had restraints imposed by their mission or their sponsor, and all have had orders that would allow for surprise, adaptation, and redirection.

What the robots did not have was a human consciousness and conscience. They knew nothing of the traditional horrors, like ship rats, that had ever accompanied long-voyaging expeditions. They would experience nothing akin to the miseries Magellan's crew faced as they sailed for "three months and twenty days without taking on board provisions or any other refreshments," during which they ate "only old biscuit turned to powder, all full of worms and stinking of the urine which the rats had made on it, having eaten the good." The crew "drank water impure and yellow. We ate also ox hides which were very hard because of the sun, rain, and wind. And we left them four or five days in the sea, then laid them for a short time on embers, and so we ate them. And of the rats, which were sold for half an ecu apiece, some of us could not get enough." The worst affliction was scurvy, which killed thirty-one of the crew. Other "maladies" crippled another twenty-five or thirty.[72]

Yet spacecraft had their own peculiar ailments. Parts broke, mechanical gears became arthritic, instruments lost sight, computers suffered hearing loss. There were leaks. Filters clogged. The critical onboard provisions for Voyager were the hydrazine required by its thrusters and the electrical power derived from the RTGs. Without hydrazine the spacecraft could not maneuver, and without power, it could execute none of its mission or even communicate. It would succumb to robotic scurvy. It would become a ghost ship, at the mercy of solar winds and gravitational currents. Earth, Mars, Venus, and the Moon were littered with wrecked vehicles. The Mars Observer had vanished in space.

Voyager knew none of this—could not fret over what might cripple it, could not leap into the breach or suddenly freeze in fear, could not imagine failure or triumph. Its designers could, and they sought to program the spacecraft to handle both the expected and the unexpected. But the only way to cope with the myriad possible hazards was to grant Voyager some capacity to respond on its own. To find its own way it needed something like its own will.

VOYAGER AS GRAND GESTURE

Still, if Voyager was less than human, it seemed more than a machine. It had symbolic value. In particular, it will likely stand as the grand gesture of the Third Age.

Such expressions are not the first bold announcements of discovery, which come early, with the shock of first discovery or first expression. Such was the case, for example, with Columbus and Dias, with the campaign to measure the transits of Venus, and with IGY, all of which proclaimed a new age. While that annunciatory first revelation can galvanize the imagination and inspire successors, it comes too soon to capture the still-inchoate features of the times, or it is too tightly bound to a particular people or project. So although the Carreira da India first launched under Vasco da Gama and became the basis for Portugal's national epic, *The Lusíads*, Spain could equally point to Columbus's four voyages; and England to John Cabot's daring sail to the New Found Lands at the same time; and France, always willing to consider history pliable in the interest of *gloire*, to Jacques Cartier. The essence of the First Age was, as J. H. Parry put it, the discovery of the sea, not simply the Ocean Sea that lay beyond the classical world or maybe encircled the lesser seas as the Styx encircled Hades, but the astonishing way in which they all connect and flow one into another. The enduring symbol of the age would highlight that fact.[73]

Grand gestures seem to follow twenty to thirty years later, after exploration and its sustaining culture have worked through the full terms of engagement, as first discovery becomes full discovery. They are the moments of exploring that more than any other capture the general imagination, that fuse place, time, discovery, and yearning in ways that seem to speak to an era's sense of itself. If they do not inform an age, they do display the vital attributes of an age as nothing else can.

Thus, for the First Age, the grand gesture belongs to the circumnavigating voyage of the *Victoria*. Ferdinand Magellan was a paragon of his time, an explorer tenacious, religious, tough beyond reckoning and ambitious beyond yearning. God, gold, and glory—all filled the mold of his soul. When the Armada de Molucca, reduced from five daunting vessels to one straggler, the Victoria, completed its ambit of the world ocean, it defined the limits of what might be done (and had, in fact, consumed Magellan, dead in the Philippines). So bold was a circumnavigation that few expeditions dared to follow. But when the Second Age geared up in the 1760s, it did so with a new wave of Earth-encircling voyages, joining the two ages as one might lay a plank between ships.

Yet however much those new circumnavigations might bedazzle the late eighteenth and early nineteenth centuries, they could not speak to the dramatic discovery or rediscovery of Earth's continents or those lush fragments of it chipped off as islands. The floating excursions of James Cook and Louis-Antoine de Bougainville had to come ashore and penetrate inland. The man who achieved that task with cultural panache was Alexander von Humboldt. Convincing Carlos IV to let him enter New Spain, he became, as his own age appreciated, a "second Columbus," in this case, the *scientific* discoverer of South America. For five years (1799–1804), accompanied by Aimé Bonpland, he explored widely, paddling up the Orinoco, traversing the Andes, climbing Mount Chimborazo, scrutinizing the archives and natural history of Mexico and Cuba. He elaborated Linnaeus's natural-history excursion into a cross section of continents. He carried the Old World's grand tour to the New World, where it could also gaze on monuments and relics of the past, not least those of nature. He gave empirical heft to the misty musings of *Naturphilosophie*. He empowered geographic science with a global reach. In the words of Ralph Waldo Emerson, he was one of "those Universal men, like Aristotle." He personified the explorer as Romantic hero.

While he was not the first European to boat the Orinoco or climb in the Andes, Humboldt was the first of a new kind of European, such that even when explorers of the Second Age revisited sites known to the First, they did so with original eyes and to novel ends. Symbolically, during a layover on his way back to Europe, he dined with Thomas Jefferson a month after Lewis and Clark's Corps of Discovery departed St. Louis. For Americans the latter was the defining moment of the new age, but for Western civilization overall, that honor belonged to Humboldt, not only because he was first but because he followed the journey with decades of exhaustive research and publication, which meant his experiences could transcend mere adventure and politics and become an exemplar for others. His trek through South America defined the grand gesture of the Second Age as the cross-continental traverse.

The task was roughly completed in the 1870s. For the Arctic and Antarctic, a journey to the pole and back became an acceptable substitute, although it never had quite the cachet, and Ernest Shackleton's celebrated and ill-fated *Endurance* expedition sought to complete the circuit by traversing Antarctica. That particular achievement had to wait until IGY; by then the hype could no longer match the mood. It had a sense of cleaning up odd jobs, not of launching bold new adventures, a bit of geographic housecleaning outfitted with Caterpillar tractors instead of sled dogs. Something else would have to define the grand gesture of the Third Age.

An era of exploration characterized by the inventory of whole planets needed something both vaster and newer than Antarctica and a deed more startling than a descent to the abysses of the world ocean. A journey to the Moon might be dramatic, but it belongs with the Norse voyaging to Greenland, or Polynesians to Easter Island, something astonishing but that leads nowhere else. The same might be said of the marvelous robotic missions to Venus and Mars, or even to Jupiter and Saturn, a brilliant expedition to a single place and theme, but not a moment that, like a parabolic mirror, concentrates all the energy around it to a focus. A grand gesture has to be something that encompasses it all, as the *Victoria's* circumnavigation did, and that like its formidable captain, embodies an age in its character; that by speaking with special force to its own time, it speaks to all times; that can travel across history as the expedition does over geography.

Voyager's Grand Tour does this. In its design, in its scope, in its reprogrammable computers, in the ability of its mission to retain the past even as it speeds beyond it, Voyager has embodied the ideas, ambitions, hopes, paradoxes, aesthetics, flaws, and energies of its time. It has made manifest the power and peculiarities of a Third Great Age of Discovery.

5. Launch

Launch is a working synthesis—the possible made plausible. It reconciles motive with machinery. It welds the propellant force of rockets to ideas and instruments. It codes vision into operating plans. It is enough for prophets to find words or images to move audiences, but engineers and managers require a more tangible expression, the contact not of ink on paper or electrons on a TV screen but of metal, wires, hydrazine, lenses, and decaying plutonium. Without such labors the Grand Tour belonged in the realm of science fiction.

Expeditions are made, they are scheduled, they occur at designated places and at specified times. They require ports of departure. They must harmonize social timing with environmental opportunities. They are time capsules of a cultural moment. The Voyagers were all this.

TITAN IIIE/CENTAUR D-1T

The Voyagers could not carry more instruments than what the allotted thrust and dimensions of the Titan/Centaur rocket and Centaur casing allowed. In their liftoff the Voyagers thus continued a long heritage of mixed-technology vessels, and in the staged sequencing of their flight they recapitulated an old history of vessels redesigned, vessels refitted, vessels shed, and vessels lost. And with unintended inspiration their ascent even emulated the multistage evolution of exploration itself.

The Titan was a two-stage rocket originally developed as an ICBM, which then evolved as an all-purpose vehicle for heavier payloads such as surveillance satellites. The first stage had two engines, and the second stage, one, all of which burned liquid fuels that fired spontaneously when mixed, and rendered "ignition" a figure of speech. To the sides were bolted two solid-fuel boosters to add initial thrust. Atop rose an aptly named Centaur rocket powered by two engines that burned by kindling liquid hydrogen and oxygen and gave the hybrid a third stage. Within Centaur nested a Voyager spacecraft attached to yet another engine for a final propulsive push. Each stage fired, and then physically disengaged and dropped away, leaving the next stage to position itself and burn unimpeded without the dead weight of the husk.

Liftoff commenced with the blast of the first stage's engines and double boosters. As the solid rockets burned out, a suite of explosive bolts and small rockets peeled them from the core. When the first stage burned out, it, too, separated, and the second stage kicked in. When that stage exhausted its fuels, it also fell away, and the third-stage Centaur shed its shroud and its own engine caught fire. Here the Centaur demonstrated its value for such missions. It had high specific impulse, it could coast and reignite repeatedly, and it contained its own avionics for navigation and control. It was, in brief, the Centaur's rocket that mediated between the brute blast of the Titans and the onboard solid-propulsion engine of the Voyagers.

For each Voyager mission Centaur fired and coasted twice, once to achieve a low Earth orbit, and then again, after cruising to the ideal spot, in order to reach escape velocity and embark on its journey beyond Earth. The first episode came as Centaur jettisoned its shroud 203 seconds after liftoff and, 4 seconds later, burned for 101 seconds. Almost 43 minutes later, Centaur repositioned itself for the next burn, which lasted 339 seconds, followed by a short coasting for 89 seconds. That, at least, was the scenario for Voyager 2. The last-stage Titan faltered during Voyager 1, the result of a leak, and threatened to abandon the spacecraft short of orbit, which would have left it to finish its combustion by burning up in the atmosphere. Fortunately, the computers aboard Centaur recognized the problem and adjusted by extending their burn. Even so, they barely had enough fuel to compensate; only 3.4 seconds of fuel remained when Centaur shut down. Had this sequence played out during Voyager 2, the mission would have failed, for it had a less forgiving trajectory; Centaur's boost of burning could not have compensated. The Voyager mission thus displayed, from liftoff, that most ineffable and most essential quality of great expeditions: good fortune. If "they had swapped the Titan booster rockets," Bruce Murray observed, "there would have been no Voyager to Neptune. Flip of the coin." "We were lucky," he concluded, "and that's important."[74]

For both Voyagers, the particular trajectories required for Jupiter demanded yet another thrust. With Centaur spent, the action moved to an augmented Voyager itself. The spacecraft had a supplementary solid-fuel propulsion module under its direction. Voyager segregated from Centaur, ignited its rocket for forty-five seconds, and then shed the booster. The mission module—the spacecraft proper—was now at sea, subject to minor corrections (or "nudge" factors) to compensate for its inherent quirks and the unseen winds and currents of gravity.

Hybrid vessels, staged launches, the practice of shedding dead weight or separating close-exploring craft from long-haul vessels—all these had ample precedents dating back to the Great Voyages themselves.

The ships of discovery were a mixed lot, the result of centuries of evolution in the Mediterranean and a recent fusion with Baltic traditions. A critical innovation was the transfer, probably from the Indian Ocean, of the lateen sail. A triangular sheet with a long, stiff edge, the lateen demanded only simple rigging, could work amid a variety of winds, and sharpened maneuverability. It became the norm for modest-size ships and those working along coasts. But it required proportionally large crews, and could not be put about easily; nor could it run with heavy loads before the wind. The solution was to look north, and adapt the bulkier, square-sailed cog typical of the Baltic and North seas an introduction that came during the Crusades. The synthesis of these two styles occurred with exquisite geographic logic in Iberia, where the Atlantic and Mediterranean converged.

Each tradition was further modified to circumstances over several centuries, and then suddenly joined one to the other during roughly two decades in the mid-fifteenth century. Shipbuilders borrowed and rearranged hull design, keels, spars, rudders, numbers of masts, and various sails, all tweaked into an ancestral barque from which subsequently descended miscellaneous and mongrel progeny. Some, such as the carrack, were large and designed for haulage. Some were built mostly for fighting. But the most celebrated was the caravel (*caravella*), a specialty of Portugal and southern Spain. Mostly Mediterranean in its genes, it morphed to accommodate a square sail and a rear rudder, and became the core ship of discovery. Small, versatile, capable of riding over waves, maneuverable around coasts and shoals, the caravel was the vessel with which Portugal mapped the coast of Africa, and along with Castile, colonized the Atlantic isles and discovered the Ocean Sea.[75]

Still, the caravel was small, and long voyages required vessels of modest crews and greater capacity, so most armadas sailed with mixed fleets, of which the caravel was a part. Da Gama had one caravel, as did Cabral, and Columbus took two on his first voyage, the *Niña* and *Pinta*. (Interestingly, it was the larger *Santa Maria*, a *nao*, that foundered on a shoal off Hispaniola.) The caravels did the close work of coasting, carried messages, tested new seas, and got emissaries and explorers to previously unknown land. Few voyages lacked at least one in their company, although the most extraordinary of all, the Armada de Molucca under Ferdinand Magellan, had none. As they acquired experience, explorers turned to smaller-size carracks, which proved more capacious for crews and goods and better suited for long voyages.

Heavy-lift rockets enjoyed a comparable evolution. They were hybrids. As with ships during the Renaissance, there were geographic traditions—in this case, with centers in Russia, Germany, and

America—and some exchange between them, catalyzed by war. The Russians favored a basic model to which they added boosters. The Americans looked to a more mixed fleet, but one largely evolved from the German V-2, a process catalyzed by the capture of German rocket scientists as the war ended (the celebrated Operation Paperclip). From the V-2 evolved the Redstone, and from the Redstone, the first American intermediate-range ballistic missile (IRBM), the Jupiter; from Jupiter came the intercontinental ballistic missiles (ICBM), Atlas and Titan, separately developed for different purposes. Outfitted with a Centaur upper stage, Atlas launched seventy-two payloads over its history, and Titan, eight, of which Voyager was the last.[76]

If such hybridization and tinkering has a long pedigree, so does the freelance, freebooter movement of those who had expertise. German scientists carried knowledge of the V-2 from Peenemünde to White Sands. During the era of the Great Voyages, Italian capital and merchants, mostly Genoese and Venetian, bonded with Iberian geopolitical enthusiasms to drive overseas expansion. Portuguese pilots, like Italian *condottieri*, were the mercenaries of discovery, serving the highest bidder. During the era of continental colonies, Germans in particular were everywhere, furnishing the technical skills in cartography and botany that locals lacked. Charles Preuss did much of the mapping for John Charles Fremont's first, second, and fourth expeditions; Heinrich Möllhausen collected natural-history specimens and illustrated for Whipple's reconnaissance through northern Arizona, and later Lt. Joseph Ives's abortive voyage up the Colorado River, where F. W. von Egloffstein joined and did the critical cartography. Exploration invited the footloose and the obsessed to join whatever party would sponsor them. The Third Age is no exception.

For exploration history add the practice of adapting vehicles developed for one purpose to another. Frijthof Nansen reworked Inuit sledges into sturdier forms for traversing rough pack ice and wrestling over pressure ridges. John Wesley Powell put modified dories into the Colorado River to descend through its succession of gorges. Captain Cook's fabled *Endeavour* was a modified collier. Charles Wilkes's flagship, the *Vincennes*, was a reconditioned sloop of war; Dumont d'Urville's *Astrolabe* was a converted corvette; James Ross's *Terror* and *Erebus* were refitted naval mortar ships. (They later went to the Arctic, where they sank off King William Island with Sir John Franklin.) The HMS *Beagle* that carried Darwin around the world began as a ten-gun brig remade into a barque and modified to slough off rougher seas. Ernest Shackleton's *Nimrod* was a forty-year-old wooden sealer; Robert Scott's *Terra Nova,* a barque formerly used for sealing and whaling.

Only Nansen's *Fram* was designed from scratch for polar exploration. Its heavy oak beams gave it a stiff pliability and its curved hull was designed to have the ship ride up as pack ice squeezed. Several explorers, however, devised boats that could be disassembled into more portable parts, and then reassembled as needed. Nathaniel Wyeth experimented with a design in the American West, and Samuel Baker and Henry Stanley did likewise in central Africa. The Ives Expedition to the Colorado River transported a disassembled steamboat. So it was that rockets for planetary flybys were adapted from ICBMs, and replaced MIRV warheads with multiple-instrumented exploring spacecraft.

Those vessels, by their launch gantries, were as mongrel as the caravel-piloted armadas of the Renaissance. The heavy vehicles had to do their work first and then fall aside, their task completed in minutes and seconds upon reaching escape velocity, while Pioneers, Mariners, or Voyagers cruised through interplanetary space for months or years. In the sixteenth century the first stage could take months, tacking across winds and currents and around continents, while actual contact might exhaust itself in a few days. For this end the vessels might include a pinnace (prefabricated and carried in the hold until needed), or tow a shallop or longboat, ships that could support geographic foraging parties, or "away teams," at new coasts, akin to surface landers dropped from orbiters. The danger was that they might be swamped during the crossing, as they often were. Except for the longest voyages, they could expect to provision themselves en route. Not least, for those expeditions that intended to finance themselves by importing spices or bullion, heavy vessels would be needed for the return, for unlike planetary spacecraft, those exploring parties had to report in person and deliver their discoveries in tangible form; they could not transmit digital data across space. Still, early-stage supply ships could be shed, discarded like empty rocket boosters, until all that remained was the pure mission module.[77]

AROUND THE CAPE

The Voyager twins departed Earth from launchpads at a site first selected only eighteen years previous.

In the past, exploration had not devised its own point of departure. Expeditions left from places that had evolved organically from sites of enterprise and lines of transport that, from time to time, outfitted parties of explorers as needed. John Cabot sailed from Bristol, long a scene for trade and fishing; Jacques Cartier, from La Rochelle, likewise a well-established natural port; Captain James Cook launched from Plymouth, and Captain FitzRoy's *Beagle,* with Charles Darwin aboard, from Devonport, both naval depots. The Lewis and Clark expedition left St. Louis, the major entrepôt of the Mississippi River. Those countries, such as Russia, that lacked ready access to the sea lagged, or turned overland, until ports were available; for the Bering expeditions to Alaska temporary ports had to be constructed. Once in the New World, Spain promptly erected ports at Isabella, Vera Cruz, Lima, and Acapulco from which new voyages could set forth.

Cape Canaveral, Florida, followed the latter pattern as a place developed specifically to fire rockets. Rocketry's hazards, and to some extent its secrecy under military sponsorship, argued for remote sites, typically deserts such as White Sands or Edwards Air Force Base or Baikonur, Kazakhstan, until their heft demanded greater domains of emptiness. By 1949 the range of the V-2's successors had lengthened sufficiently that President Harry S. Truman established a Joint Long Range Proving Ground on what was then a largely uninhabited belt of Florida shoreline.

The site had plenty of attractions. The surrounding countryside was lightly developed; missiles could be readied, and even fail in violent fireballs, without threatening communities. Launches would arc over the Atlantic, and if missiles wobbled off course, blew up, or had to be destroyed, they again posed no danger to people. The weather allowed for continual operations, save for fleeting thunderstorms and the occasional hurricane. Islands trending southeast, from the Grand Bahamas to Ascension, themselves famous as sites for past discovery, could service tracking stations. There was ample land for future development.

In 1950 the army moved its facilities from White Sands to Cape Canaveral, while the air force acquired a nearby naval air station (Banana River) to convert into its Air Force Missile Test Center. In 1955 the navy relocated its Vanguard missile program to Canaveral. In December 1959 the army transferred its facilities to NASA. When the expanding program demanded still more land, nearby Merritt Island was acquired for development into a major "spaceport," the John F. Kennedy Space Center and Eastern Space and Missile Center.[78]

The site had its quirks, as all ports do, which is why historically pilots were first and foremost versed in local lore. Canaveral's shoals and tidal bores were its weather—its thunderstorms, its frosts. Having an electrostatic match striking randomly around a tower of distilled combustibles could kindle catastrophe, and a cold snap could turn pliable O rings into brittle plastic. These were local lessons, learned over time, and they would take many decades to codify into pilotage for the Cape.

Yet in one respect it did resemble so many of its predecessor ports from which explorers had embarked: Cape Canaveral was an island, or effectively so, cut off from mainland Florida by estuaries and the Banana River. Its development stands to space voyaging as the colonization of Atlantic isles does for the Great Age of Discovery. Those isles permitted a final fitting and provisioning, and then positioned a vessel within the geography of wind and currents that would carry it to the New World or around Africa, which is what also happened at the Cape. Today's equivalent to the Canaries, astride the trade winds, is a locale closer to the equator, which can contribute more rotational velocity from the Earth to a rocket moving east (Canaveral adds 1,666 kilometers an hour). For deep-space ventures, the ideal would be a port of call beyond Earth's gravitational shackles altogether, something like an orbiting space station or a lunar base. Since neither exists, the compromise is a pause in orbit before the final stage ignites.

The Voyagers' launches were the climax to a dozen years of meticulous planning, and liftoff was almost ritualistic in its tight choreography. The larger factors were many, and rarely aligned, among them the immutable geometry of the planets, the rocket's capacity for thrust, the size of the payload, the ability to navigate, and the ambitions of the mission. Every consideration varied, and each changed with changes in the others. There could be no singular solution.

Every planet had its unique launch window based on the minimum energy trajectories first elaborated by Walter Hohmann in 1925. For Venus these came every nineteen months; for Mars, every twenty-six; for Jupiter, every thirteen. The thrust available determined velocity, which then set launch opportunities, but as payload varied, so did velocity, and as velocity changed, so did potential routes and hence launch dates. Where one launch was to lead to another through gravity assistance, the options multiplied, and a planning calendar became maddeningly complex. For the Grand Tour, a suitable collective geometry would reappear only every 176 years. Yet at each planet along the way there were sites to visit, so the prospects for routes were almost unbounded. Planners began with 10,000 potential trajectories, which they then whittled down to 100 possibilities.

Voyagers' window was tight. To preserve the Grand Tour option, launch had to occur between 1976 and 1978; to capture Jupiter's gravity, it had to obey a thirteen-month cycle; to reconcile Jupiter's and Earth's orbits, it had to happen within a month of consecutive dates within that recurring near-annual cycle, and for each day within that month, within an hour-long window. There was, as well, a cultural window, for five years earlier a Grand Tour would not have been technically possible, and five years later not politically feasible.

As in the past, ceremonies of departure had emerged. There were bleachers for dignitaries and associates, cameras to record and broadcast to the public, rites of political blessing. It had ever been so. Traditionally, ship launches were a bedlam of last-minute provisioning, the testing of anchors and ropes, the bustle of late-arriving crewmen. There were observers, whether family, dockworkers, the curious, or the emissaries of sponsors. There would be a Mass said, a service recited, a political proclamation, a poem. The expedition's orders and rules of conduct might be read.

There would also be a search heavenward for signs and portents. When Sir John Franklin departed to plot out the Northwest Passage, a white dove settled on a mast, and became for many well-wishers (including Franklin's daughter, Eleanor) "an omen of peace and harmony." As Voyager 2 rested at its gantry the day before launch, black thunderheads and lightning approached threateningly within a mile of the combustible rocket before veering off to sea. In both these cases, the portents misread subsequent events entirely.[79]

Since they had different trajectories, the Voyager twins launched separately. Their names reflected the sequence of arrival at Jupiter, not the sequencing of launch. Voyager 2 went first. Voyager 1 followed sixteen days later. They had met their launch dates and sailed with the cosmic tides.

For expeditions, time can be more powerful than place. It is always possible to reposition ships (or keel boats or entradas) for secondary departures, and this was normal; but it is tricky and often fatal to ignore the seasonal geographies of wind and wave. The need for timing could further argue for staggered embarkations. Always exploration has had its launch sequences.

These could span from hours to years. Spanish fleets from the Caribbean had to sail outside hurricane season; Russian promyshlenniki relied on frozen rivers in winter and flowing streams in summer, and shunned the mires of spring breakup. Voyages to the Spice Isles had to obey the ebb and flow of the monsoons, first from Africa to India, and then to the East Indies. Vasco da Gama caught those winds for 23 days from Mombasa to Calicut, and when he tried to defy them on his return, he nearly lost his crews to scurvy in fighting their contrary flow for 132 days. Expeditions up the Missouri River left early in the spring to reach the mountains before the snows, or else they found a valley to winter over until the following spring. In Australia, the Burke and Wills expedition managed to undertake its trek across the interior with exquisite (and fatal) mistiming, fighting brutal summer heat to Cooper's Creek, and then breasting the rainy season to the Gulf of Carpentaria. In extreme cases it might take a year or more to relocate to a site from which further exploration could proceed. The Franklin expedition to the Northwest Passage expected to winter over in the frozen Arctic before summer melt would allow further progress. Ship-borne Antarctic exploration would likewise break through the enveloping pack ice late in the summer, only to winter over in preparation for late-spring treks. Russian forays to the Pacific might demand a year's travel just to reach the coast, and another year to return, with exploration limited to fleeting opportunities in between.

But apart from seasonal or secular rhythms, there were always local considerations of tide and wind, over which the explorers had often little knowledge and less control. Many a bold expedition toasted the tide, and then sat while contrary winds kept them in port, or took to sea and had to beat against the winds for a week or more until they could properly launch. (The equivalent for rockets are technical glitches that pause or close countdowns.) Tide and winds could make for cruel embarkations, and even crueler returns. These were the launch delays of the past, when the countdown stopped, the expedition slid from élan to ennui, and the drama stalled while the stagehands replaced the faulty curtains and broken limelights. This mattered less when communications were not instantaneous and when the vagaries of earthly weather offered more flexibility than the foreordained orbits of celestial mechanics.

LIFTOFF

On August 20, 1977, at 10:29:45 a.m. EDT, Voyager 2 lifted off from Cape Canaveral. On September 5, at 8:56:01 a.m. EDT, Voyager 1 followed.

They rose atop a boiling column—a controlled explosion—of flame. If their ultimate thrust derived from a cultural combustion that mixed ambition, curiosity, greed, political posturing, and utopianism, the proximate cause was a violent collision of liquid hydrogen and liquid oxygen into a distilled, full-throated burn. It was a magnificently Promethean gesture, in its audacity—the first satellite had broken into earthly orbit only a scant twenty years before, yet here was a launch intended to traverse the solar system. But it was Promethean, too, in its choice of means, for fire is humanity's signature technology and a chemistry that has no natural presence outside Earth. Once beyond Earth's gravitational tug, the Voyagers would be beyond the realm of life, which is also the realm of fire. That reach beyond was the essence of their mission. But it seemed altogether right that they should begin those journeys to lifeless worlds and a near-eternity of vacuum upon the pillars of the fire its makers had long ago seized from the heavens.

part 2

Push off, and sitting well in order smite
The sounding furrows; for my purpose holds
To sail beyond the sunset, and the baths
Of all the western stars, until I die.

—**Alfred Tennyson, "Ulysses"**

But the way is dangerous, the passage doubtful,
the voyage not thoroughly known.

—**Richard Hakluyt,**
The Principal Navigations

Beyond Earth

6. New Moon

Two escape velocities frame the Voyager mission. The first, the escape from the gravitational pull of Earth, allowed the twin spacecraft to begin their quest through the solar system by getting them to Jupiter. The second, the escape from the gravitational pull of the Sun, happened at Jupiter and allowed them to complete the Grand Tour. That second momentum would also define the end of their quest by propelling them beyond the solar system altogether.

Those dual moments of propulsion help to bookend the mission's narrative as well, by segregating the geography of places visited from that of places shunned. Simply departing Earth's gravity was not enough, for there were two other bodies from whose psychological orbits the Voyagers also had to escape. The first was the Moon, whose tidal pull had turned minds heavenward since ancient times and whose political phases had filled the night sky of the space race. The second was Mars, the most Earth-like of planets and the obsession of a culture of colonization. Both the Moon and Mars were the scenes, either actual or imagined, for human space travel, and thus for all the rest of what the segue from exploring to colonizing implied, not least some bond to a national military. A critical fact is that Voyager bypassed both bodies with hardly a wobble. In less than a day the

Voyagers blew past the sublunary realms and began the first of their long cruises between encounters.

OUT OF ORBIT

Passage from Earth to the Moon was, for both Voyagers, little more than a heartbeat in a long marathon. When they completed their final firings, Voyager 1 and 2 had velocities in excess of 143,000 kilometers per hour and 140,000 kilometers per hour, respectively. They passed the average orbit of the Moon, roughly 384,403 kilometers from Earth, some ten hours after launch.

There were a few launch glitches, some serious, some merely annoying. The most critical occurred when Voyager 1 nearly failed to attain its mandatory velocity, which would have still sent the spacecraft to Jupiter and Saturn but would have scrubbed the Grand Tour. By contrast, Voyager 2's launch crisis involved more of an anxiety attack. This began when onboard computers detected accelerations greater than expected and overly "self-corrected"; then dust particles set in motion by vibrations sparkled and misoriented the spacecraft's tracking system. Together these events left the antenna misdirected, and hence oblivious to ground commands. For a heart-stopping moment, it seemed that the spacecraft might be lost altogether. In fact, it was working as programmed, but its programs had been written for a different set of expectations; the shaking incurred at launch exceeded those forecast conditions, and had jarred overly sensitive fault-protection algorithms into sending the spacecraft into a fetal crouch. The scare passed. When the etiology of the affliction had been diagnosed and cured, one analyst described the episode as an "anxiety attack"; another, as a kind of "vertigo," or perhaps seasickness, part of Voyager getting its sea legs. Bruce Murray observed that the "new, superautonomous robot" lacked the "repertoire of human judgment and experience," and it had "mistrusted itself" before finally being "righted by its own logic." Voyager had already begun to surprise its creators, and it had begun to learn.[1]

The anxiety attack continued in other manifestations, felt more intensely by its human controllers than by Voyaget 2. Signals indicated that the science boom had failed to deploy fully; but this was deemed a failure of the sensor, not the boom. Weirdly, a hydrazine thruster pointed wrongly at the spacecraft itself, which caused the vessel to drift off trajectory, which required more precious hydrazine, until the problem was recognized and repaired and course corrections made. Sensors began to fail (some seventy-two out of several hundred throughout the mission), all pertinent but none fatal. Then the infrared sensors deteriorated when bonding materials crystallized and distorted their mirrors after the protective sheath was removed, until a flash heater corrected the problem. There were odd pitches and yaws, never explained. As a result, several days of testing commenced before Voyager 2 could acquire its navigational guide star, Canopus. For their first two weeks both spacecraft underwent shakedown cruises in which they extended booms, tested instruments, and learned to communicate with a fast-receding Earth.[2]

Similar breakdowns continued throughout the mission and not all were mechanical; some of the worse stemmed from the failures of human controllers. The Grand Tour meant a constant negotiation between robot and human, with each learning from the other and at times compensating for the other's lapses. Voyager 2 overcame its makers' errors in failing to program for a jarring launch, and its makers overlooked the malfunction of its boom sensor and fixed its faulty thruster. Over the years that exchange deepened, though their mutual reliance, begun at launch, never disappeared.

WAXING MOON

The Moon mattered. After IGY had field-tested the technologies of the Third Age, Earth and its Moon were the place where it took its ambitions. The Earth-Moon system was to the new geography of discovery what the Atlantic isles were to the First Age, and what a resurvey of Europe's interior by naturalists was to the Second.

Proximity was an obvious explanation. The Moon was the closest as well as the dominant object in the night sky, and space travelers advanced upon it step by step. The first Earth-launched satellites were identified as "new moons." The earliest spacecraft targeted near-Earth realms and the Moon. The primary rival to (and disturber of) planetary exploration, the Apollo program, aimed at the Moon. Colonizers imagined the Moon as a port of call for the solar system akin to that enjoyed earlier by Madeira and the Canaries to the Indies and Americas. Planetary spacecraft evolved from lunar Ranger to inner-planets Mariner to outer-planets Voyager. In 1969, in the months prior to the Apollo 11 lunar landing, Mariner 6 and 7 completed magnificent flybys of Mars, and while for true believers Mars mattered as much as the Moon, public attention and politics remained riveted on a lunar landing.

So it was a waxing Moon, not Earth's planetary siblings, that dominated the political sky. For planetary discovery to thrive, spacecraft, and mission planners, had to see the satellites of far planets, and couldn't do so if their eyes were flooded with the reflected light of Earth's. Then the Apollo program, its cold war mission completed, sank into near-parody as astronaut Alan Shepard hit two golf balls down the gray-powder fairways of Fra Mauro. The glittering vision of humans leaping beyond their home planet imploded into Skylab and Soyuz, the shuttle, and a hypothetical space station. Yet even as the shuttle began to drain NASA in a slow-death hemorrhage of money and talent, the planetary program blasted into its glory years.

As the Voyagers quickly rushed beyond the orbit of the Moon, they passed by the first planetary marker on their grand traverse. When the Third Age began, the Earth-Moon nexus was its Pillars of Hercules, the limits of humanity's practical powers and its blinkered imagination.

That setting served the Third Age as Europe's bounding seas had the First Age, and as the scientific rediscovery of its internal geography did for the Second when the grand tour shifted from art and classical literature to natural history. The botanical excursions of Linnaeus replaced a pilgrimage to the ruins of Rome, and the geological collecting of Christian Leopold von Buch amid the Alps superseded oils and watercolors of Mount Etna in eruption. In effect, the eyes of discovery turned to Europe, not to witness new scenes but to see old ones with new insight. The emergence of modern biology, geology, and ethnology revived the tired geography of Ptolemy into something fresh and vibrant. That experience was the essence of the Second Age, much of which had been known in some fashion to formal learning, and only a tiny fraction of which did not have indigenous inhabitants.

Each era of exploration mingled new discovery with rediscovery. The First could celebrate Madeira, previously unknown, and the Canary Islands, known to the Ancients as the Happy Isles, and even included in Ptolemy's *Geographia* and Pliny's *Natural History*. But before becoming a critical platform for launching the Great Voyages, the isles had to reestablish contact. Both Madeira and the Canaries were later rediscovered yet again by the voyaging naturalists of the Second Age, as the Enlightenment redefined what was interesting and important about them and how a rational nature might be understood. Joseph Hooker and Alfred Wallace saw the isles with very different eyes than those of Amerigo Vespucci and Pedro Cabral.

That was how it went: the reexploration that blossomed into the Second Age had learned its craft in Europe, and then propagated throughout Europe's emerging imperium, and beyond. But it had a special catalyst, and it may be well worth pausing to examine it. Much as the Voyagers coasted in orbit in order to reposition themselves properly for the final thrust of the Centaurs' RL-10 engines, so historical narrative needs to resituate itself from time to time. The final propulsion for the Third Age came from the International Geophysical Year, which blasted the era into a trajectory the Voyagers followed across the solar system.

Meanwhile, the two spacecraft sped past the nominal lunar orbit and so broke the bonds of imagination and political bureaucracy that had shackled the early years of space travel and that subsequently tethered NASA to an orbiting shuttle that, like a parodic Moon, only went in circles around Earth. One of the three pairs of hands that had held high the embryonic space program in that canonical photo of Explorer 1, von Braun's, was dropping out, and with him the vision of the Voyagers as robotic scouts blazing a Martian trail for migrating pioneers.

THE GREAT GAME

Exploration, like war, was politics by other means. Especially when grafted to science, exploring ventures provided a cover for the more devious endeavors of the twentieth century's version of the Great Game. Yet that had been no less true for Kipling's Kim, who had found himself dodging Russian "geologists" in the Himalayas, as each imperial contestant sought less an understanding of mountains than the high ground of geopolitical advantage.

The American space program began under military sponsorship, and then was laundered through participation in the overtly civilian IGY and the creation of NASA; but by the time Voyager commenced its long trek, the program was seemingly returning to something like military oversight. In 1982, while Voyager 2 flew between Saturn and Uranus, military spending on space outstripped civilian by a widening margin. If the planetary program escaped this trend directly, as the space shuttle did not, it was a segregation more apparent than real, because so many indirect costs and breakthrough technologies built upon an infrastructure erected with military monies. The Soviet space program remained squarely under military command.

Exploration has long and often hybridized civilian and military personnel, vessels, and purposes. Most expeditions went armed, and most of those that enjoyed government sponsorship—which was the great majority of them—relied on naval vessels or army escorts and had an implicit military liaison if not an overt military purpose; overwhelmingly, expedition leaders had some military background. Not least among expeditionary goals was national security, and not least among the reasons that the peoples encountered by explorers proved so often hostile was the indigenes' suspicion that exploration proclaimed in the service of untrammeled curiosity could segue seamlessly into spying, which might announce a future invasion of soldiers, prospectors, settlers, and officials—and often did. While colonization remained the ambition of many enthusiasts, it had lost momentum in an age of earthly *decolonization*. Even *Star Trek* has imagined its exploring adventures as a benign arm of the United Federation of Planets' defense force, Star Fleet, while discarding

imperialism and keeping its military in check with a "prime directive" that makes noninterference a standing order.

The uneasy alliance of military and civilian has taken many
forms. One is simply that exploration can be a reconnaissance in
force. Since exploration in the early days had to pay for itself, exploring parties had to trade or fight, or both. The "voyages of discovery"
down the coast of Africa orchestrated by Henry the Navigator, the
titular inspiration for the opening age of discovery, were, as Malyn
Newitt observes, "openly and explicitly a series of raids designed to
obtain slaves for sale or important 'Moors' who might be ransomed."
When Vasco da Gama met resistance to his plans, he seized ships,
bombarded cities, hanged hostages, and otherwise intimidated both
potential enemies and trading partners. With sure martial instincts,
Afonso de Albuquerque directed his voyages to precisely those pressure points that regulated traffic through the Indian Ocean—Aden,
Hormuz, Molucca—all patrolled out of fortified naval bases such
as Goa. Portugal remained in open war with Morocco and a cold
war with Castile, and it is no surprise that members of military
orders commanded its expeditions; its coastal fortresses were the
military-industrial complex of their day. That sentiment extended
even into the more scientifically ambitious surveys of the Second Age.
The wide-traveling Russian explorer of central Asia Nikolai Przhevalsky openly declared himself a conquistador. "Here," he exulted, "you
can penetrate anywhere, only not with the Gospels under your arm,
but with money in your pocket, a carbine in one hand and a whip in
the other." Here, "the exploits of Cortez can be repeated."[3]

Of course not everyone went with rifle and whip. Missionary
priests fanned out along ancient routes of travel, established themselves even in venerable centers of learning such as China, became fluent in local languages, and reported on terrain, customs, and exotic
curiosities, all done with the hand on a cross instead of a carbine. The
Jesuits were founded as a missionary order, roughly the same year
Coronado returned from his entrada across the American Southwest;
and they targeted the new lands unveiled in the Indies. Francis Xavier
preached in India and Japan and was preparing to visit China when
he died; appropriately he was buried in Goa. When Charles-Marie de

La Condamine readied for his descent along the Amazon, recording exact coordinates by latitude and longitude, he was handed a map of the region by Father Samuel Fritz, a Czech Jesuit who had successfully traced out its major hydrography and settlements. Jesuit fathers, at immense personal cost, recorded the contours of the Great Lakes and Mississippi River.

The Second Age secularized these tendencies, substituting the proselytizing naturalist for the missionary friar, and found more private sponsors as old-money aristocrats and new-money industrialists occasionally funded expeditions as they might museums or universities. Some, such as John Ledyard or Thomas Nuttall, simply traveled, untethered to anything beyond their own wanderlust or obsession for plants or birds or beetles. Some accompanied private expeditions or had the wealth to sponsor themselves, such as Prince Maximilian of Wied into Brazil and later the upper Missouri. A few mounted major expeditions, of which Alexander von Humboldt's remains the exemplar and Ernest Shackleton's Imperial Trans-Antarctic Expedition a fitting valedictory. But expeditions that could not claim an attachment to national security or quick plunder were not likely to attract much support from national treasuries or commercial sponsors. Most serious expeditions had somewhere in their chain of causation at least a nudge, if not something more substantial, of military assistance.

The United States was no exception. It was a nation whose origins coincided almost precisely with those of the Second Age and whose national epic, an expansion westward, occurred through explorers outfitted with guns as well as sextants. Meriwether Lewis and William Clark were of course army officers, and their Corps of Discovery operated under military discipline. As the country grew, especially by war, the nation turned to its military to help wrestle those unknown lands into understanding if not control. The Army Corps of Topographical Engineers, organized in 1836, oversaw much of the grand reconnaissance that mapped out the bulk of America west of the Mississippi. The Corps of Engineers geared up for more in the aftermath of the Civil War, sponsoring two of the four so-called great surveys (with one under nominal civilian leadership). Moreover, in antebellum America, the United States launched fifteen major oceanic expeditions, which, however many "scientifics" they carried, were fleets under the command of naval officers.[4]

But equally significant is the peace that follows conflict. The immediate effect is a surplus of equipment and officers. The vessels will be mothballed, sold, or junked, and the officers cashiered, confined to dismal barracks duties, or placed on impossibly long lists for promotion. An obvious solution is to put them all to the service of exploration. The British Admiralty after the Napoleonic Wars sponsored globe-circling surveys for several decades. As second secretary to the Admiralty John Barrows put it: "To what purpose could a portion of our naval force be, at any time, but more especially in time of profound peace, more honourably or more usefully employed than in completing those details of geographical and hydrographical science of which the grand outlines have been boldly and broadly sketched by Cook, Vancouver, and Flinders, and others of our countrymen?" The resulting outpouring scouted from the Great Lakes of Africa to the Ross Sea of Antarctica.[5]

The United States had surpluses following the Civil War, some of which it redirected to western exploration. After World War II it donated a goodly portion of its otherwise dry-docked fleet to the service of earth and oceanographic sciences. Perhaps the most astonishing expression was the U.S. Navy Antarctic Developments Program, Task Force 68, otherwise known as Operations Highjump and Windmill, in 1946–48, in which the navy dispatched thirteen ships, including an aircraft carrier and a submarine, ostensibly to survey an unmapped Antarctica, but equally to test its fleet against polar conditions that replicated those they might face against the country's Arctic rival, the USSR.[6]

The fact is, exploration by itself cannot long command the political will and cultural commitment it needs unless it can rally deeper justifications than curiosity, appeals to a genetic imperative, hyperspace rhetoric, or very expensive (and often arcane) science. The relationship between civilian exploration and military reconnaissance, that is, has been symbiotic. Exploration has repeatedly been a means of beating swords into plowshares, and ICBMs into vessels of discovery. But a perceived need for national security, and a military infrastructure, has often proved a useful and necessary incentive to encourage exploration. It is a strategy the military has repeatedly recognized and even sought. Those plowshares can serve as sheathed swords.

There was no direct military involvement with Voyager: no funds, no seconded personnel, no secret experiments. Its singularly civilian control places it within a small fraternity of major expeditions that have been wholly autonomous from the military. But there was plenty of covert context, beginning with JPL itself.

The Jet Propulsion Laboratory that designed and oversaw Voyager could not have thrived only as a dedicated laboratory for civilian spacecraft. Its origins lay in amateur and academic enthusiasms, but it became permanent when the army endowed it as a facility for experimenting with jet propulsion and then with rockets, and its future depends on a partial rerooting in that same soil. When it transferred to NASA, funding became more episodic, which left staffing unstable and technological know-how far from cutting-edge. Repeatedly, the lab has sought outside support, almost always governmental and eventually military as the only large and relatively reliable pool of money. While defense funding never dominated the budget, it was a thumb on the scale that made the final weightings balance. JPL could assemble Voyager without military money; but beyond the Grand Tour, it could not likely survive, particularly with changes in national administrations hostile to aerospace outside Pentagon control. Military funding frames the JPL story before and after Voyager, but the plucky Voyagers slipped through unscathed, as they did the Van Allen radiation belts.[7]

As it showed with IGY and NASA, and as it had done with the U.S. Geological Survey a century before, America preferred where possible to segregate its civilian from its military institutions. When scientific inventories had greater claims than absorbing new conquests, the nation gladly turned to civilian agencies. It sublimated the cold war into an International Geophysical Year and tweaked military rocketry into NASA. By such maneuvers the Third Age relocated the Great Game from the Pacific Ocean to the Sea of Tranquility, and from the Khyber Pass and the Himalayas to the Valles Marineris and Olympus Mons. Almost always there was some military money in the chain, if only covertly.

The cold war concentrated its rivalries on Earth and its Moon, and secondarily on Venus and Mars; and by avoiding all of those bodies, Voyager seemingly escaped the implicit militarization of space. Yet it was there, its presence a perturbation in the political field, like those massive if invisible bodies that ripple through and bend gravitational fields. Voyager felt the tugs of them all. But it could bypass the ideological fixations of the inner planets, and it could escape the Sun-like attraction of the cold war. It had the pull of the Grand Tour and the push of momentum from a golden age that with an assist from Jupiter, would give it an escape velocity to take it beyond its own times.

LOOKING BACK

On September 18, two weeks after launch, some 11.65 million kilometers from its home planet, Voyager 1 turned its cameras back to its origins and took a photo of Earth and its Moon together. It was the first of the Voyagers' stunning images, and it reminded observers that however far the Voyagers traveled, whatever new worlds they might discover, they always looked homeward as well and spoke ultimately to Earth. By so doing they challenged not only the bounds of our understanding and ambition, but also our sense of what exploration itself might be.

That haunting image recalled how much Voyager shared with other exploits of its era, and how much it differed. The earliest images of Earth from space were photographic maps from weather and surveillance satellites and lunar missions. A breakthrough moment occurred with Surveyor's first lunar orbiter. While it circled the Moon to photograph potential sites for Apollo, controllers adjusted the camera to take two shots that had the Moon as foreground and Earth behind. The images were not part of mission orders, and required tinkering with the spacecraft's attitude to reorient the lens. The maneuver was a "calculated risk," and when it worked, it impressed officials powerfully. This was something the public could understand. We could see ourselves from the Moon.[8]

Apollo 8 repeated the Surveyor shots in color and created one of the genuinely iconic images of the space age. But a required change in attitude was not restricted to the spacecraft: the Apollo program to the Moon went nowhere, withdrawing to the virtual solipsism of the space shuttle and a near-Earth space station. The great images of Apollo had been scenes of self-reference. That majestic earthrise was one, the blue and white gem of a living planet looming over the horizon of a dead Moon and capturing precisely the closed-circuit character of the enterprise. From the beginning the point of discovering new worlds had been to improve the old one.

Yet the Voyagers did something different, even as it remains a truism that their messages were for us and that even their gold-plated records with a greeting to some hypothetical Other beyond the solar system were in reality a dispatch to ourselves about how we wanted to be seen. Voyager widened the perspectival field. It put Earth into a planetary context, pushed beyond the range of rediscovery, and promised a reference outside our self-image, of ourselves seeking to portray ourselves as exploring. Voyager could not take pictures of itself, nor bring back images others had made of it. When it was represented for public display, the constructed field of vision typically came from behind the spacecraft as it looked toward its discoveries, not from the discovered scene looking at a spacecraft posturing as an explorer.

That first look back was a gamble, if a benign one. It might cause an instrument failure or jam the scan platform (as a test a few months later did) in ways that could compromise the mission before Voyager even reached the edge of the Grand Tour. But perhaps the greater hazard was the potential for narcissism, that the mission might look too far inward instead of outward. This peril also passed. What spared Voyager from preciousness and self-absorption was the sheer immensity of its geographic sweep—a trek too vast to remain within the frame of Earth and its Moon—and its existence as a robot, which shifted the focal plane of its cameras from itself.

Voyager compelled us to move beyond ourselves—that is what great exploration has always done. If it occasionally turned around, the intent was to measure how far it had come and to shift our perceptual frames. Eventually it would move so far away that Earth could no longer be seen at all.

DAY 29–94

7. Cruise

Their journeys were chronicles of spasms and calms. The flurry of launch and the frenetic bustle of planetary encounters were mere moments amid long lulls in the effective void of space, ruffled only by gusts of solar wind, the stray meteorite, and the subtle nudges of gravity. The interplanetary seas probably consumed 98 percent of the voyage, and beyond Neptune, all of it. Magellan's crew had found the wearying calm of the ocean they accordingly named "the pacific" to be maddening; but the weeks of Pacific tedium were nothing compared to the emptiness of interplanetary space.

Like far-sailing ships, spacecraft had their routines, and they attended to onboard maintenance. Each Voyager took about two weeks after launch to complete its circuit of instrument tests and navigational orientations. From time to time there were midcourse corrections to realign trajectories. Voyager 1 had two during its shakedown cruise; both spacecraft continued with minor corrective burns almost monthly.

The long cruise continued. On December 15, 1977, Voyager 1 passed Voyager 2. Some 445 days remained before it would make its closest encounter with Jupiter.

CAPTAIN VOYAGER

In 1632, having crossed the South Atlantic six times and the North Atlantic twenty, sometimes as a crewman and some as a captain, Samuel de Champlain set forth his conceptions of the ideal expeditionary commander, or what he termed the good seaman. He should be "above all" a "good man, fearing God." He would not blaspheme, would attend to liturgical duties, and if possible retain a "churchman" to keep his crews "always in the fear of God, and likewise to help them and confess them when they are sick, or in other ways to comfort them during the dangers which are encountered in the hazards of the ocean."[9]

The captain should be robust, alert, inured to hardships and toil, "so that whatever betide he may manage to keep the deck, and in a strong voice command everybody what to do" and should do so as "the only one to speak, lest contradictory orders, especially in doubtful situations, cause one maneuver to be mistaken for another." He should share dangers, duties, and rewards. He should be able to eat whatever the circumstances permit. He should avoid drunkenness. He should not delegate by default. He should know everything that concerns the ship, for "great care and constant practice" are the means of safe passage. He should have practical experience "in encounters and their consequences." He should be "pleasant and affable in his conversation, absolute in his orders, not communicating too readily with his shipmates, unless with those who share the command. Otherwise, not doing so in time might engender a feeling of contempt for him." He will punish evildoers, reward achievers, and avoid occasions for envy, "which is often the source of bad feeling, like a gangrene which little by little corrupts and destroys the body," and can spark outright conspiracy or worse. He should, in brief, lead by both skill and example.[10]

The nature of geographic exploration left little slack for fumbling or fussiness; and to the extent that the perennial attraction with exploration resides with the character of the explorers, not simply with destinations reached and collections gathered, how they achieve their goals has as much interest as whether they reached them. What exploration could not tolerate was irresolution in purpose, and what leaders could not overlook was insurrection within the corps. Yet uncertainty was the norm and unrest a commonplace, the one often inspiring the other. Unable to locate the Strait where forecast, Magellan nearly fell to mutiny at Puerto San Julián in Patagonia. Henry Hudson, endlessly promising successes he could not deliver, was set adrift by crews in his eponymous Bay. Inadequate leadership was as lethal as rebellious crews; expeditions with weak captains could expect to suffer and fail like Bering's second voyage to Alaska, the crew shipwrecked and wasting away on Bering Isle, practically within sight of their destination port on Kamchatka. Expeditions led by indomitable captains were almost certain to succeed, no matter the cost, as Henry Stanley's extraordinary traverses through Africa demonstrate.

People judge exploration by the explorer as much as the things explored. The perennial fascination is not simply with destinations reached and collections gathered, but with how explorers achieve their goals. By the self-conscious end of the Second Age, even explorers openly accepted this standard. Apsley Cherry-Garrard described his intrepid band as "artistic Christians," as keen to test themselves with winter journeys around Cape Crozier as to unveil the mysteries of evolution as expressed in penguin eggs. The greatest expeditions had both great personalities and fabulous quests. Which is why the Third Age stands so awkwardly.

What is the personality of Voyager? What is the meaning of its leadership? Where is the commanding presence when a captain is called upon not to stare down a smoldering mutiny but to upload a software patch? Where is the moral drama of exploration? Where is that second, latent act of discovery, the unveiling of character? Who can be named as leader when a single Voyager of discovery will continue across a score of bureaucratic and careerist lifetimes? What might be the defining traits of great explorers—their invincible will, their curiosity, their passion for fame—was here hardwired into computers. Yet Voyager has variants of all these features.

What an act of transfiguration requires, however, is what many engineers and most philosophers disdain: anthropomorphizing a robot, even if only indirectly as a device by which to refract beliefs, passions, and intentions. It means having Voyager stand as a cipher for the hundreds of people and dozens of leaders who assembled, remotely navigated, and advised the spacecraft, and who shared its encounters with new worlds—who could supply the perception that pixilated images could merely copy. It means investing in a machine such virtues as fortitude, resolution, and discipline. There would be no impressive, fallible, undaunted explorer to stand on the quarter-deck or the mountain pass and issue commands, record first contacts, and meditate on the panorama before him. The explorer was being replaced by the public he traditionally reported back to.

Its small rebellions, blown circuits, and cranky scan platforms remind us that the Voyager spacecraft did not make itself, nor was it birthed from cyborgs. It was a very human creation, and as much as a painting or a novel or a political constitution, it embodies the flawed character of its creators. To give expression to such a machine was an act of imagination and passion, and to guide it was leadership of a high order. Ultimately it was the project managers who commanded: Harris "Bud" Schurmeier (1970–76), John Casani (1976–78), Robert J. Parks (1978–79), Raymond Heacock (1979–81), Esker Davis (1981–82), Richard Laeser (1982–87), Norman Haynes (1987–89). They got Voyager to Neptune and pointed it beyond, where another succession of project managers is today overseeing a vastly reduced crew staffing a vastly diminished vessel as it plunges into the new Sea of Darkness that lies beyond the solar system.

What was Voyager? To those who built and guided it, *they* were Voyager. They made it happen; they told it what to do and received its responses; they interpreted its discoveries. And yet Voyager was something more. It existed with or without them; they had to grant it a degree of autonomy; and they sent it where no one truly knew what it might encounter. It was capable of reprogramming, which is to say, of learning and discovering. It has lasted far beyond its life expectancy, which was guaranteed only to Saturn, but which proponents hoped would extend to Uranus, and might, just might, last to Neptune, but which is persisting through the heliosphere.

Voyager did things no one predicted, found scenes no one expected, and promises to outlive its inventors. Its autonomy did not reside solely in its primitive software and magnetic tape memory, but in its capacity to inform, and inspire, and to force us outside the ordinary. Like a great painting or an abiding institution, it has acquired an existence of its own, a destiny beyond the grasp of its handlers. If it had no consciousness of itself, it could provoke consciousness in others. The mission, with its implausibly grandiloquent Grand Tour completed, continues; the spacecraft, so obviously a piece of engineering, endures as art; a project sold as science persists as saga.

JPL AS EXPLORING INSTITUTION

The deeper threat on long voyages, however, was a loss of discipline. The problem was not so much insubordination by the onboard computers as inattention or slacking on Earth. It was one thing for a spacecraft to coast; another for its commander, in this case, mission control at JPL, to go on autopilot.

At Pasadena the sense congealed that the crisis had passed. The Voyagers were launched, they were working, they would cruise through a veritable void for eighteen to twenty-two months before beginning their first encounters with Jupiter. The tension lifted. Attention turned to the next project. Operations relaxed, planning fell behind, anomalies passed by without prompt action. In December 1977 a tricky maneuver was aborted when it demanded a management decision that no one on the flight-control quarterdeck could give. In April 1978, with mission attention directed to malfunctions in Voyager 1, the officer of the watch forgot to send the mandatory weekly message, which prompted Voyager to default to safe mode. There were good reasons why classic expeditions adopted military discipline.[11]

Such breakdowns forced a NASA-mandated reorganization upon JPL. If it was to function as an exploring institution, it had to recognize that operations were continuous, not limited to launches and encounters, and that even quasi-autonomous spacecraft required a vigilant chain of command. Orders had to be restated, adjusted to circumstances, and enforced, even if they took the form of software patches and uploads. While Voyager could not put into port for an overhaul, JPL's mission crew could. Even as the spacecraft sailed on, the administration was in effect careened and scraped.

The fact is, while the Voyagers might travel in a vacuum, they were not created in one; nor could ideas, however heroic, express themselves of their own volition into scan platforms and antennas. They were the work of people organized into institutions. With particular force, Voyager was an enterprise of the Jet Propulsion Laboratory. It may well constitute JPL's finest hour. But when JPL failed to meet routine obligations, the episode not only threatened the mission but exposed the peculiar status of JPL within NASA.

The facility began in 1936 when a small group of enthusiasts organized themselves around Hungarian émigré Theodore von Kármán, a founder of aerodynamics, then a professor at the California Institute of Technology. The Guggenheim Aeronautical Laboratory, as it became known, evolved into a major center for rocketry and, as Clayton Koppes observes, "could plausibly claim that they—not Robert Goddard or the German V-2 experimenters—laid the foundation for the development of American rocket and missile technology." In 1944 Caltech operated the embryonic facility for the U.S. Army Ordnance Corps, one of a growing archipelago of labs run by universities under military contract. The facility changed its name to the Jet Propulsion Laboratory.[12]

But while JPL developed the nation's first tactical nuclear missiles, Corporal and Sergeant, a postwar status as a military shop became less attractive, particularly granted JPL's association with Caltech. The lab's real passion was for space exploration. As early as 1945, its WAC Corporal succeeded in escaping Earth's atmosphere, a first. It supplemented missiles with payloads and, together with von Braun's group, launched Explorer 1, America's first successful satellite. Once it was amalgamated into NASA, the way to the Moon and the planets opened, and JPL sent by itself or assisted in sending Ranger, Surveyor, Pioneer 4, Mariner, Viking, and Voyager.[13]

Its partisans early appreciated that propulsion was only as good as guidance: that was the difference between a rocket and a bomb. When it was reorganized in 1944 into JPL, the lab began acquiring expertise in tracking, telemetry, and the kind of communications and electronics that made missile guidance possible. The program flourished under William Pickering, a New Zealander with a physics PhD from Caltech, then a professor in its electrical engineering faculty involved with IGY's Upper Atmosphere Research Panel and early plans for an orbiting satellite, and finally director of JPL from 1954 to 1976. When military (and later NASA) support for rockets went mostly to von Braun's group, JPL reoriented itself to emphasize satellites and guidance systems. Its research into solid-fuel rockets may have given the lab liftoff among space institutions, but it thrived by designing spacecraft and the electronics that made it possible to communicate with, guide, track, and instruct the payloads once off Earth. And travel to other worlds was what JPL's staff wanted.

As Oran Nicks recalled, JPL was from the outset "aching to begin planetary missions," and it started with imagined missions rather than with existing capabilities. It would craft technology to suit missions, not limit missions to what was presently possible. JPL soon strengthened its communication capabilities with an eye beyond the sublunary realm. (Revealingly, it was the lab's chief of guidance research, Eberhard Rechtin, who proposed a "visionary program of lunar and planetary missions" and, unauthorized, commenced improvements in antennas.) In July 1958 JPL submitted the formal request to back that vision with a "Proposal for an Interplanetary Tracking Network." Five months later JPL proposed to a still-groggy NASA that it become the agency's "major" facility for space flight, or as Director Pickering expressed it, "the national space laboratory." Shortly afterward it dispatched for NASA's approval Project VEGA, an upper-stage rocket and spacecraft, along with a bold package of probes to the Moon, Mars, and Venus; a meteorological satellite for Earth; and a small clutch of unspecified interplanetary missions. In January 1959 NASA accepted JPL's concept for a deep-space communications network, and in March it approved Project VEGA, partially substantiating JPL's bid as the prime center for extra-lunar space flights.[14]

The euphoria couldn't last. VEGA got canceled, JPL sat awkwardly within the NASA administrative matrix, and after the elation over Explorer passed, projects stumbled. The lab faced rivals both inside and outside NASA. Director Pickering might proclaim that "it is the U.S. against Russia, and its most important campaign is being fought far out in the empty reaches of space," and JPL might declare itself the nation's primary institution for pursuing that contest throughout the solar system, but the reality was that the lab faced competition within the United States, and especially within NASA, as intense as any from its Soviet counterparts.[15]

The difficulties were several, both institutional and intellectual, and they began at conception. The first lay in competing visions of "space"; but the most serious—the bureaucratic version of original sin—dated from the organic act of July 29, 1958, which created the National Aeronautics and Space Administration and forced a merger of the erstwhile National Advisory Committee for Aeronautics labs with upstart facilities, mostly military. JPL now found itself competing with NACA's old Ames Research Center, NASA's new Goddard Space Flight Center, and even Langley Research Center, all of which had charges and ambitions with regard to satellites.

Unlike the others, JPL also had a costly and confusing affiliation with a university. From NASA's perspective Caltech extracted maximum fees for minimal supervision. JPL had a managerial style that placed it outside the bureaucratic norm: its university connections, which were vital for many of its participants, conveyed a sense of academic freedom, intellectual élan, and institutional insouciance that budget-conscious and politically harassed bureaucrats at NASA headquarters found often annoying and occasionally dysfunctional. JPL's sense of itself and its mission did not always agree with NASA's. It all might be tolerated so long as JPL performed well. When Ranger spacecraft after Ranger failed, NASA stepped in. It would do so again and again, even during the Voyager mission, when it perceived that JPL's demands for autonomy and Caltech's nominal supervision interfered with programmatic needs.[16]

There was an alchemy at work, but whether of white magic or black depended on perspective. NASA wanted more programmatic discipline, JPL sought standing as an intellectual institution not simply a government job shop, and Caltech coveted the funds but worried about how to reconcile a contract lab with university purposes, particularly when military research continued at JPL, as it did, and brought with it requirements for secrecy. Defense spending would in fact increase as NASA's budget plunged, a situation that worsened when the Reagan administration sought either to shift space onto the military or to privatize it. The three parties found themselves in a state of more or less constant turmoil. Major contract negotiations occurred in 1964 and 1966 as the planetary program began to hit its stride. They continued throughout the Voyagers' traverse across the solar system.

Such confusions and contests have been common over the centuries and reflect the culture's changing understanding of what exploration means and why it is done.

The Great Voyages had commercial and geopolitical purposes. There was, on one hand, an urge to open up and unleash discovery on the theory that the first comer would grab the most spoils, while, on the other, a concern that exploration serve its society, which argued for a controlling agency. Portugal placed oversight with the Concilho da Fazenda (Treasury), into whose vaults the secret discoveries were entrusted. Spain gave primary responsibility to the Casa de Contracción in Seville. Both emphasized the commercial significance of voyaging and the implacable interest of the state. Competitors might unload duties onto chartered bodies such as East India companies, a Company of Adventurers, or outright privateers; and in the Second Age, scientific associations could become promoters and occasionally sponsors. Still, expeditions rarely diverged from government interests, nor did state-sponsored exploration stray far from military support, if not leadership. The major exception is the heroic age of Antarctic exploration that concluded the Second Age. But whether within or between countries, there was competition aplenty.

There was precedent for NASA's dilemma during the Second Age, when exploring institutions proliferated and began to trespass on one another's turf. Instead of interplanetary space, the contestants sparred over the near-nation Great Plains and intermountain space of America's unexplored West. In the nineteenth century the United States had turned over most of the responsibility for exploring its continental acquisitions to the U.S. Army, and for oceanic probes, to the U.S. Navy. From 1836 to 1863 the army created a Corps of Topographical Engineers, which organized expeditions, surveyed in the company of naturalists and artists, and prepared composite maps, until the Civil War directed its talents to other landscapes. After the war, the army was keen to renew its role, even as civilians were claiming priority for more science-based institutions. What emerged were four separate programs that became known as the Great Surveys, each with a different sponsor. They soon began to crowd into one another.[17]

King, Wheeler, Hayden, Powell—each leader's name became shorthand for his survey, and each survey conveyed a style as much as a geographic locale. One emphasized high-caliber geology, one cartography, another natural resources, and another land reform. One advertised the Yellowstone and galvanized Congress into creating America's first national park; another, Grand Canyon; another, Death Valley. They appealed to commercial lust, national security, and cultural pride; they enlisted art to promote where science couldn't. Their rivalry was ferocious, not only between military and civilian, but among civilians, and often among scientists, who disputed what constituted real geology and which group made proper maps, which institution of higher learning deserved the government's patronage and which did not, and who was a genuine scientist and who a mere celebrity. So long as the West was open and money plentiful, each survey could find popular partisans and political champions in Congress, and take to the field year after year.

But after they began to stumble over one another, after the sleaziness of the Grant administration was replaced by an emphasis on sobriety, reform, and retrenchment, and after a second, more scientific grand reconnaissance had completed its survey of the West, the exuberance for unbridled exploration waned and some consolidation was mandatory. A political brouhaha ensued, with scientists fighting as ferociously against one another as against military dominance. Each survey denounced the others as a disgrace or an outright fraud. The outcome: the establishment of the civilian U.S. Geological Survey in 1879, with Clarence King as director.

The King Survey had, in truth, proposed the better hybrid of interests, and Clarence King himself, "as Yale man, adventurer and clubman, litterateur, scientist, and exposer of the Diamond Hoax," was the epitome of "that peculiar alliance between very big business, the socially acceptable intellectuals, and the advocates of limited reform" who finally rallied behind the chosen program. That scroll should sound familiar; such were the syntheses of personality and programs that allowed a comparable compromise to proceed a century later.[18]

The similarities then and now are striking—and misleading. The greatest is timing: the U.S. Geological Survey helped close out an era of frontier exploration, while NASA helped to open one.

Consolidation in 1879 purged the resulting institution of much of the conflicts that had riven the Great Surveys; it moved the enterprise from geographical survey to formal science; its charter closed a debate that had flourished for a decade. In 1958 consolidation drove external rivalries into NASA, an agency kindled into being by impulsive reactions to Sputnik, without close argument and decades of consensus. When funding shriveled, those absorbed tensions could become unbearable. In 1879 the country was able to continue demobilizing from the Civil War. In 1958 the cold war retarded a full transfer from military to civilian operations. By the 1979 centennial of the USGS—in fact, while Voyager 1 was approaching Jupiter—the system was poised to reverse that trend, and under the Reagan administration to remilitarize America's space program. Voyager threaded through that gap as though it were a historical Strait of Magellan.

JPL had made Voyager happen. Its staff had discovered the potential for the Grand Tour, had recognized in gravity assist the propulsion to yield the necessary trajectories, had designed a durable and redundant spacecraft, had equipped the robot with the semi-autonomy required to operate at the edge of the solar system, and had granted Voyager a persona—had stamped it with a JPL style. More than anything else, JPL had simply made Voyager possible. It had argued for it, fought for it, brought it back from the dead, and ultimately willed it into being. Voyager has traveled in a JPL manner, and its trek speaks in a JPL idiom. The quirks and powers and personality of the one are those of the other.

Yet that observation can be turned around with equal force. Whatever becomes of JPL, whatever stresses tear at its peculiar institutional arrangements, whatever future missions take shape or dissolve, the Voyager saga will immortalize JPL in the history of exploration. VGR-77 is a kind of Pygmalion story in reverse: the creation, begun in very mortal flesh and then preserved in imperishable form, that will outlive its creator.

8. Missing Mars

The cruise might have ended, as so many planetary expeditions have, at Mars. More than anywhere else, Mars had fused the culture of exploration with the culture of space, distilling and distorting each. Here the boosters sang loudest, and the scorners scoffed longest. In the Viking mission to the Red Planet that preceded it by a year, Voyager had its greatest competitor and a rival vision. If the goal of the Third Age was Mars, then Viking could well stand as the era's grand gesture. But exploration had greater unknowns to plumb than the Red Planet.

In November and December 1977, the Voyagers slid past the orbit of Mars without a twitch. Their meeting with Mars was a nonencounter; but it was rich with significance nonetheless, for what Voyager did not do—was never intended to attempt—could be as revealing as its announced goals. In seeking newer worlds, it bypassed the world that has most mesmerized the imagination of space partisans, that best expresses their effort to control the direction of Third Age exploration, and that best boils down the motives of those who have most fervently wished to project exploration into space and those who have most doubted its value.

MOTIVES

The Voyagers were machines on a mission. In their choice of instruments and in their design, in the passions and intentions of their creators as coded in trajectories, they carried a legacy of Western exploration. In their motivations, too, there were continuities as well as disconnects.

The Great Voyages had expressed their times. They were as much a part of the Renaissance as its commercial bustle, flamboyant arts, endless warring, and renewed learning. Over and again, explorers and their sponsors repeated the same trilogy of reasons to justify expeditions. They went for gold, for God, and for glory. They went to get rich, and thus acquire power. They went to spread the Gospel, weaken religious rivals, and generally ennoble the spirit and enhance the intangibles that endowed life with meaning. They went for fame and status, to rise in their societies and to become known and to have the future look upon them as they did the demigods and heroes of the past. Geographic exploration was an amalgam of quest, crusade, and commerce, with discovery and new knowledge as a means to those ends. With remarkable tenacity these reasons, or their reembodiments, have persisted.

The sponsors and captains of the First Age made no effort to disguise their purposes. Henry the Navigator sought new Madeiras, the gold and slaves of Africa, and a further means to wage Portugal's perpetual conflict with Morocco. Columbus's Enterprise of the Indies was founded on a premise of gold, which is "most excellent; of gold there is formed treasure and with it whoever has it may do what he wishes in this world and come to bring souls into Paradise." Gold was the font of all other motives: Columbus promised he would find as much of it as his monarchs would "require," though the forecast lands of bottomless gold were always a bit "further west." When Vasco da Gama arrived in India, he declared he had come for co-religionists and wealth. The expedition had sailed to establish trade, by force if necessary.[19]

In his epic retelling of that voyage, Luiz Vaz de Camões includes long passages on both fame and greed. The "giant goddess Fame" was

Hot-blooded, boasting, lying, truthful,
Who sees, as she goes, with a hundred eyes,
Bringing a thousand mouths to propagandize.

But it was gold that "conquers the strongest citadels," that turned friends into "traitors and liars," debauched nobles and maidens, and that could buy "even scholarship." The blinding, mesmerizing, corrupting, all-commanding power of gold could pervert; it could also drive men to astonishing deeds. Marching with Cortés to Tenochtitlán, Bernal Diaz noted simply that they came "to serve God, and also to get rich," for "all men alike covet gold, and the more we have the more we want," and it was the dazzling gold of the Aztecs that kept them fighting.[20]

Expeditions had to pay for themselves, if not by trade, then by looting. The prospect for plunder drove Iberians across the New World in search of further Mexicos and Perus, and that example inspired repeated forays by Portugal into Africa and prodded other nations to emulate them. Richard Hakluyt, for example, recounts how "certain grave citizens of London, and men careful for the good of their country," upon "seeing that the wealth of the Spaniards and Portuguese, by the discovery and search of new trades and countries was marvelously increased, supposing the same to be a course and means for them also to obtain the like, they thereupon resolved upon a new and strange navigation," in this case three ships to discover a northern route to Asia—which ended at Muscovy, but which flung greedy would-be discoverers around the littoral of the Ocean Sea.[21]

In truth, the New World would require a couple of centuries to become commercially self-sustaining; until then, its preponderance of trade goods were luxury items, plunder, and drugs, with the occasional tourist junket. Colonization was a distraction. Fantasies dissolved upon actual contact. After the glowing visions conjured by Columbus's first voyage, for example, everyone wanted to go to Hispaniola, "a land to be desired and, seen . . . never to be left," and after his second, no one did. Trade produced wealth; colonies siphoned it off. What Europe wanted was riches, and what it sought from its explorers were routes to get them.[22]

Yet the intangibles mattered, too. They all professed to serve the Cross, or the prestige of their monarch, and their own fame. The most successful had a sense of personal destiny, of themselves as ciphers for a cosmic purpose. Gomes Eannes de Zurara, chronicler of Henry the Navigator, explained that "the reason from which all others flowed" was Henry's faith in his horoscope, which had declared he would make "great and noble conquests" and "uncover secrets previously hidden from men." Columbus gave such sentiments a Christian baptism by which he believed himself to be God's instrument, and the discovery of a new route to the Indies, his destiny. He had no choice but to proceed, for by doing well by himself he would do good for all Christendom. (A remarkably similar conviction kept a fever-stricken David Livingstone in his traces.) Their personal purposes were sanctioned by their assertion of a larger consummation that both compelled and justified their implacable ambition.[23]

Still, the sum of greed, pride, and devotion does not seem enough to kindle the fuels that amply lay about. Some other spark had to set those piles ablaze. Despite endless attempts, historians have fared no better at snaring it than Renaissance mariners did in plying the Northwest Passage. In reviewing the Great Voyages to the New World, Samuel Eliot Morison asked, "What made them do it?" Was it, he continued rhetorically, "mere adventure and glory, or lust for gold or (as they all declared) a zeal to enlarge the Kingdom of the Cross?" He could not say. "I wish I knew." But he did identify as a common theme "restlessness," a physical and perhaps spiritual disquiet that led the restive to wander afield and, in the right age and with the right backing, become explorers. Felipe Fernández-Armesto proposed a more formal explanation: that "European culture" of the era was peculiarly "steeped in the idealization of adventure," that exploration was another manifestation of a "code of chivalry." The role models for such questers were "the footloose princes who won themselves kingdoms by deeds of derring-do in popular romances of chivalry—the pulp fiction of the time—which often had a seaborne setting. The hero, down on his luck, who risks seaborne adventures to become ruler of an island realm or fief, is the central character of the Spanish versions of stories of Apollonius, Brutus of Troy, Tristram,

Amadis, King Canamor, and Prince Turian, among others, all part of the array of popular fiction accessible to readers at every level of literacy in the fourteenth and fifteenth centuries." For some, then, glory might substitute for gold. Antonio Pigafetta ingenuously opened his account of Magellan's voyage by listing as his reason for travel, "that it might be told that I made the voyage and saw with my eyes the things hereafter written, and that I might win a famous name with posterity." He did.[24]

What happened with literature happened also with geography. Fabled places of legend—prodigious with lore, wealthy beyond avarice—kept appearing just over the horizon, and when not found there, reappeared at another horizon. Moreover, "at the margins, chivalric and hagiographical texts merged"; there was a "divinization" of old legends; the romance went to sea with sword and cross in an expectation of earthly and heavenly rewards. Such romance proved impervious to facts and deathless to actual discovery. It simply reincarnated and relocated, and where adventurers went, historians have followed.[25]

The Second Age secularized those motives and laundered them through the Enlightenment. A more aggressive commerce replaced simple plundering, a generalized Civilization substituted for Christendom, and glory softened into national prestige and professional reputation. The Enlightenment allowed science standing as a justification, such that new discoveries of nature could serve as the font from which all else might flow.

Consider Captain James Cook's orders for his 1768 voyage. He is first to perform his observations for the transit of Venus, this from Tahiti, an island barely discovered before his departure. He is then to proceed southward to "make discovery" of a new "Continent" (Terra Australis), for whose existence there is "reason to imagine." If that voyage falters, he is to search for the continent westward until he either discovers it or encounters "the Eastern side of the Land discover'd by Tasman and now called New Zeland." Whatever he found he was to render into detailed surveys, complete with collections of flora and fauna, and records of its inhabitants, if any. If uninhabited, he should "take Possession for His Majesty by setting up Proper Marks and Inscriptions, as first discoverers." If inhabited, he should "cultivate a Friendship and Alliance" with the indigenes and establish "Traffick." Columbus's Golden Chersonese has morphed into Terra Australis, and gold bullion into astronomical measurements, naturalist collections, and commerce. But the ambition for prestige has endured; and science and geopolitics have converged, as religion and geopolitics had earlier.[26]

The instructions written by Thomas Jefferson for Meriwether Lewis and William Clark tacked closer to Cook than to Cortés. More and more, Enlightenment learning became the public declaration of the motives behind expeditions and the means for understanding what they discovered, even if commerce followed the tracks of the explorers closely, as the Rocky Mountain fur trade did the two captains. Still, the trend was to deepen such exploits with science, and to replace individual senses of destiny with national ones. Thus America's century of discovery ends with a sprawl of Great Surveys that managed to combine adventure, science, and geopolitics in classic fashion, as the instructions to Clarence King demonstrate: "examine all rock formations, mountain ranges, detrital plains, coal deposits, soils, minerals, ores, saline and alkaline deposits... collect... material for a topographical map of the regions traversed,... conduct... barometric and thermetric observations [and] make collections in botany and zoology with a view to a memoir on these subjects, illustrating the occurrence and distribution of plants and animals." All this is a long way from looting gold and searching out souls to save; but it is a recognizable descendant, as Przhevalsky's horse is from *Eohippus*.[27]

Where wealth of any kind was unlikely, fame could substitute, as before. The Antarctic offered only frost and struggle, and perhaps death, but there was also glory promised to explorer and sponsor. Ernest Shackleton's celebrated advertisement in the London *Times* says it all: "Men wanted for hazardous journey. Low wages, bitter cold, long hours of complete darkness. Safe return doubtful. Honour and recognition in event of success." That was the voice of pure adventuring tied to a geographical goal, a traverse across the continent through the pole; this was General William H. Ashley's corps of mountain men heading to the ice sheets.

But the Second Age had come to expect more. Apsley Cherry-Garrard stated it blandly and abstractly by calling exploration "the physical expression of the Intellectual Passion." He urged those who have "the desire for knowledge and the power to give it physical expression, go out and explore," although not everyone would accept such endeavors as worthy. They would deny glory and disdain anything without an economic payoff. "Some will tell you that you are mad," Cherry-Garrard wrote, "and nearly all will say, 'What is the use?' for we are a nation of shopkeepers, and no shopkeeper will look at research which does not promise him a financial return within a year." Yet even here, even if one had to sledge "nearly alone" across the proverbial frozen wastes, there could be expectations of social recognition and a contribution to the civilization of science.[28]

Exploration had become an entity in itself: the explorer could claim honor apart from where he practiced his craft. One of the greatest explorers of the day, and Scott's rival to the South Pole, Roald Amundsen, did no science, but he did reveal geography and personified an ascendant Norwegian nationalism. For the larger culture exploring was, as Cherry-Garrard said of the "sledging life," the "hardest test." In the end it was enough that its practitioners explored their own character, and the larger civilization, its.[29]

The Third Age was different—and the same.

With astonishing tenacity, the classic rationales have persisted, not least because exploration has become a valued enterprise the culture is unwilling to discard. Gold takes the form not of wealth discovered but of wealth created through government-sponsored jobs, near-Earth satellites, and the scientific information that serves as the precious spices and bullion of an information economy. Glory has softened into national prestige, a hazy pride, and a devalued currency of the cold war. And God has permutated into vague yearnings for Something More—explanations for the fundamentals of existence, an atonement for lost virtues, and even, for some, contact with an

Intelligence beyond the solar system. Across five centuries, while the vocabulary of exploration has changed, its syntax has remained intact.

The biggest change is economic. Explorers do not head to known markets or seek to cultivate new ones—they do not probe new routes to great entrepôts or unveil natural resources along the routes they travel. No one can even pretend to imagine an Aztec or Incan empire to sack, or a bonanza of gold waiting to pan out of the lost streams of Mars, or a "traffick" in useful goods with the far Indies of the solar system, perhaps a triangular trade between Earth, Titan, and Ganymede. Private commerce is restricted to its offshore environments, the near-Earth of satellites and the occasional tourist, and the near-ocean of continental shelves rather than the abyssal plains.

A modern Muscovy Company would not load its holds with trinkets for trade to discovered peoples and draw up rosters of what they have that we want, and what we have that they want, but would determine what instruments to send for reconnaissance. What can the planets and their moons tell us that we want to know? What traffic can exist between our instruments and their data? How much bullion must we expend to get the cinnamon and rubies of knowledge? Instead of red ocher and black coney skins, vessels sail with ultraviolet spectrometers and plasma wave detectors. But no more than the merchants of the Great Voyages do scientists know exactly what will trade best. They bring what they have.

BELIEVERS

Where there were motives, there were also motivators. Exploration has overflowed with publicists, seers, prophets, soothsayers, boosters, propagandists, the putatively all-knowing and farseeing, the promoters of fame and fortune, and the augurers of collective destiny. Through them the crassest lust for money and power could alloy with the most exalted aspirations. In some cases boosters kindled the necessary enthusiasms; but mostly they captured the sentiments of the zeitgeist and placed them into the holds of ships, on sledges, and into the software of spacecraft, for, in addition to food, water, navigational instruments, and maps, explorers needed a vision of where they were going and why.

The roster of publicists begins with the explorers themselves. Almost all were experts in self-promotion. No one believed in their mission more than Christopher Columbus and John Cabot, Henry Stanley and David Livingstone, and it was often the very intensity of their conviction that proved decisive in their convincing others. The greatest welded an unyielding faith to an iron will, the self-certainty that if the actual scheme proved wrong, their sense of destiny was right, and if destiny proved muddled, they could succeed by strength of character alone. Even when unexpected landmasses blocked passages, when rivers did not run or seas failed to appear where promoters had insisted they would, when the Isle of Brasil and the Seven Cities of Cibola migrated from one imaginary locale to another, they completed their expedition; they found what did exist and temporarily banished what did not, and returned with that knowledge. The poorest foundered on incompetence, ill luck, and the violent collision between a lofty rhetoric of inspiring visions and the hidden shoals of an indifferent geography.

Delusions could prove deadly. For every Ferdinand Magellan and Henry Stanley who simply would not be deflected from his self-assigned destiny, there was a Martin Frobisher and a William Baffin who could not force a Northwest Passage whatever their determination, and a Walter Raleigh and a William Paterson whose delusional bombast led to geographic fantasies and, for their followers, death. Even the greatest of explorers could not do what was impossible, and the impossible was as much a matter of historical timing as of principle. In prophecy, as in medicine, the toxicity resides not in the substance but in the dosage. Besides, explorers too often died; some other, more enduring mechanism had to keep the enthusiasm alive. Prophecy, too, needed its institutions.

That task fell to promoters. Someone had to persuade the monarchy or a Company of Adventurers to sponsor expeditions; someone had to rally both motives and money; someone had to speak in the media of the time to influence and inspire; someone had to record and interpret what discovery had unveiled and forecast what it might yet find. As exploration became institutionalized, it found its propagandists and publicists. During the First Age, they relied on the printing press, to which in the Second, they added newspapers and popular magazines, and in the Third, film and television. Each age, too, found distinctive ways to bond commerce and culture, to fuse and transmute mixed motivations from outright greed and vainglory to national prestige, and scholarship into a popular genre that could rouse a more general ardor without which voyages were no more than fireflies in the night. Each, that is, found a suitable Romance.

Over time the English became particularly adept at promotion. The history is worth tracing, since it leads directly to those who, apart from the Russians, have most boosted interplanetary exploration. The condensed version is this: England needed trade, which meant it needed explorers to identify places, goods, and routes.

In late medieval and Renaissance Europe, news of the earliest voyages of discovery was mixed. Some reports were quickly promulgated, such as Columbus's *Letters*; others were hoarded as state secrets. But if details were locked away, the general outlines of discovery became known, if only to ensure claims to lands, seas, peoples, and trade. At the Spanish court, Pietro Martire d'Anghiera, better known as Peter Martyr, became the official chronicler of Iberian discovery, his register updated as a series of *Decas* (*Decades of the New World*). It was Peter Martyr who appreciated, as Columbus never did, that the latter's four voyages had not made landfall on Golden Chersonese but on what Martyr termed an *otro* (or *novo*) *mundo*, a New World. The printing press helped to propagate the news of discovery, and something of its excitement, throughout the elite of Europe.

England, however, lagged. Though the first press arrived with William Caxton in 1477, it specialized in what the public wanted to read, and works of geographical discovery were not among them. Those sponsoring merchants who needed to know the latest voyages did so through other means; the reading public still preferred pilgrim guides and updated encyclopedias. Despite Bristol merchants, England's interests pointed to Europe rather than New Found Lands.

Not until 1554, with the crisis of Mary Tudor's marriage to Philip of Spain, did the *Decas* appear in English. It did so amid a political crisis, economic opportunities, and a spiritual call to arms for what would evolve into a prolonged struggle with Spain.

The critical voice was Rycharde Eden, England's "first literary imperialist." Eden began by publishing *A Treatyse of the Newe India*, arranged to have the *Decas* translated along with Martin Cortes's *The Arte of Navigation*, and urged his countrymen to learn from the major colonial powers and then expand for themselves, searching out new markets for the "commoditie of our countrie," which was wool. In dedicating the *Treatyse* to the Duke of Northumberland, Eden listed his reasons for urging travels of discovery. They could improve the national economy, they served God, and they could inspire both an entrepreneurial and an adventuring spirit essential to a robust people. Those who demurred from overseas enterprises showed, he felt, a contemptible lack of courage. The earliest endeavors focused mostly on the Northeast Passage, culminating in the Muscovy Company and trade with Russia, and then renewed interest in a Northwest Passage. As Eden's first book suggested, the Indies were the prize.[30]

As England quickened the tempo of its overseas probes, the basic rhetoric laid down by Eden endured: that only by joining the scramble overseas could England secure its future at home. Yet the governing classes and reading public remained largely apathetic. Not until 1580 did the tide begin to turn. In that year, England determined two routes to the wealth of the East: a trade treaty with Turkey and the astounding return of Sir Francis Drake from "the world encompassed," not least with the *Golden Hind* stuffed full of the plunder from unsuspecting Spanish ships and towns in the Pacific. More important, England found its great publicist of voyaging. That year Richard Hakluyt, then thirty years old, commenced his pleas for an English overseas empire of commerce and colonies.[31]

An older Hakluyt recalled that, as a much younger Hakluyt, he had chanced upon "certain books of Cosmography, with an universal Map" in his cousin's study, and that he then and there resolved that he would "by God's assistance prosecute that knowledge and kind of literature." His 1580 appeal on the occasion of Humphrey Gilbert's first try at an American colony, was followed by a 1582 compendium, *Divers Voyages Touching upon the Discovery of America*, in which he exploited historical events to argue the cause for English expansionism. *Discourse of Western Planting* followed, this time aligned with schemes by Walter Raleigh. More than a simple shill, Hakluyt was a Renaissance scholar, versed in many languages and intent on amassing accurate accounts from any source, and thus eager to talk with pilots, merchants, and captains. His masterpiece followed the year after Elizabethan England defeated the Spanish Armada.[32]

Principal Navigations, Voyages and Discoveries of the English Nation was an immense encyclopedia of travel that celebrated the new age of adventuring while seeking to establish continuities with an ancient English past. It argued that the English were, by heritage, a voyaging and trading people, that an expansion of enterprises was both possible and essential, and that accurate knowledge was the font of such inspiration. The *Principal Navigations* was in equal measure patriotic and practical. A second, expanded edition published in 1598–1600 weighed in at a million and a half words distributed over three volumes. Here was history in the service of commerce and politics.

The outcome could not help but awe and, through awe, inspire both admiration over what had been achieved and ardor to further it. Yet Hakluyt was candid about his purpose: "our chief desire is to find out ample vent for our woollen cloth, the natural commodity of this our realm, the fittest place I find for that purpose are the manifold islands of Japan and the northern parts of China, and the regions of the Tartars next adjoining." To this goal were gradually added colonies in America, where trade might be supplemented by the natural wealth of those lands. The second edition made the point even more explicit by adding "Traffiques" to the title.[33]

Others, such as Samuel Purchas (*Purchas His Pilgrimage*), were less fastidious about authenticating sources and less willing to subject readers to vast catalogues of prospective trade goods. They abridged the long chronicle into a brisker narrative, pumped up the emotional receipts relative to empirical expenditures, and bequeathed a saga that made the voyage of discovery and the planting of colonies a distinctive and necessary feature of the English identity. Complicated

accounts of commercial traffic became tales of derring-do and patriotic glory. The exorbitant costs of exploring were only apparent: the
enterprise would pay for itself many times over.

Yet for some journeys, mirages work as well as landmarks. Samuel
Eliot Morison observed that "although the French seaports had every
possible advantage for Atlantic exploration that the English had;
although the French crown gave its merchant marine more support
and encouragement than the Tudors ever did, there is one English
asset which the French lacked—a Hakluyt." France lacked that enormous compendium, the comprehensive vision, that sense of urgent
inspiration. Later French enthusiasts for a Greater France lamented
the similar lack of Robinsonades—French versions of Robinson Crusoe, popular stories of overseas adventuring.[34]

In truth, Richard Hakluyt and his counterparts did more than
chronicle an age of discovery. They placed it into a national (and civilizational) narrative, they created valences with other vigorous elements of the culture, they implanted it into the minds of the educated
and governing classes. They helped institutionalize exploration. They
ensured that the Great Age of Discovery could lead to others. Exploration became complex, and because of that cultural complexity, it
could survive. It endured in part because Western civilization could
no longer imagine itself not exploring.

During the Second Age, exploration found new prophets, new
romances, and a more popular media. Not only had books become
far more common, but also newspapers and popular magazines
abounded to spread stories of discovery widely throughout a vastly
more literate public. Particularly among former colonial societies
such as a newly independent America, now bent on its own imperial project, explorers became iconic figures, founders of a national
creation epic. They were American Aeneases, the guides and seers of
national destiny. The frontiersman became the new knight-errant of
a romance later called the Western. The explorer into unknown lands
became a Romantic hero.

Their accounts were enormously popular. Let William Goetzmann tell how the reclusive Henry David Thoreau spent days "in his

quiet study at Concord, at his cabin at Walden Pond, or stretched out under a poplar tree in his backyard behind the family pencil factory" reading exploration literature. A master of synecdoche, Thoreau could see the whole world in Walden Pond, and he could observe also in his journal that "the whole world is an America, a New World." So, too, we might have his personal absorption stand for that of his culture. He read Humboldt's *Personal Narrative*, Cook's *Voyages*, and Darwin's *A Naturalist's Voyage Round the World*. He read Alexander Henry's adventures in Canada, Thomas Atkinson's travels across Tartary, John Dunn Hunter's narrative of Indian captivity. He trekked across Africa with John Barth, Hugh Clapperton, and David Livingstone; sledged to the Arctic with Isaac Hayes and Elisha Kent Kane; traveled over China with Evariste Régis Huc; searched for Mount Ararat with Frederick Parrot; tracked down the source of the Mississippi with Giacomo Beltrami and Henry Schoolcraft; sailed down the Amazon and Orinoco with Lts. William Herndon and Lardner Gibbon; slogged along the Mosquito Coast with Ephraim George Squier; and accompanied Ida Pfeiffer on *A Lady's Voyage Round the World*. He read the five-volume narrative of the United States Exploring Expedition in its entirety, steering around Lt. Charles Wilkes's cloying prose as the USS *Vincennes* did Antarctic floes. He was, in William Goetzmann's words, "another of Humboldt's children."[35]

The alliance with Enlightenment science had created powerful incentives. What was good for science was good for empire, and what was good for empire was good for science, and both looked to exploration to advance their interests. The frontiers of science were, as its promoters never ceased to proclaim, endless. Institutions of science became boosters of geographic exploration and forums for announcing their findings, which quickly moved from the pages of obscure academic proceedings to the front pages of penny newspapers.

The prophets of exploration experienced another transfiguration for the Third Age. With renewed tenacity the old justifications were refurbished, given a high-tech gloss, and sent to explore ice, abyss, and space. A new genre of romance—science fiction, or more properly technological romance—reoutfitted the knight-errant with the armor of a spacesuit, a grail quest to find intelligence or at least life elsewhere, and adventures across galaxies. The HMS *Beagle* acquired warp drive; astronauts unveiled new Botany Bays on the moons of Saturn; a New Jerusalem arose on Mars. New media that substituted light and electrons for ink added to popular enthusiasms through film and television. The pioneering rocketeers must be numbered among the emergent seers, for so they saw themselves, and it was a vision of extraterrestrial exploration (and colonization) that drove their engineering imaginations. A Great Migration beyond Earth had inflamed both Tsiolkovsky and Goddard.

But the godfather of the Third Age in space is surely Arthur C. Clarke, who knotted together as no one else could the technical, the institutional, the literary, and the visionary. It is not just that Clarke was a type or a precursor, but that he was himself the dominant oracle for an age of space voyaging. Almost every defining feature of the space age finds echoes in his voice. As seer and revelator, his immense, and immensely successful, literary output became a kind of Testament of the Space Age. Born in Britain in 1917, he outlived all his contemporaries and even the first generation of successors. He was in Britain when V-2 rockets rained down on London, and he commented by teleconference on the Cassini mission to Saturn.

He could not afford college; he learned his craft by working and by writing science fiction in his spare time. During the Battle of Britain he served in the radar units of the RAF; after the war he earned a first-class degree in mathematics and physics at King's College London, and applied his literary talents to predictions of telecommunication satellites and space travel generally. In 1949 he committed himself to a full-time career as an author of short stories, novels, and semi-technical studies. Of necessity for one who lived by his wits, he evolved a graceful, popular style. In 1950 he wrote a technically informed but accessible book on astronautics, *Interplanetary Flight*. By then he was chair of the British Interplanetary Society, an institution devoted to promoting space travel, a successor to such Second Age organs as the African Association and Royal Geographical Society. A year later he expanded from astronautics to a survey of what might be possible not only technically but socially, and perhaps spiritually, with a foundational book, *The Exploration of Space*. In 1956 he moved to Sri Lanka, only recently unyoked from British colonial rule. A year later, Sputnik made Clarke's prophecies seem clairvoyant; within three years the first communication satellite was in orbit.

Interestingly, from his tropical island Clarke enthused over the *two* emerging realms of Third Age discovery. He became, as he put it, "amphibious." The sea beckoned. He took to underwater scuba, toured reefs, and wrote a string of sea novels that paralleled his space fiction. His motivations? He liked the experience, and after he suffered paralysis in 1962, he relished the sensation of weightlessness. He regarded the two environments, sea and space, as similar, so much so that he believed the seas could train future astronauts and serve as a nursery for space treks, since "submarine exploration is so much cheaper than space flight." It could also prepare travelers for exotic life forms and, with whales and porpoises, for encounters with alien intelligences.[36]

During the era of IGY preparation, and before the space race became dominant, Clarke wrote sea and space novels in a kind of thematic fugue, which culminated in two parallel collections of essays: *The Challenge of the Spaceship* (1959) and *The Challenge of the Sea* (1960). But the deep oceans became decoupled from colonization and popular imagination, leaving space as the more untrammeled realm for the imagination, and that is where fiction, and Clarke, went.

Clarke brought to an apex the alloy of exotic technology, latent spiritualism, and futurist settings so common to the genre. From his once-colonial island he imagined brave new worlds, bold encounters with wonders and monsters, and humanity's assisted evolution into godlike stature. With the 1968 release of the movie *2001: A Space Odyssey*, based on a Clarke story and then a Clarke–co-authored screenplay, the hard engineering of rockets met utopianism, and with his *Rama* trilogy (1973–91) he created a Romantic epic, a *Lusíads* for space imperialism. Throughout there is the specter of a humanity advancing beyond the limits of its genetics and ancestral geography, with perhaps links to alien civilizations in its distant past and unbounded spiritual promise, even immortality, in its future. This vast literary output and commentaries established Clarke in the public mind as the Delphic oracle of the emerging space age. In 2000 he was made a Knight of the British Empire. He outlived, outwrote, and out-prophesied every potential colleague and rival.

What did Clarke foresee? That "the conquest of space is possible must now be regarded as a matter beyond all serious doubt" and that "the conquest of the planets" was now both necessary and inevitable to renew the human mind and spirit.[37]

It was necessary because geographic expansion enlarged "mental horizons" and stasis contracted them. Exploration and colonization were essential because "when Man loses his curiosity one feels he will have lost most of the other things that make him human," a legacy of wanderlust that "the long literary tradition of the space-travel story" showed was rooted "in Man's nature." Like the Great Voyages, space exploration would spark a New Renaissance, "an expansion of scientific knowledge perhaps unparalleled in history"; would forge a common Earth identity and force Earthlings to perceive the "true" place of their "single small globe" amid the cosmos; and most thrillingly, would hold the "prospect of meeting other forms of intelligence," for it would address "one of the supreme questions of philosophy," whether or not "Man is alone in the Universe," and "at last learn what purpose, if any, life plays in the Universe of matter." The Earth is not world enough. The Intelligent Visitors would of course be benevolent, and they would force Earth into a Reformation before which those of the past would seem laughably puny.[38]

This entire Romantic edifice was built on the mixed sand and stone of history and literary precedent. Clarke commenced his serious space romances as the British Empire began its dissolution; he resided at one of its former colonies; and his vision that Earth's future necessarily lay in expansion—in exploration and empire, though of benign forms—was a lineal descendant of Rycharde Eden and Richard Hakluyt urging that England's future lay with far-voyaging and overseas colonies. What arguments he did not invent, he revived, absorbed, and endowed with literary expression.

In striking ways few contemporaries have added significantly to the oeuvre. Virtually the entire corpus of Carl Sagan's passionate pleas for a future in space, for example, are not only foreshadowed in Clarke but present in almost identical language: The potential of technology. The power of scientific curiosity. The significance of expansion to forestall decadence. The search for intelligence beyond Earth and the belief that it is human destiny to make contact with such intelligence. The assumption that such contact would revolutionize human civilization.

What Sagan added was a stronger argument from biology. In Clarke's day rockets were the critical motive force: they made interplanetary travel possible. In Sagan's time, rockets and gravity assist were adequate to explore the solar system, but the motives to use them needed bolstering. The search for life could serve as an intermediary to the search for intelligence. If Clarke implicitly sent a benevolent British Empire into the heavens, Sagan drafted a less chauvinistic master narrative that made the space age another link in a great chain of purposed human wandering. Significantly, the two writers' passion for planetary exploration converged on Mars.

DOUBTERS

The rhetoric for space was vibrant, loud, and, for many, compelling. But where there are arguments, there are also counterexamples, and where prophets flourish, apostates abound. For every Arthur C. Clarke and Carl Sagan, there were Cassandras and chroniclers to count the cost.

In *The Sirens of Titan*, published the year after IGY ended, as satellite after satellite lofted upward, Kurt Vonnegut mordantly observed that "the state of mind on Earth with regard to space exploration was much like the state of mind in Europe with regard to exploration of the Atlantic before Christopher Columbus set out." There were differences, of course, almost all tending to make the contemporary scene even more formidable. "The monsters between space explorers and their goals were not imaginary, but numerous, hideous, various, and uniformly cataclysmic; the cost of even a small expedition was enough to ruin most nations; and it was a virtual certainty that no expedition could increase the wealth of its sponsors." In the face of such facts only one conclusion was possible: "on the basis of horse sense and the best scientific information, there was nothing good to be said for the exploration of space." His satire places Vonnegut in a long tradition that has turned the rhetoric of prophets, in this case the siren call of space wrapped in technological romance, against itself.[39]

From the beginning the skeptics and the scoffers were at the docks, in the committee rooms, and all over the press to rebut dazzling thesis with grubby fact, and to scorn forecast bright visions of the future with recalled dark visitations from the past.

In the greatest of exploration literature they come together, as in Luiz Vaz de Camões's *The Lusíads*, which casts the founding voyage of Vasco da Gama to India within the elevated style of the classical epic. The Olympians themselves are astonished by the audacity of the Portuguese. Jupiter exclaims

Now you watch them, risking all
In frail timbers on treacherous seas,
By routes never charted, and only
Emboldened by opposing winds;
Having explored so much of the earth
From the equator to the midnight sun,
They recharge their purpose and are drawn
To touch the very portals of the dawn.

He tells a worried Venus that they will exceed even the exploits of Ulysses and Aeneas, that "Your greater navigators will unfold / New worlds to the amazement of the old."[40]

This exchange occurs while the mariners are leaving the piers at Belém, ready for their passage to the Indies, but as demanded of an epic, the tale had begun in medias res. When the text returns to narrate the fleet's departure, Camões inserts an astonishing scene, one of *The Lusíads'* most moving, in which the crew try to avert their eyes from the sight of loved ones left behind and close their ears to those petitioning them to cease. But they cannot avoid an old man, his eyes "disapproving," who harangues the departing ships from the shore, hurling prophecies and mockery from a wisdom plucked out of a "much-tried heart."[41]

One by one, the Old Man of Belém demolishes the presumptions that fill the sails of the unmoored ships. Honor is no more than "popular cant"; fame, but vainglory; "visions of kingdoms and gold-mines," delusions; bold discoveries, mere folly; idealism, a disguise for greed. Crusading zeal is better satisfied closer at hand. Adventuring will only lead to "new catastrophes" and wreck "all peace of soul and body." The glitter of gold is a seductress's call that will deplete rather than enrich. Subtly, yet "manifestly," the Carreira da India will "consume the wealth of kingdoms and empires!" The voyage is but the latest example of an interminable, tragic restlessness:

> In what great or infamous undertaking,
> Through fire, sword, water, heat, or cold,
> Was Man's ambition not the driving feature?
> Wretched circumstance! Outlandish creature![42]

There lies the meaning of the Old Man's lament: the unalterably flawed character of humanity. The founding epic is a tragedy. And so it proved. Six years after *The Lusíads* was published, with its admonition to renew the grand adventure, King Sebastian led a crusade to Morocco that destroyed his army, cost him his life, and shortly after Camões's death, drove Portugal into a reluctant union with Spain. Without the quick riches of the India trade, such foreign adventures would not have been possible, and without the elevated rhetoric of redirected romance, they could likely not have rallied the obligatory enthusiasms.

But as the Old Man knew, the ships were already unmoored and riding the tides of the Tagus out to sea. His voice has to call to them over the waters. His warning comes too late.

———

As the Great Voyages proliferated, scoffers found ample experiences to criticize. Only the incorporation of exploration into national creation stories has allowed the chronicle to tilt toward the visionaries.

Columbus proved almost delusional in his systematic inaccuracies and willful refusal to acknowledge what he had actually discovered rather than what he wished to have discovered, much less what he had promised would result from his discoveries; and this stubbornness resulted in a loss of interest in the New World, certainly among prospective colonists. Until global warming melted back the pack ice, the Northwest Passage was a fata morgana that called challengers to their death. The Castilian sagas of conquest in Mexico and Peru sent ravenous conquistadors forlornly over much of the New World in a vain, often disastrous, pursuit to find another Tenochtitlán or Cuzco, and inspired a flagging Portugal to dispatch exploring warriors to unveil fabulously rich Mexicos rumored to be hidden in the interior of southern Africa, all with ruinous outcomes. Still, the call to oars was stronger, or at least louder, than the injunction to mind one's store.

But as the First Age became moribund, as exploration was tamed into trade, the doomsayers outwrote the soothsayers. The prevailing perception among elites was that exploration was a loser's game, the geopolitical equivalent of buying lottery tickets. Many of the dominant figures of the age, if they commented at all, turned against what they regarded as irrational, wasteful, and destructive voyaging. The classics of travel literature that span the early Enlightenment and continue through Britain's Augustan age are almost all inoculated against the riotously extravagant rhetoric that accompanied the Great Voyages and ridicule the voyaging visionaries. The era begins with a cautionary tale from Daniel Defoe, passes through brutal satires by Jonathan Swift and Voltaire, and ends with a moral epistle wrapped in a story by Samuel Johnson.

Defoe's *Robinson Crusoe* is not what abridged juvenile literature today often makes it: the celebration of a bold adventurer who finds and then fashions a new world in his own image. Rather, it is a paean to destructive willfulness and wanderlust that leads to a loneliness that leaves Crusoe only a stone's throw from all-consuming despair in what he openly calls his "captivity." Appropriately, the story opens with Crusoe's father in the role of the Old Man of Belém. Sensing his son's intentions, he asks "what reasons more than a mere wandering inclination" Robinson might have to throw away his prospects. "He told me it was for men of desperate fortunes on one hand, or of aspiring, superior fortunes on the other, who went abroad upon adventures, to rise by enterprise, and make themselves famous in undertakings of a nature out of the common road; that these things were all either too far above me, or too far below me; that mine was the middle state," which he had found by long experience was "the best state in the world, the most suited to human happiness" and the one "which all other people envied." Robinson père urges his son to reconsider, to be satisfied with his station in life, and cease his footloose folly, or else he would have ample opportunity to reflect upon his heedlessness. In that, Crusoe notes ruefully, his father proved "truly prophetic."[43]

The great satirists of the Enlightenment went beyond a chronicle of misplaced ambition to ridicule outright appeals to free-floating discovery and utopian adventuring. The godfather of the genre was Jonathan Swift's classic, nominally written by a Lemuel Gulliver, *Travels into Several Remote Nations of the World* (1726; revised in 1735). In it Gulliver, a surgeon forced to turn to the sea for his livelihood, finds himself "condemned by Nature and Fortune to an active and restless life" that results in four voyages of discovery. The first takes him to Lilliput, a land of tiny people northwest of Van Diemen's Land; the second, to Brobdingnag, a land of giants east of the Moluccas; the third, to Laputa, an island magnetically levitated, and to other islands leading to Japan, all full of "projectors" and other visionaries; and the fourth, as captain of the *Adventure*, after being overthrown by mutineers, marooned in the country of the Houyhnhnms.

Gulliver's Travels turned the emerging genre of the travelogue, or more properly, the journal of a voyage, back onto itself, for what Gulliver finds are commentaries upon his own society, and a critique upon discovery as it was practiced. He was particularly disgusted with the prevailing logic by which exploration must lead to claims, and claims to conquest, since he did not believe the lands he had visited had "a desire of being conquered and enslaved, murdered or driven out by colonies, nor abound either in gold, silver, sugar, or tobacco," he did "humbly conceive they were by no means proper objects of our zeal, our valour, or our interest." He scorned travel writing as "fables" and thought it "better, perhaps, that the adventure not have taken place, or if occurring, that its discoveries remain unknown."[44]

To Voltaire outrage invited a bitter satire, the short story "Micromégas" (1752), likely inspired by the 1735 journey to Lapland under Pierre Maupertuis. Voltaire reverses the usual relationship between discoverer and discovered by imagining a giant from Sirius and a dwarf from Saturn who visit Earth. As with Swift, the obsession of the age with mathematics and travel combine to produce a work of measurements and proportions, though in the end these are not so much mathematical as moral. They become an argument for a golden mean. The real need is not to look outward with idealistic awe but to look inward with greater realism. A missionary turned entrepreneur turned visionary of colonization such as Pierre Poivre might want more stories of travelers who, like Crusoe, must create gardens on deserted isles, but most preferred, after Voltaire, to tend their own plots outside the kitchen.

The same year that those paired expeditions set out to Lapland and Ecuador was the year Samuel Johnson translated into English *A Voyage to Abyssinia* by the Portuguese missionary Father Jerome Lobo. In 1759 that project birthed *Rasselas; or, the Prince of Abissinia*. Rasselas grows up in Happy Valley, a hidden Eden in a remote valley of Amhara, in which every desire is sated. Yet the prince is restless. "That I want nothing," or "that I know not what I want," he concludes, is "the cause of my complaint." The only solution, it appears, is for him to escape and see for himself "the miseries of the world, since the sight of them is necessary to happiness." The journey begins.[45]

This of course is a moral trek, a Pilgrim's Progress, brought into alignment with the geographic travels that the past age had thrown up. The journey reverses the expected route by flowing down the Nile from its source to its delta; it thus begins with a putative paradise and ends with a knowledge of misery. The conclusion is that the travel was pointless, except to confirm what the sages had said originally.

Marooned during the Nile's flood, the party abandons the ambitions that launched its travels, the search for a scheme of happiness, and resolves to return home.[46]

But that had always been the true bullion brought back by travelers. They saw themselves and their society differently. They had to engage with Others in what could ultimately be described only as an encounter between moral worlds. They did not merely climb mountains or search out the fountains of great rivers: they had to talk with other peoples. Gulliver talks, Micromégas talks, Rasselas talks, and only after Friday arrives on his island can Crusoe cease to talk to himself and begin the real task of discovery. But for such knowledge, one did not have to sail to undiscovered worlds. Equivalent lessons existed in history, for the past, too, was "a foreign country," and the neoclassicists could argue that Pliny and Plutarch might inform as fully as the Houyhnhnms and the Laputans. This, however, was an argument for learning and languages, a scholar's plea, not a call for geographic adventuring.

Yet even as *Rasselas* the text saw print, a Second Great Age of Discovery was aborning. An inextinguishable restlessness would be channeled into a renewed era of far-voyaging. On March 31, 1776, James Boswell informed Samuel Johnson that he had found a copy of Johnson's translation of Lobo's travels, which Johnson dismissed and was content to have forgotten. Two days later Boswell described a meeting he had just had with Capt. James Cook, recently returned from the South Seas, and found Johnson "much pleased with the conscientious accuracy of that celebrated circumnavigator." Boswell then burst out that "while I was with the Captain, I catched the enthusiasm of curiosity and adventure, and felt a strong inclination to go with him on his next voyage." It was easy, he continued, to be "carried away with the general grand and indistinct notion of a Voyage Round the World." The august doctor agreed but dismissed the sentiment when he considered "how very little" one "can learn from such voyages."[47]

But the culture at large sided with Boswell, and with Joseph Banks, the aristocratic naturalist who declared that *his* Grand Tour would be a voyage around the world. The romance of exploring science would sweep the moral realism of skeptics aside and would pull literature in its train.

Once Earth had been again encompassed by the Second Age, some sought to look heavenward. The means to go wasn't there, however, and the culture meanwhile had wandered into the labyrinths of modernism. When, after World War II, technology made such travel possible, the issue rekindled, and a new generation of boosters arose. Untethered to Earth, prophets could claim a high ground of hope and idealism, new creation stories unmarred by tragedy, though to critics they might seem like the Laputans on their Floating Island. Still, the rhetoric of the future rode upward on ever-more-powerful rockets. Satire had flourished as exploration sagged; now boosters could express their fantasies in steel and rocket fuel, not merely words; critics could muster nothing equivalent. It was a great age of science fiction and, by the time Voyager sailed, of Hollywood space Westerns and costume epics.

Yet the critics persisted. The scoffers noted that boosters confused geographic exploration with the virtues with which it alloyed: that curiosity was not limited to travel but could be found in libraries and laboratories; that adventuring and hardihood did not demand untrodden geographies but could be found in rock climbing, NASCAR, and extreme-site science; that wanderlust could be satisfied by internal migrations from country to city and back, by tourism, by vagabond communities of retirees in RVs, by walkabouts in virtual worlds; that idealism did not demand a ridgeline below a setting sun but could be found by trying to make a better world through political reform or social activism; that synthetic cyberworlds might satisfy precisely those human urges that in the past could come only from hazardous travel, that they might sate curiosity as a candy bar could the craving for carbohydrates. The boost to economies, science, and technology that accompanied a government-sponsored space race could follow from *any* massive spending program, any stimulant to scientific research, and any technological investments. America as a "people of plenty" required an open society, not open lands; the economic frontiers lay with building not the space equivalent of rail-roads across the Far West but information highways spanning the world wide web. Skeptics such as Amitai Etzioni dismissed the hype of the Apollo program as a "moon-doggle" and systematically dem-onstrated how it was a "monumental misdecision" that acted as a "drag" on the larger civilization.[48]

The doubting doctors remain. Space historian Roger Launius notes that, after Apollo, the NASA budget has steadied at 1 percent of the national budget, and that popular interest waxes and wanes not with launches but with Hollywood space movies. The "inescapable lesson" of Felipe Fernández-Armesto's brisk survey of humanity's exploration of Earth was "that exploration has been a march of folly, in which almost every step forward has been the failed outcome of an attempted leap ahead." Explorers were often the "oddballs or eccen-trics or visionaries or romancers or social climbers or social outcasts, or escapees from the restrictive and the routine, with enough dis-tortion of vision to be able to reimagine reality." The exploration of space he regarded as a "gigantic folly."[49]

All true, and all more or less irrelevant. The Old Man of Belém may stalk the launchpads of Canaveral and Tyuratam, but the fleets still sail.

Yet the Third Age *is* different. The reason lies not in the ultimate rightness of the boosters and prophets, not because uncontaminated idealism and techno-utopianism can at last prevail, but because of the age's peculiar geography. Amid ice, abyss, and space it is possible to shear away the moral ugliness and ultimately tragic core of explo-ration because there is no Other to confront, and without an Other, there is no need for a human self. Robots are not only the most practi-cal explorers but the only ones that make sense of the age's distinctive terrains.

That is the tradeoff: exploration by robots of places fit only for robots. If exploration can proceed without the ethical burdens of the past, it also comes without the past's inspiration, moral drama, and narrative tension. Voyager would undergo no mutinies. It could harm no one. It reduces criticism to that of comparative costs or relative returns on cultural investment. It can find new worlds without the horrors that have marred past discoveries. All this, however, comes at the cost of a sanitized encounter cleansed of the messiness and ambiguities and tragedies that had defined the founding discourse and its supporting story.

No place had shown the ambition to revive and project the old age into the new more than Mars, and nowhere did the Voyagers demonstrate better both their mission's novelty and its purity than when they bypassed Mars without a whisper. In late November 1977, Voyager 2 crossed the Martian orbit; a month later Voyager 1 repeated the transit. But both avoided Mars itself—did not even pay respects before moving on. In shunning Mars, Voyager bypassed all the agendas, and much of the inherited apparatus of boosting and scoffing, that had waxed and waned with the Great Ages of the past.

ALWAYS-KNOWN MARS

For the space program, Mars held many attractions. After the Moon it was the obvious common goal. For geopolitics, it was a potential sphere of influence, analogous to the hinterlands of Second Age imperialism. For space science, it offered the nearest best target to extend the package of IGY instruments beyond Earth, and it might, just might, have some form of life. For spacecraft designers, it promised to extend the range of technology and ambition incrementally. And for colonizers, it was the ideal arena for migration and the test planet for experiments in terraforming. After the Moon, more spacecraft went to Mars than anywhere else. By the time Voyager launched, America had sent eight vessels to Mars (six successfully), and the USSR thirteen (none really successful). Between them they had made nineteen attempts to Venus, one to Mercury, two to Jupiter (Pioneers), and one to Saturn.

Moreover, Mars had far more cultural associations than any other planet. That was its glory—and its burden. What made it attractive to popular culture also made it potentially an exorbitant distraction, for it proved impossible to shear the fantasies from the facts, each of which was renewed after every encounter. So while Mars was actually smaller than Earth, its gravitational attraction, as measured by cultural interest, was far greater than the giant planets visited by Voyager. In fact, Voyager's rival as a grand gesture was its immediate predecessor, the 1976 Viking mission to search for life on the Red Planet. For Mars partisans, Viking proposed an alternative narrative and interpretive prism. It is worth pausing, as Voyager did not, to examine how that happened and what it meant.

For the visionaries who promoted space as the next arena of colonization, Mars had been the realm of the technological romance, the target for colonizing rockets, the founding planet. When Edgar Rice Burroughs reached beyond the landscapes of the Second Age for exotic settings, he sent Tarzan, in the person of Virginia gentleman John Carter, to Mars (which he named "Barsoom")—morphing the classic Western *The Virginian* into the science fiction pulp novel. When H. G. Wells sent imperialism beyond the sublunary realm, he projected an invasion from Mars. Over and again, Mars loomed as the specter before the kindled imagination of those who looked to space for inspiration, be they rocketeers from Robert Goddard to Wernher von Braun, or visionaries from Arthur C. Clarke to Carl Sagan, or the romancers of contemporary literature from Robert Heinlein to Ray Bradbury. Mars was the bidding siren of space-voyaging history, the challenge to technology, the test case for life beyond Earth, the first port of call for the dissemination of humanity throughout the universe. Earth-orbiting space stations, lunar bases, robotic reconnaissance—all had meaning to the extent that they contributed to the settlement of Mars.

The drumbeat began early in the postwar era. Robert Heinlein published *Red Planet* in 1949. Ray Bradbury wrote *The Martian Chronicles* in 1950. The science that such fiction demanded, however, came with Wernher von Braun's *The Mars Project*, an "algorithm of spaceflight" to establish colonies, published in 1952 (English edition in 1953). Soon afterward, *Collier's* magazine ran a series of eight features on space activities. Von Braun and journalist Cornelius Ryan argued in 1954 that such a mission was technologically possible. With television emerging as the popular medium of the time, Disney Studios made the transition from print to screen by creating three animated features for TV, aired between 1955 and 1957, the last appearing two months after Sputnik. Sandwiched between the shows, von Braun and Willy Ley assembled the *Collier's* series' arguments into a summary book, *The Exploration of Mars*. By 1962, Marshall Space Flight Center, under the directorship of von Braun, was busy projecting a future beyond the Moon. Early Manned Planetary Roundtrip Expeditions (EMPIRE) would first send a major exploratory party to Mars. Immediately after Apollo 11, von Braun submitted detailed plans that would repeat the triumph of the Moon landing on Mars by 1982. And Arthur C. Clarke wrote a short story in which he neatly framed the exploratory impulse that had been announced with the eighteenth century's expeditions to measure transits of Venus by imagining the sole survivor of an inaugural expedition to Mars who watches the transit of Earth across the Sun in 1984.[50]

Missions followed. JPL had early established a Mars group, believing that Mars was where vision and practice would converge. Mariner 4 made the first planetary flyby of Mars in 1965. By then JPL was immersed in the elaborate Martian program centered on a new spacecraft called Voyager. When that program got scrapped, the name floated free until it was reclaimed for the Grand Tour. Then came Mariner 9, in November 1971. As the spacecraft entered Martian orbit, JPL convened a panel of tribal elders and young oracles to discourse on the subject of "Mars and the Mind of Man." Bruce Murray, Walter Sullivan, Ray Bradbury, Arthur C. Clarke, and Carl Sagan—all save Murray were literary figures, journalists or novelists, and science popularizers. Mars could attract that kind of cultural event.[51]

Unsurprisingly, it was Mars that merited for planetary exploration the first experiment in big science, as the abandoned Mars Voyager mission metamorphosed into Viking. When the two spacecraft landed in July 1976, NASA Langley convened another soiree, again at JPL, expanding the theme to encompass "Why Man Explores." The panel's luminaries included James Michener, Norman Cousins, Philip Morrison, Jacques Cousteau, and Ray Bradbury. Michener tidily summarized the cultural tethers to Mars: "All my life I have followed the explorations of Mars intellectually, philosophically, imaginatively. It is a planet which has special connotations. I cannot recall anyone ever having been as interested as we are in Jupiter or Saturn or Pluto. Mars has played a special role in our lives because of the literary and philosophical speculations that have centered upon it." He concluded: "I have always known Mars."[52]

The panel veered into metaphysics, meandering poetry, and loose allusions that sought to equate exploration with curiosity. But Michener was right. Attempts to replicate the event with "Jupiter and the Mind of Man" and "Saturn and the Mind of Man" never caught fire. The literary imagination returned to where there were people, or the prospects of people, or at least the works of previous literary people to contemplate. For space philosophy, Mars was less a planet than a strange attractor, perturbing all the intellectual fields around it.

At the time, the smart money would have bet that Viking would become the grand gesture of the age. It seemed to unite perfectly the classic motives behind exploration with a modern knot. With its dual orbiters and two landers, it was Apollo come to Mars, and instead of collecting Moon rocks, its robotic astronauts sampled soil for evidence of life. Both settled into the Martian maria (or *planitia*). The first was named Chryse, and the second, Utopia. "Chryse" is Greek for gold, and "Utopia" is a word invented during the Renaissance to describe an ideal if imaginary place in the distant sea. In an appropriate if eerie way the spacecraft had carried God, gold, and glory to Mars.

The Viking mission thus fused into one expedition all the inherited parts—science, with the exotic search for life; politics and national prestige, with its landings staged to coincide with the American bicentennial; engineering and journeying encoded within its complex choreography of guiding, landing, and robotic sampling, all at the edges of technology; cultural contact, that sense of always having known Mars. Here, it seemed, was the ideal narrative for the Third Age.

Yet it never quite took, even with Sagan shilling its story, and not solely because it failed to find life or because the country at large was in a dark, sour mood—exploration had often in the past countered such gloom. A likely explanation is that what Mars gave it also took away. If the density of cultural overlays added meaning, it equally burdened the expedition. In looking forward to the human explorers who it assumed would surely and shortly follow, Viking looked back to a past that the Third Age had to selectively discard. Though Mars could join space to those futures the past had imagined, it could not fling that past into the future by itself. Besides, the mission had a target: a suite of experiments to test for life, and these were at best inconclusive. When the experiments ended, so did the Vikings' narrative.

The mantle of the Third Age would require a different kind of journey in which the trek would not end—in which the journey itself contained its drama. This demanded another kind of story, one bonded to exploration and quests, not to colonization. It is the narrative of Voyager.

Voyager could not avoid the Mars mystique altogether. In presenting the Mariner Jupiter/Saturn 1977 mission to the readership of *Astronautics and Aeronautics,* JPL authors framed their account with lengthy quotes from Arthur C. Clarke's *2001: A Space Odyssey,* which had bypassed Mars for the Jovian moon Iapetus. Yet it is doubtful that even the most addled techno-romancer believed that Voyager's journey was a prelude to settlement or the end of earthly childhood.[53]

Voyager was, instead, a modernist machine loosed onto the cosmos. The Voyagers would not be blinded by gold or the mirage of fame. They would not abandon wife or child, or enslave unwary indigenes. They could not despair, could not be crippled by loneliness, could not fight for the cross or suffer for science, would not know epiphanies or endure tropical fevers. They would lay no claims, issue no proclamations of sovereignty, raise no toasts to king or republic, sign no treaties of trade or military alliance, nor send out reconnaissance parties to lay out routes for folk migration. They conducted no conversions, collected no soil samples or ore assays, erected no missions and outposts. The Voyagers confronted no Other, or even life. Instead the Voyagers would carry a tradition of exploration—one bonded to an older and brasher tradition of vision quest—into new times and to new worlds.

For this the Voyagers had to shun Mars, as they shunned the dominant passions of Martian prophets. By the end of 1977 both spacecraft had rushed by Mars's orbit without a blink and in so doing slid past all the fantasies and utopianism that Mars has provoked. They had left one of the founding trilogy of narratives, colonization, behind.

Beyond the Inner Planets

9. Cruise

Between the orbit of Mars and the asteroid belt, the Voyagers did what they did mostly through their long trek. They cruised, and cruised, and cruised. For Voyager 1 the first full-fledged encounter, at Jupiter, would not occur until nineteen months after launch, and for Voyager 2, almost twenty-three months. Between them lay the shoals of the asteroids, the first and most visible of the hazards the Voyagers had to face. Before then, however, they had to navigate through the immensity of space.

The real hazards lay on Earth. The Voyagers did not know boredom and could not be distracted; their minders could. As programmed, the Voyagers routinely sent back information gathered about interplanetary space, and they expected only in reply JPL's weekly radio acknowledgment. If they did not receive it, they assumed their primary receiver had failed, and switched to a backup. In early April 1978 a week passed with nary an electronic whisper from JPL, and Voyager 2, as preprogrammed, switched to its secondary receiver. Controllers, now alert to the glitch, instructed the spacecraft to return to the primary, a command it ignored.

Now hardware and software began a toxic scenario in which each minor failure cascaded into another potentially more fatal one. The attempt to reconnect caused a tracking loop capacitor to fail, which meant the backup receiver could not adjust to a wide range of frequencies out of which it could automatically pluck commands, but could only tune to a precisely defined one, a frequency that Voyager 2's earthbound minders would have to search for. Identifying that required frequency is complex, because it varies with all the motions of Earth and spacecraft, along with temperature and other idiosyncrasies. A week of frantic scrambling eventually reestablished the primary receiver, but only temporarily, before a short developed that blew both the receivers' redundant fuses. After another week of scrambling, communication reverted permanently to the backup.[54]

CRUISE CONTROL

To the uninitiated, space travel might seem no more complex than sending a billiard ball across a Euclidean void. It was only necessary to avoid collisions with large hard objects, which were few and obvious. The reality was, travel beyond Earth was jarring, quirky, and often rough, with slight margins for error.

That process began with launch—a vast shaking by powerful rockets that propelled awkward payloads through a scruffy atmosphere, and for which even seconds of timing and meters of positioning could amplify across many years and millions of miles of interplanetary space. Then the spacecraft introduced imbalances as they unfolded and performed. Their ongoing navigations were no better than their sensors, thrusters, and gyros. Success depended on an exact trajectory, for which it was necessary to know as accurately as possible just where the spacecraft were and what speed they traveled at, and hence what course corrections to make.

Nor was space itself truly neutral. That interplanetary realm, which seemed like a void, actually consisted of hard and soft fields, each full of irregularities and neither fully mapped. Not all the hard geography of planetary objects was known. There were gravitational tugs from bodies unrecognized from Earth, not least undiscovered moons; the planets themselves had masses not previously measured with the accuracy required for precision navigation, and were surrounded by debris-laden rings, some visible, some only hypothesized; there were hits from dust that did little direct damage but that could nudge trajectories microscopically. The soft geography of magnetic currents and solar winds, perhaps even cosmic radiation, exerted its own subtle pressure and was occasionally aroused into tidal surges and storms. Even the minuscule movements of the spacecrafts' magnetic tapes deflected attitudes and velocity. The Voyagers required ceaseless corrections by their internal guidance systems and earthbound steersmen and pilots.[55]

Voyager's targets—planetary encounters—had relatively unforgiving windows. If the spacecraft passed too far away, its instruments might not record what observers wanted; if too close, the immensity of the giant planets would blot out readings in a blur. The spacecraft had an exact route to travel, as intricate as threading the coral-infested Torres Strait, and they could make the pass only once. There would be no second chance. There was no opportunity to pause, to put to shore or lay at anchor while plans were reconsidered or advice sought or local pilots acquired. The reliance on gravity assistance, too, demanded precise steering as to not only speed but also direction, or the Voyagers might be flung wildly into space. The Voyagers had a "delivery error" of one hundred kilometers. The Grand Tour was premised on an ability, as the prevailing metaphor put it, to tee up a golf ball in New York and sink a hole-in-one in California.

An ancient distinction exists between navigation and pilotage. Pilots guided ships through local waters they knew from long apprenticeship, perhaps assisted by logbooks or rudders that spoke to the details of maneuvering through the hazards of particular harbors. The geographic oddity that rendered Europe a peninsula broken fractally into smaller peninsulas that in turn dissolved into isles meant that pilots steered along coasts and over small seas. They crossed the Mediterranean not all at once but through a series of lesser crossings, strait by strait, sea by sea. Not until mariners undertook long traverses over blue-water oceans did navigation, or the means to determine location when out of sight of land, become essential, and pilots and navigators begin to merge. And then they again searched sea by sea and strait by strait.

The means for navigating were primitive. A compass; an astrolabe, a Davis quadrant (or backstaff), or sextant; a wooden log dragged on a knotted rope—by such means one could estimate location relative to the Earth's magnetic pole, or its cosmological setting, and perhaps something of its speed. But all were faulty, little better than calculated magic. Experience counted more than instruments. The distribution of planetary magnetism—specifically the declination of the magnetic pole from true north—was unknown. Sightings of the Sun and polestar could determine with relative ease one's latitude, which argued for sailing along fixed latitudes wherever winds and currents made such passages possible.[56]

At the onset of the Great Voyages the Portuguese assembled scholars to formalize, and if possible improve upon, known practices. To the rule of the North Star, they added the rule of the Sun, created a table for the rule for "raising the pole," and made analogous calculations for the Southern Cross, all of which were gathered into a manual of navigation and nautical almanac, the *Regimento do astrolabio e do quadrante*, taught in formal schools for navigation established at Lisbon and, later, for Spain, at Seville. The exercise did for latitude what later state sponsorship did for longitude. It was thus no accident that the rediscoveries of the New World came from voyages that traveled from east to west, with the Norse sailing from isle to isle along a rude line of latitude (and, barring storms, never more than a couple of days out of sight of land) and with Columbus following favorable trade winds that blew roughly east and west.[57]

Far trickier was to determine longitude, for which there was no practical solution until the nineteenth century. The state of learning was not merely wanting but often dangerously inept. The fact is, the Great Voyages achieved their goals without adequate navigational techniques, and the Second Age accomplished most of its task before chronometers were both accurate and abundant enough to make a calculation of longitude generally sufficient. Instead explorers relied on an artful, if not quasi-superstitious, appeal to eclectic methods and a personal alloy of experience, hunch, whim, prayer, and luck, or the unfortunately named "dead reckoning." Samuel de Champlain, one of the few explorers equally successful on both land and sea, shrugged his shoulders. He had never been able to learn from any mariners with whom he talked how they did it, "except that it be done by fanciful rules, all different, some better than others." He trusted those who had actually voyaged more than those "others who often pretend to know more than they do."[58]

The common practice was to recycle pilots, as da Gama did to double the Cape, or to seize them, as he then did at Malinda, and as Albuquerque did at Java before sailing to the Spice Isles.

By the time Voyager launched, pilotage referred to the minutely choreographed acts associated with planetary encounter; and navigation, to black-space sailing. For the latter, the Voyagers commanded a navigation team (NAV) of twelve. For the former, the spacecraft relied on an elaborate procedure for identifying the hundreds of tasks that an encounter required and then worked out a second-by-second sequence, coded it for the onboard computers, and uploaded the package.

The duties of the NAV team were three. The first was trajectory, or mission design. It tested options for routes by balancing size of payload and launch capacity with where program scientists wanted to go and what they wished to do when they arrived. There were tradeoffs, an infinity of tradeoffs. Unlike Cabot or Cabral, Voyager could not put to port to refit or replan or decide the season was too advanced to proceed or elect to revisit a site of special interest. Each planetary encounter had to be exquisitely choreographed down to seconds, which meant that the mission had to determine core trajectories well before launch, since prospective launch dates varied according to the desired routes past the planets.[59]

As chief navigator, Charles Kohlhase had overseen some 10,000 prospective trajectories for the Grand Tour, a change in any one of which could ripple through all the rest. Eventually mission planners winnowed that unruly swarm into a handful. The first charge was of course to survey Jupiter and Saturn, but behind that was the vision of the Grand Tour, such that the prospects for Voyager 2 depended on

Voyager 1. Besides the anticipated hazards of asteroids and the Jovian radiation field, the mission had to make a critical assessment of Titan and avoid the Saturnian rings. Even after launch, various possibilities abounded through midcourse corrections, but only within a single-minded, multitasking furious passage at 39,000 kilometers per hour that resembled a descent through a cataract. Still, trajectory corrections were both possible and necessary.

These—the "orbit determinations" that specified where Voyager was and the "nudges" that refined or redirected its path—were the largest of the NAV group's assignments. Orbit determination relied on both Earth-based and spacecraft-based methods. Earth-based navigation tracked the spacecraft through its telemetry, the messages it sent back to the Deep Space Network's dishes. Because a regular Doppler shift occurred, it was possible to calculate distance, and this could be done over and over across months, if desired, to know exactly where the spacecraft was and how fast it was moving. In a sense, the triangulations took the place of historic methods for determining latitude, and the Doppler shift assumed the role of onboard chronometers for determining the equivalent of longitude.

But among the unknowns that made precision trajectories so daunting was the range of uncertainty about the target planets themselves. If navigators were to steer the spacecraft within a one-hundred-kilometer window, they required more precise measurements of diameter and mass—better than those obtainable from Earth. A mistake of a thousand kilometers in the diameter of a giant planet was entirely within the range of instrumental error, yet could prove ruinous for Voyager. For such measurements, navigators needed an optical navigation apparatus housed on the spacecraft itself. Images of the planet against the background of fixed stars refined its dimensions, much as small variations in acceleration (by which the spacecraft felt the pull of the planet) honed its mass.

In this way the guidance team juggled with two numbers. One forecast distance to target, and the other, time of encounter. Both were inevitably flawed, but the magnitude of error could be trivial. Distance was the more critical, since the positioning of flyby decided what the instruments and images would record. As the spacecraft approached closer, both numbers sharpened, and argued (or not) for a final tweaking of Voyager's trajectory. Such corrections were programmed into the formalized sequencing of encounter.

The third navigational duty was to decide how to make those course corrections. The sooner the adjustments, the lesser the variance as encounter approached. Some deviations resulted from the sum of minor perturbations. Others came about as the exact specifications of time and place for encounter made for a more precise if frenetic scenario of maneuvers. But either way, the exercise was harrowing, for it demanded that the Voyagers temporarily abandon their typical mode of navigation.

In normal flight, the Voyagers, like the Mariners from which they descended, stabilized themselves around three axes. To hold the craft's position, controllers had to triangulate from two fixed points in space. One was simple: the Sun. For near-voyaging craft, the second point could be Earth itself. For far-voyaging craft, however, Earth could be confused with its Moon, and both lay too close to the Sun, so another mark was needed. The star of choice was Canopus, in the southern constellation Carina, the second brightest light in the sky. Between those two sensors, one on the Sun and one on Canopus, the Voyagers constantly recalibrated their location. But when they underwent a burn to accelerate and reposition, they had to surrender that cosmodetic baseline. They needed another means to stabilize.[60]

The procedure began by repositioning the spacecraft so its engine would propel it in the proper direction, then turning off the celestial guidance system and yielding stability to a set of three gyroscopes, one for each axis. At such times, along with a temporary loss of its navigational sensors, Voyager would no longer point its high-gain antenna to Earth; it had to surrender the thermal balance that its formal stability had allowed, and then, after the burn, rely on a small omnidirectional antenna to reacquire Earth's location while its star sensors recaptured the Sun and Canopus. Until then the spacecraft was on its own, and dependent on gyros, devices long and well understood but still machines and therefore subject to their own electrical and mechanical gremlins. The maneuver was fraught with hazards, and given the difficulties of telemetry and tracking, it might be weeks before the exact outcome could be assessed.

The Voyagers' long cruises were the ideal times to correct trajectories, for the coasting phase lacked the frenzy of encounter, and without knowing the correct velocity, both position and speed, well in advance, the encounters would fail. On his second voyage Columbus missed the westerly trades and nearly foundered. Da Gama mistimed the monsoon winds to Africa and narrowly escaped disaster.

STAR STEERAGE

Across the ages navigation had relied on mixed technologies, the search for a new celestial referent, the power of judgment, and simple trust to luck. What Voyager did was accelerate the level of technical knowledge and transfer more of the burden to the spacecraft machinery: the mission was itself a kind of midcourse correction in the trajectory of exploration history. Pilot, helmsman, rudder and log, sextant and compass metamorphosed into a complex machine over which human controllers exercised ever-shrinking capacity for tactile guidance even as the demands for precision maneuvering swelled. As with everything about Voyager, its mission fused the hoary with a high-tech modernity.

The explorer still looked to the stars for guidance. At the onset of the Great Voyages, this meant the Sun and Polaris, the polestar. Yet the latter's value lay in its constancy about the North Pole, and as the Portuguese probed southward, it fell lower toward the horizon; and beyond the equator, it disappeared. Still, one could coast along Africa, though only at the cost of dreary daily tackings that made the Indies seem more remote rather than less so. If they wished to find those distant lands of their fevered imaginations, exploring *marinheiros* would have to sail from the mundane shorelines and into the Sea of Darkness, which was now all the murkier because the travelers had left behind the lights of both familiar constellations and the polestar itself.

Yet an astounding sight greeted them. Looming up was a

striking constellation that resembled a kite or, to the eyes of the Portuguese, a cross. Instead of terrifying them with its novelties and its perhaps unknowable heavens, the southern sky seemed to beckon, as though they were crusaders. The Southern Cross summoned them to new worlds, and new possibilities, of navigation. As swaths of strange stars appeared, so would novel methods emerge to pilot mariners across those untracked seas and even an ocean an order of magnitude broader than Europe itself. Eventually Galileo's telescope unveiled the inner moons of Jupiter and made a calculation of longitude feasible; surveys of geomagnetism plotted maps that traced the deviations that made a recalibration of the compass possible. Exploration and experiment would continue, each one provoking the other to new exertions. The Voyagers now raced toward the Jovian—the Galilean—moons that had caused a revolution in cosmography and navigation and were poised to announce another.

As the Portuguese sailed south, they spied also an extraordinarily bright star that rose in prominence as they pressed on, more luminous than anything in the night sky save Sirius. With providential calculation, it seemed to circle about the southern pole. They named it Canopus.

10. Encounter: Asteroid Belt

I n late 1977 Voyager 2 entered the asteroid belt; Voyager 1 soon followed. In mid-December, as planned, some 124 million kilometers from Earth, Voyager 1, on a faster, tighter trajectory, passed its twin.

The swirl of asteroids was the first of the known hazards awaiting beyond the Earth-like planets. They were, collectively, a kind of failed planet, a vast composite of planetary particles, some, such as Ceres, as large as Texas, most smaller and more worrisome. Mission planners envisioned the cluster as a diffuse shoreline of sandlike debris that could strike with the speed of bullets. Moreover, the belt could stand, in surrogate, for the rings, both known and yet to be discovered, that encircled the giant planets. It had to be threaded or rounded for the Voyagers to find the open seas beyond. Within the barrier, the biggest blocks were mapped, and could be avoided; the others were a matter of blind reckoning and, for the frozen sandstorm of meteorites, a question of luck. The only way to know was to do it.

Fortunately, the Voyagers did not have to sail blind. A plucky pair of spacecraft, Pioneers 10 and 11, had already blazed a route to Jupiter and Saturn. Thanks to them, the passage to the Indies of the outer planets was open.

O, PIONEERS

Their names were appropriate. Pioneer was the hardy frontier scout, the first to Jupiter and Saturn, the tough traveler who discovered the pitfalls and fords, the pathfinder who made the Grand Tour possible. Voyager was the scientific sojourner, the one who rediscovered and elaborated the Jovian and Saturnian systems with rigor, and then plunged into the far unknown before overtaking the trailblazers. Pioneer was the indomitable Jedediah Smith, hunkered against the wind, crossing over South Pass; Voyager, the Pacific Railroad Surveys' grand reconnaissance of the West.[61]

The Pioneer spacecraft were designed to be simple, durable, cheap, and, if necessary, expendable. The largest difference between their design and that of the Mariner series was that they maintained stability by spinning, rather than using a three-axis arrangement of thrusters. The earliest prototypes struggled through multiple launch failures until 1960, when Pioneer 5 roamed the interplanetary domains around Venus. Pioneers 6–9 were arrayed throughout the inner solar system as a "space weather network." But the famous missions were Pioneers 10 and 11 to Jupiter and Saturn. In what they found and how they did it they not only foreshadowed the Voyagers but often led.

They were, as NASA put it, "precursor missions." They were the first spacecraft to the two giant planets, they discovered the first of the new moons that the far-traveling robots would find, they helped sharpen the communications apparatus for deep-space communication, they confirmed the capacities of gravity-assist trajectories, they demonstrated how a lead spacecraft could inform and redirect the purposes of a second, and they blazed a trail through the asteroid belt, Jupiter's lethal radiation, and Saturn's rings. They were the first spacecraft to travel beyond the orbit of Pluto, and the first to carry engraved messages to any other intelligence that might lie beyond the solar wind. Dispatched the year after Voyager, Pioneer Venus 1 and 2—the last of their breed, turning inward to spiral around Venus—concluded the golden age of American planetary exploration.[62]

———

Pioneer 10 launched in March 1972, and Pioneer 11 a year later, in April 1973. It was Pioneer 10 that first encountered Jupiter, warned of its lethal radiation, and sent back real-time images of the planet as it approached periapsis. Its instruments sketched a new cartography of the solar system, a geography of magnetism and radiation. But the reports that captivated the public were the pictures that took shape, scan line by scan line, from Pioneer's Pulsed Image Converter System (PICS). Its spin-stabilization design meant Pioneer did not have a camera, but it could broadcast data from the imaging photopolarimeter's narrow-angle telescope in strips as it rotated. These were assembled into color images by computer, which added green to the reds and blues that Pioneer sent back, and then projected the result on television.

By December 2, 1973, the images exceeded those from Earth-based observatories, and as the spacecraft approached periapsis the next day it proclaimed a new perspective on Jupiter, the greatest advance since Galileo had trained his telescope on the planet. Even more, Pioneer changed the process as well as the pictures. While there were no human eyewitnesses, as with the Apollo lunar landings, the public could see what Pioneer could as it swept around Jupiter. The images were grainy—clunky by later standards, and far from the bewitching scenes recorded by Voyager. But they came in real time, and they thrilled, and they helped announce an era of virtual exploration. For its imaging triumph, the Pioneer program even received an Emmy award.[63]

The near-death, and ultimate success, of Pioneer 10 warned JPL that Voyager had to harden its electronics and tweak its trajectories. But the Grand Tour required that the mission have similar information regarding Saturn. This task fell to Pioneer 11, which followed a trajectory to Jupiter that would also allow it the option of going to Saturn.

Pioneer 11 made its closest encounter on December 2, 1974, a third as near to Jupiter as its predecessor, and on a trajectory that gave the first views of Jupiter's poles (invisible to Earth-based observation), and then slung it to Saturn. By passing through the Jovian radiation ring vertically in this way, it would experience only a short burst of irradiation, which would allow it a nearer encounter. Then it flung around on a trajectory to Saturn in which it trekked across the solar system by passing over the plane of the ecliptic. As it approached Saturn, its controllers and scientists debated between an inside or an outside passage—whether to cross the rings sharply or swing around them altogether. Either route would reveal new knowledge, but NASA determined that the heavy scientific lifting for the planet would come from Voyager, and that Pioneer would test Saturn's shoals for the explorers to follow. As Pioneer 10 had allowed Pioneer 11 to proceed to Saturn, so Pioneer 11 would be used to allow Voyager 2, if all went well with Voyager 1, to proceed to Uranus. What Voyager required was more precise knowledge about the outside passage.[64]

On September 1, 1979, Pioneer successfully navigated through the outer rings, and then passed through them again on the other side on September 3. Along the way it dispatched five images of Titan, another target of Voyager; and through occultation, it discovered a new Saturnian moon, later validated and named Epimetheus.

That achievement was perhaps not all that Pioneer 11's most visionary proponents had wished for, but it was all the spacecraft had to do. Among routes over America's Continental Divide, South Pass is virtually inconspicuous, a rise of land in a broad plateau, rather than a rift through towering mountains like a Khyber Pass; yet it was the way west. So it was with the outside passage at Saturn. The route lay open for the Grand Tour.

Both Pioneers had yet more to do, this time probing a path that would ultimately take them beyond the solar system. The first, Pioneer 10, crossed the orbit of Uranus on July 1979, and of Pluto in 1990, completing a traverse of the solar system's hard geography. The soft geography, as defined by the solar wind, was much farther away. Moreover, it was asymmetrical, compressed in the direction of the Sun's travel and stretched in the opposite direction, leaving a long ionic tail. Pioneer 10 traveled down that tail. Despite its early launch, its slower speed and trajectory thus put it behind in the race to the frontier. Pioneer 11, meanwhile, coasted toward the heliosphere's bow shock.

Each carried two messages. One was a plaque attached to the chassis of the spacecraft that, overtly, stood as a communiqué to any future finder of the hulk. It was a kind of calling card that identified who sent the machine and from where; in this, again, it tried out what the Voyagers would elaborate. The plaques became the lasting logo of Pioneer. The second message was its radio signal to Earth. Both spacecraft continued to broadcast—Pioneer 11 up to 1995, and Pioneer 10 into 2003; and the Deep Space Network continued to tease out their ever-feebler transmissions. In this, again, Pioneer assisted Voyager by prodding and refining the DSN. As one observer remarked, the total energy from Pioneer's radio signal at the edge of the planets "would have to be collected for several million years to light a single 7.5-watt nightlight for a millionth of a second." To extract that signal from the cosmic background buzz was a daunting achievement. If the two Voyagers were to succeed—Voyager 1 blitzing to the heliopause, and Voyager 2 completing the Grand Tour—they would need extraordinary communications. Those technologies were first devised to listen to Pioneer.[65]

In June 1983, while Voyager 2 was halfway between Saturn and Uranus, Pioneer 10 slid beyond the orbit of Neptune. In 1995 Pioneer 11 suffered a broken Sun sensor, and despite some slight reserves of power, it could no longer direct its wispy transmissions to Earth, and fell silent, still heading toward the constellation Aquila. Pioneer 10 continued to broadcast, but so painfully and weakly that its scientific value was nil. It sank into a virtual coma, and on March 30, 1997, at 11:45 a.m., life support ended, as the last signals were downlinked to the DSN station in Madrid. Still, hope lingered, and Pioneer 10, oblivious to Earth, sent a signal captured by the radio telescope at Arecibo. But like a Newcomen engine in an age of diesels, the equipment required to track and interpret Pioneer was beyond obsolescence. Even heroic measures could barely sense the messages sent across 7.5 billion miles and 20 hours. On March 2, 2002, Pioneer exchanged greetings with Earth on its thirtieth birthday. On February 7, 2003, across 8 billion miles, it finally fell silent, and Pioneer 10 joined its sibling as a machine corpse hurtling through the cosmos.[66]

The tragedy of pioneering is to create conditions that eliminate the pioneers—and that was the fate of Pioneers 10 and 11. Compared with the Voyagers, the Pioneers were slow and kludgy, and despite an impressive early lead and first contacts with Jupiter and Saturn, the Voyagers overwhelmed their scientific results and their capacity to evoke wonder, and then overtook them physically in 1998 to become the most distant objects to leave Earth. Unlike the Pioneers, the Voyagers have enough power and working instruments to function until perhaps 2020. They would likely survive to pierce the veil of the heliosphere and to report that event.

The frontier belonged to Voyager.

BEYOND THE BARRIER

The hard geography proved less formidable than feared, and for mission planners, surprisingly less daunting than the solar system's soft geography.

Pioneer 10 found (and Pioneer 11 confirmed) that most of the interplanetary realm's perilous particles clustered around Earth or at the center of the asteroid belt, where they thickened to almost three times the density apparent in interplanetary space. High-velocity micrometeorites and dust particles were fewer than anticipated. Both spacecraft whisked through with hardly a scratch. Likewise, the planetary rings proved porous or thinned to the point where they could be skirted. There was only one near-collision. At Saturn, Pioneer 11 found, by occultation, a new inner moon on its approach, and then nearly collided with it upon its departure.[67]

The Voyagers threaded through the asteroids, slid around and through the rings, and avoided undetected satellites.

What did threaten Pioneer was interplanetary space's soft geography. An immense solar storm, the largest ever recorded, shook Pioneer 10 on August 2, 1972. Pioneers 6 through 9, already deployed around the inner planets to measure solar activity, had sensed and then tracked a solar wind of unprecedented power and velocity (3.6 million kilometers per hour) that exploded outward. By the time this ionic tsunami struck Pioneer 10 some three days later, it had shed half its velocity, although by transforming that energy into higher temperature, and its wind had become so diffuse that Pioneer 10 sensed its passing only through the traces it left on a battery of delicate instruments.[68]

What did nearly cripple the spunky spacecraft was its scrape with the radiation belts of Jupiter, a blast completely unanticipated by designers. As it approached closest encounter, each half-hourly data dump notched up radiation to levels that would saturate and then overwhelm its onboard instruments—more than a thousand times what theory had predicted. Then, just as unexpectedly as rates had risen, they fell. The radiation belts of Jupiter, it was soon realized, were not only far more potent than those of Earth-like planets but also more unstable, and wobbled around the gaseous giant at an eleven-degree tilt. The gusty ionic wind had veered, as it were, just enough to permit Pioneer to pass through without foundering on the magnetic reefs. Two cosmic ray telescopes became temporarily infirm, and the blast of irradiation gave fatal cataracts to the optics of the Sisyphus instrument.[69]

The Voyagers' designers hurriedly reworked the still-abuilding spacecraft to shield its sensitive instruments. Thanks to Pioneer, the hazards of space had become sufficiently well known to build protection into the Voyagers' apparatus before launch. But the Voyagers had one other enormous advantage over Pioneer: their programmable computers. They could self-analyze, receive new instructions, and operate with a degree of autonomy. Pioneer 10's flyby of Jupiter required 16,000 commands from Earth, and a flaw in any one could prove fatal. On Voyager an error could, within limits, be repaired or circumvented. Just as the Voyager Grand Tour could incorporate the lessons of Pioneer, so new lessons could become encoded into practice as the spacecraft sped across the solar system.

The asteroid belt does not track a simple orbit but those of a slushy cluster of planetoids and debris scattered across a wide swath. It took the spacecraft most of a year to traverse the full field. Voyager 1 and 2 exited the realm unscathed in August and September 1978, respectively.

11. Cruise

The Voyagers sailed on, and on. Week passed week, month passed month. Between the asteroid belt and Jupiter lay 370 million kilometers of interplanetary space. Mars was half again as far from the Sun as Earth was, the asteroid belt almost three times as distant, and Jupiter was twice that. The journey could seem endless.

The euphoria of launch had long passed, and the frenzied elation of encounter lay far in the distance. Other planetary projects beckoned, and JPL siphoned off engineers to work on those. Attention wandered. The Voyagers passed through a void of concentration, filled, when possible, by anticipation and analogy. Since there was a lot of interplanetary space, and a lot of earthly time to pass before the first, defining encounter, the Voyagers spent a great deal of time measuring and weighing analogies, and were in turn measured and weighed by them.

SPACE FOR ANALOGY

What did space mean? In practical terms the choices were those represented by von Braun, Van Allen, and Pickering as they hoisted Explorer 1 over their collective heads. It meant colonization, science, and journey as exploration, and the American space program found it hard to hold them all together. But for some partisans, the space program overall meant more. It stood for—promised to catalyze—an immense social reformation destined to transform the American commonwealth on a scale with few precedents. In the words of one techno-prophet, "the thrust into space will change the ideas and lives of people more drastically than the Industrial Revolution."[70]

As early as 1962, NASA commissioned the American Academy of Arts and Sciences to explore the "secondary" impacts of the rapidly metastasizing national investment in space, anticipating that the vaunted spin-offs would extend far beyond simple economic stimulus. Good academics, the group devoted most of its exegetical energies arguing the limitations of historical analogy in principle. In the end they opted to examine the advent of the railroad as a possible model, and again, good scholars, they so hedged their analysis with qualifiers and caveats that the analogy virtually fizzled out on the launchpad. By then, too, political realities were quelling the rush of spending; by the end of Apollo, the NASA claim on the federal budget had reached a very modest steady state. The space program would not become the transcontinental railroad of the twentieth century. Partisans for utopian revolution would have to look elsewhere.[71]

What the exercise did emphasize was the complexity of novelty amid a thriving culture. A new machine, program, or idea derived its power from the richness and intensity of its interactions with the rest of society—and the space program *was* an interaction. Had the AAAS Committee on Space shifted its attention from the startling monies funneled into NASA and the promise of endless spin-offs, a kind of political perpetual-motion machine, and turned to exploration history, it would have probed and poked at very different data sets but come to a similar conclusion. Voyages of discovery derived their power from the fullness of their cultural engagements. A new machine or idea may reform society but only after it first fits in. An enterprise such as Voyager could not inspire or remake what did not already exist.

Similarly, there was no lack of analogies to exploration history. Space travel was imagined as a stage in earthly evolution, a metamorphosis in humanity's maturation, and manifest destiny gone to Mars. The planetary program was Leif Ericson, Columbus, and Magellan. What such allusions all shared was dissociation from particular sustaining societies; they were universal. Yet what boosters and designers needed was a closer look at just how those predecessors interacted with their cultures, and for that, since the Third Age was still aborning, they might profitably have examined the founders of the Great Voyages. They might have looked, especially, at the Portuguese paradigm.

The Portuguese ignited the First Age, traveled the widest, contributed the greatest number of pilots and mariners, and established a framework of trade, conquest, and discovery that the other nations subsequently emulated or seized outright. Portugal's overseas empire was an astonishing commitment that drained perhaps a tenth of the population out of Portugal and compelled the country to defend what it quickly appreciated it could not. The flush of early wealth it acquired it soon destroyed with foreign wars. Others, notably the Dutch, picked off its best Indies holdings. But while the interlopers poached pieces, a remarkably robust imperium endured. Portugal's saga told not of an endless quest that, once launched, became unstoppable, but of a life cycle, one that expanded and then contracted.

The Portuguese experience established the default setting for exploration's software. The degree of interpenetration between geographic discovery and Portuguese society was astonishing, of which the suite of exploring ships was only a down payment. Consider the founding explorers, all of whom combined exploration with some other enterprise: affairs of state, commerce and conquest, proselytizing and poetry. Henry the Navigator, late-medieval prince, blurry-eyed speculator, who began the fusion of discovery with state policy. Vasco da Gama, merchant and administrator, representing the bonding of commerce with exploration. Afonso de Albuquerque, soldier and strategist, seizing at gunpoint the critical nodes of traffic through the Indian and South China seas. Saint Francis Xavier, tempering the sword with the cross, missionizing in India, the East Indies, and especially Japan, with plans to proselytize in China. Luiz Vaz de Camões, adventurer turned litterateur, author of *Os Lusíadas*, which cast contemporary explorers into the mode of classical heroes and which became the national epic. "Had there been more of the world," Camões wrote, his bold mariners "would have discovered it." Revealingly, the founders of the Enterprise of the Indies all died overseas.

Enthusiasm there was for expansion, but the questions of where and how and to what end kindled a furious debate amid competing claims. Nine years passed after Bartholomeu Dias rounded the Cape before da Gama headed to India, and exploring energies in the Indies were soon dissipated in Morocco. The whole enterprise began winding down within sixty years after its founding. That astonishing outrush had lasted less than two generations, exhausted by overreach and especially by heedless military adventures. The colonies took on lives of their own, populated not by fresh émigrés from Portugal but by mixed-blood societies whose ties to the metropole were largely language and faith, and ever-more-tenuous memories. And even as Camões penned his epic amalgam of triumph and tragedy, Fernão Mendes Pinto was recording a parallel, equally fabulous tale of adventure, mishap, and squandered opportunities that makes his *Peregrinicão* read as though it were an early draft of *Gulliver's Travels*. In brief, Portugal did it all, and its Great Voyages transformed it as little else could. They also destroyed it as few national undertakings might. The outcome depended on what else exploration bonded to.

Did the program that launched Voyager resemble the Portuguese paradigm? Not in its particulars; not even by analogy. What they shared was that both Voyager and its Portuguese antecedents rallied and merged many complex enthusiasms within their sustaining societies. Those exploration analogies work best that are older and more diffuse and less subject to empirical qualifications. The more remote the historical sources behind an allusion, the more nebulous are its details and the more susceptible it becomes to multiple meanings. Columbus could mean anything. Lewis and Clark could mean everything.

Where commentators also groped for analogies was to depict the terrains of the Third Age. The "new ocean" of space was one, although its use was encumbered by the presence of that real new ocean of the Third Age, the recently explored abyss. Even more elaborate was the analogy to Antarctica. To both partisans and critics Antarctica was the future. They just saw that future in diametrically opposite ways.

Antarctica was an ideal venue—the geographic and historical transition from the Second Age to the Third. Its contrast with the Arctic expresses that status perfectly. The Arctic is a sea surrounded by land; the Antarctic, a continent surrounded by ocean. The Arctic, for all its hostility, harbors life around and under it, and to some extent on it, not just random organisms but functional if spare ecosystems. For the Antarctic, save trivial oases of exposed rock, life ends at the continent's edge. Even more pronounced are their divergent human histories. The Arctic is encased by, accessible to, and hence bonded to, human history. It has its indigenous peoples, its imperial claims and colonizing epochs, its ancient economies of hunting, fishing, and trade. The Antarctic has none of this. No one has ever truly lived there; no enduring natural assets bind it to the world economy; no colonization or claims to sovereignty have global recognition. Its population is scientists; its trade, information; and only an immense expenditure of will and money has forged even these tenuous links. The Antarctic's isolation is so complete that it seems less an intrinsic feature of the planet than an extraterrestrial presence accidentally slapped onto its surface, as though an icy moon of Uranus had slammed into Earth.

It is a place that is isolated, abiotic, acultural, and profoundly passive. One goes there in defiance of natural impulses. The scene reflects, absorbs, and reduces. It acts as a geophysical and intellectual sink. It takes far more than it gives. With implacable indifference it simplifies everything: that is its essence, the synthesis of the simple with the huge. It reduces an entire continent to a single mineral taller than Mount Whitney and broader than Australia.

The scene acts on people as it does on other earthly features. There is no genuine society. There are no children, no families, no schools, no social order, and no matrix of interlocking institutions. It is more like a mining camp or those shore-based trading outposts typical of the First Age. But worse: at least the residents of earlier outposts could intermarry with indigenous peoples, and the resulting mestizo societies—pioneered, as so much of European expansion was, by Portugal—did the heavy work of exploring and settling the interiors of South America and southern Africa, and of parts of south and southeast Asia. Exploration meant a transfer of knowledge from one group to another; explorers relied on native guides, translators, hunters, collectors; and they typically adopted native clothing, if not native mores. None of this was possible in Antarctica. Yet without such cultural contact and without a true social setting there could be no great literature or art. The ultimate Antarctic saga is Douglas Mawson's solo trek, slogging alone across broken ice fields, with no guide and little direction, nothing to record but conversations with himself, nothing at all but his own will to continue.

To this sketch there are seeming exceptions. Chile maintains a small army base, complete with families, on King George Island. The Southern Ocean swarms with krill, fish, seals, whales, and penguins. There are microlichens on some exposed rocks, and bacteria in sandstone and perhaps under the ice sheet itself. Tourists visit sites on the peninsula annually. But all these activities occur along the continental fringe, or on minor outcrops along the margins or, in the case of the Chilean base, on an island outside the Antarctic Circle (roughly equivalent to the latitude of Helsinki). The social order, often quasimilitary, is akin to that of a ship, quite independent of place. America's McMurdo Station is not a Plymouth colony but a Virginia City, and Amundsen-Scott South Pole Station not a St. Louis but an icy St. Helena. Biotic fragments do not make a sustaining ecosystem. The Antarctic analogy begins only when you cross the barrier ice and step onto the ice sheet. Then you enter the Third Age.

The Antarctic analogue suggests that the Third Age will be dominated by near-Earth terrains. Exploration will happen through remote sensing and robots. Outposts may be permanently established but not permanently staffed, their inhabitants coming and going routinely, like migratory flocks or marching penguins. They will traffic in the luxury goods of an information society. The requisite rivalry that must power exploration will probably derive from the competitive character of science itself, conducted as a cultural pursuit with national prestige, not national survival, as its payoff. It will mean, in a curiously postmodernist way, talking with ourselves.

These traits identify Antarctica with the Third Age. Some of them are more intensely manifest on the Ice than elsewhere. Mars is richer in information; the Canary abyss far lusher with life. But Antarctica is accessible to people at relatively little cost compared with space travel, and can be seen without the extraordinary cocoons that shield the senses of human travelers from the environment. You can breathe on the East Antarctic plateau without special oxygen tanks. You can smell, taste, touch, and hear, as well as see (there just isn't much to smell, taste, touch, or hear). In the abyss and in space, only sight is possible, which is why robots and instruments can seamlessly replace human observers. It remains to devise programmable computers to similarly guide mechanical hands and supplement, if not supplant, the respiring brain.

To partisans of space settlement, the Antarctic analogue is a glass half full. It is the beachhead for a more remote and complex colonization. To critics, it is a glass as full as it will ever become. They note that humans have wintered over in Antarctica for more than a century and that the dynamics of such outposts have not changed significantly. For them, a Voyager, not a base at Dome C, is the future of geographic discovery.

ANALOGY'S END

Analogies fill in what we don't know. They are a form of social anticipation, of prophecy or prediction. Understanding abhors vacuums as much as nature. Certainly that adage has applied to the vacuum of space.

As Voyager moved from idea to machine to functioning spacecraft, analogies buzzed around it, all forecasting what it might do, might become, and might mean. But once it began its tasks, those analogies faded; the mission moved from prediction to history. Voyager was poised to become itself a source rather than a recipient of analogy. It was no longer something to be imagined but rather an event recorded and a source of hard data.

In June 1978 Voyager 1 began transmitting photographs of Jupiter, followed by increasingly dense recorded radio emissions, plasma wave data, and other readings. On December 10, 1978, still eighty million kilometers from Jupiter, Voyager 1 transmitted photos of the giant planet that exceeded in detail and color any ever taken from Earth.

12. Encounter: Jupiter

P lanetary encounter—this is what Voyager was made for. Jupiter was the first, and it established the pattern of sequenced phases: observation, far-encounter, near-encounter culminating in periapsis, post-encounter. That ritual cadence, with modifications, like a slow spiral of activities that quickened with approach, would repeat six times across the outer solar system. Voyager 1 initiated that astonishing series, achieving its closest approach on March 5, 1979.

Preparations began while the Voyagers were still cruising. There were course corrections, as always, and in late August 1978 both spacecraft received new programming intended to sharpen the performance of their imaging systems. In early November, a month after Voyager 2 cleared the asteroid belt, flight controllers commenced training exercises, some four months before nearest encounter. A paradox of planetary exploration was that discovery depended on an intricate scenario of preplanned maneuvers that determined the exact trajectory, decided what instruments operated for how long and in what sequence, and arranged for when data was downloaded—all this calculated to the minute or even to seconds over a 39-hour period that constituted nearest approach as an accelerating spacecraft hurled toward Jupiter at 46,000 kilometers per hour and was flung away at 86,000 kilometers per hour. Such detailed choreography required precision drilling. A rough rehearsal followed on December 12 through 14.[72]

The next day Voyager 1 left its cruise phase for its observatory phase.

VOYAGER 1

Observation commenced officially on January 4, 1979. There was some flexibility as to when it might actually begin, and once tasks were uploaded, the spacecraft could do its chores with or without close ground supervision. Originally, observation had been scheduled for December 15, but the holidays complicated matters, so rehearsals had been moved up and the official opening slipped back. This left Voyager 1 still some sixty days out from Jupiter.

Beginning on January 6, Voyager took photographs of the planet every two hours; from January 30 to February 3, it began photographing every ninety-six seconds, and did so over a one-hundred-hour period, until Jupiter became too large for its narrow-angle camera. For the next two weeks, photos came in sets of two-by-two pictures, and by February 21, three-by-three images, later assembled into mosaics. Meanwhile, Voyager directed its other instruments—the ultraviolet spectrometer, the infrared spectrometer, the polarimeter, instruments for planetary radio astronomy, and plasma waves—to absorb, scan, and record.[73]

The milestones rushed by. Ground crews waited anxiously for the bow shock, the ionic reef of Jupiter's magnetosphere. On February 10 Voyager entered into the realm of the Jovian system, crossing the orbit of Sinope, the outermost moon. On the seventeenth it photographed Callisto, and on the twenty-fifth, Ganymede. It was now scanning images every forty-eight seconds, and instruments were recording auroras, ion sound waves, and the shifting shoreline of the magnetosphere. The real payoffs, though, would follow periapsis as Voyager made close flybys of the Galilean moons. Scientists and the press began converging on JPL. On February 27, with Voyager some 7.1 million kilometers from Jupiter, public TV in the Los Angeles area began broadcasting a "Jupiter Watch" that allowed the public to view virgin images at the same time as mission scientists. On the twenty-eighth Voyager finally felt bow shock, and time-lapse movies revealed the mechanics of the Jovian atmosphere and its star performer, the Great Red Spot. On March 1, now 4.8 million kilometers away, Voyager crossed the magnetosphere, and photos of the distant satellites were released. The next day heavy rain at the Canberra Deep Space Network site blocked signals for several agonizing minutes, but ever more detailed images continued: the eyes of discovery belonged to anyone with a TV set. On March 4, the eve of near-encounter, Caltech hosted a symposium on "Jupiter and the Mind of Man." There was surprisingly little to engage, for Jupiter had never commanded interest comparable to that of Mars or Venus. Within hours, however, its cultural clout would change.[74]

Closest encounter came at 4:05 a.m. PST on March 5, 1979, some 780,000 kilometers from Jupiter, at a velocity of 100,000 kilometers per hour. The message took thirty-seven minutes to reach JPL. Voyager 1 now flung about the planet for what would be a survey of Jupiter's satellites. It crossed the orbits of the Galilean moons, one after another, and that evening took a full-frame sequence of Io. A failure at the Madrid DSN station caused a gut-wrenching loss of fifty-three minutes' worth of data, and an hour later, another eleven minutes washed away. Meanwhile, as Voyager passed through Jupiter's equatorial plane, it focused its cameras on the space between the gaseous clouds of Jupiter and its tiny rock of a moon, Amalthea. Three days later, analysis confirmed that Voyager 1 had discovered an unknown ring. Now Voyager trained its cameras on Io. At 8:14 a.m., having completed its *gran volta*, the spacecraft disappeared behind the giant planet. For an anxious two hours and six minutes, invisible on the far side of Jupiter, it could only store data, before broadcasting its hoarded information back to Earth when, an hour later, having made its closest approach to Europa, it emerged from the shadow zone altogether. Before the day ended it passed by Ganymede, and the next day, March 6, it flew by Callisto. Two days later encounter officially ended, and as JPL shut down the daily press briefings, project scientist Ed Stone said simply, "I think we have had almost a decade's worth of discovery in this two-week period."[75]

The cavalcade of wonders had stunned nearly everyone. Voyager had photographed a gallery of Jupiter's inner moons, each of them revealed as a "different world." There was Io, pocked but uncratered; Ganymede, cratered but also grooved, apparently through faulting; Amalthea, an asteroid-like body; Europa, smooth with ice and mysteriously dark-streaked; and Callisto, icy, densely cratered yet also smooth and boasting the "largest single contiguous feature" yet discovered, an immense impact crater named Valhalla. Reviewing data, scientists quickly confirmed a Jovian ring; and other, more arcane analyses tumbled out. On March 8, as encounter concluded, Voyager looked back again on Io, now a luminous crescent against the Sun. The intent was mundane, an exercise in navigational backsiting. Within several days, however, the photo became the canonical image of Voyager 1 at Jupiter. In that unexpected outcome the episode might well stand for the entire encounter.[76]

Jupiter is a miniature solar system. It is a gaseous planet with a diameter of 142,800 kilometers, one tenth that of the Sun but more than ten times that of Earth. It features the dual geography of the solar system, the hard field of planets and gravity and the soft field of electromagnetic radiation and ionic gases. It has moons the size of small planets, each distinct. It has a magnetosphere to complement the Sun's. The instruments Voyager carried could measure them all.

Both realms are dynamic, both held surprises, and Jupiter warped each. In its soft geography, researchers found lightning whistlers, mapped the rude dimensions of the Jovian magnetosphere, calculated radio emissions, documented plasmas of various ions, identified the source of exceptional radiation (sulfur from Io), and plotted the magnetic torus around Io. The dominant topic was the magnetosphere, where Jupiter's electromagnetic energies collided with the Sun's to power a kind of invisible weather of strong radiative winds and rough magnetic seas. If rounding Jupiter was akin to doubling the Cape of Good Hope, then it is worth recalling the cape's original name, the Cabo das Tormentas, the Cape of Storms.

The magnetospheric border between the Sun and Jupiter was fluid and blustery; it was not where Pioneer 10 had found it; and when Voyager 1 did cross that frontier, the spacecraft had to pass through its electromagnetic shoreline, buffeting against ionic white-caps and tides, not once but five times, as violent solar winds pressed and pushed against their strenuous Jovian rivals. The radiation blast, despite hardening against it, was sufficient to damage parts of Voyager 1's payload, notably its clock and the synchronization of the two central computers, with the result that the camera and scan platform operated on a schedule some forty seconds apart. What should have been some of the highest resolution images of Io and Ganymede returned blurred.[77]

Even where fuzzy the images of Jupiter's hard geography were what gripped public imagination. Here was revealed, for all and at the same time equally, amid a collective public gasp, the character of new worlds. While there was no solid surface to survey, Jupiter's fluid, multicolor atmosphere was ready-made for time-lapse movies. Here was the weather of another planet, all recorded in gorgeous Technicolor. Hurricanes the size of Earth's Moon that lasted for centuries; stormy eddies that roiled past like boiling Mississippis; trade winds that would shred and crush sailing ships; cloud depths that could vaporize comets. As Voyager approached, and the images sharpened, the Great Red Spot became a cosmic celebrity. A photo of tiny Io against the backdrop of overweening Jupiter spoke volumes about the majesty of the Jovian system and the awesome scales of planetary discovery. With its Mondrian hues and Pollock swirls, Jupiter became a gallery of abstract, modernist art.

But it was the inner satellites that ignited what evolved into a Voyager mystique. Unlike gaseous Jupiter, they were hard bodies, and could be imagined by analogy to familiar moons and planets. As Voyager 1 trained its cameras on them, everyone could sense that these were, as mission geologist Larry Soderblom observed, "new worlds" ready for discovery. Yet none resembled Earth or its Moon, or even Mars or Venus. None looked like the others. Amalthea, Io, Ganymede, Europa, Callisto—each had its own geological evolution, and operated on principles unlike those of the Sun's inner planets. The images were fresh, startling, spellbinding. The geology they exhibited was, at first sight, inexplicable.

Relief mingled with wonder, like the colored-thread meanders and complex eddies of Jovian clouds. What first overwhelmed observers was a sense of elation that Voyager 1 had journeyed so far and so successfully. They then surrendered to that deep wonder that is what the discovery of new worlds has always promised.[78]

VOLCANOES

As Voyager whisked beyond Jupiter, it turned and took one parting shot of Io, now 4.5 million kilometers away and a luminous crescent against the deep black of space. It was a long-exposure image intended for use with its celestial navigation system.

In processing the image, Linda Morabito, a member of the optical navigation group, noted an anomaly. A domelike cloud seemed to bubble up from the surface. Yet Io had no atmosphere. Others, meanwhile, had also spotted and begun to ponder the image. An independent discovery by John Pearl of the IRIS team led to a consensus conclusion: Voyager 1 had witnessed a volcanic eruption. An investigation of all the images over the next week identified eight such events. Io in eruption became the defining image of Voyager's encounter with Jupiter.[79]

Suddenly a dozen inexplicable oddities about the Jovian radiation belt made sense. Its exaggerated intensity and the sulfuric emissions recorded by ultraviolet instruments were the result of sulfur ions blasted into it by Io. Geologists now had an explanation for the moon's weird colors, hot spots, and gaseous bubbles. Instead of impact craters, Io had massive calderas. Io was nothing like Earth's Moon, inert and cold. It was far removed from the dead bodies expected to litter the outer solar system, far distant from what theory had predicted. Subject to Jupiter's immense tidal bellows, Io warmed, melted, and blew off eruptions of sulfur that entered into and altered the magnetosphere. At Io the hard and soft geographies of the solar system collided with a display of planetary fireworks.

Such scenes may have been what researchers secretly hoped for, but it was not what they had expected. After Io, they sensed they could only anticipate surprise. They knew the mission had become a true voyage of discovery.

That the iconic image should be a volcano seemed particularly apt. Throughout Europe's half-millennium expansion, volcanoes had been a constant feature, both as a practical referent and as a symbolic emblem of exploration. Volcanoes guided and inspired, and became themselves prime objects of inquiry. They can serve as a useful index for the Three Ages.

The shipborne First Age traveled from island to island, and the critical isles were almost all volcanic. The Atlantic isles that served both Portugal and Spain were volcanoes: Madeira, Cape Verde, the Azores, and especially the Canaries. So were their destinations, the East and West Indies. There were some notable exceptions, such as the Bahamas, where Columbus first made landfall, and those critical offshore isles that so often served as protected ports of call. But the Antilles were a chain of larger and smaller volcanoes, as were the fabled Moluccas. The very Spice Isles themselves—Ternate, Ambon, Tidor, Banda—were active volcanoes. Between them the twin peaks, Tenerife and Ternate, port of embarkation and port of destination, defined the passage to the Indies.

After Spain finally conquered the Canaries, Tenerife's Pico de Teide became the tallest peak in Europe, a land's end and a point of departure for far-voyaging mariners. The isles governed the oceanic routes west; they served as both an economic and an intellectual entrepôt for receiving and disbursing the gathered flora and fauna of Europe, Africa, Asia, and the Americas; they were the proving ground for Spanish colonization, and for the naturalists who would, over centuries, replace missionaries and conquistadors; the islands served as a standard reference by which to compare what explorers might discover elsewhere in the world. In particular, Tenerife's Teide stood as a template, a rite of passage for ambitious adventurers and a scientific stele by which all else beyond Europe might be measured and its meaning deciphered. This was where one left the Old World for worlds both newer and older. What popular lore attributed to Prince Henry's mythical college of scholars at Sagres belongs in truth to Tenerife.

Even when physically bypassed, Teide persisted as symbol. The role it enjoyed in the First Age for conquest, the Second Age revived for science. "The port of Santa Cruz is in fact a great caravanserai on the route to America and India," noted Alexander von Humboldt, in this, as in so many matters, the oracle of the Second Age. "Every traveler who writes his adventures begins by describing Madeira and Tenerife, though the natural history of these islands remains quite unknown." He promptly set out to correct that defect, scaling the mountain and recording its rocks and flora, effectively field-testing the new sciences on its slopes. By celebrating Tenerife in his *Personal Narrative*, Humboldt fixed its image in the mind of his endless imitators. Then he went further. When he created an atlas by which to compare Earth's great mountains, he implanted Tenerife at the center, flanked by the Andes and Himalayas, establishing Teide as the standard by which to measure all the others. In 1831 Charles Darwin declared that he "would never rest easy until I see the peak of Teneriffe and the great Dragon Tree." When he had the chance for his own expedition, he regretted that the HMS *Beagle* sailed from Madeira, but as it passed by the Canaries, he glimpsed Teide and recited to himself "Humboldt's sublime descriptions." Then he went on to find new icons for the era at the Galapagos, another cluster of volcanic isles.[80]

When Humboldt subsequently climbed Mount Chimborazo in Ecuador, he recapitulated his ascent of Teide in more Romantic style, and through their comparison he began to formulate his grand synthesis of plant geography. Chimborazo shone as the site where Enlightenment met exploration, the summit of Second Age discovery. It replaced Ternate, the Spice Isles, as the vision quest of journeying. The image appealed powerfully to artists, now making their Grand Tours to classical Europe and discovering in Etna and Vesuvius points where ancient history met natural history. Would-be Humboldts relocated Chimborazo wherever they traveled, using it to assert claims of cultural significance. (Heinrich Möllhausen, for example, inserted a Chimborazo, complete with blowing snow on its summit, alongside the Colorado River in the Mohave Desert.) What the *padraõ* was for the First Age, Chimborazo equivalents were for the Second.

The Third Age, too, has its Möllhausens, keen to establish continuity and parity with previous exploration. A NASA-commissioned painting of a future astronaut exploring party on Mars, for example, featured a Chimborazo looming on the horizon, exactly in the place where it appears so consistently in nineteenth-century renditions. When Arthur C. Clarke imagined his Eden on Mars, in *The Snows of Olympus,* he set it on Olympus Mons, a real if dormant volcano, and the largest then known in the solar system. He thus combined the iconography of the Great Voyages with the mythology of the Ancients.

That was literature. The eruption of Prometheus on Io was fact. So were the volcanoes, hot vents, black smokers, and dormant seamounts that dappled Earth's deep oceans and became a defining discovery for the Third Age on Earth. What these features shared was less shape, or lofty panoramas, than geologic dynamism. When Voyager launched, the expectation was still rife that the satellites of the outer planets would resemble those of the inner planets. Like Earth's Moon and Mars's Deimos and Phobos, they would be inert masses, cosmographic fossils, left from the eon of planetary origins. Active volcanoes and geysers showed otherwise: they testified to a still-vigorous geology. The moons were not dead lumps, like geologic shards left from the creation and preserved in orbit like museum pieces. They warmed, they moved, they belched. They had their own distinctive histories. They spoke to our times, not just to the solar system's antiquity. The volcanoes of Io were for space science the Ternates and Teides by which to triangulate the exploration of the interplanetary seas and new worlds beyond.

VOYAGER 2

Now came Voyager 2 to confirm and amplify its twin's discoveries, and to demonstrate that it could perform agilely enough to warrant flinging itself not only to Saturn but also to Uranus. If the spacecraft had problems, it also, after Voyager 1's traverse, had acquired some opportunities.

The problems were that its polarimeter was broken, as its twin's had been, and more seriously, its primary radio receiver was still tone-deaf and balky and could not track an Earth-broadcast radio signal through its Doppler shift. The contact frequency drifted. The DSN found tricks to work around the stickiness, but when connections were good, flight control seized the moment and sent new commands and programs, and understood that communications might blink off at critical times.[81]

The opportunities were that its trajectory should help shield it from the kind of radiation damage experienced by Voyager 1. At periapsis it would be twice as distant from Jupiter, and if comparable damage did occur, a program was uploaded that would resynchronize clocks hourly and shrink the potential slurring of programs. Two months before closest approach, a new suite of commands adjusted Voyager 2's sequencing to target topics of supreme interest raised by Voyager 1's reconnaissance. Specifically, the spacecraft would maintain a ten-hour Io volcano watch, better measure the Jovian torus near Io, listen for whistlers, watch for lightning and auroras while on the planet's dark side, and photograph the Jovian ring, which it would cross twice. It would see the inner moons differently, and most of them much closer. Overall, it would reverse the sequence of Voyager 1's trek: it would begin with the moons and then cross the planet on its dark side. The new instructions were uploaded in early April.

On April 24, 1979, seventy-six days before periapsis, Voyager 2 officially entered its observation phase. From May 24 to 27 it took long-range photos of Jupiter, now experiencing a different season of weather. On July 2 Voyager first crossed bow shock. Far-encounter commenced on July 4, some 5.3 million kilometers from Jupiter and 921 million kilometers from Earth. As before, the Jovian magnetosphere was malleable, the result of solar winds and uneven eruptions on Io, and Voyager 2 passed in and out of the billowing cloud. By July 5 it had made eleven crossings and photographed Io so that researchers might see how many of the eight identified volcanoes were still erupting. The press, however, was more interested in a space story with stronger human interest, the imminent death plunge of Skylab. The two encounters—Voyager 2's at Jupiter, Skylab's at Earth—made a media counterpoint until the space junk fell into the Indian Ocean and onto Australia on July 11. On July 6, with ample media attention, Voyager continued its surveillance of Jupiter's weather and Io's vulcanism. The Red Spot alone now demanded a mosaic of six frames.[82]

Then came the main event. Voyager photographed the Jovian ring and Callisto on July 7. Voyager 2 saw that satellite far more closely and from the opposite side than had Voyager 1, so it seemed a relatively new discovery. A last set of commands went to the spacecraft to direct its imminent near-encounter. On July 8 the final sequence commenced: the ring again and Callisto up close; then, on July 9, Ganymede, Europa, and Amalthea, followed by Jupiter's dark side and a long farewell scrutiny of Io. Each sighting offered a closer and fresher perspective than with Voyager 1. At closest approach, 3:29 p.m. PDT, Voyager 2 came within 206,000 kilometers of Jupiter and sped around the giant at 73,000 kilometers per hour, more than ten times the muzzle velocity of a .38 special.

The views were again stunning, and startling. Callisto appeared to be the most densely cratered object known. Ganymede was a geomorphic breccia of craters, grooves, ejecta blankets, and fissures. Europa—"a sort of transition body" between the solid-silica Io and the icy Ganymede and Callisto—was perhaps the most bizarre, because for all its surface crinkling, it was as smooth as a billiard ball. Larry Soderblom noted how unlike these bodies were from the realm of the inner planets, and then listed the observed superlatives: "Included in the Jovian collection of satellites are the oldest (Callisto), the youngest (Io), the darkest (Amalthea), the whitest (Europa), the most active (Io), and the least active (Callisto). Today we found the flattest (Europa)." Voyager's sequel had matched its original. Even now adulation mingled combustibly with anticipation about what Voyager might achieve. NASA associate administrator for space science, Tim Mutch, championed Voyager as "a truly revolutionary journey of exploration" and exulted that, when "the history books are written," these times would be recognized as a "turning point."[83]

Yet much remained to do even at Jupiter, and Voyager 2 was at a critical turning point of its own, a long, complex trajectory correction, timed with periapsis, that would hurl the spacecraft to Saturn, always an anxious maneuver. The episode became yet more awkward after Jupiter's radiation, far more intense than anticipated, damaged the already troubled radio receiver. On the evening of July 9, radio contact ceased, and engineers scrambled to reconnect before the scheduled course correction. Happily, the intricate commands had been previously uploaded on July 6, when contact was clear and before bursts of radiation had upset the temperamental receiver. At closest encounter, Voyager's thruster rocket began a seventy-six-minute burn calculated to maximize the gravity-assist acceleration. The combined momentum would save ten kilograms of hydrazine, and with it, the capacity to tack and steer around Uranus. Meanwhile, the instrumental recording and imaging raged on. The dark-side observations chalked up marvel upon marvel, sighting the ring, auroras, lightning, and a revealing volcano watch on Io. The forward scatter that made the Jovian ring luminous, however, was nothing compared to the foreshadowing that made nearly every mind feverish with anticipation.

Both Voyagers were sprinting to Saturn. But even as it departed, Voyager 2 left a legacy akin to Voyager 1's iconic image of Io in eruption. Careful analysis revealed a new satellite, a body closer than Amalthea and apparently associated with the ring. It was named Adrastea. Jupiter acquired its fourteenth known moon, and Voyager had discovered another world.

Others would follow.[84]

ISLANDS

The idea of a New World was a late concept, first broached around 1511 by an Italian humanist in the service of Spain, Peter Martyr, and subsequently consolidated in his posthumous *De Orbe Novo* (1530). What Europe's *marinheiros* discovered in practice were islands. The equivalents in "this new ocean" of space were moons.

The Great Voyages between Old and New worlds was most typically a voyage between islands, or from archipelago to archipelago. Those isles were portal, way station, sanctuary, and fortress. Points of departure—Madeira, the Canaries—had their counterpart in off-shore islands from São Tome to Hispaniola or in seaports that had the properties of near-islands, such as Al Mina, Goa, Zanzibar, and Mombasa. The Indies, East and West, are a concourse of islands. Even in the seventeenth century, the Spanish monarchy proclaimed the

Canaries, located at a triple junction between Europe, Africa, and the Americas, as "the most important of my possessions, for they are the straight way and approach to the Indies."[85]

So, also, islands loomed large in the imagination of explorers, schemers, and cartographers. Fantasy islands, from Atlantis to the Island of the Seven Cities, dotted the Atlantic. Real islands swelled on maps to many times their actual size. Newly discovered isles became the incentive and model for colonization. If uninhabited, like Madeira, they pitted capitalist and colonist directly against the land. If inhabited, like the Canaries, they first required conquest to tame or remove the indigenes, or to smother them by immigration. Island-hopping was progressive as new islands often drafted populations from old; perhaps 80 percent of the Canaries' population was Portuguese, many following the sugar traffic from Madeira. Islands were potentially profitable estates, less onerous than seizing holdings from the Moors, and they offered ready-made fiefdoms by which to reward enterprising knights. (Sancho Panza mockingly begs Don Quixote to reward him with the governorship of an island.) Continents such as Africa and New Worlds such as the Americas were for the early explorers barriers, not beacons.[86]

In the Second Age, as sword and cross gave way to rifle and sextant, islands testified to experiments in natural history. As had Humboldt, exploring naturalists honed their skills on Atlantic isles before venturing farther abroad, and like their voyaging progenitors, they did their business on isles as destinations. It was from their journeys among volcanic islands—the Galapagos, for one; the Malay archipelago, for the other—that Charles Darwin and Alfred Wallace independently conceived of evolution by natural selection. Interestingly, Wallace developed his idea while fever-ridden on the Spice Islands themselves, a splendid symbol of how interest in islands persisted while their cultural configuration changed. Even the exploration of Antarctica proceeded mostly from islands (and it was from Ross Island that both Ernest Shackleton and Robert Scott made their separate attempts on the South Pole).

Not least, islands offered competing visions of environmental change. As naturalists spirited around the globe, they tallied the chaotic chronicle of species gained and lost, of lands gardened and gutted, of visions still bright or hopelessly blackened. Islands returned as environmental indices: they represented semi-controlled experiments in the interplay between humanity and nature, with the circulation of species as the measure of nature's economy. For every relatively untouched isle such as Mauritius, exploring naturalists identified a St. Helena degraded into biotic dust; for every successfully colonized isle, there was one plunged into ecological chaos; for every Madeira there was a Hispaniola. A summary of an era's exploring naturalists, Alfred Wallace's *Island Life,* was a virtual compendium of colonizing ecology, documenting the often lethal competition between endemic and exotic species.

The Third Age found its isles on the continents in the guise of nature preserves (Robert MacArthur and E. O. Wilson's *The Theory of Island Biogeography* replacing Wallace), in the deep oceans in the form of seamounts and hot vents, and in space through the solar system's dizzyingly diverse satellites. Even as they were disclosed, the seamounts—lush with deep coral, hosting fisheries like diminutive Grand Banks—were being denuded by trawlers. So in the Third Age, as before, there seems to be a precarious balance between discovery and destruction, as stripped seamounts compete with momentarily spared black smokers.

And space? The giant planets resemble the barrier continents of the Great Voyages. They might be coasted or their gaseous bulks occasionally visited by a probe or two, but the real work of mapping hard surfaces and sending robotic explorers (or perhaps humans) would happen on their moons. As with islands, there were a lot of them, and they were different, enough to warrant comparative study. They formed parts of what could readily seem miniatures, talismans, and relics of the solar system. The exploration of the solar system would be primarily an exploration of moons.

For the Ages of Discovery, islands have been symbols as well as sites. They were places for imagination as much as for away teams and probes.

It was onto islands that Europe's intellectuals projected their social fantasies. From the monastic-styled Utopia of Thomas More to the bustling laboratories of Francis Bacon's New Atlantis, from the Brave New World of Shakespeare's *Tempest* to the tropical Edens portrayed by Pierre Poivre, the yet-undiscovered island was a cameo of cultural ideals. Echoing Homer, who had Odysseus narrate his tale from the isle of Scherie, Camões opens *The Lusíads* at Mozambique; but narration in medias res commanded less power than the prospect of new lands—new societies, new hopes—that could be lodged only on recently discovered or yet-unvisited islands. Columbus spoke for all such visionaries when he rhapsodized over Hispaniola—and for all scorners, when he failed to implant a society equal to that dream.[87]

By the early eighteenth century the sheen had tarnished. Daniel Defoe maroons the vagabond Robinson Crusoe on a wretched desert isle in the Caribbean; Jonathan Swift casts his voyaging cipher, Lemuel Gulliver, onto one isle after another, ending with the fantastic vision of an island metropole, Laputa, suspended in the clouds, the creation of visionary "projectors." The bright prospect of new Madeiras and Tenerifes ended with the horrors of Hispaniola and the wreckage of the Antilles; the Arcadian gardens imagined beyond the horizon collapsed into the scalped forests, goat-plagued hills, and gullied slopes that washed over the boles of felled dragon trees and the bones of extinct dodos. Instead of wistful new Gran Canarias, there were grim St. Helenas, and in place of another hypothetical Ile de France, there was Red Madagascar, destined to become a symbol of habitat degradation, ever burning and bleeding its soils into the sea. In the New World the Black Legend acquired an ecological edge. The shimmering mirage of Columbus met the bleak reality of Las Casas. Exploring utopias ended as environmental dystopias.[88]

Yet still they beckoned. And since better worlds had to be somewhere else, exploration repeatedly opened up prospects for uninhabited lands—new frontiers that might avoid the mistakes of the past. The modern founder of the genre, Thomas More, published *Utopia* in 1516. As a Platonic ideal, an updated *Republic*, Utopia did not have to be any place; but the rapid discovery of unknown lands made its literary location as a New World isle plausible, along with the use of a weather-beaten Portuguese, Raphael Nonsenso, as a protagonist and prototype for the Ancient Mariners and Old Men who would hound and hector the enterprise.[89]

The Second Age found it harder to place its utopias: there were few terrestrial locales yet unvisited. For a while Tahiti served as a tropical Teide, the first and most enduring of the Enlightenment's new Edens. Jules Verne stationed Captain Nemo on Deception Island near Antarctica, and James Hilton sited Shangri-La in the remote mountains of Tibet, but most visionaries had to turn to the past or the future. They invented modern versions of lost golden ages and former Edens, or they projected, along evolutionary trajectories, perhaps outfitted with steam power, a more perfect future. Instead of places, they turned to peoples, remote tribes as relics of a primitive virtue or exotic folk such as the Polynesians of apparent plenty and ease. Then the Third Age in space suddenly made possible a revival of place-sited utopias.

For space seers there were three possibilities. One of course was Mars, seeming to stand to Earth as the New World did to the Old, awaiting only a more benevolent terraforming. How Mars might avoid the irony of past colonization and not sink into a planetary Haiti was unclear: it would simply happen. Proponents proclaimed, in a more secular declamation to those which Franciscan missionaries had made five hundred years earlier, that scientific knowledge was great enough to guide the technology to righteous ends.

A second possibility was more Platonic, to establish a space station among the Lagrange points, specifically at L-5, at which the gravitational attraction of Earth and Moon are equal, and which would thus suspend the colony in perfect weightlessness. Here was an invented, high-tech island free from the weight of the past—a solipsistic society, though one founded on ideals and first principles. If More's ideal was a kind of monastery, Gerard O'Neill's L-5 colony Dyson sphere is a kind of space suburb absolved of the past injustices and unmarred by the pull of Earthly vices. To advocates it occupies itself a kind of historical Lagrange point: it can neither evolve nor decay. To critics it might seem like a burnished version of Laputa. Neither utopia is likely to happen.[90]

Instead, exploration will probe the third alternative, the new isles of the solar system, the moons, now revealed as diverse, fascinating, and abundant. For visionaries these places come, as they had for the Great Voyages, with a window of opportunity between discovery and full-bodied exploration. The first ignites imagination, while the second tends to extinguish those utopian flames. The places' real value lies with a more worldly if still idealistic pursuit. Here are new worlds that, if closed to prospective colonists, still hold interest for science. Here are the experiments in natural history, equivalent to those scrutinized by Wallace, Darwin, and Joseph Hooker, that might reveal fundamental truths about the origin of Earth, life, and perhaps human purpose. Here are the promises less of a New Jerusalem than of a New Galapagos. Here are the Spice Isles of an exploring science: a new Madeira among the moons of Jupiter, a new Antilles in orbit about Saturn, a new Ternate at Io.

In brief, while the moons of the outer planets could never evoke the sensuousness of the earthly tropics, nor spark an equivalent lushness of imagination, they were the best the solar system had, and a few possessed the organic molecules that might be the by-product or forerunner for life. The Third Age's answer to the tropical Edens that so enchanted intellectuals in earlier times, enticing them to imagine other worlds, would be satellites that beat to geologic rhythms different from plate tectonics or were rich with organic molecules like methane. The new Tahiti would be a place like Saturn's Titan.

TO THE SIRENS OF TITAN

That is where the Voyagers now trekked.

By now, Pioneer 11, having doubled Jupiter and sprinted across the solar system, was a scant four months away from its rendezvous with Saturn on September 1, 1979. Once there, it found a new ring and even a new moon (indirectly, through magnetic disturbances), and most of all it blazed a route outside that great reef of rings that would preserve the option for Voyager 2 to continue the Grand Tour.

Meanwhile, the colossal Jovian gravitational field that had quickened the Voyagers' velocity during their planetary fling now pulled them back; but they had still gained more than they lost. Even as they slowed, they sped along some twenty-five thousand kilometers per hour faster than before they began encounter, with Voyager 1 pulling still farther ahead. For Voyager 2 its long course correction put it at a velocity and trajectory that would save precious hydrazine for its maneuvering thrusters. The Voyagers reentered cruise phase. They would continue this way for twenty and twenty-five months, respectively, chatting with Earth, sampling the solar wind and cosmic rays, reorienting themselves by the Sun and stars.

On they sailed to Saturn, across a void over 648 million kilometers wide, like two gnats crossing the Pacific.

13. Cruise

The spacecraft now had the velocities they needed to complete their mission. Voyager 1 had entered its Jovian observation phase at 48,960 kph; it exited at 86,000 kph. Voyager 2 had begun encounter at 38,016 kph and ended at 75,600 kph. Liftoff had granted escape from Earth. Their swing around Jupiter granted them escape from the Sun. They had sufficient inertia to carry them from giant planet to giant planet.

The program, too, had a quickened purpose. The spacecraft had worked. They remained sentient. They had completed what the pilots of the First Age had termed a *gran volta*.

PORTALS AND PASSAGES

Past exploration had launched with muscle, wind, current, and tide. An exploring party might begin with nothing more than a long stride, a horse's gait, a floating coracle, or an unfurled sail. Long voyages required cracking the codes of wind and current—understanding their constancies, their seasonal variations, their propensity for storms. Discovery unfolded as those motive forces permitted and as mariners learned to harness them to their own ends.

For the North Atlantic, this meant deciphering the southwesterly trade winds, the seasonal paths of storms, and the Gulf Stream. The process began with coasting down Africa and some ventures into the Atlantic that discovered Madeira and the Azores. It proved difficult (and dangerous) to sail up and down Africa, however, and as the magnitude of the continent became slowly apparent it was obvious that while long coasting could serve cautious probes, it could never support the high-volume far voyaging demanded for trade with the Indies.

The solution was what the Portuguese called a *volta do mar largo*. This required a journey westward until, after reaching the far isles, one could turn into the westerlies and then ride them back to Madeira or the Azores. The *volta* involved a great arc by which one sailed out and then back. Over time, this pattern was enlarged until it could cross the North Atlantic altogether. In this emerging geography of wind and water, the Canary and Cape Verde islands were ideally situated to ride the southwestern trade winds to the New World, and Madeira and the Azores well sited to capture them on return. The short *volta* between near-seas became a long one over the Ocean Sea.

Crossing the equator unsettled that lore. The doldrums were a nasty mix of thunderstorms and calms. The inherited learning of the Ancients had nothing to contribute, the winds below were reversed, and even the North Star vanished. One could not travel to India coastal port by coastal port, as one could sail across the Mediterranean. Bartolomeu Dias could inch down Africa before being blown by storms southwesterly and returning around the Cape; a successor would have to find another strategy. Perhaps outfitted with some intuition that the world had to be symmetrical, that what happened in the north should, in reverse, happen in the south, probably aided with a dose of accident and happenstance, Vasco da Gama, once past the Cape Verdes and Sierra Leone, rode the trades out to sea and then turned south to capture the austral westerlies. Those powerful gales hurled him back to Africa, just above the Cape of Good Hope, which took another week to round. When Pedro Cabral did the same with the next Indies fleet, he veered still farther west and ran into Brazil; but he also rode the winds farther south and rounded—or "doubled"— the Cape. The great turn, pivoting with the winds, made the passage to India possible by flinging fleets around the gravitational mass of the Cape and into the Indian Ocean, where they would ride the monsoons to India.[91]

That was half the problem: tracing the patterns that characterized each discovered sea. But to truly sail the world ocean required discovering the links by which to get from one decoded sea to another. The brachiated peninsulas and islands that constituted Europe defined interior seas between which straits allowed passage. The Mediterranean was, for mariners, a collection of smaller seas— the Tyrrhenian, the Adriatic, the Aegean, the Ionian, the Ligurian— broader seas east and west, and innumerable gulfs. The composite had one eastern strait, the Bosporus, that joined it to the Black Sea, and one to the west, Gibraltar, that connected it to the Ocean Sea. A similar logic applied to the north, with its own complex quilt of seas, gulfs, and straits. That experience, like the creation of the volta, expanded across the earth.

The quest for the Indies that underwrote the Great Voyages was a search for passages across seas and a search for those straits that would permit passage from one sea to another. The barrier that was Africa required a southern passage; the barrier that was Eurasia, a northeast passage; the barrier that was the *novo mundo*, a strait somewhere—at its narrow middle at Panama, through its icy northwest, and ultimately around its southern extremities, the Strait at Magellan and the Drake Passage. The chronicle of discovery arranges itself around those pursuits like iron filings around the poles of a magnet.

Continental exploration obeyed a different logic, though it still began with the obligatory seaport that linked to the metropole. Beyond the coast, however, exploration depended on unlocking the geography of rivers and interior lakes.

Those lands that had rivers capable of ready access were discovered quickly; those that did not, lagged. Its enormous rivers, though they drained to the frozen Arctic, allowed Russians to cross Eurasia with breathtaking speed, by hopping from one tributary to another, like a squirrel jumping between branches. Timofeyevich Yermak crossed the Urals in 1581, roughly twenty-five years before Jamestown was founded in Virginia; by 1632, Cossacks founded Yakutsk, two years after émigré Puritans founded Boston; by 1649, Yerofey Khabarov had sailed down the Amur and established Khabarovsk, some fifteen years before the Dutch established New Amsterdam. The drainage of the Mississippi River opened up the interior of North America like a split log, and despite its snags, seasonal flows, and shallows, exploring parties habitually made the Missouri River the entry to the Rockies.

Lands that lacked access, particularly by galliot (or later, steam-boat), stalled or redirected exploration. The St. Lawrence River proved little more than an extension of its gulf, stymied by rapids and Niagara Falls, so that travel portaged to the Ottawa River in order to cross to the Great Lakes. So it was also with the Rio de la Plata, which proved a similar dead end. The one major river in Australia, the Murray, was unusable as a point of entry to the interior, causing expeditions to stagger across stony desert and sandy spinifex by foot or camel. The most curious case was Africa, which was both the first and last of the continents penetrated by Europeans. The reasons for its lag were sev-eral, not least its horrific diseases; but the absence of usable streams north and south, the endless cataracts on its major rivers, and the confusing contortions and delta of the Niger all prevented serious exploration. The world's largest river by volume, the Congo, and its longest, the Nile, were the last in each category to be navigated.

The hope for simple ways through those great landmasses sur-rendered to a search for a means across them. Commercial rivers and navigable lakes were replaced by cross sections of natural history; and the hope of finding Great Khans, Prester Johns, and the bullion of new Mexicos, by inventories of natural wealth and nature's wonders. As steam power overcame the motive geography of wind and cur-rents, so railroads replaced rivers as means of transit. By 1869 the last unknown river and mountain range in the continental United States were discovered, though not fully explored, curiously the same year as the completion of the transcontinental railroad. Within another decade cross-continental surveys had traversed Australia and Africa.

For the solar system, a still different logic governed travel, for this was a journeying geography defined by gravity. It had its equivalent to seas and straits, an imprinted dynamic of forces that one could sail with or against. The solar system had its doldrums and trade winds and, in Lagrange points, its Sargasso Seas that suspended dust and asteroids. Exploration could advance only if it found a way to harness those forces to its own ambitions, to ride over gravity's waves. For that it required a new *gran volta*.

The exploration of space could begin only by overcoming Earth's gravitational field, and it could proceed in a timely way only by navigating the gravitational fields of the outer planets. In the 1920s Walter Hohmann worked out for each planet the lowest energy speed to achieve that goal, which is to say, the trajectory that would require the least departure velocity from Earth, what became known as Hohmann transfer ellipses. For the outer planets the time required to travel would run thirty years to Neptune and fifty to Pluto. No spacecraft could survive that long, no scientist could sustain a career across so many decades without results, and no institutional program could expect to thrive over such a duration. Planetary exploration seemed doomed either to sail among the inner planets or to devise some additional propulsion beyond what an Earth-launched rocket could provide.[92]

The initial thrust, then, was to concentrate on hardware—bigger rockets were an annual event. It might be possible to strap on a snazzy new propulsion system that, once beyond Earth's gravitational field, could accelerate the spacecraft to velocities that made interplanetary flight feasible. But it was also possible that better trajectories might simplify and shorten the requirements. In the early years, when getting a payload into Earth orbit, much less to the Moon or to Venus, stretched their liftoff capabilities, engineers were eager to try anything. The best one might hope for in sustained travel was a flyby mission to Jupiter.

VOYAGER'S THREE-BODY PROBLEM

In June 1961 JPL hired a UCLA math and physics graduate student, Michael Minovitch, as a summer intern to work on some tricky calculations involving trajectories to and around planets. The work absorbed, then obsessed the twenty-six-year-old, who continued to labor over it for the next two years, not only during summers but while at school on borrowed big-computer time at both UCLA and JPL. What emerged from his analysis was the realization that as a spacecraft swung past a planet, its velocity could undergo a permanent change. Specifically, moving in the same direction as the planet could add the thrust that bigger rockets or exotic propulsion systems could not, and thus make planetary exploration accessible with existing technologies.[93]

Minovitch quickly recognized the issue as a variant of the classic three-body problem in that it involved two large objects and one small one in mutual gravitational attraction—in this case, the spacecraft, the target planet, and the Sun. A solution had bedeviled Newtonian physics since its origins; it was to celestial mechanics what Fermat's Last Theorem was to number theory. No exact solution was possible, but with the advent of computers it was feasible to generate hundreds of approximations, each of them a possible trajectory for interplanetary travel. Enthralled, Minovitch, who termed his insight "gravity propulsion," learned FORTRAN to better run endless calculations and tried to work out as many solutions as possible, defaulting to his training as a mathematician to fashion a universal set of curves. He soon appreciated the seminal status of Jupiter by virtue of both its immense mass and its sentinel location between the inner and outer planets. At summer's end he wrote up his results in a JPL technical report.[94]

The initial reaction to his study was mixed. The mathematics was formidable, and the physics, in some respects counterintuitive, since it required a shift in reference frames from Earth to the Sun. Viewed from Earth, what a planet gave by gravity to an incoming spacecraft it then took away as the spacecraft departed; but viewed from the Sun, there was a gain or loss depending on the directions in which the spacecraft came and went. With a monster planet such as Jupiter, the momentum added could be significant for the spacecraft, though infinitesimal relative to the mass of Jupiter. For Voyager 2 the impulse acquired was 35,700 kilometers per hour. For Jupiter the impulse shed was a foot of orbital velocity per trillion years.[95]

The other, more serious problem was personal. As fascination deepened into obsession, Minovitch became more secretive, speaking only to friends and his late-night IBM 7090 computers, avoiding the give-and-take of shared ideas at the lab, more and more resembling a hermetic inventor worried with equal passion that his idea might be ignored and that it might be stolen. JPL had hired him to do work to fit into existing projects, and his supervisor, with whom he did not get along, believed that his independent inquiry, subject only to his own curiosity, interfered with his project assignments, which Minovitch admitted "it did." Moreover, what Minovitch believed revolutionary the trajectory group considered evolutionary, one of many ideas about how to get spacecraft to farther planets. Other researchers (not all with JPL) were experimenting with trajectories along similar lines. The group did not immediately reconstruct its planning around what they came to call "gravity assist."[96]

The technical objections were quickly overcome, and the concept of "Free-Fall Trajectories" took its place amid the assorted inquiries of the group. In 1963, after two more summers of labor, Minovitch was encouraged to write up a summary technical report. A new, more supportive supervisor, Joe Cutting, urged him to publish his results in the *AIAA Journal*. "I hope you will be able to devote enough time to finish it up," Cutting wrote, "so it can be submitted soon before anybody else comes up with something similar." You can't patent or copyright an idea, only its expression. Still, Minovitch didn't publish.[97]

Meanwhile, Cutting decided to push the idea and see if it could apply to a real mission, not to computer-generated curves such as conic sections. He and Francis Sturms plotted a flight to Mercury— an entire profile, with real numbers and actual dates—that relied on a gravity assist from Venus. What it required, and what Minovitch had not reckoned with, was precision navigation and launch dates; others supplied them. Mariner 10 demonstrated the concept's practicality by whipping around Earth, Venus, and Mercury in 1973. Pioneer 11 then confirmed the concept at Jupiter. Well before then, however, gravity assist had become fundamental to the design of the Grand Tour. Gravity assist was both real and essential. Those who conceived it and coded it into a mission moved on to other projects and, in Minovitch's case, other institutions.[98]

Yet, even as the concept passed test after test, Minovitch brooded over what he regarded as a lack of suitable recognition compounded with imagined slights by JPL. He saw his research as a work of individual genius, unprecedented and unique. It was not enough that the trajectory group had included him on its roster, that his technical reports had entered bibliographies of subsequent studies, or that NASA had awarded him an Exceptional Service Award in 1972. He believed he had done something monumental, and indispensable, and in his estimation planetary exploration such as the Grand Tour could not have happened without him.

So when Victor Clarke, his first supervisor, applied for a joint monetary award for the trajectory group's success with gravity assist, Minovitch sensed conspiracy, an attempt by undeserving others to claim what he autonomously had done. And when a historian, Norriss Hetherington, began research for a scholarly paper on the origins of the concept by interviewing members of the group, Minovitch threatened JPL with lawsuits, ended Hetherington's study, and began a campaign to have the concept, and hence the entire planetary program since Mariner 10, follow from his lone and unfairly ignored "invention." He found collaborators in his quest; JPL invited him to return for the Neptune encounter; and he has written up his versions in several papers for the International Astronautical Federation and constructed an elaborate Web site to promote his case in the belief that, as he put it in the third person, "there may be a small group at JPL that may attempt to claim the credit for his invention after he dies."[99]

Who discovered gravity assist as a means of propulsion for planetary exploration? How the issue might be answered depends on how the question is asked. Minovitch defined his achievement in terms of a classic theme in celestial mechanics, the restricted three-body problem, and his achievement he regarded as most significant for its mathematical techniques, especially his vector equations, which when combined with the number-crunching power of computers yielded the "first numerical solution." But gravity assist was, for him, also something more. It was an "invention," like John Harrison's chronometer or James Watt's governor, that made possible a "new philosophy of space propulsion."[100]

Others saw it all differently. The personality that made Minovitch's solitary labors possible also isolated them. Upon investigation there were many antecedents for the idea of gravity perturbations; and it was almost inevitable that the idea would gain currency, if not by mathematical analysis, then by empirical observation as spacecraft ventured to nearby planets and navigational groups recorded unanticipated changes in velocity. Minovitch's claim to absolute priority stems from his sense that no one else, certainly no one at JPL, was prepared to tackle a general solution to the restricted three-body problem; and because he saw it as a mathematical topic for which only numerical estimates were possible, he had to amass all possible trajectories, with the curve of his calculations asymptotically approaching something like a proof.

But what Minovitch saw as an intellectual puzzle, the JPL trajectory group, all engineers, saw as meaningful only within the context of a mission, and its solution would not come from endless hypothetical trajectories but from scenarios in which a spacecraft had real dates, real weight, and real escape velocities, and mission control had the capacity actually to navigate around planets with the accuracy that could ensure success. In their estimation, instead of elevating the concept, his complex mathematics and endless iterations had tended to depress its pragmatic value, and other trajectory group members, who regarded those solutions as "not truly adequate," devised simpler methods, including old-fashioned manual techniques with "tabulations and graphs." JPL was not an academy of science but a laboratory for reconciling science, engineering, and politics. Gravity assist was for them not an invention but a fact awaiting discovery and then, more important, demanding confirmation, development, and expression in a traveling spacecraft.[101]

What should have shone with the brilliance of its participants has threatened to sink into mires of petty egotism. The episode reminds us that history, too, has its three-body problems. They arise with particular vehemence when someone claims priority and someone else disputes it and when third parties only perturb their interplay, and such dynamics work with special vehemence when one body is smaller than the others. In such contests there is no formal solution, only working approximations. The transfer of gravity assist from mathematical concept to working mission was one such approximation. But, then, so was Voyager.

FIRST DISCOVERY

Disputes over priority—credit for first discovery—are a constant of science, no less than for exploration, and when the two combine, the issue can be both futile and fathomless. There is no scene more common in both enterprises than a quarrel over priority, and perhaps none more unseemly or dismaying.

Both science and exploration thrive on competition. A collectively identified problem approached with shared understanding and techniques—the co-discovery of places, species, ideas, and techniques is so common as to be the norm. Without competition, the drive to discover weakens; but with it comes the spectacle of rivals converging, and then arguing endlessly over who really got there first. Both Isaac Newton and Gottfried Leibniz invented calculus, independently and more or less simultaneously. Alfred Wallace wrote a dilatory Charles Darwin, then still tinkering as he had for a decade with his ideas, and presented a fully realized articulation of evolution by natural selection. There are precious few scientific discoveries that have not come amid multiple contestants or that would not have been announced, with a slightly different accent, by another.[102]

So, too, has it been with geographic exploration. The norm is for rivals to converge, and then for explorers and their partisans to argue endlessly and with scholastic tenacity over who deserves priority. Did Portuguese (or Biscayan) cod fishermen rather than Columbus first discover the New World? And even among his small flotilla, did Columbus deserve credit for the initial sighting? On the evening of October 11, 1492, shortly before moonrise, both he and a seaman on the *Santa Maria* thought they spied a distant light, "like a little wax candle rising and falling," and others thought they did, too, or might have, before it vanished. At 2:00 p.m. on October 12, Rodrigo de Triana, aloft on the Pinta, cried out, "*Tierra! Tierra!*" Captain Pinzón confirmed the sighting, and signaled to the flagship, where Columbus agreed. Who, then, discovered the Americas? Those who saw a flickering light? The sailor who happened to be manning the *Pinta*'s lookout? The captain general of the fleet? Those who sponsored the expedition? Besides, all of these quarrelsome concerns only pertain to those who came from afar, not to those for whom the New World was an ancient homeland.[103]

Who discovered the Great Salt Lake? Fur trappers were all around the region in the mid-1820s. Etienne Provost almost certainly saw a part of it from the Wasatch Mountains in 1824. Some months afterward, to settle a bet, Jim Bridger followed the Bear River to where it entered the lake, tasted the waters, and reported as his discovery that he had found an "arm of the Pacific Ocean." Or did David Jackson, who reportedly explored the western shores in 1828–29? Or a party of fur trappers who spent twenty-four days in a bullboat on the lake, never finding the mythical outlet to the sea, the river Buenaventura? Or did discovery lie with the first published map of the enclosed sea by Capt. Howard Stansbury of the Army Corps of Topographical Engineers, after traipsing around the lake in 1849–50?[104]

Who truly reached the North Pole first? Did Robert Peary really stand at the Pole, or should his ambiguous assertion at the time, "I suppose we cannot say we are not at the pole," be taken as an admittance of failure? Did Frederick Cook beat out Peary at the last secretive moment, or commit another obvious fraud as with his earlier claim to have climbed Mount McKinley? These are sparse facts, bitter resentments, and strong personalities. Certainly Robert Peary's character inspired more critics than it did supporters. Moreover, there are institutional claims and jealousies, demands for recognition among this patron or that, this nation rather than another, and questions about whether the person or the sponsor merits special honor.

If not Peary, then who? Richard Byrd? Did he really pilot a Ford Trimotor to the pole, or turn back short? One can sympathize with those who prefer to leave the honor of first discovery to the

USS *Nautilus* and *Skate*, nuclear-powered submarines that surfaced through the polar pack during IGY. If so, then who can claim priority? The captains? The ships and crews? The U.S. Navy? To those engaged, nothing seems more vital than clearly establishing the pedigree of priorities, and to those less committed, nothing seems so pointless.

Voyager's quarrels, such as they were, lay in the realm of scientific rather than geographical discovery. Voyager was a corporate enterprise, an exercise in big science. The mission had in place explicit guidelines by which to determine if a new moon or ring was found, and methods by which to corroborate claims. Who, for example, discovered the volcanoes on Io? The first specialist to realize that an anomaly existed? Or the second, who was already moving toward independent discovery? Or the person who appreciated the anomaly for what it was? That no such quarrel bubbled up in public speaks to Voyager's sense of itself as a collective project.

Where it most differs from predecessors has to do with the peculiar character of Third Age terrains. No one lived on Adrastea, Cressida, or Proteus, so there was no tradition to guide visiting explorers, nor old accounts to translate into a new vernacular. There were no competing discoverers with rival claims or standards of substantiation. The procedures were in place, and followed. Some disputes were inevitable: they are intrinsic to discovery of any kind, and especially to the practice of modern science with which exploration had bonded.

Except for gravity assistance. It was easy, particularly in retrospect, to identify intellectual predecessors for the concept; Michael Minovitch crystallized one of them in elegant form. But the concept could enter into Voyager only by being engineered. It had to be tested against potential trajectories, had to fuse with guidance and communication systems, had to reconcile spacecraft with rockets, had to merge politics with ambition and idea. The recognition of gravity assistance did not make Voyager: by itself it went nowhere. It no more created spacecraft than the enunciation of the second law of thermodynamics created steam engines. The idea had to become a working machine. It had to be embedded in a mission. To those personally removed from it, the quarrel might seem like arguing over who invented the lateen sail that made the caravel possible, or who first identified the prospects for the *gran volta*.

Gravity assist was one of dozens of ideas—inventions, if you will—that made Voyager possible. Who invented Voyager? Who invented the Grand Tour? Without the discovery of gravity-assist propulsion, it could not have happened. But neither could it have happened without the Deep Space Network, high-speed digital computers to project trajectories, onboard computers to monitor and reset programs, and elaborate instruments and imaging; or without those complex groups, so often tedious to ambitious souls, that did the collective task of adapting, fitting, and testing to ensure that spacecraft could actually perform over long missions; or without support from NASA and OMB; or without the cold war to pry open tax dollars to compete with the Soviet Union among the planets.

Among their payloads each Voyager carried six small aluminum plates on which were engraved the signatures of all the persons who could claim to have contributed to their trek. The roster ran to nearly 5,400 names. What, or who, was Voyager, and who invented it? Many people, and no one.

ACROSS THE VOID

Having made their *gran volta*, the Voyagers commenced a long, lonely trek to Saturn. Even with a roughly 40,000-kilometer-per-hour boost in velocity, Voyager 1 needed another twenty months, and Voyager 2 another thirty, before they reached their near-encounters with what members of the space community were coming to call the Lord of the Rings. Meanwhile, the shuttle had throttled the U.S. planetary program into silence. Pioneer Venus, designed to do at Venus what Pioneers 10 and 11 had done at Jupiter and Saturn, launched in May 1978. Then nothing. The shuttle took it all. The Grand Tour was the only tour.

The Voyagers flew alone.

14. Encounter: Saturn

To the Ancients it was known as the Great Conjunction, that moment, roughly every twenty years, when the varying speeds of Jupiter and Saturn cause them to appear to unite momentarily in the night sky.

As Voyager 1 closed on Saturn, a Great Conjunction was under way, with those two giant planets joined by Venus and the star Regulus to create a brilliant predawn constellation. Such alignments had happened forever, interpreted as portents of fortune and fate. But this time the cluster included a new celestial body and it joined humanity to the planets not through astrological magic but by aeronautical engineering in that predawn of solar system exploration. A Great Conjunction now marked Voyager's encounter with Saturn.[105]

VOYAGER 1

Well before that moment, as early as January 1980, Voyager 1 began recording radio bursts emanating from Saturn on a roughly ten-hour cycle. These coincided with the rudely known rotation period for the planet; the refined transmissions allowed for a sharper determination of the precise numbers. But the anticipated spectacle was the spin not of the gaseous planet but of its rings, which had mesmerized viewers from Galileo onward. Where Jupiter stunned and dazzled with its Technicolor weather, Saturn did so with its gorgeous rings.

The observation phase commenced in October 1980. As Voyager 1 barreled toward the planet at 1.3 million kilometers per day, something like weather appeared, with lighter and darker blotches on the generally opaque surface of Saturn, and the rings revealed definitions and structures previously unviewed, a drama heightened by time-lapse movies akin to those made for Jupiter's Red Spot. Voyager photographed two inner satellites, first identified in 1966 but with properties otherwise unknown. By October 24 the spacecraft had halved its distance to Saturn, enhanced imaging beyond its narrow-angle camera, and brought its other instruments to bear, particularly its ultraviolet and infrared spectrometers. Voyager 1 officially entered its far-encounter phase.[106]

The rings betrayed not only more and more detail—grooved like a phonograph record—but also inexplicable dark "spokes" that spun among the rings. The phenomenon quickly became an object of special imaging. Analysis on October 25 and 26 led to the discovery of two satellites along the F Ring. Day by day, the resolution sharpened. Saturn displayed yellowish bands and turbulence among its cloud cover; its rings multiplied into hundreds, then thousands; its now-fourteen satellites acquired substance, rendering Saturn, like Jupiter, into a miniature solar system. Among the rings the Cassini Division revealed internal divisions. Computer enhancement and false-color imaging broke down the blurry haze of surface cloud to display a score of weather belts in the southern hemisphere alone. Titan acquired some definition and loomed as what it was: the second largest moon in the solar system. Daily, Voyager imaged the rings in a grand mosaic; every six hours it directed its full battery of instruments toward Titan, while otherwise it searched for unknown satellites and swept the scene with its spectrometers.[107]

On the evening of November 6, Voyager 1 underwent a final course correction—its ninth. The maneuver was doubly complicated because the Canopus star tracker had earlier malfunctioned, but controllers were confident that onboard redundancies would compensate. The spacecraft tilted 90 degrees, fired its rockets for 11.75 minutes, and took almost four hours before recovering sufficiently to transfer control to its gyroscopes back to celestial tracking. With its new trajectory it could speed past Titan, dip below the southern pole of Saturn, and then rise back up through the ecliptic of not only Saturn but also the Sun, and race away to the edge of the solar system. For the most part, Voyager 1 also determined Voyager 2's passage; but for now its remote, trailing twin assisted its sibling by measuring the strength of the approaching solar winds (which were high), thus allowing for better forecasts of when Voyager 1 might encounter bow shock, the turbulent, filmy border between the solar wind and the Saturnian magnetosphere. Meanwhile, the plucky spacecraft took a snapshot of Iapetus.[108]

What mattered was less the Sun's weather than Earth's. Thunderstorms pummeled Madrid and blocked out transmissions to its DSN tracking station for some six hours. Not until the Goldstone station, in California's Mojave Desert, acquired a signal could data return. When it did, Voyager revealed another new moon—the third it had discovered at Saturn—and yielded more information about the rings, Titan's atmosphere, and Saturn's magnetosphere. On November 9, sharpened images only heightened the mysteries of the rings and their spokes and of the anomalous absence of upstream bursts of electrons such as happened at Jupiter. But photos of Rhea promised another gallery of new satellite worlds. And of course there was Titan, as large as Mercury. On the eve of near-encounter, the panel of planetary wise men reassembled once more, as they had for Mars and Jupiter, to discuss "Saturn and the Mind of Man."[109]

On November 10, the air was electric with expectation. Voyager 1 would pass through Saturn's bow shock and fly past Titan, but veteran scientists and journalists readied to undergo their own bow shock of novelties. In what had become a mantra, researchers repeated that "Everything we are seeing on Saturn is brand new." That, in truth, is exactly what the partisans of Pioneer 11 had proclaimed, and both were right. Voyager saw more and saw more clearly, and it encountered a differently tilted Saturn, so that even when it revisited themes, it found them altered or it reexperienced them as though for the first time. Moreover, what Voyager had found at Jupiter did not, uninterpreted, translate to Saturn. The two planets, or planetary mini-systems, more resembled each other than they did Venus and Mars, yet they differed no less than did the inner planets. The discoveries were as fresh as the Bahamas in October 1492, or Antarctica in January 1840. The images scrolled past: Tethys, Dione, Rhea; the befuddling and mesmerizing rings; the muted weather of Saturn. Still maneuvering, Voyager acquired a new guide star while its far-encounter rapidly closed.[110]

The measurements, the images, the outburst of data—all rushed forward on the eleventh with the quickening pace of the spacecraft. For Voyager 1 there were in reality several near-encounters. The first was with Titan, some eighteen hours prior to its near-encounter with Saturn proper. As it whooshed toward Titan, the giant, enigmatic moon overflooded Voyager's narrow-angle camera, demanded three-by-three mosaics, and absorbed almost all the spacecraft's scans. Yet Titan refused to part its lofty haze; its surface remained opaque, and Voyager was forced to rely on indirect instrumentation, especially a double occultation, once as it passed behind Titan, and again after it passed out the other side. With that telemetry came the calculation that trajectory deviated from the programmed schedule: the distance, two hundred kilometers, mattered less than the timing, some forty-three seconds. (Engineers scrambled to recalibrate the sequencing before closest encounter.) Even as it swept beyond Titan, Voyager glided through the Saturnian ring plane and approached periapsis from beneath and on the dark side of the planet.[111]

On November 12 the countdown to closest encounter began with photographs of Tethys, the dark side of the rings, then Mimas and Enceladus, and the co-orbital satellites, S-10 and S-11, that Pioneer hinted at but never saw, followed by an occultation of Saturn and passage to its dark side, an encounter with Dione (which it was hoped would sweep the region clear of ring debris), followed by an exit occultation and reemergence from Saturn. Telemetry twice zipped through the atmosphere of Saturn and, ninety minutes later, danced dangerously with thunderstorms at the Madrid DSN station; but the signal came through. Still within Dione's presumed clear zone, Voyager 1 passed upward through the ring plane. Soon afterward the spacecraft made its closest approach to Rhea.

Everyone watching was stunned, and overwhelmed. They were "euphoric," exhausted, but mostly "simply flooded with new data." There was too much, and there was too much new, and too much that didn't fit theories and preconceptions. In this "strange world," as Bradford Smith, head of the imaging team, commented, "the bizarre" had become "the commonplace." He spoke particularly of fresh images of an F Ring, eccentric and braided in defiance of gravitational mechanics. But almost everything about the Saturnian system had either blurred Voyager's instruments with a gauze of haze or, if it sharpened the image, only deepened the haze of understanding. Tiny Mimas had an impact crater almost half as large it was. Tethys had a near-encircling trench. Dione hinted at internal forces. Enceladus lacked mighty craters. Iapetus had contrarian dark and light surfaces. Rhea boasted a new saturation level for impacts, all the more astonishing for what was essentially an icy rock. Saturn's inner satellites, all five, constituted "ice planets," an "entirely new class of worlds never before seen."[112]

The data analysis continued, even as Voyager turned to photograph and measure a receding, crescent Saturn. That image—Saturn's shadow streaking across its luminous rings—would be Voyager 1's Saturnian signature, as Io's volcanoes had been its Jovian. When the encounter phase officially concluded on November 13, Voyager continued to scan the scene, looking for new moons, viewing Saturn from fresh angles. It now sailed above the ecliptic, headed away from not only Saturn but also the planets altogether, for a final encounter with that nebulous boundary where the Sun's wind collided no longer with planetary magnetospheres but with those of other stars.

TITAN

Saturn's shadow had not been the expected dominant image of Voyager's encounter. That honor had been reserved for Titan, for it was hoped that Voyager 1 might penetrate the veil of Titan's atmosphere. It didn't.

From the earliest planning, Titan had loomed as a primary target. The desire for a close flyby determined the entire trajectory of Voyager 1, which is to say, the Voyager mission overall, because going to Titan meant departing the planetary ecliptic altogether. But Titan was a world in itself. Its size, nearly as large as Mars; its atmosphere, denser than Earth's and rich in methane; its proximity to Saturn, with the promise of magnetospheric dynamics between the two—all suggested that, in the words of Project Scientist Ed Stone, "an encounter with Titan" would be "the equivalent to a planetary encounter."[113]

It would, so enthusiasts noted, perhaps be equivalent to visiting an early Earth, and a world more likely than any other to have life, or at least its predecessor organics. Voyager carried those hopes and queries to the planetary borders of Titan. A week before periapsis with Saturn, the spacecraft began an imaging sequence that, with computer enhancement, allowed some hint of contrast and perhaps of surface structure. But even with false-color imaging and other tricks, Titan remained impenetrable and inscrutable. Instead of contrasting with the generally bland surface of Saturn, Titan recapitulated it. Its size overwhelmed Voyager's cameras, forcing imaging into two-by-two mosaics, and then three-by-three; there was no break in the clouds, only at best a computer-forced glaze of gloom. The cameras that had proved so illuminating on hard-surface satellites could here show close up only what telescopes had viewed from far off. The gauzy sheen screened off detail. The best that close scrutiny could discover was a haze layer, detached and hovering over the north pole, some one hundred kilometers above the impermeable primary atmosphere. The interrogation of Titan fell to instruments operating outside the spectrum of visible light.[114]

These did as they were programmed to do. The infrared spectrometer (IRIS) mapped heat, the ultraviolet spectrometer (UVS) scanned for higher-energy wavelengths, while radio astronomy tested occultation through the Titan atmosphere, and plasma wave detectors traced the anticipated interaction of magnetospheres between

Titan and Saturn. (Titan, it was discovered, lacked a magnetic field.) But there was no surface to view, and there would not be until a radar imager could be sent to penetrate the clouds. Titan shied away from offering a tangible new world, presenting only an enigmatic mist-shrouded isle to taunt and tempt.

Instead of revisiting this unpromising scene, Voyager 2 would tweak its trajectory away from Titan and toward the equally baffling but far more transparent rings.

Had those hunkered down in the windowless mission center at JPL been able to look outside, they might have found the contrast between Earth and Titan that eluded them on their monitors. As the Saturn encounter wound down, Santa Ana winds had picked up, threatening the DSN antennas at Goldstone as thunderstorms had those at Madrid and compelling JPL to rely on backup generators to ward against power failure. More strikingly, the San Gabriel Mountains were aflame.[115]

Titan's most passionate partisans were those obsessed with its organic chemistry and the prospects for life, or at least life's biochemical progenitors. Titan was Mars with methane. Voyager revealed that its atmosphere was 1.6 times as dense as Earth's and that nitrogen was, as with Earth, a major constituent. Titan offered a tantalizing prospect for a world in which methane took the place of water on Earth, with methane clouds, methane rain, and methane seas; but mostly it teased with the hope that a fluid soup of organics might reveal the cosmological foundations for life. It would offer that comparative alternative that would move life from a singularity to a statistic. What the Galapagos Islands did for the theory of evolution by natural selection, Titan might do for exobiology.[116]

That is what made those back-lot fires significant. At the time the prevailing portrayal of free-burning fire held that combustion was solely a chemical reaction shaped by physical circumstances, and that it mattered ecologically because it had been on Earth since the earliest terrestrial plants. It was a physical disturbance like hurricanes and ice storms, and affected the living world similarly. While everyone agreed that "life" elsewhere would not look like life on Earth, there had to be common features, much as the atmospheres and rings of Saturn and Jupiter, so seemingly alike, were different, and a general theory of planetary atmospheres had to accommodate both. So it would be with a theory of life. It would have to embrace both Earth and Titan. Earth chauvinism would falter before the challenges of the planetary Other.

Yet increasingly it is the conception of earthly life that has changed, a reformation for which fire may trace the emerging contours. The realization slowly grows that fire on Earth is biologically constructed; that life creates the oxygen, that life creates the hydrocarbon fuels, that life in the hands of humans is the primary source of ignition, that the chemistry of combustion is a *bio*chemistry, joining the mitochondrial Krebs cycle to the cycle of flame in chaparral. Unlike floods, earthquakes, volcanoes, or the Santa Ana winds—all of which can happen without a particle of life present, or even shards of preorganics—fire cannot exist apart from its living matrix. Fire literally feeds upon biomass.

The fires that ripped across the San Gabriels offered an insight into earthly life far more vivid than abstract appeals to hydrocarbon drizzles and smoggy screens in the upper Titan atmosphere, and they threatened not so much the electrical power that ran JPL monitors as the conceptual power that underwrote what those monitors were designed to search for. Life was indeed more pervasive and exotic than prevailing formulas allowed; but the challenges to those views would likely come from Earth. They would come when new eyes viewed seemingly old worlds afresh.

This is what exploration by Western civilization had always done. From time to time it revealed truly unknown places, but mostly it discovered places known to others or rediscovered once known places in novel ways. The Indies—the destination of the First Age—were hardly unknown: the whole point of the Great Voyages was to find a new way to get there. Charles-Marie de la Condamine surveyed the Amazon with a map in his hand produced by predecessor Jesuits, and Humboldt succeeded La Condamine in Ecuador; while across the globe the Institut d'Egypte, accompanying Napoleon's invasion, measured monuments known for thousands of years, yet saw them anew, and rendered them from obscurantist reliquaries to the measured and catalogued artifacts of science. The Second Age, after all, had begun in Europe as well as the Pacific. It was in Europe that the natural history excursion, the Grand Tour, and the new geology converged before Joseph Banks and Louis-Antoine de Bougainville took them global.

Sometimes discovery can come not by looking farther and deeper but simply by turning around.

THE PLANETARY SOCIETY

On the eve of Voyager 1's closest encounter, as had happened with Mariner 4 and Viking at Mars and with Voyager at Jupiter, a panel, now well versed in the venue, convened at JPL to discuss "Saturn and the Mind of Man." Chaired by Walter Sullivan of the *New York Times* and the author of books on IGY and Antarctica, the panel included Bruce Murray, Ray Bradbury, and Carl Sagan, all veterans of previous encounters, and Philip Morrison, returning from a stint with the Viking landing panel. Framing the session were comments by Marvin Goldberger, president of Caltech, and Jerry Brown, governor of California.[117]

The themes identified the usual suspects: imagination, curiosity, wonder, the imperative to understand our place in the cosmos. All combined science with other themes. The physicist Morrison added an emphasis on the aesthetic qualities of Saturn—its enthralling rings. Geologist, and now director of JPL, Murray commented on Voyager as a "climax of a glorious decade of exploration" and as the vanguard of a necessary era of discovery by robots. There was no alternative to semiautonomous spacecraft: the distances were too great and the velocities too speedy to allow for hands-on guidance from Earth. Astronomer Sagan managed to mingle the scientific with the prophetic, a kind of modern astrology purged of its hocus-pocus.[118]

Afterward the panel, along with many others, retired to a fundraising dinner on behalf of The Planetary Society, which Murray, Sagan, and Louis Friedman had just founded. Its originating purpose was to rally public sentiment on behalf of space exploration by providing an institutional focus for such enthusiasms, one that could speak to politics. Its stated mission: "to promote planetary exploration and the search for extraterrestrial life." By the time the organization celebrated its twenty-fifth anniversary, that charter had expanded to read: "to inspire the people of Earth—through research, education, private ventures, and public participation—to explore other worlds and seek other life."[119]

That private groups might sponsor expeditions or, more commonly, pressure governments to do so had ample precedent. In the Second Age it was possible for individuals or small groups simply to trek to the frontier and walk into the unknown. But the Great Voyages, and certainly space exploration, were vastly too expensive for private capital, or, if undertaken, came with generous concessions.

Somewhere the state would be involved as not simply a tithe collector but a player concerned with the shifting balances of power that exploration might catalyze. While Prince Henry could mingle public and private enterprise, most rulers preferred to outsource discovery to individuals or Companies of Adventurers. Cabot and Columbus, for example, could establish themselves as medieval barons on new lands, provided they ceded a fifth of the discovered wealth to the state. In this way private groups took the risk, and the state collected money and power. Later, scientific societies supplemented commercial institutions and campaigned for expeditions; think of the Paris Academy dispatching Maupertuis and La Condamine to measure an arc of the meridian, or botanical gardens sponsoring collecting naturalists, or the Royal Geographical Society and National Geographic Society sending exploring parties (usually under naval officers) to the ends of the Earth, from Lt. Verney Lovett Cameron to central Africa to Lt. Robert Peary at the North Pole. More recently philanthropy and publicity have combined to loosen the purse strings of private benefactors, leaving Antarctica, for example, endowed with the Beardmore Glacier, the Ford Mountains, and the Walgreen Coast. The idea that the state should undertake such enterprises for the sake of curiosity is a very recent innovation tied to the peculiarities of modern science and the perceived imperatives of national prestige as a subset of national security.

Perhaps the closest analogue to the Planetary Society was the African Association, or in its more fulsome title, the Association for Promoting the Discovery of the Interior Parts of Africa, organized in 1788 with Joseph Banks as chair. At the time, Banks was probably the best-known British scientist identified with exploration, was an aristocrat well placed in British society and scientific institutions (including Kew Gardens and the Royal Society), and was a keen promoter of geographic discoveries. The African Association targeted particularly a place of popular, even mythological lore, Timbuktu, and its associated river, the Niger. Under its auspices Mungo Park made two ventures to the region (the second proved fatal). More than sponsoring treks, however, the African Association kept the image of Africa and the putative value of its geographic exploration before the public eye and in the corridors of power. It lamented, as the Planetary Society did, the lapse in official enthusiasm after Park's disappearance, and it struggled institutionally after its most charismatic figure, Banks, died. It was succeeded by the Royal Geographical Society under Roderick Murchison, which bridged official and unofficial exploring as Britain lurched into imperial competition with France and later Germany during Europe's unseemly "scramble for Africa." (It was in turn succeeded in space exploration by the British Interplanetary Society.)[120]

The African Association resembled dozens of lobbying groups, all intent on directing the power of the state, with its capacity to mobilize truly impressive resources, toward their own particular exploring enthusiasms. Each would claim that, without such commitments, the nation would sink into slovenly insignificance. Each sought to keep its ambitions before the public. In Banks's day it was enough to interest the elite and select officials of the empire. But increasingly, in democracies, it was the public that either drove expeditions or allowed them to expire. That required a public medium, which in the heyday of European imperialism meant popular books, lecture tours, and especially newspapers. The press could make or break an exploring venture. It could browbeat an administration into sending an expedition, or ridicule one into remission, or even sponsor expeditions of its own, as the *New York Herald* did when it underwrote

Stanley's search for Livingstone. A race to the pole made good copy. Adventures into unknown lands sold papers.

By the time Voyager launched, however, the American public was plugged into television. The entire space program had grown up with TV: it was, in some respects, staged for TV. The press corps that came to JPL for the Voyager encounters watched the drama unfurl on TV monitors; the most gripping reports from Voyager science came from the imaging team that delivered graphic visuals suitable for rebroadcast. The "Mind of Man" that mattered was the TV-viewing public. Even as Voyager closed on Saturn, PBS was airing Carl Sagan's blockbuster series *Cosmos*, of which episode six, "Traveler's Tales," highlighted Voyager. It was masterly timing, as art and life intertwined into a Great Conjunction of exploration and culture.

VOYAGER 2

Seven months after its twin, Voyager 2 began its approach to Saturn.

It had the same instruments and was visiting the same planetary world, so much would be similar. Yet it would see Saturn differently because it flew on a different trajectory, had a superior camera (50 percent more sensitive), saw Saturn when its rings were turned higher into sunlight and its weather was more boisterous, and could target specific features that its robotic sibling had noted only in passing. But Voyager 2 had always been the troubled twin. It entered Saturn plagued with faulty receivers, and it left with a crippled scan platform. Most of all, constraining its goals was the need for a trajectory that could propel the spacecraft on a 4.5-year cruise to Uranus.

The narrative of their Saturnian encounters thus differed in their fundamentals. Fraternal twins they might be, but the two Voyagers had different historical DNA, and they had different destinies.

Voyager 2's ten-week observation period commenced on June 5, 1981. This time scientists hoped for sharper atmospheric images from Saturn, more detailed photos of the satellites, and greater refinement of the ring structure, including shots of elusive shepherding satellites along with an explanation for the baffling dark spokes on the B Ring. The cameras rolled; the images of white-ringed Saturn loomed large on screens; still photos were strung together into animated movies.[121]

Voyager 2's mechanical ills continued, however. One of the memory chips in its flight data system computer failed, which forced mission control to devise a new encounter sequence—"better" than the original, they insisted. On August 19 the spacecraft executed a final course correction, a day before the fourth anniversary of its launch. Soft geography caused problems because the solar wind was high and gusty and no trailing spacecraft could issue forecasts as Voyager 2 had for Voyager 1; even more than usual, bow shock was a frothy frontier, complicated by the planet's interaction with Titan and the magnetospheric tail of Jupiter, now in rude alignment. Yet anticipation was high, less in the hope that Voyager 2 might discover whole new phenomena than that it might help clarify the raw mysteries unveiled by Voyager 1. Much as the imaging team resorted to more false-color and computer-enhanced photos to massage out details, so the mission design sought to refine the encounter sequence to illuminate some of Saturn's more baffling revelations.[122]

Near-encounter began with a close flyby of Iapetus, the outermost of Saturn's ice moons, on August 22. Thereafter, Voyager intensified its reconnaissance of Saturn's hard and soft geographies. Although bow shock proved evasive, the spacecraft undertook a complex sequence of rolls to plot out the contours of the magnetosphere and trained its UVS and IRIS instruments on everything in sight. But the hard geography had its fugitive phenomena as well: the satellites that theory demanded be embedded in the rings could not be found. Nor could instant analysis locate any explanation for the dark spokes. What the images did reveal was an ever-multiplying number of rings, now in the thousands. Compensating for the missing moonlets, however, were brilliant images of real moons, now including Hyperion. Slight perturbations in the spacecraft caused by their gravitational pulls allowed for estimations of mass. (Iapetus, it was calculated, was nearly pure ice.) As Voyager 2 crossed bow shock for the last time, those satellites would command much of near-encounter efforts on August 25.

Guidance was nearly perfect: the spacecraft was within fifty kilometers and three seconds of schedule. The images flashed by—the rings, the moon Tethys, newly discovered satellites with orbits shared with Tethys and Dione. But the mission was science, not merely reconnaissance, and for an astonishing 2.5 hours the photopolarimeter claimed exclusive attention while it measured the occultation of the star Delta Scorpii through the rings. When it ended, with a profile of 82,000 kilometers of rings on chart paper half a mile long, the spacecraft's cameras scanned the moon Enceladus in riveting detail. Then it passed behind Saturn and plunged through the rings, and completed periapsis, not to reemerge until midnight some ninety-five minutes later. Its record of occultation through Saturn's atmosphere, its inner passage through the ring plane, and its final scans of Enceladus would not be broadcast until it reconnected with the DSN. There was only minor anxiety about the physical hazards posed by the rings, since Voyager was following the rough trail blazed by Pioneer 11. And on schedule the DNS station in Australia reacquired the telemetry signal from the spacecraft, now boldly hurtling toward Uranus.

The signal, yes. But the Voyager 2 that emerged was not the Voyager 2 that had entered.

Something had happened. A few instruments transmitted odd data, and erratically; near the ring plane some control thrusters had made unauthorized firings; the scan platform now pointed not at a receding Saturn but into black space. While fresh news to mission control, this was old news to Voyager 2. Everything had happened ninety minutes earlier. The near-imaging of Enceladus and Tethys; the planned stereo views of the F Ring; a photopolarimeter-recorded occultation of the rings; the backside view of Saturn—all were gone, irretrievably lost in space. The change in temperature caused by passing into Saturn's immense shadow had also upset the balky receiver, and mission control struggled to identify an acceptable frequency and to reengage. Each new command required multiple transmissions, which even at the speed of light would take more than ninety minutes to reach the crippled spacecraft. Gloom replaced euphoria, until the mood at mission control resembled the abrupt borders of black and white that Voyager had imaged on Iapetus.[123]

The primary goal was to spare the spacecraft further harm. Mission control sought to shut down whatever was not essential and to preserve, if possible, the option to go to Uranus. New commands placed the instruments on standby, since they recorded nothing valuable and might complicate attempts to reclaim control and diagnose the disorder. They shut down the preprogrammed command sequence for the encounter, since that sequence was anyway a shambles. And they moved the scan platform away from where it had frozen, a position that might ruin some instruments by making them directly face the Sun. It then remained to wait for the download from the Voyager's tape recorder, which had held its transmissions while the spacecraft passed behind Saturn.

That broadcast arrived on Earth at 9:00 a.m. on August 26. Here was Voyager doing what it was supposed to—sighting a magnificent scan of the F Ring, and a crescent profile of an F-Ring shepherd satellite. Then the record entered its problem phase, as the narrow-angle camera sent, instead of crisp images of Enceladus, black screens. The wide-angle camera could still capture the edge view of the rings as the spacecraft crossed through, but anything that had demanded precision targeting was gone. There were no rings, there was no Tethys. Misaligned, the camera got only a marvelous if unanticipated image of the Keeler Gap in the rings. The wide-angle lens got a snippet of a moon. Worse, the scan platform's ability to move along an azimuth was clearly deteriorating. Finally, the platform froze altogether. The cause of its malfunction remained unknown, and frenetic inquiries were stymied by the faulty receiver. The startling clarity and vigor of the early images made the subsequent losses all the more poignant.[124]

The flow of science based on the information successfully sent continued, as it would for months during which analysis would replace brute reconnaissance. There was more data from plasma waves, particularly a burst of energy a millionfold higher than normal as Voyager passed through the ring plane. And there were those brave, cold new worlds, as continued study scrutinized the major satellites of Saturn and continued to find new minor ones. But what had always characterized near-encounters—the brute flood of new data, the sheer awe of first contact and shared discovery—was gone. Voyager continued to transmit empty scenes, each frame "displayed on the monitors at JPL, complete with the commanded exposure time, filter, and so forth," and they "kept coming, one after another, all day." Unless Voyager righted itself, it might go to Uranus as a blind chunk of metal rather than a robotic explorer.[125]

So engineers continued their inquiry, at once feverish and measured, to diagnose the problem and prescribe remedies. They isolated the trouble to a stuck azimuth platform, the geared mechanism that allowed the scanning instruments to rotate in a plane and point in different directions. One by one, engineers brought back online the other instruments, successfully. The soft geography Voyager could still track; it was the hard geography of visible worlds that was threatened. Then engineers began to massage the azimuth mechanism in ten-degree increments, and they discovered that they could still control the elevation mechanism. With that, and by using the spacecraft as a platform overall, it would be possible to do some basic reconnaissance at Uranus. Step by step, mission control inched Voyager 2 back to where it might at least focus on Saturn rather than continue taking its disheartening images of empty space.

As the engineering investigation continued into August 27, E. K. Davis, project manager, and Ed Stone, chief project scientist, jointly declared that the principal objective was "to recover the scan platform capability for Uranus." The mission had nearly five years to tinker and perhaps solve the problem before a Uranus encounter, and they were not willing to do anything "to increase risk by premature activity now." When asked how much had been lost, Stone preferred to emphasize how much had been gained. The mission, he announced, had been "200 percent" successful—by so much had Voyager 2 exceeded its mandated charge. The full raft of data would take years to assimilate; and even as the spacecraft struggled to return from its passage through the dark side, project science leaders trooped forward to place the latest discoveries before the world. The odd surface of Enceladus. Titan's hydrogen torus, and apparently missing ionosphere. Plasma discontinuities created by Tethys and Dione. The ever-enigmatic rings.[126]

By August 28, diagnostics had progressed sufficiently to identify the problem and suggest, as Dick Laeser, deputy project manager, put it, that "the platform improves with use." The glitch was in part an outcome of what had earlier doomed the polarimeters: overuse. The science teams had earlier demanded more of Voyager than its engineering could guarantee. Its scan platform had tried to zip too quickly among too many targets, slewing faster than its lubricant could respond, and the apparatus had gagged. The spacecraft needed a mandatory rest, followed by a cautious program of rehabilitation. The worrisome days after the crash met that need. Within hours after identifying the source of the breakdown, on August 28, mission control hoped to get Saturn back into Voyager's field of vision. They did.

Encounter officially ended on August 30 with a bittersweet celebration. Once again Voyager 2 had come back from a near-death experience. If much had been lost, far more had been gained. But the real losses were in the future: it was as though Voyager were passing through a gap in the ring plane of American planetary exploration. It was a gap in history, and this one had no shepherding satellites. Voyager *was* the American planetary program, and would be the only mission to other worlds until the Galileo spacecraft went to Jupiter in 1989. Bradford Smith anticipated a "data gap," Ed Stone an institutional gap, and others, career gaps. However hobbled, Voyager 2 was the future for planetary exploration.[127]

By now the spacecraft had recovered enough mobility that it could exercise its right to the traditional parting shot. On September 4, Voyager 2 photographed Saturn's most distant and darkest moon, Phoebe. Probably a captured asteroid now in retrograde orbit, the moon seemed to emphasize the retrograde character of the American planetary program as it looked back. Yet there was hope, too, in that new world, and there was faith, as Voyager pointed to the dark promise of Uranus.

NAMES OF DISCOVERY

Even wonders require names, and marvels, labels. The cascade of data and images revealed worlds swarming with physiographic novelty ready for both.

Between them the Voyager twins discovered thirty-five new moons and first mapped twenty known ones; they traced the gaseous contours of Titan and the four outer planets; and they recorded hard geography surface features by the hundreds. Suddenly there were craters to name; valleys and rifts to label; volcanoes, dark splotches, and half rings to categorize; to say nothing of features for which no landscape terminology existed. They were not hollows, washes, mesas, shorelines, hills, or dales, since they expressed a different tectonism and a land sculpture purged of flowing water. They were, rather, ancient Earths, before seas and life; alternative Earths, obedient to stresses and abrasions unknown terrestrially; and simply alien worlds. Spontaneous, slangy expressions sputtered out in order for scientists to talk about just-revealed terrains, as they struggled to place odd features into familiar categories. But these would not be the names recorded on the maps and the gazetteers that would codify them formally.

Fortunately two decades of planetary exploration could build on a nomenclature and a mechanism developed for traditional planetary astronomy, which in turn reflected both centuries of geographic discovery and the rationalizing instincts of two centuries of Enlightenment exploration. As ever, there were similarities as well as differences.

All this had happened from the beginning. New places needed names, or else one could not speak of them, but also because naming was a means of possessing. The commissions dispatched under the auspices of the Spanish monarchy were thus enjoined: having arrived "by good providence, first of all you must give a name to the country as a whole, and to the cities, towns, and places." The chronicler of Juan Ponce de León's 1513 expedition recorded that "it was the custom of those who discovered new lands to give their own names to the rivers, capes, and other places; or else the name of the saint on whose day they made the discovery; or else, other names, as they wished." When Ponce de León arrived off the coast of a new land, it was Easter—"Easter of Flowers," as it was known in Spanish—and the land seemed well blossomed, so for both reasons he named it "Florida."[128]

Common sources for inspiration were legends—hence, Brazil and the Antilles, named for mythical islands in the Atlantic; California, for an island in a romance, ruled by Queen Calafía; or the Amazon River, since women there were rumored to fight like those of ancient legend. Other sources were analogues to places back home—hence, a Nuevo León, a New York, a Neuw Amsterdam—or to rivers and hills reminiscent of those from where they had come. Often some feature of the site sparked a name, as some characteristic or deed inspired a nickname. Turtles led to the Tortugas; famine, to the Starving River; snow, to the White Mountains or Sierra Nevada. Classical allusions led to recommissioned Troys, Syracuses, and Romes. Biblical terms often subjected local terms to a full-immersion baptism into Jordan Rivers and Mounts Pisgah. Mormon pioneers drafted liberally from the Book of Mormon, bestowing Deseret, Bountiful, and Kolob. Some founders, wishing to emphasize the novelty of their ambition (if not settlement), invented neologisms, perhaps from Latin or Greek, as William Penn did with Philadelphia. And not least there was the practical flattery of naming features after patrons: Virginia, for the virgin queen Elizabeth I, and Jamestown for her successor; Mount Hood, for the Lord of the Admiralty; the Jefferson River, for the sponsoring president; and Washington nearly everywhere. The explorers themselves showed varying shades of immodesty. (Cook, for example, discreetly left the inlet beside Anchorage unnamed so a junior officer might insert Cook's name.)

But few places at the time of discovery were truly unnamed because they were rarely uninhabited. Every settled place already came as thickly covered with names as with woods or flying insects. Since most explorers had native guides and interpreters, they first learned of those places through their indigenous nomenclature. Some survived, more or less intact, leaving Massachusetts, Tidbinbilla, and Rotorua. More got bent through linguistic prisms as adults struggled to mouth exotic sounds or convert them into something that sounded familiar. Nahuatl Gualé twisted into "Gualape." Algonquian *che*, meaning "big," and *sepi*, meaning "river," combined with a generic ending -*at* to become "Chesapeake," which sounded vaguely familiar, like something that might apply to a mountain. French Canadians exploring in the Plains named a river the Purgatoire, which Anglophone Americans reengineered into "Picketwire."[129]

But there were some places that seemed strikingly new, required many names for unusual features, lacked indigenous labels, and came late enough in the game that explorers invoked some system. The prime example may be the Grand Canyon. The first explorer through the gorge, John Wesley Powell, elevated the canyon from Big to Grand, and named some of the salient features of the river, particularly its rapids and their associated gorges, bestowing such memorable labels as Sockdolager and Bright Angel. But the perspective from the Canyon rim was more daunting: there were so many features, all unnamed. Clarence Dutton decided that the mesas resembled pagodas and that the Canyon deserved a spiritual aura, and so bestowed the names of Asian gods and sages. Immediately there were temples for Confucius, Shiva, Vishnu, and Zoroaster, while the rim proper got Cape Royal, Cape Final, and Point Sublime. The next major cartographer, François Matthes, favored Nordic gods, bequeathing Wotan's Throne, Freya's Castle, and Thor's Hammer. When Arthur Evans succeeded him, the Welshman insisted that figures from the Arthurian legend be immortalized, which led to Lancelot Point, Guinevere Castle, and a spire called simply Excalibur. Meanwhile the Birdseye Expedition through the gorge, an exercise in cartographic engineering, merely labeled the river's features by their mileage from Lee's Ferry (eg., Mile 128 rapid). A few vernacular terms slid into the gazetteer, such as Horseshoe Mesa and the Battleship; miners and promoters put their names on trails and select features; and the National Park Service arranged to name the main tourist overlook after its first director, Stephen Mather. Explorers ensured they got onto the map, although they found themselves clustered on Powell's Plateau, with Dutton claiming the prominent point to the southeast and army rivals such as Lieutenants Wheeler and Ives banished to less interesting western peninsulas.

To a remarkable extent this same pattern would govern the naming of planetary bodies and their landscapes.

One reason is that by the time the Canyon was fully mapped, the U.S. Board on Geographic Names had been established to oversee uniform place-names by federal agencies, particularly the U.S. Geological Survey, which was mapping the country. The board functioned to regulate usage much as a dictionary does ordinary language. The board was rechartered in 1947, and continues today to promulgate "official geographic feature names with locative attributes as well as principles, policies, and procedures governing the use of domestic names, foreign names, Antarctic names, and undersea feature names." It thus oversaw two of the three regions of the Third Age. It spread into space because the U.S. Geological Survey's Astrogeology Research Program, established in 1963, has responsibility for mapping and naming the features that planetary exploration discovers.[130]

Two traits especially distinguish space from the naming practices typical of the First and Second Ages. There are no indigenous peoples, and hence no existing names, and similarly there are no territorial claims associated with the naming process. The solution to the first issue is to create a past by appealing to ancient or traditional lore from around the Earth, much as Dutton and his successors did at Grand Canyon. The solution to the second is to rely on a neutral institution to govern naming, a task that falls to the International Astronomical Union, first established in 1919, which arbitrates and regularizes nomenclature for planetary bodies. At first this meant the Moon and Mars, as viewed by Earth-based telescopes. But as robotic spacecraft began their reconnaissance, the task expanded. In 1970 a Mars nomenclature working group was charged with designating names for the features revealed by Mariner 4 and its successors, particularly those anticipated from Mariner 9. In 1973 the IAU established a Working Group for Planetary System Nomenclature, which in turn created task subgroups for the Moon, Mercury, Venus, Mars, and the outer solar system. In 1982 Harold Masursky of the USGS Astrogeology Program and a member of the Voyager Imaging Team became president of the Working Group.

By then the Voyagers had recorded two flybys through the Jovian and Saturnian systems. In their wake were tens of thousands of photographs of new worlds overrunning with features. They needed names, or at least some did. In the end more than five hundred landmarks got them.

The naming process begins with a theme, approved by the proper IAU task group, followed by some names to prominent features. Improved images lead inevitably to more names. From the task group the names go to the Working Group for Planetary System Nomenclature, where they must again find approval. The protocol allows for a three-month period for objections before the names are recorded into gazetteers, maps, and the transactions of the IAU.[131]

In their search for themes, the working groups assembled a library of more than two hundred published or submitted sources, from the *Larousse Encyclopedia of Mythology*, *Kiowa Tales*, *Gilgamesh*, *The Indian Background of Colonial Yucatan*, *Giants*, *Tales of Yoruba: Gods and Heroes*, *Soviet Encyclopedia*, *Webster's Biographical Dictionary*, a list of radar scientists (provided by G. H. Pettengill), *Fairies*, *Zhenshchina v mifakh i legendakh* (*Women in Myths and Legends*), *Dictionary of Slavic Mythology*, and *Myths of North American Indians*, to say nothing of classic literature from Homer and Virgil to Dante and Milton.[132]

On November 16, 1980, some members of the working group for naming the outer planets met at JPL to identify the themes for naming features on Saturn's satellites. Hal Masursky thought that since they all had themed lists of potential names, they might match many-featured moons such as Rhea with the longest lists; but Tobias Owen, the chair, thought they might begin with the moons with the fewest features. That pointed to Enceladus and Hyperion. But a theme? Since Saturn was a Titan, most of the satellites were named for sibling Titans. Enceladus, however, was a giant that Athena buried under Sicily, so Masursky suggested that the craters on the moons be named for giants. Owen then noted that the IAU had criticized the nomenclature committees for taking too many names from Western civilization. The group considered using names of giants from cultures everywhere, which segued into a query about giants in the

Aeneid, and then the *Odyssey*, which free-associated into *The Tale of Genji* and then Arthurian legend. (With its sharply etched black-and-white terrains, Iapetus seemed suitable for a story of good and evil— a white crater for Lancelot, a black one for Mordred.) Then they considered naming after discoverers, but since living persons were disallowed, they could not, for example, use Rich Terrile. Instead, they decided to let him pick from a list. Returning to Enceladus, they fussed over the idea of naming features after Sicilian towns, which led back to the *Aeneid*, which then led to adjournment. In the end the full working group proposed that Tethys get its names from the *Odyssey*, Dione from the *Aeneid*, Mimas from Arthurian legend (based on Baines's translation of *Le Morte d'Arthur*), and Rhea from creation myths from around the world. Enceladus got names from people and places in Burton's *Arabian Nights*. In the end the giants lost out altogether because they tended to cluster too heavily in Nordic legends and thus found themselves buried beneath the Sicily of cultural diversity.[133]

By the time Voyager completed its flybys, the *Gazetteer of Planetary Nomenclature* recognized some fifty-one "descriptor terms" for features, almost all of which had Latin roots. These ranged from "arcus" (arc-shaped feature) to "cavus" (hollows) to "dorsum" (ridge) to "labes" (landslide). "Palus" described a swamp or small plain. "Planitia," a low plain. "Planum," a plateau. "Macula," a dark spot. "Rima," a fissure. "Rupes," a scarp. "Tessera," tile-like polygonal terrain. Matched with themes, Io's volcanoes got names from fire, sun, thunder, and volcano gods and heroes. Its catenae (chains of craters) came from sun gods; its "mensae," "montes," "paterae," and "tholi" from the Io myth or Dante's *Inferno*. Europa received names from the Europa myth or Celtic mythology. Ganymede boasted gods and heroes from the Fertile Crescent. Some small satellites, like Colorado River features, got numbers. After the space shuttle Challenger blew up, the committee resisted the impulse to name moons after the deceased astronauts.

The names rolled on, a fugue of words counterpointing the rosters of raw data. While neither names nor numbers could compete with the graphic shock of images, both were necessary means of assimilating what would never be colonized. They populated the new worlds with gods, heroes, giants, and so connected the mission with a cultural heritage that a machine could not otherwise have. They made Voyager a saga, not simply an instrument.

EYES OF DISCOVERY

To planetary scientists, Voyager was a flying lab, outfitted with instruments for recording phenomena largely invisible to the naked eye that it then transmitted back in streams of data, which researchers would pore over for years. To the public, however, Voyager was a camera, and its startling revelations were its photos. No one could see infrared or ultraviolet radiation, much less something as recondite as a bow shock. But everyone could stand amazed at crisp images of exotic worlds viewed instantly as they were displayed on monitors. For humanity at large, and for the media, those images largely defined and sustained Voyager.

The split in perception was real, however, and it dated from the very origins of the space program. Many space partisans saw scientific research in only a supporting role; and space scientists themselves disagreed about what research warranted a place on the instrument boom. Certainly in its origins planetary science had meant geophysics; of the fifteen scientists allied with Voyager, only one, Larry Soderblom, was a geologist because, as Bruce Murray put it, "there was no geology of the outer planets." IGY had been, after all, a *geophysical* year, with special focus on the upper atmosphere; and the new astronomy was shifting away from imagery based on hard bodies and visual light and toward radio, X-ray, or infrared spectra and the objects that emitted them. The first triumph of the American space program was Explorer 1's discovery of Earth's invisible radiation belts. Simple pictures of new landscapes, moons, and galaxies held little research promise; they seemed scarcely better than postcards, or tourist souvenirs, with trivial value for scientific inquiry. As early as 1962 an august group of space scientists (including Nobel laureates) had argued strenuously against putting a TV camera on satellites as a waste of precious payload. Even as Voyager 1 hurtled toward its rendezvous with Jupiter, "nowhere," observed two chroniclers of the mission, was "there any indication of the dominant role that images would play in the exploration of these new worlds."[134]

That was the vision of professional science speaking to its own. Against its bias was the steady penetration of TV into American culture. This was an age in which the word increasingly counted less than the image, and the still image less than the moving one. From its origins, the space program had been televised; Vanguard 2 had attempted to televise Earth; and beginning with Tiros 1, weather satellites beamed back photos, both startling and self-evident, to an eager public. The eyes of discovery disseminated to anyone with a TV set: nothing created so great a bond with the citizenry whose consent made the space program possible. Still photos were effectively published on TV.

Gradually, however, geophysicists came to appreciate the value of images for interpreting the hard geography of the new worlds being discovered. Even seemingly backwater sciences such as geomorphology enjoyed a revival by being able to decode from surface images past and current planetary dynamics, from once-flowing waters on Mars to subterranean renewals on Europa. The lasting image of the Apollo program was not a posturing astronaut on the Moon but Earth rising above the Moon's horizon. The camera surrogate used by Pioneers 10 and 11—painstakingly reconstructed from scans by a photopolarimeter—had enthralled viewers; but those spare, grainy images paled before the glossy, multihued thousands that Voyager broadcast back.

Their wide- and narrow-angle cameras, not their recording of whistlers on Jupiter or the unstable magnetospheric fringes of Titan, were what most bonded the Voyagers to the wider public.

That had long been true. Before printing became cheap, explorers had indulged in word paintings, and they still did, even as the Second Age made it standard practice to carry artists with expeditions. Those paired images were the ones that electrified the public.

It was one of the great convergences of the Second Age that nature became a reputable subject for art. Vast natural history paintings replaced operatic human history canvases as a source of wonder and moral instruction; portraits of parrots, beavers, turkeys, and platypuses replaced, at least in popular lore, portraiture of aristocrats, plutocrats, and ecclesiastics; mountains and blasted trees sublimated religious allegory, and then became iconic objects in their own right. Artists such as William Hodges established indelible images of Tahiti, Easter Island, and floating Antarctic ice mountains. Karl Bodmer bequeathed a brilliant, irreplaceable record of upper Missouri tribes, as aesthetics merged with ethnography. Frederic Church reproduced Humboldt's South American adventures with tropical mists, towering peaks, and erupting volcanoes in immense chromatic canvases. Artists recorded and introduced to Europe the kangaroo, the Aborigine, the baobab tree, the Ituri Forest, the Great Plains. In America, where a sublime Nature and its monuments would substitute for the absence of Antiquity and its relics, discovery and artistic representation knotted tightly together. Thomas Moran's splendiferous canvas of Yellowstone Falls and his mellifluous watercolors of Mammoth Hot Springs, painted for the Hayden Expedition of 1871, were galvanic in pushing Congress to declare Yellowstone a national park. Immediately, John Wesley Powell persuaded Moran to visit the newly unveiled Grand Canyon, and repeat the trick—which he did.

Eventually technology changed the terms of public engagement, as the camera overtoppled the brush as the most popular medium. Photographs were what primarily engaged the public; even artists used photos to help re-create paintings later in their studios. Where expeditions had to pay for themselves by lectures and publications, as Shackleton's did, photos were critical. That makes all the more gripping the moment when, on the *Endurance* expedition, knowing they had to leave the ice floes for boats, Shackleton and Frank Hurley sat down and determined which glass-plate negatives they could afford to take with them and which they could not. Shackleton smashed the rejects to forestall any attempt by expedition members to secrete the remainder among the stores.

During the interregnum between the Second and Third ages that followed, discovery became increasingly banal, or even staged by magazines such as *National Geographic*. Everyone used cameras. Expeditions sought out niche landscapes, or simply places that lent themselves to being photographed. The photogenic mattered more than the unknown. There were a few exceptions, most spectacularly the Leahy brothers, who carried a motion-picture camera on their 1930 foray into the highlands of New Guinea, filming a first-contact record never to be repeated.

By the Third Age the camera had continued as an instrument of record, but art had abandoned nature for art, and artists had plunged into a greater unknowable, themselves. No artists accompanied the major expeditions of the era, although an Earth-based art of space did evolve, and some cosmonauts dabbled in paint and pencil while enduring the ennui of Earth orbit, like sailors on long voyages carving scrimshaw. The medium of the age, however, was the moving picture. The classic episodes of exploration were recorded on TV or recapitulated in documentaries. The dominant technological romance emerged from Hollywood.

For Voyager, in particular, its long trek paralleled a revival of space movies. *Star Wars* was released in May 1977, three months before Voyager 2 launched, and *Star Trek: The Movie*, in late 1979, when the Voyagers were halfway between their encounters with Jupiter and Saturn. The real Voyagers did not have to wait for Hollywood. Among their most memorable images were time-lapse movies made of Jovian storms, Saturn ring spokes, and fast-approaching moons. Technicians completed the trend by creating animated, computer-generated movies that tracked Voyager as it flew past new worlds.

Such productions required more than normal manipulation. "Enhancement" was already a mandatory practice, however, since Voyager did not transmit canvas oils and watercolors but only electronic daubs and brushstrokes for its pixels. The published image was assembled at JPL labs.

This, too, had a long tradition. Exploring artists rarely painted their canvases on the scene and then hauled them for months on mule and keelboat. They carried sketchbooks and journals in which they did studies and executed tricky details and indicated in words what color should go where, and then collected artifacts that they could subsequently include in a reconstructed scene. Later, they relied on photographs as well. They completed their final compositions in a studio. And not surprisingly, they indulged in a degree of enhancement.

The nature of digital images made manipulation both necessary and tempting, as what began as a means to sharpen data could segue seamlessly into artistic license. It was possible to compensate for weak and distorted signals; to lighten dark blotches; to parse bland haze into false color tints based on differing electromagnetic spectra; to highlight murky rings with sharp coloration, as though the image had been washed with psychedelic drugs. Computers became palettes, and imaging labs, artists' studios. The first survey from Mars by Mariner 4 consisted of two hundred scan lines of two hundred picture elements each, a giant printout of forty thousand numbers, which were then hand-colored with crayons to produce an image the public could understand. The volcanoes on Io were effectively discovered by manipulating data into a form that highlighted the crescent domes of sulfuric gas. As with all data, the numbers had to be processed to make meaningful patterns. The imaging teams used photo software instead of statistics.[135]

Yet the scientists who initially distrusted the cameras, particularly TV, were right in their suspicions. The romantic horizon that captivated so many nineteenth-century painters had acquired a high-tech reincarnation. Perhaps the most famous distortion was the oft-reproduced image from the Magellan mission to Venus, in which the radar-measured surface of Venus was exaggerated twenty-fold to turn lumpy lava into mountains and basins. But Voyager had its enhancements, too. Some of the mission's most celebrated images were, as literary journalists might say, composites. The Voyager 1 shot of Earth and Moon began as three images with different color filters, which were then synthesized into a single composition at JPL's imaging processing lab, where the lunar scene was brightened three-fold in order to yield a more pleasing and informative contrast. The images that brought spontaneous gasps from the press were almost all manipulated in some way to enhance one or another feature; and some of those images simply charmed because they were gorgeous. The outer planets were worlds of beauty as well as data.

Once again, the sublime competed with the scientific. The software engineers at the Image Processing Laboratory were the artists of the Grand Tour.[136]

Yet the Third Age, once again, broke simple continuities. It reversed the thematic arc of the Second by which art had fastened itself to exploration. The classic grand tour of the eighteenth century had been a journey to centers of art and antiquity, but by trekking across the Alps and visiting Etnas in eruption, visitors had to confront nature as well as Old Masters, and travelers appealed to the new sciences to decipher nature's hieroglyphs and illuminate its meaning beyond what classical texts could do. Art and science together pulled the cart of travel.

Yet just as space science had changed, so had art, and so had the intrinsic character of those encountered landscapes that both science and art sought to wrestle into meaningful form, which meant the Voyagers saw differently from exploring naturalist-artists of the Second Age. This was a modernist nature: abstract, conceptual, minimal, alien to the human presence. It was a world only a robot could visit and only a robot's instruments could record. The human observer was, even at the speed of light, an hour and a half distant, with the studio banks of electronics further distancing him between the real and the reconstructed. Much as those on the grand tour sought to recreate the new into the venue of the ancient, so the imagers labored to place the Voyagers into the inherited traditions of discovery in which the wonder of first contact was an expected outcome.

But the shock of the new also spoke to a different realm of art, a comparable shift for the arts to that which the sciences were making as they refocused from hard to soft geographies. Willingly or not, the Voyagers' was a modernist art. The issue went beyond obvious visual parallels that made false-colored rings into something like a Barnett Newman painting, or the blotchy surfaces of Titan and Saturn into the abstract expressionism of Mark Rothko. It had to do with the position of the artist-explorer in the scene, and it went well beyond what computer enhancement could do.

The classic views of exploring art included observers in their foreground. The painting looked over the shoulder of the explorer. It saw not only the view of the explorer but also the explorer doing the viewing. Often, too, it attempted to imagine the explorer as seen by the explored, looking over the shoulder of Fijians or Fuegians or the putatively awed gaze of Aborigines, or it found in the wondering faces of encountered indigenes a reflection of the encountered explorer. The artist could view the expedition from the outside, or at times even place himself within the scene as viewed by an outside observer.

But no one could view Voyager. The twins were too far apart for one to image the other. There was no other platform by which to see Voyager sweep past Jupiter, Saturn, Iapetus, Titan, the rings, and the rest. This was a fundamental condition of the Third Age: there would be no Other to receive, bestow awe, or even witness. There was no one on Ganymede or Rhea, no village on the F Ring, or fishing vessel on the cloud seas of Jupiter, from whose perspective it might be possible to imagine Voyager's arrival. Its only audiences were the imaging team, the press corps, and the TV-viewing public. Yet continuity with the understood heritage of exploration seemingly required a perspective that the Third Age could not offer. Voyager might hurtle blithely through the void of interplanetary space; it could not so easily leap that looming void of solipsism, the threat posed by the missing perspective outside the spacecraft.

So when the time came to create computer movies of the flybys, the producers inserted Voyager into the frame. The animation follows the plucky spacecraft as it pitches and yaws and rotates its scan platform past exotic new worlds, just as we knew it would. Much as the camera, though initially vilified by space scientists, came to define discovery for the public, so old perspectives intruded into what might have been a purely modernist moment. That the Voyagers made the compromise allowed them to bond better with a public that regarded modernist art as something best kept in a museum. An image of the spacecraft went into the scene, rather as its curiously awkward trek went into the grand narrative of Western exploration.

There Voyager sailed, while we looked over its shoulder, and while five hundred years of exploration history looked over ours.

PARTING

The Voyagers bid farewell not only to Saturn but to each other.

So far they had been linked, with Voyager 1 breaking trail for Voyager 2, and Voyager 2 sending data on solar winds to Voyager 1, and the twins programmed to complement each other as they soared past the satellite islands and planetary continents of new worlds. Now they split. Voyager 1 left the plane of the ecliptic entirely in a rising ascent to the borders of the heliosphere. Voyager 2 careened around Saturn for a rendezvous with Uranus. They would never again share routes or pass in tandem. Almost a quarter century later they would meet termination shock separately.

They were both scarred and limping. Shortly after encounter, Voyager 1's plasma science instrument had ceased transmitting. This had happened also after Jupiter, and engineers had successfully rekindled the system by temperature cycling. This time it failed to spark. Its photopolarimeter remained broken. The scan platform stubbornly resisted slewing, although this mattered little, since its cameras were turned off on December 19. For the next decade it would transmit only data about the soft geography of the solar system.[137]

Voyager 2 also had a defective scan platform. After restoring control, engineers eventually determined that the frenzied pace of the near-encounter—the rapid rotations of the platform, almost minute by minute—had overworked the system, driven out its lubricant, and caused the mechanism to seize up. Through temperature cycling and a pause sufficient to allow some lubrication to seep back, engineers regained enough control to permit the platform to image Phoebe. Then, save for experiments to diagnose the problem, further maneuvering ceased. With enforced rest and fast-slewing prohibited, the system performed as desired. This, too, mattered little for the present, since Voyager 2's cameras were also shut down. Until it reached Uranus, it would emulate its twin and measure and map only the soft geography of interplanetary space.[138]

On September 30, 1981, the primary Voyager mission officially ended, succeeded on October 1, 1981, by the Voyager Uranus/Interstellar

Mission (VUIM). The spacecraft were well beyond their warranty, though not beyond their encoded ambitions. The goal for Voyager 1 was now to monitor the interplanetary medium preparatory to leaving the solar system and entering the interstellar realm. The goal for Voyager 2 was a flyby of Uranus, another miniature planetary system, while preserving the option to continue to Neptune.[139]

The projected mission was long and lonely, almost 4.5 years and 724 million kilometers away. Uranus was farther from Saturn than Saturn was from Earth. The gravity assists Voyager 2 had received from Jupiter and Saturn helped it pare that immense distance to a perhaps manageable stretch. But there was no way to disguise the fact that the journey was far and the risks high. The cruise phase was longer than the cycle for presidential elections. Five course corrections would be needed to steer the spacecraft through the Uranus system, a place about which only the crudest facts were known. With the euphoria of encounter over and the space shuttle hemorrhaging money, NASA demanded major budget cuts, including 60 percent of staff, which left the Voyagers to sail through solar winds and gravitational tides on something like autopilot. If a crisis developed, JPL would activate a Spacecraft Anomaly Team (SCAT), packed with Voyager veterans, to grapple with the issue. Without money, staff, and knowledge, it was daunting to plan for an encounter at a place so remote that even the simplest exchange of messages would require 328 minutes, or 5.5 hours.[140]

15. Cruise

Voyager 2's cruise to Uranus was longer than its trek from Earth to Saturn. That prolonged stint offered a chance for the spacecraft to rehabilitate, for programmers to study a poorly known planet in preparation for encounter, and for both Voyager and JPL to improve their ability to communicate. In the end, Voyager was only as good as the commands it could be given and the means available to give them. As time and distance increased, both messages and means became more arduous, which left cleverness to compensate for aging, and upgraded communication for remoteness.[141]

When they launched, the Voyagers' capacity for reprogramming and their power packs were revolutionary. Today, when computers sit on every desk and microchips make cell phones into miniature PCs, those software uploads seem as quaint as their transmitting power, about a billionth the wattage of a digital watch. When Voyager left Saturn, the first personal computers were just entering the market; for an IBM PC, the choice for RAM was either 64k or 128k, and program software ran on the same diskette as its output files. Voyager 2's computer command subsystem held a scant 2,500 words of memory for sequencing. For each instruction, one word specified the event, and the other, the time. Yet Voyagers' constraints were even more formidable: it would not be possible to swap out a new hard drive or install a new modem. But while Voyager's hardware could not be updated, the earthbound antennas for sending and receiving could.

The success of Voyager 2 at Uranus depended on the capabilities of the Deep Space Network. But, then, the DSN became what it was largely because it had to do what Voyager required.

DEEP SPACE NETWORK

The Deep Space Network performed three tasks. It assisted navigation and guidance by tracking spacecraft. It sent and received messages. And its signals could serve as an instrument of radio astronomy, particularly during occultations. But the network had to do all this on a twenty-four-hour basis; it had to receive from every spacecraft in orbit, a number that swelled yearly; and it had to connect even as spacecraft, notably Voyager, ranged farther and farther afield. In this, as in other matters, Pioneers 10 and 11 had pushed technology and procedures, forcing the DSN, further hobbled by Pioneer's antiquarian hardware and its algorithms, to its limits.[142]

These were only the known challenges. There were unknowns, too, such as the intensity of planetary radiation, which at Jupiter had caused wobbles in Voyager 2's receiver. And there were known but uncontrollable variables, related to weather both on the Sun and Earth. The solar wind caused turbulence, and passing behind the Sun overwhelmed receivers with noise. Rain in Spain caused a blackout of Jupiter data. As it had for explorers trekking for a year to distant lands to measure the transit of Venus, a wisp of cloud could wipe out the observation period.

Uranus strained both Voyager and the DSN. Even as it downloaded data from Voyager 2, the DSN had to track Voyager 1, along with Pioneer Venus and the ever-receding Pioneers 10 and 11. It had to maintain contact with the Russian Vega and European Space Agency's Giotto Halley probes. It communicated with the Japanese spacecraft MST-5 and Planet A. It transmitted and received with the

Giacobini-Zinner comet probe ICE. It still followed Helios and the earlier Pioneers (6, 7, and 9). The complexity of multisatellite tracking was daunting. But none of these issues equaled the challenge posed by Voyager's Uranus encounter.[143]

The spacecraft could not perform as it had at Saturn. It was losing power at a rate of seven watts annually. It was using fuel in the RPG, and as it aged it became less efficient with what it had. It could no longer power the IRIS flash-off heater while also transmitting on both the X band and the S band; yet all those operations were required for particular experiments. The solution was to shut down those components not absolutely needed, to turn off the IRIS heater when both transmitters were working, and to prohibit the simultaneous use of X-band and S-band transmitters in their high-power mode. By meticulous sequencing, IRIS could take its critical readings, the Uranus ring occultation measurements could proceed under high-power X band and low S band, and the planetary occultation at high S band and low X band. Another fix was to upload new software that could compress the data stream, allowing more kilobits to be sent for the same expenditure of power.[144]

Still, the signal was weakening at an exponential rate. For every doubling of distance, the strength of the signal fell by a fourth. Saturn was twice as far from Earth as Jupiter, and Uranus twice again as far as Saturn. The maximum rate of data transmission at Saturn had been 44.8 kilobits per second. At Uranus, it would be 21.6 kbps and 14.4 kbps. At Uranus, Voyager's radio signal would be "several billion times weaker than the power of a watch battery." The only way to compensate was to upgrade the DSN facilities. By a quirk of celestial geometry, the Canberra Deep Space Communication Complex in Australia could track the near-encounter for twelve hours. That was where the DSN and JPL Telecommunication Division would concentrate their efforts. The long cruise phase allowed time to consider options.[145]

A straightforward solution was to upgrade the receiving dishes; but this was unlikely since it was very expensive. NASA was investing everything in the space shuttle, and there were no other planetary missions on the books until Galileo in 1986, for which the existing arrangement sufficed. DSN would have to amplify what it had.

In 1982 it commissioned a global survey of large antenna facilities, what became known as the Interagency Array Study, which issued a report in April 1983. The study recommended as the best option to expand a technique developed for Saturn by which the several receivers at a station could be electronically linked and, in effect, establish a collective range far greater than the instruments could manage individually. Uranus, however, exceeded even these capabilities; the Canberra complex would have to link with another large dish, and the obvious candidate was the Parkes Radio Telescope, which also had a 64-meter antenna. By effectively connecting all the receivers together, the DSN had the equivalent of a 100-meter antenna, an escalation in capacity of 20–25 percent. The Voyager imaging team had wanted 330 images every 24 hours. The DSN could now guarantee 320 under ideal conditions.[146]

The other way to sharpen reception was to target the DSN array more accurately, which would reduce background noise (not a trivial concern given the lower wattage and the vast distances involved). To prevent degradation, DSN had to point its sixty-four-meter antennas to less than 6/1000th of a degree. One approach, called "blind pointing," was to estimate the location of the spacecraft and direct the antenna to the forecast spot, a technique applied during occultation and signal acquisitions. Instead of visible stars such as Canopus to assist navigation, the radio telescopes relied on radio stars for fixed points. The other strategy was to scan the estimated region in a conical sweep and acquire a signal from the spacecraft, which could then be used to track its location precisely.[147]

For Voyager 2 the two techniques were complementary, and both were necessary. To complicate the procedure, however, suitable radio stars in the region were unavailable, and the spacecraft's balky receiver demanded extra tending to locate its shape-shifting downlink signal. New software, practice drills at blind pointing, the installation of a Mark IVA system, and weekly meetings between DSN and

JPL brought the apparatus to working requirements. At Uranus the DSN could support up to 29.9 kilobits per second, improve navigation, and bolster the radio science experiments.[148]

Or it could in principle. In practice, upgrading facilities, crafting interagency agreements to bind individual antennas into arrays, and writing code had consumed time and money that would otherwise have gone into training. This was the mission cost of those sharp staff cuts after Saturn; continuities, once broken, were not easily regained. When, two weeks prior to the Uranus observation phase, the flight team conducted a dress rehearsal of near-encounter, it became clear that DSN was not sufficiently fluent; it needed more training and more people. But unearthing such outcomes was the reason behind the operational tests. DSN responded by adding technical staff and using the observation phase to conduct drills, as JPL used the information received from that period to refine targeting and the final sequencing for near-encounter, and of course to correct last-minute glitches.[149]

One such glitch emerged only shortly before closest approach, as images became marred by light and dark streaks. The first thought was that the error came from computer processing on Earth. But a scurried survey isolated the difficulty instead in a faulty memory spot in the onboard image processor. Within three days new software had been written to use an alternate location, and only six days before closest approach, the package was uploaded. The streaks vanished.[150]

There remained a final course correction, the last tweaking of a trajectory that had spanned nearly five billion kilometers. But so accurate was the spacecraft's path that no further adjustments were needed. Voyager 2 hurtled within twenty kilometers of its ideal aim point, testimony to a masterful triangulation among it, JPL, and the Deep Space Network.[151]

Compared to past exploration, Uranus was unfathomably remote in space but close in time. It could substitute speed for distance.

Lewis and Clark traveled 13,700 kilometers in 28 months; Voyager

Liftoff for America's space program. After the launch of Explorer 1 in 1958, a press conference led to one of the canonical images of the ensuing space age: William Pickering, James Van Allen, and Wernher von Braun hefting a mock-up of Explorer 1 over their heads. Each man stood for a competing version of what space might represent.

Source: NASA/JPL

Voyager spacecraft being assembled at the Kennedy Spaceflight Center. The foundational bus is clearly shown, along with the dominating high-gain directional antenna.

Source: NASA/JPL

Voyager spacecraft, assembled, as it would appear in the blackness of space.

Source: NASA/JPL

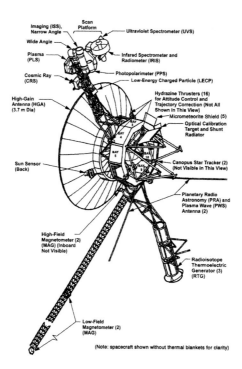

Schematic of Voyager spacecraft with instruments deployed.

Source: NASA/JPL

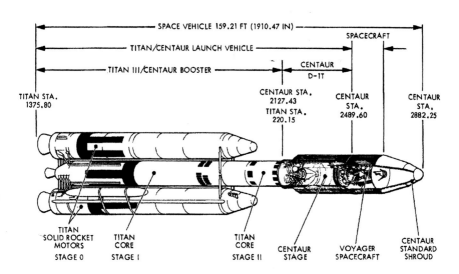

Titan IIIE-Centaur D-1T launch vehicle.

Source: R. L. Heacock, "The Voyager Spacecraft," Institution of Mechanical Engineers. Reproduced by permission.

Launch of Voyager 2, August 20, 1977.

Source: NASA/JPL

Voyager's gold-plated record.

Source: NASA/JPL

Iconic images: Voyager at Jupiter, showing technicolor clouds and orbiting moons.

Source: NASA/JPL

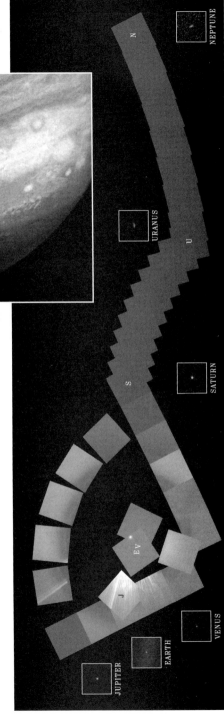

The Voyager family portrait: Voyager 1 looks back on the solar system. The panels show the panorama of imaging, and the inserts, the separate images of the planets.

Source: NASA/JPL

Voyager 1 looking back on Earth and Moon. Note: the brightness of the Moon has been enhanced to sharpen the contrast.

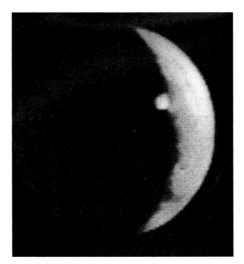

Voyager 1 looking back on Io. This is the original
black-and-white image, intended to assist navigation,
but which first showed anomalous features (center right)
eventually identified as a volcanic eruption.

Source: NASA/JPL

Voyager 1 looking back on Saturn.

Source: NASA/JPL

Voyager 2 looking back on Uranus.

Source: NASA/JPL

Voyager 2 looking back on Neptune and Triton, in a replay of Voyager 1's parting shot of Earth and its Moon.

Source: NASA/JPL

2 would take a few months longer than that to travel almost eight billion kilometers. The Corps of Discovery was basically out of contact for two years, and the collective journals were not published (and then in abridged form) for another century. At Saturn a message from Voyager took 86 minutes to reach the DSN; at Uranus, it would take 164 minutes, and as long to return. The first fruits of discovery were offered at daily press conferences during encounters, and published in scientific journals within months. While the ever-lengthening lag in electronic communications required Voyager to be semiautonomous, compared with historic precedents their correspondence and publication were practically simultaneous.

Such communications had always served to tell just where an explorer was and where he was headed. With space travel, however, the exchanges were the irreplaceable means needed to guide the spacecraft to its destination. This was a novelty. During the Great Voyages armadas had vanished over the horizon with hardly the prospect of a reply until they, or some fraction of them, returned. The last port of call was the final opportunity to exchange commands, information, personal mail, or warnings. While in the Canaries, Magellan received an alert that a Portuguese squadron was waiting to intercept him on his way to the New World, and so rerouted his voyage southward. One of his ships, the *San Antonio*, broke off and deserted near the Strait and returned with news (much false) to Spain. Otherwise, no one heard from the expedition again until, two years later, the *Victoria* limped into Lisbon. No camera watched as Columbus set foot on San Salvador, no radio message signaled da Gama's arrival in Calicut, no transmission measured Dias's occultation around the Cape of Good Hope. No one heard until someone returned, and if no one returned, no one knew what had happened or where. Lewis and Clark simply disappeared up the Missouri River, with no word about their whereabouts until they reappeared at St. Louis. When John Cabot disappeared in his search for a Northwest Passage, no one knew when or where.

Increased commercial traffic improved communication during the eighteenth century, and the telegraph boosted opportunities during the nineteenth. Humboldt sent letters to his sister Caroline in Prussia, who published them in newspapers. Dispatches from Russian American Company outposts in Alaska could take two hard years to reach Moscow and return. From Greenland, the 1845 Franklin Expedition sent letters home with the returning supply ship and military escort, though they might have used the whaler that spotted them afterward in Melville Bay; but they could not have expected any replies (and they themselves were never heard from again). Thomas Huxley on the HMS *Rattlesnake* could anticipate sending and receiving letters at Australian ports via the Royal Navy or commercial shipping. Henry Stanley had to wait until he returned to Zanzibar before he could telegraph his "discovery" of Livingstone to the *New York Herald*; but his more breathtaking traverse across central Africa down the Congo had him out of contact for three years. Newspaper rumors about his death preceded John Wesley Powell's successful run of the Colorado River through Grand Canyon. When Robert Scott's party died on their trek to the South Pole, it took two weeks for a search party to find their remains, another two months to inform the crew of the returning *Terra Nova,* and still another two weeks by ship before they could tell the world at Lyttleton, New Zealand. Seventeen years later Robert Byrd flew over the pole in a Ford Trimotor and then reported the feat by wireless radio upon his return to base at Little America.

Voyager had its missed, and mixed, messages, beginning years before, with JPL's error to send it an expected signal, which caused it to default to backup procedures, and continuing to moments when its cantankerous receiver would lose contact and when the spacecraft disappeared for painful minutes behind a planet. But it had what few prior expeditions did: a system of redundancy. As it pushed across the Outback of the solar system, it also had encoded in its protocols the wrenching history of past exploration. It could accept new orders. It could adapt new procedures. It could learn.

The immense distances meant that Voyager could not wait for commands from Earth. That it could communicate routinely with JPL was an astounding accomplishment; but the lengthening lines of communication meant that its managers had to allow Voyager more and more leeway. The velocity of encounters left no other option, for although communication—if compared to that available to Louis-Antoine de Bougainville in the Pacific or Nikolai Przhevalsky in Central Asia—was nearly instantaneous, "nearly" wasn't good enough. Voyager had to communicate with itself.

THE DARKEST WORLD

Still, Voyager 2 could only report on what it was told to examine, and Uranus was a dark world, only dimly fathomed. With Jupiter and Saturn enough had been known to predict what the scientific priorities might be. But Voyager 2 now required detailed scenarios for an encounter with a planet only first discovered in 1781, two centuries before the spacecraft had left Saturn, and a body about which almost nothing was known. Its planetary plane was tilted: that anomaly was only the most apparent of Uranus's obliquities.

During its long, silent cruise phase, Voyager's staff had sought to sharpen that blurry vision and to heighten the return of Voyager information as the spacecraft blasted through the planetary plane of an eccentrically oblique Uranus. The task was formidable. There would be no Pioneers 10 and 11 to forge trails, and no Voyager 1 to do a sweeping reconnaissance. The skewed rotational plane made trajectories stranger still, and the path to Neptune trickier. Near-encounter would have to compress almost everything into a scant six hours, roughly the time it took to exchange messages between Voyager and Earth. Long distances, limited computing power, a bottomless thirst for data, and a scarcely known target—encounter demanded an unusually intricate scenario, which is to say, advance scientific scouting and planning.[152]

That began with a conference on February 4–6, 1984, which assembled more than one hundred scientists to assess the state of knowledge regarding Uranus and Neptune. The resulting proceedings revealed ignorance about even such basic parameters as rotation periods, magnetic fields, radiation, rings, and major satellites. Remoteness and a thick methane atmosphere made Uranus's surface opaque. Nothing was known of its weather, and heating at the poles rather than the equator introduced unprecedented variables in comparison with the other gaseous planets. Five satellites were known; almost certainly there were others. Nine narrow rings had been identified; again, there were surely more. (The rings had been discovered by stellar occultation only in 1977, the year of Voyager's launch.)[153]

Necessarily, much of the expected data and anticipated measurements would draw on analogies to the two gaseous giants Voyager had already visited. But some features did not translate—that oblique rotational plane, for one, and worse, Uranus's exceptional dimness, which rendered its rings and moons among the darkest objects observed in the solar system. Since sunlight decreased with the square of the distance, Uranus received 1 unit of solar radiation for every 360 at Earth. That left Uranus plenty dark, its moons nearly invisible, and its rings, reflecting some 2 percent of even incident sunlight, with half the brightness of "ground-up charcoal."[154]

Researchers were organized into three Uranus Science Working Groups, one each for atmospheres, rings, and satellites and magnetospheres. (To assist deliberations, Bradford Smith and Richard Terrile of the Voyager imaging team conducted special observations at the Las Campanas Observatory, in Chile, to gather extra data on the rings.) Between April and May the three working groups met repeatedly and independently to identify the major themes of inquiry and then to work with the flight science office to reconcile what they wanted with what the instruments could do and how to sequence the desired observations, each of which was designated as a "link," and which collectively made a chain of encounter events that could be graphed into a timeline. Each group also prioritized its scientific goals. In July 1984 they issued their final report to the Voyager Science Steering Group. Then the three groups had to reconcile their ambitions and produce a master (if still incomplete) timeline. Iteration followed iteration, with the work lasting from February 11, 1985, to July 19, 1985.[155]

One intractable issue concerned Miranda, the principal moon of

Uranus. Planetary astronomers desperately wanted to know its mass, which would affect their calculations of the planetary system's orbits as well as the path of Voyager 2, and this required real-time tracking to detect the gravitational pull of the moon on the spacecraft. But planetary geologists wanted equally to image the surface, which required image motion compensation; that is, the spacecraft had to turn along with the camera to keep the narrow-angle lens pointed steadily on target. The first needed constant contact with Earth, while the second forced the antenna to turn away, breaking that connection; there was no way for the hardware to be in two places at the same time. But it was possible for the software to pretend otherwise. During the iteration exercise, with its successive refinements of timing, planners realized that the image requirements could be satisfied best just prior to closest approach, and the mass determination during and just after closest approach, which left a difference between the two tasks of roughly five minutes during which the antenna had to reposition itself. The hardware could run only one way, but the software could be run backward, as it were; the effect on image motion compensation was the same. And so it proved: both experiments yielded excellent returns.[156]

The experience was no less a symbolic reversal of public expectations of how Voyager actually worked. The public face was rockets and robots. The reality was software and communications.

Over and again, hardware failures—faulty platform gears, broken receivers, the need for extended imaging—were compensated for by software fixes and the ability to send them across the immensity of interplanetary space. Programs for image motion compensation tweaked spacecraft gyroscopes to allow long exposures even as the spacecraft hurtled onward. Special software compressed data, and even allowed for onboard processing, which reduced the time and burden of transmission; an onboard Reed-Solomon data encoder bolstered the accuracy of data transmission while shrinking its digital "overhead." Other programs adjusted actuators for slewing, torque, and rolls.

But the grandest software, constantly rewritten and uploaded, remained in the human brain. It was the vision of the Grand Tour, and in late 1985, made real in Voyager, it sailed boldly beyond any previous encounter and toward a world darker than any other in the solar system.

16. Encounter: Uranus

From March 26 through November 3, 1985, preparations for encounter commenced with a routine that included regular imaging of Uranus, a recalibration of instruments, and a trajectory course correction. For almost three and a half years, Voyager had run in maintenance mode; now it had to be resuscitated, and its crew retrained for the intricate tacking and close hauling executed at velocities ten times that of a bullet. Staffing gradually scaled up. There were training sessions and trial runs, a shakedown rehearsal. As it felt the gravitational tug of Uranus, the mass of the planet altered Voyager's velocity, and the quickening events bulked up time until its history, too, seemed to acquire momentum.[157]

From October 7 to November 4, over four years after leaving Saturn and eight since it broke free from Earth, Voyager 2 put its instruments, mechanisms, and procedures through a series of checks. The power system, scan slewing, maneuvers for image motion compensation and radio occultation, likely frequency drift in the spacecraft radio reception, wide-angle photography of background stars—everything that the spacecraft would have to do in less than three months when any prospect for corrections would be lost in the blistering rush past the planet was tried now. The process culminated in a full-dress rehearsal of near-encounter. The exercise revealed assorted problems, primarily in new and inadequate staff, which JPL and DSN addressed by calling up reserves and scheduling more training. Meanwhile, engineers worked feverishly to ready final adjustments, engage the so-called target maneuver that would calibrate the image science subsystem and IRIS, and upload software patches and the all-important sequence commands.

Near-encounter would last a mere 6 hours; an exchange of radio messages between Earth and Uranus would take 5.5 hours; as Voyager hurtled around Uranus in another volta, there would be no opportunity to do anything but let the program play out. Expectation and anxiety tumbled along like wood chips through a cataract.

CLOSE ENCOUNTER

On November 4, Voyager 2 entered its observatory phase.

Since July the extended scrutiny of the planet offered by Voyager's instruments had exceeded the best Earth-based sources. One after another the remote inventory of what JPL's *Voyager Uranus Travel Guide* called "our human quest to understand the world beyond Earth" began its third grand iteration. The ultraviolet spectrometer sought out gaseous emissions and the Uranian aurora. The planetary radio astronomy instruments searched for evidence of a Uranian magnetosphere. Of particular interest was timed imaging of the atmosphere; these photos were assembled into thirty-eight-hour movies (hence, two complete rotations of the planet) although the oddities of tilted Uranus meant that the imaging recorded the south pole, which allowed far less variety than comparable movies of the Jovian and Saturnian equatorial belts. Steadily, strikingly, the blue murk that was Uranus began to dissolve into features and movements, and the hard matrix that was the Uranian system resolved itself out of a starry background. The planet became real.[158]

Voyager's arcing trajectory around Uranus offered the usual occasion for occultation, with measurements of rings and planetary atmosphere, but halfway through its observatory phase, the spacecraft, as viewed from Earth, would pass behind the Sun. This solar conjunction allowed for occultation of the solar atmosphere as well, and because of the Sun's immense mass, for a test of the general theory of relativity, which predicted that the rays would bend (and therefore slow) under the influence of gravity, or more precisely, from the curved geometry of space around the Sun. This backside transit of Voyager yielded results consistent with prediction.[159]

Mostly, observation meant preparations: more measurements of the interplanetary medium, continuing instrumental calibrations, further testing of scan platforms, torque margins, and gyroscopic drifting. The various clocks had to be synchronized. Increasingly large images had to be edited into movies. Eventually an acrobatic Voyager underwent four yaws and four rolls that helped reset its magnetometer and furnished detailed star maps for precision guidance. The observatory phase ended with a final (of five) trajectory correction maneuver.[160]

After ninety-five days, observation segued into far-encounter on January 10, 1986. For the next dozen days the pace of monitoring matched the acceleration of the spacecraft. The pull of Uranus speeded up everything.

By now the bulk of Uranus could no longer fit into a narrow-angle lens; it took four such images to make a planetary mosaic; and soon the scope of the scene would overwhelm capabilities for whole-planet movies. Measuring the gravitational tug allowed for more precise calculations of planetary mass, which refined further trajectory corrections. Dormant instruments came back to life. The temperature of IRIS stabilized, readying it to transmit infrared data. The photopolarimeter revived and swept over the planet, satellites, and rings. The radio astronomy and plasma wave instruments added to particle and field measurements. New command packages, B721 and B723, were uploaded. A final "operational readiness test" put both the Voyager JPL team and the DSN through their paces. After years of mechanical hibernation, Voyager 2 was fully roused and ravenous, and on January 22 it began its near-encounter.[161]

In something like six hours Voyager threaded its way through the Uranian system, conducted more than ninety priority science experiments, and sped at still greater velocity toward Neptune. It was not simply the number of maneuvers but their condensation that astonishes. At Jupiter and Saturn, the Voyagers had sailed along the plane of planetary rotation, joining the flow of the rings and moons, faster than those other satellites but moving with and through a shared orbital plane over several days. Now Voyager 2 passed across them, almost at right angles. Everything had to happen in sharp, crisp succession. The spacecraft had to roll, which meant it had to shift its reference stars from Alkaid (in Ursa Major) to Canopus and then Fomalhaut in Piscis Austrinus and Achernar in Eridanus. Voyager soaked up so much data that it could not unload it, even with compression algorithms, except by replaying tapes over several days.

As it passed across the backside of Uranus, Voyager conducted almost continual occultation experiments with rings and atmosphere. The unblinking eyes of Voyager's instruments, especially IRIS and the radio science sensors, recorded atmospheric temperature, pressure, and chemical composition. Full-ring mosaics were composed both coming and going. Passage through the rings recorded particle impacts. Other instruments sampled the north polar region, invisible as Voyager had approached but now exposed as it swung behind the planet. The spacecraft interrogated the mysteries of the Uranian magnetosphere—whether it existed at all, and if so, with what dynamic geometry, since the south pole pointed into the solar wind. After passing repeatedly into and out of bow shock, Voyager could sketch a map of that magnetic shorescape. It imaged and studied the brightness of the five major moons—Ariel, Umbriel, Titania, Oberon, and Miranda—and used their perturbing gravitational effects on the spacecraft to measure more precisely their separate masses; of Miranda, the innermost moon, it made particularly close observations, passing within a mere 29,000 kilometers. But most complicated were the full-color and monochromatic photos of the Uranian satellites, all of which demanded image motion compensation, which required the spacecraft to pitch, yaw, and roll with intricate timing to hold the bleakly dark scenes steady while the spacecraft sped past. All this occurred amid constant moderate-rate slewing to capture as many objects as possible. And so it did: Voyager unveiled new rings and discovered ten new moons. For the largest, Puck, it captured a hurried but still usable image.[162]

There were a few snafus. A glitch at the Canberra DSN station lost some data, but engineers were able to have Voyager replay the stored information later. There were other minor "deviations" in expected performance. But for what Ellis Miner called JPL's "aging brainchild," they were "few in number and minor in consequences." Voyager had far exceeded its basic design parameters; it had twisted, measured, imaged, rolled, and reoriented its way around probably the most anomalous planet in the solar system; it had gone where no spacecraft had gone before; and when it hurtled past the far side of the Uranian system, it was on a dead course for Neptune, some thirty times farther from the Sun than Earth is, a trek that even with its once-more gravity-assisted acceleration would require 3.5 years.[163]

Uranus was a new world. It lay almost beyond the reach of Earth-based observation. No prior space probe had visited it, and only its most coarse contours had been traced. After Voyager, Uranus became, if not familiar, at least recognizable.

Every instrument of Voyager, and even the gravitational behavior of the spacecraft itself, added real knowledge: The mass of Uranus, and its aspherical distribution; the period of planetary rotation; the structure and chemistry of the atmosphere, including an abundance of helium, water, and methane, and their stratification; the eccentric energy budget, its reflectivity and reradiation, a pattern that leaves the planet much warmer than solar heating alone would permit; a unique meteorology, driven more by planetary rotation than solar radiation, with subtle differences in color and haze; an accurate geometry of the Uranian magnetosphere, including the wide divergence between magnetic and rotational poles; the confirmation of polar aurorae and lightning; radio emissions only weakly controlled by solar winds; low-density plasma filling out the magnetosphere; new rings and ring arcs—their composition, obscure reflectivity, particle size, dynamics. If images were "moderately disappointing," as one observer noted, that had to do with Uranus's hazy outer atmosphere, which blurred the kind of structure that riveted attention at

Jupiter and even Saturn, and with the baffling darkness of its hard geography of orbiting particles.[164]

Perhaps most spectacularly for both the public and even jaded scientists, Voyager 2 found miniature new worlds: it tripled the number of known Uranian moons. Because its passage through the system was so swift, its imaging hardware could not be adequately reprogrammed to photograph them all, nor because of its oblique rush through the orbital plane could its cameras view the outermost moons with the kind of resolution it had brought to the Jovian and Saturnian satellites; and to be authenticated, each revelation required at least two separate sightings, with enough lag to calculate a probable orbit.

But they came in a rush of near-epiphany. The first moon was found on December 30, 1985, sufficiently early that it could be targeted in the final flurry, sandwiched amid images of Miranda. Two more were identified on January 3; one on January 9 and another on January 13; another three on January 18; two shepherd satellites, flanking the epsilon ring, on January 20; and the last on January 21. Since its known moons had names from Shakespeare's *A Midsummer Night's Dream*, the first new discovery became Puck, and the others derived from various Shakespeare plays or from Alexander Pope's *The Rape of the Lock*. All this new discovery, moreover, happened while the five known moons were also imaged, with varying degrees of resolution, and their properties compared. The five outer moons were brighter, showed evidence of former melting, and were colder. The two most intriguing were also those with the highest resolutions. Ariel was lightly cratered, which revealed a period of post-bombardment surface flooding, or "cryovolcanic flows." Miranda was, simply, a jumbled mess, or more formally, a "geologic enigma." It seemed as though it had smashed apart, then cold-fused with whatever had splintered it, and there stayed, like a geologic Frankenstein's monster, full of odd lithic parts and thick stitches. Three days after its last discovered satellite, Belinda, Voyager slingshotted through near-encounter.[165]

Even to those experienced in Voyager's serial surprises, the capacity of the valiant spacecraft to amaze remained undiminished. However dark Uranus, Voyager 2 had shone.

On January 26, near-encounter segued into post-encounter. The Voyager team scheduled a final press conference for 8:00 a.m. on January 28, 1986, what everyone anticipated would be the celebration of a weary, wondrous quest. Instead, thirty-five minutes later, participants watched in horror as the space shuttle Challenger exploded on launch. The Uranus encounter could survive radiation, celestial mechanics, sagging power, balky actuators, particle attacks, impossibly tenuous lines of communication. It could not compete with immolated astronauts.

BREAKUP

For almost thirty years the competing factions within the American space program had united in common cause under a fulsome NASA budget and against a cold war rival. At the onset of the space race their primary contestants, symbolized by JPL's William Pickering, the University of Iowa's James Van Allen, and the U.S. Army's rocketeer Wernher von Braun, had hoisted Explorer 1 over their collective heads, and they had continued that display of public unity, if not amity, as a downsizing Apollo program and its shuttle successor cleaved the funds that kept them all in loose alliance and forced the contestants to fight for the scraps that fell from the shuttle's table.

Both NASA and space apologists wanted to isolate criticisms within the community lest any harping harm the space enterprise overall. The official line was that both programs were necessary, and that what was good for one was good for the other. NASA tried to quarantine the issue by segregating the manned and unmanned programs except at the highest administrative level. But as the competition sharpened over the years, von Braun's vision of space colonization came to dominate; Van Allen's perspective of space as a scene for science suffered, and over the years Van Allen became more vocal, expounding his criticisms to fellow space scientists, to the public and press, and to Congress. The competition was both undeniable and subtle: the sheer weight of the manned space program could shove rivals aside. During Pioneer 10's encounter with Jupiter, von

Braun had shown up at mission control and sat on a desk stuffed with terminals to watch the show. His rump hit a switch on a video terminal and turned it off, and since all the terminals were linked, the entire system crashed. The mission staff had to remove him and reboot. That episode might well stand (or sit) as symbolic of the larger rivalry.[166]

By the time Voyager 2 reached Uranus, it was obvious that NASA's three-ply composite was delaminating. The agency had consistently favored the manned over the unmanned, the aeronautical industry over the universities and research centers, and defense over science. The manned program, with its ultimate vision of extraterrestrial colonization, might fume over the slow pace of the shuttle's development and express frustration with the lack of progress toward Mars, but the shuttle, Skylab, and the space station were at least within its informing narrative. That program, and its increasing domination by the Pentagon, cut the others off in midsentence. But while the immediate aftermath of the tragedy hushed any overt criticism— one could only voice admiration for the dead astronauts and mouth determination to honor them by reflying the shuttle—the options were out in the open.

In the January issue of *Scientific American*, which ran a few weeks before the disaster, Van Allen had publicly broken ranks and questioned the value of the manned program altogether. In May he wrote an essay for *Science* in which he systematically compared the manned and unmanned programs, noting that "many space enthusiasts blithely ignore the fact that almost all the truly important utilitarian and scientific achievements of our space program have been made by instrumented, unmanned spacecraft." He mocked the "misty-eyed concept that the manifest destiny of man is to live and work in space"; scorned the "Columbus analogy" to support a manned mission to Mars as "massively deceitful"; and concluded with a "poignant juxtaposition" of the Challenger disaster and Voyager 2's flyby of Uranus. (Some years later he suggested, with tongue only partly in cheek, that NASA sell the manned space program to China.) Instead of pursuing mirages, NASA ought to develop "space applications of widespread human importance" and sponsor "major advances in human understanding" of the universe. It ought, in brief, to be a scientific research institution.[167]

It was obvious that robots were not only cheaper and safer than people, but also capable of increasingly sophisticated semiautonomous behavior, and were improving at far faster rates than *Homo*. If NASA had committed itself to robotic spacecraft, he implied, there would have been no space shuttle to drain away funding from the truly breakthrough programs and no Challenger to explode. The science fiction that seemed to animate his rivals pointed not to a usable future but to a visionary past.

Neither Van Allen nor von Braun affected Voyager directly. Van Allen, to his and others' surprise, failed to make the scientific cut and had no instrument to place on either Voyager's boom; and von Braun died two months before Voyager 2 launched. But his ghost continued to haunt NASA and hound Voyager.

As the costs of Apollo ballooned, NASA had dumped the original Voyager mission to Mars. The reincarnation of Apollo as the space shuttle in 1972 repeated that experience and soon whittled the original Grand Tour down to MJS 77. In July 1979, as Voyager 2 commenced its encounter with Jupiter, it had to compete for media attention with the death spiral of Skylab and speculation about where it might land (and on whom) and with Tom Wolfe's paean to the Mercury astronauts, *The Right Stuff.*

Then, as Voyager 2 approached Uranus, JPL realized that the proposed shuttle manifest included a launch four days before near-encounter. Such a schedule conflict could affect support and tracking, to say nothing of public attention, and JPL asked to have the shuttle delayed. Voyager 2 had spent 8.5 years getting to Uranus; the shuttle could wait 8.5 days. The request went to James Beggs, then NASA director, who denied the request. When asked why, he reportedly replied, "The White House doesn't want the launch slipped." The Reagan administration had long sought to hobble the planetary program; this final snub, however petty and unreasonable, was in keeping. As it happened, the launch schedule for the shuttle

Challenger slipped anyway, until after Voyager 2's near-encounter. It then launched under questionable circumstances and promptly blew up.[168]

The immediate reaction at JPL and among Voyager enthusiasts was shock, and grief for their mutual enterprise of space travel. There was, as Ellis Miner put it, "a spontaneous day of silence for fallen friends and blasted hopes." But the realization quickly grew that rebuilding the shuttle program would eviscerate the planetary program, not only from financial starvation but from lack of a launch vehicle. The shuttle had taken everything. NASA had put all its eggs into one basket and watched it explode. The Challenger disaster was a "temporary death knell," Miner continued, for the "continued unmanned exploration of the planets."[169]

Others were not so forgiving. "Even then," as Bruce Murray expressed it, "Fletcher [NASA director] would not acknowledge what everyone else knew—that planetary missions were intrinsically incompatible with the Shuttle." America's planetary exploration remained "hostage to the dying embers of NASA's Shuttle fantasy." Already, to pay for the shuttle and its endless delays and overruns, the United States had declined to join the international mission to Comet Halley. Now the Galileo mission to Jupiter was postponed indefinitely. Ulysses to Jupiter and the Sun, Magellan to Venus, Cassini to Saturn, the Mars Observer, the Comet Rendezvous/Asteroid Flyby—all went into suspension as NASA struggled to make its white elephant fly again. All that remained was Voyager.[170]

What is perhaps less obvious is the challenge space science, as pure science, the search for data, posed to Voyager-like missions. This was in some respects more subtle, as Van Allen's own career demonstrated.

After all, James Van Allen had been a founder of the field. He had blazed a postwar trail to the outer atmosphere with balloons, rocketoons, and rockets; had been part of the catalytic discussions that led to IGY, and had helped ensure its commitment to the geophysics of soft geography; had sent the first instrument aloft on Explorer 1, which had led to the first great discovery of the era's space science, the eponymous Van Allen radiation belts; and had outfitted the Pioneer spacecraft, including Pioneers 10 and 11, with critical instrumentation. He had grown up with the space program, and grown famous because of it. Yet his emphasis could easily divert attention away from spacecraft and onto other platforms. In particular, astronomers might well—and did—argue for Earth-orbiting telescopes, what became NASA's Great Observatories.

If science is what you want, they delivered. Within twenty years after the Grand Tour, and after its own blinkered start, the Hubble Space Telescope (HST) and other major observatories could achieve "nearly Voyager-class imaging" of the outer planets. They could crudely map Pluto and its moon Charon; they could offer evidence that the Kuiper Belt, with some two hundred million inert comets, existed; they could improve on the Voyagers' astonishing tally of discovered satellites. Altogether the Voyagers discovered twenty-six new moons among the outer planets; the HST has since found forty-eight for Jupiter alone, most the size of asteroids. The HST can peer at a planet for long periods, return to detect seasonal and orbital changes, image the same scene over and over, and combine it with sophisticated software to detect satellites and rings. It can be patient. The Voyagers flew past once, faster than the human eye could follow.[171]

If partisans of manned programs had clawed away at planetary spacecraft, so had space scientists who wanted money and institutional attention lavished on topics of interest to them, and who might well regard robotic spacecraft as a proxy for the pointless adventuring that appalled Van Allen. The most powerful institutional voices on the NAS and NASA space science boards were astronomers, who tended to view planetary science, with its discovery of icy geysers, erupting volcanoes, and whacked-out moons, as a latter-day form of field naturalist gathering the contemporary equivalent of conch shells and orchids, and they consistently undermined the case for spacecraft in favor of telescopes and their equivalents.

Of course some measurements can't be done from observatories, great or otherwise, just as some activities robots can't do as well as people. But the pace of technological innovation continues to quicken. Much as robotic exploration was much cheaper than manned, so, potentially, was near-Earth science cheaper than far-trekking spacecraft. The arguments made in favor of robots as scientists can be made equally against robots as instruments.

The Voyagers thus had to fight on two flanks. Was Voyager, as both banks of critics implied, only an interim measure, with the robots destined to succumb either to humans or to instruments? Were such spacecraft only devices to do the work of other programs, or might they have an identity of their own? Did they do what the others could not? How might Voyager answer the charge that the Grand Tour was a Great Detour?

Like all defining expeditions, the Voyager mission was a synthesis—that's what gave it stamina and cultural power. It differed from orbiting observatories in that it traveled. That's what made it exploration, not merely extreme science. It was not the gathered data, artifacts, souvenirs, loot, logs, and journals that transformed curiosity into discovery, and discovery into exploration; it was the trek. The medium—the journey—was part of the message. It mattered not solely as a means of positioning instruments but as an event in itself, one that segued into quest. An entrée of geophysics and a dash of astrobiology might be enough for academicians scornful of space-craft cameras and other seeming popularizations. It was not enough for the culture, which wanted to recreate that alchemical alloy of discovery and adventure, fused into a journey and culminating in an encounter. It wanted the personification of cultural identity, whether it be placed on a Nansen sledge or an adapted Mariner hex, whether by a character-testing Edwardian or a quasi-autonomous robot.

And it is the issue of character and encounter that most separated Voyager from traditional exploration. What it encountered did not require a human presence. At one level this is simply the argument for better instrumentation. Amid the geographic realms of the Third Age, there is no Other; not as a person, an intelligence, or a biota. People are simply a clever means to record data, which machines can do. The Mercury astronauts worried that they might be nothing more than "Spam in a can," that monkeys could do (and did do) what was required of a passenger. What, then, exactly, do people bring to the event? They know those hostile environs only through heavily intermediated suits and mechanical cocoons. They cannot smell or taste or touch or hear those scenes. They can only see them. Yet the "eyes of discovery" are available to everyone with access to a TV set or an LCD monitor connected to the Internet. The human "presence" is already mostly a machine presence. Exploration is becoming more and more virtual. As Robert Ballard said of manned submersibles, "ultimately" their "limits will become intolerable."[172]

What is lost is the inherited sense that exploration must be done by human explorers on the scene and the human drama that goes with flawed human actors. The argument, that is, is not that people are better at science, but that they are better at exaltation and tragedy, and that without the prospect for loss and strife, public interest in Third Age exploration will wane. Exploration will morph into something like normal science, which has its own competitions and motivating curiosity but is not organized as geographic travel. Here is one of the paradoxes of the Third Age. Because it does not involve contacting Others, it has purged past exploration of the moral dry rot of imperialism, but it has done so at the cost of its moral drama—the angst, the horror, the triumphalism, the fusion in a single personality of ambition and vision quest, the equally embedded internal struggle, what William Faulkner called "the human heart in conflict with itself"—that plagued past discovery and fascinated the public.

Apologists might argue with both reason and conviction that the reality of modern exploration was that it is an alloy of machines and men. "The truth," as Oran Nicks noted, "is that there were no such things as unmanned missions; it was merely a question of where man stood to conduct them." But equally, "crewed" missions were utterly dependent on semiautonomous machines and "flew" spacecraft that could be as easily flown on their own, without the genetically and morally flawed carbon bipeds. The proportions and perceptions might vary, but no human could venture into the realms of the Third Age except through an artificial habitat, and no robot could build, launch, and steer itself. We are of course drawn to the human, or to those creatures and machines that can be humanized. Even professional explorers such as Roald Amundsen and Henry Stanley have a complexity, a plexus of motives, surprises, and contradictions that robots cannot achieve. They are, after all, human, and it is the human story, the fusion of plot and character, powered by conflict, that drives the traditional narrative of exploration.[173]

But as the relative composition of human and machine has changed, so have the stakes. No one has calculated the attrition rate for exploration, or what trend it has shown, other than that exploring has come at a declining cost of lives over the centuries, largely as a result of better shipborne travel, medicine, and technology. On his epochal voyage, da Gama lost 120 of 180 men and two of three ships. Magellan's Armada de Molucca returned with 18 of 237 men, and one of five ships (although one vessel had deserted for home earlier), and Magellan himself died. The demands for long-voyage care and feeding were enormous. In the nineteenth century, Britain's Royal Navy recorded the percentages of shipboard fatalities as disease (60 percent), accident (32 percent), ship losses from fire or sinking (10 percent), and enemy action (8 percent). Substitute "exploring hazards" for "enemy action" and the statistics would likely compare.[174]

No such dangers attended Voyager. JPL engineers might labor feverishly to correct a flaw that threatened a mission, and advocates might lobby Congress and NASA with tireless resolve, but such efforts are still a far cry from the young Henry Stanley, himself temporarily roused from a deep fever, with the threats of Arab slavers ringing in his ears, resolving by candlelight to succeed in his quixotic search for the "Apostle of Africa," David Livingstone. "I have taken a solemn, enduring oath, an oath to be kept while the least hope of life remains in me, not to be tempted to break the resolution I have formed, never to give up the search, until I find Livingstone alive, or find his dead body." No living man, "or living men," he continued, "shall stop me, only death can prevent me. But death—not even this; I shall not die, I will not die, I cannot die!" No robot thought it might die. No spacecraft defied death in its quest. Machine failure in a robotic mission might dash dreams, but it would not claim lives.[175]

Antarctica again offers a point of inflection. Contemplating the tragedies and extraordinary exertions of the Terra Nova expedition, Apsley Cherry-Garrard characterized their endeavor as "running appalling risks, performing prodigies of superhuman endurance, achieving immortal renown, commemorated in august cathedral sermons and by public statues, yet reaching the Pole only to find our terrible journey superfluous, and leaving our best men dead on the ice." He proposed instead that modern technology—proper ships, aircraft, specialists—"will all be needed if the work is to be done in any sort of humane and civilized fashion." Then he came to the crux: that politicians and the public must "learn to value knowledge that is not baited by suffering and death," be it the death of the discoverer or of those discovered. Simple adventuring was insufficient; true exploration, he thought, was the "physical expression of the Intellectual Passion." There had to be some cultural purpose beyond simple travel and personal tests of character. He thought science might do. But his own bolt, he reckoned, was "shot."[176]

In the Third Age those appropriate technologies exist. They can allow millions to share in robotic discovery, in the only kind of sensory encounter that the forbidding geographies of ice, abyss, and space allow. The transformation of moral drama is still playing out. What modern exploration wants is not just shared sense data but shared meaning: not merely the eyes of discovery but its poetry. In some way, if only by literary tropes, the robots must be anthropomorphized. They must be agents and proxies, and a presence. They would then be, as Nicks observes, "reflections of their masters."[177]

Encounter, in brief, is not simply an event, the meeting of two entities, like the bow shock of ionic winds, but an exchange of minds, and ultimately a confrontation between moralities. How to find such moments, or their simulacra, amid ice, abyss, and space is the issue that confronts the sponsors who dispatch machine explorers. And it is what Voyager 2 enigmatically, brilliantly, poignantly displayed at Uranus.

FIRST CONTACT

For Voyager, planetary encounter was a programmed event. It was a prescribed ritual, written into the software commands that told the spacecraft, minute by minute, often second by second, what to do. But that did not make the event idiosyncratic to the mission, or to space exploration. What Voyager codified was five hundred years of experienced encounters.

When Columbus made landfall, the practice already had its prescriptions. The first task was to look to the safety of the ship—wait for the dawn's light, watch for shoals and rocks, find a protected harbor or lee anchorage. Then the admiral and captains would take the longboat ashore, kneel, and give thanks. As soon as possible they would try to locate natives (who typically were already watching the newcomers, and often came to the ship in boats), display emblems of authority, communicate by signs and perhaps share gifts, begin to train interpreters, and collect directions to the headmen, and, always, identify the way to wealth. Amid so many isles, the crews had ample time to drill and adapt, but behind them stood more than seventy years of Portuguese probing among Atlantic isles and African coastlines.

With further centuries of exploring, the protocol evolved, reaching something of a pinnacle in Capt. James Cook, as he made contact with island upon island. His landing party consisted of him, his chief scientist, a physician, an interpreter, a security guard of marines, and sailors to row to shore. (Eerily, this is exactly the composition of the "away teams" so beloved by *Star Trek*, save that Hollywood scriptwriters could dispense with interpreters, having disseminated universal translators, not to mention other plot apparatus deemed necessary to go where, outside Hollywood, no one was.) As Cook understood, encounters typically went bad not because of natural circumstances such as high seas but because of social ones. A native stole, a sailor was killed, a chief was seized or hostages taken, the exploring expedition retaliated; or a captain failed, a crew mutinied, an exploring party fell apart. Conflict, character, choice—these are what metamorphose adventure into drama.

What explorers most valued was the founding encounter, what popular culture has come to call first contact. Here, potentially, was exploration stripped of the qualms, morasses, and banalities into which, historically, discovery had morphed into imperialism and normal scholarship. Here, physical adventure underwent a transubstantiation into moral drama.

Few first-contact narratives speak as today's partisans might wish. They were not recorded as part of a genre they knew the future desired. But there is one extraordinary exception, because it happened in recent times, and that is the saga of the gold-seeking Leahy brothers when they trekked into the unknown interior of New Guinea in 1930. Not only were they seeking new lands, but they also were doing so as explorers, and they even carried a motion-picture camera to document what they saw and experienced.

When they passed over the summit of the Bismarck Mountains, they looked down on immense highland valleys, densely cultivated, flush with fires, awash with people unknown to them and who themselves knew nothing of the world beyond their tribal borders. The prospecting expeditions, under Mick Leahy, continued into the mid-1930s, extending discovery into valley upon valley, beyond the vales of Goroka and Asaro, and meeting tribe after tribe, pushing on to the putative source of the gold, much as Hernando Cortés kept moving inland until he found the great depository of Aztec wealth. That first expedition ended up crossing the island, a veritable microcontinent. Here was raw first contact of a sort not seen since the Great Voyages and the entradas of the New World conquistadors.[178]

In truth, it is unsettling how fully the Leahys' encounters echoed those of previous centuries. Without a common language, exchanges were limited to signs, pantomimes, and demonstrations. The Australians wanted food, information, safe passage, and, later, women and workers; the highlanders wanted shells (their equivalent to bullion), steel axes, and, later, weapons. The explorers demonstrated their firepower and their superior technologies, and in later years flew select indigenes by airplane to see coastal cities; they took youngsters who could learn their language and serve as interpreters. The highlanders sought to fit the strangers into their existing economic and political dynamics as well as their prevailing cosmology; they wanted the unbelievable wealth of shells the strangers could distribute, and they sought to exploit the newcomers to advantage in the complex balance of endless wars among neighbors. Quickly, the Leahy party evolved protocols for contact.

Yet the encounter was profoundly asymmetrical. Like Pizarro or Stanley, the explorers had come without permission or prior notice. They had simply appeared and, by their sheer presence, broke the old order. They stood outside the existing etiquette of exchange, were not subject to taboos, did not warrant traditional courtesies to travelers or pilgrims, were neither friend nor foe, just a pale Other. Their very identity was upsetting. Given the options, the highlanders labeled the newcomers as the spirits of former tribal members now returned. So, too, they sought to incorporate the cornucopia of shell wealth and the firepower of the interlopers within their existing economic and political contexts. Unsurprisingly, where communication was limited to crude signs and barter, violence was almost inevitable. The explorers were determined—believed it essential to their survival—that they demonstrate their lethal weapons. The indigenes wanted, first, to seize the wealth of the intruders and then, once they understood the folly of direct force, to steer that violence against their hereditary enemies.

In the single-mindedness of their gold lust; in claiming special spiritual powers by predicting events from eclipses to the arrival of a Junkers transport plane; in reliance on indigenous labor and local lore; in their sexual relations with native women; in their violent retaliations to theft; in the cultivation of interpreters and a common language of trade and travel (pidgin); in the white-hot rivalries occasioned by competing prospectors and the bitter quarrels over priority that followed; in their awkward relations with missionaries and colonial authorities; in their destabilizing presence; in their growing weariness over the endless violence around them and the sheer strangeness of an Otherly morality; in an exhaustion that could lead to either submersion into that order or a desire to exterminate it—the Leahys were a throwback to First-Age exploration. They recapitulated a historical scenario of the civilization they represented.

Each group was a novelty to the other. But the Leahys coped more easily. Why? They knew what they wanted, where they wished to go, and how they proposed to get what they sought. The New Guineans did not. The Leahys were surprised, but not stunned. They carried in their baggage train half a millennium of cultural tradition based on encountering new peoples in new lands. The New Guineans knew no one outside their hostile neighbors, all of whom worked to keep one another strictly in their place. They learned quickly enough; but the momentum lay with the explorers, as it had so often in the past. It was when the explorer returned that troubles so often boiled over. That had happened with Columbus, Stanley, Cook, and it happened with the Leahys. Familiarity bred not only contempt but covetousness, as each party sought to turn the other's strengths to its own advantage.

In this, however, the exploration of New Guinea marked perhaps the last hurrah of discovery before the Third Age. While the march of exploring prospectors across the highlands had its oddities, it shared with those other ages some great constants: they all had to deal, instantly and unavoidably, with the indigenes. Survival skills had less to do with hunting, tracking, making lean-tos, wrestling with grizzlies and shooting rhinos, or with more rugged nineteenth-century versions of camping out and backpacking, than with cross-cultural politics and negotiations. Explorers would succeed or fail according to their ability to deal with local peoples. They needed them as guides, interpreters, collectors, laborers, porters, assistants, and soldiers. With few exceptions—those stray desert islands such as Diego Garcia and Midway, those patches of continental terrain too empty for people and nearly for life, such as the inner Gobi, the Barren Grounds, and the interior ice sheet of Greenland—exploration was about encounters with people and, through people, places.

That was the great divide among discovered places—and it is the major divide between the Second and Third Great Ages of Discovery. When Verrazano cruised off the coast of North America, and Cook off New Zealand, they saw smoke that they interpreted as evidence of people; but the Voyagers saw nothing that spoke to life, much less to exotic hominids. When Voyager 2 zipped past Uranus, there was no one on the planet or its moons to marvel at the strange spacecraft or wonder if it signified a returned ancestor, a forecast god, or a marooned machine ready for sacrifice. There was no one to threaten harm or to offer friendship. There was no one to enlist as a guide or impress as an interpreter. There was no one to reflect back a self-image of the explorer or serve as a prism to refract visions of the future. There was no one to stand, simply as himself, for an alternative moral universe. There was no one at all.

Encounter was the great set piece of exploration, in which something happened that placed the journey beyond the routine of travel and through which narrative moved beyond tedium and banality into the essential drama of discovery. Yet it was less a simple process of reaching a goal—the source of the Nile, the North Pole—than it was an exchange between peoples whose aftershocks could affect the discoverer as much as the discovered.

While Columbus might exalt, "How easy it would be to convert these people and to make them work for us," the reality was that conversion might go either way. Europeans might themselves be forcibly converted, or simply choose to go native. The threat was present from the beginning, as Cortés discovered at Cozumel. Through an Indian interpreter named Melchior (who "understood a little Spanish and knew the language of Cozumel very well"), Cortés learned of two Spaniards who were held as "slaves" by Indians farther inland. One, Gerónimo de Aguilar, was freed, while the other, Gonzalo Guerrero, chose to remain. Aguilar told their story. They were the refugees of a voyage from Darien to Santo Domingo, brought on the wrecked ship's boat by currents to Campeche. Some fifteen men and two women had escaped the downed ship. Upon the refugees' landing, the indigenes they encountered sacrificed some "to their idols"; some died of disease; the two women had perished "of overwork"; but Aguilar and Guerrero had escaped, and now they alone survived. So far this was almost a parody of those narratives in which the indigenes found themselves under Spanish control. The climax came when the captives had to choose which society to follow.[179]

When Aguilar appeared, he squatted "in Indian fashion" and wore no more clothing than the natives. He had taken holy orders, was grateful to be rescued and reclaimed by Spain, and willingly accepted clothes and relearned Spanish. But Gonzalo Guerrero, a sailor from Palos (where Columbus had first embarked), did not wish to return to Spain. Tattooed and pierced, he was married now, a father; a Cacique and a "captain in time of war," he had been absorbed into indigenous society. Aguilar reminded him that he was a Christian and "should not destroy his soul for the sake of an Indian woman," and if necessary could take his family with him to Spanish settlements. Gonzalo refused; and "neither words nor warnings" could persuade him otherwise. He had converted.[180]

And that was the threat, that exposure to other cultures might subvert loyalty to the true faith, be it of religion, ethnicity, or enlightened science. The discoverers could not simply slide newly discovered peoples into thematic pigeonholes. Their presence challenged those categories, and more powerfully, they did so by experience and felt belief, not simply by myth and codes of conduct. Over the coming centuries the proliferation of discovered peoples and the elaboration of their cosmologies disturbed Western civilization's assumed values as fully as the bones of *Megatherium* and *Archaeopteryx* did the great chain of being.

Because so many explorers thrived to the extent that they adapted native technologies, emulated native practices, or even assumed native identities, their experiences gnawed at the ideological and ethical roots of their self-identities and those of their sponsoring culture. The experience could be corrosive. Isolated, unfettered from their own social norms, they might lose the restraints of either society, as the officers of his rear column did on Stanley's last expedition across Africa in 1887. They kidnapped or bought Manyema women for sex, became recorders (and perhaps enablers) of cannibalism, and sank into the kind of debauchery and brutality that Joseph Conrad would later characterize in *Heart of Darkness*.

More experienced in the temptations, and so tempered against their ugly seductions, Stanley offered an explanation without apology. The men had, he believed, been changed by their "circumstances." "At home these men had no cause to show their natural savagery," but suddenly transplanted "to Africa & its miseries," they became "deprived of butcher's meat & bread & wine, books, newspapers, the society & the influence of their friends." Fever "seized them, wrecked minds and bodies," while "anxiety" banished their "good nature."

The breakdown was relentless. "Pleasantness was eliminated by toil. Cheerfulness yielded to internal anguish ... until they became but shadows, morally & physically of what they had been in English society." As exploration segued into empire, the same dark unravelings threatened their sustaining society as well. [181]

Yet there was no alternative. If exploration was to happen, someone had to go, and that someone would be as affected as those he met, and would become a carrier of a cultural virus, whether malign or benevolent, back to the society to which he returned. The sustaining culture dispatched explorers to discover what it wanted—wealth, souls, allies, trade goods, beetles and butterflies, knowledge that would expand the existing cosmology of religion and science, but all ultimately an ordering of the world that was at heart moral.

Yet what the explorer often acquired—what the sensitive observer could not help but get, whether pinning it like a beetle to a collection box or getting it into his blood like malaria—was an empathy for alternative cosmologies, for understanding and often admiring the perspectives and codes of his native companions even though that appreciation might be profoundly unsettling of his own culture's existing order. The very nature of contact made such an exchange inescapable. If the discovered peoples had not wanted to be discovered, neither did the discovering peoples wish to see their own beliefs frayed and unwound. Yet that is what, inevitably, exploration did.

POST-ENCOUNTER: MODERNISM AS EXPLORER

The nature of the encountered geography and the character of its purposes as science and national prestige pushed the Third Age more and more toward machines. Remote sensing acquired its own motive power. Antarctica had robots descending into the caldera of Mount Erebus, and robotic snowmobiles traversing crevasse fields and empty ice sheets. The deep ocean had a flotilla of unmanned craft, some capable of autonomous voyaging for weeks or months. And interplanetary space had its spacecraft. The first contact with the outer planets, the first traverse through the solar system, came with robots.[182]

This went beyond naming expeditions by their transport vessels, which already had a long pedigree. The voyage of the *Beagle;* the *Challenger* expedition; the *Discovery, Nimrod,* and *Terra Nova* expeditions to Antarctica—these were signature labels that summarized the complex societies and stories they carried. So it was with spacecraft. Mariner 4 or Viking distilled an institution, a population of engineers, technicians, scientists, and bureaucrats, and a culture. A trek as long as Voyager's spanned generations. It was an easy step to go from encapsulating to anthropomorphizing, just as mariners had long invested their ships with personalities.

The culture at JPL openly disdained anthropomorphism. Engineers treated the spacecraft as they would a glitchy computer or a cantankerous vacuum cleaner. Edward Stone characterized Voyager as only "a tool," like "using a telescope; it's the same," and refused "to personalize" the spacecraft. Preparing for the first of the planetary encounters, Mariner 2 to Venus, Oran Nicks dismissed the spacecraft as "a machine that had no real consciousness." It didn't "'know'" what it was doing or why. "At the time," Nicks observed, "few of us thought about the similarities of the spacecraft to ourselves or to other living creatures."[183]

But of course anthropomorphism crept in. Voyager was not simply a prosthesis, but a projection of the personalities of its creators. They saw themselves in its history: its conduct was theirs, its triumphs and flaws their own. The Voyager mission took on a life of its own, as a work of art might: a *Moby Dick*, a *Mona Lisa*, a Ninth Symphony, distinctive of its author (in this case its complex society of authors), but somehow possessing an existence of its own. Inevitably, "Voyager" as a label went beyond the traditional shorthand of characterizing crews and support institutions by the name of the vessel.

Particularly as commentators sought to explain its trek and purpose, they did so in traditional tropes, genres, and narrative styles that had evolved out of centuries of human explorers. Whether or not Voyager was a person, it behaved like one. Voyager became a character.

Carl Sagan explained its encounter at Jupiter as another in the long legacy of "travelers' tales." Oran Nicks, speaking for those who worked on Mariner 2, "conscious of the precariousness of the enterprise and the unpredictable behavior of that historic spacecraft," concluded that it became "not so much a rudimentary automaton" as "a beloved partner, feverish and slightly confused at times, not entirely obedient, but always endearing." So, similarly, did Voyager appear to Bruce Murray: "I certainly think it has a personality." That's "perceptual," he confessed, and "in the mind of the beholder," and something that scientists, ever reaching for analogies to help explain, were more disposed to adopt as figures of speech than were engineers, whose numbers had to measure against empirical designs. It was also a tendency of those who had to interpret the mission to the public. Still, he believed that Voyager did have a "personality," a "very nasty" one for a while, "then lost it," and behaved itself.[184]

As the saga grew, so did the tendency to attribute to Voyager the character traits of its designers, operators, and interpreters. As it pushed on to newer, outer worlds, it acquired such epithets as "plucky," "valiant," "indomitable," and "enduring." It became the Little Spacecraft That Could.

The grand gestures of the three ages had each embodied what Cherry-Garrard called the intellectual passion, each attuned to its times. The voyage of the *Victoria* was to discovery as the Renaissance was to learning and the Reformation to religion. The travels of Humboldt to the New World were of a piece with European Enlightenment and imperialism. So the Voyagers were, in peculiar ways, emissaries of a Greater Modernism and its postmodern progeny. That was a second reason why people didn't need to go.

Without an Other, exploration became about the self. Encounter turned inward; dialogues simplified into soliloquies; discovery slid into self-disclosure. All this was not peculiar to exploration. It was an essential trait of modernism, which thrived on paradoxes of self-reference and self-scrutiny. Russell's paradox, Heisenberg's principle, Gödel's proof, Bohr's concept of complementarity, all built on the apparent contradictions and topological riddles that made the self into a Möbius strip. Does the set of all things include itself? Can a set be both consistent and complete? Can you know both the location and velocity of a particle with equal precision, or does the act of measuring, the presence of an observer, introduce irreducible uncertainties? Efforts to study the self yielded odd distortions of logic and meaning. And when the self had no Other, the boundary conditions dissolved into the circularity of a Klein bottle, whose inside and outside surface are the same.

Yet this is precisely what the geographies of ice, abyss, and space created. In previous ages, an explorer might stare thunderstruck, like Defoe's Robinson Crusoe, at the footprint of another man in the sand. In the Third Age, the explorer was more likely to photograph, as Apollo astronauts did, their own footprints on the lunar dust. The protocol went a step further when the Viking lander sent, as its initial image of Mars to Earth, a photo of its mechanical foot on the red sands. The constant discovery of new peoples had forced scholarship beyond its inherited taxonomies. New tribes and customs overwhelmed ethnography as new mountains did geology and new flora did biology. It demanded a distinctive scholarship, and got it with anthropology; and when the flow of exotic cultures ceased, that scholarship turned inward and shriveled. The anthropology of the Third Age is the psychology of the explorers themselves, or their virtual facsimile.

Perhaps nothing so conveys the paradox, however, as that canonical photo from Apollo 11 taken as men first walked on the Moon. The image is a portrait of astronaut Buzz Aldrin staring at a camera held by Neil Armstrong. Here, it would seem, was at least a vestige of a classic encounter, if only of one member of the party with another. Yet with the reflective visor of Aldrin's helmet lowered, the image conveyed of his face is of the photographer taking the photo. The Möbius loop is complete.

No Voyager took a photo of its twin, and no one photographed Voyager on its flybys. But Voyager took images for Earth and of Earth, and its decades-long communication might well stand as a conversation with ourselves. The Third Age was different not only because of its weird terrains, but also because of the cultural syndrome that determined what it saw and how it spoke. Without an Other, there was no reason to send a human self. That paradox any good modernist would have understood instinctively.

Even as euphoria alloyed with exhaustion and as the Voyagers' triumphs sharpened the contrast with Challenger's tragedy, they indefatigably continued their journey. Voyager 1 rose unveeringly upward toward the remote heliopause, routinely sampling the interplanetary medium. Voyager 2 still had plenty of observations to complete, and they remained squarely within the realm of geophysics, not metaphysics, even as another jolt of gravity-assisted acceleration flung it away from Uranus.

Its post-encounter phase lasted from January 26 to February 25. There was new data to gather and course corrections to make. Passage outward, after all, complemented passage inward. For the first three days Voyager 2 crossed bow shock seven times. It tracked the rotation of Uranus's magnetosphere. Its instruments sampled the dark side of Uranus. It reported more occultations. It attempted a ring movie, though the images proved too dark to discern. Its interminable record of fields and particles continued. Yaws and rolls and other maneuvers recalibrated instruments. Most critically, Voyager executed two playbacks of its near-encounter data—twice, to ensure a successful transmission; briskly, before the tapes were overwritten by further activity and because the European Space Agency's Giotto spacecraft was scheduled to rendezvous with Comet Halley within a week after Voyager's near-encounter and the DSN had to redirect its antennas. For four months Voyager 2 had enjoyed priority: Uranus was unique, and the prospects for another visit, remote. But now the other fledglings in the space science nest squawked for attention.[185]

On February 16 Voyager 2 executed a trajectory correction that propelled it to Neptune. It was a slow burn, the longest in the lengthening history of its interplanetary traverse—some three hours. When it ended, the spacecraft was sprinting toward an encounter with the outermost planet, scheduled for August 1989. The Voyager twins returned to a state of quasi-hibernation.[186]

DAY 2,636–3,829

17. Cruise

For the next forty-two months Voyager 2 cruised at 70,000 kilometers per hour toward a cold, dark planet far beyond the realm of what the naked eye could see from Earth, a world first intuited only mathematically by the quirky perturbations its gravitational presence caused in the motions of Uranus and whose first sighting was confused with a comet. It was an abstract world, posited by astronomers, outside the realm of ancient mythology, beyond Newton's classic model of the solar system. Of Neptune's particulars very little was known. It had a moon, Triton; it had some kind of ring; it was gaseous and experienced a variety of weather conditions. Much of this information came from intensive observations amassed after Voyager had launched (and conducted to better inform Voyager 2's encounter). Neptune was as little known as the abyss that its namesake ruled. At the time of encounter, Pluto's skewed path would bring it closer to the Sun than Neptune, which left the murky blue giant as the outermost planet of the solar system.[187]

Both spacecraft were well beyond their specifications and warranties. Ellis Miner likened them to a "vintage automobile" whose accumulating eccentricities its owner understood and could tweak to advantage. Yet while its mechanical aches never lessened, while its power supply relentlessly faded, and while distance magnified communication needs geometrically, the capacity of its computers for reprogramming meant Voyager 2 was in some respects a better spacecraft at Uranus than at Saturn, and would be better still at Neptune—and so were its human handlers. Without competing projects—the Challenger disaster had shut down all the others—the Voyager mission kept more of its experienced staff, and JPL understood better the demands for preparing, the procedures for crafting a master sequence for encounter, and the protocol for rehearsing. Between them the Voyager team had experienced five planetary encounters.[188]

Now they prepared for Neptune. It would be, its handlers liked to say, Voyager 2's "last picture show." It would, in effect, perform an occultation on the entire mission.[189]

OCCULTATION OF THE GRAND TOUR

Once again, readying Voyager meant managing a complex staging by which science objectives evolved, trajectories were tweaked, communications upgraded, and new software uploaded. A change in one meant a change in the others. The process of establishing guidelines for the final uplink of commands consumed over three years. But doing it previously was not the same as doing it at Neptune.

Too little was known, the planet was impossibly far, and while Voyager 2 could receive new software, it could not rebuild its aging hardware. Its power output was particularly troubling. It would broadcast at "a billionth of a billionth of a watt." At Jupiter, Voyager could transmit a maximum of 115,000 kilobits per second; at Uranus, even with clever compression coding, 21,600 kps; and at Neptune, perhaps 14,400 kps. Some new algorithms helped, but the only option was to improve Earth's capacity to hear Voyager's whisper against the background static.[190]

Fortunately, the Canberra DSN station would once more serve as primary antenna. So, again, the DSN arranged to contract for the Parkes radio telescope, and NASA agreed to allow the Voyager team to delay the spacecraft's anticipated arrival by five hours in order to maximize the time of Canberra reception. So vast were the distances, and so attenuated the signal, however, that effective communication would need much more, a virtual array the size of the Pacific Basin. The DSN thus reached northward to Japan's Usuda 64-meter tracking antenna on the island of Honshu, and to western North America as well, first to the Goldstone complex, which now included one 74-meter and two 24-meter antennas, and then to the very large array of radio telescopes at Socorro, New Mexico, operated by the National Radio Astronomy Observatory, which added the equivalent of two 70-meter antennas. The actual synthesis of data would have to occur after the flyby rather than in real time, but Earth could now hear what Voyager had to say.[191]

The other worry was identifying the roster of targets and the means to navigate to them, particularly since so little was known. Planners made their best guess, and then hedged by actually building into the scenario places for the acquisition of new data and recoding on the fly. The scientific working groups had already begun identifying targets even as they planned for Uranus, since the route past Uranus had to include a path to Neptune. And in one sense, the spectrum of interests was already hardwired into Voyager 2's instrument package, a medley of hard- and soft-geography scans. Specifically, Voyager 2 would interrogate the Neptunian atmosphere, notably its composition, energy budget, structure, and aurorae; it would map, delineate, and identify the constituent parts of the planetary rings and ring arcs; it would search out and characterize satellites, especially the planet's largest moon, Triton; it would survey the magnetosphere and its dynamics; and it would conduct an experiment close to the science working group's heart, four occultations and a close passage over the north pole that would deflect Voyager into a course as near as possible to Triton. Along the way it would record such fundamentals as the planet's rotation period, the orientation of its axis, and its precise mass along with those of its moons. And the spacecraft's master sequence would not only allow for fresh input but even anticipate it.[192]

The Neptune groups held a series of meetings between August 1986 and July 1987 to agree on a roster of wishes and to establish priorities. It submitted its final recommendations, pending further discoveries, on July 15, 1987. The process would continue up to encounter, a total of three years.[193]

Of all the Voyager encounters, Charles Kohlhase concluded, the planning for Neptune's was the "most challenging," and he likened the task to guiding the spacecraft "through an imaginary needle's eye about 100 km wide, while the spacecraft is going a blistering 27 km/sec—and they expect to predict when this will happen to within *one* second!" The final trajectory was the outcome of nearly eight years of planning, editing, refining, tinkering, a ceaseless juggling between what scientists wanted, what engineers could provide, and what the spacecraft could bear.[194]

The one ameliorating factor was that Neptune ended the Grand Tour. Voyager 2 would not have to tweak its trajectory in order to continue to another planet, so its passage around Neptune could be maximized for the values that planet offered. But the only hope for anything like the precision demanded was a good sequence of course corrections, constant refinements of trajectory based on improving data about Neptune's hard geography and its gravitational effects, and a stream of successfully uploaded commands to tell Voyager 2 how to perform its acrobatics.

Nothing in the Grand Tour, perhaps, was more daring than the hope—the planned expectation, really—that the spacecraft could in fact acquire the additional data it needed for precision guidance. The engineering term "critical late activities" disguised the audacity behind the ambition. The particular issue was that the spacecraft's navigational system could not work reliably from Canopus alone; it needed other bodies, preferably Neptunian moons, objects that were not, at the time, known to exist but whose identities were programmed blankly into Voyager's computers. If—when—such satellites were discovered and their orbital parameters measured, the additional information would be uploaded into the code. Voyager 2 needed at least one such moon; it found six. It then needed to tweak its trajectory to thread the Neptunian needle. It planned for six corrections, the first coming on February 14, 1986, a scant three weeks after the Uranus encounter. It needed only four.[195]

All this of course required smart sequences uploaded to an onboard computer command subsystem that dated to the Paleolithic age of computing by a cobbled-together array of DSN dishes that spanned from Japan to Australia to California and New Mexico. By 1989 Voyager 2's computers were nearly as creaky as its scan platform rotors, and its onboard memory was an order of magnitude less than that of even the lower-end personal computers then available. Still, JPL planned ten uploads of command sequences, the product of "high-fidelity timelines" translated into machine language and the outcome of nearly thirty-six months of intense labor.[196]

In the end, the reality was that robot and handlers would have to rely on each other—Voyager 2, that JPL could tell it what it needed; and JPL, that Voyager 2 could operate autonomously, for once the spacecraft commenced near-encounter, it would be on its own. The distance between Neptune and Pasadena was such that even a simple transmission would take 246 minutes, or over four hours, and for a full exchange, 492 minutes, assuming that a response was instantaneous. So among its programs were "failure [or fault] protection algorithms," which would allow Voyager to detect and repair many problems, or shunt into a safe mode. There were, for example, routines to have the spacecraft begin a sequence of pitches and yaws to relocate the Sun, and then roll to refix with Canopus should something break navigational contact. The computer often tested itself. Critical instruments could be shut down and then reignited in the event of voltage surges. And a "backup mission load," frequently uploaded, programmed Voyager to execute a basic survey of Neptune should something prevent the final near-encounter transfer of commands. Only at the most frenetic moments, when every fragment of memory space was needed, was the backup mission load removed.[197]

What remained was to test the system under simulated conditions. JPL and NASA had learned a hard lesson at Uranus. They could not scatter staff across other projects, or even lay them off, and then expect an instant return to service, nor could they expect that upgrades in hardware, software, or operating procedures could synchronize without practice. Beginning in October 1987, nearly all project teams underwent "operational readiness tests" to "validate and calibrate" the DSN and prepare for occultation experiments.

The Voyagers themselves experienced special "capability demonstration tests," with Voyager 1 serving as a "test-bed." Between 1988 and early 1989 both spacecraft and those communicating with them confirmed protocols and calibrations, one involving a roll-turn course correction maneuver. In May 1989 the entire operation undertook a dress rehearsal.[198]

THE LONG TREK

From near-encounter at Uranus to near-encounter at Neptune, some forty-two months passed. It had taken the spacecraft twenty-three months to reach Jupiter, another twenty-three months to reach Saturn, and a whopping fifty-three additional months to reach Uranus. Neptune was almost as far from Uranus as Uranus was from Saturn, but the additional velocity Voyager had acquired from its sling-fling around Uranus had hastened its travel. From Earth to Neptune, however, had taken almost exactly a hundred and forty-four months, or twelve years. The Grand Tour was a notably Long Tour.

Interplanetary space is in many respects a benign environment for a machine. Voyager did not experience that long passage as astronauts might: it did not become bored or restless or overcome with anxieties. It shut down most of its instruments, shrank power and hydrazine requirements, and cruised. It entered a mechanical hibernation. Unlike an earthly vessel, it suffered from no physical waves or shearing winds; nor did it have to navigate around unknown shoals. The usual stresses that assault exploring craft were absent. There were no acoustical blasts, no aerodynamic tugs and shears, no gravitational forces pulling it to extinction, no salt to corrode or rain to rot, and no organisms to chew on it. It sailed through no sargasso weeds, acquired no barnacles, endured no ship worms. And it had no human occupants for which it had to sustain an artificial environment. It felt fields and particles, but this was a soft geography, and apart from the planets and asteroid belt, or the rare meteorite, it could sail serenely on autopilot, unworried, and unafflicted by lethargy and ennui.[199]

But this was not true for its human servants. While Voyager had trekked to Neptune, the United States had experienced four presidential elections and was ten weeks away from a fifth. The Voyager mission had gone through six program managers and was preparing for a seventh. Twelve years was an academic lifetime—two full tenure-review cycles. Staffers had grown up with Voyager. They graduated, married, divorced, had children, transferred and traded jobs, retired, got cancer and injuries, healed, died. Candice Hansen remarked that people "actually remembered when their babies were born relative to encounters." Ellis Miner noted wryly that the group had been "considerably younger" in 1965, when the Grand Tour was conceived, than in 1989, when it reached Neptune. The long cruise phases were particularly trying for scientists who had to publish constantly to advance careers. Voyager could experience a rhythm of comatose cruising broken by frenzied encounters without a change in life or career. Its human tenders couldn't.[200]

While space science seemed a promising career during IGY, in truth it became risky several times over. The spasms of discovery were infrequent and too scattered to sustain regular positions and funding. It always proved easier to create a new project than to continue paying for an old one, more appealing to sponsor a new voyage of discovery than to subsidize the publication of results from returned ones. The missions themselves were too sparse to sustain a self-supporting community. A successful encounter could make its staff into celebrities; but such fame was fleeting, and a failed spacecraft or instrument could be a career-ending blow. Planetary science was a bet against long odds.

Yet the sense that scientific productivity had to accelerate continuously in every field is a recent aberration. In the past, exploration had often taken years, and its scholarly write-up could consume decades. Charles-Marie de la Condamine spent ten years measuring in the Andes before returning down the Amazon; the last member of his expedition did not return to France for thirty-eight years. Alexander von Humboldt devoted his young manhood to preparing for an exploring expedition, spent five years in the field, exhausted five decades and his inheritance distilling it into his fifty-four-volume

Voyage to the Equinoctial Regions, and died still writing his popular summary, *Cosmos*. The Institut d'Egypte, the corps of 151 savants whom Napoleon assembled to survey his conquests along the Nile and who, in the words of Gaspard Monge, would "carry the torch of enlightenment" in its *mission civilisatrice*, lost 31 members directly, a disaster that distorted the scientific establishment of France for decades afterward; the record of their findings, *The Description of Egypt*, took its members twenty-six years to complete. The U.S. Exploring Expedition—America's belated answer to Cook's voyages—soaked up ten years from first approval to actual departure, spent some four years at sea, and for nineteen subsequent years crawled toward the publication of nineteen volumes (out of twenty-eight originally conceived). By the time the expedition's findings got into print, the public had more or less forgotten about it, and the country was headed into civil war. Lewis and Clark had taken two years to cross North America, and never did see their vaunted journals published. Beginning in 1867 the Russian general and geographer Nikolai Przhevalsky conducted five major expeditions in Asia with the ultimate ambition of reaching Lhasa. Eighteen years later, he died suddenly while in the field, Lhasa still a mirage over the mountains.[201]

A successful expedition could not only make a career, it could be a career.

For oceangoing expeditions, long voyages with short encounters were the norm. Still, few could rival the saga of Vitus Bering and the discovery of Alaska.

The motive began with Peter the Great's 1724 order to Bering, a Dane in his service, to determine whether the far eastern lands of Russia's expanded empire met the western extent of North America. It took Bering four years to travel to Kamchatka, build a vessel, and sail to the straits that now bear his name. Dense fog prevented a direct sighting, but the nature of the strait and its currents strongly suggested that the two continents were not joined, and native Chukchis confirmed that fact. When he returned, Peter had died, and his successors decided that Bering had not fully answered the question, so in 1731 they sent him back, this time with the naturalist Georg Steller. He finally sailed in the spring of 1741 with two vessels, again constructed in Kamchatka, the *St. Peter* and the *St. Paul*. In July 1741 the St. Peter sighted the southern shore of Alaska (at Mount St. Elias), made landfall at Kayak Island, and subsequently wrecked off the coast of Kamchatka, where its crew spent a wretched winter at Fox Island and where Bering died in December. In August 1742 the sur- vivors reached Petropavlovsk and began the long trek across Asia to report their findings.[202]

The second expedition had lasted over ten years and granted Steller a scientific "encounter" with North America, at Kayak Island, for something like ten hours. The rhythm was eerily like that of plan- etary exploration. The difference was the immense tedium, frustra- tions, and suffering that Steller and crews endured to earn those frenzied few hours ashore.

Perhaps the closest historic analogue is the fabled HMS *Challenger* expedition of 1872–76, generally recognized as the origin of modern oceanography and a model that anticipates Third Age conditions as La Condamine's did the Second Age.

The *Challenger*'s complex voyage around the world lasted forty- two months, exactly the length of Voyager 2's traverse from Uranus to Neptune. The essential rhythm was one of long hiatuses broken by spasms of encounters with islands or ports. In many respects the cadence was also a foretaste of what Antarctic discovery would be like, as explorers broke through the barrier ice at the end of the aus- tral summer, and then wintered over under confined conditions until spring allowed for sledging forays. This was of course equally the pulse of interplanetary exploration. What made it tolerable was the presence of a large cohort of like-minded comrades, and the anticipa- tion of adventure with exotic peoples or unknown lands. Even with other cultures and strange ports of call, this is a formula for a robot. Without the prospect of those interludes, it is hard to imagine how an expedition could thrive.

Of the *Challenger*'s crew of 243, a quarter deserted out of boredom, numbed by the tedium of sounding and dredging ("drudging," as the sailors called it), and out of restlessness on the converted (and confining) corvette; 7 men died, and 26 were invalided out of service or left at hospitals. The scientific corps was marginally better. The "great adventure" across 69,000 nautical miles came at the cost of an "industrious boredom" that nearly drove even the most zealous mad. After they disembarked, the vast tedium continued as some 50 volumes, involving 100 scientists, saw print over the subsequent 20 years, concluding in 1895. Interestingly, as with so many proposals for manned space exploration, the scientific quest involved a search for life in forlorn niches; and this the *Challenger* found. But so long was the ordeal, and so complex its production, that the public and treasury lost interest, and by the time the *Challenger* expedition formally completed its task, general enthusiasms were poised to explore new lands.[203]

Still, the enterprise loomed large in its day—everyone recognized it as a vast and important undertaking, even if it could rouse only sparse popular excitement. It has remained a landmark, a historical point of reference for exploring expeditions much as Tenerife remains a geographic one. The last of the lunar modules (Apollo 17) bore its name as did the first of the space shuttle disasters, and the most successful of the deep-drilling oceanographic research vessels. Yet it has endured perhaps better as an ideal than as a practical guide. In the 1870s there was no alternative to crewed ships and their onboard "scientifics" and "philosophers." By the 1970s, when the RV *Glomar Challenger* was coring deep-ocean sediments, there was.

Among the *Challenger*'s lessons was the difficulty of sustaining research once the adventure ended. The fact is, science is long, politics short, and public interest capricious. The insistence by the "scientifics" that the expedition meant only research, and that research had to be thorough and be published according to the standards of the guild, meant that the drain on the public treasury was bound to be bottomless. Politics and public interest, however, had their own cadences.

In the past, as often as not, scientific societies or wealthy patrons had to intervene to complete the task, which could easily absorb the careers of those involved. Accounts of adventure in the guise of personal narratives were popular and could be published by subscription. The latter often helped underwrite private exploring expeditions in ways that shelves of dense reports could not. Politicians, publicists, and even sciences moved on. Where cruises lasted for years without tangible consequences, where investments were swallowed in upgrading instruments and improving staff performances for brief encounters, it was difficult to sustain much fervor.

Two years after Voyager launched, five months after encounter with Jupiter, the first *Star Trek* movie was released. It posits a later, fictional, Voyager mission that disappears into a black hole, finds a machine civilization, and then returns laden with knowledge it seeks to transmit to its "creator." Ten years later, after Voyager 2 had encountered Neptune, the fifth movie in the series, *The Final Frontier*, opened with a bored Klingon commander blasting a dead-metal NASA spacecraft, now dismissed as "space junk," for target practice. The tempo of modern society had quickened, and public expectations seemed to shorten. Even as the Galileo mission to Jupiter at last launched, after a decade during which Voyager was the only exploring vessel in action, there was only so much passion that a nominally spacefaring society could muster.[204]

Many staffers considered the Voyager mission the adventure of a lifetime. For anyone present from its conception—and they were more than a handful—the mission *was* a lifetime.

THIS NEW OCEAN

The character of the Earth's oceans set the tempo for the HMS *Challenger*'s cruise, and the properties of what partisans eagerly called "this new ocean" of interplanetary space set those for Voyager. In the Third Age, however, the densest discoveries came not from the analogous ocean of the solar system but from the true new ocean of Earth's abysses.

The deep oceans and interplanetary space were the two commanding realms of the Third Age, and their exploration proceeded in an eerie fugue. Bathyspheres were the high-altitude balloons of the sea; the bathyscaphe *Trieste* descending to the Challenger Deep in 1960 was the wet twin to Mariner 2 flying past Venus. The knowledge of the Laurentian Abyss was no better than that of the crater Daedalus on the far side of the Moon. There was putative bullion in the abyssal plains. There were schemes for undersea tourism and colonization. There was even precedent in science fiction; after all, Jules Verne had written *20,000 Leagues Under the Sea* as well as *From the Earth to the Moon*. The cold war rivalry played out beneath the waves as fully as it did beyond the clouds.

Yet a profound paradox emerged. Space captured the public and political imagination; the deep oceans did not. Space had a mystique that the abyss lacked. Arthur C. Clarke's sea novels sank; his space fiction soared. Much of what happened in the seas occurred in bureaucratically secret "black" programs, not publicly promoted and not known until the cold war ended and declassification began revealing what had happened and the technologies of submersibles and robotic probes became generally available. The high ground for military rivalry was not thermonuclear bombs in orbit but nuclear-armed submarines. The search for life that drove the post-Apollo planetary program, particularly to Mars, found nothing, and might discover it only at immense cost and in token fossils. The exploration of the oceans discovered startling realms of previously unknown life, from the largest ecosystems on Earth to exotic niches powered by chemical rather than photosynthetic metabolism. Likewise, the long-anticipated revolution in geosciences came not from other planets but from Earth's oceans, as remote sensing unveiled world-girdling mountains, faults, and seamounts. The submersible *Alvin* visiting black smokers in the East Pacific Rise (the same year Voyager launched) and plucking rocks from the Mid-Atlantic Rift provoked more change than Moon rocks brought back by Apollo astronauts. In his critique of the Apollo program, *The Moon-doggle*, Amitai Etzioni shrewdly contrasted the panicked response to Sputnik with the overlooked prospects for the oceans. The paradox was that while attention looked up, the bigger payoff came from below. The promises of the Third Age were unfolding less in the depths of space than in the depths of the Earth's seas.

The reasons are many. The oceans are closer, and cheaper to explore, and however alien to humanity's quotidian existence, the seas are continuous with humanity's world both geographically and historically.

The "void" of the deep seas is in reality a tangible medium, a watery matrix and a more plausible nursery of life than microbe-carrying meteors from Mars. While light fades below 2,400 meters, while pressure can crush anything dropped from the surface, and while nutrients either concentrate in niches or diffuse through chunks of salty seawater the size of continents, this is the place where life originated on Earth, and where life has adapted in forms more fantastic than any worlds conjured up by writers of science fiction. Organisms abound at all levels. There are biota on the abyssal plains; vast throngs of micro- and macroorganisms gliding upward and downward on daily and seasonal cycles; giant squid, jellyfish-like siphonophora, sleeper sharks, viperfish, lantern fish, a menagerie of bioluminescent browsers, and predators that thrive according to alien metabolisms and obey a different ecological logic. The migrations of pelagic species are the largest on Earth, dwarfing those on African savannas. There are ecosystems clustered to hot vents organized around chemosynthetic bacteria and symbiotic tube worms. There are deep corals and fisheries attached to seamounts, submerged versions of volcanic islands and atolls. There are worms and benthic bugs that burrow into the ooze that blankets the abyss. There are opportunistic communities that feed on fallen whales and other macrofauna.[205]

Far from being abiotic vats, only capable of supporting life at the surface, the oceans are the dominant habitat on Earth. However hostile to terrestrial life, the sea is an abode for earthly life and is continuous with it. Increasingly it appears that the rifts, submarine volcanoes, hot vents, and black smokers that parse and stitch the solid floor of the sea are fundamental to a grand geochemical cycling of planetary water, and with it the nutrients and minerals essential to a living planet. Not least, it is possible to step from land to sea and back again. The shore is a familiar boundary between the two, literally ebbing and flowing with the rhythms of earthly existence.[206]

The void of deep space is a vacuum. Nothing lives within it. It may be that organic molecules travel through the void within particles blasted off planets, but there is no ecosystem possible, and no connectivity between those spores or bio-shards and a Gaian Earth. Passage between planetary bodies is a mix of tiny violence and immense void; the fiery impact of meteorites or the flame-powered launch of rockets. The solar system may loosely resemble Earth, with its interplanetary space assuming the role of oceans, the planets that of continents, and planetary moons as islands. But contact between them requires years of travel across a vacuum. It demands power; and behind power, will; and behind will, belief. One can jump into the ocean by stepping into the surf, but into space only by a leap of faith.

Another continuity is historical. The oceans have led each age of discovery. The exploration of the world ocean virtually defined the First Age. The Second began with that outrush of circumnavigators of which James Cook, Louis-Antoine de Bougainville, Alejandro Malaspina, and Thaddeus Bellingshausen are its informing captains, and which ferried the fabled naturalists of the era, from Humboldt to Joseph Hooker, to their destinations, and made islands into scholarly ports of call. The age even attempted to extend its powerful Enlightenment science to the sea, making it an object of inquiry and not simply a means of transport. Matthew Fontaine Maury's *Physical Geography of the Sea* (1855) adapted Humboldtian techniques to map the oceans. A century after Cook, as the Second Age was completing its final continental traverses, the *Challenger* expedition applied the accumulated lessons of the Second Age to a global survey of the world ocean, even as its mountainous efforts seemed to yield a molehill of fresh science. Other nations followed, sporadically, with outcomes that seem impressive mostly in retrospect.[207]

The Third Age commenced seriously in the oceans. After World War II, naval vessels were commissioned as research ships and began mapping the solid floor of the world's seas. Submarines replaced capital ships as nuclear-armed Poseidon missiles became one leg of the American strategic triad; the need grew to know better how to navigate the deep oceans and to communicate with undersea vessels.

By the time of IGY, the USS *Nautilus* and *Skate* had surfaced at the North Pole, the Trieste was bobbing in the Mediterranean, the Mid-Atlantic Rift was rudely mapped, and it was apparent that the deep oceans were not the lifeless chemical tombs and geologically inert sinks early research and prevailing theory had indicated. By 1962 Harry Hess had published his "History of Ocean Basins," which inverted the standard geophysical model of Earth, and conceptually catalyzed what became the theory of plate tectonics within a handful of years. No less than comparative planetology, oceanography became a cold war science. As the space race heated up, the U.S. Navy found a desperate need for submersibles and poured money into their development. The *Alvin* became the naval counterpart to Apollo. The deep oceans were the first of the Third Age landscapes to be mapped, and the one that catalyzed a scientific revolution.

Not least is the similarity of debates about purpose, especially the wedge issues of human versus robotic exploration, and the ultimate vision of colonization beyond Terra. On this the oceans once again appear to lead. Costs, dangers, the relative merit of human senses versus instruments, the diminishing value of a human brain and hand on board are all propelling deep-sea exploration toward remotely operated vessels or even autonomous submersibles that can wander for weeks. The only sense available to an aquanaut, as to an astronaut, is sight, which is replicated with a richer spectrum by instrumented cameras. The pilot of the *Alvin*, Robert Ballard, a pioneer of submersibles, having used both crewed vehicles and robots for decades, has concluded that "the robots are better." So, too, early prospects for a frontier of ocean settlement died in the depths. Ocean exploration can advance unencumbered by techno-utopian colonizers and aspiring homesteaders.[208]

After roughly sixty years, the evolving contours of the Third Age suggest that the solar system will not be the primary arena of discovery, that the pattern of exploration among the planets will more resemble the pattern of exploration of the First Age, when complex armadas undertook long voyages, an era of relatively few expeditions but huge returns. Rather, the deep oceans will likely claim the variety and

vivacity of exploring, perhaps even the swarm effect that characterized the Second Age. But if so, why does "space" continue to claim
pride of place?

Secrecy is one reason. Much of the oceanic work had military
sponsorship and was not broadcast. Nor was there any overt, broad-
cast-over-TV, soap opera drama for an abyss race as there was for a
space race. There was no literature for deep sea exploration as there
was for planetary. Robert Heinlein did not write a novel titled *Submarine Troopers,* nor Ray Bradbury a *West Mariana Basin Chronicles.*
Arthur C. Clarke did not imagine *Childhood's End* happening on the
East Pacific Rise. Stanley Kubrick did not film *2001: A Sea Odyssey* or
place alien obelisks on the Valdivia Abyssal Plain. There was no Tsiolkovsky or Goddard to imagine a Great Migration to the Laurentian
Abyss, or a Percival Lowell to sketch the contours of a dying civilization on the Loihi Seamount. There was no Carl Sagan to fantasize
about cosmic connections with galactic intelligences, or rhapsodize
about chemo-spiritual liaisons with "salt stuff" shared between people and black smokers.

Over and again, the most publicly ardent proponents of planetary
exploration said they saw their endeavor as part of a larger mission to
colonize, and an astonishing number traced their enthusiasm to an
adolescent literature of technological romance in which worlds were
found and lost in space. While the oceans had their lore, and champions of the sea held fiercely to their distinctive sagas of exploration,
that tradition stayed on the surface. The utopians wanted colonies
on other worlds, by which they meant worlds that looked like planets. What the deep oceans showed, however, was that exploration was
neither confined to space nor defined by it. Geographic exploration
and space occupied separate cultural realms, though they could from
time to time intersect.

The deep oceans will likely claim the lion's share in terms of
numbers of Third Age expeditions and discoveries. The yet-unvisited
oceans may reveal more animals than the terrestrial Earth, answer
fundamental queries about the origin and character of life, and tell
us more directly than analogies to Mars or Europa about how to care
for an abused Earth. But neither numbers alone nor the robustness

of oceanographic science can determine cultural clout. Space will retain its partisans, and its promise, and it will offer in the prospects of a sweeping journey, a trek beyond, something that the deep oceans cannot. And that distinction may explain why abyssal exploration has failed to imaginatively inform the coming age. It lacks a Grand Tour. It lacks a Voyager.

18. Encounter: Neptune

On June 5, 1989, some 42 months after leaving Uranus, and nearly 142 after leaving Earth, Voyager 2 began the end of its Grand Tour.

This was the sixth time the Voyager team had met a planet, and Voyager 2 would do what it had done at each prior encounter: it would direct its instruments toward a full-body, geophysical scan of the planet and its satellites. But if the scenario had become ritualized, it had lost none of its wild alloy of awe, anticipation, and anxiety.[209]

LAST CONTACT

JPL uplinked the first of new commands that would prepare the spacecraft to do its gamut of tasks. To scan for ultraviolet emissions that might identify atmospheric chemistry. To search for radio signals birthed where Neptune's magnetic field met the solar wind and for long-wave radiation that could measure more accurately the opaque planet's rate of rotation. To measure the brightness of the Sun and of select stars pertinent for navigating through near-encounter events. To ready its infrared instruments by turning their flash heater on and then off. To continue, as it had throughout its long trek across interplanetary space, to sample fields and particles, from time to time recalibrating its instruments by rolls and yaws to allow researchers to account for the distorting influence of the spacecraft itself; to commence a series of four occultation experiments. To search for rings and satellites.

This was what discovery meant in the popular mind: the revelation of new worlds. The Voyager twins had found a covey of moons at Jupiter, Saturn, and Uranus, and there was every expectation Voyager 2 would discover even more exotic moons here at the outer fringes of the solar system. So its cameras imaged each side of Neptune, and in early July, Voyager found its first new satellite, unimaginatively dubbed 1989N1. This discovery gave the navigation team the needed coordinate by which to guide Voyager through near-encounter maneuvers. Other satellite discoveries soon followed. By the end of the month, Voyager had detected four new moons, subsequently named after figures from Greek mythology—Proteus, Larissa, Galatea, and Despina. On July 30 it captured all four in a single, mesmerizing image.

On August 6, Voyager 2 left its observatory phase behind and raced toward full encounter. A world that before Voyager had no sharper identity than that of a hazy blue Smurf ball, the third largest of the planets now beckoned at 67,000 kilometers per hour.

Everything began to surge. Commands—three new computer packets were uploaded. Imagery—Neptune was now too large to fit within a single aperture, so mosaics became the norm. Data—the extra antennas enlisted by the DSN came into play. Less than a day into far-encounter, the last dress rehearsal, a complex execution for an occultation experiment dubbed Radio Science ORT-4, ran for ten hours and identified soft spots in performance, which were quickly corrected.

The expected discoveries acquired their rhythm. The mosaics were assembled into movies of Neptunian weather; the search for moons intensified; rings, ring arcs, and shepherd satellites came into focus; IRIS recorded temperatures; PRA and PWS tracked radio waves, emitted where Neptune's magnetosphere met the solar wind. As Voyager 2 quickened its pace, estimates of the planet's hard parameters sharpened. "The uncertainties that everyone fussed over for so many years," Charles Kohlhase noted, were "dropping precipitously." Neptune's mass and position would be known three times more accurately, Triton three to six times better, and Voyager 2's time of arrival a third better. The Voyager staff would no longer find Triton's mass "a mystery." With the new data, engineers refined parameters for the final, complex roll-turn course correction that would climax near-encounter. Everyone waited for bow shock, the final hurdle before closest approach. It arrived on August 24, 1989.[210]

From August 24 to 29, an aging Voyager 2, now zipping at more than 71,000 kilometers per hour, hit its target trajectory, performed a riot of acrobatic maneuvers, amassed mountains of data, and executed nearly 90 high-priority optical and remote-sensing observations. At 8:56 PDT on August 24, Voyager passed within 29,240 kilometers of the planet's center.[211]

It photographed the surface and its wild weather. It sped through Neptune's ring plane and behind the gaseous giant, sending and receiving radio signals vital for occultation experiments. It used the star Nunki (δ Sagittarii) to occult the rings. It photographed the rings and arcs directly on both approach and departure, as illuminated on the foreside and as backlit, and merged those images into movies. It measured particle impacts. It flew over the north pole of rotation, recording auroral emissions and identifying the magnetic pole. It absorbed the soft geography of Neptune's ionic and electromagnetic fields, mapping the spongy borders of the magnetosphere. It measured the brightness, pressure, temperature, chemical composition, and cloud structure of the planetary atmosphere. Just before periapsis, Triton occluded the star Gomeisa, and then the Sun, and Voyager seized both opportunities to add to its inventory. Then, while in Neptune's shadow, it reversed its instruments and surveyed the planet's dark side. Some 110 minutes after closest approach, Voyager undertook a series of pitches and yaws, realigning from Canopus to Alkaid as a navigational referent in order to position its instruments to interrogate Triton. Relying on image motion compensation, it proceeded to create a high-resolution mosaic of the satellite's surface. At 2:10 PDT on August 25, Voyager 2 made its closest approach to Triton, some 39,800 kilometers from the moon's center.[212]

The Triton flyby—much sought by scientists—took Voyager 2 out of the plane of the Sun's ecliptic, and hurled it obliquely southward at forty-eight degrees. With that effort, Voyager had shot its bolt: it would encounter no further worlds. In fact, the odd trajectory actually caused a gravity-assisted slowdown. Some thirty-eight hours after entering bow shock, Voyager exited the magnetosphere, and continued to move in and out of bow shock amid the filmy fields for another two days. Finally, seventy-nine hours after closest approach, it turned its cameras back to the planet and its moon.[213]

The gesture had become a valued parting ritual begun by Voyager 1 when, hurrying to Jupiter, it had turned and captured Earth and the Moon in a single image. This time Voyager caught the double crescents of Neptune and Triton in an unforgettable scene: haunting, austere, radiantly lonely. It was the Grand Tour's last work of art.

Post-encounter had its usual anticlimactic aura—"like the cleaning crew that does its work the morning after an all-night party," Ellis Miner thought. The phase began officially on August 29 and didn't end until October 2, 1989, almost exactly thirty-two years after Sputnik 1 launched.[214]

This time post-encounter did not have the anxieties attendant on the need to target another planet. But Neptune's remoteness added an anxiety of its own. The immense distance, low wattage, and feeble computing capabilities meant that much of what Voyager 2 had sensed it still had to send to Earth. Its digital tape recorder had to play back the drama of near-encounter. It did so twice in order to reduce noise, fill gaps, and substitute redundancy for lost transmitting power. Even so, critical instruments continued to record and image. The far side of Neptune had its interests and its partisans, and the fields of soft geography busily reclaimed the place they had temporarily yielded to hard geography. Then the spacecraft undertook a final series of rolls and yaws to recalibrate instruments and navigational systems before beginning its final, uninterrupted cruise to infinity.[215]

TRITON

Triton was the last of Voyager's surveyed worlds, and with a fitting sense of closure, perhaps the strangest.

Almost everything about Triton proved exceptional. It combines variety with size. It has "perhaps the most diverse geological land forms found anywhere in the Solar System," the result of a complex and dynamic history. It has an atmosphere flush with ices of nitrogen, methane, carbon monoxide, carbon dioxide, and water. Among icy satellites, it has the "most spectrally diverse surface." It is the seventh largest moon, with a volume more than five times that of Titania (the eighth largest), but it is the only large satellite with an inclined, retrograde orbit, an orbit almost perfectly circular. Unlike other captured moons, it shares no features with asteroids; it more closely relates to objects from the Kuiper Belt and best resembles Pluto. How it originated—whether by capture or by co-evolution with Neptune or whether it might share some eccentric history with Pluto—is at present indeterminate. What is known is that Triton is the coldest body identified in the solar system, a scant thirty-eight degrees Kelvin above absolute zero.[216]

That made the discovery of geologic activity astounding. Studying images revealed what appeared to be transient streams or plumes of gas. In all, Voyager 2 photographed four eruptions—nitrogen geysers—that lofted emissions some eight kilometers high before shearing winds carried them one hundred kilometers beyond. The proposed explanation was that insolation, however feeble (900 times lower than on Earth), could still penetrate Triton's clear icy cap, create a greenhouse effect underneath, and build up a gaseous pressure that then vented violently back to the atmosphere.[217]

The scene offered a fitting sense of closure: the cold eruptions on Triton bracketed the hot ones on Io. The unforeseen discovery of volcanoes on Jupiter's Io had announced convincingly that Voyager would find new worlds, and now at the end of its trek, one had come to expect the unexpected. At Triton the Grand Tour's alpha had found its omega.

INFORMATION AND IDEA

That was what the Third Great Age of Discovery had done overall. Not only had it revealed unknown lands but it had intellectually remade an Earth that many believed already discovered and old. Like the First Age, it had found new lands, and like the Second, it had seen old lands with new eyes. Knowledge, after all, was relative. It was contingent not only on fresh data but on novel means of interpreting.

The Second Age had bequeathed a legacy of geographic surfaces that left the solid geography of Earth and the planets obscured by ice, seawater, and gaseous atmospheres. To probe beneath those contours required special sensors and innovative means to get those instruments to the scene. Until then the terrains of ice, abyss, and space were unknowable. Antarctica did not have its perimeter fully mapped until Operations Highjump and Windmill accomplished the task by air in 1946 to 1948, and no one had traversed the continent until the Commonwealth Trans-Antarctic Expedition did so under loose affiliation with IGY. The deep oceans had been sampled but never seen, and only vaguely understood. They were conceived as a geochemical tomb and a geophysical void, a vast sink removed from the dynamics of the planet. As for the solar system, photos of the planets and the larger moons from Earth-based telescopes existed, but the gritty inner planets and gaseous outer ones were the dregs of astronomy, which was far more fascinated by distant pulsars and quasars, white dwarfs and red giants, spiraling nebulae, cosmic rays, dark matter, and traces of the Big Bang.

The Third Age revolutionized those perceptions. Field-testing had occurred in Antarctica, and then leaped outward, much as the proposed third polar year had bulked up into the International Geophysical Year. It was, J. Tuzo Wilson wrote, "in the Antarctic, which was least known [of ice sheets], that recent efforts have produced the most marked changes in our knowledge."[218]

Before IGY the basics of Antarctica as a continent were barely appreciated: the pastiche of ice shelves and sheets, the underlying solid-earth surfaces so different between East and West Antarctica, the interconnections of south polar weather with the rest of Earth. Modern technology such as Sno-Cats and DC-4s, seismic profiling, and remote-sensing instruments gradually unveiled the nearly extraterrestrial world that was the Ice. It became both more familiar and more alien. Unlike abyss and space, this was a place where people could walk, breathe, and, along its edges, survive by hunting. With permanent bases established under the aegis of IGY, Antarctic discovery made the transition from exploration to a normal, if extreme science. It made a suitable point of intellectual departure for the discovery of those new worlds, now being exposed, where humanity could not live and would not go.

The deep oceans were, at the dawn of the Third Age, a deep mystery. A century after Maury had synthesized the known ocean in his *Physical Geography of the Sea*, Rachel Carson summarized the state of knowledge in her prize-winning *The Sea Around Us* (1951). Maury's geography appeared two decades before the *Challenger* expedition; Carson's, two decades before the revolution in earth science was distilled into the theory of plate tectonics. If her book was prophetic, it was because she believed that Earth's seas, its collective Oceanus, were the grand synthesizer of geology, climate, and life, "the beginning and end"; for "all," she insisted, "at last return to the sea." Besides, she intoned, it is "always the unseen that most deeply stirs our imagination." Her prophecy was based on an aesthetic sense. The real revolution came with hard data.[219]

A decade later, as Carson revised and reissued the book, Wilson published his personal account of IGY as viewed from the perspective of his tenure as president of the International Union of Geodesy and Geophysics. "The history of the exploration of the sea floors is brief and simple," he observed. Not until IGY was their study "first faced in an adequate manner." Preparations for IGY had forced a consolidation of existing evidence, and an IGY-inspired Special Committee on Oceanic Research perpetuated the experience. Even as Carson wrote her paean of wonder, a flotilla of war-surplus research vessels with their sparkling instruments—their hydrophones, echo sounders, fathometers, piston corers, cameras, explosion seismometers, magnetometers, dredges, and thermal probes—was stripping the veil from the abyss. That year Lt. Don Walsh and Jacques Piccard rode the bathyscaphe *Trieste* to the bottom of the Marianas Trench. The imagination no longer needed to rely on analogies, poetic tropes, and appeals to "ultimate causes": it could feast on hard data. Ideas expanded to match that empirical bounty.[220]

The modernist revolution that had swept one field of inquiry after another like rolling thunder through the early decades of the twentieth century at last rumbled across geology. As IGY closed, Wilson could ponder that "No one knows with any certainty how the earth behaves, why mountains are uplifted, how continents were formed, or what causes earthquakes. We know some anatomy of the earth, but no real physiology." Earth sciences "await" a revolution. As discoveries poured in, reformation followed. A quiet Earth became dynamic. Its sciences were reborn—renewed like its crust. Earth became the first of the planets surveyed by the remote-sensing instruments of the Third Age, and plate tectonics appeared as the founding theory of planetary science.[221]

There was little opportunity, and less need, to indulge in rhetorical tropes or incantatory musings about the "unseen" and the unfathomable. The unseen abyss had been mapped. The unfathomable had been plumbed and measured. An elevated tone, if it matches its subject, works if its voice comes well before an episode of massive change or well after one. In either setting, a few select data points, stories, anecdotes, and personalities, be they people or marine worms or fishes, can be abstracted, granted an epic aura and a poetic cast, and hold up as a narrative. But during a revolution, with new discoveries rushing like a turbidity current, they cannot. Rachel Carson's ode to Oceanus could hardly be possible after the Third Age had commenced its serious exploration: there was too much data, too many new species, too great an abundance of geologic features, a crowded, jostling, spilling-over-the-desk thesaurus of natural-history and geophysical exotica. By the 1960s there was little need to elevate rhetorically the study of the deep oceans; discovery was pouring out of the abyss and onto the continents. Thanks to the Third Age the oceans were moving to the center of Earth history. The silent abyss joined moons and distant planets as new worlds.

Something similar happened with space. Before the advent of exploring spacecraft, the solar system seemed a tired, even clichéd subject, a relic of Newtonian physics in an age of relativity and quantum mechanics. Planetary astronomy, in particular, was a backwater, and worse, one contaminated by the fantasies of Percival Lowell and techno-romance novelists. The labors of planetary astronomers, poring over photographic plates, spoke the scholarship of classicists analyzing variants of obscure texts. Here was the laboratory turned library.

Prior to the Third Age the study of the planets—of Earth, for that matter—seemed moribund, committed to ever-greater musings over untestable theories and refinements in its numbers, with august authorities such as Henry Norris Russell and Sir Harold Jeffreys recycling old themes and issuing ponderous pronouncements. When the newly created U.S. Air Force funded a summary series of books on planetary astronomy in the early 1950s, Gerard P. Kuiper of the University of Chicago's Yerkes Observatory was the world's sole professional planetary astrophysicist. When Nobel Laureate Harold Urey delivered the Silliman Lecture in 1951 on *The Planets: Their Origin and Development*, the same year Carson published *The Sea Around Us*, he devoted fifty-five pages to the "terrestrial" (inner) planets and a scant five to the "major [outer] planets and their satellites."[222]

There was some movement as astronomers occasionally directed their new instruments, from spectrometers to radio waves, toward the planets to firm up rotational periods, atmospheric chemistry, and densities; and better photographic media allowed for a trickle of discovery in planetary satellites. But the subject seemed as opaque as a gaseous giant and as dead as its. Before Mariner 2 arrived, Venus's thick clouds had screened the planet from close scrutiny; even its rotational period was uncertain. Before Mariner 4, it was believed that Mars had no craters. The major college text of the time, Robert Baker's *Astronomy*, could assert as late as 1964 that "the times of the Martian year when the dark markings change in intensity and color are such as would be expected if the changes are caused by the growth and decline of vegetation." In a volume of 557 pages, Uranus and Neptune claimed a page each, half of that devoted to grainy black-and-white photos. Mostly the text spoke to their discovery, not their properties. Kuiper lamented the lack of "reciprocity" between geosciences and planetary astronomy; the latter could only marvel at the "incredible richness of the data" the former possessed.[223]

Then exploration blasted off and the data streamed back. IGY required three world centers to hold the rising stream. Explorer 1 found the Van Allen radiation belts. Tiros 1 began imaging the dynamics of Earth's atmosphere, and even before the Apollo program was announced, it had photographed all the continents save Antarctica. Ranger spacecraft went to the Moon. Mariner 2 flew by Venus. Pioneer 6 amassed tape recordings, "shipped daily, big 9,600 foot, 17-inch reels"—"truckloads of tapes." Then came the major missions, culminating in Voyager. Writing in 1981, when the Grand Tour had just begun, and focusing only on the inner planets, three prominent geoscientists remarked that their field was "immersed in a planetary information explosion." As Voyager 2 rushed toward Uranus, JPL estimated the volume of data the mission had so far dispatched to Earth as four trillion bits, enough to "encode over 5,000 complete sets of the *Encyclopedia Britannica*."[224]

The exploring spacecraft had sparked a revolution. They not only amassed fresh data but also prompted astronomers to redirect their instruments (if not their minds) to the solid-bodied new worlds of space; and more than raw digits, the missions established a context for their comparison. Earth science became planetary science.

All this—the fevered incantation of information, dazzling scenes, novel experiences, the rhythm of trek and encounter—was the cultural and psychological drive that made planetary exploration distinct from scientific observation or technological adventuring. Here was Cherry-Garrard's Intellectual Passion leaping from Earth's miniature ice-world of Antarctica to other planets and moons. Make it new, Ezra Pound had demanded; the robots did.

So little had been known; so much was revealed. Looking back from 1985, Oran Nicks observed that "it is not easy to recapture the extent of our ignorance a quarter-century ago; *everything* we learned was new." Everything about spacecraft, everything about interplanetary voyaging, everything about the worlds the spacecraft discovered. That was true for Mariner 2 at Venus, Mariner 4 at Mars, Pioneers 10 and 11 at Jupiter and Saturn ("everything we found out at Saturn was totally new," Van Allen declared), and it was true for every planetary visitation by the Voyagers. Writing after the Neptune encounter, Ellis Miner declared simply that "no other experience is likely to come close to matching the excitement of anticipation and discovery that accompanied the Voyager Mission." Those sentiments were the hallmark of a golden age.[225]

To that astounding era, Voyager came as a climax. The twin spacecraft went to more places, sent back more data, did more varied things, and continued for the longest time. "No other mission," explained Edward Stone, "explored so many different worlds" and revealed "such unexpected diversity." After Voyager no one could see the solar system in the same way, or see Earth, or for that matter themselves, as they had before. "You only discover the solar system for the first time once," observed Larry Soderblom. "Voyager did that."[226]

GOLDEN AGE

A golden age.

All those who participated in the American planetary program from Mariner 2's flyby in 1962 to Voyager's embarkation in 1977 agreed that this was a privileged time. Spacecraft visited virtually every planet, and revisited the closest; almost every year saw a launch; and when, after the hiatus imposed by the Challenger debacle, planetary exploration revived, it built on the legacy and hibernated ideas of those epic years. It was all "the stuff of legend and myth," as space historian Roger Launius put it. Proponents differed only in their sense of the era's tempo and their reckoning of its capacity to persist. They fretted because the age depended less on engineering cleverness and scientific purpose than on the whims, wealth, and mores of its sustaining society. Voyager, Bruce Murray noted, was the last mission in which "the technical challenge was dominant. Since then it's been politics."[227]

A golden age is to history what a utopia is to geography. It is a time of the good, the just, the ideal. Good people do good things. The world works as it should. If the past can't supply a golden age, the future might. For space advocates, that forecast future lay always just over the horizon; and after World War II it seemed it might happen in their lifetimes. Then it did happen. For NASA, the golden age of manned flight was the sixties, the age of Apollo; and for planetary exploration, the seventies, when its spacecraft visited every planet save Pluto or were on their way to do so. The ideal became the expected.

At the time, those in the political trenches recognized what a close-run thing it was. Even Voyager had faced cancellation, or rechartering, and had downsized dramatically. The era seemed golden mostly in retrospect. The space shuttle siphoned and then hemorrhaged funding and energies away. The Reagan administration was hostile—wanted space, but in the hands of private companies or the military, and was eager to force the cold war to a conclusion, but not through proxy expeditions to other worlds. Office of Management and Budget director David Stockman sought to shut down planetary exploration altogether. Voyager—in some ways "really a product of the 1960s"—was, as Murray expressed it, "the last hurrah." As the twins sped across the solar system, the sentiment could easily unfold that they climaxed a golden age, now lost.[228]

Yet there was also a sense at the time, often a quiet euphoria, that space exploration would continue because it had to continue. The space program was more than an event: it embodied a movement of evolutionary importance on a planetary scale. It would transcend its sordid origins in the cold war. NASA could commission studies that likened the space program to the advent of the railroad, movies could be made of *Childhood's End*, and otherwise sober observers might declare that outer space would revolutionize humanity more than the industrial revolution. The golden age, once arrived, would stay. That was part of the promise, and the appeal of historical utopias of all kinds across all ages. It characterizes exploration no less than other cultural endeavors.

Yet it is the nature of history's golden ages to be fleeting. To those living amid them, their significance becomes apparent often only at the time they are primed to implode. Before then, too much is happening to stand aside and contemplate, but it is just as the climax comes, with a softening of urgent tasks and a fading of vision, that the recent past begins to glow.

Great outbursts of exploring enthusiasms are rare. They are possible because of distortions in the normal routine of their societies; and for that very reason they cannot be sustained. They feed off their larger nurturing culture; they can, from time to time, feed back into that culture like a self-reinforcing dynamo; but the larger dynamic comes from society, not from exploration. Geographic discovery can continue only insofar as it creates ongoing wealth. Planetary exploration expended surplus wealth; it did not create it. The great outbursts of exploring that punctuated Western history rather resemble the gravity-assisted acceleration granted by passage around a giant planet like Jupiter. Viewed from the planet, the velocity gained on approaching periapsis is also lost when the spacecraft recedes. It is only from another, more remote reference frame that the event can be seen to yield a long-term gain. So it is with the golden age of planetary exploration.[229]

Many proponents refused to accept that the golden age might end, or have urged, with a progressive urgency hedging into hysteria, that it be revived and expanded. That, too, is typical, and can segue into parody. It is present in the spectacle of Hernando Cortés's stumbling around Guatemala, Hernando de Soto's bulling through Georgia, bold knight Francisco Coronado's wandering through Kansas, and the Portuguese *degredado* (convict turned conquistador) António Fernandes's blundering around the interior of Africa—all in search of another Mexico or Peru. After the Second Age, it resurfaces with Roy Chapman Andrews's leading an expedition to Shiva Temple, an isolated mesa in Grand Canyon, to search for lost worlds and with Richard Byrd leaving Little America to live by himself at Advance Base on the Ross Ice Shelf, and nearly perishing from carbon monoxide poisoning. Today it appears in proposals to sponsor another Apollo program or a national commitment to imminently colonize Mars.

Such willful pursuits have their costs, not all dismissable as fool-ish vanity or misplaced idealism. Such obsessions can distort public discourse, and cabals dedicated to them can capture public policy and lead into costly misadventures. These can go beyond satire into darker parodies. If Don Quixote, a knight-errant mounted in a haze of imagined ideals, is a benign response to a lost golden age, the foot-loose *bandeirante*, an overland buccaneer opaque to anything other than slaving, raiding, and plundering, is his malign double. Yet it is hard to know when a golden age has crested, and when to adjust ambition to possibilities.

Most enthusiasts shun even asking such questions, because to do so suggests that the recent golden age, our age, might not revive and exceed itself. But in the late 1990s, Bruce Murray did ask.

While director at JPL, he had noted the "terrible contrast" between the technical successes of Viking and Voyager and the social failures to "reinvest" in the future. The space shuttle, in particular, he regarded as "the greatest threat to space exploration" since pre-NASA days. In April 1980 he wrote Arthur C. Clarke, several of whose books he had just finished reading, thanked him for providing "a full sup-ply of much-needed nourishment for our imaginations and spirits in this difficult period when Man seems unable to keep up with des-tiny," and invited him to JPL for Voyager 1's encounter with Saturn. He also planned to invite Freeman Dyson and others for a session on interstellar travel. As that theme suggests, Murray, like many of his contemporaries, thought the trek would continue to the stars.[230]

Then he realized it wouldn't; not in his lifetime, not outside sci-ence fiction novels. The spectacular supernova of exploring that Voy-ager had "epitomized" he came to regard as "a very brief anomaly," one that expressed a "combination of politics and economics and technology" that had allowed American society to rush through a phase at "an extraordinary rate" before hitting a limit. He raised the possibility that there would be no further escalation to the stars, that "this was the end," that it was "the end of adolescence for humanity," that "we'll have to learn to live within the space we have, physically and intellectually." In the unmanned exploration of the solar system, he thought "we've already reached the limits of what we're going to be doing. We're not going to the nearest star." Voyager, he believed, was "a symbol" and an "extraordinary historical event." But it also raised questions about whether such rates of activity were "unsupportable." Murray concluded they were: it was not possible to "keep exploring like that." There would be a falloff, which he found both depressing and impossible to stop. He wondered what such a lapse might mean for a society that "has always been expanding."[231]

Space proponents hated the meditation. Even close friends like Philip Morrison and Carl Sagan found that such prospects "violated their intuitive beliefs." But the longer the American space program continues, the longer exists the empirical record of what the public will support, and what out of the general "space" budget it will expend on genuine exploration. In 2007 the NASA budget for planetary exploration was some $3 billion. This was more than the American college textbook and resale market ($2.3 billion), and less than the estimated sales from fast food restaurants in Los Angeles ($3.4 billion). That same year, the National Football League and Major League Baseball each accrued roughly $6 billion in revenue. Those who claimed in the early 1960s that the space program would inaugurate an economic revolution had been proved wildly wrong.[232]

Planetary exploration, in particular, was a significant but niche enterprise, larger than handmade soap and self-publishing, smaller than professional sports and movies. It was, in brief, a cost that society justified as it did much scientific research and art museums. Observatories in space were on par with opera houses, and for similar reasons: they were a chosen, discretionary cultural activity, and to a large extent, an elite activity. They satisfied social needs and yearnings. They might vanish if alternate or surrogate activities could meet those desires. Society might choose instead to colonize cyberspace. It might prefer virtual exploration and extreme sports.

How does a society respond to the passing of a golden age? Some would reverse the stance of King Knute trying to halt the rising tide and stem its ebb. The danger especially exists of the quixotic turn, the determination to pursue the old glories and chivalry into new times. The scene abounds with fancied Isaiahs and aspiring Cassandras, alternately warning and threatening, all abuzz with prophecies and jeremiads. But an exploring age integrates too many activities to respond to rhetoric and vision alone.

If the social order doesn't collapse entirely, golden ages segue into silver ones. These tend to be more broadly based, less given to heroic posturing, more prone to irony and a sense of constraint. In place of new initiatives, its participants fill out the old agenda, stabilize and firm up its institutional foundations, and replace raw if grand gestures with more polished manners and elegant phrasing. The edge is off. Steady work replaces inspiration. Rude narratives become textbooks. Epic poems become eclogues and elegies. For exploration, bold traverses into the wild give way to trading posts, land surveys, and intercultural exchanges. It is not that participants are less hardy or courageous or clever; they just perform in a different context, in new settings of time and place. Besides, massive programs create a kind of wake turbulence after their passage. The institution pauses; a sequel requires a caesura.

Something like this has happened with planetary exploration. After a hard crash, programs have recovered equilibrium. Complex single missions have taken Magellan to Venus, Galileo to Jupiter, Cassini to Saturn, and Huygens to Titan, and a small fleet of rovers and orbital observers to Mars. These are brilliant, successful missions, but they necessarily lack the zest of the vision quest and the drama of first-time encounter. Perhaps from a vantage point in the distant future, everything from Mariner 2 to the New Horizons mission to Pluto and other expeditions yet to launch will all merge into a single, heroic panorama. But from the perspective of those present when Voyager completed its Grand Tour, a golden age had declined into a silver one and struggled not to sink into bronze.

PARTING, TWO

As the adage goes, it's better to be lucky than good. The Voyagers were both. They were lucky in the providential alignment of a Grand Tour and a golden age, lucky in their handlers and their determination to rescue them from a shaky launch, lucky in that their revelations beat those from orbiting telescopes. It was good in that they didn't just hit their designated target as Viking did at Mars, or orbit a planet endlessly like Pioneer Venus. They spanned the solar system.

Voyager was, in Bruce Murray's words, "a concatenation of really good people, good ideas, support by society, luck in the engineering sense and luck in the scientific sense." The mission was "always successful." And more than any other space enterprise, it has lasted. It has outlived all its competitors. It has renewed itself. It has retained the capacity to discover. "History is what you write when a mission is over," Murray observed in 1997, but "this mission keeps on going."[233]

It continued after Neptune. Voyager 1 still arced upward toward the heliosphere, one final task remaining for the Grand Tour. Voyager 2 spun downward, also on a trajectory to termination shock. Both continued to sample the interplanetary medium and report back to Earth, still going. They are still going today.

19. Cruise

Once again, the Voyager staff began to turn off instruments. Those most closely linked with hard-geography science went first, along with those most prone to guzzle power and hydrazine. But this time some would never be revived. Infrared sensors, imaging systems, the photoelectric photometer—these were instruments designed to inventory worlds, and the Voyagers had no more worlds to visit.

Even the exploration of the solar system's soft geography was reaching a terminus. Time and again, planet after planet, encounter had begun and ended with bow shock, that fluid, twisting field where the planet's magnetosphere collided with the solar wind. Now there remained one last such border, the heliopause, a thick fringe of ions and rays, where the Sun's magnetosphere met the interstellar medium. "Termination shock," its inner edge was called, and that phrase might stand not only for the clashing of electromagnetic fields but for the Grand Tour itself.

This time, too, there were no further burns or gravity assists. The trajectory each spacecraft had was the trajectory it would always have. The Voyagers' pasts set their futures.

TRIANGULATING THE THIRD AGE

Why does a society explore? For many reasons, but at base because it chooses to, and it chooses to because the enterprise appeals to felt needs. What makes exploration powerful is that it bundles those longings into compelling packages and sends them on a journey. Over time some pieces are lost and some added, and the assemblage bonds to its culture with weaker or stronger valences. When those mixings give rise to qualitative change, they can spark great ages of discovery; the Third Age is such a moment.

But how to parse the significant new from the enduring old? The space program's instinct to look back as well as ahead may help. The program had begun by looking back. It looked back to Columbus for an exploring legacy, back to America's westering frontier for a past that it could project forward, and back to the memory of a murdered president who first set the lunar lander on its way. Its most celebrated crewed and robotic missions framed their images of the future with glances back to Earth. Apollo 8 gave us earthrise, and Apollo 17 the whole Earth. Voyager framed the Grand Tour with a first look back to Earth and its Moon and a last look back at the solar system. Along the way it framed its discoveries by backsiting on the eruptions of Io and Triton, by backlighting Jupiter's storms and Saturn's rings, and by sculpted backviewing of Uranus and Neptune that transformed their cloudy murk into haunting crescents of light.

In a similar way Voyager has looked back on the long chronicle of geographic exploration by the West, and in so doing it has highlighted those features of the Third Age that are most distinctive. What they share is that the Third Age is going where no one is or ever has been. In past ages, geographic discovery *had* to be done by people. There was no other option by which to learn the languages, to record data and impressions, to gather specimens, to meet other societies and translate their accumulated wisdom. It is impossible to imagine the great expeditions of the past without considering the personality of individual explorers who inspired, collected, witnessed, fought, wrote, sketched, exulted, feared, suffered, and otherwise expressed the aspirations and alarms of their civilization. But it is entirely possible to do so now. Not only is there no encounter between people, there need not even be a human encounterer.

The geographic realms of the Third Age are not places where people learn from indigenes or live off the land. These are environs that offer no sustaining ecosystems; their geographies remain, for all practical purposes, abiotic and acultural worlds. If the Third Age has propelled exploration beyond the ethnocentric realm of Western discovery, it has also thrust it beyond the sphere of the human and, with regard to space, perhaps beyond the provenance of life. No one will live off the land on Demos, go native on Titan, absorb the art of Venus, the mythology of Uranus, the religious precepts of Mars, or the literature of Ceres. There will be no one to talk to except ourselves.

This is a cultural barrier to exploration, in comparison to which the limiting velocity of light may prove a mere technological inconvenience. The reason goes to the heart of exploration: that it is not simply an expression of curiosity but also involves the encounter with a world beyond our ken that challenges our sense of who we are. It is a moral act, one often tragic, that bonds discovery to society. It means that exploration is more than adventuring, more than entertainment, more than inquisitiveness. It means that exploration asks, if indirectly, core questions about what the exploring people are like. In the past this happened when one people met another. In the future it won't, and the explorer is most likely to be a robotic surrogate.

The good news is that the coruscating ethical dilemmas of so much earlier exploring and empire building will disappear. No group need expand at the expense of another. Ethnocentricity will vanish: there is only one culture, that of the explorer. As long as other life or cultures are not present, there is no ethical or political crisis except whatever we choose to impose on ourselves. Beyond Earth there may well be no morality as traditionally understood, that is, as a means of shaping behavior between peoples. The morality at issue is one of the self, not between the self and an Other.

The bad news is that exploration's moral power—the tension, awful and enlightening both, that is involved in a clash of cultures—also vanishes. The price of ethically sanitizing exploration is to strip it of compelling *human* drama and the kind of narrative and poetry and epic tragedy that have historically joined heart to head. Planetary probes become technical challenges, to make machines to withstand the rigors of space travel, a technological equivalent to extreme sports, like white-water kayaking in Borneo or racing in NASCAR's Daytona 500. The space enterprise may become a kind of national hobby, a jobs program, or a daytime TV soap opera.

People do not have to be physically present at the discoveries of the Third Age, and there are sound reasons for arguing that they should not be. Even if colonization is attempted, successful settlements historically followed after long gestation periods of reconnaissance with aid from indigenes. More likely is an era of space tourism or historical reenactment. A risk is that partisans will try to force the Third Age into an earlier model that no longer connects to the lived world, or that they will choose to indulge in digital or chemical surrogates, or that they might simply give up on the project altogether.

COURSE CORRECTIONS:
THE FUTURES OF EXPLORATION

As the Grand Tour faded, space exploration, too, seems to have entered a long cruise phase. Although the Voyagers have no more course corrections scheduled, some are possible—and likely—for the tradition of exploration they embody, and would point that larger enterprise to its future, which is less a spectrum of choices than a constellation of options from which various patterns might be traced. Three figurations, in particular, seem plausible. One points to cyberspace; one to a Third Age that, in closing, might also close the Great Ages; and one to an untraditional narrative in which the journey becomes its own purpose.

The first prospect assumes that exploration is a response to humans' need to know bonded to the stimulus of adventure, and asserts that it will not be possible to shut those instincts off. Technology will continue to make them possible. From its origins, in fact, space travel has exhibited just such a hybrid of people and machines. Humans must rely on an artificial habitat; and spacecraft and rovers must possess a degree of autonomy. Designers have even come to speak of an "embodied experience" with regard to Mars rovers such that robots not only behave more like people, but that people identify with, and behave more in conformity with, the robots.[234]

But this might lead to a virtualized exploration. After all, curiosity can be satisfied by many means. Literature, art, laboratory science, invention, travel, collecting—individuals and societies have filled, and overtopped, their urge for the curious (and avoided boredom) in many ways. Scholars have spent lifetimes pondering Shakespeare without exhaustion. Researches in field and lab have proved unbounded if not infinite. Geographic exploration is only one anodyne among an infinite set. Already both planetary and oceanographic discovery have apparatuses by which distant observers, far removed from the operational staff, can share in discovery by watching in real time through the same cameras. Geographic exploration is no longer something that an individual alone must do or experience; it can occur among millions simultaneously. It is only a short mutation of technology and a hop-skip of faith to have exploration venture into cyberspace altogether.

Engineers might take the process further. Science might find what physiological triggers exploration satisfies, and technology might discover ways to satisfy them without the bother and boredom of trekking, just as vitamin C can be distilled from oranges into a pill or amphetamines can bring a rush that in the past had to come from danger and adventure. The old quarrel between robots and astronauts might pale before the opportunity for virtual exploration. One could experience the ecstasy of first-contact discovery without the annoyance of first-contact mosquitoes, fevers, troublesome natives, unreliable collaborators, and a nature reluctant to yield its secrets.

Each of the motives bundled into exploration might be separately satisfied by other means. The reductionism that allows science to express itself in machines might equally be applied to disaggregate the experience of exploring and to address each urge independently of the others. It would be but a series of short steps to go from remote sensing to remote exploring to virtual exploring. Already NASA has Web sites devoted to the task. The massively multiplayer online game Second Life has an exploring option, an island named CoLab, operated by NASA Ames Research Center. Here, it is hoped, a new generation can develop a "vision for space exploration" where "participatory exploration" could emerge and where earthlings' avatars might join astronauts as they return to the Moon. The island could serve as a "portal" to new, virtual worlds. A cyber Ocean Sea has again been populated with imagined isles awaiting discoverers.[235]

Will such exercises consume the varied cultural urges that exploration has, for half a millennium, satisfied for Western civilization? Virtual reality is rolling over one frontier after another. A generation that has grown up immersed in high-tech gadgets may respond less to their ambient environment than to their digital one; their community is what they connect to electronically. Already nature enthusiasts are vocally worrying about the future of conservation as children come to experience nature not from personal contact but by digital simulacra. Will exploration be next? Could designer drugs trigger the ventral striatum to release neurostimulators such as dopamine in the absence of tangible stimuli? Could a tamed exploration-designed LSD allow "trips" through space? Could cyberspace supply the wonder without the bother? Perhaps. Almost certainly the exploring tradition will adjust. And if it does not expire, it might, like big game hunting, morph into surrogates such as nature tourism or digital voyeurism, or become ceremonial, as with reenactments of Civil War battles.

In the end exploration will remain a cultural creation, and it will assume the character of its sustaining society. How that civilization hybridizes with its technologies will shape the future of geographic discovery and decide the future cadences of cruising and encountering.

A second option points to the rhythms of great ages, and suggests not only that the Third Age, too, will wax and then wane, but that its ebb might take the ages with it. In this conception, if the Voyagers could see beyond the termination shock of the golden age, they would find a future exploration that may look a lot like the past, only different. Exploration will go back to the future, with the Third Age recapitulating the First, and then perhaps reverting to its pre-exploring ancestry.

The possibility for a rekindling of rivalries that will translate into geographic discovery exists. Political contests may boil over into space, for example, if China declares a colony on the Moon as essential to its prestige and the European Union or Japan joins the fray. There is a prospect that the search for life will take on an imaginative, even a theological cast, sufficient that a significant fraction of the culture wants to pursue it among the planets. It may happen that extreme arts, brash new sciences, an as-yet-undeveloped commerce, an astropolitics, and some critical personalities will combine to yield a Third Age echo of the Second Age. In some form or another, a virtuous cycle is possible. But it is not likely. As Damon Runyon advised, the race is not always to the swift nor the battle to the strong, but that's where you place your money.

The most plausible prognosis is that the future will resemble the past, that the Second Age's monadnock of activity will mark an axis around which the evolving contours will unfold with rough historical symmetry. The Third Age will resemble the early Second, though in reverse. Expeditions will slide toward a new steady state—for space, perhaps on the order of one or two a year. These will be complicated probes, requiring years of preparation, not unlike the expeditions launched during the Great Voyages and quite unlike the brawling swarm of state-sponsored and individually motivated treks that so inflated the Second Age. They will be targeted to some particular purpose—commercial, scientific, technological, national prowess and prestige. They are unlikely to spill out from colonization: they will rather resemble those expeditions that established trading factories on islands or episodically visited coastlines for barter or sought out new routes. If the process thrives, there will be several competitors, not some collective United Earth Space Agency; and that institutional unrest is what will keep the pot simmering. Steadily, more and more of the solar system will be visited, catalogued, mapped, assessed. Perhaps, here and there, an outpost will appear, staffed for a few years.

The Third Age will then burn itself out, as other ages have before it. Its narrative will end as exploring expeditions traditionally end: it will return to its origins. It will have a beginning, a middle, and a conclusion. It will advance from launch to journey to splashdown. Reversing this trend would require an immense, global commitment that could come only from some dark necessity or irresistible rivalry, say, the discovery amid the asteroids of some mineral absolutely vital to national existence—the equivalent of the Potosí mines of Mexico, perhaps—or from Venutians announcing that they intend to colonize Mars and the moons of Saturn, and daring earthlings to stop them.

As the Third Age winds down, it may perhaps carry the great ages of discovery with it. They were created; they may expire. The conditions that sustained them may cease altogether; they may no longer inspire interest as a tradition worthy of institutional support. One can even imagine a robotic Columbus ceremoniously announcing an end to the enterprise. If the late nineteenth century marks a bilateral middle in this saga, that passing may happen some four hundred years later, the early twenty-third century, where *Star Trek* now resides in the popular imagination. Exploration, even of space, may then exist only in literature, history, film, and popular imagination, and in a past where no one, boldly or otherwise, wishes any longer to go.

Or there is a third figuration of the future. We might create an alternative to the narrative that has characterized previous eras, as different from its cadence as Third Age terrains are from the isles and lands of previous ages.

A counter version might hold that the traditional narrative structure might not apply. Like the Voyagers, the process will simply go on and on, constantly redefined and redirected. What makes the Third Age distinctive will allow it not so much to endure as to ultimately morph into a successor. It will retain some features—enough to have it be recognizable as exploring—and discard others. That sorting process will permit it to persist. It will survive by becoming different. It will simply continue.

In such speculations the Voyagers still have something to say. Their journey may yet write a different kind of narrative, pushing through the heliosphere of a greater modernism. The Grand Tour did not end with Neptune. The Voyager mission will not end with the solar system. The Voyagers continue to surprise.

20. Last Light

Looking back.

Before the Grand Tour ended, Voyager had a chance to peer back for one last time and reflect in its lenses something of what it had accomplished. Since Saturn, Voyager 1 had cruised with its cameras shuttered, while Voyager 2 continued to assemble its brilliant photo portfolio of new worlds. Now Voyager 1 was roused from hibernation to perform a task that would, for many observers, distill the entire enterprise into an enduring, defining image.

The post-encounter phase of every planet had included backlit shots of the planet and its satellites, and often of many such scenes into a single image. The practice had begun when Voyager 1 turned around and photographed Earth and the Moon together on September 18, 1977, two weeks after launch. Now Voyager 1 was asked to turn back on behalf of the entire Grand Tour and photograph the planets as part of a grand ensemble. On February 13 to 14, 1990, it did just that.[236]

The idea emanated from Carl Sagan, who conceived it after the Saturn encounter. He wanted a space-based version of the celebrated earthrise images from Apollo. These, he thought, had revolutionized humanity's sense of itself. We could see ourselves as others might see us. Now it was time to expand that horizon, to see how we might look "to an alien spacecraft approaching the Solar System after a long interstellar voyage."[237]

But mission officials balked. Some dismissed the gesture as a stunt, far removed from engineering necessity or scientific duty. Most believed it was better to wait until the programmed tasks were done; better not to point those lenses toward a still-vibrant Sun and risk scorching sensitive instruments; better to see the whole once than to juggle commands and slew scan platforms. The hard-science crowd scoffed: this was public entertainment, more postcards, a stunt that might embarrass a real astrophysicist before his peers. But these were the same arguments by the same people who had scorned having cameras at all. They never realized that the power of Voyager lay not in its scientific role but in its cultural context. The American public did not spend $600 million to record the magnetosphere of Neptune and the rotational period of Titania. They sought the wonder of new worlds and a reflection of their own.

After Saturn, Voyager 1 had no further duties for its cameras, and after Neptune, neither did Voyager 2. JPL's Voyager staff faced a dramatic downsizing. The DSN had more urgent tasks. If the scheme was to be done, it had to be done soon. Like the alignment of planets that made the Grand Tour plausible, an alignment of planets, particularly Earth, made a parting gesture possible. NASA administrator Rear Admiral Richard Truly ordered the photos taken.[238]

On February 14, Valentine's Day, 32 degrees above the ecliptic, traveling at over 64,300 kilometers per hour, almost 6 billion kilometers from the Sun, Voyager 1 shot 39 wide-angle views and 21 narrow-angle ones that encompassed 6 of the 9 planets. Mercury and Mars were too close to the Sun to show, and Pluto too minute amid the stellar glare. Neptune and Uranus were so dark that the long exposures caused smearing. Earth, freakishly, caught a bounce of sunlight off the spacecraft that allowed it to appear "in a beam of light." Over the next three months, as the DSN schedule allowed, Voyager 1 transmitted the 640,000 pixels of each image from its magnetic tapes to Earth, then some 5.5 light-hours away. Each photo required 30 minutes. The Voyager Family Portrait, as it came to be called, thus complemented the record of Earth that the spacecraft carried.[239]

NASA spokesperson Jurrie van der Woude and Sagan quickly dismissed any special status for Earth, which only occupied 0.12 of a pixel and had to be magnified sixfold to show at all. The point of the exercise, Woude insisted, was to show "how insignificant we are." Sagan elaborated: the Earth was a mere "pale blue dot." That phrase became the title for his final book on space exploration, published in 1994. The story of Voyager's farewell photos provided the opening chapter in what Sagan proclaimed as "a vision of the human future in space." Such pronouncements, however, were the flip side of those that dismissed the exercise as merely a publicity stunt. Most participants probably echoed Candice Hansen's judgment that this was "the picture of the century." It fell to Ed Stone to craft the right alloy of poetry and science. He turned to the practice of astronomers, who call the initial imaging by a telescope "first light." This, the final use of the spacecraft's lenses, Stone labeled Voyager's "last light."[240]

It was a scene, the self-portrait, often found in exploration history.

In the past, when the portrait couldn't be photographed or painted on site, it might be done later in a studio with the explorer outfitted in full expedition regalia. It was not the place that mattered so much as the explorer positioned within it. It was a ritual act: the quest achieved, the hero returned. By the end of the Second Age, such staged events were expected. Think of the triumphant photo of Robert Peary at the North Pole, or the haggard image of exhaustion evident in the self-portrait taken by Robert Scott's sledging party at the South Pole, each in its way a concluding record of the Second Age.

In the Third Age it was not possible, either geographically or philosophically, to position a camera or an artist to record the explorer in his milieu. There was no way to include Voyager within the frame of its accomplishment. Often Voyager would appear to the side in composites, but this was a studio confection. Voyager 1's "family portrait" was in truth a self-portrait, a record of the places it had visited and of the people who had sent it. Much as its golden record was not a message to extraterrestrials but to Earth, so its gallery mosaic was less a vision of how the solar system might appear to visiting aliens than an invitation to earthlings to see themselves as others might, or perhaps more accurately as they would like themselves to appear to others. The self-reflexive event testifies that in Voyager the sojourner and the journey had become one. The encountered Other has become the exploring self. In that gesture the Grand Tour found a way to bracket its journey.

The Grand Tour, yes. But the Voyagers' journey was not yet over.

part 3

BEYOND THE UTMOST BOND:
JOURNEY TO THE STARS

And this grey spirit yearning in desire
To follow knowledge like a sinking star,
Beyond the utmost bond of human thought.

—**Alfred Tennyson, "Ulysses"**

Beyond Bow Shock

21. Voyager Interstellar Mission

On January 1, 1990, the Voyagers commenced the Voyager Interstellar Mission (VIM), a cruise without a hard encounter at its end, only the soft frontier where the solar wind buffets against and finally yields to the interstellar media.

The instruments so vital to interrogate planetary hard geography were turned off. The infrared interferometer and spectrometer and radiometer. The imaging cameras. The photoelectric photometer. While the rest could still perform usefully, they did so at greater costs, which Voyager could less and less afford. The amount of hydrazine, needed by thrusters to perform rolls for magnetometer recalibrations and to keep antennas pointed to Earth, was finite, and consumed at a rate of six to eight grams per week. The ultraviolet spectrometer remained on in order to sample hydrogen in the outer regions of the heliosphere, but then it and the scan platform were powered down to save energy. Supplemental heaters were turned off. Throughout, the power yield from the radioisotope thermoelectric generators steadily decayed; by 2001 overall production had dropped from 470 to 315 watts; by 2008, to 285. And if they were to reach bow shock, the Voyagers had a long way to go.[1]

The mission's budget was draining even more dramatically. From

May 1972, when planning began for MJS 77, up to the encounter with Uranus in 1986, with an inflationary storm in between, the Voyager mission had cost $600 million. In the favored analogy, this amounted to the price of a candy bar each year for every American citizen. Hard as it was to scrounge money for a new mission, so much harder was it to find funds to maintain an old one. The political regime that authorized a program would be long gone when the program succeeded, though it might be remembered at encounter. No one would honor those who sustained a cruise. It became harder and harder to argue for VIM when termination shock would occur years away and no new worlds might flash the event across TV screens.

As the second Bush administration projected a crewed mission to Mars (or sought to pay off cronies in aerospace, as cynics argued), money became even tighter, and the persistence of old missions such as Voyager seemed like leaches that sucked the lifeblood out of new ones. In 2005 the Voyagers still had a staff of ten (down from three hundred in 1989) and an annual budget of $2 million when NASA sought to shut down the operation along with five others. But once again Voyager survived a political threat to kill it. It would end only when its internal power finally drained away. For now, it continued to send back reports from new settings. It was doing what no other spacecraft could. Its narrative simply defied closure from Earth.[2]

The border between the solar system and the stars is broad, sloppy, and untraced. The bubble of gases, or heliosphere, that contains the solar winds has a complex structure. Its outer perimeter, the heliosheath, has two edges, one facing the solar wind and the other, the interstellar winds. At its inner border, or termination shock, the supersonic solar wind slows to subsonic speeds. This was believed to occur around eighty to ninety astronomical units (AUs) from the Sun. To reach it from Neptune would take Voyager 2 as long as it had taken the spacecraft to reach Neptune from Earth, or roughly twelve years. Within the heliosheath the pressures of solar and interstellar winds roughly balance. Its thickness varies because the entire solar system moves, which compresses the heliosheath in the direction of that movement and extends it on the downwind side, much as comets have compact heads and long tails. The outer border, or bow shock, thus ranges in thickness from 10 AUs on the windward side to 100 AUs on the lee. That geography defines the three phases of the Voyagers' Interstellar Mission. When they finally pass through the outer bow shock, they will be sailing amid the winds of stars.[3]

Voyager 1 was fastest and farthest, and at 85 AU, in August 2002, it recorded fluctuations that were reported as possible evidence of termination shock. This could not be confirmed, however; the billowing border is unstable, full of pulses and pauses from gusty solar breezes and their turmoil with interstellar winds, and the magnetic disturbances that shape them; and the plasma science instrument on Voyager 1 no longer functioned, which forced researchers to infer shock from indirect sources. But on December 16, 2004, at some 95 AU, it unblinkingly passed through termination shock and entered the heliosheath. Voyager 2 crossed that bar at 84 AU on August 30, 2007, and then reexperienced passage at least five times over the course of several days as the shock boundary twisted and bubbled.

Since the Voyagers entered the heliosheath at different places some sixteen billion kilometers apart, their encounters helped map the geography of that frontier. As predicted, the heliosphere was "squashed" on top and bottom. But the amount of variance was more than expected, and so were the temperature differences on both sides of the border; the heliosheath was far cooler than expected. Voyager, as its then program scientist Eric Christian noted, "has once again surprised us."[4]

But surprise had been a Voyager specialty since launch. On January 5, 2005, the mission surpassed 10,000 days of operation. In August and September 2007, the Voyagers reached thirty years. Measured in robot lifetimes, they were Methuselahs. They were leaving the solar system with computing power inadequate to run a cell phone, and electrical power insufficient to animate a clock radio. Yet they had much yet to survey: the dynamics of the solar wind, sunspot effects on the interplanetary medium, low-energy cosmic rays, reversals in the Sun's magnetic field, interstellar particles, radio emissions from various sources within and beyond the heliosphere, and of course the interstellar medium, if all went well. Of particular interest are their

UVS instruments in that they observe spectra no other spacecraft can.[5]

Their trek continues.

They have enough energy that, if conserved, they might still be able to transmit after passage through bow shock at the outer heliosheath. By 2015 Voyager 1 will have to shut down its data tape recorder, and Voyager 2 its gyros. A year later, Voyager 1 will cease its gyros, and after another year, Voyager 2, its data tape recorder. Steadily, in a creeping paralysis, the Voyagers will trade dead instruments for only the most basic functions—ultimately, the measurements of interstellar wind and the communication of that information to Earth. By 2016 for Voyager 2 and 2018 for Voyager 1, those few instruments still online will need to share power. By 2020, barring a sudden collapse, the robotic equivalent of a stroke or heart attack, their RTGs will no longer be able to support even a solitary instrument. The spacecraft will wither, like an organism wasting with scurvy. They might still be able to send signals, useful for tracking, but even that capacity will eventually fail. Sometime in the mid-2020s they will cease to function and become inert time capsules in a realm beyond time.[6]

For now they cruise, settling into trajectories that will propel them toward the fluid edge of the solar system and to the very borders of the Third Age.

22. Far Travelers

There are now four spacecraft headed beyond the solar system. Pioneer 10 is moving downwind toward termination shock, roughly heading to the star Aldebaran in the constellation Taurus, and at 43,000 kilometers per hour (relative to the Sun) might reach it in some two million years. Pioneer 11's long reverse trek to Saturn has pointed it toward the closer, upwind border, cruising at 41,500 kph; it will pass, within the next six light-years, by Proxima Centauri, and some 6,500 years later it will sail within four light-years of the star Ross 248. Both spacecraft have gone silent. All contact was lost with Pioneer 11 by November 1995. Shortly after its thirtieth anniversary in 2002, Pioneer 10 blinked off. The two Pioneers now sail onward, ghost ships from Earth.[7]

By comparison the Voyagers are still vigorous. They crossed termination shock with their field instruments and communications intact. And they are faster. On February 17, 1998, Voyager 1 surpassed Pioneer 10 as the most distant human-made object in space. By January 1, 2008, relative to the Sun, Voyager 1 sailed at 61,600 kph and Voyager 2 at 56,000 kph. Voyager 2 was slower because its peculiar targeting at Neptune had turned the magic of gravity assistance against it and cost it velocity—that was the price of Triton. At that date, Pioneer 10 was 94 AU distant from Earth; Pioneer 11, 75 AU;

Voyager 1, 106 AU; and Voyager 2, 85 AU. The Voyagers have become Earth's farthest explorers.[8]

In all this there is a certain symmetry. The Voyagers had begun their journeys by riding enough energy to escape Earth's gravity, and they had acquired sufficient additional energy on their travels to escape the Sun's. But there is also a profound asymmetry. They will not return. That of course has been true for many exploring expeditions, and the ships that carried them; it was a risk every explorer took; it was part of why their sustaining societies granted them special honor. But it was never an intention of design. For the Voyagers, it was.

What has been the fate of famous vessels? In the past they returned to sea and plied the waves until they sank or were scrapped. Columbus's *Santa Maria* foundered in the New World, while the *Niña* rejoined him for the second voyage, and later took him back yet again to Hispaniola. The Victoria, which first circumnavigated the Earth, was refitted and sent out for transport, until it eventually sank. That was the destiny of vessels generally: they were reconditioned, rechartered, and reworked. Very few had been originally designed for exploration; they had been refashioned, ice-strengthened, copper-plated, supplied with living quarters in place of cannons, fitted out with heaters and libraries for polar campaigns, given laboratories and collection cabinets; and when finished, they were reworked again further down the food chain until they sank or were sold for scrap. A few—the *James Caird*, lifeboat of Shackleton's *Endurance*, is an example—found themselves accidentally placed into service, yet achieved such fame that they seem to have been designed for their destiny. The *Caird* has become a museum piece, now displayed in traveling exhibitions like a painting from the Old Masters.[9]

A few might find a second wind and explore further. After serving as a flagship for the U.S. Exploring Expedition, the USS *Vincennes* was dispatched on a second tour (the North Pacific Expedition) before running out its life cycle. The HMS *Erebus* and *Terror,* having sailed with James Ross to the Antarctic, joined John Franklin's quest for the Northwest Passage, where they sank. The HMS *Beagle* was recycled into three expeditions (Darwin's was the second), before being refitted from coastal surveying to coastal patrols against smuggling, ending in the marshlands of the River Roach.

Ships were expensive: in order to endure, they had to mine a deeper vein than their legacy to exploration alone. Who frets over the fate of the *Astrolabe*? The *Mirnyy*? The *Terra Nova*? The keelboat used by Lewis and Clark? La Salle's *Griffon*? But where a richer cultural bond exists, the desire to preserve or re-create (and reenact) can thrive. Enthusiasts have rebuilt and voyaged in Norse longships; they have resurrected Columbus's *Santa Maria* and reenacted its voyage to the New World; they have reconstructed and sailed John Cabot's *Matthew* to Newfoundland; they are rebuilding the *Beagle*. Land vehicles could survive junking as well. Douglas Mawson's pared-down sledge is a museum artifact at the University of Adelaide. The *Discovery* expedition's hut at McMurdo Bay, Antarctica, is a protected historic site.

The HMS *Endeavour* began as a north-country collier, was refitted to suit Cook's first circumnavigation, and then slid back into the obscurity of the Admiralty's rosters. It was again refitted, this time as a store ship, and sold in 1775 for £615. Its subsequent history is murky, but the likely story is that, renamed the *Lord Sandwich*, it worked the Baltic trade and then was accepted into the Transport Service to carry Hessian soldiers to Rhode Island during the American Revolution. At Newport, Rhode Island, it became a prison ship and was later sunk to help blockade the harbor. In the 1960s the anchor and cannon that were lost when the *Endeavour* struck the Great Barrier Reef were recovered and put on display in Australia. In 1988, as part of Australia's bicentenary, a replica was constructed using the drawings from the 1768 refit; the project was completed in 1994, and a few years later reenactors sailed the ship around the globe before it came to rest at the Australian National Maritime Museum in Sydney.[10]

The HMS *Endeavour* was special, not only for its legacy to exploring but for its role in the national story of Australia, and it was the Australians who oversaw its partial recovery and reconstruction. The HMS *Challenger* had no such national narrative. The fifth Admiralty ship to be named *Challenger*, it was converted from a corvette in 1872, abandoned in 1880, and finally sold in 1921. It was reincarnated only in name; the seventh and eighth ships were designed for survey and research (the last sold in 1993). By then the name had been transferred to an American research vessel for deep drilling, and to a space shuttle.[11]

Only toward the end of the Second Age had exploration become sufficiently professional and self-conscious that it designed vessels for its own purpose, and considered saving them as museum pieces after their task was done. Perhaps the most famous is Frijthof Nansen's *Fram*, which survived the frozen Arctic Ocean it was designed for and then went to Otto Sverdrup for another round, and finally to the Antarctic and back with Roald Amundsen. It then dry-rotted in storage until it was reconditioned into a museum in Oslo.

The Third Age has been different—and the same. It could beat rockets designed as swords into plowshares to launch spacecraft. But the spacecraft themselves had been custom-built for their missions, and their societies have sought to memorialize them (or their facsimiles) after they completed those missions.

All this reflects the wealth of the societies that have sponsored exploration, the difficulty of recycling spacecraft, the self-consciousness with which modern exploration builds on its legacy, and the self-interest that seeks to parlay historical continuity into political conviction. No sooner do capsules return to Earth than they head to museums. Mercury Friendship 7, Gemini IV, Apollo 11—all grace the halls of the National Air and Space Museum. In place of the lost robots, curators have substituted replicas, many constructed from the spare parts left over from the originals or the reserve craft that remained on the ground, where they functioned as working models to help resolve engineering glitches, and were then available for display rather than scrapping. So the National Air and Space Museum's Milestones of Flight includes Explorer 1, Mariner 2, Viking, and Pioneer 10. Voyager resides within another exhibit, Exploring the Planets. Only the Stardust probe, returned to Earth from comet Wild 2, may be recycled into another mission.[12]

But while the Voyager simulacrum has gone into the NASM, the real Voyagers are inverting the expected relationship. Instead of fitting into an earthly museum, they are carrying a museum within them. Attached to their frame is a miniature of Earth, a distillation of the planet's sights, sounds, and stuff. It is an odd, yet oddly apropos, act of self-reflection that once again bears witness that the Voyagers are truly mechanical doubles of their creators.

23. New Worlds, New Laws

Once beyond Earth, the Voyagers would seem to have left behind earthly concerns with law and politics; and once beyond Mars, obsessions and qualms over colonization. After all, while the spacecraft carried plaques from Earth, they had neither the capacity nor the intention to deposit them on the new worlds they surveyed. Now, as they pushed beyond the Sun, they would seem to have shed such concerns altogether as mere metaphysical distractions. Even an abstract rule of law had to fade at termination shock.

But while the Third Age might go beyond Earth, it could not go beyond history. In the past, geographic discoveries had led not only to new ideas but also to new relations among peoples. Notions of sovereignty, of just wars, of the rights to rule over distant lands or remote others—all were upset and reformed as much as ideas in natural history, text-based scholarship, and the literature of travel. Exploration stretched, deformed, and remade inherited legal and political regimes. In particular it kept in constant turmoil two sets of governances. One sought to mediate among the explorers themselves. The other sought to mediate between the discoverers and those being discovered.

The Third Age skimmed over the latter. But it could not avoid the former. Like all ages, the Third was powered by rivalries, and its keenest political energies arose out of the cold war. It had to govern those passions so that exploration did not mutate into more lethal expressions. The revelations of the Third Age forced inherited institutions and ideas to evolve, and much as natural selection must act on what exists—turning a mammalian digit into a fin or a thumb, for example—so novel legal and political orders appeared that still bore the legacy of their hard-thought past.

From the onset of the Great Voyages, explorers had simply gone where they were sent or wished to go. They rarely sought permission from those being discovered.

When Vasco da Gama arrived at Calicut, for example, he was asked why he had come, and famously replied, "for spices and Christians." But the question had been posed by a Muslim trader who was neither astonished nor rapt with wonder, but dismayed and angry at the arrival of an unwanted commercial competitor. The Armada may have been a grand adventure for Portugal, but it was a destabilizing presence for the peoples it contacted. It meant fighting, treaties, forts and trading factories, a reconfiguration of commerce, and a realignment of political alliances. Was this havoc warranted so that, in modern terms, the Portuguese might exercise their inalienable curiosity and right to wander? They weren't wanted. The Indians didn't accept as justification that they were only responding to ethnic imperatives or the call of their DNA. Their choice to explore did not affect them alone. All too often trade, especially monopoly, required force, and force segued seamlessly into empire.

No one put it more succinctly than Henry Stanley at the close of the Second Age. "We went into the heart of Africa self-invited," he confessed, "therein lies our fault," and conceded that Africans certainly had an "undeniable right to exclude strangers from their country." Once having tramped into new lands, explorers might then have to fight their way out, or be rescued, or incite rivalry with another country that had also sent in exploring teams, which removed local matters into international politics. Similarly, the Institut d'Egypte's appeal to science hardly justified Napoleon's invasion, nor did the discovery of the Rosetta Stone warrant a forcible translation of institutions onto a society that didn't want them. A Stanley critic from the *Saturday Review* summarized the situation succinctly: "a private American citizen, traveling with negro allies, at the expense of two newspapers" had precipitated the deaths of indigenes "with no sanction, no authority, no jurisdiction—nothing but explosive bullets and a copy of the *Daily Telegraph*—into a country where he and his black allies are intruders and natural enemies."[13]

Of the justifications offered—science, proselytizing, the Enlightenment of commerce—only the cause of knowledge could persist into the Third Age. Instead of the call to missionize, advocates substituted a genetic hardwiring, and in place of empire, the need for national rejuvenation. Without indigenous peoples and without obvious sources of wealth, the classic competition sublimated into rivalries over science and status, or the paranoid desire to keep someone else from claiming something whether or not it had any value to the claimant. Instead, techno-romances brood over the possible contamination of newly discovered worlds; and the adventures of *Star Trek* pivot around a "prime directive" that specifically forbids interference in the affairs of discovered cultures and that prescribes protocols for contact. Apart from forcing sterilization procedures on spacecraft, these concerns have remained in the realm of fiction.

In the Third Age, as earlier, the first set of relationships, those among the exploring nations, still require regulation. There is clear value to all participants in having rules and in signing treaties that can prevent incidents from spiraling into ruinous competition or outright war.

This, too, can trace its genealogy to the Great Voyages. Between 1479 and 1494, Portugal and Spain negotiated three treaties that partitioned the discovered new worlds between them. The first divided Morocco and the Atlantic isles—Spain got the Canaries, and Portugal the rest. The most critical determinations involved the primary realm of the First Age, the ocean. The Iberians naturally wanted to rule the seas as they did isles and discovered lands; and as other nations entered the scramble, Spain and Portugal also sought to extend their monopoly over sea as well as land. In practice, however, they were unable to enforce such an edict, and the more nations that joined the contest, the more difficult it was for any one to assert unquestioned ownership.[14]

Instead of the right to a *mare clausum*, or closed sea, challengers proposed a *mare liberum*, or open sea. In 1609 the Dutch jurist Hugo Grotius codified the arguments for a mare liberum into a book of that title, establishing a body of customs and prescriptions that evolved into a generally recognized Law of the Sea. It was not an easy sell. That the Dutch were, at the time, keen competitors demonstrated the working alliance of politics, commerce, and jurisprudence. Self-interest figured as fully as idealism. Grotius was himself equally engaged in justifying various Dutch intrusions, such as seizing everything from vessels to ports, particularly against the Portuguese and English. Nations had a right to their coastal seas out to three miles (roughly, the range of a cannonball), but the idea that the high seas should be freely open to all became an enduring legacy.

Over the centuries a corpus of international law elaborated on what constituted discovery and on what basis a nation might claim rights to discoveries. When islands and coastlines were the prime realms, first sighting was deemed sufficient until other explorers demanded a more tangible act, a landing along with a formal declaration and a monument of some kind. Trading posts and colonies escalated the requirements into "effective settlement," and then into various concepts of "hinterlands," seeking to establish just how far a presence might justifiably extend into the backcountry, a judgment that had to factor in the character of the land and its inhabitants (if any). These issues were still under legal definition as late as 1933, when the international court at The Hague ruled that Norway could not claim eastern Greenland, since Denmark's two settlements on the south and west were sufficient to extend its rule over the uninhabitable ice sheet.

The Third Age required new protocols for its discovered realms. Unsurprisingly, the process began in Antarctica. In the aftermath of IGY, the nations active in Antarctica met in Washington, D.C., to establish a workable arrangement for governance.

At the time seven nations had territorial claims over the continent, three of which overlapped significantly. A large chunk of West Antarctica was unclaimed but widely recognized as the American sector, although officially American policy was to advance no formal claim and not to recognize the claims of others. During IGY, the Soviet Union carefully placed bases in each of the claimant territories. The prospect that the cold war might extend to the Ice was real. Yet IGY also demonstrated an alternative: in the name of science, it allowed for the free movement of all parties across the continent. In effect, for the duration of IGY, it treated Antarctica as high seas. The Antarctic Treaty that emerged in 1959, and entered into force on June 23, 1961, sought to continue that regime.

The treaty applied to all land and ice south of sixty degrees south. Among its articles were provisions to eliminate military activity, weapons trials, and nuclear tests or waste disposal; to allow the free movement of personnel and information; and to resolve disputes through the International Court of Justice. By adding further protocols and accords, these provisions have established a system of governance. Most interesting, perhaps, is the way the treaty has finessed the question of national sovereignty. It neither recognizes such claims, nor does it insist that by signing the treaty nations are renouncing claims. The treaty can thus mean one thing to domestic audiences and another to international, a kind of legal equivalent to Bohr's principle of complementarity. Sovereignty becomes symbolic, not operational. Modernism finds a geopolitical expression.

The deep oceans, likewise, increasingly found themselves outside a legal regime. The world sea was collecting problems as it did garbage; its concerns embraced the oft-oil-rich continental shelves as well as pollution, military traffic, nuclear waste disposal, even schemes for colonization. The more the Third Age mapped its terrain and identified its constituents, the greater the incentive for potential rivals to announce claims. The mare liberum threatened to become a submarine mare clausum. The case went to the UN in 1967, when the Malta ambassador, Arvid Pardo, warned about a cold war in the abyss, and called for a regime to govern these newly accessible but lawless regions. They should belong to no one, he insisted. They were rather the "common heritage of all mankind."[15]

In response the UN sponsored a series of conferences on the Law of the Sea. The last, convened in 1973, produced a convention ready for adoption in 1982. Unlike Antarctica, the oceans had a long history of human usufruction that was unlikely to be set aside. The resulting compromise extended the territorial seas from three to twelve miles, established an exclusive economic zone of two hundred miles, and otherwise granted the deep oceans the same freedoms as the surface seas. With one exception: adopting the "common heritage" principle, it established an International Seabed Authority, under the auspices of the UN, to oversee exploitation of the ocean floor. That principle the United States refused to recognize, and accordingly it has yet to sign the convention.

These same principles, and problems, have extended to that other realm of the Third Age: space. Again, the political promptings came from exploration, specifically the space race ignited during IGY; again, it looked to the Antarctic Treaty for inspiration. Unlike the ocean, there was little heritage of national economies connected to space at the onset. There was no fishing of the upper atmosphere, no military presence through the satellite equivalent of nuclear-armed submarines, no dredging of the solar wind or drilling for cosmic rays. As with other realms, the active parties sought to avoid a "new form of colonial competition."[16]

Addressing the UN in 1960, President Eisenhower urged that the principles enunciated in the Antarctic Treaty be adapted and extended over the solar system. Subsequently, the Limited Test Ban Treaty of 1963 removed the question of orbiting nuclear weapons from consideration; neither the United States nor the USSR argued to allow their presence in Earth orbit or beyond. Discussions continued, with one objection after another overcome, mostly along the analogous lines devised for Antarctica. In 1966 the General Assembly recommended approval of what became known as the Outer Space Treaty. In 1967 it was opened for signature and entered into force.

The treaty declared that the "exploration and use of outer space" should be conducted "for the benefit of all peoples," that such realms "shall be the province of all mankind." That phrasing looked generally to the useful ambiguities of the Antarctic Treaty and to the heritage of the open seas. An alternative, the Moon Treaty, restated the principles into the language and institutional framework of the Law of the Sea in that it relegated jurisdiction to the UN, particularly over the commercial exploitation of resources. With regard to the deep oceans, the institutions of exploitation were a matter solely of principle; almost nothing of real value then existed (save perhaps manganese nodules). But near-Earth space was rapidly filling up with satellites for commercial use or military reconnaissance, and other schemes were likely. In this case not only the United States but all the nations with launch capabilities have refused to sign the Moon Treaty. Completed in 1979 the treaty entered into force in 1984 for the thirteen nations that have acceded to it.

Complicating the picture are the inevitable ideologues, or the Third-Age equivalent to privateers and freebooters—the Cecil Rhodes and William Wallaces—who want untrammeled access to new lands and unfettered rights to claim them as private fiefdoms. Antarctica already suffers from unregulated tourism; the oceans are becoming gyres of garbage; near-Earth space is cluttered with debris from commerce and the clamber from well-heeled tourists, and its near-militarization threatens to unhinge existing treaties. The prospect of a scramble for Africa on the Moon or Mars should be enough to frighten even the most fanatic partisan.

At issue is the same question posed by Stanley except that it involves lands instead of peoples. Why should individuals have access outside any legal regime? The concern is that what people do has social consequences, that private profit will come at social costs. When an Air New Zealand DC-10 carrying tourists crashed into Mount Erebus in 1979, the U.S. Antarctic Research Program had to shut down in order to attend to the wreckage. An adventurer might go on his own, but some apparatus of government would have to rescue him. Stateless entrepreneurs among the Moon and planets might easily have the destabilizing presence of stateless terrorists. All this the Third Age has set into motion.

For Voyager, such concerns were not even hypothetical. It carried no weapons, and served no geopolitical reconnaissance. It landed on no planets. It issued no manifesto, deposited no tokens of sovereignty, proclaimed no imminent demesne, and implied no manifest destiny. It encountered no one, so was not encumbered with the moral qualms of cross-cultural contact. It made no landfalls, so was not plagued with questions of biotic contamination, state sovereignty, or corporate ownership. It was an alloy of adventure and exploration, a voyage of discovery that was in its narrative trajectory and purposes stripped of the moral and legal barnacles that encrusted and burdened the heritage that helped launch it. It did not seek new worlds to loot, colonize, or lord over.

It was an old world made new by its journey and became a new world unto itself.

Beyond Narrative

24. Voyager's Voice

The Voyagers spoke to the public primarily through images, for which words served more as captions than as stand-alone texts. Unlike past explorers, the Voyagers would write no personal narrative upon their return, nor would they address thousands on extended speaking tours, or receive medals and be toasted by kings and academies. NASA and JPL could find spokespersons to address their mission, and press conferences were important ceremonies of planetary encounter, but what they said accompanied what they showed. Without those photos, the public was left with mumblings about bow shock and occultations. What Voyager needed was someone who could speak publicly to its meaning.

That task fell to Carl Sagan. His biography and that of the space program had co-evolved: he had proposed, explained, boosted, and preserved in print, on TV, and even in gold-plated records the reasons and necessity for humanity's exploration of space. For much of the American public, he was the public face of planetary exploration, and he became, with a tenacity both particular and paradoxical, the public voice of Voyager.

The golden age of planetary discovery and Sagan's career had evolved in tandem, like binary stars. He received a master's degree in astronomy and astrophysics from the University of Chicago in 1956, the year before Sputnik; a doctorate in 1960, a scant two years before Mariner 2's flyby of Venus. He spent a summer with Gerard Kuiper at the McDonald Observatory specializing in planets and their atmospheres when those topics interested very few people. Even more revelatory, he studied biology, including work with H. J. Muller; met Harold Urey and Stanley Miller; and saw planets as arenas for life beyond Earth. These interests granted him a special niche in the natural sciences. What brought him to the public was a flair for presentation and writing. In 1966 he authored a popular-audience book titled simply *Planets*, for Time-Life, and co-authored with I. S. Shklovskii a general book on *Intelligent Life in the Universe*. The contours of his career were set: he would search for extraterrestrial life and its corollary, extraterrestrial intelligence.

He needed only a suitable vehicle, and this the planetary program provided. On several occasions Sagan marveled at the providential timing of his ambitions and the age in which he lived. "Had I been born fifty years earlier, I could have pursued none of these activities. They were all then figments of the speculative imagination. Had I been born fifty years later I also could not have been involved in these efforts, except possibly the search for extraterrestrial life." The co-evolution of his career and planetary discovery had the same kind of synchronicity of technology, politics, and astronomical alignments that had made the Grand Tour possible. The planets met their publicist.[17]

In 1971 he became a full professor at Cornell, and a year later began directing its Laboratory for Planetary Studies. Then *Other Worlds* and, with Jerome Agel, *The Cosmic Connection: An Extraterrestrial Perspective* appeared in 1973, a year before Mariner 4 arrived at Mars and three years before the Viking landing, which promised a perfect synthesis of Sagan's obsessions. The year Voyager launched, he published a popular science account of earthly intelligence, *The Dragons of Eden: Speculations on the Evolution of Human Intelligence*; it won a Pulitzer. The next year saw into print his book *Murmurs of Earth*, about the golden records that the Voyagers carried, and another collection, also on the evolution of intelligence, *Broca's Brain*. By then Voyager was well into its rhythm of encounters.

Its project scientist, Edward Stone, early appreciated that planetary exploration was "accessible to the public" in ways many sciences and topics were not. It could be presented in nontechnical terms, it contained a narrative arc inherent within the act of exploring, and it could be used to "communicate to the public" not only what such missions learned but "why scientists do what they do, and why it's interesting to be a scientist." But if JPL's press conferences could present the play-by-play account of Voyagers' mission, it was Sagan who provided the color commentary. It was Sagan, a member of the Voyager imaging team, who appeared regularly as a guest on late-night television (*The Tonight Show*), who was ideally positioned to exploit those encounters and explain them to the layman. As a writer, he did for Voyager what Eric Burgess had done for Pioneer. As a commentator, he made Voyager's saga into a romance.[18]

From the beginning he had grasped the power of the Grand Tour. It was Sagan who had most promoted the golden records, who persuaded NASA to have Voyager 1 take the emblematic photo of Earth and the Moon at the start and the planetary family portrait at its farewell, and who brought the thrill of discovery to the public. Between the time the Voyagers encountered Jupiter and the time they engaged Saturn, while Sagan joined Bruce Murray and Louis Friedman in founding The Planetary Society, he hosted the most spectacularly successful documentary series ever aired by PBS, what he modestly called *Cosmos: A Personal Journey*.

The 1980 TV series was seen by two hundred million viewers; the resulting book became the bestselling science book in English; both won awards. An episode dealing with "Traveler's Tales" featured Voyager at Jupiter. The Voyager spacecraft, Sagan declared, were "the lineal descendants of those sailing-ship voyages of exploration, and of the scientific and speculative tradition of Christiaan Huygens." The one had visited new worlds on Earth, the other wondered about possible "celestial worlds discovered," or "worlds in the planets." The Voyager spacecraft, Sagan insisted, were "caravels bound for the stars."[19]

The Voyagers could carry the public enthusiasm kindled by *Cosmos* throughout the rest of their mission: they were, in a sense, the apex of planetary exploration. But it is equally true that Sagan needed them to carry his message, which they did both physically in their golden records and symbolically by their trek beyond the solar system. Despite Sagan's enormous popularity, NASA veered from the trajectory he preferred for it. The Search for Extraterrestrial Intelligence programs were shut down; the space shuttle throttled planetary exploration; and for a dozen years there was only Voyager to supplement reruns of *Cosmos*. In 1996, as the Voyager twins pushed on toward termination shock, Sagan wrote a sequel to *Cosmos, Pale Blue Dot: A Vision of the Human Future in Space*, which opens with Voyager 1's family portrait and showcases the Grand Tour.

It was always Mars, however, that Sagan most obsessed over, and he imagined the colonization and terraforming of the planet as the critical task facing humanity as it moved from exploration to settlement. It was Mars that would reveal the extraterrestrial life that would make more plausible the reality of extraterrestrial intelligence. That discovery, Sagan assumed, would be epiphanous for Earth—"messianic" would not be too strong a term. In this he resembled Arthur C. Clarke, whom he complemented and in many ways succeeded, even writing a novel, *Contact*, whose premise is a connection with an alien intelligence.

Carl Sagan had his own psychic yearnings for an intelligent Other. He presented a curious, seemingly vulnerable, alloy of the skeptical and the wishful, ever pushing his desires before the public even as he countered them with the demands of a disciplined rationalism. Not infrequently he bonded those two sentiments together with double negatives that seemed simultaneously to allow and deny what he wanted. He was a believer in aliens, yet a critic of UFOs; he celebrated an unbounded human spirit, yet skewered religions. Famously agnostic, accepting a Spinoza-like reverence before a lawful universe, he nonetheless effectively populated those galaxies with godlike creatures—not the God of the great monotheisms, but local deities like Clarke's Overlords or the residents of a galactic Olympus or stellar Asgard. His belief that they would be benign and that encounter would be a messianic first-coming drew little support from history; but this was belief, not reason.

It was also literature. An author of Sagan's skills surely appreciated that supposing intelligent Others made encounter possible, and with encounter, something like a traditional narrative. The ideal way to convey information, even science, was through story. But what kind of story could exist if there was no Other to engage, if we talked only to ourselves? What kind of traveler's tale could be told if the traveler never returned? What kind of vision quest could be related if the hero kept going? Assuming contact allowed for an aesthetic closure as well as a thematic one.

Popular writing succeeds because it relies on popular genres. But if the Third Age changed some of the fundamentals of exploring, and especially of encountering, it perhaps required a different style of expression as well. Yet modernism, while full of self-referential paradoxes, spoke in a voice that was hardly attuned to a popular audience. Rather, it preferred to speak in ironic tones to an avant-garde about itself. The trick to expanding that realm was to package new experiences in old forms, and this is what Carl Sagan did with spectacular aplomb. As early Christian missionaries baptized pagan sites into churches, so Sagan rationalized the prophecies of Arthur C. Clarke by immersing them in a more rigorous science.

For his achievements as a popularizer he was often shunned by space scientists, who tended to equate "Saganizing" with shilling. The same group that would have denied Voyager eyes, a camera, would also have denied it a voice, the golden record; and they were prepared to punish anyone who promoted values beyond those most precious to the guild or the prescribed venues by which it expressed itself. Paradoxically, no space scientist was better known than Sagan, and none was so ostracized by his own community. Whether or not his golden records might someday connect with aliens, his books and TV appearances certainly connected in his own time with an audience for whom the subjects he addressed were often instinctively alien.

———

What makes a strength also makes a weakness. One is a distortion of the norm, and typically comes at the cost of neglecting some other trait. So it is with great popularizers.

Cosmos had the scope of an electronic epic of exploration. But it is less the work of a bard than of a propagandist. It is more animated by the vision of a Richard Hakluyt than that of a Luiz Vaz de Camões. It has no Old Man of Belem, or Moses who leads his people to a Promised Land but is himself denied entry. It shuns ultimate tragedy for a promised utopianism. (Unlike Camões, who traveled to the Indies and lost an eye fighting there, Sagan traveled in an imaginary spaceship, the whimsically named *Dandelion*.) *Contact* comes close to putting Carl Sagan's celebrated double negatives into novelistic (and very modernist) form, a contact with Others that ends with a journey to self. *Cosmos* will likely survive as one of the era's grand romances. It is unlikely to survive as its *Os Lusíadas*.

Cosmos and *Contact* are a long way from the Mars novels of Edgar Rice Burroughs, which Sagan openly confesses were the spark for his extraplanetary imagination. The chrysalis of a rigorous scientific education metamorphosed those boyish fantasies into an enduring adult passion that bonded with a hard-wrought intelligence, and granted a way to project in technological garb his longings for worlds to come. Yet origins can matter as much as futures. By looking to Homer and Virgil, Camões lapses into an imitative style that can seem contrived to modern eyes, and which leaves the poem fettered to archaic forms and an exalted language that edges into bombast; yet that structural quotation also endows the text with an aura of classical gravitas. Originating from the Tarzan-gone-to-Mars pulp fiction of Burroughs, Sagan's vision retains a juvenile joyfulness that suffuses it with an attractive zest, but perhaps never achieves the intellectual heft it needs to transcend its own circumstances and times. That may seem a harsh judgment, and perhaps an unfairly ironic one, but it may not be unearned for one whose view of the future glazed over his understanding of the past.

What endures are the tales told along the way. No one told the Voyagers' better.

25. Voyager's Record

As the Voyagers passed through termination shock, interest turned again to another of their instruments, this one prerecorded. Each spacecraft held a gold-plated copper record full of pictures, sounds, and voices of Earth. Of all the artifacts the Voyagers carried, this was the one the public most readily appreciated, and may well become the mission's signature memento.

Like many features of the Grand Tour, it built on a Pioneer prototype. The concept originated with Eric Burgess, a journalist then writing for *The Christian Science Monitor*, who eventually approached Carl Sagan, who along with Frank Drake had just designed a message suitable for communicating with aliens. They modified their ideas into a plaque, which Sagan's current wife, Linda Salzman Sagan, converted into etchings.[20]

The outcome was a collage of symbolic representations: a silhouette of Pioneer, the binary equivalent of decimal eight, the hyperfine transition of neutral hydrogen, the position of the Sun relative to fourteen pulsars and the center of the galaxy, the planets of the solar system and their binary relative distances. And there was one realistic representation, this of the male and female of the species responsible for the creation of the entity. That they were nude was a cause for some hysteria, and equal hilarity. The prospect of anyone finding the plaque was infinitesimally tiny, and of their interpreting it still more remote. But most observers, less addled by aliens and committed to cosmic liaisons, understood that the real message was aimed at Earth.

In October 1974, as Pioneer 11 began its observation phase for Jupiter, Voyager project manager John Casani coyly noted as a "concern" that there was "no plan for sending a message to our extra solar system neighbors," and recommended that the group "coordinate with Barney Oliver" and "send a message." His suggestion lay fallow until December 1976, when he contacted Sagan, who quickly organized a small committee of like-minded partisans that included Philip Morrison, Frank Drake, A. G. W. Cameron, Leslie Orgel, B. M. Oliver, and Stephen Toulmin, and "because some science-fiction writers" had been "thinking about such problems longer than most of the rest of us," he also solicited comments from Isaac Asimov, Robert Heinlein, and Arthur C. Clarke. Drake, a keen advocate of SETI and director of the National Astronomy and Ionosphere Center, suggested a long-playing phonograph record as the ideal medium. That set in motion a scramble to fill the record.[21]

The group had learned some lessons from the public outcry that had attended the Pioneer plaques. This time it sought out diversity— of peoples, of media, of senses. This plaque would display art to convey emotion, not simply exhibit mathematical and physical notations to show cleverness; the record had to "touch the heart as well as the mind." And this time NASA would not tolerate any nudity. A close working team that included Jon Lomberg, Ann Druyan, Linda Sagan, Timothy Ferris, Frank Drake, and, of course, Sagan gathered. Other consultants, such as musicologist Alan Lomax, were recruited to assist in specialty areas. In the end the record housed 118 photographs, 90 minutes of music, an "evolutionary audio essay" on "The Sounds of Earth," a roster of the U.S. senators and representatives with oversight for NASA, and greetings in 55 languages, along with statements from President Jimmy Carter and UN secretary-general Kurt Waldheim, and a "song" from a humpback whale.[22]

The group appreciated that every choice had two audiences, and that the audience on Earth was the most critical. "Great care was

taken with all the musical selections," Sagan intoned, "in an attempt
to be as fair and representative as possible in terms of geographical,
ethnic and cultural distribution, style of music, and the connection
with other selected pieces." Music ranged from Bach and Mozart
to Chuck Berry singing "Johnnie B. Goode" and Surashri Kesarbai
Kerkar performing the raga "Jaat Kahan Ho." The languages of the
greetings were spoken by 87 percent of Earth's human population.
Voyager's was an ecumenical vision, a musical and photo essay on
the Family of Man. Whether or not an alien interceptor might understand it, humans on Earth could, and to that end the outcome was a
proselytizing text.[23]

The record itself was made of gold-coated copper, and hence
both imperishable and nonmagnetic. To bolster its capacity it was
machined to play at 16 $2/_3$ revolutions per minute instead of the more
typical 33 $1/_3$. In place of a manufacturer label, it had a photo of Earth
with the caption "United States of America, Planet Earth." An aluminum cover shielded its delicate grooves from the micrometeorites
that were expected to cluster between Earth and Jupiter and through
the Oort cloud. (Calculations suggested that impacts might degrade
some 4 percent of the record's surface by the time Voyager had traveled a hundred million years, or a sixth the distance to the center
of the galaxy.) In order to date its conception, the cover was electro-
plated with uranium-238, whose regular decay makes it a radioactive
clock with a half-life of 4.51 billion years, roughly the estimated life
of the Earth.[24]

It was that other audience, however, that proved sticky. To help
an alien intelligence (or "recipient") make sense of its find, the aluminum cover had etched onto it visual instructions for using the stylus,
safely tucked behind, to play the record. A diagram demonstrated
how to decode the resulting signals into pictures. And completing
the instruction manual were two images: one, a pulsar map that
showed Earth's exact location relative to fourteen pulsars, and the
other, "two circles" depicting "a drawing of the hydrogen atom in its
two lowest states, with a connecting line and digit 1 to indicate that
the time interval associated with the transition from one state to the
other is to be used as the fundamental time scale, both for the time

given on the cover and in the decoded pictures." With these clues, a recipient could presumably play Earth.[25]

Even partisans admit the odds of discovery belong in the realm of infinite numbers, and if the record is discovered, it is questionable that the intelligent recipient might be able to decode it, or even recognize it as a message. The technology of recording has evolved like a fast-mutating virus during Voyager's long traverse. By the time Voyager reached Jupiter and Saturn, vinyl phonograph records were overtaken by magnetic tapes; by the time it reached Uranus and Neptune, tapes were fast fading before CDs; by the time it reached the heliosheath, CDs were passé compared with digital drives and iPods. The phonograph was hopelessly archaic just as the golden record reached the edge of the solar system—in technology years, barely beyond cuneiform tablets. It is doubtful that, presented with the record, even earthlings unfamiliar with phonographs could operate it.

Worse, a recipient was unlikely to decode it, and could never decipher the many languages it held. As Linda Sagan noted, there was no Rosetta Stone on board, "let alone a pocket dictionary." The recipients would know them as sound waves, assuming they had senses for sound. Carl Sagan confessed that "the most likely situation" was that "no human language will be remotely intelligible to an extraterrestrial auditor" without a previously provided "primer." And Frank Drake told the story of an experiment with a group of elite specialists in SETI, the self-styled Order of the Dolphin, who proved unable to decipher a test message. Even earthlings could make no sense of an earthling code. Still, desire begat belief. Science would provide an intergalactic language. That faith, at least, provided a context for the experiment.[26]

In the end, what advocates wanted was recognition that a cosmic Other existed. Voyager was a way of validating their belief. The deeper political agendas had to deal with harmony on Earth and support for SETI. The former value was widely recognized, and applauded. Even with Voyager as a totem, however, and with Sagan, then the most widely recognized spokesman for science, as a publicist, the latter faltered. What survived was an older variant of discovery: the received image of the discoverer. Or, in the eyes of critics, what emerged was another exercise in narcissism: *they* would want to know about *us*. (A historical note: Tom Wolfe's essay on the "Me Generation" was published a few months before the Voyager record team assembled.)

In *Murmurs of Earth*, Sagan concluded his reckoning of the Voyager golden record by imagining its encounter with "the planetary system of AC + 79 3888." The "inhabitants will of course be deeply interested in the Sun, their nearest star, and in its retinue of planets. What an astonishing finding the Voyager record, this gift from the skies, would then represent!" They would "wonder about us." They would appreciate that we were beings with "a positive passion for the future." They would be the significant Other who would affirm what we wish to believe is best about ourselves.[27]

As Voyager's recorders appreciated, the heritage of such efforts—exchanges, memorials, and hopeful first contacts—reached much further back than the Pioneer plaques. A meeting between peoples, especially when neither could speak the other's language, was awkward and could easily become violent. Accordingly, for example, when sailing down new shorelines along the coast of Africa, the usual custom was to leave goods on the beach, which the natives would take, leaving something of their own in exchange. Hard goods and hands-off gestures could substitute for greetings and common protocols. Having established one another's presence and interest, the process could scale up.

But such proceedings could not advance much further without a common language, which is why interpreters loom so large in successful exploration. The process of discovery was mostly a process of transferring knowledge from those living in the discovered lands to those who were discovering them; explorers needed interpreters as much as they needed guides and pilots; and this, too, they sought to systematize. As the Portuguese probed south, they brought Africans to Portugal, often as slaves, to learn Portuguese, and then shipped them out to contact new peoples. Bartolomeu Dias thus took two Africans with him south in the hopes that they could communicate the purpose of the expedition with the new peoples they met; they couldn't. Columbus, on his first voyage, brought an Arab interpreter, Luis de Torres, who found his linguistic skills worthless in the Antilles. Instead, Columbus took a direct approach. "As soon as I came to the Indies, at the first island I discovered I seized some natives, intending them to inquire and inform me about things in these parts. These men soon understood us, and we them, either by speech or signs and they were very useful to us." The Admiral of the Ocean Sea had tapped into a complex maritime civilization, for which discovery meant translating local lore into the scholarship of Europe. He kept his informants throughout the voyage, adding "one inhabitant of each country" to take to Castile in order "to give an account of its nature and products." Unfortunately, the group did what most indigenous peoples did: they told the newcomers what the newcomers wanted to hear, a misconstruction magnified because Europeans heard what they wanted the locals to say.[28]

As contact proliferated, interpreters arose from happenstance as much as from calculation. Survivors of shipwrecks adopted into local tribes, youthful captives, children of mixed parental cultures, slaves, and of course those simply gifted in learning tongues were all at times critical, particularly where some general language had evolved—such as hand-signing on the Great Plains or quechua along the Amazon or pidgin in New Guinea—by which basic communication was possible across a large region. Such interlocutors often became interpreters of culture and politics, not simply translators. Think La Malinche, the consort of Cortés as he moved toward Tenochtitlán; Sacajawea, as she helped Lewis and Clark thread the cultural watershed of the Missouri River and cross the Rockies; Oahu Jack, a Hawaiian, who served the Wilkes Expedition as interpreter through Polynesia and Melanesia; Tupaia, the Tahitian who accompanied Capt. James Cook and named and gave rough directions to seventy-four islands within a few days' sail. Revealingly, when Samuel Johnson and James Boswell heard Captain Cook's account of his travels, they doubted his rendering among the natives since he himself "didn't speak the local languages." They appreciated that indigenous lore could be understood only through indigenous tongues.[29]

The ideal was an interpreter who could also guide, or serve as a pilot. Where none was present, explorers were inclined to seize one, as they did translators or captives. Da Gama crossed the Indian Ocean from Malindi to Calicut by commandeering a pilot (perhaps the leading navigator of the day, Ibn Majid). At Valparaiso, Sir Francis Drake seized John Griego, a Greek pilot in the service of Spain, to navigate the *Golden Hind* to Lima. At California, after vanquishing the *Santa Anna*, Thomas Cavendish took "two young lads born in Japan, which could both write and read their own language," "3 boys born in the isle of Manila," and a "Spaniard, which was a very good pilot until the islands of Ladrones" [Guam], who knew the route between Acapulco and Manila. In 1610 Samuel de Champlain sent a young Frenchman, Etienne Brûlé, to live with the Iroquois and learn their language, and so created the progenitor of a species of frontiersman, the coureur de bois, who could broker between societies. Similar classes of mixed-race, multilingual frontiersmen sprang up everywhere. They were especially prominent around Portuguese settlements in South America and Africa, where as *bandeirantes* and freebooters they not only interlocuted but destabilized whole regions.[30]

But with the desire to learn, there was also a desire for a tangible record of the experience through souvenirs and deposited records. Portuguese *marinheiros*, for example, deposited cruciform stone *padrões* like beach flotsam around Africa. Buffeted by a storm on his return, Columbus wrote a brief account of his journey on parchment, wrapped it in waxed cloth, and stuffed it into a cask, which he committed to the sea. Lewis and Clark erected a memorial post at Fort Clatsop when they reached the Pacific. At the tidal delta of the Bella Coola River, Alexander Mackenzie painted onto stone with vermilion and grease an inscription that identified himself, the date, and his origin, "from Canada, by Land." The sorties of the Franklin Expedition left cairns with notices in six languages, along with instructions to finders to return them to Britain. Robert Peary heaped up a pyramid of ice at the North Pole before taking a photo; Roald Amundsen left a tent and flag at the South Pole.[31]

The creators of the Voyager golden record struggled to describe its significance; their singular point of agreement was the need to say something. As B. M. Oliver observed, "There is only an infinitesimal chance that the plaque will ever be seen by a single extraterrestrial, but it will certainly be seen by billions of terrestrials." There is no need to analogize, however. The urge to leave a mark and to take mementoes would seem hardwired into human travelers. The Voyagers' golden record had a long pedigree of memorials, territorial markers, messages, self-promotions, and simple graffiti. It tapped a yearning by humanity to immortalize a record of itself, and in truth the golden records buried in the vacuum of space will long survive the copies placed with the president, the Library of Congress, and the Smithsonian. They will certainly outlive their creators and may endure to the end of time itself.[32]

Whatever the bid for immortality, the public trope behind the golden record was contact with aliens. On this score, there is little evidence from past exploration to suggest that the reactions imagined by Sagan among both recipient and giver would occur. Yet it is significant that he made his appeal through the classic formula of an encounter. For that to work he had to have an Other, and granted his predisposition for an Other, he had to tell the story through the old devices. The golden record was a means to both ends.

Certainly what expeditions carried as exchange goods and memorials were always a cameo not only of what an exploring society sought from its enterprise but how it wanted to see itself—its best goods, its finest technology, its boldest emissaries. It would plant the cross, raise monuments for trigonometric surveys, deposit political tokens. In return, explorers would be received with awe and delight by the discovered Others. Almost always, however, practice proved otherwise. Explorers were troubled, and often troublesome; indigenes had their own ambitions, and rather than use encounter to transcend their society, they strove to bring the discoverers—their goods, their weapons, and their symbolic presence—into their existing world to more mundane ends.

Grand gestures such as expensive exploring expeditions plead for the ideal and the hopeful: Voyager needed to carry some kind of symbolic talisman against the fate of loss, forgetfulness, extinction, and oblivion. Almost all observers have accepted the golden record as a reasonable totem of Earth, one that however constrained, by its own time, place, values, and personalities, has tried to speak to enduring virtues of hope, perseverance, wisdom, humility, and generosity. If Voyager needed the pretext of an alien Other to so present itself, then that, too, they conceded. If aliens did not exist, it seems, we would have to invent them.

26. Voyager's Returns

For all its modifications of that tradition, the Voyager mission tapped into a heritage of exploration—that was its cultural power. But there was always to the Grand Tour a quality that went beyond normal expeditioning, a sense of the providential or, for the more literary, perhaps of the mythical. The aura would have embarrassed hardheaded engineers intent on ensuring that solders would not shake loose during launch and electronics could survive immersion in Jovian radiation. Yet it was there, a tradition that predates exploration and in fact a heritage that Western exploration itself taps into.

Myth, as Joseph Campbell has argued, is "the secret opening through which the inexhaustible energies of the cosmos pour into human cultural manifestation." Its primary purpose is "to supply the symbols that carry the human spirit forward." Myths offer a kind of transcendence, a transfiguration or transport beyond death.[33]

The endlessly mutable myths themselves seem to emerge out of a grand monomyth, the "universal mythological formula of the adventure of the hero," so fecund in humanity's multicultural imagination as to display "a thousand faces." At its core are three rites of passage that prescribe a beginning, middle, and end, or specifically, phases of separation, initiation, and return. In Campbell's summary: "A hero ventures forth from the world of common day into a region of supernatural wonder: fabulous forces are there encountered and a decisive victory is won: the hero comes back from this mysterious adventure with the power to bestow boons on his fellow man." That is not a bad formula for the classic tale of exploration.[34]

The journey has multiple stages, latent in the archetype, not all of which are present in each variant. There is a call to adventure—an appeal to depart from the pale of the mundane into a special realm of marvel. The call is sometimes refused, and the refusal must be overcome. There are helpers who outfit the hero with special devices. Then comes the initiation, the crossing of a formidable and seemingly impermeable threshold. Within the wonder world, the hero undergoes test after test, which he must overcome and by which he is measured. In popular tales these tests are physical, or the outcome of cleverness; in more religious contexts, they are moral. At last he reaches his goal. Paradoxically, that moment of climax cannot be the end, for he must return and bestow his boon—his acquired knowledge, his newfound tools—to society. He must recross the threshold, often after further struggle. Upon his return skeptics may challenge his accounts, rivals question his deeds, an apathetic public ignore his elixirs and enlightenment; and he must relearn how to live within this society. Once done, however, he ends as a celebrated hero or in apotheosis.[35]

The formula fuses journeying with seeking, and places both within a particular cultural setting that emphasizes the disruptive power of new knowledge and the terrible task of resocializing the knower. This broad formula is what the West institutionalized during the Great Voyages into its classic scenario for geographic exploration, an undertaking that goes beyond simple scientific inquiry, beyond routine touring, and beyond untethered restlessness. The journey to unknown lands and seas amalgamates them all. Time and again, exploration has echoed those erstwhile themes.

It is there in the call to go: explorers ardent with desire, possessed by visions or driven by personal demons, looking only for an outlet. The simple mythic structure, however, overlooks the history of the many called who declined to answer. The U.S. Exploring Expedition could not locate a naval officer willing to command it. Capt. Robert FitzRoy could not find a companion to accompany him on the HMS *Beagle* until an intermediate eventually proposed Charles Darwin. When a complementary expedition by the HMS *Rattlesnake* to Australia and New Guinea was proposed, Beaufort wanted the veteran surveyor-captain Alexander Vidal to lead it. But Vidal's wife had died, leaving him with a young family to raise. Much as he craved another expedition, the prospects of being away for four years were too much. The needs of family proved the greater call. He stayed—surely, the better choice. Instead, Capt. Owen Stanley assumed command, and took with him Thomas Huxley as assistant-surgeon-cum-naturalist.[36]

The explorer's return could be awkward, too. Columbus was arrested at the Azores, and after his third voyage he was later clapped in irons in Spain. Magellan, dead in the Philippines, was denounced, and credit for the return of the *Victoria* bestowed on a Spaniard, Juan Sebastián del Cano, as the Spanish state seized the official record to doctor the story. (It was only after Antonio Pigafetta, having made a duplicate of his journal, published a full chronicle, that the world appreciated Magellan's successes.) James Bruce was ridiculed as a liar for his "discovery" of the sources of the Nile. Henry Stanley was shunned as a fraud, then scorned as a "workhouse brat," and then condemned as a freebooting killer. Robert Peary returned not to accolades in a shower of ticker tape but to dismissal, since Frederick Cook had some months earlier announced his own trek to the pole and fraudulently seized the glory. Upon its completion, the voyage of the *Rattlesnake* did for Huxley what the voyage of the *Beagle* did for Darwin; but Captain Stanley died at sea. Meriwether Lewis and William Clark were lionized after their trek; but Lewis never published his journal, and ended a suicide.

It often proved difficult for both explorer and society to reabsorb each other. Instead what endured were the exploration's gathered artifacts and printed record.

The written account, too, had its formula, and this evolved along with other aspects of exploration. The earliest records were ship's logs or journals, or letters from expedition leaders to the Crown; they were often impounded and hoarded in the Treasury as state secrets. The modern version appeared in the Second Age when, not coincidentally, the novel arose as a literary genre and Romantic histories adopted a shared narrative structure. The ship's chronicle assumed a more organic form; at its core was the personal narrative, a literature that enjoyed enormous popularity during the Second Age.

Publicists, too, recognized the literary possibilities, along with their political potential. They appreciated how the personal narrative might communicate with the literate public and could get a story into the larger culture in useful ways, and knew that few explorers could also write adequately. The British Admiralty thus hired a professional writer, John Hawkesworth, to prepare James Cook's journal for publication, and commissioned him to do the same with the records of Cook's British predecessors, John Byron, Philip Carteret, and Samuel Wallis. Hawkesworth did what he was told: he effectively transfigured notes and chronologies into a master narrative. Meanwhile, Georg Forster, one of the naturalists on Cook's second voyage, further pioneered the genre with his *A Voyage Round the World*, and Alexander von Humboldt, whom Forster had inspired, helped devise the continental version with his *Personal Narrative of a Journey to the Equinoctial Regions of the New Continent*.[37]

That set the pattern of recounting: the personal narrative was the nuclear core around which details and scientific studies clustered like electrons. The success of an expedition as a cultural event was often determined by its ability to penetrate the imagination, and this meant a combination of art and literature. Many of the classic accounts had ghostwriters. John Charles Fremont relied on his wife, Bessie, to turn his adventuring into narrative and on her father, Thomas Hart Benton, senator from Missouri, into politics. Charles Wilkes refused the Navy Department's wish to hire a professional writer, and churned out five volumes that only sporadically overcame his turgid prose and crabbed personality. Particularly where subscriptions or book sales financed expeditions, literary skills mattered. Both books and lectures built on a narrative pith in which the explorer assumed the role of hero, answering the call to adventure, overcoming perils, and returning to proclaim his triumph and bestow its meaning to an admiring society. That great coda to the Second Age, Robert Scott's epistles, written as he was dying on the Ross Ice Shelf, cast his vanquished expedition in exactly that light, and made even failure fit the formula for triumph.

In the Third Age the genre split. Part went to manned exploration, where it merged with journalism. Norman Mailer would pose as Aquarius and ponder the Apollo Moon landing; Tom Wolfe's paean to the Mercury astronauts, *The Right Stuff*, appeared a decade later; and participants wrote their own personal narratives, such as Michael Collins's *Carrying the Fire*. But the larger part went into fiction and popular culture, where space travel was easy, adventure challenging, and aliens abundant. Hollywood and TV refilled the old bottles with Klingons, Martians, Overlords. In 1968, as Apollo 8 filmed the earthrise over the Moon, *2001: A Space Odyssey* brought Arthur C. Clarke to the big screen; *Star Trek*—the voyage of the *Beagle* outfitted with warp drive—discovered new worlds weekly, before also heading into the deep space of Hollywood with biennial launches; and *Star Wars* grafted high-tech special effects onto the rootstock of ancient myth.

The deeper split was between fiction and nonfiction. Without human protagonists or their alien proxies, the genre sank into formula fiction. The robots remained snugly within nonfiction, particularly journalism. They bonded insecurely to classic tropes of the quest.

Yet the saga of Voyager seemed rife for just such treatment. However much its engineers might scorn anthropomorphism, however much its scientists distrusted and dismissed the allusive, the metaphoric, and the mythical, however much politics might confound and conflate a literary imagination with simple publicity, Voyager is an artifice of human hand and heart as fully as any poem, and its journey is a narrative of adventure and aspiration that eerily echoes the template of ancient myths. Its trajectory has the arc of a hero's quest.

All the parts are there. The call to adventure: the beckoning to a unique journey, one set by the rare alignment of planets beyond mundane Earth. The initial, political refusal: the ensuing struggle to reinstate and accept, if reluctantly or provisionally, the Grand Tour. The threshold: launch, with their separate shaky initiations. The perils, overcome with the help of clever engineers. The tests—the planetary encounters—successfully met. Each adventure propelled it to another, beyond the horizon, until the explorer had journeyed beyond not merely Earth but all the earthly worlds that inhabit the solar system and then passed through a second veil, the transcendence of termination shock. Voyager's ascent to the stars seems an apotheosis.

Here the narrative arc falls apart. The hero won't return—won't return not from refusal, as often happens in the quest narrative and must be overcome, but by design. With a human actor, this would challenge the premise of exploration. As Hakluyt noted, "All this great labour would be lost, all these charges spent in vain, if in the end our travelers might not be able to return again, and bring safely home into their own native country that wealth and riches, which they in foreign regions with adventure of goods, and danger of their lives have sought for." With a robot as actor, the issue is not lost knowledge but the rent fabric of the mythological form. In Campbell's words, "The adventurer still must return with his life-transmuting trophy. The full round, the norm of the monomyth, requires that the hero shall now begin the labor of bringing the runes of wisdom, the Golden Fleece, or his sleeping princess, back into the kingdom of humanity, where the boon may redound to the renewing of the community, the nation, the planet, or the ten thousand worlds." Or, one might add, the lost megabytes of data from beyond the reach of Earth.[38]

The return is often more forceful than the departure. The fountainhead of Western civilization's adventure epics, *The Odyssey*, is the consuming story of a journey home. The grand gesture of the First Age was a circumnavigation—a voyage beyond that by design would end where it began. The Second Age sent its emissaries out and expected them to come back. Then the Third Age dispatched parties into ice, abyss, and space, and the hero quest crossed another threshold.

Until Voyager. Voyager would not return. It could send back data; it would not itself return. The "cosmogenic cycle" would remain if not broken then recast in a modernist vogue.

———

Of course plenty of explorers have failed to return, and rescue missions have from time to time enormously expanded the range of discovery. The two-decade search for the Franklin expedition effectively mapped northern Canada and the North American stretch of the Arctic Ocean. The search for the missing Burke and Wills expedition quickly fleshed out the geography of interior Australia. The search for the "lost" Livingstone launched the most famous career in African exploration. But not returning was never part of the design. The return was fundamental: it may be said that, as with narrative, the character of the ending dictated the beginning.

Clearly, Voyager has "returned" a cornucopia of images and data, and sent back (as mythic heroes do) a seemingly special lore, "a certain baffling inconsistency between the wisdom brought forth from the deep, and the prudence usually found to be effective in the light world." But the protagonist hero won't return; the narrative arc remains unfinished; the cosmogenic cycle, incomplete. Up to a point, Voyager can evade this issue: it continues to function, still probing outward, still meeting tests. But when its power burns out and its transmissions fall silent, the narrative can no longer pretend that the story fits the old forms.[39]

The Voyagers—reluctant modernists to the end—offer one solution with their golden records: they carry the return destination with them. The records avoid the dilemma, too, by the fiction that the adventure will persist and that Voyager will meet an Other, and that Other will presumably return the information to Earth (as *Star Trek I* imagined). Sagan's belief in a cosmic connection, that we are at base "star stuff," provides another closure. In this version, humanity's earthly existence is the outward journey, and spaceflight is but a return to our ultimate origin, the cosmos. Yet both visions continue to imagine, as technological romance does, the old genres filled with new adventures. They exchange an exploration narrative for an emigration one, part of a larger task of colonizing. They remake the manifest destinies of the Second Age into a destined manifest to the stars. What Joseph Campbell called the "hero with a thousand faces" could, it seems, apply equally to the genre as it morphs with the times.

Voyager's visionaries looked to the future. They thought of the Voyagers as instruments, and assumed their journey was simply another incremental moment in what would prove to be an irresistible expansion over the solar system, and beyond. The Grand Tour mission would be followed by more and better missions. They could not know that Voyager would culminate a golden age, that its trek would be unique, that it might require a distinctive narrative. Even the most culturally sensitive such as Sagan looked only outward and forward. They imagined, in Emerson's phrasing, a continued succession of "new lands, new men, new ideas."

Yet the Voyagers looked back as well as ahead. Repeatedly, their most stunning images were those taken when they turned around to review what they had passed, from the volcanoes on Io to the family portrait of the solar system. So, too, much of the Voyager mission's cultural power resided less in its future fruits than in its ancient roots as a quest narrative. The Voyagers were what they were because they looked both ways. It is then a lost opportunity, perhaps, that the two Voyagers were not dispatched one to each world, one to the great beyond of interstellar space and one to the home planet.

That thought never occurred to mission designers. The mission was a voyage of scientific discovery. It could continue only toward the new. Without astronauts the spacecraft, as instrument, had no necessity to return. The reason for return lies not in science but in the logic of the quest narrative. The character of Voyager's journey made the spacecraft more than an automated lab. The power of its mission lay in its trek, and that deserved a suitable narrative, which pointed to a quest.

Oddly, return trajectories were the original task of the JPL project that had led to Minovitch's recognition of gravity propulsion, and hence to the Grand Tour. If there was no exact narrative solution, neither was there more than an approximation of the restricted three-body problem, but that didn't stop the mission. Perhaps given its scientific tasks and engineering constraints, no trajectory would have been possible that could have allowed one of the spacecraft to be pulled back, cometlike, into an orbit around the Sun, and then around Earth. If some mechanism did exist, the journey would likely take decades or, more probably, centuries, or more plausibly still, millennia; and the spacecraft would die long before it arrived. But what a true time capsule it would have made. What a narrative of Return.

The quirks of robotic exploration might seem to have created a mechanical divide that the old formulas cannot bridge. Yet perhaps Voyager requires a change in the genre of the same sort that the Third Age has demanded in our understanding of exploration. It may be that Voyager has caught the *gran volta* of modernism, a literary doubling of the Cape in which the self relates to Other, and that it may well require a literary form, a narrative arc, that more resembles a Klein bottle than an arch.

The Voyager saga may have instinctively found a way around that omission, much as its engineers have repeatedly found software patches to work around broken hardware. That cultural patch lies in the dual plaques, gold and aluminum, that the Voyagers carry. The golden records that Sagan celebrated meant they carry their home with them. The aluminum plates that JPL quietly affixed make them a hero of 5,400 faces.

Beyond Tomorrow

Yet all experience is an arch wherethro'
Gleams that untravelled world whose margin fades
For ever and for ever when I move.

—Alfred Tennyson, "Ulysses"

The untold want, by life and land ne'er granted,
Now, Voyager, sail thou forth, to seek and find.

—Walt Whitman, *Leaves of Grass*

T

he passage through the heliosheath will be Voyagers' last measurable event. It begins with termination shock, the final veil before the sanctum sanctorum. It will end with bow shock, beyond which there can be no further encounter. There will be only void. Yet the Voyagers will sail on—*ad astra*, to the stars—without foreseeable cessation. *In saecula saeculorum.*

It is hard to imagine a nonending, like the empty echo of the Marabar Caves. Yet over time the Voyagers' power will fail, their transmissions cease. The need remains, nonetheless, to project a continuation, for even as their trajectories diverge ever wider, their histories converge, shrinking like their declining power into a common emptiness of inertia.

Because of its close targeting past Titan, Voyager 1 sails at 35 degrees northward from the ecliptic at a rate of roughly 3.5 AU a year, and because it was programmed to sweep close to Triton, Voyager 2 arcs some 48 degrees southward of the ecliptic at a rate of 3.1 AU. In 40,272 years Voyager 1 will be within 1.64 light-years of the star AC+79 3888, and 100,000 years later, within 2.35 light-years of the star DM+25 3719. Voyager 2 will pass by objects and stars with more familiar names. In some 26,000 years it will reach the

Oort cloud of ice-comets; in another 20,319 years, Proxima Centauri, then only 3.21 light-years distant, and some 310 years later, Alpha Centauri, a scant 3.47 light-years away. In a further 300,000 years it will cruise 4.32 light-years from Sirius.[40]

The Voyagers will approach their final rite of passage amid a void that no human could endure, a vacuum of meaning no less than of geography. It would seem that their trek must become a journey of movement without purpose and a narrative without events.

They will continue to coast. They won't decompose. They won't rust. They won't break down or wear out from use. With their motive power gone and their equipment switched off, they will no longer be even machines, but rather metallic statues or gangly headstones. They will move out of sheer inertia, slowed or quickened by the soft geography of the galaxy, the friction of interstellar gases, and the pull of distant gravitational fields. Light-years from now they may crash into a solid body, or vanish into a gaseous vortex. They may be captured by a planet or a star, or join the vast swirl of the Milky Way, another particle amid trillions. They will pass worlds unbounded, without a scan, a nod, or a message. They will simply persist, an endurance without sentience, record, or end, passing the black holes of space and the dark matter of time.

But while this may be the Voyagers' fate, it won't be their story.

The Third Age is yet young. It may yet last for another century or more.

Like the others it has its distinctive traits and its ideal explorer. The Great Voyages had their questing mariners and indomitable conquistadors—their pilot-admirals like Columbus and Magellan, their great captains like Cortés and Coronado, and their maritime warriors like Albuquerque. The Second Age had its far-ranging naturalists and peripatetic natural philosophers with their unquenchable curiosity, their balky instruments, and their personal narratives. It could boast of La Condamine and Humboldt, Darwin and Wallace, and ended with the unyielding wills of professional explorers such as Stanley and Amundsen. The Third Age has its machines, some staffed by people, most piloted remotely or granted some slack as semiautonomous robots. It has the *Trieste* and the *Alvin, Jason,* and *ABE,* the Autonomous Benthic Explorer. It has Mariner 2, Viking, and Voyager.

Among these new explorers Voyager may serve as synecdoche, as a testimony and a defining gesture. The Grand Tour offered the greatest possible traverse; it trekked farther and longer, saw more for the first time, spanned the entire geographic realm of the solar system, and climaxed a self-proclaimed golden age. Among that Earth-launched constellation of travelers Voyager offers the boldest silhouettes: it contrasts most starkly with the all-too-human explorers of the Second Age and the human-crewed capsules of Apollo, Cosmos, Skylab, and the fatally flawed space shuttle. The Third Age could proceed only with people and machines in sync, but as Voyager has demonstrated, people do not have to be *in* the machines. If Voyager does not perhaps offer the fullest synthesis of the age—for it did not send probes to the planets or land itself on discovered moons—if it has traded a breadth of reconnaissance for intensity of inquiry, it has coasted past the hard geography of new worlds and has cruised through the soft geography of interplanetary space as nothing else.

And if, unlike the human hero of myth, it has not apotheosized, it has become iconic and as immortal a monument as civilization might build. It will outlast the pyramids, coliseums, and the *Mona Lisa.* It will outlast its rival realms, the ice sheets and the abyssal plains, which will rise and fall under the push and pull of tectonic and climatic tides. It might perhaps outlast Earth.

Those associated with Voyager sensed from the beginning that it had a special destiny.

The allure of the Grand Tour suggested an almost mythological birth, as though the heavens had foreordained it: it could not be denied, it had to happen. And the Voyagers were lucky. Through perils and glitches and malfunctioning parts, they survived, they defied odds and manufacturing warranties, they endured to the end.

Voyager surprised, and kept surprising, and when the planetary program stalled shortly after launch, Voyager surprised everyone with its power to keep a grander vision alive. Ellis Miner noted, with almost impossible understatement, "There were more discoveries made on Voyager than I expect to ever see made on any single mission. It is probably the most successful mission ever done and likely ever to be done." As Voyager 2 approached Neptune, Dick Laeser, mission director and later project manager, said simply, "I have no desire to do much else except to ride this thing all the way out into interstellar space."[41]

Most participants found it difficult, in discussing Voyager, to avoid both the trite and the self-laudatory, and they stumbled; for them, the Voyagers' continuing trek was the spacecrafts' own narrative and statement. Professional pundits have tended to follow Carl Sagan's lead and stress both the canonical power of the Voyagers' images and the enforced vision that Earth is merely a speck in the cosmos, of scant significance, that Voyager's power lies in its capacity to humble and to offer hope of some future redemption, perhaps with interstellar contact.

Few believed that. They sensed, if they could not give voice to their sentiments, that there was little about Voyager that spoke of a mandatory meekness or frailty. Perhaps if viewed from the stellar Olympus of Clarke's Overlords or the cool mathematics of Sagan's cosmic intelligence, Earth seems trite and its inhabitants boorishly arrogant. But viewed from Earth, the Voyagers look positively Promethean, expressions of an indomitable moment when humanity returned fire to the heavens. Their power was not to humble but to inspire. Its observers recognized that Voyager's like would not come again. Norm Haynes, project manager for the Neptune encounter, explained in terms many participants recycled, "It wasn't an once-in-a-lifetime experience. It was a one-time experience." It did what couldn't be repeated. Voyager's saga was, as Edward Stone put it, injecting new juice into an old cliché, "the journey of a lifetime." The lifetime was humanity's.[42]

There are those for whom the quest for newer worlds must point outward, for whom it means the discovery and occupation of distant places. And there are those for whom the quest points inward, for whom it means the rediscovery of Earth, or further, a deeper discovery of the human heart. But all can look to Voyager with awe, pride, and faith that whatever we are, we will endure, and all can savor its journey as an expression of a shared longing that newer and better worlds are indeed possible, and that Earth might be among them.

Afterword

Voyager is not the text I set out to write. What intrigued me about the Voyager mission—apart from its sheer audacity and awe—was its long history, which is to say, a lengthy and complex narrative that I thought might braid with a general chronicle of geographic discovery by Western civilization. I hoped that I might use a stream of commentaries, drawn from the exploring past, to shepherd the story, much as Voyager's overseers used course corrections to keep it on trajectory, such that each narrative could reinforce the other. Voyager could carry the grand narrative of Western exploration, the grand narrative of Western exploration, could propel Voyager, and their collective story could have a common tempo throughout.

I couldn't make it work. One or the other had to be the primary vehicle, and I chose Voyager. That left the Great Ages of Discovery as a commentator but not a co-chronicle; and without the prospects for sustained counterpoint, I opted to replace a chattering stream of recalibrating observations with fewer but larger set pieces that could highlight particular themes of relevance to both. Accordingly, I shifted the early chapters from a continuous narrative into a format more traditional and analytical. This meant a lot of text to get Voyager to launch and a big payload to carry upward. What results is an interpretive history whose internal rhythms mimic those that led to Voyager's launch and journey.

The Great Ages will have to wait for a full-spectrum history of their own. They enter this text as an organizing principle that allows for comparisons and contrasts, that is, for context. The conceit has itself a context, however, that may be worth explicating. I wish to acknowledge my intellectual debts for its evolution.

The idea of parsing the grand sweep of exploration by Western civilization into eras derives from a 1974 graduate seminar on nineteenth-century America in which William Goetzmann read a paper that argued for a "second great age of discovery." It took no great leap of imagination to see the latter half of the twentieth century as part of a third great age. I exploited Goetzmann's phrase, if not wholly his idea, in a paper read at an AAAS meeting in 1976 and subsequently published under the title "From the Grand Canyon to the Marianas Trench: The Earth Sciences after Darwin," and then in my 1976 doctoral dissertation, written under Goetzmann's general supervision, about an American geologist and explorer, later published as *Grove Karl Gilbert* (1980). Our separate lines of inquiry converged in 1986 with his book *New Lands, New Men: America and the Second Great Age of Discovery*, and my book *The Ice: A Journey to Antarctica*.

Over the succeeding years I have tinkered with and refined the idea in a handful of papers read to conferences and occasionally published, used it as an organizing device for a course I taught on exploration history, and relied on it as an informing conceit for *How the Canyon Became Grand* (1998). It was embedded in the text I delivered on "The Future of Exploration" at the Sarton Memorial Lecture at the AAAS meeting (2002), and in "Seeking Newer Worlds," delivered at a workshop co-sponsored by NASA and the National Air and Space Museum and later published in *Critical Issues in the History of Spaceflight* (2006). By then I had decided I ought to apply these ideas directly to the space program, with Voyager as my preferred vehicle. As before, the three ages get refracted through a particular subject. In the past, these were places; here, an expedition. Even Voyager, however, has only so much narrative thrust: it cannot lift the entire Third Age, and it carries it outward to space when so much of the era will explore the depths of the oceanic abyss. But it is a start.

Several people have assisted in this project, which has too often resembled the tempo of the Voyager mission, full of frenzied activity and long voids. I would like to note particularly Julie Cooper, archivist at JPL; David Fries at NASA's History Office; Stan Seibert, who gave up scarce discretionary time to help a mathematically challenged friend check some calculations; and Lydia Pyne, who offered comments on a draft. A special thanks goes to Wendy Wolf for defibrillating parts of texts and ideas that threatened to sink into reverie, self-absorption, or obscurantism and for reminding me that the narrative really is the message. While the text, unlike the Voyager spacecrafts, cannot carry an aluminum plaque with all their names, it carries their presence.

All were thrusters, helping to stabilize and point. The primary propulsion has come as always from Sonja, who looks ever heavenward, yet always manages to have her feet planted squarely on Earth.

Brittlebush Valley, August 2009

Appendix

CHRONOLOGY OF MAJOR LUNAR AND PLANETARY MISSIONS (LAUNCH DATES FOR SUCCESSES ONLY)

1957

    USSR: Sputnik 1
    USSR: Sputnik 2

1958

    USA: Explorer 1
    USA: Vanguard 1

1959

    USA: Pioneer 4—lunar flyby
    USSR: Luna 2—lunar impact
    USSR: Luna 3—lunar flyby

1962

    USA: Ranger 4—lunar impact
    USA: Mariner 2—Venus flyby

1964

    USA: Mariner 4—Mars flyby

1965

    USA: Rangers 8, 9—lunar impact
    USSR: Luna 5—lunar soft landing

1966

    USSR: Lunas 9 and 13—lunar landers
    USSR: Lunas 10 through 12—lunar orbiters
    USA: Surveyor 1—lunar lander
    USA: Lunar Orbiter 1, 2

1967

    USA: Lunar Orbiter 3 through 5
    USSR: Venera 4—Venus probe

USA: Surveyors 3 through 6—lunar lander

USA: Mariner 5—Venus flyby

1968

USA: Surveyor 7—lunar lander

USSR: Luna 14—lunar orbiter

USSR: Zonds 5 and 6—lunar orbit and return

USA: Apollo 8—lunar orbit and return

1969

USSR: Venera 5 and 6—Venus probes

USA: Mariner 6 and 7—Mars flybys

USA: Apollo 10—lunar orbit and return

USA: Apollo 11—lunar landing

USSR: Zond 7—lunar flyby and return

USA: Apollo 12—lunar landing

1970

USA: Apollo 13—aborted lunar landing

USSR: Venera 7—Venus lander

USSR: Luna 16—lunar sample return

USSR: Zond 8—lunar flyby and return

USSR: Luna 17/Lunokhod 1—lunar rover

1971

USA: Apollos 14 and 15—lunar landings

USSR: Mars 2 and 3—Mars orbiters and landers

USA: Mariner 9—Mars orbiter

USSR: Luna 19—lunar orbiter

1972

USSR: Luna 20—lunar sample return

USA: Pioneer 10—Jupiter flyby

USSR: Venera 8—Venus probe

USA: Apollos 16 and 17—lunar landings

1973

USSR: Luna 21/Lunokhod 2—lunar rover

USA: Pioneer 11—Jupiter/Saturn flyby

USA: Skylab

USSR: Mars 4 through 7—Mars flybys, orbiters, landers

USA: Mariner 10—Venus and Mercury flyby

1974

USSR: Luna 22—lunar orbiter

1975

USSR: Veneras 9 and 10—Venus orbiters and landers

USA: Vikings 1 and 2—Mars orbiters and landers

1977

USA: Voyagers 1 and 2—Grand Tour

1978

USA: Pioneer Venuses 1 and 2—Venus orbiter and probes

USA: ISEE-3/ICE—Comet flybys

USSR: Veneras 11 and 12—Venus orbiters and landers

1981

USSR: Veneras 13 and 14—Venus orbiters and landers

1983

USSR: Veneras 15 and 16—Venus orbiters

1984

USSR: Vegas 1 and 2—Venus landers and Comet Halley flyby

1989

USA: Magellan—Venus orbiter

USA: Galileo—Jupiter orbiter and probe

USA: Hubble space telescope

USA/ESA: Ulysses—Jupiter flyby and solar orbiter

1994

USA: Clementine—lunar orbiter, attempted asteroid flyby

1996

USA: NEAR—asteroid Eros orbiter

USA: Mars Global Surveyor—Mars Orbiter

USA: Mars Pathfinder—Mars lander and rover

1997

USA: Cassini—Saturn orbiter

1998

USA: Lunar Prospector—lunar orbiter

USA: Deep Space 1—asteroid and comet flyby

1999

USA: Stardust—Comet Coma sample return

—

Source: NASA Planetary Exploration Timeline

STATUS OF VOYAGERS (AUGUST 2009)

	VOYAGER 1	VOYAGER 2
Distance from Earth:	16,387,000,000 km	13,252,000,000 km
Total distance traveled:	20,992,000,000 km	20,004,000,000 km
Velocity (to Earth):	131,389 km/hr	107,374 km/hr
Round-trip light time:	30 hr, 21 min, 14 sec	24 hr, 24 min, 18 sec
Propellant remaining:	26.63 kg	28.28 kg
Electrical output:	277.4 watts	278.7 watts

Source: JPL Voyager Weekly Operations Report http://voyager.jpl.nasa.gov/mission/weekly-reports/index.htm

THE GRAND TOUR AND ITS ENCOUNTERS

FIGURE 1   THE GRAND TOUR

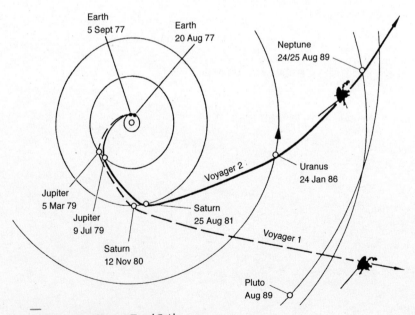

Source: *Voyager Neptune Travel Guide*

FIGURE 2   ENCOUNTER: VOYAGER 1 AT JUPITER

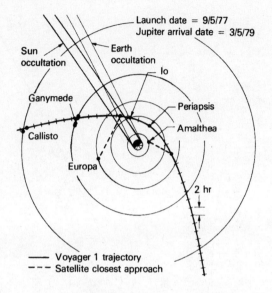

FIGURE 3   ENCOUNTER: VOYAGER 2 AT JUPITER

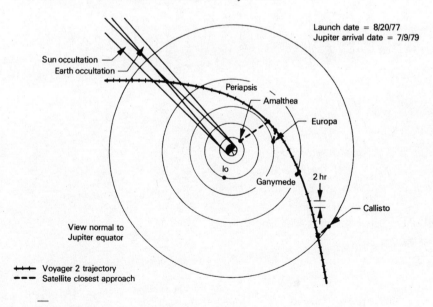

FIGURE 4 ENCOUNTER: VOYAGER 1 AT SATURN

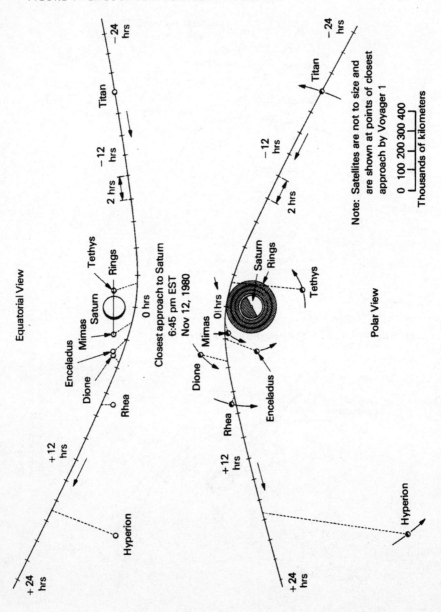

Source: NASA

FIGURE 5   ENCOUNTER: VOYAGER 2 AT SATURN

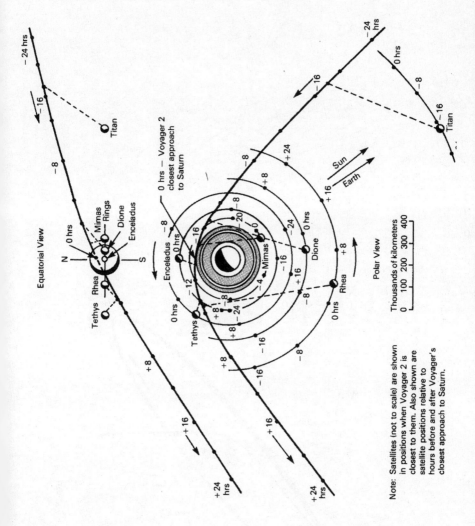

Note: Satellites (not to scale) are shown in positions when Voyager 2 is closest to them. Also shown are satellite positions relative to hours before and after Voyager's closest approach to Saturn.

Source: NASA

FIGURE 6   ENCOUNTER: VOYAGER 2 AT URANUS

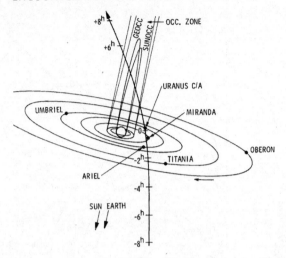

Source: NASA

FIGURE 7   ENCOUNTER: VOYAGER 2 AT NEPTUNE

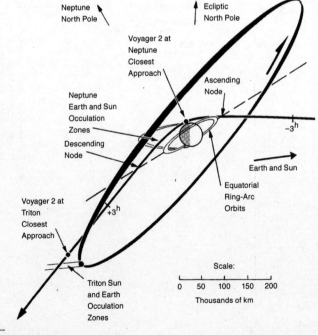

Source: NASA

FIGURE 8   VOYAGER INTERSTELLAR MISSION AND MAP OF THE FOUR
FAR-TRAVELER SPACECRAFT LEAVING THE SOLAR SYSTEM

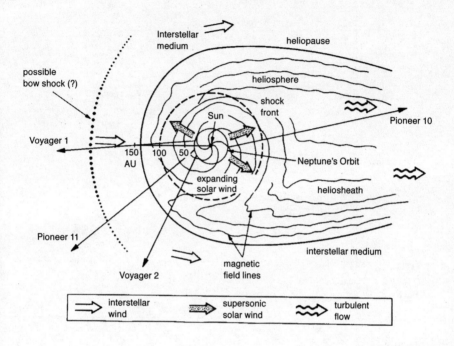

Source: *Voyager Neptune Travel Guide*

FIGURE 9   EXPLORING THE SOLAR SYSTEM: A SPACE-TIME CONTINUUM

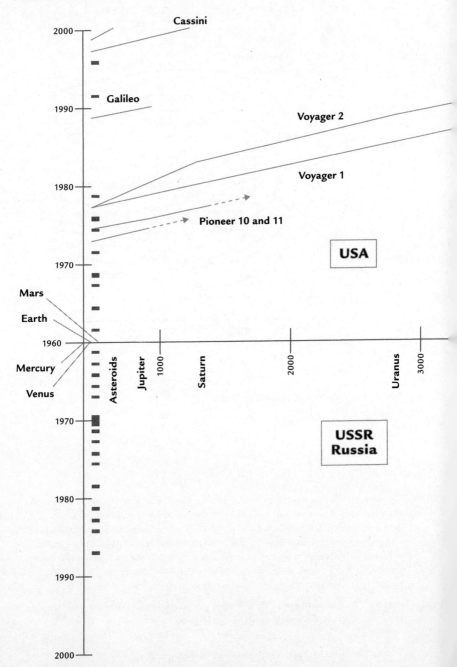

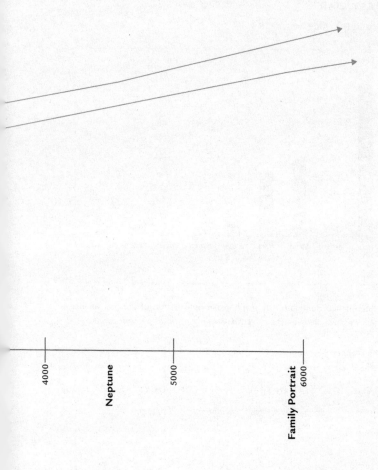

4000

Neptune

5000

Family Portrait

6000

The horizontal axis locates the planets by distance from the Sun (million km). The vertical axis gives years of launches and encounters for the United States (top) and the USSR (bottom). On this scale missions to the inner planets appear as mere hachures. It's easy to see how the immense trek of the Voyagers dominated distance, and given the long hiatus after launch, the history of planetary exploration by NASA. While the Pioneers continued their outward trek as well, their missions officially ended with Jupiter and Saturn. The Voyagers had their missions redefined as they progressed.

Note both the dominating position of Voyager spatially by encountering the outer planets and its domination of American launches for a decade.

Data source: NASA, Planetary Exploration Timeline

THE COLDEST WAR

FIGURE 10   COLD WAR FRONTIERS

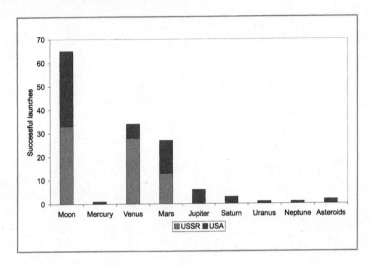

Note how the inner planets dominate. The graph shows only successful launches, or else Mars—the scene for many failed Soviet spacecraft—would appear as a higher target.

Source: NASA Planetary Exploration Timeline

FIGURE 11   THE COLD WAR IN SPACE: A CHRONOLOGY (1957 TO 2000).

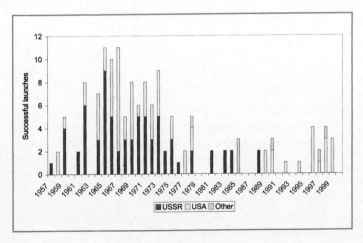

Source: NASA Planetary Exploration Timeline

Notes

MISSION STATEMENT: VOYAGER OF DISCOVERY

1. See, for example, Asif A. Siddiqi, *Deep Space Chronicle: A Chronology of Deep Space and Planetary Probes 1958–2000*. Monographs in Aerospace History, no. 24. NASA SP-2002-4524 (Washington, D.C.: NASA, 2002), and Brian Harvey, *Russia in Space: The Failed Frontier?* (Chichester, UK: Springer Praxis, 2001).

PART 1: THE BEGINNING OF BEYOND:
JOURNEY OF AN IDEA

CHAPTER 1. ESCAPE VELOCITY

1. Bruce Murray, *Journey into Space: The First Three Decades of Space Exploration* (New York: W. W. Norton, 1989), p. 15.
2. On shifting rationales, see Jacob Darwin Hamblin, *Oceanographers and the Cold War: Disciples of Marine Science* (Seattle: University of Washington Press, 2005); the introduction is a useful summary of motives, so similar to those for space.
3. An excellent study of this convergence is available in Walter A. McDougall, *The Heavens and the Earth: A Political History of the Space Age* (New York: Basic Books, 1985).

4. Expression "exploration's nation" taken from William H. Goetzmann, "Exploration's Nation," pp. 11–36, in Daniel J. Boorstin, ed., *American Civilization* (New York: McGraw-Hill, 1972).

5. Letter, W. H. Pickering to Dr. Thomas O. Paine, July 1, 1969, JPL Archives 214, no. 66.

6. Ibid.

7. Ibid. A thorough survey of the uses of exploration as justification for the space program is available in Roger D. Launius, "The Historical Dimension of Space Exploration: Reflections and Possibilities," *Space Policy* 16 (2000): 23–38.

8. Wernher von Braun, Frederick I. Ordway III, and Dave Dooling, *Space Travel: A History*, 4th ed., rev. (New York: Harper and Row, 1975), p. 281.

9. Ibid.

CHAPTER 2. GRAND TOUR

10. There are many accounts of NASA's origins; see Roger E. Bilstein, *Orders of Magnitude: A History of the NACA and NASA, 1915–1990*. NASA SP-4406 (Washington, D.C.: NASA, 1989), and Homer E. Newell, *Beyond the Atmosphere: Early Years of Space Science*, NASA History Series, NASA SP-4211 (Washington, D.C.: NASA, 1980); exchanges between George Kistiakowsky (presidential science advisor) and Lloyd Berkner, p. 124. For an excellent political history of the space age, see McDougall, *The Heavens and the Earth*. For the perspective of JPL, see Clayton R. Koppes, *JPL and the American Space Program: A History of the Jet Propulsion Laboratory* (New Haven, Conn.: Yale University Press, 1982).

11. Quote from Rocket and Satellite Research Panel in Appendix D, Newell, *Beyond the Atmosphere*, p. 427.

12. Craig B. Watt, "The Road to the Deep Space Network," *IEEE Spectrum* (April 1993): 50. JPL quotes from Henry C. Dethloff and Ronald A. Schorn, *Voyager's Grand Tour: To the Outer Planets and Beyond* (Washington, DC: Smithsonian Books, 2003), pp. 10–12, and Koppes, *JPL*, pp. 90–95.

13. Dethloff and Schorn, *Voyager's Grand Tour*, pp. 14–16; Koppes, *JPL*, pp. 102–5.

14. Lack of interest explained in Oran W. Nicks, *Far Travelers: The Exploring Machines*, NASA SP-480 (Washington, D.C.: NASA, 1985), p. 14.

15. On S-1, Dethloff and Schorn, *Voyager's Grand Tour*, p. 19; Nicks, *Far Travelers*, p. 101.

16. Nicks, *Far Travelers*, p. 17.

17. Dethloff and Schorn, *Voyager's Grand Tour*, pp. 21–22. G. W. Morgen-thaler and R. G. Morra, eds., "Unmanned Exploration of the Solar System," *Advances in Astronomical Sciences* 19 (1965); Maxwell W. Hunter II, "Unmanned Scientific Exploration Throughout the Solar System," *Space Science Reviews* 6 (1975): 601–54.

18. For a concise account of Voyager Mars, see Nicks, *Far Travelers*, pp. 170–74.

19. An excellent digest of events is available in J. K. Davies, "A Brief History of the Voyager Project: The End of the Beginning," *Spaceflight* 23, no. 5 (March 1981): 35–41, although the article's value is compromised by sloppy citations.

20. See the 1963 summary, M. A. Minovitch, "The Determination and Characteristics of Ballistic Interplanetary Trajectories under the Influence of Multiple Planetary Attractions," Technical Report No. 32-464, JPL, Oct. 31, 1963. For claims that others were also closely tracking the concepts, see M. W. Hunter II, "Unmanned Scientific Exploration Throughout the Solar System," *Space Science Reviews* 6 (1967): 601–54.

21. Flandro has given several accounts of how he arrived at the Grand Tour scheme, and of the connection (or not) to Minovitch: Gary Flandro, in David W. Swift, *Voyager Tales: Personal Views of the Grand Tour* (Reston, Va.: American Institute of Aeronautics and Astronautics, 1997), pp. 62–70; Dr. Gary A. Flandro, "Discovery of the Grand Tour Voyager Mission Profile," pp. 95–98, in Mark Littman, *Planets Beyond: Discovering the Outer Solar System* (Mineola, N.Y.: Dover Publications, 2004; rev. ed.). See also Tony Reichhardt, "Gravity's Overdrive," *Air and Space/Smithsonian* 8, no. 6 (1994): 77.

22. See Flandro in Littman, *Planets Beyond*, pp. 95–96.

23. Ibid., p. 97. G. A. Flandro, "Utilization of Energy Derived from the Gravitational Field of Jupiter for Reducing Flight Time to the Outer Solar System," *JPL NASA SPS* IV (1965): 37–35. Published version: G. A. Flandro, "Fast Reconnaissance Missions to the Outer Solar System Utilizing Energy Derived from the Gravitational Field of Jupiter," *Astronautica Acta* 12, no. 4 (1966): 329–37. See also Minovitch's update, "Utilizing large planetary perturbations for the design of deep space, solar probe, and out-of-ecliptic trajectories," Technical Report No. 32-849, JPL (December 15, 1965).

24. Flandro, in Littman, *Planets Beyond*, p. 97. Homer Joe Stewart, "New Possibilities for Solar System Exploration," *Astronautics and Aeronautics*

4 (Dec. 1966): 26–31; James Long, "To the Outer Planets," *Astronautics and Aeronautics* 7 (June 1969): 32–48. Murray quoted in Dethloff and Schorn, *Voyager's Grand Tour,* pp. 44–45.

25. Long, "To the Outer Planets," 7, quote on p. 47; William Pickering, "Grand Tour," *American Scientist* 58, no. 2 (March–April 1970): 148–55; E. M. Repic, "Outer-Planet Exploration Missions" (Part B of NAS8-24975), Final Report, Vol. 1, Summary. Space Division, North American Rockwell, S.D., 70-32-1 (January 1970). Note, however, that the NAS Space Science Board, in its report "Planetary Exploration 1968–1975," did not boost missions to the outer planets, clinging to Venus and Mars, with a flyby of Mercury (NAS-NRC, July 1968). Note: See JPL Archives, 122; item no. 2 is the basis for the popular article distilled by Long (1969). Some critical memos trace the very interesting thinking (and the complexity of choices among alternatives) that led to the Grand Tour. See, in particular, Fred H. Felberg to F. E. Goddard et al., Interoffice Memorandum OPP 68-102, May 23, 1968, Subject: Review of AST Candidates, JPL 230, no. 28; and Letter, W. H. Pickering to D. P. Hearth, March 2, 1970, JPL 214, no. 74.

26. See Long, "To the Outer Planets," pp. 33–34. An excellent, balanced survey of the evolution of the Grand Tour is available in Andrew J. Butica, "Voyager: The Grand Tour of Big Science," chapter 11, in Pamela E. Mack, ed., *From Engineering Science to Big Science.* NASA SP-4219 (Washington, D.C.: 1998). See also David Rubashkin, "Who Killed Grand Tour?" ms., NASA History Office, Historical Reference Collection.

27. Several sources for funding: Dethloff and Schorn, *Voyager's Grand Tour;* J. K. Davies, "A Brief History of the Voyager Project," *Spaceflight* 23, no. 3 (March 1981): 35–41; Bruce Murray, *Journey into Space,* pp. 138–42.

28. Schurmeier quoted in Dethloff and Schorn, *Voyager's Grand Tour,*" p. 45.

29. A good account available in Butica, "Voyager: The Grand Tour of Big Science." Quotes from Ellis D. Miner, *Uranus: The Planet, Rings, and Satellites* (New York: Ellis Horwood, 1990), pp. 101–2. See "The Grand Tour," draft manuscript, 11-1-69, JPL Archives 214, no. 70, for a simplified version of the early conception, and Advanced Planetary Mission Study Team, "Grand Tour Definition Study, Vol. 1. Mission Analysis, March 15, 1971," JPL Archives 122, no. 1, for the fuller, final draft.

30. National Academy of Sciences, "The Outer Solar System: A Program for Exploration," report of a study by the Space Science Board, June 1969 (Washington, D.C.: NAS, 1969).

31. There are several published accounts of these events, but Butica, "Voyager: The Grand Tour of Big Science," is a very handy synopsis.

32. I follow Dethloff and Schorn, *Voyager's Grand Tour*, pp. 52–57; quote on budget, p. 56.

33. Space Science Board, "The Outer Solar System: A Program for Exploration," p. 5.

34. Fletcher quotes from Fred H. Felberg to Memorandum to Record, Interoffice Memorandum OPP 72-45, February 24, 1972, JPL Archives 230, no. 51.

35. Quotes from preface, which contains a good summary of preceding studies, NAS-NRC Space Science Board, "Priorities for Space Research, 1971–1980: Report of a Study on Space Science and Earth Observations Priorities" (Washington, D.C.: National Academy of Sciences, 1971), pp. 17–18. "Satellite imaging" quote from NAS-NRC Space Science Board, "Outer Planets Exploration 1972–1985" (Washington, D.C.: National Academy of Sciences, 1971).

36. As always, the details are more complicated than the inherited explanations imply. Fletcher spoke to JPL in February 1972 and offered his own thoughts. The Grand Tour, as originally conceived, did not have support from either OMB or the White House, but a stripped-down version to Jupiter and Saturn for 1977 did, and would likely be considered in the next budgetary round. He also listed two "lessons" from his time as NASA administrator: that any specific decision makes enemies but few friends, and that there was, in reality, little occasion to trade dollars from one NASA program to another; each had to be justified on its own. Source: Fred H. Felberg to Memorandum to Record, Interoffice Memorandum OPP 72-45, February 24, 1972, JPL Archives 230, no. 51.

37. The Mariner study commenced immediately after the SSB report; see F. H. Felberg, Interoffice Memorandum OPP 71-117, "Mariner Outer Planets Missions Study," JPL Archives 230, no. 47. For a good chronology of the revival, see Dethloff and Schorn, *Voyager's Grand Tour*, pp. 60–64.

38. Pickering quote: F. H. Felberg to R. J. Parks, Interoffice Memorandum OPP 71-124, September 16, 1971, JPL Archives 230, no. 47.

39. See Harris M. Schurmeier to MJS Review Board, November 6, 1974, JPL Archives, Flight Collections, Folio 54.

40. Dethloff and Schorn, *Voyager's Grand Tour*, p. 88, for Final Spacecraft; Casani quote, p. 106.

41. On the reconstituted design, see Roger D. Bourke et al., "Mariner Jupiter/Saturn 1977: The Mission Frame," *Astronautics and Aeronautics*

(Nov. 1972), pp. 42-49. For a detailed internal review of final trajectory trade-offs, see Letter, J. R. Casani to R. A. Mills, "MJS77 Flight Trajectory Selection and Rationale," June 22, 1976, JPL Archives 36, no. 60.

42. Dethloff and Schorn, *Voyager's Grand Tour,* pp. 106-7. An excellent summary of the Voyager preparations as viewed by an insider is Miner, *Uranus,* chapter 6; quotes from p. 105.

43. Dethloff and Schorn, *Voyager's Grand Tour,* p. 105.

44. The story of naming preserved in oral interviews, the results of two published as: Charles Kohlhase, in Swift, *Voyager Tales,* p. 85, and Dethloff and Schorn, *Voyager's Grand Tour,* pp. 105-7. See also Nicks, *Far Travelers,* pp. 170-73, which is better on the antecedent history. On final choice and NASA approval, see J. R. Casani, Interoffice Memo, MJS77-JRC-77-63, Subject: Project Name, March 4, 1977, NASA History Office, Historical File 005566.

45. Malyn Newitt, *A History of Portuguese Overseas Expansion, 1400–1668* (New York: Routledge, 2005), p. 58.

CHAPTER 3. GREAT AGES OF DISCOVERY

46. This analysis of three ages of discovery is an adaptation of "Seeking Newer Worlds: An Historical Context for Space Exploration," pp. 8-35, in Steven J. Dick and Roger D. Launius, eds., *Critical Issues in the History of Spaceflight,* NASA SP-2006-4702 (Washington, D.C.: NASA, 2006). As the common title suggests, this entire book before you is an attempt to extend and elaborate the arguments of that essay, and by focusing on the Voyager mission to find a more focused mode of expression for the ideas within it. I note here, as in the afterword, that the idea of a Second Age of Discovery belongs to William H. Goetzmann, who developed it most fully in *New Lands, New Men: America and the Second Great Age of Discovery* (New York: Viking, 1986).

47. I have relied on that doyen of the founding age of discovery, J. H. Parry. Among his many works are three that serve especially as syntheses: *The Establishment of the European Hegemony, 1415–1715,* 3rd ed., rev. (New York: Harper and Row, 1966); *The Discovery of the Sea* (Berkeley: University of California Press, 1981); and *The Age of Reconnaissance: Discovery, Exploration and Settlement, 1450–1650* (New York: Praeger, 1969).

48. Parry, *The Discovery of the Sea,* op cit.

49. Harry Wolf, *The Transits of Venus: A Study of Eighteenth-Century Science* (Princeton, N.J.: Princeton University Press, 1959), p. 83.

50. See William H. Goetzmann, "Exploration's Nation: The Role of Discovery in American History," in Daniel J. Boorstin, ed., *American Civilization: A Portrait from the Twentieth Century* (New York: McGraw-Hill, 1972).

51. As a useful way to summarize this explosion, see the flawed but indispensable, J. N. L. Baker, *A History of Geographical Discovery and Exploration* (New York: Cooper Square Publishers, 1967).

52. J. Tuzo Wilson, *I.G.Y: The Year of the New Moons* (New York: Alfred Knopf, 1961), p. 324. Chapman characterized IGY's mission as learning "more about the fluid envelope of our planet—the atmosphere and oceans—over all the earth and at all heights and depths." But this was academic abstraction. Wilson came closer to the mark when he observed that it was the yet-unvisited places that mattered, that IGY proposed a planetary inventory as conceived by geophysicists. The founding geophysicists fretted most over the outer boundary of Earth, which is where they most wanted IGY to go. Chapman, in *IGY Annals* 1 (Jan. 28, 1957): 3.

53. Wilson, *I.G.Y,* pp. 275, 320, 324, 219–25 passim.

CHAPTER 4. VOYAGER

54. The best summary is Raymond L. Heacock, "The Voyager Spacecraft," Institution of Mechanical Engineers, *Proceedings 1980,* 194, no. 28 (1980). Digests are available in most books on Voyager; for example, Ellis D. Miner, *Uranus: The Planet, Rings and Satellites* (New York: Ellis Horwood, 1990), pp. 119–32. See also Nicks, *Far Travelers,* pp. 15–17.

55. Mark Wolverton, *The Depths of Space: The Story of the Pioneer Planetary Probes* (Washington, D.C.: Joseph Henry Press, 2004), pp. 58–61.

56. S. E. Morison says "c. 55 feet" in *The Great Explorers: The European Discovery of America* (New York: Oxford University Press, 1978), p. 385. A more detailed study by Eugene Lyon recommends sixty-seven feet; *"Niña:* Ship of Discovery," in Jerald T. Milanich and Susan Milbrath, eds., *First Encounters: Spanish Explorations in the Caribbean and the United States, 1492–1570* (Gainesville: University of Florida Press, 1989).

57. Gilbert data: Arvid M. Johnson and David D. Pollard, transcribers, "Part of the Field Notes of Grove Karl Gilbert for the period 20 June 1875 to 24 November 1876 taken during his study of the Henry Mountains and Areas to the West," School of Earth Sciences, Stanford University (1977), pp. 87–88, for list of items carried. On HMS *Challenger,* see the published deck plans (available online at www.19thcenturyscience.org/HMSC/HMSC-INDEX/Deck-Plans.html; accessed October 13, 2008).

58. Nicks, *Far Travelers*, p. 71. On dimensions, see Heacock, "Voyager Spacecraft."

59. Nicks, *Far Travelers*, pp. 80-82.

60. A good digest of robotic needs is found in Roger D. Launius and Howard E. McCurdy, *Robots in Space: Technology, Evolution, and Interplanetary Travel* (Baltimore, Md.: Johns Hopkins University Press, 2008), pp. 140-45.

61. Casani, in Swift, *Voyager Tales*, pp. 118-19. Statistics: Voyager Mission Planning Office Staff, *The Voyager Uranus Travel Guide* JPL D-2580 (August 15, 1985), p. 107.

62. Casani, in Swift, *Voyager Tales*, p. 119.

63. Raymond Heacock, in Swift, *Voyager Tales*, p. 152; Nicks, *Far Travelers*, p. 80.

64. Raymond Heacock, in Swift, *Voyager Tales*, p. 152.

65. Quote from Morison, *The Great Explorers*, p. 563.

66. Quote from William H. Goetzmann, *Exploration and Empire: The Explorer and Scientist in the Winning of the American West* (New York: Alfred A. Knopf, 1967), p. 58.

67. Casani, in Swift, *Voyager Tales*, p. 120.

68. Good summary of early history in James E. Tomayko, *Computers in Spaceflight: The NASA Experience.* NASA Contractor Report 182505 (March 1988). But an excellent distillation is available in Raymond L. Heacock, "The Voyager Spacecraft," *The Institution of Mechanical Engineers, Proceedings 1980* 194, no. 28 (1980): 221-22.

69. Tomayko, *Computers in Spaceflight*, chapter 6; Miner, *Uranus*, p. 118.

70. Quotes from Ben Evans, with David M. Harland, *NASA's Voyager Missions: Exploring the Outer Solar System and Beyond* (Chichester, UK: Springer Praxis, 2004), p. 67.

71. Nicks, *Far Travelers*, p. 253.

72. Antonio Pigafetta, *Magellan's Voyage: A Narrative Account of the First Circumnavigation*, trans. and ed., R. A. Skelton (New York: Dover Publications, 1994), p. 57.

73. See J. A. Parry, *The Discovery of the Sea* (Berkeley: University of California Press, 1981).

CHAPTER 5. LAUNCH

74. Murray quoted in Swift, *Voyager Tales*, p. 215.

75. Account of ship technology from the inestimable J. H. Parry, *The Age of Reconnaissance*, chapter 3, and *The Discovery of the Sea*, chapter 1.

76. Rocket history from Wernher von Braun and Frederick I. Ordway III, *Rocket's Red Glare* (Garden City, N.Y.: Anchor Press, 1976), and Wernher von Braun, Frederick I. Ordway III, and Dave Dooling, *Space Travel: A History* (New York: Harper and Row, 1985; 4th ed).

77. On pinnaces and longboats, see Morison, *The Great Explorers*, p. 16.

78. Cape Canaveral information from NASA, "Kennedy Space Center Story," www.nasa.gov/centers/kennedy/about/history/story/ch1_prt.htm; accessed August 30, 2007.

79. On Franklin's dove, see Owen Beattie and John Geiger, *Frozen in Time: The Fate of the Franklin Expedition* (Toronto: Greystone Books, 1987), p. 16. On the storms around Voyager, see Bruce Murray, *Journey into Space: The First Thirty Years in Space* (New York: W. W. Norton, 1989), p. 143.

PART 2: BEYOND THE SUNSET: JOURNEY ACROSS THE SOLAR SYSTEM

CHAPTER 6. NEW MOON

1. On Voyager malfunctions, I rely on several accounts: J. E. Davies, "A Brief History of the Voyager Project: Part 2," *Spaceflight* 23, no. 5 (May 1981): 71-72; Bruce Murray, *Journey into Space: The First Thirty Years of Space Exploration* (New York: W. W. Norton, 1989), pp. 143-47. A good summary exists in Miner, *Uranus*, pp. 108-12. For Voyager 2, see Swift, *Voyager Tales*, especially John Casani, pp. 119-20; "Anxiety attack" and "Superautonomous" in Murray, *Journey into Space*, pp. 146-47.

2. Miner, *Uranus*, pp. 108-12. A good journalistic account of Voyager woes, beginning with the faulty Centaur rocket, is available in Joel Davis, *Flyby: The Interplanetary Odyssey of Voyager 2* (New York: Atheneum, 1987), pp. 42-46. For detailed accounts of malfunctions, see Davies, "Brief History," and Heacock, "The Voyager Spacecraft."

3. Malyn Newitt, *A History of Portuguese Overseas Expansion, 1400–1668* (New York: Routledge, 2005), pp. 15-16; Donald Rayfield, *The Dream of Lhasa: The Life of Nikolay Przhevalsky: Explorer of Central Asia* (Columbus: Ohio University Press, 1976), p. 69.

4. Best summary is in Goetzmann, *New Lands, New Men*, chapter 6; number of expeditions, p. 266.

5. Quote from Fergus Fleming, *Barrow's Boys* (New York: Grove Press, 1998), p. 1.

6. See Lisle A. Rose, *Assault Against Eternity: Richard E. Byrd and the Exploration of Antarctica, 1946–47* (Annapolis, Md.: Naval Institute Press, 1980).

7. An excellent institutional history that addresses this issue directly is Peter J. Westwick, *Into the Black: JPL and the American Space Program 1976–2004* (New Haven, Conn.: Yale University Press, 2007); a distilled synopsis is available on pp. 309–13.

8. Nicks, *Far Travelers*, pp. 154–55.

CHAPTER 7. CRUISE

9. Sieur de Champlain, "Treatise on Seamanship and the Duty of a Good Seaman," Appendix II, in Samuel Eliot Morison, *Samuel de Champlain: Father of New France* (Boston: Atlantic Monthly Press, 1972).

10. Ibid.

11. My analysis follows the criticisms summarized in NASA's review of JPL oversight of Voyager, reproduced in Dethloff and Schorn, *Voyager's Grand Tour*, pp. 141–42. The fullest account of the April 1978 communications breakdown is in Miner and Wessen, *Neptune*, pp. 76–77.

12. Quote from Clayton R. Koppes, *JPL and the American Space Program: A History of the Jet Propulsion Laboratory* (New Haven, Conn.: Yale University Press, 1982), p. ix. My analysis follows closely this excellent study.

13. Again, I follow Koppes, *JPL*, closely, pp. ix–x.

14. Craig B. Watt, "The Road to the Deep Space Network," *IEEE Spectrum* (April 1993): 50. Nicks, *Far Travelers*, p. 17. Other JPL quotes from Koppes, *JPL*, pp. 90–95.

15. Pickering quoted in Koppes, *JPL*, p. 112.

16. This is a primary theme of two outstanding institutional histories: Koppes, *JPL*, op. cit., and Peter J. Westwick, *Into the Black: JPL and the American Space Program 1976–2004* (New Haven, Conn.: Yale University Press, 2007). It is present in all of the published accounts of Voyager, although the liveliest and most informative is Murray, *Journey into Space*.

17. There are several accounts of the Great Surveys. I follow Goetzmann, *Exploration and Empire*, chapters 12–16. The other prime contenders are Wallace Stegner, *Beyond the Hundredth Meridian* (Boston: Houghton Mifflin, 1953), which hedges into Powell hagiography, and Richard A. Bartlett, *Great Surveys of the American West* (Norman: University of Oklahoma Press, 1962).

18. Quote from Goetzmann, *Exploration and Empire*, p. 589.

CHAPTER 8. MISSING MARS

19. See Carl O. Sauer, *The Early Spanish Main* (Berkeley: University of California Press, 1966), pp. 46, 138; and Morison, *The Great Explorers*, pp. 390–91.

20. Camões, *The Lusíads*, 9:44 and 8:98. Díaz in Bernal Díaz, *The Conquest of New Spain*, trans. by J. M. Cohen (New York: Penguin Books, 1963), p. 274.

21. Richard Hakluyt, *Voyages and Discoveries: The Principal Navigations, Voyages, Traffiques, and Discoveries of the English Nation*, ed. and abridged by Jack Beeching (New York: Penguin, 1973), p. 60.

22. Columbus quote from Cecil Jane, trans. and ed., *The Four Voyages of Columbus: A History in Eight Documents* (New York: Dover Publications, 1988), p. 12. The Spanish phrasing reads: "esta es para desear, e, v [ista], es para nunca dexar."

23. Felipe Fernández-Armesto, *The Pathfinders: A Global History of Exploration* (New York: W. W. Norton, 2006), p. 131; for a better take on Henry's career overall, see Peter Russell, *Prince Henry "The Navigator": A Life* (New Haven, Conn.: Yale University Press, 2000). Morison, *The Great Explorers*, pp. 390–91.

24. Columbus, in Morison, *The Great Explorers*, pp. 390–91, and quotes from p. xvi. Fernández-Armesto, *The Pathfinders*, p. 145–47; Pigafetta, *Magellan's Voyage*, p. 37.

25. Fernández-Armesto, *The Pathfinders*, p. 145.

26. Orders quoted in Newby, *The Rand McNally World Atlas of Exploration*, p. 134.

27. Best summary of purposes and practices of the American exploration throughout the century is Goeztmann, *Exploration and Empire*; Ashley quote, p. 105; King Survey quote from p. 437.

28. Apsley Cherry-Garrard, *The Worst Journey in the World: Antarctic 1910–1913* (New York: Penguin Books, 1970, reprint), pp. 642–43.

29. Ibid., p. 643.

30. John Parker, *Books to Build an Empire* (Amsterdam: N. Israel, 1965), p. 39.

31. Ibid., p. 102.

32. Hakluyt, *Voyages and Discoveries*, p. 31.

33. Ibid., p. 38.

34. Morison, *The Great Explorers*, p. 127. See Richard H. Grove, *Green Imperialism: Colonial Expansion, Tropical Island Edens, and the Origins of Environmentalism, 1600–1860* (Cambridge, UK: Cambridge University Press, 1995), p. 249.

35. This paragraph is a close paraphrase and partial quote from Goetz-mann, *New Lands, New Men*, pp. 229–30.

36. For a distillation of his thoughts, see "Which Way Is Up?" pp. 124–33, in Arthur C. Clarke, *The Challenge of the Spaceship* (New York: Ballantine, 1961).

37. Clarke, *Exploration of Space* (1951), pp. 183–85.

38. Ibid., pp. 186–87, 194–95.

39. Kurt Vonnegut Jr., *The Sirens of Titan* (New York: Dell, 1959), p. 30.

40. *Lusíads*, 1:27, 2:45.

41. Ibid., 4:94–95.

42. The Old Man's soliloquy runs from 4:94 to 4:104.

43. Daniel Defoe, *Robinson Crusoe* (New York: Charles Scribner's Sons, 1920), pp. 2, 4, 368.

44. Swift, *Gulliver's Travels*, pp. 359–60.

45. Bertrand H. Bronson, ed., *Samuel Johnson: Rasselas, Poems, Selected Prose* (New York: Holt, Rinehart and Winston, Inc., 1958), p. 511.

46. "Of these wishes that they had formed they well knew that none could be obtained": Bronson, ed., *Samuel Johnson*, p. 612.

47. James Boswell, *The Life of Samuel Johnson* (Garden City, N.Y.: Doubleday and Co., Inc., 1946), p. 355.

48. Amitai Etzioni, *The Moon-Doggle* (Garden City, N.Y.: Doubleday and Co., Inc., 1964), pp. ix, 111.

49. The statistic comes from an outstanding general survey of motives in Roger Launius, "Compelling Rationales for Space Flight: History and the Search for Relevance," pp. 37–71, in Steven J. Dick and Roger D. Launius, eds., *Critical Issues in the History of Spaceflight*. NASA SP-2006-4702 (Washington, D.C.: 2006). Fernández-Armesto, *Pathfinders*, p. 399. Two other useful articles on popular support (and funding) are Roger D. Launius, "Public Opinion Polls and Perceptions of U.S. Human Space-flight," *SpacePolicy* 19 (2003): 163–75, and Howard E. McCurdy, "The Cost of Space Flight," *Space Policy* 10, no. 4 (1994): 277–89.

50. The weight of literature on Mars could sink the International Space Station. A concise summary of the major events, at least for the American program, is Thor Hogan, *Mars Wars: The Rise and Fall of the Space Exploration Initiative*, NASA SP-2007-4410 (Washington, D.C.: NASA, 2007), pp. 1–21. "Algorithm" quote from Thomas O. Paine, in foreword of Wernher von Braun, *The Mars Project* (Springfield: University of Illinois Press, 1991; reprint of 1953 edition), p. vii.

51. Ray Bradbury et al., *Mars and the Mind of Man* (New York: Harper and Row, 1973).

52. The Saturn and Jupiter events were recorded and are available in poor-quality DVDs from JPL.

53. Roger D. Bourke et al., "Mariner Jupiter/Saturn 1977: The Mission Frame," *Astronautics and Aeronautics* (Nov. 1972): 42–49.

CHAPTER 9. CRUISE

54. Miner, *Uranus*, pp. 110–11. A complete account of the episode is also available in Miner and Wessen, *Neptune*, pp. 76–77.

55. For a succinct summary of what Voyager navigation involved, see Robert Cesarone interview, in Swift, *Voyager Tales*, pp. 262–73. A good account of adjustments is available in J. K. Davies, "A Brief History of the Voyager Project," *Spaceflight* 23, no. 5 (May 1981): 72–73.

56. Major sources: Lloyd A. Brown, *The Story of Maps* (New York: Dover Publications, 1977); Parry, *The Discovery of the Sea*, and *The Age of Reconnaissance*; and for a concise distillation, Samuel Eliot Morison, *The Great Explorers*, pp. 26–32.

57. The description follows Parry, *Discovery of the Sea*, pp. 147–50.

58. Morison, *Champlain*, pp. 256, 267.

59. For the specific makeup of the NAV group and its techniques, see Miner, *Uranus*, pp. 117–18. The best general accounts of navigation in principle and as practiced for Voyager are Robert John Cesarone, pp. 261–73, and Charles E. Kohlhase, pp. 83–100, in Swift, *Voyager Tales*; and Nicks, *Far Travelers*, esp. pp. 22–24, 29–30, 41, 56.

60. I found Nicks's explanation in *Far Travelers* the most enlightening, and have followed his accounts, although most deal with earlier spacecraft and handle Voyager especially for the complicated maneuvers around Saturn.

CHAPTER 10. ENCOUNTER: ASTEROID BELT

61. The Pioneer bibliography is appropriately long. A good summary is Mark Wolverton, *The Depths of Space: The Story of the Pioneer Planetary Probes* (Washington, D.C.: Joseph Henry Press, 2004). Two overlapping but lively surveys by some of the principal participants and the project's best-known journalist are available in Richard O. Fimmel, William Swindell, and Eric Burgess, *Pioneer Odyssey*, NASA SP-396 (NASA, 1977), and an updated version, in Fimmel, et al., *Pioneer*, op. cit.

62. Quote by John Naugle, in Wolverton, *Depths of Space*, p. 140, which also distills Pioneer's achievements on p. 4.

63. See Fimmel et al., *Pioneer*, pp. 84–85, with a more detailed explanation of the imaging system on pp. 251–52.

64. The story of the choice of routes is told in all the Pioneer accounts. The most elaborate is in Wolverton, *Depths of Space*, pp. 140–49. But see also, Robert S. Kraemer, *Beyond the Moon: A Golden Age of Planetary Exploration 1971–1978* (Washington, D.C.: Smithsonian Institution, 2000), pp. 77–78.

65. See Fimmel et al., *Pioneer*, pp. 248–50. Burgess offers a more detailed account in Eric Burgess, *Far Encounter: The Neptune System* (New York: Columbia University Press, 1991), pp. 57–58. Wolverton, *Depths of Space*, pp. 184–85.

66. Wolverton gives an eloquent eulogy in *Depths of Space*, pp. 199–209 and 224–25.

67. Kraemer, *Beyond the Moon*, pp. 71–72; Wolverton, *The Depths of Space*, pp. 95, 98. A good description of the asteroid belt problems, anticipated and real, is in Richard O. Fimmel, James Van Allen, and Eric Burgess, *Pioneer: First to Jupiter, Saturn, and Beyond*. NASA SP-446 (Washington, D.C.: NASA, 1980), pp. 91–92.

68. Wolverton, *Depths of Space*, pp. 97–98.

69. Kraemer, *Beyond the Moon*, pp. 73–74; Wolverton, *Depths of Space*, pp. 112–15.

CHAPTER 11. CRUISE

70. Quoted in Bruce Mazlish, ed., *The Railroad and the Space Program: An Exploration in Historical Analogy* (Boston, Mass.: MIT Press, 1965), p. 4.

71. Ibid.

CHAPTER 12. ENCOUNTER: JUPITER

72. By far the best account for encounter is David Morrison and Jane Samz, *Voyage to Jupiter*, NASA-SP-439 (Washington, D.C.: NASA, 1980); for above details, see p. 56. I have followed this text closely, largely doing what any collage does, namely, deface the original to make a new whole.

73. Ibid., pp. 58, 60.

74. Ibid., pp. 60, 63.

75. Ibid., pp. 74–86; Stone quote on p. 86.

76. Ibid., pp. 74–86; Callisto quote quote on p. 86.

77. Ibid., p. 75.

78. Ibid., Soderblom quote on p. 67.

79. Ibid., pp. 86–91.

80. Alexander von Humboldt, *Personal Narrative of a Journey to the Equinoc-tial Regions of the New Continent*, abridged and translated by Jason Wilson (London: Penguin Books, 1995), p. 26. Darwin quoted in Jason Wilson, introduction to Humboldt, *Personal Narrative*, p. xxxvi. Charles Darwin, *The Voyage of the Beagle*, ed. Leonard Engel (Garden City, N.Y.: Doubleday, 1962), pp. 2–3.

81. I again follow, in this entire section, Morrison and Samz, *Voyage to Jupiter*, pp. 97–99.

82. Ibid., pp. 101–2.

83. Soderblom quote from ibid., p. 106; Mutch quote, ibid., p. 108.

84. Cited in ibid., pp. 114–15.

85. Felipe Fernández-Armesto, *The Canary Islands After the Conquest: The Making of a Colonial Society in the Early Sixteenth Century* (Oxford: Clarendon Press, 1982), p. 205, fn 6. For a general consideration of the Canaries within early European expansion, see Fernández-Armesto, *Pathfinders*, pp. 122–51.

86. Fernández-Armesto, *The Canary Islands After the Conquest*, p. 15; on San-cho Panza: from Fernández-Armesto, *Pathfinders*, p. 145.

87. See Columbus, *Four Voyages*, p. 12.

88. For an introduction to the tropic island as Eden and the role of traveling naturalists generally, see Grove, *Green Imperialism*.

89. Thomas More, *Utopia*, trans. Paul Turner (Baltimore, Md.: Penguin Books, 1965), pp. 38, 42.

90. An excellent survey of space-based utopias is available in DeWitt Doug-las Kilgore, *Astrofuturism: Science, Race, and Visions of Utopia in Space* (Phil-adelphia: University of Pennsylvania Press, 2003), which includes an insightful chapter on O'Neill. I have also found very useful the excellent summary in Roger D. Launius and Howard E. McCurdy, *Robots in Space: Technology, Evolution, and Interplanetary Travel* (Baltimore, Md.: Johns Hopkins University Press, 2008), chapter 2.

CHAPTER 13. CRUISE

91. Sources: Morison, *The Great Explorers*, pp. 353–54; Fernández-Armesto, *Pathfinders*, pp. 174–78; and for an especially lively account, Alfred W. Crosby, *Ecological Imperialism: The Biological Expansion of Europe, 900–1900* (Cambridge, UK: Cambridge University Press, 1986), pp. 113–19.

92. Charles Kohlhase, ed., *The Voyager Neptune Travel Guide*. JPL Publication 89-24 (Pasadena, Calif.: JPL, 1989), pp. 103–4.

93. I rely on several accounts, listed in these notes. Of particular value is Tony Reichhardt, "Gravity's Overdrive," *Air and Space/Smithsonian* 8, no. 6 (1994): 72–78. Details of Minovitch's work are difficult to extract from JPL sources, ostensibly because they are covered by privacy guidelines governing personnel disputes, but likely because of threatened lawsuits. Some of the major documents are posted on Minovitch's Web site (www .gravityassist.com). The responses of his JPL supervisors are unavailable. On JPL's inability to furnish details, I quote Julie Cooper, archivist, who helped as much as she could: "The correspondence about Minovitch was denied clearance on the grounds that it is personnel related—like correspondence about any dispute between an employer and employee. Our clearance procedures at JPL have changed since the documents were processed back in the early 1990s, so they weren't separated from the rest of the collection, as discreet records should be. So, the correspondence won't be available to any other researchers, and you won't be able to use those documents again." E-mail to author, Oct. 6, 2008.

94. M. A. Minovitch, "A Method for Determining Interplanetary Free-Fall Reconnaissance Trajectories," JPL Technical Memo no. 312-130 (August 23, 1961). Earlier memos that summer had inquired into conic trajectories of various kinds.

95. Figures from Reichhardt, "Gravity's Overdrive," p. 76. Inner versus outer planet contributions from G. A. Flandro, "Fast Reconnaissance Missions to the Outer Solar System Utilizing Energy Derived from the Gravitational Field of Jupiter," *Astronautica Acta* 12, no. 4 (1966): 334.

96. For the evolution of publications, see M. A. Minovitch, "The Determination and Characteristics of Ballistic Interplanetary Trajectories Under the Influence of Multiple Planetary Attractions," JPL Technical Report no. 32-464 (1963); M. A. Minovitch, "Utilizing Large Planetary Perturbations for the Design of Deep-Space, Solar-Probe, and Out-of-Ecliptic Trajectories," JPL Technical Memo no. 312-514 (1965). For a general survey of efforts, see Richard L. Dowling et al., "The Origin of Gravity-Propelled Interplanetary Space Travel," 41st Congress of the International Astronautical Federation, IAA-90-630 (1990), pp. 1–19. For a parallel project, outside JPL, see Maxwell W. Hunter II, "Unmanned Scientific Exploration Throughout the Solar System," *Space Science Reviews* 6 (1967): 601.

97. Cutting quote: Joe Cutting to Mike Minovitch, interoffice memo, Jan. 21, 1964, JPL, p. 2 (accessible at www.gravityassist.com).

98. Reichhardt, "Gravity's Overdrive," pp. 76–77.

99. I follow Tony Reichhardt, "Gravity's Overdrive," pp. 72–78; Kohlhase, ed. *The Voyager Neptune Travel Guide*, pp. 103–9. Quote from Minovitch Web site home page, www.gravityassist.com; accessed September 1, 2007.

100. Richard L. Dowling et al., "The Origin of Gravity-Propelled Interplanetary Space Travel," *41st Congress of the International Astronautical Federation* (1990), IAA-90-630, p. 16.

101. On the limitations of Minovitch's methods, see Gary Flandro in Littman, *Planets Beyond*, p. 97.

102. See Robert Merton, "Singletons and Multiples in Scientific Discovery," *Proceedings of the American Philosophical Society*, vol. 105, no. 5 (October 1971), pp. 470–86. Einstein's general theory of relativity is an exception.

103. Account from Morison, *The Great Explorers*, p. 400.

104. I follow William H. Goetzmann, *Exploration and Empire*, pp. 117–20, 276–78.

CHAPTER 14. ENCOUNTER: SATURN

105. My account of the Voyagers' encounter follows closely the excellent narrative in David Morrison, *Voyages to Saturn*, NASA SP-451 (Washington, D.C.: NASA, 1982). He describes the coincidence of the Great Conjunction on page 50.

106. Ibid., pp. 50–56.

107. Ibid., pp. 56–61.

108. Ibid., pp. 62, 65.

109. Ibid., pp. 67–68, 94.

110. Quote from Bradford Smith, in Morrison, *Voyages to Saturn*, p. 69, and for Pioneer 11, from James Van Allen, in Wolverton, *The Depths of Space*, pp. 150, 154.

111. Morrison, *Voyages to Saturn*, pp. 70–76.

112. Details from ibid., pp. 78–85. Quotes: Bradford Smith, p. 84; Larry Soderblom and Morrison, p. 85.

113. Stone quoted in Morrison, *Voyages to Saturn*, p. 86.

114. Ibid., pp. 59, 67, 70–71.

115. Ibid., pp. 89–90.

116. Summary of findings from ibid., p. 93.

117. The event was advertised as a "planetary festival" that would extend the three days before encounter and would include symphony orchestras, lectures, educational activities, and an invitational black-tie dinner at $150 per plate to which members of Congress would also be invited. This would be the last planetary encounter for years, but acceptance

rates had "traditionally run low." See Memo, Lynne Murphy to Terry Finn, July 15, 1981, NASA Historical Reference Collection, File 005580.

118. Summary of session in Morrison, *Voyages to Saturn*, p. 94. The session was not transcribed or published, but was filmed for possible TV broadcast. The tape is available through JPL.

119. Bruce Murray and Louis D. Friedman, "Our Founders: The Planetary Society Founders' Statement," www.planetary.org/about/founders, accessed December 23, 2007.

120. For a synopsis, see William Sinclair, "The African Association of 1788," *African Affairs* 1, no. 1 (1901): 145–50.

121. Again I follow the chronology of events laid out in Morrison, *Voyages to Saturn*, pp. 96–135.

122. Quote from ibid., p. 100.

123. Ibid., pp. 117–21.

124. Ibid., pp. 119–21.

125. Quote from ibid., p. 123.

126. Quoted in ibid., p. 127.

127. Quotes from ibid., p. 133.

128. My historical analysis is a mere gloss of George R. Stewart's classic, *Names on the Land: An Historical Account of Placenaming in the United States*, 4th ed. (San Francisco: Lexikos, 1982); quotes from pp. 11–12. Columbus quote from J. M. Cohen, ed. and trans., *The Four Voyages of Christopher Columbus* (London: Penguin Books, 1969), p. 2.

129. Stewart, *Names on the Land*, pp. 23, 315.

130. Charge quoted from USGS Board on Geographic Names Web site: http://geonames.usgs.gov, accessed December 30, 2007.

131. For the procedure, see "How Names Are Approved," USGS Astrogeology Research Program, http://planetarynames.wr.usgs.gov/approved.html, accessed December 31, 2007.

132. "Sources of Planetary Names," USGS Astrogeology Research Program: http://planetarynames.wr.usgs.gov/jsp/append4.jsp, accessed December 30, 2007.

133. This synopsis distills a wonderful, dialogue-rich passage in Henry S. F. Cooper, Jr., *Imaging Saturn: The Voyager Flights to Saturn* (New York: Holt, Rinehart and Winston, 1982), pp. 99–103.

134. Incident reported in Nicks, *Far Travelers*, p. 76. Quote on "no geology" from Bruce Murray, in Swift, *Voyager Tales*, p. 217. End quote from Dethloff and Schorn, *Voyager's Grand Tour*, p. 145.

135. Nicks, *Far Travelers*, p. 121.

136. On Voyager 1 photo: Ben Evans with David M. Harland, *NASA's*, caption for color plate 1.

137. Best account is Miner, *Uranus*, pp. 153-54.

138. Ibid., pp. 141-43.

139. Ibid., pp. 156-57. The critical official documents are found in JPL, "Voyager: Project Plan, Part 2: Voyager Uranus/Interstellar Mission," PD 618-5, Part 2 (July 22, 1981), JPL Archives. The option had long been retained; see, for example, Decision Paper, AD/Deputy Administrator to S/Associate Administrator for Space Science, October 29, 1975, Selection of a Uranus Mission Option, in which "one spacecraft is launched on a trajectory that retains the Uranus targeting option."

140. The most useful document is JPL, "Voyager: Project Plan, Part 2"; quotes from p. 3-1. For a brief assessment of what the reduced staffing meant, see Ellis Miner, in Swift, *Voyager Tales*, p. 309.

CHAPTER 15. CRUISE

141. For background on the DSN, see Craig B. Waff, "The Road to the Deep Space Network," *IEEE Spectrum* (April 1993): 50-57, and "The Struggle for the Outer Planets," *Astronomy* 17, no. 9 (Sept. 1989): 33-52, and for a good general survey, Douglas J. Mudgway, *Uplink-Downlink: A History of the Deep Space Network 1957-1997*. NASA SP-2001-4227 (Washington, D.C.: NASA, 2001). Also useful for contemporary status, Roger Ludwig and Jim Taylor, "Voyager Telecommunications," JPL DESCANSO, Deep Space Communications and Navigation Systems, Design and Performance Summary Series (n.d.). On the role of Pioneer, see Wolverton, *The Depths of Space*, pp. 184-85.

142. See Mudgway, *Uplink-Downlink*, pp. xliv-xlvi; Nicks, *Far Travelers*, pp. 157-58.

143. JPL, *The Voyager Uranus Travel Guide*, p. 24.

144. I follow Miner, *Uranus*, p. 178.

145. Ibid., pp. 178-80. Quote on watch battery: Ben Evans with David M. Harland, *NASA's*, p. 172.

146. Miner, *Uranus*, pp. 180-81; Douglas J. Mudgway, *Uplink-Downlink*, pp. 193-96.

147. Mudgway, *Uplink-Downlink*, p. 200.

148. Ibid., p. 201.

149. Ibid., pp. 202-3.

150. Miner, *Uranus*, p. 182.

151. Mudgway, *Uplink-Downlink*, p. 203.

152. Miner, *Uranus*, pp. 177–86.

153. Jay T. Bergstralh, ed., *Uranus and Neptune: Proceedings of a Workshop Held in Pasadena, California, February 6–8, 1984*, NASA Conference Publication 2330 (Washington, D.C.: NASA, 1984).

154. I follow Miner, *Uranus*, p. 186. Quote from JPL, *The Voyager Uranus Travel Guide*, pp. 9, 6; on ring discovery, p. 17.

155. Miner, *Uranus*, pp. 186–89. For a more accessible review, see JPL, *Voyager Uranus Travel Guide*, pp. 19–24, and for a copy of the master timeline, p. 77.

156. Miner, *Uranus*, pp. 288–89.

CHAPTER 16. ENCOUNTER: URANUS

157. JPL, "Voyager. Project Plan: Part 2," pp. 3–4, 5–6. See also Miner, *Uranus*, p. 195.

158. Miner, *Uranus*, pp. 195–96.

159. Ibid., p. 196.

160. JPL, *The Voyager Uranus Travel Guide*, Voyager Project Document no. 618-150 (Pasadena, Calif.: Caltech, 1985), p. 6. The projected record of what Voyager 2 might find is in *The Voyager Uranus Travel Guide*, pp. 79–94, and the actual record of results is in Miner, *Uranus*, pp. 190–93, 195–96.

161. Miner, *Uranus*, pp. 297–98.

162. Ibid., pp. 198–200, 203. For an interesting comparison, see how deeds matched expectations in JPL, *Voyager Uranus Travel Guide*, and JPL, "Voyager. Project Plan. Part 2: Voyager Uranus/Interstellar Mission."

163. Miner, *Uranus*, pp. 201–202, 207; quote from p. 202.

164. Ibid., pp. 210–78. For the best quasi-popular summary, see the special issue of *Science* 233 (July 4, 1986): 39–107; E. D. Miner and E. C. Stone, "Voyager at Uranus," *Journal of the British Interplanetary Society* 41 (1988): 49–62.

165. Miner, *Uranus*, pp. 282–84; names on pp. 282–83; descriptions from pp. 285–319, and quote from p. 319. For fuller technical account, see also published articles, especially the special issue of *Science*.

166. Von Braun story in Wolverton, *The Depths of Space*, p. 127.

167. James Van Allen, "Space Science, Space Technology, and the Space Station," *Scientific American* 254 (January 1986): 32–39, and "Myths and Realities of Space Flight," *Science* 232 (May 30, 1986): 1075–76.

168. JPL efforts to avoid conflict and Beggs's response reported by Charles Kohlhase in *Voyager Tales*, p. 96.

169. Miner, *Uranus*, pp. 207–8.

170. Murray, *Journey into Space*, p. 235. The contest among competing space interests has a long trail of literature. An interesting survey of public opinion is Roger D. Launius, "Public Opinion Polls and Perceptions of US Human Spaceflight," *Space Policy* 19 (2003): 163–75. For particulars cited in text, see the following: for Apollo's oversize profile, see Etzioni, *The Moon-Doggle*, pp. 13–14; for Skylab competition, see Morrison and Samz, *Voyage to Jupiter*, p. 101; Kraemer, *Beyond the Moon*, pp. xvi–xviii.

171. Miner and Wessen, *Neptune*, pp. 265–67.

172. Robert D. Ballard, *The Eternal Darkness: A Personal History of Deep-Sea Exploration* (Princeton, N.J.: Princeton University Press, 2000), p. 227.

173. See Nicks, *Far Travelers*, esp. pp. 190, 245–48, 250; quote from p. 245.

174. Statistics from Newby, *The Rand McNally World Atlas of Exploration*, p. 135.

175. Quote from Tim Jeal, *Stanley: The Impossible Life of Africa's Greatest Explorer* (New Haven, Conn.: Yale University Press, 2007), p. 111.

176. Cherry-Garrard, *The Worst Journey in the World*, pp. 606, 613, 642.

177. Nicks, *Far Travelers*, p. 254.

178. The story is told with fascinating detail and empathy in Connolly and Anderson, *First Contact*. For a rawer version, see Leahy and Crain, *The Land That Time Forgot*.

179. Columbus quote from Morison, *The Great Explorers*, p. 403. Díaz, *The Conquest of New Spain*, pp. 59, 64–65.

180. Diaz, *Conquest*, pp. 60–61.

181. Quotes from Jeal, *Stanley*, pp. 358–59.

182. For an interesting survey, see James G. Bellingham and Kanna Rajan, "Robotics in Remote and Hostile Environments," *Science* 318 (Nov. 16, 2007): 1098–1102.

183. Stone quote in Swift, *Voyager Tales*, p. 57. Nicks quote from Nicks, *Far Travelers*, p. 32.

184. Carl Sagan, *Cosmos* (New York: Random House, 1980), p. 125; Nicks, *Far Travelers*, p. 32; Murray, quoted in Swift, *Voyager Tales*, pp. 210–11.

185. Miner, *Uranus*, pp. 202–3.

186. Ibid., pp. 206–7.

CHAPTER 17. CRUISE

187. On sources of Neptune information at the time, see Miner and Wessen, *Neptune*, pp. 1–62.

188. My sources for this phase of the journey are Miner and Wessen, *Neptune*, with Miner quote from p. 147, and "better spacecraft" quote, p. 157;

Kohlhase, ed., *The Voyager Neptune Travel Guide*; and Evans with Harland, *NASA's*. On staffing: see Ellis Miner, p. 309, and Charles Kohlhase, p.89, in Swift, *Voyager Tales*.

189. Quote from Miner and Wessen, *Neptune*, p. 147. The phrase refers to a Larry McMurtry novel of that name, released as a Hollywood movie in 1971.

190. Jay T. Bergstralh, ed., *Uranus and Neptune*. On staffing: see Ellis Miner, p. 309, and Charles Kohlhase, p. 89, in Swift, *Voyager Tales*. Quotes from Evans with Harland, *NASA's*, pp. 204, 206, and Kohlhase, *Voyager Neptune*, pp. 123-29, 136 (this book is probably the best single source). Transmission numbers from Miner and Wessen, *Neptune*, p. 147.

191. Miner and Wessen, *Neptune*, pp. 147-49; Kohlhase, *Voyager Neptune*, pp. 78-80; Evans with Harland, *NASA's*, pp. 202-4.

192. Miner and Wessen, *Neptune*, pp. 158-60.

193. Evans with Harland, *NASA's*, pp. 204-6. Best summary is in Miner and Wessen, *Neptune*, pp. 158-66.

194. Kohlhase, *Voyager Neptune*, p. 72.

195. Best account is in Evans with Harland, *NASA's*, p. 206. Eight years reference and quote: from Kohlhase, *Voyager Neptune*, p. 68. Miner and Wessen, *Neptune*, p. 167; Evans with Harland, *NASA's*, p. 206.

196. See Miner and Wessen, *Neptune*, pp. 154-56. See also Kohlhase, *Voyager Neptune*, pp. 73-74, 89.

197. Miner and Wessen, *Neptune*, pp. 155-56.

198. Best summary in Kohlhase, *Voyager Neptune*, pp. 77-78.

199. For partial listing of stresses, Dethloff and Schorn, *Voyager's Grand Tour*, p. 141.

200. Quoted by Charles Kohlhase, in Swift, *Voyager Tales*, p. 88. Miner quote from Swift, *Voyager Tales*, p. 311.

201. On Humboldt, see Helmut de Terra, *Humboldt: The Life and Times of Alexander von Humboldt 1769-1859* (New York: Octagon Books, 1979); on the Institut d'Egypte, see Nina Burleigh, *Mirage* (New York: HarperCollins, 2007); on the *Challenger* expedition, see Richard Corfield, *The Silent Landscape: The Scientific Voyage of the HMS Challenger* (Washington, D.C.: Joseph Henry Press, 2003).

202. There are many accounts available; a good popular version that grants special attention to Steller is Corey Ford, *Where the Sea Breaks Its Back* (Anchorage: Alaska Northwest Books, 1966).

203. Numbers from Eric Linklater, *The Voyage of the Challenger* (Garden City, N.Y.: Doubleday, 1972), p. 270, and quotes from p. 24. For a good com-

parison with modern oceanographic discoveries, see Corfield, *The Silent Landscape*, op. cit.

204. The plaque briefly flashed onto the screen before the spacecraft blasts off appears to identify it as one of the Pioneers.

205. The story of oceanic research has become a growth industry. I found particularly helpful as a compendium of recent discoveries Tony Koslow, *The Silent Deep: The Discovery, Ecology, and Conservation of the Deep Sea* (Chicago: University of Chicago Press, 2007). For a detailed examination of one career as it evolved through the broader field, see Henry Menard, *The Ocean of Truth: A Personal History of Global Tectonics* (Princeton, N.J.: Princeton University Press, 1986), and for the larger research context, Jacob Darwin Hamblin, *Oceanographers and the Cold War: Disciples of Marine Science* (Seattle: University of Washington Press, 2005).

206. See Ballard, *The Eternal Darkness*, p. 5.

207. The *Challenger* story has been oft-told. Koslow, *Silent Deep*, op. cit, provides a useful sketch. For accounts both more thorough and more popular, see, respectively, Corfield, *The Silent Landscape*, and Linklater, *The Voyage of the Challenger*.

208. Ballard, *The Eternal Darkness*, pp. 225-31, and in "The Explorers," *The Universe Beneath the Sea* (Beverly Hills, Calif.: Oxford Television Co., 1999).

CHAPTER 18. ENCOUNTER: NEPTUNE

209. My account closely follows Miner and Wessen, *Neptune*, pp. 174-76. For the official documentation, see JPL, "Voyager. Project Plan: Part 3: Voyager Neptune/Interstellar Mission. Revision A," JPL Archives 44, no. 48.

210. Miner and Wessen, *Neptune*, pp. 174-76; Kohlhase quote and estimates from Kohlhase, ed., *Voyager Neptune Travel Guide*, p. 89.

211. While most encounters were given in local time at JPL, this one was recorded officially in UTC (coordinated universal time), which results in 3:56 UTC on August 25, or 11:56 EDT August 24. The usual date for the encounter is thus listed as August 25, 1989. See E. C. Stone and E. D. Miner, "The Voyager 2 Encounter with the Neptunian System," *Science* 246 (December 15, 1989): 1418.

212. I follow Miner and Wessen, *Neptune*, pp. 176-81.

213. Ibid., p. 181.

214. Ibid.

215. Ibid., pp. 181-82.

216. Information and paraphrases from Miner and Wessen, *Neptune*, pp. 255-61.

217. Source: ibid., p. 259.

218. Wilson, *I.G.Y*, pp. 162-63.

219. Rachel Carson, *The Sea Around Us*, rev. ed. (New York: New American Library, 1961), pp. 196, 123.

220. Wilson, *I.G.Y*, p. 245. For an overview of exploring marine geology, see H. William Menard, "Very Like a Spear," in Cecil Schneer, ed., *Two Hundred Years of Geology in America: Proceedings of the New Hampshire Bicentennial Conference on the History of Geology* (Hanover, N.H.: University Press of New England, 1979), p. 21. Menard published a fuller, book-length personal survey of the revolution with *The Ocean of Truth: A Personal History of Global Tectonics* (Princeton, N.J.: Princeton University Press, 1986).

221. Wilson, *I.G.Y*, p. 190.

222. Useful summary of field in Dethloff and Schorn, *Voyager's Grand Tour*, pp. 146-53; Kuiper identification on p. 147. On the USAF series, see G. P. Kuiper, ed., *The Solar System*, 4 vols. (Chicago: University of Chicago Press, 1953-62). Also: Harold C. Urey, *The Planets: Their Origin and Development* (New Haven, Conn.: Yale University Press, 1952).

223. Robert Baker, *Astronomy*, 8th ed. (New York: D. Van Nostrand Co., 1964), p. 209. G. P. Kuiper, ed., *The Earth as a Planet*, Vol. 2: *The Solar System* (Chicago: University of Chicago Press, 1954), p. v.

224. On Pioneer 6, Wolverton, *The Depths of Space*, p. 126. On Voyager: JPL, *The Voyager Uranus Travel Guide*, p. 106; Bruce Murray, Michael Malin, and Ronald Greeley, *Earthlike Planets* (San Francisco: W. H. Freeman, 1981), p. xi. Any modern text will demonstrate the changes, but for a handy digest, see David J. Stevenson, "Planetary Science: A Space Odyssey," *Science* 287, no. 5455 (Feb. 11, 2000): 997-1005.

225. Nicks, *Far Travelers*, p. 219; Miner and Wessen, *Neptune*, p. xix; Van Allen quoted in Wolverton, *The Depths of Space*, p. 154.

226. Stone quoted in Swift, *Voyager Tales*, p. 38. Soderblom quoted in JPL video *And Then There Was Voyager*. I have confirmed his use of the quote and its original source by personal interview. The expression also appears in a slightly different version by Edward Stone, in Swift, *Voyager Tales*, p. 28.

227. For "legend and myth" quote: Roger Launius, foreword, in Kraemer, *Beyond the Moon*, p. x. Murray quoted in Swift, *Voyager Tales*, p. 215.

228. Murray, in Swift, *Voyager Tales*, p. 214.

229. Careful readers will note the irony of my criticizing one analogy by creating another. So be it.

230. Murray, in Swift, *Voyager Tales*, p. 212; Letter, Bruce Murray to Sir Arthur C. Clarke, April 23, 1980, JPL Archives, 223, no. 45.

231. Murray, in Swift, *Voyager Tales*, pp. 212-13.

232. Ibid., p. 213. On the federal budget, see Roger D. Launius, "Public Opinion Polls and Perceptions of US Human Spaceflight," *Space Policy* 19 (2003): 163-75. Data sources: Web sites for NASA, MLB, and NFL. For publishing and restaurants: "The 24-Billion-Dollar Question," PublishingTrends.com, www.publishingtrends.com/copy/batch0one/ 3-00-24billion.html (20 June 2008).

233. Murray, in Swift, *Voyager Tales*, pp. 215, 210.

CHAPTER 19. CRUISE

234. See Janet Vertesi, "'Seeing Like a Rover': Embodied Experience on the Mars Exploration Rover Mission," CHI 2008, April 5-10, 2008, Florence, Italy. I thank Valerie Olson for alerting me to this item and sending me a copy. On symbiosis between explorers and machines, see Nicks, *Far Travelers*, p. 94, and Ballard, *The Eternal Darkness*, pp. 299-311.

235. "NASA investigates virtual space," BBC News: http://news.bbc.co.uk/go/ pr/fr/-/2/hi/technology/7195718.stm, published 2008/01/18. I would like to thank Valerie Olson for correspondence early in this project in which she alerted me to the question of virtual exploration.

CHAPTER 20. LAST LIGHT

236. Several accounts exist. I follow Charlene Anderson, "Voyager's Last View," on the Planetary Society's Web site: www.planetary.org/explor/ topics/space_missions/voyager/family_portrait.html, accessed June 23, 2008; and the account given in Carl Sagan, *Pale Blue Dot* (New York: Ballantine, 1994), pp. 1-7; and the detailed recollection of Candice Hansen, in Swift, *Voyager Tales*, pp. 323-25. Constance Holden, "Voyager's Last Light," *Science* 248 (1990): 1308, gives the date as the "evening of candice 13 February 1990." Granted the long process, it spilled over into February 14, which is what has been generally reported.

237. Quote from Sagan, *Pale Blue Dot*, p. 5.

238. For an interesting account of the competing interests, see Candice Hansen, in Swift, *Voyager Tales*, p. 324.

239. Quote from Sagan, *Pale Blue Dot*, p. 5. An interesting UPI story by Rob Stein dates the event to February 13, 1990, a day earlier; see NASA Historical Collection, File 005578.

240. Woude and Hansen quoted in Stein, NASA Historical Reference Collection, File 005578; Stone quoted in John Noble Wilford, "From Voyager 1, a Space Snapshot of 6 Planets," *New York Times*, June 7, 1990.

PART 3: BEYOND THE UTMOST BOND:
JOURNEY TO THE STARS

CHAPTER 21. VOYAGER INTERSTELLAR MISSION

1. Best summaries: Miner and Wessen, *Neptune*, pp. 182-84, and Kohlhase, ed., *The Voyager Neptune Travel Guide*, pp. 151-54.

2. On costs: JPL, *Voyager Uranus Travel Guide*, pp. 105-6. On prospects for shutting down: Andrew Lawler, "NASA Plans to Turn Off Several Satellites," *Science* 307 (March 11, 2005): 1541; Tony Reichhardt, "NASA's Funding Shortfall Means Journey's End for Voyager Probes," *Nature* 434 (March 10, 2005): 125, which lists the costs as $4.2 million annually. The discrepancy seems to derive from the cost of both spacecraft and data analysis.

3. Sources on heliosheath are many. Good diagram and brief explanation on NASA JPL Web site: www.voyager.jpl/nasa.gov/mission/mission .html, accessed June 22, 2008. For what mission planners expected, see Kohlhase, ed., *The Voyager Neptune Travel Guide*, pp. 151-54, and Miner and Wessen, *Neptune*, pp. 182-84.

4. Christian quoted in "Voyager 2 Proves Solar System Is Squashed," JPL Voyager Web site: www.voyager.jpl.nasa.gov/news/voyager_squashed .html, accessed June 22, 2008.

5. See Kohlhase, *Voyager Neptune Travel Guide*, p. 153.

6. Timetables: Miner and Wessen, *Neptune*, p. 184; Kohlhase, *Voyager Neptune Travel Guide*, p. 155, and 155-67 passim.

CHAPTER 22. FAR TRAVELERS

7. Sources: Wolverton, *The Depths of Space*; data, p. 225. See also the NASA Pioneer Web site for technical information and dates. Velocity calculations from JPL Web site on Solar System Dynamics, Horizon System: http://ssd.jpl.nasa.gov/?horizons.

8. Calculations from JPL Web site on Solar System Dynamics, Horizon System: http://ssd.jpl.nasa.gov/?horizons. Other information from Wolverton, *Depths of Space*, p. 225, and NASA Pioneer mission Web sites.

9. On the fate of Columbus's ships, see Morison, *The Great Explorers*, on the *Niña*, p. 386. The *Caird* was preserved at Dulwich College, South London, then did a stint at the National Maritime Museum before returning to Dulwich and a career of exhibitions.

10. The best composite account is in Wikipedia; accessed June 25, 2008.

11. Vessel history from ibid.

12. Alicia Chang, "New tasks given to old NASA spacecraft," AP, reported on *Yahoo! News*, July 3, 2007. Plans include redirecting the Deep Impact spacecraft into use as an observatory, although this was part of its two-phase mission.

CHAPTER 23. NEW WORLDS, NEW LAWS

13. Direct quotes and intervening passages (paraphrased) are from Jeal, *Stanley*, p. 225.

14. Best source on Portuguese expansion is Newitt, *A History of Portuguese Overseas Expansion*; for the origins, see p. 41.

15. The story of Arvid Pardo and the "common heritage" concept is a well-told tale, but see George V. Galdorisi and Kevin R. Vienna, *Beyond the Law of the Sea: New Directions for U.S. Oceans Policy* (Westport, Conn.: Praeger, 1997), p. 25 for the observation that the concept, and nearly the language, was in American policy, additional fallout from the Antarctic Treaty.

16. "Treaty on Principles Governing the Activities of States in the Exploration and Use of Outer Space, including the Moon and Other Celestial Bodies," U.S. Department of State; www.state.gov/t/ac/trt/5181.htm, accessed June 26, 2008.

CHAPTER 24. VOYAGER'S VOICE

17. Sagan quoted in Tom Head, ed., *Conversation with Carl Sagan* (Jackson: University of Mississippi Press, 2006), p. xvii.

18. Stone quoted in Swift, *Voyager Tales*, p. 39.

19. Carl Sagan, *Cosmos* (New York: Random House, 1980), pp. 120–21.

CHAPTER 25. VOYAGER'S RECORD

20. See Fimmel et al., *Pioneer*, pp. 248–50. Burgess offers a more detailed account in Burgess, *Far Encounter*, pp. 57–58.

21. Casani quote: October 16-17, 1974, Mariner Jupiter/Saturn 1977, Mission and Systems Design Review, Concern/Action Control Sheet, JPL Archives 36, no. 29. Quotes from Sagan, "For Future Times and Being," in Carl Sagan, et al., *Murmurs of Earth: The Voyager Interstellar Record* (New York: Random House, 1978), p. 11. My account of the golden record derives primarily from this source.

22. Sagan et al., *Murmurs*, preface, pp. 146, 162.

23. Sagan, "For Future Times and Beings," p. 37.

24. Sagan, et al., *Murmurs*, epilogue, p. 234; Sagan, "For Future Times and Beings," p. 37.

25. Sagan, "For Future Times and Beings," p. 37.

26. Linda Sagan, "A Voyager's Greetings," in Sagan et al., *Murmurs*, p. 125; Carl Sagan, "For Future Times and Beings," p. 23; F. D. Drake, "Foundations of the Voyager Record," pp. 47-53.

27. Sagan, *Murmurs*, epilogue, p. 236.

28. Christopher Columbus, *The Four Voyages*, pp. 118, 80.

29. Boswell, *The Life of Samuel Johnson*, p. 355.

30. Hakluyt, *Voyages and Discoveries*: Drake, p. 177; Cavendish, pp. 287-88. On Brûlé, see William H. Goetzmann and Glyndwr Williams, *The Atlas of North American Exploration* (New York: Prentice Hall, 1992), p. 59.

31. The Columbus story comes from Morison, *The Great Explorers*, p. 422.

32. Oliver quoted in Sagan, "For Future Times and Beings," p. 11. On the disposition of the records, see Letter, Robert A. Frosch to S. Dillon Ripley, Dec. 19, 1977, NASA History Office, File 005580. Interestingly, Sagan and Casani were denied copies. One might also note the slightly blasphemous associations possible between the Voyager golden record and Joseph Smith's golden plates, dug up across the Finger Lakes from Sagan's Laboratory for Planetary Studies—both metal tablets that record an era and identify its originators, subsequently buried deeply to preserve that memory, a record to be found ages hence, written in a peculiar language surely unintelligible to its eventual finder, save with a special apparatus by which to interpret it, a message ultimately that speaks to the character of its creators. The Voyager golden records and the gold plates of Moroni—the prophet of the space age channeling the prophet of Mormonism? Would an alien intelligence confronted with the association be a lumper or a splitter?

CHAPTER 26. VOYAGER'S RETURNS

33. Joseph Campbell, *The Hero with a Thousand Faces,* 2nd ed. (Princeton, N.J.: Princeton University Press, 1968), p. 3.
34. Ibid., pp. 11, 21, 30.
35. Ibid., pp. 245, 38.
36. Jordan Goodman, *The Rattlesnake* (London: Faber and Faber, 2005), pp. 18–19.
37. Stories on Hawkesworth and Forster from Lynne Withey, *Voyages of Discovery: Captain Cook and the Exploration of the Pacific* (Berkeley: University of California Press), pp. 175, 312–13.
38. Campbell, *Hero,* p. 193; Hakluyt, *Voyages and Discoveries,* p. 163.
39. Campbell, *Hero,* p. 217.

BEYOND TOMORROW

40. I follow the scenarios sketched in Kohlhase, ed., *The Voyager Neptune Travel Guide,* pp. 151–67. Other versions exist on the JPL Voyager Web site, particularly the projected scenario for shutting down instruments.
41. Miner quoted in Douglas Fulmer, "Memories of Voyager," *Ad Astra* (July/August 1993): 48. Laeser quote in Kohlhase, ed., *Voyager Neptune Travel Guide,* p. 205.
42. Haines quoted in Fulmer, "Memories of Voyager," p. 48; Stone, in Swift, *Voyager Tales,* p. 57.

Sources

Voyager: Seeking Newer Worlds in the Third Great Age of Discovery is a study—call it perhaps a meditation—about context. It is not a scholarly reconstruction based on original archives but one that seeks to achieve insights by arranging facts, many of which are common knowledge, and observations, few of which come from unexplored sources. It strives to generate new understanding by emphasizing comparisons, contrasts, and continuities.

Still, some work in archives was useful, and necessary. I have consulted only two such sets of primary documents: the JPL Archives and the NASA Historical Reference Collection at the NASA History Office. Each has guides accessible online. For NASA resources, see also Stephen J. Garber, compiler, *Research in NASA History: A Guide to the NASA History Program* (Washington, D.C.: NASA, June 1997), and the fine line of monographs the NASA History Office has sponsored.

Most of my research derives from published accounts. These fall into three general areas. Some—quite a few—deal specifically with Voyager, and I am happy to defer to them on matters of design, construction, and operations. Some pertain to exploration generally. Some are specific to the era under examination, particularly its institutions. Those works that I found most pertinent I have listed here. Since exploration is among the most heavily chartered historical literature around, I include only major works that I reviewed for several purposes, or to help establish general concepts. Books or articles consulted for a single fact or purpose are included in the notes where and when they are cited.

BOOKS (AND MAJOR ARTICLES) WHOLLY OR SIGNIFICANTLY ABOUT VOYAGER

Burgess, Eric. *Far Encounter: The Neptune System* (New York: Columbia University Press, 1991).

———. *Uranus and Neptune: The Distant Giants* (New York: Columbia University Press, 1988).

Butrica, Andrew J. "Voyager: The Grand Tour as Big Science." In Pamela E. Mack, ed. *From Engineering to Big Science: The NACA and NASA Collier Trophy Research Project Winners*. NASA SP-4219 (Washington, D.C.: NASA, 1998).

Cooper, Jr., Henry S. F. *Imaging Saturn: The Voyager Flights to Saturn* (New York: Holt, Rinehart and Winston, 1982).

Davies, J. K. "A Brief History of the Voyager Project," Part 1: *Spaceflight* 23 (March 1981); Part 2: *Spaceflight* 23 (March 1981); Part 3: *Spaceflight* 23 (May 1981); Part 4: *Spaceflight* 23 (Aug.–Sept. 1981); Part 5: *Spaceflight* 24 (Feb. 1982); Part 6: *Spaceflight* 24 (June 1982).

Davis, Joel. *Flyby: The Interplanetary Odyssey of Voyager 2* (New York: Atheneum, 1987).

Dethloff, Henry C., and Ronald A. Schorn. *Voyager's Grand Tour: To the Outer Planets and Beyond* (Washington, D.C.: Smithsonian Institution Press, 2003).

Evans, Ben, with David M. Harland. *NASA's Voyager Missions* (Chichester, UK: Springer Praxis, 2004).

Heacock, Raymond L. "The Voyager Spacecraft," Institution of Mechanical Engineers, *Proceedings 1980*, 194, no. 28 (1980).

JPL. *Voyager: The Grandest Tour: The Mission to the Outer Planets*. NASA CR-197708 (Pasadena, Calif.: JPL, 1991).

Kohlhase, Charles, ed. *The Voyager Neptune Travel Guide*. JPL Publication 89-24 (Pasadena, Calif.: JPL, 1989).

Kraemer, Robert S. *Beyond the Moon: A Golden Age of Planetary Exploration 1971–1978* (Washington, D.C.: Smithsonian Institution Press, 2000).

Littmann, Mark. *Planets Beyond: Discovering the Outer Solar System* (Mineola, N.Y.: Dover Publications, 2004; reprint of 1990 ed.).

Miner, Ellis D. *Uranus: The Planet, Rings, and Satellites* (Chichester, UK: Ellis Horwood, 1990).

Miner, Ellis D., and Randi R. Wessen. *Neptune: The Planet, Rings, and Satellites* (Chichester, UK: Springer Praxis, 2002).

Morrison, David. *Voyages to Saturn.* NASA SP-451 (Washington, D.C.: NASA, 1982).

Morrison, David, and Jan Samz. *Voyage to Jupiter.* NASA SP-439 (Washington, D.C.: NASA, 1980).

Murray, Bruce. *Journey into Space: The First Thirty Years of Space Exploration* (New York: W. W. Norton, 1989).

Sagan, Carl. *Pale Blue Dot* (New York: Ballantine, 1994).

Sagan, Carl, et al. *Murmurs of Earth: The Voyager Interstellar Record* (New York: Random House, 1978).

Stone, E. C. "Voyager Mission: Encounters with Saturn," *J. Geophys. Res.* 88, no. A11 (Nov. 1983): 8639–42.

———. "The Voyager Mission Through the Jupiter Encounters," *J. Geophys. Res.* 86, no. A10 (Sept. 1981): 8123–24.

Stone, E. C., and A. L. Lane. "Voyager 1 Encounter with the Jovian System," *Science* 204, no. 4396 (June 1, 1979): 945–48.

———. "Voyager 2 Encounter with the Jovian System," *Science* 206, no. 4421 (Nov. 23, 1979): 925–27.

Stone, E. C., and E. D. Miner. "Voyager 1 Encounter with the Saturnian System," *Science* 212, no. 4491 (Apr. 10, 1981): 159–63.

———. "Voyager 2 Encounter with the Saturnian System," *Science* 215, no. 4532 (Jan. 29, 1982): 499–504.

———. "Voyager 2 Encounter with the Uranian System," *Science* 233 (1986): 39–43.

———. "Voyager 2 Encounter with the Neptunian System," *Science* 246, no. 4936 (Dec. 15, 1989): 1417–21.

Swift, David W. *Voyager Tales: Personal Views of the Grand Tour* (Reston, Va.: AIAA, 1997).

Voyager Mission Planning Office Staff. *Voyager Uranus Travel Guide.* JPL D-2580 (Pasadena, Calif.: JPL, August 1985).

BOOKS ABOUT EXPLORATION, INCLUDING SPACE EXPLORATION

Atlas of Exploration (New York: Oxford University Press, 1997).

Baker, J. N. L. *A History of Geographical Discovery and Exploration* (New York: Cooper Square Publishers, 1967).

Ballard, Robert D. *The Eternal Darkness: A Personal History of Deep-Sea Exploration* (Princeton, N.J.: Princeton University Press, 2000).

Broad, William J. *The Universe Below: Discovering the Secrets of the Deep Sea* (New York: Simon and Schuster, 1997).

Burrows, William. *Exploring Space: Voyages in the Solar System and Beyond* (New York: Random House, 1990).

——. *This New Ocean: The Story of the First Space Age* (New York: Random House, 1998).

Carson, Rachel. *The Sea Around Us* (New York: Oxford University Press, 1951; rev., 1961 ed.).

Clarke, Arthur C. *The Exploration of Space* (New York: Harper and Brothers, 1951).

Dick, Steven J., and Roger D. Launius, eds. *Critical Issues in the History of Spaceflight*. NASA SP-2006-4702 (Washington, D.C.: NASA, 2006).

Fernández-Armesto, Felipe. *Pathfinders: A Global History of Exploration* (New York: W. W. Norton, 2006).

——, ed. *The Times Atlas of World Exploration* (New York: HarperCollins, 1991).

Fimmel, Richard O., James Van Allen, and Eric Burgess. *Pioneer: First to Jupiter, Saturn, and Beyond*. NASA SP-446 (Washington, D.C.: NASA, 1980).

Foerstner, Abigail. *James Van Allen: The First Eight Billion Miles* (Iowa City: University of Iowa Press, 2007).

Goetzmann, William H. *Exploration and Empire* (New York: Knopf, 1966).

——. *New Lands, New Men: The United States and the Second Great Age of Discovery* (New York: Viking, 1986).

Hakluyt, Richard. *Voyages and Discoveries: The Principal Navigations, Voyages, Traffiques and Discoveries of the English Nation*. Ed. and abridged by Jack Beeching (New York: Penguin, 1973).

Harvey, Brian. *Russia in Space: The Failed Frontier?* (Chichester, UK: Springer Praxis, 2001).

——. *Russian Planetary Exploration: History, Development, Legacy and Prospects* (Chichester, UK: Springer Praxis, 2007).

Kilgore, DeWit Douglas. *Astrofuturism: Science, Race, and Visions of Utopia in Space* (Philadelphia: University of Pennsylvania Press, 2003).

Koppes, Clayton R. *JPL and the American Space Program* (New Haven, Conn.: Yale University Press, 1982).

Koslow, Tony. *The Silent Deep: The Discovery, Ecology, and Conservation of the Deep Sea* (Chicago: University of Chicago Press, 2007).

Launius, Roger D. *Frontiers of Space Exploration*, 2nd ed. (Westport, Conn.: Greenwood Press, 2004).

Launius, Roger D., and Howard E. McCurdy. *Imagining Space: Achievements, Predictions, Possibilities 1950–2050* (San Francisco: Chronicle Books, 2001).

——. *Robots in Space: Technology, Evolution, and Interplanetary Travel* (Baltimore, Md.: Johns Hopkins University Press, 2008).

Lewis, Richard S. *From Vinland to Mars: A Thousand Years of Exploration* (New York: Quadrangle Books, 1976).

Logsdon, John M., ed., with Amy Paige Snyder, Roger D. Launius, Stephen J. Garber, and Regan Anne Newport. *Exploring the Unknown: Selected Documents in the History of the U.S. Civil Space Program, Volume IV: Exploring the Cosmos*. NASA SP-4407 (Washington, D.C.: NASA, 2001).

Logsdon, John M., ed., with Dwayne A. Day, and Roger D. Launius. *Exploring the Unknown: Selected Documents in the History of the U.S. Civil Space Program, Volume II: External Relationships*. NASA SP-4407 (Washington, D.C.: NASA, 1996).

Logsdon, John M., ed., with Linda J. Lear, Janelle Warren Findley, Ray A. Williamson, and Dwayne A. Day. *Exploring the Unknown: Selected Documents in the History of the U.S. Civil Space Program, Volume I: Organizing for Exploration*. NASA SP-4407 (Washington, D.C.: NASA, 1996).

Logsdon, John M., ed., with Ray A. Williamson, Roger D. Launius, Russell J. Acker, Stephen J. Garber, and Jonathan L. Friedman. *Exploring the Unknown: Selected Documents in the History of the U.S. Civil Space Program, Volume II: External Relationships*. NASA SP-4407 (Washington, D.C.: NASA, 1999).

Logsdon, John M., ed., with Roger D. Launius, David H. Onkst, and Stephen J. Garber. *Exploring the Unknown: Selected Documents in the History of the U.S. Civil Space Program, Volume III: Using Space*. NASA SP-4407 (Washington, D.C.: NASA, 1998).

Logsdon, John M., ed., with Stephen J. Garber, Roger D. Launius, and Ray A. Williamson. *Exploring the Unknown: Selected Documents in the History of the U.S. Civil Space Program, Volume VI: Space and Earth Science*. NASA SP-4407 (Washington, D.C.: NASA, 2004).

McDougall, Walter A. *The Heavens and the Earth: A Political History of the Space Age* (New York: Basic Books, 1985).

Menard, Henry. *Islands* (New York: Scientific American, 1986).

——. *The Ocean of Truth: A Personal History of Global Tectonics* (Princeton, N.J.: Princeton University Press, 1986).

Morison, Samuel Eliot. *The Great Explorers: The European Discovery of America* (New York: Oxford University Press, 1978).

Mudgway, Douglas J. *Uplink-Downlink: A History of the Deep Space Network 1957–1997*. NASA SP-2001-4227 (Washington, D.C.: NASA, 2001).

Newell, Homer E. *Beyond the Atmosphere: Early Years of Space Science*. NASA SP-4211 (Washington, D.C.: NASA, 1980).

Newitt, Malyn. *A History of Portuguese Overseas Expansion, 1400–1668* (New York: Routledge, 2005).

Nicks, Oran. *Far Travelers: The Exploring Machines*. NASA SP-480 (Washington, D.C.: NASA, 1985).

Parry, J. H. *The Age of Reconnaissance: Discovery, Exploration, and Settlement, 1450–1650* (New York: Praeger, 1969).

——. *The Discovery of the Sea* (Berkeley: University of California Press, 1981).

Pyne, Stephen J. *How the Canyon Became Grand: A Brief History* (New York: Viking, 1998).

——. *The Ice: A Journey to Antarctica* (Iowa City: University of Iowa Press, 1986).

——. "Seeking Newer Worlds: An Historical Context for Space Exploration," pp. 7–36. In Steven J. Dick and Roger D. Launius, eds., *Critical Issues in the History of Spaceflight* (Washington, D.C.: NASA, 2006).

Roland, Alex, ed. *A Spacefaring People: Perspectives on Early Space Flight* (Washington, D.C.: Government Printing Office, 1985).

Scammel, G. V. *The World Encompassed: The First European Maritime Empires c. 800–1650* (Berkeley: University of California Press, 1981).

Siddiqi, Asif A. *Deep Space Chronicle: A Chronology of Deep Space and Planetary Probes 1958–2000*. Monographs in Aerospace History, No. 24. NASA SP-2002-4524 (Washington, D.C.: NASA, 2002).

Westwick, Peter J. *Into the Black: JPL and the American Space Program 1976–2004* (New Haven, Conn.: Yale University Press, 2007).

Wilson, J. Tuzo. *I.G.Y.: The Year of the New Moons* (New York: Alfred Knopf, 1961).

Wolfe, Harry. *The Transits of Venus* (Princeton, N.J.: Princeton University Press, 1959).

Wolverton, Mark. *The Depths of Space: The Story of the Pioneer Planetary Probes* (Washington, D.C.: Joseph Henry Press, 2004).

USEFUL WEB SITES (ALL ACCESSED NOVEMBER 1, 2008)

JPL

JPL maintains two sites that are particularly pertinent, one on Voyager itself and one on solar system dynamics (Horizons) by which it is possible to calculate the ephemeris for both spacecraft.
On Voyager: http://voyager.jpl.nasa.gov/index.html
Horizons: http://ssd.jpl.nasa.gov/?horizons

NASA

NASA has several useful sites on Voyager and on historical research.
For Voyager: http://www.nasa.gov/mission_pages/voyager/index.html
and http://nssdc.gsfc.nasa.gov/planetary/voyager.html
For historical publications, archives, and services, see:
http://history.nasa.gov/series95.html

THE PLANETARY SOCIETY

See: http://www.planetary.org/explore/topics/space_missions/voyager/

USGS ASTROGEOLOGY RESEARCH PROGRAM

See: http://astrogeology.usgs.gov/Missions/Voyager/

Index

PERFECT

PERFECT RIGOR

A Genius *and the* Mathematical
Breakthrough *of the* Century

MASHA GESSEN

HOUGHTON MIFFLIN HARCOURT • BOSTON / NEW YORK • 2009

For information about permission to reproduce selections from this book, write to Permissions, Houghton Mifflin Harcourt Publishing Company, 215 Park Avenue South, New York, New York 10003.

www.hmhbooks.com

Library of Congress Cataloging-in-Publication Data
Gessen, Masha.
Perfect rigor : a genius and the mathematical breakthrough
of the century / Masha Gessen.
p. cm.
Includes bibliographical references and index.
ISBN 978-0-15-101406-4
1. Perelman, Grigori, 1966–   2. Mathematicians—Russian (Federation)—
Biography.   3. Poincaré conjecture.   I. Title.
QA29.P6727G47   2009
510.92–dc22 [B]   2009014742

Book design by Brian Moore

Printed in the United States of America

DOC 10 9 8 7 6 5 4 3 2 1

Contents

A Problem for a Million Dollars

Numbers cast a magic spell over all of us, but mathematicians are especially skilled at imbuing figures with meaning. In the year 2000, a group of the world's leading mathematicians gathered in Paris for a meeting that they believed would be momentous. They would use this occasion to take stock of their field. They would discuss the sheer beauty of mathematics—a value that would be understood and appreciated by everyone present. They would take the time to reward one another with praise and, most critical, to dream. They would together try to envision the elegance, the substance, the importance of future mathematical accomplishments.

The Millennium Meeting had been convened by the Clay Mathematics Institute, a nonprofit organization founded by Boston-area businessman Landon Clay and his wife, Lavinia, for the purposes of popularizing mathematical ideas and encouraging their professional exploration. In the two years of its existence, the institute had set up a beautiful office in a building just outside Harvard Square in Cambridge, Massachusetts, and had handed out a few research awards. Now it had an ambitious plan for the future of mathematics, "to record the problems of the twentieth century that resisted challenge most successfully and that we would most like to see resolved," as Andrew Wiles, the British number theorist who had famously conquered Fermat's Last Theorem, put it. "We don't know how they'll be solved or when: it may be five years or it may be a hundred years. But we believe that somehow by solving these problems we will open up whole new vistas of mathematical discoveries and landscapes."

As though setting up a mathematical fairy tale, the Clay Institute named seven problems—a magic number in many folk traditions—and assigned the fantastical value of one million dollars for each one's solution. The reigning kings of mathematics gave lectures summarizing the problems. Michael Francis Atiyah, one of the previous century's most influential mathematicians, began by outlining the Poincaré Conjecture, formulated by Henri Poincaré in 1904. The problem was a classic of mathematical topology. "It's been worked on by many famous mathematicians, and it's still unsolved," stated Atiyah. "There have been many false proofs. Many people have tried and have made mistakes. Sometimes they discovered the mistakes themselves, sometimes their friends discovered the mistakes." The audience, which no doubt contained at least a couple of people who had made mistakes while tackling the Poincaré, laughed.

Atiyah suggested that the solution to the problem might come from physics. "This is a kind of clue—hint—by the teacher who cannot solve the problem to the student who is trying to solve it," he joked. Several members of the audience were indeed working on problems that they hoped might move mathematics closer to a victory over the Poincaré. But no one thought a solution was near.

True, some mathematicians conceal their preoccupations when they're working on famous problems—as Wiles had done while he was working on Fermat's Last—but generally they stay abreast of one another's research. And though putative proofs of the Poincaré Conjecture had appeared more or less annually, the last major breakthrough dated back almost twenty years, to 1982, when the American Richard Hamilton laid out a blueprint for solving the problem. He had found, however, that his own plan for the solution—what mathematicians call a program—was too difficult to follow, and no one else had offered a credible alternative. The Poincaré Conjecture, like Clay's other Millennium Problems, might never be solved.

Solving any one of these problems would be nothing short of a heroic feat. Each had claimed decades of research time, and many a mathematician had gone to the grave having failed to solve the problem with which he or she had struggled for years. "The Clay Mathematics Institute really wants to send a clear message, which is that mathematics is mainly valuable because of these immensely difficult problems, which are like the Mount Everest or the Mount Himalaya of mathematics," said the French mathematician Alain Connes, another twentieth-century giant. "And if we reach the peak, first of all, it will be extremely difficult—we might even pay the price of our lives or something like that. But what is true is that when we reach the peak, the view from there will be fantastic."

As unlikely as it was that anyone would solve a Millennium Problem in the foreseeable future, the Clay Institute nonetheless laid out a clear plan for giving each award. The rules stipulated that the solution to the problem would have to be presented in a refereed journal, which was, of course, standard practice. After publication, a two-year waiting period would begin, allowing the world mathematics community to examine the solution and arrive at a consensus on its veracity and authorship. Then a committee would be appointed to make a final recommendation on the award. Only after it had done so would the institute hand over the million dollars. Wiles estimated that it would take at least five years to arrive at the first solution—assuming that any of the problems was actually solved—so the procedure did not seem at all cumbersome.

Just two years later, in November 2002, a Russian mathematician posted his proof of the Poincaré Conjecture on the Internet. He was not the first person to claim he'd solved the Poincaré—he was not even the only Russian to post a putative proof of the conjecture on the Internet *that year*—but his proof turned out to be right.

And then things did not go according to plan—not the Clay Institute's plan or any other plan that might have struck a mathematician as reasonable. Grigory Perelman, the Russian, did not publish his work in a refereed journal. He did not agree to vet or even to review the explications of his proof written by others. He refused numerous job offers from the world's best universities. He refused to accept the Fields Medal, mathematics' highest honor, which would have been awarded to him in 2006. And then he essentially withdrew from not only the world's mathematical conversation but also most of his fellow humans' conversation.

Perelman's peculiar behavior attracted the sort of attention to the Poincaré Conjecture and its proof that perhaps no other story of mathematics ever had. The unprecedented magnitude of the award that apparently awaited him helped heat up interest too, as did a sudden plagiarism controversy in which a pair of Chinese mathematicians claimed they deserved the credit for proving the Poincaré. The more people talked about Perelman, the more he seemed to recede from view; eventually, even people who had once known him well said that he had "disappeared," although he continued to live in the St. Petersburg apartment that had been his home for many years. He did occasionally pick up the phone there—but only to make it clear that he wanted the world to consider him gone.

When I set out to write this book, I wanted to find answers to three questions: Why was Perelman able to solve the conjecture; that is, what was it about his mind that set him apart from all the mathematicians who had come before? Why did he then abandon mathematics and, to a large extent, the world? Would he refuse to accept the Clay prize money, which he deserved and most certainly could use, and if so, why?

This book was not written the way biographies usually are. I did not have extended interviews with Perelman. In fact, I had no conversations with him at all. By the time I started working on this project, he had cut off communication with all journalists and most people. That made my job more difficult—I had to imagine a person I had literally never met—but also more interesting: it was an investigation. Fortunately, most people who had been close to him and to the Poincaré Conjecture story agreed to talk to me. In fact, at times I thought it was easier than writing a book about a cooperating subject, because I had no allegiance to Perelman's own narrative and his vision of himself—except to try to figure out what it was.

1

Escape into the Imagination

A S ANYONE WHO has attended grade school knows, mathematics is unlike anything else in the universe. Virtually every human being has experienced that sense of epiphany when an abstraction suddenly makes sense. And while grade-school arithmetic is to mathematics roughly what a spelling bee is to the art of novel writing, the desire to understand patterns—and the childlike thrill of making an inscrutable or disobedient pattern conform to a set of logical rules—is the driving force of all mathematics.

Much of the thrill lies in the singular nature of the solution. There is only one right answer, which is why most mathematicians hold their field to be hard, exact, pure, and fundamental, even if it cannot precisely be called a science. The truth of science is tested by experiment. The truth of mathematics is tested by argument, which makes it more like philosophy, or, even better, the law, a discipline that also assumes the existence of a single truth. While the other hard sciences live in the laboratory or in the field, tended to by an army of technicians, mathematics lives in the mind. Its lifeblood is the thought process that keeps a mathematician turning in his sleep and waking with a jolt to an idea, and the conversation that alters, corrects, or affirms the idea.

"The mathematician needs no laboratories or supplies," wrote the Russian number theorist Alexander Khinchin. "A piece of paper, a pencil, and creative powers form the foundation of his work. If this is supplemented with the opportunity to use a more or less decent library and a dose of scientific enthusiasm (which nearly every mathematician possesses), then no amount of destruction can stop the creative work." The other sciences as they have been practiced since the early twentieth century are, by their very natures, collective pursuits; mathematics is a solitary process, but the mathematician is always addressing another similarly occupied mind. The tools of that conversation—the rooms where those essential arguments take place—are conferences, journals, and, in our day, the Internet.

That Russia produced some of the twentieth century's greatest mathematicians is, plainly, a miracle. Mathematics was antithetical to the Soviet way of everything. It promoted argument; it studied patterns in a country that controlled its citizens by forcing them to inhabit a shifting, unpredictable reality; it placed a premium on logic and consistency in a culture that thrived on rhetoric and fear; it required highly specialized knowledge to understand, making the mathematical conversation a code that was indecipherable to an outsider; and worst of all, mathematics laid claim to singular and knowable truths when the regime had staked its legitimacy on its own singular truth. All of this is what made mathematics in the Soviet Union uniquely appealing to those whose minds demanded consistency and logic, unattainable in virtually any other area of study. It is also what made mathematics and mathematicians suspect. Explaining what makes mathematics as important and as beautiful as mathematicians know it to be, the Russian algebraist Mikhail Tsfasman said, "Mathematics is uniquely suited to teaching one to distinguish right from wrong, the proven from the unproven, the probable from the improbable. It also teaches us to distinguish that which is probable and probably true from that which, while apparently probable, is an obvious lie. This is a part of mathematical culture that the [Russian] society at large so sorely lacks."

It stands to reason that the Soviet human rights movement was founded by a mathematician. Alexander Yesenin-Volpin, a logic theorist, organized the first demonstration in Moscow in December 1965. The movement's slogans were based on Soviet law, and its founders made a single demand: they called on the Soviet authorities to obey the country's written law. In other words, they demanded logic and consistency; this was a transgression, for which Yesenin-Volpin was incarcerated in prisons and psychiatric wards for a total of fourteen years and ultimately forced to leave the country.

Soviet scholarship, and Soviet scholars, existed to serve the Soviet state. In May 1927, less than ten years after the October Revolution, the Central Committee inserted into the bylaws of the USSR's Academy of Sciences a clause specifying just this. A member of the Academy may be stripped of his status, the clause stated, "if his activities are apparently aimed at harming the USSR." From that point on, every member of the Academy was presumed guilty of aiming to harm the USSR. Public hearings involving historians, literary scholars, and chemists ended with the scholars publicly disgraced, stripped of their academic regalia, and, frequently, jailed on treason charges. Entire fields of study—most notably genetics—were destroyed for apparently coming into conflict with Soviet ideology. Joseph Stalin personally ruled scholarship. He even published his own scientific papers, thereby setting the research agenda in a given field for years to come. His article on linguistics, for example, relieved comparative language study of a cloud of suspicion that had hung over it and condemned, among other things, the study of class distinctions in language as well as the whole field of semantics. Stalin personally promoted a crusading enemy of genetics, Trofim Lysenko, and apparently coauthored Lysenko's talk that led to an outright ban of the study of genetics in the Soviet Union.

What saved Russian mathematics from destruction by decree was a combination of three almost entirely unrelated factors. First, Russian mathematics happened to be uncommonly strong right when it might have suffered the most. Second, mathematics proved too obscure for the sort of meddling the Soviet leader most liked to exercise. And third, at a critical moment it proved immensely useful to the State.

In the 1920s and '30s, Moscow boasted a robust mathematical community; groundbreaking work was being done in topology, probability theory, number theory, functional analysis, differential equations, and other fields that formed the foundation of twentieth-century mathematics. Mathematics is cheap, and this helped: when the natural sciences perished for lack of equipment and even of heated space in which to work, the mathematicians made do with their pencils and their conversations. "A lack of contemporary literature was, to some extent, compensated by ceaseless scientific communication, which it was possible to organize and support in those years," wrote Khinchin about that period. An entire crop of young mathematicians, many of whom had received part of their education abroad, became fast-track professors and members of the Academy in those years.

The older generation of mathematicians—those who had made their careers before the revolution—were, naturally, suspect. One of them, Dimitri Egorov, the leading light of Russian mathematics at the turn of the twentieth century, was arrested and in 1931 died in internal exile. His crimes: he was religious and made no secret of it, and he resisted attempts to ideologize mathematics—for example, trying (unsuccessfully) to sidetrack a letter of salutation sent from a mathematicians' congress to a Party congress. Egorov's vocal supporters were cleansed from the leadership of Moscow mathematical institutions, but by the standards of the day, this was more of a warning than a purge: no area of study was banned, and no general line was imposed by the Kremlin. Mathematicians would have been well advised to brace for a bigger blow.

In the 1930s, a mathematical show trial was all set to go forward. Egorov's junior partner in leading the Moscow mathematical community was his first student, Nikolai Luzin, a charismatic teacher himself whose numerous students called their circle Luzitania, as though it were a magical country, or perhaps a secret brotherhood united by a common imagination. Mathematics, when taught by the right kind of visionary, does lend itself to secret societies. As most mathematicians are quick to point out, there are only a handful of people in the world who understand what the mathematicians are talking about. When these people happen to talk to one another—or, better yet, form a group that learns and lives in sync—it can be exhilarating.

"Luzin's militant idealism," wrote a colleague who denounced Luzin, "is amply expressed by the following quote from his report to the Academy on his trip abroad: 'It seems the set of natural numbers is not an absolutely objective formation. It seems it is a function of the mind of the mathematician who happens to be speaking of a set of natural numbers at the given moment. It seems there are, among the problems of arithmetic, those that absolutely cannot be solved.'"

The denunciation was masterful: the addressee did not need to know anything about mathematics and would certainly know that solipsism, subjectivity, and uncertainty were utterly un-Soviet qualities. In July 1936 a public campaign against the famous mathematician was launched in the daily *Pravda*, where Luzin was exposed as "an enemy wearing a Soviet mask."

The campaign against Luzin continued with newspaper articles, community meetings, and five days of hearings by an emergency committee formed by the Academy of Sciences. Newspaper articles exposed Luzin and other mathematicians as enemies because they published their work abroad. In other words, events unfolded in accordance with the standard show-trial scenario. But then the process seemed to fizzle out: Luzin publicly repented and was severely reprimanded although allowed to remain a member of the Academy. A criminal investigation into his alleged treason was quietly allowed to die.

Researchers who have studied the Luzin case believe it was Stalin himself who ultimately decided to stop the campaign. The reason, they think, is that mathematics is useless for propaganda. "The ideological analysis of the case would have devolved to a discussion of the mathematician's understanding of a natural number set, which seemed like a far cry from sabotage, which, in the Soviet collective consciousness, was rather associated with coal mine explosions or killer doctors," wrote Sergei Demidov and Vladimir Isakov, two mathematicians who teamed up to study the case when this became possible, in the 1990s. "Such a discussion would better be conducted using material more conducive to propaganda, such as, say, biology and Darwin's theory of evolution, which the great leader himself was fond of discussing. That would have touched on topics that were ideologically charged and easily understood: monkeys, people, society, and life itself. That's so much more promising than the natural number set or the function of a real variable."

Luzin and Russian mathematics were very, very lucky.

Mathematics survived the attack but was permanently hobbled. In the end, Luzin was publicly disgraced and dressed down for practicing mathematics: publishing in international journals, maintaining contacts with colleagues abroad, taking part in the conversation that is the life of mathematics. The message of the Luzin hearings, heeded by Soviet mathematicians well into the 1960s and, to a significant extent, until the collapse of the Soviet Union, was this: Stay behind the Iron Curtain. Pretend Soviet mathematics is not just the world's most progressive mathematics—this was its official tag line—but the world's only mathematics. As a result, Soviet and Western mathematicians, unaware of one another's endeavors, worked on the same problems, resulting in a number of double-named concepts such as the Chaitin-Kolmogorov complexities and the Cook-Levin theorem. (In both cases the eventual coauthors worked independently of each other.) A top Soviet mathematician, Lev Pontryagin, recalled in his memoir that during his first trip abroad, in 1958—five years after Stalin's death—when he was fifty years old and world famous among mathematicians, he had had to keep asking colleagues if his latest result was actually new; he did not really have another way of knowing.

"It was in the 1960s that a couple of people were allowed to go to France for half a year or a year," recalled Sergei Gelfand, a Russian mathematician who now runs the American Mathematics Society's publishing program. "When they went and came back, it was very useful for all of Soviet mathematics, because they were able to communicate there and to realize, and make others realize, that even the most talented of people, when they keep cooking in their own pot behind the Iron Curtain, they don't have the full picture. They have to speak with others, and they have to read the work of others, and it cut both ways: I know American mathematicians who studied Russian just to be able to read Soviet mathematics journals." Indeed, there is a generation of American mathematicians who are more likely than not to possess a reading knowledge of mathematical Russian—a rather specialized skill even for a native Russian speaker; Jim Carlson, president of the Clay Mathematics Institute, is one of them. Gelfand himself left Russia in the early 1990s because he was drafted by the American Mathematics Society to fill the knowledge gap that had formed during the years of the Soviet reign over mathematics: he coordinated the translation and publication in the United States of Russian mathematicians' accumulated work.

So some of what Khinchin described as the tools of a mathematician's labor—"a more or less decent library" and "ceaseless scientific communication"—were stripped from Soviet mathematicians. They still had the main prerequisites, though—"a piece of paper, a pencil, and creative powers"—and, most important, they had one another: mathematicians as a group slipped by the first rounds of purges because mathematics was too obscure for propaganda. Over the nearly four decades of Stalin's reign, however, it would turn out that nothing was too obscure for destruction. Mathematics' turn would surely have come if it weren't for the fact that at a crucial point in twentieth-century history, mathematics left the realm of abstract conversation and suddenly made itself indispensable. What ultimately saved Soviet mathematicians and Soviet mathematics was World War II and the arms race that followed it.

Nazi Germany invaded the Soviet Union on June 22, 1941. Three weeks later, the Soviet air force was gone: bombed out of existence in the airfields before most of the planes ever took off. The Russian military set about retrofitting civilian airplanes for use as bombers. The problem was, the civilian airplanes were significantly slower than the military ones, rendering moot everything the military knew about aim. A mathematician was needed to recalculate speeds and distances so the air force could hit its targets. In fact, a small army of mathematicians was needed. The greatest Russian mathematician of the twentieth century, Andrei Kolmogorov, returned to Moscow from the academics' wartime haven in Tatarstan and led a classroom full of students armed with adding machines in recalculating the Red Army's bombing and artillery tables. When this work was done, he set about creating a new system of statistical control and prediction for the Soviet military.

At the beginning of World War II, Kolmogorov was thirty-eight years old, already a member of the Presidium of the Soviet Academy of Sciences—making him one of a handful of the most influential academics in the empire—and world famous for his work in probability theory. He was also an unusually prolific teacher: by the end of his life he had served as an adviser on seventy-nine dissertations and had spearheaded both the math olympiads system and the Soviet mathematics-school culture. But during the war, Kolmogorov put his scientific career on hold to serve the Soviet state directly—proving in the process that mathematicians were essential to the State's very survival.

The Soviet Union declared victory—and the end of what it called the Great Patriotic War—on May 9, 1945. In August, the United States dropped atomic bombs on the Japanese cities of Hiroshima and Nagasaki. Stalin kept his silence for months afterward. When he finally spoke publicly, following his so-called re-election in February 1946, it was to promise the people of his country that the Soviet Union would surpass the West in developing its atomic capability. The effort to assemble an army of physicists and mathematicians to match the Manhattan Project's had by that time been under way for at least a year; young scholars had been recalled from the frontlines and even released from prisons in order to join the race for the bomb.

Following the war, the Soviet Union invested heavily in high-tech military research, building more than forty entire cities where scientists and mathematicians worked in secret. The urgency of the mobilization indeed recalled the Manhattan Project—only it was much, much bigger and lasted much longer. Estimates of the number of people engaged in the Soviet arms effort in the second half of the century are notoriously inaccurate, but they range as high as twelve million, with a couple million of them employed by military research institutions. For many years, a newly graduated young mathematician or physicist was more likely to be assigned to defense-related research than to a civilian institution. These jobs spelled nearly total scientific isolation: for defense employees, burdened by security clearances whether or not they actually had access to sensitive military information, any contact with foreigners was considered not just suspect but treasonous. In addition, some of these jobs required moving to the research towns, which provided comfortably cloistered social environments but no possibility for outside intellectual contact. The mathematician's pencil and paper could be useless tools in the absence of an ongoing mathematical conversation. So the Soviet Union managed to hide some of its best mathematical minds away, in plain sight.

Following Stalin's death, in 1953, the country shifted its stance on its relationship to the rest of the world: now the Soviet Union was to be not only feared but respected. So while it fell to most mathematicians to help build bombs and rockets, it fell to a select few to build prestige. Very slowly, in the late 1950s, the Iron Curtain began to open a tiny crack—not quite enough to facilitate much-needed conversation between Soviet and non-Soviet mathematicians but enough to show off some of Soviet mathematics' proudest achievements.

By the 1970s, a Soviet mathematics establishment had taken shape. It was a totalitarian system within a totalitarian system. It provided its members with not only work and money but also apartments, food, and transportation; it determined where they lived and when, where, and how they traveled for work or pleasure. To those in the fold, it was a controlling and strict but caring mother: her children were well nourished and nurtured, an undeniably privileged group compared with the rest of the country. When basic goods were scarce, official mathematicians and other scientists could shop at specially designated stores, which tended to be better stocked and less crowded than those open to the general public. Since for most of the Soviet century there was no such thing as a private apartment, regular Soviet citizens received their dwellings from the State; members of the science establishment were assigned apartments by their institutions, and these apartments tended to be larger and better located than their compatriots'. Finally, one of the rarest privileges in the life of a Soviet citizen—foreign travel—was available to members of the mathematics establishment. It was the Academy of Sciences, with the Party and the State security organizations watching over it, that decided if a mathematician could accept, say, an invitation to address a scholarly conference, who would accompany him on the trip, how long the trip would last, and, in many instances, where he would stay. For example, in 1970, the first Soviet winner of the Fields Medal, Sergei Novikov, was not allowed to travel to Nice to accept his award. He received it a year later, when the International Mathematical Union met in Moscow.

Even for members of the mathematical establishment, though, resources were always scarce. There were always fewer good apartments than there were people who desired them, and there were always more people wanting to travel to a conference than would be allowed to go. So it was a vicious, backstabbing little world, shaped by intrigue, denunciations, and unfair competition. The barriers to entry into this club were prohibitively high: a mathematician had to be ideologically reliable and personally loyal not only to the Party but to existing members of the establishment, and Jews and women had next to no chance of getting in.

One could easily be expelled by the establishment for misbehaving. This happened with Kolmogorov's student Eugene Dynkin, who fostered an atmosphere of unconscionable liberalism at a specialized mathematics school he ran in Moscow. Another of Kolmogorov's students, Leonid Levin, describes being ostracized for associating with dissidents. "I became a burden for everyone to whom I was connected," he wrote in a memoir. "I would not be hired by any serious research institution, and I felt I didn't even have the right to attend seminars, since participants had been instructed to inform [the authorities] whenever I appeared. My Moscow existence began to seem pointless." Both Dynkin and Levin emigrated. It must have been soon after Levin's arrival in the United States that he learned that a problem he had been describing at Moscow mathematics seminars (building in part on Kolmogorov's work on complexities) was the same problem U.S. computer scientist Stephen Cook had defined. Cook and Levin, who became a professor at Boston University, are considered coinventors of the NP-completeness theorem, also known as the Cook-Levin theorem; it forms the foundation of one of the seven Millennium Problems that the Clay Mathematics Institute is offering a million dollars to solve. The theorem says, in essence, that some problems are easy to formulate but require so many computations that a machine capable of solving them cannot exist.

And then there were those who almost never became members of the establishment: those who happened to be born Jewish or female, those who had had the wrong advisers at their universities, and those who could not force themselves to join the Party. "There were people who realized that they would never be admitted to the Academy and that the most they could hope for was being able to defend their doctoral dissertation at some institute in Minsk, if they could secure connections there," said Sergei Gelfand, the American Mathematics Society publisher, who happens to be the son of one of Russia's top twentieth-century mathematicians, Israel Gelfand, a student of Kolmogorov's. "These people attended seminars at the university and were officially on the staff of some research institute, say, of the timber industry. They did very good math, and at a certain point they even started having contacts abroad and could even get published occasionally in the West—it was hard, and they had to prove that they were not divulging state secrets, but it was possible. Some mathematicians came from the West, some even came for an extended stay because they realized there were a lot of talented people. This was unofficial mathematics."

One of the people who came for an extended stay was Dusa McDuff, then a British algebraist (and now a professor emeritus at the State University of New York at Stony Brook). She studied with the older Gelfand for six months and credits this experience with opening her eyes to both the way mathematics ought to be practiced—in part through continuous conversation with other mathematicians—and to what mathematics really is. "It was a wonderful education, in which reading Pushkin's *Mozart and Salieri* played as important a role as learning about Lie groups or reading Cartan and Eilenberg. Gelfand amazed me by talking of mathematics as though it were poetry. He once said about a long paper bristling with formulas that it contained the vague beginnings of an idea which he could only hint at and which he had never managed to bring out more clearly. I had always thought of mathematics as being much more straightforward: a formula is a formula, and an algebra is an algebra, but Gelfand found hedgehogs lurking in the rows of his spectral sequences!"

On paper, the jobs that members of the mathematical counterculture held were generally undemanding and unrewarding, in keeping with the best-known formula of Soviet labor: "We pretend to work, and they pretend to pay us." The mathematicians received modest salaries that grew little over a lifetime but that were enough to cover basic needs and allow them to spend their time on real research. "There was no such thing as thinking that you had to focus your work in some one narrow area because you have to write faster because you had to get tenure," said Gelfand. "Mathematics was almost a hobby. So you could spend your time doing things that would not be useful to anyone for the nearest decade." Mathematicians called it "math for math's sake," intentionally drawing a parallel between themselves and artists who toiled for art's sake. There was no material reward in this—no tenure, no money, no apartments, no foreign travel; all they stood to gain by doing brilliant work was the respect of their peers. Conversely, if they competed unfairly, they stood to lose the respect of their colleagues while gaining nothing. In other words, the alternative mathematics establishment in the Soviet Union was very much unlike anything else anywhere in the real world: it was a pure meritocracy where intellectual achievement was its own reward.

In after-hours lectures and seminars, the mathematical conversation in the Soviet Union was reborn, and the appeal of mathematics to a mind in search of challenge, logic, and consistency once again became evident. "In the post-Stalin Soviet Union it was one of the most natural ways for a freethinking intellectual to seek self-realization," said Grigory Shabat, a well-known Moscow mathematician. "If I had been free to choose any profession, I would have become a literary critic. But I wanted to work, not spend my life fighting the censors." Mathematics held out the promise that one could not only do intellectual work without State interference (if also without its support) but also find something not available anywhere else in late-Soviet society: a knowable singular truth. "Mathematicians are people possessed of a special intellectual honesty," Shabat continued. "If two mathematicians are making contradictory claims, then one of them is right and the other one is wrong. And they will definitely figure it out, and the one who was wrong will definitely admit that he was mistaken." The search for that truth could take long years—but in the late Soviet Union, time stood still, which meant that the inhabitants of the alternative mathematics universe had all the time they needed.

2

How to Make a Mathematician

N THE MID-1960S Professor Garold Natanson offered a graduate-study spot to a student of his, a woman named Lubov. One did not make this sort of offer lightly: female graduate students were notoriously unreliable, prone to pregnancy and other distracting pursuits. In addition, this particular student was Jewish, which meant that securing a spot for her would have required Professor Natanson to scheme, strategize, and call in favors: in the eyes of the system, Jews were even more unreliable than women, and convoluted discriminatory anti-Semitic practices carried the force of unwritten law. Natanson, a Jew himself, taught at the Herzen Pedagogical Institute, which ranked second to Leningrad State University and so was allowed to accept Jews as students and teachers—within reason, or what passed for it in the postwar Soviet Union. The student was older—she was nearing thirty, which placed her well beyond the usual Russian marrying-and-having-children threshold, so Natanson could be justified in assuming that she had resolved to devote her life entirely to mathematics.

Natanson was not entirely off the mark: the woman was indeed wholly devoted to mathematics. But she turned down his generous offer. She explained that she had recently married and planned to start a family, and with that she accepted a job teaching mathematics at a trade school and disappeared from the Leningrad mathematical scene for more than ten years.

Ten or twelve years was nothing in Soviet time. There was a bit of new housing construction in Leningrad, and some families were able to leave the crowded and crumbling city center for the new concrete towers on its outskirts. Clothing and food continued to be in short supply and of regrettable quality, but industrial production picked up a bit, so some of the new suburban dwellers could actually buy basic semiautomatic washing machines and television sets for their apartments. The televisions claimed to be black-and-white but showed mostly shades of gray, thereby providing an accurate visual reflection of reality. Other than that, little changed. Natanson continued to teach at the Herzen, which itself grew only more crowded and crumbling. His former student Lubov found him in his office. She was older and a bit heavier. She reported that she had indeed had a baby all those years ago, and now this baby was a schoolboy who exhibited a talent for mathematics. He had taken part in a district math competition in one of those newly constructed concrete suburbs where they now lived, and he had done well. In the timeless scheme of Russian mathematics, he was ready to take up where his mother had left off.

It all must have made perfect sense to Natanson. He himself hailed from a mathematical dynasty: his father, Isidor Natanson, was the author of the definitive Russian calculus textbook and had also taught at the Herzen, until his death, in 1963. Lubov's boy was entering fifth grade—the age at which he could begin appropriately rigorous mathematical study in a system that had been constructed over the years for the making of mathematicians. Natanson had his eye on a young mathematics coach to whom he could direct the boy and his mother.

So began the education of Grigory Perelman.

Competitive mathematics is more like a sport than most people imagine. It has its coaches, its clubs, its practice sessions, and, of course, its competitions. Natural ability is necessary but entirely insufficient for success: the talented child needs to have the right coach, the right team, the right kind of family support, and, most important, the will to win. At the beginning, it is nearly impossible to tell the difference between future stars and those who will be good but never great.

Grisha Perelman arrived at the math club of the Leningrad Palace of Pioneers in the fall of 1976, an ugly duckling among ugly ducklings. He was pudgy and awkward. He played the violin; his mother, who had studied not only mathematics but also the violin when she was a child, had engaged a private teacher when Grisha was very young. When he tried to explain a solution to a math problem, words seemed to get tangled at the tip of his tongue, where too many of them collected too quickly, froze momentarily, and then tumbled out, all jumbled up. He was precocious—a year younger than the other children at his grade level—but one of the other kids at the club was even younger: Alexander Golovanov had packed two grades into every year of school and would be finishing high school at thirteen. Three other boys beat Grisha in competitions for the first few years in the club. At least one more—Boris Sudakov, a round, animated, curious boy whose parents happened to know Grisha's family—showed more natural ability than Grisha. Sudakov and Golovanov both carried the marks of brilliance: they seemed always to be rushing forward and bubbling over. They naturally fought for dominance in any room, and mathematics was simply one of many things that got them excited, one of the ways to apply their excellent minds, and one of the tools to showcase their uniqueness. Next to them, Grisha was the interested but quiet partner, almost a mirror; he was a joy for them to bounce their ideas off, but he himself rarely seemed to exhibit the same need. He formed relationships with the math problems; these relationships were deep but also, it seemed, deeply private: most of his conversations appeared to be mathematical and to take place inside his head. A casual visitor to the club would not have singled him out from the other boys. Indeed, even among the people who met him many years later, not one that I encountered described him as brilliant; no one thought he sparkled or shone. People described him, rather, as very, very smart and very, very precise in his thinking.

Just what manner of thinking this was remained something of a mystery. Crudely speaking, mathematicians fall into two categories: the algebraists, who find it easiest to reduce all problems to sets of numbers and variables, and the geometers, who understand the world through shapes. Where one group sees this:

$$a^2 + b^2 = c^2$$

the other sees this:

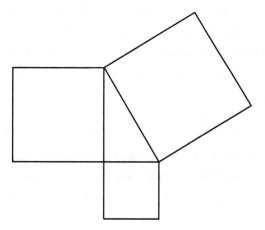

Golovanov, who studied and occasionally competed alongside Perelman for more than ten years, tagged him as an unambiguous geometer: Perelman had a geometry problem solved in the time it took Golovanov to grasp the question. This was because Golovanov was an algebraist. Sudakov, who spent about six years studying and occasionally competing with Perelman, claimed Perelman reduced every problem to a formula. This, it appears, was because Sudakov was a geometer: his favorite proof of the classic theorem above was an entirely graphical one, requiring no formulas and no language to demonstrate. In other words, each of them was convinced Perelman's mind was profoundly different from his own. Neither had any hard evidence. Perelman did his thinking almost entirely inside his head, neither writing nor sketching on scrap paper. He did a lot of other things—he hummed, moaned, threw a Ping-Pong ball against the desk, rocked back and forth, knocked out a rhythm on the desk with his pen, rubbed his thighs until his pant legs shone, and then rubbed his hands together—a sign that the solution would now be written down, fully formed. For the rest of his career, even after he chose to work with shapes, he never dazzled colleagues with his geometric imagination, but he almost never failed to impress them with the single-minded precision with which he plowed through problems. His brain seemed to be a universal math compactor, capable of compressing problems to their essence. Club mates eventually dubbed whatever it was he had inside his head the "Perelman stick"—a very large imaginary instrument with which he sat quietly before striking an always-fatal blow.

Practice sessions at mathematics clubs the world over look roughly the same. Kids come in to find a set of problems written on the blackboard or handed to them. They sit down and attempt to solve them. The coach spends most of his time sitting quietly; teaching assistants check in with the students occasionally, sometimes prodding them with questions, sometimes trying to nudge them in different directions.

To a Soviet child, the afterschool math club was a miracle. For one thing, it was not school. Every morning Soviet children all over the country left their identical concrete apartment blocks a little after eight and walked to their identical concrete school buildings to sit in their identical classrooms with the walls painted yellow and with identical portraits of bearded dead men on the walls—Dostoyevsky and Tolstoy in the literature classrooms, Mendeleev in the chemistry classroom, and Lenin everywhere. Their teachers marked attendance in identical class journals and reached for identical textbooks that they used to impart a perfectly uniform education to their charges, of whom they demanded uniformity in return. My own first-grade teacher, in a neighborhood on the outskirts of Moscow that looked just like Perelman's neighborhood on the outskirts of Leningrad, actually made me pretend my reading skills were as poor as the other children's, enforcing her own vision of conforming to grade level. The first time I spent an afternoon solving math problems—around the same time Perelman was doing it, four hundred miles to the north—I sat for what seemed like an eternity, holding a pencil over a drawing of some shape. I do not remember the problem, but I remember that the solution required transposing the shape. I sat, unable to touch my pencil to paper, until a teaching assistant came by and asked me a very basic question, something like "What might you do?"

"I might transpose it, like this," I answered.

"So do it," he said.

Apparently, this was a place where I was expected to think for myself. A wave of embarrassment covered me; I hunched over my piece of paper, sketched out the solution in a couple of minutes, and felt a wave of relief so total that I think I became a math junkie on the spot. I did not drop the habit until I was in college (and was actually busted for illegally replacing a required humanities course with advanced calculus). The joy of feeling my brain rev up, rush toward a solution, reach it, and be affirmed for it felt like love, truth, hope, and justice all handed to me at once.

The particular math club where Perelman landed was a barebones operation. The coach with whom old Natanson decided to place his protégé by proxy was a tall, freckle-faced, light-haired loudmouthed man named Sergei Rukshin. He had one very important distinguishing characteristic: he was nineteen years old. He had no experience leading a club; he had no teaching assistants. What he did have was outsize ambition and a fear of failure to match. By day, he was an undergraduate at Leningrad State University; two afternoons a week, he put on a suit and tie and impersonated an adult math-club coach at the Palace of Pioneers.

In the quiet, dignified mathematics counterculture of Leningrad, Rukshin was an outsider. He had grown up in a town near Leningrad, a troubled kid like any troubled kid anywhere in the world. By the age of fifteen, he had racked up several minor juvenile offenses, and the only thing he liked to do was box. He was on a clear path to trade school, then the military, followed by a short life of drink and violence—like most Russian men of his generation. The prospect terrified his parents so much that they begged and pleaded and possibly bribed until a miracle happened and their son got a spot at a mathematical high school in the city. There, another miracle happened: Rukshin fell in love with mathematics and turned all his creative, aggressive, and competitive energies toward it. He tried to compete in mathematics olympiads, but he was outmatched by peers who had been training for years. Still, he believed he knew how to win; he just could not do it himself. He formed a team of schoolchildren who were just a year younger than he and trained them, and they did better than he had. He started training upperclassmen all over Leningrad. Then he became a teaching assistant at the Palace of Pioneers, and barely a year later, when the coach with whom he had been apprenticing left for a job assignment in a different city, he became a coach himself.

Like any young teacher, he was a little scared of his students. His first group included Perelman, Golovanov, Sudakov, and several other boys, all of whom were just a few years younger than he but poised to become successful competitive mathematicians. The only way he could prove he deserved to be their teacher was by becoming the best mathematics coach the world had ever seen.

Which is exactly what he did. In the decades since, his students have taken more than seventy International Mathematical Olympiad medals, including more than forty gold ones; in the past two decades, about half of the competitors Russia has put forward have come from Rukshin's now-sprawling club, where they were trained by either him or one of his students, who use his unparalleled training method.

What exactly made his method unparalleled was not entirely clear. "I still don't understand what he did," admitted Sudakov, now an overweight and balding computer scientist living in Jerusalem, "even though I know a thing or two about the psychology of these things. We would come in and sit down and we would get our problem sets. We would solve them. Rukshin would be sitting there at his desk. When somebody solved one of the problems, [that student] would go over to Rukshin's desk and explain his solution and they would discuss it. There! That's all there was to it. Eh?" Sudakov looked at me across the table of a Jerusalem café, triumphant.

"That's what everyone does," I responded, as expected.

"Exactly! That's what I'm talking about!" Sudakov fidgeted happily as he talked.

I observed practice sessions at the club Rukshin still ran a quarter century later. It was now called the Mathematics Education Center; it included a couple of hundred children eleven and older. Just like Perelman's group, they spent two afternoons a week at the club. At the end of each session—which lasted two hours at the lower grade levels and could stretch into the night for upperclassmen—the students got a list of problems to take home. Rukshin claimed that one of his unique strategies was adapting the list of problems to the class during the course of the session: the instructor had to go in with several possible lists and choose among them depending on what he learned about the students' progress over the next couple of hours. Three days later, the students brought in their solutions, which, one by one, they explained to teaching assistants for the first hour of the session. In the second hour, the instructor went over all correct solutions at the blackboard. As they grew older, the students gradually transitioned to explaining their own solutions at the blackboard themselves, in front of the entire group.

I watched the younger kids struggle with the following problem: "There are six people in the classroom. Prove that among them there must be either three people who do not know one another or three people who all know one another." Teaching assistants encouraged them to start with the following diagram:

Two of the half dozen children working on the problem managed to doodle their way to the fact that the diagram can develop in one of three possible ways:

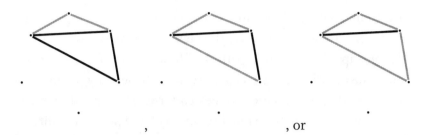

, or

The challenge, to which two children successfully rose, was to explain that this was a graphical—and therefore irrefutable—way to show that there must be at least three people who either all know or all do not know one another. Listening to the children struggle to put this into words, battling an entire short lifetime of inarticulateness, was painful.

Mathematicians know this as the Party Problem; in its general form, it asks how many people must be invited to a party so that at least m will know one another or at least n will not know one another. The Party Problem refers back to Ramsey theory, a system of theorems devised by the British mathematician Frank Ramsey. Most Ramsey-type problems look at the number of elements required to ensure a particular condition will hold. How many children must a woman have to ensure that she has at least two of the same gender? Three. How many people must be present at a party to ensure that at least three of them all know or all do not know one another? Six. How many pigeons must there be to ensure that at least one pigeonhole houses two or more pigeons? One more than there are pigeonholes.

The Mathematics Education Center children—some of them, at least—would learn about Ramsey theory in time. For the moment, they had to learn to express a way of looking at the world that would ultimately make them interested in Ramsey theory and in other methods of observing order in a chaotic environment. To most individuals, children in a classroom or guests at a party are just people. To others, they are the elements of an order and their relationships the parts of a pattern. These others are mathematicians. Most mathematics teachers seem to believe some children are born with the inclination to seek patterns. These children must be identified and taught to nurture this skill, the peculiar ability to see triangles and hexagons where others see only a party.

"That's my biggest know-how," Rukshin told me. "I discovered this thirty years ago: every child must be heard out on every problem he thinks he has solved." Other math clubs had children present their solutions to the class—which meant that the first correct solution ended the discussion. Rukshin's policy was to engage every child in a separate conversation about that child's particular successes, difficulties, and mistakes. This was perhaps the most labor-intensive instruction method ever invented; it meant that none of the children and none of the instructors could coast at any time. "In the end we teach children to talk," said Rukshin, "and we teach the instructors to understand the students' incoherent speech and direct them. Rather, I should say, to understand their incoherent speech and their incoherent ideas."

As I listened to Rukshin and watched him teach, I struggled to place the feeling his club sessions communicated. What made them different—more emotionally engaged but also more tense than any other math, chess, or sports practice session I had ever seen? It took months for my mind to locate the analogy: these sessions felt most like group therapy. The trick really was to get *every* child to present his or her solution to the *entire* group. Mathematics was the most important thing in these children's lives; Rukshin would not have it any other way. They spent most of their free time thinking about the problems they had been given, investing all the emotion and energy they had—not unlike a conscientious twelve-stepper who stayed connected with the program between meetings by writing out the steps. Then, at the meetings, the children laid bare their minds before the people that mattered most to them by telling the stories of their solutions in front of the entire group.

Did this explain Rukshin's unprecedented coaching success? Like many insecure people, Rukshin tended to oscillate between self-effacement and self-aggrandizement, now telling me that he was no more than a mediocre mathematician himself, now telling me for the fifth time in three days that he had been offered a job with the Ministry of Education in Moscow (he turned it down). Similarly, he told me several times that his teaching methods could be reproduced, and had been, to rather spectacular results: his students made money by training math competitors all over the former Soviet bloc. But other times he told me he was a magician, and these were the times he seemed most sincere. "There are several stages of teaching," he said. "There are the student, apprenticeship stages, like in the medieval guild. Then there are the craftsman, the master—these are the stages of mastery. Then there is the art stage. But there is a stage beyond the art stage. This is the witchcraft stage. A sort of magic. It's a question of charisma and all sorts of other things."

It may also have been that Rukshin was more driven than any coach before or since. He did some research work in mathematics, but mathematics seemed to be almost a sideline of his life's work: creating world-class mathematics competitors. That kind of single-minded passion can look and feel very much like magic.

Magicians need willing, impressionable subjects to work their craft. Rukshin, who was so wrong for the job of mathematics teacher for so many external reasons, cast about not just for the most likely child genius but also for the best way to prove he could make a mathematician out of a child. He focused his attention not on the loudest boy, or the quickest-thinking boy, or the most fiercely competitive boy, but on the most obviously absorbent boy.

Rukshin claims not to have appreciated the power of Perelman's mind right away. He had helped judge some of the district competitions in Leningrad in 1976, reading through many sheets of graph paper with ten- to twelve-year-olds' solutions to math problems. He was on the lookout for kids who might amount to something mathematically; the unwritten rules of math clubs allowed them to recruit but not poach, so an unknown like Rukshin had to look for kids early and aggressively. Perelman's set of solutions went on the list; the child's answers were correct, and he arrived at them in ways that were sometimes unexpected. Rukshin saw nothing in those solution sets that would have placed the child head and shoulders above the rest, but he saw solid promise. So when Professor Natanson called and said the child's name, Rukshin recognized it. And when he finally saw the boy, he recognized in him the promise of something bigger than a good mathematician: the fulfillment of Rukshin's ambition to be the best math coach who had ever lived. Adjusting his judgment of Perelman so quickly must have required something of a leap of faith for Rukshin, but it also promised the reward of making a singular discovery—that a child who seemed as capable as dozens of others would surpass them all.

"When everyone is studying math and there is one person who can learn much better than others, then he inevitably receives more attention: the teacher comes to the home, he tells him things." Alexander Golovanov spoke from experience: not only had he spent years studying mathematics alongside Perelman, but he had spent most of his adult life coaching children and teenagers for mathematics competitions. He was Rukshin's anointed heir. And now he explained to me just what it meant to have a favorite student, or to be one. As in any human relationship, love can engender commitment, which can engender investment, which in turn deepens the commitment and perhaps even the love. "So that is one definition of a favorite pupil, and Grisha was that: a favorite pupil because he had been given more. Another aspect, a very important one, is that anyone who teaches [competitive mathematics] has a very clear idea of how much he has done—what he can and cannot take credit for. Say, there are kids who have been to the [all-Russian] olympiad three or four times—and I can say that if I hadn't taught them, they would have made it two rather than three times. So I wasn't the main reason. And then there are people about whom I can say that yes, I was the main reason. That doesn't mean they were pathetic and I put a brain in their heads. What it means is love. And what I think is that Rukshin feels that way about Grisha. And I also think he is right." There was a third aspect too, said Golovanov, one that had to do with pure closeness. Rukshin was a hypochondriac whom the erudite Golovanov compared to Voltaire. Over the months when I was in contact with Rukshin, he spent no less than a third of his time in hospitals. "So there was one time when Rukshin was going blind," Golovanov remembered. "It was during summer camp, and he and Grisha were sharing a room." Perelman was then a university student working as a teaching assistant to Rukshin. "And one morning Rukshin said he'd felt great joy upon awakening because he saw Grisha lying in the other bed. And there was no telling what pleased him more: that he could see in general or that he could see Grisha in particular."

At some point, the care and teaching of Perelman became the thing that gave meaning to Rukshin's life; Rukshin, for his part, strove to insert meanings into Perelman's head. He got Grisha to quit the violin—and the derision with which he spoke of it almost thirty years later impressed me. "It's the shtetl dream." He scowled. "Learn the fiddle and play at weddings and funerals."

Like every competitive sports coach, Rukshin disliked it when his boys spent their time doing anything else. He claimed that he'd kicked Alexander Khalifman, the future chess world champion, out of his club for failing to choose math over chess. And like many coaches, he claimed his sport was the fairest, truest, and most beautiful sport of all. Also like many coaches, he saw it as his mission to shape not only his students' competitive skills but their entire personalities. When they grew older, Rukshin hounded any boy who was sighted doing something as undignified and distracting as kissing a girl—and he caught them with such regularity that the boys began to suspect he had spies shadowing them. Perelman never disappointed his teacher in this way; as Rukshin repeatedly told me, "He was never interested in girls."

Two evenings a week Rukshin, accompanied by his math boys and a couple of girls, walked from the Palace of Pioneers to the Vitebsk Railroad Station, where he and Grisha boarded the same train. Rukshin, who had married very early, lived with his wife and mother-in-law outside the city in the historic town of Pushkin; Grisha lived with his mother, father, and baby sister on the far southern outskirts of the city, in a dreary concrete apartment block in the Kupchino neighborhood. Rukshin and his pupil rode the subway together to Kupchino, which was the last stop, where Grisha would get off and walk home and Rukshin would switch to a commuter train with hard wooden seats and ride another twenty minutes to Pushkin. Along the way, Rukshin discovered things about Grisha. He learned, for example, that Grisha would not untie the earpieces of his fur hat while riding the subway. "It's not just that he would not take the hat off," recalled Rukshin. "He would not even untie the ears, saying that his mother would kill him because she told him never to untie the hat or he'd catch cold." The subway car was generally heated to normal room temperature, but the compactor in Grisha's brain left no room for the nuance of circumstance. Rules were rules.

When Rukshin criticized Grisha for not reading enough—Rukshin saw it as his duty to introduce the children not only to mathematics but to literature and music—Grisha asked why he should be reading books. To Rukshin's argument that reading was "interesting," Grisha responded that anything that needed to be read would be included on the school's required-reading list. Rukshin had better luck with music. When Grisha came to the club, his taste was limited to clear and precise classical instrumental music, generally with a violin solo. While solving a problem, he often engaged in what his club mates alternately called "howling" and "acoustic terror," but when he was asked, Grisha explained that he was humming Camille Saint-Saëns' *Introduction and Rondo Capriccioso,* a composition for violin and orchestra remarkable for both its clarity and the prominence of a virtuoso violin soloist. However, at one of the summer camps, Rukshin succeeded in interesting his pupil in vocal music, through which Grisha proceeded to move systematically: he accepted the lower-range voices first, then gradually moved through to the sopranos, but he drew the line at Rukshin's attempt to introduce him to the singing of castrati, which he deemed "unnatural" and therefore "uninteresting."

Far from being disappointed in his student, Rukshin seemed to rejoice in Perelman's lopsided nature. In this love pairing of teacher and student, each continuously got to be the other's better half. Perelman could be the competitor Rukshin never was, while Rukshin could interact with the outside world on Perelman's behalf and shield his student from it at the same time. They—or, rather, Rukshin—created situations in which they complemented each other in more practical ways too. At summer camp, where fifteen-year-old Perelman lived away from his mother for the first time in his life, Rukshin took care of his day-to-day needs. Personal hygiene was tricky, but Rukshin occasionally managed to get Perelman to change his socks and underwear and pack the soiled items away in a plastic bag, since he refused to wash them—as, often, he refused to wash himself. He also refused to go swimming with the rest of the boys, both because he disliked the water and, more important, because he did not see the point of such a nonintellectual and noncompetitive pastime (he did play Ping-Pong, and was very good at it, and very competitive). So Rukshin used him as an extension of himself: Rukshin got in the water with the children and swam in the deep end, using his own body to mark the line the children were not allowed to cross; Perelman sat on the shore and kept a constant head count, making sure no one went missing. As time went on, Rukshin found other ways to use Perelman's brain as a more efficient extension of his own. As a university student, for example, Perelman would sift through thousands of math problems to select problem sets for training. "It's work that I could have done and spent, say, t amount of time on it," Rukshin told me. "Grisha did it in t over five. Now these problem sets are club classics and no one remembers at this point what was done by me and what was done by Perelman."

It was a match made in mathematical heaven.

3

A Beautiful School

A S PERELMAN MATURED, he learned to take the words that bunched up in his mouth and combine them to form sentences—beautiful, precise, correct sentences—but his narrative remained tangled and personal. The reigning star of the club for the first three or four years, a boy named Alexander Levin, would, said Rukshin, "explain his solution with the idea of helping people understand how to solve these sorts of problems. Perelman told the story of his own personal communication with this particular problem. Imagine the difference between a doctor filling out a medical history and the patient's mother talking about sitting by her child's bedside, wiping his brow and listening to his labored breathing. So did Grisha tell the story of his own journey through the problem. And if the solution could have been different or even shorter, Grisha would still only tell the story of how he had solved it. After he talked, I often had to go up to the blackboard and point out what was important and what could have been cut or simplified—not because he did not see it himself but because he was not the one who would do it."

It is remarkable that Perelman learned to explain as well as he did. Imagine how unmanageable everyday language is for someone given to understanding things literally. Language is not just a frustratingly imprecise way of trying to navigate the world but also a willfully and outrageously inaccurate one. The psychologist and linguist Steven Pinker observed that "language describes space in a way that is unlike anything known to geometry, and it can sometimes leave listeners up in the air, at sea, or in the dark as to where things are." In speech, noted Pinker, objects have primary and secondary dimensions, ranked by importance. A road is imagined as one-dimensional, as is a river or a ribbon—all of them consist of length only, like a segment in geometry. "A *layer* or a *slab* has two primary dimensions, defining a surface," continued Pinker, "and a bounded secondary dimension, its thickness. A *tube* or a *beam* has a single primary dimension, its length, and two secondary dimensions, plumping out its cross-section."

Even greater trouble with language begins when we split up objects into their contents and their boundaries. We describe a stripe as the boundary of a plate, and we portray both objects as two-dimensional, and to a literal mind, all of this is wrong: the stripe is not the actual boundary of the plate (the plate's edge is), and the plate has three dimensions. At the same time, words like *end* and *edge* are used to denote shapes that have anywhere from zero to three dimensions. What is worse, the sloppy way of describing objects coexists in language with an extreme wealth of names for actual shapes. There may be as many as ten thousand shape-names in English; and in all human languages, the number of shape nouns far exceeds the ability to define them. To a literal mind, this is an outrage: how can we use words for things that we not only cannot define properly but insist on defining incorrectly?

Take the Möbius strip, the length of ribbon famously twisted before being reconnected to itself. Language is stumped by the Mö-bius strip. Does something move *along* the strip, as with a one-dimensional object; *around* the strip, as with a two-dimensional object; or, as in the title of a 2006 animated film, *"thru"* the strip—suggesting a three-dimensional object? For a literal mind, salvation lies in the geometry that lives in the imagination—where every shape is clearly defined. In fact, geometry as it is studied in secondary school, with its basic theorems and its precise meas-urements, represents a marked improvement over everyday speech, but it is topology that is the quintessence of geometrical clarity. Not coincidentally, the Möbius strip, which evades casual understanding, is among the earliest known objects of topological inquiry. *Clearly defined,* in the case of topology, does not mean that every shape can easily be visualized. Quite the opposite: it means that every shape has only those qualities that its definition grants it. A shape has a certain number of dimensions; it may be bounded; it may or may not be smooth; and it may or may not be simply con-nected, which is to say, it may or may not have holes. An object in topology may be a sphere—that is, all of its constituting points are an equal distance from the center—but a topologist notes that the essential qualities of a sphere do not change if the sphere is dented; the sphere can easily be reshaped, so its temporary change in imag-inary appearance may be disregarded. Not so if a hole appears in the sphere: the sphere is no longer a sphere but a torus, an object with a different relationship to that which surrounds it and one that cannot easily be reconstituted as a sphere. The topological universe has no use for silly riddles like those of which Pinker is fond: "What can you put in a bucket to make it lighter?" "A hole!" This is not funny to the literal mind. You cannot *put* a hole any-where. Moreover, a hole—or an additional hole—means the shape is no longer what it was; the bucket would not be made lighter be-cause it would no longer be a bucket.

Normally, even mathematicians do not begin to study topology until they have entered college; the discipline has traditionally been considered too abstract to present to children. But a mind like Grisha Perelman's, an undeniably mathematical mind that was at the same time neither visual nor numeric—a mind that thought in systems, that traded in definitions—was a mind born for topology. Starting roughly when Perelman was in eighth grade (when he was around thirteen), visiting lecturers at the math club sometimes taught a class in topology. Topology called to Perelman from beyond the more traditional geometry he had already navigated, the same way the lights of Broadway call to the child who moves the audience to tears in a middle-school production of *Annie*. Grisha Perelman would grow up to live in the universe of topology. He would master all its rules and definitions. He would be a lawyer in the court of shapes, eventually able to argue precisely and articulately why a three-dimensional, simply connected closed object would always be a sphere. Rukshin would light Perelman's way there; he came to Perelman as an emissary from his mathematical future, and his implicit promise was that he would make Perelman's life in Leningrad as safe and as ordered as his life in the imagination.

For this, there was Leningrad's Specialized Mathematics School Number 239.

The summer Grisha Perelman turned fourteen, he took the train from Kupchino to Pushkin every morning and spent the day being tutored by Rukshin in the English language. The plan was to cover four years' worth of English in one summer so that in September Perelman could enter Leningrad's Specialized Mathematics and Physics School Number 239. This was the shortest path to engaging with mathematics fully, with minimal outside disturbances.

The strange story of the specialized math schools goes back to Andrei Kolmogorov. Having been so essential to the war effort dur-

ing World War II, Kolmogorov alone among the top Soviet mathematicians avoided being drafted into the postwar military effort.
His students always wondered why—and the only likely explanation seems to be Kolmogorov's homosexuality. His lifelong partner,
with whom he shared a home starting in 1929, was the topologist
Pavel Alexandrov. Five years after the couple started living together, the Soviet Union criminalized male homosexuality, but
Kolmogorov and Alexandrov, who exercised minimal discretion—they called each other "friends" but made no secret of the
life-shaping nature of their relationship—apparently had no trouble with the law. The academic world accepted them as a pair, if
not a couple: they generally requested academic appointments together, booked their accommodations together at Academy of Sciences resorts, and made donations to military relief efforts together. In his last interview, recorded for a documentary film about
his life, the eighty-year-old Kolmogorov asked the filmmaker to use
Johann Sebastian Bach's Double Violin Concerto—a baroque composition based on the interplay of two violins—when showing the
home he had made with Alexandrov.

Whatever the reason, his not being a part of the military effort left Kolmogorov free to devote his considerable energies to
creating the world for mathematicians that he had envisioned
since he was a young man. Kolmogorov and Alexandrov both hailed
from Luzitania, Luzin's magic land of mathematics, and they
sought to re-create it at their dacha outside of Moscow, where they
would invite their students for days of walking, cross-country skiing, listening to music, and discussing their mathematical projects.

"The way our graduate group interacted with Kolmogorov was
almost classically Greek," said one of the countless memoirs published by his students; virtually everyone who had contact with
Kolmogorov seemed to have been moved to write about him.

"Through the woods or along the shore of the Klyazma River the muscular mathematician would be moving briskly, on foot or on skis, surrounded by young people. The shy students would be rushing behind him. He talked almost without stopping—although, unlike perhaps the ancient Greeks, he talked less of mathematics and more of other things." Kolmogorov believed that a mathematician who aspired to greatness had to be well versed in music, the visual arts, and poetry, and—no less important—he had to be sound of body. Another of Kolmogorov's students wrote in his memoir that he was singled out by the teacher for wrestling well.

The mix of influences that shaped Kolmogorov's idea of a good mathematical education would have been an odd combination anywhere, but in the Soviet Union in the middle of the twentieth century, it was extraordinary almost beyond belief. Kolmogorov hailed from a wealthy Russian family that founded a school of its own in Yaroslavl, a town about a hundred and fifty miles north of Moscow. There they published a children's newspaper to which Kolmogorov, along with other family members, contributed. Here is a math problem he authored at the age of five: How many different patterns can you create with thread while sewing on a four-hole button? Don't try solving this one until you have some time; I know two professional mathematicians, both students of Kolmogorov's, who each came up with a different response.

In 1922, Kolmogorov—nineteen, a student at Moscow University, and already an emerging mathematician in his own right —started teaching mathematics at an experimental school in Moscow. Incredibly, the school was modeled after the Dalton School, the famous New York City institution immortalized by, among others, Woody Allen in the film *Manhattan*. The Dalton Plan, which lay at the foundation of both the Dalton School and the Potylikha Exemplary Experimental School where Kolmogorov taught, called for an individual instruction plan for every student. Each child would map out his own path for the month and proceed to work independently. "So every student spent most of his school time at his desk, or going to the small school libraries to get a book, or writing something," Kolmogorov recalled in his final interview. "The instructor would be sitting in the corner, reading, and the students would approach him in turn to show what they had done." This might have been the first sighting of the figure of the instructor reading quietly behind his desk; decades later, the math-club coach would take up this position.

It was always a boys' club. Kolmogorov himself referred to his students affectionately as "my boys," reporting to Alexandrov, in a letter from a trip taken with his students in 1965, "In just three hours at an elevation of 2400 meters all my boys got so badly sunburned (parading around in their swimming trunks or without them) that they could barely sleep for two nights following." The casual happy homoeroticism of Kolmogorov's view of his students seemed to come from an entirely different time and place. Before the Iron Curtain sealed off the Soviet Union from the rest of the world, Kolmogorov and Alexandrov had done some traveling. Alexandrov, who was seven years older, had traveled extensively before the two met, but the pair spent the 1930–1931 academic year abroad, some of it together. They started out in Berlin, where all culture, and gay culture in particular, was flourishing. They imported all they could: books, music, ideas. "Interesting that this idea of a truly beloved friend seems to be purely Aryan: The Greeks and the Germans seem always to have had it," Alexandrov wrote to Kolmogorov in 1931, a few years before the reference to Aryans would have had a different connotation. "The theory of a lone friend is a difficult one to fulfill in the contemporary world," Kolmogorov lamented in response. "The wife will always have pretensions to that role, but it would be too sad to consent to this. In Aristotle's times, these two sides of the issue never came into contact:

The wife was one thing, and the friend quite another." Kolmogorov brought back from Germany collections of verse by Goethe, who would always be his favorite poet. In all their letters to each other, Kolmogorov and Alexandrov included detailed reports of concerts attended and music heard, and when vinyl records became available, they started collecting them. Alexandrov hosted weekly classical-music evenings at the university; he would play records and lecture on the music and the composers; after Alexandrov's death, Kolmogorov—already nearing eighty and crippled by Parkinson's disease—took over as host.

Classical music and male bonding, mathematics and sports, poetry and ideas added up to Kolmogorov's vision of the ideal man and the ideal school. At the age of forty, Kolmogorov wrote up a plan "of how to become a great man should I have sufficient desire and diligence." The plan called for completing his research work by the age of sixty and devoting the rest of his life to teaching secondary school. He followed the plan: in the 1950s he enjoyed a second creative flowering, publishing as prolifically as he had in his thirties—very unusual for a mathematician—and then he stopped and turned his full attention to teaching children.

In 1935, Kolmogorov and Alexandrov organized the first Moscow mathematical competition for children, helping to lay the foundation for what would eventually become the International Mathematical Olympiad. A quarter century later, Kolmogorov teamed up with Isaak Kikoin, an unofficial kingpin of Soviet nuclear physics who had run similar competitions in physics. Since the only value the State seemed to assign their sciences was military, the two conspired to make Soviet leaders believe that elite, specialized math-and-physics high schools could supply the country with the brains it needed to win the arms race. The project was championed by a young Central Committee member named Leonid Brezhnev—then five years away from becoming the Soviet leader. The Soviet of Ministers issued a decree creating the school in August 1963, and it opened in December of that year. Half a dozen similar schools soon opened in Moscow, Leningrad, and Novosibirsk. Kolmogorov's students ran most of them, and he personally oversaw the shaping of the curriculum.

That August, Kolmogorov organized a summer mathematics school in a town outside of Moscow. Forty-six high-school seniors who had done well in the All-Russian Mathematical Olympiad attended. Kolmogorov and his graduate students taught workshops, lectured the boys in mathematics, and took them hiking in the surrounding woods. In the end, nineteen boys were chosen to attend the new mathematics-and-physics boarding school in Moscow.

They landed in a strange new world. Kolmogorov, who had been dreaming up the school for forty years, had developed not only a method of individual instruction based on the Dalton Plan but an entirely new curriculum. Lectures in mathematics—a number of them presented by Kolmogorov himself—aimed to introduce ideas from the world of real research while taking into account the students' varied backgrounds, for Kolmogorov emphasized choosing students who exhibited the presence of what he called "a spark from God" rather than a thorough knowledge of high-school mathematics. In addition, the boarding school was probably the only one in the Soviet Union that offered a high-school course in the history of antiquity. The curriculum also included more hours of physical education instruction than regular Soviet schools did. Finally, Kolmogorov himself lectured the students in music, the visual arts, and ancient Russian architecture. He also took the boys on boating, hiking, and skiing trips. "We liked the trips and the poems," one of the students wrote in a memoir. "And few of us understood the music: that required at least some background. Fortunately, [Kolmogorov] kept quiet on the importance of the social sciences." In other words, Kolmogorov not only rushed to impress his students with his version of Renaissance values but also shielded them from the Marxist indoctrination to which they had been subjected in secondary school and which they would be forced to endure once again at the university.

Kolmogorov's goal was not just to create a handful of elite institutions for talented mathematicians but also to teach real mathematics to as many children as could learn it. He developed a curriculum that took schoolchildren out of the business of adding and subtracting and getting confused, and into the business of thinking about mathematics in clear and interesting ways. He oversaw a curriculum-reform effort that introduced the use of simple algebraic equations with variables and of computers as early as possible. In addition, Kolmogorov sought to revamp the secondary-school understanding of geometry, opening the way to comprehending non-Euclidean ideas. In the mid-1970s I attended one of the schools chosen to try out the new textbooks (this was not a specialized math school but an "experimental" school open to a much broader range of children). It must have been in third grade that I shocked my father, a computer scientist, with my understanding of the concept of congruence. It made perfect sense to me: two triangles, for example, were considered congruent if they were exactly the same in every way. The word *equal*, which older textbooks had used, was clearly less precise.

Bizarrely, it was the subject of introducing congruence to schoolchildren that forced Kolmogorov's first serious confrontation with the Soviet system—something he had avoided for decades, through luck and care. In December 1978 the seventy-five-year-old Kolmogorov was dressed down at a general meeting of the mathematics section of the Soviet Academy of Sciences. One after another, Kolmogorov's colleagues rose to criticize him for the term *congruence*, for a difficult new definition of *vectors* used in the textbooks he oversaw, and for the introduction of set theory as the cornerstone of the math curriculum. These, the speakers claimed, were examples of a larger failing: the reform—and its authors—were evidently anti-Soviet. "These things can provoke nothing but disgust," opined Lev Pontryagin, one of the leading Soviet mathematicians. "This is a disaster. This is a political phenomenon." Newspaper denunciations followed: authors of the curriculum reform were exposed as having "fallen under a foreign influence of bourgeois ideology" of set theory. They had a point. Education reform just then under way in the United States and, indeed, throughout the Western hemisphere mirrored Kolmogorov's efforts. The New Math movement brought actual mathematicians into active involvement in secondary schools; set theory was introduced in early grades and formed a basis for teaching all of mathematics. The Harvard psychologist Jerome Bruner observed at the time that it had "the effect of freshening [the student's] eye to the possibility of discovery." At the third-grade level, mathematics finally became accessible enough to be dragged through the pages of the Soviet newspapers—and Kolmogorov was exposed as what he most certainly was: an agent of Western cultural influence in the Soviet Union.

The aging Kolmogorov never recovered from the scandal. His health deteriorated catastrophically; he developed Parkinson's and lost his sight and, eventually, speech. Some of his students believed the illnesses were set off by the public disgrace and by a head trauma that resulted from what may have been an attack: walking through a university building, Kolmogorov was struck by a heavy door that he thought might have been swung deliberately by someone he then saw rushing away. As long as Kolmogorov was able, and perhaps a little longer, he continued to lecture at the boarding school. He died at eighty-four, speechless, blind, and motionless, but surrounded by his students, who for the preceding couple of years had taken turns providing round-the-clock care at his house.

The ideological conflict that made Kolmogorov's proposed reforms impossible was real. His plan called for dividing high-school students into groups depending on their interest and abilities in mathematics, allowing the most talented and motivated to get farther faster. The entire Soviet system of secondary education was based on the concept of uniformity: everyone was to be taught the same thing at the same time, using the same textbooks. But the Soviet Union still craved international prestige—in fact, that need became more and more pronounced as the technological rivalries of the second half of the century heated up. Just as the world of adult mathematics had to cultivate a certain number of geniuses to showcase at international conferences, so a small world of talented children had to be allowed to exist in a sort of greenhouse setting, if only for the country to field competitors at international math and physics olympiads. And just as it was in the world of adult mathematicians, in the world of student mathematicians, the space for comfortable existence was too small to accommodate all whose talents warranted inclusion; to get in, a Jewish child had to be twice as good as a non-Jewish child and four times as good as the child of an apparatchik.

Possibly because there were so few schools, they were all fairly similar, shaped in the Kolmogorov mold of increased emphasis not only on math and physics but also on music, poetry, and hiking—in no small part because Kolmogorov's students influenced most of these schools directly. They were all subject to heightened scrutiny: Kolmogorov's boarding school was visited frequently by ideology inspectors, who became especially vigilant following the denunciation of his curriculum reform. School supporters were often called upon to defend it before the authorities, who claimed that "elite education is not allowable in our society"; Moscow's School 2 was apparently the object of many denunciations—written by concerned parents and outraged Soviet-issue teachers—that eventually had its cofounders fired; and School 239 lost some of its most popular teachers to KGB pressure while its principal was frequently reprimanded for admitting too many Jewish children (according to historical lore, two out of four Leningrad math schools were shut down in the 1970s for having too many Jewish students). And the feature that united all the math schools was the sheer concentration of student brainpower, teacher talent, and intellectual urgency: the children had only two or three years to spend at the school, which was always on the verge of being discovered and shut down by the authorities.

The selection of teachers assembled at these schools matched that of the best Soviet universities. In fact, for the most part, they were the same people. Kolmogorov brought his students to teach at his school, and those students, in turn, drafted their own students. Some teachers came because their children attended the school; some were strong-armed for the same reason. School 2 graduates recalled that when members of Moscow's intellectual elite flocked to the school, the director set the price of admission: those parents who were college instructors had to offer electives at the school. As a result, the school's bulletin boards overflowed with announcements of elective courses offered by some of the top names in various fields—more than thirty courses at one time. Clearly, if there had been more schools like these, the concentration of outstanding instructors at them would not have been so high. By trying to keep the number of schools low, the Soviet authorities had in fact created hotbeds of freethinking.

"What made the school different was that the students' talents and intellectual achievements made them more popular and significant," remembered a Boston computer scientist who graduated from a Leningrad math school in 1972. In the world outside the school, peers respected one another for athletic achievements while the establishment rewarded proletarian provenance or Komsomol (the Communist youth organization) eagerness. Inside the school, the ideological demands of the outside world were flouted:

some schools allowed students not to wear uniforms (though they were still required to put on a jacket and tie and keep their hair cropped); some teachers read forbidden works of literature aloud in class (though they avoided naming the author or the work). "What can be more beneficial at sixteen or seventeen than not having to lie?" author Mikhail Berg wrote in a memoir of his years at a Leningrad math school. "You had an interview, you were admitted, and you became a member of a community in which the percentage of anything Soviet was many times lower than outside of it. You had to pay for the opportunity to breathe in this microclimate: Every day, spine bent, you had to deliver gifts to the altar of the idols—the two sisters Mathematics and Physics and their mother, Logic. Mathematics and rigid logic simply left no space for ideology: It could mix with logic no more than water can mix with kerosene." Granted, these were still Soviet schools, complete with Komsomol organizations, denunciations, and "primary military training" classes, but compared with the rest of the country, the boundaries placed on speech and thought had been broadened so much as to seem almost nonexistent. The schools managed to create a bubble that resisted the pressure of the Soviet state. It protected both the students who paid mathematical dues in order to gain a measure of intellectual freedom, like Berg, and those who paid intellectual dues—studying antiquity, for example—in order to gain the freedom to study mathematics, like Perelman.

The schools taught children not only how to think but also that thinking was rewarded—and rewarded fairly. In other words, they reared people who were very ill-suited for life in the Soviet Union —or, one could argue, for life in the real world anywhere. The schools produced freethinking snobs. A graduate of Kolmogorov's boarding school recalled studying with Yuli Kim, one of the Soviet Union's best-known dissident singer-songwriters, who taught literature at the school (until his firing was forced by the KGB in

1968): "Because of him, we felt like gods: We lived our lives and had our accomplishments, and we had our own Orpheus to sing our praises."

The Soviet system, fine-tuned to all shades of difference, rejected these kids and put every possible obstacle in their way once they graduated. The year I would have graduated from math school in Moscow (had my family not emigrated to the United States), none of the graduates would be admitted to Moscow University's Mechanics and Mathematics department—and the teachers made a point of warning us about this. Leningrad's School 239, most of whose graduates were convinced—some say rightly—that they could easily sleep through their freshman year at any university and still ace the exams, saw so few of its students allowed into Leningrad University that it had to forge a relationship with a second-tier college that would take its kids, overeducated and overconfident as they were. They may have believed they were gods, but when they emerged from high school, they found themselves outside the well-organized and well-guarded mainstream of Soviet mathematics. Not all of them—perhaps not even a majority—would become mathematicians, but those who did were destined for the very strange world of the alternative mathematics subculture.

Kolmogorov himself was no stranger to the official mathematics establishment. He was eccentric for an insider, protected in large part by his larger-than-life standing in international mathematics, earned early and maintained with apparent ease for decades. Still, he spent months and years of his life negotiating teaching hours and salary increases and apartments for assorted members of the Academy. He was, by all accounts, extremely careful in what he said and did—and he made no secret of his fear of the secret police (and indeed hinted at a cooperative relationship with them)—

but in 1957 he was fired as dean of Moscow University's Mechanics and Mathematics department following dissident rumblings among his students.

Daily exigencies of life within the establishment notwithstanding, Kolmogorov held to the ideals he passed on to his students. He parted with his ideas with famous ease: after doing a few weeks' work on the foundation of a problem, he would give it to one of his students, who might spend months or a lifetime working on it. He claimed little interest in the authorship of solutions as long as the great problems of mathematics were indeed solved. In other words, even when he was recognized and celebrated by the establishment as the greatest Russian mathematician of his age, he espoused every ideal of the Soviet mathematical counterculture. His numerous students were that culture's leaders, and Kolmogorov himself its guiding light.

His vision was gospel to his students and their students and their students' many students. Kolmogorov had envisioned a world without dishonesty or backstabbing, without women and other undue distractions, with only math and beautiful music and just rewards for all; several generations of Russian mathematical boys believed in it. Wrote Mikhail Berg: "Many of us would have wanted to take the school with us after graduation, like a turtle's armor, because we could feel comfortable only within the confines of its precise and logically understandable rules."

A life within the confines of logical and understandable rules was what Rukshin offered Perelman in exchange for the heroic feat of learning English in a summer. For his part, Rukshin would get to realize his own project. Math clubs are to math schools what after-school band practice is to the High School of Performing Arts: one is a respite from the rest of school life but might produce brilliant professionals; the other offers total immersion and a vision of the future. They are two different, if related, worlds. Now, if Rukshin had his way, the two worlds would meld. For the first time in the history of Leningrad math clubs, virtually all suitably aged members of the club would go to high school together. Ordinarily, they had to apply—and be accepted—to receive their last two years of secondary education at either of the two Leningrad math schools, and they were spread among different classes so as not to skew math instruction too much in any particular class. It was generally expected that the club mathematicians, like professional athletes among talented amateurs, would spend some of their time at the math schools being bored and waiting for others to catch up. Rukshin had a radically different idea: create a class that consisted mostly of math-club members, add some kids from a physics club, fill it out with the help of other exceptionally gifted and motivated children, and—most important, he thought—keep everyone else out. No one who was not obsessed with mathematics, or at least with the sciences, should be allowed into the class "lest the rot catches on and spreads" was how Rukshin put it to me a quarter of a century later. When he was in a more generous mood, he explained that he'd wanted his charges to be surrounded by other kids with similar interests, since "there wasn't an Eton School for them." Plus, there were organizational issues: "They could all come to the club together, it wouldn't be like one was getting out of school at one and another at four. I could make arrangements with their teachers regarding what they would be studying in mathematics and physics at school and what I would cover at the club. And concerted action is always better where it comes to gifted kids. Many of them were black sheep, and this way they could have a teacher who would shield them the same way I did." Once the coach, and his math club, became the center of these children's lives, he was not going to budge.

The only snag in the plan to create a bigger and better cocoon for Perelman and his ilk was the foreign-language issue. Soviet schools generally offered either English, German, or French starting in fifth grade, and transferring from school to school was contingent on a language match. School 239 offered English and, if enough students required it, German; Perelman had been studying French for four years. Rukshin claimed his own English was bad and to illustrate this offered, "My knowledge of English leaves very much to be desired," pronounced with the queen of England's accent. This was vintage Rukshin: either his English was excellent and he was just fishing for compliments, or his English was as poor as he claimed but he had memorized that one phrase. Whatever the case, it was Rukshin and his bizarre English-learning project that took over Perelman's life the summer he turned fourteen.

Perelman's mother allowed her son to submit to this taxing regimen without protest, as she had done with all of Rukshin's demands—even though this meant keeping the family, which now included a toddler named Lena, in the city for the summer instead of going to the dacha like all the other Leningrad families that belonged to what might have been called the Soviet middle class. Rukshin's own mother-in-law, he said, was furious: "Not only had her daughter married a poor mathematician but now he was dragging his Young Pioneers home." Since they were not welcome in the apartment, Rukshin and Perelman spent their days walking the numerous scenic pathways in the town's huge historical parks, first following textbooks and then teaching themselves conversational English by conversing in it. Once again, Rukshin proved to be an outstanding coach. At the end of the summer, Perelman was fit to study at School 239. Years later, he wrote in excellent English, not only correct but idiomatic—and while that was partly a result of the couple of years he'd spent in the United States as a postdoc, it rested on the foundation he received from Rukshin during those walks in the parks.

Now all of Rukshin's "black sheep" could go to school together. Twenty-seven years later I spoke with a Russian Israeli psychologist who was married to Boris Sudakov, one of Perelman's club mates and, later, classmates. Boris had suggested I talk to her because she had seen something off balance in Perelman when he visited Israel in the mid-1990s. I wondered if she'd noticed something then that had been a portent of his later oddness. "Come on," she said, apparently irritated. "I'd seen Boris's other classmates, and they are all like that. Weird. It's like they are made of different stuff." The literal translation of the Russian expression she used is "made of different dough," which is particularly appropriate for the pudgy, pale boys who grew up into pale, doughy men.

Collecting these kids in a single classroom struck many of the teachers at School 239 as a crazy idea. "They'd speak up at the meetings, they'd say that it would just be too hard," recalled current principal Tamara Yefimova, who had been the vice principal back in those days. "I mean, there was this boy, for example, he was so talented, and his teacher would come to me almost in tears, and I'd ask the boy what happened, and he'd say, 'Tamara Borisovna, I left home on time, but then I just got to thinking.' And they were just like that, so difficult to understand: they'd be sitting in the back of the class, she'd be saying her thing, and who knows what they were doing back there, maybe thinking again." The principal, a short, stout woman with a crewcut, looked and sounded more like everyone's favorite gym teacher than the head of an elite school that imagined itself to be a Russian Dalton or Eton. In her youth she had run a secondary school on a military base someplace she still tried not to name. She had been sent down to School 239 by the Party to keep watch over the school's exceedingly liberal atmosphere and was apparently accepted there as a reasonable evil: She clearly possessed a genuine admiration for the intellectuals she found herself commanding. She finessed the endless Party inspections to which the school was subjected, and she succeeded in accomplishing things none of her more cultivated predecessors had pulled off—like repairing the leaky roof and restoring the school's magnificent auditorium. But her support for a math-club class apparently struck some of the teachers as a misguided expression of her fondness for intellectualism; she claimed that several teachers actually left in protest. Still, in September 1980, the first club class entered School 239.

Some people are born to be schoolteachers. I have met a few, and they are an unusual breed: supremely sensitive, thin-skinned like the children or adolescents to whose needs they are so finely attuned, yet secure in the understanding that their best students will develop into adults who are smarter and altogether better educated than they are. Valery Ryzhik was born, in 1937, to teach mathematics. He was twenty-five when he started teaching at School 239, where he helped create the mathematics curriculum, and he had been teaching mathematics for twenty-eight years when, over his vocal objections, he was handed the club class of Rukshin's creation. His job was to teach them math and also to serve as the class teacher, something like a homeroom teacher at an American high school.

Ryzhik had the idea that teaching School 239's average students —who had been top students at other schools, but not the exceptionally gifted sort—was best accomplished by teaching the very best students in such a manner that the rest got pulled along. Students recalled that in ordinary years he picked five top students at the start of the school year and focused all his attention on them while the others learned by watching. "There would be inspectors criticizing me for not working with the average kids," Ryzhik recalled in 2008, when he had been a practicing schoolteacher for nearly half a century. "And I would say, The issue is not working with the average kids; the issue is working with the gifted kids —and that's really hard, because, for one thing, they are all different. Another is, if you teach them in a way that's not interesting for them, they can tolerate it for a day or two and then they get bored and start wondering what they are doing at this school. And that can't happen. You have to make their eyes light up, and I can't explain to you how you do that."

Having a group of ten exceptionally gifted students thrown at him along with twenty-five other adolescents presented Ryzhik with an apparently insurmountable challenge. The club kids were all different. Alexander Golovanov, the wunderkind, sat up front "and wouldn't let anyone get a word in," Ryzhik remembered. "Such a little boy." Grisha Perelman sat in the back. He never spoke up unless a solution or an explanation required a correction. "And then he would raise his hand." Ryzhik mimicked the movement, lifting his hand off his desk only slightly. "You could hardly see it. His was the final word." Still, Perelman never did what other exceptional students did: he never let himself grow distracted and, say, fiddle with a different problem during class. He sat and listened to discussions that were of no pragmatic use to him; rules were rules, and if one came to class, one listened.

Ryzhik had met kids like Perelman before. "We got someone like that every year," he told me. "What's curious is that they were all marked by an extraordinary modesty, a schoolchild's reserve. There is never any conceit, and I think that's one of the necessary conditions for something extraordinary in the future. I have seen kids like Golovanov too, but I've never known them to do something outstanding in mathematics—they stop at the professorial level. The ones who make it beyond are a different kind of person." With his trained teacher's eye, Ryzhik spotted an awe-inspiring student.

Ryzhik attempted to form a personal relationship with Perelman—partly at the request of Grisha's mother. She came in early in the school year to ask Ryzhik to try to ensure two things: that Grisha ate something while at school and that he tied his shoelaces. A Western mother might have bought her son slip-on shoes to wear, but Soviet stores offered no such option for the absent-minded schoolchild. Ryzhik never succeeded at either task: Perelman walked around with his laces flopping about, and he would not eat. "Maybe he could not get distracted," suggested Ryzhik. "Maybe his entire nervous system was so tuned to the learning process that he could not stray from it. Or maybe it was a blood pressure issue—he might have felt that if he ate, his thinking would not be as precise." Another possibility was that school food was too varied for Perelman; the cafeteria had a different menu for each day of the week. In the math-club group, every boy had his own pronounced food preference. So in the afternoons, when they made the walk from the school to the Palace of Pioneers, they made quick pit stops for the refueling of each club member. Naturally, Perelman's system was the simplest and the fastest: he would go to the bakery on Liteyniy Prospect, less than halfway between the school and the club, and buy a Leningrad loaf, a large piece of wheat bread with raisins on the inside and crushed peanuts on top. Perelman did not eat peanuts, so Golovanov would scrape them off and eat them. Sometimes the ebullient Golovanov would try to help himself to the raisins also, whereupon Perelman would slap his hand hard.

Mondays Perelman would stay at school after class and play chess in Ryzhik's chess club. They played fast chess, a game that is believed to require more intuition than calculation, but Perelman did very well, even winning twice against Ryzhik himself—probably because what chess players call intuition is in fact the ability to grasp complex systems in a single take, which was exactly Perelman's strength. But in all the weekly afternoons together, the tactful and awestruck Ryzhik never tried to venture into more personal territory with Perelman, never broached a subject that reached beyond school, chess, and mathematics. Nor did he choose him as one of the students he regularly addressed in the classroom; rather, he kept him as his "command reserve," as he put it, for particularly difficult problems.

To the general troops, Ryzhik tried to be an all-encompassing leader. On Sundays—the only day of leisure for Soviet schoolchildren at the time—he would take his class out of the city for hikes and orientation races. Summers, he would take groups of children on weeks-long trips in difficult terrain in the Caucasian mountains or the Siberian forests. Perelman never went. Ryzhik believed this was because he was a homebody, though he apparently did submit to the requisite math-school culture hikes organized by Rukshin for his club kids; his out-of-school self belonged to Rukshin. Both Rukshin and Ryzhik practiced the Kolmogorovian approach: while dragging the children on long and grueling walks, they tried to shape them into the human beings they wanted to see—with Rukshin focusing more on literature, music, and all-around erudition, and Ryzhik on chivalry, honesty, responsibility, and other universal values. Ryzhik had been doing this for more than twenty years, but with the club class of 1982, he felt he failed.

"The class split into two groups," recalled Ryzhik. "One was a group of learners, and the other had different values. And I never did manage to connect them." The math-club boys formed the heart of the learners' contingent. During one of the Sunday hikes in their second and final year at School 239, one of the math-club students got a nonclub classmate involved in a chemistry experiment. He handed him a substance but failed to warn him it was highly explosive if heated. When the boy approached the campfire, the stuff blew up in his hand, severing it at the wrist. "The boy survived—thank god for that," said Ryzhik. "And then I recall I had a talk with the kids. I remember it well. I said, 'Imagine we are on a trip. And say, we have set up camp somewhere for the night. And say there is a lake there, and I do not like the look of the lake and I judge the approach to be unsafe, so I tell you not to go there without my oversight under any circumstances. And now imagine that one of you has decided to go for a swim during the night anyway. Who will wake me up to tell me what's happening?' No one! And I said, 'Do you see what's happening? A child might die! You may not understand this, but I do. And still, based on this silly child-corporate-value system of yours, you are going to keep quiet. That means that story with the explosion taught you nothing. You still don't get it.'"

Rukshin's club-class experiment upset the delicate balance that existed at School 239 and at other math schools, as well as in the adult Soviet world, where the mathematics counterculture was allowed to exist quietly so long as it did not take its ideas to the streets. In Ryzhik's class, the usual rules of nonconfrontation between the geniuses and the rest no longer applied: the genius contingent was too large, too male, and too adolescent for that. It was war, and Ryzhik was right in thinking he had failed to convince the students it was wrong. A quarter of a century later, the student who had slipped his classmate the bomb referred to the incident occasionally in his blog, recalling it with a clear lack of remorse. There is no single explanation for what happened. Perhaps Rukshin's boys perceived their classmates as representatives of the system that had humiliated them at other schools; perhaps they had already grown to perceive anyone outside their small circle as the enemy. In any case, as always happens in war, the two sides saw each other as less than human. Ryzhik discontinued the hikes following this conversation. The following year, he cut his class time down to one day a week so he could focus on finishing a geometry textbook that he had been test-driving with his students. The year after, when he tried to return to full-time teaching at School

239, Ryzhik was turned away, apparently because the principal had come under increased pressure to cut the number of Jewish teachers.

By the time I met Ryzhik, he was seventy, teaching again—at a new elite physics-and-math school—playing chess in the afternoons, and given to looking back kindly on his life, which had been lived largely in the shadow of the Soviet compromise. He had been denied entry to Leningrad University because he was Jewish. "They did not even manage to find a problem I couldn't solve: I sat for three hours after the exam was over, I solved them all, and still they failed me. I was just a boy. I went home and cried." He graduated from Herzen, the second-tier college, and was later cut from its faculty because there were too many Jews. He never managed to defend his doctoral dissertation, which was based on the geometry textbook he coauthored and was criticized for violating every rule of Soviet teaching methodology. In the hours I spent with him, the only regret he expressed concerned his failure to bring together the very strange experiment of a class in which Grisha Perelman had been his student.

The drama of this teacher surely passed Perelman by, as did most of what surrounded him at School 239. He never attended the literary Tuesdays, which contained poetry and generally reached beyond the mandatory school reading list. He probably did not follow the story when the School 239 principal Viktor Radionov was fired amid charges of pedophilia. He was surely oblivious to the countless ideological inspections, which required the teachers and the more attuned students to be on their best Soviet-school behavior, which came naturally to Perelman anyway. He almost certainly never posted a question on the supposedly anonymous question-and-answer board run by the history teacher Pyotr Ostrovsky, who impressed students with his willingness to entertain even risky political questions and who was later exposed as a KGB informant who tracked down those tricky questioners and denounced them and their parents.

While careers teetered and entire lives were ruined, and while some children thrived in the liberal math-school atmosphere and others labored anxiously to keep up, Perelman studied mathematics. A classmate recalled seeing Perelman and Golovanov stop about halfway between the underground station and the school to write formulas frantically on the sidewalk in front of what happened to be the U.S. consulate. In all likelihood, Perelman did not notice the consulate, or the popular movie theater that was housed in the church building to which the school was adjacent, or the school's grand semicircular marble staircase and the white marble boards with the names of national olympiad prize takers, on which Perelman's own name would eventually appear in gold. To his classmates, he appeared a sort of math angel: he sounded his voice only if a solution required his intervention; looked forward to Sundays, sighing happily and saying that he could "finally solve some problems in peace"; and if asked patiently explained any math issue to any of his classmates though apparently utterly unable to conceive of anyone not comprehending such a simple thing. His classmates repaid him with kindness: they recalled his civility and his mathematics, and none ever mentioned to me that he walked around with his shoelaces undone—not a particularly uncommon occurrence at the school anyway—or that by the time he was in his last year of school, his fingernails were so long they curled.

Other School 239 graduates thanked the school for opening their minds; for teaching them that intelligence, erudition, and civility were rewarded; and for giving them a head start in their higher education. If it ever occurred to Perelman to thank anyone for something so intangible, he should have thanked School 239 for leaving him alone. One suspects that Rukshin's entire club-class design worked for only two people: Rukshin and Perelman. It was destructive for other kids, and it was tragic for Ryzhik, but it allowed the symbiosis of Perelman and Rukshin to continue unchallenged and Perelman's view of the world to remain undisturbed—but also unexpanded. Like all protective bubbles, the environment of the math school served not only to shield but also to isolate its inhabitants. It ensured that Perelman's relentlessly logical approach to life was never challenged, allowing him to concentrate on mathematics to the exclusion of—literally—almost everything else. It let him avoid confronting the fact that he lived among humans, each with his or her own ideas and thoughts, to say nothing of emotions and desires. Many gifted children realize with a start as they mature that the world of ideas and the world of people compete for their attention and their energy. Many make a difficult choice in favor of one or the other. Not only did School 239 spare Perelman the choice; it kept him from noticing that the tension between people and mathematics even existed.

4

A Perfect Score

SOMETIME DURING THE FINAL year of school, Ryzhik would have difficult, delicate talks with some of his students' parents. He would ask them to think about their child's chances for university admission. Ryzhik, who himself had cried when he was turned away for being Jewish, endeavored to warn parents who he felt had not given the issue enough thought. There were subtleties in the admission process, of which he was acutely aware. Leningrad University's Mathematics and Mechanics department had a quota of two Jews admitted per year, which was enforced strictly but not zealously: unlike its Moscow counterpart, the Mathmech, as it was known, did not delve into the family histories of applicants in an effort to root out hidden Jewish relatives. At the same time, Mathmech turned away non-Jewish applicants burdened with Jewish-sounding surnames.

"I had a student named Filipovich," recalled Ryzhik. "It's not a Jewish name, but it might sound Jewish, so just in case, they did not accept her. Olga Filipovich got run over by the system." Parents had to be warned and then directed to schools with more liberal admissions policies, if need be. Ryzhik had two rules: he did not talk to the students directly about this, preferring that they learn the facts from their parents, and he talked to the parents only when he judged it absolutely necessary. He said he hated meddling, and he surely must have hated acting as the unwilling agent of an absurd and cruel system of discrimination. But when he had to, he engaged the parents in what he called "a standard conversation: that you have to be mindful of what you are doing to spot the child, and you have to have a plan for what you are going to do if it doesn't work out. And how are you going to explain this to the child? I had been through it all myself."

The children in question were not that young—Soviet schools generally graduated seventeen-year-olds—but the stakes were indeed too high for many adolescents to understand and to handle. The Soviet system of college admissions was based on a set of four or five exams, generally a combination of oral and written formats, for which the applicant had to be physically present at the college. Therefore, a high-school graduate could apply to two colleges, at most, in one summer. If he was male and he failed to gain admission, he would be drafted into the military. When Perelman was graduating, the Soviet Union was in the third year of its war in Afghanistan; roughly eighty thousand conscripts were serving there at any given time, and conscription was what every parent feared most.

For a Jewish adolescent who was exceptionally gifted in mathematics, there were only three available college strategies: choose a college other than Leningrad University, with less discriminatory admissions policies; bank on being one of only two Jews accepted in a given year; or become a member of the Soviet team at the International Mathematical Olympiad—members of the team, which numbered four to eight people each year, were admitted to the colleges of their choice without having to take the entrance exams. Boris Sudakov, a boy Rukshin had believed was no less naturally talented than Perelman but who had performed erratically in competitions, chose the first strategy. Alexander Levin, the reigning number two at the math club, chose the second strategy. By the time Perelman was in his last year of secondary school, he had one silver and one gold medal from the All-Soviet Math Olympiad to his name, and it seemed a certainty to him and to everyone around him that he would travel to the international competition and return triumphant, assured of a place at the Mathmech. It was a relief for Ryzhik, who was particularly loath to meddle in the life of a student he respected so highly, especially since trying to prove the anti-Semitic nature of admissions policies to either Grisha or his mother might very well have been an impossible task. Lubov Perelman, it seemed, had an extraordinary gift for denying the obvious, and she had passed this gift along to her child.

The basic questions of parenthood—what to tell your child, when, and how much—are tinged with fear in a totalitarian society, where dissidence is punished. What if the child says the wrong thing at the wrong time, exposing the family to danger? My own parents, active consumers and sometime producers of samizdat, chose to give me unfettered access to information, occasionally admonishing me to keep my mouth shut. On several occasions I spilled more than I should have, and this fortunately went unnoticed—but while I am ever grateful to my parents for treating me like an adult, the risk they took was probably unwise. Most other parents kept to a policy of never exposing their children to anything that could not be safely repeated at school. Lubov Perelman seems to have pursued an even more radical strategy: she taught her son that the world worked exactly as it should.

"He never believed there was anti-Semitism in the Soviet Union," Rukshin told me on a couple of occasions, repeating this observation with the kind of joyous wonder with which he had informed me that Grisha was never interested in girls, as though the denial of anti-Semitism too were evidence of Perelman's unparalleled purity.

When I asked Golovanov, who also happened to be Jewish, whether this was true, he was uncharacteristically stumped. No, he had never discussed the topic with Perelman, but how could anyone in his right mind believe there was no anti-Semitism in the Soviet Union? "He was not stupid," Golovanov assured me.

How can one not believe in something as evident as Soviet anti-Semitism? This raises two other questions: What is belief? And what is evidence? Soviet anti-Semitism was not quantifiable. Nor was it absolute: for example, the number of Jews accepted to Mathmech appeared to vary from year to year. Never was discrimination practiced so openly as to be articulated: when a Jew was turned down for a job or for university admission, a reason other than the person's Jewishness was generally cited. When Perelman was thirteen, all the boys who took prizes at the Leningrad citywide math olympiad at his grade level were Rukshin students and Jewish; the surnames of prize takers and honorable-mention recipients included Alterman, Levin, Perelman, and Tsemekhman. This was worse than just four Jewish boys; this was four *obviously* Jewish boys. As Rukshin remembered it, the university professor who chaired the city jury that year, himself a Jew, looked at the list and sighed. "We ought to have fewer of these sorts of winners."

Starting in the eighth grade, those who took first and second places in the city olympiad would advance to another round of competition to select the city representative for the national competition. Predictably, the winners that year came from Rukshin's club: Alexander Vasilyev and Nikolai Shubin took first place; Perelman, along with two more boys and a girl from Rukshin's club, took second place. The rules dictated that the six teenagers advance to the selection round, but all six were Jewish. Still, the names of the two top-prize takers were not as obviously Jewish as Perelman was: Vasilyev was a Slavic surname, and Shubin, while Jewish, did not sound quite as offensive as Perelman did to those who were offended by the Jewishness of others. So, apparently in an attempt to avoid reprimands, the organizers suggested scrapping the selection round and simply sending either Vasilyev or Shubin to the nationals. Rukshin waged a fight to have a selection tour and to have Perelman take part in it. Rukshin's ambitions as coach melded with his indignation on behalf of his favorite student, and he succeeded —almost: the organizers agreed to hold a selection round, but only between top scorers Shubin and Vasilyev. "I pleaded, I swore, I screamed, and I threatened," recalled Rukshin. In the end Perelman was not allowed to compete, but the organizers said he could attend the selection round to practice solving problems if he so wished.

Except that Perelman did not want to attend the selection round. "He kept saying, 'But I really didn't solve as many problems as Shubin and Vasilyev,'" said Rukshin. "I mean, if ever the Soviet regime could rear a Jewish boy who believed that man was always rewarded in accordance with his accomplishments, here he was." Finally, Rukshin strong-armed Perelman into attending, and Perelman ended up solving seven out of seven problems—the next-best result was three out of seven—and going to the nationals. Rukshin chalked up another strategic victory in the battle against anti-Semitism even as Perelman demonstrated that the existence of anti-Semitism could not be proved. So why should he believe in it? That would be like believing an object was a sphere just because it looked round only to discover that it had a tiny hidden hole.

My own father had cried following his first round of university admissions exams, just as Ryzhik had. My mother had walked out of her exam when she saw the word *Jewess* in black ink next to her name on a sheet of paper on the examiner's desk. Both of my parents had been warned about anti-Semitic admissions policies and had decided to trust their abilities to break through. As long as I can remember, they talked of the prospect of my own college entrance exams with dread—what I now understand to be the chilling dread of trying to explain to your child that some of the world is so unfair as to make all hope futile. I know that this dread was a large part of the reason for my parents' decision to emigrate.

Lubov Perelman acted as though reality corresponded to the rules—and for the moment, reality accommodated her, albeit with a lot of help from Grisha Perelman's small phalanx of supporters.

Sometime in the fall of 1981 Alexander Abramov, the young coach of the Soviet IMO team, traveled to Leningrad to ask Rukshin who among his students would likely be joining the team. Rukshin's reputation as a brilliant coach had already been established, so it was certain he would be offering someone. He named two people: Perelman and Levin. Both were graduating from high school that year, making it the last year they were eligible to compete.

Members of the math club believed Perelman to be the undisputed and unreachable number one and Levin his distant but stable and also hardly reachable number two. City competition results bore this out, and, in the self-absorbed way of adolescents in general and members of Rukshin's club in particular, the students believed Perelman and Levin were the top two mathematics competitors in the whole huge country. In Rukshin's opinion, Levin's potential indeed equaled or even exceeded Perelman's. But in this competition, Levin had too many disadvantages. "His parents did not understand what it was to be a mathematician," explained Golovanov. "Grisha's mother understood it very well, while Levin's parents thought studying mathematics might be useful if one wanted to become an engineer." In other words, they failed to see the value of the single-minded devotion Rukshin inspired in his students. Levin's parents apparently insisted he pay as much attention to his schoolwork as to the math club. "He was too good a student at the school, consequently he did not always attend the club, and that was his silly accident, the gate that had been left open, so Alik was done in by his conscientiousness," said Golovanov, referring to the fortress gate that, legend has it, brought down Constantinople in the fifteenth century. "At the All-Soviet competition he solved all the problems with the exception of the one that had actually been solved at the club." It was a freak accident: only very, very rarely and contrary to all rules and logic was a problem used in the All-Soviet competition one that had been floated elsewhere. But since every math problem had a human author and an idea behind it, no one could guarantee uniqueness. And in this particular case, in April 1982, a problem that was offered to competitors in the All-Soviet Mathematical Olympiad was one whose solution had been written down neatly by every member of Rukshin's math club—at least, everyone who had shown up. Alexander Levin had not come to the club that particular day. He did not solve the problem in the competition, and he did not make the Soviet IMO team. And though surely this was not intended by Levin, Rukshin, or even Perelman, it was fitting; that year only Rukshin's favorite, brightest, singular student went to the IMO. Rukshin had worked for this for six years, shaping Grisha into the ideal competitor.

The Leningrad city competition looks very much like any session of a Petersburg math club: competitors sit in classrooms solving problems, and when one considers a problem solved, he raises a hand to call attention to himself; a pair of judges then escorts the competitor out of the classroom to listen to his solution and make a judgment on the spot on its quality; the competitor then returns to the classroom to either rework his solution or go on to another problem. As Rukshin recalled, at the selection round Perelman was explaining his solution to one of the problems. He had talked his way through one of the possible outcomes when the two judges who were his audience turned to leave, saying that his solution was correct. "Wait!" he shouted, grabbing one of them by the tail of his suit jacket. "There are three more possible outcomes."

Two key Perelman traits were displayed here. One was that, as Rukshin put it, "he was deliriously honest even at moments when what was important was that he could have saved time." *Delirious* is a wonderful word, conjuring up the drive of someone organically incapable not only of telling an untruth but of telling an incomplete truth. But what if Perelman was wrong? What if the part he had explained was correct and represented the complete solution while the rest was superfluous? In math olympiad slang, a solution—or part of a solution—that looked right to its author but was wrong was called a *lipa*, a general Russian slang term for *fake* that literally means "linden" but is probably best translated as *lemon*. Everyone who spoke to me about Perelman specifically mentioned this trait of his: he had no lemons. None. Ever. Such was the precision of his mind: not only was he incapable of telling a lie—he was even incapable of making an honest mistake.

Mathematicians make mistakes. This is part of what they do. Unlike humanities scholars, they cannot allow for the possibility of more than one truth. But unlike natural scientists, they cannot check their hypotheses against empirical truths. So they have only the resources of their own minds—and those of their colleagues—with which to subject their imaginary constructions to sets of imaginary rules, to see if they still hold up. This makes the peer-review process in mathematics even more important than it is in any other academic discipline, and it also explains the importance of having the two-year waiting period imposed by the Clay Institute before it awards one of its Millennium Prizes. Even so, mathematicians make mistakes that sometimes take years to catch. Occasionally they catch them themselves—as Poincaré did when he realized that he had not proved his own conjecture. Sometimes the mistakes are discovered by referees, as when Andrew Wiles released his original attempt to prove Fermat's Last Theorem. The solution turned out to contain a serious flaw, which Wiles fixed himself but not until two years later. Young mathematicians, less adept at subjecting their own solutions to scrutiny, make mistakes more frequently than older ones. It is not surprising that Grisha Perelman could not conceive of himself making mistakes; what is surprising is that he actually did not make them.

So it must have been all the more upsetting to him that when he finally made it to his first national competition that year, he took second place. Both of his coaches—Rukshin and Abramov—claimed that it was after the All-Soviet Olympiad in Saratov that Perelman got mean. He set about ensuring he would never lose to anyone again. "He had now tasted the blood of a freshly killed competitor" was how Rukshin put it. "And his ambitions far exceeded his accomplishments." Here Rukshin's ornate language seemed to get the better of his understanding of Perelman. It seems that what bothered Perelman in Saratov in 1980 was what would always bother him about the world: things had not gone logically. If Perelman was so good that he had never had a lemon, if his mind was so powerful that it had never encountered a problem it could not crack, then why had he not taken first place? The only possible answer lay in unforgivable human failure: Grisha Perelman had not practiced enough. From then on he practiced ceaselessly. While for other kids life was divided into school and leisure, for Perelman it was split into time devoted to solving problems without disruption and the rest of the time.

The 1982 IMO team was to have four members; that meant six would be chosen, so there would be two alternates. In January 1982

Abramov collected a dozen potential members of the team at a school in the science town of Chernogolovka, about fifty miles north of Moscow. The national chemistry and physics coaches were gathering their potential competitors at the same time and in the same place, so about forty of the country's brightest high-school seniors were there, bunking four to a room in the school's dormitory, located in the same building as the school. They were fifteen- to seventeen-year-olds—seventeen being the standard age for a graduating student. But several of these competitors were, like Perelman, precocious; at fifteen and a half, Grisha was not the youngest. So they were not quite grownups, and though several of them lived away from home at specialized schools, they later remembered the odd sensation of being on their own in Chernogolovka. One student recalled waking up in the morning and seeing that water in a jar on the windowsill had frozen because a pane of glass was broken; though the room was nonetheless adequately heated, he felt shocked and depressed by the sight. Another recalled arriving by bus in Chernogolovka in the dark evening—which in January is any time after four in the afternoon—and then, unable to find the school, wandering the empty and poorly lit streets of the town carrying a suitcase with clothes and books and a mesh bag of food supplies that were so heavy they hurt his glove-less hands. Grisha Perelman certainly remembered nothing so traumatic because he traveled to Chernogolovka with his mother. Other trainees thought that was odd and slightly humiliating for a male adolescent, even if he was a math prodigy, but Perelman was apparently oblivious.

As he was oblivious to the grueling physical routine to which the trainees were subjected. In full accordance with Kolmogorov's ideals, the boys were expected to train not only in their chosen sciences but also in athletics—a custom that set the Soviet math-competition training system sharply apart from those of Western countries, which also gathered potential team members for training sessions. "They would collect all the mathematicians, physicists, and chemists—that's more than thirty people right there—in one gym," recalled Alexander Spivak, who eventually made the team. He was a student at the Kolmogorov boarding school in Moscow, where athletics was stressed as an important part of the study program, but as he recalled, he had never been subjected to anything so physically taxing. "To give us all something to do, first they made us run around the perimeter of the gym, and run, and run. And then there were these long benches there, and there was the gym coach and his imagination, which determined what could be done with them. You could do pushups off them. You could lift them over your head. You could jump over them back and forth. And you do all this. And all you see is this bench in front of your eyes. The whole time it's the bench, the bench, the bench."

Spivak recalled that one of the boys fainted, and at one point the others simply stopped and sat down on a bench, all of them in a row. What he remembered about Grisha Perelman was that he was "heroic," which in that case meant that, unlike the other boys, he did not protest, stage a sit-down strike, or generally show any dissatisfaction with the proceedings. He could not have enjoyed the exercise or found it easy: Perelman had a terrible time in gym class at school, and despite everyone's best efforts, he never managed to fulfill the Preparedness for Labor and Defense of the USSR requirements, which called for an upperclassman to run, swim, perform pull-ups, and shoot a small-caliber rifle. Nor did he manage to get above a C-level grade in physical education, which accounted for the only nonperfect grade on his graduating transcript. But rules were rules, and if Grisha was told to hop back and forth over a bench as part of his training for the international mathematics competition, hop he did.

His behavior at the gym may partly explain why some of his fellow trainees remembered Perelman as athletic. "He wasn't formally athletic, as if he had trained in tennis or something like that," recalled Sergei Samborsky, who made the team reserve. "But we all tended to ignore gym class and be shapeless while he was fit, in shape. And if you asked me what kind of sport I would associate with him, I'd say it was boxing." Over the course of a quarter of a century, Samborsky's memory had probably melded the deep impression left by Perelman's competitiveness and confidence with the recollection of Perelman's physical being. Perelman was pale, slightly overweight, and much shorter than his teammates; he was no boxer. But he was a math fighter, certain he would never again be defeated.

He was cocky. "One time one of the coaches reproached him by saying, 'You know, Grisha, everyone else knows derivatives and you don't,'" recalled Samborsky. "That was a part of mathematical analysis, and strictly speaking, as a secondary-school student, he wasn't required to know. But he responded, 'So what, I'll solve the problems without it.' It sounded brazen, but in essence, he was right." And then Samborsky added something that showed he remembered Grisha Perelman perhaps more accurately than he himself realized: "I suspect he knew a lot more than he let on." In fact, he probably knew derivatives. But he left this information out because he was there to solve problems, not to prove anything to the coaches.

Everyone got the point anyway. Coach Abramov remembered Perelman as being the only student who had never seen a competition problem he could not solve. And Samborsky put it simply: "He was better at solving problems—so much better, in fact, that one could say he was better than the rest of us put together. There was Grisha, and then there were the rest of us."

Out of the rest of them, at the end of the winter training camp, five more members of the team were tentatively chosen. The trainees were ranked according to the number of problems solved in the course of the camp. Number six was fifteen-year-old Spivak. An ethnic Russian who came to Moscow from a village in the Urals to study at the Kolmogorov boarding school, he hadn't known he had a Jewish-sounding last name. So he had no way of making sense of things when he was suddenly bumped off the list in favor of an ethnic Ukrainian who ranked seventh.

To the trainees, the winter camp was a succession of problem-solving competitions designed to resemble the actual olympiad; grueling gym sessions; lectures by renowned mathematicians, many of whom were living legends in the boys' world; and a nagging but tolerably quiet buzz produced by various education ministry and Party officials who hovered around the camp and occasionally cornered the trainees to remind them that it was the honor of the great Union they would be defending at the IMO. To the coaches, however, the camp was equal parts training and evaluating the boys and neutralizing the buzzing officials. They chose their battles. Even the obvious, inevitable inclusion of the extraordinary Perelman on the team required that the coaches put up a fight, for a competitor with a surname like that spelled trouble for the ministry minders; the coaches used up all of their fighting points, and the sixth-ranked Spivak, with his suspicious last name, was sacrificed.

When I met Spivak a quarter of a century later, he was an overgrown math boy: huge, with a disheveled head of graying hair, dressed in mismatched multicolored knits, he pleaded with me to relieve him of the social discomfort of a café, and he came to be interviewed at my apartment instead. He was working as a math instructor at one of Moscow's specialized schools, and he had spent much of his life putting together collections of math problems for gifted children. His manner of answering questions was disarmingly direct:

"So do you remember arriving in Chernogolovka?" I asked. "Was it morning, daytime, or evening?"

"I don't see why that's interesting," he responded. "It would be so much more interesting to ask me where everyone was now."

"Indeed it would be," I admitted. "Where is everyone now?"

"I don't know," he answered simply.

I fared barely better with questions regarding the connections that team members had made with one another: Spivak claimed he didn't see what was so special about the experience that it would have made the boys bond. When I argued that stress was a great unifier, he launched into a discussion of the comparative levels of complexity of the problems in different competitions. But he had a striking, emotionally charged memory of his experience of trying to get on the team. He had known that he had to make it in order to gain admission to a university. Even if he was unaware of the suspicious sound of his surname, he had judged—rightly, in all likelihood—that he would be unable to write the essay that was part of the entrance exams. "I just knew that I would be spending two years in the army, and I didn't know what would happen to me there," he told me. He had to claw his way to the IMO. He begged and pleaded, and he caused the coaches and ministry officials to scream at one another, and in the end, while he remained the seventh-ranking competitor, he was allowed to work on the take-home problem set, a small book that filled the potential competitors' time between the January camp and the All-Soviet Olympiad in April.

April saw all the boys in Odessa, a once-grand city on the Black Sea. They spent two days at a seaside resort solving the hardest problems they had ever faced: the consensus was that the All-Soviet problem sets were harder than those at the IMO. Spivak, who felt the rest of his life was at stake, took nothing for granted —he worked frantically, desperately, filling two entire composition books with textbook proofs that formed merely a part of the basis of his solutions and that he should have claimed were well established. Had Perelman perceived the world as the unfair place it was, he also would have had reason to think the rest of his life was at stake. But his confidence in himself and in the order of things was unshakable. He did what he always did: he read the problem, closed his eyes, leaned back, rubbed his pant legs with his palms with growing intensity, then rubbed his hands together, opened his eyes, and wrote down a very precise and very succinct solution to the problem. When solving the more difficult problems, he hummed softly. He filled only a couple of pages with his solutions. Both he and Spivak had perfect scores.

On the final day of the competition, as the jury gathered to grade the results, the top seven contenders—now including Spivak—were chosen to accompany Kolmogorov, who was visiting the national competition for the last time, on a walk through Odessa. Neither Spivak nor Samborsky remembered what Kolmogorov discussed with them—in any case, he was already afflicted with Parkinson's, and making out what he said must have been difficult—but both recalled that at a certain point he commanded the entire group to head for the beach. "The wind from the sea was piercing," recalled Samborsky. "We had to stay by his side because we'd been warned never to leave him alone since he couldn't see well. And Kolmogorov decided to go swimming. He undressed and went into the sea, and I was scared even to look at it; it was so cold it was almost like there were slabs of ice still floating. Waves the color of lead, foaming, wind so strong it could knock you off your feet. None of us followed him." Presently a guard emerged and told the boys to "rescue the grandpa," who surely could not fare well in the sea in this weather. The boys refused—either because none of them could swim well enough, as Spivak remembered, or because none of them dared confront Kolmogorov, as Samborsky recalled.

In either case, the following picture emerges. On a cold gray afternoon in the second half of April 1982, the greatest Russian mathematician of the twentieth century, making his last mathematical journey, went for a swim in the freezing water of the Black Sea while the greatest Russian mathematician of the twenty-first century sat impassively on shore and looked on. He had come because he was instructed to watch over "grandpa"; he had little use for all the walking and small-talking that was tacked onto the body of mathematics, and he had a distinct dislike for the water in which Kolmogorov was now enjoying what was left of his physical strength. The exuberant, expansive era of Russian mathematics was ending; a time of closed, secretive, concentrated individualism was beginning. Of course, no one could know this yet.

While Perelman waited for Kolmogorov on the beach, the All-Soviet Mathematical Olympiad jury worked out the final results of the competition, and Rukshin, Abramov, and several others began the final leg of the long and arduous process of ensuring Perelman would travel to Budapest for the IMO. The previous year, the IMO had been held in Washington, D.C. The Soviet Union's number one that year had been a Kiev high-school senior named Natalia Grinberg, a Jewish girl. This was a year after the United States had boycotted the Olympic Games (not the mathematics variety) held in Moscow. It was a year when Ronald Reagan's Evil Empire rhetoric defined U.S. policy toward Moscow. It was also the year when the Soviet Union de facto ended Jewish emigration. There was no way Soviet officials were going to let a Jewish girl represent the country at an IMO held in Washington: U.S. media coverage of her participation as envisioned by Moscow, as well as the possibility that she would defect—and the publicity surrounding that—added up to unacceptable risks. Grinberg was picked for the team—she had to be—but shortly before the planned trip she was told that her travel documents could not be processed in time. The USSR fielded six competitors instead of the eight required that year—another member of the team also had so-called problems with his documents—

and took ninth place with 230 points; every country that beat the Soviets that year had fielded eight competitors. Abramov was proud of that achievement: he had made sure that the Soviet team was set back no more than the 84 points the two missing members could have brought it.

Natalia Grinberg emigrated to Germany and became a professor of mathematics at Karlsruhe University. Her son, Darij Grinberg, represented Germany at the IMO three times between 2004 and 2006, winning two silver medals and one gold. Upon learning, during the judging of the IMO, that her son had apparently won the gold, Natalia Grinberg congratulated him and the team on a math forum and signed her post, "Natalia Grinberg, former number 1 in the 1981 USSR team, who was not allowed (in the last minute) to quit the beloved motherland to participate at IMO in Washington." For this professor, twenty-five years had clearly not assuaged the pain and insult of having been denied a prize for which she had worked most of her childhood and young adulthood.

As usual, Perelman was lucky and unaware of it. After placing ninth in Washington, the Soviet Union needed to restore its IMO status. The 1982 competition would be held in Budapest, the capital of Hungary, which was a part of the Soviet bloc and so, from a Soviet official's perspective, posed fewer publicity and security concerns than Washington. Nonetheless, competitors would still have contact with students from other parts of the world, including the United States. Further, the IMO was set up in such a way that competitors had next to no adult supervision: since all coaches were engaged in the judging process, teams and their adults had to have separate accommodations and keep contact to a minimum. To ensure that the Soviet competitors performed appropriately in every way, the boys were subjected to regular pep talks by ministry officials reminding them that they were representing the honor of their great land, and the adults were forced to prove to a dozen different officials that their charges were ideologically reliable. And still the risks, in the eyes of the officials, were formidable. Just four years earlier, when the IMO was held in Communist Romania, the Soviet Union had fielded no team at all—because, rumor had it, every single member of the team would have been Jewish.

To be allowed to travel, a Soviet citizen had to be granted a foreign-travel passport—no ordinary person was allowed to hold one as a matter of course—and an exit visa. This required clearance by local officials, travel authorities, and the secret police. To be allowed to travel on official business, representing the country, one also had to be cleared by the Party at every level, working one's way up from the local precinct to the district and, finally, to the federal level. At any of these stages, the documents of someone like Perelman could be stalled indefinitely by an overly cautious bureaucrat. "So Abramov and I made a pact," recalled Rukshin. "He worked on it in Moscow. I worked in St. Petersburg, pushing his documents through. After all, you know, I'd had many students in the club who were the children of someone powerful." Rukshin called in every chip he had; he used his connections to a secret police officer who was the father of one of his students, a local Party boss who was the father of one of his classmates, and another Party boss who was the husband of another classmate. Meanwhile, in Moscow, Abramov made regular visits to the education ministry begging officials there to keep tabs on the bureaucratic progress of the Soviet Union's great mathematical hope.

The six teammates—four members and two alternates—spent the month of June back in Chernogolovka. Incredibly—or, rather, it would have been incredible if they had been six regular teenagers thrown together in close quarters for a month instead of these six boys supremely gifted in mathematics—they did not socialize; they did not bond. They trained for days on end, breaking only for games of volleyball, visits with mathematical luminaries, and the inevitable Party pep talks. By July all four members of the team had their travel documents. They were Spivak; Vladimir Titenko from Belarus; Konstantin Matveev from Novosibirsk; and Perelman, the only Jewish member of the team.

The Soviet team arrived in Budapest on July 7. The competitors were taken to a hotel where each country's team of four had its own room. The students were now on their own; their coach had arrived in Hungary a couple of days earlier to take part in the final preparations—approving the translations of competition problems and assigning points to parts of each solution—and now the ministry handler who had accompanied the boys on the flight was also gone.

The competition lasted two days: July 9 and 10. Each day the 120 participants spent four and a half hours solving a set of three problems. Each problem was worth seven points for a complete solution, and anywhere from one to six points could be awarded for starting off in the right direction without making it to the end. The judging process—a complicated dance of negotiation and sometimes outright haggling involving judges from the host country, adjudicators from the countries where the particular problems originated, and coaches representing the competitors' interests— took three days following the competition.

During that time, the competitors were left to the care of local handlers. They were charged with the task of being good guests and worthy representatives of their countries—social tasks for which they were ill-suited. They submitted to touring around Budapest, taking a boat ride down the Danube, traveling to Balaton Lake for sightseeing and a swim, and visiting Ernő Rubik, inventor of the cube and other torturous mathematical toys that were then enjoying worldwide popularity. For the most part, they traveled speechlessly, though Rubik managed to elicit some questions, mostly concerning the minimum number of moves required to solve his puzzle and the possibility of devising an algorithm for a universal Rubik's Cube solution. Perelman showed no interest in the sights, declined to swim, and had no questions for the great Rubik.

A final social responsibility with which the Soviet team was burdened had to do with a bag of buttons. These had been handed to the team by a ministry official, who had talked of their duty to the motherland, of their responsibility as both competitors and diplomats, and of international friendship. And then she had pulled out the bag of buttons—the tourist variety, with pictures of Moscow and Leningrad on them—and, apparently zooming in on the most vulnerable of the boys, shoved the bag into Spivak's hands. Spivak, who had already done what he could for his country mathematically (he would be awarded a bronze medal), now had to figure out what to do with the souvenirs. He tried to draft his fellow team members into the effort but failed. So he took the bag and headed out into the hotel corridors.

"The order had to be carried out, even if we were not being supervised," Spivak told me. "So I went and tried to hand them out, though I barely spoke English, which made it very difficult, and then I went to the American team's room. And the way they fled the Evil Empire. I mean, they literally climbed under their beds. You would totally get the impression I was about to open fire on them. I tried to say something about friendship and that sort of thing, but I realized it was just too hard." Spivak left the room and disposed of the buttons someplace where he assumed they would not be found.

On July 14, the last day of the 1982 IMO, Perelman collected his trophies: a gold medal, shaped like an elongated hexagon that year; a special award certificate sponsored by Team Kuwait (last place) given to competitors who earned the maximum number of points —forty-two out of forty-two; a giant whip, which the Hungarians gave each medal winner; and a Rubik's Cube, which Grisha gave away when he returned to Leningrad. These were the prizes; Perelman's actual rewards for years of single-minded training were automatic admission to a university and, more central to his needs, the right to be left alone for another five years.

5

Rules for Adulthood

THE UNIVERSITY, FOR PERELMAN, began with long train
trips, long lines, and paperwork. Roughly ten members of
Rukshin's math club traveled as a pack. As Rukshin saw it, the
path to Mathmech had been blazed by Perelman, whose right to be
admitted without entrance exams had either forced or allowed the
university to exceed its usual two-Jews-per-year quota and accept
at least three people who, for the purposes of admissions discrimination policies, were Jewish in every way: their surnames sounded
Jewish, and their identity documents stated they were Jewish. One
additional Jewish student in an entering class of roughly three
hundred and fifty may seem like a drop in the bucket, but for Rukshin, who got to send three rather than two of his Jewish students
off to Mathmech, it felt like a victory and even, perhaps—if he was
to be believed when he spoke about it a quarter of a century later—
a revolution. The other members of the math club who made it to
the prestigious mathematics department were either ethnic Rus-

sians or, like Golovanov, Jews who through marriage or other circumstances had lucked into Russian surnames and Russian identity documents.

The large entering class was split into groups of about twenty-
five people each. Perelman and several others from Rukshin's math
club and from Leningrad's other specialized math schools were assigned to the same group, and those who were not arranged to be
transferred to it. In the end the group represented a sort of elite
learning center within Mathmech, singled out much as its members had been when they were schoolchildren. Most of them traveled daily from the city; in the 1970s Leningrad University had
moved its science departments to Petrodvorets, a suburb about
twenty miles west of the city. What had been conceived as an ambitious project, a campus that was a city unto itself like a sort of
Russian Cambridge University, had fizzled, turning the newly built
glass-and-concrete math, physics, and science buildings into a very
inconveniently located commuter school (the rest of the university
remained in Leningrad). The students took unheated suburban
trains with wooden seats, invariably having to run to catch the one
that would deliver them to school in time for the day's first lecture
and often risking missing the last city-bound train, which left before midnight.

Russian universities offered a highly specialized education.
Mathmech was geared toward producing professional mathematicians or, if that failed, mathematics instructors and computer
programmers. Detours into what might be considered liberal arts
were minimal, while detours into Marxist theory, though not as
demanding as they were at the humanities departments, still included required courses in dialectical materialism, historical materialism, scientific communism, scientific atheism, the political
economics of capitalism, and an entire course entitled A Critique
of Certain Strands of Contemporary Bourgeois Philosophy and

Anti-Communist Ideology, which was taught by a young philosophy professor who managed to sing all the requisite praises of Marxist-Leninist philosophy, brand other contemporary philosophers rotten, and then proceed to tell the students what they had always wanted to know but were afraid to ask about Nietzsche and Kierkegaard. "So this was a class we actually attended," Golovanov told me. Otherwise, most students attempted to devise ways to avoid showing up not only to the ideological classes but also to the large lecture courses and, in most cases, courses that fell outside the area in which they planned to specialize. There was, naturally, one exception: Grisha Perelman attended everything, including the large lectures from which he was exempt because his grades never dipped below a four on a five-point scale.

Golovanov called the Marxism courses "the crazy disciplines." Perelman accepted them as part of the learning package and used the great compacting brain of his to the benefit of all his classmates. "Grisha's clarity of mind was very helpful here," recalled Golovanov. "The thing about all this stream-of-unconsciousness is that you either have to process it all or ignore it completely. The former is impossible for ordinary humans, and the latter is fraught with danger. Grisha somehow managed to find the strands of thought, if you can call it that, in those disciplines. So his notes on all the crazy disciplines were of great value to us all."

What no doubt helped Perelman plow through the dense nonsense of Marxist theory as it was then being taught was his genuine disregard for politics of any sort. "In Grisha's lexicon *politics* was always a swearword," said Golovanov. "Say, if I wanted to organize something to make things better, some campaign aimed at helping our beloved Sergei Rukshin even, he would say, 'That's politics, let's focus on solving problems instead.' And you have to understand that this was a genuine position: he disliked all sorts and directions of politics equally." The traditional Russian intellectual's queasiness at the political process had less to do with Perelman's position than did the fact that he was truly uninterested in anything that was not mathematics. While other students may have felt insulted or excited, Perelman remained dispassionate; none of the issues discussed in these courses had a connection to anything that mattered. His notes on Marxist theory were purely systematizing exercises, performed with his unique efficiency.

The ideology courses notwithstanding—and they were, after all, fewer than at many other departments—Mathmech was what in the Soviet Union passed for a liberal institution of higher learning. Those who wanted to get through its five-year course with minimal effort and minimal knowledge had to suffer through the first year with a heavy learning load and afterward could proceed to coast. Those who wanted to specialize early could tune much of the rest of mathematics out. Perelman represented the rarest breed of Mathmech student: one who sought to be universally educated in mathematics.

Most mathematically ambitious students had for years known their specialization was preordained: they had one sort of brain or the other. The algebraists might then look for the most promising problems of algebra while the geometers might cast about for the most interesting geometer with whom to study, but in general, their directions were set. Perelman's brain was made to embrace all of mathematics. In retrospect, one might suppose that topology ultimately attracted him as the quintessence of mathematics—the province of pure categories and clear systems, with no informational interference—but as a first-year student, he was barely exposed to topology. Most mathematicians remember their one freshman course in topology for teaching them the mental exercise of turning an inner tube inside out using a tiny hole; it is that mind-bending quality of topology that most recall, not its streamlined clarity. Perelman did not have the other usual motivation to specialize early: he had no reason to try to save time by studying only the mathematics in which he planned to work. He was not rushing anywhere. He was living for mathematics and by doing mathematics.

He attended lectures and seminars across mathematical disciplines without much apparent concern for the quality of instruction offered. The effect could be comical. In his fourth year at the university Perelman attended a course in computer science taught by an instructor who had earned the reputation of being one of the department's worst lecturers. "Normal people did not attend this," said Golovanov. Perelman did. And he generally sat at the front of the room, which was probably why he caught the eye of the instructor, who at one particular moment became agitated about the state of mathematical knowledge among Mathmech students in general. "Our fourth-year students can't even solve the simple Cauchy Problem," he declared. He wrote out the classic differential-equation problem on the board and turned to Perelman. "Can you tell me how this problem is solved?"

Perelman approached the board calmly and wrote out the solution.

"Yes," said the instructor. "This student solved the problem correctly."

Where Perelman and his crowd came from, a high-school student who could not produce the solution to the Cauchy Problem on request would be disdained as an imbecile—"and rightly so," commented Golovanov. Still, when the instructor was in a position of authority, Perelman seemed willing to submit to ridiculous exercises without protestation. Later, what he perceived as the need to prove his worthiness to his peers or to academic authorities infuriated him instantly, but within the confines of the university, he apparently gave professors almost unlimited license. This particular computer-science instructor also had the bizarre custom of nailing his students' notes to their desks—to ensure that students actually attended the sessions rather than borrowed one another's notes. Perelman tolerated this indignity too and helped the rest of his group by verbally summarizing the notes.

He was loyal to his group as long as no one broke the rules as he perceived them. A Mathmech custom dictated that students help peers who found themselves stuck during a written test. Outright cheating was impossible, since every student had an individual problem set, drawn at random from a large pool. But if one was stalled desperately, one could generally pass a note to another student that briefly summarized the issue. The response was never a solution but often something along the lines of "Try this tack." Perelman, the universal problem-solver, the fastest thinker in his age group in the Soviet Union and perhaps the world, would have been the best person to answer these sorts of questions. He was, however, unwilling to entertain them, and he let his disapproval of the practice be known: everyone had to solve his own problem for himself.

Somewhere in the transition from adolescence to adulthood, Perelman seemed to have found a way to relieve the tension between prevailing social mores, which he perceived as illogical, internally inconsistent, and perpetually shifting—and they certainly were all of these things—and his idea of how the world should work. He derived a set of his own rules based on the few values he knew to be absolute and proceeded to follow them. As new situations presented themselves, he figured out the rules that applied to them—this too may have seemed inconsistent and shifting to an observer, but only because the observer did not know the algorithm. Naturally, Perelman expected the rest of the world to follow his rules; it would not have occurred to him that other people did not know them. After all, the rules were based on universal values, honesty being primary among them. Honesty meant always telling the whole truth, which is to say, all of the available accurate information—much as Perelman did when he supplied his proofs with information extraneous to the actual solution. Clearly, in the case of a student taking a Mathmech test, supplying *all of the available information* would have included naming the person with whom the idea for the solution had originated, and that would truly have been inconsistent with the rule that every student must do his own work. Later, he would view, say, sloppy footnoting, as practiced by many mathematicians, as plagiarism. It is possible too that a bit of the competitor's habit shaped his perception of the written tests; after all, they did look and, perhaps for Perelman, feel a bit like the olympiad, and it would have been inconceivable for a competitor to ask his fellow problem-solvers for hints.

In the third year, each Mathmech student chose a specialty that would presumably take him through graduate school and into a research career. Golovanov chose number theory. It was a natural choice for a boy who could be knocked out of competitions upon encountering a geometry problem and who seemed to relate to numbers as others did to people. Perelman chose his own destiny. He had picked geometry, he told his group cryptically, because he wanted to go into a field populated by a few remaining dinosaurs so that he might also become one of them. In the 1980s in Leningrad, geometry seemed like an anachronism: it had none of the flair of computer science and none of the romance of numbers, and its practitioners were indeed a few larger-than-life old men. One of his classmates, Mehmet Muslimov, remembered that Perelman's declaration had not sounded pretentious. If anything, it sounded logical: here was a person from another time and place, odd and differently minded even in an environment as full of eccentrics as a university mathematics department; it was only reasonable that he would consciously fashion himself into a dinosaur.

What Perelman may also have been telling his classmates was that he felt quite exasperated with his fellow humans and their ways, and his chosen field seemed to attract the few people whose internal codes of conduct were as strict as his own.

Perelman needed someone to guide him along his path to dinosaurhood—or at least someone who would not get in his way and who would shield him from others if necessary. He was strongly drawn to Viktor Zalgaller, a geometer then in his sixties.

I interviewed Zalgaller in early 2008 in Rehovot, about twenty miles south of Tel Aviv. The town was built around the Weizmann Institute, a mathematics research facility with which Zalgaller was affiliated though he did all his work at his apartment, where his wife lay nearly motionless in the final stages of Alzheimer's disease. "The woman no longer manages the house," Zalgaller said apologetically as he welcomed me in. It was a messy place, lived in awkwardly, with Zalgaller's crumpled bedding on the living room couch, and a clutter of books, papers, and teacups where apparently a homey order had once reigned. Zalgaller himself was similarly unkempt: unshaven, wearing a crewneck sweater over gray pajamas, but entirely coherent and pointedly businesslike in his manner. He spoke of Perelman with awed affection, which was what he had always felt for him: "I had nothing to teach him from the beginning," he claimed.

Zalgaller was a World War II veteran, a charismatic teacher who had almost single-handedly shaped the mathematical curriculum and teaching style of School 239 (in the 1960s he had taken time off from research and university teaching to do this), and he was an incomparable storyteller. All of this had made him popular around the university and at the Leningrad Mathematics Institute, but none of those qualities held any special appeal for Perelman. "He liked me, I have no doubt about it," Zalgaller told me. "It may have had something to do with ethics. What I thought about what people must do." When I asked him to elaborate, Zalgaller claimed, "He liked my style of communicating with students. He must have known that I would not be strict and that studying with me would be interesting." In fact, it seemed Perelman had fairly little concern for the teaching style of his instructors. What must have drawn him to Zalgaller was a more particular aspect of the way he related to the world, exemplified by a story Zalgaller told me but forbade me to tape, apparently because it concerned him, and not Perelman—Zalgaller thought it improper to talk about himself. I wrote it down from memory as soon as I left his apartment.

Like most Soviet men of his generation, Zalgaller joined the Red Army in the early days of World War II, and like a very lucky few he spent the entire four years of the war in the service and survived with nary a scratch. He graduated Leningrad University in the late 1940s, just as Stalin's anti-Semitic Campaign Against Cosmopolitans was getting in full swing and Jews all over the Soviet Union were finding themselves universally turned down by colleges, graduate schools, and employers. Zalgaller was one of five Jews from his graduating class who applied to stay on in graduate school. All were deserving, thought Zalgaller, but when the list of those accepted for graduate study was posted at the university, Zalgaller found his own name on it—and none of the other Jewish students. So he turned the graduate school down.

The old man saw that I now expected him to tell me that he was unwilling to play by rigged rules, that he wanted to stay on in graduate school but could not if he felt he was doing it at another student's expense. "I was no fighter against anti-Semitism," he said, correcting my unspoken misconception with evident irritation. "I just didn't want to be dependent on those people." If he was the only Jew accepted, he would be in receipt of a favor—and that was what he turned down.

Zalgaller proceeded, stubbornly and almost miraculously, to construct a career on his own terms, accepting only those favors he was certain he could repay and conducting himself in accordance with a code that was not only more confining than that of others but also—perhaps equally important to Perelman—often indecipherable to anyone but Zalgaller himself. In the early 1990s, when Soviet researchers started having to write their own funding proposals, Zalgaller devised an ingenious way to solve the perceived dilemma of making the direction of his research contingent on the preferences of funders: he applied for money for projects he had already successfully completed but had not published and then used that money to finance his next project. Surely it was this complicated but internally coherent set of ethical perceptions and behaviors that appealed to Perelman, who asked Zalgaller to be his thesis adviser.

"I had nothing to teach him," Zalgaller repeated. "So what I did was just give him small problems that had evaded solution. Once he solved them, I saw to it that they were published. So by the time Grisha graduated from university, he already had several published papers." In other words, he continued to feed Perelman's brain, continuing what Rukshin had done and ever so gently helping Perelman find his way as a self-declared dinosaur.

Perhaps the single most fateful incident in Perelman's lifetime was the appearance, in Perelman's first year at Leningrad University, of a larger-than-life presence in the form of a small old man with a square gray beard. His name was Alexander Danilovich Alexandrov (his patronymic was generally used, in order to distinguish him from numerous other Alexander Alexandrovs); he was a living legend, and miraculously and almost ridiculously, he was teaching geometry to first-year Mathmech students.

Alexandrov had started out as a physicist but dropped out of graduate school in the 1930s because, he once explained, "I can't promise that I'll always do what I'm expected to do." One of his two advisers, the physicist Vitaly Fok, reportedly said to him, "You are too decent." The other, the mathematician Boris Delone, added, "You are too much not a careerist." He went on to defend two dissertations by the time he was twenty-five, receive a number of prestigious prizes, and in 1952 become president of Leningrad University at age forty.

"Alexandrov had a great influence on Grisha," claimed Golovanov, who had witnessed the beginning of their relationship firsthand: he too attended Alexandrov's freshman geometry course that year. "He was just the type, psychologically, who could exert that kind of influence. To sum up who Alexandrov was, briefly: he was a Young Pioneer of colossal intellectual might. I know quite a lot about him, and I think he is a person who never once in his life wanted to do something bad. Naturally, with this sort of approach to things, he committed bad deeds on an industrial scale—but he never once wanted to." Golovanov was fully aware that his description fit his friend Perelman just as well as it did their teacher. "There is a wonderful [Latin] saying," he continued, "that people consider incorrect, for some reason: *Vos vestros servate, meos mihi linquite mores*, 'I will go my own way and let others stick to theirs.' From a moral standpoint, this position is unassailable. And I think you know at least one other person who acts in accordance with this motto—he just happens not to be a university president," unlike Alexandrov. He happened to be Grisha Perelman.

Alexandrov owed his appointment as president of the university to his background as both a physicist and a mathematician: the two sciences had grown so important during the Soviet nuclear push that physicist-mathematicians had been chosen over Party functionaries to run the Leningrad and Moscow universities in the early 1950s. He was also a member of the Communist Party and remained one, in his true-believer style, until his death in 1999. He was by no means a loyalist, however. His most remarkable accomplishment as president of Leningrad University was preserving the study of genetics—a science banned under Stalin. While geneticists who had worked elsewhere were either jailed or reduced to employment at animal farms at best and menial jobs at worst, he ensured that seminars in genetics continued at his university. After Stalin's death, he even managed to get international geneticists to speak there, long before official Soviet science began its slow reacceptance of genetics. In the 1950s, he played a key role in protecting mathematics from a similar destructive campaign that had seemed to be taking shape. He managed, almost single-handedly, to reframe it as a movement to protect the prestige of Soviet mathematics from imagined Western efforts to denigrate Soviet achievements.

Alexandrov also risked his career—and ultimately lost his post as university president—by supporting mathematicians who came under attack for being either ideologically unreliable or Jewish. In 1951, the year before he became university president, he managed to intervene when the university's department of mathematical analysis was in danger of dissolution because it was staffed primarily by Jews. The department's members had exhausted all their appeals—no one felt powerful or brave enough to help. Then one of the mathematicians dared ask Alexandrov to step in, which was a desperate move on her part, since she had previously made an enemy of Alexandrov by mocking his sideline studies in philosophy. Alexandrov responded and devised a way to stem the attack by replacing the department chair. Almost forty years later, Alexandrov would play a key role in securing Perelman's academic career in the face of anti-Semitic discrimination, and another ten years after that, Olga Ladyzhenskaya, the daring mathematician from that department of mathematical analysis, would become the last person who successfully shielded Perelman from the world of real-life mathematicians.

Alexandrov was a believer—a literal one. He had engineered Leningrad University's move out of the city, and when a former student reproached him for this years later, as he was traveling to the university on one of the overcrowded commuter trains with hard bench seats, Alexandrov shouted for the entire train car to hear: "I believed in the Party program! It said in the appendices that Leningrad would be developing southward and the center would move southward! And then they started building northward." The former student, a very prominent mathematician, commented in a later memoir that by the 1960s everyone knew Party documents were not to be believed. He was probably missing the point: Alexandrov, like Perelman, lacked the disbelieving gene; he had the ability to reject, resist, and even hate, but he could not disbelieve.

Alexandrov was fired as the president in 1964 and proceeded to spend the next two decades in what still amounted to exile of the not-entirely-self-imposed variety in Siberia, helping to create a science town there. In his seventies, he returned to his university with what turned out to be a vain hope of reclaiming a place there: he wanted to fill a vacant chair in geometry. In the run-up to the chair election, he taught a first-year course and charmed students in part because of his openness about the absurdity of his predicament. He was given to quoting, among other things, the numerous poems Mathmech students made up about him. Poems like this one:

> Danilych labored in the math field
> Danilych rose every morning
> Too bad his efforts could but yield
> A course the students found boring

Eventually Alexandrov's hopes of obtaining the chair in geometry were dashed by academic and Party authorities, and he moved to a position at the Leningrad mathematical research institute—

but not before he had chosen Grisha Perelman as his protégé. While other students might have been drawn by Alexandrov's legendary status, his informal approach to teaching, and his intellectual expansiveness, Perelman gravitated not to Alexandrov's style but to his essence, contradictory and rigid as it was.

Indeed, had it not been for Alexandrov's bizarrely fearless management of the university, Perelman's career might have taken an entirely different path. As it happened, the study of topology was barely represented at the university until the early 1960s. When Alexandrov looked for a person who might launch the field in Leningrad, he stumbled upon Vladimir Rokhlin, a student of Kolmogorov's and Pontryagin's who was then eking out an anchorless existence in Moscow. He had served time in the Gulag, was still under surveillance, and was generally considered unhirable. Alexandrov brought Rokhlin to Leningrad and managed to provide him not only with a teaching job at the university but also with an apartment. In Leningrad, Rokhlin would see twelve of his students' dissertations to completion, including that of Mikhail Gromov, one of the world's leading geometers today and the man who would be largely responsible for introducing Perelman to the international mathematics community.

Perelman likely did not know much of this about Alexandrov, and if he had known, he might have disregarded what amounted to Alexandrov's heroism as mere politicking. Nor could he have predicted the role Alexandrov would play in his career. What certainly attracted Perelman to Alexandrov were his approaches to mathematics and to life in general.

On one hand, Alexandrov came from the academic school of unbounded generosity. "He would give topics and promising ideas away to his students," wrote Zalgaller, who was a student of Alexandrov's. On the other hand, he viewed mathematics as one long problem-solving marathon. A student recalled walking into Alexandrov's office.

"'So have you proved it?' Alexandrov asked.

"'What should I have proved?'

"'Anything!'

"It would be difficult to overestimate the influence of such constant expectation of results," wrote the former student. "From that point on I aimed to be prepared for this question."

Alexandrov was the undisputed king of geometry in Leningrad and, possibly, in all of the Soviet Union. Another student recalled Alexandrov's reaction to a request to write a history of Soviet geometry. "That would be immodest," Alexandrov had said. "There was no one there but me." Another student wrote that he had chosen to become a geometer after hearing another professor's words to the effect that "Alexandrov has discovered whole new worlds in mathematics and is now inhabiting them all by his lonesome." Perelman's dinosaur remark referred mostly to Alexandrov.

Around the time Perelman met him, Alexandrov was said to have made the following comment at a geometry seminar: "Everyone is a bastard, everyone is bad, with the possible exception of Jesus Christ. Einstein is bad too, because he did not leave America after the nuclear bomb was detonated over his objections." He once wrote, "In the end, through the general interconnectedness of events, a person becomes, in some way or another, to a greater or lesser extent, party to everything that happens in the world, and if he can exert any influence whatsoever on any event, then he becomes responsible for it." This view of individual responsibility squared perfectly with Perelman's concept of honesty, so he adopted Alexandrov's criteria as his own and would later apply them to everyone he encountered.

When Perelman entered the university, he became, at the advanced age of sixteen, practically an official adult. A more conventional teenager might have celebrated this transition by reassessing the rules, reshuffling authority figures, or claiming more independence. Perelman made the rules stricter, and added Zalgaller and Alexandrov to his pantheon of unassailable authority figures, where they joined his mother and Rukshin. Perelman adopted more-formal signs of his new status as a grownup: he stopped shaving, and in the math-club world, he went from being a student to being a teacher.

Following the established Kolmogorovian tradition, Rukshin sought to turn his first math-club graduates into the first math-club instructors who came from within. He chose Perelman and Golovanov—Perelman being his favorite student and Golovanov showing, even at fourteen, the potential to become a great teacher in Rukshin's mold. Rukshin took both to summer camp as instructors. Neither experiment proved fully successful. Golovanov, it turned out, was just a boy and generally acted like one; this would pass with age, and he would indeed grow into a math coach second in mastery and charisma only to Rukshin. Perelman turned out to be Perelman, which is to say, rigid, demanding, and hypercritical; these qualities would only intensify with age, ultimately making it impossible for him to be any kind of teacher or, indeed, communicator.

Early on in his career as an instructor—either during or right after his first year at the university—Perelman observed, in conversation with Golovanov, that the basic military training that was among Mathmech's required courses had proved useful because the military bylaws he had had to memorize could be applied directly to the running of the math club. "He said this with a smile, of course, because he is very smart," recalled Golovanov. "But one could tell that the share of humor in this supposed joke was no more than ten percent."

At camp following his first year, Perelman served as an instructor to a remarkable group of mathematicians two years younger than he. They included Fedja Nazarov, now a professor at University of Wisconsin; Anna Bogomolnaia, now a professor at Rice University; and Evgeny Abakumov, now a professor at the Université de Marne-la-Vallée in Paris. Every morning Perelman gave them a set of twenty problems—roughly double the club's usual semiweekly dose. The problems were extremely difficult, and the level of difficulty was increased with little regard for the students' actual abilities and achievements. "The general concept always was that the carrot should be hanging just barely above the level to which the rabbit could jump," Golovanov explained to me. "But Grisha believes that the rabbit should always be jumping higher and higher." A student who failed to solve at least half of the problems by midday was told he or she could not have lunch. "They still got lunch, of course," recalled Golovanov. "But undeservedly."

What was the seventeen-year-old Perelman thinking about his fifteen-year-old charges? Did he suspect that despite all of their considerable accomplishments and their desire to learn, as evidenced by their presence at the math camp, they were secretly intellectually lazy? Possibly. "He certainly thought that they did not take things seriously enough," said Golovanov. "It's also possible that he was so noble that he could not fathom they were just not smart enough—and anyway, considering what they grew into, those kids probably were smart enough." More likely, this was a classic theory-of-mind problem. The seventeen-year-old Perelman —university student, olympiad champion, and universal problem-solving machine—did not and could not imagine that these math-club teenagers, who had two years' fewer problem-solving and competition experience and who simply lacked his problem-crunching skills, could not do what he could if they really, really put their minds to it.

When depriving his hapless students of lunch failed, he started banishing them from the study room. "We tried to explain to Grisha that if a child has been accepted into camp, he cannot be held outside class for days at a time, that this was not punishment but total craziness," recalled Rukshin. "He responded that he would not let the child into class until the child solved such-and-such. It was really hard." Those banished included Bogomolnaia, Nazarov, and Konstantin Kohas; in another dozen years, Kohas would hold the chair in mathematical analysis at Mathmech.

So why did Rukshin keep Perelman, whose lectures could be borderline incomprehensible and whose behavior was clearly abusive? Part of the answer was surely that Rukshin loved Perelman, and having him near—this seems to have been the summer when the two shared a room at the camp—filled his time, and his teaching, with additional meaning. But it also may be that Perelman's limitations as a teacher suited Rukshin's perceptions of how things ought to work. Here is how Rukshin described the situation to me, using terminology from Laurence Peter and Raymond Hull's *The Peter Principle:* "Perelman was a brilliant teacher for super-competent students, a good one for competent students, and a mediocre one for those who were moderately competent. You see, a cobalt-alloy drill bit is a wonderful instrument. But you cannot use it to drill a piece of glass: the glass will crack and crumble. Whereas a bullet will leave a neat little round hole in a piece of glass but absolutely cannot be used to drill metal. A knife and an ax perform similar jobs, but one is far superior for sharpening a pencil while the other is a better tool for felling an oak tree. A teacher is a tool. For a limited group of super-strong students, where discipline is not an issue—I mean, where it came to the organizing duties of a teacher, Perelman did not do as well. But at camp, we have always had this tradition: we do not hire a separate person for making sure the kids are clean and fed and go to bed on time, and a separate teacher who teaches them things. The Holy Trinity is a single being: a teacher, a counselor, and the boss. Because these kids would never have respected some random camp counselor anyway.

They had respect for the kind of teacher who took them hiking, got wet in the rain with them, sweated in the heat, did mathematics, and discussed books—especially since back then I wasn't much older than my students." Rukshin was nine years older than Perelman and ten to twelve years older than most of his students, and, as his diction indicates, he clearly thought he was not just a beloved teacher but God himself. His students turned teachers were therefore angels, and as such, in his mind they had the right to be not only of clearly circumscribed utility but also unreasonable, capricious, and outright childish.

The conflict came, naturally, once the students who had borne the brunt of Perelman's military-style mathematical discipline grew old enough to encounter him as equals. It must have been just before the summer camp season of 1985 when Perelman declared he would not teach summer camp if Nazarov and Bogomolnaia were teaching there too. Twenty-plus years later, Rukshin either could not or would not recall the nature of Perelman's objections to the two younger teachers. It seemed Perelman found Bogomolnaia generally objectionable—because she was a girl who did not wear skirts, for example, and because he had somehow discovered that she did not always tell the truth.

"Did he catch her lying to him?" I asked Rukshin.

"No, he just found out she did not tell the truth at all times," said Rukshin. "I tried to explain to him—I mean, only idiots tell the truth at all times, but I did not tell him that. What I did say was, Grisha, what you are describing is not a part of a human being but a feature of his relationships with others. There are people I would never lie to, and there are people to whom I have no moral obligations. I would prefer not to lie to them, but I cannot exclude the possibility that I would distort the truth or not tell the truth. He would not accept this point of view." In fact, he probably could not; the idea that a behavior—especially a behavior he found unacceptable—was not an inherent quality but a function of something as intangible as a particular human relationship was, in all likelihood, entirely incomprehensible to him. Plus, he knew at least one person who claimed always to tell the truth and to have done so his whole life, thereby giving the lie to Rukshin's basic premise. That person was Alexander Danilovich Alexandrov, whose gravestone in St. Petersburg is inscribed with words that translate to "The truth is the only thing to be worshipped."

Bogomolnaia couldn't recall the incident either, but she remembered the world of math clubs, summer camps, and Rukshin as conflict-ridden. "We were young, we were all difficult to get along with, and it was hard to work alongside one another," she explained, and she continued in a detached tone of voice but using vocabulary that conveyed residual bitterness—mostly, I gathered, toward Rukshin. "In our little snake pit, people would come into conflict with one another for reasons that seem utterly insignificant now that I'm forty."

Generally, Bogomolnaia thought, Perelman was poorly suited for teaching: "He just didn't quite have the temperament—I mean, you have to do something in addition to pure mathematics when you teach." But rather than simply drift away from teaching, he left in a rage—a rage, it seemed, that was fostered in part by Rukshin, who did anything but discourage conflict among his little stable of math angels. "I held discussions with every teacher who had agreed to teach at camp that summer," he told me. "We discussed it and decided that we could not take Grisha with us in light of his ultimatum."

So it was that when Perelman was nineteen, his world began its inexorable narrowing. He lost the social setting that had nurtured him since he was ten years old. At roughly the same time, in the middle of his third year at the university, he picked his specialty, which meant that his path and Golovanov's began to diverge; after

almost nine years of traveling to every class and math club together, occasionally stopping to write formulas in chalk on the
sidewalk, they now had different schedules. Here began the road
that would take Perelman through the next twenty years of his life
and to the point where he was speaking regularly to only his
mother and Rukshin, who still got to play God in his student's life,
now without the diluting and mitigating effects of the angels.

6

Guardian Angels

W HEN HE WAS GRADUATING, his mother came to see me," recalled Zalgaller. "She said it was his dream to stay on at our institute." She meant the Leningrad branch of the Steklov Mathematics Institute of the Russian Academy of Sciences. Apparently Zalgaller did not think there was anything particularly strange about the mother of a grown man going to his adviser to discuss her son's graduate-study prospects. Both Zalgaller and Lubov Perelman probably had good reason to believe that intervention was required, because Grisha himself was unwilling and unable to do what it took to stay on for graduate study.

Little had changed in graduate-school admissions policies since Zalgaller found his name on the roster in the late 1940s: graduate work was still very nearly off-limits to Jews. The Steklov Institute was particularly odious. An open letter circulated by a group of American mathematicians at the world mathematical congress in Helsinki in 1978 stated, "The Steklov Mathematical Institute is a prestigious institution in the field of mathematics. For the last thirty years its director has been academician I. M. Vinogradov, who is proud of the fact that under his leadership the Institute has become 'free of Jews.' . . . The key positions in mathematics nowadays are occupied by people who are not only unwilling to protect the interests of science and scientists in the face of the authorities, but who go even beyond official guidelines in their policies of political and racial discrimination."

Ivan Vinogradov, the number theorist who ran the Steklov for nearly half a century, turned the Soviet policy of anti-Semitic discrimination into a personal crusade. By the time Perelman was nearing university graduation, Vinogradov had been dead four years—not long enough to make a dent in the legacy of fifty years of anti-Semitic policies, which Vinogradov's successors continued with greater or lesser enthusiasm but always in full accordance with basic Soviet policies. Perelman's situation was further complicated by the fact that all Steklov decisions were made in Moscow, with the leadership of the Leningrad branch exercising little influence. In addition, the new director of the Leningrad branch, Ludvig Faddeev, scion of an aristocratic and slightly eccentric (the mathematician was named for Beethoven) St. Petersburg ethnic Russian family, had never indicated whether he personally opposed the anti-Semitic policies of his institution. "I wasn't sure what Faddeev would think of the idea," recalled Zalgaller—"the idea" being to offer a graduate research spot to one of the most gifted and diligent students ever seen at the Mathmech. "So I consulted Burago." Yuri Burago was a former student of Zalgaller's who at that time ran a lab at the Leningrad branch of the Steklov.

Together Zalgaller and Burago concocted a plan. Perelman's application to the Steklov would be preceded by a preventive heavy-artillery strike. Alexander Danilovich Alexandrov would write a letter to the Steklov leadership asking that Perelman be allowed to do his graduate work at the Leningrad Steklov under Alexandrov's supervision. The incongruity of the request—a full member of the Academy of Sciences, the man at the center of all of Soviet geometry, writing a letter on behalf of a lowly university senior—was exactly what would ensure the operation's success. Alexandrov was not a man who either accumulated or tallied favors, but this was a case where his sheer status promised a positive outcome.

"If it had been just Burago wanting to take him on as his student, they wouldn't have let him," Aleksei Verner, a student and coauthor of Alexandrov's, told me. "But they couldn't say no to Alexandrov." Valery Ryzhik, who was sitting next to Verner during this conversation, readily concurred and added that Alexandrov had personally told him what the letter had said, "that this was just the kind of exceptional situation when ethnicity should be ignored." Leaving aside the assumptions behind this recollection—particularly the idea that Alexandrov or Ryzhik or both believed that, ordinarily, ethnicity *should* be taken into account—what was really striking about this story was that it seemed that everyone in the Leningrad mathematics community was in on it. Everyone, that is, except Perelman.

"I was sure Grisha would have problems with admission," recalled Golovanov. "His papers said he was Jewish; mine, as it happened, did not. So the issue was taken up at the highest level, a level that at the time seemed beyond the clouds to me. That was pretty funny in itself. I mean, yes, Grisha is Grisha, but he was still just an aspiring graduate student. And here he had members of the Academy going to do battle for him."

Was Grisha engaged in the effort to get him into graduate school, I asked, or was he oblivious to it? "Being engaged and being oblivious are not the sole possibilities." Golovanov leaned back in his chair and, with a satisfied grin, reiterated a phrase he used continuously throughout our conversations: "Grisha is very smart, I keep repeating this. This is a statement that has no relationship to his mathematical talent, which is recognized by everyone. Grisha is a very smart person. That means I cannot imagine he was oblivious to the process. But I have to admit that we never talked about it at the time."

In other words, Golovanov and Perelman, who had known each other for more than ten years, who had received the bulk of their mathematical education side by side, and who were sitting together for their graduate-school admission exams (there were two: one in their chosen mathematical disciplines and one in the history of the Communist Party), diligently avoided discussing the elephant in the room. Golovanov's motivation was clear: he was an exaggeratedly polite man, almost painfully aware of his friend's potential sensitivities—and in 1987, he was also acutely aware of the unfair advantage he enjoyed simply because his documents did not label him Jewish. Perelman's behavior was also entirely in character. The system of graduate admissions, byzantine and discriminatory as it was, could not possibly have fit Perelman's view of the mathematics world as fair and meritocratic. He might have been not just unwilling but unable to talk about the uncertainty of his future in mathematics and the scheming undertaken to save it.

In effect, Perelman's approach to the graduate-admissions problem was a mirror image of Zalgaller's. The older man so loathed the idea of being indebted to anyone that he had removed himself from the corrupt and corrupting system, literally crossing himself off the list. Perelman, who similarly could not have entertained the idea of being indebted to someone, ignored the behind-the-scenes aspect of his graduate-admissions process, as though crossing out that part of the narrative. In the grand scheme of things as it had been imparted to him by his teachers, Perelman, of course, was right: the indignities to which the Soviet system subjected its scholars, especially the Jews among them, had no relationship to the practice of mathematics and could lay no claim to the mathematician's mind. Traditionally, in the second half of the twentieth century, Soviet mathematicians accepted that those who wished to practice mathematics as it ought to be practiced would be relegated to the world of unofficial mathematics, where they would have the scholarship without the perks. Those who belonged to the world of official mathematics got the office space and the salaries, the apartments apportioned by the Academy of Sciences, and even the occasional trip abroad—but had to abide the ideology, the discrimination, and the corruption. Perelman's totalizing mind could entertain no such dichotomy; he would practice mathematics the way it ought to be practiced in the place where it ought to be practiced—the Leningrad branch of the Steklov Mathematics Institute. The benevolence of colleagues who intervened on his behalf and the kindness of friends who did not push the issue in conversation allowed him to do just that: continue living in the world as he imagined it.

In the fall of 1987 Grigory Perelman became a graduate student at the Leningrad branch of the Steklov. Alexander Danilovich Alexandrov was officially listed as his dissertation adviser—making Perelman the last mathematician who would be so honored—but in fact Perelman took up residence in Burago's lab. No one knew this then, but there had never been a better time and place for a mathematician to start his research career.

Just over a year before Perelman graduated from Leningrad State University, Communist Party general secretary Mikhail Gorbachev announced a sweeping series of reforms, which he dubbed *perestroika*. At the end of 1986, physicist Andrei Sakharov, Nobel Peace Prize recipient and the Soviet Union's leading human rights activist, was allowed to return to Moscow from the city of Gorky, where he had been under house arrest. By early 1987, all Soviet political prisoners had reportedly been released. The year 1988, just after Perelman became a graduate student, saw the dawn of the era of glasnost, the Soviet intellectuals' brief golden age, when the readership of thick intellectual journals shot into the millions and a national public conversation about the future of Russia commenced. In 1989, the year Perelman wrote his dissertation, the entire country was glued to its TV screens watching the first semi-democratic elections and then the first open parliamentary debates that occurred in their lifetimes. So sweeping was the excitement of the time, not even someone as disdainful of politics as Perelman could resist the spirit entirely.

It was an extraordinary stroke of luck that Perelman began his career several years before the economic reforms of the early 1990s impoverished research institutions and condemned Russian academics to either precarious research-grant-to-research-grant existences or moorless lives of shuttling back and forth between teaching gigs abroad and research positions at home. In the late 1980s, in Golovanov's estimation, a graduate student's stipend still placed him "ten rubles a month above the salary level at which one could exist." At the same time, the most important change in how Soviet academic institutions worked was already under way: the Iron Curtain was lifting. Soviet scholars were starting to travel abroad, foreign researchers could come and go unimpeded, censorship of foreign academic journals was lifted (but the economic crisis had not yet caused library subscriptions to lapse), and communication through letters and phone calls became as accessible as it should have been all along. What this meant for institutions such as the Steklov was a daily sense that change and intellectual opportunity were in the air. What it meant for Perelman was that his path to membership in the international mathematical elite would be natural and straightforward—and his view of the world would not be challenged. Plus, he would meet Mikhail Gromov.

After a certain point, Mikhail Gromov's name becomes linked to just about every important thing that Perelman did. Everyone I interviewed to trace Perelman's trajectory past graduate school mentioned Gromov: he recommended Perelman for this or that academic position, he brought him to this conference, he coauthored a paper with him.

Zalgaller called Gromov "the best thing Leningrad University ever produced." Gromov defended his PhD dissertation there in 1968, at the age of twenty-five; his adviser was Vladimir Rokhlin, the topologist whom Alexander Danilovich Alexandrov had saved from persecution. Gromov, whose mother was Jewish, despaired of getting a research position at the Steklov or even a less desirable, to him, professorial appointment at Leningrad State, and in the late 1970s he emigrated to the United States, where he worked at the Courant Institute at New York University. Later, having established himself as one of the world's leading geometers, he started dividing his time between the Courant and the extraordinarily prestigious Institut des Hautes Études Scientifiques, outside of Paris.

I interviewed Gromov in Paris at the Institut Henri Poincaré, the part of the Université Pierre et Marie Curie reserved for conferences and seminars in mathematics and theoretical physics. So said the university's website and so said laminated signs placed on the large round wooden tables in the institute's cafeteria: RE-SERVED FOR THE USE OF MATHEMATICIANS AND THEORETI-CAL PHYSICISTS. As I arrived in the cafeteria, I saw Gromov engaged in an animated discussion with the American topologist Bruce Kleiner, whom I had interviewed in New York a couple of months earlier. Kleiner rose to leave when I approached the table but seemed too agitated by the discussion to say hello to me. Instead, he turned back to face Gromov and said that a science in which nothing had to be proved was no science at all. Gromov responded that an alternative system could still be consistent. "Have you ever talked to a street person?" Kleiner demanded, apparently infuriated. "They have some great ideas." I think he meant to say something about every crazy person having an internally consistent system to offer, but Kleiner had become too upset to articulate the idea. Gromov too became enraged, waving his arms and saying, "No, no!" He looked very much like a street person himself: his clothes hung loosely and awkwardly on his very thin frame; his black belted jeans were stained; his light green button-down shirt had thinned on the chest and frayed at the cuffs; and both his gray beard and his gray hair stuck out haphazardly in every direction.

Kleiner stomped off, and Gromov turned to me, apparently still irritated. First, he bristled at my questions about his reasons for leaving the Soviet Union. "Why not?" he asked, speaking Russian that was distinctly affected by the three decades he had spent away from the mother country. "Everyone was leaving, and I left too. I was offered a job in America and went there, and then I was offered a job here and came here." I already had enough information to know he was not exactly telling me the truth, but I also knew not to push: he was obviously in no mood to talk about the long-ago hardships of Jewish emigration from the Soviet Union.

"I understand you are the person who brought Perelman to the West," I attempted.

"I took part in it," Gromov responded, still annoyed. "But it was Burago's initiative."

"A lot of people have told me that you were the one who came and said there was this great new mathematician."

"Burago told me that. I may have mentioned it to other people."

"And what had Burago told you?"

"He said he had this good young mathematician."

"Who needed to be brought here?"

"Yes, it had to be arranged for him to come here."

Gromov arranged for Perelman to spend a few months at IHES as soon as he defended his dissertation at the Steklov in 1990. At IHES Perelman began working on Alexandrov spaces, a topological phenomenon named for Alexander Danilovich Alexandrov. The old man had abandoned this topic in the 1950s, but now three of his mathematical descendants—Burago, Gromov, and Perelman— had come together to work on it.

In 1991, Gromov helped bring Perelman to the Geometry Festival, an annual event held on the East Coast of the United States at a different location each year. That year it was at Duke University. Perelman gave a talk on Alexandrov spaces that the following year became his first major published work, coauthored with Gromov and Burago. Gromov mentioned Perelman to all the right people to ensure that he would be invited to do postdoctoral research in the United States.

As Gromov and I talked, I began to understand Gromov's motivation—or, rather, the depth of his commitment to the Perelman project. "When he entered geometry," Gromov said, "he was, at the time, the strongest geometer. Before he went underground, he was certainly the best in the world."

"What does that mean?"

"He did the best work," Gromov responded with perfect precision. I immediately remembered a joke told to me by a mathematician: A group of people taking a ride in a hot-air balloon get carried away by the wind. After drifting some distance, they spot a man below and shout to him, "Where are we?" The man, who happens to be a mathematician, responds, "You are in a hot-air balloon."

But as we talked more, I realized Gromov thought Perelman was actually the best *man* in the world—not just the best geometer, but the best human being involved in mathematics. Gromov compared Perelman to Isaac Newton, then immediately amended the comparison to say, "Newton was a rather bad person. Perelman is much better. He has some faults, but very few." His faults, Gromov explained, sometimes led him to attack his friends, but these conflicts were minor compared to Perelman's overwhelming natural goodness. "He has moral principles to which he holds. And this surprises people. They often say that he acts strange because he acts honest, in a nonconformist manner, which is unpopular in this community—even though it should be the norm. His main peculiarity is that he acts decently. He follows ideals that are tacitly accepted in science."

In other words, Perelman was what a mathematician—and a man—ought to be. Later that day I walked around Paris with a French mathematician and historian of science who bemoaned the state of French mathematics, the commercialization of science, and the unprincipled participation of people like Gromov who, this man claimed, stood by while IHES printed up vapid fundraising brochures. I realized that Gromov probably wished he could be as principled as Perelman, as resolutely removed from the institutionalization of mathematics, and as sincerely disdainful of empty recognition. Which was clearly why Gromov had adopted Perelman as a cause—and also why he resisted taking credit for having helped him.

So continued the line of Perelman's guardian angels: Rukshin shepherded him into competitive mathematics, Ryzhik coddled him through high school, Zalgaller nurtured his problem-solving skills at the university and handed him off to Alexandrov and Burago to ensure that he practiced mathematics uninterrupted and unimpeded. Burago passed him on to Gromov, who led him out into the world.

7

Round Trip

HAD GRIGORY PERELMAN been born ten or even five years earlier than he was, his career may well have ground to a halt around the time he finished writing his dissertation: it would have been difficult, if not outright impossible, for a Jew to defend his dissertation at the Steklov and stay on in a research position there; even the intervention of someone as influential as Alexander Danilovich Alexandrov might not have guaranteed success. Had Perelman been born ten or even five years later than he was, he might never have entered graduate school at all: State anti-Semitism would no longer have been an issue, but his family would likely have been unable to afford to keep him in school at a time when a graduate student's stipend barely bought three loaves of black bread. But Grisha Perelman was born at just the right time, and when he completed his dissertation, he was in exactly the right place: a country that was collapsing, which freed its citizens to travel abroad for the first time in seven decades. He belonged to the luckiest generation of Russian mathematicians. Like millions of other Soviet citizens, Perelman began a new life sometime around 1990, a life out in the world. So fortuitous was the timing of this change that Perelman might be forgiven for believing the world worked exactly as it should. Just when Perelman needed to broaden his circle of mathematical communication, the opportunities to do so presented themselves.

In this new part of Perelman's life, a new cast of characters appeared. Whether they knew it or not—and most likely they did not, for Perelman was as reserved with them as he was with most people—and whether he cared or not, they would play important roles in the development of his career. In addition to Gromov, these included Jeff Cheeger, Michael Anderson, Gang Tian, John Morgan, and Bruce Kleiner.

Cheeger is an important American mathematician, a generation older than Perelman. He works at the Courant, in a large sparse office in a high-rise building on the NYU campus. Like other American acquaintances of Perelman, Cheeger seemed to find him both sympathetic and inscrutable, if occasionally slightly infuriating, and he spoke carefully, hoping to avoid offending him. Cheeger recalled that he first heard about Perelman from Gromov: "He came back and mentioned that he had met this young fellow who was extraordinarily impressive." In 1991, Cheeger saw Perelman at the Geometry Festival at Duke. And then Perelman came to the Courant as a postdoctoral fellow in the fall of 1992. He was still working on Alexandrov spaces.

By the time Perelman arrived in the United States, he was twenty-six, no longer pudgy but tall and apparently fit. His beard had passed out of its extended awkward-tuft stage and was thick, black, and bushy. His hair was long. He did not believe in cutting hair or fingernails—some people thought they remembered his saying something about the unnaturalness of such trimming, but no one can vouch for this recollection and chances are at least as good that Perelman found the conventions of personal hygiene and appearance both taxing and unreasonable. "He was very, you know, known as eccentric," said Cheeger, citing the nails, the hair, the habit of wearing the same clothes every day—most notably a brown corduroy jacket—and his holding forth on the virtues of a particular kind of black bread that could be procured only from a Russian store in Brooklyn Beach, where Perelman walked from Manhattan.

Structurally, the life of a postdoc in the United States differed little from the life of a graduate student in Russia. Perelman was left largely to his own devices, but he apparently saw no reason not to spend most of his time at the Courant. The institute was conveniently located in a concrete-block tower as square and impersonal as anything that had been built in Russia in the previous thirty years. It looked out on Washington Square Park, a place as flat, geometrical, and ceremoniously architectural as any park in St. Petersburg or Paris, where Perelman had just spent several months. To complete his sense of familiarity, Perelman had to travel to the outer reaches of Brooklyn to get his bread and fermented milk— and by making the journey on foot, he ensured that he had both solitude and the usual measure of physical hardship. After a while, he had his mother waiting for him at the other end of the journey to Brooklyn; she had followed him to the United States and was staying with relatives in Brighton Beach. Within Courant Institute itself, Perelman did not find the social demands taxing; the typical regimen of mathematics seminars was accompanied by a familiar array of faces, since Gromov, Burago, and other St. Petersburg mathematicians were occasional residents there.

Perelman made a friend at Courant. I am not sure Gang Tian knew he was Perelman's friend, but Viktor Zalgaller, Perelman's old teacher in Israel, was certain he was. "He made a friend there, a young Chinese mathematician," he told me. "They suited each other." This they certainly did. I went to see Tian at the Institute for Advanced Study at Princeton, one of the world's most prestigious mathematical institutions, where Tian now occupied another cold concrete box. He spoke very softly and sadly, if not as reluctantly as Cheeger. He had already made the mistake of speaking to the media, and he believed this was why Grisha had not responded to his letters in several years. Tian did not think he and Perelman had been friends. "We talked quite often," he acknowledged, but it was all about math. "I don't think we talked much other than that. There are probably other people with whom he was friendly and talked more about other things. He did talk about bread. He somehow cared a lot about bread. He found a place to buy good bread in Brooklyn and near the Brooklyn Bridge." What kind of bread was it? I asked. "I'm not so sure," responded Tian, "because I'm not that fond of bread. I eat bread but I don't really care which one." Aside from the bread issue, Tian and Perelman really were perfect for each other: both were interested in little outside of mathematics, and their mathematical interests were shared.

It was with Tian that Perelman started going to lectures at the Institute for Advanced Study at Princeton. Cheeger came along too. During one of these visits Perelman surprised Cheeger by joining a game of volleyball after a lecture. "You look at him and think this is something he'd have no interest in or couldn't do," recalled Cheeger. "But I remember one time watching it, the game, and he said, you know, 'Well, I think I could do that.' And you know, he was pretty good." I nodded. My lack of surprise surprised Cheeger. I explained that Perelman had had to take part in numerous games of volleyball while he was training for the International Mathematical Olympiad as well as when he was at the math camps. Then Cheeger looked slightly annoyed. Even on this small score, he had been misled by Perelman's habit of underplaying both his abilities and his interest. This was, of course, the same man who later told no one he was working on the Poincaré Conjecture and who posted his solution on the Internet without claiming it was in fact the solution. It was only after someone asked him if he had proved the conjecture that he said he had. Most likely, if Cheeger had asked him directly whether he had had much volleyball practice, Perelman would have said yes. He still believed in telling the entire truth—but only when asked. He just didn't see the utility of volunteering information, especially information about himself. I suspect he also took some pleasure in demonstrating that he could solve any problem he picked—even a game of volleyball.

Another Perelman incident that surprised Cheeger during the New York period was harder to explain. In 1993 Cheeger and Gromov went to a conference in Israel that had been convened in part to celebrate their fiftieth birthdays. Perelman came, as did his mother—but that was not what surprised Cheeger. What he found startling was that he saw Perelman renting a car at the airport, using a credit card. I have talked to no one else who ever witnessed Perelman drive a car—indeed, some people claimed he rejected cars as "unnatural"—but it is conceivable he could have obtained a driver's license and a credit card during his first semester in New York. The reason he might have done this was that, for a fleeting moment, Perelman seems to have planned to move permanently to the United States.

"You see, it often happens that when someone crosses the border with Russia in any direction, he has a very strong reaction," Golovanov explained to me. "In Grisha's case, it was the only time he experienced something resembling political enthusiasm. As soon as he ended up there, he started sending letters decreeing that the entire family had to move." The entirety of the family remaining in St. Petersburg at this time was Grisha's younger sister,

Lena, who had just graduated from high school. Their father had emigrated to Israel, and their mother was in New York hovering over Grisha, so in essence, he was campaigning for his sister to go to college in the United States. Lena decided to move to Israel, where she obtained her PhD in mathematics from the Weizmann Institute in 2004.

To the best of Golovanov's recollection, Perelman did not try to make a case for the move: he "decreed" it, as Golovanov put it, in accordance with his understanding of his role in the family, which was to "know what is right." Making an argument to his little sister may also have seemed to him to be beneath his dignity or, in any case, a waste of time. When he talked to colleagues, however, he made the argument that Western mathematicians, while suffering from too narrow a focus compared with their Russian counterparts, organized their research more effectively and accomplished more. This may have been a classic solipsism, for in 1993 Perelman did exactly what postdoctoral researchers who are unencumbered by formal academic obligations and are at the height of their creative and mental abilities are supposed to do at that stage in their lives: he solved an important long-standing problem, and he did it in a way that, to mathematicians, possessed breathtaking beauty.

Twenty years before Perelman arrived at Courant, Cheeger and his coauthor Detlef Gromoll had published a paper outlining a way of deducing the properties of certain mathematical objects from small regions of these objects, which they called the *soul* of the objects, for, like the imaginary human soul, the imaginary soul of the imaginary mathematical object also possessed all the qualities that made the whole what it was. Cheeger and Gromoll proved part of what they set out to show, and this became known as the Soul Theorem, but they could only suppose the rest, and this became known as the Soul Conjecture. It remained a conjecture—that is, a mathematical supposition without proof—until Perelman showed that it was true. His paper was four pages long.

"It seemed to be extraordinarily hard," Cheeger told me. "At least a couple of people had written very long and technical papers on it. And they only proved part of it. And he realized that everyone had been missing the point, you could say. And he made a very short proof of it. He used something—something nontrivial, but something that had been in the public domain since the late seventies."

This was the trick Perelman's friends at the math club had called his "stick": absorbing the problem in its entirety and then boiling it down to an essence that proved simpler than everyone had assumed. "Part of it was that the problem was not as difficult as people had thought it was," Cheeger continued. "Part of it was, you could say, the force of his personality. I mean when you talked to him it was clear you were dealing with an unusually penetrating and powerful mind. A personality that's very forceful in a certain direction, very believing in his own insights. You could say almost stubborn in a way, not aggressive, but you could almost say a little arrogant."

You could certainly say that. Cheeger encountered this aspect of Perelman's personality when he tried to convince the younger mathematician to expand one of his papers to allow more exposition of his ideas. "One of the papers he wrote while he was here was very short; it was a mixture of power and arrogance. It was very striking. I read it and admired it a lot. But I felt it was a little bit too terse, a little bit not making the insights as manifest as they could be. So I said this to him and he said he would consider it. But I couldn't really get him to change. I don't know. Have you seen the film *Amadeus*?" The scene Cheeger was recalling was the one in which Mozart presents an opera he has written and the emperor suggests the piece is wonderful but not perfect: it has too many notes. "Just cut a few and it will be perfect," he says. "Which few did you have in mind, Majesty?" responds Mozart. By 1992, Perelman was apparently quite certain he was the Mozart of contemporary mathematics. No one, not even an outstanding mathematician twenty-three years his senior, was going to tell him what to do or how to present his ideas to the world.

For the spring semester of 1993, Perelman went to the State University of New York's Stony Brook campus—one of the best American graduate programs in mathematics. Located just sixty-five miles from New York City, Stony Brook was probably as different from St. Petersburg and New York as any place Perelman had ever visited. Its architecture was square, and its landscape consisted of parking lots, low buildings, and large fields. Its railroad station was a tiny two-room structure across the tracks from campus. To an outsider—and Perelman would always be an outsider, wherever he went—it must have felt utterly desolate.

Mike Anderson, a geometer Perelman had met earlier—currently the director of SUNY Stony Brook's graduate math program —helped Perelman find an apartment. Perelman's criteria were "quiet and small," and he found a studio apartment that cost roughly three hundred dollars a month. He slept on a futon he borrowed from the Andersons. The pay for a postdoc at the time was about thirty-five to forty thousand dollars a year, and Perelman, who lived on bread and yogurt, put most of that money away in his bank account. His mother stayed in Brooklyn but came to visit frequently.

Perelman continued to wear the same brown corduroy jacket. People continued to notice his long hair and fingernails. His personal hygiene may have deteriorated slightly; he gave the impression of someone who bathed regularly, but the futon on which he slept took on a smell so strong that the Andersons had to throw it out when he returned it. His extraordinary long nails, however, remained clean.

Perelman taught a course on Alexandrov geometry. The following summer, he traveled to Zurich to speak on Alexandrov spaces at the International Congress of Mathematicians. It was a prestigious opportunity; the congress took place just once every four years, and that year only fifty-five of the world's top mathematicians, most of them significantly older than Perelman, had been invited to speak—four Fields Medalists, past and future, among them. With his proof of the Soul Conjecture, Perelman had become an undisputed young star. In Zurich, he spoke on the paper he had coauthored with Gromov and Burago. His first talk at the congress probably attracted people who wanted to see the twenty-eight-year-old who, if Gromov was to be believed, was doing the best work in the world in his field. But Perelman apparently exhibited the worst of his public-speaking habits during the talk. He started by sketching something on the board and then began pacing back and forth as he talked. His speech seemed vague and disconnected and essentially incomprehensible.

If Perelman was true to his habit of describing his personal relationship with the problem rather than the problem itself, it might explain why his Zurich talk was a disaster. He had lectured on this paper before—at the Geometry Festival at Duke in 1991, and at a couple of American universities immediately following the festival. He had been clear at the time—as the geometer Bruce Kleiner, who heard him speak at both Duke and the University of Pennsylvania that year, recalled, it was obvious that "the mathematics was very, very good." But by 1994, his relationship with Alexandrov spaces had grown complicated.

After a semester at Stony Brook, in the fall of 1993, Perelman moved to the West Coast to take up a two-year Miller Fellowship—an enviable position at the University of California at Berkeley that offered generous funding for research in one of the basic sciences without any teaching responsibilities. In fact, the conditions of the fellowship stated explicitly that fellows were "granted more independence than other postdocs on campus" and could participate in the lives of their host departments as much or as little as they desired. This was the kind of setting for which Perelman had been raised by his early mathematical mentors—the kind of setting he had praised in his conversations with Russian colleagues—but it did not work. Or something didn't work. Perelman had been trying to press on with Alexandrov spaces, and he had gotten stuck.

"That's normal," Gromov told me. "Out of everything you try, most things don't work out. That's just the way life is." Gromov might have been talking about life in mathematics or life in general, but in either case, he was speaking from experience, which Perelman, even in his late twenties, simply did not have. Improbably, with the possible exception of his second-place showing at the All-Soviet Math Olympiad at the age of fourteen, he had never failed to accomplish what he had set out to accomplish, or to receive what he was due, or to solve a problem he had taken on. Moreover, all the hours of practice and all the behind-the-scenes anxiety and intrigue notwithstanding, in the eyes of observers, he had accomplished everything with ease. At this point, following the Soul Conjecture proof and the international congress, he had more mathematical eyes trained on him than ever before—and he was facing the unfamiliar experience of failure.

Kleiner spent the 1993–1994 academic year at Berkeley too, and he and Perelman "had several math conversations during that year," he recalled. Perelman occasionally ventured into areas adjacent to Alexandrov spaces. He talked about the Geometrization Conjecture, a long-unsolved problem that included the Poincaré Conjecture; that is, if someone proved Geometrization, Poincaré would also be proved along the way. He talked about the possibility of applying Alexandrov spaces to Geometrization, and "there was no obvious way or scheme," said Kleiner. Perelman also considered dipping into Ricci flow, an approach invented by another mathematician to prove the Poincaré Conjecture—but that mathematician had himself gotten stuck years before. Perelman wondered out loud whether Ricci flow might be applied usefully to Alexandrov spaces. Had there been any indication that Perelman might actually take up the Poincaré and Geometrization conjectures? No —but, recalled Kleiner, "he was not very open about what exactly he was working on or thinking about. He was no more reticent than many people would be in a similar situation. It's not necessarily a good idea to share your ideas openly because, unless you really know the person and trust them, they could start working on it themselves or they could pass information on to a third party who might start working on it. You'll find someone competing against you using your same ideas, which is not a very comfortable situation." Kleiner's own area of research lay quite near Perelman's, so Perelman's reticence seemed reasonable to him.

But there was probably another reason for the reticence, one that Perelman articulated in a conversation with Cheeger in 1995. As Cheeger recalled, Perelman stopped by his office while he was briefly in New York City and they discussed some issues related to Alexandrov spaces but not to the specific aspects Perelman had studied in the past. This time, however, Perelman was very interested and even referred to one of the questions as the "holy grail" of the subject. "And I ask him, 'Didn't you say you had no interest in it?'" Cheeger recalled. "And he said, 'Well, whether a problem is interesting depends on whether there's any chance of solving it.'" As pompous as that statement sounds, Perelman was probably telling an important emotional truth about himself: he could become engaged with a problem only if he could fully grasp it—and if he grasped a problem fully, down to the nature of every minute technical complication, he could certainly solve it. What had happened between Perelman and Alexandrov spaces was that he had come up against technical difficulties he could not penetrate, and so he had grown emotionally disengaged. Hence the nebulous, rambling talk at the congress.

Perelman's term as a Miller Fellow ended in the spring of 1995. His paper on the Soul Conjecture had come out the previous year, and he had spoken at the International Congress of Mathematicians, so it is not surprising that even though he put no effort into securing an academic position after Berkeley, he was courted by several leading institutions. He turned all of them down, and the way he did it—specifically, the way he rejected Princeton—has become part of American and Russian mathematical lore. I had heard about it on both sides of the Atlantic before I asked one of the immediate participants what had happened, and his account differed little from what I had been told.

Peter Sarnak, a Princeton professor who became chair of the mathematics department in 1996, first heard of Perelman from Gromov, who, Sarnak recalled in an e-mail message, had said Perelman was "exceptionally good." In the winter of 1994–1995, Perelman came to Princeton to give a talk on his proof of the Soul Conjecture. Few people showed up, but the math department's brass was there: distinguished professor John Mather, then–department chair Simon Kochen, and Sarnak all attended. Perelman gave a great lecture: clear, precise, and engaging—probably because his personal relationship with the Soul Conjecture had been brief and satisfying and was resolved. "After the lecture the three of us approached Perelman saying we would like to arrange for him to come to Princeton as an assistant professor," recalled Sarnak. Legend has it—though Sarnak did not remember it—that at this point Perelman asked why they would want to bring him to Princeton when no one there was interested in his areas of research—an impression perhaps intensified by the nearly empty auditorium and which, Sarnak acknowledged, was an accurate reflection of the situation, "which we were eager to change." Sarnak remembered Perelman making clear "that he wanted a tenured position, to which we responded that we would have to look into that and in any case we need some information from him such as a CV. He was surprised by the latter, saying something like 'you have heard my lecture, why would you need any more information?' Given that he wasn't interested in a tenure track position we didn't pursue this any further. History has proven that we made a mistake in not being more aggressive in recruiting him."

Perelman told several people at the time that he would settle for nothing less than immediate tenure—an audacious position for a twenty-nine-year-old mathematician with few publications and only a semester's worth of teaching experience. But Perelman's own logic was impeccable. He was not out looking for work, so the job offers were coming from institutions—or, rather, people—who, as Cheeger put it, "knew how terrific he was." In other words, they knew what Perelman and Gromov knew: that he was the best in the world. Why, then, would they want to put him through the conventional paces of earning his full professorship? Why even make him submit his CV before they offered him his well-deserved job? It would not have occurred to Perelman that his well-intentioned interlocutors did not perceive his place in the mathematical hierarchy quite the same way he did and simply did not realize that his would be a star presence in any university mathematics department. Or his insistence on immediate tenure might merely have been a way of setting the bar so high as to cut off any further discussion of his staying in the United States. The University of Tel Aviv, where Perelman's sister was by then a student, actually offered him a full professorship, and Perelman, as Cheeger recalled, "ended up turning them down or not responding at all." So Sarnak might take some consolation in the knowledge that even if Princeton had been more aggressive, it probably would not have succeeded in drawing Perelman.

Getting ready to return to Russia, Perelman told his American colleagues he could work better back home—the exact opposite of what he had told his family in Russia three years earlier but in all likelihood the exact same sort of solipsism. Back when breakthroughs came easily to him, his American environment had seemed to be on his side; now that he was stuck, a return to Russia held the promise of rejuvenation, a renewed ability to work. What it was he was working on, no one knew. The questions he asked Cheeger when he was passing through New York on his way to St. Petersburg in 1995 seemed to indicate he was broadening his focus on Alexandrov spaces—in a way that, in retrospect, may have meant he was edging closer to tackling the Poincaré Conjecture.

Back in St. Petersburg, Perelman took up residence in Kupchino with his mother and reclaimed his spot in Burago's laboratory at the Steklov Institute. He would not have any teaching responsibilities—or, for that matter, any obligations at all. By the mid-1990s, institutions of the Russian Academy of Sciences had fallen into physical disrepair and organizational chaos. Researchers no longer had to submit regular reports on their work or account for their time in any way; institute rolls gradually filled up with dead souls —or, in any case, long-absent émigré souls. Buildings, which had been maintained at architectural subsistence levels in the Soviet era, literally began to crumble after about five years of neglect. The Steklov building in St. Petersburg, a once-lovely low-rise structure on the Fontanka River in the very center of town, grew increasingly cold and drafty. Researchers' salaries were so far out of sync with inflation as to be laughable; many people did not even bother showing up at their institutes to pick up the wads of worthless cash that was their pay. They sought sources of income elsewhere —mostly in the West, where many stayed all the time while others created complicated schedules of semester-on/semester-off teaching. But none of this bothered Perelman. At the institute, there was heat, and there was electricity, and the phone lines worked—most days, anyway. At home, his mother catered to his ascetic needs. The subway continued to run from the center of town to Kupchino. And Perelman had saved tens of thousands of dollars while he was in the United States; in 1995, a family of two in St. Petersburg could live well enough on less than a hundred dollars a month. It seemed he would never again have to worry about anything but mathematics. With the distraction of exams, competitions, dissertation, and teaching behind him, he would lead the life he had been raised to live: the life of the pure mathematician.

Whatever patience he had once had for distractions was now gone. In 1996, the European Mathematical Society held its second quadrennial congress in Budapest and awarded prizes to mathematicians under the age of thirty-two. Gromov, Burago, and St. Petersburg Mathematical Society president Anatoly Vershik submitted Perelman's name for his work on Alexandrov spaces. "I was always interested in making sure that our young mathematicians looked good," Vershik explained to me. "They decided to award it to him, but as soon as he learned about it—I don't remember whether I was the one who told him or if it was someone else—he said he did not want it and would not accept it. And he said that he would create a scandal if it was announced that he was a recipient of this prize. I was very surprised and very upset. He had in fact known that he was up for the award and had said nothing about this. I had to have some emergency communication with the chairman of the prize committee, who was an acquaintance of mine, to make sure they did not announce the prize."

A dozen years after the incident, Vershik, a soft-spoken, bearded man in his early seventies, still seemed to feel betrayed by Perelman's behavior. He told me he would rather refrain from trying to find the reason for Perelman's rejection of the prize. If Perelman was opposed to prizes on principle, this was news to Vershik: in the very early 1990s the Mathematical Society had awarded Perelman a prize, which Perelman had accepted; he even gave a talk on the occasion. Later Perelman apparently told someone that the European Mathematical Society had no one who was qualified to judge his work, but Vershik did not recall hearing anything of the sort then—and with Gromov and Burago on board, that would have seemed an odd argument. "He did say one thing to me at the time, and it actually sounded convincing. He said the work was not complete. But I said there were reviewers and the jury had decided he deserved the prize." Still, the idea that anyone might be better suited than he was to judge whether a paper of his deserved a prize could only have infuriated Perelman.

Unlike Vershik, Gromov thought Perelman's behavior entirely acceptable, even though Gromov had been one of the three mathematicians who had submitted Perelman's name for the prize. "He believes he is the one who decides when he should be getting a prize and when he should not be," Gromov told me quite simply. "So he decided that he had not fulfilled his program and they can just take their prize and stuff it. And, of course, he also wanted to show off." Or at least show that he wanted to be left alone.

He continued to accept invitations to take part in mathematical community events, especially ones involving children. Apparently this was not so much because he had any affection for children as it was that he had respect for the tradition of the clubs and competitions in which he had been reared. But Perelman grew increasingly resistant to entertaining any questions concerning his projects. His American colleagues soon discovered he did not answer e-mail messages. In 1996, Kleiner went to St. Petersburg for a conference on Alexandrov spaces that Perelman also attended. Even though the two men had had a few mathematical conversations at Berkeley a couple of years earlier, Kleiner could not find a way to approach Perelman with questions about his current research. A friend of Kleiner's, a German mathematician named Bernhard Leeb, who had met Perelman at the International Mathematical Olympiad, did manage to ask a question—but not to get an answer. As Kleiner recalled twelve years later, Perelman said to him, "I don't want to tell you." Leeb's own recollection differed in tone if not substance. "I did ask him what he was working on," he wrote to me. "He told me that he would be working on some topic in geometry but he did not want to become specific. I find this attitude very reasonable. If one is working on a big problem like the Poincaré Conjecture, one is well advised to be extremely reluctant to talk about it."

No one knew what was occupying Perelman's mind. Even Gromov heard nothing from him and assumed he was still stuck on Alexandrov spaces—in other words, that he had joined the sizable ranks of talented mathematicians who did brilliant early work and then disappeared into the black hole of some impossible problem.

In February 2000, Mike Anderson at Stony Brook suddenly received an e-mail message from Perelman. "Dear Mike," it began. "I've just read your paper on generalised Lichnerovicz thm, and there is one point in your paper that disturbs me." Perelman went on to describe the nature of his doubts in one long, perfectly constructed sentence and finished with: "Am I missing something? Best regards, Grisha." There were no unnecessary niceties one might expect in a letter like this—nothing along the lines of "I hope this finds you well" or "It has been a long time." But the letter was perfectly polite, and Perelman's English—presumably disused for more than five years—all but impeccable.

Anderson responded the next day with a letter that by the standards of the mathematical world was downright effusive:

Dear Grisha,

It was a surprise to hear from you again—a pleasant surprise. I often ask people who I see from St. Petersburg if they know how you are and what you are thinking about these days.

I just returned from a short trip, and so haven't been able to think yet in detail about your remarks on my stationary paper. But I see your points, and agree I have made an error here. I don't think these two errors effect [sic] the results, and that the proofs require only minor modifications. I will think this through in the next couple of days and report back to you.

I'd also like to hear how you are, and what kind of mathematical or other issues you are concerned about these days.

Best regards to you,

Mike

Three days later, Anderson sent Perelman a more detailed e-mail message, outlining a fix for the mistakes Perelman had found. Again, he inserted a note of personal and professional interest: "I thank you very much for spotting these errors. Are you becoming interesting [sic] in these areas yourself?" Anderson also complained that so few people were working in his area—geometrization—that he had no one to double-check his ideas. He asked if Perelman had looked at his other two papers on related topics.

Perelman replied the next day. He thanked Anderson for his prompt response but ignored every single one of his questions. He wrote only that Anderson's paper had drawn his attention because it was "tangentially related" to Perelman's own current interests—and also, he noted, because it was short. He did not invite further communication. Nor did he promise he would look at Anderson's other papers—he wrote that he had them but had not read them. In fact, it seems likely that he subsequently read the papers but, finding no errors, saw no reason to write to Anderson again.

Anderson still tried to pursue the dialogue. He sent Perelman a file containing a more detailed fix for his paper. Perelman responded by saying he could not open the file without somebody's help ("I do not know computers at all," he claimed) and explained that his sister had helped print out the original Anderson papers when he visited her in Rehovot, where she was a graduate student. He proceeded to write that sending the file to a Steklov computer to open there might make it accessible to other people, so in the end he would rather wait until Anderson published the paper. In other words, he had gotten all he needed from this exchange with his colleague.

The message was a curious document in other respects. It seems that in the five years since leaving the United States, Perelman had drifted far from the practical aspects even of mathematics: he didn't seem to know how to use his office computer to log onto the SUNY e-mail account he used to correspond with Anderson or how to forward the file to a Web-based address no one else could access. At the same time, Perelman was using his lack of technical expertise to close the conversation, which had evidently outworn its usefulness to him. After all, when he actually needed Anderson's preprints, he had been resourceful enough to ask his sister for help. It is remarkable too how casually Perelman shared the details of his life and his sister's. It was never his intention to hide his family life or refuse to discuss himself or his relatives; it was just very rarely relevant to any conversation he found worth having.

It would be two and a half years before Mike Anderson heard from Perelman again.

8

The Problem

"T HE VERY POSSIBILITY of mathematical science seems an insoluble contradiction." So, more than a century ago, wrote Henri Poincaré, known among mathematicians as the last universalist, for he excelled in all areas of mathematics. If the objects of study are confined to the imagination, "from whence is derived that perfect rigor which is challenged by none?" And when rules of formal logic have replaced the experiment, "how is it that mathematics is not reduced to a gigantic tautology?" Finally, "are we then to admit that . . . all the theorems with which so many volumes are filled are only indirect ways of saying that A is A?"

Poincaré went on to explain that mathematics was a science because its reasoning traveled from the particular to the general. A mathematician who conducted his mental experiments with sufficient rigor could derive the rules that governed the rest of the imaginary terrain he shared with other mathematicians. In other words, he not only proved that A was A but also explained what made A quintessentially an A and where other A's might be found or how they might be constructed. "We know what it is to be in love or to feel pain, and we don't need precise definitions to communicate," wrote an American mathematics professor who, after authoring many academic books, undertook to explain topology to a general audience. "The objects of mathematics lie outside common experience, however. If one doesn't define these objects carefully, one cannot manipulate them meaningfully or talk to others about them." This may or may not be so. Most of us are, in fact, perfectly satisfied with our casual understandings of distances long and short, of slopes smooth and steep, and of lines and circles and spheres. We're satisfied with a gut feeling that puncturing a hole can sometimes but not always change the nature of an object—that is, a punctured balloon is entirely different from an intact one, while, say, a jelly-filled doughnut without a hole is, to us, essentially similar to a doughnut with a hole in the middle, with or without jelly. All of these things are in their simplest forms parts of our common experience. But in the disjointed world of the mathematician, shifting understandings and imprecise coordinates muddle the picture intolerably. In his world, nothing is like anything else unless proven similar; nothing is familiar until thoroughly defined; nothing—or very nearly nothing—is self-evident.

At the dawn of mathematics, Euclid attempted to start with things that were self-evident. He began his *Elements* with thirty-five definitions, five postulates, and five common notions, or axioms. Definitions ranged from that of a point ("that which has no parts, or which has no magnitude") to that of parallel straight lines ("such as are in the same plane, and which being produced ever so far do not meet"). Then he made a series of statements such as "things that are equal to the same thing are equal to one another." And the five postulates were:

1. "A straight line may be drawn from any one point to any other point" (interpreted to mean that only one straight line may be drawn from any point to any other).

2. "A terminated straight line may be produced at any length in a straight line" (in other words, a segment may be extended indefinitely into a straight line).

3. "A circle may be described at any center, at any distance from that center."

4. "All right angles equal one another."

5. "If a straight line falling on two straight lines makes the interior angles on the same side less than two right angles, the two straight lines, if produced indefinitely, meet on that side on which are the angles less than the two right angles."

To a true classifier, even these five statements take too much for granted. "I had been told that Euclid proved things, and was much disappointed that he started with axioms," wrote Bertrand Russell of his first childhood encounter with the *Elements*. "At first, I refused to accept them unless my brother could offer me some reason for doing so, but he said, 'If you don't accept them, we cannot go on,' and so, as I wished to go on, I reluctantly admitted them."

As a place to start, the first four postulates struck Euclid, his contemporaries, and the generations of mathematicians to follow as indeed self-evident. Since they are confined to a space we can not only visualize but actually *see*, the postulates could be checked empirically by drawing with a straightedge or a compass or by stretching a piece of string. As a segment grew in length or a circle in radius, even past the point where a human eye might be able to grasp it, it would not change essentially, and this was as close as anything could get to being obvious and not requiring further proof. But the fifth postulate made claims on the imagination. It said that if two lines were not parallel, they had to cross eventually.

Conversely, it said that two parallel lines would never cross, no matter how far they traveled. It was also interpreted to mean that for any straight line, only one parallel could be drawn through any given point not on the original line. This was not obvious; it could not be verified. And because it could not be verified, it had to be proved. For centuries mathematicians struggled to find proof of this claim, and found none.

The eighteenth century saw two mathematicians' attempts to prove the fifth postulate by first assuming that it was not correct. The objective of such an exercise is to build on an assumption until it grows evidently absurd, thereby debunking the original premise. But the examples failed to show themselves wrong; the exercises produced internally consistent pictures that settled in the imagination quite comfortably and quite separately from Euclid's fifth. Both mathematicians deemed this ridiculous and abandoned their efforts. After another century, three different mathematicians—the Russian Nikolai Lobachevski, the Hungarian János Bolyai, and his teacher the German Johann Karl Friedrich Gauss—decided that other, non-Euclidean geometries could exist where four of the postulates obtained but the fifth did not. But what does it mean that they *could* exist? Do they exist? They do, as long as mathematicians can find no holes or, rather, internal contradictions in them. Can we see them the same way we can see a line segment and a circle? Sure, no less and no more than we can see a strictly Euclidean geometry. So how do we know which is right? The great American mathematician Richard Courant (for whom the Courant Institute of Mathematical Sciences at New York University is named) and his coauthor Herbert Robbins, then a professor at Rutgers University, wrote that for our purposes it did not matter and we might as well choose Euclid: "Since the Euclidean system is rather simpler to deal with, we are justified in using it exclusively as long as fairly small distances (of a few million miles!) are under consideration. But we should not necessarily expect it to be suitable for describing the universe as a whole."

But how about describing a small piece of the universe? Say, the planet Earth. Or an apple. Remember this for future reference: the Earth and an apple are essentially the same. Let us think about the surface of the Earth, or of an apple, as the plane we are studying. Take an apple and draw a triangle on it. Now, if Euclidean geometry obtained for the surface of the apple, the sum of the angles of this triangle would equal 180 degrees. But because the surface of the apple is curved, the sum of the angles of the triangle is greater. This would mean that the fifth postulate is not true for this surface. Indeed, it is easy to see that on this surface, any two straight lines—a straight line being the extension of a segment that connects two points in the shortest possible way—will cross. All straight lines on the apple, or on the Earth, are "great circles" with their centers at the center of the sphere.

It was the nineteenth-century German mathematician Bernhard Riemann who developed a geometry of curved spaces, where straight lines are called geodesics and any two of them will cross. The geometry is called elliptic, or simply Riemannian, geometry, and it is the geometry used in Einstein's general theory of relativity.

Euclid's world, limited to his immediate surroundings, was, for all intents and purposes, flat. Our world is curved. Humans now routinely travel distances great enough to make the curvature of the Earth part of our lived experience. Not all of us travel so far all the time, but in the imagination—the very place where mathematics resides—the shortest distance between two points is the trajectory described by an airplane, which generally lies along a geodesic, even if we have never heard the word. These straight lines do not go on forever but, being circles, inevitably close in on themselves. And, of course, they cross, any two of them. What seemed absurd in the eighteenth century is now an accurate reflection of the way we experience the world.

In other words, our world has grown bigger. But that raises two questions: How much bigger can it get? and What does *bigger* mean? Here, allow me formally to introduce topology, an area of mathematics born in St. Petersburg in 1736, when the Swiss mathematician Leonhard Euler, who was teaching there, freed geometry of the burden of measuring distances. He published a paper on the solution to the Königsberg bridge problem, which had been posed by the mayor of the eponymous city, who had wanted Euler to devise a walking tour that would have an individual pass through each of Königsberg's seven bridges exactly once. Euler concluded that this could not be done. He also showed, first, that in any city with bridges, such a walking tour could be designed if and only if an odd number of bridges led to two areas of the town or to no areas, and, second, that it could not be designed if an odd number of bridges led to one area or to more than two. The third thing that Euler did while solving a problem where locations, not distances, were important was herald a new area of mathematics, which he termed "geometry of position."

In this new discipline, size—distance—in the familiar sense of the word did not matter. The number of steps that made up the walking tour made no difference; it was the way these steps were taken. What made an object lesser or greater in this new field was the amount of information required to locate it; to be precise, it was the number of coordinates needed to describe it. A single point has dimension zero; a line segment has one dimension; the surface of something such as a triangle or a square or a sphere has two dimensions. That is correct: the surface of something that we envision as flat and the surface of something that we envision as solid are, for the purposes of topology, the same. This is because when topologists talk about the surface of a sphere, or, say, an apple, they mean *just* the surface, with no regard for the solid internal space of the apple. Put another way, a topologist is like a tiny bug crawling on the apple, or like Euclid walking on the Earth: neither the bug nor Euclid has much reason to suspect that a triangle he describes will have angles amounting in sum to more than 180 degrees or that the straight line he is walking will not go on forever but will eventually close in on itself, describing a great circle. The curved nature of the surface is a function of the third dimension, of which neither of them has any experience.

We modern humans, who know firsthand that the Earth is a sphere and that its surface is therefore curved, live in three dimensions. But there is a fourth dimension—we know there is—and it is called time. We cannot move ourselves back and forth in time, so we cannot observe our three-dimensional habitat the way we can observe, by being lifted up into the air, the two-dimensional habitat of lesser animals. We are reduced to exploring the space that surrounds us and making guesses as to what it would look like from a vantage point we can suggest but cannot experience or, really, imagine. This is the nature of the Poincaré Conjecture: the last universalist supposed that the universe was shaped like a sphere—a three-dimensional sphere.

The young mathematician who gave me topology lessons for this book—who watched as I painfully tried to wrap my mind, like so many tight rubber bands, around the basic concepts of topology —cringed whenever he encountered references to the Poincaré Conjecture describing the shape of the universe. It would be more accurate to state that the proof of the Poincaré Conjecture will probably aid science greatly in learning the shape and properties of the universe, but this was not the issue Grigory Perelman tackled: he attacked a simply stated, much discussed mathematical problem that had gone unsolved for more than a century. Just like my young tutor and many other mathematicians I met along the way, he emphatically did not care about the physical shape of the universe or the experience of people who inhabited it; mathematics had given him the liberty to live among abstract objects in his own imagination, which was exactly where this problem had to be solved.

In 1904 Henri Poincaré published a paper on three-dimensional manifolds. What is a manifold? It is an object, or a space, existing in the mathematician's imagination—whether or not something like it can actually be observed in reality—that can be divided into many neighborhoods. Each neighborhood, taken separately, has a basic Euclidean geometry or can be explained through it, but all the neighborhoods together may add up to something much more complicated. The best example of a manifold is the Earth as portrayed through a series of maps, each showing only a small part of its surface. Imagine a map of Manhattan, for example: its Euclidean nature is obvious. When maps are put together in an atlas, their parallel lines continue not to cross and their triangles maintain their 180-degree nature. But if we used the maps to try to replicate the actual surface of the Earth, we would start with something that looked like a many-many-faceted disco ball, and then we would smooth out the edges and ultimately get a globe that reflected the Earth's curved complexity—and if we extended Manhattan's First Avenue and Second Avenue, they would cross. These concepts—*maps, atlases,* and *manifolds*—are basic to topology.

What makes one manifold different from another is its having a hole, or more than one hole. To a topologist, a ball, a box, a bun, and a blob are essentially the same. But a bagel is different. The key to this is the rubber band, an instrument as important to the topological imagination as the atlas. The imaginary rubber band is placed around the imaginary object and allowed to do its rubber-band thing, which is contract. If a rubber band—a very tight rubber band—is placed around a ball, it will find a way to contract and slip off the ball. It is significant that this will happen no matter where on the ball the band is placed. A bagel, however, is different: if one end of your imaginary rubber band has been threaded through the hole in the bagel and then reconnected to itself, it will stay around the bagel, never slipping off no matter how tight it is. A rubber band can be slipped off any place on a ball, a box, a bun, or a blob without a hole, which makes them all essentially similar or, in the language of topology, diffeomorphic to one another. This means you can reshape any one of them into any other and then back again.

This more or less brings us to the point where we can understand the Poincaré Conjecture. A bit more than a hundred years ago, Poincaré posed an innocent-sounding question: if a three-dimensional manifold is smooth and simply connected, then is it diffeomorphic to a three-dimensional sphere? *Smooth* means that the manifold is not twisted (you can imagine that twisting something would cause some problems with the papering-over map project). *Simply connected* means that it has no holes. And we know what *diffeomorphic* means. We also know what *three-dimensional* means: a three-dimensional manifold is the surface of a four-dimensional object. Let us also pause to consider what a *sphere* is. A sphere is a collection of points that are all equally far from a given point—the center. A one-dimensional sphere (a circumference in regular school geometry) is all of these points in a two-dimensional space (a plane). A two-dimensional sphere (the surface of a ball) is all of these points in a three-dimensional space. What makes spheres particularly interesting to topologists is that they belong to a category called hypersurfaces—objects that have as many dimensions as is possible in a given space (one dimension in a two-dimensional space, two dimensions in a three-dimensional space, and so on). The three-dimensional sphere that so interested Poincaré was the surface of a four-dimensional ball. We cannot imagine this thing, but we just might inhabit it.

Topologists often tackle problems by trying to solve them for a different number of dimensions. The equivalent of the Poincaré Conjecture for two dimensions—the understanding that the surfaces of a ball, a box, a bun, and a blob without a hole are essentially the same—is basic to topology. But in three dimensions—when we actually get to the conjecture itself—it gets tricky. Mathematicians struggled with the Poincaré Conjecture in its original three dimensions for the better part of a century, but the first breakthroughs came from a different place—or, rather, in higher dimensions.

At the dawn of the 1960s, several mathematicians—exactly how many and under what circumstances is still a matter of some dispute—proved the Poincaré Conjecture for dimensions five and higher. One was the American John Stallings, who in 1960 published a proof of the conjecture for seven dimensions or more just a year after he received his PhD from Princeton. Next was the American Stephen Smale, who probably completed his proof earlier than Stallings but published it several months later; he, however, proved the conjecture for dimensions five and higher. Then the British mathematician Christopher Zeeman extended Stallings's proof to dimensions five and six. A fourth man in the mix was Andrew Wallace, an American mathematician who in 1961 published a proof essentially similar to Smale's. There was also a Japanese mathematician named Hiroshi Yamasuge who published his own proof for dimensions five and higher in 1961.

So, more than fifty years after it was originally posed, the Poincaré Conjecture started to give—ever so slightly. All of these mathematicians, like countless others who were far less successful, had hoped to prove the conjecture itself—for the three dimensions for which it was stated. And while they will probably be remembered for their groundbreaking contributions to the cause of cracking the conjecture, at least one of them seemed to think himself most remarkable for the contribution he did not make. John Stallings, a professor emeritus at Berkeley, listed only a few of his papers on his personal website. The first published paper he mentioned dated back to 1966, and it was called "How Not to Solve the Poincaré Conjecture."

"I have committed—the sin of falsely proving Poincaré's Conjecture," Stallings began. "Now, in hope of deterring others from making similar mistakes, I shall describe my mistaken proof. Who knows but that somehow a small change, a new interpretation, and this line of proof may be rectified!" That is the spirit of hope against hope, at once conscious of the futility of efforts and obsessively incapable of giving up, that characterized the nearly hundred-year battle against the conjecture.

It was twenty years before the conjecture yielded slightly once again. In 1982 the young—he was thirty-one at the time—American mathematician Michael Freedman published a proof of the conjecture for dimension four. The accomplishment was hailed as a breakthrough; Freedman received the Fields Medal. But the conjecture for dimension three remained unproven. None of the methods used in the higher dimensions worked for dimension three; there was not enough room in this dimension to allow topologists to wield the tools they used in higher dimensions. It seemed to call for a revolutionary approach, something Poincaré himself could not have envisioned or even suspected.

Perhaps one of the problems with four-dimensional spaces is that, unlike higher-dimensional ones, they are not quite abstractions; it seems that we humans may very well inhabit a three-dimensional space embedded in four dimensions, even if most of us cannot wrap our minds around it. But experts say there is one living man, the American geometer William Thurston, who can imagine four dimensions. Thurston, they say, is possessed of a geometric intuition unlike that of any other human. "When you see him or talk to him, he is often staring out into space and you can see that he sees these pictures," said John Morgan, a professor at Columbia University, a friend of Thurston's, and a coauthor of one of several books written about Perelman's proof of the Poincaré Conjecture. "His geometric insight is unlike anyone I've ever met. So can there be a type of mathematician like Bill Thurston? How can someone have that kind of geometric insight? You know, I've got a fair amount of mathematical talent myself but I don't approach the human conclusions he does."

Thurston talked of three-dimensional manifolds in four-dimensional spaces as though he could see and manipulate them. He described the ways they could be cut up, and what would happen if they were. To a topologist, this was a very important exercise; complex objects are usually studied through their simpler composite parts, and understanding the nature of these parts and their relationships is essential to understanding the larger object. Thurston suggested that all three-dimensional manifolds could be carved up in particular ways that yielded objects that belonged to one of eight specific varieties of three-dimensional manifolds. It would not be quite right to call Thurston's conjecture a step toward proving Poincaré's. Indeed, it was even more ambitious, if a bit less famous. If Thurston had proved his conjecture, Poincaré's would automatically have followed. But he could not prove it.

"I watched Bill make progress," Morgan recalled. "And when he didn't get it, I thought, 'I'm not going to get it, nobody is going to get it.' Just as Jeff [Cheeger] said one time, 'It just gets too complicated to keep practicing the Poincaré Conjecture.'"

While other mathematicians wisely chose to direct their energies elsewhere, a Berkeley professor named Richard Hamilton persisted in tackling the Poincaré and then the Thurston conjectures. The standard journalistic description of Hamilton usually contains the word *flamboyant,* which seems to mean, basically, that he is interested not only in mathematics but also in surfing and in women. He is sociable, charming, and absolutely brilliant—for it was he who devised the way to prove both of the conjectures.

In the early 1980s Hamilton proposed something that can sound deceptively obvious. The surface of a sphere in any dimension has a constant positive curvature; this is a basic quality of the object. So if one could find a way to measure the curvature of an unidentifiable, unimaginable three-dimensional blob and then start reshaping the blob, all the while measuring its curvature, then one might eventually get to the point where the curvature was both positive and constant, whereby the blob would definitively be proven to be a three-dimensional sphere. That would mean that the blob had been a sphere all along, since reshaping does not actually change the topological qualities of objects—it just makes them more recognizable.

Hamilton devised a way of placing a metric on the blob to measure the curvature, and he wrote an equation that showed the way the blob, and the metric, would change over time. He proved that as the blob was molded, its curvature would not decrease but would necessarily grow—and this helped him demonstrate that the curvature would indeed be positive. But how to ensure that it would be constant? Hamilton got stuck.

Think about a simple function of the sort you studied in high school. Say, $1/x$. A graph of this function would look like a smooth line until it got to the point where $x = 0$. Then things would get crazy, because you cannot divide by zero. The line of your graph would suddenly soar toward eternity. This is called a singularity.

The process of transforming the metric described by the equation devised by Hamilton is called the Ricci flow. As the flow worked its theoretical magic on the imaginary metric on the unimaginable blob, every so often, a singularity would develop. Hamilton suggested that the singularities could be predicted and disarmed by stopping the function—the Ricci flow—fixing the problem by hand, and resuming the flow. When a mathematician says that he has fixed something "by hand," he actually means that he has devised a different function for the problem piece. An example is something that often happens in computer programming, where different functions are used depending on the conditions. When, say, your function is equal to x for all cases where x is equal to or greater than o, and equal to $-x$ for all cases where x is less than o. In topology, where imaginary hands intervene in the imaginary transformation of an object, this intervention is called *surgery*. So the process that Hamilton envisioned was Ricci flow with surgery.

Hamilton was not the first mathematician who thought he knew how to prove the Poincaré Conjecture. He was also not the first to encounter insurmountable obstacles on his way to a proof. In order for his program—as mathematicians call it—to work, several things had to be true. First, the curvature he was attempting to measure had to have a constant limit, a sort of uniform boundary; if he assumed this was true, the proof would probably work—but how could he know that his assumption was correct? Second, while Hamilton devised Ricci flow with surgery and could show that it would be effective in some cases, he could not prove that it could be used effectively no matter what kind of singularity developed. He could theorize about the sorts of singularities that would appear, but he could not find a way to tame all of them or even claim to have identified all of them. Here was another man who "made progress and then didn't get it." Here was another man for whom, as Morgan quoted Jeff Cheeger as saying, it got "too complicated to keep practicing the Poincaré Conjecture."

Twenty-five years later, two things are perfectly clear. First, Hamilton did indeed create the blueprint for proving both the Poincaré and the Geometrization conjectures. Second, his personal tragedy was as great as his professional achievement: at the age of forty, Hamilton became stuck and, apparently, remained stuck.

The point at which Hamilton got stuck is roughly the point at which Perelman began to engage the Poincaré Conjecture. It was also the point at which Perelman began to disappear; he went to fewer seminars, gradually reduced his hours at the Steklov so that he really only appeared when it was time to pick up his monthly pay. He slowed his e-mail correspondence to such a degree that most acquaintances assumed he had become yet another mathematician who had once shown promise but then met a problem and was crushed by it, reduced to mathematical nonexistence.

We know now that this was not the case. Rather, Perelman had completed his mathematical education and began to apply it. As it happened, the process of being educated—or, perhaps more precisely, the desire he had for mathematical knowledge that could be imparted by others—was what had kept him connected to the outside world. Now that world was more or less used up; its utility was negligible, and its demands therefore incomprehensible and even more irritating than before. Perelman, naturally, turned his back on the world and faced the problem.

What the world had given Perelman was the habit of honing the power of his incomparable mind on a single problem. What Hamilton had essentially done was turn the Poincaré Conjecture into a super mathematical-olympiad problem. He had, in a sense, taken it down a notch. In the world of top mathematicians, the intellectual elite are people who open new horizons by posing questions no one else has thought to ask. A step down are the people who devise ways to answer those questions; often these are members of the elite at earlier stages in their career—a few years after obtaining their PhDs, for example, when they are proving other people's theorems before they start formulating their own. And finally, there are the rare birds, those who take the last steps in completing proofs. These are the persistent, exacting, patient mathematicians who finally lay down the paths others have dreamed up and marked out. In our story, Poincaré and Thurston represent the first group, Hamilton the second group, and Perelman the one who finished the job.

So who was he? He was the man who had never met a problem he could not solve. Whatever he had been trying to do with Alexandrov spaces at Berkeley might have been an exception—he might indeed have gotten stuck—but then it might also have been the only time he tried to do something that fell into the second or even the first category of mathematical work rather than the third. The third category is essentially similar to solving a mathematical-olympiad problem: it has been clearly stated, and restrictions have been placed on its solution—the path to proof had been marked out by Hamilton. This was a very, very complicated olympiad problem; it could not be solved in hours, or weeks, or even months. Indeed, it was a problem that perhaps could not be solved in any amount of time by anyone—except Perelman. And Perelman was a man in search of just such a problem, one that would finally utilize the full capacity of the supercompactor that was his mind.

Perelman managed to prove two main things. First, he showed that Hamilton did not need to assume that the curvature would always be uniformly bound; in the imaginary space in which the proof unfolded, this simply would always be the case. Second, he showed that all the singularities that could develop stemmed from the same root; they would appear when the curvature began to "blow up," to grow unmanageable. Since all the singularities had the same nature, a single tool would be effective against all of them—and the surgery originally envisioned by Hamilton would do the job. Moreover, Perelman proved that some of the singularities Hamilton had hypothesized would never occur at all.

There is something peculiar and slightly ironic in the logic of Perelman's proof. He succeeded because he used the unfathomable power of his mind to grasp the entire scope of possibilities: he was ultimately able to claim that he knew all that could happen as the matrix grew and the object reshaped itself. Knowing it all, he was able to exclude some of the topological developments as impossible. Speaking of the imaginary four-dimensional space, he referred to things that could and could not occur "in nature." In essence, he was able to do in mathematics what he had tried to do in life: grasp at once all the possibilities of nature and annihilate everything that fell outside that realm—castrati voices, cars, anti-Semitism, and any other uncomfortable singularity.

9

The Proof Emerges

Date: Tue, 12 Nov 2002 05:09:02 -0500 (EST)
From: Grigori Perelman
To: [multiple recipients]
Subject: new preprint

Dear [Name],
may I bring to your attention my paper in arXiv math.DG 0211159.

Abstract:
We present a monotonic expression for the Ricci flow, valid in all dimensions and without curvature assumptions. It is interpreted as an entropy for a certain canonical ensemble. Several geometric applications are given. In particular, (1) Ricci flow, considered on the space of riemannian metrics modulo diffeomorphism and scaling, has no nontrivial periodic orbits (that is, other than fixed points); (2) In a region, where singularity is

forming in finite time, the injectivity radius is controlled by the curvature; (3) Ricci flow can not quickly turn an almost euclidean region into a very curved one, no matter what happens far away. We also verify several assertions related to Richard Hamilton's program for the proof of Thurston geometrization conjecture for closed three-manifolds, and give a sketch of an eclectic proof of this conjecture, making use of earlier results on collapsing with local lower curvature bound.

Best regards,

Grisha

About a dozen U.S. mathematicians received this message. It said that the day before, Perelman had posted a paper on arXiv.org, a website hosted by the Cornell University Library and created for the express purpose of facilitating electronic communication among mathematicians and scientists. The preprint was the first of three papers that contained the results of Perelman's seven-year attack on the Poincaré and Geometrization conjectures.

"So I start looking at the paper," Michael Anderson told me. "I'm not an expert on Ricci flow—nevertheless, looking through it, it became clear that he had made huge advances, that the solution to the Geometrization Conjecture and therefore the Poincaré Conjecture was within sight." Every recipient of the e-mail had been on his own crusade against one of the problems for many years. Every one of them had a conflicted reaction to the news: if Perelman had indeed proved the conjectures, this was a mathematical accomplishment of monumental proportions, and it had to inspire a sense of triumph—but it was someone else's triumph, and it dashed many mathematicians' hopes for their own breakthroughs. Anderson had been working on Geometrization for almost ten years and was, as he told me, "getting bogged down in technical issues. I was still hoping that I'd have some insight or some breakthrough but really came to the conclusion that it wouldn't happen.

But if anybody was going to do it, good that it was Grisha. I liked him. So the next day I invited him to come here, and a day later I was really surprised that he said yes."

Meanwhile, a flurry of e-mails began to travel among American and European topologists. Mike Anderson sent out a few that read as follows:

Hi [Name],

Hope all is well with you. I don't know if you've noticed yet but Grisha Perelman has put up a paper on the Ricci flow at mathDG/0211159 that you and your friends working in the area may want to look at. Grisha is a very unusual and also very bright guy—I first met him about 9 years ago, and we used to talk about Ricci flow and geometrization of 3-manifolds a fair amount in the early 90's. Out of the blue he sent me an e-mail yesterday informing me of his paper.

Basically, I know very little about the Ricci flow, but it seems to me he has answered, in this paper, many of the fundamental problems that people have been trying to solve. It may be that he is even very close to the solution of Hamilton's goal, i.e. proving Thurston's conjecture. The ideas in the paper appear to me to be completely new and original—typical Grisha. (He solved a number of other outstanding problems in other areas in the early 90's and then "disappeared" from the scene. It seems he has now resurfaced.)

Anyway, I wanted to inform you of this, and also ask if you could keep me "in the loop" on discussions/rumors regarding this work . . . Of course, what I'd really like to know is how close one now is to solving Thurston's conjecture—since this affects some of my work a lot. I'm assuming here that his paper is correct—which to me is a reasonable bet, knowing Grisha.

I'm sending a similar message to a few other friends I know working on Ricci flow.

Best regards, Mike

Someone who had never heard of Perelman might be forgiven for not taking the paper seriously: work claiming to prove the Poincaré Conjecture appeared regularly, yet in almost a hundred years, no one had solved the problem. Everyone, including mathematicians of great repute—indeed, including Poincaré himself—had made mistakes. Purported proofs appeared every few years, and all of them had been debunked—some sooner, some later. One had to know Perelman—be aware that he never produced lemons, as his math-club mates used to say, and have a sense of his propensity for the well-prepared gesture—to know just how seriously this particular attempt at the Poincaré should be taken.

But how was one to determine whether it was in fact correct? The paper pulled together techniques and even problems from several distinct specialties inside mathematics; they were not even all limited to topology. In addition, Perelman's presentation was so condensed that a judgment on his proof would first require, in essence, deciphering his paper. Nor did he help by stating up front what he proposed to do and how. He did not even claim he had proved the Poincaré and Geometrization conjectures until he was asked the question directly. Anderson's e-mails were some of the first steps in starting this process of verification. *This guy should be taken seriously,* he was saying, *and please let me know whether he has done what I think he has done.* Anderson wrote this e-mail message at 5:38 in the morning the day after he'd received Perelman's e-mail alerting him to the preprint.

Within a few hours, Anderson started getting responses from geometers who apparently had also stayed up all night reading the paper. They reported that what the mathematicians called "the

Ricci flow community" was in a frenzy—and noted that none of them had heard of Perelman before.

None of the topologists with whom Perelman had been acquainted in the United States belonged to the Ricci flow community, which centered around Richard Hamilton—the most important addressee of Perelman's e-mail announcement and, in a sense, of his entire paper. As the e-mails flew back and forth among geometers, Hamilton remained conspicuously silent. "Has there emerged yet any impressions of Perelman's work?" Anderson wrote to another Ricci flow-er a few days later. "Are some of you in Hamilton's group going over the paper? Does Hamilton know about it? Any ideas how close [Perelman] may be to finishing the program?"

Hamilton knew about the paper, the correspondents reported. The paper appeared very important indeed.

In fact, it took Perelman less than half of his first paper to get past the point at which Hamilton had been stuck for two decades. No wonder Hamilton was silent. One can only imagine what it must have felt like to see one's life's ambition hijacked and then fulfilled by some upstart with unkempt hair and long fingernails. One can imagine, that is, if one understands that ambition, competitiveness, and a sense of professional self-worth are what likely motivates human behavior—not, say, the best interests of mathematics. Grisha Perelman did not have that understanding.

Indeed, one of the most remarkable aspects of the story of Perelman's proof is the number of mathematicians who temporarily set aside their own professional ambitions to devote themselves to the deciphering and interpretation of his preprints. In November 2002, Bruce Kleiner was traveling in Europe. Just as he was about to begin a lecture at the University of Bonn, Ursula Hamenstaedt, a local professor who was in the audience, asked him: "Oh, by the way, did you see the preprint that Perelman just posted with proof of the geometrization of the Poincaré Conjecture?" At least, this was what he remembered her saying. She might in fact have been more cautious in her assessment—but Kleiner knew just how seriously Perelman was to be taken.

"Nobody who knew his papers or had listened to his lectures had ever suggested he made claims that would later collapse, or would say things that he hadn't thought through carefully," Kleiner told me. "And here he was posting something on the arXiv, which is a very public forum. So, unless there was some personality change that had taken place since the early nineties, I thought there was a very good chance there was something there or maybe he had solved it completely." And this meant that Kleiner's professional life was taking a sudden turn. Like Anderson, Kleiner had for years been working on an aspect of the Geometrization Conjecture, though using an entirely different approach. Unlike Anderson, he did not yet suspect that his pursuit would prove fruitless. He did know that, as he put it, "it was a high-risk project," a famous conjecture with which someone else might succeed sooner, but he was hardly prepared to hear, just before his own lecture, that his project was effectively over. For the next year and a half, Kleiner would be working on Project Perelman.

Perelman, meanwhile, was preparing for his trip to the United States. He had received invitations from Anderson at Stony Brook and Tian, now at MIT, and he decided to spend two weeks at each place. He had told Anderson at the outset that he would be in the United States no more than a month because he could not leave his mother alone for longer. The plan later changed to include his mother on the journey, but Perelman stuck to the original length of the trip.

Perelman now seemed fully re-engaged with the world. He handled the U.S. visa formalities—burdensome even for people seasoned in dealing with bureaucracies—on his own, securing visas for himself and his mother. He bought his tickets himself, apparently using money still left in his American bank account. He had been living frugally the past seven years, using his postdoc savings—he even added a footnote to that effect to his first preprint, obsessively true to his ideal of giving credit where credit was due, however irrelevant it was to the matter at hand. He corresponded with Anderson and Tian regarding the scheduling and logistics of his travels, including medical insurance, an issue that apparently concerned him a great deal.

Perelman's re-emergence from his near hermithood did not seem to impair his ability to continue writing up his proof. He submitted the second of his three preprints to the arXiv on March 10, 2003, while he was in the process of obtaining his U.S. visa. At twenty-two pages, this one was eight pages shorter than the first installment. He had apparently formulated the proof so clearly in his mind that distractions, minor and major, did not take away from his ability to devote a couple of weeks at a time to these concentrated write-ups (that spring he would tell Jeff Cheeger that it had taken him three weeks to write the first paper—less time than it had taken Cheeger to read and understand it).

Perelman arrived at MIT at the beginning of April 2003. To Gang Tian, he looked more or less as Tian had remembered him: lean, long-haired, and with long fingernails, although without the brown corduroy jacket. To those who were seeing him for the first time, Perelman looked striking but entirely within the weirdness bounds of mathematicians. At his lecture, the hall was packed. A number of people in the audience had been reading Perelman's first paper and writing their own notes on it; several of them were doing this in a seminar started by Tian. But a majority were curious mathematicians who had come to look at the man who might have made the biggest mathematical breakthrough in a century. These mathematicians were qualified to follow the narrative line of his lecture but would certainly have been unable to ask meaningful questions after the lecture—which made them, to Perelman, uninteresting at best and annoying at worst. He had banned videotaping of the lecture and had made it clear he did not want any media publicity, but a couple of journalists made it into the audience that day anyway.

Almost incredibly, those who had come hoping for a mathematical spectacle got one. In sharp contrast to his speech at the 1994 international congress, Perelman presented an organized, lucid, and at times even playful narrative. He was at the peak of his relationship with the Poincaré Conjecture. If the Poincaré Conjecture were a person, this might have been the moment when Perelman would have chosen to marry it: a time when he could see their entire history together clearly, and when he was most free of doubt and most certain of the future.

Almost daily for two weeks after his first presentation, Perelman gave talks on his work to smaller audiences. He spent several hours a day answering questions, mostly about the Geometrization Conjecture. In the mornings before his lectures, Perelman made a habit of stopping by Tian's office to talk, mostly about mathematics. He may have been looking for new problems to tackle; he asked Tian about his own research and even floated some ideas related to Tian's specialization at the time rather than to geometrization. Tian, unlike Anderson and Morgan—who regularly attempted to draw out Perelman—rarely ventured outside the narrow discussions of mathematical problems. "He was focused and very single-minded," Tian told me. "I respect that he can ignore many things other people pay attention to and focus on doing mathematics."

Perelman seemed so relaxed and friendly during this visit that in one of their morning talks Tian broached the subject of Perelman's staying at MIT. The university was interested in making an offer, and some colleagues of Tian's had approached Perelman the previous evening and attempted to convince him that the resources of MIT would allow him to work more productively. Tian asked Perelman for his reaction. Whatever Perelman said to him in response, the polite, exceedingly soft-spoken Tian would not repeat to me. "He made some comments," Tian allowed. "I don't want to say them." The problem was not just that this time Perelman had no interest in staying on in the United States. It was that the idea of being rewarded now with a comfortable university position insulted him. He had expected a full professorship eight years earlier. His brain had been the same then as it was now; he had been just as deserving; and yet they had wanted him to prove that he was good enough to teach mathematics. Now they acted as though he had finally proved it, when in fact he had proved the Poincaré Conjecture, which was its own reward.

The two returned to their civilized discussions of manifolds, metrics, and estimates. Perelman's irritation surfaced just once more in their discussions. The first of what Tian called "incidents" must have occurred April 15, toward the end of Perelman's stay at MIT, when the *New York Times* published an article titled "Russian Reports He Has Solved a Celebrated Math Problem." Just about every word in the title was an insult to Perelman. He had "reported" nothing; he had been careful to make his claims only in response to direct queries. To call the Poincaré Conjecture "celebrated," and to do so in a mass-circulation newspaper, was, from Perelman's standpoint, unconscionably vulgar. And the story itself heaped on the insults. The fourth paragraph of the article began, "If his proof is accepted for publication in a refereed research journal and survives two years of scrutiny, Dr. Perelman could be eligible for a $1 million prize." This seemed to imply that Perelman had taken on the problem in order to win the million dollars—that he had any interest in the money at all—and that he would actually submit his work for publication in a refereed journal. All of this was demonstrably untrue. Perelman had started working on the conjecture years before the Clay prize was created. While he used money and had some appreciation for it, he felt little need and, certainly, no desire for it. Finally, his decision to post his proof on the arXiv had been an intentional revolt against the very idea of scientific journals distributed by paid subscription. And now that he had solved one of the hardest problems in mathematics, Perelman would not be asking anyone to vet his proof for publication.

Before coming to the United States, Perelman had made it clear to those who asked—and Mike Anderson, for one, was very careful to ask—that at that point he did not want any publicity outside the mathematics community. Perelman did not say he never wanted publicity; he made it clear he did not think the time was right for it. And as strict as he was on the issue of speaking to journalists, he took a relaxed attitude toward publicizing his lectures and his work among colleagues: he was happy to let the organizers of his lectures use their professional mailing lists, or not, as they saw fit. He had an implicit trust in mathematicians of many stripes, and he had just as instinctive a mistrust of journalists. The *New York Times* article not only reinforced his suspicions of journalists—the author misinterpreted events and motivations in all the ways Perelman had probably feared—but also undermined his trust in his colleagues; one of the reporter's two quoted sources was a mathematician who had attended Tian's seminar and Perelman's talks. Thomas Mrowka was no idle observer, yet he had offered an appraisal that served as the perfect kicker for the article and likely made Perelman cringe: "Either he's done it or he's made some really significant progress, and we're going to learn from it."

On the day Perelman left MIT, he and Tian went across the river to Boston's historic Back Bay to have lunch, which Perelman seemed to enjoy. Perelman even talked of the possibility of returning to the United States; he said he had offers from Stanford, Berkeley, MIT—in fact, by that point he could have had any terms he desired at any mathematics department in the country. In a perfectly Bostonian flourish, the two mathematicians followed the lunch with a walk along the Charles River. Perelman's relaxed state must have given way to anxiety, for he confided to Tian that things had gone sour between him and Burago—and, more generally, between him and the Russian mathematical establishment. Tian, again, would not reveal the details to me—saying only that he doubted that his friend was right this time—but the rupture was so much discussed in St. Petersburg that the details were easy to obtain. The conflict involved another researcher at Burago's laboratory, one whose footnoting practices, Perelman believed, were so sloppy as to border on plagiarism. The man followed a generally accepted footnoting practice of referencing the latest appearance of an item rather than providing all the available truth on its origins. Perelman had demanded that the notoriously tolerant Burago subject his researcher to all but a public scientific whipping. In Perelman's estimation, Burago's refusal made him an accomplice to what amounted very nearly to a crime; Perelman's screaming at his mentor had been heard in the halls of the Steklov. Perelman left Burago's laboratory and found refuge in the lab of Olga Ladyzhenskaya, a remarkable mathematician who was old enough, wise enough, and woman enough to accept Perelman just as he was. Everyone else—including Burago and Gromov, who generally saw Perelman as nearly faultless—seemed willing to forgive him, but they were incapable of seeing his approach to footnoting as anything but capricious at best and meanly ridiculous at worst.

Following his lectures at MIT, Perelman went to New York City, where his mother was once again staying with relatives. He stayed the weekend and traveled to Stony Brook by train on Sunday evening. Mike Anderson picked him up at the station and delivered him to the dormitory where he was staying; Perelman had explicitly requested that his accommodations be "as modest as possible." He started lecturing the following day, establishing a consistent schedule for the next two weeks: morning lectures followed by afternoon discussion sessions. To those attending, these sessions seemed nothing short of a miracle. Here was a man some of them had never heard of and others had believed had vanished who had slain the Poincaré and now exhibited fantastic clarity in his lectures and unparalleled patience during the discussions.

This was how Perelman had been taught mathematics should be practiced. He went to the lecture hall every day to fulfill his destiny, and this explained both his clarity and his patience. But in the world outside the Stony Brook classrooms, things increasingly diverged from his expectations. On the day he arrived at Stony Brook, the *New York Times* published another article. This one too started out by stating, inaccurately, that Perelman claimed to have proved the Poincaré Conjecture and linked that solution to the million-dollar prize, and it then went on to quote a single source: Michael Freedman, who had received the Fields Medal after solving the Poincaré for dimension four, and who was now working at Microsoft. Freedman, incredibly, called Perelman's achievement "a small sorrow" for topology: Perelman had solved the biggest problems in the field, which made it less attractive, he reasoned, and so "you won't have the brilliant young people you have now."

This was probably a fairly serious insult. After Perelman's falling-out with Burago, his reference group, which was small to begin with, had shrunk to include just a few people who were in a position to understand his proof. Back at MIT, he had told Tian he thought it would take a year and a half or two years for his proof to be understood. But someone like Freedman might have been expected to have an immediate overall grasp of the elegance—and the correctness—of Perelman's solution. For Freedman to frame Perelman's proof as a setback for their once-shared area, and do so in an interview with a newspaper whose readership would never understand the problem or the solution, had to be hurtful—all the more so because Freedman's reaction seemed so illogical.

If anyone could speak authoritatively on what Perelman had done—particularly on what he had laid out in his first paper—it was Richard Hamilton. After all, Perelman had followed Hamilton's program. One of the oddest and most tragic aspects of this story is the extent to which Perelman's and Hamilton's orbits missed each other. Perelman did not belong to what Anderson and others called the "Ricci flow community," which had grown up around Hamilton in the two decades he had been trying to force the matrix to conform to the conjecture. Perelman had apparently approached Hamilton twice—once following a lecture of his, and once in writing, after Perelman had returned to St. Petersburg. Both times, Perelman was asking for a clarification of something Hamilton had said or written. On the second occasion, Hamilton failed to respond—something Perelman might have understood perfectly if he held others to the same standards of behavior to which he held himself. Indeed, for reasons that were probably entirely different from Perelman's—Hamilton, by all accounts, was an atypically sociable mathematician—Hamilton tended to be elusive, occasionally reclusive, and usually very slow to respond to letters and calls. But rather than recognize familiar patterns, Perelman probably felt significantly frustrated by Hamilton's silence; he generally expected his own needs, few as they were, to be met.

Now, too, Hamilton was keeping his silence. That he had not attended Perelman's lectures at MIT might have been disappointing but was understandable. But when Perelman began his stint at Stony Brook, just an hour and a half from New York City, where Hamilton was teaching at Columbia University, Hamilton's absence became conspicuous. Other mathematicians from New York attended. One of them, John Morgan, asked Perelman to lecture at Columbia over the weekend. Perelman agreed, and then agreed to give another lecture that weekend at Princeton.

On Friday, April 25, Perelman lectured at Princeton. The university again made him an offer. Perelman turned it down. On Saturday, he lectured at Columbia. Hamilton came and stayed for the discussion after the lunch break—until the only people in the room were he, Perelman, Morgan, and Gromov, who was then at Courant. "Everybody was waiting for Richard to say either he got it or he doesn't get it," Morgan told me. "It's his theory, his idea. This is the way to do it. He's the obvious person to pass judgment."

And did he? This is where it gets tricky. "Richard from the beginning was willing to and did acknowledge that what was in the first paper was correct and it was a huge advance," said Morgan, now trying to tread carefully so as not to offend a colleague. The first paper dealt solely with Ricci flow, which was Hamilton's invention and his area of total confidence. The second paper dealt with Ricci flow with surgery, which was also Hamilton's invention but which in Perelman's treatment intermingled with Alexandrov spaces and the work Perelman had done with Gromov and Burago. Hamilton was less of an expert here, and that may have made him both less confident and, perhaps, more hopeful that Perelman had failed. "I think maybe he thought, *Well, this is a mistake,*" said Morgan, "*and if it's a mistake, that would leave room for me to produce something more that I wanted to contribute.* So I think he was sort of withholding judgment, waiting to see." If there was a chance that Perelman had taken things in the wrong direction with his second paper, then someone else—most logically, Hamilton himself—could build on the breakthroughs of Perelman's first paper. All of this, however, is conjecture: when Hamilton spoke of Perelman's work publicly, he always did so graciously; he just did it far less frequently than many—including Perelman—might have expected.

That day at Columbia, as Morgan remembered it, "It was proper but distant. There didn't seem to be any overt tension. Grisha was not going to aggressively approach anybody. If you looked at it from the outside, it looked like any other math conversation: ideas coming in and going out. In other words, whatever Richard's private feelings were about his distance, in this conversation at least, he was sort of normal about it."

Morgan invited Perelman to come to his house for brunch the following morning. "And he said, 'Well, who would be there?' I said, 'Oh, my wife, my daughter, I may invite a couple other people.' He said, 'Oh, no. I don't think so.' So my take on that is, had it been a mathematical gathering, maybe he would have come. But a social gathering he was not at all interested." That day, Perelman walked around New York with Gromov and talked to him about the Poincaré Conjecture and about his conflict with Burago. Then he went back to Brighton Beach, where his mother was staying, planning to return to Stony Brook the following night for another week of lectures and discussions.

Perelman went back to Stony Brook discouraged. He told Anderson he was disappointed at the level of questions Hamilton had asked him: it seemed the inventor of Ricci flow had not taken the time to delve deeply into Perelman's proof. In all likelihood, the reasons for this were complex: Hamilton was conflicted about engaging Perelman's work, and, in addition, it may have been both psychologically and mathematically difficult to absorb a sudden break in the wall against which he had been beating his head for twenty years. But, just like twenty years earlier, while Perelman could be endlessly patient in reiterating his explanations to interested listeners, he could not imagine that anyone might have a difficult time with something that seemed, to Perelman, transparent and nearly self-evident.

Perelman was annoyed too with Princeton's insistent courtship attempts. Someone from that university called Anderson following Perelman's lecture to ask for help in recruiting Perelman. At Perelman's request, Anderson declined to help, but Princeton got a formal offer in the mail to Perelman anyway—and this he found upsetting. "They are being pushy," he told Anderson. Among Perelman's many rules of behavior, articulated and perhaps even formulated a couple of years after the Princeton offer, was the rule that "one should never force oneself on anyone." Princeton, which had offended Perelman by asking him to apply for a job, now offended him by being too persistent in its affections.

Anderson, who in addition to his genuine admiration for Perelman also seemed to have a keen sense of Perelman's boundaries, apparently managed not to offend Perelman while pursuing the same agenda as all of Perelman's other American hosts: to convince him to stay at his university and to draw him out socially. Anderson daily took great pains to convince Perelman to go out to dinner, and occasionally he succeeded. He also held a party for Perelman at his house, which, in retrospect, seemed a bit of a disaster: Anderson and his friend Cheeger got into a loud argument over the U.S. invasion of Iraq, which Cheeger supported and Anderson did not. Anderson remembered getting very angry. "Grisha just listened," he recalled. "He didn't seem to have an opinion." Except, of course, for the firmly held opinion that the discussion of politics was beneath the dignity of a mathematician.

Anderson took Perelman to meet Jim Simons, the extraordinary man who had transformed the Stony Brook math department into one of the top such departments in the country and then become a hedge-fund manager and amassed impressive wealth, which he shared with many charities as well as with the university at Stony Brook. "So Simons made it clear that he'd like Grisha to come here—any terms he wants, any salary, or even one month a year," said Anderson, "because Simons has the influence and money to make this possible. Grisha says, 'Thank you, that's very nice, but I don't want to talk about this now. I have to go back to St. Petersburg to teach high-school students.' He had a commitment in fall 2003."

Perelman's answer might have been fully understood only by Perelman himself. A popular Russian joke tells of an actor courted by a major Hollywood studio. The actor is going to star in a film, and he is very excited, until he finds out that the filming is scheduled for December. "I can't do it," he says. "I have New Year's parties," meaning that he is scheduled to play Grandfather Frost (Santa's Russian cousin) at children's parties—and since he values this gig, he will have to pass up the opportunity of a lifetime. Perelman's excuse sounded equally absurd and touching—but apparently it was just an excuse. From what I could tell, his sole commitment in the fall of 2003 was to attend a daylong math competition at a physics-and-math school in St. Petersburg, which he did, but which in no way would have precluded his accepting any of the many offers American institutions were making. The real reason he didn't was simple: he abhorred the idea of being some department's prized possession.

Perelman went back to Russia at the end of April. He submitted the third and last in his Poincaré series of preprints on July 17; this time, it was just seven pages. The discussions went on without him. In June, Kleiner and his University of Michigan colleague John Lott started a Web page where they posted their notes on Perelman's first paper. Toward the end of the year, the American Institute of Mathematics in Palo Alto and the Mathematical Sciences Research Institute in Berkeley held a joint workshop on the first preprint; Kleiner, Lott, Tian, and Morgan were its most active participants. In the summer of 2004, all four attended a workshop at Princeton sponsored by the Clay Institute, which, as the administrator of the million-dollar prize, had a stake in encouraging the appraisal of Perelman's proof. Around the time of the Clay workshop, the four mathematicians most involved in closely reading the papers seemed to dispense with any residual doubts that the proof was correct. There were some mistakes, it seemed, and there were many gaps in the narrative Perelman presented, but none of this any longer seemed to challenge the assertion that Perelman had proved the Poincaré Conjecture and, probably, the Geometrization Conjecture (consensus on geometrization would come a bit later). Just as Perelman had predicted, this understanding came about a year and a half after his colleagues started studying his proof.

Following the summer 2004 workshop, Tian and Morgan decided to collaborate on a book about Perelman's proof; it was eventually published by the Clay Institute, which also funded Kleiner and Lott's work. In the summer of 2005, the institute sponsored a month-long workshop on the proof. The study of Perelman's preprints was turning into a mathematical cottage industry, which was just as it should be; many of the mathematicians involved had spent significant portions of their professional lives attacking these conjectures, and now each sacrificed the hope of a starring role for the opportunity to play a supporting part in the greatest mathematical production of the age.

Had Perelman followed the more traditional route—had he written a conventional paper or papers and submitted them to a mathematical journal—his work could hardly have been subjected to any more scrutiny. A journal would have sent his papers to be reviewed by his peers—who, the world of topology being so small, would have been some of the same people who pored over his preprints now. The difference is that, as reviewers, they would have read the papers in private, not in a seminar, workshop, or summer-school setting, and they would have revealed the results of their examination in a letter to the journal rather than in notes posted on the Web for all interested parties to see. The process Perelman set in motion by posting his proof, in highly concentrated form, on the Web probably involved as many people as journal publication would have, but it turned out to be far more collaborative and public than the traditional procedure. It was also faster: before going public, Perelman did not take the typical months or years to frame his results in a traditional mathematical narrative. Perelman's revolt against the conventions of scientific publishing was not based on an ideology; he simply had no use and therefore no regard for them.

But outside of a traditional publishing framework, what were the roles of people like Kleiner, Lott, Tian, and Morgan, who had set out not only to understand but also to explain Perelman's proof? In a sense, they became his coauthors. Perelman had coauthored one of his most important early papers in a similar manner. When I asked Gromov what it had been like to write an article with Perelman, he said, "It wasn't like anything. I didn't actually interact with him. Burago came here and we talked, and then Burago went back and they talked, and I guess Perelman wrote it up."

"So you didn't look at the manuscript?" I asked, incredulous.

"No."

"But wasn't there the risk that someone would have gotten something wrong along the way?"

"There is, there always is. It often happens that somebody writes part of the work and someone else writes another and it actually doesn't come together. Some very well-known mathematicians have had bad articles like that."

"But that's not a reason to read the manuscript?"

"The manuscript? Of course not. It's not interesting to read about work that you've already done. You do it—and you forget about it."

This was Perelman's school. While Perelman was lecturing at

Stony Brook, Kleiner and Lott found him as approachable and willing to engage in conversation about his proof as any mathematician could be. But when, toward the end of Perelman's stay, Kleiner
and Lott asked him whether he would look over their notes once
they were done, Perelman said he would not. "He could have spent
a half-hour sort of looking through and making some comment,"
said Kleiner, who five years later still seemed perplexed by Perelman's reaction. "That would be sort of the typical thing one might
expect at the minimum. But, you know, he's not a typical guy." As
Kleiner recalled, Perelman had explained that looking at their
notes would make him in some way responsible for the work
Kleiner and Lott had done. This was a perfect combination of
Perelman's exaggerated sense of personal responsibility and his
equally solipsistic perception of the importance of any given mathematical problem. At the center of the universe in which Perelman
stood, the Poincaré Conjecture was fading into the past. As Gromov said, "You do it—and you forget about it." Perelman knew that
months later, once Kleiner and Lott had finished their notes, he
would no longer be interested in discussing the Poincaré.

Kleiner and Lott went on to work on Perelman's papers without
Perelman. They found some problems along the way—at one
point, in fact, Kleiner was convinced that they had found a serious,
possibly fatal flaw, but Lott disabused him of this idea—and they
found that even in the highly condensed preprints, Perelman had
stayed true to his manner of relaying not so much the solution to
the problem as the history of his own relationship with the problem. As Kleiner and Lott's exploration moved toward the end of
the first preprint, they realized that some of the earlier sections of
the paper were self-contained pieces that had no bearing on the
eventual trajectory of the proof.

In September 2004, following the Clay workshop, Tian sent
Perelman an e-mail note "saying that we now understood the

proof." He pointed out that a year and a half had passed since their walk along the Charles River. Tian asked him if he would be publishing his preprints, for he and Morgan were now thinking of a book. Perelman did not respond. "He may think that he had done enough for publication by posting his preprints on the arXiv," Tian suggested when he talked to me. "Or he could be already uncomfortable with me by that time. I tried to avoid talking to reporters, because first, I didn't really enjoy talking to reporters; secondly, it takes time." But in the spring of 2004 Tian had, at a friend's request, broken his silence and talked to a freelance reporter for *Science* magazine—and now he suspected that Perelman was aware of this breach and had not written back for this reason. Most likely, though, Perelman simply had nothing to say. His prediction about the proof had come true, and he had never planned to publish his preprints—why would any further comment be necessary?

Morgan had better luck with Perelman. In the Tian-Morgan tandem, it was Morgan who wrote to Perelman to ask mathematical questions. He was consistently amazed with the precision of the responses he received. "I would ask him a mathematical question and I would almost immediately get back the answer I was looking for," Morgan told me. "Now a much more typical mathematical interchange is: You ask a question, the person you ask it to either doesn't quite understand what you're asking or because he's coming at it from inside a different point of view answers it slightly obliquely from what you're looking for. So then you ask it again. You reformulate it; refine it. And then maybe you get back an answer that is really what you're looking for. That never happened with Perelman, I'd ask him a question and it was like he knew exactly what point I was confused about or didn't understand, and exactly what I needed in order to clarify the situation."

So Morgan tried his luck with other questions. He had several sets of pressing ones. First, he wanted to see Perelman's preprints in published form—for the historical record if for no other reason. He suggested he would edit them himself and place them in a journal he coedited. He also invited Perelman to Columbia University: "Would you like to come for a week, a month, a semester, a year, for the rest of your life?" Morgan inserted these sorts of questions carefully between his mathematical requests. "And I would get back responses like: 'The answer to question one is that; here's the answer to question two. I have no answers to your other questions.' So he did acknowledge them, which is more than he did with most people." But he certainly did not answer them. After a while, Morgan ran out of mathematical questions.

When Morgan and Tian completed their manuscript in 2006, they mailed it to Perelman. The package came back stamped SERVICE REFUSED.

10

The Madness

PERELMAN RETURNED TO St. Petersburg in May of 2004. Late spring is the only time Petersburg becomes not just livable but attractive; its usual grayness gives way to a soft, cool light that refuses to dim well into the night. The city's residents pour out onto its sidewalks and embankments and start taking all the strolls they did not take in the cold, wet winter months. Perelman, who always walked, and Rukshin, who made a point of doing all things beautiful in St. Petersburg, went for a walk. The weather must have been much the same as it had been in Boston weeks earlier, when Perelman had walked along the Charles with Tian. He said many of the same things too, but more emphatically this time—or Rukshin heard them more clearly and louder than Tian had heard them. Perelman said he was disappointed in the world of mathematics.

"It took him eight or nine years to solve the Poincaré," Rukshin told me, recalling that conversation. "Now imagine that for eight years you did not know whether your child, who was born ill, would survive. You have spent eight years caring for him day and night. And now he has grown strong. From an ugly duckling, he has turned to a fine swan. And now someone says to you, 'Why don't you sell your baby to me? Here is some grant money, for half a year, or perhaps a year, we could publish the work together, we'd make this a joint result.'"

Normally, when you're having a conversation with a mathematician, pointing out logical errors will enrich the exchange. This was clearly not the case here. First, no one sends a child into the world at the tender age of eight, nor would one perceive it as offensive if, say, one's eighteen-year-old child were offered a spot at university. The thing was, even if Rukshin twisted the logic of what Perelman had said to him, he was likely still conveying the emotions correctly. In a sense, the point was precisely that this was a bad comparison: Perelman's proof of the Poincaré Conjecture was not as vulnerable or as valuable as a human child, but Perelman's experience of the incongruity of his accomplishment and the rewards he had been offered was like that of a doting parent who had been offered money for his baby. Rukshin, who was highly suspicious of the world in general and given to feeling slighted, surely added his own interpretations to Perelman's emotional charge. This was how, in the retelling, offers of professorial appointments turned into not-so-veiled attempts to buy the right of coauthorship of the proof; and how in Rukshin's and perhaps Perelman's imaginations, Kleiner and Lott's, and later Tian and Morgan's, work on interpreting the proof turned into attempts to usurp credit for it.

Concluded Rukshin: "The world of science—the science that Perelman had considered the most honest of the sciences—had turned its other side to him. It had been soiled and turned into market goods."

Perelman presented similarly charged recollections of his lecture tour to several other St. Petersburg colleagues. They too embellished his narrative with details that served to justify his anger and pain. For example, one person told me that Perelman had been hurt when Hamilton "walked out of the lecture, stomping his feet." When I asked for clarification, my interlocutor conceded, "I added the part about his stomping his feet. But from what I have been told, he did leave demonstratively."

When Perelman spoke to two *New Yorker* writers in the summer of 2006, he told them that Hamilton had shown up late for his lecture and asked no questions during the discussion session or the lunch—a recollection that is at odds with Morgan's. In all likelihood, Hamilton had asked no questions that indicated to Perelman that the older mathematician had made a serious effort to understand his work. "I'm a disciple of Hamilton's, though I haven't received his authorization," Perelman told the *New Yorker* and added, "I had the impression he had read only the first part of my paper."

The more Perelman talked about his disappointment with the mathematical establishment, and the more his acquaintances decorated his stories with demonizing details, the more Perelman's sense of betrayal deepened. His world, which had begun narrowing in his first university year and then broadened slightly both times he had traveled to the United States, was now headed for its final, disastrous narrowing. Like a rubber band slipping inexorably off a sphere, his world was about to shrink to a point.

From the moment Perelman entered Rukshin's math club at the age of ten—or perhaps from a much earlier point, when his mother told her professor she was leaving mathematics to have a baby—Perelman had been a human math project. He was raised by his mother, reared by Rukshin, coddled by Ryzhik, coached by Abramov, directed by Zalgaller, protected by Alexandrov, tended by Burago, and promoted by Gromov so that he could do pure mathematics in a world of pure mathematics. Perelman repaid his teachers and benefactors by doing just that: solving the hardest problem he could find—and by devoting himself to this process fully. And when he was done, he expected certain things. Just as he had been convinced that he should not untie his hat and had always, against all evidence, believed in meritocracy, so now he had in his head a perfect picture of how things should go. He had, in essence, a script. This script apparently indicated that Hamilton would attend all of Perelman's lectures at Stony Brook, possibly even his first lecture at MIT, and Hamilton and the whole Ricci flow community would delve deeply into Perelman's proof, making every effort to understand it. Other mathematicians would do this too; this would be their natural way of responding to his contribution and of showing mathematical appreciation.

Perelman's disappointment in Hamilton was all the more painful because he had apparently perceived Hamilton as a member of the pure-mathematician caste. In his conversation with the *New Yorker* journalists, Perelman recalled his first encounter with Hamilton, at Princeton, in a way that made this clear: "'I really wanted to ask him something,' Perelman recalled. 'He was smiling, and he was quite patient. He actually told me a couple of things that he published a few years later. He did not hesitate to tell me. Hamilton's openness and generosity—it really attracted me. I can't say that most mathematicians act like that.'" So striking and stable was this image of Hamilton in Perelman's memory that he seemed to have ignored Hamilton's nonresponse to his initial letter regarding Ricci flow and Hamilton's nonreaction to the first preprint—and so he kept expecting that Hamilton would stick to the script during the lecture tour.

The script also contained rules, obvious ones. People should not talk about things they do not understand; if it was going to take a year and a half for anyone to understand the proof, no one should talk about the proof until then. Great mathematical achievement should be rewarded with professional recognition, which can take only one form: the form of studying and understanding the work that the person has done. Money is no substitute for work. In fact, money is insulting. If you think it is natural for a university to offer money to someone who has solved a huge problem even though no one at this university understands the solution, imagine the following parallel: a publisher approaches a writer, saying, "I have not read any of your books; in fact, no one has gotten to the end of one, but they say you are a genius, so we want to sign you to a contract." This is a caricature. There was no place for caricatures in Perelman's script.

Back in the summer of 1981, the first year Sergei Rukshin managed to organize a summer mathematics training camp, Grisha Perelman lived away from home for the first time. Rukshin transported a score of his club members, age thirteen to sixteen, to a pioneer camp outside of Leningrad, a grouping of low stone buildings situated scenically in a mixed wood with easy access to a cold lake. Rukshin's agenda called for roughly four hours of problem-crunching per day, diluted with some swimming, hiking, walking through the woods listening to Rukshin recite poetry, and resting indoors listening to classical music. The arrangement with camp officials stipulated that the mathematicians would be a unit within the camp; they would have their own sleeping quarters and their own schedule, but they would have to wear Young Pioneer uniforms—white or blue button-down shirts and red neckerchiefs— and participate in some campwide activities, like politics lessons.

So it was at the beginning of the camp season that Rukshin's boys attended a lecture on foreign affairs. "The international situation," said the speaker, a young Komsomol worker, "is particularly tense today." The entire mathematics contingent broke out laughing. It is particularly tense today! Get it? It is like it was not at all tense yesterday but is *particularly* tense *today.*

If you do not find that especially funny, then chances are you do not have Asperger's syndrome. The condition got its name from the Austrian pediatrician Hans Asperger, who was long believed to have been the first to define it, in the 1940s. In fact, it seems it was the Soviet child psychiatrist Grunya Sukhareva who first grouped the symptoms, in the 1920s; she, however, called the syndrome a schizoid personality disorder, which may partly account for why it has not become a popular diagnosis in Russia. Asperger's is a disorder that's part of the autism spectrum. Unlike most autistics, Aspergians tend to have normal or high IQs, but their mental development still proceeds in ways that are markedly different from neuronormals', as people in Aspergian circles call them. Hans Asperger observed that these children's social maturity and social reasoning were delayed, and some of their social abilities remained, as he kindly put it, "quite unusual" for life. They had difficulty making friends; they had trouble communicating—the tone, rhythm, and pitch of their speech were often odd and off-putting to others; they had trouble understanding and controlling their emotions; and many of them needed profound assistance in organizing their lives, so they were often dependent on their mothers for their day-to-day functioning.

More than forty years after Hans Asperger, a British psychologist named Simon Baron-Cohen came to study autism and Asperger's syndrome and figured out several things that seem to me to be very useful in understanding Grigory Perelman. First, Baron-Cohen suggested that the autistic brain was lopsided in a particular way. Where a neuronormal brain has the ability to both systemize and empathize, the autistic brain might be excellent at the former but is always lousy at the latter—causing Baron-Cohen to dub the autistic brain "the extreme male brain." Baron-Cohen defined systemizing as "the drive to analyze and/or build a system (of any kind) based on identifying input-operation-output rules" and theorized that great systemizers might be at increased risk for autism. When he tested this theory on a population of Cambridge University undergraduates, it turned out that the mathematicians among them were three to seven times more likely than other students to have a diagnosis of an autistic condition. Baron-Cohen also developed the AQ, or the autism-spectrum quotient, test, which he administered to adults with Asperger's or high-functioning autism as well as to randomly selected controls and Cambridge students and winners of the British Mathematical Olympiad. The correlation between math and autism and/or Asperger's was proved again: mathematicians scored higher than other scientists, who scored higher than students in the humanities, who scored roughly the same as the random controls. I took the AQ test too when Baron-Cohen e-mailed it to me, and scored as high as Baron-Cohen would probably expect a former math-school student to score, which is very high. Grigory Perelman, as far as I know, never took the AQ test and certainly cannot be diagnosed by someone who has not talked to him, though after I spent an hour on the phone describing Perelman to Baron-Cohen, the famous psychologist volunteered to fly to St. Petersburg to evaluate the famous mathematician—who sounded so very much like many of his clients—thus joining the long list of people who had volunteered help that Perelman did not welcome.

Had Baron-Cohen chosen Russian rather than British mathematicians as his subjects, the results would probably have been either the same or even more clearly pronounced. After all, Russian mathematical prodigies are often grouped with others of their kind in environments that are especially tolerant of their particular brand of weirdness. The tradition of forgiving mathematicians their autistic rudenesses dates back as far as anyone can remember. Many memoirs of Kolmogorov cite his peculiar manner of walking away in midconversation, demonstrating both his utter disregard for social convention and his pragmatic approach to socializing, which is typical of Aspergians: once he had received the information he sought, he had no further use for communication. In one instance, Kolmogorov, then a dean at Moscow University, was accosted in a hallway by a man who said repeatedly, "Hello, I am Professor Such-and-Such." Kolmogorov did not answer. Finally, the professor said, "You do not recognize me, do you?" Responded Kolmogorov: "I do, and I realize that you are Professor Such-and-Such." In the Aspergian world, conversations are exchanges of information, not exchanges of pleasantries. Most of Kolmogorov's students cited another of their teacher's typically Aspergian traits: what they called his "temper" and what were actually frightening episodes of apparently uncontrollable rage. That Kolmogorov's marked social problems did not impair his career is a measure of the degree to which a sort of Aspergian culture was built into the larger Russian culture of mathematics.

Baron-Cohen's other key insight is the concept that people with autism do not have a "theory of mind"—that is, the ability to imagine that other people have ideas, perceptions, and experiences that are different from one's own. In a striking experiment, Baron-Cohen tested normally developing children, children with autism, and children with Down syndrome. All children watched a brief play involving two dolls and a marble. One of the dolls placed the marble in a basket and left the room. While she was gone, the other doll moved the marble. When the first doll returned, the experimenter asked the children where she would look for the marble. The mentally retarded Down syndrome children and the normal children did equally well on the test: they realized that the doll would look for the marble in the basket, where she had left it. But sixteen out of twenty autistic children were certain she would look for the marble where it really was, not where the doll would have believed it to be. These children were believers in a single truth, utterly incapable of adjusting for human limitations.

Another world authority on Asperger's syndrome, an Australian psychologist named Tony Attwood, believes it is the theory-of-mind impairment that causes Aspergians to interpret everything they hear literally. In one of his books he described a child who sketched a picture at the end of an essay because the teacher had told students to "draw their own conclusions." The belief that people mean exactly what they say is what can lead Aspergians to laugh at a political lecture that to them sounds like a weather forecast ("the political situation is tense *today*"). It also leads them to believe that things work exactly as they are said to work. "I suspect that many 'whistle-blowers' have Asperger syndrome," wrote Attwood. "I have certainly met several who have applied a company's or government department's code of conduct to their work and reported wrongdoing and corruption. They have subsequently been astounded that the organization culture, line managers and colleagues have been less than supportive."

So it is perhaps no accident that the founders of the dissident movement in the Soviet Union were mathematicians and physicists. The Soviet Union was not a good place for people who took things literally and expected the world to function in predictable, logical, and fair ways. But the math clubs, such as the one run by Rukshin, provided a refuge. Rukshin saw it as his mission to shelter the black sheep of Soviet schoolchildren, and he saw a certain posture of social withdrawal as the mark of a gifted mathematician. The first time I interviewed Rukshin, he had a later appointment with an eleven-year-old boy; the child's mother was bringing him "to be looked at," which meant that Rukshin would spend an hour or two or three giving the boy math problems in order to decide whether to accept him to the club. At the appointed time,

Rukshin opened his office door to see if the boy had shown up yet. He had, and was sitting quietly in the lone armchair in the hallway. "I can tell he is gifted," Rukshin said, closing the door. "I can spot them." I knew exactly what he meant: the boy was pale and awkward, and he looked absent. If Attwood and Baron-Cohen had looked at him, they probably would have seen familiar signs as well: physical awkwardness and inappropriate facial expressions are among the outward signs of Asperger's syndrome.

Virtually everything people have recounted to me about Perelman's behavior, starting from the time when he joined the math club, fits the typical picture of a person with Asperger's syndrome. His apparent disregard for the conventions of personal hygiene is common to Aspergians, who perceive it as a nuisance forced upon them by the incomprehensible world of social mores. The trouble he had with articulating his solutions to problems is also classic. "People with Asperger often put in far too much detail," said Baron-Cohen. "They don't know what to leave out. They are not taking into account what the listener needs to know." That is the theory-of-mind problem: the point of telling is not to get a point across but solely to tell. Schoolmates told me Grisha was always willing to answer questions about mathematics; the problems arose if the questioner did not understand the explanation. "He was very patient," a former classmate recalled. "He would just repeat the exact same explanation, again and again. It was as though he could not imagine that somebody found it hard to understand." She was probably exactly right: he really could not imagine it.

His trouble with relating his solutions may also be interpreted in this light. If Perelman has Asperger's, the lack of an ability to see the big picture may be one of his curious shortcomings. British psychologists Uta Frith and Francesca Happé have written on what they call "weak central coherence," a quality that characterizes the thinking of people with autism-spectrum disorders, who focus on detail to the detriment of the big picture. When they are able to arrive at a big picture, it is usually because they have arranged elements—say, the elements in the periodic table—in a pattern, which systemizers find extremely satisfying. "The most interesting facts are those which can be used several times, those which have a chance of recurring," Henri Poincaré, one of the great systemizers of all time, wrote more than a hundred years ago. "We have been fortunate enough to be born in a world where there are such facts. Suppose that instead of eighty chemical elements we had eighty millions, and that they were not some common and others rare, but uniformly distributed. Then each time we picked up a new pebble there would be a strong probability that it was composed of some unknown substance . . . In such a world there would be no science . . . Providentially it is not so."

Aspergians learn the world pebble by pebble, ever grateful for the periodic table that allows them to recognize patterns of pebbles. Discussing the existence of Aspergians in the social world, Attwood used the metaphor of a "jigsaw puzzle of 5000 pieces," where "typical people have the picture on the box of the completed puzzle," which accounts for their social intuition. Aspergians do not have that picture and have to painfully assemble the puzzle by trying to fit the pieces together. Perhaps rules such as "never untie your fur hat" and "read the books on the school's reading list" were Grisha Perelman's attempts to envision the missing picture on the box, elements of his periodic table of the world. Only by sticking to them could he live his life.

The amount of human interaction in which Perelman engaged had been dwindling for eight years. Whatever social skills he had once had—he had exercised them in graduate school and as a postdoc, and they had been adequate, though minimally nuanced—had grown rusty with disuse. So had his tolerance for the behavior of others. Aspergians, it appears, are by and large capable of adjusting to social relationships, though this does not come naturally to them, as it does to neuronormals. John Elder Robison, the author of a memoir of life with Asperger's, described the process as a tradeoff: socialization seemed to rob the person of some of his extraordinary powers of systemizing concentration. Conversely, intense concentration over the course of several years seemed to have robbed Perelman of any social skills he had had. One can imagine how grating he had found the heated political argument between Cheeger and Anderson at Anderson's party, how disinclined he was to engage in anything superfluous and how completely unwilling to entertain any ironies, real or imagined, connected with his work—such as the idea that his proof might drive people away from topology. And he had had such high expectations. He had given mathematics something great, something truly valuable. Mathematics had responded feebly, trying to convince him to accept substitutes for true recognition. No wonder he was disappointed in mathematics.

For the moment, though, Perelman's disappointment was limited to the international mathematics establishment. The Steklov Institute was exempt, or rather his laboratory, his safe harbor after the falling-out with Burago, was exempt. Perelman resumed his activities, such as they were, at the institute: he attended seminars, sometimes several times a week, and he occasionally went by to check his e-mail. In the months before he had left for his lecture tour, he had maintained an even relationship with Ladyzhenskaya, the head of his new lab. She had died in January 2004, at the age of eighty-two, and after that Perelman rarely talked to anyone. As soon as Perelman returned, he wrote up the final installment of his proof, which he posted on the arXiv in June, and then he seemed to be exploring other problems. He was reticent, as usual, to talk about them, but he had apparently moved closer to Ladyzhenskaya's research interests.

Perelman got a promotion at the Steklov: he now held the title of lead researcher. Russian academic institutions assign their researchers to one of four levels, lead researcher being the top. Simple PhDs rarely hold this title; Russia maintains a two-tier dissertation system, in which the first dissertation—the one Perelman had written at the end of his graduate studies and that qualified him as a doctor of philosophy in the United States—ranks one as a candidate, while a second dissertation entitles one to be called Doctor. Steklov well-wishers kept telling Perelman to write his second, doctoral dissertation. The process required a traditional publication, and a defense. Perelman, naturally, scoffed at the idea. "He didn't think he needed it," Steklov director Sergei Kislyakov told me in a slightly puzzled tone of voice. Kislyakov seemed to personify the attitude that grated on Perelman the most: he liked Perelman and wished him well, but Kislyakov sincerely thought rules were the same for everyone, and this meant that a lead researcher should really get his act together and write and defend a second dissertation. Perelman, of course, also thought that rules were rules—but by now this applied only to rules of his choosing and, increasingly, of his own invention. He considered other rules to be sorts of impostors, all the more offensive for pretending to be real rules.

Meanwhile, the Russian Academy of Sciences was putting its house in order, trying to restore itself, after the chaos of the 1990s, to its former buttoned-down glory. On the one hand, Academy property was gradually being repaired—the Steklov got a decent paint job and new plumbing—and salaries were going up; a lead researcher's pay had gone from what literally amounted to pennies in the early 1990s to about four hundred dollars a month in 2004 (though Perelman would have made more had he secured his doctorate). On the other hand, the Academy was now demanding paperwork, reports on research and publishing activity. Perelman, predictably, bristled at the very idea of filling out paperwork to justify his mathematical existence. Ladyzhenskaya's successor, Grigori Seregin, shielded Perelman, ensuring his continued peaceful existence at the Steklov.

In late 2004 Perelman even traveled to Moscow to represent the St. Petersburg branch of the Steklov at a year-end Academy meeting. He gave a talk on the Poincaré. When he returned to St. Petersburg, he was unable to file his expense report. Russian law required that a person dispatched by an institution on official business have his documents stamped at his final destination in order to qualify for reimbursement. Surely someone who just a few months earlier had navigated the U.S. visa maze could easily have managed the Russian business-trip maze. In fact, Perelman had not had his documents stamped on principle: "I cannot go robbing the institute," he told the staff at the accounting office back in St. Petersburg. The accountant had to mail Perelman's documents to the Academy in Moscow so they could be stamped and returned. Still, Perelman would not accept the reimbursement money until the accountant had shown him the books proving that the reimbursement would come out of a special travel fund that was entirely separate from the Steklov's salary budget. Clearly, Perelman's rules on handling money had grown as exacting and as convoluted as his rules on footnoting. And as with footnotes, while the standards were known only to Perelman himself, he believed they were universal—and if he caught anyone violating them, he was merciless.

Merciless he was in the summer of 2005, when he showed up at the Steklov accounting office to ask why he had been paid more than his usual monthly salary. By this time the Steklov was depositing its researchers' pay directly into their accounts, so Perelman had made his discovery at a bank machine. The accountant, a short, overweight woman in her fifties who had seen a lot of mathematician weirdness in her nearly thirty years at the Steklov, confirmed that Perelman had been paid eight thousand rubles—a bit less than three hundred dollars—over his usual monthly amount, thereby receiving almost double his normal monthly pay. The reason was no mystery: his lab had completed a project and had some grant money left over. In keeping with the usual practice, Seregin, the head of the lab, had instructed the accounting office to divide the leftover funds among the staff of his lab. He had made one mistake. Perelman's previous bosses had known he did not approve of the practice—much as he had not approved of exam-time cooperation at the Mathmech, another generally accepted activity that could probably be seen as violating the letter of the law—and so they had always left him off the list of beneficiaries. Seregin did not know of Perelman's position and so placed him on the list.

Perelman asked the accountant to name the exact amount he had been overpaid. He then left the institute and returned a short time later with eight thousand rubles in cash. He wanted to give the money back to the accounting office. The accountant suggested he take it to the lab, where Seregin could decide how to dispose of it. Perelman insisted on returning the money directly to the institute. This is probably the point in the conversation where, as some Steklov staff members later reported, Perelman's shouting could be heard in the hallways. The accountant, however, denies that there was yelling—though over her years at the Steklov she may have grown accustomed to extreme and unexpected expressions of human emotion. Perelman finally prevailed: he convinced the accountant to write a receipt saying she had accepted the money.

The grant story, absurd and telling as it is, is famous in St. Petersburg and among mathematicians elsewhere. In fact, I heard it for the first time in the United States. But the first three or four times I heard it, it was purported to be the story of how Perelman left the Steklov. He refused to take the money and walked out, slamming the door behind him, the story went. That would be a very neat narrative, but it was not what happened. Perelman quit his job at the Steklov half a year later, in early December 2005, for no apparent reason. He came to the Steklov and tendered his resignation letter to the secretary. She ran to the director to alert him. Kislyakov asked Perelman to come in. Perelman went into the director's long rectangular office, with its endless polished-wood conference table, and said calmly, "I have nothing against the people here, but I have no friends, and anyway, I have been disappointed in mathematics and I want to try something else. I quit."

Kislyakov suggested it might be a good idea for him to stay until the end of the month, so he would be able to draw the traditional December bonus—four hundred dollars or so. Perelman declined. He canceled his e-mail account at the Steklov and left mathematics by walking out through the heavy oak double doors that led onto the embankment of the Fontanka River and into the oppressing grayness that masqueraded as daylight in St. Petersburg in winter.

"Something just snapped," Kislyakov told me, shrugging. He had no idea what had snapped. There was a chance that Perelman encountered a difficulty with a problem he was tackling—but then, he had encountered difficulties before and they had not caused him to reject mathematics. Anyway, he was certainly a marathoner. There was a possibility that his final disappointment had to do with the second anniversary of his posting the first Poincaré preprint. Perhaps he had given the mathematical establishment a grace period. After all, the Clay Institute's rules said the million-dollar prize could be awarded two years after publication. (In fact, the rules said a committee to administer the prize could be appointed two years following a *refereed* publication, but Rukshin, for one, willfully ignored the subtleties when he spoke to me about the Clay prize, claiming to represent Perelman's position.) November 2005 may have been the mathematical establishment's last chance to redeem itself in Perelman's eyes. By ignoring the superfluous parts of the rules that made no sense to Perelman and observing only the rules that did make sense, the Clay Institute could have declared Perelman the winner of its million-dollar prize. The money was, as ever, not the issue; the recognition was—and the recognition had to be as singular as Perelman's achievement. He would have been the first person ever to receive the Clay prize. He would have received it alone. And he would have received it on his own terms.

This did not happen.

What happened next was very strange. The June 2006 issue of the *Asian Journal of Mathematics* came out. The journal's entire three hundred pages were devoted to an article by two Chinese mathematicians, Huai-Dong Cao and Xi-Ping Zhu, titled "A Complete Proof of the Poincaré and Geometrization Conjectures—Application of the Hamilton-Perelman Theory of the Ricci Flow." At first glance, this might have appeared to be another explication of Perelman's proof, along the lines of what Kleiner and Lott and Morgan and Tian had been doing—with the important distinction that Cao and Zhu had not been public about their work and had not participated in any of the seminars and workshops sponsored by Clay. They had worked under the tutelage of Shing-Tung Yau, a Harvard professor, Fields Medalist, close friend of Hamilton's, one of the most powerful mathematicians in both the United States and China, and the editor of the *Asian Journal of Mathematics*. Yau had been among the recipients of Perelman's e-mail message drawing attention to his first preprint. He had not responded in any way save for telling *Science* magazine that he thought Perelman's proof might contain a fatal flaw connected with the number of surgeries required to complete the flow.

The abstract of the Cao and Zhu paper read more like a marketing pitch than perhaps any mathematical abstract ever written. In fact, there was nothing obviously mathematical about it. It said, in its entirety: "In this paper, we give a complete proof of the Poincaré and the geometrization conjectures. This work depends on the accumulative works of many geometric analysts in the past thirty years. This proof should be considered as the crowning achievement of the Hamilton-Perelman theory of Ricci flow." The authors appeared to be claiming that Hamilton and Perelman had laid the groundwork for the proofs of the Poincaré and Geometrization conjectures but the last mile had been covered by the Chinese mathematicians, hence the breakthrough—and, it would seem to follow, the fame, glory, and the million dollars—rightfully belonged to them. Such is the law of mathematics: the person who takes the final step gets all the credit for the proof. The difference between taking the final step and providing the explication of the proof is substance, and substance can be a difficult thing to measure. Yau held a press conference at his mathematics institute in Beijing on June 3, and the acting director of the institute declared, "Hamilton contributed over fifty percent; the Russian, Perelman, about twenty-five percent; and the Chinese, Yau, Zhu, and Cao et al., about thirty percent" (there had apparently been a miracle of arithmetic, among other things, and Yau has disputed this account, which was originally printed in a Chinese paper and later reproduced in the West).

A week later, Yau held a conference in Beijing that was headlined by Stephen Hawking. Though most of the several hundred people in attendance were physicists, Yau used the occasion to announce Cao and Zhu's putative breakthrough, saying, "Chinese mathematicians should have every reason to be proud of such a big success in completely solving the puzzle."

Yau was frantically creating a chronology to support his narrative, in which Cao and Zhu were the mathematical heroes. In an article he published in June 2006, Yau painted the following picture: "In the last three years, many mathematicians have attempted to see whether the ideas of Hamilton and Perelman can hold together. Kleiner and Lott (in 2004) posted on their web page some notes on several parts of Perelman's work. However, these notes were far from complete. After the work of Cao-Zhu was accepted and announced by the journal in April, 2006 (it was distributed on June 1, 2006) [sic]. On May 24, 2006, Kleiner and Lott put up another, more complete, version of their notes. Their approach is different from Cao-Zhu's. It will take some time to understand their notes which seem to be sketchy at several important points." In fact, it appears Yau rushed the Cao-Zhu paper through to publication, effectively forgoing the review process and preempting previously scheduled content, specifically so the authors could claim not to have read Kleiner and Lott's notes—which stated clearly, at the outset, that the proof explicated was Perelman's.

The race was on, because the end of the summer would see the International Congress of Mathematicians—the first such gathering since Perelman started posting his preprints. The Poincaré proof—and the million-dollar prize that went with it—would certainly be the main topics of the congress.

The ICM in Madrid began on August 22. On the morning of the opening, publications all over the world received a press release —embargoed until noon that day, when the information would be made public—announcing that Perelman would be awarded the Fields Medal "for his contributions to geometry and his revolutionary insights into the analytical and geometric structure of the Ricci flow." The document went on to explain, "As of the summer of 2006, the mathematical community is still in the process of checking his work to ensure that it is entirely correct and that the conjectures have been proved. After more than three years of intense scrutiny, top experts have encountered no serious problems in the work." In other words, the official press release stopped short of giving Perelman credit for proving the Poincaré. On the same day, the new edition of the New Yorker went on sale; it included an article called "Manifold Destiny," written by *A Beautiful Mind* author Sylvia Nasar and science journalist David Gruber. The article traced the story of Perelman's proof, Cao and Zhu's paper, and Yau's promotion of the Chinese scientists' authorship of the proof, and it even contained excerpts from a conversation with Perelman, whom the authors had convinced to speak with them in St. Petersburg. The article quoted Anderson, who said, "Yau wants to be the king of geometry. He believes that everything should issue from him, that he should have oversight. He doesn't like people encroaching on his territory." It also quoted Morgan, who contradicted Cao and Zhu's claim that Perelman's proof had contained catastrophic gaps that they had filled in. "Perelman already did it and what he did was complete and correct," Morgan told the *New Yorker* writers. "I don't see that they did anything different."

"It was so much fun," one mathematician told me. "It came out right during the congress, and the copy machines immediately started working at full capacity. I might have been bored there otherwise, but as it was, it was really fun."

On August 29, the day after the *New Yorker*'s cover date, the daily ICM newsletter published back-to-back interviews with Cao and Jim Carlson, head of the Clay Institute. Cao extolled Hamilton and Perelman, saying that they "have done the most important fundamental works," and adding, "They are the giants and our heroes!" But he stopped conspicuously short of saying that it was Perelman who had proved the Poincaré and Geometrization—indeed, he made both Hamilton and Perelman sound like giants from the past on whose shoulders modern-day mathematicians had stood to construct the ultimate proof. Carlson, on the other hand, was decisive: "Perelman fulfills all the requirements of the Millennium Prize," he said, naming the work of Kleiner and Lott, Morgan and Tian, and Cao and Zhu as the papers that completed the Clay Institute's refereed-publication requirement.

Mathematicians are not accustomed to controversies this heated

and publicity this broad. There had been arguments over authorship and credit before—including one involving a Russian topologist, Alexander Givental, and Yau and one of his students, who
claimed to have completed a proof Givental had begun—but they
had never spilled over into the mainstream media. Unlike social
scientists or even doctors, mathematicians whom Nasar and Gruber interviewed had no experience talking to the press. When they
saw their words in print—and copiously reproduced for their colleagues' entertainment—they were aghast. Yau engaged a lawyer,
who wrote a letter to the *New Yorker* demanding a correction and
an apology, because, Yau now claimed, he had never tried to wrest
credit away from Perelman. Three mathematicians quoted in the
article wrote what amounted to letters of apology to Yau and allowed them to be posted on various websites. Anderson was among
those who claimed to have been quoted out of context. And when I
spoke to him a year later, he was extremely reluctant to go on the
record. He also tried to convince me that the Yau controversy had
been unnecessarily exaggerated by nonmathematicians.

Perelman likely did not follow this story. He had positioned
himself outside the mathematics community, and he had never
been much of a Web surfer. But Rukshin, who was expert at scouring blogs and tracing links, was in his element following this unprecedented mathematical scandal. It would have given him satisfaction to report back to Perelman what both had long suspected:
the mathematics community did not stand up for its own, not even
for one who had given mathematics its biggest gift in a hundred
years.

The mathematics community in the United States, and even in
the world, is very small and very peaceful. "And that's one of the
great joys of being a mathematician," John Morgan told me about a
year after the controversy. "It's not like sociology or history, where
it does become quite political. And maybe that's another reason

why people shy away from these controversies, hoping they'll go away. You know, you start having war in camps and then suddenly the department explodes. The X supporters are separated from the Y supporters and the anti-Y supporters and, you know, that doesn't do anybody any good. Keep it a pleasant place to do the work. So few people understand what we do, appreciate what we do, it's nice. This community is actually a community of people who respect each other and treat each other decently." Most of the people, most of the time, that is. In a community this small, one cannot afford to burn bridges. Yau, with his academic positions and his army of professor-students on two continents, is not only extremely powerful institutionally but also central to a large and vibrant intellectual community, being shut out of which would amount to a tragic loss for most mathematicians.

The contemporary Western mathematics community acts like a corporation, albeit a very small one: it protects its own from the outside world, and it depends on peace, cooperation, and communication to function. But being a very small corporation, it also sometimes acts like a family, sacrificing ideals and principles for shared history and interdependence. Perelman had almost as little use for family, outside of his mother, as he did for corporations. He simply did not understand either. And he did not like to deal with things he did not understand. In fact, he refused to deal with them.

About a year before all hell broke loose in the summer of 2006, the ICM program committee sent Perelman a letter inviting him to give a lecture at the Madrid congress. The program committee and the medal committee worked independently; the members of both were kept secret until the congress, and only the names of the chairs were released. Perelman did not respond to this letter or to subsequent others. A committee representative then called

Kislyakov—Perelman was still on staff at the Steklov then—and Kislyakov called Perelman at home. Perelman explained to Kislyakov that he had not responded to the letters precisely because the names of committee members were kept secret. He would not, he said, deal with conspiracies.

Kislyakov conveyed Perelman's reasoning back to the committee, which followed with another letter, this time disclosing the names of its members. Perelman again did not respond; the committee again requested Kislyakov's intervention; and the Steklov director again called Perelman at home. Perelman explained that the committee's disclosure was too little, too late—and he would not entertain further discussion.

Perelman's refusal to deal with the program committee, which amounted to his refusal to speak at the congress, was an almost debilitating blow to the ICM organizers. It was obvious that the topic of the Poincaré Conjecture would dominate the congress. At the same time, the Fields Medal committee had decided that Perelman should be one of the recipients. The Fields Medal, often called the Nobel Prize of mathematics (there is, in fact, no Nobel Prize for mathematics), is awarded every four years to two to four mathematicians age forty or younger. Perelman would turn forty just before the congress, making it the last year he would be eligible. And although by the summer of 2005 a consensus had formed among topologists that Perelman had indeed proved the Poincaré—and the committee was aware of this consensus, because Jeff Cheeger was one of its members—final certainty was lacking. Kleiner and Lott and Morgan and Tian were not yet done with their explorations of the proof, so no one could guarantee that a major flaw—or even a fatal one, as Yau had implied—would not emerge. The committee drafted a carefully worded invitation to Perelman to accept the Fields Medal—an invitation that, much like the press release a year later, did not state that he had proved the Poincaré Conjecture.

Normally the names of Fields Medalists are not released to any-one, including the laureates themselves, until they are announced at the ICM. Naturally, though, the medal recipients are usually present at the congress and already scheduled to give speeches. But Perelman had refused to speak, and this was what necessitated the special invitation. Imagine Perelman's reaction. Was this all the mathematics community had to offer him, after all he had contrib-uted? Recognition along with three other mathematicians, none of whom had accomplished anything as momentous as the proof of the Poincaré? And recognition that was carefully worded so as to avoid giving Perelman true credit for what he had done! If ever Perelman had seen mathematics taking on the worst traits of poli-tics, it was then.

To ensure that Perelman would agree to attend the congress and accept the medal, the Fields Medal committee dispatched its chair-man—president of the International Mathematical Union, Oxford professor Sir John Ball—to St. Petersburg. This was an unprece-dented mission, but then, there had never been as difficult a prob-lem as the Poincaré Conjecture or as difficult a medal recipient as Grisha Perelman. The week before Perelman was due to be awarded the medal, he and Ball spent hours speaking at a conference center in St. Petersburg. Perelman would not accept the medal. Ball of-fered him a number of alternatives, including the delivery of the medal to St. Petersburg—as had been done decades before when Soviet mathematicians were not allowed to travel to the ICM and the medal had been awarded whenever it could physically meet its recipient—but Perelman refused.

On August 22 in Madrid, during the ICM opening ceremony, John Ball announced the names of the four Fields Medal recipi-ents. They were Andrei Okounkov, a Russian mathematician work-ing at Princeton; Perelman; Terence Tao, a onetime Australian wunderkind now at the University of California at Los Angeles; and the French mathematician Wendelin Werner. Perelman came second on Ball's list, as the list was arranged alphabetically. "A Fields Medal is awarded to Grigory Perelman, of St. Petersburg, for his contributions to geometry and his revolutionary insights into the analytical and geometric structure of the Ricci flow," said Ball. "I regret that Dr. Perelman has declined to accept the medal."

When the *New Yorker* writers visited Perelman earlier that summer, he told them it was the prospect of being awarded the Fields Medal that had forced him to make a complete break with the mathematics community: he was becoming too conspicuous, getting roped into the limelight. He might have been engaging in a bit of justification postdating: when he had quit the Steklov in early December 2005, declaring on his way out that he was abandoning mathematics altogether, the Fields Medal, while certainly a predictable possibility, was not yet a subject of discussion. "At a certain level you could say he lives absolutely by his principles," Jeff Cheeger said to me almost two years later. "But he is certainly not entirely open about his motivations, and in particular I believe he's quite an emotional person. And he uses his powerful mind to sort of explain his emotions after the fact."

The Fields Medal debacle seems to have tried Cheeger's patience with his brilliant younger colleague. "It's sort of like he is above it and maybe there is something wrong with practitioners in general," Cheeger told me, trying as hard as he could to choose words that would not offend Perelman, on the infinitesimal chance that he ever reads this book. "His behavior was supposed to be purer than pure, but it wound up having the effect of essentially focusing all the attention on him—not just because of the extraordinary importance of what he had done, but seemingly paradoxically. To the relative exclusion of all the other Fields Medalists."

If part of what insulted Perelman about the Fields Medal was the suggestion of his sharing with three other mathematicians what he felt should have been a singular honor, then by rejecting the medal, he set himself firmly apart. The same way that Perelman's refusal to accept the European honor in 1996 had hurt Vershik, now a number of his colleagues felt slighted, insulted, or at least misunderstood and puzzled by Perelman's behavior. Only Gromov claimed to understand Perelman's reasoning perfectly and to support it fully.

"When he got the letter from the committee inviting him to give a talk, he said he wouldn't talk to committees," Gromov recounted for me. "And that is absolutely the right thing to do! There are all sorts of things that we accept that we shouldn't accept. And he looks extreme only against the backdrop of conformism that is characteristic of mathematicians in general."

"But why shouldn't one talk to a committee?" I asked.

"One doesn't talk to committees!" Gromov exclaimed, exasperated. "One talks to people! How is it possible to talk to a committee? Who is on that committee? It might be Yasir Arafat is on it."

"But they sent him the list of committee members and he still refused to talk," I objected.

"After the way it started, he was right not to talk to them," Gromov persisted. "The moment the community begins to act like a machine, you have to stop dealing with it—that is all! The only strange thing is that more mathematicians don't act that way. That is the strange thing! Most people are perfectly content to talk to committees. They are satisfied to travel to Beijing and accept a prize from the hands of Chairman Mao. Or the king of Spain, which is the same thing."

Why, I pleaded, was the king of Spain undeserving of the honor of hanging a medal around Perelman's neck?

"Who the hell are kings?" Gromov was really cranked up now. "Kings are the same kind of crap as communists. Why should a king give a mathematician his prize? Who is he? He is nothing. From a mathematician's point of view, he is nothing. Same as

Chairman Mao. So one of them seized power like a robber while the other got it from his father. That's no difference." In contrast to these people, Gromov explained, Perelman had actually made a real contribution.

Following my interview with Gromov, I walked around Paris with a French mathematician who had refashioned himself as a historian of science. I had met Jean-Michel Kantor at a conference on mathematics and philosophy. Here was a classic French intellectual, a short, disheveled man who had to rush off to an editorial meeting of a highbrow book-review journal following our walk. As we walked, he criticized Gromov. The geometer, he said, had stood idly by as French mathematics sank into the abyss: mathematical institutions now issued fundraising brochures, blatant appeals for money that contributed nothing to the mathematical discourse. And professors shamelessly entered into salary negotiations, sometimes even making their plans contingent on the remuneration. Where was their love of the science and their will to sacrifice material comforts for the common cause of mathematics?

What this man was describing was the Americanization of French mathematics. And what I found invaluable about his perspective was that he still managed to see the money-centric, marketing-driven messages of the mathematical establishment as outrageous rather than obvious and expected, as they are in the United States. To someone like this—and to someone like Gromov, who seemed sensitive to criticism that he was becoming a capitalist conformist—Perelman, with his disregard for money and aversion to institutions, appeared very much like the Platonic ideal of a mathematician.

In 2006, the ICM went forward without Perelman. John Lott gave what would ordinarily have been the laudation but was instead a presentation devoted to Perelman's mathematical career trajectory and the trajectory of his proof. Two hours later, Richard Hamilton led a discussion of the Poincaré Conjecture. The announcement of this session in the program, presumably submitted by Hamilton, adopted a virtuoso approach to apportioning credit: the program for the solution, it said, had been invented by Hamilton and Yau, followed by Perelman, who supplied an important part of the solution and "announced the completion of the program," crowned by Cao and Zhu's paper, which Hamilton called "a full exposition." Such wording did not suggest that Cao and Zhu deserved credit for the proof, but it also did not state that Perelman did—only that Perelman himself believed so. During the actual discussion in Madrid, however, Hamilton was as gracious when speaking of Perelman as he had ever been. One participant recalled that Hamilton said he had not originally believed Perelman's claims that he had resolved the problems with his Ricci flow program and taken it to its completion but on closer inspection had seen that Perelman was right. "It was an expression of real admiration," recalled Jeff Cheeger. "Even more so because his initial reaction was 'this guy has got to be crazy!'"

By the end of the congress, the international mathematics community had fully accepted the majority topologists' position: Perelman had completed the proof of the Poincaré Conjecture. The Clay Institute would now use the ICM as the starting point for its countdown to the prize.

Any lingering idea that Cao and Zhu deserved ultimate credit was quietly put to rest the following fall, when a pdf file started circulating among mathematicians. Its left column contained excerpts from Kleiner and Lott's notes on the first Perelman preprint, which had been posted on the Web in 2003; the right column contained excerpts from Cao and Zhu's later paper. Sizable passages appeared to match verbatim. In an erratum note they submitted to the *Asian Journal of Mathematics*, Cao and Zhu claimed they had forgotten they had copied the material into their notes three years earlier. In early December, Cao and Zhu posted a revised version of their article to the arXiv. Now it was called "Hamilton-Perelman's Proof of the Poincaré Conjecture and the Geometrization Conjecture," and the abstract no longer claimed to give the complete proof or be the "crowning achievement." It now read almost contrite: "In this paper, we provide an essentially self-contained and detailed account of the fundamental works of Hamilton and the recent breakthrough of Perelman on the Ricci flow and their application to the geometrization of three-manifolds. In particular, we give a detailed exposition of a complete proof of the Poincaré conjecture due to Hamilton and Perelman."

Following the ICM and the *New Yorker* article, a frenzy broke out where it could hurt Perelman most: the Russian media. Journalists from all sorts of newspapers, including tabloids with press runs of more than a million copies, began calling constantly. Some days, School 239 seemed engaged in a nonstop press conference. Perelman's old teachers weighed in on the subjects of his sanity and his relationship with the mathematics community. Channel 1, which reached more than 98 percent of Russian households, reported that Perelman had turned down the million-dollar prize. Tamara Yefimova, the director of School 239, told a tabloid newspaper that Perelman had not attended the ICM in Spain because he did not have the money to buy a ticket. Alexander Abramov, his old coach, contributed an article to a highbrow Moscow weekly, arguing that there was "no Perelman mystery," just the failure of Russian academic institutions to recognize his achievements. Channel 1 called Perelman at home and broadcast the conversation, in which he said he was no longer doing mathematics and had not been since he left the Steklov Institute. "You could say I'm engaged in self-education," he said. "I cannot predict what I am going to be doing." A camera crew from a Channel 1 tabloid-style talk show burst into his apartment, pushing his mother out of the way on camera in order to film an unmade bed. People began recognizing him in the street and at the opera. He took to saying he was not Grigory Perelman. Strangers snapped pictures of him with their mobile phones and posted them on the Internet.

Politicians joined in the madness too. The St. Petersburg city council considered stationing guards outside the apartment he shared with his mother. It seemed that everyone wanted to give him money. A cabinet member asked to talk to him. Perelman wanted no part of this. Elderly teachers of his, approached by powerful, respected men, agreed to act as intermediaries and called him. He shouted profanities, which the teachers would not repeat. They told me only that he had been rude, very rude. On one occasion, a private Moscow foundation in cooperation with Rukshin cooked up a scheme to give money to his mother, a sort of reward for nurturing a genius son. Perelman overheard her speaking on the phone and ripped the receiver out of her hands, shouting. The once meek, conspicuously well-behaved Jewish boy had, cornered, turned into a domestic tyrant. If the world was not going to respect his seclusion, he would consider the world—the whole world—his enemy.

A year later, when I asked Rukshin to get a copy of Morgan and Tian's new book to Perelman, Rukshin demurred; the last time he had tried to pass on a gift from a foreign admirer, he said, Perelman had lobbed the gift—a classical-music CD—at Rukshin's head.

11

The Million-Dollar Question

WHEN JIM CARLSON was in elementary school, he found arithmetic tedious; his mind wandered. His mother had to tutor him with flash cards to prevent a failing grade. When Carlson was in his senior year of high school, his mathematics teacher handed him a typewritten sheet of paper and sent him to the back of the room. The sheet contained the names of a dozen books on mathematics that the teacher thought Carlson would find interesting—and he could study them on his own time in the back of the room so long as he got his other work done. The list included Courant and Robbins's classic *What Is Mathematics?*, where Carlson read about irrational numbers, among other things, for the first time. When Carlson started college at the University of Idaho in 1963, he planned to major in either physics or psychology. He never took a course in psychology; physics fared a little better, but by the time Carlson was a sophomore, he was doing graduate-level work in mathematics.

He received his PhD from Princeton in 1971, taught at Stanford and Brandeis, and finally settled at the University of Utah, where he spent a quarter of a century, eventually becoming chair of the mathematics department. Then he left for Cambridge, Massachusetts, to run the Clay Mathematics Institute. He had taken the job for a variety of reasons, including the fact that the schedule suited his personal circumstances, but the mission suited him as well. His job was to promote mathematics. Part of that job was to ensure that children and young people would enter mathematics in more elegant ways than he had—that is, through the back of the mathematics classroom. In a sense, he had to give American mathematics some of the luster and streamlined institutionalization that distinguished Russian mathematics. And one of the tools he was handed for popularizing mathematics was the ambitious and extremely well-funded Millennium Prize project. Though truth be told, Jim Carlson did not expect to be wielding that sort of money; he did not think any of the Millennium Problems would actually be solved in his lifetime.

Carlson assumed his position as president of the Clay Institute in the summer of 2004, just as the controversy that would eventually surround Perelman's proof and his prize started to brew. I always had the impression that to be who he was and do what he did, Carlson had to constantly keep at bay great, potentially overwhelming shyness. He was soft-spoken, retiring, exceedingly polite, and the last person one could imagine at the center of a controversy. Fortuitously, when he began his tenure as president of the Clay Institute, he did not know enough to expect the kind of media storm that ultimately surrounded the award. "I heard reports [about Perelman's preprints]," Carlson recalled when he talked to me. "I actually remember thinking, 'My goodness, isn't this fantastic that perhaps there will be a solution to the Poincaré Conjecture?' And of course I started thinking about the Millennium Prizes. And of course, isn't this remarkable, it will certainly be the only one in my lifetime that anyone will receive. But you know, one really doesn't know. I liken it to an earthquake: You know it when it happens. And maybe you could say that tension is building up in the rocks, but no one has successfully been able to predict earthquakes. And nobody knows when somebody will find that breakthrough idea that leads to a solution."

That was what Carlson thought a couple of months before he took the reins at the Clay Institute. He knew that Perelman had posted his preprints on the arXiv—not an unusual circumstance these days; many mathematicians post their articles as soon as they submit them to journals, to spur mathematical discussion before the peer-review process is over. But it was becoming apparent that Perelman had not submitted his papers to any journals and had no intention of doing so. What had seemed a perfectly innocuous and self-evident condition of the Millennium Prizes was emerging as a potential sticking point.

Carlson steered the Millennium boat gracefully and skillfully, funding workshops on Perelman's proof and on Kleiner and Lott's and Morgan and Tian's work explicating it. When he talked to me, he likened Perelman's work to a "flash of light that allows you to get through the forest." Sure, "there is a lot of work to be done, you have to cut down a lot of trees and climb over some boulders and stuff, but it's finding that new way that is so difficult. And if you can't find that, it doesn't matter how much work you do, it will be in vain. And this is what Perelman did." The projects undertaken by those who wrote the explications were clearly much less rewarding than the original solution, and this too filled Carlson with admiration—both for the mathematicians and for the mathematical system, which somehow bent itself to the unusual conditions set by Perelman to deliver the kind of examination and explanation his proof required.

Carlson opened his MacBook Air to read aloud a passage he had found particularly striking, from Kleiner and Lott's published notes on Perelman's proof: "Here it is. 'We did not find any serious problems, meaning problems that cannot be corrected using the methods introduced by Perelman.' I think that is a very accurate statement of what happened. You know, there was a very substantial amount of work to be done to ensure this was correct and complete. But the key thing is that there were no 'serious problems, meaning problems that cannot be corrected using the methods introduced by Perelman.' And there were many methods and ideas. It's always hard to communicate these to a general audience, but I hope you can do that when you write your book." What he wanted me to say, in other words, was that Perelman was the indisputable author of the proof, and that Kleiner and Lott had affirmed this in a way that Carlson greatly admired.

The months leading up to the ICM in Madrid, with the Cao and Zhu paper and the unfamiliar media attention, had been nerve-racking. But the ICM seemed to settle the score, and the evidence of plagiarism that emerged in the fall of 2006 rendered the issue of authorship entirely moot. The publication of Morgan and Tian's book on the proof followed; the Clay Institute commenced the two-year waiting period required by the rules of the Millennium Prizes. At the end of that time it will appoint a committee, which could make its recommendations by fall 2009. Barring the emergence of an error in the proof or some other unforeseen and highly improbable disaster, the committee will recommend that the million-dollar prize be given to Grigory Perelman. Which leaves only one question: Then what?

If Perelman's reasoning on prizes, awards, and honors were consistent, he might accept the Clay million if it was offered to him. After all, his stated objection to the European prize had been that it would have been given for work he did not consider complete. Nothing of the sort could be said of the Poincaré proof. Not only did other mathematicians consider it complete but Perelman himself clearly believed he had completed his project this time. His objection to the Fields Medal, though never stated as clearly, seemed to have been twofold: first, he no longer considered himself a mathematician and hence could not accept a prize intended for the encouragement of midcareer researchers; and second, he wanted no part of the ICM, with all the attendant publicity, speeches, ceremony, and king of Spain.

The Clay prize, however, was designed to be awarded for a particular achievement; there was no stipulation that the recipient had to continue practicing mathematics. Nor did it necessarily require any ceremony. It was an honor bestowed on a mathematician by his colleagues, with no nonmathematical royalty involved. And it was different from both the European prize and the Fields Medal in another very important respect: it represented recognition of Perelman's singular achievement. He could not be compared with any other recipients, concurrent or past—indeed, there was some likelihood that no one alive today would see another Millennium Prize bestowed.

"I think he might have a plan," Alexander Abramov, Perelman's former olympiad coach, told me. "He may have decided that when he is awarded the Clay prize, he will actually accept it because it will be a sign of total recognition and then he could live however he wants to live and not be dependent on anyone." Abramov paused. "But you see, that's just because one needs to come up with some sort of reasonable hypothesis here." That is, one needed to contemplate happy-ending scenarios for Perelman because otherwise, if one cared about Perelman, one might be scared for him, as Abramov was. "I fear this is a situation that will end badly," he said. "He is too full of stuff and too alone." Abramov was yet another person who gave up on calling Perelman after Perelman had grown abrasive on the phone. Before that happened, Abramov had called occasionally, offering support, both moral and financial. For example, he had suggested that if Perelman wanted no part of prizes, he could write an article for *Kvant,* the popular-science magazine founded by Kolmogorov and at which Abramov was now an editor, and receive money for it. Perelman turned down all offers, including Abramov's offer of his friendship. "He told me," Abramov recalled, "that one of his principles was 'One should not force one's friendship on anyone.' So I asked him if he knew the story of Kolmogorov and Pavel Alexandrov's friendship, and he showed a sudden interest in this topic and we talked about it for about ten minutes. He was most interested in the story of Kolmogorov slapping Luzin" —the time Kolmogorov attacked his and Alexandrov's former teacher after Luzin failed to cast a promised vote to induct Alexandrov into the Academy of Sciences. Happy to locate any common ground with his former student, Abramov offered to send Perelman a book on Kolmogorov and Alexandrov. "I'm not reading anything," said Perelman, using the excuse he used to reject all offers of books, including books on his own proof. Abramov was inclined to see some hope in the exchange he had had with Perelman: "At least he has not lost all interest in all things." But I am inclined to interpret it differently. It seemed that Perelman was then getting ready finally to end his last remaining close personal relationship outside of his mother, that with Rukshin. Sometime in the winter or spring of 2008, Perelman cut off all contact with his former teacher.

But before Perelman stopped speaking to Rukshin, the two spent some time talking about the million-dollar prize, and apparently they jointly worked out their approach to it. Just like the rest of the world of mathematics, they believed, the Clay Institute had betrayed Perelman. Rukshin even suggested to me that Clay had

changed its rules along the way, introducing the refereed-
publication requirement and the two-year waiting period just to
delay giving Perelman the money, or possibly to avoid giving it to
him altogether. There is in fact no evidence of any changes being
made to the Clay Millennium rules after the prizes were instituted,
in 2000. Indeed, someone in Jim Carlson's position might find
himself wishing for a way to postpone the decision and the subsequent probable failure to convince Perelman to accept it and then
the uneasy publicity that would accompany the award. This series
of events would certainly not be the story of mathematical triumph
and glory that the Clays had envisioned, and while it would fulfill
the stated goal of attracting the public's attention to mathematics,
it would hardly qualify as the fairy tale meant to inspire droves of
young people to pursue mathematical careers. Jim Carlson might
well have wished to put off navigating this tricky terrain. But there
is no evidence that he did. In fact, he did everything in his power
to speed up the process, driven mostly by the desire to fulfill his
weighty mission by helping to affirm Perelman's achievement, but
also a little bit by the hope of meeting Perelman himself.

In the spring of 2008, Carlson was planning a trip to Europe. He
decided to take a detour to St. Petersburg. It seemed as good a time
as any: the controversy had died down, there was no lingering
doubt about Perelman's proof, and the moment when someone
—probably Carlson himself—would have to ask Perelman to accept a million dollars was very clearly approaching. It was time to
start talking to Perelman.

Carlson was perhaps hoping for a conversation much like the
one John Ball had had with Perelman—long and in-depth, if fruitless. He had little reason to expect the conversation would end any
differently, but he had to hope for this nonetheless.

Carlson called Perelman from his hotel room on his first day in

St. Petersburg. He introduced himself and proceeded to explain the Clay prize timetable to Perelman. He repeated all the things Perelman surely knew—that two years had to pass following refereed publication, and that Morgan and Tian's book had provided the starting point for the countdown. He said the committee would likely be appointed as soon as May 2009 and might report back in August 2009.

Perelman listened politely.

Carlson did not ask whether Perelman would accept the money if offered. "The way the conversation was going," he explained to me, "I didn't think it was appropriate." A wave of shyness, held back for so long, may have broken through. Or perhaps Carlson simply wanted to hold off on asking the question, allowing himself another year of slim hope that Perelman might accept the prize. "I didn't get the sense that the door is completely closed," Carlson told me.

At the end of the conversation, Perelman said, "I don't see any point in our meeting."

The next day, I found Carlson at the Steklov, visiting with his old friend Anatoly Vershik, chairman of the St. Petersburg Mathematical Society and the man who once nominated Perelman for the European prize he later turned down. Vershik and Carlson were having tea. Yau's name came up; he was apparently holding a conference to celebrate his fifty-ninth birthday. "I don't understand it," Vershik grumbled. "I know Gian-Carlo Rota held a conference to celebrate his sixty-fourth birthday, but sixty-four is two to the sixth power—and what is fifty-nine? A prime number!" This was mathematicians gossiping.

Carlson spent the rest of his three-day visit seeing old mathematics friends, practicing his cello—a special, highly geometrical travel model—in his hotel room, and thinking about Perelman and the prize. He concluded that no matter what Perelman decided, the Clay prize could be used for the benefit of mathematics. In fact, it already had been. "It's good to explain to the public that there are unsolved mathematical problems," he told me when we went out for some exotic midday vodka at a café called the Idiot. "Surprisingly, a lot of people don't know that."

It is true, Carlson admitted, that a lot of mathematicians criticize monetary prizes for their superficiality; some find it offensive. His friend Vershik had published a piece criticizing the Clay Millennium Prize on these exact grounds. But Carlson told me he had many conversations with undergraduates who wanted to know what these million-dollar problems were. In a way, the buildup to the prize had brought unexpected benefits: "To spend no money to get mathematics in the public eye is not a bad accomplishment," Carlson boasted. Perelman had been his unwitting accomplice: "There is more interest in the public eye in a person who has no interest in the money."

Carlson was not simply putting on a brave face, though he was certainly doing that. He clearly felt that, in an awkward way, he was helping to draw attention to an accomplishment that deserved it. In all my conversations with Carlson, I never perceived any resentment of Perelman, which set him slightly apart from other mathematicians I interviewed: unlike Kleiner, Carlson had not had to cede any of his professional ambition to Perelman's achievement; unlike Tian, he had not been personally slighted by Perelman. He did not understand Perelman—or claim to understand him. All he had was abiding respect for him.

The only person who not only claimed to understand Perelman but at times seemed to channel him was Gromov.

"Do you think he'll accept the million dollars?" I asked Gromov.

"I don't think so."

"Why not?"

"He has his principles."

"What principles?"

"Because Clay is a nothing, from his point of view—why should he take his money?"

"Okay, Clay is a businessman, but it's Perelman's colleagues who are making the decision," I objected, using a word that in Russian meant both "decision" and "solution."

"Those colleagues are playing along with Clay!" Gromov was very irritated now. "They are deciding [solving]! He has no use for any of their solutions! He has already solved the theorem, what's there left to solve? No one is solving anything! He solved the theorem."

Acknowledgments

Notes

Index

Acknowledgments

I owe a special debt of gratitude to all the sources in this book. Writing about a man who does not wish to be written about is an unusual undertaking, and the decision to talk to me could not have been easy for some of Perelman's friends and teachers. In particular, Alexander Golovanov, Viktor Zalgaller, and Sergei Rukshin went to great lengths to try to make me understand their friend and student, and I hope that this book reflects at least some of their insights. I am also very grateful to Jim Carlson, Sergei Gelfand, and especially Leonid Dzhalilov for doing what they could to ensure I wrote about mathematics in a way that made sense. Any mistakes are, of course, still mine. Finally, many thanks to my agent, Elyse Cheney, and my editors Becky Saletan and Amanda Cook, for making this book much better than it would otherwise have been.

Notes

Prologue

page

viii *Millennium Meeting descriptions and quotes: The CMI Millennium Meeting,*
documentary, directed by François Tisseyre (New York: Springer, 2002).

1. Escape into the Imagination

2 *"The mathematician needs no laboratories or supplies":* A. Ya. Khinchin,
"Matematika," in F. N. Petrov, ed., *Desyat Let Sovetskoy Nauke* (Moscow:
N.P., 1927).

3 *"Mathematics is uniquely suited to teaching":* "Sudby matematiki v Rossii,"
a lecture by Mikhail Tsfasman, http://www.polit.ru/lectures/2009/01/30
/matematika.html, accessed February 1, 2009.
The movement's slogans were based on Soviet law: Alexander Yesenin-Volpin,
interview,http://www.peoples.ru/family/children/alexander_esenin-volpin/,
accessed January 31, 2009.

4 *His article on linguistics:* I. V. Stalin, "Marxism i voprosy yazykoznaniya,"
Pravda, June 20, 1950, http://www.philology.ru/linguistics1/stalin-50.htm,
accessed January 31, 2009.
Stalin personally promoted: V. D. Yesakov, "Novoye o sessii VASKhNIL 1948
goda," http://russcience.euro.ru/papers/esak940s.htm, accessed January 31,
2009.

One of them, Dimitri Egorov: J. J. O'Connor and E. F. Robertson, "Dimitri Fedorovich Egorov," www-history.mcs.st-andrews.ac.uk/Biographies/Egorov.html, accessed December 27, 2007.

6 *Luzin case descriptions and quotes:* S. S. Demidov, V. D. Yesakov, "'Delo akademika N. N. Luzina' v kollektivnoy pamyati nauchnogo soobshestva," *Delo Akademika N. N. Luzina* (St. Petersburg: RKhGI, 1999).

7 *As a result, Soviet and Western mathematicians:* Dennis Shasha and Cathy Lazere, *Out of Their Minds: The Lives and Discoveries of Fifteen Great Computer Scientists* (New York: Springer, 1998), 142.

A top Soviet mathematician: Lev Pontryagin's entire memoir is devoted to the backstabbing and intrigue in which this outstanding mathematician personally took part. Lev Pontryagin, *Zhizneopisaniye Lva Semenovicha Pontryagina, matematika, sostavlennoye im samim* (Moscow: Komkniga, 2006), 134.

"It was in the 1960s": Sergei Gelfand, interview with the author, Providence, RI, November 9, 2007.

8 *Three weeks later, the Soviet air force was gone:* Richard Overy, *Russia's War: A History of the Soviet War Effort: 1941–1945* (New York: Penguin, 1998), 73–85.

9 *The greatest Russian mathematician of the twentieth century, Andrei Kolmogorov:* This work by Andrei Kolmogorov is classified, so the published results, apparently called *Strelyaniy sbornik,* are not available. The information comes from Alexander Abramov, his student and biographer, interview with the author, Moscow, December 5, 2007, and from *Etikh strok begushchikh tesma,* ed. A. N. Shiryaev (Moscow: Fizmatlit, 2003), 355, 500.

by the end of his life he had served as an adviser on seventy-nine dissertations: Mathematics Genealogy Project, http://genealogy.math.ndsu.nodak.edu/id.php?id=10480, accessed January 22, 2008.

it was to promise the people of his country that the Soviet Union would surpass the West: Cited in Roger S. Whitcomb, *The Cold War in Retrospect: The Formative Years* (Westport, CT: Praeger Publishers, 1998), 71.

The effort to assemble an army of physicists and mathematicians: Zhores A. Medvedev, *Soviet Science* (New York: Norton, 1978), 46.

10 *Estimates of the number of people engaged in the Soviet arms effort:* Clifford G. Gaddy, *The Price of the Past: Russia's Struggle with the Legacy of a Militarized Economy* (Washington DC: Brookings Institution Press, 1998), 24–25.

11 *official mathematicians and other scientists could shop at specially designated stores:* Etikh strok, 293, 467.

Sergei Novikov, was not allowed to travel to Nice to accept his award: Pontryagin, 169.

12 *Leonid Levin, describes being ostracized:* Leonid Levin, "Kolmogorov glazami shkolnika i studenta," in *Kolmogorov v vospominaniyakh,* 168–69.

Cook and Levin, who became a professor at Boston University, are considered coinventors: Shasha and Lazere, 139–56; Leonid Levin's homepage at Boston University, http://www.cs.bu.edu/~lnd/, accessed January 29, 2008; description of the P versus NP problem http://www.claymath.org/millennium/P_vs_NP/, accessed January 29, 2008.

13 *One of the people who came for an extended stay was Dusa McDuff:* Dusa McDuff, "Advice to a Young Mathematician," in *Princeton Companion to Mathematics,* ed. Timothy Gowers, June Barrow-Green, and Imre Leader (Princeton, NJ: Princeton University Press, 2008), 1007.
   "It was a wonderful education": Dusa McDuff, "Some Autobiographical Notes," http://www.math.sunysb.edu/~tony/visualization/dusa/dusabio .html, accessed March 19, 2009.

14 *Mathematicians called it "math for math's sake":* Vladimir Uspensky, "Apologiya matematiki, ili O matematike kak chasti duhovnoy kultury," *Noviy Mir* 11, 2007.
   "If I had been free to choose any profession": Grigory Shabat, professor at the Russian State Humanities University, interview with Katerina Belenkina, Moscow, April 2007.

2. How to Make a Mathematician

18 *Alexander Golovanov:* Alexander Golovanov, interview with the author, St. Petersburg, October 18 and October 23, 2008.
   Three other boys beat Grisha in competitions: According to Rukshin, these three were Nikolai Shubin, who went on to become a chemist, and Alexander Vasilyev and Alexander Levin, both of whom became computer scientists.
   Boris Sudakov: Boris Sudakov, interview with the author, Jerusalem, December 31, 2007.

20 *he hummed, moaned, threw a Ping-Pong ball against the desk:* Sergei Rukshin, interview with the author, St. Petersburg, October 17 and October 23, 2007, and February 13, 2008; Alexander Abramov, interview with the author, Moscow, December 5, 2007.
   he never dazzled colleagues with his geometric imagination, but he almost never failed to impress them: John Morgan, interview with the author, New York City, November 9, 2007; Yuri Burago, phone interview with the author, February 26, 2008.

22 *loudmouthed man named Sergei Rukshin:* Rukshin interview.

23 *I observed practice sessions:* I visited the Mathematics Education Center in St. Petersburg on February 13, 2008.

25 *Mathematicians know this as the Party Problem:* http://mathworld.wolfram .com/PartyProblem.html, accessed March 19, 2009.

the *Ramsey theory, a system of theorems:* Ronald Graham, Bruce Rothschild, Joel Spencer, *Ramsey Theory* (New York: John Wiley and Sons, 1990).

30 *When they grew older, Rukshin hounded:* Golovanov interview.

3. A Beautiful School

34 *Steven Pinker observed:* Steven Pinker, *The Stuff of Thought: Language as a Window into Human Nature* (New York: Viking, 2007), 177.
"A layer or a slab has two primary dimensions": Ibid., 179–80.
words like end and edge are used: Ibid., 180.

35 *the Möbius strip . . . is among the earliest known objects of topological inquiry:* Richard Courant and Herbert Robbins, *What Is Mathematics? An Elementary Approach to Ideas and Methods,* 2nd ed., revised by Ian Stewart (New York: Oxford University Press, 1996), 235.

37 *His students always wondered why:* V. M. Tihomirov, "Geniy, zhivushchiy sredi nas," in Alexander Abramov, ed., *Yavleniye chrezvychaynoye: Kniga o Kolmogorove* (Moscow: FAZIS, 1999), 73. Tihomirov notes that Ivan Vinogradov, Nikolai Luzin, and Pavel Alexandrov also avoided being drafted into top-secret work but explains that their research had no apparent military application at the time; the same could not be said of Kolmogorov's.
with whom he shared a home starting in 1929: Andrei Kolmogorov, "Vospominaniya o P. S. Alexandrove," in A. N. Kolmogorov, *Matematika v yeyo istoricheskom razvitii* (Moscow: LKI, 2007), 141.
they generally requested academic appointments together: The donation, food for people held in the siege of Leningrad, is described in *Etikh strok begushchikh tesma,* ed. A. N. Shiryaev (Moscow: Fizmatlit, 2003), 332. Issues of joint appointments and accommodations appear throughout the correspondence published in *Etikh strok,* for example, on page 80.
Kolmogorov asked the filmmaker to use Johann Sebastian Bach's Double Violin Concerto: "Posledneye interview," in *Yavleniye,* 205.

38 *"Through the woods or along the shore of the Klyazma River":* R. F. Matveev, "Vspominaya Kolmogorova . . . ," in Albert Shiryaev, ed., *Kolmogorov v vospominaniyakh uchenikov* (Moscow: MTsNMO, 2006), 170.
Another of Kolmogorov's students wrote in his memoir: M. Arato, "A. N. Kolmogorov v Vengrii," in *Kolmogorov v vospominaniyakh,* 31.
a math problem he authored at the age of five: Alexander Abramov, interview with the author, Moscow, December 5, 2007.
two professional mathematicians: These are Alexander Abramov and Vladimir Tihomirov.
In 1922, Kolmogorov: "Avtobiografiya Andreya Nikolayevicha Kolmogorova," in *Matematika,* 21.

The Dalton Plan: http://www.dalton.org/philosophy/plan/, accessed January 23, 2008.

39 *"So every student spent most of his school time at his desk":* "Posledneye interview," 186.

"In just three hours at an elevation of 2400 meters": Vladimir Arnold, "Ob A. N. Kolmogorove," in *Kolmogorov v vospominaniyakh,* 40.

the pair spent the 1930–1931 academic year abroad: Kolmogorov, "Vospominaniya," 143.

all culture, and gay culture in particular: Harry Oosterhuis, *Homosexuality and Male Bonding in Pre-Nazi Germany: The Youth Movement, the Gay Movement, and Male Bonding Before Hitler's Rise* (New York: Haworth Press, 1991).

"Interesting that this idea": Etikh strok, 63.

"The wife will always have pretensions to that role": Ibid., 430.

40 *after Alexandrov's death, Kolmogorov:* A. V. Bulinsky, "Shtrihi k portretu A. N. Kolmogorova," in *Kolmogorov v vospominaniyakh,* 114–15.

At the age of forty, Kolmogorov wrote up a plan: Albert Shiryaev, ed., *Zvukov serdtsa tihoe eho: Iz dnevnikov* (Moscow: Fizmatlit, 2003), 110–11.

In 1935, Kolmogorov and Alexandrov organized: B. V. Gnedenko, "Uchitel i drug," in *Kolmogorov v vospominaniyakh,* 131. Kolmogorov did not invent the format; the first competition actually occurred a year earlier, in Leningrad. He was, however, instrumental in taking the competitions national. See N. B. Vasilyev, "A. N. Kolmogorov i matematicheskiye olimpiady," in *Yavleniye,* 168.

Kolmogorov teamed up with Isaak Kikoin: "Istoriya olimpiady," http://phys.rusolymp.ru/default.asp?trID=118, accessed January 24, 2008.

The Soviet of Ministers issued a decree: Abramov interview.

41 *That August, Kolmogorov organized:* Alexander Abramov, "O pedagogicheskom nasledii A. N. Kolmogorova," in *Yavleniye,* 105.

nineteen boys were chosen: A. A. Egorov, "A. N. Kolmogorov i kolmogorovskiy internat," in *Yavleniye,* 163.

Lectures in mathematics: Abramov, 107.

what he called "a spark from God": Egorov, 164.

a high-school course in the history of antiquity: Alexander Prohorov, interview with the author, Moscow, December 8, 2007.

more hours of physical education instruction: Abramov, 111.

Kolmogorov himself lectured the students in music: Egorov, 165.

He also took the boys on boating, hiking, and skiing trips: Gnedenko, 149.

"And few of us understood the music": L. A. Levin, "Kolmogorov glazami shkolnika i studenta," *Kolmogorov v vospominaniyakh,* 167.

42 *He oversaw a curriculum-reform effort:* A. S. Monin, "Dorogi v Komarovku," in ibid., 182.

Kolmogorov sought to revamp the secondary-school understanding of geometry: Alexander Abramov, *"O polozhenii s matematicheskim obrazovaniyem v sredney shkole" (1978–2003)* (Moscow: FAZIS, 2003), 13.

43 *"These things can provoke nothing but disgust":* Ibid., 40.

authors of the curriculum reform were exposed: R. S. Cherkasov, "O nauchno-metodicheskom vklade A. N. Kolmogorova," in *Yavleniye,* 156.

The New Math movement brought actual mathematicians: David Klein, "A Brief History of American K-12 Mathematics Education in the 20th Century," from James Royer, ed., *Mathematical Cognition.* Preprint version at http://www.csun.edu/~vcmthoom/AHistory.html, accessed January 25, 2008; Patrick Suppes and Shirley Hill, "Set Theory in the Primary Grades," *New York State Mathematics Teachers' Journal* 13 (1963): 46–53.

"the effect of freshening [the student's] eye": Quoted in Klein.

Some of his students believed the illnesses were set off: Abramov, 54; Abramov interview.

his students, who for the preceding couple of years had taken turns: Prohorov interview.

44 *everyone was to be taught the same thing at the same time:* Abramov, 48.

"elite education is not allowable in our society": Egorov, 166.

Moscow's School 2 was apparently the object of many denunciations: Leonid Ashkinazi, "Shkola kak fenomen kultury," *Himiya i zhizn* 1 (1991): 16.

School 239 lost some of its most popular teachers to KGB pressure: Mikhail Ivanov, principal of the Physics in Mathematics Lyceum and former teacher at School 239, interview with the author, St. Petersburg, October 23, 2007.

45 *its principal was frequently reprimanded for admitting too many Jewish children:* Tamara Yefimova, principal of School 239, interview with the author, St. Petersburg, October 17, 2007.

two out of four Leningrad math schools were shut down: Tatyana Hein, education activist and Leningrad School 317 graduate, interview with Katerina Belenkina, Moscow, April 2007.

those parents who were college instructors: Aleksandr Krauz, "Zapiski o vtoroy shkole," http://ilib.mirror1.mccme.ru/2/07-krauz.htm, accessed September 16, 2008.

the school's bulletin boards overflowed with announcements: Ashkinazi.

"What made the school different": Boris Levit, interview with Katerina Belenkina, April 2007.

46 *some schools allowed students not to wear uniforms:* Arkady Tsurkov, Israeli mathematician and former Soviet dissident, interview with Katerina Belenkina, April 2007.

some teachers read forbidden works of literature aloud in class: Ivanov.

"What can be more beneficial at sixteen or seventeen": Mikhail Berg, "Tridtsat

let spustya," http://litpromzona.narod.ru/berg/30let.html, accessed September 16, 2008.

47 *"Because of him, we felt like gods"*: Viktor Kistlerov, Moscow computer scientist, interview with Katerina Belenkina, April 2007.
forge a relationship with a second-tier college: Yefimova interview.
he made no secret of his fear of the secret police: Arnold in *Kolmogorov v vospominaniyakh*, 37; Abramov interview.

48 *in 1957 he was fired as dean:* Arnold in *Kolmogorov v vospominaniyakh*, 45.
He parted with his ideas with famous ease: Prohorov interview.
He claimed little interest in the authorship of solutions: "Posledneye interview," in *Yavleniye*, 191.

51 *I spoke with a Russian Israeli psychologist:* Viktoria Sudakova, phone interview with the author, Jerusalem, December 31, 2007.

52 *her support for a math-club class apparently struck some of the teachers:* Yefimova, Rukshin, Ivanov interviews.
Valery Ryzhik: Valery Ryzhik, interview with the author, St. Petersburg, Russia, February 28, 2008; biographical information retrieved from a website devoted to the memoirs of School 239 teachers and graduates, http://club.sch239.spb.ru:8001/club/htdocs/teach_page/ryzhik/, accessed March 23, 2008.
Students recalled that in ordinary years he picked five top students: Natalya Alexandrovna Konstantinova, recollections, http://club.sch239.spb.ru:8001/club/htdocs/teach_page/ryzhik/words.shtml, accessed March 23, 2008.

54 *he would go to the bakery on Liteyniy Prospect:* Golovanov interview.
what chess players call intuition is in fact the ability to grasp complex systems in a single take: Jonah Lehrer, *How We Decide* (Boston: Houghton Mifflin Harcourt, 2009), 44.

55 *Rukshin focusing more on literature, music, and all-around erudition:* Sergei Rukshin, interview with the author, St. Petersburg, October 17 and October 23, 2007, and February 13, 2008.
Ryzhik on chivalry, honesty, responsibility, and other universal values: Ryzhik interview; Yelena Vereshchagina, a former classmate of Perelman's, interview with the author, St. Petersburg, February 13, 2008.

56 *the student who had slipped his classmate the bomb:* For example, see http://scholar-vit.livejournal.com/159422.html?thread=5221566#t5221566, accessed February 7, 2009.

57 *turned away, apparently because the principal had come under increased pressure to cut the number of Jewish teachers:* Ryzhik, Yefimova, Vereshchagina interviews.
criticized for violating every rule of Soviet teaching methodology: Golovanov interview.

Viktor Radionov was fired amid charges of pedophilia: Yefimova, Golovanov, Rukshin interviews.

impressed students with his willingness to entertain even risky political questions: Vereshchagina interview.

later exposed as a KGB informant: Memoir of 1970 graduate Alexander Kolotov, http://club.sch239.spb.ru:8001/club/HTDOCS/teach_page/ostrovsk/alternative.shtml, accessed March 23, 2008.

58 *patiently explained any math issue to any of his classmates:* Vereshchagina interview.

by the time he was in his last year of school, his fingernails were so long they curled: Rukshin interview.

4. A Perfect Score

60 *Mathmech anti-Semitism:* Valery Ryzhik, interview with the author, St. Petersburg, Russia, February 28, 2008; Alexander Golovanov, interview with the author, St. Petersburg, October 18 and October 23, 2008.

61 *roughly eighty thousand conscripts were serving there at any given time:* G. F. Krivosheev, ed., *Rossiya i SSSR v voynakh XX veka*, website of Zabytiy Polk, http://www.polk.ru/pl/afg1.php, accessed March 27, 2008.

63 *all the boys who took prizes at the Leningrad citywide math olympiad at his grade level:* In 1979 first place went to Alexander Levin and Grigory Perelman; second place went to Boris Sudakov and Nikolai Shubin; all four were members of Rukshin's math club. In addition, Alterman (his first name is unknown) and Vadim Tsemekhman, who had taken first and second place respectively the preceding year, had honorable mentions. Information supplied by Dmitry Fomin, historian of the St. Petersburg/Leningrad mathematics olympiads, in an e-mail to the author, March 14 and 15, 2008.

those who took first and second places in the city olympiad would advance to another round of competition: See http://www.mathcenter.spb.ru/history/fomin.html, accessed March 14, 2008.

Alexander Vasilyev and Nikolai Shubin took first place: Fomin e-mail, March 14, 2008.

65 *He named two people: Perelman and Levin:* Alexander Abramov, interview with the author, Moscow, December 5, 2007.

66 *Alexander Levin had not come to the club that particular day:* Sergei Rukshin, interview with the author, St. Petersburg, October 17 and October 23, 2007, and February 13, 2008; Golovanov interview.

Competition description: Fomin, "Istoricheskiy ocherk."

67 *"Wait!" he shouted:* Rukshin interview.

68 *The solution turned out to contain a serious flaw:* Simon Singh, *Fermat's*

Enigma: The Epic Quest to Solve the World's Greatest Mathematical Problem (New York: Anchor, 1998).

for Perelman it was split into time devoted to solving problems: Yelena Vereshchagina, interview with the author, St. Petersburg, February 13, 2008.

69 *One student recalled waking up in the morning:* Alexander Spivak, 1982 Soviet IMO team member and later mathematics teacher, interview with the author, Moscow, February 7, 2008.

Another recalled arriving by bus in Chernogolovka: Sergei Samborsky, 1982 Soviet IMO team reserve member and later computer scientist, interview with the author, Moscow, February 14, 2008.

70 *Preparedness for Labor and Defense of the USSR requirements:* http://russian-sport.narod.ru/files/norms_gto.html, accessed April 1, 2008.

the only nonperfect grade on his graduating transcript: Yefimova interview.

74 *Both he and Spivak had perfect scores:* Abramov, Spivak interviews.

75 *shortly before the planned trip she was told that her travel documents could not be processed in time:* Abramov interview.

76 *took ninth place with 230 points:* Information from the official IMO website, http://www.imo-official.org/year_country_r.aspx?year=1981, accessed April 7, 2008.

a professor of mathematics at Karlsruhe University: http://www.mathematik.uni-karlsruhe.de/iag1/~grinberg/en, accessed April 7, 2008.

represented Germany at the IMO three times between 2004 and 2006: http://www.imo-official.org/participant_r.aspx?id=7901, accessed April 7, 2008.

"Natalia Grinberg, former number 1": http://www.mathlinks.ro/Forum/viewtopic.php?t=101785, accessed April 7, 2008.

78 *1978 IMO team:* http://www.imo-official.org/year_country_r.aspx?year=1978, accessed April 7, 2008; rumor comes from Rukshin interview.

The students were now on their own: A. Abramov and A. Savin, "XXXIII mezhdunarodnaya matematicheskaya olimpiada," *Kvant* 12 (1982): 46–48, http://kvant.mirror1.mccme.ru/1982/12/XXIII_mezhdunarodnaya_matemati.htm.; Spivak interview.

The judging process: Abramov, Savin; Spivak interview.

79 *Perelman showed no interest in the sights:* Abramov, Spivak interviews.

80 *Perelman's results:* See http://imo-official.org/participant_r.aspx?id=10481, accessed April 16, 2008.

5. Rules for Adulthood

82 *the group represented a sort of elite learning center:* Alexander Golovanov, interview with the author, St. Petersburg, October 18 and October 23, 2008; Mehmet Muslimov, interview with the author, St. Petersburg, February 27,

2008. (Back in his university and math-club days Muslimov had been known as Aleksei Pavlov, but he later converted to Islam and took a new name, in addition to becoming a linguist.)

in the 1970s Leningrad University had moved its science departments: http://www.naukograd-peterhof.ru/peterhof-history.html, accessed April 17, 2008.

86 *He was, however, unwilling to entertain them:* Muslimov interview.

88 *He was strongly drawn to Viktor Zalgaller:* Golovanov interview.

I interviewed Zalgaller: Viktor Zalgaller, interview with the author, Rehovot, Israel, March 16, 2008.

Zalgaller was a World War II veteran: Mikhail Ivanov, ed., *Sbornik vospominaniy o 239 shkole*, unpublished manuscript.

90 *Alexander Danilovich Alexandrov:* Biography of A. D. Alexandrov at http://www.univer.omsk.su/LGS/#s2, accessed April 24, 2008.

A. D. Alexandrov and graduate school: O. A. Ladyzhenskaya, "Ocherk o zhizni I deyatelnosti A. D. Aleksandrova," in G. M. Idlis, O. A. Ladyzhenskaya, eds., *Akademik Aleksandr Danilovch Aleksandrov. Vospominaniya, publikatsii, materialy* (Moscow: Nauka, 2002), 7.

91 *He was also a member of the Communist Party and remained one:* A. M. Vershik, "A. D., kakim ya yego znal," http://www.pdmi.ras.ru/~vershik/B22.pdf, accessed April 24, 2008.

92 *He managed, almost single-handedly, to reframe it:* Idlis, Ladyzhenskaya, 8–10.

Then one of the mathematicians dared ask Alexandrov: Ibid., 74.

93 *The former student, a very prominent mathematician:* Vershik.

still amounted to exile: Idlis, Ladyzhenskaya.

he wanted to fill a vacant chair in geometry: Vershik.

Alexandrov's hopes of obtaining the chair in geometry were dashed: Ibid.

94 *was generally considered unhirable:* Lev Pontryagin, *Zhizneopisaniye Lva Semenovicha Pontryagina, matematika, sostavlennoye im samim* (Moscow: Komkniga, 2006), 113.

managed to provide him not only with a teaching job: Ladyzhenskaya, "Borba," 75–76.

Rokhlin would see twelve of his students' dissertations to completion: Mathematics Genealogy Project, http://www.genealogy.math.ndsu.nodak.edu/id.php?id=42580, accessed April 24, 2008.

the man who would be largely responsible for introducing Perelman: Zalgaller interview; Jeff Cheeger, New York University professor, interview with the author, New York City, April 1, 2008.

"He would give topics and promising ideas away to his students": V. A. Zalgaller, "Vospominaniya ob A. D. Alexandrove i yego leningradskom geometricheskom seminare," in Idlis, Ladyzhenskaya, 16.

95 *"So have you proved it?" Alexandrov asked"*: A. V. Kuzminykh, "Pamiati uchitelya," in ibid., 120.

Alexandrov's reaction to a request to write a history of Soviet geometry: M. A. Rozov, "Lev v kresle," in ibid., 155.

he had chosen to become a geometer after hearing another professor's words: Yu. G. Reshetnyak, "Vospominaniya o nashem uchitele: A. D. Aleksandrov i yego geometricheskaya shkola," in ibid., 40.

Alexandrov was said to have made the following comment: O. M. Kosheleva, "My otvetstvenny za vsyo," in ibid., 125–26.

"In the end, through the general interconnectedness of events": Quoted in ibid., 126.

96 *Fedja Nazarov:* Nazarov's faculty page at http://www.math.wisc.edu/~na zarov/, accessed April 27, 2008.

97 *Anna Bogomolnaia:* Bogomolnaia's faculty page at http://www.ruf.rice .edu/~econ/faculty/bogomolnaia.html, accessed April 27, 2008.

Evgeny Abakumov: Directory of French mathematicians, http://wwwmaths .anu.edu.au/people/past_visitors.html, accessed September 23, 2008.

98 *Those banished included Bogomolnaia, Nazarov:* Rukshin interview.

Konstantin Kohas: Kohas's faculty page at http://www.math.spbu.ru/user /analysis/pers/kohas.html, accessed April 27, 2008.

terminology from Laurence Peter and Raymond Hull's The Peter Principle: Laurence J. Peter, Raymond Hull, *The Peter Principle* (New York: Buccaneer Books, 1996), 46.

100 *"He just didn't quite have the temperament"*: Anna Bogomolnaia, telephone interview with the author, April 18, 2008.

6. Guardian Angels

102 *An open letter circulated by a group of American mathematicians: Khronika tekushikh sobytiy* 51, December 1, 1978, http://www.memo.ru/history/DISS /chr/XTC51-60.htm, accessed July 31, 2008; quoted according to G. A. Freiman, *It Seems I Am a Jew: A Samizdat Essay,* trans. and ed. Melvyn B. Nathanson (Carbondale, IL: Southern Illinois University Press, 1980), 87.

103 *Zalgaller and Burago concocted a plan:* Viktor Zalgaller, interview with the author, Rehovot, Israel, March 16, 2008.

104 *Aleksei Verner:* Aleksei Verner and Valery Ryzhik, interview with the author, St. Petersburg, February 27, 2008.

108 *his adviser was Vladimir Rokhlin:* Mathematics Genealogy Project, http: //www.genealogy.math.ndsu.nodak.edu/id.php?id=14999, accessed August 4, 2008.

Gromov . . . despaired of getting a research position: Olga Orlova, "Pochemu ucheniye prodolzhayut uezzhat' iz Rossii," an interview with Anatoly Vershik, http://www.svobodanews.ru/Article/2007/11/22/20071122161321910 .html, accessed August 4, 2008.

So said the university's website: http://www.ihp.jussieu.fr/, accessed August 4, 2008.

As I arrived in the cafeteria: Mikhail Gromov, interview with the author, Paris, June 24, 2008.

110 *Geometry Festival:* http://www.math.duke.edu/conferences/geomfest97 /PreviousSpeakers.html, accessed August 4, 2008.

his first major published work: G. Perelman, Yu. Burago, M. Gromov, "Aleksandrov Spaces with Curvatures Bounded Below," *Russian Math Surveys* 47, no. 2 (1992): 1–58.

Gromov mentioned Perelman to all the right people: Jeff Cheeger, New York University professor, interview with the author, New York City, April 1, 2008.

111 *a French mathematician and historian of science:* Jean-Michel Kantor, mathematician at the Institut Mathématiques à Jussieu, Université de Paris.

7. Round Trip

113 *Gang Tian:* Gang Tian, interview with the author, Princeton, NJ, November 9, 2007.

117 *Lena . . . obtained her PhD in mathematics from the Weizmann Institute:* http: //www.weizmann.ac.il/acadaff/Scientific_Activities/2004/feinberg_degrees .html, accessed August 9, 2008.

Western mathematicians, while suffering from too narrow a focus: Andrei Minarsky, interview with the author, St. Petersburg, October 23, 2008.

Cheeger and his coauthor Detlef Gromoll: Jeff Cheeger and Detlef Gromoll, "On the Structure of Complete Manifolds of Nonnegative Curvature," *Annals of Mathematics* 96 (1972): 413–43.

118 *His paper was four pages long:* Grigory Perelman, "Proof of the Soul Conjecture of Cheeger and Gromoll," *Journal of Differential Geometry* 40 (1994): 209–12.

119 *one of the best American graduate programs in mathematics:* U.S. News & World Report rankings, http://grad-schools.usnews.rankingsandreviews .com/grad/mat/items/45094, accessed August 14, 2008.

Michael Anderson: Faculty page at http://www.math.sunysb.edu/~anderson/, accessed August 14, 2008; Michael Anderson, interview with the author, Stony Brook, NY, November 8, 2007.

120 *Alexandrov spaces at the International Congress of Mathematicians:* G. Perelman, "Spaces with Curvature Bounded Below," http://www.ams.org/math web/icm94/04.perelman.html, accessed August 9, 2008.

fifty-five of the world's top mathematicians: List of speakers at http://www
.ams.org/mathweb/icm94/, accessed August 14, 2008.

four Fields Medalists, past and future: Richard Borcherds (1998), Gerd
Faltings (1986), Maxim Kontsevich (1998), and Jean-Christophe Yoccoz
(1994).

His speech seemed vague and disconnected: Two of the mathematicians
quoted elsewhere in this book told me this, but neither one wanted the
opinion attributed to him.

geometer Bruce Kleiner: Bruce Kleiner, interview with the author, New York
City, April 9, 2008.

121 *the conditions of the fellowship stated explicitly:* Miller Fellowship description, http://millerinstitute.berkeley.edu/page.php?nav=11, accessed August 14, 2008.

123 *Peter Sarnak:* Peter Sarnak's CV at http://www.math.ias.edu/media/Sar
nakCV.pdf, accessed August 15, 2008.

Sarnak recalled in an e-mail message: Peter Sarnak, e-mail to the author,
June 1, 2008.

124 *Perelman told several people at the time:* Jeff Cheeger, New York University
professor, interview with the author, New York City, April 1, 2008; Sarnak
e-mail.

126 *the European Mathematical Society held its second quadrennial congress:* History of the European Mathematical Society at http://www.btinternet.com/
~d.a.r.wallace/EMSHISTORY99.html, accessed September 25, 2008.

Anatoly Vershik submitted Perelman's name: Anatoly Vershik, interview with
the author, St. Petersburg, May 24, 2008.

128 *"I did ask him what he was working on":* Bernhard Leeb, e-mail to the author,
July 7, 2008.

"I've just read your paper": Grigory Perelman, e-mail message to Michael
Anderson, February 28, 2000.

129 *"Dear Grisha":* Michael Anderson, e-mail to Grigory Perelman, February
29, 2000.

He asked if Perelman had looked at his other two papers on related topics: Michael Anderson, e-mail to Grigory Perelman, March 2, 2000.

130 *Perelman responded by saying he could not open the file:* Grigory Perelman,
e-mail to Michael Anderson, March 20, 2000.

8. The Problem

131 *"The very possibility of mathematical science seems":* Henri Poincaré, "Science and Hypothesis," in *The Value of Science: Essential Writings of Henri
Poincaré* (New York: Modern Library, 1999), 9.

132 *"We know what it is to be in love or to feel pain":* Donal O'Shea, *The Poincaré*

Conjecture: In Search of the Shape of the Universe (New York: Walker and Company, 2007), 46.

"that which has no parts, or which has no magnitude": Isaac Todhunter, *The Elements of Euclid for the Use of Schools and Colleges: Comprising the First Six Books and Portions of the Eleventh and Twelfth Books; with Notes, an Appendix, and Exercises* (New York: Adamant Media Corporation, 2003), 1.

"such as are in the same plane, and which being produced ever so far do not meet": Ibid., 5.

"things that are equal to the same thing are equal to one another": Ibid., 6.

133 *postulate 1 and interpretation:* http://alepho.clarku.edu/~djoyce/java/ele ments/bookI/post1.html, accessed June 18, 2008.

postulates 2 and 3: Todhunter, 5.

postulates 4 and 5: Book I of Euclid's *Elements,* http://www.mathsisgoodfor you.com/artefacts/EuclidBook1.htm, accessed June 18, 2008.

"I had been told that Euclid proved things": Bertrand Russell, *The Autobiography of Bertrand Russell* (New York: Routledge, 1998), 31. (My attention was drawn to this passage by William Dunham's *Journey Through Genius: The Great Theorems of Mathematics.*)

134 *"Since the Euclidean system is rather simpler to deal with"*: Richard Courant and Herbert Robbins, *What Is Mathematics? An Elementary Approach to Ideas and Methods,* 2nd ed., revised by Ian Stewart (New York: Oxford University Press, 1996), 223.

135 *The geometry is called elliptic:* Ibid., 224–27.

136 *Euler and the invention of topology:* George Szpiro, *Poincaré's Prize: The Hundred-Year Quest to Solve One of Math's Greatest Puzzles* (New York: Dutton, 2007), 54–56; J. J. O'Connor, E. F. Robertson, "A History of Topology," http://www-groups.dcs.st-and.ac.uk/~history/HistTopics/Topology _in_mathematics.html, accessed June 20, 2008.

140 *proof of the conjecture for seven dimensions or more:* J. Stallings, "Polyhedral Homotopy Spheres," *Bulletin of the American Mathematical Society* 66 (1960): 485–88.

just a year after he received his PhD from Princeton: Mathematics Genealogy Project, http://www.genealogy.math.ndsu.nodak.edu/id.php?id=452, accessed June 29, 2008.

he, however, proved the conjecture for dimensions five and higher: S. Smale, "Generalized Poincaré's Conjecture in Dimensions Greater than Four," *Annals of Mathematics* 74 (1961): 391–406.

extended Stallings's proof to dimensions five and six: E. C. Zeeman, "The Poincaré Conjecture for n ≥ 5," in *Topology of 3-Manifolds and Related Topics* (Englewood Cliffs, NJ: Prentice Hall, 1962).

published a proof essentially similar to Smale's: A. Wallace, "Modifications and Cobounding Manifolds," II, *Journal of Applied Mathematics and Mechanics* 10 (1961): 773–809.

There was also a Japanese mathematician: Szpiro, 163.

141 *John Stallings:* Stallings's website, http://math.berkeley.edu/~stall/, accessed June 29, 2008.

"*I have committed—the sin*": John R. Stallings, "How Not to Prove the Poincaré Conjecture," http://math.berkeley.edu/~stall/notPC.pdf, accessed June 29, 2008.

Michael Freedman published a proof of the conjecture for dimension four: M. H. Freedman, "The Topology of Four-Dimensional Manifolds," *Journal of Differential Geometry* 17 (1982): 357–453.

The accomplishment was hailed as a breakthrough: Szpiro, 169–71.

142 *John Morgan:* John Morgan, interview with the author, New York City, November 6, 2007.

9. The Proof Emerges

153 *He had told Anderson at the outset:* Grigory Perelman, e-mail message to Michael Anderson, November 20, 2002.

He handled the U.S. visa formalities: Ibid., March 31, 2003.

154 *he even added a footnote to that effect to his first preprint:* The footnote read, in part: "I was partially supported by personal savings accumulated during my visits to the Courant Institute in the Fall of 1992, to the SUNY at Stony Brook in the Spring of 1993, and to the UC at Berkeley as a Miller Fellow in 1993–95. I'd like to thank everyone who worked to make those opportunities available to me." Grisha Perelman, "The Entropy Formula for Ricci Flow and Its Geometric Applications," http://arxiv.org/PS_cache/math/pdf/0211/0211159v1.pdf, accessed August 29, 2008.

He submitted the second of his three preprints: Grisha Perelman, "Ricci Flow with Surgery on Three-Manifolds," http://arxiv.org/abs/math/0303109, accessed August 28, 2008.

156 *the* New York Times *published an article:* Sara Robinson, "Russian Reports He Has Solved a Celebrated Math Problem," *New York Times,* April 15, 2003.

157 *an intentional revolt:* Mikhail Gromov, interview with the author, Paris, June 24, 2008.

he was happy to let the organizers: Grigory Perelman, e-mail to Michael Anderson, April 2, 2003.

158 *Perelman's screaming at his mentor had been heard:* Mathematician Nikolai Mnev, interview with the author, St. Petersburg, April 22, 2008.

old enough, wise enough, and woman enough: Alexander Golovanov, interview with the author, St. Petersburg, October 18 and October 23, 2008.

they were incapable of seeing his approach to footnoting as anything but: Gromov interview; Viktor Zalgaller, interview with the author, Rehovot, Israel, March 16, 2008; Yuri Burago, phone interview with the author, February 26, 2008.

159 *"as modest as possible":* Grigory Perelman, e-mail to Michael Anderson, March 31, 2003.

exhibited fantastic clarity in his lectures and unparalleled patience during the discussions: Anderson interview.

the New York Times *published another article:* George Johnson, "The Nation: A Mathematician's World of Doughnuts and Spheres," *New York Times,* April 20, 2003.

163 *"one should never force oneself on anyone":* Grigory Perelman, telephone conversation with Abramov in 2007, in which Perelman told Abramov that this was one of his principles.

164 *to attend a daylong math competition at a physics-and-math school:* Andrei Minarsky, interview with the author, St. Petersburg, October 23, 2008.

He submitted the third and last in his Poincaré series of preprints: Grisha Perelman, "Finite Extinction Times for the Solutions to the Ricci Flow on Certain 3-Manifolds," http://arxiv.org/abs/math/0307245, accessed August 31, 2008.

Kleiner and his University of Michigan colleague John Lott: The product of that website is now posted on the arXiv, http://arxiv.org/PS_cache/math /pdf/0605/0605667v2.pdf, accessed August 31, 2008.

a joint workshop on the first preprint: Allyn Jackson, "Conjectures No More? Consensus Forming on the Proof of the Poincaré and Geometrization Conjectures," *Notices of the AMS* 53, no. 8 (September 2006): 897–901.

10. The Madness

172 *When Perelman spoke to two* New Yorker *writers:* Sylvia Nasar and David Gruber, "Manifold Destiny: A Legendary Problem and the Battle Over Who Solved It," *New Yorker,* August 28, 2006.

174 *The arrangement with camp officials:* Sergei Rukshin, interview with the author, St. Petersburg, October 17 and October 23, 2007, and February 13, 2008.

175 *The entire mathematics contingent broke out laughing:* Boris Sudakov, interview with the author, Jerusalem, December 31, 2007.

it was the Soviet child psychiatrist Grunya Sukhareva: V. Ye. Kogan, "Preodoleniye: Nekontaktniy rebyonok v semye," http://www.autism.ru/read.asp ?id=29&vol=2000, accessed March 3, 2008. Tony Attwood, in *The Complete Guide to Asperger's Syndrome* (London: Jessica Kingsley Publishers, 2006), 36, erroneously identifies the psychiatrist as Ewa Ssucharewa.

Hans Asperger observed that these children's social maturity: Attwood, 13.

British psychologist named Simon Baron-Cohen: Simon Baron-Cohen, telephone interview with the author, February 18, 2008.

"the extreme male brain": Simon Baron-Cohen, *The Essential Difference: Male and Female Brains and the Truth about Autism* (New York: Basic Books, 2003).

176 *When he tested this theory on a population of Cambridge University undergraduates:* Simon Baron-Cohen, Sally Wheelwright, Amy Burtenshaw, and Esther Hobson, "Mathematical Talent Is Linked to Autism," *Human Nature* 18, no. 2 (June 2007): 125–31.

mathematicians scored higher than other scientists: Simon Baron-Cohen, Sally Wheelwright, Richard Skinner, Joanne Martin, and Emma Clubley, "The Autism-Spectrum Quotient (AQ)," *Journal of Autism and Developmental Disorders* 31 (2001): 5–17.

177 *once he had received the information he sought, he had no further use for communication:* Lev Pontryagin, *Zhizneopisaniye Lva Semenovicha Pontryagina, matematika, sostavlennoye im samim* (Moscow: Komkniga, 2006), 22.

Kolmogorov . . . was accosted in a hallway by a man: Alexander Abramov, interview with the author, Moscow, December 5, 2007.

what they called his "temper": Ibid.

"theory of mind": Simon Baron-Cohen, Alan M. Leslie, and Uta Frith, "Does the Autistic Child Have a 'Theory of Mind'?" *Cognition* 21 (1985): 37–46.

178 *a child who sketched a picture:* Attwood, 115–16.

"I suspect that many 'whistle-blowers' have Asperger syndrome": Ibid., 118.

the founders of the dissident movement in the Soviet Union: "Yesenin-Volpin Alexander Sergeevich," *Novoye zerkalo hronosa,* http://www.hrono.ru/bio graf/bio_we/volpin.html, accessed February 23, 2008.

179 *a nuisance forced upon them by the incomprehensible world of social mores:* Michelle G. Winner, founder and director of the Center for Social Thinking in San Jose, CA, telephone interview with the author, February 1, 2008.

"He was very patient": Yelena Vereshchagina, interview with the author, St. Petersburg, February 13, 2008.

"weak central coherence": Francesca Happé and Uta Frith, "The Weak Coherence Account: Detail-Focused Cognitive Style in Autism Spectrum Disorders," *Journal of Autism and Developmental Disorders* 36 (January 2006): 5–25.

180 *"The most interesting facts are those which can be used several times":* Henri Poincaré, *Science and Method,* trans. Frances Maitland, unabridged republication of the 1914 edition (Mineola, NY: Dover Publications, 2003), 17.

"jigsaw puzzle of 5000 pieces": Attwood, 92.

181 *socialization seemed to rob the person:* John Elder Robison, *Look Me in the Eye: My Life with Asperger's* (New York: Crown, 2007).

182 *"He didn't think he needed it":* Perelman's last few years at the Steklov described primarily by Sergei Kislyakov, Steklov Institute director, interview with the author, St. Petersburg, April 21, 2008.

183 *he was unable to file his expense report:* Tamara Yakovlevna, Steklov accountant, interview with the author, St. Petersburg, April 22, 2008.

186 *The journal's entire three hundred pages were devoted to an article:* Huai-Dong Cao and Xi-Ping Zhu, "A Complete Proof of the Poincaré and Geometrization Conjectures—Application of the Hamilton-Perelman Theory of the Ricci Flow," *Asian Journal of Mathematics* 10, no. 2 (June 2006): 165–492.
telling Science *magazine that he thought:* Dana Mackenzie, "Mathematics World Abuzz Over Possible Poincaré Proof," *Science*, April 18, 2003.

187 *Yau held a press conference:* Nasar, Gruber.
Yau used the occasion to announce Cao and Zhu's putative breakthrough: Nasar, Gruber; George Szpiro, *Poincaré's Prize: The Hundred-Year Quest to Solve One of Math's Greatest Puzzles* (New York: Dutton, 2007), 238.

188 *"In the last three years, many mathematicians have attempted to see whether the ideas":* Shing-Tung Yau, "Structure of Three-Manifolds—Poincaré and Geometrization Conjectures," http://doctoryau.com/papers/yau_poincare .pdf, accessed October 4, 2008. Date of publication obtained from http: //www.mcm.ac.cn/Active/yau_new.pdf.
Yau rushed the Cao-Zhu paper through to publication: Following much criticism, Yau described the process himself in a letter to the newsletter of the American Mathematics Society. He wrote that he had unilaterally reviewed and approved the paper for publication in his journal. Shing-Tung Yau, "The Proof of the Poincaré Conjecture," *Notices of the AMS*, April 2007, 472–73, http://www.ams.org/notices/200704/commentary-web.pdf, accessed June 13, 2009.
stated clearly, at the outset, that the proof explicated was Perelman's: Bruce Kleiner and John Lott, "Notes on Perelman's Papers," http://arxiv.org/PS _cache/math/pdf/0605/0605667v2.pdf, accessed October 4, 2008.
"for his contributions to geometry and his revolutionary insights": http://www .icm2006.org/dailynews/fields_perelman_info_en.pdf, accessed October 4, 2008.

189 *"It was so much fun":* Sergei Gelfand, interview with the author, Providence, RI, November 9, 2007.
ICM newsletter published back-to-back interviews: ICM 2006 Daily News, Madrid, August 29, 2006.

190 *Yau engaged a lawyer:* "Harvard Math Professor Alleges Defamation by *New Yorker* Article; Demands Correction," press release, September 18, 2006, www.doctoryau.com, accessed September 9, 2008.

192 *The committee drafted a carefully worded invitation:* Jeff Cheeger, New York University professor, interview with the author, New York City, April 1, 2008.

194 *"A Fields Medal is awarded to Grigory Perelman":* International Congress of Mathematics 2006, opening ceremony, http://www.icm2006.org/proceed ings/Vol_I/2.pdf, accessed September 11, 2008.

196 *John Lott gave what would ordinarily have been the laudation:* John Lott, "The Work of Grigory Perelman," talk at the 2006 ICM, http://www.icm2006 .org/v_f/AbsDef/ts/Lottlight-GP.pdf, accessed September 11, 2008.

197 *Two hours later, Richard Hamilton:* ICM 2006 schedule, http://www .icm2006.org/v_f/fr_Resultat_Cos.php?Titol=O, accessed September 12, 2008.

The announcement of this session in the program: Ibid.

The Clay Institute would now use the ICM: James Carlson, interview with the author, Boston, August 27, 2007.

a pdf file started circulating: http://www.cds.caltech.edu/~nair/pdfs/Cao Zhu_plagiarism.pdf, accessed September 12, 2008.

198 *Cao and Zhu claimed they had forgotten they had copied the material:* Denis Overby, "The Emperor of Math," *New York Times,* October 17, 2006.

"In this paper, we provide an essentially self-contained": Huai-Dong Cao and Xi-Ping Zhu, "Hamilton-Perelman's Proof of the Poincaré Conjecture and the Geometrization Conjecture," http://arxiv.org/PS_cache/math/pdf/0612 /0612069v1.pdf, accessed September 12, 2008.

Channel 1 . . . reported that Perelman: "Rossiyskiy matematik razgadal za-gadku, kotoraya muchayet uchenykh uzhe 100 let," transcript of television broadcast, http://www.1tv.ru/owa/win/ort6_main.print_version?p_news_ title_id=92602, accessed September 12, 2008.

he did not have the money to buy a ticket: "Perelman igraet v pryatki," *MK v Pitere,* August 30, 2006, http://www.mk-piter.ru/2006/08/31/022/, accessed September 12, 2008.

Alexander Abramov, his old coach, contributed: Alexander Abramov, "Zagadki Perelmana net," *Moskovskiye Novosti,* September 1, 2006.

"You could say I'm engaged in self-education": http://www.youtube.com /watch?v=jG-DGAdughs, accessed September 12, 2008.

11. The Million-Dollar Question

200 *Jim Carlson:* James Carlson, interviews with the author on numerous occasions, including Boston, August 27, 2007, and St. Petersburg, May 24 and May 25, 2008.

207 *he was apparently holding a conference to celebrate his fifty-ninth birthday:*

"International Conference in Honor of the 59th Birthday of Shing-Tung Yau!" http://qjpam.henu.edu.cn/home.jsp, accessed October 5, 2008.

"I know Gian-Carlo Rota held a conference to celebrate his sixty-fourth birthday": That conference was actually organized by Rota's students. A mention is contained in a Rota obituary, http://www.math.binghamton.edu/zaslav/Nytimes/+Science/+Math/+Obits/rota-mit-obit.html, accessed October 5, 2008.

208 *Vershik had published a piece:* Anatoly Vershik, "What Is Good for Mathematics? Thoughts on the Clay Millennium Prizes," *Notices of the AMS,* January 2007, http://www.ams.org/notices/200701/comm-vershik.pdf, accessed October 5, 2008.

Index

The Enough Moment

The

Enough
Moment

Fighting to End Africa's
Worst Human Rights Crimes

John Prendergast *with* **Don Cheadle**

Three Rivers Press / New York

Published in the United States by Three Rivers Press, an imprint of the Crown
Publishing Group, a division of Random House, Inc., New York.
www.crownpublishing.com

Three Rivers Press and the Tugboat design are registered trademarks of
Random House, Inc.

This work contains brief excerpts from the following articles: "Obama's
Opportunity to Help Africa" by George Clooney, David Pressman, and John
Prendergast, *The Wall Street Journal*, November 22, 2008; "Obama Can Make
A Difference in Darfur" by Jim Wallis and John Prendergast, *The Wall Street
Journal*, April 13, 2009; and "At War in the Fields of the Lord" by Ryan Gosling
and John Prendergast, ABC News, March 1, 2007.

Grateful acknowledgment is made to Omekongo Dibinga for permission to
reprint his poem "Honorata."

Library of Congress Cataloging-in-Publication Data
Prendergast, John, 1963–
The enough moment : fighting to end Africa's worst human rights crimes /
by John Prendergast with Don Cheadle.
p. cm.
1. Human rights—Africa. 2. War crimes—Africa. 3. Crimes against
humanity—Africa. 4. Social movements. 5. Political participation.
I. Cheadle, Don. II. Title.
JC599.A35P74 2010
364.1'38096—dc22   2010007642

ISBN 978-0-307-46482-8

Printed in the United States of America

Design by Elizabeth Rendfleisch

Map on page vi by Ellen McElhinny
Maps on pages 174–175 by The Enough Project

10 9 8 7 6 5 4 3 2 1

First Edition

We are not guaranteeing the end of all human rights crimes in Africa if you follow the advice in these pages. And we certainly do not claim to possess all the answers to the complex problems we address here. But we can be sure that if war criminals everywhere face an ocean of people with Braveheart-like commitment standing up in support of peace and human rights, the odds improve that the world will be a better and safer place for millions of people. So we dedicate this book to all the folks on the front lines of this fight, and to a future in which these most heinous human rights crimes no longer exist.

John and Don
May 16, 2010
Los Angeles, California

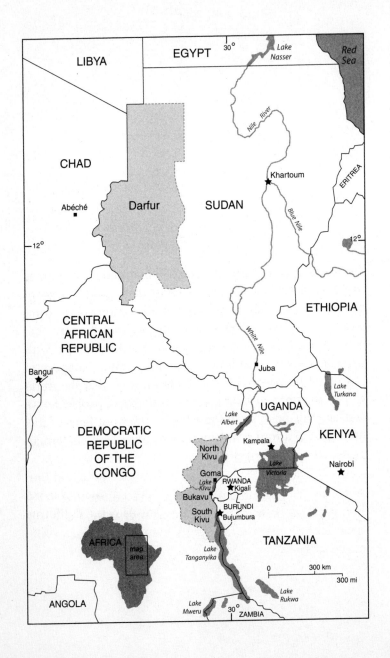

Authors' Note

We believe this book should be a living document, so we've created a place online—www.enoughmoment.org—where you can connect with others, see how to get involved, watch inspiring videos, write letters, sign petitions, and get real-time updates on what's happening in the countries and crises we discuss. There's a wealth of information there, including some amazing Enough Moments from Upstanders around the world. Share your Enough Moment with others, and read the inspiring things people are doing every day all over the world in the fight to end Africa's greatest human rights crimes.

A portion of the authors' earnings will be donated to the Enough Project (www.enoughproject.org) at the Center for American Progress in its efforts to end the human rights crimes discussed in this book.

Contents

Introduction

Don and John and the Enough Moment

Dateline, Las Vegas.

It is a few hours after the successful conclusion of another Ante Up for Africa charity poker tournament to raise funds and awareness for Darfur. Two years have passed since our first book, *Not On Our Watch,* was published. But it is the immediate future that consumes us on this boiling Las Vegas night: there is an impossibly short time before our next book is due to the publisher. If you are not reading this, it didn't happen. The tape recorder is turned on . . .

JOHN PRENDERGAST: Buddy. The deadline for this book is coming at us like a runaway train, and we have the grand total of a vague outline. Some people hate endings. I seem to be unable to cope with beginnings.

DON CHEADLE: Well, nothing concentrates the mind like a crushing deadline. But, frankly, I really hate committing anything to tape.

1

JOHN: The post–Richard Nixon Syndrome? I can take lots of notes, and we can shut this thing off . . .

DON: Naah, let's play through. It seems surreal that our last book came out two years ago.

JOHN: My God, my life is careening by. I'm a dinosaur, man.

DON: A fossil.

JOHN: A museum exhibit. So the idea here is that part of this book we can talk through, and part of it I can write. Our conversations can be the narrative spine that links the chapters together, the Mississippi River that winds its way through the middle of the book and keeps everything flowing. Branching off our conversations will be stories and testimonies of Upstanders from the wars' front lines, from amazing everyday activists, and from celebrities and other prominent folks, as well as everything you ever wanted to know about why genocidal tactics and other human rights crimes are used and how we can stop them. Geez, I have the sudden, chilling feeling that it won't work.

DON: Of course it will work.

JOHN: Who are you, the conductor of the *Titanic* string band?

DON: So can we hit rewind and tape over some of the parts of this conversation we don't like?

JOHN: How many times a day do I wanna just hit the rewind button, extract my foot out of my mouth, and re-record? What a great thing to have in life. A much more pressing issue, however, requires reiteration. This publisher is gonna have to send the literary bounty hunters after us to get this book, brother, if we don't get our act together.

DON: Umm, I thought you were kidding about this deadline?

JOHN: (Silence)

DON: This is the mother of all Hail Marys.

JOHN: We are going to redefine the concept of Hail Mary.

DON: No, this is the exact definition of a Hail Mary. I'm sure there's an opt-out clause in the contract.

JOHN: Or at least some kind of extension based on incompetence or desperation, for which we qualify and will no doubt utilize more than once on this one. So much pressure. Is that tape really rolling? Can you check?

DON: It's rolling. I pressed start. Someone had to take charge.

JOHN: Oh, it is moving . . . Oh, God . . .

DON: That tape is a metaphor for something. If we were real writers, we'd think of something insightful to write here.

JOHN: Real writers? I'm the nomadic son of a frozen foods salesman, and you're Iron Man's accomplice. I hope people aren't expecting too many fancy metaphors from us. But we do have a purpose here that we've been talking about for the last few months now. The essence of our discussions has been this concept of the "Enough Moment."

DON: Yeah, after all the "Never Again" speeches by all of these politicians, as genocide and other horrible human rights crimes continue, and all this attention for Darfur and the Congo and other places, we can't just sit by and not respond to them. Enough is enough.

JOHN: Exactly. So the point of writing another book is to focus on this concept of the "Enough Moment," when a potentially perfect storm is gathering for real action in response to some of the worst atrocities in world history. For the first time we've seen the creation of an anti-genocide constituency, around Darfur, while the genocide was still happening. For the first time a global effort is being developed to counter rape as a war weapon, with the tip of the iceberg in the Congo. And for the first time we have a young people's movement forming to protect other young people half a world away who are being forced to become child soldiers, in the attempt to stop the Lord's Resistance Army. These are three of the most heinous and despicable ways to fight a war, and the objective of this growing movement is to eradicate their use from the face of the earth.

DON: And helping to fuel all these efforts is this incredible new engine: these social networking tools. Every day there are new innovations. You learn from a sixteen year old what the new thing is.

JOHN: And we aren't done yet. Finally, we have an administration in Washington, a cabinet full of people who have really made a mark in their previous positions as vocal human rights advocates, as anti-genocide crusaders.

DON: From the president to the vice president to the secretary of state to the UN ambassador. We have had interactions with all of them, and we could see it firsthand, that all of them have been committed to doing much more to bring these nightmares to an end.

JOHN: And though we might have been inclined to give them a pass during the first year and a half on the job, by now they've all had sufficient time to adjust to their executive branch jobs and really live their principles. So if there ever were one, this is the Enough Moment, potentially, for these human rights issues. And that's just on the macro level. There is also the micro level, the individual level. Anyone who has stepped up to become an advocate for other people in less fortunate circumstances has had his or her own personal Enough Moment. These Enough Moments originate from all kinds of things. Like when you see a picture that personalizes someone's suffering, or you hear a story, or someone tells you about a particular issue.

DON: Or you see a movie, a TV show, or hear a song, and something registers. It could be for a million different reasons that it registers.

JOHN: You may have had a teacher or an experience as a kid that triggers some level of compassion and desire to act. Or it could have been a parent, or a role model.

DON: You heard the bell toll.

JOHN: Yeah, it's like in that Sinatra/Denzel movie, when the chip gets switched on . . .

DON: Oh, yeah, *The Manchurian Candidate*, but in this case the light gets switched on for good instead of evil.

JOHN: The light goes on, and you are like, okay, now I gotta go and do something. I can no longer be a bystander. I have to become an Upstander, to use Samantha Power's term. What I am going to do I may not know immediately, but I know

I must do something. So these auditoriums full of people who show up for events and film screenings, for people who buy books like this, for people who come to rallies and demonstrations, for folks who get online and sign petitions and write letters to public officials . . .

DON: They all have had some kind of Enough Moment that led them to decide to be part of something bigger for something beyond themselves.

JOHN: It is fascinating to explore what makes people care about these issues. I think some people have their Enough Moment because they genuinely are driven or touched or affected by the suffering of others, and they feel in some way, shape, or form that there is some kind of responsibility . . .

DON: Cosmic responsibility . . .

JOHN: The concept of being my brother's or sister's keeper. And I think some people are driven by an imperative that is found in any faith to reach out and provide assistance to those less fortunate. Action is very clearly an essential element of any faith. I was just at a service on Sunday, and the sermon was all about the imperative to work for peace. And then, of course, there is the common security threat—you know, if we don't deal with some of these issues, then they might bounce back on us. Whether it is terrorism, disease, or environmental degradation, the issue of enlightened self-interest also can be the catalyst for involvement.

DON: It will always be my hope that people will care beyond themselves, and they will want to do more. That's going to be an imperative a lot more quickly than we think it is, as some of these problems that seem so far away are going to rebound back here on us. So we are going to need to link arms with people all over the world against a greater common enemy involving environmental destruction and the ensuing lack of resources, water, and food. I mean, we cannot continue to waste as we have as a world and expect that there will be no consequence. So you need to be able to flex the muscle of altruism and humanitarianism and brotherhood and fellowship in a very necessary way. Or you know, get a bunch of guns, and hunker down and hope you got enough people with you that you can stave off the masses when they come to try to take your stuff, because it's one or the other—stand apart . . . united we . . .

JOHN: Hang together, or all hang separately.

DON: Exactly. Any one of those concepts. So I think that people will come to the realization that it's not just necessarily saying "I want to stop genocide in Sudan" but rather "We HAVE to stop genocide. We have to stop rape as a war weapon, or it will spread and some day rebound directly on us."

Ultimately, what are we doing this for? What's the point? What's gonna make some senator get off his ass, walk down the steps, get in his car, drive to the White House, and say, "No, I gotta get in now. No, move, I gotta talk to the president now." "What's the problem, senator?" "This is the problem, and we have to do something about it now."

What is the gear that has to be shifted to make that happen? There has to be a political benefit to taking meaningful action for some politicians. How do we translate altruism into something that is maybe less idealistic and more visceral for the people we are asking to act, so that there is a reward, a real reward, and a recognition, for being an Upstander?

Because we, as ordinary citizens, can feel good just knowing that we have done something, that we have tried to do something. But I don't think that is always what motivates politicians. I think there are many more people that they have to answer to, and there is sort of a bottom line in all the policies they put into place that has a big quid pro quo element to it and a big concern with staying in that seat of power for as long as they can. So in order to break through the barrier of inaction and inertia that exists in halls of power in D.C. and around the world, we're gonna have to be more creative in going beyond the usual reasons why people care.

JOHN: Recently I was in Washington, and we had an event with a group called Invisible Children, which is an organization led by young people and focused on stopping the recruitment of child soldiers by the Lord's Resistance Army of Uganda. We were having a lobby day.

So we get the word out, and we have no idea how many people are gonna be willing to fly or bus or drive to D.C. to be part of this thing on behalf of kids half a world away. Frankly, I'm thinking a hundred or so will straggle in on their own dime. I mean, they're students, so this kind of unanticipated expense isn't easy to absorb.

So I arrive at the auditorium that morning, and what do you know: there are 1,500 young people already there from all over the country, ready to descend on Capitol Hill. The number of congressional cosponsors for the legislation we had worked on quadrupled in something like six hours, because there is a light at the end of the tunnel. The bill ended up having the most cosponsors of any freestanding bill on Africa ever.

DON: When you and I went to northern Uganda a few years ago, nobody in the United States had even heard of the Lord's Resistance Army.

JOHN: It's incredible. So the point is that we have these growing people's movements focused not on responding to the symptoms of human rights abuses but on ENDING genocide, on ENDING child soldier recruitment, and on ENDING rape as a war weapon. And we finally have a group of people in government whose careers have in part been committed to ENDING these scourges as well.

DON: And we need to remind them every day of their commitment.

JOHN: You ain't kiddin'. But the news gets even better. It turns out that when political will is generated, and it is combined with smart, game-changing, inspired, effective policies, wars can end, and problems can get solved.

DON: You're always talking about "blood diamonds."

JOHN: Yep, perfect example. A multifront movement was created that sought an end to the connection between diamond purchases and terrible human rights abuses in places like Sierra Leone, Liberia, and Angola. When the political will was generated and consumer pressure got hot enough, corporations and governments did the right thing and filtered blood diamonds out of the interational market. And now, less than a decade later, all three of those countries are at peace.

DON: When you look at this history, the possibility for transformation can be dramatic. But supporting that transformation requires focus, attention, commitment, drive, and innovation.

JOHN: And imagination. People have to believe peace and justice are possible, and they have to imagine the roadmap required to get there. It was an Enough Moment for those countries and that issue. Now the time has come for the Enough Moment for the issues you and I have worked on together, some of the most dramatic human rights issues of the last century: genocide, child soldier recruitment, and rape as a tool of war.

CHAPTER ONE

Enough Is Enough

Building a People's Movement Against Genocide,
Child Soldier Recruitment, and Rape as a War Weapon

A human wave in support of the world's most forgotten people is building. We're not surfers, but we love how surfers describe the perfect wave. The wave builds to a crescendo, you're in awe of it, you approach and ride it, and it carries you safely home to your destination. The formation of this human wave was not predicted. A decade ago, few people even knew what a "Darfur" was, how our cell phones directly contributed to making Congo the most dangerous place in the world to be a woman or a girl, or who the "invisible children" of Uganda were. Ten years ago, an event regarding genocide or other crimes against humanity would have attracted perhaps a dozen or so hardy souls, wearing their sandals and psychedelic t-shirts, prepared, if necessary, to break out into a stanza or two of "Kumbaya."

But today a strange and beautiful cocktail of hope, anger, citizen activism, social networking, compassion, celebrities, faith in action, and globalization are all coming together to produce the beginnings of a mass movement of people against these crimes and for peace. And this is happening at the very time that an American administration is populated by a number of people who have been the leading elected officials to have stood up against genocide, child soldier recruitment, and rape as a war weapon. We call the sheer possibility inherent in this confluence of factors the Enough Moment, and it means that our feeling that Enough Is Enough might actually get translated into real action for change.

These are three of the great scourges of our world, of our time. Genocide, mass rape, and child conscription are the most deadly and diabolical manifestations of war, with the gravest human consequences imaginable. Nearly 10 million fresh graves have been dug as a result of these tactics in East and Central Africa alone over the last twenty years, and countless millions of refugees have been rendered homeless. Sudan and Congo, in fact, are the two deadliest conflicts in the world since the Holocaust.

The stakes remain enormous. And this is by no means an Africa-only phenomenon. The kinds of tactics used by warring parties globally are increasingly targeted at civilian populations who are usually defenseless and largely disconnected from the perpetrators of the violence. As a result, the ratio of civilians to soldiers who die at times runs as high as nine to one. Because of this targeting of civilians, over 100 million people died violent deaths during the twentieth century's wars and genocides. This exceeds the death count of all pre-twentieth-century wars and massacres combined.

At this juncture of human history, and because of the distortion and delay in Africa's own historical trajectory created by the European colonial era, it turns out that the global epicenter of this kind of targeted violence is currently playing itself out on African soil, with weapons that come largely from America, Europe, and Asia. And these are therefore the places most in need of a global people's movement and smart U.S. policies to ensure an appropriate global response in support of peace.

This is also the continent we know best, and we have committed ourselves to making a difference there.

The Enough Moment

> *In times of tragedy the United States of America steps forward and helps. That is who we are. That is what we do. . . . When we show not just our power but also our compassion, the world looks to us with a mixture of awe and admiration. That advances our leadership. That shows the character of our country.*
>
> —PRESIDENT BARACK OBAMA[1]

Strong and true words indeed from President Obama. But words unmatched with deeds can sometimes be worse than no words at all. Politician after politician, and UN resolution after UN resolution, have made promise after promise to end these crimes without doing what is necessary to give their words teeth.

But now a politically potent constituency forming through mass campaigns is raising awareness of these crimes, and it's time to translate intention into action. There is an increasing opportunity to democratize our foreign policy-making and to widen and deepen people's stake in international issues. We've finally got a president and a cabinet that have made huge pledges to act. Before they took office in 2009, President Obama, Vice President Biden, and Secretary of State Clinton were all major anti-genocide campaigners in the U.S. Senate, as was U.S. Ambassador to the United Nations Susan Rice in her previous think tank capacity. They all have formidable track records, demonstrating that being a bystander has never been an option for them. Now in the executive branch, they have the opportunity to act.

Now is the time to make this our collective Enough Moment—the day when we say "Enough" to the atrocities happening to our brothers and sisters in these war-torn regions. We have the opportunity to say "Enough Is Enough" and have these words become something tangible.

Historically, when we have decided that we are indeed our brother's and sister's keepers, we have acted. There are cases around the world of this resolve, such as global efforts to stop genocides in Kosovo and in East Timor. Africa has its own examples:

- When a genocide was about to occur in northeast Congo in 2003, the world said ENOUGH and stopped it from happening by deploying a European-led force to protect people and disarm militias.
- When terrible wars fueled by blood diamonds ripped Sierra Leone, Liberia, and Angola apart, the world said ENOUGH and stopped buying the blood diamonds, which helped cut off the fuel for the war, providing the opening for the wars to finally end.
- When South Africa was ruled by a racist white supremacist government that put Nelson Mandela in Robben Island prison for decades, the world said ENOUGH, and governments imposed—at the request of the people of South Africa—biting comprehensive sanctions until the racist system and government were dismantled completely and Mandela was freed (and elected president).

Now it is the moment to say Enough death in Darfur. Enough rape in the Congo. Enough children turned into fighting machines in northern Uganda and the surrounding region. Enough.

JOHN: There are so many great examples and great stories in Africa that people hardly know anything about. There was this kid, Arnold, that I met on my last trip to Congo, who had been forcibly recruited a few times as a child soldier, but he escaped and he is now going to university. He went through all this counseling, and he recently started his own nongovernment organization (NGO), Youth and Human Rights, advocating for the importance of justice and accountability. Instead of succumbing to the crushing circumstances he had endured, the kind of trauma that would destroy most of us, and then instead of being a bystander, Arnold decided to stand up and be a leader. That is utterly remarkable.

DON: It was amazing when we were making *Hotel Rwanda*. In one of the scenes where women were being brutalized, a lot of the extras had actually been through it in real life. And I just remember asking one of the women, "How could you go through it again like this, even in a movie scene?" And she said, "It's very important that the story be told again, and in the right way. And I want to be part of that." And I was like, "Wow."

JOHN: That is a strength that is just immeasurable, man. I remember this one Darfurian fellah that Samantha Power and I met on our first trip together into the rebel-held areas of Darfur. One night early on in our trip, out under a thousand stars, with everyone in their sleeping bags, this gentleman began telling us the story of Darfur and why his people are fighting for freedom. With a flashlight and his finger, he illustrated everything with drawings and diagrams in the sand. He spent hours on the nuances, the grievances, the rationale for what he argued is a just war in Darfur. The people in Darfur, he

told us, are not helpless or passive victims. Most are struggling, indeed, but many are fighting for their rights and for
peace. Under that starry canopy, he was telling us that there are
REASONS for the conflict in Darfur, and therefore there
are SOLUTIONS that the Darfurian people are trying to
contribute to by supporting the rebellion with their sons and
their sustenance. And the reason he said he was risking his
life to travel with us is because the solution won't come without telling the real story of Darfur to America and the world,
and he is hoping that enough people in what seemed to him
to be an indifferent world will stand up and lend a hand in the
solution.

The good news is that over the last few years, there have
been huge rallies, large numbers of people joining advocacy
groups, lobby days, petition drives, massive postcard and
letter writing campaigns, major congressional interest, and
bold pronouncements by all the major candidates for president in 2008. And even our previous book became a top-five
New York Times bestseller. It's still available, by the way. I'm
just saying.

DON: Please focus.

———————

The task is clear. We as caring citizens need to catalyze
and build an even bigger and stronger people's movement
for change. We need to assemble an unusual coalition and
force better policies through popular demand. The political will for real change will come from the bottom up. This
is our chance. There may never again be an opportunity
like this. We must seize this Enough Moment, and seize
it now.

Why This Book

Africa is a continent full of promise, with identifiable solutions to these human rights crimes. Genocide has, in some places, been successfully prevented or ended. Child soldier recruitment has, in some places, been stopped, and the children affected have been rehabilitated. Rape as a tool of war, in some places, has been neutralized. Wars have been resolved. Understanding that there are answers is empowering. Demonstrating that the answers usually involve partnerships between Frontline Upstanders in the war zones and Citizen Upstanders in the United States and around the world is crucial to showing that there is a connection between the activism of ordinary citizens and the ending of wars and massive human rights crimes.

If we can build a broader and deeper people's movement against these kinds of crimes against humanity, our political system will become more motivated and effective in responding to and ultimately in preventing these crimes. Unless there is a political cost for inaction, we will get inaction. The growing people's movement is attempting to create a political cost for inaction, for lip service, for turning away from people in need of a hand. We hope to see a world where the penalties for committing these atrocities are so severe and the diplomacy to prevent them so deft and automatic that their recurrence becomes a subject relegated to our museums and history books.

We want to ring the bell for the seven-alarm fire that is raging in Africa's deadliest war zones. The 10 million deaths in the countries on which we are focused is a modern-day holocaust that demands a response. This book is the call to your Enough Moment.

People's Movements

If we take a hard look at the last century, we see both politicians and great ideas come and go. But the ingredients that time and again have really changed the world are the people's movements we know so well: the women's movement, the civil rights movement, the labor movement, the peace movement, the environmental movement, the anti-apartheid movement. They all show how change is possible—even when conventional wisdom is stacked in opposition—when organized groups of people come together around an issue they care enough about to move aside the forces of the status quo.

Finally, for the first time ever, we have a popularly based anti-genocide movement. We have a growing chorus of voices focused on stopping the destruction of women in the Congo. There is a renegade, underground phenomenon, called Invisible Children, that is sweeping through college campuses and that is dedicated to finding a solution to the child soldier travesty in northern Uganda and the surrounding region. Building the scale and scope of these efforts provides a unique and historic opportunity to help alter the course of history in those areas.

When we hear about Africa, it is often in the context of war, genocide, or famine. These phenomena are not inevitable. They can be stopped, and even prevented. Enlightened government policies focused on solving these challenges have proven successful. Unfortunately, so much of the effort and resources are focused on the shocking symptoms of war, leading to multi-billion-dollar outlays for emergency aid and military observers. There needs to be an equal emphasis on dealing with the causes led by competent peace processes, which are perhaps the most cost-effective tool we have in the international arsenal for dealing with crises. The truth is, though, government action in support of addressing the causes that will lead to an end to these crises will be deployed earlier and be more consistent only when there is a larger and deeper people's movement focused on ending these tragedies.

We need to shift the paradigm away from simply responding to the symptoms of these wars to focusing on ending them. The best way to end genocide, child soldier recruitment, and rape as a war weapon is to end the wars in which these strategies run wild and to impose a significant cost on those who utilize these deadly strategies.

This is where you come in. People's movements have two functions: to place pressure on our government to care about these kinds of issues that are often at the bottom of the list, and to ensure that our government is actually pursuing lasting cures for these crises, rather than just treating their symptoms. In other words, we don't want just action. We want smart action.

There are reasons why the world hasn't "saved" Darfur. The genocide there raged long beyond the time it could have been stopped. The reason is that the governmental policies that were pursued regarding Darfur were not focused on ending the crisis. Instead, the policies mostly addressed only the symptoms, which they treated with humanitarian aid and peacekeeping forces, for which billions of taxpayer dollars have been and are being spent. This symptoms-based approach represented a failure of nations like the United States, but it also represented the Darfur anti-genocide movement's early overemphasis on UN peacekeeping troops, when the emphasis should have been on a peace deal backed by serious consequences for continued human right crimes.

Humanitarian aid is a necessary bandage, provided to keep people alive and address their acute emergencies presumably while solutions are being sought. Peacekeeping forces are sent in primarily to observe and report on the actions of the parties to a conflict or a ceasefire, sometimes before a peace deal has even been signed. Inexplicably, it usually takes years of a crisis burning before there are systematic attempts to END the crisis that generate the need for aid and peacekeepers. That is what the people's movement must do: demand that government and UN policies be designed to focus early on dealing with root causes and ending these crises in a sustainable way. This Enough Moment today may be the best chance we will ever have to do so.

The people's movements against genocide, child soldier recruitment, and rape as a war weapon are composed of people from all walks of life and from many different motivations. Students, faith-based groups, and a diverse constituency of concerned citizens throughout the world have come together to express the sentiment that the destruction of human life on the basis of identity, gender, or age is simply not acceptable in the twenty-first century.

Significant constituencies are being constructed for each of these major human rights crimes:

- The anti-genocide movement for Darfur (also marked by efforts to prevent further crimes throughout Sudan) continues to advocate in the United States and in other countries, and Humanity United's Sudan Now campaign was constructed in mid-2009 to reenergize advocacy efforts of the movement and take them to the next level.
- There are rapidly expanding worldwide efforts to protect and empower the women of eastern Congo, who are subjected to violence more extreme than anywhere else globally. (The V-Day campaign led by Eve Ensler and the Enough Project's Raise Hope for Congo campaign work on parallel tracks and cooperate closely.)

- Similar efforts have been expended to protect the children of northern Uganda and the surrounding region (the How It Ends campaign spearheaded by a partnership between Invisible Children, Resolve Uganda, and Enough) who have experienced the highest abduction rates in the world at the hands of the Lord's Resistance Army.

In 2007, Gayle Smith and John founded the Enough Project to contribute to catalyzing this movement to focus on ENDING these kinds of human rights abuses rather than just responding to their symptoms with humanitarian aid, peacekeeping forces, and "Never Again" speeches and press releases. The Enough Project and other groups are attempting to create foreign policy literacy and trying to move the discussion beyond just getting involved to actual participation in tactics and strategy for change, especially when the "right" way is not always so clear. The objective is to not just shed light on the big policy solutions but to also help people understand why, and give people the tools for participating in an informed way. We want a smarter movement because compassion and dedication have exponentially more impact when they are applied strategically.

"What distinguishes the Enough Project is that it doesn't say, 'Hey, we've built this house, come and live in it with us,'" notes Karen Murphy of the organization Facing History and Ourselves. "Instead, Enough is showing people how to build it out, make it stronger. People feel prepared, inspired, successful, ready to take on something. Belonging is an essential human need. Enough provides that for these causes. You inspire people to say 'I want to belong to that,' or 'I want to do that,' and even 'I can do that.' People make this essential connection because they are informed and feel like they are part of something."

"Obama's Opportunity to Help Africa"

—George Clooney, David Pressman,
and John Prendergast, *Wall Street Journal*,
November 22, 2008

Rahm Emanuel, the White House chief of staff, recently reminded us that in the midst of crisis, there is great opportunity. For Congo and Sudan, we see three big reasons for hope.

The first is China. Because of China's nearly $9 billion investment in the oil sector in Sudan, and its recent $5 billion deal for Congolese minerals, China increasingly has a vested interest in peace and stability in these two countries. President Obama could send a powerful message and take a meaningful step by sending a high-level envoy to Beijing, early in his first 100 days, to explore ways to work together to help bring peace to these African countries. With all that divides the United States and China, these are issues we can and should unite on.

The second reason for hope is the [president] himself. Mr. Obama has offered the world a renewed American commitment to global citizenship. In both Congo and Sudan, as is the case in countries around the world, there is an extraordinary eagerness to see this global phenomenon engage positively in their crises. However intangible, the president-elect's ability to inspire and lead is as real as any other point of leverage. He can make the case for peace to those controlling the flow of money and munitions into Congo and Sudan. And he can raise the cost of continuing the status quo through multilateral measures to economically and politically isolate the spoilers.

The third reason for hope may be the most potent of all. The American public, especially our younger generation, is increasingly interested in what happens outside of our borders, and particularly in Africa. While we have all participated in our own way in building an advocacy movement around Darfur, it has been the high school and college students who have made Darfur a political issue too important to be ignored, and who are now preparing similar campaigns for Congo. It is these same young Americans who voted in large numbers for the new president. They are now ready to be led by a President Obama to build a safer world and a safer Africa.

Why Activism Matters

By mid-2009, many critics had looked at Darfur's continuing crisis and pronounced activist efforts aimed at stopping it a failure.

Not so fast.

Activists helped put the issue on the map for politicians on both sides of the aisle in Congress and on the presidential campaign trail in 2008, forcing them to address a situation that would have otherwise been lost in a sea of competing domestic and foreign policy priorities. But activists have done much more than simply garner attention for this cause.

Let's look at what has actually been accomplished in part due to activist efforts:

1. **Saving Lives:** It is no exaggeration to say that hundreds of thousands of Darfurians are alive today because of the anti-genocide activist movement. In the absence of the extraordinary global effort to shine a light on what is happening in Darfur, the death toll would have been far higher. Look back in history—to a time when there was *not* a mobilized and active anti-genocide constituency—at what the Sudanese regime did in southern Sudan during the twenty-year war there: tens and sometimes hundreds of thousands of

southerners perished each time the regime cut off access for humanitarian aid, until the death toll reached two and a quarter million. There was never a strong enough public outcry in the United States or elsewhere to force politicians to confront the Sudanese regime in a way that would prevent large-scale deaths. But now, because of the globalization of the genocide prevention movement, it is impossible for the Sudanese regime to cut off the flow of aid in Darfur without a huge international outcry from activists, journalists, and governments. In the spring of 2009, when the regime threw out over a dozen aid agencies from Darfur, the response was swift and united, and although many of the groups weren't allowed back in, the lost capacities were in part replaced as quickly as possible by other groups, thus avoiding a large increase in death rates. Additionally, activist-driven initiatives on the ground in Darfur—such as pressing for the establishment of focused patrols allowing women to collect firewood in the absence of a substantial peacekeeping presence around displaced camps and providing solar cooking stoves to reduce the number of trips outside protected areas—continue to save lives and reduce the rate of sexual violence.

2. Supporting Peacemaking: At the beginning of the Bush administration's time in office, before the Darfur war erupted, many Christian organizations, human rights activists, and committed members of Congress pressed for a robust response to the deadly north-south Sudanese war. Particularly in response to the faith-based constituency, the Bush administration led a complex and protracted peace process that resulted in the Comprehensive Peace Agreement (CPA) in 2005 ending that war. Furthermore, Darfur activist efforts around the time of the 2006 Washington, D.C., rally resulted in President Bush's sending a top diplomat to attempt to negotiate an end to the Darfur war. However, the negotiators' poorly conceived proposals and hurried negotiations left the resulting deal dead on arrival. These two examples—though only one resulted in an actual peace deal—of activist-led pressure triggering government-led peacemaking efforts are promising illustrations of what activists have already helped to achieve for Sudan.

3. **Indicting War Criminals:** The Bush administration's strong opposition to the International Criminal Court nearly doomed an effort by the United Nations Security Council to refer the case of Darfur to the court. However, a major push by activists and congressional allies led the Bush administration to step aside and let the referral pass. The resulting investigation has led to an arrest warrant for President Omar al-Bashir and other officials charged with war crimes and crimes against humanity, an important step toward real accountability.

4. **Deploying Peacekeepers:** Despite consistent pledges by Sudanese government officials that they would never allow UN peacekeeping troops in Darfur, over 15,000 troops were sent to be part of a UN and African Union combined force attempting to provide some measure of monitoring and protection to Darfuri civilians. Woefully inadequately equipped, this peacekeeping force was ill fated from the start as it was sent to keep a peace that didn't exist. Activists were able to generate the necessary political will to get troops authorized and deployed, but in the absence of a peace deal, the effectiveness of the peacekeepers remains compromised. Nevertheless, many Darfuri civilians have been protected from further attacks simply because of the presence of these peacekeeping forces, directly attributable to activist pressures.

5. **Removing Genocide from Stock Portfolios:** A student-led activist initiative spearheaded by the Sudan Divestment Task Force and supported by the Save Darfur Coalition has resulted in numerous institutions' selling their stock holdings

of companies doing business with the Sudanese government and thereby helping indirectly to finance genocide. As of the Spring of 2010, over 60 universities and colleges have divested, along with 27 state pension funds and 23 cities.

Activism does matter. We know that ultimately the conflicts in Africa will be solved because of the efforts of African people themselves. But the rest of the world has a major role to play in promoting solutions. Our roles as interested citizens and activists are to urge our political leaders to invest in achieving peace and ending human rights atrocities and to remind these officials that doing so is in the political and strategic interests of the United States. These crises are complex, and they will not be solved quickly or without sustained negotiations and engagement between multiple parties. We must resist the temptation to jump at overly simplistic or ineffective solutions and proceed with appropriate humility, while continuing to act with the knowledge that our efforts as activists are a crucial component to achieving peace and ending human rights abuses in Africa.

In towns and cities around the United States hang banners that read: "Darfur, A Call to Your Conscience." They are spot on. Responding to the crises of genocide, rape as a war weapon, and child soldier recruitment is fundamentally about our responsibility to affirm our belief in the value of human life and call on our government to promote policies that reflect our nation's core values. The Save Darfur Coalition pulled together 180 organizations, and it has been at the center of keeping grassroots constituencies informed and active. On the student side, the Genocide Intervention Network oversees the student anti-genocide organization STAND as well as the Sudan Divestment Task Force, and it helped focus young people's attention on the issue. Working with the Enough Project, these organizations were joined by many other localized groups—such as Jewish World Watch, the Massachusetts

Coalition to Save Darfur, and the San Francisco Bay Area Coalition to Save Darfur—as well as faith-based organizations—like the National Council of Churches, the National Association of Evangelicals, the American Jewish World Service, and Religious Action Center for Reform Judaism—in the quest to bring an end to the suffering of the people of Sudan.

The increasingly interconnected nature of the world means that the well-being and security of Americans are inextricably linked to the lives of people thousands of miles away. Terrorism, insurgencies, organized crime, drug trafficking, infectious diseases, environmental crises, refugee flows, and mass migrations can spill over into neighboring states, destabilizing entire regions. Our world is often like a gigantic spider web: touch one part of it and you set the whole thing trembling.

It is increasingly understood that failed states or ungoverned regions can become incubators for extremism, terrorist recruitment, and other cross-border threats. The United States cannot afford to ignore these crises. But it shouldn't ignore them anyway because achieving peace there could lead to positive spillover effects in the surrounding countries.

———

JOHN: More than anything else, it has been people's movements that have altered the course of history. When you look back at the last century of American history, and our interaction with the world, the real shifts have usually occurred in response to growing tidal waves of popular resistance or support for some kind of monumental change. So an interesting argument here is that with most of these movements, there were huge social forces arrayed against change and in favor of the status quo.

DON: Yep, all these movements faced tremendous resistance, but to varying degrees, they have succeeded. An advantage today is that we'd be hard-pressed to find anyone who would say that he or she is for child soldiers.

JOHN: We don't have a bunch of K Street lobbying firms in D.C. supporting genocide.

DON: Not openly anyway . . .

JOHN: Whoa, whaddya mean?

DON: I mean you don't have to be explicit in your "complicit." Special interests often dictate relationships among governments and/or corporations, and the result is silence or inaction in the face of some of the worst human rights crimes.

JOHN: Ahh, I see. That's true, and that is precisely why we have to recruit as many people as possible to make as much noise as possible. We can't have any illusions. This is a battle. There are forces that would use the most inhuman tactics to maintain power or to make money. You know, when we were working with some senators to introduce a bill on the Congo's conflict minerals, the electronics industry spent $15 million to try to kill the bill before it was even introduced. But all those letters and e-mails and calls from voters convinced the senators to move ahead anyway. And now we have a bunch of senators who have become champions on this issue because it is right and because they heard from their constituents that the issue matters. This is a fight. And it is winnable.

CHAPTER TWO

Enough with the Misconceptions

Africa as a Continent of Hope and Upstanders

JOHN: To have your Enough Moment, you have to know that your efforts are not in vain, that there is the potential for success. We want people to know about the success stories of countries that have transformed from seemingly hopeless cases to peaceful democracies, sometimes very quickly.

DON: Right. You want to know that you aren't throwing your efforts into a hole.

JOHN: And by telling the stories of Sierra Leone, Liberia, Angola, Mozambique, South Africa, and many others, we can demonstrate that increased activism by concerned citizens, finally combined with the right policies, can actually make a difference. In fact, activism has made a difference in so many things.

DON: It really has. Each of these conflicts was supposedly intractable, but the right combination of actions and interventions actually had an effect, moving the bar, in a very substantive way.

JOHN: So one of the things we want to do with these successful cases is to demonstrate that these issues like genocide, crimes against women, and child soldiers are not hopeless and that there are solutions.

DON: At the end of the day, let's say you convince me—if I'm Joe Public—to write this letter to my senator or attend that rally. And I make a real commitment to this cause, and I even make a donation even though I'm struggling, and I put in some energy and some time. And let's say our efforts are able to bring about a ceasefire, and the African boy in the refugee camp gets to go home, and he is able to have access to clean water, and there is a school nearby that he can go to. What's to say that the conflict isn't going to come storming back, and we aren't going to have to do this again in two years?

JOHN: That's exactly why we're writing this chapter. We need to demonstrate how the success stories don't just stop wars but actually transform societies. We want people to know that these kinds of problems are solvable and that these countries and people's plights aren't hopeless at all.

The Untold Story of Africa

There is a lingering, omnipresent phenomenon that helps paralyze individual and global responses as we contemplate what to do about Sudan and Congo. It is the widespread belief that Africa is a hopeless continent, filled with war and famine and basket-case countries marked by tribal divisions and aging dictators.

While it is true that there are still some countries in

Africa that are trapped in cycles of conflict and crisis, and this book is dealing directly with the biggest ones, the larger truth is that the majority of the continent is largely peaceful and striving to build democratic institutions and traditions. If we don't combat this perception of Africa as a hopeless continent, we will have much more trouble rallying support for our cause: ending the human rights crimes that occur within the context of the remaining conflicts, and preventing future ones.

From the headlines and the occasional television show, Africa sure *seems* hopeless. But remember the media mantra: If it bleeds, it leads. And if Hollywood's rendition of Africa were any guide, certainly we would think of Africa as a huge chasm of despair and savagery. Let's look at four movies and contrast the image being presented with the reality today of the country being portrayed. While it is positive that these kinds of movies are being made to highlight otherwise obscure crises, in the absence of more elaborate postscripts at the end of the films, as you'll see below, they can help feed stereotypes of Africa as a hopeless place:

1. **Leonardo DiCaprio stars in *Blood Diamond* (2006),** which depicts Sierra Leone as a hell on earth, with drug-crazed child soldiers who hack off people's limbs. Some of that actually happened in the 1990s and early the following decade. But it would have been good if at the end of *Blood Diamond* there had been a more elaborate postscript informing the viewer that Sierra Leone today is not only a country at peace but also a country that boasts positive economic growth rates and democratic elections that reflect the will of the people. The postscript could also have added that some of the rebel leaders who press-ganged the kids into military service and forced them to commit terrible atrocities are now facing justice for their crimes. And perhaps most importantly given the theme of the movie, the postscript could have educated

viewers that Sierra Leone's former blood diamonds are now, for the most part, clean diamonds, no longer fueling one of the most violent wars in African history.

2. **Nicholas Cage plays the lead role** in a movie called *Lord of War* (2005) about an arms dealer who sells some of his merchandise in Liberia, which is depicted as a land of savage violence that Cage's character at one point proclaims "God has forsaken." Liberia's civil war was indeed violent. But again, at the end of the film, it would have been better to add a postscript explaining that Liberia is a country now at peace. In fact, it has held democratic elections that resulted in the first elected female president—Ellen Johnson Sirleaf—in all of Africa, a president who is regularly invited to Europe and North America to lecture about how to heal divided societies. The postscript could have said that thousands of former child soldiers have gone through rehabilitation programs and that the man most responsible for the violence, the former president Charles Taylor, is now in The Hague on trial for crimes against humanity.

3. **Forrest Whitaker portrays the Ugandan dictator Idi Amin's** reign of terror in *The Last King of Scotland* (2006). Indeed, Amin was right out of central casting as one of postcolonial Africa's most murderous strongmen. But again there was no postscript at the end of the film explaining that Uganda is a country that has emerged from this period to see peace consolidated in the center and south of the country. There was no postscript explaining that the north is stabilizing now that the Lord's Resistance Army has been driven out of Uganda into the surrounding region. Without a postscript, most of the movie viewers wouldn't know about Uganda's successes with economic growth and HIV/AIDS reduction and its robust press and civil society sector. Most of Uganda has moved far beyond those dark days of Idi Amin.

4. **A certain actor by the name of Don Cheadle** portrays hotel manager-turned-rescuer Paul Rusesabagina in *Hotel Rwanda* (2004). The film realistically depicted the most dark and extreme moment in the country's history by using Paul's story. Though the film was phenomenal in educating people about the genocide, it would have been even more helpful if there had been a longer postscript at the end of the film letting the viewers know that Rwanda—a mere decade and a half after the genocide—is now a country that is for the most part at peace internally, though unresolved Rwandan issues bleed across the Congolese border and rebound negatively on the people there. A postscript could have referenced the positive, ongoing work regarding postgenocide justice and reconciliation—as well as the diversity of legislative representation, with the highest percentage of female parliamentarians in the world—helping to lay the groundwork for the possibility of a different future in Rwanda if transparency and inclusivity are stressed.

The point here is that Africa is NOT a continent of despair, or hopelessness. Scratch a little beneath the surface, and there is much hope. Most of Africa is at peace—democratizing and growing economically. To us, Africa's capacity for transformation seems limitless.

Is Africa Really that Different?

In fact, Africa is not only full of hope but its history actually isn't all that different from the rest of the world's history, which by contrast did not have twenty-four-hour cable news coverage of every problem experienced. Most African countries have been independent from European colonial rule for only fifty years or so. Let's not forget, before we judge Africa as different, that Europe fought its own wars of state formation for five centuries—from the Renaissance to World War II and the Holocaust—to determine its borders. And it still isn't finished: There is continuing instability in the Balkans and on Russia's periphery.

And where was the United States fifty years into its independence? Well, among other things there was a massive ethnic cleansing campaign against Native Americans. Look at this account of an attack by English Puritans led by John Mason in Connecticut on the Pequot Indians: "Those that escaped the fire were slaine with the sword; some hewed to peeces, others run through with their rapiers, so they were quickly dispatchte, and very few escaped. It was conceived they thus destroyed about four hundred at this time. It was a fearful sign to see them thus frying in the fyre, and the streams of blood quenching the same, and horrible was the stincke and sente thereof, but the victory seemed a sweete sacrifice."

There was also, of course, a transatlantic slave trade that led to the abduction of 30 million Africans who were sold into bondage, a phenomenon that helped catalyze America's economic juggernaut. At fifty, the United States hadn't even yet fought its own Civil War, one of the bloodiest conflicts in history.

It turns out that Africa is just going through its wars of governance and state formation at a later period in history than Europe, North America, and other continents because of the interruption of its natural historical cycle due to colonialism.

Africa's own course of state building was grossly undermined by Europe's colonization of the continent, leaving legacies of economic exploitation, slavery, and elitist governments that require much more work to overcome. Additionally, Africa has had to deal with major weapons dumping by China, Russia, and the United States and with having their tribulations catalogued on CNN for all the world to see, and judge.

And we need to tell the story of the genocide survivors of Sudan, the rape survivors of Congo, and the child soldier survivors of the Lord's Resistance Army, and tell people that it is their turn to rise now.

If we accept the notion that wars can be resolved in Africa, that Africa is not different from the rest of the world, and that Africa is full of transformative examples of hope, then the effort required to give peace a chance becomes a whole lot more viable, and even attractive.

COUNTRY UPSTANDERS:
African War to Peace Success Stories

LIBERIA

Not too long ago, to even mention Liberia was to evoke images of some of the worst atrocities in the world: drugged-up child soldiers, wide-scale use of rape as a weapon of war, and brutal battles for control of natural resources like diamonds and timber. Today, however, Liberia is at peace, having held democratic elections that brought Ellen Johnson Sirleaf to the presidency.

When Charles Taylor, a former Liberian cabinet official and escapee from a U.S. prison, invaded northwest Liberia in 1989 with a few hundred fighters, he was quickly able to mobilize much of the country against the regime of a U.S.-supported dictator named Master Sergeant Samuel Doe.

Taylor's invasion was the beginning of years of brutal conflict. He broke chilling new ground in his use of children as weapons of war, whom he would drug, indoctrinate, and use to commit brutal atrocities. Pro- and anti-Taylor factions perpetrated horrific atrocities on the civilian population while fighting for control of Liberia's substantial natural resources. Eventually, anti-Taylor elements began to coalesce. These rebel factions brought additional pressure on Taylor, as did his indictment for war crimes in June 2003 by the Special Court for Sierra Leone—a tribunal jointly administered by the United Nations and the government of Sierra Leone. Facing mounting international pressure to step down and courageous internal human rights organizing, often led by women (see the extraordinary 2008 documentary film *Pray the Devil Back to Hell*), Taylor departed for exile in Nigeria on August 11, 2003. A week later the factions signed a peace agreement that paved the way for a transitional government and a UN peacekeeping mission. A two-year transitional period cleared the way for disarmament, the return of refugees and displaced persons, and national elections.

It was never predetermined that Liberia would successfully emerge from war. A heroic combination of goodwill, good governance, and good luck helped Liberia to manage its transition. Donor governments like the United States brought significant sums of aid to the table, thanks in no small part to an active and organized Liberian Diaspora community that effectively pressured Capitol Hill. Fed up with the looting of reconstruction aid by the fighting factions, international donors devised a new system to administer aid transparently, putting international experts and respected Liberian civil servants jointly in control of those parts of the government that had been funnels for corruption. After Liberia's first free elections, Ellen Johnson Sirleaf, a former World Bank official who had supported Taylor but was later imprisoned by him, became the first democratically elected female president of an African state.

ELLEN JOHNSON SIRLEAF, LIBERIAN UPSTANDER

President Ellen Johnson Sirleaf is known in Liberia as "the Iron Lady" for her iron will and determination, qualities that are well reflected in her career. Johnson Sirleaf became Liberia's first female minister of finance in 1979, just before Doe's coup. She avoided the fate that met most of Liberia's ministers when Doe executed thirteen of them on the beach after seizing power. Johnson Sirleaf spent the Doe years in and out of Liberia, with stints at the World Bank, Citibank, and the United Nations. But in 1985, when she turned her criticism toward Doe and his associates, she was imprisoned and threatened with rape. She went into exile for more than a decade.

When Charles Taylor launched his assault on Liberia in 1991, Johnson Sirleaf initially supported him, a decision that would prove controversial. But she went on to oppose Taylor, and she later contested the 1997 elections, coming in second. Once he became president, Taylor charged her with treason, forcing her once again into exile. As one supporter put it to the BBC, "It would have been much easier for her to quit politics and sit at home like others have done, but she has never given up."[2]

Following her own election, she pledged to bring the "motherly sensitivity and emotion to the presidency" needed to heal the problems that plague Liberia after years of violence and warfare.[3] She has continued to fight graft by firing corrupt officials and demanding transparency in contracts, and she has appointed experienced women to run the ministries of finance, justice, and commerce.

SIERRA LEONE

Children as young as eight being forcibly conscripted by rebels; women getting their arms cut off because they voted for the wrong presidential candidate; diamonds being traded for guns to perpetuate war. This was Sierra Leone, a small, coastal country in west Africa, about half the size of Illinois, in the 1990s. When all was said and done, over 50,000 people had been killed, and 4,000 people had their arms or legs cut off by rebels. And yet nearly ten years later, Sierra Leone is at peace. The warlords that were behind its conflict are either on trial or are deceased, and its people are picking up their lives to rebuild. How did this happen?

Sierra Leone's war lasted ten years, and its main victims were the civilian population. In 1991 when the war began, there was large-scale opposition to the government because of deep corruption, but the rebel Revolutionary United Front (RUF) that sprung up quickly became unpopular itself. Rather than mobilize popular support, its two main leaders—ex-junior army officer Foday Sankoh and his former colleague, warlord rebel leader and future president of Liberia Charles Taylor—were a deadly duo, intent on gaining personal power and monetary gain for themselves at any cost. Sometimes in collaboration with units from the national army, the RUF raided villages to loot for food and goods, and they killed uncooperative civilians in very brutal ways, such as using machetes to behead local chiefs.

Far from mindless violence, these were deliberate, rational strategies used by the RUF's leaders to gain power. The brutal killings and raids—called "population-clearing guerrilla tactics" by military strategists—spread fear like wildfire, causing civilians to flee from their homes in droves. One in five people in Sierra Leone—1 million in total—became homeless as a result of the war, either forced to flee to other areas of the country or to neighboring Guinea or the Ivory Coast. (One of those 1 million was Ishmael Beah, the extraordinary author of *A Long Way Gone*.) The RUF was then able to operate out of the newly emptied villages and stage attacks on the next area.

Finally, the international community, led by the United Kingdom, the former colonial power, decided to invest seriously in resolving the crisis. The keys were an international campaign to deal with the blood diamonds fueling the war and a focused military strategy that understood the motivations of the rebel leaders. In addition, the United Nations sent in a large peacekeeping force of 17,000 troops. But in May 2000, 500 of its soldiers were taken hostage, and the RUF began a last-gasp invasion of the capital again.

Great Britain, bolstered by a cacophony of protests and shocking CNN-aired footage from the war zone, responded by sending in troops who secured Freetown in May 2000 and began a massive retraining and restructuring of the Sierra Leone army. With operational and planning support from the British troops, the Sierra Leonean army then launched several campaigns to disarm the RUF, and these campaigns were ultimately successful. Importantly, the United Kingdom and other donors also began a ten-year program to help reconstruct Sierra Leone, committing significant aid to roads, police restructuring, and other efforts to rebuild the country's infrastructure, thereby ensuring that its investment in peace would quickly be put to good use.

The British intervention worked because it was bolstered by three other initiatives:

- *Local activism:* Sierra Leonean civil society played a critical role that has often gone unmentioned. The community leaders, women's groups, and chiefs provided accountability to the warlords.
- *Sanctions:* UN sanctions on blood diamonds as well as

on timber and travel by the RUF's top leaders helped financially squeeze the rebels at a key point in 1999 and 2000. The RUF's demise accelerated when the UN Security Council sanctions were imposed on Charles Taylor. Further, RUF leader Foday Sankoh was captured in 2000 after being ousted because of financial arguments with other RUF leaders, in large part a result of the sanctions.

- *Justice:* The Special Court for Sierra Leone was set up to prosecute those most responsible for the atrocities. It has had a very successful track record and has indicted thirteen of the top militia leaders, including Charles Taylor, who went on trial at the end of 2009.

Overall, Sierra Leone remains at peace today, a remarkable success story in which the transformation from atrocities to reconciliation occurred very rapidly. There is no question that the country is still threatened by continuing corruption, illiteracy, and poverty, and it is the poorest country in the world, according to the United Nations.[4] But thanks to a concerted, coordinated effort by international and local Upstanders, people are no longer under threat of having their villages burned or their children abducted by a rebel group.

For more on how the blood diamonds movement helped end the crisis in Sierra Leone, go to www.enoughmoment.org.

SORIOUS SAMURA, SIERRA LEONEAN UPSTANDER

It's as if the war in Sierra Leone had its own Enough Moment. With the country spiraling out of control after nearly ten years of war, the rebels were about to invade the capital. Governments around the world were debating what to do in early 2000. In the midst of the crisis, one brave Sierra

Leonean thought he could change the debate and catalyze serious peacemaking. Sorious Samura was a documentary filmmaker living in London, but he decided to give up his safe haven from the war and go back to his country.

After seeing footage of individuals filming the war in Kosovo, Samura packed his new video camera and flew to Freetown, Sierra Leone's hot, humid capital city. "If only people could see what is happening in Sierra Leone, then they'd realize they have to do even more than what they did in Kosovo. I thought I should do something, to go back and film." Almost immediately after touching down, the rebels invaded Freetown, and he was trapped in a building. But he couldn't be dissuaded from heading out to find the facts. "I said to myself, 'If I stay in here, I'm possibly a dead man. If I go out there, I'm possibly dead too.' Rather than stay in the house and die here, I decided to go out."

He started to film killings in the street, and then he found himself in the rebel RUF camp and he managed to shoot for three days. Filming in the rebel compounds was unprecedented and extremely dangerous for Samura, but he went on. "These boys in the RUF, they were permanently drunk or on drugs. They were totally unpredictable. I walked into the middle of a humiliating rape, and they told me to clap. If I didn't, they would have killed me. But they allowed me to film many things which had never gotten out in the Western media."

When Samura returned to London, media outlets didn't want to air his tapes. The footage was too shocking for a British or American audience to bear, they said. But in the end, his message was too powerful, and CNN agreed to air his documentary *Cry Freetown* in February 2000. Immediately after the broadcast, Samura was invited to brief the United Nations. The United Kingdom intervened shortly thereafter with a powerful military and political presence that was a catalyst for ending the war. "I know that my footage wasn't the only thing that led to the end of the conflict, but I hope it helped," said Samura humbly.

MOZAMBIQUE

In 1977, just two years after the country's independence from Portugal, Mozambique entered a brutal civil war that ravaged the country for the next sixteen years. The war was largely a struggle between the government of Mozambique, supported by the Soviet Union, and rebels supported by the apartheid regime in South Africa and white-ruled Rhodesia (now Zimbabwe). South Africa and Rhodesia were looking to ensure white minority rule in southern Africa, and they spent large sums of money to destabilize Mozambique by supporting the rebel group Renamo.

Renamo committed horrific atrocities against civilian populations, mutilating victims and leading Mozambique to have one of the highest amputee rates in the world. Renamo set standards in human cruelty later matched by the Lord's Resistance Army, Darfur's Janjaweed, and the genocidal Rwandan militias. By the time the Mozambique war ended in 1992, roughly 1 million people had been killed, and 5 million had been forced to flee from their homes. The economic costs reached $15 billion, an enormous amount of money for one of the poorest places on earth.

In mid-1990 President Joaquim Chissano began negotiations with Renamo, looking to end his country's civil war. Chissano offered major concessions to the Renamo fighters, including space and assurances for Renamo as a political party, the ability to join the country's army, and, perhaps most remarkably, forgiveness for crimes committed. By the end of 1990, Chissano was able to lead the process of enacting of new constitution that enabled a multiparty system and an open market. President Chissano's negotiations led to the 1992 Rome General Peace Accords that officially ended the Mozambican Civil War.

In 1994, President Chissano won Mozambique's first multiparty elections. By mid-1995, more than 1.7 million refugees who had fled famine and war had returned. Another estimated 4 million of the people displaced within Mozambique had returned home. President Chissano was reelected in 1999, and he decided to step down at the end of this term despite the fact that the constitution allowed him a third term. Since leaving office, Chissano has been a negotiator in other peace processes in Africa.

Mozambique had one of the highest growth rates in the world from 1994 to the present, with growth rates consistently averaging between 8 and 11 percent annually. The country has no oil and no mining, but it does have extremely good governance and the rule of law, despite its emerging from a deadly war so recently.

GRAÇA MACHEL, MOZAMBICAN UPSTANDER

For human rights advocate Graça Machel, life has always been about "try[ing] to fight for the dignity and the freedom of my own people."[5] Machel grew up in a poor Mozambican peasant family, and she later studied in Lisbon and trained as a freedom fighter in the Mozambican Liberation Front (Frelimo).[6] After the tragic death in 1986 of her then husband, President Samora Machel, she dedicated her life to the cause of education, especially for women and young girls, and later to solving conflicts around the world.

In 1994 the secretary general of the United Nations asked Machel to undertake a study of the impact of armed conflict on children. The *Machel Report*, released in 1996, concluded that the inability to defend children's rights "represents a fundamental crisis of our civilization." Her report proposed practical ways to stem the involvement of children in armed conflict. Machal is also a member of The Elders, an independent group of global leaders that includes her husband Nelson Mandela, Archbishop Desmond Tutu, former Irish president Mary Robinson, former UN Secretary General Kofi Annan, and Jimmy Carter. In this role she has been involved in a number of peacemaking efforts around the world, including those in Sudan, Zimbabwe, and Burma. Her latest initiative is to sponsor the education of underprivileged women in South Africa with a scholarship program. Humble as ever, she has said, "Of course, what I'm doing is only a drop in the ocean, but I feel I have to do something."[7]

ANGOLA

In Angola, a brutal civil war began in the winter of 1974, and it lasted for almost three decades. In total, fighting killed almost 2 million people and forced almost 4 million to leave their homes. Soldiers planted over 10 million landmines—many of which were manufactured in the United States—throughout Angola's central highlands. The war created armies of child soldiers.[8] Driven by the exploitation of conflict diamonds and oil, Angola's crisis was intimately tied to natural resources. However, the end of the conflict diamonds trade paved the way for lasting peace. Angola remains imperfect, but the story of its journey from war to peace is a testament to those tireless advocates in Angola and around the world who spent decades working for change.

War in Angola came in the wake of the colonial Portuguese authorities' withdrawal in 1974. Fighting was bloody and pitted neighbors against one another. Child soldiers were recruited on all sides and fought on the front lines for decades.[9] Rufino Satumbo was eighteen when he was drafted into the army of the main rebel group, UNITA, about which he narrates a typical day:

> When we went into the villages, sometimes we set fire to them, while the people we knew to sympathize with the MPLA were killed. . . . [T]he women were for the leaders, who picked them out in the villages. They chose girls of 12, 13, 14, and 15 years old; those who didn't come by themselves were tied up. . . . [M]any starved of hunger because the nourishment was not good.[10]

UNITA's leader Jonas Savimbi carefully cultivated an image that appealed to American "Cold Warriors" intent on fighting Soviet power abroad,[11] and the enormous value he placed on his relationship with the United States is well documented. Between 1986 and 1991, the United States provided UNITA with an estimated $250 million dollars.[12]

Angola's natural resource wealth lay at the center of the violence throughout the brutal war. The government controlled the massive oil reserves, and UNITA's trade in conflict diamonds was critical to financing the group's predations. Between 1992 and 1994, UNITA made an estimated $3.7 billion from diamonds.[13] Most diamonds were smuggled into what is now the Congo (then called Zaire) and purchased by the company De Beers.

It took Savimbi's death in a firefight and the end of the Angola's conflict diamonds trade to stop the violence.

Today, Angola is becoming a stable African regional power. It has surpassed Nigeria as the continent's largest oil producer. Angola still has major challenges to overcome, such as endemic corruption and lack of democracy, but the country has hope and more stability than ever. The cycle of violence and chaos, which was intimately tied to the trade in diamonds throughout the conflict, is ending, and Angolans are slowly but surely rebuilding their lives.

SOUTH AFRICA

More than fifteen years after Nelson Mandela was elected president of South Africa, the awe-inspiring end of the apartheid era is beginning to recede into history. Although South Africa never experienced a full-scale civil war, the process leading to the end of apartheid could have led to one.

Beginning in 1948, South Africa's minority white government introduced the racist system known as *apartheid*, decreeing that black and white people should live separately and tearing apart the fabric of South African society to enforce this discriminatory system. Through a series of infamous laws, the government uprooted hundreds of thousands of people. Resistance began with the African National Congress (ANC) party, originally formed to protect the rights of mine workers but which shifted gears to oppose the ruling National Party and promote equality through mass protest. The ANC's Youth League was started by activists like Nelson Mandela and Walter Sisulu. When the government banned the ANC in 1961, its members went underground and adopted violent opposition.

The apartheid regime successfully stifled resistance for much of the 1960s and 1970s, opening fire on peaceful protestors at Sharpeville in 1960, arresting Nelson Mandela in 1962, and gunning down student protestors in Soweto, a township near Johannesburg, in 1976. But the violence and oppression of the apartheid government, which brutally cracked down on domestic resistance and also lashed out at its neighbors, funding violence in Angola, Zimbabwe, and Mozambique, contributed to its growing international isolation, as much of the world recoiled from the regime's racism. Even the United States, which had pursued a policy of "constructive engagement" with the South African government as an ally during the Cold War under the Reagan administration, eventually came around to the objective of economically isolating the regime. In 1986, Congress passed the Comprehensive Anti-Apartheid Act over President Reagan's veto, which imposed comprehensive economic and diplomatic sanctions on the apartheid regime.

Within South Africa, elements from across South African society—including student groups, trade unions, and faith-based communities—developed new means of resistance, including school boycotts and industrial sabotage. These tactics increasingly threatened the economic base of the ruling party. In 1990, F. W. de Klerk became prime minister, and he committed to ending the apartheid system. On February 11 of that year he released Nelson Mandela from prison and opened a series of negotiations culminating in South Africa's first democratically held elections in April 1994.

South Africans developed an unprecedented and influential institution: the Truth and Reconciliation Commission. Chaired by Archbishop Desmond Tutu, the Truth and Reconciliation Commission heard testimony from victims of political violence on all sides, and it allowed perpetrators to admit what they had done and request amnesty from prosecution. The commission is frequently held up as a model for similar reconciliation processes around the world. However, of the similar commissions established elsewhere, few have been perceived to be as inclusive or successful as South Africa's.

Although South Africa continues to struggle against severe social challenges, including an HIV/AIDS epidemic, economic inequalities, and rising crime rates, it has nonetheless managed to institute sound democratic practices and significant economic reforms, as well as carve out a leadership role on the African continent.

DESMOND TUTU, SOUTH AFRICAN UPSTANDER

Archbishop Desmond Tutu has spent most of his life fighting for racial equality, justice, and peace, a fight that began in Johannesburg, where he grew up. When he was about twelve, Tutu and his mother, a housekeeper and cook, passed a white man in the streets of Johannesburg. The man was wearing priest's clothing, and he greeted his mother politely. Tutu expressed his shock at seeing a white man greet a working-class black woman. Tutu formed a relationship with the priest who had greeted his mother, and, from then on, the priest played a significant and formative role in Tutu's life.

Tutu joined the Anglican priesthood in 1960. Congregations at this time were mostly white, but he was determined to speak out against the injustices faced by black Africans. Tutu became increasingly outspoken about apartheid while simultaneously pleading for reconciliation. After the end of apartheid, Tutu went on to chair the Truth and Reconciliation Commission. "The Arch," as his friends affectionately call him, has continued to speak out forcefully against injustice throughout the world and to work for peace both as an individual and as a member of The Elders. His voice is a beacon of truth that lights a path for those working for human rights in zones of conflict and dictatorship around the world.

OTHER AFRICAN UPSTANDERS

The heroic actions of many African Upstanders go unmarked and unnoticed by the rest of the world. But the work of some of these Upstanders who grace the world stage cry out for recognition due to the enormity of their achievements, and their courage.

KOFI ANNAN, GHANAIAN UPSTANDER

Although he couldn't have known it at the time, Kofi Annan's preparation for his position as the seventh secretary general of the United Nations began as a young boy in Ghana, where he grew up observing his grandfathers and his uncle, all of whom served as tribal chiefs, and his father, who was governor of Ghana's Asante province. Annan completed studies in Ghana and the United States, and he worked with the World Health Organization (WHO) and the Economic Commission for Africa in Addis Ababa before returning to Ghana in 1974 to find that the country had become politically unstable and rife with military coups. According to Annan, "I wanted to make a contribution to Ghana but I found [myself] constantly fighting the military, so I went back to the UN." Annan returned to the United Nations, and he was later chosen to be the UN secretary general, a post he took up in 1997.

As UN secretary general, Annan presided over peacekeeping operations around the world, and he advocated for increased assistance for developing countries fighting the HIV/AIDS pandemic. After his term as UN secretary general, Annan continued his peacemaking efforts. He has played an integral role in spearheading peace efforts, especially in Africa. In the aftermath of a disputed presidential election in Kenya that had left more than 1,000 people dead, Annan led successful mediation efforts that prevented the killings and rioting from escalating into an even deadlier war. He continued to stay involved after the deal was brokered in order to monitor its progress and assist with reforming Kenya's constitution and institutions.

International mediators who watched the peace deal unfold agreed that the unexpected resolution was a testament to Annan's diplomatic skills and the respect he commands across the globe. In the summer of 2009, when the Kenyan leaders hadn't lived up to their pledges on accountability, he presented a list of names of war crimes suspects to the chief prosecutor of the International Criminal Court, demonstrating that justice must be a part of any lasting peace.

BETTY BIGOMBE, UGANDAN UPSTANDER

In 2004, Betty Bigombe was a consultant with the World Bank, working on development in African countries, when she started a journey to rejoin the fight for peace in her native Uganda. She remembers having her own Enough Moment after seeing a television broadcast that reported that an LRA massacre in Uganda had left 259 people dead.

It was at that point in time that Bigombe decided, " 'No, it can't go on anymore. I can't stay here anymore. . . . People are dying. Children are not going to school.' So I decided to go right back and take it on."[14]

Bigombe worked tirelessly for the next eighteen months as the chief mediator between the government of Uganda and the LRA, this time as an impartial broker rather than a government minister, a post she had held twenty years before during her first efforts at bringing an end to the LRA insurgency. She arranged the first ever face-to-face meeting between the Ugandan government and LRA. She then helped create a multipronged peace effort that included traditional leaders, women, youth, and the international community in a dramatic push to end the twenty-year-old war. This initiative helped lay the foundation for the peace talks between the government and the LRA held in Juba, southern Sudan, that resulted in a final proposed deal that LRA leader Joseph Kony ultimately decided not to sign. Although no peace was forged, the international community united around the understanding that military operations would have to be undertaken to stop the LRA, since Kony clearly had no interest in peace.

Bigombe has the true craft of a peacemaker, trying to walk in each side's shoes and base negotiations on this thorough, deeper understanding. She continues to work on issues of mediation, peace building, transitional justice, and the empowerment of youth in northern Uganda, and she has provided support to the Juba peace talks. In addition, she works with international donors and local NGOs to equip the people of northern Uganda with tools for achieving sustainable peace.

WANGARI MAATHAI, KENYAN UPSTANDER

Growing up in rural Kenya, Wangari Maathai pursued education in her home country and later the United States, eventually returning to Kenya as a professor of veterinary medicine. Throughout the course of her work, Maathai was profoundly affected by her exposure to her homeland's ills: endemic ethnic patronage, discrimination against women, and shocking changes wrought on the Kenyan landscape by environmental degradation. Rather than viewing the environment, women's rights, and politics as separate problems, Maathai understood the interconnected nature of these issues as they related to everyday life: "I listened to women saying that deforestation was forcing them to walk farther and farther to find firewood for cooking, that they couldn't grow enough on depleted soil to feed their families, that they had no money to buy food."[15]

Maathai soon developed the idea that would later spawn a movement: planting trees. The Green Belt Movement, which began in 1977, was a grassroots effort to reduce poverty and promote environmental conservation by planting trees. The movement would go on to plant more than 20 million trees on farms, schools, and church compounds in Kenya. The movement's supporters built hundreds of tree nurseries and provided more than 100,000 jobs, mostly to women. In 1986, the Pan African Green Belt Network took the movement across the continent, launching similar initiatives in Tanzania, Uganda, Malawi, Lesotho, Ethiopia, and Zimbabwe.

At home, Maathai encountered increasing hostility from the Kenyan government of longtime ruler Daniel Moi:

> *The former Government was completely against the Green Belt Movement and our work of mobilizing women into groups that could produce seedlings and plant them. The Government was also against the idea of educating and informing women. It didn't want citizens to know that sometimes the enemy of the forests and the environment was the Government itself, which was supposed to be protecting the environment. If citizens saw the linkages, they would put pressure on the Government to improve governance, to create democratic space, to help them protect their environment, and to be responsible managers on citizens' behalf. When we were beaten up, it was because we were telling the Government not to interfere with the forests. We were confronted by armed police and guards who physically removed us from the forests as we sought to protect these green spaces from commercial exploitation. Sometimes in the process we got hurt, arrested or thrown into jail.*[16]

Since winning the Nobel Peace Prize in 2004, Maathai has become even more directly involved in peacemaking, following the outbreak of postelection violence in Kenya in 2007, speaking out strongly on behalf of reconciliation and accountability.

LAZARO SUMBEIYWO, KENYAN UPSTANDER

Lazaro Sumbeiywo was the chief of staff of the Kenyan army, not the typical background for a peace mediator. But in 2001, he was named the lead mediator for the north-south war in Sudan. Sumbeiywo immersed himself in Sudan's notoriously intricate peace process, demonstrating the patience and tirelessness crucial to being an effective mediator. It took more than six months just to organize the first meeting between the parties, a meeting that was followed by a series of disagreements and setbacks.

Nonetheless, Sumbeiywo persevered, and his approach laid the groundwork for talks in Machakos, Kenya, which produced a crucial breakthrough: a single negotiating text (this was a point that Sumbeiywo learned from Jimmy Carter, who used the same approach at Camp David). The result was the Machakos Protocol signed on July 20, 2002, which granted the south the right to a referendum on self-determination following a six-year interim period, dictated that sharia law would remain in force only in the north, and provided the framework for the future final peace deal, which was finally struck in January 2005. Sumbeiywo remains modest about his achievements and attributes much to his faith in God and what he learned from his father, a chief in the rural village of Iten in Kenya's Rift Valley: "He used to settle a lot of conflict. I learnt a lot from him, not from formal teaching so much as simply watching him work."[17]

CHAPTER THREE

Saying Enough to Genocide

DON: So we are talking about stopping genocide, a concept against which there isn't any real opposition, and yet strangely there still is a shocking lack of success when it comes to the twenty-first century's first genocide: Darfur. What has been tried so far doesn't seem to be moving the ball very far forward at all. And although the Janjaweed militias aren't burning villages much anymore, because most of the villages they wanted to burn are ashes now, we are still talking about millions of people displaced from their ancestral homes, dying from diseases they shouldn't be, being raped in appalling ways and numbers, and being completely disenfranchised. They've been driven out of their homes, and they have lost family members. They have no feeling of security or safety, and they live under the thumb of a dictator who's been indicted as a war criminal. The Arab nations are really doing nothing, and no one has truly come forward to correct the situation, even though the world collectively is saying this cannot stand.

JOHN: Yes, there are definitely reasons why Darfur has continued to churn. There hasn't yet been an Enough Moment for Darfur because although we had one-half of the equation in place—the people's movement—the other half of the equation—smart policies—were nowhere in evidence. You gotta have both for success. The intention was right. President Bush was personally invested, and I think he was personally affected by the large-scale citizens' movement that was urging him to do something about the suffering. But he was crushingly undermined by a few officials in his administration who pursued the wrong policy track, totally at variance with the issues and history at play in Darfur and with how previous success stories actually worked. Now we have Obama in the same position. When I met with him in the White House in the spring of 2009, he said all the right things and evinced a clarity about what needed to be done that was extraordinary. Then his envoy on Sudan promptly goes out and undermines so much of what Obama had told us. Very frustrating.

DON: The years between 2004 and 2007 were especially remarkable to watch. All these people were asserting that the crisis in Darfur must be brought to an end: President Bush, Secretary Rice, the U.S. Congress, a significant portion of NATO, the European Union, President Sarkozy, Prime Minister Blair, the Arab League, the African Union, the United Nations. All of these leaders were saying that Darfur is a horror, whether they used the "g-word" or not. How could we still be here today?

JOHN: The most remarkable thing was the size of the movement that formed so quickly about a place, Darfur, that no one had ever heard of before. We have seen huge rallies, frankly unprecedented, in New York and Washington. Our first book got to the top five on the bestseller list after a number of publishers had passed on it because they said there was no market for an issue like this. Crazy. And your film *Darfur Now* came out in the theaters, while Clooney's movie *Sand and Sorrow* racked up great ratings on HBO. There is seemingly endless positive celebrity involvement and strident leadership from members of Congress. President Obama then gets elected on a platform that includes pretty aggressive statements from him, Vice President Biden, and Secretary of State Clinton about what they would do about Sudan if elected.

If someone would have told us a couple years ago, as we sat down to write our first book, that all these things were going to happen . . .

DON: We'd have said, "Wow, this is great. There surely won't be a need for a second book."

JOHN: I mean, how could this NOT succeed? How do we even react and respond to that as participants and observers?

DON: Well, it's obviously beyond frustrating. There seemed to be a momentum that was hurtling toward a lasting solution that we were just a small part of. And then there was the International Criminal Court's indictment of Bashir right on the heels of Obama's taking office. If that wasn't the moment of opportunity, I don't know what would be. But the lack of support for that indictment was remarkable. It suddenly felt like there was only one person out there, Ocampo the ICC's chief prosecutor, and he was looking around, and nobody was responding to this call. It's very frustrating. And you find yourself asking, "What is it going to take for the people of Darfur—such as the Fur, Masalit, and Zaghawa—to get some real justice and some protection?"

JOHN: Maybe we need another *Hotel Rwanda*. A "Hotel Darfur" or something. *Blood Diamond* sure put that story on the map.

DON: I carry around ideas for scripts, plays. And when I bring it up, if I have an idea, the reaction is always blah blah blah blah blah. Somehow it kinda went outta fashion.

JOHN: We gotta bring it back into fashion, and we can't quit until there is a lasting solution.

Genocide

As Samantha Power explains in her book *A Problem from Hell: America in the Age of Genocide,* before 1948, the crime of genocide had no name and no definition. In 1948, in the aftermath of World War II, a fledgling and shell-shocked United Nations passed the Genocide Convention, which established the legal definition of genocide as targeting a group of people for total or partial destruction on the basis of their identity, whether racial, national, ethnic, or religious.

But legal documents and international conventions are only one aspect of the tragic story of genocide in our time. There are complex reasons why genocide has happened and continues to occur. And these factors can be ignited by any number of triggers, with horrific consequences—an estimated 1.7 million people dead in Cambodia, more than 800,000 dead in Rwanda, and more than 300,000 dead and 3 million more people displaced in Darfur. But one of the most chilling themes in this disturbing history of genocide is the undeniable failure of the international community to act to *end* them, and to end the suffering of the people who are targeted.

The Genocide in Darfur, Sudan

Sudan is the largest country in Africa, and it has been torn apart by conflict since its independence in 1956. One key dynamic has been at the heart of every one of Sudan's current and past conflicts, and it is a root cause of the widespread suffering that Sudan's people have endured: the hoarding of wealth and power by ruling elites in the capital, Khartoum.

The Sudanese government has been ruled since 1989 with an iron fist by a president who, in March 2009, became the first sitting head of state in the world to be charged with war crimes and crimes against humanity by the International Criminal Court. President Omar al-Bashir's government has at various times during its brutal reign in Sudan targeted particular ethnic groups for attack and starvation, supported militias who use sexual violence and slave raiding as weapons of war in these campaigns, and directed proxy militias to destroy villages and force people from their homes.

And it has evolved from a scorched-earth military campaign to a low-intensity conflict marked by sexual violence, aid cut-offs, and growing levels of displacement. As in other mass death crises, the vast majority of mortality in Darfur has been due to diseases and malnutrition directly resulting from the displacement caused by the village burnings of 2003 to 2005.

To accomplish its task, the Sudanese regime armed and organized the Arab militias collectively known as the Janjaweed. The Janjaweed are Darfur's Ku Klux Klan. The regime knew that the Janjaweed would be far more ruthless and draconian than their own army, and they gave the militias instructions to burn, loot, and kill anything or anyone in their path. Like the KKK today in America, the Janjaweed represent only a very small percentage of the most extreme racial sentiment in Sudan. But they have enormous firepower, courtesy of the Sudan government. And they have gone about their work with deadly efficiency. They have burned over 2,000 villages to the ground. This was not just a divide-and-conquer operation. It was divide-and-destroy.

Maintaining Power by Any Means Necessary

The strategy was to drain the water to catch the fish: the old-est counterinsurgency strategy known to humanity. The re-gime targeted three ethnic groups: the Fur, Zaghawa, and Masalit. We often hear that the rebels are the main problem in Darfur. There is no question that the multitude of Darfu-rian rebel factions are some postapocalyptic version of the keystone cops. Some have stolen from humanitarians, raided villages, and stonewalled peace efforts. But understand the context. Since the rebellion erupted in 2003, the Khartoum regime has systematically bought off certain rebel leaders as Benedict Arnolds and used them to attack other rebel groups and rival ethnic communities, spurring cycles of intra-Darfur violence that are usually labeled "anarchy" by diplomats visit-ing Darfur for the day. Continuing support by the regime for the Janjaweed militias has further stoked inter-communal fires, and it has led many Darfurian armed groups to fight neighbors or rivals rather than the government, playing right into the regime's hands and leading to a phenomenon of war-lordism among some of Darfur's rebel leaders.

The officials in power are getting rich from the oil money, and any threat to their absolute authority elicits an over-whelming response. They will maintain power by any means available to them. It is megalomaniacal, murderous behavior, but it is not irrational or random. And now, years later, the sands of the Sahara Desert have swallowed much of the evi-dence of their horrific crimes.

To this day, millions of Darfuris have yet to return to their homes because insecurity and instability reign in the places they once called home, and many of their lands are occupied by government-supported Arab groups. And at the time of this writing, ominous signs are emerging from southern

Sudan pointing to a return to these same divide-and-destroy tactics that the ruling party in Khartoum used to such deadly effect in the south during the 1990s.

The ruling National Congress Party has been responsible directly or indirectly for the deaths of over two and a half million Sudanese civilians in Darfur and the south. If one actually reads the relevant international conventions, one could conclude that the genocide is not over for those millions of Darfurians still homeless from earlier attacks and facing targeted rapes and aid cut-offs based on their identity.

If you're looking for the root cause of the problem in Sudan, you have to go to the ruling party headquarters in Khartoum to find it. Until there is a willingness to deal firmly with a genocidal regime, then Sudan's cycle of deadly conflict will continue.

The U.S. Response to Darfur

As has been the case in its response to other genocides globally, the United States' involvement has been too little and too late. The Bush administration lurched back and forth between intensifying cooperation with the Sudanese government on counterterrorism, strong engagement in support of negotiating—but not then of implementing—a peace deal in southern Sudan, and feckless diplomatic efforts on Darfur. Without an integrated all-Sudan strategy, the Darfur crisis has continued to burn, with total impunity for its architects.

During the 2008 presidential campaign, Hillary Clinton, John McCain, Joe Biden, Mike Huckabee, Barack Obama, and the other candidates battled each other over many issues, but on the issue of Darfur, the candidates were in lockstep agreement. In May 2008, Clinton, McCain, and Obama declared in a remarkably clear joint statement: "We wish to make clear to the Sudanese government that on this moral issue of tremendous importance, there is no divide between us." On the stump, the three talked tough, pledging to bring real pressure to bear on the Sudanese government and help deploy UN peacekeepers to join the faltering African Union mission.

"We can't say 'never again' and then allow it to happen again," Obama said of Darfur during the campaign. "And as president of the United States, I don't intend to abandon people or turn a blind eye to slaughter."

After Obama's victory, Darfur activists watched the beginnings of a veritable human rights dream team fall into place. Representing Obama at the United Nations would be Susan Rice, a former assistant secretary of state for African affairs under President Clinton. Rice had experienced her own Enough Moment as a midlevel White House staffer during the Rwandan genocide in 1994, when she watched as 800,000 Tutsis and moderate Hutus were exterminated in cold blood—and the Clinton administration stood by and did nothing. Now, from her perch in New York, she swore: "If I ever faced such a crisis again, I would come down on the side of dramatic action, going down in flames if that was required."[18]

Vice President Biden brought a rich legislative résumé to the mix and harsh words on the campaign trail. During the vice presidential debate, he called for a no-fly zone in Darfur to stop the aerial bombing, similar to the no-fly zone in Iraq that protected the Kurds and Shiites after the first Gulf War. Biden's position was more strident than those of the majority of Darfur activists and advocacy organizations. "I don't have the stomach for genocide when it comes to Darfur," he said during the vice presidential debate.

Secretary of State Clinton was also a leading voice on Darfur during her tenure in the Senate. She advocated frequently for a no-fly zone and other measures that would go far beyond current policy.

On Obama's National Security Council staff would be Gayle Smith and Samantha Power, two of the leading voices in the anti-genocide movement. Other human rights champions were spread throughout the administration, including Harold Koh, Eric Schwartz, Melanne Verveer, Tony Blinken, Mike Posner, and David Pressman.

Of course, a few anti-genocide warriors sprinkled around the executive branch doesn't guarantee action. After a lengthy delay, multiple congressional entreaties, and even an urgent visit from George Clooney to the White House, President Obama finally chose his Sudan envoy: Scott Gration. A former Air Force major general, Gration's boosters had a clean and plausible set of talking points. He had grown up in East Africa, the son of missionaries, and he spoke Swahili (though Swahili is not spoken in Sudan). As a military man, he might add a measure of gravitas to negotiations and command the respect of the Khartoum government. And as an advisor to the president, his calls back to Washington from the field were more likely to be answered.

However, a number of high-profile miscues and disputes ensued throughout 2009, as General Gration began articulating positions that directly contradicted the previous words and pledges of Obama, Clinton, and Biden. A slow-burn Sudan policy review had been creeping along within the bureaucracy, so Gration moved into the vacuum with some of his contrarian opinions, damaging the clarity of the president's pledges.

But this wasn't just an internal U.S. policy debate about policy toward one country. President Obama, like President Bush before him, had called Darfur an ongoing genocide. The policy on Sudan would have global ramifications because it was the president's first chance to articulate his policy on responding to genocide.

Twenty years of empirical evidence have demonstrated

that it has been sustained pressure and the credible threat of meaningful sticks that had previously led the Sudanese government to make compromises and change its behavior. For example, a diverse set of meaningful pressures combined with deeper engagement had led directly to the north-south peace deal, the end of government-sponsored slave raiding in the south, and the diminishment of the role of the regime in supporting international terrorist organizations. Now, with Obama, Clinton, Rice, and Biden, we hoped there would be swift and decisive action based on this clear and compelling evidence of cause and effect in the past. Instead, the president's envoy argued the opposite position, and the administration lost its first year and a half in terms of its clear direction on a Sudan policy consistent with Obama's campaign rhetoric.

Why the World Hasn't Stopped the Darfur Crisis—Yet

Sudan is a unique country. We run right smack into three of the great global issues of our time when trying to understand why the response to Darfur has not been appropriately potent: Iraq, counterterrorism, and energy security.

- *Iraq:* Coincidentally, the war in Darfur exploded at the same time as the United States began its invasion of Iraq. Most of the world's energy and attention was riveted on the overthrow of Saddam Hussein and its aftermath. Being so overwhelmed by the difficulties of the Iraqi intervention compromised the ability of the United States and other countries to respond to the genocide in Darfur.
- *Counterterrorism:* Osama bin Laden lived in Sudan from 1990 to 1996 as a guest of the Sudanese government.

He incubated the al Qaeda commercial infrastructure in Khartoum during this period. When the United States invaded Afghanistan after 9/11 and overthrew the Taliban government there, the Sudanese regime became very nervous because the United States was clearly casting around for further targets with links to al Qaeda. Although bin Laden had left five years before in response to coordinated pressure by the UN Security Council, the Sudanese government still retained some ties with terrorist organizations. Concerned about what the United States might do, the Khartoum regime decided to cut most of those ties and begin an active cooperation on counterterrorism issues with the United States. The expanding security relationship made it awkward for the Bush administration to act decisively against its new counterterrorism partner in Khartoum, even as it was committing genocide.

- *Energy security:* China is the biggest investor in the oil sector in Sudan, with perhaps $8 billion committed so far. In return for taking the dominant position in Sudan's energy development, China supports Sudan in all international bodies, most importantly the UN Security Council. This makes it very difficult for significant multinational pressure to be placed on Sudan for human rights or peace issues because China works to block or threatens to veto any action it deems unfavorable to the Sudanese regime.

Furthermore, the peace process itself in Darfur was failing because of specific variables. First, diplomats have consistently displayed a lack of understanding of and patience for the complexity of the Darfur case. Second, key variables of any successful peace process—including leadership by a full-time envoy with gravitas, well-resourced mediation structures involving full-time experts and diplomats, unanimous support from the international community for one process, and having a diplomatic strategy to deal with the spoilers and others who benefit from war and dictatorship—were not being utilized in Darfur. Third, the countries that have influence with the government of Sudan and other combatants have chosen not to use it in support of the compromises necessary for peace, handcuffed by competing priorities and interests. Finally, perhaps the biggest reason why there has been no end to the cycle of war in Sudan is that there have been no consequences for those perpetrating human rights crimes. This has left the warring factions with the clear signal to continue with business as usual.

Rather than walking softly and carrying a big stick, for years the United States has been walking loudly and carrying a toothpick. The Sudanese regime has seen right through this, and it has realized that it can literally get away with mass murder.

What the United States Could Do to End It

As is the case with the other conflicts discussed in this book, Darfur and its related crises in Sudan may seem at first glance to be insoluble. This is simply not true. On the contrary, we have already seen that when the Obama administration devotes real leadership to addressing a complex problem, these high-level efforts can bear fruit. And we have learned from history that smart policies coupled with people's movements are the answer to the world's seemingly most intractable conflicts—the success stories of South Africa's anti-apartheid movement and the campaign to end the trade of "blood diamonds" provide solid proof of the power of activists to influence policy change from the grassroots up.

There is no silver bullet or magic formula to confronting and eradicating the scourges of genocide and mass atrocities. But there is a strategic one. Ending the crisis in Darfur, addressing the root causes of Sudan's conflicts, and preventing these crimes from happening in the future in Sudan should be addressed within a framework we call the three P's: peace, protection, and punishment.

Peace: At the time of writing this, nearly seven years into the Darfur crisis, the most damning indictment of the U.S. and international efforts on Sudan is that there has not yet been an effective peace process for Darfur that addresses the real root causes of continuing conflict. At the time of writing this book, another poorly conceived international mediation effort is playing itself out, and the outcomes do not look encouraging. In the absence of a real international investment in peacemaking marked by more competent and strategic U.S. leadership, in which the interests of the people of Darfur and the south are protected and championed, Sudan's crisis will only deepen.

There is an answer, and the lessons come right from within Sudan. The twenty-year north-south war was resolved not with peacekeeping forces and not by billions in humanitarian aid. It was resolved by a good old-fashioned investment in diplomacy, led by full-time U.S. diplomatic teams working with teams from other countries, and backed by significant incentives and pressures. That is how things get done in response to most crises.

What is needed is a concerted, sustained peace surge for Sudan focused on making and implementing peace deals, both in Darfur and in the south. The objective would be sustainable peace marked by democracy and accountability. This is doable. A handful of U.S. diplomats plus a few regional and issue experts should be deployed to Africa to staff a diplomatic peace cell that would help staff the processes and implementation efforts around the clock in the manner they deserve. The United States should make a more concerted outreach effort to China in order to make the compelling case that

Chinese oil assets are at risk if the north-south peace deal collapses. The United States should also make clear that this is a real opportunity for the United States and China—the two countries with the most influence in Sudan—to work together at a time when other issues are dividing Beijing and Washington.

Protection: The Sudanese government has repeatedly abdicated its responsibility to protect its own people, and in fact, it has become the principal abuser. Pressure from the international community on the Sudanese government is part of the solution, but another essential element is building the capacity of the peacekeeping missions in Darfur (UNAMID) and southern Sudan (UNMIS) to protect people as much as is physically possible.

Punishment: There is total impunity in Sudan. Untold thousands of women have been raped. During both the Darfur genocide and the north-south civil war, millions of people have been forced out of their homes and into exile in neighboring countries such as Chad and Ethiopia. By and large, ordinary people have been unable to seek redress for the crimes they have suffered. Sudan will simply be unable to move forward toward a more inclusive, free, and peaceful future unless the fundamental right to justice is promoted, starting now.

The ICC's arrest warrant for Bashir—the first arrest warrant issued by the court for a sitting president—is a step firmly in the right direction. At present, there is no other legal mechanism powerful enough to enable the Sudanese people to seek the justice they deserve. The United States should provide greater support for the ICC indictments, work with other countries to build a coalition to expand the targeted sanctions, go after the assets of the top officials, deny debt relief, enforce the arms embargo, and plan for targeted military action in the event of a major upsurge in killings or in response to humanitarian aid cut-offs. We need to create a legal, financial, and political cost to committing genocide and other crimes against humanity, just as the international community is building its own protection against terrorism. If there is any hope for protecting people in Sudan, it will be in part through a concerted multilateral effort to impose consequences on those most responsible for the violence, while at the same time ramping up peace efforts.

JOHN: During the eight trips I've taken to Darfur since the genocide began in 2003, I've found that displaced and war-affected Darfuris don't see a tension between justice and peace. They unite the problem in the simplest and purest of ways. How can you have peace, they ask, without justice? We need to understand that respect for human rights is an essential ingredient of sustainable peace, which requires elements of justice. As I was watching Bashir and his cronies mock his ICC arrest warrant, I couldn't help but be reminded of the fates of other indicted leaders with names such as Charles Taylor, Slobodan Milosevic, Radovan Karadzic, Augusto Pinochet, and Saddam Hussein. Hopefully Bashir will be added to this growing list of now imprisoned, exiled, or deceased war criminals, which would give his country a real chance for the peace its long-suffering people deserve.

DON: There is a huge opportunity if the world gets tough with this regime. The north-south peace agreement proves that emphatically.

JOHN: Exactly. There was a credible threat of serious consequences for the regime if it did not resolve the war in the south, and so it did. That is the lesson. But the lesson has been ignored because we don't like imposing real consequences for human rights crimes. Instead, our political system gravitates toward nonconfrontation and noncontroversy. Fighting human rights crimes, it turns out, is messy and inconvenient.

Call to Action

Responding to the lack of political will to do what is necessary to end this genocide and others in the future that may fall off the radar screen of "traditional" U.S. foreign policy concerns. But this is exactly where the growing anti-genocide movement must come in. The movement has proven successful at demonstrating to elected officials in the United States that genocide is occurring on *our* watch and that ending the genocide in Darfur must be a political priority for the United States.

Jim Wallis and John wrote in the *Wall Street Journal* on April 13, 2009:

> The United States needs to lead the international community in presenting Sudanese regime officials with a choice. If they allow access to aid organizations, sideline their indicted president, and secure peace for Darfur and the south, then they will be offered a clear path toward normal relations with the United States and other coalition partners. But if those officials use starvation as a weapon, allow Mr. Bashir to remain defiant, and make no progress toward peace, then there will be escalating costs in the form of targeted economic sanctions, diplomatic isolation, and potential military action. The crisis is not a new one. The refrain regarding international crises is often, "If only the world had known, we would have done something." The people of Darfur know that we know. What they are waiting to find out is if we care enough to act. When the dust clears and the bodies are buried, burned or left to rot in forsaken camps, the world will mourn for what it did

*not do. What Darfur needs is not a future apology, but
steps today that offer hope.*

This is the Enough Moment for ending the genocide in
Darfur and bringing peace to Sudan.

**To take action to help end Sudan's cycles of violence,
go to www.enoughmoment.org.**

CHAPTER FOUR

Upstanders for Darfur

Darfurians aren't waiting to be saved. They are fighting back against the forces committing human rights crimes and the forces of anarchy in many different ways. Thousands have picked up guns, for better or worse, and joined rebel groups to fight against the Khartoum regime. Thousands of others have joined organizations that help provide sustenance to the survivors of the violence. Still others risk their lives to report on continuing human rights violations, to provide legal aid to victims, or to organize local groups to advocate for their rights. They are redefining the word *hero*, fighting on the front lines in Darfur, being tear-gassed or beaten in the streets in Khartoum, and providing comfort to the survivors in the displaced camps in Darfur and the refugee camps in Chad.

It is these Frontline Upstanders who are risking their lives every day to bring change to their country who are the building blocks of a truly globalized human rights movement. They need our support. They need to know we stand with them and that we find it unacceptable that solutions are not found.

And standing with them in greater and greater numbers, a continent away in the United States, Citizen Upstanders are working tirelessly on behalf of people they've never met and places most will likely never visit. And their numbers are enhanced and their cause magnified by Famous Upstanders who are fighting for peace and human rights as well. Why? Read on and find out when Enough became Enough for these committed human rights and peace advocates, and their courageous Darfurian counterparts.

FRONTLINE UPSTANDERS:
Genocide Survivors Who Are Making a Difference

ABDEL AZIZ ADAM, TEACHER,
DJABAL REFUGEE CAMP

The Koranic Call of Duty

"Unto whom wisdom is given, he had indeed been blessed with a great treasure" is a verse found in Al-Baqarah, the eighth chapter of the Koran. This Koranic verse inspires and sustains Abdel Aziz, a Darfur refugee, in his current profession as teacher and headmaster of the Obama School in the Djabal refugee camp on the Chad-Sudan border, where hundreds of thousands of Darfurians fled after the genocide.

Abdel Aziz's journey to headmaster of the Obama School is an unlikely one because he was not always set on a trajectory of becoming a teacher, let alone a headmaster of a school. In fact, when Abdel Aziz completed secondary school in 2004, he returned home to his village in West Darfur unsure about his future but determined to use his newly acquired skills to develop his hometown. However, shortly after he returned to his village of Furbaranga, the Janjaweed attacked his village, killing men, women, and children indiscriminately. Some of Abdel Aziz's family members were killed, and others fled to displaced-persons camps in Sudan. Abdel Aziz and his immediate family walked over fifty miles to the Chadian border, where UNHCR, the UN refugee agency, moved them into a refugee camp further inside Chad.

For the past six years, the Djabal refugee camp has been home to Abdel Aziz and roughly 19,000 Darfuri refugees, most of whom are children. Since they have lived in the refugee camps for years now, with no prospect of returning home until there is peace, the children in the camps desperately need access to quality education or over time they will become severely undereducated relative to their peers in Sudan.

Abdel Aziz saw immediately that there were very few qualified teachers in the refugee camps. The very small number of qualified adults in the camps often fail to respond to the call to teach because of a lack of training and the low wages. Abdel Aziz notes that "most qualified adults in the camps have forgone the teaching profession and have opted to join NGOs or even rebel groups because of the low wages."

For Abdel Aziz, the Koranic verse is significant because he believes he was given the gift of education (wisdom) in Darfur and is responsible for passing this gift on to the next generation. As a result, Abdel Aziz accepted the duty of not only being a teacher but also a headmaster. During each school year, Abdel Aziz is responsible for the welfare of 900 students in Grades 1 through 8 at Obama School.

Obama School is one of six primary schools in the Djabal refugee camp, all of which are being supported by the Darfur Dream Team's sister school's program. According to Abdel Aziz, his primary school is proudly named after President Obama because the "Darfuris feel a direct tie to America's first African American president, and they are sure he will help the people of Darfur to find a solution to the crisis in Darfur."

TEHANI ISMAIL

Keeping Their Memories Alive

Tehani Ismail, a Darfuri woman, was born and raised in Nyala, the capital of South Darfur. Tehani's parents separated when she was young so she was raised by her single mother. The eldest of three sisters, Tehani was studying at the University of Khartoum when the violence in Darfur erupted. As reports of the violence reached Khartoum, Tehani and her Darfurian classmates in Khartoum sat paralyzed listening to the news stories.

With her family and friends still in Nyala, Tehani decided to go home and see with her own eyes what was happening. She traveled to Nyala and volunteered to work with a local organization. On her first field visit with the group, Tehani and her colleagues traveled by car to the countryside just north of Nyala. Tehani recalled that when she had been there before the war, it was the lushest area of South Darfur. "It was a place where any crops grew and all animals grazed." But this time, when they arrived, the area was still smoldering from the fires. They encountered dead bodies of men, women, and children strewn everywhere and homes completely ransacked. There were very few survivors of the attack. They encountered burned village after burned village until they reached Muhajiriya, where they saw signs of life again.

When they reached Muhajiriya, Tehani remembers being overwhelmed by what she had seen. "What happened to the people, animals, and land that she had always admired?" She then realized that "this is not just collateral damage of warfare but rather systematic killing of people and a violation of their human rights. If the people of Darfur aren't aware of their rights," she concluded, "then the government of Sudan could keep violating them."

That was Tehani's Enough Moment. She decided she would forgo getting a four-year university degree and would work with an organization to raise awareness and educate her fellow Darfuris about their human rights.

Tehani joined the Sudan Social Development Organization (SUDO) as a human rights worker in 2004. SUDO is dedicated to the promotion of human rights and international development. While at SUDO, Tehani faced harassment and watched her colleagues disappear to detention centers. Sudanese government security agents had begun targeting SUDO staff and shutting down their operations in 2003. Intimidation tactics used by Sudan security operatives included going to Tehani's mother and sister and advising them that they should tell her that "what she is doing is dangerous and her safety is not guaranteed." Both Tehani and her mother, a public health worker, were prevented from going to work by the security officials.

In spite of this, Tehani continues to be a human rights advocate and is now a correspondent for Radio Dabanga in Nyala. Tehani is currently mobilizing women's groups in South Darfur. The groups have established the Riaheen el-Salam for Maternity and Childhood center, and it is focused on addressing gender-based violence. Tehani notes she has seen the "worst of the worst" cases in her work: women who were raped, who have lost everything, and who must begin picking up the pieces of their lives. Tehani now documents their cases and provides counseling and comfort so they can begin the healing process. Several of Tehani's close friends have died because of the violence in Darfur. Initially, Tehani was always thinking of her lost friends while doing her work and constantly searching of ways to keep their memories alive. Tehani has found the best way is to work with the survivors.

AWATEF ISAAC, JOURNALIST

Telling Darfur's Story

It is said that the sibling bond, particularly among sisters, can be the most significant relationship a person will ever have. Born six years apart in El-Fasher, the capital of North Darfur, Awatef Isaac and her sister Afaf shared a close bond. Afaf, the older sister, was the trail blazer in the family. She attended El-Fasher High School for Girls and dreamed of publishing a newspaper to tell the story of their town. While at El-Fasher High School, Afaf started *Al-Mustakbal* (The Future) newspaper. The newspaper was handwritten on A4 paper and pinned on the tree in front of the high school.

Afaf suddenly died due to complications in her pregnancy in 1998 at the age of twenty-two, and Awatef vowed to carry on her legacy. Awatef continued to publish Afaf's newspaper by hand, but she changed the name to *Al-Rahil* (The Journey) in order both to acknowledge the forced migrations of the Darfurians and to commemorate her sister's eternal journey. She began posting the paper outside her house. The newspaper took on added significance when the genocide engulfed Darfur in 2003. Though somewhat insulated from the violence by virtue of living in the main town, Awatef saw her family and friends directly affected by the violence in Darfur; her grandfather was forced to seek refuge in a displaced-persons camp where he later died. Awatef began writing about and publishing accounts of the violence in Darfur instead of solely focusing on local issues in the town of El-Fasher. The newspaper now focuses on the conflict, including cases of rape. Awatef also includes political jokes and commentary on women in politics and Sudanese society.

Al-Rahil has transformed how people in El-Fasher get information about the government-supported attacks in Darfur.

The tree outside Awatef's house has become a gathering place for the community. As soon as the weekly paper is posted on the tree, residents of El-Fasher crowd around to read it. The newspaper is published locally in Arabic, but Awatef recently began to provide accounts of the humanitarian situation in Darfur geared toward a broader external audience.

Four years after her sister Afaf's death, Awatef began to put together an exhibit of her sister's old newspapers to honor her work. The exhibit also included old editions of Awatef's own newspaper. But before the exhibit opened to the public, the government of Sudan officials shut down the exhibit and confiscated the newspapers.

Although she has continued to receive threats, Awatef has had significant support from her community in El-Fasher and the people of Sudan. Many groups, including the government of southern Sudan, have commended Awatef for her efforts. After the *Washington Post* and *Agence de France Presse* featured articles about Awatef, an anonymous individual opened a bank account in Awatef's name with a modest contribution. She has also received a camera, computer, and printer so she can publish *Al-Rahil* electronically and print free copies. Members of the sudaneseonline.com website have been an instrumental base of support for Awatef and are trying to make *Al-Rahil* available to the world online.

Awatef, now in her mid-twenties, is called the "The Girl-Journal" in reference to a poem by Sudanese poet Mustapha Sayyid entitled "The Garden-Girl." She continues to publish her newspaper despite continuing threats. After a trip to The Hague during which her picture was taken with Luis Moreno-Ocampo, the International Criminal Court's chief prosecutor, her return to Sudan was delayed because of the picture, and her family has been harassed since. Awatef remains undeterred from her mission of telling the truth about what is happening in Darfur and maintaining the legacy of her sister.

ADEEB YOUSEF

"I Will Work for Darfur Even If It Costs Me My Life"

Adeeb Yousef is a human rights advocate from Zallengi, West Darfur. Adeeb comes from a large family with twenty-two children. He remembers his hometown as an island of peace, where the Fur people and their Arab neighbors lived together, and intermarriage and even property exchange between the Fur and Arab ethnic groups was common. Adeeb's family owned a large orchard, with fruits such as mangoes and oranges. He remembers many instances in which his father would turn over his cattle to an Arab friend for safekeeping. Each year, his father's Arab friend would then return to their home for a large feast, and they would discuss the welfare of the cattle. If a cow had died, his father's friend would bring the leather as proof.

This idyllic life is what Adeeb left behind when he completed secondary school and went to Dongole University in North Sudan. While at Dongole, Adeeb, like Tehani, became involved with the Sudan Social Development Organization (SUDO). After he completed his university degree, Adeeb returned to Zallengi to open a regional office for SUDO. Adeeb was charged with managing and coordinating all of SUDO's Darfur activities with the main office in Khartoum, the capital of Sudan.

In 2002, Adeeb heard about attacks in the rural areas of Darfur. Adeeb began documenting the various attacks and providing support to the displaced persons in the area, who were streaming into Zallengi from the rural areas. Most were camping in schools, and some were living on the streets. Since there were no relief agencies providing support to those driven from their homes at that time, Adeeb reached out to the local community, especially the merchants, for support. The merchants agreed to provide food, and SUDO helped set up a local committee to give out the food to the people each morning.

As a result of his work with the displaced people, Adeeb's profile was heightened, and the Sudan security forces began harassing him. Eventually he was arrested. Adeeb vividly remembers the day he was first arrested: Friday, January 2, 2004. Adeeb had gone about his day as usual. He had visited the homeless and had gone to prayers, and he was at his father's pharmacy to check on the business. At around 2 p.m., Sudan national security forces came to his father's pharmacy and arrested him. For four months, government security officers tortured and questioned Adeeb. "I was beaten, tortured, and humiliated daily. I lost over fifteen pounds while I was in jail, and my spirit was nearly broken."

When he was released from jail in April 2004, Adeeb had his own Enough Moment. He realized that nothing had changed while he had been in jail. In fact, the situation had deteriorated, and there were more people rendered homeless, without access to food, shelter, or protection. Adeeb painfully notes, "If you see with your naked eye what I saw, you will never stand by. I saw the stomach of a woman cut, and the child inside was stabbed. I saw people burned in their homes, people whose names I knew. I will work for Darfur even if it costs me my life."

After his release from jail, Adeeb redoubled his efforts to document the human rights abuses in West Darfur for SUDO. The first town he visited after his release was Delge, a town 85 kilometers from the town of Zallengi. In Delge, Adeeb and the SUDO team encountered a horrific massacre. Several children, mostly boys, were tied together and shot in the head.

Adeeb was again arrested when he was visiting Khartoum

for a training workshop. He was taken to a detention center and held for seven months. He was beaten and repeatedly interrogated. Adeeb lost consciousness six times in the detention center. To draw attention to his wrongful arrest, Adeeb went on a hunger strike and had to be taken to Amal hospital. While at the hospital, an individual whom Adeeb believed to be a human rights lawyer convinced him to stop the hunger strike so that he would be released from jail. But as soon as Adeeb broke his hunger strike, he was thrown back in jail and kept in solitary confinement.

Sudanese organizations made noise about Adeeb's wrongful arrest. Prominent international groups such as Human Rights Watch and Amnesty International sent letters to Sudan's vice president, Ali Osman Taha, calling for Adeeb's release. Adeeb was finally released in April 2005, and he continued his work with SUDO, but he still faced harassment from national security forces.

Adeeb has had the opportunity to learn about the reconciliation process communities undergo in the aftermath of crimes against humanity. Adeeb was able to travel to South Sudan to attend the Rift Valley Institute's Sudan course in Rumbek; he also traveled to Rwanda, northern Uganda, and even the United States to learn more about how communities are dealing with reconciliation. Upon his return home from the United States in September 2007, Adeeb was once again harassed by Sudanese government security officers. His family and friends were also being monitored and harassed as well, and they advised him to leave Sudan. With a heavy heart, Adeeb finally left Sudan in August 2008, and he is now in the United States seeking asylum. He is presently getting a master's degree in international relations at the University of San Francisco. Adeeb feels that with an education he can be of better use to the people in Darfur and Africa.

CITIZEN UPSTANDERS:
Darfur's Champions in America

ETHAN BARHYDT

A Choice

In the seventh grade, Ethan took a class at his Jewish congregation on the Holocaust. Rather than focusing on mere dates and facts, Ethan's instructor, Dick Strauss, attempted to explain what might have happened if the United States and neighboring countries had stepped in before the Holocaust took so many lives. What could have happened if people had chosen to say ENOUGH?

Ethan's instructor ended the class with a one-question final exam: "Your final exam is how you conduct the rest of your lives. Can it happen again? The answer is up to YOU and to YOUR CHOICES. Will YOU CHOOSE to get involved, or will you be a bystander?"

It was that exact moment when Ethan decided he would no longer remain a bystander but would instead make a life-long commitment to help end mass atrocities and crimes against humanity. In 2007, Ethan created the organization Youth United for Darfur in the Chicago area. This organization was a coalition of ten student groups, which until then had not been collaborating very much. Being able to work together, the Youth United for Darfur organized a conference focused not only on educating students about genocide but also on providing effective advocacy techniques.

By January 2009, their efforts had expanded to forty student organizations. It was then that Youth United for Darfur decided to host the Darfur Rally in Chicago. Reaching out to political figures, musical groups, high schools, and colleges, the rally became the biggest rally for Darfur in the United

States outside of Washington, D.C., and New York that year. With thousands of students supporting the rally, they gathered in Chicago to advocate for peace in Sudan and celebrate their month-long fundraising campaign that had raised $17,000 for Illinois' Sudanese Community Center and the Darfur Dream Team's Sister Schools Program.

Ethan graduated from high school in 2009, deferred enrollment to Macalester College, taught English to middle school students in Tibet for a semester, and then headed to Washington, D.C., to join the Darfur Dream Team. Ethan stresses that he has learned the value of fostering relationships to promote awareness and action, and to bring people together for a common purpose.

LEE ANN DE REUS

"I Tapped the Very Core of My Meaning"

"People often ask me why I do this type of work and how I got started. I tell them there's no short answer and that I'm not entirely sure I understand it myself! I have no single childhood trauma to offer as a compelling reason, or great religious conviction—but rather a strong feeling of moral obligation and sense of fairness that years of therapy might eventually connect to any number of personal insecurities or a fear of who knows what. What I do know is there's a drive I can't deny. This took me first to work for years in the Dominican Republic and Tanzania.

"It was a student who came to me about her interest in 'doing something' about the genocide in Darfur. I shared her passion and seized the opportunity to work with a like-minded soul. We organized our first event and managed to get 'the' John Prendergast to make an appearance! Unbelievably, his beloved Aunt Mary, who was a longtime activist herself, was my neighbor. As this issue of genocide became ever more real to me and the gravity began to sink in, so did my need to get involved. But to advocate with any authority, for me, meant having some direct experience and connection with the people and issues. I knew I was returning to Tanzania. Could I possibly get to the Darfur refugee camps in Chad? I was already going to be on the continent, so . . . *why not?* I knew my decision would depend on John's opinion. So I made certain it was I who drove him from the airport to our event venue. Little did he know how significant his words in the car would be. When I asked John if he thought I could pull off the trip, he said unequivocally, 'Yes!' It was the only endorsement I needed! That was April 1, 2007. By June 30, I was in a refugee camp in Chad with a Penn State student and a colleague.

"In other words, this is ALL John's fault.

"Our travel to and from the Gaga refugee camp was actually against all odds. And at times I was worried I'd gotten my companions—Lorraine (a colleague) and Wendy (a returning adult student)—and me in over our heads. Despite our advanced planning, the unpredictability, instability, and chaos we encountered in Chad proved almost impossible to navigate. To travel within the country, we had to 'hitch' rides on eight-seater UN World Food program planes. The unpredictability of when we might fly and whether we'd have to split up added to the vulnerability we already felt. The night before we finally arrived at the camps, a guard for an NGO was shot and killed, raising the local security level and anxieties. Four UN vehicles had been hijacked in the previous weeks, requiring us to travel by convoy. On our ninety-minute drive to Gaga, we passed an unexploded bomb on the side of the road. The temperature was 130 degrees. Water cost $4.50 per bottle and tasted like gasoline as petroleum leached from the plastic. Getting cash was next to impossible and had to be exchanged on the black market. At one point we were banned from UN flights due to a misunderstanding. And while we had an interpreter for part of the trip, we knew little French and no Arabic. We all took a turn at being violently sick, and in the end, we missed our international flight home.

"But as we sat on mats with the women of Gaga, listening to their powerful stories, Lorraine, Wendy, and I knew, through our shared tearful glances, that it had all been worthwhile. Our frustrations and inconveniences were miniscule compared to what the women had experienced. What a privilege it was for us to connect with them emotionally for a brief moment. We all laughed at our absurd attempts to communicate via sign language, felt a shared delight as we bounced their babies on our laps, and enjoyed serving each other sweet tea. I have never been more profoundly humbled or moved.

"This was truly my Enough Moment. Through my connection with these survivors, I had tapped the very core of my meaning and realized a depth of purpose I'd known previously in only small, fleeting glimpses. But now, the self exposed and a mystery revealed, there was no turning back from the gift the women of Gaga gave me. My hope is that in some small way their gift is paid forward and a gift is returned with the telling of their stories."

REVEREND MIKE SLAUGHTER

Darfur in the Middle of an Ohio Corn Field

Ginghamsburg Church is a United Methodist congregation in Tipp City, Ohio, a small city of 9,300 people just north of Dayton, in the heart of the "rust belt." When the Reverend Michael Slaughter arrived at Ginghamsburg thirty years ago, he inherited a 104-year-old small country church on a quarter of an acre, with fewer than a hundred members and an annual budget of $27,000. The population of the Miami Valley region, in which Ginghamsburg is located, has declined by more than 20,000 people since Pastor Mike's arrival because of the region's dependence on, and the national decline of, the automobile industry. In August 2008, *Forbes* magazine named Dayton one of the ten fastest-dying cities in America. Today, however, roughly 4,500 people worship, attend class, serve, or find community each week on the church's campus.

One Sunday afternoon in 1998, Pastor Mike was reading the *Dayton Daily News* when his eye caught an ad featuring a new luxury sedan, a BMW, for lease. Being a car fan, Mike found himself checking out the various features to compare them to his current vehicle. Then, his eye was drawn to a picture on the opposing page of a clearly emaciated child featured in an article about famine in the Sudan and the tragedies of the civil war between north and south Sudan. Mike was stunned by that juxtaposition of the sedan, the heart of our culture, versus the Sudan, the heart of God as he saw it, and the fact that he knew many things about the luxury vehicle and nothing about the conflict in this large African country. Although that afternoon did not yet lead Mike to action, the image and the challenge stayed in his heart.

In the fall of 2004, Pastor Mike was reading one of the very few news stories published in that entire year about the crisis in Darfur. He clearly felt God's urging to engage the Ginghamsburg faith community, "no holds barred" as he says, into serving the needs of the survivors of the Darfur war. That Advent season, he reminded Ginghamsburg attendees, "Christmas is not your birthday. It's Jesus' birthday!" and he challenged everyone to have a simple Christmas that year. All were asked to spend only half as much on their own Christmas as they would normally spend and to give the rest as a "Christmas Miracle Offering" to serve the people of

Darfur. That same challenge has been issued in all subsequent Advent seasons. In an area of the United States badly hurt by the recession and the decline of the auto industry, these appeals have raised a total of nearly $4.5 million for humanitarian relief in Darfur from 2005 through 2009, going for sustainable agriculture, water, sanitation, and education programs.

In addition to Ginghamsburg's humanitarian relief focus, Pastor Mike has encouraged social activism by Ginghamsburg attendees, other churches, college students, and community groups. In April 2006, a bus of Ginghamsburg activists traveled to Washington, D.C., to participate in the rally for Darfur on the National Mall. Ginghamsburg is actively represented in Dayton for Darfur, and it participated in the Dayton-based rally in the spring of 2008. The church has also partnered in educational initiatives about the crisis with Central Ohioans for Peace, based out of Columbus. Congregants are encouraged to participate in Darfur petition drives and to write to congressional representatives, ambassadors, and the U.S. president in support of action on Darfur.

Pastor Mike and other members of the Ginghamsburg team frequently speak on college campuses, United Methodist "schools of mission," and in other venues to advocate on behalf of their sisters and brothers in Darfur. In the spring of 2009, Pastor Mike partnered with the Christian Communications Network (CCN) and the Enough Project to host on Ginghamsburg's campus a live simulcast called "Not On Our Watch" to hundreds of churches around the country.

In his second trip to Darfur in June 2007, Mike took with him his only son, Jonathan, who served as the trip photographer. Mike says that one of his most emotionally and spiritually significant moments as a parent was when he spent Father's Day on the ground in Darfur with Jonathan at his side.

Mike has reminded the people of Ginghamsburg Church, an ordinary church surrounded by corn fields in the rust belt of Ohio, that the true greatness of any local church is measured by how many people are serving the marginalized and, as he says, by how many of us are willing to live more simply and sacrificially so that other people can simply live.

GABRIEL STAURING

Because It's Personal

"During the week of the tenth anniversary of the 1994 Rwanda genocide, I was driving around Orange County, California, visiting homes for my job as a counselor for abused children and their families. National Public Radio had a week-long series on the horrors of Rwanda in which they shared very personal accounts of what happened to victims and survivors. During that week, I went through a series of strong emotions, starting with shock at the numbers, then anger at the world's inaction, sadness at the lives lost, and—finally—guilt at not having lifted a finger ten years before, when I saw the reports of what was happening in that tiny nation that seemed so far away and completely removed from me as a person.

"In the weeks and months that followed, I would have regular conversations with my then nine-year-old daughter, Noemi, about how we had to do more for others. She would ask me where and how, and I did not have an answer. Then I started to hear about Darfur. I knew I had to act. Without knowing where to start, I began with what I know best, my own family and community. I started telling them about Darfur. I then looked around for what others were doing and found that it was difficult for anyone to connect with something as huge and shocking as genocide. It is easier for people to turn the other way and feel, 'There is nothing I can do.' I never could have imaged that a year later I would be walking in a refugee camp in an effort to put a face on the numbers.

"For two years, I continued working full time as a counselor for abused children here in the United States, but I also worked on creating a team that facilitates relationships between children and families that have seen horrors none of us can imagine and people around the world that are in a position to help. I now work full time on this, and my Stop Genocide Now i-ACT (www.stopgenocide.org) team is made up entirely of regular citizens that feel a need to embrace responsibility and do all in our power to make a difference in the lives of the very real human beings that are the victims of mass atrocities and genocide. It is very personal. I do this for all the children I have met on my now eight trips to refugee camps, but I also do it for my own children."

MARV STEINBERG

Never Too Late to Say ENOUGH

Marv is a seventy-eight-year-old retired educator who had open-heart surgery a decade ago and retired soon thereafter from his job as the superintendent-principal of a small one-school district. In May 2005 his thirty-eight-year-old daughter passed away from complications related to multiple sclerosis. For the last eighteen months of her life, Marv spent much of his time caring for her. She was living in the Seattle area, and because of her illness, she was hospitalized for over three months. She then moved home and was finally able to live independently again. She required a great deal of assistance so when she passed away, not only was Marv devastated but there was also a real void in his life.

In March 2006 Marv was once again hospitalized with suspected heart problems. Before going in for a heart scan, he had some time to reflect on his life. "I had a long conversation with God," Marv told us. "I had witnessed a series of reports by Ann Curry on the situation in Darfur, and I thought about my experiences growing up Jewish in San Francisco. I reflected on the many reports by Rabbi Burstein of Temple Beth Israel on what was happening to the Jews in Europe. I knew that family members had been lost in the Holocaust, but I never knew anything about them. As I went in for the test that would determine whether I needed heart surgery, I talked to one of our pastors and told her that if I made it I was going to turn my attention to Darfur."

Luckily, Marv's health was fine, and the next Sunday he spoke to members of his congregation at the First Methodist Church in Redding, California, at all three services, inviting them to join him in praying for the people of Darfur and for peace in Sudan and Chad, to learn more about Darfur, and to participate in a "Day of Conscience for Darfur" in San Francisco later that month. Out of those simple talks was born an initiative called Genocide No More—Save Darfur, a coalition of several churches and other groups in Shasta County. Since then the coalition has raised over $30,000 for humanitarian relief and sponsored many informational events, including speakers, films, and forums.

At his church, Marv has twice led a Bible study class utilizing the *Not On Our Watch Christian Companion*. Emerging from that class came a petition campaign in support of the International Criminal Court and justice for the perpetrators of the genocide in Darfur. The class also helped form an action group within the church.

Marv's local group also worked closely with their representative in Congress after marching on his office twice to get his attention. This member of Congress had been rated a D by the Genocide Intervention Network's Darfur Scores. "He received an A for the year after we 'worked' with him," Marv reported. Marv's group also sponsors Camp Kounoungo, and it is currently in the process of raising money for a library-classroom for the camp. High school students have made PowerPoint presentations to the Redding City Council, which adopted a resolution of support, and to other agencies in the area. Clubs from two area high schools have raised over $3,000 at benefit concerts in 2008 and 2009. They have also worked with other nonprofits in his area—People of Progress and the Women's Shelter—in fundraising efforts, and they now have a substantial contact list. The last Friday of each month the group has been sponsoring Interfaith Prayer Vigils on the Calatrava-designed Sundial Bridge. They have also been sponsoring monthly Letter Writing Parties, they have been meeting the first Monday of the month for planning meetings, and they have launched a spin-off group called the Darfur Action Group, all at the First Methodist Church.

LESLIE THOMAS

"Humanity Does Not Stop with Borders"

"My son was six months old, and I was holding him in the middle of the night reading an article by Nicholas Kristof about Darfur. The column described a young boy who had been killed because of his ethnicity, and looking down at my child, I realized that this was simply not acceptable, that it was not right that my son should be 'safe' while another boy was not.

"I then found a photo of Mihad Hamid taken by U.S. Marine Brian Steidle. She was a beautiful one-year-old child from Darfur who was shot from a government helicopter and who most likely died some hours after her photo was taken. Looking at the computer screen, I sat and cried for hours—bereft at the idea that we have created a world where this is feasible. I got angry and got started trying to work on the problem.

"To this day I would love to believe that Mihad survived, that somehow she is walking free in this world, though I know that this is likely to be impossible. But her beauty and grace shadow me even now, and she and the little boy will always be my inspiration.

"The photo exhibit we created, DARFUR/DARFUR, started out of my incredible despair at what was happening to a group of people in Sudan and Chad. It was going to be a one-night event in which we would talk about an issue, raise money, and try to help. Three years, multiple human rights projects, forty exhibitions, and three zillion cups of coffee later, we are an organization with plans to work on as many human rights abuses as we can.

"Over 500,000 people have seen the DARFUR/DARFUR exhibition, and more importantly thousands of them have been introduced to the incredible advocacy and humanitarian organizations that have been represented at the installations. It has been used in support of divestment and international diplomacy. Another exhibit, Congo/Women, has been presented on Capitol Hill twice where it was exhibited in support of a successful request for significant funding for women in the Congo. But the most rewarding feeling is getting an e-mail at three o'clock in the morning from a student in a small Texas college town who wants to bring an exhibition to his or her community because he or she feels it will help generate mass support for action.

"When we started DARFUR/DARFUR, I didn't know any photojournalists, film editors, or museums. Or have any money. You need all these things to make such a project work. But somehow it all came together. After things took off, we realized that we had a methodology that we wanted to apply to other issues so we built Art Works Projects backward. First we did a project, then we built an organization. Everyone would tell you to do it the other way around—as someone said today, 'You're trying to build the plane while you are flying.' The other hurdle is that I haven't slept in three years.

"Genocide would be unacceptable here in the United Sates, and it is no less so for being thousands of miles from my home. We are all global neighbors. Humanity does not stop with borders."

We have many other testimonials that we just didn't have room for in the book, so go to www.enoughmoment.org to read more inspiring stories of activism and to find out what you can do. If you have stories of your own or of Upstanders that you know, please send them in, and we'll include them on the site.

FAMOUS UPSTANDERS:
Highlighting Darfur through Celebrity Activism

MADELEINE ALBRIGHT

"We Have a Stake in What's Happening in Other Countries"

JOHN: When was your first Enough Moment?

DR. ALBRIGHT: Well, let me just take a little step back. As you know, I was born in Czechoslovakia. So all through the Cold War period, I watched what the various dissidents were doing, and I wrote my dissertation on the period of relative openness that occurred in 1968 and that became known as Prague Spring. I cared deeply about human rights and democracy in Central and Eastern Europe and in Russia, but I was just a professor and an ordinary citizen, so all I could really do was talk, teach, and write. Then, in 1993, as part of the Clinton administration, I was given the chance to serve as America's permanent representative to the United Nations. It so happens that my Enough Moment really came just before that. I certainly knew about genocide, given what had happened in Europe when major powers like Great Britain, France, and the United States didn't act early enough to prevent it. So I was shocked when, in 1991 and 1992, we began seeing pictures of Bosnians and Croats being put on trains and shipped to concentration camps, and pictures of whole families being driven from homes in which their families had lived for centuries. I thought, I can't believe it. These looked like pictures we had seen in history books of World War II. I remember seeing those pictures and thinking that this was impossible to accept. It also happened that I knew Yugoslavia well because my father had been the Czechoslovakian ambassador there when I was young. So I reacted to the violence there with considerable passion.

When I became U.S. ambassador to the United Nations, Bosnia was at the top of our agenda, along with Iraq. Unfortunately, it was easier to say that what was happening in the Balkans was unacceptable than to actually stop it. We began with a disadvantage because the previous administration had encouraged the Europeans to take the lead on Bosnia. The Clinton administration was divided, with some of us wanting to adopt a firmer line than others. The interagency process within the administration was slow, and we had many meetings where nothing was decided. I was on what I call the "diplomatic front line" because I saw representatives from more countries than any other American diplomat. There were the ambassadors from Bosnia and Croatia at the United Nations, as well as representatives from all the various Muslim countries. Every day someone would come up to me and say, "Aren't you going to do something about this?" During that period one of the UN votes I'm most proud of established the War Crimes Tribunal for former Yugoslavia. But I'm also proud that I was able, along with others, to persuade the administration to eventually stand up to what was happening, persuade NATO to act, and bring the war to an end. I'd had my Enough Moment, and I was fortunate to be in a position to do something about it.

JOHN: What sustains you? What's the cocktail inside that motivates you?

DR. ALBRIGHT: First of all, I saw in Bosnia and later on in the halting of the ethnic cleansing in Kosovo that if you properly marshal your arguments and figure out how to move the process, you can make an enormous difference. People ask me, "What are you proudest of as secretary of state?" It really was ending the terror in Kosovo. I had seen how long Bosnia had taken, and I thought, "Now I'm secretary of state, and I can't let this happen again in Kosovo." Looking back, both Bosnia and Kosovo provide interesting case studies of how to mobilize the U.S. government, NATO, and the world community to implement a humanitarian intervention. Now that I am a professor again, I see value in offering my experience as an example of what works and what might not work in the future. If I can inspire my students to believe in their own ability to achieve change, that is extremely worthwhile.

The other thing that has really made me understand the need to keep a light shining on human rights problems, and on freedom and democracy, has been my conversations with Nobel Peace Prize winner Vaclav Havel. This matters because those of us who are on the outside often wonder whether our criticisms on human rights abuses help or hurt democratic leaders such as Burma's Aung San Suu Kyi or the people of Darfur. If we keep talking about these issues, does that actually make life worse for the people who are at risk? Havel said to me, "The thing that's most important is you have to keep talking about these issues. It helps us if the light is shining on us." That's a very important message. It isn't just that we're helping ourselves. It's that we're giving the victims who are suffering some hope, and it certainly shows the people who are inflicting the pain that outsiders care. That has made a huge difference in how I view my own role.

The other part I feel strongly about is that it took me a very long time to find my voice. I did not have a high-level position in government until I was in my midfifties. Now that I have a platform from which to speak, I'm not going to be quiet. That's true when it comes to promoting democracy, and it's true with respect to upholding human rights. That's why I was so pleased recently to serve as cochair with former Defense Secretary Bill Cohen on the Task Force to Prevent Genocide. The task force made a series of recommendations that I hope the U.S. government and the world community will take steps to fulfill.

JOHN: With all the students you have, how do you get and keep young people interested in genocide and human rights? What are the most effective ways of widening the scope of the population that's willing to get involved?

DR. ALBRIGHT: I have found students these days to be very interested and involved. After 9/11, there was more and more of a sense that we were not an isolated nation that could just sit here and not be involved with what was happening abroad. I have had quite a number of students in my classes who see

Darfur as a clear example of where the "Never Again" philosophy should be applied.

JOHN: The Enough Moment.

DR. ALBRIGHT: Yes. The Darfur movement began with students who really felt that they could make a difference. I think that the more we help students to understand that, there but for the grace of God, this could be happening to them, the more they will identify with the people who are in danger. I was born in Czechoslovakia at the time it was being threatened by the Nazis. When British Prime Minister Chamberlain came back from Munich and said, "Why would we want to help people in a far-away country with an unpronounceable name?" one of the people he was talking about was me. My parents taught me to believe that every individual counts—and my experience has taught me that we have a stake, a national interest, in what's happening in other countries. It's easy to pretend that people in poor circumstances become accustomed to suffering and therefore don't feel the pain, but that's nonsense both morally and biologically. I often think about this when I go somewhere and people are living in abject poverty with flies in their eyes. I think to myself, "I can't stand flies in my own eyes. Why would I think that that person would?" Something I'll never forget was when I was in Ethiopia on International HIV/AIDS day. I was sitting next to a little boy who was an AIDS orphan. I had a ballpoint pen in my pocket that I gave to him, and he said, "No—food, shoes." He was the same age as my grandchildren. I think that personal identification is so important.

JOHN: Thank you for your extraordinary dedication.

DR. ALBRIGHT: Thank *you* for your extraordinary dedication.

ANN CURRY

"An Obligation to Care"

JOHN: What is your motivation for being such a forceful advocate for the rights of people from Sudan, Congo, and other forgotten war zones around the world?

ANN: When I look at people and I decide who is going to be my friend, I don't look at their bank accounts, how famous they are, how beautiful they are, or what they can do for me. I look at, Who are they *really* in the worst of circumstances? What kind of a human being might they be? Would they stand up against evil? Would they stand up to do the right thing? Are they the people who watch someone drown because they are too afraid to call 911? Or are they the people who throw in the life raft? Or the people who jump in to save the person in the water who is drowning? This question I think is a fundamental core question, and it deals with who we are and what makes us who we are.

It can be how we were raised. It can be ideas we let percolate in our brains. For me, it was early on as a young person discovering injustices and discovering that there were people who enlist themselves to make things right. So when as a child I discovered, for example, there was a Holocaust, that was enough to interest me. But then I realized there were people who risked their lives to save people from the Holocaust, and that was mind-blowing. And then what really made my eyes open up was when I realized that people not only risked their lives but they also risked their children's lives, and in some cases their children were killed trying to save Jews. And I thought to myself, "How much love is there when you risk the thing you love the most, your child? What must be within you to do that?"

So that launched an investigation about this question that I have really been conducting my entire life. This idea of who we are and what we're made of, I think, is a key question because it is what will define who we will be. What we pivot into as we evolve, as we continue to evolve into a species that is moving toward greater compassion, greater understanding of each other. That argument I may need to make because most people may not agree with that argument. But if you look back through the scope of history at everything you've learned about history—even if you have to factor in the injustices of, say, the wars in Sudan, Congo, the genocide in Rwanda, and about what's happened to civilians in Iraq and Afghanistan—you have to acknowledge that the very fact that we are outraged, that we move against these injustices speaks to the rise of empathy. And we can see that even though we once did so, we are not today allowing children at the age of five to run around homeless on the streets of Manhattan. And we no longer consider the killing of civilians to be just a factor of war but rather the crime against humanity that it is. And we can elect a black president given the racist history of this nation. All of these things speak to the rise of empathy.

So that argument now made, I believe that when you have this kind of thinking in your mind, it's not even a question as to whether you should stand against anything that smells like inhumanity. Anything that looks like a crime against our human family. Nothing makes me angrier than when one human being purposefully just puts down, hurts, diminishes, kills, or tries to frighten another human being for no other reason except that one has power and the other does not. One is of one race, the other is of another. One is a man and one is a woman. One is an adult and one is a child. Injustice is something we should never tolerate, and I think we are moving toward being a species that will no longer tolerate it.

You never know if you can be that person who, in the midst of the Holocaust, would step forward and have your child walk Jews to a place where they can be safe. You never know who you will be when you are faced with this question. But you can practice, and you can attempt to learn to grow this part in you. And I believe that if you do, you are more likely to step up.

JOHN: What helps sustain you and reinforce your commitment?

ANN: There is a degree of trauma associated with reporting about injustice. There is a degree of trauma that anyone involved with that has to endure, whether you are an aid worker or whether you are someone who is working for the State Department going into Congo, or whether you are a soldier who faces it, or whether you are even a perpetrator. And reporters, any reporters, who tell you they are not to some degree traumatized by some of the kinds of things that we witness when we cover these kinds of stories are liars. I have a tribe of people that I work with—photojournalists, newspaper reporters, television journalists, thinkers. We gather, not very often, sometimes once a month and sometimes once every six months, but we gather and we are all on that same page. They are people that can barely speak to their own families or their best friends about what they have seen because it is unfathomable. It is not describable. I think most anyone who has gone and seen this stuff firsthand can describe it to people who have no connection or experience, and they can't get past the fact that you were in Darfur, that you were in Congo, or you were some other one of these places. So when you are able to be with your sisters and brothers who choose to do this kind of work, there is a kind of comfort, a kind of acceptance, a kind of listening that I think all people need who are in this kind of work.

I think that the most inspiring, most foundational thing in this is my core belief in the future and my core belief that I have an obligation and that each one of us has an obligation to work in some way to make this world better. I'm not saying everybody has to go to a war zone, but I do think every one of us has an obligation to care, that's the first thing. We live in a country where if people care, things change. What Americans care about affects the world.

I think that's the first step. And that to me is enough. If people care enough to be activists, that's gravy, but the fact that they care, that to me is transformative. That's an investment in the future of our world because once you care you have got to acknowledge. You can care only if you acknowledge that no matter whether someone is sitting in a hospital having been brutally raped in Goma, Congo, or suffering third-degree burns in Darfur, or is blinded and will never see again because a Janjaweed put a bayonet in their eyes—that that person matters. And when you say that and acknowledge it, then it's an investment in the future. Then we are all brothers and sisters. That is the way the world is going, and if we don't have that connection then I don't think we've left the world a better place.

We can teach our children this kind of idea. It comes from your own decision making about who you are and what your place is in the world. I think it also comes from your family, and that is where the foundation is laid. When I asked him what should I be when I grow up, my father always said the same thing: "Ann, no matter what you do, do something that is of some service to someone else. Because then, on your last day, on your dying day, you'll know that it mattered that you were here." This idea of living your life so that you can be proud of who you've been, that's a key lesson for our children.

We are not in this life running around and just going from one experience to another. We are going to come to an end some day. Who do we want to see ourselves as having been? I think that is a great wall or an edge to feel and know about as you look to the decisions you make in your life. I frankly do not want to look back and feel that I had not done everything I could to be useful to other people in this world. I do not want to look back and feel ashamed that there was something I might have done to ease suffering and I didn't. I never want someone to accuse me of having been insensitive to a great tragedy in this world or thoughtless to another human being's suffering. I never want that to happen, and so I guard against it looking, feeling for that edge of my dying day.

JOHN: In all of your travels, is there one particular story that stands out that helps sustain you, that helps keep you going when your strength is flagging?

ANN: There is a sea of faces, and they all stay with you, but I think that probably the one in my mind the most right now is Sifa. I found her in a hospital in Congo with her legs in stirrups as she was being repaired for having been so broken up inside. She had been so brutally raped that she was incontinent. She was eighteen, stunning, and in any other world she would have been a model. She's so beautiful. Her hand was shaking, and she stared at me, frightened as the surgery was about to begin. I had been led in there by the doctor, and I held her hand for a bit and then backed out. The next day I came to speak with her. I introduced myself and explained to her that it was her decision as to whether I would continue talking to her. I asked her if she would tell her story, which she did. And what she told me just broke my heart.

She was sixteen or seventeen when she watched Congolese rebel troops slaughter her mother and father. The troops kidnapped her, tied her to a tree, kept her for weeks, and raped her so that she could no longer walk. Then they left her for dead because she didn't mean anything, she didn't matter. She got loose and crawled until someone found her and took her back to the village and nursed her back to health, except that she was broken up inside. She discovered she was pregnant, but of course couldn't keep the baby because of all the damage that had been done. I asked her, "Do you want revenge? Do you want those men who killed your parents and raped you, made you pregnant, and broke you up—do you want them to be punished?" And she said, "No. All I want is to rise from this bed so I can thank the people who took care of me. All I want to do is rise from this bed and work for God and try to be good in this world. All I want is maybe to feel a mother's love. Maybe someone will help me feel that."

That is what is possible in human beings. The ability to rise above suffering into greatness. I have discovered that only with adversity is there greatness.

I have become a great admirer of humankind, even despite seeing some of the worst in human behavior, the worst in humanity. It has never ceased to amaze me that no matter how terrible some of the acts are in our human family, I am still in awe of the greatness of what's possible in that same humanity. That is, more than anything else, what pushes me forward.

JOHN: What is the most effective way that we can communicate that these things are occurring in the world in ways that can grab people and make them want to do something to help change things?

ANN: Empathy. I think what people don't realize is a fundamental truth. The only way out of your own suffering is to take up somebody else's. The only way to stop being self-absorbed and sad and broken by what has happened to you in your life or what you think you didn't get in your life or why you're not satisfied, the only real way out of that I have found is to turn your eyes outside yourself and look into someone else's life and you can feel empathy. What I still don't get is why more people don't understand this very selfish thing. It is so rewarding when you see someone who needs a hug or needs a thought . . . just today I met a twelve-year-old boy in a crowd outside the *Today* show. He for some reason told me that he was living with his parent's divorce. They got divorced when he was six, and he looked at me. There was this whole crowd around him—his parents weren't even with him, they were across the way. And he looked at me, and I either had that opportunity to say something to him or not. You damn bet you I did. I jumped right in there and told him that life was going to become amazing. Every sadness that he has in his life is going to become the fire that is going to propel him like a rocket into life and opportunity. Oftentimes, when we don't have a challenge, we don't have that fire, and he's got it. And everything he wants to make happen he can make happen. You damn bet you grab that opportunity.

ANNIE DUKE

Living the Message

JOHN: What motivated you to get involved?

ANNIE: It is important when you are in a situation where you have so much, that you stand up and recognize it, "I have been very lucky in life, and I have a lot, and I certainly have a voice to protect myself." I just felt that, at that point, if I could, I should do something to help in whatever way to protect people who didn't have a voice to protect themselves.

That's where Don and I came together. I play all these poker tournaments that make so much money, and I thought

"Why don't we try to do something for Darfur?" Obviously I knew he was passionate about Darfur as well. I think that, as I got deeper into it and started working on it, my passion grew.

It was really a slow process. I think that part of it came from the fact that one of the things I'm very vigilant about with my children is the idea that often we have this attitude that when we do well, it's through hard work and we deserve it, which is fine. But then I think people infer the flip side, which is when we are not doing well, and things aren't going well for us, that somehow we don't deserve to succeed and we're not hard-working. That is not true. Not doing well in life is not the reverse.

In looking at what is happening around the world, certainly Darfur is one of the most in-your-face cases of people wanting a better life, but how are they supposed to have one? Certainly one of the key ingredients to having a good life is that you are in a place where you feel protected by the people who are supposed to be protecting you, namely, your government. If your government isn't protecting you, what kind of hope do you have? If you are living in a tent trying to find out how to get firewood and you could be raped or murdered along the way, you tell me how you would improve your life? I don't care how smart you are or how hard-working you are or how diligent you are or any of those things. It's just not going to happen. So I always felt that if I was going to send that message to my children, then I should live that message.

JOHN: Where does this feeling of responsibility come from?

ANNIE: First of all, I credit my parents. When I was younger, my mom was politically active. She worked with the Democratic Committee in New Hampshire. We had McGovern posters on our wall. One of my first memories is in our den with wall-to-ceiling bookshelves, because my dad was an English professor. They were covered one year with posters of McGovern. I think I was six years old.

They were very active, but they were also very diligent about teaching us a sense of social responsibility. They are real flaming liberals. In our political views, my brother, my sister, and I ended up being a lot more fiscally conservative than my parents are, but on the social side we are completely in line with them. We feel that social responsibility and social activism are really important.

JOHN: How do you sustain people's interest over time? How do you keep them in the game?

ANNIE: The interesting dilemma is that the real help comes from the policy side, and the policy side is a harder public relations sell. It is harder to say, "Aren't we excited because we had another hearing or there was another vote?" I think that generally it's just hard for people to get excited about policy and working toward policy change. That's the catch-22 here because it's the change in policy and political pressure that will actually create lasting change in the region. So that's the thing that people really need to be paying attention to, but the good public relations sell is the starving children and aid to the refugees. The key, at least the approach that Ante Up for Africa has taken, is to do both. Clearly the Darfurians need direct aid, and so Ante Up is going to direct quite a bit of our resources toward aid and helping people in Darfur, which I think is the piece that the general population can get really passionate about. Then on the other side we are going to donate a significant portion of our resources to getting policy changed so we can get some kind of lasting solution as well. It's harder to sell the lasting solution and keep people excited about that.

DAVE EGGERS

*"By Feeling and Acting Obligated
to Our Fellow Humans, We Are Freed"*

"I have a strange personal theory about when and why we act on certain issues, on needs and injustices. For me, it's being confronted with the problem through first-person contact, and then having the means of addressing it readily available.

"This is how I got involved in Sudanese issues: One day in 2002 I got a letter in the mail. It was from Mary Williams, who had started an organization, the Lost Boys Foundation, to help the acclimation of Sudanese refugees in the United States. She basically said, there are thousands of young men who need help, so would you like to write a book about the Lost Boys of Sudan—and about Valentino Deng in particular—thus bringing attention to their plight and to the millions who have died and are still dying in the Sudanese civil war? That was all pretty much in the first paragraph.

"It was quite a letter.

"I'm a journalist by training, so my interest was piqued. I thought I had to at least meet Mary and Valentino. So I went to Atlanta, and I met Mary and Valentino at a celebration, a birthday party actually, for all the Lost Boys in the region. When they were processed as refugees in Ethiopia, the UNHCR had given them all, thousands of boys, the same birthday, January 1, and so once a year they celebrated this faux birthday. At the party, there was food and dancing, and even an inspirational lecture from Manute Bol, the famous basketball player who had donated most of his NBA earnings to the plight of the people in his native country, Sudan. Valentino and I talked briefly amid the hubbub, knowing that we had all weekend to get acquainted.

"After the event, I was introduced to Manute Bol. Someone

told him that I was a writer and that I was in Atlanta to learn more about the civil war and the state of Sudan. He got very serious, and he grabbed my arm. 'You have to do this,' he said. 'You have to bring this story to a Western audience!' Now, Manute Bol is a very big guy, almost eight feet tall, and he has very intense eyes. I hadn't decided what exactly I would do with Valentino and Mary, but Manute's directive stuck with me.

"Over the next few days, Valentino and I spent a dozen or so hours talking in his apartment, and I recorded the basic outline of his life story. What he had seen, what his family had endured, and the immeasurable injustices visited upon the southern Sudanese people by its government in Khartoum were beyond comprehension. I was outraged, and I agreed that the story needed to be told, and as soon as possible. 'We need to do this!' I told Valentino. 'We need to tell this story, and now.' I was so full of righteous fury that I promised him we could publish the book within a year.

"So I went back to San Francisco, and in the cold light of day, I wondered what the hell I was doing. All I knew about Sudan I'd learned from a few articles, and from what Valentino himself had told me. I was starting from scratch. And when I really thought about it, I realized that the book wouldn't take a year, it would take many. It would entail trips to Sudan. It would entail hundreds of hours of interviews. And it would entail feeling an obligation to do justice to the story—not just of one man but of the thousands who had shared his journey, who had seen the indescribable things he had seen. So I hesitated. I didn't tell Valentino I was hesitating, but damned straight, I was thinking twice about all this.

"But then again, I thought, what else was I doing with my time? What was more important than this work? I'm no believer in fate or any kind of determinism, but hadn't this man, Valentino, come into my life at a moment when I was actually in a position to help? I had written a few books before, and so while I wasn't confident I would do the story justice, I felt that I could probably bring a new audience to the story of Sudanese immigrants like Valentino. I could help, in some way, to tell a few more people, in a few new ways, about what had happened and what was happening, so the horror and suffering—and also the individuals and their losses and triumphs—would never be forgotten. So what excuse could I possibly have for not doing it?

"I worked on the book for the next four years, mainly because it all conformed to the theory I mentioned at the beginning. I had been apprised of a need through personal contact, and when my help was asked for, I had the tools available to provide that help. I didn't ever again overcomplicate it from there. When you're walking down the street holding a ladder, and someone needs a ladder, you hand over that ladder. It's almost a relief, to have a tool in hand and meet someone who needs that very tool. There is such comfort, life-affirming comfort really, in feeling useful. We go through life, most days, unsure of our usefulness, unsure why we're here and for how long, and so to have a purpose guiding your days, well, there is liberation there. It's strange but true: by feeling and acting obligated to our fellow humans, we are freed."

CONGRESSMAN KEITH ELLISON (D-MINNESOTA)

Keeping the Focus

"Darfur is a tragedy of enormous proportions. I have followed this issue since 2002, and I am committed to preventing an escalation of this crisis. My visit to Darfur was a haunting experience. How can people inflict such pain and suffering on their fellow human beings? I visited the Zam Zam refugee camp in Darfur where tens of thousands of people struggle for their daily survival and fear further attacks from the Janjaweed. Darfur's humanitarian crisis has not passed. The situation could worsen—millions of people remain displaced and scattered in refugee camps, most of which are overcrowded and underresourced.

"We simply cannot let Darfur fall off the world's radar screen as so many other human tragedies have. Continue to write e-mails, make phone calls, and protest the horrific conditions in Sudan. We must be ever vigilant until the last refugee walks safely home."

MIA FARROW

With Knowledge Comes Responsibility

"Who among us is not haunted by the genocide in Rwanda? Its components define us, condemn us, demand better of us, and pose profoundly wrenching questions. My country, my Church, the United Nations, and all the nations of the world did nothing to halt that nine-month rampage in which a million people were slaughtered. Collectively and individually, we must bear the burden of our abysmal failure. We failed to protect our brothers and sisters in their darkest hour, even as we failed our most essential selves.

"In that context, a 2004 *New York Times* op-ed piece by Samantha Power stopped me in my tracks. On the tenth anniversary of the Rwandan genocide, Ms. Power wrote that another genocide was unfolding in a remote region of Sudan. This time it was an Arab government attempting to eliminate the non-Arab populations of the remote Darfur region.

"Now, I have always told my children that 'with knowledge comes responsibility.' This time, I thought, I could not stand by. And so I first went to Darfur in 2004. Sudanese government aircraft and their proxy militia, the Janjaweed, were busy. They were attacking village after village, raping, mutilating and murdering, stealing livestock, torching crops and food stocks, and poisoning wells with butchered corpses of people and animals. Traveling through Darfur I encountered dazed and terrified survivors, sheltering under scrawny trees or walking across the parched terrain in search of food, water, and safety.

"Aid workers were there too, struggling to sustain the massive numbers of people displaced since the killing began in 2003. Hundreds of camps had been hastily assembled throughout Darfur and across the border in neighboring Chad. They were hauling water bladders on the backs of trucks, setting up latrines, drilling bore holes, and distributing grain and plastic sheeting to more than 1 million traumatized desperate people, mostly women and children, and the number was swelling. It would eventually approach 3 million.

"The camps were, as they are today, deplorable places where the inhabitants are barely surviving. Food and water are minimal; medicines minimal; sanitation minimal to nonexistent; education minimal to nonexistent; hope minimal to nonexistent. And they offer little safety. While I was visiting Kalma camp, it was invaded by Janjaweed. When the women leave the camps to gather firewood needed to cook the sorghum donated by the World Food Program, they are often raped. The Janjaweed are never far away.

"In one such camp a woman named Halima told me about the day her village was attacked. It had been an ordinary morning. Halima was preparing breakfast for her family. Without warning, planes and helicopters filled the sky, raining bombs upon homes, upon people as they slept, as they prayed, as they scattered in all directions. Halima tried to gather her children, and holding her infant son, she ran for her life. But then militia swarmed the village. On camels and horseback they came, shouting racial slurs and shooting.

They chased Halima, and before they raped her, they tore her baby from her arms and bayoneted him before her eyes. Three of her five children were similarly killed that day, and her husband too. 'Janjaweed,' she told me. 'They cut them and threw them into the well.' Halima clasped both of my hands saying, 'Tell people what is happening here. Tell them we need help. Tell them we will all be slaughtered.'

"As I traveled from camp to camp, I met many people, and they were eager to talk to me. Their stories of loss and terror, of torture and rape, of beloved homes and carefully tended fields ablaze, of lives destroyed are with me always. Like Halima, they begged me to tell people what was happening there. They hoped that the world would hear their cries and that the United Nations would send forces to protect them.

"Darfur in 2004 was an inferno for which no words seemed adequate. On the plane trip home, I tried to process all I had seen and learned. With knowledge comes responsibility. An inescapable knowledge of Darfur was now mine. As a mother, an actor, and a citizen on this earth, I knew only that I must honor my promise to Halima and the other courageous people of Darfur. I would do my best to 'tell the world what is happening' there.

"I didn't know then what my 'utmost' would mean. I couldn't know that over the next five years I would return to the Darfur region and to refugee camps in eastern Chad eleven times. I would write scores of op-ed pieces that appeared in publications around the world. My photographs too found their way into print in newspapers and magazines. I, who had shirked interviews all my life, would now do at least a thousand. I went on every TV or radio show that would have me. I would speak to students on countless campuses, to U.S. leaders at congressional and senate hearings. I set up my own website, (miafarrow.org) so that people could inform themselves and access the photos and articles as well as the links to the best Darfur-related sites I could find.

"A relentless focus on the crisis revealed that revenues from Chinese oil purchases fund a majority of Khartoum's assaults upon Darfur's civilians and its instruments of destruction: bombers, assault helicopters, and small arms. The vast majority of weapons are of Chinese origin. Beijing has repeatedly used its place on the UN Security Council to obstruct international efforts to curtail the slaughter.

"I found myself at the front of a national movement urging investment firms to divest in companies that have holdings in the Chinese oil companies. Colleges, universities, and dozens of states divested. On a hugely popular women's TV show, my message was that we must all be responsible for our own savings and retirement accounts. I urged people to send a clear message to our investment advisors that we refuse to have our savings used to slaughter innocent people. Every day of that week 45,000 people visited my website.

"On April 27, 2009, I began a fast of water only in solidarity with the people of Darfur and as a personal expression of outrage at a world that is somehow able to stand by and watch innocent men, women, and children needlessly die. My blood sugar dropped to dangerous levels after thirteen days. But my fast was taken up by others; by members of Congress, celebrities, business tycoons, sports figures, and ordinary folks in thirty-three countries. And incredibly, after four months it continued, unbroken.

"I have begun my own project, the Darfur Archives. I am filming the traditional ceremonies, songs, dances, and stories of the tribes of Darfur. Their culture was a rich one. 'But we don't do the ceremonies any more,' the leader—or Oumda—of one tribe told me. 'We are suffering. We are in mourning.' I promised the refugees that when peace comes, I will build a museum in Darfur, and this footage will be there for their children and their children's children. It is for them. I just operate the equipment. And so in the thousands they came each day, and they brought forth their treasures. I filmed in the camps for four weeks. The task isn't finished, but I'm on my way. I have some forty hours of footage and a bonus: the refugees gave me almost 200 artifacts, everyday items they used before their lives were destroyed.

"Until we can have the museum in Darfur, I will be uploading their testimony on the Darfur Archives website. I believe seeing the ceremonies and hearing the stories will bring Darfur's people into focus in a new way. Its primary importance is for the Darfuris in the future, but also, at this point in advocacy, it will serve as an important tool to show the world what extraordinary people we have been talking about and how rich and meaningful their customs and traditional way of life once were.

"I think this is how I will spend the rest of my life. As I write this, violence has torn apart traditional ways of life in the Democratic Republic of Congo; in the Central African Republic; in Somalia. I will continue to archive, to try to preserve the cultures and tell the stories of victims of genocide and mass atrocities.

"Did I actually make a difference for the people of Darfur? Maybe not. But I can help to preserve their culture. In that one sense, perhaps Darfur can be saved. And the old Oumda eventually rewarded me bountifully when he said, 'Thank you for reminding us to remember.' "

SENATOR JOHNNY ISAKSON (R-GEORGIA)

Fulfilling an Obligation

"I first became aware of the atrocities in Darfur in 2004 while serving in the U.S. House of Representatives. Since becoming a U.S. senator, I have cosponsored many pieces of legislation aimed at stopping the violence and achieving peace in Darfur. Most recently, I traveled to Sudan to engage with officials from the government of Sudan on many issues including Darfur, as well as to visit an internally displaced person (IDP) camp in el Fasher, North Darfur.

"I believe that I have an obligation as a husband, father, grandfather, and U.S. senator who is the ranking member on the Senate Foreign Relations Subcommittee to ensure that innocent women and children in Africa are protected from conflict and violence. My official travels have allowed me to see firsthand much of the violence and suffering taking place in Africa, and I do not believe that any person should have to live in such deplorable situations.

"While the issue of Darfur is always on my radar, I do have many constituents who contact me on a regular basis to express their views on the current situation there. Constituents affiliated with groups such as Save Darfur and the Darfur Urgent Action Coalition of Georgia regularly contact my office and meet with me and my staff. While my position on the Senate Foreign Relations Subcommittee on African Affairs keeps me well aware of what is going on in Sudan, in particular Darfur, it is very beneficial to me to hear from my constituents who are working toward ending the violence in Darfur."

BIG KENNY

"I Don't Want a World Like That for My Son to Grow up In"

Kenny Alphin is one-half of the country duo Big and Rich, but he is also a tireless advocate for the people of Sudan. We caught up with him right before he was going on stage in Big Flat, New York. There was a bit of a storm, so the concert manager delayed his act. Perfect time for Big Kenny to tell his story . . .

"Let me first say that having a child myself, I couldn't stand the thought that something like what is happening to the kids in Sudan could happen to my boy. I would hope that if something like that happened to him, someone somewhere would reach out and help him. Secondly, it seems to me that we can always break barriers with music. We can develop a common understanding between people. We are all the same, even if there might be some cultural differences.

"For some reason, I've always watched what is happening in Sudan, even when I was a kid reading *National Geographic*. I've always considered myself a common man. I was raised on a cattle farm in Virginia. My father taught us the lesson of stewardship. We don't own what we are given here on earth. We keep it and improve it for future generations.

"Living down in Nashville, I was asked by a local anti-genocide group to bring a guy down to speak to the people there. That was Brian Steidle [the U.S. Marine captain who worked for the United Nations in Darfur and blew the whistle on the unfolding genocide], who is deeply committed to educating people about what is happening there. Brian came to my house and showed me his pictures. I saw schoolgirls shackled and burned alive. Horrible things. Children should not be allowed to live through that. I don't want a world like that for my son to grow up in.

"So I started reading everything I could get my hands on to try to understand what was going on in Sudan. Then Gloria White-Hammond, the dynamic founder of My Sister's Keeper and former board chair of the Save Darfur Coalition, came to Nashville, and after I heard her speak I was on a mission. My band had a fifty-foot banner up on our stage for a year after that at every one of our shows.

"I decided to buy a bunch of supplies and take them to

Sudan. We brought twenty military-sized crates of educational and medical supplies from Nashville, plus 300 refugee survival kits. A doctor came with us to help treat the kids. We also dedicated a school that My Sister's Keeper had funded. There are 550 girls in that school. They have a school now! My first check from my first number 1 song went straight to My Sister's Keeper. I learned so much at that school from those kids. I can be an instigator to get more education for kids in Sudan, and to raise awareness of what is happening there over here in America.

"We went back to Sudan again and I brought eighteen people with me this time, including doctors and filmographers. I remember one day we saw a little two and a half year old kid. The doctor in the clinic thought he was gonna die. But we had brought rehydration fluids. They hooked the kid up to an IV, and within a day he was playing with the other kids. We can do so much with so little. I want to see the way paved with flowers for these children."

NICHOLAS KRISTOF

Addiction and Inspiration

"When I first went to Darfur in early 2004, I never imagined I'd become a frequent visitor or a regular commenter on genocide. Frankly, genocide is a lousy issue for a newspaper columnist: you want to be stimulating, surprising, and counterintuitive in a column, and criticizing genocide in a remote part of Africa that no one cares about isn't surprising at all. Indeed, it's essentially a recipe for the reader to turn the page.

"The problem was that the story just grabbed hold of me and wouldn't let go. On my first visit, I reached the Chad-Sudan border and was blown away by what I found.

Darfuris had been driven from their villages and were in hiding, but they were in desperate need of drinking water to stay alive. The only sources of water were wells scattered across the landscape, and members of the Janjaweed militia were camped at the wells. When men showed up to get water, the Janjaweed would shoot them. When women showed up, the Janjaweed would rape them.

"So I watched these Darfuri families sending their little children, ten-year-olds, with donkeys across the desert toward the wells to fetch water, because the Janjaweed often didn't bother the children. The parents were terrified when they sent their children, and I couldn't imagine sending my children into danger that way. But there was no alternative. Unless the little children went, the entire families would die of thirst.

"I returned from Darfur to the comfort of America, but those scenes haunted me. I went on to writing about other topics—Iraq, domestic policy, and so on—but I knew that those Darfuri families were still in hiding, still sending their children on these crazy missions to get water.

"Frankly, those Darfuris seemed to need my help more than other people I might write about.

"People often think that newspaper columns are powerful, but in fact that influence is often overstated. If I write about topics that people already have thought about and have a view on—health care, capital punishment, abortion—I change very few minds. People who start out agreeing with me think that I'm brilliant, and those who start out disagreeing think that I've completely missed the point. Yet where we as journalists truly do have power is when we shine our spotlight on an uncomfortable truth and force the public and policy makers to take account of it. In other words, our power doesn't lie in shaping the issues that are already on the agenda but in helping place certain issues on the agenda.

"So as the months passed, and I grew increasingly

frustrated that nothing was happening about Darfur, that others in the news media weren't covering the story. I began to think that maybe I should make a return trip. Darfur nagged at me. So I returned three months later, and then again three months after that—and then I couldn't shake the addiction.

"People often ask if it isn't incredibly depressing to go again and again to Darfur and talk to survivors. Yes, at times it is. You go to Darfur, or Congo, or similar spots, and you encounter the worst atrocities imaginable. But the worst of humanity also tends to bring out the best, in other people. In places like Darfur, I'm truly humbled and awed when I see local people, aid workers, and elders risking their lives on behalf of other people.

"In New York, some people don't want to comment on an issue because they can't be bothered. In Darfur, I interview rape victims who allow me to use their names and show videos of them, despite enormous stigma and risk, because they say it is the only way they can fight back against the rapists. They express their humanity by risking their own safety and honor to protect other women—and that's inspiring, not depressing. In contrast, I come back to the United States and see young people who can find no higher way to express their humanity than to have the hottest cell phone or coolest car.

"And that's what's truly depressing."

TRACY McGRADY

"How Can We Stand By?"

Every summer off from his grueling basketball season, Tracy McGrady would take a vacation overseas. Something moved him in 2007 to talk with his manager, Elissa Grabow, about doing something different than the usual recreational vacation to Cancun or wherever. So they literally called Amnesty International's main number and eventually got to Bonnie Abaunza, who at the time was coordinating Amnesty's work with artists and athletes. Bonnie called John, and they conspired with Tracy and Elissa for a trip to the Darfur refugee camps in Chad.

Dorothy, we're not in Cancun any more.

Tracy and Elissa went with John, Darfurian activist Omer Ismail, and a film crew led by documentarian Josh Rothstein. The stories Tracy heard were like nothing he had ever encountered, and they moved him to tears, and to life-changing action.

We met Isaac, a young man whom we met sitting on a mat in a humble community center in one of the refugee camps we visited. We listened closely to his story to understand why a government would try to wipe out entire groups of its own people such as Isaac.

Before late 2003, Isaac was a student in a high school in West Darfur. His village wasn't wealthy, but his family lived well, growing all kinds of crops, nurturing large orchards of fruit trees, and raising goats and a few cows. He had heard about a few battles between the Sudan government and some rebel groups based in Darfur, but he was concentrating on his schooling and hoped it wouldn't disrupt that.

But on December 1, 2003, everything changed.

Isaac had just left a wake at his mosque when his village came under attack. The Sudanese government and their main militia allies, the Janjaweed, came into town on horseback and trucks, hunting all the males in the village, whether children, adults, or elderly. At least 150 males were killed that morning, including 42 children. The village was looted, and most of the houses were burned to the ground. Isaac lost two uncles, two aunts, and two brothers.

Dazed and devastated, the survivors hid in the orchards

outside the village. For the next two months, the Janjaweed scouted out their locations and warned them, "If you don't want to turn to ashes, you better leave this place." But for Isaac and the others, "this place" was their home, and they didn't want to leave.

But on February 13, 2004, the Janjaweed and government forces attacked again. Many more were killed, and this time many of the women who were trying to hide were raped.

It took Isaac and some of his neighbors three months to find their way to the safety of the refugee camp in Chad. There we found him, three years later, trying to make sense of his ordeal.

He told us that the government of Sudan had decided to destroy the communities like Isaac's from which rebels were being recruited, even though no rebels lived in his village. And he said the Janjaweed want their land, so they have to get rid of the people on it. This is why there is an alliance between the government and the Janjaweed to destroy the non-Arab communities of Darfur.

We met dozens of people from both Sudan and Chad with stories like Isaac's. All of them told us that they just want to go home. They said that to get there, three things were necessary: a fair peace deal, a UN force to protect them, and punishment for those who had driven them from their homes."

These "three Ps" inspired Tracy to change the number on his Rockets uniform to 3, and it is the name of the documentary that resulted from the trip.

But something bigger emerged from this visit as well. On their last night in the refugee camps, the team came up with the idea for a sister schools program that could connect students in U.S. schools with students from Darfur in the refugee camp schools. The Darfur Dream Team's Sister Schools Program (www.darfurdreamteam.org) resulted, and it now has hundreds of schools in the United States actively involved in raising funds and awareness for the refugee camp schools. A number of basketball stars have joined in as supporters, including Derek Fisher, Baron Davis, Luol Deng, Etan Thomas, and Jermaine O'Neal. And most importantly, just as Tracy did, the students are connecting directly with the students in the camps, thus putting a human face on war and investing young Americans personally in helping to find a solution to the Darfur crisis.

Tracy concluded about his trip and the aftermath:

> As I was hearing more about Darfur, something inside me needed to learn more about the conflict. I was filled with questions and was compelled to get answers. But as my journey brought me to the refugee camps, I realized that there are no easy answers, just more questions. How can we stand by and allow this to happen to these innocent people? How can the world be aware and do nothing? After looking into the eyes of my brothers and sisters who sit in those camps, I made a promise to tell their stories, to share what I saw, and to help in any way that I can. If I put a hand out in aid, then maybe, just maybe, it will inspire another to do the same.

CONGRESSMAN FRANK WOLF (R-VIRGINIA)

"To Whom Much Is Given, Much Is Required"

"I have long been interested in Sudan—having traveled there five times since 1989. My most recent visit to Darfur was in July 2004 when I led the first congressional delegation with Senator Sam Brownback. I witnessed the unfolding nightmare with my own eyes. I spoke to women who had been raped and brutalized by the Janjaweed. I saw burned out villages, decimated by war. I visited with families living in makeshift camps. The misery that we saw demanded action—the status quo was simply unacceptable.

"Defending human rights, thereby giving a voice to the voiceless, has long been a priority during my service in Congress. I believe that in order for America to truly be the 'shining city on a hill' envisioned by our founders, we must continually affirm that we stand for the defenseless, champion liberty, and confront injustice the world over. Further, my faith teaches that to whom much is given, much is required. America has faced its share of difficulties, but as a nation, we have been richly blessed. This reality leads me to seek to draw attention and prompt action to confront human rights abuses in places like Darfur.

"In my experience, members of Congress get involved in these types of issues for a variety of reasons. Sometimes they have a large diaspora community in their district from a particular country that takes an active interest in events of their home country. Sometimes they've traveled to these regions and personally witnessed something that stirred them to action. My own travels to places like Sudan, Sierra Leone, and Ethiopia have served to inspire policy recommendations and other congressional action upon my return.

"With advances in mass communication, I have seen a dramatic uptick in the amount of constituent mail, specifically e-mail, in my nearly thirty years in Congress. E-mail makes it easier for constituents to share their views with me. But often times we receive huge numbers of form letters, with identical text, simply cut and pasted into an e-mail. This is obviously one way for constituents to share their opinions, but when someone has taken the time to write a personalized letter in his or her own words detailing their thoughts about any given issue, that certainly stands out."

CHAPTER FIVE

Saying Enough to Child Soldier Recruitment

DON: One of the most harrowing experiences I've ever had, outside of visiting Darfur, is when you and I visited that rehabilitation camp of former child soldiers in northern Uganda, run by World Vision. It was particularly overwhelming, especially sitting there with my daughter, who was not much younger than the child I was talking to, who was telling us the story of how he had to kill his best friend so that he would not be killed by the Lord's Resistance Army commander. What a horrifying choice to have to make.

JOHN: For anyone. But especially for a kid.

DON: This isn't the first time something like this has happened in history. You think of the Khmer Rouge in Cambodia and how they press-ganged kids into military service. You think of the Hitler Youth. You think of the exploitation of completely undeveloped human beings and the most horrific way they could be employed and how that changes the individuals forever. How are you rehabilitated out of that? How do you ever find peace if you have been made to do some of the things these kids have been made to do to survive?

JOHN: Just as incredible as the LRA problem is, equally extraordinary is the fact that a solution has been within reach for a long time, but the world has barely lifted a finger to implement it. There are many precedents, many successful models. Sierra Leone was one of the most violent wars in the world for a decade. A murderous rebel leader named Foday Sankoh kidnapped thousands of kids and forced them to commit terrible atrocities. Finally, the world woke up. An international strategy was developed thanks to the blood diamonds campaign and the willingness of the British and Nigerians to intervene, and Foday Sankoh was captured. His rebel group collapsed. Today, Sierra Leone is a democracy, completely at peace.

DON: And Idi Amin, the Ugandan dictator back in the 1970s, was taken out by a military intervention by neighboring countries, right?

JOHN: Yep, Tanzania led it. And for decades the wars in Angola were some of the most violent in the world. A rebel leader named Jonas Savimbi terrorized the country and forcibly recruited kids to be his foot soldiers. Finally, after the blood diamond campaign undermined rebel diamond revenues and led to some serious internal rifts among its leadership, a bullet ended Savimbi's life, and his rebel group ceased fighting almost immediately. Angola today is a country at peace.

DON: This is often how these situations seem to get "resolved."

JOHN: It's time for something like this for Joseph Kony and the LRA. Two million rendered homeless in four countries.

Tens of thousands of innocents kidnapped to be child soldiers and sex slaves. Enough Is Enough.

DON: Are you saying that killing him is the solution?

JOHN: I think a credible military strategy that focuses on apprehending Kony and the other LRA leaders is where our efforts should be focused. Attack the roots of the problem. And yes, war can be messy, and it is possible in an operation like this Kony could be killed.

DON: When we were there, there were sporadic peace efforts.

JOHN: Each time Joseph Kony has shot down any chance of a peace deal.

DON: So one guy says no, and thousands more kids get abducted?

JOHN: It doesn't have to be that way. As always, there is a solution. And frankly, I'm a tree-hugging peace advocate. I belong in sandals, a Grateful Dead t-shirt, and a pony tail. So when someone like me advocates for a military solution, you can rest assured all other peaceful means have been exhausted, and I was personally involved with some of those ill-fated peace efforts. As with so many of these armed groups that abduct kids to fight for them, the LRA is not fighting for a cause. Kony is not a rebel leader in the classic sense. His methods and tactics end up terrorizing the people he claims to represent rather than liberating or protecting them.

DON: The LRA is like a mafia.

JOHN: And Kony is like the worst mafia don imaginable, with his dozens of "wives" and child soldier home guards. The LRA's sole rationale is to sustain itself through looting and abducting more children as soldiers and sex slaves. The answer is to arrest Kony, to execute the ICC warrants, and end this mafia insurgency once and for all.

Child Soldiers

History is full of examples of the use of child soldiers. The term *infantry* is derived from the Italian phrase *enfanteria*, which described boys who followed knights into battle during the Renaissance. However, the modern era has seen an unprecedented increase in the use of children in war. At any given time, more than 300,000 children, some as young as eight, are exploited in armed conflicts around the world. That's a staggering number; more than three times the number of people that the biggest football stadium could accommodate. Children living in almost any conflict zone around the world are vulnerable to recruitment into war.

In his book *Innocents Lost,* investigative journalist Jimmie Briggs—who has spent more than a decade reporting and writing about children in war—notes that child soldiering is the result of "a breakdown in society, making the youngsters vulnerable to war's abuses with daunting odds of escape."[19] Child soldiers have served in significant numbers on almost every continent in the world. From Sri Lanka, to Colombia, to Sudan and Sierra Leone, children have been exploited and have suffered unimaginable trauma.

One of the primary methods of recruiting children is through abduction from their homes, schools, or communities. In countries mired in conflict, children are often kidnapped or abducted during village raids. Groups that rely on children to carry out the gruesome realities of war often go about recruitment systematically and intentionally. Some groups set quotas for the minimum number of children who must be recruited into war. The LRA, for instance, sets numeric goals for child recruits and raids villages with the intent of capturing a specific number of children.[20] In Sri Lanka, the Tamil Tigers reportedly maintained computer databases that guided their recruitment efforts.[21] The kidnapped children who meet physical size requirements, usually determined by their ability to carry a weapon, are deemed ready to fight in combat. Those who are unable to fight are forced to serve as scouts, porters, sex slaves, cooks, or spies. Some child soldiers claim to have joined combat "voluntarily," but, most likely, these children have been driven to join out of desperation and the need to flee extreme poverty, abuse, or discrimination. Once they are under the control of armed groups, child soldiers are subject to brainwashing, abuse, and sexual exploitation. These children see things no one should ever see, and experience things no one should ever experience. They are deprived of their innocence and their freedom, and the world has an obligation to stand up and fight as hard as they can to end their suffering.

Child Soldier Recruitment by the Lord's Resistance Army

The Grimm Brothers could not have concocted a fairy tale as surreal as that of northern Uganda. For many years, each night before the sun set, tens of thousands of Ugandan children would march in grim procession along dusty roads that would take them from their rural villages to larger towns. The children were afraid to sleep in their beds, terrified that they would be abducted by a madman who would force them into a marauding guerrilla army that would hunt down their friends, families, and loved ones. The fleeing children would sleep in churches, empty schools, makeshift shelters, and alleyways. And every morning at sunrise, the children would walk home, free for another day.

This was no make-believe fairy tale though. It was not the creation of some imaginative writer intending to scare his or her audience and then create a hero to rescue the children. No, this was the reality of northern Uganda's two-decade conflict, where nearly everyone at some point has been rendered homeless and where there existed for years the highest rate of child abductions in the world.

The rebels, in what may be the most ironically titled insurgency in the history of war, call themselves the Lord's Resistance Army. They are led by a self-proclaimed messiah named Joseph Kony, a man rooted in a grotesquely distorted view of the Old Testament. He likens himself to Moses bringing the Ten Commandments to a people who are largely deaf to his message. He believes—or says he believes—he is instructed by God to punish anyone who collaborates with the Ugandan government, and he accuses everyone from northern Uganda of collaboration, so everyone is therefore, conveniently, a potential target.

Kony, his few disciples, and an army comprised largely of kidnapped, tortured, and brainwashed child soldiers fight not for a cause but rather to maintain their warlord existence and to embarrass the Ugandan government by undertaking spectacular attacks that usually involve sadistic mutilations. Driven out of northern Uganda by the Ugandan government army, the LRA has spread to three neighboring countries, bringing along its continued reliance on child abductions for recruits and sadistic mutilation for terror. For lack of better term, the LRA is a mafia that has run amok.

Stealing Children by Any Means Necessary

Rarely in human history has such a small group of people caused so much suffering for so many. The LRA is a militia of 1,000 to 1,500 mostly child soldiers headed by the indicted war criminal Kony. The organization has no clear political agenda. Its support comes from what it plunders, and at times from its patrons in the government of Sudan in Khartoum. This small but ruthless force has caused havoc in northern Uganda, southern Sudan, eastern Democratic Republic of Congo, and the Central African Republic.

The LRA's toolbox of war tactics includes murder, torture, mutilations, rape, sexual slavery, and widespread child abductions. Since 1986, the LRA has abducted as many as 40,000 children in northern Uganda and thousands more in neighboring countries. In an effort to prevent looting and abductions, the Ugandan government created "protected villages." Sadly, these were often overcrowded, unsanitary, dangerous camps for the internally displaced, and most of the camps' inhabitants were forced by the government to enter these camps against their will. In 2002, Uganda launched Operation Iron Fist in an attempt to definitively defeat the insurgency, but the operation sparked more intense and violent attacks by the LRA—and instigated the LRA's return from southern Sudan to northern Uganda. The military operation dramatically increased the number of internally displaced people, and it failed to end the war. At the height of the conflict, nearly 2 million northern Ugandans were living in displaced-person camps.

Throughout late 2005 and early 2006, the LRA shifted its base of operations into northeastern Congo, where no state existed and the jungle terrain offered a perfect sanctuary for Kony. Around the same time, the International Criminal Court (ICC) unsealed arrest warrants for five senior LRA leaders, including Kony. The ICC's actions, coupled with increasing pressure on the battlefield, pushed the LRA to agree to peace talks with the Ugandan government, and these negotiations began in July 2006 in Juba, southern Sudan. While many Ugandans, activists, and diplomats were hopeful that a deal might be struck, talks fell apart late in 2008,

with Kony repeatedly refusing to sign a deal that his delegation had helped draft.

The U.S. Response to the LRA

The word terrorism *is used loosely by governments around the globe. In northern Uganda, touring through displaced camps and centers for war-affected children, we hear story after story of spectacular violence, the aim of which can only be to terrorize. "We are awaiting death," one young man in a displaced-person camp told us. "Will it be the LRA or hunger that takes us?"*
—RYAN GOSLING AND JOHN PRENDERGAST FOR *ABC NEWS*

In late 2008, after nearly four months of renewed LRA attacks, the armies of Uganda, Congo, and southern Sudan—with the support of the United States—launched Operation Lightning Thunder, a joint military operation in Kony's Congo hideout. Though the offensive weakened the LRA by cutting off food stores and other supplies, it also forced the LRA back into its familiar and highly advantageous position as a highly mobile insurgent force that knows the terrain and lives off the backs of the people it loots and pillages. The LRA also retaliated with brutal attacks against Congolese villages.

Why the World Hasn't Succeeded in Stopping the LRA—Yet

Operation Lightning Thunder was seriously flawed and was unable to end the LRA insurgency. The aerial bombardment of LRA hideouts in northeastern Congo and sub-
sequent ground operation did not achieve their initial goal of surprise, and ensuing military incursions have been indiscriminate—endangering children previously abducted

by the LRA and creating significant risks for civilians in the region. Scattered LRA units were dispersed and stretched across hundreds of kilometers, able to conduct hit-and-run attacks against their pursuers. It is likely that many of the children who were forcibly abducted to become soldiers are too traumatized and sometimes drugged to envision a life beyond the LRA.

After the failure to capture any of the top LRA commanders, most of the Ugandan soldiers returned home to Uganda, and military operations against the LRA were reduced, with disastrous consequences for civilians throughout central Africa. An angry, hungry, and violent LRA remained on the loose, preying on civilians with frightening efficiency. As a result of the LRA's predations in the first half of 2009 alone, over 1,000 people were killed and 200,000 people were forced out of their homes and into squalor, mostly in southern Sudan and northeastern Congo, with millions of dollars spent on humanitarian operations to help clean up the mess. The LRA began abducting en masse again at the beginning of 2010, and it also started to train children again. Children abducted in the Central African Republic fight in Congo, and vice versa. As of the time of this writing, LRA units had been spotted in Darfur, receiving sanctuary from the government of Sudan. The longer that the regional and international powers wait to figure out what to do next, the more time the LRA will gain to regroup and rebuild, particularly if the Sudanese regime resumes large-scale support.

The United States had a major role in encouraging and supporting regional military operations against the LRA, and the U.S. military was directly involved in planning Operation Lightning Thunder. For years, the U.S. Army has been training Ugandan Special Forces for operations such as this. The United States provided the Ugandans with the equipment to listen in on the LRA's satellite phones and triangulate the group's positions. U.S. military advisors provided the

Ugandans with satellite imagery and maps to plan out the operation.

What the United States Could Do to End It

This is the Enough Moment for redoubling and reinvigorating international and regional efforts to finally bring an end to the LRA's devastating reign of death and destruction. Closing the book on this nightmare requires a more comprehensive approach than just occasional military operations, as called for in the congressional bill signed into law by President Obama in May 2010. Once again, the effective common three P's strategy can lead to success by promoting peace, providing civilian protection, and ensuring punishment of the perpetrators.

Peace: A peace process in Juba unraveled in April 2008, despite intense and lengthy negotiations, when Kony failed to come to the table to sign the final deal. The LRA exploited a year of negotiations to stave off international pressure, collect food and money from donors, and buy time to abduct, train, and equip new combatants. This failed peace effort, however, was not entirely without reward. Many Ugandans as well as governments around the world had long called for peace talks rather than justice initiatives or military strikes to end the LRA insurgency. But now it has been proven beyond a shadow of a doubt that this particular militia leader, Joseph Kony, has no interest in a peace deal. Consequently, Ugandans throughout their country and governments around the world are increasingly supportive of bringing Kony to justice, even if his apprehension requires targeted military operations.

However, there is still much room for peacemaking. A great deal of investment must be made in long-term reconciliation in and rehabilitation of northern Uganda to address the conditions that might lead potentially to a future Lord's Resistance Army II. Furthermore, support for the reintegration of former child soldiers—both economic and psychosocial—is imperative for long-term peace. Putting together a credible reintegration program that supports the children as well as their home communities will create a further incentive for the LRA child soldiers to try to escape and go home.

Ryan Gosling and John, on their trip to northern Uganda together, heard the story of Bosco, a former abducted child soldier, who stood up one day in primary school and in a frightening moment announced, "I have killed eighty-two people." He lunged for the boy next to him, proclaiming, "You will be the eighty-third!" He was physically restrained, and the school sent him for psychosocial counseling through a local NGO. Bosco is now successfully attending secondary school and planning for his future.

Ryan and John also met Sarah, who was abducted by the LRA in 1996 at the age of eight. She was trained to fight, and she was part of a group that killed thirty people. She told us that if she had not participated in those killings, she would have been killed by her commander, the infamous Okot Odhiambo, one of the ICC indictees. She became a rebel's "wife" at the age of thirteen in a forced arrangement, and the next year had a child. "If I said no, I would have been killed," she told us. She escaped during a Ugandan army raid. After going through counseling, Sarah is now attending school full time, studying and deciding what she would like to do for a career. Uganda's children are full of hope. They just need a helping hand. Supporting the former child soldiers is a crucial element to a broader peace building agenda in northern Uganda.

Protection: While northern Uganda is finally experiencing relative peace, civilians throughout the broader central African region are at risk and have increasingly fallen victim to LRA attacks. As one international official told us, "If the people resist, as they did in Uganda, you can be sure the LRA will massacre them, as they did in Uganda."[22] And if increasing numbers of civilians resist, the numbers of casualties will grow. It is thus critical that efforts are made now to ensure the protection of civilians from this increasingly dangerous regional threat posed by the LRA. Additional protection should come from the government armies and peacekeeping forces in the region, bolstered by logistical and training support from the United States and other capable countries, as well as military justice when those forces commit human rights abuses of their own.

But frankly, the best defense is a good offense, and the answer to protecting civilians is ultimately to neutralize the source of their problems, the LRA. More effective and better internationally resourced military operations focused on ending the threat of the LRA are still at the core of the answer. But such operations require a shift from a battle with the LRA generally to a much more targeted and focused mission that isolates and takes the LRA leadership off the battlefield, which will crater the organization.

Punishment: Most of the LRA's leaders have never been held accountable for their crimes, though efforts are ongoing to bring them to justice. Kony and two of his key commanders are wanted by the International Criminal Court, for war crimes and crimes against humanity. (Two other commanders that were originally indicted are now dead.) In July 2005, the ICC issued arrest warrants for Kony and four other key LRA commanders: Raska Lukwiya, Okot Odhiambo, Dominic Ongwen, and Vincent Otti. Formerly Kony's second-in-command, Otti was killed on Kony's orders in late 2007, and Lukwiya was shot during a battle with the Ugandan army. Kony, Odhiambo, and Ongwen remain at large. Bringing them to justice or otherwise removing them from the battlefield will end this nightmare. Also investigating the sources of support for the LRA from the Sudanese government and a small segment of the Ugandan diaspora around the world would diminish Kony's prospects.

A structural problem that exists today in the quest for improved global justice is the lack of an international strategy and force to apprehend those that are indicted for war crimes. After Kony and his main henchmen were indicted on multiple counts of crimes against humanity, the ICC's global backers—most notably a number of European governments—did nothing to enhance the prospects that the warrants would have any chance of execution. No plan was developed concurrent with the issuance of the warrants that would set forth the strategy for apprehending the suspects. And of course there is no world police force that would automatically be tasked with tracking and arresting Kony and his cohorts. The legislation in the U.S. Congress that the Enough Project, Resolve, and Invisible Children successfully promoted requires President Obama to create such an apprehension strategy for Kony and his henchmen.

Call to Action

Despite the fact that the LRA has survived by feasting on children, women, and defenseless villages for over twenty years in northern Uganda and the surrounding region, this is one of the easiest wars in the world to resolve. Dependent solely on its charismatic leader Joseph Kony for strategy and survival, if he were somehow neutralized, the LRA would collapse.

Here's the challenge, and why success is likely: in Congo, there may be upwards of 150,000 men and boys under arms. In Sudan, the number is only slightly less. By contrast, the LRA has perhaps 1,000 troops at any given time. That is the entire scope of the threat. The fact that the world has not yet dealt with this mafia militia full of abducted children is a legacy of failure that may well be unmatched anywhere globally.

When Ryan Gosling and John were visiting northern Uganda together with author Jimmie Briggs, they met a young Acholi woman named Margaret. She asked with fire in her eyes, "What level of suffering do we have to experience here before you come to help us?" This is the question we have to ask President Obama and our members of Congress: "What level of human suffering do the people of Central Africa have to endure before you act?"

The brutal nature of the violations against the "invisible children" of northern Uganda and the surrounding region has put this issue on the global map. We can help these children become visible to the entire world, and with the right effort we can make sure these beautiful, precious, very visible children can soon all go home in peace.

**To help end the scourge of child soldiers,
go to www.enoughmoment.org.**

CHAPTER SIX

Upstanders for Northern Uganda

Just as in Darfur, there are Frontline Upstanders in northern Uganda, survivors of the LRA's worst atrocities, who have had their own Enough Moments and have been working on behalf of their communities and other former child soldiers to help make things better. They are joined by ordinary citizens and celebrities who have taken up the cause and are doing what they can to help make a difference.

FRONTLINE UPSTANDERS:
Former LRA Child Soldiers Who Are Making a Difference

JACOB

"Please Help Us Make Sure the Rebels Do Not Return"

If you meet Jacob today, he seems like the most jovial, hopeful person in northern Uganda. He greets you with a wide smile, introduces you to his family of five, and tells you about how a community farming group that he manages expanded to farm thirty new acres this year. Excited about his successes, he even offers to take you to the farm on the new bicycle he just bought with his portion of the proceeds from the project. And yet behind this façade lies a deeper story that makes you wonder how anyone could live through such an experience, let alone flourish the way Jacob has.

"I was eleven. The rebels came to Olwal, our village. They burned many huts, and they found me. I spent the next one and a half years with them." Jacob was abducted by the LRA in northern Uganda.

"I fought in five major battles and had to kill many people. They thought I was strong, even though I was young. I lost three brothers to the rebels. My family had lost hope."

Then one day the rebels camped near the Paico River, and Jacob was sent to collect materials to build a shelter for the night. As he walked out into the woods, he saw a window of opportunity when no one was looking, and he took it. Jacob was finally free, and his family was ecstatic to lay eyes on him one more time.

But just a few months later, the rebels came again. This time, Jacob tried to employ skill to avoid being seen by the LRA fighters. But the troops were too many, and they re-abducted him. At this point, Jacob felt as though he would never live a normal life again. But thankfully, just two days later an opening came, and Jacob managed to get out, never to return to rebel life again.

Since coming back home, Jacob has faced many challenges. His home community in Olwal turned into an enormous camp for people displaced because of the war. At the height of the war, over 25,000 people lived in the overcrowded camp, with the entire camp population sharing only three boreholes as toilets.[23] He also got married, and taking care of his four children has been a challenge.

But Jacob wasn't going to give up the fight. Under tutelage from Tom Okello, Olwal's inspirational camp leader, and a partnership with the NGO Grassroots Reconciliation Group,[24] Jacob helped set up a group of twenty-five former child soldiers and community members to aid reconciliation in the community. "We faced a lot of stigmatization when we got back from the bush [captivity with the LRA]. It wasn't good; people called you a mad person, and you felt bad. We wanted to do something about this, so we formed this group," explained Jacob. He called it "Pok ki Lawoti," or "Share with a Colleague" in the local Acholi language.

Jacob and Tom started the group out with a brick-making project, aimed at both providing income and helping the other former child soldiers better integrate with the community. "We work together every week, and the differences [between ex-combatants and local community members] become much less," he explained. On its own initiative, the group established a microlending program with profits from their projects. Along with several other group members, Jacob was able to take out a loan and set up a small retail shop that sells groceries in the community. The revenues from the shop now help him feed his family. Jacob's group also has a contingency fund to take care of community problems. In 2008, when one of its members' children got sick with tuberculosis, Pok ki Lawoti paid for the child's medical treatment out of this fund. Because of the treatment, the child's life was saved.

In 2009, Jacob talked to other fellow group members, and they decided to start a farming project. The success has been rapid. "We started with five acres with a startup from the Grassroots Group, but we then expanded the land to thirty acres and hired workers to farm it." The group earned over $400, a substantial amount in local terms, and they reinvested it by buying goats, which they plan will in turn yield even more income for the group.

ROBERT

A Long Walk Home

Three weeks. Twenty-one days. Five hundred and four hours. That is how long Robert spent walking back home as a child after escaping from captivity in the Lord's Resistance Army in northern Uganda. In his seemingly endless two years with the rebels, he was forced to kill, abduct young children, and walk over 300 miles, usually in dense jungle without shoes. And yet now just three short years later, he is leading a successful community project to help his fellow former child soldiers to generate income and reintegrate back into society.

"The LRA is terrible. They make you do terrible things, and then these memories stay with you," Robert explains. Making a bad situation worse, abductees often carry a stigma when they return home, despite the fact that they were forced by the rebels to carry out crimes against their will. The home community is often angry at the former child soldiers, since some of those who were killed or maimed by the LRA often have come from the local community.

Even after his incredible journey back home, Robert also faced this stigma upon his return. It nearly broke his strength. "When I came back home, people said I had evil spirits. I felt as if I was being chased away, and people would bring back those horrible memories from the bush [from the time I spent with the LRA]. Anyone who was angry would vent his or her anger on me, because of what I was forced to do in the bush." Approximately 66,000 youth have been abducted by the LRA over the years, and many thousands of them have expressed similar sentiments.[25]

But these bad experiences didn't stop him. The situation in northern Uganda was changing at the time in 2006: the rebels were moving out of northern Uganda into the surrounding region, leaving Robert's home area more stable than it had been in two decades. The peace process seemed to be moving forward, and people were starting to rebuild. Robert knew that he had to pick up the pieces and move on. He had a family to take care of—he now had three children of his own.

Not only did Robert move on, he led. "I wanted to take my bad experiences and turn them into good," he explained. He wanted to help his family, his community in Alokolum, and the people who were abducted with him. "They don't deserve those bad things. We need to rebuild together."

Last year, Robert became chairman of the group "Can Bwone" (pronounced Chan Bwon-ay, meaning "Poverty requires humility"), a community group formed two years ago with the support of the Grassroots Reconciliation Group. Robert explained "Can Bwone" to us in his own words: "We have twenty-five people, and half of them are returnees [former LRA child soldiers and concubines], and we work together three times per week on a farming project. When we are working hard like that on our project, we are transforming ourselves. We sensitize the community to not stigmatize other returnees, so that they won't call them names or bring back the bad memories."

The new opportunity has not only changed his life but it has also transformed the community's perception of him. "Being in this group has helped erase the bad memories from the bush, because we interact very well and socialize often. Now people don't say that I have those evil spirits any more. They say I have a humble, good character. That is why they chose me to become a group leader."

Robert then took initiative and went even further. "Last year I also organized our group to form a cultural drumming and dancing group, and I entered us into a regional dancing competition. The music and dancing helps our community heal, especially the returnees. We are like a family."

Not stopping there, Robert is already making plans to help his fellow former child soldiers and his community rebuild in additional ways. "I also now started a small fish-selling business from the profits we made from the farming project. This helps me support my family and pay school fees for my children. This year I want to help Can Bwone start a microfinance project from the profits of the farming project, so I can supplement my business and help other returnees and others in the community with small businesses. We need that boost. I want to help give it."

NELSON OCHAYA

Making Life Better for Others

Nelson lived in a village near Gulu, the main town of northern Uganda. He was twelve years old at the time of his abduction by the LRA. He had heard the LRA was in his village, so he ran away and hid with his father. When they were on their way home, they ran into the rebels. He and his father were tied up. But he knew that if he admitted that he was with his father, he would be forced to kill him so he wouldn't run away and return to his village. So he denied that his father was beside him.

They took Nelson away and told him that he must be caned so that "civilian behaviors" would be beaten out of him. The rebels brought heaps of sticks and he lay down on the ground. Five rebels caned him ferociously; his hand was so swollen that if he pressed it, it would crack. If he survived they said it meant he was very strong.

Nelson was anointed with oil to show he was now part of the LRA. He recovered from his caning and began his military training in southern Sudan. He was trained to use a gun, lay an ambush, and loot for food. Nelson was taken to a Sudanese government barracks in Juba to receive artillery training. He trained for six months and was given the rank of sergeant. He was then ordered to attack an outpost of southern Sudanese rebel soldiers and cut a male organ to prove his talent. He succeeded and this got the attention of the rebel high command. Nelson was then sent to Uganda to abduct a group of girls from a boarding school.

Nelson finally escaped from the LRA after a battle. He was too traumatized to be taken to his father, who was still alive. But a generous Frenchman provided counseling for him and helped him get treatment for a gun wound he had sustained. Nelson's parents were very poor and could not afford an education for him. He stayed at a World Vision rehabilitation compound for nine months, and he was still wearing army combat uniforms.

One day he went to see where his mom lived, and he told her that he wanted to go to school. But he still had "rebel hair" (dreadlocks) that distinguished him from the other students. Most of the students kept away from him when he started attending the local school. The teacher at the school was so scared that she couldn't teach—she kept repeating herself—and everyone in the classroom was looking at him, so he left the school.

After these experiences, Nelson wanted to do something to change perceptions and to support his fellow abductees. He joined with a few other former child soldiers to create the War Affected Children's Association (WACA) to help his friends who were in captivity like him. WACA provides former child soldiers with formal and vocational education to help them reintegrate back into their home communities in northern Uganda. He hopes to help other people and his colleagues who are still there in the bush. He wants to be a good example to them.

Nelson is happy working with WACA, although he is "still traumatized" by what he experienced in the LRA. He is gradually feeling better about himself and working with WACA has helped. He is helping other former child soldiers, and he wants to be a good mentor and example to them, to assist in any way that he can. He hopes that life will get better in northern Uganda, and he wants to do what he can to help his fellow former child soldiers so that a better life can be possible for all of them.

VICTOR OCHEN

Justice and Reconciliation, One Person at a Time

"I was born and raised in northern Uganda, in the village of Abia, which is the location of one of northern Uganda's camps for displaced people. It is also near a former command post of the LRA. On February 4, 2004, the LRA attacked Abia. Under the command of Vincent Otti and Okot Odhiambo, the LRA massacred hundreds of people.

"My childhood was very painful. I witnessed all sorts of human rights abuses. Together with my family, I often survived on just one meal a day and sometimes had to go without food. Education in the displaced-persons camps in which I lived was a nightmare. My brother and I burned charcoal and sold it in order to pay for our school fees. Because we chose not to pick up guns or join the army, we became targets for abduction by the LRA. Some of my classmates felt such desperation and helplessness that they deliberately allowed themselves to be abducted by the LRA.

"We suffered immeasurable burdens, miseries, and inequalities. Sometimes I have trouble believing that I made it through all these challenges. But we remained with our loving parents and hoped that one day, the war would end and we would all be fine.

"In 2003, the LRA abducted my elder brother and my cousin. I blamed myself for not learning how to shoot a gun so that I could protect them, and I contemplated picking up a gun to try to get them back. To this day, no one knows what happened to them. I have a feeling that if my brother were alive, he would have escaped and come back by now, but I still hope to see him some day.

"What has happened in northern Uganda over the last twenty years is shocking and unbelievable, but it has happened. Nothing can cool down the burning feelings of the people pained and hurt by this war. One young girl described her parents and others being killed and cooked, and other abductees were forced to eat their bodies. She told me, 'Every time I try cooking using the pot, I see my parents inside the pot.' She has wept too bitterly and suffered too much, and it's sad to witness many people like her whose situation only worsens without assistance. It haunts me that I have been unable to help people like this young girl escape circumstances that leave them vulnerable.

"Today I work with the communities affected by the war. I meet and hold in-depth discussions with victims, and these help me to help them help themselves. I am the director of an organization called the African Youth Initiative Network, or AYINET. We work with the victims of the war; we deliver life-saving health assistance and help to promote tolerance, reconciliation, forgiveness, and development. AYINET strongly believes that justice for the victims is necessary to prevent new atrocities in the future.

"A year ago, I had a trying moment during an interview with a formerly abducted child. I discovered that this person was one of the ex-combatants who was ordered to tie up my brother during his abduction. To date, he doesn't know that it was my brother whom he was talking about to me. I felt tortured, but I never told him and never will, and not even any one from my family will get to know him. It was very hard for me to concede this, but I feel that this ex-combatant is innocent since he was forced to do that.

"Given my experience working with victims from northern Uganda and at a time of crisis, I am confident that rehabilitating northern Uganda is not possible without rendering justice for those who have suffered the grave crimes committed by the LRA."

MORRIS OKWERA

Becoming a Role Model

In February 2004, the LRA launched one its most gruesome massacres of the entire war in the northern Ugandan displaced camp called Barlonyo. Out of the camp's population of nearly 12,000 people, the LRA killed and abducted around 700 people in one night, according to local sources. The people in the camp had expected the government to provide sufficient forces to protect them in this confined area, but the Ugandan army didn't deploy and instead recruited local children to serve as "local defense forces." Some were as young as fourteen years old. On the day of the attack, fewer than forty of these local defense forces were in the barracks. The camp was burned to the ground. LRA commander Okot Odhiambo, one of the three living LRA commanders indicted by the International Criminal Court in 2005, led this attack.

On the day of the attack, Morris Okwera was on his way back to Barlonyo when he heard gunshots and ran into his house. A bomb landed in the compound, and Morris started feeling faint, but he didn't know exactly where he was wounded. He ran to another camp nearby to get some medicine. He came back to Barlonyo in the morning to find his mother had been killed and his father had been shot in the leg and was in bad condition. His sister had a bayonet wound through the temple of her head, and she died in the hospital. When he found his mother dead, it seemed as though she may have been tortured but he was not certain. "Even now," Morris said, "I sometimes feel like somebody who doesn't have life again."

Morris had been in captivity for one and a half years, and he had finally escaped from the LRA and come home one week before this massacre happened.

The LRA had abducted Morris from Barlonyo camp in 2003, while he was in "senior 3," at the age of fourteen. He was on his way back from secondary school because he didn't have the money to pay for his school fees. He went home and heard the rebels were coming. He hid, but then he heard it was actually government soldiers, not rebels, so he returned. He went into his house, and he didn't know the LRA had laid an ambush. His brothers started yelling that the rebels had come—Morris found them at his door with a gun. His brothers took off, but he was unable to escape. They tied up Morris along with three or four other abductees and made them carry the food, and they kept looting as they moved. As he was leaving Barlonyo camp with the LRA rebels and the new abductees, three newly abducted elders from his community were killed because they were too slow and old. This was meant as a lesson to Morris and the other child soldiers that they must behave well and be strong. In the group of LRA rebels he was with, the new abductees were each attached to a rebel, and during ambushes this made it very difficult to move when shots were fired, and the abductees had to struggle to keep up.

There were many rebels, and they started dividing the abductees. They wanted more abductions, and they asked their new abductees where the government soldiers were. Morris thought he knew and told them. Shortly after moving, they ran into a government ambush—and it was clearly his fault for misdirecting them. A killing spree began, and Morris was beaten and punished because the LRA was angry with him for misguiding them.

Morris and the other boys were trained as soldiers all day and were beaten frequently. The new abductees were told, "If anyone tries to escape, they'll be shot." When one young abductee tried to escape, he was caught and brought back to the camp and the other kids all had to join in beating him up, and then they slit his throat. All of the children had to beat him and then jump over his body. "This was part of the process of making it as a soldier—beating the dead body and then jumping over it to the 'next level.' "

Morris was supposed to loot every day so he could eat during his life in captivity. He took what he could each day to survive, and he carried as much food as he could steal with him because he never knew how long a fight would last and when he would be able to eat again. "Life was full of looting." The biggest problem was the lack of water. There was no water, just muddy, stagnant water that he would try to strain through his clothes.

On many occasions he had to kill a number of people. The young soldiers were given guns and put on the front lines, and they would shield the commanders, who stood just behind them with guns pointing at their backs. The commanders would say, "If you don't shoot we will shoot you." He was forced to beat and kill people his own age. But in most cases he killed elders. When any of the child soldiers tried to run away, they were all forced by the commanders to kill the escapee.

Finally he had a chance to escape. When Morris made it

back to Barlonyo, he realized the attitude of the community toward former child soldier abductees: "Formerly abducted people are useless and aggressive." That was the stigma he felt. He wanted to be a part of his community again, and he wanted to learn about peace and development. He wanted to show that formerly abducted people like him "could do something."

He became a community counselor with AYINET, the African Youth Initiative Network, which aims to improve relations and build trust between the community and former child soldiers. Initially, he was not trusted, but over time, as he continued to work hard, he showed them that "I am from here, and I am part of this suffering also." As a former child soldier, he can support fellow soldiers as they also attempt to reintegrate into his community.

CITIZEN UPSTANDERS:
Anti-LRA Champions in the United States

LAREN, JASON, AND BOBBY

Invisible Children's Founding Fathers

In 2003, nineteen-year-old engineering student Laren Poole and his good friend Bobby Bailey followed their friend Jason Russell, a recent University of Southern California film school graduate, to Africa. They found themselves in northern Uganda in 2003, and their lives were changed when they saw the car in front of them on the road near Gulu attacked by the LRA.

Ending up in Gulu town, the guys then met Jacob, a Ugandan student who had been abducted by the LRA. The friendship between Jacob, Laren, Bobby, and Jason grew, and the group stayed with Jacob for over a month. While with Jacob, the guys saw firsthand how children walked to towns nightly to escape the predations of the LRA.

Jacob and their experiences in Gulu inspired the friends to return to the United States in order to do whatever they could to end a conflict that very few people seemed to know about or were working to stop. The result of their interest and activism was the creation of the organization Invisible Children, which has helped develop a grassroots constituency of activists in the United States intent on ridding Central Africa of the LRA. Their movement has succeeded in dramatically raising the profile of an issue that had previously been swept under the rug.

From its humble beginnings as a rough documentary, Invisible Children quickly grew to a movement of hundreds of thousands of young people. Captivated by the compelling stories of night commuting and child soldiers, a generation has rallied behind Invisible Children, attending major events each year to highlight the LRA crisis. Volunteers tour across North America with the documentary and other films produced by the team, bringing the story to classrooms and churches with educated representatives. In only four years, over 250,000 young people had taken part in Invisible Children rallies and events. Even Oprah spoke with the Invisible Children guys on her show after they gathered thousands of activists in front of the Chicago studio where she films.

In the summer of 2009, Laren and the rest of the Invisible Children team joined with the Enough Project and Resolve Uganda to host a series of lobby days in Washington, D.C. The team called the event and ensuing campaign "How It Ends." The three groups then launched a political campaign primarily directed at President Obama. Invisible Children developed a nationwide, awareness-raising tour ultimately converging on Washington, D.C. To make as much noise as possible, they held call-in days and delivered a citizens' arrest warrant for Kony, aimed at bringing him to justice. This "Hometown Shakedown" aimed at having activists meet with their elected officials back in their home district offices ended up doubling to fifty-one the number of senators cosponsoring legislation aimed at apprehending Joseph Kony from mid-November to the end of 2009. On one day in November, thirty-two meetings were held in different Senate offices throughout the country. This represented the most cosponsors for any stand-alone Africa-related bill in the U.S. Senate since 1973.

The three founders of Invisible Children each came to the issue in different ways:

Bobby Bailey: He had no idea that their first trip would lead to the formation of their own nonprofit focused on children in northern Uganda. When they got back, they started small, with a bracelet campaign and their first film. Now, their programs employ hundreds of Ugandans, and their grassroots movement involves hundreds of thousands of American youth. As Bobby says, "Media shapes the way we view our lives." He worked on the first film because he saw the impact it could have on young people across the country. He is driven by a desire to give the children of northern Uganda the same opportunities he and his friends have had. The chance to inspire the youth of America to take a stand, Bobby says, has shown him that life is more meaningful when you're giving your time and talent to something bigger than yourself.

Laren Poole: He was an engineering student at the University of California at San Diego when he first learned about Joseph Kony and the LRA. Since his trip to Uganda, Laren has used his interest in filmmaking and activism to highlight the LRA in documentary films that are seen by thousands of students and activists across the country. He also funnels his interest in new media into working on the Invisible Children's website and other multimedia products.

Jason Russell: He credits a church group trip to Kenya in 2000 for transforming his mindset and fomenting his interest in Africa. His ultimate goal is "to raise enough money to build a refuge for the children of northern Uganda so they may grow up in peace." Until he traveled to Uganda in 2003, Jason had planned to make Hollywood musicals once back in the United States. Instead, he has devoted himself to telling the stories of the children he met on that trip. The first step was producing the documentary *Invisible Children: Rough Cut.* Since his first trips to Africa, Jason has married and had a child. Fatherhood has only strengthened his resolve to do all that he can to help end the scourge of the LRA.

BRITTANY DEYAN

Finding Her Voice

"I am from Orange County, California, a place overly stereotyped for its focus on materialism, wealth, and the quest to obtain the unnecessary. This had been all I had known for most of my childhood. I was very much naïve to the world around me. I credit this upbringing to my initial shock in hearing about the travesties taking place in northern Uganda.

"The fall semester of my senior year of high school was a defining moment for me. A teacher with whom I was very close handed me a documentary entitled *Invisible Children,* telling me she thought I would like this film. I sat there and watched it with her in her classroom. I didn't understand. I was watching a film about three young guys from San Diego, not much older than me, traveling to Uganda, a country I had hardly heard of. In the film, I saw children holding guns, being brainwashed and destroying land—all for the desires of a crazy warlord. It didn't make sense to me. I was living a very comfortable life, and these children woke up each day fearing what the day entailed. At the end of the film, the three young filmmakers said they needed help: they wanted to see an end to the war in Uganda, and they wanted me, a seventeen-year-old girl from Orange County, to help them.

"Much about what we know of what is going on in the world, especially in Africa, is communicated through starving children and feelings of extreme desperation. And sadly, oftentimes that is a reality. However, *Invisible Children* tells the story of a crisis taking place a world away from a different angle. They expose the tragedy of war and poverty, but additionally, they expose joy; and most importantly, they give you a specific call to action in how you can help.

"The fact that *Invisible Children* has not only engaged but has also relied on a very young demographic might seem crazy. Perhaps even more crazy is that they are relying on us as young people to end a war, to stop a warlord, to put kids in schools, to facilitate an end to displacement, to pressure the U.S. government to make this a political priority, to help the rehabilitation of brainwashed child soldiers, and ultimately, to raise the profile of this issue. It seems crazy, and it is crazy, but putting the onus on us to make a difference is also empowering.

"At the end of the film they asked for my time, talent, and money. Three boys with a goal of ending (at that time) a twenty-one-year-long war, and I immediately knew that I was going to try and help them. At that time, however, I just didn't realize how much impact I could really make.

"My journey from the day almost three years ago when I saw that film has been a whirlwind. I became an Upstander because at seventeen I felt, for the first time, that I, as a young person, was empowered to have a profound impact on this world. I was standing up for something I believed in, and still believe in: pursuing peace in northern Uganda.

"Since 2007, I have realized that if you are committed and work hard, anything is possible: I started two clubs at my high school and university campuses, raising a total of about $90,000. I traveled to northern Uganda to meet the people and understand the situation firsthand. I traveled to Washington, D.C., on two separate occasions to participate in Ugandan Lobby Days and lobby my congressman to make ending the scourge of the LRA a priority. I taught a class at UC Berkeley for fifty students on the power of social activism and the rise of social movements toward international issues with a focus on specifically what is taking place in Uganda through Invisible Children. I helped in founding a women's university-level scholarship that has currently put over 100 women in universities in northern Uganda through Invisible Children. The first recipient was the friend I made on my trip to Uganda who, more than anything, wanted to pursue a higher education in order to emerge as a female leader of some kind in Gulu.

"Perhaps most importantly, I have found my voice and have begun to understand the impact that I as a seventeen-year-old—well, now a twenty-year-old—can truly make in helping to end Africa's longest-running war."

JOSHUA DYSART

Telling the Story in Different Ways

For many comic book artists and aficionados, comics are a form of escapism, but comic book writer Joshua Dysart is interested in how comics might interact with the real world. This interest in bringing together his creativity and his keen sense of social justice are what eventually led to the creation of a comic book teaching readers about the predations of the LRA.

After first learning about the LRA, Dysart spent years reading whatever he could get his hands on, trying to understand how exactly it was possible that such a small group could be responsible for so much bloodshed and violence. Learning and understanding the crisis was an important part of his life, and an opportunity from DC Comics (best known as the home of Superman and Batman) opened the door for a revolutionary new project. When DC Comics approached him with the concept of re-creating the character from the World War II comic called the Unknown Soldier, Dysart immediately saw the opportunity to use his art to raise awareness about the LRA by setting his book in northern Uganda. Dysart created a series of comic books about Dr. Lwanga, a fictional doctor who as the Unknown Soldier returns home to Uganda and does all he can to ameliorate the suffering of those victims of LRA atrocities.

When talking to Dysart about his work and its juxtaposition with efforts to end the conflict, the first thing he does is offer a caveat. "It's violent," he says, "very violent." But that is Dysart's medium, and he conceded that it very consciously uses some "pulp, mainstream action beats" to accidentally educate. In fact, Dysart stays awake some nights in fear that he is exploiting those who have endured atrocities committed by the LRA. In order to learn for himself, he spent more than a month in Uganda talking with anyone and everyone willing to speak with him. He spent nights in IDP camps and visited AIDS hospices and found himself inside the lives of people who persevere despite unimaginable hardship.

While Dysart continues to worry and work tirelessly to ensure that he is doing his best not to exploit the situation, he has begun to see the fruits of his labor. "When a sixteen-year-old wealthy white kid comes up to me and knows who the president of Uganda is," he says, "I feel good."

FAMOUS UPSTANDERS:
Highlighting the LRA Crisis through Celebrity Activism

SENATOR RUSS FEINGOLD (D-WISCONSIN)

Letters Matter

"I have been a member of the Africa Subcommittee since I came to the Senate in 1993, and I have been chairman of that subcommittee for five of those years. It is my job in that capacity to follow human rights crises very closely, and I take that job very seriously. I also learn more about these crises from constituents—and even my daughters, in the case of the LRA—who care about these issues and raise them in letters, phone calls, or the listening sessions I hold throughout Wisconsin each year.

"Through my work as chairman of the Africa Subcommittee, I have come to believe strongly in the strategic importance and vast potential for the United States to partner with Africans so as to advance both our security and shared prosperity. At the same time, we have a proud tradition of social justice in Wisconsin, and I believe the United States has a responsibility to do what we can to prevent and respond to genocide and mass killings wherever they take place. My trips to eastern Congo, northern Uganda, and many other areas affected by conflict have only strengthened that conviction.

"It makes a big difference when my constituents raise issues at the listening sessions I hold throughout Wisconsin—seventy-two of them a year. Personal letters and phone calls also let me know that people care about these issues and want to see specific actions."

RYAN GOSLING

"If You Make a Big Enough Noise, They Will Listen"

JOHN: I know you're self-critical about how much you are actually doing, but you've done a lot, going to Africa twice, and lobbying on Capitol Hill and at the United Nations. What made you initially get involved?

RYAN: It was around the time that I met Don Cheadle. I had worked with him on a movie. So I went to see the *Hotel Rwanda* premiere. And Paul Rusesabagina, the gentleman that the film was based on, was there.

First of all, I was really impressed with the film, and with Don, not only for his performance but also because he had become so involved with the issue afterward. And he just seemed to have such a sense of purpose. Not that he didn't have one before, but he had come alive after that experience. Angelina Jolie gave a really powerful speech at the premiere about what was going on in Darfur. I ended up talking to her about the film she was making, and she asked me if I would go to Chad to film something for her movie. I don't think that was actually my Enough Moment, but I think I was going more out of curiosity, just to see what all of this was about.

I had a moment when I went to the first camp, which had thousands of kids, and I had been briefed on what they had probably been through, a list of things. I tried to prepare myself for that. I wanted to be respectful, and I didn't want to be too prying. I wanted to try to figure out how to be in the situation. I ended up being surrounded by something like a hundred kids, who were all looking at me with this look in their eyes, as if they were thinking that if I just flew away at that moment, it wouldn't surprise them.

It was really quiet. They were all just following me and watching me. And there was this one little girl who was kind of getting crushed, squeezed, by the group that was trying to be close. And I said, "It's okay, it's okay." And in that exact tone, they tried to mimic me and say, "It's okay, it's okay." A hundred kids at the exact same time. And then, I kind of laughed, and I said something else, and they mimicked it. And I realized the potential of this. So I kinda taught them that part to "Sweet Caroline, Bah, bah, bah." And I started singing the song. So when I pointed to them, and they would sing the "Bah, bah, bah!" We ended up having a really fun day after that. We made little films together. I gave them the camera, and they filmed each other. They were just really cool. One kid made sunglasses out of a piece of unexposed negative film, and so when he looked through the glasses, he could see pictures. Another kid made a hat out of vodka bottle labels. They were just really creative, and cool. And I liked them. And so, when I left, they weren't just these faceless kids anymore. There was a small group of them that I felt I got to know. And so I felt invested in them after that experience.

When I got back, I began to try and figure out more of what they had been through. And I found this book, *Innocents Lost,* written by Jimmie Briggs, and it was all about child soldiers. I was really impacted by those stories. I didn't even know that that was going on, and so I started doing a lot of research on it. I found their perspective on what they had been through compelling. Most of the kids from Uganda didn't seem to have any bitterness about what had been done to them. There were no revenge fantasies. The fight had been taken out of them. Not in the sense that they weren't willing to fight for their freedom, or they weren't fighting to keep their spirits hopeful, but they weren't interested anymore in physical fighting.

They were able to forgive each other in a really amazing way. Or at least it was amazing to me that I had heard stories about kids sharing the same bunks in rehabilitation camps after they had been in the jungle together, and you know the kid on the top bunk had been forced to rape and kill the mother of the kid on the bottom bunk. And beaten him to an inch of his life. Yet they were able to be best friends as soon as they got out. Because they both had the understanding that this was something they had to do, and had they not, they wouldn't have survived. There isn't a lot or resentment there, although it's not completely idealistic. These kids are very traumatized, and so sometimes they act up. And it's not always that way, but it seemed to be the major theme of most of the interviews I was reading. It was so different from how I think I would experience that, so much more evolved. Just so different from us. We are so revenge-fantasy driven. I was compelled by them.

I really wanted to go back. During that process, I met you. So when you and I started plotting, I was very inspired by you. And it's difficult to do this because you asked me what keeps me inspired, what keeps me going, and the truth is that it's you. Haha. I'm truly grateful for that. You are that kick in the ass for me, and for a lot of people. And you should be proud of that.

JOHN: Thanks, bro. Let's go back to this whole issue of why you said yes to Angelina, not that anyone would say no to Angelina. You said it was curiosity that made you decide to go to Africa. What was piquing your interest?

RYAN: I just felt compelled to do it. It's not because I felt as though I would be of any service. But it's just not that often that people are given an opportunity like that. Most people hear about these things, but they don't have someone saying, "I'll fly you there, and I'll connect you with all these aid agencies and workers, and they'll give you a tour and access." It was a once-in-a-lifetime opportunity that would be stupid to turn down. But I had no idea how to be effective, if I could be effective, or any of that. I wasn't really educated on the situation. I didn't know what I was getting into. And when I got there, I was kind of struck with the reality of it. We landed kind of in the middle of the desert, and we had to take a two-hour detour because two days before, the UN vehicles had been shot at by Janjaweed militia. We couldn't take the main road. We realized how immediate the danger was when we got there. It was not relatable to home. We were right in it, and there was a real sense of fear among the aid workers because these vehicles had been shot at. And they were wondering if they should be there, let alone us, and so we hit the ground running when we got there.

A lot of the stories that you hear, although they are incredible, they aren't real to you. You don't have a personal connection to those people. But now that I have gone there, and I've been able to hang out with these kids, getting to know them, I can plainly put into perspective what they have been through. Suddenly it all became possible. It seemed impossible before I went. It seemed like a fairy tale. You and I have used this analogy before, but the child soldiers and the night commuters in Uganda were kind of like something out of a Grimm Brothers fairy tale. It was hard to understand how this could be real.

JOHN: In the Darfur refugee camps, were there people you connected with? Was there any particular story that impacted you in any way?

RYAN: There were two sisters, twins. Zena was the girl I got to know. We were set up to interview them. And when we came into the tent to interview them, they were afraid of us. This was the last thing we wanted to do, to add any stress to them, so we left. We didn't want to impose on them. But one of the girls told an aid worker that she was protecting her sister because her sister was afraid of us, but that she would be willing to talk to us. But I didn't want to interview her, and have her relive her experiences, even if she has been asked to do so a thousand times.

So we just kind of gave her a camera, and I asked Zena if she would be my camera person. She could film her friends, and it would give viewers more of a sense of what their lives are like if they were to just film each other. So I got to spend the day just with her. Not talking very much, just shooting. Asking her to shoot something, her pointing, asking to shoot something. She started wearing my sunglasses, wearing my buddy's hat. Over the course of the day, her personality totally came out. You could tell she was a real character, you know? She was just really dynamic, completely aware, so fast and smart, just a really impressive young lady. And I didn't really know what had happened to her until the day was over. I asked the refugee camp worker about Zena as we were leaving, after we had spent the day together: "So what's the story? How did they get here?" And the camp worker told me that the girl and her sister had been raped by a bunch of the Janjaweed militia and left for dead. But they had found a way to escape this village. And they walked by night, in the direction of Chad, hoping to find the refugee camp because everyone in their village had been killed. They were traveling by night so that they wouldn't be seen in the day by the Janjaweed. And it was a miracle. They picked the right direction and landed into this camp.

JOHN: How old was Zena?

RYAN: Maybe twelve or thirteen.

JOHN: Whom do you remember from northern Uganda?

RYAN: Patrick was this guy from northern Uganda. He was a young guy, really cool and funny. And he was showing us around. And it wasn't until a few days into it that I found out his story. And it was a really crazy story. He was one of Joseph Kony's bodyguards in the LRA. The first time Betty Bigombe, the Ugandan mediator whom we were with, met Patrick, he was pointing a machine gun in her face, and now she was employing him. She basically hired him to show us around. I was asking her, "So how did you and Patrick meet?" And she said, "Well, he had a machine gun in my face.'"

Patrick had heard about some fellow rebels in the LRA setting a little girl on fire, where they killed a family in a car and set the car on fire, and this little girl Joyce, I think she was two or three, crawled out of the car when it was on fire, and she was on fire. And they threw her back in the car, but somehow she got out again. So the rebels wrapped her in a carpet and set the carpet on fire. Somehow she was able to hold out long enough for the government army to arrive, and they fought off the rebels and rescued her. She had 80 percent of her body covered in burns.

Patrick heard this story, and he decided that this was his Enough Moment, which is probably the one we should really be talking about, because he did this really amazing thing where he escaped from the LRA, which is punishable by a pretty brutal death. And I'm sure Patrick had been a part of doling out some of those punishments, so he knew what he was risking, but he escaped and found her. And he decided he was going to spend his life taking care of her. Because her father was an army soldier for the government, he decided he would be her substitute dad.

So when we met him, he kept telling us, "I want you to meet Joyce, I want you to meet Joyce," and we were so busy and overwhelmed, that we kept saying, "Yeah, yeah, yeah," though we didn't really make a plan to do it. And then we finally showed up to see Joyce, and we saw this beautiful little girl, just covered in burns, and he told us her story. So that became our focus. She was very sick, and we tried to take her to the hospital. It was an interesting but very frustrating process because you could see why it's difficult for people living in a displaced-person camp in Africa to stay healthy. Thousands of people all just stacked up on top of each other. There is literally no room. They are just packed into this place. And they are not starving to death, but they are certainty malnourished. And disease spreads so rapidly.

Joyce was just so sick. So we took her to the hospital. I think we waited for like a whole day, and we couldn't find a doctor to look at her. It was just so unorganized, so we took her to another place the next day and found out she had bronchitis. We had to take her to another doctor, and I just can't convey how frustrating it is, how many lines we waited in. You get there, and it's like they are selling tickets to some show. . . . It's not even a line for the doctor. And, you know, it ended up taking weeks to get her blood tests to figure out the diagnosis. And we were on our second to last day when we got the blood tests back and found out she had HIV, which was a total shock obviously to us. But it was even more of a shock to Patrick, who now just really didn't know what to do. It was because she had received so many blood transfusions for her burns. She had received contaminated blood. The next day we went to see her, and she had a bloody nose. And she was playing with a bunch of kids, and they were all wiping the blood off her nose. You can see how difficult it is to stay healthy there.

We tried to put her in a hospital. And we got her a room, and all these things. And at night, she and her family would sneak out and go back to the displaced-persons camp, because for them, from what I understood, community and family were everything. Isolating her from her family and community to keep her healthy was our intention, but for her and her family, there was no point in living if she could not be with her community. They are a unit; they aren't individuals. I'm not trying to speak for the whole culture, but that is the experience we had with this particular family. And there was a certain point we reached when we said to ourselves, "What do we do? It's not our place." Joyce should have had a doctor looking over her. And at the same time, for the other kids, they can contract either bronchitis, or potentially HIV, and a ripple effect comes from that.

JOHN: With all the communication tools that the new information age provides, what are the most promising things out there that can help make it easier to teach people about what's happening and connect them to these communities, to these people?

RYAN: I think that the Internet is going to play a huge part. Not just in this but in everything. In the future. Haha.

JOHN: Very profound insight.

RYAN: And from what I understand, there are kids who have pen pals, iChat pals, kids from the United States who can iChat with kids in the camps. So I think people in these kinds of situations are now so much more accessible, and that's definitely something that you can build on. It's going to keep growing. There are ways to build personal relationships without having to travel all the way to Africa. It seems to me that there is a shift and that people are becoming more globally minded—because we must be and because we are so accessible to one another now. The borders have sort of all come crashing down because we have access to everyone and everything, to all information, whenever we want it. So I hope that this will help.

JOHN: It would be a grotesque failure, through the media that exist now—through the pictures, and stories, and videos, and everything that exists—if we could not resolve these crises. Does anything stick out in your mind from all those experiences that might have wider relevance to people and give them hope that our voices can actually make a difference?

RYAN: Yeah, that experience when we lobbied Congress was really great because we got a crew together and we walked around Capitol Hill and knocked on doors, and we talked to quite a few representatives and senators. We explained the issues of northern Uganda and what we had seen. The reaction from the representatives was fascinating. Voters think that these officials don't get their calls or letters, but they do get them. It was interesting to actually see that they do have an office. And if you have sent a letter to that office, they have received it. And if they get 100 letters in that office, they pay attention to that. A few of the representatives said, "Look, it would be embarrassing for me if I got 100 letters in my office and I didn't deal with the issue." So it was nice to go and put perspective on this place that seemed so inaccessible to me before and to realize it is just a building with a bunch of people in it, and yeah, if you make a big enough noise, they will listen.

CONGRESSMAN DONALD PAYNE (D-NEW JERSEY)

Hold Your Representatives Accountable

"Regarding the LRA, it was around the time that I came to Congress in 1989 that Kony began wreaking havoc in northern Uganda. I knew Uganda well, having traveled there in 1973 to meet with Idi Amin to protest the expulsion of the

Asians. In the late 1990s and early 2000s, the media's spotlight was shown on the recruitment of children by Kony and the LRA, and it was really then that the world began to learn about the phenomenon of the night commuters—hundreds, maybe thousands, of children who had to leave their homes in rural parts of northern Uganda for the town centers to take shelter and sleep for the night.

"I decided to take this issue up personally because I had been involved in the civil rights movement in the United States during my high school and college days, and I have been a fierce fighter against injustice. As an extension of my work internationally, when I became involved in the world-wide YMCA movement and became chair of the World Council of the YMCA in 1973, I started to focus attention internationally the way that I had domestically.

"People often think lobbyists hold so much power because they can influence lawmakers. It is true that lobbyists have a great deal of influence, but at the end of the day, it is the people—the constituents—who are the most effective and have the greatest potential to influence lawmakers. Members listen to constituents and will side with them over lobbyists if they assert themselves and hold their representatives accountable. Church groups and advocacy organizations can be particularly effective."

CONGRESSMAN ED ROYCE (R-CALIFORNIA)

"Bringing One Man to Justice Can Lead to Peace"

"I have served on the Foreign Affairs Committee since I came to Congress in 1993. I chaired the Africa Subcommittee for eight years, starting in 1997. I traveled to Uganda with President Clinton. Uganda is a bit deceptive, in that many sections, including the capital of Kampala, are free of violence and enjoy relative prosperity. Because the violence occurs in rural areas, and because Uganda has been celebrated as an 'African success,' the spotlight on LRA atrocities and its recruitment of child soldiers hasn't been so bright. Frankly, without advocacy NGOs, this would be a forgotten conflict.

"I fought very hard to bring to justice the president of Liberia, Charles Taylor, who threw his region into war. My efforts included a well-timed *New York Times* op-ed that I wrote pressuring the president of Nigeria, Obasanjo, to turn over Taylor, then exiled in Nigeria. Many opposed me, arguing that the apprehension of Taylor would destabilize the region, or alternatively, would be inconsequential. Today Taylor is being tried for war crimes, and the two countries are at peace. Bringing one man to justice can lead to peace, whether it's Charles Taylor, Joseph Kony, Omar Bashir, or an indicted Congolese warlord. Indeed, imposing accountability can work wonders, while unaccountability guarantees conflict. I'm committed to resolving these conflicts because they're not irresolvable. There is hope.

"I meet with many constituents interested in these issues, both in Washington and in my Orange County district. They also write my office. I always learn from them. Step 1 is simply calling or writing your local member of Congress, requesting a meeting in his or her district office. In July 2009, Resolve Uganda, the Enough Project, and Invisible Children organized a lobbying day on Capitol Hill, encouraging members of Congress to support my bill on northern Uganda. Having a physical presence in Washington is very effective. I think it's great that there are so many activists, including young people, concerned about human suffering in Africa."

CAST FROM NBC'S *THE WEST WING*

"Art Can Be a Bridge to Understanding"

A group of actors, led by Melissa Fitzgerald, from the television series *The West Wing* have committed themselves to telling the stories of people affected by LRA attacks and abductions.

Martin Sheen: "It was when I saw the film *Hotel Rwanda* that I was able to witness from afar what had happened there. I learned more about what was happening in Uganda when Melissa Fitzgerald went there to volunteer. When she returned and shared her experiences with me, I offered to help and support her work there. As artists, we can make choices that speak to the great issues of our time, and if we don't, what we do is a waste of time. We can shine light on the horrible human rights abuses and the increasingly terrible situations we witness going on today. George Clooney, Don Cheadle, Mia Farrow: I am proud to be in the same profession."

Allison Janney: "About ten years ago, my dear friend Melissa recruited me for Voices in Harmony, a Los Angeles theater program for at-risk teenagers. Over the past decade, I've witnessed firsthand the life-changing impact this program has had on these teens—giving them confidence and empowering them to take on the challenges they face. It's been a privilege to be a part of this effort. So when Melissa asked me to help her adapt Voices for teenagers in the displacement camps of northern Uganda, it was a no-brainer. Of course I wanted to be involved. Voices in Harmony has had such a powerful impact on American teenagers that it was my personal hope that we could replicate that experience with the teens in northern Uganda.

"And we have. I've watched some of the video footage from the Voices program in Uganda. Watching these teenagers flourish and shine has been amazing. I was particularly moved by one of these teens, an orphan who had been abducted by the rebels and forced to be a child soldier. He had escaped and returned to the camps, but he still clearly struggled with the nightmare his life had been. While Voices is certainly not a cure-all, watching this teenager participate in the theater program, watching him gain confidence, I could see the hope bubble up in him, and it was both heartbreaking and inspiring.

"I think art can be used to enlighten, to be a bridge to understanding. So I was thrilled when Melissa asked me to perform a monologue based on interviews of women who have suffered tremendously because of the war. I was asked to do what I know how to do: share stories. And it has been an honor to travel around the country and try to give voice to these beautiful, heartfelt, and, ultimately, hopeful stories.

"There is so much injustice, pain, and suffering in the world. At times it feels overwhelming. But by making a small contribution to help even one person, it no longer feels overwhelming and I feel hopeful. My mother has always been an inspiration in this regard—throughout her life, she has given so much to so many people. She has worked often behind the scenes for everyone from Planned Parenthood to the Dayton Ballet to Muse Machine, an organization that educates teachers about the arts. I am thankful for all that I have in my life, and with that comes an obligation. I believe if you can make a difference, you should. I hope I have made some small difference for the teenagers Voices has worked with here in Los Angeles and in Uganda."

Janel Moloney: "I remember looking at pictures from Melissa's trip after she returned from Uganda. There was this one, a picture of her holding a small, sick child from northern Uganda. I found it so moving. There was my friend Melissa, the same friend that drove me to the hospital when I was sick, that hugged me when I was happy, that listened when I was sad—that same friend was a world away, holding this child in her arms. When I saw that picture, my eyes stung and I got a lump in my throat . . . and I couldn't look away.

"I hadn't known much about northern Uganda, but I knew it was ravaged by war and that the United States and most of rest of the world were doing nothing. I was guilty too. I did nothing. It was thousands of miles away. How could I do anything? But then I saw that photo of Melissa holding that child, a child who's known more brutality and loss in his young life than all of my friends and family are ever likely to know. And I realized that I don't have to save the whole country or stop the war, but I could do something, right? After all, there was Melissa, helping that child.

"Sometimes, we can't see beyond what's familiar to us. Beyond our immediate family and friends. But seeing that child in my friend's arms, I could feel the weight of his little body through her arms and hear his voice through her ears, and just like that, I knew him. He was my nephew, my neighbor, my child. And then, it was obvious. You know what to do. You reach out, and you do your best to help. So that's what I've tried to do in whatever little way I can."

Dulé Hill: "My grandparents left a legacy of helping those in need. They came from Jamaica, so this meant being there for family in good times and bad. For me, this goes beyond my immediate or blood family. We are all one big family. We are all brothers and sisters.

"I am grateful for this legacy and saddened that so many children in northern Uganda have lost their grandparents and parents to war. I have been blessed to be raised by a wonderful family, but I can't receive this blessing without trying to bless others. I can't just take in and never give out. I've got to keep it moving.

"Melissa asked me to participate in Voices of Uganda by performing a monologue about what was happening there. She wasn't dropping me off in the middle of northern Uganda and saying, 'Hey Dulé solve all the problems here!' She asked very little of me. But I think, if we all do a little, we can achieve great things.

"One of our *West Wing* writers, Josh Singer, wrote the monologue I perform. It is based on one of the boys in the Voices of Uganda theater program. Through the monologue, this boy drew me in. He's a kind, thoughtful boy, wise beyond his years, living in poverty, his father killed by rebel soldiers. Being an African American young man, I feel a kinship with him. Knowing that he is out there in the world, the least I can do is give voice to his story.

"There is an immovable mountain made of a billion little stones. I can't move the mountain, but I can lift a stone. If you join me, we can move twice as many stones. And if we get more people to help, one by one, we will move those billion little stones. Together we can move that immovable mountain."

Melissa Fitzgerald: "I am an actor and an activist. I like to call myself an 'actorvist.' The common thread? Act. To act is to do. It is not to sit around and wait for the spirit to move you to do something or to hope someone else does it. It is not to wait for the perfect time to do it. It is not to wait until you have enough money to do it. It is not to say you don't have enough to offer to do it. It is simply to do it. I think this is as true about life as it is about acting.

"So in 2006, after I learned about the brutal rebel war in northern Uganda from International Medical Corps (IMC), I knew I had to do something—to act. So a few weeks after we wrapped the final episode of the *West Wing*, I was on a plane to northern Uganda to volunteer with IMC.

"That summer, I was allowed to join a field team working with malnourished children and their mothers in camps for internally displaced persons. The mostly Ugandan field team welcomed me with open arms, especially a wonderful woman, let's call her Josephine. She was kind and patient despite what fate had dealt her. Her father died of malaria; her sister and brother-in-law were killed by the LRA, leaving three sons who Josephine now cares for. Her brother was abducted twice by the LRA. Both times they captured him for over a year before he was able to escape. The second time he escaped, Josephine told me he was so abused and malnourished when he got home that he almost died. He is unable to work or do anything, so in addition to caring for her sister's three sons, she has also cared for her brother.

"Josephine and I worked closely together every day for several weeks. We were the same age, and although the circumstances of our lives were completely different, the things we hoped for, the love we had for our friends and families, seemed much bigger, deeper, and more significant. I couldn't help feeling that the only difference between Josephine and me was that I had the good fortune to have been born in the United States to a family that was able to care for me, educate me, and support me, whereas Josephine was born in northern Uganda and her life was torn apart by war.

"I had done nothing to earn this; it was luck, the luck of birth. I won the lottery, and I didn't even have to buy a ticket. I have been given so much, and with that comes an obligation to share some of that with others.

"In 2007, I went back to northern Uganda with my friend and producing partner, Katy Fox, and a small group of actors, writers, and filmmakers. We went to work with fourteen teenagers living in a displaced-persons camp on a theater program and documentary film. We collaborated with the teens to turn their personal stories into dramatic plays about HIV/AIDS, peace building, and reconciliation. These plays gave the teens the opportunity to share their voices and stories with over a thousand of their friends and neighbors in their camp. We returned home with documentary film footage from the program, dramatic monologues based on interviews with war-affected northern Ugandans, and a strong commitment to help resolve the desperate situation facing its people.

"Recently, I received a letter from one of the young men who participated in Voices of Uganda, and in it he wrote, 'The USA is the signal for freedom and equality of all humanity. I can't imagine anything more noble than that.' Please join us in making sure he is right."

Conflict Minerals Supply Chain

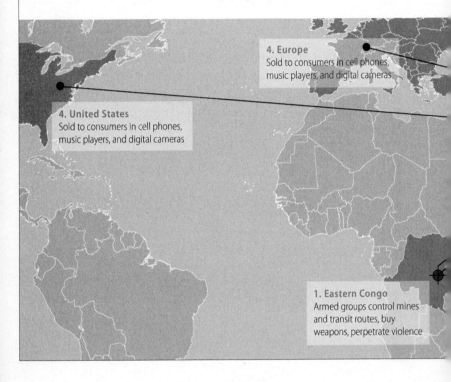

4. Europe
Sold to consumers in cell phones, music players, and digital cameras

4. United States
Sold to consumers in cell phones, music players, and digital cameras

1. Eastern Congo
Armed groups control mines and transit routes, buy weapons, perpetrate violence

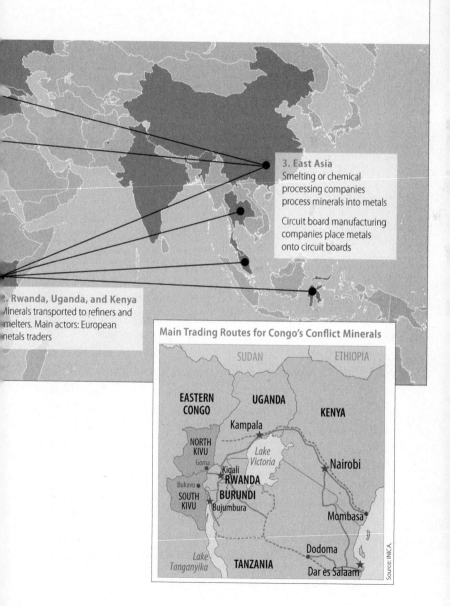

3. East Asia
Smelting or chemical processing companies process minerals into metals

Circuit board manufacturing companies place metals onto circuit boards

. Rwanda, Uganda, and Kenya
Minerals transported to refiners and melters. Main actors: European metals traders

Main Trading Routes for Congo's Conflict Minerals

SUDAN ETHIOPIA

EASTERN CONGO UGANDA KENYA

Kampala

NORTH KIVU
Goma
Lake Victoria
Nairobi
Kigali
RWANDA
Bukavu
SOUTH KIVU
BURUNDI
Bujumbura
Mombasa

Dodoma

Lake Tanganyika TANZANIA Dar es Salaam

Source: INICA.

CHAPTER SEVEN

Saying Enough to
Rape as a War Weapon

JOHN: We as an "international community" have failed so far to address three of the great human rights challenges of our time. We've failed to check a genocide in process in Darfur. We've failed to stop a little insurgent group from Uganda that has been able to kidnap thousands of kids and force them to become child soldiers and sex slaves. And perhaps worst of all, we've failed to counter the highest rate of sexual violence in the world in the Congo. This is all the more amazing given all this goodwill out there. Do you get the feeling, as an informed observer, that it's more a lack of attention or more a lack of the right policies that has caused this?

DON: I think it's both, and I think that one feeds the other. They're difficult, complicated, convoluted problems. I think very few people at any level, whether they are government officials or normal everyday human beings, get involved in trying to address something as devastating as the issue of violence against women. For politicians, it helps if there is some kind of political payoff on the other side for them somehow. For others, it is the humanitarian or altruistic impulse that keeps them in these issues. And the really committed have to wonder what they are going to get out of this. If I go risk life and limb and commit all this time and energy, and even maybe contract malaria, and have to run away from a militia in a Jeep while people are shooting at me, . . . it's like, what, why would I do this? And it's sad, such as when the police used to harass me and my friends over nothing. I would complain, and some people would say, you know, the police are just human beings too, and they get frustrated and overworked. But I say you shouldn't pick up the badge at the police academy when you promise to serve and protect because when you put the uniform on, the badge on, you are saying, "I'm not just a person anymore. I'm the guy that comes in when people are just being people, and I need to be a little more than just people. I've sworn to protect and help and serve." So I don't give you that out. And I feel the same way with these government officials who have stood up to be de facto leaders on the ideals of their nations or communities. They are standing up and saying, "I am the focal point of what we should be doing, and what is right, and what is correct, and what is just." And yet there is an insufficient response to some of the greatest injustices in the world, like what is happening in the Congo.

What is the altruism that produces the commitment, the desire to say, "Okay, I'm going to get my hands messy. I'm going to get involved in a situation that I may not be able to fix in five minutes. That I am going to really commit and throw some resources into the mix, and I'm really going to get some of the brightest minds on this, and not just force something down a community's throat but also to try and get from them their brightest minds and resources, and work together to find a solution." I think if you look at that and say, "I don't have a lot of hope for success," then it becomes a fait accompli—and why even go into it? If I may walk out of this without a success, then all I have is all that work and frustration and it led to nothing. And everyone points to me and says, "That's what you did with our time, our resources? THAT?" So I think that it's regrettable, but it seems like leaders are incentivized to go after objectives for which they can get a quick solution.

JOHN: Yeah, that's the essence of politics. And that's why I think that even though we can draw cynical conclusions, we can also derive a great deal of hope from this because it means that doing the right thing politically can be incentivized somehow, that doing good in this space can actually be rewarded politically. And that's why, ultimately, if we can succeed in really creating a constituency of conscience, a genuine mini-movement of people, not just some grandiose aspiration, but if we can marshal just a few hundred people per congressional district all across the United States, then we can move mountains politically. At the end of the day, if a president or other elected officials believe that there will be some kind of a political reward, that they will be perceived to be Upstanders, that they'll be credited to have solved a problem and will be rewarded by a small but important and dedicated constituency in favor of that issue, then they're going to look at the best way of getting that done. And one of the best things about our political system is that when that kind of incentive exists, then the elected officials will bring the best minds together. There is a real commitment to try and fix things, to solve problems.

I think this juncture in history might be an embryonic Enough Moment for Africa in the sense that we have a growing political constituency, partially because of what Bono and his organization ONE, as well as (Product) RED, have achieved. We saw faith-based groups help fuel a dramatic increase during the Bush administration for aid to Africa, particularly in how they moved President Bush from opposition to AIDS funding to having one of the largest increases in foreign assistance outside of the Marshall Plan in the history of the United States focused on fighting AIDS in Africa. I mean, it was a politically driven thing that was incentivized. If you do good, there will be this constituency of folks that will reward you, and it's the right things to do, so let's find the policies and resources to do it.

DON: Then again, with HIV/AIDS, you are talking about something that everyone realizes can touch them. It can be in your family, and it can happen to you. I think that, again, people are more incentivized to move on to things that have a more direct impact on their lives. I think that people don't really have a spiritual, visceral, or sort of kinesthetic understanding of what some genocide 15,000 miles away might have to do with them, sitting on their couches. I think people understand it on an idealistic level, but I think that people are understandably consumed—and it's not their fault—with their everyday lives. "I have a mortgage that went into default." "I'm trying to pay my rent." "I can't afford my car payments." "I have terrible health care, and my mother is sick. What do I do?"

JOHN: Especially now, in how the American economy broke badly for so many folks out there.

DON: In so many ways. So the challenge is to get people to think beyond their own particular circumstances and to think in a much bigger way about something that is the right thing to do because if mass rape goes unchallenged in Congo, then how long does it take before you start seeing it spread and get closer to home? There are no barriers around it, no walls. Things of this nature do not stand still. I think that if people feel that an issue is too far away geographically, and if they don't have some kind of a visceral connection to it, and they don't know anyone from there, anyone who has been killed, then it is easier to turn away.

JOHN: That is exactly why we launched the Congo "conflict minerals" campaign, to highlight the connection between our consumer demand for cell phones and laptops and the mineral exports from Congo that are fueling the worst sexual violence in the entire world.

DON: So you were just down there in Congo with *60 Minutes*. I know you ran into some real trouble.

JOHN: Being held at gunpoint by thirty drunk and angry militiamen in the middle of the night on a deserted road in one of the most dangerous war zones in the world was not our plan when we started out that day. But we were digging into the links between the mines and the militias, so we didn't expect a walk in the park. We had visited a gold mine contested by some of the most vengeful armed groups on the planet earlier that day, and the militia that had lost the mine wasn't happy about the result. So when we limped by on the road on a slowly deflating tire, they saw their chance to strike. After hours of negotiations, guns poked into ribs, and death threats, and being taken to a remote militia barracks lit only by the full moon, we emerged relatively unscathed and a few hundred dollars poorer. Congolese civilians, however, are usually not so fortunate.

Rape as a War Weapon

Rape has long been used in wartime because of its ultimate power to demoralize the enemy. Literature and historical documents from the Old Testament to the *Iliad*[26] suggest that rape has been viewed as a common spoil of war or even an impetus for going to battle. Research indicates that the opposite can be true as well—that wartime rape is not driven by sexual desire but rather is employed systematically by commanders as a weapon to control populations[27] and as a tool of retribution. More recent examples of the vicious practice indicate that rape is also used as a method for achieving the ultimate end goal of some of today's most sinister conflicts: the genetic obliteration of a group of people.

In recent decades the use of rape as a weapon of war has increased in scale, organization, and brutality around the world, according the UN Development Fund for Women, leading a former UN force commander to declare, "It has probably become more dangerous to be a woman than a soldier in armed conflict."[28]

Systematic rape was used to carry out ethnic cleansing and genocidal campaigns in the former Yugoslavia, Rwanda, Sierra Leone, Sri Lanka, and Darfur, prompting renewed attention to the use of rape as a weapon of war. Sexual violence in the former Yugoslavia set the stage for how modern rape is deliberately utilized as a weapon, often with the most heinous tactics. As the region descended into war, a group of senior Serbian officers adopted a military strategy proposed by psychological experts that concluded that Muslim communities "can be undermined only if we aim our action at the point where religious and social structure is most fragile. We refer to the women, especially adolescents, and to the children."[29] The judgment continued that raping women and girls would evoke panic among the Muslim populations, forcing them to flee, thus creating *ethnically cleansed* regions. A similar strategy was employed in Sierra Leone after the rebel Revolutionary United Front (RUF) was on the brink of losing a conventional civil war against the government. In 1993, the RUF transformed into a guerrilla insurgency using rape as a means of removing populations from the diamond mines that would come to finance the brutal war.[30]

Rape as a Tool of War in Congo

Over the past decade, waves of violence have continuously crashed over eastern Congo, the world's deadliest war since World War II, with nearly 6 million new graves dug as a result of the conflict. The human wreckage that washes ashore in Congolese camps for displaced people has few parallels globally in terms of pure human suffering. Eastern Congo is Africa's Ground Zero. Over a thousand people die every day there due to the legacy of war. Continuing attacks on villages, the highest rate of sexual violence in the world, child soldier recruitment, village attacks, looting, and forced labor all lead to cycles of displacement, frequent health epidemics, lack of health care, persistent malnutrition, and spiraling impoverishment. As in Darfur, it isn't violence itself that causes the majority of Congo's war-related fatalities. It is the disease and malnourishment that result from the displacement caused by the violence.

The stories that survivors from Congo tell defy comprehension. How does one even begin to fathom the experience of one teenage girl who was brutally gang raped when she was thirteen years old and now has a baby boy whom she cares for alone—because her parents were killed in a massacre in her village—even though the child reminds her every day of the horror she endured?[31] Or the fifty-three-year-old woman whose husband and children were killed in front of her eyes before members of a local militia took turns ramming guns into her vagina and raping her, who wakes up at night thinking of her family and wishing she too had died that night?[32]

Rape is often used as a tool of war in Congo, but its motivations vary. Systematic rape has evolved over the last dozen years of war in the Congo as a tool of vengeance, social control, and collective punishment against civilian populations deemed supportive of opposing armed groups. As one Congolese woman activist named Solange told us, "When they rape the women, they send a message to the men and the community that they have the power and the control. It is designed to humiliate and to spread HIV/AIDS. And if they capture an area that was under the control of a competing group, they rape and say they are punishing the women because they were spies."[33]

Congo analyst Jason Stearns further points out, "Rape is also used by commanders to indoctrinate and socialize new recruits and also occurs opportunistically [i.e., without orders] amongst soldiers who have developed a highly chauvinist and sexist military culture."

There's no way of knowing how many women in Congo have been raped. Societal taboos dissuade women from discussing their experiences and often lead to the rejection of rape survivors by their own husbands, family members, and villages. But by any account, we're talking about numbers in the hundreds of thousands of rape survivors, many of whom lack the basic support network that would enable them to treat the wounds they sustained during the rape, cope with resulting pregnancies, and overcome the accompanying emotional trauma.

Making Money by Any Means Necessary

We are blessed with all kinds of technical advances and creature comforts that we often take for granted. But the lives we have inherited or created are often based—unbeknownst to us—on a great deal of misery and suffering by others a half a world away. Nowhere is this truth more searing than in Congo. Once you burrow down to the cause of the suffering, suddenly there is a simple clarity that emerges, something we all understand: greed.

To understand why conflict in eastern Congo continues to boil with devastating consequences for civilian populations, we have to follow the money trail. Greed ensures that these conflicts remain violent and unsettled.

Mass rape in Congo is a direct result of the war, perpetrated by a number of armed groups over the years, including the Rwandan FDLR militias, the Congolese Army, the Rwandan army, and an assortment of Congolese militias and rebel groups. This surge in sexual violence began when the perpetrators of the genocide in Rwanda sought refuge over the border into Congo. While the conflict has numerous roots, the primary fuel for the violence is greed: over $180 million a year from trading in minerals, according to estimates by Enough Project researchers David Sullivan and Sasha Lezhnev. The various armed groups compete violently for control of the mines, mineral transport, taxation of the minerals, and smuggling of the minerals across the border. At times, bizarrely, some of the armed groups that compete on the battlefield will collude for the profits of war.

Deep underneath the picturesque landscape of Congo sleep the very minerals upon which modern circuitry relies: in particular, gold and the three T's: tin, tungsten, and tantalum (known as *coltan*). All of these minerals are conductive, meaning that they are the veins through which information on a circuit board flows. It is unlikely that you are reading this book in a room void of circuit boards: they are in your computer, your cell phone, your landline, your appliances, your televisions, and your MP3 devices. A good portion of these minerals are smuggled out of the country through mafia networks linked to the armed groups, which use the money to buy more arms and keep the war on a slow, agonizing burn.

The mines themselves are an ongoing human calamity: men and boys work endless hours in mine shafts that go sometimes thirty feet or more into the ground. Many of these laborers are forced by the armed groups to work in these mines and to pass pans of dirt from hand to hand out of the scorched earth. Then the soil is panned for trace elements that are eventually melted into tiny pieces and collected for sale. A worker normally makes $1 to $5 a day for his labor, which is not enough to feed, clothe, and house himself or a family.

The reason why we are focusing on the conflict minerals is that they provide the fuel for the war. Take the fuel away, and the original causes of the conflict—involving land, ethnic identity, and power—are much easier to resolve. In the current context of illegal mining, it serves the interest of all the armed groups, including the government army, to maintain an unstable, violent status quo because profits become privatized and the guys with the biggest guns enrich themselves. If that is taken away, the current logic of war will be replaced by a more normalized incentive for stability, investment, and properly compensated labor force. The way to get there is to cut off the fuel for the current illegal system.

The government army is one of the worst abusers of all the armed groups, given that the army possesses the biggest guns, and it is a major culprit committing rape in eastern Congo.[34] Through a series of peace deals, the army has absorbed thousands of fighters from numerous predatory militia factions, thus reducing further any discipline or respect for the rule of law within the ranks of the armed forces. In fact, the deputy commander of the army's military operation in 2009 was Jean-Bosco "The Terminator" Ntaganda, a former rebel commander and a wanted war criminal by the International Criminal Court for recruiting child soldiers, including using thirteen-year-old girls as his personal bodyguards. Many army officers are enriching themselves off corruption and the minerals trade.

The vampires are in charge in eastern Congo and up through the supply chain.[35] It is a Vampire's Ball, a feeding frenzy designed to suck the lifeblood out of the Congo for the enrichment of the leaders of armed groups and companies in Africa, Asia, Europe, and North America.

Vampires take many forms in Congo. They are the armed group leaders who control or tax the mines and who often use mass rape as a means of intimidating local populations, punishing civilians for perceived support of competing militias, and driving people away from areas they want to control. Vampires also include some of the middlemen based in neighboring countries or Europe, Asia, and the United States who arrange for the purchase and resale of Congo's resources to international business interests, run by people who are often accomplices. They need to acquire minerals like tin and gold to be able to satisfy the insatiable demand for these products in North America, Europe, and Asia. It leads them to ask no questions about how the minerals end up in their hands. Then there are consumers like us—completely unaware that our purchases of cell phones, computers, and other products are helping fuel a shockingly deadly war halfway around the world, not comprehending that our standard of living is in some ways based on the suffering of others.

The U.S. Response to the Congolese Crisis

Actions to address the conflict in eastern Congo have largely been reactive and incommensurate to the scale of the problem. The international community has spent billions on elections and peacekeeping, but despite the extensive documentation of the Congolese war economy by an ongoing UN group of experts, existing peacemaking efforts have failed to address the economic drivers of the conflict. There hasn't been a coherent approach to alter the incentive structures of the Congo's conflict mineral trade and its devastating impact in helping to keep the Congo's institutions weak and dysfunctional.

Efforts to date have focused either exclusively on sanctioning individual malfeasance or on piecemeal capacity building for institutions. Some of these initiatives have the potential to contribute to developing much-needed legitimate economic opportunities in eastern Congo, but they have thus far sorely lacked the coherence and diplomatic momentum necessary to alter the status quo.

In 1999, the United States and other UN Security Council members authorized the UN peacekeeping mission known by its French acronym MONUC (later renamed MONUSCO) to help implement a peace agreement. Since 2000, MONUSCO has had a mandate that enables it to use force if necessary to protect civilians, though it is erratically utilized. Despite being the largest and most expensive UN peacekeeping mission in the world and despite its having overseen the country's first national elections in forty years in 2006, violent conflict never actually ceased in the eastern part of the Congo. Congolese people most commonly cite rape as the war tactic that they feel is most unacceptable.[36] Yet despite MONUSCO's presence, sexual violence is still on the rise.[37] To truly end the use of rape as a weapon of war requires a shift from managing the conflict's symptoms to ending the war itself.

Sadly, MONUSCO's attempts to move in that direction have been a complete disaster. MONUSCO supported a bloodbath of a Congolese military operation in 2009 against the Rwandan FDLR militia with logistics and firepower, which resulted in nearly 1 million people being forced to flee their homes, at least 1,100 civilians killed, and over 7,000 girls and women raped.[38] The United Nations' own Group of Experts on Congo reported that the operation was a failure and actually resulted in the FDLR's regrouping and recruiting new fighters.[39] In one horrific case during the MONUSCO-supported operation in the village of Shalio, the Congolese army massacred at least ninety-six civilians, raped dozens of women, and cut off women's breasts.[40]

During its first year in office, the Obama administration

talked about Congo, but it took no game-changing initiative that activists hoped the new team would bring. Deeds have yet to match words. President Obama invoked Congo and rape as a weapon of war in his address to the Ghanaian parliament on his first trip to the continent in June 2009: "It is the ultimate mark of criminality and cowardice to condemn women to relentless and systematic rape."[41] He also referred to Congo in his acceptance speech for the Nobel Peace Prize. As with Sudan, activists want to see his rhetoric backed by more significant action to end these scourges about which he talks so eloquently.

In May 2009, the U.S. ambassador to the United Nations, Susan Rice, visited the Congo with a UN Security Council delegation, and while there, she visited a hospital that cares for victims of sexual violence. She later recalled a story of one victim who pulled her aside: "She asked me, with tears in her eyes, to do everything that I could do, and that we could do, to end this horrible systematic violence that she and so many others had experienced. And I gave her my word that I would."[42]

In August 2009, Secretary of State Hillary Clinton visited Goma, a provincial capital in eastern Congo. In a meeting with Congolese President Joseph Kabila, Secretary Clinton raised the issue of the use of rape as a weapon of war. Recalling the discussion, Secretary Clinton stated: "We believe there should be no impunity for the sexual and gender-based violence, and there must be arrests and punishment because that runs counter to peace." Secretary Clinton made some of the strongest remarks to date of any official worldwide when she spoke out about the fuel for the war—conflict minerals—and the need to prevent profits from the mineral trade from continuing to fuel the violence. Long-time women's rights advocate Melanne Verveer, in her newly created post as U.S. ambassador at large for global women's issues, led efforts following up on Secretary Clinton's pledges on the issue of sexual violence, and Under-Secretary of State Robert Hormats is leading the policy process on conflict minerals.

The U.S. government will need to do much more to back up its rhetoric. It all starts with meaningful action on conflict minerals. There is a huge role for the United States to play. The growing activist movement will help focus the administration's attention on the need to do more.

What the United States Could Do to End Rape as a War Strategy

The United States—pressed by the growing people's movement in support of women in the Congo—can decisively alter these dynamics by focusing attention on the international dimension of the trade in conflict minerals and by ensuring that peacemaking efforts address the long-neglected political economy of the conflict.

A comprehensive approach to ending mass atrocities must be put in place. The three P's—peace, protection, and punishment—are the essential ingredients, and they should be the rallying call for activists and policy makers. Ending the conflict is the most direct way to end the conscience-shocking sexual violence in Congo.

Peace: Although an internationally backed peace process led to the official end of a near decade long war and the Congolese elections in 2006, relations between Congo and its neighbors—particularly Rwanda—have until recently remained severely strained. Early 2009 saw a thawing in this frigid rapport when the two countries did some horse trading and agreed to work together to arrest or fight each other's enemies. What is needed now is deeper diplomatic engagement by the United States and the European Union aimed at the further improvement of the relationship between Rwanda, Congo, Uganda, and Burundi.

Shining daylight on the illicit mineral trade that crosses the borders between this quartet of countries will be a key component of this regional engagement, as Congo's conflict minerals are currently smuggled through Rwanda, Uganda, and Burundi. Creating a mechanism to certify that the minerals that go into our electronics products are conflict free will help lay the groundwork for peace efforts in Congo. A campaign like the one waged against blood diamonds is underway and is necessary to stop the trade in conflict minerals from the Congo.

Protection: The violence in Congo is deliberately targeted at civilians, and therefore it is vital that UN peacekeepers take the lead on providing civilian protection. Of course, this role should, by definition, fall to Congo's own army, but in light of the army's collusion in the conflict minerals trade, which requires instability and violence to continue enriching the armed groups, the UN mission should play the temporary lead role in protection efforts. Civilian protection must be one of the essential building blocks of a comprehensive peace in Congo. Efforts to establish a lasting peace will be consistently stymied as long as armed groups—including the Congolese army—target civilians.

At the same time, donors and governments with military expertise should work with the Congolese government to forge a major multilateral, diplomatically supported, decade-long commitment conditioned on human rights to help reform the Congolese army so that it evolves from being a predator on civilians to being a protector of civilians. One Congolese civil society leader told us, "If our government and army were stronger and more responsible, then neighbors and corporations couldn't take advantage of Congo. If we paid our soldiers and fought impunity, no neighboring country would invade or try to take our mineral resources."

Punishment: The Congolese justice system is sorely in need of a sweeping overhaul to reverse what is now an accountability-free zone. Donors should increase investment in the long-term reform of the Congolese justice system so that it prosecutes the warlords who use rape, village burning, and other attacks on civilians as tools of war. This should include both civilian and military justice.

The United States and European Union should make ending violence against women and girls a central part of their diplomatic engagement and aid conditionality with the governments in Congo and Rwanda, instead of confining the issue into a gender-programming category. The Congolese government should be held accountable by donors and diplomats for its army's abuses of women and girls, and Rwanda should be held accountable as well for its abuses of civilians—particularly women and girls—in the context of its incursions into Congo and its support for any future Congolese rebel groups.

In 2004 Congolese President Joseph Kabila referred the crisis in eastern Congo to the ICC. In September 2009, the first case that included the charge for wartime rape went to trial. Two alleged Congolese rebel commanders, Germain Katanga and Mathieu Ngudjolo Chui, have been charged with rape as a war crime and a crime against humanity. This case and other high-profile ICC prosecutions have the potential to send a powerful message to current or would-be perpetrators of rape, tackling head on the impunity that fuels rape in the Congo.

The International Criminal Court should further target its investigatory efforts on sexual violence in eastern Congo, focusing on the command structure within the various armed combatants who encourage rape as a weapon of war. The UN Security Council and countries with influence such as the United States should focus on countering the incentives for violence as the means of achieving wealth and power in the Congo through the application of sanctions, asset freezes, ICC prosecutions, targeted military operations, diplomatic isolation, focused arms embargo enforcement, and resource export control mechanisms. This should apply to the leadership of nonstate armed groups as well as key officials in the Congolese and neighboring governments that, for their own economic enrichment, continue to undermine peace and protection objectives in the mineral-rich east.

The People's Movement in Defense of Congo's Women and Girls

Over a century ago, thousands of people across the globe joined together in what became the twentieth century's first great international human rights movement. That movement focused on protesting the bloody reign of Belgium's King Leopold II over the Congo. In a murderous effort to exploit the vast natural resources of the country, half of the Congo's population was decimated by King Leopold's predatory rule—an estimated 10 million people. When the atrocities were revealed by a public investigation by British diplomats in 1903, it set off an activist movement from Britain to Belgium to the United States called the Congo Reform Association, led by former shipping clerk E. D. More. Two years later, the Belgian parliament forced Leopold to set up an independent commission to investigate the abuses, and in 1908 Leopold was stripped of his personal power over Congo.

A century ago, this public outcry helped curb the worst abuses of that period. This was before the Internet. Before television. Before the widespread use of telephones. A century later, the people of the Congo are hearing about the beginnings of a new popular movement to end the atrocities once and for all, atrocities that continue to be fueled by our demand for the Congo's natural resources. It is up to us.

Since women and girls have become the primary targets in the economic war of attrition between the Congolese armed groups, the Congo's transformation must begin with them.

We have the power to demand an end to the horrible crimes in the very place where the term "crimes against humanity" was invented a century ago. We have the power to decide when enough is really enough. That power is our voice.

There are two primary campaigns focused on ending the violence against women and girls in Congo, and they cooperate closely, aiming at different audiences with different modes of outreach.

The first campaign was conceived by Eve Ensler and her organization V-Day. In 2007, V-Day, in partnership with UNICEF, launched the global campaign Stop Raping Our Greatest Resource: Power to the Women and Girls of the Congo (www.vday.org). The campaign has been raising awareness about the level of sexual violence in Congo, and it is building the City of Joy in the eastern Congolese city of Bukavu. The City of Joy is a place where V-Day "will turn pain to power, healing and supporting survivors of violence to become the next leaders of the Congo." And personally, Eve Ensler has partnered with Dr. Denis Mukwege from Panzi Hospital and other Congolese activists to educate and activate thousands of people around the world about the atrocities being committed in eastern Congo.

The other campaign is RAISE Hope for Congo, and it is being coordinated by the Enough Project. RAISE Hope for Congo (www.raisehopeforcongo.org) is also raising awareness, but it is focusing its primary work on ending the scourge of Congo's conflict minerals trade. By calling for conflict-free phones and other electronic products, the hope is that consumer demand will influence corporate ethics and change the way minerals used in these products are obtained.

There needs to be action by both governments and corporations. The Enough Project and other nongovernmental organizations have worked with leading members of Congress to introduce legislation that requires companies to trace, audit, and declare whether conflict minerals are entering their supply chains. We are campaigning for Congress to stand up and pass a legal framework within which to audit minerals supply chains. Corporations need to take the lead in demonstrating that they will produce conflict-free products. So the RAISE Hope for Congo campaign is pressing companies to make verifiably conflict-free electronics by tracing, auditing, and certifying their chains. Since gold is the trickiest of the conflict minerals, we are, in addition, calling for jewelry companies and Central African governments to lead a regional certification process for gold that would help cut out conflict gold from the world market.

Call to Action

There is no silver bullet solution to Congo's conflict. The United States and other countries have largely avoided responsibility for addressing the economics that perpetuate the conflict. A new strategy must tackle the political economy of the conflict head on.[43] If the Congolese and regional governments, the international community, and the private sector can align their efforts on the common goal of a legal and peaceful mineral trade in eastern Congo, it would have a major impact in resolving the conflict now and preventing future outbreaks of violence.

There are many Congolese community leaders, churches, politicians, human rights activists, women's organizations, and others who are struggling to create a future Congo that is defined by peace and security. We can play an important role in supporting these Congolese heroes and institutions that will be the vanguard of change.

And let's not forget our direct complicity in the cause and our direct capacity to influence the solution. If we deal with the fuel for the violence, we have a good chance of ending the war. Consider the evidence:

- In Liberia, when the UN Security Council imposed sanctions on the illegal sale of timber out of Liberia, and it began moving on the illegal diamonds being smuggled out of Liberia. That economic pressure made it much easier to end the war there.
- In Sierra Leone, the long blood diamonds campaign began to make it more difficult for the RUF rebels to trade diamonds that were mined there for arms. That helped put a financial squeeze on the rebels. That helped contribute to the eventual defeat of the rebels and an end to the war.
- In Angola, a UN commission focused attention on the illicit trade in diamonds that was funding the rebels there. The commission's actions helped to divide and weaken the rebellion, which eventually catalyzed an end to the war after the main rebel leader was killed.

Literally millions of precious human lives are at stake in the Congo. When you log onto your laptops, remember they might not work as easily or cheaply without minerals from the Congo. When you answer your cell phone, remember the women of the Congo who have survived sexual attacks. We must tell our politicians that we cannot allow such crimes against humanity to continue. We need to tell these phone and computer companies that we demand conflict-free products, and that we'll reward the ones that give them to us with our business. Conflict-free products, in which Congo's conflict minerals no longer fuel violence there, is the game changer the women and girls of Congo need.

To take action, go to www.enoughmoment.org and find out how you can help advocate for conflict-free phones and rape-free computers.

CHAPTER EIGHT

Upstanders for Congo

As the violence continues and even intensifies, Congo's survivors themselves are saying "Enough Is Enough." For the Congolese people living in the midst of a war—in which they have lost family members, dealt with the trauma of having people they are close to raped or killed—it's an impressive feat to rise above the human-driven destruction and reach out to others around them in need. Some of these remarkable heroes are survivors of sexual violence themselves, and they have had their own version of an Enough Moment, when despite what they have endured, they decide they need to go back and help those left behind in the war's wreckage. These exceptional individuals are working miracles in Congo today, and with the help of citizens and celebrities who can amplify their stories and an international community that listens to their recommendations, we're convinced these unsung heroes will be the driving force behind a lasting peace in eastern Congo.

FRONTLINE UPSTANDERS:
Congolese Rape and Violence Survivors Who Are Making a Difference

FRANCINE'S STORY

The Puppet Maker

Francine (not her real name) is a beautiful young lady, with a soft spoken voice and a shy smile, and she is from the Walungu territory in eastern Congo. When we first met her, the only indication that something might be wrong was her noticeable limp as she walked up the stairs. She was wearing a bright colored scarf, and a yellow band in her hair.

Francine began her story by saying, "Sometimes when I think of these things, it makes me sad in my heart." One night in 2005, Francine's husband went to bed while she stayed up to bathe her sick baby girl—the youngest of four—when she heard a knock on the door.

She told her husband to answer the door, saying, "Your friends are here to see you." He was tired so he told her to tell them to come back tomorrow. Without thinking, she opened the door to tell the friends to return the next day. Instead of familiar faces, there were numerous men outside. Francine screamed and tried to close the door, but she was holding the baby, and they easily forced the door open. Eight men entered with blinding flashlights, and they asked where her husband was. She claimed he was traveling, but they quickly found him under the bed. They lined them up against the wall and had them remove their clothes. Then they asked her husband why he married her, and he said because he loved her. They then asked Francine why she married him, and she also said because she loved him. The invaders told the two of them to look at each other, and they said this is the last time you will ever consider her your wife because she will now become our wife.

Francine's husband begged for mercy and asked what they could give as an offering or bribe. The men said, "Give us two picks, a radio, and clothes," and then they went through the house looting, ultimately demanding a further $100.

"We don't have $100, only $5," Francine told them. They told her it was not enough and asked her to lay down. She refused and her husband said he wouldn't abandon her even if she were raped. But one of the men forced her down and raped her.

The men were speaking Kinyarwanda, the language of Rwanda, and they took turns. Her husband protested, and they shot him, the blood spurting on her and the rapist. She cried out and they told her to be quiet. She kept crying so they shot her through both legs, multiple times.

At some point the attackers left and the children came out of hiding to get help from their neighbors, who brought Francine to a local hospital. She was later transported to Panzi Hospital in Bukavu. When she finally regained consciousness, she learned that one of her legs had to be amputated and that due to the trauma to her uterus, the doctor had to abort an early-term pregnancy of which she had been unaware. Her husband had not survived. Worse still, she didn't know where her children were. The nurse took the names, and word was put out on the radio. They found the children being protected by a Congolese priest.

When she finally left the hospital with her children, she didn't know where to go. Panzi Hospital staff gave her money to get an apartment. The family faced difficult circumstances, and they just had enough money for the house. She became a street beggar, and her children became street beggars. (She wept at this point but insisted she could go on.) It was very hard for her, and she wondered how her children would survive. She only had one leg, and she didn't know what would happen. She started begging on the corner. She couldn't believe that she would have to sit on the side of the road and ask people she didn't know for help. Eventually they were kicked out of their apartment and had no money.

They went to a bad neighborhood to try to see if there was anywhere they could live. A woman had mercy on her and let the family sleep on her living room floor at night. Francine's children were selling water. A staff person from the international organization Women for Women would regularly pass her on the road and give her small things. The staff person told her about Women for Women, and she made an appointment.

Francine enrolled, started training, and got sponsored with $20. She didn't know what to do with the money. "Should I rent an apartment, buy clothes, food?" In Panzi, she learned small things there, like how to make dolls and puppets. So she made eight puppets with the $20. A man she met took two of the puppets to his boss, and he bought them for $40. She rented a house, and she invested the rest of the money in more material, with which Francine made more puppets. She received training from Women for Women in culinary arts and how a woman can survive and transform her life, as well as in running a small business. She learned how to budget.

Francine now makes puppets and cooks pastries. Now she has money, and she is looking for a place to live that is more permanent. She makes forty puppets per month, and the pastries sell quickly. Her children are going to school. She goes around and sells the puppets.

When asked about her dreams for her family, Francine replied, "My hope is that God will provide assistance in helping me be strong and sending me people to buy my goods so I'll be able to send my four daughters to school and that they will be able to take care of me when I get old. And I also dream of my own house because they are always changing the rent."

When asked about her dream for her country, she said, "We need a good president. The government is not good; Congo hasn't changed. My dream is to find the right leader to bring change to Congo. President Obama should talk to President Kabila and ask him to change his mind so that killing and raping will end. I want the opportunity to meet Kabila and tell him my story if it can help. I'm a widow, and I don't have a leg, which is only because of war. We need peace, and to stop shooting and stop raping. Please talk to Kabila and to America, and tell them there are so many children living in the streets. Tell them we need peace."

HONORATA'S STORY

From Teacher to Human Food and Back

Honorata (her real name, which she insists on using because she wants her story told) looks at us with faraway eyes, and a hard smile. She has a very expressive face and wears a beautiful leopard-print dress. She is a fifty-seven-year-old woman from Shabunda province who is married with seven children.

Honorata was a teacher who was paid so little that she would go to the mines in Shabunda to sell salt on the weekends to make extra money. On one fateful day in 2001, she reached the mine at around 4 p.m. There was a Rwandan FDLR militia unit there looting and shooting. The soldiers abducted her and other women and took them into the forest and made them wander for hours. The soldiers wanted the women to be confused as to where they were so they wouldn't try to escape. The women were eventually taken to an FDLR camp in the forest. The FDLR soldiers in the camp said, "We are happy, the food has arrived."

The food they were referring to was the women.

The soldiers said they would kiss and hug, but for them they really meant that they were going to beat the women. They beat Honorata, knocking her bottom front teeth out. After this, four men spread her out, holding her arms and legs down while a fifth man raped her. When he was done, he took a gun and put material on the barrel, putting it in her vagina to "clean" it. This process was repeated by the other four soldiers as well. One of the soldiers noticed her wedding ring and cut it off, damaging her finger. He said, "Now you are not married, you are the wife of everyone, you are the food of everyone."

She was held captive from October 2001 until January 2003 when she escaped. During captivity, Honorata and the other women would go to a new location every three months to meet new FDLR soldiers. She was raped the same way in each of these locations. She could not count the total number.

She got so angry—she was a wife, a teacher, and now she was "food."

She felt that she could not do anything because they had guns and could do anything they wanted. Some FDLR groups were fighting each other over mines, which is why Honorata and the other women moved around so much. One day during heavy fighting, they decided to escape. There were women held captive for sexual slavery, but there were also men who were captured to cut firewood and perform other chores. They all fled, but villagers were afraid to help them because they feared reprisals from the FDLR.

A male nurse decided to protect them. He had a small residence in the forest with a farm. He hid the twenty escapees, mostly women. During the time Honorata spent in the forest, they learned the passwords that allowed people to go safely from one area to another. If they didn't know the passwords, they were killed. The nurse always had them go with people who knew the passwords. Sometimes they had to wait a week until they could move safely. They walked 350 kilometers in the forest to get to Bukavu, battling heat, rain, and wind. When Honorata reached Bukavu, her family refused to welcome her, rejecting her because she had had sex "with those who cannot be called human."

Fortunately, she met a sailor who had a house in Bukavu but was traveling. She and four other women were able to stay in the house, another in a long list of kindnesses from strangers that helped keep Honorata going. In order to survive, Honorata would serve as a porter for merchants. Two of the other four women were pregnant so she had to assist them. She continued on this way until June 2004. Rwandan soldiers came to the house and broke the door in. Two of the soldiers stayed outside and five entered the house. They asked the women where their husbands were. Though the women said they had no husbands, the soldiers accused them of being the wives of mai-mai militias. They told the women that they would have many husbands. They had to take their clothes off and lay down. They said there are no old women in Congo. All seven men raped all five women. Honorata didn't know how they had the stamina for that. She and the other women begged them not to rape the two small women who were pregnant, but they were ignored. As a result, one of the two ladies aborted her baby and the other had surgery after the rape. Because of the rape, her baby died.

Honorata spent two weeks bleeding after the rapes. A nun took her to a health center to be treated, and then she was transferred to Panzi Hospital in Bukavu. She had five infectious diseases and spent three months in treatment. After her treatment, Honorata was enrolled in a small crafts course. She was physically present, but was not really there. She was utterly traumatized.

When the owner of the house returned, he kicked them out saying they brought bad luck. But Honorata had taught a man back in Shabunda who had a brother in Bukavu who gave her a room. With her first money of sponsorship through the American nonprofit organization Women for Women, she started selling bananas and avocados. Her life began changing. Her son went to school as a result of the money she made, while her other children remained in Shabunda with their father.

Honorata began teaching other women in the program. She taught twenty-six topics for an entire year, two classes per month. She taught health, rights, education, and nutrition, and many others. Her son entered university and was studying agronomics and environmental science. She never returned to Shabunda, as she was too traumatized to cross the forest after what she had experienced. "They are still in the forest," she whispered, referring to the FDLR militia.

Honorata has never spoken to her husband since the first attack. If she went back, she is sure she would be rejected. Her husband never asked if she was alive. Now a telephone service has been connected to Shabunda, so she is going to try to talk to him. She doesn't think that he is remarried. She is very excited by the prospect of speaking with her children. Two of her children are now in Bukavu. When she is in Bukavu, Honorata lives with her children. Otherwise, she lives in Fizi territory, working as a teacher and counselor in the Women for Women office there. She believes she should help other survivors because they experienced the same problems as she did and she can use the training that changed her life to change others' lives. She wants their lives to change as hers did.

When asked what gives her hope, she replied, "The work I do gives me hope, and the exchange of ideas with women gives me hope." When asked about her dreams for Congo, she demanded, "Rape should end in Congo. It is a big disease that is devastating Congo, a calamity. I dream of peace and the development of Congo."

The following is a poem written by a Congolese poet in honor of Honorata, titled, "Honorata's Story: From Teacher to Human Food and Back."

HONORATA
BY OMEKONGO DIBINGA

5 million screams falling on deaf ears
Fatherless children fathered by foreign soldiers
Homes with no husbands
Husbands with no honor
Rape as a tool for much more than power
Pregnant women's legs spread
Aborted by their own community
Thus another rape committed
Another violation unforgiven
Another lifeless life lived by abandoned women
But on behalf of men worldwide
I ask you to stand with pride
Because your screams were never silent
We were never compliant in these acts so violent
Across oceans we cried for you when you ran out of tears
Incapable of international intervention to assuage your fears
Your stories became our poems
Your horrors inhabited our homes
But now you must hear that we are here for you
I implore you to forgive the world for having ignored you
As they raped you they said "today you will have husbands . . ."
But as we embrace you I say "today you will have brothers"
For all of my Congolese sisters, daughters, and mothers
Your perseverance is appreciated
Your persistence respected
Though human interest has depreciated
I'll ensure you're no longer neglected

Let the world be your pillow to comfort your despair
And let the love of this one man show you that men do care

IMMACULÉE BIRHAHEKA

Advocating for Rights in the War Zone

Immaculée Birhaheka is a pioneering voice for women's rights in the Congo. For many years, Immaculée has shown remarkable courage in her efforts to challenge authorities and expose human rights abuses, particularly wartime rape. She began advocating for women's rights two decades ago, a nascent concept at the time. In 1992 she founded the organization PAIF, which stands for "promotion and support of women's initiatives," in Goma, the provincial capital of North Kivu.

In the early 1990s, Immaculée became acutely aware that the perspective of women was completely absent in both the public square and in family matters. Girls were not being raised to dream big and excel. Instead, they were being raised to eventually return to the kitchen to care for the husband. Through PAIF, Immaculée organized women to start advocating for political space for women in the public sphere. They focused on educating women about the law and enabling them to confront political authorities and discuss issues. They also began sensitizing the authorities about international law and human rights.

It wasn't long before Immaculée started to see positive results from her work empowering women. After canvassing many women, Immaculée learned that the main problems women faced at the time had more to do with social rights than political rights. In particular, they complained of limited to nonexistent access to water in Goma, which meant that girls had to venture out to the lake to get water. So PAIF set out to educate and organize local women on the issue. They met with the governor, the companies that provided the utilities, as well as international NGOs, and eventually they succeeded in getting water pipes installed and local markets built for women.

Despite the increasingly insecure environment in which Immaculée was working, she continued to fight relentlessly for women. Following the 1994 genocide in Rwanda, Goma endured two violent armed invasions and became inundated with waves of displaced civilians who had been forced to flee their homes. It was around this time that Immaculée started to realize just how many women had been raped in the crossfire of the conflict. And then, through the course of her work, she met a family in which the grandmother, mother, and daughter had all been raped, independently, on three separate occasions. It was this family's story, which she still remembers to this day, that drove Immaculée to start focusing her efforts on rehabilitating rape survivors and publicly denouncing rape as a weapon of war.

Because of her outspokenness, Immaculée continues to receive death threats and has been arrested numerous times. Yet despite the risks, she is tireless in her efforts—she has held peace rallies, she has met with Congolese authorities, and she has consulted with international NGOs. She has even taken her cause to the African Union to denounce the epidemic of sexual violence. Believing that the Congolese authorities must act where the international court does not, Immaculée led a successful campaign to secure passage by the parliament of a stringent law on rape in 2006. This law not only specifically criminalized, for the first time, acts of sexual violence, such as sexual mutilation and slavery, and introduced stiff penalties for these crimes, it also demarcated the rights of the victim. Finally, the law began to recognize that rape is a crime and that survivors are not themselves criminals or condemnable.

More recently, PAIF built a safe house for women in Goma, which provides programs specifically for severely traumatized women, many of whom have been rejected by their families, to help them get medical and psychosocial support. At the center, women also learn how to build new livelihoods, whether through sewing, cooking, or selling other goods, and they receive microcredit to help them get started.

Despite the challenges and risks that she faces on a daily basis, Immaculée still has hope for her country and its women. It's this hope that drives her to keep pushing for peace and the empowerment of Congolese women. Even more importantly, the thousands of women who dream for a better future for themselves and their children, and whose lives she has touched, find hope in Immaculée.

CHOUCHOU NAMEGABE, JOURNALIST

"What If It Were Me?"

When war broke out in eastern Congo in 1996, fueled by the influx of fighters who had crossed into Congo after carrying out the Rwandan genocide, Chouchou Namegabe was a journalist-in-training at Radio Maendeleo, a popular local community radio station in South Kivu. As violence engulfed her hometown and horrific accounts of sexual violence—shared in hushed tones—became more and more frequent, Chouchou found that her microphone and skills as a fearless journalist gave her the unique ability to speak out for women silenced by the unspeakable crimes committed against them.

Chouchou earned a reputation as a journalist with expertise in women, health, and human rights, and she was offered a full-time reporting position at Radio Maendeleo in 2002. A year later, she founded the South Kivu Association of Women Journalists, known by its French acronym AFEM. The same conviction that had led her to radio broadcasting—that the airwaves are the most effective way to reach the masses in Congo—also provided a compelling reason for her to do outreach through the radio to women affected by sexual violence. Her words could reach them in their homes where they coped with the vivid memories and often physical scars of the violence they had endured.

Chouchou's broadcasts have spotlighted sexual violence in Congo and empowered women to share their stories, breaking the curtain of silence that cultural norms and the interests of the perpetrators have imposed over the gruesome practice.

To further spread the message to Congolese women that "you are not alone," AFEM now distributes handheld radios in rural areas so that women can tune in to the programs and catch news updates, connecting Congolese women to the world beyond their remote villages.

Chouchou attributes the shocking prevalence of sexual violence in Congo to the fight by rebel groups and the Congolese army to exploit Congo's mineral riches. "The rebels want to control the mines definitively," Chouchou explains. "Why do they fight on women's bodies? Because they know that women are the heart of the community. Through these women they send a message, a strong message: Leave!" A million people in eastern Congo are currently displaced from their homes, many of whom now live in barebones camps where they are dependent on international aid to meet their basic needs.

Beyond giving voice to survivors of sexual violence, AFEM works to cultivate an active network of women journalists in Congo with the goal of increasing women's representation in the media and mentoring female journalists who will then be able to draw attention to issues important to women through their reporting. AFEM pairs this work with outreach to men in the same communities, raising awareness about sexual violence and combating the societal belief that a woman who has been raped is somehow culpable. AFEM counters society's damaging viewpoint about sexual violence by encouraging men to take a firm stance against the abuse of women in their communities and to provide support to women in their families who fall victim to sexual violence. AFEM's outreach to men also focuses on challenging gender roles in Congo, emphasizing that empowering women does not destroy the household.

"I always say that change will come from women," Chouchou asserts. "When Congolese women have the power to make decisions in our country, we'll see the Congo change."

Certainly, powerful forces in Congo have an interest in silencing Chouchou and the women with whom she works. When we met with Chouchou in Congo in mid-2009, she reported that two journalists had recently been shot and that nearly all journalists who seek to expose the crime of sexual violence live with harassment and the fear that they might be abducted. Chouchou frequently receives threats from people who say they will come for her in the night, but she feels the work is too important for her to be deterred.

"What if it were me? That is a question I ask myself sometimes," Chouchou said. "What if it were me?"

JOSEPH

A Man Who Stands Up for Women

Joseph is the name this peace advocate requested as a pseudonym for his own protection. He is a very passionate and generous person, and he is a fierce advocate for peace. The seemingly unending cycle of violence in Congo has left a very personal mark on Joseph. His parents were shot and killed by soldiers during the war a decade ago. Then, three years ago, his two cousins were kidnapped as sex slaves in the forests near Walungu. When they finally escaped, he took them in to his own home in Bukavu. It was then that he saw firsthand the stigma attached to survivors of rape in Congo and the unparalleled challenges they face.

A few years ago, Joseph was working as a fixer and translator for an American journalist in Congo when he got the idea to start the Kivu Sewing Workshop. No stranger to the struggles faced by orphans and survivors of sexual violence, Joseph understands firsthand the obstacles faced by all marginalized people in society. So he decided to create a program that would give some sliver of hope to people who often slip through the cracks in eastern Congo.

When he got started, Joseph rented a small shack in the middle of town and invested in a few sewing machines, all on his own meager salary as an interpreter for a humanitarian aid organization. In a small, cramped space no bigger than the size of an average walk-in closet in the United States, Joseph, his wife, and a few other trainers have been teaching women how to sew and provide a support network for people who are on the fringe of Congolese society. Since founding the workshop, Joseph has expanded his organization, Actions for the Welfare of Women and Children in Kivu, to also provide small microcredit loans to women. The organization also identifies children who have dropped out of school for lack of funds or familial support, and help them reenroll in school. He specifically targets war orphans and disabled children to minimize their risk of facing discrimination. Despite the generosity of a few supporters, Joseph funds these programs mostly out of his own pocket.

Though these programs are small, they mean the world

to the people Joseph helps. One such person is Justine (also a pseudonym), a widow whose husband was murdered, leaving her to care for their seven children alone. Joseph brought Justine into the workshop and gave her a microloan of $200. With this money, she has been able to sell flour, beans, and palm oil. The money she has been earning is not sufficient, but without it she would have nothing. Joseph's program also helps Sara (another pseudonym), a teenage girl who was brutally gang-raped when she was only thirteen years old and has a baby boy as a result of the rape. Her parents were killed, leaving this new mother—who is still a child herself—without any support network. Sara's child reminded her of the pain and suffering she had endured. Joseph brought her to the workshop, and thanks to the support of the workshop and the generosity of Joseph, she has begun to come alive again and care for her child. She wants to be a teacher one day and hopes that her child will have an education and a better future.

Though he has seen ethnic rivalries tear apart his country and the broader region, Joseph fiercely believes that nationalities and ethnicities should be able to live peacefully, and for that he has paid a steep price. When two Rwandan women were brought to his attention because they needed help, he invited them to participate in the workshop. His generosity to these Rwandan women was not viewed favorably by many Congolese, who blame Rwanda for the violence that continues to plague eastern Congo. One evening in mid-2009, Joseph, his wife, and his six children were sitting in their living room when they heard their neighbors shouting that their house was on fire. They all escaped the house just before it burned to the ground, along with all their possessions and most of Joseph's savings. The subsequent investigation indicated that his house had been firebombed, in retaliation for the generosity he had shown to the Rwandan women.

Despite the challenges he faces, Joseph continues to

support his organization and the workshop, and he continues to dream of expanding his programs so that he can better support those who are most marginalized in society. He is working to build a better future for Congo, one person at a time. He has already helped so many, with so little himself.

CITIZEN UPSTANDERS:
Congo's Champions in the United States

The war in Congo, and the devastating effect it is having on women and girls in particular, only rarely makes the front pages of newspapers or the nightly news in the United States. But a growing and increasingly agitated community of activists throughout America has responded to this horrific reality in eastern Congo by getting engaged—by staying vigilant about the evolving situation on the ground and putting their talent and commitment to use to sound the alarm.

REVEREND DEBRA HEFFNER

"I Knew I Had to Do Something"

Reverend Heffner is the cofounder and executive director of the Religious Institute on Sexual Morality, Justice, and Healing, a nonprofit organization dedicated to advocating for sexual health, education, and justice in faith communities and society. It wasn't until 2008 when Reverend Heffner attended V-Day's tenth anniversary celebration in New Orleans that she decided to address the situation in Congo and fight to end rape as a weapon of war. A tireless advocate for sexual justice and reproductive rights, Reverend Heffner brought her mother and daughter along to learn more about V-Day, and they all walked out with so much more than she had expected.

After hearing the speech of Panzi Hospital's Dr. Denis Mukwege, during which he recounted stories of the violence and crimes against Congolese women, Reverend Heffner recalled, "I was so incredibly moved that I knew I had to do something." Even though it was her first time hearing about the crisis in Congo, Reverend Haffner took it upon herself to find a way to help. She contacted Eve Ensler and shared her desire to help gather religious voices around ending rape as a weapon of war.

She created the Congo Sabbath campaign, an initiative to call on faith communities to respond to the violence against women in the Congo and participate in a "Congo Sabbath" day. Congo Sabbath is a day when congregations might sponsor an educational program on the crisis, raise funds to provide medical services to Congolese women and girls, or include a prayer during worship for the Congolese people. Local communities are encouraged to host Congo teach-ins, film screenings, prayer groups, and anything else they can think of to show their support to help end rape as a weapon of war in the Congo.

Reverend Heffner developed an interfaith dialogue on sexual justice, reproductive rights, and protection of women from sexual violence in the Congo. She personally reached out to religious leaders and organizations and secured over fifty endorsements for the Congo Sabbath from national religious leaders of various denominations and religions. With these endorsements, her institute launched a viral campaign with letter writing samples, religious bulletin inserts, language for newspaper articles, and online resources for its members. She held meetings and workshops with local clergy to discuss the ways faith leaders could support the quest to end rape and sexual violence against Congolese women.

In less than a year, the Congo Sabbath reached 156

congregations across the United States and helped to raise $4,000 for the Panzi Hospital through small fundraisers throughout the country. As a result of the response to Congo Sabbath, the institute received a grant from the UN Foundation, and it will continue to focus on ending sexual violence in Congo.

LISA JACKSON

Breaking the Greatest Silence

Emmy Award–winning producer and director Lisa Jackson had been tracking the horrors unfolding in the Congo for many years, mostly through anecdotal accounts from friends working in the area for the United Nations. She decided to travel to eastern Congo in 2006 to see for herself if what she had been hearing—that Congo was the "rape capital of the world"—was actually true and, if so, how and why this could be happening.

Lisa went with a video camera hoping to find a rape survivor who would talk with her about her experiences. But what she found was not one survivor but hundreds of women who would often wait in lines for hours just to speak with someone who would listen to their stories with compassion and without judgment. She spoke with rape survivors in their eighties and young girls not yet in their teens. She interviewed activists, ministers, peacekeepers, physicians, and even the perpetrators themselves, traveling alone to homes, hospitals, churches, and to remote villages in the jungles of eastern Congo to meet rape survivors who have often been shamed and abandoned.

Lisa realized that no one was covering this story in any meaningful depth and that these women wanted and needed to have their voices heard. So she resolved to make a feature-length film, and she returned to Congo three more times to fill out the story. Jackson was gang-raped in 1976, and she shared her experience with the survivors she interviewed. These women in turn recounted their stories to Lisa with honesty and immediacy.

She traveled and filmed in Congo entirely alone, struggling with language barriers and other challenges. She also encountered incredible resistance from authority figures, and at one point she spent four hours in jail for having an allegedly forged filming permit. Not to mention the terror of interviewing armed rapists in the middle of the bush and the logistical hurdles of traveling through a war zone during a monsoon on some of the world's worst roads.

Lisa distinctly recalls two Enough Moments that she experienced while in Congo. On her first visit to Panzi Hospital, where many rape survivors are treated, she was stunned and sickened by not only the hundreds of women who were in beds recovering from the surgeries required to repair their mutilated genitals but also by the hundreds more who were waiting for beds to become available. She thought to herself, "Why isn't the world tearing its hair out at the horror of this?" She decided that the world had to know and to see.

Her second Enough Moment occurred when she interviewed soldiers in the Congolese army who nonchalantly—and without fear of reprisal—confessed to her camera that they had committed dozens of rapes. Here were men admitting to war crimes, and when the interviews were over, they just melted back into the bush, and none would ever be held accountable for what they had told her. It hit her like a ton of bricks: women in the Congo have no justice. None. Something had to change.

Little did Lisa know how much of an impact her commitment would have. Her resulting film *The Greatest Silence* inspired the U.S. ambassador to the United Nations to vigorously support UN Security Council Resolution 1820, which finally recognized rape during conflict as a crime of war and as a destabilizing force for families, societies, and nations. The UN passed Resolution 1820 unanimously in May 2008. The film aired on HBO, and it has been screened in the U.S. Senate, the U.K. House of Commons, and in the Congolese National Assembly, and it has also spurred hundreds of grassroots awareness and fundraising efforts by individuals and college campuses around the world.

LYNN NOTTAGE

"Because I Had To"

"I am a storyteller by trade. I remain committed to telling the stories of women of the African diaspora, particularly those stories that don't often find their way into the mainstream media. Sexual violence against the women of Congo is one of the great human rights crises in the world today, and I am using the tools that I have at my disposal to raise awareness and draw attention to the situation; those tools are my imagination and my storytelling skills. I feel the onus is on all of us who have the ability to reach audiences to try and bring an end to the scourge. I cannot bear to live in a world where such horrific things are happening to my African sisters without doing whatever I can to help them. Silence is complicity. I believe that. Our silence on this issue sends a message to the Congolese government that it can continue to rape the land and its people with impunity. Our silence on this issue means that every time we use our cell phones, we are inadvertently fueling a war that is being fought on the backs of women.

Why did I go to Africa to collect their stories? Because I had to."

When Lynn Nottage, the playwright of the 2009 Pulitzer Prize–winning play *Ruined*, first traveled to Central Africa to interview Congolese women seeking refuge in Uganda, she originally intended to write a modern version of Bertolt Brecht's famous pre–World War II play *Mother Courage*, about "a wily businesswoman who does whatever it takes to survive a seemingly endless war," as Nottage explains. But when she began hearing the testimonies of women who had survived rape in Congo, Nottage said she realized that she had the makings of a poignant story that deserved being told in its own right. "In listening to the narratives of the Congolese, I came to terms with the extent to which their bodies had become battlefields. I felt that my play had to deal with the reality in a bold and direct way. The subject matter was not easy, but rape had become part of the vocabulary of war in Congo, and thus became a central theme in my play."

Nottage credits her time working at Amnesty International in New York as a young adult with teaching her that shining a focused light on an injustice can actually lead to tangible change. While at Amnesty International, Nottage began writing a book with Filipina author and human rights activist Ninotchka Rosca with the goal of making the case that women's rights are human rights. Over the course of several years, they gathered testimonies and interviewed numerous women from around the world. Although the book was never completed, Nottage says that the intrepid, strong, and resilient women she encountered forever changed her. "I think that *Ruined* exists because of the journey that I took while at Amnesty International," she said. Nottage concluded: "The power of the theater is that it can peel back layers of emotion to reveal human truths that often get lost in clinical human rights reports and detached news stories. In many societies you'll find that theater is at the vanguard of change. The communal nature of the medium allows us to explore difficult and troubling subject matters that ultimately lead to some form of collective catharsis for the audience."

JACKIE PATTERSON AND STEPHANIE JOLLUCK

Social Entrepreneurship for Positive Change

When retailers and long-time friends Jackie Patterson and Stephanie Jolluck decided they wanted to get more involved in the causes they cared about, they focused on what they knew best: selling merchandise to raise awareness and funds. As entrepreneurs, they felt they could use their creativity, initiative, and passion for positive social change in raising awareness with a unique approach to activism.

A few years ago, Stephanie received the book *Not On Our Watch* as a Christmas gift from her sister. As a social entrepreneur working in Guatemala with indigenous populations, she was already involved as an activist in social causes, but reading *Not On Our Watch* opened an entirely new world of activism to her. In reading the book, she discovered the power of using her voice to create change through the media and the power of holding her elected representatives accountable. It was then that she told her friend Jackie that she had to read this book. Wanting to somehow incorporate advocacy into their current businesses, Jackie and Stephanie partnered with NGOs like the Enough Project and created t-shirts with a social message. Soon their activities evolved into spearheading local advocacy and fundraising efforts after learning more about the causes. They realized that to make the kind of sustainable impact they were seeking, they needed to engage people with various perspectives and talents to "start a dialogue" about genocide and crimes and against humanity, as well as other global social injustices.

Since getting started, Stephanie and Jackie have hosted many fundraising and awareness-raising events, and they've sold thousands of activist t-shirts and other merchandise. They hosted a "Yoga for Congo" workshop in honor of International Women's Day 2009 in Atlanta, during which students dedicated an afternoon to the women of the Congo. The participants learned how to "open their hearts, cultivate compassion, and to take their yoga off the mat and into the world." They've also invited experts to come speak at awareness-raising dinners in their hometowns, and they've started partnering with local universities to engage students in their efforts.

As Stephanie has pointed out, "Contributing in this way is not a job for us, and we aren't paid for this work. It's our passion." Jackie added, "We want to dedicate our free time and energy to creating positive social change in the world."

KIMBERLY PINKSON AND CHRISE DETOURNAY

Eco-Moms Embrace Congo

When thinking about the concept of "going green," most people wouldn't automatically think of human rights. But San Francisco natives Kimberly Pinkson and Chrise DeTournay do, and that's what drew these two eco-activists to the cause of protecting and empowering Congolese women.

Raised with a sense of global stewardship and interconnection, Kimberly attended a UN World Environment Day a few years ago and was inspired to build a global network of women working together to create a healthy and sustainable future. Thus was born the EcoMom Alliance, and she brought friend and fellow eco-activist Chrise on board as executive director. Chrise was automatically attracted to the concept, having spent the majority of her childhood summers on a Native American reservation in Arizona, witnessing huge financial disparities. Since then, Kimberly and Chrise have grown the EcoMom Alliance from just a concept to a worldwide movement with EcoMom Leaders in communities from Mumbai to Minneapolis.

Fortuitously, fellow environmentalist and friend Robin Wright invited them to a screening of the documentary film *The Greatest Silence: Rape in the Congo* in the winter of 2008. This powerful film hit them both at their core. As they listened to Robin and John Prendergast during the discussion following the film, Kimberly and Chrise both got this strong sense of being in the right place at the right time. The speakers appealed to the audience, suggesting that if anyone had a group that they convened, such as gatherings at homes where information was shared, those events would be the perfect place to raise awareness about the tragedy that had been unfolding for over ten years in the Congo. Kimberly and Chrise looked at each other, and it all clicked—this is what EcoMom does. With the launch of their new EcoMom Market, an online store that offers sustainable, fair-trade, and environmentally sensitive goods, they realized that they could also help women in Congo with skills training to produce saleable items for their members and beyond. The fit was uncanny, and they put the project, which they called Sowing Hope, into motion immediately.

The project moved quickly from an idea to a campaign, in just a few weeks. Following the film's screening, Kimberly and Chrise teamed up with Robin to begin raising awareness about their project and hosting fundraising events. With this newfound sense of purpose, donations have been made, house parties have been thrown, and women have been sponsored through Women for Women International. As Kimberly always says, "There is no force of nature more powerful than a network of women."

LISA SHANNON

A Simple Run

Lisa Shannon's plan was to be in Paris for her thirtieth birthday. Instead, she caught strep throat and had to cancel her trip. About a week before her birthday, she wound up sprawled on her couch watching the *Oprah Show,* where she learned about the conflict in Congo. In her report, journalist Lisa Ling called Congo "the worst place on earth . . . and the most ignored." Lisa was dumbfounded. The deadliest war since World War II had been raging for more than ten years. The same guys responsible for the Rwandan genocide were still out there killing people, and she had never even heard of it? So she did what was suggested on the show: she signed up to sponsor a "sister" through Women for Women International.

But what she had seen in Ling's report continued to haunt Lisa. On her birthday, she was in an airport and spotted *O, The Oprah Magazine.* They had run a companion story with personal accounts of Congolese women. One woman had written about an attack. She was being dragged away to the forest, the militia was about to rape or kill her, so she begged for her life. One of the militia responded, "Even if I kill you, what would it matter? You are not human. You are like an animal. Even if I killed you, you would not be missed."

Lisa just sat in the airport crying, thinking that in many ways the world agrees with that guy. She knew she had to figure out some way to send the opposite message: these people do matter. Lisa tried to rally her friends into throwing a fundraising party or doing a walk . . . anything. But none of them had heard of Congo, and they thought there surely must be a reason no one was talking about it to the extent that they were talking about Darfur. So Lisa decided she would have to do it alone. All she could think of was running. Since many people make fundraising runs, it would have to be bold enough to get the attention of her friends and family. So she set a goal: she would run a thirty-mile trail to raise thirty sponsorships for women in Congo through Women for Women International.

Lisa didn't consider herself to be a good runner, and she had never done any public speaking or fundraising before. But she figured the only qualification she needed was that she cared, and she decided to figure out the rest as she went along. On her first lone run, Lisa raised eighty sponsorships (about $28,000). We asked her, "Did you succeed because you are compelling and charismatic and just so darned good at all of this?" No, she replied. The success stemmed simply from that fact that she had created an opportunity for people to learn about what was happening in Congo, and she had given them a way to do something about it.

Word spread, and before long, Lisa was at the helm of her new organization: Run for Congo Women. In the second year of Run for Congo Women, people participated in the run by themselves or in groups in ten states and four countries. They received press coverage in *Runner's World, Fitness Magazine,* and *O, The Oprah Magazine.* And the runs have continued. Thousands have run, walked, baked, swum, hiked, and biked for Congo's women. Lisa's appearance on the *Oprah Show* in 2009 spread the word to millions of new people. Women for Women International's Congo program grew by 100 percent because of the *Oprah Show,* which doubled the number of women being helped. More than 6,000 Congolese women were enrolled in the program as a direct result of the show. Women for Women International's Congo program now serves more than 12,000 women per year. As a stand-alone project, Run for Congo Women has raised more than $600,000 and has sponsored more than 1,200 women in the Congo.

But to Lisa, there has been no greater sense of success than going to Congo and meeting face to face the women her organization has sponsored. She was shocked at how much they depend on personal connections with women around the world. They carry letters from their American "sisters" in pouches, hung around their necks, tucked under their shirts, like their most prized possessions. Just because someone cared and reached out to them as human beings. Of course they had endless stories of the atrocities they've lived through. But they also had endless success stories of the Women for Women program—stories of buying land, protecting their families, building businesses, and becoming community leaders. What Lisa heard in almost every women's group was, "I feel like a human being again."

FAMOUS UPSTANDERS:
Highlighting the Congo Through Celebrity Activism

BEN AFFLECK

Defying Stereotypes

"If I can lay claim to an Enough Moment, it would be in the course of reading a book about Sudan. I had been asked to participate in activism on Darfur, and, insecure about being a dilettante, I hastily began researching the issue. While ticking off the grim statistics concerning western Sudan, the book made brief, parenthetical mention that the number of deaths paled in comparison to the 5 million Congolese who had died since 1998 in eastern Congo. The conflict in Congo, sparked in part by the 1994 Rwandan genocide, has become a maze of militias, regional influences, and mining interests that have continued to catch the people of eastern Congo in their crossfire.

"I was shocked by the magnitude of the tragedy and ashamed that I'd never even heard of it (not to mention that at that time I had difficulty locating the Democratic Republic of Congo on a map).

"I declined the offer to participate in Darfur-related advocacy, gauging that Sudan had a surfeit of advocates dedicated to raising awareness about the war crimes going on there—certainly relative to eastern Congo. Instead, I decided to commit myself to do what I could to raise the visibility of the people and issues of Congo—where the paucity of news coverage, international attention, and general awareness was surely contributing in some measure to the crisis.

"I became acutely aware of the complexity of the situation in Congo—and even more so of how poorly I understood it. If the goal was to raise awareness, the danger was in raising the wrong kind, spreading misinformation or—at worst—fostering a cultural arrogance that has often characterized Western relations with Africa.

"So I set out first to learn. One of the advantages of celebrity is access, and I used it to meet or speak with every Congolese, Rwandese, Burundian, northern Ugandan, and southern Sudanese expert that I could find in an effort to understand the 'conflict matrix' in the region—the way the nations' histories are interwoven and continue to affect one another.

"I read every book that was recommended, particularly on Rwanda and Congo—whose histories and present are thoroughly interlocked.

"Then I traveled—four times over a year and a half to north and south Sudan, Kenya, Tanzania, Rwanda, northern and western Uganda, and Congo.

"On the ground I spoke with hundreds of people—refugees, the internally displaced, doctors, genocide survivors, child soldiers, rape survivors, artisanal miners, aid workers, politicians, Genocidaires, Mai Mai militia, warlords, UN soldiers, Congolese and Rwandese army spokesmen, presidents, dissidents, rebel leaders, think tank analysts, participants in genocide trials, mediators from the Goma and Juba peace talks, and countless others.

"What struck me most powerfully from this collection of experiences—though it ranged from the good and the great to the notorious—were the everyday people. The people I met who had taken it upon themselves to improve their lives and the lives of their neighbors. I suppose when I started traveling to Africa, I carried with me the subconscious image of people lying on their back, flies in their eyes, bodies like sticks tied together with wire, and hands raised waiting for rescue. Nothing could be further from the experiences I have had across the continent.

"Even during the worst of the fighting in eastern Congo, the regional capital city, Goma, was alive with people going about their lives, selling goods, and doing what they had to do to care for their families, make money, and make do. A volcano had nearly destroyed the whole city a few years before—leaving it covered in gray, hardened rock lava—and yet people simply chopped it up, made houses from it, and carved roads through it. I often had cause to reflect on how in the United States, it is common to hear uproarious, riotous complaining at the airport from people whose flights have been delayed or canceled, and yet in Goma there would be a family of five on a motorbike, carrying rocks to build a house with a war going on—and more often than not with a measure of serenity and grace, often even with a smile.

"However, more important than the spirit with which people dealt with their own adversity was how much they confounded the other aspect of the stereotype: no one I saw in eastern Congo was waiting for a handout. And the most effective help wasn't coming from the West. It was coming from their own communities.

"There are amazing community-based organizations in eastern Congo, funded and run by the Congolese people themselves. Whether it's running hospitals or clinics, counseling rape survivors, or negotiating the release of child soldiers and placing them in communities who will care for them, these people are spectacular. They run peace and reconciliation activities and art workshops, start radio stations hosted by women talking about rape and justice, provide job training and support farmers to grow better, more profitable crops . . . the list goes on. You can read more of their remarkable stories by visiting our Eastern Congo Initiative website at www.easterncongo.org.

"The dynamic nature of the way the Congolese are solving their own problems inspired me and changed the context through which I view aid. Western NGOs and governments can do great things, but I believe we would do well to support many of the existing community-based organizations already doing excellent work solving African problems with African solutions. If they can function with virtually no money, imagine what they could do with our support.

"So often the person has been considered wise who, when speaking about aid in Africa, has said, 'Give a man a fish and he will eat for a day, but teach a man to fish and he will eat forever.' I found, speaking humbly from my own experience, that this aphorism doesn't apply to what I have seen in eastern Congo. I never met an African who couldn't fish already. They just don't have any fish to catch. The people of eastern Congo (and in many countries across Africa) need a stocked pond—basic infrastructure to support small and regional business, stable microfinance and community banking, basic health care for families, and the ability for women and children to live without the constant fear of violence. The people of eastern Congo are no less determined or talented or hopeful than you or I. With fish in the water, the people of eastern Congo will have the resources to provide for themselves so that they can focus on peace and stability, growth and prosperity. This means investing in their vision, their solutions, and in their security."

KEN BAUMANN

With True Modernity Comes True Responsibility

> *This is the beginning of true modernity: to experience your own cultural background as ultimately contingent, irrelevant.*
>
> —SLAVOJ ZIZEK

"The quote above, from one of the most provocative thinkers alive, has stuck with me since the first time I read it. Maybe it resonated with me because of my upbringing; my family raised me without instilling any sort of preconceived notion of who I was supposed to be, what I was supposed to believe in, and what groups, if any, I was supposed to belong to. I was left to explore and make independent decisions with their loving support. So now, even though I would call myself American, and fill in 'Caucasian' in the census, I feel I belong more so to an unbound family. I feel that I belong to people. I feel that I belong to the world.

"And the day I learned about the war in the Congo, I was heartbroken. I had failed, was failing, at being a responsible person, as I was totally unaware of a horrendous crime against humanity being committed right now. The scale of atrocity seems unimaginable. I was shocked that I hadn't known about the conflict earlier. And I wanted to help.

"With the encouragement and participation of John Prendergast, Bonnie Abaunza, Patrick Welborn, and countless others, I organized an event in Los Angeles to benefit Raise Hope for Congo and to educate my friends and family about the conflict and what we can all do as individuals, as Americans, and as consumers to end the conflict. But that was only a small step. What is needed now is massive action, massive media pressure on the electronics companies that use minerals mined from the Congo, massive consumer demand for 'conflict-free' technology, and massive support for our brothers and sisters who are suffering, as well as support for those who champion their safety and freedom.

"I continue to help because with true modernity comes true responsibility."

SENATOR BARBARA BOXER (D-CALIFORNIA)

"Help Bring It to an End"

"I have learned the most about the horrible conflicts in Darfur, the Congo, and northern Uganda from the hundreds of individuals who have traveled to Capitol Hill to shed light on these atrocities—many who have experienced the violence firsthand and others, including many young people, who are determined to make sure these crises get the attention they deserve.

"Over the course of my life and career, I have been saddened and disheartened by the cruel treatment of women and children. What we see on television or read about in the news is just a small snapshot of the horrors that many endure each and every day across the world.

"That is why I am deeply honored to be the chair of the first-ever Senate subcommittee to focus specifically on global women's issues. In this role, I am determined to shine a spotlight on brutality against women and girls and help bring it to an end. In May 2009, I held the first hearing of my subcommittee to examine the use of violence against women as a tool of war in Sudan and the Democratic Republic of Congo. Shortly thereafter, Secretary of State Hillary Rodham Clinton announced a new series of initiatives for Congo.

"The voices of these women have been ignored for far too long. Historians and economists on the right and the left will tell you the same thing: no country will move ahead in today's global economy if half its people are left behind.

"With so many problems in the world, it is more important than ever for my constituents to keep up the drumbeat for action. I am proud that my constituents in California have been very engaged in human rights issues at a grassroots level. From holding massive advocacy events to organizing letter writing campaigns to lobbying elected officials in Washington, these advocates do an amazing job of promoting public awareness."

EMMANUELLE CHRIQUI

"My Personal Wake-up Call".

JOHN: What spoke to you about these human rights issues and inspired you to get involved?

EMMANUELLE: I heard you and your friend from Darfur, Omer Ismail, and your level of commitment and passion, and it literally moved me to tears. I think that's what I was searching for. My personal wake-up call. And to be in a space that was intimate enough to really feel and understand what everybody was saying and to be affected by it. That was really the trigger point for me. What was most inspiring of all was the acknowledgment that there was a lot to learn. It wasn't like from one day to the next, I suddenly would become this massive activist. I needed to learn about the issues. I knew that I was moved, but I needed to understand what was going on. I needed to learn how to speak about what's going on. I can't bite off more than I can chew. That was a tough one because initially when you get involved in activism, you feel as though you want to do more, that you're not doing enough.

I started to brainstorm and thought, "My creative side can really help in all of this." So it continues to be this ongoing learning process that ebbs and flows. I'm at the point where I see the impact that we've already made, just in regard to Congo because that's the issue I really stepped up behind. Stopping the violence against women and girls was something that really resonated with me. How fortunate am I to be a woman with so many freedoms?

JOHN: Where does your desire to become involved like this come from?

EMMANUELLE: I come from a great family where spirituality and awareness are really important. When I watched the film *The Greatest Silence*, I remember being amazed by the strength and courage of these women. And I remember that it was initially a massive driving force for me. Like a wake-up call. That feeling that even on a really bad day, I am one of the luckiest people on the planet. To watch the stories of the Congolese women, seeing how spiritual they are, their sense of community, and the support system that they create among themselves in their villages is mind-boggling to me. That's the story that needs to be told.

In the film, a woman told a story about the worst atrocities I've ever heard that can be done to a woman. She was one of the women who started the group of women speaking at that church, almost like a therapy session. Each and every woman spoke about forgiveness and the presence of God in her life. Forgiveness? Presence of God? These women had the worst things happen to them. It was just the biggest strength of character I have ever *ever* heard of. It makes everything else seem so trivial. We learn from these women.

JOHN: In terms of the Internet tools, what has the most potential for spreading the word?

EMMANUELLE: Getting people to sign and pass on the online pledges or letters or petitions is important. This is going to go to the president so let's gather as many names as we can. I know that when we did that a few months back, we got thousands and thousands of names. It was so easy: "Take this and put it on your e-mail list. Write a letter to your representative from your heart." That's what I did. I wrote a letter from my heart basically saying I rarely do this. I am moved to do this. If you would take two minutes to follow these directions, you will be making such a huge step helping humanity. It's so easy. It's already organized for us. We just need to take the few minutes out of our days to start.

SHERYL CROW

The Responsibility That Comes with Knowledge

JOHN: When did you first realize that these issues mattered to you enough that you decided to do something?

SHERYL: My Enough Moment occurred when I traveled to Bosnia with the first lady at that time, Hillary Clinton. She asked me if I would go and entertain the troops, and I have always been 100 percent behind entertaining our soldiers. So I educated myself as to what we were doing in Bosnia and what that war was about. When we went, I was heavily impacted by what I saw in that war-torn area and by our commitment to ending the Bosnian war. But when I came home, there was so much coverage about the genocide in Rwanda, and nothing was being done to stop it. I was ruminating and reflecting on my trip to Bosnia, but everything I kept seeing on TV was about Rwanda. I could not get it out of my head that the perpetrators demolished entire communities in Rwanda—a full-on genocide—and we didn't do anything but turn a blind eye. Yet we were spending all this money in Bosnia. And I didn't understand the difference. In both places, people were suffering, but we were responding only in one place. Here was a whole country torn apart by genocide. And we didn't do anything.

Much later on, I was at a birthday party for President Clinton, and he spoke about Rwanda, about how it was the one thing during his time as president from which he could not escape his guilt. Feeling as though he had had an opportunity to stand up, but instead the issue got swept under the rug. I feel that it's just such a dark spot on our history, the fact that we didn't step up and do something about the genocide in Rwanda. So watching what's happening in the Congo now, I feel we just can't let that happen again. Especially when we know what we know. And I think everyone has that Enough Moment, when you know what you know, and you have a choice to go forward and ignore what you know, or to do something about it. And there is a lot of responsibility with knowledge, but it's what creates the urgency to act.

JOHN: What brought you back into these issues a dozen years after that trip with Hillary Clinton?

SHERYL: I got the opportunity to hear a Congolese refugee speak at an event we did at the House of Blues in Los Angeles. Her name is Rose Mapendo, and she spoke about her experience there, which was devastating. And you talked that night about the electronic gadgets we use every day and their connection to the violence in Congo. And I couldn't feel good about carrying a gadget that is causing someone else's pain or devastation unless I was prepared to do something about it.

JOHN: Many people can hear about these things, or read this, and say, "Yeah, the world's a messed up place, so sorry to hear that," and then turn away. But other people say, "Oh, wow, really? Okay, I want to try and do something." What do you think—in your family, your character, your past—made you actually become an Upstander on this issue?

SHERYL: I think there is a huge commitment that goes along with trying to reconcile spirituality and consciousness and the everyday living experience. This is why I think there is a grander interest in issues among people from all walks of life. This is why we go buy t-shirts from The Gap that make us feel good about where our money is going. It is entering our consumer culture. And people are starting to take responsibility for the things they buy and the things they support. And maybe it's because of all of the images we see on TV, or maybe it's the amount of product saturation that we are hit over the head with. This phenomenon in the Congo is different because it's not something that has been a huge issue despite the numbers of dead. Living the kind of life I am living, I generally feel that I have a responsibility to people who do not have as much as I do. I have a family, I have food, I have transportation. I think that there is a movement across the board where we are feeling much more conscious about the fact that millions of people are suffering and we have a responsibility to respond.

JOHN: It's an incredible concept because it becomes more possible that these kinds of issues and activist activities and social awareness become more integrated into our daily existence than they ever were in our past.

SHERYL: Yes. Integration of our spirituality into our everyday living experience.

JOHN: So it is spirituality that plugs you into a larger ethical or moral universe?

SHERYL: It's compassion-based decision making. I read this great article by George Harrison. He felt that spirituality was really simple: that one must manifest peace within to manifest peace throughout. I think that once people start becoming conscious of goodness with compassion, then it becomes very difficult to not factor that in when making decisions. If you know wrong from right, then you know when you are making a wrong decision. And people are becoming much more conscious about what it means to live in spiritual alignment. It becomes not only motivating but also a part of the way you choose to live.

JOHN: I love that. People can take meaningful action within the context of their daily lives that impacts people halfway around the world. They can actually make a difference in opposing genocide or mass violence against women. And the actions you take will not be outside the framework of your daily life but rather, integrated thoroughly into it. If that idea can be sold or internalized en masse, we could build a much bigger movement of people who would advocate for compassion as a basic element of our foreign policy.

SHERYL: I think it is being sold. Look at the RED campaign, which is a great example of marketing—even consumerism—

that is actually doing good at the same time products are being sold. And I think people are much more aware of where they spend their money, and what effect their purchases can have. And that's why I keep thinking that something's got to happen on the conflict minerals front in the Congo. If I can buy a cell phone that is conflict free, then I am going to opt to do that over buying the one that is going to cause someone else distress. So it's just got to happen. We gotta make it happen.

JESSE DYLAN

Organizing for Change 101

"It is a fallacy to think you can dictate a top-down approach to community organization. People don't want to do what you want them to do. So you have to give people tools by which they can come up with their own ideas about how to do it. You need to elucidate a very clear problem, a very clearly articulated plan about how to solve that problem, an organizing principle to get people to participate with really specific goals, and then an action on a specific day. A specific goal.

"So you go to the people in your community, you get them on a list, and you ask, 'What are some ideas that we can do?' Give them the power to choose in the same way that the *Yes We Can* video was a small part of a bigger movement. Find new ways of arranging information. People can record themselves performing a song. That's an idea that can bring people together because people can take their piece of the song and put it in there. You need to have places for people to go because they want to be there. I don't think you need millions of people. You need a group of people who are really dedicated. They will find you if you have a place that's welcoming.

"You've got to ask people to participate initially, and then all the technologies and all the other stuff can be built on top of it. But it's got to start that way. In the Sudan 2 million people are being slowly starved to death, over a long period of time, in order to kill them a little bit at a time, and the most effective thing that was said about that was not throwing numbers at people. It was, 'If it were your family, what would you want to do about it?' That's a very powerful thing because you're creating empathy. You want to make the world smaller. How do you get people to care about Africa if they are really far away?

"So there are ways of doing it. Simple things. Like a book club with women in Michigan and women in Rwanda reading a book and talking about it. So it's not about aid—it's about making the world smaller. The website is the greatest democratizing tool ever invented. That's the power of smaller communities banding together. It's all about people who care most about this issue finding each other. If they can find each other, they can change the world. The question is how you make the tools that make it possible for them to do it. The answer is not to think of the answer but for you to give people the tools to come up with their own answers. It's how you get people to participate in these things. It's how you get individuals to decide that this is their issue and then work for it. Because there are so many things that need help. You need a clear, stripped-away message, and then you need to get people involved to help you tell that message. Give people a way to sign up and give them the way to come up with ideas for what they want to do.

"You have to organize an army of people who are really passionate about this issue. That requires superclarification for them and a network that has rules but allows personal expression. Get computer programmers and challenge them to actually build programs and applications. Create small prizes and Facebook and MySpace applications. That information can spread all over the world. A song can spread all over the world like that. Give prizes for creative ways to educate people about these issues and to activate them. Create five different strategies of innovation at the same time, and one of them may work. I think if you have materials that make it possible for people to understand what the issue is in the shortest number of sentences possible with the least amount of the extra stuff, that goes a long way.

"It's really good old-fashioned organizing. So it's short content; it's not an hour-long documentary. It's literally a one-minute film that says, 'This cell phone that you have in your hand came from this mine, and that money went to this person and this person hacked to death these other people. . . . Are you Okay with that?' How outrageous do you want to be? Because you follow the value chain right back up and you make that transparent. They *will* address it because it's a big fat stain. You can take those videos and just have a meeting with a phone company and say, 'Listen, I just want you to know, this is what I'm putting out. It's going to go to a million people on Friday. Are you cool with that?' And you will see change. Because corporations don't want those things out there; transparency is what they don't want. But it's not one thing; it's lots of little pieces of content that are just knocking at their door. And you have to make it entertaining enough that people will actually watch it and it doesn't feel like it's a wooden 'public service announcement.'

"Corporations have to still make money. You can't say to them, 'Listen, we're not going to buy this stuff.' What you are going to say is that you have to be a good corporate citizen and make sure that people are protected. You'd like them to have business ethics. You know corporations have to be beaten to have any ethics at all. You have to make it an anvil.

"When you have a strategy, simplicity is sophistication. The simpler the message is, the easier you make it for people to understand what it is and really make it clear. Boil it down. When you're going to tell people stuff (I make content all the time), if you try to say six things to somebody in a commercial, you're lucky if you can get one idea across clearly.

"Who's going to tell you that you can't do it? Is this the same person who's going to tell you that Ghandi would never make it in India? Social movement isn't about people telling you what's possible. It's about your seeing the vision of what you want to do."

MARISKA HARGITAY

"Your Healing Is Our Priority"

"Rape never played a significant role in my life before 1999. That's when I started playing a sex-crimes detective on *Law & Order: Special Victims Unit*, and the worst of what people do to each other became the vocabulary of my days. The show operates in the world of fiction, and I am fortunate that I can close my dressing room door at the end of those days and go home to comfort and safety. But the show's fictions are based in facts, and the facts are terrible.

"When I was preparing to shoot the appropriately titled episode 'Hell' in the spring of 2009, I encountered a category of facts far beyond terrible. Comparing suffering—'This experience is worse than that experience'—is complex territory. I can say, however, that the realities my research revealed were some of the worst I have ever encountered. The story revolved around an eleven-year old girl who had been held as a sexual slave by the Lord's Resistance Army, one of the militias that has brought terror and suffering to Central Africa.

"I read and watched films about the atrocities being perpetrated in Congo, Uganda, and Sudan. I learned of gang rapes, internal mutilations, amputations, and rape as an instrument of war. I learned of women who had been raped so violently and left so internally destroyed that they can no longer control their bowels. I learned of government, military, and social systems that not only fail to prosecute those committing these acts but fail to condemn them and, worse still, harbor, protect—*and sometimes include*—the perpetrators. I learned of hundreds of thousands of women imprisoned in a silence of fear and shame.

"Holocaust survivor Jean Améry titled his book about his experiences at Auschwitz, Buchenwald, and Bergen-Belsen *At the Mind's Limits.* Reading and seeing the stories of Central Africa's women, that is where I found myself: in a realm of facts that were beyond what my mind could comprehend.

"Améry describes how his most terrible wounds, more enduring than the physical ones, came from the experience of having been in the presence of people who were impervious to human suffering. That, he states, is what makes survivors lose 'trust in the world.' He concludes, 'Whoever has succumbed to torture can no longer feel at home in the world.'

"I remember my shock when, in my research for my role, I first encountered the U.S. rape statistics. In response, and because of survivors who began reaching out to me through my work on the show, I started the Joyful Heart Foundation.

"It was my moment of saying Enough to the shame, suffering, and isolation of rape survivors. Joyful Heart runs retreat and community programs to heal, educate, and empower survivors of sexual assault, domestic violence, and child abuse. We are also seeking to engage in a cultural conversation that will shed light into the darkness that surrounds these issues.

"What we envision is a community that seeks to reverse Jean Améry's conclusion. Such a world community says to the women of Congo, 'We are not impervious to your suffering. We will not add our indifference to what you have suffered already. We will give you our ears if you wish to speak of your anguish, we will lend you our voices if you cannot find yours, we will give you our most courageous and informed action to advocate on your behalf before those who have the ability to bring about an end to your plight. We will hold you within our hearts and our minds. Your healing is our priority.'

"In my work on behalf of rape survivors, I am sustained by the experience of seeing courageous souls find their way back to lives of hope, possibility, and joy. Or, in the words of Judith Herman in *Trauma and Recovery*, 'Something in herself that the victim believes to be irretrievably destroyed is reawakened.' A participant in one of our programs once said it was the first time her body hadn't felt like a crime scene. I have the same ambition for the women of Congo: their bodies are not only crime scenes but war zones. And they have suffered enough."

EMILE HIRSCH

Into the Congo

JOHN: What got you involved in Congo in the first place?

EMILE: I got a call from Oxfam America, and they asked me if I wanted to go to Congo. Immediately my pulse just went racing. I had worked on the film *Into the Wild*. And in the movie, Chris McCandless gave his life savings to Oxfam America before he went on his journey into Alaska. I was supposed to go with a couple other actors. And I was on my way to the airport when I got the call that everyone else had dropped out.

I knew almost nothing about Africa. At the airport, I met Liz from Oxfam, and I asked, "How safe is it?" and she said, "Well, there was this little incident last week in which these people were attacked at one of the refugee camps, and thirteen people were killed." This was when my pulse really started to go. The danger of what I was about to get into hadn't really sunk in until then.

The whole time I was on the plane, I was reading the packet over and over again, and just trying to learn. It is just such an incredibly complex situation in Congo—you have the 1994 Rwandan genocide, and all these people from the genocide going over and crossing the borders and the militias are staying there. And raping and looting. And then you have other militias trying to take these militias out, and they are raping and looting. And everyone is getting rich off the mines.

We went to the Synergie clinic, one of the main women's health clinics and rehabilitation centers in eastern Congo. I learned that over 7,000 rapes had been reported, but only sixty-three people had been convicted of the crime. How many people do you think served a day in jail? She said zero, and I would believe it. We went into a room with two little beds, totally dark, and there was this girl named Kamani. She had been there about a month, and I don't think I had ever seen someone as skinny as this girl, in person, in my whole life. And she told us she had been out in the fields one day with her two-year-old son, and these two soldiers came out of the bush and raped her at gunpoint, in front of her kid. Afterward, she had to take her kid and walk home. And there, her husband found out she had been raped, and he rejected her. And then she was basically an outcast, and she got really sick. This woman was right at death's door. I would be surprised if she weighed more than sixty or seventy pounds. But she was beginning to recover at the clinic.

The Synergie clinic gives these women the chance to hope. They band together, they build baskets, which is one of the activities that they do. I was walking through the compound, and I saw all of these women sitting, because most of them have had fistulae, where the tissue between the vagina and the rectum gets ripped when they are raped, and they can't really walk for a month. So most of them are sitting and weaving baskets. And they sell the baskets. And it's productive for them.

The women nursed Kamani back to health. I was just blown away that Kamani was able to recover. She hadn't stood up in a long time. She was so excited, with our presence and talking to her, that she actually stood up.

You can be cynical and tell yourself that you can't change the world, but at the end of the day, for most people, that's not reality. That's just your own cynicism or personal baggage. Because at the end of the day, you know, if you support these kinds of causes, you can really make a difference. And even if it's just affecting one person like Kamani, I think that is a really big deal, and really important. Especially from a place like the United States, where we are all so fortunate, it's not hard to help these people, it's really not. It doesn't take that much effort. So, that's just a little piece of when I was there.

JOHN: Where are you gravitating toward in terms of your efforts?

EMILE: People are using rape as a weapon of war, but the perpetrators are just the pawns. Who is really the master chess player? We need to find who is responsible. And the violence is really fueled by these mines. All of the money and wealth that is in the Congo, and the government and militias are making that money by keeping the country in a state of chaos.

JOHN: It's not just shady unknown corporations. It's the companies we all know.

EMILE: Yeah, like the ones that make our computers and cell phones.

JOHN: The minerals that come from the Congo are inside all the electronics products we use. That's just the way the market is structured. They all go in one big pot until the companies change it. And they won't change it till we demand that change.

EMILE: I think that we are obligated to try and help the Congo and all the people suffering because we are directly implicated in their suffering. And I think the first step really is raising awareness. Just letting people know what is even going on. And from there, people can think creatively and work through their own ways. But until they know what's really going on, they can't do anything. They're in the dark. It's sad to think that we live in a world where that happens. But we also live in a world where that doesn't have to happen if people act.

JOHN: It's not like we have to sell everything we have.

EMILE: Though we could! We could move to Congo! Drop everything!

JOHN: All right, Chris McCandless. Alternatively, you can accomplish a lot just sitting in your living room and writing to these companies, and writing to your senators, and to President Obama, and asking them, "What are you doing about this?"

EMILE: There is so much that we can do.

JOHN: Like that incredible organization Run for Congo Women. People all over the country sponsor runs and raise money for women like Kamani.

EMILE: Or a jog.

JOHN: Very reasonable. A jog for Congo's women.

EMILE: Or a power walk. Then you have an alliteration: a walk for women.

JOHN: What else, Mr. Innovator?

EMILE: Just regularly search Congo on Google news and learn about what's actually going on. This is something I've started doing since I got back. I think that when you start to learn more and more about the current situation and it's not like you're flipping through a history book, you'll see stuff that's happening that day or yesterday, and it will seem more real for you and you will get more invested in it.

IMAN

"Because I Am One"

JOHN: You have this extraordinary beginning that no one else could possibly compare with because of where you came from. As a refugee from your home country of Somalia, how did it feel? What was it like to be separated from your home and then from your culture, and then from everything that you knew?

IMAN: I could never forget how dehumanizing it feels to be helpless. To see my dad in that condition as a refugee literally broke my heart. He didn't know how he was going to be able to take care of us, so my brothers and I tried to pretend to be so strong, so that he didn't feel that we were so upset. There were six of us in one little hut. Stand in line for food, and you didn't get three meals a day. The humility and the loss of everything—my parents left with one picture of each of us. One picture. We left our families, we left our friends, we left our heritage, culture. I didn't go back to Somalia for twenty years, until the civil war started. And to be in a foreign country where, most of the time, people look at you as if you are looking for a handout, or you are lazy and you just want to take what the government gives you. They think you don't want to work or you don't want to do anything.

Most refugees don't ever want to leave their countries. Ever. They leave because of persecution, they leave because of fear for their lives. They don't live in a happy way. . . . Nobody willingly leaves his or her country and walks and lives in a hut and asks for a handout. Most refugees try as best as they can to become really productive members of the societies that take them in. So I've always tried to really make people understand what refugees are. Because I am one.

JOHN: Where did you sleep?

IMAN: On the floor.

JOHN: Was it in a building?

IMAN: No, no. It was homemade, like a hut.

JOHN: And how did you eat? Did you have some supplies with you?

IMAN: No, we didn't have any supplies; they were given in the refugee camp. But it was an eye opener to not know. And mind you, we had left only with the clothes on our backs because we had to cross the border by foot, so we couldn't take anything with us.

JOHN: After your own personal experience as a refugee, what struck you about the Congo that compelled you to do something, even with all your other charitable commitments?

IMAN: It goes back to how I feel about women and children. It's not lost on me that what sustains the continent of Africa really starts with women. And the fabric of that is being destroyed. The Congolese conflict, and what it's doing morally—the sexual violence, the rape of women and children—is the rape of a whole continent. When families and communities are destroyed in that way, there is a moral issue at stake. We need an Enough Moment for Congo. We all need to say, "Enough of this now." Whether we say it as an international community, or whether they say it in Congo, family by family. It's a front line.

JOHN: There are various elements to the response—such as the empowerment of women who are not just people to be saved but agents of their own destiny, and the transformation of the Congolese culture and society.

IMAN: Exactly. And taking care of themselves. Congolese women know what they need. It's not for us on the outside to decide what they need. We can structure for them what is available, so they can start again their communities. Obviously, one thing is to stop the violence against women and children. But also, it is building communities, infrastructure, small businesses for themselves, which has been shown to be life transforming, especially for women.

JOHN: I think so many people don't understand—no, it's not that they don't understand. It's that they don't know this because it's presented that these women are victims, that they're beaten down, that they have to be saved. But the truth is that every woman I've met in Congo is fighting for her family, fighting for her community. And as you're saying, it's just a small little support that we can provide that can help her blossom.

IMAN: Exactly. And most of the time it is asking them, exactly, what do they need. Because what's needed in Congo definitely is not the same thing as what is needed in South Africa or Kenya.

JOHN: Another aspect of the situation, beyond empowerment, is protection. I think we would agree that protecting women and children ought to be the number 1 priority of the United Nations in Congo.

IMAN: To rape women and children is actually the destruction of a community. It's how to morally and emotionally destroy people. And that's what one group uses against another. So protection is entirely warranted, as much as it would be in a situation of ethnic cleansing.

JOHN: It turns out that inadvertently our thirst for consumption of electronics products like cell phones and laptops is fueling the war in Congo.

IMAN: This is the kind of issue that needs a people's movement. I was part of something close to this. We all have heard about blood diamonds. I was asked to be under a contract as the face of De Beers. I went to South Africa, and I talked to Mandela to find out exactly what I would be representing. How come I didn't know anything about these blood diamonds? But I knew I would have a clear conscience if I wasn't part of it—so I terminated my contract. So what I'm saying is that it's very easy for everybody, if they really want to utilize their consciences, to just ask. Make that call, and ask that we want our phones to not be part of the conflict in Congo. It takes a conscience. And singularly, one person's conscience. I couldn't live with myself. Can you? Pick up the phone and tell companies you want a conflict-free phone.

JOHN: One of the amazing things that I've found is how meaningful it is to refugees when they learn that there are people back in the United States who are working to try to help them go home. That is a direct lifeline to people surviving in these situations.

IMAN: I cannot stress enough the importance of writing letters to our representatives. Whether one is a celebrity or not, it doesn't matter because of the direct impact you can make on somebody who is stuck, somewhere far away, to help them and give them hope that either they can go back home or start anew where they are. It is beyond amazing. Because it has happened for me. I saw it myself and continue to see it.

ANGELINA JOLIE

Finding Hope

In the fall of 2003, Angelina and John traveled together to Congo. After they returned, the U.S. Holocaust Memorial Museum produced a web-based photo exhibit of their trip. Below are excerpts from Angelina's journal of their trip that remain relevant today.

Bunia Internally Displaced Persons Camp
I am introduced to a woman who is starting a committee in a camp. She thanks me for coming so far away to see them. In that statement, I think how much a simple

*gesture, just visiting, means. No one here knows what I do
for a living, my name, or if I have money. They just know
that I came from a more fortunate country. That I'm a
foreigner who cares how they are and wants to hear what
they have to say.*

Bunyakiri, a town in South Kivu

*We enter a room of all women. It is dark inside the ce-
ment room. Many hold babies, and some are breastfeed-
ing. Most of them are in their early twenties. We ask them
to speak freely about what they have been through during
the war. No one speaks. No one moves. We say, "You can
tell us your story in general, if you wish. It does not have
to be very personal."*

[They say,] "We are the women of Bunyakiri. We have
suffered a lot. We thank you for hearing us. Our homes were
looted and burned. We slept in the forest. Many women died,
and many were killed. It feels as if the war was against us.
The rape was the most shocking. They made us cook, then
stole our food and brutally raped us. We had to plant in areas,
and we worked hard; they would steal all our crops. If we
got sick, we had no way to get to the hospital. We had no
funds. We are displaced. We have nothing. As a result of the
violence, many of us have STDs. Our families after the rape
have banished us, and we cannot afford to send our children
to school."

What is interesting here is that the Congolese people on
the ground are working toward peace themselves. The local
people and the local NGOs, with no outside help, are broker-
ing their own peace deals in their areas. It's amazing, and
they deserve support.

As we fly out of the Congo, I think of the hundreds of
thousands living in the camps on the border dreaming of one

day being able to live at home in Congo. I believe I am right in saying that peace here would not just stop the killing but begin to give hope to all of Africa.

JOEL MADDEN AND NICOLE RICHIE

Integrating Activism into Family Life

JOHN: What was it that made you two decide to stand up for the women of the Congo?

NICOLE: First of all, I just want to say that it is very easy nowadays to kinda turn it all off. So I don't think it is necessarily ignorance that is the problem here. I just think there is a lot going on, lots of competition for our attention. Between computers, television, and cell phones, it is so easy to just become distracted. But if you just take ten or twenty minutes to listen to someone's story, like the stories of some of the women from Congo, I think it is absolutely impossible to turn away.

The first time that I became aware of these issues was when I actually met a refugee camp survivor. I was at a small gathering of about forty people at someone's house, and I listened to a Congolese refugee named Rose Mapendo speak. Rose lives in Arizona now. She spoke of women being raped. It was overwhelming. Children being killed in front of the mothers. And when I looked into her eyes, she was a complete hero to me. And she is right here among us. And she is alive, and she is strong. And she wasn't asking for pity. She was just telling us about the reality she lived through in Congo. And it's unacceptable that this situation exists. Completely unacceptable. She wasn't saying, "Feel bad for me." She was saying, "This is my reality. This is what I go through.

This is what my friends go through." I just can't imagine what that's like.

JOHN: Anyone who heard that would be horrified, but what actually led you to do something about it? What chord did it strike?

NICOLE: It is so easy to complain about the hardships of your own life. I can't imagine what it's like for Rose. Rose talked about the things that had been done to her body, without her consent, and she just had to live with it, her womanhood being just stripped from her. It was completely taken away. And I wasn't okay with just letting that happen. I wasn't okay with hearing about the young girls who are getting raped as well. I still can't even really think about. I still have to separate myself to even be able to get involved with something like this because I cannot imagine it fully.

JOHN: So how did your caring about these issues actually lead you to doing something about them?

JOEL: Actually, meeting you. Most people care when they hear about these things, but they don't act on their concerns. But if they are presented with the opportunity to do something about these things, they will. I think many people don't feel self-empowered. But if you present them with the opportunity, or the moment, to say something or do something, they will.

NICOLE: Most people just need someone to walk them through it—how to get involved, what they can do.

JOEL: I also think that people need to be held accountable in some way to connect how they feel to how they then act in response. And that's what people like you do, and what I have started to do. We help hold people accountable. We are obligated, and we are responsible for our children, our brothers and sisters, and mothers and daughters. When you become a parent, you start to realize not only the value of human life but how precious all people are. It's like the old saying, "There but for the grace of God go I." We are here in our shoes, and not theirs. There is no explanation for why we got dropped here and they got dropped there, why we were born here and they were born there. So we aren't talking about aliens or people without real feelings. We are talking about real human beings, with the same needs, the same feelings, the same happiness, and the same sadness as us. And I think the important thing for me is showing the human side to it all. This is your mother, this is your daughter. These are your children. One problem is that when people hear the numbers of dead, of displaced, they turn away. I hate the way it's being presented to people on TV, because . . .

NICOLE: It seems too big.

JOEL: Millions of faceless beings. We are talking about the deadliest war since World War II, and it's almost invisible because there are not enough faces to it. What made me want to make a difference there, or just try to raise consciousness, or decide to go there? You know, I don't think I would have ever ended up in Africa if I weren't a parent. When you shake people's hands, and you hang out with them, and you live with them, you can feel what great people they are, and how they are living in these difficult situations. And I wanted to bring that back with me. And when it became that to me, it became something I will not ever let go of until it's solved. Until that war is over.

JOHN: When did you first hear about these issues?

JOEL: I met a group of guys from the Invisible Children organization a couple years ago. It was the first time I ever even looked into what was going on in Africa. And that was what sort of sparked my interest. Someone said, "Hey, some friends of mine are doing an event for children in Africa, and you should come." And I went and checked it out, by chance.

I met this little boy who had been a child soldier. They brought him over to LA, to the event. And the kid was like twelve years old. And he was one of the children that had been a child soldier and had escaped, and he was hiding out. He was one of these kids that the group was supporting and fighting for. I love it when I see people who have made it their life's mission to make these kids' lives better. So I said, "Hey, why don't you bring the kid over to my house this week," and my brother Benji and I got to hang out with him. And I fell in love with him. He was such a sweet kid. And I had no clue about the causes. I was utterly clueless. There were all of these different steps along the way, and we met you, and it's just been this journey that's been really cool.

What Nicole and I have tried to do together is to integrate these issues into our lives. It's very important that you pace yourself. And you have to, just like anything else you do in your life. It's just gotta become a part of your lifestyle, that you commit this amount of time and energy to whatever you want to change. Like the work I do with UNICEF and the work I do with Enough—I try to find a way to make it all work together, make it all a part of my life. So that you stay the course. So that hopefully in ten years, we can turn around and say, "It's cool that I got to see that change happen firsthand, and I was a part of it." But it's important for people to understand that we aren't going to solve it overnight. It's more about joining the momentum of something, and spreading the word, raising consciousness.

It's important for us as a family, not only for Nicole and me but for and with our kids, to integrate these issues into our family life. So it becomes something that is normal. If you can raise your kids to be the opposite of ignorant, the opposite of unaware, and the opposite of unconscious, then they are going to be, hopefully, part of the solution, as opposed to part of the problem. For us, it's been more about a lifestyle, integrating it into our family and lives. And now it is very normal. Our kids are going to know what's going on, and they are going to know how to respond. It's already normal for them to hear us talking to other people about it. We have the opportunity to change what we are putting out there to the world, and consciousness is everything.

I'm not an intelligent or elegant speaker at all.

JOHN: Are you kidding? You should write a book, not me.

NICOLE: Our kids are also fortunate enough to be born and raised during a time when these issues and opportunities are so out there in the open. So they are not going to have the same experience as our generation, where we have been so shocked and taken aback by some of the world's problems. They will have the access to address these issues and reach out to people thousands of miles away. That is going to be part of their life. They are not going to be shocked the way our whole generation was.

JOEL: When I was in Africa, I was with these volunteer doctors, people with PhDs, giving their entire lives to live in dirt-poor conditions and to do something. That's where my heart has led me, because my faith holds me to do the right thing as well. This work is an expression of my faith because it's the only place I feel like my actions and intentions are received purely.

CONGRESSMAN JIM MCDERMOTT
(D-WASHINGTON)

"One Has to Be a Stone Not to Be Moved"

"Tragically, I've known about rape as a weapon of war since my days in the State Department in the 1980s. After seeing it firsthand, how could you not be moved to action? I visited a hospital in Goma and saw the wounded. I walked through the refugee camps in the Chadian desert and had letters with pleas for help placed into my hands by innocent people who had lost everything. And I met towering heroic figures—men, women, and children—who were unwilling to yield to the finality of death even as they clung to life. One has to be a stone not to be moved by this. There's a world war going on in Central Africa that most people are unaware of because there is no television coverage by and large and most people get their information from television. These are far-off places and not often covered on television.

"The group in Seattle that reached out to me also reached out across the community to close the information gap. So my advice is straightforward: Get people together, and show one or more of the many excellent documentaries that have been made. One picture is worth a thousand words, and one person can make a difference."

ROBIN WRIGHT

"We All Deserve the Same. Justice. And Life."

JOHN: Why did you say, "I'm going to do something about this"? Why Congo?

ROBIN: Well, it was meeting you. You brought to my attention the gravity of this issue. The violence in the Congo involves a direct attack on women, this weapon of war the armed groups are using. It's that unacceptable Enough Moment in us, in humanity. We as individuals have had enough of feeling that unacceptable moment. And that's what triggered me to be proactive. I feel like I can help get the word out to the public. Society needs to understand where this is coming from. Where are we positioning ourselves as individuals so that we can help?

JOHN: In your own background, history, view of the world, how did you gravitate to this?

ROBIN: Ever since I was four or five, I had this dream that I would work in a refugee camp. I would be a doctor, saving people's lives. Bringing people to safety and sustainable lives. A few years ago I read a script by Erin Dignam. And in that script, you have two people that have the same core beliefs, which are that unacceptable suffering must end, and we must help it end. I felt aligned with one of the characters who wants to get at the root causes of the war in which she is a refugee camp doctor.

JOHN: So you decide to go to Senegal to research the role. What did you take away from your trip to Africa?

ROBIN: It is important that we are able to look at another and say, "We are all one." We all deserve the same. Justice. And life.

Last Word on Upstanders

There are many other Famous Upstanders working on the issues of Sudan, Congo, and northern Uganda who are not reflected in this book. Andie MacDowell does film screenings all over her native North Carolina. George Clooney is an indefatigable advocate for Darfur. Ashley Judd has traveled to Congo and stays closely engaged in developments there. Matt Damon and Brad Pitt work with Don and George on the board of Not On Our Watch in support of Darfur. Julianne Moore, Julianna Margulies, Sandra Oh, Mary-Louise Parker, Saffron Burrows, Jeffrey Dean Morgan, and Brooke Smith have all done videos on Congo. Rosario Dawson and Kerry Washington have worked closely with Eve Ensler on Congo. Forrest Whitaker has visited Uganda and supported schools there. Mira Sorvino has spoken at numerous events and lobbied Congress on Darfur. Sonya Walger and Wim Wenders were judges on a major YouTube contest on Congo. Damien Rice, Mos Def, Norah Jones, and other musicians have contributed songs for a CD in support of the women and girls of the Congo (see www.raisehopeforcongo.org). If top-rated television shows could be Upstanders, *60 Minutes* (thanks to Scott Pelley and his all-star producers) and *Law & Order: Special Victims Unit* (thanks to its creator Neal Baer) would qualify for their ongoing programming focused on these issues.

If you want to learn more about the work of many of these Upstanders, you can visit www.enoughproject.org and go to the celebrity activism section.

CHAPTER NINE

The Menu for Change

Renewing Our Enough Pledge and
Helping You Make Yours

JOHN: This concept of an Enough Moment at the individual level isn't just a one-off deal or a one-time affair, clearly. We all have different challenges or issues that pop up constantly that allow us to recommit and reenter the fray. There are multiple moments when the opportunity arises to be an Upstander again, and we have that choice, over and over again. Look at the last few years of your life: you were in *Hotel Rwanda*, you took a trip to Africa, and then another one, you did all kinds of public events, you helped start the aid organization Not On Our Watch, you helped found Ante Up for Africa poker tournaments with Annie Duke and Norman Epstein, you did the film *Darfur Now*, you designed a boot with Timberland to "Stomp Out Genocide," you are writing your second book with me—hey, didn't we swear never to write another book together?—the list goes on and on. Basically, it comes down to renewing your pledge, your "Enough Pledge."

DON: Hmmm, what makes us continue to renew our pledge? I like that, great way to say it. Your responsibility doesn't end with one action. Like Ante Up for Africa, it is an annual event, so we come back every year. You and I continuously come back to each other with questions—what are we doing now to move the cause forward? What should we do now? It's what you have dedicated your life to, and it's what I continue to recommit to in various ways. During the year when these various events are coming together, every time I'm on the phone with these guys, Brad and George and Matt, it is often a subject of discussion. Mainly because the Sudanese people aren't yet dancing in the streets of Khartoum saying, "We're free."

JOHN: I remember when I was working for President Clinton and we were working closely with Nelson Mandela on the Burundi peace process. People would get discouraged, and President Mandela would remind us—sometimes sternly—that no situation, no matter how bleak the snapshot may look, is actually hopeless. He would tell us stories of his own experiences, being in prison for decades and then coming out and becoming president, to demonstrate how things can change. We just have to stay positive because the worm will turn. One of my favorite stories in our previous book is about your visit to UCLA's campus when you had that torn ACL in your knee, and you had to limp all the hell over the campus all day. You guys started with about fifteen people, and you were like, "Oh no, this is a bust," but the word kept spreading throughout the day, and by the end there, you had well over a hundred students, and you all went in to the hearing room and convinced the university regents to sell all the stocks in the university portfolio that are related to Sudanese investments. That was invigorating. At the end you wrote, "Sore as I am, my battery has been recharged. What's next?" That's an example, if there ever were one, of renewing one's Enough Pledge.

DON: Don't remind me. I still can't beat my man off the dribble because of that injury.

JOHN: I can't beat my man even if I didn't dribble and just ran with the ball. It has all slipped away so quickly.

DON: We had our day. At least we can still walk.

JOHN: Oh, that's what that is called, when you painfully move under your own power from point A to point B?

DON: Speaking of pain . . . I had to write a lot more of my personal stories in the last book, my Enough Moments. I thought you got off a little light. I think it's your turn to really spill the beans and tell us more about how you've stayed in the game for over twenty-five years now, how you've been able to keep renewing your Enough Pledge, fighting the good human rights fight.

JOHN: I'll admit, I've had my share of disappointments and hopes, failures and successes, narrow escapes and lucky misses, lost friends, and found allies . . .

DON: What, are you gonna sing a song or answer the question?

JOHN: Sheesh, tough crowd. All right all right. I was born in Indianapolis, Indiana, to a frozen foods salesman and a social worker.

DON: Please fast forward.

JOHN: Okay. I can't even count the significant forks in the road I've encountered, but it all really started when I was twenty-one years old, sitting in my favorite old Archie Bunker Lazyboy chair with my ankle in a cast from yet another basketball injury, and in the middle of the night, footage comes on from the famine in Ethiopia and Eritrea. I had a choice. I could have given a few bucks. I could have changed the channel if I had a remote control clicker. I could have maybe tried to learn more about what was happening there. But I decided in that instant, when confronted with pictures of human misery like none I had ever countenanced before, I decided to just go to Africa and see for myself and figure out where I fit into the whole thing.

A couple years later, another fork presented itself to me. I was in Somalia and witnessing how a U.S.-backed dictator was destroying his own country. I had started down a career track that was focused on the delivery of humanitarian and development assistance, and it promised to be a fascinating life full of adventure and meaningful work. But as I watched the American government—in its pursuit of cold strategic interest—help inadvertently underwrite the destruction of a country and its people, I decided to go another way. I decided that I needed to come back to the United States and use my one comparative advantage, my U.S. citizenship, to help re-form American policy in Africa so it wasn't solely designed to use Africa and its people to achieve U.S. foreign policy and economic security objectives.

Don! Don! Wake up!!

DON: I'm listening! Whaddya want, minute-by-minute validation?

JOHN: Okay, just checking. Another fork came a decade later. After years of rabble rousing as a long-haired outsider activist, content with making bold pronouncements about U.S. policy in Africa to anyone who would listen, I was presented with the opportunity to put my time where my mouth was and come join the U.S. government to help make its Africa policy. So I went to the barber, got a genuine haircut and not just a "trim," bought one suit from a great thrift store, reinvented myself as a diplomat and peace negotiator, and showed up at the White House the next day to work for Susan Rice and the president of the United States, Bill Clinton.

After I left government, I reinvented myself again as a policy wonk. I spent a few years just working inside the system, inside the Beltway, doing think tank conferences and presenting long and probably boring papers to like-minded people in a circular process that had little effect on actual policy making and the broader public's role in shaping it. I realized that if anything was going to change STRUCTUR-ALLY in terms of U.S. policy toward and interest in Africa, it would only be through a much more informed citizenry shaping those changes. So I reinvented myself again and became a populist campaigner.

In all these years of working on these issues, I have never had a boring day or even a dull moment. And the various paths have been so incredibly unpredictable.

I couldn't have imagined so many of the things that I have since experienced when I had my first Enough Moment at the age of twenty-one.

I was utterly petrified of public speaking when I was younger. I couldn't have imagined that twenty years later I would be doing over one hundred speeches a year, sometimes in front of crowds in the thousands.

I have been a tech phobe all my life. I couldn't have imagined that one of the main things I am doing now is focusing on how to build campaigns using the latest social networking functions, even though I myself don't have any idea how to use them.

Sitting in that Lazyboy at the age of twenty-one, I had never read a book on Africa, or peacemaking, or even foreign policy for that matter. I couldn't have imagined then that fifteen years later I would be helping to broker peace deals in different parts of Africa, including contributing to an end to a deadly war involving Ethiopia and Eritrea, the places that had originally brought me to Africa.

I watched in awe of what musicians led by Bono, Bob Geldof, and Sting were able to do to generate attention for the cause of the Ethiopian and Eritrean famine shortly after I went to Africa the first time in the 1980s. I couldn't have imagined then that twenty years later I would be regularly working with musicians and other artists to raise awareness.

During my college years, as I bounced from school to school, I had been an amateur student of the civil rights movement. I couldn't have imagined that a couple decades later I would be sitting in a D.C. jail cell with John L. Lewis, one of the original Freedom Riders in Mississippi, as we were arrested together for trespassing on the property of the Sudan Embassy and refusing to leave during one of our protest marches.

When I was in my early twenties, no one would hire me full time because I had no experience because no one would hire me, a vicious catch-22. I couldn't have imagined that a decade and a half later I would be sitting elbow to elbow with Nelson Mandela strategizing with him on how to bring peace to some of Africa's war-torn countries.

I moved to Washington, D.C., at the age of twenty-four to take an internship, and I was living in a condemned building because I couldn't afford rent. I couldn't have imagined that sixteen years later I would be traveling around Congo with Angelina Jolie, or that I would move so quickly from renegade outside critic to director for African affairs at the White House, or that I would get the chance to help shape U.S. policy in Africa.

I loved watching the Ben Affleck and Matt Damon movies like *Good Will Hunting* and *Rounders* in which they would team up using their real-life chemistry. I couldn't have imagined that I'd eventually be working with them—and you—raising money for Darfur and awareness for Congo.

DON: What, you don't like my movies?

JOHN: I'm sorry, were you in *Good Will Hunting* as well? Well, what I'm saying is that part of the process of renewing my Enough Pledge has been remaining open to all possibilities and being willing to take less traveled paths. By being an Upstander for others and dreaming big dreams, some of them actually have come true on the road to trying to make the world a little bit better. But it hasn't been all Bill Clinton, Angelina Jolie, and Emmy Awards for *60 Minutes*. Over the years, my mind and focus have been concentrated by some near misses, some real close calls:

- From the side window of a small plane I was in over southern Sudan, I watched a shoulder-to-air missile get launched in our direction, and after evasive measures, I saw the rocket fly a few dozen feet past our plane.
- In a long convoy of trucks in Angola, I watched the vehicle ahead of me explode as it drove over a land mine planted in the road.
- In one of the most dangerous neighborhoods in Mogadishu, the capital of Somalia, a mortar round hit the building I was in, and half the building collapsed (but not the half that I was in).
- On the border of Rwanda and Congo after the genocide, a child soldier all drugged up by his superiors stuck a gun in my mouth and threatened to kill me at a roadblock, but then ended up walking away muttering to himself.
- In both Zimbabwe and southern Sudan, I was arrested and detained for human rights reporting. In the former case I was roughed up and deported. In the latter, I was left in a hut that doubled as a jail for four days in a remote village with little food and water until I was released after having been "taught a lesson."

- In Congo I was stopped at a roadblock, and a couple dozen machine gun–wielding militia emerged from the woods and began threatening my travel companions and me, poking guns in my stomach and simulating a throat slash. We were taken to the militia barracks in the middle of the night, and a debate ensued about what to do with us. We finally were released when we convinced the militia leader we'd put in a good word for him with the U.S. military.

DON: The grim reaper is camped outside your doorstep permanently, it seems.

JOHN: It comes with the territory. Luckily, not everyone who wants to be an Upstander has to experience these kinds of close calls to make a difference . . .

Your Enough Moment Is Calling: How Do You Answer?

DON: So now we're at the point in the book where people hopefully are like, okay, we got all that. Now tell us what we can do. How can we get involved in a way that might really make a difference? And I think at the core of this is the recurring theme of the importance of creating connections. Finding the personal connection between us and them, you and me, so that these artificial barriers dissolve.

JOHN: And I think there are some road-tested ways to do that. One way is by telling personal stories of survivors. People connect to individuals, all the research shows that. It is much harder to connect to 6 million dead in the Holocaust than it is to connect to Anne Frank.

DON: Another way is creating these school-to-school or student-to-student ties. Like what your Darfur Sister Schools Program has done. When young people in the United States get the chance to personally connect to young people in Darfur or another far-off place, the distance between them gets a lot shorter, and you start to see concepts of mutual responsibility play themselves out right in the classroom.

JOHN: I wish every school, every classroom, could have these kinds of connections. Yet another way to establish connections and invest people in activism is by demonstrating the economic linkages. That is why we focused on the conflict minerals in the Congo, to demonstrate to people that this wasn't some ancient tribal feud that led to the highest death toll since the Holocaust. The war there is fueled directly by our demand for electronic products. By demonstrating the links, we show people that there are solutions, and we can even use these electronic devices themselves to catalyze change through texting, call-in, and e-mailing campaigns.

Making a Difference in the Twenty-First Century

The incredible thing in the twenty-first century is that you can raise your voice and fight genocide, mass rape, and child abductions right from your laptop in the comfort of your living room. And that's good because now, more than ever, our voices are needed if we're going to help bring about the change we'd like to see.

Americans are a generous and pragmatic people. We've seen that over and over: Haiti, Hurricane Katrina, the tsunami. When someone is in need, they will help, but usually only if they can see a chance for success or that their help can actually make a difference. We want to help people wade into some of the most difficult issues and broken societies of our time and find the hope, the humanity, and then connect it back here to us, to America's rightful place in the world as a beacon for peace and human rights.

Here's a menu you can choose from, a menu of fourteen (nice round number) life-saving and life-affirming actions, all of which can make a real difference in the battle for a more just and peaceful world. We've learned a lot since *Not On Our Watch* about what is needed to influence policy makers and build a genuine people's movement, so this menu is more elaborate and offers more choices than the one in our earlier book. All of the actions below can be found updated on www.enoughmoment.org. Just start with one of them!

1. **First, Join the Movement!** Get off the bench and get in the game, and recruit your friends and family members as well. It turns out that the most effective tool for inspiring action isn't a fancy ad campaign or a huge rally. It isn't a celebrity endorser. It's when a friend or family member asks a friend or family member to help him or her solve a problem that matters personally. Everyone has social networks and communities both online and offline that are much bigger and more powerful than we might realize. So join an organization like Enough, STAND, Invisible Children, V-Day, Amnesty International, Save Darfur Coalition, or other groups in this movement that stand up for what you stand for. Get involved in one of the ongoing campaigns, like Enough's Raise Hope for Congo, Humanity United's Sudan Now, or Invisible Children's How It Ends. Sign up for action alerts and newsletters, and get your friends and family members to join you and take action.

2. **Contact Your Senator or Representative.** The bedrock of our democracy lies in the fact that your elected officials work for you. Despite all of the new tools at our fingertips, and despite all the special-interest money, policy is ultimately changed the old-fashioned way, and it is a supply and demand system.

If you demand it, our government will supply it. If you don't vote, and you don't write to pressure your elected officials, you don't count. But if you do those things, then you count disproportionately to the one body you inhabit because of all the other complainers who are sitting it out. So get in touch with your elected officials by calling, writing, e-mailing, or even going to meet them when they come to your hometown looking for votes. You are their employer. Tell them what you want them to do for you as their constituent. Thank them when they do what you ask, and hold them accountable when they don't. And in the age of technological protest, where members of Congress can be overwhelmed by huge amounts of electronic communications from large-scale well-financed campaigns, there is no substitute for sending your representative a handwritten letter (neatly written; don't be a loon!) or putting together a unique coalition of folks at the district level and making an appointment to see your representative personally when he or she is holding office hours. Our issues are ones where the greatest political opponent we face is usually apathy, but apathy can easily be overcome with enough concerted political pressure.

3. Call the White House. It takes only a few minutes to let our president know that it matters to you as a voter that he (or in the future, she) makes fighting these human rights crimes a priority. It's easy; you may not even have to write this number down anywhere. The Genocide Intervention Network has a number that you can call to get a short briefing and talking points before forwarding you to the White House switchboard. The number is 1-800-GENOCIDE (1-800-436-6243). Use it, recruit your friends and family to call it, and call back often. They don't have caller ID so don't be shy about calling multiple times. One single call to the White House or your elected officials might not make much of an impact by itself, but a community or constituency can make a world of difference by calling regularly and keeping the pressure on until progress is made.

4. Get Local Media. In the world of newspapers and local television and radio, it is again a supply and demand equation. If a producer or editor gauges that people are interested in a particular subject, he or she will provide that content. So write or call your local radio and television networks, and urge them to cover stories about these human rights crimes in Africa, and the positive stories as well. Ask for a meeting with your paper's editorial board, and make a compelling case for an editorial on Sudan or the conflict minerals trade in Congo. Write a letter to the editor about a newsworthy item related to these issues. Media networks need our help too with content to cover these issues. There are lots of good people who care about these issues working in the media, and they need popular, quantifiable support in the form of letters, phone calls, and e-mails that demonstrate that there is an audience for stories about war and peace and human rights beyond Iraq and Afghanistan. At a time when broader foreign media coverage is rapidly declining, it is often up to us to keep these issues in the news by creating the need to cover it.

5. Get Involved in Corporate Campaigning. Although governments are usually the main players in supporting solutions to complex international problems, private sector entities can also be influential. We currently have two big opportunities here. In the case of Congo's conflict minerals, the Enough Project is spearheading a campaign to influence the behavior of the top electronics companies. We want them to stop buying from suppliers that get their raw materials in a way that fuels war and atrocities, and instead produce conflict-free phones, laptops, and other electronic products. They produce the technology that we all use, but we can use that same technology to organize and raise our collective voices to change their behavior. Visit www

.raisehopeforcongo.org and find out the latest initiatives in which to get involved.

Another great opportunity for corporate engagement comes through organizations like the Conflict Risk Network (CRN) and Investors Against Genocide (IAG). In the case of the Darfur genocide, the Sudan Divestment Task Force (now CRN) forged a campaign to get big institutional investment funds to sell the stock of companies doing business in Sudan in ways that strengthened the government there. Congress passed the Sudan Accountability and Divestment Act, which authorizes and encourages state and local divestment. Twenty-seven state pension funds, over sixty universities and colleges, twenty-three cities, the retirement fund TIAA-CREF, and even Warren Buffett's Berkshire Hathaway have divested from these targeted stocks. Thirteen international companies have ceased operations in Sudan or have developed exit plans as a result of divestment efforts. Get involved with these organizations, and stay informed about how you can influence corporations to do their part to help stop the violence.

6. Join the Darfur Dream Team's Sister Schools Program. This initiative links middle schools, high schools, colleges, and universities in the United States with schools in the Darfur refugee camps and helps fund the refugee camp schools. Video links between schools there and here will allow students to get to know each other and build connections to people directly affected by the atrocities in Sudan. NBA players act as spokespersons and supporters of the program, and they are helping to carry this new program to a wide audience. The more human linkages that can be established connecting good-hearted people with those for whom they are advocating, the more sustainable the movement will be to ensure that the Darfurian students and their families can one day go home in peace. Go to www .darfurdreamteam.org to sign up or donate.

7. Get on the Bus and Attend an Event! Enough, Invisible Children, the Save Darfur Coalition, STAND chapters, Resolve Uganda, V-Day, Jewish World Watch, and many other organizations regularly organize local events to galvanize support, educate the community, and publicly demonstrate that this movement's strength is not just in Washington, D.C., but in grassroots actions carried out across the country. Attending or organizing an event is one of the most important things activists can do because these demonstrations get local press and show our elected officials that their constituents care about these issues at a local level. So get on a bus! Attend an Invisible Children movie screening, support a local STAND chapter, or go to a conference or a lobby day!

8. Use Your Social Media for Social Good. The tools of social media are undoubtedly important in their ability to make us all neighbors in one interconnected global marketplace of ideas and actions. However, the connections made on Facebook, the knowledge gained through tweets, and the opportunities uncovered in communities of interest are only the first step. For social media to mean social good, you must go further.

Start using your online identity to make a footprint on the issues in this book and that you care about. Use your virtual soapbox on Facebook to promote news articles covering the stories that need to be told. If you care deeply about issues like the ongoing violence against women in the Congo, tell somebody! Start a blog, and cover the story in ways that the mainstream media are missing. Write your favorite bloggers like Daily Kos or FiredogLake and ask that they start providing more coverage of these crimes against humanity. Use whatever platforms you can to raise the profile of these tragedies. We can all work to highlight the issues that otherwise aren't getting enough attention.

Finally, make the online world count in the offline world. Use easy and lightweight tools like TweetUps or Facebook groups to bring people together in the real world for viewing parties, discussion groups, or other events that can help promote the importance of making an impact with those less fortunate. Check out social media platforms like TakePart. com, SocialVibe, and Causecast as ways to get further involved and become part of a larger online community.

9. Make a Video! With the popularity of video-sharing websites and an abundance of affordable, easy-to-use cameras on the market, spreading your message via video has never been easier—or more essential. In the past, presidents made weekly addresses on the radio. But President Obama posts his weekly address on YouTube. And there's a reason for that: it's where the eyeballs are.

Creative video doesn't necessarily have to be time-consuming or elaborate (although that doesn't hurt either!). The beauty of video is that it allows you to add your face to a movement simply by firing up the camera, looking into the lens, and speaking your mind. Share your video online, and encourage your friends to join you. A visual chorus of people calling for change is difficult to ignore.

10. Get Off Your Ass and RUN! Run for Congo Women is a grassroots run (or walk, bike, swim, bake, pray . . . you get the point, just get creative!) fundraiser for Women for Women International's Congo Program (www.women forwomen.org). So far, the group has raised more than $600,000, and it has sponsored well over 1,200 women in Congo. And those women are raising more than 5,000 children. You can visit www.runforcongowomen.org to find out if there's a run scheduled near you or to get tips on organizing your own run. Who knew that exercising could be so meaningful?

11. Host a Movie Screening. Consider hosting a screening of one of the amazing films that have been produced about the issues addressed in this book: Don Cheadle's *Darfur Now*, George Clooney's *Sand and Sorrow*, Tracy McGrady's *3 Points*, Brian Steidle's *The Devil Came on Horseback*, Emmanuel Jal's *War Child*, Lisa Jackson's *The Greatest Silence*, and Invisible Children's various films. Whether you host something at your house or a local venue, this is a great way to get your friends and community more informed and passionate about taking action.

12. Organize a Teach-in at Your School or Your Child's School. V-Day, Enough, and STAND have teamed up to create materials to teach a class about the conflict in Congo. Facing History and Ourselves has a curriculum for Darfur based on the film *Darfur Now* and our book *Not On Our Watch*. Use one of these existing resources or create your own to educate those around you. Let's make sure no one can say he or she did not know about these issues as a reason for inaction. We have to get out and educate our communities and schools about what we know.

13. Involve Your Local Faith Community. Faith-based groups have a great history of being powerful forces for change in areas of human rights—from helping to end slavery to pressuring the U.S. government to lead in creating the Comprehensive Peace Agreement for Sudan in 2005, which brought the twenty-year civil war to a halt. Two great resources for the Christian community are a Bible study series called the *Not On Our Watch Christian Companion* (a resource by Greg Leffel and Bill Mefford, whose inspiring Enough Moment is captured in the Internet companion to this book) as well as a version specifically based on Catholic Social Teaching. (See www.enoughproject.org for these materials.) American Jewish World Service has developed

Jewish prayers and Passover materials to incorporate into Jewish services (www.ajws.org). These tools are just an idea to get you started. Regardless of your particular denomination or background, people of all faiths are called to speak out against injustice. Help organize your local faith groups, and call them to action.

14. Make a Difference on the Ground. While there are many actions we must take to urge our own leaders to take steps toward bringing peace, we must also support and connect to the people we are fighting for. Omer Ismail's and Suliman Giddo's Darfur Peace and Development Organization (www.darfurpeace.org) is a Darfurian-run group that provides education and life-saving aid to those displaced by the genocide. Organizations like Women for Women International work to empower women in conflict and postconflict environments to transition from victim to survivor to active citizen, through programs that address their unique needs. Enough's RAISE Hope for Congo campaign partners with local Congolese organizations that work at community, national, and/or international levels. Together they work to provide a wide range of services, including medical and psychosocial support, child soldier demobilization, skills training, political empowerment, grassroots organizing, and legal counseling. You can find out how to contribute to these organizations by visiting www.raisehopeforcongo .org/partners.

JOHN: Ultimately, all the greatest policy ideas in the world don't mean squat if we don't have a permanent constituency of people behind the ideas, demanding that our elected officials do something about some of the world's worst human rights abuses. I think that the deepening of a popular movement against mass atrocities could literally help change the fate of millions of people.

DON: The truth is, I have doubts all the time about whether we can succeed. I know I drive you crazy with my questions and my skepticism as to whether change can occur in the face of difficult odds. But what I do know is that we can get involved and do something. And there are many things that we can do if we do an inventory of our own skills, our own networks, our own areas of creativity, our own communities. So hopefully this book can provide some examples, some knowledge, some tools, and some inspiration.

The crises in Sudan, Congo, and elsewhere in Africa may seem unresolvable. But real leadership from the Obama administration in Washington—applying lessons from previous success stories of hope, and supported and prodded by the continuing development of a people's movement focused on these issues—provides great hope that the crimes focused on in this book can be ended in the places where they are occurring now and eventually prevented from ever occurring again.

There was a small meeting in New York in early 2004 at which Elie Wiesel and John spoke. This group of people were outraged by the reports of mass slaughter beginning to trickle out of a place few people had ever heard of, and they had gathered in order to discuss what to do. The group didn't seem like much at the time, but the members pooled their resources and the Save Darfur movement was born from that little meeting. Now over a million people are working to end the suffering in Darfur, and it is front and center on the Obama administration's radar screen. Little meetings like that occur all the time on important issues, and you never know what is going to catch fire within the larger population when a small, creative, and committed group of people are backing it. Don't forget what Margaret Mead said:

Never underestimate the power of a small group of committed people to change the world. In fact, it is the only thing that ever has.

Well, here we are.

And if that quote doesn't do it for you, how about the pre-eminent historian Howard Zinn:

If there is going to be change, real change, it will have to work its way from the bottom up, from the people themselves. That's how change happens.

And now it is up to you.

It took ten years to build a successful blood diamonds campaign that helped end the wars in Sierra Leone, Liberia, and Angola. People on the receiving end of genocide, rape as a war weapon, and child soldier abduction don't have another ten years to wait. Your friends, your networks, your schoolmates, your sorority or fraternity, your family members, your union, your club, your team, your church or synagogue or spiritual center—all these are the small groups that are part of world-changing movements. We have a chance through our efforts to support the peace that the survivors of these human rights crimes so desperately crave. How lucky are we to have the chance to do this together.

Standing up is key. You will have so many opportunities in the years ahead to seize an Enough Moment. To be someone who

- takes the road less traveled,
- dives into the deep end,
- loves being an Upstander,
- takes the chance,
- goes for the cake AND the icing,

- trusts yourself and believes anything is possible, and finally
- just goes for it.

When you live like this, especially on behalf of other people less fortunate than you, incredible things can happen. Remember the words of John Donne:

Any man's death diminishes me because I am involved in mankind. Therefore never send to know for whom the bell tolls, it tolls for thee.

Let's remember: Smart, solution-oriented policies plus people's movements together are the answer. They are the indispensable elements of change. But the people's movements, a veritable legion of hope, can't just wish that their good intentions are translated into effective policy responses. Activists must pursue coordinated messages that are more nuanced than just "stop it." A degree of sophistication in the campaigning is required, to gain the attention and respect of policy makers as well as to foster inevitability toward the correct policy choices. And Internet-based mass advocacy requires different approaches that go beyond the old-school notions of sending a prepared postcard to your representative in Congress. The new media have created new opportunities for much wider and deeper education and more creative and participatory mobilization than ever before on issues affecting people halfway around the world.

This is the Enough Moment for us as individuals, as communities, as constituents, as voters, as church or synagogue or mosque members. This is the moment to stand up and be counted as someone who has had ENOUGH with inaction in the face of the world's greatest human rights crimes. In the words of Paul Hawken, "Don't be put off by people who know what is not possible. Do what needs to be done, and check to see if it was impossible only after you are done."

If we fail to get policy makers to stand up, hundreds of thousands, maybe millions, more lives will be extinguished. On our watch.

But if we are successful, if we can make the wheel squeak loudly enough, if we can make enough noise:

- Millions of people will NOT remain homeless in desolate camps.
- Hundreds of thousands of women and girls will NOT be raped.
- Tens of thousands of children will NOT be abducted to be soldiers or sex slaves.

Throughout our lives, we will constantly have choices and opportunities to either become Upstanders or bystanders. If ENOUGH of us choose to be Upstanders, we can help change the course of history. That is the Enough Moment. ENOUGH of us, with ENOUGH commitment, will lead the change.

This is a people's movement worth building. The truth is, it takes fifteen minutes a week to become a full-fledged, card-carrying member of the people's movement to end genocide, or child soldier conscription, or rape as a war weapon. Or all three.

Here's what this all means for you: if the world your own children will inherit someday will NOT be engulfed by environmental destruction, violent wars, preventable diseases, racial and religious discrimination, human rights abuses, and other scourges of our age, it will be because YOU organized, YOU led, YOU believed in yourself, YOU didn't sleep through the revolution, YOU were an Upstander, and YOU made sure your life was a beacon that lit a path for all those seeking a better world!

Epilogue: One Last Word Before We Go

DON: I think often if you look at the totality of it, if you look at the level of despair and inequity that these people are experiencing, it can sometimes feel overwhelming to the point of paralysis, where it is maybe easier to just look away than to try and address in it any way that is substantive. We may be doing the issues a disservice in some strange way when we frame them as massive, complex problems. There is so much noise to cut through and have people say, "Oh, I see you." We are talking about issues that are very difficult to try and get your mind around, and maybe even harder to figure out how to solve them. So it's vital that the movement continue to generate innovative ways to attract attention and draw people to it. And no, it's not about telling people what the answer is. It's letting them know that you need them for the answers and for spreading the word. But even to come up with that, as you guys have come up with on Congo, even to frame it in that context, you have to have a person, a group of people, say, "This is what we need from you." We have done a lot of the heavy lifting in terms of research and policy solutions, but we need you to plug into that and help push in the right direction.

JOHN: Damn, that's so interesting. And it's so contrary to what so many campaigns and causes do, which simply tell people to send this letter now or sign this petition without giving their members or activists any room for creative input. With the issues we're addressing, at the end of the day, it's such a tantalizing and frustrating moment because we have all the pieces in place for a winning campaign. We have policy initiatives or legislation on Sudan, the Congo, and the LRA, we have the knowledge of what has worked in the past in response to mass atrocities—the three P's of the solution: peace, protection, and punishment—that once they are together will help produce a transformed situation. And we have millions of people who have manifested themselves as desirous of becoming activists on these issues. We have Famous Upstanders who care about these things, who show up and do something. We have committed legislators in D.C. and all over the country and even in some other countries. We have corporations that have made changes in regards to divestment. All these pieces, but what appears to be missing at the very core is a way to organize the innovation, the creativity, the challenge to people's initiative that will allow for the most important element of the whole thing: the people's movement applying political pressure and offering political rewards for doing the right thing, for solving a problem. I think what's missing is the level of organization that allows, in some sort of decentralized way, for real creativity on the part of the movement to grow and support the leadership of local activists from Portland to Little Rock to Kansas City, and somehow reward that innovation and local leadership.

DON: And I believe that there ought to be a lot more of "What can you do?" as opposed to "I have something for you guys, do this."

JOHN: Yeah, we need that, we gotta encourage that. The way the world works with issues and causes that are in our direct interest is much easier. Take the National Rifle Association or the American Association of Retired Persons. They send their message out to their constituents with very clear directions: write to this senator with this specific message, and do it this way, or don't bother. It's a very top-down hierarchical thing. And they have the built-in constituencies because they are dealing with things that matter personally to people, so these organizations can just tell their members exactly what to do and when to do it. But as you said earlier, if it doesn't affect your daily life, you better come up with a different model that inspires people to become involved. You have to come up with something that allows them to have a stake in it through their own creative involvement. And I think that the Darfur efforts, for example, probably lost a lot of time by not fully comprehending this necessary way of maintaining momentum and commitment.

DON: People want to feel like we felt with the Obama campaign. You sent the five bucks in via text or e-mail, they hit you back with a creative thank you, and you're like, "Damn, I really did something. I didn't think doing that would have an impact." We usually don't get that kind of feedback. You kind of feel like your action is out in space. "What happened with that money? What did my action do?" There is a "disconnection," which results in a kind of "dis-concern" about the result. So if the feedback part isn't happening, you feel like you might be throwing your time or money into the ocean. You don't feel like there is much more required of you other than "Just give us more money." You still have to somehow figure out a way to make the activist or concerned citizen feel validated, feel necessary.

JOHN: I saw a fund-raising envelope with a starving baby on it recently, and frankly I didn't even open it. You know where they are coming from. It's the same Pavlovian response they are looking for. But if you get a message that gives you some way to be part of the solution, then it becomes interesting. From ground floor construction, to opening the front door when it's finished. I care about schools in refugee camps, but I think more is required to make a connection with someone here. If I met a kid through a video profile or video blogging in his school in the refugee camp he lives in, and I took responsibility for textbooks for his class with my own classmates, then sooner or later I'm gonna want to make sure that this kid has a chance to be able to go home some day, which then would lead me to take action politically. How much more compelling is it going to be for me to be a part of seeing change happen if I have a personal link to someone there, rather than just seeing e-mails that tell me to stop the genocide by giving $5. We need to invest in these folks who have survived these crises, make connections with them, and then ask people here for their ideas on how to make sure these solutions are implemented. I think that's the future of advocacy.

> *I do not pretend to understand the moral universe, the arc is a long one, my eye reaches but little ways. I can calculate the curve and complete the figure by the experience of sight; I can divine it by conscience. But from what I see I am sure it bends toward justice.*
>
> —THEODORE PARKER

We think the speed with which that arc bends toward justice can be dramatically influenced by people getting together to try to make a difference. That is the point. There will always be injustice, driven by greed, bigotry, power. But the degree to which injustice is thwarted and countered and reversed is up to us. The battle is joined. We hope you will choose to be part of it. Millions of lives hang in the balance.

See the interactive companion to this book on the Enough Project's website at www.enoughmoment.org for up-to-date ideas for getting involved in your own community.

Resources

Here's a list of the great Upstanding organizations we discussed throughout the book. We thought we'd put them all in once place for your reference.

Africa Youth Initiative Network (AYINET), www.ayinet.or.ug

American Jewish World Service, www.ajws.org

Amnesty International, www.amnestyusa.org

Ante Up for Africa, www.anteupforafrica.org

Central Ohioans for Peace, www.centralohioansforpeace.org

Christian Communications Network, www.ccn.tv

Darfur Dream Team, www.darfurdreamteam.org

Darfur Peace and Development, www.darfurpeace.org

Eastern Congo Initiative, www.easterncongo.org

EcoMom Alliance, ecomomalliance.ning.com

Enough Project, www.enoughproject.org

Facing History and Ourselves, www.facinghistory.org

Grassroots Reconciliation Group, www.grassrootsgroup.org

Humanity United, www.humanityunited.org

i-ACT, www.i-act.org

Invisible Children, www.invisiblechildren.org

Jeunesse et Droits Humains, www.jdhrdcongo.unblog.fr

Jewish World Watch, www.jewishworldwatch.org

Man Up Campaign, www.manupcampaign.org

Massachusetts Coalition to Save Darfur, www.savedarfurma.org

Mia Farrow's website, www.miafarrow.org

My Sister's Keeper, www.mskeeper.org

National Association of Evangelicals, www.nae.net

National Council of Churches, www.ncccusa.org

Not On Our Watch, www.notonourwatchproject.org

- Raise Hope for Congo Campaign, www.raisehopeforcongo.org

Religious Action Center of Reform Judaism (RAC), www.rac.org

Resolve Uganda, www.resolveuganda.org

Run for Congo Women, www.runforcongowomen.org

San Francisco Bay Area Darfur Coalition, www.darfursf.org

Save Darfur Coalition, www.savedarfur.org

STAND, www.standnow.org

Stop Genocide Now, www.stopgenocidenow.org

Sudan Divestment Task Force, www.sudandivestment.org

Sudan Now, www.sudanactionnow.com

Sudan Social Development Organization, www.sudosudan.org

The Elders, www.theelders.org

V-Day, www.vday.org

Voice of Uganda, www.voicesofuganda.org

- Women for Women, www.womenforwomen.org

Youth United for Darfur, www.youthunitedfordarfur.org

Acknowledgments

We are very grateful for the contributions of the following people to moving this book from a vague concept to a reality: Bonnie Abaunza, Nikki Alam, Semhar Araia, John Bagwell, Victoria Bosselman, Hacer Bozkurt, Zack Brisson, Rebecca Brocato, Molly Browning, Summer Buckley (ESPECIALLY Summer Buckley), Katherine Carson, Maggie Fick, Elissa Grabow, Laura Heaton, Alex Hellmuth, David Herbert, Corrine Irish, Omer Ismail, Stella Kenyi, Candice Knezevic, Sasha Lezhnev, Daniel Maree, Ellen McElhinny, Will McElhinny, Russell Moll, Robert Padavick, Larissa Peltola, Gitanjali Prasad, Dylan and Michael Prendergast, Meghna Raj, Eileen Read, Jenny Russell, Sia Sanneh, Courtney Schoenbohm, Barb Scott, Julia Spiegel, Jason Stearns, David Sullivan, Andrew Sweet, Whitney Williams, Meg Whitton, Lindsey Wood, Nate Wright, and Katherine Wycisk. Finally, Heather Lazare was an incredible editor, and Sarah Chalfont ably agented us to the right home at Random House.

Endnotes

1. *Newsweek*, January 25, 2010, p. 20.

2. *BBC Profile*, "Liberia's 'Iron Lady,'" November 23, 2005, http://news.bbc.co.uk/2/hi/world/africa/4395978.stm.

3. *CBC News*, "Ellen Johnson Sirleaf: Liberia's 'Iron Lady,'" March 28, 2006, http://www.cbc.ca/news/background/liberia/sirleaf.html.

4. Integrated Regional Information Networks, "Sierra Leone: Still Last on Human Development Index," December 18, 2008, http://www.unhcr.org/refworld/publisher,IRIN,,SLE,494b62d427,0.html.

5. *BBC Profile*, "Graca Machel," July 18, 1998, http://news.bbc.co.uk/2/hi/africa/135280.stm.

6. Headliners, "Don't Call Me Mrs. Mandela," 2001, http://www.headliners.org/storylibrary/stories/2001/dontcallmemrsmandela.htm?id=33728183847079258416978.

7. Times Online, Interview, Graca Machel, September 2, 2007, http://www.timesonline.co.uk/tol/news/world/africa/article2367072.ece.

8. David Birmingham, "Angola," in Patrick Chabal, *A History of Postcolonial Lusophone Africa*, Indiana University Press, Bloomington, 2002, p. 138.

9. Rufino Satumbo, "Testimony from UNITA Deserters," in William Minter, *Operation Timber: Pages from the Savimbi Dossier*, Africa World Press, Trenton, N.J., 1988, p. 111.

10. In 1983, twenty-four-year-old Satumbo was captured by the MPLA and forced to testify during a series of public hearings in Luanda. William Minter, *Operation Timber: Pages from the Savimbi Dossier*, Africa World Press, Trenton, N.J., 1988, p. 110.

11. Samantha Power, *A Problem from Hell: America and the Age of Genocide*, Basic Books, New York, 2002, p. 269.

12. Human Rights Watch, http://www.hrw.org/sites/default/files/reports/ANGOLA94N.pdf.

13. http://www.africaaction.org.

14. *PBS Wide Angle*, "Lord's Children: Aaron Brown Interview with Betty Bigombe," July 29, 2008, available at www.pbs.org.

15. *O Magazine*, Interview, available at http://www.greenbeltmovement.org/a.php?id=114.

16. Green Belt Movement website, http://greenbeltmovement.org/c.php?id=6.

17. Harriet Martin, *Kings of Peace, Pawns of War*, accessed through Google books.

18. Samantha Power, "Bystanders to Genocide," *Atlantic Monthly*, September 2001.

19. Jimmie Briggs, *Innocents Lost: When Child Soldiers Go to War*, Basic Books, New York, 2005, p. xiii.

20. P.W. Singer, *Children at War*, University of California Press, Berkeley and Los Angeles, 2006, p. 58.

21. Ibid.

22. E-mail correspondence with Enough Project staff, April 2008.

23. For a profile on Olwal, see UN Office for the Coordination of Humanitarian Affairs, "Uganda: Humanitarian Challenges of the Northern Crisis," *IRIN News*, 2006, available at http://www.irinnews.org/InDepthMain.aspx?InDepthId=23&ReportId=65777/.

24. For more on Jacob's project, see Grassroots Reconciliation Group at www.grassrootsgroup.org.

25. Jeannie Annan and Chris Blattman, "Survey of War-Affected Youth (SWAY) Research Brief 1, The Abduction and Return Experiences of Youth in Uganda," April 2006, available at www.sway-uganda.org.

26. *See* Catherine N. Niarchos, "Women, War, and Rape: Challenges Facing the International Tribunal for the Former Yugoslavia," *Women's Rights: A Human Rights Quarterly Reader*, edited by Bert B. Lockwood, 1995.

27. *See* Ruth Siefert, "War and Rape: A Preliminary Analysis," *Mass Rape: The War against Women in Bosnia-Herzegovina*, edited by Alexandra Stiglmayer, University of Nebraska Press, Lincoln, 1994, p. 55; and

Joshua Goldstein, *War and Gender: How Gender Shapes the War System and Vice Versa*, Cambridge University Press, Cambridge, United Kingdom, 2001, p. 363.

28. United Nations Development Fund for Women, "Preventing Wartime Rape from Becoming a Peacetime Reality," June 24, 2009.

29. Beverly Allen, *Rape Warfare: The Hidden Genocide in Bosnia-Herzegovina and Croatia*, University of Minnesota Press, Minneapolis, 1996, p. 57.

30. Sierra Leone Truth and Reconciliation Commission, *Witness to Truth: Final Report of the Sierra Leone Truth & Reconciliation Commission*, 2007, ch. 1, para. 25.

31. Candice Knezevic, "Congo's Courageous Men," blog post, August 6, 2009, http://www.enoughproject.org/blogs/congos-courageous-men.

32. From the *Sydney Morning Herald* special report on sexual violence in eastern Congo, http://www.smh.com.au/interactive/2009/congo/.

33. From John Prendergast and Noel Atama, "Eastern Congo: An Action Plan to End the World's Deadliest War," Enough Project Report, July 16, 2009.

34. Human Rights Watch, "DR Congo: Hold Army Commanders Responsible for Rapes," July 16, 2009, http://www.hrw.org/en/news/2009/07/16/dr-congo-hold-army-commanders-responsible-rapes.

35. Javier Bardem and John Prendergast, "Stop the Vampires in the Congo," CNN.com, October 22, 2008.

36. International Committee of the Red Cross, *Our World: Views from the Field: Democratic Republic of the Congo*, June 23, 2009.

37. Enough Project, *A Comprehensive Approach to Congo's Conflict Minerals*, Enough Strategy Paper, April 24, 2009.

38. Human Rights Watch, "DR Congo: Civilian Cost of Military Operation Is Unacceptable," October 13, 2009, available at http://www.hrw.org/en/news/2009/10/12/dr-congo-civilian-cost-military-operation-unacceptable.

39. United Nations Security Council, *Final Report of the Group of Experts on the Democratic Republic of the Congo*, November 23, 2009, S/2009/603.

40. Human Rights Watch, "You Will Be Punished," December 13, 2009, http://www.hrw.org/en/reports/2009/12/14/you-will-be-punished.

41. President Barack Obama, "Remarks to the Ghanaian Parliament," Accra International Conference Center, Accra, Ghana, July 11, 2009.

42. Ambassador Susan Rice, remarks during an Open Security Council Debate, August 7, 2009.

43. Enough Project, *A Comprehensive Approach to Conflict Minerals.*

Discussion Guide

1. What inspired you to pick up this book? Would you recommend it to a friend or relative?

2. Discuss the thoughts and feelings you had about Africa before reading *The Enough Moment*. Have any of your preconceived notions changed? Why or why not?

3. Have you ever had an Enough Moment? Can you describe it?

4. Did you know anything about child soldier abduction before reading this book? If so, where did you learn about it? How does it make you feel?

5. There are some very vivid testimonials in this book. Which testimonials were particularly moving or inspiring to you?

6. What are the three P's? Do you think this is an effective way to view the problems and resolutions in Africa?

Discuss the Congo, northern Uganda, and Sudan and how the three P's apply to each.

7. Which of the Upstanders did you connect with the most? Were you surprised by any of the testimonials from Famous Upstanders? Who and why?

8. Describe some of the things you might do to become an Upstander.

9. Of the menu of fourteen actions listed in Chapter Nine, which are you most likely to take?

10. Are there actions we haven't thought of?

SLAVES AND MASTERS
IN THE ROMAN EMPIRE

Slaves and Masters in the Roman Empire

A *Study in Social Control*

K. R. Bradley

New York   Oxford
OXFORD UNIVERSITY PRESS
1987

Published in 1984 by
Editions Latomus
18, av. Van Cutsem, B. 7500 Tournai, Belgium

Published in 1987 in the United States by
Oxford University Press, Inc.
198 Madison Avenue, New York, New York 10016-4314

Oxford is a registered trademark of Oxford University Press

Library of Congress Cataloging-in-Publication Data

Bradley, K. R.
Slaves and masters in the Roman Empire.
Originally published: Bruxelles : Latomus, revue
d'études latines, 1984.
Bibliography: p.
Includes index.
1. Slavery—Rome.   2. Social control.   3. Rome—
Social conditions.   I. Title.
HT863.B72   1987   306'.363'0937   87-15331
ISBN 0-19-520607-X

6 8 10 9 7

Printed in the United States of America
on acid-free paper

For
Diane Elizabeth

PREFACE TO THE OXFORD EDITION

I wish to express my gratitude to William P. Sisler of Oxford University Press for making this new printing possible, and to the editors of *Collection Latomus* for agreeing to its appearance. The original manuscript was completed early in 1982. Since that time various items of scholarship germane to its contents have been published, and for the convenience of readers I append a supplementary bibliography.

Winter, 1986   K.R.B.

PREFACE

My object in this essay is to offer some broad explanation of how the Roman system of slavery maintained itself in the imperial age, and to describe thereby some of the adverse conditions under which I believe the majority of slaves in the Roman world to have spent their lives. I have not attempted a full history of slavery at Rome (if such is at present possible), but have been more content to try to examine a few facets of the slave experience. Although the views which result are partial, I hope they may prepare for a more balanced understanding of Roman slavery than is often found elsewhere.

I am happy to acknowledge the help I have received as my work has progressed. Drafts of the book were read and significantly improved by John Drinkwater, Erich Gruen, A. N. Sherwin-White, Gordon Shrimpton and Susan Treggiari. While none of these scholars necessarily agrees with all (or anything) I have tried to say, all have given support and encouragement, and for their generosity of time and interest I am deeply thankful. My debts to other scholars who have earlier dealt with the topics covered will be clear from the citations in notes and bibliography. Preparation of the manuscript has been greatly facilitated through the efforts of A. Nancy Nasser, whose superb typing skills have been an enormously valuable resource to have at one's disposal. And completion of the project has been aided by research awards made to me by the University of Victoria.

Special thanks must be given to Marsh McCall, who not only read my manuscript, but also gave help of a more valuable sort ; for the circumstances under which the book was begun proved far from conducive to its rapid completion, and the fact that there is a book at all (whatever its interest) is very much due to a friend's encouragement to press on in times of adversity. The brunt of the burden of that adversity, however, fell upon my wife, Diane Bradley, and it is she who deserves my greatest thanks. Mere words are inadequate to express my gratitude for her noble and patient willingness to endure and to tolerate it all ; and through the dedication of my book I offer what can never be more than a frail token of all I owe to her. Finally I wish to thank the editors of *Collection Latomus* for publishing my work in their series of monographs.

Spring, 1982   K.R.B.

CONTENTS

ABBREVIATIONS

Authors and works are cited in ways which should be easily understood. The following list comprises abbreviations used for legal, inscriptional and papyrological sources, for journals and works of reference.

AE	*L'Année épigraphique.*
AJAH	*American Journal of Ancient History*
AJP	*American Journal of Philology*
ANRW	*Aufstieg und Niedergang der römischen Welt*, ed. H. Temporini
BGU	*Aegyptische Urkunden aus den Staatlichen Museen zu Berlin, Griechische Urkunden*
CAH	*Cambridge Ancient History*
CE	*Chronique d'Egypte*
CIL	*Corpus Inscriptionum Latinarum*
CJ	*Codex Iustinianus*
Coll.	*Collatio Legum Mosaicarum et Romanarum*
CP	*Classical Philology*
CPL	*Corpus Papyrorum Latinorum*, ed. R. Cavenaile
CQ	*Classical Quarterly*
CSCA	*California Studies in Classical Antiquity*
CTh.	*Codex Theodosianus*
Dig.	*Digesta Iuris Romani*
FIRA	*Fontes Iuris Romani Anteiustiniani*[2], ed. S. Riccobono *et al.*
HSCP	*Harvard Studies in Classical Philology*
ILS	*Inscriptiones Latinae Selectae*, ed. H. Dessau
Instit.	*Institutiones Iustiniani*
JAC	*Jahrbuch für Antike und Christentum*
JEA	*Journal of Egyptian Archaeology*
JRS	*Journal of Roman Studies*
LCL	Loeb Classical Library
MAAR	*Memoirs of the American Academy at Rome*
P. Ant.	*The Antinoopolis Papyri*, ed. C. H. Roberts *et al.*
Pap. Lugd. Bat.	*Papyrologica Lugduno-Batava*
Paul. Sent.	*Pauli Sententiae*
P. Bour.	*Les Papyrus Bouriant*, ed. P. Collart

PBSR	*Papers of the British School at Rome*
PCPhS	*Proceedings of the Cambridge Philological Society*
P. Dura	*The Excavations at Dura-Europos ... Final Report V*, Part 1, *The Parchments and Papyri*, ed. C. Bradford Welles *et al.*
P. Fouad.	*Les Papyrus Fouad I*, ed. A. Bataille *et al.*
P. Grenf.	*New Classical Fragments and Other Greek and Latin Papyri*, ed. B. P. Grenfell, A. S. Hunt
P. Hamb.	*Griechische Papyrusurkunden der Hamburger Staats- und Universitätsbibliothek I*, ed. P. M. Meyer
PIR	*Prosopographia Imperii Romani*
P. Lips.	*Griechische Urkunden der Papyrussammlung zu Leipzig*, ed. L. Mitteis
PLRE	*The Prosopography of the Later Roman Empire I*, ed. A. H. M. Jones *et al.*
P. Meyer	*Griechische Texte aus Äegypten*, ed. P. M. Meyer
P. Mich.	*Papyri in the University of Michigan Collection*, ed. C. C. Edgar *et al.*
P. Oxy.	*The Oxyrhynchus Papyri*, ed. B. P. Grenfell *et al.*
P. Ross.-Georg.	*Papyri russicher und georgischer Sammlungen*, ed. G. Zereteli *et al.*
P. Ryl.	*Catalogue of the Greek Papyri in the John Rylands Museum, Manchester*, ed. A. S. Hunt *et al.*
PSI	*Papiri greci e latini*, ed. G. Vitelli *et al.*
P. Strass.	*Griechische Papyrus der Kaiserlichen Universitäts- und Landesbibliothek zu Strassbourg*, ed. F. Preisigke
P. Tebt.	*The Tebtunis Papyri*, ed. B. P. Grenfell *et al.*
P. Wisconsin	*Papyri at the University of Wisconsin*
P. Vindob. Boswinkel	*Einige Wiener Papyri (Pap. Lug. Bat. II)*, ed. E. Boswinkel
RD	*Revue historique de droit français et étranger*
RE	*Real-Encyclopädie der classischen Altertumswissenschaft*
REL	*Revue des études latines*
RSA	*Rivista storica dell'antichità*
SB	*Sammelbuch griechischer Urkunden aus Äegypten*, ed. F. Preisigke, *et al.*
SO	*Symbolae Osloenses*
SPP	*Studien zur Palaeographie und Papyruskunde*, ed. C. Wessely

StudClass	*Studii Classice*
TAPA	*Transactions of the American Philological Association*
ZPE	*Zeitschrift für Papyrologie und Epigraphik*
ZSS Rom. Abt.	*Zeitschrift des Savigny-Stiftung für Rechtsgeschichte, Romanistische Abteilung*

INTRODUCTION

The purpose of this study is to explore some of the means by which slaves were controlled by their masters in the imperial period of Roman history and to define some of the conditions under which slaves spent their lives as a result. Since the very concept of control is related to the question of the long duration of slavery as an institution in the Roman world, and since Rome can be called a genuine slave society from the third century B.C. (¹), the subject undoubtedly requires examination from a Republican as well as an imperial perspective (²). But concentration on the imperial period alone seems legitimate in view of the fact that Roman slavery, as much else, was affected and altered by the arrival, with Augustus, of imperial peace, so that in what follows the approximate chronological limits of enquiry are marked by the reigns of Augustus and Constantine (³). Even for this timespan, however, some explanation is required for the practical maintenance of slavery over time.

It must be stated at once that the picture of servile life to be drawn is impressionistic and partial : impressionistic because many of the topics discussed could be better understood if the evidence available were capable of quantitative measurement, which is not usually the case ; and partial in the sense that the study will deliberately dwell on the negative side of the slave-master relationship. It is of course very true that at times slaves and masters in Roman society enjoyed a surprising degree of intimacy (⁴), and that simple, constant animosity between slave and slave-owner is too naive a concept to have had universal applicability or meaning. But although the harmonious relations attested between some slaves and their masters should not be lost sight of, they were not in all

---

(1) Cf. FINLEY (1973), 69 ; HOPKINS (1978), 99ff. ; FINLEY (1980), 86. On slavery at Rome before the third century see particularly WATSON (1975), 81ff.

(2) The statement at PLAUT. *Curc.* 300, *ita nunc seruitiumst : profecto modus haberi non potest*, contains in my view a fundamental insight.

(3) I stress the word 'approximate' because evidence from beyond these limits will be freely used when considered appropriate.

(4) TREGGIARI (1975), 48ff. ; VOGT (1975), 103ff.

likelihood characteristic of the Roman slavery system as a whole ([5]). Thus attention will focus on what is conceived to be the essential brutality of the slave experience in the Roman world and especially on the kinds of harsh pressures to which slaves were constantly exposed as a normal part of their everyday lives. There is a danger here that moral judgement on the Roman practice of slavery may seem implied, but such is not consciously intended. Rather the historical reality of Roman slavery must be understood for what it was : to the extent that many of the accomplishments of the upper classes depended upon the leisure time which accompanied the exploitation of a servile labour force, slavery was a fundamental component of Roman society ([6]), and in order to put aristocratic accomplishments into perspective it is vital to understand something of the less elevated, less humane side of Roman social relations, of which the depressed conditions under which most slaves lived provide abundant illustration.

No attempt will be made to give a narrative history of slavery under the Roman Empire. Thus it is necessary by way of introduction to delineate some general features of the Roman slavery system and to make clear some assumptions about it so that they can be kept in mind as the main object is pursued.

Under the Roman Empire slavery did not remain a static institution. Among historians there is general agreement that after the great Republican wars of expansion, first in Italy and then in the Mediterranean world at large, as a result of which huge numbers of war captives were brought to Italy as slaves for use predominantly in agriculture and pastoral farming but also increasingly for domestic service, the imperial period gradually gave way, as wars of conquest declined in frequency, to a system whereby slaves were either bred domestically or else were supplied by dealers (in order to keep up numbers), until both numbers and

---

(5) See in general FINLEY (1980), 93ff. ; TREGGIARI (1979a), 73ff. illustrates the complexity of owners' attitudes towards human property which might occur.

(6) This is not to imply that the Roman world was overwhelmingly dependent on slave labour to the exclusion of other types of compulsory labour, or that other social groups were free from control exercised from above. These are not matters of concern here, however, despite their importance otherwise and will be omitted ; and since the primary emphasis of study falls on slavery as a social institution, detailed economic questions are also omitted. On the profitability of slavery, however, see WHITE (1970), 370 ; FINLEY (1976), 821 ; (1980), 91 ; cf. HOPKINS (1978), 106ff.

the institution itself withered in late antiquity [7]. This dynamic element in the history of slavery is important and the social relations with which this study is concerned were affected by it. But the decline in slave numbers and the withering of the institution should not be exaggerated [8], so that attention here will be devoted to the interaction over time between slaves and masters in what is considered to be a firm, enduring system.

The neat cleavage between masters and slaves, between those who were free and those who were not, should not lead to any belief that slaves in the Roman world ever formed a rigid social class, in the modern sense of that term, with a recognisable consciousness of itself and a concomitant programme for its own amelioration [9]. An enormous variety of functions in enormously different circumstances was performed by slaves, perhaps the most miserable being those of workers in mines and mills to judge from descriptions given by Diodorus Siculus and Apuleius [10]. In particular, slave miners seem to have been consumed as so much human energy with little concern for their needs or wellbeing, and life for these people can have been little more than a grim and meaningless existence. At the other end of the scale, however, were the slaves, both male and female, who belonged to the domestic estates of wealthy Roman magnates. In the luxurious townhouses and country villas of the rich, such people were probably better off materially than many of the free poor, while slaves who belonged to the Roman emperor could enjoy both political influence and relatively high social esteem [11]. For some, that is, slavery may well have had distinct advantages [12]. In between the two extremes, slaves provided labour in a broad range of

(7) See WESTERMANN (1955), 60ff. ; 84ff. ; FINLEY (1979), 137ff. ; JONES (1968), 7ff. ; BRUNT (1971), 121ff. ; MILANI (1972), 193ff. ; BURFORD (1972), 49 ; FINLEY (1973), 84f. ; MARÓTI (1976) ; HOPKINS (1978), 8ff. ; FINLEY (1980), 67ff. ; 123ff.

(8) Cf. FINLEY (1980), 123f., citing M. BLOCH, *Comment et pourquoi finit l'esclavage antique* in *Annales* 2 (1947), 29ff. at p. 30.

(9) VOGT (1975), 83ff. ; contra, D. KONSTAN, *Marxism and Roman Slavery* in *Arethusa* 8 (1975), 145ff. at p. 169 n. 77.

(10) DIOD. SIC. 5.38.1 ; cf. 3.12-13 ; APUL. *Met.* 9.12.13. On mining conditions see BURFORD (1972), 73ff., and on mills see L. A. MORITZ, *Grain-Mills and Flour in Classical Antiquity*, Oxford, 1958, 67f. ; 97ff.

(11) TREGGIARI (1969), 106f. ; WEAVER (1972), passim.

(12) The importance of the guarantees of food and shelter enjoyed by slaves belonging to large households should not be minimised ; many slaves, by virtue of their location in such households, must have been in relatively favourable economic circumstances. But in general terms such conditions do not appear to have encouraged slaves to remain slaves if an alternative were available, as will become clear later.

contexts, agriculture and pastoral farming, industry and commerce, domestic and private service, medicine and education, even, occasionally, the military ; there can in fact have been few economic areas in which labour and expertise were not provided by slaves at one time or another. But because a miner in Spain can have felt little in common with a herdsman in Italy or with the hairdresser of a grandee in the capital, it is clear enough that distinctions of function led to distinctions of status among slaves (distinctions which were reinforced additionally by intense job-specialisation along the servile scale and by differences of origin), and that in consequence no organisation of group solidarity emerged ([13]).

The circumstances of slave-owners varied almost as much as those of slaves. On one level there was the smallscale owner of a mere handful of slaves, something of the norm in the province of Egypt, though common elsewhere too : Horace for example probably had no more than three domestics at Rome and eight labourers, with a *uilicus*, on his farm outside ([14]). On a far different level, however, there was the Roman aristocrat, a man such as L. Pedanius Secundus, a senator of the mid first century, whose domestic entourage alone comprised a minimum of four hundred slaves, or a woman such as the Christian noblewoman Melania, who is said to have owned, in the early fifth century, the amazing number of twenty-four thousand slaves ([15]). Whatever the plausibility of this latter figure, it is beyond doubt that thousands of slaves, scattered throughout the Empire, were owned by the emperor, who was himself the greatest slave-owner of all ([16]). The incidence of slave-owning similarly varied

(13) For specialisation among slave miners see *FIRA*[2] III no. 105 ; in the rural context, *Dig.* 33.7.12.5 ; in domestic service, TREGGIARI (1975). Cf. CIC. *Para. Stoic.* 5.36-37 and, in general, FINLEY (1980), 77. For the conditions of public slaves see ROULAND (1977).

(14) HOR. *Sat.* 1.6.116 ; 2.7.118 ; *Epist.* 1.14.1. For Egypt see BIEZUNSKÁ-MAŁOWIST (1977), 93ff. ; cf. J. A. STRAUS, *Le statut fiscal des esclaves dans l'Egypte romaine, CE* 48 (1973), 364ff. BURFORD (1972), 50, believes smallscale ownership the norm.

(15) TAC. *Ann.* 14.43.4 ; *PLRE* s.v. 'Melania 2' for the relevant texts. The wife of Apuleius of Madaura, Pudentilla, also owned at least four hundred slaves, APUL. *Apol.* 93 ; cf. 43-45 ; 17 (on small numbers owned). MART. *Epig.* 12.86 mentions thirty boys and girls in one household. For alleged gigantic holdings ATH. 6.272e ; *HA Firm. Sat. Proc. Bon.* 12.1. Cf. H. FURNEAUX, *The Annals of Tacitus*[2], Oxford, 1907 *ad* TAC. *Ann.* 14.43.4. Statistics given by ancient sources are notoriously untrustworthy, but there has to be an eventual limit to suspicion.

(16) Since imperial slaves constituted a particularly distinct status group whose circumstances were often far different from those of other slaves they will not generally be considered in this study. For background, see WEAVER (1972) ; BOULVERT (1970) ; G. BOULVERT, *Domestique et fonctionnaire sous le haut-empire romain*, Paris, 1974. Imperial slaves, however, were no less an exploited group despite their difference in status.

from region to region within the Empire, which, from an economic standpoint, cannot be described as a slave society in its totality [17]. Yet because slavery was entirely absent from no province, even such remote areas as Britain and the northerly provinces along the Danube, and because some evidence is available from those regions where slavery cannot be thought to have constituted the principal means of production, there is no reason to avoid provincial situations completely, or such evidence from them which may be of value for comprehending slave-master relations in the heartland of the Empire where slavery did predominate [18]. Problems of control, that is, were not necessarily dependent upon huge concentrations of slave numbers in all places.

In spite of these variables among both slaves and slave-owners it does not seem perverse to examine relationships between the two main groups. The distinction between slavery and freedom was not meaningless, and no matter how relatively privileged some slaves may have been they nonetheless remained the juridical peers of those less fortunate [19]. Indeed, Cicero gives important expression to the idea that whereas slaves

(17) Although there is general agreement that slavery in the Roman world declined during the imperial age, there are insufficient figures available to allow certain knowledge either of the precise number of slaves in any one place or time or of the proportion of slaves in the overall population in any one place or time. For a recent estimate of the situation in Italy in the late Republic see, with reference to previous calculations, HOPKINS (1978), 101 ; cf. 68 (cf. also FINLEY (1980), 79f.) : two million slaves equalling about 35 % of the full population. It may be valid to insist on a minimum slave percentage in the population at large in order to describe a given society as a slave society (HOPKINS (1978), 99 : 20%) when economic concerns are paramount. But the view taken here is that wherever slavery existed, no matter what the absolute numbers involved, problems of control might be anticipated.

(18) Cf. R. P. DUNCAN-JONES, *Age-rounding, Illiteracy and Social Differentiation in the Roman Empire* in *Chiron* 7 (1977), 333ff. at p. 347 : 'Some of the practices of Roman Egypt reflect and illuminate for us conditions in parts of the Empire where documentation is much less explicit'. The importance of this statement will become clear in subsequent chapters. For information on slavery in some provincial areas see BODOR (1963) 45ff. ; J. J. WILKES, *Dalmatia*, Cambridge, Mass., 1969, 196ff. ; 235 ; A. DAUBIGNY, F. FAVORY, *L'Esclavage en Narbonnaise et Lyonnaise* in *Actes du Colloque 1972 sur l'esclavage*, Paris, 1974, 315ff. ; A. ALFÖLDY, *Noricum*, Cambridge, Mass., 1974, 127ff. : A. MOCSY, *Pannonia and Upper Moesia*, Cambridge, Mass., 1974, 151 ; 216 ; 241 ; 322 ; P. D. A. GARNSEY, *Rome's African Empire under the Principate* in P. D. A. GARNSEY, C. R. WHITTAKER, edd., *Imperialism in the Ancient World*, Cambridge, 1978, 223ff. at pp. 236ff. ; E. M. WIGHTMAN, *Peasants and Potentates : An Investigation of Social Structure and Land Tenure in Roman Gaul* in *AJAH* 3 (1978), 97ff. ; A. BIRLEY, *The People of Roman Britain*, London, 1979, 145ff. ; BIEZUNSKÁ-MAŁOWIST (1977).

(19) For the juridical situation see BUCKLAND (1908), 2f. ; that situation was an important expression of class attitude. Contrast, however, HOPKINS (1967), 173.

themselves may have been conscious of their own distinct statuses, from the master's point of view they were all servile regardless [20] : the broad categorization could not be altered and was something more than the merely juridical. Moreover, as a form of property, to be set alongside land and livestock, all slaves were commodities to be used to slave-owners' maximum advantage, adding as well to the latters' social prestige if owned in sufficient quantities. No slave, in other words, was exempt from the forces of social and economic exploitation, a notion which is inextricably bound up with the Roman practice of slavery as a whole. Because of this exploitative element, and because slavery by definition is a means of securing and maintaining an involuntary labour force by a group in society which monopolises political and economic power, it follows of necessity that tensions between slave and free could be expected in the Roman world. Hence a need for control mechanisms is also to be expected if the maintenance over time of slaves in coerced subjection is to be explained.

The historian who wishes to penetrate the lives of slaves in antiquity is confronted by an insuperable obstacle : the absence in extant classical texts of anything that can be called a slave literature, works written by slaves or ex-slaves about their experiences in slavery [21]. He is instead under the great disadvantage of being compelled to draw either on sources which for the most part reflect slave-owners' views and attitudes exclusively, or else on terse and often fragmentary documents whose usefulness is circumscribed by the relatively small amount of information they convey (precious as that information is). Consequently many of the suggestions to be made here are expressed tentatively, as little more than suggestions, not because they are unarguable or implausible but because, given the nature of the evidence on which they depend, they are ultimately incapable of full verification. The evidence itself comes from inscriptional, legal and papyrological sources, all of which contain particular limitations as well as the general constraints just mentioned. The literary evidence, for example, tends to be mainly anecdotal, and allowance has to be made for this as well as for the literary genre

---

(20) Cɪᴄ. *Para. Stoic.* 5.36, *atque ut in magna familia seruorum sunt alii lautiores ut sibi uidentur serui sed tamen serui* ... On Cicero see Mɪʟᴀɴɪ (1972), 204ff. and cf. also Fɪɴʟᴇʏ (1976), 819, 'granted that slavery includes a spectrum of types, it is a fallacy to conclude ... that the institution cannot be examined as such'. Cf. below, p. 35.

(21) But see Appendix F.

supplying it. But with caution in mind it has not seemed inappropriate even to draw on such an author as Plautus to explain some of the conventions about slaves perceptible in later literature [22]. The papyri from Roman Egypt can also be useful, not because what may be learned from them is necessarily relevant elsewhere, but because what may be learned is suggestive for other parts of the Roman world for which similar evidence is less copious [23]. The papyri illustrate well the importance of using material from diverse geographical areas, in spite of the regional variations outlined earlier, both because of their suggestive quality, and because slaves throughout the Roman world were subject to their owners' control. The sources as a whole, no matter what their weaknesses from the modern point of view, certainly permit something of the problem of control to be seen, as too the practical solution to it which slave-owners used. Likewise, the implications of that solution for servile life can be sensed at least, and it is with an exposition of those implications that the following pages are concerned.

The historiography of ancient slavery has been traditionally apologetic in one way or another and it is not until recent times that the realisation has begun to set in among scholars that there is something distinctly unpalatable about slavery in antiquity [24]. Indeed in some quarters apologetic influences are still at work. Two of the chapters which follow are concerned with the family lives of slaves and the prospects of emancipation that slaves had before them. Both take a bleak view of their subjects, and form a reaction against the line of thinking which can characterise servile familial life as relatively secure and dignified, and which can regard the achievement of manumission by slaves as a relatively easy process [25]. Doubtless at times individual slave-owners allowed their slaves to live in family units and set their slaves free for what would now be called humanitarian reasons. But if it is kept in mind that the Roman slavery system as a whole was by nature oppressive and

---

(22) On the use of Plautus as historical evidence see below, p. 29 n. 33.

(23) Above, n. 18.

(24) The influences affecting the historiography of ancient slavery are set out at length in FINLEY (1980), 11-66. For the harsher aspects see recently HOPKINS (1978), 118-123 ; FINLEY (1980), 93-122.

(25) Susan TREGGIARI, *"Contubernales" in "CIL" 6* in *Phoenix* 35 (1981), 42-69 at p. 61 (and cf. below p. 52 n. 18); ALFÖLDY (1972), on which cf. now Peter GARNSEY, *Independent Freedmen and the Economy of Roman Italy Under the Principate* in *Klio* 63 (1981), 359-371 at pp. 361-364.

was maintained for the benefit of the privileged only, the behaviour of such individuals appears exceptional and explains little of the actual conditions governing servile family life or servile emancipation on a day to day basis [26]. Moreover, the belief that slaves comprised a labour force easily managed and compelled to work requires examination [27], and this is done at the outset. Whatever the humanitarian concern for slaves occasionally visible, it must be assumed that slave-owners deliberately manipulated the lives of their slaves to a very substantial degree if the system of slavery itself were to retain its exploitative character across time, which it clearly did.

(26) See FINLEY (1980), 122, quoted below, p. 22 n. 6.
(27) HOPKINS (1978), 108 ; 111, quoted below, p. 25 n. 23.

CHAPTER I

LOYALTY AND OBEDIENCE

The Roman agricultural writer Columella provides in his work, the *Res Rusticae*, important information on the subject of how to manage and to treat slave labourers on the farm ([1]). His remarks must be set out in detail because the questions which they raise are fundamental for the purpose of this study.

At first sight an apparent humanitarianism emerges from Columella's recommendations on how the owner of a farm should treat his slaves. He urges careful attention to sick slaves on the part of the *uilica*, and recommends the availability of a large kitchen in the *rustica pars* of the villa which can serve as a resting place for the members of the slave household. The individual cells in which chained slaves are housed should be built so as to admit some sunlight, while the *ergastulum*, although subterranean, should be well lit and as healthy as possible. (With the provision, however, that its windows be beyond hands' reach.) Sturdy clothing for the slaves is advised, and the whole *familia* should be allowed to bathe − at least on holidays, since Columella believed frequent bathing to be physically impairing. For the slave *uilicus* even marital life is catered for ([2]).

Random details such as these afford something of a glimpse of the everyday living conditions of rural slaves in Italy in the mid first century ; and it would be tempting to associate Columella's rather generous remarks which supply them with what has been perceived to be a broad humanitarian concern for slaves in the early imperial period ([3]). Indeed,

(1) On Columella in general see Brockmeyer (1968), 137ff. ; White (1970), 26ff. ; 332ff. ; Martin (1971), 289ff. ; (1974), 267ff., and on slave terminology in the *RR*, R. Günther, *Kolonen und Sklaven in der Schrift 'de re rustica' Columellas* in R. Stier, H. E. Stier (edd.), *Beiträge zur Alten Geschichte und deren Nachleben* I, Berlin, 1969, 505ff.

(2) *RR*. 1.6.3 ; 1.6.19-20 ; 1.8.5 ; cf. 12.3.7.

(3) For example, Westermann (1955), 109ff. ; Duff (1958), 34f. ; Kajanto (1969), 53ff. ; Milani (1972), 200 ; cf. with greater caution, rightly, Griffin (1976), 268ff. and see below, pp. 126ff. Cizek (1972), 49 states that Columella counselled humane treatment of slaves because free society continued to scorn manual labour. This is only true in part.

the source of Columella's attitude has been found precisely in the Stoic influence allegedly exercised upon him by his contemporary and fellow countryman, the philosopher Seneca [4]. But there is no more compelling evidence for this view than for the notion that Columella and Seneca were on intimate terms [5]. The possibility of disinterested humanitarianism should never be discounted as a factor which influenced the kindly treatment of slaves when such is visible [6], yet the true basis of Columella's recommendations was one very practical in nature and far from disinterested, as his own words make clear.

According to Columella himself sick slaves were to be given medical attention so that they would become more reliable in response, and sturdy clothing was to be provided by the owner of the farm so that his slaves could work every day, no matter how bad the weather. The *uilicus* was to be allowed a wife so that she could, in part, keep her husband in order, while the hands were to be consulted by the owner because they would thereby become more enthusiastic about their work if they thought their opinions actually carried some weight [7]. In sum, 'Such justice and consideration on the part of the owner', Columella states, 'contributes greatly to the increase of his estate' [8].

It is thus quite clear that Columella's recommendations on the treatment of slaves were designed to promote servile efficiency as the key to economic productivity in a situation where the owner's profit from agricultural production was a dominating principle [9]. Columella recognised the problem of how to extract work from a labour force which was by nature involuntary, and understood that the solution lay in the provision of incentives towards and rewards for good performance from his slaves. Purely and simply, therefore, apparent generosity was in reality dictated by the economic motive of making the farm profitable, and what becomes visible in Columella's work accordingly is a set of variations on the theme of slave manipulation.

---

(4) Cizek (1972), 128.

(5) See Appendix A.

(6) What requires emphasis here is the 'sharp distinction between more or less humane treatment of individual slaves by individual masters and the inhumanity of slavery as an institution'; Finley (1980), 122.

(7) *RR*. 1.8.9 ; 1.8.15 ; 12.1.6 ; 11.1.21.

(8) *RR*. 1.8.19, Loeb translation.

(9) Cf. White (1970), 26f.

Columella's attitude was by no means unique. He wrote in fact in a long tradition of proposals and recommendations which stretched back through the works on agriculture of his predecessors Varro and Cato ultimately to the *Oeconomicus* of Xenophon, all of which he knew first hand ([10]). Varro, for example, had advised his readers in an important section of his *De Re Rustica* that slave foremen on the farm should be rewarded with a *peculium* and at least a semblance of family life; consultation of the better hands by the farm owner was also suggested as a means of making the slaves believe their master regarded them well; and a supply of extra food or clothing was intended to restore servile goodwill (*beneuolentia, uoluntas*) at times when harder work than usual or some form of punishment became necessary ([11]). In a much earlier age Cato had similarly stated that the *uilicus* had the responsibility of commending good work in slaves so as to elicit the same from others ([12]). It was thus a long-time understanding of farm owners that gentle treatment of their slaves worked to their advantage in a very direct way.

The distinction of Columella, however, lies in the fact that he devotes far more attention to the topic of slave management than his forerunners, and he gives advice suggesting a particular need for the application of common sense to such management. Cato's recommendation that old and sickly slaves should be sold off by the owner makes little sense if, like Plutarch ([13]), one wonders who would be willing to purchase such property, and it is equally difficult to see the point of putting sick slaves on rations, again as Cato had advised ([14]). By comparison Columella's recommendation was more beneficial to master and slave alike. Moreover, Columella admits the prospect of freedom for the slave, the ultimate incentive and reward ([15]), whereas it is significantly absent elsewhere.

Further, there is an urgency about Columella's material on slave management not immediately obvious in the works of Cato and Varro.

---

(10) *RR*. 1.1.12; 11.1.5, etc. Columella makes clear that the catalogue of his predecessors was greater than that now available. For the background see Brockmeyer (1968), 103; 137; K. D. White, *Roman Agricultural Writers I : Varro and His Predecessors* in *ANRW* 1.4 (1973), 439ff.

(11) Varro, *RR*. 1.17.5-7. Cf. Maróti (1976), 120.

(12) Cato, *De Ag*. 5.2; cf. 5.4; 5.6

(13) Plut. *Cato* 4.5.

(14) Cato, *De Ag*. 2.4; 2.7; cf. Astin (1978), 264f., not fully convincing on the reservations attached to the two passages cited.

(15) *RR*. 1.8.19.

He was aware of the dangers of slave ownership, of slaves' potential for revolt, of the need to rule by fear (*metus*) (16) as well as by kindly treatment, and his suggestions assume something of a prison-camp mentality, for all is seen in terms of security, control and containment as far as the servile labour force is concerned. Almost in a preoccupied manner, he states that the cautious master will himself monitor conditions in the *ergastulum*, will even ask the chained slaves how their overseers are treating them, will allow grievances to be expressed, and he writes that ox-drivers and shepherds are to be quartered close together so that they can observe the extent of each others' diligence (17).

If the need for close supervision of rural slaves is made very clear by Columella, one question which is raised immediately by the *Res Rusticae* is whether, in the imperial period, close supervision of non-rural slaves was also considered important and necessary by slave-owners. There is of course no handbook of regulations for the management of a Roman urban household comparable to the *Res Rusticae*. Yet incidental remarks can be summoned from various authors which do indeed suggest a similar concern with slave management in the domestic sector. According to Tacitus, for instance, one of the reasons which lay behind Augustus' institution of the city prefecture was the need to discipline slaves at Rome itself, while the assassination of the senator L. Pedanius Secundus by a slave in Nero's reign produced the argument that slaves in the city had to be ruled by fear, particularly in view of the foreign element (18). In both instances domestic slaves were the objects of interest. Domestics owned by the younger Pliny were permitted to make their own wills, and his observation of their provisions resulted, so he says, in a certain community of feeling among them (19). But such a feeling also eliminated potential for unrest. In most general terms, but terms which must be understood to include domestics again, Seneca argued that harsh treatment produced disaffection among slaves and, in rhetorical fashion, he contrasted a more satisfactory past age with the present, when enlightened, humane treatment had made slaves loyal to their masters

---

(16) *RR*. 1.8.17-18 ; 1.2.1. Cato and Varro did of course recognise that supervision was required ; Cato, *De Ag.* 5.1-5 ; cf. 142 ; Varro, *RR*. 1.13.1-2. Cf. Brockmeyer (1968), 112 ; Biezunská-Małowist (1973b), 370f. ; Maróti (1976), 117.

(17) *RR*. 1.8.16 ; 18 ; 1.6.8.

(18) Tac. *Ann.* 6.11.3 ; 14.44.5.

(19) Plin. *Epp.* 8.16.1-2 ; cf. Sherwin-White (1966), 467 ; Duncan-Jones (1974), 22.

even under torture ([20]). Dio Chrysostom will also have had domestics in mind when he offered the injunction, 'The wise master will give orders to slaves that benefit slaves as well as masters' ([21]), a statement in which the realisation is unmistakable that slaves performed better if consideration of their interests were forthcoming on the owner's part. Even Cato had been able to see the practical value to himself of allowing male and female domestics to consort with each other : intransigence in the household was thereby reduced ([22]).

Owners of both rural and urban slaves were thus aware, it seems, that close supervision of their property was required, both to encourage work and to diminish the possibility of servile disaffection. Slaves could not simply be forced to work by virtue of their subject status ([23]), but instead their social contentment had to be secured as a prelude to work efficiency and general loyalty. Columella, it must be emphasised, was writing for an audience which would presumably identify strongly with his remarks on slave management, which, together with the fact that congruent statements appear in diverse authors less directly concerned with the subject of slavery, makes it incontrovertible that slave management was a wide-spread issue in Roman imperial society as a whole.

As noted already, Columella gives some indication of the means by which social contentment among slaves might be elicited : the provision of decent living conditions, of time off from work, the fostering of family life among slaves, the prospect of emancipation from slavery. Such means acted as incentives and rewards in the lives of slaves, and this fact has always been recognised ([24]). But what is not at all clear is how such acts of

(20) Sen. *Epp.* 47.4 ; on Seneca and slavery see Milani (1972), 212ff. ; Griffin (1976), 256ff.

(21) Dio Chrys. *Or.* 14.10 ; on Dio and slavery see Creţia (1961) ; Brunt (1973), 18f.

(22) Plut. *Cato* 21.2, according to which a fee was levied on the male slaves ; cf. Astin (1978), 263 for explication.

(23) Cf. Hopkins (1978), 108 ; 111 : 'slaves ... could be forced to work long hours throughout the whole year' ; '... high productivity which could be forced out of them (i.e. slaves) on larger farms'. These assertions seem to me to gloss over the difficulties of extracting work from slaves. It may be true, potentially, that 'no other system (i.e. than slavery) offers such undivided loyalty as well as such absolute rights of control and discipline' (Finley (1976), 819), but potential could only be realised with effort on the part of slave-owners. Loyalty and high productivity cannot be assumed to be naturally forthcoming from slaves.

(24) A complete list of works in which the point has been made would serve no useful purpose, but note especially the comments made by Treggiari (1969), 18f. ; White (1970), 352f. (rather inaccurate) ; Martin (1974), 290ff. (distinguishing between material

generosity actually affected the daily lives of slaves, especially on those two fronts which may be presumed to have been most important to slaves themselves, and which are introduced by the agricultural authors, their family lives and their prospects of manumission. What was the precise contribution of these inducements to the maintenance of Roman slavery, what refinements can be established, what recourse was available if and when they did not work successfully ? These questions, while forming the basis of present enquiry, are grounded on the belief that a problem of controlling slaves existed in the Roman world, a problem which is certainly below the surface of the material so far presented, but which requires further description before they can be examined in detail. For to assume a problem of control would be legitimate only if tensions, more or less constant, could be demonstrated between slaves and their masters in Roman society, and while it could with all reason be maintained that expressions of the need for slave management of the kind already mentioned are in themselves evidence of such tensions, there is other important evidence to be brought out.

If attention is turned first to the topic of how slave-owners generally regarded their slaves, a beginning can be made with the depiction in literary sources, which of course represent the views of the slave-owning elite above all, of the slave as a criminous being. Columella again offers abundant material on the theme of the essential criminality of the slave as perceived by the slave-owner, and his overall attitude towards slaves is one of disdainful superiority about which there is nothing unusual. In a lament on the condition of contemporary agriculture he states that farming has been abandoned by the landowning class (with which he naturally identifies himself) to the worst of its slaves, as though to the hangman for punishment. He recognises that the *uilicus* had an important function on the estate as far as management of the *familia* is concerned, but he says that he can be effective only insofar as the servile nature allows. The need to have agricultural slaves kept at work in chains and quartered in an *ergastulum* at night causes him no disquiet. Deprecating statements are extended to urban slaves who, Columella says, cannot provide a suitably qualified *uilicus* for the farm because they are too accustomed to the pleasures and vices of the city, of which a lengthy catalogue is given. He launches into a tirade against the practice whereby the slave doorkeeper of an urban houshould controls access to his master and profits from it. And the highest indignity a slave-owner can suffer, Columella remarks, is to grow so old and lax that his slaves come to despise him [25].

It thus causes no surprise that the *Res Rusticae* also gives ample expression to the owner's view of slaves as an intransigent property. The work contains a liberal sampling of the excesses of which Columella considered slaves capable, or which he had himself observed, as the following itemised list shows :

> They let out oxen for hire, and keep them and other animals poorly fed ; they do not plough the ground carefully, and they charge up the sowing of far more seed than they have actually sown ; what they have committed to the earth they do not so foster that it will make the proper growth ; and when they have brought it to the threshing-floor, every day during the threshing they lessen the amount, either by trickery or by carelessness (*uel fraude uel neglegentia*). For they themselves steal it and do not guard against the thieving of others, and even when it is stored away they do not enter it honestly in their accounts. (*RR*. 1.7.6-7, Loeb translation).

These were some of the servile crimes and misdeeds (*flagitia, maleficia*) which Columella elsewhere reports or assumes. Slaves not under the watchful eye of their owner, being corruptible, were more intent on damage (*rapinae*) than farming. The chained slaves used in viticulture had to be sharp-witted in their work, but all intelligent slaves were classed together as wicked (*improbi*). It was the responsibility of the *uilicus* to get lazy slaves to work, to be aware of their time-wasting and delinquency ; and the *uilica* had to be alert for any shirkers indoors. Columella realised that all slaves could not be tarred with the same brush : in his list of the shortcomings of city slaves it is implicit that all were not considered abject, though nothing more than this appears. He showed personal attention (*comitas*) to those who comported themselves well, took note of the greater loyalty of unchained slaves, and saw that some slaves had to be described as industrious and thrifty. But by and large the representation of servile behaviour found in the *Res Rusticae* is in unequivocally negative moralistic terms : apart from *fraus* and *neglegentia*, the actions of slaves

(25) *RR*. 1 *praef.* 3 ; 1.8.10 ; 1.6.3 ; 1.7.1 ; 1.8.1-2 ; 1 *praef.* 9-10 ; 1.8.20.

are characterised by greed, cruelty, avarice and idleness (*rapacitas,
saeuitia, auaritia, desidia, pigritia*) ([26]).

It must be stressed that it is servile behaviour of which Columella
speaks so much and not servile labour, which on the whole Columella
must have believed productive enough ([27]). But be that as it may, some
explanation is required of why such a negative presentation predominates
in Columella's work, and one solution would be to take simple recourse in
the longstanding literary convention of the criminous slave ([28]). This,
however, merely raises the question of why such a convention existed at
all, and to answer that question the origins of the convention itself must be
approached.

Negative servile behaviour is first met in Latin literary sources in the *De
Agricultura* of Cato and in the comedies of Plautus his contemporary,
though in obviously different ways. Several sections of Cato's treatise, for
which there were no Latin models, imply that the agricultural slaves with
whom he had had personal experience before the work was composed
were difficult to contain and that surveillance was imperative ([29]). Flight,
fractiousness, mischief, pilfering and perhaps malingering, all are referred
to incidentally as marks of the slave but with the cumulative impact of
suggesting a general intractability as the slave's chief characteristic ([30]). In
Plautine comedy the *seruus callidus* is by common consensus one of the
most successful comic figures of all, appearing ubiquitously in the form of
domestic slaves ([31]), yet it is equally agreed that the *seruus callidus* is not a
stock character taken over by Plautus from Greek comedy, but an

(26) *RR*. 1.1.20 ; 11.1.27 ; 1.9.4 ; 11.1.14, 16, 21, 23 ; 12.3.7 ; 1.8.1-2 ; 1.8.15, 18 ;
1.9.1 ; 11.1.12, 19, 25 ; 1.3.5 ; 1.6.8 ; 1.7.6 ; 1.8.17 ; 7.4.2 ; 9.5.2. Pliny's complaint about
tenant farmers (*Epp*. 9.37.2, *rapiunt etiam consumuntque quod natum est, ut qui iam
putent se non sibi parcere*) is not really comparable (cf. FINLEY (1980), 126) : debt was the
motive for the tenants' actions, which cannot have been true of slave workers.

(27) Cf. BIEZUNSKA-MAŁOWIST (1973b), 367. CIZEK (1972), 49 totally misrepresents *RR*.
1.7 as evidence of servile inefficiency, a text which does not refer to *uilici* ; MARÓTI (1976),
121f.

(28) The corollary of this convention was that of the good or faithful slave, on which
see further below, pp. 33ff.

(29) Cf. ASTIN (1978), 265.

(30) CATO, *De Ag*. 2.2 ; 4 ; 5.1 ; 67.2 (cf. 66.1).

(31) On the slave in Plautus see E. FRAENKEL, *Elementini Plautini in Plauto*, Florence,
1960, 223ff. (revised edition of *Plautinisches im Plautus*, Berlin, 1922) ; George E.
DUCKWORTH, *The Nature of Roman Comedy*, Princeton, 1952, 249ff. ; 288ff. ; SPRANGER
(1961).

innovation and creation of his own ([32]). This fact, taken in conjunction with the prevalence of language associating slaves with deceitfulness, suggests that the behaviour of Plautus' slave characters was based on real historical experience of the sort sketched by Cato and which contemporary audiences could be expected to understand ([33]). In other words, while it is of course unnecessary to believe that the schemes with which Plautus' slaves become involved are realistic in any way, the trickery essential to those schemes makes sense only if it were developed from a popular conception that slaves, in reality, were deceitful and conniving, and such a conception can have only derived from the observed behaviour of slaves in everyday life. The troublesomeness which appears directly in Cato has thus been converted by Plautus into innocent entertainment, but for present purposes that hardly minimises the historical substratum from which the playwright was working.

It is true that there are passages in the *Res Rusticae* which stamp Columella firmly as a moralistic writer, working in a tradition not unlike that of Roman historiography. He complains that women in his own day were so given to luxury and idleness that domestic responsibilities had been forgotten, and he offers a recurring idea in Roman literature at large that rural discipline had been superseded by the attractions of the city ([34]). But whatever Columella's debts to his predecessors in the sphere of agronomy in particular or to conventional literary stereotypes in general, a purely literary approach does not provide a complete explanation of

---

(32) This is not to deny that Plautus may have drawn on Greek models ; cf. SPRANGER (1961), 57, 'So darf man wohl mit gutem Recht in dem griechischen Großstadtsklaven den Prototyp des servus callidus sehen'. But the degree of 'inflation' (Fraenkel) seems unmistakable.

(33) Cf. especially PLAUT. *Asin*. 256-7, *serua erum, caue tu idem faxis alii quod serui solent, / qui ad eri fraudationem callidum ingenium gerunt ; Bacch*. 639-660. The vocabulary of deceitfulness in Plautus includes terms such as *mendacium, seruilis schema, fallaciae, fraudatio, audacia, astutia, dola*, etc. The question of realism in Plautus is of course thorny, but there seems to me to be enough of an unchallengeably realistic element to justify the generalisation of the text. The enslavement of war captives, the manumission of slaves, the availability of the *peculium*, the buying and selling of slaves, child exposure, the existence of professional slave dealers, the practice of hiring out slaves − all of these details (and there are more) in the comedies conform with historical reality and serve to establish a sufficiently realistic basis. (Contrast SPRANGER (1961), 52ff.) Cf. D. C. EARL, *Political Terminology in Plautus* in *Historia* 9 (1960), 235ff. for an aspect of Plautus' topicality, and WATSON (1971), 43ff. for use of Plautus as an historical source.

(34) *RR*. 12 *praef*. 9 ; 1 *praef*. 13ff. ; cf. BROCKMEYER (1968), 139 and on similar expression in Dio Chrysostom cf. BRUNT (1973), 10f. ; JONES (1978), 56.

negative servile behaviour, when the stereotype of the slave can be seen to have had a basis in historical reality and when there is no reason to assume significant alteration of that reality by Columella's time. In any case, the *Res Rusticae* is not in the strictest sense a 'literary' work intended for the personal improvement of its readership, with an inherent moralistic foundation imposed by the canons of genre. Rather, it is a practical manual like that of Cato, designed to give pragmatic instruction to the landowner. As such it deals on a level of everyday reality that only the technical handbook can, and thus has no need of any formal literary devices or preconceived notions dictated by convention. Consequently when Columella speaks of servile criminous behaviour there is no alternative but to accept what he says as a literally genuine reflection of his own experiences in agriculture and farm management : criminous acts were to be expected from slaves because this was in the order of things. Moreover, if Columella were to be understood by his readership, it must be assumed that his remarks reflect a widespread difficulty for slave-owners of containing servile recalcitrance.

It would be tedious to compile a full catalogue of slave-owners' statements on this recalcitrance. It is enough to point out, when Columella or Cato (or Plautus) utter such statements, or when Dio Chrysostom similarly remarks on the anxieties a slave-owner felt over the possibility his slaves might steal from him or commit some other act of mischief [35], that expression is being given to slave-owners' tensions about the stability of the slavery system upon which they themselves economically depended. There was simply no guarantee that the system could or would indefinitely perpetuate itself without effort. Furthermore, although the actual record of servile insurrection in the imperial age is not (as far as can be seen) very strong, slave-owners were very much alive to the fact that slave-owning carried with it the automatic corollary of personal danger to themselves. The famous Roman proverb that the number of one's enemies equalled the numbers of one's slaves is an important indication of both the antagonism with which slaves were regarded en masse by their masters and of the latters' fears for their own safety, fears which were occasionally realised with alarming effect [36]. Seneca's report of the senate's fearful dismissal of a proposal that slaves should be compelled to wear distinctive

(35) Dio Chrys. *Or.* 10.12.
(36) Festus, *De uerb. signif.* p. 314 Lindsay ; Sen. *Epp.* 47.5 ; Macrob. *Sat.* 1.11.13 ; cf. Milani (1972), 204.

clothing again illustrates the corporate apprehension about their security felt by slave-owners [37].

To turn to the demonstration of tensions from the opposite side, that of slaves, it can be stated at once that what was regarded by slave-owners as servile recalcitrance or misbehaviour was not necessarily perceived in the same way by their practitioners. Indeed, since it is obvious that slaves were not usually content to remain slaves when the opportunity of freedom presented itself, it is legitimate to believe that 'negative' actions were in fact forms of servile resistance against or opposition to the social system of which slaves themselves were the victims. What avenues of resistance and opposition were in fact available?

Perhaps the most obviously cogent demonstration of slaves' unwillingness to accept their underprivileged status and conditions comes from their occasional resort to open revolt, though in the imperial age, as already noted, this is a very rare phenomenon [38]. In the approximate period from 140 B.C. to 70 B.C. there were of course three major insurrections of slaves with which Rome had to deal, two taking place in the province of Sicily, the third (most memorable of all due to the leadership of Spartacus) in Italy itself [39]. The relative absence of revolt in the imperial age, however, is in itself no indicator of general servile contentment or passivity : revolt incorporated great risks for slaves, was subject to betrayal, demanded great courage, and depended on expert organisation and leadership, a combination of circumstances which did not often manifest themselves. There is reason to believe, moreover, that the eventual scale of the Republican risings was more fortuitous than preconceived [40]. Nonetheless, the possibility of revolt was always available.

(37) SEN. *Clem.* 1.24.1, *Dicta est aliquando a senatu sententia, ut seruos a liberis cultus distingueret ; deinde apparuit, quantum periculum immineret, si serui nostri numerare nos coepissent.* Cf. GRIFFIN (1976), 267ff., and for legal texts showing concern with safety see JONKERS (1934), 243 n. 6.

(38) Outbreaks are attested at TAC. *Ann.* 4.27 ; *Hist.* 3.47 ; *ILS* 961, but may have been more common than the sources suggest ; cf. GRIFFIN (1976), 267 and E. A. THOMPSON, *Peasant Revolts in Late Roman Gaul and Spain* in *Past & Present* no. 2 (1952), 11ff. at p. 12 (slaves included in 'peasant' revolts).

(39) For the Republican slave wars see P. GREEN, *The First Sicilian Slave War* in *Past & Present* no. 20 (1961), 10ff. (and cf. *Past & Present* no. 22 (1962)) ; VOGT (1975), 39ff. ; FINLEY (1979), 137ff.

(40) See Appendix B.

Individual acts of violence by slaves against their owners constitute a
second category of opposition. The murder of L. Pedanius Secundus
under Nero has already been mentioned, but a similar attack on a certain
Larcius Macedo early in the second century can also be noted as an
example of the extreme lengths to which some slaves were at times
driven [41]. Again, however, violent resistance of this sort included danger
for the slaves involved and this must have acted as a deterrent against a
high incidence of violent outbursts.

A more prevalent form of resistance, and one commonly attested
throughout imperial history, was the tendency of slaves to abscond, and
nothing illustrates better the lengths to which owners went to prevent
flight than the surviving iron collars worn by slaves, which contained
instructions for the return of a captured fugitive [42]. Further, in Roman
law special rules were addressed to cases of flight by slaves, and in the
early imperial period professional slavecatchers (*fugitiuarii*) came into
existence to help contain the problem [43]. In spite of its pervasiveness,
however, fugitivism also imposed certain risks upon the slaves who
attempted it : separation from family members might be involved, for
example, while recapture meant certain punishment.

Finally, the type of dilatoriness and poor work performance of which
Columella complained so vigorously can also be interpreted as a form of
resistance, in the sense of deliberate sabotage by slaves of their masters'
property and economic interests. Naturally it is impossible to measure the
incidence of such activity, but the frequency with which servile idleness is
referred to must be taken as a firm indication of its prevalence [44].

In spite of uncertainties about their exact frequency, all of the activities
mentioned are on record (together with other, probably less common acts
such as slave suicide) [45] and they combine to show the expression by

(41) PLIN. *Epp.* 3.14 ; cf. 8.14 (Afranius Dexter).
(42) See for example *ILS* 8726-8733, and cf. PLAUT. *Capt.* 357 for a much earlier
period. On flight in general cf. BELLEN (1971).
(43) When a slave was sold, Roman law required the seller to guarantee to the
purchaser that the slave was not prone to running away ; *Dig.* 21.1.1.1 ; GELL. *NA.* 4.21 ;
CIC. *De off.* 3.7.1. Surviving documents show that the requirement was maintained ;
*FIRA*² III nos. 87, 88. But the law also contained elaborate regulations concerning actual
cases of flight ; *Dig.* 11.4. On *fugitiuarii* see D. DAUBE, *Slave-Catching* in *Juridical Review*
64 (1952), 12ff.
(44) In PLAUTUS, *Pseud.* 139-158 ; *Merc.* 715 ; *Most.* 15-33 ; 789 ; *Stich.* 58-67.
(45) HOR. *Sat.* 2.4.78-79 (stealing) ; DIO CHRYS. *Or.* 10.8-9 (self-neglect) ; on slave
resistance cf., briefly, MARTIN (1974), 294f. ; HOPKINS (1978), 121. DAUBE (1972), 53ff. puts

slaves of dissatisfactions with the servile condition. In and of themselves they constitute decisive proof of tensions, and it is not too much to conclude that containment of those activities was a constant preoccupation of the Roman slave-owning classes over time and place and for all manner of slaves.

One of the responses of the slave-owning classes to this situation was to hand down from generation to generation a firm view of the kind of behaviour which they ideally desired (rather than expected) from their slaves, a view summed up in the words *fides* (loyalty) and *obsequium* (obedience) [46]. It is self-evident but nonetheless true that if slaves could be kept acquiescent and compliant the privileged world of the ruling elite stood to gain most, so the emphasis in literary sources on servile loyalty and obedience is not at all surprising and comes to take on a certain conventionality [47]. Nonetheless, some of the relevant material requires exposition because the underlying social attitudes form an essential part of the background against which the practical rewards and incentives have to be seen.

An emphatic demonstration of the association between loyalty, obedience and the slave is found in the works of the great historian Tacitus, for it is the maintenance or denial of loyalty and obedience which governs Tacitus' interest in slaves [48]. At the beginning of the *Histories* he writes :

forward the very interesting idea that slaves demonstrated opposition through 'verbal attack' and sees the fables of Phaedrus as significant examples. For the fable as a form of servile self-defence see PHAEDR. *Fab.* III prol. 33-37, and cf. Appendix F.

(46) Evidence on the topic of the faithful slave is compiled by VOGT (1975), 129ff. The following references to *obsequium* in the text are to be distinguished from the legal use of the term as applied to the relationship between freedman and patron, on which see DUFF (1958), 36ff., TREGGIARI (1969), 68ff. ; cf. also below n. 62, and J. HELLEGOUARC'H, *Le Vocabulaire latin des relations et des partis politiques sous la République*, Paris, 1963, 23ff. ; 217.

(47) VOGT (1975), 129ff. is concerned with illustrating the topos of the faithful slave in literature, with showing that some slaves were indeed faithful, and with showing that Christianity introduced resignation to their status among slaves. This, however, does not seem to go to the more important question of why the topos was a topos, i.e. of why so many authors thought it worthwhile enough to include the motif in their writings. The notion of an aristocratic common view of slaves may be of more help here than that (simply) of literary conventionality, not just for the origin of the topos but for its maintenance as well.

(48) On Tacitus and slavery in general see KAJANTO (1969), rather underestimating the importance of the loyalty theme.

> However, the period was not so barren of merit that it failed to teach some
> good lessons as well. Mothers accompanied their children in flight, wives
> followed their husbands into exile. There were resolute kinsmen, sons-in-
> law who showed steadfast fidelity, *and slaves whose loyalty (fides) scorned
> the rack*. (*Hist*. 1.3 translation, K. Wellesley).

Tacitus was not writing for a servile, but for an elite audience, and it is
consequently significant that the elite in society had to be reminded from
history of the 'correct' behaviour to be cultivated in their slaves : it was
important to speak of traditional social norms in order to preserve them in
the present and for the future.

Tacitus deals with slaves as the main object of concern in several
sections of the *Annals* and *Histories*. Disturbances are described in Italy in
the year 16, disturbances caused by a slave's impersonation of Agrippa
Postumus. A rebellion of *pastores* in Apulia in 27 is mentioned, the
murder in 61 of L. Pedanius Secundus, the appearance in 69 of a 'false
Nero', a man who was either a slave or a Pontic freedman. Finally two
uprisings are included, one led by a fugitive slave in Istria in 69, the other
also in 69 but in Pontus and led by a slave or freedman of the former king
Polemo ([49]).

These events were recorded in the first place because they were judged
matters of historical importance by Tacitus. But clues from the language
he uses to recount them allow something of the aristocratic attitude
towards slaves to emerge clearly. The murder of Pedanius Secundus is
called an 'outstanding crime' ; a certain sense of relief is apparent in the
account of the miraculous termination of the Apulian revolt, 'as if by
heaven's gift' ; the adventure of Agrippa Postumus' impersonator is
attributed to the 'brazenness of a slave' ; the episode in Pontus allows
Tacitus to comment on the treacherousness of barbarians, similar to that
of slaves, and the whole tone of the section on the Istrian episode is hostile
to the events outlined ([50]). This uniform disapproval of slaves depends on
the fact that all the events mentioned are examples of 'non-virtue' ([51]), and
they are such because of their common absence of slave loyalty either to
individual masters or else to society at large. Tacitus' adverse bias means
that no sympathy is extended by him to the slaves' point of view of the

---

(49) TAC. *Ann*. 2.29-30 ; 4.27 ; 14.42-45 ; *Hist*. 2.8-9 ; 2.72 ; 3.47-48.
(50) TAC. *Ann*. 14.40.1, *insignia scelera* ; 4.27.1, *uelut munere deum* ; 2.39.1, *mancipii
unius audacia* ; *Hist*. 3.48, *fluxa, ut est barbaris, fide* ; cf. 4.23, *fluxa seruitiorum fides*.
(51) WEAVER (1972), 10.

events described and little attention is given to consideration of servile motivations.

This is not to deny, however, that Tacitus ever portrays slaves in a favourable light. The slave of L. Piso, governor of Africa in 70, who impersonated his master to save the latter's life, is credited with an 'outstanding lie'. When the maidservants of Nero's wife Octavia were tortured for false evidence against their mistress, Tacitus is explicit that some refused to betray her, and one is even allowed a defiant outcry against the infamous Tigellinus. The corpse of Galba, according to Tacitus, was buried by a slave who can only be regarded as dutiful [52]. Tacitean approval of slaves' behaviour is forthcoming here, implicitly at least, but only because loyalty has been maintained by them, no matter what the personal cost involved. Approval thus depends upon the manifestation of a proper moral attitude laid down by the slave-owning establishment, of which Tacitus himself was of course a representative.

Slavery as an institution posed no problems for Tacitus, moral, intellectual or otherwise. There is a firm commitment visible in his writings to the social status quo : slaves owed their first responsibility to their owners and deserved commendation only if this were apparent. If the obligation were not maintained, slaves became the object of criticism without any concern for the human reasons which led to breaches of the obligation. And since slaves constituted the lowest stratum in society there was a strong tendency to equate low with base ; low in a social sense became low in a moral sense, an illogical step but one which reinforced the prejudice, exemplified by the preponderance of unfavourable over favourable slave references, and which permitted no differentiation among slaves [53].

There was in Tacitus' thinking something of a composite, perhaps even stereotyped slave personality, in which certain features − recklessness, cowardice, criminality − are shown as common to all slaves. There is little reason to doubt in all of this that Tacitus departed from views that were typical of his peer group [54], upper class Romans whose wealth and

---

(52) TAC. *Hist.* 4.50, *egregio mendacio ; Ann.* 14.60 ; *Hist.* 1.49.

(53) Cf. above, p. 18.

(54) See TAC. *Ann.* 1.17.1 ; 2.12.4 ; 2.39.2 ; 6.10.3 ; 12.4.1 ; 13.46.4 ; 14.40.1 ; 15.45.5 ; *Hist.* 1.46 ; 1.48 ; 2.59 ; 2.92 ; 3.32 ; 5.9. Cf. TREGGIARI (1969), 265ff. for descriptions of freedmen as slaves by Cicero for perjorative reasons. Among historians other than Tacitus, Appian may be noted especially for his interest in servile loyalty and disloyalty. The fourth book of his *Civil War* is replete with late Republican examples of

position in society made them impervious to the circumstances of those less privileged. The book, for example, of Valerius Maximus on memorable deeds and sayings contains a section entitled 'On the Loyalty of Slaves' [55]. In it the author provides a catalogue of examples taken from late Republican history in which slaves demonstrated loyalty to their masters at moments of crisis and at cost to themselves. Possibly the most poignant is the tale of a slave belonging to a certain Antius Restio, who, although previously brutalised (he had been shackled and branded), nevertheless saved his proscribed owner from assassination by building a funeral pyre and burning on it the corpse of an old man he claimed to be his master. To Valerius Maximus, this was an instance not just of *fides*, but of goodwill (*beneuolentia*) and dutifulness (*pietas*) too [56]. A repository of such anecdotes about slaves must have been generally available to writers, because Seneca used the same kind of examples as Valerius to prove his point that a slave could confer a benefit (*beneficium*) on his master [57]. In a totally different context, however, the biographer Suetonius records that the future emperor Caligula, while at Capri with Tiberius, showed so much *obsequium* that he could be described as the ideal slave [58]. In his comparison of Trajan's reign with that of Domitian, the younger Pliny argued that social and moral normality had returned to Rome once the emperor was no longer using slaves as informants against their masters : *obsequium* had been restored to slaves, 'who are to respect, obey and preserve their masters' [59]. According to two passages in the *Historia Augusta*, Marcus Aurelius armed gladiators whom he called the *obsequentes*, and Aurelian discouraged by imperial letter servile obedience among the soldiery [60]. Even under the changing conditions of the late imperial age loyalty and obedience still remained the desired servile ideal

---

both, and Appian's attitude is clear enough : having described Cinna's massacre of slaves who had earlier plundered and murdered, he comments, 'Thus did the slaves receive fit punishment for their repeated treachery to their masters' (*BC* 1.74, Loeb translation). Note also, much later, Amm. Marc. 18.3.2ff. ; 19.9.4ff.

(55) Val. Max. 6.8, *de fide seruorum*.

(56) Val. Max. 6.8.7. Valerius' contemporary, Velleius Paterculus, referring again in a lugubrious passage to events of the late 40's B.C., similarly thought it noteworthy that some servile loyalty had been preserved towards proscribed masters (2.67.2, *fidem ... aliquam*).

(57) Sen. *Ben.* 3.18-27.

(58) Suet. *Cal.* 10.2.

(59) Plin. *Pan.* 42.2.

(60) *HA Marc.* 21.7 ; *Aurel.* 7.8.

to judge from Macrobius, who, in the first book of the *Saturnalia*, introduced through his character Praetextatus a further string of anecdotes illustrating slave virtues, some of them familiar from previous authors [61]. It is significant that despite their conventionality such stories could still circulate at the turn of the fifth century with their collective emphasis on loyalty and obedience.

The historicity of the stories about slave loyalty and disloyalty which have been referred to is unimportant here. What is striking and worth emphasis is the consistent attitude over time and among diverse authors towards what was thought to be desirable and commendable behaviour in slaves, because that attitude stood for the maintenance of the established social order and against any resistance to it from the servile element. Naturally this attitude catered to the interests of the aristocracy which perpetuated it, and this is one reason why it receives so much attention in literature. Moreover, loyalty and obedience of slave to master was only one form in Roman society, where categories of social status and role were heavily demarcated by patriarchal and aristocratic tradition, of the manner in which obligations were imposed on various social groups. The kinds of family loyalties considered desirable in free society, for instance, are illustrated in the quotation above from Tacitus, while the loyalty of freedman to patron and of wife to husband are analogous [62]. Servile loyalty and obedience, therefore, belonged to a wider nexus of social obligations imposed downwards from the upper levels of society, obligations which of course by the beginning of the period were established concretely. It is the 'correctness' of this behaviour, however, which is the main point.

What effects did the perpetuation of what might be called this aristocratic ideology of loyalty and obedience have ? In many ways servile acquiescence seems to have followed as a matter of course from the mere process of inculcation. The historical cases of maintained loyalty reported

(61) MACROB. *Sat.* 1.11.16-46.

(62) See DUFF (1958), 36ff. ; TREGGIARI (1969), 68ff. ; BOULVERT (1970), 101 (though *Dig.* 37.15.9 is inapposite) ; WILLIAMS (1958), 16ff. ; JONES (1978), 24 (on the submissiveness expected by aristocrats from their social inferiors). For the notion of total subservience implicit in *obsequium* see SUET. *Aug.* 21.1 (the obedience of defeated enemies) and TERT. *Spect.* 1 (*obsequium* as the Christian's obedience to God) ; and on the related term *oboedientia* see CIC. *Para. Stoic.* 5.35, *oboedientia fracti animi et abiecti et arbitrio suo carentis* (defining *seruitus*) ; cf. 5.41. See also *ILS* 8034, 8401, 8430, 8430a, 8473.

by Tacitus, for instance, show that obedience was displayed without question by some slaves at some times. More significantly, inscriptional dedications made by owners to deceased slaves who were described as 'most faithful', and dedications to owners set up by their slaves provide a firmer indication of servile compliance over long periods of time, compliance which is underscored by the virtual ordinariness of these commemorative texts [63]. Furthermore, the 'normality' of the slave's deferential attitude towards his master in society at large is well illustrated from Christian, that is non-aristocratic, literary sources. Since Christianity in its earliest stages was a religion which appealed to and spread among the lower orders of society, it is not surprising to find injunctions to slaves from the teachers of the new doctrine [64]. The stress contained in these injunctions on servile obedience is remarkable for a religion which taught the spiritual equality of all mankind, and what this reflects is an unqualified acceptance of the existing social structure in which they found themselves by early Christians [65]. The brotherhood of man inherent in the teachings of Christianity anticipated equality not in the present world but in the world to come, and for slaves the important point was to be able to withstand one's condition and to fulfill its obligations in expectation of a better life ahead. Thus the emphasis beneath the reiterated instruction, 'Servants, obey your masters', was on preserving and reaffirming current social norms, which for slaves was a state of passivity and compliance to the will of the slave-owner. Early Christian literature, it can thus be said, seems to show how ingrained and pervasive this state had become as a result of the steady downward imposition of aristocratic values.

As already intimated, the association of the slave with loyalty and obedience has a long literary history, its first expression appearing again in the Plautine corpus [66]. The *seruus callidus* of Plautus' comedies is

(63) For example, *ILS* 7370, 7371, 7376, 7378, 8421. VOGT (1975), 131, states that 'Educated Roman society was sufficiently open-minded in the second century B.C. to recognize that such devoted servants and assistants possessed that part of the moral personality embraced in the concept of *fides*'. Rather, the aristocratic desirability of *fides* had been created by that date.

(64) *Tit.* 2.9-10 ; I *Cor.* 7.20-24 ; *Coloss.* 3.22-4.1 ; *Ephes.* 6.5-9 ; I *Tim.* 6.1-2 ; I *Pet.* 2.18-20 ; *Did.* 4.11 ; *Barn.* 19.7.

(65) Cf. *Matt.* 10.24-25 ; *Luke* 6.40 ; *John* 13.16 ; 15.20 ; JONKERS (1934), 247ff. ; STE. CROIX (1975). For the revolutionary potential of Christian teaching, J. MORRIS, *Early Christian Orthodoxy* in *Past & Present* no. 3 (1953), 1ff. at p. 5.

(66) For the type, SPRANGER (1961), 16. For the language of obedience, note PLAUT. *Bacch.* 993 ; *Capt.* 195-200 ; 349 ; 363 ; 428 ; 438 ; 716 ; *Cas.* 449 ; *Epid.* 348 ; *Merc.* 156 ; *Most.* 785 etc.

often a *seruus fidus*, Tyndarus in the *Captiui* perhaps representing the noblest example of the type. It would of course hardly have been appropriate for Plautus to create slave characters for the stage openly inimical to their masters' interests, but servile devotion to their owners must be taken as a reflection of what free society hoped for in reality and sometimes achieved. Yet there is a sequence of soliloquies spoken by slave characters in the plays which are disquisitions, from the servile point of view it must be emphasised, on the meaning of loyalty and obedience, and which are very revealing [67]. Faithfulness and diligence are shown to be not automatic, selfless responses from slaves to their condition, but rather means of avoiding physical punishment or gaining some reward from their owners. In other words, Plautus provides a hint of the disparity between owners' and slaves' interpretations of *fides* and *obsequium*. It is obvious that by Plautus' day Roman slave-owners had created the ideal of loyal behaviour from their slaves, but it would be surprising if slaves themselves had accepted this, and the subservience which accompanied it, as an ideal of their own choosing and without question [68]. The expression in aristocratic literature of a desirable form of servile conduct was after all the expression only of an ideal wish for social stability between slave and free, and it is clear from what has already been said that the ideal did not always coincide with reality. No society in which one section of the population is held in subjection by another can expect social relations to be constantly stable, and that is implicit, for Roman society, in the opening statement of Valerius Maximus' work previously referred to : 'It remains for me to relate the loyalty of slaves to masters, *which is all the more deserving of praise because least expected*' [69].

Incentives and rewards thus functioned as mechanisms for the attainment of the ideal on a practical level. Social stability, as expressed in the moral terms *fides, obsequium, beneuolentia, pietas*, or through the absence of servile *flagitia* and *maleficia*, could be secured by directly catering to and accommodating the human interests of slaves. In other words, the use of incentives and rewards by slave-owners points to a process of social control at work in the Roman Empire, a process which

(67) PLAUT. *Amph.* 959ff. ; *Aul.* 587ff. ; *Rud.* 918ff. ; *Pseud.* 1103ff. ; *Most.* 859ff. ; *Men.* 966ff. The significance of the motives expressed in these passages is highly distorted by VOGT (1975), 131.

(68) Note PLAUT. *Asin.* 380, flight as an *officium* of the slave, and cf. above n. 63.

(69) VAL. MAX. 6.8 *praef., Restat ut seruorum etiam erga dominos quo minus expectatam hoc laudabiliorem fidem referamus.*

operated to preserve existing social differentials and which was dictated by the elite, whose object was to create servile loyalty and obedience so that its privileged existence was not threatened from below ; and expression of the object, as has been seen, continued throughout the imperial age. In order to illustrate the meaning of these statements in more detail, one specific type of generosity can be examined, the practice of masters periodically granting holidays to their slaves.

Holidays for slaves are attested from at least the time of Cato until the late imperial period [70]. The annual number of these occasions was never excessive, but it seems nevertheless to have been fairly well-defined and protected. As a general rule slaves were barred from the ceremonial aspects of religious festivals – the origin of all holidays – because they were thought to be a defiling or polluting influence [71]. Yet the Roman calendar prescribed nonetheless a specific number of annual holidays from which slaves were not excluded on religious grounds. Thus a holiday was included in the Matronalia of March 1 ; slaves took part in the festival of Fors Fortuna on June 24 ; August 13 was a holiday for slaves alone, not the free population ; and slaves also participated in the two major celebrations at the turn of the year, the Saturnalia (December 17-23) and the Compitalia (January 3-5) [72]. Moreover in a papyrus apprenticeship contract from Roman Egypt for a female slave about to learn the trade of weaving, a provision is included for eighteen days annual holiday on account of festivals [73]. A number of other such contracts is known with similar provisions but in which the apprentice is freeborn not servile [74]. The highest total of holidays allowed in these

(70) What follows is adapted from K. R. BRADLEY, *Holidays for Slaves* in *SO* 54 (1979), 111ff. ; cf. also ASTIN (1978), 265.

(71) PLUT. *QR* 16 (with ROSE *ad loc.* ; cf. *Camillus* 5.2) ; SUET. *Claud.* 22 ; Zos. *Hist. Nou.* 2.5.1 ; cf. PLUT. *Aristides* 21.2 ; ATH. 6.262b ; R. M. OGILVIE, *The Romans and Their Gods in the Age of Augustus*, New York, 1969, 91f.

(72) Matronalia : MACROB. *Sat.* 1.12.7 ; LYDUS, *De Mens.* 3.22 ; Fors Fortuna : CIC. *De Fin.* 5.70 ; OVID, *Fasti* 6.771ff. ; AUGUST 13 : PLUT. *QR* 100 ; FESTUS, *De Verb. Signif.* p. 460 Lindsay ; Saturnalia : SEN. *Ep.* 47.14 ; ATH. 14.639b ; IUST. 43.1.4 ; DIO CASS. 60.19.3 ; LUC. *Sat. passim* ; Compitalia : DION. HAL. 4.14.3-4. Cf. in general J. MARQUARDT, *Römische Staatsverwaltung* III, Leipzig, 1878, 197ff. ; 548f. ; 554f. ; 562ff. ; J. G. FRAZER, *The Golden Bough³ Part VI, The Scapegoat* (reprint) London, 1966, 306ff. ; K. LATTE, *Römische Religionsgeschichte*, Munich, 1960, 254 ; G. DUMÉZIL, *Archaic Roman Religion*, Chicago, 1970, II 618.

(73) *P. Oxy.* 1647.

(74) *P. Oxy.* 725 (twenty days) ; 2586 (eleven days) ; *P. Fouad* 37 (thirty-six days) ; cf. also *P. Oxy.* 2971 ; and *P. Wisconsin* 5, where a female slave hired out as a weaver is given

documents is thirty-six, but one is close to the arrangement for the slave apprentice and one is lower. If the arrangement for the female slave was common it might be that a greater number of holidays was given to a more valuable or potentially more accomplished slave ; that is, distinctions may have been drawn depending on the status of the slave, for from Varro it seems that the *uilicus* might be more favoured than ordinary hands [75], although this cannot be certain.

It is equally difficult to say whether slaves enjoyed holidays other than those already mentioned for which clear testimony exists. For Rome itself the possibilities are governed by the number of religious festivals and of games (*ludi*) held during the year, on which some statistics are available. Through the late Republic and early Empire the number of days marked *feriae* gradually increased until Marcus Aurelius imposed a limit of one hundred and thirty-five, while by the mid fourth century the number of days on which *ludi* were given had similarly increased from seventy-seven in the time of Augustus to one hundred and seventy-seven [76]. Some of these of course overlapped. Now although legal and other official business could not be conducted on days marked *feriae* most of the free population, especially at the lower levels of society, probably went about its business much as usual [77]. Even in the case of the free poor a distinction has to be drawn between *feriae* which called for little more than religious observance by priests, and festivals which constituted major periods of holiday. For slaves accordingly it should be true in general that they were required to fulfill their functions on these as on other days. Apart from the matter of their religious exclusion it seems doubtful that they can have shared entirely whatever free time was available at holiday periods, for in the case of the games the full working day was not lost for those who did attend, an obvious limit was set on the number who could attend at any one time, and tickets cannot have been easily accessible to slaves [78]. If they happened to attend with their owners, this could have meant only a limited form of respite at most.

---

at least eight days holiday a year. Cf. Herbert C. YOUTIE, *The Heidelberg Festival Papyrus : A Reinterpretation* in P. R. COLEMAN-NORTON ed., *Studies in Roman Economic and Social History in Honor of Allan Chester Johnson*, Princeton, 1951, 178ff.

(75) See above, p. 23.
(76) BALSDON (1969), 245ff.
(77) BALSDON (1969), 244 ; cf. BRAUN (1959), 57 ; 68ff. ; 81ff.
(78) BALSDON (1969), 248 ; 268.

For rural slaves it is implied by both Cato and Columella in random passages that local holidays were kept. Columella indeed speaks of a period of forty-five days when no ploughing was possible because of bad weather and holidays as well as a period of thirty days given over to rest once the sowing season was over (⁷⁹). Cato gives a list of jobs which could be done by slaves on local and private holidays, and Columella follows suit, in even fuller detail, with a whole catalogue of chores which, if adhered to, could have produced no more than partial relief from work (⁸⁰). There is no way of telling how representative of other slave-owners' attitudes Cato and Columella were, whether for urban or rural slaves, and in reality much must have depended on the personal inclinations of individual masters. But the demands of labour, especially in agriculture, did not disappear at holiday times and the indications are that slaves enjoyed only a small number of specifically designated days' relief from work.

Two considerations must be made at this point to put into higher relief the unusual character of slave holidays. First, the servile population of Rome and Italy was far greater in late Republican and early imperial times than in the early historical period when the holidays first came into existence (⁸¹). This being so, it seems rather curious at first sight that a depressed element in Roman society should have been periodically permitted irregular freedom of movement and action when the potential for various unsavoury acts that existed among slaves might be realised. Of special note in this connection is the emphasis found in the sources on the licence (*licentia*) of slaves at the Saturnalia (⁸²). Secondly, and in contrast, the holidays continued over time to provide opportunities for the demonstration towards slaves of generosity on the part of slave-owners, apart from whatever free time from work was allowed. At the Matronalia mistresses gave their slaves special meals as part of the holiday, and the same was done by masters at the Saturnalia (⁸³). At both Compitalia and Saturnalia even Cato had prescribed an increase of rations for field hands (⁸⁴). Again at the Saturnalia normal restraints were removed from

(79) Cato, *De Ag.* 132.1 ; 140 ; Col. *RR.* 1.8.5 ; 11.1.19 ; 2.12.9 (cf. 11.2.95-6 ; 98).
(80) Cato, *De Ag.* 2.4 ; 140 ; Col. *RR.* 2.21.
(81) See Brunt (1971), 121ff.
(82) Cf. Dio Cass. 27.93 ; Macrob. *Sat.* 1.7.26 ; Plut. *Sulla* 18.5 ; Luc. *Sat. passim.*
(83) Sen. *Ep.* 47.14 ; Solin. 1.35 ; Ath. 14.639b ; Iust. 43.1.4 ; Luc. *Sat. passim.* ; Macrob. *Sat.* 1.7.37 ; 12.7 ; 24.22-3.
(84) Cato, *De Ag.* 57.

slaves to the extent that they might gamble and address their masters more frankly than usual ; and at the Compitalia signs of servitude were removed from slaves [85].

If attention is now turned to accounting for the continued maintenance of these holidays it must be stated first that since all Roman holidays were in origin days of religious observance, religious traditionalism must form part of any explanation. The habits of centuries could not be simply set aside. But it is questionable to what extent by the imperial period the original reasons for all religious ceremonies were remembered or considered valid. It was of course long remembered in Roman lore that the Saturnalia recalled an age of gold during the reign of Saturn when a natural abundance of material needs made slavery an unnecessary institution ; all men were then free and equal [86]. Less assurance, however, is visible in the sources which speak of the origin of the holiday for slaves alone on August 13. This was thought by Festus to mark the foundation of the temple to Diana on the Aventine by Servius Tullius, who had been born a slave, whereas Plutarch believed that the same day commemorated Tullius' birthday [87]. More strikingly, Plutarch was at a complete loss to explain the peculiar hairwashing ritual of women on August 13 : 'Why is it that ... the women are in the habit of washing and cleansing their hair on that day in particular ? ... Did the headwashing start from the slave-women in consequence of their holiday and spread to free women ?' [88] No positive answer can be given. Again, while the ability of slaves to take part in the ceremonies of the Compitalia and of Fors Fortuna was also attributed to Servius Tullius, this does not explain the statement of Dionysius of Halicarnassus that in his day, the Augustan age, all traces of their condition were removed from slaves at the Compitalia [89].

It seems, therefore, that the religious-mythological origins of slave holidays gradually became obscured but, as has been seen, the holidays

(85) Hor. *Sat.* 2.7 ; Mart. *Epig.* 4.14.7ff. ; 5.30.7f. ; Epict. *Diss.* 1.25.8 ; Dio Cass. 60.19.3 ; Luc. *Sat. passim.* ; Dion. Hal. 4.14.4.

(86) Luc. *Sat.* 7 ; Iust. 43.1.3 ; Macrob. *Sat.* 1.7.26 ; cf. Braun (1959), 58ff. ; 76ff. Braun argued that the various taboos associated with all holidays preserved a collective memory of a golden age ; but he gave no evidence of traditional connections between specific holidays and a golden age, except for the Saturnalia.

(87) Festus, *De Verb. Signif.* p. 460 Lindsay ; Plut. *QR* 100.

(88) Plut. *QR* 100 translated by H. J. Rose, *The Roman Questions of Plutarch*, Oxford, 1924.

(89) Ovid, *Fasti* 6.771ff. ; Dion Hal. 4.14.3-4.

themselves were not dispensed with. It is preferable in consequence to set these occasions in the context of master-slave relations outlined above and to regard them as a vehicle of social control, a view for which there is important corroborative literary evidence in Solinus and Macrobius, authors who have explicit statements on the connection between slave holidays and social stability. They remark that slaves were given banquets (*cenae*) on March 1 and at the Saturnalia by their owners in order to foster *obsequium* for the immediate future or as compensation for work completed in the recent past : 'so that at the beginning of the year they might incite their slaves to steadfast obedience through reward' or 'as it were pay off the account for work completed' ([90]). Even though these writers were aware of the antiquity of the custom of providing meals for slaves, no religious association or explanation occurs in the passages referred to. Instead what is discernible is a motivation on the part of owners to keep their slaves under control through the use of sparing rewards or incentives. Dionysius of Halicarnassus has a further relevant observation : commenting on the Compitalia he writes that signs of slavery were removed then 'in order that the slaves, being softened by this instance of humanity, which has something great and solemn about it, may make themselves more agreeable to their masters and be less sensible of the severity of their condition' ([91]). What emerges, therefore, is a desire by slave-owners to appease slaves, to make the servile condition more tolerable by providing temporary but periodic respites from it.

In summary, then, it has been maintained in this chapter that the institution of slavery presented a conflict between the unwillingness of slaves to accept passively their position of social inferiority in the Roman world and the desire of slave-owners to maintain the institution for their own continuing benefit. Servile opposition to the Roman social system was demonstrated by means of flight, deliberate inefficiency at work and, occasionally, violent revolt, activities which ran counter to the ideal of servile loyalty and obedience which owners handed down from

---

(90) SOLIN. 1.35 ... *ut honore promptius obsequium prouocarent ... quasi gratiam repensarent perfecti laboris* ; MACROB. *Sat.* 1.12.7 ... *ut ... ad promptum obsequium honore seruos inuitarent ... quasi gratiam perfecti operis exsoluerent* ; the language suggests either the use of the former by the latter or else the use by both of a common source. These texts seem decisive in establishing a connection between holidays and management ; contrast MILANI (1972), 199, however, who sees holidays as a sign of the flexibility of the barrier between slavery and freedom, perhaps too simplistically.

(91) DION. HAL. 4.14.4 (Loeb translation). Cf. CIC. *De Leg.* 2.19 ; 29.

generation to generation. In order to resolve the conflict, to negate the potential for servile resistance and to achieve the ideal of compliance – in other words, to secure social stability – slave-owners granted various incentives and rewards which catered to their slaves' interests, and, to an extent, diminished the severity of slavery. These included holidays, whose function as a device for reducing tensions between slave and free can be satisfactorily perceived.

In the following chapters detailed examination will be made of how two of the incentives and rewards mentioned by Roman authors, family life and manumission, actually functioned in the everyday lives of slaves. It will then be shown how masters reinforced this system of relatively generous treatment with a constant counterpoint of violence in order to secure their ends. Together the generosities and climate of fear which can be seen to surround servile life help to explain the survival over time of the Roman slavery system.

CHAPTER II

THE SLAVE FAMILY

In the Roman imperial age, as in other periods of classical history, the family constituted the basic social unit among the free [1]. To the elite the traditions of the family and the importance attached to preserving and continuing them were sometimes so strong that it was considered more satisfactory that they be assumed by adopted descendants, if there were no alternative, than that they die out altogether [2]. Given this predominant norm, it could be assumed that slaves would wish to establish and live in their own family units if conditions were to allow, even though marriage between slaves, and hence the existence of a slave family, was technically a legal impossibility [3]. But three types of evidence prove the assumption correct, that from literary sources, that from legal sources, and that from sepulchral inscriptions, the last being especially important since it comes directly from slaves themselves.

Servile familial arrangements are incidentally alluded to in all kinds of literature from the imperial period. Martial, for example, expresses the hope of a lasting union between two slaves about to marry, and Juvenal refers to one of his own domestics as the son of slave parents on his farm at Tibur ; Tertullian assumes the normality of slave marriages in his rhetorical statement that discipline among slaves is better if they marry within the same household, and Ammianus Marcellinus tells of a slave who informed against his master after his wife (*coniunx*) had been flogged [4]. From Christian literature a parable in Matthew's Gospel is worth special note. According to the story a slave unable to repay a debt to his master on request was eventually forgiven, but proved far less lenient in his own treatment of a fellow slave who in turn owed him

(1) Weaver (1972), 95. For an indirect affirmation of the value of marriage and family life, see Dio Chrys. *Or.* 7.133 ; 135, on prostitution.
(2) Cf. Veyne (1961), 221.
(3) Buckland (1908), 76.
(4) Mart. *Epig.* 4.13 ; Iuv. 11.146ff. ; Tert. *Ad ux.* 2.8.1 ; Amm. Marc. 28.1.49.

money. Once the master discovered this, he punished the slave. Obviously the story is fictional, but if it were to have been comprehensible when originally told the story must have had a recognisable basis in historical reality. This being so, it is of some significance that the master's first order, before his act of forgiveness, had been that the slave, his wife and children (and property) be sold to make good the debt (⁵).

Legal sources show that offspring from slave women was anticipated as a matter of course. References to female slaves and any issue they may have are common in the *Digest* and other major codes, as well as the more localised *Gnomon of the Idiologus* from Roman Egypt (⁶). For its suggestiveness one legal ruling can again be noted particularly : in the early fourth century the emperor Constantine imposed a ban on the compulsory separation of slave families in Sardinia as a result of land redistribution, and ordered the reuniting of families already broken up in this way (⁷).

From evidence of this sort, spread over different times and places, it cannot be doubted that slave families existed in the Roman world, or that there was anything unusual about the fact. And epigraphic material simply confirms this view. Among the great mass of sepulchral inscriptions which have survived from the imperial age, many commemorate a deceased spouse and in so doing use formulaic expressions of the surviving partner's feelings. A bereaved husband would record that he had lived with his wife for a certain number of years 'without any complaint' and the partner would be spoken of in endearing terms (⁸). The phraseology was doubtless highly conventional, much like its modern counterpart, but it suggests all the same a view of marriage based at least in part on mutual feelings of love, intimacy and respect (⁹). Moreover, the inscriptions refer to marriages which were terminated not

(5) *Matt.* 18.23-34 ; cf. Vogt (1975), 142, for the essential statement that δοῦλος in the Gospels means 'slave'.

(6) E.g. *Dig.* 33.7.12.7 ; 27.1 ; *Instit.* 2.20.7 ; 16 ; *Gnom. Id.* 61. E. J. Jonkers, *Economische en sociale Toestanden in het romeinsche Rijk*, Wageningen, 1933, 113, gives a long list of legal texts which refer to *partus ancillarum* ; cf. also Treggiari (1979b), 194ff.

(7) *CTh.* 2.25.1 ; *CJ* 3.38.11 ; see also *Dig.* 33.7.27.1 (Africa) and cf. Finley (1980), 76.

(8) For formulae and examples of terms of endearment see Richmond Lattimore, *Themes in Greek and Latin Epitaphs*, Urbana, 1962, 277ff.

(9) For a more cautious view see Hopkins (1965) ; contrast Hopkins (1980), 325. Cf. in general Richard I. Frank, *Augustus' Legislation on Marriage and Children* in *CSCA* 8 (1975) 41ff. ; Brunt (1971), 558ff. ; Flory (1978), 83ff.

by divorce or some other personal factor, but only by the death of one of the partners. All in all, the implication is strong that marriage was often regarded, once entered upon, as a binding and permanent union until the intervention of death ([10]).

It is not always possible to identify with absolute certainty the social status of the individuals mentioned in this great wealth of inscriptions, whether freeborn, freed or slave. But it is generally understood that all three categories are included in the material as a whole ([11]) ; marriages, that is, between slaves, or between persons who were slaves when their marriages began (they may have been subsequently set free), are definitely commemorated. What is important in such cases is that the phraseology and terms of endearment used are exactly the same as for persons of totally non-servile status, and not only the terms of affection but also the designative terms of reference such as *coniunx* (spouse) and, though less commonly, *uxor* (wife) and *maritus* (husband) as well ([12]), despite the fact that they were strictly inappropriate. Whatever the precise degree of romantic intimacy involved in marriages among the lower orders in Roman society, the evidence of the epitaphs suggests that servile attitudes towards marriage did not differ appreciably from those of the rest of society, that relationships were entered upon which slaves probably regarded as permanent arrangements, that such relationships endured over time, and that married slaves thought of each other as 'husband' and 'wife'. From marriages children followed, and the epitaphs show that slaves referred to one another as mother and father, son and daughter, brother and sister ([13]), again just as free members of society did. There is

---

(10) For the significance of women being married only once see WILLIAMS (1958) ; Marjorie LIGHTMAN and William ZEISEL, *'Univira'. An Example of Continuity and Change in Roman Society* in *Church History* 46 (1977), 19ff.

(11) For identification of slaves in inscriptions see the nomenclature principles outlined in WEAVER (1972), 42ff. and TREGGIARI (1975b), 393ff.

(12) E.g., *ILS* 7393 ; 7402 ; 7423 ; *CIL* 8.20084 ; etc. ; cf. ROULAND (1977), 264ff. ; TREGGIARI (1979b), 195. Presumably slaves who married marked their unions by some kind of marriage ceremony, but this is only a guess. PLAUT. *Cas.* 68, *seruiles nuptiae*, is suggestive but difficult to interpret ; the phrase could mean that ceremonies were common, or that the very idea of such was preposterous ; see generally J.-H. MICHEL, *Le Prologue de la "Casina" et le mariage d'esclaves* in *Hommages à Léon Hermann, Collection Latomus* 44, Brussels, 1960, 553ff. But note the expectation that Olympio and Casina will have children if married (*Cas.* 256 ; 291). The precision with which the duration of slave marriages was commemorated at least indicates that the wedding day was significant.

(13) E.g. *ILS* 7379 ; 7384 ; 7401 ; 7431 ; etc.

thus no cause to doubt that in the slave consciousness the family was anything but a perfectly natural and normal concept. The extent to which slave families existed at any one time or in any one place cannot be measured precisely, but the impression that the slave family was a common phenomenon is incontrovertible ([14]).

However, because slaves were technically not permitted to marry and could thus not produce legally recognisable families, the relationships which are attested in the sources must be considered concessions to slaves from their owners : it cannot be imagined, in light of owners' omnipotence over their slaves, that servile marriages occurred and lasted, or that children were born to married slaves, without the connivance if not express permission of masters ([15]). In turn this implies that owners benefited from condoning servile familial relationships, a view which can be corroborated in principle from certain passages in Varro and Columella which suggest that Roman slave-owners encouraged slave families because their interests in preserving social and economic order were thereby served. First Varro :

> As to the breeding of herdsmen ; it is a simple matter in the case of those who stay all the time on the farm, as they have a female fellow-slave in the steading, and the Venus of herdsmen looks no farther than this. But in the case of those who tend the herds in mountain valleys and wooded lands, and keep off the rains not by the roof of the steading but by makeshift huts, many have thought that it was advisable to send along women to follow the herds, prepare food for the herdsmen, *and make them more diligent*. (*RR*. 2.10.6, Loeb translation).

Varro assumes here, and perhaps approvingly, that mating between and reproduction by slaves will occur spontaneously and he offers what appears to be a common view of slave-owners on the need to supply females to slave *pastores* on the trail not just for the practical purpose of preparing their food but to 'make them more diligent' (*assiduiores*)

---

(14) Cf. Finley (1976), 820. Veyne (1978), believes that between the end of the Republic and the Antonine age a moral transformation occurred as part of which marriage and the concept of conjugal love became more characteristic of Roman society than in earlier ages. If true this might mean that the importance of the family to slaves increased in the period of concern here. But Veyne's reluctance to present much evidence means that his hypothesis is difficult to evaluate. It seems, however, that the slave family was not a discovery of the Principate, and it is doubtful that Columella can be used to support the view that agricultural slaves of the first century lived in promiscuity.

(15) Cf. similarly Finley (1980), 75.

also ([16]). The same assumption of spontaneous sexual relationships among slaves appears in that passage from Columella in which he makes recommendations on the treatment of slaves drawn from his own experience :

> To women, too, who are unusually prolific, *and who ought to be rewarded* for the bearing of a certain number of offspring, I have granted exemption from work and sometimes even freedom after they had reared many children. For to a mother of three sons exemption from work was granted ; to a mother of more her freedom as well. (*RR*. 1.8.19, Loeb translation).

Both authors speak of the farm bailiff (*praefectus, uilicus*) and his family :

> The foremen are to be *made more zealous by rewards*, and care must be taken that they have a bit of property of their own, and mates from among their fellow-slaves to bear them children. (Varro, *RR*. 1.17.5, Loeb translation). But be the overseer what he may, he should be given a woman companion *to keep him within bounds* and yet in certain matters to be a help to him. (Col. *RR*. 1.8.5, Loeb translation).

Moreover, the passage from Tertullian already referred to ([17]), in which a connection is made between slaves marrying within the same household and order (*disciplina*), indicates that it was not the agricultural writers alone who understood the value of allowing slaves at least a semblance of family life.

It seems clear, then, that in many circumstances it was considered normal for slave families to exist, that the attitudes of slaves towards family life did not differ in essence from those of other sections of society, and that Roman slave-owners recognised the principle that permitting marital and familial associations among their slaves could contribute positively to the preservation of social and economic order. What now needs to be explored is the extent of familial stability in their lives that slaves might expect. How secure, in fact, were the relationships which they created ? The question is important because in everyday reality several factors arising from the ordinary practices of slave-owning acted

---

(16) Cf. also Varro, *RR*. 2.1.26, *quod in hibernis habent in uillis mulieres, quidam etiam in aestiuis, et id pertinere putant, quo facilius ad greges pastores retineant, et puerperio familiam faciunt maiorem et rem pecuariam fructuosiorem.*

(17) *Ad ux.* 2.8.1, *Nonne etiam penes nationes seuerissimi quique domini et disciplinae tenacissimi seruis suis foras nubere interdicunt. Scilicet ne in lasciuiam excedant, officia deserant, dominica extraneis promant.* See Appendix C for remarks on Cato's attitude.

against the maintenance of familial stability and adversely affected the quality of servile life, yet such factors have hardly been taken into consideration in earlier estimates of slaves' family conditions ([18]). Nonetheless, it must be emphasised that slaves were basically a form of property, and as commodities they were hence disposable. Slaves could be sold by one person to another, or left as part of a legacy without any obligation on the owner's part to take into account his slaves' domestic relationships. The arrangement of a marriage in free society might involve movement of slaves who were included in a dowry ([19]). Slaves could even be loaned by one person to another, or given away as gifts as when the historian Appian sent two slaves to Fronto, the confidant of Marcus Aurelius ([20]). Martial is found apparently seeking a slave from a patron for sexual reasons as if this were quite common ([21]). The mechanics of the slave-owning system thus involved forcible transference of slaves from place to place and from owner to owner, and since slaves themselves had no control over such transference it was at times inevitable that their family conditions and arrangements be endangered. Some of these factors can be examined in detail.

The ability to be sold was the slave's most compelling reminder of his status as a sheer commodity, a point to be stressed since the frequent allusions to sales of slaves in the literary sources encourage a certain disregard of the dehumanising nature involved in the process of human exchange ([22]). Turnover of slaves appears always to have been brisk, even in the later imperial age to judge from the schedule of slave prices contained in Diocletian's Edict on Maximum Prices of 301 ([23]). But particularly rich information on sales is available from Roman Egypt in the form of records of actual transactions and this material is worth

---

(18) For generally favourable and optimistic views of servile family life see WESTERMANN (1955), 119 ; BIEZUNSKÁ-MAŁOWIST (1969), 95 ; BURFORD (1972), 51 ; BIEZUNSKÁ-MAŁOWIST (1973a), 88. The views of RAWSON (1966), 71ff., are more realistic : from the sepulchral evidence of Rome, she suggests common separation of slave children from their parents, at early ages ; it is not necessary, however, to believe that the parents of such children were engaged only in transitory unions. See also FLORY (1978), 88f.

(19) *P. Oxy.* 265 ; 496 ; APUL. *Apol.* 92 ; cf. PLAUT. *Asin.* 86.

(20) MART. *Epig.* 2.32 ; 8.52 ; FRONTO 1.264-9 (Haines, LCL).

(21) MART. *Epig.* 8.73. For the violent theft of a slave from her owner, see *P. Oxy.* 1120.

(22) On this aspect see further below, pp. 115ff.

(23) J. M. REYNOLDS, M. CRAWFORD, *The Aezani Copy of the Prices Edict* in *ZPE* 34 (1979), 163ff. at pp. 177 ; 198.

careful attention (²⁴). The papyrological evidence from Egypt on slave sales extends from the first to the early fourth century, so that its seeming abundance is offset by its diffusion over time. But the legal framework of the relevant documents is fairly standardised throughout, and this allows some general observations to be made. First, the overwhelming majority of attested sales concern individual slave transactions, a fact long since recognised but the social significance of which has not been properly brought out. Of the few multiple transactions, most deal with sales of mothers and young children. Secondly, perhaps the most surprising fact which emerges is that the Egyptian evidence offers no example at all of the sale together of a husband and wife, or of a husband, wife and children. So on the assumption that the extant papyri are representative of the typical patterns of slave sales in Roman Egypt, it seems on statistical grounds alone that slave-owners were not affected when they sold slaves by any interest in preserving whatever familial ties their slaves had formed, with one or two exceptions (²⁵). Given this predominant pattern of individual sales and the absence in the documentation of any full family group, it must follow that in all recorded instances there was a strong possibility of family disruption among slaves when they were sold.

Consideration of the ages at which slaves were sold substantiates these views. In Table I some recorded ages at which female slaves were sold are listed (²⁶). The span ranges from a minimum of age four to a maximum of age thirty-five with a fairly even distribution in between. If children are separated from adult women, the dividing line occurring at age fourteen (²⁷), the range of ages at which the latter were sold is that when

---

(24) The following remarks are developed from K. R. BRADLEY, *The Age at Time of Female Slaves* in *Arethusa* 11 (1978), 243ff. ; see also Andrew K. DALBY, *On Female Slaves in Roman Egypt* and K. R. BRADLEY, *Response* in *Arethusa* 12 (1979), 255ff. For transactions see Tables I and II.

(25) E.g. *P. Oxy.* 375 ; 1209.

(26) The sales records which supply ages constitute only a proportion of a longer catalogue of similar transactions where ages are not given. For full information see O. MONTEVECCHI, *Ricerche di sociologia nei documenti dell'Egitto greco-romano : I contratti di compravendità* in *Aegyptus* 19 (1935), 11ff. ; JOHNSON (1936), 279ff. ; OATES (1969) ; STRAUS (1971) ; MONTEVECCHI (1973), 211f. ; BIEZUNSKÁ-MAŁOWIST (1975).

(27) Age fourteen is chosen because literary evidence suggests that menarche in antiquity was believed to begin in the fourteenth year ; see Darrel W. AMUNDSEN and Carrol Jean DIERS, *The Age of Menarche in Classical Greece and Rome* in *Human Biology* 41 (1969), 125ff. ; cf. HOPKINS (1965), 310ff. Although that age may seem low, it is supported by direct evidence of teenage motherhood in Egypt ; see, for example, *P. Oxy.* 1638, a female slave aged about twenty-five having a daughter aged about ten ; *P. Brux.* E

TABLE I*

No.	Date	Age at Sale	Remarks	Source
1	18/19-44/45	4		*BGU* 864 (987)
2	c.30	6		*P. Mich.* 278-9
3	108/116	7 (?)		*P. Strass.* 505
4	77	8		*P. Oxy.* 263
5	207	11	Pamphylian slave probably bought outside of Egypt	*P. Mich.* 546
6	180/192	13	Pontic slave	*SB* 9145
7	268/270	13		*SPP* XX 71
8	225	14		*P. Vindob. Bos.* 7
9	89	14	Fractional sale	*P. Oxy.* 332
10	3rd century	15	Libyan slave	*P. Ross.-Georg.* III 27
11	143	15	Fractional sale	*SB* 6291
12	252	17	Osrhoenian slave bought outside of Egypt	*P. Oxy.* 3043
13	37	17		*P. Mich.* 264-5
14	late 1st c.	18		*P. Lugd. Bat.* XIII 23
15	1st/2nd c.	18		*P. Oxy.* 1648
16	206	20	Lycian slave probably bought outside of Egypt	*BGU* 913
17	c.300	20		*SB* 8007
18	293	20	Cretan slave	*P. Lips.* 4-5
19	251/3	21	Slave sold with infant	*P. Oxy.* 1209
20	215	24	Asiatic slave	*P. Oxy.* 1463
21	138	24		*BGU* 805
22	early 2nd c.	24		*BGU* 2111
23	49	25		*P. Oxy.* 2582
24	234	25		*PSI* 182
25	129	25		*P. Oxy.* 95
26	late 1st c.	27	Fractional sale	*P. Lugd. Bat.* XIII 23
27	79	30		*P. Oxy.* 380
28	1st century	32		*P. Mich.* 281
29	Augustan	35		*BGU* 1059
30	1st century	35	Slave sold with two children	*P. Oxy.* 375

* Not included here are the slave girl in Oates, (1969), whose age was below 19 ; and the infant in *PSI* 1228, whose age is given in Straus (1973), no. 25 as c. 2.

females reached the peak of their physical maturity. This is hardly surprising and would indeed be logical, since a prospective buyer would presumably be concerned above all with his purchase's capacity to undertake the work he needed to be done [28]. Additionally, however, it should be noted that in the age span of fourteen to thirty-five female reproduction could most be expected [29], and given ancient views on the accidence of menopause [30] there is no example on record of a female slave being sold who might not have been expected to bear children after sale. A correlation thus seems indicated between the age of adult female slaves at time of sale and the period of expected reproductivity. If true, this can hardly be accidental, and it is generally agreed that one of the principal means of maintaining the servile population in the imperial age was through the breeding of slaves [31]. To what extent slave-owners were able to breed new slaves systematically, if at all, is a question which cannot be definitively answered, yet the indications from Egypt are that reproduction by slaves was encouraged at least [32]. And the present data suggest that female slaves may have been bought and sold with their potential for breeding acting as a prime consideration for buyers and sellers, which means in turn that economically the traffic in female slaves was not motivated solely by the slave's labour potential. Naturally the

7360, a free female aged about twenty-six having three children by a slave father, of whom the oldest is eight. Moreover, the common appearance in documents of the provision that any children born to a female slave after sale are to belong to her purchaser (see Taubenschlag (1955), 76), can be taken as a sign of biological maturity, or virtually so. For the appearance of the provision in a document referring to a fourteen year old, see *P. Vindob. Boswinkel* 7. The two thirteen year olds in Table I might still qualify as adults since no single age for menarche will apply in every instance. The high prices of these two slaves should be noted, as also the provision concerning future offspring in *SPP* XX 71.

(28) For occupations performed by female slaves in Egypt see Straus (1977); Biezunská-Małowist (1977), 73ff.

(29) The average age of slave women giving birth in Egypt has been computed to be 23 years and 45 days ; see M. Hombert and C. Préaux, *Recherches sur le recensement dans l'Egypte romaine* (*Pap. Lugd. Bat.* V, 1952), 171.

(30) Menopause in antiquity was thought to have occurred on average between ages forty and fifty ; see Darrel W. Amundsen and Carrol Jean Diers, *The Age of Menopause in Classical Greece and Rome* in *Human Biology* 42 (1970), 79ff. For some examples of childbearing by women in their thirties see Biezunská-Małowist (1977), 113f.

(31) E.g. Gsell (1932), 398 ; Westermann (1955), 84ff. ; Jones (1968), 12 ; I. M. Biezunská-Małowist and M. Małowist, *La Procréation des esclaves comme source de l'esclavage* in *Mélanges offerts à K. Michalowski*, Warsaw, 1966, 275ff. ; Brunt (1971), 708 ; R. Meiggs, *Roman Ostia²*, Oxford, 1973, 225.

(32) Biezunská-Małowist (1977), 113ff. See further below.

slave's capacity to reproduce cannot have been the only reason for the imposition of an upper age limit for the purchase of slaves, because if an earlier average age of death in antiquity than in the modern world can be assumed, the older the slave when acquired the greater the chance of a quickly diminishing return on the price invested in the property by the purchaser. Nevertheless, the reproduction factor was there.

The documentary evidence on slave sales does nothing to show how frequently they took place ; the impression simply remains that sale was common. The ability of females to provide their owners with new slaves may imply that at times the chances of establishing a stable family unit were good. But from the servile point of view the conclusion seems inescapable that any female slave could reasonably expect to be sold during her childbearing years because it was then that she was of greatest economic value to buyers and sellers alike, when interest in producing new slaves as well as the need for labour or capital were making themselves felt among owners. Presumably that expectation might have diminished as the slave advanced in years, but it must always have formed part of the female slave psychology ([33]).

The Egyptian evidence on ages of male slaves at time of sale as listed in Table II extends from a very young age of two years up to forty years with few examples of men being sold over the age of thirty. As is to be expected, adult males were again bought and sold in their prime, between ages fourteen and forty, and it is hardly likely that slaves over thirty had a great life expectancy left to them, probably few reaching what seems from one document to have been the 'retirement' age of sixty ([34]). Any purchase of a slave represented a considerable financial investment on the part of the buyer and, as with the females, return on the investment obviously diminished in proportion to the age of the slave when acquired. It might be believed, therefore, that slaves in the age span twenty-five to thirty, both men and women, could expect to go through their final transference as a result of sale and that their prospects of some years of relative familial stability increased about this time in their lives. This is not to say,

(33) What is envisaged is a situation where one owner no longer needed fertile women and was prepared to sell to another who did in return for hard cash. It can be noted that the ages of adult females when sold are comparable to those when free women might expect marriage to disrupt their lives. But that does not affect the rigours of disruption experienced by slaves.

(34) *P. Oxy.* 1030. For fourteen as the age of male majority and tax liability see JOHNSON (1936), 245 ; 248 ; and on life expectancy see references given below, p. 96 n. 53.

however, that such prospects were immune from the disruptive effects of other factors over which, as with sale, slaves had no control, and again the possibility of sale itself beforehand must have influenced men as well as women.

TABLE II

No.	Date	Age at Sale	Remarks	Source
1	c. 30	2	Sold with 6 yr. old girl	*P. Mich.* 278-9
2	1st/2nd c.	3		*BGU* 859
3	1st/2nd c.	3	See no. 4	*P. Oxy.* 1648
4	1st/2nd c.	4		*P. Oxy.* 1648
5	166	7	Mesopotamian slave	*P. Lond.* 229
6	136	8		*BGU* 193
7	143	8	Sold with 15 yr. old female	*SB* 6291
8	237	8	Macedonian slave	*PSI* 1254
9	116	8		*SB* 7573
10	250	13	Pontic slave	*BGU* 937
11	359	14	Gallic slave	*BGU* 316
12	154	17		*SB* 7555
13	212?	19		*P. Oxy.* 2777
14	198	19		*P. Antin.* 187
15		25		*SB* 7533
16	83	30	Sold with 40 yr. old male	*P. Oxy.* 94
17	late 1st c.	30		*P. Oxy.* 327
18	186	30		*P. Oxy.* 716
19	91/2	32		*P. Oxy.* 2856
20	91/2	38		*P. Hamb.* 63
21	83	40	Sold with 30 yr. old male	*P. Oxy.* 94

Familial disruption through sale is further implied by the evidence of sales of children who when sold were not accompanied by an adult. The material collected in Tables I and II implies that for sale children were compulsorily separated from their parents (and siblings) ; even the sale of children with mothers implies separation from fathers. It is possible of course that such separation had already taken place beforehand, following exposure as infants ([35]) or previous transference of the children's parents, but in such cases as these sale might now mean severance from familiar surroundings and whatever surrogate attachments had been formed in a new household in the interim ([36]).

Although children could and did work ([37]), they obviously cannot have been as productive as adults because of their physical immaturity, and at first sight the traffic in slave children seems consequently odd. One explanation of the practice is that the low cost to the owner of maintaining a child after purchase, even over a period of years, was financially more attractive than the expenditure of a much larger capital sum for the acquisition later on of an adult slave ([38]). But it might also be the case that children were bought for short-term speculative advantage as well as for long-term investment reasons, for this seems indicated by the case of a fourteen year old girl, who, when sold at that age, had already been sold at least three times previously in her young life ([39]). How typical this case was cannot be said, but it is not an isolated example ([40]), and a process of

(35) On the prevalence of child exposure throughout the Roman empire see HARRIS (1980), 123 ; exposure, however, was not synonymous with infanticide, for one view of which see ENGELS (1980) ; contrast W. V. HARRIS, *The Theoretical Possibility of Extensive Infanticide in the Graeco-Roman World* in *CQ* 32 (1982), 114ff.

(36) Cf. WATSON (1968), 291ff. on the separation of slave mothers and children which resulted from Republican legal rulings on usufruct. When slaves were sold only locally they may have been allowed or secured access themselves to family members elsewhere, but the extent of this is hard to judge (see further below). This is true too for cases of unions between slave women and free men (on which cf. BIEZUNSKÁ-MAŁOWIST (1977), 115f.) where paternity of children was not acknowledged. For the sense of community engendered among slaves by their households see in general FLORY (1978). A newly published papyrus, *P. Turner* (=*Papyri Greek and Roman... in Honour of Eric Gardner Turner*, London, 1981) 22, records the individual sale of a ten year old girl from Galatia at Side in Pamphylia in 142.

(37) For slave children working at early ages see BIEZUNSKÁ-MAŁOWIST (1969), and (1973a). For children in farming, VARRO, *RR*. 2.10.1 ; 2.10.3 ; 3.5.15 ; 3.17.6 : COL. *RR*. 8.2.7 ; 11.2.44.

(38) BIEZUNSKÁ-MAŁOWIST (1969), 96 ; (1973a), 84. The cost of 20dr. given by DIODORUS SICULUS (1.80.6) for the maintenance of a child until adulthood is of no value. In *BGU* 859 a man buys a three year old boy whose mother he had purchased two and a half years earlier ; the baby actually stayed with his mother, so the buyer deducted 200 dr. from the purchase price of 300 dr. as expenses for having previously supported the child.

(39) *P. Vindob. Boswinkel 7*, dated 225. There is some obscurity over the exact number of earlier sales ; cf. BIEZUNSKÁ-MAŁOWIST (1977), 39f.

(40) Cf. *P. Mich*. 546 where an eleven year old girl is being sold for probably the second time ; *P. Oxy*. 3054 where a male slave is being sold for the fourth time, though his age is unfortunately missing. The girl probably came from Paphlagonia ; STRAUS (1971), 363ff.

frequent exchange would of course have greatly intensified the degree of social disruption in slave children's lives.

The possibility of being sold away from family members always then threatened to disturb the personal lives of slaves. But that disturbance must have been exacerbated further by the distance involved in the transfer of the slave property. The papyrological evidence from Egypt illustrates the forced geographical mobility to which some slaves were exposed, and from this the potential for deracination in the lives of all slaves can be better understood. Many of the sales recorded in Roman Egypt appear to have concerned local transactions only, so that separated slaves may have found it possible to visit each other if owners agreed and vast distances did not have to be covered to do so. At Oxyrhynchus, which naturally supplies a large amount of information, the buyer and seller of a slave often both belonged to the town, and in such a small community it may not have been unduly difficult for slaves to contact one another, whether or not with the owners' permission. But while even this circumstance should not be taken to minimise the effects on family life that separation entailed, there remain nevertheless graphic examples of sales where transfer over substantial distances was, or had been, necessitated by one or a succession of transactions, especially so in cases where a slave in Egypt had been imported from outside the country. In order to demonstrate a process constantly at work throughout the imperial period, the following cases can be particularly noted.

In 49 a twenty-five year old woman named Demetrous, a homeborn slave from the village of Taamechis in the Heracleopolite nome, was purchased by a woman from Oxyrhynchus. In 129 another woman, Dioscorous, also aged twenty-five, was bought by a resident of Oxyrhynchus from a man who had earlier bought the woman from an Alexandrian citizen. Sotas, an eight year old boy, was sold in 136 by a woman from Ptolemais Euergetis to another woman whose husband was also a citizen of Alexandria. In 151 a Phrygian slave named Sambatis was sold to an Alexandrian, the transaction occurring at Side in Pamphylia. In 215 a woman from Oxyrhynchus wished to purchase a twenty-four year old female slave named Tyrannis from the present owner who lived at Choinothis in the Heracleopolite nome ; if the sale were concluded, movement to Oxyrhynchus would not have been the first dislocation in the slave's life, since she was of Asiatic origin. A thirteen year old boy, Karos, was sold in 250 at Heracleopolis Magna, the home of both buyer and seller ; although no great distance could have been involved in this transfer, the boy had somehow come to Egypt from Pontus. In 252 a seventeen year old female, Balsamea, who appears to have been born in Osrhoene, had arrived by unknown circumstances at Tripolis in Phoenicia, where she was sold to a man from Oxyrhynchus who took her back and locally registered his purchase. Also in the mid-third century the purchase of a male slave named Prokopton was registered at Oxyrhynchus, the sale having taken place at Bostra in Arabia where Prokopton had already had three previous owners in succession, in the house of the first of whom he had been born. In 267 a female slave named Nike passed from the ownership of one soldier to another, the exchange occurring in Alexandria although the woman was Arabian in origin. Finally, from a document which eventually found its way to Hermopolis there is the example from 293 of a twenty year old female slave originally from Crete who was sold to a man from Antinoopolis by a citizen of Alexandria ([41]).

In cases such as these it is not possible to tell how many of the slaves had started life as exposed infants and had lost their parents this way. But when transfer over considerable distances occurred, there can have been little hope of slaves maintaining contact with their places of birth or earlier residence where personal relationships might have been formed. The examples which have been cited all concern individual sales only, so there is no likelihood that adult women were kept with any children born to them before sale. A homeborn slave in Egypt had a certain advantage in knowing that sale out of the country was unlikely (it was illegal) ([42]), but being homeborn was no protection in and of itself against the threat of sale and movement within Egypt. Apart from the evidence of the sales of mothers and children together, no more than a handful of the full number of recorded sales, it seems that slave-owners were little troubled about breaking servile familial ties when economic considerations made sale of their slaves attractive or necessary.

---

(41) The examples in this paragraph are respectively from *P. Oxy.* 2582 ; *P. Oxy.* 95 ; *BGU* 193 ; *P. Oxy.* 1463 ; *BGU* 937 ; *P. Oxy.* 3053 ; *P. Oxy.* 3054 ; *P. Oxy.* 2951 ; *P. Lips.* 4 and 5. For background see STRAUS (1971) ; BIEZUNSKÁ-MAŁOWIST (1975), and on Oxyrhynchus in particular see E. G. TURNER, *Roman Oxyrhynchus* in *JEA* 38 (1952), 78ff. ; *Oxyrhynchus and Rome* in *HSCP* 79 (1975), 1ff.

(42) Export of slaves from Egypt was controlled, as known from *Gnom. Id.* 65-67 ; but sections 67 and 69 suggest that despite the law exports did sometimes take place. Egyptian slaves in other parts of the Roman world are known.

The documentary evidence on slave sales in other parts of the Roman world is far less copious than for Egypt, but it cannot be doubted that the generally negative picture for the stability of servile familial arrangements which the Egyptian records give was not applicable elsewhere as well. A small number of (individual) sales documents from Dacia belonging to the second century include the exchange of a six year old girl named Passia, of a Cretan woman named Theudote, and of a Greek boy, Apalaustus [43]. From Dura-Europus there are records of the sale of a twenty year old male between two brothers in 180 and of a twenty-eight year old woman in 243 [44]. And an exchange of a seven year old boy named Abbas (Eutyches) in Syria in 166 is also known [45]. None of this material is at odds with the evidence from Egypt. Moreover, the existence of a substantial body of Roman law governing sales of slaves [46] and the frequent allusions to sales and slave-dealers in the literature of the imperial age [47] are strongly suggestive of a brisk turn-over among owners, of slaves suffering separation from kin, and of considerable distances being covered as a result of sale. The younger Pliny, for instance, is found

(43) *FIRA*² III no. 87 (139) : no. 89 (160) ; no. 88 (142).

(44) *P. Dura* 25 ; 28.

(45) *FIRA*² III no. 132. Cf. VEYNE (1961), 215 for the presumption of common sale of children throughout the Empire, and note the accounts of L. Caecilius Iucundus from Pompeii in FRANK (1940), 255. In PLAUT. *Merc.*, the plot involves purchase of a slave girl in Rhodes who is transported to Athens to be sold again. Despite the fiction, the circumstances of compulsory movement and frequent change of ownership (in this case a two year interval is involved ; cf. 534-7) are the same as shown above from the documentary sources. The geography of the slave trade outside Egypt is much illuminated by HARRIS (1980), 125ff., who clearly demonstrates as well considerable movement of slaves from one region of the empire to another.

(46) For the law see BUCKLAND (1908), 39ff. The following extract from the Edict of the Curule Aediles (c. 129) is representative : 'Whoever sells slaves shall inform the buyers what sickness or defect each slave has, who is a runaway or a vagabond or is not free from noxal liability ; and when they sell the said slaves they shall announce openly and correctly all the said points. If any slave is sold contrary to these regulations or if whatever the buyer alleges must be properly performed in this regard is contrary to the statement or the promise made when he was being sold : we shall grant an action to him and to all persons to whom the matter pertains in six months from the time when first there is an opportunity to try the matter by law, that this slave may be returned'. Translation from A. C. JOHNSON, P. R. COLEMAN-NORTON, F. C. BOURNE, *The Corpus of Roman Law (Corpus Iuris Romani), Volume II, Ancient Roman Statues*, Austin, 1961, no. 245. Cf. also D. DAUBE, *Forms of Roman Legislation*, Oxford, 1956, 92ff.

(47) On slave-dealers see HARRIS (1980) and below, pp. 114ff. For incidental slave sale references, see HOR. *Epist.* 2.2.1-19 ; SEN. *Epp.* 80.9 ; IUV. 6.373 ; 11.147 ; QUINT. *Inst.* 2.15.25 ; APUL. *Apol.* 45 ; 92 ; 93 ; GELL. *NA* 6.4 ; 4.2.1.

buying slaves, anxious only about their reliability ([48]). The elder Pliny tells of the infamous dealer Toranius who, for a good price, sold two slave boys to the triumvir M. Antonius as twins, despite the fact that one came from Asia and the other from Gaul ([49]). The story has an amusing aspect, but it also hints at the harshness of separation more directly visible in the case of a slave family owned by Juvenal. The poet speaks of a boy in domestic service at Rome who had been taken from his parents on Juvenal's farm at Tibur, apparently to the boy's great distress ([50]). Even more vivid is the depiction on the funeral stele ([51]) of the slave-trader A. Kapreilius Timotheus from the Black Sea of a train of chained slaves being led away for disposal by sale, almost a photographic capture of what must have been a common sight in antiquity since slave-trading was ubiquitous throughout the Roman Empire ([52]). A recent hypothesis has been advanced that the Roman government of the Augustan age expected some 250,000 sales of slaves among Roman citizens each year ([53]) and although the accuracy of the figure is hardly verifiable, it certainly conforms with impressions left by various kinds of evidence. As far as the sale of female slaves is concerned, nothing conflicts with what has been suggested on their attractiveness to purchasers as providers of future slaves, and an important item from the *Digest* may indeed be taken to confirm the high value of women in their childbearing years : it was a common legal opinion that pregnancy was no barrier to the sale of a woman, because reproduction was her greatest responsibility ([54]). Breeding certainly took

(48) PLIN. *Epp.* 1.21.2.

(49) PLIN. *NH* 7.56.

(50) IUV. 11.146ff. ; cf. G. HIGHET, *Juvenal the Satirist*, Oxford, 1954, 131 ; 237. Observe the separation of a slave apprentice from his mother in TREGGIARI (1979b), 191.

(51) For which see J. ROGER, *Revue Archéologique*[6] 24 (1945), 49ff. : *AE* 1946, no. 229. It should be noted that besides the eight chained slaves, the scene on the stele also includes two women and two children who are not in chains. Whether these people were also slaves and related to the men or the family of the dealer himself cannot be stated.

(52) HARRIS (1980), 126ff.

(53) HARRIS (1980), 121.

(54) *Dig.* 21.1.14.1, *Si mulier praegnas uenierit, inter omnes conuenit sanam eam esse : maximum enim ac praecipuum munus feminarum est accipere ac tueri conceptum.* This opinion appears to have superseded that given by VITRUVIUS (2.9.1) in the Augustan age. Cf. VEYNE (1978), 55. The objection might be made that since the importance of slavery in the economy of Egypt was substantially less than in that of Italy (slaves were barely used in Egyptian agriculture), the evidence of the Egyptian papyri is irrelevant for practices elsewhere in the empire. Yet if insistence is made on the point that slavery as a social institution is the main object of concern here, then the principles of the detailed Egyptian material are not at all irrelevant for other areas ; cf. above p. 17 n. 18. TREGGIARI (1979b),

place, and the results were highly prized [55].

A certain tension can thus be perceived between the fact that slaves married and produced children when conditions allowed and the fact that certain factors operated in their lives which were beyond their control. Although owners encouraged servile familial life when it was in their interests to do so, those narrow interests did not permit any deep concern for the human relationships their slaves formed to intervene in their thinking when sale was decided upon.

From Roman Egypt many examples have also survived of bequests of property [56] which sometimes included slaves, and this material can be used to add to knowledge of slaves' expectations. In general terms a low possibility for the retention of family connections upon transfer of this type arises from the point that in Egypt itself slave households tended to be small in comparison with the establishments of wealthy aristocrats at Rome [57]. A document recently published suggests ownership of perhaps one hundred slaves by a single individual in Alexandria early in the second century [58], but such a large household would be very much an exception to the rule. Thus, if a slave-owner had several heirs and his property were divided at his death more or less equally among them, the chances had to be high that servile relationships would suffer as a result. It often happened that slaves were fractionally divided among heirs (and not just in Egypt but elsewhere too), a rather curious arrangement whose practical effects are not at all properly understood [59]. Additionally, slaves

187f. comments on the attractiveness of female slaves for breeding purposes visible in legal sources on sale, but doubts, on the basis of *Dig.* 5.3.27 pr., that breeding was 'the *main* function of women slaves' (her emphasis, p. 188). Complementary functions, however, do not require primacy of one over the other, and it is only to be expected that owners who did purchase slaves with their breeding potential in mind would have exercised due caution beforehand, as the text from the *Digest* suggests.

(55) Cf. STAERMAN-TROFIMOVA (1975), 17f. ; TREGGIARI (1979b), 187ff. ; HARRIS (1980), 120f. ; FINLEY (1980), 130. 'Breeding' of slaves is a difficult term to define because the conscious element on the slave-owner's part in it could obviously not be the same as in the breeding of livestock on the farm. This problem is reflected in Varro who certainly speaks of *fetura humana pastorum* (*RR.* 2.10.6) and who can recommend the most suitable kind of women for *pastores* (*RR.* 2.10.7), but who is unable to devote the same amount of space to the topic as with animals.

(56) See generally BIEZUNSKÁ-MAŁOWIST (1977), 116ff. ; cf. MONTEVECCHI (1973), 207ff.

(57) See above, p. 16.

(58) *P. Oxy.* 3197 (see introduction to the text by J. D. Thomas) ; cf. BIEZUNSKÁ-MAŁOWIST (1977), 96f., who believes the household may have included more than a hundred slaves ; BIEZUNSKÁ-MAŁOWIST (1976).

(59) See in general I. M. BIEZUNSKÁ-MAŁOWIST, *Les Esclaves en copropriété dans*

could be and were sold off by the new owner to pay the testator's debts or burial expenses, or a surviving wife might be allowed to control a minor's inheritance until the latter's coming of age [60]. Provisions such as these were again likely to have an impact on the lives of the property being handled.

The complications that arose from the death of a slave-owner, as well as the lack of certain knowledge of how transmitted slaves subsequently fared, can be demonstrated by reference to a number of specific documents. First, in a papyrus from the late third century [61] property and land are divided between the two families of a deceased man who had been married twice during his lifetime. Seven children had been born to the two wives, respectively two and five, among whom four slaves were now equally apportioned (i.e. fractionally) in the father's will. Thus the children of the first family, a brother and sister, received two-sevenths of the four slaves, the remainder going to the other five children, three of whom were minors. What the de facto arrangements the heirs made were is not at all clear, but they may have been less confused than the formal situation suggests. If in actuality the three minors were too young to have had effective supervision of their share of the property, the solution may have been that two slaves went to the children of the first marriage (even though they did not have full legal title), while the two other slaves went to the two older children (brothers) of the second marriage. Three of the slaves' names are recorded in the papyrus and they include those of a twenty-five year old woman and her ten year old daughter ; it may have happened that mother and daughter were kept together under the new arrangements, but little more than the bare possibility can be stated.

A second document tells of a father who again bequeathed four slaves, this time to three sons [62]. Three of these slaves were female and apparently still of an age to reproduce. The two older sons each received one slave, respectively a man and a woman, while the youngest son was given two slaves ; of these, however, one was lame and the use of the

---

l'Egypte gréco-romaine in *Aegyptus* 48 (1968), 116ff. On the tendency to divide property equally, HOPKINS (1980), 322.

(60) *P. Oxy.* 493 ; *P. Ryl.* 153. For the element of uncertainty which affected slaves note also *Instit.* 2.20.22, *Si generaliter seruus uel alia res legetur, electio legatarii est, nisi aliud testator dixerit.*

(61) *P. Oxy.* 1638.

(62) *P. Mich.* 323-325 + *PSI* 903 = A. S. HUNT, C. C. EDGAR, *Select Papyri* I, LCL, 1932, no. 51 (47).

other was reserved for the former owner's wife. No provision for joint ownership was made, and it is not known whether the sons already had their own independent households or still all resided together. In either case it is difficult to see how the three female slaves could have reproduced, as seems expected [63], unless access were available to men other than the one member of the original household.

Even more perplexing on the question of sexual balance, or imbalance, among slaves is that document already mentioned [64], which lists a large number of slaves from one household who were divided equally among three sons after their father's death. Some forty-five slaves are named in the papyrus, but it appears that some of these were effectively owned by the sons while their father was still alive. All the slaves allotted, however, were men, which led the editor of the text to estimate a possible total number of one hundred slaves for the full establishment since females must have been included, and the text is not complete. One son already had possession of a female slave and two others are mentioned in order to differentiate their homonymous sons (Alexander son of Anabasis and Alexander son of Gemella). Further, the text speaks of other slaves, not listed, remaining the common property of the heirs, which might mean females. A total of one hundred slaves, however, would be an exceptionally large sized household for Roman Egypt, as already seen, and it may perhaps be doubted that the number of women equalled that of the men. No ages of the slaves are provided, so how many of the named males were children (presumably some were) cannot be known. The division among the three brothers was supposed to take place by lot, but it is worth noticing that one of the heirs received three slave brothers, one of whom was called Gemellus and so just possibly the brother of the Gemella who had a son Alexander. Alexander, himself, however, went to a different heir.

A third example which deserves attention is a document from the mid first century which is rather unusual in view of the detailed information it gives concerning the distribution of a slave household on the owner's death [65]. The text is by no means free from ambiguity but it allows for a tentative interpretation at least. The circumstances were that eighteen

---

(63) The clause concerning anticipated future offspring from females (above n. 27) appears in this document.

(64) *P. Oxy.* 3197 ; see n. 58 above.

(65) *P. Mich.* 326 ; cf. BIEZUNSKÁ-MAŁOWIST (1977), 119f.

slaves were divided among six heirs, brothers and sisters [66], five of whom had belonged to the children's father, the remaining thirteen to their mother [67]. The paternally owned slaves are as follows : Agathous, Herakles, Euphrosynon, Epaphras and Leontas. Of these Agathous was the mother of Herakles and Euphrosynon who were thus brother and sister [68]. The list of maternally owned slaves runs thus : Herakleia, Narkissos the barber, Sarapas, Euphrosynon, Nike, Thermouthis, Serapous, Euphrosynos, Helene, Thaubas, Ganymas, Athene, and Narkissos the muleteer. The document is clear that Herakleia had a certain number of children, who seem to extend in the list from Narkissos the barber to, and including, Serapous, that is a total of six, although Serapous might have to be excluded [69]. In turn, however, Serapous is described as the mother of the following Euphrosynos who may consequently have been Herakleia's grandchild. Helene definitely did not belong to the family of Herakleia because her mother was a certain Herous who already had been sold away from the household, unless she was related by marriage. But a three-generational slave family may nonetheless be in evidence here, comprising a mother, her six children and a grandson. Among the remaining slaves Thaubas was the mother of Ganymas and Athene. So from the total of eighteen slaves three families are partially represented at least, though fathers and husbands cannot be safely identified from the text as it stands. The following chart shows how the full complement of slaves was allocated to the heirs according to the terms of the division.

P. Mich. 326

Herakleides the elder	Maron	Herodes
Herakles*	Leontas	Agathous*
Serapous† +	Herakleia†	Euphrosynon I*
Euphrosynos +	Ganymas Ø	Epaphras
	Narkissos the muleteer	

(66) Their names were Herakleides the elder, Maron, Herodes, Didymus, Herakleides the younger, Herakleia.

(67) Clearly, however, the document is concerned with a united household.

(68) P. Mich. 326 line 7.

(69) P. Mich. 326 lines 8-9. The text makes the exact number of Herakleia's children uncertain : Ἡράκλειαν τὴν καὶ Τααρμιῶσιν καὶ ταύτης τέκνα Νάρκισσον κουρέα καὶ Σαραπᾶν καὶ Εὐφρόσυνον καὶ Νίκην καὶ Θερμοῦθιν καὶ Σεραποῦν καὶ ταύτης τέκνα Εὐφρόσυνον καὶ Ἑλένην ἔγγονον Ἡροῦτος ἐκ τῆς προπεπραμένης ἔτι πάλαι. Some scholars assume a break before καὶ Σεραποῦν, to give Herakleia only five children ; Biezunská-Małowist (1977), 119 ; Harris (1980), 135 n. 39. But this cannot be certain and a reading with no break is preferred here.

Didymus	*Herakleides the younger*	*Herakleia*
Euphrosynon II†	Thaubas Ø	Narkissos the barber†
Thermouthis†	Athene Ø	Nike†
	Sarapas†	Helene

Sigla denote certain and possible familial connections

Although the ascription of family ties is to a large extent tentative, it seems from the allocations that Thaubas and her daughter were kept together, but that Thaubas' other child Ganymas was separated from her ; that Agathous was kept with her child Euphrosynon, but that her other child Herakles was also separated from the mother ; that Herakleia was separated from all her children, though among the latter siblings remained together on two occasions, while Serapous and Euphrosynos also stayed together. Only Sarapas and Herakleia were not put with another family member, and in the newly formed groups only one contains no obvious continuation of a family tie of some sort.

Unfortunately the document gives no information on the ages of these slaves. If indeed Herakleia was a grandmother she must by ancient standards have been quite elderly, and the two men named Narkissos might be presumed to be adults since specific occupations are assigned to them. Many of the females must have been adult or close to adulthood either because they had already given birth to children (Agathous, Thaubas, Serapous) or because future offspring from them was anticipated (Nike, Thermouthis, Helene, Athene) [70]. Since Serapous was of childbearing age her siblings may have been close to adulthood or even older. Under the terms of the division Serapous may conceivably have been 'paired' with Herakles, Agathous with Epaphras, Helene with Narkissos the barber, Thaubas' with Sarapas. But Athene, Thermouthis and Nike apparently had no access to men, unless the possibility of brother-sister couplings is brought into the picture [71].

Highly speculative as this reconstruction is, it may nonetheless give some slight indication that attention was given to the preservation of familial connections among slaves when they were divided up after their owners' deaths. Similarly, another document from the mid second century shows that of six slaves who were divided between two heirs (a

---

(70) Again the clause concerning future offspring is applied to these women (above n. 27).

(71) On which in general see HOPKINS (1980).

brother and sister), a woman was kept with her two children on one hand and a second woman apparently set free retained custody of her ten-month old twins (still slaves) on the other [72]. But the extent of this concern should not be exaggerated. In the last example the twins were to return to their new owner six months after weaning, so that the original failure to separate mother and children appears to have had a practical purpose behind it, while with a family as large as that of Herakleia appears to have been it was virtually inevitable that some family connections be maintained in the division. Moreover, Serapous and her child might also have been kept together for practical reasons. It cannot be known whether the divided families had access to each other once the new groups had been formed, or whether these groups came to constitute totally distinct entities. Nor can it be known whether the six heirs already owned slaves other than those they now received who might have served as possible wives and husbands for the new batches. At most, therefore, concern was limited, and from the cases which have been presented the general impression prevails that interest in the disposal of property as property prevailed over sentiment or sympathy for the emotional wellbeing of the slaves who composed it.

Although the provisions of documents of the kind considered so far were often intricate enough, further complications could set in if the provisions were subsequently overturned, and it is clear that on occasions certain heirs did act contrary to the directions given in wills. The result was further difficulty for the slave. A papyrus from the late third century [73], for example, reveals the inability of a young woman to secure title to her apparent share of bequeathed slaves who were being held by two of the woman's uncles. An appeal was addressed to the governor of Egypt, but the outcome, and the fate of the slaves, is unknown. Again in the third century a claim of false ownership of slaves was brought by a man against his great-uncle's heirs : two children had been born to a slave woman owned by the petitioner's mother (now dead) and had been fraudulently claimed by the great-uncle ; although the mother had resecured ownership while alive, the heirs of the great-uncle, once he died, had again claimed the slaves, which led to the present appeal for redress [74]. The struggle was obviously one for property and nothing else.

(72) *P. Strass.* 122.
(73) *P. Oxy.* 2713.
(74) *P. Oxy.* 1468.

Finally, the case can be noted of a similar struggle in the early second century between two brothers on one hand against a third party on the other : the brothers claimed ownership of a female slave by virtue of inheritance, but obviously did not have such ownership. Once more the issue was so involved that the strategus of the nome referred it to the governor ([75]).

Once the papyrological material from Roman Egypt is set aside, there is virtually no other documentary evidence from elsewhere to show slaves being bequeathed to new owners, an indication of the paucity of surviving sources. Yet again it cannot be imagined that the problems and complexities which have been seen in the Egyptian material were unique to one part of the Roman world. Roman legal sources make clear that slaves were property which could be left by will to new owners and the application of Roman law was not of course confined to Italy alone ([76]). The well known will of Dasumius, belonging to 108, seems to show the process in operation at Rome itself of slaves being willed to heirs, though details are obscure because of the highly fragmentary nature of the text ([77]). In literary sources, however, incidental remarks provide confirmation, such as Varro's statement that inheritance gave full legal ownership of slaves, Petronius' reference to a chef who had been left by will to Trimalchio (to Trimalchio's ignorance), or Apuleius' statement that Pudentilla had made over to her sons some four hundred slaves ([78]), remarks which are of interest because of their ordinary nature. And an inscription from Rome is suggestive of the emotional upheaval which might be presumed in the lives of slaves when owners' wishes affected their relationships : a woman named Furia Spes, apparently a freedwoman, made a dedication to her deceased husband, L. Sempronius Firmus, apparently a freedman, in which she recorded that wife and husband had loved each other since childhood, had married, but then after a short interval had been involuntarily separated 'by an evil hand' ([79]). When

---

(75) *P. Oxy.* 97.

(76) See BUCKLAND (1908), 15ff. ; cf. BOYER (1965), 357f. ; 366 ; 370f. ; 387 ; 400 ; TREGGIARI (1979a), 69ff. ; (1979b), 196ff. Servile *agnomina* also indicate transference of slave property ; cf. WEAVER (1972), 212ff.

(77) *FIRA²* III no. 48.

(78) VARRO, *RR.* 2.10.4 ; PETR. *Sat.* 47.11-13 ; APUL.. *Apol.* 93 ; cf. PLIN. *Epp.* 10.104-105, Pliny left as the patron of Junians.

(79) *ILS* 8006. The full circumstances of the couple are not clear, and *a manu mala diseparati sumus* may, however, mean separation by death.

property was left by one person to another with slaves on it, it may be that at times no changes occurred in the personal lives of the slaves concerned. But all in all the conclusion seems justified that the death of a slave-owner must have been a difficult time indeed for his slaves because the world which they had created for themselves was threatened with possible extinction ([80]). Anxiety about or fear of severance can never have been far from the minds of those slaves who had been able successfully to form family units.

The possibility of disruption following sale or bequest was a pressure to which all slave families were exposed. A further circumstance and constraint can now be outlined which must have had a more restricted application, but which was nonetheless important for those affected by it and which continues the theme of economic exploitation overpowering emotional concern. The evidence again in the first instance comes from papyri.

In contracts for the hire of wet-nurses, several of which still remain ([81]), the stipulation is commonly found that the nurse was not to sleep with a man or become pregnant during the period covered by the contract, an interval which ranged from a minimum of six months to a maximum of three years, with two years being that most frequently found ([82]). The

---

(80) It must be remembered here that slaves could be set free in their owners' wills (see below, pp. 97ff.), though manumission was not universal in this situation. Also, there should be no inference that all slave-owners all of the time were universally indifferent to their slaves' situations ; this cannot have been the case. But in light of what is detectable from the documentary papyri on sales and bequests the statement that the 'creation of a slave family... could not be ignored by masters with any degree of feeling' (WEAVER (1972), 191) may be considered questionable.

(81) Examples are collected in BRADLEY (1980), 321ff., from which the following remarks are derived and in which other secondary references are available ; cf. additionally BIEZUNSKÁ-MAŁOWIST (1977), 24ff. ; 104f. ; and for a new document see S. M. E. VAN LITH, Lease of Sheep and Goats. Nursing Contract with Accompanying Receipt in ZPE 14 (1974), 145ff.

(82) 'So long as she is duly paid she shall take proper care both of herself and of the child, not injuring her milk nor sleeping with a man nor becoming pregnant' ; BGU 1107, translated by A. S. HUNT, C. C. EDGAR, Select Papyri I, LCL, 1932 no. 16. See also BGU 1058 ; 1106 ; 1108 ; 1109 ; SB 7607 ; 7619, P. Bour. 14 ; P. Ross.-Georg. II 18 ; XVI ; LXXIV ; ZPE 14 (1974), 148. The following periods are specified as indicated : six months, P. Meyer 11 ; eight months, BGU 1110 ; ten months, BGU 1109 ; twelve months, BGU 1112 ; fifteen months, BGU 1108 ; sixteen months, BGU 1107 ; eighteen months, BGU 1106 ; two years, BGU 297 ; 1058 ; SB 7619 ; PSI 203 ; 1065 ; P. Bour. 14 ; P. Oxy. 37 and 38 ; 91 ; P. Ross.-Georg. II 18 ; LXXIV ; ZPE 14 (1974), 148ff. ; two years, six months, SB 7607 ; three years, P. Tebt. 399.

reason for this provision was a concern to protect the nurse's supply of milk for the nursling [83], a view supported by Soranus' recommendation of sexual abstinence for wet-nurses on both physical and emotional grounds :

> For coitus cools the affection toward < the > nursling by the diversion of sexual pleasure and moreover spoils and diminishes the milk or suppresses it entirely by stimulating menstrual catharsis through the uterus or by bringing about conception [84].

Under these conditions a great degree of self-control seems to have been required in the private lives of wet-nurses, even for the minimum contractual period known. Wet-nurses could be free or slave women, but distinctions of status did not affect the obligation to sexual abstinence to which they were bound [85]. Some of the attested free nurses were married [86], and the implication follows that while nursing normal marital arrangements had to be discontinued. While slave nurses could not of course have had legal marriages, it seems reasonable to imagine that for them too some personal relationships may well have been affected once a contract was entered upon, whether with a slave or free partner [87], since a wet-nurse must have given birth herself in order to fulfill her function. Quite obviously the degree to which such interruptions were experienced depended upon the extent to which the provision was maintained, a factor which cannot be measured. But the nursing contracts contained stringent penalty clauses against breach and in the case of slave nurses their owners were required to return any sums of money received for nursing services and to pay an additional fine as well [88]. The owners were concerned above all to exploit the potential of a labour force at their disposal and producing income lay behind the agreements that were made. This could give reason consequently for

---

(83) See for example *SB* 7619 : καὶ [μὴ] ἀνδροχοιτεῖν πρὸς τὸ μὴ διαφθαρῆναι [τὸ γάλα ...

(84) SORANUS, *Gynaecology* 2.19, translated by O. TEMKIN, *Soranus' Gynecology*, Baltimore, 1956.

(85) Slave nurses appear in *BGU* 1058 ; 1109 ; 1111 ; 1112 ; *PSI* 1065 ; *P. Oxy.* 91 ; *P. Tebt.* 399.

(86) See *BGU* 297 ; 1106 ; 1110 ; *SB* 7607 ; 7619 ; *PSI* 203 ; 1131 ; *P. Meyer* 11 ; *P. Ross.-Georg.* II 18 ; LXXIV ; *ZPE* 14 (1974), 149f. ; where the nurse's husband appears as *kyrios* in the contracts.

(87) For relationships between slave women and free men see BIEZUNSKA-MAŁOWIST (1969) ; (1977), 115f.

(88) See for example *BGU* 1107 ; 1109.

believing that in general the provisions of the contracts were not usually disregarded because the financial losses to be incurred were too great a liability and the nurses may also have feared punishment from their owners.

Broad assertions about private behaviour, however, are perhaps best avoided when they cannot be corroborated, especially since the relevant documents extend over a large span of time which may have provoked varying forms of response [89]. The possibilities, however, can be simply stated : the provision against sexual activity was either observed by slave wet-nurses or it was not. If it was, it follows that sexual continence formed a staple element in the life of the nurse and that at any moment in time a certain number of slave women were obliged to make some alteration in the normal marital situation which could be inferred, in some instances at least, from the birth of their own children. If it was not, then the danger of an unwanted pregnancy must have led to the use of some kind of birth control [90]. In either case a not inconsiderable burden was imposed on the slave women and their male partners. Moreover, because it was the decision of the nurse's owner, not of the nurse herself, which led to the restrictions suggested there was no element of choice for the woman involved here but rather one of compulsion. In consequence the nursing contracts, as far as slave wet-nurses are concerned, seem to provide some illustration of how in antiquity the owner's absolute authority extended into the most intimate areas of his slaves' lives and behaviour [91]. The economic basis of the employment of slave nurses, which has to do with the owner's development of resources at his disposal more than with anything else, led to the overriding of concern for the finer feelings of the nurses who were hired out.

Moreover, wet-nursing was probably a widespread occupation for women of low social status throughout the Roman world. Literary sources again suggest this, while for Rome itself a certain amount of epigraphic material is available to show nursing of infants of all social levels [92]. Further, if it is true to believe that the *columna lactaria* in the

(89) The nursing papyri, which include receipts for services as well as contracts for employment of nurses, extend from 15 B.C. (*BGU* 1111) to A.D. 305 (*P. Grenf.* 75).

(90) See further Bradley (1980), 323f.

(91) On the sexual abuse of slaves see further below, pp. 117f.

(92) Cf. Dio Chrys. *Orat.* 7.14 ; Gell. *NA* 12.1 ; Tac. *Dial.* 28-29 ; for the epigraphic evidence see Treggiari (1976), 88f.

Forum Holitorium was so-called because infants were commonly brought there to be nursed [93], another indication of the common nature of the job emerges. It is plausible to believe, therefore, that the compulsive effect argued from the Egyptian evidence was experienced on a broad scale.

Up to this point certain factors which threatened interference in servile familial life have been illustrated from the relatively detailed evidence provided by Egyptian papyri and the probability of their application elsewhere, at least in principle, has been stated. The estimate of slaves' prospects for successful family life can next be taken further by considering in conjunction, and on a wider geographical scale, information on the nature of the households to which slaves belonged and on the balance of male to female slaves in different locations. One of the points to emerge from the Egyptian documents is that it is seldom apparent where slaves found partners who might become their husbands or wives since slave holdings were small and the availability of partners must often have been consequently restricted [94]. A certain proportion of slave infants must always, without doubt, have been the product of casual relationships, voluntary or otherwise, between female slaves and the free members of their owners' households, relationships which can in general only have been an impediment to slave familial stability [95]. But the question of access by slaves of one sex to another requires further comment.

In the great aristocratic households of Rome itself, where slaves numbered in the hundreds, women's availability to men was probably higher than in the rural areas of Italy, a circumstance likely to have been true for the urban-rural division in the Roman world at large and one which marks in part the generally favoured status of urban slaves. Even at Rome, however, male slaves appear to have preponderated over females : an investigation of the burial sites of three aristocratic households from the early imperial age has revealed a ratio of two male slaves to every

---

(93) FESTUS, De uerb. signif., p. 118 Lindsay ; cf. PLATNER, ASHBY (1929), s.v.

(94) In Egypt it is difficult to identify slave fathers ; see P. Brux. E 7360 and P. Ryl. 178, two examples where slave men had free wives. Paternity of infant slaves did not of course have to be officially recorded, a fact which indicates an attitude of general relevance : an owner was under no constraint, legal or otherwise, to recognise the existence of a slave family. But it does not follow that 'fatherless' slave children were always the product of casual sexual relationships, as perhaps implied for an earlier period by P. M. FRASER, Ptolemaic Alexandria, Oxford, 1972, I p. 85.

(95) See above, n. 87.

female, though the imbalance may not have been representative of conditions in the city, or other cities, as a whole ; although many infant females were kept and raised for later work in the domestic entourages of their owners, others were exposed, either to be left to die or to be claimed by whoever might want them, because it was uneconomic to have excessive numbers of young females in the household [96]. Nonetheless female slaves there certainly were, since the private retinues of Roman grandees required substantial numbers of both men and women to perform the needed highly specialised services and to add to the lustre of the magnate [97]. Slave women were also involved to some extent in the commercial life of Rome [98]. The result may well have been that there was a certain competition among male slaves for the number of potential wives available when marriage was being contemplated, a factor which may, on the male side, have sharpened the value of a successfully achieved union. Furthermore, the relative shortage of female slaves may offer one reason why such women were very young, by modern standards, when they married, their husbands usually being much older than themselves [99]. However that may be, men and women were able in their selection of a partner to benefit both from the huge size of urban households and from the proximity of such households to one another. It has been shown that slaves tended to marry from the same household [100] and the reasons for this pattern are not hard to find : the slaves enjoyed a greater chance of spending time together than if they were from separate households, while sanction of marriage from the owner could be expected since he would benefit materially from any offspring the slaves might produce (whether it was kept or sold). Yet to a lesser degree marriages between slaves of separate households are attested [101], and that fact presupposes a certain willingness on the part of owners to cater to servile interests.

(96) TREGGIARI (1975b), 395. See also Appendix C for earlier information.

(97) Cf. DION. HAL. 4.24. On services in the grand *familiae* see TREGGIARI (1973) ; (1975a) ; (1976), 76ff.

(98) Susan TREGGIARI, *Lower Class Women in the Roman Economy* in *Florilegium* 1 (1979), 65ff.

(99) On the age at which females married see HOPKINS (1965) ; WEAVER (1972), 184 ; 186.

(100) WEAVER (1972), 192 ; cf. also FLORY (1978). Some male slaves owned their female slaves, *uicariae*, regarded presumably as wives on occasion ; see for example *ILS* 7981a ; 7981b.

(101) WEAVER (1972), 191 ; TREGGIARI (1975b), 398.

Accurate proportions cannot be given, but it is probably true to believe that male slaves engaged in farm work of one kind and another far outnumbered those found in the cities [102]. And little is heard of female slaves in the rural sector : in the works of the agricultural writers, for example, they scarcely appear at all, with the exception of the *uilica*. But this silence should not be taken to signify a total absence of slave women from rural society, a point which requires emphasis [103], because in spite of the absence of prolific epigraphical testimony characteristic of Rome and other cities there are indications that opportunities for servile family life in the country were far from hopeless. For a period as early as the late second century B.C. there is evidence that slaves who had been imported to Italy from overseas to meet labour demands in Italian agriculture had reproduced in sufficient numbers so as to become a cause of public alarm [104]. There is no reason to doubt this information, which strongly implies the availability to slave men of women since the status of a child followed that of the mother [105]. Indeed, legal sources point towards the presence of women on farms, and it is significant that a catalogue of traditional occupations for slave women given by Plautus includes shepherding [106]. Nearer the beginning of the imperial age Virgil tells a tale of an Italian *pastor* who, late in life, exchanged a spendthrift female companion, seemingly of long-standing, for one more frugal, a story told without any sign that the relationships mentioned were extraordinary [107]. In Petronius' *Satyricon*, the realistic substratum of which is certain, Trimalchio receives news of servile births on his estates at Cumae ; the married couple on Juvenal's farm outside Rome has already been mentioned, and a passage in the *Digest* indicates availability of slave

(102) The majority of the population in antiquity was always occupied in agriculture ; cf. VEYNE (1961), 228 ; HOPKINS (1967), 166f.

(103) It has been claimed that the 'Roman writers of treatises on agriculture imply that in the period of expansion agricultural slaves were usually male and celibate' ; HOPKINS (1978), 106 (see also HOPKINS (1967), 170 ; 171 : 'on plantations, certainly, male slaves were kept apart, without families'). This view seems to minimise the texts from Varro and Columella referred to at the beginning of the chapter and is to be questioned. Contrast MARTIN (1974), 290, 'La procréation des esclaves ruraux était loin d'être un phénomène négligeable'.

(104) APP. *BC* 1.7, though this does not mean of course that breeding fully met labour requirements ; cf. HARRIS (1979), 84.

(105) BUCKLAND (1908), 397f.

(106) See BRUNT (1971), 144 n. 1 ; 707, citing *Dig.* 33.7.12.5 especially, and TREGGIARI (1979b), 196ff. on *fundus cum instrumento* ; PLAUT. *Merc.* 509.

(107) VIRG. *Ecl.* 1.27-32.

women on estates in Africa ([108]). Moreover, there are some inscriptions which record slave marriages and families in rural contexts : a male slave described as an *actor et agricola* who died at the age of forty was commemorated by his surviving slave wife on a stone from Velitrae, while an inscription from Gaul referring to a husband, wife and son who were all slaves commemorates the husband and father, dead at forty-one, a man who had also been a rural *actor* ([109]). Finally, there is some evidence of slave child labour in the country, young people who might reasonably be assumed to have been born there, especially in view of Varro's statement that births increased the farm owner's estate ([110]).

In any case the silence of Varro and Columella on slave women is not total, as already seen, and is explicable : it can be attributed to the fact that the labour skills of women were not suited to the farm work with which the agricultural writers were principally concerned ; the domestic and commercial skills provided by slave women in cities were not required to the same degree in the country. All the same there will have been a need for clothes-making, cooking, cleaning, tending children and so on, occupations strictly outside of the interests of Varro and Columella, but when the context is appropriate remarks are forthcoming ([111]). Moreover, in order to explain the preponderance of male over female slaves in Rome, the attractive suggestion has been made that girls were deliberately taken away from the urban households in which they were born and put on farms precisely for the purposes of domestic work and subsequent childbearing ([112]). Altogether, therefore, there is no cause for believing that slave marriages and families did not exist in rural situations ([113]), only for believing that female availability as wives for men was far more limited

(108) Petr. *Sat.* 53.2 ; Iuv. 11.146ff. ; *Dig.* 33.7.27.1 ; cf. Gsell (1932), 401, and see also Mart. *Epig.* 12.18 (Bilbilis) ; Tibullus 2.1.23, *turbaque uernarum, saturi bona signa coloni.*

(109) *ILS* 7451 ; 7452.

(110) See above n. 37 for Varro, and note particularly *RR*. 2.1.26, cited in n. 16 ; cf. Brunt (1958), 166.

(111) Varro, *RR*. 2.10.7 on the best kind of women to have for the mates of the *pastores*. Col. *RR*. 12.3.6 has been taken to suggest the common presence of women on farms (e.g. Martin (1974), 290) but this text is arguable ; (cf. also Col. *RR*. 8.2.7).

(112) Treggiari (1975b), 400 ; (1979b), 189f. This view becomes even more useful if it is true to believe that deaths resulting from female infant exposure were minimal ; cf. above n. 35. Moreover, country life was good for human reproduction, according to Apul. *Apol.* 88.

(113) Contrast Finley (1976), 820 ; Harris (1980), 119f.

than in cities and that the feasibility of achieving marriage and producing children was consequently more difficult. Not that all male agricultural labourers were themselves suitable for the concession of family life : those dangerous or uncompliant enough to warrant being housed in the *ergastula* can presumably have had little expectation of normal family life. In turn, the exclusion or deprivation of some may once more have increased the value of marriage and children to those fortunate enough to have had them.

The lowest expectations of family life were faced by male slaves who worked in the mining districts of the Empire. The work itself, gruelling and dangerous, allowed for no female presence in the labour force ; the turn-over of male labourers seems to have been rapid due to a high mortality rate [114] ; and the criminal penalty of condemnation to the mines was not applied to women [115]. None of these conditions favoured the formation of family units, let alone maintenance of stability within them. It would perhaps be too sweeping to claim that the slave family did not exist at all among mining slaves. Diodorus Siculus' description of the gold mines in Egypt contains references to women and children, and the charter of Vipasca, a mining community in Spain formally organised in the reign of Hadrian, has a provision for the use by women of the public baths [116]. But Diodorus is describing Egypt before its annexation by Rome and the women referred to in the charter of Vipasca are more likely to have been the free residents of the community than slaves. On balance the family will have been a rare phenomenon among slaves who worked in mines.

A factor which worked in favour of servile familial stability was manumission, the acquisition of freedom by slaves, which brought among other things release from anxieties about separation from family members [117]. From inscriptional evidence it is possible to see various stages of the securing of freedom by family units which had come into being after two people had married while slaves, but which had been affected by the death of one of the principals. A male slave may have been set free by his owner, for instance, and have subsequently gained his

---

(114) See O. DAVIES, *Roman Mines in Europe*, Oxford, 1935, 14ff.

(115) On *metallum* see in general GARNSEY (1970), 131ff.

(116) DIOD. SIC. 3.12.2-13.2 ; *ILS* 6891.

(117) Since manumission is the subject of Chapter III the remarks here are restricted to the relationship between family life and freedom.

wife's freedom so that he became her patron. The pattern is illustrated by the example of a slave named Heracla who took his former master's praenomen and nomen upon manumission to become L. Volusius Heracla ; his wife Prima later took her husband's nomen, becoming Volusia Prima, and on Heracla's death she made a dedication to her *coniunx* and *patronus* ([118]). The children of parents such as these might themselves have also been set free, as seems to have happened with a brother and sister named Cn. Racilius Fructuosus and Racilia Fructuosa, whose mother, Racilia Eutychia, also set up a memorial to her deceased *patronus* and *coniunx*, Cn. Racilius Telesphorus ([119]). In instances of this sort both children and parents had escaped the dangers of familial severance and emotional disruption. But not all were so fortunate. Of the family of L. Volusius Hamillus, clearly a freedman, his wife Ianuaria and son Hamillus were still slaves apparently (to judge from the single names) when their husband and father died ([120]), and their future together will still have been theoretically uncertain. All kinds of permutations were possible. A generous owner might have liberated a married couple simultaneously ; a slave woman might have been set free before her husband, or have become her freed husband's patron, or the patron of her children ([121]). It is well understood that masters were agreeable to setting slave women free before the formally required age in order for them to marry ([122]), yet at the same time it remains true that the majority of slaves in the Roman slavery system never achieved manumission at all ([123]).

The evidence of the inscriptions thus illustrates the movement of slave families along a sliding scale, as it were, from totally servile status for the whole group to totally free status. The important point, however, is that any progress along the scale depended on the willingness of the owner to liberate one or several family members, a variable which was always beyond absolute prediction. Slave family members were set free and

---

(118) *ILS* 7413.

(119) *ILS* 8219. It is possible that the children had been born after the manumission of the parents which would automatically have made them freeborn. In this instance the couple had been married for more than twenty-one years, and the son, who died before his father, had not survived to the age of eleven.

(120) *ILS* 7405.

(121) E.g. *ILS* 8162 ; 8259 ; 8388.

(122) Weaver (1972), 186 ; Harris (1980), 120.

(123) Hopkins (1978), 118 ; 139. Examples of no family members achieving freedom at the time principals were commemorated appear in *ILS* 7404 ; 7423 ; 7430.

families could reach a level of stability ; but when two slaves first married they had no way of assuring or controlling their future family life. The advantages which manumission brought the slave family were constantly the prerogative of the master, and that knowledge must again have always formed another aspect of the slave mentality and consciousness which in turn modified the behaviour of the slaves themselves [124].

The encouragement of slave family life by owners and their willingness to separate the members of slave families when necessary form two opposing but not mutually inconsistent tendencies. Given the complexity of the Roman slavery system, indeed, it would be surprising if historical analysis of it could be reduced to neat and fully congruent lines. Slaves in the Roman world attached as much importance to family life as other sections of society and they desired if possible to create and maintain their own family units. In many cases this was achieved, both across time and space, but always through the agency of their owners, who understood directly the principle that allowing the formation of slave families contributed to the achievement of contentment and hence acquiescence among their slaves. Stability in slave families, however, was shaped, and to some extent undermined, by factors arising from the mechanics of the slave-owning system, which constantly exposed slaves to the danger of familial disruption because of their disposable nature as a form of property. Owners exhibited no reluctance or qualms about causing separation when occasion demanded because the purpose of the slave family had been served up to the time of disposal and separation, while for the new owners of transferred property other avenues of manipulation were available [125].

The value slaves attached to family ties was high, and owners were able to exploit to their advantage the element of uncertainty in slave life which was produced by the inevitable transference of slaves in normal social and economic circumstances. Opportunities for marriage and family life were far from equal among slaves but depended in part on their location within

(124) If the manumission of one partner in a slave marriage entailed departure from the household, then freedom would have had a negative impact on his family life ; this must have happened sometimes (cf. Treggiari (1969), 209) but as always its precise extent is difficult to evaluate.

(125) It may be true that 'The legal attitude to slave families became gradually more humane under the empire' ; Treggiari (1979b), 196. But this view seems to me to be overly generous ; in any case, the opinions of jurists are not necessarily an accurate index of historical reality.

the range of servile statuses, in part on the type of household to which
they belonged, in part on the availability of marriage partners, in part on
owners' readiness to manumit. Those factors in themselves perpetuated
divisions among the slave population at large and thus served the interest
of maintaining the social status quo. All in all the family life of slaves
fortunate enough to enjoy it was always precarious until the complete
family had acquired emancipation, and indirectly it was in this element of
precariousness that owners' psychological control over their property was
able to make itself felt most forcefully. The response of slaves to this
reality, it might be imagined, was to demonstrate attitudes of acquiescence
and passivity in order to protect and preserve as far as possible the familial
associations they were able to bring into existence.

CHAPTER III

MANUMISSION

Manumission was always a distinctive feature of the Roman slavery system and has a history that stretches back well before the imperial period ([1]). Roman masters were indeed relatively liberal in the extent to which they conferred freedom on their slaves, and at any moment innumerable ex-slaves throughout the Roman world demonstrated by their mere existence that slavery was not of necessity a permanent state but one from which release was possible. The freedmen and freedwomen of Roman society provided for those still in slavery an example to follow and emulate.

It should be noted immediately, however, that when slaves were set free they did not in consequence find themselves absolved of all responsibilities towards their former owners, now patrons. Instead, as a condition of release from servile status the freedman might find himself bound to his patron by a nexus of obligations, summed up in the legal term *operae*, as a result of which he continued to discharge various services for the patron for a certain length of time ([2]). This device was convenient to both parties, because it meant that the social status of the slave could improve dramatically but without the automatic accompaniment of economic loss to the owner who still benefited from the freedman's efforts on his behalf. To some degree the system of *operae* explains the prevalence of manumission in Roman society as a whole ([3]).

In spite of these restrictions it is absolutely clear that slaves coveted freedom and were anxious to become whenever possible part of the great mass of ex-slaves. The advantages were obvious : in theory at least all subjection to the whim of the slave-owner disappeared, the acquisition of

---

(1) Cf. DION. HAL. 4.24.1-4 and see in general WATSON (1971), 43ff. ; (1975), 86ff.

(2) For *operae* see DUFF (1958), 44ff. ; TREGGIARI (1969), 75ff.

(3) For a recent account of Roman manumission practices see HOPKINS (1978), 115ff., which may not, however, be compelling in all respects ; cf. K. R. BRADLEY, *CP* 76 (1981), 82ff.

Roman citizenship brought political and legal rights, descendants had
before them the prospect of upward social mobility. In reality the ex-slave
forfeited upon manumission the economic support of his former master
and henceforward had to rely on his own efforts in order to provide basic
necessities ; it was possible, therefore, that hardship in the former slave's
life could replace a certain material security, as shown by the following
passage from the philosopher Epictetus, himself an ex-slave :

> Then he (the slave) is emancipated, and forthwith, having no place to which
> to go and eat, he looks for someone to flatter, for someone at whose house
> to dine. Next he either earns a living by prostitution, and so endures the
> most dreadful things, and if he gets a manger at which to eat he has fallen
> into a slavery much more severe than the first ; or even if he grows rich,
> being a vulgarian he has fallen in love with a chit of a girl, and is miserable,
> and laments, and yearns for his slavery again. "Why, what was wrong with
> me ? Someone else kept me in clothes, and shoes, and supplied me with
> food, and nursed me when I was sick ; I served him in only a few matters.
> But now, miserable man that I am, what suffering is mine, who am a slave
> to several instead of one !" (Epict. *Diss.* 4.1.35-37, Loeb translation).

But as far as can be told slaves seem in general not to have been
deterred by this possibility, which must often have been realised, from
seizing the new status once it was within their grasp. Indeed inscriptions
from slaves who had successfully escaped their original servile condition
illustrate the importance they attached to the acquisition of freedom.
There is a certain pride visible, for instance, in dedications recording the
discharge by free men of vows undertaken as slaves, in dedications 'on
behalf of freedom', and in a plain but emotive expression of the type 'C.
Ducenius Phoebus, freedman of Gaius, son of Zeno, was born at Nisibis
in Syria and became a free man at Rome' [4].

Since no precise statistics on the total population of the Roman world
and on the servile proportion of it exist, the extent of manumission in
different times or places cannot be measured ; obviously, however,
variations should be expected depending, as far as numbers are
concerned, on the relative incidence of slave-owning throughout the

---

(4) *ILS* 3427 ; 3491 (cf. 3819) ; 3526, *ob libertatem* ; 3944, *C. Ducenius C. lib. Phoebus,
filius Zenonis, natus in Suria Nisibyn, liber factus Romae* ; cf. also *CIL* 6.663, a prayer to
Silvanus, *ob libertatem*. For evidence from an early date that slaves aspired towards
freedom see PLAUT. *Amph.* 462 ; *Aul.* 817 ; 824 ; *Capt.* 119f. See also PHAEDR. *Fab.* II 5 for
servile degradation encouraged by the hope of manumission.

empire ([5]). Yet the motives which led masters to confer freedom on slaves seem to have remained consistent over time and place : owners were concerned to attract the esteem of their peers through acts of apparent kindliness, to act generously for its own sake (not to be minimised), or else to reward slaves in return for meritorious service and the personal demonstration of loyalty and obedience over the years ([6]). Again these are factors which contribute to understanding why so many slaves in the Roman world were set free, but it is with the notion of freedom as an incentive and reward in the life of the slave that attention here is concerned, a notion illustrated in Columella's statement, quoted earlier, that he had rewarded with freedom a slave woman who had borne at least four sons for her owner ([7]). Not only had the woman added to the number of slaves in Columella's overall possession, but during the years in which her children were being produced she must also have demonstrated little opposition to her servile status. After her reward, it is easy to see how her life can have operated as a prototype for her fellow-slaves − acquiescence to the will of the owner would bring similar compensation in time, or so it could be hoped.

Columella was not of course the only slave-owner to appreciate the value of emancipation, or its prospect, as an incentive towards or reward for compliant behaviour in slaves. The principle was understood throughout society and from an early date : the understanding that freedom could be used both to bribe and repay slaves is apparent first in Plautus and then all manner of literary sources ([8]). But the fact remains that in spite of Rome's liberal practices most of the servile population probably never achieved freedom at all ([9]). Thus the conditions under which slaves might anticipate freedom and the circumstances under which freedom actually proved to be forthcoming need to be delineated so that their connection with the maintenance of stability in Roman society

(5) See ALFÖLDY (1972), 110ff. Even the exhaustive study of manumission practices at Delphi in the last two centuries B.C. given by HOPKINS (1978), 133ff. does not permit knowledge of absolute numbers. For regional variations in slave-owning see above, pp. 16f.

(6) See in general Treggiari (1969), 11ff. Emphasis must again be laid on the point that acts of generosity by owners were exceptional not the rule ; cf. FINLEY (1980), 122, and HOPKINS (1978), 117 : 'Roman society was not marked by altruism'.

(7) COL. *RR*. 1.8.19 (see above, p. 51), itself no evidence of disinterested generosity.

(8) E.g. PLAUT. *Cas*. 283f. ; 291ff. ; *Merc*. 152 ; *Poen*. 134 ; SEN. *Ben*. 3.23.2-4 ; *Dig*. 40.2.9.

(9) HOPKINS (1978), 118 ; 139.

can be better understood. Freedom was the greatest reward a slave could be given, and the factors which governed its acquisition are of cardinal importance for comprehension of the master-slave relationship.

Manumission was controlled by law, and at the very beginning of the imperial period Augustus was responsible for the passage of new regulations which are germane to the subject at hand. In turn, Augustus' legislation formed a response to circumstances under which slaves had been set free in the late Republic, so something of that background must be described before the law itself is examined. As noted above, the Roman tradition of freeing slaves was very old, but in the last century or so of the Republic that tradition had been ruthlessly exploited by aspirants to political power : the revolutionary period had created a climate in which slaves in Rome and Italy could be and were offered their freedom, randomly and opportunistically, by men immersed in war and politics who needed all possible support to further their public ambitions. While it would be superfluous to list all the relevant examples, from the tribunate of Gaius Gracchus until the battle of Actium, a few may be mentioned to show the tendency at work by which slaves were offered freedom at moments of crisis and upheaval in return for their political or physical support ([10]). Thus, Gaius Gracchus and his associate C. Fulvius Flaccus are said to have made an offer to slaves at Rome in the tumult which preceded their own deaths ; in 89 B.C. the senate en bloc offered freedom as a reward to any slaves who would bring information to light on the assassination at Rome of the praetor A. Sempronius Asellio ; at the battle of the Colline Gate slaves were offered freedom for their support of the Marians against Sulla, who himself was later said to have liberated ten thousand men to serve as his own personal bodyguard ; and L. Cornelius Cinna twice offered slaves their freedom at times of civil commotion ([11]). In a later era Sex. Pompeius used the offer of freedom for slaves' help against their masters in Africa ; the members of the second triumvirate offered the rewards of freedom and cash to slave informants ; and

(10) For the background see H. KÜHNE, *Zur Teilnahme von Sklaven und Freigelassenen an den Bürgerkriegen der Freien in I. Jahrhundert v.u. Z. im Rom* in *StudClas* 4 (1962), 189ff. ; cf. WESTERMANN (1955), 66f. The significance of offers of freedom is highlighted by the contrast with economic pressures which could be applied to tenant-farmers, but which could not be used with slaves ; cf. M. I. FINLEY, *Private Farm Tenancy in Italy before Diocletian* in M. I. Finley, ed., *Studies in Roman Property*, Cambridge, 1976, 103ff. at pp. 115f.

(11) APP. *BC* 1.26 ; 54 ; 58 ; 65 ; 69 ; 74 ; 100.

Octavian was said to have liberated some twenty thousand slaves to serve as rowers in the campaign against Pompeius, claiming himself in the *Res Gestae* to have restored to their owners thirty thousand slaves who had absconded to fight in the late civil wars on the promise of manumission [12].

It is possible that in the often confused political and military circumstances of the late Republic slaves took the opportunity to liberate themselves without direct provocation from the ruling elite, for at the time of the Catilinarian conspiracy it is likely that slaves outside Rome who were not actively recruited for rebellion used the occasion of civil unrest to make themselves free [13]. However that may be, it is very clear that these offers of freedom, of which there were many more than those mentioned, acted as powerful motivating forces, and they offer strong evidence of slave-owners' awareness of the importance of freedom in the servile mentality. The offers were not always taken up by the slaves [14] : over successive generations slaves periodically showed themselves not altogether devoid of political acumen by realising that promises of freedom could not always be guaranteed. But the final result was that the frequency with which the offers were made destroyed whatever balance there might otherwise have been between masters and slaves as far as manumission was concerned and confusion was substituted for it : there was no stable basis on which slaves could put their expectations and the impact on slave psychology must have been severe. Despite Cicero's famous remark that slaves might expect to be manumitted after seven years of enslavement, there are no grounds for believing the statement to be generally valid [15].

At the close of the Republic then, there was a long history of strained relations between masters and slaves, the outcome of the formers' abuse of manumission for self-interested reasons, of which, it should be observed, Augustus himself had firsthand experience. This situation was aggravated further in the period of Caesar's ascendancy through the early years of Augustus' principate by new accretions to the servile population

---

(12) App. *BC* 4.7 ; 11 ; 36 ; 95 ; 131 (cf. 73 ; 81) ; Suet. *Aug.* 16.1 ; Caes. *BC* 1.57 ; Dio 41.38.3 ; *RG* 25.1 ; Oros. 5.12.6.

(13) See K. R. Bradley, *Slaves and the Conspiracy of Catiline* in *CP* 73 (1978), 329ff.

(14) E.g., App. *BC* 1.26 ; 54 ; 58 ; 65.

(15) Cic. *Phil.* 8.11 ; the text contrasts strongly with other evidence (see below, pp. 110f.), and Cicero's description of the slaves needs to be noted, *captiui serui frugi et diligentes*, as another illustration of the expectation of servile acquiescence. Cf. Weaver (1972), 97.

which followed from the military campaigns Rome waged abroad on a vigorous scale and which produced great numbers of captives. During the campaigns in Gaul Caesar took phenomenal numbers of prisoners, over four hundred thousand according to one source [16]. In 25 B.C. forty-four thousand members of the Alpine Salassi are said to have been sold into slavery for a minimum period of twenty years ; in 22 B.C. members of the Cantabri and Astures in Spain were enslaved ; in 12 B.C. the future emperor Tiberius reduced a revolt in Pannonia and sold the men of military age into slavery ; in 11 B.C. members of the Thracian Bessi were also enslaved [17]. The subsequent history of all of these people is not certain, and it should not be automatically assumed that all were imported to Rome and Italy [18]. But there is a strong likelihood that many were : Dio is specific that the Pannonians enslaved by Tiberius were to be deported from their country and Suetonius reports that under Augustus enslaved captives were to remain in servitude for at least thirty years and were not allowed to stay in any country near their own [19]. The contemporary witness Strabo himself saw British captives in Rome [20].

These new acquisitions of relatively unsophisticated slaves from predominantly western and Danubian sources can have done little to improve the insecure relations between masters and slaves in the last decades of the first century B.C. With the gradual establishment of the Augustan peace, however, the uncertain political conditions of the late Republic receded, allowing thereby for the prospect of a new stability between slaves and their owners and in particular for the creation of fixed standards for the award of freedom to slaves. It is in this context that Augustus' legislation on slaves should be seen, and some attention can now be given to this aspect of Augustus' achievement, which represented an effort to establish an official, public set of standards for the granting of

---

(16) VELL. PAT. 2.47.1 ; cf. PLUT. *Caes*. 15.5 ; APP. *Celt*. 1.2 ; cf. VOLKMANN (1961), 51f.

(17) STRABO 4.6.7 ; DIO 53.25.4 ; 54.5.2 ; 31.3 ; 34.7 ; cf. VOLKMANN (1961), 34 ; 50. Enslavement in the East under Augustus was minimal ; see WESTERMANN (1955), 84.

(18) At later times war captives were sometimes sent to work in mines outside Italy ; for example, Jewish prisoners were sent to Egypt after the war against Rome that began in Nero's reign (Jos. *BJ* 6.418) and captives from Trajan's campaigns in Dacia may have been sent to mines in Dalmatia (see BODOR (1963), 45ff.). For captives as a continuing source of slaves under the empire see STAERMAN-TROFIMOVA (1975), 13ff. ; HARRIS (1980), 121f.

(19) DIO 54.31.1 ; SUET. *Aug*. 21.2.

(20) STRABO 4.5.2.

freedom to slaves to be followed by individual owners in their own households. Once the public posture has been outlined, the more realistic circumstances which lay behind manumission can be compared.

In 2 B.C. the *lex Fufia Caninia* introduced a sliding scale to govern the proportion of slaves in a single household that could be set free at the owner's death ; the proportion declined as the size of the household increased and in no circumstances could more than one hundred slaves be manumitted [21]. The thrust of the *lex Aelia Sentia* of A.D. 4 was to fix a minimum age of thirty for a slave and of twenty for a slave-owner before manumission with the Roman citizenship could be accepted by one or conferred by the other, though there were some exceptions in both cases [22]. A third law, the *lex Junia*, formalised the half-way status between slavery and full emancipation by allowing freedom without citizenship ; it remains unclear, however, whether this enactment belongs to the reign of Augustus or that of Tiberius [23].

What was the purpose of this legislation ? In his biography of Augustus, Suetonius offers the following general statement :

> Considering it also of great importance to keep the people pure and unsullied by any taint of foreign or servile blood, he was most chary of conferring Roman citizenship and set a limit to manumission (Suet. *Aug.* 40.3, Loeb translation) [24].

(21) For the sources of the *lex Fufia Caninia* see *RE* 12 cols. 2355-2356 (R. Leonhard). A full account of the Augustan slavery legislation from the strictly legal point of view is provided by BUCKLAND (1908), 537ff. ; cf. also ATKINSON (1966) ; STAERMAN-TROFIMOVA (1975), 216ff. ; ROBLEDA (1976), 149ff. For Augustus' use of intermediaries in lawmaking see DIO 55.13.4.

(22) For the sources of the *lex Aelia Sentia* see *RE* 12 cols. 2321-2322 (R. Leonhard).

(23) For the sources of the *lex Junia* see *RE* 12 cols. 910-923 (Steinwenter) ; cf. also SHERWIN-WHITE (1973), 328ff. ; ROBLEDA (1976), 135ff. For arguments in favour of an Augustan date see LAST (1934), 888ff. ; ATKINSON (1966), 361ff. ; and in favour of a Tiberian date SHERWIN-WHITE (1973), 332ff.

(24) *Magni praeterea existimans sincerum atque ab omni colluuione peregrini ac seruilis sanguinis incorruptum seruare populum, et ciuitates Romanas parcissime dedit et manumittendi modum terminauit.* The generalisation has been doubted by BRUNT (1958), 164, who makes the important observation that freedmen were encouraged by Augustus to propagate (cf. JONES (1970), 133f.), a relevant consideration for estimating the views of LAST (1934) on the Augustan slavery legislation (see Appendix D). Suetonius' text, *ab omni colluuione peregrini ac seruilis sanguinis*, is the only evidence which could possibly be taken to suggest a racial motive behind the slavery laws, but it contains no hint of specific races and cannot support the construction of Last and his followers. It is far more natural to take the text in a social and moral sense.

This is subsequently illustrated first with instances of Augustus' reluctance to make viritim grants of citizenship and then with details on the slavery legislation :

> Not content with making it difficult for slaves to acquire freedom, and still more so for them to attain full rights, by making careful provision as to the number, condition, and status of those who were manumitted, he added the proviso that no one who had ever been put in irons or tortured should acquire citizenship by any grade of freedom. (Suet. *Aug.* 40.4, Loeb translation) [25].

These passages show with certainty that Augustus did not object to the principle of manumission itself, and, given the force of existing Roman tradition and practice, any notion of completely stopping manumission would of course have been impossible. Instead, insistence was made on the suitability of those slaves who could be considered for the citizenship which full freedom brought. In one of the two examples Suetonius gives of Augustus' refusal to grant the *ciuitas*, stress is firmly laid on the point that the person concerned, a Greek client of Tiberius, was not qualified : there were no justifiable grounds for it [26]. The same thought is apparent at the end of the second quotation above [27] : the Roman citizenship was not to be defiled by being bestowed on criminous slaves. It was obviously important in Augustus' thinking to preserve the moral respectability of the *ciuitas*, a view confirmed both by Suetonius' later comments on Augustus' treatment of his own slaves and freedmen who did not know their place [28], and by the evidence of Dio on the slavery legislation.

According to Dio Augustus established minimum ages for slave and master at the time of manumission and instituted rules to govern

---

(25) *Seruos non contentus multis difficultatibus a libertate et multo pluribus a libertate iusta remouisse, cum et de numero et de condicione ac differentia eorum, qui manumitterentur, curiose cauisset, hoc quoque adiecit, ne uinctus umquam tortusue quis ullo libertatis genere ciuitatem adipisceretur.*

(26) Suet. *Aug.* 40.3, *Tiberio pro cliente Graeco petenti rescripsit, non aliter se daturum, quam si praesens sibi persuasisset, quam iustas petendi causas haberet.*

(27) A reference to the provision in the *lex Aelia* concerning *dediticii* ; Gaius, *Inst.* 1.13 ; 14 ; 26.

(28) Suet. *Aug.* 67. On the idea of moral personality see also *Dig.* 40.4.46. Cf. Brunt (1958), 164 on Augustus' wish 'to limit the flow of new citizens to the extent that their *cultural* absorption could be achieved' (Brunt's emphasis). It is not clear whether this means before or after conferment of the *ciuitas*, though from Suetonius and what follows proof of moral responsibility was plainly desired beforehand.

treatment of slaves by their former owners and by the general public [29].
Dio principally (though briefly) refers here to the *lex Aelia*, and his reason
for the initiatives is worth noticing : too many people were freeing their
slaves indiscriminately [30]. His statement should not be taken simply in a
numerical sense but also from a qualitative point of view : there was no
barrier to servile emancipation once the requisite qualification had been
achieved and it was the moral fibre of the slave to which attention had to
be given.

This point has to be spelled out because modern scholarship on the
Augustan legislation has been dominated by the idea that in the pre-
Augustan era too many slaves, simply, were being manumitted and that
Augustus merely wished to halt the numerical flow of emancipations [31].
A passage from Dionysius of Halicarnassus has been customarily invoked
in support of the traditional interpretation [32], but in actuality its main
concern is the same as that already seen in Suetonius and Dio. Pausing in
his account of the reign of the king Servius Tullius, Dionysius digresses on
the early practice of manumission at Rome and finds nothing to criticize
in that very early period of Roman history. He then contrasts what he
considers to be the more lax and unjustifiable procedures of his own day :
slaves, he says, now buy their freedom from the proceeds of criminal
acts ; they are set free for having served as their masters' accomplices and
confidants in crime, or to allow owners to benefit from public largesse or
to display their owners' liberality at death [33]. Again Dionysius shows no
sign of opposition to manumission itself, only disapproval of manumission for the wrong reasons ; and he makes the constructive suggestion of
screening ex-slaves, in the manner of the censorial review of senators and
equestrians, to ensure that they maintain a proper moral status [34].

Dionysius is not likely to be inventing false facts in his lament on the
manumission procedures of the late first century B.C. ; something of the
background due to political factors has already been seen. But
qualification must certainly be applied to the literal statement of the extent
of 'corruption' in Roman society. First, Dionysius speaks of only a

---

(29) DIO 55.13.7.
(30) πολλῶν τε πολλοὺς ἀκρίτως ἐλευθερούντων ; cf. ATKINSON (1966), 367.
(31) See Appendix D.
(32) DION. HAL. 4.24.1-8.
(33) DION. HAL. 4.24.4 ; STAERMAN-TROFIMOVA (1975), 216f. emphasise savings the
state could make from the distribution of largesse if manumissions were reduced.
(34) DION. HAL. 4.24.8.

minority of slaves for most people, he says, disapprove testamentary manumission for reasons of social ostentation : it is *some* slaves who purchase freedom with illicitly gained cash, *others* who assist their masters in crime ; *some* who are freed for the sake of largesse, *others* for their owners' display. But nowhere does Dionysius complain of *all* slaves being criminals or being set free for defective reasons ; rather he speaks of deviation from morally accepted standards by an unspecified, and unspecifiable, number of people. Secondly, the whole digression is a rhetorical topos on the decline of moral standards of Rome, a comparison of a corrupt present with a better past, the nature of which is purely conventional in Roman literature [35]. In consequence Dionysius should not be taken too seriously. The point is that his text contains no objection to the numerical extent of manumission once the correct kind of behaviour has been exhibited by those slaves to be set free.

It cannot of course be denied that the *lex Fufia* shows some concern with slave numbers, but in spite of Suetonius' comments on restricting manumissions it is not really known if the limits were severe or liberal in comparison with practices in individual households before the law was passed [36], and it is difficult to see how its provisions can have had a great impact on the absolute numbers of slaves being set free after its passage because other methods than testamentary manumission continued to be available. The way was still open for an owner, technically at least, to set free all of his slaves before his death if he wished, a fact which makes it hard to believe that the *lex Fufia* was conceived with a numerical problem alone behind it. Moreover, the *lex Fufia* cannot be interpreted as an attempt to deal with manumission by will and the *lex Aelia* with manumission during the owner's lifetime with an emphasis once more on sheer numbers of slaves [37], because the lapse of six years between the two measures is too great to make any sense of what was a foreseeable situation after the passage of the first law. Had Augustus been driven by no more than a wish to make drastic reductions in the numbers of slaves being freed in 2 B.C., it is far more plausible to imagine that all forms of emancipation would have been dealt with at one fell swoop. Nor, finally,

---

(35) See WILLIAMS (1968), 630f. on moral decline, and cf., for example, COL. *RR*. 12 *praef.* 8-9 ; AMM. MARC. 14.6.16-17. On the numbers question cf. HOPKINS (1978), 128.

(36) Apart from the evidence given in n. 30, Dio says nothing concerning reduction of the numbers of manumissions.

(37) As in DUFF (1958), 31f. ; LAST (1934), 433 ; *RE* 12 col. 2321 (Leonhard).

are there any justifiable grounds for believing that testamentary manumission was more common than other methods [38] ; otherwise passage of the *lex Aelia*, which applied to manumission during the owner's lifetime as well as by his will [39], would have been superfluous.

The *lex Fufia* governed testamentary manumission and it is the precise occasion of this form of conferring freedom on slaves which is of most relevance to understanding its intent. The contemporary evidence of Dionysius just summarised, for all its rhetoric, reveals a tendency on the part of the Roman elite to free slaves by will as a form of social ostentation, which in actuality cost the owner nothing, the rationale being to have all think well of the deceased from a final act of generosity. It is known that Augustus endeavoured to regulate other kinds of ostentatious behaviour among the Roman upper classes by sumptuary laws, which placed limits on private spending, extravagance and bribery, and to set a new moral tone in society not least by his legislation on marriage [40]. The *lex Fufia* is best understood in consequence as one of a series of efforts to amend the luxurious and unpalatable practices of the ruling classes by imposing reasonable, but not necessarily stringent, limits on the numbers of slaves who could be freed by will. This is not to deny that some effect may have been subsequently felt on the absolute numbers of slaves who were set free, but if so this was of no more than secondary importance.

A common interest, however, between the two slavery laws can still be perceived. For those slave-owners who were to adhere to the dictates of the *lex Fufia* without setting free their slaves en masse while still alive, a principle of selectivity, imposed from without, must henceforward have made itself felt as they listed in their wills the names of those slaves who would become free once the wills were implemented. When looked at from the servile point of view, one of the effects of the *lex Fufia* was to give testamentary emancipation something of the character of a competition, the rules for which had to be compliant behaviour, loyalty and obedience. The beginnings of a set of standards by which

(38) This is a common view among scholars ; see, for example, Buckland (1908), 442 ; 460 ; Duff (1958), 25 ; Robleda (1976), 121 ; but it is hardly plausible ; cf. Atkinson (1966), 368 ; Treggiari (1969), 27.

(39) Gaius, *Inst.* 11.17 ; 18.

(40) Gell. *NA* 2.24.14 (cf. 15) ; Suet. *Aug.* 34.1 (cf. 89.2) ; cf. Dio 54.16.3-5. On the marriage legislation see references at p. 48 n. 9. Note that according to *Dig.* 40.2.16 the *lex Aelia* was designed to prevent manumission for reasons of *luxuria*. For the elite luxury of the age see Jasper Griffin, *Augustan Poetry and the Life of Luxury* in *JRS* 66 (1976), 87ff.

manumission could be achieved thus become visible and with the *lex Aelia* the standards at large become much clearer.

The conferment of freedom together with the *ciuitas* is the most significant feature of the *lex Aelia* because in theory the new law did not prevent liberation of slaves below the age of thirty but simply denied them access to fully freed status [41]. The law, it can be emphasised, showed a concern with protecting the moral character of the citizenship but not with delimiting the actual extent of manumission in the sense of merely setting slaves free. It may be in fact that the establishment of an arbitrary age for full manumission, with the citizenship, encouraged servile agitation for it once the requisite age had been reached, since the law was creating reasonable expectation of full emancipation at a definite point in the slave's life. What is of more consequence, however, is that the *lex Aelia* made full manumission a reward to the slave who reached a deserving age, or, once the exceptions to the main rules are examined, a slave who displayed conformity to the established values of free society. Full freedom below thirty was possible in cases involving a blood relationship between master and slave, cases where the slave was the teacher of the owner's children, a potential wife or *procurator* for the owner, or an *alumnus* [42]. In this regard the law exhibited no repressiveness at all but rather encouraged conventional domestic relationships within the household. Moreover, the absolute denial of the citizenship upon emancipation in all circumstances to those slaves to be categorised as *dediticii* by the *lex Aelia* had the corollary effect of instituting a penalty in the absence of meritorious servile conduct [43]. Slaves who, at the time of emancipation, had ever been put in chains, branded, found guilty of a crime after torture, consigned to fight in the arena, or put in the gladiatorial schools, could never achieve full citizen status because the law judged them guilty of moral disgrace (*turpitudo*), though freedom itself was not denied them [44]. It can be plainly stated that the *lex Aelia* conceived of both reward and penalty in moralistic terms (the force of *turpitudo* should be noted especially) and set up a code of

---

(41) GAIUS, *Inst.* 1.17 ; 18.
(42) GAIUS, *Inst.* 1.19 ; 39.
(43) GAIUS, *Inst.* 1.15.
(44) GAIUS, *Inst.* 1.15, *Huius ergo turpitudinis seruos quocumque modo et cuiuscumque aetatis manumissos, etsi pleno iure dominorum fuerint, numquam aut ciues Romanos aut Latinos fieri dicemus, sed omni modo dediticiorum numero constitui intellegemus.*

desired behaviour for the slave, behaviour at once dictated to and fostered in the slave by the slave-owning classes.

It is implicit in the law that slaves wished to acquire the *ciuitas* as much as simple release from slavery, and this is only to be expected as a true reflection of real historical circumstance. Without full freedom the ex-slave might find his condition tenuous, the status and prospects of his children dubious, participation in the life of the community to which he belonged difficult. Under the terms of the law, however, if slaves were to achieve full emancipation they had to ensure for a substantial amount of time, especially those who were homeborn slaves, that all criminal involvement were avoided. Thus the potential reward of Roman citizenship conferred by free society became, from the slaves' point of view, an inducement to sound moral behaviour during the period of enslavement or, in other words, to assimilating themselves within the existing social status quo. This preempted, at least in theory, their participation in acts of rebellion, escape by flight, or any other means of securing freedom not condoned by free society. It may be suggested consequently that the purpose of the *lex Aelia* was to inform slaves as much as their owners of the qualifications required for citizenship, and to create potential for harmony between privileged and non-privileged sections of Roman society by offering slaves the prospect of eventual release from their condition in a way which meantime guaranteed without resistance the continuation of the servile system on which the elite so heavily depended [45].

The provisions of the *lex Junia* may be taken to confirm this view. The creation of Junian status as a half-way step towards full citizenship carried the liability that Junians were debarred from directly benefiting from wills, from making wills of their own, or from being appointed tutors in wills [46]. The converse of these restrictions was the reward that Junians

---

(45) The ideas of reward and penalty in the *lex Aelia* have of course always been recognised ; see for example H. F. JOLOWICZ and Barry NICHOLAS, *Historical Introduction to the Study of Roman Law*[3], Cambridge, 1972, 345 ; SHERWIN-WHITE (1973), 327ff. ; (and cf. LAST (1934), 429, 'moral fitness'). But the question of why such ideas were carried into law has not been given a great deal of attention, though it becomes all the more urgent once alleged motives of numerical restriction of manumissions in and of itself and of avoiding racial fusion are downplayed, as clearly they must be ; see Appendix D.

(46) GAIUS, *Inst.* 1.23. As with the *lex Aelia*, however, an easing of these restrictions meant that Junians could receive legacies through the complicated rules of *fideicommissum* ; GAIUS, *Inst.* 1.24.

could acquire full status through what has been called the 'benefit of paternity', meaning marriage and the procreation of children ([47]). Here the notions of reward and penalty are again quite explicit : the capacity to receive and to dispose of property is considered by the law as something befitting a citizen only, and the further notion is implicit that additional passage of time after acquisition of Junian status is necessary before the former slave is ready to assume all the citizen's responsibilities. Similarly, the law is liberal to the Junian once commitment to established social values, marriage and the raising of a family, is demonstrated, but once more only after the passage of a certain interval of time, the reaching of age one by a child ([48]). From the Junian's point of view, therefore, full citizen rank was made an incentive to greater acceptance of social conformity as imposed downwards from the upper reaches of society, whereas its rejection resulted in the retention of inferior social grade. Junian status was in itself a sign that progress in the social order was possible, but the law continued to protect the citizenship until its recipients were morally suitable for it.

If passage of the *lex Junia* preceded that of the *lex Aelia*, it might perhaps be possible to speak of a broad system devised by the Augustan government to mould the behaviour of slaves and ex-slaves in society as a whole. But if the *lex Junia* is of Tiberian date, it should then be viewed as an extension of a principle first laid down in the *lex Aelia* ([49]). Nevertheless, it is true that over the course of the first century and beyond the principle of the *lex Aelia* was gradually extended, as far as Junians were concerned, into a much wider network of incentives which led to full citizen status in return for service to the community which represented thereby further attachment to free Roman values. Service in the *Vigiles* for six years, the furnishing of grain ships, the building of houses at Rome, working in a mill for three years at Rome, all these circumstances were covered in successive enactments up until the reign of Trajan as means of arriving at fully freed status ([50]). The consequence of the scheme introduced by the *lex Aelia* and the *lex Junia* was that their

(47) The phrase is from SHERWIN-WHITE (1973), 332 and elsewhere. This is to equate the *Latini* of GAIUS, *Inst.* 1.29 with Junians, which seems necessary.

(48) GAIUS, *Inst.* 1.29 ; ULP. 3.3. It should be noted that the *fideicommissum* provision shows that there was no objection by the makers of the law to ex-slaves receiving legacies ; it merely had to be done by a clumsy and penalising method.

(49) See n. 23 above for sources on the date of the *lex Junia*.

(50) GAIUS, *Inst.* 1.32b-34 ; ULP. 3.1-6 ; cf. SUET. *Claud.* 18.2 ; TAC. *Ann.* 15.43.3.

promulgators, who naturally represented the slave-owning section of society, were deliberately attempting through the use of the law to perpetuate the established social status quo by appealing for the support of slaves and former slaves, whose eventual reward, after the passage of time and proof of acceptability, was assimilation within it.

Something of the background against which the Augustan legislation was passed has already been seen. It can be emphasised finally, however, that it was precisely those new slaves who continued to arrive in Rome and Italy from tribal settings who were most in need of the acculturative programme of incentives, rewards and penalties laid down by the law. By A.D. 4 war captives who had earlier been enslaved for periods of twenty or thirty years would be nearing the time when manumission may have been becoming a real possibility for those who had survived. Yet it is perfectly credible that the Roman authorities still felt the need to guard against admission to the *ciuitas* of elements which had not yet achieved a demonstrable degree of commitment towards Rome and its values. The *lex Aelia*, and possibly the *lex Junia* too, was passed with the social legacy of earlier military conquests in mind as a form of social control in its own right and in a very direct sense.

The Augustan legislation, then, set public standards or conditions for the emancipation of slaves and, although later modified, it remained in effect for centuries, until the time of Justinian in fact [51]. But the difficulty which underlay the slavery laws, as indeed all Augustus' social enactments, was one of enforcement : the creation of public conditions for manumission could not provide any guarantee that in everyday reality they would be met by slaves or maintained by slave-owners. At this point, therefore, an attempt must be made to see how the process of manumission actually operated in the lives of slaves and their masters. It will become clear in the end that the main condition prescribed for slaves by the *lex Aelia*, attainment of age thirty, was only one of a series of barriers to freedom which had to be successfully crossed before emancipation could become a reality.

The first point to make is that it cannot be imagined that waiting for the arrival of age thirty was a simple waiting process for the slave. The unfulfilled anticipation of freedom is recorded in melancholy fashion on an inscription from Venafrum which refers to a slave *uilicus* who died too

(51) *Instit.* 1.5.3 ; 7.

young to be manumitted : *debita libertas iuueni mihi lege negata morte immatura reddita perpetua est* [52]. Although there is no accurate means of calculating life-expectancy for antiquity, it is indisputable that thirty was a far more advanced age than in the modern world, particularly so at the lower levels of society which, in the cities especially, were most affected by overcrowding, disease, poor health facilities and other social misfortunes, and life-expectancy at birth for slaves is not likely to have been much more than twenty years [53]. The survival of a slave to age thirty cannot have been regarded as automatic or easily predictable, and this consideration only reinforces the notion apparent in the *lex Aelia* that manumission was a long-term reward for many years of devoted service from the slave.

Secondly the slave's acquisition of freedom never became a right, no matter what reasonable expectations the law fostered, but depended ultimately on the willingness of the owner to agree to manumission ; as such freedom was subject to the owner's caprice and an owner on his death-bed might be as inclined towards severity as generosity, towards the lash as towards largesse [54]. From a survey of epigraphic evidence from the western provinces of the Empire, it has been contended that slaves between the ages of thirty and forty had a very good chance of being set free [55], but even if this were true there was still no certainty of the fact ; and the mass of tombstones from which servile expectations have been inferred tells only of those slaves who in later life secured sufficient wealth to be able to make some commemoration of themselves and their family members. It cannot be assumed that such expectations presented themselves to all points of the servile compass at all moments in time, and it is more plausible to believe that the majority of slaves was never set free at all [56]. No doubt location to some degree determined slaves' prospects

---

(52) *CIL* 10.4917.

(53) Sepulchral inscriptions which record ages of death have been shown to be of no value for calculating life-expectancy in spite of their abundance ; see M. K. HOPKINS, *On the Probable Age Structure of the Roman Empire* in *Population Studies* 20 (1966), 245ff., who nonetheless argues for the whole population an expectation of life at birth of below thirty but over twenty years ; this estimate is conventionally accepted ; cf. BRUNT (1971), 132f. ; ENGELS (1980), 116ff. ; HARRIS (1980), 118 ; (see also HOPKINS (1978), 34 n. 44). On urban problems see P. A. BRUNT, *The Roman Mob* in *Past & Present* no. 35 (1966), 3ff. = M. I. FINLEY, ed., *Studies in Ancient Society*, London, 1974, 74ff.

(54) Cf. TAC. *Ann.* 16.19.4, *seruorum alios largitione, quosdam uerberibus adfecit.*

(55) ALFÖLDY (1972), 114f.

(56) See above n. 9.

of emancipation ([57]), but in all cases agreement of the master had to be gained beforehand and this was a factor always subject to denial or withdrawal. As a passage in Tacitus makes clear, the conferment of freedom on a slave was a *beneficium* which followed evidence of servile *obsequium*, an act of generosity which resided in the control of the master alone, not of the slave ([58]).

Although the evidence is limited in quantity, enough documentary records of manumission are available to illustrate the element of personal inclination at work on the master's part, to the disadvantage of the slave. The will of Dasumius, first of all, provides a glimpse into the liberation of household slaves by a member of the Roman upper crust early in the second century. The text is too fragmentary to allow the total number of manumitted slaves to emerge but that is relatively unimportant. What is remarkable in the will is the express ban on the setting free of a certain group of slaves at any future point in their lives after Dasumius' death, a prerogative which was, indeed, formally sanctioned by the law ([59]) : 'I ask', Dasumius writes, 'that Menecrates and Paedaros not be manumitted but kept in the same occupation as long as they live ... because they have given me great offence by their lack of merit' ([60]). It was observed earlier that the *lex Fufia* is likely to have imposed a principle of selectivity upon owners intending to manumit slaves by will, but in this particular instance the master went beyond that constraint to leave certain members of his household little hope whatever of ever leaving their servile condition.

As a complete contrast to the harsh attitude of Dasumius, the generosity of an anonymous slave-owner from Egypt appears in a fragment of his will, appropriately governed, it is clear, by the *lex Fufia*, in which he asks that some of his slaves be set free despite the fact that they had absconded ([61]). It may perhaps be doubted that slave-owners were regularly prepared to overlook such recalcitrant behaviour in their households since efforts were often made to recapture and punish fugitives ([62]), and it was

---

(57) See further below, pp. 103ff.

(58) Tac. *Ann*. 13.26.4-5.

(59) *Dig*. 40.1.4.9 ; 40.1.9.

(60) *FIRA*² III no. 148, lines 80ff., *Menecraten et Paedaro[tem rogo ne manumittas, sed in eodem o]pere illos habeas donec ui[uent, quo habui ego ... quoniam n]ullo merito meo tam ualde [offenderunt...].*

(61) *P. Hamb*. 1.72 = *CPL* no. 174 ; for the legality of the procedure, *Paul. Sent*. 4.14.3. For manumission documents from Egypt see Biezunská-Małowist (1977), 145.

(62) See, for instance, *P. Oxy*. 1422 ; 1423 ; 1643 ; cf. above, p. 32.

probably more normal that slaves were liberated 'on account of their goodwill and affection' towards the owner, a phrase which appears in Egyptian documents that highlight the demonstration of appropriate servile conduct before conferment of the reward (⁶³). But when freedom was bestowed the master was still able if he wished to impose restrictions on it. For example, in the will dating from the mid second century of Acusilaus (⁶⁴), a resident of Oxyrhynchus, five female slaves were set free but subject to the condition that their services and earnings were to remain after Acusilaus' death at the disposal of his wife as long as she survived, while his son was given claim to any children borne by the women in the future. Not all of Acusilaus' slaves were liberated in the will : some went again to the son, though the wife had a right to sell or mortgage them if she wished. Inevitably, the reading of a will must have brought a certain disappointment to those not fortunate enough to be on the manumission list.

In the well-known will of a veteran of the Roman fleet which belongs to the late second century (⁶⁵), C. Longinus Castor gave freedom to two female slaves, Marcella and Cleopatra, both of whom are described as being over thirty and who in actuality were to become Castor's heirs, as well as to Cleopatra's daughter Sarapias. Four other individuals are named in the document, probably slaves, but nothing is said of their emancipation. In a case such as this it is likely that the slaves knew in advance of their impending manumission, once the owner died that is : in Petronius' novel, indeed, Trimalchio announces his intention to his favourite slaves of setting them free in his will and of giving them property (⁶⁶). Wills were by no means the last minute dictates of slave-owners but were often drawn up years before death finally occurred. Longinus Castor's will was made in 189 and opened in 194, Acusilaus' was made in 156 and opened in 165, while the younger Pliny refers to a

---

(63) κατ᾽ εὔνοιαν καὶ φιλοστοργίαν ; *P. Oxy.* 494 ; *P. Tebt.* 407 ; cf. BIEZUNSKA-MAŁOWIST (1977), 116f.

(64) *P. Oxy.* 494 = A. S. HUNT, C. C. EDGAR, *Select Papyri* I (LCL 1932), no. 84. For forms of manumission in Egypt under local as well as Roman law see TAUBENSCHLAG (1955), 96ff. ; MONTEVECCHI (1973), 201f. ; cf. also M. W. HASLAM, *Notes on Deeds of Manumission* in *ZPE* 20 (1976), 58ff.

(65) *BGU* 326 = A. S. HUNT, C. C. EDGAR, *Select Papyri* I (LCL 1932), no. 85 = *FIRA²* III no. 50.

(66) PETR. *Sat.* 71.1-3.

will made eighteen years before implementation [67]. To earn the initial favour of the master, however, and thus to become a candidate for testamentary manumission, total subordination of the slave to the interests of the master was required, subordination which could then be maintained by the owner through making known in advance the contents of his will. This procedure resulted in a guarantee of continued compliance on the part of the slave, extending over an indefinite interval of time and which for the slave meant more years of waiting before freedom became a reality. Slaves who hoped for liberation in this way had to ensure that they became the 'dearest' slaves within the household [68], whether or not genuine sentiment was involved, and that they remained so by continued self-denial and conformity. Even so, changes made in wills when periodically revised could still confound expectations, and there was also always the chance that wills could be disregarded : in the late second century in Egypt a letter was sent by a certain Marsisuchus to his wife and daughter threatening them not to interfere with arrangements he had made for setting free a number of slaves [69].

In the last resort of course slaves were able to commit acts of violence against their owners if they believed their own interests had been injured, though this does not seem to have happened frequently to judge from the surviving literary record [70]. What might take place, however, is illustrated by Tacitus' famous account of the murder of the city prefect L. Pedanius Secundus at the hands of a slave in 61 [71]. Tacitus did not know the precise cause of the attack on Pedanius Secundus but he gives as a possible motive the explanation that an agreement on a price for manumission had been made between the prefect and the slave, but that Pedanius had reneged on the contract at the last minute [72]. It is of some significance that this could occur to Tacitus as a rational account of the episode since presumably it would also have been comprehensible and

---

(67) Plin. *Epp.* 8.18.5 ; cf. 5.5.2 ; the contents of an old will did not always reflect the testator's final wishes.

(68) Tac. *Ann.* 15.54.2, *carissimi*.

(69) *P. Tebt.* 407 ; the wife and daughter may have already had some claim on some of the slaves (Biezunská-Małowist (1977), 95). Cf. Sherwin-White (1966), 320, on revising wills.

(70) See below, p. 113.

(71) Tac. *Ann.* 14.42-45.

(72) Tac. *Ann.* 14.42.1, *seu negata libertate cui pretium pepigerat*. Cf. *Dig.* 40.1.5, the slave was supposed to seek redress before the city prefect or provincial governor when his owner reneged on a manumission agreement.

acceptable to his readers ; as such the explanation might suggest that Pedanius' behaviour was not all that unusual. What was abnormal was the slave's recourse to violence, when resignation to the master's decision would perhaps be more normally forthcoming.

If the passage of time and the caprice of the master were circumstances beyond the direct control of slaves, there were also other practical hurdles to be confronted and crossed before the process of manumission could be brought to completion. For formal emancipation during the lifetime of the owner to be valid, both master and slave had to appear before a Roman magistrate for the ceremony of liberation to take place [73]. The magistrate concerned could be a consul or, more usually, a praetor at Rome, and in the provinces a proconsul or imperial legate, or even an imperial procurator [74]. In Egypt the local agoranomus of a town was often involved with manumissions subject to Greco-Egyptian rather than Roman law [75]. Certain legal texts suggest that these occasions could be very casual affairs and this has been taken as a sign of the frequency with which manumissions occurred [76]. Thus Gaius states : 'Slaves over thirty can usually be set free at any time, so that they are manumitted for instance when the praetor or proconsul is en route to the baths or the theatre' (*Inst.* 1.20). But the context of this passage shows that Gaius is drawing a contrast with the fixed days on which slaves below the age of thirty were able to appear before the appropriate board to prove their grounds for exemption from the normal rules in order to be set free, and it is equally clear that Gaius' text was copied wholesale or adapted by subsequent jurists, which means that mere repetition of the statement does not give it any greater force as a piece of historical evidence [77]. At most, therefore, the legal texts should be taken to signify the constant potential availability of manumission, but they are not in themselves evidence of constant frequency of manumission.

---

(73) See BUCKLAND (1908), 451ff. on manumission *uindicta*.

(74) BUCKLAND (1908), 453 (under some circumstances local officials were acceptable).

(75) TAUBENSCHLAG (1955), 97f. ; cf. A. H. M. JONES, *The Cities of the Eastern Roman Provinces*², 1971, 317ff.

(76) GAIUS, *Inst.* 1.20 ; *Dig.* 40.2.7 ; *Instit.* 1.5.2 ; ALFÖLDY (1972), 105f.

(77) GAIUS, *Inst.* 1.20, *in prouinciis ... idque (consilium) fit ultimo die conuentus ; sed Romae certis diebus apud consilium manumittuntur. maiores uero triginta annorum serui semper manumitti solent, adeo ut uel in transitu manumittantur, ueluti cum praetor aut pro consule in balneum uel in theatrum eat.*

The agreement of the master always had to be secured for emancipation and then the relevant magistrate approached. This may have been relatively straightforward in Rome itself when local slaves and their owners did not have to travel a great distance to find the urban praetor, who, however, even in the imperial period had other responsibilities than presiding over manumissions [78]. But outside the city the situation was rather different. The younger Pliny provides a case in point in a letter addressed to his wife's grandfather L. Calpurnius Fabatus [79], who apparently wished to complete the manumission of a number of Junians on his estate in northern Italy but was hampered by the lack of a suitable magistrate. Pliny wrote that his friend Calestrius Tiro was about to assume a governorship of one of the Spanish provinces and could be persuaded to visit Calpurnius Fabatus for the purpose on his way out. In the sequel Calestrius complied and the operation was brought to a successful conclusion [80]. But the fortuitous set of circumstances required for this to happen – Pliny's initial willingness to intervene on the Junians' behalf (there was certainly no compulsion to do so) and the subsequent willingness of a magistrate to make himself available when he happened to be in the vicinity of Calpurnius Fabatus' estate – is revealing : it was not necessarily easy for the administrative apparatus of manumission to be set in motion. Pliny also later assisted three other Junians whose patron he had become through the will of another friend by requesting full emancipation for them from Trajan ; again the outcome was successful, though Pliny deliberately overlooked the claims to full freedom of other Junians from the same estate [81]. A forty year old Jewish woman who was set free with her two young children at Oxyrhynchus in the late third century through the process of *manumissio inter amicos* was again fortunate to be ransomed from slavery through the efforts on her behalf of the membership of a local synagogue [82].

In the provinces, indeed, the administrative complications were great. Formal manumissions were part of the regular round of business of the provincial governor : in the political crisis of 68 the future emperor Galba distracted himself from affairs of state by presiding over manumission

---

(78) See Th. MOMMSEN, *Römisches Staatsrecht* II³, Leipzig, 1887-88, I, 193ff.

(79) PLIN. *Epp.* 7.16 ; cf. SHERWIN-WHITE (1966), 420f.

(80) PLIN. *Epp.* 7.32.1.

(81) PLIN. *Epp.* 10.104-105 ; cf. SHERWIN-WHITE (1966), 714f. Cf. MART. *Epig.* 9.87.

(82) *P. Oxy.* 1205 (291).

cases, having issued an edict to appoint a day on which individual manumissions would be granted [83]. But access to the governor by the slave was not possible at any given moment. In the imperial period it was the governor's practice during his term of office to make circuit tours of his province, residing temporarily in those cities which had the status of an assize centre, so that administrative and judicial business was handled locally but only for a relatively short interval in each place [84]. Several months might pass before a slave who had been promised freedom could expect the governor to be on hand for the formal ceremony to occur, and even then it was not automatic that his case would be taken up because the governor had a great deal of latitude in deciding to which matters he would give attention [85]. In addition not every city in a province was an assize centre ; so candidates for emancipation might be compelled to travel with their owners to an appropriate city when they were not themselves resident in an assize centre, and it may be wondered how often owners were willing to sacrifice time, money and effort on travel and indefinite attendance on the governor for the purpose of formally setting free their slaves. Popular complaints about the inconveniences caused by the circuit tour system were not unknown [86]. The whole operation was thus unpredictable and in bringing it to a successful end from the servile point of view, any number of adverse factors might intervene to scotch the whole process. Application of these factors is likely to have intensified when a slave who claimed to be free and who found his claim disputed took the option theoretically open to all imperial subjects and presented a petition to the emperor himself for resolution of his situation. A compilation of evidence from the major law codes has revealed that in the Antonine and Severan periods especially successive emperors certainly dealt with such petitions, and for the most part decisions were handed

(83) SUET. *Galba* 10.1 (cf. 9.2) ; PLUT. *Galba* 5.1.

(84) SHERWIN-WHITE (1966), 640 ; BURTON (1975), who examines the practices of proconsuls only, though it should not be doubted that imperial legates also conducted assize tours, as Pliny in Bithynia (even though Pliny's was an unusual imperial appointment). Note the inclusion in *Dig.* 40.2.7. of *legatusue Caesaris* and in *Instit.* 1.5.2 of *praeses*, in contrast to Gaius' omission (*Inst.* 1.20) ; and for the prefect of Egypt's tour see G. FOTI TALAMANCA, *Ricerche sul processo nell'Egitto greco-romano* I, Milan, 1974, with *Dig.* 40.2.21 for the prefect's ability to preside over manumissions (from the time of Augustus).

(85) BURTON (1975),100f.

(86) DIO CHRYS. *Orat.* 35.17.

down in favour of the slave petitioners [87]. But the volume of such appeals is never likely to have been large, because access to the emperor by any subject was drastically limited by considerations of space, time and money, the social status of the petitioner, and the emperor's selection of business items [88].

In the way, seen earlier, that the family lives of slaves were to some degree governed by their geographical and occupational location, so too were slaves' prospects of acquiring freedom. It should be expected that urban domestic servants, who had close contacts with their owners, would be able to win the attention and favour of owners and thus present good claims for emancipation, especially if their jobs were rather more than simply menial. In his biographies of Roman grammarians Suetonius presents one type of slave who could benefit from the value attached to literary accomplishments and he preserves the information, for example, that Staberius Eros, a Thracian slave, was set free 'on account of his zeal for literature', and Lenaeus, a freedman of Cn. Pompeius, 'on account of his wit and learning' [89]. The use of ex-slaves in positions of responsibility and slaves' acquisition of freedom from the basis of such occupations as nurse, pedagogue and doctor are features of the Roman slavery system too familiar to warrant elaboration [90]. Manumission of agricultural slaves, who did not have the same kind of proximity to their owners, often absentees, is less well attested and as far as can be told even the *uilicus* on the farm was probably a slave more often than a freedman [91]. One reason

---

(87) PIGANIOL (1958); cf. MILLAR (1977), 10f. Piganiol showed the tendency for freedom to be ratified when circumstances were dubious and explained it in terms of humanitarian, philosophical influences on the Antonine and Severan emperors. This may be doubted and it is alternatively possible that verdicts favourable to slaves were given for reasons of creating good public relations. If imperial decisions were continually given against petitioners the result would have been general servile antagonism ; instead it was more important that freedom be seen to be attainable. Nothing was lost by the conferments while the benefit to society at large was considerable. Cf. the practice of habitual manumission in the circus at Constantinople, AMM. MARC. 22.7.2.

(88) MILLAR (1977), 465ff. ; cf. WYNNE WILLIAMS, *The 'Libellus' Procedure and the Severan Papyri* in *JRS* 64 (1974), 86ff.

(89) SUET. *Gramm.* 13, *propter litterarum studium manumissus* ; 15, *ob ingenium atque doctrinam gratis manumissus*.

(90) DUFF (1958), 89ff. ; VOGT (1975), 103ff.

(91) WHITE (1970), 352 is perhaps overly cautious about manumission among rural slaves (contrast p. 358) ; see also TREGGIARI (1969), 106ff., who did not have to mention Columella's reference to emancipation of the prolific slave-woman. On *uilici* see MARÓTI (1976), 115ff., and Rhona BEARE, *Were Bailiffs Ever Free Born* ? in *CQ* 72 (1978), 398ff., who gives *CIL* 3.7147 (Tralles) and *ILS* 7372 (Atina) as examples of bailiffs being set free.

why little is heard of rural emancipation will be that those who gained it will have been probably less able, for financial reasons, to commemorate themselves with inscriptions than freedmen in cities, though the odd example survives, such as that of a freed *pecuarius* mentioned on a stone from Moguntiacum, and although Virgil's Tityrus is a fiction, its basis cannot be totally unrealistic [92]. Even slaves who worked in the harsh conditions of the mines, and who can rarely have escaped, had the possibility of emancipation before them, to judge from the charter of Salpensa in Spain (belonging to the eighties of the first century) in which detailed provisions for local manumission are set down in such a context that mining slaves must be understood to be catered for [93]. While, therefore, gradations of expectation of freedom are indisputable, it was important that hope of freedom be made available to all slaves, no matter what their status, so that during slavery their behaviour could be regulated and exploited.

Location was also important for the slave's personal accumulation of cash with which freedom might be purchased from the owner, but before that theme is pursued the importance in the Roman slavery system of manumission in the provinces can be underscored from examining some details about the tax collected by the Roman state when formal emancipation took place, the *uicesima libertatis*. This tax has a very long history indeed, extending from the mid fourth century B.C. as far as the fourth century A.D., which in itself is a reflection of the value of the tax as a continuing source of public revenue over the centuries. Many aspects of the administration of the tax are no more than imperfectly understood, but it is clear enough that in the imperial age it was collected on an empire-wide basis. The find-spots of inscriptions which commemorate persons involved with the *uicesima libertatis* should not perhaps be automatically regarded as evidence of tax collection in those areas, but it is likely that most inscriptions were set up in places where tax-agents had worked, and once these areas are set alongside those for which the evidence of collection is unquestionable, it can scarcely be doubted that all formal manumissions were subject to the *uicesima* in all regions where Roman law prevailed. The evidence covers Spain, Gaul, Bithynia-Pontus-

(92) *ILS* 8511 ; Virg. *Ecl.* 1.27-35 ; cf. Eleanor Windsor Leach, *Virgil's Eclogues*, Bloomington, 1974, 119ff. ; Williams (1968), 307ff. ; note also *Dig.* 40.4.52, *testamenta paganorum*.
(93) *ILS* 6088.28.

Paphlagonia, Egypt, Dacia, Achaea, Germany, Africa, Asia, and of course Rome and Italy [94].

There is something of a tendency in recent scholarship on slavery to stress that from an economic standpoint at least only classical Italy, not the Roman empire *in toto*, can be accurately categorised as a genuine slave society [95]. While such emphasis has value in certain respects, it has the corollary effect of minimising the significance of slaves elsewhere which in other respects was considerable. The fact that slaves in Roman Egypt constituted less than twenty percent of the full population [96], for example, may mean that Egypt was not a true slave society, but it can hardly follow that formally manumitted slaves in Egypt, or anywhere else, were of no consequence as far as Roman financial administrators were concerned. Roman government did not differentiate between genuine and non-genuine slave societies within the overall empire, but from the fiscal point of view regarded all slaves everywhere in an identical manner.

It is also noteworthy that the manumission tax was still being collected in the fourth century when slavery as a system of compulsory labour was being overtaken by the colonate [97]. It is not difficult to see why when there still remained great numbers of slaves in the Roman world and when manumission was still being practised. The apparent liberation of some eight thousand slaves by the Christian Melania early in the fifth century may not have been a typical event [98], but the proceeds of even lesser acts of generosity will still have been worth collecting. The action of the emperor Caracalla in temporarily doubling the *uicesima libertatis* and the sense of urgency apparent in a letter concerning the tax written by a prefect of Egypt in the second century [99] suggest that Rome was always interested in collecting revenue from manumissions and that money was always there to be collected. The long chronological duration of the tax

---

(94) See Appendix E for evidence on the chronology and collection of the *uicesima libertatis*.

(95) Hopkins (1978), 99 ; Finley (1980), 9 ; 79.

(96) Hopkins (1978), 99 ; (1980), 329f.

(97) For the background see A. H. M. Jones, *The Roman Colonate* in *Past & Present* no. 13 (1958), 1ff. = *The Roman Economy* (ed. P. A. Brunt, Oxford, 1974), 293ff. ; Finley (1980), 123ff.

(98) Finley (1980), 123, rightly emphasising previous underestimation of the slave population in the later imperial period.

(99) Dio 77.9.4 ; *P. Oxy.* 2265.

and its geographical dispersal can be seen as means by which the Roman state exploited slavery to its own advantage, in this instance purely pecuniary.

Sustained collection of the *uicesima* implies that formal emancipations continued to take place, in the provinces and at Rome, despite the difficulties involved. That is not in contention of course, though the difficulties are not thereby made less in trying to form an estimate of slaves' thinking about and securing of manumission. Indeed, in cases where slaves themselves were responsible for paying the manumission tax ([100]), a financial obstacle to freedom was imposed upon them, which in many instances was added to the problem of accumulating money required for the purchase of manumission itself. It was remarked earlier that testamentary emancipation did not entail financial loss to the slave-owner (though his heirs of course may have been affected). But the situation was rather different when masters freed slaves during their own lifetimes, because they lost both property and the revenue from it. In part the loss was offset by the obligations towards the patron by which the slave was bound on emancipation ([101]), and in wealthy households, where a constant supply of servile births helped keep up the numerical level of the establishment, it is doubtful that Roman magnates suffered unduly in economic terms. Yet even men of senatorial rank needed to be careful about their finances. The younger Pliny was most concerned that a group of slaves he was considering for purchase be inexpensive to maintain ([102]), so in cases of smallscale slave ownership the freeing of slaves can be supposed to have incorporated a certain loss of capital. It consequently causes no surprise that slaves sometimes received their freedom at a price, a mechanism which was obviously designed to compensate the owner. In theory the system was not unreasonable from both points of view : on one hand the slave had before him the incentive of freedom towards which he could aspire through diligence, industry and frugality ; on the other the owner benefited from the collaborative efforts of the slave while a slave and then received a cash dividend when the slave was set free. In practice, however, the system is likely to have been weighted in the interests of the owner, as can be seen to some extent from considering actual costs of emancipation.

(100) See Appendix E for the evidence.
(101) See above n. 2.
(102) PLIN. *Epp.* 1.21.2 (*frugi*, cf. CIC. *Phil.* 8.11).

Very few manumission figures have been preserved by the sources and their typicality is thus open to question. But they allow some slight indication of the financial burden to slaves which the acquisition of freedom might involve. Petronius gives HS4,000 as one figure ; HS10,000 was paid by a dancer named Paris who belonged to an aunt of the emperor Nero ; and HS50,000 was paid by a slave doctor who subsequently took the name P. Decimius Eros Merula ([103]). These are considerable sums and fall within the range of attested purchase prices for slaves ; indeed, the cost of manumission probably came close to or was a little higher than the market price of slaves, known for Rome and Italy to have extended from a minimum of HS600 to a maximum of HS700,000 ([104]). Purchase prices must have varied according to the skills and ages of the slaves concerned and the same variation is likely to have applied to manumission costs. But it is difficult to see how the vast majority of slaves ever had opportunities to acquire substantial sums of money because most never found themselves in contexts where cash on the grandscale was readily forthcoming. On a recent estimate HS1,000 could provide basic rations for one man for a period of four to eight years, and in the second century the Roman legionary soldier received annual pay of only HS1,200 ([105]). This kind of information gives a useful comparison for the manumission figures and strongly suggests that sums of cash had to be accumulated over very lengthy periods before enough was on hand to buy freedom. The chances for saving must have depended on the nature of the slave's occupation or of the household to which he belonged or both. The examples of Paris and Merula indicate that attachment to a large household or expertise in a specialised occupation could produce wealth of considerable dimensions, and slaves who worked as doorkeepers, actors, doctors, prostitutes and so on had jobs which gave a potential for collection of tips and other windfall gifts ([106]). Moreover,

---

(103) See DUNCAN-JONES (1974), 349f. ; add PLIN. *NH* 7.128-129 (credible ?). It may perhaps be doubted that sums paid by the slave for manumission were as vital to the Roman slavery system as suggested by HOPKINS (1978), 131 ; 147 ; 160 ; 170 ; cf. K. R. BRADLEY, *CP* 76 (1980), 82ff.

(104) DUNCAN-JONES (1974), 349f. ; HOPKINS (1978), 134 ; WESTERMANN (1955), 36 ; for prices in Egypt see STRAUS (1973) ; BIEZUNSKÁ-MAŁOWIST (1977), 165ff. The range of prices now available in Diocletian's Price Edict is between 10,000 denarii and 30,000 denarii ; *ZPE* 34 (1979), 177.

(105) DUNCAN-JONES (1974), 10 ; 12.

(106) Cf. COL. *RR*. 1.9-10 ; HOR. *Sat*. 1.2.55-56 ; 9.57 ; TAC. *Ann*. 16.11.3. Contrast MART. *Epig*. 2.68, a claim that freedom was purchased at the cost of *totis sarcinis*.

some slaves received wages for their work, a fact illustrated by a papyrus
from the late second century which records the arrangements made
between a female slave-owner in Oxyrhynchus and a local weaver who
was to teach the woman's slave his craft [107]. Whereas the owner
assumed responsibility for feeding and clothing her slave during the four
years of the apprenticeship, the slave was to be paid a regular wage by the
weaver, the amount increasing each year. Technically the wages must
have belonged to the owner who could have reimbursed herself for her
slave's expenses ; but it may also be that the slave was allowed to keep
some of the money, perhaps to be saved for eventual manumission. But
most slaves fell outside these circumstances, especially those in agriculture
and mining, and their prospects of acquiring money were consequently
restricted. The importance of the element of time involved here seems to
be shown by two documentary examples of manumission again from
Egypt : in one, from the late first century, a homeborn female slave
named Euphrosyne was set free by her owner (Aline) on payment of a
ransom sum (plus tax) at the age of thirty-five, while in the second,
another woman named Zosime was manumitted by her owner
(Tasucharion) in the late second century, after payment of ransom, at the
age of forty-four [108]. Neither act of emancipation is likely to have been
motivated by pure kindness on the part of the owners.

Monies acquired by the slave became part of his *peculium*, and in
estimating the likelihood of slaves' capacity to buy freedom it is relevant to
consider briefly this feature of the Roman slavery system. In the imperial
age the term *peculium* had come to refer specifically to cash or property at
the disposal of the slave [109]. Technically the *peculium* belonged to the
slave-owner, but in practice the slave usually had complete use and
control of its contents [110], which varied enormously : cash, food,
livestock, land, clothing, moveables, other slaves, even grazing rights are
all attested [111]. And there was no limit on the type of slave who might
have a *peculium* ; in exceptional circumstances even slaves in relatively
humble occupations were able to build up impressive holdings : on his

(107) *P. Oxy.* 1647. For similar documents cf. BIEZUNSKÁ-MAŁOWIST (1977), 85ff.

(108) *P. Oxy.* 2843 (see also *P. Oxy.* 48) ; *SB* 6293.

(109) BUCKLAND (1908), 187ff. ; CROOK (1967), 188f. ; see also FINLEY (1973), 64f.

(110) BUCKLAND (1908), 187 ; CROOK (1967), 189.

(111) VARRO, *RR*. 1.17.5 ; 2.10.5 ; *Dig.* 15.1.7.4 ; cf. *RE* 19 cols. 13-16 (W. von Uxkaill).

arrival at Constantinople in 361 the emperor Julian was amazed at the extravagant attire of a palace barber who, on request, accounted for his 'income' as follows − the equivalent each day of twenty times the daily supply of food for himself and for pack animals, besides an annual salary and other perquisites ; according to the barber, the palace cooks and other servants did just as well [112].

From the evidence of the agricultural writers it could be said that the *peculium* was in its own right a further instrument by which servile interests were met and which contributed towards the creation of good relations between slave and free [113]. The uninterrupted control of cash and property represented a concessive attitude from the master who as always was not obliged to permit existence of the *peculium*, which itself gave the slave some sense of responsibility and some taste of independence. Yet this was not mere and indiscriminate generosity for its own sake on the part of slave-owners : much of the commercial life in Roman society was conducted by slaves exploiting their *peculia* on behalf of their owners, while the diversity of wealth ownership among slaves, comparable and related to the diversity of their statuses and occupations, aided the prevention of any sense of corporate identity among them [114].

Moreover, the slave's *peculium* cannot have been in many cases a bonus, as it were, but a vital part of his basic needs. Although it was the master's responsibility to feed and clothe his slaves, this was not always an easy task for those of relatively modest means [115]. Varro refers to animals kept by slaves on the farm as a means of their being more easily able to maintain themselves, and presumably the animals could provide a source of clothing as well as of food [116]. Thus, an ex-slave who wrote on an epitaph that he was wealthy in spirit even though his *peculium* was small must have been typical of many others at large [117]. Further, it cannot be

---

(112) AMM. MARC. 22.4.9-10 (cf. G. W. BOWERSOCK, *Julian the Apostate*, Cambridge, Mass., 1978, 72) ; VARRO, *RR*. 1.17.5 ; 2.10.5 ; ATH. 6.274d ; VIRG. *Ecl.* 1.27-35. Cf. TREGGIARI (1979b), 200 on *peculium ancillae*. WHITE (1970), 359 doubts the possibility of rural slaves having the *peculium* in Cato's time, but note PLAUT. *Asin.* 539-41, *Etiam opilio qui pascit, mater, alienas ouis, aliquam habet peculiarem, qui spem soletur suam.* When a slave was set free by will, it was possible that his *peculium* was given him by his owner ; for the technical details see BOYER (1965), 360ff.

(113) VARRO, *RR*. 1.17.5.

(114) FINLEY (1973), 64.

(115) SEN. *Ben.* 3.21.2 ; IUV. 3.166-167.

(116) VARRO, *RR*. 1.19.3 ; cf. DIO CHRYS. *Orat.* 7.32.

(117) *ILS* 8436.

imagined that freedom was the only item on which slaves would spend whatever money they had. From epigraphic evidence it appears that at times they spent what must have been substantial sums on commemorative epitaphs and even public monuments ; and money could always be squandered on such luxuries as prostitutes ([118]). Nevertheless, when essential and other needs had been met, whatever additional cash could be saved by the slave could go towards the cost of his freedom. Literary sources suggest that slaves went to some lengths to secure cash, as in the case of Tityrus, Virgil's shepherd figure who sold sacrificial animals and cheeses he had made in a local town ; selling off surplus food from the master's table seems to have been possible for domestics, to judge from a story in Apuleius ; and Seneca refers to slaves deliberately starving themselves in order to increase their personal incomes ([119]). The proceeds of the *peculium* thus gave the long-term prospect of freedom established by law a short-term immediacy and reality, because cash savings in hand at any one time were a tangible reminder of that distant prospect. The *peculium* acted to reinforce the incentive aspect of manumission.

All in all, however, the simple fact of the slave's ability to purchase his freedom conceals the difficulties actually involved in raising the cash, with the result, again, that freedom was more easily realised by some slaves than others, even though the law, in setting up the abstract conditions under which freedom was to be granted, did not differentiate between one category of slaves and another. Naturally slaves might find themselves rewarded with manumission in return for exceptional acts of loyalty, or the reverse, sooner than anticipated, and the tendency to emancipate women for the purpose of marriage has already been noted ([120]). Yet it may be suspected that the kind of career illustrated by the fictional Trimalchio was far closer to the level of reality on which many slaves lived. Trimalchio had come to Italy as a boy from an indeterminate part of Asia and had remained in slavery for fourteen years before, so it seems, he was manumitted in his owner's will, manumission having

(118) Iuv. 3.131-134. For the costs of monuments see DUNCAN-JONES (1974), 79ff. ; 127ff. ; note *ILS* 8265, *Hoc monumentum ex mea frugalitate feci*.

(119) VIRG. *Ecl.* 1.27-35 ; APUL. *Met.* 10.13-14 ; SEN. *Epp.* 80.5 ; cf. also TER. *Phorm.* 43-44.

(120) See above, p. 92. By the early imperial period certain stories about manumission for exceptional acts of loyalty had become canonical (above, pp. 36f.) ; that did not exclude the possibility of other similar eventualities. For offers of freedom for untoward purposes, note APUL. *Apol.* 46, freedom in return for perjury. Cf. *Dig.* 40.2.9.

depended on his ability to secure the favour of both master and mistress during the period of enslavement [121]. Subsequently the way was open for seeking a fortune, though in reality this did not always lead to the sort of financial success Trimalchio encountered. One ex-slave who is commemorated on an inscription from Naples was set free at the age of thirty-one – on his deathbed ; another who received freedom at the age of thirty in his owner's will survived for little more than a year to enjoy his new condition [122].

As far as freedom and manumission are concerned, it can be said that the life of the slave in the Roman world was controlled on two planes : one, the official climate of opinion created by the legislation of Augustus which was developed and maintained by his successors ; the second, the more immediate world of the slave as shaped by his own environment. The law set up rules by which the slave could live his life under the expectation that freedom would be forthcoming once the requirements of age and moral suitability, synonymous with the espousal of Roman values, had been met. Freedom was a long-term prospect, but one that was not wholly beyond reach. In actuality, however, and distinct from the qualifications stipulated by law, the achievement of manumission depended on factors well beyond the slave's control. The elements of time involved – having to survive until the requisite age, having to await the death of the master for testamentary emancipation, having to wait for the accumulation of cash within the *peculium* to buy freedom ; the location of the individual slave in the spectrum of servile statuses ; and above all, the caprice of the slave-owner ; all of these factors conditioned the eventual acquisition of liberty and made it a far more difficult proposition than the strict letter of the law suggests. The fact of the extensive practice of manumission does not alter the situation that manumission was a real but fragile prospect for slaves, and it conceals the years of hardship that preceded its attainment.

From the point of view of the slave-owning establishment, the dual system of control operated in such a way as to maintain acquiescence

(121) Petr. *Sat.* 75-76 (cf. in general Veyne (1961)) ; cf. the biography of the eunuch Eutherius in Amm. Marc. 16.7.5.

(122) *ILS* 7842 ; 1985. It should be remembered that a slave whose freedom was purchased may not have paid the money himself ; it may instead have been paid for him by a family member already free ; this was probably a common phenomenon, but it did not minimise the waiting factor.

among slaves, who did not wish to prejudice their chances of acquiring freedom, and to perpetuate the slavery system to its own advantage. Everything combined to produce subordination in the slave to the master during slavery and to create a situation in which total domination over and exploitation of the slave were feasible. The long-term incentive of freedom did not automatically convert itself for the slave into the final reward, and was not necessarily supposed to, so that as with the family lives of slaves, it was the element of uncertainty which surrounded manumission which made freedom an effective form of social manipulation ([123]).

(123) An incentive does not always have to be applied in order to be effective from the instigator's point of view ; cf. E. J. HOBSBAWM, *The Age of Capital 1848-1875*, New York (Mentor edition), 1979, 239, 'The promise of the field-marshal's baton in every private's knapsack was never intended as a programme for promoting all soldiers to field-marshals'.

CHAPTER IV

FEAR, ABUSE, VIOLENCE

In preceding chapters some examples have been examined of ways in which Roman slave-owners might treat their slaves with various forms of generosity, and certain restricting factors which affected their application have been noted. Generosity in and of itself, however, was not enough to secure the elite ideal of servile *fides* and *obsequium*, that is to guarantee social stability, a fact perhaps most blatantly demonstrated to owners on those occasions when slaves became so discontented that they resorted to the ultimate means of defiance and physically attacked their owners. 'No master can feel safe because he is kind and considerate', the younger Pliny aptly commented, on the death in 108 of the praetorian senator Larcius Macedo, who had been assaulted by his slaves while bathing in his villa at Formiae [1].

No slave-owner wished to be murdered by his slaves, in his bath or elsewhere. Instead it was desirable that slaves stand in fear of their masters [2]. Generosity had to be tempered with either force or the threat of force in order for control to be maintained, and a climate of fear over those of subordinate social position had to be created. The principle was well understood in Roman society : Cicero stated bluntly that 'severity must be employed by those who keep subjects under control by force – by masters, for example, towards their slaves, if no other way is possible' [3]. Fear in the slave produced greater loyalty, so it was said [4], and Columella thus pragmatically advised the prospective buyer of an estate to make a

(1) PLIN. *Epp.* 3.14. For similar episodes compare the murders of L. Pedanius Secundus in 61 (TAC. *Ann.* 14.42-45) and of Afranius Dexter in 105 (PLIN. *Epp.* 8.14). On Pliny's accounts see SHERWIN-WHITE (1966), 246ff. ; 461ff.

(2) Cf. CIC. *Para. Stoic.* 5.41, *omnis animi debilitati et humilis et fracti timiditas seruitus est* ; FINLEY (1976), 820.

(3) CIC. *Off.* 2.24, *Sed iis, qui ui oppressos imperio coercent, sit sane adhibenda saeuitia, ut eris in famulos, si aliter teneri non possunt.* SEN. *Epp.* 4.4 suggests that masters' behaviour could drive slaves to suicide.

(4) PROPERT. 3.6.6, *maioremque timens seruus habere fidem.*

purchase which would allow him to arrive unexpectedly, because his slaves would stay at work because of the fear (*metus*) which resulted ([5]). Similarly Tacitus attributes to the jurist C. Cassius in the senatorial debate which followed the servile murder of L. Pedanius Secundus the argument that fear (*metus*) was especially needed among slaves in Nero's reign in view of the admixture of foreigners ([6]). All of this was merely a variation on the broad theme, 'Experience teaches that fear is the most effective regulator and guide for the performance of duty', words found in the preamble to Diocletian's Edict on Maximum Prices ([7]). Moreover, the all-pervasive quality of this attitude is reflected in early Christian writings, for the reiteration in Apostolic and post-Apostolic literature that slaves should obey their masters 'with fear and trembling' ([8]) simply shows how Christian leaders absorbed and indirectly supported the ideology of the slave-owning classes in Roman society at large. In this chapter, therefore, some of the ways in which fear might make itself felt in the life of the slave will be presented through describing various forms of abuse and violence to which the slave was exposed as part of everyday normality, the psychological impact of which can subsequently be compared with the results of apparently generous and humane treatment already seen.

Certain kinds of maltreatment which were not punishments but which essentially depended on the exploitation of the slave as a marketable commodity were associated with the slave-dealer (*mango*), and they can be introduced first. In view of his disreputable stock character the slave-dealer is not a figure well represented in surviving literary or other sources, but individuals such as the Toranius Flaccus and A. Kapreilius Timotheus already encountered must have been far more numerous and far more vital a part of the economic life of the Roman world than the sparse record suggests ([9]). One reason for their relative obscurity is that, like Trimalchio, men who trafficked in slaves did not necessarily confine

(5) COL. *RR*. 1.2.1.

(6) TAC. *Ann*. 14.44.

(7) *et semper praeceptor metus iustissimus officiorum inuenitur esse moderator* ; line 130 of the preamble in the edition of Marta Giacchero (Genoa, 1974), I p. 136, though the words are outside the narrow context of the master-slave relationship. The origin of the fable is ascribed by PHAEDRUS (*Fab*. III prol. 33-37) to slaves' fears of speaking openly before masters in case of punishment ; see Appendix F.

(8) *Eph*. 6.5 ; *I Pet*. 18 ; *Did*. 4.11 ; *Barn*. 19.7. For slaves and fearfulness in PLAUTUS, see *Amph*. 291ff. ; *Pseud*. 1103ff. ; *Most*. 859ff. and below, p. 136.

(9) Cf. above, pp. 61f. Evidence is collected in *RE* 14 col. 1107 (Hug), and an inventory of actual dealers is given by HARRIS (1980), 129ff.

themselves to dealing in one commodity alone but combined slave-dealing with other ventures ([10]). In consequence, and given the constancy over time of a regular trade in slaves ([11]), it can safely be inferred that the abuses for which dealers became notorious, and which restricted their individual self-advertisement, were practised on a wide scale and affected the lives of considerable numbers of slaves.

Slave-dealing was a profitable enterprise ([12]), and anything which might increase his profit was attempted by the dealer. Slaves put up for sale on the auction block were not always physically excellent specimens, and because the potential purchaser was able to inspect the merchandise before buying ([13]), dealers tried to disguise defects in order to complete a transaction. For example, a false but healthy looking complexion could be produced in a slave by painting his face, and a thin slave could be artificially fattened up by rubbing an ointment made from terebinth resin over his body so that his skin became loose and enabled a greater intake of food (or so it was believed) ([14]). Among other indignities slaves on the block might find themselves being examined for epilepsy, having to appear naked, having their feet whitened with chalk to show their foreign origin, or being obliged to carry placards advertising their own qualities ([15]). Moreover, the dealers also catered to the market for slaves as homosexual partners, boys who had to be especially presentable when up for sale. Thus special depilatories were used for the removal of body hair, the growth of which (again so it was believed) could even be prevented ([16]). Similarly, ants' eggs, blood from the testicles of castrated lambs and the bodily application of hyacinth bulb dipped in sweet wine were considered to restrain the onset of puberty ([17]). Most tellingly of all,

(10) Petr. *Sat.* 76.6 ; Harris (1980), 129.

(11) M. I. Finley, *The Black Sea and Danubian Regions and the Slave Trade in Antiquity* in *Klio* 40 (1962), 51ff.

(12) Cf. Cic. *Orat.* 232. No distinction is made here between primary and secondary dealers, for which see J. P. V. D. Balsdon, *Romans and Aliens*, London, 1979, 78f.

(13) Sen. *Epp.* 80.9.

(14) Quint. *Inst.* 2.15.25 ; Plin. *NH* 24.35.

(15) Plin. *NH* 35.199 ; 201 ; cf. Propert. 4.5.52 ; Iuv. 1.111 ; cf. *Dig.* 21.1.31.21. Sen. *Epp.* 80.9 ; Apul. *Apol.* 44 ; Suet. *Rhet.* 1.

(16) Plin. *NH* 32.135. On the connection between homosexuality and slavery see Beert C. Verstraete, *Slavery and the Social Dynamics of Male Homosexual Relations in Ancient Rome* in *Journal of Homosexuality* 5 (1980), 227ff.

(17) Plin. *NH* 30.41 ; 21.170.

dealers were associated with the practice of castration despite successive laws forbidding it ([18]).

It is impossible of course to measure the actual extent of any of these practices and trade secrets, especially those at first sight seemingly outrageous but not for that reason to be dismissed. Yet taken together they illustrate the level of sheer personal humiliation, if not physical despoliation, to which slaves could be subjected when they passed through the market. The evidence on slave-dealers is strong enough to show activity throughout the Empire, and slave-markets are also attested on a wide basis ([19]). Thus it can scarcely be doubted that personal degradation from the process of sale was a common servile experience, while for those who had been conveyed to Rome or Alexandria ([20]) or some other major city from remote areas of the Mediterranean world, sale and all that it involved was only the culmination of a train of experiences likely to have had both physically and emotionally debilitating effects : capture, forced migration, deracination. As seen already ([21]), the possibility of being sold was a contingency with which any slave might have to contend, and that possibility is as important as the reality itself for understanding the psychological conditions under which slaves lived.

Secondly, since slaves by definition were at the complete disposal of their owners it follows that they might become the object of capricious sexual abuse ([22]), as the practice of castrating young boys confirms. It has already been suggested that the sexual behaviour of slave wet-nurses was adversely affected by the economic interests of their owners ([23]), and similarly the sale of slaves as prostitutes, both male and female, suggests further another form of degradation founded on economic motives, incorporating not only the trauma of sale but also continuous sexual exploitation for as long as the slave-owner wished ([24]). The process is

(18) E.g. MART. *Epig.* 9.6 ; Iuv. 6.373A&B ; for the legislation see below, pp. 128f.

(19) HARRIS (1980), 126ff. For sales at Rome itself cf. SEN. *Const.* 13.4, ... *aliquis ex his, qui ad Castoris negotiantur nequam mancipia ementes uendentesque, quorum tabernae pessimorum seruorum turba refertae sunt.*

(20) For Alexandria and the slave trade, see BIEZUNSKA-MAŁOWIST (1976).

(21) See above, pp. 52ff. Something of the fear in servile life which the prospect of sale aroused may be guessed at from the question 'Am I to be sold ?' put to an oracle as recorded in *P. Oxy.* 1477 = A. S. HUNT, C. C. EDGAR, *Select Papyri* I (LCL 1932), no. 195.

(22) Cf. FINLEY (1976) ; (1980), 95f.

(23) See above, pp. 70ff.

(24) Some information on prostitution is assembled in Fernando HENRIQUES, *Prostitution and Society ; A Survey, Vol. I,* London, 1962, 89ff. ; cf. also Hans HERTER, *Die*

illustrated in principle, despite its comic setting, in the auction and sale to a brothel-keeper of the character Tarsia in the *Historia Apollonii Tyriensis*, and Tarsia's subsequent exposure to a string of clients willing to pay for her services ; Tarsia's ability to protect herself by eloquence, however, is not likely to have been the fate of many prostitutes in real life [25]. The number of slaves who functioned as prostitutes appears to have been great, though the information available is mainly anecdotal ; nonetheless rules on the registration and taxing of prostitutes, and the notoriety of an area such as the Subura in Rome itself must be taken to indicate widespread profiteering at the expense of slaves in no position to choose the nature of their work [26].

It is even more probable, however, that slave-owners gratified their own appetites from among the slaves of their households with no thought of financial gain in mind, and from this perspective the poems of Martial prove to be of interest because they are full of allusions to casual sexual relations between owners and slaves, both heterosexual and homosexual. Thus, the outcome of intrigues between one of Martial's addressees, Quirinalis, and this man's maidservants (*ancillae*) was 'homeborn gentlemen' (*equites uernae*), and another addressee, Cinna, is ridiculed by the poet because his seven 'children' had all in fact been fathered by different male slaves in his household [27]. In other poems, a woman uses her dowry to redeem her lover from slavery, relationships between a master and his *uilica* and maidservants, and between a mistress and her litter-bearers are mentioned, young boys and girls are purchased expressly to serve as sexual partners [28].

Soziologie der antiken Prostitution im Lichte des heidnischen und christlichen Schrifttums in *JAC* 3 (1960), 106ff. and (briefly) Sarah B. POMEROY, *Goddesses, Whores, Wives, and Slaves*, New York, 1975, 192 ; 201. Note PLAUT. *Pseud.* 188ff., for the possible contemporary political allusiveness of which see A. ARCHELLASCI, *Politique et religion dans le «Pseudolus»* in *REL* 56 (1978), 115ff. at pp. 119ff.

(25) *Hist. Ap. Tyr.* 33-36 (cf. B. E. PERRY, *The Ancient Romances*, Berkeley and Los Angeles, 1967, 314f. ; DUNCAN-JONES (1974), 253f.) ; cf. also SEN. *Controu.* 1.2.3 ; MART. *Epig.* 6.66 ; APUL. *Met.* 7.9 ; DIO CHRYS. *Or.* 7.148.

(26) E.g., TAC. *Ann.* 2.85.1-4 ; SUET. *Cal.* 40 ; T. FRANK, ed., *An Economic Survey of Ancient Rome, Vol. IV*, Baltimore, 1938, 253 (F. M. Heichelheim). HOR. *Epod.* 5.58 ; PROPERT. 4.7.15 ; MART. *Epig.* 2.17.1 ; 6.66.2 ; 11.61.3 ; 11.78.11. Note also PLAUT. *Poen.* 339f. ; HOR. *Epist.* 1.14.21 ; MART. *Epig.* 3.93.14f. ; AMM. MARC. 28.4.9. For Egypt see BIEZUNSKA-MAŁOWIST (1977), 91ff.

(27) MART. *Epig.* 1.84 ; 6.39.

(28) MART. *Epig.* 2.33 ; 3.33 ; 4.66 ; 6.71 ; 11.70 ; 12.58 ; 12.96.

The practices referred to evoke no comment of disbelief from Martial [29], but if in actuality the historicity of his anecdotes and allusions may be dubious, that is not an important matter. Rather it is the underlying assumptions which are revealing, because Martial takes for granted the fact that slaves of both sexes and of all ages were objects of casual sexual pleasure, and that the contexts of his poems will reflect reality sufficiently to be understood by his readers. Likewise the Stoic Musonius Rufus makes similar assumptions in criticising the master's lack of self-control in his relationships with slave girls [30]. It is possible, therefore, that many slaves in close proximity to their owners had to accept with a certain fatalism that they might be required to cater to their owners' sexual demands. Some may even have welcomed the situation, seeing in it a chance to win their owners' approval and their own freedom as a result. This was the claim of Trimalchio concerning his former master and mistress, and it helps explain why the concubines kept in aristocratic households, such as those of Larcius Macedo, were willing to tolerate their position [31]. It is equally possible that some slaves became involved in relationships with their owners which were founded on genuine sentiment : marriage between an ex-slave and her patron is accepted as normal in the social legislation of Augustus (though the patron himself might well be an ex-slave) [32]. Yet it remains true that slaves were automatically deprived of individuality and self-respect when they could anticipate becoming their owners' involuntary lovers. Sexual abuse was to be expected by them just as much as other forms of maltreatment, and even in a society where sexual relationships were regarded with a great deal of openness and lack of guilt, there is likely to have been in consequence much dehumanisation at work in slave life about which nothing is heard in conventional sources.

The most direct way in which violence appeared in the life of the slave was through physical chastisement, the normal prerogative of the slave-owner to which there was practically no limit, and few owners would have disputed the axiom that 'one must punish one's slaves according to

(29) BARBU (1963), 67ff. believes that Martial has a certain sympathy for abused slaves, is genuinely indignant about their condition, and that the poems (as Juvenal's) are essentially realistic in their description of servile conditions.

(30) MUSONIUS, p. 66 Hense. See in general TREGGIARI (1979b), 192ff.

(31) PETR. Sat. 75.11 ; PLIN. Epp. 3.14.3 ; cf. also SUET. Vesp. 3 ; HA Marc. 29.10 ; see in general RAWSON (1974).

(32) See above, p. 92.

their deserts' [33]. Physical punishment was taken for granted and largely unquestioned, a fact revealed implicitly in Tacitus' description of slave-owning customs in Germany, where punishment was surprisingly rare, explicitly by Seneca's broad statement that slaves were treated 'not as if they were men, but beasts of burden' [34]. In Seneca's view, indeed, owners were in general 'excessively haughty, cruel and insulting' towards slaves, and that made servile respect for the master, as opposed to fear of him, difficult to achieve [35]. Seneca's apparent distaste for this state of affairs was virtually exceptional [36], so it is not surprising that Roman literature is replete with examples of slaves being punished, and by describing merely a few of them it is easy to see what the principal kinds of punishment were, what offences led to them, and what kinds of slaves received them. The unhistorical nature of some of the literary stories again does not deprive them of significance when it is remembered that authors wrote in the belief that their readers would recognise common elements in the master-slave relationship in their works.

Flogging was a widespread punishment for which, it seems, little justification was required. Juvenal shows slaves being flogged by professional employees as a result of their mistress' pique for her husband, and he offers also a scene of a slave-owner standing over his slaves, whip in hand, as they clean the house [37]. Less sensationally Varro advised that farm-hands should only be beaten by the *uilicus* if words did not achieve the desired effect, but Tacitus refers to slaves being flogged as their owner lay on his deathbed and Ammianus Marcellinus reports that owners in his day might have slaves beaten three hundred times for an offence as trivial as being slow to bring hot water [38]. In Diodorus' description of servile conditions in the mines in Spain, moreover, beating is a staple ingredient [39]. The prevalence in the first century of *ergastula* for housing

(33) ATH. 6.265a ; cf. SEN. *Clem*. 1.18.2, *in seruum omnia liceant*.

(34) TAC. *Germ*. 25.2 ; SEN. *Epp*. 47.5. Cf. Ps. PLUT. *De lib. ed*. 12 : physical punishment is fit only for slaves.

(35) SEN. *Epp*. 47.11 ; 17-19.

(36) Cf. however EPICT. *Diss*. 1.13.2, and cf. CREŢIA(1961),373f., MILANI (1972), 222f., and BRUNT (1973), 18f. on Dio Chrysostom ; on Seneca and slavery see MILANI (1972), 212ff. and GRIFFIN (1976), 256ff., and for Roman attitudes towards cruelty in general see LINTOTT (1968), 35ff.

(37) IUV. 6.474ff. ; 14.60f. ; cf. BARBU (1963), 68.

(38) VARRO, *RR*. 1.17.5 ; TAC. *Ann*. 16.19.4 ; AMM. MARC. 28.4.16 ; cf. also PLUT. *Cato* 21.3.

(39) DIOD. SIC. 5.38. In the *Satyricon*, the heroes on entering Trimalchio's house find themselves confronted by a desperate domestic who entreats them to rescue him from a

rural slaves can be assumed from Columella's recommendations on their upkeep and from the elder Pliny's complaints of the low quality of work performed by their inmates ([40]). According to Suetonius these men at the beginning of the imperial age were so dangerous at large as brigands that Augustus was compelled to take coercive action against them ; that hints at a problem of control, as too the supposed abolition of the *ergastula* by Hadrian ([41]). Detention in these places involved permanent shackling, and some agricultural workers appear to have been regularly kept in chains during the daytime ([42]). No small wonder, then, that the threat of being sent to the country as punishment was held over the heads of urban slaves ([43]), yet shackling was frequent elsewhere as well : Augustus, for example, put in chains a certain Cosmus for having made some insulting remarks, and the penalty was considered mild ([44]). Equally, slaves were branded in punishment, for an offence according to Juvenal as slight as stealing a couple of towels ([45]), and the elder Pliny's reference to the branding of slaves' faces lends credibility to the ruse of Eumolpus in the *Satyricon* whereby the heroes' foreheads were covered with false inscriptions to make authentic their disguise as slaves ([46]). Finally, the

steward whose clothes have been stolen, and Trimalchio himself has a slave beaten for bandaging his bruised arm with white instead of purple wool (PETR. *Sat.* 30.7-11 ; 54.4). On Trimalchio's doorpost there was an inscription reading, 'Any slave leaving the house without the master's permission will receive one hundred lashes' (PETR. *Sat.* 28.7) ; cf. COL. *RR*. 11.1.23, servile absence from the farm only under extreme conditions, and for the connection between flight, theft and flogging, HOR. *Epist* 1.16.46f. On incidental allusions to cruelty in literature, cf. HOPKINS (1978), 118.

(40) See above p. 21 ; PLIN. *NH* 18.36 ; cf. 21 ; on the history and meaning of the term *ergastulum* see R. ETIENNE, *Recherches sur l'ergastule* in *Actes du Colloque 1972 sur l'esclavage*, Paris, 1974, 249ff. and J. C. FITZGIBBON, *Ergastula* in *Echos du monde classique / Classical News and Views* 20 (1976), 55ff.

(41) SUET. *Aug.* 32.1 ; *HA Hadr.* 18.10 ; cf. the difficulty of restraining the *pastores* of southern Italy (TAC. *Ann.* 4.27 ; 12.65.1), on the background to which see T. P. WISEMAN, *Viae Anniae* in *PBSR* 32 (1964), 21ff. ; Brunt (1971), 551ff. According to *HA Seu. Alex.* 27.1-3, Severus Alexander wished to have slaves wear distinctive dress to allow easy recognition and to cut down disorder (*ne quis seditiosus esset*). In spite of Hadrian's alleged suppression, the term *ergastulum* appears in Apuleius (*Apol.* 47 ; cf. *Met.* 9.12) as if still in common use.

(42) COL. *RR*. 1.6.3 ; 1.9.4 refer to slaves working in vineyards as the *uincti* or *alligati* ; cf. MART. *Epig.* 9.23 and contrast PLINY (*Epp.* 3.19.7), who avoided chain-gangs, unusually.

(43) HOR. *Sat.* 2.7.118 ; IUV. 8.179f. ; cf. PLAUT. *Bacch.* 365 ; *Asin.* 341f.

(44) SUET. *Aug.* 67.1.

(45) IUV. 14.15ff.

(46) PLIN. *NH* 18.21 ; PETR. *Sat.* 103 ; cf. also MART. *Epig.* 8.75 ; DIO CHRYS. *Or.* 14.19 ;

practice was common of compelling slaves to wear iron collars which bore their owners' names or addresses so that fugitives could be appropriately returned on capture ([47]).

The omnipotence of the master over the slave was such that the way was open not just for the exercise of these, as it were, standard types of physical punishment and treatment, but also for the devising of exceptional acts of cruelty in which sadistic tendencies on the part of some owners stand out clearly. In this respect Roman emperors figure prominently in the literary record. For example, a slave who had stolen a piece of silver plate at a banquet given by Caligula is said, upon detection, to have been handed over at once by the emperor to a *carnifex* : his hands were cut off and hung around his neck, and he was then paraded around the dining hall with a placard giving the reasons for his misfortune ([48]). Such an atrocity cannot be attributed solely to Caligula's possible derangement. Augustus had the legs of a slave named Thallus broken for taking a bribe, while the *paedagogus* and other attendants of his grandson C. Caesar were thrown into a river with weights tied around their necks for having too precipitately anticipated their master's death ([49]). While similar stories surround other emperors ([50]), they are not confined to the imperial house alone. Larcius Macedo represents the type of the cruel master, *superbus alioqui dominus et saeuus* ([51]), whose enormities against slaves there was little to prevent, such as the decision of the infamous Vedius Pollio to feed to his lampreys a boy who had broken a crystal cup ([52]). Seneca portrays a gourmand at dinner surrounded by a retinue of slaves whose slightest murmurs − coughs, sneezes and hiccups − were suppressed with the rod, and Juvenal describes the cruel Rutilus

Ovid, *Trist.* 4.1.5 ; *Pont.* 1.6.31. Constantine abolished branding of the face as a criminal penalty, reserving it for hands and legs only ; *CTh.* 9.40.2.

(47) Examples available at *ILS* 8726-8733 ; the practice was not mitigated by Christianity ; cf. G. Sotgiu, *Un collare di schiava rinvenuto in Sardegna* in *Archeologia Classica* 25-26 (1973-74), 688ff. The collars may be one of the stigmatising signs of slavery referred to at Dion. Hal. 4.14.4.

(48) Suet. *Cal.* 32.2.

(49) Suet. *Aug.* 57.1-2.

(50) Hadrian is said to have stabbed a slave in the eye with a stylus in a fit of anger (Galen 5.17-18, Kühn) ; Macrinus had a particular reputation for flogging slaves (*HA Macr.* 13.3) ; and Valentinian killed off slaves in Germany to eliminate a security threat (Amm. Marc. 29.4.4.) ; cf. also *HA Hadr.* 21.3.

(51) Plin. *Epp.* 3.14.1 ; cf. Petr. *Sat.* 107.4, *saeui quoque implacabilesque domini* ; Amm. Marc. 25.4.2, *rabiosus ... dominus et crudelis*.

(52) Sen. *Ira* 3.40.2 ; cf. *Clem.* 1.18.2 ; Dio 54.23.1-4 ; Plin. *NH* 9.77.

delighting in the infliction on his slaves of flogging, branding and incarceration [53].

It is thus indisputable that physical coercion from the owner played a large part in servile life in one way or another and that subjection to brutality was a basic component of slavery. It may readily be allowed that some of the literary stories referred to attracted the attention of writers because they were extreme examples of cruelty ; and it was of course the case that outrages were perceived and not necessarily condoned : 'If one were to crucify a slave who, when bidden to take away a dish, has greedily licked up the half-eaten fish and its sauce, now cold, sane men would call him more insane than Labeo,' Horace wrote, and again, 'If you were to take to pelting stones ... at your own slaves, for whom you've paid in cash, all would hoot at you as mad' [54]. But any thought that the anecdotal nature of the literary evidence makes that evidence totally suspect is shattered by the testimony of an inscription from Puteoli, which gives details of the duties of a public official (manceps) in charge of local burials, duties which included the torture and execution of slaves. If a private citizen wished to punish a slave (male or female), he could on payment of a fee have public facilities (crux, patibulum, uerberatores) put at his disposal, the manceps having to see that all the necessary apparatus was provided. Local officials could have slaves tortured free of charge, and again the manceps had to ensure availability of instruments and personnel, and to take care subsequently of the removal of corpses [55]. The point is that there was no real restraint on the slave-owner, other than his own temperament or conscience, to prevent outrage or extremity if circumstance led to it : any slave who offended his owner could expect not only punishment but severe punishment, the penalty apparently often exceeding the transgression, especially in cases of sheer accidents. The threat of punishment always overhung servile activities and since

---

(53) SEN. Epp. 47.2-3 ; IUV. 14.15ff.

(54) HOR. Sat. 1.3.80-82 ; 2.3.128-130, Loeb translation. While there are notorious instances of brutality in the literary record, the most common forms of punishment were perhaps not such as to destroy the slave property. Limits on masters' severity must have been imposed by the realisation that frequent excessive punishment acted against their own best economic interests ; cf. BURFORD (1972), 42f. Men such as Vedius Pollio and Larcius Macedo were doubtless extreme.

(55) AE 1971 no. 88, II 8-14 ; cf. Lucio BOVE, Due inscrizione da Pozzuoli e Cuma in Labeo 13 (1967), 22ff. ; Francesco DE MARTINO, I "supplicia" dell'inscrizione di Pozzuoli in Labeo 21 (1975), 210ff. ; FINLEY (1980), 95.

penalties could be inflicted either by the owner or an underling there was often more than one person to fear. While it should not be thought that all slaves in Roman society were being physically violated all the time, it is nevertheless true that all slaves were under the constant pressure of exposure to punishment and that such pressure formed another aspect of the servile mentality [56].

Moreover, even from the limited amount of material considered so far, it is clear, and requires stress, that servile distinctions of status, function, age or sex gave no protection against arbitrary punishment. It may be an accident of the sources that more details are preserved on the harsh treatment of domestic than other slaves : Juvenal's evidence contains references to a woolmaid, a litter-bearer, a maidservant, and indeed the full domestic household ; Martial adds a hairdresser and a cook [57] ; Caligula's slave must have been a waiter ; Thallus was obviously some kind of secretary. Agricultural and mining slaves were certainly exposed to the same climate of violence and even children were not spared, but urban domestics were more visible to their owners than their rural counterparts and they were thus at a particular disadvantage as far as the infliction of punishment was concerned. In view of their relative advantages in the areas of creating families and achieving manumission, this point is valuable for offsetting the common belief that the conditions of urban slaves were always more favourable than those of slaves elsewhere.

In what ways could the slave find protection against arbitrary cruelty from the master ? As seen already, excess led at times to slaves' own physical retaliation against their owners, though this must have been an extremely dangerous undertaking. But there were other means, notably through the law, which were at least theoretically available to slaves, mechanisms whose purpose was perhaps to prevent the possibility of physical danger and injury to owners from retaliating slaves. At Rome it was the responsibility of the city prefect (*praefectus urbi*) to hear slaves' complaints of cruel treatment, perhaps from the inception of the office under Augustus and certainly soon thereafter [58]. In the provinces the

(56) For the relationship between physical punishment and the absence of servile *dignitas* see Lintott (1968), 46.

(57) Mart. *Epig.* 2.66 ; 8.23.

(58) *Dig.* 1.12.1.1 ; 8 ; Sen. *Ben.* 3.22.3 ; cf. Bellen (1971), 66ff. ; Griffin (1976), 269f. ; (cf. 460f.).

same function was filled by the governor ([59]). Yet it is questionable how often, from the servile point of view, these procedures were successfully applied. Roman law as a whole favoured the interests of the elite over those of the lower social orders ([60]) and it might thus be thought unlikely that slave-owning officials would have been genuinely open and impartial to slaves who appeared before them. A slave who wished to seek legal redress had to face the problem of the official's availability, which as in the case of obtaining formal manumission must always have been unpredictable. At Rome there appears to have been a special site where the city prefect could be found, though how often is not known, while in the provinces the limiting conditions of the circuit tour again prevailed ([61]). And the slave's very decision to seek help from the authorities is likely to have involved desperate action on his part before access to officials was even gained : since the slave-owner could to some degree control the slave's movements ([62]), and cannot be expected usually to have given permission to leave the household or estate for complaints to be made against himself, the slave was compelled to abscond and to take refuge often at a place of asylum ([63]). This is not to say that the slave's position was hopeless, but it is to emphasise the risks and difficulties which attended appeal ([64]).

In the early imperial age the right of asylum, originally a Greek rather than Roman convention, came to be associated with temples and representations of the emperor both at Rome and in the provinces ([65]). Under Tiberius, sanctuary before a statue of Augustus was claimed in Crete ; it had become a capital offence to beat a slave near such a statue ;

(59) GAIUS, *Inst.* 1.53 ; *Dig.* 1.6.2 ; *Instit.* 1.8.2 ; this evidence refers to rulings of the emperor Antoninus Pius, but the governor was probably hearing slaves' appeals earlier since rights of asylum (see below) were already in existence.

(60) GARNSEY (1970), passim. ; cf. also *Legal Privilege in the Roman Empire* in M. I. Finley, ed., *Studies in Ancient Society*, London, 1974, 141ff.

(61) *Dig.* 1.12.1.1 with BELLEN (1971), 66f. ; above, pp. 101ff. JONKERS (1934), 243 perhaps overestimates the ease with which complaints were made.

(62) Cf. COL. *RR.* 11.1.23.

(63) He did not thereby become a fugitive, however, technically at least ; *Dig.* 21.1.17.12.

(64) According to *HA Pert.* 9.10, slaves who had brought false charges (*calumniae*) against their masters were crucified by Pertinax ; how the *calumniae* were established is not made clear by the text.

(65) See for example DIO 47.19.2 ; TAC. *Ann.* 3.36 (cf. 3.60) ; SUET. *Aug.* 17.5 ; SEN. *Clem.* 1.18.2 ; BELLEN (1971), 64ff. ; St. WEINSTOCK, *Divus Julius*, Oxford, 1971, 242f. ; cf. DAUBE (1972), 57f. ; HOPKINS (1978), 221ff.

and even statues of the living emperor were deemed to afford protection [66]. Among those who could legitimately draw on the safety of asylum were slaves who had complaints against their owners, protection which was certainly drawn upon [67]. Even so it is not altogether clear whether a fair hearing of the complaints followed : in circumstances admittedly exceptional, right of asylum was simply violated when Augustus executed the sons of M. Antonius and his wife Fulvia, who had taken refuge at a statue of the deified Julius [68]. Nor is it safe to assume that access to an official was always automatic once asylum had been sought : refuge at a busy time of day in order to compel attention and a hearing, when public awareness of the situation was intense, was urged to the elder Agrippina and Nero Caesar under harassment from Sejanus again in Tiberius' reign [69]. The younger Pliny dealt with a fugitive in Bithynia who had sought refuge before a statue of Trajan, but it should be noted that the slave had earlier appeared before other, presumably municipal, magistrates [70], a circumstance which may at other times have hindered access to the governor's tribunal. All in all the frequency with which slave suppliants were able to come before Roman magistrates and to be heard sympathetically cannot be determined, but it is doubtful that the law and reality often coincided equitably. And even in the event of a successful hearing the benefit which accrued to the slave was no more than sale to a new owner, to judge from a ruling of Antoninus Pius [71], whereby the slave became exposed to new possibilities of abuse.

Again in theory and to some extent in practice the emperor himself was available to slaves for appeal, as he was to other members of society. Petitions were received from slaves and emperors gave responses, but as seen earlier factors of time, distance, cost and imperial temperament meant that this source of redress was unusual for slaves rather than a common occurrence [72]. Moreover, the majority of attested imperial responses to servile petitions concern questions of slaves' status and not

---

(66) TAC. *Ann.* 3.63 ; SUET. *Tib.* 58 ; (cf. PLIN. *Epp.* 10.74).

(67) PLIN. *Epp.* 10.74, and legal texts cited in n. 59. On asylum as protection against sexual abuse see TREGGIARI (1979b), 192.

(68) SUET. *Aug.* 17.5.

(69) TAC. *Ann.* 4.67.

(70) PLIN. *Epp.* 10.74.1.

(71) *Dig.* 1.6.2 ; cf. BELLEN (1971), 66ff. ; GRIFFIN (1976), 269f. ; WILLIAMS (1976), 76f.

(72) See above, pp. 102f. with references.

questions of abuse or maltreatment [73]. On the other hand Hadrian is known to have relegated for five years a woman who had harmed her maidservants (*ancillae*) [74] ; yet the details of the episode – the precise nature of the charges and how the emperor came to be involved – are beyond recovery. An incident between Augustus and Vedius Pollio, however, suggests that imperial intervention could be totally fortuitous, for Augustus, while at dinner with Vedius Pollio, is reported to have saved from the man-eating fish a slave who made a timely appeal to him, and then to have rebuked the slave's owner [75]. To say the least Augustus' location was highly convenient for this particular individual and there can have been few other slaves fortunate enough to obtain the emperor's clemency in this fashion at such personally critical moments.

The conclusion follows, therefore, that a significant dichotomy existed between the potential of legal relief for slaves who had unduly suffered from their owners and the realisation of that potential, an imbalance which operated firmly in the interests of slave-owners and against those of slaves : according to a ruling of Constantine a slave-owner whose slave had died after punishment was not himself subject to a penalty unless the slave's punishment had been immoderate [76]. Yet this view, which many might regard as overly cynical, would seem to be vitiated by the knowledge that in the imperial period a series of laws was enacted which ostensibly brought about a great improvement of servile conditions. Whereas in technical terms the master's power over his slaves, including the power of life and death, remained constant, in actuality a number of legal developments had the effect of bringing slaves more and more under the control of the state [77]. For instance, the slave-owner's ability to consign slaves to wild beasts in the arena was abolished (the *lex Petronia*) ; sick slaves who were abandoned by their owners but who subsequently recovered were not returned to their owners but were set free ; the master

---

(73) See the items collected in Piganiol (1958).

(74) *Dig.* 1.6.2 ; *Coll.* 3.3.4.

(75) Sen. *Ira* 3.40.2 ; cf. *Clem.* 1.18.2 ; Dio 54.23.1-4 ; Plin. *NH* 9.77 seems to equate the feeding to fish with the penalty of *bestiae*. On Pollio see R. Syme, *Who was Vedius Pollio* ? in *JRS* 51 (1961), 23ff. = *Roman Papers*, Oxford, 1979, II 518ff. Is it possible that the episode between Pollio and Augustus influenced the creation of the office of *praefectus urbi* ?

(76) *CJ* 9.14.1. The loophole for the master is obvious.

(77) See in general Buckland (1908), 36ff. ; Westermann (1955), 114f. ; Griffin (1976), 268f.

who killed a slave became subject to trial for homicide, and the master was required to give up a slave proved to have suffered excessive brutality. Castration of slaves was also banned [78].

The usual interpretation of this legislation is that it reflects the growth of a humanitarian concern for slaves in the imperial age [79], a notion which, although perhaps containing some truth, is beyond proof and inconsistent with what can be determined of actual practice as seen so far. It could be said that protection against cruelty to slaves was given more attention than in the past by the various emperors who were responsible for rulings ; but pronouncements were not necessarily matched by compliance, and not only do the limitations already described on the slave's capacity to secure redress have to be kept in mind here, but the degree of amelioration of the slave's conditions contained in the law can be shown to have been not really all that great. Claudius' grant of freedom to abandoned sick slaves who recovered their health is the only certain case in which genuine protection against future abuse and violence can be allowed : freedom permitted change because subjection to the will of a slave-owner was fully eradicated, though it should be noted that the slave was not given full freedom but only Junian status [80]. But in the ban, established by the *lex Petronia*, on masters arbitrarily assigning slaves to the wild beasts of the amphitheatre, the law continued to uphold that penalty if the slave-owner were able to prove just cause against his slave [81], a rather obvious loophole. And given an inferable identification of social status and general interest between owner and magistrate, it may be doubted that the latter frequently pronounced in favour of the slave in cases of this sort. At any rate, the *lex Petronia* did nothing to diminish the severity of other forms of physical punishment, nor did the laws on homicide and castration, and again, significantly, in cases where a slave was able to show excessive cruelty − which must have been difficult since the right of the master not to be accused by his own slave was preserved [82] − the law allowed only for his sale to a new owner, the

---

(78) *Dig.* 48.8.11.1-2 ; 18.1.42 ; 40.8.2 ; 1.6.1.2 ; Suet. *Claud.* 25.2 ; Gaius, *Inst.* 1.53 ; *Instit.* 1.8.2 ; cf. *HA Hadr.* 18.7 ; for castration see below, pp. 128f.
(79) E.g., Westermann (1955), 116f. ; Burford (1972), 50 ; contrast Griffin (1976), 268f.
(80) Buckland (1908), 37. Cf., however, Tert. *Apol.* 39. 6.
(81) *Dig.* 48.8.11.2, *iusta querella*.
(82) *Dig.* 1.12.8, *nisi ex causis receptis*.

value of which for future protection can hardly be said to have been great ([83]).

The law on castration requires special attention because it illustrates particularly well the problems of enforcement which can be presumed to have applied to all the 'ameliorative' legislation, and because it shows how insubstantial improvement really was. Within roughly fifty years around the turn of the first and second centuries castration was legislated against on three occasions : Domitian first forbade castration of slaves on Roman soil ; Nerva then followed suit, fixing the penalty at *publicatio* of half the guilty party's estate ; and in a rescript to a Spanish governor Hadrian finally made offenders liable to the *lex Cornelia de sicariis et ueneficiis* ([84]). The action of Nerva implies that Domitian's original order had had little effect, and Hadrian's ruling implies the same for Nerva's law, which indeed is clear from the banishment of an offender for five years by the Spanish governor to whom Hadrian wrote ([85]), as well as from allusions, which belong after Domitian's death, to the castration of slave boys in Juvenal's poems ([86]). Although the homosexual market for eunuchs was supplied in part by imports from beyond the borders of the Roman Empire ([87]), it seems implausible to believe that castration within the borders was impeded by Hadrian's ruling any more than by those of his predecessors. The slave-dealer who castrated boys was not as exposed to the possibility of future retaliation as the cruel master who repeatedly abused his slaves, because he disposed of his property relatively quickly (and at a profit) and did not have to worry over the problem of a lengthy relationship with the slaves he sold. Impressive evidence is available from late antiquity to show the ubiquity of eunuchs in the Empire ([88]), and that

(83) *Dig.* 1.6.2 ; cf. n. 71. According to *HA Hadr.* 18.8 ; 10, Hadrian abolished *ergastula*, but unsuccessfully (above, n. 41 ; cf. BUCKLAND (1908), 37 n. 4), and banned the sale of female and male slaves to pimps and gladiatorial entrepreneurs respectively, but with the proviso, *causa non praestita* ; the action did nothing to stop slave prostitution ; cf., e.g., *CTh.* 15.8.1. The information of *HA Hadr.* 18 is reliable (see Richard BAUMANN, *Legislation in the Historia Augusta* in *ZSS Rom. Abt.* 94 (1977), 43ff. at pp. 45ff.), but a distinction still persists between passage and enforcement of legislation.

(84) SUET. *Dom.* 7 ; Dio 67.2.3 ; 68.2.3 ; MART. *Epig.* 2.60 ; AMM. MARC. 18.4.5 ; *Dig.* 48.8.4.1-2 ; 48.8.5-6 ; *Paul. Sent.* 5.23.13.

(85) *Dig.* 48.8.4.1.

(86) IUV. 6.373, which belongs near the transition from Trajan to Hadrian ; see E. COURTNEY, *A Commentary on the Satires of Juvenal*, London, 1980, 1 ; cf. also R. SYME, *Juvenal, Pliny, Tacitus* in *AJP* 100 (1979), 250ff.

(87) HOPKINS (1978), 172ff.

(88) HOPKINS (1978), 172ff.

suggests that earlier legislation against castration had simply become a dead letter. The ability of the slave to set in motion the legal machinery of redress, the chances of detection, trial and punishment were not great enough to restrict the practice of castration as long as it was profitable, and to that extent servile conditions did not improve.

What may have been genuinely compassionate motivations on the part of the individual emperors responsible for legislation on slavery should not be unnecessarily impugned. But as already seen humanitarianism does not have a great bearing on the master-slave relationship in Roman society as a whole, and improvement of servile conditions for its own sake may not have been the real or only cause of the various enactments to which reference has been made. In a rescript to a provincial governor handed down by Antoninus Pius, obedience (*obsequium*) was ordered in slaves and mild treatment of them by their masters commanded, under the threat of the governor's intervention, 'in case greater danger should arise' [89]. This suggests that ameliorative legislation was intended less to afford protection to slaves than to restrain the owner from excess for the sake of maintaining order among the servile population, eventually to the benefit of the master, a view consistent with the fears of slave resistance seen earlier, the overall tendency of Roman law to favour higher social interests, and no more than minimal literary evidence from the imperial period of true humanitarian concern for slaves [90]. The arbitrary physical abuse of slaves cannot be said to have been dramatically alleviated by legislation of an improving kind.

Under Roman law slaves were subject to criminal penalties just as other segments of the population, and in this respect they were not exposed to a particular form of treatment which was not experienced by other social groups as well. The inherent bias of the Roman legal system meant, however, that lower social categories were discriminated against as far as the application of punishment was concerned [91], and slaves, as the lowest category of all, suffered the most severe types of criminal penalty : 'Our ancestors have in every penalty punished slaves more

(89) *Coll.* 3.3.5-6, *ne quid tumultuosius contra accidat* ; cf. WILLIAMS (1976), 77.

(90) Cf. BRUNT (1973), 18 on Stoic philosophers, 'Of course Stoics urged masters to treat their slaves justly and kindly ... But one constantly feels that Stoics were concerned rather with the moral evil involved in injustice than with the sufferings of the slaves'.

(91) Cf. GARNSEY (1970), 121 ; 152.

severely than free men' so a passage from the *Digest* states [92]. Thus, for example, conviction under the *lex Cornelia de falsis* brought deportation for a free person but death for a slave [93]; and in the regulations governing the mines at Vipasca in Spain, the crime of stealing ore was punishable by a fine of HS1,000, though 'If a person who steals ore is a slave, the procurator shall have him beaten and shall sell him on the condition that he shall be kept in chains for ever and that he shall not remain in any mining camps or mining district' [94]. Slaves were consequently exposed to stronger pressures by the criminal legal system, pressures which remained constant over time since criminal liability itself remained constant.

Of course slaves were not unique in receiving harsh penalties. In the army the ancient punishment of decimation was still at times practised in the imperial period, and individual miscreants were flogged, occasionally even executed, or else subjected to other ignominious penalties [95]. Josephus was able to comment upon the element of fear in military training and its connection with military discipline [96], a fitting analogy for the relationship between fear and servile discipline. Moreover, a distinct trend can be perceived under the early Empire towards the infliction of what traditionally had been servile punishments only (*seruilia supplicia*) to the broad social group that came to be classified as *humiliores* [97]. It may be in consequence that before the law slaves gradually became less and less of a distinct group, and certainly the simple division between slave and free is of no use for a discussion of criminal

(92) *Dig.* 48.19.28.16, *maiores nostri in omni supplicio seuerius seruos quam liberos ... punierunt.*

(93) *Instit.* 4.8.17.

(94) *FIRA*² III no. 104, translation from A. C. JOHNSON, P. R. COLEMAN-NORTON, F. C. BOURNE, *The Corpus of Roman Law* II, Austin, 1961, no. 233. Cato executed slaves after trial, PLUT. *Cato* 21.4.

(95) See G. R. WATSON, *The Roman Soldier*, London, 1969, 117ff. for details.

(96) Jos. *BJ* 3.102-104, 'By their military exercises the Romans instil into their soldiers fortitude not only of body but also of soul ; fear, too, plays its part in their training. For they have laws which punish with death not merely desertion of the ranks, but even a slight neglect of duty ; and their generals are held in even greater awe than the laws. For the high honours with which they reward the brave prevent the offenders whom they punish from regarding themselves as treated cruelly. This perfect discipline makes the army an ornament of peace-time and in war welds the whole into a single body' ; (Loeb translation).

(97) P. D. A. GARNSEY, *Why Penalties Become Harsher : the Roman Case, Late Republic to Fourth-Century Empire* in *Natural Law Forum* 13 (1968), 141ff.

penalties (⁹⁸). But while the criminal treatment of slaves should not be seen outside the context of criminal penalties as a whole, military discipline and the depression of *humiliores* are largely irrelevant for present purposes because these matters did not affect the impact on actual servile expectations as far as the criminal law was concerned : slaves knew at all stages of imperial history that criminal conviction entailed extreme physical suffering for them.

The death penalty was used no more than sparingly for upper-class offenders, with the exception of cases of treason (*maiestas*), and simple decapitation, or even the alternative of voluntary exile, was then the mode of punishment. In strong contrast persons of low social rank, including slaves, were subject to punishment by death for many offences and in several forms : burning alive (*crematio*), crucifixion (*crux*), and exposure to wild animals in the amphitheatre (*bestiae*) (⁹⁹).

According to Callistratus *crematio* was the penalty for slaves who had conspired against their owners, and presumably it was applied against the households of the men known from literary sources to have been attacked in the first and early second centuries, L. Pedanius Secundus, Larcius Macedo and Afranius Dexter, and indeed against the whole households – in the Pedanius Secundus affair, a total number of four hundred slaves, according to Tacitus, including women and children – not simply those who had committed the assaults (¹⁰⁰). In situations such as these the law exempted from punishment slaves whose connivance was logically impossible, but it showed no other tendency towards mildness (¹⁰¹). Consequently many slaves who even contemplated an act of violence against their owners must have been well aware that action would have opened not only themselves to the possibility of grim execution but also friends and family members in their various households. This danger might then well account for the relative shortage of recorded attacks by slaves on their owners if the literary record is indeed a genuine reflection of reality.

Death by crucifixion is well-attested in the central periods of Roman history (¹⁰²). Its use by the triumvir M. Crassus to punish the slave rebels

---

(98) Cf. GARNSEY (1970), 103ff.
(99) GARNSEY (1970), 105ff. ; 111ff.
(100) *Dig.* 48.19.28.11, *igni cremantur* ; TAC. *Ann.* 14.43.4 ; 45.1.
(101) BUCKLAND (1908), 95 ; SHERWIN-WHITE (1966), 463.
(102) See M. HENGEL, *Crucifixion in the Ancient World*, Philadelphia, 1977, 51ff. ; GARNSEY (1970), 127.

who had followd Spartacus ([103]) is perhaps comprehensible, a drastic end to a drastic episode, but far lesser crimes than armed rebellion drew the punishment. Caligula is said to have crucified an ex-slave who knew of his role in Tiberius' death ; Domitian crucified the secretaries of Hermogenes of Tarsus for having transcribed their master's questionable history ; and Severus Alexander supposedly crucified a eunuch for venality ([104]). In Trimalchio's gazette the crucifixion of a slave named Mithradates is announced following his slander of Trimalchio, while in Juvenal crucifixion is made to appear the prerogative of the master without any semblance of a trial at all, or even of a crime ([105]). It is a reasonable supposition that the execution of slaves in the area on the Esquiline at Rome which was specially reserved for the punishment of slaves was a common sight ([106]).

Condemnation to wild beasts in the amphitheatre must have entailed an even more grisly form of execution. Again in Petronius a realistic detail emerges in the record of the sentencing of a slave to *bestiae* for having committed adultery with a freeborn woman ([107]). But perhaps the most vivid accounts of this penalty appear in the records of early Christian martyrdoms, which included both slaves and free persons ([108]). Thus a female slave Blandina, one of a group of Christians martyred at Lugdunum in the reign of Marcus Aurelius, was first exposed to animals in the local amphitheatre, then hung on a stake as bait, scourged and exposed to animals a second time, put on a burning seat and tied up in a net before a third and final exposure, which resulted in her death ([109]). Blandina's treatment is known from a source highly sympathetic to her and Christians of servile status were not the only ones to be executed in this manner ([110]). But there seems little cause to doubt the details of

(103) App. *BC* 1.120.

(104) Suet. *Cal.* 12.2 ; *Dom.* 10.1 ; *HA Seu. Alex.* 23.8.

(105) Petr. *Sat.* 53.3 ; Iuv. 6.219ff.

(106) Tac. *Ann.* 15.60.2 ; cf. Platner, Ashby (1929), s.v. 'Sessorium'.

'(107) Petr. *Sat.* 45. Note that Aurelian allegedly punished with death a maidservant who had committed adultery with a fellow slave ; *HA Aur.* 49.5.

(108) Evidence collected in H. Musurillo, *The Acts of the Christian Martyrs*, Oxford, 1972. The literature on martyrology is of course immense, but for the background see especially W. H. C. Frend, *Martyrdom and Persecution in the Early Church*, Oxford, 1965.

(109) *Mart. Lug.* (1) 36 ; 41 ; 56 (Musurillo) ; cf. also the slave Felicitas, *Mart. Lug.* (1) 18 (Musurillo).

(110) See Garnsey (1970), 129ff. for other examples. The point, again, is that while *bestiae* came to be used against non-servile groups, for slaves it remained a constant form

Blandina's death, and her execution may serve as a paradigm for the penalty of *bestiae* whether or not in a Christian context.

The prospect of capital punishment cannot have affected the quality of servile life in the same way as that of capricious punishment from the individual slave-owner : in contemplating or planning a crime slaves were able to foresee the possible result of personal physical suffering, but this was a risk open to calculation. In one respect, however, namely with regard to torture, the law was arbitrary, and although in the imperial period the use of torture to extract evidence for criminal proceedings from free persons is documented, for slaves it was traditional and their liability again remained constant and without variation ([111]). Even so, the amount of psychological pressure exercised by the prospect of torture varied among slaves in relation to their proximity to their owners. Those who formed part of their owner's retinue, accompanying him wherever he went, or those who attended in some other personal capacity − for example, waiters, dressers, barbers − were much better situated for picking up incriminating information than non-domestics. The domestic staffs of Roman senators, men directly engaged in politics, were especially prone to torture at moments of conspiracy, real or imagined, against the emperor. And whereas slaves were theoretically prevented by the law from being tortured to provide evidence against their owners, devices were concocted to circumvent the law, as when, under Tiberius, the slaves of C. Iunius Silanus were compulsorily sold during his trial so that they could be appropriately interrogated ([112]). In spite of the availability of torture for all slaves, therefore, once more the better living conditions of domestic slaves in prominent urban households were offset by the increased likelihood of physical abuse in a legally institutionalised form.

The severity and constancy of servile criminal penalties are quite clearly consistent with attitudes towards slaves revealed by methods of private correction, but in degree they often exceeded what might be considered standard forms of private punishment. Part of the explanation for this must lie in the nature of the social status of the slave criminal, for while an upper class offender could find his social rank impaired on criminal

of execution. Christian slaves could be confronted with the expectation of *bestiae* on a double count eventually.

(111) GARNSEY (1970), 141ff.

(112) BUCKLAND (1908), 88 ; TAC. *Ann.* 2.30.3 ; cf. VAL. MAX. 6.8.1. For slaves as betrayers of their masters' secrets cf. IUV. 9.102ff. ; and for some cases of torture see SUET. *Aug.* 19.2 ; *Galba* 10.5 ; TAC. *Ann.* 1.23.3 ; 3.14.3 ; 3.50.1 ; 4.29 ; 14.60.4.

conviction, through the loss of citizenship or property as a sequel to exile ([113]), the slave, as a member of society with no technical rights or privileges, could not suffer any reduction of his status at all. Extreme physical punishment of the slave was thus the only avenue open to the law, which exhibited no moral qualms about the infliction of brutality on slaves ([114]). In addition, it could be believed that the anticipation by slaves of severe physical punishment had a deterrent effect upon them : Horace wrote that fear of penalty restrained the slave from crime and C. Cassius, in his speech in the senate after Pedanius Secundus' murder, referred to the effect of 'exemplary punishment' on the servile population ([115]). In the view of Epictetus the suffering which resulted from punishment meant that slaves did not commit the same mistake twice ([116]). Harsh penalties were prescribed and upheld by the law, therefore, because they afforded the most basic means of containing slaves and of eliciting subordination among them, or, in other words, of achieving *disciplina* ([117]). Although individual masters came to lose certain formal prerogatives under the Empire with regard to the indiscriminate punishment of slaves, the conditions of the latter did not significantly improve because the law, subsuming to itself more and more of the master's role, retained and perpetuated physical penalties as harsh as anything seen in the private sector. The intent of the law above all was to intimidate slaves into a state of passivity and acquiescence.

One of the most unusual ways in which violence manifested itself in servile life was that of a slave himself being required to commit a violent act at the instigation of his owner or some other member of free society. The emperor Nero, for example, ordered the death by drowning of his

---

(113) Cf. GARNSEY (1970), 112.

(114) In view of the maintenance of torture and the forms of execution mentioned above, as well as their extension to *humiliores* at large, the ameliorative slave legislation discussed earlier cannot jeopardise this statement.

(115) HOR. *Epist.* 1.16.53 ; TAC. *Ann.* 14.44.4.

(116) EPICT. *Diss.* 3.25.9-10 ; note also 1.29.59.

(117) See TAC. *Germ.* 25.2 on the connection between punishment and *disciplina* and *seueritas* ; cf. above p. 130 (military discipline). The dividing line between the needs of *disciplina* and the satisfaction of sadistic impulses could be very narrow : Aurelian is said to have had criminal slaves executed in his own presence either to keep up discipline or else to accommodate a lust for cruelty ; *HA Aur.* 49.3-4 ; cf. also PLAUT. *Capt.* 752-753, *ego illis captiuis aliis documentum dabo, ne tale quisquam facinus incipere audeat.* There is much on the need of violence to extract work from slaves in Ballio's speech at PLAUT. *Pseud.* 133ff., and the presentation of a genuine point of view is not to be doubted despite the comic context.

stepson Rufrius Crispinus through the agency of Crispinus' slaves, but assistance in suicide was perhaps more to be expected, as when C. Iunius Silanus asked his slaves to despatch him after his trial [118]. Such assistance was considered by the slave-owner to be an obligation of the slave, an act indeed of obedience to the master's will (*obsequium*) [119]. Examples in the literary record of slaves being manipulated to commit unsavoury acts usually allude to their corruptible nature : slaves by definition, as it were, were so base that they could easily be enticed by their owners to carry out any number of atrocities [120]. Such representation, however, conceals the tension which individuals must have encountered and experienced when confronted by the demand to perform. It might readily be suspected that there was always a certain type of slave to whom such demands came only too willingly, since the use of force under sanction, against any free member of society, would have had a certain inherent attraction. But it must nonetheless be recognised that for others the demands of loyalty and obedience could be stretched unbearably, because their choice lay between a violent act committed out of dutifulness but which might have entailed moral or physical problems on one hand, and a refusal to act which automatically exposed them on the other hand to their owners' anger and reprisal. Whether this was the actual dilemma in which some slaves periodically found themselves, the slave as an agent of violence remains over time a fixed element in literary sources and to that extent the expectation of direct violence in servile life was a condition of life itself [121].

The same is true of course from all the forms of abuse and punishment which have been described so far, as well as such a totally unpredictable eventuality as being kidnapped [122]. There was much of which to be afraid, and an equation between fear and compliance is consequently not

(118) Suet. *Nero* 35.5 ; Tac. *Ann.* 2.31.1-2.

(119) Plin. *Epp.* 8.14.12. According to the law, however, the slave was supposed to prevent his owner's suicide if at all possible ; *Dig.* 29.5.1.18 ; 22. For other cases of suicide, *HA Hadr.* 24.8 ; Tac. *Ann.* 16.15.4.

(120) On slave corruption see above, pp. 26ff.

(121) See for example Tac. *Ann.* 2.80.2 ; 13.47.4 ; 14.61.3 ; *Hist.* 1.33 ; 2.68 ; 3.64. A slave required to commit a violent act could of course disobey and use his ingenuity to conceal the fact. A story is told of a bath attendant who, on being consigned to the furnace by the young Commodus for having drawn too cool a bath, was rescued from his fate by the slave entrusted to carry out the execution. The latter substituted a sheepskin for the intended victim in the furnace ; *HA Comm.* 1.9.

(122) For cases of abduction, *P. Oxy.* 283 (45) ; *P. Oxy.* 1120 (third century).

difficult to posit. Unfortunately the absence of a real slave literature makes it exceedingly hazardous to estimate the psychological impact (upon individual slaves) of the climate of fear in which they lived, for here even the evidence of sepulchral inscriptions is of no value. The most suggestive material comes from Plautus, dangerous to rely on wholeheartedly by definition, but nonetheless of some value. In *Amphitryon*, for example, there is a long scene between the slave Sosia and Mercury (who has assumed Sosia's identity), the comedy of which depends on the slave being duped by the god. Whatever the contrived or even derivative nature of the encounter, it seems significant that the scene depends for its effect on Sosia being filled with fear of Mercury who at first threatens and finally delivers to the slave a sound thrashing ; the language of fear and beating is unmistakable [123]. In *Pseudolus* the slave Harpax gives a disquisition on how the good slave should conduct himself, namely by maintaining attention to duty even when the master is absent, an attitude which is governed by the slave's fear of his owner [124]. Similarly, Strobilus in *Aulularia* states that utter devotion to and unquestioning obedience of his master is motivated by the desire to avoid physical punishment [125]. The product of this attitude, in the words of Phaniscus in *Mostellaria*, is that 'Slaves who fear a beating, even when they have no cause to fear, are usually their masters' most useful slaves' [126]. Once all allowance is made for comic exaggeration and irony in the plays which provide this material, it seems inconceivable that they are not grounded on true servile fears of slave-owners, fears which continued across time as long as slavery persisted in the Roman world. The fear which the prospect of torture could elicit is illustrated in Eusebius' account of the Christian persecution in which Blandina died, when slaves faced with the danger of tortures they had seen already applied to their Christian owners were prepared to make false accusations against the latter in order to save themselves [127]. Likewise, Epictetus' comments on fugitives' alarms in the theatre on mention of the word 'master' strike a realistic note [128]. The accounts are credible ; the fears of suffering comprehensible.

(123) PLAUT. *Amph.* 291ff.
(124) PLAUT. *Pseud.* 1103ff.
(125) PLAUT. *Aul.* 587ff.
(126) PLAUT. *Most.* 859ff.
(127) EUSEB. *HE* 5.1.14.
(128) EPICT. *Diss.* 1.29.59.

The conditions of life which produced fear of their owners in slaves were thus numerous and all-embracing. The exploitable nature of slaves as commodities led to personal humiliation, notably at the hands of slave-dealers, and their subjection to sexual abuse by their owners led to a similar degradation. The impression is firm that physical punishments meted out to slaves by their owners were consistently brutal, showed little change in the course of time, and were not altered by any distinctions of status among the servile population as a whole. The Roman legal system contained the means by which slaves might seek redress against harsh treatment, yet a strong distinction existed between the theory of the law and its application in real circumstances, because slaves who wished to complain of cruelty were confronted by a string of practical difficulties inimical to their impartial treatment, and because the law contained loopholes detrimental to their interests. The state, as represented by the law, did little to improve servile conditions in the imperial period, but arrogated to itself certain prerogatives which had previously belonged exclusively to slave-owners. By penalties handed down against them, the law thus institutionalised the use of violence against slaves, who were persistently discriminated against because of their very status.

Moreover, Roman slave-owners understood well the deterrent value of punishment and the fact that force could be used to control subordinates when other tactics of manipulation failed or were lacking. Force was deliberately exploited to aid the repression of the slave classes. The overall result was that the frequent recourse to physical coercion produced pain and hardship in the lives of countless slaves over successive generations of which virtually nothing is heard in conventional sources. Slaves were never in a position to predict when the wrath of an owner would descend upon them and their lives were thus conditioned by this perennial fear of physical abuse and maltreatment. Within that element of fear lay owners' capacity for the permanent control of their slaves.

EPILOGUE

CONTROL

Among the forms of compulsory labour which emerged in classical antiquity, chattel slavery ranked at the bottom of the scale insofar as the sheer rightlessness of slaves and masters' expectations of their total obedience to authority were concerned [1]. Chattel slavery was an extreme type of compulsory labour. From this conceptual standpoint it would be tempting to assume that slave-owners were able to control their slaves, to secure loyalty and to extract work from them, with relative ease [2] ; for it was certainly in the nature of slavery in the Roman world that the master had absolute authority over the slave, who was always a dependent being, and that the conditions under which the slave spent his life were laid down either by the owner or else the state, in the form of law, which represented his interests. It must be remembered, however, that despite slaves' inherent rightlessness and no matter what ideal expectations of servile deference and obedience owners entertained, slavery itself always remained a form of *compulsory* labour, which implies two things : on one hand the unwillingness of slaves to remain in servitude if an alternative were available, and on the other hand the need for owners to exercise continuous coercion, of one kind or another, if slaves were to remain socially content and economically productive. It was characteristic of slaves as human property that they were able to demonstrate human reaction to and even opposition against their condition of inferiority, and evidence of such behaviour has been seen. It may also have been essential for slaves' own survival that they accommodate themselves to their condition [3], but such accommodation was also required by slave-owners in order that their world of privilege might be sustained, and it cannot be allowed that servile accommodation was an automatic, natural sequel to

(1) Finley (1973), 67ff. ; (1980), 68ff.
(2) See references at p. 25 n. 23, and cf. also Finley (1980), 77 ; 104.
(3) Finley (1980), 116.

the mere state of enslavement ; instead accommodation had to be elicited by catering to slaves' interests or imposed by overriding them. In spite of the diversity of slave statuses in the Roman slavery system, therefore, and in spite of the absence of overt class consciousness among slaves, it was the case that deliberately contrived methods of controlling and manipulating them were obligatory on the part of the ruling classes. Roman slave-owners were well aware of this reality, and the information of the Roman writers on agriculture particularly implies that control of slave property was impossible without conscious effort on their part to that end.

In view of the restrictions outlined at the outset of this essay any conclusions arrived at must remain tentative, even hypothetical. But from the certain framework that slaves in Roman society were varyingly the recipients of generous and not so generous forms of treatment from their owners, certain observations, at least, can be presented. First, and on one basic level, it seems that the life of the slave alternated between rewards and punishments which depended on the proclivities of individual slave-owners. Immediate rewards such as holidays and privileges of a deeper significance such as the capacity to establish and maintain a family or to aspire towards and achieve manumission were offset by slaves' periodic subjection to physical pain and suffering. It follows from this state of affairs that the slave was never able to take anything for granted, so that in consequence his submission to and acquiescence before the owner were guaranteed : rewards and privileges provided incentives towards compliant industry, punishment added the spur when necessary and quite literally beat down the slave's independence. In many respects, therefore, it could be said that the greater the slave's compliance to the will of his owner the better the conditions of his life would become ; greater lenience and fewer doses of the lash could be expected in proportion to the degree of demonstrated and observed loyalty and obedience. At this level control of the Roman slave population and continuation of the Roman slavery system were made possible through the maintenance by owners of a balance between generosity and its opposite towards slaves, a balance of which recognition clearly appears in Columella's statement, which may be presumed to be typical in thought of Columella's peers, that control of subordinates requires avoidance by superiors of excessive indulgence and of excessive cruelty (⁴). Admittedly much of the physical violence in slave

(4) Col. *RR*. 11.1.25.

life seems to have been capriciously inflicted, erratic and lacking in justification ; and the granting of freedom, especially by will, might also have been equally arbitrary. But at the same time enough evidence survives to make clear that privileges and punishments were consciously recognised and consciously employed as vehicles of social control, even if individual slave-owners at times overstepped the limits of what was utilitarian in their application of them.

Secondly, however, beyond this mechanism of alternating treatment and at a far more abiding level there is another observable aspect which governed the servile mentality. The rewards and privileges which masters allowed their slaves were not all of equal value : a distinction obviously existed between the single concession of a brief holiday and those of maintaining a family or being granted freedom from servitude. No slave was about to find his life irreparably shattered if an anticipated period of release from work were suddenly denied him by his owner for whatever reason (though he may have been temporarily irked). But because family life and liberty were of considerable importance to slaves, to judge from the evidence which is available, the emotional distress and suffering are likely to have been enormous at those times when the slave found his family involuntarily broken up or if freedom which had been promised him were suddenly and arbitrarily closed off. It has been contended that servile family life and the path towards the acquisition of freedom were surrounded by a number of adversative factors beyond the immediate control of the slave which rendered security in slave life minimal. The prospect of sale among slave family members was a particular constant cause of anxiety, and the actual conferment of freedom on slaves was relatively uncommon. In order to protect privileges already acquired, therefore, or in the hope of gaining them, it might be said that the safest policy for slaves was to comply with and conform to the wishes of their owners, the product being the semblance of harmony between slave and master or continuing social stability between slave and free. Because slaves knew the hardships and dangers which characterised their familial lives and their pursuit of freedom, the element of fear which they experienced from the amount of physical abuse and violence in their relationships with their owners extended also, and penetrated deeply into the enjoyment of privileges they had been conceded. Under these circumstances masters' potential for psychological domination over their slave property was intensified beyond that which stemmed from the simple, but arbitrary fluctuation between kindliness and severity.

Since no accounts written by slaves of their experiences during slavery exist, the extent of this posited emotional factor in servile life cannot be adequately evaluated. It is not capable of measurement. But some support is available in the form of analogy, even though analogy cannot be used as absolute proof in and of itself for the generally bleak conditions of Roman slaves which have been suggested. Nonetheless it has been proposed from a purely psychological perspective that the existence of a predominant climate of fear and the use of coercive power by a superior on a subordinate may well lead to compliant and submissive behaviour in the subordinate, perhaps of childlike quality, and, given his will to survive adversity, even to an adoption by him of the superior's values, although within this corporate response there may be great variations of behaviour from individual to individual [5]. This theory was proposed by a historian of slavery in the New World, and far more elaborately than the crude summary statement just given, in an effort to explain the conventional image of the black slave as Sambo held by slave-owners in the Southern states of America. The argument depended in part on a psychological study of prisoners-of-war in Nazi concentration camps, where a submissiveness and docility akin to putative features of the black slave personality were visible. Among modern historians this view has generated intense debate, not yet over, which has included vigorous attack and denial, on the grounds for example that the comparison of the concentration camps was defective or that one predominant image of black slaves in the United States never existed [6]. Yet with due allowance being made for overstatement and due caution being invoked, something useful for what has been seen of the experiences of slaves in the Roman world may still be salvaged from the essential hypothesis.

(5) Stanley M. ELKINS, *Slavery : A Problem in American Institutional and Intellectual Life*[3], Chicago, 1976, 81ff. ; the book first appeared in 1959. Cf. John W. BLASSINGAME, *The Slave Community : Plantation Life in the Antebellum South*[2], New York, 1979, 284ff. ; first published in 1972.

(6) The literature on modern slavery which has appeared since, and in response to Elkins is immense ; for a survey of developments see D. B. DAVIS, *Slavery and the Post-World War II Historians* in *Daedalus* 103 (1974), 1ff., as well as Elkins' own treatment in chapter six of the third edition of his book (above, n. 5). A collection of papers which discuss Elkins' views appear in Ann J. LANE, ed., *The Debate over Slavery : Stanley Elkins and his Critics*, Urbana, 1971. Cf. also M. I. FINLEY, *Slavery and the Historians* in *Histoire sociale / Social History* 12 (1979), 247ff ; Kenneth M. STAMPP, *The Imperilled Union*, New York, 1982, 164ff.

In the imperial period of Roman history slaves did not, as far as can be told, organise a great number of revolts or commit a great number of violent acts against their owners. Instead, on the surface at least fidelity was more forthcoming than not. This situation, however, cannot be taken as an index of slaves' true, inner thoughts and feelings, in the sense that they can automatically be assumed to have been satisfied with their social inferiority and were in consequence content to display undivided loyalty to their owners for its own sake (though some undoubtedly were). Rather, as a result of the fears and anxieties which conditioned the life of slaves as described earlier, it may be suggested that the role of the slave desired by the slave-owner became internalised within him to such a degree that it created the response of apparent obedience, variously sincere or disguised according to the individual slave's wish to safeguard himself and his privileges and to preserve some sense of individuality through means of resistance less obvious and dangerous than those of overt rebellion. If this is right, the leverage for manipulation and exploitation which thereby accrued to the slave-owner was immense.

There must be no confusion here. No suggestion is being made that slaves in Roman society did not, in significantly large numbers and over time, successfully enjoy family life or acquire release from slavery and other privileges. It is plainly the case that they did. Nor should it be doubted that these privileges occasionally followed from the benign interest of slave-owners in their slaves. But until the slave had obtained freedom, and in the case of those with families until freedom was acquired for the full group, there could not be any guarantee, even for those slaves in the most favourable circumstances, of release from the climate of fear which characterised the period of actual enslavement in an all-embracing manner. Above all, therefore, it is this absence of psychological and emotional security in slave life which offers the key to understanding the continuing ability of Roman slave-owners to control and keep in subjection their slaves. The capacity of masters to control the minds of their slaves contributes, so it may be proposed, to explaining the endurance of slavery across time within the Roman world.

APPENDICES

A. The biography of Columella constructed by C. Cichorius (*Römische Studien*, Stuttgart, 1922, 411ff.) remains standard ; cf. *PIR*² I 779 ; Griffin (1976), 89, 290f. Of the few known facts of his life, Columella's Spanish origin has been grossly overvalued in attempts to tie him to L. Annaeus Seneca. On one view Columella was an 'adepte de Sénèque', 'qu'il admira avec ferveur', belonged to a politico-literary group headed by Seneca, and attended meetings given by Seneca's nephew, Lucan (Cizek (1972), 61, 128, 290, 370 ; cf. also Martin (1971), 290, 363). Less extreme but equally tenuous are the suggestions that Columella may have 'sought out' Seneca when he came to Rome and that Seneca acted as Columella's literary patron (Griffin (1976), 253 ; 290f. ; cf. *JRS* 62 (1972), 1ff.). The sole item of firm evidence on which such views depend is Columella's polite description of Seneca as *uir excellentis ingenii atque doctrinae* (*RR*. 3.3.3). Seneca's brother, L. Iunius Gallio, is also mentioned by Columella (*RR*. 9.16.2) in such a way as to leave no doubt that he did act as Columella's patron. But the terms of reference are quite distinct : Gallio is *Gallio noster*, as *M. Trebellius noster* (*RR*. 5.1.2), whereas the notice on Seneca is formal and purely passing. It does not seem enough on which to build a close relationship between Columella and Seneca.

B. The major slave wars which occurred in Sicily and Italy between 140 B.C. and 70 B.C. are important events because of their general exceptionality. Although the source material for these events is notoriously full of difficulties, one undoubted aspect of the exceptionality is the eventual scale of the risings : vast numbers of slaves became involved, and the dangers they posed to established society were genuine. But the rebels did not formulate any specific, programmatic goals which they hoped to implement, other than their own escape from slavery. 'The slave revolts of the ancient world ... struggled for some kind of perceived restoration and lacked the material base and concomitant ideology for the projection of a new and economically more advanced society' (E. D. Genovese, *From Rebellion to Revolution*, Baton Rouge and London, 1979, 82). It is sometimes maintained that the slaves in Sicily set up hellenistic styled kingdoms (on the particular model of the Seleucids ; see especially Vogt (1975), 39ff. ; cf. Milani (1972), 197f.), their object being 'to invert society' (Vogt (1975), 54 ; cf. 58f.). But the organisation which is visible in the account (mainly) of Diodorus Siculus should not be regarded in my view as an object in and of itself, only as a means of maintaining the momentum of rebellion once escalation of numbers had started to occur. In all three wars events began on a low scale. In the first Sicilian revolt, a small number of slaves looked to the Syrian wonderworker Eunus for sanction of their murderous revenge against a single master, Damophilus, in one household (Diod. Sic. 34/5.2.10-11 ; Florus, 2.7.4ff., attributes outbreak of rebellion solely to Eunus and has no mention of Damophilus ; Diodorus (34/5.2.4 ; 37) mentions slave discussions of revolt and murder before the actual outbreak, but no careful planning on the grandscale is indicated ; it should not be odd that slaves at any time discussed the *idea* of revolt). In the second episode Diodorus tells of revolts in two households, but there is no sign of coordination between them (Diod. Sic. 36.3.4-6 ; 4.1-2 ; cf. Florus, 2.7.9ff. ; respectively thirty and eighty slaves were involved). Spartacus' rebellion, finally, began with two hundred gladiators' resentment of their status, and when plans for escape were betrayed, a successful break was made by some seventy-eight of them (Plut. *Crassus* 9.4 ; cf. Livy, *Per.* 95 ; App. *BC* 1.116). This suggests strongly that the early rebels did not intend their actions to expand in the way that happened, rather that their initial successes sparked off the widespread potential for rebellion that always existed. Important factors in this were the first-generation nature of many of the slaves, their common geographic origins, and the emergence of competent leaders who were able to impose some organisation on the rebels (though Spartacus quickly lost control). It should not be surprising that the principals assumed the trappings of kingship in order to assist the process of organisation, but this does not indicate any programme of long-term import based on political ideology and with the prime object of raising grandscale rebellion. The rebel leaders used whatever means were at their disposal to maintain order among the snowballing numbers of their adherents, means which were influenced (but no more, and not unexpectedly) by the established institutions with which they were familiar (cf. Diod. Sic. 36.2.2ff. on T. Minucius ; and C. L. R. James, *The Black Jacobins*, New York, 1963 edition, 93f. on Toussaint L'Ouverture). Yet there is no basis for believing that a great proliferation of slave numbers, which automatically invited the predictable response of Roman military retaliation, was sought by those responsible for the initial outbursts ; instead, the accidentally acquired strength of rebel numbers became their ultimate (and fatal) weakness.

   C. According to Plutarch (*Cato* 21.2) it was the elder Cato's practice to charge his male slaves a fee for the privilege of entering the quarters of his female slaves and to confine servile relationships within his own household. The intention was to prevent disaffection among the slaves ; but the anecdote suggests that slaves' needs for sexual release, if not for the establishment of families, was recognised by slave-owners from an early point in the history of Roman slavery. Moreover, the contemporary evidence of Plautus gives some basis for believing that slave families were indeed in existence in Cato's day, if it can continue to be assumed that a realistic basis underlies Plautus' comedies. At *Amph.* 365, for example, the slave Sosia is able to identify his father ; at *Capt.* 888 the slave Stalagmus refers to his wife (*uxor* ; cf. also *Miles* 1008 ; *Stich.* 433 ; and for *uernae* note *Rud.* 218 ;

Miles 699). Note that Cato's wife is said to have nursed the children of her slaves herself (Plut. *Cato* 20.3 τὰ τῶν δούλων παιδάρια).

The frequency, however, with which slaves were able to enter into familial relationships in the mid Republic was obviously governed by the numbers of slave women available to serve as wives for male slaves. The huge importations of war captives in Rome's expansionist era are usually assumed to have consisted overwhelmingly of men (e.g. Harris (1979), 84 n. 2), an assumption which must be essentially correct : slaves were required most of all to replace Italian peasants consumed by warfare and men were far more suitable for the purpose than women. Yet there are several indications that slave women were not as rare as is conventionally imagined. The story above about Cato shows clearly enough that he owned female domestics and Cato can hardly have been unique in this respect. References to female slave quarters at Plaut. *Most.* 756, 758, 908 suggest that Cato's practice of sexual segregation may not have been unique, whereas the expectation that slave women should form part of a domestic entourage is clear from *Miles* 1339. Again according to Plutarch (*Cato* 21.1) Cato habitually bought young slaves on the open market to be trained in domestic service, and these may have comprised girls as well as boys (as too the infants nursed by his wife) : Plaut. *Epid.* 43 contains a reference to the acquisition of a female slave *ex praeda* and *Epid.* 210f. a reference to the return of soldiers from campaign with male and female slaves in tow (cf. *Merc.* 415 for Syrian and Egyptian women). Moreover, the list of traditional female slave occupations at Plaut. *Merc.* 396ff. (weaving, grinding grain, cutting wood, spinning, house cleaning, cooking for the *familia*, cf. 509, shepherding) can be nothing but a reflection of historical circumstance (cf. Brunt (1971), 144) and the ubiquitous appearance in Plautus of female slave-prostitutes and of kidnapped women should not be attributed to literary convention alone.

It must be accepted that in all probability some slaves did reproduce in the earliest phase of Rome's developed slavery system, which means in turn that female as well as male infants will have appeared in the next generation (cf. Watson (1968), 291ff. on the acceptance of such by Republican jurists). Although the issue of infant female exposure has to be taken into consideration, it would be nonsense to assume that some females were not raised for domestic service at least, females who would in due course provide wives for slave men on reaching adulthood. It may be the case that there were more females in domestic occupations in cities than in the country at large and that the possibilities for slave family life were better in cities in consequence. Even so, there is no reason why Treggiari's view that certain numbers of infant females were sifted off from the city to be raised on farms (see above, p. 76) should not be applied retroactively for the age of Cato. The comparatively low level of fertility in the Roman slave population is not to be attributed alone to the insufficiency of slave women for purposes of reproduction.

D. For more than forty years the standard account of Augustus' social programme has been that of Last, and of necessity something was said about the slavery legislation (Last (1934), 429 ff.). Because Last's views have been so influential, and because they are not followed here, it may be of value to describe them in some detail and to show their impact in subsequent scholarly work.

A single thread, essentially, runs through Last's account : the Romans' need to avoid contamination of their stock by excessive manumission of Eastern slaves. Emphasis was put on the double danger of too many manumissions and of the pollution of the Roman and Italian peoples by Eastern elements — hence a racial theme and a numerical theme. 'If the population of Italy was only maintained by immigration, it must soon become a nondescript farrago, with the Roman element too weak to leaven the whole lump'. Thus Augustus 'was involved in measures which, by arresting the extension of the Roman *ciuitas* and above all by setting limits to the numbers of those Greeks and Orientals who, coming to Italy as slaves, were merged on manumission into the general body of Roman citizens, would preserve that material from uncontrolled contamination' (Last (1934), 429). Last wrote of 'the threat made to the character of the Roman people by the numbers in which slaves were set free' ; of damning 'one of the broadest channels by which foreign blood flowed into the community of Roman citizens' ; and of 'the infiltration of foreign blood' being 'brought under control' by legislation (Last (1934), 432 ; 433 ; 464). Although other factors were considered, these quotations reflect Last's principal ideas.

Before Last, Duff showed the same concern for the numbers and racial origins of manumitted slaves (Duff (1958), 30ff. ; cf. Last (1934), 949). But Last's influence in particular has been extensive. Thus R. Syme (*The Roman Revolution*, Oxford, 1939, 446), speaking of Rome's 'readiness to admit new members to the citizen body' in Republican history, spelled out the 'grave' result that 'slaves not only could be emancipated with ease but were emancipated in hordes. The wars of conquest flooded the market with captives of alien and often inferior stocks ... Augustus stepped in to save the race, imposing severe restriction upon the freedom of individual owners in liberating their slaves'. Less emotively H. H. Scullard (*From the Gracchi to Nero*[4], London, 1976, 240 unchanged since the first edition of 1959) wrote that 'Augustus wished not only to increase the Italian element in the Roman citizen body, but also to limit the foreign element that was mixing with it, especially as a result of manumission'. And Jones (1970), 133, wrote of the 'excessive and indiscriminate manumission of slaves, or rather the massive influx of freed slaves into the citizen body' as a 'social problem' confronting Augustus. (Cf. also Westermann (1955), 89f. ; Crook (1967), 43).

The connection between and insistence on numbers and race has continued down to the present with little sustained questioning, though Brunt (1958), 164 briefly stresses the incentive of full freedom for reasons to do with economic efficiency rather than with social harmony ; cf. also E. M. Staerman, *Die Blütezeit der Sklavenwirtschaft in der römischen Republik*, Wiesbaden, 1969, 274f., who sees the Augustan laws as an attempt to soften the relations between the free and unfree urban plebs, relations that were dangerous to the ruling classes (but the laws were not restricted to Rome alone) ; and Burford (1972), 50, who suggests that Augustus wished to protect heirs' interests with the *lex Fufia* (which takes no account of the *lex Aelia*). Yet the conventional account raises difficulties. For example, what evidence is there that Augustus really feared racial contamination of the Roman body politic ; that he was ill-disposed to its assimilation of Eastern or any foreign elements ; or that he believed slaves were being set free in excessive numbers ? Recent scholarship suggests, in fact, no sign of racial antipathy from Augustus towards Greeks and the Greek world (G. W. Bowersock, *Augustus and the Greek World* (1965), 41 ; 61) and that racial prejudice, as currently understood, was a notion scarcely visible in antiquity (A. N. Sherwin-White, *Racial Prejudice in Imperial Rome*, Cambridge, 1967). Extension of the citizenship to peregrine communities under Augustus is well established (Sherwin-White (1973), 225 ff.). And, while precise measurement is impossible, there is no justification for assuming a glut of Greek and Oriental slaves at Rome in the Augustan era to overwhelm the state (see E. S. Gruen, *The Last Generation of the Roman Republic*, Berkeley and Los Angeles, 1974, 360f. with references to earlier work). Last did not consider other sources of slave supply immediately before Augustus' legislation, nor did he provide direct evidence for his theory of racial contamination. And too much emphasis was put on Dionysius, at least as interpreted above.

E. According to Livy (7.16.7) the *uicesima libertatis* was instituted in 357 B.C. at a time when the senate was anxious to create a new source of public revenue, since the reserves of the *aerarium Saturni* were depleted. By 209 B.C. (Livy 27.10.11-12) some four thousand pounds of gold had accumulated from the proceeds of the tax, although there is no way of telling how long it had taken for the reserve to build up, or the number of manumissions thereby represented (cf. Brunt (1971), 549 f. ; Westermann (1955), 71). Cicero has a passing reference to the tax (*Att*. 2.16.1 ; 59 B.C.), whose proceeds Caesar may have drawn on ten years later (Brunt (1971), 549f.), but otherwise little else is heard of the *uicesima* under the Republic. Subsequently Caracalla is reported to have doubled the tax, Macrinus to have quickly restored it to its original level (Dio 77.9.4 ; 78.12.2). The common view is that the *uicesima* survived until the age of Diocletian and Constantine, whose fiscal reforms brought about its demise as an independent tax (e.g. Cagnat (1882), 156 ; Hirschfeld (1905), 109 ; *RE* 8 col. 2478 (G. Wesener)). But this can no longer be certain in view of *P. Mich.* 462 (as restored by J. F. Gilliam, *AJP* 71 (1950), 437f. = *CPL* no. 171), which, whether pre- or post-Constantinian, provides evidence of continued collection of the tax in fourth century Egypt, and renders invalid the view that 'In the second century, when the number of slaves decreased, the tax dwindled to unimportant dimensions' (Frank (1940), 50).

Detailed knowledge of the organisation of the *uicesima* cannot be obtained from literary sources. Livy (27.10.11-12) says that proceeds were maintained *in sanctiore aerario*, and scholars have assumed only for emergency purposes, as in 209 B.C. (thus Cagnat (1882), 154 ; Frank (1940), 50 ; Westermann (1955), 71 ; Cl. Nicolet, *Le Métier de citoyen dans la Rome républicaine*, Paris, 1976, 230) ; but this is in fact unlikely ; see Brunt (1971), 549f. The tax was sometimes paid by slaves, sometimes by their masters (Epict. *Diss.* 2.1.26 ; 4.1.33 ; Petr. *Sat.* 5.8.2 ; 71.2) ; hence the theory that the *uicesima* was paid by the slave if he bought his freedom following agreement with his owner, but by the owner if freedom was granted as a generosity, for example by testament (Cagnat (1882), 168ff. ; A. Berger, *An Encyclopedic Dictionary of Roman Law*, Philadelphia, 1953, s.v. 'vicesima manumissionum' ; for unambiguous cases of testamentary provision of the *uicesima* see *FIRA*² III no. 48 lines 53-4 ; no. 47 lines 36-7). But it remains uncertain when such a convention developed, and whether it was ever legally ratified.

Inscriptional evidence indicates the predictable : that in the late Republic and early Empire the *uicesima* was farmed out to the *publicani* (e.g. *CIL* 11. 5435 ; 5.164 ; 10.3875), and that under the Empire its administration eventually fell within the purview of the emperor (see *RE* Supp. 6 col. 1034 (Westermann) for a *procurator XX libertatis* before 79). For a time *publicani* and imperial procurators must have collected the tax contemporaneously (cf. *CIL* 3.7729 with Dessau *ad ILS* 4241 ; *CIL* 3.6753 with Weaver (1972), 57 ; 3.4827 with *PIR*² A 1469), which is not impossible ; cf. Millar (1977), 624f. Reorganisation by Septimius Severus also seems likely ; see H.-G. Pflaum, *Les Carrières procuratoriennes équestres sous le haut-empire romain*, Paris, 1960, 94f. On the assumption that their find-spots reflect activity in those areas, inscriptions reveal collection of the *uicesima* on an empire wide basis in the imperial period ; see *CIL* 5.3351 ; 2.4187 ; 12.2396 ; 3.6753 ; 3.7729 ; 3.7287 ; 13.7215 ; 8.7099 ; *AE* 1930 no. 87 ; add *P. Oxy.* 2265 to *CPL* no. 171 for Egypt. The history of the *uicesima libertatis* is worth further treatment.

F. At *Fab.* III prol. 33-37, Phaedrus accounts for the origin of the fable as follows :

> *Nunc, fabularum cur sit inuentum genus,*
> *breui docebo. seruitus obnoxia,*
> *quia quae uolebat non audebat dicere,*
> *affectus proprios in fabellas transtulit,*
> *calumniamque fictis elusit iocis.*

Seruitus here might mean servitude of any kind, such as political servitude under a despotic form of government (e.g. the Principate, the sense understood by J. Wight Duff, *A Literary History of Rome in the Silver Age*³, London, 1964, 113f. and *Roman Satire* (Berkeley and Los Angeles, 1936, 110). But the word may equally mean the condition of being a slave, which would then suggest that the origin of the fable should be ascribed to slaves and stories told by them in such a way that the true meaning was disguised so as to spare slaves punishment from their masters. If true this explanation would be of great importance, especially in view of the prevailing absence of a slave literature in antiquity, because it would point to the existence of an oral form of servile protest otherwise unknown. Can the explanation be accepted as plausible ?

The fable has an extremely long history in the ancient world and the question of its origins cannot be resolved by recourse to one determining factor (for the complications see K. Meuli, *Herkunft und Wesen der Fabel, Gesammelte Schriften*, Basel/Stuttgart, 1975, II 731ff. ; M. Nøjgaard, *La Fable antique I*, Copenhagen, 1964 ; B. E. Perry, *Introduction* to the Loeb edition of Babrius and Phaedrus (1975)). Moreover, it is clear from the hints of literary pretension that Phaedrus did not address himself solely, if at all, to a servile audience, and many of his fables have no relevance, by any stretch of the imagination, to servile situations.

On the other hand Phaedrus himself had of course been a slave before, as an imperial freedman, he turned to the literary composition of fables, and so might be presumed to have had an interest in any expression of servile points of view. And there is no reason simply to dismiss out of hand the notion that the fable could function as a vehicle of servile protest and indirect criticism of slave-owners, whether at a very early date, in Phaedrus' own lifetime, or beyond ; indeed, fables have served this purpose in other slave societies (cf. E. D. Genovese, *Roll, Jordan, Roll*, Vintage ed. New York, 1976, 582). The subject has apparently received little attention from scholars, though Daube (1972), 53ff. has accepted the reality of slave stories contributing to the tradition of the fable and has pointed to two examples from Phaedrus which fit the context of servile protest (making allowance at the same time for embellishment by the author himself) : in *Fab.* I.15 Daube sees a 'rather hefty incitement to disloyalty, to not caring a hoot' and in *App. Per.* 17 a 'recommendation of deceitfulness'. Cf. also M. Nøjgaard, *La Fable antique II*, Copenhagen, 1967, pp. 174 ff.

The explanation is thus plausible, and the question naturally arises of whether other fables told by Phaedrus seem suitable for explication along the lines of servile protest or statement. The following are examples which, without too great an imposition on credulity, appear consistent with themes and subjects dealt with in this study.

1. I.6 : Jupiter enquires why the Frogs are upset at the prospect of the Sun's marriage ; he is told that the Sun dries up the Frogs' pond as it is and causes their deaths ; so what will happen when the Sun procreates ? This fable fits the background of slaves' fears of masters' cruelty, and may be taken as an expression of slaves' anxieties about the coming to maturity of owners' children and the additional threats of abuse they represent.

2. I.8 : a Crane and a Wolf strike a bargain for the extraction of a bone from the Wolf's throat ; once the Crane has performed the operation, the Wolf refuses to pay up, claiming the Crane was lucky not to have had its head bitten off beforehand. This is reminiscent of the striking of compacts between slave and master for manumission, as in the Pedanius Secundus affair (above pp. 99ff. and cf. Plaut. *Pers.* 192), on which the master always might renege, and the use of a potential reward as an inducement to compliance is also noticeable. The fable expresses the slave's realisation that a slave-owner cannot, ultimately, be trusted, and that a trusting slave only harms himself.

3. I.28 : an Eagle carries off a Fox's cubs as food for her young ; the Fox seeks the cubs' release but is rebuffed by the Eagle ; the Fox then prepares to burn the tree which houses the Eagle's nest, and under the threat of losing her own young the Eagle returns the cubs. This story suits the context of slaves being separated from family members at the dictate of the master, and threatens retaliatory violence in a manner which obviously could not be stated openly but which might nonetheless make slave-owners aware of the dangers to themselves from slaves if pushed too far (cf. above pp. 113f.) : *Quamuis sublimes debent humiles metuere, / uindicta docili quia patet sollertiae.* Yet given the real problems slaves faced in taking vengeance against owners (cf. above pp. 31f.), and the common fact of family separation among slaves, the story may have functioned more as a consolation for slaves rather than as an expression of true intent. The same is true of II.16, which is on the same theme, an individual's *superbia* and lack of *humanitas* towards others may lead to his discomfiture. Here the agricultural writers' recognition of the need for kindly treatment of slaves may be compared, together with the stereotype of the cruel master represented by Larcius Macedo (above p. 121). The 'craftiness' common to I.28 and III.16 recalls the type of the cunning slave (above pp. 28f.).

4. II.8 : a hunted Stag takes refuge in an ox-stall on a farm ; it goes unnoticed by the *bubulcus*, other *rustici*, and even the *uilicus* ; but when the farm owner (*dominus*) arrives to inspect his cattle, he first notices signs of servile neglect – insufficient fodder and bedding for the animals, cobwebs everywhere – and then discovers the Stag, which is killed before the assembled *familia*. The point of the fable, *dominum uidere plurimum in rebus suis*, is especially appropriate for a servile audience as a reminder of the need to beware the master ; but the references to dilatoriness echo complaints of slovenliness seen elsewhere (above pp. 27f.) and so reflect slaves' recognition of their ability to cause the owner annoyance, at least, which provides humour in the re-telling of the story among them. Perhaps a satirical note is directed towards the *dominus*.

5. III.7 : in return for his vigilance as a nightwatchman, a Dog is well fed by his master (*dominus*) and has a place to live ; during the daytime, however, he is chained up, has no freedom of movement, and his neck bears the mark of his collar ; a Wolf rejects the offer of joining the Dog's household, preferring his

liberty, even at the cost of hunger and no shelter. The point of this fable, *quam dulcis sit libertas*, has obvious relevance to slave circumstances and slaves' aspirations towards freedom (cf. above, p. 82), but its details recall the use of slave collars and the *ergastulum* as well. The story, from the servile point of view, is a lament that the material comforts of slavery do not compensate the absence of freedom. An expression of such dissatisfaction, however, clearly could not be articulated openly.

6. IV.4 : Boar and a Horse are involved in a dispute ; the Horse secures the aid of a Man, who kills the Boar but then reduces the Horse to slavery (*seruitus*) ; the moral, *inpune potius laedi quam dedi alteri*. This has application to the process by which a slave might secure redress against injury done to himself by the master from a magistrate (cf. above, pp. 123ff.), and can be understood as a protest against the inequity of the legal system which merely handed over the slave to a new owner if his case were upheld, or else as a consolation, since it was scarcely worthwhile to seek help. Cf. I.15, which could be taken to mean that one slave-owner is no better than another and that nothing is to be gained from the 'award' of a new master. Cf. also I.30, a fatalistic response to the civil wars of the Late Republic ?

7. V.10 : a Hunting-Dog, always successful and efficient in the past, is now too old to work for its Master (*dominus*) ; after failing to secure a boar, the Dog is reprimanded, but puts up a spirited self-defence : *Non te destituit animus, sed uires meae. / quod fuimus lauda, si iam damnas quod sumus*. This fable is particularly interesting because Phaedrus does not explain its meaning, claiming that the significance is obvious. It recalls the sources which speak of the abandonment by owners of old and sickly slaves (though contrast Columella's recommendation of good medical treatment ; above p. 22), and may be understood as the response of slaves to the onset of old age and the fear of abandonment it brought. The story is a statement to the slave-owner that long years of loyalty should be rewarded with humane treatment when high work performance can no longer be maintained. Perhaps defiantly so.

The ideas expressed about these fables do not prove that the fable had servile origins or that the fables themselves circulated among slaves or spoke to servile circumstances. The viability of a fable depends after all on its applicability to many and different situations. But without undue strain, the applicability to slave circumstances of the fables referred to above is fairly clear, which supports the view that fables were at least influenced by forms of slave protest-statements.

SELECT BIBLIOGRAPHY

This list contains works cited more than once ; full details of other items will be found in the notes.

ALFÖLDY, G. (1972), *Die Freilassung von Sklaven und die Struktur der Sklaverei in der römischen Kaiserzeit* in *RSA* 2, 97-129.

ASTIN, A. E. (1978), *Cato the Censor*, Oxford.

ATKINSON, Kathleen M. T. (1966), *The Purpose of the Manumission Laws of Augustus* in *The Irish Jurist* 1, 356-374.

BALSDON, J. P. V. D. (1969), *Life and Leisure in Ancient Rome*, London.

BARBU, N. I. (1963), *Les Esclaves chez Martial et Juvenal* in *Acta Antiqua Philippopolitana*, Serdica, 67-74.

BELLEN, H. (1971), *Studien zur Sklavenflucht in römischen Kaiserreich*, Wiesbaden.

BIEZUNSKA-MAŁOWIST, I. M. (1969), *Les Enfants-esclaves à la lumière des papyrus* in *Hommages à Marcel Renard, Collection Latomus* 101, II, Brussels, 91-96.

BIEZUNSKA-MAŁOWIST, I. M. (1973a) *L'Esclavage dans l'Egypte gréco-romaine* in *Actes du Colloque 1971 sur l'esclavage*, Paris, 81-92.

BIEZUNSKA-MAŁOWIST, I. M. (1973b), *L'Opinion que les anciens avaient du travail servile* in F. C. LANE, ed., *Fourth International Congress of Economic History, Bloomington*, 1968, 366-372.

BIEZUNSKA-MAŁOWIST, I. M. (1975), *La Traite d'esclaves en Egypte* in *Proceedings of the XIV International Congress of Papyrologists*, London, 11-18.

BIEZUNSKA-MAŁOWIST, I. M. (1976), *L'Esclavage à Alexandrie dans la période gréco-romaine* in *Actes du Colloque 1973 sur l'esclavage*, Paris, 293-312.

BIEZUNSKA-MAŁOWIST, I. M. (1977), *L'Esclavage dans l'Egypte gréco-romaine, Seconde Partie : Période romaine*, Wroclaw.

BODOR, A. (1963), *Dacian Slaves and Freedmen in the Roman Empire* in *Acta Antiqua Philippolitana*, Serdica, 45-52.

BOULVERT, G. (1970), *Esclaves et affranchis impériaux sous le haut-empire romain*, Naples.

BOYER, Laurent (1965), *La Fonction sociale des legs d'après la jurisprudence classique* in *RD* 43, 333-408.

BRADLEY, K. R. (1980), *Sexual Regulations in Wet-Nursing Contracts from Roman Egypt* in *Klio* 62, 321-325.

BRAUN, Pierre (1959), *Les Tabous des "Feriae"* in *L'Année sociologique*[3], 49-125.

BROCKMEYER, N. (1968), *Arbeitsorganisation und ökonomisches Denken in der Gutwirtschaft des römischen Reiches*, Bochum.

BRUNT, P. A. (1958), Review of Westermann (1955), *JRS* 48, 164-170.

BRUNT, P. A. (1971), *Italian Manpower*, Oxford.

BRUNT, P. A. (1973), *Aspects of the Social Thought of Dio Chrysostom and of the Stoics* in *PCPhS* 19², 9-34.

BUCKLAND, W. W. (1908), *The Roman Law of Slavery*, Cambridge.

BURFORD, Alison (1972), *Craftsmen in Greek and Roman Society*, London & Ithaca, N.Y.

BURTON, G. P. (1975), *Proconsuls, Assizes and the Administration of Justice under the Empire* in *JRS* 65, 92-106.

CAGNAT, M. R. (1882), *Etude historique sur les impôts indirects chez les Romains*, Paris.

CIZEK, E. (1972), *L'Epoque de Néron et ses controverses idéologiques*, Leiden.

CREŢIA, P. (1961), *Dion de Pruse et l'esclavage* in *StudClas* 3, 369-375.

CROOK, J. (1967), *Law and Life of Rome*, London & Ithaca, N.Y.

DAUBE, D. (1972), *Civil Disobedience in Antiquity*, Edinburgh.

DUFF, A. M. (1958), *Freedmen in the Early Roman Empire*, Cambridge.

DUNCAN-JONES, Richard (1974), *The Economy of the Roman Empire : Quantitative Studies*, Cambridge.

ENGELS, Donald (1980), *The Problem of Female Infanticide in the Greco-Roman World* in *CP* 75, 112-120.

FINLEY, M. I. (1973), *The Ancient Economy*, Berkeley & Los Angeles.

FINLEY, M. I. (1976), *A Peculiar Institution ?* in *Times Literary Supplement*, July 2, 819-821.

FINLEY, M. I. (1979), *Ancient Sicily to the Arab Conquest*, London (revised edition).

FINLEY, M. I. (1980), *Ancient Slavery and Modern Ideology*, New York.

FLORY, Marleen B. (1978), *Family in "Familia" : Kinship and Community in Slavery* in *AJAH* 3, 78-95.

FRANK, Tenney (1940), *An Economic Survey of Ancient Rome : Volume V, Rome and Italy of the Empire*, Baltimore.

GARNSEY, Peter (1970), *Social Status and Legal Privilege in the Roman Empire*, Oxford.

GRIFFIN, Miriam T. (1976), *Seneca : A Philosopher in Politics*, Oxford.

GSELL, St. (1932), *Esclaves ruraux dans l'Afrique romaine* in *Mélanges Gustave Glotz* I, Paris, 397-415.

HARRIS, William V. (1979), *War and Imperialism in Republican Rome*, Oxford.

HARRIS, William V. (1980), *Towards a Study of the Roman Slave Trade* in *MAAR* 36, 117-140.

HIRSCHFELD, O. (1905), *Die Kaiserlichen Verwaltungsbeamten bis auf Diocletian*², Berlin.

HOPKINS, Keith (1965), *The Age of Roman Girls at Marriage* in *Population Studies* 18, 309-327.

HOPKINS, Keith (1967), *Slavery in Classical Antiquity* in A. DE REUCK, J. KNIGHT edd., *Caste and Race : Comparative Approaches*, Boston, 166-191.

HOPKINS, Keith (1978), *Conquerors and Slaves : Sociological Studies in Roman History I*, Cambridge.

HOPKINS, Keith (1980), *Brother-Sister Marriage in Roman Egypt* in *Comparative Studies in Society and History* 22, 303-354.

JOHNSON, A. C. (1936), *Roman Egypt* = TENNEY FRANK ed., *An Economic Survey of Ancient Rome, Vol. II*, Baltimore.

JONES, A. H. M. (1968), *Slavery in the Ancient World* in *Economic History Review*[2] 9 (1956), 185-199 = M. I. FINLEY, ed., *Slavery in Classical Antiquity*, Cambridge & New York, 1-15.

JONES, A. H. M. (1970), *Augustus*, London.

JONES, C. P. (1978), *The Roman World of Dio Chrysostom*, Cambridge, Mass.

JONKERS, E. J. (1934), *De l'influence du Christianisme sur la législation relative à l'esclavage dans l'antiquité* in *Mnemosyne* 1, 241-280.

KAJANTO, I. (1969), *Tacitus on the Slaves* in *Arctos* 6, 43-60.

LAST, H. (1934), *The Social Policy of Augustus* in *CAH* X, 425-464.

LINTOTT, A. W. (1968), *Violence in Republican Rome*, Oxford.

MARÓTI, Egon (1976), *The Vilicus and the Villa-System in Ancient Italy* in *Oikumene* 1, 109-124.

MARTIN, R. (1971), *Recherches sur les agronomes latins et leurs conceptions économiques et sociales*, Paris.

MARTIN, R. (1974), *"Familia Rustica" : Les esclaves chez les agronomes latins* in *Actes du Colloque 1972 sur l'esclavage*, Paris, 267-297.

MILANI, Piero A. (1972), *La schiavitù nel pensiero politico dai greci al basso medio evo*, Milan.

MILLAR, Fergus (1977), *The Emperor in the Roman World*, London.

MONTEVECCHI, Orsolina (1973), *La papirologia*, Turin.

OATES, J. F. (1969), *Rhodian Auction Sale of a Slave Girl* in *JEA* 55, 191-210.

PIGANIOL, A. (1958), *Les Empereurs parlent aux esclaves* in *Romanitas* 1, 7-18 = *Collection Latomus* 133, Brussels, 1973, 202-211.

PLATNER, S. B. & ASHBY, T. A. (1929), *A Topographical Dictionary of Ancient Rome*, London.

RAWSON, Beryl (1966), *Family Life among the Lower Classes at Rome in the First Two Centuries of the Empire* in *CP* 61, 71-83.

RAWSON, Beryl (1974), *Roman Concubinage and Other De Facto Marriages* in *TAPA* 104, 279-305.

ROBLEDA, Olis (1976), *Il diritto degli schiavi nell'antica Roma*, Rome.

ROULAND, Norbert (1977), *A propos des servi publici populi Romani* in *Chiron* 7, 261-278.

SHERWIN-WHITE, A. N. (1966), *The Letters of Pliny : A Historical and Social Commentary*, Oxford.

SHERWIN-WHITE, A. N. (1973), *The Roman Citizenship*², Oxford.

SPRANGER, P. P. (1961), *Historische Untersuchungen zu den Sklavenfiguren des Plautus und Terenz*, Wiesbaden.

STAERMAN, E. M. & TROFIMOVA, M. K. (1975), *La schiavitù nell'Italia imperiale*, Rome.

STE. CROIX, G. E. M. DE (1975), *Early Christian Attitudes towards Property and Slavery* in *Studies in Church History* 12, 1-38.

STRAUS, J. A. (1971), *Le Pays d'origine des esclaves de l'Egypte romaine* in *CE* 46, 363-366.

STRAUS, J. A. (1973), *Le Prix des esclaves dans les papyrus d'époque romaine* in *ZPE* 11, 289-295.

STRAUS, J. A. (1977), *Quelques activités exercées par les esclaves d'après les papyrus de l'Egypte romaine* in *Historia* 26, 74-88.

TAUBENSCHLAG, R. (1955), *The Law of Greco-Roman Egypt in the Light of the Papyri*², Warsaw.

TREGGIARI, S. M. (1969), *Roman Freedmen during the Late Republic*, Oxford.

TREGGIARI, S. M. (1973), *Domestic Staff at Rome during the Julio-Claudian Period* in *Histoire sociale/ Social History* 6, 241-255.

TREGGIARI, S. M. (1975a), *Jobs in the Household of Livia* in *PBSR* 43, 48-77.

TREGGIARI, S. M. (1975b), *Family Life among the Staff of the Volusii* in *TAPA* 105, 393-401.

TREGGIARI, S. M. (1976), *Jobs for Women* in *AJAH* 1, 76-104.

TREGGIARI, S. M. (1979a), *Sentiment and Property : Some Roman Attitudes* in A. PAREL, T. FLANAGAN edd., *Theories of Property : Aristotle to the Present*, Waterloo, Ont., 53-85.

TREGGIARI, S. M. (1979b), *Questions on Women Domestics in the Roman West* in *Schiavitù, manomissione e classi dipendenti nel mondo antico*, (Università degli Studi di Padova, Pubblicazioni dell'instituto di storia antica 13), Rome, 185-201.

VEYNE, P. (1961), *Vie de Trimalcion* in *Annales* 16, 213-247.

VEYNE, P. (1978), *La Famille et l'amour sous le haut-empire romain* in *Annales* 33, 35-63.

VOGT, J. (1975), *Ancient Slavery and the Ideal of Man*, Cambridge, Mass.

VOLKMANN, Hans (1961), *Die Massenversklavungen der Einwohner eroberter Städte in der hellenistisch-römischen Zeit*, Wiesbaden.

WATSON, Alan (1968), *Morality, Slavery and the Jurists in the later Roman Republic* in *Tulane Law Review* 42, 289-303.

WATSON, Alan (1971), *Roman Private Law Around 200 B.C.*, Edinburgh.

WATSON, Alan (1975), *Rome of the XII Tables*, Princeton.

WEAVER, P. R. C. (1972), *Familia Caesaris*, Cambridge.

WESTERMANN, W. L. (1955), *The Slave Systems of Greek and Roman Antiquity*, Philadelphia.

WHITE, K. D. (1970), *Roman Farming*, London & Ithaca, N.Y.

WILLIAMS, G. W. (1958), *Some Aspects of Roman Marriage Ceremonies and Ideals* in *JRS* 48, 16-29.

WILLIAMS, G. W. (1968), *Tradition and Originality in Roman Poetry*, Oxford.

WILLIAMS, Wynne (1976), *Individuality in the Imperial Constitutions, Hadrian and the Antonines* in *JRS* 66, 67-83.

SUPPLEMENTARY BIBLIOGRAPHY

K.R. Bradley, 'Slave Kingdoms and Slave Rebellions in Ancient Sicily', *Historical Reflections/Réflexions Historiques* 10 (1983), 435ff.

K.R. Bradley, 'Child Labour in the Roman World', *Historical Reflections/ Réflexions Historiques* 12 (1985), 311ff.

K.R. Bradley, 'Seneca and Slavery', *C&M* 37 (1986), 161ff.

J. Christes, 'Reflexe erlebter Unfreiheit in den Sentenzen des Publilius Syrus und in den Fabeln des Phaedrus. Zur Problematik ihrer Verifizierung', *Hermes* 107 (1979), 199ff.

Hervé Duchêne, 'Sur la Stèle d'Aulus Caprilius Timotheos, *Sômatemporos'*, *BCH* 110 (1986), 513ff.

Jane F. Gardner, *Women in Roman Law and Society* (London 1986).

M. Garrido-Hory, *Martial et l'esclavage* (Paris 1981).

Orlando Patterson, *Slavery and Social Death: A Comparative Study* (Cambridge, Mass. 1982).

Beryl Rawson, ed., *The Family in Ancient Rome: New Perspectives* (London 1986).

Olivia Robinson, 'Slaves and the Criminal Law', *ZSS Rom. Abt.* 98 (1981), 213ff.

A.J.B. Sirks, 'Informal Manumission and the Lex Junia', *RIDA* 28 (1981), 247ff.

A.J.B. Sirks, 'The *lex Junia* and the Effects of Informal Manumission and Iteration', *RIDA* 54 (1983), 211ff.

G.E.M. de Ste. Croix, *The Class Struggle in the Ancient Greek World* (Ithaca 1981).

Alan Watson, 'Roman Slave Law and Romanist Ideology', *Phoenix* 37 (1983), 53ff.

Thomas E.J. Wiedemann, 'The Regularity of Manumission at Rome', *CQ* 35 (1985), 162ff.

INDEX

ALSO BY CARL SAFINA

A SEA IN FLAMES

A SEA IN FLAMES

The Deepwater Horizon Oil Blowout

CARL SAFINA

CROWN PUBLISHERS
NEW YORK

All rights reserved.
Published in the United States by Crown Publishers,
an imprint of the Crown Publishing Group,
a division of Random House, Inc., New York.
www.crownpublishing.com

CROWN and the Crown colophon are registered trademarks
of Random House, Inc.

Library of Congress Cataloging-in-Publication Data
Safina, Carl, 1955–
A sea in flames : the Deepwater Horizon oil blowout / Carl Safina.
  p.   cm.
1. BP Deepwater Horizon Explosion and Oil Spill, 2010—Environmental
aspects. 2. BP Deepwater Horizon Explosion and Oil Spill, 2010—Social
aspects. 3. Oil spills—Mexico, Gulf of. I. Title.
GC1221.S24 2011
363.738'20916364—dc22   2010051455

ISBN 978-0-307-88735-1
eISBN 978-0-307-88737-5

PRINTED IN THE UNITED STATES OF AMERICA

Book design by Elizabeth Rendfleisch
Jacket design by David Tran
Jacket photograph by U.S. Coast Guard/Getty Images

1   3   5   7   9   10   8   6   4   2

First Edition

To the memories of the people who died.

To their families.

To those who survived.

To the creatures that suffered.

To those who anguished.

To those who did their best.

And to those who continue asking what will come out of this well.

CONTENTS

Know Before You Go

Crucial mistakes, disastrous consequences, the weakness of power, unpreparedness and overreaction, the quiet dignity of everyday heroes. The 2010 Gulf of Mexico blowout brought more than oil to the surface.

This is not just a record of a technological event. It's also a chronicle of a season of anguish and panic, deep uncertainties, and the emotional topography of the blowout. It is the record of an event unfolding, a synthesis of personal experience, news, rumors, and the rapidly shifting perspectives about how bad things were—and how bad they were not.

There are roughly three parts to this event, and to this book: what caused this particular well to blow out; the varied technological, biological, and emotional responses during the months the oil was flowing; and a little more calmness, clarity, and insight after the flow of oil was stopped.

I've chosen to convey my impressions as they occurred over a season that was intense, chaotic, and seemingly interminable. In the turmoil, it was easy to form the wrong impressions and follow blind alleys. And I did.

Over the months, information and understanding improved significantly. Later, after the flow of oil was stopped, we calmed down, and those with cooler heads began to see more clearly.

This book is not a definitive treatise; it's a portrait. The story will continue unfurling. Some aspects, we'll never fully understand.

In trying my best to get it right, I am sure that nearly all of what I've written is reasonable, most of it is true, and some of it is wrong. It's not less than that, and not more.

It's easy to criticize people in charge. It's much harder to be the person in charge. I was angry at the Coast Guard for weeks, until I began to realize that its ability to respond was largely dictated by the laws that confined it. If officials such as Admiral Thad Allen rankled me at times, it may say more about me than about them. But it remains part of the portrait of this whole event.

In truth, such people deserve not just our admiration but also a little slack. During the blowout, perfection wasn't an available option. I've left my first impressions in place to show how my perceptions changed as my initial rage—and I felt plenty of rage—subsided. Admiral Allen, as the most visible federal official and the man in charge, gets the brunt of my exasperation. But he never fully deserved it. I could not have done the job he did.

Admiral Allen, Dr. Jane Lubchenco, and others in our government gave us their very best under months of intense pressure, heavy responsibility, and public scrutiny. They were doing a nearly impossible job on behalf of us all. I didn't always appreciate that right away, especially during my summer travels through the Gulf region, when I was often both angry and grief-stricken. In truth, they deserve our thanks and praise.

But it's not all about them. It's about us. We all contributed to this event, and we're all trapped in the same situation. We all use too much gasoline and oil, because we've painted ourselves into a corner when it comes to energy.

For clarity I have lightly cleaned up or slightly condensed some of the verbatim testimony and quotes. Verbal exchanges during the hours leading up to and including the initial disaster on the drilling rig derive from recollections of those who endured that trauma. Because they are subject to the fog of crisis, some testimony conflicts; we may never know how to resolve those contradictory recollections.

In the end, this is a chronicle of a summer of pain—and hope. Hope that the full potential of this catastrophe would not materialize, hope that the harm done would heal faster than feared, and hope that even if we didn't suffer the absolute worst, we'd still learn the big lesson here.

We may have gotten two out of three. That's not good enough. Because: there'll be a next time.

Carl Safina
Stony Brook, New York
November 2010

PART ONE

DISASTER CHAIN

BLOWOUT!

April 20, 2010. Though a bit imprecise, the time, approximately 9:50 P.M., marks the end of knowing much precisely. A floating machinery system roughly the size of a forty-story hotel has for months been drilling into the seafloor in the Gulf of Mexico. Its creators have named the drilling rig the Deepwater Horizon.

Oil giant BP has contracted the Deepwater Horizon's owner, Transocean, and various companies and crews to drill deep into the seafloor forty-odd miles southeast of the Louisiana coast. The target has also been named: they call it the Macondo formation. The gamble is on a volume of crude oil Believed Profitable.

Giving the target a name helps pull it into our realm of understanding. But by doing so we risk failing to understand its nature. It is a hot, highly pressurized layer of petroleum hydrocarbons—oil and methane—pent up and packed away, undisturbed, inside the earth for many millions of years.

The worker crews have struck their target. But the Big Payback will cut both ways. The target is about to strike back.

A churning drill bit sent from a world of light and warmth and living beings. More than three miles under the sea surface, more than two miles under the seafloor. Eternal darkness. Unimaginable pressure. The drill bit has met a gas pocket. That tiny pinprick. That pressure. Mere bubbles, a mild fizz from deep within. A sudden influx of gas into the well. Rushing up the pipe. Gas expanding like crazy. Through the open gates on the seafloor. One more mile to the sea surface.

The beings above are experiencing some difficulty managing it. A variety of people face a series of varied decisions. They don't make all the right ones.

Explosion.

Fireball.

Destroyed: Eleven men. Created: Nine widows. Twenty-one fatherless kids, including one who'll soon be born. Seventeen injured. One hundred and fifteen survive with pieces of the puzzle lodged in their heads. Only the rig rests in peace, one mile down. Only the beginning.

Blowout. Gusher. Wild well. Across the whole region, the natural systems shudder. Months to control it. Years to get over it. Human lives changed by the hundreds of thousands. Effects that ripple across the country, the hemisphere, the world. Imperfect judgment at sea and in offices in Houston, perhaps forgivable. Inadequate safeguards, perhaps unforgivable. No amount of money enough. Beyond Payable.

Deepwater exploration had already come of age when, in 2008, BP leased the mile-deep Macondo prospect No. 252 for $34 million. By 1998 only two dozen exploratory wells had been drilled in water deeper than 5,000 feet in the Gulf of Mexico. A decade later, that number was nearly three hundred.

With a platform bigger than a football field, the Deepwater Horizon was insured for over half a billion dollars. The rig cost $350 million and rose 378 feet from bottom to top. On the rig were 126 workers; 79 were Transocean employees, 6 were BP employees, and 41 were subcontractors to firms like Halliburton and M-I Swaco. None of the Deepwater Horizon's crew had been seriously injured in seven years.

Operations began at Macondo 252 using Transocean's drilling platform Marianas on October 6, 2009. The site was forty-eight miles southeast of the nearest Louisiana shore and due south of Mobile, Alabama. As the lessee, BP did the majority of the design work for the well, but utilized contractors for the drilling operation. Rig owner Transocean was the lead driller. Halliburton—formerly headed by Dick Cheney, before he became vice president of the United States under George W. Bush—was hired for cementing services. Other contractors performed other specialized work.

The initial cost estimate for the well was approximately $100 million. The work cost BP about $1 million per day.

They'd drilled about 4,000 feet down when, on November 8, 2009, Hurricane Ida damaged Marianas so severely that the rig had to be towed to the shipyard. Drilling resumed on February 6, 2010, with BP having switched to Transocean's Deepwater Horizon rig.

By late April, the well would be about $58 million over budget.

Being a deepwater well driller—what's it like? To simplify, imagine pushing a pencil into the soil. Pull out the pencil. Slide a drinking straw into that hole to keep it open. Now, a little more complex: your pencil is tipped not with a lead point but with a drilling bit. You have a set of pencils, each a little narrower than the last, each a little longer. You have a set of drinking straws, each also narrower. You use the fattest pencil first, make the hole, pull it out, then use the next fattest. And so on. This is how you make the hole deeper. At the scale of pencils-as-drills, you're going down about 180 feet, and the work is soon out of sight. As you push and remove the pencils, you slide one straw through another, into the deepening hole. You have a deepening, tapering hole lined with sections of drinking straw, with little spaces between the hole and each straw, and between the sections of straw. You have to seal all those spaces, make it, in effect, one tapering tube, absolutely tight.

And here's why: the last, narrowest straw pokes through the lid of a (very big) pop bottle with lots of soda containing gas under tremendous pressure. As long as the lid stays intact and tight, there's no fizz. But only that long. Everyone around you is desperate for a drink of that pop, as if they're addicted to it, because their lives depend on it. They're in a bit of a hurry. But you have to try to ignore them while you're painstakingly working these pencils and straws. And you'd better keep your finger on the top of the straw, or you're going to have a big mess. And you'd better seal those spaces between sections of straw as you go down, or you're going to have a big mess when you poke through that lid. And before you take your finger off the top of the straw, you'd better be ready to control all that fizz and drink all that pop, because it's coming up that straw. And if, after poking a hole in this lid that's been sealed for millions of years, you decide you want to save the soda for later, then you'd better—you'd better—have a way to stopper that straw before you take your finger off. And you'd better have a way to block that straw if the stopper starts leaking and the whole thing starts to fizz. If it starts to fizz uncontrollably, and you can't regain control, you can get hurt; people can die.

The real details beggar the imagination of what's humanly and technologically possible. Rig floor to seafloor at the well site: 5,000 feet of water, a little under one mile. Seafloor to the bottom of the well: about 13,360 feet—two and a half miles of drilling into the seabed sediments. A total of 18,360 feet from sea surface to well bottom, just under three and a half miles.

Equally amazing as how deep, is how narrow. At the seafloor—atop a well 2.5 miles long—the top casing is only 36 inches across. At the bottom it's just 7 inches. If you figure that the average diameter of the casing is about 18 inches, it's like a pencil-width hole 184 feet deep. Nine drill bits, each progressively smaller, dig the well. The well's vertical height gets lined with protective metal casings that, collectively, telescope down its full length. At intervals, telescoping tube of casing gets slid into the well hole. The upper casing interval is about 300 feet long. Some of the lower ones, less than a foot across, are 2,000 feet long. The uppermost end of each casing will have a fatter mouth, which will "hang" on the bottom of the previous casing. You will make that configuration permanent with your cementing jobs. The casings and drill pipes are stored on racks, awaiting use. Casings are made in lengths ranging from 25 to 45 feet; the drill pipe usually comes in 30-foot joints. They are "stacked" in the pipe racking system. You assemble three at a time and drop approximately 90 feet in, and then repeat. When you get ready to put the casing in, you pull all the drill pipe out. Rig workers also remove the drill pipe from the hole every time the drill bit gets worn and needs changing or when some activity requires an open hole. Pulling the entire drill string from the hole is called "making a trip." Making a trip of 10,000 feet may take as long as ten or twelve hours. When you want to start drilling some more, you have to reassemble the drill pipe and send it down.

On drillers' minds at all times is the need to control the gas pressure and prevent gas from leaking up between the outside of the casings and the rock sides of the well. At each point where the casing diameter changes, the well drillers must push cement between the casings and the bedrock wall of the well. This cements the casings to the well wall. It controls pressure and eliminates space.

Drillers continually circulate a variety of artificial high-density liquid displacements or drilling fluids, called "mud," between the drill rig and the well. The circulating fluid is sent down the drill pipe. It causes the drill bit to rotate, then leaves the drill bit and comes up to the surface, carrying the rock and sand that the drill bit has ground loose. Because the well is miles deep, the fluid creates a miles-high column of heavy liquid. (The drilling fluid is heavier than water. Imagine filling a bucket with water and lifting it; then imagine that the bucket is three miles tall. It's heavy.) That puts enormous downward pressure on the entire well bore. As the drill digs deeper, the drilling "mud" formulation is made heavier to neutralize the higher pressures in the deepening depths. But that heavier fluid can exert so much pressure on the shallower reaches of the well (where the ambient pressure is less) that it can fracture the rock, damage the well, seep away, and be lost into the rock and sand. Steel casings can protect weaker sections of rock and sand from these fluid pressures.

Because things fail and accidents happen, a 50-foot-high stack of valves sits on top of the well on the seafloor. Called a "blowout preventer," it is there to stop the uncontrolled release of oil and gas when things go wrong in a well. If something goes seriously wrong below, the valves pinch closed, containing the pressure. The blowout preventer is relied on as the final fail-safe.

Designs vary. This rig had a 300-ton blowout preventer manufactured by Cameron International. A blowout preventer's several shutoff systems may include "annulars," rubber apertures that can close around any pipe or on themselves; "variable bore rams," which can seal rubber-tipped steel blocks around a drill pipe if gas or oil is coming up outside it; "casing shear rams" or "super shear rams," designed to cut through casing or other equipment; and "blind shear rams," designed to cut through a drill pipe and seal the well. Blind shear rams are the well-control mechanism of last resort. Though often designed with redundant equipment and controls, blowout preventers can fail. On occasion, they have. Neither casing shear rams nor blind shear rams are designed to cut through thick-walled joint connections between sections of drill pipe. Such joints may take up as much as 10 percent of a pipe's length. So having redundant shear rams ensures that there is always one shear ram that is not aligned with a tool joint.

The drilling fluid is the primary stopper for the whole well. If you're going to remove that stopper, you'd better have something else to hold the pressure. Usually, that something else is several hundred feet of cement. On the night of the explosion, as rig workers were preparing to seal the well for later use, drillers were told to remove the drilling fluid and replace it with plain seawater—in essence, to pull out the stopper. The cement did not hold. And in the critical moment, the blowout preventer failed. The consequent gas blast was the blowout.

That's what went wrong. But so many things had gone wrong before the blowout that assistant well driller Steve Curtis had nicknamed it "the well from hell." Curtis, thirty-nine, a married father of two from Georgetown, Louisiana, was never found.

❧

Right from the start—beginning with Hurricane Ida forcing the Marianas rig off the well location—various things didn't proceed as planned, or struck people as risky.

The Deepwater Horizon, built at a cost of $350 million, was new in February 2001. In September 2009, it had drilled the deepest oil well in history—over 35,000 feet deep—in the Gulf of Mexico's Tiber Field.

It was a world-class rig, but it was almost ten years old. The wonderful high-tech gadgets that were state of the art in 2001 did not always function as well in 2010. Equipment was getting dated. Old parts didn't always work with new innovations. Manufacturers changed product lines. Sometimes they had to find a different company to make a part from scratch.

The world has changed a lot since the rig was built. So has software. More 3-D, a lot more graphics. Drillers sit in a small room and use computer screens to watch key indicators. Depth of the bit, pressure on the pipe, flows in, flows out. But on this job, the software repeatedly hit glitches. Computers froze. Data didn't update. Sometimes workers got what they called the "blue screen of death." In March and April 2010, audits by maritime risk managers Lloyd's Register Group identified more than two dozen components and systems on the rig in "bad" or "poor" condition, and found some workers dismayed about safety practices and fearing reprisals if they reported mistakes.

Risk is part of life. And it's part of drilling. Yet drilling culture has changed, with much greater emphasis on safety than in the past. Many people still working, however, came up the ranks in a risk-prone, cowboy "oil patch" culture. A friend of mine who worked the Gulf of Mexico oil field in the 1970s says, "It was clear to me that I was way underqualified for what I was doing. Safety didn't get you promoted. They wanted speed. If we filled a supply boat with five thousand gallons of diesel fuel in twenty-five minutes, they'd rather you disconnect in a big hurry and spill fifty gallons across the deck than take an extra three minutes to do it safe and clean. I'd actually get yelled at for stuff like that. Another thing that was clear: if you could simply read or write, you could pretty much run the show. They actually gave oral exams to workers who couldn't read. I was still a kid, but pretty soon I was put in charge of a supply boat because I could read and write. That was the culture then." Another friend, now a tug captain, says, "Never in the four years I worked the rig did I hear anyone say, 'Let's wait for better sea conditions.' We were always dragged into situations we didn't want to be in, doing things I didn't think were safe. Now it's a lot better. It used to be the Wild West out there."

When you pump drilling fluid down the well, it comes out the bottom of the drill pipe and circulates up between the drill pipe and the wall of the well, and comes back to you. For every barrel of drilling fluid you push down, you'd better get a barrel back. If you get more—that's really bad, because gas and oil are coming up in your fluid. If you get less—that's really bad, too. Drillers call it "lost returns." It means the returning fluid has lost some of its volume because fluid is leaking into the rock and sand of the well's walls, sometimes badly. Sometimes there are fractures in the rock and the fluid's going there. When it's leaking like that, you can't maintain the right pressure in the well to tamp down the pressure of oil and gas that wants to come up from below.

In a March 2010 incident, the rig lost all of its drilling fluid, over 3,000 barrels, through leaks into the surrounding rock and sand formation into which they were drilling.

BP's onshore supervisor for this project, John Guide, later testified, "We got to a depth of 18,260 feet, and all of a sudden we just lost complete returns."

BP's senior design engineer, Mark Hafle, was questioned on this point:

Q: "Now, lost returns, what does that mean in plain everyday English?"

Hafle: "While drilling that hole section we lost over 3,000 barrels of mud."

Three thousand barrels is a lot of barrels. At over $250 per barrel for synthetic oil-based mud, that's $750,000.

A high-risk pregnancy is one running a higher than normal risk for complications. A woman with a high-risk pregnancy needs closer monitoring, more visits with her primary health-care provider, and more careful tests to monitor the situation. If BP can be called the birth parent, this well was a high-risk pregnancy.

Several times, the well slapped back with hazardous gas belches called "kicks," another indication that the deep pool of hydrocarbons did not appreciate being roused from its long sleep.

At around 12,000 feet, the drill bit got stuck in rock. The crew was forced to cut the pipe, abandon the high-tech bit, and perform a time-consuming and costly sidetrack procedure around it to continue with the well. The delays cost a week and led to a budget add-on of $27 million.

The work had fallen forty-three days behind schedule, at roughly $1 million a day in costs. At a "safety meeting," the crew was informed that they'd lost about $25 million in hardware and drilling fluid. Not really safety information. More pressure to hurry.

High-risk pregnancy, added complications. On April 9, 2010, BP had finished drilling the last section of the well. The final section of the well bore extended to a depth of 18,360 feet below sea level, which was 1,192 feet below the casing that had previously been inserted into the well.

At this point, BP had to implement an important well-design decision: how to secure the final 1,200 or so feet and, for eventual extraction of the petroleum, what kind of "production casing" workers would run inside the protective casing already in the well. One option involved hanging a steel tube called a "liner" from the bottom of the previous casing already in the well. The other option involved running one long string of steel casing from the seafloor all the way down to the bottom of the well. The single long string design would save both time (about three days) and money.

BP chose the long string. A BP document called the long string the "best economic case." And though officials insist that money was not a factor in their decisions, doing it differently would have cost $7 to $10 million more.

BP's David Sims later testified, "Cost is a factor in a lot of decisions but it is never put before safety. It's not a deciding factor."

Sims was John Guide's supervisor. Guide described the long string design as "a win-win situation," adding that "it happened to be a good economic decision as well."

Guide insisted that none of these decisions were done for money.

Q: "With every decision, didn't BP reduce the cost of the project?"

Guide: "All the decisions were based on long-term well-bore integrity."

Q: "I asked you about the cost of the project. Didn't each of these decisions reduce the cost, to BP, of this project?"

Guide: "Cost was not a factor."

Q: "I didn't ask if it was a factor. I asked if it reduced the cost. It's a fact question, sir. Did it not reduce the cost, in each case?"

Guide: "All I was concerned about was long-term well-bore integrity."

Q: "I just want to know if doing all these decisions saved this company money."

Guide: "No, it did not."

Q: "All right; what didn't save you money?"

Silence.

Q: "Which of these decisions that you made drove up the cost of the project, as opposed to saving BP money? Can you think of any?"

Guide: "I've already answered the question."

Q: "What was the answer?"

Guide: "These decisions were not based on saving BP money. They were based on long-term well-bore integrity."

Some people called the long string design the riskier of two options. Greg McCormack, director of the University of Texas at Austin's Petroleum Extension Service, calls it "without a doubt a riskier way to go."

But others disagree. Each of the two possible well casing designs represented certain risk trade-offs. One called for cement around casing sections at various well depths, providing barriers to any oil flowing up in the space between the rock and casing. The other called for casing sections seamlessly connected from top to bottom with no outside barriers except the considerable bottom cement. Investigators would later focus lasers on this aspect of the well design for weeks after the well blew. The cost savings led many to believe that this was a cut corner that resulted in the blowout. Months later, however, it became clear that this decision was not a direct cause of the disaster.

Final hours. In the eternal darkness of the deep sea, the well is dug, finished. All that's needed: just seal the well and disconnect. The plan was for a different rig to come at some later date and pump the oil for sale.

At BP's onshore Houston office, John Guide is BP's overall project manager for this well. He has been with BP for ten years, has overseen more than two dozen wells. Mark Hafle is BP's senior design engineer. With twenty-three years at BP, Hafle created much of the design for this well. Brian Morel, a BP design engineer involved in many of the key meetings and procedures in the final days, splits his time between Houston and the rig. Out on the drilling rig itself, BP's supervisors, titled "well site leaders," are often called the "company men." They oversee the contractors. Because a drilling rig operates twenty-four hours a day, BP has two well site leaders aboard, working twelve-hour shifts: Don Vidrine and Bob Kaluza. Vidrine is in his sixties. Kaluza in his fifties. Vidrine has been with the rig for a while. Kaluza is new.

Because the Deepwater Horizon was both a drilling rig and a vessel, rig owner Transocean has two separate leadership roles. When moving, the rig is under the authority of the captain; when stationary at the well site, an offshore installation manager, or OIM, is in charge. Jimmy Harrell, OIM, managed the drilling. He'd been with Transocean since 1979 and on the Deepwater Horizon since 2003. Curt Kuchta was the Deepwater Horizon's captain.

Managers play an important part in the decision process, but the drilling team executes the plan. At the top of the drilling personnel chart are the "tool pusher," who oversees all parts of the drilling process, and the driller, who sits in a high-tech, glass-paneled control room called the "driller's shack" and leads the actual work. Many people work under the direction of the tool pusher and driller.

On duty on the evening of April 20 were Transocean's tool pusher Jason Anderson and driller Dewey Revette. Thirty-five years old, Jason had worked on the Horizon since it launched, in 2001, and was highly respected by his crewmates. At home before the explosion, Jason had been concerned about putting his affairs in order. He wrote a will and gave his wife, Shelley, instructions about things to do if anything were to "happen to him." Jason told his father that BP was pushing the rig operators to speed up the drilling. In telephone calls from the rig before the explosion, Jason told Shelley he could not talk about his concerns because the "walls were too thin," but that he would tell her about them later, when he got home. Jason had just been promoted to senior tool pusher. He had been due to leave for his new post aboard the Discoverer Spirit on April 14, but was persuaded to stay aboard the Deepwater Horizon for one more week. He was scheduled to be helicoptered to his new job at 7:00 A.M. on April 21. By then, he had died in the explosions and the rig was an inferno.

At the closing of a well, it might seem you'd want the team members most familiar with the well and one another to be present. But approaching the critical juncture of closing up the well they'd been drilling for months, one of BP's company men, with thirty-three years of experience as a well site leader, was sent off the rig to take his mandatory biannual well-control certification class. Just four days before the explosion, his replacement, Bob Kaluza, appeared on the rig. A *Wall Street Journal* article said of Kaluza, "His experience was largely in land drilling," and he told investigators he was on the rig to "learn about deep water," according to Coast Guard notes of an interview with him. We don't have a better feel for Kaluza because he has exercised his Fifth Amendment right not to provide testimony that could incriminate himself.

Transocean's onshore manager responsible for the Horizon, Paul Johnson, testified that he was troubled by the timing in BP's switch of well site leaders. "I raised my concerns," he noted. "I challenged BP on the decision. We didn't know who this gentleman was. I wasn't making any assumptions on him, I just—I heard he come from a platform, so I was curious about his deepwater experience in a critical phase of the well. They informed me that Mr. Kaluza was a very experienced, very competent well site leader, and it wouldn't be a concern."

Kaluza showed a tendency toward appropriate caution, but the simple fact that he was new seemed to get in the way. At a critical juncture, Kaluza was uncertain enough about a crucial procedure called a "negative pressure test" that he sought out Leo Lindner, a drilling fluid specialist with the company M-I Swaco. Lindner, who'd worked on the rig for over four years, was in charge of the different types of fluids used during the negative test, an important role.

"Mr. Bob Kaluza called me to his office," Lindner testified. "He wanted to go over the method. I briefly explained to him how the rig had been conducting their negative tests and he just wanted—." Lindner interrupted himself to note, "Bob wasn't the regular company man on the Horizon."

So, competence aside, there were working dynamics, team cohesion. It was a time for familiar faces and an almost literally well-oiled team. But it felt like BP was taking out its quarterback during the fourth quarter of a playoff game.

And on the morning of April 20—the day the rig exploded—BP

engineer Brian Morel departed the rig, creating space for visiting company VIPs. Wrote one industry analyst later, "Let's face it; the timing of that VIP visit was terrible. It could not have been at a worse time."

A difficult pregnancy, new doctors, altered procedures: BP decided to turn this exploratory well into a production well. Usually, the purpose of an exploratory well is to learn about the geological formation and what the oil and gas–bearing production zone contains. Then the well is closed out. Engineers use the information to decide where to drill a production well, perhaps in a nearby spot. If you decide to turn an exploratory well into a production well, you obviously save a fair amount of drilling expense. But is an exploration crew going to be familiar with production technology? BP's drilling and completion operations manager David Sims testified that the decision was not a major technical issue. Yet veteran well site leader Ronnie Sepulvado who'd been on the rig for eight and a half years had a different take: "We're in the exploration group, so we hardly ever set production strings. We did maybe a handful of wells that was kept for production."

Added complications. The oil and gas—in the pay zone, or "production zone"—lay between 18,051 and 18,223 feet. The well was drilled to below the zone, to 18,360 feet below the sea surface, which allowed cement to be placed under the oil and gas reservoir as well as around it.

Because this was an exploratory well, the idea was to find the oil, then seal the well shut so a different rig could later tap it for commercial production. Cement is the main barrier for preventing the pressurized oil and gas from entering the well. So it was crucial that the cement job at the bottom of the well absolutely seal off the oil and gas reservoir from the well casing. A bad cement job could let oil and gas into the well.

The environment at that depth means cementing is not a matter of getting a few bags of concrete from the hardware store. Temperatures and pressures at the bottom of a well like this—it's hotter than boiling, 240° Fahrenheit—make cementing a highly technical endeavor, requiring calculations and tests to select several chemical mixtures, which will be used in layers.

Earlier heavy losses of drilling fluid told technicians that they could be into very loose rock and sand. If you are nervous about a soft zone, you also worry that when you insert cement to seal the well bottom, your cement may ooze into the loose stuff. This complicated the cementing deliberations. John Guide: "The biggest risk associated with this cement job was losing circulation. That was the number one risk."

If you're worried that the well walls may be so porous that they'll suck in cement pumped under pressure, you might add some nitrogen gas to the cement mixture, to get it to form foamy bubbles; this would prevent the cement from leaking into the loose spots.

From the well's training resources document: "Foamed cement is more expensive than regular cement and it works better than regular cement in some applications. One of the advantages is that the bubbles stiffen the wet cement so that it is less prone to being lost into a zone or being invaded by fluids in a zone. A remote analogy is that when a sink is drained after washing dishes, the water flows out the drain while the soap bubbles remain in the sink." But, the document notes, while foamed cement is good at sealing off shallow areas, "use of nitrogen foam is less common for deep high-temperature, high-pressure zones."

Halliburton cement specialist Jesse Gagliano first proposed including nitrified cement. After some back-and-forth, BP agreed. But because nitrified cement is usually used for shallower jobs, the depth created concern on the rig.

Transocean offshore installation manager Jimmy Harrell: "That nitrogen, it could be a bad thing. If it gets in the riser, it will unload the riser on you. . . . Anything can go wrong."

There were three parts to the cement and three formulations. "Cap cement" topped the cement in the space between the casing and the oil-bearing rock and sand formation of the well's sides. Below that, the nitrified "foamed cement" filled the rest of the narrow space outside the casing and along the formation. "Tail cement" filled the "shoe track" at the bottom and was used inside the lower part of the casing itself.

So in various ways this was going to be a difficult cement job. As late as the afternoon of April 14, BP was still reconsidering the chosen long string casing design, with its heavier reliance on the integrity of the cement deep at the well bottom. And the porous surrounding rock was on everyone's mind. Cement has to be pumped in under some degree of excess pressure in order to fully fill the gap and get a good bond to the rock and sand on one side and to the outside of the production casing on the other. You need enough pressure both to keep the hydrocarbons contained and to force the cement against the sides, but too much pressure will inject the cement into the sand, and you'll lose it. The team spent days determining how to approach the cement job. BP engineer Mark Hafle testified to this: "We were concerned that the pore pressure and frac gradient was going to be a narrow window to execute that cement job. That's why we spent five days." BP's Brian Morel apologized to a colleague for asking yet another question about the design in an April 14 e-mail that he ended with this resonant comment: "This has been a nightmare well." Hafle added, "This has been a crazy well for sure."

When BP won the lease to this piece of seabed, it held an in-house contest to name it. The winner, "Macondo," came from the mythical town hewn from a "paradise of dampness and silence" in Gabriel García Márquez's novel *One Hundred Years of Solitude.* In the novel, Macondo is an accursed place, a metaphor for the fate awaiting those too arrogant to heed its warning signs. What had seemed a nice literary allusion now carries ominous portent.

More complications. Part of Jesse Gagliano's task was to model the cement's likely performance in this well and design a procedure that would get the cement to the proper locations. On April 15, he discovered some problems. This space between the casing and the wall of this well was very narrow. And the previous experience with lost drilling fluid indicated soft walls, requiring a low cement-pumping rate.

These conditions contributed to a model predicting that if the casing moved too close to one side of the well-bore wall, drilling fluid could get left behind, creating pockets or channels where the cement would not distribute uniformly. That is, it wouldn't fill in all of the space it needed to fill.

To prevent a casing from getting too close to one side of a well bore, drillers slip flexible metal spring devices called "centralizers" over the casing so that it will stay centered in the well bore. By keeping the casing centered, centralizers help achieve good, even, thorough cementing between the casing and the well's geological wall. In this case, BP had six centralizers. That number concerned Gagliano. On April 15 Gagliano e-mailed BP saying he'd run different scenarios "to see if adding more centralizers will help us."

BP's Brian Morel replied, "We have 6 centralizers. . . . It's too late to get any more to the rig. Our only option is to rearrange placement of these centralizers. . . . Hopefully the pipe stays centralized due to gravity."

But Jesse Gagliano continued his calculations. He determined that twenty-one centralizers should create an acceptably safe cement flow.

And it wasn't really too late. On April 16, BP engineering team leader Gregg Walz e-mailed BP project manager John Guide, saying that he'd located fifteen more centralizers that could be flown to the rig in the morning with "no incremental cost" for transporting them. "There are differing opinions on the model accuracy," he wrote to Guide, "but we need to honor the modeling." He added, "I apologize if I have overstepped my bounds."

The centralizers made the helicopter trip to the rig.

But Guide expressed dismay at these particular centralizers' design, the addition of new pieces "as a last minute decision," and the fact that it would take ten hours to install them. He wrote, "I do not like this," adding that he was "very concerned about using them."

Walz backed off.

Later that afternoon BP's Brian Morel wrote to his colleague Brett Cocales, "I don't understand Jesse's centralizer requirements."

Cocales replied, "Even if the hole is perfectly straight, a straight piece of pipe in tension will not seek the perfect center of the hole unless it has something to centralize it." And then he added this: "But who cares, it's done, end of story, will probably be fine and we'll get a good cement job."

That was on April 16. It seems to suggest a certain willingness to add risk.

That's not how BP's managers saw it. Guide later testified: "It was a bigger risk to run the wrong centralizers than it was to believe in the model."

But months later in September, BP's own internal investigation concluded, "The BP Macondo team erroneously believed that they had received the wrong centralizers."

In late July 2010, examiners from BP contractors Anadarko, Transocean, and Halliburton questioned Guide on his decisions.

Q: "That left you several days to get whatever centralizers you felt might be needed."

Guide: "I didn't feel they were needed."

Q: "So what you're telling me is that there was just no discussion among you between you and Mr. Walz about just waiting for the right centralizers? None, zip, zero, true?"

Guide: "That subject never came up."

Q: "You still had time between the 16th and the 20th—"

Guide: "Well, we didn't know if we could find them. That subject never came up."

Q. "Sir, can you tell us the number of times, that you have personal knowledge of, that BP did not follow the recommendations of Halliburton in connection with the cementing of any of its jobs, if any?

Guide: "I don't know of any."

Well, perhaps we know of one. Halliburton's Gagliano accepted BP's decision and, on April 17 and 18, developed the specific procedure for pumping the cement. Gagliano created and sent one final cementing model out to the team on the evening of April 18.

The model would later cause a firestorm for a particular page that no one at BP seems to have looked at. That page said that using only six centralizers would likely cause channeling; it also noted: "Based on analysis of the above outlined well conditions, this well is considered to have a SEVERE gas flow problem." But with twenty-one centralizers, it added, "this well is considered to have a MINOR gas flow problem."

This report was attached to an e-mail sent to Guide on April 18, but it went unopened because the casing with just the six centralizers was already down the hole. Although BP had had days to get the centralizers, it was now too late to read the e-mail predicting severe gas-flow problems. Guide later testified: "I never knew it was part of the report."

The cement job will fail. But a few months later, in September 2010, BP's own investigation will conclude, "Although the decision not to use twenty-one centralizers increased the possibility of channeling above the main hydrocarbon zones, the decision likely did not contribute to the cement's failure."

That's BP's executives exonerating themselves, so season it with a grain of salt. But numerous industry analysts think centralizers are not the smoking gun. We'll get back to that question later, but for now, it's important to understand the distances involved. The recommended twenty-one centralizers were meant to keep the bottom 900 feet of casing evenly centered in the well. If the workers had had all twenty-one, they would have put fifteen above the span containing the oil and gas, four in the zone that held the oil and gas, and two below that zone.

BP placed the six centralizers so as to straddle and bisect the 175 vertical feet of oil and gas–bearing sands deep in the well, at depths of around 18,000 feet. They placed two centralizers above the oil and gas zone, two in the zone, and two below it.

But even if centralizers won't be the smoking gun, the e-mail exchanges over the centralizers convey the sense that the BP team isn't treating this endeavor with the utmost care. When red flags go up, BP's decision makers seem rushed, rather than thorough.

BP e-mails suggest that its personnel believed that any problem with cement could be remediated with additional cement. And actually, that's often what's done; well cement jobs sometimes do fail. The reason why they fail is seldom precisely ascertained. Usually the failure is not catastrophic and the fix is to pump more cement in, then test it again. For this reason, the industry has developed several ways of testing the soundness of cementing jobs.

But detecting problems assumes, of course, that the cementing job will be properly tested.

The crew did their cementing over a five-hour period, starting at 7:30 P.M. on April 19. When they finished, at around 12:30 A.M., the calendar had turned over to April 20.

Testing. More complications: when wells lose drilling fluid—as this one did weeks earlier—one possible solution is to send down a special mixture of fluids to block the problem zones in the well bore. Think of the stuff made to spray into a flat tire to seal it enough to get you home. A batch of this mixture is called a "kill pill." It is a thick, heavy compound (16 pounds per gallon, compared to 14.5 for drilling fluid and 8.6 for seawater).

Two weeks before the accident, when the rig had its serious 3,000-barrel loss of drilling fluid, the fluid specialists made up a kill pill and pumped it down to the problem zone. It didn't seem to work, so they mixed up another batch: 424 barrels of a combination of two materials. But just as they were preparing to send this second kill pill down the hole, the losses stopped.

They now had a thick, unused 424-barrel kill pill sitting in an extra tank, taking up space on the rig. To dispose of it they had two options: take it onto shore and treat it as hazardous waste or use it in the drilling process. The second choice would allow them to skirt the land-based disposal process and dump the compound directly into the ocean.

The drilling fluid specialists got the bright idea of using the unused kill-pill material in a "spacer." A spacer is a distinct fluid placed in between two other fluids. When you're pushing different fluids down a well, you'll often decide to use a spacer between the different fluids—between displacement fluid and drilling fluid, for instance—so that they won't mix and so you can keep track of where things are. A spacer also creates a marker in the drilling flow, which allows the rig team to watch the fluid returns, to ensure that flow in equals flow out.

Because BP didn't want to have to dispose of the thick kill-pill material, they mixed it with some other fluid to create a spacer. BP's vice president for safety and operations, Mark Bly, later said that using such a mixture was "not an uncommon thing to do." The rig's drilling fluid specialist, Leo Lindner, put it differently, saying, "It's not something that we've ever done before." At a government hearing in August, BP manager David Sims was asked if he had ever used a similar mixture as a spacer. "No, I have not," Sims said.

Down the hatch it goes. Just like that.

Q: "What if you hadn't used it that way, what would the rig have had to do; hazardous waste disposal, right?" ·

Lindner: "Yes."

Q: "When these pills are mixed, have you ever heard anybody characterize it as looking like snot?"

Lindner: "It wasn't quite snotty."

Q: "But it was close?"

Lindner: "It was thick. It was thick, but it was still fluid."

Q: "So it was very viscous?"

Lindner: "Yes."

Q: "And really the only reason for putting those two pills down there was just to get rid of them; is that your understanding?"

Lindner: "To my knowledge—well, it filled a function that we needed a spacer."

Chief engineer Steve Bertone later recalled that after the explosion, "I looked down at the deck because it was very slick and I saw a substance that had a consistency of snot. I can remember thinking to myself, 'Why is all this snot on the deck?'"

Back on the rig, Transocean installation manager Jimmy Harrell outlines the well-closing procedure. BP's company man (later testimony is conflicting as to whether Kaluza or Vidrine was speaking) suddenly perks up. Interrupts. Says, "Well, my process is different. And I think we're gonna do it this way." Chief mechanic Douglas Brown will later testify that BP's company man said, "This is how it's going to be," leading to a verbal "skirmish" with Transocean's Jimmy Harrell, who left the meeting grumbling, "I guess that's what we have those pincers for" (referring to the blowout preventer). Harrell will later testify that he was alluding to his concerns about risks inherent in the cementing procedure, but would say, "I didn't have no doubts about it." He'll claim he had no argument but that "there's a big difference between an argument and a disagreement." Chief electronics technician Mike Williams, seated beside BP's company man, will later recall, "So there was sort of a chest-bumping kind of deal. The communication seemed to break down as to who was ultimately in charge."

This is certainly not the time for chest bumping or blurred authority. If you're gonna release the parking brake, you'd better agree on who's gonna be in the driver's seat. And whoever grabs the wheel better know how to drive.

High-risk pregnancy enters labor. To determine if the cement job has worked and the well is sealed, rig operators can choose from several tests. On the Deepwater Horizon the engineers decide to do two kinds of pressure tests. In a "positive pressure test," they introduce pressure in the well; if it holds, it means nothing's leaking *out* from the well into the rock. They do this test on the morning of April 20, between about 11:00 a.m. and noon, roughly eleven hours after the cement job ends. It goes well; it seems nothing's leaking out.

But the reason nothing's leaking out may be that there's pressure from oil and gas pushing to get in. So the engineers prepare to do a "negative pressure test." A negative test is a way of seeing if pressure is building in the well, indicating that gas and oil are leaking in. That could mean the cement has failed.

To do a negative test, they close the wellhead, then reduce the downward pressure on the well by replacing some heavy drilling fluid with lighter water. Then they look at pressure gauges. If the pressure increases, hydrocarbons are entering, exerting upward pressure from below. What they want to see is zero pressure.

Until the negative pressure test is performed successfully, the rig crew won't remove the balance of the heavy drilling mud that stoppers the well; that's their foot on the brake.

Between 3:00 P.M. and 5:00 P.M., about fifteen hours after the cement job was finished, they start reducing the pressure by inserting seawater into the miles-long circulating-fluid lines. To make sure the drilling fluid and the seawater don't mix, they precede the seawater with a spacer. The spacer they use contains that extra kill-pill material, the "snot." And though a typical amount of spacer is under 200 barrels, this time it's over 400 barrels because, remember, they're trying to get rid of that leftover stuff.

There are various places all this fluid is getting to, because there are various lines and pipes going into and out of the blowout preventer. One such line is called the "kill line." Another is the drill pipe.

A little before 5:00 P.M., they work for a while to relieve any residual pressure and are looking for the fluid to stabilize at zero pressure, indicated by a reading of zero pounds per square inch, or psi. They've got the pressure down to 645 psi in the kill line, but it's at 1,350 psi in the drill pipe. So they try bleeding the system down, venting off some of that pressure. They achieve zero in the kill line. The drill pipe retains 273 psi. They need zero.

Over six minutes right around 5:00 P.M., the drill pipe pressure increases from 273 psi to 1,250.

The engineers tighten the blowout preventer's rubber gasket and add 50 barrels of heavier-than-water fluid.

So the lines are filled with a variety of different fluids snaking through in segments: there's a stretch of drilling fluid, or "mud," a stretch of the unusual spacer material, followed by plain seawater. At this point in the circulation of the various fluids, the spacer—the "snot"—should be above the blowout preventer. But some of it has found its way into the blowout preventer and has entered one of the lines being tested.

The engineers see pressure building in the drill pipe, zero pressure in the kill line. They're unsure what to make of that, so they repeat the test procedure several times. From shortly after 5:00 to almost 5:30, they get the pressure in the drill pipe down a little, from 1,250 to almost 1,200.

The Deepwater Joint Investigation panel asked Dr. John R. Smith, whose PhD is in petroleum engineering, to describe a negative test:

"If it's a successful test, there's no more fluid coming back. You've got a closed container. There's no hole in the boat. There's no fluid leaking in through the wall of the container or the casing. It just sits there. If you have an unsuccessful test, external pressure is leaking through the wall of the system somewhere. Through the wall of the casing, past the casing hanger seals, up through the float equipment in the casing—. Somewhere there's a leak from external pressure into the system. You'd expect to continue to see some fluid coming back."

To reach for an analogy: if you did a negative test in a swimming pool, you'd empty the pool. If the pool stayed dry, you'd have a successful test. If you had a problem, the pool would start filling itself through leaks in its walls. A well 18,360 feet deep is a bit trickier to test than a swimming pool. Even though you're reducing the pressure, you still have to keep enough downward pressure on the well to control any oil and gas that might start entering. And you must check specific pipes for indications of pressure.

Wells come in many different sizes and shapes and pipe setups. So, somewhat surprisingly, there isn't a "standard" negative test.

Q: Do you know if there's any standard negative test procedure that the industry follows?

Dr. John Smith: I was unable to find a standard.

The Minerals Management Service's permit specified that this negative test be conducted by monitoring the kill line above the blowout preventer. John Guide: "And that was really the only discussion, was to make sure that we did it on the kill line so that we would be in compliance with the permit."

Drilling fluid specialist Leo Lindner had spent four years on Deepwater Horizon.

Q: "And what is a good negative test?"

Lindner: "Where you don't have any pressure up the kill. Of course . . . I haven't been a witness to that many negative tests."

And that's another thing: negative tests are not routine on exploratory wells. The Deepwater Horizon mainly drilled exploratory wells. This well was unusual, because it was an exploratory well that was being converted to a *future* production well that would later be reopened and tapped. Not all the crew were familiar with all these steps and procedures.

Dr. John Smith: "Before they ever started the test, they've got enormously high pressure on the drill pipe." That should have been, he noted, "a warning sign right off the bat."

Leo Lindner: "They decided to go ahead and try to do the first negative test. They bled off some pressure from the drill pipe and got fluid back. They attempted it again and got fluid back."

But as Dr. Smith had said: "If it's a successful test, there's no more fluid coming back."

The crew had been replacing heavier fluid with seawater. But Lindner was sufficiently worried by the initial results that at around 5:00 P.M., he ordered his coworker to stop pumping drilling fluid off the rig. He wanted to keep his foot on the emergency brake.

At 5:30, Transocean's subsea supervisor Chris Pleasant comes on duty in the drill shack. "My supervisor was explaining to me that they had just finished a negative test. Wyman Wheeler, which is the tool pusher, was convinced that something wasn't right. Wyman worked to 6:00 P.M. By that time his relief come up, which is Jason Anderson, which is a tool pusher as well."

It was a bad time to change guards.

But now it's approximately ten minutes till 6:00. Bob Kaluza, the BP company man, tells Jason Anderson, "We're at an all stop."

Kaluza's relief, BP company man Don Vidrine, is scheduled to come on at 6:00 P.M.

Chris Pleasant: "Jason Anderson, he's convinced that it U-tubed. Where that U-tube's at, I don't know. But, you know, I guess we never really had a clear understanding. Anyway Jason is telling Bob that, 'We want to do this negative test the way Ronnie Sepulvado does it.' And Bob tells Jason, 'No, we're going to do it the way Don wants to do it. So, probably five minutes after 6:00 or something Don comes to the rig floor. Him and Bob talks back and forth for approximately a good hour.'"

They discuss possible causes for the fact that they're reading pressure on the drill pipe but not on the kill line. Don Vidrine believes that if the pressure in the drill pipe was evidence of a surge of gas deep in the well, they would be seeing similar pressure in the kill line.

Later question: "Based on industry standard ways of reading negative tests, you're looking for something pretty simple, right? A zero on the drill pipe and a zero on the kill line; right?"

Dr. John Smith: "Right."

Q: "And if you don't see that, you need to be very concerned; right?"

Smith: "Yes." Dr. Smith further says, "We know there's all this heavy spacer mud stuff in the well below the blowout preventer. Likely that mixture is what's going back up into the kill line, holding the pressure back."

Smith adds, "We're doing a test with a line that's got this dense stuff in it. So, the symptoms are a successful test, but the reality is— it's not a test at all. My opinion."

In other words: the only reason they've got zero pressure showing on the line they're relying on is that the thick spacer material has gotten in; the line is clogged.

After thirty minutes of staring at zero pressure on the kill line, the team is convinced that they've completed a successful negative test. Never mind that the drill pipe has 1,400 psi on it. They've convinced themselves that this was due to something Jason Anderson was calling a "bladder effect."

BP well site leader trainee Lee Lambert was later examined on this point.

Q: "What was Mr. Anderson saying about the bladder effect? Can you tell us?"

Lambert: "That the mud in the riser would push on the annular and transmit pressure downhole, which would in turn be seen on your drill pipe."

Q: "Was Mr. Anderson explaining why they were seeing differential pressure on the drill pipe versus the kill line?"

Lambert: "Yes."

Q: "Okay. And did anyone say anything or disagree with Mr. Anderson's explanation?"

Lambert: "I don't recall anybody disagreeing or agreeing with his explanation. At the time it did make sense to me. My lack of experience—. After learning things after the incident, it did not make sense to me, because the kill line and the drill pipe are open up to the same annulus, so in theory should see the same pressure."

Q: "And since then have you had an opportunity to study this so-called 'bladder effect'?"

Lambert: "I have not found any studies on the bladder effect."

In September 2010, BP's internal investigation concluded: "According to witness accounts, the toolpusher proposed that the pressure on the drill pipe was caused by a phenomenon referred to as 'annular compression' or 'bladder effect.' The toolpusher and driller stated that they had previously observed this phenomenon. After discussing this concept, the rig crew and the well site leaders accepted the explanation. The investigative team could find no evidence that this pressure effect exists."

After the negative pressure test, Vidrine tells Bob Kaluza, "Go call the office. Tell them we're going to displace the well." They're about to remove their fluid and replace it with seawater. Poised on a mountaintop, over an oil volcano, they're about to release the brake.

They're in a bit of a hurry. But what about the cement job; had it cured correctly already? The negative test helped convince them that it had. But that was only because the kill line was clogged and they chose to explain away the pressure they were seeing on the drill pipe.

The industry standard for judging the success of cement work, to best try to ascertain whether the cement is bonding to everything properly, is called a "cement bond log test." Halliburton, which did the cement job, will later tell a Senate committee that a cement bond log test is "the only test that can really determine the actual effectiveness of the bond between the cement sheets, the formation and the casing itself."

Of course, because Halliburton did the cement job, its people would like to blame BP for not using the definitive test. They don't want anyone focusing on their cement itself.

Using sonic tools, a cement bond log test makes 360-degree representations of the well and can show where the cement isn't adhering fully to the casing and where there may be paths for gas or oil to get in. In reality, even a cement bond log test is not perfect. But it is the best test going.

Perhaps the most skilled people to do a cement bond log test work for the rig-servicing company Schlumberger. They're on the rig on the morning of April 20, ready to get to work.

BP decides instead to just rely on the pressure tests and other indicators that say that all's well with the well. BP tells the Schlumberger workers that their services won't be needed after all, and arranges for them to leave.

John Guide explains: "Everyone involved on the rig site was completely satisfied with the job. You had full returns running the casing, full returns cementing the casing. Saw lift pressure, bumped the plug, floats were holding. So really all the indicators you could possibly get. So it was outlined ahead of time in the decision tree that we would not run a bond long if we saw these indicators. So the decision was made to send the Schlumberger people home."

As the Schlumberger folks board a helicopter and lift off the rig, oil and gas are already trying to get into the well, pushing hard on the cement. At 11:00 A.M., as the helicopter flies out of sight, eleven men on the rig have eleven hours left to live.

The main critical error was in not recognizing that the drill pipe pressure they were reading during the pressure test indicated that gas was already getting in—and, therefore, that the cement job had failed.

Why did it fail? People will speculate for months. Some will suggest that the cement was not allowed to set adequately before BP began altering the well pressure during the positive and negative pressure tests. Others will see that as irrelevant. Even the time required for the cement to harden at the pressure and temperature deep in the well will be subject to controversy.

Not until September and October did some of the most important pieces of this puzzle start to fit into a clearer glimpse of what happened.

First, as promised, let's revisit the centralizers. In late September 2010, when the relief well finally intersects the original well, it will find no oil outside the casing above the oil-bearing zone in the rock. This will confirm that the oil and gas flowed first out of the sand, then down more than 80 feet outside the casing, then into the well casing and up through 189 feet of "shoe track" cement within the casing. This entire 270-foot run—down outside, then up inside the casing— was supposed to be filled with cement. It's astonishing that the cement in the casing failed. The inner cement was designed to be a solid seven-inch-diameter, 189-foot-long plug.

Though Halliburton had recommended twenty-one centralizers to help ensure a good cement job, BP used only six. But the other fifteen would have been placed *above* the zone bearing the oil and gas. Above that hydrocarbon zone where the other fifteen centralizers would have gone, the engineers poured 791 feet of cement into the gap between the casing and the well wall. That upper cement, above the oil and gas, remained sound. Cement failed in and *below* the main hydrocarbon zone. The part of the cement job that failed was where the centralizers were, and in the reach below them, and *inside* the casing. The flow of gas and oil was not up outside the casing but out of the sand, then *down* to the bottom of the well, then up inside the casing—despite the cement there—and then out to the surface.

This seems to acquit the centralizers. So was there something wrong with the cement formulation itself?

In its September 8, 2010, investigative report, BP will blame the cement. They'll offer several reasons why the cement could have failed: contamination with drilling or spacer fluids, contamination among the three cement parts, or "nitrogen breakout," in which the nitrogen breaks out of the foam and forms big gas pockets.

BP will have a third party make cement samples designed to resemble Halliburton's and test them in a lab. (They could not get cement samples from Halliburton because those are impounded as legal evidence.)

BP's report will claim that Halliburton's foamed cement would have broken down in the well. BP will say Halliburton used a mixture containing 55 to 60 percent nitrogen, and that lab results indicate that "it was not possible to generate a stable nitrified foam cement slurry with greater than 50% nitrogen by volume at the 1,000 psi injection pressure." The investigation team will conclude that "the nitrified foam cement slurry used in the Macondo well probably experienced nitrogen breakout, nitrogen migration and incorrect cement density. This would explain the failure. . . . Nitrogen breakout and migration would have also contaminated the shoe track cement and may have caused the shoe track cement barrier to fail."

Of course, BP's investigation is suspect of pro-BP bias. But even if the BP report is self-serving and finger-pointing, this we do know: the cement did fail.

Just before Halloween 2010, the president's Oil Spill Commission will make its own explosive announcement: Halliburton officials knew weeks before the fatal explosion that its cement formulation had failed multiple tests—but they used the cement anyway.

On March 8, 2010, Halliburton e-mailed results of one failed test to BP, but sent only the numbers; there's no evidence that Halliburton specified that the numbers indicated failed testing. BP had overlooked

Transocean's warning of "severe gas flow," and might also have not understood it had been given information predicting that the cement would fail.

Halliburton altered the testing parameters, but the cement failed several tests. Finally, just days before the blowout, one last test indicated that the cement would remain stable. But Halliburton may not even have received the results of that final test before pouring the cement on April 19. BP definitely did not get notified that one of the formulations tested successfully. In other words, when Halliburton pumped cement into the BP well, both companies apparently possessed lab results indicating that what they were doing was unsafe.

After the blowout, Halliburton will refuse to give its exact cement formulation to BP for independent testing for its September report. But in coming weeks the president's Oil Spill Commission's chief counsel, Fred H. Bartlit Jr., will persuade Halliburton to hand over its cement formulation by reminding its officials that anything they withhold from federal investigators will enlarge the Justice Department's billowing civil and criminal charges. He'll then ask Chevron to create a batch and test the mixture under various conditions. In all nine tests, the cement formulation will prove unstable. The unstable cement solidifies into a firm indictment of Halliburton and BP liability.

At the stupendous pressures acting upon the oil and gas in the surrounding strata, even small cracks in the cement are enough to allow the flow rates that would send 60,000 barrels of oil a day out of the well.

Something called a "float collar" enters the discussion. These flapping one-way valves were situated far down the well casing. Rig workers had a hard time getting them to close. They may not have sealed properly, and the fact that the oil and gas shot up the well casing indicates that the float collar's valves also failed.

Having mistakenly concluded that no hydrocarbons are coming into the well, the workers declare success at 7:55 P.M. on April 20.

At 8:02 they begin displacing all the remaining heavy fluids with seawater. This will take over an hour. They know they're near completion when the spacer comes back up to the surface.

Returning fluids are usually directed into "pits" on the rig. This time, when the spacer reaches the surface, the crew directs the material directly overboard. This was their way, remember, of avoiding the requirement to bring it ashore and dispose of it as hazardous waste. While the material is being dumped overboard, certain flow meters, or "mudloggers," are bypassed. In fact, they may have also been bypassed for much of the day as valuable returning drilling fluids were directed onto a waiting ship, before the spacer was just dumped directly overboard.

BP's September investigation will conclude: "The investigation team did not find evidence that the pits were configured to allow monitoring while displacing the well to seawater. Furthermore, the investigation team did not find evidence that either the Transocean rig crew or the Sperry-Sun mudloggers monitored the pits from 13:28 hours (when the offloading to the supply vessel began) to 21:10 hours (when returns were routed overboard)."

Consultant Dr. John Smith will later testify that bypassing the flow-out meter amounted to "eliminating all conventional well control monitoring methods. That's essentially in direct violation of the Minerals Management Service rules."

There's another major wrinkle. Typical spacers are 180 to 200 barrels in volume, an amount that can be pumped out in fifteen to twenty minutes. But because the crew was trying to get rid of all the unused kill-pill material and bypass the solid-waste requirements by using unwanted material, this spacer was over 400 barrels. That meant that the rig crew had to spend an extra fifteen to twenty minutes or so pumping it overboard.

This extra fifteen minutes occurred between 9:15 and 9:30. Had any crewmates been monitoring the flow through the meters, they would have seen some very irregular pressure and flow readings. Those fifteen minutes, fifteen crucial minutes of not monitoring the volume of their fluids, ended at 9:30 P.M., when they so clearly should have realized they had a problem. Those fifteen minutes could have saved the rig.

Halliburton's cement. M-I Swaco's spacer. Transocean and BP's misinterpretation of the negative pressure test. BP's push to replace all the heavy fluid with seawater. An observation comes to me via this e-mail from a friend: "My ex-brother-in-law was up for the weekend. He was a mud engineer on rigs all over the world, offshore and on. He says there are no excuses, the company man's supposed to be in charge of everything. One thing he was very insistent on is that there's no such noun as 'drill' on the rig. You can have drill bit, drill string, drill pipe, but a drill is what you use to find the lifeboats."

Now the crew is bypassing their monitors as their excess spacer is being dumped overboard.

They'd slowed the pumps at approximately 8:50 P.M. in anticipation of the returning spacer. Slowing meant they should have seen reduced flow coming out, but the flow out actually increased. This was another indication that pressurized oil and gas were entering the well.

Starting at approximately 9:01 P.M., without a change in pump rate, the drill pipe pressure increased from 1,250 psi to 1,350 psi. Another indicator. The pressure should have decreased at this time, not increased, because they were replacing fluid weighing 14.17 pounds per gallon with 8.6-pounds-per-gallon seawater. This increase should have gotten the rig crew's attention.

Over the ten-minute period from 8:58 to 9:08, they gained 39 barrels of fluid, the result of upward pressure in the well.

BP's September report will note: "No apparent well control actions were taken until hydrocarbons were in the riser." In other words, gas had already gotten past the blowout preventer and was rushing the final mile to the surface.

Now the rig crew begins sending returning fluids into a mud-gas separator with limited capacity. They may have thought this was just a "kick," a belch.

In fact, an enormous volume of methane was streaming into the well, shooting upward from miles below, expanding as the surrounding pressure lessened, pushing out the fluid above it, gathering itself into an accelerating blowout. In an awful irony, *this* would have been the time to send all the returning material overboard.

BP's report says that they'd gained 1,000 barrels of liquid volume before anyone tried to activate the blowout preventer. The report adds, "Actions taken prior to the explosion suggest the rig crew was not sufficiently prepared to manage an escalating well control situation."

The gas quickly overwhelms the separator's capacity and mud begins flowing onto the rig floor.

The blowout preventer is attached to the wellhead at the seafloor and to the riser pipe that connects to the rig at the surface. Its many components are often used during routine operations like pressure testing, sealing around drill pipe, and pressure control in the well. It doesn't just sit there unless there's an emergency. And it is tested routinely. It was tested just a few days before the explosion.

The blowout preventer is controlled from the rig through two cables connected to two redundant control "pods"—blue and yellow—and with a hydraulic line. Remotely operated vehicles can also control the blowout preventer by directly operating the pods.

The BP investigation team will conclude that, if the blowout preventer had been closed at any time prior to 9:38 P.M., the flow of hydrocarbons to the riser and up to the surface would have been reduced or eliminated.

They missed it by four minutes.

Remember, by pumping the extra 200 barrels of spacer fluid just to save disposal costs, they'd wasted fifteen minutes.

At 9:42, the crew did try to activate the blowout preventer, tightening a gasket against the drill pipe. At first it did not seal. It does appear that the blowout preventer was sealed around the drill pipe at approximately 9:47. The part of the blowout preventer that they closed simply tightened a rubber gasket against the pipe, a chokehold. What they needed was to close the blind shear rams and sever the pipe—to chop its head off and seal the well.

It was too little. And then, it was too late.

Randy Ezell, a Transocean senior tool pusher, was asleep when his room phone rang. He recalled,

Well, I hit my little alarm clock light and, according to that alarm clock, it was ten minutes till 10:00. And the person at the other end of the line there was the assistant driller, Steve Curtis. Steve opened up by saying, "We have a situation." He said, "The well is blown out." He said, "We have mud going to the crown." And I said, "Well—." I was just horrified. I said, "Do y'all have it shut in?" He said, "Jason is shutting it in now." And he said, "Randy, we need your help." And I'll never forget that.

And I said, "Steve, I'll be— I'll be right there."

So I put my coveralls on; they were hanging on the hook. I put my socks on. My boots and my hard that were right across that hall in the tool pusher's office. So I opened my door and I remember a couple of people standing in the hallway, but I kind of had tunnel vision. I looked straight ahead and I don't even remember who those people were.

I made it to the doorway of the tool pusher's office when a tremendous explosion occurred. It blew me probably twenty feet against a bulkhead, against the wall in that office. And I remember then that the lights went out, power went out. I could hear everything deathly calm. My next recollection was that I had a lot of debris on top of me. I tried two different times to get up, but whatever it was it was a substantial weight. The third time something like adrenaline had kicked in and I told myself, "Either you get up or you're going to lay here and die." My right leg was hung on something; I don't know what. But I pulled it as hard as I could and it came free. I attempted to stand up. That was the wrong thing to do 'cause I immediately stuck my head into smoke. And with the training that we've all had on the rig

I knew to stay low. So I dropped back down. I got on my hands and knees and for a few moments I was totally disoriented on which way the doorway was. And I remember just sitting there and just trying to think, "Which way is it?"

Now there was mud shooting out the top of the rig and the loud and continuous *whoosh* of surging gas. More explosions followed, igniting a high-intensity hydrocarbon fire fueled by incoming gas and oil.

Up until the explosions, the crew had two different ways to activate the shear rams that could cut the pipe and seal the well. They did not activate them. Then the explosions damaged the control cables and hydraulic line to the blowout preventer, costing the rig crew the ability to control the blowout preventer.

The loss of connections should have triggered the blowout preventer's automatic emergency mode—and closed the blind shear rams. However, the yellow pod had a defective solenoid and the blue pod's batteries were weak, so the blind shear rams did not activate.

Sensors for fire, gas, and toxic fumes were working; any irregularities appeared on a screen. But their audio alarms were inhibited. This is understandable, but many rigs don't allow it. The Deepwater Horizon had hundreds of individual fire and gas alarms. Having the general alarm go off for local minor problems would cost workers sleep, a safety concern. And people would start ignoring alarms—also a safety concern. The idea was: have a person monitoring the computer, and let them control the general audio alarm. Sound it only when conditions require.

But chief electrician Mike Williams has asserted that inhibiting alarms also prevents the computer from activating emergency shutdown of air vents and power. Such a shutdown could have prevented the rig's diesel generator engines from inhaling the gas and surging wildly.

The over-revving engines send surges of electricity that make lights and computer monitors begin exploding. The engines spark, igniting the gas, triggering explosions.

Transocean's chief mechanic, Doug Brown, knew there was a manual engine shutdown system. He also understood that he was not authorized to activate it. He later said, "If I would have shut down those engines, it could have stopped as an ignition source."

Mike Williams hears loud hissing. Hears the engines revving. Sees his light bulbs getting "brighter and brighter and brighter," knows "something bad is getting ready to happen," hears "this awful whoosh."

He reaches for a door that's three inches thick, steel, fire-rated, supported by six stainless steel hinges. An explosion blows the door from those hinges, throwing him across the shop. When he comes around, he's up against a wall with the door on top of him. He thinks, "This is it. I'm gonna die right here."

When he crawls across the floor to the next door, it too explodes, taking him thirty-five feet backward, smacking him up against another wall. He gets angry at the *doors;* he feels "mad that these fire doors that are supposed to protect me are hurting me." He crawls through an opening. He thinks, "I've accomplished what I set out to accomplish. I made it outside. I may die out here, but I can breathe."

Williams can't see. Something's pouring into his eyes. "I didn't know if it was blood. I didn't know if it was brains. I didn't know if it was flesh. I just knew I was in trouble."

There's a gash in his forehead. He's on one of the rig's lifeboat decks. He's got two functioning lifeboats, right there. But he thinks, "I can't board them. I have responsibilities."

He hears alarms, radio chatter, "Mayday! Mayday!" Calls of lost power. Calls of fire. Calls of man overboard. People jumping from the rig.

Transocean's subsea supervisor Chris Pleasant wants the rig's master, Captain Curt Kuchta, to activate the emergency disconnect system, or EDS. With the blowout preventer unresponsive, the last-ditch response is: disconnect the rig from the pipe that is delivering the gas that's feeding the fire. Kuchta replies, "Calm down! We're not EDSing." Jimmy Harrell, Transocean's man in charge of all drilling operations, has just had his quarters destroyed in explosions while he was in the shower; he now comes running, partially clothed, partially blinded by fine insulation debris. He tells Chris Pleasant to activate the emergency disconnect system. Pleasant tries it. All attempts to disconnect the pipe fail.

Having survived the explosions and freed himself from entrapment in debris, Randy Ezell is trying to get his bearings from where he sits, stunned. "Then I felt something and it felt like air," he later recalled. He says to himself, "Well, that's got to be the hallway. So, that's the direction I need to go. That leads out." Crawling over debris, he makes it to the doorway. But then he realizes, "What I thought was air was actually methane and I could feel, like, droplets; it was moist on the side of my face. So he continues crawling down the dark hallway. Suddenly he puts his hand on a body. He hears a groan. In the dark, Ezell can't see who it is. (It's Wyman Wheeler.) Next, he sees a wavering beam of light. Someone is coming down the hallway, their light going up and down as they duck debris hanging from the ceiling and make their way around jutting walls and over a buckled floor. As the approaching person rounds the corner, Ezell recognizes Stan Carden. While they are pulling debris off of Wyman Wheeler, another flashlight arrives, wielded by Chad Murray. Ezell and Carden ask Murray to find a stretcher while they continue removing debris from Wheeler. Thinking it might be quicker to try to help Wheeler walk out, Ezell helps him to his feet, but, after just a couple of steps with his arm around Ezell's shoulder Wheeler, overcome by pain, says, "Set me down. Set me down." So Ezell lets him back down. Wheeler says, "Y'all go on. Save yourself." To which Ezell replies, "No, we're not going to leave you."

Suddenly Ezell hears another voice saying, "God help me. Somebody please help me." He looks. Where their maintenance office had been, all he sees is a pile of wreckage over a pair of feet. Removing that debris requires the efforts of all three: Ezell, Carden, and Murray. When they get the debris off, they realize it's Buddy Trahan, one of Transocean's visiting dignitaries. Trahan's injuries are worse than Wheeler's, so he gets the first stretcher.

Stan Carden and Chad Murray convey Trahan all the way to the lifeboat station. Ezell stays back. "I stayed right there with Wyman Wheeler because I told him I wasn't going to leave him, and I didn't," he recalled later. "And it seemed like an eternity, but it was only a couple of minutes before they came back with the second stretcher."

Carrying Wheeler outside of the living quarters, Ezell notices that the main lifeboats are gone. Then he notices a few people starting to deploy a raft. The men carrying Wheeler continue down the walkway to the raft and set the stretcher down. "And after several minutes," Ezell will recall, "we had everything deployed and got in the life raft. But the main thing is, Wyman was there, you know—he didn't get left behind."

But unbeknownst to those in the boats, others are left behind.

Mike Williams, who minutes earlier could have had both now-departed lifeboats to himself, watches eight other survivors drop an inflatable raft from a crane.

In weekly lifeboat drills they'd practiced accounting for everyone. There is no longer such a thing as "everyone."

Now left watching are Williams, another man, and twenty-three-year-old Andrea Fleytas. Williams experiences several more blasts that he'll later describe as "Take-your-breath-away explosions. Shake-your-body-to-the-core explosions. Take-your-vision-away explosions."

Fire spreads from the derrick to the deck itself.

Williams sees in Andrea's eyes that she seems resigned to death. He says, "It's okay to be scared. I'm scared, too." She says, "What are we gonna do?" Williams outlines the choice: Burn up or jump down.

From where they are, it's ten stories to a black ocean. Bloodied, backlit by raging fire, Williams takes three steps and jumps feet-first. "And I fell for what seemed like forever," he later recalled. He thinks of his wife, their little girl. "A lotta things go through your mind."

Love conquers all. But only sometimes.

He crashes into the sea and the momentum takes him way, way beneath the surface. He pops up thinking, "Okay, I've made it." But he feels like he's burning all over. He's thinking, "Am I on fire?" He just doesn't know.

He realizes he's floating in oil and grease and diesel fuel. The smell and the feel of it. He sees that the oil that has become the sea's surface beneath the rig is already on fire.

Says to himself, "What have you done? You were dry, and you weren't covered in oil up there; now you've jumped and you've landed in oil. The fire's gonna come across the water, and you're gonna burn up." He thinks, "Swim harder!" Stroke, kick, stroke, kick, stroke, kick, stroke, kick. As hard as he can until he realizes: he feels no more pain. He thinks, "Well, I must have burned up, 'cause I don't feel anything, I don't hear anything, I don't smell anything. I must be dead."

He hears a faint voice calling, and next thing, a hand grabs his lifejacket and flips him over into a boat. Then the boat finds one more survivor. Andrea.

A ship that had been tending the rig, the *Bankston*, retrieves those in lifeboats. Not aboard the *Bankston*: Jason Anderson, of Midfield, Texas, thirty-five, father of two, tool pusher, the supervisor on the floor at the time of the accident who'd worried aloud to his wife and dad about safety on the rig and who'd spoken of the "bladder effect" causing the pressure discrepancies they were seeing; Aaron Dale Burkeen, thirty-seven, of Philadelphia, Mississippi, father of a fourteen-year-old daughter, Aryn, and a six-year-old son, Timothy; Donald Clark, forty-nine, an oil industry veteran married to Sheila, living in Newellton, Louisiana; Steven Ray Curtis, thirty-nine, the driller who'd named this the "well from hell"; Roy Wyatt Kemp, twenty-seven years old, who lived in Jonesville, Louisiana, with his wife, Courtney; Karl Kleppinger Jr., thirty-eight, of Natchez, Mississippi, Army veteran of Operation Desert Storm, leaving behind a wife and son; Keith Blair Manuel, fifty-six, father of three daughters, avid supporter of Louisiana State University sports teams, and engaged to be married to his longtime love, Melinda; Dewey Revette, forty-eight, of State Line, Mississippi, having been with Transocean for twenty-nine years, and leaving a wife and two daughters; Shane Roshto, just twenty-two, of Liberty, Mississippi, husband to Natalie and already father to three-year-old son Blaine Michael; Adam Weise, twenty-four, of Yorktown, Texas, a former high school football star who loved the outdoors; Gordon Jones, twenty-eight, of Baton Rouge. A few days after Gordon died, his widow, Michelle, gave birth to their second son.

Mike Williams says, "All the things that they told us could never happen, happened."

For two days, a fireball. So hot it appears to be melting some of the rig. Which finally sinks.

Accusations: BP's own report will later say, "A complex and interlinked series of mechanical failures, human judgments, engineering design, operational implementation and team interfaces came together to allow the initiation and escalation of the accident. Multiple companies, work teams and circumstances were involved." BP's recap: The cements failed to prevent the oil and gas from entering the well. Staff of both Transocean and BP incorrectly interpreted the negative pressure test by tragically explaining away the pressure they were seeing on one gauge. This led them to release the downward fluid pressure on the well by replacing the heavier fluid with seawater in a well that they falsely believed—because the kill line was clogged with the "snotty" spacer—was not exerting upward pressure. It was. The pressure in the drill pipe, which they chose to ignore, was telling them that the cement had failed. They didn't notice other warning signs because they bypassed gauges and routed displacement fluid and their irregularly concocted spacer overboard. But as gas reached the rig, when the crew might have prevented disaster, they routed the flow to a mud-gas separator whose capacity was soon overwhelmed. Gas flowing directly onto the rig got sucked into generators, causing them to surge and spark, igniting a series of explosions. Fire and gas emergency systems that should have prevented those explosions failed. The blowout preventer should have automatically sealed the well but it, too, failed.

Unlike a tanker running aground and spilling oil—a simple cause-and-effect accident—this is a chain disaster. Each of the distinct failures of equipment and judgment, combined, was required to cause the event. And if any single component had not failed, or had been handled differently, this blowout never would have happened. And we're not done yet, because a failure of preparedness to deal with a deepwater blowout will cost many pounds of cure over the coming months.

APRIL

The Coast Guard's Gulf region chief, Rear Admiral Mary Landry, who, we are told, is "leading the government's response," says, "You're getting ahead of yourself a little when you try to speculate and say this is catastrophic. It's premature to say this is catastrophic."

Though eleven men died and the rig sank.

She's just much too cool. Right off the bat, her statements set my confidence in the Coast Guard on a wobble. I realize immediately that it's going to be one of those events where, from all sides, the truth gets pinballed back and forth among bumpers of spin and flippers of distortion. And other than herself, who's Landry kidding? The immediate impressions: (1) she's still wait-and-seeing; and (2) because of No. 1, the official response is slow.

President Barack Obama says the federal response to the disaster is "being treated as the number one priority." He may think so, but it doesn't feel that way. It seems as though no one is prepared for oil shooting from a mile-deep pipe.

Oddly, just one day after the rig sinks, one major press agency is calling the *Exxon Valdez* spill "vastly bigger than the current one in the U.S. Gulf." That may be because right after the rig sank, Rear Admiral Landry said that no oil appeared to be leaking from the wellhead and nor was there, at the surface, "any sign of a major spill." Landry said at the outset that most of the oil was burning off with the fireball, leaving only a moderate rainbow sheen on the water.

The impression given: fuel oil had *spilled* from the rig, but from the well no oil was *leaking.* She said, "Both the industry and the Coast Guard have technical experts actively at work. So there's a whole technical team here to ensure we keep the conditions stable."

Stable.

Even if this isn't "Obama's Katrina," she sounds like Obama's Michael Brown. Heckuva job, Brownie. And now the real Michael Brown comes out of his hole. President George W. Bush's infamous FEMA chief claims that Obama is purposely dragging his feet, wanting the oil leak to worsen so he can shut down offshore drilling. "This is exactly what they want, because now he can pander to the environmentalists and say, 'I'm gonna shut it down because it's too dangerous,'" Brown says, adding, "This president has never supported Big Oil, he's never supported offshore drilling, and now he has an excuse to shut it back down."

How very odd of Brownie to say that, considering that less than a month ago Obama alienated environmentalists with a blindsiding announcement that he was opening millions of acres for new offshore oil development.

Rewind: March 30, 2010. President Obama lays out an offshore drilling plan. He decides to open 167 million acres of ocean to oil and gas exploration. Candidate Obama had attacked John McCain's proposal to expand offshore drilling, saying, "It would have long-term consequences for our coastlines but no short-term benefits since it would take at least ten years to get any oil. . . . When I'm president, I intend to keep in place the moratorium." With this March announcement, President Obama erases that promise. He ends a longstanding moratorium on oil exploration along the East Coast from the northern tip of Delaware to the central coast of Florida. For environmentalists, this leaves a very bad impression. Something like betrayal. Buried in the announcement—because the administration wants it to look like he's into offshore oil—is that President Obama canceled the plans, scheduled by President G. W. Bush, for four lease sales off Alaska in the Beaufort and Chukchi Seas. But he left 130 million acres of those seas open to exploration. Obama's decision keeps the entire West Coast closed to oil and gas leasing. He also takes Alaska's Bristol Bay off the table from any future speculation, thereby keeping its teeming salmon flowing. Obama: "There will be those who strongly disagree with this decision."

Right again. Greenpeace: "Is this President Obama's clean energy plan or Sarah Palin's?" The envirogroup Center for Biological Diversity says, "All too typical of what we have seen so far from President Obama—promises of change and ultimately, adoption of flawed and outdated Bush policies." Republican congressman John Boehner slams the president anyway for not going far enough; he wants to give Big Oil more access. Piling on from the opposite side, Democratic senator Frank Lautenberg rails, "Giving Big Oil more access to our nation's waters is really a 'kill, baby, kill' policy: it threatens to kill jobs, kill marine life, and kill coastal economies that generate billions of dollars. Offshore drilling isn't the solution to our energy problems. I will fight this policy and continue to push for twenty-first-century clean energy solutions."

Obama says his policy is "part of a broader strategy that will move us from an economy that runs on fossil fuels and foreign oil to one that relies more on homegrown fuels and clean energy." And that's exactly what's needed. But other pieces of the strategy are not in place; Congress isn't into clean energy. So Obama's nuance is lost on everyone. The public impression will cost Obama's administration the moral high ground, and will seem to translate—another impression, admittedly—into weeks of lost momentum and lagging leadership after the rig explosion.

Who likes Obama's announcement? Why, it's Obama's former opponent for the presidency, Senator John McCain, who Twitters, "Drill baby drill! Good move."

And it doesn't exactly sound like pandering to enviros when White House spokesman Robert Gibbs says that sometimes accidents happen; loss of the Deepwater Horizon is no reason to back off the president's recent decision to expand offshore drilling.

Yet that face-saving will turn butt-biting.

And this from rig owner Transocean itself: "The U.S. Coast Guard has plans in place to mitigate any environmental impact from this situation." The world's largest offshore drilling contractor, with a fleet of 140 mobile offshore drilling units, seemingly sees scant need to further trouble itself. And well owner BP says, "We are working closely with BP Exploration & Production, Inc. and the U.S. Coast Guard to determine the impact from the sinking of the rig and the plans going forward."

Between that line and this one, you can read the following: they have no response plan; they're unprepared and have no real idea of what to do.

The Coast Guard searches for the lost men. They'll keep searching "as long as there is a reasonable probability of finding them alive." There was never a reasonable probability of additional survivors, and the horror of eleven killed begins to sink in.

Rear Admiral Mary Landry's statement that there's "no apparent leak" notwithstanding, leaking it is. First estimate: 1,000 barrels per day (a barrel is 42 gallons, so 42,000 gallons). The Macondo well's oil is not leaking from the wellhead, or from the blowout preventer. It's leaking from the former umbilicus between rig and well, a kinked pipe broken off when the rig sank, now lying mangled on the seafloor one mile down. The only shard of luck—if that term applies here—is that the hulking mass of the drilling rig itself did not land atop the wellhead, blocking all access to it.

A remotely operated vehicle is sent to shut the leak at the blowout preventer.

Fails.

A few days ago, the gushing oil was termed "manageable." Now BP executives say at least two to four weeks to get it under control. We don't hear them say "at least." We still can't believe the phrase "four weeks." (That estimate, too, will get several resets. Four months from now, we'll wish it had been "four weeks.") Ideas, anyone?

I did not want to come to the Gulf. It seemed like a good situation to avoid. But I also don't feel that the information I'm getting from officials and the news media is fully reliable. So I want to see things for myself. I've resisted initial predictions of ecological disaster, believing that the natural systems will more or less continue functioning. Yet as you'd guess from a statement like that, I was also in a bit of denial; I could not fathom that stopping the leak might require more than a few days. That just couldn't happen. But the new reality is settling in: this won't be quick. Now a lot will depend on what will, indeed, become a months-long question: How much oil will come out of that hemorrhaging stab wound in the seafloor?

Dawn on the coast. Shell Beach, in southeast Louisiana, is the end of the road, the edge of the marsh, the beginning of the Gulf. A man is sitting in his car next to a stone memorial engraved with the names of dozens of local Katrina victims. I feel like I'm interrupting a private moment just glancing at him, but he says hello and seems to want to talk. He says he's not in the seafood business, but he lives here among the fishing families. "The small-timers in the seafood business," he says, "people make fun of them because they don't know the answers to intelligent questions. Maybe they don't know the name of the First Lady of the United States, but that's not what they care about. What they care about is that their motor starts in the morning and that they go out, and go to work. And out there, they're professionals that nobody can compete with; they're scientists at their jobs."

The oil now raises the question of whether an enduring way of life is truly endangered, or whether an endangered way of life will endure.

The sheriff has already erected a guard post to close the road into Shell Beach because the National Guard is building a dock for ferrying materials. The guy in the booth tells me no cars, but he lets me walk through.

He's tall, thin, black, talkative, fortyish, worried. "This'll make Katrina look like a bad day," he says. "Because Katrina did what it did.

Then you picked up and got back to your way of life. But this, I mean—it's disheartening to say it, but I think the parish has pretty much had it. Once that oil comes in, it won't leave. There'll be no people workin' for a *long* time. Years. And every time it rains, we'll get a sheen. And every time we get a sheen, they'll shut fishin'. These fishermen makin' money, spendin' money. That's gone. There's *nothing* that's gonna replace that income. I mean, you probably had ten, twenty thousand sacks of oysters goin' outta this place a day. There's one crab buyer I know, he probably averages thirty, forty thousand pounds a day when the crabs are running good. That's just one buyer. See what I'm sayin'? The average working fisherman that fishes hard, I'd say they gross at least a hundred thousand dollars a year. Minus expenses, but BP can't replace their income forever. Not the rest of their lives."

He tells me to look around at the places that sell bait, fishing gear. "These boats. See what I'm sayin'? That's all gone. You look around at these weekend fishing houses. This is serious money. The average place back here, they got five hundred thousand dollars invested. There's people had camps on order; they already canceled. What are you gonna build a fish camp for, if you can't catch fish? But some's got hundreds of thousands already invested in a new place they won't be able to give away."

He says the parish still runs a tax deficit of $1 million a year. Aftereffects of Katrina. "A lot of people had to leave the parish. Some people say, 'Oh, try to get a Walmart—.' You can have all the stores you want. People got the same amount of money to spend no matter how many stores you have. We can't draw from anywhere anymore. The whole surrounding area was devastated. Before, a lot of the people came from the Ninth Ward to shop. We just don't have that anymore; it's depressed all through there. This oil's gonna cripple us here in St. Bernard Parish. But it goes much farther than St. Bernard. It ain't gonna be good."

One week in, the slick already covers 1,800 square miles. Larger than Rhode Island.

One week in, BP plans to lower a large dome. A dome to capture the oil. To capture the oil, then pump it through pipes. To pump it through pipes to a vessel on the surface. First engineers have to design it. Then workers have to make it. Could have used Better Planning. Bereft of Preparedness.

We will now play a game called BP Says. BP says it'll do this; BP says it'll try that; BP says it has ideas; BP says it needs a month—. Perhaps its leaders don't want to raise any expectations. BP spokesman, he says: "That kind of dome-pump-pipe-ship system has been used in shallow water." BP spokesman, he says: "It has never been deployed at five thousand feet of water, so we have to be careful."

Careful.

Here's how careful: "From the air, the oil spill reached as far as the eye could see. There was little evidence of a major cleanup, with only a handful of vessels near the site of the leak," writes the Associated Press on April 27.

Louisiana governor Bobby Jindal asks the Coast Guard to use containment booms, "which," he notes, "float like a string of fat sausage links to hold back oil until it can be skimmed off the surface." Oh, the innocent optimism of those early days.

The letting go of optimism. One week in, we learn the phrase "relief well." The pressure driving oil and gas out of the well may overcome any attempt to stop the blowout by pumping material in from the top. That's like trying to stuff pudding into a fire hose. So BP might decide to drill a whole other well. More likely, two. A parallel well could let workers pump material into the original well near the bottom, increasing the chances that they can clog and seal the well. No guarantees. BP says it will be a $100 million effort. We are so grateful for their generosity. And we're told that the relief wells could take an inconceivable two months. Actually, it will require twice that time. Meanwhile, they're going to try some other things. They don't know what.

The newly arriving pessimism. "You will have off-flavors that would be a concern," the oyster farmer says.

Misreported: "If the well cannot be closed, almost 100,000 barrels of oil, or 4.2 million gallons, could spill into the Gulf before crews can drill a relief well to alleviate the pressure." It's noted that the *Exxon Valdez*, the United States' worst oil spill to date, leaked 11 million gallons into the waters and onto the shores of Alaska's Prince William Sound in 1989. Compared to that, the forecast 4.2 million is meager. But the Associated Press is guessing one hundred days based on us being told three to four months, at 1,000 barrels a day.

Soon the estimate of the flow below gets quintupled. On April 28, Coast Guard rear admiral Mary Landry reports that federal experts have concluded that 5,000 barrels a day are leaking. BP had estimated—or at least said—only 1,000. Landry says BP officials are "doing their best."

If that's BP's best, well, maybe it is.

As if New Orleans doesn't have enough problems. As if shrimpers and fishermen, already staggered, need an oil spill that will finish them. Five *thousand* barrels a day. That's 200 barrels an hour. When will it end? Now I'm hearing, "It could eclipse the *Exxon Valdez*." And if the oil reaches shore—.

I read, "A BP executive on Thursday agreed with a U.S. government estimate that up to 5,000 barrels a day of crude could be spilling into the ocean."

They *agreed?* Or got busted?

Mary Landry had said there was "ample time to protect sensitive areas and prepare for cleanup should the oil impact this area."

She makes the mobilization feel like a Kabuki dance.

And now that government scientists are saying "multiply by five," the reassuring lullabies evaporate. There is snarling. Fingers pointed. Blame to go round. Now Landry warns that if not stopped, the spill could end up being among the worst in U.S. history. Now it's *mature* to say it's catastrophic. Now President Barack Obama says he'll deploy "every single available resource." He orders his disaster people, his environmental people, to the Gulf in person.

Why'd it take so long?

Five thousand barrels a day, roughly 200,000 gallons. A few of those gallons—more than anyone would like—begin lightly touching shore here and there in Louisiana. We begin hearing the name Billy Nungesser. The president of a place called Plaquemines Parish, Nungesser says a sheen of oil has reached the fragile wetlands of South Pass. (South Pass is one of the artificial mouths of the Mississippi River that was created by destroying fragile wetlands.) We begin hearing of a place called the Chandeleur Islands. On those isles of fabled fishing and abundant birds, a light sheen of oil plays touch-and-go.

Officials immediately halt fishing in a large area. A group of shrimpers sues for damages. For all the people affected by fisheries closures—everyone from people who grow oysters to people who build weekend homes—the fishing closures answer the question "How bad will this get?" by pushing the needle all the way. At least for the foreseeable future, it has just gotten as bad as it could get. They are suddenly completely out of business. People whose lives are about getting up and going to work are no longer going to work. A certain shock settles in.

Trying to regain footing on the moral high ground, a White House spokesman acknowledges that the administration might revisit the president's announcement on expanding offshore drilling.

Rear Admiral Mary Landry has repeatedly asserted that BP is the responsible party and will shoulder the costs and organizational duties associated with the cleanup effort while the Coast Guard monitors and approves things. But BP's interests are not fully in line with the public's interests. The public wants to know; wants to see.

We don't normally put the criminal in charge of the crime scene. The perpetrator's interests are different from the victim's. Certainly, as far as damages and people out of work, they'd Better Pay. But many people (including me) think the government should push BP out of the way on everything else. The company had a permit to drill. Not a permit to spill. They're on our property now. BP should be made to focus exclusively on stopping the eruption. All the big oil companies should now be convened in a war room for their best expertise. Our government should direct the efforts on everything else.

But the government keeps deferring to BP. Obama does not federalize the situation. Maybe he's afraid this will become—as people have been wondering out loud—"Obama's Katrina." Maybe he, too, wants to reserve all the blame for BP.

Today's vocabulary word: "dispersants." Use it in a sentence: "Most oil floats, but it dissolves into the sea if you apply *dispersants*." By April 30, BP has begun sending dispersants down a mile-long tube from a ship. Releasing such chemicals on the deep seafloor—rather than spraying them on surface oil—has never been done before. It's a secondary toxic leak, this one intentional, sent from above to meet the oil coming from below.

If you're BP, if part of your liability will depend on *how much oil*, it's in your financial interest to do everything you can to: (1) say you think it's leaking at a much smaller rate than it is and (2) hide as much of it as possible and (3) in as many ways as possible, try to prevent people from seeing the parts you can't hide. If you're BP, will you let people see and measure a sea of Billowing Petroleum? Not if you can avoid it.

Dispersed oil stays in the ocean. Because it dissolves into the sea, it's impossible to see or measure. Like a cake "hides" a rotten egg mixed into the batter, dispersants hide the oil. It's still a rotten egg, but now you can't retrieve it.

Dispersants are basically like dishwashing detergents, which dissolve oil and grease. And by dissolving oil concentrated at the surface, they ensure pollution of water that is home to fish larvae, fish eggs, and plankton. At certain concentrations, dispersants are toxic to those fish larvae, fish eggs, and plankton.

And what do the dolphins think? Does it burn their eyes? What is its smell to them now? What taste is conferred to their big, aware brain? Capacity for reason, ability to express; they alone in the sea can use syntax, the building blocks of language. Do they have words for this? I don't.

A week in, as the sheer unstoppable quantity of oil breeches the confines of our ability to imagine what to do, the idea of skimming up most of the oil gives way to a desire to get rid of the oil, no matter how. Landry talks about burning it off the sea. Lighting the sea on fire. In 1969, the Cuyahoga River in Ohio caught fire. So shocked was America to see its *waters* on fire that the incident—along with an oil leak off Santa Barbara, California, the same year—helped precipitate the explosion of environmental laws that Republican president Richard Nixon signed in the early 1970s.

(Note to the young: If you wonder why we need a Clean Water Act—a reasonable question, since you're lucky enough not to have seen America's waterways as they were before—consider that the Cuyahoga River had ignited about ten prior times in the last century, and also consider this description from *Time* magazine, August 1, 1969:

> Some river! Chocolate-brown, oily, bubbling with subsurface gases, it oozes rather than flows. "Anyone who falls into the Cuyahoga does not drown," Cleveland's citizens joke grimly. "He decays." . . . The Federal Water Pollution Control Administration dryly notes: "The lower Cuyahoga has no visible signs of life, not even low forms such as leeches and sludge worms that usually thrive on wastes." It is also—literally—a fire hazard.

Now Landry explains about burning this oil off the surface of the Gulf. She uses the term "controlled burns," and says they would be done far from shore. As if nothing that breathes air lives out in the Gulf of Mexico. No turtles, say. No whales. She says that crews would make sure marine life and people were protected and that work on other oil rigs would not be interrupted. But can they protect sea turtles? Can they avoid interrupting dolphins and whales?

Two decades after the *Exxon Valdez* ran aground, its oil can still be found under rocks along Prince William Sound. Scratch and sniff.

There's that terror here—that it will never be back to normal. Or that in the years it takes, communities will die and families disintegrate. But others begin saying maybe not. This isn't Alaska crude. Gulf crude is "sweet crude"—gotta love these funky terms—while the *Exxon Valdez* disgorged heavy crude. This isn't Prince William Sound. It's hot here. What's different is different.

"You have warm temperatures, strong sunlight, microbial action. It will degrade a lot faster," says Ronald S. Tjeerdema, a University of California toxicologist who studies the effects of oil on aquatic systems. "Eventually, things will return to normal."

But how long is eventually? One summer? A year? Five? Twenty? People know that before it returns to normal they are hurtling toward a time like no other, when everything they know and love is suddenly at risk.

We're all aware that there'll be oiled birds, dead turtles, the like. Some people ask, How bad? Most simply believe it will be real bad. Now we wait.

The Gulf of Mexico had gotten its own personal warning call in June 1979, when the Mexican drilling rig Ixtoc I blew out in about 160 feet of water. In the nine months required to stop the flow, it released 140 million gallons of crude oil into the Gulf, the world's largest accidental release up to then. It killed hundreds of millions of crabs on Mexican beaches and 80 percent of the invertebrates on Texas beaches. But other than that, its effects were poorly studied.

And since then, there's been no new preparedness. No new techniques. No prefabricated deep-sea oil-capture technology.

What's new is the depth of this well. A blowout this deep is new. But we shouldn't be so surprised.

DÉJÀ VU, TO NAME BUT A FEW

March 1967. The supertanker *Torrey Canyon,* whose captain took a shortcut to beat the tide, strands in the Scilly Isles, spilling 35 million gallons of Kuwaiti oil. People watch in horror as oil kills about 25,000 seabirds and coats the shores of Cornwall and Brittany. There is no containment or cleanup equipment, no capacity to aid wildlife or even assess the spill. It's the world's first massive marine oil-pollution event.

January 28, 1969. A blowout at a drilling rig six miles off Santa Barbara, California, sends 4 million gallons of crude oil into the Santa Barbara Channel, where it fouls beaches in the Channel Islands and exclusive parts of the mainland coast. Residents and the country are horrified by the sight of thousands of dying seabirds, elephant seals, sea lions, and other wildlife. The disaster creates significant awareness of the vulnerability of nature, as well as an impetus for the major environmental legislation that followed in the 1970s. It remains the third-largest U.S. marine spill.

September 1969. A tugboat towing the oil barge *Florida* from Rhode Island to a power plant on the Cape Cod Canal snaps its towline. The barge runs aground on boulders, spilling 180,000 gallons at West Falmouth and killing lobsters, scallops, clams, crabs, marine worms, and fish such as tomcod and scup. Though relatively small compared to some other spills, this is among the best studied. Four decades later, oil still forms a visible layer four inches below the marsh surface. Burrowing fiddler crabs still try to avoid the oil, and react slowly to startling motions such as a predator might make.

December 15, 1976. The *Argo Merchant*, which has been involved in more than a dozen incidents, including a collision and two groundings, runs aground again, this time off Nantucket, Massachusetts, and sinks. Its 7.7 million gallons of spilled oil cause a slick 100 miles long, 50 miles wide. The ship's résumé earns it a place in Stephen Pile's 1979 *Book of Heroic Failures,* "written in celebration of human inadequacy in all its forms."

March 1978. Oil again spoils the shores of Brittany, after the *Amoco Cadiz* loses its steering, snaps the towing cables of a rescue tug, and spills 69 million gallons of Iranian crude, which besmirches 400 miles of the French coast and destroys thousands of acres of oyster beds and thousands of fish, shellfish, and seabirds. Fish starve as their prey die, and fish populations remain depressed for two years. Where French authorities scrape oiled marshes, most never come back. Where they leave marshes alone, the ecosystems recover.

June 3, 1979. Ixtoc I, a Mexican drilling rig in about 160 feet of water, blows out and blows up, igniting an explosion and a fireball. The rig sinks. By the time two parallel relief wells plug it with 3,000 sacks of cement, it has hurled 140 million gallons of crude oil into the Gulf of Mexico, the world's largest petroleum accident up until that time. Oil eventually decimates mollusks and intertidal vertebrates along the Texas coast. An American graduate student and a Mexican biologist airlift 10,000 endangered sea turtle hatchlings to an oil-free part of the Gulf.

Late 1970s. President Jimmy Carter envisions a future array of energy sources and represents this vision with solar panels on the White House roof. After Carter's one-term presidency, Ronald Reagan has the solar panels dismantled and junked. By the end of 1985, when Reagan's administration and Congress have allowed tax credits for solar homes to lapse, the dream of a solar era has faded. Solar water heating has gone from a billion-dollar industry to peanuts overnight; thousands of sun-minded businesses have gone bankrupt. "It died. It's dead," says one solar-energy businessman of the time. "First the money dried up, then the spirit dried up."

1988. Occidental Petroleum's North Sea production platform Piper Alpha produces about a tenth of all North Sea oil and gas. When it explodes on July 6, it kills 167 men.

March 1989. The 987-foot supertanker *Exxon Valdez* has just been loaded with 50 million gallons of crude oil piped across the vastness of Alaska from the North Slope to a terminal near the tiny village of Valdez, on Prince William Sound. After altering course to avoid ice, the crew fails to get the ship to respond to efforts to resume course. Bligh Reef opens the vessel's belly, spilling at least 11 million gallons, which eventually reach beaches 400 miles—equivalent to the distance from Connecticut to North Carolina—from the grounded ship, fouling wilderness shores and killing extraordinary numbers and kinds of wildlife, from barnacles to salmon to killer whales, including roughly 2,000 sea otters and a quarter million seabirds. Hundreds of harbor seals die of disorientation and from brain lesions caused by inhaling toxic fumes. In many ways, the *Valdez* spill remains the world's most devastating and traumatic.

February 1996. The Norwegian-owned, Liberian-flagged, Russian-crewed *Sea Empress* grounds on the coast of Wales, spilling about 24 million gallons near densely populated seabird nesting rookeries, likely killing over 50,000 birds.

March 23, 2005. An explosion at BP's Texas refinery kills fifteen people. Determined: "willful negligence." BP's $108 million in fines fail to return any of the workers to their family dinner tables but stand as the United States' highest-ever workplace safety fines. Those record-setting fines represent less than 2 percent of BP's $6 billion profits for the first three months of 2010.

2005. Great Britain's Health and Safety Executive issues a warning about a Transocean-owned rig leased by BP in the North Sea, saying the rig's remote blowout-preventer control panel had not been "maintained in an efficient state, efficient working order and in good repair." The office also accuses Transocean of bullying and intimidating its North Sea staff.

2006. BP spills 200,000 gallons of oil in Prudhoe Bay. The North Slope's biggest spill, it is caused by corrosion in poorly maintained equipment. BP is eventually ordered to pay $20 million in fines.

September 14, 2007. In a letter, the Fish and Wildlife Service agrees with the Minerals Management Service's conclusion that deepwater drilling in the Gulf of Mexico poses no significant risk to endangered species like the brown pelican and the Kemp's ridley sea turtle. The agencies consider only spills totaling 1,000 to 15,000 barrels. And they say such spills would have less than a one-in-three risk of oiling the critical habitat for either of the endangered species.

October 2009. An environmental assessment for an area of the Gulf covering the site of the Deepwater Horizon blowout (Lease Sale 213) says, "The effect of proposed Lease Sale 213-related oil spills on fish resources and commercial fishing is expected to cause less than a 1 percent decrease in standing stocks of any population, commercial fishing efforts, landings, or value of those landings." It concludes thus: "There would be very little impact on commercial fishing."

November 2009. A BP pipeline ruptures in Alaska, releasing about 46,000 gallons of oily gunk onto the tundra.

January 2010. In a letter to the president of BP Exploration (Alaska), Congressmen Henry Waxman and Bart Stupak refer to "a number of personnel incidents involving serious injury or death" and question whether proposed BP budget cuts might threaten the company's ability to maintain safe operations.

March 4, 2010. President Obama lays out a Gulf Coast plan, "to deal with the catastrophic dangers of rising sea levels, hurricanes, and erosion, and invest in restoring barrier islands and wetlands in Mississippi and Louisiana." The White House adds, "Unless we stem the rapid rate of loss, Gulf ecosystems and the services they provide will collapse." And the Department of the Interior adds, "Finally, a president that has said we are going to take charge of this." This is not about concern over oil leaks. The concern: the Mississippi River Delta has been slowly falling apart for more than half a century. Causes: levees and flood controls built since the 1930s also starve marshes of the sediments and nutrients that created and maintained them; 14 major ship channels have been gouged through the wetlands to inland ports to facilitate Mississippi River commerce; and countless canals and channels have been dug by oil companies for boats, pipelines, and oil-rig servicing.

March 25, 2010. Three U.S. senators—Massachussetts Democrat John Kerry, South Carolina Republican Lindsey Graham, and Connecticut switch-hitter Joe Lieberman—are trying to draft bipartisan climate-change legislation capable of getting sixty votes to overcome a filibuster. It's the year of filibusterphobia. Graham's main concern is that depending on foreign oil is a security threat. The environment isn't uppermost in his mind. Considering these things, their bill includes environmental compromises so big, oil rigs could sink in them. So those three senators get a letter from ten Democrat senators. The ten warn that expanded offshore drilling could put their states at risk from oil spills, threatening fisheries, tourism, and the coast—a "national treasure that needs to be protected for generations to come." Senator Bill Nelson of Florida says the letter means "in a nutshell: No oil rigs off protected coastal states." Florida's beaches are its white gold. The senators' letter says the best way to lower oil costs is through energy efficiency and conservation.

April 4, 2010. The 700-plus-foot Chinese-owned coal carrier *Shen Neng 1* slams into Australia's Great Barrier Reef at full speed. The impact ruptures the vessel's fuel tanks. It's carrying 300,000 gallons of heavy fuel oil to run its engines while hauling 65,000 tons of coal.

First week of April 2010. The Government Accountability Office reports to Congress that the federal Minerals Management Service's Alaska office hasn't developed any guidelines for determining whether proposed developments comply with federal law. The GAO complains of "absence of a process."

April 14–15, 2010. The Interior Department's Minerals Management Service approves a series of permit changes that will help BP speedily conclude its over-budget drilling operation being conducted on Transocean's Deepwater Horizon drilling platform. BP has already secured a "categorical exclusion" from environmental review under the National Environmental Policy Act.

2010. Another BP platform, called Atlantis, has been operating with major apparent safety irregularities. One man who called attention to them has been laid off. He is suing BP. He says, "I've never seen this kind of attitude, where safety doesn't seem to matter and when you complain of a problem and try to fix it, you're just criticized and pushed aside." In 2008 a manager wrote an e-mail warning of "potential catastrophic operator errors" and said that operating the rig while "hundreds if not thousands" of critical engineering drawings for its operation were never finalized is "fundamentally wrong." The Atlantis well is capable of pumping a lot of oil, estimated at 800,000 barrels per day when fully operational. Says the man who's been laid off, "If something happens there, it will make the Deepwater Horizon look like a bubble."

PART TWO

A SEASON
OF ANGUISH

MAYDAY

Perhaps no pause has ever been as pregnant. Before May Day, hotel owners, fishermen, and restaurateurs—and most of the rest of the country—begin an anxious watch of satellite images and maps of how the oil is spreading, and models of how the oil could spread. The mere thought. The fear that it could all be lost. The fun, the wildlife—and the revenue they represent—ruined.

It begins looking like it could wash ashore heavily within days, coating fragile wetlands, ruining the Gulf's famous oyster beds, and redacting the whiteness from heretofore dazzling beaches. In fact, our minds spoil those beaches before any oil reaches them. The siege mentality seizes up our thinking.

So by May Day, a certain passion play has been written: the greed of men, the sacrifice of life, utter unpreparedness compounded by inability to respond, and a blanketing dread.

"I am frightened for the country," says the assistant chief of the National Ocean Service, David Kennedy. "This is a very, very big thing, and the efforts that are going to be required to do anything about it, especially if it continues on, are just mind-boggling." And Florida's Governor Charlie Crist wonders if anyone, really, could be doing enough in this situation. "It appears to me," he said, "that this is probably much bigger than we can fathom."

A New Orleans businessman who loves the bayou and loves his fishing tells me, "We got hit with the country's worst natural disaster; now we're getting hit with the worst man-made disaster. We were finally getting past the Katrina aftermath and the stigma, with the Saints winning the Super Bowl, and many businesses finding the stimulus dollars well spent." He tells me, "We just had this great glow going. And now it's just starting to dawn on folks what this oil might mean. It's the rest of *my* lifetime, anyway."

He says that people are "hugely frightened" of both the disaster itself and the media's ability to exacerbate the situation.

"This is the worst possible thing that could happen to the Mississippi Gulf Coast," says a man in the tourism business. "It could kill family tourism. That's our livelihood."

The person I'm staying with overnight in New Orleans says, "Everyone's deeply vested in the enjoyment and all the livelihoods and businesses that have been made. This is an outdoor lover's paradise. *Everything* revolves around seafood, wild food, the marshes, the coast. I mean, people are *very* scared that it will change a way of life. You've got to get outside this city, go down to those areas. You've got to feel that."

And so, I do.

I am now bouncing around the southern Louisiana delta region, through the mixture of poverty and affluence (mostly poverty) and the many visible reminders of Katrina. People who'd been rebounding post-Katrina now feel truly scared that their economy and their future are ruined forever. It's quietly horrifying.

Seeing families in small boats, local people crabbing in the canals, and the enormous pride with which people rebuilt waterside fishing retreats that Katrina had wholly swept away, I feel many connections between the people here and my own loves.

For all its self-image as the laid-back land of the Big Easy, the Gulf Coast of Louisiana is a brutal and brutalized place. The work hard, the options few, the stakes high, the damage and the scars deep.

Docked near Shell Beach lies a red-hulled trawler named *Blessed Assurance.* These communities could always depend on the marshes and waters and fishes and shellfish, no matter what. But now, that blessed assurance is suspended indefinitely. Human dignity is its own justification, and many people here, citizens of our imperfectly united country, feel that they may have just lost theirs.

"I'd hate to think that the hurricane didn't kill me and an oil spill did," says the sixty-eight-year-old survivor who'd rebuilt his century-old bait-and-fuel business from scratch after Katrina utterly destroyed it. Says his forty-one-year-old son, "This marsh is going to be like a big sponge, soaking up the oil. It's going to be bad." Captain Doogie Robin, eighty-four, oysterman, says, "Katrina really hit us hard. And this here, I think this is going to finish us now. I think this will wipe us off the map." A seafood dealer in Buras, Louisiana, says, "When you kill that food chain, nothing's going to come back to this area." A woman in Hopedale says, "If it gets in the marsh, it could be a year, it could be two years, it could be ten years." She adds, "It all depends on what happens."

What happens: By the first week of May, fishing is suddenly a thing of the past in 6,800 square miles of federal waters. More people whose lives depend on fishing realize they're out of work. Just like that. And the effects ripple further. A restaurant owner catering to fishermen worries, "How is a fisherman going to be able to afford to eat if he doesn't have a job?"

Meanwhile, the spokesman for the Louisiana Seafood Promotion and Marketing Board is working to—y'know—promote Louisiana seafood, assuring the public that Louisiana seafood remains available and safe. In 2008, the federal government had estimated the annual volume and value of Gulf-caught fish and shellfish at 1.3 billion pounds, worth $661 million. "We should be fine unless this thing gets totally out of control," the seafood promoter says.

"What BP's doing is throwing absolutely everything we can at this," says a senior vice president for the corporation.

Does that sound like a response plan or like this thing is totally out of control?

On May 2, BP begins drilling the first of those two relief wells. I say "BP begins drilling," but actually BP doesn't actually own any drilling equipment or *do* any drilling. As always, it simply hires someone else. It's just the Big Payer. Incredibly, these relief wells are planned to go straight down to around a mile below the seafloor (two miles from the surface), then *angle* in toward the blowing-out well, whereupon they will hit it 13,000 feet below the seafloor—where it is seven inches in diameter. They're capable of doing this—but they can't stop a leaking pipe lying on the seabed.

BP says it will spend a week making a 74-ton, concrete-and-metal box to put over the leak. "It's probably easier to fly in space than do some of this," says a BP spokesman.

Florida's Governor Charlie Crist says, "It's not a spill, it's a flow. Envision sort of an underground volcano of oil and it keeps spewing."

Twenty or so dead sea turtles wash ashore along thirty miles in Mississippi. None with oil on them, but the number's unusual. They could have eaten oil blobs, a frequent health problem for sea turtles. Or been overcome by fumes. Or drowned in shrimp nets. Fingers get pointed each way. Shrimpers say no way, impossible; they're required to use turtle-escape devices in their nets. The suspicious say panicked shrimpers tied the turtle-escape flaps shut to get every last shrimp. I'm going with the shrimpers on this one. I think it was the oil. A few years ago, off South Carolina, where there had not been any spills noted, veterinarians showed me how ingesting oil suppresses turtles' white blood cell counts, their immune system, and makes them unhealthy.

May 7. Along with the oil comes a new vocabulary of silly names for half-baked ideas. Today's password: "dome." Use it in a sentence: "BP has constructed a four-story containment dome intended to control and capture the largest of the leaks (yes, the pipe is leaking elsewhere, too).” But even as the dome was lowered, crews discovered that the opening was becoming clogged by an icy mix of gas and water—why didn’t the engineers foresee this?—so they set the 74-ton steel contraption down on the seabed 650 feet away from the leak, “as officials decide how to proceed.” New definition of “decide”: to scratch one’s head in wonder and confusion.

Foreseeing vast costs for cleanup and damage, investors Begin Pummeling, wiping about $30 billion off BP’s value in the first two weeks of the blowout. Outrage spreads. Momentum billows for lifting the recklessness-inducing $75 million cap on oil firms’ damage liability to a more realistic $10 billion.

It doesn’t take long to connect the most obvious dots: The *Economist* argues that “America’s distorted energy markets, not just its coastline, need cleaning up.” America needs a real energy policy. We need more diversified, cleaner, more competitive energy.

Easier said.

Meanwhile the *New York Times’* Thomas Friedman writes that there is only one meaningful response to the horrific oil spill in the Gulf of Mexico and that is for Congress to pass an energy bill that will create an American clean-energy infrastructure and set our country on a real, long-term path to ending our oil addiction. The obvious beneficiaries: our environment, our national security, our economic security, innovators, entrepreneurs. “We have to stop messing around,” writes Friedman, “with idiotic ‘drill, baby, drill’ nostrums, feel-good Earth Day concerts and the paralyzing notion that the American people are not prepared to do anything serious to change our energy mix.” He says this oil spill is like the subprime mortgage mess, a wake-up call and an opportunity to galvanize “radical change that overcomes the powerful lobbies and vested interests that want to keep us addicted to oil.”

It all sounds so obvious, and too familiar. And that’s the problem: the things that should have us on fire demanding change somehow fail to rouse we, the people, to the passion that could free us from our dependence on our pushers.

———

Senator John Kerry, one of the first sponsors of the Senate's energy bill, back before the blowout, seems to share such sentiments. He believes America is confronting three interrelated crises: an energy security crisis, a climate crisis, and an economic crisis. He says our best response to all three "is a bold, comprehensive bill that accelerates green innovation and creates millions of new jobs as we develop and produce the next generation of renewable power sources, alternative fuels and energy-efficient cars, homes and workplaces."

But ironically, because some Republican governors—such as Florida's Charlie Crist and California's Arnold Schwarzenegger—are withdrawing support for expanding drilling off their coasts, Republican support for an energy bill—wafer thin at its apogee—is dissolving faster than dispersant-drenched oil. Obama paid the price of reaching for that support by opening new areas, but the blowout has coastal politicians shrinking back in horror. The bill dies. Most proponents say the bill in Congress had been decorated with so many gifts and compromises that it had become a bad bill anyway. That's an apt balm. It was like the bill had eaten so much fat that it collapsed of arterial blockage.

Even though it's a matter of physics that carbon dioxide makes the planet warmer, and even though, because of burning oil and coal, our atmosphere now contains a third more carbon dioxide (and climbing) than it did at the start of the Industrial Revolution, many people just won't believe we have a big problem. People have a lot of kooky notions, but many who are disconnected from reality on this issue are running or aspiring to run the government of the United States of America.

Ron Johnson, a Republican candidate for the U.S. Senate from the great dairy state of Wisconsin, doesn't "believe" that carbon dioxide is causing climate change, "not by any stretch of the imagination." With his head still in his dairy air, he's going to Washington. In a few months, Johnson, steeped in tea party support, will beat Democratic incumbent Russ Feingold. "I think it's far more likely," Johnson opines of the causes for global warming, "that it's just sunspot activity."

When U.S. senators are offering the same explanation for climate change that were used to explain UFOs in the 1950s—watch out.

Here is a *real* conservative, one I admire: Congressman Bob Inglis, Republican of South Carolina:

As a Republican, I believe that we should be talking about conservation, because that's our heritage. If you go back to Teddy Roosevelt, that's who we are. And after all, there are very few letters different between conservatism and conservation. People asked me if I believe in climate change. And I tell them, no, I don't believe in climate change. It's not big enough to be a matter of faith. My faith informs my reaction to the data. But the data shows that there is climate change and that it stands to reason that it is in part human caused. And so, therefore, as responsible moral agents, we should act as stewards. Unfortunately, a clear majority of the Republican conference does not accept human causation in climate change. It's definitely not within the orthodoxy of conservatism as presented by, you know, Sarah Palin and folks like her. So you don't want to stand against that. And the result is that some people are sort of cowed into silence. . . .

It's really about national security. We are dependent for oil on the region of the world that doesn't like us very much. We need to change the game there. It's also about free enterprise, letting the free enterprise system actually solve this problem. Right now, the reason that free enterprise can't solve the problem is that petroleum and coal have freebies. Accountability, by the way, is a very bedrock conservative concept, even a biblical concept. We insist on accountability. So do we want to persist in a situation where we need to land the Marines in order to make sure that we have, in the future, the access to this petroleum that we must have? Or do we want to use the strength of America, the free enterprise system and the innovativeness of entrepreneurs and investors here to break that dependence? So our choice is, do we play to our strengths? Or do we continue to play to our weakness, which is playing the oil game?

Anyone expecting thunderous applause for such a rousing call to patriotism isn't paying attention. Asked what happens to Republicans who respond positively to science, Inglis says, "People look at you like you grew an extra head or something. You're definitely seen as some kind of oddball, and perhaps even a heretic."

Congressman Inglis lost his bid for reelection in the 2010 *primaries.* Too "moderate."

The fact that politicians, media talking heads, and too much of the electorate lost the ability to differentiate between science and ideology is one of the causes of America's decline. But if Americans don't understand science, is it really fair to blame Big Oil?

The government's main office for gathering all the scientific data on climate change and informing the U.S. Congress, more than a dozen federal agencies, and the American people is called the Global Change Research Program. Rick Piltz was a senior officer there from 1995 to 2005. Soon after George W. Bush took over the White House after losing the "popular vote"—which in other countries is called the "election"—Piltz was putting together a major report for Congress. "We were told to delete the pages that summarized the most recent IPCC report and the material about the National Assessment of climate change impacts that had just come out," he recalled in 2010. The IPCC is the international scientific body that collects and assesses all the climate research from around the world. The National Assessment was a similar report covering research by U.S. scientists. They'd both concluded that climate change was happening and that human activity was accelerating it.

But the Bush White House put its fingers in its ears and sang, "La-di-da." Piltz says the experts had made "pretty clear and compelling statements. And to say that you didn't believe it was to say that you did not want to go along with the preponderance of scientific evidence." Until he left, four years later, from almost every report Piltz and his team compiled, the White House deleted references to climate change or carbon emissions. Many of those deletions were made by a guy named Philip Cooney. He was chief of staff for the Bush White

House's Council on Environmental Quality. His previous job had been as a lawyer and lobbyist for the American Petroleum Institute, and his next job was with ExxonMobil.

And when we so crucially need campaign finance reform and publicly funded elections to get the money out of politics, in the 2010 Citizens United case, the Supreme Court overturned a century of precedent, and effectively destroyed the McCain-Feingold campaign finance reform legislation. McCain-Feingold banned the broadcast or transmission of "electioneering communications" paid for by corporations or labor unions from their general funds in the thirty days before a presidential primary and in the sixty days before the general elections. By doing away with that, the Supreme Court opened the floodgates to corporate election-distorting money and made it easier for the sources of that money to remain anonymous. All five of the Court's "conservatives" joined together to overturn a sixty-three-year-old ban on corporate money in federal elections and twenty-year-old and seven-year-old precedents affirming the validity of such corporate electioneering bans. They ignored the protests of their four more moderate (actually conservative, in other words) dissenting justices. Writing ninety pages for the dissenters, Justice John Paul Stevens noted: "Today's decision is backwards in many senses. The Court's opinion is a rejection of the common sense of the American people, who have recognized a need to prevent corporations from undermining self government since the founding, and who have fought against the distinctive corrupting potential of corporate electioneering since the days of Theodore Roosevelt. It is a strange time to repudiate that common sense. While American democracy is imperfect, few outside the majority of this Court would have thought its flaws included a dearth of corporate money in politics."

President Obama called the decision "a major victory for big oil, Wall Street banks, health insurance companies and the other powerful interests that marshal their power every day in Washington to drown out the voices of everyday Americans."

This "Joke of the Week" arrives in my in-box: "The economy is so bad, Exxon-Mobil just laid off 25 congressmen."

⚘

I hop onto a small boat that's already pulling away from the dock in Shell Beach, Louisiana. The captain, Casey Kieff, was a fishing guide until the oil blowout caused an indefinite fishing closure. Now he's taking some photographers out to have a look at Breton Sound. On board is a reporter from Reuters, a crew from Russian state television, a photographer working for Getty Images, and several others. The captain names a fair price and I jump on, too, wondering if this is his last week of work—and what price could really be fair to him. For decades he's been guiding people who want to sport-fish for speckled sea trout and redfish. No matter how bad the oil gets, the media attention will wane. Guiding reporters won't be a new career. So he's got a lot on his mind.

We go to Hopedale to pick up a couple of other people. The cops have the road into here closed, but by the grace of boats we have free range of the place. The waterfront is bustling with trucks carrying miles and miles of boom, all kinds of boats getting into the act for a day's uneasy pay. The National Guard, wildlife enforcement people— all kinds of busyness intent on oil-containment plans that are at worst futile and at best high-risk. There seems both a lot of organization and a lot of confusion.

In Kieff's overpowered outboard, we blast through a sliver of the astonishingly vast and intricate wetlands of Louisiana.

The first thing that really impresses me is the immensity of Louisiana's marshes and coast. Marshes as far as you can see, to all points of the compass. Bewildering mazes of channels.

How could this whole coast be protected? And if oil comes, it could never be cleaned by people. It's a wet, grassy sponge from horizon to horizon.

The skeletons of oak forests stand starkly on marsh islands now subsiding, too low and too inundated to sustain trees. They're dying back, and the marshes themselves are eroding away.

But still, there are miles and miles of marshes before one gets to the open waters of Breton Sound. As we head toward the Gulf, I notice a few bottlenose dolphins rolling as they snatch air in the mud-murked channels.

When we reach open water, the horizon is dotted with gas rigs and a few boats that have piled their decks with booms.

After a long, pounding ride through a stiff chop, our captain steers us to one of the inner islands, Freemason, a barely emergent ridge of sand and shell about a mile long. The innermost of the Chandeleur chain, the island is maybe a mile long. (Katrina dissolved several miles of these islands.)

The island isn't well known to people. But it is to birds. Brown pelicans, laughing gulls, herring gulls, black skimmers, and least, Sandwich, and royal terns rest by the dozens. They're joined by a few itinerant ruddy turnstones, sanderlings, and black-bellied plovers migrating toward their Arctic nesting grounds.

In some ways, a catastrophe of this magnitude could not have happened in a worse place. Or at a worse time of year.

The Gulf is a large region, but its natural importance is even more outsized, disproportionate to its area. The Gulf is the hourglass pinch point for millions of migrating creatures that funnel in, and then fan out of it to populate an enormous area of the hemisphere's continents and coasts. Anything that affects living things inside the Gulf affects living things far outside it.

In the Gulf in May, with the oil gushing, are loons, gannets, various kinds of herons and others that have spent the winter here but will soon leave to migrate north. Depending on the species, they'll breed all along the coast from the southern states to as far north as the Maritimes and lakes across much of Canada. Some of the longest-distance migrants on Earth are various sandpipers, plovers, and other shorebirds, many of which winter as far south as Patagonia and breed as far north as the high Arctic. Perhaps a million cross the Gulf in May, and when they reach the U.S. coastline, they must stop to rest and feed. Problems with habitat and food supply have reduced many of their populations 50 to 80 percent in the last twenty years. And now this.

Oil is just starting to smudge some of the birds. Even among those that do not get heavily oiled, some will not make it. The birds' energy budgets will not bear the cost of feathers sticking and functioning inefficiently, and many such birds will likely drop out on their way north. Migrating peregrine falcons traveling north from South American wintering areas, destined for nesting sites as far as Greenland, are also crossing the Gulf's marshes. Preferentially picking off birds whose flight seems compromised, falcons could end up getting disproportional doses of oil.

Certain animals that normally inhabit the open Atlantic travel to the Gulf to breed. The world's most endangered sea turtle, the Kemp's ridley, ranges throughout the western Atlantic as far north as New England. But it breeds only in the Gulf. Adults are now heading there to lay their eggs on remote beaches. So are other sea turtles. Adults are vulnerable, but hatchlings will likely have an even harder time. And whether from oil or fishing nets, disproportionate numbers of turtles continue turning up dead.

A magnificent frigatebird—that's not my description; it's the species' name: magnificent frigatebird—patrols overhead. It shares the airspace with a couple of helicopters and a C-130 military cargo plane, newcomers in its eons-old realm. And it feels the place more deeply than anyone aboard those aircraft.

Booms designed to keep away oil have been placed along one side of Freemason Island. But they don't run the whole length of even one side of the island. And on the side where they were placed, the wind and chop have already washed them ashore in places and partly buried them in sand and shell. In other words, segments of the boom barrier have already been rendered useless by a couple of days' wave action.

We'd had some news that part of the oil slick was eight miles southeast of the islands in the open Gulf. But the water is too rough for us to continue on to the main Chandeleur Islands or beyond. Indeed, some of the fishing boats carrying booms are headed back in. Over the radio they tell us they were sent toward port due to the rough water.

So far, I see oil only on the heads and bellies of a few Sandwich terns. Just a few little brown smudges; but it's unmistakably oil. I fear much worse is coming. Diving into water—that's how they eat. Oil is famously hazardous to waterbirds. It's a chronic thing: a few oiled birds are always showing up around harbors and ports, and I once saw a tropicbird in the middle of the ocean whose immaculate pearl plumage was stained with considerable oil from somewhere—probably a ship that had discharged dirty bilgewater.

People have been counting dead birds from major spills for years. In 1936, 1,400 oiled birds washed ashore near Kent, England. In 1937, a ship collision sent 6,600 oiled birds onto the coastline of California. Five thousand ducks on the East Coast in a 1942 mishap; 10,000 ducks killed by oil in the Detroit River in 1948; an estimated 150,000 eiders off Chatham, Massachusetts, after two ships collided in a 1952 winter gale; 30,000 ducks off Gotland, in the Baltic, in 1952, and 60,000 more in the same place in three successive spills over the next four years. In 1955 the wreck of the *Gerd Maersk* killed an estimated 275,000 scoters and other ducks and waterbirds near the mouth of Germany's Elbe River. Kills of several thousand birds remained quite common throughout the 1960s. As Japan industrialized, its first large oil spill, in 1965, killed large numbers of kittiwakes, shearwaters, and other birds. Between 1964 and 1967, worldwide there were 19 tanker groundings, with 17 large spills, and 238 supertanker collisions, resulting in 22 more large spills. Though thousands of birds continued to be killed in various oil-related mishaps, improved safety and environmental regulations resulted in fewer accidents and reduced wildlife deaths, until the *Exxon Valdez* set new records.

Birds that are lightly oiled, like the ones here today, often raise fewer, slower-growing chicks than normal.

Some oiled animals may eventually be rescued and cleaned. Less possible to cleanse is the anguish on the faces and in the hearts of fishing families.

Casey wants to say hey to a relative, James Kieff, who's been an oysterman for thirty-five years. "We outta work," James says disbelievingly from the deck of his forty-eight-foot boat, *Lady Jennifer,* as he motors along carrying 3,000 feet of boom to the outer edge of one of the marsh islands. "Now we workin' for BP. They don't know these waters. We do." A moment later he adds, "The stress is in the not knowing. Katrina came and went. We knew what to do. If the oil stays offshore, we could be okay. But that's a big if."

I watch him and other boats laying booms along the marshes. They work hard. I see men and women who know water, boats, and work, bending seriously to their task. And despite never having handled booms before, they do the job well.

The only problem: No one believes the booms can work. Any medium wave action will push oil over them. And despite miles and miles and miles of booms, miles and miles and miles and miles and miles and miles of marsh remain utterly naked and undefended. It's a fool's errand. (During the *Valdez* catastrophe, Exxon's CEO was apparently audiotaped saying he didn't care if the booms contained the oil; he just wanted pictures of them in the water.)

The only saving grace is that there is no oil in sight yet. And that hardly helps. Because the people have no jobs after this. As always, it's a matter of who people are at the mercy of how people are.

But for this frantic moment, with oil rigs in every direction and the oil coating everyone's mind, it's boom boom boom.

A Louisiana State University professor says the oil could entirely wipe out many kinds of fish, and notes, "We may very well lose dozens of vulnerable fish species." A toxicologist says, "We'll see dead bodies soon. Sharks, dolphins, sea turtles, whales; the impact on predators will be seen in a short time because the food web will be impacted from the bottom up." Another Louisiana State University professor says oil pushed inland by a hurricane could affect rice and sugarcane crops. A meteorologist says there's a chance that the oil could cause explosive deepening of hurricanes in the Gulf. The *Christian Science Monitor* asks whether hurricane-blown oil could make coastal towns permanently uninhabitable. The *Monitor* then quotes a Pensacola Beach solar energy salesman (bias alert) who took a hazardous materials class as saying, "In these classes, they basically tell you that swallowing even a small amount of the oil or getting some on your hands and then having a smoke could be deadly."

Well, holy cow; somebody needs to warn auto mechanics, boat owners, auto-lube attendants, heating-oil delivery people, gas station attendants, and anyone with a car or lawn mower *not to move* because they're about to *explode!*

In the Florida Keys, Miami, and beyond, people begin worrying about the "Loop Current" (vocabulary term). It flows out of the Gulf of Mexico to become the Gulf Stream, and might carry oil throughout the Keys' reefs and then up the East Coast. "Once it's in the Loop Current, that's the worst case," says a Texas A&M University oceanographer. "Then that oil could wind up along the Keys and get transported out to the Atlantic." I begin hearing worries from Long Island's Hamptons—and, indeed, as far away as *Ireland*—that in a few months, oil from the blowout will ruin beaches there. Florida senator Bill Nelson warns, "If this gusher continues for several months, it's going to get down into the Loop Current. You are talking about massive economic loss to our tourism, our beaches, to our fisheries, very possibly disruption of our military testing and training, which is in the Gulf of Mexico."

Another scientist from Texas A&M University says, "The threat to the deep-sea habitat is already a done deal, it is happening now." He adds, "If the oil settles on the bottom, it will kill the smaller organisms, like the copepods and small worms. When we lose the forage, then you have an impact on the larger fish."

Yeah, maybe. But "a done deal"? Really? How much oil would have to settle? How densely?

I'm a professional environmentalist and conservationist; I'm really angry about the recklessness that caused this, and the inanity of the response; I am deeply distressed about the potential damage to wildlife and habitats—but I find myself becoming uncomfortable with all the catastrophizing. "A done deal"—that's not very scientific. Especially for a scientist. Many scientists—and as a scientist it hurts to say this—are being a little shrill. Cool heads are not prevailing.

But it's not a time of calm. With the situation out of control, everyone wants to know what's gonna happen. Even the normally cautious are prone to overspeculating.

And then there are those never burdened by caution. Enter the crazies. Some say this was done on purpose: Obama and BP have conspired to make money from this; someday, they claim, we'll get to the bottom of how. Some believe this will merely kill the entire ocean; others think it will kill the whole world.

Something called Yowusa.com posts an article based on warnings it says are from an Italian physicist. (The site also features predictions made by Nostradamus, including his "proven" prediction that a giant tsunami will destroy New York City.) We read, "The Loop Current in the Gulf of Mexico has stalled as a consequence of the BP oil spill disaster. The effects have also begun to spread to the Gulf Stream. If natural processes cannot re-establish the stalled Loop Current, we could begin to see global crop failures as early as 2011." Yow, indeed.

The Web begins amplifying a blogger-posted article called "How BP Gulf Disaster May Have Triggered a 'World-Killing' Event." In another post the same blogger writes, "The giant oil company is now quietly preparing to test a small nuclear device in a frenzied rush against time to quell a cascading catastrophe." On the same site (whose slogan is: "Where Knowledge Rules") we find several entries under the heading "How the Ultimate BP Gulf Disaster Could Kill Millions." The first click gets me "A devastating eruption of methane gas, buried deep beneath the sea floor, could absolutely decimate the region. Even worse, this eruption could inundate the low lying coast line with a tsunami." The entry unleashes a tsunami of speculation and dire conclusion that surges across the Web.

Sparked by very legitimate fears and fanned by wild speculation, a certain simmering siege mentality, peppered with panic, begins bubbling across the region. The sky begins falling a little.

As gallop horsemen of the Apocalypse, so also ride a few doubters of disaster. "The sky is not falling. It isn't the end of the Gulf of Mexico," says the director of a Texas-based conservation group. While many are predicting a thousand ruined miles of irreplaceable wetlands and beaches, fisheries sidelined for seasons on end, fragile species shattered, a region economically crippled for years, and tongues of oil lashing beaches up to Cape Cod, others shrug.

It's still the first inning in a nine-inning game. "Right now what people are fearing has not materialized," says a retired professor and oil spill expert from Louisiana State. "People have the idea of an *Exxon Valdez,* with a gunky, smelly black tide. . . . I do not anticipate this will happen here." Others point out that the Ixtoc leak seemed largely to vanish in about three years. (Even if it did, three years would be a very long time in a fishing community that can't go fishing.)

Still others note that this isn't so bad compared to all the other bad stuff that happens to the Gulf every day: scores of refineries and chemical plants from Mexico to Mississippi pouring pollutants into the water, pollution from all the ships, the degrading marshes, the dead zone caused by all the Midwest's farm runoff flowing down the Mississippi River. It's hardly a pristine Eden.

"The Gulf is tremendously resilient," says the cool-headed director of the Texas-based conservation group. But he adds, "How long can we keep heaping these insults on the Gulf and having it bounce back? I have to say I just don't know."

No one knows. The not knowing thickens a gumbo of fear.

Meanwhile, BP executives admit to Congress behind closed doors that the leak could reach 60,000 barrels per day, sixty times what they'd been saying.

Now, about that Loop Current. There're kernels of truth in both the fear that it could take oil across the Keys reefs and into the Gulf Stream and the observation that it's "stopped." Normally, the Loop Current flows a bit like a snaking conveyor belt; it does have the potential to take the oil and move it past the Florida Keys. But that conveyor has just pinched itself off. As sometimes happens, a meander has bent itself into an enormous eddy that's just pinwheeling in the Gulf. This greatly blunts the likelihood of the oil getting into the Gulf Stream and up the East Coast. "This is the closest thing to an act of God that we've seen," says Dr. Steve Murawski of the National Oceanic and Atmospheric Administration. Well, maybe—whatever. But another way of looking at it is that the Gulf will be stuck with all the oil. And I'm about to get a pelican's-eye impression of how much oil is currently in the Gulf.

⚗

"My name's Dicky Toups," says the pilot before he starts the engine of the seaplane I'm climbing into. "But they call me Captain Coon-ass."

We overfly the emerald maze of the vast Mississippi Delta. Captain Coon-ass points, saying, "There's a big ole gator."

To the far points of view, America's greatest marshes lie dissected, bisected, and trisected, diced by long, straight artificial channels and man-angled meanders, all aids to access and shipping. For the vast multimillion-acre emerald marshes, they are death by a thousand cuts.

The sign had said, "Welcome to Louisiana—America's Wetland." Pride and prejudice. People here depend on nature or the control of nature—or both. Keep an eye on nature; it can kill you here. But people can kill the place itself.

Since the 1930s, oil and gas companies have dug about 10,000 miles of canals through the oak and cypress forests, black mangrove swamps, and green marshes. Lined up, they could go straight through Earth with a couple thousand miles to spare. The salt water they brought killed coastal forests and subjected our greatest wetlands to steady erosion. Upstream, dams and levees hold back the sediment that could have helped heal some of that erosion. Starved on one end, eaten at the other. How to kill America's wetlands. Long after this oil crisis is over, this chronic disease will continue doing far more damage than the oil.

All these Delta-slicing channels cause banks to dissolve, swapping wetlands for open water. Those channels also roll out red carpets for hurricanes. Incredibly, this has all cost Louisiana's coast about 2,300 square miles of wetlands. Marshland continues to disintegrate at a rate of about 25 square miles a year. The rise in sea level due to global warming is also helping drown watery borderlands. Oil leak or no leak, these things, all ongoing, constitute the most devastating human-made disaster that's ever hit the Gulf. Bar none.

Only slowly does the muddy Mississippi lose itself to the oceanic blue of the open Gulf, a melding of identities, a meeting of watery minds. And also the drain for sediments, agricultural fertilizers, and dead-zone-generating pollutants from the entire Midwest and most of the plains. Even before the oil blowout, this was a troubled place—a troubled place whose troubles have now escalated to a whole new level.

Two boats are tending booms around an island densely dotted with nesting pelicans. As I've noticed from the ground—but it's even more striking from up here, at 3,500 feet—most of the coast is bare of booms and undefended. Where booms have been placed along the outer beach, many have already washed up onshore, already useless.

The sea-surface breeze pattern is interrupted by a marbling of slicks. Often such a pattern is perfectly natural, so I look carefully. It's brown.

"Oil," says Captain Coon-ass.

One of those slicks has nuzzled against the shore. There's a boat there and some people are walking along the beach, inspecting a long boom that the wind has washed ashore.

The nearshore waters and beyond are dotted with drilling rigs for oil and gas, some abandoned. Like bringing coals to Newcastle, many of the rigs stand surrounded by floating oil.

Offshore, longer slicks ribbon their way out across the blue Gulf. As we follow them, the light slicks thicken with dark streaks that look from the air like wind-driven orange fingers, then like chocolate pudding. An ocean streaked with chocolate pudding.

A few miles out, the streaks grow darker still. Yet there remains far more open water than oil slick.

That changes. Blue water turned shiny purple. A bruise from a battering. The sea swollen with oil.

As the water darkens and the slicks widen, Captain Coon-ass points to a small plane below us, saying it's on a scouting run for the C-130s that will follow to spray dispersants. More chemicals on a sea of chemicals.

Yet plenty of the oil—and I mean plenty—is not dissolved. Blue water turned brown.

"This is some pretty thick stuff right here," Captain Coon-ass says. The crude is now drifting in broad bands that stretch to the horizon. "We're lookin' at twenty miles of oil right here."

We're directly over the source of the blowout. Below, two ships are drilling the relief wells that we've been told will take months. A dozen ships drift nearby, most with helicopter landing pads on them. What they're all doing, heaven knows.

A fresh breeze puts whitecaps on the nonoiled patches of the black-and-blue sea. As the C-130 comes out, we turn northeast.

We're headed toward the Chandeleurs, the line of sandy islands that have been much in the news for their at-risk bird rookeries. Soon we're over Breton Sound, where a couple of days ago, from a boat, I saw no oil.

But now there is plenty of oil, moving in between the main coast and the islands.

Out to intercept the oil is a fleet of shrimp boats towing booms from the outriggers that would normally tow their nets. The idea appears to be that they will catch the oil at the surface, the way they catch shrimp at the seafloor.

Dozens of boats tow booms through the oil, but as they do, water and oil simply flow over them. Far from corralling it, they're barely stirring it. As they pass, the oil—seemingly all of it—remains.

Louisiana lives by oil and by seafood. But oil rules. Fishing has nothing like the cash, the lobbyists, the destructive sophistication of the pusher to whose junk we're all addicted. But Florida lives largely by the whiteness of its sand. It has long eschewed oil. And the difference in what politicians will and won't say about oil is stark.

Florida's Governor Charlie Crist returns from a little airtime over the Gulf. His message: "It's the last thing in the world I would want to see happen in our beautiful state." He adds, "Until you actually see it, I don't know how you can comprehend and appreciate the sheer magnitude of that thing. It's frightening. . . . It's everywhere. It's absolutely unbelievable." Where oil money rules, governors are not at liberty to disclose such impressions. They're probably not at liberty even to think them.

"The president is frustrated with everything, the president is frustrated with everybody, in the sense that we still have an oil leak," says a White House spokesman.

But we've only just begun.

When Obama announced that he was opening up large new areas for offshore drilling, he said, "Oil rigs today generally don't cause spills. They are technologically very advanced." That's exactly right. Leaks, spills, and blowouts are never expected. Yet we know they happen. That should make us thorough in preparedness. But the human mind lets down its guard if big danger seems rare and remote.

And so we did. In 2009, the Interior Department exempted BP's Gulf of Mexico drilling operations from a detailed environmental impact analysis after three reviews concluded that a massive oil spill was "unlikely." Oil rig operators usually must submit a plan for how they'll cope with a blowout. But in 2008, the Bush administration relaxed the rules. In 2009, the Obama administration said BP didn't need to file a plan for how it would handle a blowout at the Deepwater Horizon. Now a BP spokesman insists, "We have a plan that has sufficient detail in it to deal with a blowout."

Obviously, they don't. Obviously, they aren't.

"I'm of the opinion that boosterism breeds complacency and complacency breeds disaster," says Congressman Edward Markey, a Democrat from Massachusetts. "That, in my opinion, is what happened."

Bush and Cheney's ties to big oil and their destruction of Interior over-sight are infamous. But Obama's Interior secretary's ties to big energy also make environmentalists uneasy. As a senator from Colorado, Ken Salazar accepted some of BP's ubiquitous campaign contributions. In 2005, Senator Salazar voted against increasing fuel-efficiency stan-dards for cars and trucks, and voted against an amendment to repeal tax breaks for ExxonMobil and other major petroleum companies. In 2006, he voted to expand Gulf of Mexico drilling. And then as Interior secretary, he pushed for more offshore drilling. The Interior secretary now says there have been well more than 30,000 wells drilled into the Gulf of Mexico, "and so this is a very, very rare event." The oil from those offshore rigs accounts for 30 percent of the nation's domestic oil production, he notes, adding, "And so for us to turn off those spigots would have a very, very huge impact on America's economy right now."

Probability, however, tells us that the spill's a very, very inevitable event. *Especially* with 30,000 wells drilled and roughly 4,000 wells currently producing oil in the region. In 2007, the federal Minerals Management Service examined 39 rig blowouts that occurred in the Gulf of Mexico between 1992 and 2006. So a blowout every four and a half months. I guess most are quickly controlled. Why aren't we ready for one that isn't? A car accident is a rare event, but we use our seat belts and we like to know we have air bags.

Rather than plan for the worst, Big Petroleum has indulged in—and been indulged by—a policy of waving away risks. In a 2009 ex-ploration plan, BP strongly discounted the possibility of a catastrophic accident. A Shell analysis for drilling off Alaska asserts that a "large liquid hydrocarbon spill [hydrocarbon meaning oil and gas] . . . is re-garded as too remote and speculative to be considered a reasonably foreseeable impacting event."

Foresee this: if you think it's difficult to clean up oil in the warm, calm Gulf of Mexico, imagine trying to do it in Arctic waters with icebergs, frozen seas, and twenty hours of darkness.

Speaking of the cold and the dark, "Drill, baby, drill" queen Sarah Palin just has to say *something* about all this. So she says we shouldn't trust "foreign" oil companies such as BP. She says, "Don't naively trust—verify." Verified: her husband worked for BP for eighteen years. Palin blames "extreme environmentalists" (c'mon, Sarah, is there any other kind?) for causing this blowout because they've lobbied hard to prevent new drilling in Alaska. If you follow what she has in place of logic, it could seem she'd rather that this had happened in her home state.

In and out of the comedy of horrors strides BP CEO and court jester Tony Hayward. "I think I have said all along that the company will be judged not on the basis of an accident that, you know, frankly was not our accident." That's what he actually says. Highlighting the failed blowout preventer, Hayward says, "That is a piece of equipment owned and operated by Transocean, maintained by Transocean; they are absolutely accountable for its safety and reliability."

Transocean's president and CEO says drilling projects "begin and end with the operator: in this case, BP."

Take that.

He says that Transocean finished drilling three days before the explosion. And he says there's "no reason to believe" that the blowout preventor's mechanics failed. That's what *he* actually says.

Halliburton's spokesman says his company followed BP's drilling plan, federal regulations, and standard industry practices.

In sum, BP has blamed drilling contractor Transocean, which owned the rig. Transocean says BP was responsible for the well's design and pretty much everything else, and that oil-field services contractor Halliburton was responsible for cementing the well shut. Halliburton says its workers were just following BP's orders, but that Transocean was responsible for maintaining the rig's blowout preventer. And the Baby Bear said, "Somebody's been sleeping in *my* bed."

By the end of the first week of May, a heavy smell of oil coming ashore along parts of Louisiana's coast begins prompting dozens of complaints about headaches, burning eyes, and nausea.

Meanwhile, I hear on the radio that in an effort to *do* something, "People from around the world have been giving the hair off their heads, the fur off their pets' backs, and the tights off their legs to make booms and mats to mop up the oily mess spewing out of the seabed of the Gulf of Mexico." Whether any of this stuff was ever actually used, I can't say. I never saw any; that I can say.

By May's second week, heavy machinery, civilian and military dump trucks, Army jeeps, front-end loaders, backhoes, and National Guard helicopters are pushing up and dropping down sand to keep an impending invasion of oil from reaching the marshes in and around Grand Isle, at the tip of Louisiana. Much of the mobilization falls to the Marine Spill Response Corporation, formed in 1990 after the *Exxon Valdez* disaster and maintained largely by fees from the biggest oil firms. Its vice president of marine spill response says that most of its equipment, including booms and skimmers, was bought in 1990. She says, "The technology hasn't changed that much since then."

"This is the largest, most comprehensive spill response mounted in the history of the United States and the oil and gas industry," crows BP's CEO Tony Hayward, sounding proud when he ought to be aghast and horrified by the scale of the mess and the upheaval.

Workers farther inland are diverting fresh water from the Mississippi River into the marshlands, hoping the added flow will help push back any oily water that comes knocking. "We're trying to save thousands of acres of marsh here, where the shrimp grow, where the fin-fish lay their eggs, where the crabs come in and out," says the director of the Greater Lafourche Port Commission. Enough Mississippi River water to fill the Empire State Building is now rushing into southeastern Louisiana wetlands *every half hour.* "We have opened every diversion structure we control on the state and parish level to try to limit the oil approaching our coasts," says the assistant director of the Office of Coastal Protection and Restoration, "nearly 165,000 gallons every second."

"It can't hurt," says a wetlands ecology professor at Ohio State University and an authority on the Mississippi's interaction with the Gulf of Mexico. Oh, but it can.

———

New fear factor: hurricane season. The image: hurricanes that could "churn up towering black waves and blast beaches and crowded cities with oil-soaked gusts." The news stories carry attributions such as "experts warned." And precise-sounding imprecision like: "As hurricane season officially starts Tuesday . . ." and "Last month, forecasters who issue a closely watched Colorado State University seasonal forecast said there was a 44 percent chance a hurricane would enter the Gulf of Mexico in the next few months, far greater than the 30 percent historic average."

To the ambiguity and imprecision, add unnecessary intonations of worrisome complexity: "The high winds may distribute oil over a wide area," says a National Hurricane Center meteorologist, adding, "It's a complex problem that really needs to be looked at in great detail to try to understand what the oceanic response is when you have an oil layer at the sea surface."

To most normal people faced with the real event of an out-of-control mess, especially people who've survived hurricanes, that kind of noninformation stokes anxiety, provokes fear—and gives no one a clear clue about what to do. Does one make decisions based on the difference between 30 and 44 percent? News you can use, it isn't. It's news that can help ruin your health.

Insult to injury: "Safety first," says a BP spokesman. "We build in hurricane preparedness, and that requires us to take the necessary precautions."

By mid-May, something like 10,000 people are Being Paid for cleanup efforts around the Gulf. BP has little choice. Anything less, there'd be riots. Most are fishermen riding around looking for oil, dragging booms that don't collect much oil, or putting out booms that can work only on oil that hasn't been dissolved by dispersants. About a million and a half feet—roughly 300 miles—of boom is already out along the coast. Other people are out picking oil off beaches with shovels.

How much oil are we dealing with? This gets good: Purdue professor Steve Wereley performs computer analyses on the video of the leaking oil to see how far and how fast particles are moving (a technique called particle image velocimetry). His conclusion: the well is leaking between 56,000 and 84,000 barrels daily. His other conclusion: "It's definitely not 5,000 barrels a day."

Just a few days ago, during congressional testimony, officials from BP, Transocean, and Halliburton estimated a "worst-case" scenario maximum flow of 60,000 barrels a day. Yet a BP spokesman says the company stands by its estimate of 5,000 barrels per day. There's "no way to calculate a definite amount," he says, adding coyly, "We are focused on stopping the leak and not measuring it."

That's Bull Poop. As the director of the Texas A&M University's geochemical and environmental research group points out: "If you don't know the flow, it is awfully hard to design the thing that is going to work."

Killing the well is proving difficult. Killing public confidence is easier. The fact that the real flow will turn out to be sixty times what BP was first saying, and twelve times the Coast Guard's most oft-repeated estimate, does the trick handily.

LATE MAY

Another discovery, another debate, more resistance from BP about disclosing how much oil is leaking. Scientists from the University of Georgia, Louisiana University, and elsewhere, aboard the research vessel *Pelican*, report finding—well, let them tell you: "There's a shocking amount of oil in the deep water, relative to what you see in the surface water," says Samantha Joye, a researcher at the University of Georgia. "There's a tremendous amount of oil in multiple layers, three or four or five layers deep in the water column." "Tremendous" meaning plumes as large as 10 miles long, 3 miles wide, and up to 300 feet thick. She reports methane concentrations up to 10,000 times higher than normal.

Dr. Joye says oxygen near some of the plumes has already dropped 30 percent because of oxygen-using microbes feeding on the hydrocarbons. In an e-mail, Joye calls her findings "the most bizarre-looking oxygen profiles I have ever seen anywhere." She notes, "If you keep those kinds of rates up, you could draw the oxygen down to very low levels that are dangerous to animals." Some parts of the plume had oxygen concentrations just above levels that make areas uninhabitable to fish, crabs, shrimp, and other marine creatures. "That is alarming," she says, adding that some of the Gulf's deepwater corals live directly below parts of the oil slick, "and they need oxygen."

But what are "plumes"? We don't quite get from the scientists an indication of how dense they are. Are we talking murky clouds? Tiny amounts detectable only with instruments? Enough to kill plankton? Small fish? Even a 10-by-3-mile plume is only a fraction of the Gulf. Are there other, more widespread plumes?

Plume definition: something flowing within a different medium.

The farther from the source of the blowout, the less concentrated the oil and gas hydrocarbons in the plume. Currents determine where plumes go. Dispersants also break up oil. If oil gets broken into very small droplets, say 1 micron in size, it no longer floats but dissolves into the seawater. "Clean" seawater contains oil concentrations less than 1 part per billion; in every billion drops of seawater there's less than one dissolved drop of oil. A polluted place, like a city harbor, may have between 100 and 800 drops of oil for every billion drops of seawater. You can also think of it as, say, 100 to 800 gallons of oil in every billion gallons of seawater. A billion gallons occupies about 5,000 cubic yards, or a space 100 yards long, 50 yards wide, and 1 yard deep. Two hundred gallons of oil would take up one cubic yard.

A bit of comparison. The Ixtoc blowout discharged a maximum of about 30,000 barrels per day. The present blowout is leaking perhaps twice that amount, so at any given distance from the blowout, our concentrations should be higher. Within a few hundred yards of the Ixtoc blowout, oil was 10,000 parts per billion. About 50 miles away, it was 5 parts per billion. Because the concentration gets lower and lower as oil travels away from the blowout, nobody knows much about how toxic the plumes of oil are.

They used to say "dilution is the solution to pollution," and sometimes that's right. If you think of a pollutant as anything that overwhelms the environment's ability to harmlessly absorb it, dilution can work. (Animals' bodies, though, often reconcentrate pollutants, much to their harm, so dilution isn't always the solution.)

BP's chief operating officer continues insisting that there exist no underwater oil plumes in "large concentrations." He says that this may depend on "how you define what a plume is here."

The way University of Georgia researcher Dr. Samantha Joye defines a plume, one large concentration of hydrocarbons from the blowout stretches at least 15 miles west of the gushing oil well, 3,600 feet beneath the sea surface, 3 miles wide, and up to 1,500 feet thick. The way University of South Florida researchers define a plume, there's an even larger plume stretching more than 20 miles northeast of the oil well, with the hydrocarbons separated into one layer 1,200 feet below the surface and another 3,000 feet deep.

"The oil is on the surface," says BP's somnambulant CEO Tony Hayward. "There aren't any plumes." That's certainly interesting, coming from someone whose company is blasting dispersants into the oil right at the seafloor as it emerges from the broken pipe, to keep the oil below the surface, and sending planes to carpet-bomb the slicks with more dispersant to sink the oil that has risen.

So how do *you* define plumes? In some places there's enough oil to discolor the water. But in most places, water samples come up clear. Yet the dissolved hydrocarbons show up vividly on instruments, and in some samples you can smell them. That's plumes.

Plumes are more evidence that there's more oil leaking than we're seeing. Because the Purdue University estimate and these reports of massive plumes seem so at odds with BP's continual 5,000-barrel-a-day drumroll, scientists want to send sophisticated instruments to the ocean floor to get a far more accurate picture of how much oil is really gushing from the well.

"The answer is no to that," a BP spokesman says. "We're not going to take any extra efforts now to calculate flow there."

That's just outrageous. Now I'm really angry. How does BP get to decide who can have access to the seafloor? The corporation has a permit to drill, and a responsibility to clean up its mess. Why does the government keep deferring to it? Why is it allowed to dictate what does and doesn't happen on public property? Why do our public agencies keep allowing it do whatever it wants?

There's at least one quite likely explanation for the discrepancy between what the Purdue scientist measured from the video of the leaking pipe and what BP is saying about what's on the surface.

And here it is: "It appears that the application of the subsea dispersant is actually working," says BP's chief operating officer. "The oil in the immediate vicinity of the well and the ships and rigs working in the area is diminished from previous observations."

And, considering that all the oil we can't see is polluting the Gulf, we can reasonably ask, In what way is that "working" for BP?

"The amount of oil being spilled will help determine BP's liability," confirms retiring U.S. Coast Guard admiral Thad Allen. But despite "overseeing the operation" on our behalf, Allen seems to be doing nothing—incredibly enough—to ensure that we actually send down some instruments designed to get the best possible estimate of *how much oil.*

I am not impressed with the Coast Guard so far. Admiral Thad Allen becomes to me a one-dimensional government talking head: the Thadmiral. Does he deserve to be a caricature? Of course not; does anyone? But in my anger, that's what happens.

Under the Clean Water Act, penalties are based on the number of barrels deemed spilled. Those penalties range from $1,100 to $4,300 a barrel, depending on the extent of the company's negligence. At, say, 5 million barrels, and if BP were found willfully negligent, it could face a fine of over $20 billion. So, yes, the dispersant is "working." Get it?

Dispersants begin accumulating well-deserved criticism. When broken up by dispersants, "The oil's not at the surface, so it doesn't look so bad," says Louisiana State University veterinary medicine professor Kevin Kleinow, "but you have a situation where it's more available to fish." By breaking oil into small particles, dispersants make it easier for fish and other sea life to soak up the oil's toxic chemicals. That can impair animals' immune systems, gills, and reproductive systems.

Marine toxicologist Dr. Susan Shaw says the dispersant "is increasing the hydrocarbon in the water." Dr. Samantha Joye says, "There's just as good a chance that this dispersant is killing off a critical portion of the microbial community as that it's stimulating the breakdown of oil." Louisiana State University environmental chemist Ed Overton is of the opinion that "we've gone past any normal use of dispersants." LSU's Robert Twilley wryly observes, "There are certain things with dispersants that are of benefit, and there are negatives, and we're having problems evaluating those trade-offs."

News flash! A new study shows that dispersant is no more toxic to aquatic life than oil alone. Okay, thanks, but that's not the question. The question is this: Is the mix more toxic to marine life than either alone? Part of the answer to that is: Yes, the mix is more toxic than dispersant alone, at least in lab tests. On the other hand, will dispersant, as its proponents insist, help speed the oil's degradation into harmlessness? Maybe; but will it also speed oil-caused mortality first? The problem is, no one really knows what will happen out in the complex Gulf. Everyone's guessing, and at best there are, indeed, trade-offs.

"This is what we call the Junk," Captain Keith Kennedy says derisively as he steers us from Venice, Louisiana, through the Industrial Canal. It's hard to imagine a more awful waterfront, and the whole place smells like petroleum. That's one reason a good chunk of southern Louisiana is called Cancer Alley.

The angled light, yellow through the heavy haze of moist air, joins the sounds of gulls and engines to make a Gulf morning. Once upon a time there was a wild coast here. Must have been magnificent.

Until a couple of weeks ago, Kennedy fished for redfish, "specs"—sea trout—and tarpon.

"When I first heard about the blowout, I didn't really think much about it. These things do happen. I figured they'd have it under control pretty quick. Their big metal thing didn't seem to work. I have to believe they're doing the best they can."

There is no single Mississippi River mouth. The mighty, muddy Mississippi speaks in tongues; her song is a chorale, her delta is a polyglot of channels. We're gonna run down via the channel called the Grand Pass, and from there through the Coast Guard Cut to East Bay, directly confronting the open Gulf of Mexico.

We pass a swimming alligator. A river otter pops its head up briefly.

A peregrine falcon comes high over the distant marsh, assessing the shorebirds for any weakness.

If oil comes into any of these channels, there is no way people can clean it from the intricate intimacy of these marshes.

One area with many resting birds is boomed. But birds fly. We're seeing pelicans, gulls, and terns diving. There's a slick near the diving birds. It could be natural. I don't see or smell any oil. There's no rainbow sheen or scent. It's very thin on the water, and at first Kennedy and I both think it's a slick from a school of fish below.

But then he spots some floating flecks that don't look familiar. Using a bait net, Captain Kennedy collects one, then a larger blob. The stuff's a bit gooey, the consistency of peanut butter but stickier. It smells like petroleum. It doesn't dissolve in water. It's hard to get off our hands. This is our first actual contact with the actual crude oil. It's nasty stuff. Let's hope we don't explode.

We pass a shack called Paradise, and another called Happy Ending. By now everything seems laden with portent; every sight and sign seems ominously like some metaphor of the all too real.

A rather gratifying amount of public and media interest arises over the fate of the magnificent bluefin tuna, which grows to over half a ton and whose numbers have been demolished by overfishing. Swimming at highway speeds, they tunnel throughout the whole Atlantic, but when spawning on our side of the ocean they migrate into the Gulf of Mexico. And this is spawning season. And though they can live for decades and grow to fifteen hundred pounds, they start out by hatching from millions of minute eggs to begin life as tiny drifting larvae. At the Gulf Coast Research Laboratory, a biologist opines, "This places the young larvae, I think, in a precarious position in respect to the location and magnitude of the spill." A tuna plankton expert here adds, "Large numbers of bluefin tuna larvae on the western edge of the Loop Current might be impacted by the oil spill as they move northward through the loop." Finding and counting fish larvae is painstaking work. They'll have to compare this year's numbers to prior and subsequent years. It'll take a while to learn more.

Understanding accrues slowly. Reactions happen at a different tempo. In the third week of May, the government suddenly closes 46,000 square miles to fishing, or about 19 percent of the Gulf of Mexico's federal waters.

The Louisiana Seafood Promotion and Marketing Board whistles in the dark that seafood from the areas not closed is still both available and safe; and more than half the state's oyster areas remain open. But as a local seafood market owner says, "Perception is everything."

And here's a different perception of the whole situation. The delta's Native Americans include the Pointe-au-Chien tribe. A century ago, Natives like them, isolated, illiterate, non-English-speaking, unable to get to New Orleans, missed the opportunity to claim land and territory after the Louisiana Purchase, in 1803—even though it had for millennia all been theirs. Much of southern Louisiana was claimed by the federal government, which auctioned a lot of it to land companies in the 1800s. Later, oil companies bought much of southern Louisiana. They swindled the Natives out of any crumbs they'd gotten.

Native Americans have in the past accused land grabbers and oil companies of seizing waterlands that rightfully belonged to them. They sued to regain vast tracts now owned by big landholding and energy companies. Needless to say, they lost.

"If you see pictures from the sky, how many haphazard cuts were made in the land, it blows your mind," says Patty Ferguson of the Pointe-au-Chien tribe. "We weren't just fishermen. We raised crops, we had wells. We can't anymore because of the saltwater intrusion." Sixty-year-old tribal elder Sydney Verdin feels a tingle of vengeful satisfaction. "I'm happy for the oil spill. Now the oil companies are paying for it the same way we've had to pay for it," says Verdin. "I can't think of one Indian who ever made any money from oil."

May 16. Out of the galaxy of goofy ideas, one that seems positively prosaic: they'll stick a tube into the leaking pipe. Why didn't any of us think of that? (Actually, of course, we did.) But their leaky tube is half-assed and it less-than-half works.

Incessant national airing of live video shows a lot of oil streaming past the mile-long tube sucking some of the oil from the ruptured pipe up to a waiting ship. BP is in an interesting bind. They say they're collecting 5,000 barrels a day through the tube. But for weeks they've been saying the well is leaking 5,000 barrels a day. Yet we can all see clearly on TV that most of the gushing oil isn't going into the tube. Busted!

A BP spokesman washes clean, sort of, fessing, "Now that we are collecting 5,000 barrels a day" through the tube, "it [the amount coming out of the pipe] might be a little more than that."

A *little* more? It's *twelve times* more.

Spin cycle: "From the beginning," intones the BP spokesman, "our experts have been saying there really is no reliable way to estimate the flow from the riser, so we have been implementing essentially a response plan." Anyone Buying Propaganda?

It gets better. Two days later, BP decides to announce that it is *not* collecting 5,000 barrels through the tube. "We never said it produced 5,000 barrels a day," says BP's chief operating officer. "I am sorry if you heard it that way." Oh, it's *our* mistake; we all heard it wrong. He says the tube is scarfing more like 2,000 barrels a day.

Lying? I don't know. But, well, actually, yes, since they *did* say, "we are collecting 5,000 barrels a day."

It would make BP look better if its spin doctors can convince us they're collecting less than 5,000 daily, whether it's true or not. Trouble is, we can't tell. Question is: Can we trust BP?

"We cannot trust BP," says Congressman Edward Markey. "It's clear they have been hiding the actual consequences of this spill." Purdue Professor Wereley, who'd estimated that the flow is more like 56,000 and 84,000 barrels daily, says, "I don't see any possibility, any scenario under which their number is accurate."

Ian MacDonald of Florida State University, an oceanographer who was among the first to question the official estimate, concludes that BP is obstructing an accurate calculation. "They want to hide the body," he says. Notes Congressman Henry Waxman, who chairs the

House Committee on Energy and Commerce: "It's an absurd position that BP has taken, that it's not important for them to know how much oil is gushing out."

During the third week of May, Tony Hayward says, "Everything we can see at the moment suggests that the overall environment impacts of this will be very, very modest."

When CNN's Candy Crowley asks Thad Allen for his response, the admiral responds, "Obviously they are not modest here in Louisiana. We don't want to perpetuate any kind of notion at all that this is anything less than potentially catastrophic for this country."

Crowley responds with what most of us are thinking: "Well, this is why people don't really trust BP, because here is the CEO of the company out there saying, 'We think the environment impact will be very modest.'"

Allen adds, "We're accountable. And we should be held accountable for this. We are taking this very, very seriously."

Thank you, Thadmiral. It's about time we got a government message in a plain-paper wrapper, and that we got to hear you come right out and say that.

In brown and orange globs, in sheets thick as latex paint, oil begins coating the reedy edges of Louisiana's wetlands. As crude oozes in the entrances, hope flees out the back door.

The worst fears of environmental disaster are, it seems, being realized. "Twenty-four miles of Plaquemines Parish is destroyed," rages a despairing Billy Nungesser, head of the parish. "Everything in it is dead. There is no life in that marsh. It's destroying our marsh, inch by inch." And because this is not a spill but an ongoing eruption, his prognosis: more of the same, coming ashore for weeks and months. Louisiana's governor says, "This is not sheen, this is heavy oil." He also fears that "this is just the beginning." He wields the statistics at stake: 60,000 jobs in Louisiana's $3 billion fishing industry; that Louisiana produces 70 percent of the Gulf's seafood, nearly one-third of the continental United

States' seafood. In addition, throughout the Gulf of Mexico region in a typical year, commercial fishermen usually catch more than 1 billion pounds of fish and shellfish, and nearly 6 million recreational fishermen make 25 million fishing trips. (One cannot help wondering whether the sea creatures would rather face our oil or our nets and hooks.)

The EPA tells BP: you have a twenty-four-hour deadline to choose a less toxic chemical dispersant. Dispersants have gotten our attention, but plenty of other chemicals—many of them similar—drain from America's Heartland to America's Wetland and beyond. Soaps, dish-washing liquids, and industrial solvents are all oil dispersants. Down the drain they go. Household cleaners, ingredients used to make plastics, and pesticides. Medical residue that goes from body to potty to Gulf. Livestock waste and traces of the drugs they've been given. Enough estrogen from birth control pills to bend genders and mess the sex of fish. Caffeine. Herbicides toxic to aquatic animals, by the thousands of tons. And good old (actually new, synthetic) fertilizers that cause algae populations to skyrocket, leading to an explosion of the bacteria that decompose them, which depletes the deeper water's oxygen, killing everything. That's the "dead zone" that happens every year in the Gulf (and now in hundreds of other coastal places around the world and is coming soon to a river mouth near you). The Gulf dead zone holds the distinction of first and worst, and this year it's set to break a record: it's about 8,000 square miles, the size of New Jersey. Or Massachusetts. (Some of us remember when it was a cute little dead zone no bigger than Delaware.) There's actually a federal goal of shrinking it to less than 1,900 square miles by 2015. Agencies planned to accomplish that by getting midwestern farmers to put less fertilizer into the river system. But good luck. "It's getting bigger over the years, and it's extending more into Texas," says Nancy Rabalais, director of the Louisiana Universities Marine Consortium. So one more thing is killing the Gulf, and it's a big one: agriculture. Modern, industrialized, artificialized, corporatized, heavily lobbied agriculture. When the oil is gone, the water of the mighty Mississippi will remain all too fertile for the Gulf's good.

For vigilance, we the people pay taxes that support our government's defense of our interests. Among the vigilant defenders is that government agency called the Minerals Management Service, a branch of the Interior Department. Its mission, if it decides to accept it: make sure extraction of oil and other nonliving resources is done well, done safely, and done to certain specified standards. And yet in at least one region—though there's no evidence that this was an issue in the Gulf—the MMS got a little too informal when it mattered. In 2008, it came to light that eight MMS employees had accepted lavish gifts and had partied with—and in some cases had sex with—employees from the energy companies they regulated. A formal investigation found the agency's Denver office rife with "a culture of substance abuse and promiscuity." The report further noted, "Sexual relationships with prohibited sources cannot, by definition, be arms-length."

On May 19, Interior Secretary Salazar announces that he's dividing the disgraced Minerals Management Service into three units. One might say he's dispersing the agency. The agency had been created by Ronald Reagan's infamous Interior secretary James Watt. That explains some things. The current agency's three missions—energy development, enforcement, and revenue collection—"are conflicting missions and must be separated," Salazar says. Applause. No more sex, drugs, and rock-and-oil. In a few days the agency's chief will quit under pressure.

The agency has been collecting royalties from the companies it regulates. That lowers the incentive for strict safety oversight. The new idea: there'll be a Bureau of Safety and Environmental Enforcement (this one will inspect oil rigs and enforce regulations), a Bureau of Ocean Energy Management, Regulation and Enforcement (this one will oversee offshore drilling leasing and development), and an Office of Natural Resources Revenue (to collect the billions of dollars in royalties from mining and drilling companies extracting resources from American territory).

In Grand Isle and Barataria Bay, Louisiana, hideously oiled gulls and pelicans struggle to keep the life they'll lose. Parent birds have brought to their eggs coatings of oil, blocking oxygen from entering the shell. Chicks that manage to hatch will know only a short life on the gummy surface of a petroleum-coated planet. Behind the lines of useless boom, oil coats the marsh cane.

"It took hundreds of years to create this," one fisherman says, lowballing the time required by about six thousand years. "And it's gone just like that."

Meanwhile, President Obama announces that automakers must meet a minimum fuel-efficiency standard of 35.5 miles a gallon by 2016. Savings over the five-year phase-in: 1.8 billion barrels of oil. That means saving a million barrels of oil daily, about seventeen times faster than it's leaking from the blowout.

Gulf breezes smell of oil. Marshes smell of oil. And "All systems are go" for the seventy-fifth annual Louisiana Shrimp and Petroleum Festival. Says the festival's director, "We will honor the two industries as we always do."

On May 24 in Port Fourchon, Louisiana, seven Greenpeace members board the ship *Harvey Explorer* that's heading north in July to support drilling operations in the Arctic. In oil from the blowout, they write, "Is the Arctic Next?" on the hull. They're all charged with *felonies.*

No one from BP, Transocean, or anyone else has been charged with anything. That's our government Bullying People. (It'll take about three months for the squeaky wheels of justice to dismiss the charges.)

A house divided: Coast Guard admiral Thad Allen says on May 23 that BP's access to the mile-deep well means the government could not take the lead to stop the leak. Yet a few hours later outside BP's Houston headquarters, a tough-talking Interior secretary Salazar (who early in the crisis vowed to "keep the boot on the neck" of BP) says, "If we find they're not doing what they're supposed to be doing, we'll push them out of the way." This prompts the Thadmiral to wonder out loud to reporters, "To push BP out of the way would raise the question of, 'replace them with what?'" He adds, "They have the eyes and ears that are down there."

Okay, at least now he's pretty much acknowledged who's really in charge. Fact is, the government, as the *Christian Science Monitor* puts it, is "incapable of taking over from BP at the wellhead and unwilling to displace the web of contractors leading the cleanup at BP's behest."

Allen remarks about BP, "They are necessarily the modality by which this is going to get solved."

In my experience, people who use the word "modality" never quite get to the point.

He gets to the point: "They're exhausting every technical means possible to deal with that leak. I am satisfied with the coordination that's going on."

I'm not. Nor is anyone else I know. A few days later, even the president will say he regrets not realizing that oil companies did not "have their act together when it came to worst-case scenarios." He will add a stern admonishment: "Make no mistake, BP is operating at our direction."

It's a mistake I will continue to make—often—in the upcoming weeks. Meanwhile, enraged over BP's stonewalling and its refusal to entertain new ideas and alternate solutions—or to make any seemingly sincere attempt to collect oil at the surface—Plaquemines Parish president Billy Nungesser rails, "BP has taken over the Gulf of Mexico, and we're doing nothing to stop them."

Indeed, it feels to many as if the Coast Guard has handed BP the keys to our car and climbed into the back seat.

Louisiana's governor declares a commercial fisheries' failure to trigger aid. Within a week, the fisheries disaster declarations spread to include Alabama and Mississippi. Aid means tax dollars. Aid means that oil is not as cheap as it seems at the pump. We pay anyway.

Here's who doesn't get dispersants: the head of the EPA. Lisa Jackson, Environmental Protection Agency chief, exclaims, "Oh my God, it's so thick!" as she assesses a cupful of the oily mess dipped from the mouth of the Mississippi. "At a minimum what we can say is dispersants didn't work here," Jackson actually says. She adds, "When you see stuff like this, it's clear it isn't a panacea."

Panacea? As if perfection would be to just send all the oil out of sight, out of mind? Isn't that BP's dream scenario, to make it all seem to just go away by sinking it all below the surface? I don't agree. At a minimum, what we *can* say is that dispersants don't work if your goal is to avoid polluting the water on a massive scale.

Panacea? Dr. Susan Shaw of the Maine-based Marine Environmental Research Institute says, "The worst of these dispersants—sold by the name Corexit 9527—is the one they've been using most. It ruptures red blood cells and causes fish to bleed. With 800,000 gallons of this, we can only imagine the death that will be caused." But that's the problem: we can only imagine. It causes harm in laboratory tests at certain concentrations, but the dose makes the poison, and we have no clarity on what it's doing in the Gulf.

Panacea? The *Exxon Valdez* disaster is what first linked Corexit to respiratory, nerve, liver, kidney, and blood disorders. *Exxon Valdez* cleanup workers reported blood in their urine. EPA data shows Corexit more toxic and less effective than other approved dispersants.

A BP spokesman calls Corexit "pretty effective," adding, "I'm not sure about the others." BP's main reason for continuing to use Corexit appears to be its close ties to the manufacturer.

Panacea? Dr. Shaw writes in the *New York Times* after actually diving in part of the dispersant-and-oil mixture, "What I witnessed was a surreal, sickening scene beyond anything I could have imagined." She describes the murky mixture drifting a few meters down, then concludes, "The dispersants have made for cleaner beaches. But they're not worth the destruction they cause at sea, far out of sight. It would be better to halt their use and just siphon and skim as much of the oil off the surface as we can. The Deepwater Horizon spill has done enough damage, without our adding to it."

The pressure seems to be pushing the EPA. Its officials finally obtain and make public a list of the concoctions' ingredients. One version of Corexit ("corrects it"; get it?) contains benzene and 2-butoxyethanol, linked to destruction of red blood cells and cancers in lab studies of monkeys, rats, mice, rabbits, and dogs, which can lead to kidney, spleen, or liver damage. Also it caused breathing difficulties, skin irritation, physical weakness and unsteadiness, sluggishness, convulsions, birth defects, and fewer offspring in mammals. This stuff, you *don't* want to swallow. The head of the Louisiana Shrimp Association calls Corexit "the Gulf's Agent Orange."

Now EPA administrator Lisa Jackson orders BP to take "immediate steps to scale back the use of dispersants" by 50 to 75 percent. (Well, which one is it?) While the government had approved the use of dispersants before this blowout, no one had anticipated that they'd ever be used at this scale and in these quantities.

My question is: Why are they using dispersants at all? As the incessant video shows, the entire leak is erupting from one small pipe. It's not like a massive tanker spill, where it's all in the water already and there's no ongoing "source." This is very different. They have their hands around this whole thing at that pipe. It seems to me it could *all* be captured. After all—*it's an oil well.*

And now: voider of her own election, former Alaska governor turned national misfortune Sarah Palin comes out of her nutshell again to say that—to make a long story short—Obama's response has been slow. It's another signature blast of her sound-and-fury insight. And it prompts White House spokesman Robert Gibbs to suggest that Palin needs her own personal blowout preventer.

Granted, the administration's response does seem slow. And the Coast Guard, in my estimation, has been disappointing. Our president disagrees with the likes of Palin and me, saying, "Those who think we were either slow on the response or lacked urgency, don't know the facts."

———

In a late-May press release, a group called Public Employees for Environmental Responsibility alerts us to the details and particulars of the BP response plan. Basically, there aren't any. Plus, it's so full of nonsense that apparently no regulator read it seriously.

Dated June 30, 2009, the "BP Regional Oil Spill Response Plan—Gulf of Mexico" covers all of the company's various operations in the Gulf. The plan lists "Sea Lions, Seals, Sea Otters, and Walruses" as "Sensitive Biological Resources" in the Gulf. None of those animals live there (at least not since the Caribbean monk seal went extinct in the 1950s). BP has obviously just cut-and-pasted from documents written for drilling in Alaska. The document also gives a Japanese home-shopping website as a "primary equipment providers for BP in the Gulf of Mexico Region for rapid deployment of spill response resources on a 24 hour, 7 days a week basis." The sea turtle expert you're supposed to call is a researcher who's been dead for five years. And the 600-page plan *never discusses how to stop a deepwater blowout.*

By May's last waning days, some fishermen hired to do cleanup by BP say they have become ill after working long hours near oil and dispersant. Headaches, dizziness, nausea. Difficulty breathing. Burning eyes. The EPA's air monitoring has detected odors strong enough to cause sickness. The EPA's website warns coastal residents that these chemicals "may cause short-lived headache, eye, nose and throat irritation, or nausea."

BP says it's unaware of any health complaints.

That's because: "You don't bite the hand that feeds you," says the president of the Commercial Fishermen's Association. Many fishermen have told *him* about feeling ill. "You left in the morning, you were OK. Out on the water, you've got a pounding headache, throwing up." And yet, he says, "BP has the opinion that they are not getting sick."

Maybe time for a second opinion.

On May 26 BP subjects us to two new vocabulary terms. Of all the kooky names for dopey ideas, these two take the cake: "junk shot" and "top kill." Let's use them in one sentence: "They don't work either." The rodeo names reflect the rodeo thinking that got us here. One half-baked idea after another.

The Bright Ploy this time: attempt to stop the upward flow of oil by sending heavy drilling fluid down the well. Workers have triggered the original blowout and explosion by *removing* the heavy drilling fluid that had, in fact, been holding down the oil. So we might call this the "oops" strategy, as in "Oops, let's go back to what was working before we caused the blowout."

It's *way* too late now, though. As the University of Texas's Petroleum Engineering Department chairman says, "You have the equivalent of six fire hoses blasting oil and gas upward and two fire hoses blasting mud down. They are at a disadvantage."

BP pegs its chance of success at 60 to 70 percent. (New definition of "pegged": made up, fabricated.) "We're doing everything we can to bring it to closure, and actually we're executing this top kill job as efficiently and effectively as we can," says BP chief operating officer Doug Suttles.

I don't know what to make of the word "actually" there. Is he surprised? Or does he know that we know that he's just BS-ing us?

The University of Texas's Petroleum Engineering Department chairman watches a live video and says, "It's not going well."

"I wouldn't say it's failed yet," says BP's chief operating officer. With dramatic flair that seems oblivious to the sheer irresponsibility it implies, BP reminds us that the method *has never been tried before at such depth.* "This is the first time the industry has had to confront this issue in this water depth," gushes BP's CEO, the ever-perspicacious Tony Hayward, "and there is a lot of real-time learning going on."

"We've never tried this before in water this deep" is a bad answer when you've been *drilling in water this deep.*

"It's a wait-and-see game here right now; so far nothing unfavorable. . . . The absence of any news is good news," says the chipper Thadmiral.

Thad Allen was a hero in the Hurricane Katrina disaster, yet I find myself unable to believe what he's telling us. Not entirely fair, but my anger is stoking my cynicism. The impression given—at least the impression I form—is that Admiral Allen is up to his neck in oil and over his head in this debacle. In my mind he becomes government chief of useless statements.

Next, Thad Allen begins talking enthusiastically about BP's planned "junk shot." "They're actually going to take a bunch of debris, shredded-up tires, golf balls, and things like that and under very high pressure shoot it into the preventer itself and see if they can clog it up and stop the leak."

There's that word "actually" again.

It all fails.

Obviously, Admiral Allen has been bugging me. But to be honest, I'm not sure how much of that is him—and how much is me. It's difficult to maintain one's objectivity amid so much subjective confusion. The drilling rig wasn't his responsibility, and he certainly didn't cause the blowout.

BP announces that it has spent $930 million responding to the spill. The company is acting like an emotionally distant husband seeking appreciation from his wife and children by telling them how much his bills cost.

And rather belatedly, Tony Hayward calls the blowout "a very significant environmental crisis" and a "catastrophe." After he'd earlier said the oil leaked has been "tiny" compared with the "very big ocean," his media coaches are earning their fees. But he should try telling us something we *don't* already know.

So far, about 26,000 people have filed damage claims.

Researchers on the University of South Florida College of Marine Science vessel *Weatherbird II* report discovering a massive amount of oil-polluted water beneath the Gulf of Mexico, in a layer hundreds of feet thick, down to a depth of well over 3,000 feet, drifting in a several-miles-wide plume stretching twenty-two miles from the leaking wellhead northeast toward Alabama. Chemical oceanographer David Hollander makes this announcement, saying with all due scientific caution that it's likely oil from the blown-out well.

But really, what else could it be? Let's review: Oil is gushing from a well. One end of the plume is in the vicinity of that well. And the company running the drilling operation has been spraying dispersants on the seafloor and at the surface to keep as much of the oil underwater as is humanly possible. Scientists have detected oil underwater, ergo—what else could it be from?

"This is when all the animals are reproducing and hatching, so the damage at this depth will be much worse," says Dr. Larry McKinney of the Harte Research Institute for Gulf of Mexico Studies. "We're not talking about adults on the surface; it will impact on the young—and potentially a generational life cycle. At the depth that these plumes are at, the sea will be toxic for God knows how long."

The federal government closes more fishing areas, to the west and south, on May 25. The closed area now: 54,096 square miles, over 22 percent of the Gulf of Mexico's federal waters. "This leaves approximately more than 77 percent still open for fishing," our National Marine Fisheries Service adds with silver-lining turn-a-frown-upside-down think-positiveness.

Meanwhile, U.S. Geological Survey director Marcia McNutt says the oil leaked in the last five weeks totals somewhere between 18 million and 39 million gallons. That's way past *Exxon Valdez*'s 11 million gallons. (So it's said; others insist the total was much more than Exxon ever admitted.)

And speaking of Alaska, Shell Oil has been poised to start exploratory drilling this summer as far as 140 miles off Alaska's coast. But now the Obama administration suspends proposed exploratory drilling in the Arctic Ocean until 2011. *Alaska politicians are pissed!* They have to be—about 90 percent of Alaska's general revenue comes from the petroleum industry. It's what helps get them elected. They're like sled dogs who start the day with a big bowl of oil and then get harnessed up to pull Petroleum's sled.

※

"I was certain I was going to die," Deepwater Horizon survivor Stephen Stone tells a congressional hearing panel. He says the April 20 blast was "hardly the first thing to go wrong." He testifies, "This event was set in motion years ago by these companies needlessly rushing to make money faster, while cutting corners to save money." More than a day after the explosion, Stone was finally back on land. "Before we were allowed to leave, we were lined up and made to take a drug test. It was only then, 28 hours after the explosion, that I was given access to a phone, and was allowed to call my wife and tell her I was OK."

Then, a few days later, a representative of rig owner Transocean asked him to sign a document "stating I was not injured, in order to get $5,000 for the loss of my personal possessions." He declined to sign.

These are the kinds of people we're dealing with.

Eight workers airlifted to a Louisiana hospital this week were released. That's the good news. One fisherman hospitalized after becoming ill while cleaning up oil—severe headaches, nosebleeds, and so on—files a temporary restraining order in federal court against BP. He wants BP to give workers masks and not harass workers for publicly voicing their health concerns. He also says, "There were tents set up outside the hospital, where I was stripped of my clothing, washed with water and [had] several showers, before I was allowed into the hospital. When I asked for my clothing, I was told that BP had confiscated all of my clothing and it would not be returned."

A lot of fishermen are reluctant to complain. Making as much as $3,000 a day cleaning up the oil, they fear losing their jobs with BP. If it's partly hush money, BP's plan for them is working.

Of course, a BP spokesman says there have been no threats against workers for speaking out. He adds, "If they have any concerns, they should raise them with their supervisors."

In the space after that statement, I hear "and not with anyone else." When I ask one worker a question, he says to me, "No comment." When I ask him if his supervisors have told him to say that, he says, "Yeah."

"The only work fishermen can get right now is with BP," affirms the fisherman seeking the restraining order.

A fisherman's wife says her husband called her from a boat, saying, "This one's hanging over the boat throwing up. This one says he's dizzy, and he's feeling faint." She says they were downwind of it and the smell was "so strong they could almost taste it."

In addition to concern over oil, many fear the *million* gallons of dispersant served so far. The dispersant's own manufacturer states that people should "avoid breathing vapor" and that when this product is present in certain concentrations in the air, workers should wear masks.

The fisherman's wife says her husband came home so sick he collapsed into a recliner without eating dinner or saying hello to her or their children. After three weeks of coughing and feeling weak, he agreed to go for medical help. His wife's been trying to get BP to give the workers masks.

BP says workers who want to wear masks are "free to do so"—as long as they receive instructions from their supervisors on "how to use them."

A spokesman for the shrimpers' association insists that BP has told workers they are not allowed to wear masks: "Some of our men asked, and they were told they'd be fired if they wore masks." Environmental groups offering free masks to workers have been told by BP that they can't do that. If you wear a respirator you have bought with your own money, if you wear a respirator someone has given you—you're fired.

And here's why: oil is not their problem. Their problem is that they are eating. At least, that's what BP says. BP's CEO and chief harlequin Tony Hayward actually says, "Food poisoning is clearly a big issue." He adds, "It's something we've got to be very mindful of. It's one of the big issues." He himself seems to be suffering from foot-in-mouth disease.

"Headaches, shortness of breath, nosebleeds—there's nothing there that suggests foodborne illness," said Dr. Michael Osterholm of the University of Minnesota School of Public Health. "I don't know what these people have, but it sounds more like a respiratory illness."

The fisherman's wife has better data. She says there's no way her husband and the other men had fallen victim to food poisoning—they were on eight different boats and didn't eat the same food.

The director of Louisiana's Department of Health and Hospitals says, "It's hard to understand if nausea or dizziness or headache is related to the oil or to working in 100-degree heat." (I wonder why BP didn't think of that.) Wearing respirators could help unpack that. No, never mind; we're told that respirators could add to heat stress.

There's another reason the suffering workers aren't using respirators. But get ready for some tortured logic: the head of the federal Occupational Safety and Health Administration (OSHA) says the toxins in the Gulf air aren't concentrated enough to require workers to wear respirators. Based on that, BP says there are no health threats to workers. After public-health advocates criticize both of them, OSHA's head tells C-SPAN that he wouldn't advise using his agency's "out-of-date" guidelines. Confused? It can take your breath away.

Who else can't breathe? A Dauphin Island Sea Lab study finds a dramatic decline in dissolved oxygen near the ocean bottom at sites twelve and twenty-five miles off Alabama. The study's senior scientist, Dr. Monty Graham, announces, "Oxygen is dropping out offshore. We got minimum dissolved oxygen values of 1.7 micrograms per liter." Dissolved oxygen levels below 2 micrograms per liter are considered too low for almost everything that depends on oxygen for normal living. The values found are less than a fifth of normal. Dauphin Island Sea Lab director Dr. George Crozier says, "This is the kind of unexpected consequence that I warned BP representatives of on May 3rd, after they announced the successful application of dispersant at 5,000 feet."

And yet—. Other scientists will find the oxygen depletion rather moderate. And a federal panel of about fifty experts recommends continued use of chemical dispersants, saying populations of the underwater animals likely to be killed have a better chance of rebounding quickly than birds and mammals on the shoreline.

That's probably true, if you decide to be unconcerned about turtles, whales, and dolphins, and if you write off the possibility of effectively capturing floating oil. And at the heart of the matter are two things: dispersants are easy; dispersants make things look better. Plus, no one really knows for certain what would happen here with or without dispersants. There's a lot of guessing on the details.

On the final day of May, engineers begin trying to fit a new "top hat." The dome weighed 100 tons; this cap weighs two tons (further evidence that their shrinking thinking is all over the map). The idea now is that a diamond-bladed pipe cutter will create a smooth cut of the mangled pipe, right at the blowout preventer, to facilitate a tight fit.

Drawback 1: kinks in the pipe have been slowing the rate of leak; cutting the pipe will facilitate a higher flow. Before the pipe is cut, the government has estimated that the oil is flowing at 12,000 to 19,000 barrels a day—meaning at least 20 million gallons since April 21. Now BP says that cutting the kinked pipe will increase the flow by as much as 20 percent. (It'll be more like 300 percent.)

Coast Guard admiral Thad Allen says, "If we don't get as clean a cut as we want, then we'll put something called a 'top hat' over it, which is a little wider fitting, but you have an increased chance that some oil will come out around the sides." Definition of "increased chance": 100 percent certainty. And note: "we," thrice. Quite the sense of camaraderie, the admiral and BP. Boot on their neck or feather boa?

And that brings us to Drawback 2: the diamond blade gets stuck, and a pair of remotely operated hydraulic shears finish a rougher-than-intended job.

"It is an engineer's nightmare," says a Louisiana State University professor. "They're trying to fit a 21-inch cap over a 20-inch pipe a mile away using little robots. That's just horrendously hard to do." Tulane Energy Institute's associate director says it's like trying to place a tiny cap on an open fire hydrant.

BP is doing all it can. "No one wants this over more than I do," says BP CEO Tony Hayward. "I'd like my life back."

So would the families of the people who died on the rig. So would everyone in the Gulf region. Hello.

Meanwhile, an oil spill in Alaska has caused a shutdown of the Trans-Alaska Pipeline. And in a piece headlined "That Was Then, This Is Then," MSNBC's *Rachel Maddow Show* points out that in June 1979, an Alaska spill shut the pipeline at the same time oil gushed for months from a blown-out Mexican well in the Gulf of Mexico. "If you close your eyes and listen to the news reports from back then," she says, "you'd be forgiven for thinking you were listening to today's news." Back then, the well was being drilled by the same company that later changed its name to Transocean. Its blowout preventer had failed. The responses included spreading chemical dispersants, putting out booms along shorelines, and burning floating oil. People worried about "underwater plumes" and the possibility that currents would carry oil to Florida. Being Mexican, they did not have a "top hat"; they tried a "sombrero." When that failed, they tried forcing stuff down the top and pumping metal balls into the well to jam it up. And when that failed, a pair of *relief wells* finally stopped the blowout. Maddow's summation: "The stuff that did not work then is the same stuff that does not work now: same busted blowout preventer, same ineffective booms, same toxic dispersant, same failed containment domes, same junk shot, same top kill; it's all the same." Point being: nothing's changed in preparedness or response. What's changed is the depth. Ixtoc was in about 160 feet of water; the present blowing well starts a mile down. "All they've gotten better at," Maddow notes, "is making the risks worse."

Congress has certainly played a role—and been played—in encouraging risky drilling. One trend has been to undo the tapestry of prior protections. In 1995, Congress "decided" to reduce the government's royalties on oil and gas extracted from deep water (you can bet the idea came from Big Oil in an envelope marked "Campaign

Contribution"). The goal and result: more drilling encouraged. Okay, fine; bringing more of our oil under domestic production *is* good for national security. But other nations charge more. Oil taxes and royalties in the United States are considered much lower than elsewhere in the world. Our country should benefit financially, as the oil companies do. And what else isn't fine is that this encouraged more and riskier drilling but not more safety. Industry assurances that deepwater drilling was "safe" rocked a willing Congress to sleep on the issue. The fact that accidents are rare and unpredictable has substituted for the obvious truth and certainty that accidents do happen.

In 2001 the president's National Energy Policy report (it was actually the vice president's; the first page is Dick Cheney's submittal letter to George W. Bush) ordered agencies to increase oil production and remove "excessive regulations." The report has a lot of good ideas. For instance, it says, "A primary goal of the National Energy Policy is to add supply from diverse sources. This means domestic oil, gas, and coal. It also means hydropower and nuclear power. And it means making greater use of non-hydro renewable sources now available." But in practice, federal agencies didn't get past the first sentence on that list. Maybe they never really intended to; I don't know.

In 2005, despite high oil prices and even President George W. Bush saying oil companies needed no further drilling incentives, the Republican-dominated Congress again lowered the royalties oil companies are required to pay our national Treasury. That's nonsensical, especially in an era of massive federal deficits, but part of the ideology appears to be a desire to starve the government so there is scant money for wasteful social programs like education, health, and environmental protection. And while, yes, there are excessive regulations, there is also excessive greed. Regulations don't threaten business; they threaten greed, the greed that threatens both us and our nation's economy. In 2006, Louisiana's congressional delegation supported giving a share of oil royalties to states that allowed drilling. This means using national oil revenue directly to achieve state policies that benefit Big Oil. Nice giveback. Clever.

And while calling for more incentives to drill, baby, Congress slashed those annoying safety regs. From 2002 to 2008, Congress approved budgets reducing regulatory staff by over 15 percent. So we got more complex, deeper drilling, higher-volume oil pools, no further safety. In 2000, the Interior Department had voiced concerns that industry's extensive use of contractors and inexperienced offshore workers in deep water created new risks. *And* a 2004 Coast Guard study—repeatedly cited by Congress's own Congressional Research Service—warned, "Oil spill response personnel did not appear to have even a basic knowledge of the equipment required to support salvage or spill clean-up operations." Lawmakers slept peacefully. Environmental groups focused on maintaining the existing moratorium on new drilling, not operational safety or response. Consequently, regulatory proposals often drew fewer than ten "public" comments, but most came from the oil industry.

With democracy working on half of its cylinders, the Interior Department politely filled the public-interest vacuum with a new tendency to better serve, rather than better monitor, the oil companies. The person in charge of offshore drilling for Interior boasted that he "oversaw a 50 percent rise in oil production." But he was supposed to be a regulator, not a fixer. Ergo: deep blowout preparedness = zero.

EARLY JUNE

A *dead dolphin* rots in the shore weeds; an oil-stained gull stands atop its corpse. "When we found this dolphin, it was the saddest darn thing to look at," says the cleanup worker who is taking a news team on a surreptitious tour. "There is a lot of cover-up for BP. They specifically informed us that they don't want these pictures of the dead animals." The shore is littered with oiled marine creatures, some dead, others struggling. "They keep trying to clean themselves," the guide says. "They try and they try, but they can't do it. Some of the things I've seen would make you sick." He mentions that he recently found five turtles in oil. Three were dead. Two were dying. He says, "Nature is cruel, but what's happening here is crueler. No living creature should endure that kind of suffering."

News crews are now being barred from and escorted away from public beaches and public roads. The cops acknowledge that they're taking orders from BP. No one can figure out how or why this is being allowed, but as far as anyone can tell, it seems the Coast Guard is abetting BP.

On the first day of June 2010, BP is trying to cover the leak with the new top hat. Akin to applying condoms after they're pregnant. To defeat ice formation this time, technicians will inject heated water and methanol into the cap. To capture more oil, they begin closing the vents.

The Coast Guard Thadmiral tells us the goal is to gradually capture more of the oil. For anybody who didn't grasp that, he compares the process to stopping the flow of water from a garden hose with your finger: "You don't want to put your finger down too quickly, or let it off too quickly." A rather odd analogy. What does he mean?

After robots place the cap, video shows *plenty* of escaping oil still billowing around the cap's lip. "A positive step but not a solution," says the Thadmiral. "Even if successful, this is only a temporary and partial fix and we must continue our aggressive response operations at the—"

Okay, never mind. The plan is to capture most of the spewing oil and bring it up to a surface ship.

The Thadmiral says the "ultimate solution"—relief wells—is not likely till August.

Relief wells, alternate take: "The probability of them hitting it on the very first shot is virtually nil," says the president of the American Association of Petroleum Geologists, David Rensink, who spent thirty-nine years in the oil industry, mostly in offshore exploration. "If they get it on the first three or four shots they'd be very lucky."

BP shares lose 15 percent of their value on news that its attempted stop-from-the-top hasn't worked, indicating that the leak—and BP's liabilities for economic and environmental damages—will likely continue mounting for months.

The Justice Department announces criminal and civil investigations into the Gulf oil disaster. "All possible violations of the law," including the Clean Water Act, Oil Pollution Act, Endangered Species Act.

About 15,000 barrels of oil a day begin finding their way out the high end of the pipe and into the ship *Discoverer Enterprise.*

BP's Tony Hayward, sounding like he's trying to convince even himself, says the cap will likely capture "the majority, probably the vast majority" of the gushing oil. Ever the cheerleader for the sheer magnificence of the enterprise, he himself gushes, "It has been difficult to predict because all of this is a first. Every piece of this implementation is the first time it's been done in 5,000 feet of water, a mile beneath the sea surface."

Yes, Tony, that's what people mean when they say "total lack of preparedness."

As for BP's statement that the present cap might be capturing "the vast majority" of the spew, Purdue's Professor Wereley—who'd initially busted BP and the Coast Guard with his estimate that the blowout was spewing at least 56,000 barrels daily—says, "I don't see that as being a credible claim. I would say to BP, show the American public the before and after shots of the evidence on which they're basing that claim."

Similarly, a University of California researcher says, "I do not know how BP can make that assertion when they don't know how much oil is escaping." He believes that cutting the kinked riser pipe in order to install the cap increased the flow by far more than the 20 percent BP and government officials had predicted. He speculates it may be spewing what BP had called the "worst case": a 100,000-barrels-a-day blowout. He says the video feed now appears to show "a freely flowing pipe," adding, "From what it looks like right now, it suggests to me they're capturing a negligible fraction."

BP says "the vast majority," the academic says "a negligible fraction." Let's see if the Thadmiral can mediate. Ready? Go: "They continue to optimize production," Allen tells reporters. Then, digging himself an alternate escape route, he adds, "I have never said this is going well. We're throwing everything at it that we've got."

BP intends to hook up a new, tighter cap, with more pipes that will attach to more vessels. Its Bigger Plans include four collection vessels passing oil to two tanker ships. The collection vessels can process a combined total of between 60,000 and 80,000 barrels per day.

The discerning reader may note this subtlety: there's a slight difference among that planned capacity, the 1,000 barrels per day BP had first announced, its grudging acknowledgment and later insistence that 5,000 barrels were leaking, and its refusal to engage on the question of "how much" after Purdue professor Steve Wereley estimated 56,000 to 84,000 barrels. Yet BP plans to collect essentially the very same amount the professor estimated. What does that tell you?

Meanwhile, the Thadmiral says that within the next week all these activities "could take leakage almost down to zero." Says he's ordered a special task group to work up new estimates on how much oil is still gushing out. (It's about time.) Says, "I'm not going to declare victory on anything until I have the numbers." He adds for emphasis, "Show me the numbers."

Here's the only number we need: zero. Show us zero.

On June 9, BP shares hemorrhage an incredible 16 percent, to $29.20. BP shares have lost half their value, wiping off $90 billion in market capitalization, since the blowout began.

On June 10 the official government-accepted rate of leakage gets doubled. The U.S. government's flow rate assessment team announces, "The lowest estimate that we're seeing that the scientists think is credible is probably about 20,000 barrels, and the highest is probably a little over 40,000." Twenty-five thousand, near the low-end estimate, is over 1 million gallons a day. The *Exxon Valdez* tanker leaked an estimated 11 million gallons.

"I think we're still dealing with the flow estimate. We're still trying to refine those numbers," says—guess who—Coast Guard admiral Thad Allen. Almost certainly the rate is changing; it may be increasing, because once oil starts flowing out of a geologic formation, the rock erodes with the flow and the channels enlarge.

The Gulf isn't the only thing hemorrhaging; BP stock closes down 6.7 percent, hitting its lowest level since 1997. The company's market value has spilled billions. Its share price has collapsed more than 40 percent since the blowout began, leading some to raise the possibility of bankruptcy.

It occurs to me that this would be a time to buy, if I hadn't sworn off fossil fuel stocks. Bankruptcy is just wishful thinking. BP is the third-largest oil company in the world, after ExxonMobil and Royal Dutch Shell, with 80,000 employees, sales of $239 billion in 2009, and a market value—even after the recent losses—of more than $100 billion. BP is multinational, traded on both the New York and the London stock exchanges, with Brits and Americans on its board of directors, and extensive U.S. holdings. In 1998 it merged with the American oil company Amoco. About 40 percent of its shares are held by American investors. Its Texas City refinery is one of the world's largest, and BP owns 50 percent of the Trans-Alaska Pipeline.

Sarah Palin calls BP a "foreign company" because, well, she's a little behind in her current events. The White House knows better, but it, too, is whipping up anti-foreign sentiment by consistently calling BP by its former name, British Petroleum. And so in Britain—where BP is, in fact, an evocation of the glory of the empire, a huge tax contributor, and thus beloved—Conservative peer Lord Tebbit calls the American response "a crude, bigoted, xenophobic display of partisan, political, presidential petulance." He may think America's response is much too crude, but from our vantage, BP has provided America with too much crude.

The fisheries closures continue expanding. Now totaling 88,522 square miles. About 37 percent of the Gulf's federal waters. Federal waters begin three miles from shore, but most state waters are also closed. More than half the Gulf remains open to fishing, but buyers are canceling orders. "I've had guys saying, 'If it's from the Gulf, we don't want it,'" says a New York City seafood distributor. The celebrity chef says, "People are really wondering if we're getting safe fish." In Chicago and elsewhere, restaurants display signs declaring, "Our Seafood Is Not from the Gulf of Mexico." "They believe it's toxic," a New York chef says. "So let me be clear," says the president of the United States. "Seafood from the Gulf today is safe to eat." The New Orleans sales rep who ships fish nationwide says, "They're not ordering anything. Not a one. They know we're not selling tainted fish. But their customers? No way. They don't want seafood from Louisiana at all."

"Everybody is so stressed here. We're just sitting here waiting and they're not telling us anything because they don't know," says a Grand Isle restaurant owner who may soon be out of business. "I had four people who came yesterday crying." A fisherman says, "My wife cried and cried over this. Just the other night she told me, 'Thank God there isn't a loaded gun in this house.'"

In Gulf Shores, Alabama, thick oil washes up at a state park, coating the white sand with a thick, red stew. "This makes me sick," says one resident, her legs and feet streaked with crude. "I've gone from owning a piece of paradise to owning a toxic waste dump." Says a fishing guide, "I don't want to say heartbreaking, because that's been said. It's a nightmare. It looks like it's going to be wave after wave of it and nobody can stop it."

Meanwhile, dozens of oil-drenched pelicans float around Louisiana's Grand Terre Island. People have found more than 500 tarred-and-feathered birds dead, and have rescued about 80 oiled birds and nearly 30 mammals, including dolphins. Most showed no obvious oil; maybe something else killed them. But oil ingestion and fumes could have caused this.

The sight of animals struggling in oil moves me to tears more than once. But the numbers here are small compared with the avian toll of the *Exxon Valdez*. After that spill, workers immediately found more than 35,000 birds; by reasonable estimates, approximately 250,000 died. That was because of the density of the oil, the temperature of the water, and the fact that coastal Alaska is home to enormous numbers of aquatic birds of whole family types that (like sea lions) don't live in the Gulf.

That doesn't mean the rescue efforts are going well.

"This is the worst screwed-up response I've ever been on," says Rebecca Dmytryk, who has worked with oiled birds in Louisiana, California, and Ecuador, and founded a group called WildRescue. Experienced wildlife rescuers have complained that they've been prevented from going out to look for live oiled birds in the most likely places, sidelined, or never called in at all. A guy with the U.S. Fish and Wildlife Service says that rescuing oiled birds is a task for "our trained biologists." But experienced rescuers complain that the job of rescue went to inexperienced government employees—fisheries biologists, firefighters—who had never touched a bird before. "I'm just at a loss for why this was allowed," says Lee Fox of Save Our Seabirds, who has written a manual on handling oiled birds.

Jay Holcomb of the International Bird Rescue Research Center has been saving birds from oil spills for thirty years, on three continents. During the *Exxon Valdez* event, he oversaw the entire bird search and rescue program in Prince William Sound, the largest ever attempted, involving dozens of boats and thousands of birds. But here, that's not good enough for the officious officials. "We've been assigned to take hotline calls," he complains, "completely kept out of it."

BP hired a four-year-old Texas company called Wildlife Response Services to oversee the rescue and rehabilitation of birds, turtles, and any other animals hurt by the spill. Its owner says Holcomb and the other wildlife rehabilitation experts "didn't have the personnel to go out and rescue all the birds." She says the system she set up has worked well, adding, "I don't know why anyone would question that."

Four months ago, she did call Lee Fox and tell her to get ready. Fox says, "I've never heard another word. I'm up to my nostrils drowning in frustration." Dmytryk says she and her coworkers begged for permission to go out into the Gulf to look for sick and injured birds that were too weak to make it to shore. But they were turned down. Sharon Schmalz of Wildlife Rehab and Education in Texas, who has over twenty-five years' experience working spills Gulf-wide, says, "We were told to stay put." "They said for safety reasons we couldn't do it," Holcomb says. "There was not a lot of interest in using our expertise."

Meanwhile, a blowout in Pennsylvania: a well blows natural gas and drilling fluid seventy-five feet into the air. It does not ignite and no one is hurt but it takes sixteen hours to control.

The government now estimates that 500,000 to 1 million gallons of crude—12,000 to 24,000 barrels—are leaking daily.

Our Thadmiral tells us, "This spill is just aggregated over a 200-mile radius around the wellbore, where it's leaking right now, and it's not a monolithic spill. It's an insidious war, because it's attacking, you know, four states one at a time, and it comes from different directions depending on the weather." He adds with a dash of frustration, "This spill is keeping everybody hostage."

Hostages: A BP rep tells residents gathered at a church, "We are all angry and frustrated. Feel free tonight to let me see that anger."

Residents aren't buying it. " 'Sorry' doesn't pay the bills," says one. "We're sick and tired of being sick and tired."

Sick. And tired. In Louisiana, seventy-one people suffer throat irritation, cough, shortness of breath, eye irritation, nausea, chest pain, and headaches following exposure to emulsified oil and dispersant. Most are briefly hospitalized.

The stress of anger is giving way to the hopelessness of depression. Without fishing, what's lost is not just vocation, but also what life means, what life is, and people's understanding of who they are. What's lost is pride. What's gained is fear of losing everything. What's creeping in around the edges: The search for answers at the bottom of a bottle. The thought that suicide may end the pain.

In two weeks spanning the last week of May and the first week of June the Louisiana Department of Health and Hospitals counseled 749 people having symptoms that could lead to destructive behavior. Experts say the region should brace for long-term psychological strain. Are they making matters worse by announcing that?

One fisherman, stricken by the sight of fish floating dead, frets over whether he will be able to pass on his trade to his children, a thirteen-month-old son and ten-year-old daughter. His wife, who has sought counseling, says, "My husband went from a happy guy to a zombie consumed by the oil spill." He replies, "If you're not out there in it, you can't comprehend what this is about. We're going to be surrounded by it." Says one town council member, her voice trembling, "We're not going to be okay for a long, long time."

HIGH JUNE

The flow BP is getting good at stopping is the flow of news. When folks at Southern Seaplane, in Belle Chasse, Louisiana, call the local Coast Guard–Federal Aviation Administration command center for routine permission to fly a photographer from the *Times-Picayune* over part of the oily Gulf, a BP contractor answers the phone. His swift and absolute response: Permission denied. "We were questioned extensively. Who was on the aircraft? Who did they work for?" recalls Rhonda Panepinto, who co-owns Southern Seaplane with her husband, Lyle. "The minute we mentioned media, the answer was: 'Not allowed.'"

A spokeswoman for the Federal Aviation Administration says the BP contractor who answered the phone was there because the FAA operations center is in one of BP's buildings. "That person was not making decisions about whether aircraft are allowed to enter the airspace," the spokeswoman spoke.

Why is the FAA in a BP building when BP is the cause, and is under criminal investigation? No other office rental spaces in the four-state region? And they're sharing phone lines?

Across the Gulf, I as well as various photographers, journalists, filmmakers, and environmentalists trying to understand and document the spreading oil are now having real problems. We're getting turned away from public areas affected by the oil—and being threatened with arrest—by private guards, sheriffs, cops, and the Coast Guard.

Senator Bill Nelson, Democrat of Florida, planned to bring a small group of journalists with him on a trip he was taking through the Gulf on a Coast Guard vessel. The Coast Guard agreed to accommodate the reporters and photographers. At about 10:00 P.M. on the night before the trip, someone from the *Department of Homeland Security* called the senator's office to say that no journalists would be allowed.

What lame excuse did they have? "They said it was the Department of Homeland Security's response-wide policy not to allow elected officials and media on the same 'federal asset,'" said a spokesman for the senator. "No further elaboration."

A reporter and photographer from New York's *Daily News* were told by a BP contractor that they could not access a public beach on Grand Isle, Louisiana, one of the areas most heavily affected by the oil spill. The contractor summoned a local sheriff, who then told the reporter, Matthew Lysiak, that news media persons had to fill out paperwork and then be escorted by a BP official to get access to the public beach. "For the police to tell me I needed to sign paperwork with BP to go to a public beach?" Lysiak said. "It's just irrational."

BP is obviously a company with a lot to hide. But how it's staged a coup of the Gulf and gained control of government—*that*, I don't get.

"Our general approach throughout this response," says yet another of the seemingly dozens of faceless BP spokesmen, "has been to allow as much access as possible to media and other parties without compromising the work we are engaged on or the safety of those to whom we give access."

They *allow?* To whom *they* give access? How did a corporation succeed in suppressing U.S. citizens trying to see and talk about what's going on, and *why* are any of our law enforcers, who should be guarding the coast against BP, so thoroughly and sickeningly capitulating, deferring, and letting themselves Be Played? Obama wanted to know "whose ass to kick"? The answer's so blindingly obvious. How is that even a question?

When CBS News reports that one of its news crews was threatened with arrest for trying to film a public beach where oil had washed ashore, the Coast Guard says it is disappointed to learn of the incident.

Signs announce imaginary lines, but the real landscape changes slowly from Louisiana to Mississippi to Alabama to Florida. And so does the light. Green fields. Blue skies. Black cows. Red barns. Sentinal mockingbirds. Amber waves of wheat. Hay for sale while the sun shines. Modest houses with wide lawns and the shade of big trees. Chairs on porches. Mimosas in bloom. Spreading palms, tall pines. The proudness of corn. A few unlucky armadillos. The Roadkill Cafe, the Elberta Social Club. Antiques and collectibles. Live bait and crawfish at the hardware store and at the grocery store. At the garden store: "Ten Percent Off All Firearms." The tank guarding the veterans memorial. Signs directing our attention to pizza, the control of pests, and eternal salvation. A Baptist church advises, "Do Your Work Today As If There Is No Tomorrow." Dopey advice; all work is about tomorrow. Tomorrow, opposable thumbs, and the ability to ignite oil are what make us human.

But for fishermen and anyone dependent on tourist dollars, perhaps yes, now's not a time to wreck your head over tomorrow; too many unknowns. Take it one day at a time. On the other hand, to get you through this, the most important thing is to keep imagining a better tomorrow. Another church and a sign a bit more to the point: "Forgive Us, Lord." That covers the multitude of sins, serves up the Big Prayer.

Nighthawks and chimney swifts. Small bridges. Their rivers and bays lined with emerald summer. Troops of pelicans flying west. I've come from the west. West is where the Oil is coming from. It dominates even my sense of direction. Coats my mental compass.

The scenery, changing slowly. Tractors for sale. Tractors at work. Signs advertise the services of those who weld, those who build docks. "Deep Sea Fishing: 4.4 miles." Close by but already in the past. A man named Twinkle is running for office.

One of life's simple pleasures: driving with the radio on. I hear that the wife of one of the eleven killed says BP will never feel the pain the survivors feel. But how could it? It is not a person. Where a heart would be, it has only money.

The Supreme Court disagrees with me; five of its justices say a corporation *is* a person. Does a corporation have a belly button? That's one's passport down through ages, a living link in the one eternal chain of being, life to life. BP is no person. Person: a two-legged primate with thoughts, feelings, blood ties, dreams. Not something for courts to trifle with. Not, in truth, subject to their opinion. A sacred matter, of the greatest of mysteries.

First glimpse of Mobile, Alabama, includes too many oil rigs to count easily. One reason I've so seldom returned to the Gulf is the rigs' visual blight. They're the wide horizon's piercing reminder of oil's stranglehold on us, our cheap-energy addiction. The rigs flare their gas from their long arms like Lady Liberty's torches. We are all victims, all perpetrators. What goes around comes apart.

The shorelines of Mobile Bay are confettied with orange boom. It's hot. The sun raises an ocean haze. Right now here, the Oil is mostly an idea, the coming thing. The booms await it. The rigs foreshadow it.

On the corner, the BP station. I still have half a tank.

Scientists continue to plague us with pesky reports of massive plumes of undersea oil. Woods Hole Oceanographic Institution researchers working aboard the National Science Foundation's ship *Endeavor* beginning in mid-June confirm the presence of drifting oil deep below the surface. Using 5,800 separate measurements, they find a hydrocarbon plume over a mile wide, over twenty miles long, hundreds of feet thick, detectable down to 3,300 feet, and extending itself at a little over four miles a day.

People envision a river of oil. But Woods Hole chemist Chris Reddy will explain, "The plume was not a river of Hershey's syrup." The water samples collected at these depths had no odor of oil and were clear. The dilute oil was detected by instruments. "But that's not to say it isn't harmful to the environment," he adds.

And in perhaps the world's first case of plume envy—or whatever you'd call it—the University of Georgia's Samantha Joye says her plume is bigger than theirs; she says Woods Hole's plume "doesn't hold a candle to the plume we saw."

Whether like syrup or seltzer, the thought of massive plumes of under-sea oil is disturbing. So from what corner shall come the next volley of fresh reassurance? National Oceanic and Atmospheric Administration (NOAA) officials call the academic scientists' announcements of their discovery of plumes "misleading, premature and, in some cases, inaccurate."

Note: "in some cases." Interesting phrase. An exception big enough for a wiggly pig. Means—it would seem—that "in some *other* cases" it *is* accurate to say there are giant undersea plumes of hydrocarbons now drifting in the Gulf.

NOAA says oxygen depletion in the waters surrounding plumes is not "a source of concern at this time." NOAA says critics blaming dispersants for the plumes have "no information" to back their claims up. NOAA administrator Dr. Jane Lubchenco, whom *Newsweek*—in a carefully crafted phrase—calls "a respected oceanographer when President Obama tapped her to lead the agency," says there are no "plumes," only "anomalies."

Now, wait a minute. Don't tell me "no information." Obviously, the oil is coming out of the seafloor. The dispersants are designed to keep it underwater. It's *coming* from beneath the surface. It's *being dispersed* beneath the surface. And when it surfaces, it's being hit with dispersants that dissolve it to make it *sink*. Beneath the surface is where a lot of it is—obviously.

I've known Jane Lubchenco for close to twenty years, and in the late 1990s I spent a lot of time with her when we were part of a team traveling to various cities to tell people about how the ocean is changing. I respect her very much. But there comes a time when political pressures cause a person to try to distinguish between "plumes" and "anomalies," though those are two words for the same thing. One can parse language into droplets so small that the facts dissolve to difficult-to-detect dilutions; one can disperse truth itself. People get confused, get the wrong impression. Sometimes that's the goal. So it's better to stand with the truth. Political situations come and go. What begins and what ends, and what follows a person forever after, is the truth. Obviously the oil is in the water. It comes from somewhere, it has to go somewhere, and the water is where.

A scientist at Columbia University's Lamont-Doherty Earth Observatory says that even without dispersants, oil originating with such force at this depth and pressure breaks into zillions of droplets that stay suspended in the water.

Not as visually shocking as dead pelicans, but much more basic, is the plight of the minute clouds of life at the base of the food chain. The things that grow the fish that magically become leaping dolphins and plunging seabirds—tiny things living deep, almost beyond the reach of human acknowledgment—are probably having a pretty hard time right now across large swaths of the Gulf.

The deep sea contains a galaxy of little animals—everything from planktonic beasts to jellies to billions of small fishes called lanternfishes (myctophids). They all live in a layer of life that twice a day performs the greatest animal migration on Earth, from the darkness of deep daytime waters to the darkness of shallow nighttime waters, and back again. This zone of life is like a flying carpet throughout an astonishingly large portion of the world ocean. On a moving ship, it is extraordinary to watch it on the sonar as it slowly rises and dives over the course of the day, even while your ship is covering hundreds of miles. Proponents of dispersants contend that by dissolving the oil, microbes can more easily feed on it. But before that happens, these billowing toxic clouds will roll through this zone of life in the Gulf, where the damage will likely never really be assessed.

I'm not saying it's utter catastrophe for all of them. I'm not saying they won't bounce back. I'm saying, Let's not fool each other. Let's attend to the matters to which the researchers are calling our attention. Let's not be in denial of science, logic, and sense. That's indecent.

BP's CEO, Tony Hayward, insists there's "no evidence" of hydrocarbon plumes in the Gulf. There are wiggly pigs, and then there are liars. For an alternate take, we turn to Florida State University oceanographer Ian MacDonald: "These are huge volumes of oil, in many cubic kilometers of water."

The National Oceanographic and Atmospheric Administration acknowledges that it has "confirmed the presence of very low concentrations of sub-surface oil at depths from 50 meters to 1,400 meters." In other words, from shallow waters down to around 4,000 feet. But they say it's in "very low concentrations," less than 0.5 parts per million. The thing is, a concentration of hydrocarbons in the range of less than 0.5 parts per million—say 0.4—is in the range of a notably polluted place like Boston Harbor. So one person could say, "It's not going to kill everything," and another could say, "The oil is polluting an enormous volume of water in the Gulf of Mexico." They'd both be right.

From the federal government, we get both a little more minimizing—"We have always known there is oil under the surface"—and this honest admission of ignorance: "The questions we are exploring are where is it, in what concentrations, where is it going, and what are the consequences for the health of the marine environment?" So asks NOAA administrator Dr. Jane Lubchenco.

Those are the questions. If the oil stays suspended it will eventually dissipate throughout the world ocean in rather harmless concentrations—the dose makes the poison—or be dismembered by microbes. Another possibility is that the dispersed oil might sink to the seafloor. A fisherman I know on the West Coast e-mails me: "During the 1969 Santa Barbara blowout dispersants were used extensively. Several years later, some of the oil that had settled to the bottom eventually formed large clumps. In the early/mid 1970s I was working on drag boats in the SB Channel and we would periodically hit one of the clumps, which would render the net completely worthless. No way to clean that shit off the net. Union Oil wound up paying for a lot of nets, although not willingly. No one knows the effects on bottom life, although the English sole disappeared for years."

At a press conference, Lubchenco, sounding like a bomb-sniffing canine working in a political minefield, says, "The bottom line is that yes, there is oil in the water column. It's at very low concentrations." That sounds like she's minimizing it. But in her next breath she adds, "That doesn't mean that it does not have significant impact."

Taken together, a true enough picture. Depends on your definition of "significant," but I'm satisfied. Even if she didn't hit a home run, she touched the three bases of truth in this mess: it's there; it's at low concentrations except near the source; and it could still be a problem. I think that's really as much as anyone knows. This isn't a home-run situation.

Dauphin Island, Alabama. A pretty place. A mixture of fishing village and resort. A beach place with pines tall enough to cast shade across the road, a place that welcomes you with a sign proclaiming, "Fishing, Beaches, Bird Sanctuary." The Oil welcomes you with a sign saying, "BP Claims Center."

It's June 8; today is World Oceans Day. I'm having a bit of a hard time, emotionally speaking, with that.

Away from the pines and alongside the sea oats, by 10:00 A.M. the sun is uncomfortably hot, its glare unrelenting, resolute.

I'm with filmmaker Bill Mills, a real pro who's done a lot of work with *National Geographic* films and many others. He wants to interview a few people, and he's toting his movie camera as we walk from the parking lot toward the water. Someone in the shade of one of BP's little sun awnings starts yelling at us. Bill doesn't even turn around. I glance over my shoulder. An arm-waving man, too lazy to come our way, demanding we come his way. Public beach, so screw him.

A light, ribbony slick gift-wraps the shoreline like a Big Present. A few hundred people are still putting a brave face on beachgoing. Determined to have their beach day. In their swimsuits. On their blankets. The sun still works for them. Admirable fortitude.

Not surprised to see oil globs splattering the beach. Surprised to see some kids in the water.

Didn't see the sign that said no swimming? It's easy to miss: tiny, smaller than a stop sign. "The Public Is Advised Not to Swim in These Waters Due to the Presence of Oil-Related Chemicals."

Just a small cover-your-ass sign in a community reluctant to admit that it's ruined. Ruined at least for now. It could be much worse. Just go to Louisiana's beaches. But what's arrived here now is quite enough to spoil things.

A mom: "We come here a *lot*. It's *killin'* me to see this."

BP workers in white suits rummage among the beachgoers like foraging chickens pecking at oil. Near the tide line they shovel oil blobs and oil-stained sand into plastic bags.

An old man says he was a newscaster for forty years, that's enough of being on camera, so no photos, please. Now he casts a fishing line. "Other day I went fishing over there, where I've fished for thirty-five years. The place was full of tar balls and the fish I caught smelled like gasoline. I *just had to leave!*"

Tar balls I believe; there's plenty. A fish that smells like gasoline? I'd have to smell that myself. Healthy skepticism is how I like to think of it. It means that, at least sometimes, I'm seeing through my anger.

Ashore, a wet boy, nineish, looks bewildered. Won't go back in. "You feel it all over your skin," he says. Another family's kids are body-boarding, looking perfectly content.

Other creatures continue to work their world, their side of things. Least terns diving along the shore. The small fish. A school of mullet nose the surface. A small ray swims past: another hazard to swimmers. It's a very alive place. That's the point. The people and the others that live here. Everything that lives here.

A man emerges. I ask him if he can feel and taste oil. He says, "Oh, I can feel it on me. But as far as tastin' it or anything, no, nothin' like that."

Mike, thirty-nine, wears American flag swim trunks. He stands with his well-tattooed arms folded. Feet oil-stained. "We come with the family on weekends. I'm worried this is the last time. Forget this oil; go solar power."

You can clean a beach, but every wave brings a little more. The oil is still gushing, and there's plenty more to come. Every day, oily sand goes out in bags. Bags and bags. Bag People.

The BP workers wander near. I ask what kind of work they would be doing if not for the Oil. "I have no comment," they regurgitate.

"They tell you not to talk to anyone?"

"Yes, that's right."

The Oil is a big secret. Okay, I wouldn't want my employees talking to anyone while on the job, either. But there's a motive here: minimize the scope of information and opinion. Aren't we really quite past the point where that can help even BP? What might these people say that we don't already know? That the genie's blown his cork, Pandora's opened the coop, and the cats are out of their bags all over the region? Basic Privacy is no longer this company's prerogative, and the pettiness does less to hide the facts than it does to expose the corporation's desire to hide facts.

In a cloudless sky, a Coast Guard helicopter passes.

Outside one of the local churches, I meet Reverend Chris Schansberg. He's forty-three, soft-spoken. "The first Sunday after the explosion," he says, "I told our people, 'Let's get together and pray that the oil won't hit the island.' I don't know why we focused on our island, but we did. And I was talking to the mayor later, and he didn't know we'd prayed, and he said, 'Y'know, it's really remarkable that oil hasn't hit the island.' I know it hit the far west end. But on the oil-flow charts on the evening news, people were saying, 'Now, look at Dauphin Island; there's a seven-mile buffer between it and the oil.' And apparently—to the glory of God—oil's been flowing around us. Now, that's a great victory. But of course, you have to answer, Well, why is it on the shores from Louisiana to Pensacola? That's a deeper question." Brief pause. "The oil cleanup workers come from everywhere, from Washington to New York State, Puerto Rico. I've seen loneliness, isolation, boredom—. Many of them have never seen heat like this. We have seen this as an opportunity to reach out toward them, sharing God's love, giving out frozen Popsicles—.

"Someday, if not now, the people who've done this will be judged. I'm not saying it's unforgivable. But they *are* accountable to God. If they tried to cut corners, if they failed in their stewardship, they will be accountable on the Day of Judgment. The Bible promises that when Jesus returns he will make all things right. And it really means everything. So if we still have oil in the Gulf when he returns—that's it."

Fifty House Democrats begin calling for BP to suspend its planned dividend payout, stop its advertising campaign, and instead spend the money on cleaning up the ongoing Gulf of Mexico oil spill. Congressional Representative Lois Capps says, "Not a single cent" should be spent on television ads. If BP is so concerned about its public image, "it should plug the hole." Yes, but—. Suspending a dividend payment would save BP something like $10 billion. The loss of prestige and stock value is a strong deterrent for not paying a dividend. But for BP, the silver lining would be pretty convenient cost savings. And it could simultaneously deflect its shareholders' anger over plummeting stock value by blaming the mean old U.S. congressional Democrats.

The depth of 2009's global recession sent global energy consumption down for the first time in twenty-seven years, but only by 1 percent. In the same year, China's carbon dioxide emissions from fossil fuels rose by 9 percent. Global wind and solar generation rose by about 30 percent and 45 percent, respectively, enormous gains. Who says? A BP energy report says. The world's oil reserves (including yet-to-be-developed Canadian "tar sands") appear sufficient to last—at 2009 production rates—for forty-five years; gas will last about sixty-five years, and coal will last 120 years. After that, what? Do you or does someone you love plan to be alive forty-five years from now? This is our wake-up call. Don't touch that snooze button.

By mid-June the cap is ferrying about 10,000 barrels of oil a day up to a tanker on the surface. The well is leaking much more than that.

Revisiting the basic question: How much oil? A team of researchers and government officials is finally studying the flow rate. Team member and Purdue University professor Steve Wereley says it's probably somewhere between 798,000 and 1.8 million gallons—roughly 20,000 to 40,000 barrels—daily. He says, "BP is claiming they're capturing the majority of the flow, which I think is going to be proven wrong in short order."

Meanwhile, at the start of the second week of June, the tide begins leaving a splattering of oil blobs on Florida Panhandle beaches, from Perdido to Pensacola. Signs warn: Don't swim. Don't wade. Avoid skin contact with oily water. Avoid dead sea animals. Notes one: "Young children, pregnant women, people with compromised immune systems and individuals with underlying respiratory conditions should avoid the area."

Some people are in the water anyway. I wouldn't want to get in where I can see a sheen, but it's probably not very toxic in small amounts for short intervals.

Tourism, though, has been completely poisoned. In Mississippi, Governor Haley Barbour angrily blames the news media for scaring away tourists and making it seem as if "the whole coast from Florida to Texas is ankle-deep in oil."

The fact is, he's right; it isn't the same everywhere. As Thad Allen intones, "We're dealing with an aggregation of hundreds of thousands of patches of oil that are going a lot of different directions. It's the breadth and complexity of the disaggregation of the oil that is now posing the greatest clean-up challenge." And so, some places are ankle-deep and some, barely freckled.

Pensacola Beach, Santa Rosa Island, Florida. The sand here makes the "white" sand back home on Long Island seem battleship gray. In bright sun it can be blinding. Workers have picked up the day's dark tar balls. Mostly.

High-rise hotels and condos loom over the low-slung beach. They shimmer in the sunset. A huge restaurant with a huge fake crab is overbuilt and tacky. The whole place is not my cup of tea. But it's not *my* home.

Listen to people whose home it is: "So, this is Santa Rosa Sound," she says, as if presenting it as a gift. "Really precious." Then, almost under her breath: "I don't know, it may be twenty years before it ever looks like this again. The oil's just a few miles offshore. Oh look—a dolphin." A moment's silence, then: "There's no plan to help the dolphins."

The evening breeze is still warm enough to raise a sweat. The clouds paint with pastels. A guy with a floppy hat, a waddling walk, arrives, sighs, "I'd like to take one last look at my heaven."

BP's full-page ad promises to invalidate their fears. "We Will Make This Right," it announces, projecting confidence. But just below the horizon, flying under the radar, on everyone's minds, on their nerves: oil blobs stalk.

At public faucets, moms rinse sand from kids' toes. News vans, their satellite dishes turned to heaven as if in prayer, stand like military hardware on the eve of invasion. Ready to report attack. We breathe the parked vans' continuous exhaust, their engines running their air conditioners and electronics.

A Big Protest is scheduled for here, now, this moment. But so sparse are the protesters—fewer than twenty, among several hundred beachgoers—that even the organizers cannot locate them.

Finally, the protesters. There they are. Here they come. They have signs—"Save the Dolphins"—and a little theater; a woman wears a black veil of mourning. They group up and knock on a media van. There're enough of them to fill a frame. Passable for local news. Dutifully reported. Story filed: "Local People Do Not Like Oil on Beaches." Basically Pointless.

One police car stands idling, its occupant utterly relaxed, a bit bored. The woman beneath the veil says, "We already got the *police* here—and I ain't even showed my ass yet."

Oh boy. Time to go.

Restaurant. "The oysters are from—?"

"Texas," says the waiter. "We might have a month left there."

Realtor, late forties, energetic blonde, clear blue eyes, too much Sunshine State sun, a tough cookie: "People come for the beaches. If they can't put their feet in sand, they won't come." She's already refunded 75 percent of this season's rental down payments. Her home sales are in cardiac arrest.

Activist folksinger to me: "Do you think we can save the dolphins?"

"If it gets down to them needing to be saved? No."

"There should have been a plan." She wipes her face, gazes out toward the dock. "It's weird to fight as you're grieving the loss of your own place. With global warming, you feel some distance. But this. When the rig sank on Earth Day, I cried myself to sleep. We take turns picking each other up."

Others chime in. "If the wind tonight was off the Gulf like last night, we couldn't sit here. The smell was thick. We've all been exposed."

"People are sick. More people are gonna get sick. I took two reporters out and they both got sick. One was in the hospital. Karen right there's got chemical burns from picking up four dead turtles."

"This is war. This is all-out war. This is a story that has to be told. And a powerful, very *powerful* group does not want this story told. I'm just me. I've been helping where I can. But my phone's having problems. My sister's been helping, too, and her e-mails are getting kicked back to her. I'm not paranoid, but what if somebody's interfering with our communications? Do you know how I could find out? Since the day the president came through, my phone really hasn't worked very well. I don't know. But that's what's happened."

"Every time the oil moves, they change the no-fly zone. They don't want us to see."

"How many notebooks do you fill up before you have a book?"

"Karen's trying to get her kids out of town. There's nothing for them to do. Everything we do is sailin', crabbin', boatin', shrimpin', surfin'."

"I'm really worried about Lori; these dolphins are like her children."

"If a kid says the water tasted soapy, is that dispersant?"

This is the conversation now.

But while we talk, the water still looks fine. The pelicans unruffled. Gulls galore. Dolphins roll within a hundred yards of the restaurant deck. All looks safe. Nothing feels safe.

The real estate agent says, "If this keeps up much longer, we're dead. I have people who, if they can't rent their houses, they'll get foreclosed. They don't have the money to refund deposits. And they can't sell; who's gonna buy anything now? Everybody's hit. The gas stations. The laundry services. Even the hairdressers depend on tourists. Gonna be a ghost town."

Another volley of comments from around the table. "I never thought this could happen."

"I'm stayin' to the end. Till they make me leave. This is my home."

"This was my *dream*. I'm *really* mad. I'm upset enough to have dessert."

On the futility and utility of helping wildilfe, a debate: More than a thousand birds in the Gulf region have been collected alive with visible oil. Serious question: Should they be cleaned or killed? Two years after a 1990 spill in southern California, fewer than 10 percent of oiled brown pelicans that had been cleaned remained alive, and they showed no signs of breeding. "If nothing else, we're morally obligated to save birds that seem to be savable," says one bird worker. Several hundred Gulf sea turtles are also getting aid. But a University of California professor who worked to save animals after the *Exxon Valdez* spill in 1989 says cleaning wildlife gives a false impression that something can be done. To which the director of the International Bird Rescue Research Center retorts, "What do you want us to do? Let them die?"

In mid-June, another vocabulary word hits Alabama: "mousse." Think of it as crude oil the consistency of chocolate pudding. But remember, it's not pudding. If you step in it, you can't wash it off. You need some kind of solvent. If it's just a little, you can maybe rub until you've gotten most of it. If it's on clothes, throw them away. If your kids or dog track this stuff into the house, you need a new rug or maybe a new couch.

On June 14, 300 birds get coated with oil—in Utah.

Car radio: ". . . We've just been hearing from Riki Ott, author of *Not One Drop: Betrayal and Courage in the Wake of the* Exxon Valdez *Oil Spill.* She was heavily involved in the *Exxon Valdez* disaster. If you have any questions for Riki Ott about what's going on in the Gulf, give us a call. . . ."

I once met Riki Ott; I've been in her home, actually. She lives in Cordova, Alaska. Former salmon fisherman with a PhD. Unusual woman.

"Riki, you've been saying—"

"In this country, we've made the decision to depend on the oil industry for cleanup. We put the spiller in charge. In Norway, the government nationalizes the spill; they have the equipment, they do the cleanup. In this country, we put the irresponsible party in charge."

"So we say, 'You're irresponsible, now you're in charge—'"

"Right. We've been trying to get the workers respirators. Something as simple as respirators. We need federal air-quality monitoring. Because if we rely on BP's monitoring, it will end up where Exxon's air-monitoring data ended up: disappeared—sealed into court records until 2023."

"You were saying earlier that there's some trouble with just getting to the sites."

"The oil companies learned a heck of a lot more than the citizens in the wake of the *Exxon Valdez.* And what the oil companies learned is this: control the images. No cameras. No evidence. No problem—right?"

A royal tern and a brown pelican watch Captain Cody McCurdy pull the *Gray Ghost* from its pilings at Orange Beach, Alabama. Tommy Gillespie, mate, wears old tattoos on weather-beaten arms, a Confederate bandanna, two packs of cigarettes in his T-shirt. Fishermen. Until last week or so.

"I don't see a way out," Cody says, but he means it literally.

The marine police are enclosing the inlet with boom. Various boats stand by in case they're needed to deploy more boom. There's not enough for all to do. The Oil inflicts a certain aimlessness.

All boats, many of them recreational boats, are now "workboats." BP's money flows like oil. BP's managers can't turn *it* off, either, or they'll trigger another eruption: people's anger. They know that to keep people Busy and Paid—no matter how useless the errand—serves their bigger purpose: to quell, to calm, to keep the masses anything but idle. The people are Being Pacified. This busywork is theater. And to that extent, BP is now the Gulf's biggest patron of the arts. The obvious calculation: paying for theater to suppress rage is well worth it.

The folks on the boats don't see themselves as being manipulated. They are desperate for the income, and it's enough that they're getting what they've Been Promised. They can't afford to look behind that curtain. Many feel—deeply—that they are defending their home waters and wetlands, defending the most important and meaningful thing in their lives.

While we wait to see if we can get out of here, I notice that everyone aboard all the other boats wears a silly little orange life jacket, the uniform of Being Paid, even in water calm enough to reflect one's tightening anger. Most professional fishermen have probably never in their lives worn a life jacket on a boat. But of course BP wants to ensure *safety on the job.* Unlike while drilling in mile-deep water amid risks galore.

Even ashore, I see fishermen walking the docks—their *own* docks—in their little orange life jackets. Part of how Being Paid wipes away their autonomy, their adulthood, their discretion, their individuality; infantilizes them.

Fishermen are famously talkative, but now the vest wearers "have no comment." I pity their sorry slavery. But I can afford my anger; I can go home.

We are the *only* boat on the water not drawing a BP check. We wear no orange vests; we have signed no waivers. I can abstain indefinitely.

My companions, their options narrowed to the Breaking Point, can't. They're going to lose their bet that the gusher will end soon enough for them to salvage their sense of self. They just got their hazmat training and say they're hoping to start working the oil cleanup response soon.

Can't blame 'em; everyone's under Big Pressure to make a day's pay.

On the tide in the pass: lumps of oil.

Basic Problem: The marine police, blue lights flashing, say that if we go out, we won't be allowed back in.

Cody says his boss knows the cops. His boss makes some calls and rings back, saying, "They aren't letting anyone back in here. They don't know why."

A well-planned, well-coordinated, well-executed plan is all that's lacking. Speculation remains open. Reason is closed. The officious are expert at Being Petty.

Cody says screw it, we'll go. "Open up."

We's takin' our chances, betting on the unreliability of the marine police's advice, on inconsistency, on lack of coordination. Those guys may be off their shift by the time we get back. The next guys may say something else. And maybe it's easier to say no to a boat leaving than to one coming back? We'll see. They all seem to be making it up as they go.

One thing's certain: opening a line of boom to let a boat back in makes zero difference as far as the Oil is concerned. This boom is useless against it. You might as well stretch dental floss across your bathtub to hold soapy water to one side.

They lower the boom on our wake. So much effort, applied so diligently, so earnestly—and so unequal to the task at hand.

At 9:00 A.M. the sun squints my eyes. How do the locals stand such heat?

Our mission: find the oil before it finds us. Get a sense of where. How far. How heavy. Paul Revere with outboard power.

Pelicans and helicopters. Ospreys and helicopters. Royal terns and Coast Guard helicopters.

Looking back from three miles off. High-rise condos line the shore. Ugly as hell. No boats out here, just helicopters. All fishing, even catch-and-release, is closed. A fishing boat may not possess fishing gear. That's to *protect* us.

Safe from fishermen, the fish must fend for themselves in the dispersant-and-oil seawater. In the low-oxygen end of the pool. For them it's always either frying pan or fire.

We head to a great fishing spot fifteen miles from shore. Rumors are: someone saw dead fish at the surface there. We are fishing for rumors, fishing for dead fish.

There's enough wind for a light chop, but the water is calm. Too calm. A bit slick. An ocean normally shows many natural slicks, caused by the bodily oils from schools of fishes, by water of different densities—nothing to do with petroleum. I ask Cody if he thinks these slicks are natural. He says, "What slicks?" I point.

"Naw, this is just—" He waves it away.

From the back of the boat Tommy yells, "A lot of oil here."

We're suddenly sliding past coin-sized oil blobs. By the thousands. Then, none.

Schools of tuna-cousins called little tunny shred the surface chasing small-fish prey. A couple of porpoises, far off. Blue sky. Blue-green sea. A light whiff of oil. Not as bad as I've heard tell.

When I ask Cody where he fishes—fished—for tuna and marlin, he points left and says seventy to ninety miles thataway. The big fishes' address is the names of three oil rigs way out there. The rigs float on half a mile of water. The fish like rigs. "When them things light up at night, it's like a city. Them lights draw the fish like crazy." Natural is long gone. "It's a lotta fun out there at night," Cody says. We remember fun.

Tommy was born here. Cody, from Tennessee, came for the fishing.

Tommy shrimped for twenty-five years. "Hard work, the open Gulf is. You're up three days straight, takin' heads off shrimp. You're just sittin' there poppin' heads, packin' anywheres from ten to twenty boxes a day." A box is one hundred pounds. How many shrimp?

"Depends on what sizes you're catchin'. You get anywhere from forty-fifties to ten-fifteens. That's how many to make a pound." About the Oil: "I ain't no scientist or anything like that, but I don't think it's gonna be okay in a year. It'll be years, prob'ly. That's just my opinion. It'll be parked a *long* time there."

"That's too scary to think about," Cody says. "I depend on these coming two months for a large portion of my living."

Let's reminisce: "Best snapper fishin' in the world, right off our coast," Cody proudly crows. "Red snapper's our bread and butter. They average five to ten pounds. We also catch vermillion snapper, triggerfish, grouper, amberjack—"

Enough reminiscing. What does he think of the booms and stuff? "A waste of time."

Our boat rocks and growls forward. Our boat is slow and loud. Its noise helps cancel my thoughts. A good thing here, not thinking is. Not thinking about how much I always loved being at sea.

Cody spots a loggerhead turtle that seems fine. It dives. A helicopter passes.

Cody says that a few days ago, there was a slick here that ran for miles. Not here now. It's a stealthy adversary.

Our boat scratches the sea, and on the breeze a whiff of hydrocarbons. Scratch and sniff. Twenty miles into the Gulf we enter a wide mosaic of mazelike slicks freckled with blobs of crude. In the beating heat of the sun, each blob bleeds its own mini-slick into the overall sheen, like pats of butter melting in a skillet.

Under that buttery petroleum coating I am surprised to see small living fishes. I am surprised to see fish alive in the ocean.

A few flyingfish leap through the oil. I wonder how long they can last. Surely they ingest it. Surely their gills are getting gummed. More little tunny chase the small fish in a froth of white explosions that slice the rainbow sheen to ribbons. Life as always, the eternal sea, now with a twist: Can it last, can it stand it? I can't.

Cody says last week, seven miles from shore, he saw oil blobs the size of cars. He was out for opening day of a fifty-seven-day red snapper season. It lasted two days before the government closed the waters.

Heavy lines of crude like ten-foot anacondas, like cobras with hoods spread, for miles now. And snake oil on the breeze.

Cody says, "It was just an accident. You know, we gotta have that oil. It's a necessary evil."

LATE JUNE

In a rather extraordinary breaking of ranks during a congressional hearing on June 15, oil executives distance themselves from BP. "We would not have drilled the well the way they did," says ExxonMobil's CEO. Chevron's chief says, "It certainly appears that not all the standards that we would recommend or that we would employ were in place." Shell's CEO: "It's not a well that we would have drilled in that mechanical setup." In a seemingly sincere apology, BP's chairman says, "This tragic accident should never have happened." Then he manages to offend everyone in the Gulf region by adding, "We care about the small people."

And all across the Gulf, tongues flicker with phrases like "They're no greater than us," "We don't bow down to them," and "We're human beings."

Big People, small people. How sad.

On June 16, a new and improved containment system hooked directly into the blowout preventer begins carrying 5,000 to 10,000 additional barrels per day to another vessel called the *Q4000*, which has no storage capacity and wastefully burns off all that oil and gas. By late June they're either taking or flaring off as much as 25,000 barrels of oil daily. But plenty of oil continues billowing into the sea throughout all this. A third vessel, the *Helix Producer*, is scheduled for hookup to another valve on the blowout preventer by around the end of June. It can burn 25,000 barrels of oil a day. What a waste of everything. What a mess.

Tony Hayward gets a fourteen-page letter from Democratic Congressmen Henry Waxman and Bart Stupak. The letter contains nothing he hasn't already heard and everything he won't affirm. "Time after time, it appears that BP made decisions that increased the risk of a blowout to save the company time or expense," the lawmakers write. "If this is what happened," they venture, "BP's carelessness and complacency have inflicted a heavy toll on the Gulf, its inhabitants, and the workers on the rig."

President Obama visits the Gulf for a fourth time, trying to boost tourism by eating in local restaurants. He acknowledges the tragedy and—responding to public criticism—speaks more harshly about BP.

The White House is also pressuring BP to put tens of billions of dollars into an escrow account. As one of the world's three largest oil companies, BP generates $8 billion to $9 billion every *quarter*. It spends $5 billion to $6 billion a quarter. The difference—$2 to $4 billion—is its average profit every three months. Under the corporation-shielding federal liability cap, BP is legally on the hook for just $75 million— which, for perspective, is 1.25 percent of BP's $6 billion *first quarter* profit this year. If Obama can simply strong-arm billions out of BP, it will be a stunning and masterful coup.

But, needless to say, many Senate Republicans are accusing Democrats and the White House of trying to exploit the oil "politically." They also accuse Democrats of using the calamity in the Gulf to push "a job-killing climate change bill." It's a terrible irony that the blowout has dampened—not whetted—what little appetite there had been in the U.S. Senate to cap greenhouse gas emissions. That's a shame, because we really need an energy bill that puts people to work in new jobs, building the energy future. Without taking from this event a propelling motivation toward new jobs for new energy, the whole blowout becomes simply a calamity, with no lessons learned, no up-side, no value added in honor of the lives lost and the lives so changed. South Carolina Republican senator Lindsey Graham had worked on a climate-change bill for months, but has pronounced it hopeless.

How much oil? The company is now funneling about 16,000 barrels a day from its leaky containment cap to a collecting ship. Federally convened experts currently estimate that the well has been spewing 35,000 to 60,000 barrels a day. Every new official estimate is higher than the previous one. Asked how much he thinks is leaking, our Thadmiral demurs: "That's the $100,000 question." He later adds that he believes the figure is closer to the low end of the new estimate, 35,000 barrels. Of course, for weeks he'd acquiesced to 5,000. BP's chief operating officer now says that by the end of June, BP plans to be able to capture more than 50,000 barrels a day.

Meanwhile, oil blobs and slicks coming ashore between eastern Alabama and Pensacola provoke Orange Beach's mayor to rail, "BP isn't giving us what we need. We're screaming for more. We want to skim it before it gets here."

A year after the *Exxon Valdez* ran aground, lawmakers passed the federal Oil Pollution Act to ensure a quick and effective response to oil spills. Every region of the country was required to have a tailored contingency plan.

But the plans amount to what the oil industry says on paper, not a demonstration of what it can do—or what might be needed. The Gulf plan considers a blowout of 240,000 barrels a day into the Gulf for at least one hundred days, far worse than the current leak—yet it declares that "no significant adverse impacts are expected" to beaches, wetlands, or wildlife.

The Minerals Management Service approved that plan. The Thadmiral now says the response has been "adequate to the assumptions in the plans." He adds, "I think you need to go back and question the assumptions."

Thank you, Thadmiral. That's been tried. A 1999 Coast Guard report recommended that equipment like booms, skimmers, and absorbent materials should be increased by 25 percent. But over the next several years, lobbyists for oil companies pushed to keep the existing standards in place—and emphasized the cheaper alternative: chemical dispersants.

In August 2009, the Coast Guard effectively overruled its 1999 report, declining to require the substantial increase in the amount of mechanical response equipment.

"BP could fire all their contractors because they're doing absolutely nothing but destroying our marsh," rages Billy Nungesser, the president of Plaquemines Parish. Weeks in, he says, "I still don't know who's in charge; is it BP? Is it the Coast Guard?" "The boom has been a disaster from the beginning," Florida senator Bill Nelson tells a Senate hearing. "You have a big mess, with no command and control." Florida's attorney general says he's "absolutely appalled." The mayor of Orange Beach, Alabama, says it's "a very discombobulated and discoordinated effort."

By now people have found more than 350 dead or moribund loggerhead turtles along the Gulf Coast since the blowout began—including 20 carcasses in a single day. More than 60 have been covered in oil. Fishing gear remains suspect for some of the deaths. Meanwhile, more than 70 human Louisiana residents have reported oil-related illness to the state's Department of Health and Hospitals.

Morning. Another day of this. I've driven from the Florida border, across Alabama and Mississippi, and into Louisiana, and I'm watching dawn rise in the rearview mirror. What an awful night. In the last couple of weeks our dog, Kenzie, had lost her appetite. Yet just a couple of days ago she was walking with her tail high, giving us hope that she'd get better. After I left for the Gulf she weakened rapidly, and last night she was suddenly unable to walk. Patricia called me at midnight and took her to an all-night veterinary clinic. They found a tumor in her spleen and blood in her body cavity. The vet said that operating would not guarantee success even in the short term, and partly because of Kenzie's age, approximately thirteen, he recommended euthanasia. Pat sat with Kenzie for a while, then called me tearfully at 2:00 a.m. to say our dog was gone. I will always remember our walks on the beach and watching her run so far along the ocean, or alongside us as we biked around Lazy Point; and, more recently, helping us herd our new chickens back into their coop, and being so interested yet gentle with the infant raccoon that fell to earth in our yard. I regret that I was not home for this crisis. I regret that Patricia had to shoulder the burden alone. I regret being here. Busyness hurts relationships.

Dew and low fog hang heavy on the grass. Eighty-three degrees by 6:30. Roads lined with pines and worry.

Radio news: Louisiana's Governor Bobby Jindal is accusing BP of dragging its feet on paying claims; President Obama will meet today with grieving relatives of workers killed in the explosion. The president wants to include deepwater drilling "as part of a comprehensive energy strategy." The radio says wildlife workers are picking up birds on islands. There's concern about oiled pelican nests.

I think they should destroy all the nests and try to frighten the adults away; that would break the adults' motivation to keep returning and continuing their exposure. For the population's future, saving breeders is more important than trying to save eggs or even chicks. If adults die or get immobilized and rescued, their eggs and chicks are doomed anyway. That's uncomfortable to say, but it's true.

Along the interstate, signs for a concert venue advertise coming headline acts: Liza Minnelli (still?), Ringo Starr (still), the O'Jays (really?). The highway reaps its constant harvest of armadillos; our most heavily armored surviving mammal cannot survive our daily onslaught. More to pity. An alligator with an urge to roam has had its ambitions crushed. Glad I wasn't in that car.

The sign reminds travelers, "Welcome to Louisiana—America's Wetland." Almost immediately the land seems lusher, greener, lower, wider. The rest area is stocked with pamphlets for tourists: fishing, seafood. Oh, well.

Radio talk show: A guy who runs a parasailing business calls to say, "Congratulations, BP. Today you've accomplished something hurricanes couldn't do, banks couldn't do, and even the greed of Wall Street couldn't do: you've put me out of business." He has made more than eighty phone calls trying to get BP to respond to his financial claims.

Three congressional hearings today. Five yesterday.

Kevin Costner has a solution to the oil; for years he's invested in a machine to separate oil from water. There are thousands of other people making suggestions, promoting their ideas, hawking their own products. There seems no clear route for these things to get evaluated.

Time to have another look as the frigatebird sees it. Wheels defy gravity at Belle Chasse, Louisiana, a little after 10:00 a.m.

Our twenty-four-year-old pilot is Corey Miller. Up over the marshes, we're oil hunters once more. Soon we're flying in and out of clouds, and this makes me nervous. Increased air traffic in the last few days has brought planes close enough to blow kisses.

The curious and the dispersant dispensers and the helicopters crowd the sky. Slip-sliding by. Up here at these speeds, gaps close fast. You want good vis. We have bad vis.

Sometimes we're whited out for minutes. Cat-and-mouse with other planes. Corey talks to his headset constantly. Young and alert, I hope; not cocky. Seems on the ball.

A rather alarming number of wildlife biologists get raked off in small-plane crashes. Do a computer search with the words "biologist plane crash" and you'll see what's on my mind right now. Once, in Honduras, I was about to board a small plane to an outer island, but agreed to go later so some other people could get back to the mainland first. During their flight the engine quit, and the plane crashed into the sea and sank. Luck put them close enough to land that someone saw the plane plummet and raced to pick up survivors. But I'd planned a much longer water crossing, and if we'd done my trip first, we'd probably never have been found.

Yet right now, I'm not worried about our plane. I'm worried about other planes. Our current destination, directly above the blowout, is also of much interest to the other fliers. Corey tells me they've worked out altitude separations for the different aircraft. I tell him good, thanks. I gaze down, and think of home.

Headed to 3,500 feet, for safety's sake. A little high for seeing details well, but you see more if you're alive. The clouds let us play peekaboo with the ocean. They also cast Rorschach-test shadows. We see: barges, boats. Oil rigs, of course. Muddy troughs of river water slinking seaward, soils of the Great Plains, carrying their fertilizers and pesticides, maintaining the Gulf's chronic illness. Like I said: problems besides petroleum.

The shimmering sea pea green now. The engine noise. When we open a side window for photos, the flapping wind.

Shrimp boats continue towing boom through thick and thin oil with no significant effect on it. Most oil spills over their U of boom. Slicks greet the boats' bows, slicks are their wake. They've been wasting time like this for weeks now.

We apply more altitude to defeat the thickening clouds. A worse and safer view of a sea streaked widely with oil. The sea keeps appearing and disappearing, blue sky appears and disappears. The one constant: oil.

Miles and miles of streaks, tendrils, fingers. Oil coats the ocean brick orange. Brown. Differing densities under varying light. Miles, miles, miles.

With his small camera, Corey is taking pictures. I remember being twenty-four. So will he.

At 11:30 we're flying ellipses over ground zero. The clouds break nicely, revealing a couple of *dozen* ships. Ships large and smaller. The relief well drillers. The flare of burning gas. Choppers touch ships' helipads like dragonflies grasp reeds.

The blue water looks like mere cracks between heavy brown billows of used motor oil. An absolute mess. The horizon-gobbling *scale* of this now.

My camera loads image upon image to its buffer before I give it a chance to save. Maybe I can get it all, take it all out of the ocean.

Corey's had my headset turned off while he's been talking to planes and air-traffic control. He hits a button and says to me, "A photo makes it look like one area. Until you get up here and see that it's as far as you can see in all directions. You can't get that in a picture."

Picture that.

At 12:15 P.M. more or less, we're back over the shoreline. Thick blobs near the shore. Waves lap darkly. The beach is stained. The emerald marsh, bordered black.

But only bordered. I sense the marshes' restorative power. Nature hurls hurricanes, droughts followed by floods, diseases, famine. But in the long haul—and this will require time—nature is what can get us out of the trouble we keep getting ourselves into. They call it Mother because, though she can punish, she's why we're here in the first place. She's the hope we have while we're so hopelessly juvenile.

As the heat of June soars, anger mounts over the Obama administration's recently declared six-month moratorium on exploratory deepwater drilling. The president is in a no-win spot, with people both demanding that he do more and condemning him for what he is doing. The goal was to give the government time to review the rules for oversight of such wells. Many Americans horrified by the blowout welcomed the shutdown.

But here, the moratorium on new drilling is deeply unpopular. Various people are calling it things like "a death blow to Louisiana" that "has and will continue to destroy tens of thousands of lives," creating "an economic ripple effect that will be catastrophic to our entire region."

Those working in the petroleum industry see the moratorium as a bigger threat than the spewing oil. Many of the affected rigs will seek to drill in other countries, imperiling an estimated 800 to 1,400 jobs per rig, including third-party support personnel. As many as 50,000 jobs may be affected, though the industry and Louisiana's elected officials provide the highest estimates.

"From 1947 until 2009, there were 42,000 wells drilled in state and federal waters in the Gulf of Mexico and 99 days ago one of them blew up," rages Democratic senator Mary Landrieu of Louisiana. "But no matter how horrible that is, you don't shut down the entire industry." She says that a temporary ban on drilling, even if it lasted for only a few months, could affect as many as 330,000 people in just Louisiana.

I'm not downplaying the dilemma here, but I don't trust her numbers or her hyperbole. The Louisiana Economic Development department estimates that the six-month moratorium will cause the loss of up to 10,000 jobs within a few months. State figures show that the area's whole oil and gas industry—not just the deep exploratory drilling that is temporarily banned—supports 320,000 jobs, $12.7 billion in wages, and $70.2 billion in business sales.

To the industry, its supporters, and its congressional backers and lobbyists, a moratorium doesn't make sense when more than 30,000 other wells have been drilled in U.S. waters, 700 of which are as deep as or deeper than the one the Deepwater Horizon was drilling. And they argue that the incentives are already there to avoid the fate of this ill-fated well; no one wants the kind of mess BP now has all over its hands. One rig worker says, "For us to stop drilling in the Gulf is like ending our lives as far as the way we live. It's really that scary." That's what fishermen say about their inability to keep fishing. (The administration will lift the drilling moratorium on October 12.)

President Obama signals what might be the first inflection point from unmitigated disaster to silver linings. It's part rhetoric, part counterbalance to the panic. He promises, "Things are going to return to normal." Not only that, but: "I am confident that we're going to be able to leave the Gulf Coast in better shape than it was before." He declares seafood from the Gulf's open fishing areas safe to eat. And he announces that he's pried from BP an agreement to set up a compensation fund that will run into "the billions of dollars."

In the same span of days, the biggest mess to come ashore so far is heavily coating Louisiana's enormous Barataria Bay. Birds sodden in syrupy crude, stranded sea turtles, beaches blanketed in brown goo, marshes bathtub-ringed in oil produce some of the most heart-wrenching photos yet of the blowout.

"This was some of the best fishing in the whole region, and the oil's coming in just wave after wave. It's hard to stomach, it really is," says one fishing guide. A resident adds, "We got little otter families that swim in and out, we got coons, all that good stuff, man. It's good for the kids out here. They swim, work on the boats, fish." They did.

Day and night, the well continues injecting more of the same into the oily Gulf. It feels like a siege. Like it's hopeless.

Because I'd wanted to fly right over the blowout, we had to stay high. But in a different part of the Gulf, author David Helvarg and conservationist John Wathen were low enough to see wildlife. Their video is the most affecting thing I've seen yet about the blowout's ongoing effects. In a TV interview on MSNBC, Wathen, in a mellow Mississippi drawl, describes seeing dolphins mired in oil. "You can see the sheen for miles and miles and miles to the horizon. We figure we saw over a hundred dolphins that were in distress. Some were obviously dead, belly-up in the water. And others, they looked like they were in their death throes." He talks about seeing the Gulf set aflame, the towering columns of smoke.

Still ninety-three degrees at 5:00 p.m. Everything here is far from everything else. Grand Isle, on the seacoast side of Barataria Bay, is about a two-and-a-half-hour drive from New Orleans. The road runs along canals for many, many miles, the roadside vegetation beautiful, lush, green, summery. I especially enjoy seeing the draping Spanish moss hanging from trees. And those black vultures in that robin's-egg-blue sky, effortlessly circling.

Lots of modest to run-down homes. Not a thriving place. Looks like money is tight. Beauty salons in people's homes; their signs on the lawn. A sign advertises frogs' legs and turtle meat. "Ducks for Sale." Live minnows, live crabs. Docks every now and then. Boats. *Bayou Queen, Lady Catherine, Captain Toby,* looking both proud and forlorn, tied up, underemployed. "For Sale: Black Angus Bulls and Heifers." Mitch's Garden Center. Doc's Body Shop. The Flower Pot florist. Debra's Movie World. Tiresome billboards picturing real estate agents, insurance agents, car salesmen. A funeral home's hand-painted sign. Austin's Fresh Seafood bears a smaller hand-painted placard: "Closed Due to BP."

Up over the Intracoastal Canal.

And now displays of grief and rage come bubbling to the surface. At one intersection, murals. Obama's portrait and the words "What Now?" A Grim Reaper identified as BP, captioned, "You Killed Our Gulf. You Killed Our Way of Life." A grim statue of a person holding a dead fish, accompanied by a child whose head is bowed, painted as though oil-drenched, labeled, "God Help Us All."

On the main road, with a speed limit of fifty, I suddenly notice I'm doing eighty. It's not that I'm in a hurry to get there. It's that I'm in a hurry to get this over with so I can leave. I'd better watch my speed; a cop is occupied with someone who didn't watch his.

The road narrows to one lane. The paralleling channel widens as I near the coast. Thirty miles to go. There are some pretty big ships here now. More port facilities for oil rig tenders and the like. More industrial plants related to oil and gas. Not quaint.

At the bridge to Grand Isle, the horizon is punctured by derricks, giant antenna towers guy-wired into the marsh, petrochemical tanks, helicopter pads, warehouses on stilts, tugboats and rig tenders. Chevron's aircraft operations has its own small airport for helicopters.

While I'm driving through Leeville, the radio conveys that "BP said it was unaware of any reason for the stock price drop."

I'm on a road paved right through an immense marsh that stretches from horizon to horizon. How many millions of wildfowl must once have swarmed into here. I've stopped in three places looking for a road map. No one sells them. But in each place stood a line of guys buying beer. I guess that's what there is to do.

Contrast: In places like Shell Beach and Hopedale, the fisherfolk seem woven into the place like vines grown up on netting. Can't be uprooted. Transplantation would be wrenching, possibly impossible. The rig workers, different. Just a job. Could be anywhere. Might as well be. Looking displaced. Their workplace distant and forsaken from whatever counts to them as home. Painful to witness. Everything here in pain, or bored.

It's hard to imagine that anything but oil could have made it worth the time and money to build a raised roadbed and pave it. This road seems so tenuous, so vulnerable to harsh weather. All the houses here are on stilts. A Forster's tern dives into a creek. Surprisingly, pleasantly, there are plenty of white, un-oil-stained egrets here.

And suddenly a cheerful "Welcome to Grand Isle." Stylish roadside sign, letters three feet high. Blue stylized waves harken back to when the ocean was that color. Artful and colorful, of cut steel, with colorful steel marlin and redfish and tarpon swimming across it. Flanked by planted palms. Pretty and proud.

Anxious for a quick glance at the water, I turn where it says, "Welcome to Elmer's Island. Open Daily." When a sign warns, "Access at Your Own Risk," I take it at its word. Where the sign says, "Beach Closed," I continue.

Before reaching the telltale lineup of Porta Potties that have become BP's major expression of Gulf architecture, I get repelled by security guards incredulous that police did not intercept me sooner. (Who'd have thought that Portosans, so innocuous at Woodstock, so reliable during the Age of Aquarius, would turn ominous and foreboding so soon into this millennium?)

"If you come back here, you'd have to get a BP representative to come with ya. This is a BP safety area. You need a hard hat, steel-toed shoes, safety glasses—"

Another impressive display of BP's near obsession with keeping everyone *safe*. In the wrong ways, at the wrong time, sweating the meaningless small stuff.

"They got containers full of oil. You get a whiff of that crap—I don't know; they just don't want nobody passed out, y'know?"

No, I don't. Because hard hats, steel shoes, and safety glasses won't protect you from fumes. This is the company that refuses respirators. Talk to anyone with an ID badge, you can't help feeling every word is bullshit. It's not always their fault. Sometimes they're just regurgitating the bullshit they've been overfed. Some of the bullshitters are nice: "If you get one of them BP guys to come with ya, you can come back," he offers as I'm turning around. And some, less so.

This is a miserable purgatory of a place. The channels cut straight in a place where water naturally meanders. The raised roads trespass into low country where boats would belong. And now there's oil where water belongs. Oil where honesty belongs. Everything at odds with the place's soul.

It's a contest for the worst kind of possession, the one that diminishes what it acquires, harms what it strives to hold.

Grand Isle is grand indeed, many miles long. Marshes and power lines on the north, sandy Gulf beach on the south. A horizon pierced and pincushioned by cranes. A weathered sign says, "Jesus Christ Reigns over Grand Isle," but another new "Beach Closed" warning indicates that BP reigns now. I pass sheriffs and a couple hundred day laborers climbing aboard school buses in a big lot full of Porta Potties.

I duck down a road. On the beach: Porta Potties. Little shade shelters spaced evenly along miles of shoreline. Stacked cases of water. It's already after quitting time, 7:00 P.M., so no one's here. It's still hot, and a bottle of water would be nice. Perhaps BP owes me a little *clean* water. I forbear. I don't actually want anything of BP's. As far up and down the beach as I can see the dry sand is thoroughly crisscrossed with tire tracks. Was a beach, is a disaster site. BP's D-Day.

There's no one here to watch the sunset, stroll hand in hand, look for shells, or take an evening dip as the day releases its hot irons of heat. One woman leads her small son along the sand. Having a hard time negotiating the corrugated ridges and dips of tire tracks in soft substrate but trying to make a go of it, he follows like a toddling bear cub. She tells me she can last a year like this; after that they don't know. Says we can be here, but can't go past the berm to the water. It's patrolled. I see one distant vehicle moving on the sand. When she leaves, I walk over the berm anyway; I need a closer look. Nearer the water the *entire* beach is oiled. Long, dark band of stain. Fresh blobs and splatters.

Rather surprisingly, the water seems like water. Where the waves lap, there's some clarity to it. And I can see some crabs, alive. The Oil comes and goes in great waves. Unpredictable foe.

A few days ago, oil slurped the shore so thickly here that pelicans looked cast in bronze. Horrible. That massive murk has moved. The water from the shore outward remains slicked and splatter-dappled, but it's not a black lapping mat right now.

Two middle-aged women get out of their car. Just drove sixty miles. "I never thought I'd see anything like *this!* It used to be a sand beach. You could come out and have parties and picnics and swim. This is really—"

"You think *God* would do something about this."

"The hurricane season, it could pick up all that oil out there and put it all over everything."

A small band of souls come out to set up their volleyball net in the tire tracks. Resolute, jaws set for fun.

Outside a cottage, a sign: "BP Headquarters." Its arrow points directly down into an actual toilet bowl.

Closer to the east end of the island and on the north side, mullet jump. Gulls loaf. They look okay. Terns fishing along the bridge offer cheer that even here life continues. Overhead, those pelicans are all soiled. But still flying, at least. At least for now.

Speckled Trout Lane. Bayside Circle. Redfish Lane. Pete's Wharf Lane. Sunset Lane. A place for sun and fun. Was. News networks, their trucks parked at cottages, provide some owners with summer rental income. At other cottages, camouflaged fat-wheeled trucks. Varied contractors and the National Guard.

Overhead, a frigatebird. *Really* brown pelicans. Distinctly dingy, they skim over the slick surface. I fear for them.

On a lawn, a graveyard of white crosses memorializes these departed: "Beach Sunsets," "Sand Between My Toes," "Marlin," "Sand Castles," "Dolphins," "Bluefin Tuna," "Crabbing," "Shrimp," "Sailing," "Beach Sunrises," "Summer Fun," "Sea Turtles," "Picnics on the Beach," "Floundering," "Flying a Kite," "Sand Dollars," "Oysters on the Half Shell," "Boogie-Boarding"; there're about four dozen more.

Nearby, a much larger cross says, "In Memory of All That Was Lost; Courtesy of BP and Our Federal Government." Another cross marks the passing of "Our Soul." Another roadside sign: "BP— Cannot Fish or Swim. How the Hell Are We Suppose to Feed Our Kids Now?" Signed by the owner. A hurting, hurting place.

Based on the latest flow rate estimates of up to 60,000 barrels per day, the fine for the escaping oil alone could be $260 million *per day*. Anyone still doubt that BP has been trying to hide the body? Criminal penalties, if fully imposed, could cause the costs to balloon to more than $60 billion, dwarfing an escrow account the White House wants BP to establish for paying claims of economic loss.

The government will likely use BP's prior criminal record, such as BP's guilty plea in the 2005 refinery explosion that killed fifteen people in Texas City, to argue that the Deepwater Horizon disaster resulted from a corporate culture that lets hurrying and cost-consciousness jeopardize safety.

BP's carefully crafted public image of friendliness belied its egregious record for serious safety problems. The *Economist* reports that between June 2007 and February 2010, BP received an astonishing 97 percent of all operational safety and health citations for "willful" and "egregiously willful" breaches of the rules at American oil refineries, adding that this is "a remarkable share even allowing for close scrutiny after Texas City."

But the laws that would be brought to bear generally don't have felony provisions that would lead to jail time for executives, and where they do, prosecutors would have to directly connect a defendant with a crime.

On Capitol Hill, congressional Democrats Henry Waxman and Ed Markey blast the heads of ExxonMobil, Chevron, ConocoPhillips, BP, and Shell Oil for producing "virtually identical" disaster response plans. All discuss how to protect those famous walruses in the Gulf of Mexico. The congressmen excoriate the oil titans' "cookie-cutter plans," citing sections that have "the exact same words," indicating an investment of "zero time and money."

It will turn out that five giant oil companies all got their response plans from the same tiny Texas contractor. The firms all assured the government that they could handle oil spills much *larger* than the one now threatening the region's environment and economy. And each time, the Minerals Management Service approved the plan and gave the go-ahead for drilling.

In its exploration plans for Alaska, Shell has analyzed the prospect of only a 2,000-gallon diesel fuel spill. It asserted that a larger crude oil spill would be unlikely because the water is shallow. The Minerals Management Service skimmed up this assumption without questioning it. Shell is relying on a single company based about three hundred miles from its intended Chukchi Sea drilling sites. Anything goes wrong there, Shell would have available only a tiny fraction of the resources BP called up in the Gulf.

Big ol' jet airliner. I doze, then rouse. That's Sandy Hook, New Jersey. I glance at the ocean and reflexively look for streaks of oil. The stain in my brain.

On Long Island, when an egret flies over my house, I absentmindedly check it for signs of oil, as has become my habit. At our local marina, they're talking the Oil. At the beach, it's sun lotion and the Oil. It sticks to everyone's minds. Follows everywhere. You can't wash your thoughts of it.

At the marina's outdoor bar, the loud ones blame environmentalists. (That's what their favorite broadcasters have told them to say.) "There's no reason not to get the oil that's in Alaska." "Because they won't let them." "It's the enviros." "The enviros pushed them to this; BP was pushed into this by the enviros." "Big guvvamint." "Can't do nuthin' anymore."

In his first and much-anticipated address to our nation from the Oval Office, President Obama called for a new "national mission" to wean the United States off fossil fuels. "The tragedy unfolding on our coast is the most painful and powerful reminder yet that the time to embrace a clean energy future is now. Now is the moment for this generation to embark on a national mission to unleash American innovation and seize control of our own destiny."

Perfect!

But why isn't Obama throwing all his weight behind the new energy bill unveiled by Senators John Kerry and Joe Lieberman? Because the Kerry-Lieberman bill includes fees on carbon emissions, and the White House is afraid Republicans will ride the slogan "carbon tax" to multiple victories at the midterm elections.

It's hard to see how America can accomplish anything as long as two parties locked in a death battle can't see past two-year congressional cycles. But I think Obama should press it, because he will never win his opponents over, but by not acting boldly he is losing the enthusiasm of his supporters.

Thomas Friedman had written that this is not Obama's Hurricane Katrina; it's his 9/11—one of those rare seismic opportunities to energize the country to do something really important that is too hard to do in normal times. But as Bush blew 9/11's possibilities, Obama is blowing this blowout. To Americans wanting to do something for the country they love, Bush told a few to go fight and the rest of us to go shopping.

Boosting new energy technology and building new energy infrastructure would seem to line up with the mood among those who elected Obama to bring sweeping reforms. Yet Obama is chary, and a well-oiled moment is slipping through his fingers.

Obama, having already asked congressional Democrats to make a hard vote on health care, seems to feel he can't ask them for another. He isn't publicly deploying his assembled brain trust, including Nobel Prize–winning Energy secretary Steven Chu, to rally Americans who are waiting to be enlisted, ready to be rallied.

When people ask me, "What can I do to help the Gulf?" I don't know what to tell them. There are no real opportunities for the public to just go down and help out, and for the Big Picture, we haven't been given a concrete presidential vision that we can get behind.

"Mr. President," Friedman offers, "Americans are craving your leadership on this issue. Are you going to channel their good will into something that strengthens our country?—'The Obama End to Oil Addiction Act'—or are you going to squander your 9/11, too?"

In a similar but much more enjoyable vein, MSNBC's Rachel Maddow assumes the role of fake president just long enough to deliver the speech she wishes the president had given. Among other things, she wishes he'd said:

> Never again will any company be allowed to drill in a location where they are incapable of dealing with the potential consequences. . . .
> I'm announcing a new federal command specifically for containment

and cleanup of oil that has already entered the Gulf of Mexico. . . . I no longer say that we must get off oil like every president before me has said. We will get off oil and here's how: The United States Senate will pass an energy bill. This year.

When the benefits of drilling accrue to a private company, but the risks of that drilling accrue to we the American people, whose waters and shoreline are savaged when things go wrong, I as Fake President stand on the side of the American people, and say to the industry: From this day forward, if you cannot handle the risk, you no longer will take chances with our fate to reap your rewards.

Maybe Maddow will someday throw her sombrero into the presidential ring. And if she wins, she will join every president since the 1970s in saying that America must get off oil. Richard Nixon, Gerald Ford, Jimmy Carter, Ronald Reagan, George H. W. Bush, Bill Clinton, George W. Bush, Barack Obama. And Rachel Maddow.

But until the country realizes that our Congress and our courts must serve people with belly buttons, not multinational corporations . . .

More congressional hearings and briefings. The Interior Department's acting inspector general, Mary L. Kendall, tells a congressional panel that in the Gulf region the Minerals Management Service has only sixty inspectors to oversee about four thousand drilling facilities. Inspectors in the Gulf operate "with little direction as to what must be inspected, or how." Yet on the Pacific Coast, ten inspectors cover only twenty-three facilities. She says the minerals service has a difficult time recruiting inspectors because the oil industry tends to pay a lot more.

The sargassum weed, whose yellow floating mats provide cover and nursery habitat for many kinds of sea life in the open Gulf, is dying. Most people have never seen or even heard of sargassum, but it shelters and feeds uncountable numbers of fish and young sea turtles. Tunas, mahimahi, billfish, mackerels, and others often haunt its edges. Blair Witherington, a research scientist and sea turtle expert with the Florida Fish and Wildlife Conservation Commission, says, "Ordinarily, the sargassum is a nice, golden color. You shake it, and all kinds of life comes out: shrimp, crabs, worms, sea slugs. It is really just bursting with life. It's the base of the food chain. And these areas we're seeing here by comparison are quite dead." He speaks of seeing flyingfish land on rafts of oil and get stuck right there. He says the jellies are dying. "These animals drift into the oil lines and it's like flies on fly paper," Witherington relates. "As far as I can tell, that whole fauna is just completely wiped out." Of dispersants, he says the thinking is "just keep the oil out at sea; the harm will be minimal. And I disagree with that completely." Of his beloved turtles, he says, "We've seen the oil covering the turtles so thick they could barely move, could hardly lift their heads."

It's hard to imagine a turtle in the ocean catching fire, but after all, it's hard to imagine any of this. And so today's vocabulary word from the theater of the absurd is "burn box." Noun: an area of corralled oil set on fire. Contractors are staging mass burns of some of the floating oil mats, setting the sea aflame. Some people allege they're burning up sea turtles along with the oil. I'm dubious. But then again, a lot of little turtles could be clinging to weed mats. The turtle rescuers want to pick up as many turtles as they can find, for fear they'll be incinerated. They find eleven, all of them heavily speckled with oil.

I read that only 3 percent of the slick is thick enough to catch and hold a flame on the surface of the sea. But there is so much oil that the fires and their towering billows of thick smoke are horrendous.

Workers will light more than three hundred fires at sea, sending thick plumes of smoke, carbon dioxide, and hydrocarbons toward heaven. They'll burn more oil than the *Exxon Valdez* spilled. A man employed to ignite floating oil will brag, "No one can deny this is a success."

John Wathen, who spoke of seeing dolphins dying in thick oil, says he witnessed other dolphins, lined up with their heads out of the water, watching the astonishing sight of their ocean in flames.

Various people report seeing sharks, mullet, crabs, rays, and small fish in unusual numbers close to shore. Are they fleeing the oil? Could be. But the Gulf has long had its dead zone of low oxygen, which worsens in summer. Large numbers of fish moving into shallows where there's more oxygen isn't unheard of. The latest figures of dead wildlife total about 800 birds, 350 turtles, and 40 mammals. It's not clear whether the oil killed them all. Even people cruising Louisiana's heavily besmirched Barataria Bay see dozens of dolphins frolicking in oil-sheened water, and oil-smudged pelicans feeding their young.

In some areas still open to fishing, fishers report large catches of red snapper, grouper, king mackerel, and amberjack. Are the fish congregating after fleeing the oil or are they unaffected by it? Are the large schools of fish locals see hanging around piers there because the fishing ban has given the fish a huge break? No one knows. But it's seeming that much life in the Gulf has resilience enough to resist the oil.

After many days of very public pressure from President Obama and many hours of private negotiations, BP finally agrees to divert $20 billion into an independent fund to pay claims arising from the blowout. The company will also suspend paying shareholder dividends for the rest of the year and will set aside an additional $100 million as compensation for lost wages for oil rig workers affected by the Obama moratorium on deep exploratory drilling. The president stresses that the amount is not a ceiling on BP's obligations. Suspending dividends delivers another blow to BP's reputation and its shareholders, but for the company's accountants it's a godsend that saves BP something like $10 billion. The president had earlier alluded to his determination to step in and do "what individuals couldn't do and corporations wouldn't do." For the president and the Gulf, it's a stunning coup.

To Obama, this is a rebalancing after two decades in which multinationals sometimes acted like mini-states beyond government reach, while influencing the government to, as he says, "gut regulations and put industry insiders in charge of industry oversight." The president had no legal basis for the demand. (Remember, BP is legally on the hook for just $75 million.) The deal follows an extraordinary four-hour White House meeting that was punctuated by breaks as each side huddled privately. BP will pay into the fund over four years, at $5 billion a year. Last year, BP generated profits of $17 billion. After the announcement, BP shares close up 1.4 percent, at $31.85.

While the president may have been walking a fine line, at least one member of Congress was blocking the intersection. Republican congressman Joe Barton of the great oiligarchy of Texas rails that Obama acted illegally, and—during a congressional hearing—Barton apologizes to BP executives for our president's "shakedown" of their company. That rumbling is the sound of jaws dropping across America. Even though Barton had reportedly gotten $1.5 million in campaign donations from oil companies, his outburst is bizarre enough to quote at length: "I am ashamed of what happened in the White House yesterday, that a private corporation would be subject to what I would characterize as a shakedown," said Barton. The fund, he said, "amounts to a $20 billion slush fund that is unprecedented in our nation's history" and "sets a terrible precedent for the future." He continued, "I apologize . . . I do not want to live in a country where any time a citizen or a corporation does something that is legitimately wrong it is subject to political pressure that amounts to a shakedown." Keep in mind, this guy was in charge of the Energy and Commerce Committee before the Democrats won the House majority in 2006. And as the political pendulum swings, he'll likely be the chairman again. One thing we agree on: I don't want him to live in this country, either.

On June 17, a *New York Times* editorial opines that BP's CEO, Tony Hayward, has just given Congress "a mind-bogglingly vapid performance." Congressmen Waxman, Stupak, and others spent hours trying to pry answers out of Hayward about what went wrong. Mostly, he deflected and sidestepped the grilling and frustrated the congressmen and the American public. "I was not part of that decision-making process" was his frequent answer to questions. But fair enough; that's true. To Texas Republican congressman Michael Burgess, who was taken aback by the idea that Hayward had no prior knowledge of this well, Hayward answered, "With respect, sir, we drill hundreds of wells a year around the world." To which Burgess shot back: "That's what's scaring me now." During the seven-hour hearing, something like 735,000 gallons of oil leaked into the Gulf.

Rather to its credit, I grudgingly admit, BP releases $25 million of a pledged half billion dollars over ten years to support several universities' research into the effects of the blowout. To make recommendations on which institutions will receive funds, BP appoints an expert panel chaired by environmental microbiologist Rita Colwell, who formerly headed the National Science Foundation and is now a distinguished professor at Johns Hopkins University. Sounding so refreshingly out of character that the cynic in me has trouble figuring out BP's motivation, BP CEO Tony Hayward says in a press release, "It is vitally important that research start immediately into the oil and dispersant's impact, and that the findings are shared fully and openly. We support the independence of these institutions and projects, and hope that the funding will have a significant positive effect on scientists' understanding of the impact of the spill."

So, summing: BP has agreed to pay $20 billion, pledged $500 million for a ten-year research program to study the blowout's lasting effects, agreed to contribute $100 million to support rig workers idled by the administration's deepwater drilling moratorium, and paid over $50 million to promote Gulf tourism.

And yet, doesn't it always seem that no good deed goes unpunished? The House is lining up to pass a drilling overhaul bill that, inter alia, would bar any company from drilling on the outer continental shelf if: more than ten fatalities had occurred at its offshore or onshore facilities or if, in the last seven years, it's paid fines of $10 million or more under the Clean Air or Clean Water Acts.

BP is the only company that currently meets that description.

Coincidence? "The risk of having a dangerous company like BP develop new resources in the Gulf is too great," said Daniel Weiss, Representative George Miller's chief of staff. "Year after year after year, no matter how many incidents they're involved in, no matter how many fines they've had to pay, they never changed their behavior. BP has no one to blame but themselves."

BP's bargaining chip: it says that if it can't drill, then maybe it won't be able to pay. Our bargaining chip: in about two weeks the House will, in fact, pass that company-banning language, helping guarantee BP's continued attention.

This, I think, is true: BP, which gets more than 10 percent of its global production out of the Gulf of Mexico, needs us more than we need it. There are other companies that would send the same oil ashore.

Seeming to recognize that fact, BP is—for once—on its best behavior. Not only is its $20 billion escrow agreement with the White House voluntary, but "We have committed to do a number of things that are not part of the formal agreement with the White House," notes a BP spokesman, in case America really hadn't noticed. "We are not making a direct statement about anything we are committed to do. We are just expressing frustration that our commitments of good will have at least in some quarters been met with this kind of response."

I receive this inane e-mail:

> To help clear the toxins from the water, we will be using the energies of love and appreciation, and a special prayer related by Dr. Masaru Emoto. Dr. Emoto is the Japanese scientist who has done extensive research on how the energy of love and appreciation can change the molecular structure of water at the quantum level. The Process: Stand near, or in, the Gulf of Mexico. Or, imagine that you are standing

there. Direct your thoughts and energies to feelings of love and appreciation. When you are filled with loving thoughts, speak the following prayer: "To whales, dolphins, manatees, pelicans, seagulls, and all aquatic bird species, fishes, shellfish, planktons, corals, algae, and all ion creatures in the Gulf of Mexico, I am sorry. Please forgive me. Thank you. I love you." Join us in prayer. We are one, and the One will join us together in this great work from wherever we are!

So there you have it.

Back on planet Earth, the total count of sea turtles recovered dead, injured, and oiled is up to about 460. The number of turtles coming up to nest has gone down, but the cold winter could have translated into a late spring for them.

Diane Sawyer, ABC News, has this report:

"Who is in charge of the cleanup? For four days we have been asking that question and we have not been able to get an answer. David Muir was with two frustrated governors today. David?"

"This barge should be out in the Gulf sucking up oil. But sixteen of these barges are docked here, all under orders not to move."

Louisiana Governor Jindal: "The Coast Guard stopped them from going to work."

David Muir: "And then today, word from the Coast Guard saying, 'Go ahead.' This kind of confusion is everywhere. Who's in charge here?"

Alabama's Governor Bob Riley: "Great question."

Diane Sawyer: "Two governors saying they cannot get straight answers."

But alongside the video on the Web, the print version of the story says, "The Coast Guard needed to confirm that the boats were equipped with fire extinguishers and life vests." Well, I've been critical of the Coast Guard, but let's be fair: that *is* a straight answer.

On June 20, Tony Hayward "steps down" from being BP's gusher usher (after he was stepped *on* for making so many trips over his own feet). One day later, he has his life back. Off the Isle of Wight he attends yachting races with his son, while BP PR races to defend his right to do so. "No matter where he is, he is always in touch with what is happening within BP," the BP spokesman says of Mr. Hayward, the very man who'd told the U.S. Congress that he was not aware of the Macondo well as Deepwater Horizon was drilling it because "with respect, sir, we drill hundreds of wells a year around the world."

The events prompted Senate Republican Minority Leader Mitch McConnell to say, "All of these guys could use a better PR adviser."

Yes, Tony Hayward has his life back, but Gulf people are saying things like "I see my life ruined. There ain't no shrimping, there ain't no crabbing, there ain't no oystering. Well, the only thing I know is shrimping. That's all I know. Now, you tell me: Where do I go from here?" The owner of a seafood company that normally ships fifteen million pounds a year gets up in the morning, walks to his empty warehouse, trudges back again, sits down in front of the TV, and stares at CNN's oil spill coverage; then he heads back to the warehouse. "I'm just walking around in a circle," he says. "I never been this confused in my life." In the U.S. House of Representatives, while speaking to the House Energy and Commerce Committee, a Lousiana congressman breaks down in tears. He's not alone. A fisherman in his fifties explains, "We start talking, and before you know it, we're all crying. Tough men, you know? Tough as they come. Just break down and cry."

Fisherman: "The first thing I'd like to do is punch that CEO in the mouth. That'd make me feel a little bit better, I guess."

Social worker: "There's breaking points for people. You look at some of these people and you wonder, when is that person going to snap?"

People snap differently. In Alabama, at least one fisherman, despondent, chooses to make his final exit while sitting aboard his beloved boat.

And as one takes his life and one gets his life back, BP decides that an American, Bob Dudley, will replace Tony Hayward. Dudley spent much of his childhood in Mississippi.

Various people in the news media continue to complain about hassles with BP's private guards and about cops and sheriffs' departments doing BP's bidding in clear violation of public rights of freedom of movement on public property. Weeks ago, on June 6, Thad Allen had told ABC News, "I put out a written directive and I can provide it for the record that says the media will have uninhibited access anywhere we're doing operations, except for two things: if it's a security or safety problem. That is my policy. I'm the national incident commander." So there you have it. He's the decider.

The memo, signed by Allen on May 31 and sent to various government entities and to BP, says: "In any matter whatsoever, and at any level of the response, the media shall, at all times, be afforded access to response operations and shall only be asked to leave an area when their presence is in violation of an existing law or regulation, clearly violates the written site safety plan for the area or interferes with effective operations."

Allen's memo says, "the media." I'd have preferred it to also say the public, because people who work for conservation groups, scientists, book writers, freelance or part-time photographers, fishermen who know the area, and folks like that don't have media IDs. Later down the memo says, "No contractor, civilian employee or other responder involved in the Deepwater Horizon response has the authority to deny media access to operations except as noted in paragraph one." That's pretty clear. And the intent is clear.

Okay, great. Now let's see the directive in action. On June 22, weeks after Allen's "uninhibited access" order, *Mother Jones* magazine's website posts a video of a "law officer" hassling a guy from the American Birding Association for filming the exterior of a BP office building from across the street. Andrew Wheelan was not on BP's property at the time, but the law officer nevertheless carries out BP's intimidation program:

Wheelan: "Am I violating any laws or anything like that?"

Guard: "Um . . . not particularly. BP doesn't want people filming."

Wheelan: "Well, I'm not on their property so BP doesn't have anything to say about what I do right now."

Guard: "Let me explain: BP doesn't want any filming. So all I can really do is strongly suggest that you not film anything right now. If that makes any sense."

Let's make the rapid trip from no sense to incensed: Shortly thereafter, Wheelan got into his car and drove away, but he was soon pulled over. It was the same cop, but this time he was with a guy whose badge read "BP Security." The cop stood by as "BP Security" interrogated Wheelan for twenty minutes, asking him who he worked with, who he answered to, what he was doing, why he was down here in Louisiana. Mr. BP Security phoned someone and, just to be mean, confiscated Wheelan's bird-helper volunteer badge. Eventually, he "let Wheelan go." But bear in mind, this is a private security guard, pulling a citizen off a public road.

It gets better. "Then two unmarked cars followed me," Wheelan says. "Every time I pulled over, they pulled over." This went on for twenty miles.

Bye-bye, God bless America; hello, corporate police state. So easy. And no blood.

Coda: the "law officer" was an off-duty sheriff's deputy for Terrebonne Parish. Off duty—and working in the private employ of BP. The deputy failed to include the traffic stop in his incident report. In other words, he abused his authority and then hid the fact. But he had support from higher up: a major in the sheriff's office tells the magazine's writer, Mac McClelland, that an off-duty deputy using his official vehicle to pull someone over while working for a private company is "standard and acceptable practice" because—get ready—Wheelan *could have been a terrorist.*

Of *course* he could. It's not like BP is at the epicenter of a giant oil blowout and someone with a video camera might want to post an image of BP's headquarters, with its huge logo, on the Web, or anything like that. It's much more likely that a terrorist would be standing across the street with a video camera and a magazine writer in broad daylight, talking to BP's guards.

Ergo, back to Thad Allen: "The media will have uninhibited access anywhere . . . except . . . if it's a security or safety problem." And it's *always* a security or safety problem—because that's all they ever have to say to do anything they want.

It could be a cleanup; it could be a cover-up. You can't tell. You can't tell because the Big People are undermining our ability to ask. But let's make it simple, people: Either there's freedom of speech or there isn't. Either there's freedom of assembly or there isn't. Either there's freedom of movement or there isn't. Either there's freedom. Or not.

And what there is here and now is: bullying and lying at the speed of sound. Illegal, sure; but when law enforcers agree, it gets very hard to deal with. Why they agree, why they get turned against the public, I'm not sure. Something about the liberal media? Something against outsiders? Boredom and a chance to throw their weight around with impunity? It's all a little dose of "the banality of evil" (a phrase originally coined in reference to the Nazis). The idea: it doesn't take terrible people to do bad things in an official capacity. It takes average people. Average people who want to do a good job for their superiors, want to be loyal, who know how to go along to get along, and who like to avoid any risk to themselves. Unfortunately, that's all it takes. Average people.

Who are the "terrorists"? Who are the ones acting against America's principles? The people who don't want you to see the pictures, or those who do? The people who abuse their authority, or the ones they abuse? The people whose reckless rush risked hurting all "the little people," or the people with little, who stand tall?

And here's the main thing: even if the Coast Guard has taken the spirit of Allen's media-access memo to heart and fully embraced his directive (I said "if"), BP and local law enforcers are ignoring it. They're doing whatever they want when they feel like pushing people around. And this is America. These companies are multinational. Imagine what they do elsewhere.

What they do: In Nigeria, an amount of oil roughly equivalent to that lost by the *Exxon Valdez* spills into the Niger Delta every year. It has destroyed farms and forests, contaminated drinking water, driven people from their homes, and ruined the nets and traps of fishing people. On May 1, 2010, a ruptured ExxonMobil pipeline spilled more than a million gallons into the delta over seven days. Local people protesting say security guards attacked them. Thick tar washed ashore along the coast. Said Bonny Otavie, a member of Parliament, "Oil companies do not value our life; they want us to all die."

Nigerians can scarcely believe the efforts to stop the Gulf oil leak and to protect the Gulf shoreline. When major oil spills happen in the Niger Delta, Nigerian writer Ben Ikari observes, "The oil companies just ignore it." The Nigerian government says there were more than 7,000 spills between 1970 and 2000. Nearly one-tenth of the oil America imports comes from Nigeria.

Shell says that 98 percent of all its oil spills in Nigeria are caused by vandalism, theft, or sabotage. Local communities and environmental groups insist that the problem is rusting facilities and apathy. Similar stories come from the Amazon, Ecuador, and elsewhere. Nigerian environmentalist Nnimo Bassey says, "In Nigeria, they have been living above the law. They are now clearly a danger to the planet."

By the start of the third week of June, one-third of the Gulf's federal waters, 81,000 square miles, remain closed to fishing.

And the *Economist* estimates that BP is on the hook for eventual cleanup costs and damages of $20 billion, plus fines up to $17 billion. But BP's market-value plummet is two to three times as great. BP stock has melted off nearly $90 billion worth of value. Investors fear that compensation claims are spiraling out of control. I think they're overreacting. BP, I am willing to say, will probably be fine.

Big Oil has long enjoyed the milk and honey of tax-fed privileges ranging from massive subsidies to supreme dispensation. Exxon led the small communities of Prince William Sound in a grimly choreographed death dance that ended in 2008. When a huge penalty was levied against Exxon, the oil giant got the U.S. Supreme Court to hear its case nearly two decades after *Valdez* ran aground. Chief Justice John Roberts began his inquiry by asking, "Isn't the question here how a company can protect itself from unlimited damages?"

No, John, that isn't the question. The question is: how can *people* be protected from unlimited damage?

A jury had awarded $5 billion in damages, but the Bush-wacked Supreme Court said, "No, it'll be more like ten percent of that." Thanks to the antisocial, pro-corporate ideology of certain "justices" still seated on the Court for life, the oil titan paid just $507 million (10 percent) of the $5 billion damage settlement that a lower, better court had arranged, and just $25 million (17 percent) of its $150 million initial fine. The payments were a tiny, momentary blip on Exxon's profit spreadsheets—and a second catastrophe for the real lives of real people of actual communities. Nineteen years after the *Exxon Valdez* ran aground on Bligh Reef, some plaintiffs received their final payment. Others had already died.

And today the Court remains stacked with Bush appointees as thoughtless, more heartless, and more pro-business than it was then.

The aftermath of the *Exxon Valdez* spill—its devastating effect on the region's wildlife, its long-lasting depression of fish prices, the social and economic strains that followed, Exxon's antisocial behavior and the way the Supreme Court swam with it into the toilet—set the bar so low, it's as if someone dug a trench and threw the bar in. One nation under oil. The *Exxon Valdez* spill was more than a tragedy, more than a crime. It remains a national stain and a national trauma. The fear that this Gulf blowout will be "as bad as the *Exxon Valdez*" will remain in hearts, on minds, and on lips throughout.

Back on May 6, President Obama had declared a three-week moratorium on exploratory oil drilling in the Gulf of Mexico, to give his administration time to review safety regulations and the quality of government oversight. While drilling technology has exploded—poor word choice—*improved* incredibly in the last thirty years, allowing location and extraction in ever-deeper, harder-to-reach regions, cleanup equipment has gone nowhere. Since the Ixtoc blowout, since the Exxon spill, it's the same old booms, skimmers, dispersants, and guys with shovels. They make money from oil, so they put money into oil. They don't make money from cleanup, so they ignore cleanup. Big mistake, because accidents can be costly—but it's obvious how little they've cared.

Nearly two hundred miles from shore, a $3 billion floating oil platform much larger and more complex than the Deepwater Horizon straddles the deep ocean like a giant steel octopus. Named Perdido (Spanish for "lost"), this colossus pumps oil from dozens of wells in water nearly two miles deep—while simultaneously drilling new ones. The pipelines flowing from wells to rigs like this can be tens of miles long. Compared to this monster, the Deepwater Horizon was a simple little rig with the luxury of focusing on one task in relatively shallow water. Meet the new wave: *ultra-deep* platforms.

It's safe, of course. Accidents are rare, as we've seen. And also, of course, the stakes—and the risks—increase as the rigs get larger and more complicated.

"Our ability to manage risks hasn't caught up with our ability to explore and produce in deep water," says Edward C. Chow, a former oil executive now with the Center for Strategic and International Studies. Perdido, for example, lies twenty hours away from supply-boat help. It lives in a realm of hundred-mile-an-hour hurricanes and mountainous walls of angry, battering-ram waves. Its delicate underwater equipment and many pipelines feel the insistence of currents and mud slides, but lie far beyond human reach in their own underwater metropolis populated by unmanned submarines and robots. Down there, it's *Dune*—but without people.

In 2005, Hurricanes Rita and Katrina damaged or destroyed hundreds of offshore platforms and pipelines. (About thirty thousand miles of pipeline crisscross the Gulf of Mexico seafloor.) The gulf's oil and gas production shut down for weeks. I hope we don't someday look back at that as a quaint time of heroic people. Meanwhile, new rigs have recently arrived in the Gulf that can drill in water 12,000 feet deep.

"Going to the moon is hazardous. Going to Mars is even more

hazardous," says University of California professor Robert Bea. "The industry has entered a new domain of vastly increased complexity and increased risks."

On May 27, Obama had extended the ban on deep exploratory drilling for six months. Today, June 22, a federal judge strikes down the moratorium, saying, "Are all airplanes a danger because one was? All oil tankers like *Exxon Valdez*? All trains? All mines? That sort of thinking seems heavy-handed, and rather overbearing."

Of course, that's not the point. When a plane crashes, hundreds of thousands of people don't get put out of work, nor do they perceive their communities, livelihoods, and self-identities threatened; an entire region doesn't lose tens of billions of dollars. That's a difference. The judge says the six-month moratorium would have an "immeasurable effect" on the industry, the local economy, and the U.S. energy supply. Maybe *he* can't measure it, but economists should be able to tell us how many jobs, what overall effects, things like that. All those big robes and that big bench don't guarantee much. Beware the man behind the curtain.

And yet, I have to admit that even I'm not sure that the Obama moratorium is necessary. It seems that regulators could greatly improve rules and tighten oversight without a moratorium. But I just don't like the judge's juvenile logic. His silly comparisons are off base. Rather than blind justice at work, I see a certain blindness. Like most everyone in this mess, he doesn't grasp the big picture: this isn't like a plane crash; it's like aviation safety procedures. There are systemic problems to fix.

In response, the Interior secretary says he will order a *new* moratorium, one designed to eliminate doubt that it is appropriate. Salazar says he expects oil companies to complain that the coming regulations are too onerous. "There is the pre–April 20th framework of regulation and the post–April 20th framework," he'll say, "and the oil and gas industry better get used to it."

———

Wherever you turned, the Oil shadowed.

Suddenly, the Gulf seemed to betray all prior promises.

For weeks, much of the Gulf resembled abstract oil paintings.

In the beautiful blue Gulf, the blowout meant a massive brownout.

Directly over the blown-out well, crews drilled relief wells while one rig collected oil and flared gas.

Oil drifting inexorably onto undefended Louisiana shoreline.

Intimate, intertwined relationships create human reliance
on the Mississippi Delta marshes.

The marshes have for decades suffered death by a thousand cuts and,
oil aside, they still do.

Booms, booms, booms.

Workers collect sand
splattered with oil while
a few beachgoers remain,
determined to enjoy
themselves.

Booms rendered useless by a little
wave action.

Booms could not prevent birds
from flying to oiled areas.

Booms towed by shrimp boats seemed to leave as much oil behind as there was ahead.

Oil-splattered beaches kept tourists away in droves.

On Dauphin Island, Alabama, wetlands were destroyed to mine sand to build oceanfront berms.

Were the multimillion-dollar berms really to hold back oil, or were they a desperate attempt to shield real estate from the next big hurricane?

A sea turtle nest. Protected?

Around the taped-off turtle nest, all beach-holding vegetation was destroyed for berms that would likely wash away, and any turtles that hatched had a near-zero chance of detecting the direction to the sea.

Happy Independence Day

By the dawn's oily light, kids had slick fun on the Fourth of July.

Spontaneous art expressing roadside rage.

One Mississippi River Delta resident's opinion.

On a private lawn in Grand Isle, Louisiana, grief.

On a southern Louisiana intersection, despair during a summer of anguish.

Despite the judge's ruling, BP stock drops 2.7 percent. The better bet: shrimp. Imported shrimp prices are up 13 percent, and Thai shrimp import poundage is up 37 percent. And Gulf shrimp prices have gone jumbo, up a whopping 43 percent. About 60 to 70 percent of oysters eaten in the United States come from the Gulf, and oysters now cost about 40 percent more, too.

On June 23 the feds reopen fishing over more than 8,000 square miles. Their reason: "because no oil has been observed there." So why'd they close it? Other parts of the Gulf with no observed oil were never closed. Still closed: roughly 75,000 square miles, about 32.5 percent of the Gulf's federal waters. Their smiley face: "That leaves more than two-thirds of the Gulf's federal waters available for fishing." People have now found more than 500 sea turtles dead or dying around the Gulf.

During the last days of June, Tropical Storm Alex thickens the air with sheets of rain that pound so heavily on my car that several times, unable to see, I have to pull over. Seven- to ten-foot seas lash the coast. Beach cleanup is halted, most work disrupted, most people scurrying for shore; hundreds of vessels steam for ports. Waves are pushing most booms ashore. Movement of the surface oil accelerates; winds push the crude turds northwest, toward heretofore oil-unsoiled Texas beaches.

Thad Allen says the weather could suspend operations for two weeks. It "would be the first time and there is no playbook," he says with dramatic flourish. No playbook because the BP Gulf plan mentions walruses, but doesn't mention tropical storms or hurricanes.

One of the bigger worries: if they have to make the capture vessels disconnect from their supply lines, all that oil just resumes leaking full-on into the sea. Upgraded to a hurricane, Alex is the strongest June storm since 1966, with sustained winds of more than one hundred miles an hour. But its main winds pass wide of ground zero, and the rigs stay connected. The winds, though, splatter oil onto the beaches of South Padre Island, Texas, and Galveston.

On June 30, 2010, every Republican in the House of Representatives votes no on a bill that would require corporations to disclose the money they give to American elections.

Also on June 30, Coast Guard admiral Thad Allen becomes retired Coast Guard admiral Thad Allen. He joins the Department of Homeland Security and will continue managing the federal oil spill response.

Meanwhile, the widows of workers killed in the Deepwater Horizon explosions are being told that Transocean plans to argue that its liability for damages owed is limited by the Death on the High Seas Act and the Jones Act. Shelley Anderson, whose husband, Jason, was a tool pusher on the rig, says, "Why would the damages to a family be different if a death occurs on the ocean as opposed to on land?" Well, Ms. Anderson, it's not that the damage to your family is different. It's just that, having caused your husband's death, the corporation doesn't want to pay you. That's just the kind of people their executives are. Remember, no belly button; they've got their wallets in their chest pockets, where their hearts should be, and are bereft of pulse.

In the true heart of the delta, what land there is lies like giant snakes resting in shallow water, each snake just wide enough for a road, a few docks, some homes. That's all. The people and communities seem as aquatic as muskrats.

Things have changed in the last two months. When I first came, people were in shock. Now most people have worn a slight groove in their situation.

The first place I'd visited was Shell Beach, Louisiana. So now I'm going back. This time I have a little company for a change. Mandy Moore works for the National Wildlife Federation. Blond, twenty-nine, slight of build, she's from around here, knows the place. So she's driving. I'm in the passenger seat eating peanuts and some cherries.

"We won't go to the staging area," she says. "They won't let us down that road at all. That part's gotten a lot worse."

Other road. Another sheriff booth. We'll park before it, plan to walk through. Our calculus on their psychology is that walking is less confrontational, somehow, than driving on a public road. That's how distorted things are. Mandy tells the guard we've gotta talk to Frank Campo. Dropping a name earns us permission to walk on a public road.

Just a little bit down the road is an open-air fishing station with a corrugated aluminum roof, a dock, tanks for live bait, fuel pumps. Fishing's been closed for a couple of months.

Campo's ancestral ethnicity is Spanish via the Canary Islands to Louisiana. His fishing station normally sells bait, fuel, and ice to commercial and recreational fishermen. He's spent a lot of time in the sun.

Hurricane Katrina sent twenty feet of water through here. "There's only two things here that's old, besides me," Campo says, pointing, "That post, and a piece of pipe in the front. The rest, Katrina destroyed. The whole parish was destroyed. You couldn't buy anything. You couldn't get here to work because the road was destroyed. All them power poles, they were all gone. They never rebuilt the gas lines, not for the few people here. We knew we were gonna rebuild, but the question was 'Where the hell do you start.' My dad was dead. But I asked him, 'Dad, where the hell do we start?' And we talked about it and he said, 'We have to rebuild; this is what we do.'" It took about a year to get back in business. Campo's son Michael, late thirties, is fourth-generation in this family business. Michael says he's "tryin' t' stay positive." So much of this is psychological warfare.

Campo the elder says, "When I first heard about the oil, to be quite honest, I didn't think much of it. Rigs blow up all the time, y'know. Then I saw that eleven people lost their lives. That really bothers me. That's not good. You got kids? I sure wouldn't want to be rubbed out because somebody did something stupid. I mean, I got grandkids and I know I'm not gonna be here forever; but I wanna be here, y'know, as long as I can. So I feel really bad for the people who lost their husbands and their fathers.

"Katrina destroyed us—but it didn't kill us. A hurricane takes everything, but you know you're gonna come back. You know you're gonna have the seafood, sport fishing—. I mean, it takes a while, but you know you're gonna be back on top of the ball again. But the oil really bothers me. The oil could take all this away from us. What do you do then? And *where* we gonna go? What's the use of coming here if you can't fish?

"I *fish*, y'know what I mean? Louisiana produces most of the seafood that's eaten in the country. They got shrimp comes outta other states but they ain't no good; I wouldn't eat 'em. Our shrimp are *so* good, it's not even funny.

"I've fished out of so many places, I got friends all over the doggone country. Biloxi, Gulfport, Houma. I've been all over. I got friends in Texas. I didn't have to punch a clock. And I didn't have to drive. I went with the boat, everywhere.

"This fishin' is a learnin' process. You get to meet interesting people. And you learn a lot from everybody. When I started, you used a trawl. Well, all right. Then they started using what they call a tickler chain ahead of the net. It makes the shrimp jump up. Well, that improved the catch—greatly.

"As we travel through the jungle, you gotta change with the times. But now—. I don't know *what* we're gonna do. Because if the oil moves in, it could kill the marsh. I don't feel confident we'll survive this. This is a significant threat to our well-being. This is not something to take lightly. This is very serious. This could destroy a way of life for everybody in this part of the world. If they don't stop it, then we'll be dead. Eventually, this is gonna go away. Whether it's going to take everybody with it, that I don't know."

Over on the *Ellie Margaret* we find Charlie Robin—"S'posed to say Ro-*ban*," he acknowledges, "but it's Robin." His boat, designed for shrimping, is laden with that elongated pacifier of the Gulf summer of 2010: boom. But Robin isn't quite pacified yet. He's mad as a buzzworm. Angrily, but amiably—he knows who his enemies are *not*—he sits astride the side of his battered boat. Not a lean man. Talkative. Worried. On top of it all, mechanical problems. Hit some leftover hurricane debris. Bent the propeller. "Destroyed it." Broken exhaust. Clothes covered in grease. Hands full of grease. Last week, he cut his finger off in a winch. "Dat little-bitty winch right there? Cut it off." Reattached, heavily bandaged.

Gesturing to the boom on his deck, he says, "Ninety percent of the boats here are workin' de erl. Nevvah thought it would still be comin' out in July. . . . Gettin' my flares. Gettin' all my safety equipment. Dat's what I'm doin'. Dat way we's good t' go. We been practicin' in a lake. We pull two twenty-four-inch booms. And we tow at, like, one knot. You got t' go a certain speed. Don't want the erl to go over, don't want it under. So you go *slow*. Other boat's behind you; he skims it. Pumps it on a barge. That's the way you go. Mop it up. Exactly what we doin'. So, pretty cool. I'm excited about it. Because I know it's gonna help our fisheries out. Anything we do to save our land, save our area, it's good. I'm five generations. If I go shrimpin' and de erl comes in, I'm screwed, right?

"We don't *know* what's the effect all this gonna be. Dat's de scary part. Dat's the part we feah de mos'. *No one* not knowin'. Hurricane comes in, we clean up, lick our wounds, go back workin'. We might bust a few nets on debris, but we back to livin'. But this?" His voice drops to an emphatic whisper: "We don't know the *outcome* of this. We don't know, we don't know.

"The ground you standin' on been in de family a hundred and fifty yeauhs. My great-grandfather lived on it. It means a *lot* to me. And it's worth savin'. This place goes, what we gonna do? Is BP gonna give us back owah culture? *Hell* no. There's not enough money in the world to pay for five generations of freedom. You don't *buy* dat.

"And to give you fresh seafood, Mother Nature's home brew— instead of some farmed frozen foreign chemical-raised shrimp. You follow dat? Okay.

"Well, *dat's* how we feel. Dat's how *angry*. Their ignorant mistake— is gonna cost all this. To try to save a million bucks. Dat's a penny to us. Now I'm gettin' mad. I'm sorry."

As we're walking out, back up the road to Mandy's car, we pass a handful of young people hanging out, leaning against a parked car. One, in his early twenties, is wearing the little orange life vest of the body snatchers. (He's on land, mind you—safety!)

Just after we pass he yells, "Hey. *Hey. HEY!*" Apparently he's "working," but doesn't know the difference between adolescence and a job.

We're walking *out*, on the public road, and he's yelling at us. Mandy has the courtesy to stop, so I turn around, too.

He suspects we're "from the media."

Mandy says we're not "the media."

"Then what's *that*," he demands. She happens to be carrying a folder bearing the business card of a *Los Angeles Times* reporter. Seeing that, the guy believes he's caught her lying to him. These are the banal ways the Gulf becomes a police state.

As if he deserves any answer, as though he has any scrim of real authority, Mandy calmly tells him that, no, it's someone else's business card. It's a good thing he's talking to her (that's an easy choice for him, of course) and that she's doing the talking, because I can feel my next breath forming the words *Go fuck yourself.*

As oil speckles Mississippi beaches, Governor Haley Barbour complains of not being given adequate resources. A Democrat congressman says he's "dumbfounded by the amount of wasted effort, wasted money and stupidity that I saw."

Oil spreads. Pain deepens. "Seeing everything that you've been used to for years kind of slowly going away from you, it's overwhelming," says a boat captain. His family wants answers he doesn't have. His wife says she cries. A lot. "I haven't slept. I've lost weight," says Yvonne Pfeiffer, fifty-three. "The stress has my shoulders up to my ears."

Oil floats. Shares sink. BP's stock price drops 6 percent, to $27.02, on June 25. Lowest value in fourteen years.

Oil floats. Turtles fly. The U.S. Fish and Wildlife Service is coordinating collection of about 70,000 sea turtle eggs from around 800 beach-buried nests from the Florida Panhandle to Alabama. The fear:

hatchlings will head into a toxic sea and be fatally mired as they seek food and shelter in oil-matted seaweed. The dilemma: nobody's ever done this before at such a scale. There's a lot of guessing. And any hatchlings that survive will almost certainly not return to the Gulf as adults, because they'll imprint on the east coast of Florida beaches where they'll be released. The turtles could squeeze out a win. But for the Gulf, it's a loss either way. It's not that anyone thinks this is a great idea. It's that the people involved don't want to just sit back; they want to help.

Halfway around the world is a man who wants so very much to help, he has sent us a giant, unsolicited gift. And so now, in the center ring, we have for you: the World's Largest Skimming Vessel. That's right, ladies and gentlemen. This massive beast, the awkwardly named *A Whale*, has crossed the Pacific flying a Taiwanese flag to go head-to-head, mano a mano, with the slick. How many football fields is it? you might ask. Three and a half! Ten stories high! It's a tanker newly converted at its owner's expense for just this purpose. And what a guy he must truly be. It has never been tested, but it's the thought that counts. And this whole season is about testing technology and people as never before.

The radio theater of the absurd tells us that "officials" hope the vessel will be able to suck up as much as 21 million gallons of oil-fouled water per day! But that's not quite true. That's what the *owner* hopes. Remember, it hasn't been tested. And the key phrase there is "oil-fouled water." Nobody thinks it could collect that much sheer oil.

Officials are doing their usual bit: being skeptical and mulling whether to grant access. And so the ship's mysterious and "reclusive" owner has sent a representative from a PR firm to "unleash a torrent of publicity and cut through red tape."

Turns out, "officials" are inclined to deny the ship permission to work, citing the fact that after it skims water and separates out the oil, the water it returns will still have some oil in it—*and it's illegal for a ship to discharge oil.* Never mind that there are skimmers all over the

Gulf right now doing just that. "BP and the Coast Guard still have concerns about the ship," one official says.

I continue to have a concern: Why does it keep sounding like "BP and the Coast Guard" are one team? How is it that BP gets to say *anything* about what and who goes into the federal waters of the United States? Especially when we the people of the United States sit helplessly watching BP fill the Gulf to the brim with oil and dispersants?

Finally, finally, finally, after about a week, the giant skimmer ship is allowed to do its thing.

It doesn't work.

On the final day of June, oil is scoring a touchdown on the Mississippi coast. On the radio, Governor Barbour says they had a great plan six weeks ago that isn't working very well now. Not enough skimmers, not enough equipment.

He is asked by the radio host whether this tests the philosophy that he and many Republicans champion: smaller government, less regulation, more freedom for industry. "The idea that more regulation is good is, I believe, a very suspect idea," Barbour answers. "In the case of this well, I think that if existing regulations were followed, it wouldn't have blown out. I think if there was somebody from Minerals Management Service on the rig that day making sure the regulations were properly followed, that would've made a difference. Now I think every oil company in the world is looking and thinking they wouldn't want to be paying $100 million a day like BP. That's how I believe the market system works."

And why *wasn't* the "Minerals Management Service on the rig that day making sure the regulations were properly followed"? Precisely because of people who champion smaller government, less regulation, more freedom for industry. Let's face it: most people who think they're "conservatives" these days are mainly phonies, radical front people for big business dedicated to removing public safeguards and safeguarding private greed. The missed point about whether government should be small or big, strong or weak is: it's *our* government. It should be accountable *to us*. Real conservatives would tell corporations to go to hell when they try to contribute campaign money, when they work to influence elections. By allowing themselves to become obsessed with the demand for "small government," "deregulation," and taxes, in effect they mostly represent big corporations that pocket profits and dump their risks and the costs onto other people. Some of the other people are too angry to realize that there's a shell game going on. The rest of us are simply too comfortable. "The best lack all conviction," Yeats said, "while the worst are full of passionate intensity."

It's hot. And because it's so hot, BPs beachside cleanup workers— 30,000 of them—are told to work for twenty minutes and rest for forty. For $12 an hour, the work is sweaty and uncomfortable, but not overly taxing. To save their backs, workers are not allowed to put more than ten pounds of oily sand in a bag. That's not much sand. Hundreds and hundreds of plastic bags, each with its little dollop of the besmirched beach—where are the hundreds of thousands of plastic bags, oily absorbent materials, and hundreds of tons of oily trash going? Landfills. Mixed with regular trash. Because it has to go somewhere. Don't worry: BP says that "tests" have shown that the material is not hazardous.

Someone on the radio is saying, ". . . To get near oil on the beaches, people need special training. But BP has troops . . . *thousands* of workers, who have received such training. . . ."

They make oil sound so *special*. It's *oil*. Gasoline's more dangerous. Ever fill your car's tank? Ever change your car's oil? You don't need special training. For anyone with a pair of old sneakers and a shovel, it should be no Big Problem to pick up a little oil if they want to.

Out on the water, some of the workforce sits idle. About 2,000 vessels are supposedly involved in the cleanup efforts. But many captains sit aboard their boats, awaiting instructions. For this, BP pays them, say, $1,000 a day (the fee varies with the size of the boat). Meanwhile, thousands of people from around the country want to drop everything and come help. But there's nothing for them to do. And their calls don't get returned. Forty-four nations have offered to help. For the most part, their calls don't get returned, either.

"The clean-up effort has not been perfect," BP's new American spokesmouth, Bob Dudley, acknowledges. But, seeking to assuage fears in the only language known to multinational corporate brains, he adds that BP remains a "very strong company in terms of its cash flow."

Science bulletin: an astonishing congregation of dozens of the world's largest fish—whale sharks—have been discovered in the Gulf of Mexico. One aerial photograph showed about ninety of the behemoths together, about sixty miles from the oil. "It blew my mind," says the University of Southern Mississippi's Eric Hoffmayer. The bad news? You guessed it: some of them have also been seen in heavy oil. They eat tiny creatures that they strain from the water. Their feeding technique includes skimming the surface and moving almost 160,000 gallons of seawater through their mouths and gills per hour as they feed on tiny fish and plankton. Watching them, you get the impression that their feeding method is the worst possible technique for surviving an oil slick. "This spill's impact came at the worst possible time and in the worst possible location for whale sharks," Hoffmayer says. "Taking mouthfuls of thick oil is not conducive to them surviving."

Science bulletin: scientists with the University of Southern Mississippi and Tulane University report finding petroleum droplets on the fins of small larval fish. "Their fins were encased in oil," says Harriet Perry, director of the Center for Fisheries Research and Development at the Gulf Coast Research Laboratory. "This is one route up the food ladder," she speculates. "Small fish will eat the larvae, bigger fish—you know how it goes."

Laboratory studies and field experience with wildlife shows that oil can cause skin sores, liver damage, eye and olfactory irritation, reduced growth, reduced hatching success, fin disintegration, and, of course, death. In heavily oiled areas, some animals can move away. Fish eggs and larvae cannot move. The *Argo Merchant* oil spill killed 20 percent of nearby cod eggs and almost half of pollock eggs. The *Torrey Canyon* killed 90 percent of the eggs of a fish species called pilchard. Similar death rates followed the *Exxon Valdez.* Other species seem far less affected. Of oiled fish eggs that hatched, larvae often had deformed jaws, spinal problems, heart problems, nerve problems, and behavioral problems.

However, under normal circumstances in clean water, natural mortality rates of eggs and larvae are so colossal, and such a tiny fraction survive to adulthood, that even the near-total destruction of one whole year-class of fish eggs by an oil spill might have a difficult-to-notice effect on adult populations.

In Prince William Sound during the months following the *Exxon Valdez* spill, herring eggs and larvae in oiled areas died at twice the rate they did in unoiled areas. Larval growth rates were half those measured in other North Pacific populations. Herring larvae also suffered malformations, genetic damage, and grew slower than ever recorded anywhere else. Those problems were gone by the following year.

But it's not that simple. Different things get hurt at different rates for differing periods of time. Oil that works its way into sediments and under boulders remains toxic and available to living things. In Prince William Sound after *Exxon Valdez,* oil hiding beneath mussel beds continued to find its way into the region's animals and their food web. For years, ducks and otters suffered chronic exposure to oil. For at least four years, the eggs of pink salmon, which spawn in the lower reaches of streams, near seawater, failed at abnormally high rates. Young sea otters born for several years after the spill survived at unusually low rates. After sea otters had received protection from hunting for their fur, their population increased 10 percent annually. But after the oil spill, they recovered at only 4 percent per year. In heavily oiled areas, their numbers did not increase at all for at least a dozen years. Shellfish—which sea otters (and people) eat—concentrate oil hydrocarbons quickly and metabolize them slowly. For at least several years, black oystercatchers fed their chicks more mussels but achieved less growth than normal. Harlequin ducks (probably the world's most exquisitely beautiful sea duck, which is saying something) for many years suffered low weight as their bodies tried to fight the toxic effects of the petroleum hydrocarbons they were getting in their food. In parts of Prince William Sound, they died at rates of 20 percent annually for over a decade. A study published in the April 2010 issue of *Environmental Toxicology and Chemistry* finds that harlequin ducks are still ingesting *Exxon Valdez* oil. Biopsy samples show their livers containing the enzymes they produce when their body is wrestling with oil.

Everywhere I've been, there's boom. Boom along the shore, boom under bridges, boom in roadside canals. Boom, boom, boom. You can't avoid it. And almost everywhere I've been, there's been the chronic low-level hassling of camera-toting types like me, by sheriffs and orange-vested private guards on public roads and alongside waterways.

And today, the Coast Guard takes the situation one giant step in the wrong direction. They make it a crime in southern Louisiana to get within seventy feet of boom. You risk a $40,000 fine. And if you do it "willfully," that's now a felony.

A *felony?* Impossible. Can the Coast Guard *make* a law? But it's true. Here is their press release:

> June 30, 2010 16:51:40 CST
> Coast Guard establishes 20-meter safety zone around all Deepwater Horizon protective boom operations taking place in Southeast Louisiana.
>
>   The Captains of the Port for Morgan City, La., New Orleans, La., and Mobile, Ala., under the authority of the Ports and Waterways Safety Act, has [*sic*] established a 20-meter safety zone surrounding all Deepwater Horizon booming operations and oil response efforts.

Vessels must not come within 20 meters of booming operations, boom, or oil spill response operations under penalty of law. . . .

Violation of a safety zone can result in up to a $40,000 civil penalty. Willful violations may result in a class D felony.

This, after weeks of people screaming for transparency and complaining about interference and petty bullying by people getting paid by BP. When I do a Google search with the words "media access Gulf oil," I find plenty of other people complaining. One Web commentator says, "Never in my lifetime could I imagine that a foreign company could dictate my ability to move freely and openly in American territorial waters."

America should be able to show that in a crisis we are at our finest, our most American. But wow. I can barely contain the rage I feel at the Coast Guard and its Thadmiral.

The highway to Venice, Louisiana, is sixty miles of levee sandwich, a corridor of road between corridors of water. Heavy shipping lanes gouged through wetlands. Dying trees in subsiding marshes. Herons. Cormorants. A least bittern; nice bird. They're all nice. Egrets still immaculately white, offering the hope of the living even as they feel the squeeze.

Captain Jeff Wolkart is telling me, "Two weeks into the spill, we were at Pelican Island fishing under birds in about five feet of water, which is a common way of fishing this time of year. And a dolphin kept coming around. Its body was covered in that brownish oil, that tannish-colored crude. And he was trying to blow out his blowhole, and he was struggling. Porpoises scare fish, so I moved off a hundred yards. It followed. I kept doing that and it kept coming back, coming to us, hanging right alongside the boat. That's very unusual. They're pretty intelligent, and it seemed to want help. But eventually I had to leave."

———

Dawn. Helicopters soon join the gulls. The drone of engines is as incessant as the industries of swallows that affix their nests to the I-beams of waterfront warehouses.

The media invasion is pulling away, leaving a low-level occupation. So many were they—many of them urban northerners—that the dockside burger-and-fries joint I'm in was compelled to add a "healthy platter." BP, its contractors, its security guards, and more than a few sheriffs understand the media as spies, prying eyes for a public prone to unwieldy concern if well informed.

The watermen seem a bit severed by the constant traffic of contractor vans and trucks and the private guards. It's not their place anymore. How are they finding the strength?

Here's how: all the watermen are choosing to work for BP. There's money now, work moving stuff, bringing stuff, towing stuff. Two grand a day. For now. After that, they don't know.

Charter captains meeting: fishermen—former fishermen, for now. A young man, twenties, asks, "Where will I take my kids fishing?" He has no kids yet. I hope he becomes CEO of an oil company. They could use his concern for kids.

All these guys know what it was like a couple of months ago, before the Big Problem. Few know, as the head of this association knows, what it was like way back. "You young guys, you'll never see it like me and Billy saw it," he says. I follow his eyes to where Billy's gray hair flows from under a baseball cap. "The place is a small fraction of what it was. It's infinitesimal compared to what it was."

The place is about water, cane, tides, mud, crabs, fish, birds, shrimp. All the pesky things an engineer overlooks while making "America's Wetland" bear the tasks of shipping, industrial access, flood control.

This isn't just a working coast. It's an overworked coast. Watermen feel stalked by disintegrating marshes. And everywhere the towering hardware of oil and gas prickles the horizon and brings down the sky. Henry Ford first used biodiesel. Standard Oil lobbied for Prohibition so there'd be no ethanol available. Ford was forced to switch to petroleum gasoline.

Outside, the oil complex confronts the eye with pipes, stacks, tubes. "It's so ugly," my companion says, "but it's jobs." A moment later she adds, "Ports, rigs; the oil is just the face of how the whole place—nature and people—have been so disrespected."

LIKE A THOUSAND JULYS

By the beginning of July, this blowout achieves peerdom, in sheer volume, with the Ixtoc disaster. That had been the largest accidental release of oil ever. Until now. Something like 140 million Macondo gallons have hemorrhaged into the Gulf.

Way back on May 26, the Environmental Protection Agency ordered BP to cut dispersant use roughly 75 percent *from the maximum.* But the maximum was 70,000 gallons in one day. The EPA now says it wants to keep dispersant use down to 18,000 gallons per day. CNN reports that BP is still averaging about 23,250 gallons. Such are the games.

EPA administrator Lisa Jackson said weeks ago that she was "dissatisfied with BP's response." Her agency set a deadline for BP to stop using two particular Corexit dispersant formulations (including one banned in Britain).

In mid-June BP announced that one, Corexit 9527, is "no longer in use in the Gulf." The manufacturer will say that the alternative, Corexit 9500, does not include the 2-butoxyethanol linked to the long-term health problems of *Exxon Valdez* cleanup workers.

BP seems to get away with shrugging its shoulders. When it only partially complies, there are no fines and no one goes to jail. I know what would happen to, say, me if I took a boat into the Gulf and radioed the Coast Guard to announce that I was about to dump one barrel of chemical dispersant.

And at the beginning of July, more than two months into the blow-out, the Environmental Protection Agency comes out with new findings on the dispersants: They're "practically non-toxic."

Because of the early "not leaking; too early to say catastrophe" statements by the Coast Guard, because of the tone implied by "anomalies, not plumes," because of the BP–Coast Guard marriage and the chronic official bullying, because the EPA seems to let BP shrug off even weak directives, because, because, because—nobody believes "them" when they say the dispersants are "practically" non-toxic. Whether they're right or wrong is beside the point. The point is: "they" have a credibility problem; they've lost the people's trust. No one is sure who to believe. There is no real source of reliable information, and people continue to believe, think, and feel a lot of things that aren't true. But some are true. It creates confusion.

So, rightly or wrongly, people remain concerned that the dispersants will kill plankton, fish, and other marine life. People are concerned they'll taint seafood. People are concerned that they'll break up millions upon millions of gallons of oil so that it pollutes vast swaths of the Gulf, making the oil unrecoverable, rendering millions of feet of boom useless on principle, bathing fish eggs and larvae, making things die, getting long-term into commercial fish, shrimp, and oysters, and taking bolt cutters to the food chain.

Certainly all that is "true" in a strict sense, but the important questions are: How much, for how long? Will it kill a lot of plankton? Will it seriously taint seafood? Or, in the vastness and chemical complexity of the Gulf, will the effects be trivial and temporary? It's so hard to know.

An EPA spokesperson: "Before making any alterations to the current policy of allowing heavy dispersant use, we will need to have additional testing of the dispersants plus the oil."

Allow it, then do tests. Isn't that completely backward? They're allowing the whole region to become a laboratory of lives.

St. Tammany Parish president Kevin Davis isn't having any of this. He simply calls on the Coast Guard commander to immediately end use of dispersants. "Breaking the oil down so that it travels underwater and resurfaces is creating a situation where we can neither see it nor fight it," Davis says. "This is not a prudent course of action."

Comedy Central's Jon Stewart tells us that BP has had 760 "willful, egregious safety violations" over the last three years. ExxonMobil, by contrast, has had one. "Exxon," explains Stewart, "could get seventy times the willful, egregious safety violations and still be ninety percent safer than BP."

A few days after the Coast Guard declares "willfulness" a felony, BP generously decriminalizes free speech in America, encouraging workers to talk to the press if they wish to. About that, a shrimp boat captain says, "Yeah, I saw that notice. But our contract still says our people on our boat can't talk to anyone."

With a perceived crisis in oil supply not just from the blowout but also from Obama's drilling bans and moratoriums, I expect a surge in gasoline prices. But the price of gasoline is going *down.* Is this because calls to get beyond oil might galvanize political pressure to move away from fossil fuels and do more for clean energy— so gasoline prices are getting fixed? It's as if, just when we're waking up to fight the bad guys, they give us another shot of muscle relaxant.

Do you remember the "ultimate solution," relief wells? By the first week of July the first relief well is about 1,000 feet vertically from its targeted point of interception with the blowing well—a target, remember, seven inches wide, 18,000 feet below the Gulf's surface. In scale, the drill pipe is like a wet hair extending thousands of feet from the drilling rig, through the ocean, and deep into the seafloor. How can they know where it is, where it's headed, and where it needs to go?

It's very high-tech. To determine the inclination (angle) and azimuth (compass direction), accelerometers and magnetometers send binary pulses through the drill pipe to the drill rig. If the drill bit has strayed, it can be steered back on course by pressure pads that change the bit's direction. Magnetometers sense the seven-inch target of the original well by detecting an electromagnetic field created by an electric current that engineers send through the blown-out well's casing. In addition, devices resembling torpedoes up to 30 feet long bear sensors and processors that measure gamma radiation emitted by rock, the electrical resistance of any fluids within, and even the magnetic resonance of hydrocarbon atoms. Thus drillers know whether they are drilling through sand or rock, or oil and gas.

But no one makes booms capable of effectively corralling oil in open water. Incredible sophistication—and abject stupidity.

And a whiff of an end: the Coast Guard is talking of a new cap in the works. We also hear that the relief well is ahead of its early-August schedule. Don't hold your breath. The Thadmiral says, "I am reluctant to tell you it will be done before the middle of August because I think everything associated with this spill and response recovery suggests that we should underpromise and overdeliver."

Overdeliver? The only thing they've overdelivered is oil and polluted water. That's the part that has vastly exceeded all expectations. (There will not be a relief well in early August. Or mid-August. Or late August. Or early September. Nor by the ides of September.)

In July's first week, BP reports that nearly 95,000 claims have been submitted and the company has made more than 47,000 payments, totaling almost $147 million. So far, total, it has paid out about $3.12 billion.

Meanwhile, the federal government extends fishing closures to cover more than 80,000 square miles, a third of the Gulf's federal waters.

Says a fisherman, "Everything we've ever known is different now. Anything I ever built, it's gone: the business, my client base, my website—." Another says, "In bed, I feel safe. It feels like everything is okay and I'm away from all this. When I get up in the morning, it is just very depressing."

✎

July 2. Headed to Alabama. Downpours overcome by blue sky. Big lofting clouds.

Lots of churches. And their creepy billboards: "Oil Now, Blood Later.—Revelation 8:8." "The second angel sounded and the third part of the sea became blood." What were they smoking? I like my Bible's translation better: "The second angel blew his trumpet, and something like a great mountain, burning with fire, was thrown into the sea." That does sound a bit like the Deepwater Horizon, doesn't it?

Car radio: ". . . If it were up to me, I'd let them try it, because, let's face it, nothing BP and the Coast Guard are doing is doing much good out there."

"BP has received so many suggestions, it's created a *hotline.*"

A *hotline.* Imagine.

A BP hotline operator in Houston asserts that the spill hotline is just "a diversion to stop callers from getting through." She adds, "Other operators do nothing with the calls. They just type, 'blah blah blah,' no information, just 'blah blah blah.'"

BP denies this, saying, in effect, blah blah blah.

Hand-painted signs on utility poles advertise "Snapper," "Grouper," "Flounder," "Shrimp." Bait and tackle every little while. That's all archival now.

Local news: "Mississippi officials have closed the last portion of the state's marine waters. Any fish caught must now be returned to the waters immediately. Officials say tar balls, patties, mousse, and oil residue [such ugly terms] will continue to wash ashore for two months after the oil stops gushing." As Eskimos are said to have many words for differing kinds of snow and ice, the Gulf now has a vocabulary of oil.

The local news also says, "Oil is now building on Mississippi's shoreline, but officials say the major batch of oil is still twenty miles south."

Officials say. Officials say do this; officials say do this; officials say do this; officials say do this; do this. Out. Out. "Officials say . . . Unified Command says . . ."

I say, Unified Command my ass.

". . . all commercial and recreational fishing has been shut down in Mississippi Sound."

Officials say.

National news: "I'm Michele Norris." "And I'm Melissa Block. Computer modeling suggests that Miami and the Florida Keys are actually more at risk from oil than much of the state's Gulf coast. But all that depends on a fickle phenomenon known as the Loop Current—"

Click.

Really, I just need a few minutes of quiet. Let my head settle.

Pelicans remain much in evidence wherever the view embraces water. Terns. Laughing gulls. Salt marsh, rather pretty, at least for now. Occasionally a mullet jumps. I wonder whether they'll be here in these numbers next year.

I should hear what they're saying, so I turn on the radio again. ". . . They collected wind and current data from the last fifteen years, added an oil gusher, and ran it again and again to see where the oil would likely go. Oil ended up on the Atlantic coast of Florida more often than not. But the model could be wrong. The Loop Current usually pushes oil out of the Gulf and along the east coast of Florida, but it's not doing that right now. On the other hand, it looks like this could be a record-breaking year for tropical storms in the Gulf. This week's storm has delayed oil cleanup activities. What actually happens to the oil will depend on the weather. So keep watching those weather forecasts. . . ."

That's news you can't use. All that matters: Is the oil still gushing or stopped? Still gushing. That's all that matters.

A sign says, "Taking Oysters Beyond This Point Prohibited." The syntax raises the image of escorting oysters out into the bay. They need the word "from" between "oysters" and "beyond." At any rate, a few weeks ago, oyster rakers freckled the wide water. Now there are none.

Boom in channels. Boom under bridges. A long crescent boom arcs out from the shoreline, then simply ends. Protects nothing. The inescapable visual dominance of oil rigs. And this fiasco. I've never before seen a coast I hated.

Cedar Point Pier is on the north side of the bridge to Dauphin Island. Last time I was here the place was open. Now there's a hand-painted sign saying, "Closed."

A middle-aged woman named Jo is feeding the cats. Doesn't want "them to be victims, too." Takes me inside the store next to the empty piers. Shelves empty. "This is what's left." She's known me for two minutes, but she gives me a soft drink and a candy bar and won't let me pay.

On June 10 at 9:30 P.M., while several dozen people were fishing from the pier, police officers came onto the property to announce that the waters were closed to fishing and the place was "closed immediately." Not just the fishing. The whole business, bait shop, snacks and drinks, everything.

When the seventy-four-year-old proprietor came out to get an explanation, the six-foot-five officer knocked him to the ground to handcuff him, sending his face into a fence post on the way down and landing him in the hospital for two weeks. "Ambulance people could not believe the officer wouldn't uncuff him," Jo tells me. Word is that the officer had a prior problem controlling himself.

"When it's all over," she says, "it'll be bad for everyone."

While we wait to see when it'll be over, we pause for this word from the United Nations: a new report says that large modern corporations are "soulless" and threaten to become "cancerous" to society. The author of those comments, Pavan Sukhdev, is on sabbatical from Deutsche Bank and is working at the United Nations on a report called "The Economics of Ecosystems and Biodiversity." Reading between the lines, I infer that one goal of the report is to install an artificial heart in the treasure chest of multinational corporations. "We have created a soulless corporation that does not have any innate reason to be ethical about anything," he says. "The purpose of a corporation is to be selfish. That is law. So it's up to society and its leaders and thinkers to design the checks and balances that are needed to ensure that the corporation does not simply become cancerous." This doesn't come as news. But checks and balances—isn't that liberal code for regulations and taxes? In a famous report in 2006, British economist Nicholas Stern argued that the cost of tackling climate change would be 1 to 2 percent of the global economy, while the cost of doing nothing would be five to twenty times as great. Sukhdev says that failure to put a dollar value on nature's services—things like flood protection and crop pollination and carbon take-up by forests—is causing widespread destruction of whole ecosystems and of life on Earth.

"Arrogant and in denial." That's how a safety specialist who helped BP investigate its own refineries after the deadly 2005 explosion at its Texas City facility describes the company.

BP had grown into the world's second-largest oil company, behind only ExxonMobil. The company struck bold deals in shaky places like Angola and Azerbaijan, and drilled high in Alaska and deep in the Gulf of Mexico. It did "the tough stuff that others cannot or choose not to do," as BP CEO Tony Hayward once boasted.

When Hayward became BP's chief executive in 2007, he did away with fancy affectations, replacing art in the company's headquarters with photographs of BP service stations, platforms, and pipelines. A geologist by training, Hayward dispensed with the limousine used by his socially prominent predecessor. "BP makes its money by someone, somewhere, every day putting on boots, coveralls, a hard hat and glasses, and going out and turning valves," Hayward said in 2009. "And we'd sort of lost track of that." He vowed to make safety BP's "No. 1 priority."

But Hayward's predecessor, John Browne, had gone after the most expensive and potentially most lucrative ventures. And that record of risk translated to success. BP's share price more than doubled; its cash dividend tripled. Browne was knighted.

As Browne was reaching, he was also cutting. He outsourced. He fired tens of thousands of employees. Among them, many engineers. He kept rotating managers into new jobs with tough profit targets. The Texas City refinery, for example, had five managers in six years before the blast that killed fifteen people.

Built in 1934, that plant was poorly maintained even before BP acquired it. "We have never seen a site where the notion 'I could die today' was so real," a consulting firm hired to examine the plant wrote two months before the accident. The explosion was "caused by organizational and safety deficiencies at all levels of BP," the U.S. Chemical Safety Board concluded. The government ultimately found more than 300 safety violations. BP paid $21 million in fines, a record at the time. A year later, 267,000 gallons of oil leaked from BP's corroded pipes in Prudhoe Bay, Alaska. BP eventually paid more than $20 million in fines and damages.

Revisiting Texas City in 2009, inspectors from the U.S. Occupational Safety and Health Administration found more than 700 safety violations and proposed a record fine of $87.4 million. Most of the penalties, the agency said, resulted from BP's failure to live up to the previous settlement.

In March 2010, OSHA found 62 violations at BP's Ohio refinery. An OSHA administrator said, "BP told us they are very serious about safety, but they haven't translated their words into safe working procedures, and they have difficulty applying the lessons learned." On May 25, 2010, in Alaska—during the Gulf blowout—BP spilled about 200,000 gallons of oil. It was the Trans-Alaska Pipeline System's third-largest spill.

"In effect, it appears that BP repeatedly chose risky procedures in order to reduce costs and save time and made minimal efforts to contain the added risk," wrote Representatives Bart Stupak, Democrat of Michigan, and Henry A. Waxman, Democrat of California. "BP cut corner after corner to save a million dollars here and a few hours there," Waxman said. "And now the whole Gulf Coast is paying the price."

BP's executive overseeing the Gulf response, Bob Dudley, says it's unfair to blame cultural failings at BP for the string of accidents. "Everyone realized we had to operate safely and reliably, particularly in the U.S., to restore a reputation that was damaged by the accident at Texas City," he notes. "So I don't accept, and have not witnessed, this cutting of corners and the sacrifice of safety to drive results." He's about to become Tony Hayward's successor.

Dauphin Island, Alabama. Salt marshes on the north side. Egrets here look fine, miraculously immaculate. As do gulls. Adult pelicans—unlike those dingy birds near Grand Isle, Louisiana—retain the whiteness of their heads. Wherever they've been foraging, it's the safe place to be now.

On the main island, palmettos and cicadas. Full-on summer. In the entrance to a bed-and-breakfast hangs a big, framed prayer:

> We pray for your protection, Lord
> From the oil that is on the sea.
> We ask that you keep it far away
> And our island safe and free . . .

Standard selfishness directed skyward. How about asking the Lord to *stop* the blowout. And why would any God of mercy whose eye misses not the falling sparrow actually need to be asked?

Marion Laney, a part-time real estate agent here, says, "Every day something happens that makes you say—y'know—'What the fuck?' Stuff that doesn't make sense, at any level."

How's business? "I'm on the verge of bankruptcy in so many ways it's almost funny." Fourth of July weekend coming up. Last year one local company rented one hundred and eleven units for the holiday weekend. This year: ten. House values have fallen by half.

We park in the driveway of someone he knows. They're away. He wants photos of the four bucket loaders currently digging enormous amounts of sand from the north side of the island. The sand's being trucked to the ocean side, where other machinery patty-cakes it into ten-foot berms. Sand castles of woe. Also, unbelievably expensive.

They're digging a series of pits about one hundred yards long, fifty yards wide, twelve feet deep. Destroying whatever habitat was there. Scale of digging, scale of sand removal, scale of vegetation ruination: astonishing. Likelihood that this will deter oil in a hurricane: zero.

I'm guessing the idea is: attempt to replace sand dunes washed away by the last decade's major hurricanes. In other words, a subterfuge; the town is gouging BP while trying to fix an issue not related to oil.

Terns carrying fish circle the site; they seem to be looking for lost nestlings. Word is the permit was expedited. Loss of wetlands? What wetlands?

My other guess: BP doesn't care what excuse municipalities use to tangle themselves in BP's money. Money's how they gain control. Money's what they have. And all they have. Reasonable people might disagree with me. Unreasonable people surely would.

Also on the bay side, National Guard workers are replacing the natural shoreline with hard walls, armoring the shore against—what are they thinking? It all seems part of a "can-do" attitude that can't do the job of distinguishing whether the cure aids the ailment or kills the patient.

Anyway, when a car pulls into the driveway, Laney tensely breathes, "Car coming." He's afraid it's BP's Bully Police. How quickly the chill sets in. How easily. How thoroughly. When he recognizes the person, he says, "It's okay; I know them."

But it's okay either way, because all we're doing it taking photos from the deck of his friend's private house.

On the ocean side, a man is visiting a friend; he's brought along his family. His vacation home is in Gulf Shores, but Gulf Shores is closed. "And anyway, your kids go a couple hundred yards, then track tar all in your house and ruin everything you've got." He gestures with his chin. "These berms, they're useless."

He's part owner of an RV park. Recent acquisition. Bad timing. No tourists, no business, but it costs him twenty-three grand a month to pay his note. And in the midst of renovations, his contractors quit to work for Better Pay. "We have $3.2 million invested, and I just had to lay off all our help. In six months, we'll probably lose the place."

Right on the public beach where there's almost no vegetation left, I see a little puff of green near the end of a miles-long berm. Around this vegetation, a little string fence and a few small signs announce that a sea turtle's clutch of eggs lies incubating below the sand. All the other vegetation on the beach has been removed. If the nest hatches, the dark shape of the berm will look to the night-emerging baby turtles like land. Instead of marching to the sea, they'll march away from the berm, inland, and die.

At a pile of sand forty feet high, I climb to take photos. A guy in a truck from a company called Clean Harbors, from Albany, New York, gets out. I'm sure he's going to hassle me. Instead he says, "It's okay to park here. How can I help you today?" I say he already has, just by being such a breath of fresh air. I ask if his company is contracted by BP. "I really can't comment." Okay, something less threatening: I wonder out loud how much it's costing to make these miles-long berms. Just small talk. I'm not really asking him. He says, "I really can't talk about any of that. I could get fired for talking." The First Amendment protects corporations' free speech, but not the free speech of people who work for those corporations.

It's the Fourth of July. Two hundred and thirty four years ago, the United States won its independence from, guess who: the British.

Not so fast.

At the end of the road is a public park clearly marked "Open." It's noon when, on foot, I approach what looks like a little temporary trailer-style guard station at the entrance.

A young guy with a clipboard straightens up and walks quickly to the threshold of the park entrance. The power play is immediate. He's joined by an older guy, sixties, who takes over the interaction.

"I assume this park is open," I say, "since the sign says 'Open.'"

"No."

"Then why does the sign say 'Open'?"

"Because they haven't taken it down."

"Why would they take it down if it's a public park that's 'Open'?"

"It's closed."

"Why is it closed?"

"Because there are operations going on here connected to the oil spill. It's been taken over by the National Guard. The National Guard is operating down here."

"And they've closed the public park, even though it says it's 'Open'?"

"Yes. The city has closed it."

"Does that seem right to you?"

"I have no comment on that, sir. All I know is, it's closed to the public."

"And who do you work for?"

"I work for Response Force One security."

"What is Response Force One? I've never heard of that."

"A security company."

"And you're hired by who?"

"Response Force One."

"Yes, but who are they hired by?"

"BP," he says with a lift of his chin, as though those two letters are the big trump card of the whole Gulf region. A foreign-based corporation has hired American citizens to keep other Americans off public property clearly marked "Open" on our national holiday. These are not even real cops. They're what we used to call rent-a-cops, private security guards, the kind appropriate for guarding private property like office buildings and department stores. The kind who have no real legal authority. Local police or sheriffs, as I understand it, can grant authority to private security guards, but I can't check whether they've officially done so here, since, after all, it's a holiday. These guys, however, are not guarding the park or public property. They're guarding, well, I can't really see; looks like more booms and Porta Potties.

"So BP closed the public park?"

"No. The *town* has closed it. Because there are operations going on here."

The parking lot behind the guard is pretty empty, and the equipment is idle. It's a holiday, after all. "I don't really see any operations *going on* here," I say.

"Sir," he says, starting to lose his cool, "I'm tellin' ya—it's closed. Okay?"

"Okay, and I'm asking why."

"Because there are operations going on. It's a secure area."

"So, it's the Fourth of July, Independence Day, and—"

"Sir," he interrupts, now getting exasperated, "if you have any questions about the beach being closed, I'm gonna suggest that you contact somebody from the Town of Dauphin Island."

"Okay. Who can I contact?"

"Anybody in the city. Contact the mayor."

"Do you have their phone numbers?"

"They're not working today. It's a holiday."

"But do you have phone numbers, any contact information?"

"No, I don't." Now he's pretty fed up with me. Feeling's mutual, I'd estimate. The eye contact between us is turning hostile. I ask if I can take a picture of him and the younger guard at their booth and, not surprisingly, he says, "No."

"But you're on public property," I point out again. I assume he'd have a private right not to have his photo taken. Since he's saying he's acting in an official government capacity, however, I'm pretty sure I'd be within my rights taking a photo of an "official." But this is not a discussion on the fine points of the Constitution. We're miles and miles from the fine points. This, after all, is the Oil.

"*I said, NO!*" he yells. I see hatred in his eyes and he's starting to shake with rage. I guess he's not accustomed to being challenged. Most cars coming to the park just turn around upon seeing the guard booth. He usually doesn't even have to talk to anyone. His mere presence is enough to repel people. Everyone can see it's closed, never mind the sign. And obviously, I've come with an attitude about this. I hate all of it. I feel myself pointlessly returning his glare of rage.

He reaches for his radio in a threatening way, as if to warn, "I'm going to call Daddy." He's got his finger on the key.

I should make him call some real police, who work in tax-paid uniforms and drive a real cop car. But I presume they'll side with him and we'll all get angry. I turn and leave.

Later, I do find a sheriff and ask how private security guards can keep people off public property, especially where the sign very clearly says a park is "Open."

"I don't know," he says. "The park is closed; that's true. But right now there's a lot of screwy things on this island. I don't understand it all myself."

I guess you can't explain something that doesn't make sense.

Lunchtime. Shootin' the breeze over a beer with Marion Laney. He says, "There's a weird difference between what the government says to do and what this corporation does." He can't understand why, when the U.S. government tells BP to do something, BP seems to have the luxury of deciding whether to comply. "If this was a Venezuelan drilling company—or a *Cuban* drilling company," he chuckles, "I wonder what the government tone would be."

He's spoken to some of the fishermen whom BP is paying in the idiotically named Vessels of Opportunity program. Laney says, "Guys who'll talk when there's no camera around say they just putter around, not getting much done; say there's no real plan of attack. It's just, like, get in your boat, get out there, come back at quitting time."

He adds, "I hate to be a conspiracy theorist, but I think it's all just a big show. They're spending a lot of money. But either they're totally incompetent or there's some reason behind putting a lot of people out there and getting very little done."

Cooking up conspiracy theories here is easy as cereal and milk. Laney thinks BP wants the fishermen's mouths zipped—everybody just stay calm—and for a day's wages, they comply. But with bills to pay, what other option do they have? I think it's exactly that simple.

On docks where no one would think to wear life preservers just to walk to and from the boats they've run for decades, everyone wears life preservers. Former captains of their fate now march to rhythms not their own. Second childhoods in their own prime. Fishing boats lie stacked with white absorbent pads, like the diapers for whole communities suddenly severed from the normal progression of a life's memories.

At the marina, no one's in the store; they're not expecting customers. When a fisherman wearing a life preserver enters, we surprise each other. I'm not expecting "Abandon ship!" on land; I just want a few snacks. He calls a thirtyish woman, who takes her place behind the counter.

With a chuckle, she says, "We could be unemployed in the blink of an eye. Everyone's working for BP. That's all there is now. No one can think past next week." She says, "Everyone's worried in every way you can imagine."

I can't imagine. I get to go home.

Because it's a holiday weekend, Marion wants to see if he can get any shrimp. In the seafood shop over which he presides, Gary Skinner sweeps back his golden hair. He's a large man who describes his age as "fifty-nine, going on a hundred." He'd been a jeweler and watchmaker. "Got to be a dead trade," he says. "Cheap imports. Now we got cheap imported shrimp. That's why we had to open this shop up, to survive shrimpin'. Couldn't survive on wholesale prices."

We get a little tutorial on shrimp. A connoisseur, Skinner says, "The pink shrimp is probably the prettiest shrimp. It's beautiful. It's got this unique little black spot on the back of it; the shell is firm, it peels real good, it's real sweet. It's just a good shrimp. They're all good, but I think it's just the best."

He's had the shop for six years. He's been shrimping since 1975.

His two shrimp boats supply his shop. Except now they're working for BP.

"My big boat, last week they scooped up about forty barrels of oil. That's, like, sixty seconds' worth of what's comin' out that well."

He tells me, "At first, my wife said, 'There's gonna be a big slick comin' this way.' I said, 'Aw, they'll stop it in a coupla days.' When a week went by—. They started shuttin all the fishin' down. I mean, they *had* to, or you'd be getting oil all over your net, contaminatin' your whole catch.

"Right now, BP's actually payin' *more* than shrimpin' pays," Skinner says. He explains that the shop's business has grown 20 to 40 percent each year, including 20 percent in the 2009 recession. It's been a big success. "BP has figured in what our profit would have been this year, and what they've been giving me has been accurate," he reports. "They're payin' on time, so it looks like that's not gonna be a problem."

The problem: "Business has really fell off since this oil. This weekend—and this is a big holiday—it's down about 80 percent. Normally we have tourists, we have fresh shrimp off my boats. We'd sell forty or fifty ice chests full of shrimp for backyard parties.

"There's been a lot of sleepless nights," he acknowledges. "The money's one thing. Mainly it's been hard watching the business going down. What are we gonna do if they find out everything's contaminated, that it's killin' the nurseries inside, where shrimp grow. Or it's on the bottom offshore, where the shrimp spawn. It could be all over with. If they get it stopped, there might be some light at the end of the tunnel. Nobody knows, man. This is new for everybody."

His daughter-in-law works in the shop, with her babies calling and crying. His sons are running his boats. He comments, "My own two little boys started coming out on the boat when they were three years old. Now they're captains." He says he built the business to leave to his grandkids, "if they want to go fishin.' If they want to go to college and be a doctor, I support that, too." He adds, "People say, 'Oh, how can you keep doing this?' Well, we've had a good life. Money's not everything. We've had a lot of good times."

But we're not having good times today. This is the sorriest Fourth of July I've ever seen, and—because I like boats, I guess—it seems saddest at the boat ramp. Fishing is closed, but boating is allowed. Yet right now, the boat launch is empty when it should be packed.

Marion says, "Normally, there'd be dozens of boats here, jockeying for position, launching, hauling, standing off waiting to get in or out. It would be a madhouse. Normally there would have been hundreds of boats launched this morning, hundreds coming in at day's end."

There's not one single boat. No motorboats, not a single sail anywhere in view.

Dauphin Island has canceled its official fireworks. I guess no one is feeling sufficiently independent. I hear that BP offered ten grand toward fireworks but the town had the pride to decline.

Plenty of private fireworks, though. *Zip—pop!*

I get myself invited to a deck party. Lots of locals and a lot of great food on the grill. Nice view of the ocean, the sunset. Bottle rockets, Roman candles. *Zoom. Boom.* Firecrackers crackling by the pack—a regular good time after all, maybe.

We solemnly drink a shot of tequila to sundown. The whole scene is beachy enough to shake the fog of oil for a little while. Like, thirty seconds. It's all anyone is talking about. And here, where the blowout has turned things upside down, most people are thoroughly confused.

"How deep is the well?"

"I think it's eighteen thousand feet."

"It's seventeen *hundred* feet. The well itself starts five thousand feet from the surface."

"No, it's a lot more than seventeen hundred."

"I think it's seventeen thousand."

"I think that's right."

"Or it's seventeen thousand feet from the surface—"

"Maybe it's seventeen thousand from the surface to the bottom of the bore?"

"No, no; from the *floor* of the sea, it's seventeen thousand—. Uh, wait; you're right. Correct, correct."

"I don't understand these numbers; how can they do this drilling?"

"There's *nobody* in the Coast Guard who knows—I mean, the oil companies are *secretive*. You can't find out *anything* from the oil companies."

"That's—to me—the government should be keeping the transparency."

"Y'know, we put observers on fishing boats."

"We had observers in *Iraq*."

"Observers do visit, but—"

"They should have observers on *all* these rigs. And they should *report* to the public what's going on."

"Instead, Minerals Management Service, literally in *bed* with them; what I hear."

"That whole department needs to be washed out. Start over."

"BP's hiring for a lotta different things. Look for oil, put out boom, check boom, move boom around—a lotta different stuff."

"What do they tell you *not* to do?"

"Can't pick up birds; gotta call them in."

"And they got, like, a gag order. They tell you anything you find is the property of BP."

"These past weeks have felt like months. You *know* it's gonna really hit. You're pretty sure, anyway. You don't know when. But with these onshore winds, you know it's coming. Don't quote me; I have a contract. Been to training. Got my yellow card. Got my credential card. Hopin' to get called."

A diesel mechanic says, "*All* the work's slowin' down. People don't use their boats, nothing breaks."

"Recently I went for three days' fishing in the blue water, about a hundred twenty-five miles from shore. These guys I was with are very knowledgeable about catching fish. We caught one dolphin and a barracuda. Normally at this time of year, we should've loaded the boat. We should've had lots of yellowfin tuna, wahoo, a *bunch* of dolphin-fish, prob'ly hooked a blue marlin. It shoulda been *phenomenal*. This is a *very* good time of the year. We were shocked. We did not see oil—but the fish are *gone*."

A man named Jack, retired after thirty years of working seafood safety for the Food and Drug Administration, says in frustration, "If only the guys from Transocean had said, 'Y'know, we've got a problem with one of the gauges not working right and we feel like we shouldn't remove the fluid from the well,' and the BP guy had said, 'Let's take a couple of extra days and do it right.' That's all they had to say. None of this would have happened. But they did the exact opposite. They forced this catastrophe on everybody."

"And the second wolf said, 'I can save you money by . . .'"

By the bottle rockets' red glare, I shake hands with a guy who says he was in Vietnam in 1968. I say, "That must have been unspeakable." He says it was. He says, "What kills me about this present atrocity with the oil is that when you've had an investment in this country like I have made, seeing the lack of mobilization is staggering. I can't believe this has been allowed to happen to the United States. I can't believe that the United States allowed this to happen to itself."

On July 7, the Thadmiral tells America via CNN.com that a relief well is "very close" to being completed, adding that he expects it to intercept its target in a mere month to five weeks.

I'm going to keep breathing.

The same CNN article informs us that Christian, Jewish, and Muslim clergy joined "in prayer and commitment to the communities most affected by the BP oil disaster," while "wives of current and former major league baseball players also fanned out across southern Louisiana to draw attention to the people and creatures affected by the disaster." Whatever it takes.

Louisiana's Governor Bobby Jindal, appearing to both lubricate his cake and eat it, complains that the oil has already ruined the seafood industry and depressed tourism, and now Obama's ban on deep exploratory drilling is costing thousands of Louisianans their jobs. When such wanting-it-both-ways rhetoric actually makes some sense—as this does—you know we're really in trouble. Stuck because we've built no options.

Bobby must therefore be pleased when, on July 8, a federal appeals court in the heart of New Orleans affirms a lower court's June 22 decision that there should be no drilling ban. Two of the judges on the appeals panel—both appointed by Ronald Reagan—had represented the oil and gas industries as private lawyers. Judge Jerry E. Smith's clients included ExxonMobil, ConocoPhillips, and Sunoco. Judge W. Eugene Davis represented various companies involved in offshore drilling. Blind justice.

Plaquemines Parish president Billy Nungesser, who's been outspoken throughout this ordeal, is apoplectic about the rule criminalizing getting within seventy feet of booms. Nungesser says the only way to maintain public confidence in the cleanup is to make it as transparent as possible.

I appreciate that sentiment, but I don't fully agree. In my opinion, if everyone really saw what a rope-a-dope circus this "cleanup" really is, they'd acquire scant reason for confidence.

But, actually helping address the confidence chasm, out of the ashes of the former Minerals Management Service, some fresh resolve. The former federal prosecutor who now heads the Obama administration's newly created Bureau of Ocean Energy Management, Regulation and Enforcement outlines for us his planned approach: "I'm not going to say you can't drill, but if people don't get the message that we are really stressing regulation and enforcement to an unprecedented degree they will have problems with me," he says. "There's a reason why we renamed the agency by putting regulation and enforcement in the name."

Just a few days after the appeals court affirmed the overturn of the administration's ban on exploratory drilling, Interior Secretary Ken Salazar issues a *new* moratorium. Rather than basing the ban on depth, which the courts called arbitrary, he bases it on what he should have based it on in the first place: "evidence that grows every day of the industry's inability, in the deep water, to contain a catastrophic blowout, respond to an oil spill and to operate safely." Salazar adds, "The industry must raise the bar on its deepwater safety." It sounds like what I want to hear: our government working to protect us.

Of course, the head of the American Petroleum Institute says the only thing he can say within the narrow confines of his job script: that the ban is "unnecessary and shortsighted," that it will "shut down a major part of the nation's energy lifeline," that it "threatens enormous harm to the nation." In other words, all the usual hype.

And, speaking of hype, a White House senior adviser this week calls the blowout the "greatest environmental catastrophe of all time." He adds that he's "reasonably confident" that all of the oil can be contained by the end of July.

If only *all* great catastrophes will be over in a week. Sad fact: this is *far* from the "greatest environmental catastrophe of all time." Actually using oil is the far greater environmental disaster; oil and coal are changing the world's climate, swelling the rising seas, and turning the oceans acidic. And in the Gulf itself, *getting* the oil has destroyed far more of the Mississippi River Delta's world-class wetlands than the blowout ever will.

Congressional briefing, Capitol Hill. Testimony. National Wildlife Federation president Larry Schweiger likens the response to inventing fire trucks and building a fire department for a house that's already in flames. He relates his recent experience aboard a boat in the Gulf amid "oil an inch-and-a-half thick in places" and "fumes overwhelming."

Another witness at the briefing says that a sixty-nine-year-old man with sixty-nine cents in the bank called into Larry King's Gulf telethon and pledged $10 on his credit card. Why doesn't such decency come in corporate proportions?

Courts have ruled that a corporation's first and foremost "responsibility" is maximizing profits for shareholders. But what if the courts had said instead—in consideration of the fact that a corporation's profitability benefits from military, copyright, and patent protections of the United States government—and by being ensconced in a great and technologically sophisticated country made stable by its laws and the peace its taxes buy—that corporations must budget 10 percent of profits (in the age-old tradition of tithing) to doing social good? What would the world look like then?

But *that* would be big government, interfering with *business.* Burdensome regulation! Meddling with the market. Happy to enjoy the meal and loath to wash the dishes, oil companies and other multinationals slurp their market-distorting taxpayer-funded subsidies like spaghetti. But this prevents new energy technologies and new companies from getting a toehold in a real market.

Sorry; the mind drifts.

Next witness. Brittin Eustice. Charter boat captain, about thirty. He takes people fishing for fun. Rather, took. Like the guy I talked to on Dauphin Island, Eustice says he recently fished an area about eighty miles south of Port Fourchon, Louisiana. Lookin' for the big boys: marlin, huge yellowfins. It was "very dead." They got one small blackfin and one dolphinfish in three days of fishing. "Usually that's what you catch in the first ten minutes," he says; usually you see lines of live floating weed and a lot of flyingfish. It was, he testifies, "extremely unusual." About the Oil and his life, he tells the assembled congressional folks, "No one knows what's the plan, what the effects will be. How can I plan anything?"

National Wildlife's Schweiger has the closing comment: "America needs clean energy . . ." He elaborates while my mind drifts again, because, of course, this is the most obvious message of the blowout. But before that locomotive can start moving, more fundamental things need to happen, things about money in politics.

On July 10, a Saturday, crews use undersea robots to yank six 52-pound bolts and remove the existing flange. They remove the ill-sealed cap installed five weeks ago. Oil resumes gushing. Next task: install-ing a 12-foot high, 15,000-pound piece of equipment that will eventu-ally attach to the remaining hardware on the ocean floor and, on its other end, allow attachment of an 18-foot-high, 150,000-pound series of hydraulic seals that—engineers hope—will allow them to fully di-rect all the oil up to collection ships.

In a procedure taking several days, they install this new tighter-fitting cap, which features valves like a blowout preventer's. On a positive note: it is possible that the cap can also close the well like the blowout preventer was supposed to do, stopping the flow of oil altogether.

It appears that BP is actually getting serious about stopping the flow of oil. Not just collecting some of it. Not just marking time while waiting for relief wells that require more weeks of drilling.

Cleverly—how refreshing to be able to say that—this new cap has a perforated temporary pipe above the valves. Rather than trying to simply cap the enormous pressure, the perforations allow the pressur-ized oil to continue escaping through the open valves while workers fully tighten the cap into place.

By July 14, on the eighty-fourth day of the blowout, nearly 5 million barrels—something like 200 million gallons of oil—have spewed into the Gulf. And the well is still flowing unchecked. This blowout now clearly outranks Ixtoc I's 3.3-million-barrel blowout.

Engineers have been trying to determine if it's safe to close the cap's vents and let the pressure build. The worry is that pressurized oil could rupture another channel for itself right through the seafloor. If that happens, there'd be no way of controlling it. They're also afraid that the blowout might find its way into the relief wells, blowing them out, too. These fears cause BP to suspend digging the relief wells that we've been told for months are the "ultimate solution." Meanwhile, oil keeps gushing into the Gulf.

Finally they're ready to see if this cap is going to work. They begin closing a trio of ram valves. They monitor the pressure gauges. If the pressure holds, it means the cap is holding. If the pressure falls, it means the oil has found another route out.

New vocabulary term: "static kill." Definition: using a device that should already have been invented, built, tested, and warehoused for this purpose before the blowout ever happened.

The Thadmiral tells us that BP tells *him* that the test of the pressure will last six to forty-eight hours "or more, depending."

And as if our expectations could be lower, BP tells us to hold our applause, that such a cap has "never before been deployed at such depths" and that its ability to contain the oil and gas cannot be assured.

The pressure builds.

And so on July 15, a seismic shift: at about 3:00 in the afternoon, it looks like the new cap, with its valves shut, is holding the pressure. They've gotten control of the upward surge.

In other words, they've stopped the leak.

But no one celebrates. Everyone is holding their breath. No one knows whether the pressure will hold indefinitely. In the days to come, the pressure appears lower than expected, suggesting the possibility of leaks. Word of leaks near the well begins seeping out in the media. BP wants to leave the well capped and the valves shut. The Thadmiral wants BP to hook up the collection lines and let the oil go into waiting vessels at the surface. That would lessen the pressure, lowering the chances of a rupture through the nearby seafloor.

But it seems there are no leaks; they leave the cap closed.

This is how the blowout is over. It's the end of the beginning.

Eighty-six days. Two thousand and sixty-four hours.

Kill the well, slay the dragon, conquer the demon. But it's only liquid under miles and miles of the pressure of the Earth. Prick of a needle. That's all it ever was. The real fire-breathing dragon, the real dangerous demon, lurking on the surface all along, can be located in the mirror.

It's been the world's largest accidental release of oil into ocean waters. Twenty times the volume spewed by the *Exxon Valdez*. They'd told us 1,000 barrels a day; then 5,000; then 12,000 to 19,000; then upward from there. Now the best estimate: 56,000 to 68,000 barrels per day. From April 22 to June 3, oil had spurted from a jagged break in the riser pipe at about 56,000 barrels, or 2.4 million gallons, per day. After June 3, when robots cut the riser, oil spewed into the ocean even more freely for a time, around 68,000 barrels—approaching 3 million gallons—per day, or 2,000 gallons per minute.

The Gulf got an estimated 4.9 million barrels, about 206 million gallons: 99,700 gallons per hour, 1,662 gallons per minute, about 30 gallons per second. Roughly 25 gallons each and every time your heart sent a pulse of blood up your aorta, for nearly three months.

But the beat goes on and the usual pumping and burning continues; we in the United States burn over 20 million barrels of oil a day, about the same as Japan, China, India, Germany, and Russia—*combined.* Per person, Americans burn more fossil fuels and emit more carbon dioxide than anyone else; 4 percent of the world's population uses 30 percent of its nonrenewable energy.

Just as some of the hysteria was misplaced, now a false calm ensues. BP seems to be saying it's all finished; the oil is gone. All gone. That is also hype, a kind of information junk shot, pumping smoke and mirrors into the media stream to jam the flow of clarity.

BP's stock price rises.

LATE JULY

For a crisis begun so spectacularly, it's a murky, uncertain ending. We begin the next phase with an enormous amount of floating oil, and Gulf waters polluted by deep oil and dispersant. What now?

Of course, turtles, birds, fish, shrimp, crabs, shellfish, dolphins, and all their habitats have been affected. And creatures that range widely but funnel through the Gulf to migrate or to breed are of hemispheric importance. How many of these creatures, and what proportion of their populations, were damaged or spared? That, no one can say.

So far, the dead wildlife found and collected total about 500 sea turtles, 60 dolphins, and nearly 2,000 birds. It's not at all clear that oil killed most of them. But it's also not at all clear how many were killed by oil and never found. One dolphin's ribs were broken—a boat strike. But dolphins are usually nimble enough to avoid boats. A necropsy found what looked like a tar ball in its throat. Affected by oil, then hit by a boat; it's a reasonable conclusion. But not certain.

Every oiled carcass found may suggest ten to one hundred undetected deaths. Birders are reporting the disappearance of black skimmers, pelicans, royal terns, least terns, Sandwich terns, laughing gulls, and reddish egrets from several Louisiana islands, including Raccoon Island, Cat Island, Queen Bess Island, and East Grand Terre Island.

But it's also true that there remain along Gulf shores and marshes many clean-looking pelicans, gleaming gulls, and egrets with no re-grets. A silver lining for animals with gills is that they got a season's break from fishing, which typically kills millions of adult fish, shrimp, and crabs, probably far more than this blowout did.

Some say the floating oil is blocking light needed by the plankton that are the base of the whole food web. Some say oil will settle on the bottom and continue washing up for years. Some say microbes will eat it. Some say those microbes will also rob regional waters of oxygen, killing nearly everything for miles. Some say no one knows what its effects will be, or how long they'll last.

As a naturalist, I find that the effects on wildlife remain hard to grasp.

People, though, have taken deep and immediate hits. Closures have meant an end to fishing, the cessation of a way of life and of the way thousands of people understand who they are. No one knows whether the seafood and tourism and fisheries will be clean and healthy again next year or in a decade.

So even with the leak stopped, there's hardly a sigh of relief.

"Just because they kill the well doesn't mean our troubles go away," says the crab dealer in Yscloskey, Louisiana. Another fisherman says, "As soon as BP gets this oil out of sight, they'll get it out of mind, and we'll be left to deal with it alone."

"We're not going anywhere" is the reassurance offered by NOAA chief Dr. Lubchenco. But official reassurances do little to dispel such deep anxiety. Many residents don't know who to believe, or what to believe. Many simply believe that the oil isn't going away anytime soon, whatever anyone says.

But they do believe that help is going away. During a public forum, Louisiana fishermen hear an Alaskan seafood spokesman describe how after the 1989 *Exxon Valdez* accident, the perception was that oil affected all seafood from the state. "It took ten-plus years to get out of that hole," he says. "We put in a request directly to the oil companies to fund a marketing effort. They gave us zero, absolutely nothing."

An estimated 45,000 people and 6,000 vessels and aircraft have by now been involved in the response. Now even the *retreat* of oil manages to become bad news for fishermen. For many fishermen idled by the oil, responding to the oil has become their livelihood. As the crude ebbs, many face being left with nothing to do but wait for the government to reopen fishing areas, and for consumers to show confidence in their seafood. And there are no guarantees that they will be able to resume fishing soon.

"This whole area is gonna die," bemoans a fifth-generation fisherwoman in Buras, Louisiana. "Down here, we have oil and we have fishing," she says. "We are water people. Everything we do involves the sea, and the spill has taken it all away from us. I've been contemplating suicide to the point of making myself a hangman's noose, honest to God. Then I decided that's not going to do anything, apart from shut me up."

The manager of a BP decontamination site for cleanup workers says he gets calls "every day" about people who want to commit suicide.

I can't help noticing it's only the victims who want to kill themselves.

On July 19, while a tanker is offloading oil near a Chinese port, two oil pipelines explode, sending flames 60 feet into the air and an estimated 11,000 barrels of oil into the Yellow Sea. Local media reports a 70-square-mile slick, which workers try to break up with chemical dispersants and with oil-eating bacteria.

On July 21, a federal judge stops companies from developing oil and gas wells on billions of dollars' of leases off Alaska's northwest coast. He says the federal government sold drilling rights without following environmental law. Alaska Native groups and environmentalists insist that no one could ever clean up an oil spill in Arctic waters, especially if there's sea ice. The Arctic is much more remote than the Gulf of Mexico. It's far from harbors and airports. The nearest Coast Guard base lies many horizons away.

"That spill in the Gulf, it could have been our ocean," says Daisy Sharp, mayor of Point Hope, an Inupiat Eskimo community of seven hundred people on the Chukchi Sea. "It's sad to say, but in a way I'm glad it happened. Maybe now people will take a closer look at offshore oil drilling."

Caroline Cannon, Native president of the village, says the decision brought tears of joy: "The world has heard us, in a sense. We're not on the corner of the back page. We exist and we count."

Well, Ms. Cannon, you guys exist as far as I'm concerned, but oil greases Alaska. Alaska's governor and other politicians love oil, because the petroleum industry pumps more than 90 percent of the state's revenue into Alaska's budget. And that judge didn't void the leases, but merely ruled that the federal government must analyze the environmental impact of development. For the oil companies, it's not over.

For the people, it might be. "Our ancestors had seen the hunger for oil when the Yankee whalers came in the nineteenth century," says village council vice president Steve Oomittuk. "They came for the whale oil and wiped out the whales." Whole villages that had relied on whales for food disappeared, Oomittuk says. He adds, "Then six years ago we saw the hunger for oil coming back. We started to think, 'This time *we* will go extinct.'"

But a whale might think, "Thank God for petroleum." Without it, as Oomittuk implies, we would have destroyed the whales. And thank heaven even more for the power of the sun, the wind, the tides, the heat in the heart of the Earth, the oils in the algae that feed the whole sea, these eternal energies that drive our world and all its life. Without them, we might have overheated the planet and acidified the ocean. But I'm getting way ahead of the story; we're not there yet. Not even close. As the whalers were stuck in their remorseless havoc, so we have stuck ourselves, with oil.

As we burn the easy oil and tap the deep oil to the limits of technology, sources that hadn't been worth it are getting attention. Enter: "oil-sands," "tar sands," "shale oil," and other relatively meager sources that are now worth money. Of Canada's northern Alberta—a province I remember as beautiful when it was younger—I read that as the Athabasca River and several of its tributaries flow past facilities gouging at oilsands (one ugly word), heavy metal neurotoxins like lead and mercury are entering the water at levels hazardous to fish. Add to them cadmium, copper, nickel, silver, and seven other metals considered priority pollutants by the U.S. Environmental Protection Agency. First, workers bulldoze the trees and strip the soil. "As soon as there was over 25 percent watershed disturbance we had big increases in all of the contaminants that we measured," one scientist tells us. What's he mean by "big increases"? In places, cadmium levels ranged between thirty and two hundred times over the guideline set by the Canadian Council of Ministers of the Environment to protect marine ecosystems. Silver levels were thirteen times higher than recommended at one site, and copper, lead, mercury, nickel, and zinc were five times the suggested limit.

And then there's "fracking," wherein engineers actually pump fluids at high pressure to shatter rock formations up to several miles underground to get the gas they contain. This practice is increasing because the resources are getting depleted. It's a long way from tapping surface seeps. In the East, the big target is the Marcellus Shale, which underlies states from Virginia to New York and into Canada. Its recoverable gas has been estimated at 49 trillion cubic feet, about two years' total U.S. consumption, worth about $1 trillion.

If you've already heard of fracking, here's a new vocabulary word: "proppant." In a sentence: "Proppant, such as grains of sand of a particular size, is mixed with the treatment fluid to keep the fracture open when the treatment is complete." This is all injected deep into the Earth. In shales they use oil-based drilling fluids when they're getting down to the reservoir, and then the fracturing fluids pumped down contain a multitude of sins—proppants, gels, friction reducers, breakers, cross-linkers, and surfactants similar to those in cosmetics and household cleaning products. These additives are selected to improve the "stimulation operation" and the productivity of the well. The fluids are 99.5 percent water, but it's the other .5 percent that matters. The

New York State environmental impact statement for drilling to frack the Marcellus Shale has six pages of tables listing the many components of fracturing fluids.

You can begin to imagine the above-ground mess and risk of all this fluid. Then there is the little issue of drinking water. Experts say it's not a problem. The New York State environmental impact statement reads, "Regulatory officials from 15 states have recently testified that groundwater contamination from the hydraulic fracturing procedure is not known to have occurred despite the procedure's widespread use in many wells over several decades."

The Environmental Impact Statement says that there is a vertical separation between the base of any aquifer in New York (850 feet) and the target shales (below 1,000 feet, although it also, confusingly, gives this depth as above 2,000 feet). It says the rock between the target shales and the aquifers is impermeable, so it should be an effective migration barrier.

Go ahead and take a big sigh of relief.

Now get worried again. The big case everybody cites is Pavillion, Wyoming, where gas fracking has been happening for a while. After several years of complaints by residents, the U.S. Environmental Protection Agency sampled nineteen drinking-water wells and, in August 2010, confirmed in eleven the presence of 2-butoxyethanol phosphate (probably from frac fluids), plus adamantane compounds (definitely from fracking) in four wells, and methane in seven. This is the first confirmed case of frac fluids getting into groundwater. It's possible that the fluid contaminants got into the wells—into people's drinking water—from surface spills; but the methane is conclusively from the underground reservoir. The final EPA Pavillion report is recent and is the smoking gun for opponents of fracking.

And now a dash of good news, a step toward the techno prep that was needed in the Gulf all along: ExxonMobil, Chevron, ConocoPhillips, and Royal Dutch Shell announce plans to voluntarily contribute $250 million each to build what they should have had warehoused already: modular containment equipment that would be on standby, capable of capping a blow-away well or siphoning and containing up to 100,000 barrels of oil daily in the next leak or spill. (BP is not included initially but will join in September 2010.)

Ulterior motive: the companies want Obama to lift his ban on deep exploratory drilling. They also realize that the gushing hemorrhage of bad publicity is detrimental to their stranglehold on what should be a national discussion about our energy future.

"It's doubtful we will ever use it, but this is a risk-management gap we need to fill in order for the government and the public to be confident to allow us to get back to work," the oil spokesman says. It could be sixteen months before the system is completed, tested, and ready to be used. In a blowout, it could still take weeks to stop the flow. Drawings of the proposed system show a cap and a series of undersea pipes and valves and a piece of equipment that would pump dispersant. Lines would be hooked up to vessels on the surface.

If it doesn't work, there's still no good plan for capturing oil.

The oil companies say this initiative is the product of *four weeks* of intensive efforts involving forty engineers from the four companies. And, of course, they want to deflate the momentum for a series of congressional bills that aim to bring more safety, more oversight, and more unwelcome lawmaker meddling.

One bill they don't like, for instance, would force companies to drill a relief well alongside any new exploration well. Oil executives argue that this would double the risk because a relief well would be just as likely to blow out. They don't mention that this would be true only if they drilled the relief well all the way into the hydrocarbon zone—or that they don't like the fact that it would cost them a bundle more.

But what about that slippery and elusive bigger picture?

In 1969, Senator Gaylord Nelson was so moved by seeing the devastation following the oil blowout off Santa Barbara that he called for a national day to discuss the environment. After the resulting establishment of Earth Day the following year, Republican President Richard Nixon created the Environmental Protection Agency and signed the National Environmental Policy Act and the Clean Air Act into law. Congress followed that burst of legislation with the Clean Water Act, the Endangered Species Act, the Coastal Zone Management Act, the Toxic Substances Control Act, and other giant strides of high-minded lawmaking that invented environmental protection and put the United States ahead of any nation on Earth.

Though the Gulf eruption far exceeds Santa Barbara's ten-day, 100,000-barrel blowout, when President Barack Obama pushes for clean energy, Republicans accuse him of trying to exploit the Gulf tragedy for political gain. Liberals fault him for failing to specifically push for a cap on carbon dioxide emissions.

Santa Barbara's leak originated much closer to shore, covering miles of California beaches with thick crude oil. Pictures of dead seals, dolphins, and thousands of birds horrified the country. I myself had never imagined a bird coated in oil, and in my mind I still see vividly the television image that shocked me. Santa Barbara's psychological effect was huge. And the country was more cohesive. We hadn't yet had thirty years of anti-government propaganda and deregulatory chaos, so we set our government to work passing laws to address the problems.

That was then, this is now. South Carolina republican senator Lindsey Graham worked on a climate-change bill for months before pronouncing it hopeless. And now, in July's last week, legislation to reduce climate-warming greenhouse gases from fossil fuels implodes in the Senate, derailing the year's top environmental goal. Not even this disastrous blowout could create a national consensus to move America off dirty fossil fuels and into clean, eternal energy.

Lois Capps, now a Democratic congresswoman representing Santa Barbara and the central coast, was a young stay-at-home mother in 1969. She reminds us that Gaylord Nelson's speech came eight months after the January 1969 blowout. The resulting Earth Day didn't happen until April 1970. Not until 1981 did Congress impose a ban on offshore drilling along most of the nation's coastal waters, an action rooted in the memories of the Santa Barbara spill, more than a decade earlier. (That congressional moratorium endured for a quarter century; Congress lifted it in 2008.) "It doesn't happen overnight," Capps says.

Agreed, but it's now been 40 years—14,600 nights—and we still don't have a clean, eternal-energy economy. My friend Sarah Chasis, who started working at the Natural Resources Defense Council while I was still a college undergrad, says, "I think we're going to see a really significant response to what happened in the Gulf play out over time. I think it's going to affect people's thinking and the way they approach issues for a long time."

I'd like to think so. An Associated Press poll in June 2010 found that 72 percent of Americans rate the environment as "extremely important" or "very important," up from 64 percent in May and 59 percent in April. But that's the problem. We care when it's headlined, but it's toast when it's redlined.

We're better than we were in 1969 on important issues like civil rights, women's equality, even on the environment. But that's mainly because of what was accomplished *then.* Since then, we've increasingly given our economy and our government to the kinds of people who care more about themselves than they do about our economy or our government. They've stagnated our energy policy, shipped our manufacturing jobs overseas, and racked up enormous national debt. Why? What was accomplished for America? Mainly, very rich people became extremely rich. Which would be fine, but the widening gap in the middle is very harmful to most Americans. And that gap is where moderation would lie, and from where a sane, enduring, future-forward energy policy would emerge. Thoughtful planning doesn't come from people who think only of themselves and only of today, traits shared by both the needy and the greedy.

In the deep earth's wings, the relief wells continue grinding along toward their seven-inch target, the intention still being to "kill" the well at its bottom.

On July 22, the National Oceanic and Atmospheric Administration reopens commercial and recreational fishing in 26,388 square miles of Gulf waters, or about one-third of the 83,927 square miles of Gulf of Mexico federal waters that had been closed to commercial and recreational fishing—which itself had been over a third of all of the Gulf of Mexico federal waters.

Fishing means seafood means consumer confidence. So to rebuild consumer confidence, the government hires people to *sniff* seafood for oil. We're told the sniffers' identities will be kept secret to prevent harassment. That seems ludicrous, but then again, this is the blowout. So only the nose knows.

Inanity 101: A professor shows us how to sniff seafood: "Take small bunny sniffs," she says. No, really.

After the first clean samples, the professor demonstrates with a bowl of shrimp intentionally tainted with a small amount of ammonia. One small bunny sniff, and the verdict?

"It's pungent and putrid. It smells bad. Eww."

Well, *you put ammonia* in it. You didn't even put actual petroleum in it.

"I didn't want to use the actual oil with some of the volatile hydrocarbons that are in there just, you know, for safety purposes."

Oh, *puleeez!* We who run our lives with gasoline and heat our homes with oil and methane and propane will have our safety compromised by a bunny whiff of *oil?* We *live* in the stuff.

The whole idea of sniffing as a test of seafood safety seems iffy. But a deputy from NOAA seeks to reassure us by saying, "If you think about your ability to detect something in your refrigerator, if it has an off odor, you can detect it at very, very low levels."

So scientific. Don't you feel confident now?

We're told that if the sniffers *don't* find oil, the samples they've sniffed will get chemically analyzed. I hope so, because I have zero confidence in sniffing as a way to ensure the safety of massive quantities of seafood.

And get this: we're told that the sniffers will "detect whether a sample is normal by testing it against a baseline of seafood caught before the spill." In other words, seafood that's been frozen for more than three months will be sniff-compared with fresh-caught seafood, to see which smells better.

We're told, "The experts can detect contamination of one part per million. Newer, less experienced state screeners, up to ten parts per million—that's a single drop in a gallon of water." We're told, "You have known experts who are in the room who, in fact, can help direct the trainees towards this sort of smell you should be getting. You might get it in your tongue. You might get it in the back of your nasal cavity. You might feel it right here."

I feel like I'm back in the Middle Ages. And while we're sniffing, I'd like to know why we aren't using dogs. Do we have agency experts sniffing for dope and bombs in airports? Do expert hunters chase rabbits with their expert noses to the ground? C'mon.

We're told, "NOAA officials are on high alert to prevent any seafood containing oil from being caught and sold." The professor says, "Believe me, I don't believe someone would go ahead and attempt to eat something that is tainted, because it is very aromatic and it's quite unpleasant."

Really? Is that all you've got? Sorry; I have a lot of respect for professors, but I don't believe her. If tainted food always smelled bad, people wouldn't get sick from eating tainted food.

We're told that in addition to using sniffers, the agency sends hundreds of samples to a lab in Seattle for chemical analysis. So far, just one sample came back tainted. *That*, I believe. I'd reserve small bunny sniffs for detecting, say, carrots.

Despite splotches of brown crude that continue washing up here and there, Louisiana plans an early August opening of state waters east of the Mississippi to catching fish like redfish, mullet, and speckled trout. Shrimping season will begin in mid-August. But oysters and blue crabs will remain off-limits. "I probably would put oysters at the top of the concern list and I don't think there's a close second," says Dauphin Island Sea Lab director George Crozier.

What about seafood in general? The oil contaminants of most health concern, polycyclic aromatic hydrocarbons, or PAHs (which can cause cancer), also show up in other everyday foods, such as grilled meat. A NOAA spokesman says the levels in Gulf seafood "are pretty typical of what we see in other areas." That's because they're common in oil, vehicle exhaust, food grown in polluted soil, tobacco smoke, wood smoke, and meat cooked at high temperatures. NOAA found that Alaskan villagers' smoked salmon contained far more PAHs than shellfish tainted by the *Exxon Valdez* spill. Live fish metabolize PAHs rather than store them.

For instance, the highest level of the PAH naphthalene found in fish from recently reopened Florida Panhandle waters was 1.3 parts per billion, well below the federally considered safe limit of 3.3 parts per billion. Federal regulators say they're sure the fish will be safe. They say that of the more than 3,500 samples taken from the Gulf during the spill, none contained enough oil or dispersant to be harmful to people.

In fact, regulators did not turn up a single piece of seafood that was unsafe to eat—even at the height of the eruption. Unlike certain contaminants, such as mercury, which accumulates in fish, fish quickly metabolize the oil's most common cancer-causing compounds. Crabs and oysters metabolize these chemicals more slowly. So far, shellfish testing is just beginning, and many shellfish areas remain closed.

It's not appetizing to think about eating a fish that's been neutralizing cancer-causing chemicals, no matter how promptly and efficiently. But I'm confident that an occasional meal, or a bit more, would be safe. Safety is a relative term, of course. I drive a car—the most dangerous thing most of us do routinely. We live in a world of hazards, including some pretty awful artificial chemicals and food containing God knows what. On the other hand, we have higher average life expectancies than ever in history, especially if you subtract people who eat too much and who smoke.

So if the feds say the seafood is safe, I would be willing to put a little initial squeamishness aside. Others have their own analysis. "It tastes like fish," a fisherman says. "I'm not dead yet. If the government tells me it's unsafe, I won't eat it. But I'm not going to worry about it. They're the experts, I'm just a fisherman." A tourist finds a different source of confidence. "Restaurants aren't going to sell the shrimp if they're bad," she says. "These are decent American people down here. They're not going to lie about it."

You'd think anyone in the fish biz would be delighted at the openings, but some think it absurd to open fishing grounds so soon. Some fishermen and their families worry that if any seafood diners wind up with a tainted plate, it will be a knockout blow. "I wouldn't feed that to my children without it being tested—properly tested, not these 'Everything's okay' tests," says a shrimp boat owner from Barataria, Louisiana. She and her husband are sufficiently skeptical of the government's assurances that they will not go shrimping when the season opens, at least not initially. Gotta respect them for that.

For the owner of a Venice shrimp and crab processing dock, it's the not knowing. "Will there even be a market for Louisiana seafood?" he wonders. "What is the impact on crabs and shrimp over the long haul? It's impossible to know."

In the short haul, part of the answer is possible to know. Keath Ladner's Gulf Shores Sea Products has a steady customer who buys two million pounds of shrimp a year. They've canceled their entire order. "The sentiment in the country is that the seafood in the Gulf is tainted," Ladner says. "People are scared of it right now."

Dawn Nunez's family is also in the shrimp business, but she dismisses the reopenings as premature, "nothing but a PR move. It's going to take *years* to know what damage they've done," she denounces. "It's just killed us all."

July 28 is day 100. Louisiana gets a new small oil spill just after midnight when a barge being pulled by a tugboat crashes into an inactive well in Barataria Bay, sending a mist of oil and gas a hundred feet into the air, creating a mile-long slick.

Two days later, a ruptured pipeline gushes as much as a million gallons of oil into Michigan's Kalamazoo River, sending federal and state government officials scrambling to stop the oil from reaching the Great Lakes.

On July 30 Dr. Caz Taylor of Tulane University copies me on an e-mail saying, "We have been seeing droplets of what could be oil or dispersant (or both) in crab larvae, from Pensacola, FL, all the way down into Galveston, TX. We haven't yet confirmed what these droplets are but if they are oil-spill related, then we have been seeing effects of the oil spill in places where oil is not visible for a while now. So the (welcome) news that the surface oil is receding does not greatly change my perception of the magnitude of the effects of the spill. There is still a lot of oil out there. If the oil and/or dispersant has entered the food web then the effects will be felt throughout the Gulf although they may take months, or longer, to manifest themselves."

Here is what most people read in something like that: "We have been seeing droplets of oil and dispersant (both) in crab larvae from Florida to Texas. So we have been seeing effects of the oil spill even where oil is not visible. The (dubious) news that the surface oil is receding does not greatly change the magnitude of the effects. There is still a lot of oil out there. It has entered the food web and the effects will be felt throughout the Gulf for months, or longer."

Here's what a scientist reads: "We have been seeing droplets of what could be oil or dispersant in crab larvae, but we haven't yet confirmed what these droplets are. If the oil and/or dispersant has entered the food web, then the effects may take months, or longer, to manifest themselves. That's a big 'if.'"

Here's what the media actually writes and what most everyone reads: "University scientists have spotted the first indications oil is entering the Gulf seafood chain—in crab larvae—and one expert warns the effect on fisheries could last 'years, probably not a matter of months' and affect many species."

———

Meanwhile, engineers are in the process of pumping drilling fluid that, under miles of its own weight and pressure, can push the petroleum and methane back into its genie bottle three more miles to the bottom of the well. This not only holds the pressure in, it neutralizes it.

Success arrives quietly on August 5, after they've followed the drilling fluid with tons of cement, which seals off the well's walls and once again isolates the oil and gas back in its cave, where it had slept for millions of years, away from the living world.

At the end of July, BP posts a quarterly loss of $16.9 billion. BP must now coordinate the drudgery of picking up 20 million feet (3,800 miles) of boom.

With the spigot capped, talk of relief wells ebbs. Two relief wells were supposed to be completed by early August, which, in May, seemed unendurably far into the future. Now the latest tropical storm, which has again forced evacuation of offshore crews, has everything further delayed.

PART THREE

AFTERMATH

DOG DAYS

When I was a kid, we were told that oil formed from dead dinosaurs. The idea is so easy to visualize, it had persisted since the early twentieth century. But back in the 1930s, a German chemist, Alfred E. Treibs, discovered that oil harbored the fossil remains of chlorophyll; the source appeared to be the planktonic algae of ancient seas, blizzards of microscopic sea life gently falling into the depths over the ages. Covered with sediments, cooked by the geothermal energy of the planet's hot heart, dead microscopic algae became oil.

Some of the waters that made the planet's oil still exist, like the Gulf of Mexico, which has long received the flows and nourishment of big rivers draining the continent, as the Mississippi does today. Meanwhile, the seas that produced other massive oil fields, such as the Middle East's, are gone.

For over half a billion years, incompletely decayed plant and animal remains from countless quintillions of tiny organisms buried under layers of rock have been percolating in the pressures and boiling heat of the Earth. Since the Paleozoic era, roughly 540 to 245 million years ago, organic material has been slowly moving to more porous layers of sandstone and siltstone, accumulating there and pooling where it has become trapped by impermeable rock and salt layers. A typical petroleum deposit includes oil, natural gas, and salt water. Crude oil is a mixture of different hydrocarbons with different boiling points that facilitate their separation into materials like asphalt, heavy and light oils, kerosene, light and heavy naphtha (from which gasoline is made), gas, and other components. It gets further refined and blended with other products to make fuels, solvents, paints, plastics, synthetic rubber, soaps, cleaners, waxes and gels, medicines, explosives, and fertilizers.

Petroleum seeps to the surface in many places, most famously the La Brea tar pits in Los Angeles, which for tens of thousands of years captured mastodons, saber-toothed cats, giant ground sloths, lions, and wolves, and today continues to claim pigeons and squirrels. In the early days of Spanish California, settlers used La Brea's asphalt for roofing.

Though the world has relied on petroleum as a major industrial fuel for only a little over a century, people have been using petroleum for over six thousand years. The Sumerians, among others, mined shallow asphalt for caulking boats and for export to Egypt, where it was used to set mosaics to adorn the coffins of great kings and queens. In about 330 B.C., Alexander the Great was impressed by the sight of a continuous flame issuing from the earth near Kirkuk, in what is now Iraq; it was probably a natural gas seep set ablaze. People being what we are, the potential for petroleum-based weapons was recognized early on. Arabs used petroleum to create flaming arrows used during the siege of Athens in 480 B.C. The Chinese, around A.D. 200, used pulleys and muscle labor to pump oil from the ground, send it through bamboo pipes, and collect it for fuel. Not until the 1800s did the West catch up to this level of oil drilling. The Byzantines in the seventh and eighth centuries hurled pots filled with oil ignited by gunpowder and fuses against Muslims. Similar bombs used at close range nearly destroyed the fleet of Arab ships attacking Constantinople in 673. Bukhara fell in 1220 when Genghis Khan hurled pots of naphtha at the city gates, where they burst into flame.

During the Renaissance, oil and asphalt from shallow pools discovered in the Far East found their way to Europe, and traders soon established routes to the West. By the 1600s, petroleum was lighting streets in Italy and Prague. By the end of the Napoleonic Wars, asphalt was being used extensively to build roads.

In the New World, natives in what is now Venezuela used petroleum to caulk boats and baskets and for lighting and medicines. In 1539, a barrel of Venezuelan oil was sent by ship to Spain to soothe the gout of Emperor Charles V. In North America, certain natives used oil in rituals and for making paints.

The modern commercial petroleum era began in 1820, when a lead pipe was used to bring gas from a natural seep near Fredonia, New York, to nearby consumers and a local hotel. In 1852, Polish farmers in Pennsylvania asked a local pharmacist to distill oil from a local seep. They were hoping to make vodka, but the result was undrinkable. It burned, though, and so they invented kerosene. The invention of the kerosene lamp two years later created a mass market for commercial kerosene, and soon towns everywhere were glowing with the light of petroleum. In 1858, Colonel Edwin Drake pounded a well sixty-nine feet into the ground near Titusville, Pennsylvania. It produced a continuous flow of oil, and within a short time kerosene replaced whale oil for lighting lamps. In the 1880s, the first oil tanker began carrying oil across the ocean. By the 1970s, the seas began bearing thousand-foot-long supertankers capable of containing 800,000 tons of oil. Today oil accounts for over half the tonnage of all sea cargoes.

Petroleum didn't really get big until the internal combustion engines of the twentieth century and the autos, tractors, trucks, and, eventually, aircraft they powered. Middle East oil ramped up rapidly in the late 1940s. Oil was discovered in Iran in 1908, in Iraq in 1927, and in Saudi Arabia in 1938. By the 1970s, the oil fields of the Middle East were producing about half the world's oil. Between 1950 and 1970, annual world oil production surged from 500 million to 3 billion tons. Today there are more miles of petroleum pipelines than of railroads.

Saudi Arabia is now by far the world's largest oil producer. (The United States is the Saudi Arabia of coal.) The Organization of Petroleum Exporting Countries (OPEC) has the greatest oil reserves. Its member countries include some notable enemies of the United States, and some friends the likes of which make enemies unnecessary.

In many parts of the world, depletion of land-based oil has forced drillers to the continental margins and beyond. In 1947, the first in-water oil well began operating from a wooden platform in sixteen feet of water off Louisiana.

Today one of the most innovative and promising ideas for a new liquid fuel to replace petroleum involves extracting energy from the oil in genetically engineered algae. Algae make oil that can be converted to biodiesel; they can be used to make ethanol; they can be converted to biogas; and they take carbon dioxide out of the air. It may seem surprising that algae create long-chain hydrocarbons resembling petroleum crude oil, but it shouldn't. Energy from the oil in algae, it turns out, is pretty much what we've been using. Algae is, though, vastly better than petroleum in terms of risks and consequences. Unlike such other fuel sources as corn, soybeans, and sugarcane, algae do not compete with our food supply or, like palm oil, cause farmers to cut down tropical forests. And because algae absorb carbon dioxide—the main pollutant from burning fossil fuels—their use as fuel could actually help reduce global warming. Algae naturally produce about half of the oxygen we breathe. And they can produce a much larger harvest per acre than other energy crops.

ExxonMobil said in 2009 that it would invest $600 million over the next few years to produce algae fuels comparable to fuels refined from conventional crude oil. So the tiny organisms that produce petroleum may be the liquid fuel of the future—without us having to wait, say, 300 million years.

Sounds good. Why aren't we rushing to do this? Why isn't this a national priority?

For a very short course on oil's influence in Louisiana politics, meet Professor Oliver Houck. In a Tulane University Law School office with well-stocked bookshelves and a small aquarium, the floor piled with documents organized for a new book he's writing, Houck sits back casually in his swivel chair.

He sees Louisiana as a petro-state, its petro-dictators propped up by oil money spread across parties. No candidate can really stand up against oil and gas. Louisiana, in too deep, is stuck.

Houck notes, "There's a kind of toilet mentality in states where resources are abundant. There's no ethic of conserving. In a timber state, the feeling is there's nothing wrong with clear-cutting. In Wyoming, it's a crime to say something bad about coal. In Texas, you can't say something about beef. Florida's never been oil-dependent; it's dependent on white-sand beaches. Oil impregnated Louisiana politics a long time ago."

But we are a union of fifty states. Nationwide, might this blowout eventually change the mood on energy?

"In the people, yes. In Congress, no. And there's no connection. Nationally there's a feeling of being fed up with oil; that the oil companies can't be trusted. I think the people would strongly support an energy bill that would go far beyond anything now in Congress. But they're not passionate about it. So members of Congress don't fear getting tossed out by voters based on their record on energy. And in Louisiana we have two of the most sorry-ass senators in Congress. They're hacks. But they're hacks with enormous power, because whatever party is in the majority is there by just a razor-thin margin. So suddenly they're swing hacks with enormous influence."

You will not be surprised to learn that Louisiana's congressional representatives have tried to get rid of Houck and this law clinic. "The only reason I'm not gone," Houck explains, "is that I'm at a private university."

On TV, Congressman Ed Markey is complaining that the oil companies "basically owned and operated their regulator but [the blowout] will catalyze Congress to create legislation to end this. We cannot continue to allow their cozy complacency between regulator and regulated." It's so much worse than he says. Oil companies basically own the whole Gulf region.

Republican tea-bagging superstar and knucklehead Senator Jim DeMint is putting a hold on a bill that would let the commission investigating the blowout subpoena needed information. DeMint says, "When Obama says, 'Yes we can,' we'll say, 'No you won't.'" He doesn't care "what," only "not." DeMint appears to be doing his personal best to "shrink government," and government could hardly get smaller than having senators like him. When men like him cast large shadows, it must be pretty late in the day.

⚭

When a certain tugboat captain—a man I've known for several years—comes ashore after an extended stay in the waters of the open Gulf, he's got a few frustrations to relay.

"We were never given a big-picture speech about what we were all trying to accomplish," he says, "where we each fit in. It was just, like, Okay, go out to here and drive around for a while."

"Nobody really knew what they're doing," he continues. "It was very half-assed. The guy in charge of our task force, he's a nice guy, but he was lost. He's got all these shrimp boats and charter boats, and we tried to organize them into search patterns so we could know what we did. We said to the guy, 'Do you want us to give these boats courses and legs to run searches on?' And he's like, 'Sure, if you know how to do that.' He added, 'I have no idea; I'm a shore-based guy.' As far as running an effective vessel group, he was overwhelmed. I don't think he was trained. When we started talking about 'search pattern grids' and stuff like that, it was right over his head.

"We were towing four 50,000-barrel-capacity double-hulled barges. Our job was to be a receptacle for skimmed oil. The need for us was wildly optimistic. With 200,000-barrel capacity, we came back with about 1,000 barrels of oil-water mix.

"The oil we traveled fifteen hundred miles to help recover was mostly not recoverable. We saw little patches here, little blobs there, pancakes, palm-sized pieces, pennies, dimes, nickels everywhere. Most of the stuff is just broken up into tiny droplets. And it's in suspension, so there's no way you can skim it.

"So we're constantly driving around looking for something we may be able to do something with, and almost never finding it, not really accomplishing anything. I'm sure we used more oil as fuel than the amount of oil we recovered.

"On the radio you'd hear frustration from other boats. Southerners attracted to working on boats and oil rigs have a very powerful work ethic; nobody wants to feel like they're wasting their time.

"To compound it, every time we find a large enough mass to actually be able to do some productive skimming, they just hit it with dispersants. One day we were in water with a heavy sheen on top. The air stank of the crude, and there were millions of little blobs of what has become known as 'peanut butter,' or weathered crude. It was also scattered throughout the water vertically. I couldn't tell how far down it went. It lasted mile after mile, as far as the eye could see.

"This is my second major spill response—I was one of the volunteer idiots power-washing rocks after *Exxon Valdez* back in '89—and as bad as *Valdez* was, the scale of this one simply takes my breath away.

"In this horrible mess was the biggest herd of dolphin I've ever seen, about sixty to ninety, I estimated. They stayed with us for about two hours, until I changed course. As the day progressed the oil got heavier and heavier, and by sunset I thought that the next day we'd get to do some real skimming and recovery.

"About four in the morning they called and told us all to get out of there and go north of twenty-nine degrees, ten minutes latitude. They kicked all the boats out of the area by dawn, then they bombed the whole area with dispersants from planes. I said, 'What the hell do they want to do that for? We finally found it in a concentration we might have picked up, and these assholes go and spray it.'

"I don't know if those dolphins were around for that or not. I don't know if the pilots would have aborted the mission if they had spotted them in the target area. Probably not, I imagine. I only hope the dolphins somehow knew what was going to happen and got the hell out of there. I don't even want to think about what would have happened to them if they didn't."

Splotches of crude are still washing up here and there along Louisiana's coast, but in early August NOAA releases a five-page report called "Deepwater Horizon/BP Oil Budget: What Happened to the Oil?"

It's got a nifty pie chart that describes the fate of the estimated 4.9 million gallons of oil, broken into seven categories. Designed to be simple and communicate clearly, it becomes a major public relations mess because: (1) some high-ranking government officials apparently can't read; (2) that's partly because there is one major thing in the report that really is pretty confusing; and (3) some reporters also apparently can't read. And what the confused officials say confuses the media totally.

Here's what the report says; you can read it for yourself:

> In summary, it is estimated that burning, skimming and direct recovery from the wellhead removed one quarter (25%) of the oil released from the wellhead. One quarter (25%) of the total oil naturally evaporated or dissolved, and just less than one quarter (24%) was dispersed (either naturally or as a result of operations) as microscopic droplets into Gulf waters. The residual amount—just over one quarter (26%)—is either on or just below the surface as light sheen and weathered tar balls, has washed ashore or been collected from the shore, or is buried in sand and sediments. Oil in the residual and dispersed categories is in the process of being degraded. The report below describes each of these categories and calculations. These estimates will continue to be refined as additional information becomes available.

The report explains what "dissolved" means with this line: "molecules from the oil separate and dissolve into the water just as sugar can be dissolved in water." Just as sugar. Isn't that nice? Facts aside, that reassuring tone makes many people feel they're being snowed. And that undermines credibility by keeping people on their guard. It's not that NOAA's scientists are giving the wrong information; it's that they're striking the wrong tone.

"I think it is fairly safe to say," remarks White House spokesman Robert Gibbs, "that many of the doomsday scenarios that we talked about and repeated a lot have not and will not come to fruition."

That's easy to say if you're not living it. Psychologically, his statement is a serious miscalculation. Most people in the Gulf want empathy, not reassurance. They want to know that their government *cares.* That's an emotion, not a desire for facts or official opinions. And because the most lingering bad taste that the nation had after Katrina was that the Bush administration seemed not to care enough, the Obama people should have understood that it was more important to show concern than to show pie charts.

Gibbs should have avoided the temptation to sound an "all's well" so early, and waited for academic experts to determine what has or hasn't come to pass *after* a relief well does its thing, when the blown-out well is officially declared good and dead. The federal government's most visible officials are misjudging people's need to *grieve.*

Even worse, some of the political folks don't seem able to read a simple pie chart. High on the list of those needing personal blowout preventers is Carol Browner, director of the White House Office of Energy and Climate Change Policy, who blurts: "The vast majority of oil is gone."

Just like that. She's totally wrong. And many people rightly jump all over her. Browner's glib comment, which rises to the definition of plain stupid, utterly undermines—yet again—public confidence in what "the government" (defined with a broad brush dipped in crude oil) is telling us.

So, for the benefit of Ms. Browner, let's review what NOAA's report actually says: "burning, skimming and direct recovery from the wellhead removed one quarter (25%) of the oil." That means, according to this estimate, that human intervention took only a quarter of the oil *out* of the system. "One quarter (25%) of the total oil naturally evaporated or dissolved . . ."

Whoa, wait a minute. Evaporated *or* dissolved? Those are very different things; evaporated means it went bye-bye in the sky; dissolved means it's asleep in the deep, still very much in the Gulf. Lumping together two very different categories that collectively account for 25 percent of the oil is another big blunder that helped make this seem very confused.

". . . and just less than one quarter (24%) was dispersed (either naturally or as a result of operations) as microscopic droplets into Gulf waters." The term "naturally dispersed" refers to oil that shattered into fine microdroplets from the sheer physical forces of being shot from a hot well into cold seawater. Twice as much is estimated to have naturally dispersed—if you call that natural—than was dispersed by chemical dispersants.

"The residual amount—just over one quarter (26%)—is either on or just below the surface as light sheen and weathered tar balls, has washed ashore or been collected from the shore, or is buried in sand and sediments. Oil in the residual and dispersed categories is in the process of being degraded." Here again, the report is confusing because oil that's been collected is no longer in the Gulf system, but at least with this category you know that the amount of residual oil in the Gulf is *not more* than they're estimating. You do know that, right?

So how much oil are they saying is in the Gulf now? Well, let's see: there's the 24 percent that's dispersed, the (up to) 26 percent that's either on or near the surface or washed ashore or is buried, plus whatever is the "dissolved" part of the 25 percent that's "evaporated or dissolved." That means the pie chart is telling us that up to 75 percent of the oil is in the Gulf. And if more of it evaporated and we split the difference, it's saying that perhaps two-thirds of the oil is still in the Gulf.

But so annoyed and upset are a lot of people—especially by the White House misstatements—that various independent scientists want a do-over. Louisiana State University oceanography professor Jim Cowan tosses the pie chart into NOAA's face, saying, "It looks like a nice neat diagram, but I have no confidence in it whatsoever." The Georgia Sea Grant program, itself part of an NOAA-sponsored university network of ocean and coastal researchers, releases an "alternative report" claiming that most of the oil that leaked into the Gulf is still present and estimating that between 70 percent and 79 percent of the oil remains in the Gulf ecosystem.

And yet, look: that's not too far off from what the original pie chart says.

Some people don't seem to care how much oil is where. Ronald J. Kendall, who directs Texas Tech University's Institute of Environmental and Human Health, says, "Even if all the oil were gone tomorrow, the effects of the spill on species such as sea turtles, bluefin tuna and sperm whales may take years to understand."

Trying to keep the message on point, the report's lead author, NOAA chief Dr. Jane Lubchenco, notes, "No one is saying that it's not a threat anymore. I think the view of most scientists is that the effects of this spill will likely linger for decades." She observes, "There's so much noise out there now saying the Gulf is dead or the Gulf will come back easily. The truth is in the middle."

Despite her attempts to recenter the discussion, the media reports on this are all over the place. One leading newspaper says, "Roughly one-third of the oil that gushed from the wellhead is out of the system: recovered directly or eliminated by burning, skimming, or chemical dispersion operations." Nope, wrong; dispersed oil is very much *in* the system.

The Associated Press, a stalwart of steady-as-she-goes reporting, publishes an article with this strikingly sarcastic (and inaccurate) headline: "Looking for the Oil? NOAA Says It's Mostly Gone."

The *New York Times* writes that federal officials are saying that only about 26 percent of the oil is still in the water or onshore. (No, see above.) Britain's *Independent* says, "Only about one-quarter of the oil remains as a residue in the environment, according to the US National Oceanic and Atmospheric Administration. The other three-quarters no longer poses a significant threat to the environment, the NOAA scientists said." The writer knows that the NOAA people said no such thing; in the same article he *quotes* Dr. Lubchenco as saying, "Dilute and out of sight does not necessarily mean benign, and we remain concerned about the long-time impacts both on the marshes and the wildlife but also beneath the surface."

Another British newspaper, the *Guardian*, says that NOAA scientist Bill Lehr "appeared to contradict the official report that he wrote" by saying, "Most of the oil is still in the environment." The paper goes on: "His statement is bound to deepen a sense of outrage in the scientific community that the White House is hiding data and spinning the science of the oil spill." But the report says what he said: that most of the oil is still in the environment. It's the media that's getting it wrong and spinning it.

Independent and academic scientists label the report misleading. "The oil has not left the building," says Ian MacDonald of Florida State University. He says the federal report gives the impression that most of the oil is no longer in the water because it was dissolved, dispersed, or degraded. "That only means it's still in the ocean, but in different forms," he points out. "It's still in the water."

University of Miami marine scientist Jerald Ault points out, "All those toxins that were injected into the Gulf, and remain in the Gulf, can be deadly to eggs and larvae and the young life stages of these species like giant bluefin tuna, yellowfin tuna, the billfishes and marine mammals, and many others. When you inject that volume of oil and dispersants into this life web, changes will echo through the system for a very long time. This is a long way from being over."

That's reasonable speculation. But it's speculation. Really, nobody knows. The stuff can be toxic, but how toxic at what concentrations, and for how long? It's continually being diluted and degraded. Its toxicity yesterday isn't the same tomorrow. And yet there must have been—I speculate—tremendous damage to sheer numbers of those eggs and larvae. We should also bear in mind, however, that the numbers of eggs and larvae are always far in excess of what the system can support. The competition and struggle for existence is so intense that under normal, healthy circumstances, only one fish egg in millions wins the lottery ticket for becoming an adult. That is where a lot of the resiliency comes from. There may be enough survivors to let the Gulf recover quickly.

So yes, this is a long way from being over. But I think it's the people and communities that will have the longest and hardest time recovering. Again, that's my speculation. But I'd bet on it.

Patches of oil are still washing up in the marshes and coastal areas of Louisiana, tourists remain skeptical and elusive, and waters remain closed to fishing.

"For technological disasters, unlike natural disasters, we see long-term impacts to communities, families, and individuals," says University of South Alabama sociologist Steven Picou. He has studied the impacts of both the *Exxon Valdez* spill and Katrina. In a natural disaster, he says, "People quit blaming God, usually after two weeks; then they come together with purpose and meaning to rebuild, so your social capital in a community grows after a natural disaster." But, he notes, "What we found in Alaska was that communities tended to lose their social capital. Their trust in local institutions and state and federal institutions, and their social networks, tends to break down. Everyone is angry and people get tired." The resiliency coast residents showed after Katrina may help them overcome the blowout, too, he says—but this will be a marathon, not a bounce-back.

And as for misjudging people's emotions, few can rival BP, which is saying it might someday go back to Plan A and use the well for commercial purposes. Tony Hayward said in June that the reservoir was believed to hold about 2.1 billion gallons of oil. Roughly 200 million gallons have leaked out, leaving about 1.9 billion gallons, over 45 million barrels. At the current per-barrel value of $82, what remains is still worth $3.7 billion. Now BP's chief operating officer, Doug Suttles, is saying—and you have to wonder why in the world he thinks it necessary to bring this up before the well is even deemed fully secured—"We're going to have to think about what to do with that at some point."

It happens to really bother some people that a company with revenues of $147 billion in the first half of 2010 would commercialize a grave site. A fifty-four-year-old real estate agent from Mississippi, her voice cracking, says, "People died out there on that rig. They can find another place. Leave that one alone."

BP still has lease access to a roughly three-by-three-mile block of seafloor there. They'll be back.

In another stroke of public relations insight, BP is now hedging about how the relief wells will be used. BP officials had insisted for months that the relief wells were the only surefire way to end the oil leak, but now they're saying that what they've already done might do the trick.

BP is now refusing to commit to pumping cement down the relief well and into the bottom of the blown-out well. But why? Maybe their reason is a good one. Or maybe they think they'll use it to produce oil. Or they want to save a little money. Thing is, we don't know. They're so inept at PR, they manage to murk up the plan that for months they've touted as their best way to finally bring closure to the blown-out well.

But Thad Allen will have none of BP's vacillating. He makes it clear that the gusher will have to be plugged from two directions to be sure it's permanently dead. "I am the national incident commander and I issue the orders," he insists. "This will not be over until we do the bottom kill." He adds, with some urgency, "The quicker we get this done, the quicker we can reduce the risk of some type of internal failure." He assures us that a relief well will inject cement into the well deep below the seafloor. "There should be no ambiguity about that," Allen says. "I'm the national incident commander and this is how this will be handled."

"I wouldn't put it as 'government versus BP,'" says one of BP's interchangeable vice presidents. "This is just about some really smart people debating about what's the best way to do things."

When people refer to themselves as really smart, my confidence in them—if I have any—declines.

Perhaps sensing certain limits, BP's CEO now (again) confirms that BP plans to use the 18,000-foot relief well to seal the blown-out well with drilling fluid *and* cement.

But stay tuned.

Maybe BP is getting distracted by the 300 lawsuits piling against it like snowdrifts. Transocean, close behind with 250 lawsuits, claims it's not responsible and has the gall to ask a court to limit its liabilities to a piddling $27 million.

Central to BP's legal strategy will be the need to rebuff claims that the company acted with "gross negligence." The difference between "gross negligence" and regular garden-variety negligence for BP, in this case, could be more than $15 billion in additional civil penalties under the Clean Water Act. Consequently, BP does what any negligent company would do: blames its partners. "Halliburton should have done more extensive testing and signaling to BP," says BP. To which Halliburton retorts, "The well owner is responsible for designing the well program and any testing."

While the principals engage in a foot-eating contest and continue to antagonize one another, the media, and us, we have a bit of luxury in asking the real questions: How much? How long? How bad? A big part of this—maybe all of it now—turns on the questions, How toxic? What will die?

Easy questions, hard to answer. People are still measuring, analyzing, writing up their findings. A fuller picture hasn't yet emerged. And so there's a tug-of-war between those who see the changing Gulf situation as a glass half empty, those who see it as half full, and those who see it as half-assed.

We can begin with brief comparisons. Oil from the *Exxon Valdez* remains obvious in the sands of Prince William Sound. Oil spilled four decades ago in a well-studied Cape Cod marsh lingers a few inches below the surface. But the Ixtoc blowout sent more than 3 million barrels into the Gulf of Mexico. That's a lot; it's more than half the total of the 2010 blowout. Ixtoc did a lot of damage, yet by most accounts, most things were pretty much back to normal a few years after Ixtoc blew.

Because an estimated couple thousand barrels of oil enter the Gulf daily from thousands of small natural seeps, the Gulf is well populated with bacteria that can eat oil. (Thank God for evolution.) Like a living inoculation, their existence gives the Gulf some powers of natural recuperation, even from such an enormous shock as this blowout. They're part of the Gulf's resilience, its flex. Microbiologist Ronald M. Atlas, formerly a president of the American Society for Microbiology, says, "I believe that most of the oil will not have a significant impact. That's been the story with spills that stay offshore." Texas A&M University professor emeritus Roger Sassen says that because the Gulf is "preadapted" to crude oil, "The image of this spill being a complete disaster is not true."

One way of seeing if invisible oil-eating microbe populations are active and growing is to measure oxygen, since microbes use up oxygen. So one research team notes that oxygen levels haven't declined much, implying that the oil down deep is degrading slowly (it's cold down there—40° Fahrenheit). Until more puzzle pieces start coming in, it's a bit puzzling.

Everyone agrees that oil is toxic, but the plain truth is, no one can say how toxic it is out in the Gulf. That's because the concentrations vary from place to place and continually change. Laboratory tests are usually done by putting organisms such as shrimp or fish larvae in a mixture of water and the chemical they're testing, and seeing what concentration kills half the organisms in forty-eight hours. Researchers want results, so the concentrations are fairly high. But they want acute results—death. Doing experiments on the effects of very low concentrations means needing more samples and much more time, which translates into money. Too expensive, so seldom done.

And real ecosystems are so much more complicated that a laboratory experiment doesn't help us understand the fate of chemicals in the Gulf's living communities. If a research team finds oil and dispersant chemicals in the Gulf at concentrations a hundred times lower than the concentrations that killed half the larvae during two days in the laboratory, does that mean half the shrimp and fish larvae will die in two hundred days instead of two? No, it doesn't. But that also doesn't tell you whether the lower chemical concentrations will hamper the organisms' ability to continue finding food, grow normally, avoid predators, migrate, fight off infections, and so on. So when a scientist says, "We don't know how toxic it is," that's the truth.

But let's ask it another way. Let's look at trends. Is stuff dying? What isn't dying? What about recovery—are any components of the Gulf or its coastal marshes showing signs of bouncing back? Or not?

Now, here's the thing: though there's still a lot of disagreement, suggestions that the oil is rapidly disappearing are beginning to come from various independent sources. Even before July rolls over to August, the floating oil mats that covered thousands of square miles of the Gulf are largely gone. Remaining oil patches are quickly breaking down in the warm surface waters.

"Less oil on the surface does not mean that there isn't oil beneath the surface, or that our beaches and marshes are not still at risk," says NOAA chief Dr. Jane Lubchenco. "The sheer volume of oil that's out there has to mean there will be some very significant impacts. Dilute does not mean benign."

That's true. But it might also be fair to bear in mind that dilution is what pollution passes on the way to benign. In other words, the trend seems good.

My friend the tugboat captain is heading back to shore from another trip into the Gulf. This time he's off Florida, approaching Pensacola. And this time he's got good news: he's seeing numerous schools of the tuna cousins called little tunny. Because he's driving a boat in open water, he's got plenty of time to talk.

What are his impressions?

Despite the fish, "a lot of the water just looks off," he says. "What it usually looks like and what it looks like now are two different things. I know that's very subjective. I haven't seen any obvious slicks recently; it just looks off. It's like an old piece of Plexiglas; it just doesn't have that clarity like when it was new. Ever so slightly opaque.

"And I've pulled up a bucket of water that seemed perfectly clean, but it feels slimy. Like I say, the closer to the well, the worse that was. I'm accustomed to seeing large areas of sargassum. I've seen none of that. What you see is little bits, like it was run through a food processor, nowhere near the amount I would normally see, and no big patches. And I'm looking for it on purpose. The coloring is usually bright yellow, but it was gray; that's something that really jumped out at me. Sea turtles, a few, but nowhere near what I'd expect.

"And once or twice a day, twenty to sixty miles out, I saw isolated large shrimp swimming on the surface. Not near a weed line or near any protection. And also blue crabs, way offshore on the surface. I've never seen shrimp on the surface, and I've never seen blue crabs so far offshore. These were not small shrimp; I could see them from the wheelhouse, clearly alive, snapping their tails for locomotion. No other shrimp with them and no shelter, so what they were doing there, I've got no idea. I've seen this about a dozen times in the last ten days. I saw no sign of obvious distress. They were just very much out of place. What to attribute it to, I don't know. Except we've had this enormous event, and then you see behavior you've never seen before.

"And I could count on one hand how many flyingfish I've seen. That's extraordinary; I'm used to seeing them everywhere. They've got to be one of the more vulnerable animals to the oil.

"The dolphins, they're there, but I have seen, I'd guess, less than a third of what I'd expect, and other than that one enormous herd I saw the day before they dropped dispersants near us, they're pretty scarce and the groups are smaller. They seem more common to the east, away from the leak site. I haven't seen a lot of seabird activity except farther east near Pensacola, where the little tunny are. And I only saw this once, but the action was fast and furious: two or three spinner sharks leaping out after prey—spectacular—with multiple twists before they splashed down."

When I ask if he's going back out, he tells me he's not sure. "I don't know if they're going to keep us on the job much longer," he says. "We're not doing anything. It's just wasteful to keep us on the payroll. They should just give the fishermen the money instead of paying us to run in circles."

There's a pause on the line—it's not like him to stay quiet long—and then he adds this coda: "I can honestly say I have spent the whole summer doing absolutely nothing productive at all, and burning an enormous amount of fuel in the process. We just put a lot of miles and a lot of hours on the boat, for absolutely nothing. We accomplished no work, helped no one, produced no seafood, saved no lives, nothing. The only thing I have from all this is, at least I got to see it."

On August 10, NOAA reopens federal waters off a portion of the Florida Panhandle. The modification applies to fish only. No crabs. No shrimp.

Fraud alert: BP discovers that the numbers of commercial fishing licenses sold since April is up by 60 percent compared with last year. Fishing was *closed*. "There was an approach by two individuals asking me to sign that they had worked for me, that they had been deckhands for me," says one boat captain. "I had never seen these two individuals before in my life." One guy charged with filing false public records and theft by fraud faces possible prison time, large fines, and even hard labor if convicted. But like dead birds, for every one you find, there could be ten out there.

Legal alert: BP is prepping for its rootin' tootin' rodeo of legal wrangling. University of South Alabama's Bob Shipp says BP's lawyers tried to hire his whole Department of Marine Sciences to do research for them. "They wanted the oversight authority to keep us from publishing things if, for whatever reason, they didn't want them to be published," Shipp says. "People were to be muzzled as part of the contract. It's not something we could live with."

Tulane law professor Mark Davis reminds us that BP is doing what other oil, tobacco, and pharmaceutical companies have done in the past: hiring scientists to do research they want kept secret. "When the best scientists have evidence that would work against you, but they're not able to present it to the public, well then, you've essentially bought some silence."

LATE AUGUST

Relief well? Cement? No cement? Just a week ago BP stopped hedging on whether it would send cement into the bottom of the blown well. Its people have reconfirmed that yes, they will cement the thing using the relief well they've been digging for three and a half months. Our adamant commandant the Thadmiral has resolutely insisted that he gives the orders and that the endgame equation is: relief well = bottom kill = pumped cement = final victory.

Now, what's this? BP *and* the feds are back to wondering whether the bottom kill is even necessary.

The Thadmiral can't really be telling us that the blown-out well may not need to have heavy fluid and cement pumped into it through the relief well after all, can he? I guess he is. He's saying, "A bottom kill finishes this well." Then he adds, "The question is whether it's already been done with the static kill."

I don't get it.

This statement seems—what's a good word?—it seems *evasive.* How could no one have even hinted at this possibility all along? What's *up?* The relief well is late, they've been hemming and hawing, and now this.

It appears that after the relief well intersects its target—assuming it does, eventually—BP wants to check to see whether the cement pumped in through the top of the blown-out well went all the way down the casing, went out through the bottom of the well, and came up far enough between the casing and the rock to have plugged the whole shebang to secure satisfaction.

If so—spokesmen now say—sending cement in near the bottom might not be necessary. But as the Associated Press puts it, this new idea "would be a hard sell to a public that's heard for weeks that the bottom kill is the only way to ensure the well is no longer a danger to the region."

Exactly.

What is Allen thinking? The Thadmiral has zero to gain by even introducing this as a question now. It once again undermines the perceived credibility of everything he and other federal officials have been saying for months—even if what he's saying is perfectly reasonable. Sometimes you just gotta do what you've been promising.

I admire Thad Allen's willingness to reassess and to change course accordingly. It's a sign of intelligence. A foolish consistency indicates a small mind. He may be right, and he's certainly being reasonable.

But people don't want to feel reasoned with. They want to feel safe. This whole disaster is psychological almost as much as it is physical—and America hates flip-floppers. To suddenly open this as a question scratches the scab just forming over this gaping wound. For all of us who've been assured for months that a relief well that pumps cement is the only assurance, it feels excruciating.

Emotions. The public mood is at least as big an issue as the oil. I don't think the officials have realized this. If they have, they haven't dealt with it skillfully.

Emotions dominated the region while the oil flowed. Yes, there is real blame for what caused the blowout and for the utter unpreparedness to anticipate and deal with a blowout one mile deep. Some places, like Grand Isle, received awful coatings of oil. Wildlife suffered, and there is damage to natural habitats (though, luckily, less than feared).

But the two most devastating social and economical consequences of the blowout—the region-wide tourism meltdown, the vast fisheries closures—have been, in much of the wider region, emotional responses to aesthetics and perceptions, rather than necessary responses to real dangers. That's been true even where little oil reached. Panic, blind anger, and the months-long inability to know how long the oil would continue flowing have dominated people's responses to the event— including my own—especially in the months from late April until early August, when the leak was finally stopped.

Now that the oil has stopped flowing, we can begin to assess the extent of the event, the damage done, the prospects for recovery—and we can begin to calm down.

We've seen what caused this well to blow out, and the varied responses during the chaotic months while the oil was flowing. Now we can afford ourselves a little more calmness, clarity, rationality, and insight.

So what is the main observable effect to date, and what has taken the biggest hit—marshes, fishes, birds, water quality? It doesn't seem that way. Many Gulf Coast beaches are now free of both oil *and* tourists. The tourism industry projects losses in the $20 billion range. Both the tourism and the seafood industries see themselves as battling negative perceptions more than actual oil at this point, and perception may turn out to be the most costly of consequences.

There's still a lot of oil out in the Gulf. The twin fears for deep-sea oil plumes have been that billows of toxic hydrocarbons would roll through plankton communities, causing massive damage, and that the dissolved oil and gas would trigger a population explosion of oil- and gas-eating microbes that would burn up most of the surrounding oxygen, strangling nearby life.

NOAA and the EPA now report on dissolved oxygen at some 350 sampling stations. Bottom line: no oil-caused dead zones developed; none are expected. The average normal oxygen level in the Gulf at plume depths is 4.8 milliliters per liter. The average in-plume level was 3.8. The depressed oxygen level indicated bacteria eating oil.

But for the water to be a dead zone, the level would have to be below 1.4. Modeling indicates that dead zones have not developed because of oil mixing with nearby water. In other words, it's a relatively small amount of oil in a big ocean.

"We're seeing very few, if any, moderately or heavily oiled turtles," says sea turtle biologist Blair Witherington. Until the blowout was capped, the floating mats of sargassum weed that young turtles must spend years in had collected their own mats—of oil. Many young turtles must have perished unaccounted for. But the sargassum habitat is revitalizing, the oil dissipating from it. The blackened sargassum of early summer is being replaced by clean new growth teeming with crabs and other recovering creatures, and accompanied by turtles either clean or so lightly oiled that they can be cleaned on the spot and released. Says veterinarian Dr. Brian Stacy, "I personally didn't anticipate such a dramatic change so quickly."

Louisiana State University professor emeritus Edward Overton observes, "The Gulf is incredible in its resiliency and ability to clean itself up. I think we are going to be flabbergasted by the little amount of damage that has been caused by this spill."

But remember the oil and dispersant droplets in the larval crabs, showing that the spill was already climbing up the food chain? A pretty explosive find. Yet we haven't heard more about it. So a reporter from the *Orlando Sentinel* followed up, asking one of the scientists about it.

"That was a mistake," she said.

But what about the droplets seen in the crab larvae?

"We don't know what it is," she said. "It could be natural."

The owner of a bait-and-fuel dock peers into the marina's clean-looking water and says, "The spill isn't as bad as the media has suggested."

A charter boat captain who's been fishing several times a week since his area reopened says, "The perception is, everything down here is absolutely slap covered in oil. But that's not true. You could drive around all day and not find it." He's back to catching redfish and speckled sea trout.

Even in Louisiana's Barataria Bay, where two months ago grue-some scenes of oil-clotted pelicans horrified America, by mid-August green shoots began appearing in oil-blackened grass and mangroves and cane started to regrow. The Gulf region does indeed appear to have escaped the most dire predictions of spring. It could have been a lot worse.

Of the oil that reached the coast, most was stopped by the marsh itself. Marshland closest to the Gulf took the worst of the spill, ab-sorbing oil more thoroughly than all the boom in BP's checkbook, and preventing it from moving farther into thousands of square miles of marshes. Estimates of how much of Louisiana's vast marshes have been affected are remarkably small. The Associated Press calculates that, over hundreds of miles of Louisiana coastline, at most 3.4 square miles of marshland got oiled. There are roughly 7,000 square miles of marsh.

It's tempting to shout, "The marsh is coming back!" But it's just that the vegetation is regrowing. The *marsh* is disappearing.

In Shell Beach, Louisiana, a man saw me staring at all the dead trees standing in the marsh. "When I was a kid," he said, "this chan-nel wasn't here. And all of this was woods, all cypress and oak and other hardwoods. Everything behind us was cattle pasture. Now it's water. The channel let salt water pour in. Now you see all these dead trees. Those all died in the last ten years. The road leading up to the bridge you came over? That road was canopied with trees. It was real nice. So it gives me bad memories. Everything tries to live. Two feet above the water, a tree will grow. Everything wants a chance to sur-vive. The land is subsiding. Anyway, yeah, it was a paradise. Everyone got told they were all gonna be rich when the channel came. Look at any other state. Their coasts continue to thrive. This one died."

"We were anchored," writes Louisiana outdoor columnist Bob Marshall three weeks after the leak has been stanched, "watching redfish push wakes in clear water as they raced along a bank lined with very green and very healthy *Spartina* marsh. Shrimp were leaping from the water in attempts not to become redfish dinners. Blue claw crabs were riding the outgoing tide toward the Gulf of Mexico. Pelicans were diving on mullet schools. Mottled ducks were puddle jumping, and sand flies were taking their pint of blood from my ankles.

"One of the planet's most vibrant and dynamic ecosystems seemed the picture of health. Of course, like most wetlands sportsmen, I knew better. That's because I know these marshes are turning into open water at the rate of 25 square miles per year."

The delta originally covered something like 8,500 to 10,000 square miles, and has lost about 20 percent of that area, or very roughly 1,800 square miles of marsh, with recent loss rates around 20 to 40 square miles a year. All these estimates vary, as do the actual loss rates. Hurricanes Katrina and Rita alone dissolved over 200 square miles of marsh to open water, but much of that had been already degraded marsh. The Mississippi River is the main source of the delta's nourishment, but engineering projects have almost completely isolated the river from its own delta. The projects include levees built for ships and against floods, thousands of miles of channels sliced through the mazes of marshes, and the dredging and deepening done for shipping, and oil drilling, and the ships and traffic buzzing to and fro to service the rigs. The delta is disintegrating because the sediment that washes from the heartland now gets shot straight out into the open Gulf. It never gets a chance to build the marshes. Oil and gas pumping have also helped the marshes subside. The rise in sea level isn't helping.

A lot of marsh remains, but the amount lost—and with it the lost wildlife, recreation, and fisheries productivity—is staggering. The marshes are one big reason the Gulf produces more seafood than any other region in the lower forty-eight states. But some estimates say they'll largely vanish by 2050.

A certain irony is not lost on Dr. Felicia Coleman, who runs Florida State University's Coastal and Marine Laboratory. "There's a tremendous amount of outrage with the oil spill, and rightfully so," she notes pointedly. "But where's the outrage at the thousands and millions of little cuts we've made on a daily basis?"

BP has indeed been the subject of national rage all summer. One of the greatest fears was that the oil would destroy a great swath of marsh. Yet the things that are really destroying the marsh are all intentional. They could be fixed.

BP may end up saving more wetland than the oil ever harmed. The new national focus on the Gulf has helped bring attention to the delta's disintegrating marshes. Some of the billions BP is expected to pay in fines could bankroll restoring critical wetlands and reengineering projects that Congress hasn't bothered to fund. The Obama administration seems to grasp this. Navy secretary and former Mississippi governor Ray Mabus, having been tasked by the president to draft a long-term restoration plan for the Gulf, says he envisions spending some of the money from BP's anticipated fines on repairing wetlands. In one sense, it's a way for BP to give back for using all those wetland-killing canals and ship channels dug throughout the marshes to serve the oil rigs.

On August 16, Louisiana shrimpers go back to work—their real work, not dragging useless booms. Seventy-eight percent of federal waters—up from 63 percent—are open. On August 18, wildlife rehabbers release the first turtles back into the Gulf. And on August 20, the Louisiana Wildlife and Fisheries Commission reopens recreational fishing in all state waters that had been closed.

If that doesn't help people's mental health a little bit, BP announces that it's going to give $52 million to five behavioral health-support and outreach programs. "We appreciate that there is a great deal of stress and anxiety across the region, and as part of our determination to make things right for the people of the region, we are providing this assistance now to help make sure individuals who need help know where to turn," says a BP spokesman.

BP's $52 million for mental-health care doesn't by itself solve the material basis of problems like sleeplessness, anxiety, depression, anger, substance abuse, and domestic violence. To put it plainly, money will be the only anxiety cure for people like Margaret Carruth, who lost her hairstyling business and then her house when tourists stopped coming and locals cut back on luxuries like haircuts. Now she sleeps on friends' couches or on the front seat of her blue pickup. For people like her, the blowout continues to wreak its damage full-force.

In fact, people's mental health may get worse as the financial strains persist. A Louisiana husband and wife who both work in the seafood business and have seven children say they've received only $5,000 in claims payments since May. One single mother of four who worked as a sorter on a shrimp boat used to earn about $4,000 a month. Her BP payments: less than $1,700 monthly. "I worry about my kids seeing me this way," she says, "and them getting sad or it affecting their schoolwork."

At a day-care center in Grand Bay, Alabama, preschoolers whose parents were left jobless by the blowout are lashing out, their caregiver reports, by "throwing desks, kicking chairs. It's sad. With this," she continues, "people do not have hope. They cannot see a better time."

Top kill. Bottom kill. Junk shot. Dome. Riser. Skimmer. Annular. Cap. Relief well. Negative test. Blind shear ram. Centralizer. Drilling mud. Spacer. Blowout preventer.

None of those words refer to a woman sleeping in her truck or a child throwing a desk. And yet, of course they do.

For the rest of us, here's a new reason to seek mental help: the Thadmiral says he's no longer giving timetables for the final plugging of the now-quiescent well. He says he'll give the order to complete the relief well operation when he is ready. He doesn't want to give timelines anymore because, he says, if he has to change them—*it could cause a credibility problem.*

On August 27 NOAA reopens to commercial and recreational fishing over 4,000 square miles off of western Louisiana. Ten times more than that remains closed, about 20 percent of the federal waters in the Gulf. At the disaster's height, 37 percent of Gulf federal waters—88,000 square miles—were closed.

Meanwhile, with much fanfare, Canadian prime minister Stephen Harper announces a new protected area for beluga whales at the mouth of the Mackenzie River, in the Beaufort Sea. The Beaufort Sea region is home to one of the world's largest summer populations of belugas, which go there to feed, socialize, and raise their calves. In the remote town of Tuktoyaktuk, Northwest Territories, Harper proclaims, "Today we are ensuring these Arctic treasures are preserved for generations to come." But the government has already granted licenses to two companies that have proven the existence of about $6.6 billion in oil and gas reserves next to the beluga protection area. And the government will allow the companies to "continue to exercise their rights." Member of Parliament Nathan Cullen says with apparent disgust, "This is a protected area that protects nothing except oil and gas interests. It's some insane notion that we can draw a line in the water and drill right beside it."

Taking a leaf—as the saying goes—from Obama's book, Indonesia demands $2.4 billion in compensation from a Thai oil company for a blowout in the Timor Sea that lasted three months, spread a 35,000-square-mile slick, and was eventually plugged with a relief well. Indonesia says the oil damaged seaweed and pearl farms and hurt the livelihoods of 18,000 poor fishermen.

Taking a leaf from Exxon's book, the Thai-owned oil company rejects Indonesia's demand.

There's been a lot about BP to quite rightly criticize. All the good money it's now throwing around is certainly self-serving. We are right not to let the corporation simply buy our goodwill; in important ways, it doesn't deserve it. But when, in the wake of the *Exxon Valdez* spill, the Congress of the United States of Corporate America passed the Oil Pollution Act of 1990, it sent squeals of delight through the petroleum industry by capping an oil company's liability at a measly $75 million. Despite its ability to do unlimited damage, Big Oil has, ever since, operated with that congressional promise of impunity.

And so we must acknowledge that BP has voluntarily waived that protection. Compared to the way Exxon turned on the people of Prince William Sound, there's no comparison. In the wake of this blowout—and I say this with no disrespect to the families of those who died on the Deepwater Horizon—BP has done some honorable things for the people of the Gulf and America. More honorable, one might observe, than the U.S. Supreme Court, when the Court basically let Exxon off the hook. How sad is that?

EARLY SEPTEMBER

Morgan City, Louisiana. "Yes!" the sign says. "We Are Having Our 75th Annual Shrimp and Petroleum Festival."

"We still need both," says Lee Darce, assistant director of the festival. "That's what makes our community. That's our lifeblood." Mayor Tim Matte is aware that the festival can seem pretty weird to outsiders. "But we've always thought it's unusual that they think it's unusual."

Fire engulfs an oil production platform one hundred miles off the Louisiana coast. Though the fire started in living quarters and there is no loss of life, to a region whose nerves are so frayed the news comes like fingernails on a chalkboard. The same day, from Panaji, India: "Thick and dark layers of oil being deposited with each lapping wave along the sun-kissed beaches of Goa could be another ill omen for the Goa tourism industry."

On September 2: NOAA reopens fishing and shrimping in over 5,000 square miles of water stretching from Louisiana to Florida. NOAA throws open another 3,000 square miles of fishing area on September 3.

Festivals notwithstanding, there is a big difference between what fishers need and what oil companies need. Oil companies need oil. If it was on land, they'd get it there. And they did. That's why they're going into deeper and deeper water. They don't need marshes, clean water, or vibrant wildlife populations. If the whole ocean was suddenly empty of fish or the marshes vanished or the Gulf's water all evaporated, they'd still be there for the oil.

Fishermen really need the place, and they need it to be working and pretty intact.

Of about 8,500 water samples so far taken by NOAA from Mississippi to Florida, only two—both from Florida's Pensacola Pass—came back positive for oil. NOAA scientist Gary Petrae reports, "We are not finding anything, and even when we're suspicious of oil being present, we're finding that we're wrong. We're doing the best we can—and we can't find it." NOAA scientist Janet Baran says, "We haven't seen any oiled sediments." Her crews have looked at more than 100 sediment samples from federal waters more than three miles offshore, including near the well. "All the sediments we have taken," she adds, "have no visible oil on them."

That's the good news.

But while she says, "We haven't seen any oiled sediments," the University of Georgia's Samantha Joye says, "I've never seen anything like this." Joye describes layers of oily sediment two inches thick. Below the oily layer, she says, she finds recently dead shrimp, worms, and other invertebrates. And University of South Florida researchers see what they believe are droplets of oil on the seafloor. "It wasn't like a drape, like a blanket of oil, don't get me wrong," says David Hollander. "It looked like a constellation of stars that were at the scale of microdroplets."

What are we to make of such different findings? Different samples, different times, in different parts of the Gulf where heavy oil did or didn't go. Pieces of a puzzle.

Greenpeace says it's still easy to find oil just a few inches down in the sand on beaches that had been obviously oiled a few weeks back. That's believeable, and the videos look convincing.

Less convincing is that Louisiana's Governor Bobby Jindal is still trying to get his one hundred miles of sand berms built. BP has agreed to pay a hefty $360 million for them. But the Environmental Protection Agency is urging the Army Corps of Engineers to turn down the state's sand berm project, saying berms don't do anything and can harm wildlife. Ostensibly they're to stop oil from contaminating shores and marshlands. Using a May permit, the state spent tens of millions of dollars to build four miles of berms.

Here's a good line of BS: one of the governor's aides says the berms they built received "some of the heaviest oiling on Louisiana's coast." So what are they, oil *magnets?* He reportedly says the Louisiana National Guard has picked up at least a thousand pounds of oily debris from the berms. You know how much oil and sand it takes to make a thousand-pound pile? Very, very little. Let's put it this way: one cubic yard of sand weighs 2,700 pounds. He says, "Now is not the time to stop protective measures that have proven their effectiveness." Actually, now might be a good time.

I suspect that this desire for berms stems from a fear of hurricanes, not oil. Is my suspicion misplaced? Says Grand Isle's mayor, "What is wrong with us dredging and building these islands back up?"

On September 8, BP's just-released internal investigation spreads the blame widely, declares the disaster—lawyers and jurors, please take note—a "shared responsibility," blames "no single factor," and adds, "Rather, a complex and interlinked series of mechanical failures, human judgments, engineering design, operational implementation, and team interfaces came together to allow the initiation and escalation of the accident. Multiple companies, work teams, and circumstances were involved."

Oh, and also, even after all the stuff leading to the blowout went wrong, the blowout preventer should have activated automatically, sealing the well. BP says the device "failed to operate, probably because critical components were not working."

Self-serving as all that is, it's also probably all correct. But there's "shared responsibility" and then there's "shared responsibility." It certainly does seem that multiple workers from multiple companies made multiple errors. But whether BP shares or owns "responsibility" will largely come down to legal definitions of said term. I once got a ticket for an undersized fish that was caught on my boat but that I did not catch and did not measure and did not put in the cooler myself (it was a quarter-inch short and the mismeasurement was a friend's honest mistake). But as captain, I was responsible. I got the ticket. Sometimes that's the way it is; the crew messes up, but the captain pays.

⚓

The sign at Pensacola Beach proclaims "World's Whitest Beach." And still, it pretty much is.

People here say they dodged a bullet. Workers are keeping the main beaches almost clean. Fort Pickens National Park maintains a plentiful complement of pelicans, gulls, nesting terns, herons, plovers, dolphins. So lovely. A few well-weathered tar balls here and there are easily coped with. One heron has a smudge of oil on its throat. Other than that, it looks nice and seems certain to survive.

And that worries me. On my first trip to the Gulf after the explosion, I feared the worst case would be that the blowout would ruin the Gulf's marshes and beaches and fisheries and wildlife for years to come. Now a new worst-case scenario arises: What if it doesn't? What if, having looked catastrophe in the pupils, we decide the worst blowout ever is simply not so bad? What if we think that wherever, whenever the next one comes, we can just deal with it? What if we do, in fact, hit the snooze button? And nothing changes. Then this was all for nothing; it was just an unredeemed sacrifice, an unmitigated disaster.

The thing about having dodged a bullet is: if you just keep staring, you get shot.

⚓

Engineers are preparing to start the delicate remote-control work of detaching the temporary cap that first stopped the gushing oil, so they can raise the failed blowout preventer the mile from seafloor to surface. There's concern that in the process, the crane may accidentally drop the 50-foot, 300-ton device onto the wellhead. So my question: What's the rush? Why not wait for the relief well to securely seal the well bottom? Why the hurry to do this now? Didn't we learn that hurrying wasn't the right thing to do with this well?

Allen is holding his cards tight, but the relief well must be close, right?

After four months and another recent delay for bad weather, the relief well drill bit is now churning nearly 18,000 feet beneath the rig. The task is a bit like hitting a dartboard three miles away. Except the dartboard is under a mile of water and two and a half miles of rock, and it's not a straight shot.

Drilling the final stretch is a slow, exacting process. The drillers dig about twenty-five feet at a time, then run electric current through the relief well. The current creates a magnetic field in the pipe of the blown-out well, allowing engineers to calculate distances and make fine adjustments.

To guide the relief well to its target, BP has picked John Wright, who, after four decades of work drilling forty relief wells around the world, can say, "We've never missed yet. I've got high confidence."

Well, okay; that's the kind of guy we want.

THE NEW LIGHT OF AUTUMN

On *September 17, 2010,* the long, long-awaited relief well—one of them, anyway—reaches and breaches the quiescent blown-out well.

"Five agonizing months," as the Associated Press puts it. The next step: drive the long-awaited cement stake deep into its black heart, plugging it up for good.

BP's website has this announcement:

Release date: 17 September 2010 HOUSTON—Relief well drilling from the Development Driller III (DD3) re-started at 7:15 A.M. on Wednesday, and operations completed drilling the final 45 feet of hole. This drilling activity culminated with the intercept of the MC252 annulus and subsequent confirmation at 4:30 P.M. CDT Thursday. Total measured depth on the DD3 for the annulus intercept point was 17,977 feet. Operations conducted bottoms up circulation, which returned the contents of the well's annulus to the rig for evaluation. Testing of the drilling mud recovered from the well indicated that no hydrocarbons or cement were present at the intersect point. Therefore, no annulus kill is necessary, and the annulus cementing will proceed as planned. It is expected that the MC252 well will be completely sealed on Saturday. Once cementing operations are complete, the DD3 will begin standard plugging and abandonment procedures for the relief well.

Saturday, September 18. While the final cementing is under way out in the Gulf, Coast Guard admiral Thad Allen, the man the *Washington Post* called "perhaps the least-excitable person in American public life," walks into a Washington, DC, coffee shop looking so casual and relaxed that—though I've seen him on television enough times and I'm expecting him—at first I don't recognize him. He's just been mandatorily retired from the Coast Guard at age sixty, so he's out of uniform—wearing a casual short-sleeved shirt—and so he's free to accept my offer to buy him a cup of coffee and his almond croissant. Dr. Jane Lubchenco, NOAA administrator, is here too. But when I make the same offer she pats my shoulder and says, "That's nice of you, Carl, but I'll pay for my own, thanks."

Lubchenco leads us out the back of the shop, into a nice garden area with tables under the shade of a grape arbor. It's a perfect September morning. "We got lucky with the weather," she says. "Grape arbors wouldn't work so well in rain."

"First off," I say, "how much time do we have?"

"About an hour," Lubchenco answers. "I'm leaving this afternoon for meetings in Europe."

"An hour's good," Allen says.

Because the long-heralded final cement is getting pumped down the relief well as we take our seats, I'm sure Allen's got plenty of other things on his mind today. So I appreciate that on such a momentous morning, he's decided to peel off some valuable time for breakfast.

Recently, I happened to catch a long interview with Allen on *Charlie Rose.* Allen, who's beefy, with a military-style crew cut, took time to describe how much his participation in releasing several rehabilitated sea turtles had meant to him. I resonated. He seemed centered and insightful, and kind. And I started feeling an uncomfortable twinge— more than a twinge—that my summer-long simmering mental caricature of him was off base. Yes, I didn't like some things he'd said and done. But he'd worked to lead the region through two major disasters, Katrina and this. I could not think of anyone else who'd quite done that. And I was surprised to find myself thinking that if a hero is someone who steers events during a national crisis, Allen's as much a national hero as anyone I could think of. Well, *that* was certainly a startling thought. I've been critical all summer. But for everything there is a season. A time to cast stones, and a time to gather stones together.

A few days ago, Dr. Lubchenco was the surprise guest speaker at a National Geographic event honoring the famed ocean explorer Dr. Sylvia Earle. Someone tapped my shoulder and said to meet him at a nearby restaurant, and when I did, I was surprised to find myself sitting next to both Jane Lubchenco and Sylvia Earle. I knew that Lubchenco had worked a lot with Thad Allen recently, and after dinner, as we were saying our good-byes, my twinge prompted me to tell her that I'd been writing critically of him, and I was getting the feeling that this might be unfair. "Oh," she said, "that *would* be terribly unfair. He's a good guy. You should meet him."

And so as we sit down, Lubchenco, a coastal ecologist by profession, explains by way of introduction that Allen's understanding goes beyond the law he must enforce and includes the ecology, the science, the regional culture, and oil drilling technology.

"I stay up late at night studying," says Allen quite matter-of-factly. "I had to do the same during Katrina. You have to convert it to something the public can understand. If you don't put a public face on these disasters, you'll fail immediately. That's what happened during Katrina. Mike Brown went and hid, y'know—"

Katrina was then, this is now. Because we're pressed for time, I want to get down to it. So, I say, if the problem during Katrina was that the federal face was hiding, the problem this time was that the Coast Guard seemed to be guarding *against* public understanding and access. "How in the world," I demand, "was declaring a felony for getting near booms—"

"I can explain." Allen takes a sip of his coffee, a bite of his croissant, and says, "My policy was open access, except where safety and security were issues. Early on, right over the site, we had eight midair near collisions. People thought our flight restrictions were to stop the press; but it was simply to prevent collisions. Regarding boom, there were people vandalizing it to get boats in and out. That wasn't illegal. So, like you can't give a parking ticket unless you make parking illegal, we did it to have something to enforce. It was to keep people from damaging the boom. Things happen in the fog of war. But would we go and arrest someone just sitting near a boom? No. That was misunderstood."

I say, "It had a bad effect on people's perceptions—including mine—about whose side you were on."

"Yeah, I understand that," he says. "But I can tell you there was no untoward intent."

And why such heavy reliance on booms anyway? I ask. They obviously weren't up to the job.

"Oil was getting under and through the boom," Allen acknowledges. "Boom is easily defeated."

"So why—?"

Lubchenco begins, "The Oil Pollution Act directs NOAA to do research on cleanup, response, these kinds of things, and—"

"Budget casualties," says Allen, beating her to the punch line. "We stopped doing research and development, so we never advanced beyond skimming and burning and dispersants."

Lubchenco offers, "Every time they tried to put it in the budget; I wasn't there then but I'm told—"

"I was budget director for the Coast Guard," Allen asserts. "This stuff was defunded in the nineties and never got back into the budget. You can quote me on that."

I know we're pressed for time and I don't want to keep you, I say, but that gets to the other peeve: such heavy reliance on dispersant chemicals.

"This is really important," Allen explains. "Because the Oil Pollution Act of 1990 was Congress's response to *Exxon Valdez*, legislators were producing regulations aimed at tanker spills. But drilling technology was going to deep water. We lost it on the technology."

I comment that what people saw was the Coast Guard building a fire truck while the house was in flames.

"If you're faced with building the fire truck," Allen says, accepting the premise, "you can't deploy a response system that doesn't exist. You can't spend time investigating what happened. You can't get bogged down measuring what's happening if your urgent goal is to stop it. You optimize what you've got. After you're done, you analyze. We did get better over the weeks—. I don't think the response was ever optimized. The availability of tools, the weather, how fast we could get ramped up—"

Allen explains that the Coast Guard's role is to enforce and implement laws and regulations. The Oil Pollution Act of 1990 laid out a spill response called the National Oil Spill Contingency Plan. That creates limitations, but he says it's worked well—until now.

"This thing went off the scale," he adds. Allen explains that the oil spill contingency plan had protocols allowing dispersants and surface burning, and when this blowout happened, events triggered the protocols. "But," he says, "two things went off the scale: one was the total amount of oil; the other was that when the protocols were written, no one envisioned injecting dispersants at depths of five thousand feet.

"And we had what I call 'the social and political nullification' of the National Contingency Plan," he says. In other words, the public and politicians weren't buying the constraints of the law. Main case in point: "The National Contingency Plan says the spiller is the 'responsible party.' That means they have to be there with you. But having BP with us created cognitive dissonance with the public. People didn't understand; how could BP be part of the command structure? But that was what the law required."

He thinks it would be best to have a third party—not the oil company, not government—in charge of spill response. "Too much perception of conflicts of interest otherwise," he says.

Another problem: "BP's efforts to just keep writing checks to state and local governments—you can describe it any way you want— allowed those folks to act outside of federal coordination. Perfect example: the people of Plaquemines Parish decided they wanted to put boom out in Barataria Bay. That should have been coordinated with us. But they independently went out and did it. And to keep the boom in place, they hired a contractor who drove PVC pipe into marshland— every twenty feet. They did that with BP money. Obviously not good for the marsh. The law says it has to be federally coordinated, but that was hard when the law was politically, socially, and economically nullified. There were other plans to close off estuaries with rock jetties so oil wouldn't get in. But that would basically destroy the ecosystem."

"We were very insistent on preventing people from trying to clean marshes," Lubchenco adds. "That just pushes the oil into the sediment, and then later it keeps coming up." After the spill from the *Amoco Cadiz*, some oiled marshes were bulldozed; those are the areas that haven't recovered. Marsh recovery seems to depend a lot on not disturbing the plants' roots. With the *Exxon Valdez*, the mistake was to pressure-wash tidal zones with hot water. Hard clams are still diminished in washed areas because the structure of sediments was disrupted.

Following up on BP's unusual eagerness to write checks—thinking again of Exxon—I ask for their thoughts on why BP agreed to fund a $20 billion account when no law required that.

"Early on," Allen replies, "BP was saying yes to just about anything. It's safe to say BP thought the situation was an existential threat to their corporation and their industry."

"But—early on, too," Lubchenco says turning to Allen, "BP wouldn't let us get the video. That was a case where they had to be ordered to—"

"But even there," Allen replies, "I don't think they were trying to hide anything. Their position on live video was that with several remotely operated vehicles being very delicately maneuvered near each other, they didn't want the operators under the added stress of being watched real-time."

"That's reasonable," I say.

"It is reasonable," Allen affirms. "But you know what? I said no. I said, 'At this point—you lose that.' I told them, 'You've had a market failure and you're responsible. So you lose discretion and things get dictated. That's the way it is.'"

Allen adds that in dealing extensively with BP's senior management, he sensed "*no* indication of any ulterior motives other than to re-establish their credibility, do what they had to do, and be responsible."

Seeing my face turn skeptical, he continues: "Put it this way: there's a difference between what seems like foot-dragging and obfuscation—and competence. BP is an oil company; they're very good at getting oil out of the ground, but they absolutely suck at retail. One-on-one inter-actions with people—they don't have a clue. You cannot hire consul-tants to give you compassion and empathy. A lot of things people got upset about and viewed as bad intent on BP's part were, in my view, a lack of competency, capability, and capacity. But it produces inaction and people get the same perception."

Speaking of inaction and perception, I ask how Coast Guard rear admiral Mary Landry could have said—after the whole rig sank, with eleven lives—that it was too early to call this a catastrophe and that no oil was leaking. Why didn't they act immediately as if this obvious catastrophe would produce a worst-case blowout, and hope they were wrong?

Lubchenco insists that this is what they did. That the president said in his very first briefing, "I want everybody prepared for worst-case scenarios"; that within hours, her agency began generating models of currents, predicting where oil would be going. "Our folks mobilized anticipating the worst. Right from the beginning our efforts were in-credibly intense."

But how, I persist, could the Coast Guard have said immediately that it didn't seem oil was leaking?

Allen replies that for two days after the rig sank, there was so much silt kicked up that the remote vehicles had a hard time seeing any-thing. "You've gotta remember, this is a place where there's no human access. Everything has to be done remotely. It took almost seventy-two hours to understand what was going on. Initially there were leaks in three places where the pipe was kinked. It took a few days before the abrasive sand and everything coming out finally ground a larger hole in it."

"You can do Monday-morning quarterbacking," Lubchenco says to me a bit pointedly, "but at the time there was extraordinary effort. We mobilized ships and planes and people, assuming that it would be really bad."

"How," I posit, "is it possible to assume it's really bad when you kept putting out flow estimates that were one-sixtieth of the—"

Allen interrupts: "I was irritated over the early declarations about whether this was one or five thousand barrels. I listened to that and I thought, 'This is crazy—*nobody* knows.'"

Lubchenco wants me to appreciate that "for weeks and weeks, the primary focus was stopping the flow." She adds, "We all thought the early estimates were very low, but we didn't have a way of getting better estimates initially. In every other spill, the amount of oil was estimated from the surface. But this time a lot of oil was staying deep. We were really frustrated early on because BP said, 'No, we don't want anybody else down there.'"

"They were just focused on stopping the oil," says Allen. "That's when it's our job to say, 'Here's our national priorities; here's how we're gonna do it.' With the amount of remotely operated vehicles moving around down there, it is stunning we didn't have a major accident. We had ROVs bump into one other and knock things off; that happened twice, almost with major consequences. It's like the eight near midair plane collisions. There was an unbelievable amount of stuff going on within one square mile; that never happened before. The area where oil was coming to the surface sometimes had thirty-five vessels all in one square mile. But at one point," he adds, "I said, 'We're gonna establish an independent estimate of flow rate.'"

Lubchenco continues: "Thad ordered them to let the group go down and make those measurements."

Allen takes another sip of his coffee and glances at his watch. I know we don't have a ton of time left. He poses the next question himself: "Could we have stopped it sooner? In hindsight, we might have saved two to three weeks. But we were operating with an abundance of caution."

"We had very good reason to believe," Lubchenco informs me, "that the well had been damaged. The concern was, if we built too much pressure in it, the oil would start breaking out through the seafloor. And *then*—it would be completely uncontrollable."

"That's the Armageddon we all feared," Allen adds. "So we had eighty-five days of a different spill coming to the surface in a different way in a different place every day, depending on winds and current conditions. We had a hundred thousand different patches of oil from Louisiana to Florida. Because the oil spill contingency plan didn't call for enough equipment, we were behind the power curve for six or seven weeks. We had three kinds of responses to the oil: skim it, burn it, or disperse it."

I point out that *all* of the oil was coming out of one pipe: "You had your hands around it right there at the source, and you let it get away."

"We just did not have the ability to capture it at the source," Lubchenco replies. "And we didn't have the boats, skimming equipment, right weather—or the kind of oil—to let us just put a ring around it and capture it at the surface. It sounds like that should have been easy," she says. "But it was *not*."

"When the Deepwater Horizon's pipe broke," Allen affirms, "there was nothing capable of capturing that oil. A system should have been in place, but it wasn't, because we were focused on tanker spills. Oil spill response in this country is based on *Exxon Valdez*."

"That's *painfully* obvious," Lubchenco concurs.

"The assumption was, 'We'll never have a failed blowout preventer.'"

But we know blowouts happen, I insist. What they finally installed on July 15 to stop the leak, they should have already had in a warehouse before April 20.

"I couldn't agree more," Lubchenco affirms.

"We're not gonna sit here and defend the fact that it wasn't there," Allen says.

Of the kinds of things that *were* there, Lubchenco says that she hadn't anticipated how much their response options depended on weather. "I mean, skimming just doesn't work in rough water."

"But in rough water you can disperse," Allen points out, "and the motion helps mix the dispersant and oil so it's not just laying on top of it."

"Oil is toxic and nasty," Lubchenco says. "There are no choices that are risk-free."

"No right choices," Allen agrees. "Nothing good happens when oil gets into water."

"Skimming and burning were just very ineffective. That wasn't getting us very far," Lubchenco says.

"The Hobson's choice was," Allen says, "accept the fate of the oil in the ocean, or accept the fate of the oil along the shore. There was no easy answer."

"So," Lubchenco says, "the decision was made—not by me; on the advice of our scientific support people—that, on balance, using dispersants was the right thing to do."

But the thing that sticks in people's ribs, I say, is this: dispersed oil is still oil. And it's still in the waters of the Gulf.

"Agreed," says Lubchenco.

"The dispersants don't make the oil go away," Allen acknowledges.

"And that's problematic," Lubchenco points out. "So let me continue. Now, the thing is, dispersed oil is available to be biodegraded much, much faster." That's because the crude's surface area gets vastly increased, facilitating microbial attachment, basically cutting it into little pieces that bacteria can more easily eat. "And that's the *whole* rationale for using chemical dispersants," she says.

"But," she adds, "twice as much was dispersed physically as chemically. When such hot oil, being shot out under pressure, suddenly hits such cold water, it fractionates into microscopic droplets. 'Dispersed' *doesn't mean* it hasn't had impact. I think it has likely had. Early on we got ships out there to get baseline data of things like plankton and bluefin tuna larvae—as much as possible. When this disaster happened, just-spawned shrimp and crabs and fish were in the drifting plankton. The plankton, I think, could have been very seriously affected. Something like eighty to ninety percent of the economically important fish populations in the Gulf depend on the marshes and estuaries for part of their lives; they move back and forth. For them, this could not have come at a worse time. But it's next to impossible to document—so far—what's happened to them."

"So," she sums up, "1.25 million barrels of neutrally buoyant chemically and physically dispersed oil ended up drifting in the water at depths between thirteen hundred to forty-three hundred feet. And *that*—that's not good. I mean, oil is inherently really toxic. We won't know for a while—we really won't know for decades—but it's likely it's had very serious impacts."

I'm surprised that Lubchenco seems to think things will likely turn out worse than I'm betting they will. And that she's saying so. I might have expected her to downplay the long-term effects while I insisted that things were likely worse. How odd that we're not following that script. It's in her best professional interest for the long-term effects of this to be minimal. Because the results won't be in for a long time and some damage may never be known, Jane's got the option of hiding behind uncertainty to make herself look better. She could easily put on a game face and say she thinks the Gulf will bounce right back. That she's not doing this suggests both admirable integrity and a cool hand on the tiller.

"Even if the oil degrades pretty rapidly," Lubchenco says, "and is gone in, like, a year, its impact on populations may already be very, very substantial. I have very grave concerns about impacts this has had for populations that were already depressed and longer-lived species."

"So," adds Allen, "since Kemp's ridley turtles don't start breeding until they're twelve years old, we won't know for twelve years what happened with this year's hatchlings."

Kemp's ridleys were probably the most at-risk of the Gulf's wildlife. "This was a critically endangered population finally coming back because of turtle excluders in fishing nets and better protection of their nesting beaches in Texas and Mexico," Jane notes. "They were really coming back. And then with this, they were hit very, very hard—they were *hammered*."

What about dolphins? "It doesn't look like many died," Lubchenco says, brightening a bit. "We brought some people in to tag them. And from the tagging we can see them still moving around, alive and seeming to behave normally."

Corals? Oyster beds?

"So far we haven't seen oil in corals," Lubchenco says, "though we haven't finished looking everywhere yet. But oysters—they're toast."

"In Louisiana," says Allen, "they decided to send so much fresh water through the delta to keep the oil outside the marshes, they committed oystercide—or whatever you'd call it."

In May, Louisiana's Governor Bobby Jindal, supported by local parish officials, ordered technicians to open giant valves on the Mississippi River, releasing torrents of fresh water with the idea of pushing any oil off the coast. The fresh water largely demolished southeastern Louisiana's oyster beds, killing far more oysters than did the oil.

"Again, that's local officials doing what they think is expedient. Oyster beds have to be reseeded and started over again."

(In September, it seems as if shallow-water coral reefs may escape oil damage. But in November 2010, researchers on one of NOAA's ships will find dead deep-water corals seven miles southwest of the Macondo well, 4,500 feet deep, where researchers last spring had discovered drifting hydrocarbon plumes. The expedition's chief scientist, Charles Fisher of Pennsylvania State University, will comment, "We have never seen anything like this at any of the deep coral sites that we've been to, and we've been to quite a lot." Dr. Lubchenco will say, "This is precisely why we continue to actively monitor the Gulf.")

Lubchenco starts to gather her things and says, "I really have to get going, but we've been talking about the ecological dimensions of this disaster, and yet the human disaster here is very, *very* real."

"We on the government side need to get better at making it known that we understand that people's emotional reactions—the passion and the angst—*are* the right way to feel about this," Allen adds. "This is *grieving*."

"So many communities, so many individuals are just devastated," Lubchenco points out. "The federal government did an insufficient job communicating real compassion. Not that those in government didn't care, but it didn't come across to people as compassion."

"I'll give you a good example of the problem here," the admiral says. "We are not allowed under the Oil Pollution Act of 1990 to use money from the Oil Spill Liability Trust Fund to do anything about behavioral health."

Lubchenco shakes her head and breathes, "Isn't that *just* ridiculous?"

"It's not allowed," Allen says. "Nor was BP, the responsible party, required to do anything for mental wellness."

"A *lot* of changes need to be made," Lubchenco says, though her agency's charge is oceans and weather forecasting, not emotional health.

Of course, that's the space between angst and suicide.

"So we had a charter boat captain in Alabama who did commit suicide," Allen says somberly. "So I went to BP and said, 'You have to give money to these states to set up an 800 number for suicide prevention counseling.' This had nothing to do with my job as national incident commander. But it's what the country expects out of the whole government response. And that's a conversation we have to have."

This conversation is coming to a close. We've been here for two hours; Jane's got a plane to catch. We rise and shake hands, and I thank them for their valuable time.

Allen begins to turn away, then suddenly turns back to me and says, "One last thought: large corporations and the government are usually not capable of the conspiracies that are attributed to them. A lot of what seems like conspiracies has to do with just plain culture, capacity, and ineptness."

Lubchenco nods and agrees: "I can't *believe* all the conspiracy theories I've heard." She rolls her eyes and smiles, and says, "It's been hell."

❧

On Sunday, September 19, with the cementing done, Admiral Allen declares America's worst oil leak "effectively dead."

Two months after the oil stopped flowing, currents and oil-eating microbes continue steadily dissipating and degrading the oil. NOAA's Dr. Steven Murawski says that even to the most sensitive instruments, the oil deep in the open Gulf is fading to levels barely detectable, making the underwater plumes "harder and harder to find." The oil is becoming, Murawski says, "like a shadow out there."

In the last week of September and the first week of October, NOAA will reopen fishing in almost 17,000 square miles of Gulf federal waters. BP ends its boat employment, and Jane Lubchenco's agency—in an unusual move—opens fishing for the hugely popular red snapper as a boost to tourism and to anglers who've missed a whole spring and summer's fishing. If fish could think, they might find themselves feeling nostalgic for the summer of *pax petroleum.*

Those fish that got a few months' peace—oil notwithstanding—remain to be caught in numbers anglers are not accustomed to. "Red snapper are unbelievable right now," says one fisherman. "You could put a rock on the end of a string and they'll bite it."

What are scientists finding?

"It's not what you would have guessed," says Dauphin Island Sea Lab senior marine scientist John Valentine. "You would have expected something horrible, but that's not what we're seeing." Ironically, the blowout's most powerful environmental effect seems to be both indirect and positive: the fishing closures. Fishing is designed to kill things living in the sea, and it does so effectively. It's been by far the major agent of change in the world's oceans until now. And if all of us use petroleum, most of us also eat seafood. Valentine's finding about three times as many fish now compared to before the blowout, and they're bigger.

Likewise, Sean Powers of the University of South Alabama finds that even some coastal Alabama shark populations have tripled in number, and a lot of that comes from this year's young. Normally, shrimp nets kill a lot of small sharks. "It's just been amazing how many more sharks we are seeing this year," he says. "I didn't believe it at first. What's interesting to me," he adds, "we are seeing it across the whole range, from the shrimp all the way up to the large sharks." Ken Heck, also of the Dauphin Island Sea Lab, says species whose young live in sea-grass meadows also appeared robust. "It's quite amazing. Everyone speculated that an entire year class of larvae and young might have been lost, smothered in oil," Heck says. "That hasn't happened."

Oddly, this seems almost troubling to researchers wishing to understand the effects of oil itself. "The problem with the fishing closure is, that impact is so large it is probably going to swamp any impact of the oil spill," Powers says. "We're not saying we didn't lose any fish to the spill. We're saying it is going to be harder to detect any smaller changes due to oil spill contamination. We'll have to look carefully."

Valentine notes, "This was the first time we've ever seen such a large-scale cessation of fishing." I note, nature's resilience is truly magnificent.

Well, what does all that tell us? It tells me that restoring a healthy ocean must also involve mixing fishing into the big-picture strategy. An oil lease is a piece of seafloor specially set aside for oil extraction. Why don't we also set aside other places, to restore a better ocean? If it's in the national interest to produce oil and gas, it's as much in the national interest to protect other social and economic and living interests. There are more than eight thousand active oil and gas leases on America's outer continental shelf. In addition to setting those places aside for taking oil and gas, why don't we insist on setting special places aside for protection? Right now, less than 1 percent of all federal waters of the United States have been protected as national marine sanctuaries or any other safeguarded areas.

In an e-mail to various folks, the indefatigable Dr. Sylvia Earle exhorts:

To compensate the Gulf, and provide hope for recovery, actions should be taken ASAP to identify and protect areas that are still in good shape. Obama has the power to do as Presidents T. Roosevelt and G. W. Bush have done in the past—under the Antiquities Act— to declare National Monuments. What better way to "give back to the Gulf," and to the people whose livelihoods depend on a healthy Gulf, than to protect the deep reefs and string of "topographic highs" in the Northern Gulf, the spawning areas for tuna, the critical places for menhaden, grouper, snapper, shrimp and others, as well as the vital—but neglected—seagrass meadows of Florida's Big Bend area. Respect for the importance of the floating forests of sargassum and their role in providing nursery areas, food and shelter—as well as taking up carbon and generating oxygen—might be considered in an overall recovery plan. This could be the moment to act to secure protection for Pulley Ridge, the extraordinary system of deep reefs 150 miles offshore from Sarasota. And time is of the essence. Maybe now is the time, when the need is so obvious, to act.

When BP announces it has spent $9.5 billion cleaning up its mess (a helium-filled figure that will keep floating upward over the next weeks and months), I'm not sure how I feel about it. It's nice of BP, but they could have saved themselves and all of us the trouble by saying, "Wait a minute" when they saw pressure on the gauge during the afternoon of April 20. Maybe next time they won't keep driving when the oil light comes on.

But what will the next time be? Just as the federal response plan failed this blowout because it was designed to fight the next *Exxon Valdez*, we're gonna need something that doesn't just plan to fight the last war. Some added thought is called for. Some vision. What might be the next big problem in the tapping and transport of oil, the one nobody is anticipating?

More than 27,000 abandoned wells lurk beneath the Gulf of Mexico. With some abandoned as long ago as the 1940s, deteriorating sealing jobs may already be failing. About 13 percent of them are categorized in government records as "temporarily abandoned." Temporarily abandoned wells are supposed to be plugged within a year. That's routinely ignored. Many "temporarily abandoned" wells have been sitting since the 1950s and '60s. No one—not the oil companies, not the government—is checking whether they are leaking. Meanwhile, cement and pipes never intended to last so many years are aging in the seafloor. All this raises the possibility that old wells may spontaneously blow out.

If that happens, it seems unlikely that companies will rush forward to accept responsibility. BP alone has abandoned about 600 wells in the Gulf. "It's in everybody's interest to do it right," says a spokesman for Apache Corporation, which has abandoned at least 2,100 wells in the Gulf. But early on, the rules were less strict than they are today, and many—tens of thousands—of wells are poorly sealed.

Texas alone has plugged more than 21,000 abandoned wells to control pollution in state waters. Other places have similar problems. California has resealed scores of abandoned wells. But in deeper federal waters, the U.S. Minerals Management Service has typically inspected only the paperwork, not the real job. Over five years, from 2003 through 2007, the MMS fined seven companies a total of only $440,000 for improper plug-and-abandonment work.

The Government Accountability Office, which does congressional investigations, warned as early as 1994 that leaks from offshore abandoned wells could cause an "environmental disaster." The GAO pressed for inspections of abandonment jobs, but nothing was done. A 2001 Minerals Management Service study noted concern that "some abandoned oil wells in the Gulf may be leaking crude oil."

Nothing came of that, either. In 2006 the U.S. Environmental Protection Agency said, "Well abandonment and plugging have generally not been properly planned, designed and executed." The EPA was talking about wells *on land*, where wells abandoned in recent decades have leaked so routinely that dealing with the problem is called "replugging" or "reabandonment." The GAO estimated that 17 percent of the nation's land wells had been improperly plugged. If offshore wells are no worse, thousands of wells in the Gulf of Mexico alone are badly plugged.

Various people, from the president on out, have called this blowout "the worst environmental catastrophe in American history." Some simply said "in history."

Well, no. I heard a lot of catastrophizing on both ends. I read everything from how the Deepwater Gulf blowout would trigger a massive seafloor methane release that would kill the whole world (actually, global warming is beginning to trigger a massive methane release), to BP's Tony Hayward saying it's nothing much, really. Usually the truth is somewhere in the middle. But this time, the truth is closer to one end of those extremes.

BP's Tony Hayward became the most hated man in America for saying that the amount of oil leaked was "tiny" compared with the "very big ocean." He might have been making excuses for BP; I'm certainly not. BP, Transocean, Halliburton, and others had to screw up big-time half a dozen different ways to get this well to blow. And in order to be 100 percent unprepared, Big Oil and our own anti-government government regulators had to ignore Ixtoc and the world's other blowouts, cut and paste walruses into their response plans, and do the sloppiest, most cynical job money can buy. BP, Transocean, and Halliburton's legal, fiscal, and public relations nightmare is far from over, and that's fine by me. But whether he realized it or not, in one sense Hayward was right.

In the blowout, 206 million gallons of oil mixed with the Gulf's 660 quadrillion gallons of water. That volume of water could greatly dilute the oil. But the carbon dioxide we're adding to the atmosphere isn't getting diluted; it's building up.

The oil that is getting into the ocean has everyone's attention. It was supposed to be refined to help power civilization, not spew waste and devastation. But Plan A, *burning* the oil—and coal, and gas—in our engines is continually adding carbon dioxide to the atmosphere at the inconceivable rate of a thousand tons a second, billions of tons a year. *That* spill is invisible. Rather than washing up on one coast and scaring tourists, this spill, spread in time and space, is slowly coating the whole world. There is no single company at which to point fingers.

In this, we are all involved. Our everyday use of fossil fuels is changing the atmosphere, ruining the world's oceans. The top-tier journal *Science* has published a special issue called "Changing Oceans" that summarizes major changes being seen in marine life and ocean function—and the significant implications for human health and the food supply. Calling the world's oceans the heart and the lungs of the planet, one of the authors says, "It's as if the Earth has been smoking two packs of cigarettes a day." The oceans produce about 50 percent of the oxygen we breathe, but absorb 30 percent of the carbon dioxide our burning produces, and also absorb more than 85 percent of the extra heat trapped by carbon dioxide and other greenhouse gases. Carbon dioxide isn't just warming the world; it's making seawater more acidic.

Because we've bet the house on burning oil, coal, and gas, our atmosphere's concentration of carbon dioxide is a third higher now than at the start of the Industrial Revolution. As environmental catastrophes go, that dwarfs the Gulf blowout of 2010. That's just a fact, and, again, I state it with no intended disrespect to the people of the Gulf whose lives were so horrendously distorted by the blowout.

The worst environmental disaster in history isn't the oil that got away. The real catastrophe is the oil we *don't* spill. It's the oil we run through our engines as intended. It's the oil we burn, the coal we burn, the gas we burn. The worst spill—the real catastrophe—is the carbon dioxide we spill out of our tailpipes and smokestacks every second of every day, year upon decade. *That* spill is changing the atmosphere, changing the world's climate, altering the heat balance of the whole planet, destroying the world's polar systems, killing the wildlife of icy seas, killing the tropics' coral reefs, raising the level of the sea, turning the oceans acidic, and dissolving shellfish. And as the reefs dissolve and the productivity of oceans and agriculture destabilizes, so will go the food security of hundreds of millions of people.

———

Fossil fuels are great fuels. They are very energy-dense for their size and weight. You can't eat them, so their use as fuel doesn't compete with people's needs for food or farmland. (If the entire U.S. corn crop went to make ethanol, it would replace only 15 percent of America's gasoline usage.) Clean renewables have drawbacks. A coal plant can keep producing energy whether or not the sun is shining or the wind is blowing. Wind is clean, but many people object to the sight of turbines (they should see how the oil rigs dominate the view in the Gulf), to their sound, or to the fact that they kill birds and bats. Large-scale solar projects need a lot of land.

But fossil fuels have drawbacks, too. One, they're not eternal and won't last forever. Their production is likely to peak in a few decades. Two, in the process of getting them, workers die and dictators thrive. Three, they're hurting the world's life-support capacity.

It is hard to imagine how solar power or wind or algae could power all of civilization. But not so very long ago, the present scale and difficulty of coal mining, oil drilling, and civilization itself—for that matter—was impossible to envision. Even though fossil fuels elicited giddy attraction, ramping them up to dominance took the better part of a century. No matter how good a fuel is, it takes time to create the technology to produce it, the infrastructure to transport it, and the consumer demand for it.

We have to do something. The Gulf of Mexico accounts for almost a third of America's oil production and most new discoveries. Most of the world's land has been sucked dry, especially in the United States. And elsewhere, it's being put out of reach by autocratic, self-protecting governments.

Many people say—*and they have a point*—that if Americans do not want to hand even more money and clout to the likes of Iran, Saudi Arabia, Russia, and Venezuela (I certainly don't), we should drill more at home. I would add: and America should harness *all* our domestic sources of energy. We should get on an emergency war-footing crash

program for creating the jobs and building the infrastructure to surpass China and northern Europe's renewable-energy race, summon
the determination to lead the world into the eternal-energy economy,
and emerge again as the greatest country on Earth. You'll hear me say
this again, because, really, that's the Big Picture here.

In America, there hadn't been a big offshore oil well leak in forty
years. Underwater pipeline leaks declined from an average of 2.5 million gallons per year in the early 1980s to just 12,000 gallons a year in
the early '00s, according to the Congressional Research Service. The
National Research Council estimates that offshore drilling, tankers,
and pipelines account for 5 percent of the oil that gets into in U.S.
waters, while shipping accounts for 33 percent, and 62 percent comes
from natural seeps (natural seeps send perhaps 1,000 to 2,000 barrels
of oil into the northern Gulf daily, though estimates vary a lot).

This leads us to a question. What's the worst part of America's
oil addiction: funding foreign dictators, warming the air and acidify-
ing the seas, or drilling holes? Perhaps we should not, after all, keep
America's waters closed to our thirst for oil. Perhaps we should just
drink a wider variety of energies that are better for us, better for everything. Americans pay a fraction of the full cost of a gallon of gasoline,
if you count the costs of pollution and wars to maintain access. Not at
the pump, anyway.

The best way to respond to the Gulf disaster? Not washing oil off
birds, picking up turtles, spraying dispersants, or cleaning beaches.
Rather, pulling the subsidies out from under Big Petroleum. Since we
pay those subsidies in our income taxes and lose sight of them, it'd be
better to put them right in our gasoline and oil taxes and let ourselves
be shocked at the pump by the true cost we're paying—and hurry
toward better options.

We have a shortage of time and a long way to go. Considering how
much damage carbon dioxide is doing to our atmosphere and ocean, it
would be unwise to simply assume we won't need nuclear energy. We
in the United States already get about a fifth of our electricity from nu-

clear, and nuclear plants provide similar proportions for several other countries. (In one sense, all our energy is nuclear, since the sun itself derives its energy from hot nuclear fusion reactions similar to those in a hydrogen bomb.) It might be necessary to accept the drawbacks of more nuclear as a bridge to cleaner energy. But the dangers with nuclear's spent fuels and potential weapon-building materials make nuclear hard to swallow. The economics are difficult, too: construction and decommissioning costs remain quite high, likely too high. Things can go wrong with nuclear in ways that simply can't happen with other zero-carbon-emissions sources. (Terrorists can't do much with windmills and solar panels.) Reasonable people can reach different conclusions about nuclear energy. My conclusion is that our attention ought be firmly focused on clean renewables.

Solar energy delivers power enough to meet our projected future energy demands all by itself. But today solar electricity is just 0.1 percent of total world electricity production and solar heating, a similar 0.1 percent of world energy production. For wind to generate 20 percent of U.S. electricity, we'd need almost ten times the capacity we currently have and we'd need to build 100,000 new turbines.

Replacing just half the power generated today by oil, coal, and gas would require 6 terawatts; renewable energy sources now generate only half a terawatt. But transitions have always been forced by shortages. Necessity is the mother of innovation. During the War of 1812, wood shortages around Philadelphia prompted residents to experiment with burning coal. When Edwin Drake drilled the first oil well in the United States, in 1858, whale oil was already getting harder to come by.

One problem with clean fuels is the perception that "they don't offer new services; they just cost more," as one analyst has said. Wrong on both counts, but the statement reveals our inability to understand the effects and costs of energy. The new services are the elimination of toxic pollution, risk, and the climate change and ocean chemistry change that fossil fuels cause. The costs of those things are enormous. The fact that the costs are not in the fuels' at-pump price is a failure of our economics, not a drawback of clean fuels. We are already paying, and we will pay enormous future costs for the effects of climate change on agriculture, coastal cities, coral reefs and fisheries, security, and the abundance and diversity of wildlife worldwide.

Those costs are serious. A moral and practical answer is to engineer the transition. Shifting massive and guaranteed subsidies away from fossil fuels and into clean renewables would be a big part of the way to accomplish what's needed.

But because we don't understand the difference between price, cost, and value, we can't seem to get our minds unstuck and move beyond or around the idea that we simply don't want to "pay more" for better energy. On June 20, 2010, at the height of the agony in the Gulf, a CBS News / New York Times poll found that 90 percent of people agreed that "U.S. energy policy either needs fundamental changes or to be completely rebuilt" but that just under half of them—49 percent of people responding—supported new taxes on gasoline to fund new and renewable energy sources. If people don't want to pay more at the pump, the best thing we can do to save money *and* buy time until we have better options would be to conserve energy and improve efficiency. Who are the losers there? Everybody wins. But boosting efficiency, too, runs into political trouble.

If we could build the infrastructure to capture and transport energy from renewable sources, the energy itself—sunlight, wind, tides, geothermal heat—would come for free. That's what "clean, eternal" means. But we hear that energy that comes for free is too expensive. Who tells us clean, eternal energy is too expensive and that it would "wreck the economy"? Why, it's none other than the big brothers: Big Oil and Big Coal! We've crossed that bridge before. There was another time when people vehemently insisted that changing America's main source of energy would wreck the economy. The cheapest energy that has ever powered America was slavery. Energy is always a moral issue.

Big Oil and Big Coal maintain our addiction to their elixirs. But we allow it, rather than freeing ourselves to a more diverse, decentralized, cleaner, stable array of fuel sources.

The real tragedy is that for thirty years we've known that for reasons of national security and patriotism alone, we need to phase out our dependence on oil, coal, and gas. Our foreign dependence, the jobs we're missing out on, the pollution, the worker-killing explosions, the way we enrich dictators and terrorists—we've known all that since the politically induced oil shocks and gasoline lines of the 1970s. I remember those lines with some fondness, because I waited on them as a young high school buck and proud new owner of a used hippie van. But those lines were all we needed to learn that security for the United States, and the globe, requires a future largely free of fossil fuels.

And since the late 1980s, we've known that fossil fuels are also destabilizing the world climate. But Big Oil and Big Coal, using the subsidies we pay them, maintain the weakest government money can buy. So most Republicans and a few indebted Democrats scoff at energy efficiency.

Multinational corporations are by definition not patriotic; they can't afford to be. But we can't afford for them not to be. Their interests are not our interests. For the main reason behind America's decline—in manufacturing, jobs, technological innovation, and moral leadership—we need look no further. Multinational corporations have strangled innovation in its crib. Killed all our first-born ideas and sent the entrepreneurs who could have saved us fleeing to places like China.

China understands its moment. Today China is rapidly becoming the world's leader in wind and solar energy, electric cars, and high-speed rail. It's also the world's greatest lender of money to the United States; we have yoked ourselves to interest payments to the world's biggest totalitarian government, while forking over union jobs, technological leadership, and the American Dream. It's been said that empires are not destroyed from the outside; they commit suicide.

Every president since Nixon has talked about our need to kick our oil addiction. Some were serious. But by failing to sweep money out of politics, we disenfranchise ourselves from control of our own government, our own country.

And yet we simply won't be able to maintain civilization by digging fossil energy out of the ground and burning it. There's not enough. By the middle of this century, well within the life span of many people already born, we are scheduled to add to the world another two billion people—nearly another China plus another India's worth of people. Of the truly great human-caused environmental catastrophes, foremost is the human population explosion. The forests, the fishes, and fresh water are collapsing under the weight of the number of people on Earth right now. All the other global environmental, justice, human development, energy, and security problems either start with or are made worse by the sheer crush of our numbers. The projected growth will squash human potential as billions of poor get poorer, while flaring tensions and igniting violence. Being concerned about overpopulation isn't anti-people; not being worried about it is anti-people.

We run civilization mainly on the energy of long-ago sunlight, locked away in oil and coal. It's time we step into the sunlight itself and phase in an energy future based on harnessing the eternal energies that actually run the planet. Whoever builds that new energy future will own the future. And the nation that owns the energy future will sell it to everyone else. I'd rather that nation be the United States of America. Did we really wage a decades-long Cold War just so we could anoint China the world's Big Box Store? So we could be indebted to China for generations? Did we really hand world leadership to the largest autocratic nondemocracy in the history of the world because all it can offer is low wages, no unions, and cheap goods? Is that all it takes to secure our surrender? Where are the patriots?

New details about the Gulf blowout of 2010 will continue to bubble up for quite some time. As the birds of autumn begin rowing through the air near my Long Island home, I begin seeing gleaming white gannets on their way south after nesting in Canada. Last spring, the first oiled bird whose image made news was a gannet that had spent its winter in the Gulf. I realized that the bird would never return to its Canadian nesting grounds, meaning the oil would create problems reaching far beyond the Gulf of Mexico. Juvenile gannets can spend several years in the Gulf, and now I get word that Suncoast Seabird Sanctuary, near

Tampa, is still nursing about eighty gannets it received during the summer, debilitated by oil but alive. That means hundreds of gannets died. In Canada, seabird biologist Bill Montevecchi says that his tagging studies suggest that the oil posed a threat to as many as a third of Canada's gannets. Even if all goes well from now on, it will take a few years for the population, nesting well over two thousand miles from the Gulf, to replace those birds lost to the Gulf oil slicks. And that's just gannets.

The blowout is both an acute tragedy and a broad metaphor for a country operating sloppily, waving away risks and warnings, a country that does not use care in stewarding its precious gifts, a country concerned only about the next little while, not the longer time frames of our lives or our children's futures.

In the meantime, we are left with the Gulf itself. Regardless of how fast the Gulf's waters, wildlife, and wetlands recover from this blowout, Gulf residents will be left with scars and years-long pain. The stamp of this will be on lives, families, marriages, and children for quite a while to come.

During the last week of September, "moderate to heavy oil" washes onto almost one hundred miles of Louisiana's shoreline. And when Louisiana State University scuba divers go for a look into the waters off of St. Bernard and Plaquemines Parishes, they see "oil everywhere."

REFERENCES

BLOWOUT!

4 *Deepwater Horizon size, and insured for over half a billion dollars* S. Mufson, "Gulf of Mexico Oil Spill Creates Environmental and Political Dilemmas," *Washington Post*, April 27, 2010. *See also* "Deepwater Horizon," at Wikipedia.org; accessed on November 12, 2010.

4 *No serious injuries in seven years* "Blowout: The Deepwater Horizon Disaster," CBS News, May 16, 2010; http://www.cbsnews.com/stories/2010/05/16/60minutes/main6490197.shtml.

5 *Drilling progressed to about 4,000 feet* "Oil Spill Postmortem: BP Used Less-reliable, but Cheaper Drilling Method on Deepwater Horizon," McClatchy-Tribune News Service, May 23, 2010.

5 *$58 million over budget* "AFE Summary for the Macondo Well," http://www.deepwaterinvestigation.com/external/content/document/3043/914919/1/AFE%20Summary%20for%20the%20Macondo%20Well.pdf.

7 *Casing and drill pipe and "making a trip* M. Raymond and William Leffler, *Oil and Gas Production in Nontechnical Language* (Tulsa, OK: PennWell Corp., 2006), p. 104.

9 *It was a world-class rig* "Deepwater Horizon's Cementing Plan Is Under Scrutiny." The well-drilling description is based on schematic and notes from the *Times-Picayune*, 2010; see schematic at http://media.nola.com/2010_gulf_oil_spill/photo/oil-halliburton-cement-052010jpg-e618a2271a66c847.jpg.

9 *The rig was getting dated, and Lloyd's findings* R. Brown, "Oil Rig's Siren Was Kept Silent, Technician Says," *New York Times*, July 23, 2010, p. A1; http://www.nytimes.com/2010/07/24/us/24hearings.html?_r=1&hp.

10   *The rig lost all its fluid*   I. Urbina, "BP Used Riskier Method to Seal Well Before Blast," *New York Times*, May 26, 2010, p. A1; http://www.nytimes.com/2010/05/27/us/27rig.html?_r=2 .

10   *"We got to a depth of 18,260 feet"*   "USCG/BOEM Marine Board of Investigation into the Marine Casualty, Explosion, Fire, Pollution, and Sinking of Mobile Offshore Drilling Unit Deepwater Horizon, with Loss of Life in the Gulf of Mexico," April 21–22, 2010," testimony of John Guide, transcript p. 87, lines 1–25, July 22, 2010; http://www.deepwaterinvestigation.com/go/doc/3043/856503/.

11   *"While drilling that hole section we lost over 3,000 barrels of mud"*   "USCG/MMS Marine Board of Investigation into the Marine Casualty, Explosion, Fire, Pollution, and Sinking of Mobile Offshore Drilling Unit Deepwater Horizon, with Loss of Life in the Gulf of Mexico 21–22 April 2010," testimony of Mark Hafle, transcript pp. 42–43, lines 1–25, 1–5, May 28, 2010;http://www.deepwaterinvestigation.com/go/doc/3043/670171/ .

11   *At over $250 per barrel*   P. Parsons, "The Macondo Well: Part 3 in a Series About the Macondo Well (Deepwater Horizon) Blowout," *Energy Training Resources, LLC*, July 2010, pp. 17, 15; http://www.energytrainingresources.com/data/default/content/Macondo.pdf. *See also* M. J. Derrick, "Cost-Effective Environmental Compliance in the Gulf of Mexico," *World Energy Magazine* 4, No. 1 (2001); http://www.derrickequipment.com/Images/Documents/wemdvol4no1.pdf.

11   *Delays cost a week and led to a budget add-on of $27 million*   "AFE Summary for the Macondo Well," http://www.deepwaterinvestigation.com/go/doc/3043/914919.

11   *Forty-three days behind*   R. Brown, "Oil Rig's Siren Was Kept Silent, Technician Says," *New York Times*, July 23, 2010, p. A1; http://www.nytimes.com/2010/07/24/us/24hearings.html?_r=1&hp.

11   *Crew is informed they'd lost $25 million,*   "Blowout: The Deepwater Horizon Disaster," a *60 Minutes* report that features Mike Williams, CBS News, May 16, 2010; http://www.cbsnews.com/stories/2010/05/16/60minutes/main6490197.shtml.

11   *The final section of the well bore extended to 18,360 feet*   U.S. Congress, House Committee on Energy and Commerce, June 14, 2010, letter from Henry Waxman and Bart Stupak to Tony Hayward, 111th Congress: p. 4; http://energycommerce.house.gov/documents/20100614/Hayward.BP.2010.6.14.pdf.

12   *"Cost is not a deciding factor"*   "USCG/MMS Marine Board of Investigation into the Marine Casualty, Explosion, Fire, Pollution, and Sinking of Mobile Offshore Drilling Unit Deepwater Horizon, with Loss of Life in the Gulf of Mexico," April 21–22, 2010, testimony of David Sims, May 26, 2010; http://www.deepwaterinvestigation.com/go/doc/3043/670067/.

12   *"a win-win situation"*   USCG/BOEM Marine Board of Investigation into the Marine Casualty, Explosion, Fire, Pollution, and Sinking of Mobile Offshore Drilling Unit Deepwater Horizon, with Loss of Life in the Gulf of Mexico," April 21–22, 2010, testimony of John Guide, transcript p. 397, lines 18–23, July 22, 2010; http://www.deepwaterinvestigation.com/go/doc/3043/856503/.

12 *"With every decision, didn't BP reduce"* "Video: Deepwater Horizon Joint Investigation Footage," July 22, 2010, Part 36, posted on July 24, 2010; http://www.dvidshub.net.

13 *"without a doubt a riskier way to go"* I. Urbina, "BP Used Riskier Method to Seal Well Before Blast," *New York Times*, May 26, 2010, p. A1; http://www.nytimes.com/2010/05/27/us/27rig.html?_r=2.

14 *Jason Anderson's concerns over safety* "BP Toolpusher Jason Anderson Feared for His Life," June 3, 2010; http://seminal.firedoglake.com/diary/52541\. *See also* "Deepwater Horizon Victim—Jason Anderson," http://www.awesomestories.com/assets/deepwater-horizon-victim-jason-anderson. *See also* R. Arnold, "Son Warned of Trouble on Doomed Rig," August 16, 2010; http://www.click2houston.com/news/24652197/detail.html. *See also* T. Junod, "Eleven Lives," *Esquire*, August 16, 2010; http://www.esquire.com/features/gulf-oil-spill-lives-0910. *See also* J. Carroll and Laural Brubaker Calkins, "BP Pressured Rig Worker to Hurry Before Disaster, Father Says," Bloomberg, May 27, 2010; http://www.bloomberg.com/news/2010-05-28/bp-pressured-oil-rig-worker-to-hurry-before-fatal-gulf-blast-father-says.html.

15 *"His experience was largely in land drilling"* B. Casselman and Russell Gold, "BP Decisions Set Stage for Disaster," *Wall Street Journal*, May 27, 2010; http://online.wsj.com/article/SB10001424052748704026204575266560930780190.html?KEYWORDS=negative+test.

15 *"I raised my concerns"* "USCG/BOEM Marine Board of Investigation into the Marine Casualty, Explosion, Fire, Pollution, and Sinking of Mobile Offshore Drilling Unit Deepwater Horizon, with Loss of Life in the Gulf of Mexico," April 21–22, 2010," testimony of Paul Johnson, transcript p. 205, lines 7–17, August 23, 2010; http://www.deepwaterinvestigation.com/external/content/document/3043/903575/1/USCGHEARING%2023_Aug_10.pdf.

15 *"Mr. Bob Kaluza called me to his office"* "USCG/BOEM Marine Board of Investigation into the Marine Casualty, Explosion, Fire, Pollution, and Sinking of Mobile Offshore Drilling Unit Deepwater Horizon, with Loss of Life in the Gulf of Mexico," April 21–22, 2010, testimony of Leo Lindner, transcript pp. 272 and 313, July 19, 2010; http://www.deepwaterinvestigation.com/go/doc/3043/856483/.

16 *"Let's face it"* W. Semple, e-mail to Mark Loehr, September 19, 2010.

16 *"We're in the exploration group"* "USCG/BOEM Marine Board of Investigation into the Marine Casualty, Explosion, Fire, Pollution, and Sinking of Mobile Offshore Drilling Unit Deepwater Horizon, with Loss of Life in the Gulf of Mexico," April 21–22, 2010, testimony of Ron Sepulvado, transcript p. 63, lines 5–6, July 20, 2010; http://www.deepwaterinvestigation.com/go/doc/3043/856499/.

16   *Production zone between 18,051 and 18,223 feet*   BP's Deepwater Horizon Accident Investigation Report, September 8, 2010; http://www.bp.com/liveassets/ bp_internet/globalbp/globalbp_uk_english/incident_response/STAGING/local _assets/downloads_pdfs/Deepwater_Horizon_Accident_Investigation_Report .pdf.

17   *"The biggest risk associated with this cement job"*   "USCG/BOEM Marine Board of Investigation into the Marine Casualty, Explosion, Fire, Pollution, and Sinking of Mobile Offshore Drilling Unit Deepwater Horizon, with Loss of Life in the Gulf of Mexico," April 21–22, 2010, testimony of John Guide, transcript p. 87, lines 2–4, July 22, 2010; http://www.deepwaterinvestigation.com/go/doc/3043/ 856503/.

17   *Nitrified foamed cement*   P. Parsons, "The Macondo Well: Part 3 in a Series About the Macondo Well (Deepwater Horizon) Blowout," *Energy Training Resources, LLC*, July 15, 2010; https://www.energytrainingresources.com/data/default/ content/Macondo.pdf.

17   *The depth created concern*   D. Hammer, "Deepwater Horizon's Ill-Fated Oil Well Could Have Been Handled More Carefully, Hearings Reveal," May 29, 2010, *NOLA.com;*   http://www.nola.com/news/gulf-oil-spill/index.ssf/2010/05/hammer -hearings-cg.html.

17   *"That nitrogen, it could be a bad thing"*   "USCG/MMS Marine Board of Investigation into the Marine Casualty, Explosion, Fire, Pollution, and Sinking of Mobile Offshore Drilling Unit Deepwater Horizon, with Loss of Life in the Gulf of Mexico," April 21–22, 2010, testimony of Jimmy Harrell, transcript p. 72, lines 20–22, May 27, 2010; http://www.deepwaterinvestigation.com/go/doc/3043/670139/.

18   *"We were concerned"*   "USCG/MMS Marine Board of Investigation into the Marine Casualty, Explosion, Fire, Pollution, and Sinking of Mobile Offshore Drilling Unit Deepwater Horizon, with Loss of Life in the Gulf of Mexico," April 21–22, 2010, testimony of Mark Hafle, transcript p. 45, lines 8–12, May 28, 2010; http:// www.deepwaterinvestigation.com/go/doc/3043/670171/.

18   *BP held an in-house contest*   A. G. Breed, "The Well Is Dead, but Gulf Challenges Live On," Associated Press, September 19, 2010.

19   *"To see if adding more centralizers will help," and related discussion*   U.S. Congress, House Committee on Energy and Commerce, June 14, 2010, letter from Henry Waxman and Bart Stupak to Tony Hayward, 111th Congress, p. 7; http:// energycommerce.house.gov/documents/20100614/Hayward.BP.2010.6.14.pdf.

20   *"It was a bigger risk to run the wrong centralizers"*   "USCG/BOEM Marine Board of Investigation into the Marine Casualty, Explosion, Fire, Pollution, and Sinking of Mobile Offshore Drilling Unit Deepwater Horizon, with Loss of Life in the Gulf of Mexico," April 21–22, 2010, testimony of John Guide, transcript p. 307, lines 1–25, July 22, 2010; http://www.deepwaterinvestigation.com/go/doc/3043/ 856503/.

20 *"The BP Macondo team erroneously believed"* BP's Deepwater Horizon Accident Investigation Report, p. 35, September 8, 2010; http://www.bp.com/liveassets/bp_internet/globalbp/globalbp_uk_english/incident_response/STAGING/local_assets/downloads_pdfs/Deepwater_Horizon_Accident_Investigation_Report.pdf.

20 *"That subject never came up"* "USCG/BOEM Marine Board of Investigation into the Marine Casualty, Explosion, Fire, Pollution, and Sinking of Mobile Offshore Drilling Unit Deepwater Horizon, with Loss of Life in the Gulf of Mexico," April 21–22, 2010, testimony of John Guide, transcript p. 307, lines 1–25, July 22, 2010; http://www.deepwaterinvestigation.com/go/doc/3043/856503/.

20 *"Well, we didn't know if we could find them"* "USCG/BOEM Marine Board of Investigation into the Marine Casualty, Explosion, Fire, Pollution, and Sinking of Mobile Offshore Drilling Unit Deepwater Horizon, with Loss of Life in the Gulf of Mexico," April 21–22, 2010, testimony of John Guide, transcript p. 205, lines 1–25, July 22, 2010; http://www.deepwaterinvestigation.com/go/doc/3043/856503/.

20 *"I don't know of any"* "USCG/BOEM Marine Board of Investigation into the Marine Casualty, Explosion, Fire, Pollution, and Sinking of Mobile Offshore Drilling Unit Deepwater Horizon, with Loss of Life in the Gulf of Mexico," April 21–22, 2010, testimony of John Guide, transcript p. 356, line 22, July 22, 2010; http://www.deepwaterinvestigation.com/go/doc/3043/856503/.

21 *"I never knew it was part of the report"* "USCG/BOEM Marine Board of Investigation into the Marine Casualty, Explosion, Fire, Pollution, and Sinking of Mobile Offshore Drilling Unit Deepwater Horizon, with Loss of Life in the Gulf of Mexico," April 21–22, 2010, testimony of John Guide, transcript p. 269, lines 7–8, July 22 2010; http://www.deepwaterinvestigation.com/go/doc/3043/856503/.

21 *"Although the decision not to use twenty-one centralizers"* BP's Deepwater Horizon Accident Investigation Report, p. 35, September 8, 2010; http://www.bp.com/liveassets/bp_internet/globalbp/globalbp_uk_english/incident_response/STAGING/local_assets/downloads_pdfs/Deepwater_Horizon_Accident_Investigation_Report.pdf.

22 *Kill pill as spacer, and quotes about using it* D. Hilzenrath, "Credibility of BP Oil Spill Study Is Challenged," *Washington Post*, September 11, 2010; http://www.washingtonpost.com/wpdyn/content/article/2010/09/11/AR2010091104579.html.

23 *Spacer fluid abnormally used, and that spacer could have affected the blowout preventer, and "would have required disposal," and "snot on the deck"* D. Hammer, "Finger-Pointing over Deepwater Horizon Explosion Grows Heated," July 19, 2010, NOLA.com;   http://www.nola.com/news/gulf-oil-spill/index.ssf/2010/07/finger-pointing_over_deepwater.html. *See also* M. Kunzelman, "Federal Hearings Resume in Oil Spill Probe," Chron.com, July 19, 2010; http://www.chron.com/disp/story.mpl/ap/tx/7115149.html.

23 *"To my knowledge—well, it filled a function"* "USCG/MMS Marine Board of Investigation into the Marine Casualty, Explosion, Fire, Pollution, and Sinking of

Mobile Offshore Drilling Unit Deepwater Horizon, with Loss of Life in the Gulf of Mexico," April 21–22, 2010, testimony of Leo Lindner, transcript p. 321, lines 12–15, July 19, 2010; http://www.deepwaterinvestigation.com/go/doc/3043/856483/.

23 *"Why is all this snot on the deck?"*   "USCG/MMS Marine Board of Investigation into the Marine Casualty, Explosion, Fire, Pollution, and Sinking of Mobile Offshore Drilling Unit Deepwater Horizon, with Loss of Life in the Gulf of Mexico," April 21–22, 2010, testimony of Steve Bertone, transcript p. 41, lines 1–4, July 19, 2010; http://www.deepwaterinvestigation.com/go/doc/3043/856483/.

24 *Douglas Brown's statements and disparity about whether Vidrine or Kaluza said they'd do it a certain way*   J. Harkinson, "The Rig's on Fire! I Told You This Was Gonna Happen!" *Mother Jones*, June 7, 2010; http://motherjones.com/blue-marble/2010/06/rigs-fire-i-told-you-was-gonna-happen.

24 *"I didn't have no doubts about it"*   "USCG/MMS Marine Board of Investigation into the Marine Casualty, Explosion, Fire, Pollution, and Sinking of Mobile Offshore Drilling Unit Deepwater Horizon, with Loss of Life in the Gulf of Mexico," April 21–22, 2010, testimony of Jimmy Harrell, transcript pp. 57–58 and 74. He later says he doesn't recall the remark: transcript p. 80, May 27, 2010; http://www.deepwaterinvestigation.com/posted/3043/May_27_PDF.670139.pdf.

26 *"If it's a successful test"*   "USCG/BOEM Marine Board of Investigation into the Marine Casualty, Explosion, Fire, Pollution, and Sinking of Mobile Offshore Drilling Unit Deepwater Horizon, with Loss of Life in the Gulf of Mexico," April 21–22, 2010, testimony of John Smith, transcript p. 267, lines 1–3, July 23, 2010; http://www.deepwaterinvestigation.com/go/doc/3043/856507/.

26 *"And that was really the only discussion"*   "USCG/BOEM Marine Board of Investigation into the Marine Casualty, Explosion, Fire, Pollution, and Sinking of Mobile Offshore Drilling Unit Deepwater Horizon, with Loss of Life in the Gulf of Mexico," April 21–22, 2010, testimony of John Guide, transcript p. 156, lines 13–14, July 22, 2010; http://www.deepwaterinvestigation.com/go/doc/3043/856503/.

27 *"I haven't been a witness"*   "USCG/BOEM Marine Board of Investigation into the Marine Casualty, Explosion, Fire, Pollution, and Sinking of Mobile Offshore Drilling Unit Deepwater Horizon, with Loss of Life in the Gulf of Mexico," April 21–22, 2010, testimony of Leo Lindner, transcript pp. 286 and 288, July 19, 2010; http://www.deepwaterinvestigation.com/go/doc/3043/856483/.

27 *" a warning sign right off the bat"*   "USCG/BOEM Marine Board of Investigation into the Marine Casualty, Explosion, Fire, Pollution, and Sinking of Mobile Offshore Drilling Unit Deepwater Horizon, with Loss of Life in the Gulf of Mexico," April 21–22, 2010, testimony of John Smith, transcript p. 279, line 10, July 23, 2010; http://www.deepwaterinvestigation.com/go/doc/3043/856507/.

27 *"They attempted it again and got fluid back"*   "USCG/BOEM Marine Board of Investigation into the Marine Casualty, Explosion, Fire, Pollution, and Sinking of Mobile Offshore Drilling Unit Deepwater Horizon, with Loss of Life in the Gulf of Mexico," April 21–22, 2010, testimony of Leo Lindner, transcript p. 274, lines 3–4, July 19, 2010; http://www.deepwaterinvestigation.com/go/doc/3043/856483.

27–28 *My supervisor was explaining,"* and *"Where that U-tube's at,"* and *"Bob tells Jason, No,"* and *"approximately a good hour"* "USCG/MMS Marine Board of Investigation into the Marine Casualty, Explosion, Fire, Pollution, and Sinking of Mobile Offshore Drilling Unit Deepwater Horizon, with Loss of Life in the Gulf of Mexico," April 21–22, 2010, testimony of Chris Pleasant, transcript pp. 115–116 and 264, May 28, 2010; http://www.deepwaterinvestigation.com/go/doc/3043/670171.

28 *Don Vidrine believes* J. C. McKinley Jr., "Documents Fill in Gaps in Narrative on Oil Rig Blast," *New York Times*, September 7, 2010, p. A18; http://www.nytimes .com/2010/09/08/us/08rig.html?_r=2&hpw=&pagewanted=all.

28 *"And if you don't see that, you need to be very concerned, right?"* and *"So the symptoms are a successful test"* "USCG/BOEM Marine Board of Investigation into the Marine Casualty, Explosion, Fire, Pollution, and Sinking of Mobile Off-shore Drilling Unit Deepwater Horizon, with Loss of Life in the Gulf of Mexico," April 21–22, 2010, testimony of John Smith, transcript p. 392 and pp. 289–90, July 23,2010; http://www.deepwaterinvestigation.com/go/doc/3043/856507/. *See also* "Video: Deepwater Horizon Joint Investigation Footage, July 23rd, Part 35," posted on July 25, 2010; http://www.dvidshub.net. *See also* "USCG/BOEM Marine Board of Investigation into the Marine Casualty, Explosion, Fire, Pollution, and Sinking of Mobile Offshore Drilling Unit Deepwater Horizon, with Loss of Life in the Gulf of Mexico," April 21–22, 2010, testimony of Lee Lambert, transcript pp. 290, 357, and 395, July 20, 2010; http://www.deepwaterinvestigation.com/go/doc/3043/856499/.

29 *"The investigative team could find no evidence"* BP's Deepwater Horizon Accident Investigation Report, p. 40, September 8, 2010; http://www.bp.com/liveassets/ bp_internet/globalbp/globalbp_uk_english/incident_response/STAGING/local _assets/downloads_pdfs/Deepwater_Horizon_Accident_Investigation_Report .pdf.

29 *"Go call the office"* "USCG/MMS Marine Board of Investigation into the Marine Casualty, Explosion, Fire, Pollution, and Sinking of Mobile Offshore Drilling Unit Deepwater Horizon, with Loss of Life in the Gulf of Mexico," April 21–22, 2010, testimony of Chris Pleasant, transcript p. 118, May 29, 2010; http://www .deepwaterinvestigation.com/go/doc/3043/670191/.

30 *Cement bond log test's importance and decision not to use it* D. Hammer, "Costly, Time-Consuming Test of Cement Linings in Deepwater Horizon Rig Was Omitted, Spokesman Says," NOLA.com, May 19, 2010; http://www.nola.com/news/gulf-oil -spill/index.ssf/2010/05/costly_time-consuming_test_of.html.

30 *"Everyone on the rig was completely satisfied"* "USCG/BOEM Marine Board of Investigation into the Marine Casualty, Explosion, Fire, Pollution, and Sinking of Mobile Offshore Drilling Unit Deepwater Horizon, with Loss of Life in the Gulf of Mexico," April 21–22, 2010, testimony of John Guide, transcript p. 43, lines 24–25, July 22, 2010; http://www.deepwaterinvestigation.com/go/doc/3043/856503/.

32   *BP's discussion of Halliburton's cement*   BP's Deepwater Horizon Accident Investigation Report, September 8, 2010; http://www.bp.com/liveassets/bp_internet/globalbp/globalbp_uk_english/incident_response/STAGING/local_assets/downloads_pdfs/Deepwater_Horizon_Accident_Investigation_Report.pdf.

32–33   *Halliburton and BP had prior knowledge that the cement failed tests*   J. M. Broder, "Panel Says Firms Knew of Cement Flaws Before Spill," *New York Times*, October 28, 2010, p. A1. *See also* D. Cappiello, "Critical Test Not Done on Cement Before Blowout," Associated Press, October 29, 2010. *See also* D. Hammer, "Oil Spill Commission Finds Halliburton's Cement Was Unstable, Failed Several Tests Before Deepwater Horizon Disaster," *Times-Picayune*, October 29, 2010. *See also* "BP, Halliburton Knew Oil Disaster Cement Was Unstable," Agence France-Presse, October 29, 2010.

33   *Even small cracks*   PumpCalcs, Orifice flow calculator: http://www.pumpcalcs.com/calculators/view/103/.

33–34   *Events after 8:00 P.M. on April 20*   BP's Deepwater Horizon Accident Investigation Report, p. 92, September 8, 2010; http://www.bp.com/liveassets/bp_internet/globalbp/globalbp_uk_english/incident_response/STAGING/local_assets/downloads_pdfs/Deepwater_Horizon_Accident_Investigation_Report.pdf.

34   *"eliminating all conventional well control"*   "USCG/BOEM Marine Board of Investigation into the Marine Casualty, Explosion, Fire, Pollution, and Sinking of Mobile Offshore Drilling Unit Deepwater Horizon, with Loss of Life in the Gulf of Mexico," April 21–22, 2010, testimony of John Smith, transcript p. 409, July 23, 2010; http://www.deepwaterinvestigation.com/go/doc/3043/856507/. *See also* "Video: Deepwater Horizon Joint Investigation Footage, July 23rd, Part 49," posted on July 25, 2010; http://www.dvidshub.net.

36   *"Rig crew was not sufficiently prepared"*   BP's Deepwater Horizon Accident Investigation Report, p. 108, September 8, 2010; http://www.bp.com/liveassets/bp_internet/globalbp/globalbp_uk_english/incident_response/STAGING/local_assets/downloads_pdfs/Deepwater_Horizon_Accident_Investigation_Report.pdf.

37   *Randy Ezell*   "USCG/MMS Marine Board of Investigation into the Marine Casualty, Explosion, Fire, Pollution, and Sinking of Mobile Offshore Drilling Unit Deepwater Horizon, with Loss of Life in the Gulf of Mexico," April 21–22, 2010, testimony of Randy Ezell testimony of Miles Ezell transcript, pp. 283–288, May 28, 2010; http://www.deepwaterinvestigation.com/go/doc/3043/670171.

38   *Mud shooting out the top*   BP's Deepwater Horizon Accident Investigation Report, p. 126, September 8, 2010; http://www.bp.com/liveassets/bp_internet/globalbp/globalbp_uk_english/incident_response/STAGING/local_assets/downloads_pdfs/Deepwater_Horizon_Accident_Investigation_Report.pdf.

38   *Alarm inhibition*   R. Brown, "Oil Rig's Siren Was Kept Silent, Technician Says," *New York Times*, July 23, 2010 p. A1; http://www.nytimes.com/2010/07/24/us/24hearings.html?_r=1&hp.

39 *"If I would have shut down those engines"* R. Arnold, "Testimony: Safety System 'Inhibited' on Doomed Rig," Click2Houston.com, July 23, 2010; http://www .click2houston.com/news/24373880/detail.html.

39 *Mike Williams's description of events* "Blowout: The Deepwater Horizon Disaster," *CBSNews.com,* May 16,2010; http://www.cbsnews.com/stories/2010/05/16/ 60minutes/main6490197.shtml. *See also* R. Brown, "Oil Rig's Siren Was Kept Silent, Technician Says," *New York Times,* July 23, 2010, p. A1; http://www.nytimes.com/ 2010/07/24/us/24hearings.html?_r=1&hp. *See also* "Deepwater Horizon Joint Investigation Hearings Testimony Videos for July 23, 2010," August 4, 2010; http://www .deepwaterinvestigation.com/go/doc/3043/834139/.

40 *Interchange between Pleasant and Kuchta* D. Hammer, "Deepwater Horizon's Ill-Fated Oil Well Could Have Been Handled More Carefully, Hearings Reveal," NOLA.com, May 29, 2010; http://www.nola.com/news/gulf-oil-spill/index.ssf/ 2010/05/hammer-hearings-cg.html.

40 *Disconnect failed* "USCG/MMS Marine Board of Investigation into the Marine Casualty, Explosion, Fire, Pollution, and Sinking of Mobile Offshore Drilling Unit Deepwater Horizon, with Loss of Life in the Gulf of Mexico," April 21–22, 2010, testimony of Jimmy Harrell, transcript p. 58, May 27, 2010; http://www .deepwaterinvestigation.com/go/doc/3043/670139.

43–44 *Summary of the things that went wrong* "Oil Spill: BP Engineers Partly Responsible," ComodityOnline.com, September 10, 2010; http://www .commodityonline.com/news/Oil-Spill-BP-engineers-partly-responsible-31641-3-1 .html.

APRIL

45 *"leading the government response"* C. Woodward, "A Containable Accident, Then Suddenly a Crisis," Associated Press, April 30, 2010.

45–46 *April 23 quotes from Obama, the Coast Guard (except Landry), BP, and Transocean, and the misreported amount of oil* "Major Oil Spill as Rig Sinks off US Coast," Agence France-Presse, April 23, 2010; http://www.physorg.com/news191218312 .html.

46 *Michael Brown quotes* D. Sweet, "Michael Brown: Obama Let Oil Spill Get Worse on Purpose," *Raw Story,* May 4, 2010; http://www.rawstory.com/rs/2010/05/ michael-brown-obama-wanted-oil-spill.

46 *Obama drilling decision* A. Koppelman, "Is There Anyone Who Likes Obama's Drilling Decision?" Salon.com, March 31, 2010; http://www.salon.com/ news/politics/war_room/2010/03/31/drilling_reacts. *See also* J. M. Broder, "Obama to Open Offshore Areas to Oil Drilling for First Time," *New York Times,* March 30, 2010; http://www.nytimes.com/2010/03/31/science/earth/31energy.html.

47–48 *Landry quotes about no apparent leak, plus Robert Gibb and sometimes accidents happen* C. Woodward, "A Containable Accident, Then Suddenly a Crisis,"

Associated Press, April 30, 2010; http://abcnews.go.com/Business/wireStory?id
=10513415.

48   *Manageable*   F. Grimm, "Vast Oil Spill May Alter Debate on Gulf Drilling,"
Miami Herald, April 27, 2010; http://www.miamiherald.com/2010/04/26/1599498/
vast-oil-spill-may-alter-debate.html.

48   *Two to four weeks*   S. Mufson, "Oil Spill in Gulf of Mexico Creates Dilemmas
in Nature and Politics," *Washington Post*, April 27, 2010; http://www.washingtonpost
.com/wpdyn/content/article/2010/04/26/AR2010042604308.html.

50–51   *Relief well, 1,800 square miles, dome, "we have to be careful," "far as the eye
could see," off-flavors, and Jindal asked for booms*   C. Burdeau, "Oil Leak from Sunken
Rig off La. Could Foul Coast," Associated Press, April 26, 2010; http://abcnews.go
.com/Business/wireStory?id=10480828.

51   *Relief wells could take two months and that the relief well will cost $100 million*   H.
Mohr and Cain Burdeau, "Coast Guard Considers Lighting Oil Spill on Fire," Associated Press, April 28, 2010; http://minnesota.publicradio.org/display/web/2010/
04/28/oil-spill-gulf/.

51   *Misreported: 4.2 million barrels could spill*   C. Burdeau, "La. Gov Declares
Emergency over Gulf Oil Spill," Associated Press, April 29, 2010; http://www.salon
.com/news/2010/04/29/us_louisiana_oil_rig_explosion_5.

52   *A BP executive agreed on 5,000 barrels a day*   "Shrimpers, Fishermen File Suit
over US Oil Spill," Agence France-Presse, April 30, 2010; http://www.mysinchew
.com/node/38400.

52   *Going from "manageable" to "emergency," Landry's "ample time"*   C. Woodward, "A Containable Accident, Then Suddenly a Crisis," Associated Press, April
30, 2010; http://abcnews.go.com/Business/wireStory?id=10513415.

53   *"Shrimpers sue"*   "Shrimpers, Fishermen File Suit over US Oil Spill," Agence
France-Presse, April 30, 2010; http://www.mysinchew.com/node/38400.

53   *Administration might revisit president's drilling announcement*   C. Woodward,
"A Containable Accident, Then Suddenly a Crisis," Associated Press, April 30, 2010;
http://abcnews.go.com/Business/wireStory?id=10513415.

55   *"Controlled burns," and the relief well will cost $100 million*   H. Mohr and Cain
Burdeau, "Coast Guard Considers Lighting Oil Spill on Fire," Associated Press,
April 28, 2010; http://minnesota.publicradio.org/display/web/2010/04/28/oil-spill
-gulf/.

56   *"Eventually, things will return to normal"*   H. Mohr and Cain Burdeau, "Gulf
Businesses Wait as Oil Creeps Toward Coast," Associated Press, April 29, 2010;
http://www.chron.com/disp/story.mpl/business/deepwaterhorizon/6978731.html.

56 *Ixtoc killed hundreds of million of crabs*   J. Achenbach and David Brown, "In Gulf Oil Spill's Long Reach, Ecological Damage Could Last Decades," *Washington Post*, June 6, 2010; http://www.washingtonpost.com/wpdyn/content/article/2010/06/05/AR2010060503987.html?hpid=topnews.

DÉJÀ VU, TO NAME BUT A FEW

57   *Histories of antecedent oil spills, in part, from:*   Joanna Burger, *Oil Spills*, New Brunswick, NJ: Rutgers University Press, 1997.

58   *Amoco Cadiz*   J. Achenbach and David Brown, "In Gulf Oil Spill's Long Reach, Ecological Damage Could Last Decades," *Washington Post*, June 6, 2010; http://www.washingtonpost.com/wp-dyn/content/article/2010/06/05/AR2010060503987.html?hpid=topnews.

59   *"First the money dried up"*   A. Allen, "Prodigal Sun," *Mother Jones*, March–April 2000; http://motherjones.com/politics/2000/03/prodigal-sun.

59–60   *Exxon Valdez otter, bird, and seal deaths*   C. H. Peterson et al., "Long-Term Ecosystem Response to the *Exxon Valdez* Oil Spill," *Science* 302, December 19, 2003: 2082–86.

60   *Great Britain's Health and Safety Executive warning to Transocean*   R. Mason, "Transocean Denies Bullying Oil Rig Workers over Safety Fears," *Daily Telegraph* (London), September 8, 2010; http://www.telegraph.co.uk/finance/newsbysector/energy/7987815/Transocean-denies-staff-bullied-over-safety-fears-in-North-Sea.html.

61   *September 14, 2007, letter*   L. Kaufman, "2010 Agency Is Faulted for Saying Oil-Spill Risk to Wildlife Was Low," *International Herald Tribune*, July 6, 2010; http://www.highbeam.com/doc/1P1-181710108.html.

61   *October 2009 environmental assessment*   K. Sheppard, "License to Drill," *Mother Jones*, June 2010; http://motherjones.com/environment/2010/06/new-drilling-leases-gulf-of-mexico.

62   *Waxman and Stupak letter to BP*   B. Bohrer, "Congressmen Cite 'Significant' BP Issues in Alaska," Associated Press, May 6, 2010; http://abcnews.go.com/Business/wireStory?id=10567540.

62   *Obama's coast plan and the Mississippi Delta*   "Obama Administration Officials Release Roadmap for Gulf Coast Ecosystem Restoration Focused on Resiliency and Sustainability," White House Press Release, March 4, 2010; http://www.whitehouse.gov/administration/eop/ceq/Press_Releases/March_4_2010.

62–63   *The senators' letter on energy efficiency and conservation*   R. Schoof, "10 Senate Democrats Oppose Climate Bill If It Expands Coastal Drilling," McClatchy-Tribune News Service. March 25, 2010; http://www.mcclatchydc.com/2010/03/25/91107/10-senate-dems-oppose-climate.html.

63   *Chinese-owned coal carrier Shen Neng 1*   J. M. Glionna, Ju-min Park, and Kenneth R. Weiss, "Oil Leak Threatens Barrier Reef; Australia Rushes to Protect the Sensitive Ecosystem from a Stranded Chinese Ship Carrying Heavy Fuel," *Los Angeles Times*, April 5, 2010.

63   *Minerals Management Service's Alaska office hasn't developed any guidelines* K. Murphy, "Agency Faulted over Alaska Oil Drilling Policy," *Los Angeles Times*, April 7, 2010; http://articles.latimes.com/2010/apr/07/nation/la-na-alaska-drilling8 -2010apr08.

63   *Minerals Management Service approves permit changes*   J. Barry, "Oil Spill Disaster Marked by BP Mistakes from the Outset," *St. Petersburg Times*, June 2, 2010; http://www.tampabay.com/news/environment/water/oil-spill-disaster-marked-by -bp-mistakes-from-the-outset/1099273.

64   *"I've never seen this kind of attitude"*   "Blowout: The Deepwater Horizon Disaster," CBSNews.com, May 16, 2010; http://www.cbsnews.com/stories/2010/05/16/ 60minutes/main6490197.shtml.

MAYDAY

67   *"I am frightened for the country," and Crist's "bigger than we can fathom"*   C. Woodward, "A Containable Accident, Then Suddenly a Crisis," Associated Press, April 30, 2010; http://abcnews.go.com/Business/wireStory?id=10513415.

68   *"This is the worst possible thing"*   H. Mohr and Cain Burdeau, "Coast Guard Considers Lighting Oil Spill on Fire," Associated Press, April 28, 2010; http:// minnesota.publicradio.org/display/web/2010/04/28/oil-spill-gulf.

69   *"I'd hate to think" and related quotes*   "Oil Leak Poses Risk of a Lost Generation on Louisiana Coast," Agence France-Presse, May 3, 2010; http://www.terradaily .com/reports/Oil_leak_poses_risk_of_a_lost_generation_on_Louisiana_coast _999.html.

69   *Captain Doogie*   H. Allen G. Breed and Holbrook Mohr, "Another Week at Least of Unabated Gulf Oil Geyser," Associated Press, May 3, 2010; http://abcnews .go.com/Business/wireStory?id=10531316

69   *"When you kill that food chain," and "We should be fine"*   K. McGill, "A Murky Picture as Seafood Industry Eyes Oil Slick," Associated Press, May 3, 2010; http:// abcnews.go.com/Business/wireStory?id=10536472.

69   *Volume and value of Gulf catch*   "Mobile Baykeeper Says BP Spill Could Destroy Most Productive Fishery in the World," *Energy Weekly News*, May 14, 2010; http://www.prnewswire.com/news-releases/mobile-baykeeper-says-bp-spill-could -destroy-most-productive-fishery-in-the-world-92497804.html.

69–70   *"What BP's doing is throwing," and "It's probably easier to fly," and "It's not a spill, it's a flow," and twenty dead turtles*   H. Mohr and Allen G. Breed, "Another

Week at Least of Unabated Gulf Oil Geyser," Associated Press, May 3, 2010; http://abcnews.go.com/Business/wireStory?id=10531316.

71 The Economist *argues, and statistics attributed to the Congressional Research Service and National Research Council* "Deep Trouble: The Oil Spill in the Gulf of Mexico," *The Economist*, May 8, 2010; http://www.economist.com/node/16059948.

71 *Thomas Friedman writes* T. Friedman, "No Fooling Mother Nature," *New York Times.* May 4, 2010; http://www.nytimes.com/2010/05/05/opinion/05friedman.html.

72 *John Kerry quote and Republican governors withdrawing support* C. Babington, "Bid to Enact Energy Bill Might Survive Gulf Spill," Associated Press, May 6, 2010; http://abcnews.go.com/Business/wireStory?id=10569505.

72–73 *Republican climate science denial, and Bob Inglis quoted* "GOP Victory May Be Defeat for Climate Change Policy," NPR's *All Things Considered*, October 23, 2010; http://www.npr.org/templates/transcript/transcript.php?storyId=130776747.

79 *History of tanker wrecks affecting birds* Joanna Burger, *Oil Spills*, New Brunswick, NJ: Rutgers University Press, 1997.

80 *Exxon's CEO didn't care if the booms contained the oil* *Countdown with Keith Olbermann*, MSNBC, June 14, 2010.

80 *"We may . . . lose dozens of vulnerable fish species"* "Dozens of Fish Species in Danger in US Oil Leak," Agence France-Presse, May 31, 2010; http://www.seeddaily.com/reports/Dozens_of_fish_species_in_danger_in_US_oil_leak_expert_999.html.

80 *"We'll see dead bodies soon"* E. Dugan, "Oil Spill Creates Huge Undersea 'Dead Zones,' " *Independent,* May 30, 2010; http://www.independent.co.uk/news/world/americas/oil-spill-creates-huge-undersea-dead-zones-1987039.html.

80 *Could affect rice and sugarcane* R. School and Chris Adams, "Gulf's Future Looks Grim," *Sun News*, May 31, 2010; http://www.thesunnews.com/2010/05/31/1505058/gulfs-future-looks-grim.html.

80 *Hurricane effects* J. Masters, "What Would a Hurricane Do to the Deepwater Horizon Oil Spill?" *Weather Underground*, May 26, 2010; http://www.wunderground.com/blog/JeffMasters/comment.html?entrynum=1492.

80 *The* Christian Science Monitor *asks* P. Jonsson, "Gulf Oil Spill: Could 'Toxic Storm' Make Beach Towns Uninhabitable?," *Christian Science Monitor*, June 26, 2010; http://www.csmonitor.com/USA/2010/0626/Gulf-oil-spill-Could-toxic-storm-make-beach-towns-uninhabitable.

81 *"Once it's in the Loop Current"* C. Burdeau and Harry R. Weber, "Deep Beneath the Gulf, Oil May Be Wreaking Havoc," Associated Press, May 6, 2010; http://abcnews.go.com/Business/wireStory?id=10558496.

81   *Senator Bill Nelson quoted*   "Disaster of a New Dimension Looms in Gulf of Mexico Spill," Agence France-Presse, May 9, 2010; http://www.grist.org/article/ 2010-05-09-disaster-of-a-new-dimension-looms-in-gulf-of-mexico-spill.

81   *"The threat to the deep-sea habitat"*   C. Burdeau and Harry R. Weber, "Deep Beneath the Gulf, Oil May Be Wreaking Havoc," Associated Press, May 6, 2010; http://abcnews.go.com/Business/wireStory?id=10558496.

82   *The Web begins amplifying*   T. Aym, "How BP Gulf Disaster May Have Triggered a 'World-Killing' Event," Helium.com; http://www.helium.com/items/1882339 -doomsday-how-bp-gulf-disaster-may-have-triggered-a-world-killing-event. *See also* T. Aym, "Why BP Is Readying a 'Super Weapon' to Avert Escalating Gulf Nightmare," *Helium.com*; http://www.helium.com/items/1889648-bp-preparing-super -weapon-to-avert-escalating-gulf-nightmare.

83   *Fears not materializing, things not so bad*   J. M. Broder and Tom Zeller Jr., "Bad. But an Apocalypse?" *New York Times,* May 4, 2010; http://query.nytimes.com/gst/ fullpage.html?res=9A05E7DF113FF937A35756C0A9669D8B63.

83   *Leak could reach 60,000 barrels*   J. M. Broder et al., "Amount of Spill Could Escalate, Company Admits," *New York Times,* May 5, 2010; http://www.nytimes.com/ 2010/05/05/us/05spill.html.

85   *Louisiana's coastal wetlands have lost 2,300 square miles*   C. Burdeau and Harry R. Weber, "Deep Beneath the Gulf, Oil May Be Wreaking Havoc," Associated Press, May 6, 2010; http://abcnews.go.com/Business/wireStory?id=10558496.

87   *"It's the last thing in the world"*   B. Farrington, "Gulf Spill Gives Gov. Crist Pause over Drilling," Associated Press, April 28, 2010; http://abcnews.go.com/US/ wireStory?id=10488587.

87   *"The president is frustrated"*   H. J. Hebert and Harry R. Weber, "Political Patience Wanes as Gulf Oil Spill Grows," Associated Press, May 12, 2010; http://www .cbsnews.com/stories/2010/05/12/national/main6475125.shtml.

87   *In 2009 the Interior Department exempted BP's Gulf of Mexico drilling*   J. Eilperin, "U.S. Exempted BP Rigs from Impact Analysis; Prior Reviews Concluded That a Large Oil Spill in the Area Was Unlikely," *Washington Post,* May 5, 2010; http://www .washingtonpost.com/wp-dyn/content/article/2010/05/04/AR2010050404118.html.

87   *"Boosterism breeds complacency"*   D. Usborne, "US Oil Regulator 'Gave in to BP' over Rig Safety," *Independent,* May 7, 2010; http://www.independent.co.uk/ news/world/americas/us-oil-regulator-gave-in-to-bp-over-rig-safety-1965611.html.

88   *Salazar's "very, very rare event"*   "Gulf Oil Spill: Interior Secretary Says Spill 'Very, Very Rare Event,' " *Los Angeles Times,* May 2, 2010; http://bit.ly/buSoSo.

88 *39 rig blowouts in the Gulf of Mexico*   R. Gold and Ben Casselman, "Drilling Process Attracts Scrutiny in Rig Explosion," *Wall Street Journal,* April 30, 2010; http://online.wsj.com/article/SB10001424052748703572504575214593564769072 .html.

88–89 *Sarah Palin*   N. Allen, "Foreign Oil Firms Not to Be Trusted, Says Sarah Palin," *Daily Telegraph,* May 7, 2010; http://www.telegraph.co.uk/news/world-news/northamerica/usa/7686978/Gulf-of-Mexico-oil-slick-Sarah-Palin-fuels-anti-British-sentiment.html.

89 *"I think I have said all along"*   D. Usborne, "US Oil Regulator 'Gave in to BP' over Rig Safety," *Independent,* May 7, 2010; http://www.independent.co.uk/news/world/americas/us-oil-regulator-gave-in-to-bp-over-rig-safety-1965611.html.

89 *Transocean's president, Halliburton's spokesman*   H. J. Hebert and Harry R. Weber, "Political Patience Wanes as Gulf Oil Spill Grows," Associated Press, May 12, 2010; http://www.cbsnews.com/stories/2010/05/12/national/main6475125 .shtml.

89 *Blame among BP, Transocean, and Halliburton*   CNN Wire Staff, "Congressman to Launch Inquiry on How Much Oil Is Gushing into Gulf," CNN.com, May 14, 2010; http://articles.cnn.com/2010-05-14/us/gulf.oil.spill_1_bp-oil-spill -dispersants?_s=PM:US.

89–90 *"People from around the world"*   "Hair, Fur, Nylons Join Fight to Hold Back US Oil Spill," Agence France-Presse, May 9, 2010; http://www.terradaily .com/reports/Hair_fur_nylons_join_fight_to_hold_back_US_oil_spill_999.html.

90 *Activities in and around Grand Isle*   H. R. Weber and John Curran, "Oil Spill Swells to 4M Gallons," Associated Press, May 11, 2010; http://www.cbsnews.com/ stories/2010/05/11/national/main6471488.shtml.

90 *"The technology hasn't changed that much"*   J. C. McKinley and Leslie Kaufman, "As Oil Spreads, a Call for Industry's 'Plan B,' " *New York Times,* May 11, 2010; http://www.boston.com/news/science/articles/2010/05/11/as_oil_spreads_a_call _for_industrys_plan_b.

90 *"This is the largest, most comprehensive"*   H. R. Weber and John Curran, "Oil Spill Swells to 4M Gallons," Associated Press, May 11, 2010; http://www.cbsnews .com/stories/2010/05/11/national/main6471488.shtml.

90 *Workers diverting freshwater*   "More River Water Sent into Marshes to Fight Oil," Associated Press, May 10, 2010; http://www.nola.com/news/gulf-oil-spill/ index.ssf/2010/05/more_fresh_river_water_sent_in.html.

91 *The looming hurricane season*   J. C. Olivera, "Hurricane Could Worsen Huge US Oil Spill," Agence France-Presse, May 12, 2010; http://www.google.com/ hostednews/afp/article/ALeqM5jf8KgVCVcikaoZArKPqnF1Rrbheg.

91 *BP's "Safety first"*   C. Krauss, "BP Tries Again to Divert Oil Leak with Dome," *New York Times*, May 31, 2010; http://www.nytimes.com/2010/06/01/us/01spill.html.

91–92 *Purdue professor's computer analysis*   "Congressman to Launch Inquiry on How Much Oil Is Gushing into Gulf," CNN.com, May 14, 2010; http://articles.cnn.com/2010-05-14/us/gulf.oil.spill_1_bp-oil-spill-dispersants?_s=PM:US.

92 *"If you don't know the flow"*   S. Goldenberg, "Scientists Study Ocean Footage to Gauge Full Scale of Oil Leak: Independent Researchers Press BP to Telease Film," *Guardian*, May 14, 2010; http://www.guardian.co.uk/business/2010/may/13/bp-oil-spill-ocean-footage.

LATE MAY

93 *"There's a shocking amount"*   J. Gillis, "Giant Plumes of Oil Forming Under Gulf," *New York Times*, May 15, 2010; http://www.nytimes.com/2010/05/16/us/16oil.html.

93 *She reports methane, and "the most bizarre-looking"*   M. Brown and Ramit Plushnick-Masti, "Gulf Oil Full of Methane, Adding New Concerns," Associated Press, June 18, 2010; http://www.cbsnews.com/stories/2010/06/18/national/main6594500.shtml.

93 *Deepwater corals*   J. Dearen and Matt Sedensky, "Deep Sea Oil Plumes, Dispersants Endanger Reefs," Associated Press, May 17, 2010; http://abcnews.go.com/Business/wireStory?id=10665749.

93–94 *Plumes and related discussion, "The answer is no to that," and "It appears that the subsea dispersant is actually working"*   J. Gillis, "Giant Plumes of Oil Forming Under Gulf," *New York Times*, May 15, 2010; http://www.nytimes.com/2010/05/16/us/16oil.html.

94 *Plume science compared to Ixtoc oil*   P. D. Boehm and Davld L. Flest, "Subsurface Distributions of Petroleum from an Offshore Well Blowout; The Ixtoc I Blowout, Bay of Campeche," *Environmental Science and Technology* 16, no, 2 (1982): 67–74.

95 *"The answer is no to that"*   Justin Gillis, "Giant Plumes of Oil Forming Under the Gulf," *New York Times*, May 15, 2010; http://www.nytimes.com/2010/05/16/us/16oil.html.

96 *Penalties under the Clean Water Act*   "The Oil Well and the Damage Done," *The Economist*, June 19, 2010; http://www.economist.com/node/16381032.

96 *"It appears that the application of the subsea dispersant"*   Justin Gillis, "Giant Plumes of Oil Forming Under the Gulf," *New York Times*, May 15, 2010; http://www.nytimes.com/2010/05/16/us/16oil.html.

96 *Dispersant making oil available to fish*   M. Brown and Jason Dearen, "New, Giant Sea Oil Plume Seen in Gulf," Associated Press, May 27, 2010; http://www.msnbc.msn.com/id/37384717/ns/gulf_oil_spill.

96–97   *Quotes by Shaw, Joye, Overton, and Twilley*   "Debates Rage over Impact of Oil Dispersants in Gulf," *Hindustan Times*, July 12, 2010; http://www.dnaindia.com/scitech/report_debates-rage-over-impact-of-oil-dispersants-in-gulf_1408787.

97   *The mix is more toxic*   M. J. Hemmer et al., "Comparative Toxicity of Louisiana Sweet Crude Oil (LSC) and Chemically Dispersed LSC to Two Gulf of Mexico Aquatic Test Species," U.S. Environmental Protection Agency Office of Research and Development, July 31, 2010; http://www.epa.gov/bpspill/reports/phase2dispersant-toxtest.pdf.

98   *Bluefin tuna*   "USM Scientists Head Out for Bluefin Tuna Larvae," Associated Press, May 17, 2010; http://www.bettermsreport.com/2010/05/ap-scientists-from-usm-seek-tuna-larvae.

99   *Native Americans*   C. Burdeau, "Spill Reinforces Oil Bad Will for American Indians," Associated Press, May 18, 2010; http://abcnews.go.com/US/wireStory?id=10673076.

100   *"We never said it produced 5,000"*   M. Winter, "Oil Update: Spill to Harm Europe, Arctic Wildlife; Hurricane Season Looms," *USA Today*, May 21, 2010; http://content.usatoday.com/communities/ondeadline/post/2010/05/oil-update-spill-to-harm-europe-arctic-wildlife-hurricane-season-looms/1.

100   *"We cannot trust BP," and "I don't see any possibility," and "it might be a little more," and "an absurd position"*   "BP Accused of Cover-up as Size of Slick Remains Unknown," Agence France-Presse, May 20, 2010; http://www.terradaily.com/reports/BP_accused_of_cover-up_as_size_of_slick_remains_unknown_999.html.

101   *"They want to hide the body"*   J. Gillis, "Scientists Fault Lack of Studies over Gulf Spill," *New York Times*, May 20, 2010; http://www.nytimes.com/2010/05/20/science/earth/20noaa.html.

101   *Interview with Admiral Thad Allen*   C. Crowley, interview with Thad Allen, *CNN's State of the Union with Candy Crowley*, May 23, 2010; http://transcripts.cnn.com/TRANSCRIPTS/1005/23/sotu.01.html.

101   *Brown and orange globs*   K. McGill and Vicki Smith, "A Month in, Outrage over Gulf Oil Spill Grows," Associated Press, May 21, 2010; http://blog.al.com/live/2010/05/a_month_in_outrage_over_gulf_o.html.

101   *Billy Nungesser, and the Louisiana governor, and his statistics, also EPA's deadline*   "Louisiana Marshes Hit by Gulf Oil Slick," Agence France-Presse, May 21, 2010; http://www.channelnewsasia.com/stories/afp_world/view/1058133/1/.html.

102   *"This is not sheen"*   J. C. McKinley and Campbell Robertson, "Oil Is Fouling Wetlands, Official Says," *New York Times*, May 20, 2010; http://www.nytimes.com/2010/05/20/us/20spill.html.

102   *Dead zone*   C. Burdeau, "Dead Zone in the Gulf One of the Largest Ever," Associated Press, August 2, 2010; http://www.cbsnews.com/stories/2010/08/02/tech/main6736957.shtml.

102   *Nancy Rabalais quoted*   C. Burdeau and Seth Borenstein, "Scientists Think Gulf Can Recover," Associated Press, August 6, 2010; http://www.msnbc.msn.com/id/38582049/ns/us_news-environment/

103   *Requirements to submit plans, and a "culture of substance abuse and promiscuity*   M. Kunzelman and Richard T. Pienciak, "Rule Change Helped BP on Gulf Project," Associated Press, May 6, 2010; http://abcnews.go.com/Business/wireStory?id=10568369.

103   *Salazar dividing the Minerals Management Service*   J. C. McKinley and Campbell Robertson, "Oil Is Fouling Wetlands, Official Says," *New York Times*, May 20, 2010; http://www.nytimes.com/2010/05/20/us/20spill.html. *See also* M. Daly, "Minerals Management Service to Be Divided into 3 Parts," Associated Press, May 19, 2010; http://www.huffingtonpost.com/2010/05/19/minerals-management -servi_0_n_582248.html.

104   *"It took hundreds of years"*   J. Dearen, "Month into Gulf Spill, Fishermen See Bleak Future," Associated Press, May 21, 2010; http://www.boston.com/news/nation/articles/2010/05/21/month_into_gulf_spill_fishermen_see_bleak_future.

104   *Meanwhile, President Obama announces*   B. Walsh, "Obama to Tighten Fuel Economy Etandards," *Time*, May 19, 2010; http://www.time.com/time/health/article/0,8599,1899534,00.html.

104   *"All systems are go"*   C. Robertson, "Despite Leak, Louisiana Is Still Devoted to Oil,". *New York Times*, May 22, 2010; http://www.nytimes.com/2010/05/23/us/23drill.html.

104–105   *A house divided and related quotes*   I. Urbina, "Despite Moratorium, Drilling Projects Move Ahead," *New York Times*, May 23, 2010; http://www.nytimes.com/2010/05/24/us/24moratorium.html. *See also* P. Eckert, "Fishery Disaster Declared in Three Gulf States; U.S. Officials Vow to Impose Fines on Energy Giant," *Ottawa Citizen*, May 25, 2010; Via Reuters; http://www.reuters.com/article/idUSTRE64N5TT20100524. *See also* "BP and the Damage Done," energyboom.com, May 29, 2010; http://www.energyboom.com/policy/bp-and -damage-done.

105   *The president will say he regrets*   T. Raum and Jennifer Loven, "Fixing Oil Spill My Responsibility, Obama Says," Associated Press, May 28, 2010; http://abcnews.go.com/Business/wireStory?id=10766709.

106   *Shaw on Corexit 9527*   E. Dugan, "Oil Spill Creates Huge Undersea 'Dead Zones,' " *Independent*, May 30, 2010; http://www.independent.co.uk/news/world/americas/oil-spill-creates-huge-undersea-dead-zones-1987039.html.

106 *BP's close ties to Corexit's manufacturer* "Corexit," SourceWatch, August 7, 2010; http://www.sourcewatch.org/index.php?title=Corexit.

106 *Dr. Shaw writes* S. Shaw, "Swimming Through the Spill," *New York Times*, May 28, 2010; http://www.nytimes.com/2010/05/30/opinion/30shaw.html.

107 *Corexit and illness* "Corexit," SourceWatch, August 7, 2010; http://www .sourcewatch.org/index.php?title=Corexit.

107 *Butoxyethanol in Corexit* K. Zeitvogel, "Dispersants: Lesser Evil Against Oil Spill or Gulf Poison?" Agence France-Presse, June 7, 2010; http://www.physorg .com/news195106476.html.

107 *Sarah Palin says Obama's too slow* G. Bluestein and Matt Brown, "Heat on White House to Do More About Gulf Spill," Associated Press, May 25, 2010; http:// www.foxnews.com/politics/2010/05/25/heat-white-house-gulf-spill/

108 *The BP response plan* "Did Anyone Actually Read BP's Oil Spill Response Plan?," Targeted News Service, May 25, 2010; http://www.commondreams.org/ newswire/2010/05/25-0

108 *Fishermen saying they're getting sick, EPA air monitoring, and related quotes* N. Santa Cruz and Julie Cart, "Oil Cleanup Workers Cite Illness," *Los Angeles Times*, May 26, 2010; http://www.sott.net/articles/show/209299-Gulf-oil-spill-Cleanup-workers-report-illness.

109 *Doug Suttles's "doing everything we can" and Thad Allen's "no news is good"* B. Nuckols and G. Bluestein, "Gulf Awaits Word on Latest Bid to Plug Oil Leak," Associated Press, May 27, 2010; http://www.delcotimes.com/articles/2010/ 05/27/business/doc4bfe3b8e0c221649103327.txt.

109 *"I wouldn't say it's failed yet," and "They're actually going to take"* "Disaster of a New Dimension Looms in Gulf of Mexico Spill," Agence France-Presse, May 9, 2010; http://www.grist.org/article/2010-05-09-disaster-of-a-new-dimension-looms -in-gulf-of-mexico-spill.

109 *"This is the first time the industry"* J. C. McKinley Jr. and Leslie Kaufman. "New Ways to Drill, Old Methods for Cleanup," *New York Times*, May 10, 2010; http://www.nytimes.com/2010/05/11/us/11prepare.html?_r=2.

110 *$930M and 26,000 people, Hayward quotes* J. Resnick-Ault, "BP Uses 'Junk Shot,' Calls Oil Spill a 'Catastrophe,'" Bloomberg, May 28, 2010; http://www .bloomberg.com/news/2010-05-28/bp-uses-junk-shot-to-plug-well-that-s-spilled -more-oil-than-exxon-valdez.html.

110 *Hayward's "tiny" in a "very big ocean"* T. Webb, "BP Boss Admits Job on the Line over Gulf Oil Spill," *Guardian*, May 14, 2010; http://www.guardian.co.uk/ business/2010/may/13/bp-boss-admits-mistakes-gulf-oil-spill.

110   *Discovery of plume by* Weatherbird II   M. Brown and J. Dearen, "New, Giant Sea Oil Plume Seen in Gulf," Associated Press, May 27, 2010; http://www.msnbc .msn.com/id/37384717/ns/gulf_oil_spill/.

111   *"This is when all the animals"*   E. Dugan, "Oil Spill Creates Huge Undersea 'Dead Zones,' " *Independent*, May 30, 2010; http://www.independent.co.uk/news/ world/americas/oil-spill-creates-huge-undersea-dead-zones-1987039.html.

111   *Oil leaked totals between 18 and 39 million gallons*   T. Raum and Jennifer Loven, "Fixing Oil Spill My Responsibility, Obama Says," Associated Press, May 28, 2010; http://abcnews.go.com/Business/wireStory?id=10766709.

111   *Obama suspends exploratory drilling in the Arctic*   M. Daly, "Salazar Delays Arctic Ocean Drilling," Associated Press, May 27, 2010; http://abcnews.go.com/ Business/wireStory?id=10755614.

112   *"This event was set in motion years ago"*   R. Simon, "Gulf Oil Spill: Companies Were 'Rushing to Make Money Faster,' Survivor Says," *Los Angeles Times*, May 27, 2010; http://latimesblogs.latimes.com/greenspace/2010/05/gulf-oil-spill-companies -were-rushing-to-make-money-faster-survivor-says.html.

112   *Workers taken ill and arguments over what their problems are*   E. Cohen, "Fisherman Files Restraining Order Against BP," CNN, May 31, 2010; http:// articles.cnn.com/2010-05-31/health/oil.spill.order_1_bp-oil-rig-oil-spill?_s=PM :HEALTH.

113   *A fisherman's wife, and BP spokesman comment that air monitoring shows no health threats*   E. Cohen, "Fisherman's Wife Breaks the Silence," CNN, June 3, 2010; http://articles.cnn.com/2010-06-03/health/gulf.fishermans.wife_1_shrimping -exxon-valdez-oil-spill-cell-phone?_s=PM:HEALTH.

114   *"It's hard to understand if nausea"*   F. Tasker and Laura Figueroa, "How Dangerous Is Oil to Human Health?," *St. Petersburg Times*, June 27, 2010.

114   *There's another reason workers aren't using respirators*   Elana Schor, "OSHA Chief to Face Hot Seat over Cleanup-Worker Health," *Environment and Energy Daily*, June 21, 2010.

114   *Who else can't breathe?*   "Dauphin Island Sea Lab Scientists Report Drop in Oxygen on Alabama Shelf," June 9, 2010; http://press.disl.org/6_9_10oxygenBP .htm.

114–115   *A federal panel of fifty experts*   N. Schwartz, "Panel Recommends Continued Use of Oil Dispersant," Associated Press, June 5, 2010; http://abcnews.go.com/ Technology/wireStory?id=10828517.

115   *If we don't get as clean a cut"*   "Gulf Oil Closes in on Florida, Containment Efforts Hit Snag," Agence France-Presse, June 3, 2010; http://economictimes .indiatimes.com/news/international-business/Gulf-oil-closes-in-on-Florida -containment-efforts-hit-snag/articleshow/6007598.cms.

115 *"Engineer's nightmare," and a tiny cap on a fire hydrant* G. Bluestein and B. Skoloff, "Oil Closes in on Fla. as BP Tries Risky Cap Move," Associated Press, June 2, 2010; http://abcnews.go.com/Business/wireStory?id=10802853.

115–116 *Congress has certainly played a role, and Congress approved budgets reducing regulatory staff, and a 2004 Coast Guard study warned* D. S. Abraham, "A Disaster Congress Voted For," *New York Times*, July 13, 2010, p. A27.

117 *Other nations charge more* J. Wardell and Robert Barr, "BP Not Spearheading Oil Industry Move Back in Gulf," Associated Press, November 2, 2010.

117 *It was actually the Vice President's* National Energy Policy Development Group, *Reliable, Affordable, and Environmentally Sound Energy for America's Future: National Energy Policy Report*. Washington: GPO, 2001.

118 *Congress approved budgets reducing regulatory staff, and a 2004 Coast Guard study warned* D. S. Abraham, "A Disaster Congress Voted For," *New York Times*, July 13, 2010, p. A27.

EARLY JUNE

119 *Dead dolphin, surreptitious tour, and news crews escorted from public places* M. Lysiak and Helen Kennedy, "The Hidden Death in the Gulf," *Daily News*, June 2, 2010; http://www.nydailynews.com/news/national/2010/06/02/2010-06-02_the _hidden_death_in_the_gulf.html.

119 *BP tries again to cover the leak* C. Krauss, "BP Tries Again to Divert Oil Leak with Dome," *New York Times*, May 31, 2010; http://www.nytimes.com/2010/06/01/ us/01spill.html?th&emc=th.

120 *Allen's garden hose analogy* H. Mohr and John Flesher, "Gulf Containment Cap Closely Watched in 2nd Day," Associated Press, June 7, 2010; http://www .cbsnews.com/stories/2010/06/06/national/main6553587.shtml.

120 *"A positive step but not a solution"* G. Bluestein, "Cap Placed atop Gulf Well; Oil Still Spewing," Associated Press, June 4, 2010; http://seattletimes.nwsource .com/html/businesstechnology/2012017723_apusgulfoilspill.html.

120 *"The probability of them hitting it"* M. Brown, "Relief for Gulf Is 2 Months Away with Another Well," Associated Press, June 1, 2010; http://abcnews.go.com/ Business/wireStory?id=10786704.

120 *BP shares lose, and Justice Department investigations* B. Winter and Kevin Johnson, "Justice Department to Launch Oil Probe," *USA Today*, June 2, 2010; http:// www.usatoday.com/news/nation/2010-06-01-criminal-probe-of-oil-spill_N.htm.

120–121 *"The majority, probably the vast majority," and "I don't see that as being a credible," and "They continue to optimize production"* "Scientists Challenge BP Containment Claims," MSNBC, June 9, 2010; http://www.msnbc.msn.com/id/ 37573643/ns/disaster_in_the_gulf.

122   *"could take leakage almost down to zero," and "I'm not going to declare victory"*   "US Sets Deadline for BP as Mistrust Grows," Agence France-Presse, June 10, 2010; http://dalje.com/en-world/us-sets-deadline-for-bp-as-mistrust-grows/308972.

122   *BP shares hemorrhage an incredible 16 percent*   F. Ahrens, "BP Stock Crashes; Oil Giant Trading Below Book Value," *Washington Post*, June 9, 2010; http://voices.washingtonpost.com/economy-watch/2010/06/bp_shares_crash_oil_giant_trad.html.

122   *Estimate of the leak gets doubled*   "US Doubles Gulf Oil Flow Estimate," Agence France-Presse, June 11, 2010; http://www.dailystar.com.lb/article.asp?edition_id=10&categ_id=2&article_id=115861#axzz16gupLzQJ.

122   *"Still dealing with the flow estimate"*   S. Borenstein and Harry R. Weber, "New Oil Numbers May Do More Harm to Fish, Wildlife," Associated Press, June 11, 2010; http://www.fox8live.com/news/local/story/New-oil-numbers-may-do-more-harm-to-fish-wildlife/56mU8Qat2kCx5d5H_7-hSA.cspx.

122   *BP is the third-largest oil company*   S. L. Yall and Julie Werdigier, "U.S. Fury at BP Stirs Backlash Among British," *New York Times*, June 10, 2010; http://dealbook.nytimes.com/2010/06/11/u-s-fury-at-bp-stirs-backlash-among-british/.

123   *"I've had guys saying"*   B. Anderson, "Nationally, Chefs Stand by Gulf Seafood, but Customers Are Turning Their Backs," *Times-Picayune*, June 20, 2010; http://www.nola.com/news/t-p/frontpage/index.ssf?/base/news-14/1277020369237720.xml&coll=1.

124   *"Thank God there isn't a loaded gun"*   S. Saulny, "Cajuns on Gulf Worry They May Need to Move On Once Again," *New York Times*, July 19, 2010; http://bbedit.sx.atl.publicus.com/apps/pbcs.dll/article?AID=/20100719/NEWS0107/7190374/1159&template=print.

124   *Gulf Shores, Alabama*   H. Mohr and John Flesher, "Gulf Containment Cap Closely Watched in 2nd Day," Associated Press, June 7, 2010; http://www.cbsnews.com/stories/2010/06/06/national/main6553587.shtml.

124   *Dozens of oil-drenched pelicans*   "Dozens of Heavily Oiled Pelicans off La. Coast," Associated Press, June 3, 2010; http://www.fox10tv.com/dpp/news/gulf_oil_spill/heavily-oiled-pelicans-off-la-coast.

124   *Birds and mammals rescued*   "25 Live Sea Turtles Rescued, at Least 12 Oiled," Associated Press, June 2, 2010; http://www.mysanantonio.com/news/environment/25_live_sea_turtles_rescued_at_least_12_oiled_95493429.html.

124–125   *"This is the worst screwed-up response," and quotes by frustrated bird rescuers*   C. Pittman, "Bird Experts Left Waiting in Wings," *St. Petersburg Times*, September 5, 2010; http://www6.lexisnexis.com/publisher/EndUser?Action=UserDisplayFullDocument&orgId=574&topicId=100020423&docId=l:1256619892&start=7.

125   *A blowout in Pennsylvania*   M. Levy and Jennifer C. Yates, "Marcellus Gas Well Blows Out in Pennsylvania; Gas, Drilling Fluid Shoot 75 Feet into Air," Associated Press, June 4, 2010; http://www.pressconnects.com/article/20100604/NEWS01/6040353/Marcellus-gas-well-blows-out-in-Pennsylvania-gas-drilling-fluid-shoot-75-feet-into-air.

125   *"This spill is just aggregated over a 200-mile radius"*   "US Oil Spill Spread Around 200-mile Radius," Agence France-Presse, June 6, 2010; http://www.heraldsun.com.au/news/breaking-news/us-oil-spill-spread-around-200-mile-radius-official/story-e6frf7jx-1225876240262.

126   *BP tells residents in a church*   G. Bluestein, "Cap Placed atop Gulf Well; Oil Still Spewing," *Associated Press*, June 2010; http://seattletimes.nwsource.com/html/businesstechnology/2012017723_apusgulfoilspill.html.

126   *Seventy-one people suffer*   "Gulf Oil Spill Sickens More Than 70 People in Louisiana," Agence France-Presse, June 9, 2010; http://www.terradaily.com/reports/Gulf_oil_spill_sickens_more_than_70_people_in_Louisiana_999.html.

126   *Department of Health counsels 749 people, and related quotes*   M. Navarro, "Spill Takes Toll on Gulf Workers' Psyches," *New York Times*, June 16, 2010; http://www.nytimes.com/2010/06/17/us/17human.html?th&emc=th.

HIGH JUNE

127   *BP good at stopping the flow of news*   J. Peters, "Efforts to Limit the Flow of Spill News," *New York Times*, June 9, 2010; http://www.nytimes.com/2010/06/10/us/10access.html?th&emc=th.

130   *Using 5,800 separate measurements*   R. Camilli et al., "Tracking Hydrocarbon Plume Transport and Biodegradation at Deepwater Horizon," *Science* 330, no. 6001, August 19, 2010: 201–4; http://www.sciencemag.org/content/330/6001/201.short.

130   *Researchers finding plumes, and BP responses*   J. Gillis, "Plumes of Oil Below Surface Raise New Concerns," *New York Times*, June 8, 2010; http://www.nytimes.com/2010/06/09/us/09spill.html.

130   *"Not a river of Hershey's syrup"*   "WHOI Scientists Map and Confirm Origin of Large, Underwater Hydrocarbon Plume in Gulf," Woods Hole Oceanographic Institution News Release, August 19, 2010; http://www.whoi.edu/page.do?pid=7545&tid=282&ct=162&cid=79926.

130   *"doesn't hold a candle"*   R. Kerr, "Report Paints New Picture of Gulf Oil," *Science*, August 19, 2010; http://news.sciencemag.org/sciencenow/2010/08/report-paints-new-picture-of-gul.html.

131   *NOAA confirmed the presence of undersea oil*   "NOAA Completes Initial Anal-

ysis of *Weatherbird II* Water Samples," NOAA, June 8, 2010; http://www.noaanews
.noaa.gov/stories2010/20100608_weatherbird.html.

131–132   *NOAA's response to undersea plumes, and oil breaking into zillions of droplets*   S. Begley, "What the Spill Will Kill," *Newsweek,* June 6, 2010; http://www
.newsweek.com/2010/06/06/what-the-spill-will-kill.html.

132–134   *Hayward's "no evidence," "These are huge volumes," and "The bottom line
is that yes"*   J. Resnick-Ault, "Toxic Plumes Lurk Throughout Gulf," Bloomberg,
June 9, 2010; http://www.businessweek.com/news/2010-06-08/toxic-undersea-oil
-plumes-lurk-in-gulf-of-mexico-update2-.html.

137   *Energy statistics according to BP*   S. Foley, "World Needs Gulf of Mexico's
Oil, Says BP," *Independent,* June 10, 2010; http://www.independent.co.uk/news/
business/news/world-needs-gulf-of-mexicos-oil-says-bp-1996097.html.

137   *The cap is now collecting 10,000 barrels*   "No End in Sight; the Gulf Oil Spill,"
The Economist, June 12, 2010; http://www.economist.com/node/16322752.

138   *Wereley's estimate of 798,000 to 1.8 million gallons*   R. Henry et al., "Gulf Oil
Leak May Be Bigger Than BP Says," Associated Press, June 9, 2010; http://www
.salon.com/news/feature/2010/06/08/gulf_oil_spill_bigger.

138   *Signs warn*   M. Nelson, "Florida Posting 1st Signs Warning Swimmers
About Oil," Associated Press, June 9, 2010; http://www.foxnews.com/story/
0,2933,594242,00.html.

138   *"It's the breadth and complexity"*   J. Berger et al., "Dispersal of Oil Means
Cleanup to Take Years, Official Says," *New York Times,* June 8, 2010; http://www
.nytimes.com/2010/06/08/us/08spill.html.

141   *The futility and utility of helping wildlife*   J. Flesher and Noaki Schwartz, "Rescuing Oiled Birds: Poignant, but Is It Futile?," Associated Press, June 10, 2010;
http://www.msnbc.msn.com/id/37627833/ns/disaster_in_the_gulf/.

142   *Coated with oil—in Utah*   "Oil Coats 300 Birds Near Salt Lake After Pipeline Breach," *Los Angeles Times,* June 13, 2010; http://latimesblogs.latimes.com/
greenspace/2010/06/oil-coats-300-birds-near-salt-lake-after-pipeline-breach.html.

LATE JUNE

148   *Oil executives break ranks with BP*   J. Broder, "Oil Executives Break Ranks in
Testimony," *New York Times,* June 15, 2010; http://www.nytimes.com/2010/06/16/
business/16oil.html?ref=politics.

149–150   *BP's profits, and also estimates about oil*   P. Nicholas et al., "Stakes Rise
for Obama and the Gulf," *Los Angeles Times,* June 15, 2010; http://articles.latimes
.com/2010/jun/15/nation/la-na-oil-spill-obama-20100615.

149   *Blowout dampening appetite for greenhouse gas caps*   J. Broder, "Oil Spill May Spur Action on Energy, Probably Not on Climate," *New York Times,* June 12, 2010; http://www.nytimes.com/2010/06/13/science/earth/13climate.html.

150   *"That's the $100,000 question," and Orange Beach's mayor*   J. Lebovich et al., "BP Promises Swifter Attack Against Oil Spill," *Miami Herald,* June 15, 2010; http://www.miamiherald.com/2010/06/15/1680757/bp-promises-swifter-attack-against.html.

150–151   *A year after the* Exxon Valdez, *and, "I still don't know who's in charge"*   C. Robertson, "Efforts to Repel Gulf Spill Are Described as Chaotic," *New York Times,* June 15, 2010; http://www.nytimes.com/2010/06/15/science/earth/15cleanup.html.

151   *Senator Bill Nelson, the mayor of Orange Beach*   D. Brooks, "Trim the 'Experts,' Trust the Locals," *New York Times,* June 18, 2010; http://www.nytimes.com/2010/06/18/opinion/18brooks.html.

151   *More than 70 human residents*   E. Schor, "Health Consequences of Oil, Dispersant Chemicals Take Center Stage," *Environment and Energy Daily,* June 14, 2010; http://www.eenews.net/eed/2010/06/14.

155   *In mid-June, anger mounts*   "Anger Mounts over Moratorium as Obama Tours Spill Zone," Agence France-Presse, June 15, 2010; http://www.lankabusinessonline.lk/fullstory.php?nid=1038762547. *See also* K. Zeitvogel, "Lift 'Reckless' Oil Drilling Ban, Gulf Residents Plead," Agence France-Presse, July 27, 2010; http://www.google.com/hostednews/afp/article/ALeqM5g33v9-JoE_SLNstMjQ5AqOy9DGJw.

156   *Rigs will seek to drill in other countries*   T. Zeller Jr., "Drill Ban Means Hard Times for Rig Workers," *New York Times,* June 17, 2010; http://www.nytimes.com/2010/06/18/business/18rig.html.

157   *Also in mid-June, President Obama signals*   E. Werner, "Obama: Gulf to Be 'Normal,'" *Associated Press,* June 15, 2010; http://www.huffingtonpost.com/2010/06/14/obama-gulf-coast-visit-th_n_611788.html.

157   *"This was some of the best fishing"*   C. Burdeau and Brian Skoloff, "Oil Spill Spreads in La.'s Big, Rich Barataria Bay," Associated Press, June 14, 2010; http://abcnews.go.com/Business/wireStory?id=10909228.

162   *Based on the latest estimates*   J. Schwartz, "With Criminal Charges, Costs to BP Could Soar," *New York Times,* June 16, 2010; http://www.nytimes.com/2010/06/17/us/17liability.html?th&emc=th.

163   *The* Economist *reports*   "The Oil Well and the Damage Done," *The Economist,* June 19, 2010; http://www.economist.com/node/16381032.

163   *Congressional Democrats Waxman and Markey*   "Oil Estimate Raised to 35,000-60,000 Barrels a Day," CNN, June 15, 2010; http://articles.cnn.com/2010-06-15/us/oil.spill.disaster_1_bp-oil-disaster-oil-flow?_s=PM:US.

163 *It will turn out that five giant oil companies, and Further, the companies consistently downplay* S. Mufson and Juliet Eilperin, "Lawmakers Attack Companies' Spill Plans," *Washington Post,* June 16, 2010; http://www.washingtonpost.com/wp -dyn/content/article/2010/06/15/AR2010061501700.html.

164 *Obama's first and much-anticipated address from the Oval Office* "Obama Warns of Oil Spill 'Epidemic' in Oval Office Address," Agence France-Presse, June 16, 2010; http://www.channelnewsasia.com/stories/afp_world/view/1063563/ 1/.html.

165 *Friedman on Obama and the oil spill* T. Friedman, "Obama and the Oil Spill," *New York Times,* May 18, 2010; http://www.nytimes.com/2010/05/19/opinion/ 19friedman.html.

165–166 *Rachel Maddow's fake president's speech* "Rachel Maddow Gives Fake Obama Oil Speech, Lunches with Obama," *The Rachel Maddow Show,* MSNBC, June 17, 2010; http://voices.washingtonpost.com/44/2010/06/rachel-maddow-gives -fake-obama.html.

166 *Mary L. Kendall* J. Calmes and Helene Cooper, "BP Chief to Express Contrition in Remarks to Panel," *New York Times,* June 16, 2010; http://www.nytimes.com/ 2010/06/17/us/politics/17obama.html.

167 *Blair Witherington* K. Murphy, "Death by Fire in the Gulf," *Los Angeles Times,* June 17, 2010; http://articles.latimes.com/2010/jun/17/nation/la-na-oil-spill -burnbox-20100617.

167 *Workers lighting fires at sea* B. Drogin, "Teams Resume Burning Oil in Gulf of Mexico," *Los Angeles Times,* July 12, 2010; http://articles.latimes.com/2010/jul/ 12/nation/la-na-0712-burn-box-20100712.

168 *People report seeing sharks, mullet* J. Reeves et al., "Sea Creatures Flee Oil Spill, Gather Near Shore," Associated Press, June 17, 2010; http://www.physorg .com/news195978510.html.

168 *BP agrees to pay $20 billion* J. Calmes and Helene Cooper, "BP Chief to Express Contrition in Remarks to Panel," *New York Times,* June 16, 2010; http://www .nytimes.com/2010/06/17/us/politics/17obama.html.

169 *"mind-bogglingly vapid"* "A Bad Day for BP and Mr. Barton," editorial, *New York Times,* June 17, 2010; http://www.nytimes.com/2010/06/18/opinion/18fri3 .html.

170 *Oil leaked during the hearing* D. Barry, "Looking for Answers, Finding One," *New York Times,* June 17, 2010; http://www.nytimes.com/2010/06/18/us/18land .html?th&emc=th.

170 *BP releases $25 million* J. Cillis, "New Estimates Raise Amount of Oil Flow," *New York Times,* June 15, 2010; http://www.nytimes.com/2010/06/16/us/16spill .html.

171 *BP's frustration that its acts of goodwill have not been met with goodwill* C. Krauss and John M. Broder, "BP Says Limits on Drilling Imperil Spill Payouts," *New York Times*, September 2, 2010; http://www.nytimes.com/2010/09/03/business/03bp .html.

172 *The total count of sea turtles* "Reporting Oiled Sea Turtles," press release from Sea Turtle Restoration Network, June 18, 2010; http://www.gctts.org/node/557.

173 *"All of these guys could use"* "US Lashes Out at BP as Gulf Oil Spill Reaches Two-Month Mark," Agence France-Presse, June 21, 2010; http://www .hurriyetdailynews.com/n.php?n=us-lashes-out-at-bp-as-oil-spill-reaches-two -month-mark-2010-06-21.

173 *Things Gulf people are saying* K. Murphy, "Oil Spill Stress Begins Taking Its Toll," *Los Angeles Times*, June 20, 2010; http://articles.latimes.com/2010/jun/20/ nation/la-na-oil-spill-mental-health-20100621.

174 *Thad Allen had told ABC News* "Allen Has Ordered 'Uninhibited Access' to Oil Spill Operations," ABC News, June 6, 2010; http://bit.ly/904Giz.

174 *The directive in action* M. McClelland, "La. Police Doing BP's Dirty Work," *Mother Jones*, June 22, 2010; http://bit.ly/cFER9Q.

176 *Information on Nigeria* J. Vidal, "Nigeria's Agony Dwarfs the Gulf Oil Spill," *Observer*, May 30, 2010; http://www.guardian.co.uk/world/2010/may/30/oil-spills- nigeria-niger-delta-shell.

177 *Nigerian fraction of U.S. oil imports* "Petroleum," U.S. Energy Information Administration; http://www.eia.gov/oil_gas/petroleum/info_glance/petroleum.html.

177–178 *The* Economist's *estimates, and John Roberts quote* "The Oil Well and the Damage Done," *The Economist*, June 19, 2010; http://www.economist.com/node/ 16381032.

178 Exxon Valdez's *devastating effects* A. Symington, "Spill Waters Run Deep," *New Statesman*, October 4, 2010; http://www.newstatesman.com/environment/ 2010/10/oil-spill-liability-gulf.

178 *Obama's May 6 moratorium* M. Kunzelman, "Judge Lifts Offshore Drilling Ban as 'Overbearing,' " Associated Press, June 22, 2010; http://www.heraldsun .com/view/full_story/8016622/article-Judge-lifts-offshore-drilling-ban-as -%E2%80%98overbearing%E2%80%99?instance=homesixthleft.

179 *Perdido and related quotes* J. Mouawad and Barry Meier, "Risk-Taking Rises as Oil Rigs in Gulf Drill Deeper," *New York Times*, August 29, 2010; http://www .nytimes.com/2010/08/30/business/energy-environment/30deep.html.

180 *"There is the pre-April 20th framework of regulation and the post-April 20th framework"* "What Have They Learned?" editorial, *New York Times*, October 5, 2010; http://www.nytimes.com/2010/10/05/opinion/05tue1.html.

181 *The better bet*   R. Huval, "Miami Distributor Turns to Imported Shrimp to Replace Gulf's," *Miami Herald,* June 23, 2010; http://www.miamiherald.com/2010/06/23/1695008/miami-distributor-turns-to-imported.html.

181 *Statistics about oysters*   "Oil Catastrophe Cracks Gulf of Mexico Oyster Industry," Associated Press, June 23, 2010.

181 *Hurricane Alex strongest since 1966*   T. Breen and Jay Reeves, "World's Largest Oil Skimmer Heads to Gulf Spill," Associated Press, July 2, 2010; http://www.foxnews.com/us/2010/07/02/worlds-largest-oil-skimmer-heads-gulf-spill/.

186 *" dumbfounded by the amount of wasted effort"*   M. Hennessy-Fiske and Richard Fausset, "Mississippi Officials Blast BP, U.S. Government as Oil Hits Coast," *Los Angeles Times,* June 29, 2010; http://articles.latimes.com/2010/jun/29/nation/la-na-oil-spill-20100629.

186 *"Seeing everything that you've been used to," and "I haven't slept"*   J. McConnaughey and Mitch Stacy, "Gulf Oil Spill's Psychological Toll Quietly Mounts as Tragedy Drags On," *Ledger* (Lakeland, FL), June 27, 2010; http://www.theledger.com/article/20100627/news/6275086.

186 *Turtle eggs moved*   B. Skoloff, "Some 70,000 Turtle Eggs to Be Whisked Far from Oil," Associated Press, June 30, 2010; http://www.physorg.com/news197118448.html.

189 *Where oily absorbent materials are going*   F. Barringer, "As Mess Is Sent to Landfills, Officials Worry About Safety," *New York Times,* June 14, 2010; http://www.nytimes.com/2010/06/15/science/earth/15waste.html.

189 *Some of the workforce sits idle*   T. Breen, "Volunteers Ready but Left Out of Oil Spill Cleanup," Associated Press, July 2, 2010; http://www.njherald.com/story/news/a1237-BC-US-GulfOilSpill-9thLd-Writethru-07-01-1624.

190 *"The clean-up effort has not been perfect"*   "BP Boss Takes Spill Questions in Open Internet Event," Agence France-Presse, July 1, 2010; http://www.muzi.com/news/ll/english/10101675.shtml?q=&cc=26416&a=on.

190 *Appearance of whale sharks*   B. Raines, "Whale Sharks Unable to Avoid Oil Spill," Alabama Local News, June 30, 2010; http://blog.al.com/live/2010/06/whale_sharks_unable_to_avoid_o.html. *See also* J. McConnaughey, "Threatened Whale Sharks Seen in Gulf Oil Spill," Associated Press, July 1, 2010; http://www.ajc.com/news/nation-world/threatened-whale-sharks-seen-562061.html.

190 *"the worst possible time" for whale sharks*   B. Handwerk, "Whale Sharks Killed, Displaced by Gulf Oil? The Gulf Oil Spill Occurred in Crucial Habitat for the World's Largest Fish," *National Geographic News,* September 24, 2010; http://news.nationalgeographic.com/news/2010/09/100924-whale-sharks-gulf-oil-spill-science-environment/. *See also* "Whale Shark Tagging in the Gulf of Mexico," a scene from *Mission Blue.* Insurgent Media, June 22, 2010; http://www.youtube.com/watch?v=zVd7aRFaDqY.

190 *Scientists with the University of Southern Mississippi and Tulane University* G. Pender, "Oil Found in Gulf Crabs Raises New Food Chain Fears," *Biloxi Sun Herald*, July 1, 2010; http://www.mcclatchydc.com/2010/07/01/96909/oil-found-in-gulf-crabs-raising.html.

190–191 *Effects of oil on fish eggs and larvae* Joanna Burger, *Oil Spills*. New Brunswick, NJ: Rutgers University Press, 1997.

191 *Herring egg and larval mortality following Exxon Valdez* M. D. McGurk and Evelyn D. Brown, "Egg–Larval Mortality of Pacific Herring in Prince William Sound, Alaska, After the Exxon Valdez Oil Spill," *Canadian Journal of Fisheries and Aquatic Science* 53, no. 10 (1996): 2343–54. *See also* B. L. Norcross et al., "Distribution, Abundance, Morphological Condition, and Cytogenetic Abnormalities of Larval Herring in Prince William Sound, Alaska, Following the *Exxon Valdez* Oil Spill," *Canadian Journal of Fisheries and Aquatic Science* 53, no. 10 (1996): 2376 –87. *See also* J. E. Hose et al., "Sublethal Effects of the *Exxon Valdez* Oil Spill on Herring Embryos and Larvae: Morphological, Cytogenetic, and Histopathological Assessments, 1989–1991," *Canadian Journal of Fisheries and Aquatic Science* 53, no. 10 (1996): 2355–65.

191 *Different things get hurt at different rates* C. H. Peterson et al., "Long-Term Ecosystem Response to the *Exxon Valdez* Oil Spill," *Science* 302, no. 5653, December 19, 2003: 2082–86.

192 *Harlequin Ducks still ingesting Exxon Valdez oil* S. Dhillon, "Exxon Oil Showing Up in Alaskan Wildlife 20 years After Spill, Research Shows," *Canadian Press*, April 14, 2010.

192 *Felony announced for getting near booms* C. Kirkham, "Media, Boaters Could Face Criminal Penalties by Entering Oil Cleanup 'Safety Zone,'" *Times-Picayune*, July 1, 2010; http://www.nola.com/news/gulf-oil-spill/index.ssf/2010/07/media_boaters_could_face_crimi.html.

193 *"Never in my lifetime"* G. Nienaber, "Facing the Future as a Media Felon on the Gulf Coast," Huffington Post, July 3, 2010; http://www.huffingtonpost.com/georgianne-nienaber/facing-the-future-as-a-me_b_634661.html.

LIKE A THOUSAND JULYS

196 *BP's dispersant use and cutback* E. Lavandera, "Dispersants Flow into Gulf in 'Science Experiment,'" CNN, July 2, 2010; http://articles.cnn.com/2010-07-02/us/gulf.oil.dispersants_1_corexit-dispersant-bp?_s=PM:US.

196 *EPA and BP's tussle over dispersant policy* E. Rosenthal, "In Standoff with Environmental Officials, BP Stays with an Oil Spill Dispersant," *New York Times*, May 25, 2010; http://www.nytimes.com/2010/05/25/science/earth/25disperse.html.

196 *Corexit 9527 "no longer in use in the Gulf"* E. Schor, "EPA Vows to Push Dispersant Makers After Posting Corexit Ingredients," *Greenwire*, June 10, 2010.

198 *Jon Stewart* "BP's Latest Plan Succeeding, but May Make Spill Worse (for

Now)," *Newsweek*, June 2, 2010; http://www.newsweek.com/2010/06/02/first-stage -of-new-bp-plan-succeeds-will-mean-more-oil-in-the-short-term.html#.

198   *BP decriminalizes free speech*   J. Reeves, "BP to 40,000 Oil Spill Workers: Talk Away to Media," Associated Press, July 2, 2010; http://abcnews.go.com/US/ wireStory?id=11075912.

198   *Relief well very high-tech*   H. Fountain, "Hitting a Tiny Bull's-Eye Miles Under the Gulf," *New York Times*, July 5, 2010; http://www.nytimes.com/2010/07/ 06/science/06drill.html.

199   *The new cap, relief well schedule, Pensacola tourism, and related quotes*   F. Tasker, "Officials Offer Glimmer of Hope in Containing Gulf Oil Spill," *Miami Herald*, July 2, 2010; http://www.miamiherald.com/2010/07/02/1712046/rough -seas-still-stymie-oil-spill.html.

200   *Hotline operator calls it a diversion*   *Countdown with Keith Olbermann*, MSNBC, June 14, 2010.

202   *Modern corporations are "soulless"*   J. Jowit, "'Big Business Needs Biodiversity' Says UN," *Guardian*, July 12, 2010; http://www.guardian.co.uk/environment/2010/jul/12/soulless-corporations-hurt-environment-pavan-sukhdev.

203   *"Arrogant and in denial," and the associated BP management and accident history and related quotes*   S. Lyall, "In BP's Record, a History of Boldness and Costly Blunders," *New York Times*, July 12, 2010.

215   *On July 7, the Thadmiral tells America*   "Crews Connecting Oil Vessel to Ruptured Well as Leaders Pray for Gulf," AC360 blog, July 7, 2010; http://ac360.blogs .cnn.com/2010/07/07/crews-connecting-oil-vessel-to-ruptured-well-as-leaders -pray-for-gulf/.

216   *Two of the judges on the panel, and appeals court affirms lower court*   J. M. Broder, "Court Rejects Moratorium on Drilling in the Gulf," *New York Times*, July 8, 2010; http://www.nytimes.com/2010/07/09/us/09drill.html.

216   *"I'm not going to say you can't drill, but"*   M. Daly, "New Drilling Chief Promises Balance," Associated Press, July 12, 2010; http://abcnews.go.com/Business/ wireStory?id=11141138.

216   *Salazar issues a new moratorium, and quote from American Petroleum Institute*   F. J. Frommer, "Obama Hopes New Drilling Moratorium Can Survive," Associated Press, July 13, 2010; http://www.philly.com/philly/business/20100713 _ap_govthopesnewdrillingmoratoriumcansurvive.html?c=0.6657310272741187 &posted=n.

217   *the head of the American Petroleum Institute says*   "Obama Team Issues New Deepwater Drilling Pause," Frank James, NPR, July 12, 2010; http://npr/igbyaD.

217   *White House senior adviser this week calls the blowout the "greatest environmental catastrophe . . ."*   Richard Fausset, "BP Says It's Closer to Oil Containment," *Los Angeles Times*, July 12, 2010; http://lat.ms/gcj9Te.

217   *"greatest environmental catastrophe"*   R. Fausset and Nicole Santa Cruz, "Gulf Oil Spill: Containment Cap May Be in Place by Day's End," *Los Angeles Times*, July 12, 2010; http://latimesblogs.latimes.com/greenspace/2010/07/gulf-oil-spill-containment-may-come-by-days-end.html.

220   *News of leaks and BP wanting to leave the well capped*   C. Long and Harry R. Weber, "BP, Feds Clash over Reopening Capped Gulf Oil Well," Associated Press, July 19, 2010; http://abcnews.go.com/Business/wireStory?id=11190544.

LATE JULY

222   *Dolphin with broken ribs and a tar ball*   S. Dewan, "Sifting a Range of Suspects as Gulf Wildlife Dies," *New York Times*, July 15, 2010; http://www.nytimes.com/2010/07/15/science/earth/15necropsy.html.

222   *Disappearance of birds*   C. Burdeau, "Reported Number of Bird Deaths Grow on Gulf Coast," Associated Press, July 23, 2010; http://abcnews.go.com/US/wireStory?id=11231013.

223   *"Just because they kill the well"*   H. R. Weber and Greg Bluestein, "BP Begins Effort to Permanently Seal Gulf Gusher," Associated Press, August 4, 2010; http://www.boston.com/news/nation/articles/2010/08/04/bp_begins_effort_to_permanently_seal_gulf_gusher.

223   *"we'll be left to deal with it alone"*   G. Bluestein and Tamara Lush, "Crush of Mud Finally Plugs BP's Well in the Gulf," Associated Press, August 5, 2010; http://abcnews.go.com/Business/wireStory?id=11320455.

223   *"We're not going anywhere"*   L. Neergaard, " 'CSI' for Seafood: Gulf Fish Gets Safety Tests," *Ledger* (Lakeland, FL), August 16, 2010; http://abcnews.go.com/Health/wireStory?id=11407762.

223   *"They gave us zero"*   C. Kirkham, "Seafood Facing a Tainted Image," *Times-Picayune*, August 9, 2010; http://nola.live.advance.net/news/t-p/frontpage/index.ssf?/base/news-15/1281334817130300.xml&coll=1.

224   *An estimated 45,000 people and 6,000 vessels*   D. Helvarg, "Obama Signs on for the Sea: A Promising New Commitment to Ocean Protection," *E Magazine*, June 2010; http://www.emagazine.com/view/?5262.

224   *"This whole area is gonna die," and suicide calls*   "Faced with Oil Spill, Gulf Residents Fight Mental Pain," Agence France-Presse, July 22, 2010; http://www.rawstory.com/rs/2010/07/faced-oil-spill-gulf-residents-fight-mental-pain.

224   *Chinese pipeline explosion*   S. McDonell, "Oil Spews from Exploded China

Pipeline," Australian Broadcasting Corporation, July 19, 2010; http://www.abc.net
.au/news/stories/2010/07/19/2957868.htm.

224–225 *A federal judge stops companies, and Caroline Cannon quote* D. Joling,
"Judge Halts Oil, Gas Development on Chukchi Sea," Associated Press, July 22,
2010; http://www.msnbc.msn.com/id/38352548/.

225 *Daisy Sharp and Steve Oomittuk quoted* "Gulf Spill Focuses Fear of Drilling
Disaster in Arctic Villages," *Anchorage Daily News*, August 31, 2010; http://www
.adn.com/2010/08/31/1432664/gulf-spill-focuses-fear-of-drilling.html.

225–226 *Oil sands* B. Weber, "Toxic Oil Sands Threat to Fish," *Kamloops Daily
News* (British Columbia), August 31, 2010.

226 *Definitions of proppant and fracking fluids* Schlumberger Oilfield Glossary;
http://www.glossary.oilfield.slb.com.

227 *The New York State Environmental Impact Statement* "Draft Supplemental Generic Environmental Impact Statement on the Oil, Gas and Solution Mining Regulatory Program," *New York State Department of Environmental Conservation*, October
26, 2009; http://www.dec.ny.gov/energy/58440.html.

227 *The final EPA Pavillion report* "Pavillion Area Groundwater Investigation, Pavillion, Fremont County, Wyoming," United States Environmental Protection Agency: Contract No. EP-W-05-050, TDD No. 0901-01, see p. 37,
August 30, 2010; http://www.epa.gov/region8/superfund/wy/pavillion/Pavillion
_GWInvestigationFSP.pdf.

228 *"It's doubtful we will ever use it"* J. Mouawad, "4 Oil Firms Commit $1 Billion
for Gulf Rapid-Response Plan," *New York Times*, July 21, 2010; http://www.nytimes
.com/2010/07/22/business/energy-environment/22response.html.

228 *Sixteen months before completion of containment equipment* H. R. Weber,
"Oil Industry Has Yet to Adopt Lessons of BP Spill," Associated Press, October 4, 2010; http://www.timesherald.com/articles/2010/10/05/news/
doc4caab57b10006826476498.txt.

228–230 *Gaylord Nelson, Santa Barbara, Earth Day, Lois Capps, and the Associated Press poll on Americans and the environment* F. J. Frommer, "Gulf Spill Lacks
Societal Punch of Santa Barbara," Associated Press, July 29, 2010; http://abcnews
.go.com/Business/wireStory?id=11275571.

231 *Seafood sniffers* Y. Q. Mui and David A. Fahrenthold, "Gulf Seafood Must Pass
the Smell Test; Government Trains Inspectors to Sniff Out Contaminated Catch,"
Washington Post, July 13, 2010; http://www.highbeam.com/doc/1P2-25347383.html.

231 *"Take small bunny sniffs," and "If you think about your ability to detect," and sniff-
related quotes* K. Lohr, "Gulf Fish Cordoned Off for Seafood Sniffers' Inspection,"
NPR's *Weekend Edition*, July 18, 2010; http://www.npr.org/templates/story/story
.php?storyId=128600385.

233   *PAHs in seafood and oysters at the top of the concern list*   "Gulf Seafood Undergoes Intense Testing," Associated Press, August 16, 2010; http://www.huffingtonpost.com/2010/08/16/gulf-seafood-undergoes-in_n_682935.html.

233–234   *Federal regulators say they're sure, and Dawn Nunez quoted*   J. Dearen and Greg Bluestein, "Gulf Seafood Declared Safe; Fishermen Not So Sure," Associated Press, August 2, 2010; http://www.rdmag.com/News/FeedsAP/2010/08/energy-gulf-seafood-declared-safe-fishermen-not-so-sure.

233   *The 3,500-plus samples were safe*   D. A. Fahrenthold and Juliet Eilperin, "Unallayed by Tests, Fishermen Greet Start of Gulf Shrimp Harvest with Suspicion," *Washington Post*, August 17, 2010; http://www.washingtonpost.com/wp-dyn/content/article/2010/08/16/AR2010081605471.html.

233–234   *"It tastes like fish," and "These are decent American people"*   C. Robertson, "In Gulf, Good News Is Taken with Grain of Salt," *New York Times*, August 4, 2010; http://www.nytimes.com/2010/08/05/us/05gulf.html.

234   *"I wouldn't feed that to my children"*   D. A. Fahrenthold and Juliet Eilperin, "Unallayed by Tests, Fishermen Greet Start of Gulf Shrimp Harvest with Suspicion," *Washington Post*, August 17, 2010; http://www.washingtonpost.com/wp-dyn/content/article/2010/08/16/AR2010081605471.html.

234   *"Will there even be a market"*   B. Boxall et al., "BP Jams Gulf Well with Drilling Mud," *Los Angeles Times*, August 5, 2010; http://articles.latimes.com/2010/aug/05/nation/la-na-oil-spill-20100805.

234   *"People are scared of it right now"*   S. Dewan, "Questions Linger as Shrimp Season Opens in Gulf," *New York Times*, August 17, 2010; http://www.nytimes.com/2010/08/17/us/17gulf.html.

234   *Barge crashes into inactive well*   R. Adams, "Barge Hits Abandoned Oil Well off Louisiana Coast," *Wall Street Journal*, July 27, 2010; http://online.wsj.com/article/SB10001424052748703977004575393672718018794.html.

235   *"University scientists have spotted"*   G. Pender, "Oil Found in Gulf Crabs Raises New Food Chain Fears," *Biloxi Sun Herald*, July 1, 2010; http://www.mcclatchydc.com/2010/07/01/96909/oil-found-in-gulf-crabs-raising.html.

236   *BP quarterly loss of $16.9 billion, and 3,800 miles of boom*   A. Gully, "100 Days in, Gulf Spill Leaves Ugly Questions Unanswered," Agence France-Presse, July 28, 2010; http://www.google.com/hostednews/afp/article/ALeqM5invct2td Mai2ExWeQaGJwFmdt9Xg.

DOG DAYS

239   *Origins of oil*   W. J. Broad, "Tracing Oil Reserves to Their Tiny Origins," *New York Times*, August 3, 2010; http://www.nytimes.com/2010/08/03/science/03oil.html.

240   *History of early oil uses and extraction*   Joanna Burger, *Oil Spills*, New Brunswick, NJ: Rutgers University Press, 1997.

242   *Potential in algae*   "Slimy Scum May Hold the Key to Freedom from Oil," Editorial: *Canberra Times*, August 4 2010; http://www.canberratimes.com.au/news/opinion/editorial/general/slimy-scum-may-hold-the-key-to-freedom-from-oil/1903354.aspx.

242   *Benefits of algae as fuel*   R. H. Wijffels and M. J. Barbosa, "An Outlook on Microalgal Biofuels," *Science* 329, no. 5993 (2010): 796–99.

246–247   *"I think it is fairly safe to say"*   S. Borenstein, "Looking for the Oil? NOAA Says It's Mostly Gone," Associated Press, August 5, 2010; http://abcnews.go .com/Technology/wireStory?id=11328193.

248   *Jim Cowan quoted*   B. Boxall et al., "BP Jams Gulf Well with Drilling Mud," *Los Angeles Times*, August 5, 2010; http://articles.latimes.com/2010/aug/05/nation/la-na-oil-spill-20100805.

248–249   *Georgia Sea Grant's alternative report*   A. Miles, "Scientists Wary of U.S. Report That Says Only 26 Percent of Spilled Gulf Oil Left," *Times-Picayune*, August 17, 2010; http://www.nola.com/news/gulf-oil-spill/index.ssf/2010/08/scientists_wary_of_us_report_t.html.

249   *Ronald J. Kendall quoted, and Lubchenco's "I think the view"*   B. Boxall et al., "BP Jams Gulf Well with Drilling Mud," *Los Angeles Times*, August 5, 2010; http://articles.latimes.com/2010/aug/05/nation/la-na-oil-spill-20100805.

249   *"The truth is in the middle"*   D. Fahrenthold and Leslie Tamura, "Majority of Spilled Oil in Gulf of Mexico Unaccounted for in Government Data," *Washington Post*, July 29, 2010; http://www.washingtonpost.com/wp-dyn/content/article/2010/07/28/AR2010072806135.html.

249   *"Roughly one-third of the oil"*   A. Miles, "Scientists Wary of U.S. Report That Says Only 26 Percent of Spilled Gulf Oil Left," *Times-Picayune*, August 17, 2010; http://www.nola.com/news/gulf-oil-spill/index.ssf/2010/08/scientists_wary_of_us _report_t.html.

249   *Only about 26 percent of the oil is still in the water or onshore, and Carol Browner quote*   J. Gillis, "U.S. Finds Most Oil from Spill Poses Little Additional Risk," *New York Times*, August 4, 2010; http://www.nytimes.com/2010/08/04/science/earth/04oil.html.

249–250   *"Only about one-quarter of the oil," and Lubchenco's "Dilute and out of sight"*   S. Connor, "How Did Five Million Barrels of Oil Simply Disappear?" *Independent*, August 6, 2010; http://www.independent.co.uk/news/science/how-did-five-million-barrels-of-oil-simply-disappear-2044817.html.

250   *Bill Lehr statement*   S. Goldenberg, "US Scientist Retracts Assurances over State of BP Spill," *Guardian*, August 20, 2010; http://www.guardian.co.uk/environment/2010/aug/19/bp-oil-spill-scientist-retracts-assurances.

250 *Quotes from McDonald, Condrey, and Ault*   B. Marshall, "Don't Kid Yourself, Oil Isn't Gone," *Times-Picayune*, August 8, 2010; http://www.nola.com/sports/t-p/index.ssf?/base/sports-47/1281336612181230.xml&coll=1.

251 *"We're going to have to think about what to do"*   "BP Says It Might Drill Again in Gulf Reservoir," Associated Press, August 6, 2010; http://www.usatoday.com/communities/greenhouse/post/2010/08/bp-oil-spill-gulf-1/1.

252 *"People died out there," and BP hedging about relief wells*   H. R. Weber, "To Seal or Sell? BP Has Options on Remaining Oil," Associated Press, August 6, 2010; http://abcnews.go.com/Business/wireStory?id=11328201.

252 *"I am the national incident commander"*   H. R. Weber and Greg Bluestein. "BP Begins Effort to Permanently Seal Gulf Gusher," Associated Press, August 4, 2010; http://www.boston.com/news/science/articles/2010/08/04/bp_begins_effort_to_permanently_seal_gulf_gusher/.

252 *BP hedging about relief wells and Allen's response*   J. Dearen and Greg Bluestein, "Crude Still Coats Marshes and Wetlands Along Gulf," Associated Press, August 6, 2010; http://www.signonsandiego.com/news/2010/aug/06/crude-still-coats-marshes-and-wetlands-along-gulf/. See also "BP Says It Might Drill Again in Gulf Reservoir," Associated Press, August 6, 2010; http://www.usatoday.com/communities/greenhouse/post/2010/08/bp-oil-spill-gulf-1/1.

253 *Transocean asks for a liability limit of $27 million*   "Partner Says BP Hiding Oil Spill Documents," Agence France-Presse, August 19, 2010; http://www.google.com/hostednews/afp/article/ALeqM5hE2vTYfDJqNnNj8r3reXXT6fZ7wg.

254 *Gulf is well populated with bacteria*   T. C. Hazen et al. "Deep-Sea Oil Plume Enriches Indigenous Oil-Degrading Bacteria," *Science* 330, no. 6001, August 24, 2010: 204–8.

254 *Ronald Atlas and Roger Sassen quoted*   W. J. Broad, "Oil Spill Cleanup Workers Include Many Very, Very Small Ones," *New York Times*, August 4, 2010; http://www.nytimes.com/2010/08/05/science/earth/05microbe.html.

255 *Floating oil mats largely gone, and Lubchenco quotes*   J. Gillis and Campbell Robertson, "On the Surface, Oil Spill in Gulf Is Vanishing Fast," *New York Times*, July 27, 2010; http://www.nytimes.com/2010/07/28/us/28spill.html.

257 *Fraud alert*   D. Usborne, "BP Believes 10% of Oil Spill Claims Are Fraudulent," *Independent*, August 12, 2010; http://www.independent.co.uk/news/world/americas/bp-believes-10-per-cent-of-oil-spill-claims-are-fraudulent-2050309.html.

257–258 *Bob Shipp and Mark Davis quoted*   T. Smith, "By Hiring Gulf Scientists, BP May Be Buying Silence," National Public Radio, July 31, 2010; http://www.npr.org/templates/story/story.php?storyId=128892441&sc=17&f=1001.

LATE AUGUST

259   *BP wondering if bottom kill is necessary*   T. Breen and Harry R. Weber, "Gulf Leaders Wary over Wavering on Final Plug," Associated Press, August 12, 2010; http://www.indianexpress.com/news/gulf-leaders-wary-over-wavering-on-final -plu/659395/.

259–260   *"A bottom kill finishes this well," and "a hard sell"*   T. Breen, "Decision Expected on Plug for BP's Broken Oil Well," Associated Press, August 13, 2010; http://abcnews.go.com/Business/wireStory?id=11390638.

261   *No oil-caused dead zones developed*   J. Raloff, "No 'Dead Zone' from BP Oil," *Science News*, September 7, 2010; http://www.sciencenews.org/view/generic/id/ 63103/title/No_dead_zone_from_BP_oil.

262   *Sargassum recovering*   M. Hirsch, "Fewer Turtles Being Found Soaked in Oil, Researchers Say," *Times-Picayune*, August 11, 2010; http://www.nola.com/news/ gulf-oil-spill/index.ssf/2010/08/fewer_turtles_being_found_soak.html. *See also* L. Kaufman and Shaila Dewan, "Luck and Ecology Seem to Soften Impact of Gulf Oil Spill," *International Herald Tribune*, September 14, 2010; http://www.highbeam .com/doc/1P1-184098210.html.

262   *"The Gulf is incredible"*   "Nearly 80 Percent of Gulf Spill Oil Still in Water: Experts," Agence France-Presse, August 18, 2010; http://www.independent.co.uk/ environment/nearly-80-percent-of-gulf-spill-oil-still-in-water-experts-2055910 .html.

262   *Oil and dispersant droplets in the larval crabs*   M. Thomas, "Oil-in-Seafood Reports; Do They Hold Water?" *Orlando Sentinel*, August 12, 2010.

262   *"The spill isn't as bad," and "The perception is"*   C. Robertson, "In Gulf, Good News Is Taken with Grain of Salt," *New York Times*, August 4, 2010; http://www .nytimes.com/2010/08/05/us/05gulf.html.

263   *Green shoots appearing, and Associated Press calculates 3.4 square miles*   C. Burdeau and Jeffrey Collins, "Signs of Regrowth Seen in Oiled Louisiana Marshland," Associated Press, August 12, 2010; http://www.boston.com/news/science/articles/ 2010/08/12/signs_of_regrowth_seen_in_oiled_louisiana_marshland/.

263   *"We were anchored"*   B. Marshall, "Don't Kid Yourself, Oil Isn't Gone," *Times-Picayune*, August 8, 2010; http://www.nola.com/sports/t-p/index.ssf?/base/ sports-47/1281336612181230.xml&coll=1.

264   *Very roughly 1,800 square miles*   K. Wells, "Collapsing Marsh Dwarfs BP Oil Blowout as Ecological Disaster," *BloombergBusinessweek*, August 18, 2010; http://www.businessweek.com/news/2010-08-18/collapsing-marsh-dwarfs-bp-oil -blowout-as-ecological-disaster.html. *See also* S. Borenstein and Cain Burdeau, "Scientists Think Gulf Can Recover," Associated Press, August 6, 2010; http://abcnews .go.com/Technology/wireStory?id=11337200.

264 *Marsh losses*   J. W. Day Jr. et al., "Restoration of the Mississippi Delta: Lessons from Hurricanes Katrina and Rita," *Science* 315, no. 5819, March 23, 2007: 1679–84. *See also* L. D. Britsch and Joseph B. Dunbar, "Land Loss Rates: Louisiana Coastal Plain," *Journal of Coastal Research* 9, no. 2, Spring 1993: 324–38; http://www .jstor.org/stable/4298092.

264 *Felicia Coleman quoted*   C. Robertson, "Gulf of Mexico Has Long Been Dumping Site," *New York Times,* July 30, 2010; http://query.nytimes.com/gst/ fullpage.html?res=9A04E4D8133AF933A05754C0A9669D8B63.

264 *Mississippi marsh loss*   C. Burdeau and Jeffrey Collins, "Signs of Regrowth Seen in Oiled Louisiana Marshland," Associated Press, August 12, 2010; http:// www.boston.com/news/science/articles/2010/08/12/signs_of_regrowth_seen_in _oiled_louisiana_marshland/.

265 *Navy secretary Ray Mabus*   H. R. Weber and Dina Cappiello, "Obama Endorses Using Fines for Gulf Rehabilitation," Associated Press, September 29, 2010; http://news.yahoo.com/s/ap/20100929/ap_on_bi_ge/us_gulf_oil_spill_restoration.

265 *Louisiana shrimpers go back to work*   D. A. Fahrenthold and Juliet Eilperin, "Unallayed by Tests, Fishermen Greet Start of Gulf Shrimp Harvest with Suspicion," *Washington Post,* August 17, 2010; http://www.washingtonpost.com/wp-dyn/ content/article/2010/08/16/AR2010081605471.html.

265 *BP's money for mental health*   "Plumes of Gulf Oil Spreading East on Sea Floor," AC360 blog, August 17, 2010; http://ac360.blogs.cnn.com/2010/08/17/ plumes-of-gulf-oil-spreading-east-on-sea-floor.

266 *Margaret Carruth, a Louisiana husband and wife, and "throwing desks, kicking chairs"*   J. Reeves, "Oil Gusher Is Dead, but Not Residents' Anguish," Associated Press, September 27, 2010; http://news.yahoo.com/s/ap/20100927/ap_on_re_us/us _gulf_oil_spill_mental_health.

266 *Allen wanting to avoid timelines*   H. R. Weber, "Feds: No Timeline for Completing Gulf Relief Well," Associated Press, August 18, 2010; http://www.physorg .com/news201364019.html.

267 *Beluga whales*   A. Mayeda, "Whale Sanctuary Open to Oil Drilling; Small Portion Put Aside for Exploration," *Calgary Herald,* August 28, 2010; http:// www.calgaryherald.com/technology/Whale+sanctuary+open+drilling/3454789/ story.html.

267 *Indonesia demands $2.4 billion*   "Indonesia Demands 2.4 Billion Dollar Payout over Oil Spill," Agence France-Presse, August 31, 2010; http://www.thenewage .co.za/Detail.aspx?news_id=288&cat_id=1026&mid=53.

267 *Thai-owned company rejects Indonesia's demand*   "Thai Firm Rejects Indonesia's 2.4-Billion Oil Spill Claim," Agence France-Presse, September 3, 2010; http:// www.thejakartaglobe.com/home/thai-firm-rejects-indonesias-24-billion-oil-spill -claim/394363.

EARLY SEPTEMBER

269 *"Yes!" the sign says*   R. Fausset, "Shrimp and Oil Are Still King at This Louisiana Festival," *Los Angeles Times,* September 6, 2010; http://articles.latimes.com/2010/sep/06/nation/la-na-petroleum-festival-20100906.

269 *Oil near Panaji, India*   "Goa on Slippery Slope as Mystery Ship Dumps Oil," *Pioneer* (India), September 2, 2010; http://www.dailypioneer.com/280374/Goa-on-slippery-slope-as-mystery-ship-dumps-oil.html.

270 *"We are not finding anything"*   M. Newsom, "Officials Say No Submerged Oil Found," *Biloxi Sun Herald,* September 10, 2010.

270 *"We haven't seen any oiled sediments"*   C. Burdeau, "NOAA Says Sediment on Gulf Floor Not Visibly Oiled," Associated Press, September 30, 2010; http://www.wkrg.com/gulf_oil_spill/article/noaa-says-sediment-on-gulf-floor-not-visibly-oiled/994300/Sep-30-2010_3-30-pm/.

270 *"I've never seen anything like this"*   R. Harris, "Scientists Find Thick Layer of Oil on Seafloor," National Public Radio, September 10, 2010; http://www.npr.org/templates/story/story.php?storyId=129782098.

270 *"It wasn't like a drape"*   "Experts See Oil in Gulf as Threat to Marine Life," *Los Angeles Times,* August 18, 2010.

270–271 *Jindal's berms*   C. Burdeau, "EPA: Louisiana's Sand Berms Not Stopping Much Oil," Associated Press, September 10, 2010; http://www.dailycomet.com/article/20100910/FEATURES12/100919996.

273 *Raising the failed blowout preventer*   H. R. Weber, "Engineers Prepare to Remove Gulf Well's Cap," Associated Press, August 28, 2010. *See also* H. R. Weber, "Risks Remain with Gulf Well Cap Coming Off," Associated Press, September 2, 2010; http://news.yahoo.com/s/ap/20100902/ap_on_bi_ge/us_gulf_oil_spill.

273 *John Wright, and drilling the final stretch*   J. Collins, "Gulf Relief Well Down to Final, Tricky 100 Feet," Associated Press, August 9, 2010; http://www.scpr.org/news/2010/08/09/gulf-relief-well-down-final-tricky-100-feet.

THE NEW LIGHT OF AUTUMN

274 *The cement stake*   A. G. Breed, "The Well Is Dead, but Gulf Challenges Live On," Associated Press, September 19, 2010.

285 *Freshwater largely demolished Louisiana's oysters*   J. C. Rudolf, "For Oysters, a 'Remedy' Turned Catastrophe," *New York Times,* July 21, 2010; http://green.blogs.nytimes.com/2010/07/21/for-oysters-a-remedy-turned-catastrophe/.

285 *Dead deep-water corals*   J. C. Rudolf, "Dead Coral Found Near Site of Oil Spill," *New York Times,* November 5, 2010; http://www.nytimes.com/2010/11/06/science/earth/06coral.html.

287   *"effectively dead"*   "BP Oil Well Declared 'Dead.' " *Washington Post*, September 21, 2010; http://www.washingtonpost.com/wp-dyn/content/article/2010/09/20/AR2010092005835.html.

287   *"like a shadow out there"*   C. Morgan, "Study: Oil from Spill Has Not Become a Drifting Cloud of Death," *Miami Herald*, September 8, 2010; http://www.miamiherald.com/2010/09/07/1813032/study-oil-from-spill-has-not-become.html.

287   *"Red snapper are unbelievable"*   S. Borenstein and Cain Burdeau, "Scientists Lower Gulf Health Grade," Associated Press, October 19, 2010; http://news.yahoo.com/s/ap/20101019/ap_on_sc/us_gulf_survival.

287   *What are scientists finding?*   B. Raines, "Researcher: Fish Numbers Triple After Oil Spill Fishing Closures," *Mobile Register*, November 7, 2010; http://blog.al.com/live/2010/11/researcher_fish_numbers_triple.html.

289   *More than 27,000 abandoned wells*   J. Donn and Mitch Weiss, "Gulf Awash in 27,000 Abandoned Wells," Associated Press, July 7, 2010; http://www.msnbc.msn.com/id/38113914/ns/disaster_in_the_gulf.

291   *The oil has everyone's attention*   A. Revkin, "While Oil Gushes, Invisible Ocean Impacts Build," Dot Earth blog, *New York Times;* http://dotearth.blogs.nytimes.com/2010/06/18/while-oil-gushes-invisible-ocean-impacts-build/.

292   *The heart and lungs of the planet*   D. Smith, "Alarm at Speeding Sea Change," *Age* (Melbourne, Australia), June 18, 2010; http://newsstore.theage.com.au/apps/viewDocument.ac?page=1&sy=age&kw=deborah+smith&pb=all_ffx&dt=selectRange&dr=6months&so=relevance&sf=text&sf=author&sf=headline&rc=10&rm=200&sp=nrm&clsPage=1&docID=AGE100618C649UFM4JOH.

292   *Science has just published a series*   J. Smith et al., "Changing Oceans," *Science* 328, no. 5985, June 18, 2010: 1497.

295   *Drawbacks of renewable energy sources, and "they don't offer new services"*   "Scaling Up Alternative Energy," special section of *Science* magazine 329, August 13, 2010: 779–803.

296   *A CBS News / New York Times poll*   "Poll: Vast Majority Say U.S. Energy Policy Needs Major Changes," CBCnews, June 21, 2010; http://www.cbsnews.com/8301-503544_162-20008368-503544.html.

298–299   *Gannets*   "BP Spill Threatens a Third of Canadian Gannets," CBCnews, October 21, 2010; http://www.cbc.ca/technology/story/2010/10/21/nl-montevecchi-gannets-1021.html.

299   *"oil everywhere"*   S. Davis, "La. Coast Hit by More Oil," *Advocate*, September 25, 2010.

ACKNOWLEDGMENTS

Mark Loehr's herculean devotion to getting the story of what happened in the well and on the rig absolutely right has immensely benefitted both this book and me. As a researcher, he stands in a class of his own. I believe it is likely that for most of the summer Mark understood the totality of what happened to cause the blowout, the specific details of events, and the role of different personnel in the various companies better than any other single person, period. I could never have truly afforded him.

On the science side, John Angier was exceptionally generous, prompt, and entertainingly attuned to debunking hype and hysteria and setting records straight. I thank also William Semple for his expertise and insight.

Admiral Thad Allen, the national incident commander, and Dr. Jane Lubchenco, the chief of the National Oceanic and Atmospheric Administration—neither of whom had time to spare and both of whom had much better things to do—generously gave me two hours of their time, during which they efficiently conveyed months of experience and years of wisdom.

In and around the Gulf region, I benefited from the generous assistance of the National Wildlife Federation's Karla Raettig, Amanda Moore, Emily Guidry Schatzel, and Larry Schweiger.

Jo Billups, a singer and activist, was extremely generous in helping arrange my aerial perspective and in welcoming me into her home and community. I also thank filmmaker Bill Mills, Marion Laney, Frank Campo, Charlie Robin, Jeff Wolkart, James Fox, Gary Skinner, Reverend Chris Schansberg, and Julian MacQueen of the Hampton Inn in Pensacola Beach. George Brower graciously hosted me on my first night in New Orleans. I thank Campbell Robertson for introducing me to Oliver Houck. For other logistical assistance, I thank the Gulf Restoration Network, especially Jonathan Henderson. And photographer Jeffrey Dubinsky. Jennifer Godwin of the Suncoast Seabird Sanctuary, near Tampa, told me about the gannets.

All season long, my understanding of the Gulf-wide picture benefitted greatly from the constant stream of reporting from the dedicated professional journalists at the *New York Times*, the Associated Press, the *Washington Post*, the *Los Angeles Times*, Agence France-Presse, and elsewhere, whose importance to society is now so undervalued. If not for the news they uncover and deliver, there'd be little to huff about. I thank Connie Murtagh of SeaWeb for sending hundreds of articles my way.

Sylvia Earle and Charlotte Vick provided continual encouragement. I was first persuaded to overcome my initial reluctance to go to the Gulf by Steve Dishart and Myra "Just go" Sarli. As always, the indefatigable and always reliable Megan Smith arranged and backstopped my logistics. I thank also Kate McLaughlin, Alan Duckworth, and the staff of Blue Ocean Institute for their patience in my absence. Jesse Bruschini provided feedback and feed. For interest and encouragement and discussion, I thank the faculty and staff of Stony Brook University's School of Marine and Atmospheric Sciences and School of Journalism's Center for Communicating Science. I thank Judy Bergsma for introducing me to Mark Loehr. When I bemoaned my deadline, Joanna Burger provided her usual "you can do it" encouragement. I thank Jack Macrae for his graciousness, Jean Naggar for her diligence, and John Glusman for his confidence.

For their interest in my impressions and opinions, I thank congressional representatives Ed Markey, Lois Capps, and their able staffs, as well as the hosts and staffs of *Democracy Now,* PBS's *Need to Know,* CNN, and, particularly, Richard Galant, MSNBC's Keith Olbermann, *Audubon* magazine, the Blue Ocean Film Festival, the organizers and participants at the TEDxOilSpill conference, and Stephen Colbert and the producers of *The Colbert Report.*

I thank my family, Patricia and Alexandra, for dealing with a serially difficult summer on the home front. Being seventeen is not for the faint of heart, but as the saying goes, what doesn't kill us makes us stronger, and Alex has made us proud. Things were at times more difficult because of my absences and, at times, because of my presence. Not least, while I was in the Gulf, Pat had to deal alone with a middle-of-the-night decision to end the life of our dog, Kenzie. Sad though that was, we were again touched by the healing powers of the new young furred and feathered creatures who came—and literally fell—into our lives this year. Each time I returned home drained after confronting the grief in the Gulf, those young lives were my smile factory. The topography of life includes much rough terrain. When big things go off the rails, it's the little things that keep one sane.

INDEX

Carl Safina has studied the ocean as a scientist, stood for it as an advocate, and conveyed his travels among the sea's creatures and fishing people in lyrical nonfiction. His first book, *Song for the Blue Ocean,* was chosen as a *New York Times* Notable Book of the Year, and in 2000 he won the Lannan Literary Award for nonfiction. Dr. Safina's second book, *Eye of the Albatross,* won the John Burroughs Medal for the year's best nature book; it was chosen by the National Academies of Science, Engineering, and Medicine as the "Year's Best Book for Communicating Science." The *New York Times* selected both his *Voyage of the Turtle* as well as *The View from Lazy Point: A Natural Year in an Unnatural World* as "Editors' Choices." Safina is founding president of Blue Ocean Institute and adjunct professor at Stony Brook University, where he is involved with its School of Marine and Atmospheric Sciences and its Center for Communicating Science. He has been named among "100 Notable Conservationists of the Twentieth Century" by *Audubon* magazine.

El nuevo libro de Stephen Stran[g]... parte sobre George Soros y su ope[...] que, ciertamente, es un reportero [...] miendo el libro más reciente de S[...] obligatoria en tiempos en que son [...] cido gobierno en la sombra.

FUNDADOR/PRESIDENTE, *THE CHRISTIAN BROADCASTING NETWORK INC.*
ANFITRIÓN, CLUB 700

Si escribiera una canción para los de Izquierda, que capturara su conducta frenética sobre los últimos dos años, definitivamente la titularía: "El síndrome de la locura Trump". Desde abogados especiales con casos falsos, construidos en un "expediente" sin verificar, hasta la censura de los medios sociales; desde las voces conservadoras hasta acosadores liberales que atacan a los miembros de la administración, incluyendo a mi propia hija, en público ninguno es inmune a la tensión. Los norteamericanos sienten que ver las noticias se ha convertido en un asiento de primera fila para la batalla por nuestra nación. Entre los medios populares, se le da poco crédito al Presidente por sus logros y su postura firme por los valores y libertades conservadoras, pero este libro importante, que sostiene en sus manos, deja las cosas claras sobre el presidente Trump y también provee ideas en los aspectos espirituales de la presidencia de Trump. Escribí el prólogo del último libro de Stephen Strang, *God and Donald Trump*, y ahora recomiendo incondicionalmente su nuevo libro, *El temblor después de Trump*, y le animo a que lo lea.

—MIKE HUCKABEE
AUTOR DE ÉXITOS DE VENTAS DEL *NEW YORK TIMES*
ANFITRIÓN, HUCKABEE EN TBN

En un crucero reciente hacia Alaska, una señora sentada a mi mesa hacía alarde sobre el libro anterior de Stephen Strang, *God and Donald Trump* con una dama al otro lado de la mesa. Sin saber que yo conocía a Stephen y que también había publicado mi libro más reciente con su empresa, ella continuaba hablando. "Es una lectura obligatoria", decía, "¡No podía dejar de leerlo!". Me hizo sentir orgullosa de conocer a Stephen y ser entrevistada por él para su siguiente libro, el cual usted sostiene ahora en sus manos. *El temblor después de Trump* revela magistralmente por qué importa la presidencia trascendental de Donald Trump, porque es una lucha para preservar los valores y las libertades judeocristianos de nuestra gran nación para la futura generación. Si se preocupa por el futuro de nuestro país, necesita leer este libro.

—BRIGITTE GABRIEL
AUTORA DE ÉXITOS DE VENTAS DEL *NEW YORK TIMES*
FUNDADORA, ACT PARA AMÉRICA

Cuando mi amigo Stephen Strang escribió su libro anterior, *God and Donald Trump*, no podía esperar a tenerlo como invitado en mi programa de televisión para hablar sobre él, ya que temía que demasiadas personas creían las mentiras en los medios de comunicación dominantes, y quería ayudar a que las personas entendieran la verdad sobre Donald Trump. Es por eso por lo que estaba tan contento de que Stephen hubiera escrito este nuevo libro, *El temblor después de Trump*, porque la tergiversación de los medios de comunicación acerca de nuestro presidente y su agenda solo ha empeorado después de su elección. El libro de Stephen es uno de los únicos libros que conozco que aclaran las cosas desde una perspectiva cristiana. *El temblor después de Trump* es una lectura obligatoria para los cristianos con mentalidad política, quienes toman en serio los valores y las libertades religiosas, quienes creen que por fin tenemos a alguien en la Oficina Oval que apoya esos valores, y quienes están orando que estos eventos provoquen que nuestra gran nación regrese a Dios.

—JIM BAKKER
PIONERO DE LA TELEVISIÓN CRISTIANA
ANFITRIÓN, *THE JIM BAKKER SHOW*

Por décadas, Stephen Strang, como periodista y editor distinguido, ha estado muy consciente de los sucesos en Estados Unidos. En su nuevo libro, él documenta hábilmente el impacto poderoso que el presidente Trump ha tenido en la cultura de la nación. La pregunta es, ¿qué sucede después? Y Stephen entrega un vistazo contundente de hacia dónde se dirige la nación.

—TODD STARNES
CANAL *FOX NEWS*
BROOKLYN, NUEVA YORK

En los años 60, Estados Unidos sufrió un temblor cuando fueron asesinados los tres K: John F. Kennedy, Robert Kennedy, y Martin Luther King. Después, el país experimentó una rebelión: el movimiento "Dios está muerto", la revolución sexual y las drogas, *Roe contra Wade*, y otras señales de decadencia moral. El país, entonces, tuvo un encuentro con otro "temblor" cuando, contrario a las encuestas de opinión liberal, Donald Trump fuera elegido como presidente. Stephen Strang ha escrito un libro fantástico que captura el impacto de la presidencia extraordinaria de Trump en nuestra nación y en el mundo, y le animo a leerlo.

—MIKE EVANS
AUTOR DE ÉXITO DE VENTAS DEL *NEW YORK TIMES*
FRIENDS OF ZION HERITAGE CENTER, JERUSALÉN

¡Stephen Strang lo hizo de nuevo! En *El temblor después de Trump*, Strang captura con genialidad periodística el cambio sin precedentes e impacto desplegado por la presidencia de Donald J. Trump. Strang no solo nos informa de lo que ha cambiado, sino que nos dice por qué las cosas han cambiado. Cualquier persona interesada en descubrir por qué el 81% de los evangélicos votó por él y continúa apoyando a Donald Trump, deben leer este libro.

—SAMUEL RODRÍGUEZ
PRESIDENTE, CONFERENCIA NACIONAL DE LIDERAZGO CRISTIANO HISPANO
PASTOR PRINCIPAL, *NEW SEASON*

Me alegra que mi amigo Stephen Strang haya escrito este libro, *El temblor después de Trump*, el cual aclara los logros de la administración Trump y la oposición muy real que enfrenta. Stephen no solo es un autor; también es un periodista que dirige una empresa cristiana de medios de comunicación y en la que podemos confiar como fuente de noticias que afectan nuestra vida diaria. Necesitamos más voces como la de Stephen quien no tiene miedo de comunicar la verdad. No crea las mentiras de los medios sociales. Busque hechos de fuentes cristianas confiables tales como la de Stephen Strang, *Charisma News*, y libros como este. Nuestro Presidente está sacudiendo las cosas. Él necesita nuestro apoyo. Es tiempo de que nosotros lleguemos a estar informados, unidos y que exijamos el fin de las investigaciones de cacería de brujas, las noticias falsas y la retórica llena de odio de aquellos cuya agenda es causar el fin de este presidente y alejar de Dios a nuestra gran nación.

—ROBERT JEFFRESS
PASTOR PRINCIPAL; *FIRST BAPTIST DALLAS*
DALLAS, TEXAS

El temblor después de Trump es una guía simple, aunque profundamente incisiva e informativa a través del terremoto político, cultural y espiritual generado por la elección del presidente Trump y su presidencia. Cualquier persona que verdaderamente busque un conocimiento profundo de la turbulencia extraordinaria generada por la elección del presidente Trump encontrará en este libro un recurso que no tiene precio.

—DR. RICHARD LAND
PRESIDENTE, *SOUTHERN EVANGELICAL SEMINARY*
CHARLOTTE, CAROLINA DEL NORTE

Un despertar un levantamiento algo grande está sucediendo y la cultura estadounidense y la Iglesia nunca serán las mismas.

Estoy de acuerdo con Stephen Strang que "si nuestra nación puede empezar a confiar verdaderamente en Dios y a permitir que su luz guie nuestros pasos; entonces, después de todo, ese será el temblor más grande".

—TIM CLINTON
DIRECTOR EJECUTIVO, *JAMES DOBSON FAMILY INSTITUTE*
PRESIDENTE, *AMERICAN ASSOCIATION OF CHRISTIAN COUNSELORS*

El temblor después de Trump definitivamente es una exposición "para un tiempo como el de hoy". El presidente Donald Trump es verdaderamente una persona influyente, provocando que las personas se arrodillen en asombro o en oración dependiendo de la perspectiva. Felicidades a Stephen Strang por articular el temblor de la elección de Trump de una forma directa y honesta. Él tiene el valor de trabajar el ministerio del escriba de nuestros tiempos.

—EVANGELISTA ALVEDA C. KING
SOBRINA DEL DR. MARTIN LUTHER KING JR.
ATLANTA, GEORGIA

¡Mi amigo Stephen Strang lo ha hecho de nuevo! Si pensó que la cobertura de la elección de Trump en *God and Donald Trump* fue profunda, le encantará leer este nuevo libro, *El temblor después de Trump*, da una perspectiva reveladora de nuestro cuadragésimo quinto presidente y su extraordinaria agenda y logros.

—JIM GARLOW
PASTOR PRINCIPAL, *SKYLINE CHURCH*
SAN DIEGO, CALIFORNIA

Stephen Strang ha escrito la narrativa definitiva de los inicios candentes de la presidencia de Donald Trump. Aquí hay una crónica indiscutible del Presidente que, a pesar de sus críticos, ha cumplido sus promesas a Estados Unidos. La experiencia periodística de Stephen Strang y su absoluta devoción a la exactitud hacen de este recurso una lectura obligatoria para cada ciudadano. Yo especialmente lo recomiendo también para personas con pensamientos de Izquierda. Este libro deja las cosas claras. Finalmente, los seguidores de Jesús y la Iglesia son desafiados a no abandonar la plaza pública. Tome este libro y ármese con el arma de la verdad.

—DR. RON PHILLIPS
PASTOR EMÉRITO, *ABBA'S HOUSE*
CHATTANOOGA, TENNESSEE

Desde la isla de Gran Bretaña he vivido y observado la presidencia de Trump, y comparto su sentir. El nuevo libro de Stephen Strang, *El temblor después de Trump*, es una historia escrita maravillosamente, capturando todo lo que he visto. Lo que atrajo mi atención es que hubo revelación en su escrito. Es un comentario muy detallado, y de nuevo, él produjo un documento histórico. Además, es una lectura fascinante de principio a fin.

Mi parte favorita fue la definición de Ronald Reagan de *statu quo*, el latín que significa "el lío en el que estamos".

—MARTIN CLARKE
PRESIDENTE, *THE MARTIN CLARKE GROUP OF COMPANIES*
LONDRES, INGLATERRA

Stephen Strang es un investigador cuidadoso que, en este nuevo libro, *El temblor después de Trump*, provee material documentado para el observador que desea una verdad objetiva sin sesgo progresista. Strang también es la voz profética que desafía al lector a trabajar y a orar por un avivamiento en un día de oportunidad sin precedentes. Como el libro concluye, Strang le recuerda al lector: "Si nuestra nación puede empezar a confiar verdaderamente en Dios y a permitir que su luz guie nuestros pasos, entonces, después de todo, ese será el temblor más grande". Dios ha escuchado la oración de su pueblo y ha dado prueba de que hay esperanza para Estados Unidos. Este no es el tiempo para que la Iglesia se albergue en un refugio subterráneo construido por el temor, sino que se levante y afirme su identidad.

—LARRY SPARGIMINO, PhD
PASTOR, *SOUTHWEST RADIO CHURCH*
OKLAHOMA CITY, OKLAHOMA

EL TEMBLOR

DESPUÉS DE

TRUMP

STEPHEN E. STRANG

CASA
CREACIÓN

El temblor después de Trump por Stephen E. Strang
Publicado por Casa Creación
Una compañía de Charisma Media
600 Rinehart Road
Lake Mary, Florida 32746
https://www.facebook.com/casacreacion

Visite la página web del autor: trumpsftershock.com

Traducido por: Yvette Fernández-Cortez | www.truemessage.co
Revisión de traducción: Nancy Carrera
Director de Diseño: Justin Evans
Diseño de portada por: Justin Evans

Originally published in English under the title:
Trump Aftershock
Published by FrontLine
Charisma Media/Charisma House Book Group
600 Rinehart Road
Lake Mary, FL 32746 USA

Library of Congress Control Number: 2018962342
ISBN: 978-1-62999-439-0
E-Book ISBN: 978-1-62999-440-6

Aunque el autor hizo todo lo posible por proveer teléfonos y páginas
de internet correctas al momento de la publicación de este libro, ni la editorial
ni el autor se responsabilizan por errores o cambios que puedan surgir
luego de haberse publicado. Además, la editorial no tiene control ni asume
responsabilidad alguna por páginas web y su contenido de ya sea el autor o
terceros.

Impreso en los Estados Unidos de América
18 19 20 21 22 * 6 5 4 3 2 1

ÍNDICE

PRÓLOGO

DURANTE MÁS DE dos años ya, la gente me ha estado preguntando por qué apoyé a Donald Trump como candidato para presidente de Estados Unidos y por qué sigo apoyándolo ahora en su papel como jefe ejecutivo de nuestra gran nación. Después de todo, yo era uno de los pocos del campo evangélico que respaldaba al Sr. Trump aun antes de los *caucus* de Iowa. Yo determiné tempranamente lo que aquejaba a Estados Unidos requeriría más que relaciones públicas y una política de alivio temporal. Y si Trump fuera electo, él necesitaría más que un apoyo temporal y ruidoso.

Pero, para responder la pregunta sobre mi apoyo, mucho de mi motivación vino de mi trasfondo en los negocios. Mi padre venía de una familia de gente de negocios que no era cristiana, incluyendo a mi abuelo. Sin embargo, una serie de tragedias personales resultaron en su muerte prematura, a la edad de cincuenta y un años. Mi padre, tenía solamente quince años en ese entonces, y él se volvió cristiano debido a esos eventos tristes. Creo que él pudo haber entrado al negocio familiar si aquellas cosas no hubieran sucedido. El punto es que, aunque el mundo conoce el nombre Falwell mayormente en el contexto de mi padre, un clérigo famoso, la mayoría de los Falwell han sido emprendedores exitosos: hombres y mujeres de negocios.

Aun en el contexto de la organización sin fines de lucro, tal como la universidad Liberty, he sido testigo de lo que aplicar principios de negocios puede hacer para salvar una organización. A finales de los años ochenta y los noventa, cuando los donativos se agotaron, tuvimos que crear un modelo de negocios que pudiera mantener viva la Universidad. Al final, no solo eliminamos la deuda; también prosperamos lo suficiente que ahora hemos alcanzado muchas de las visiones originales que mi padre tuvo para esta universidad. Sin embargo, el éxito de Liberty no llegó a través de un liderazgo opaco o perezoso.

Así que esa es la razón por la que apoyé a Donald Trump al inicio, porque Estados Unidos se está ahogando en una deuda de veintiún billones de dólares. Trump es un hombre de negocios. No hemos tenido muchos hombres de negocios que se hayan convertido en presidentes. En su lugar, hemos tenido políticos de carrera que tienen poco pensamiento transformador y una larga carrera política que quieren preservar. Aunque Trump no había siquiera decidido cuáles eran sus puntos de vista políticos en ese entonces, yo sabía que un hombre de negocios pragmático, con sentido común, llegaría al lado correcto de los problemas. Trump quería hacer lo que era mejor para el país. Y si usted empieza con ese deseo, hacer lo que es mejor para el país y para el hombre común, entonces no tiene otra opción sino la de ser conservador. Es así de simple.

Estoy muy orgulloso de haber apoyado a Donald Trump. Y desde que él entró a la Casa Blanca, he estado en contacto cercano con él, hablando con él casi una vez al mes. Ha llegado a ser una amistad cercana. Estoy muy complacido de la manera en que él ha cumplido su promesa. Ha asignado jueces en las cortes de primera instancia y en la Corte Suprema, y creo que son personas que defenderán la Constitución. En cuanto a temas relacionados con la libertad de culto, el Presidente ha sido un enviado de Dios. Y sus estrategias de liberalización han traído prosperidad a los negocios y al trabajador estadounidense. Él ha hecho todas las cosas que ofreció que iba a hacer, incluso con todos los de la izquierda que no se detendrían ante nada para derrocar a un presidente debidamente electo.

Mire, necesitamos a alguien resuelto y que tenga agallas. Los republicanos y los demócratas, los partidos se han vuelto tan parecidos que uno no puede realmente notar la diferencia. Muchos de ellos estaban, y todavía están, tan asustados por la crítica y la sombra de la prensa que se andan por las ramas en todos los asuntos. Levantan el dedo para ver hacia dónde sopla el viento.

Sin embargo, Trump solo marcha hacia adelante. A él no le importa cuánta crítica le hagan. Y a la gente tampoco le importa. La gente ya no le da importancia a lo que diga la prensa porque ellos han perdido la credibilidad. Eso es lo que los estadounidenses han anhelado ver en su presidente: alguien que defienda al país, defienda lo que es recto y justo y que no se amedrente frente a la adversidad.

Tal como lo hace Stephen Strang en este libro, yo comparo a Trump con Winston Churchill durante la Segunda Guerra Mundial. Todo parecía perdido frente a la arremetida del poder militar de Hitler. Churchill tenía que tomar la decisión para avanzar de alguna manera y no rendirse. Eso es lo que veo en Donald Trump, y creo que es por lo que la gente lo apoya a pesar de todas las cosas negativas que dicen de él.

En este libro nuevo, escrito por mi amigo, Stephen Strang, usted llegará a tener un mayor entendimiento de todo lo que ha estado sucediendo desde la noche electoral. Strang muestra cómo el presidente Trump ha excedido las expectativas de quienes lo apoyan. Y Strang revela cómo la Izquierda, en lugar de reconocer el éxito genuino de la administración Trump, está incrementando su antipatía hacia el Presidente. Se rehúsan a reconocer la economía pujante y a renovar el sentido de optimismo y el orgullo nacional, algunos de los izquierdistas (y algunos de los derechistas) sucumben ante "el Síndrome del trastorno Trump". Y así, la grieta entre la Izquierda y la Derecha se ha vuelto más profunda y nuestra política nacional más polarizada que nunca.

Sin embargo, el libro de Strang toca un punto sensible de esperanza porque él cree (y yo también) que estos días son unos de los tiempos más extraordinarios en la vida de nuestra nación. Usted disfrutará *El temblor después de Trump*. Pero, aún más, este lo animará a orar y a trabajar en su propia comunidad para "hacer a Estados Unidos grande otra vez".

–Jerry Falwell Jr.
Presidente de la Universidad Liberty
Lynchburg, Virginia

SACUDIDOS HASTA EL NÚCLEO

L A ELECCIÓN DE Donald Trump fue inesperada. Incluso para quienes trabajaron más duro por su elección, darse cuenta de que el multimillonario de Nueva York realmente había ganado azotó como un terremoto, sacudiendo todo y a todos. Si usted leyó el libro *God and Donald Trump* sabe que yo creía que él *podría* ganar, así que volé a Nueva York para la fiesta de la noche de su elección. Sin embargo, admito que estaba nervioso. Pero estando allí, en esa noche histórica, vi que incluso sus más ardientes admiradores apenas podían creerlo a medida que los informes iban ingresando. Y ese era solo el principio.

Los impactos han continuado desde la investidura, afectando políticas, negocios, relaciones exteriores y la cultura en muchas maneras nuevas y sorprendentes. El pánico que siguió a la mañana del 9 de noviembre de 2016 se debía principalmente al hecho de que nadie en ninguno de los partidos había pensado mucho en cómo sería el mundo si Hillary Clinton perdiera la elección. Durante meses, las encuestas y los reporteros habían estado diciendo que ella lo tenía en la bolsa. Que finalmente había atravesado el techo de vidrio que le impedía llegar a ser la primera presidenta de Estados Unidos. Luego, repentinamente, todo cambió.

Todos esos grandes planes nunca llegaron a fructificar, y los demócratas se encontraron viendo de cara a una realidad nueva y áspera: ellos estaban fuera del poder, y el candidato que la Izquierda le temía más que ningún otro, estaría haciéndose cargo de la Casa Blanca. La era Obama había terminado, y el mundo pronto lo veía, a él y a su presidencia, bajo una nueva luz. Hoy día, todavía estamos lidiando con esa realidad, descubriendo secretos y travesuras ocultas en la oscuridad por mucho tiempo y haciendo nuestro mejor esfuerzo para lidiar con los impactos que acompañan a esas revelaciones sorprendentes.

En los primeros dos años de Trump en el cargo, la economía, después de décadas de ir en picada, no solo dejó de caer, sino que marcó tantos récords que el *New York Times* tuvo que admitir que se había "quedado sin palabras" para describir el éxito increíble de la economía bajo el liderazgo de Trump. Las cifras de empleo se han disparado superando los 220,000 empleos nuevos en el mes de mayo de 2018, con una caída del desempleo del 3.8 por ciento en general, la más baja en dieciocho años. Al mismo tiempo, el desempleo en la comunidad negra disminuyó en 5.9 por ciento, un récord histórico,[1] y las empresas anunciaron que estaban dando miles de dólares en bonos a más de un millón de trabajadores.[2] A pesar de los contraataques del liderazgo demócrata, los estadounidenses estaban extasiados, y los medios de comunicación convencionales estaban en *shock*.

Los medios estaban a favor del otro lado desde el primer día, pero Trump fue llevado al cargo por una ola roja de ciudadanos promedio que estaban hartos de la manera en que Washington estaba administrando. Estaban cansados de los reporteros liberales pregonando sus valores y creencias, y ya no iban a soportarlo más. Los observadores políticos reportaron que la gente estaba tan frustrada con la intromisión inoportuna del gobierno en su vida que estaban a punto de una revuelta a gran escala. Ellos podían sentir que el país descendía en espiral apartándose de su grandeza previa.

La nación estaba llegando al punto donde algo tenía que hacerse, y ese algo resultó ser Donald Trump. Tal como el gobernador Mike Huckabee me dijo en una entrevista para este libro: "Muy francamente, el objetivo de los votantes no era enviar a alguien a Washington que pudiera arreglar algo. A ellos no les importaba cuáles eran nuestras soluciones. Ellos querían que alguien fuera y quemara todo, y Trump era el hombre que parecía tener una lata de gasolina y un encendedor cada vez que iba en campaña. Él estaba listo para quemarlo todo, y eso emocionaba a la gente".

Resultó que los votantes de ambos lados concluyeron que no había esperanza de encontrar intereses comunes. Algunos de ellos, particularmente los obreros, decidieron cambiar en vez de luchar y se pasaron a la derecha. Sin embargo, también vimos confrontaciones sin precedentes y un nivel de hostilidad que no se había visto en este país desde la Guerra Civil. Las batallas sobre inmigración, control de armas, impuestos, servicios de salud, aborto, derechos, el ambiente y todo lo demás estaban llevando a los partidos al borde. Las emociones hervían en las comunidades en todo el país cuando las pandillas de ladrones y anarquistas izquierdistas trataron de forzar su participación en la conversación. Pero el hecho es que, el presidente Trump ganó las elecciones de 2016 a la antigua, ganando los votos de más de sesenta millones de ciudadanos y ganando los votos electorales de treinta estados.

Parece que la sorpresa más grande en esta historia en desarrollo era que durante la campaña, la administración del presidente saliente, apoyado por el Departamento de Justicia, el FBI, la CIA y una red de espías y operativos encubiertos, condujeron una misión de búsqueda y destrucción contra la campaña Trump. Durante varios meses, estos hombres y mujeres pusieron una trampa elaborada para que en el remoto caso de que Trump, de alguna forma, arrebatara la victoria de los brazos de Hillary Clinton, él no duraría mucho tiempo para poder causar suficiente daño. El hecho de que esta intentona golpista profunda ha fallado y que el Presidente ha defendido exitosamente su administración es casi un milagro tan grande como la elección en sí.

CONTRA TODO PRONÓSTICO

Donald Trump fue un candidato extraordinario que vino en un tiempo inesperado en nuestra historia. El desafío para el presidente Trump, como sucesor del primer organizador comunitario inspirado por Saul Alinsky, sería enorme; sin embargo, él tenía el apoyo entusiasta de millones de votantes en todo el país, y ellos lo cuidaban, así como él prometió cuidar de ellos. La elección fue evidencia del cambio en el estado de ánimo de los votantes estadounidenses. Nunca había sucedido algo como eso. Los simpatizantes de Trump eran de todas las razas, credos, trasfondos socioeconómicos y de partes del país de las que nunca se había oído que apoyaran a un republicano conservador para la presidencia. Nada pudo haber comprobado mejor que la nación había alcanzado un punto de inflexión.

Cuando Trump anunció inicialmente su plan de ser candidato presidencial, yo, como muchos, me preguntaba si él era realmente un conservador. Él había sido demócrata y republicano e independiente varias veces. Él estaba a favor del aborto antes de estar en contra. Era volátil e impredecible, y muchos se preguntaban si él podía ser alguien que dispara ante la más mínima provocación y llevarnos a la guerra. Como cristiano evangélico, me preguntaba si se podría confiar en que él cumpliría sus promesas de proteger la libertad de culto y ayudar a millones de cristianos perseguidos alrededor del mundo.

Desde entonces, el presidente Trump ha excedido toda expectativa. Ha comprobado tener un rasgo de carácter que no comparten muchos políticos: él realmente cumple sus promesas. Él ha usado la consigna "Promesa hecha, promesa cumplida" y una vez dijo bromeando que había cumplido más promesas de las que había hecho. Tal como lo señaló Michael Goodwin en el *New York Post*, la popularidad de Trump ha hecho cambios sísmicos en tantas áreas que el *Big Mo* (el momentum) ha cambiado de lado, de la izquierda a la derecha. Una gran razón, dice, es debido a la resolución reciente de la Corte Suprema a favor de las políticas de Trump. "La primera confirmación: su corrección a la prohibición de viajar para varias naciones de mayoría musulmana, diciendo que estaba dentro de su autoridad ejecutiva. Lo que reprendió a los jueces de las cortes de primera instancia, quienes habían creído la falsa noticia partidaria de que era una 'prohibición musulmana'. Sus fallos inválidos contrastaban duramente con las simples lecturas de la ley", dice Goodwin, "y demostró que son tretas empujadas por el viento político".[3]

La segunda resolución impidió que los sindicatos municipales obligaran a sus trabajadores a pagar cuotas sindicalistas. Esto se convertiría en un corte impositivo para los trabajadores y daría un golpe mayor al partido Demócrata en Nueva York, Nueva Jersey y otros estados azules. "El nexo entre los sindicatos y los demócratas convirtió a esos estados en feudos de un solo partido", escribe Goodwin, "y resultó en contratos sindicalistas que los contribuyentes no podían pagar". Ambas resoluciones se decidieron con 5 a 4 votos, donde el juez Anthony Kennedy proveyó el voto decisivo. Luego, con el retiro del juez Kennedy, el presidente pudo nominar a Brett Kavanaugh como su sucesor; y muy probablemente tendrá la oportunidad de consolidar su legado designando a un segundo o hasta un tercer juez antes de terminar su mandato. Decapitar el dominio liberal en la corte podría reducir las estrategias de la Izquierda a escombros y proveer un muro defensivo para los principios conservadores para las generaciones venideras.

EL PORQUÉ DE ESTE LIBRO

Este libro es mi intento de documentar lo que ha estado sucediendo desde la victoria de Trump en una forma que ayuda a los lectores a comprender mejor las dimensiones políticas, emocionales y espirituales de la elección que nos trajo a un líder así de complejo, impredecible y evidentemente dotado. Mirando en retrospectiva los encabezados, los videos y las noticias de los años ochenta y de los noventa, es irónico ver cómo Trump era amado por los medios cuando era un hombre de negocios extravagante y mujeriego. El *New York Times* dijo que Trump en su apogeo recibió más solicitudes de entrevistas que nadie en Nueva York. Sin embargo, cuando fue candidato presidencial como republicano, los liberales de la Costa Este y sus amigos en los medios hicieron un giro a la izquierda tan fuerte que tuvo que crearse una nueva frase para describirlo: *El síndrome del trastorno Trump.*

Sin embargo, una vez instalado en la Casa Blanca, Trump no cambió. En vez de eso, se propuso demostrar que él tenía soluciones verdaderas y funcionales. Se puso a trabajar rápidamente y alcanzó más que de lo que nadie pudo imaginar. Él sorprendió a muchos con la profundidad de su entendimiento y su fuerza de voluntad. Pero, tal como lo he atestiguado y lo documentaré en estas páginas, los medios no han estado dispuestos a darle el crédito por sus logros. Así que él usa sus asambleas y su cuenta de Twitter para jugarle la vuelta a los medios, y está funcionando. Los medios de comunicación saben que su base de apoyo más firme es la comunidad evangélica, y a ellos nada les encantaría más que poner una barrera entre el presidente y su base; cualquier cosa para debilitarlo a él y a su presidencia.

Durante mis apariciones en las redes noticieras liberales (a las cuales Trump llama redes de noticias falsas), me han pedido que explique por qué los cristianos evangélicos, quienes afirman ser tan morales, podrían ser tan hipócritas como para votar por un pecador como Trump. A veces me siento como si estuviera entrando a la cueva de los leones para defender al Presidente. Aunque yo fui capacitado como un periodista secular y trabajé en los medios seculares al inicio de mi carrera, tengo que estar de acuerdo con Trump en el apodo de "noticias falsas". La prensa secular se niega a darle a Trump el crédito por algo. Mi amigo Russell McClanahan me dijo una vez: "Si a Donald Trump inventara la cura para el cáncer, sus críticos dirían que él estaba quitándoles los negocios a los doctores". Mientras tanto, Barack Obama está dirigiendo un partido oponente fundado por izquierdistas radicales, como George Soros, tratando de imponer su voluntad socialista en la nación, y los medios principales tienen poco o nada que decir sobre eso.

La brecha entre la Izquierda y la Derecha se ha vuelto tan profunda que parece como si Estados Unidos estuviera en guerra contra sí mismo, y yo he escrito sobre eso en este libro con más detalle. Trump tiene una marca de potencia muscular única, lo que trajo a los coreanos del norte a la mesa de negociaciones, convenció a nuestros socios comerciales en Europa y China a revisar sus políticas tarifarias y ayudó a forjar nuevas alianzas con el Medio Oriente. Hoy, Israel y Arabia Saudita, quienes tienen en común a Irán como enemigo, se están hablando y compartiendo recursos entre sí. ¿Quién pudo haber imaginado tal cosa solo diez años atrás? Y la decisión de Trump de trasladar la embajada americana a Jerusalén fue un paso enorme y una bendición, no solo para la comunidad judía, sino para los cristianos sionistas como yo.

En mi libro *God and Donald Trump* mi objetivo era ver más de cerca la mano de Dios sobre el hombre que todos percibíamos como un líder imperfecto. Solo sobrevivir el temible reto de la nominación, vencer a dieciséis candidatos altamente calificados, fue un milagro. Como ya he mencionado, volé a Nueva York para la celebración de la victoria en la noche de las elecciones. Lo que me dio una perspectiva singular, pero la historia no terminó allí, tal como la mayoría de Estados Unidos pensó que sería. Las sorpresas continúan hasta el día de hoy a medida que los temblores del milagro de Trump ganan, siguen estremeciendo y enviando cambios sísmicos a través de la cultura y del mundo. Creo que Dios no solamente está sacudiendo al gobierno y a la cultura, sino que, además, está sacudiendo a la iglesia, lo que exploro al final de este libro.

Estoy convencido de que Dios está usando a Donald Trump de manera excepcional y sin precedentes, similar a la forma en que usó a Winston Churchill y hasta al general estadounidense George Patton cuando parecía como si los nazis iban a tomar control de toda Europa y el mundo estaba en la cuerda floja. Mientras investigaba y escribía este libro, en muchas ocasiones tuve la sensación de que estaba documentando la historia de una de las etapas más extraordinarias en la vida de nuestra nación.

Se han escrito muchos otros libros sobre este hombre, con mucho más porvenir. Sin embargo, mi objetivo ha sido ofrecer una perspectiva que, de otra manera, el lector promedio no podría ver. Haber escrito desde una cosmovisión cristiana que ve la mano de Dios en acción, espero haber podido proveer nuevos conocimientos y darle a usted algo en qué pensar y orar mientras continuamos, juntos, en esta aventura increíble y completamente inesperada.

–Stephen E. Strang
St. Augustine, Florida,
30 de junio de 2018

PARTE I

TEMBLOR Y ASOMBRO

PSICOSIS CAPITAL

ESDE LA ELECCIÓN 2016 y el ascenso de Donald Trump a la Casa Blanca, la Washington oficial y el establecimiento político ha estado en pandemonio perpetuo. Hay días cuando la vida de la capital de la nación parece más como un circo de tres pistas con actos de animales, domadores de leones y grupos de acróbatas haciendo su número en la cuerda floja, desafiando a la muerte. Incluso hay uno o dos tragafuegos, sin mencionar a los payasos y al eventual oso danzarín. Sin embargo, ya sea esta un simple teatro político o un surgimiento de locura genuina, el melodrama nunca deja de entretener. Es un espectáculo sin igual.

Todos los días, el mundo despierta con nuevas sorpresas, anuncios impactantes y revelaciones que dejan sin aliento. Las redes de cable y la internet arden constantemente con las afirmaciones atroces e igualmente apasionadas negaciones. Y las tormentas en el Twitter del Presidente determinan frecuentemente el ciclo de las noticias del día. Sin importar lo que cualquiera de nosotros piense o diga respecto a la figura central de este drama diario, el presidente Donald J. Trump es el epicentro indiscutible de la atención, y a él le encanta.

Para cuando Trump entró en la carrera, en junio de 2015, descendiendo por las escaleras en Trump Tower al ritmo del éxito musical de Neil Young, *Rockin' in the Free World*, él ya se había vuelto una figura polarizante, que inspiraba medidas iguales de admiración y angustia. Pero lo ame o lo odie, este presidente ha iniciado ondas de impacto de una magnitud que Washington nunca había visto, exponiendo las rupturas en nuestras fallas geológicas de política y cultura y sacudiendo la situación actual.

Intensificando la sensación de drama, está el hecho de que el electorado estadounidense ha estado cambiando en maneras extraordinarias, negándose a aceptar las promesas vacías de las administraciones previas. En la contienda final, larga y controvertida, de las elecciones de 2016, millones de votantes de la región central encontraron su voz, formando nuevas coaliciones y grupos de interés y convirtiéndose en una fuerza más volátil en el proceso político. Repentinamente, los miembros del Congreso fueron confrontados por un nuevo nivel de escrutinio público, junto con una gran dosis de justo enojo. Tanto demócratas como republicanos se vieron forzados a adaptar, ajustar y a mejorar sus tácticas para este ambiente nuevo y más exigente.

Inspirados por la promesa de campaña de Trump "hacer a Estados Unidos grande otra vez", millones que nunca habían votado, o que votaban rutinaria y predeciblemente por los demócratas, jalaron la palanca por el equipo Trump. Como resultado, Trump y los republicanos pudieron celebrar una victoria sorprendente, tomando el Congreso y la Casa Blanca por primera vez en más de una década. Pero esto era solo el principio. Aunque los demócratas sufrieron una derrota aplastante, y a pesar de las deserciones inesperadas en la base, la lucha apenas empezaba. En medio de las festividades después de las elecciones empezaron a aparecer, casi cada hora, desafíos nuevos y siniestros, y las amenazas a la nueva administración se volvieron más frecuentes e intensas durante las semanas y meses siguientes.

Como pronto descubriría el nuevo presidente, el pantano dentro de la circunvalación está lleno de peligros. Allí hay asesinos, saboteadores, cazarrecompensas y operativos clandestinos a la vuelta de cada esquina con la misión de debilitar, atrapar y someter a su presa. Plagados de filtraciones en el transcurso de los primeros meses en el cargo, el Presidente y su equipo empezaron a registrar en el poder ejecutivo para exponer a los miembros del personal que eran infieles o aparentemente vulnerables. La rampa de salida de la Casa Blanca pronto se convirtió en una vía pública para los una vez confiables aliados, incluyendo a Michael Flynn, Sean Spicer, Anthony Scaramucci, Steve Bannon, Sebastian Gorka, Rob Porter, Gary Cohn y Hope Hicks, entre muchos otros.

El vicepresidente, Mike Pence, por otro lado, permaneció como un partidario leal y confiable. Sin embargo, su lealtad al Presidente, junto con su franca fe cristiana, expuso al excongresista y gobernador de Indiana a los ataques incansables de la Izquierda. En marzo de 2018, el cómico del ala izquierda, John Oliver, hasta hizo un ataque de mal gusto contra la hija de Pence, Charlotte, en HBO, burlándose del libro infantil que ella había escrito para obras benéficas.

Desde la investidura, los medios principales han mantenido una campaña inagotable de rechazo al Presidente, su familia y sus consejeros clave con lo que solamente puede describirse como fervor partidario extremo. En septiembre, en un reporte del primer año del presidente en el cargo, el *Washington Post* reportó que el 91 por ciento de la cobertura de noticias durante el verano de 2017 fue negativa.[1] El artículo estaba basado en una investigación hecha por el *Media Research Center* (MRC),[2] que llegó casi a la misma conclusión después de un estudio de la cobertura de noticias de principios de 2018. En los primeros dos meses de 2018, las redes de televisión rara vez informaron sobre los logros de Trump. El crecimiento de la economía y los empleos alcanzaron solo doce minutos, y el impacto positivo de los cortes de impuestos, aprobados en diciembre de 2017, recibieron solamente nueve minutos de cobertura. El éxito militar en la guerra contra Al Qaeda e ISIS recibió solamente ochenta y tres segundos de cobertura.[3]

El análisis de los noticieros nocturnos en ABC, CBS, y NBC durante enero y febrero 2018, revela que, una vez más, el 91 por ciento de las noticias relacionadas con el Presidente fue negativo. Casi el 63 por ciento fue dedicado a escándalos como la investigación de Rusia (204 minutos), alegatos de violencia doméstica contra el auxiliar de la Casa Blanca, Rob Porter (54 minutos), y el chisme del libro de Michael Wolff (mucho del cual se ha determinado que está equivocado y confuso) acerca de la Casa Blanca y Trump (53 minutos).[4] Las redes creen aparentemente que su cobertura no debería diluirse enfocándose en cualquier asunto donde Trump estuviera teniendo éxito. El propósito de los principales medios, tal como el reporte de la MRC lo sugiere, ya no es el periodismo objetivo, sino el apoyo a la resistencia liberal Trump y la campaña para obstruir, avergonzar y, en última instancia, (con miras a la gloria de Bob Woodward y Carl Bernstein) desacreditar al presidente.

CONSTANCIA OFICIAL

Una historia objetiva poco común y sorprendente, publicada por *Newsweek* en el primer aniversario de la victoria electoral de Trump, ofreció a los lectores un recordatorio de algunos de los arrebatos más notables por parte de las celebridades y comentaristas anti-Trump. Todos reaccionaron un poco diferente, admitió el escritor, pero la reacción de la contingencia liberal era uniformemente predecible e implacable. "Trump envió a la Izquierda en picada", decía el artículo, "mientras demostraba que las encuestas y los comentaristas estaban equivocados y consiguió más de 300 votos del Colegio Electoral. Y aunque algunas de las preocupaciones de unos liberales de alto perfil pueden haber sido justificadas muchas de sus reacciones fueron un poco dramáticas". [5]

Durante los meses previos a las elecciones, la presentadora de la MSNBC, Rachel Maddow, le había asegurado a su público enfática y frecuentemente que Donald Trump nunca podría superar la ventaja dominante de Hillary Clinton. Señalando los mapas de colores brillantes que mostraban los patrones cambiantes en el terreno de batalla de los estados y los resultados de las encuestas nacionales que le daban a Clinton una ventaja clara, Maddow le dijo a sus seguidores: "Si hacen los cálculos relacionados con todos los votos electorales de todos los estados… y entonces digamos que Donald Trump tiene el mejor día en todo el mundo y supera completamente las expectativas y gana en todos los estados donde hay incertidumbre, gana esos cinco estados y el voto del Colegio Electoral en Maine que él persigue… aun si Donald Trump ganara en todos los estados inciertos, aun así, él perdería".[6]

Sin embargo, ya tarde en la noche de las elecciones, la historia era diferente. Una vez aclarado que Trump tenía la victoria en la mano, se compartió ampliamente un clip de octubre de la reportera de MSNBC porque parecía comunicar su reacción demasiado dramática ante los resultados electorales. "Están despiertos, por cierto", una Maddow desanimada les dijo a sus televidentes. "No están teniendo una pesadilla terrible. Tampoco están muertos, y no se han ido al infierno. Esta es su vida ahora". Hubo otros que tuvieron reacciones similares. Reconociendo que la administración y la agenda enfrentaban un cambio sustancial, el exconsejero de Obama, David Axelrod, reaccionó sobre la elección de Trump en CNN, diciendo: "Este fue un alarido primitivo de parte de muchos votantes que están desencantados con la situación actual".[7] Y tenían mucha razón.

Mientras tanto, el lanzallamas liberal Keith Olbermann, dijo: "Me gustaría empezar por felicitar al FBI por su operativo contra el proceso electoral de Estados Unidos de América. Ustedes han estado trabajando en uno de estos durante un tiempo ya, jóvenes, y sé que todos en el Bureau están muy contentos de que la "F" ahora también significa 'Fascista'".[8] La ironía de las palabras de Olbermann sería evidente cuando nos enteramos más y más de que el director del FBI, James Comey, y sus principales lugartenientes trabajaban de encubierto para debilitar al Presidente.

El libertario, autor y *blogger*, Andrew Sullivan, en su propio berrinche de desconsolación, escribió: "Los Estados Unidos ahora se han lanzado por el despeñadero constitucional…Hoy, estos son Estados Unidos de Trump. Él controla todo de ahora en adelante. Él ha ganado esta campaña en una manera tan decisiva que no le debe nada a nadie. Él ha destruido el Partido Republicano y lo rehízo a su imagen. Ha humillado a las élites y a la élite de los medios. Ha avergonzado a todos los encuestadores y a todos los opositores. Él se ha vengado de Obama. Y en las semanas venideras, probablemente Trump no se contentará con disfrutar de una vindicación".[9]

No todos los comentaristas fueron tan generosos. Sin embargo, el periodista y *blogger*, Jeff Jarvis, no pudo disfrazar su preferencia elitista cuando proclamó: "Yo lo diré: Esta es la victoria de los incultos y los ignorantes. Ahora, más que nunca, eso parece imposible de arreglar. Ellos gobiernan ahora".[10] Y el cineasta izquierdista, Michael Moore, nunca a favor de la sutileza, exclamó: "Tomen el control del Partido Demócrata y devuélvanselo al pueblo. Nos han fallado miserablemente… Despidan a todos los críticos, pronosticadores, encuestadores y a todos los demás en los medios que tenían un discurso que no querían soltar y se negaban a escuchar o reconocer lo que realmente estaba sucediendo. Esos mismos, que hablan pomposamente, ahora nos dirán que debemos 'sanar las heridas' y 'unirnos'… Sáquenlos".[11]

Entre las reacciones más coloridas, la comentadora política de CNN, Ana Navarro, dijo: "Hay que emplumar a todos los encuestadores. A cada uno de ellos. La próxima vez que alguien me muestre una encuesta, la voy a usar para empacar pescado".[12] Mientras tanto, en ABC, Joy Behar, coanfitriona de *The View*, expresaba su sorpresa y desencanto de que la Cámara, el Senado y la Casa Blanca estarían en manos republicanas. "Y entonces", exclamó, "el FBI ha metido su naricita asquerosa en medio de esto. Es más, la Corte Suprema, ¿quién sabe a dónde va a llegar eso? Así que el único sistema de control y equilibrio somos nosotros, *The View*, ¡Es todo!".[13]

Apoyar a su elegido

Quizás lo más desconcertante para los adversarios de Trump es el hecho de que, independientemente de lo que él diga o haga, y sin importar qué escándalos o fiascos logren reunir los medios, la base ha permanecido leal y continúa apoyando al Presidente y su agenda a toda costa. De hecho, pareciera haber un patrón insólito para los desastres de los medios que incluyen a Trump. Ya sean sus tuits sobre la Acción Diferida para los que llegaron en la infancia, los jugadores de la NFL que se arrodillan al momento del himno nacional, o sus críticas al grupo de jóvenes en Parkland, Florida, que protestaban contra las armas; cada intento de presentar al Presidente como rudo, insensible o, simplemente, equivocado cae en oídos sordos. Y, lo peor es que, en cuestión de días u horas, un evento grande aparece para confirmar que Trump lo hizo como se debe y que sus acusadores perdieron la oportunidad.

Estas vueltas del destino tienen a los críticos rascándose la cabeza. Yo experimenté personalmente su exasperación cuando varios entrevistadores de los noticieros nacionales empezaron por pedirme que explicara cómo los evangélicos podían pasar por alto los reportes de infidelidad y, aun así, apoyar al Presidente. En esencia, estos periodistas estaban diciendo: "¿Qué se necesitará para que los seguidores evangélicos de Trump lo abandonen finalmente?". En un editorial para el *Washington Post*, Gary Abernathy, columnista invitado y editor de periódico de Ohio, abordó esta pregunta. "A lo largo de los años", dijo, "ha sido comúnmente aceptado que todos los candidatos presidenciales dirán lo que sea con tal de ganar, y una vez en el cargo, esas promesas son abandonadas o ignoradas. Sin embargo, ese no es el caso con este presidente, quien 'ha permanecido tan constante como la estrella del norte'". Luego, el escritor dijo: "¿Trump se ha comportado realmente, de alguna manera nueva, que no estuviera completamente demostrada durante la campaña? Los tuits extravagantes, las jactancias, el autoengrandecimiento, los insultos, Trump el comandante en jefe es virtualmente idéntico a Trump el candidato neófito".[14]

Aun mientras él exhibe lo que los críticos consideran como atributos negativos, Trump ha trabajado diligentemente para cumplir sus promesas de campaña, incluyendo lo siguiente:

- Nombrar a un juez conservador en la Corte Suprema para reemplazar a Antonin Scalia

- Hacer de la seguridad fronteriza una máxima prioridad

- Promulgar recortes impositivos de gran alcance y ampliamente populares

- Revocar *Obamacare*

- Empoderar la manufactura y la producción energética estadounidense

- Reconocer a Jerusalén como la capital de Israel y ordenar que la Embajada de Estados Unidos fuera trasladada para allá.

"Nadie que haya apoyado a Trump como candidato, con todos sus defectos", escribe Abernathy, "ha recibido razones para abandonarlo".[15]

Entre todos sus errores, el único que muchos pensaron que llevaría la candidatura de Trump a un alto repentino fue la cinta cinematográfica *Access Hollywood* y la denuncia de varias mujeres de que Trump las había agredido sexualmente. "Sin embargo", dice Albernathy, "de lo que muchos liberales no se habían percatado era el hecho de que los medios ya habían declarado, durante la presidencia de Bill Clinton, que tales historias ya no eran relevantes". Los demócratas ya habían ganado ese debate desde mucho tiempo atrás. Consecuentemente, Trump era inmune a ese tema, y, tal como hice la referencia en varias entrevistas de los medios, ni *Access Hollywood*, ni el enredo más reciente de Stormy Daniels sería suficiente para desacelerar su *momentum*. Los votantes entienden que todos tenemos esqueletos en nuestros armarios, y el columnista añade: "La puerta del armario de Trump ha estado bien abierta desde hace mucho. Ninguna revelación nueva sobre su vida personal iba a sorprender o a sacudir a sus seguidores".[16]

Sorprendentemente, la corresponsal de BBC Estados Unidos, Katty Kay, parece haber llegado a una conclusión similar. "Para entender por qué aproximadamente entre el 35-38 por ciento de los estadounidenses aprueba consistentemente el trabajo que el Sr. Trump está haciendo, uno necesita volver a enmarcar la manera en que ve a sus votantes. Lo que importa no es lo que ellos aprueban, sino lo que ellos rechazan. Entonces, no es que un tercio de los votantes de Estados Unidos esté fervientemente del lado de Donald Trump "lo que es más relevante es que ellos están obstinadamente en el lado opuesto a una guerra cultural que ha estado gestándose aquí desde los años ochenta".[17]

Kay continua: "El Sr. Trump está contra el establecimiento político (los medios, el Partido Republicano, los grandes políticos como los Bush y los Clinton) y el cambio (que acompaña todo lo que uno tuvo, pero teme estarlo perdiendo) y está en contra del mundo (que se ha llevado trabajos y enviado inmigrantes a conquistar Estados Unidos). Las raíces de esta guerra cultural pueden rastrearse hasta la mayoría moral de Ronald Reagan. Incluso, los historiadores pueden retroceder hasta las explosiones cívicas de los años sesenta. Si cree que Estados Unidos está comprometido en una batalla de vida o muerte por su identidad, donde el pasado se ve dorado y el futuro, bueno, algo café, entonces, Sr. Trump, parece que él está de su lado".[18]

Un asunto de confianza

"Todo esto", dijo la presentadora", "explica por qué los abusos de Trump contra los medios de comunicación y la prensa liberal ganan puntos importantes con el electorado. "Por mucho tiempo, los conservadores en la zona central de Estados Unidos han creído, y con cierta justificación, que no pueden obtener una audiencia imparcial en la prensa estadounidense, la cual consideran como arrolladoramente costera y liberal. Creen que la prensa les ha hecho imposible ganar las elecciones". La fuerza de su resentimiento pudo verse en una encuesta de la Universidad Quinnipiac en noviembre de 2017 mostrando que el 80 por ciento de los republicamos confiaba más en Trump que en los medios. "No es de sorprenderse que sea su enemigo favorito", escribe Kay, "son las noticias falsas".[19]

Una confirmación similar de la perspectiva de esta comentadora viene de la revista semanal con base en Londres, *The Economist*, que comisionó a la encuestadora YouGov a muestrear opiniones republicanas sobre los medios. En la encuesta de mil quinientos estadounidenses, hallaron que la mayoría de los republicanos confían más en el Presidente que en los medios. Cuando se les preguntó por qué confiaban en Trump más que en el *New York Times*, el *Washington Post* o *CNN*, al menos el 70 por ciento estuvo del lado del Presidente. Un poco menos del 15 por ciento eligió a los medios. (El 15 por ciento restante estaba indeciso).

Los republicanos también prefirieron a Trump por encima de las publicaciones del Movimiento anti-Trump, el *Weekly Standard* y el *National Review*. En general, entre todos los noticieros, *Fox News Channel* fue considerado el mejor; no obstante, el 54 por ciento de los republicanos encuestados dijo que confiarían en el Presidente en vez de en la cadena Fox si llegara a haber un conflicto de opinión.[20]

Una acotación más del locutor Michael Medved podría aclarar el porqué del abismo entre la Izquierda y la Derecha en cuanto a los asuntos morales (lo que es algo que he tratado de explicar en CNN, MSNBC y Fox News cuando se dio a conocer la historia de Stormy Daniels). Una encuesta de *The Economist/YouGov* que exploraba opiniones discrepantes, les preguntó a sus encuestados si ellos estarían dispuestos a apoyar "a un candidato presidencial que hubiera cometido actos inmorales en su vida privada".[21] De manera sorprendente, los demócratas fueron menos indulgentes que los republicanos. El 48 por ciento de los republicanos estaría dispuesto a respaldar a un candidato con fallas morales, mientras que solo el 19 por ciento de los demócratas lo haría. "Después de tres décadas de obsesión con los profundamente imperfecto Bill y Hillary", escribe Medved, "esto cuenta como un shock".[22]

Sin embargo, más adelante, la encuesta *YouGov* también confirmó que, con relación a los asuntos morales, tales como aborto, matrimonio homosexual, sexo libre y el suicidio con ayuda médica, la mayoría de los demócratas tenían una opinión muy tolerante. "Estas cosas son sencillamente asuntos de elección personal", dijeron. Sin embargo, el hallazgo más sorprendente fue que el 82 por ciento de los demócratas cree que "cazar a un animal por deporte" está moralmente mal.[23] Si esto refleja su preocupación genuina por todos los seres vivos, uno pensaría que un infante humano, en el vientre de su madre, sería digno de protección. "Aun si alguien no considera que un bebé sea completamente humano antes de nacer", señala Medved, "con toda seguridad un niño no nacido merece tanto respeto como, digamos, un venado. Aun así, los demócratas hallan al aborto más aceptable que la cacería por un margen de tres a uno".[24]

LIBERTAD DE CONCIENCIA

En gran parte, la amargura y la hostilidad en la política contemporánea está centrada en estos asuntos, lo que hace que la moralización de la izquierda sobre los pecados del Presidente sea mucho más sorprendente. Y como mencioné antes, lo más desconcertante que contribuye a la angustia existencial entre los miembros del partido liberal es el enigma del apoyo incansable que los cristianos evangélicos le dan a Trump. Fui entrevistado por CNN, MSNBC y Fox News precisamente sobre este tema, el cual discutiré más a fondo en un próximo capítulo. A pesar de todas las revelaciones sucias sobre sus malas acciones del pasado, la calificación de preferencia por el Presidente entre los evangélicos permanece, hoy en día, tan alta como siempre. Más del 80 por ciento de los evangélicos blancos votó por Trump en el 2016, y ese nivel de apoyo alto ha cambiado muy poco. Incluso las revelaciones más lujuriosas aparentemente no han tenido un efecto a largo plazo en los fieles.

Se han escrito muchos libros y artículos en el intento de darle sentido a este enigma. Concluyeron falsamente que los cristianos evangélicos son fanáticos de cualquier líder franco con encanto carismático. Afirman que Donald Trump atrae a los evangélicos porque él es el líder carismático e iconoclasta de un movimiento grande y franco. En otras palabras, ellos lo siguen instintivamente como un substituto de la figura de Cristo. Nada ilustra mejor el disparate de los secularistas afirmando comprender el corazón de creyentes sinceros.

Jonathan Wilson-Hartgrove, un escritor de religión presentado en la revista *Time*, declaró que los evangélicos son seguidores de una religión esclavista que condena y subyuga negros, mujeres, homosexuales, ateos y creyentes de todas las otras religiones.[25] Aun así, otros comentaristas, tal como un antiguo escritor de discursos de la Casa Blanca, Michael Gerson, explotó en la expresión escrita afirmando que el apoyo de los cristianos por Donald Trump ha llevado a una crisis de evangelismo.[26] La suposición es aparentemente que votar por un hombre con un pasado ciertamente imperfecto es un acto de hipocresía, equivalente a una herejía rotunda. Sin embargo, como he tratado de señalar, los fieles no han vendido sus almas; más bien, han tomado una posición calculada con base en las alternativas políticas y su entendimiento de que todos los seres humanos son pecadores.

He publicado historias sobre evangélicos durante los últimos cuarenta años, así que conozco bien la historia. Ellos han visto, sin remedio, como sus costumbres y creencias religiosas han sido asaltadas por la institución educativa, los medios de comunicación, y los que más daño han hecho, las cortes federales. Los fallos de la Corte Suprema en los años sesenta, arrancaron a la oración y la lectura bíblica de las escuelas públicas. No hubo protestas, ni marchas. En vez de eso, los creyentes permanecieron en silencio, temiendo que no había nada que pudieran hacer. Sin embargo, ese era solo el principio. En las escuelas y en otros lugares públicos, se prohibieron los Diez Mandamientos junto con inscripciones, símbolos y la sabiduría acumulada de los patriotas estadounidenses que habían adornado cortes y monumentos por décadas. Hoy día, reposteros cristianos, floristas y organizadores de bodas, junto con propietarios de restaurantes, hoteles y lugares de descanso, están bajo la amenaza constante de perder su sustento, sus casas y su libertad de simplemente guiarse por los principios de su fe de larga tradición.

Para monitorear estos desarrollos, el *Family Research Council*, con base en Washington, emitió un reporte en 2014 titulado *"Hostility to Religion: The Growing Threat to Religious Liberty in the United States"*. El estudio documenta varios ejemplos de hostilidad evidente hacia la fe en Estados Unidos en cuatro áreas: (1) ataques a la expresión religiosa en la vía pública; (2) ataques a la expresión religiosa en las escuelas; (3) censura de las opiniones religiosas respecto a la sexualidad; y (4) supresión de opiniones religiosas sobre sexualidad usando leyes no discriminativas. Ese catálogo de violaciones, permaneciendo durante diez años, contiene noventa incidentes separados donde los valores y las prácticas cristianas han sido reprimidas, llevadas a juicio y penalizadas.[27] (Para ser transparente, también hubo algunos casos de hostilidad contra otras religiones).

"Para quienes se preguntan por qué los cristianos han favorecido consistentemente a Donald Trump, a lo largo de sus muchos desafíos", escribe Hugh Hewitt, "esta es la razón principal. Específicamente, se reduce a los enfrentamientos ejemplificados por el caso de *Masterpiece Cakeshop, Ltd. vs. Colorado Civil Rights Commission* discutido ante la Suprema Corte de Estados Unidos en diciembre de 2017. En este caso, el estado de Colorado resolvió que Jack Phillips, el dueño de *Masterpiece Cakeshop*, estaba violando la ley estatal al negarse a diseñar un pastel de bodas para celebrar ceremonias de matrimonio entre parejas del mismo sexo. La buena noticia es que, el 4 de junio de 2018, la Corte Suprema revirtió el juicio contra el dueño de la pastelería por una votación sorprendente de siete a dos bajo el argumento de que la Comisión de derechos civiles de Colorado había sido claramente hostil a la fe de Phillips en el caso inicial. El juez Anthony Kennedy presentó la opinión mayoritaria y el juez Neil Gorsuch, junto con el juez Samuel Alito, y la juez Elena Kagan, acompañados del juez Steven Breyer, presentaron opiniones concurrentes apoyando la decisión de la Corte.[28] Sin embargo, este es solo un ejemplo de cómo las cortes liberales han intentado usar leyes políticamente correctas para castigar a la gente de fe y restringir su libertad de consciencia.

Hewitt pregunta: "¿Se les permitirá a los estadounidenses practicar sus creencias religiosas sin temor a la ruina por parte de los absolutistas seculares? En la opinión de estos votantes, las élites creen que toda rodilla debe doblarse ante su credo secular, no solo en cuestiones relacionadas a la intimidad sexual, sino también en asuntos sobre cuando la vida empieza y cuando la muerte tiene que ser opcional. Mucha gente de fe está convencida de que su capacidad para creer, proclamar y practicar sus convicciones de fe genuinas está en peligro, no solo de ser ridiculizada sino también de ser castigada. Se escuchan a sí mismos de manera rutinaria e injustamente a los racistas intolerantes".[29]

El descontento es algo que Donald Trump entiende, y es también la razón por la que su compromiso de nombrar constitucionalistas fuertes en las cortes federales se convirtió en un incentivo muy importante para los votantes conservadores y cristianos. "Para muchos millones de personas de fe", explica Hewitt, "Trump es la última línea de defensa evitando que tengan que elegir entre sus creencias religiosas y la participación completa en la comunidad y en los negocios… Este se mantiene como un país profundamente religioso, y muchos de sus creyentes más apasionados desconfían de las cortes federales y de los productores de opinión a tal grado, que formarán una causa común con aquellos que protejan su libertad de consciencia. El derecho al "libre ejercicio" no es solamente uno de muchos derechos importantes para ellos; es el principal".[30]

DRENAR EL PANTANO

Durante la campaña presidencial larga y contenciosa de Donald Trump, quizás ninguna cosa era más aplaudida más consistentemente y con más fuerza que su promesa de "drenar el pantano". Gracias a muchos años de decepciones, derrotas y promesas rotas, los votantes entendían que sus intereses habían sufrido debido a la interferencia de fuerzas poderosas en Washington que trabajaban tras bambalinas. Como originario de Florida, conozco y entiendo los pantanos. Hay un pantano de quinientos mil acres al final de mi calle, y de ese pantano salen osos, coyotes, panteras y lagartos. Además, yo he sido un demócrata registrado y un republicano en diferentes ocasiones. Al igual que Ronald Reagan, yo no abandoné el partido Demócrata; el partido Demócrata me abandonó a mí. Aun así, muchas veces me siento incómodo con republicanos que hacen campaña como conservadores y gobiernan como liberales. Si acaso, muchos republicanos son tan parte del pantano como cualquier otro en Washington.

El candidato Trump dijo que entendía la ansiedad pública y prometió expulsar a los jugadores sigilosos de sus cómodos puestos de vanguardia. Fue un movimiento inteligente; sin embargo, ninguna cosa pudo haber hecho más para fortalecer a la resistencia afianzada contra él entre la legión de los abogados, cabilderos y grupos de intereses especiales de la *K-Street* acostumbrados al acceso privilegiado a la sede del poder.

"Ya sea que uno apoye al presidente Trump o no", escribe James Strock, "la nación tiene interés en su éxito en la transformación de la manera en que Washington funciona. Esta es un área donde hay un amplio acuerdo fuera de la capital". Quitarles la sonda alimenticia a los que habitan en el pantano es una iniciativa arriesgada, pero es uno de los pasos más importantes que Trump puede tomar para sacudir la cultura burocrática. Y es el medio más saludable para demoler lo que Strock llama "el sistema autosostenido de políticos, burócratas y su equipo de cabilderos, periodistas, intelectuales expertos y abogados que los apoyan".[31]

Aun con el amplio consenso, drenar el pantano podría demostrar ser el mayor desafío de Trump, tal como los opositores y los *anti-Trump* fueron raudos en señalar. Sin embargo, incluso el liberal *New York Times* está de acuerdo en que sería un error ignorar la importancia de este asunto. La necesidad de desenredar alianzas entre los operativos políticos ocultos y los legisladores y burócratas que les sirven rutinariamente es muy real, y el público está rotundamente de acuerdo. "Para muchos votantes que se cambiaron de partido", dijo el *Times*, "esto fue lo que los llevó a las urnas". El artículo, escrito por Brink Lindsey y Steve Teles, continuaba diciendo:

> Uno no puede hallarle sentido a su victoria sorprendente del año pasado sin hacer referencia a la caída en espiral de la fe pública en las élites gobernantes e instituciones establecidas. Años de salarios estancados, combinados con prospectos futuros desvaneciéndose, prepararon a los votantes para el mensaje de que el sistema estaba "arreglado" y que solamente alguien ajeno, no comprometido con la institución corrupta, podía limpiarlo
>
> La imagen del pantano comunica una verdad profunda sobre la economía estadounidense... Un factor importante es el acaparamiento de los sistemas políticos estadounidenses por parte de los infiltrados poderosos "grandes negocios, profesionales de élite, propietarios pudientes" que solían afianzar su propio poder económico. Al hacerlo, se protegían a sí mismos de la competencia, engordaban sus cuentas bancarias con dinero malversado y atrasaban la destrucción creativa que conduce al crecimiento económico.[32]

La imagen que estos escritores evocan no está lejos de la verdad. Incluso antes de su Informe Presidencial de enero de 2018, la administración Trump se había metido en el pantano y empezado el proceso de limpieza, abrazando completamente el 64 por ciento de los enunciados de agenda propuestos por la conservadora *Heritage Foundation* para cambiar la manera en que funciona Washington.

Sacar a Estados Unidos del Acuerdo de París sobre el cambio climático resultó ser una gran victoria de relaciones públicas para el Presidente, enviando una salva de advertencia al afianzado *lobby* del cambio climático en DC y ganándose los aplausos de parte de su base antiglobalista. Terminando con las regulaciones de la era Obama sobre la neutralidad de la red, fue otra. Luego, proponer y pasar un paquete de reforma tributaria por primera vez en una generación, por encima de las objeciones de los legisladores de ambos partidos, fue una secuela importante que llevó a, contrario a las advertencias de algunos medios, que los trabajadores estadounidenses llevaran a casa una paga más alta y bonos. Aprovechando las provisiones del *Congressional Review Act*, la administración trabajó con el Congreso para eliminar catorce regulaciones adoptadas en los días decrecientes de la administración Obama. El Presidente dejó en claro su intención de lidiar una batalla contra la regulación excesiva y empezó por quitar la suspensión de Obama sobre el usufructo del carbón en tierras federales. Luego, instruyó a todas las agencias ejecutivas a revisar las nuevas reglas, con el propósito de eliminar dos regulaciones por cada nueva que surgiera. Antes del fin de año, la administración había retirado, retrasado o inactivado mil quinientas regulaciones propuestas, ahorrando más de US$8 mil millones de costos vitalicios regulatorios netos, con la promesa de aumentar los ahorros a US$9.8 mil millones con el corte de costos regulatorios en 2018.[33]

Otra prioridad de la agenda del presidente Trump es la nominación y confirmación de jueces constitucionales conservadores, quizás mejor ilustrada por el nombramiento de los jueces Neil Gorsuch y Brett Kavanaugh a la Corte Suprema de los Estados Unidos. Trump también nominó y ganó la confirmación de doce jueces de circuito de los tribunales de apelación antes del final de este primer año en el cargo. Este fue el número más grande de jueces de apelaciones confirmado durante el primer año de gobierno de cualquier otro presidente estadounidense. Sin embargo, el desafío se volvería más complicado el año siguiente, mientras más de noventa de las nominaciones del Presidente fueron bloqueadas por el Senado.

Ya que la mayoría de los casos se resuelven a nivel de apelación, nombrar y confirmar a los constitucionalistas estrictos al estrado federal es un paso importante para reducir los enredos burocráticos tal como lo ha señalado repetidamente el equipo Trump. Cada año, se presentan hasta ocho mil casos ante la Corte Suprema, lo cual es mucho más de lo que cualquier corte puede considerar. La revisión plenaria, con debates orales por parte de los abogados de ambas partes, se concede en aproximadamente ocho casos por término, y hasta cien casos podrían ser resueltos sin una revisión plenaria. Solamente uno de cada setecientos casos escuchados por el tribunal de apelación podrá llegar a la Corte Suprema; así que, reducir el número de jueces activistas, eliminar la burocracia innecesaria y resolver las disputas tan pronto como sea posible es una victoria para la ley.[34]

RESISTENCIA Y OBSTRUCCIÓN

Como secuela de las elecciones presidenciales de 2016, las calles de Manhattan, Washington, Chicago, Filadelfia, Portland y San Francisco muchas veces parecían zonas de guerra, con un estallido de vandalismo y violencia, incluyendo ataques verbales y físicos contra el presidente recién electo y cualquiera que haya votado por él. Tal como lo reportó *Los Angeles Times*, muchos de los manifestantes eran jóvenes que protestaban por primera vez en su vida. En algunos casos, las multitudes fueron organizadas y manipuladas por agitadores profesionales financiados por los grupos izquierdistas y las organizaciones anarquistas internacionales.

Las imágenes televisadas mostraron miles de personas, jóvenes en su mayoría, marchando frente a la *Trump Tower* gritando: "¡Nueva York te odia!" y "¡No eres mi presidente!". Durante varios días, hubo manifestaciones contra Trump por todo el país mientras los activistas de izquierda y los jóvenes en las instalaciones universitarias coreaban "resistencia y obstrucción", jurando dificultar, si no imposibilitar, que la presidencia de Trump tuviera éxito. Esta resistencia tomaría muchas formas, pero ninguna ha sido más perturbadora que el esfuerzo de bloquear los nominados de Trump a las cortes.

Cuando el Presidente empezó el proceso de nominación para los cargos judiciales, habían más de cien vacantes que llenar, pero no había mucha duda de que el partido minoritario montaría un contraataque intenso para bloquear tantos nombramientos de Trump como fuera posible. Valiéndose de varias maniobras políticas y judiciales, el Senado republicano evitó exitosamente que la administración Obama saturara las cortes con juristas liberales. Los partidarios de Trump celebraban la victoria, pero los planes de la nueva administración de regresar las cortes a la derecha pronto se encontrarían con una resistencia igualmente fuerte por parte de los demócratas usando tácticas políticas que el *U.S. News & World Report* describió como comparable a "una contienda guerrillera".

Aunque se valieron de reglamentos legislativos secretos, retenciones de aprobación de los nominados locales y obstrucción a los nominados de Trump en todas las maneras posibles, no pudieron evitar que Trump obtuviera más jueces confirmados a los tribunales de apelación que cualquier otro presidente. Los demócratas estaban determinados a desgastar la agenda judicial del presidente hasta detenerla. El éxito de estas tácticas dejó al sistema judicial con tantas vacantes que los analistas legales de ambos bandos empezaron a decir que era una crisis judicial. "Tenemos a los demócratas viendo sus intereses personales y colocando barricadas enormes para obstaculizar la confirmación", dijo Carrie Severino, el jefe del consejo y director de políticas de la conservadora *Judicial Crisis Network*. "Están tratando de usar toda táctica de proceso que puedan para bloquear a los jueces [de Trump]".[35]

En particular, los demócratas se han esforzado en bloquear a los nominados que expresaron sus puntos de vista fuertemente conservadores o cristianos. Sin embargo, Trump no ha renunciado a su plan de instalar constitucionalistas estrictos en el estrado federal y continúa presionando al Congreso para obtener resultados. Para cuando cumplió seis meses en el cargo, el presidente ya había nominado dieciocho personas para las vacantes en las cortes de distrito, catorce para los tribunales de circuito y el Tribunal de Demandas Federales, y veintitrés fiscales federales. Tal como reportó *Business Insider*, "Durante ese mismo lapso, en el primero periodo del presidente Barak Obama, él había nominado solo cuatro jueces de distrito, cinco jueces de tribunales de apelación y trece fiscales federales. En total, Trump nominó 55 personas y Obama, solo 22".[36]

Sin embargo, el ritmo de las nominaciones, junto con la negativa de Trump para cambiar de dirección, solamente provocó que los demócratas intensificaran su resistencia. Los liberales temían que la confirmación de tantos jueces jóvenes y conservadores en los tribunales federales de todo el país tuviera un impacto a largo plazo en el sistema de justicia, poniendo en peligro la agenda progresista para las generaciones venideras. No obstante, la desventaja de la estrategia demócrata es que el nivel de obstrucción ha creado una crisis de procedimiento para los tribunales y el sistema de justicia en general. Casos importantes que tienen que ser escuchados y resueltos se están retrasando por un tiempo inadmisible, y algunos podrían quedar en el limbo por años.

La obstrucción sistemática ha hecho casi imposible que muchos individuos bien preparados puedan soportar el proceso de confirmación. Tal como Trump tuiteó el 14 de marzo de 2018, "Cientos de personas buenas, incluyendo embajadores y jueces muy importantes, están siendo bloqueados y/o lentamente acompañados por los demócratas en el Senado". Y él añadió: "Muchos cargos importantes en el Gobierno no se han podido llenar debido a esta obstrucción. ¡La peor en la historia de Estados Unidos!".[37] La agencia liberal de verificación de hechos, *PolitiFact*, en el *Tampa Bay Times*, confirmó que, al momento del tuit de Trump, solamente el 57 por ciento de los nominados por Trump había sido confirmo. Lo cual está por debajo de Obama (67 por ciento), George W. Bush (78 por ciento), Bill Clinton (81 por ciento) y George H. Bush (81 por ciento).[38]

"Las últimas dos semanas, hemos estado destacando los esfuerzos históricos de los demócratas en el Senado para obstruir la capacidad del gobierno para funcionar. Un sorprendente 43 por ciento de los nominados, altamente calificados, del presidente aún está esperando a ser confirmado en el Senado", dijo la secretaria de prensa de Trump, Sarah Sanders, durante una sesión informativa para la prensa el

7 de marzo de 2018. "Las tácticas autorizadas por el líder de la minoría del Senado, Chuck Schumer, añadió ella, "han derivado en 102 confirmaciones menos que la administración más cercana siguiente".[39] "Posteriormente", dijo un portavoz del líder de la mayoría del Senado, Mitch McConnel, "los demócratas se han tomado muchas molestias a fin de bloquear incluso a los nominados más altamente calificados que el presidente ha presentado y esto ha provocado un retraso innecesario para nuestro servicio exterior y la seguridad nacional en todo el mundo".[40]

Las reglas diseñadas para que el Senado sea más efectivo han logrado todo lo contrario. Durante la administración de Obama, los demócratas se quejaban de la obstrucción de los republicanos; sin embargo, repentinamente, la obstrucción y la resistencia son elogiadas como la única reacción razonable a la agenda legislativa del presidente. Bajo las reglas para cierre de debates del Senado, cualquier miembro del Senado puede retrasar un voto de confirmación por hasta treinta horas de debate mínimo. Durante esas treinta horas, no se finaliza ningún trabajo y ninguno de los nominados del presidente puede avanzar.

Sin embargo, el senador James Lankford (republicano, Oklahoma) ha llamado la atención al incremento dramático en el número de votos de debate sobre las nominaciones en el Senado durante la última década. Hubo un total de diecinueve intentos de cierre de debates en nominaciones en el Senado entre 1949 y 1992; era una señal de una atmósfera más restringida en el Senado en aquel tiempo. Hubo ocho intentos de cierre de debate en el 2005, y luego, por lo menos nueve cada año desde 2009 a 2012. En el 2017, sin embargo, hubo sesenta y siete intentos de cierre. "En el 2013, cuando Obama controlaba la Casa Blanca", escribe la columnista Debra J. Saunders, "los republicanos del Senado ayudaron a pasar una resolución para reducir el tiempo de debate post cierre de treinta a ocho horas para la mayoría de los nominados al poder ejecutivo. Lankford quiere que el Senado apruebe otra medida igual para detener las trabas hasta el 2018, y permitir que los nominados asuman con 51 votos o pierdan sin ellos".[41]

PROGRESAR EN EL CAOS

Desde el primer día, los temblores de su elección han continuado, y la presidencia Trump ha estado inmersa en la controversia. Algunos observadores de Trump se han preguntado por qué este presidente se encuentra en tantas disputas. Ya sea que esté acaparando los medios de comunicación tradicionales, expulsando diplomáticos extranjeros o despidiendo a otro jefe de personal, él está muchas veces en medio de una batalla tras otra. Para quienes siguen su *Twitter* a diario, con frecuencia parece que el Presidente está en guerra con el mundo. Donald Trump es polémico por naturaleza. Es un negociador dotado y un ejecutivo de negocios astuto que siempre espera ganar. Sin embargo, tal como señala Saunders, muchas personas creen que esta atmósfera de conflicto y caos no es casualidad; en realidad es parte de una estrategia deliberada. Trump es un hombre que progresa en el caos y a quien le encanta la emoción de la confrontación directa. Tal como el exsecretario de prensa de la Casa Blanca, Sean Spicer, dijo una vez "yo creo que él no retrocede ante una pelea".[42]

"Está claro que él prospera en el caos", dice la estratega del Partido Republicano, Alice Stewart. Ella añade que cuando Trump grita "noticias falsas", o reenvía un tuit con videos contra los musulmanes, "eso encuentra claramente eco en su base y los entusiasma y motiva, y hace que ellos presionen a sus congresistas". Mientras el presidente presiona al Congreso y, también, avanza en su agenda legislativa. "Pero la realidad es que su base no lo abandona. Ellos van a estar con él sin importar lo que pase".[43]

Cuando Trump despidió a su primer jefe de personal, Reince Priebus, y lo reemplazó con John Kelly, muchos pensaban que el ex general de la Marina iba a moderar la tormenta *Twitter* de Trump. Sin embargo, eso no sucedió. En vez de eso, Kelly pronto descubrió que la cuenta de *Twitter* de Trump estaba por encima de su control, y que había más que suficientes batallas diarias y desafíos de personal en que preocuparse. Kelly dejó en claro que su objetivo era sencillamente administrar el tráfico en la Oficina Oval.[44] La atmósfera de conflicto e incertidumbre es aparentemente un síntoma de la vida cotidiana en la Casa Blanca, pero también puede ser un reflejo de lo que se ha vuelto la política en el siglo veintiuno.

Tal como Kristen Soltis Anderson escribe en el *Washington Examiner* "Somos una nación dividida, e incluso estamos divididos en cuanto a *por qué* estamos divididos. Pero si hay algo que nos une, es que hay un sentido generalizado, a través de las líneas ideológicas y partidistas, de que algo en relación con la manera en que vivimos hoy día sencillamente parece insostenible… Estamos experimentando un desgaste de nuestra nación que dificulta imaginar que cualquiera de los otros grandes problemas, como el costo de la vida o la seguridad nacional, ver mejoras Más del 75 por ciento de los estadounidenses piensa que estamos muy divididos, una cifra que es la más alta registrada en décadas".[45]

Los votantes demócratas están enojados. Si no pueden hacer que Trump sea desacreditado, el objetivo sería bloquearlo en cada paso del camino. Excepto por los demócratas, la mayoría de los votantes no necesariamente quieren más estancamiento ni más conflicto. Según los datos de encuestas recientes, la mayoría de los votantes no quiere que el Congreso abra audiencias de destitución contra el Presidente; sin embargo, el 70 por ciento de los demócratas sí.[46] Cuando les preguntaron si querían tener un Congreso demócrata como un "sistema de control y equilibrio" sobre Trump, los votantes demócratas dijeron casi unánimemente que sí; sin embargo, solamente el treinta por ciento de los independientes estuvo de acuerdo, y un veintiuno por ciento de independientes dijo que preferirían un Congreso republicano para apoyar al Presidente.[47]

"Lo que la base demócrata quiere que haga su partido en el Congreso es sencillo: oponerse a Trump en cada vuelta", dice Anderson, "y si fuera posible, desacreditarlo... Si lo que los demócratas están promoviendo es más división y más estancamiento, le estarán dando un regalo enorme a los republicanos".[48]

Por su propia naturaleza, el sistema estadounidense de dos partidos que ha sido aclamado como un modelo, para el mundo es un campo de batalla donde las actitudes, ideologías y cosmovisiones chocan habitualmente. El debate es esencial y el desacuerdo es natural en nuestra forma de gobierno; sin embargo, también debería haber espacio para la cooperación y la reconciliación. Para muchos en ambos partidos, la elección de Donald Trump llegó como un impacto. Algunos en la derecha fueron igualmente antagonistas como los de la izquierda, y han estado luchado con las secuelas desde entonces. Sin embargo, lo que sea que suceda en los meses y años siguientes, y hacia donde quiera que la clase política trate de guiarnos, nunca debemos olvidar lo que tenemos en común. A pesar de las convicciones profundas que tenemos y que nos separan políticamente, compartimos una historia notable, y nuestro legado de fe, familia y libertad permanece como un modelo para el mundo. Republicano, demócrata o independiente, tenemos una herencia digna de ser defendida a cualquier costo.

EL PUNTO DE INFLEXIÓN

L OS TITULARES CELEBRANDO la victoria de Barak Obama en las elecciones de 2012 apenas acababan de ser publicados cuando los candidatos empezaron a alinearse para la campaña presidencial de 2016. Después de varios meses de tantear el terreno y de coquetear con donantes de mucho dinero, Hillary Clinton anunció su candidatura el 12 de abril de 2015. El senador socialista de Vermont, Bernie Sanders, surgió poco después, haciendo su primera declaración en televisión el 30 de abril de 2015. Sanders estaba convencido de que los demócratas fieles estaban preparados para algo completamente diferente. No lo estaban. Sin embargo, nunca hubo duda de que Hillary sería la campeona de los estados azules el día de las elecciones, a pesar de que llevaba la carga de la era Clinton y de que una mujer nunca había sido nominada ni elegida presidenta.

Los Clinton tienen un apetito insaciable por el poder, y la creencia común era que Hillary había hecho un pacto con Obama después de su derrota en las primarias de 2008. Ella estaba en su segundo período como senadora demócrata del estado de Nueva York y si tan solo se apartaba y cooperaba, Obama se aseguraría de que ella recibiera una cita estratégica. Por consiguiente, ella fue nombrada secretaria de Estado el 1 de diciembre de 2008, y confirmada solamente siete semanas después, prometiendo un apoyo incondicional al Presidente hasta que llegara su momento.

El gobernador de Maryland, Martin O'Malley, anunció su campaña presidencial en mayo de 2015, seguido por el gobernador de Rhode Island, Lincoln Chafee, en junio, y el senador de Virginia, Jim Webb en julio. Todos eran apenas conocidos más allá de sus estados de origen, aun así, cada uno hizo una carrera determinada en la candidatura demócrata, encabezada por más de una docena de aspirantes menos conocidos que nunca sobresalieron. Sin embargo, los oponentes de Clinton le ofrecieron un poco más que argumentos de pautas trazadas por el partido sobre temas que variaban desde control de armas de fuego hasta el cambio climático, lo que llevó al *New Republic* a concluir: "A los estadounidenses les encantan los que llevan las de perder; pero no Lincoln Chafee, Jim Webb ni Martin O'Malley".[1]

En comparación, el campo republicano se veía más como el Derby de Kentucky: una carrera de caballos a todo galope, postulando a dieciséis hombres y a una mujer, todos eran figuras muy conocidas públicamente, y acostumbrados, durante mucho tiempo, a ganar grandes carreras. Entre este grupo grande estaban nueve gobernadores actuales o previos, cinco congresistas actuales o previos, un expresidente corporativo y un médico distinguido.

De los diecisiete candidatos, conocí a cinco de ellos o hice campaña para ellos, así que empecé a preguntarme a quién apoyaría. ¿Sería a Mike Huckabee, para quien recaudé dinero cuando quedó en segundo lugar para la nominación de 2008? ¿O, tal vez, a Marco Rubio, a quien apoyé en el 2010 cuando se postuló para su larga carrera por el Senado de los Estados Unidos? Conocí a Rick Santorum después de apoyarlo en el 2012, y él me solicitó personalmente apoyo en 2016. Luego, en el 2015, asistí a una reunión de oración en Baton Rouge, Louisiana, y me invitaron a cenar a la Mansión del Gobernador y luego orar por Bobby Jindal, quien estaba por decidirse si debiera postularse para presidente. Finalmente, conocí y entrevisté al senador Ted Cruz de Texas y decidí respaldarlo.

Yo sabía que él era un cristiano devoto. Sin embargo, mientras veía la campaña desarrollarse, me di cuenta de que pude haber apoyado a cualquiera de los diecisiete en la competencia contra la candidata demócrata, solo basándome en la diferencia en las plataformas políticas.

Todos hicieron sus discursos con diversos grados de aplauso y triunfo, pero ninguno logró capturar la imaginación del público. El candidato que ocupó el centro del escenario en cada evento fue el único hombre que todos los otros candidatos estaban determinados a vencer. Era Donald Trump contra el mundo, y estaba haciendo un espectáculo.

A pesar del alto nivel de descontento con Washington y la demanda del público por un fuereño rudo y agresivo, la mayoría de la gente estaba sorprendida cuando Donald Trump lo oficializó y entró en la contienda. El neoyorquino extravagante había insinuado muchas veces entrar a la contienda electoral; pero muchos, incluyéndome, lo vimos como una caricatura. Él era una estrella de un *reality show*, un fanfarrón, un propietario de casinos y un mujeriego. Difícilmente alguien lo tomó en serio hasta que hizo realmente el anuncio. Luego, como candidato, Trump empezó a articular un mensaje que hizo eco poderosamente con los votantes descontentos en el centro del país, las multitudes en sus mítines a lo largo de las planicies fructíferas creció a decenas de miles y, repentinamente, el candidato con menos posibilidades estaba a la cabeza de la contienda electoral.

El Comité Nacional Republicano le dio su bendición al exgobernador de la Florida, Jeb Bush, pero los votantes no estaban impresionados. Aunque Bush no fue un mal gobernador, yo no sentía que él estuviera listo para guiar a la nación. Resulta que la gente arduamente trabajadora del centro de Estados Unidos tampoco estaba interesada en el hijo menor de la familia Bush. Mientras que hubo coqueteos breves con Cruz, Rubio, John Kasich y uno o dos más, el cortejo no duró. Los votantes conservadores estaban buscando un agente de cambio que fuera duro, que no solo cambiaría el equilibrio del poder en Washington, sino que, además, alteraría la institución en ambos partidos políticos. Ellos querían un presidente que pudiera soportar el calor y drenar el pantano de los burócratas atrincherados en políticas que estaban llevando al país en la dirección equivocada y hundiéndolo más en la deuda.

Muchos estadounidenses sintieron que la nación estaba en una situación precaria, al borde del desastre o posiblemente de la guerra civil, debido a los cambios radicales que Obama había impuesto durante los seis años anteriores. Haciendo uso de órdenes ejecutivas, comunicaciones oficiales y "otros asuntos regulatorios oscuros", Obama había eludido los procedimientos legislativos habituales para implementar directivas poco populares que nunca hubieran pasado la asamblea del Congreso ni de los tribunales.[2]

Al final de su segundo mandato, Obama había emitido 276 órdenes ejecutivas; sin embargo, tal como lo reportara la revista *Forbes*, estas ni siquiera fueron las más preocupantes de los principales decretos de la administración. Las comunicaciones confidenciales y las publicaciones de "orientación" serían las más problemáticas para la administración entrante. Es posible que las directivas menos conocidas nunca aparezcan en el *Registro Federal*, y puede ser difícil descubrirlas y rescindir de ellas. Esto les permite dirigir las políticas de burócratas secretos e irresponsables en los años venideros.[3]

Como escribí en otra parte, el encumbramiento de Donald Trump a la presidencia de Estados Unidos fue un acto desesperado por parte del electorado. Él no era la clase de persona que esperábamos como presidente estadounidense, pero eso comprobó finalmente ser su mayor ventaja. Él no era un político. Él no pertenecía a ninguna entidad del gobierno federal. Él era un candidato de campaña electoral, una bola de demolición y, fiel a su palabra, estaba haciendo temblar las ventanas en la Casa Blanca aun antes de llegar.

Nunca olvidaré la noche en que Trump fue electo, y puedo decirle que para el partido que estaba siendo expulsado de la Casa Blanca, la elección de Trump impactó como un terremoto enviando ondas de asombro a través de las entidades políticas, los medios y los observadores de Washington en todo el mundo. Sin embargo, nadie estuvo más devastada que la rival demócrata de Trump, quien corrió a esconderse en la noche de las elecciones, negándose a dirigirse a los medios o a admitir que había sido rotundamente derrotada. Sin embargo, Clinton no fue la única sacudida por la victoria de Trump; y las recriminaciones y señalamientos apenas empezaban cuando las legiones izquierdistas tomaron las calles y la aversión del anarquismo y el movimiento de la resistencia empezaron con toda su fuerza.

Para el 9 de noviembre de 2016, los batallones de tropas de la ofensiva izquierdista, acompañados por multitudes de viajeros simpatizantes fácilmente manipulables fueron movilizados a ciudades y pueblos por todo el país. Los grupos anarquistas dieron a conocer sus intenciones con letreros, pancartas y banderas impresas profesionalmente, impulsados por miles de fanáticos de alquiler transportados para atacar las calles de Nueva York, Filadelfia, Los Ángeles, Portland y Washington, D.C., cuando se les diera la orden. Tan pronto como empezaron las manifestaciones, los medios de comunicación liberales celebraban el nacimiento de un movimiento representando falsamente como un desahogo espontáneo de resistencia por estadounidenses comunes decepcionados por la victoria republicana.

Sin embargo, estos manifestantes eran de todo menos ordinarios. Ocultando sus rostros tras capuchas, gorras pasamontañas, cascos de motocicleta y vestidos completamente de negro, los anarquistas aseguraron que estaban allí para "resistir y obstruir" cada movimiento que hiciera el nuevo presidente, su gabinete y el Congreso republicano. Pero las turbas, en algunos casos incitadas por activistas europeos Antifa, también tenían hambre de violencia. Quebraron las ventanas de las tiendas, voltearon vehículos y los quemaron, y hubo asaltos sangrientos a civiles inocentes. Avergonzados por su propia incapacidad de leer el estado de ánimo de la nación o de pronosticar lo que acababa de suceder, a los principales medios de comunicación les parecía que la violencia era aparentemente una reacción perfectamente natural. ¿Se imagina si los republicanos hubieran reaccionado de esta manera en la elección de Obama en el 2008? Los medios habrían condenado rotundamente a esa o a cualquier otra que el bando perdedor organizara en cualquier elección debidamente calificada.

LA MANO INVISIBLE

Las pandillas callejeras y los anarquistas del bloque negro pueden haber sido el rostro del movimiento, pero la mano que guiaba detrás esta insurrección planeada cuidadosamente fue un hombre que muchos asumían que estaba fuera del proceso electoral. El multimillonario húngaro György Schwartz, mejor conocido como George Soros, no era un observador pasivo, tal como lo documento a profundidad más adelante en este libro. Como quizá el mayor donante del partido democrático, él gasto US$27 millones para derrotar a George W. Bush en el 2004, y dio más de US$ 25 millones para financiar la campaña de Hillary Clinton en el 2016, junto con otros candidatos y causas demócratas.[4]

Él canalizó miles de millones para grupos de izquierda como *MoveOn.org*, *Media Matters*, el *Center for American Progress*, la *Democracy Alliance*, la *Open Society Foundations* y muchos otros. Y según un reporte de 2011 del Centro de Investigación de Medios, Soros tiene vínculos directos con treinta organizaciones de medios, seguramente para influir y manipular la cobertura de noticias a favor de políticos liberales e izquierdistas.[5] Está claro que esto no es filantropía.

Soros hizo gran parte de su fortuna como depredador financista, devastando la economía europea más de una vez y destruyendo virtualmente la moneda en varias naciones. En el libro *More Money Than God*, el escritor financiero, Sebastian Mallaby, revela como Soros usó los activos de su fondo *Quantum* en 1992 para provocar la caída de la libra esterlina y embolsarse mil millones de dólares. Él fue condenado por un tribunal francés en el 2002 por obtener más de US$2.3 millones en 1998 por medio de la explotación de información privilegiada y la manipulación de acciones del banco francés *Société Générale*. Sus apelaciones subsecuentes ante el Tribunal Europeo fallaron y fue multado con 2.2 millones de euros, equivalentes a la cantidad que obtuvo.[6]

Sin embargo, nada de esto le impidió a Soros crear y financiar grupos izquierdistas para debilitar instituciones democráticas, el sistema capitalista y el gobierno de Estados Unidos. Soros ha contribuido US$32 mil millones para financiar la *Open Society Foundations*, la cual funciona en más de cien países alrededor del mundo y que promueve una agenda de fronteras abiertas. En el pasado, nadie parecía comprender el peligro que representa Soros o los grupos que él apoya. Más recientemente, los conservadores saben ampliamente que la política de fronteras abiertas de tales grupos es en gran parte, responsable de la debacle inmigratoria que ha devastado a Europa Occidental y que amenaza con hacer lo mismo en Estados Unidos. Después de la elección de Trump, se informó que Soros dio US$18 mil millones a la Fundación para una acción inmediata contra el Presidente; lo que significaba más manifestaciones y violencia si fuera necesario.

Aunque asegura ser una organización independiente de investigación objetiva, *Media Matters* es mejor conocida como una máquina izquierdista de desprestigio cuya misión es desacreditar conservadores por cualquier y todos los medios necesarios. La organización está fundada por Soros y otros activistas de izquierda a través de la Alianza Demócrata, compuesta por cerca de cien millonarios y multimillonarios con tendencia izquierdista y organizaciones activistas 501(c)4 relacionadas. Tal como lo describen los autores David Horowitz y Richard Poe:

> George Soros es el arquitecto de un "Partido en la sombra", el cual funciona de manera muy parecida a una red de empresas de control que coordinan las distintas ramas de este movimiento, tanto dentro como fuera del Partido Demócrata, y las dirige con el propósito de asegurar el poder estatal. Una vez alcanzado, ese poder se usará para efectuar una transformación mundial: económica, social y política.[7]

Aunque algunos en el Partido Demócrata estarían impresionados por el grado al que este partido en la sombra ha infiltrado y manipulado su comunidad, un gran número de demócratas leales han sido involucrados como participantes voluntarios y defensores de un ataque revolucionario a los valores tradicionales. Gran parte del vituperio dirigido a Donald Trump y el Partido Republicano es resultado directo de la retórica acalorada que surge de individuos y grupos que repudian la historia auténtica de este país. Financiados por ideólogos y radicales megarricos, estos grupos y soldados rasos que ellos han facultado trabajan metódicamente para transformar la nación en algo que nuestros ancestros nunca reconocerían y que lamentarían profundamente.

Al igual que muchos de los votantes que apoyaron a Donald Trump en 2016, yo estuve comprometido con otros candidatos al principio de la contienda, pero llegamos aquí porque hemos visto más que suficiente de la llamada "agenda progresiva". Pudimos ver lo que lo políticamente correcto y la idea de diversidad y tolerancia de la Izquierda estaban haciéndole al país. Trump tenía pocas posibilidades cuando entró a la contienda, pero él decía lo que los votantes conservadores y de clase media querían escuchar, y una gran franja del electorado se dio cuenta que la visión de Clinton para Estados Unidos sería solamente más de la misma "esperanza y cambio" radical que sufrieron durante los últimos ochos años.

Trump era audaz, franco, abrasivo e imparable, pero comprendía las emociones de los hombres y mujeres estadounidenses promedio. Y él entendía la importancia del voto cristiano, reuniéndose desde el 2012 con líderes evangélicos, la mayoría de ellos carismáticos, para pedirles que oraran para saber si él debía postularse para la presidencia. Él había crecido en un hogar presbiteriano y era amigo del Dr. Norman Vincent Peale. Sin embargo, él era conocido como un *playboy* multimillonario, no como un cristiano escrupuloso. Sin embargo, tal como lo describí en mi primer libro, él empezó a ver televisión cristiana a principios de la década de 2000, y hasta llamó a mi amiga, Paula White Cain, cuyo programa él veía. Recuerdo a Paula contándonos a mi esposa y a mí, durante una cena, que su oficina había recibido una llamada de una celebridad de nombre Donald Trump, quien le preguntó si se podía reunir con él para discutir algunas preguntas espirituales que él tenía. Una década después, con el consejo de Paula, él se acercó a líderes cristianos, y prometió hacerse cargo de los problemas que preocupaban a la gente de fe. La candidata demócrata, por otro lado, se refirió a los partidarios evangélicos de Trump como una "canasta de deplorables" e ignoró por completo a la comunidad de fe.

Los principales medios de comunicación estaban totalmente de acuerdo con la campaña de Clinton; sin embargo, una ola de apoyo de los votantes hartos de la manera en que Washington hace las cosas llevó a Donald Trump rápidamente al cargo. Ellos no le estaban poniendo atención a los medios de comunicación liberales y tampoco estaban respondiendo sus encuestas. Habían alcanzado el punto de inflexión, y no iban a seguir aguantando. Tal como señaló Malcolm Gladwell en su éxito de ventas *The Tipping Point: How Little Things Can Make a Big Difference*, el cambio revolucionario muchas veces llega repentinamente y sin aviso previo. Sucede en la naturaleza y también puede ocurrir en la gente. Leí ese libro cuando recién acababa de salir y lo recomendé a otros porque ayuda a explicar por qué sucede lo inesperado.

Cuando un grupo suficientemente grande llega a un nivel de frustración suficientemente alto, con frecuencia hay una combustión espontánea. Al principio, los miembros del grupo ignorado y privado del derecho al voto tratan de hablar. Pero, si no se les presta atención a sus intereses o si son rechazados, y si no hay indicios de mejoría, puede haber una explosión repentina e irresistible de resentimiento que lleve a un cambio de dirección sin precedentes. Esto es obviamente lo que sucedió en el movimiento de los derechos civiles, y creo que explica en gran parte el temblor que hemos experimentado desde las elecciones de 2016.[8]

Las revoluciones no suceden simplemente. Suceden a causa de la frustración, las decepciones, los insultos y las provocaciones de muchas clases que impulsan a la gente a responder en maneras revolucionarias. Ya sea que sucedan en política o en alguna otra área de la sociedad, las revoluciones siempre son un fenómeno volátil. Pueden suceder después de años de estrés e ira, pero nunca se tratan de una sola cosa. Resultan de un listado largo de ofensas, percibidas y reales, que preparan una cadena natural de reacción que rápidamente se vuelve irreversible. La liberación repentina de presiones continuas es explosiva y frecuentemente lleva a consecuencias impredecibles.

Millones de estadounidenses sienten que la nación ha estado yendo en la dirección equivocada. La retórica que escuchamos en los medios de comunicación, en la internet o de los amigos y familiares refleja la tensión que se está acumulando en nuestra sociedad. Por todo el país, estadounidenses promedio están uniendo fuerzas y haciendo donativos para los candidatos que han prometido desafiar la dirección en la que nuestros líderes nos han llevado durante los últimos cuarenta años. Tal como escribe Richard G. Lee en *The Coming Revolution*:

> En su mayoría, todos estos son ciudadanos promedio, hombres y mujeres de toda clase social, y personas que nunca han estado políticamente involucradas de esta manera. Sin embargo, a través de sus esfuerzos combinados, están expresándose con un nuevo sentido de urgencia, determinados a terminar con lo que millones ahora perciben como un comportamiento arrogante y depredador por parte de los burócratas de Washington y otros funcionarios electos y no electos que ejercen demasiado poder.[9]

No hay que confundir la emoción ni la intensidad de aquellos que claman por un cambio. En la comunidad cristiana, millones estaban orando. Grandes reuniones, como las de *The Call*, dirigida por mi amigo Lou Engle, no protestaban por nada, sino que intercedían públicamente por nuestra nación y la necesidad de un avivamiento en Estados Unidos. En el 2016, Donald Trump fue el beneficiario de la indignación del público y una respuesta a las oraciones de los cristianos. Los encuestadores y los críticos no lo habían entendido; ellos reportaban lo que querían creer en vez de lo que realmente sucedía en el corazón del país y, por esta razón, el mundo reaccionó con conmoción y asombro después de la elección. Había sido manipulado y engañado.

Desde la toma de posesión, el presidente Trump ha estado en una batalla campal con los defensores del régimen anterior. Agitación en el Departamento de Justicia, acusaciones de conspiración con Rusia, las filtraciones de su propio personal en la Casa Blanca y funcionarios de alto nivel en el Departamento de Estado y el Pentágono han creado una situación inestable. Todo esto ilustra no solo las divisiones que agitan a la nación hoy día, sino el grado en que los antagonistas dentro de la de burocracia permanente, junto con los subversivos del "subgobierno" (también conocido como el "estado profundo") trabajan para debilitar la legitimidad del Presidente y guiar a la nación, consciente o inconscientemente, al borde de una guerra civil.

Enfrentarse al mundo

En su discurso a los delegados en el Foro Económico Mundial en Davos, Suiza, en enero de 2018, el presidente Trump entró en lo que muchos conservadores describirían como "el campo enemigo". Sin embargo, cuando llegó, fue casi rodeado por una multitud de simpatizantes, uno de ellos le entregó un ejemplar del libro *God and Donald Trump*. Mientras docenas de espectadores fotografiaban y grababan con sus celulares cada uno de los movimientos de Trump, él sostenía el libro en alto; por supuesto, eso fue algo que me sorprendió y me agradó cuando vi las fotografías en los medios sociales. Aunque inicialmente él no fue invitado a esta confabulación de agentes mundiales de poder, el Presidente viajó a Davos para hacer una declaración, para manifestar entusiastamente que "Estados Unidos está listo para hacer negocios". Él dijo que estaba allí para ofrecer una mano de amistad y una oportunidad económica al mundo. Y en una acotación enfática, dijo: "El mundo está atestiguando el resurgimiento de un Estados Unidos fuerte y próspero... Somos competitivos otra vez".[10]

Como lo mencionaron los reporteros del *New York Times* y otros medios de comunicación presentes, su discurso de "una de las reuniones de mayor escala mundial" no fue lo que cualquiera hubiera esperado.[11] Un comentario de Reuters indicaba que muchos temían que el discurso de Trump fuera un "choque de civilizaciones".[12] Después de todo, este era, por excelencia, un territorio de George Soros, territorio de los Bilderberg y otras reuniones secretas de élite. Sin embargo, Trump estaba allí para hablar de cómo las políticas económicas implementadas desde su elección estaban haciendo de Estados Unidos un mercado más atractivo para los inversionistas internacionales.

"Estoy aquí hoy", dijo, "para representar los intereses del pueblo estadounidense y para afirmar la amistad y la asociación de Estados Unidos en la construcción de un mundo mejor. Al igual que todas las naciones representadas en este gran foro, Estados Unidos espera un futuro donde todos puedan prosperar y cada niño pueda crecer sin violencia, pobreza y sin temor". Mientras que evitaba tocar temas candentes, tales como el cambio climático, geopolítica o cualquiera de los desafíos específicos en la diplomacia internacional, Trump les dijo a los delegados que él "siempre pondría a Estados Unidos en primer lugar, de la misma manera en que los líderes de otros países deberían poner su país en primer lugar también. Sin embargo, Estados Unidos primero no significa Estados Unidos a solas. Cuando Estados Unidos crece, el mundo también crece".[13]

Tal como reportó el *New York Times*, "los oradores del Foro Económico Mundial generalmente celebran la globalización, elogian la diversidad y denuncian el cambio climático. Así que el discurso del viernes por el presidente Trump, quien a veces ha expresado su escepticismo en las tres posturas, fue cautelosamente esperado por la asamblea de líderes empresariales y de gobierno".[14] Sin embargo, para esta ocasión, ninguno de esos temas estaba en la agenda del Presidente. En cambio, entregó un fuerte respaldo a la reciente legislación tributaria republicana, pronosticando una oleada de optimismo cuando comenzaran las reducciones de impuestos y los aumentos de sueldo.

El Presidente les aseguró a los líderes empresariales y gubernamentales que él favorece el libre comercio, en tanto las prácticas comerciales abusivas hacia Estados Unidos sean reducidas y eliminadas. A principios de la semana, el Secretario de Comercio, Wilbur Ross, había advertido que Estados Unidos estaba harto de "ser una presa fácil" en el comercio internacional y que las tarifas en importaciones eran una posibilidad perceptible.[15] Sin embargo, con solo una referencia implícita a China, Trump dijo: "Los Estados Unidos ya no se harán de la vista gorda ante las prácticas económicas injustas, incluyendo el robo masivo de la propiedad intelectual, los subsidios industriales ni la planificación económica generalizada dirigida por el estado.

"Estos y otros comportamientos depredadores", añadió, "están distorsionando los mercados mundiales y perjudicando a empresas y trabajadores, no solo en Estados Unidos, sino alrededor del mundo".[16] Luego, el Presidente enfatizó "la importancia de elevar la prosperidad de todos los estadounidenses, mencionando particularmente al bajo desempleo entre los afroamericanos… Dijo que Estados Unidos estaba 'levantando comunidades olvidadas' y cumpliendo los sueños de los estadounidenses por 'un excelente trabajo, un hogar seguro y una vida mejor para sus hijos'".[17]

El impacto de las palabras del Presidente fue visible casi inmediatamente en el repentino aumento de las acciones en el mercado de valores, tanto en el país como en el mundo.[18] *The Irish Examiner* informó que "impulsado por un discurso del presidente de Estados Unidos, Donald Trump, que se consideró más moderado y presidencial, y que ayudó a aliviar los impresionantes resultados del fabricante de chips Intel, los mercados bursátiles europeos subieron y muchas acciones estadounidenses alcanzaron niveles récord".[19] Trump señaló que el mercado bursátil estadounidense ya estaba "rompiendo un récord tras otro".[20] Durante la semana previa, el *Dow Jones Industrial Average* había superado la marca de veintiséis mil por primera vez en la historia. Los niveles máximos me recordaron un artículo en el *New York Times* escrito por Andrew Ross Sorkin que había leído la semana antes de las elecciones. Sorkin escribió: "Suponga, por un momento, que Donald J. Trump gana la presidencia... desde el primer momento, el mercado bursátil caería precipitadamente".[21]

Luego, al día siguiente de las elecciones, el economista graduado de la universidad Princeton, Paul Krugman, escribió en el *New York Times* que los mercados se estaban hundiendo, y, "si la pregunta es cuándo se van a recuperar los mercados, la respuesta de primer paso es 'nunca'". Él también predijo una "recesión mundial" después de la derrota electoral de Hillary Clinton, "sin que se vislumbre un final".[22] Curiosamente, no se ha escuchado mucho de ninguno de ellos desde la explosión del mercado de valores.

Los récords máximos históricos fueron buenas noticias para la mayoría de los inversionistas, pero no lo que George Soros estaba preparado a escuchar, tal como lo dejó en claro durante sus propios comentarios en Davos un día antes, asegurando que Trump estaba empujando al mundo hacia una guerra nuclear y tratando de establecer una dictadura derechista en Estados Unidos. Él dijo:

> Sin duda, Estados Unidos está en curso hacia la guerra nuclear al negarse a aceptar que Corea del Norte se ha convertido en un poder nuclear. Esto crea un incentivo fuerte para que Corea del Norte desarrolle su capacidad nuclear con toda la velocidad posible, lo que, a su vez, inducirá a Estados Unidos a usar su superioridad nuclear preventivamente, en efecto, para empezar una guerra nuclear a fin de evitar una guerra nuclear, una estrategia que obviamente se contradice.[23]

Además, Soros dijo que Trump estaba tratando de instituir un "estado de mafia" en Estados Unidos, pero no había podido "porque la Constitución, otras instituciones y una sociedad civil dinámica no se lo permitirían". Por otro lado, el multimillonario de ochenta y siete años, dijo que está usando a *Open Society Foundations*, la organización a la que acababa de darle otros US$18 mil millones para "[proteger] los logros demócratas del pasado". Y agregó: "No solo la sobrevivencia de la sociedad abierta, sino la sobrevivencia de toda nuestra civilización está en juego".[24]

Mientras muchos estadounidenses celebraban el salto de los precios en las acciones, después de la elección de Trump, Soros había perdido hasta mil millones de dólares. Él había invertido fuertemente esperando una victoria para Clinton, pero apostó por el caballo equivocado. Aprovechando su discurso en Davos, pasó a hacer lo que algunos periodistas percibieron como "una amenaza encubierta contra el Presidente",[25] diciendo: "Claramente, considero a la administración Trump un peligro para el mundo. Sin embargo, la veo como un fenómeno puramente temporal que desaparecerá en el 2020, o incluso antes".[26] Soros ha estado en modo de pánico desde las elecciones, diciendo poco después: "Tenemos que hacer algo para revertir lo que está pasando aquí" debido a que "las fuerzas de las tinieblas se han despertado".[27]

UNA GUERRA DE COSMOVISIONES

¿Qué sucede cuando chocan las cosmovisiones? Quizás no haya mejor ejemplo que la controversia por la que atraviesa la legislación en la capital de la Nación hoy día. El sistema de gobierno bipartidista es antagonista por naturaleza, lo que provee un vehículo para que los votantes con opiniones y creencias diferentes puedan estar del lado del partido político que mejor represente sus intereses. Sin embargo, en los años recientes, la división filosófica se ha vuelto más profunda y arraigada; y, a pesar de que los votantes atribulados frecuentemente piden el bipartidismo, eso sería lo último que los votantes quieren realmente.

Los partidos Demócrata y Republicano de hoy representan opiniones tan altamente polarizadas sobre casi todo que hay muy poca esperanza de encontrar intereses comunes, lo que significa que es casi imposible promulgar una legislación aceptable para ambas partes. Este es obviamente el caso en las batallas presupuestarias y las amenazas de cierre de gobierno que ahora suceden con regularidad predecible. Los desacuerdos sobre temas tales como inmigración, aborto, control de armas de fuego, impuestos, cuidado de la salud, derechos, medio ambiente, y mucho más ha apartado a los partidos cada vez más y creado una hostilidad profunda y permanente en el Congreso y en las comunidades en todo Estados Unidos. Algunos de mis familiares se niegan a hablar con los otros familiares que apoyan a Trump. Posiblemente, usted ha experimentado lo mismo en su familia.

Un investigador de la *Brookings Institution*, Thomas E. Mann escribe que mientras dos partidos sean los "actores principales" en el gobierno, los legisladores tienden a responder más a su base activista que a los votantes que los eligieron. Esto explica parcialmente el porqué "la aprobación pública del Congreso y la confianza en el gobierno se han hundido en profundidades récord". Sin embargo, considerando las diferencias extremas en actitudes, creencias y cosmovisiones de ambos partidos, la polarización es inevitable. Tal como lo escribe Mann, el nivel de polarización creciente refleja más que solo diferencias ideológicas:

La paridad hostil entre los partidos nutre una competencia intensa por el control de la Casa Blanca y el Congreso. Hay mucho en juego porque las diferencias ideológicas son grandes, y porque ambos partidos tienen una oportunidad realista de ganar o mantener el control. Esto lleva a establecer una agenda estratégica y de votos, aun sobre temas con poco o ningún contenido ideológico y un tribalismo que ahora es una característica muy prominente de la política estadounidense.[28]

Muchas veces, los demócratas y republicanos están en desacuerdo mutuo sencillamente porque se niegan a llegar a un acuerdo con la contraparte en todo. Para tener una perspectiva, podía ser útil recordar que la división entre la Izquierda y la Derecha no empezó aquí. Los términos Izquierda y Derecha, y la división institucional entre partidos, en realidad data de la Revolución Francesa en 1789, cuando los miembros de la división antimonárquica, incluyendo a los jacobinos, en la Asamblea Nacional Francesa, se trasladaron al lado izquierdo de la cámara para expresar desprecio por los leales defensores del rey, quienes se sentaban al lado derecho.

Los jacobinos eran pensadores libres y políticos radicales. Junto con otras facciones rebeldes, rechazaron los valores tradicionales, especialmente a la Iglesia Católica, y dirigieron la campaña para erradicar a los aristócratas adinerados, al clero y a la nobleza francesa. La erupción violenta que se llevó a cabo el 14 de julio de 1789, conocida como el Día de la Toma de la Bastilla llevó en el debido curso hacia lo que se llegó a conocer como "El Reino del Terror", donde cuarenta mil leales, empresarios, nobles y clérigo fueron ejecutados en 1793 y 1794. La Revolución Francesa provee una advertencia oportuna acerca de las consecuencias de la polarización extrema.

Las disputas entre los funcionarios de gobierno han llevado a contiendas amargas en el pasado, el duelo entre Aaron Burr y Alexander Hamilton es un ejemplo notable, no obstante, la mayoría de los debates hoy día no llegan a la violencia física. Pero los reportes de los noticieros nocturnos dejan en claro que los estándares del discurso civil están desmoronándose, y los debates entre la Izquierda y la Derecha ya no son simplemente académicos.

Recuerdo que este tipo de anarquía fue apoyada durante la época de la Guerra de Vietnam, y que vi que algunas de las protestas en la Universidad de Florida se volvieron violentas. Creo que las raíces de los problemas actuales empezaron en aquel entonces. No obstante, hoy día es mucho peor.

El anfitrión de programas radiales, Dennis Prager, recientemente observó que el temor número uno en Estados Unidos hoy día es el temor a la violencia de la Izquierda. "Desafortunadamente", dice, "ya está aquí":

Pero, por ahora, viene solamente de una dirección. Los matones izquierdistas se involucran en violencia y amenazas de violencia con impunidad absoluta. Callan a los oradores en las universidades; bloquean carreteras, puentes y aeropuertos; toman el control de edificios universitarios y oficinas; ocupan capitales de estado y aterrorizan a las personas en sus hogares. Para entender por qué podría venir más violencia, es esencial entender que las multitudes izquierdistas casi nunca son detenidas, arrestadas o castigadas. Las universidades no hacen nada para detenerlas y las autoridades civiles tampoco las detienen en las instalaciones o en ninguna otra parte.[29]

En muchos casos, los policías son simples espectadores mientras observan a estas "pandillas izquierdistas saquear tiendas, quebrar ventanas de negocios y vehículos, y hasta apoderarse de las capitales estatales". "La única conclusión que uno puede sacar", sugiere Prager, "es que los alcaldes, jefes policiales y presidentes universitarios no tienen interés alguno en detener esta violencia". Los funcionarios izquierdistas tienden a simpatizar con los infractores de la ley. Y mientras la policía local podría tener poca simpatía por los matones y tratar en general de evitar la ideología tanto de la Izquierda como la de la Derecha, se les ha ordenado retirarse en situaciones inestables. Los funcionarios locales corruptos los han emasculado efectivamente.

Fui testigo de cómo los anarquistas trataron de provocar tensiones raciales después de la trágica muerte del joven de diecisiete años, Trayvon Martin, en de febrero de 2012, en Sanford, Florida, a pocos kilómetros de donde yo vivo. Cuando sucedió, la comunidad negra local realmente no conocía a Trayvon porque él estaba de visita y venía de Miami. Inicialmente no estaban airados. Luego, los izquierdistas agitadores de fuera de la ciudad aparecieron diciendo que Trayvon había sido asesinado por un blanco racista llamado George Zimmerman y que la policía lo había dejado ir. Después de un juicio difícil, visto por toda la nación, se consideró que Zimmerman (quien, a pesar de su apellido, realmente es hispano) actuaba en defensa propia y que las autoridades lo dejaron ir porque las leyes en Florida permiten el uso de la fuerza en defensa propia.

Primero, el veredicto de los radicales predijo que Sanford sería quemado totalmente si Zimmerman no fuera condenado. Luego, los comentarios del presidente Obama inflamaron la situación aún más. Yo, en lo personal, estuve involucrado en ese periodo con otros líderes cristianos locales que trabajaron para aliviar las tensiones raciales. Cuando Zimmerman fue absuelto en julio de 2013, hubo manifestaciones y disturbios menores en otras partes del país; pero, gracias a la oración, no hubo violencia en Sanford.

Después de que los medios de comunicación azuzaran las llamas sobre la muerte de Trayvon Martin, la plataforma quedó lista para un escándalo y cobertura mayor a lo normal un año después cuando un policía en Ferguson, Missouri, le disparó a un joven negro que lo estaba atacando. Y, por supuesto, las cosas escalaron con otros incidentes en Baltimore, Maryland, y otros lugares. Para cuando Trump fue elegido, estos anarquistas y sus patrocinadores en los medios de comunicación estaban listos para más disturbios civiles cuando las elecciones no resultaron como ellos querían.

Los liberales en el gobierno y los medios de comunicación aseguraban que la elección de Donald Trump creó la crisis en el diálogo civil. Señalando las "tormentas en Twitter" del Presidente y los ataques verbales a los proveedores de las llamadas noticias falsas, los demócratas creían que la fuerte retórica política y el antagonismo generado por los republicanos había llevado a un colapso del orden civil. Una encuesta de opinión pública hecha por el *Pew Research Center* halló que los republicanos y demócratas están más divididos ahora que en cualquier otro momento de las dos últimas décadas,[30] y que la división partidista es más profunda y más extensa que nunca. Desde la elección del presidente Trump, la polarización se ha vuelto más profunda e intensa.

Así como en la Revolución Francesa, hace más de dos siglos, la Izquierda política en este país está menos inclinada a responder a un desacuerdo político y filosófico a través del diálogo y el debate. Especialmente para los jóvenes adultos y los liberales jóvenes, los medios de respuesta preferidos son las protestas masivas, las manifestaciones, los boicots y la retórica violenta de los líderes que no tienen pelos en la lengua. La quema de una gran figura de Donald Trump en Los Ángeles, en la noche después de las elecciones, seguida meses después por la comediante Kathy Griffin sosteniendo una réplica de la cabeza cortada y ensangrentada de Trump, así como los ataques verbales implacables sobre la marcha de los políticos demócratas Maxine Waters y Nancy Pelosi, han energizado la base e indicado el nivel de ira que se desborda sobre la Izquierda. Los comediantes nocturnos, desde Bill Maher y Jimmy Kimmel hasta Stephen Colbert y Samantha Bee, han enfocado virtualmente todo su repertorio en difamar al Presidente.

Daniel Lattier, vicepresidente de un comité de expertos de Minnesota, cree que algo de esta ira se conduce por el flujo constante de malas noticias por parte de los medios de comunicación nacionales. Las emociones ya están desgastadas, y muchas personas siguen el ejemplo de los noticieros y luego, en defensa propia, reaccionan con ira. "En este ambiente", dice, "muchas personas han llegado a ver la ira como una virtud y un mecanismo de defensa natural". Él señala la frase que usaron los organizadores liberales: "Si no estás enfadado, entonces, simplemente no estás poniendo atención".[31] En este sentido, la ira se ve como un signo de consciencia política y cultural. Es como los "liberales responsables" hacen política. Repito, he sido testigo de las consecuencias de la cobertura desmedida y el escándalo extremo por la muerte de Trayvon Martin.

Pero también hay un patrón de división en el lado conservador. El exrepresentante republicano de Nueva York, Chris Shays, dice que, durante sus veintidós años en el Congreso, muchas veces cruzó el pasillo para trabajar con los demócratas. "Cuando me eligieron para el Congreso, a uno lo habrían expulsado si no podía trabajar con el lado contrario", dijo. Sin embargo, muchos miembros del Congreso hoy día "nunca han conocido un Congreso donde demócratas y republicanos trabajen juntos por el bien del país". Shays culpa del problema a los líderes de ambas partes que intentan eliminar del partido a los moderados. El resultado es que ambos partidos están siendo empujados a los extremos.[32] Sin embargo, muchos de los conservadores creen que ceder con la Izquierda es la causa de muchos de sus fracasos sociales y legislativos, y la elección de Donald Trump estaba destinada a ser una parte relevante de la solución.

GOBERNAR LO INGOBERNABLE

La amargura y la ira que ahora están muy extendidas en el gobierno han dificultado más que nunca que nuestros representantes puedan llevar a cabo los asuntos de la nación. La atmósfera de luchas internas y la deslealtad hace surgir serias dudas sobre el futuro del sistema democrático. ¿Cómo puede cualquier funcionario electo esperar gobernar efectivamente cuando la oposición, auxiliada por un medio de comunicación condescendiente y las pandillas de mercenarios radicales, es capaz de interrumpir impunemente las iniciativas nuevas? Para ser más específicos, ¿cómo puede el presidente Trump cumplir las promesas que le hizo a los estadounidenses cuando sus adversarios en el partido de la oposición y los renegados en el partido propio lo bloquean, se burlan de él, lo traicionan y lo contradicen en todo momento?

Claramente, este ha sido el objetivo de la resistencia demócrata desde el primer día; resistir y obstruir la agenda del Presidente para evitar que el Congreso republicano alcance el éxito en cualquier área. La trágica ironía de esta situación, tal como lo señaló el columnista del *Washington Times*, Charles Hurt, es que la trampa para enredar y distraer al Presidente fue tendida mucho antes de que Donald Trump fuera electo. El estándar estadounidense para elegir un presidente ha sido anunciado como un modelo para el mundo, como "el máximo experimento vivo de autogobierno". Pero ¿qué sucede cuando el presidente es debilitado y atacado salvajemente a diario en la prensa y se le impide llevar a cabo los deberes del cargo? Tal como dice Hurt:

> Un hombre puede atravesar la tormenta contra más de veinte políticos profesionales y salir triunfante. Puede ganar más de cuarenta primarias republicanas y vencer a todos los activistas políticos profesionales allí, ganando los votos de más de catorce millones de republicanos. Seguidamente, puede enfocar su atención para vencer

a la maquinaria política de Estados Unidos más poderosa y arraigada que se ha visto en casi medio siglo… Pero, luego, la poderosa burocracia establecida tiene que realizar una investigación masiva, extensa e ilimitada sobre todos los aspectos del presidente que elegimos.[33]

"El presidente Trump ganó la presidencia con todas las de la ley, obteniendo los votos de más de sesenta millones de estadounidenses", señala Hurt, "ganando los votos electorales de los treinta estados que necesitaba para tomar la Casa Blanca. Sin embargo, en el momento culminante de la campaña, parece que la administración del presidente saliente le dio poder a una red masiva de espías, subversivos y saboteadores con órdenes de llevar a cabo operaciones clandestinas contra los candidatos del otro partido. Así que, espiaron, transigieron y expusieron todo lo que pudieron hallar y tendieron una trampa elaborada solo por si acaso el pueblo estadounidense pudiera realmente elegir a Donald Trump como su próximo presidente".

"De esa manera, la investigación interminable que llevó a cabo el abogado especial Robert Mueller, en busca de un crimen que nunca sucedió no debería sorprendernos", escribe Hurt. "Fue preparado mucho antes de que el Sr. Trump ganara las elecciones", y continua como el caso de tortura con agua más prolongado del mundo. Pero esto es aparentemente "el nuevo estándar para el 'autogobierno' en Estados Unidos". El pueblo puede elegir a quien quiera, pero los que se ganan la vida descubriendo escándalos, los detractores y los difamadores harán todo lo que esté a su alcance, incluyendo inventar escenarios extraños para la intriga internacional, para forzar al otro equipo a dejar el cargo. Hasta ahora, el esfuerzo ha sido efectivo, arruinando las obras, "pero esta gente", dice Hurt, "no tiene idea de cuánto la desprecian realmente los votantes y los contribuyentes".[34]

James Strock, al escribir en el diario de Washington *The Hill*, ha llegado a una conclusión similar. Desde que Donald Trump subió al estrado en Washington con la confianza de un vencedor, declarando que había llegado a "drenar el pantano", ha sido un blanco de la Izquierda. "A veces", sugiere Strock, "el Presidente tiene que 'preguntarse si el lodo le llega hasta la rodilla'".[35] Su administración ha estado sumida en el caos desde la investidura. Gracias a la obstrucción de los demócratas del Senado, muchos nombramientos importantes del gabinete y jueces federales permanecen sin cubrirse después de meses de disputas. Los abogados y las demandas son ahora las noticias del día, mientras que los asuntos de la nación están siendo ampliamente ignorados. Comencé en la carrera periodística durante la era del *Watergate*. En ese entonces, los medios de comunicación odiaban al presidente Richard Nixon y tuvieron éxito en sacarlo del cargo (con mucho menos daño del que los demócratas hicieron en las elecciones de 2016). Los medios de comunicación despreciaron casi de la misma forma a Ronald Reagan y a George

W. Bush. En menor medida, se opusieron a Gerald Ford y a George H. W. Bush. Una prensa libre es importante para responsabilizar a los que están en el poder. Fui capacitado en la más alta ética del periodismo en la Universidad de Florida. Me entristece ver cómo la prensa en gran parte no es objetiva y se ha convertido en el brazo publicitario de la extrema Izquierda. Creo que la prensa se ha vuelto parte del problema, de lo que Donald Trump llama "el pantano", al cual prometió drenar.

Ningún presidente puede drenar el pantano de la noche a la mañana, y quizá el Presidente debería haber sabido que su amenaza a la vasta red invisible de habitantes de los pantanos podría convertirse en una experiencia que altera la vida. "No obstante", escribe Strock, "el presidente Trump puede 'cambiar el clima de la política de Washington' llevando a la batalla a las fuerzas dispuestas en su contra y poniendo el enfoque sobre los miembros del Congreso. Un paso importante sería hacer cumplir las regulaciones que obligan a aquellos que hacen nuestras leyes a ser responsables ante el pueblo al que gobiernan. A través de regulaciones obligatorias y voluntarias, el Presidente puede regresar el enfoque sobre el Congreso e introducir medidas capaces de crear un ambiente en el que el gobierno pueda volver a funcionar como previsto.[36]

Independientemente de la afiliación a un partido, debería ser obvio que la nación tiene un interés en la capacidad del presidente para tener éxito en su trabajo. Debería ser igual de obvio que la obstrucción lastima, no solo al presidente, sino a toda la nación. Drenar el pantano significa restaurar la autoridad de los líderes y funcionarios clave electos para hacer su trabajo y eliminar la capacidad de los operativos dentro del "estado de interés especial" para interferir y obstruir. El sistema que permite a los políticos, burócratas, cabilderos, periodistas, comités de expertos, y abogados abrumar a la administración con cargos difamatorios ha ayudado a crear un ambiente tóxico en el que casi nada importante puede lograrse. ¿Puede imaginarse tratando de hacer su trabajo con esta cantidad de oposición llegándole diariamente? Aun así, el presidente Trump es único en su capacidad para restarle importancia a las críticas más duras y simplemente ignorarlas.

Strock señala varias áreas donde los cambios regulatorios podrían marcar una gran diferencia; por ejemplo: abolir el sistema de pensiones para los expresidentes y los exmiembros del Congreso, prohibiendo el uso de los fondos de los contribuyentes para subsidiar acuerdos secretos de acciones contra los funcionarios electos, remover los subsidios de *Obamacare* y el trato especial para los miembros del Congreso y su personal, y prohibir la recaudación de fondos de campaña mientras el Congreso está en sesión. Estos son algunos lugares donde la acción ejecutiva puede ayudar a que el gobierno sea más responsable, pero en conjunto, las iniciativas de esta clase iniciarían el proceso de reorientar al gobierno y hacer que nuestros líderes sean más receptivos con los ciudadanos a los que representan.

Poner la carga sobre el Congreso para cumplir con las mismas reglas que todos los estadounidenses deben cumplir, envía un mensaje a los votantes de que la administración está velando por los intereses de ellos, y pone al Congreso sobre aviso de la demanda de que los miembros o se ponen las pilas o se callan. Sin embargo, eso no significa que las operaciones encubiertas vayan a cesar repentinamente. No necesariamente restaurará ninguna semejanza de compañerismo entre los miembros de los partidos opositores. Y tampoco significa que los enemigos declarados, como George Soros, Tim Gill, Tom Steyer, y la liga de los cien izquierdistas multimillonarios abandonará repentinamente su campaña para desprestigiar o debilitar al Presidente. Pero es un paso en la dirección correcta cuando se necesita grandemente algún tipo de contraofensiva.

Según los documentos obtenidos por *Judicial Watch* a través de la Ley de Libertad de Información, la administración Obama estaba entregando activamente el dinero de los contribuyentes a un grupo de extrema Izquierda dirigido por George Soros. Los documentos muestran que la Agencia de EE. UU. para el Desarrollo Internacional (USAID, por sus siglas en inglés) canalizó US$9 millones del dinero de los contribuyentes a través de su *Civil Society Project* para apoyar las operaciones de *Open Society Foundations* en Albania. Estas operaciones estaban designadas para darle al gobierno socialista del país mayor control sobre el poder judicial.[37] Por decepcionante que sea la noticia, lo que realmente muestran tales descubrimientos es la magnitud a la que la administración anterior y que el "estado profundo" llegarían para perpetuar la agenda izquierdista.

El informe también muestra que un grupo de senadores le escribió al entonces secretario de estado, Rex Tillerson, solicitando una investigación sobre las denuncias que el gobierno de Estados Unidos estaba enviando el dinero de los contribuyentes para financiar las operaciones de Soros en Albania. El presidente de *Judicial Watch*, Tom Fitton, dijo: "George Soros es un multimillonario y no debería estar recibiendo el apoyo de los contribuyentes para llevar a cabo su agenda izquierdista radical para debilitar la libertad aquí y en el extranjero".[38] Pero, al mismo tiempo, el ambientalista multimillonario, Tom Steyer, está promoviendo campaña "Necesidad de impugnar" con la esperanza de enredar al Comandante en jefe en asuntos legales, muy similar a la manera en que Richard Nixon fue incapacitado durante la era *Watergate*.

Según un informe, Steyer envió por correo una "guía para impugnar" a 5,171 candidatos demócratas en todo el país para ser usada como punto de conversación en sus campañas políticas. "Consideramos que evitar la impugnación es un error estratégico" les dijo a los reporteros del sitio liberal de internet *Axios* el estratega de Steyer, Kevin Mack. "Es lo que enciende a la base demócrata".[39] En el lanzamiento de sus planes, Steyer y compañía, se acercaron a la juventud adulta con la esperanza de inscribir a los votantes demócratas antes de las elecciones intermedias de 2018. Ellos afirman tener ya más de cinco millones de simpatizantes; sin embargo, muchos candidatos demócratas han optado por ignorar las guías de impugnación por temor a las repercusiones por parte de los votantes en sus distritos locales.

Tal como lo informara Breitbart.com, algunos observadores creen que los esfuerzos de Steyer realmente son un intento de preparar el terreno para su propia campaña presidencial en el 2020.[40] Pero la intensidad de todos estos esfuerzos de los miembros del Congreso y de las fuerzas invisibles para bloquear y obstruir la agenda del Presidente y para paralizar a la administración han incrementado la intensidad de la lucha en Washington y creado un entorno en el que puede suceder cualquier cosa. ¡Quién sabe cuándo llegará el próximo desastre, y quién sabe cuándo la siguiente bomba mediática provoque una explosión de furia y venganza partidista!

Creo que Dios levantó a Donald Trump en este momento de inflexión en nuestra historia. Hubo expresiones políticas en el estado de ánimo cambiante del país. Pero creo que algo estaba sucediendo espiritualmente. Los cristianos oraban para que las cosas cambiaran y el magnate de bienes raíces de Nueva York era realmente una respuesta a la oración. Nada similar a eso había sucedido, y el surgimiento de una coalición de votantes de tantas creencias y de tantas partes del país fue un fenómeno. Y en las primeras horas del 9 de noviembre de 2016, quedó en claro que la nación había llegado a su punto de inflexión.

Ninguno de los partidos anticipó completamente lo que podía suceder si Clinton perdía las elecciones. Los demócratas estaban seguros, animados por docenas de encuestas, de que habían ganado. Ya habían completado sus listas de los secretarios de gabinete y jefes de departamento para la administración entrante de Clinton. Pero, repentinamente, ambos partidos tuvieron que enfrentar el hecho de que el candidato menos probable había ganado. Hoy, vivimos en los resultados de esa revelación. Esperamos y rogamos a Dios que disminuyan las tensiones y que la nación pueda volver a funcionar como siempre, pero quién puede predecir lo que sucederá si el espectáculo por el que atraviesa el gobierno continúa en la misma dirección demente en la que ha estado yendo.[41]

LA AGENDA DE RÁPIDO INICIO DE TRUMP

Uno de los hechos que se ha vuelto dolorosamente claro para los líderes políticos tanto de la Izquierda como de la Derecha es que Donald Trump no creó la crecida electoral que lo impulsó al cargo en las elecciones de 2016. Sino más bien, él fue el beneficiario de un movimiento grande y amorfo compuesto por millones de votantes enojados e insatisfechos de ambos partidos políticos y quienes buscaban un candidato en el que pudieran confiar.

Fue precisamente porque Trump era tan franco, tan poco ortodoxo, tan "no de Washington" que los votantes le respondieron de la manera que lo hicieron. Él fue animado, pero también fue examinado cercanamente con un escepticismo considerable hasta que los votantes comprendieron que este era su elegido; luego, fue elevado a su alto cargo sobre una ola de expectación cautelosa.

Según una encuesta del estado de ánimo general del país, de abril de 2015 a octubre de 2016, por lo menos el 68 por ciento y como máximo el 79 por ciento de los estadounidenses estaba insatisfecho con la manera en que iban las cosas.[1] La ira y el resentimiento de los votantes por la humillación que habían soportado durante los ocho a diez años previos ardía lentamente justo bajo la superficie. Ellos estaban al borde, y aquellos con la campaña de Clinton estaban tan confiados en su mandato liberal que se les pasó por alto completamente. Pero si la elección de Donald Trump como el presidente número cuarenta y cinco de Estados Unidos muchos la sintieron como un terremoto, el temblor posterior fue más como un desplazamiento de las placas tectónicas.

En los primeros días de su presidencia, Trump empezó a rescindir las órdenes ejecutivas de Obama. En los primeros seis meses, él aseguró la confirmación de un juez conservador de la Corte Suprema, puso fin a la Asociación Transpacífica, anunció su intención de separar a Estados Unidos del Acuerdo de París, y firmó cuarenta y dos propuestas convirtiéndolas en leyes, incluyendo la ley de Responsabilidad de Asuntos de Veteranos y la Ley de Protección a los Denunciantes. Hacia el final de su primer año en el cargo, él había acumulado uno de los listados más impresionantes de logros de cualquier presidente en la historia y dejado claro que él apenas estaba empezando.

Trump fue electo porque fue visto como un agente de cambio. Él prometió detener la carrera precipitada de la administración Obama hacia la globalización, desmantelar el estado profundo y arrancar de raíz la clandestinidad izquierdista transformando de manera encubierta a la república en una oligarquía socialista. Sin embargo, esta elección fue de muchas maneras una anomalía. Ambos candidatos ignoraron la guía de sus respectivos líderes del partido, escuchando más atentamente a sus bases.

Para Clinton, esto fue desafortunado, ya que su base era fuerte y ferozmente agresiva. A medida que la carrera se encendía, Clinton se volvió "hiperagresiva",[2] "chillona"[3] y "fastidiosa".[4] El periodista Bob Woodward en el programa *Morning Joe* supuso que ella "no estaba cómoda consigo misma".[5] Por otro lado, Trump permaneció calmado, provocativo, sorprendentemente ingenioso y completamente involucrado con las multitudes en sus mítines. Su promesa de hacer que Estados Unidos volviera a ser grande capturó los sentimientos de los votantes que temían que algo único y maravilloso se había perdido.

"La consigna de la campaña de Trump", escribe Francis Wilkinson en el *Denver Post*, "fue elaborada con destreza por sus seguidores principales. Comunica nacionalismo, nostalgia y profundo pesimismo e inseguridad acerca del estado actual de la nación, tres pilares de la candidatura de Trump, junto con la acción implicada requerida para revertir el curso".[6] La consigna era sencilla y directa y atractiva para nuestra naturaleza competitiva. Según un vuelco de *WikiLeaks* de los correos electrónicos de la campaña de Clinton, su equipo analizó ochenta y cinco ideas de consigna antes de quedarse finalmente con "Juntos somos más fuertes", una frase que Obama había usado repetidamente en sus discursos.

Desde el principio de la campaña, Trump cortejó el voto religioso y se reunió en privado con pastores, aunque varios de sus oponentes primarios eran evangélicos fuertes y dividieron inicialmente el voto evangélico. En contraste, Trump hablaba con fluidez limitada en el lenguaje de los fieles, además, había vivido la mayor parte de su adultez como un mujeriego multimillonario. Sin embargo, tal como lo documenté en *God and Donald Trump*, a principios de la década de los dos mil, Trump empezó a ver televisión cristiana y se acercó a Paula White Cain, diciéndole que tenía algunas preguntas sobre temas espirituales. Cuando él consideró postularse para presidente en el año 2012, le pidió a Paula que reuniera a algunos de sus amigos predicadores "que supieran cómo orar" sobre si él debía postularse, y recibió sus oraciones con gratitud. Estos líderes vieron que él era un hombre cambiado y que se había convertido en un defensor de sus causas en una manera en que John McCain y Mitt Romney nunca lo fueron. Y, al momento de la postulación en las elecciones generales de 2016, él era recompensado con la mayor participación evangélica desde que las encuestas de salida empezaron a incluir a los evangélicos blancos; el 81 por ciento de los evangélicos blancos accionó la palanca en favor de Trump en noviembre, lo que le dio el margen de victoria.

Él aceptó el respaldo de individuos y organizaciones con quienes había tenido grandes diferencias de opinión, pero creyendo en el adagio "el enemigo de mi enemigo es mi amigo" él pudo formar una coalición formidable para ayudar a abordar algunos de los problemas más difíciles imaginables.

Un nuevo alguacil en el pueblo

La agenda de Trump, detallada casi diariamente vía *Twitter* a sus más de cincuenta y tres millones de seguidores y admiradores, se enfocaba en fortalecer la economía, restaurar la integridad de las cortes federales, detener la oleada abrumadora de inmigrantes ilegales, renovar al ejército y elevar la posición de Estados Unidos en el mundo. Este era un cambio de 180 grados de la agenda progresiva de la administración Obama, a la cual se le conoce como "dirigir desde atrás". Temiendo que sería perder lo ganado con los jueces activistas liberales, un gobierno más y más grande, y la tendencia general del país hacia la Izquierda en los últimos cuarenta años, la oposición liberal estaba determinada a oponerse a la agenda de Trump y a desestabilizar a la nación a toda costa. El objetivo era desacreditar y, finalmente, impugnar a Donald Trump sin importar el costo o las repercusiones.

El nuevo presidente heredó un listado largo e intimidante de los problemas diplomáticos sin resolver por las administraciones anteriores, tales como: Corea del Norte, el Medio Oriente, la OTAN, y los déficits comerciales, que se remontan hasta los años de Reagan. Aun así, desde su primer día en el cargo, él empezó a tomar acciones dramáticas para restaurar la funcionalidad del gobierno. Una de las primeras acciones de su administración, unas horas después de su investidura, fue emitir un memorándum ordenando un congelamiento sobre las nuevas regulaciones gubernamentales.

Para finales del año 2016, la administración Obama había aumentado el *Registro Federal* a 97,069 páginas de reglamentos y regulaciones, más de 10,000 páginas más extenso que cualquier otra administración previa. Esto representaba 3,853 regulaciones nuevas o corregidas, el mayor número en once años. La orden enviada por Reince Priebus de parte del presidente Trump instruía a todos los departamentos a "no enviar ninguna regulación a la Oficina del Registro Federal... hasta que un jefe de departamento o agencia, nombrado o designado por el Presidente en la tarde de 20 de enero de 2017, revisara y aprobara la regulación".[7]

Desenredar la red administrativa tomaría tiempo, pero Donald Trump quería dejar en claro que había un nuevo alguacil en el pueblo. Él fue un hombre de negocios y empresario, justificadamente orgulloso de su destreza como negociador; pero, tal como lo señaló Víctor Davis Hanson, él no poseía el temperamento diplomático para lidiar con políticos y negociantes que habían pasado toda su carrera inmersos en los protocolos de diplomacia.[8] Tal como Trump lo deja en claro en su libro *The Art of the Deal*, su estilo es más personal, más directo, más intimidante. Muchos de los temas que él tendría que confrontar tenían mucho tiempo de existir y aparentemente insolubles, pero para Donald Trump, la paciencia nunca había sido una virtud.

El líder de Corea del Norte se jactó de que podía atacar a Estados Unidos continentales con misiles nucleares. La economía de China estaba en auge a expensas de la economía estadounidense porque los chinos no solo violaron los acuerdos comerciales, sino que obligaron a las empresas estadounidenses a entregar su tecnología patentada como precio por hacer negocios con China. Cuando las quejas de los funcionarios del Departamento de Estado fueron rechazadas, en lugar de amenazar con sanciones o tarifas, se quedaron callados y regresaron a casa. Solo negocios, como de costumbre.

Desde 1949, Estados Unidos había sido cargado con un porcentaje significativo del presupuesto de la OTAN, mientras que las fuerzas militares de Estados Unidos fueron obligadas a defender el continente europeo. Al mismo tiempo, México se estaba enriqueciendo con las remesas de millones de inmigrantes ilegales que habían estado atravesando nuestras fronteras por décadas. Los trabajadores extranjeros residiendo en Estados Unidos estaban contribuyendo aproximadamente US$30 mil millones al año a la economía mexicana. Cuando Estados Unidos se quejó, los funcionarios mexicanos respondieron afirmando racismo, xenofobia y nativismo. Una vez más, el gobierno estadounidense no hizo nada.

Hay temas comunes en todos estos impases internacionales, y como lo señala Hanson: "Las sutilezas diplomáticas han resuelto poco. El descuido de Estados Unidos se ha visto como una ingenuidad de que aprovecharse, no como concesiones generosas que deben ser retribuidas en especie".[9] Estos, y muchos otros, problemas han estado pudriéndose por años, y ni los Clinton, ni los Bush, y tampoco la administración Obama pudieron hacer progresos. Pero ese no era el estilo de Trump. A él se le ha descrito como "un toro en una tienda de figuras de porcelana", pero él aprende rápido, es extraordinariamente perceptivo, seguro de sí mismo y tenaz.

"El estilo de Donald Trump", dice Hanson, "es abordar tales problemas de manera muy parecida a como Alejandro Magno lo hizo en la historia del nudo gordiano. Según la leyenda, el nudo de Gordio era imposible de desatar, y quien pudiera desatarlo se convertiría en el rey de Asia. A pesar de muchos intentos, nadie tuvo éxito; sin embargo, cuando se le presentó el desafío a Alejandro, él sencillamente sacó su espada y cortó el nudo. Posteriormente, como rey de Macedonia y Persia, "estableció el imperio más extenso que el viejo mundo había visto".[10]

La analogía es lo suficientemente clara. Hanson escribe: "Antes de la llegada de Trump, la diplomacia estadounidense sutil y la habilidad política no habían desatado ninguno de estos nudos. Pero, al igual que Alejandro, el foráneo Trump no estaba comprometido con ninguno de los protocolos acostumbrados sobre desatarlos. En cambio, el sacó su espada proverbial y empezó a cortar".[11]

En respuesta a la amenaza de Kim Jong-un de presionar el botón nuclear, Trump envió un tuit: "¡Yo también tengo un botón nuclear, pero es mucho más grande y poderoso que el de él, y mi botón sí funciona!", y luego se burló de él como "el pequeño hombre cohete".[12] A la vez, ordenó al Departamento de Defensa de Estados Unidos que empezara a expandir nuestro arsenal nuclear y a fortalecer los sistemas de defensa antimisiles de Estados Unidos. El estilo de Trump fue "ganar por intimidación" y la amenaza de Kim es muy parecida a la misma manera en que ha amenazado a otros.

Debido a que la política comercial de China es tan compleja y engañosa, sería difícil desatar ese nudo por medio de la diplomacia tradicional, así que Trump decidió tomar el mismo acercamiento por la fuerza con el presidente chino, Xi Jinping, anunciando en marzo de 2018 que Estados Unidos empezaría a imponer tarifas sobre las importaciones chinas. La tarifa de 25 por ciento sobre US$34 mil millones de productos chinos entró en efecto el 6 de julio de 2018; y China respondió de igual manera, implementando una tarifa de 25 por ciento sobre US$34 mil millones en los productos estadounidenses. Algunos temen una creciente guerra comercial entre los dos países, pero el presidente del Comité de Medios y Formas de la Cámara de Representantes, Kevin Brady, apoya los esfuerzos del presidente Trump para desafiar a China y considera que los dos líderes deben reunirse en persona para lograr el mejor resultado. Brady le dijo a *Fox Business*: "Confío en que esta reunión presidencial cara a cara con el presidente Xi pueda nivelar el terreno de juego, crear un nuevo conjunto de reglas comerciales para ambos países".[13]

Los problemas con la OTAN eran igualmente antiguos, y los estrategas de la defensa estadounidense querían saber por qué Estados Unidos debían pagar más de una quinta parte de todo el presupuesto para defender a Europa si los otros veintiocho países miembros no cumplieron con su parte. En el 2017, solamente cuatro de los veintiocho países cumplieron con su compromiso de gastar al menos el 2 por ciento de su producto interno bruto en la defensa.

Cuando habló en la central de la OTAN, en Bruselas, en febrero de 2017, el Secretario de la Defensa, Jim Matis, les dijo a los delegados: "Estados Unidos cumplirá con sus responsabilidades, pero si sus naciones no quieren ver que Estados Unidos modere su compromiso con la alianza, cada una de sus capitales debe demostrar su apoyo a nuestra defensa común".[14] Poco después, el presidente Trump confrontó a los delegados de la OTAN diciendo: "Durante los últimos ocho años, Estados Unidos gastó más en defensa que todos los otros países de la OTAN combinados".[15] Nadie dudó hacia dónde se dirigía el debate, y luego, el 27 de mayo de 2017, Trump tuiteó: "Muchos países de la OTAN han acordado aumentar considerablemente sus pagos, como deberían hacerlo. El dinero empieza a llegar: la OTAN será mucho más fuerte".[16]

Mientras escribo este libro, Estados Unidos ha empezado a levantar un muro en los tramos largos de la frontera sur. Los agentes del Servicio de Inmigración y Control de Aduanas (ICE, por sus siglas en inglés) han empezado a llevar a cabo redadas en todo el país, reuniendo inmigrantes indocumentados, delincuentes conocidos y los que rebasan su estadía; y Estados Unidos ha estado apoyando los esfuerzos del ejército mexicano para atacar el flujo de drogas y opioides que ingresan a este país. Desde la Oficina Oval, el 27 de agosto de 2018, el presidente Trump anunció su plan para terminar el Tratado de Libre Comercio entre Estados Unidos y México. Agradeció a los negociadores de ambas naciones por su arduo trabajo en las revisiones de un acuerdo de veinticuatro años de existencia que él había criticado constantemente como "uno de los peores tratos que se hayan hecho". Además de ser "un gran día para el comercio", fue una más de las promesas de campaña que él cumplió. También anunció que empezaríamos de inmediato negociaciones similares con Canadá.[17]

Más allá de México y Canadá, Estados Unidos está en un alejamiento comercial con la Unión Europea y China. Pero el propósito de Trump es reducir el déficit y resolver los problemas de comercio a favor de Estados Unidos. Aunque los otros países están tomando represalias, el presidente de Estados Unidos se rehúsa a dar marcha atrás poniendo los intereses de Estados Unidos por encima de los intereses mundiales.

PRIMERO LO PRIMERO

Para muchos de los simpatizantes de Trump, incluyéndome, nominar a un conservador digno de confianza para reemplazar al fallecido Antonin Scalia en la Corte Suprema era la primera orden del día. Trump había prometido en la campaña electoral que iba a nominar a un constitucionalista acérrimo. En marzo de 2016, dijo que probablemente tendría una oportunidad para reemplazar varios de los jueces liberales de mayor edad con conservadores escogidos. Disfrutando la oportunidad para provocar a sus rivales, dijo: "Déjenme decirles que, si no ganan, probablemente tendrán cuatro, o hasta podrían ser cinco, jueces de la Corte Suprema aprobados que nunca permitirán que este país sea el mismo. Tomaría 100 años".[18]

El 31 de enero de 2017, once días después de la investidura, Trump cumplió su promesa nominando a Neil Gorsuch como juez asociado de la Corte Suprema. A medida que los medios de comunicación y la institución legal empezaron a hurgar en sus logros, encontraron que Gorsuch tenía calificaciones académicas eminentes y excelentes credenciales, habiendo trabajado para los jueces Anthony Kennedy y Byron White y servido en la Corte de Apelaciones del Décimo Circuito. Gorsuch podría convertirse en el primer juez en ser ubicado en la corte con un juez con el que había trabajado.

Luego, en julio del 2018, Trump nominó al segundo juez de la Corte Suprema, Brett Kavanaugh, quien a los cincuenta y tres años es ligeramente mayor que Gorsuch. Y, al igual que Gorsuch, él trabajó para Anthony Kennedy, a quien reemplazará en el tribunal superior.

El primer nominado de Trump fue confirmado el 7 de abril, en solo un poco más de dos meses. Y, a la edad de cuarenta y nueve años, al momento de su confirmación, Gorsuch sería el miembro de la corte más joven, llevando un apoyo muy necesario para los tres constitucionalistas sirviendo actualmente.

Tan pronto como presentó la nominación de Gorsuch, el Presidente pasó a una larga lista de nominados para llenar más de cien vacantes en los tribunales federales. Repito, el objetivo era nominar candidatos jóvenes, altamente calificados, que tuvieran principios conservadores fuertes para proteger los derechos constitucionales por muchas décadas futuras, incluyendo especialmente la libertad de culto y el derecho a la vida. Predeciblemente, los demócratas usaron cualquier truco disponible para bloquear a los nominados judiciales, ejecutivos y diplomáticos del Presidente.

Para enero de 2018, ellos habían rechazado cerca de cien nominaciones cuidadosamente seleccionadas y evaluadas por la Casa Blanca. Esto fue además de los muchos puestos de embajadores que están siendo detenidos en el Senado. Para abril de 2018, solamente setenta y cinco de las vacantes del Departamento de Estado se habían cubierto.[19] Sin embargo, en respuesta a la obstrucción del proceso de confirmación por parte de los demócratas, el Presidente propuso que se le requiriera al Senado que permaneciera en sesión los siete días de la semana hasta que sus nominados políticos y judiciales estén confirmados.

Una de las acciones ejecutivas más importantes del Presidente fue ampliar las exenciones religiosas y de conciencia al mandato de anticoncepción de *Obamacare* para incluir tanto las organizaciones lucrativas como no lucrativas, lo que era muy importante para la comunidad evangélica. En relación con lo mismo, ordenó al Departamento de Salud y Servicios Humanos que creara una División de Consciencia y Libertad Religiosa para proteger los derechos de los doctores, enfermeras y trabajadores del cuidado de la salud que se negaran a realizar abortos u otros procedimientos que de otra manera violarían sus objeciones religiosas o de consciencia. Además, él ordenó al Departamento de Justicia que publicara guías para más de cuatrocientos departamentos, agencias y subagencias en el gobierno federal requiriéndoles que salvaguardaran la libertad de culto de las partes en todas las acciones legales ante el gobierno.

El 19 de enero de 2018, el Presidente dio otro paso audaz al dirigirse a la cuadragésima quinta anual Marcha por la Vida, vía satélite, desde el Jardín de las Rosas de la Casa Blanca, diciéndoles que estaba especialmente orgulloso de ser el primer presidente en hacerlo. Les aseguró a los asistentes: "Estamos protegiendo la santidad de la vida y de la familia como el fundamento de nuestra sociedad".[20] Durante sus comentarios, el Presidente anunció que había restablecido la Mexico City Policy (Política de la Ciudad de México) que requiere que todas las organizaciones estadounidenses funcionando en el extranjero certifiquen que no "realizarán ni promoverán activamente el aborto como un método de planificación familiar".[21]

Además, dijo que había anulado la regulación de la era de Obama que prohibía que los estados impidieran que los proveedores de servicios de abortos siguieran recibiendo fondos, y enfatizó que "los estadounidenses están cada vez más a favor de la vida… De hecho, solamente el 12 por ciento de los estadounidenses apoya el aborto solicitado en cualquier momento del embarazo". Añadió: "Bajo mi administración siempre defenderemos el primer derecho en la Declaración de Independencia, y ese es el derecho a la vida".[22]

El Presidente mencionó luego otros logros de su administración. "Mañana será exactamente un año desde que tomé el juramento al cargo. Y diré que a nuestro país le está yendo muy bien. Nuestra economía es quizá la mejor de la historia. Vemos los números de empleo, vemos a las empresas invirtiendo en nuestro país; vemos el mercado de valores en un máximo histórico; el desempleo en su punto más bajo en diecisiete años. El desempleo de los trabajadores afroamericanos es el más bajo en la historia de nuestro país. El desempleo de los hispanos, el registro más bajo en la historia. El desempleo de las mujeres, piensen en esto, la marca más baja en dieciocho años".[23]

El 12 de octubre de 2017, la Casa Blanca anunció que Trump estaba poniendo fin a los pagos de costo compartido para los seguros de salud bajo *Obamacare*, y durante una reunión de gabinete en la Casa Blanca, el 16 de octubre de 2017, Trump añadió: "*Obamacare* está acabado. Está muerto. Se fue. Ya no existe; ustedes ni deberían mencionarlo. Se acabó. Ya no existe tal cosa como *Obamacare* Es un concepto que no podría haber funcionado. En sus mejores días no podría haber funcionado".[24]

Además, el 12 de octubre de 2017, el Presidente firmó una orden ejecutiva requiriendo nuevas regulaciones para animar el establecimiento de planes de salud más baratos que puedan comprarse a través de las líneas estatales y que permitan a los propietarios de negocios pequeños formar coaliciones y asociaciones con grupos del sector y otros para comprar seguros de salud. Los planes podrían ser diseñados para cubrir las necesidades de cada empleador y las organizaciones asociadas y no se requeriría que ofrecieran planes de medicamentos recetados ni ciertos beneficios adicionales.

Una de las características más importantes del proyecto de ley de reforma fiscal del Senado aprobada el 1 de diciembre de 2017, es la eliminación del mandato individual que penalizaba a los contribuyentes por optar no comprar seguro de salud. Después de semanas de un debate muy reñido, dentro y fuera de la sesión, el Senado votó cincuenta y uno a cuarenta y nueve para aprobar el proyecto de ley republicano. La nueva ley reduce permanentemente la tasa de impuesto corporativo de 35 a 21 por ciento y reduce las tasas para individuos y familias. Pone un tope de diez mil dólares en deducciones para impuestos estatales y locales, pero lo más importante es que la ley le atraviesa una estaca al corazón de *Obamacare*.

El Presidente dijo que la ley impulsará la economía, promoverá nuevos negocios e inversiones industriales, y animará a las empresas a hacer negocios en el extranjero para traer a sus trabajadores a casa y hacer negocios en Estados Unidos. A raíz de estos y otros cambios, la Casa Blanca fue impulsada por una encuesta de la Universidad de Michigan publicada en marzo de 2018 mostrando que la confianza del consumidor había alcanzado la máxima marca en catorce años.[25] Mejoras en la economía, niveles de ingreso crecientes y la fortaleza general de las finanzas personales contribuyeron al optimismo de los consumidores que respondieron la encuesta.

TEMAS DE POLÍTICAS MAYORES

Durante la campaña, Trump había prometido tomar acción definitiva contra ISIS y el califato de Irak. Para octubre de 2017, el Pentágono pudo anunciar que la "capital del terrorismo", en Raqqa, Siria, había caído ante las fuerzas de coalición lideradas por Estados Unidos. Rex Tillerson, el entonces secretario de Estado dijo que la caía de la capital del estado islámico fue acelerada por las decisiones tomadas por el presidente Trump. "En enero, ISIS estaba planeando activamente ataques terroristas contra nuestros aliados y nuestra patria en Raqqa", informó Tillerson. "Nueve cortos meses después, está fuera del control de ISIS debido a las decisiones críticas que el presidente Trump hizo para acelerar la campaña".[26]

En diciembre de 2017, los oficiales militares informaron que ISIS había perdido el 98 por ciento del territorio que una vez poseyó, y que las evaluaciones de inteligencia indicaban que el número de combatientes de ISIS, que ascendía a cerca de cuarenta y cinco mil cuando el califato islámico subió al poder durante la administración de Obama se había reducido a poco menos de mil en menos de un año después de la elección de Trump. La caída del califato demostró será un golpe certero para el estado islámico.

Pocos podrían dudar de su determinación. Cuando se le preguntó a Trump, en una entrevista en el 2011, cómo lidiaría con los piratas somalíes que estaban atacando barcos de Estados Unidos y otras naciones en el Océano Índico, su respuesta fue: "Los borraría de la faz de la tierra".[27] Luego, cinco años después, durante un mitin de campaña en Ohio, en septiembre de 2016, prometió que como presidente él "destruiría completamente a ISIS" en Irak. "Vamos a tomar una acción rápida y fuerte para proteger a los estadounidenses del terrorismo islámico radical", dijo.[28]

Como comandante en jefe, el Presidente les advirtió a las fuerzas islámicas en

Siria e Irak sobre su determinación de erradicar la amenaza de ISIS. El 13 de abril de 2017, él autorizó al Pentágono para dejar caer a la madre de todas las bombas, el arma no nuclear más grande en el arsenal de Estados Unidos, en los túneles y fortalezas de ISIS en Afganistán. Ese evento envió un mensaje escalofriante de que este presidente hablaba en serio. Mientras el califato islámico estuviera creciendo, ganando nuevos reclutas y expandiendo su territorio, los líderes de la facción militar podrían convencerse de que los religiosos del yihad del siglo dieciocho eran invencibles y que Alá estaba de su lado. Sin embargo, con el califato desaparecido y el liderazgo decapitado, el mundo entero podría ver la tragedia y la locura de ese desafortunado engaño.

Según los encuestadores que monitorean las preocupaciones de los votantes, la promesa central de la campaña de Trump, y el problema que con más frecuencia aparecía en la cima de las encuestas, es la construcción de un muro en la frontera sur para detener el flujo de inmigrantes a este país. Para empezar el proceso, el Presidente empezó a presionar al Congreso para financiar la construcción del muro fronterizo durante sus primeras semanas en el cargo; sin embargo, no fue sino hasta la aprobación del proyecto de ley de gastos diversos, lo que contribuyó a ahorrar US$1.6 mil millones para los tramos del muro, que él tuvo fondos suficientes para comenzar la construcción.

Cuando firmó el proyecto de ley, el 23 de marzo de 2018, el Presidente emitió una orden ejecutiva incrementando el número de agentes de la patrulla fronteriza y de funcionarios de aduanas para acelerar las deportaciones. Se necesitaría financiamiento adicional para completar el muro, pero el Presidente estaba firme en su promesa de "hacer que México pague por él", ¿y quién sería lo suficientemente valiente para creer que no podría hacerlo?

La Aduana y la Protección Fronteriza de Estados Unidos reportaron un 23.7 por ciento de reducción en el ingreso de inmigrantes ingresando al país de manera ilegal durante el año fiscal 2017, y esto fue sin que el muro esté terminado. Estaba quedando claro para los aspirantes a inmigrantes y la comunidad internacional en general que este presidente estadounidense hablaba más seriamente acerca de reducir la inmigración ilegal que sus predecesores. Tal como lo prometió durante toda la campaña, Trump estaba poniendo realmente a los estadounidenses en primer lugar, y el temor de lo que podría suceder bajo la nueva administración Trump hizo que muchos de los que potencialmente cruzarían la frontera decidieran que era mucho más seguro quedarse en casa.

Richard Baris, también informa que el 92 por ciento de los extranjeros ilegales arrestados por la ICE desde la elección de Trump, tenía condenas o cargos criminales pendientes o ya era fugitivo de ICE u ofensor reincidente. Contrario a lo que los medios sensacionalistas informan acusando a la administración de criminalizar a los soñadores y permitiendo que los funcionarios aduanales traten barbáricamente a quienes cruzan la frontera, "arrancando a los bebés de los brazos de sus madres" los hechos dejaron perfectamente aclarado que estos no eran víctimas inocentes, y que la narrativa de los medios de comunicación eran poco más que teatro barato.[29]

Continuando su lucha contra las fuerzas a favor de la inmigración dentro de Estados Unidos, el Presidente emitió una orden ejecutiva requiriendo que el Departamento de Justicia y la Seguridad Nacional les retuvieran los "fondos federales, excepto por mandato de la ley", a cualquier ciudad o municipalidad que se declarara ser "una ciudad santuario".[30] Él había hablado mucho de las ciudades santuario en su recorrido de campaña, y muchos estadounidenses estaban complacidos de verlo tomar acciones contra estas ciudades sin ley.

El Presidente también había prometido hacer de la política energética un tema importante en su administración, y empezó por abrir el Refugio Nacional para la Vida Silvestre del Ártico (ANWR, por sus siglas en inglés) para el desarrollo energético. Durante décadas, los republicanos habían prometido permitir la perforación petrolera en ANWR, pero la fuerte oposición de la Izquierda bloqueaba sus esfuerzos. Sin embargo, más adelante, cuando la perforación en ANWR en el proyecto distintivo de ley tributaria del Presidente, hubo solo una resistencia limitada. Los defensores del proyecto de ley argumentaron que perforar en ANWR sería beneficioso para los productores de petróleo y gas nacional y permitiría que Estados Unidos importara menos de fuentes hostiles, como Rusia, Venezuela y el Medio Oriente. Mientras tanto, el Comité de Recursos Naturales de la Cámara de Representantes informó que desarrollar los recursos naturales en ANRW ayudaría a generar cerca de 130,000 empleos nuevos y US$440 mil millones en ingresos públicos.

Según el escritor político, Mason Weaver, el presidente Trump dio un gran golpe con la firma del proyecto de ley de gastos diversos, persuadiendo básicamente al Congreso para que liberara miles de dólares en "financiamiento discrecional" que le daría al poder ejecutivo amplios poderes para financiar y dejar de financiar una variedad de iniciativas. Para obtener el apoyo de los demócratas del Senado, el Presidente aceptó ciertas medidas contra las que él se oponía fuertemente, tales como permitir que *Planned Parenthood* fuera elegible para financiamiento federal durante un año más. Eso era algo a lo que él se había resistido fuertemente, pero obstruir el problema habría alargado las deliberaciones y arriesgado un obstáculo mayor hacia otros asuntos vitales.

El debate acalorado sobre el proyecto de ley de gastos diversos se estaba convirtiendo en una obstrucción y en un juego político que el Presidente quería evitar, así que él trabajó para obtener el mejor trato posible. El Congreso, no el Presidente, está a cargo del financiamiento federal, por lo que él terminó aceptando estas medidas y firmó el proyecto de ley. "Sin embargo, el Presidente tiene la capacidad de dirigir la manera en que se usa el dinero", dice Waver, "y él tiene la autoridad discrecional para gastar o no gastar cantidades que de otra manera no hay requerimiento legal en cuanto a cómo gastarlo". [31]

El gobierno federal tiene que pagar por los programas sociales obligatorios tales como el Seguro Social y *Medicare*. Sin embargo, las agencias como el Departamento de Energía, el Departamento de Vivienda y Desarrollo Urbano, el Departamento de Educación, el Departamento de Defensa y el Departamento de Estado, todos se pagan por medio de fondos discrecionales. El Presidente disfruta de amplios poderes para determinar cómo, o incluso si, estos fondos se gastan. Para que el Presidente obtenga lo que él quiere a través del Congreso, generalmente tiene que aceptar una serie de cosas que él no quiere. Durante el alboroto del proyecto de ley de gastos diversos, tanto amigos como enemigos del Presidente aseguraban que él había cambiado de bando. Él estaba permitiendo que se financiaran medidas que una vez había declarado inaceptables. "Pero", dice Weaver, "el presidente Trump los derribó a todos".[32]

Trump tuiteó, poco después de la firma del proyecto de ley de gastos, "Construir un muro fronterizo, con drogas (veneno) y combatientes enemigos invadiendo nuestro país, se trata de la Defensa Nacional. ¡A construir un muro a través de M!".[33] Lo que estaba diciendo era que iba a usar una porción del dinero designado en el proyecto de ley para que el ejército construyera el muro, y el Pantano, para su disgusto, acababa de financiarlo.

Aunque los países como Corea del Norte, China y Rusia han demostrado ser hostiles a los intereses de Estados Unidos en el mundo, el Congreso de Estados Unidos ha aportado consistentemente ayuda y comodidad a estas naciones enemigas, a veces, por medio de políticas comerciales injustas que penalizan los negocios estadounidenses. Cuando el presidente Trump firmó el proyecto de ley de gastos diversos, exigiendo incrementos sustanciales para el ejército, fue en el entendido de que él podría aportar ese dinero para hacer el mayor bien, defender a la nación no solo en las batallas extranjeras, sino en nuestras propias fronteras.

"El Cuerpo de Ingenieros del Ejército de Estados Unidos", dice Weaver, "es la organización principal de construcción en el mundo. Puede construir, mantener y establecer proyectos en cualquier parte y bajo cualquier circunstancia. Está involucrado en más de 130 países. Los militares responden a los desastres naturales como huracanes, incendios y otros desastres naturales. Si puede construir carreteras, edificios y escuelas en Irak y un muro fronterizo entre Afganistán y Pakistán, el sur de Texas y los desiertos del condado de San Diego no serán un problema para ellos".[34]

HACER GRANDE A ESTADOS UNIDOS

Debido a la importancia de una economía fuerte y creciente, la primera gran reunión del Presidente fue con un grupo de los principales ejecutivos corporativos de la nación para discutir las prioridades de la administración Trump y la importancia de hacer negocios en Estados Unidos.

Entre los asistentes se encontraban los presidentes ejecutivos de la *Ford Motor Company*, *Lockheed Martin*, *Dow Chemical*, *Dell Technologies*, *US Steel*, *Whirlpool* y seis más. El Presidente le contó al grupo de los cortes tributarios para las empresas y que la eliminación de regulaciones punitivas innecesarias sería una prioridad principal de su administración, y animó a los fabricantes con operaciones en el extranjero a regresar los negocios a casa. "Habrá ventajas para las compañías que verdaderamente fabriquen sus productos aquí", dijo.[35]

Después de la reunión, el presidente ejecutivo de la *Dow Chemical*, Andrew Liveris, le dijo a CNBC durante una entrevista en vivo que él y los demás estaban entusiasmados por el fuerte apoyo de Trump. "Todo lo que percibí de esta administración en los 30 días trabajando con ellos es una urgencia en el aspecto comercial. Ellos realmente quieren quitar las barreras del camino", dijo. "Si supera la caída, yo estaría asombrado". La derogación de *Obamacare* puede ser una prioridad mayor, dijo, pero la reforma tributaria estaba "a la altura". Liveris también dijo que "todos los presidentes ejecutivos que estaban aquí hoy y en la reunión anterior, están muy animados por las políticas en favor del comercio del presidente Trump y su Gabinete". Él añadió, "algunos de nosotros hemos dicho que esta es la administración que ha estado más a favor del comercio desde los Padres Fundadores. No hay duda de que el lenguaje de negocios se da en la Casa Blanca".[36]

Desde que Trump asumió el cargo, el mercado de valores tuvo un auge, el cual discutiré más a fondo en el capítulo 7, "La economía en auge de Trump". Aunque el mercado se desplomó repentinamente en febrero de 2018, algunos analistas creen que el evento fue orquestado por adversarios multimillonarios del Presidente, quienes manipularon transacciones grandes para distraer de las ganancias recientes del mercado. Los funcionarios de la administración Obama habían proyectado una desaceleración a largo plazo y dijeron que el dos por ciento de crecimiento sería "la nueva normalidad". Sin embargo, de hecho, el Promedio Industrial *Dow Jones* alcanzó niveles récord setenta veces en el 2017. Los valores promedio de los 401(k) individuales, en junio de 2017, fueron 9.6 por ciento mayores al año anterior, y un analista del Bank of America predijo que el S&P 500 y el Compuesto NASDAQ subiría otro 12 y 16 por ciento, respectivamente, en el 2018.

Hacia el cuarto trimestre de 2017, se proyectó que la economía alcanzaría el 3 por ciento de crecimiento. La Asociación Nacional de Fabricantes observó que, en el segundo trimestre de 2018, "según el *Manufacturers' Outlook Survey*, un sorprendente 95.1 por ciento de los fabricantes registró una perspectiva positiva para su compañía, el nivel más alto registrado en los 20 años de la historia de la encuesta".[37] Richard Baris dice: "Las políticas de Trump han estimulado los niveles históricos de optimismo entre consumidores y comerciantes".[38]

Tal como lo había prometido, el primer año de Donald Trump en el cargo fue uno de los inicios más rápidos para cualquier administración en la historia estadounidense, no solo creando y facultando medidas nuevas, sino terminado otras que les estaban costando millones de dólares a los contribuyentes. Por ejemplo, él ordenó a todas las agencias federales que cortaran dos regulaciones por cada regulación nueva. El punto era reducir el número de regulaciones, lo que, a su vez, reduciría el costo neto de ejercer los intereses de la gente. Una de las mejores maneras de ayudar a la economía es quitándoles los grilletes a las empresas estadounidenses al reducir los trámites burocráticos y simplificar y modernizar al gobierno.

A los pocos días de asumir el cargo, el Presidente ordenó un congelamiento de todas las contrataciones federales, excepto el ejército, la seguridad nacional y el personal de seguridad pública. Luego, ordenó que el Departamento de Justicia retirara una política de la administración Obama que permitía que los estudiantes transgéneros "usaran el baño con el que ellos se identifican". El propósito era que todos los asuntos de este tipo quedaran en manos de los estados.

Entre otras iniciativas importantes, la agencia de Protección del Medioambiente, bajo el liderazgo de Scott Pruitt, desmanteló las Aguas de Estados Unidos y el Plan de Energía Limpia, que había sido implementado por las regulaciones de Obama. La Comisión Federal de Comunicaciones, bajo la dirección de Ajit Pai, terminó con el esquema peligroso y falso de neutralidad de red. Y el Departamento de Educación, bajo el liderazgo de Betsy DeVos, rescindió la orientación de la administración de Obama sobre cómo las escuelas deben manejar los abusos sexuales bajo la ley federal del Título IX, que había creado "tribunales canguro" que negaban los derechos de los acusados a la defensa y muchas veces destruyen la vida de los individuos sin el beneficio del debido proceso.

El 21 de marzo de 2017, todavía dentro de sus primeros cien días en el cargo, el presidente Trump firmó el Acta de Autorización de Transición de la Administración Nacional de Aeronáutica y del Espacio de 2017. El programa del transbordador espacial finalizó en el 2011, convirtiendo esencialmente a la NASA en un programa alcance. La administración de Obama incluso le dijo al jefe de la NASA que hiciera de "alcanzar al mundo musulmán" una de las prioridades principales de la agencia espacial.[39] Al restaurar a la agencia a su función legítima, la ley de Trump exige un presupuesto US$19.5 mil millones para la NASA y pide que la agencia espacial llegue a Marte antes de 2033. En respuesta, el administrador interino de la NASA, Robert Lightfoot, dijo que el proyecto de ley "garantiza que el programa espacial de nuestra nación continuará siendo el líder mundial vanguardista de nuevas fronteras en exploración, innovación y logros científicos".[40]

En la misma línea, el presidente Trump también firmó la Directiva 2 de la Política del Espacio de la Casa Blanca, el 11 de diciembre de 2017, apoyando la investigación y el desarrollo para el transporte de humanos a la luna, Marte y otros destinos celestes. El programa, que es una sociedad pública/privada desarrollada por científicos de investigación independiente, es un ejemplo del apoyo de la administración a la tecnología y la innovación y a la investigación científica de pensamiento futurista, encaminada a renovar el liderazgo estadounidense en la exploración espacial. Este programa fue creado por el apoyo unánime del nuevo Consejo Nacional del Espacio, presidido por el vicepresidente Mike Pence.

Si Donald Trump no hubiera hecho nada más que detener a Hillary Clinton, quien es —en mi opinión— la candidata más corrupta que jamás se haya postulado para presidente, él habría tenido éxito, a mi parecer. Pero cuando dijo que él quería hacer a Estados Unidos grande una vez más, no solo era una consigna, sino una visión que impulsó a este presidente a alcanzar más de lo que cualquiera de nosotros habría imaginado. Al ver el éxito de las políticas presidenciales durante los primeros dos años de su administración, es difícil no estar impresionado. Solo los casos enumerados en este capítulo forman una lista impresionante de logros. En cada listado recopilada por los medios de comunicación que monitorean el éxito o fracaso de las promesas de campaña de Trump, él está bateando muy por encima de .500. Ya sea que estemos viendo su primer día, su primer mes, sus primeros cien días, o incluso su primer año en el cargo, el presidente Trump ha podido alinear el apoyo necesario para lograr casi todos sus objetivos. Esto es extraordinario cuando uno considera que él ha estado librando una batalla continua con los medios de comunicación y manteniéndose firme contra un Congreso recalcitrante.

Gran parte del tiempo, su propio partido ha sido tan problemático como la resistencia demócrata, y la buena noticia que celebra sus triunfos ha sido reportado solamente por unas pocas fuentes: la Oficina de Prensa de la Casa Blanca, la red Fox, unas pocas publicaciones amigables y los propios tuits del presidente. Sin embargo, el pueblo estadounidense ha estado observando. Al igual que durante la campaña, está intrigado por este hombre. Tiene esperanza y, con el tiempo, el pueblo será el juez que determine el legado de la administración de Donald Trump.

EN EL FOSO DE LOS LEONES

LOS MEDIOS DE comunicación liberales en este país estaban enfocados en derribar a Donald Trump desde el día en que el anunció por primera vez que estaba postulándose para la presidencia. Empezó durante las primarias. Cuando los analistas políticos y los presentadores de redes tomaron a broma la posibilidad de que Trump ganara la nominación, nunca pensaron que él podía ganar en realidad. Las cosas extravagantes que decía y tuiteaba no eran políticamente correctas. "Con seguridad", pensaron, "la nueva atrocidad que salga de la boca de Trump será la gota que derrame el vaso".

Como periodista, soy parte de los medios de comunicación, así que estaré compartiendo algunas experiencias personales en este capítulo. Pero primero, permítame darle un panorama general. En el mundo de la élite mediática, los críticos liberales y los comentaristas son los guardianes. Ellos controlan el acceso al público, y determinan ganadores y perdedores con base al tipo de cobertura que deciden darles. Saben que cualquier paso en falso, enfatizado y repetido interminablemente, podría ser suficiente para acabar la carrera de un candidato aspirante. Después de todo, sucedió en 1987 cuando un bombardeo mediático intensivo terminó con la campaña presidencial del senador Gary Hart solamente una semana después de que los reporteros descubrieron que él había pasado el fin de semana con Donna Rice. Y, antes de eso, en 1972, el senador Edmund Muskie perdió su competencia por la presidencia cuando los reporteros notaron lágrimas en su rostro (él aseguraba que era nieve derretida) después de que él y su esposa fueron criticados. Había sido el favorito, pero el informe del senador que lloraba abiertamente lo arruinó políticamente. Y la candidatura de Muskie fue antes de los días de las noticias por cable, 24 horas, 7 días a la semana, y los noticieros por la internet transmitiendo noticias de última hora en tiempo real.

¿Y qué hay de John Edwards, el senador rubio de Carolina del Norte que estaba en la boleta con John Kerry en el 2004? Después de la derrota ante George W. Bush, Edwards decidió postularse por su cuenta en el 2008, pero los tabloides y luego los medios principales de comunicación revelaron que él había estado involucrado en un amorío de largo plazo con una trabajadora de la campaña mientras que su esposa moría de cáncer de mama. Más tarde, él admitió haber engendrado una hija con la mujer. No solo su carrera política se destruyó, sino que se le imputaron cargos de haber usado el dinero de la campaña para silenciar todo. Uno de los cargos fue retirado, los otros terminaron en un juicio nulo, después de lo cual el gobierno abandonó el caso.

Todos los políticos están preocupados de cometer una indiscreción en un debate o dar un paso en falso en la campaña electoral. El más mínimo detalle podría ser lo suficiente para anular al candidato. Y en el mundo de lo políticamente apropiado una mala elección de palabras puede ser fatal. Así que cuando Donald Trump descendió por la escalera en *Trump Tower* para anunciar su candidatura el 16 de junio de 2015, y habló rápidamente sobre los problemas con los inmigrantes ilegales y los planes para construir un muro, los críticos predijeron que su campaña sería abortada antes de arrancar. "Después de todo", dijeron, "no es políticamente correcto criticar a los 'inmigrantes indocumentados'".

Sin embargo, Trump sobrevivió esa arremetida, tal como lo hizo cuando comentó sobre el senador John McCain, diciendo que se le consideraba un héroe solo porque había sido prisionero de guerra en Vietnam. Cuando Trump dijo: "Me gusta la gente que no fue capturada",[1] los críticos estaban seguros de que finalmente lo tenían en sus manos. Pero, una vez más, eso no sucedió. No obstante, el vaivén a continuado en su presidencia donde cada paso en falso percibido que el presidente haga es reportado por los medios como la última gota.

Antes de la elección, los críticos mediáticos de Trump estaban seguros de que su ignorancia de la política exterior demostraría ser su punto débil. Entonces, cuando desafió a Rusia e Irán, y amenazó con desatar un santo infierno sobre ISIS y los yihadistas en Irak, estaba claro para los reporteros en CNN, MSNBC, y todos los noticieros liberales que Trump estaba acabado. Pero, dentro de las cuarenta y ocho horas siguientes, Rusia e Irán estaban hablando de la posibilidad de una reconciliación, y poco tiempo después, las fuerzas armadas estadounidenses en Irak estaban aplastando a yihadistas en Mosul y en Kirkuk.[2]

Avancemos hasta finales de 2017. Después de sobrevivir una controversia tras otra, y mientras que lograba evitar las arremetidas diarias de la investigación de Mueller sobre la supuesta conspiración con los rusos, los medios de comunicación estaban aferrándose a cada pequeño hilo. El abogado demócrata y exprofesor de leyes en Harvard, Alan Dershowitz, señaló que aún si hubiera evidencia de conspiración, no hay estatuto federal que la prohíba. Sin embargo, las redes de clave no podían dejar de hablar sobre la investigación rusa, el "Dossier de Steele" (lo que ha sido completamente desacreditado), y la posibilidad de una investigación exhaustiva que lo llevara a la destitución.

Pero la esperanza brota eternamente, y justo cuando *Rusiagate* parecía desvanecerse, Stormy Daniels apareció de la nada, ¡y se volvió todo un *Twitter* nocturno! Las afirmaciones de Daniels sobre una aventura de una noche con Trump, en el 2006, se convirtieron repentinamente en los titulares del día. No importaba que el pasado de mujeriego de Trump no hubiera marginado su campaña o su elección. Si las cintas magnéticas de *Access Hollywood* que grabaron a Trump haciendo comentarios vulgares sobre las mujeres no lo retrasaron, es difícil imaginar que algo de naturaleza sexual fuera a detenerlo. Surgieron varias mujeres, ninguna parecía tener una historia creíble, y una por una desaparecieron en las sombras en cuestión de días.

Stormy Daniels aparecía en todos los noticieros durante semanas, pero sus acusaciones no parecían lastimar al Presidente. Cuando se reveló que el exabogado de Trump, Michael Cohen (quien se declaró culpable de varios cargos de fraude fiscal y de violación de campaña), le había pagado a Daniels para que se callara, la estrella porno volvió brevemente a los titulares, pero parecía cada vez más como si Trump estuviera blindado. Mientras los medios de comunicación se abalanzaban más sobre él, excavando canaletas en busca de cualquier escándalo que pudieran encontrar, los simpatizantes de Trump lo defendían con más fuerza. Es difícil imaginar que cualquier revelación nueva podría haberles hecho cambiar de parecer.

El argumento de la historia de los medios era este: ¿Cómo puede un hombre así de inmoral merecer servir como presidente? Los medios afirmaban que todos los cristianos que apoyaban a Donald Trump eran hipócritas. Sin embargo, en realidad, la hipocresía se fue por el lado contrario. Después de un empecinamiento constante de "¡Es solo sexo!, y ¡El sexo entre adultos que acceden no es un crimen!", durante los años de Clinton, ¿de dónde viene este repentino estallido de indignación por el hecho de que Trump no se adhería a los estándares morales recién hallados de los medios?

La prensa nunca pareció estar preocupada cuando John Kennedy y Bill Clinton tuvieron múltiples amoríos mientras servían en la Casa Blanca. ¿Por qué no? Claro, todos conocemos la respuesta: Kennedy y Clinton eran demócratas, y Trump es un republicano conservador. Ese tipo de comportamientos ya sea por parte de Trump o de cualquier otra persona, no pueden ser aprobados por los cristianos bibliocéntricos, y mucho menos por mí. Yo no apoyé inicialmente a Trump debido a preocupaciones sobre su estilo de vida. Apoyé a Ted Cruz hasta que él abandonó la carrera. Sin embargo, aunque no estoy de acuerdo con los *anti-Trump* que no creen que Trump ejemplifique los estándares de comportamiento bíblico, sea en el dormitorio o en su cuenta de Twitter, sí estoy de acuerdo en que los cristianos debemos mantener los estándares bíblicos en nuestra cultura, incluso mientras la cultura en general los ha rechazado en su mayoría.

DEFENDER LO INDEFENDIBLE

Un *anti-Trump* me atacó en Facebook durante las elecciones porque yo había respaldado a Donald Trump. Ella enumeró sus muchas transgresiones. Generalmente, no respondo a esas publicaciones, pero esa vez sí lo hice. Acepté que lo que ella decía sobre Trump era verdad, pero que eso era como una mota en su ojo en comparación al leño en el ojo de Hillary Clinton. No solo Clinton sí respaldo la postura de los izquierdistas sobre el aborto de nacimiento parcial y el matrimonio entre personas del mismo sexo, sino que ella era probablemente la persona más corrupta que se haya postulado a la presidencia. Después del escándalo de los correos electrónicos; después de que su campaña le pagara más de US$1 millón a *Fusion GPS* por una investigación de la oposición sobre Trump, lo cual resultó en un expediente de treinta y cinco páginas; y después de que muchos creyeran que su participación era una estrategia de soborno con Rusia, concretamente, el trato *Uranium One*, ¿por qué estos cristianos, bibliocéntricos, santurrones, no estaban siendo "*anti-Hillary*"?

En algún punto durante la campaña, empecé a ver que Trump había cambiado, y que aquellos comportamientos parecían estar en el pasado. En ese punto, lo respaldé de todo corazón, no porque aprobara su reputación de mujeriego, sus múltiples matrimonios, o su involucramiento en el juego (entre otras cosas), sino en parte debido a su contrincante en la carrera por la presidencia. Cuando explotó el escándalo de Stormy Daniels, los críticos decían que Trump perdería finalmente el apoyo que recibió de los carismáticos y los evangélicos. Abrir una brecha entre Trump y su base era importante para la Izquierda, especialmente si sus simpatizantes evangélicos podrían ser vistos como hipócritas. Ellos tenían un argumento. Ahora, todo lo que necesitaban era un contingente de líderes evangélicos que les pudiera dar los extractos publicitarios que necesitaban.

En ese tiempo, la firma de relaciones públicas que representa a mi compañía había estado insistiéndome, con poco éxito, que apareciera en algunos de los programas en vivo de las redes para discutir mi libro *God and Donald Trump*. Sin embargo, el día en Stormy Daniels le contó su historia mediocre a Anderson Cooper, recibí una llamada de CNN diciendo que querían entrevistarme sobre el tema en menos de tres horas antes de la entrevista con la estrella porno altamente promocionada por Cooper.

¿Qué iba a hacer? Era un domingo por la tarde y yo acaba de regresar de estar fuera del país y no había estado viendo las noticias. Además, me preguntaba, ¿Qué pasa cuando un escritor conservador entra al estudio con los medios liberales antes de que una entrevista popular, diseñada para desacreditar y, quizá, destruir a un presidente en funciones? ¿Cómo tratarían ellos a alguien como yo dentro y fuera de cámaras? Para empeorar las cosas, mi esposa, quien no es fanática de CNN, me advirtió que no lo hiciera, comparando a la red con un foso de víboras. Sin embargo, yo quería poder hablarle de mi libro a un público nuevo y, con suerte, hablar francamente sobre temas de la fe, tratando de explicar por qué la mayoría de los evangélicos apoyan a Trump a pesar de los problemas de su estilo de vida.

Estaba haciendo algunas diligencias cuando sonó mi celular con la solicitud de entrevista de nuestra firma de relaciones públicas. Dije que me tomaría veinte minutos llegar a casa y por lo menos media hora en estar listo, y que era un trayecto de cuarenta y cinco minutos al estudio al otro lado de Orlando. No había manera de que yo pudiera manejar la logística con un periodo tan corto de tiempo. Le pedí a la persona de relaciones públicas que les dijera que me encantaría ser invitado en otra ocasión, esperando completamente que nada se materializara. Pero para mi sorpresa, al día siguiente me dijeron que CNN quería entrevistarme, pero que no sabíamos qué día. ¡Eso me dio mucho tiempo y mucho de qué preocuparme! ¿Me vería como un tonto tratando de defender un comportamiento que es indefendible? ¿Era CNN realmente tan malo como la mayoría de los conservadores pensaba, incluyendo al presidente Trump? ¿Podría decir algo que pudiera usarse fuera de contexto para hacer ver mal a los evangélicos?

Hace muchos años decidí que, sin importar las consecuencias, estaría dispuesto a entrar por las puertas que el Señor abriera para mí. Así que, después de consultar con un par de amigos y orar por ello, decidí entrar por esta puerta, incluso si era una puerta hacia un pozo de víboras. Decidí que lo peor que podía pasar es que esa gente se riera de mí o que la experiencia sería tan negativa que nunca querría hacer otra entrevista con CNN. Sabía que iba a un territorio desconocido, pero al menos lo habría intentado.

Mientras esperábamos para saber qué día querían hacer la entrevista, sintonicé el programa matutino de CNN, *New Day*, para tener una idea de lo que podía esperar. Los presentadores, Chris Cuomo y Alisyn Camerota, estaban entrevistando a un conservador, y parecían ser respetuosos. No eran tan agresivos como yo esperaba. Cuando la invitación llegó finalmente, los productores me pidieron que fuera al estudio un miércoles, durante la Semana Santa. Tendría que levantarme a las 4:00 a.m. para llegar antes de las 6:00 a.m., y estaría al aire aproximadamente a las 6:50 a.m.

He hecho muchas entrevistas en televisión, pero casi siempre en programas cristianos. Así que, como las entrevistas eran amigables, la experiencia me ayudaba a relajarme, a ser yo mismo, a prestarle atención al entrevistador y a olvidar todo lo demás. Y, sobre todo, mi esposa me dijo después de ver uno de los programas, "¡Sonríe, Steve! Diles que te da gusto estar allí". Pero también sentía que había un propósito mayor para que yo estuviera al aire, y no era acerca de mí o de mi libro. Entonces, decidí solo ser yo mismo, ser amigable, y tratar de dar respuestas positivas sin importar cómo me trataran.

Me habían dicho que hablaríamos de Stormy Daniels y Trump y de por qué los evangélicos todavía lo apoyan. Antes de ir al estudio, hice mi propia encuesta, preguntándoles a amigos y colegas si ellos sentían que este escándalo dañaría seriamente a Trump. Yo creía que no, y ellos tampoco. Mientras que mi encuesta no tenía nada de científica, me dio la confianza de que estaría hablando por la mayoría de los evangélicos.

Camerota me entrevistó. Ella empezó el segmento diciendo: "Explícanos, otra vez, cómo es que los evangélicos están dispuestos a pasar por alto estos reportes de infidelidad y otras cosas para apoyar al presidente Trump".[3]

"Eso es fácil para mí", le dije. "Donald Trump ha tenido una reputación como mujeriego que se remonta a la década de los ochentas". "Yo no apoyé a Donald Trump durante mucho tiempo porque no aprobaba, ya saben, lo que yo sabía de su estilo de vida".

Camerota preguntó, "Entonces, ¿qué fue lo que cambió?", lo que me dio la apertura que yo esperaba.

Yo dije: "Creo que él cambió. Realmente lo creo. Y hablo de esto en mi libro *God and Donald Trump*. Lo entrevisté en el 2016 y esperaba algo como la personalidad ostentosa que uno ve en los medios". Añadí: "Hallé que es respetuoso, que es en realidad un poco modesto".

"Y la gente sabía que él no era perfecto. Menciono eso en mi libro, una y otra vez, porque nosotros, los cristianos, sabemos que uno tiene que ser perdonado y que Dios puede cambiar vidas y que los líderes de quienes leemos en la Biblia, empezando por el rey David, no eran perfectos en ninguna forma, manera o tamaño".

Ella replicó: "Pero para recibir perdón, ¿no se tiene que confesar sus pecados? … ¿No es un principio bíblico? Es decir, ¿no tiene que reconocer estas cosas? Ya sabe, es muy conocido que Donald Trump dijo que nunca le pidió perdón a Dios".

Obviamente, ella me estaba haciendo preguntas de "te atrapé", esperando por un extracto que CNN pudieran transmitir una y otra vez, demostrando su premisa predeterminada de que los evangélicos estaban empezando a darle la espalda a Donald Trump.

En ese momento, no sentí que Camerota me estuviera confrontando; yo tenía mi atención centrada en dar respuestas convincentes y hacer que se viera como una conversación, aunque ella estaba en la ciudad de Nueva York y yo en un estudio oscuro en Orlando, Florida, tratando de relacionarme con la lente de una cámara como si fuera el entrevistador que no podía ver. Pero, cuando vi el video después, parecía estar confrontándome y pude ver cómo trataba, una y otra vez, de que yo mordiera el anzuelo. Pero no lo logró. En cambio, traté de llevar la discusión de regreso a lo que los cristianos creen o lo que la Biblia dice.

Cuando ella preguntó lo que la Biblia dice sobre el perdón, ¡enfaticé que me daba gusto que ella estuviera citando la Biblia! Giré la discusión hacia las políticas de Donald Trump que le agradan a los evangélicos. Después, los amigos que vieron la entrevista me felicitaron por mis "puntadas". En realidad, en ese momento, no lo vi como una puntada, tampoco como un punto particularmente importante. Fui a la entrevista deseando solamente responder sus preguntas, no para debatir ni para hacerlos ver mal. Había rogado que el Señor me diera las palabras a decir.

Más tarde, Camerota me preguntó si los evangélicos estábamos volteando la mirada intencionalmente cuando se trataba del pasado sexual de Trump. Creo que el Señor me motivó a decir que, si ese fuera el caso, no era peor que cuando los medios principales de comunicación volteaban la mirada cuando el presidente John Kennedy y, después, el presidente Bill Clinton tuvieron múltiples amoríos mientras ocupaban la Casa Blanca. Ni siquiera había pensado en eso antes de ese momento como una línea probable de interrogación o tema de discusión que debía repetir.

Curiosamente, Camerota no discutió mi punto más que para referirse al hecho de que yo estaba haciendo lo que la prensa hizo, voltear la mirada. Le recordé que yo también soy periodista. Ella probablemente está acostumbrada a lidiar con pastores evangélicos, no con alguien que tiene un grado en periodismo y que ha entrevistado a cuatro presidentes. Me sentí bien acerca de cómo fue la entrevista. Lo estaba haciendo más para hablar del Señor y para intercalar, a mi manera, el significado espiritual de lo que está sucediendo en nuestro país y la conversión de los eventos que nos llevaron a elegir a Donald Trump, y no solo a vender más libros. Para ese momento, mi libro ya había estado en los listados de los libros cristianos de mayor venta desde el mes en que se lanzó.

Por lo general, cada vez que hago una entrevista en los medios, vemos un incremento en las ventas de Amazon, por parte de quienes se enteraron del libro por la entrevista. Ellos van a sus computadoras y lo piden en línea. Después de esta aparición, sin embargo, vimos muy poco incremento en ventas. Al principio, me sorprendió, pero luego, me di cuenta de que el público de CNN no es propenso a leer un libro sobre Dios y Donald Trump como lo son los espectadores de los medios cristianos, donde aparezco generalmente. Más tarde, un amigo me recordó que los *ratings* de CNN son tan bajos que quizá no muchas personas estaban viendo el canal a las 6:50 a.m., cuando yo estaba al aire.

Cuando me entrevistaron en *Fox&Friends*, dos meses antes, yo estaba recibiendo textos y correos electrónicos antes de salir del estudio. Los amigos que casualmente tenían la televisión encendida no esperaban verme allí, y me enviaron notas de felicitación. Recibí muy pocos comentarios así después de mis dos apariciones en CNN y MSNBC. Quizá sea porque mis amigos normalmente ven Fox y no esas otras redes de televisión.

VOCES PROFÉTICAS

Anteriormente, había hecho muchas entrevistas de radio y televisión para promover mi libro *God and Donald Trump*. Mientras lo hacía, me di cuenta de que, sin planearlo necesariamente, yo repetía ciertos temas. Uno de ellos era el hecho de que varios profetas modernos habían predicho que, contra todo pronóstico, Donald Trump sería el próximo presidente de Estados Unidos. Esto había ocurrido desde el año 2007, y es algo que yo documenté en el libro. Meses antes de las elecciones, yo había escrito sobre las voces proféticas en la revista *Charisma*, tanto en la versión impresa como digital.

Esas profecías pueden haber sonado ridículas o imposibles para algunos, pero Trump fue electo, tal como lo dijeron los profetas. Las profecías fueron una razón por la que tuve la confianza de viajar a Nueva York para la fiesta de la noche de las elecciones. Sé que parece una locura, pero, de alguna manera, de algún modo, Dios intervino en esas elecciones y nos libró de que "Hillary, la corrupta" se convirtiera en presidenta.

Cuando los entrevistadores me preguntaron cómo los evangélicos podían votar por un hombre tan imperfecto, me encontré diciendo que millones de cristianos estaban orando para que, de alguna manera, Dios cambiara la dirección en que iba esta nación. Dije que Dios respondió nuestras oraciones de una manera que no esperábamos, con una persona que no nos agradaba necesariamente. Sin embargo, una vez Trump empezó a implementar sus políticas, estuvimos seguros de que habíamos elegido correctamente.

Como ya lo he mencionado, yo no apoyaba inicialmente a Trump por la misma razón que algunos evangélicos todavía no lo apoyan: su estilo de vida y su comportamiento ostentoso no era lo que los cristianos esperan de sus líderes nacionales. Lo he dicho en muchas ocasiones.

Yo respaldé públicamente a Ted Cruz y lo apoyé hasta el día en que abandonó la carrera. Para entonces, ya estaba consciente de las comparaciones entre Donald Trump y el rey persa, Ciro el Grande, un pagano que fue usado por Dios para que los israelitas salieran del cautiverio y regresaran a Jerusalén.

La Escritura dice en Isaías: "Así dice el Señor a Ciro, su ungido,… te he llamado por tu nombre; te he honrado, aunque no me conocías" (45:1-4). Oí esto por primera vez de mi amigo Lance Wallnau, pero documenté en *God and Donald Trump* que otros habían hecho la misma comparación.

En mi caso, tenía sentido que, si Dios podía usar al rey Ciro para cumplir sus propósitos, Él definitivamente podía usar a Donald Trump. Claro está, también le di mi respaldo debido a su apoyo declarado por los intereses cristianos, lo que era contrario a lo que su oponente decía y creía. Sin embargo, no fueron solo los profetas carismáticos quienes hicieron la comparación Ciro-Trump. Las organizaciones del Templo acuñaron una "moneda del templo" a principios de 2018 con el perfil de Trump, y justo detrás de él hay una representación del rey Ciro. La mayor parte de la escritura está en hebreo, pero también dice en inglés: "Declaración de Cyrus-Balfour-Trump 2018".[4]

Por supuesto, a la prensa secular no le importan las comparaciones con los reyes del Antiguo Testamento. Sin embargo, están obsesionados con la "hipocresía" de los cristianos que van a la iglesia, creen en la Biblia y apoyan a un mujeriego de Nueva York.

ORAR INTENSAMENTE

Ya que nunca había estado en CNN antes, me sorprendí cuando recibí una segunda invitación para entrevistarme el Domingo de Resurrección, esta vez en un programa vespertino de CNN presentado por Ryan Nobles. Él fue menos polémico que Camerota, pero hizo algunas buenas preguntas. Por ejemplo: cuando preguntó sobre el comportamiento de Trump y citó a Franklin Graham diciendo que, del momento de esos supuestos amoríos hasta ahora, Trump es un hombre cambiado. Nobles me dio la mejor oportunidad de cualquiera de mis entrevistas para hablar en favor del Señor.

"Tú sabes, toda la esencia del cristianismo", dije, "es que Dios puede cambiar a las personas a través del poder del evangelio".[5] Le dije que en mi libro yo había documentado que, a principios de la década de 2000, Trump empezó a sintonizar programas de televisión cristiana, viendo a ministros como Paula White cain. Y yo mencioné cómo él permitió que pastores y demás se reunieran alrededor de él y le impusieran manos y oraran al estilo Pentecostés.

Le dije que Trump parecía disfrutar las oraciones. Incluso fui lo suficientemente audaz para añadir un comentario que probablemente no tuvo sentido para Nobles: "Me han contado que disfruta que los cristianos lo llamen 'el ungido'". Claro, ese comentario era una cápsula, y no tuve tiempo para describir o explicar cómo, durante la elección, Trump hablaba en mítines en Ohio, que muchas veces se llevaban a cabo en iglesias carismáticas, y cómo él estaba presente cuando esas personas adoraban y oraban en su estilo carismático usual, frecuentemente dirigidos por el pastor Frank Amedia de Canfield, Ohio, quien es un amigo personal. Cuando los cristianos oran y hay una sensación de que el Señor está presente en ese lugar, los pentecostales llaman a eso "la unción". Es algo que uno siente cuando adora profundamente. Amedia, quien tenía un acceso considerable al candidato, y luego, presidente Trump, me dijo que Trump le pedía que "orara intensamente" porque Trump parecía disfrutar esa presencia.

Cuando pasé por las puertas de las entrevistas de los medios seculares que Dios había abierto, empezaba a ver que podía defender el evangelio y que ellos no me contradecían, aun si era solo porque estábamos en Semana Santa. En una entrevista el Viernes Santo con Craig Melvin en MSNBC, él me preguntó: "Además del confirmar a Neil Gorsuch en la Corte Suprema, ¿Qué más señalan los evangélicos como un triunfo de este presidente desde un punto de vista legislativo o de políticas?'". Entonces, giré la discusión de vuelta al hecho de que hay "millones cristianos evangélicos que creían que el país iba en dirección equivocada, y oramos. Rogamos a Dios que, de alguna manera, hiciera algo para cambiar la dirección de nuestro país, y él levantó a un hombre que a nosotros no necesariamente nos agradaba, en la forma de Donald Trump. Él ha hecho más por la libertad de culto y ayudado a los cristianos perseguidos y al tipo de causas que los cristianos sienten que son importantes que cualquier otro presidente, creo, en mi vida".[6]

Yo cité: proteger la libertad de culto, ayudar a los cristianos perseguidos; y el hecho de que él cree que la Enmienda Johnson al Código del ISR, que limita a las iglesias y organizaciones sin fines de lucro a respaldar candidatos –una clara violación de sus derechos de la Primera Enmienda–, debería ser derogada por el Congreso. Mientras tanto, el Presidente giró una orden ejecutiva para que la Enmienda Johnson no se hiciera cumplir hasta que se pudiera cambiar la ley.

Como era de esperar, Melvin dijo algo sobre la separación de la iglesia y el estado. Cuando vi el programa, más tarde, me di cuenta de que pude haber dicho algo acerca de esa falacia. Las palabras *separación de la iglesia y del estado* no aparecen en la Constitución. Es una frase conveniente que Thomas Jefferson se sacó de la nada para asegurarle a un grupo bautista en Connecticut que el gobierno no haría ninguna ley restringiendo su libertad de culto. Esto es lo que la enmienda dice en realidad: "El Congreso no deberá hacer ley alguna con relación a una institución religiosa o que prohíba el libre ejercicio de la misma", y luego, el documento añade que el Congreso no puede abreviar "la libertad de expresión o de prensa; ni el derecho del pueblo de reunirse pacíficamente, y solicitar al Gobierno un resarcimiento de los daños".[7]

Cuando los medios citan la Primera Enmienda, generalmente se refieren a la libertad de prensa, lo que apoyo fuertemente. Sin embargo, note que la libertad de culto, la cual el gobierno no puede prohibir "el libre ejercicio de la misma", viene antes de las otras libertades.

Luego, Melvin citó una encuesta que parecía demostrar su punto de que Trump estaba perdiendo el apoyo evangélico. Dudo de la encuesta porque probablemente fue hecha por las mismas personas que predijeron que Hillary Clinton ganaría por una avalancha. Pero no había oído hablar de eso, así que cité mi propia "encuesta" basada en las declaraciones de todas las personas con las que he hablado, indicando que ninguno de ellos ha cambiado de opinión acerca de Trump. "Ha habido muchas, muchas oportunidades para cambiar de modo de pensar sobre Trump", le dije, "pero él no ha fallado. Se mantiene fuerte. Está tratando de hacer grande a Estados Unidos otra vez, y la mayoría de los cristianos evangélicos, como yo, estamos orando para que, de alguna manera, Estados Unidos se vuelva grande moral y espiritualmente otra vez".

Los principales medios de comunicación no parecen entenderlo. Los cristianos conservadores quieren una gran nación espiritual, y si bien estamos interesados en los recortes tributarios y en la política exterior, para nosotros, el verdadero problema es si las políticas ayudarán o lastimarán a la comunidad cristiana y si estas están llevando a nuestro país en la dirección correcta. Desde la elección de Donald Trump, creo que las cosas van en la dirección correcta. Creo que Donald Trump toma en consideración nuestros intereses, o si no, no lo defendería como lo hago.

Resalté el mismo punto con Camerota. Dije: "El tema para mí y para millones de evangélicos es sus políticas. Él apoya el tipo de políticas que nosotros creemos que son importantes".[8] El experto político, Marc A. Thiessen, a quien admiro por su claro comentario en el canal de noticias Fox, estuvo de acuerdo conmigo cuando escribió un artículo de opinión en el *Washington Post,* publicado el 23 de marzo de 2018, titulado "Por qué los cristianos conservadores se apegan a Trump".

Thiessen escribió: "Él es un hombre con muchos defectos. Sin embargo, Trump ha demostrado una cualidad moral como presidente que merece admiración: Él cumple sus promesas. Durante la campaña de 2016, Trump prometió defender la libertad de culto, defender la vida de los no nacidos, y nombrar juristas conservadores para la Corte Suprema y los tribunales federales de apelación. Y ha hecho exactamente lo que prometió".[9]

"Mayor prueba de que él está respaldando los asuntos cristianos, tales como reducir el aborto, pueden hallarse en la literatura y los anuncios de cabildeo proaborto de NARAL (National Abortion Rights Action League)", Thiessen añade, "que se quejan de que Trump ha sido 'implacable' sobre esos frentes, y declaran a su administración 'la peor que hayan visto'".

Thiessen da un largo listado de logros documentados en otra parte de este libro y concluye su artículo de opinión diciendo: "Nadie defiende a Trump como un ejemplo moral. Él no es el presidente más religioso que hayamos tenido, pero puede ser el presidente que más ha estado a favor de la religión. Los cristianos conservadores no juzgan a Trump por su fe, sino por sus obras. Y en lo que se refiere a la vida y la libertad, sus obras son buenas".

La elección de Donald Trump fue "impactante y asombrosa" para el *statu quo* y la dirección de la nación, tal como lo he descrito en la Parte 1. Pero ese era solo el principio. Para hacer a Estados Unidos grande otra vez, Donald Trump ahora "va a la ofensiva".

PARTE II

IR A LA OFENSIVA

EL PÚLPITO INTIMIDANTE DE TRUMP

A LO LARGO DE los años 80 y 90, Donald Trump fue una sensación para los medios. Extravagante, ingenioso y fabulosamente rico, él fue uno de los magnates de los bienes raíces más exitoso en Nueva York y de la nación, y los medios no se cansaban de él. Las revistas, los periódicos, la radio y la televisión; él estaba por todas partes. Era un multimillonario, casado y con un hijo, y una figura pública muy buscada en 1980 cuando fue invitado a los estudios de la NBC en Manhattan para una entrevista con el famoso presentador, Tom Brokaw, en el *The Today Show*.

"Sr. Trump, ¿qué le falta en la vida?", preguntó Brokaw. "Tiene 33 años, y todo ese dinero. Usted dijo que no había dicho que quería valer mil millones de dólares".[1] A Trump se le había descrito como ostentoso y egoísta. Él creció en distrito de Queens, luego obtuvo un título universitario en la *Ivy League* de la *Wharton School* y siguió los pasos de su padre millonario en los negocios. Él tenía razón para ser vanidoso, y él claramente disfrutaba su éxito. No veía su riqueza con timidez y seguramente creía que pronto sería un multimillonario. Sin embargo, él siempre era amable en las entrevistas y, como lo señaló *The Atlantic*, incluso algo humilde.

"No, realmente no lo hice", le respondió a Brokaw. "Solo quería mantenerme ocupado y activo y estar interesado en lo que hago. Y eso es todo en la vida en lo que a mí concierne". Poco a poco, y una cápsula tras otra, el apuesto joven promotor inmobiliario de la ciudad de Nueva York se estaba convirtiendo en una celebridad nacional y en un personaje famoso.[2] Haber completado las reparaciones en la pista de patinaje sobre hielo Wollman de *Central Park* en tiempo récord y US$750,000 por debajo del presupuesto, después de que el contratista original se había pasado del presupuesto y del tiempo, elevó dramáticamente su estatus de celebridad con los neoyorquinos.

Recuerdo haber leído cómo humilló a la municipalidad de Nueva York al completar la pista de patinaje sobre hielo de Wollman cuando la municipalidad no pudo hacerlo. Pero, en general, no me impresionó su reputación de mujeriego, y no tenía interés en observar el desarrollo de su carrera. Nunca hubiera soñado que treinta años después él sería electo el cuadragésimo quinto presidente de Estados Unidos.

Las fortunas de Trump aumentaron y disminuyeron repetidamente a través de la década de los noventa, pero para el 2004, él estaba en acción, con tres concursos de belleza televisados a nivel nacional, un libro de mayor venta, una cadena de casinos, y su propio programa de televisión, *El Aprendiz*, que apenas estaba empezando su impresionante décimo quinta temporada. Su propiedad distintiva, *Trump Tower*, completada en 1983 sobre la Quinta Avenida, en el corazón de Manhattan, fue la sede mundial del imperio creciente de Trump. Una presentación por James Traub en la revista *New York Times*, decía: "Trump probablemente recibe más solicitudes de entrevistas que cualquier otro ciudadano privado en Nueva York".[3]

"Las normas que rigen a otros, simplemente no se aplican a Trump", afirmó Traub. "Con él, es la celebridad la que genera el éxito en vez de ser al revés. Y Trump nunca había sido una celebridad más grande de lo que es ahora, gracias al éxito impresionante de *El Aprendiz*, que ha sido nominado para cuatro premios *Emmy* y empezó su segunda temporada la semana pasada". Y para rematar, dijo, el libro "*The Art of the Deal*, que fue publicado en 1987, vendió 835,000 ejemplares solamente en tapa dura".[4] La Organización Trump resistió su cuota de problemas, incluyendo quiebras y juicios de diversos tipos, pero el éxito de su libro y la exposición semanal en televisión, le estaban dando a Donald una audiencia mucho mayor. Tal como lo escribe Traub:

> Más de cuarenta millones de personas vieron el último episodio de la primera temporada...cuando Trump ungió al ganador. El programa fue la nueva serie mejor valorada y empató con *The West Wing* por atraer a la demografía más acaudalada del horario estelar de la televisión. "El Aprendiz" casi por sí solo rescató las fortunas en decadencia de la NBC, la red que lo transmitía.[5]

Con todo su éxito, Trump había llegado al Olimpo de la cultura de la celebridad, donde reinaban personas como Oprah, Martha Stewart, Ralph Lauren, y el artista *hip-hop* P. Diddy. "Ahora viene Donald, con su propio programa de televisión exitoso, sus propios cambios de golf y su propia revista: *Trump World*, cuyo primer ejemplar acaba de llegar a los quioscos, y su colección de camisetas, corbatas, trajes, y una fragancia que llevan su nombre. Los trajes y la fragancia eran algo seguro, y sobre lo demás, solo tiene que dar la orden".[6]

Pero como dicen, *tempus fugit* ("el tiempo vuela"), y para muchos jóvenes votantes, todo esto describe a un Donald Trump que no conocían. Para los medios principales de comunicación, en particular, el brillo de la estrella en ascenso se ha evaporado, y el hombre que se convertiría en el cuadragésimo quinto presidente de Estados Unidos se ha vuelto un objeto de desprecio. Sin embargo, la pregunta existencial es: ¿Cómo es posible que alguien con tanto éxito, carisma y reconocimiento público pudo volverse repentinamente la persona más controversial y divisoria sobre el planeta? ¿Qué cambió?

Creo que Donald Trump cambió. Como lo describí en otra parte, él empezó a ver la televisión cristiana y a hacer preguntas a los líderes cristianos como Paula White Cain. En el proceso, sus políticas cambiaron. Él se convirtió en opositor del aborto y abrazó las causas conservadoras. ¿No es de extrañar un poco que a la élite de los medios no le gusta el nuevo Trump conservador más de lo que les gustaba aquellos en Estados Unidos a quienes, como Barack Obama famosamente dijo, "apéguense a sus armas o a la religión?".[7]

Tal como lo han demostrado las multitudes en sus mítines de campaña presidencial en las ciudades y pueblos por todo Estados Unidos, Donald Trump aún es celebrado y admirado por millones de estadounidenses comunes. No obstante, a la vez es maldecido y vilipendiado con igual medida de temor y odio por Hollywood, la academia y las élites de Nueva York. Su índice de preferencia, superando el 50 por ciento a principios de 2018, fue ligeramente mejor que el de hostilidad.[8] Sin embargo, entre liberales, progresistas y los principales medios de comunicación no hay palabras para describir el odio que hierve y surge dentro de ellos cuando se menciona el nombre de Trump.

DAR A CONOCER A ESTADOS UNIDOS

El día que anunció su candidatura, Trump le dijo a la multitud reunida en el vestíbulo de la Trump Tower, "necesitamos a alguien que pueda tomar la marca de Estados Unidos y volver a hacerla grande…Necesitamos a alguien que, literalmente, tome este país y lo haga grande otra vez. Podemos hacerlo…Así que, damas y caballeros, me postulo oficialmente para la presidencia de Estados Unidos".[9] En ese momento, el *Washington Post* informó: "Trump entra en la carrera con un reconocimiento de nombre casi inigualable y una marca inmobiliaria poderosa, pero con una reputación de temperamento rápido y de acaparar la atención de las contiendas de las celebridades".[10]

Es cierto que Trump había tenido un intercambio de palabras con personas como Ariana Huffington, Rosie O'Donnell, Cher, Mitt Romney y otros. Él nunca fue tímido para decir lo pensaba. Sin embargo, la contienda más provocativa y que más lejos llegó sucedió en el 2011 cuando Barack Obama decidió burlarse de Trump en la cena anual para los corresponsales de la Casa Blanca. En medio de la controversia de natalidad, remontándose a la campaña de Obama en el 2008, los analistas de documentos encontraron inconsistencias en el certificado de nacimiento de Obama, y Trump dijo más de una vez que él sospechaba que el documento era falso. Los medios y los políticos de ambas partes negaron las afirmaciones, pero Obama no estaba satisfecho con eso.[11]

Durante la cena, con Donald Trump sentado a solo unos cuantos pasos, Obama bromeó: "Nadie está más orgulloso de dar por terminado este asunto del certificado de nacimiento que Donald. Y eso es porque finalmente puede volver a concentrarse en cosas importantes, como: ¿falsificamos el aterrizaje lunar? ¿Qué pasó realmente en Roswell? ¿Y dónde están Biggie y Tupac?". Claramente disfrutando de la risa a costa de Trump, el Presidente añadió: "Digan lo que quieran, el Sr. Trump de seguro traerá algún cambio a la Casa Blanca".[12] En ese momento, la imagen de la Casa Blanca, remodelada para parecerse a un casino extravagante de Las Vegas, fue proyectada en la pantalla de video del salón de recepción.

El golpe de Obama alcanzó el objetivo, y el video del evento muestra a un Donald serio y con el rostro endurecido tratando lo mejor que pudo de contener sus instintos naturales. Sin embargo, muchos observadores políticos creen que ese fue el momento preciso cuando Trump decidió postularse para la Casa Blanca. No obstante, el enfrentamiento entre Trump y Obama no quedó allí. En agosto de 2012, en medio de la segunda campaña de Obama, Trump tuiteó: "una fuente extremadamente confiable llamó a mi oficina y me dijo que el certificado de nacimiento de @BarackObama es un fraude".[13] Luego, solo unas semanas antes de las elecciones intermedias de 2014, Trump envió otro tuit: "Estoy empezando a pensar que hay algo seriamente malo con la salud mental del presidente Obama… ¡psicópata!".[14]

El episodio de 2011 aún resuena fuertemente en los individuos al centro del conflicto, particularmente a la luz de la sorprendente sentencia de los organizadores de la Cena de corresponsales de la Casa Blanca de 2018. El ataque vulgar y de mal gusto a la secretaria de prensa, Sarah Sanders y al Presidente, por parte de la comediante Michelle Wolf simplemente enfatizó el nivel de odio en el corazón de la división Izquierda-Derecha. Los seguidores y liberales en los medios celebraron el ataque de Wolf, pero Donald Trump no carece de recursos propios.

Desde que se convirtió en presidente y ocupó la Casa Blanca, él ha hecho historia con su cuenta de Twitter. Como el columnista, James Lewis, señala: "Donald Trump es el único presidente desde Ronald Reagan que puede sortear a los medios para llegar directamente al corazón de los estadounidenses".[15] Utiliza Twitter a menudo, para disgusto de su equipo de asesores, no solo para felicitar a ciudadanos privados por su heroísmo y servicio público, sino como su primer arma de defensa contra la prensa antagonista. Al explicar sus motivos, Trump, dijo: "uso los medios sociales, no porque me guste, sino porque es la única manera de luchar contra una 'prensa' deshonesta e injusta, a la que ahora se le conoce como los Medios de Noticias Falsas. Las 'fuentes' falsas e inexistentes se están utilizando más que nunca. ¡Muchas de las historias e informes son pura ficción!".[16]

Tan pronto como fue identificado como un posible candidato republicano,

Trump se convirtió en un blanco de la Izquierda. Cada palabra, cada acción y cada paso fueron examinados y detectados por reporteros ansiosos de obtener una primicia. Pero, a pesar de la animosidad casi compulsiva que genera en la Izquierda, Trump está en su mejor momento. Él es el titular de todos los noticieros, y les guste o no, él es la fuente de ingresos de los medios.

En un artículo que escribió para la revista *Fortune*, Mathew Ingram cita un estudio hecho por el analista de televisión Andrew Tyndall durante la campaña de 2016 que descubrió que Trump estaba recibiendo la mayor parte de la cobertura de noticias en la cadena, un total combinado de 327 minutos en ABC, CBS y NBC en el 2015. Compare esto con Jeb Bush y Ben Carson, quienes obtuvieron solamente 57 minutos cada uno; Marco Rubio, quien obtuvo aproximadamente 22 minutos; y Ted Cruz, quien recibió solo 21 minutos de cobertura. Y eso no incluye la cobertura que Trump estaba recibiendo prácticamente a toda hora en las redes de cable.

Una razón por la que Trump es fácil de cubrir: "Él es efectivamente una máquina de medios de una sola persona, especialmente a través de su cuenta Twitter", dice Ingram, "donde escoge peleas y lanza granadas a todos, desde los otros candidatos hasta a Taylor Swift". Como Tim Dickinson, un escritor para los *Rolling Stone* señaló en una tormenta de tuits: "los 6.5 millones de seguidores de Trump lo hacen como del mismo tamaño que el noticiero nocturno de CBS…Él es su propia entidad mediática".[17]

Claro está, el número de seguidores de Trump ha incrementado muchísimo desde la campaña, y su influencia solamente ha crecido. Pero por mucho que no les agrade a los medios, no pueden vivir sin él. " ¿Necesitan aumentar su tráfico?", dice Ingram. "Pase un par de historias más de Trump con algunos tuits en ellas, y está bien… Aunque él es una entidad mediática por sí solo, el candidato confía en las redes de televisión y los periódicos y los sitios web no solo para darle cobertura, sino para proveerle de un buen lugar para desahogarse cuando critica a los ortodoxos liberales y cómo ellos no lo entienden a él".[18]

EL PUNTO CIEGO DE LOS MEDIOS

Según la encuesta de encuestas compilada por *RealClearPolitics*, que incluye un promedio estadístico de múltiples encuestas de popularidad, el promedio de aprobación del trabajo del Presidente, en mayo de 2018, estaba alrededor del 43 por ciento,[19] lo que aparentemente es un enigma para los críticos de Trump. A pesar de sus mejores esfuerzos, las fuerzas combinadas con los medios principales de comunicación, la DNC, los liberales de Hollywood y toda la entidad progresista, Trump sigue siendo relevante e inmensamente popular con los votantes de Estados Unidos continental. Nada podría ser más desconcertante. Pero este es el punto ciego de los medios. No solo están enojados por el resultado de las elecciones, sino que, además, están avergonzados de haber fracasado en atraer a la nación a su punto de vista liberal.

Los analistas expertos de la red leyeron repetidamente mal el pulso de la nación durante todo el ciclo de las elecciones de 2016 y, aparentemente, tuvieron poco o ningún impacto en los índices de popularidad de Trump. Ellos aún no pueden comprender cómo el hombre al que denigraron por meses pudo ganar los votos de sesenta y tres millones de estadounidenses. Esto podría explicar por qué James Acosta, de CNN, un crítico del Presidente, de mucho tiempo y que suele ser un perturbador, concluyó que los estadounidenses carecían de inteligencia para ver a través del acto de Donald Trump. Tal como Acosta declaró durante una entrevista con *Variety*: "Ellos no tienen todas sus instalaciones, en algunos casos su elevador puede que no llegue a todos los pisos" (Paráfrasis: No están en todos sus cabales).[20]

Vi personalmente esta hostilidad hacia Trump en CNN cuando me entrevistaron dos veces acerca de Stormy Daniels, en la Semana Santa de 2018. Como lo dije en otra parte de este libro, ellos solo estaban interesados en interrogarme sobre cómo era posible que evangélicos devotos pudieran respaldar a alguien tan inmoral como Donald Trump, incluso al compararlo con Harvey Weinstein. Yo dije que no aprobamos esos asuntos de su estilo de vida pasada; nosotros le damos más importancia a las políticas de Trump.

Durante más de dos años, los medios han conducido un bombardeo permanente al aire del carácter, los motivos y la inteligencia del presidente, mientras que ignoran, y generalmente malinterpretan, sus logros con la economía, lo laboral, lo tributario, la política exterior, el ejército y la seguridad fronteriza. La impresión entre la mayoría del público en general es que el enfoque de los medios de comunicación se basa casi en su totalidad en los puntos de conversación y en los aspectos generales proporcionados por el DNC. "Lo que tenemos aquí", escribe John Nolte, "son más pruebas de que los medios ya no pueden influir en la opinión pública ni alterar el rumbo. Mientras la aprobación del trabajo de Trump se mantiene al 43 por ciento, la confianza en los medios está solo al 41 por ciento. Pero aun ese 41 por ciento está sesgado. Solo los demócratas apoyan a los medios en un nivel respetable del 62 por ciento".[21]

La antipatía detrás de la agresión constante de los medios no se ha perdido en el público. Tal como informó Gallup en enero de 2018, el 43 por ciento de los estadounidenses cree que los medios de comunicación apoyan nuestra democracia "mal" o "muy mal", mientras que el 28 por ciento dice que apoya la democracia "bien" o "muy bien". Y menos de la mitad de los estadounidenses en la encuesta (44 por ciento) pudo nombrar al menos una fuente de noticias objetiva. Adicionalmente, Gallup descubrió que los estadounidenses de todas las persuasiones políticas creen que la difusión de información inexacta en la internet también es un problema importante, con el 76 por ciento de republicanos, 71 por ciento de demócratas y 75 por ciento de independientes que comparten esta opinión.[22]

Mientras tanto, solo el 14 por ciento de los republicanos cree que los medios de comunicación entienden los hechos bien. Y que solo el 37 por ciento de los independientes, un grupo objetivo crítico para ambos partidos dijo que los medios entienden los hechos bien.[23] En otras palabras, fuera de los precintos sólidamente demócratas del Este y los liberales de la Costa Oeste, la mayoría de Estados Unidos ya no cree en los medios. Y como Nolte dice: "¿Por qué deberían hacerlo?". Los medios son una fábrica de noticias falsas que, por casi dos años, nos han dicho una mentira tras otra sobre Trump conspirando con Rusia; y, ahora, nos hemos enterado de que era un enorme y asqueroso fraude fabricado por el subgobierno, CNN y BuzzFeed".[24]

Durante más de medio siglo, desde al menos el final de la Segunda Guerra Mundial, las encuestas han mostrado que lo que la mayoría de los estadounidenses desean realmente es paz y prosperidad. Hacia el final de su segundo año en la Casa Blanca, la mayoría de los estadounidenses cree que Donald Trump ha cumplido con sus promesas. Los niveles de ingresos han aumentado constantemente, los impuestos están más bajos, la nación no está en un peligro inmediato de guerra, y los estándares de vida en Estados Unidos son unos de los mejores en el mundo. A principios de 2018, Nolte especulaba que, muy probablemente, los votantes juzgarán a Trump sobre esa base en las futuras elecciones generales y de medio término. Pero, en su mayor parte, escribe Nolten, "ellos pueden ver a través del humo de las mentiras de los medios y la histeria de los críticos, y ellos empiezan a entender que 'las fuentes no dicen' es el equivalente en el griego a 'estas son noticias falsas'".[25]

Los ejemplos de los errores y los lapsus de los medios no son difíciles de encontrar. Durante un mitin en Florida, el 19 de febrero de 2017, Trump se refirió a las noticias de los ataques recientes en Suecia, y dijo: "Miren lo que está sucediendo en Suecia. Suecia, ¿quién iba a creerlo? Suecia. Ellos recibieron a un gran número [de inmigrantes]. Están teniendo problemas como ellos nunca se imaginaron". Al día siguiente, el liberal británico *The Guardian* aseguró que él se lo había inventado y dijo: "Trump cita ataque terrorista inexistente".[26]

De hecho, Trump se refería a los comentarios hechos por el cineasta Ami Horowitz, quien había sido entrevistado por Tucker Carlson la noche anterior en *Fox News*. Él dijo que hubo "un aumento repentino, tanto en la violencia con armas de fuego como en violaciones sexuales en Suecia una vez que comenzaron con esta política de puertas abiertas". Él continuó hablando sobre las "zonas prohibidas" de Suecia, diciendo: "Estas son áreas donde los policías nunca entran porque es demasiado peligroso para ellos".[27] Posteriormente, *The Guardian*, CNN, y otros noticieros tuvieron que informar que el Presidente no había inventado la historia, sino que estaba refiriéndose a los comentarios del cineasta.

El 20 de enero de 2017, mientras la administración Trump todavía estaba mudándose a la Casa Blanca, el reportero, Zeke Miller, de la revista *Time* tuiteó, diciendo que el busto de Martín Lutero había sido removido de la Oficina Oval; seguramente una señal de la opinión racista de Trump. Claro está, Miller tuvo que disculparse al día siguiente, después de que Sean Spincer tuiteara una fotografía del busto del Dr. King sobre su pedestal en la Oficina Oval. Resulta que alguien estaba parado enfrente del busto cuando Miller estuvo en la Oficina Oval y él ni se molestó en verificar.[28]

En el caos que rodea el despido del Asesor de Seguridad Nacional, Michael Flynn, el corresponsal de ABC TV, Brian Ross, reportó durante una transmisión en vivo que Flynn estaba preparado para testificar que Trump le había ordenado contactar a operativos rusos sobre asuntos de política, mientras Trump aún era un candidato. Debido al indicio de que Trump podría ser destituido si la evidencia de conspiración se confirmaba, el reporte de Ross envió ondas de shock a través de la comunidad financiera y el *Dow Jones* se desplomó en 350 puntos. Más adelante, fue demostrado que Trump ya estaba en el cargo al momento del incidente en cuestión y no era un candidato. Luego, la red corrigió el reporte, y Ross fue públicamente avergonzado y se le dieron cuatro semanas de suspensión.[29] Él después renunció en deshonra.

LAS GUERRAS DE TRUMP EN TWITTER

En medio de las acusaciones, amenazas e insinuaciones de parte de los medios principales de comunicación, el Presidente estaba lidiando una guerra propia, tomando el ataque directamente a las principales redes y organizaciones noticieras de cable por promulgar "noticias falsas". Durante un informe por Jeff Zenely, en el programa de CNN *The Lead With Jake Tapper*, que salió al aire el 29 de mayo de 2017, se mostró un tuit de Trump diciendo: "Es mi opinión que muchas de las filtraciones que provienen de la Casa Blanca son mentiras fabricadas inventadas por los medios de noticias falsas". Él añadió que: "Las noticias falsas de los medios trabajan duro en desdeñar y degradar mi uso de los medios sociales porque ¡ellos no quieren que Estados Unidos oiga la verdadera historia!".[30]

En junio de 2017, Trump tuiteó: "Lo siento amigos, pero si tuviera que confiar en las noticias falsas de CNN, NBC, ABC, CBS, *Washington Post* o *New York Times*, habría tenido CERO oportunidad de ganar la Casa Blanca".[31] Ese mensaje fue reenviado casi 25,000 veces y recibió 102,000 "me gusta".

Ese mismo día, un poco más temprano, él fue criticado por castigar al alcalde de Londres, Sadiq Khan, en la víspera de una serie de ataques terroristas en esa ciudad; Trump tuiteó: "Las noticias falsas de MSM están trabajando muy duro para tratar de que yo no use los medios sociales. Ellos detestan que yo pueda enviar los mensajes honestos y sin filtros".[32] Luego, diez días después, él tuiteó:

"Los medios de noticias falsas detestan cuando uso lo que ha resultado ser mi medio social muy poderoso, ¡más de 100 millones de personas! ¡Yo puedo darles la vuelta [a los medios]!".[33]

Cuando uno compara a los seguidores de Trump (105 millones[34] a julio de 2018) con los de los principales noticieros, está claro que él no necesita a los medios para enviar su mensaje. La red de telenoticieros que más se ha visto por cable durante dieciséis años consecutivos es *Fox News*, con un promedio de audiencia en hora estelar de 2.4 millones de televidentes (Sean Hannity es el líder con un promedio de 3.368 millones de televidentes por su programa a las 9:00 p. m.); CNN Noticias de Última Hora es "la cuenta de noticias con más seguidores en Twitter", con 54.5 millones de seguidores; y el *New York Times* a la cabeza de la categoría de periódicos con 41.6 seguidores en Twitter.[35] Trump los opaca a todos.

A medida que los medios se apilaban, muchos de sus críticos aparentemente se sintieron ofendidos por Trump, no tanto por su agenda política, como por defenderse con Twitter y sus comentarios públicos francos. Sin embargo, Trump se negó a detener sus ataques verbales. Respondiendo a un informe de *NBC News* del 30 de abril de 2018, citando varias fuentes anónimas asegurando que el jefe de personal de la Casa Blanca, General John Kelly, había llamado "idiota" al presidente, Trump contraatacó: "Las noticias falsas se están volviendo locas inventando historias falsas y usando solo fuentes sin nombre (las cuales no existen). Están totalmente trastornados, y el gran éxito de esta administración está haciéndolos hacer y decir cosas que ni siquiera ellos creen lo que están diciendo. ¡Gente verdaderamente mala!".[36]

Poco tiempo después, el Presidente tomó una oportunidad en la investigación de Mueller y buscó una posible conspiración con los rusos, diciendo: "La Casa Blanca está funcionando muy bien a pesar de la falsa cacería de brujas, etc. Hay una gran energía y una resistencia inagotable, ambas necesarias para hacer que las cosas sucedan. Estamos logrando lo impensable y estableciendo récords positivos mientras lo hacemos. ¡Las noticias falsas se vuelven locas!".[37] No cabe duda de que parte del enojo que provocó los tuits del Presidente en esta ocasión fue generada por el escándalo que explotó dos noches antes. El 28 de abril, la comediante Michelle Wolf había tomado la plataforma en la cena de corresponsales de la Casa Blanca y desatado un diatriba vulgar no solo contra el Presidente sino, también, contra la secretaria de prensa de la Casa Blanca, Sarah Sanders, quien estaba sentada en la tarima a unos pasos de distancia. Sanders se mantuvo tranquila y actuó con decoro, así como lo hace durante las sesiones informativas, acaloradas, diarias con la prensa o cuando se le pidió hace algunos meses que se retirara de un restaurante en Virginia porque al dueño y algunos de los trabajadores no les gustan las políticas del presidente Trump.

Wolf no mostró piedad ni tolerancia con sus blancos, y muy poco humor, atacando la personalidad, apariencia y profesionalismo de Sanders. En su monólogo,

Wolf llamó a Sanders un "Tío Tom, pero para las mujeres blancas", y dijo que pensaba en la secretaria de prensa como la Tía Lydia, uno de los personajes más oscuros de la serie de televisión *El cuento de la criada*. Entre sus bromas mordaces, dijo: "Cada vez que Sarah sube al podio, me emociono porque no estoy realmente segura de lo que vamos a obtener, ya saben, un informe de prensa, un montón de mentiras o cualquier otra cosa. A mí realmente me cae bien Sarah, creo que es una persona muy ingeniosa. Ella quema los hechos, y luego usa esas cenizas para crear un maquillaje perfecto. Como si quizá nació así, quizá sean mentiras".[38]

A favor de ellos, algunos de los que asistieron a la cena y otros que vieron el evento o escucharon de ello, reprendieron a la comediante y pidieron una disculpa de parte de la Asociación de Corresponsales de la Casa Blanca por el sermoneo ofensivo de Wolf. La comentadora de *NBC News*, Andrea Mitchell, que no es amiga de la Casa Blanca, tuiteó: "Se le debe una disculpa a la Secretaria de prensa y a los demás que fueron groseramente insultados por Michelle Wolf durante la Cena de Corresponsales de la Casa Blanca, la cual comenzó con un discurso inspirador y sincero por Margaret Talev; la comediante fue la peor desde que Imus insultó a los Clinton".[39] El exjefe de personal de la Casa Blanca, Reince Priebus, lo llamó "un espectáculo clasificado R/X que empezó de mala manera y terminó en el fondo del cañón. Otra victoria para @realDonaldTrump por no asistir y proveer su opinión una vez más. El salón estaba incómodo. Los que aman a Trump e incluso un gran número de los que lo odian se sintieron muy mal".[40]

La misma noche, el gobernador Mike Huckabee se dirigió a Wolf y a los organizadores por haber humillado a su hija, señalando que la hipocresía de los liberales, quienes aseguran que "el discurso de odio" no es lo mismo que la libertad de expresión. "Aquellos que piensan que la agresión corriente y de mal gusto que se dio en la Cena de Corresponsales de la Casa Blanca fue un ejemplo de la Primera Enmienda nunca deberían condenar la agresión, los comentarios peyorativos, la aspereza racista o el discurso de odio". Y el excandidato presidencial republicano añadió: "Las personas deben tener libertad de expresión, pero debe responsabilizárseles por ella".[41]

Yo estaba particularmente horrorizado por este trato porque conozco a Sarah desde que estuve involucrado en la infructuosa campaña presidencial primaria de su padre en el 2008. Sarah era una joven impresionante en aquel momento, y ha crecido a pasos agigantados desde entonces. Ella tiene uno de los empleos de mayor presión en Washington, y lo lleva a cabo mientras hace malabares para criar a tres niños pequeños.

Obviamente, el presidente Trump estaba sorprendido de que su secretaria de prensa, quien asistió a la cena como su representante, se hubiera convertido en el chivo expiatorio para los ataques despiadados de Michelle Wolf. Cuando él tuiteó su respuesta al día siguiente, dijo: "La Cena de Corresponsales de la Casa Blanca fue un fracaso el año pasado, pero este año fue una vergüenza para todos los relacionados a ella. La 'comediante' asquerosa fue un fracaso a lo grande (ni siquiera pudo dar su mensaje, muy parecido al débil desempeño de Seth Meyers). ¡Suspendan la cena permanentemente, o empiecen de nuevo!".[42]

Más tarde, enfatizó que él siempre lo había dicho, que los medios de comunicación están irremediablemente en contra de él y de su administración. "'La Cena de corresponsales de la Casa Blanca' ha dejado de existir como la conocíamos", dijo. "Fue un desastre total y una vergüenza para nuestro gran país y para todo lo que representa. ¡Los medios de noticias falsas están bien y fueron hermosamente representados el sábado en la noche!".[43] En respuesta a las reacciones de enojo que ella y los organizadores del evento estaban recibiendo, Margaret Talev, presidenta de la Asociación de Corresponsales de la Casa Blanca, admitió que el desempeño de Wolf no estuvo a tono con "el espíritu" del evento anual de los medios.

"El programa de anoche tenía la intención de ofrecer un mensaje de unidad sobre nuestro compromiso común hacia una prensa vigorosa y libre y, a la vez, honrar la cortesía, el buen periodismo y a los ganadores de becas, no para dividir a las personas", dijo en una declaración preparada enviada a la prensa. "Desafortunadamente, el monólogo de la comediante no fue según el espíritu de esa misión". Cuando le preguntaron cómo respondía a las "bromas" de Wolf, Talev dijo: "Algunas de ellas me hicieron sentir incómoda y no personificaron al espíritu de la noche".[44]

No hay duda de que Talev estaba ansiosa de subsanar las diferencias, pero la periodista de *Fox News*, Liz Peek discrepó de sus comentarios. "La señora Talev está equivocada", dijo y enfatizó que "el ataque estuvo muy en línea con la forma en que los medios liberales ven a la Casa Blanca. Ellos detestan al presidente Trump, y el sentimiento es mutuo. CNN, el *New York Times*, MSNBC y el resto no pueden perdonar al presidente Trump por haberle negado a Hillary Clinton su 'inevitable' presidencia". Luego, la escritora añadió:

> Hillary no era la única que acariciaba la idea de estar en la Oficina Oval; el mundo de los medios esperaba cuatro, ¡quizás ocho!, años más de una administración con la que tienen el mismo parecer, con quien podrían elaborar historias, puliendo los resultados y enterrando las desagradables realidades. Con quien los medios podrían darse el gusto de tener pequeñas discusiones sabiendo que ellos controlaban el mensaje, y la dirección del futuro del país.[45]

Diferencias irreconciliables

Un estudio conducido por dos investigadores del *Reuters Institute* en la universidad de Oxford, examinó la desconfianza creciente del público sobre los medios. Sus hallazgos indicaron que aquellos que no confían en los medios de noticias, lo que llegó a ser el 25 por ciento de la muestra, acusaron a los medios de sesgo, de inventar historias y de intenciones ocultas. La investigación informó que "una porción significativa del público siente que los poderosos están usando a los medios para empujar sus propios intereses políticos o económicos, en vez de representar a los lectores o televidentes promedio. En muchos países, particularmente en Estados Unidos y el Reino Unido", dicen ellos, "algunos noticieros son vistos como quienes toman partido, animando un creciente set de opiniones polarizadas". Con base a sus hallazgos, el informe de Reuters sugiere que "los periodistas y los que publican noticias deberían estar mucho más abiertos sobre sus prejuicios y más claros sobre distinguir las noticias de la opinión y las noticas". [46]

Sin embargo, basándose en los factores más inmediatos, tales como la cena de corresponsales y la guerra continua de palabras entre el Presidente y sus adversarios en los medios de comunicación, una reconciliación de cualquier tipo parece altamente improbable. Los estadounidenses consumen más noticias hoy día que en cualquier otro momento en la historia, y según un artículo de investigación del Dr. Neil Johnson, un físico del grupo interdisciplinario de Complejidad de la Universidad de Miami, el flujo constante de noticias negativas ha empujado a la nación hacia "un estado de polarización pura". Y el investigador agregó que "el tamaño de los extremos de la Izquierda y la Derecha son tan grandes ahora, que superan en número a los que están en el medio". [47]

Como científico, Johnson le dijo al *Miami Herald* que él generalmente espera que las encuestas produzcan resultado en la forma de una curva de campana; es decir, las respuestas tienden a agruparse en el rango medio, con las respuestas externas tendiendo a uno u otro lado. Sin embargo, cuando exploró el grado de polarización política y social sobre la población general de la actualidad, descubrió que las respuestas fueron mayores en los extremos opuestos; "lo que significa" dijo él, "que el simple acto de absorber las noticias que todos los demás están viendo, causa un efecto polarizante". Cuando se le preguntó si había esperanza de que las cosas cambiaran y estimularan un mayor consenso y moderación, Johnson respondió: "en realidad, no". [48]

La realidad de las diferencias irreconciliables entre la Izquierda y la Derecha se pueden ver casi siempre en las confrontaciones diarias en cable TV, en los tuits de Trump, y en las batallas verbales que se llevan a cabo en los pasillos del Congreso. Vi esta hostilidad la mañana después de las elecciones en Nueva York. Me fui a acostar hasta después de la fiesta de victoria de Trump, más o menos a las 4:00 a. m., así que desayuné tarde, justo antes de que empezaran a servir el almuerzo. Una joven, sentada a unos cuantos pasos, veía en su teléfono inteligente, un video contra Trump que tenía lenguaje soez. Yo no quería escucharlo durante mi desayuno, así que le pedí que le bajara el volumen. No se dijo nada acerca de Trump. Ella debe haber pensado que yo parecía un republicano porque empezó un alegato en mi contra que hizo que todos en el restaurante voltearan a ver. Ella también insistió en irse a otra parte del restaurante. Ese fue mi encuentro con la fuerte crítica a la investidura que veríamos por todo el país desde el resto de ese día hasta el presente.

Aunque la hostilidad es genuina, los combatientes no están luchando en un campo de juego nivelado. Los principales medios de comunicación tienen la ventaja de la tecnología y noticias veinticuatro horas al día, cada día de la semana, y comentarios por una bandada de comentadores inmaculadamente personalizados transmitiendo por las ondas aéreas y la internet a los hogares. Sin embargo, el Presidente tiene su púlpito intimidante.

El presidente Theodore Roosevelt usó el término *púlpito intimidante* en un discurso en 1909, diciendo: "Supongo que mis críticos llamarán a eso predicar, ¡pero tengo un púlpito tan intimidante!". Él se refería a la influencia extraordinaria de la que disfrutaba como presidente de Estados Unidos.[49] (Por si sirve de algo, Theodore Roosevelt es uno de los presidentes que más admiro, y creo que es un primo lejano mío). Para Donald Trump, su púlpito intimidante consiste principalmente en el poder sin precedentes de su cuenta de Twitter y de su capacidad singular para estar en los titulares sin importar lo que diga o haga.

Tal como explica Victor Davis Hanson, Donald Trump es peligroso para la agenda progresiva. "En términos militares, él es un B-52 estratégico en una misión profunda. Trump apunta a la patria del enemigo, incluso mientras los ejércitos expedicionarios, remotos y débiles de sus oponentes se atascan en el extranjero". El poder que el Presidente maneja no necesariamente se halla en el éxito de sus maniobras políticas, sino en sus notables poderes de persuasión. Los 63 millones de estadounidenses que votaron por Donald Trump lo enviaron a Washington con un mandato, y encuesta tras encuesta revelan que ellos están convencidos de que él está cumpliendo con su parte del trato. Estoy de acuerdo con Hanson, quien escribe:

> Más de la mitad de la nación ha perdido la confianza en el progresismo, el estado administrativo, y la jerarquía y la institución republicana... Sienten que la mayoría de sus objetivos se lo merecían y que el caos resultante, dentro de ciertos límites, es una purga muy necesaria. Fuera del dilema diario, Trump, no obstante, ha logrado hasta ahora alcanzar una prosperidad mayor en el país y una estabilidad en el extranjero en comparación a Obama, mientras que la reputación de los medios habitualmente perjudicada está hundiéndose rápidamente. Donde los críticos ven caos, es probable que algunos votantes vean claridad y escarmiento.[50]

Además, Hanson dice que el bombardeo implacable de malas noticias y los ataques personales por parte de los medios han animado a Trump a volverse aún más combativo y excéntrico. "En el pasado, cuando un progresista etiquetaba a un político republicano, como una especie de fanático irreversible o despreciable, él a menudo se hacía a la izquierda en busca de penitencia o para evitar más ataques".[51] Sin embargo, ese nunca ha sido el estilo de Trump. Él arremete con más fuerza, con más de la mitad de la nación animándolo. Según la conservadora *Heritage Foundation*, para enero de 2018, el Presidente ya había completado el 64 por ciento de su agenda en cerca de dos tercios de los 334 objetivos políticos recomendados en su Mandato de liderazgo, el cual ha sido publicado como una guía para las administraciones presidenciales entrantes desde 1981.[52] Y lo ha hecho mientras lucha constantemente en una acción de retaguardia defensiva contra la protesta de la Izquierda sobre sus políticas.

La *Heritage Foundation* siente que los destacados en el listado de logros de Trump incluyen lo siguiente:

- Salir del Acuerdo Climático de París
- Derogación de la neutralidad de la red
- Negociar un incremento de US$54 mil millones en gastos militares
- Restablecer la Política de la Ciudad de México sobre el aborto
- Eliminar las restricciones sobre el desarrollo de los recursos naturales de Estados Unidos
- Retirarse de la UNESCO, una organización costosa e ineficaz
- Ordenar reformas dramáticas en una amplia gama de agencias gubernamentales costosas e ineficaces.

"Estas son todas las políticas que apoya la gran mayoría de los estadounidenses, y si al público le gusta o no el lenguaje y comportamiento del Presidente", escribe Hanson, "los votantes de Trump aún creen que el mensaje mayormente positivo importa más que los defectos del mensajero".[53]

TENTAR A LA SUERTE

A pesar del hecho de que Trump es un neoyorquino, no es fácil para los liberales de Nueva York entender, no digamos apreciar, que la mayoría del resto de Estados Unidos no esté de acuerdo con ellos. Eso me recuerda la portada simbólica del ejemplar de 29 de marzo de 1976 de la revista *New Yorker*. Mostraba un acercamiento de Manhattan desde la perspectiva de la Novena Avenida, viendo al oeste hacia la Décima Avenida y más allá hacia un ancho río Hudson y un diminuto Estados Unidos continental con solo unas pocas montañas y, más allá de eso, el Océano Pacífico, con solo Japón, China y Rusia a la distancia.[54] Muestra cuán provincial era el pensamiento neoyorkino (tanto de la revista como de la gente) incluso en aquel entonces.

Cuando Salena Zito, una escritora para el *New York Post* hizo un viaje fuera de Manhattan para ver las actitudes de los hombres y las mujeres del medio oeste, estaba sorprendida de encontrar un amplio apoyo para el Presidente, aún en los condados del noreste de Ohio previamente controlados por los demócratas. Uno de los votantes que ella entrevistó en su serie de dos partes no votó por Trump, no obstante, se había vuelto un admirador y seguidor. "Si él continúa apegándose a sus armas y haciendo lo que está haciendo", dijo, "votaré por él si se postula de nuevo". A él no le gustaba Trump como candidato, pero estaba "disfrutando un montón su presidencia".[55]

Pero eso no es todo lo que la reportera descubrió. El hombre le dijo que él está frustrado por la manera en que los medios tratan al presidente Trump, especialmente en comparación con la manera que adulaban al presidente Obama: "Ellos no le dan realmente a Trump su justa parte", dijo. El sesgo percibido contra Trump ha cambiado la manera en que lo ve a él, y "en vez de [que eso] lo aleje del Presidente, está más intrigado por él".[56]

Zito dice que las opiniones que encontró en esta y en otras partes del centro del país desafían la sabiduría convencional de los noticieros nacionales. Los medios principales parecen incapaces de captar el hecho de que la base de Trump no lo va a dejar o de que ellos creen que su liderazgo ha sido exitoso en general. Pero aún más problemático para los leales demócratas son los resultados de una encuesta del *Washington Post-ABC News* publicada en abril de 2018 mostrando que muchos votantes de Clinton sienten remordimientos por su apoyo a la candidata demócrata. Es más, la encuesta sugiere que, si las elecciones se repitieran hoy, Trump ganaría no solo el colegio electoral, sino también el voto popular. Los investigadores hallaron que el 15 por ciento de los votantes de Clinton votaría por un candidato diferente si las elecciones se llevaran a cabo de nuevo. Por otro lado, solamente el 4 por ciento de los votantes de Trump dijeron que cambiarían su voto. [57]

La encuesta también mostró que, mientras el 58 por ciento de los estadounidenses piensa que Trump está desfasado, la mayoría de los encuestados sienten que el Partido Demócrata está aún más desfasado que Trump o que el Partido Republicano. El 67 por ciento expresó la opinión de que los demócratas están desfasados, incluyendo casi la mitad de los encuestados que se identificaron como demócratas.[58] Cuando Zito le preguntó a su entrevistado por qué pensaba que los medios fallaban tanto, él dijo: Los medios nacionales sencillamente no entienden a la gente que cubren. No lo hicieron el año pasado. Todavía no lo hacen". Ella dijo que una entrevista tras otra, los votantes le dijeron que ellos no ven sus opiniones expresadas en ninguna parte en los medios nacionales. Ellos entienden que no son el centro del universo, pero quisieran ser incluidos en la cobertura.[59] Una de las razones por las que escribí *God and Donald Trump* y este libro es para contar las historias sin contar de las elecciones y Trump que algunos en la élite de los medios nunca cubrieron.

"Para la gente en los pueblos pequeños de Estados Unidos", escribió Zito en su artículo complementario para el *Post*, "el clima político de hoy es difícil de comprender". Ellos ven la manera en que los medios hablan de Trump y sus seguidores. Posiblemente no les guste todo de ellos, pero les gusta la consigna: "Hacer a Estados Unidos grande otra vez". Es inspiradora y mira hacia adelante, algo más grande que ellos mismos". Luego, Zito hace referencia a una encuesta de Quinnipiac de abril de 2018 que indica que el 58 por ciento de los votantes blancos, sin grado universitario, aprueba el desempeño del trabajo de Trump, con el 44 por ciento aprobándolo fuertemente. Resumiendo lo que aprendió en su recorrido exploratorio, Zito dice:

> La verdad es que todavía es el 8 de noviembre de 2016 en este país. Si votó por Trump, usted está, en su mayor parte, optimista sobre lo que él pueda hacer en el futuro. Y si no votó por él, todavía cree que no es digno de la presidencia. Ninguna cartelera corporativa elegante va a cambiar el modo de pensar de nadie. Nadie sabe a dónde irán sus seguidores, pero ya que ellos son una fuerza a tener en cuenta dentro de la política moderna, ¿no deberíamos dejar de tratarlos como estudios antropológicos y empezar a escuchar lo que ellos tienen que decir?[60]

Como muchos observadores de ambos lados de la cerca han afirmado, en muchas partes del país se está formando una reacción contra los medios de comunicación. "Los principales medios de comunicación han tentado su suerte con sus ataques incesantes y venenosos sobre Donald Trump", escribe Darrell Delamaide para *MarketWatch*. "Él, por supuesto, ha azuzado las llamas con sus burlas petulantes; pero, después de todo, son los medios los que han desperdiciado su credibilidad. Su obsesión con una posible conspiración rusa con la campaña de Trump, incluso en ausencia de evidencia sólida, no solo ha bloqueado la agenda de Trump, sino que ha impedido que los demócratas y otros oponentes ofrezcan algo como alternativa constructiva".[61] Se ha llegado al punto, dirían muchos, que las "noticias de última hora" de los medios consisten principalmente de informes vagos de funcionarios de la administración reuniéndose con figuras sombrías, consideradas sombrías principalmente porque no hay fuentes confiables. Tal como Donald Trump ha argumentado siempre, las historias de las noticias falsas son "muy numerosas para contarlas", dice Glen Greenwald en *The Intercept*, cuando cita numerosos ejemplos de las publicaciones de los medios principales tales como el *Washington Post*, MSNBC, Slate, *The Guardian*, y el *New York Times*.[62]

Ya que la prensa es por lo general insensata, raras veces admite estar equivocados a menos que estén contra la pared. A principios de mi carrera, recuerdo que una reportera del *Washington Post* llamada Janet Cooke ganó un premio Pulitzer por un artículo desgarrador sobre un niño de ocho años, llamado Jimmy, en Washington, DC, que era adicto a la heroína y posteriormente murió. Fue una mentira total, y ella devolvió el Pulitzer, la única persona que lo ha hecho.

Algo que me afectó mucho fue la historia triste de Jack Kelley de *USA Today*, a quien yo conocí en la década de los ochentas como un cristiano comprometido, uno de los pocos en los medios seculares. Él fue nominado para un Pulitzer en el 2002. Sin embargo, en el 2004 renunció avergonzado cuando se reveló que había inventado historias durante años, incluyendo una historia de una página en 1999 donde él informaba sobre una orden mecanografiada del ejército yugoslavo para "limpiar" una aldea en Kosovo.

Avanzando hasta el 2016 y la presidencia de Donald Trump, hay una nueva generación de periodistas que, para todos los efectos y propósitos, están inventando historias en el intento de acabar con él. "Los periodistas tras estas historias aparentemente se consideran como la nueva generación de héroes del periodismo, reflejando las hazañas de Bob Woodward y Carl Bernstein al exponer el escándalo de Watergate y derrocar al presidente Richard Nixon", dice Delamaide. Pero incluso Woodaward considera que la persecución de Trump es exagerada y recientemente pidió más "imparcialidad" en sus reportajes.[63]

Hablando con un presentador de Fox, Sean Hannity, sobre "la retórica violenta" en los medios, la feminista liberal, Camille Paglia, dijo: "No queda nada de periodismo. ¿Qué ha pasado con el *New York Times*? ¿Qué ha pasado con las redes principales? Es un escándalo". La exreportera de CBS, Sharyl Attkisson, quien escribió el sensacional nuevo libro *The Smear: How Shady Political Operatives and Fake News Control What You See, What You Think, and How You Vote* dice que el ataque constante de los medios sobre el Presidente y su administración ha hecho que pierdan credibilidad con la mayoría del público. "Queremos cubrir de manera crítica y cuidadosa a nuestras instituciones y políticos poderosos", dijo. "Pero cuando uno lo hace en tal forma que el público ya no cree que lo que recibe es toda la verdad, o a veces, ni siquiera un mínimo de verdad, uno se debilita a sí mismo porque llegaremos a un área donde la gente difícilmente crea cualquier cosa que escuchen a primera vista".[64]

Este ha sido el mensaje de Donald Trump desde que entró en campaña, y si, tal como escribió Shakespeare, el pasado es el prólogo de lo que ha de venir, las provocaciones continuarán, las batallas se propagarán y el púlpito intimidante del Presidente estará tan ocupado como siempre.

DIPLOMACIA MUSCULOSA

Hablando de reporteros fuera de la Casa Blanca, el 8 de junio de 2018 poco antes del encuentro G7 en la provincia canadiense de Quebec, el presidente Trump dijo que estaba muy emocionado por su reunión con el líder de Corea del Norte, Kim Jong-un, programada para el 12 de junio. El presidente les aseguró a los reporteros que estaba bien preparado para la reunión. "Yo siempre he creído en la preparación", dijo, "pero he estado preparándome toda mi vida".[1] Trump había participado en una serie de discusiones verbales con los líderes del G7 durante su breve estadía en Canadá y se había ido un día antes, omitiendo la discusión del medio ambiente y el cambio climático para poder volar a la isla Sentosa de Singapur, donde él y Kim iban a discutir el fin del programa de armas nucleares del remoto régimen.

Un tiempo después, los corresponsales de la Casa Blanca y los oponentes políticos se burlaron de los comentarios de Trump diciendo que era una exageración afirmar que se había estado preparando toda su vida para negociar con el dictador coreano. Pero, luego, salió un video de octubre de 1999, que apareció en YouTube donde el fallecido Tim Russert entrevistaba al futuro presidente en el programa *Meet the Press* en NBC. Durante la conversación, Russert dijo: "Usted dice que, como presidente, estaría dispuesto a lanzar un ataque preventivo contra la capacidad nuclear de Corea del Norte". A lo que Trump respondió: "Primero, negociaría y me aseguraría de que tratamos de obtener el mejor trato posible. En tres o cuatro años", dijo, "Corea del Norte podría tener armas nucleares apuntando hacia todo el mundo y específicamente hacia Estados Unidos". Luego añadió:

> El problema más grande que tiene este mundo es la proliferación nuclear, y nosotros tenemos un país, allá, Corea del Norte, que parece medio loco, pero no son un montón de sonsos, y van a salir, y están desarrollando armas nucleares. Y no lo hacen porque les divierte. Lo están haciendo por alguna razón. ¿No sería bueno sentarse y negociar algo realmente? Y sí quiero decir negociar. Ahora, si esa negociación no funciona, es mejor resolver ese problema ahora

que resolverlo después, Tim. Y usted lo sabe, y todo político lo sabe, y nadie quiere hablar de eso.[2]

Repentinamente, quedó claro que, durante por lo menos dos décadas, Donald Trump había estado pensando en cómo lidiar con un tirano como Kim Jong-un. Y afortunadamente su reunión cara a cara con Kim demostró ser todo lo que él esperaba. Hablando con reporteros después, dijo que él estaba esperanzado por los prospectos de paz, pero advirtió que ese encuentro era solamente "el principio de un proceso arduo". Él dijo que las sanciones sobre Corea del Norte se mantendrán en pie hasta que los objetivos de la negociación se hayan cumplido. "El pasado no tiene que definir el futuro", dijo. "Los conflictos del ayer no tienen que ser la guerra del mañana… No hay límite para lo que Corea del Norte puede lograr cuando entregue sus armas nucleares y abrace el comercio y el compromiso con el resto del mundo".[3]

Cuando se le preguntó sobre el vergonzoso récord de abusos a los derechos humanos de Corea del Norte, Trump dijo que los norcoreanos estarían "haciendo algo" para mejorar la situación. Luego, le preguntaron cómo podía elogiar a Kim Jong-un cuando el norcoreano era un dictador brutal, él habló de Otto Warmbier, el estudiante estadounidense de veintidós años, quien fue detenido por los norcoreanos y encarcelado por tomar una pancarta de propaganda. Warmbier sufrió una herida cerebral devastadora mientras estuvo en custodia, pero fue liberado el 12 de junio de 2017, bajo la intensa presión de Estados Unidos.

Fue evacuado médicamente hacia Estados Unidos el 13 de junio de 2017, y murió seis días después, sin haber recuperado la conciencia. Pero el Presidente dijo que fue el cautiverio, la herida y la muerte de Warmbier lo que finalmente dio paso al encuentro en Singapur. "Otto no murió en vano", dijo. La trágica muerte del joven inspiró a ambos lados a luchar por la paz. "Otto Warmbier es una persona muy especial y estará en mi vida por mucho tiempo. Sus padres son buenos amigos míos… Un joven especial. Y debo decir, padres especiales, personas especiales". Y él dijo, además, "Creo que, sin Otto, esto no hubiera sucedido".[4]

El Presidente dijo posteriormente que el Departamento de Estado no quitaría las sanciones sobre Corea del Norte sin que hubiera una "mejoría significativa" sobre los derechos humanos. Él indicó que había discutido el tema del secuestro de ciudadanos japoneses con Kim, pero lo conversado específicamente no se incluyó en el documento que firmaron debido a cuestiones de tiempo. Sin embargo, sí llegaron a un acuerdo sobre la repatriación de los restos de soldados estadounidenses perdidos en acción durante la Guerra Coreana, diciendo que el proceso empezaría inmediatamente. Además, él indicó que Estados Unidos dejaría de hacer prácticas militares en conjunto con Corea del Sur si los norcoreanos cumplían las promesas de Kim.[5]

En la conclusión del encuentro, los dos líderes se dirigieron a la multitud de por lo menos dos mil quinientos periodistas de todo el mundo. "Estamos muy orgullosos de lo que se llevó a cabo hoy", dijo Trump. "Creo que toda nuestra relación con Corea del Norte y la Península Coreana va a ser una situación mucho más diferente de lo que ha sido en el pasado". Durante la ceremonia televisada, donde el presidente y el dictador coreano firmaron una declaración de acuerdo conjunto, Kim Jong-un agradeció a Trump por hacer posible una conversación cara a cara. "Hemos tenido un encuentro histórico y decidido dejar el pasado atrás", dijo, añadiendo que "el mundo verá un cambio grande".[6]

UN TIEMPO DE DESPERTAR

En la mañana después del encuentro, había una sensación de que el mundo había cambiado sobre su eje y que todo estaba de cabeza, en un muy buen sentido. El presidente Trump lo había logrado. Se reunió con Kim Jong-un en un lugar neutral, se estrecharon las manos, y firmaron un acuerdo comprometiéndose a la eliminación de las armas nucleares en la península coreana. Ningún otro presidente estadounidense en funciones había hablado jamás, ni siquiera por teléfono, con el líder de Corea del Norte desde el principio de la Guerra Coreana, hace casi setenta años. Pero Donald Trump tomó el riesgo, y el mundo fue repentinamente un lugar mejor y más seguro, y el presidente estadounidense era su líder más poderoso.

Al concluir las negociaciones, incluso los principales medios tuvieron que admitir que Donald Trump, su presidencia y toda la comunidad internacional habían alcanzado un hito importante. Alrededor del mundo había alivio y agradecimiento. La exestrella de la NBA, el provocativo Dennis Rodman jugó una parte también. Luciendo orgullosamente su gorra MAGA [hacer a Estados Unidos grande otra vez, por sus siglas en inglés], le aseguró al presidente que Kim Jong-un estaba listo para hablar. Rodman había desarrollado una amistad inusual con el dictador coreano y rogado, con lágrimas en sus ojos, para que Trump le diera una oportunidad al encuentro. En cuestión de horas, la espada que había amenazado al mundo, y especialmente a las naciones asiáticas, desde que las hostilidades empezaron en 1950, había sido levantada.

Los medios pasaron por alto varios paralelos espirituales fascinantes entre Trump y Kim mientras que los periodistas se concentraban en los aspectos políticos del encuentro. En 1907, un avivamiento cristiano en Pyongyang, Corea, tuvo tal impacto que los misioneros llamaron a la ciudad la "Jerusalén de Asia".[7] De hecho, el tatarabuelo de Kim Jong-un se volvió pastor, y el bisabuelo de Kim, un anciano que crio a su hijo, el futuro dictador, como presbiteriano. Durante casi cuatro décadas, el cristianismo era mucho más fuerte en Corea del Norte que en Corea del Sur. Sin embargo, Kim Il-sung, el dictador que llevó el comunismo a Corea del Norte no solo rechazó el cristianismo, sino que hizo de Corea del

Norte uno de los regímenes más opresivos sobre la tierra, aplastando la libertad de expresión y los derechos religiosos.

Cuando empezó la Guerra Coreana, había treinta y cinco iglesias en Corea del Norte. Hoy día, hay dos iglesias oficiales, para propósitos de propaganda, y hasta 120,000 cristianos confesados retenidos en campos de trabajo.[8] Más de 100,000 refugiados norcoreanos residen actualmente en China, en espera de la oportunidad para ser repatriados a Corea del Sur, pero menos de 100 pueden ser evacuados cada mes. Los grupos que apoyan el esfuerzo han dicho que, si uno de cada 140 de los 14 millones de surcoreanos cristianos se uniera para evacuar a solo un refugiado cada uno, lo atrasado podría evacuarse.[9] Hay millones de personas orando por la reconciliación, pero el progreso ha sido dolorosamente lento.

Curiosamente, el presidente Donald Trump fue criado presbiteriano por su madre, una nativa de las Islas Hébridas Exteriores en Escocia, donde hubo un tremendo avivamiento espiritual de 1948 a 1952; irónicamente casi exactamente los mismos años de la Guerra en Corea. El avivamiento estaba tan ampliamente esparcido y era tan inspirador que las Hébridas durante un tiempo fueron conocidas como la "Jerusalén de las Islas Británicas".[10] Según fuentes escocesas familiarizadas con los eventos y los individuos involucrados, dos hermanas, Peggy y Christine Smith, de ochenta y dos y ochenta y cuatro años, oraron durante años para ver el mover de Dios en sus pequeñas aldeas de pescadores en la isla de Lewis, y sus oraciones fieles ayudaron a iniciar el avivamiento. El movimiento siguiente se dispersó por todo Escocia y la Mancomunidad de naciones.[11] Varias fuentes han informado que las dos hermanas ancianas eran tías abuelas de Donald Trump. Al investigar para este libro, no pude verificar que ellas fueran sus tías abuelas, pero independientemente de eso, su familia hubiera sido impactada por el avivamiento de alguna manera.

El encuentro de 2018 en Singapur fue una respuesta a la oración de miles de surcoreanos que han estado orando fervientemente por la reunificación de Corea y por el avivamiento en el norte. El presidente Moon Jae-in de Corea del Sur dijo en los días previos al encuentro que la gente de su país estaba orando por Trump para "que se creara un resultado milagroso".[12] He visitado Corea del Sur varias veces, y cada vez, he asistido a servicios de oración enormes, donde me di cuenta de que ellos oraban por su vecino del norte, aun mientras la represión parecía crecer y la hambruna diezmaba a la población.

El líder de Corea del Sur, Jeffrey Yoon, director de *Church Growth International* en Seúl, me dijo que los coreanos cristianos han estado orando no solo por los cristianos de Corea del Norte, sino también por la reunificación de las dos naciones desde que terminó la Guerra Coreana, y oran para que Dios abra las puertas de Corea del Norte. En mayo de 2018, cuando el encuentro de Singapur no se había definido, mi amigo y mentor Alex Clattenburg estaba en Seúl para asistir a una reunión de consejo de *Church Growth International* y él fue testigo de esto otra vez.

Alex, quien es el pastor líder de *Church in the Son* en Orlando, Florida, ha servido en la junta, fundada por el famoso pastor coreano David Yonggi Cho.

Alex asistió a un mitin el 18 de mayo de 2018, en el *Seoul World Cup Stadium*, con una capacidad para 66,700 personas. La reunión de oración entusiasta, de seis horas de duración, ("lo más cercano al cielo que yo haya experimentado", me contó) estaba enfocada en la reunificación de Corea y el avivamiento en Corea del Norte. "Confiamos en que Dios ha estado haciendo algo y estamos seguros de que sucederá y tendrá éxito", dijo Jeffrey Yoon.

A pesar de su herencia cristiana, Corea del Norte se ha convertido en uno de los gobiernos más represivos sobre la tierra, implementando el infame "sistema *songbun*" donde toda la población ha sido clasificada en clases sociales según la lealtad percibida al socialismo y al régimen. Tal como lo informó la organización *Liberty* en Corea del Norte:

> El régimen silenciaba con detrimento extremo a cualquiera que se opusiera al sistema. La libertad de expresión se volvió una ofensa sancionable con prisión y hasta con la muerte. Peor, cuando alguien era arrestado, hasta tres generaciones de su familia serían enviadas a los campos de prisión políticos. El régimen instruía a los niños a denunciar a sus padres y a los vecinos a denunciarse entre sí. Bajo estas condiciones, la gente de Corea del Norte se volvió temerosa y desconfiada unos de otros.[13]

En el 2016, la revista *Christianity Today* informó que los cristianos en Corea del Norte enfrentaban violación sexual, tortura, esclavitud y estaban siendo asesinados por su fe en las maneras más inhumanas. Según un informe de *Christian Solidarity Worldwide*, la libertad de culto ha sido "inexistente por mucho tiempo" durante las tres generaciones de la dictadura de la familia Kim. "Las creencias religiosas son vistas como una amenaza a la lealtad exigida por el Líder Supremo, así que cualquiera que tenga estas creencias es perseguido severamente", dice el informe. "Los cristianos sufren significativamente a causa de las etiquetas de anti-rrevolucionario e imperialista que les pone el liderazgo del país".[14]

La mayoría de los occidentales sabe que no hay mucha libertad en Corea del Norte, pero la mayor parte de la atención en los años recientes se ha enfocado en la capacidad nuclear de Corea del Norte, especialmente con la tendencia de Kim para disparar misiles que, según él, podrían llevar una ojiva nuclear. Él incluso alardeó de que podría enviar misiles tan lejos como la costa oeste de Estados Unidos. Sin embargo, tal como Russel Goldman escribió en el *New York Times*, los esfuerzos de Estados Unidos para contrarrestar las ambiciones nucleares de Kim no empezaron cuando el presidente Trump amenazó al régimen coreano con "fuego y furia". Goldman escribe: "Durante décadas, los predecesores del Sr. Trump se han metido en el lodo diplomático, tratando de amenazar o persuadir a la familia gobernante para que abandonen los programas de armas del país. Cada uno ha fracasado".[15]

Goldman informa que, durante la década de los noventas, Bill Clinton quitó las sanciones que habían estado allí por décadas, suplió cinco mil toneladas de petróleo por un año y proveyó US$4 mil millones en ayuda. Nada de esto disuadió a Corea del Norte de desarrollar su capacidad nuclear.

El presidente George W. Bush tomó una táctica diferente al confrontar a los norcoreanos. Recuerdo el discurso de Bush al Estado de la Unión en el 2002, en el cual se refirió a Corea del Norte, Irak e Irán como un "eje del mal". El objetivo de Bush era castigar a Corea del Norte con sanciones hasta que se derrumbara. Pero eso tampoco funcionó.

Luego, el presidente Obama optó por una política de "paciencia estratégica", al decidir esperar a la nación ermitaña hasta que se diera cuenta de que era ventajoso hacer un esfuerzo de buena voluntad para renovar las conversaciones de paz. En vez de eso, Goldman dice: "El Norte prosiguió su programa de armas y lanzó una serie de ataques cibernéticos a las empresas estadounidenses".[16] Mientras Obama era presidente, Kim Jong-un, nieto del fundador del país, fue declarado líder después de la muerte de su padre, Kim Jong-il, supuestamente diez días antes de su vigésimo octavo cumpleaños.

Los diplomáticos estadounidenses inicialmente tuvieron la esperanza de que Kim Jong-un se apartara de las políticas de sus predecesores; pero, en vez de eso, él tomó una posición más agresiva. En septiembre de 2016, probó la ojiva nuclear que, según afirmó, podría estar conectada a un misil de largo alcance, y luego amenazó que podía atacar, no solo a Japón y a Guam, sino también al continente norteamericano. Muchos temían que Kim estaba lo suficientemente loco para hacerlo. Sin embargo, el presidente Trump no se lo iba a permitir, y en vez de "paciencia estratégica", respondió con amenazas de "fuego y furia" en agosto de 2017. "Mejor si Corea del Norte no sigue amenazando a Estados Unidos", les dijo Trump a los periodistas en su club en Bedminster, Nueva Jersey. "Se encontrará con fuego y furia como el mundo jamás ha visto".[17]

Poco después, empezó a llamar al dictador norcoreano "Pequeño hombre cohete", haciendo que sus críticos gritaran que Trump estaba en riesgo de una guerra nuclear y que debería ser más diplomático. En vez de guerra nuclear, Kim aceptó ir a la mesa de negociaciones. Pero cuando Kim empezó a fanfarronear de los términos que le ofrecieron, Trump canceló la reunión. En cuestión de horas, el Viceministro de Relaciones Exteriores de Corea del Norte envió una declaración conciliatoria; y unos días después, Kim envió un emisario a Washington, DC, con una carta para Trump solicitando oficialmente que la cumbre se reestableciera. Este fue otro ejemplo del liderazgo fuerte de Trump y su capacidad de negociación, incluso si fue demasiado agresivo en su acercamiento.

Trump le dijo a Sean Hannity de *Fox News* en Singapur, después de que terminó la cumbre, que él se sentía ridículo y detestaba haber tenido que usar una retórica áspera para condenar a Corea del Norte y a Kim Jong-un, pero sentía que tenía que reunir a los dos países. Esto implica que el acercamiento excesivamente agresivo en sus tuits era estratégico. También demuestra que el Presidente está dispuesto a sacrificar su reputación por lo que él considera que es mejor para el país.[18]

UN DESTELLO DE ESPERANZA

Al concluir las reuniones en Singapur, los reporteros le preguntaron al Presidente que, si durante las sesiones a puerta cerrada, había hablado con Kim sobre la difícil situación de los cristianos perseguidos. "Nosotros… lo trajimos a colación muy fuertemente", dijo, añadiendo que "Franklin Graham pasaba y pasa una tremenda cantidad de tiempo en Corea del Norte. Él lo lleva en su corazón. Sí surgió el tema, y las cosas estarán cambiando".[19] Luego, de regreso en Washington, un reportero de CNN le preguntó por qué no había confrontado a Kim más directamente por los abusos del régimen a los derechos humanos, y el Presidente dijo: "no quiero ver que un arma nuclear lo destruya a usted y a su familia".[20] La implicación era que vendrán cambios, pero la negociación todavía era delicada en esta fase temprana como para presionar más a Kim.

Franklin Graham es mejor conocido por su importante obra con el grupo de asistencia cristiana *Samaritan's Purse*, pero su familia ha estado involucrada en actividades misioneras en China y Corea durante más de cien años. Sus abuelos maternos, el Dr. L. Nelson Bell y Virginia Leftwich Bell, sirvieron como médicos misioneros en China durante veinticinco años, de 1916 a 1941, y los tíos de Franklin, Virginia Bell Somerville y el Dr. John Somerville, siguieron sus pasos, sirviendo como médicos misioneros presbiterianos en Corea del Sur durante muchos años más. Además de la influencia de su padre, el evangelista Billy Graham, y su ministerio práctico en muchas partes del mundo, la preocupación de Franklin por la gente de Corea es profunda y multigeneracional.

Bajo el liderazgo de Graham, *Samaritan's Purse* ha provisto ayuda y ministerio en Corea del Norte al "distribuir alimentos, suministrar ayuda agrícola, brindar alivio por inundaciones, mejorar las instalaciones médicas, equipar centros de tratamiento contra tuberculosis y proveyendo clínicas móviles".[21] En respuesta a la inundación severa en Corea del Norte en el 2007, Graham y su equipo ministerial llevaron un avión Boeing 747 cargado con setenta y cinco toneladas de alimentos y suministros médicos de emergencia, valorados en más de US$8 millones, a la ciudad capital de Pyongyang. La nación había sido golpeada por la peor inundación en décadas, lo que ocasionó un desastre humanitario por todo el país. Un aproximado de seiscientos norcoreanos murieron o desaparecieron, y más de cien mil quedaron sin hogar. "A pesar de las diferencias políticas que dividen a nuestros dos países", dijo Graham en ese momento, "necesitamos hacer todo lo que podamos para cuidar de la gente en Corea del Norte".[22]

En la conclusión de la cumbre de Singapur, Graham expresó su gratitud al Presidente y publicó su reacción en Facebook, diciendo: "Gracias, Sr. Presidente, Mike Pompeo y todos los consejeros de la administración por estar dispuestos a trabajar por la paz. Les debemos nuestro apoyo y gratitud en este esfuerzo. La Biblia nos dice 'busca la paz, y síguela' (Salmo 34:14). Millones de personas cubrieron las reuniones de Singapur con sus oraciones: estadounidenses, norcoreanos, surcoreanos, había personas orando en todo el mundo. Roguemos a Dios que siga trabajando en el corazón y la mente de estos líderes".[23]

Open Doors USA, el grupo de vigilancia cristiano fundado por el líder cristiano, holandés, conocido como el Hermano Andrew, de quien era bien sabido que introducía ilegalmente Biblias en la antigua Unión Soviética y en Europa Oriental durante muchos años, ha calificado a Corea del Norte como el perseguidor número uno de cristianos durante los últimos diecisiete años. Según David Curry, presidente de *Open Doors*, "la decisión del presidente Trump de abordar las atrocidades a los derechos humanos en Corea del Norte fue diplomáticamente audaz, y estamos particularmente complacidos de escuchar al Presidente decir que trajo a colación la difícil situación de más de 300,000 cristianos que enfrentan persecución, e incluso la muerte, bajo el régimen de Kim Jong-un".[24]

"En Corea del Norte", dijo que hasta "120,000 cristianos ya han sido confinados a campamentos de prisioneros, donde las condiciones siguen siendo deplorables... Mantengo viva la esperanza de que los derechos humanos y la desnuclearización en Corea del Norte no tengan que ser esfuerzos mutuamente excluyentes". Él añadió: "Por esta razón, estamos en oración y cautelosamente optimistas por nuestros compañeros cristianos en Corea del Norte, para quienes ahora hay al menos un destello de esperanza que no existía antes de las reuniones del presidente Trump con el dictador".[25]

En un artículo para nuestro servicio de noticias en línea, CharismaNews.com, la directora de noticias Jessilyn Justice reportó que los cristianos en el norte son severamente perseguidos, y que solamente pueden practicar su fe en secreto. Para evitar sospechas, las reuniones de oración tienen que ser discretas y en lugares secretos, muchas veces con no más de dos o tres adoradores a la vez. Si fueran descubiertos, los cristianos están sujetos a detención y encarcelamiento en campamentos prisioneros, donde se les imputan delitos contra el estado. El castigo en estos campamentos podría incluir asesinato extrajudicial, esclavitud, trabajo forzado, tortura, violación y violencia sexual, y otros actos inhumanos.

Los informes de testigos oculares documentados por los fugados hablan de que los cristianos son colgados en cruces y suspendidos sobre un fuego, son aplastados bajo una aplanadora, empujados desde los puentes para caer en abismos rocosos y aguas profundas, e incluso son pisoteados por guardias militares y otros. Y, tristemente, muchos cristianos norcoreanos, quienes logran escapar a China, son repatriados por la fuerza a Corea del Norte, donde posteriormente son encarcelados y sometidos a las formas más brutales de represalia y tortura.[26]

La organización de intervención y ayuda *Christian Solidarity Worldwide* ha dicho que Estados Unidos y sus aliados no pueden darse el lujo de eludir el mandato moral de responsabilizar al dictador coreano, Kim Jong-un, por los abusos de su régimen a los derechos humanos. Para los cristianos coreanos, quienes han sido encarcelados, torturados y sujetos a formas de ejecución espantosas, su único crimen fue expresar su fe en Dios y tener creencias distintas a aquellas aprobadas por el régimen comunista. Tal como lo informa *Open Doors*:

> Durante tres generaciones, todo en el país ha estado enfocado en idolatrar a la familia Kim. Los cristianos son vistos como los elementos hostiles de la sociedad que tienen que ser erradicados. Debido al adoctrinamiento constante que impregna todo el país, los vecinos e incluso miembros de la familia están muy atentos e informan a las autoridades de cualquier actividad religiosa sospechosa.[27]

"Si bien las imágenes amigables del presidente Trump y Kim Jong-un pueden ser reconfortantes y aunque tenemos la esperanza de que estas negociaciones puedan ofrecer un camino hacia la desnuclearización", dice Vernon Brewer, CEO y fundador de *World Help*, "los cristianos norcoreanos no están más seguros hoy de lo que estaban antes de la Cumbre de Singapur".[28] El Presidente no puede dejar de presionar a Kim para que haya cambios en las prácticas totalitarias del régimen.

Brewer también dice: "Creer en Jesús sigue siendo un crimen que puede llevar a un seguidor de Cristo a un campamento de trabajo o a la cárcel, lo que, en muchos casos, equivale a una sentencia de muerte. Sin embargo, esto es lo más maravilloso: ¡la Iglesia subterránea de Corea del Norte sigue creciendo! Los creyentes siguen arriesgando su vida para obtener una Biblia. Al celebrar la reunión conjunta de los líderes de Estados Unidos y Corea del Norte, no podemos olvidar a nuestros hermanos y hermanas norcoreanas. Tenemos que seguir hablando y orando por ellos; quienes todavía están esperando su propia victoria".[29]

World Help ha estado utilizando una variedad de medios clandestino para proveer Biblias para los cristianos norcoreanos. Aunque Trump dijo que la desnuclearización era la máxima prioridad de sus reuniones de la cumbre con Kim, él dijo que el líder norcoreano reaccionó muy bien cuando le preguntó sobre tomar medidas para eliminar los abusos a los derechos humanos en su país. "Creo que es una situación difícil allá", dijo Trump. "No hay duda de ello. Y nosotros la discutimos hoy muy fuertemente. Quiero decir, sabiendo que el propósito principal de lo que estábamos haciendo es: *desnuclearizar*. Pero lo discutimos con bastante amplitud. Estaremos haciendo algo al respecto... Es difícil en muchos lugares, por cierto. No solo allí. Pero es difícil, y continuaremos eso. Y creo que, con el tiempo, estaremos de acuerdo en algo. Pero fue discutido extensamente fuera de la situación nuclear, uno de los temas principales".[30]

Trump también dijo que pondría un alto a los ejercicios militares que se llevan a cabo regularmente por las fuerzas armadas de Estados Unidos y Corea del Sur en tanto las negociaciones mantengan el rumbo, y dijo que Kim Jong-un también estuvo de acuerdo en que trabajadores internacionales recuperen los restos de los soldados estadounidenses muertos durante la Guerra Coreana. Refiriéndose a lo que sigue en las negociaciones durante una entrevista después de la Cumbre en *Fox News*, Trump dijo: "yo solo creo que vamos a empezar el proceso de desnuclearización con Corea del Norte, y creo que a su regreso empezará virtualmente de inmediato; y él ya lo indicó".[31]

Orar por un milagro

En otro reportaje para la revista *Charisma*, el escritor y evangelista, Lee Grady, predijo que, con todos los cambios increíbles que están sucediendo hoy día en todo el mundo, Kim Jong-un pronto estaría "abriendo de par en par las puertas [de Corea del Norte] al cristianismo y se uniría al siglo 21". Muchos lectores criticaron la idea, me dijo Grady, ya sea porque no creen en las motivaciones o en la honestidad de Kim, o posiblemente porque temían que el escritor de *The Art of the Deal* podría no estar a la altura del desafío. "Pero me atengo a mi predicción", dijo Grady. "Yo creo personalmente que el futuro de Corea del Norte no está en las manos de Kim, Trump o cualquier otro ser humano. Creo que el soberano Señor de las naciones está dirigiendo este milagro".[32]

Si damos un paso atrás y pensamos por un momento en cuán extraño es para Corea del Norte estar considerando cualquier tipo de cambio a sus barbaries, después de setenta años de represión brutal, tendríamos que ver que algo milagroso está sucediendo. Grady dijo que el mundo está al borde de un avance verdaderamente histórico, que los prospectos de una reversión de las suertes que hace temblar a la tierra podrían estar mucho más cerca de lo que sabemos, y los cambios de tal magnitud son desesperadamente necesarios.

"Hasta tres millones de norcoreanos murieron de hambre en la década de los noventa", dice Grady. "La economía es tan pobre que más de 6 millones de personas están desnutridas hoy día, y un tercio de todos los niños norcoreanos están atrofiados por la inanición. La persona promedio gana US$1,800 al año, lo que hace de Corea del Norte uno de los países más pobres en la tierra. Sin embargo, tiene un ejército de 1.2 millones de soldados, el doble del tamaño del ejército de Corea del Sur". Aunque el fundador del régimen totalitario, Kim Il-sung, murió en 1994, el gobierno le otorgó "el cargo de la presidencia eterna", y es adorado como un dios por los seguidores de la religión Juche.

Hoy día, hay más de treinta y cuatro mil estatuas de Kim Il-sung en el país, una estatua por cada setecientos cincuenta norcoreanos. El cuerpo embalsamado del líder está en exhibición en el Palacio del Sol de Kumsusan, el sitio turístico más popular del país. Todos los ciudadanos de Corea del Norte están obligados a portar una insignia que muestra el rostro de Kim Il-sung. Es más, escribe Grady, en Corea del Norte no es el año 2018. Es el 107, lo que, según el calendario Juche norcoreano, conmemora el nacimiento de Kim Il-sung en 1912. A los norcoreanos nacidos el 8 de julio o el 17 de diciembre no se les permite celebrar su cumpleaños porque Kim Il-sung y su hijo, Kim Jong-il, murieron en esas fechas.

Los súbditos leales al actual dictador, Kim Jong-un, creen que él puede controlar el clima. Su biografía oficial, publicada por el gobierno, dice que Kim aprendió a caminar y a hablar antes de los seis meses de edad y que él puede controlar el clima con sus estados de ánimo. El ministerio de propaganda del régimen también convenció a la gente de Corea del Norte que una estrella nueva apareció en el cielo el día que Kim Il-sung nació. Las escuelas en el norte son centros de adoctrinamiento donde a los niños se les lava el cerebro desde los primeros grados. Se les enseña la canción "No tenemos nada que envidiarle al mundo" y se espera que ellos lleven sus propios escritorios y sillas a la escuela. Además, los niños son obligados a hacer trabajo gubernamental durante las horas escolares, pero si los padres pueden pagarlo, se les permite sobornar a los maestros para evitar que los niños realicen trabajos forzados.

A diferencia de las condiciones en Corea del Sur, la cual es una sociedad avanzada y tecnológicamente sofisticada, la red eléctrica en Corea del Norte es tan inadecuada que la mayoría de la gente no tiene luz en sus hogares. Las imágenes nocturnas tomadas por satélites desde el espacio muestran un país inmerso en la oscuridad; sin embargo, los visitantes del Norte han informado que las personas han llegado a amar la oscuridad porque les da la única privacidad que pueden experimentar. Sin embargo, viajar es increíblemente difícil, Lee Grady escribe, porque solamente el 3 por ciento de las carreteras en Corea del Norte están pavimentadas. Aun así, los civiles raramente usan las carreteras ya que muy pocos poseen vehículos privados. Un grupo pequeño, de élite, de norcoreanos tienen acceso a la internet, pero el gobierno filtra todo el contenido en línea.

Los granjeros tienen poco o ningún acceso a los fertilizantes químicos, así que el gobierno requiere que la gente de Corea del Norte produzca cierta cantidad de desechos humanos. De hecho, muchas familias ponen candados en sus baños al aire libre para evitar que sus vecinos roben los desechos para cumplir con la cuota del gobierno. Los cristianos son a menudo ridiculizados, dice Grady, porque creemos que los demonios son reales y que las fuerzas demoníacas trabajan tras bambalinas para afectar los eventos mundiales.

"¿Por qué es tan difícil de creer?", dice. "No puedo entender cómo alguien puede ver la sombría situación en Corea del Norte y no creer que el diablo existe.

Afortunadamente, la Biblia también dice que Cristo venció el poder de Satanás a través de su muerte y resurrección, y que el reino de Dios se expandirá dondequiera que se predique el evangelio". Por eso, dice Grady, que está esperando ver milagros en Corea del Norte.[33]

Paz por medio de la fortaleza

Como escritor y editor cristiano, le doy alta prioridad a la libertad de culto para todas las personas. Pero es solo una de las muchas maneras en que el presidente Trump está marcando la diferencia más allá de las fronteras de Estados Unidos. Como he discutido antes, Trump está presionando a nuestros aliados de la OTAN a pagar su parte del costo de defender a Europa después de muchas décadas de lento cumplimiento. Él también se reunió en Helsinki con el presidente ruso, Vladimir Putin, en julio de 2018. Aunque su conferencia de prensa con Putin en la cumbre provocó conmociones de especulación política y mediática, una cosa es segura: Donald Trump no adopta un enfoque convencional en nada, incluyendo la diplomacia. En vez de apresurarse a emitir juicios como muchos en los medios y en las arenas políticas, creo que a largo plazo habrá un progreso significativo para Estados Unidos como resultado de las reuniones y tácticas de política exterior de Trump, ya sea con Rusia, Siria, Irán, Corea del Norte, China, Ucrania, o en algún otro lugar.

A veces, pareciera que el presidente Trump tiene a líderes mundiales, como el presidente chino Xi Jinping y el presidente francés Emmanuel Macron, comiendo de su mando, y él se ha enfrentado directamente con las élites en Davos, Suiza, en el Foro Económico Mundial. Todo eso, como él ha dicho, es parte de "hacer grande a Estados Unidos otra vez", restaurar el espíritu del excepcionalismo estadounidense y poner a Estados Unidos en primer lugar en el escenario mundial. Esta es su pasión, la cual parece estar guiando todo lo relacionado a su política, tanto doméstica como internacional.

La mentalidad determinada de Trump me recuerda una historia que James Watt me contó cuando él era el Secretario del Interior de Estados Unidos bajo la presidencia de Ronald Reagan. Tuve el privilegio de entrevistar al secretario Watt en su oficina en Washington, DC, y escribí un artículo de portada sobre él en la revista *Charisma* en 1983. Me dijo que la prioridad número uno de Reagan era derrotar el comunismo soviético. Ahora bien, esos fueron los días cuando la mayoría de los estadounidenses, incluyéndome, asumimos que tendríamos que coexistir con el comunismo durante toda nuestra vida.

Tengo la edad suficiente para recordar la crisis de misiles cubanos de 1962 y cómo algunos floridanos hasta construyeron refugios antibombas porque había tanto temor de guerra con los soviéticos. También recuerdo que Reagan heredó una economía horrible de Jimmy Carter. La inflación fue del 14 por ciento en

1980, y puedo recordar haber pagado tasas de interés de hasta 20 por ciento, cuando empecé mi empresa de medios a principios de la década de los ochenta. La recesión de 1981–82 fue la peor desde la Gran Depresión.

Entonces, ¿qué debía hacer el Presidente si quería derrotar a los soviéticos cuando parecía casi imposible? Primero, él necesitaba un ejército fuerte. Para tener un ejército fuerte, él necesitaba una economía saludable. Para tener una economía saludable, él tenía que administrar mejor los recursos de nuestro magnífico país. Allí fue donde entró James Watt. El Departamento de Interior es más que el departamento que supervisa los parques nacionales y los edificios en Washington. Puede otorgar arrendamientos para la perforación de petróleo y gas natural. Decide cuánta madera puede extraerse en determinado momento. Watt sabía que tenía que hacer bien su trabajo para que la economía pudiera crecer, lo que permitiría que Estados Unidos tuviera un ejército fuerte que pudiera arrodillar a los soviéticos. Cuando la Unión Soviética se disolvió una década después, recordé lo que Watt me dijo.

El presidente Trump cree que, para volver a hacer grande a Estados Unidos, tenemos que reestructurar nuestro ejército. Y para tener una perspectiva clara de lo que está sucediendo en el ejército, contacté a mi amigo, el general retirado Jerry Boykin. Durante su carrera de treinta y seis años, él pasó trece años en la Fuerza Delta y estuvo involucrado en varias misiones de alto perfil, incluyendo el incidente de *Black Hawk Down* en Mogadishu, Somalia. Él también se desempeñó como subsecretario adjunto de defensa para inteligencia bajo el presidente George W. Bush. Se le conoce como un líder cristiano franco que ahora se desempeña como vicepresidente ejecutivo del Family Research Council (Consejo de Investigación Familiar) en Washington, DC.

Cuando le pregunté al general sobre los cambios en el ejército desde que el presidente Trump fue electo, él citó al general Douglas MacArthur, quien les dijo a los cadetes en West Point en 1962, "su misión permanece fija, determinada, inviolable. La cual es, ganar nuestras guerras", añadiendo que la misión no ha cambiado. El general cree que el presidente Obama fracasó en entender ese sencillo concepto y, por lo tanto, estuvo dispuesto a permitir que la preparación militar languideciera, alcanzando con el tiempo un estado donde ya no se podía esperar que el ejército ganara las guerras de la nación.

Tal fallo de juicio creó un riesgo crítico de seguridad nacional. El objetivo de Donald Trump ha sido restaurar la preparación militar, y lo está cumpliendo. Él liberó al ejército para que cumpliera su responsabilidad. En poco menos de un año, las fuerzas armadas iraquíes y sirias apoyadas por una coalición guiada por Estados Unidos recuperó la mayor parte del territorio en Siria e Irak que ISIS tenía capturado, reduciendo significativamente su capacidad para organizar la guerra y cometer actos de terrorismo en otras partes del mundo.

Mientras que Al Qaeda existía en Irak antes de Obama, el surgimiento de ISIS se debió a una disputa entre Osama bin Laden y un líder renegado iraquí llamado Abu Bark al-Baghdadi, quien se convirtió en el jefe de ISIS y lo expandió a Siria. ISIS, después de todo, significa estado islámico de Irak y Siria [por sus siglas en inglés] lo que denotaba su deseo por un imperio sin fronteras, un califato que los fanáticos musulmanes creían que un día cubriría todo el mundo. Debido a eso, algunos radicales lo llaman "el estado islámico", lo que sugiere que el califato es mucho más grande que solo Siria e Irak. En un tiempo, ISIS parecía imparable ya que expandió su territorio exponencialmente.

Aunque Estados Unidos había estado empantanado en la guerra con Irak durante más de una década y había estado luchando en Afganistán desde el 2001, parecía que no podíamos ganar. "Pero luego llega Trump, y en un año, Trump, como comandante en jefe, a través de su ejército, ha recuperado el 90 por ciento del territorio que ISIS controlaba en Irak y Siria", me relató Boykin. "Entonces, ¿qué pasó? Él le dio a nuestro ejército reglas de combate que le permitieron ganar. La administración Obama nunca habló de ganar. Repito, remontémonos a MacArthur su misión es ganar las guerras de nuestra nación".

Uno de los mayores obstáculos para ganar las guerras fue el embargo, una disposición de la Ley de Control Presupuestario de 2011 que imponía recortes de gastos global si el Congreso y la Casa Blanca no podían ponerse de acuerdo sobre las reducciones específicas destinadas a reducir el déficit presupuestario. Trump hizo campaña para deshacerse del embargo y aumentar el presupuesto militar, y él ha hecho exactamente eso, lo que ha marcado una gran diferencia en poder equipar a nuestro ejército. "Ahora tenemos un presidente que comprende el concepto de ganar: incluirlo en tiempo de guerra, en combate". Obama nunca lo entendió Él tenía gente en el campo de batalla solo para jugar, no para ganar", Boykin dijo. "Solo piense en cuánto tiempo peleamos contra ISIS y cuán poco éxito tuvimos contra ISIS en la administración Obama", me dijo.

Para un tiempo como este

El general cree que el nuevo comandante en jefe cambió las reglas de combate y está en el proceso de darle al ejército los recursos que necesita, lo que Boykin siente que ha sido el logro más significativo de Trump. Esto ha puesto a las fuerzas armadas estadounidenses en el curso correcto para poder ganar las guerras de la nación. Boykin predijo que Trump pasará a la historia como el presidente que le dio a nuestro ejército todo lo necesario para tener éxito contra nuestros adversarios en el campo de batalla, y la prueba es el hecho de que ISIS ahora ha perdido más del 90 por ciento de su territorio.[34]

"La falta de voluntad para luchar fue solamente una de las formas en que Obama lastimó al ejército", dijo. Mientras que las guerras en el Medio Oriente iban lentamente, Obama decidió que era tiempo de terminar la política "no pregunte, no diga" y les dijo a los homosexuales que podían desempeñarse abiertamente en el ejército. Luego, dijo que el ejército pagaría por el tratamiento hormonal y la cirugía para reasignación de género para aquellos en el ejército que sentían ser transexuales.

"Obama usó nuestro ejército para probar un experimento social; eran casi como ratas de laboratorio", Boykin dijo. "Y luego viene el Sr. Trump que dice: 'Esto no tiene sentido para mí, en lo absoluto, y no vamos a hacer esto', y expulsa a los transexuales del ejército. Ahora bien, con lo que él tiene que lidiar, que es un asunto serio, es ¿qué hace uno con aquellas personas que salieron durante la administración Obama, de buena fe, creyendo que su gobierno iba a apoyar su compromiso de permitirles hacerlo público?".

Boykin señaló que la sabiduría convencional dice: "Tienes que dejarlos continuar sirviendo o darles incentivos enormes para que vayan y háganlo público por su propia cuenta. Pero si quieren quedarse, tienes que dejarlos porque es un asunto que se hizo en buena fe". Esta era la posición oficial, dijo Boykin, pero hay más qué considerar. "¡Espere!", él me dijo. "¿Cómo contribuye eso a la preparación en el ejército? Está trayendo gente que uno sabe que no podrá ser movilizado en un momento cuando necesitamos a cada hombre y mujer totalmente capaz de ser movilizados y peleando y ganando las guerras de la nación. Siempre regresa al problema de ¿podemos ganar las guerras de la nación en nuestro ejército?". "Así que ahora", él dijo, "tienes una situación donde estás trayendo gente que sabes que no podrás movilizar por algún periodo de tiempo, además vas a usar el dinero de los contribuyentes, que podría ser usado para alimento y municiones para nuestro ejército y lo estás gastando para darle terapia hormonal a una persona y cirugía transexual, ¿qué lógica hay en eso? ¿Cómo va a contribuir en hacer a nuestro ejército capaz de ganar las guerras de la nación? Y la respuesta es, no contribuye", dijo él. Y por eso, el Presidente tomó la decisión ética y sensata de restringir los reclutamientos militares.

Mientras tanto, tres jueces no electos en el sistema judicial federal decidieron que las acciones de Trump eran inconstitucionales, y para mediados de 2018 ese caso todavía estaba tratando de llegar a los tribunales. Pero el general Boykin pregunta: "Como comandante en jefe, bajo el artículo 2 de la Constitución, si el Sr. Obama tuvo la autoridad para decir que pueden salir y desempeñarse abiertamente, ¿por qué el Sr. Trump no tiene la misma autoridad para poder decir 'estoy cambiando esa política'? Ya que el presidente de Estados Unidos es responsable del ejército como comandante en jefe, el estado de la preparación de nuestro ejército".

Pero este no fue el único experimento social, me dijo Boykin. En el 2010, la administración Obama derogó la política "no pregunte, no diga". Siempre ha habido homosexuales sirviendo en el ejército; la pregunta era si ellos podrían servir abiertamente. Obama hizo el compromiso de anular la derogación de la política "no pregunte, no diga", y lo hizo. También decidió poner mujeres en la infantería y en operaciones especiales. Boykin dijo que Obama lo consideraba una cuestión de imparcialidad el poner a las mujeres en puestos de combate en tierra, algo que nunca se había permitido. "Pero, repito", dijo él, "¿cómo contribuye eso a la preparación? Y la respuesta es, en realidad no contribuye. Sin embargo, ese fue otro de sus experimentos".

El general Boykin dijo que está absolutamente convencido de que Donald Trump ha sido "levantado para un tiempo como este". Y añadió, "creo que es igual a Winston Churchill, quien salvó al mundo de ser aniquilado o subyugado por el régimen nazi". "Churchill nunca habría cumplido los estándares de un cristiano evangélico", él dijo; y Donald Trump quizá tampoco. No obstante, él cree que Donald Trump fue escogido para este trabajo en este tiempo. "Él no habla el idioma de los evangélicos, pero está en deuda con los evangélicos porque sabe que, lo que sea que ellos tengan, es real. Y creo que Dios lo está utilizando de una manera muy poderosa para darle a Estados Unidos la oportunidad de actuar juntos y cambiar esta nación por completo a través del liderazgo de Donald Trump".

Siento que esas fueron palabras reafirmantes de un soldado y patriota que sabe lo que significa estar listo en toda situación, sin importar los riesgos ni las consecuencias potenciales. Parece estar claro que la paciencia del presidente Trump con Kim Jong-un se basa en su evaluación estratégica de esas mismas cosas: el riesgo de no tomar medidas y la consecuencia potencial de presionar demasiado durante las primeras etapas críticas de las negociaciones. Es un equilibrio delicado y no una señal de debilidad o indecisión.

Según un informe del canal *Fox News*, dos legisladores noruegos han nominado oficialmente al presidente Trump para el Premio Nobel de la Paz 2019 como resultado de su histórica reunión en la Cumbre de Singapur con Kim Jong-un. La historia, que salió al aire por televisión, durante la transmisión de Sean Hannity el 13 de junio de 2018, indica que los políticos del populista Partido Progreso, de Noruega, anunciaron su decisión a las pocas horas de que Trump se reuniera con el dictador comunista y elogiaron al Presidente por su capacidad para llevar al líder norcoreano a la mesa de negociaciones. El presidente Obama recibió un reconocimiento en el 2009 antes de que hubiera tomado alguna acción diplomática significativa, basado en la esperanza del comité Nobel de que él sería un defensor de la paz mundial, pero su administración estuvo plagada de guerras a lo largo de su presidencia.

No hay duda de que la gente de Corea del Norte necesita y merece un defensor dedicado al proceso de paz. Ellos necesitan bienes materiales, alimentos, esperanza y libertad para expresar sus creencias abiertamente. Sin embargo, el desafío es inmenso, y la paz solo se logrará si el presidente Trump, el Secretario de Estado, Mike Pompeo, y sus equipos de negociadores y operativos pueden, de alguna manera, convencer al dictador norcoreano que es mejor para él deshacerse de sus armas y abrir las puertas de par en par al reino ermitaño. Si el presidente Trump puede lograr esa hazaña, definitivamente se merecerá su lugar en la historia. Pero si van a suceder cambios de esa magnitud, será a través del poder de una diplomacia musculosa apoyada por el poder de la oración fiel e imparable.

LA ECONOMÍA FLORECIENTE DE TRUMP

S IN IMPORTAR CUÁN duro traten los medios liberales, de reconcentrar la atención del mundo en otros asuntos, las buenas noticias que vienen de la economía floreciente del presidente Trump son difíciles de ignorar. Tome, por ejemplo, este análisis sobre la abrasadora economía de *U.S. News & World Report*: "*Wall Street* abrió el 2018 con una nota ganadora el martes, y ofreció a Nasdaq su primer cierre en la historia por encima de 7,000 puntos, luego de un repunte en las acciones de tecnología. Al momento del cierre, el índice compuesto de Nasdaq, rico en tecnología, había saltado 1.5 por ciento al final de la primera sesión del año en 7,006.90. La S&P 500 también registró un récord, ganando 0.8 por ciento para cerrar en 2,695.79, mientras que el promedio industrial Dow Jones subió 0.4 por ciento a 24,824.01, aproximadamente 13 puntos por debajo de su récord histórico".[1] Todo esto está realmente sucediendo, y todo al mismo tiempo.

Tal como el analista económico, Peter Roff, explica en su reporte especial, esto significa que "Estados Unidos está hasta la nariz de buenas noticias económicas". El Dow saltó a 26,000 en su primer día de negociaciones del año nuevo. El desempleo disminuyó a 3.75 por ciento en junio 2018, el número más bajo desde 1969, y el desempleo en la comunidad negra estuvo en su punto más bajo de lo que había estado desde que la Oficina de Estadísticas Laborales empezó a llevar un récord en 1972.

Bajo Barack Obama, el desempleo en la comunidad negra alcanzó un pico de 16.5 por ciento. Para junio de 2018, inspirado por el clima pronegocios creado por la administración Trump, había bajado al 5.9 por ciento. Animado por todas las buenas noticias, el mercado laboral añadió 223,000 empleos el mismo mes, de los cuales 218,000 fueron en el sector privado, y el pago promedio por hora subió de $26.84 a $26.92.[2] Pero las buenas noticias solo continuaban llegando.

En el índice mensual de *Economic Optimist*, una colaboración del *Inverstor's Business Daily* y *TechnoMetrica*, mide la confianza de los consumidores, trabajadores e inversionistas en la fortaleza general de la economía. Un punto por encima de cincuenta indica optimismo, mientras que un punto por debajo de cincuenta indica pesimismo. Como informó *Investor's Business Daily*, la escala de optimismo saltó a más del 6 por ciento en enero de 2018 (a 55.1). El mes siguiente, el índice llegó a 56.7. Para el 1 de junio de 2018, aun el *New York Times* se sintió movido a decir: "Nos quedamos sin palabras para describir cuán buenos están los números laborales", añadiendo que "la economía está en su mejor punto, con un crecimiento sostenible y amplia mejoría en el mercado laboral".[3]

Esta fue la clase de crecimiento que Donald Trump había prometido a lo largo de la campaña y la confirmación que su administración había estado esperando. Al celebrar el momento, el Presidente tuiteó el 4 de junio:

> ¡En muchas maneras, esta es la mayor economía en la HISTORIA de Estados Unidos y el mejor momento de la HISTORIA para buscar empleo![4]

Claro está, no pasó mucho tiempo para que los negativos aparecieran, y Bloomberg protestó ligeramente que: "etiquetar a una sola era económica como la más grande de la historia es subjetivo porque no hay una métrica acordada". Pero luego, añadió: "Juzgar únicamente por el producto doméstico bruto, quizás es la manera más simple para medir el progreso de una nación, las décadas posteriores a la Segunda Guerra Mundial fueron las más calientes en la historia estadounidense. La demanda acumulada del consumidor, el auge de la vivienda y el vibrante sector manufacturero, todo fundido en la Era de Oro de la economía".[5]

Nadie puede negar que la era postguerra fue un periodo de crecimiento único para la nación, pero eso fue hace sesenta años, y el entusiasmo de Trump hoy está siendo avivado por el hecho de que más estadounidenses que nunca están encontrando empleos buenos y productivos y mejorando sus estilos de vida. El empleo en la mayoría de los sectores está en el punto más alto de la historia, y los despidos a lo largo de la nación están bajos, hasta donde estuvieron en diciembre de 1990. Además, el gasto corporativo en bienes capitales está en el alza, y el crecimiento en el producto interno bruto (PIB) ha alcanzado el 4.1 por ciento. Con informes económicos tan sólidos, las empresas empiezan a aumentar salarios, a pagar bonos y a anunciar planes de expansión.

El PIB es la mejor manera para medir si la economía está creciendo, y la Reserva Federal proyectó que el PIB, para el segundo trimestre de 2018, sería un alto 4.8 por ciento. "Ese número no se había visto desde los días de Reagan", dijo el columnista Wayne Allyn Root. "Estados Unidos ha regresado al primer lugar en el mundo en el índice económico mundial de competitividad. Gracias a los cortes tributarios masivos del presidente Trump y la eliminación de regulaciones, ahora estamos por delante de economías florecientes como Singapur, Hong Kong y Suiza".[6]

"Pero si no ha escuchado ninguno de estos números", dice Peter Roff, "no debería sorprenderse mucho". Los medios principales de comunicación se niegan rotundamente a darle al Presidente el crédito que él y su administración merecen por su economía que está rompiendo récords. "Lo que está sucediendo", dice, "es "similar a una conspiración de silencio que intenta garantizar que nadie le dé el crédito por el giro económico al presidente Donald Trump".[7]

He escuchado a los reporteros liberales de la televisión por cable decir que la economía es buena solo debido a la forma en que el presidente Obama se la dejó preparada a Trump con lo que Obama llamaba su "pala preparada" al plan de estímulos en el 2009. Sin embargo, yo estoy de acuerdo con lo que Ross, un experto cuyo análisis respeto, escribió: "Si Obama tuvo algo que ver con los números buenos", eso empezó antes de las elecciones, fue solo porque el mercado estaba reaccionando al hecho de que, sin importar quién ganara en noviembre 2016, Obama y "su feliz banda reguladora de planificadores centrales progresistas pronto se irían".[8]

En su artículo destacado en el sitio web de *U.S. News & World Report*, Roff dice que puede ser difícil de aceptar que los números así de buenos se deban solamente a las políticas de Trump, pero son lo que son. Como prueba, él cita a Patrice Lee Onwuka del Foro de Mujeres Independientes, diciendo que el desempleo para los negros en Estados Unidos ha declinado de 7.9 por ciento en diciembre de 2016, a 6.8 por ciento al final de 2017, lo cual "es un logro significativo".

La economía, según Onwuka la ve, "está mejorando para los afroamericanos y debería seguir mejorando a medida que las políticas sobre procrecimiento y profamilia expanden nuestros recursos y brindan mejores oportunidades".[9] Sin embargo, la verdadera pregunta puede ser: ¿Cómo es posible que esto no esté en primera plana en las noticias?

> ¿Cómo es que las redes de cable de 24 horas están dispuestas a dedicar horas de programación al impacto de lo que el presidente Trump dijo o pudo haber dicho en reuniones privadas con senadores discutiendo la política de inmigración no están teniendo ayuntamientos televisados y llevando a las mejores mentes económicas en el país para explicar por qué el tema del desempleo en la comunidad negra, la cual muchos han relegado al cementerio de problemas sin solución, ha dado repentinamente un giro para bien?[10]

Roff escribe que lo que sucede es más que solo un sesgo mediático. Los medios parecen pensar que los presidentes Reagan y Bush fueron muy bobos para hacer el trabajo. Él dice que con Trump es más que eso:

> Es una hostilidad abierta contra el hombre reflejada en una negativa para cubrir cualquier cosa buena que él hace y cualquier cosa

buena que pueda suceder debido a las políticas que él ha puesto. La misma gente que nunca pudo aceptar que él ganara la nominación, cuando todos ellos decían que era improbable que él ganara la presidencia, a pesar de sus proyecciones y encuestas que mostraban que sería imposible que él lo hiciera, están tan arraigados en probar que al final tenían la razón que, no solo están empeñados en que él fracase, sino que están tratando de hacer que suceda.[11]

Aun si Trump invita una cierta cantidad de abuso por parte de los medios liberales por su tono adversario y el lenguaje fuerte que usa en sus tuits, la batalla no es justa. Por una razón, Donald Trump no es el tipo de persona que le tema al confrontamiento; de hecho, parece disfrutarlos. Y gracias a sus tuits, comentarios públicos y aun las filtraciones ocasionales de sus comentarios privados, el público comprende la naturaleza de la batalla, y no están ciegos ante el éxito que tiene su administración con la economía. Todos pueden ver el impacto que todas estas buenas noticias están teniendo en el mercado y, a pesar del criticismo y la negativa incesante de los medios y los políticos liberales en ambos partidos, sus índices de preferencia están muy altos.

Desafortunadamente, la política no se trata realmente de lo que es bueno para el país. Con demasiada frecuencia se trata de lo que es bueno para el partido. Así que, cuando empresas como AT&T, Wells Fargo y Visa anunciaron que estarían dando un bono, incrementos salariales o incrementos en beneficios para los empleados y le dieron el crédito a la legislación fiscal del Partido Republicano en diciembre de 2017, la líder de la minoría demócrata en la Cámara de Representantes, Nancy Pelosi, se lanzó al ataque y calificó de "migajas" a las bonificaciones proyectadas de mil dólares. Ella dijo: "en cuanto a las bonificaciones que las corporaciones estadounidenses recibieron versus las migajas que están dándoles a sus trabajadores como para congraciarse, es muy patético". Luego, cuando Walmart, que había sido blanco de mala prensa por muchos años y de huelguistas debido a los salarios bajos, anunció que la empresa aumentaría el pago mínimo por hora a once dólares y ofreció a los empleados antiguos un bono de mil dólares, los críticos de los medios y demócratas de Trump llamaron a eso un ardid publicitario.[12]

Pero la reacción a raíz de los comentarios de Pelosi y las críticas a los patrones que estaban ofreciendo bonos en efectivo fue rápida y furiosa. Los trabajadores de todo el país criticaron a Pelosi por la arrogancia y falta de sensibilidad de sus comentarios. En entrevistas instantáneas televisadas, muchos indicaron que mil dólares extras no son migajas para la mayoría de las familias trabajadoras y que, para una multimillonaria como Pelosi, decir algo tan grosero y desconsiderado solo demuestra que vive en un mundo irreal. En un discurso durante un retiro congresista en West Virginia, el 1 de febrero de 2018, el presidente contraatacó. "Para los mineros de West Virginia y los empleados de las fábricas, mil dólares significan muchísimo, y el comentario de Pelosi", dijo, "fue tan delicado como la afirmación de Hillary Clinton de que la mitad de los seguidores de Trump eran una "canasta de deplorables".[13]

HACER LA ECONOMÍA GRANDE OTRA VEZ

A lo largo de su campaña, Donald Trump prometió liberar la economía para que hiciera lo que es mejor: aumentar la prosperidad de todos los estadounidenses. "Por supuesto, eso fue exactamente lo que sucedió", escribió el economista Andy Puzder. Cuando se redujeron los impuestos y eliminaron las regulaciones contra las empresas, el crecimiento del PIB escaló durante los primeros tres trimestres de Trump a un promedio de 3.1 por ciento, y la tasa de desempleo cayó a una baja que no se había visto desde el año 2000. Obama predijo confiadamente en el 2010 que el PIB podría "exceder el 4 por ciento anual de 2012 al 2014".[14]

Sin embargo, Obama nunca tuvo ni siquiera un año de 3 por ciento de crecimiento en el PIB. En el 2016, dice, Puzder, el crecimiento de promedio del PIB fue un deplorable 1.5 por ciento, y agregó que las personas designadas por Obama implementaron políticas agresivas y regulaciones contra las empresas que hicieron que la economía fracasara en "producir suficientes empleos bien pagados, mientras que la gente abandonaba la fuerza laboral, los salarios se estancaron, los caminos a la clase media se cerraron y la desigualdad de ingreso creció". Puzder dice que era predecible que esas "políticas económicas progresistas produjeran exactamente los mismos problemas" que la administración aseguraba querer evitar.[15]

A principios de 2017, la administración Trump pronosticaba un crecimiento de 3 por ciento en el PIB, pero el economista de Obama, Lee Branstetter, aseguró que era "matemática y esencialmente imposible obtener el crecimiento del que hablaban". El economista de la administración Obama, Jason Furman, pronosticó diez años de crecimiento en el PIB de "aproximadamente 2 por ciento al año". El economista de Obama, Larry Summers, dijo que creer en el pronóstico de Trump de 3 o 4 por ciento de crecimiento en el PIB era como creer "en cuentos de hadas y la ridícula economía de la oferta". Pero los progresistas adivinaron mal. Con un crecimiento promedio del PIB del 3.1 por ciento durante más de tres trimestres, la Oficina de Presupuesto del Congreso pronosticó una tasa aún mayor de 3.3 por ciento en el 2018. A eso, Puzder dijo:

> Con la economía liberada de la mano dura del gobierno, el optimismo económico es palpable. La Asociación Nacional de Fabricantes informó recientemente que el 93 por ciento de los fabricantes estadounidenses están optimistas por el futuro. Esa es la cifra más alta en las encuestas de los últimos 20 años; un incremento que supera al 56.6 del año pasado. El índice de optimismo para marzo

de la Federación Nacional de la Pequeña Empresa y Negocios Independientes alcanzó su décimo sexto mes consecutivo de estar el cinco por ciento superior en 45 años de leer encuestas[16].

Para enero 2018, más estadounidenses formaban parte de la fuerza laboral que en cualquier otro momento de la historia nacional. Según la Federación Nacional de Negocios Independientes, el problema más grande que enfrentan las empresas hoy día ya no son los impuestos o las regulaciones; es encontrar trabajadores calificados. Puzder dice: "Algunos podrían llamar a eso una revancha capitalista. Sin embargo, no es una sorpresa para aquellos de nosotros que, parafraseando al presidente Kennedy, apreciamos cuán rápido la creciente marea del capitalismo puede levantar todos los barcos".[17]

El pueblo estadounidense está consciente de los cambios que se están llevando a cabo. En marzo, una encuesta de Gallup informó que apenas un tercio de los estadounidenses estaban muy preocupados por la economía, y menos de un cuarto estaban grandemente preocupados por el desempleo; los números más bajos desde que Gallup empezó a reportar los datos en el 2001. La disminución más significativa en ambas medidas sucedió después de que el Presidente Trump asumió el cargo. Desde ese punto de vista, dice Puzder, "sería bueno sí, por una vez, esos en la Izquierda progresista pudieran dejar de lado el desdén por el Presidente durante el tiempo suficiente para ver el capitalismo estadounidense por lo que es: una máquina sin igual para crear prosperidad y oportunidad, facultando a los consumidores en lugar de a las élites y ofreciéndole a la gente de todos los trasfondos un buen empleo y una mejor vida".[18]

Los estadounidenses saben que a la economía le va mucho mejor bajo el presidente Trump que durante los ocho años de estancamiento que experimentamos bajo Obama. La política económica durante la administración anterior estaba basada en el incremento de los impuestos sobre aquellos que generan riqueza para crear programas de gobierno que les permitieran a los demócratas redistribuir el dinero y los beneficios a los potenciales votantes demócratas. Construyendo un apoyo a través de "mensajes breves de propaganda falsa sobre la imparcialidad y la decencia", dice Puzder, hubo muy poco tiempo o interés para crear políticas que pudieran realmente motivar el crecimiento económico.

El presidente Clinton ha admitido que él aumentó demasiado los impuestos durante su presidencia. Con el aporte y asesoramiento de la Cámara de Representantes Republicana y el orador Newt Gingrich, Clinton aceptó recortar los impuestos sobre las ganancias de capital, reformar la beneficencia, desregular los bancos, equilibrar el presupuesto y reducir el tamaño del gobierno. Durante su discurso al Estado de la Unión en 1996, dijo lo que ya todos sabían, "la era del gobierno grande ha terminado". Desafortunadamente, ese no es el mensaje que viene de los demócratas en la actualidad. Para los demócratas progresivos, el crecimiento económico ocupa el segundo lugar después de expandir el tamaño y poder del gobierno.

Como presidente de la cadena de restaurantes CKE, durante los años de Obama, Puzder dijo que los periodistas lo confrontaban a menudo preguntándole "¿Cómo podían los restaurantes emplear personas a medio tiempo y en puestos básicos con salarios tan bajos para sostener a una familia? La discusión se convertía invariablemente en un salario mínimo de US$15 la hora, automatización o 'avaricia corporativa'". Sin embargo, las dinámicas han cambiado desde entonces, y gracias a la economía floreciente de Trump, la tasa de desempleo es ahora la más baja en casi dos décadas. A pesar del récord de 155 millones de personas en la fuerza laboral en marzo de 2018, hubo un récord alto de 6.6 millones de empleos disponibles. Según Puzder:

> El número de personas trabajando en construcción está en su nivel más alto desde junio de 2008, y hubo 248,000 puestos vacantes adicionales en ese mes. El número de personas trabajando en fábricas está a su nivel más alto desde diciembre de 2008, con 391,000 puestos vacantes adicionales.
>
> Según una encuesta reciente por la Asociación Nacional de Fabricantes, el 72 por ciento de los fabricantes estaba incrementando los salarios y beneficios de los trabajadores, mientras que un 77 por ciento estaba contratando más trabajadores.[19]

Desde que Barack Obama dejó el cargo, la economía ha dado una vuelta de 180 grados, yendo de una situación "donde el problema era que los trabajadores no podían encontrar empleos bien pagados hacia una economía donde el problema es que las empresas no pueden encontrar trabajadores para llenar empleos bien pagados.

Puzder dice que esto sucedió debido al compromiso del presidente Trump de "reducir los impuestos y disminuir el tamaño del gobierno a través de la desregulación. No fue el resultado de impuestos más altos ni de programas de gobierno expandidos. De hecho, el número de estadounidenses que dependen de los beneficios del gobierno está disminuyendo. El promedio mensual de las solicitudes de beneficios por desempleo inicial está en lo más bajo que se ha visto desde hace cuarenta y cinco años. El número de personas recibiendo beneficios SNAP (estampas para alimentos) también ha bajado, en más de 2.5 millones de personas desde que el presidente Trump tomó el cargo".[20]

El enfoque del Presidente hacia la economía, según su hijo Donald Trump Jr., está diseñado para ayudar a la clase trabajadora "olvidada" en el centro del país, en vez de las élites costeras y "los ricos" como han asegurado los oponentes del Presidente. Trump Jr., quien ha asumido las operaciones del día a día de la

Organización Trump junto con su hermano menor, Eric, dijo que las cifras de empleo más recientes que muestran un 3.8 por ciento de desempleo y el récord más bajo de desempleo para los negros, hispanos y las mujeres son un indicativo del éxito de las políticas del presidente Trump; un nivel de éxito que ha dejado a los medios antagonistas casi sin habla. "Y, una vez más", dijo Trump Jr., "si el *New York Times* está diciendo que ellos no tienen palabras para describir cuán buenos son estos números, no lo están haciendo con alegría".[21]

Tal como lo dijo su padre durante la campaña presidencial de 2016, el objetivo es hacer posible que los obreros promedio triunfen, y eso es lo que está sucediendo. "Los hombres olvidados a quienes dirigimos nuestra campaña, ellos están obteniendo el verdadero beneficio de eso", dijo. "Eso no está ayudando a los multimillonarios ni a las historias que están tratando de vender. Eso está ayudando a los patriotas estadounidenses, verdaderos, obreros que se esfuerzan duro. Ellos están recibiendo mejores salarios. Hay más demanda por su trabajo. Ellos pueden hacerlo. Pueden sostener mejor a sus familias. Eso ayuda a la estructura familiar. Todo, quiero decir, esto es para lo que hicimos campaña. Para esto se postuló mi padre. Esto es ayudar a la gente en lo que era la tierra olvidada, todas partes entre la ciudad de Nueva York y Malibú, que la institución del Partido Demócrata ha olvidado por décadas".[22]

Trump Jr. añadió que cumplir con las promesas de campaña es inusual para un presidente, pero que su papá no es como la mayoría de los políticos. Él está comprometido con ver a Estados Unidos triunfar. "Esa era la tesis de toda su campaña, y ¿adivinen qué? En realidad, lo está llevando a cabo… Promesas hechas, promesas cumplidas. Una y otra vez. Eso no viene de los que son seguidores de Donald J. Trump. Eso viene de gente como el *Washington Post* que están diciendo: "Oye, Trump está cumpliendo con sus promesas de campaña".[23]

"Veo el nuevo giro demócrata", dijo. "'Vamos a estar a favor de los empleos'. ¿De veras? ¿Dónde han estado durante los últimos treinta años?". Este presidente ha creado más empleos que cualquiera antes que él en la misma cantidad de tiempo. Ahora los demócratas están diciendo que se van a enfrentar a él en las elecciones del Congreso y en el 2020 ¡con los mismos conceptos: impuestos opresivos, sobrerregulación ridícula y todas las políticas progresistas que ahora son los fundamentos básicos de su partido! "Eso no tiene sentido en absoluto", dijo Trump Jr., "pero tenemos que recordar que", y él añadió que, si Trump gana un segundo mandato en el 2020, la administración puede realmente volver a encarrilar el país. "Es realmente increíble, y es una oportunidad increíble que no podemos desperdiciar".[24]

EL PRONÓSTICO ECONÓMICO

Con base a una amplia gama de indicadores clave, el pronóstico económico de Estados Unidos es muy fuerte. Se espera que la tasa de crecimiento del PIB se mantenga entre 2 y 3 por ciento, lo cual es "el rango ideal" según los analistas en TheBalance.com. Se pronostica que el desempleo continúe a un ritmo natural, y que los riesgos tanto de la inflación como la deflación sean moderados y estén muy dentro del rango normal. Eso es lo que la mayoría de los expertos en el mercado y las finanzas llamarían "una economía de Ricitos de Oro", dicen ellos. No muy fuerte, no muy débil, pero justo en su punto. El presidente Trump había pronosticado un crecimiento económico del 4 por ciento durante la campaña (una cifra que después fue templada por el Jefe de la Tesorería, Steven Mnuchin, porque muchos analistas creen que el crecimiento a una tasa tan alta puede llevar a inversiones demasiado confiadas cuando la prudencia es la mejor política en un cambio económico). Sin embargo, a Trump no se le persuade fácilmente de sus objetivos para un crecimiento sin precedentes, y el 27 de julio de 2018, cuando el informe del PIB para el segundo trimestre de 2018 salió, el crecimiento había subido al 4.1 por ciento, señalando un giro económico histórico y otra promesa de campaña cumplida. Trump tuiteó las cifras como "maravilloso" y "terrífico" y con mucha razón.[25]

Tasas de interés en préstamos a corto plazo "la tarifa principal para los préstamos bancarios, *London InterBank Offered Rate* (LIBOR), la mayoría de los préstamos con tasa ajustable y los de interés solamente, y las tasas de las tarjetas de crédito, son controlados por la tasa de fondos federales. El Comité Federal de Mercado Abierto aumentó la tasa de los fondos federales a 1.5 por ciento en diciembre de 2017, con la expectativa de aumentarla a 2.1 por ciento en el 2018, 2.7 por ciento en el 2019, y 2.9 por ciento en el 2020. La última vez que los federales elevaron las tasas fue en el 2005, y el incremento repentino en esa ocasión contribuyó a la crisis de hipotecas de alto riesgo. Algunos observadores en la industria de la vivienda han sugerido que los mercados inmobiliarios podrían colapsar en un par de años. Sin embargo, las diferencias entre el mercado de la vivienda hoy día y la situación en el 2007 hace que un escenario tan sombrío sea altamente improbable.[26]

Mi buen amigo, Joe Bert, un profesional financiero certificado en Longwood, Florida, a quien le confío mis propias inversiones, revisó este capítulo a petición mía y señaló que, mientras el mercado de valores es el calibrador que la persona promedio usa para juzgar la salud de la economía, no es ni de cerca tan válido como otros muchos elementos discutidos en estas páginas. Él me dijo: "Nadie puede predecir el movimiento de corto plazo en el mercado de valores, pero los peldaños y logros que mencionas en tu libro son un buen augurio para una tendencia positiva al alza a largo plazo". Yo tomo eso como un estímulo fuerte.

Aunque la economía se ve realmente fuerte mientras escribo este libro a mediados de 2018, eso podría cambiar, y podría haber una caída en el mercado de valores. Si eso sucede, mantenga la calma. Ese es el mejor consejo para cualquiera que invierta en el mercado de valores porque los mercados bajan y luego vuelven a subir. Claro está, las correcciones son inevitables, pero cuando los precios de los productos básicos, como el oro, el petróleo y el café se desploman, los expertos le dirán que siempre vuelven a la media. A medida que la nación avanza hacia los efectos de los años mediocres de Obama, la economía floreciente de Trump ha hecho de este un gran momento para reducir la deuda, acumular ahorros y mejorar las posiciones financieras personales en una manera práctica, no especulativa.

Sin embargo, siendo todas estas noticias tan buenas como lo han sido para la administración Trump, aún hay una nube oscura que ha flotado sobre el bienestar financiero de la nación durante más de un siglo, desde la presidencia de Woodrow Wilson y aún más: la deuda nacional. Posiblemente no hay amenaza más grande para el futuro financiero del Estados Unidos y la seguridad nacional que el crecimiento ininterrumpido de la deuda nacional durante los últimos cincuenta años.

Según del Departamento del Tesoro, "el término *deuda nacional* se refiere a las responsabilidades financieras directas del gobierno de Estados Unidos".[27] Su sitio de internet explica los diferentes conceptos que pueden referirse a la deuda nacional:

- **Deuda pública** proviene de los títulos de deuda pública emitidos por la Tesorería de Estados Unidos. Estos consisten principalmente en valores negociables, tales como letras del Tesoro, pagarés y bonos; bonos de ahorro de Estados Unidos en posesión de inversionistas individuales; y una larga lista de títulos emitidos a gobiernos estatales y locales.

- **Deuda en posesión del público** excluye la porción de la deuda pública en posesión de las cuentas gubernamentales.

- **Deuda federal bruta** se compone de los títulos de deuda pública y una pequeña cantidad de títulos emitidos por las agencias gubernamentales. [28]

"Deuda en posesión del público", dice el Departamento del Tesoro: "es el más significativo de estos conceptos y mide el monto acumulado pendiente que el gobierno ha prestado para financiar déficits".[29] El Congreso y la Casa Blanca han estado obligados a liquidar esta responsabilidad por generaciones; sin embargo, la deuda nacional continúa aumentando, y poco se ha hecho para resolver la crisis de deuda que se cierne sobre nuestra cabeza.

En su testimonio ante la Comisión Selecta del Senado sobre Inteligencia el 13 de febrero de 2018, el director de Inteligencia Nacional de Estados Unidos, Dan Coats, dijo a los legisladores que él cree que nuestra deuda nacional creciente es la única amenaza más grande para la seguridad nacional de Estados Unidos. Coats, quien se desempeñó como senador republicano de Indiana durante dieciséis años, describió una serie de amenazas crecientes mundiales y cibernéticas que Estados Unidos enfrenta de parte de sus adversarios, como Corea del Norte, Rusia, Irán y

China. Sin embargo, él también advirtió contra la amenaza interna más grande, la cual, dijo, podría debilitar la economía estadounidense y la seguridad nacional. Él dijo: "Estoy preocupado por nuestro proceso político cada vez más agitado, particularmente en lo que respecta al gasto federal, está amenazando nuestra capacidad de defender adecuadamente a nuestra nación tanto a corto plazo y especialmente a largo plazo. El hecho de no abordar nuestra situación fiscal a largo plazo", dijo, "ha incrementado la deuda nacional por encima de los US$20 billones y continúa creciendo".[30]

Los comentarios del director de inteligencia son un eco de la advertencia que el almirante Michael Mullen, expresidente del Estado Mayor Conjunto hizo siete años antes, el 22 de septiembre de 2011, cuando dijo: "Yo creo que la única amenaza más grande a nuestra seguridad nacional es la deuda".[31] Según el congresista de Arizona, Andy Biggs, estos dos expertos de defensa de alto rango lo entendieron bien. Estados Unidos enfrenta muchas amenazas existenciales, dijo, desde ISIS, naciones corruptas tales como Irán y Corea del Norte, inmigración ilegal y mucho más. Sin embargo, el único peligro más grande para la paz y la seguridad de Estados Unidos es nuestra incapacidad de poner bajo control nuestra deuda nacional.

Al 4 de mayo de 2018, la deuda pública era de US$21,037,962,909,322.34. En menos de un año, Estados Unidos vio una deuda que sobrepasó los US$20 billones en septiembre de 2017 y US$21 billones en marzo de 2018. Durante el año fiscal 2018, el Congreso aprobó siete proyectos de ley para gastos a corto plazo, incluyendo el paquete de gastos diversos por US$1.3 billones firmado por el Presidente en marzo. Ninguna de estas propuestas de ley de gastos equilibró el presupuesto federal ni redujo el gasto. Aún peor, al aprobar estas resoluciones continuas de corto plazo, el Congreso desestimó el "orden regular", que habría permitido que los congresistas consideraran enmiendas a las propuestas de ley.

En lugar de recortar el gasto, el Congreso extendió el techo de la deuda para acomodar los requisitos de gasto capital proyectado. En consecuencia, dijo el congresista, estamos en riesgo de incumplir las obligaciones actuales de la deuda y de poner en peligro nuestra estabilidad económica. Los analistas de *Moody's Financial Metrics* dijeron en agosto de 2017 que "el aumento de los costos de asistencia y el incremento en las tasas de interés provocarán que la posición fiscal de Estados Unidos se erosione aún más durante la década siguiente; a menos que se tomen medidas para reducir esos costos o para aumentar los ingresos adicionales".[32] Nuestra nación tiene que enfrentar este desafío.

Durante un discurso dirigido a los funcionarios militares y gubernamentales en enero de 2018, el Secretario de Defensa, James Mattis, advirtió que "ninguna nación en la historia que no haya sido económicamente viable ha mantenido a su poder militar sin mantener su casa en orden". Y el Director de Inteligencia, Dan Coats, declaró: "nuestro endeudamiento continuo es insostenible y representa una grave amenaza futura para nuestra economía y para nuestra seguridad nacional".

El Representante Biggs también advirtió que "Estados Unidos está en una carrera hacia un precipicio fiscal", y el Congreso está haciendo muy poco para salvar a la nación de un destino de ruina. Sin embargo, afortunadamente el presidente Donald Trump y su administración están conscientes de la urgencia de esta crisis y están comprometidos a encontrar una solución responsable, añadió Biggs.[33]

"En su Estrategia de Seguridad Nacional", dijo Biggs, "el Sr. Trump resaltó la necesidad de reducir la deuda a través de la responsabilidad fiscal". Nadie niega las consecuencias severas que podrían ocurrir en la nación si, por alguna razón, incurriéramos en incumplimiento de esta deuda. Sin embargo, Biggs cree que la administración Trump ve a la amenaza constante por lo que es, aun si muy pocos en el Congreso reconocen el peligro. "Ya se pasó la hora para que mis colegas se tomen en serio el hecho de equilibrar nuestro presupuesto y hacer cortes significativos al gasto federal", dice. "Si no cambiamos nuestro curso, seremos parte de una de las peores catástrofes que esta nación haya experimentado: el colapso de la economía estadounidense y la desaparición de una superpotencia".[34]

¿QUIÉN TIENE LA CULPA?
Porcentaje de incremento en la deuda pública por presidente

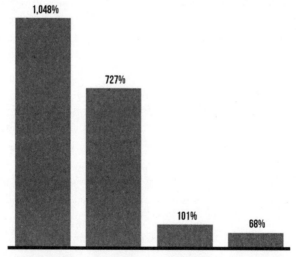

Para tener una mejor idea de cómo llegó el gobierno a este punto y cómo varios presidentes han lidiado con el problema de la deuda, es informativo saber cuáles administraciones añadieron más a la deuda nacional. Como era de esperar, el presidente Franklin D. Roosevelt (FDR) fue quien porcentualmente incrementó más la deuda. Tal como lo informa Kimberly Amadeo de *The Balance*, FDR solamente añadió US$236 mil millones a la deuda, lo que parece poco según los estándares actuales, pero fue un 1,048 por ciento de aumento de US$23 mil millones de deuda que su predecesor había dejado. Las causas fueron: la Gran Depresión, la cual disminuyó los ingresos y creó incontables agencias y programas para ayudar a los desempleados, y la Segunda Guerra Mundial. El gasto de guerra fue la contribución más substancial de Roosevelt a la deuda, añadiendo US$209 mil millones, según Amadeo.[35]

Woodrow Wilson, presidente durante la Primera Guerra Mundial, está en segundo lugar porcentualmente hablando, añadiendo US$21 mil millones, un 727 por ciento de incremento en deuda sobre los US$2.9 mil millones que dejó el presidente Taft.

Barack Obama llega en quinto lugar de incremento porcentualmente hablando (un 68 por ciento de incremento durante siete años), pero él es el número uno en el aumento de la deuda nacional monetariamente hablando. Él añadió US$7.917 billones, según la investigación de Amadeo.[36]

La segunda cantidad más alta de dólares añadida a la deuda nacional llegó durante la presidencia de George W. Busch, quien, según Amadeo, añadió US$5,849 billones a la deuda (el cuarto incremento más largo en porcentaje). Al igual que Wilson y Roosevelt, financiar una guerra fue un factor importante en el incremento durante el mandato de Bush. En su caso, los ataques terroristas del 11 de septiembre lanzaron la Guerra al Terror tanto en Afganistán como en Irak. El presidente Busch también lidió con la recesión de 2001 al aprobar enormes cortes tributarios que redujeron los ingresos públicos aún más e incrementaron la deuda nacional.

Con base a los planes actuales, el presidente Trump el presupuesto proyectado del año fiscal 2019 es por un incremento de 41 por ciento, de los US$20.245 billones en deuda que Obama dejó, añadiendo US$8.282 trillones a la deuda nacional. Si esto sucede, concluye Amadeo, Trump reemplazará a Bush como el segundo en la cantidad en dólares más alto en la historia, y él añadirá en un término casi tanto como Obama añadió en dos.[37] Sin embargo, el Presidente tiene una estrategia alternativa para lidiar con la crisis de deuda que se está desarrollando.

EL APUESTA AUDAZ DE TRUMP

Estados Unidos está posado sobre una bomba de tiempo financiera. Todo el mundo lo sabe; sin embargo, los miembros del Congreso no pueden forzarse a reducir los gastos. "¿Por qué?", pregunta Garland Tucker. "Porque el público estadounidense se niega a exigir acción de parte del Congreso". Tucker, un alto miembro de la Fundación John Locke, dice que hay "dos aspectos primarios para la crisis de gasto: la asombrosa explosión de la deuda federal" y la creciente dependencia del gobierno por millones de estadounidenses. El debate sobre tales cosas está siempre centrado en los problemas financieros, dice, pero el núcleo de este asunto es realmente un tema moral, y ya va siendo hora de que la nación lidie con los problemas antes de que nuestros pecados financieros nos alcancen".[38]

Según Tucker: "Desde el inicio de la Guerra de la Pobreza de la Gran Sociedad a mediados de la década de los sesenta, Estados Unidos ha gastado más de US$15 billones en programas de asistencia económica. Entre 1960 y 2010, el gasto por derecho federal incrementó de 19 a 43 por ciento del gasto federal anual... Estos programas, estaban diseñados no solo para eliminar pobreza, sino para erradicar sus causas. ¿Los resultados? El índice general de pobreza en 1966 se mantuvo en 14.7 por ciento, mientras que en el 2013 se mantuvo en 14.5 por ciento". En otras palabras, nada cambió. "Según cualquier estándar de medición", dice Tucker, "estos programas fueron una inversión desastrosa".[39]

El gobierno de Estados Unidos redistribuía el ingreso en escala masiva, y desde entonces el gasto era financiado con déficits más y más grandes, la carga de la deuda pasó a las generaciones de estadounidenses que aún no nacen. Esto es ahora un asunto moral para el pueblo estadounidense. Tal como el exdirector de presupuesto de Estados Unidos y gobernador de Indiana, dijo en una ocasión al hacer eco de la advertencia atribuida al historiador escocés del siglo XVIII, Alexander Tytler: "Como pueblo, hemos descubierto la capacidad de votarnos a nosotros mismos como generosidad del tesoro federal en cantidades tan vastas que estamos destruyendo nuestras propias oportunidades de prosperar". O en las palabras del presidente del *American Enterprise Institute*, Arthur Brooks, "nos hemos convertido en una nación de tomadores, no de hacedores".[40]

Sabemos que el presidente Trump firmó un proyecto de ley de gastos diversos por US$1.3 mil millones en marzo de 2018. Tal como Tucker lo señala: "Con este último abono al triste descenso a la crisis fiscal y moral de Estados Unidos, nuestro déficit proyectado alcanzará US$850 mil millones para el 2018". El orador de la Cámara, Paul Ryan, dijo que él estaba determinado a enfrentar el gasto en derecho, pero el Senado y el Presidente tendrían que unirse si algo productivo sucediera.[41] O, como Jesse Hathaway, un investigador del Instituto *Heartland*, lo explica: "Hay un sonido de tictac ominoso en el fondo de este agujero fiscal. Si nuestros representantes en Washington, DC, no lo escuchan y siguen empujando a la nación hacia un desastre más profundo, el pueblo estadounidense, especialmente los niños, son los que terminarán sufriendo más por la inminente explosión de la deuda".[42]

La apuesta audaz de Donald Trump es su inamovible fe de que los niveles actuales de crecimiento económico continuarán y que un ingreso público incrementado de los impuestos y el costo disminuido del gobierno debido a reducciones substanciales en la burocracia y regulaciones costosas, junto con un ingreso incrementado de las tarifas de bienes internacionales, empezarán el proceso de reducir la deuda a un nivel sostenible. Tal como lo señaló el columnista de Bloomberg, Conor Sen, el Presidente está llevando a cabo un experimento riesgoso al permitir que el gobierno dirija uno de los déficits presupuestarios más grandes de cualquier nación, fuera del tiempo de guerra o de una recesión, con la esperanza de que esto, de alguna manera, impulsará el crecimiento económico a un nivel mucho más alto. "Tan irresponsable como parece", dice, "en realidad tiene un poco de sentido".[43]

"A la larga, el crecimiento económico es una función de dos variables: población y productividad. Durante décadas, Estados Unidos ha tenido suficiente de ambas. Las tasas de crecimiento fueron amplias, y cualquier mano de obra adicional podría ser atraída [de otros lugares si fuera necesario]. De 1947 al 2007, la producción por hora de los trabajadores creció a un promedio anual de 2.3 por ciento. Así que, en su mayor parte, los presidentes estadounidenses podrían centrarse en mejorar en vez de reactivar el crecimiento". Pero después de la recesión de 2008, las variables cambiaron. El crecimiento de la fuerza laboral empezó a disminuir a medida que los nacidos entre 1946 y 1965 alcanzaban la edad de jubilación. Al mismo tiempo, la productividad también empezó a declinar.

"La administración Obama aceptó la nueva realidad", escribe Sen. El informe presupuestario anual de la administración en el 2016 proyectaba un crecimiento inflacionario ajustado del PIB a solo 2.2 por ciento para la siguiente década. En vez de abordar la inminente crisis de la deuda, los economistas de Obama ofrecieron "ideas tradicionales tales como la reforma migratoria, más comercio transfronterizo, gastos en infraestructura e inversión en educación".[44]

Donald Trump, por otro lado, ha tomado una aproximación mucho más agresiva, proyectando una tasa de crecimiento anual de 3 por ciento durante la próxima década, lo cual es alto, pero saludable. Este tipo de crecimiento no vendrá de la población, particularmente con los planes de la administración para restringir la inmigración, lo que significa que la productividad tendrá que aumentar tremendamente, dijo Sen. Los aranceles sobre importaciones, tales como el hierro y el aluminio y los automóviles fabricados en el extranjero traerán nuevo ingreso, pero, al mismo tiempo, podría hacer la producción local más cara. Para mediados de 2018, los planes para implementar los aranceles en las importaciones principales aún estaban sujetos a cambio, pero la administración dejó en claro que la balanza comercial a largo plazo que favorecía a China y a otras naciones tendría que cambiar, y mientras que las tasas arancelarias podrían cambiar, la política de Trump favorecería a las empresas estadounidenses.

Aunque la organización Bloomberg ha expresado duda sobre los aspectos del plan de Trump, el proyecto de ley de gastos diversos en marzo de 2018 y los cortes tributarios firmados como ley en diciembre de 2017, animaron a las empresas de todos tamaños y en todos los segmentos del mercado a comprometerse con mayores inversiones de capital, aumentando el tamaño de la fuerza laboral y salarios más altos, lo que atrae a más y mejores trabajadores. Como el escritor dice, no hay seguridad sobre cómo las reducciones tributarias de Trump ayudarán a largo plazo o cuándo durará el impulso actual en la economía. Pero, hasta ahora, las perspectivas son muy buenas, y el Presidente está usando su púlpito intimidante para ayudar a animar a los empresarios y a sus empleados a aprovechar el clima económico próspero.

La apuesta de Donald Trump es que el crecimiento económico y la productividad recibirán un impulso de los recortes tributarios y los planes de gasto del gobierno. El secretario del Tesoro, Steven Mnuchin, dijo durante una entrevista en Bloomberg el 22 de febrero de 2018: "Hay muchas maneras de tener un crecimiento económico… Uno puede tener inflación salarial y no necesariamente tener preocupaciones sobre la inflación en general".[45] Los datos al inicio de ese mes mostraron un gran salto inesperado en salarios, lo que asustó a los mercados globales por un momento. Los nuevos datos alimentaron las preocupaciones de que los salarios en rápido aumento empujarían la inflación al alza más rápido de lo esperado y obligarían a la Reserva Federal a subir las tasas de interés más rápido de lo previsto, pero no fue así; y la subida de los mercados empezó a ser lenta pero constante.

La idea de que las políticas de Trump "podían llevar a un crecimiento salarial sin inflación" es sorprendentemente similar a las políticas presentadas por Bernie Sanders durante la campaña de 2016. "Al controlar la economía y hacer la mano de obra más cara, el gobierno puede inducir a las empresas a invertir más de lo que lo harían en una economía normal. Desde la crisis financiera, una economía débil ha desanimado la inversión en muchas empresas, llevándolas a un crecimiento productivo más débil. Así que ¿por qué probar lo opuesto?". La apuesta de Donald es "una teoría que no ha sido probada en décadas", escribe Sen, pero es una idea intrigante, y él pregunta:

> ¿Cuáles son los riesgos y reconocimientos potenciales? Quedarse con el *statu quo* promete más de la misma desilusión; un crecimiento anual real de aproximadamente 2 por ciento. El experimento del déficit tiene dos resultados posibles. En el mejor caso, Estados Unidos obtiene alguna forma de milagro productivo. En el otro, la inflación creciente obliga a los federales a elevar las tasas de interés para enfriar la economía, provocando una recesión.[46]

La inflación de dos dígitos, como la que experimentamos durante la década de los setenta, no es lo que les preocupa a los inversionistas, economistas y legisladores de hoy. En las economías avanzadas, dice el escritor, los bancos centrales ahora tienen mejores herramientas para lidiar con la inflación de ese tipo. Sin embargo, una productividad débil continúa siendo una preocupación importante para las economías con poblaciones de edad avanzada y la necesidad de proveer niveles más altos de apoyo para el adulto mayor y otros segmentos de la sociedad.

Mientras los republicanos y los demócratas ciertamente estarán en desacuerdo sobre la mejor manera de lidiar con déficit y gastos, las opciones que Trump ofrece son intrigantes y posiblemente hasta inspiradas.[47]

El modelo Obama estaba basado en aumentos de impuestos, inversiones en infraestructura y educación, y gasto militar reducido (aunque el gasto militar aumentó cada año hasta el 2011 antes de decrecer). Era una política de bajas expectativas y bajo retorno de inversión. Por otro lado, el modelo Trump pide aceleración de la economía a todo galope, reducir los impuestos, estimular el empleo y la productividad, y animar al mercado desde su púlpito intimidante.

El equilibrio de los riesgos, como el columnista de Boomberg concluye, apunta hacia tomar el riesgo de Trump. Ya sea que resulte ser Trump o el próximo jefe ejecutivo quien salga con un plan brillante, alguien va a tomar ese riesgo, y el beneficio a largo plazo no será solo una lista más grande e impresionante de ganadores, sino una oportunidad para hacer retroceder la deuda nacional a un nivel más manejable. Y sabiendo lo que sabemos de este presidente, ¿quién dudaría que una cosa así pueda suceder realmente?

MULTIMILLONARIOS RADICALES

Cientos de limosinas con chofer, al menos doscientos helicópteros, más de mil aviones privados y más de metro y medio de nieve descendieron en Davos-Klosters, conocida como la ciudad más alta en los Alpes suizos, para la reunión anual del Foro Económico Mundial. La lista de invitados incluía a más de tres mil de los banqueros, líderes de compañías y empresarios, junto con diplomáticos y jefes de estado de casi setenta países. Fuera del círculo interno de élites de multimillonarios, rondaba una partida de estrellas pop y celebridades ansiosas de promover sus credenciales activistas y codearse con los hombres y mujeres más ricos y más poderosos del mundo.

La agenda para la semana del evento, del 23 al 26 de enero de 2018, incluía más de cuatrocientas sesiones y paneles de discusión enfocados en el cambio climático, ecología de los océanos, tecnología, internet, crecimiento económico, energía, sostenibilidad, educación, geopolítica, pobreza, fronteras abiertas y migración mundial", pero el principal objetivo de este foro, como lo ha sido cada año desde que el evento empezó en 1971, era construir un consenso sobre cómo las élites globales podían superar el impulso populista y "mejorar el estado del mundo".[1]

Aunque su asistencia fue ampliamente publicitada por los organizadores del foro y vigorosamente discutida por los medios, Donald Trump no era un invitado oficial al principio. De todas maneras, él fue porque Estados Unidos es la nación más poderosa en el planeta, dijo, con una máquina económica como ninguna otra, y era importante que él estuviera allí. El Presidente le dijo a *Wall Street Journal* que él iba a Davos como un animador para la economía estadounidense, para llamar la atención a los éxitos económicos de su administración.[2] CNN *Money* lo describió como "Trump vs. la élite mundial, en el terreno de ellos".[3]

El discurso del presidente fue recibido con críticas variadas. Muchos de los asistentes estaban predispuestos a denunciar sus comentarios, sin importar lo que dijera. Sin embargo, otros estaban agradablemente sorprendidos por el tono moderado y diplomático de su presentación. Él empezó diciendo: "Es un privilegio estar aquí en este foro donde por muchos, muchos años se han reunido líderes de empresas, ciencia, arte, diplomacia y asuntos mundiales para discutir cómo podemos fomentar prosperidad, seguridad y paz. Estoy aquí hoy para representar los intereses del pueblo estadounidense y afirmar la amistad y la colaboración de Estados Unidos para construir un mundo mejor".[4]

Él prosiguió diciendo que la economía de Estados Unidos ha creado más de US$7 billones de nueva riqueza desde que fue electo, junto con 2.4 millones de empleos. "El mercado de valores está rompiendo un récord tras otro", dijo. Al mismo tiempo, la confianza de consumidores, empresas y fabricantes está a su nivel más alto en décadas, y el desempleo para los trabajadores afroamericanos y los hispanos está en su récord más bajo. Su mensaje al mundo fue que "Estados Unidos está dispuesto a hacer negocios, y somos competitivos una vez más".[5]

Incluso, el irreflexivamente crítico *New York Times* observó: "Surgió un consenso áspero sobre sobre la visita de dos días del Sr. Trump de que su administración había demostrado ser más pragmática de lo promocionado. Muchos estuvieron inclinados a ver las posturas más extremas del Presidente como actitudes de negociación agresiva".[6] Después del discurso, una multitud de delegados curiosos y entusiastas rodeó al presidente de Estados Unidos en busca de *selfies*, autógrafos o unas cuantas palabras con él. En un punto, mientras saludaba a las personas que se acercaban, alguien le dio una copia de mi libro *God and Donald Trump*. Con solo un breve vistazo a la portada que mostraba su imagen, él levantó el libro por encima de su cabeza para que todos lo vieran. No hace falta decir que ese fue un momento memorable y una sorpresa para mí.

Después de su discurso, durante la sesión de preguntas y respuestas moderada por el ingeniero alemán Klaus Schwab, el fundador y presidente ejecutivo del foro, el presidente estuvo relajado y cordial. Pero cuando le preguntaron sobre su relación con los medios, él dijo: "Como hombre de negocios, siempre fui muy bien tratado por la prensa. Y no fue sino hasta que me volví un político que me di cuenta cuán ruin, cuán infame, cuán despiadada y falsa puede ser la prensa".[7]

Prediciblemente, esos comentarios desataron un coro de abucheos de parte de los miembros de la prensa internacional que estaban parados al fondo del salón. Pero, sin importar lo que cualquiera piense de Donald Trump, no puede haber duda de que la prensa ha sido agresivamente antagonista contra él desde el primer día. Los medios principales se han involucrado en lo que el columnista Victor Davis Hanson describe como "un verdadero esfuerzo en cámara lenta para destituir a una presidencia electa". Si bien los tuits de Trump pueden ser groseros o insensibles, Hanson dice: "ningún nombre es una isla", y en muchos casos el Presidente está sencillamente defendiéndose contra una avalancha de cargos difamatorios. "Trump puede ser impulsado por el ego y tener una sensibilidad a flor de piel", dice, "pero incluso la piel de un rinoceronte se irrita bajo el odio de los medios por su persona, su familia y su presidencia".[8]

MIL TENTÁCULOS

Ya que fui capacitado como un periodista secular, he visto con interés la animosidad de la prensa durante la campaña y el primer término. Cuando empecé mi carrera durante la era de *Watergate*, vi a la prensa acosar a Richard Nixon y sacarlo del cargo por hacer mucho menos que Hillary Clinton, a quien los medios le dieron un trato notable. Hace varias décadas, empecé a comprender que, a pesar de lo que se ve, hay fuerzas en acción que muchas veces son malévolas. Como cristiano, creo en un mundo espiritual que a menudo se manifiesta en el mundo político. Así que, cuando Donald Trump empezó a hablar de drenar el pantano y la gente empezó a hablar de un estado profundo, no me costó creerlo.

Sabía que esto tenía que ser abordado en cualquier libro sobre las consecuencias de la elección de Donald Trump. Aunque mi experiencia se centra más en el funcionamiento interno de la comunidad evangélica y la historia de la Iglesia que en los globalistas que se están trasladando a un gobierno mundial, algo que no me cuesta creer a la luz de mi visión escatológica de la historia. Cuando llegó el momento de escribir este capítulo, me preguntaba si debía incluirlo. Si bien he recibido retroalimentación de los lectores de *God and Donald Trump* agradeciéndome por atreverme a enfatizar la manera en que Trump está sacudiendo la agenda globalista, razón por la cual recibe tanta oposición. Ya que no soy un experto, me da gusto haber tenido investigadores y editores para ayudarme a escribir este capítulo difícil, pero importante. Además, la internet da acceso a tantas cosas escritas acerca del globalismo y Trump y a lo que yo veo como fuerzas siniestras tras bambalinas.

Para entender por qué los medios se han vuelto muy agresivos contra Trump, puede ayudar saber que los multimillonarios de la extrema Izquierda, incluyendo a George Soros, al ex alcalde de Nueva York, Michael Bloomberg; el gurú de fondos de inversión pública, Tom Steyer; el fundador de eBay, Pierre Omidyar; y el super inversionista Warren Buffett, han estado en una maratón de gastos durante los últimos quince años, comprando periódicos, financiando sitios web y creando una falange de grupos de apoyo sin fines de lucro para promover políticas ultraliberales y para debilitar a los conservadores y sus organizaciones.

Según un proyecto de investigación de varios años, hecho por el *Media Research Center* (MRC), estos multimillonarios, junto con Jonathan Soros, hijo de Soros, han contribuido más de US$2.7 mil millones desde el año 2000, para los grupos que impulsan el aborto, el alarmismo en el cambio climático y el control de armas, y han apoyado a una larga lista de políticos liberales selectos. Por su lado, Soros ha gastado al menos US$52 millones construyendo una red de periódicos, organizaciones nuevas e instituciones periodísticas.[9]

Pero los tentáculos de este pulpo no están limitadas a las conexiones multimillonarias con las organizaciones de noticias como ABC, NBC, el *New York Times* y el *Washington Post*. Tal como lo informa el MRC, el *Columbia Journalism Review* (CJR) provee una lasta larga de proyectos de investigación financiados por las fundaciones de Soros. Entre ellos están los grupos activistas como ProPublica, el *Center for Public Integrity*, el *Center for Investigative Reporting*, y *The Lens* de Nueva Orleans, todos fundados, a su vez, por la *Open Society Foundations*, financiada por Soros. La *Columbia School of Journalism*, la cual produce CRJ, considerada como el estándar de oro cuando yo estaba estudiando periodismo hace cuatro décadas, ha recibido al menos US$600,000 de parte de Soros, según revela el informe del MRC.

La facultad de periodismo más reconocida en la nación no es lo único que Soros financia. Él usa su fortuna para influenciar asociaciones en la industria del periodismo tales como la Federación Nacional de Radios Comunitarias, la Asociación Nacional de Periodistas Hispanos y el Comité para la Protección de los Periodistas. También apoya a la Organización Defensora de Noticias que enumera a cincuenta y siete miembros y miembros retirados de organizaciones de revistas y noticias de todo el mundo:

"Un defensor de noticias", declara su sitio web, "recibe e investiga quejas de los lectores o de la audiencia de los periódicos, o los televidentes o los radioescuchas, sobre la exactitud, imparcialidad, equilibrio y buen gusto en la cobertura de las noticias".[10] Sin embargo, cualquiera con el mínimo conocimiento de Soros y su agenda izquierdista solo se pregunta cuál es la objetividad y el equilibrio del grupo.

El dinero de Soros también se destina a *Investigative News Network* y a la fundación James L. Knight, la cual tiene oficinas en ocho ciudades grandes y de tamaño mediano, y a dieciocho más pequeñas, y está asociada con la antigua cadena de periódicos Knight.[11]

Warren Buffett, a quien muchos ven solo como su amigable multimillonario del vecindario, tiene uno de los portafolios más agresivamente liberales en la nación. "Buffett empezó a comprar periódicos pequeños y medianos en 2012, gastando millones en una industria que la mayoría de las personas creía que estaba muriendo. Para julio de 2014, cuarenta y seis de setenta y cinco periódicos que él poseía", informa el MRC, "fueron estratégicamente ubicados en los cruciales estados en disputa de Iowa, Virginia, Carolina del Norte y Florida".[12] Mientras tanto, la fundación Susan Thompson Buffett, nombrada por su difunta esposa, donó al menos US$1.2 mil millones para apoyar el aborto y la anticoncepción mundialmente.

El ambientalista activista radical, Tom Steyer, y los Soros más jóvenes han financiado las noticias liberales o los sitios web relacionados a las noticias, tales como el Centro para la Integridad Pública, *Media Matters*, el Centro de Información Ecológica, y el Centro para el Progreso Estadounidense. Steyer, cuyo super comité de acción política gastaron casi US$100 millones para apoyar a los demócratas durante la campaña del 2016, también ha gastado US$20 millones para una campaña publicitaria de *"Need to Impeach"* [es necesario destituir], que muchos observadores ven como la primera etapa de la candidatura de Steyer para la presidencia en 2020. Y estos son solo algunos de los radicales multimillonarios que trabajan para debilitar al Presidente y la voluntad del pueblo estadounidense.

Al explicar el impacto de dicha generosidad, un informe del 2017 del *Capital Research Center* dice:

> Cuando los medios de comunicación cubren noticias en el momento de las elecciones y tratan de explicar algún punto político complejo, el financiamiento generoso de Soros significa que siempre hay un grupo ligado a la *Open Society Foundations* preparado para responder las llamadas y los correos electrónicos de los reporteros sobre casi cualquier asunto concebible. Solo en Estados Unidos, la *Open Society Foundations* está otorgando subvenciones en muchas áreas clave, entre ellas: justicia, política de drogas, igualdad, democracia, progreso económico, seguridad nacional y derechos humanos.[13]

No debería haber duda sobre qué tipo de respuestas están recibiendo los reporteros de parte de la fundación financiada por los Soros. Compartiendo un modo de pensar parecido al de Soros, están: Steyer, Michael Bloomberg y el fundador de Amazon.com, Jeff Bezos, de quienes se rumorea que son socios del grupo conocido como Alianza Demócrata, fundado por Rob Stein después de la victoria en la reelección del presidente George W. Busch. George Soros y Peter B. Lewis, el fallecido presidente de la aseguradora *Progressive*, se destacan entre los socios más conocidos. La alianza está formada por aproximadamente 110 donantes adinerados y activistas liberales que financian a los llamados grupos y políticas "progresistas". Para ser parte del grupo, los socios tienen que firmar un acuerdo de confidencialidad y consentimiento para contribuir con al menos US$200,000 al año a causas y grupos que la Alianza Demócrata recomienda. No obstante, muchos de los socios contribuyen muchísimo más que eso. La alianza ha ayudado a distribuir más de US$500 millones para las organizaciones liberales desde que se fundó en 2005.

Según los reporteros del *Washington Post*: "Este club de donantes exclusivo incluye millonarios tales como Susie Tompkins Buell y su esposo, Mark Buell, principales partidarios de la senadora Hillary Rodham Clinton" cuando ella hizo campaña por el senado en el 2008. Bernard L. Schwartz, jefe ejecutivo retirado de *Loral Space & Communications Inc.*, es otro donante de la alianza, quien dijo que se unió al grupo porque eso "es lo más útil para los donantes grandes que no tienen tiempo para examinar de cerca sus opciones de inversión política". Fred Baron, un abogado litigante, donante demócrata de mucho tiempo y miembro de la alianza, estuvo de acuerdo: "La pieza que siempre ha faltado en nuestros donativos son inversiones en infraestructura a largo plazo".[14]

Los reporteros en el *Post* dijeron: "Además, hay unos cuantos 'inversionistas institucionales' tales como la *Service Employees International Union* (SEIU), que paga una tarifa anual de US$50,000 y acepta gastar US$1 millón en esfuerzos respaldados por la alianza".[15] Soros también financia fundaciones que, a su vez, financian otras fundaciones, incluida la *Tides Foundation*, y hasta doscientos grupos de extrema izquierda, como la *Alliance for Global Justice* y organizaciones asociadas con Antifa, a su vez, a una larga lista de anarquistas y causas ultraliberales. *MoveOn.org*, *Black Lives Matter* y *Planned Parenthood* son las favoritas de Soros. Solo en el 2015, la Fundación Soros para promover *Open Society* dio un total de US$431 millones en contribuciones y subvenciones a grupos de extrema izquierda, llamados causas "antifascistas" y a otras causas alrededor del mundo.[16]

Las cantidades que estos grupos pagan, y que pueden obtenerse de formularios de impuestos e informes de noticias, probablemente se quedan cortas en comparación a lo que reciben realmente. Sería difícil de recabar un conteo completo porque muchas de las operaciones financiadas por los Soros incluyen sus propios medios y subgrupos de acción directa.[17]

Asra Q. Nomani, quien ha escrito para el *New York Times*, informó que muchos de los disturbios "espontáneos" que se produjeron después de las elecciones de noviembre, en realidad fueron comprados y pagados por la red de acción directa de grupos radicales negros de los Soros. Virtualmente, todas las organizaciones involucradas en las manifestaciones contra Trump que agitaron a Nueva York y a otras ciudades en enero de 2017 tenían vínculos con Soros. Y Nomani señaló que Soros también tuvo vínculos con más de cincuenta grupos de protesta involucrados con la *Women's March* en Washington, DC, la que tuvo lugar con publicidad masiva el día después de la elección de Trump. Todos estos grupos fueron financiados por organizaciones relacionadas con Soros.[18]

EL PODER DE LA PERSUASIÓN

Debería ser aparente que el impacto de estos grupos no está limitado a su influencia en ABC, CBS, NBC, o el *New York Times* y el *Washington Post*. CJR, quien se promociona a sí misma como "un guardián de los medios", enumera varios proyectos de periodismo investigativo financiados por una o más de las fundaciones Soros. La *News Frontier Database*, organizada por la Escuela de Periodismo Columbia, incluye siete proyectos de investigación diferentes financiada por la *Open Society Institute* de Soros.

Junto con el grupo liberal y perro guardián *ProPublica*, Soros financia el Centro para la Integridad Pública, el Centro para el Reportaje Investigativo y *New Orleans' The Lens*. Sin embargo, desde cualquier punto de vista, la *Democracy*

Alliance ha comprobado ser la creación más poderosa y más peligrosamente efectiva de Soros. Según el *Washington Post*:

> La *Democracy Alliance* trabaja esencialmente como una cooperativa para donantes, permitiéndoles coordinar sus donaciones para que estas tengan más influencia. Para convertirse en "socio", ya que los miembros son referidos internamente, se requiere una tarifa de ingreso de US$25,000 y pagos anuales de US$30,000 para cubrir las operaciones de la alianza, así como también algunas de sus contribuciones para la iniciación de grupos liberales. Más allá de esto, los socios también aceptan gastar al menos US$200,000 anualmente en organizaciones que han sido endosadas por la alianza. Esencialmente, la alianza sirve como la agencia de acreditación para los grupos políticos de apoyo.
>
> Este proceso de acreditación es la raíz de la influencia de la *Democracy Alliance*. Si un grupo no recibe la bendición de la alianza, docenas de los contribuidores políticos más adinerados de la nación quedan fuera del límite para propósitos de recaudación de fondos. Muchos de estos contribuyentes, donan mucho más que el requerimiento de US$200,000 el 45 por ciento de los socios da US$300,000 o más en la ronda inicial de subvenciones [en octubre 2005], según una fuente familiarizada con la organización.[19]

Para julio de 2018, el fundador de Amazon.com, Jeff Bezos, quien compró el *Washington Post* en 2013, es ahora el hombre más rico en Estados Unidos, con una fortuna estimada en los US$147 mil millones. El fundador de Microsoft, Bill Gates, quien fue el primero durante los últimos veinte años, quedó en segundo lugar, con US$96 mil millones en 2018, y Warren Buffett era el tercero, con una fortuna de US$83.2 mil millones.

El fundador de Facebook, Mark Zuckerberg, es el cuarto hombre más rico en Estados Unidos, con US$68.4 mil millones, y el cofundador de Oracle, presidente ejecutivo y director en jefe de tecnología, Larry Ellison, es el séptimo estadounidense más rico, con activos de US$54.2 mil millones. Mientras tanto, los infames hermanos Koch, Charles y David, quienes son atacados frecuentemente en la prensa por su apoyo a las causas conservadoras, clasifican en el décimo segundo y décimo tercer lugar en la lista de multimillonarios de Bloomberg, con activos de US$47 mil millones cada uno.[20]

La fundación Bill & Melinda Gates ha invertido miles de millones de dólares en programas dedicados a terminar con la pobreza e incrementar el acceso al cuidado de la salud en países en desarrollo. Por un discurso que él dio en octubre de 2017, Gates está comprometido con la iniciativa en educación *Common Core* y está involucrado en desarrollar planes de estudios y desarrollo profesional alineado con *Common Core*. El heredero de Taco Bell, Rob McKay, quien se desempeñó previamente como presidente de la Alianza Demócrata, era uno de los primeros partidarios del programa de organización comunitaria de Barack Obama, Organizing for America, ahora conocido como Organizing for Action.

El petrolero multimillonario, George Kaiser, quien apostó y perdió una fortuna en la debacle energética *Solyndra*, ha invertido fuertemente en la política en Oklahoma y fue un recaudador de fondos para la campaña presidencial de 2008 de Barack Obama. Junto con Drummond Pike, el creador de la *Tides Foundation*, y Tim Gill, el mega donante que financia el movimiento LGBT y los partidarios del Partido Demócrata, casi todos estos multimillonarios han estado involucrados en el esfuerzo para resistir y obstruir la agenda conservadora del Presidente y destruir el derecho religioso. Gill fue citado en una entrevista para la *Rolling Stone* en junio 2017 diciendo: "Vamos a castigar al malvado".[21]

Un programador de software que se hizo rico durante el auge de las puntocom, Gill dijo que sus esfuerzos por bloquear los proyectos de ley de la libertad de culto en los estados sureños realmente han dado fruto. Usando amenazas y tácticas de mano dura, la Fundación Gill convenció a más de cien corporaciones, incluyendo a Coca-Cola, Google y los hoteles Marriott a sacar sus negocios del estado de Georgia como protesta por la Ley de Restauración de la Libertad Religiosa, la cual había pasado, provocando que el gobernador republicano, Nathan Deal, la vetara. Gill ha donado más de US$400 millones para ayudar a financiar el movimiento LGBT.

Hoy en día, la fundación de Gill está llevando a cabo operaciones similares por todo el sur, con operaciones como el ataque al gobernador de Carolina del Norte, Pat McCrory, quien firmó una ley estatal regulando los baños públicos, los vestidores y otras instalaciones sobre la base del género biológico. En este caso, los operativos de Gill pusieron presión sobre organizaciones como: PayPal y la Asociación Nacional de Basquetbol para que se retiraran del estado. Consecuentemente, el gobernador McCrory perdió su candidatura a la reelección en 2016 a pesar del fuerte apoyo de los cristianos en Carolina del Norte al fiscal general demócrata del estado, Roy Cooper, quien había asistido a reuniones en Nueva York con un grupo de donantes de Izquierda. En ese momento, Gill dijo que la carrera del gobernador de Carolina del Norte era un "tiene que ganar" para el movimiento LGBT.[22] Tristemente, ellos ganaron en esta ocasión.

LA RESPUESTA CRISTIANA

Pocos conservadores estadounidenses, no digamos los cristianos que creen en la Biblia, están conscientes de la magnitud de las fuerzas que se oponen no solo a Trump, sino a los valores básicos judeocristianos sobre los que fue construida nuestra nación. Ellos podrían haber escuchado algunas cosas y están (espero) empezando a despertar ante las amenazas; tengo la esperanza de que incluso este libro pueda estimular alguna acción responsable para detener lo que son esencialmente tácticas terroristas contra nuestra manera de vivir.

Considere a Gill queriendo "castigar al malvado": eso es usted y yo. Debido a que creemos en que la Biblia dice que cualquier relación sexual fuera del matrimonio, incluyendo la homosexualidad, está mal, ahora se nos etiqueta como "malvados". Incluso, hay una ley que espera la concurrencia de enmiendas en la legislatura de California que penalizaría la ayuda a la gente que quiere cambiar su orientación sexual. Mientras que la ley ha sido enmendada para prohibir específicamente "promover, ofrecer para la venta, o vender servicios constituyendo esfuerzos para cambio de orientación sexual", aun declara explícitamente, "Este proyecto de ley intenta dejar en claro que los esfuerzos para cambiar la orientación sexual es una práctica ilegal",[23] lo que deja la puerta abierta para que los libros que dicen que la homosexualidad es un pecado o que hablar en contra de la homosexualidad desde el púlpito sea considerado criminal. Los que respaldan esta ley horrible dicen que la prohibición no incluye vender la Biblia, la cual claramente dice que la homosexualidad es pecado. Sin embargo, yo creo que a menos que haya un contragolpe, y que la ley fracase, ya sea en la legislatura de California o en las cortes (porque es una violación muy descarada de la libertad de culto constitucional), es solo una cuestión de tiempo hasta que la Biblia sea prohibida como un "discurso del odio".

Creo que estas personas que odian a Trump lo odian solo porque él está defendiendo el tipo de valores que los cristianos creemos que son correctos. Y él perturba la agenda izquierdista, la cual no solo es política, sino que se opone a Dios. Para mí, esto es igual a Sanbalat y Tobías, quienes se opusieron a Nehemías, mientras él reconstruía Jerusalén; o Amán, quien quería matar a los judíos. Siempre ha habido quienes se oponen a Dios. Y muchas veces parecen ganar, al menos en el corto plazo. Yo creo que Dios está levantando un estandarte contra esto, pero en lo natural, la situación no se ve bien.

Por ejemplo: parece que la mayoría de los multimillonarios son izquierdistas, y que están invirtiendo sus millones para promover agendas infames, del aborto a temas de LGBT a reglamentos políticos, tales como fronteras abiertas y socialismo. Gracias a Dios que hay algunos multimillonarios, como la familia Cathy, propietarios de Chick-fil-A, y la familia Green, dueños de Hobby Lobby, que son ejemplo de valores piadosos. Pero ellos forman solamente una fracción de los multimillonarios de Estados Unidos.

Considere, también, la diferencia entre la influencia de la iglesia, y el dinero y la influencia de estos radicales multimillonarios en la cultura. Si bien hay muchos ministerios buenos, y algunos de ellos son grandes, aun los más grandes son pequeñitos en comparación con la clase de números que estamos describiendo aquí. Y gracias a Lyndon Johnson, quien presentó una enmienda al código tributario en

1954 diciendo que las entidades sin fines de lucro que respaldan a los candidatos podrían perder su estatus de exentos de impuestos, las iglesias han tenido una mordaza por más de seis décadas. Lo cual ha tenido un efecto espeluznante más allá de la regulación en sí, en el sentido de que los pastores y otros líderes religiosos son dóciles y no intentan hablar sobre temas morales para no ser considerados políticos. Afortunadamente, el presidente Donald Trump ve esto como una violación a la libertad de expresión de los pastores y otros cristianos y ha emitido una orden ejecutiva para no aplicar la Enmienda Johnson; mientras tanto, él trabaja con el Congreso para cambiar la ley permanentemente.

Como he dicho tantas veces, no estamos luchando contra carne ni sangre, sino contra principados y potestades y el mal en las regiones celestes. Esto es guerra espiritual, y espero que este libro sea un llamado para que los creyentes luchen contra estas fuerzas en el reino espiritual. La razón por la que incluyo tantos detalles es para documentar lo que está sucediendo, para que nuestros ojos estén abiertos. Aquellos que atacan nuestras instituciones políticas e incluso al presidente Trump tienen una agenda aún más insidiosa que es demoníaca en su médula. Y la viva imagen de esta agenda vil y engañosa es George Soros, quien ha sido el cabecilla indiscutible de esta camarilla.

Nacido como György Schwartz, el 12 de agosto de 1930, en Budapest, Hungría. Soros vino de una familia de judíos no practicantes que se cambiaron el apellido durante el surgimiento de Adolfo Hitler para integrarse en la población cristiana de la ciudad. Para mediados de la década de los cuarenta, cuando los nazis invadieron el país y empezaron la exterminación sistemática de los judíos húngaros, Soros trabajaba con un hombre, después identificado como su padrino, cuyo trabajo era confiscar propiedades de los judíos que estaban siendo enviados a los campos de concentración.

A los catorce años, Soros era el ayudante de su padrino, confiscando la propiedad de las víctimas del Holocausto. Cerca de medio millón de judíos húngaros fueron enviados a su muerte en ese tiempo. Durante aquella infame entrevista con Steve Kroft en el programa *60 Minutos* de CBS TV, en 1998, Soros dijo que su experiencia "no le creó ningún problema". Sorprendido por su frialdad, Kroft preguntó: "¿Ningún sentimiento de culpabilidad?". A lo que Soros respondió: "No".[24] En otra entrevista, Soros se refirió a su tiempo como colaborador nazi como "el año más feliz de mi vida".[25]

Durante un corto tiempo después de la guerra, Soros luchó para ganarse el sustento y vendía *souvenirs* costeros. Con el tiempo, fue admitido en *London School of Economics*, luego obtuvo un empleo con la casa de inversiones *Singer & Friedlander* en Londres en 1954 como dependiente. Soros ha dicho que fue contratado porque el director administrativo era húngaro.[26] En 1956, se mudó a Nueva York donde trabajaba como analista de valores y comerciante mientras hacía la solicitud para convertirse en un ciudadano estadounidense naturalizado. Fundó *Soros Fund Management* en 1970, donde consolidó su fortuna.

Soros es mejor conocido en Europa como "el hombre que hizo quebrar el Banco de Inglaterra". Al apostar fuertemente sobre la devaluación de la Libra esterlina, ganó mil millones de dólares en una sola transacción y virtualmente colapsó la economía inglesa. Según el sitio de internet de su *Open Society*, "George Soros lanzó su obra filantrópica en Sudáfrica en 1979. Desde entonces, él ha donado más de US$32 mil millones para financiar la *Open Society Foundations*, la cual funciona en más de 100 países alrededor del mundo".[27] Pero no se equivoque; el objetivo de los defensores de "fronteras abiertas" es eliminar los estados nación como los conocemos, junto con sus leyes individuales, costumbres, monedas y tradiciones para facultar una estructura global de élites educadas y progresistas para gobernar a toda la gente.

En su libro de 2006, *The Shadow Party*, David Horowits y Richard Poe revelan que la filantropía privada de Soros provee financiamiento para organizaciones que apoyan no solo las fronteras abiertas, sino: derecho de aborto, ateísmo, legalización de drogas, educación sexual, eutanasia, feminismo, control de armas, globalización, inmigración en masa, matrimonio homosexual y otros experimentos radicales en la ingeniería social".[28] Un listado de las muchas organizaciones sin fines de lucro que reciben fondos de Soros puede hallarse en DiscoverTheNetworks.org.[29]

La Izquierda religiosa

Soros gasta una indecible cantidad de millones de dólares presionando su agenda de fronteras abiertas e inmigración ilegal para lograr lo que la Izquierda ve como una "mayoría permanente progresiva". La presión por amnistía y derecho de voto para los ilegales es un parte fundamental de sus planes de sociedad abierta para derrumbar las fronteras y crear lo que equivale a un solo gobierno mundial dirigido por una élite global. Sin embargo, Soros sabe que los votantes conservadores y cristianos nunca estarán dispuestos a apoyar esos objetivos, así que usa su fortuna para movilizar cientos de organizaciones militantes izquierdistas para protestar, crear disturbios y levantar tanto caos y temor que quienes no estén de acuerdo con sus objetivos estarán demasiado intimidados para resistir.

Sin embargo, como Rebecca Hagelin escribe para Townhall.com, va mucho más allá porque Soros también cree que si se les lanza suficiente dinero, aun los más ardientes tradicionalistas pueden ser comprados. Y esto es particularmente cierto para ministros liberales y de inclinación izquierdista, tales como el reverendo Jim Wallis, quien fundó la organización de justicia social cristiana *Sojourners* en 1971 y se desempeña como fundador y presidente de la revista liberal *Sojourners*.[30] Entre 2004 y 2007, la organización *Sojourners* recibió subvenciones de los grupos financiados por Soros por un total de US$325,000 según un informe del

National Review por Jay Richards, que son parte de por lo menos cuarenta y nueve subvenciones de fundaciones entre 2003 y 2009 totalizando US$2,159,346. "Ninguno de estos", Richards descubrió, "proviene de una fundación discerniblemente conservadora. Muy pocas son de fundaciones discerniblemente cristianas".[31]

El padre Robert Sirico, presidente del Instituto *Acton*, informó en el *Washington Times* que la *Open Society Policy Center* financiada por Soros, había hecho donativos totalizando US$650,000 a dos organizaciones basadas en la fe. Si cualquiera fuera a concluir que Soros ha encontrado religión, dice Sirico, pronto descubrirían que "la motivación de la filantropía es mucho más banal". Si están "basadas en la fe" es un asunto discutible, pero las organizaciones *Faith in Public Life* (FPL) y PICO *National Network* (cuyo nombre cambió a *Faith in Action* en 2018) son en realidad redes de acción política de base. En su financiación inicial de estos grupos, Sirico descubrió, a través de una revisión de documentos filtrados, que Soros estaba intentando movilizar diez mil voluntarios para influenciar a la Iglesia Católica durante la visita del Papa Francisco a Estados Unidos en 2015. Sobre la superficie, él dice, las donaciones parecían benignas. Sin embargo:

> Lo que desconcierta es la burda intención política de manipular a los líderes de la iglesia que es evidente en los documentos filtrados. Uno tiene la impresión de que el Sr. Soros y sus compañeros de viaje ven al liderazgo de la comunidad religiosa en general y a la Iglesia Católica, en particular, como simples bobos útiles para ser manipulados a fin de promover su propia agenda política y, francamente, secularista.[32]

En un artículo para el *Capital Research Center*, Neil Maghami informa que el FPL se promueve como una red de líderes de la fe y es identificado en el sitio web de la organización como "una red nacional de casi 50,000 clérigos y líderes de la fe unidos en una búsqueda profética de justicia y bien común. Con personal en cuatro estados y creciendo, trabajamos de cerca con nuestros miembros para tomar una acción estratégica moral que dé forma a la política local y nacionalmente. Creemos que los líderes de la fe tienen un poder moral único para influenciar debates públicos y edificar comunidades más justas y equitativas".[33] Fundada en 2005 y situada en Washington, DC, la FPL recibió aproximadamente US$1.7 millones en subvenciones de parte de la Fundación para Promover la Sociedad Abierta entre el 2012 y 2015 y reportó una utilidad de US$2.252 millones en 2015.[34]

Al frente de la acusación contra la Derecha religiosa, está la reverenda Jennifer Butler, quien se desempeña como directora ejecutiva de FPL y es la expresidenta del *Council on Faith and Neighborhood Partnerships* para la administración Obama. La FPL se ha involucrado en un ataque vigoroso y constante al presidente Trump y a su agenda a favor de: Estados Unidos, el comercio y la fe. El 23 de noviembre de 2016, la FPL hizo circular una carta firmada por mil quinientos clérigos condenando al "gabinete de fanatismo" del presidente Trump, llamándolos "embajadores del odio, el fanatismo y la intimidación".[35]

El 9 de enero de 2017, la reverenda Butler y sus asociados organizaron una marcha de protesta de doscientos "líderes morales" en *Capital Hill* para oponerse a la nominación presidencial del senador Jeff Sessions como fiscal general. Poco tiempo después, la FPL hizo circular una página de opinión escrita por el director del grupo católico de alcance, John Gehring, la cual decía: "La gente de fe que quiera dar cobertura moral a las acciones de Trump le da la espalda a Jesús".[36] Luego, el 23 de febrero, la organización emitió un comunicado de prensa sobre la carta firmada por cuatro mil clérigos condenando "cualquier cambio de política que bloquee a los refugiados con base a su religión o nacionalidad", refiriéndose a la prohibición de Trump sobre los refugiados musulmanes.[37]

El 6 de marzo de 2017, la FPL emitió un enunciado de prensa sobre una conferencia de prensa para "condenar la orden ejecutiva del presidente Trump prohibiendo la entrada de inmigrantes y visitantes de los países de mayoría musulmana".[38] Luego, en abril, emitieron un comunicado de prensa sobre una vigilia de oración en la capital de la nación "para urgir al Congreso a rechazar la propuesta presupuestaria federal pecaminosa e inmoral de Trump, la cual hace recortes profundos y destructivos a los programas dirigidos a las necesidades humanas a fin de incrementar el gasto del Pentágono".[39] Para promover su agenda izquierdista, la FPL también publicó una guía para el votante: "Fe, valores y las elecciones 2016: Hacia una política de la regla de oro", respaldada por unos doscientos líderes religiosos representando varias organizaciones cristianas, judías y musulmanas. Como era de esperarse, la guía se enfocaba en: calentamiento global, inmigración, control de armas, justicia racial, seguridad nacional y economía, con muy poca mención de la fe en realidad.

En junio de 2013, Maghami informa, otra intervención por parte de la FPL en los asuntos católicos que tomó la forma de un panfleto titulado "¿No tenga temor?". El panfleto critica a la *Catholic Campaing for Human Development*, la una vez confiable fuente de financiamiento para "bases de organización comunitaria", por ceder a la presión de los "activistas católicos conservadores y sus aliados ideológicos sobre el derecho político" y evitar, por razones políticas, que varias organizaciones recibieran fondos.[40] Un artículo de la *Foundation Watch* ofrece un análisis útil para esta situación.[41]

Los autores del panfleto afirmaron que el recién nombrado obispo de la diócesis de Santa Rosa, California, fray Robert Vasa, tenía una participación en la negación de fondos para el *North Bay Organizing Project* en esa ciudad. Vasa expresó disgusto por el "estilo de organización Alinsky" del grupo".[42] La referencia al mentor de Hillary Clinton, Saul Alinsky, escritor de *Rules for Radicals* y un notorio organizador marxista, tiene que haber disparado las alarmas para cualquiera que entienda las verdaderas intenciones de los seguidores de Alinsky.

La otra organización, *Faith in Action*, está activa en más de veinte estados. El sitio web de la organización y alguna literatura identifica a *Faith in Action* como "una red nacional de organización comunitaria basada en la fe trabajando para crear soluciones innovadoras a los problemas que enfrentan las comunidades urbanas, suburbanas y rurales".[43] Fue fundada en 1972 por fray John Baumann, SJ, entre su primer y segundo año de seminario. Mientras hacía trabajo de campo en Chicago, Baumann tenía contacto con Alinsky. Baumann dice que quedó profundamente impresionado por los argumentos y la actitud del organizador radical. En una entrevista en 2014 publicada por *Holy Names University*, Baumann describe cómo la reunión con Alinsky cambió su vida, promoviendo su dedicación al activismo comunitario.[44]

De 2012 a 2015, la FPL recibió un poco menos de US$1.9 millones de parte de la *Foundation to Promote Open Society*. Pero estas no son las únicas organizaciones de orientación religiosa que están a favor de Alinsky en la lista de beneficiarios de la *Open Society*. También está la *Gamaliel Foundation*, que ha recibido US$550,000 de la *Foundation to Promote Open Society* desde 2012. Para tener una idea de los vínculos de la Fundación con el organizador comunitario Barack Obama, el artículo "*The Gamaliel Foundation: Alinsky-Inspired Group Uses Stealth Tactics to Manipulate Church Congregations*", en el ejemplar de julio de 2010 de la revista *Foundation Watch*, provee un acercamiento a la manera en que se usa el dinero de Soros.[45]

Sin embargo, la guerra contra los valores cristianos no está limitada a aquellos en la extrema Izquierda, tales como FPL y *Faith in Action*. En el programa matutino dominical de CBS, *Face the Nation*, al columnista del *Washington Post*, Michael Gerson, un evangélico liberal, le pidieron que comentara sobre los líderes evangélicos que apoyaron al Presidente durante el escándalo de Stormy Daniels. El antiguo escritor de discursos para el presidente George W. Bush, respondió: "Bueno, ellos están actuando como, usted sabe, falsos operativos políticos, no líderes morales. Están esencialmente diciendo, para obtener beneficios para ellos, de alguna manera —hablan sobre libertad de culto y otros temas— pero para beneficiarse ellos mismos, están dispuestos a guiñar el ojo a Stormy Daniels, y guiñar el ojo a la misoginia, y guiñar el ojo al nativismo".[46]

Mi amigo Tony Perkins, el presidente del *Family Research Council*, quien fue acusado de duplicidad moral por Gerson en un artículo para *The Atlantic*, respondió diciendo que su decisión de apoyar a Donald Trump se debió al contraste dramático entre dos candidatos y el bien que la agenda conservadora de Trump haría. "La libertad de culto está siendo restaurada", dijo, "las políticas provida están siendo fomentadas, la infraestructura del gobierno izquierdista está siendo desmantelado. Por eso es por lo que Gerson y la Izquierda están muy airados".

El Dr. Robert Jeffress, pastor de *Dallas' First Baptist Church*, y un consejero del presidente, estuvieron de acuerdo: "Estamos apoyando a este presidente por sus políticas".[47]

Mientras tanto, el Dr. Richard Land, presidente del *Southern Evangelical Seminary*, dijo que los evangélicos "se sienten cultural y políticamente asediados" y "sienten como si su gobierno ha sido convertido en un arma en contra de ellos". Durante una entrevista de radio, Land dijo, "En un mundo caído y pecaminoso, a veces nos vemos forzados a elegir entre el menor y el mayor de los males. Y si no optamos por ayudar a que el menor de los males triunfe sobre el mayor de los males, nos volveremos moralmente responsables por el predominio del mayor mal". Él añadió: "Da igual cuán inmoral piense usted que es Donald Trump, la Sra. Clinton es más inmoral". Él añadió que los evangélicos liberales, como Mike Gerson, no han entendido.[48] No podría estar más de acuerdo, y lo he descrito en alguna otra parte en que he hecho ese mismo punto, no solo en mi libro *God and Donald Trump*, sino también en varias entrevistas en los medios.

EVALUAR EL IMPACTO

David Horowitz y Richard Poe concluyen en su poderosa exposición de George Soros y el *Shadow Party*, diciendo:

> Usando el poder para su gran bolsa y su visión institucional brillantemente manipulativa, Soros ha construido un partido, un *Shadow Party*, diferente de cualquier otro en la historia estadounidense. No es un partido al estilo Estados Unidos que rinda cuentas al pueblo y esté sujeto a su voluntad, sino que es más como un partido de vanguardia Leninista, completamente así de conspiratorio y justamente igual de irresponsable ante el pueblo. Es más, este es un partido increíblemente construido por un magnate financiero, hábil en la manipulación de la moneda y los mercados.[49]

Soros diseñó y construyó la conspiración de fronteras abiertas por "elementos institucionales arrancados de cada nivel de la jerarquía social existente". En el proceso, él ha ayudado a movilizar "el partido de rebeldes", dicen, "pero también el partido de los gobernadores, una unidad corporativa de capital y trabajo", usando los recursos de algunos de los hombres y mujeres más ricos y poderosos del mundo. Y, día a día, esta oligarquía de radicales multimillonarios está siendo "insinuada dentro del corazón del sistema estadounidense".[50]

En otra evaluación del impacto de los radicales multimillonarios y su marca de activismo izquierdista, *Investor's Business Daily* observa:

Este es el mundo verdadero de la política progresista: Multimillonarios, peces gordos, infiltrados, élites de Washington, sindicatos grandes, todos conspirando para fracturar en pedazos nuestra democracia y poner a un grupo de estadounidenses en contra del otro, por un poder y beneficio político máximo. Para este fin, dan cientos de millones de dólares para el Partido Demócrata, ignorando o insultando la Constitución y tratan al sistema político de Estados Unidos como un juguete personal con el cual cambiar radicalmente la estructura misma de nuestra nación.[51]

Claramente, el daño que puede infringirse sobre una república constitucional por actores a este nivel es inmenso. Por eso es muy importante para los conservadores y los cristianos estadounidenses oponerse a la agenda de la Izquierda radical y, al mismo tiempo, apoyar a la alternativa política.

En sus comentarios de cierre para los miembros del *World Economic Forum* en Davos, el presidente Trump señaló que el éxito es más que dinero y más que estrategia política. "Para ser exitoso", dijo, "invertir en nuestra economía no es suficiente. Tenemos que invertir en nuestra gente. Cuando la gente es olvidada, el mundo se fractura. Solo al escuchar y responder a las voces de los olvidados podemos crear un futuro brillante que todos comparten verdaderamente". Y en contraste dramático a la filosofía de "un solo mundo" de los activistas de fronteras abiertas, el Presidente dijo: "La grandeza de una nación es más que la suma de su producción. La grandeza de una nación es la suma de sus ciudadanos: los valores, el orgullo, el amor, la devoción y el carácter de la gente que lo llama hogar".[52]

Viendo alrededor del salón a los ricos y poderosos que habían llegado a ver las intenciones de Donald Trump, dijo:

En este salón están representados algunos de los ciudadanos más notables de todo el mundo. Ustedes son líderes nacionales, titanes del comercio, gigantes industriales y muchas de las mentes más brillantes en muchos campos. Cada uno de ustedes tiene el poder de cambiar corazones, transformar vidas, y forjar el destino de sus países. Sin embargo, con ese poder viene una obligación: el deber de lealtad hacia la gente, los trabajadores y los clientes que han hecho de ustedes lo que son.[53]

Al cerrar, dijo: "Propongámonos usar nuestro poder, nuestros recursos y nuestra voz, no solo para nosotros mismos, sino para nuestra gente: para quitar sus cargas, elevar su esperanza y dar poder a sus sueños; para proteger a sus familias, a sus comunidades, sus historias y su futuro". Por eso es por lo que tomé la decisión de postularme para el cargo, y eso es lo que está sucediendo en

Estados Unidos ahora. Al escuchar a la gente y trabajar por sus intereses, dijo, los resultados han sido sorprendentes. "Es por eso por lo que nuevos negocios e inversión nueva están entrando a raudales. Es la razón por la que nuestra tasa de desempleo está en su nivel más bajo en décadas. Es la razón por la que el futuro de Estados Unidos nunca ha sido más brillante". Y él les pidió a los multimillonarios de Davos ser parte de "este futuro increíble que estamos construyendo juntos".[54]

En 2016, a medida que las elecciones presidenciales de noviembre se acercaban rápidamente, el sitio web *Politico* reportó que George Soros estaba políticamente más activo de lo que había estado en años, motivado, según decían, por su temor a los triunfos recientes de la agenda política conservadora y particularmente por Donald Trump, a quien Soros acusaba de "'estar haciendo el trabajo de ISIS' al aumentar temores". Más que cualquier otro donante liberal, dijeron los escritores, Soros tiene el mayor "potencial para catalizar donaciones de otros activistas ricos".[55] Considerando que sabemos del poder y la influencia de los radicales billonarios, la observación casual del sitio web tiene que ser un llamado a despertar. Si hay algo que aprender al observar más de cerca a los hombres y mujeres que están financiando hoy día a la Izquierda, es la importancia de entender quiénes son estas personas, lo que han dicho y dónde están invirtiendo su tesoro.

Si bien hay razón para alarmarse en lo que los radicales multimillonarios están diciendo y haciendo, también hay una razón para que los cristianos se regocijen. Mientras que los radicales acusan a Donald Trump de suscitar "temores", son ellos los que están temerosos de que las victorias izquierdistas que han logrado durante medio siglo puedan estar en peligro y que su lado gane no es una conclusión precedente. Eso debería ser un estímulo, pero acordémonos que la lucha no ha terminado y que debemos seguir orando, especialmente porque el hombre que personifica el cambio radical reciente hacia la Izquierda, mucho más que cualquiera de estos desconocidos multimillonarios, es Barack Obama. Y él continúa teniendo una agenda aún después que su mandato terminó.

EL TERCER MANDATO DE OBAMA

CUANDO BARACK OBAMA ganó su lugar en el Senado en 2004, él era un exprofesor de derecho de cuarenta y tres años que ganaba US$85,000 al año. Para cuando salió de la Casa Blanca, en 2017, él tenía una fortuna de aproximadamente US$20 millones. Según una revisión de dieciséis años de declaraciones de impuestos de Obama y de registros financieros, hecho por la revista *Forbes*, tres cuartas partes de eso vino de venta de libros. Solo US$3.7 millones provenían de los salarios del antiguo presidente. Tal como Dan Alexander escribe:

> El presidente anterior no perdió mucho tiempo para aprovechar su historia una vez que llegó a la capital de la nación. En enero 2005, el mismo mes en que se unió al Senado, recibió aprobación de su comité de ética por un anticipo de US$1.9 millones contra las regalías con *Random House* por dos libros de hechos reales y un libro para niños. Los Obama, quienes habían ganado menos de US$300,000 cada año, desde 2000 hasta 2004, ganaron un promedio de US$2.4 millones anualmente durante los siguientes cuatro años, incluso antes de que Barack fuera electro presidente.[1]

Para ese tiempo, Michelle Obama era vicepresidenta de comunidad y asuntos externos en la *University of Chicago Hospitals*, donde devengó US$317,000 en 2005 y US$274,000 en 2006. Su ingreso personal fue disminuyendo durante la campaña presidencial de Obama, relata *Forbes*. "Luego vino el buen dinero". Cuando los Clinton dejaron la Casa Blanca en 2005, Hillary aseguró que ellos estaban "sin un centavo", pero desde ese tiempo ellos han tomado más de US$240 millones, principalmente provenientes de discursos altamente pagados y acuerdos de libros.[2] Siguiendo el ejemplo de ellos, y con la ayuda de sus partidarios, los Obama sin duda tendrían una oportunidad para pescar mucho más.

Tal como lo ha explicado el autor de libros de mayor venta, Peter Schweizer, el dinero es una gran parte del juego en la política de Washington. "Para muchos, desempeñarse en el Congreso es el mejor trabajo que tendrán en su vida. Aparte del ingreso, son premiados con poder y responsabilidad. Pero, cada vez más, los miembros están tomando ventaja de ese poder y responsabilidad para crear riqueza también Bajo un capitalismo de compadrazgo" dice él, "el acceso a los funcionarios gubernamentales que pueden repartir subvenciones, exenciones fiscales y subsidios es una ruta alterna a la riqueza".[3] Y no es solo el Congreso. Sin embargo, a pesar de cuánta riqueza puedan acumular nuestros legisladores mientras están en el cargo, a aquellos en la cima de la cadena alimenticia les va definitivamente mucho mejor.

Desde que los días rebeldes de Tammany Hall, hace más de un siglo, la manipulación de los fondos gubernamentales por los políticos corruptos ha sido una realidad. Sin embargo, canalizar el dinero de los contribuyentes a los amigos y partidarios, nos dicen los investigadores, ha incrementado exponencialmente en los años recientes. Con los gastos federales alcanzando los US$3 billones, los funcionarios de gobierno tienen "oportunidades extraordinarias para obtener un pedazo de la acción".[4] La mayoría de los estadounidenses estarían asombrados ante el número de cheques gubernamentales que se pagan a algunos de los estadounidenses más ricos. Desenvainar millones puede ser complicado, escribe Schweizer. Sin embargo, los gastos se presentan ante el público como un "plan de estímulo económico" que crea empleo, entonces los programas como las argucias de "energía alternativa" de Obama permiten a los funcionarios de gobierno distribuir miles de millones al selecto grupo de dignos empresarios.

De hecho, Washington ha repartido miles de millones en efectivo y garantías de préstamos a individuos favorecidos en el negocio de la energía alternativa. Cuando Obama se mudó a la Casa Blanca, en enero de 2009, empezó inmediatamente a hablar sobre la necesidad de miles de millones de dólares para un "estímulo económico" para arrancar la economía que estaba en dificultades. Luego, por supuesto, se necesitaron más miles de millones para expandir el acceso a internet y crear una "red inteligente" para garantizar recursos de energía seguros. Schweizer dice:

> Los medios de comunicación casi no informan el hecho de que una cantidad abrumadora de este dinero ha sido dirigido a los partidarios financieros adinerados del presidente Obama y el Partido Demócrata… Muchos beneficiarios se desempeñaron en el comité de finanzas del presidente, o fungieron como *bundlers* de los donativos de campaña (coordinadores de contribuciones individuales que pueden ser combinadas en donativos grandes) o fueron donantes mayores. En resumen, ellos recaudaron y donaron *millones* para la campaña de Obama en el 2008 y, a cambio, las compañías que ellos poseían o dirigían han recibido *miles de millones* en préstamos respaldados por el gobierno y subvenciones incondicionales.[5]

Obama les aseguró a los contribuyentes que la distribución del dinero sería con base al mérito, en lugar de amistades políticas. Sin embargo, tal como lo relata Schweizer, eso no es lo que sucedió.

Una gran proporción de ganadores del programa de estímulos, subvenciones y préstamos del *Department of Energy* (DOE) eran empresas con las que la campaña de Obama tenía conexiones. Varios miembros del comité financiero de Obama fueron seleccionados para recibir préstamos garantizados, y los políticos que apoyaron a Obama lanzaron empresas de energía alternativa y obtuvieron grandes subvenciones del gobierno.

Solo en un programa, las 1705 empresas conectadas con Obama recibieron más de US$16.4 billones de la asignación total del programa de préstamos respaldados por el gobierno. Todas estas firmas pertenecían o eran dirigidas primordialmente por los patrocinadores financieros de Obama. Tal como dice Schweizer: "Su generosidad política es probablemente la mejor inversión que hayan hecho en energía alternativa. Les trajo dividendos con creces a su inversión".[6] Estas fueron las iniciativas DOE; sin embargo, memoranda interna muestra que el DOE no manejó solo el proceso de revisión de subvenciones. Se requería que todos los préstamos y las subvenciones fueran revisadas por la Casa Blanca antes de ser aprobados.[7]

El retorno por parte de las administraciones de inversiones en energía alternativa, sin embargo, no era lo que el público había sido guiado a creer. Para 2015, diez años después, la *Government Accountability Office* informó en su auditoría que más de US$800 millones en préstamos ya estaban asignadas, por defecto, bajo el *Energy Department Program*.[8] Y dicho, en los años fiscales 2010 y 2011, hubo 345 iniciativas federales diferentes que apoyaban la energía solar, y solo 65 de esas iniciativas representaban más de 1,500 proyectos de energía solar administrados por seis agencias federales.[9] El gasto de 2009 a 2014 fue estimado en un exceso de US$150 mil millones en energía solar y otros proyectos de energía renovable. El IRS informó que las exenciones fiscales para las iniciativas de energía alternativa le costaron al país cerca de US$9 mil millones en ingresos perdidos.

Solo una pequeñísima parte, más o menos el 2.2 por ciento, de la electricidad de los estadounidenses fue generada por el viento y el sol, y aún entonces, esta no era poco confiables, poco práctica y cara, según un análisis de la revista *Forbes*. "Todo lo que ganamos realmente por el esfuerzo y el gasto es la creación de una institución de energía solar formada por burócratas, intelectuales y corporaciones en busca de créditos, cuyo principal interés no es generar energía, sino embolsarse los recursos públicos… Con tan poco que mostrar por tantas iniciativas costosas, debería estar claro para el observador objetivo que los esfuerzos federales para la energía solar no han sido un uso productivo ni prudente de los preciados dólares tributarios".[10]

CONTINGENCIAS POSTPRESIDENCIALES

En las semanas posteriores a la sorprendente victoria de Donald Trump, cuando los miembros del círculo interior de Obama se encontraron cara a cara con la realidad de su derrota electoral, aquellos que fueron los más cercanos al expresidente durante los ocho años anteriores no podían dejar de sentir que "así no era como debía de haberse desarrollado la trama. Así no era como se suponía que los años de Obama tenían que terminar". Sin embargo, el corresponsal político, Jason Zengerle, en un artículo de la revista GQ, del 17 de enero de 2017, señaló que este no iba a ser el final. En vez de eso, sería el principio del tercer mandato de Obama.[11]

Puedo recordar cuando Harry Truman se convirtió en un amado anciano estadista, pero se mantuvo fuera de la política después de haber dejado el cargo. De la misma manera fue con los presidentes Eisenhower, Johnson, Nixon y Ford. Solamente Jimmy Carter ha permanecido en el centro de atención, pero eso se debe principalmente a proyectos positivos como *Habitat for Humanity*. Ronald Reagan, los dos Bush e incluso Bill Clinton han estado fuera de la atención política. Al igual que todos los otros jefes ejecutivos que terminaron su época en el escenario más grande de la nación, los Obama encontrarían maneras para relajarse, disfrutar de otras vacaciones en Hawái sin duda y decorar su nueva casa en el vecindario exclusivo de Kalorama, en Washington DC. Sin embargo, este iba a ser un cambio mucho más grande de lo que ellos o cualquiera de sus amigos, consejeros y confidentes habían anticipado. Con una victoria de Clinton, Obama había continuado influenciando la política nacional durante otros diez años o más. Él habría tenido un papel estelar. Pero si algo de esa naturaleza fuera a suceder ahora, en las sombras de la administración Trump y el Congreso controlado por republicanos, requeriría un juego de reglas diferente. Tendría que llevarse a cabo tras bambalinas.

Tal como el exconsejero de Obama, Dan Pfeiffer, le explicó a Zengerle: "Para este momento, en ocho años, cuando Obama busque consolar a los estadounidenses atravesando un evento traumático, él sabe que, en el fondo, su vida ha cambiado irrevocablemente. Este tiempo no es un pueblo en Oklahoma aplanado por un tornado; es él". Pfeiffer dijo que el legado de Obama podría haber continuado durante generaciones si los demócratas hubieran ganado tres mandatos, uno tras otro. Todos en el círculo de Obama creían que la victoria de Clinton podría garantizar el legado de Obama. Luego, él añadió: "Algunas de las batallas que pudieron haberse resuelto con una victoria de Clinton ahora continuarán durante los próximos cuatro o veinte años".[12]

Otro consejero de Obama le dijo al escritor que había una contingencia de cómo sería la postpresidencia de Obama, dependiendo de que Clinton obtuviera la victoria. "Luego, Trump obtuvo la victoria y eso desarmó el plan por completo. Ahora, es momento del Plan B". La nueva contingencia demandaba una realineación de la estrategia. Todo el que lo conoce, Zengerle escribe, sabe que Obama nunca estaría conforme con quedarse al margen, así como lo han hecho Bush y Clinton. En vez de eso, él estaría buscando el momento oportuno para volver a la acción: "para poder así alcanzar el máximo impacto".[13]

El resultado más probable, según aquellos que lo conocen mejor, sería involucrarse en una contienda contra Trump sobre algún asunto importante de política, tal como el esfuerzo de eliminar *Obamacare*, el trato con Irán, o cualquiera de las diferentes iniciativas EPA que su administración promocionó. El intento de erradicar el último vestigio del legado de Obama podría fácilmente provocar una batalla política mayor. La pregunta más grande que confronta a Obama, sostiene el artículo de *GQ*, podría ser cuándo y cómo atacar. Pfeiffer le dijo al escritor que los antiguos funcionarios de la Casa Blanca no están ilusionados por el porvenir. "Nadie lo vería como suficiente como para quedarse al margen". Al igual que su jefe, el antiguo equipo de la Casa Blanca ya estaba preparado para la batalla que apenas empezaba.[14]

El jefe de organización comunitaria

El expresidente, un organizador comunitario, se ha instalado a la sombra de la Casa Blanca. Según el autor e investigador Paul Sperry, exbecario de medios de la *Hoover Institution*, Barack Obama está librando una insurgencia política tras bambalinas, financiando y entrenando grupos radicales de protesta para oponerse a las políticas de Trump y tramando voltear a la mayoría del Partido Republicano al volver azules a los estados rojos. Sperry escribe:

> Desde su oficina en crecimiento en DC, cerca de la Casa Blanca, donde tiene bajo su cargo a 20 empleados de tiempo completo, Obama ha llevado a cabo reuniones regulares con legisladores demócratas, así como con el jefe de la DNC, Tom Pérez, a quien él ayudó personalmente a instalarse para dirigir el Partido Demócrata. Obama también se ha reunido con su fiscal general, Eric Holder, para elaborar una estrategia para volver a dibujar los mapas de distrito del Congreso a favor de los demócratas, según *Politico*. *Holder* ahora dirige el *National Democratic Redistricting Committee*, el cual Obama ayudó a su viejo amigo a lanzar.[15]

La organización que él creó estando aún en el cargo, *Organizing for Action* (OFA), ahora se ha convertido en el centro de organización y entrenamiento de la resistencia contra Trump, dice Sperry. Ha ayudado a organizar protestas por todo el país contra las políticas fronterizas de Trump. Si bien se describe a sí misma como una "organización fundamentalista no partidista", la OFA es la

Casa Blanca post Obama, trabajando para continuar la agenda izquierdista del expresidente. La OFA es dirigida, de hecho, por los exconsejeros de campaña y exfuncionarios de la Casa Blanca durante el mandato de Obama. El problema no es que Obama esté trabajando tiempo extra para defender su agotado legado, sino que él está usando la riqueza e influencia de los agitadores izquierdistas, tales como Soros y Steyer, para desestabilizar al país.

"La OFA", dice Sperry, "se ha asociado formalmente con uno de los grupos de resistencia más violentos, *Indivisible Project*, el cual ha sido criticado por usar tácticas de protesta extremadamente agresivas contra los republicanos en las reuniones municipales". *Indivisible Project* estaba detrás de los ataques de los agitadores entrenados por la OFA que irrumpieron en los distritos republicanos durante el receso del Cuatro de julio en un intento de cerrar las "políticas racistas de Trump", tal como el sitio web *Indivisible* lo admite. Obama ha apoyado a la OFA a obtener entre US$6 y $14 millones en donativos al año, informa Sperry, y está parcialmente financiada por la *Democracy Alliance*, que es la liga de corredores del poder izquierdista que apoyan a la *Open Society Foundations* de Soros.[16]

A propósito, la OFA está conectada a grupos radicales que han enviado agitadores a protestar fuera de los hogares de los funcionarios de la administración, incluyendo a la secretaria de seguridad del país, Kirstjen Nielsen, cuya privacidad fue invadida en junio del 2018 por protestantes enmascarados haciendo sonar a todo volumen grabaciones de niños inmigrantes llorando, mientras coreaban: "¡Sin justicia no se duerme!" durante toda la noche. Estas no son las acciones de los ciudadanos en una república democrática y tampoco el tipo de política que la mayoría de los estadounidenses apreciarían.

Muchos, quienes se beneficiaron de los años de Obama estaban más que listos para que empezara la batalla. Entre los partidarios acérrimos de Obama estaba el comentador del PBS, Bill Moyers, ex secretario de prensa de Lyndon Johnson y graduando del Seminario Bautista, a quien conocí cuando fue invitado a dar un discurso a un grupo de editores evangélicos. En ese momento, supe que él estaba un poco más centrado a la Izquierda; sin embargo, con el paso de los años, él se ha dado a conocer por vituperar a conservadores y evangélicos. Moyers estaba tan consternado por la derrota de Clinton que, junto con su escritor, Michael Winship, redactó un borrador de discurso inaugural para que la candidata derrotara anunciara la inauguración de un nuevo "gobierno alternativo de la oposición" para contrarrestar y debilitar la presidencia de Trump.

Lo que Moyers proponía era un movimiento radical atraído por legiones de partidarios de Obama enojados y humillados, quienes se encontraban repentinamente sin país. El objetivo era rastrear cada plan y cada propuesta de la administración Trump para levantar alarma y desacuerdo y luego trabajar las obras y tomar acción directa, cuando fuera necesario, para derrotar la agenda de

Trump a cada momento. Toda propuesta y toda acción ejecutiva tendría que ser retada, independientemente del daño hecho al país.

A la cabeza del ataque estaría un grupo central de políticos internos que saben cómo funciona Washington, junto con "alcaldes, legisladores estatales, servidores públicos, activistas y organizadores que conocen las necesidades de nuestros municipios, condados y estados por todo el país". Trabajando tras bambalinas, este nuevo gobierno tendría su propio gabinete ejecutivo, secretarios de estado, tesorero, educación, salud y servicios humanos, y todo lo demás, para hacer frente a las consecuencias, para proveer un liderazgo verdadero, y para aliviar los sentimientos de desesperanza que han tomado la nación desde la derrota de Clinton.[17]

Claro está, Hillary jamás dio ese discurso. Quizá nunca lo haya leído. Sin embargo, en retrospectiva, la propuesta fantasiosa de Moyers no parece simplemente tonta sino rebelde. Moyers afirmó que la propuesta era una gran tradición que aún mantienen los partidos que actualmente están fuera del poder en Gran Bretaña. No obstante, ni en la ley ni en la tradición estadounidense hay cabida para un "gobierno alternativo de la oposición", y las incursiones realizadas por exfuncionarios de gobierno, como las reuniones no autorizadas del exsecretario de estado, John Kerry con los líderes de Irán, que no solo son potencialmente ilegales, sino también extremadamente peligrosas y podría llevar a consecuencias serias. Sin embargo, Moyers cree que es vocero del gran contingente de refugiados desorientados de los años de Obama, quienes creen que su misión no ha terminado.

¿UN PARALELO BÍBLICO?

Si Moyers hubiera puesto más atención en su clase de escuela dominical bautista cuando era niño, él podría haber aprendido las lecciones del rey Acab y su malvada reina, Jezabel. En lugar de inclinarse hacia la izquierda, como lo ha hecho de adulto, él pudo haber entendido que en la historia de Acab y Jezabel hay un presagio de Estados Unidos modernos. Este paralelo fue traído a luz por Jonathan Cahn en su libro revelador "El paradigma". Cahn, un rabino mesiánico y autor de libros de mayor venta del *New York Times*, cuyos libros he tenido el privilegio de publicar, vio una similitud entre los Clinton y Acab y Jezabel, así como entre Barack Obama y Joram (el hijo de Acab y Jezabel), muy similar a los paralelos entre el antiguo Israel y los eventos del 11 de septiembre sobre los cuales escribió Cahn en *El presagio*.

"El paradigma" vale la pena que lo lea quien quiera ver cómo la mano de Dios ha estado no solo sobre el antiguo Israel sino también en Estados Unidos modernos. Los paralelos son sorprendentes. Acab estuvo en el poder veintidós años. Él tenía una esposa hambrienta de poder, Jezabel, quien llevó a Israel a adorar a Baal, lo que incluía el sacrificio de bebés, una práctica que no es diferente al aborto de hoy día. Bill Clinton también estuvo en el poder veintidós años, desde cuando fue el gobernador de Arkansas hasta cuando terminó su mandato presidencial. Su esposa hambrienta de poder, Hillary, permaneció en el poder político como senadora, secretaria de estado y candidata presidencial fracasada. Esto es similar a Jezabel, quien permaneció en el poder después del reinado de Acab hasta que un extranjero rebelde e impredecible llamado Jehú apareció en escena, derribó la adoración de Baal y devolvió a Israel la adoración del único y verdadero Dios. ¿Ve algún paralelo con Donald Trump?

Entre los reinados de Acab y Jehú, Israel fue gobernada por el rey Joram, quien estuvo en el poder por doce años, tal como lo estuvo Obama. Joram continuó la adoración de Baal. Y cuando se enfrentó a Jehú en batalla, Joram dijo: "¿Hay paz, Jehú?". Jehú respondió: "¿Qué paz, con las fornicaciones de Jezabel tu madre, y sus muchas hechicerías?" (2 Reyes 9:22). Entonces, Jehú lanzó una flecha y mató a Joram, y luego mandó matar a Jezabel. En aquel entonces, el reinado de una persona terminaba con su muerte. Hoy día, tenemos elecciones democráticas o límites al mandato que terminan el reinado de alguien. Pero ¿es posible que, de algún modo, Trump terminará con la influencia de Obama en el proceso cultural y político? Solo el tiempo lo dirá, pero como estudiante de la Biblia, me encantan los paralelos. Si bien parece que la especulación (incluyendo la de Moyers) anda desenfrenada, raramente acudimos a la Biblia para ver qué está sucediendo.

Por otra parte, Obama todavía es una influencia importante, y muchos no creen que su influencia haya terminado. Mientras tanto, Obama dirigió su atención a la organización comunitaria y al activismo político, donde él empezó. En su ampliamente publicitada entrevista con el príncipe Harry de Gran Bretaña para la BBC, Obama dijo: "Estoy verdaderamente obsesionado ahora con entrenar a la siguiente generación de líderes que podrán dejar su huella en el mundo. Una manera en que lo he descrito es que yo creo que cuando uno está directamente en la política, entonces es un jugador en el campo, y allí hay algún elemento de ello que uno nunca podrá duplicar, la emoción y el entusiasmo, y a veces, la agonía que acompaña el estar en el campo. Y ahora estoy pasando por esa transición en algún grado como un entrenador. Y eso tiene sus propias demandas y responsabilidades, así como su propio impacto".[18]

El expresidente había dado la pauta, más de una vez, de que si hubiera suficiente apoyo popular para organizar un reto a la Décimo Segunda Enmienda, la cual limita al presidente a dos mandatos, él estaría dispuesto a postularse por un tercer mandato. Incluso llegó hasta a decírselo al analista de CNN, David Axelrod, en diciembre de 2016 que él podría haber derrotado a Trump si hubiera podido postularse para un tercer mandato.[19] El público nunca le aceptó la oferta, pero tal como Jason Zengerle señaló, todo lo que él necesitaba era el momento y la oportunidad oportuna para un retorno. Según un informe de enero 2018 en Politico. com, Obama había estado preparándose para un papel más significativo. Había hablado en mítines políticos, grabado una llamada automática y hecho algunos refrendos. Él no ocultó sus planes a largo plazo para ser un activista, ayudar a movilizar a la siguiente generación de líderes demócratas y continuar disertando sobre sus creencias medulares. Él incluyo ha puesto en blanco y negro un trato por varios años con Netflix para producir películas, series y otros proyectos que "capacitan a la siguiente generación de líderes aquí en Estados Unidos y alrededor del mundo".[20] En algún punto, declara el informe de *Politico*: Él activará su asociación de exalumnos de campaña por las causas y los candidatos que él apoye, incluyendo los 40 que están postulándose para el cargo. Él ya está haciendo estrategias tras bambalinas".[21] Hay señales de él ha estado cambiándose a un nivel mayor en espera del momento oportuno para volver a la contienda.

UNA DESAVENENCIA CRECIENTE

Para Donald Trump, la contienda empezó en diciembre de 2016, cuando se reveló que los funcionarios de inteligencia reportaron al Congreso que ellos tenían evidencia que indicaba que los operativos rusos trataron de interferir en las elecciones presidenciales de Estados Unidos, supuestamente para apoyar la campaña de Trump. Poco después de que el mandato de Obama terminara, él pidió un reporte sobre la situación y pidió sanciones contra las organizaciones de inteligencia rusas y varios individuos. Como parte de la respuesta de la administración Obama, el Departamento de Estado expulsó treinta y cinco diplomáticos rusos y cerró dos de sus instalaciones de inteligencia en Estados Unidos.

En ese momento, creo que el anuncio repentino de la sospecha de una conspiración unos días antes de la investidura fue un poco extraña. Algo no estaba bien sobre el reporte o el tiempo de las revelaciones. Es más, insultar a los rusos en esa manera sobre la base de puras conjeturas no fue un acercamiento muy diplomático. Para mí, y para muchos otros estadounidenses, toda esta situación olía mal, y Donald Trump estaba justificadamente receloso. Así que el presidente electo solicitó una reunión informativa de inteligencia para confirmar lo que se le había dicho. Apenas dos semanas antes de tomar el juramento para el cargo, se le informó a Trump que la reunión informativa, programada para el martes, 3 de enero, sería pospuesta hasta el viernes, 6 de enero; en ese momento, Trump tuiteó que él estaba decepcionado de que las agencias de inteligencias estuvieran tan mal preparadas.

> La reunión informativa de "Inteligencia" sobre la llamada "piratería
> rusa" fue retrasada hasta el viernes, quizá necesitan más tiempo para
> construir un caso. ¡Muy extraño![22]

Cuando el líder de las minorías en el Senado, vio una copia del tuit de Trump durante una aparición en el programa de televisión de Rachel Maddow, él comentó que Trump estaba tomando un gran riesgo con la crítica. "Permítame decirle", dijo, "uno se enfrenta a la comunidad de inteligencia, y a partir del domingo, ellos tienen seis maneras de vengarse. Así que, aun para un hombre de negocios práctico y aparentemente duro, él está siendo muy bobo al hacer esto". Durante la discusión posterior, Schumer dijo, "Por lo que me han dicho, están muy molestos con la manera en que él los ha tratado y la forma en que ha hablado de ellos".[23]

Subsecuentemente, un funcionario de la CIA debatió la afirmación de Trump de que había habido un retraso en enviar el informe y dijo que se había arreglado una reunión para el presidente electo con varios de los funcionarios de alto nivel en la Inteligencia de Nueva York. Trump recibió un informe parcial el martes, como planificado, pero el informe completo no se iba a entregar hasta el viernes, 6 de enero. Tal como reportado por el *Washington Post*, los funcionarios que tomaron parte en esa reunión incluían al director de la Inteligencia Nacional, James Clapper, al director de la CIA, John Brennan, al director del FBI, James Comey, y al director administrativo de la Agencia de Seguridad Nacional (NSA, por sus siglas en inglés), Mike Rogers. Sin embargo, antes de que pudiera tener acceso a la revisión exhaustiva, le dijeron a Trump que el documento tendría que ser revisado por Obama.[24]

El equipo que estaría informando al presidente electo era un grupo notable de personajes, reconocidos por su falta de restricción investigativa. Todos menos uno (el almirante Rogers) que se había visto involucrado en revelaciones sobre el escándalo de los correos electrónicos de Clinton. Un informe de la Oficina del Inspector General indicaba que el director adjunto del FBI, Andrew McCabe, les había mentido a los investigadores federales en lo concerniente a su manejo de la investigación del correo electrónico de Clinton.[25] Los miembros de la comunidad de Inteligencia saltaron en defensa de McCabe; sin embargo, él sería despedido por el fiscal general, Jeff Sessions, el 16 de marzo de 2018, por recomendación del inspector general y la Oficina de Responsabilidad Profesional del FBI.

Pero McCabe no estaba solo. El director del FBI, James Comey, había mentido al Congreso cuando testificó que él no había escrito un informe sobre el escándalo antes de interrogar a Hillary Clinton. El exdirector de la Inteligencia Nacional, James Clapper, y el exdirector de la CIA, John Brennan, ambos mintieron al Congreso. Brennan mintió sobre el espionaje de la CIA al personal del *Senate Intelligence Committee*, y Clapper mintió sobre que la NSA estuviera recolectando información sobre millones de estadounidenses. Los tres disputaron las acusaciones, y en 2015, el *Accountability Board* de la CIA recomendó que Brennan no fuera responsabilizado por las irregularidades.

Brennan ha evitado ser procesado y aparentemente creía que mentir al Congreso por el personal de la CIA era una ofensa excusable, lo que podría explicar su ataque verbal sin provocación al presidente Trump cuando McCabe fue despedido dos días antes de su retiro esperado. No se disputaba el hecho de que McCabe había mentido al Congreso y que probablemente enfrentaría cargos; sin embargo, Brennan atacó al presidente en Twitter, diciendo:

> Cuando se conozca la amplitud de su deshonestidad, bajeza moral y corrupción política, usted tomará su justo lugar en el basurero de la historia como un demagogo avergonzado. Pudo hacer de Andy McCabe un chivo expiatorio, pero no destruirá a Estados Unidos. Estados Unidos triunfará sobre usted.[26]

Nuevamente, el exdirector de la CIA fue raudo en defender a un miembro del círculo interno que había quebrantado la ley repetidamente. Pero hay más en la historia. El republicano de Ohio, Jim Jordan, un miembro de la *House Judiciary Committee*, le dijo a la presentadora de noticias de *Fox News*, Laura Ingraham, "Él no mintió solo una vez; mintió cuatro veces". El congresista dijo: "Él mintió a James Comey, mintió a la Oficina de Responsabilidad Profesional, y le mintió dos veces, estando bajo juramento, al inspector general".[27]

La invectiva de Brennan causó un revuelo breve, pero aún el consejo editorial del *New York Times* percibía la locura de sus comentarios intempestivos. En un editorial anónimo, publicado dos días después del tuit de Brennan, escribieron:

> Las declaraciones como estas pueden ser importantes de hacer y gratificantes de leer, pero realmente no deberían provenir de aquellos cuya integridad depende de que ellos permanezcan fuera de la contienda política, aun en estos tiempos descabellados. Para empezar, ellos facilitan que el Sr. Trump y sus defensores argumenten, como ya lo hacen, que los testigos cruciales en la investigación del consejero especial, Robert Mueller, sobre los posibles vínculos de la campaña de Trump con Rusia estén sesgadas en contra del Presidente.[28]

Allí estaba. La objetividad de los tres funcionarios de alto rango asociados con la investigación en la conspiración rusa con la campaña de Trump se estaba volviendo un asunto preocupante. Schumer había advertido al Presidente sobre el daño que la comunidad de Inteligencia podía causarle a cualquiera que se atreviera a cuestionar sus tácticas. Claramente, la sospecha de Trump sobre la objetividad de los jefes partidarios de la agencias de inteligencia estaba garantizada, y se hizo aún más evidente después de que el seleccionado a fiscal general, Jeff Sessions, se negó a tomar parte en la investigación sobre la influencia rusa.

La recusación de Sessions era sospechosa, pero él dijo que lo había hecho voluntariamente debido a la Regla28 CFR45.2, que establece que el personal del

DOJ no puede participar en una investigación criminal ni en un proceso judicial si tienen una relación personal o política con cualquier persona u organización que pueda estar sujeta a investigación.[29] Ya que él había sido un asesor para la campaña de Trump, pasó la investigación a su substituto, Rod Rosenstein, quien entonces nombró al consejo especial para la investigación.

UN SENDERO DE DEVASTACIÓN

Estaba claro, para cualquiera que estuviera familiarizado con esta red muy cerrada dentro de las agencias, que este era un conflicto de interés enorme y una violación a la misma regla que Sessions había citado para su recusación. El equipo de abogados e investigadores que Mueller reunió está, en su mayoría, formado por demócratas e incluye a muchos colaboradores de Clinton. Uno de los abogados del DOJ ha representado a la *Clinton Foundation*, y otro asistió al evento de Hillary Clinton la noche de las elecciones en Nueva York.

Rosenstein fue el funcionario que recomendó que el presidente Trump quitara a James Comey de su cargo como el director del FBI por el pobre manejo de la investigación de Hillary Clinton, aun así, la mayor parte de la indignación después del despido de Comey calló sobre el Presidente. Rosenstein hizo que pareciera que respaldaba al Presidente, pero, luego, nombró a su amigo cercano, Robert Mueller, como consejero especial para investigar al Presidente y a otros asociados con la campaña Trump.

Mire cómo ninguno de los jefes de agencia estaba interesado en perseguir a Clinton por su mal uso de los documentos secretos del gobierno, por su servidor de correo electrónico no autorizado que había sido comprometido por intrusos rusos y chinos, ni por eliminar más de treinta mil correos; uno de los escándalos más obvios y descarados en la historia de Estados Unidos. Sin embargo, ir tras el presidente electo, basándose en un documento salaz pagado por la campaña de Clinton y un grupo de partidarios con mucho dinero, no mencionados, era otro tema. ¿Debería alguien estar preocupado?

El congresista, Louie Gohmert, exjefe de justicia del *Twelfth Circuit Court of Appeals*, dejó claro que él está preocupado. En abril de 2018, publicó un informe detallado de cuarenta y ocho páginas, titulado: *"Robert Mueller: Unmasked"*, el cual detalla la "historia larga y despreciable de seleccionar personas inocentes ilegalmente". En el informe, Gohmert dice que el asesor especial "carece de juicio y credibilidad para dirigir la acusación de alguien". Gohmer añade que todo el que examine el registro de Mueller en el FBI será confrontado por un padrón largamente establecido de condena a personas inocentes, forzándolas a ir a la bancarrota al elevar sus costas legales.[30]

Uno de los trucos favoritos de Mueller, dice Gohmert, es ir tras la familia de sus objetivos, amenazándolos con acusarlos y forzando a las personas que son su objetivo a que se declaren culpables para proteger a los miembros de su familia. Esto es posiblemente cómo el FBI pudo obligar a confesar al exconsejero de seguridad nacional, el teniente general Michael Flynn por mentirle al FBI. Flynn no había quebrantado ninguna ley, pero al perseguir al hijo de Flynn, Mueller atrapó a su presa y disfrutó los elogios de los medios liberales.

En 2003, el entonces fiscal general adjunto, James Comey, convenció al fiscal general, John Ashcroft, a quien yo entrevisté muchas veces cuando era gobernador de Missouri y senador estadounidense de Missouri, a excusarse de la investigación en la filtración de recursos que revelaban la identidad de la agente de la CIA, Valerie Plame. Comey nombró al exabogado estadounidense Patrick Fitzgerald, el padrino de uno de los hijos de Comey, como consejero especial. Mueller, Comey y Fitzgerald supieron al principio de la investigación que el secretario de estado adjunto, Richard Armitage, era la persona que había filtrado la identidad de Plame, pero ellos no estaban interesados en Armitage. Ellos querían ya sea al vicepresidente, Dick Cheney o al consejero de Bush, Karl Rove.

Al final, se conformaron con el jefe de personal de Cheney, Lewis "Scooter" Libby. Le ofrecieron a Libby una oportunidad de cambiar con su jefe, pero cuando él se negó, fue acusado, enjuiciado y condenado en 2007 por perjurio y obstrucción de la justicia. Ese fue otro ejemplo de hasta dónde los partidarios defensores de la ley y el orden llegarían para destruir a un hombre inocente. Ocho años después de la condena de Libby, Judith Miller, la reportera del *New York Times*, cuyo testimonió fue instrumental para la condena de Libby, se retractó de su historia. George W. Bush había reducido la sentencia de Libby y el 13 de abril de 2018, el presidente Trump lo perdonó, diciendo: "Yo no conozco al Sr. Libby, pero durante años he escuchado que ha sido tratado injustamente. Espero que este perdón completo le ayude a enmendar una parte muy triste de su vida".[31]

El mismo tipo de acusación fue usado contra el senador de Alaska, Ted Stevens. El senador, quien había representado fielmente a su estado desde 1968, fue acusado por el Departamento de Justicia en 2008 con cargos falsos relacionados al pago de una cabaña rural. "Uno pensaría que antes de que el gobierno de Estados Unidos procurara destruir a un Senador estadounidense en funciones", dijo Ghomert, "no habría duda alguna de su culpabilidad. Uno estaría completamente equivocado si pensara así cuando el director del FBI es Robert Mueller".[32]

Durante el debate congresal sobre la controversial propuesta de ley de *Obamacare* durante la administración Obama, Stevens, el senador que más tiempo se ha desempeñado en la historia de Estados Unidos, dejó saber que él votaría contra la propuesta de ley. Ese voto podría ser la diferencia entre si la propuesta pasaba o no. Sin embargo, la acusación del FBI, basada en testimonio fraudulento, se aseguró de que el voto de Stevens no fuera contado.

Mucho después, una investigación independiente descubrió que el enjuiciamiento contra el senador Stevens estaba "impregnado por el ocultamiento sistémico de evidencias exculpatorias significativas, lo que fue corroborado independientemente por la defensa del senador Stevens y su testimonio, y que dañó seriamente el testimonio y la credibilidad" del testigo colaborador del FBI.[33] Se demostró que, en vez de mentir sobre los pagos de su cabaña, Stevens en realidad había pagado un 20 por ciento demás.

"Alguien debería haber ido a la cárcel por esta ilegalidad dentro de la agencia principal de la nación en cuanto al cumplimiento de la ley", escribe Gohmert. "En cambio, el senador Stevens perdió su curul, y sorpresa, sorpresa, el FBI de Mueller ayudó a otro republicano electo a caer en la trampa".[34] El senador Stevens fue exonerado y devuelto a su vida civil, pero murió trágicamente en un accidente aéreo en agosto 2010.

El informe de Gohmert ofrece un listado largo y perturbador de la actividad ilícita y la manipulación del sistema de justicia por parte de Mueller, Comey y sus equipos investigadores. La destrucción del congresista de Pennsylvania, Curt Weldon es otro ejemplo de ellas. Durante los resultados de los ataques terroristas del 11 de septiembre, el representante Weldon se atrevió a señalar que el FBI había ignorado la evidencia de la investigación de Able Danger, que advertía que una célula de Al Qaeda que incluía a Mohammed Atta había sido identificada. Bajo el liderazgo de Mueller, el FBI eligió ignorar la evidencia que pudo haber evitado esa tragedia nacional.

Pero aquí, nuevamente, la advertencia de Chuck Schumer para el Presidente entra en juego. En la mañana del 16 de octubre de 2005, las cámaras de los noticieros televisados capturaron la redada del FBI a la casa de la hija de Weldon, supuestamente para ver si Weldon había ayudado a su hija a ganar inapropiadamente contratos de consultoría. Fue un espectáculo manipulado para un impacto máximo. "La redada temprano en la mañana por el FBI de Mueller con todos los medios afuera, obviamente alertados por el FBI, había logrado su propósito de conspiración para abusar el sistema de justicia federal y silencia a Curt Weldon al acabar con su carrera política. El FBI de Mueller funcionó de maravilla".[35]

Estas y otras revelaciones proveen una imagen devastadora del abuso de autoridad del asesor especial durante muchos años y hace que surjan preguntas importantes sobre los motivos, tácticas y objetivos de los individuos y grupos presionando duramente por la investigación de la conspiración rusa. "La gente dice que ese tipo de cosas simplemente no suceden en Estados Unidos", escribe Gohmert. "Ellos definitivamente parecían que sí cuando Mueller estaba cargo del FBI, y ciertamente también parecen serlo mientras él se Asesor Especial".[36]

El inminente choque de trenes

El columnista e historiador Victor Davis Hanson ha escrito extensivamente sobre el teatro político que rodea la eterna investigación de la conspiración rusa y pronosticó en abril 2018 que la nación estaba por atestiguar un choque de trenes. Viniendo de un lado, dijo, está la investigación de Robert Mueller, en busca de cualquier cosa concebible para dañar o destruir la presidencia de Donald Trump. Del otro lado, viene una serie de investigaciones del Congreso, referencias del Departamento de Justicia, e informes del inspector general centrados en el comportamiento impropio o ilegal del FBI y DOJ durante las elecciones 2016. Ambas máquinas locomotoras de alto poder están corriendo a toda velocidad dirigiéndose hacia una colisión dramática.

"¿Por qué están a punto de chocar?", pregunta Hanson. "Por haber presentado cargos contra el consejero de seguridad nacional Michael Flynn por haber mentido al FBI, Mueller enfatizó que aun la apariencia de falso testimonio es un comportamiento delictivo. Si así fuera, entonces el DOJ probablemente tendrá que presentar cargos contra el exdirector adjunto del FBI, Andrew McCabe, por perjurio o faltas relacionadas".[37] Según Hanson:

> El exdirector del FBI, James Comey, también pudo haber mentido al Congreso cuando testificó que él no había escrito su reporte sobre el escándalo del correo electrónico de Hillary Clinton antes de interrogarla. El exdirector de Inteligencia Nacional, James Clapper y el exdirector de la CIA, John Brennan, mintieron estando bajo juramento al Congreso sobre asuntos relacionados con la vigilancia. Las asesoras de Clinton, Cheryl Mills y Huma Abedin posiblemente mintieron cuando les dijeron a los investigadores del FBI que no tenían ni idea de que su jefa en aquel entonces, Hillary Clinton, estaba usando un servidor de correo electrónico privado ilegal para la correspondencia oficial. Ambas se habían comunicado con Clinton al respecto.[38]

Por lo menos en cuatro ocasiones, escribe Hanson, los funcionarios del FBI y el Departamento de Justicia engañaron a la gente al decir que el expediente ruso recopilado por el espía británico, Christopher Steele, era la fuente de información utilizada en las solicitudes a la *Foreign Intelligence Surveillance Court*. El Asesor Especial aún está revisando la posibilidad de la conspiración con Rusia. Pero, si el objetivo del FBI es descubrir y procesar la conspiración, el Departamento de Justicia tendrá que analizar más detenidamente la campaña de Clinton, que le pagó a Christopher Steele para desenterrar tanta suciedad como fuera posible encontrar en la campaña de Trump para producir evidencia de interferencia rusa.

Si cuando la conspiración venga, los socorristas tendrán que hacer mucha limpieza de emergencia. Mientras este libro va a impresión, el exgerente de la campaña de Trump, Paul Manafort, ha sido condenado por ocho cargos de fraude financiero. Un jurado no pudo llegar a un veredicto sobre otros diez cargos, y el juez declaró juicio nulo sobre dichos cargos. Sin embargo, tal como escribió el columnista Jed Babbin en el *American Spectator*, mientras Manafort era todavía "un testigo colaborador" en la investigación de Mueller, fue sorprendido por una redada previa en su casa por orden de Mueller: "una táctica dura", dice Babbin, "normalmente reservada para los asesinos en serie, traficantes de drogas y jefes de la mafia que podrían destruir la evidencia".[39]

Los abogados de Manafort insistieron en que los cargos relacionados al fraude bancario y otros asuntos deberían ser retirados porque estaban fuera de la autoridad que se le otorgó a Mueller para investigar la evidencia de conspiración. Mueller logró acusar y condenar al teniente general Flynn por mentirle a los agentes federales a pesar del hecho de que, como lo reveló la *House Permanent Select Committe on Intelligence*, Comey, el exdirector del FBI, testificó que los agentes del FBI que interrogaron a Flynn no vieron evidencia de que él estuviera mintiendo. Después de eso, otros dos oficiales menores de la campaña de Trump, Rick Gates y George Papadopoulos, se declararon culpables de mentirles a los investigadores, y varios cargos más fueron presentados.

Tres condenas, todas por delitos procesales y ninguna de ellas relacionada con el asunto de la conspiración rusa. Pero para demostrar que no había olvidado el porqué de su contratación, Mueller acusó a tres empresas rusas y a trece ciudadanos rusos, exigiéndoles que se presentaran para interrogarlos. Obviamente, esto fue un truco publicitario. Los abogados del DOJ sabían que el gobierno ruso nunca presentaría acusaciones de una corte de Estados Unidos a sus ciudadanos, pero Mueller y compañía fueron tomados por sorpresa cuando una de las empresas rusas, *Concord Management and Consulting*, decidió comparecer ante la corte para responder a los cargos. Cuando recibieron la noticia, los abogados del DOJ solicitaron una demora para poder construir un caso, pero el juez Dabney Friedrich, del *US District Court*, negó la solicitud y programó una audiencia para el miércoles siguiente. En una audiencia sobre el caso de Paul Manafort, el juez T.S. Ellis III, de la *US District Court*, amonestó a los abogados del gobierno diciéndoles algo que muchos estadounidenses habían estado pensando desde hace algún tiempo.

El juez Ellis dijo que la descripción del caso que dieron los abogados del DOJ era falsa y que equivalía a: "Dijimos de qué se trataba esta investigación, pero no estamos obligados legalmente y estamos mintiendo". Él añadió: "A ustedes no les importa verdaderamente el Sr. Manafort. Lo que realmente les importa es qué información puede darles el Sr. Manafort que los guíe al Sr. Trump y a una destitución o cualquier otra cosa".[40] El equipo del DOJ fue sorprendido, pero no disuadido por el desplante.

Aunque estos contratiempos pueden no haber estropeado la investigación, sí levantaron dudas sobre la fortaleza del caso de Mueller. Dada la preocupación creciente y el escrutinio del trabajo de Mueller, tal como lo señala *Politico*, "incluso los contratiempos pequeños son buenas noticias para una Casa Blanca que está en busca de evidencia de que la investigación de Rusia ha llegado demasiado lejos".[41] Antes de la condena de Manafort, dos jueces federales cuestionaron la autoridad de Mueller para presentar cargos sobre asuntos no relacionados con las elecciones presidenciales, incluyendo las denuncias contra Manafot. En respuesta a las acciones honestas y alentadoras de los jueces federales, Trump tuiteó:

> Los 13 demócratas enojados a cargo de la cacería de brujas rusa están empezando a descubrir que hay un sistema de tribunales que verdaderamente protege de las injusticias a la gente.[42]

El número trece en el tuit del presidente se refiere a trece de los diecisiete miembros del equipo de Mueller que son demócratas registrados.[43]

La lucha interminable

Con cargos de conspiración, mentira y manipulación de ambos lados, así como el uso de tácticas Orwellian por parte del FBI para forzar las confesiones de los oficiales de la campaña de Trump, no es de extrañar que muchos hayan expresado su preocupación sobre la existencia de una entidad burocrática funcionando tras bambalinas en la capital de la nación. Según una encuesta de marzo 2018, hecha por la *Monmouth University*, más del 70 por ciento de los estadounidenses, de ambos partidos políticos, cree que un "subgobierno" de funcionarios de gobierno no electos controla el gobierno.[44]

Aunque muchos de los encuestados no estaban familiarizados con el término *estado profundo* al principio, cuando se les dio la definición: "Un grupo no electo de funcionarios de gobierno y militares que manipula o dirige secretamente la política nacional", la mayoría de ellos creen que tal institución sí existe. Además, el 60 por ciento dijo que cree que los burócratas no electos tienen demasiado poder en lo que se refiere a formar la política de gobierno.[45]

Al comentar sobre los resultados, Patrick Murray, el director del *Monmouth University Polling Institute*, dijo: "Generalmente esperamos que las opiniones sobre la operación del gobierno cambien dependiendo de qué partido esté a cargo. Pero hay un sentimiento amenazante, tanto en los demócratas como en los republicanos, de que un 'subgobierno' de operativos no electos están controlando el poder".[46] El presidente Trump usó el término en un tuit, de enero 2018, acusando al "subgobierno" Departamento de Justicia de escudar a la asistente de Hillary Clinton, Huma Abedin, que utilizó una cuenta de correo privada, no segura, mientras realizaba asuntos gubernamentales.

> La asistente principal de la corrupta Hillary Clinton, Huma Abedin, ha sido acusada de ignorar los protocolos básicos de seguridad. Ella puso las contraseñas clasificadas en manos de agentes

extranjeros. ¿Recuerdan las fotografías de los marineros en el submarino? ¡Cárcel! ¿El subgobierno, el Departamento de Justicia tiene que actuar finalmente? También sobre Comey y los otros.[47]

La encuesta de Monmouth también resaltó temores de vigilancia gubernamental, con el 82 por ciento de los encuestados que cree que el gobierno espía activamente a los ciudadanos privados. "Este es un hallazgo preocupante", dijo el director de la encuesta. "La fortaleza de nuestro gobierno descansa sobre la fe pública en la protección de nuestras libertades, que no es particularmente sólida. Y no es un asunto demócrata o republicano. Estas preocupaciones abarcan todo el espectro político".[48]

Cuando el denunciante de la CIA, Edward Snowden, reveló la existencia de un programa de vigilancia masivo, dirigido por la NSA y otras agencias aún más clandestinas, tales como la sede de comunicaciones del gobierno del Reino Unido, la nación fue advertida del hecho de que todo estadounidense está potencialmente vulnerable al espionaje del gobierno. Entonces, millones de personas se dieron cuenta de que no hay manera segura de proteger información privada y confidencial o de evitar que las computadoras de la casa y de la oficina sean intervenidas ilegalmente por organizaciones secretas trabajando bajo la cubierta de la oscuridad. Snowden reveló que la NSA estaba espiando a docenas de millones de estadounidenses, recolectando registros telefónicos y de la internet. Luego, nos enteramos de que Facebook, Google, Yahoo, Instagram, Twitter y una gran cantidad de sitios web de medios sociales estaban haciendo lo mismo y vendiendo la información que reunían.

Durante una reunión privada en su estado natal de Pensilvania, el representante Mike Kelly le dijo a un grupo de partidarios y amigos que estaba preocupado de que el expresidente se hubiera instalado en DC no solo para que su hija menor, Sasha, pudiera graduarse de la escuela secundaria, sino para administrar la operación para desacreditar y destrozar al presidente Trump. "El propio presidente Obama dijo que iba a permanecer en Washington hasta que se graduara su hija", dijo Kelly. "Yo creo que deberíamos colaborar para que él se vaya a otro lado porque está allí con un solo propósito y es el de dirigir un gobierno paralelo que va a alterar totalmente la nueva agenda".[49]

Cuando el video de esa reunión fue proporcionado secretamente a los medios de comunicación, la oficina de Kelly fue asediada con preguntas. En la respuesta oficial, su personal dijo que el congresista no cree que Obama esté dirigiendo "personalmente" un gobierno paralelo. Sin embargo, dijeron, "él sí cree que sería útil para la nueva administración si el expresidente exigiera personalmente que se terminen todas las filtraciones y la obstrucción por parte del personal de su administración que actualmente se desempeña en el poder ejecutivo bajo el presidente Trump". La declaración señaló que Kelly había hecho sus comentarios ante una audiencia de republicanos privada, y que él estaba "compartiendo la frustración de todos los que estaban en el salón sobre cómo creen que ciertos remanentes de la administración de Obama, que están dentro de la burocracia federal, están intentando alterar la agenda del presidente Trump".[50]

Preocupaciones legítimas

Como lo señaló la publicación de DC, *The Hill*, Kelly no es el único en sospechar que los remanentes de Obama estén amenazando la agenda de Trump. El entonces secretario de prensa de la Casa Blanca, Sean Spicer, dijo que es razonable creer que algunos empleados federales puedan estar tratando de continuar con la agenda de Obama. "Yo creo que no hay duda de que, cuando uno tiene ocho años de un partido en el cargo, haya personas que permanecieron en el gobierno, que están asociadas con la agenda de la administración anterior y continúan apoyándola". Durante su información diaria a la prensa, Spicer dijo: "No creo que deba sorprendernos que haya personas que se incrustaron en el gobierno durante los ocho años de la última administración y que hayan creído en esa agenda y quieran continuar procurándola".[51]

Durante una entrevista en febrero 2017, con CNN, el representante de Kentucky, Thomas Massie, dijo que él cree que el estado profundo, controlado por una red de individuos en la burocracia permanente, es una amenaza legítima para la nación. Él no está de acuerdo con quienes creen que exista una alianza de exfuncionarios de la administración Obama tratando de debilitar a la administración Trump, pero dijo que el estado profundo es una preocupación legítima. Obama no es la fuente del movimiento del estado profundo, dijo, sino que él ha sido integrado a él y usado para cumplir sus propósitos mientras estaba en el cargo.[52]

Cuando le preguntaron sobre su preocupación principal, Massie dijo: "Me preocupa que sea algo más profundo que eso. Estoy preocupado de que sea un esfuerzo de parte de quienes quieren una provocación con Rusia u otros países para tratar de forzar al Presidente en una dirección. Así que no creo que sea Trump vs. Obama; creo que en realidad es el subgobierno vs. el Presidente".[53]

En un comentario publicado un año después de la investidura del presidente Trump, el escritor político de *Newsweek*, Sam Schwarz, predijo que, si Trump y el Partido Republicano planeaban defender sus mayorías en la Cámara y en el Senado en las votaciones a mitad de legislatura de 2018, tendrían que competir contra un factor mayor: Barack Obama. "El expresidente disfrutó de un año ocupado desde que salió de la Casa Blanca, pero se ha mantenido en gran parte bajo el radar", escribió Schwartz. "Sin embargo, él siempre sostuvo que nunca dejaría la política". Antes de que terminara su mandato, Obama dijo que estaría políticamente activo, trabajando con candidatos que procuraran preservar su legado y sus logros".[54]

Obama criticó las políticas de Trump en varias ocasiones en 2017, especialmente en lo relacionado a temas como los esfuerzos para derogar *Obamacare* y deportar a los *Dreamers*. También criticó a Trump por su decisión de retirarse del Acuerdo de París. Durante la mayor parte de 2017, la popularidad del expresidente entre su electorado principal permanecía alta. Una encuesta de septiembre del 2017 mostró que el 52 por ciento de los encuestados deseaba que Obama estuviera todavía en el cargo.[55]

Si escuché el término *estado profundo* antes del 2016, no lo recuerdo. Pero en mis pocos tratos con Washington, a los largo de los años, empecé a tener una sensación de que algo estaba sucediendo tras bastidores porque no hubo mucho cambio cuando el otro partido político obtuvo el control de la Casa Blanca o el Congreso. *Aparentemente*, muchos estadounidenses se sentían de la misma forma, si una encuesta de la *Monmouth* University es correcta, porque más del 80 por ciento de los estadounidenses tienen un temor legítimo de lo que el estado profundo pueda estar haciendo para debilitar e interferir en la manera en que Washington funciona. Si ese fuera el caso, Trump y los republicanos podrían tener mucho más de qué preocuparse que solo la aparición del expresidente en el recorrido de la campaña. Hay un patrón para todo esto y un sendero que lleva a la Casa Blanca, al Departamento de Justicia, al Departamento de Estado y a los corredores del Congreso. Si Victor Davis Hanson tiene razón sobre las dos fuerzas imparables acercándose en direcciones opuestas, hay un choque de trenes en el horizonte, y solo Dios sabe a dónde puede llevar eso.

Con todas estas fuerzas malévolas locales y extranjeras, el presidente Trump tiene su trabajo definido. Sin embargo, él no es de los que se encojen de hombros cuando se trata de enfrentar situaciones difíciles. Tal como lo veremos en la siguiente sección, él monta una defensa fuerte.

TERCERA PARTE

UNA DEFENSA FUERTE

ESTADOS UNIDOS EN GUERRA (CONTRA SÍ MISMO)

L A ELECCIÓN DE Donald Trump no causó la división política y social que está desgarrando a Estados Unidos. Las fuerzas alineadas a la derecha y a la izquierda ya lo estaban haciendo mucho antes de que Trump u Obama o George W. Bush entraran en la arena política. Sin embargo, el conflicto ha explotado desde que la victoria de Trump y la derrota de Hillary Clinton sacó a luz el abismo que nos divide más dramáticamente que cualquier evento en los últimos 150 años.

Los estadounidenses difícilmente se acuerdan del eslogan que adorna nuestra moneda: "E Pluribus Unum". Recuerdo haber enseñado esta frase en latín en una escuela como ejemplo de los sueños de unidad nacional que hicieron nacer la idea de "De muchos, uno". Hoy día, esos sueños casi han desaparecido. El eslogan que una vez celebró el nacimiento de una república nueva, construida sobre intereses mutuos y nuestra herencia común, junto con una devoción casi universal a la fe, la familia y la libertad. Pero ese vínculo ya no existe. En cambio, estamos involucrados en una disputa amarga sobre valores y creencias fundamentales. ¿Quiénes somos y qué representamos? Las generaciones de estadounidenses ya no parecen saberlo.

Raras veces escuchamos sobre la guerra cultural que dominaba los titulares hace unos años. Aparentemente, ya pasamos ese punto; y la cultura común está en un estado de decadencia avanzada, siendo desgarrados de adentro hacia afuera. El eslogan nacional: "En Dios confiamos", que aparece no solo en nuestra moneda, sino en las paredes de los juzgados y monumentos de todo tipo, se ha convertido una fuente de controversia. Estamos envueltos en una batalla sobre creencias fundamentales y convicciones morales, y el resultado de esta lucha de varias décadas es una polarización peligrosa de la sociedad entre extremos políticos. Hay muy poco terreno en el medio. En cada manera concebible, somos una nación dividida, la cual veo no solo en términos políticos, sino en términos de aspecto espiritual, lo cual trataré más adelante.

El énfasis sobre el globalismo promovido por élites académicas y políticas es un repudio bien demarcado de la cultura común. El concepto de sociedad abierta es el enemigo de la nación estado. Significa derrumbar las fronteras y rechazar las leyes y las costumbres que han mantenido a salvo a Estados Unidos y lo han hecho una nación única. En vez de celebrar nuestros logros históricos, estamos siendo presionados para ir más lejos y más profundo en nuestra cultura relativista, caos social y el gobierno de burócratas no electos.

La lucha dista mucho de haber terminado, claro está, y la elección de Trump ha traído un brote de entusiasmo refrescante para los principios e ideales conservadores. Pero gracias al apoyo incansable de los medios por la ideología y las tácticas de la Izquierda, los valores y la jurisprudencia tradicionales de la civilización occidental están recibiendo una paliza. Los monumentos de nuestra historia colectiva están siendo derribados y removidos, mientras que los defensores de instituciones y tradiciones establecidas están siendo catalogados como intolerantes, racistas, homófobos y cosas peores. Bajo la tiranía de lo políticamente correcto, la libertad de expresión es virtualmente imposible, la libertad de culto está amenazada y las conversaciones diarias pueden ser riesgosas y, a veces, hasta letales.

Durante siglos, hombres y mujeres de todo continente, toda raza y todo trasfondo socioeconómico llegaron a este país para escapar de la segregación; sin embargo, el liberalismo moderno ha logrado regresar el debate a la raza, clase, género e identidad de grupo. Como resultado, Estados Unidos se está fragmentando en una colección de campos de batalla. Los comportamientos peligrosos y antisociales son aceptados, y hasta elogiados, por los medios liberales. Aquellos que gritan más fuerte acerca del odio y la intolerancia son, muchas veces, los más odiosos e intolerantes, usando el lenguaje como arma de guerra y atacando los pocos fragmentos que quedan del orden social.

Una encuesta del *American Culture and Faith Institute* ofrece un vistazo informativo a la profundidad de la división. En una entrevista sobre el estudio, George Barna discutió cómo algunos estadounidenses tienen temor de hablar abiertamente sobre su amor al país o de discutir sus puntos de vista políticos públicamente.[1] Portar una gorra de beisbol que hace una declaración política, tal como "Hacer a Estados Unidos grande otra vez", puede empezar una revuelta. Las etiquetas adhesivas en los parachoques se han convertido en una invitación abierta para el vandalismo. Las empresas como Starbucks, Target, Chick-fil-A, y Hobby Lobby están repentinamente en el centro de la controversia debido a las políticas y valores sociales a las que están suscritas. Y al permitir que los jugadores de futbol americano expresen su desprecio por la nación y la bandera, el emblema más visible de nuestro orgullo nacional, la *National Football League* ha hecho de sí misma un saco de boxeo tanto para la Derecha como para la Izquierda.

LOS NÚMEROS REVELAN MUCHO

La encuesta nacional del *American Culture and Faith Institute* llevada a cabo en octubre y noviembre 2017 descubrió dos definiciones de patriotismo impresionantemente distintas en Estados Unidos del presente. Hay una confusión generalizada, dice la encuesta, acerca de lo que significa ser patriota. Según Anne Sorock, directora ejecutiva de *Ear to the Ground Listening Project*:

> Los hallazgos revelan una fisura en nuestra cultura, las oportunidades para reunirse alrededor del patriotismo como un valor compartido, y también, las preocupaciones acerca de las definiciones fluidas. Estas sugieren que estamos más divididos que nunca, y ni la Izquierda ni la Derecha están conformes de ceder el patriotismo al otro.[2]

Si bien la mayoría de los estadounidenses cree que el país se está volviendo menos patriótico, tienden a creer que las otras personas son el problema: ellos están bien, dicen, pero sus vecinos no son patriotas, lo que podría explicar por qué solo el 22 por ciento de los encuestados dice sentir fuertemente que estaría seguro al portar una gorra de "Hacer a Estados Unidos grande otra vez".[3] Esta es la manera en que la gente respondió cuando se le preguntó si el patriotismo estaba aumentando en Estados Unidos:

PATRIOTISMO DEL PAÍS

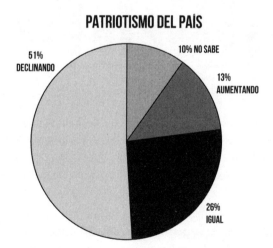

51% DECLINANDO

10% NO SABE

13% AUMENTANDO

26% IGUAL

Casi la mitad de los encuestados (46 por ciento) dijo que sería exacto describirse como "orgulloso de ser estadounidense". Así es como eso se divide entre conservadores, republicanos, moderados, independientes, liberales y demócratas:

ORGULLOSO DE SER ESTADOUNIDENSE

En general, la "libertad de expresión" demostró ser el indicador más significativo del nivel de patriotismo entre los encuestados, con casi nueve de cada diez adultos (87 por ciento) diciendo que, para ellos, en lo personal, era muy significativo. Como es de esperar, el partido y la ideología política marcan la diferencia en lo que es importante para los diferentes grupos. Según los analistas: "Los demócratas y los independientes tuvieron niveles similares y significativamente más bajos de apreciación por la bandera estadounidense, el himno nacional, el juramento de lealtad, la Biblia y el derecho a portar armas",[4] tal como lo ilustra la siguiente gráfica:

SIGNIFICATIVIDAD DE LOS TEMAS PATRIÓTICOS

Según la encuesta, los conservadores dicen que las organizaciones y los individuos más patrióticos incluyen a: la *National Rifle Association*, Chick-fil-A, el Partido Republicano, *Fox News*, y Hobby Lobby. Las organizaciones menos patrióticas según la mayoría de los conservadores son: CNN, el *New York Times*, la NFL, *Planned Parenthood*, Target y Starbucks. Solo entre el 6 y el 9 por ciento de los conservadores consideraron a Colin Kaepernick, Michael Moore, Rachel Maddow, y Al Sharpton como personas patrióticas.

Por otro lado, los liberales indicaron que las instituciones y las personas más patrióticas son: el Partido Demócrata, Kaepernick, la Corte Suprema de Estados Unidos, *Planned Parenthood*, Moore, el *New York Times*, y la NFL. Y, como era de esperarse, los menos patriotas para los liberales son Chick-fil-A, *Fox News*, y Hobby Lobby.

Para el organizador de encuestas George Barna, "la controversia de la NFL 'doblar una rodilla' era un punto crítico cultural demandando a la ciudadanía y a los líderes a tomar una posición".[5] La encuesta mostró que los conservadores están ofendidos por la NFL, en tanto los liberales están emocionados por la valentía de los que están adoptando una postura. "Trump hizo lo correcto al intervenir", dice Barna, "como líderes electos tienen la responsabilidad de darle sentido a la realidad que se desenvuelve a su alrededor".[6]

El noventa y uno por ciento de los conservadores religiosos, políticamente activos, fue a votar en las elecciones presidenciales en 2016, y el 93 por ciento de ese grupo dijo que votó por Trump. Quizá más revelador es el hecho de que solamente el 9 por ciento de los conservadores religiosos, políticamente activos apoyaban a Trump en junio de 2015; sin embargo, el 93 por ciento de ellos votó por él en noviembre de 2016. Barna dice que también es interesante observar que mientras el 58 por ciento de todos los estadounidenses votó, todo un 91 por ciento de los votantes basados en la fe votaron. Aunque muchos indicaron que aún no eran grandes admiradores del presidente Trump, estaban llegando a estar más cómodos con él en algunos temas, incluyendo sus restricciones sobre el aborto y el nombramiento de jueces constitucionalistas.[7]

Conozco a Barna desde hace muchos años. No puedo pensar en un líder cristiano de alto perfil que haya escrito más sobre cosmovisión que él. Barna cree que la cosmovisión de una persona es la única consideración más importante al evaluar a los prospectos para el futuro de la nación; sin embargo, los debates acalorados sobre las cosmovisiones y las opiniones básicas sociales y políticas están separando a nuestro país. Como sociólogo, Barna concluye que las actitudes acerca de Dios, religión y el papel de la fe en nuestra vida diaria son los indicadores más confiables de la capacidad de los estadounidenses para sobrevivir y progresar como una nación.

Los liberales y sus políticas progresistas han estado librando una guerra cultural y lingüística en nuestras escuelas, iglesias, familia, los medios y el gobierno durante décadas. Los liberales encuestados en la encuesta de Barna dijeron que la libertad de expresión es muy importante para ellos, aun así, hay una intolerancia creciente dentro del debate civil, y los liberales son los que más fácilmente se ofenden por los puntos de vista que difieren de los propios. "Los marxistas culturales han estado ganando (en nuestras instituciones y cultura)", dice Barna, "pero la batalla no ha terminado". Barna, quien ha estado llevando a cabo encuestas sobre la opinión nacional pública desde la década de los setentas, siente que el debate cultural hoy día está más encendido que nunca, razón por la cual fundamos el *American Culture and Faith Institute* para concentrarnos en lo que puede hacerse para cambiar las cosas.[8]

Durante más de dos décadas ya, la polarización política ha sido una de las fuerzas más poderosas en el discurso político dominante. Según las encuestas conducidas por el *Pew Research Center*, en junio y julio de 2017, los republicanos y demócratas están mucho más fuertemente divididos sobre los temas como el papel del gobierno, el medio ambiente, la raza, la inmigración que sobre demografía, religiosidad y diferencias educacionales. Sin embargo, lo que encuentran más sorprendente, dicen los analistas, es cuán pocos puntos en común hay en los dos lados opuestos.

Parte de la razón para el cambio, dicen, es que los demócratas inscritos se han movido cada vez más lejos hacia la Izquierda sobre temas clave, mientras que los puntos de vista de los republicanos y los que tienen inclinación republicana se han cambiado muy poco desde mediados de la década de los noventas. Los cambios más grandes en varios años anteriores han sido los puntos de vista en relación con la raza y el papel del gobierno de los demócratas y los independientes con inclinación demócrata; los analistas sienten que eso explica por qué los puntos de vista expresados por el público en general han tomado una postura más liberal. Según sus hallazgos:

> En el nuevo estudio (llevado a cabo antes de las manifestaciones violentas en Charlottesville, Virginia, y las protestas recientes por parte de los jugadores de la NFL), el 41% de los estadounidenses opinan que la discriminación racial es la razón principal por la que los negros no pueden salir adelante, hasta un 18% en 2009, y el nivel más alto remontándose a 1994. Virtualmente todo el cambio ha venido de entre los demócratas, con un récord de 64% diciendo que la discriminación racial es la barrera principal para que los negros salgan adelante. Entre los republicanos y los de inclinación republicana ha habido menos cambio desde 2009 (9% en ese entonces, 14% en el presente). La brecha entre partidarios se está ampliando sobre cuánto debe hacer el gobierno para ayudar al necesitado. La mitad de los estadounidenses hoy día dicen que el gobierno debería hacer más para ayudar al necesitado, incluso si eso significara endeudarse más, mientras que el 43 por ciento dice que el gobierno no puede pagarlo. Este cambio hacia más apoyo para el necesitado está siendo conducido por el 71 por ciento de los demócratas que expresó este punto de vista, un incremento dramático desde el 2011. Solo casi una cuarta parte (24 por ciento) de los republicanos está de acuerdo.[9]

Los encuestadores hallaron, además, que los demócratas están ahora más propensos a favorecer un rol global activo para Estados Unidos, mientras que hace tres años los republicanos y los demócratas se sentían igualmente escépticos sobre que Estados Unidos jugara un papel activo en los asuntos mundiales. Si bien el 54 por ciento de los republicanos dijo que Estados Unidos debería prestarles menos atención a los problemas extranjeros y enfocarse más en los locales, una mayoría de demócratas (56 por ciento) dijo que el país debería estar mundialmente activo, lo que subió del 38 por ciento en una encuesta similar en 2014.[10]

La encuesta también indica que la aceptación del homosexualismo está en los niveles más altos hoy día. Setenta por ciento de los encuestados están de acuerdo en que el homosexualismo debería ser aceptado. Este es el porcentaje más alto en más de veinte años y la primera vez que tanto demócratas (83 por ciento) y republicanos (54 por ciento) favorecen la aceptación del homosexualismo.[11]

Brecha partidaria más amplia sobre el trabajo de Trump que sobre cualquier presidente en seis décadas [12]

% de aprobación del trabajo del Presidente durante el primer año

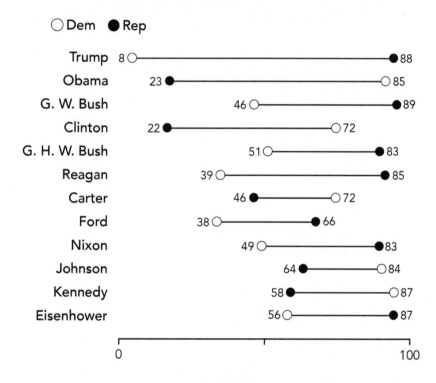

Basado en las encuestas conducidas por el *Pew Center* en la primera mitad de 2017, los índices por el trabajo del presidente Trump en el primer año están más polarizados que con cualquier otro presidente remontándose a 1953, tal como lo revela la gráfica. Generalmente hablando, podemos ver una tendencia a la baja en los índices de aprobación para el presidente de cualquier partido que no esté en la Oficina Oval.[13] Incluso después de toda la controversia alrededor de la cumbre de Helsinki en julio 2018 con Vladimir Putin, el índice de aprobación de Trump subió según una entrevista de NBC News/*Wall Street Journal*.[14]

DOS MUNDOS DISTINTOS

Puede ser que no haya un indicador más grande de la disparidad entre la Izquierda y la Derecha en Estados Unidos hoy día que la comparación entre las actitudes demócratas y republicanas hacia los valores tradicionales y la fe religiosa. Según una encuesta de NBC News/*Wall Street Journal* de septiembre de 2017, las fisuras entre republicanos y demócratas sobre temas culturales, tales como: matrimonio entre personas del mismo sexo y religión se han vuelto consistentemente más amplias a lo largo de los últimos años. Al menos un 77 por ciento de los demócratas, dijo, estar "cómodos con los cambios sociales" de los años recientes; mientras que solo un 30 por ciento de republicanos siente lo mismo. Cuarenta y dos por ciento de los republicanos encuestados apoyan la definición tradicional del matrimonio entre un hombre y una mujer, mientras que solo el 17 por ciento de los demócratas está de acuerdo. Y, en caso de que alguien se lo estuviera preguntando, los resultados demócratas fueron probablemente el doble de los republicanos al decir que nunca han asistido a un servicio eclesiástico.[15]

Según un análisis del *Wall Street Journal*, las divisiones en Estados Unidos "llegan mucho más allá de Washington a la cultura, la economía y el entramado social de la nación". El análisis dice que, si bien el alto nivel de polarización empezó mucho antes de la presidencia de Donald Trump, las elecciones del 2016 contribuyeron a solidificar las opiniones y las actitudes de ambos lados más que cualquier otro evento. Estos hallazgos ayudaron a clarificar cuán enredadas se han vuelto las diferencias culturales. Ellos escriben que los hallazgos "ayudan a explicar por qué las divisiones políticas son más difíciles de cubrir en el presente. La gente que se identifica con alguno de los partidos está crecientemente en desacuerdo no solo con la política; ellos habitan en mundos separados de distintos valores sociales y culturales y hasta ven su perspectiva económica a través de un lente partidista".[16]

Abordando temas similares, una encuesta de *Washington Post*, en cooperación con la *University of Maryland*, descubrió que casi tres cuartas partes de los estadounidenses creen que Estados Unidos está tan dividido ahora como lo estuvo durante la era de Vietnam; algo que yo recuerdo vívidamente como un estudiante de periodismo. ¿Quién puede olvidar la violencia en la convención demócrata de 1968 o el asesinato no solo del presidente John Kennedy en 1963, sino el de su hermano Robert a quien asesinaron a balazos cinco años después mientras él se postulaba para presidente? Y el más trágico de todos fue el asesinato de Martin Luther King Jr., a quien desde entonces se le ha idolatrado como uno de los que trajeron los derechos civiles a millones a través de sus métodos de protesta no violenta.

Todo el 77 por ciento de adultos mayores de sesenta y cinco años, eso es más de tres cuartos de la gente que estaba viva y recuerda la guerra de Vietnam, dijo que las divisiones del presente son tan grandes como lo fueron durante la Guerra, el 65 por ciento de adultos jóvenes, edad entre dieciocho y veintinueve años, dijo lo mismo. La encuesta también reportó que el 60 por ciento cree que el sistema político de Estados Unidos es disfuncional, y un 36 por ciento dijo no estar orgullosos de la manera en que funciona la democracia hoy día. Este fue un incremento sorprendente proveniente de los hallazgos en encuestas similares donde la gente respondía que no estaban orgullosos de la manera en que la democracia funcionaba en 1996 (16 por ciento), 2002 (9 por ciento), 2004 (10 por ciento) y 2014 (18 por ciento).[17]

En otra investigación, los encuestadores también han notado divisiones significativas dentro de los partidos políticos y aun una más profundas entre los votantes rurales y urbanos. Según un informe de junio 1017, "La división política entre el área rural y el área urbana en Estados Unidos es más cultural que económica, arraigadas en los residentes rurales hay dudas profundas sobre la demografía rápidamente cambiante de la nación, su sensación de que el cristianismo está bajo asedio y su percepción de que el gobierno federal cubre la mayor parte de las necesidades de la gente en grandes ciudades".[18]

La encuesta *Kaiser Family Foundation* del *Washington Post* halló que cerca del 70 por ciento de los residentes rurales cree que sus valores son diferentes de los de la gente que vive en grandes ciudades. Y aproximadamente el 40 por ciento indicó que sus valores son "muy diferentes". Entre los encuestados del área urbana, la mitad de ellos dijo que sus valores son diferentes a los de quienes viven en el área rural o suburbana, y solo menos del 20 por ciento de los encuestados urbanos dijo que sus valores son "muy diferentes".[19]

No hay duda de que Estados Unidos está envuelto en una guerra de cosmovisiones. Las diferencias entre la Derecha y la Izquierda son de toda la vida y sustanciales, con poca esperanza de cambio o de arreglo. Viendo a algunas de las razones tras esta enorme división cultural, el columnista y escritor John Hawkins ofreció una lista de siete indicadores culturales de que Estados Unidos ya no está unido y que la guerra de cosmovisiones podría volverse mucho más que solamente un debate religioso o político si las cosas continuaran como están.

Muchos conservadores están convencidos de que Estados Unidos se ha salido del curso y que puede dirigirse hacia una separación mayor, o posiblemente hasta a una guerra civil. Tan solo veinte años atrás tal cosa habría sido impensable, hasta risible. "Hoy día, la broma ya no es tan divertida", Hawkins dice, "debido a que estamos en una sociedad profundamente enferma con un gobierno disfuncional y por todo nuestro dinero, éxito y etapas históricas, parece que estamos en un recorrido cada vez más peligroso". ¿Por qué? "Por una cosa", dice Hawkins, "los liberales ya no creen en la Constitución".[20]

Aunque lo niegan, esto es realmente de lo que la idea de una "Constitución viva" se trata. "Se la inventan en el camino".[21] Los Fundadores se negaron intencionalmente a establecer el gobierno de Estados Unidos como una democracia pura, por esta razón: debido a que ellos reconocieron la inestabilidad que podría venir inevitablemente de confiar en los caprichos de la opinión pública. Se nos recuerda la respuesta de Benjamin Franklin a la mujer que preguntó al final de la Convención Constitucional en 1787: "Bien, Doctor, ¿qué es lo que tenemos, una República o una Monarquía?". A eso, él replicó: "Una República, si puede mantenerla".[22] Lo que los Fundadores nos dieron fue una república representativa; sin embargo, hoy día muchos estadounidenses se preguntan si podemos, de hecho, mantenerla.

Un segundo factor que amenaza nuestra unidad nacional es a lo que Hawkins se refiere como "tribalismo", lo cual se presenta de modo impresionante en la adicción de la nación a los medios sociales. Ambos lados tienen su medio favorito y sus argumentos preferidos para usarlos contra el otro lado. Los conservadores escuchan a personas como Rush Limbaugh, Sean Hannity, Ann Coulter y Donald Trump. Los liberales, por otro lado, escuchan a personas como Elizabeth Warren, Hillary Clinton, Stephen Colbert y Bill Maher y piensa que cualquiera que esté en desacuerdo con ellos es un racista, intolerante, supremacista blanco o peor y tiene que ser silenciado para que la sociedad avance. Esto hace que el diálogo sea difícil. "Cuando cada problema es una guerra de suma cero, donde una tribu tiene que ganar o perder", escribe Hawkins, "un montón de gente, muy comprensiblemente, pregunta: '¿Qué ganamos al permanecer aliados a esta otra tribu?'".[23]

Otros problemas que nos empujan hacia la disolución son cosas como el tamaño y poder del gobierno federal. Como todos sabemos, los valores culturales en las costas orientales y occidentales son muy diferentes de aquellos en el centro de la nación. Sin embargo, las leyes recientes y las manifestaciones sociales han impuesto agresivamente valores costeros sobre la gente que vive en lugares donde esos valores no son deseados. "Cuando la gente está innecesariamente forzada a vivir bajo las reglas que considera aberrantes debido a que el gobierno federal se ha convertido en un pulpo que ha incrustado sus tentáculos en cada fisura ínfima de la vida estadounidense", escribe Hawkins, "eso crea descontento a gran escala". Él añade: "Si la mayoría de los estadounidenses quisiera vivir como la gente en San Francisco, viviría en San Francisco".[24]

Todo esto es perturbador, pero los problemas que tienen el mayor potencial para rasgar el entramado de nuestra unidad nacional son la moral en constante decadencia dentro de nuestra cultura y la falta de valores compartidos. Muchas veces, escuchamos quejas de que el pueblo estadounidense está perdiendo sus modales. No es solo niños ruidosos e indisciplinados en los restaurantes, sino padres y adultos de todas las edades y en todo tipo de lugares públicos. También vemos el colapso del carácter y la disciplina moral en los políticos que elegimos.

Al ver los "principios, modales y virtudes" de los estadounidenses hoy día, Hawkins dice, "tenemos que preguntarnos cómo pudo nuestra nación lidiar con los tipos de retos que las generaciones anteriores enfrentaron, tales como la Segunda Guerra Mundial, la Gran Depresión, o la Guerra Civil. Pocos, si acaso, jóvenes entre los veinte y treinta años pudieron decirle por qué esos eventos fueron así de desafiantes en primer lugar, o por qué importaban. El filósofo George Santayana dijo lo que todo mundo sabe: "Aquellos que no pueden recordar el pasado están condenados a repetirlo".[25] Sin embargo, en nuestra condición actual de colapso cultural, educativo y moral, no hay garantía de que la república que los Fundadores nos dieron pueda sobrevivir.

La verdad es, los estadounidenses no comparten su admiración por nada ni nadie en estos días. Los conservadores y los liberales ya no están de acuerdo en política, religión, los medios ni lo que califique como libertad de expresión. Estamos en un punto, tal como lo vemos muy frecuentemente en las noticias del día, en que el punto de vista de un hombre sobre la libertad de expresión es lo que otro hombre define como discurso de odio. La Primera Enmienda a la Constitución de Estados Unidos dice: "El Congreso no podrá hacer ninguna ley con respecto al establecimiento de la religión, ni prohibiendo la libre práctica de la misma; ni limitando la libertad de expresión, ni de prensa; ni el derecho a la asamblea pacífica de las personas, ni de solicitar al gobierno una compensación de agravios".[26] Pero todas esas cosas han sido desafiadas por la institución liberal, razón por la cual muchos están pidiendo por una Convención Constitucional para redefinir quiénes somos y qué creemos como nación. Esto podría ser un desastre para muchos de los derechos básicos que hemos dado por sentados durante los últimos dos siglos. Quién sabe cómo sería una nueva constitución. Pero para quienes intentan cambiar nuestro país para que sea más ateo y socialista, les ayudaría a alcanzar sus objetivos.

LA DIFERENCIA ESENCIAL

Afirmar, como muchos lo hacen, que los liberales son antirreligiosos o anticristianos es una cosa, pero demostrar que los demócratas creen que las iglesias tienen un impacto negativo en la sociedad es un par de pasos más allá de una simple sospecha. Sin embargo, eso es precisamente lo que el departamento de *Politics & Policy* del centro *Pew* descubrió cuando examinó las opiniones liberales y conservadoras de la iglesia y de otras instituciones importantes en el país.

En un informe de julio 2017, *Pew* halló que el 36 por ciento de los demócratas cree que el impacto de la iglesia en la sociedad es negativo. Solamente el 14 por ciento de los republicanos sostuvieron ese punto de vista, pero entre los demócratas el 44 por ciento ve a las iglesias como una influencia negativa, mientras que el 50 por ciento de los demócratas en general vio a las iglesias como influencia positiva.[27]

Amplias diferencias partidistas sobre el impacto de instituciones mayores en el país [28]

% de quien dijo que cada una tiene un efecto positivo/negativo en la manera en que van las cosas en el país

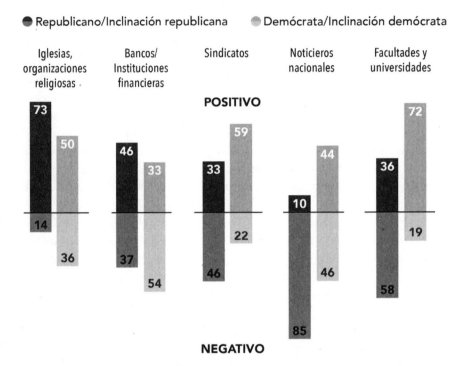

● Republicano/Inclinación republicana   ● Demócrata/Inclinación demócrata

El estudio *Pew* reveló que el 46 por ciento de aquellos que no están afiliados con ninguna religión creen que las iglesias tienen un impacto negativo sobre la sociedad, tal como lo cree el 43 por ciento de aquellos que raras veces o nunca asisten a servicios religiosos. A manera de contraste, la encuesta de junio de 2017, de 2,504 adultos reportó que el 85 por ciento de los republicanos cree que los noticieros nacionales impactan negativamente a la sociedad. Solamente el 46 por ciento de los demócratas sostuvo ese punto de vista.[29]

"Entre los republicanos", dijeron los investigadores, "las opiniones negativas de los noticieros son compartidas por grandes mayorías, tanto de republicanos conservadores (87%) y moderados y republicanos liberales (80%)".[30] Reaccionando al informe, Mark Tooley, con el *Institute on Religion and Democracy* en Washington, DC, dijo que él cree que el Partido Demócrata está rápidamente en camino a convertirse en el partido opositor de la iglesia cristiana en Estados Unidos. "Nosotros nunca hemos tenido un partido político, como lo hacen muchas naciones europeas, con oposición a la iglesia", dijo, "y con suerte, nunca lo tendremos, pero la tendencia muestra ser que mucho del Partido Demócrata, una pluralidad, parece dirigirse en esa dirección".[31]

Sería una gran ironía histórica si la nación fuera a terminar con un sistema de dos partidos que fuera esencialmente un partido político a favor de la religión y un partido político contra la religión yendo en directa oposición en Estados Unidos, un recuerdo conveniente de la Guerra Civil Inglesa, con los parlamentarios protestantes versus los realistas Cavaliers, lo que llevó a la eventual decapitación del monarca de turno. Con suerte, ese destino nunca sucederá aquí, pero "podría ser potencialmente peligroso si uno de los partidos se vuelve casi exclusivamente un partido a favor de la religión y el otro partido se vuelve un partido secular, lo que ha sucedido a veces en Europa", dijo Tooley.[32]

"Así que, mucho de esto es solo ignorancia", dijo Tooley. Él añadió que "muchos liberales ideológicamente son muy estadistas en su manera de ver a la sociedad, así que, para ellos, la Iglesia y otras instituciones en la sociedad civil podría parecer secundaria, o innecesaria, ya que el gobierno puede hacerlo todo por sí mismo". Además, dijo que muchas personas hostiles a la religión dejan de apreciar completamente el impacto que las instituciones religiosas puede tener para bien en una sociedad.[33] Sin embargo, un número sustancial de estadounidenses aparentemente han cambiado de pensar, decidiendo que la etiqueta de "No religión" describe mejor su sistema de creencias.

Esto es claramente la implicación de un reporte *Pew* ampliamente publicitado de 2012 titulado: "Nones en aumento", el cual mostraba un declive inclinado en el número de estadounidenses que se identificaban como protestantes. En la encuesta nacional de 2,973 adultos, *Pew* preguntó: "¿Cuál es su religión actual, si tiene? ¿Es usted protestante, católico romano, mormón, ortodoxo sea griego o ruso, judío, musulmán, budista, hindú, ateo, agnóstico, algo más, o nada en particular?". El número que se identificó como protestante fue un 48 por ciento, menor al 53 por ciento de hace cinco años. Este estaba en duro contraste a una encuesta similar de 1960 en la que dos tercios de los adultos se identificaba como protestante.[34] Los católicos mostraron solamente un descenso modesto de 1 por ciento, mientras que los ortodoxos y los mormones se mantuvieron firmes y el número que indicaba "otra fe" mostraba un incremento del 2 por ciento. El porcentaje de quienes se identificaban como "no afiliado religiosamente" (o "ninguno") aumentó del 15.3 por ciento en 2007 a 19.6 por ciento en 2012.[35]

Si la categoría "ninguno" ha tenido o no mucha tracción desde el informe de 2012, *Pew Research Center* hizo un descubrimiento aún más extraordinario en una encuesta de 2017 buscando en el componente racial de la fe. Los encuestadores hallaron que "si bien los demócratas blancos son menos propensos a ser religiosos que los republicanos", los demócratas de otras étnicas, generalmente negros o hispanos, están mucho más cerca de los republicanos que los demócratas liberales en un montón de temas, incluyendo creer en el Dios de la Biblia.[36] Así es como los analistas de *Pew* ilustraron sus hallazgos:

En su creencia en Dios, los demócratas no blancos se parecen más a los republicanos que a los demócratas blancos [37]

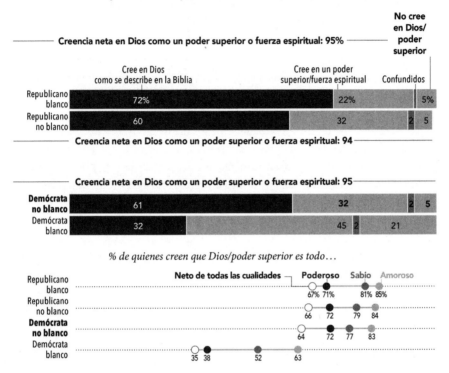

% de quienes creen que Dios/poder superior es todo...

Nuestra nación fue fundada sobre principios cristianos. Muchos inmigrantes (incluyendo algunos de mi propia familia) vinieron por la libertad de culto. Si bien muchos considerarían a Estados Unidos una sociedad "postcristiana", donde aquellos que son realmente "nacidos de nuevo" ya no son la mayoría de nuestros ciudadanos, esa creencia básica en Dios está aún fuerte entre los estadounidenses. El estudio *Pew* más reciente de estos temas informa que "la creencia en Dios, como está descrita en la Biblia está más pronunciada entre los cristianos estadounidenses. Sobre todo, ocho de cada diez personas que se autoidentifican como cristianos dicen que creen en el Dios de la Biblia, mientras que uno de cada cinco no cree en la descripción bíblica de Dios, pero sí creen en un poder superior de algún tipo. Muy pocos de los que se autoidentifican como cristianos (solo el 1%) dicen que no creen en ningún poder superior en lo absoluto".[38]

El estudio de participación religiosa de *Pew* de 2014 concluyó que los demócratas no blancos están tan religiosamente comprometidos como los republicanos en lo que se refiere a orar y asistir a la iglesia.[39]

Sobre asistencia religiosa, oración y la importancia de la religión, los demócratas no blancos son más similares a GOP que a los demócratas blancos[40]

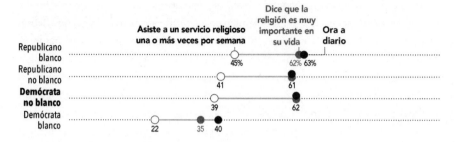

Cuando usted reduce la encuesta para incluir solamente a los demócratas negros, ellos están aún más religiosamente comprometidos que los republicanos. Casi la mitad (47 por ciento) de los demócratas negros dicen que asisten a la iglesia por lo menos semanalmente, y aproximadamente tres cuartas partes oran a diario (74 por ciento) y dicen que la religión es muy importante en su vida (76 por ciento). Hay algunas maneras en que los republicanos y los demócratas no blancos no se parecen entre sí, como sus opiniones sobre el aborto: 58 por ciento de los demócratas no blancos y 57 por ciento de los demócratas negros dijeron que el aborto debería ser legal en todos o en la mayoría de los casos, mientras que solo el 38 por ciento de republicanos sostuvo esta opinión.[41]

Cuando se trata del lugar donde adoran, los analistas dicen, puede ser que allí no haya mucho traslape. Según el más reciente *National Congregations Study* (2012), si bien las congregaciones de Estados Unidos se están constantemente volviendo más diversas racial y étnicamente, el 86 por ciento de las congregaciones estadounidenses "permanecen abrumadoramente blancas o negras o hispanas o asiáticas".[42]

UN CAMBIO CULTURAL SÍSMICO

Ningún tema define tanto la batalla llevándose a cabo en la cultura estadounidense que el problema del aborto. Desde la decisión de la Corte Suprema en 1973, en el caso *Roe vs. Wade*, que legalizó el aborto en todos los cincuenta estados, la información provista por los *Centers for Disease Control and Prevention* y el *Alan Guttmacher Institute*, que favorece el aborto, indican que se han llevado a cabo más de sesenta millones de abortos en este país en el transcurso de los últimos cuarenta y cinco años.[43] Una encuesta en 2014 halló que aproximadamente 926,000 abortos se llevan a cabo en este país cada año.[44] Según el *Guttmacher Institute*, el 4.6 por ciento de las mujeres americanas tendrán un aborto para cuando tengan veinte años de edad, el 19 por ciento de las mujeres en Estados Unidos tendrá un aborto antes de los 30 años de edad y casi una cuarta parte (23.7 por ciento) habrá abortado antes de los cuarenta y cinco años de edad.[45]

Esto es una tragedia nacional de cualquier manera razonable en que lo veamos, pero el problema se ha vuelto tan polémico en las últimas cuatro décadas que define virtualmente a los dos partidos políticos, con los demócratas estando abrumadoramente a favor del aborto a solicitud y los republicanos estando abrumadoramente en contra. Aunque los grupos como NARAL y *Planned Parenthood* aseguren lo contrario, las mujeres de todas las edades, tanto casadas como solteras, usan habitualmente al aborto como el último recurso en anticoncepción. Y a pesar de que se afirme lo contrario, un porcentaje muy pequeño incluye la vida de la madre, la salud del niño o las víctimas de incesto o violación sexual.

La renuncia del juez Kennedy en 2018 encendió una chispa de esperanza en muchos conservadores por la oportunidad de anular *Roe vs Wade*. Y la nominación de Brett Kavanaugh de parte del presidente Trump está avivando esa llama. Sin embargo, a pesar de la triste historia de la decisión desastrosa de la Corte Suprema en 1973, el hecho más esperanzador en el debate del aborto es la noticia de que una mayoría de los estadounidenses, incluyendo demócratas, ahora tienen una tendencia en favor de la vida.[46]

Tendencia a favor de la vida de la mayoría de los estadounidenses, incluyendo demócratas

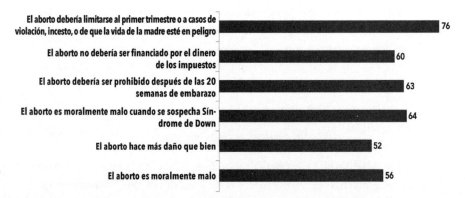

La encuesta halló que mayorías fuertes de republicanos (92 por ciento), independientes (78 por ciento) y demócratas (61 por ciento) sienten que el aborto debería estar limitado al primer trimestre de embarazo o para casos de violación sexual, incesto, o peligro de la vida de la madre. Una mayoría de los que se identifican como a favor de elegir (60 por ciento) también están de acuerdo con esta instancia, informó la encuesta.[47]

Estos descubrimientos fueron publicados justo a tiempo para la *March of Life* anual el 19 de enero de 2018. La marcha, que se lleva a cabo en Washington, es el evento provida más grande del mundo y, este año hizo alarde de un grupo impresionante de oradores, incluyendo al *Speaker of the House*, Paul Ryan, varios legisladores y líderes ministeriales, y al presidente Donald Trump en vivo vía satélite.

"Desde su primer día en el cargo, el presidente Trump se ha mantenido firme en las promesas de su campaña a la causa provida y ha trabajado activamente para proteger a los niños no nacidos", dijo Jeanne Mancini, quien es la presidenta de *March for Life*. "Durante el año pasado", dijo, "la administración Trump ha promovido significativamente la política provida, y es con gran confianza que, bajo su liderazgo, esperamos ver otros logros provida en los años venideros".[48] Las noticias de este tipo son alentadores para los votantes religiosos y conservadores que están entre los partidarios más apasionados, pero los temas sobre la vida también se han vuelto parte de una preocupación mayor para muchos en el Partido Demócrata y aparentemente están atrayendo a los que habían votado por el otro lado durante años.

Temas como el aborto, matrimonio homosexual, control de armas e inmigración ilegal son complicados y aún debatidos acaloradamente, pero hay indicios de que la agenda conservadora de Trump está alcanzando victorias en cada área de disputa. Tal como lo mencioné en mi introducción, el 1 de junio de 2018, el *New York Times* dijo que "se habían quedado sin palabras" para describir el éxito increíble de la economía bajo el liderazgo de Trump.[49] Los demócratas francos, tales como los líderes mayoritarios, Nancy Pelosi y Chuck Schumer aseguraron que la legislación tributaria, aprobada en diciembre 2017, dispararía un Armagedón financiero; sin embargo, los resultados demostraron ser exactamente lo opuesto. En el capítulo 7, donde discutí la economía floreciente, mencioné que el *Bureau of Labor Statistics* mostrando que el empleo aumentó en 223,000 plazas, en el informe de empleos, con el desempleo cayendo al 3.8 por ciento, la cifra más baja en los últimos dieciocho años. Al mismo tiempo, el desempleo en la población negra bajó a 5.9 por ciento nacionalmente, un récord histórico.

Muchas empresas dieron bonos de US$1,000 o más, y los medios principales de comunicación se vieron forzados a informar que millones de estadounidenses estarían recibiendo un recorte tributario.[50] Como Rich Lowry sugirió en *Politico Magazine*, los demócratas pudieron haber tentado a la suerte al presionar un mensaje propagandístico de extrema Izquierda para dañar a Trump, cuando, de hecho, la nación cree que los logros de Trump están realmente haciendo a Estados Unidos grande otra vez. "Trump es el conejo de la pista de carreras que mantiene a los demócratas corriendo en un circuito perpetuo de ira", dice Lowry. "Pero un partido que se encuentra en un estado perpetuo de histeria y, encima de eso, opera contra el trasfondo de una economía con 4.1 [4.0 a junio 2018] por ciento de desempleo, podría hallar más difícil de lo esperado salir adelante con sus trucos viejos".[51]

CON LOS OJOS BIEN ABIERTOS

Añadiendo insultos a la herida, la estrategia a largo plazo de los demócratas para el cambio social y la victoria en las encuestas ha resultado ser un fracaso total. Durante al menos la última década, ellos creían que eran los beneficiarios de una "un reloj demográfico apocalíptico" que les otorgaba poder perpetuo. El reloj, descrito en el libro *The Emerging Democratic Majority*, publicado en 2002, argumenta que las tendencias demográficas cambiantes, el flujo de inmigrantes y el colapso de la clase blanca media garantizaría una estadía demócrata permanente en la Casa Blanca.[52] Después de la reelección de Obama en 2012, el *Huffington Post* proclamó: "El presidente Barack Obama no solo ganó la reelección esta noche. Su triunfo es una señal del triunfo irreversible de un nuevo Estados Unidos del siglo 21: multirracial, multiétnica, mundial en perspectiva y dejando atrás siglos de tradición racial, sexual, marital y religiosa".[53]

El escritor celebraba a un "Estados Unidos nuevo" y a una nueva coalición multiétnica que incluía "una buena porción del voto blanco (aproximadamente un 45 por ciento en Ohio, por ejemplo); el 70 por ciento más o menos del voto latino en todo el país, según los expertos; 96 por ciento del voto afroamericano; y, en grandes proporciones el de asiático-americanos y polinesios".[54] En el liderazgo demócrata, nadie dudaba del control permanente de la Casa Blanca y el dominio total del debate cultural durante los años venideros. Luego, de la nada, Donald Trump apareció, y todo con lo que la Izquierda contaba salió volando por la ventana proverbial, y el Partido Republicano surgió repentinamente más fuerte de lo que había estado en más de un siglo.[55]

Confundir la carrera de ocho años de Obama como una alineación masiva fue un error estratégico, tal como lo argumentó el columnista Sean Trende en un artículo para *RealClearPolitics*.[56] De hecho, Obama destruyó virtualmente al Partido Demócrata como institución. Muchas de las pérdidas electorales de los demócratas en 2016 pueden atribuirse directamente a las políticas "progresistas" exageradas de la administración Obama. "El hambre resultante por el cambio en 2016 era tan fuerte", escribe Hayward, "que solo Hillary Clinton y su equipo de campaña (que, claro está, incluye a muchos de los medios principales de comunicación) no lo escucharon. Los demócratas descartaron las votaciones parciales de 2010 y 2014 considerándolas anomalías cuando debieron haberlas visto como una evidencia sólida de que no se había producido ninguna gran realineación".[57]

El desempeño de Trump con los votantes negros e hispanos también sorprendió a los medios, aunque no debería haberlo hecho, debido a que lo que Trump dice realmente de estos grupos es muy diferente de la imagen caricaturesca presentada por los medios. Los votantes negros, quienes están fuertemente de acuerdo con Trump en los temas morales y sociales, se han trasladado lenta, pero perceptiblemente hacia la Derecha. Y el voto hispano se está volviendo más republicano con cada ciclo electoral. Estos fueron puntos importantes que comuniqué en un capítulo completo dedicado al voto minoritario en mi libro *God and Donald Trump*.

Mientras tanto, los votantes blancos están cansados de los ataques llenos de odio de la Izquierda. "Hay un punto", dice Hayward, "donde cualquier grupo de personas determinado se cansará de que se le diga que son la fuente de todos los problemas, sin importar cuánta culpa les lance el bullicio cultural y educativo". [58]

"Los críticos de ambos lados trataron de avergonzar a los votantes evangélicos que apoyaban a Trump en las primarias de 2015 y las elecciones de 2016, pero los votantes evangélicos apoyaron al candidato republicano por una muy buena razón", dice Hayward: "Ocho años de proselitismo progresivo respaldado por el gobierno los convenció de que necesitaban un protector más fuerte, y lo vieron en Trump. Ponga a los evangélicos y la clase trabajadora juntos, añada unos cuantos latinos que quieren ser totalmente estadounidenses, y obtiene una llave inglesa lo suficientemente grande para destruir la Máquina Apocalíptica Demográfica Demócrata durante mucho tiempo por venir".[59]

Independientemente de cuánto puedan intentar los medios desacreditar al Presidente, sus logros están acumulándose. Incluso el liberal *New Republic* estaba sorprendido de cuánta tracción han perdido los demócratas entre los votantes negros. Mientras se centraba la atención sobre la manera en que los demócratas podían atraer a los votantes de la clase trabajadora, los nuevos datos mostraron que el apoyo para el Partido se estaba deslizando entre sus votantes más confiables: las mujeres negras votantes, quienes le habían dado a Hillary Clinton el 94 por ciento de su apoyo en 2016. Sin embargo, el apoyo de esta base confiable ha disminuido significativamente desde entonces. Una encuesta de la *Black Women's Roundtable/ESSENCE* de 2016 descubrió que el 85 por ciento de las mujeres negras dijo que el Parido Demócrata aún representa sus intereses; sin embargo, para 2017, la cifra expresando esa opinión había caído al 74 por ciento.[60]

Para empeorar las cosas, varias deserciones destacadas del Partido Demócrata se han producido desde la elección. El famoso abogado Alan Dershowitz, aunque sigue siendo liberal, se ha vuelto un colaborador de *Fox News* y un partidario franco de Trump. El exconsejero de Clinton y ejecutivo de Microsoft, Mark Penn, intervino en la investigación de Mueller diciendo, en diferentes ocasiones, que el Partido Demócrata se había desviado muy lejos hacia la izquierda y que la cacería de brujas de Mueller tenía que terminar. Sin embargo, quizá lo más impresionante, a la luz del papel que ella desempeñaba en el caso Benghazi y el cargo posterior de que estuvo involucrada en desenmascarar objetivos de las investigaciones del FBI, es la noticia de que el hijo de Susan Rice, John David Rice-Cameron, ha sido electo presidente del *College Republicans* en *Stanford University* y se desempeña como el director de activismo del estado de California *College Republicans*.[61]

Una vez *Fox News* describió a la exembajadora de las Naciones Unidas, Susan

Rice, como "una de las funcionarias de la administración Obama más poco populares entre los conservadores y los republicanos".[62] Una reputación que se ganó cuando intentaba culpar a un video de YouTube ofensivo del ataque al complejo de la Embajada de Estados Unidos en Benghazi, Libia, en 2012. Rice participó en el acuerdo de 2014 en el que Obama liberó cinco talibanes de alto rango y terroristas de alto valor a cambio del desertor del ejército de Estados Unidos, Bowe Bergdahl. Además, se ha informado que ella fue la persona que emitió la orden de espera a los funcionarios del *National Security Council* que desarrollaban planes para responder a la injerencia rusa en las elecciones presidenciales en el 2016.[63] Ella fue consistentemente una de las defensoras de Obama más determinadas.

Seguramente, debe haberse impresionado cuando su hijo decidió ir en otra dirección. Para promover la membresía en el grupo *Standford Republican*, su hijo ayudó a organizar un evento "Hacer a Standford grande otra vez" en el campus. El anfitrión del grupo Robert Spencer, un experto controversial sobre el islam radical; presionó por la renuncia de un profesor vinculado con Antifa; presionó a la facultad para revertir la decisión de prohibir banderas estadounidenses en las camisetas; y fue el anfitrión de los presentadores del conocido *Turning Point USA*, Charlie Kirk y Candace Owens para que dieran un discurso en el evento. De hecho, fue a raíz de la discusión lúcida de Owens sobre los principios conservadores que la sensación del rap, Kanye West, dijo que admiraba a Trump, y es posible que eso haya sido lo que lo llevó a enfrentar lo que fuera y se unió a Trump.

Cuando le preguntaron qué lo impulsó su conversión política, Rice-Cameron dijo: "Esta cosmovisión y los principios me hicieron promover las ideas conservadoras en Stanford y más allá. Me impulsa una sensación fundamental de urgencia sobre el hecho de que los estadounidenses están perdiendo lentamente su libertad, y creo que esa libertad está siendo valorada cada vez menos. Yo quiero cambiar la corriente, las instalaciones universitarias son cruciales en esto". Cuando se le preguntó cómo hizo el cambio, habiendo crecido en un hogar liberal; él respondió que cambió después de escuchar otros puntos de vista en un programa de radio conservador. Fueron palabras e ideas que él nunca había escuchado y, repentinamente, sus ojos se abrieron.[64]

Si bien es demasiado temprano para declarar la victoria para cualquiera de los bandos o asumir que la batalla por el corazón y la mente de los estadounidenses ha terminado, historias como estas ofrecen un rayo de esperanza. Inscrito sobre la puerta que data de 1881 en *Harvard University*, a través de la cual los estudiantes y el alumnado de la *Ivy League* han pasado durante más de cien años, están las palabras: "Conoceréis la verdad y la verdad os hará libres". La fuente no se menciona, pero son las palabras de Jesús. E incluso si Harvard ya no reconoce la verdad de la inscripción, o a quien la dijo, estas palabras ofrecen la esperanza de que algunos escucharán la verdad, y, tal como le sucedió a John David Rice-Cameron, sus ojos serán abiertos y, repentinamente, lo comprenderán.

La guerra verdadera

Como cristiano, no creo que esta lucha en Estados Unidos sea solamente entre la Izquierda y la Derecha, o los demócratas contra los republicanos. Creo que es entre la luz y las tinieblas, entre el bien y el mal. Hay una naturaleza espiritual en este conflicto, lo que los evangélicos llaman "guerra espiritual". Esto no es solamente entre personas. De hecho, la Biblia dice: "No tenemos lucha contra sangre y carne, sino contra principados, contra potestades, contra los gobernadores de las tinieblas de este siglo, contra huestes espirituales de maldad en las regiones celestes" (Efesios 6:12).

El 19 de agosto de 2018, mi amigo John Kilpatrick predicó un sermón a su congregación en *Church of His Presence*, en Daphne, Alabama, y les dijo que la brujería se había desatado sobre Donald Trump. Él usó la referencia en 1 Reyes 19, cuando Jezabel desató el espíritu de brujería contra el profeta Elías, el profeta más poderoso del Antiguo Testamento, y lo dejó corriendo por su vida y sintiéndose totalmente desanimado. Alguien puso un videoclip del final del servicio, cuando Kilpatrick estaba llamando a la congregación a orar por el Presidente. En una semana, casi un millón de personas lo había visto.

Normalmente, la prensa y la cultura en general parecen ignorar todo lo que la Biblia diga acerca de tales cosas. Sin embargo, cuando el sermón se hizo viral, la prensa de todo el mundo empezó a publicar sus historias. El sitio de internet *Newsweek* dijo: "Pastor ora por Trump para derrotar la 'brujería' del subgobierno, habla en lenguas".

Newsweek escribió: "Kilpatrick conectó el actual flagelo de 'brujería' de Estados Unidos que está atacando al Presidente con una lucha bíblica en la que se encuentra Trump estando en un careo de poder con las sombras del subgobierno. En el video, se puede ver a Kilpatrick gritando y hablando en lenguas mientras ora para que Trump derrote los poderes malvados de la 'brujería'". Luego, *Newsweek* citó a Kilpatrick diciendo: "No sé si lo saben, y no sé si me van a creer cuando se los cuente, pero lo que está sucediendo ahora en Estados Unidos es brujería, está tratando de apoderarse de este país", provocando una respuesta audible de su público.[65]

Kilpatrick continuó diciendo:

> No estoy siendo político, pero no veo cómo el presidente Trump soporta el peso. Él es más fuerte que ningún otro hombre que yo haya visto. Pero esto es lo que el Espíritu Santo me dijo anoche y esto es lo que me dijo que les dijera. Él dijo: "Dile a la iglesia que hasta ahora Trump ha estado lidiando con Acab. Pero que Jezabel está preparándose para salir de las sombras". Eso es lo que el Señor me dijo… Él dijo: "Ora por él ahora, porque está por haber un cambio, y el subgobierno se manifestará, y va a ser un careo que no podrán

creer". Así que vengo a ustedes como profeta, como un hombre de Dios, y les digo, es hora de orar por el Presidente.[66]

Dos días después, el 21 de agosto de 2018, Paul Manafort fue condenado sobre varios cargos en un caso presentado en su contra por la investigación Mueller. El mismo día, el exabogado de Trump, Michael Cohen, se declaró culpable de unos cargos menores. Repentinamente, el Presidente tenía más agua al cuello de lo normal. Parecía que algo se había desatado. Y dos días antes, había sido predicho por este pastor en Alabama, quien es mejor conocido en los círculos cristianos como el pastor del avivamiento que duró cinco años en *Brownsville Assembly of God* (también llamado el *Pensacola Outpouring*), que atrajo a más de cuatro millones de personas.

De alguna manera, lo que Kilpatrick dijo hizo eco en los cristianos de todo el país. Ellos percibían que algo estaba muy mal, pero no podían identificarlo. Así que cuando Kilpatrick dijo que era guerra espiritual y les dijo que oraran, ellos entendieron lo que se esperaba que hicieran.

"Algo ha sido desatado en nuestra nación", Kilpatrick me dijo cuando lo entrevisté para un blog que yo estaba escribiendo sobre el tema. "Es como si todo el mundo estuviera en un estupor espiritual. Es hora de que Estados Unidos vuelva y se arrepienta. Esto es más que solo diferencias políticas. Los espíritus han sido desatados, pero si nos humillamos a nosotros mismos y oramos, Dios destruirá a ese espíritu".

El tiempo dirá si los cristianos prestarán atención al llamado a orar y si, tal como Kilpatrick predijo, el avivamiento llegará a Estados Unidos para sanar sus heridas, o si Trump será derrotado por estas fuerzas invisibles enormes. Pero para mí y para millones de otros cristianos tratando de entender dónde está Dios en todo esto, lo que Kilpatrick predijo explica, en términos espirituales, la guerra que parece estar desgarrando a este país.

FE Y CONFIANZA RESUELTAS

UNA DE LAS primeras indicaciones de que Donald Trump iba a ser una clase de presidente diferente a sus predecesores llegó el 20 de enero de 2017, el Día de Investidura. Para empezar su presidencia, la Casa Blanca invitó a cuatro ministros evangélicos, un rabino judío, un arzobispo católico, representando diversas religiones y comunidades étnicas, para ofrecer oraciones por el nuevo presidente y la nación. Este sería el número más grande de oraciones ofrecidas en una investidura y una indicación de que el nuevo jefe ejecutivo comprendía la importancia de la fe para la gente de este país. El propósito de la ocasión era invocar la bendición de Dios sobre la nación, así como también, una declaración del firme compromiso de la administración Trump con la libertad de culto.

A lo largo de la campaña, Trump ganó acceso a las emociones de sus simpatizantes al darles la esperanza de que los días de gloria de Estados Unidos no habían quedado atrás. Energizó a su base al garantizarles su apoyo, y las multitudes en sus mítines aumentaban más en cada evento. Él se reunió con los líderes comunitarios y religiosos y escuchó sus preocupaciones asegurándoles que el mensaje lo había recibido fuerte y claro. Los evangélicos de toda la nación le dijeron que estaban hartos del irrespeto que experimentaban por parte de los medios seculares. Estaban preocupados por las políticas del gobierno relacionadas con el aborto, matrimonio homosexual y el derecho de los empresarios de determinar a quién le venden. Ellos querían un líder que defendiera sus intereses y tomara una posición para la libertad de consciencia, y Donald Trump dejó en claro que él era el hombre que buscaban.

Después de las elecciones, muchos analistas concluyeron que fue la gran participación nunca vista e inesperada de la comunidad evangélica la que le dio a Trump la victoria. Ochenta y uno por ciento de los evangélicos que votaron movieron la palanca a favor de Trump, impresionando a los pronosticadores de ambos partidos políticos. La noche previa a las elecciones, el *New York Times* recopiló los sondeos de seguimiento que mostraban que las oportunidades de ganar de Trump estaban en solo 15 por ciento, 8 por ciento, 2 por ciento, e incluso menos del 1 por ciento.[1] Los simpatizantes de Clinton estaban furiosos cuando el gurú de las encuestas,

Nate Silver, se atrevió a sugerir, antes de que terminara la noche, que Trump tenía un 29 por ciento de posibilidad de ganar el colegio electoral.[2]

Los medios y los encuestadores liberales nunca dudaron que Clinton se estaría mudando a la Casa Blanca, pero ellos leyeron incorrectamente la orden de los votantes por un cambio, y la religión resultó ser gran parte de ello. Clinton estaba muy segura de que sería la nueva presidenta. Hasta compró una casa de US$1.6 millones en Chappaqua, Nueva York, para ser utilizada por el personal y el equipo de seguridad durante sus retiros presidenciales.[3] Resultó que no la iba a necesitar, y hoy día, la casa que Clinton compró es una casa de campo para huéspedes.

El 21 de enero de 2017, su primer día completo en el cargo, el presidente Trump y el vicepresidente Pence asistieron a un servicio interconfesional en la Catedral Nacional de Washington, una tradición que data de la presidencia de George Washington. Al evento asistieron más de dos docenas de líderes religiosos de varias fes. No hubo discursos, ni comentarios políticos solo oraciones y lecturas. Y aunque la mayoría de los visitantes provenían de la comunidad evangélica, también asistieron los representantes de las tradiciones: católica romana, judía, ortodoxa, mormona, musulmana, sikh, budista y bahá'i.

Cuatro meses después, Trump animó los espíritus de los evangélicos cuando hizo un fuerte llamado durante el Día Nacional de Oración para volver a Dios y por una restauración de la libertad de culto. Ese evento convenció a muchos evangélicos que estaban en busca de confirmación del compromiso de Trump, de que este presidente daría su apoyo a los temas que más les importan a ellos. Creyeron que sus palabras eran más que solo retórica. En su proclamación para ese evento, dijo:

> Estamos unidos en oración, cada uno según su propia fe y tradición, y creemos que, en Estados Unidos, la gente de toda fe, credo y religión debe ser libre para ejercer su derecho natural de adorar de acuerdo con su consciencia. También somos reafirmados y se nos recuerda que todos los seres humanos tienen el derecho, no solo de orar y adorar de acuerdo con sus consciencias, sino de practicar su fe en sus hogares, escuelas, caridades y negocios en privado y en la plaza pública libres de coerción, discriminación o persecución por parte del gobierno.[4]

"La religión", dijo, "es más que un ejercicio intelectual. Es una expresión práctica de nuestras creencias y de nuestro compromiso para cuidar de aquellos en necesidad y defender a quienes sufren por su fe en el presente en muchas partes del mundo. "Incluso los muchos prisioneros alrededor del mundo que son perseguidos por su fe pueden orar privadamente en sus celdas", dijo Trump. "Sin embargo, nuestra Constitución exige más: la libertad de practicar la fe propia públicamente".[5]

Este fue un contraste impresionante a las políticas de Barack Obama, quien emitió proclamaciones, pero nunca celebró un *Día Nacional de Oración* en la Casa Blanca. Otros presidentes anteriores lo observaron en varias formas: Bill Clinton llevaba huéspedes a la Casa Blanca para orar durante el *Día Nacional de Oración*, y Ronald Reagan lo celebraba en el *Rose Garden*. El primer presidente Bush organizó un "desayuno de oración" en mayo 1989 en el *State Dining Room*. Yo tuve el privilegio de asistir a ese evento y sentarme a la misma mesa con el Presidente. Conversamos mucho sobre la oración durante el desayuno, pero me pareció extraño que en el *Día Nacional de Oración* no hubiera oración, excepto dar las gracias antes de la comida.

En 1952, el presidente Harry Truman estableció un día de oración como un evento nacional. En 1988, Reagan aprobó la resolución de observar el *Día Nacional de Oración* el primer jueves de mayo, cada año, y desde entonces, cada presidente ha reconocido el Día con una proclamación. Durante sus ocho años en el cargo, George W. Bush celebró el evento con un servicio en la Sala Este de la Casa Blanca, pero el presidente Obama decidió no celebrar una ceremonia en la Casa Blanca y pidió un *Día Nacional de Oración* "atenuado".[6]

Becky Armstrong, quien fue la vocera del *Día Nacional de Oración* del Cuerpo Especial en ese momento, dijo: "No parece que vayan a aprobar nuestra solicitud [para participar]". "Pero" añadió, "la Casa Blanca es una pequeña parte de lo que se trata el Día Nacional de Oración. Mañana, se llevarán a cabo docenas de eventos en la capital de nuestra nación y los gobernadores de todos los cincuenta estados ya han emitido sus proclamaciones reconociendo el *Día Nacional de Oración*". La presidenta del Cuerpo Especial Shirley Dobson dijo que estaba decepcionada por la falta de participación del Presidente y añadió que "en este momento en la historia de nuestro país, esperaríamos que nuestro presidente reconociera más plenamente la importancia de la oración".[7]

Pero Obama no rechazó la oración completamente. Durante los años siguientes, él le pidió a la nación que orara durante los desastres naturales, tales como el huracán Sandy, y que oraran por los hombres y mujeres valientes que estaban tomando parte en los esfuerzos de respuesta y recuperación. Si Hillary Clinton estaba interesada o no en conmemorar el día de oración mientras su esposo era presidente no lo sabemos, pero sí sabemos que lo ayudó a iniciar la cena de Ramadán como una tradición de la Casa Blanca en 1996. Hillary Clinton alojó 150 musulmanes invitados a la Casa Blanca y dijo que se había enterado de este ritual por su hija, Chelsea, quien había estudiado historia islámica en la escuela.

El presidente George W. Bush fue anfitrión de la cena de Ramadán cada año durante sus dos mandatos, incluyendo poco después de los ataques del 11 de septiembre. En la cena, él dijo que los estadounidenses luchan contra el terrorismo, no contra el islam. La administración Trump no llevó a cabo la cena en 2017, en cambio, envió un mensaje personal: "De parte del pueblo estadounidense, Melania y yo enviamos nuestros cariñosos saludos a los musulmanes mientras celebran Eid-al-Fitr". Él dijo, "durante esta celebración, recordamos la importancia de la misericordia, la compasión y la benevolencia".[8] En su saludo, al inicio del Ramadán, en mayo 2018, Trump dijo: "Nuestra Constitución asegura que los musulmanes puedan observar el Ramadán según se los dicte su consciencia y sin que el gobierno se los impida". Él, luego, concluyó sus comentarios con la despedida tradicional, *"Ramadan Mubarak"*.[9]

A TÍTULO PERSONAL

Entonces, ¿qué es lo que esto significa para los cristianos evangélicos, quienes han sido la médula del apoyo de Trump? Claramente, el Presidente es intencional en mantener sus promesas para salvaguardar la libertad de culto y la libre expresión para hombres y mujeres de toda fe. En el Rose Garden, la ceremonia para honrar el *Día Nacional de Oración*, en mayo de 2018, él anunció que estaría firmando una orden ejecutiva estableciendo una iniciativa de Fe y Oportunidad en la Casa Blanca. Esto aseguraría que las comunidades basadas en la fe y organizaciones relacionadas tienen un apoyo fuerte en la Casa Blanca y que la libertad de culto y de consciencia están protegidas a lo largo de todos los departamentos del gobierno federal.

El Presidente dio un discurso el 13 de octubre de 2017 en la *Value Voters Summit* en Washington, DC, y les aseguró a los asistentes que la libertad de culto sería una prioridad en su administración. Esta promesa llegó una semana después de que el Departamento de Justicia, siguiendo las instrucciones del Presidente, emitiera un listado de veinte principios de libertad de culto.[10] Luego, en enero 2018, el Departamento de Justicia creó el perfil de los casos de libertad de culto al designar un punto de contacto de libertad de culto para todas las oficinas de abogados de Estados Unidos.

El Departamento de salud y servicios humanos anunció cambios importantes de política ese mismo mes. Dicha entidad formó la División de consciencia y libertad de culto, la cual le permite a la agencia enfocarse en hacer cumplir efectivamente las leyes existentes que protegen la libertad de culto y los derechos de consciencia.

Como he mencionado en capítulos previos, en menos de cuatro meses de su mandato como presidente, Donald Trump dejó en claro que él es defensor de la libertad de culto al restaurar los ideales que han afianzado la libertad y prosperidad de la nación desde su fundación. El 4 de mayo de 2017, él trató con dos de los casos más problemáticos para las iglesias de Estados Unidos:

1. Terminar con la aplicación de la llamada *Johnson Amendment,* la cual amenazaba a las iglesias y las organizaciones sin fines de lucro con la pérdida del *estado* de exención de impuestos si respaldaban a cualquier candidato a un cargo público.

2. Reinstituir la Política de la Ciudad de México, la cual evita el financiamiento de la industria de aborto mundial con US$9 mil millones de ayuda extranjera.

El 13 de abril de 2017, el presidente Trump anuló la regulación de la administración Obama que prohibía a los estados detener el financiamiento a las instalaciones de abortos. Además, los nuevos bocetos declaraban que los fondos tributarios no podían utilizarse para cubrir abortos en los planes de intercambio de *Obamacare.* La administración Trump actuó para defender organizaciones como la *Little Sisters of the Poor,* asegurando que no fueran forzadas a cumplir con el mandato de contraceptivos de *Obamacare,* el cual viola sus creencias religiosas. El Presidente puso fin a la política de la era de Obama que impedía que las iglesias recibieran ayuda por desastres en tiempos de crisis.

El presidente Trump ha apoyado públicamente a la gente de fe y a quienes abogan por la santidad de la vida, como lo mencioné antes, él se convirtió en el primer presidente en dirigirse al encuentro *March for Life* en vivo, vía satélite. Mike Pence se convirtió en el primer vicepresidente en funciones en dirigirse a la marcha personalmente. La administración Trump también ha apoyado en la defensa de la libertad de culto al respaldar a los dueños de empresas pequeñas, tales como el repostero Jack Phillips de Colorado. Meses antes de que la Corte Suprema anulara la decisión contra Phillips, el DOJ de Trump presentó un escrito en su nombre, acordando que a él debería permitírsele operar su negocio según sus convicciones personales y sus creencias religiosas.[11]

Uno de los mejores ejemplos del apoyo de Trump a la libertad de culto es la manera en que él hizo del encarcelamiento de un misionero evangélico estadounidense en Turquía un incidente internacional. Andrew Brunson, quien pastoreaba una iglesia pequeña en Izmir, fue arrestado en 2016, uno de los miles arrestados, incluyendo periodistas, activistas y oponentes del presidente Recep Tayyip Erdogan. Él fue acusado de espionaje con vínculos con el proscrito Partido de los Trabajadores del Kurdistán y con un imán musulmán con sede en Estados Unidos, Fethullah Güllen, a quien las autoridades turcas culpan del intento de golpe. En una conferencia del Departamento de Estado sobre libertad de culto, a la que asistió la hija de Brunson, Jacqueline Furnari, Mike Pence dijo que Brunson había sido acusado de "dividir y separar Turquía por al simplemente difundir su fe cristiana", según la revista *Time.*[12]

En julio, el vicepresidente Pence, tuiteó que Turquía debería "liberar al pastor

Andrew Brunson AHORA o prepararse para enfrentar las consecuencias".[13] Ese mismo día el presidente Trump tuiteó, "Estados Unidos impondrá enormes sanciones sobre Turquía" por detener a Brunson, a quien él llamó: "Un gran cristiano, padre de familia y ser humano maravilloso. Él está sufriendo muchísimo. Este hombre de fe, inocente, ¡debería ser liberado inmediatamente!".[14] Mientras este libro va a impresión, Brunson aún no ha sido liberado, pero después de que las sanciones fueron impuestas, el mercado de valores de Turquía se desplomó, perdiendo más de US$15 mil millones de valor negociado durante agosto 2018, y la moneda turca, la lira llegó a su récord más bajo en la historia.

Durante décadas, muchos estadounidenses han temido la intromisión del gobierno federal en sus vidas, forzándolos a aceptar políticas que contradicen la tradición largamente establecida y violan nuestras creencias religiosas históricas. Como mencioné en la introducción de este libro, el gobernador Mike Huckabee me dijo que él cree que Donald Trump representa esa parte de Estados Unidos que está cansada de recibir golpes. Una razón por la que muchos conservadores apoyaron a Trump fue que ellos lo vieron a él como el tipo de persona que contraataca.

En su mayor parte, el presidente Trump ha cumplido con las expectativas. Él es un luchador, y quiere restaurar el honor y el prestigio de Estados Unidos alrededor del mundo. Los críticos aseguraban que él era solo un hombre de negocios sin habilidades diplomáticas. Él no tenía conocimiento ni experiencia en asuntos exteriores y que nos llevaría a la tercera guerra mundial. Sin embargo, desde su primer visita oficial a Europa, China, Japón, y el Medio Oriente, muchos lo han aclamado como a un héroe. Sus discursos en Rihadh, Arabia Saudita; Varsovia, Polonia; París, Francia; y Davos, Suiza, fueron altamente aclamados por la mayoría. Él estaba, y está, haciendo lo que muchos expertos aceptan que es una diferencia tremenda en asuntos internacionales, diciéndole al mundo que "Estados Unidos está de vuelta en el negocio".

En el frente interno, él ha revertido las regulaciones que restringen el libre comercio, el desarrollo energético y el uso de los recursos naturales de Estados Unidos. Tal como se relató en otros capítulos, el Presidente está empezando a drenar el pantano en Washington y se ha hecho cargo del subgobierno al hacer cambios dramáticos a la burocracia permanente. Nada de esto ha sido fácil, y a las batallas les falta mucho para terminar, pero Donald Trump ha demostrado que él es un luchador y espera ganarlas todas.

LAS INFLUENCIAS DE TRUMP EN EL REINO

A pesar de la evidencia de la postura firme del Presidente por los valores religiosos y morales, los periodistas liberales y los críticos de los medios han acusado repetidamente a los evangélicos de hipocresía por apoyar a una persona con un pasado muy escabroso. Muchos afirmaron que el respaldo de Trump al exjuez de la Corte Suprema de Justicia de Alabama, Roy Moore, quien fue acusado de salir con adolescentes, fue descarado y sus simpatizantes evangélicos fueron culpados de duplicidad moral.[15]

Nadie apoya todo lo que Trump ha dicho o hecho, sus múltiples matrimonios, las cosas negativas que ha dicho sobre los inmigrantes ilegales, o sus batallas por Twitter con celebridades y oponentes políticos. Sin embargo, el tamaño de su base evangélica, la cual es grande y continúa creciendo, es evidencia de que la gente de fe ha decidido que sus creencias y sus motivos son buenos en general. Ellos creen que él los protege, y, tal como señalado en el capítulo anterior, los votantes evangélicos tomaron una postura calculada basada en las alternativas políticas y su entendimiento de que todos los seres humanos son pecadores.

Claro está, eso no es suficientemente bueno para los que están en la Izquierda. Como ejemplo, Randall Balmer, un sacerdote episcopal y catedrático de religión en *Dartmouth College*, recientemente concluyó que la comunidad evangélica ha perdido la confianza en la moralidad bíblica. Escribiendo en el periódico liberal inglés *The Guardian*, Balmer dice: "La total aceptación de los religiosos de la Derecha al Partido Republicano y a Donald J. Trump, tanto como candidato y como presidente, ha requerido una reescritura de la ética evangélica".[16]

El profesor asegura que los evangélicos creen aparentemente que "mentir está bien en tanto sirva para un propósito mayor", "la vulgaridad es una señal de fortaleza", "los inmigrantes son basura", y "la vida de los blancos importa (mucho más que otras)".[17] Los liberales, como Balmer, no entienden que Donald Trump era la única opción responsable para los conservadores y para la gente de fe en las elecciones de 2016. Ellos entienden demasiado bien lo que habrían significado cuatro años de un Clinton en la presidencia. Con una cultura que se está volviendo cada vez más secular, y más hostil a la fe cristiana, los evangélicos se dieron cuenta que elegir a Hillary Clinton habría sido infinitamente peor que elegir a Trump, con todas sus imperfecciones.

En las guerras culturales, lo que la Izquierda ha estado fomentando durante los últimos cuarenta años, los evangélicos buscaban un agente de cambio que sacudiera el *statu quo*. Ellos vieron a Donald Trump como alguien que defendería sus intereses y apoyaría sus valores. Por eso es por lo que le dieron a Mitt Romney, un mormón, que nunca se había acercado a la comunidad evangélica, el 79 por ciento de sus votos en 2012. Eso es aproximadamente el mismo porcentaje que le dieron a George W. Bush y a John McCain. Si Romney se hubiera acercado a los evangélicos y apoyado los valores conservadores como Trump lo ha hecho, ellos lo habrían apoyado con el mismo entusiasmo, y creo que él habría derrotado a Barack Obama y ganado la Casa Blanca. Sin embargo, muchos evangélicos se quedaron en casa, y Romney perdió por 4.98 millones de votos, o 3.9 por ciento, lo que era el margen evangélico.

Después de luchar durante dos mandatos bajo Obama, quien cambió drásticamente sobre el matrimonio gay y se convirtió en defensor de *Planned Parenthood* y la industria del aborto, millones de evangélicos y otros de benevolencia, estaban desesperados por un defensor. Diecisiete republicanos se postularon para el trabajo, incluyendo varios con destacados credenciales evangélicos. Mike Huckabee, expastor bautista, hizo un caso fuerte, al igual que el exgobernador de Luisiana, Bobby Jindal y el senador Ted Cruz, a quien apoyé inicialmente. Otros como el senador Marco Rubio y el Dr. Ben Carson hablaron abiertamente sobre su fe cristiana fuerte. Ellos tenían muchos simpatizantes dedicados, pero ninguno de estos candidatos captó la imaginación de los votantes.

La pregunta era: ¿Quién era lo suficientemente fuerte para derrotar a la aplanadora Clinton? Tal como documenté en mi libro anterior *God and Donald Trump*, la mayoría de las instituciones evangélicas líderes apoyaban inicialmente a Ted Cruz. El apoyo de Trump vino principalmente a los cristianos pentecostales y carismáticos en las primeras etapas de la campaña; en parte, debido a la influencia de la pastora Paula White Cain y, en parte, debido a las profecías de que Dios estaba levantando un líder como el Ciro, el rey persa, un pagano usado por Dios para permitir que los judíos regresaran del cautiverio babilonio a Jerusalén.

Con el tiempo, Trump convenció a la amplia comunidad evangélica que él hablaba en serio y ganó la participación evangélica más grande en la historia. Como me dijo el Dr. Jerry Falwell Jr., presidente de *Liberty University*, en una entrevista para la revista *Charisma*: "Lo he dicho una y otra vez: No estamos eligiendo a un pastor. Estamos eligiendo un presidente. Cuando usted elige a un doctor, elije al mejor que encuentra."[18] El gobernador Huckabee, quien escribió el prólogo para *God and Donald Trump*, me dijo que él había intentado explicarle muchas veces a los reporteros que "nadie en el mundo cristiano, ciertamente no en el mundo evangélico, tenía expectativa alguna de que Donald Trump fuera uno de nosotros". Él dijo que dudaba que Trump pudiera encontrar Juan 3:16 (el texto cristiano primordial) en un Nuevo Testamento marcado.

En una entrevista para este libro, el exgobernador me dijo: "Incluso podría ser solo su instinto. Pero creo que eso es lo que produce su afinidad entre el presidente Trump y la comunidad evangélica. Ellos ven en él a alguien que ve el mundo con claridad, y eso no es algo que hayan visto en la mayoría de sus líderes políticos". Lo que nunca deja de sorprenderme, dijo, es el respeto sincero y la admiración por la comunidad evangélica del presidente. "Creo que parte de eso se debe a que los evangélicos y Donald Trump ven las cosas en términos binarios. Bueno o mal. Correcto o incorrecto. Arriba o abajo. Ellos no ven nada en… cincuenta tonos de gris. Lo ven más en términos de opciones muy claras, y Donald Trump se vuelve muy directo con ellos. Él ve las cosas completa y claramente. No es un diplomático, alguien que se queda de brazos cruzados que diga 'Ah, puede ser esto, pero quizá deberíamos considerar aquello'. Él llega rápido a una conclusión".

El Dr. Robert Jeffress, respetado pastor de *First Baptist Church of Dallas*, dijo que en 2016 el electorado estaba harto del *statu quo*. Jeffress me dijo: "La gente en ambos lados del pasillo sabe que somos un desastre. Se requirió de alguien de afuera, como Donald Trump, para ganar las elecciones porque él demostró que tiene la voluntad y el liderazgo necesario para revertir la trayectoria cuesta abajo de esta nación".

El evangelista James Robison, una de las personalidades de los medios evangélicos más respetados en Estados Unidos, no apoyaba inicialmente a Trump, pero terminó siendo su mayor partidario e incluso un confidente del candidato Trump. Él explicó a Trump así: "Dios tiene solo un hijo perfecto: Jesús. Todo el resto de nosotros somos imperfectos. La Biblia no blanquea a ninguno de los personajes o héroes de la fe. Todos ellos tienen defectos y fallaron trágicamente, incluso cuando estaban procurando hacer la voluntad de Dios. Incluso el apóstol Pablo se refirió a sí mismo como 'el mayor de los pecadores'. Ninguno debería estar sorprendido cuando un contratista neoyorquino habla como contratista neoyorquino".

Robison dice que Jesús quiere que se haga su voluntad "en la tierra como en el cielo". Es "no de este mundo", pero está aquí ahora. Eso se debe a que la gente con mentalidad del reino, quienes están orando sabe que solo *el* Pastor puede guiarnos a pastos más verdes, pero Él puede guiar a cualquier líder apropiadamente, dijo Robison. "Eso es por lo que la gente ha estado orando, sin creer jamás que alguien como Donald Trump, un hombre de negocios de Nueva York, podría en realidad contribuir a la corrección positiva". Robison me dijo que él cree que vienen cambios positivos debido a la "influencia del reino" sobre este presidente.

Como he intentado explicarles a los medios seculares, la mayoría de los evangélicos nacidos de nuevo sabe que Dios cambia vidas, incluso las propias, y entendemos que nadie es perfecto. El poeta y dramaturgo irlandés, profano, Oscar Wilde, dijo lo que todos sabemos: "La única diferencia entre el santo y el pecador es que todo santo tiene un pasado, y todo pecador tiene un futuro".[19] No tengo duda de que él aprendió esa lección por las malas. Sin embargo, fue esencialmente este razonamiento lo que le permitió a muchos evangélicos ver por encima de las indiscreciones de Donald Trump. Una vez que hicieron las paces con su pasado, la única pregunta era: ¿Podría él impedirle a Hillary Clinton su victoria inevitable? Contra todo pronóstico, las profecías que decían que Trump ganaría se volvieron realidad. Mientras había preocupación en la Izquierda, la Derecha religiosa estaba extasiada, sintiendo que "Dios nos ha dado un indulto". Jeffress dijo: "Yo creo que Dios puso a Donald Trump en el cargo para darle a la iglesia más libertad para compartir el evangelio de Jesucristo".

RESPONDER A LOS ESCÉPTICOS

Con Donald Trump cumpliendo tantas promesas que incluyen lo que la mayoría de evangélicos cree que es importante, algunos preguntarían: ¿Por qué un segmento de la iglesia evangélica se identifica como "Trump jamás"? Considerando que solo el 20 por ciento de los evangélicos no votó por él en 2016, yo hubiera esperado que estos individuos cambiaran de modo de pensar y apoyaran a Trump, como lo hice yo en 2016, después de que empezaron a ver lo que el Presidente ha logrado realmente.

Para comprender esto, entrevisté a Mark Galli, editor en jefe de la revista *Christianity Today*. Si bien *Christianity Today* no apoyó a los candidatos de ninguno de los partidos, por sus editoriales uno puede darse cuenta de que ellos no eran admiradores de Trump. Me enteré de que Galli no lo apoyaba a ninguno cuando él y yo fuimos entrevistados por el *New York Times* durante la semana en que el juez Roy Moore perdió su elección al Senado. La escritora del *Times*, Laurie Goodstein, me entrevistó el día de las elecciones y trató de hacerme decir que los evangélicos estaban manchando su reputación. Según Goodstein, apoyar a alguien tan imperfecto como Trump y su amigo, Roy Moore, era traicionar nuestros principios.

He conocido y admirado a Galli por muchos años cuando llegó a las filas de *Christianity Today*. La entradilla de Goodstein decía que él no necesitaba esperar a que los votos fueran contados para publicar un ensayo diciendo: "Quienquiera que gane, ya hay un perdedor: la fe cristiana". Ella citó a Galli diciendo: "Nadie creerá una palabra de lo que digamos, quizá durante una generación. La integridad cristiana está severamente manchada". Ella agregó: "La visión de los votantes blancos evangélicos en Alabama dándole su apoyo abrumador a Roy S. Moore ha preocupado profundamente a muchos cristianos conservadores, que temen que la asociación con gente como el Sr. Moore esté dándole mala fama a su nombre. La angustia ha llegado a ser tan profunda, dijo el Sr. Galli, que él sabe de 'muchos evangélicos afiliados' que están listos para abandonar la afiliación".[20]

El *New York Times* citó luego a Ed Stetzer, director ejecutivo del Billy Graham Center en *Wheaton College*, una facultad evangélica prominente en Illinois, diciendo: "Me entristece. No quiero que 'evangélico' signifique gente que apoyaba candidatos con acusaciones en su contra significativas y creíbles. Si evangélico significa eso, tiene serias consecuencias para la obra de los cristianos y las iglesias".[21]

Como reportero que soy, me di cuenta de que Goodstein tenía un argumento y estaba buscando algunas citas jugosas para respaldarlo. No estaba de acuerdo en darle las cápsulas que ella quería; en cambio, traté de explicar que con la forma en que el país se había dirigido durante el último medio siglo, necesitábamos a alguien que fuera perturbador. "Yo creo que Dios respondió nuestras oraciones en una manera que no esperábamos, por una persona que no era precisamente de nuestro agrado", ella me citó correctamente diciendo que me identificaba como el autor de *God and Donald Trump* y el fundador de Charisma Media".[22]

"Los cristianos creen en la redención y en el perdón, así que están dispuestos a darle una oportunidad a Donald Trump", seguí diciendo. Luego, añadí que el apoyo de los cristianos nacidos de nuevo no puede darse por sentado. "Si él resulta ser un libertino como Bill Clinton", dije, "o deshonesto en alguna manera, en una manera que sea demostrada, usted verá que el apoyo se desvanece tan rápidamente como llegó". Eso fue citado bastante bien, pero en una entrevista de una hora de duración, yo traté de explicar que Jesús dijo que "no todos los que dicen Señor, Señor, entrarán en el reino de los cielos", y hay algunas personas que se identifican como cristianos, pero no aceptan las doctrinas esenciales de la fe. Yo estaba sencillamente planteando la pregunta de si los "Trump jamás" y otros que odian a Trump son realmente creyentes.[23]

Durante la entrevista, la escritora nunca mencionó a Mark Galli o a Ed Stetzer. Ella me entrevistó el día de las elecciones y entrevistó a otros dos del día después. Cuando la historia apareció impresa, Goodstein citó a Galli y a Stetzer como teniendo profundas reservas sobre el juez Moore y Donald Trump, y citó a Galli como diciendo que el nombre de los evangélicos estaba "manchado". Ella me citó después: "El Sr. Strang dijo que los que dicen que el Sr. Trump está manchando el nombre de los evangélicos 'no son creyentes realmente, no están con nosotros, en ninguna manera".[24]

Aunque sí lo había dicho, mis palabras fueron tomadas fuera de contexto. Yo había planteado la idea hipotéticamente sobre personas no mencionadas. Aun así, mi comentario creó un frenesí breve en Twitter, donde la gente me atacaba como que yo hubiera dicho que todo el que no estaba de acuerdo conmigo no era un creyente. Peor que eso, me hizo parecer como si yo hubiera dicho que Mark Galli y Ed Stetzer, a quienes respeto y considero mis amigos, no eran creyentes. Cuando leí el artículo en línea, el 14 de diciembre de 2017, bajo el titular: "Efectos colaterales para los evangélicos después de elecciones caóticas", quedé anonadado. Inmediatamente llamé a ambas personas y les dije que mis palabras habían sido citadas fuera de contexto y que yo nunca dije que los líderes cristianos no eran creyentes debido a diferencias políticas. Afortunadamente, ambos aceptaron mi explicación y aprendí a ser cauto la próxima vez que hable con un reportero del *New York Times*.

Meses después, cuando entrevisté a Mark Galli para este libro, lo hice para probar y comprender el patrón de pensamiento de un "Trump jamás". Galli dejó en claro que él nunca ha sido uno de ellos, aunque no votó por él y probablemente no votará por él en 2020. Él mencionó varios logros de Trump: nombrar a Neil Gorsuch para la Corte Suprema, defender la libertad de culto, llevar a Corea del Norte a la mesa de negociación, y garantizar la puesta en libertad de tres coreanos cristianos, reconociendo cada una de esas cosas como victorias importantes para los cristianos. Trasladar la embajada de Estados Unidos en Israel a Jerusalén fue un movimiento audaz. Él reconoció que, a veces, los líderes hacen movimientos audaces que todos creen que están mal, pero que después resultan ser correctos. "Uno no puede culpar a Trump por no hacer movimientos audaces", dijo.

Él también quería aclarar las cosas sobre algo del artículo de *New York Times*.

Por ejemplo: Él no dijo específicamente que el nombre de los evangélicos estuviera "manchado". Él me dijo: "Mi intención fue esta: para la gente de la Izquierda, el apoyo evangélico para Trump hace que ellos respeten menos a los evangélicos. Eso es una realidad. Por otro lado, apoyar a Trump no ha manchado el nombre de los conservadores que votaron por Trump".

Si Galli y aquellos que concuerdan con él tienen un problema es lo que veo ahora como una diferencia fundamental en estilo. Ellos consideran a Trump descarado, jactancioso y populista. "Existen segmentos diferentes de la vida estadounidense a los que simplemente no les gusta el populismo o los líderes del movimiento populista", me dijo Galli. "Ellos piensan que los populistas son peligrosos... solo a unos pasos de convertirse en un Hitler o un Stalin". En cambio, Galli dijo que él prefiere que el liderazgo sea sutil, que hable con suavidad.

Le pregunté si él creía que el flirteo de Trump con una estrella porno hace una docena de años, disminuía sus éxitos políticos obvios. Respondió: "Cuando él está lidiando con Arabia Saudita o Corea, dudo que estén pensando una o dos veces sobre si él tuvo un amorío con Stormy Daniels o no". Sin embargo, él continuó y dijo que, a la larga, queremos que nuestros presidentes sean un ejemplo de nuestros ideales, personas a quienes nuestros hijos y nietos puedan admirar, y él siente que Trump no es eso. El verdadero enigma, dijo, es cómo tantos evangélicos lo apoyan cuando él ha tenido un pasado tan escabroso. "Durante mucho tiempo, los evangélicos han dicho que el carácter de nuestros líderes es uno de los aspectos más importantes del liderazgo. Y ahora han tomado una postura y dicho: 'Eso no es tan importante en tanto sus políticas se lleven a cabo...' Los evangélicos conservadores han tomado un tiempo para obtener el respeto de la plaza pública. Y ellos quieren ser vistos como jugadores legítimos en un mundo de cultura y política... entonces llega Donald Trump, y rompe todas esas reglas... Desde la perspectiva de nuestra reputación internacional", Galli dijo enfáticamente, "Trump es una vergüenza para nuestro país".

Aunque respeto a Mark Galli y honro su opinión, nosotros no estamos de acuerdo en un montón de cosas, incluyendo doctrinas teológicas. Sin embargo, podemos estar de acuerdo en que lo más importante para los cristianos, tanto de la Izquierda como de la Derecha, es que hay un reino más alto. En cierto modo, entiendo por dónde vienen Galli y quienes comparten sus opiniones. Durante veinte años fui un demócrata registrado, lo que significó que no pude votar en las primarias republicanas cuando Pat Robertson se postuló para la presidencia en 1988. Pero cuando me registré para votar, la decisión *Roe vs Wade* de 1973, permitiendo el aborto aún no había sucedido. Los problemas más grandes que dividían a la nación en ese momento eran la Guerra de Vietnam y las manifestaciones por los derechos civiles en el Sur. Yo proclamé la igualdad racial en aquel entonces y ahora, pero mis opiniones políticas sufrirían un cambio mayor.

¿En quién confía?

Debido a que el movimiento pentecostés surgió de la experiencia de la iglesia negra, y ya que las iglesias carismáticas están entre las más integradas en la nación, como cristiano carismático, siempre he creído que mi lugar está a la vanguardia del llamado por la unidad racial. He usado a la revista *Charisma*, la cual fundé en 1975, como un púlpito intimidante durante cuatro décadas, pidiendo la unidad en el Cuerpo de Cristo. Sostuve mi registro de votante en el Partido Demócrata de Florida hasta que el partido dio un giro brusco hacia la Izquierda y aceptó el aborto y los derechos homosexuales en la plataforma partidista. Eso me envió al Partido Republicano, el cual está ahora mucho más cerca a los valores tradicionales y conservadores cristianos en comparación al Partido Demócrata del presente.

Mark Galli me ayudó a entender otro punto importante, también, con relación a las actitudes de los evangélicos que aún critican al Presidente. A causa de los comentarios groseros y ofensivos de Trump, especialmente aquellos que denigran a varios grupos étnicos, estos individuos no creen que Trump ejemplifique los rasgos de las personas más refinadas; eso es, aquellos con ingresos más altos y mejor educación (en otras palabras, las "élites"). Ellos no sienten afinidad por una personalidad perturbadora como la de Trump. En cambio, quieren a alguien que pueda "codearse junto con el *statu quo*", lo cual no es el estilo de Trump.

El pastor Jeffress me recordó que Ronald Reagan dijo una vez que el término *statu quo* es el latín de "el caos en el que estamos".[25] Y ese podría ser el punto crucial de la división entre el 80 por ciento, al que llamo "evangélicos rojos", y el 20 por ciento, que tiende a ser "evangélicos azules". Uno tiene que preguntarse, "¿es el *statu quo* lo suficientemente bueno a medida que el país se tambalea hacia la Izquierda, o si es un perturbador lo que necesitamos realmente para traer la muy necesaria corrección de curso? El pastor Jeffress dice que él prestó atención a las encuestas en *Christianity Today* durante la campaña para ver a quién estaban apoyando la mayoría de los líderes evangélicos, y solamente uno de cada dos apoyaba a Donald Trump. "Se les pasó", me dijo, "y creo que un montón de esos líderes cristianos estaban disgustados de tener tan poca influencia sobre las bases evangélicas que no los escuchaban y votaron por Trump de todos modos".

Como lo escribí en otra parte, los medios seculares parecen interesados en los evangélicos solo si pueden encontrar evidencia de hipocresía y fanatismo. He tenido docenas de entrevistas de radio y televisión desde la publicación de *God y Donald Trump*, pero la razón por la que CNN y MSNBC querían hablarme de Trump casi no tenía que ver con mi libro, sino cómo los cristianos evangélicos podían defender a Donald Trump después de la erupción del escándalo de Stormy Daniels.

La NPR tenía preguntas similares para Stephen Mansfield, un evangélico que escribió el libro *Choosing Donald Trump*, que examinaba si los evangélicos y sus líderes, que apoyaban expresivamente a Trump le habían infringido un daño duradero a su testimonio cristiano. "Sí", dijo Mansfield. "Creo que van a perder influencia especialmente entre los adultos jóvenes, quienes están fuertemente orientados hacia la justicia social, y las encuestas indican que la gran mayoría de ellos tienen muchas sospechas de Donald Trump.

"Tienen una situación inusual aquí", continuó, "donde los líderes de la Derecha religiosa no solo tienen que rendirle cuentas a un mundo que observa por qué comprometieron su mensaje religioso para apoyar a Donald Trump, sino que van a tener alguna repercusión de parte de la misma gente que la Derecha religiosa está tratando de alcanzar. Exactamente la misma gente que estos pastores tratan de alcanzar: los jóvenes, la gente de color, etc., yo creo que los han perdido y, en algunos casos, de manera permanente".[26]

Mientras los liberales y quienes cortejan la aprobación liberal les gusta presentar acusaciones de hipocresía con respecto a los cristianos y todos los demás que no está de acuerdo con sus perspectivas izquierdistas, Tucker Carlson, el anfitrión de *Tucker Carlson Tonight* en el *Fox News Channel* tiene una opinión diferente. Como episcopal, Carlson no se identifica como evangélico, pero entiende a la Izquierda y a sus actitudes. A los liberales les encanta acusar a los cristianos de ser "más santos que vosotros", dice, "pero el término le queda mucho mejor a las élites liberales y, yo añadiría, que también a los evangélicos de "Trump jamás".

Cuando el fiscal general de Nueva York, Eric Schneiderman renunció en mayo de 2018 debido a múltiples acusaciones de conducta sexual inapropiada, Carlson dijo: "La hipocresía no es solo un distintivo del liberalismo moderno. Es el corazón del liberalismo moderno". Hablando de Schneiderman, él dijo: "Algunos de sus amigos de mucho tiempo en la Izquierda están manifestando *shock*. Usted los ha oído. 'No podemos creerlo' dicen. '¿Cómo un hombre tan comprometido públicamente con el feminismo golpea mujeres? No tiene sentido'. Pero, por supuesto, que tiene perfecto sentido. La superioridad moral es siempre una señal de repugnancia secreta. La gente que más grita es generalmente la que más oculta".[27] Carlson añadió:

> Tenga eso presente la próxima vez que escuche a algún político demócrata sermoneándolo sobre su inferioridad moral. Ese es el hombre al que debe observar cuidadosamente. Es posible que él esté haciendo algo horrible a puerta cerrada… ¿Se ha preguntado alguna vez cómo un defensor del aborto puede decir que está en defensa de los niños? ¿Cómo un movimiento que demoniza a una raza entera asegura oponerse al racismo? Del mismo modo, Al Gore puede viajar en avión privado mientras trata de prohibir su vehículo todoterreno. Porque la consistencia no le importa a la Izquierda. La virtud es lo único que importa. Somos gente buena; por lo tanto,

debemos gobernar. Ustedes no lo son; por lo tanto, tienen que obedecer. Al Gore no cree que él sea un hipócrita. Eric Schneiderman probablemente tampoco piensa que lo es. Uno no puede cometer pecado si las intenciones son puras. Y los liberales creen que sus intenciones son las más puras.[28]

En ese punto, Carlson hace una observación que se encuentra en el centro del conflicto entre la Izquierda y la Derecha, y entre secularistas y conservadores cristianos. Él dijo que el liberalismo es una religión tratando de desplazar al cristianismo en la cultura estadounidense:

Si eso suena como teología, y no política pública, es porque es teología. El liberalismo moderno es un reemplazo del cristianismo protestante que la Izquierda trabajó muy duro para debilitar y destruir. Los liberales están hablando el lenguaje de la fe; aunque sea una fe sin Dios. Esta es la razón principal por la que la Derecha y la Izquierda habla una sobre la otra, la razón del porqué nuestros debates públicos son tan extraños e insatisfactorios. Un lado llega con hechos, estadísticas y argumentos. El otro presume de su decencia. Un lado está tratando de convencer; el otro lado trata de convertir. Usted puede derrotar a un liberal en un argumento, pero nunca podrá convencerlo de que usted ganó. A él le importa mucho más profundamente que a usted y, por lo tanto, sabe que tiene razón. Por definición. Y nada puede convencerlo de lo contrario.[29]

Es difícil estar en desacuerdo con su lógica. Carlson continuó diciendo: "En alguna parte, esta noche, Eric Schneiderman se está marinado en su vergüenza. Probablemente sin afeitarse y solo. Su carrera ha terminado. Su reputación está destruida. Enfrenta años de potenciales acciones legales. Es un hombre quebrantado. Está agonizando". Luego Carlos concluyó: "Y, aun así, en algún grado, a pesar de todo eso, Eric Schneiderman todavía sabe que él es una mejor persona que usted".[30]

El pastor Samuel Rodríguez, quien oró en la investidura de Trump, cree que las cosas están polarizadas políticamente más que nunca. Me dijo que él cree que el Partido Demócrata se ha trasladado tan lejos hacia la Izquierda que, si Hillary Clinton se postulara de nuevo, sería considerada por los demócratas fieles como demasiado conservadora para obtener la denominación. Mientras tanto, los republicanos se han acercado más al centro, lo que los hace ampliamente interesante para los obreros demócratas que votaron por Trump.

El pastor Rodríguez es el presidente de la Conferencia Nacional de Liderazgo Cristiano Hispano y ha visto de cerca el cambio entre los votantes latinos. Los hispanos apoyaron a Donald Trump en un nivel mucho más alto de lo que se esperaba, casi 30 por ciento. Para los hispanos evangélicos y los católicos que asisten a la iglesia, el porcentaje fue 66 por ciento. Cuando el habló con el candidato Trump, me contó, que él dijo que los hispanos estaban interesados en cinco cosas: la Corte Suprema, la libertad de culto, las oportunidades educativas, la unidad racial, y la reforma migratoria, en ese orden. Los hispanos prestaron mucha atención a los casos de la Corte Suprema incluyendo a *Sisters of the Poor*, Hobby Lobby y otros, dijo él, y cree que Obama le hizo más daños a la libertad de culto que todos los cuarenta y tres presidentes previos combinados.

CONFIAR EN SUS CREENCIAS PRINCIPALES

¿Qué es lo que los líderes cristianos piensan realmente del presidente Trump? Entrevisté a varios que lo han visto a él de cerca. Jerry Falwell Jr., quien estuvo entre los primeros partidarios de Trump y sus aliados más cercanos, le dijo a Martha Raddatz en ABC: "Una de las razones por las que lo apoyé es porque él no dice lo que es políticamente correcto; él dice lo que está en su corazón, lo que él cree y, a veces, eso lo mete en problemas".[31]

El evangelista James Robison está de acuerdo. "Este es un hombre que no será intimidado ni manipulado. Él no será intimidado por ninguna forma de precisión política ni algún ataque manipulador de los medios. Él simplemente no se inmuta. La iglesia necesita dejar de escuchar a la gente que procura la controversia y el conflicto, en los medios y en la iglesia".

Los medios han presentado a Trump como arrogante, ostentoso y un poco loco. Esto era lo que yo esperaba cuando entrevisté al candidato Trump durante la campaña, en agosto 2016. Pero eso no fue lo que vi. Hallé que él tiene una voz gentil, que es respetuoso y hasta humilde. Desde entonces he hablado con otros líderes cristianos que opinan lo mismo. Tras bambalinas, él es simpático y les simpatizó a todos. Sin embargo, eso fue antes de las elecciones, cuando los políticos dirían y harían casi cualquier cosa por obtener su apoyo. Pero resulta, que el presidente Trump es casi igual al candidato Trump. Y para los líderes de su *Faith Leaders Initiative*, él no solo es el mismo, sino que quizás hasta ha mejorado desde que se rodea de consejo cristiano sabio.

Como Falwell me contó: "Él es agradable. Le encanta la gente. Creo que esa es una de las pruebas verdaderas de un cristiano, si le encanta la gente o no, toda la gente, no importa quiénes son. Yo soy solo el hijo de un predicador que se convirtió en presidente de una universidad, pero él todavía responde su teléfono cada dos o tres semanas cuando lo llamo, y no tiene que hacerlo. Pero él es sociable y creo que trata a las personas comunes de la misma manera en que trata a los multimillonarios y de la misma manera en que trata a los famosos. Y creo que ese es un indicador de su fe también".

Jerry Falwell y Robert Jeffress, ambos me dijeron que el Presidente está abierto a las personas de fe e invita a líderes evangélicos a la Casa Blanca y les permite que oren por él en la Oficina Oval. Cuando Jeffress le dijo a Trump que la gente quería saber de su fe personal, el Presidente le dijo que respondiera que su fe es muy importante y muy personal para él. Así que Jeffress lo dejó así. Cuando yo le pregunté a Falwell sobre la fe personal de Trump, él me respondió así: "Tú sabes lo que dijo Jesús: 'ora en tu closet, y Dios que te ve en privado te recompensará en público'. Yo creo que eso es lo que Donald Trump hace. Creo que él dice lo que piensa. Lo admiro por eso. Pero sí creo que él mantiene su fe en privado, y creo que no es de esas personas que es bueno explicando sus creencias y no se siente cómodo hablando de ello públicamente. Y él tiene derecho a esa decisión".

En cuanto a su carácter, Falwell dijo: "Nunca he sabido que sea alguna otra cosa, excepto cien por ciento sincero, y es un hombre de palabra. Lo que me haya prometido en el pasado, lo ha hecho". Trump puede haber sido injuriado por más gente que ningún otro presidente desde Abraham Lincoln, y la presión sobre él es inmensa. Aun así, eso no parece molestarle. Jeffress dijo que él ha estado con el Presidente en la Oficina Oval en momentos donde había muchas distracciones externas, y que él siempre quedaba impresionado por cuán calmado y sereno podía estar el Presidente bajo las circunstancias más adversas. "Yo creía que tenía que animar al Presidente", me contó, "pero él estaba tranquilo y jovial, tan enfocado como lo he visto siempre. ¿No es este el tipo de persona que usted querría en esa silla en la Oficina Oval?".

Falwell me dijo que cada vez que llama al Presidente, él dice: "¿Qué puedo hacer? ¿Hay algo que pueda hacer para ayudarle, Sr. Presidente? Por favor, no se rinda. No se desanime. No renuncie". Y él dijo que el presidente Trump siempre le responde: "No te preocupes por mí, Jerry. Y no voy a echar marcha atrás". Falwell explica: "Yo solo quiero darle ánimo… Ya sabes, él es el único en medio de este país y el tipo de liderazgo que tuvimos durante los últimos, qué se yo cuántos años, republicano y demócrata, y él es el único que está a favor de la persona promedio, que pone a Estados Unidos en primer lugar. Él es el único que tiene las agallas para oponerse a los atacantes y disidentes", dijo Falwell, "y la gente que miente acerca de él y el subgobierno. No hemos visto ese tipo de liderazgo en ningún presidente desde Ronald Reagan. Quizás desde antes de eso. Yo solo pienso que necesitamos hacer todo lo que podamos como cristianos para orar por él".

Hablando de personas que mienten acerca del Presidente, mientras estaba terminando las correcciones finales de este libro, el libro de Omarosa Manigault Newman, *Unhinged*, salió a la venta. Cuando ella estuvo en el personal de la Casa Blanca, la Izquierda y los medios la difamaron, al decir que ella estaba traicionando a los afroamericanos; como si los negros deberían uniformemente oponerse a Trump solo porque la mayoría son demócratas. Aun así, cuando ella le dio la espalda a Trump al escribir un libro negativo sobre él y criticándolo en las entrevistas de los medios, ella se volvió la querida de los mismos medios de comunicación, incluso si la atención fue breve.

Conocí a Omarosa en la fiesta de elección de Trump en el New York Hilton en Manhattan. Al principio de la noche, cuando no había muchas personas en el salón, vi a Omarosa rodeada de admiradores. Estaba vagamente familiarizado con ella como si fuera alguna celebridad. Ya que tuve la oportunidad, entablé una conversación con ella, sin siquiera soñar que ella se volvería controversial o que yo estaría escribiendo sobre el tema dos años después. Hablamos por un buen rato, y yo estaba impresionado de cuánto ella apoyaba a Donald Trump. Ella compartió cómo Trump le había ayudado al tenerla en *The Apprentice*. Rápidamente me di cuenta de que ella tenía una amistad de mucho tiempo con el candidato. Esa noche, estaba muy emocionada de que su amigo, por quien había hecho campaña, estaba ganando. Tuve la impresión de que ella hasta obtendría un empleo en la Casa Blanca. Así que estaba impresionado cuando le dio la espalda después de que la despidieran de la administración de la Casa Blanca.

A medida que la controversia sobre su nuevo libro, las grabaciones secretas y los comentarios desagradables sobre el Presidente en las redes de televisión empezaron a salir a luz, no podía olvidar cuán positiva había sido acerca de Donald Trump. Luego, vi algunas de las entrevistas que ella dio cuando aún apoyaba al Presidente. O estaba mintiendo entonces, o está mintiendo ahora. Pero una cosa es cierta: la gente que busca oportunidades en los medios puede simplemente criticar a Trump y obtener toda la atención que quiere.

En mi conversación con el gobernador Huckabee, él me dijo que "Donald Trump es único en su capacidad para sacudirse las críticas más ásperas y sencillamente ignorarlas". Él dijo: "Nunca he visto a nadie como él con relación a esto. Es decir, la mayoría de las personas que están tan completamente bajo asedio como lo está él probablemente estarían escondiéndose bajo el escritorio en la Oficina Oval y acurrucándose en posición final porque estarían simplemente pensando 'no puedo siquiera salir y enfrentar al mundo. Tengo todas estas acusaciones'. Ni siquiera solo políticas, la destemplanza del corazón. Se trata de todas estas cosas si es Stormy Daniels, o alguna otra mujer que hace quince años dijo que había tenido una aventura con él.

"La mayor parte de ese tipo de cosas haría que una persona quisiera solamente decir: 'Tengo que huir. No puedo quedarme aquí'. Y ¿sabe dónde termina él? Él fija su mirada en la cara de sus acusadores y los desafía. Y vi eso durante la campaña. Es una de las razones por las que al principio dije: '¿Sabes?, yo creo que este tipo va a ganar'. Todos los demás decían 'No tiene oportunidad. No hay manera'. Yo dije, 'Muchachos, no están entendiendo bien'.

"Cuando la gente dice 'No puedo creer que él haya dicho eso en el mitin', yo diría, 'Tú no entiendes. Lo que él dijo en el micrófono, en el pódium, fue lo que cuatro hombres sentados a la mesa en un restaurante económico, inclinándose para acercarse, dijeron lo mismo esa mañana, en el desayuno. Ellos estaban pensando que necesitaban ser cuidadosos, para que nadie los escuchara; pero, luego, Trump va y lo dice en el micrófono, y ellos están allí, sentados, diciendo: "¡Sí! ¡Ahora hay alguien que habla nuestro idioma!". Y eso está totalmente fuera del alcance de la mayoría de las personas que estaban cubriendo la campaña para las redes de noticias".

Según aquellos que lo conocen mejor, Donald Trump es un hombre con una fe y confianza resueltas. Él ha sido probado una y otra vez, y él ha sufrido muchos reveses y contratiempos a lo largo del camino. Se necesitaría una confianza en sí mismo monumental para levantarse por encima de las piedras y las flechas que han sido apuntadas a él. Pero este presidente tiene la fortaleza para vencer esos retos, y él tiene la confianza para creer en sus convicciones. Tal como Falwell me dijo, Donald Trump es un hombre que toma sus propias decisiones en todo. "Creo que escucha a mucha gente", dijo, "pero no creo que permita que nadie le diga qué hacer. He notado eso acerca de él. Recibirá el concejo de todos, y escuchará a todos, pero nadie le dice qué hacer. Nadie influye indebidamente en él. Nunca he visto a nadie como él. Todos los demás políticos con quienes he hablado pueden ser persuadidos e influenciados, pero él realmente no puede. Él es su propio hombre, y yo realmente respeto eso".

LA BATALLA POR JERUSALÉN

L
A INTRANQUILIDAD EN el Medio Oriente y las guerras que Estados Unidos
está peleando en otras partes del mundo están vinculadas a un tema de política exterior que puede tener el mayor significado a largo plazo, que es lo que
hay que hacer respecto a Israel y Palestina. Desde que Israel recapturó el territorio
que los judíos llaman Judea y Samaria, pero otros lo llaman el Cisjordania, ha
habido un enfrentamiento divisivo y muchas veces violento sobre si debiera haber
una solución de un estado o de dos estados. Los liberales en Israel y de Estados
Unidos tienden a optar por una solución de dos estados. Los conservadores de
línea dura y los sionistas cristianos evangélicos, por otro lado, creen que Dios les
dio la tierra a los judíos, y que ese es el fin de la ecuación.

Sin embargo, incluso entre los evangélicos hay desacuerdo. Algunos evangélicos, especialmente aquellos hacia la izquierda del centro, creen que debería ser
una solución de dos estados y a menudo critican al gobierno israelí, que ellos consideran que no tiene significado religioso. Muchos de los que se asignan a la falsa
doctrina llamada "teología de reemplazo", frecuentemente asociada con la teología
reformada, creen que Dios ignoró a los judíos cuando Él decretó el nuevo pacto
con los creyentes cristianos, expandiendo su pacto con Abraham. Por lo tanto,
ellos creen, que no es necesario apoyar al Estado judío, y que hasta podría ser
moralmente equivocado hacerlo. La doctrina pudo haber tenido algún sentido
antes del establecimiento del Estado judío en 1949, pero es claramente incompatible con las Escrituras y malinterpreta seriamente la realidad del Medio Oriente
hoy día.

Uno de los problemas más controversiales, en algunos círculos, es si Jerusalén debería ser la capital de Israel y si el presidente Trump estaba justificado
al trasladar la embajada de Estados Unidos allí. El Congreso aprobó de manera
abrumadora tal traslado en 1995 en la ley de la Embajada en Jerusalén, lo que
reconocía a Jerusalén como la capital de Israel y requería que se mantuviera como
una ciudad indivisible. El primer ministro Benjamín Netanyahu y el presidente
Trump discutieron esto en una reunión importante pocos meses después de que
Trump asumiera la presidencia como parte del recorrido multinacional del Presidente por Europa y el Medio Oriente. Ellos discutieron no solo la Ley de la

Embajada en Jerusalén, sino además Irán y Siria y cómo asociarse para pelear contra los terroristas en el Medio Oriente.

El propósito de la Ley de la Embajada en Jerusalén era apartar fondos para la reubicación de la Embajada de Estados Unidos de Tel Aviv a Jerusalén antes del 31 de mayo de 1999. Aunque la propuesta de ley se convirtió en ley, cada uno de los presidentes Clinton, Bush y Obama aprobaban exenciones cada seis meses durante sus mandatos de ocho años retrasando la implementación de la ley bajo el argumento de la "seguridad nacional". Imitándolos, Donald Trump también aprobó exenciones, pero el 6 de diciembre de 2017, anunció: "Aunque los presidentes previos hicieron de esto una promesa de campaña mayor, no la cumplieron. Hoy, yo estoy cumpliendo. He determinado que este curso de acción está en los mejores intereses de Estados Unidos de América y en la búsqueda de la paz en Israel y los palestinos. Este es un paso muy esperado para avanzar el proceso de paz y trabajar hacia un acuerdo duradero".[1]

Sería difícil de decir quién estaba más contento si los israelíes, quienes durante mucho han esperado que Estados Unidos tome esta acción monumental, o los sionistas cristianos evangélicos para quienes esto era prioridad máxima. Cuando el Presidente hizo el anuncio, un miembro de su *Faith Leaders Initiative* me contó: "Creo que él lo hizo por nosotros. Él sabe que confiamos en él. Sabe que es un asunto importante para nosotros. Y creo que es una de las razones por las que lo hizo. No creo que lo hayamos presionado o persuadido a hacerlo, pero sí creo que él lo sabía desde el principio, durante las primarias. Tuvimos esta discusión con ellos, respecto a temas principales. La número uno es la santificación de la vida. La segunda, Israel. Él sabía exactamente su posición en esos dos temas, y él cumplió su promesa en ambos".

El pastor Frank Amedia de Ohio lo ve de una manera un poco diferente. Poco después de que Trump fue declarado el ganador de la presidencia, en noviembre de 2016, Amedia se sintió guiado a empezar una red de oración llamada POTUS *Shield* para buscar el favor de Dios y su guía para el nuevo líder. Él hizo campaña a favor de Trump e incluso le dio una palabra profética en una ocasión. "Trump admite que no tuvo un entendimiento previo del apoyo apasionado para Israel por los cristianos conservadores", Amedia me dijo. "De hecho, él era de la opinión, por sus experiencias en Nueva York, de que los judíos y los cristianos estaban profundamente divididos sobre Israel".

Pero algo sucedió mientras se preparaba para hablar en un evento de *American Israel Public Affairs Committee* (AIIPAC) a principios de 2016, y el candidato Trump se atrevió a seguir el consejo de su asesor para presentar un plan para Israel de cinco puntos que incluían reconocer a Jerusalén como su capital y reubicar la Embajada de Estados Unidos allí. "Debido a que él dio el paso para bendecir Israel", me dijo Amedia, "la fuerza y el favor de Dios estaban sobre él, y a través de él, el favor de Dios se elevó más alto. ¡Quienes bendicen a Israel serán bendecidos!".

Cuando se tomó finalmente la decisión de trasladar la embajada de Tel Aviv a Jerusalén, el presidente Trump le dio instrucciones al Departamento de Estado para "empezar el proceso de contratación de arquitectos, ingenieros y planificadores para que la nueva embajada, cuando estuviera completada, fuera un tributo magnífico para la paz".[2] Pero cuando se enteró de que tomaría varios años y casi mil millones de dólares construir la embajada planificada, él decidió trasladar temporalmente la embajada al Consulado de Estados Unidos ya existente en Jerusalén y hacerlo para el septuagésimo aniversario de la independencia de Israel. Después de ese evento ceremonial importante, los arquitectos y los ingenieros contarían con tiempo suficiente para construir la nueva embajada.

"El presidente Trump no tiene el deseo de participar en la construcción de una nación en la región ni de pelear una guerra tradicional. Él se opuso firmemente a la guerra de Irak. Las nuevas guerras del siglo veintiuno son representativas, económicas, mediáticas e ideológicas", el Dr. Mike Evans, amigo mío de muchos años y el fundador y presidente del *Jerusalem Prayer Team*, lo dijo en febrero 2017 en un artículo de *Charisma News*. "Israel es el defensor sustituto indiscutible del mundo. El islam radical ha etiquetado a Israel como 'El pequeño Satanás'. Estados Unidos ha sido coronado como 'El gran Satanás'".[3] Y estas dos naciones son ahora percibidas en algunos lugares como los enemigos indiscutibles de los palestinos y de aquellos que se oponen a la autonomía de Israel en todo el mundo.

Durante la dedicatoria de la embajada, Mike Evans fue el anfitrión de una fiesta de gala en el Waldorf Astoria. Trescientos setenta y cinco de los líderes más poderosos del mundo estaban allí, incluyendo a Jared e Ivanka Trump Kushner, senador Lindsey Graham, senador Ted Cruz, exsenador Joe Lieberman, y el Secretario del Tesoro Steven Mnuchin. Al dar su discurso en la fiesta de gala, Evans dijo que el presidente Donald Trump había cumplido sus promesas, a diferencia de los presidentes previos que se negaron a hacerlo. Trump ha colocado un fundamento para un proceso de paz genuina.

Cuando Menachem Begin era el primer ministro de Israel, él le mostró a Evans un plan estratégico que estaba preparando para presentárselo al presidente Ronald Reagan a principios de la década de los ochenta. "La conclusión de Israel", dijo Evans, "era que Estados Unidos no podía ganar efectivamente las guerras en el Medio Oriente. Las guerras se pelearon durante un periodo muy largo. Para cuando Estados Unidos llegaba a la región para luchar, la guerra ya había terminado". Sin embargo, ese entendimiento reveló una nueva alineación y un nuevo aliado en la lucha mundial contra el terrorismo. Tal como lo escribe Evans:

> La realidad es que, durante la era comunista, Israel, un representante de Estados Unidos, disuadió estratégicamente a los comunistas en el Medio Oriente. Ahora, Israel se convertirá en un representante contra el islam radical. No hay información en la región que

se compare a la Inteligencia israelí. La nación tiene ojos y oídos en la tierra en cada país árabe. Irán es zona de impacto para el terrorismo mundial. Sus representantes están desestabilizando a todo el Medio Oriente. Está en la mira de ambos, Trump y Netanyahu. Israel es incapaz de destruir efectivamente los reactores nucleares solo, razón por la que Netanyahu nunca avanzó en esa operación.[4]

La perspectiva de un interno

Para darle una mirada más cercana al conflicto en el Medio Oriente y la batalla por Jerusalén, contacté a una mujer que nació en medio de la lucha y sobrevivió el temor y peligro constantes antes de venir a Estados Unidos a advertirnos de las consecuencias de no hacer algo. Desde entonces, ella se ha convertido en una de las más conocidas disertantes y activistas por Israel y los cristianos occidentales. Como lo indicara el sitio web de su organización, Brigitte Gabriel es la fundadora de ACT por Estados Unidos. Ella ha disertado en las Naciones Unidas y se ha reunido con miembros del Congreso, el Parlamento Británico, el Primer Ministro de Australia, funcionarios superiores del Pentágono, el Comando de Operaciones Especiales de Estados Unidos, el FBI y muchos otros respecto a la amenaza del islam radical. Ella recibió el espaldarazo en Europa en 2016 por sus esfuerzos en la lucha contra el terrorismo y por defender los valores occidentales judeocristianos.[5]

Cuando ella tenía apenas diez años, los islamistas radicales dispararon cohetes y destruyeron su casa. Ella fue herida seriamente. Después, la familia fue forzada a vivir durante varios años en un refugio subterráneo antibombas que medía unos ocho por diez pies, muchas veces sobrevivían de la maleza. Gabriel tenía que gatear a través de la zanja de un drenaje para conseguir agua de un manantial cercano mientras eludía a los francotiradores islámicos. Con el tiempo huyeron del Líbano a Israel, pero después se mudaron a Estados Unidos y se convirtieron en ciudadanos. Aquí, ella ha sido reconocida como una de las principales expertas en terrorismo en el mundo.

Gabriel es una invitada regular en el *Fox News Channel*, CNN, MSNBC y numerosos programas de radio. Ella se desempeña en la junta de consejeros de *Intelligence Summit* y es la autora de dos libros de mayor venta en la lista del *New York Times*: *Because They Hate: A Survivor of Islamic Terror Warns America*, y *They Must Be Stopped: Why We Must Defeat Radical Islam and How We Can Do It*. Al crecer en una familia cristiana libanesa, ella atravesó horrores indescriptibles. Al haber visto sus entrevistas en televisión, admiro su valentía. Me siento honrado de publicar su nuevo libro: *Rise: In Defense of Judeo-Christian Values and Freedom*, que se publicó poco antes de este libro. Recientemente, la entrevisté para el Charisma Podcast Network y me enteré de primera mano de lo que se trata la lucha en esa región del mundo tan disputada. Durante nuestra conversación para el podcast le pregunté: "Brigitte, tal como hemos atestiguado recientemente en Singapur, Donald Trump está dando pasos audaces en favor de la paz, y sus políticas están sacudiendo las cosas. Como experta en el conflicto en el Medio Oriente, ¿cuáles cree que serán los efectos de la presidencia de Trump en esa parte del mundo?". Su respuesta y una transcripción del resto de nuestra conversación son como sigue:

GABRIEL: Donald Trump está haciendo del mundo un lugar más seguro y mejor a través de sus fortalezas. Nuestros enemigos saben que no pueden incomodar a este presidente. Él habla en serio, y termina lo que empieza. Si él traza una línea roja, eso significa una línea roja. Vemos que los líderes corruptos alrededor del mundo ya se están dando cuenta. Por eso es por lo que Corea del Norte está viniendo a la mesa de negociación. Por eso es por lo que estamos viendo a los sauditas y los egipcios y los israelíes trabajando juntos contra un enemigo común. Y por eso es por lo que vemos cómo está reforzando las políticas fronterizas para proteger el país. Así que, en definitiva, él está haciendo al mundo un lugar más seguro.

STRANG: En el Medio Oriente están sucediendo cambios sísmicos; donde, por primera vez, los musulmanes sunitas se están aliando con Israel contra los musulmanes chiitas en Irán. ¿Cuáles son las perspectivas para nuestro interés en la región con base a estas nuevas relaciones, y cómo se relaciona eso con la lucha que usted tiene contra el terrorismo?

GABRIEL: Creo que es el tiempo perfecto porque los sauditas y los israelíes empezaron a hablarse, aun cuando el presidente Obama estaba en el cargo. Excepto que el presidente Obama estaba más interesado en formar una amistad con los iraníes que en apoyar y proteger a nuestros aliados en el Medio Oriente. Hoy día, el presidente Trump está aprovechando la voluntad de los sauditas, quienes básicamente tienen un enemigo común con los israelíes. Es en su mayor beneficio unirse y trabajar juntos, y por eso los sauditas permiten que los israelíes usen su espacio aéreo, porque los sauditas saben que Irán está construyendo un arma nuclear, e Irán quiere tener domino sobre el Medio Oriente. Por eso, ellos están dispuestos a unirse y trabajar con Estados Unidos e Israel para facilitar verdaderamente un contrapeso fuerte ante Rusia e Irán...

STRANG: ¿Cuál es la importancia de trasladar la Embajada de Estados Unidos a Jerusalén? Ahora, otros países están haciendo lo mismo, desmintiendo a los negativos que predijeron violencia en el Medio Oriente. ¿Cuál es su sentir acerca de todos estos cambios?

GABRIEL: La importancia de trasladar nuestra embajada a Jerusalén es que, básicamente, estamos demostrando con nuestra acción que hablamos en serio sobre defender a nuestro aliado. Y que estamos dispuestos a ir y luchar contra el mundo pronunciándonos e implorando el derecho de Israel para existir como un Estado judío con Jerusalén como su capital, y Estados Unidos va a poner una embajada allí, y muchos países lo están imitando.

STRANG: Con ISIS diezmado en Siria e Irak, ¿qué impacto ha tenido eso sobre el terrorismo internacional o la amenaza futura de terrorismo?

GABRIEL: Tiene una repercusión enorme, y todo es para mejor. Ahora bien, todavía no estamos fuera de peligro con ISIS porque, aunque ellos perdieron territorio físico, el califato de ISIS en el internet sigue desarrollándose, y ellos continúan reclutando. El temor ahora mismo es que casi una tercera parte de los europeos, que dejaron el país para ir a pelear con ISIS en Siria, han vuelto a casa incluyendo mujeres y niños. Así que la amenaza está evolucionando en formas diferentes. Ya no luchamos contra ISIS con su territorio, sino que ahora estamos luchando contra mujeres que están de regreso en Europa, que se ven como europeas, que tienen pasaportes europeos, que están allí con sus hijos, que han sido insensibilizadas para matar.

Pero en general, estas mujeres no podrán llevar a cabo un ataque terrorista en una escala masiva ni organizar un ejército como lo organizan los líderes de ISIS. Así que la amenaza en general está disminuyendo…

STRANG: La postura fuerte de Trump sobre asegurar las fronteras ¿impactará el riesgo de terrorismo islámico en nuestro país? En otras palabras, ¿qué peligro ha provocado que los terroristas entren ilegalmente a través de la frontera sur?

GABRIEL: Hemos estado lidiando con los terroristas islámicos que entran a escondidas a través de la frontera sur por más de quince años ya. Hablé de eso en mi libro en 2006, titulado *Because They Hate* (Porque ellos odian), donde discuto cómo nuestro gobierno en ese entonces estaba identificando algunos terroristas por nombre, llamándolos en ese tiempo OTM ("Other Than Mexicans" que significa "Otros aparte de los mexicanos"). Y a lo que se referían era básicamente terroristas islámicos entrando a hurtadillas por la frontera mexicana.

Hoy día, el presidente Trump está haciendo lo correcto al asegurar nuestras fronteras…El riesgo ahora es que Irán ha estado preparando grandes centros Hezbollah por toda Centro América y Latinoamérica. Y están proveyendo centros culturales. Están reclutando y entrenado gente de Centro América porque se parecen a los del Medio Oriente. Ellos pueden mezclarse, pueden aprender el idioma, y luego, pueden escabullirse a través de la frontera sur.

Ya hemos arrestado operativos de Hezbollah quienes han entrado por la frontera mexicana, habilitados y facilitados por el cartel de la droga. Y, entonces, al asegurar la frontera y específicamente construir un muro, y avanzando agresivamente en la construcción de un muro, eso reducirá el tipo de personas que atraviesan nuestra frontera, incluyendo a los terroristas. No solo criminales están viniendo aquí, que van a quitar los empleos y los beneficios y que hasta son un peligro para el resguardo y la seguridad de los estadounidenses, sino también terroristas. Y él está haciendo lo mismo para controlar la visa de inmigración, todos esos tipos de migraciones en cadena, y el resultado sería un Estados Unidos más resguardado y seguro.

STRANG: ¿Cuál diría usted que es la mayor amenaza terrorista para Estados Unidos hoy día?

GABRIEL: La Izquierda radical. Sin duda alguna…Lo que capacita a los terroristas islámicos es la Izquierda radical, que está silenciando y saboteando y actuando como grilletes alrededor de los tobillos de quienes tratan de mantener a salvo a nuestra comunidad, empezando por nuestros oficiales de policía y nuestros servicios de emergencia. Ahora mismo, Estados Unidos está bajo el ataque de gente dentro de Estados Unidos, que odia a Estados Unidos tanto que está dispuesta a dar ayuda y a ser cómplice de nuestros enemigos, quienes comparten un objetivo común con ellos, el cual es la destrucción de Estados Unidos, la manera en que personas como usted y yo vemos a Estados Unidos, como un país fuerte, patriota, que ama a Dios, que teme a Dios, que fue fundado sobre principios judeocristianos por grandes Padres Fundadores…La nueva Izquierda quiere ver a Estados Unidos derribada en el mundo, estar al mismo nivel que cualquier otro país en el mundo con fronteras abiertas, inmigración abierta, transexuales en cada servicio sanitario, confundiendo las líneas entre cualquier cosa que a la que fuimos acostumbrados como el Estados Unidos que fue fundado por nuestros Padres Fundadores y este nuevo Estados Unidos de hoy. Así que yo diría que la Izquierda radical es la amenaza más grande para Estados Unidos ahora mismo.

STRANG: El levantamiento palestino [sucediendo en Israel hoy] ¿es más pequeño de lo que escuchamos en Irak y Siria, pero es el terrorismo que ejecutan o inspiran los palestinos una amenaza mayor?

GABRIEL: Lo que estamos viendo en este momento con el terrorismo alrededor del mundo es básicamente lo que los palestinos han perfeccionado y ahora está siendo elaborado por ISIS. Así que la amenaza del terrorismo palestino, quienes básicamente iniciaron los carros bomba, las bombas suicidas, asesinatos, linchamientos, los estallidos de niños, ahora estamos viendo ese juego en todo el mundo.

Estamos viendo una nueva resurrección en los territorios palestinos bajo Hamas, con este odio venenoso contra los israelíes y la justificación de asesinar incluso al más joven de ellos, incluso infantes, porque en los ojos de los palestinos, los infantes crecen para ser soldados. Ellos siempre permanecerán como una amenaza mientras tengan líderes lavándoles el cerebro con odio contra el Estado de Israel y los judíos en general a nivel mundial.

STRANG: ¿Quién está financiando la mayor parte de la violencia por grupos extremistas alrededor del mundo?

GABRIEL: En este momento, Irán es el mayor financista del terrorismo. Hezbollah ha cometido ataques en cinco continentes. Después de Irán, estamos viendo a diferentes Estados islámicos, especialmente de los Estados del Golfo y Arabia Saudita, debido a la riqueza petrolera que les permite apoyar a las organizaciones terroristas islámicas. En todo el mundo, ya sea Al-Shabaab o Al-Nusra, no importa qué país es. Están siendo apoyados por islamistas de similar cosmovisión que comparten la misma ideología. Y lo que estamos viendo también en ciertas áreas es que Irán incluso ha apoyado elementos de Al Qaeda. Irán incluso está financiando Hamas, aunque Hamas es un grupo sunita. En lo que se refiere a que se unan y luchen contra sus enemigos, a ellos no les importa de dónde viene el dinero para apoyar las actividades occidentales contra Israel y Estados Unidos porque ellos son el enemigo común. Así que el flujo del dinero al terrorismo mundial viene en ambas direcciones:

la dirección sunita, que sale de Arabia Saudita y diferentes países en los Estados del Golfo y también de Irán.

STRANG: ¿Hay alguna evidencia de algún grupo que no sea islámico o no musulmán que financie el terrorismo internacional?

GABRIEL: No que yo sepa, directamente. No en pos del terrorismo y el asesinato de civiles inocentes. Ellos podrían financiar a la Izquierda moderada o lo que ellos perciben como el ala moderada en el Occidente, la cual es el movimiento *Muslim Brotherhood*. Debido a que, bajo Obama, él no veía al movimiento *Muslim Brotherhood* como una organización o grupo terrorista. Así que veamos los operativos de *Muslim Brotherhood* en el Occidente, organizaciones como el *Council on American-Islamic Relations*, o la *Islamic Society of North America*, o ahora mismo están viendo a Linda Sarsour, quien es una palestina activista y antisemita, ahora básicamente es la colíder para la *Women's March* y lidera el movimiento de mujeres que es muy corrupto en Estados Unidos, y está siendo financiado por gente como el *Southern Poverty Law Center*, el ACLU, *Planned Parenthood* y George Soros.

Así que tienen a las fundaciones de Soros canalizando dinero para estos grupos izquierdistas, incluyendo los grupos islámicos que están supuestamente operando en un movimiento pacífico en el Occidente, aunque son básicamente el brazo sigiloso de la *Muslim Brotherhood*. Ellos podrían no estar llevando a cabo sus ataques, pero están llevando su ideología y ejecutando los proyectos de *Muslim Brotherhood* para el mundo...Y estas organizaciones están recibiendo financiamiento de gente como George Soros y las organizaciones izquierdistas.

STRANG: ¿Qué es lo que la administración Trump va a hacer para lidiar con la amenaza del terrorismo?

GABRIEL: La administración Trump está golpeando y golpea con fuerza inmediatamente cuando sabe que se ha cometido terrorismo. Por ejemplo: el presidente Trump no dudó en atacar a Siria, dos veces ya en su primer año en el cargo. El primer ataque fue inmediatamente después de asumir la presidencia, básicamente enviando el mensaje de que Estados Unidos no va a tolerar ese comportamiento bárbaro ni el asesinato de gente inocente. Él ha ido agresivamente tras ISIS, matando ISIS, y por eso ISIS está perdiendo su territorio, o prácticamente ha perdido la mayor parte de su territorio.

Lo que el presidente Trump está haciendo es básicamente atacando inmediatamente donde él necesita atacar, y lo está haciendo físicamente, no con palabras. Estamos lidiando con un enemigo que no entiende palabras, pero sí entiende y respeta la fuerza y las acciones. Y el presidente Trump está actuando en fuerza con sus palabras, así como con sus acciones…

STRANG: ¿Hay algo más que debamos saber acerca de amenazas diplomáticas o militares en otros lugares, tales como Corea del Norte, Europa o Europa del Este?

GABRIEL: Lo maravilloso del presidente Trump es que él está poniendo a Estados Unidos en primer lugar, antes que otros países como Afganistán o Irak. Antes, nuestra política era básicamente ganar corazones y mentes. Fuimos y empezamos a edificar naciones. Estábamos prestando dinero de China, entrando en una deuda terrible. Poniendo la deuda como un grillete en el cuello de nuestros hijos para poder básicamente construir escuelas y carreteras en Afganistán para gente que nos aborrece y no les importa en lo absoluto lo que estemos construyendo para ellos.

El presidente Trump está cambiando todo eso. El presidente Trump es de la filosofía de entren, peleen contra el enemigo, salgan y dejen que ellos se arreglen dentro de ellos. Y eso es muy importante porque envía un mensaje a nuestro enemigo de que será destruido, y no vamos a reconstruirlos porque no estamos desperdiciando nuestro valioso dinero en ustedes mientras se lo quitamos a nuestros hijos y nos endeudamos al hacerlo. Y los países están tomando nota. Y por eso el presidente Trump está tomando todos los pasos correctos al lidiar con terroristas, especialmente el terrorismo islámico, y especialmente en esa parte del mundo, tal como el Medio Oriente, Siria e Irak. Especialmente ahora con los ojos del mundo sobre Siria, preguntándose si Estados Unidos se va a involucrar en la guerra.

En lo que se refiere a Corea del Norte, el presidente Trump trató con tal fuerza a Corea del Norte, y esto es lo que forzó a Corea del Norte a venir a la mesa de negociaciones. Mientras que los medios principales de comunicación hablaban de que el presidente Trump nos iba a llevar a una guerra nuclear, él en realidad salvó al mundo de una guerra nuclear y forzó a los norcoreanos a venir a la mesa de negociación al hacerles saber básicamente: "¡Ustedes no quieren hacerme enojar porque no saben lo que les voy a hacer!". Y eso frenó estamos volviendo a la misma filosofía de palabras fuertes para disuadir a nuestros enemigos en la manera que lo ejercimos con la Unión Soviética durante la Guerra Fría

El presidente Trump permanece fuerte. Él está firme en reconstruir a nuestros aliados en todo el mundo, ya sea en Japón, ya sea en el Medio Oriente, ya sea incluso en trabajar las relaciones con China. Y lo que él está por hacer con Irán es enviar todos los mensajes correctos sobre nuestras políticas extranjeras. Y teniendo el equipo soñado, o lo que yo llamo el equipo soñado, Pompeo y Bolton, a su lado, ahora ellos podrán terminar las cosas.

En unidad de propósito

No se requiere mucha imaginación para ver que, excepto por un milagro bien hecho, el Medio Oriente seguirá siendo un punto problemático y un hervidero de violencia e insurrección durante los años venideros. Israel es nuestro aliado más fuerte en el Medio Oriente, y debido a que también es la nación más pequeña en la región, 8.8 millones (6.5 millones de ellos son judíos) rodeados de aproximadamente 400 millones de musulmanes, depende del apoyo de Estados Unidos y de nuestra promesa de defensa. "Con Estados Unidos como socio y aliado", escribió Mike Evans, "Israel siente que puede soportar las amenazas militares. Y no solamente pueden ser neutralizados los reactores nucleares de Irán, sino que el hostil gobierno chiita hasta puede ser empujado a la bancarrota. Un movimiento así garantizaría virtualmente un cambio de régimen y una reducción en la tensión de la región.

"Este fue el mismo tipo de revolución que se llevó a cabo bajo el Shah de Irán", dijo él. "Siria se ha convertido en un pantano infestado de serpientes, lleno de los terroristas más infames del mundo. Ambos asuntos, el sirio y el iraní, pueden ser resueltos en su debido curso, pero necesitará el apoyo de un aliado mundial además de Estados Unidos e Israel. Ese sería Rusia", dijo Evans, "lo que explica la negativa de Donald Trump para enemistarse con Vladimir Putin".[6]

Evans me dijo que él se convirtió en el primer amigo cristiano sionista del Primer Ministro Netanyahu cuando ambos empezaban a rebasar los treinta años. A lo largo de los años Evans ha recaudado millones de dólares de sus donantes para proyectos en beneficio de Israel, incluyendo su museo de Amigos de Sion, y escrito docenas de libros, muchos de ellos acerca de Israel. En Estados Unidos, Evans es considerado uno de los cristianos sionistas de más alto perfil, y él cree que no solo Netanyahu ha logrado su más grande victoria con la presidencia de Trump, sino que también lo ha logrado Trump con Netanyahu, y él cree que los mejores días de Israel están por venir, gracias a la alianza Netanyahu-Trump. Finalmente, Estados Unidos tendrá "una base naval en el Puerto de Haifa, donde las tropas estadounidenses puedan estar protegidas, y puedan entrar y salir en operativos especiales para decapitar al islam radical".[7] Y una razón más por la que las dos cabezas de Estado están tan cerca: ellos comparten dos de los mismos héroes: Winston Churchill y Ronald Reagan.

Cuando Evans estaba construyendo su coalición por Israel, en la década de los ochenta, el enfoque estaba específicamente en la oración. Su ministerio compró la casa en Haarlem, Holanda, conocida como "The Hiding Place", que es donde Corrie ten Boom y su familia escondieron judíos antes de transportarlos a un lugar seguro, fuera de Holanda. Ningún judío fue capturado allí, pero varios miembros de la familia ten Boom murieron en manos de los nazis. Corrie fue milagrosamente liberada poco después de la muerte de su hermana, Betsie, y pudo contar su historia por todo el mundo.

Hubo en grupo de oración que se reunió en esa casa durante un siglo completo, de 1844 hasta 1944, para orar por el pueblo judío y por la paz de Jerusalén, y el objetivo de Evans era volver a empezar con el *Jerusalem Prayer Team*. Él también fijó una meta audaz de cien millones de intercesores orando por la paz de Jerusalén. Él asegura tener cuarenta y dos millones de intercesores ahora y dice que el número llegará a los cien millones en 2020, en gran parte a través de las redes sociales. Esto se ha convertido en la base para que Evans procure sus objetivos. Israel está contantemente peleando guerras ideológicas, pero ya que es una nación pequeña no puede esperar ganar guerras de ideas, necesita amigos que puedan ayudar. Así que Evans empezó a crear las redes sociales que lo llevaron a construir el museo Amigos de Sion en Jerusalén.

Debido a mi amistad con Mike Evans, supe de su deseo por construir el museo mucho antes de que se convierta en una realidad. Admito que estaba escéptico al principio porque conocía a Evans lo suficientemente bien como para saber que a él ni siquiera le gustaba ir a museos. También sabía de la gran historia del sionismo cristiano que antecede incluso al sionismo judío. David Brog, director ejecutivo de *Christians United for Israel*, escribió un libro fantástico, en 2006, que yo tuve el privilegio de publicar, llamado *Standing With Israel*, el cual documenta esto. Sin embargo, la mayoría de los cristianos incluso muchos evangélicos que aman Israel, no conocen esta historia maravillosa ni tampoco la conocen los judíos israelíes. Así que yo sabía que documentar esta relación especial con un museo en Jerusalén era un objetivo digno.

Cuando visité el *Friends of Zion Heritage Center*, también conocido como el museo Amigos de Sion poco antes de que abrieran oficialmente, en 2015, estaba maravillado por la narrativa sobre el sionismo. Se dijo que era el primer "museo inteligente" en Israel, combinando tecnología 3D, pantallas digitales y partituras originales y obras de arte de más de 150 artistas israelíes, con sonido envolvente en cada una de sus siete exhibiciones. Aunque he publicado libros, escrito y disertado sobre sionismo cristiano, aprendí un par de cosas nuevas y me conmovió el amor genuino por el pueblo judío que se hace patente en el museo. Hoy día el *Friends of Zion Heritage Center* es un lugar obligatorio para decenas de miles de turistas cristianos que visitan Jerusalén cada año. De manera interesante, cerca de la mitad de quienes visitan los museos son israelíes, la mayoría de los cuales no sabe cómo los cristianos han hecho amistad con los judíos a lo largo de los años.

Cuando el presidente Trump visitó Jerusalén por primera vez, fue recibido con pancartas colocadas por Amigos de Sion (o por sus siglas en inglés, FOZ, como se etiquetan ellos). Evans dijo que era una "maravillosa oportunidad para promover nuestro museo y nuestra iniciativa y, al mismo tiempo, reconocer a un presidente que aboga por la justicia". Así que, Evans colocó pancartas por todo Jerusalén. Casi la mitad de ellas decía "Trump es un amigo de Sion" y la otra mitad decía "Trump hace grande a Israel". Y como Evans dijo: "Él definitivamente ha hecho ambas cosas".

Unos días después, Trump anunció en diciembre de 2017 que estaría trasladando la Embajada de Estados Unidos a Jerusalén, Evans le entregó a Trump el galardón de Amigos de Sion en la Oficina Oval. Él le había dado el galardón al presidente George W. Bush, al príncipe Alberto II de Mónaco, y al expresidente de Bulgaria, Rosen Plevneliev. Él prometió otorgarlo a cualquier jefe de estado que trasladara su embajada a Jerusalén. Hasta ahora, adicionalmente al presidente Trump, él lo ha otorgado a los presidentes de Paraguay y Guatemala.

Channel i24 (una estación en inglés en Jerusalén) envió a un reportero a visitar el museo. "No es de sorprenderse que todas las tres delegaciones se encontraran allí, en el museo Amigos de Sion para aprender más de la historia del sionismo cristiano y por qué la relación entre el Estado judío y los cristianos alrededor del mundo es ahora más importante que nunca", el reportero de televisión, Mike Wagenheim, hablaba efusivamente mientras informaba favorablemente sobre esta nueva atracción turística de Jerusalén. "Muchos críticos dicen que fue la base evangélica del presidente de Estados Unidos, Donald Trump, la que finalmente lo convenció de trasladar la Embajada de Estados Unidos a la Ciudad Santa".[8]

El museo Amigos de Sion colocó pancartas por todo Jerusalén cuando la visita de Donald Trump coincidió con la celebración del septuagésimo aniversario de Israel en 2017, solo unos pocos meses después de haber tomado posesión. Sin embargo, Trump no anunció lo que muchos esperaban que hiciera, que Estados Unidos trasladaría su embajada allí. Ese anuncio vendría seis meses después. "Un montón de gente estaba molesta por eso", me contó Evans en una entrevista para este libro, "[pero] yo creía que Donald Trump cumpliría su palabra. En realidad, en el comité donde me desempeño en la Casa Blanca...varios [miembros del comité] estaban molestos...Ellos dijeron que él no lo haría. Y yo dije: 'Él lo hará. Él no prometió que lo haría en su primer año, pero lo va a hacer'. Así que yo siempre creí que Donald Trump haría exactamente eso".

Cuando el vicepresidente Mike Pence visitó Jerusalén en enero 2018, colocó pancartas por toda la ciudad, y lo hicieron nuevamente cuando la Embajada de

Estados Unidos abrió oficialmente en Jerusalén el 14 de mayo de 2018. Cada vez, el grupo colocaba no solo pancartas, sino también *"wraps"* en los autobuses municipales que conducen por la ciudad, e incluso pancartas atrás de los camellos. "Era muy gracioso ver a un árabe caminando a un camello con un rótulo que decía "Trump hace a Israel grande"", dijo Evans. Pero eso fue lo que sucedió.

Durante las festividades, Evans me enviaba fotos y artículos de la prensa israelí, y yo los compartía y publicaba algunos de ellos en nuestra página CharismaNews.com. Las pancartas estaban en inglés (para que Trump pudiera leerlas), pero Evans dijo que muchos israelíes hablan inglés lo suficiente para entender lo que decían las pancartas. "Ahora, lo interesante sobre las pancartas", me dijo, "es donde las pancartas [fueron] impresas en Ramallah. Todas nuestras pancartas fueron impresas por palestinos…Cuando tenemos pancartas rotas, arrancadas generalmente por judíos izquierdistas que odiaban a Donald Trump tenemos árabes palestinos que las imprimen nuevamente en Ramallah y nosotros las colocamos otra vez".

¿Cuál es la importancia de todo esto? Evans cree que muchos israelíes no saben todavía quiénes son sus amigos. Hay aproximadamente dos mil millones de cristianos declarados en el mundo, de los cuales seiscientos millones creen en la Biblia. "Hemos tenido cuatro o cinco países diferentes que se acercan a nosotros", dice Evans, "debido a nuestro enfoque hacer amigos, defender el Estado de Israel, pelear guerras ideológicas, pelear batallas espirituales, guerras de oración. Hasta guerras económicas. Debido a que lo que podemos hacer a través de nuestra red social es fantástico". En realidad, Facebook fue fundada en las instalaciones de una universidad, pero las instalaciones universitarias se han convertido en zonas de guerra contra Israel. Así que queremos llevar nuestro mensaje a las instalaciones universitarias utilizando las mismas herramientas que el mundo usó para pelear estas guerras. Es un proyecto grande", me contó Evans.

A los eventos que rodeaban la dedicación de la nueva Embajada de Estados Unidos asistieron muchos sionistas cristianos estadounidenses, quienes experimentaron una sensación de euforia. Uno de los que asistieron fue el pastor Jim Garlow de *Skyline Church* en el área de San Diego, quien ha visitado Israel dieciséis veces. Su esposa, Rosemary Schindler Garlow, ha estado allí ¡cincuenta y cinco veces! Los Garlow llegaron temprano al evento, y el describió una sensación de "casi euforia" en Jerusalén. "A medida que la gente empezaba a llegar, había tanto gozo, casi cautivante", me dijo. "El deleite del momento era increíble. Orador tras orador se refirieron a la Escritura".

Una de las cosas más maravillosas para Garlow, quien es parte de la *Faith Leaders Initiative* del Presidente, es que Trump en realidad cumple su palabra en las promesas que hace. "Para ser alguien que no es realmente 'uno de nosotros', las políticas de Trump son tan ciertas y correctas, especialmente sobre salvar la vida de los bebés no nacidos u honrar a Israel. Él está en el lado correcto en un asunto tras otro. Además, tiene el temperamento y la personalidad únicos para soportar la arremetida de criticismo que recibe. Estamos viendo algo que no puede explicarse. Él es verdaderamente como un Ciro", dijo Garlow.

Ciro fue el antiguo rey persa que, aunque no creía en el Dios hebreo, fue usado por Dios según el profeta Isaías para permitir al pueblo judío el regreso a Jerusalén. En mi libro *God and Donald Trump*, aporto pruebas sobre la manera en que algunos líderes cristianos usaron esta comparación con Trump para explicar cómo Dios podría usar a alguien tan imperfecto como Trump para sus propósitos. La comparación no pasó desapercibida para los líderes del *Mikdash Educational Center*, una organización educativa judía que acuñó una "moneda del templo" portando la imagen del presidente Trump, junto con una imagen del rey Ciro, para honrar el reconocimiento de Trump a Jerusalén como la capital de Israel. Mil copias de la moneda, que también menciona la declaración Balfour, fueron acuñadas. Mil copias de la moneda, que también menciona la declaración de Balfour, fueron acuñadas. Una segunda moneda de la serie Cirus-Trump ha sido acuñada también. Estas monedas no pueden comprarse como dinero extranjero, pero puede comprar una con un donativo.

Jonathan Cahn, a quien mencioné en el capítulo 9, también ve una conexión. Él me dijo: "La proclamación de Trump con referencia a Jerusalén, tiene paralelos impresionantes con el decreto del rey persa, Ciro, como lo registra la Biblia". Él continuó explicando que "cada proclamación reconoce el derecho del pueblo judío a la tierra y a Jerusalén como la capital de Israel. El resultado del decreto de Ciro fue la reconstrucción de Jerusalén después de setenta años. El resultado del decreto de Trump fue la inauguración de la Embajada de Estados Unidos en Jerusalén después de setenta años de la existencia de Israel, ¡*en la fecha exacta!*".

Cuando el pastor John Hagee, el director nacional de *Christians United for Israel*, se reunió con el presidente Trump poco antes de la apertura de la embajada, él dijo lo mismo sobre el presidente siendo Ciro y subió la apuesta al comparar a Trump con Harry Truman, quien reconoció el Estado de Israel en 1948, once minutos después de que fuera declarada la existencia de la nueva nación y, como todos sabemos, él dijo de sí mismo: "Soy Ciro". Hagee le dijo a Breitbart News: "Le dije 'en el momento que haga eso, creo que usted entrará a la inmortalidad política, porque está teniendo la audacia para hacer lo que otros presidentes no tuvieron el valor de hacer'". [9]

El Primer Ministro, Benjamín Netanyahu, fue aún más específico cuando se reunió con el presidente Trump en Washington. "Quiero decirle que el pueblo judío tiene una muy buena memoria. Así que recordamos la proclamación del gran rey Ciro el Grande, el rey persa. Dos mil quinientos años atrás, él proclamó que los exiliados judíos en Babilonia podíamos regresar a reconstruir nuestro templo en Jerusalén. Recordamos, cien años atrás, que Lord Balfour, quien emitió la Proclamación Balfour que reconocía los derechos del pueblo judío en nuestra tierra ancestral.

"Recordamos [setenta] años atrás, que el presidente Harry S. Truman fue el primer líder en reconocer el Estado judío. Y recordamos cómo unos cuantos años atrás, el presidente Donald J. Trump reconoció a Jerusalén como la capital de Israel. Sr. Presidente, esto será recordado por nuestro pueblo a través de las eras. Y, tal como usted acaba de decir, otros hablaron de esto. Usted lo hizo".[10]

NUEVAS SOLUCIONES ESPERANZADORAS

Uno de los problemas más escabrosos en el Medio Oriente es si la Autoridad Palestina (PA) debe conformarse en un estado separado, lado a lado con Israel. Algunos en la Izquierda todavía sostienen que Israel está ocupando la tierra que tomaron de lo que había sido parte de Jordania en la Guerra de los Seis Días en 1967. Desde entonces, Israel ha hecho las paces con Jordania, pero muchos árabes que viven en la franja de Gaza, así como lo que es llamado el West Bank en el occidente y Judea y Samaria en Israel demandan reconocimiento. Lentamente, la oportunidad para una solución de dos estados ha ganado fuerza, tanto entre los liberales en Israel como también entre los diplomáticos estadounidenses.

Luego, una recomendación para una solución de un solo estado ha venido de una fuente poco común: el *Messianic Jewish Movement* en Estados Unidos y su brazo de cabildeo en Washington, DC, la *Alliance for Israel Advocacy*. He estado cubriendo a *Messianic Jews* desde que el movimiento surgió del *Jesus Movement* de finales de la década entre los sesenta y setenta. Estos son los judíos que creen en Jesús (Yeshua, en hebreo) fue y es el Mesías prometido (de allí el nombre Mesiánico), aunque continúan identificándose como judíos, muchas veces celebrando las fiestas judías y llamando a sus líderes religiosos "rabinos". Los carismáticos y evangélicos que aman a Israel, generalmente, reciben a los judíos mesiánicos como compañeros creyentes; sin embargo, la comunidad judía tradicional los considera generalmente un anatema, diciendo que los mesiánicos se han convertido al cristianismo, lo cual ellos consideran que es no ser judío e históricamente hostiles a los judíos. Esto ha resultado en una percepción de que los judíos mesiánicos se han unido a los perseguidores históricos de la comunidad judía y, por lo tanto, deben ser tratados como traidores y rechazados como compañeros judíos.

Así que, cuando el rabino Paul Liberman, director ejecutivo de la *Alliance for Israel Advocacy* y Joel Chernoff, secretario general de la *Messianic Jewish Alliance of America*, propusieron su solución de un solo estado, estaban sorprendidos de lo bien que los recibieron los miembros del Congreso de Estados Unidos, así como los líderes israelíes, incluyendo a uno de los aliados más cercanos del Primer Ministro Netanyahu, Tzachi Hanegbi, quien es el ministro de la cooperación regional en Israel. Adicionalmente, Lieberman ha sido invitado a tres reuniones en la Casa Blanca para discutir su plan audaz y viable.

Mientras reviso y entiendo esta propuesta, es un plan muy sencillo. Habrá un solo Estado judío, Israel, y a los casi un millón de árabes que viven en Cisjordania se les daría un incentivo financiero para reubicarse voluntariamente a los países árabes vecinos, lo cual también sería incentivado financieramente para recibirlos y asistirlos a reubicarse. La solución de un estado único visualiza que esto suceda a lo largo de un periodo de diez años. Si tiene éxito, este plan cambiaría el equilibrio demográfico entre los judíos y los árabes viviendo en Judea y Samaria (Cisjordania), avanzando así hacia el día en que Israel pueda incorporar apropiadamente a Judea y Samaria sin perder su población de mayoría judía, de ahí el carácter judío. Esos árabes que queden en Cisjordania, se les darán derechos completos de ciudadanía, excepto el derecho a votar. ¿Pero, estaría la población palestina en Cisjordania dispuesta o aceptaría este arreglo? Una encuesta independiente y acreditada reciente, hecha por la *Alliance for Israel Advocacy* en Cisjordania, ha establecido que una gran mayoría de los palestinos que viven allí están tan insatisfechos con la terrible calidad de vida bajo la PA que recibirían con agrado tal oportunidad.

Entonces ¿cómo se financiará esto? En este momento, Estados Unidos presupuesta más de US$600 millones anualmente para la PA (con los que la PA financia a las familias de los terroristas) y la *United Nations Relief* and *Works Agency* para los refugiados palestinos (cuya función primordial es reubicar a los palestinos refugiados, lo cual se niega a hacer). En esencia, este dinero sería redirigido a reubicar a esos palestinos que están ahora deseando un nuevo comienzo en los países árabes vecinos, una alternativa mucho más productiva y constructiva para el uso de esos fondos. El presidente Donald Trump y su embajadora asignada a las Naciones Unidas, Nikki Haley, ya amenazaron con retirarle esos fondos a la PA cuando los palestinos se negaron a cooperar con los esfuerzos de Estados Unidos para arrancar las conversaciones de paz entre Israel y Palestina, después de que él declaró a Jerusalén la capital de Israel en diciembre de 2017. Por ciento, desde 1994, Estados Unidos les ha provisto a los palestinos US$5.2 mil millones a través de la USAID, según *The Times of Israel*. Trump tuiteó, en enero de 2018, que Estados Unidos está pagándoles a los palestinos cientos de millones de dólares al año "por nada" y se quejó de que, además, Estados Unidos no ha recibido "ninguna apreciación ni respeto" a cambio.[11]

Así que, hagamos cuentas. Durante diez años, eso es US$6,000 por cada millón de árabes, aunque hay 2.7 millones de árabes en Cisjordania y en Gaza, otros 1.4 millones de árabes que viven en el resto de Israel. Compare eso con solo 5.9 millones de judíos que temen ser superados en número, con las tasas de natalidad entre los árabes siendo altas y entre los judíos, más o menos bajas.

Obviamente, hay mucho por hacer. Y los países árabes cercanos tendrían que aceptar estos inmigrantes, y los palestinos tendrían, por supuesto, que querer mudarse. Pero, al menos, es un paso en la dirección correcta. Y, para mí, es proféticamente significativa que la idea venga de la comunidad mesiánica judía. Mientras este libro está en impresión, la propuesta de ley para la solución de un solo estado ha sido aprobada por la Cámara de Consejo Legislativo y está en espera de un congresista que proponga formalmente la iniciativa de ley para que pueda dársele un nombre y un número, convirtiéndose así en una pieza viva de la legislación congresual.

Entonces, ¿qué significa todo esto? Según Mike Evans, el pueblo de Israel ahora tiene esperanza, llevada por la decisión del presidente Trump de trasladar la Embajada de Estados Unidos a la ciudad santa de Jerusalén. "El pueblo judío se sentía solo, así como se han sentido siempre, a lo largo de la historia, durante miles de años, hasta que Donald Trump valientemente se levantó y con osadía reconoció a Jerusalén como la capital de Israel. Eso les dio una esperanza excepcional".

Evans dijo que el jefe sefardita, rabino de Israel, Yitzhak Yosef, articuló lo que muchos israelitas creyeron. Dos días antes de la apertura de la Embajada, el rabino oró en la fiesta de gala organizada por Amigos de Sion, en la cual él llamó a Estados Unidos la "nación de la gracia" y al presidente Trump, el "rey de misericordia". Él luego dijo dramáticamente que "el reconocimiento de Jerusalén por parte de Estados Unidos puede ahora abrirle paso al Mesías". Cuando invité a Evans a disertar en uno de nuestros eventos *Nights to Honor Israel* en Orlando, Florida, hace algunos años, él sorprendió a la multitud con su entusiasta apoyo a Israel. Su mensaje es aún inspirador, pero nada puede jamás ser más inspirador para los creyentes evangélicos y carismáticos que la idea de que los judíos fieles y los cristianos creyentes estarán unidos al fin en la celebración del Mesías de Israel.

EL SACUDIR DE LA IGLESIA

¿Qué vamos a obtener de todos los cambios que se están dando en el mundo hoy? Estamos en medio de una revolución cultural, y no es ningún secreto que los valores morales tradicionales están siendo lastimados. Viendo el panorama de los últimos veinte años, y la creciente cantidad de delitos que llenan los titulares de los periódicos, es difícil ignorar el sentimiento de que quizás hemos llegado demasiado lejos. La cultura se ha salido de los límites y está fuera de control. La retórica llena de odio y las amenazas de violencia física de la Izquierda revelan cuán profundamente divididos estamos como nación, tan divididos que parece haber poca esperanza de llegar algún día a estar de acuerdo en lo que se debe hacer al respecto.

Como escribí poco después de la publicación de mi libro *God and Donald Trump*, algunas personas afuera de las cuatro paredes de una iglesia le prestan mucha atención a lo que Dios está haciendo en el mundo. Para ellos, los "actos de Dios" es lo que la gente llama tormentas y huracanes. Sin embargo, ¿es posible que Dios tenga un plan para este país? ¿Es posible que Él tenga un plan para su pueblo? En ese libro cité varios ejemplos de personas que sentían que la elección de Trump era una señal de que se nos estaba dando una segunda oportunidad.

Para poner las cosas en contexto, quizás vale la pena notar que no todo está bien en la iglesia hoy en día. No solo hay divisiones entre denominaciones sino hay desacuerdos intensos sobre la forma de la alabanza, la música, la estructura y el orden del servicio, la liturgia, la preparación y el rol del clero, y no menos importante, sobre la integridad doctrinal. Algunas iglesias son más como clubes sociales en donde se toleran los vicios y el evangelismo anticuado se prohíbe virtualmente. Otros, ofrecen cultos más grandes, más ruidosos, más a la moda, menos amenazantes, descartando dos mil años de la historia de la iglesia para ser más "relevantes" a personas no religiosas o de alguna forma sin interés. Obviamente, dichos desacuerdos poseen una amenaza letal a la comunidad de creyentes.

Los pasajes proféticos de la Escritura, tales como el libro del Antiguo Testamento de Amós y el libro del Nuevo Testamento, Segunda Timoteo, advierten sobre la caída de los últimos días y la sacudida de la iglesia que puede ser una devastación o un avivamiento, dependiendo de cómo responden las personas. Este país fue fundado sobre principios cristianos, y fuimos dirigidos por generaciones de hombres y mujeres con carácter excepcional e integridad moral. Pero a la luz de la caída y la lucha interna entre los fieles, tenemos que preguntarnos si la iglesia aún puede marcar la diferencia en la vida de las personas. O si la fe de nuestros padres está tan fracturada que nuestra herencia moral está llegando a ser irrelevante.

He defendido que Donald Trump ganó el voto evangélico por el margen más grande de la historia porque los cristianos creyeron que solo él tenía las destrezas de liderazgo y la perseverancia para revertir la espiral de la muerte en que está envuelto el país. Él no es teólogo, ni siquiera evangélico, pero siempre que ha expresado su preocupación sobre la decadencia moral en Estados Unidos, ha sido satirizado por los medios de comunicación como hipócrita y fanático. Mientras tanto, hombres y mujeres de la Izquierda están saliendo a las calles en defensa del aborto y celebrando el derecho de quitarle la vida a un niño no nacido incluso hasta en el momento mismo del nacimiento. Están felices de que el matrimonio entre el mismo sexo sea validado por la Corte Suprema y que la marihuana sea legalizada de estado en estado. Y cuando se trata de la moralidad a la antigua, el mantra de la cultura secular simplemente es "todo es válido".[1] Esto también es una señal del juicio bíblico.

Sin embargo, la mayoría de los estadounidenses reconocen los problemas. No hay que ser religiosos para percibir que algo está mal con la forma en que está avanzando el país. A dos años en su presidencia, muchos de ambos lados todavía están sorprendidos de que Trump ganara la elección, pero están impresionados por lo que él ha logrado hacer en tan corto tiempo, no solo con la economía sino en los tribunales, en la cultura, en la política externa, y en todo el sentido del bienestar. Mientras los demócratas desanimados aún están furiosos por la elección y haciendo todo lo que pueden para alterar su agenda, para muchos estadounidenses se siente como si se nos ha dado un indulto.

MANTENER LA FE

Considerar la magnitud del temblor que golpeó a la nación en las elecciones de 2016, millones hoy en día sienten como si la investidura de Donald Trump fue un punto de inflexión en la historia. El mundo político dio la vuelta completa, la agenda de la Izquierda fue interrumpida, quizás permanentemente. De repente, en lugar de que un presidente que defendía a los países del tercer mundo contra Estados Unidos, y que declaró el 28 de junio de 2006 que "ya no somos un país cristiano",[2] tenemos un presidente que ha prometido restaurar nuestra herencia nacional y defender fuertemente la libertad culto. Las personas de fe están felices de saber que él cubre nuestras espaldas y que él estará usando su púlpito intimidante y la autoridad de su alto cargo para defender la libertad de culto. Somos lo suficientemente sabios para saber que la lucha acaba de empezar.

El compromiso de Donald Trump con la herencia de fe de Estados Unidos fue inmediatamente visible en su Día de Investidura cuando el Presidente y la Primera dama asistieron al servicio en la iglesia episcopal St. John's. Todos los presidentes de turno de Estados Unidos desde James Madison han asistido a un servicio en St. John's por lo menos una vez. Una multitud de cincuenta o sesenta personas se reunieron en la esquina de las Calles Dieciséis e I esperando tener un vistazo del presidente Trump y de Melania cuando llegaran. La primera pareja fue saludada con gritos de "¡Trump! ¡Trump! ¡Trump!" mientras el séquito y un pequeño grupo de líderes religiosos e invitados se abrían paso hacia la iglesia. A cierta distancia había un grupo de jóvenes adultos y protestantes amontonados en las calles y atrás de las puertas de seguridad para "hacer una declaración", llevaban pancartas que decían "No es mi presidente". Sin embargo, adentro del templo la historia era diferente.

El sermón que el presidente escuchó en esa ocasión fue compartido por el Dr. Robert Jeffress de *Dallas' First Baptist Church*, quien había apoyado al Presidente durante toda su campaña. Jeffress dijo en parte:

> Presidente electo Trump, usted ha tenido su cuota de crítica desde el día en que anunció que iba a postularse para presidente, pero los ha frustrado en cada intento. Primero, ellos dijeron que usted no podría ganar la nominación y terminó ganando con más votos que cualquier republicano en la historia. Después, dijeron que fue casualidad y que no podría ganar las elecciones. Y fácilmente derrotó a su oponente. Ahora sus críticos dicen que no puede ser posible que tenga éxito con su agenda.[3]

Inspirándonos en la historia de Nehemías, del Antiguo Testamento, quien fue llamado por Dios para reconstruir los muros derribados de Jerusalén, Jeffress aconsejó al Presidente que permaneciera fuerte, como Nehemías, enfrentando la resistencia y los obstáculos aparentemente insuperables. En cierto punto, los adversarios de Nehemías lo desafiaron: "Debes detener el proyecto y bajar del muro para reunirte con nosotros". Y Jeffress dijo: "La respuesta de Nehemías fue clásica: 'Estoy haciendo un gran trabajo…¿por qué debería detener el trabajo e ir a ustedes?'".[4]

Entonces Jeffress continuó: "Presidente electo Trump, usted, vicepresidente electo Pence, y su equipo han sido llamados por Dios y han sido elegidos por el pueblo para hacer un gran trabajo. Es un trabajo muy importante como para detenerse y responder a sus críticos". Ya cerca del cierre, él dijo:

> Señor Presidente electo, yo no creo que alguna vez hayamos tenido a un presidente con muchos dones naturales como los suyos. Como sabe, la razón por la que le apoyé unas semanas después de que

anunció que iba a postularse fue porque creí que usted era el único candidato que poseía las destrezas de liderazgo necesarias para revertir la trayectoria en descenso de nuestro país. Y empezando con el vicepresidente electo Pence, un hombre bueno y piadoso, usted ha reunido un grupo increíblemente talentoso de asesores a su alrededor. Sin embargo, los desafíos que enfrenta nuestro país son tan grandes que requerirá más tiempo de lo normal poder resolverlos. Necesitamos el poder sobrenatural de Dios. [5]

El pastor Jeffress siguió diciendo que el mismo Dios que facultó a Nehemías hace casi dos mil quinientos años, está disponible hoy para todos aquellos que están dispuestos a humillarse a sí mismos y pedirle al Señor que les ayude. Él agregó: "Cuando el presidente Ronald Reagan se dirigió a la Convención Republicana Nacional en mi ciudad de Dallas en 1984, él dijo: 'Estados Unidos necesita a Dios más de lo que Dios necesita de Estados Unidos. Si alguna vez olvidamos que somos "una nación bajo Dios" entonces seremos una nación que se ha ido para abajo'".[6]

El día de la investidura, el séquito presidencial hizo una pequeña visita a la Catedral Nacional de Washington para un servicio interconfesional ceremonial de oración, el cual ha sido una tradición para los nuevos presidentes desde la investidura de George Washington en 1789. Trump no habló en el servicio, sino que se sentó tranquilamente en la primera fila, con sus hijos y nietos sentados detrás de él, y siguió todo el programa, cerrando sus ojos en oración y meditación por un largo período de tiempo cuando cada uno de los líderes religiosos ofrecía una oración o una lectura.

Algunos feligreses de la congregación más liberal del noroeste de DC habían expresado su desaprobación de ofrecer un servicio de oración para Trump y Pence, pero el Presidente, aun así, saludó a quienes asistieron amablemente y escuchó con respecto mientras más de veinticinco líderes de fe de muchas tradiciones religiosas ofrecían oraciones y hacían breves lecturas en honor de la ocasión. Entre los oradores, mi amigo el Obispo Harry Jackson de *Hope Christian Church* en Beltsville, Maryland, quien se desempeña en la *Faith Leaders Initiative* del presidente Trump, oró para que Dios le diera al nuevo presidente y a su administración "sabiduría y gracia en el ejercicio de sus deberes". Y él oró para que el presidente Trump pudiera ser capaz de "servir a todas las personas de este país y de promover la dignidad, así como la libertad de cada persona". [7]

UN GOLPE DE ESTADO DIGITAL

A lo largo de la campaña, Trump dijo que él estaba comprometido a apoyar la libertad de culto y a defender los derechos de los cristianos que eran perseguidos alrededor del mundo. Durante una entrevista en *Fox & Friends* el 21 de enero de 2018, se le preguntó al Rev. Franklin qué pensaba del Presidente en su primer año de funciones, a lo cual Graham respondió: "Él defiende la fe cristiana más que cualquier otro presidente en toda mi vida". El hijo del fallecido Rev. Billy Graham expresó admiración por el presidente Trump y dijo: "Sencillamente estoy agradecido con el Presidente. Veo que él es una persona honesta".[8]

En cuanto al apoyo del Presidente a los temas de la fe, Graham dijo: "Veo que es una persona que se preocupa por la libertad de culto de los estadounidenses, pero no solo de nosotros aquí en este país. Él también está preocupado por la libertad de culto de las personas en otros países". Continuó diciendo: "Aplaudo lo que ha hecho en el primer año, aunque ha sido atacado desde el primer día. La Izquierda está tratando de destruir a este hombre. Es como si estuviéramos en un golpe de estado digital. Y eso es lo que es, es un golpe de estado digital. Quieren forzarlo a renunciar. Quieren tener el control de nuestro gobierno. Necesitamos orar por este hombre si [el presidente Trump] tiene éxito, todos tendremos éxito". Agregó: "Si él cae, nosotros caemos".[9]

Una medida legal que capturó la atención del Presidente a inicios de su campaña fue la Primera Enmienda de la Ley de Defensa (FADA, por sus siglas en inglés), la cual fue escrita para defender los derechos de los creyentes religiosos para practicar su fe sin restricción indebida. Fue promovida por el senador Mike Lee, con 37 copatrocinadores en el Senado y el republicano Raúl Labrador, con 171 copatrocinadores en la Cámara.

Los medios de comunicación y la comunidad LGBT reaccionaron asustados, pero cuando se le preguntó si apoyaría la propuesta de ley, Trump dijo: "Si soy electo presidente y el Congreso aprueba la FADA, la firmaré para proteger las creencias profundamente religiosas contenidas de los católicos y las creencias de los estadounidenses de todas las fes".[10] Aún falta ver si la ley FADA sobrevivirá en el Congreso con partidarios de ambos bandos actualmente alineados para debatir los temas. Los argumentos en pro y en contra son predecibles, e independientemente de cómo la ley avance en el Senado, este es un tema que no va a ir a ningún lugar pronto. El problema simplemente es muy grande como para ignorarlo.

Pero la promesa de apoyo de Trump no podría cambiar la mente de sus críticos conservadores, incluyendo muchos oponentes francos dentro de la comunidad de fe. Desde que él anunció su candidatura en el 2015, líderes religiosos de todas las creencias han estado disparando críticas a Trump, llamándolo de todo, excepto caballero. El *Huffington Post* liberal publicó una lista de evangélicos que estaban "firmemente contra Trump" en ese entonces, incluyendo al presidente del *Southern Baptist Convention's Ethics & Religious Liberty Commission*, Russell Moore; expresidente Jimmy Carter, el escritor de discursos del expresidente George W. Bush, Peter Wehner; fundador de *Sojourners* Jim Wallis; el autor célebre y pastor evangélico Max Lucado, y un par de otros.[11]

Durante una entrevista en *Christian Broadcasting Network* (CBN), Moore difícilmente pudo ocultar su hostilidad por el Presidente. Él dijo que Donald Trump está "cambiando el carácter moral de las personas" y aseguró que las personas que apoyaban a Trump "tenían que disculpar las cosas por las que nunca se habían tenido que disculpar". Demasiados cristianos han estado "silenciosos y con temor" dijo, y no se pronuncian.[12] En otra ocasión, Moore dijo que cualquiera que apoyara a Donald Trump era culpable de un error serio. "El derecho religioso", agregó, "resulta ser las personas que el derecho religioso nos advierte".[13] No todos en su denominación estuvieron de acuerdo con Moore o apreciaban sus observaciones, y a los medios de comunicación liberales no les bastaba la aparente división entre los líderes evangélicos.

Wehner, un miembro principal de *Washington's Ethics and Public Policy Center*, vituperó a Trump en viarias columnas en el *New York Times*, incluso comparándolo con el filósofo alemán Friedrich Nietzsche, quien influenció al líder nazi Adolf Hitler. La filosofía de Trump, Wehner dijo, prioriza la fuerza y el poder sobre la preocupación por los pobres e indefensos. Él agregó que el acoso a sus adversarios y su falta de compasión representa una cosmovisión que es "incompatible con el cristianismo". Y dijo que "al reunirse alrededor de Trump, los evangélicos han caído en la trampa".[14]

Estas eran las clases de ataques que alegrarían a los votantes demócratas amargados, ver a los fieles volverse contra los de su propia clase. Wehner criticó a Jerry Falwell Jr., el presidente de *Liberty University*, quien colmó de elogios a Trump durante la campaña, y dijo en una ocasión que él creía que "Donald Trump es el hombre de Dios para liderar nuestro país". Al mismo tiempo, Wehner dijo, Eric Metaxas, el autor cristiano de biografías famosas de William Wilberforce y Dietrich Bonhoeffer, "se entusiasmó por el señor Trump y argumentó que los cristianos 'deben' votar por él porque él es 'la última y mejor esperanza para evitar que Estados Unidos cayera en el olvido'". Él también acusó al pastor Robert Jeffress de decir que "cualquier cristiano que se sentara en casa y no votara por el candidato republicano" está "movido por el orgullo y no por principio".[15]

Para Max Lucado, el tema de preocupación fue aparentemente que Trump no parecía cristiano. "Soy pastor", dijo en un blog, una versión que fue publicada en el *Washington Post*. "Yo no respaldo candidatos ni pego calcomanías en el parachoques en mi auto; sino que yo protejo la fe cristiana", dijo. "Si un personaje público recurre a Dios un día y llama a alguien 'tonto' al día siguiente, ¿no está mal? ¿Y hacerlo, no solo una vez, sino repetidas veces, sin arrepentimiento ni remordimiento? ¿Acaso no deberíamos esperar un tono que dé un buen ejemplo para nuestros hijos?"

"Luchamos contra la intimidación en las escuelas", Lucado dijo, "¿no deberíamos hacer lo mismo con la política presidencial?" Agregó: "Cuando se trata del idioma, el señor Trump habita en su propio nivel. Algunos de mis amigos me dicen que su forma de hablar es una virtud. Sin embargo, yo respetuosamente me separo de mis colegas que atribuyen su naturaleza abrasiva a la franqueza".[16] Esta era justamente la clase de retroalimentación que los *anti-Trump* y los medios de comunicación liberal estaban esperando escuchar.

UNA PERSPECTIVA DIFERENTE

Durante una entrevista con Scott Ross en el Club 700 de CBN el 21 de junio de 2018, Anne Graham Lotz, hija de Billy Graham y hermana de Franklin Graham, estuvo de acuerdo en que la selección de palabras de Trump no siempre es lo que ella y otros cristianos preferirían escuchar. "Yo sé que tenemos problemas con la manera en que él se expresa", dijo ella. "Sin embargo, sus políticas han apoyado increíblemente los valores cristianos. Justo ahora él tiene mi aplauso y mis oraciones porque creo que está en un lugar muy peligroso, se puede sentir al enemigo tratando de hacerlo pedazos, incluyendo a sus políticas que defienden los valores bíblicos".[17]

Hablando de estar a la deriva en la fe cristiana en muchas partes del país hoy en día, Ross preguntó, "¿Hemos perdido nuestro temor a Dios?" Lotz respondió: "Sí, sí, lo hemos perdido dentro de la iglesia y fuera de la iglesia. Es increíble. Vivimos nuestra vida como si Él no fuera santo, como si Él no fuera poderoso, como si Él no fuera puro y el temor a Dios es eso. Es tener temor a Dios en un sentido sano. Eso nos mantiene alejados del pecado, nos mantiene justos delante de Él.

"Así como mi padre", dijo, "yo, cuando era niña y estaba creciendo, le temía a mi padre. Yo no quería hacer algo que lo desagradara o que lo enojara. Así que el temor a Dios está arraigado en el amor por Dios. Ustedes no quieren herirlo, quieren desagradarlo y por lo tanto hay reverencia. Dios es Dios y nosotros somos nosotros. Y esa es una gran diferencia".[18]

Al abordar la aparente falta de fe en la generación joven, Lotz dijo que ella sentía que parte del problema es que "los padres cristianos no les han compartido a sus hijos la verdad que conduce a la fe. Quizás le dejamos la responsabilidad a las iglesias o a los profesionales y no lo hicimos nosotros mismos", ella dijo. "Hay algo desconectado porque en lugar de que el país sea mejor, hemos empeorado. Nos hemos apartado de la Palabra de Dios. Y eso podría ser que, en respuesta a lo que mi padre hizo, hablando de la lucha espiritual, [el diablo] viene como una inundación para tratar de deshacer cualquier impacto del ministerio de mi padre y de los ministerios de otras personas o de la iglesia. Pero sabemos que al final, todos saldremos triunfantes".[19]

Recuerdo haber visto el funeral de Billy Graham en la televisión y los conmovedores panegíricos que cada uno de sus hijos pronunciaron. Especialmente, recuerdo las palabras que Lotz pronunció ese día, enfatizando que ella sentía que la fecha en que su padre falleció había sido estratégica desde la perspectiva celestial. Ella dijo: "el 21 de febrero de 2018 es el día cuando los judíos se enfocaron en la lectura de la Escritura que habla de la muerte de Moisés. Moisés fue el gran libertador. Él liberó al pueblo, a millones de personas de la esclavitud, los llevó al borde de la Tierra Prometida y Dios lo llevó al cielo, luego Dios puso a Josué para que los llevara a la Tierra Prometida, a su hogar". [20]

Ella continuó explicando: "Mi padre también es un gran libertador. Él libertó a millones de personas de la esclavitud del pecado, y él nos lleva al borde del cielo, al borde de la tierra prometida, y ahora Dios lo ha llamado a su hogar". Después, ella desafió a quienes estaban escuchando: "¿Será que Dios va a traer a Josué para conducirnos hacia la tierra prometida para llevarnos al cielo, y saben qué significa el nombre de Josué en el Nuevo Testamento? Es Jesús, y creo que esto es un tiro al otro lado del arco. Creo que Dios está diciendo: ¡Despierta Iglesia! ¡Mundo despierta! ¡Despierta Anne! Jesús viene, Jesús viene'".[21]

En la entrevista de CBN Ross continuó con la discusión sobre el famoso padre de Lotz, preguntando: "¿Estaba él decepcionado de las cosas que han estado sucediendo en Estados Unidos o en el mundo?". Ella dijo que había visto el impacto de la predicación de su padre en todo el mundo. Vidas habían sido cambiadas, millones se habían acercado a la fe, y muchas de esas personas estaban en el ministerio hoy en día. Sus vidas son mejores, ella agregó, "pero en el impacto en nuestro país, ya saben, algo falta, ¿cierto?".[22]

Proveniente del mundo de los negocios y del desarrollo de bienes raíces, Donald Trump no estaba familiarizado con la jerga y las costumbres de la comunidad evangélica cuando llegó a la Casa Blanca. Aunque había sido amigo cercano y simpatizante del fallecido Dr. Norman Vincent Peale en Nueva York y asistió a los servicios en *Marble Collegiate Church*, él estaba repentinamente siendo expuesto a diferentes perspectivas y a una clase diferente de experiencia religiosa. A través de su amistad con líderes evangélicos tales como Paula White Cain, James Robison, Robert Jeffress y algunos otros, él estaba adquiriendo un aprecio más profundo por las preocupaciones de millones de votantes evangélicos, quienes le dieron el margen crucial de la victoria.

Muy a principios de su administración, el Presidente empezó a formar a su gabinete de asesores de líderes de fe con quienes él se podría reunir de vez en cuando y quienes estarían disponibles por teléfono para ofrecerle consejos sobre temas de preocupación en las iglesias. Luego a mediados de julio de 2017, él invitó a un grupo de dos docenas de líderes evangélicos para reunirse con él en la Oficina Oval durante algunos minutos antes de una larga reunión con la oficina de relaciones públicas (OPL, por sus siglas en inglés). Como reportó CBN, el grupo discutió una gran variedad de temas con la OPL, enfocándose especialmente en la libertad de culto, la reforma de justicia penal y el apoyo de Estados Unidos a Israel.[23]

Entre los líderes que asistieron, estuvieron Tony Perkins de *Family Research Council*; Paula White Cain de *New Destiny Christian Center* en Apopka, Florida; ex diputada Michele Bachmann; Ralph Reed de *Faith and Freedom Coalition*; Gary Bauer de *America Values*; Robert Jeffress de *First Baptist Church* en Dallas; Jack Graman de *Prestonwood Baptist Church* en Plano, Texas; Jim Garlow de

Skyline Church en La Mesa, California; Rodney Howard-Browne de *River* en *Tampa Bay Church*; Mike Evans, fundador del *museo Amigos de Sion* en Jerusalén; y Richard Land del *Southern Evangelical Seminary* en Charlotte.

La reunión fue organizada por una asistente especial del Presidente e incluía un tiempo de oración, al cual, como varios miembros del grupo reportó, el Presidente fue excepcionalmente receptivo. Después Perkins les dijo a amigos y simpatizantes de su organización que la administración de Trump estaba "genuinamente interesada y sensible a las preocupaciones de la comunidad evangélica". Después de catorce años en Washington, él dijo: "Estoy más que optimista que podemos cambiar el curso de este país".[24]

Tony Suárez, vicepresidente ejecutivo de la Conferencia Nacional de Líderes Cristianos Hispanos, dijo que había estado preocupado por la falta de acción de Washington en cuanto al tema de la reforma migratoria y dijo: "Yo no culpo a la Casa Blanca. Culpo al Congreso". Agregó que la reunión con Trump había sido relajada y sin prisa, "como una reunión de amigos".[25] Es cierto, el Presidente ha sido un amigo para la comunidad cristiana. Mi amigo, el exdiputado Bob McEwen, quien trabaja como director ejecutivo del *Council for National Policy*, le dijo a un grupo de cristianos políticamente activos, en una reunión a la que asistí en Washington, el año que fue el primer período de Trump, que si ustedes no pueden "ver la mano de Dios en Donald Trump, son sordos, mudos y ciegos".[26] En este punto de su presidencia, una mayoría de cristianos y conservadores de ideas afines probablemente estarían de acuerdo.

UNA NACIÓN EN RIESGO

Una de las razones por las que escribí el libro *God and Donald Trump* fue para dar un vistazo cercano al fenómeno que se llevó a cabo en las elecciones de 2016. Cómo era posible, me preguntaba, que Donald Trump fuera capaz de ganar tal victoria sorprendente cuando los medios de comunicación, las encuestas y la institución política entera estaba en contra de él. Resulta que no fue porque los rusos habían pirateado las elecciones, no fue porque James Comey había reabierto la investigación del correo electrónico de Clinton, ni tampoco fue porque los hombres le estaban diciendo a sus esposas que votaran por Trump, como la Izquierda nos quería hacer creer. Así que, para mí, surgió la pregunta: ¿Era posible que Dios, viendo la espiral moral en la que estábamos, levantara a alguien a quien no le importara lo políticamente correcto ni el protocolo político, sino que tenía un temperamento y convicciones para hacer grande a Estados Unidos de nuevo?

Toqué este punto cuando fui entrevistado en CNN y MSNBC. Ellos querían saber cómo los evangélicos que creen en la moralidad y en la vida justa podrían apoyar a Donald Trump después de que surgiera el escándalo de Stormy Daniels. Dije que la mayoría de los cristianos no lo hacían responsable de sus indiscreciones pasadas sino que Dios ya se ocuparía de eso, pero la pregunta me abrió una puerta para hablar de problemas más grandes y para decir que los cristianos estaban orando por el Presidente y que creemos que Dios respondía nuestras oraciones, dándonos un líder fuerte y capaz quien, a pesar de sus fallas, tenía una visión clara del futuro y estaba defendiendo las políticas y los estándares en los que creemos.

ORACIÓN POR UN DESPERTAR

El Dr. James Dobson ha sido un conductor de televisión famoso y altamente respetado por más de cuarenta años, y como psicólogo cristiano influyente y autor, él ha ayudado a millones de familias estadounidenses con sus preguntas sobre el conflicto entre la cultura contemporánea y los temas de la fe. Durante mi entrevista con él para este libro, quería escuchar sus pensamientos sobre los cambios sísmicos ocasionados por la elección del presidente Trump y cómo los cambios que se llevaron a cabo han afectado la institución de la familia, así como a la comunidad evangélica y al país.

> STRANG: Muchas gracias Dr. Dobson por apartar un tiempo para compartir sus pensamientos en los cambios que se están dando en el país desde la elección de Donald Trump. Sé que ha tenido contacto personal cercano con varios presidentes de Estados Unidos como asesor y amigo. Así que tengo curiosidad por escuchar sobre eso, y especialmente me gustaría saber cómo compara al presidente Trump con otros presidentes que ha conocido.

> DOBSON: Al haber trabajado con cinco presidentes de Estados Unidos en los últimos treinta y ocho años, he tenido la oportunidad de considerar las filosofías y prioridades de cada uno. El primero fue Jimmy Carter, quien me pidió que participara en sus Conferencias sobre las familias en la Casa Blanca. Luego fui consultor durante cinco años con Ronald Reagan, quien empezó nuestra relación preguntando: "¿Qué puede hacer mi administración para fortalecer las familias del país?". Eso fue seguido por conversaciones poco frecuentes en la Casa Blanca con [George] Herbert Walker Bush, y su hijo George W. Bush. Ahora tengo el privilegio de servir a Donald Trump como uno de sus asesores de fe en numerosos asuntos, desde enfermedades mentales hasta adicciones a drogas. Esta historia personal me ha dado la perspectiva para responder a su pregunta hoy.

> Descubrí que cada uno de estos presidentes eran hombres honorables que estaban dedicados al bienestar del país y de sus familias. Los respeté a todos en su mandato. Sin embargo, los cinco eran "vasos con defectos" así como lo es cada ser humano que haya vivido

en la tierra. En su mayor parte, cada presidente trabajó incansablemente para servir a su país en lo que resultó ser una tarea compleja e imposible. Ellos tuvieron que aprender a vivir con críticas constantes de quienes querían humillarlos y desmotivarlos. Como la Rana René dijo en Plaza Sésamo: "No es fácil ser verde".

STRANG: ¿Cómo califica al presidente Trump en temas de preocupación para los cristianos conservadores?

DOBSON: Hasta hoy, en el primer período de Donald Trump, creo que ha estado más dedicado a santificar la vida humana y el bienestar de la familia que ninguno de sus antecesores. Su lenguaje algunas veces es crudo, y su récord como "hombre de familia" ha sido lamentable. Sin embargo, él parece entender que "así como funciona la familia, así funciona el país". Si duda de eso, pregúnteles a sus hijos adultos. Cada uno de ellos lo elogia con entusiasmo como hombre y como padre.

Desde su investidura en 2017, el presidente Trump luchó y logró el recorte de impuestos más grande de la historia del país. Él nominó al gran Neil Gorsuch en la Corte Suprema de Justicia, quien parecía estar comprometido con la conservación de la vida y la protección constitucional de la libertad de culto. Trump ha presionado para que la mayoría de los miembros republicanos del Congreso dupliquen el crédito tributario por hijos, lo que beneficiará a las familias en dificultades en todas partes. Mientras hablamos, la Casa Blanca está trabajando en medidas de licencia de paternidad y en otros numerosos esfuerzos legislativos para ayudar a las familias.

De hecho, Trump ha cumplido casi cada promesa que les ha hecho a las comunidades profamilia y provida, incluyendo un esfuerzo enérgico, ahora en marcha, a reducir los problemas epidémicos de opioides y otras drogas ilícitas. Él es el primer presidente en la historia en celebrar eventos sobre el Día Nacional de Oración (DNO) en el *Rose Garden*, aunque George W. Bush celebró el NDO con servicios en la Casa Blanca cada año durante sus ocho años en el poder. Yo podría escribir un libro describiendo las otras razones por las que apoyo a Donald J. Trump. A pesar de que no es perfecto, estoy agradecido de tenerlo como nuestro Presidente, pese al incesante odio que se le ha lanzado hasta ahora.

STRANG: La elección nacional de 2016 claramente dividió a la nación en dos campos de guerra, con conservadores y liberales siendo cada vez más hostiles unos con otros. ¿Qué sugiere que nosotros, como cristianos, hagamos para unir a los estadounidenses de nuevo?

DOBSON: Yo no creo que haya una solución rápida para el conflicto político y social que en este momento nos está dividiendo. Estados Unidos no ha estado así de agitada internamente desde que la esclavitud dividiera a la nación en trozos en los años previos a 1860. ¿Qué podría haber enfrentado a hermano contra hermano de esta manera y hacer que estuvieran dispuestos a matarse y mutilarse mutuamente? Las pasiones que se desataron durante ese tiempo fueron demasiado grandes para controlarlas por compromiso o negociación. El abismo entre ellas era demasiado grande como para poderlas unir. El resultado fue una masacre que persigue nuestra memoria nacional hoy en día.

No estoy sugiriendo que Estados Unidos de nuevo marche hacia otra guerra cruel. Definitivamente oro porque no sea así. Creo, sin embargo, que los sistemas de creencias contrastantes de hoy en día están poderosamente arraigados y son impresionantemente peligrosos. Algunos comentadores sugieren que nuestros líderes solo deben "caminar por los pasillos" y restaurar la armonía. Eso es simple y ridículo. Aunque el acuerdo mutuo en algunos temas es imposible, los principios medulares que nos están separando están demasiado arraigados para ser "discutidos".

Tomemos el tema del aborto, por ejemplo, y la guerra cultural que ha provocado. Ha causado furia por más de cuarenta y seis años. El aborto debe ser prohibido; no puede ser reconciliado. No debemos olvidar los asesinatos brutales de sesenta millones de bebés, sin final a la vista. ¿Podemos aceptar la redefinición del matrimonio impuesto en nosotros por la Corte Suprema? El matrimonio empezó con un pronunciamiento por el Creador en el Jardín del Edén. Él dijo, como lo dice Génesis 2:24: "Por tanto, dejará el hombre a su padre y a su madre, y se unirá a su mujer, y serán una sola carne". Después de por lo menos cinco mil años como la norma, hemos abandonado su plan para la familia. ¿Hemos olvidado que el matrimonio entre el hombre y la mujer es una metáfora para la relación entre Cristo y su Iglesia? ¿Podemos desechar esa enseñanza en un montón de ceniza de la historia?

STRANG: Como usted dice, existen estos problemas fundamentales, y todos en el país serán afectados de alguna u otra forma por la manera en que la cultura, y los cristianos en particular, responden a las amenazas en curso a la libertad de culto. Entonces me gustaría preguntarle: ¿Cuál es su receta para las personas de fe que reconocen los riesgos y quieren defender sus derechos como cristianos y como ciudadanos de este gran país?

DOBSON: Viendo hacia el futuro, ¿estamos dispuestos a abandonar los principios de libertad de culto como se nos garantizaron en la Constitución? ¿Debemos consentir cuando las escuelas públicas desvergonzadamente adoctrinan a nuestros hijos con tentaciones sexuales libertinas y con otras creencias que contradicen las enseñanzas bíblicas que se enseñan en el hogar? ¿Podemos olvidar los esfuerzos de un expresidente para "cambiar fundamentalmente" los principios inspirados por Dios que nos fueron entregados por nuestros Padres Fundadores? Y finalmente, ¿daremos la espalda a nuestro Señor y Salvador, Jesucristo, cuyo nombre genera indignación y odio por parte de los defensores de la extrema Izquierda? Recuerde que Él dijo: "No he venido a traer paz, sino espada".

¿Cuáles de estos valores medulares estamos dispuestos a sacrificar en la búsqueda vana de la unidad y la utopía? Ruego porque no sea así. Si nosotros los cristianos nos sentimos seguros de ciertas cosas que son muy importantes para nosotros, usted puede estar seguro de que quienes están del otro lado son igualmente apasionados desde su propia cosmovisión. Están peleando por sus creencias. Pero debemos hacer lo mismo si las generaciones futuras han de comprender y seguir las enseñanzas bíblicas. Así, adheridos a cada perspectiva, Derecha e Izquierda, están en conflicto por discrepancias en creencias que no parece que estarán en armonía pronto.

STRANG: ¿Entonces cuál es la solución a la guerra cultural intensa que está a nuestro alrededor?

DOBSON: Yo reconozco que, en su base, el conflicto que enfrentamos hoy es de naturaleza espiritual. La mayoría de los problemas polémicos que nos dividen están arraigados en la Escritura y la teología. Aquellos de nosotros, en el lado conservador, no estamos tratando solamente con diferencias de opinión. Estamos tratando de vivir estándares que son eternos e "inspirados por Dios". Esos principios no son negociables. Sin embargo, debemos defenderlos dentro del contexto del amor por nuestros semejantes. Eso es un regalo para los seguidores de Jesucristo. Nuestra tarea es defender nuestras creencias sin insultar ni herir a las personas con quienes estamos en desacuerdo.

Para resumir mi perspectiva, la paz y la armonía, como un pueblo, solo se lograrán mediante otro gran despertar que arrase a la nación en un espíritu de arrepentimiento y compromiso. ¿Ocurrirá esto a la luz de las iglesias menguantes y de una generación de jóvenes adultos que parece estar menos interesada en temas de fe que sus abuelos y antepasados? Yo no sé. Sucedió dos veces en tiempos pasados. Esta debe ser nuestra oración por Estados Unidos y el mundo.

El candidato del caos de Dios

El Dr. Michael L. Brown, quien es uno de los pensadores más articulados en el mundo carismático, está de acuerdo con Dobson sobre las cosas buenas que el presidente está haciendo. "Algunas veces, vemos a través de los ojos espirituales, que son inmaculados; es decir, que tenemos dificultad en reconocer cómo Dios podría usar a alguien con demasiados defectos Mientras sostenemos estándares altos para los líderes de las iglesias y cosas así, uno tiene que reconocer que, en crisis nacionales de vida o muerte, Dios puede usar personas [que son] aparentemente incompatibles". Entonces, Donald Trump es, como otros han dicho, "una bola de demolición divina, o el candidato del caos de Dios, [porque] él es uno de esos hombres a quienes en verdad no les importa la apuesta política".

Media hora después de que Trump fuera declarado el ganador de las elecciones, Frank Amedia, pastor de *Touch Heaven Church* en Ohio, sintió que el Señor le estaba diciendo que creara un escudo protector alrededor del nuevo presidente. Como mencioné brevemente en un capítulo anterior, él lo llamó el POTUS *Shield*, reflejando no solo como un compromiso para orar por el Presidente, sino que Frank dijo que el acrónimo se refería al Orden Profético de Estados Unidos. Como lo explicó: "Ser una fuerza profética, humilde y poderosa de intercesores dotados para colocar un escudo de oración, profecía, unidad y fe alrededor de nuestro presidente y vicepresidente, y para ser una punta de lanza de fuerza espiritual para transformación de nuestro sistema judicial federal y de nuestro país. No hay límites geográficos, no hay límites políticos, no hay más límites que estar fundamentados en la Palabra de Dios y darle gloria.

Frank me dijo que cree que el Presidente tiene lo que él llama una "unción que rompe" que atrae a los desafíos como un imán. Esto le da la habilidad de descubrir la procedencia de sus enemigos y de derribarlos y resistir sus bombardeos sin temor. Ahora bien, no es un secreto que Trump se nutre de la adversidad. A él le encantan los desafíos. "Lo hacen más fuerte, más audaz, más determinado", Frank me dijo, "y actúa para probar sus causas a sí mismo, desde donde se hace aún más persistente. Tiene la determinación de un guerrero experimentado y la tenacidad de un competidor feroz".

He conocido a Frank desde que nos encontramos en el Muro de los Lamentos en Jerusalén, en 2007. Ambos asistimos a la celebración cristiana de la Fiesta de los Tabernáculos, a la que los judíos llaman Sucot. El último día es Simjat Torá y es una celebración al final de un año de lectura de la Torá y el nuevo inicio de otro año en Génesis. Había por lo menos diez mil personas en el Muro de los Lamentos ese día, la mayoría eran judíos ortodoxos. Fue increíble verlos danzando, llevando los rollos de la Torá sobre su cabeza. En esa multitud masiva, Frank y yo teníamos amigos mutuos que nos presentaron y, a través de los años, hemos seguido en contacto debido a nuestro amor mutuo por Israel.

Cuando los medios de comunicación, las encuestas y todos los demás estaban diciendo que Donald Trump nunca podría ganar la presidencia, Frank me dijo que él sabía que Trump ganaría. Él no solo profetizó esto sino estuvo involucrado en su campaña. Como cité en mi libro *God and Donald Trump*, Frank tenía acceso a los asesores de Trump y persuadió a Corey Lewandowski que le entregara una profecía escrita al candidato Trump cuando estaba subiendo al avión para regresar de Ohio a Mar-a-Lago. La profecía decía básicamente: "Si te humillaras delante de mí (es decir, del Señor), tú serás el próximo presidente de Estados Unidos". Solo podemos especular, y creo que Trump leyó la profecía y se humilló a sí mismo, de la manera que él sabía hacerlo. Y desde entonces el Presidente ha sido un defensor de los valores tradicionales y un defensor de la libertad de hombres y mujeres alrededor del mundo para adorar según sus propias creencias y tradiciones.

DEFENDER A LA IGLESIA

El Presidente dejó claro, incluso antes de entrar a la carrera presidencial, que él usaría el poder e influencia de Estados Unidos para defender los intereses de hombres y mujeres en la comunidad de fe. Desde ese entonces, él se ha interesado por la difícil situación de los cristianos que sufren persecución alrededor del mundo. De acuerdo con David Curry, el presidente y CEO de *Open Doors USA*, que trabaja en favor de los cristianos perseguidos, la libertad de culto será uno de los temas más fundamentales que enfrentará la administración Trump en los próximos años. Señaló: "Es el tema central con el que van a tratar ya sea si lo ve desde el punto de vista de inmigración, o si lo ve desde el punto de vista del terrorismo".[27]

Ya que *Open Doors* y otras agencias de ayuda parecidas lo han indicado, el extremismo islámico es una de las amenazas más grandes para los cristianos en otros países. Curry dijo que "oficialmente el año 2016 fue el peor año de persecución de cristianos, con un número impactante de 215 millones de cristianos experimentando algunos niveles de persecución debido a su fe". Los gobiernos tales como Corea del Norte, Somalia, Afganistán, Pakistán y Sudán están activamente comprometidos en la represión y persecución de creyentes. Agregó que "casi uno de cada doce cristianos en el mundo hoy vive en un área o en una cultura donde el cristianismo es ilegal, prohibido o castigado. Y aún hoy, gran parte del mundo está en silencio ante la ola impactante de intolerancia religiosa".[28]

La evidencia de que el presidente tomó en serio el desafío fue el nombramiento del exsenador de Estados Unidos y exgobernador de Kansas Sam Brownback, el 26 de julio de 2017, como embajador independiente para la Libertad Religiosa Internacional. Mientras los demócratas criticaban los valores cristianos tradicionales de Brownback, especialmente en lo relacionado con la comunidad LGTB, los evangélicos vitorearon su récord en la libertad de culto. Se necesitaría un voto de desempate del vicepresidente Pence, quien se desempeña como presidente del Senado para asegurar la confirmación, pero el nombramiento recibió un gran elogio en la comunidad de fe.

"La confirmación de Sam Brownback como el embajador independiente envía un mensaje al mundo", dijo el senador de Oklahoma, James Lankford, "de que la libertad de culto es prioridad para el gobierno de Estados Unidos".[29] Y señaló que el presidente será un defensor de la libertad de culto en todo el mundo. Muchos en la comunidad de fe habían estado esperando ver más evidencias de apoyo por la libertad de culto del Departamento de Estado. Algunos días antes Brownback fuera confirmado, la Casa Blanca emitió una declaración del presidente diciendo: "La fe respira vida y esperanza en nuestro mundo. Diligentemente debemos guardar, conservar y valorar este derecho inalienable".[30]

En enero de 2018 la administración Trump colocó a Pakistán en su lista de observación especial debido a sus violaciones severas de la libertad de culto. Al hacerlo, la administración defendió la libertad de culto alrededor del mundo. También designó otros diez "países de mayor preocupación". Entonces, en mayo de 2018, la oficina del Departamento de Estado de Libertad Religiosa Internacional, publicó el informe anual de 2017. El secretario de Estado, Mike Pompeo, quien había sido confirmado en su cargo un mes antes, convocó a una conferencia de prensa para anunciar la publicación del nuevo informe. Posteriormente, el embajador Brownback dio un resumen especial de este informe, el cual cubría doscientos países y territorios.

"Este informe es un testamento del rol histórico de Estados Unidos para conservar y defender la libertad de culto alrededor del mundo", dijo el secretario Pompeo.[31] La Ley de Libertad de Culto Internacional, que se convirtió en ley en 1998, garantizaba que la libertad de culto sería un tema de preocupación en la política externa de Estados Unidos. En sus observaciones, el secretario Pompeo les aseguró a los asistentes que el presidente Trump y el vicepresidente Pence apoyarían "a quienes anhelaban la libertad de culto". Después de anunciar que el Departamento de Estado celebraría la primera "reunión ministerial para promover la libertad de culto" y que se trataría de "acción", no solo de un grupo de discusión, el secretario dijo:

> La libertad de culto es ciertamente un derecho humano universal por el que lucharé; uno por el que nuestro equipo en el departamento

seguirá luchando y uno por el que yo sé que el presidente Trump continuará luchando. Los Estados Unidos no permanecerán como espectadores. Entraremos al cuadrilátero y permaneceremos solidarios con cada persona que busca disfrutar de su derecho humano más fundamental.[32]

Cuando la administración se estaba preparando para su primer cumbre mundial sobre la libertad de culto, en julio de 2018, *Pew Research Center* reportó que el 28 por ciento de todos los países en el 2016 tuvo un "alto" o "muy alto" nivel de restricciones gubernamentales sobre religión, más que el 25 por ciento del año anterior. Entre todas las naciones, "China tenía los niveles más altos de restricciones gubernamentales sobre religión, mientras que India tenía los niveles más altos de hostilidad social que involucraba religión. Ambos países tenían los niveles más altos de restricciones en esas categorías respectivamente, no solo entre los 25 países más poblados, sino también, en el mundo en general".[33]

Como grupo, los gobiernos de Oriente Medio y África del Norte fueron los peores violadores de la libertad de culto a nivel regional, seguido de la región Asia-Pacífico, Europa, África subsahariana y América, según *Pew*.[34] En sus observaciones sobre la publicación del Informe del Departamento de Estado de 2017 sobre la Libertad Religiosa Internacional, el secretario Pompeo llamó libertad de culto "un derecho que le pertenece a cada persona en el mundo", y agregó que "la libertad de culto era vital para el inicio de Estados Unidos. La defensa es importante para nuestro futuro".[35]

El presidente Trump y el vicepresidente Pence han establecido como prioridad mantener un diálogo abierto con las iglesias de Estados Unidos y líderes eclesiásticos, y el vicepresidente reafirmó ese compromiso en sus observaciones a más de once mil miembros de la convención bautista sureña, quienes asistieron a la reunión anual en Dallas el 13 de junio de 2018. Primero, él habló sobre el avance que ha tenido la administración protegiendo la vida, conservando la libertad de culto, ayudando a la iglesia perseguida y defendiendo a Israel. Pero esos logros, dijo, no se pueden sostener sin los estadounidenses comprometidos que asisten a la iglesia.

Durante sus observaciones, él dijo: "Creo que su voz, su compasión, sus valores y sus ministerios se necesitan más que antes Y ustedes también deben saber que reconocemos que el trabajo más importante de Estados Unidos no sucede en la Casa Blanca o en algún lugar en Washington, D.C.". Después dijo:

> Sabemos que el trabajo más importante, el trabajo más transformador, sucede donde ustedes viven, donde impactan los ministerios: en los corazones y mentes de los estadounidenses. La verdad es que el presidente Trump o yo estaremos detrás de un púlpito, pero habrá más impacto en los púlpitos en donde ustedes se ponen de

pie cada domingo en la mañana. Ninguna política promulgará más significado que los ministerios que ustedes dirigen. Y ninguna acción será más poderosa que sus oraciones.[36]

Para un presidente cuya administración empezó una ola de impacto monumental, y cuyas palabras y hechos continúan provocando impactos alrededor del mundo, puede ser impactante, incluso en una magnitud más amplia, que su administración se haya convertido en una defensora sólida de la libertad de culto. Pero para las personas de fe, en realidad no es una sorpresa. Uno de los más famosos eventos en la historia bíblica es el relato acerca de los riesgos y recompensas por defender la libertad de culto es la historia de la reina Ester, quien arriesgó su vida al acercarse al trono del Rey Asuero para explicar que el general Amán estaba mintiéndole al rey para destruir a los esclavos hebreos que vivían en Persia.

Cuando el primo de Ester le pidió que se acercara al rey para decirle la verdad, él hizo una de las declaraciones más impresionantes en la literatura bíblica, diciendo: "Si te quedas callada en un momento como este, el alivio y la liberación para los judíos surgirán de algún otro lado, pero tú y tus parientes morirán. ¿Quién sabe si no llegaste a ser reina precisamente para un momento como este?». Entonces Ester envió la siguiente respuesta a Mardoqueo: «Ve y reúne a todos los judíos que están en Susa y hagan ayuno por mí. No coman ni beban durante tres días, ni de noche ni de día; mis doncellas y yo haremos lo mismo. Entonces, aunque es contra la ley, entraré a ver al rey. Si tengo que morir, moriré»" (Ester 4:14-16, NTV). Providencialmente, el rey escuchó a Ester, y su pueblo fue liberado, y Amán se convirtió en la víctima de su propia conspiración.

La historia de la reina Ester es un tributo conmovedor al poder de la lealtad y el valor abnegado que ha sido celebrado por familias judías durante innumerables generaciones. Sin embargo, como el general Jerry Boykin me dijo en un capítulo anterior: "Estoy absolutamente convencido de que él fue levantado para un tiempo como este". La analogía es válida porque las consecuencias del fracaso en ambos casos son monumentales.

Al llevar este capítulo a su final, no puedo ofrecer una mejor declaración de lo que creo que se trata *El temblor después de Trump*. Quién sabe si Donald Trump ha sido levantado para ayudar a este país a evitar, o por lo menos a retrasar, un desastre inminente. Él no es un hombre perfecto, y nosotros tampoco somos personas perfectas, pero para muchos en la familia de la fe, el presidente Trump ha sido elegido para un tiempo como este. La única pregunta ahora es ¿cómo responderá Estados Unidos?

UN CAMBIO RADICAL SÍSMICO

E L TEMBLOR MÁS grande de las elecciones 2016 podría ser que el pueblo estadounidense se ha hecho más sabio bajo la tutela de Donald Trump. La mayoría de los estadounidenses ya no confían en los medios de "noticias falsas" o de los que se hacen llamar "expertos". Ahora todos somos escépticos. Obtenemos nuestras noticias de fuentes múltiples y alternativas, tales como la internet, la radio y Fox News. Ya no necesitamos a los críticos liberales para que nos interpreten los hechos. Con buena información proveniente de fuentes objetivas, ahora podemos hacer eso por nosotros mismos.

No es ningún secreto que los medios principales de comunicación ya no reportan las noticias. Las buenas noticias acerca de nuestra economía prospera o el hecho de que las políticas de Trump están dándole a los negocios estadounidenses un impulso muy necesario es, aparentemente, mucho que pedir. En cambio, los noticieros se interesan por los errores percibidos de Trump, veinticuatro horas al día, mientras que ignoran las noticias que la gente realmente quiere saber. Por consiguiente, los índices de audiencia de CNN, MSNBC y otros noticieros liberales están en el bote. Por otro lado, los índices para el único canal que ofrece una imagen equilibrada de lo que en realidad está sucediendo son excelentes. Los presentadores en el *Fox News Channel* son precisos y bien informados e invitan opiniones contrarias. Las audiencias se han pasado a la única red honesta, lo que es una señal de que el público está diferenciando muchos más estos días y que la complacencia del pueblo estadounidense ha desaparecido para siempre.

Durante muchos años el fallecido presentador de noticias de CBS, Walter Cronkite, terminaba sus transmisiones diarias diciendo "y así es como es". Sin embargo, aun entonces, las noticias transmitidas por las tres redes grandes no eran en realidad como decían. Hubo mucha jugarreta en los noticieros de Estados Unidos, y Cronkite era tan parte de eso como cualquier otro. Los noticieros de los medios principales están constantemente quejándose sobre los tuits de Trump y sus invectivas por todo lo alto contra la prensa. Etiquetar los informes de CNN y otras redes de cable como "noticias falsas" los vuelve locos; pero, lo han demostrado varias encuestas, la crítica del Presidente sobre los medios está realmente marcando puntos importantes con los votantes. Los conservadores en el centro del país han estado convencidos por años de que ellos no pueden tener una oportunidad equitativa de parte de la prensa liberal, haciendo más difícil elegir candidatos conservadores y es casi imposible que sus creencias sean reportadas imparcialmente.

Como mencioné anteriormente, una encuesta de Quinnipiac de 2017, descubrió que el 80 por ciento de los votantes republicanos confiaba más en el presidente Trump que en los medios. Una encuesta similar de los votantes estadounidenses por la publicación británica *The Economist* informó que los votantes confían en Trump más que en el *New York Times*, el *Washington Post* o CNN por un margen del 70 por ciento. Poco menos del 15 por ciento estaba a favor de los medios. Quizá el descubrimiento más sorprendente es que cuando se le preguntó a los encuestados si ellos estarían dispuestos a apoyar "a un candidato presidencial que hubiera cometido actos inmorales en su vida privada", los votantes demócratas son menos perdonadores que los republicanos. Todo un 48 por ciento de los republicanos dijo que estaría dispuesto a respaldar a un candidato con fallas morales en el pasado, mientas que solo el 19 por ciento de aquellos en el partido de Bill y Hillary Clinton dijo que apoyaría a una persona así. La política tiene mucho que ver con eso, pero mientras los votantes demócratas estaban enfocados en difamar al Presidente, los votantes conservadores y cristianos fueron mucho más perdonadores porque entienden que todos los seres humanos somos pecadores.

En su mayor parte, el presidente Trump ha cumplido con las expectativas. Él es un luchador y quiere restaurar el honor y el prestigio de Estados Unidos alrededor del mundo. Sus críticos aseguran que es un hombre de negocios egoísta, sin conocimiento de política, economía o diplomacia. Él tiene tan poco conocimiento de los asuntos extranjeros, dicen, que terminará metiéndonos en la Tercera Guerra Mundial. Pero cuando él hizo sus primeras visitas diplomáticas a Israel, Europa, China, el Medio Oriente y luego la cumbre en Singapur, la mayoría lo aclamaba como un héroe. Él habló en Arabia Saudita, París y Varsovia, y ocupó los titulares en el *World Economic Forum* en Suiza, donde explicó su agenda a favor del comercio en el territorio de las élites internacionales. Los medios hicieron su mejor esfuerzo para minimizar su éxito en la plataforma mundial, pero era obvio que el Presidente estaba haciendo un trabajo fantástico.

De regreso en Washington redujo los impuestos, ordenó la terminación de miles de regulaciones redundantes y restrictivas, expandió el libre comercio con nuestros socios en todo el mundo, y sacó a Estados Unidos del Acuerdo de París, el cual penalizaba la industria estadounidense y financiaba extremistas ambientalistas. Lento pero seguro, él está empezando a drenar el pantano y reorganizando la burocracia permanente en Washington y dándole al subgobierno su merecido. No ha sido fácil, y falta mucho para que termine, pero Donald Trump es un luchador, y ¿quién se atrevería a apostar en su contra?

Nadie apoya todo lo que él ha dicho o hecho. Los medios de comunicación han presentado a Trump como arrogante, ostentoso y vulgar, y esa fue probablemente la persona que esperaba encontrar cuando entrevisté al candidato Trump durante la campaña 2016. Pero eso no fue lo que encontré. Él tiene una voz suave, es respetuoso y un verdadero caballero, y desde entonces, he hablado con otros que opinan lo mismo de él.

Después de que ganó la presidencia, él demostró ser exactamente la misma persona que yo vi en el recorrido de la campaña, solo quizás un poco más enfocado en los asuntos rutinarios para guiar a una gran nación.

CAMBIOS CULTURALES SÍSMICOS

Mi objetivo al escribir este libro ha sido aportar pruebas de los cambios sísmicos que han sucedido desde que el terremoto que llevó a Donald Trump a la Casa Blanca y lanzó a Hillary Clinton a su interminable recorrido de pedir disculpas. Este libro ha sido escrito con el entendimiento de que las cosas pueden cambiar. Tal vez no obtengamos todo lo que queremos, y puede ser que tome más tiempo del que quisiéramos para cumplir todas las políticas y planes de Trump. Pero algunas cosas no volverán a ser como eran. Dentro de unos años, Neil Gorsuch y Brett Kavanaugh aún estarán en la Corte Suprema, los impuestos seguirán siendo más bajos, las resoluciones de la Corte Suprema defendiendo a los reposteros y los floristas estarán todavía vigentes, y miles de regulaciones gubernamentales sofocantes estarán fuera de los libros para siempre.

Si bien he tratado de registrar la manera en que el Presidente ha estimulado la economía, levantado al ejército, y entregado una marca de diplomacia musculosa verdaderamente extraordinaria, no hay garantía de que esto continúe. Una cita atribuida a Yogi Berra lo tenía claro: "Es difícil hacer predicciones, especialmente acerca del futuro". Existen fuerzas en juego que pueden hacer que algunos de los logros del Presidente se vean menos exitosos; ese es definitivamente el objetivo de sus oponentes políticos. Esto le sucedió a la presidencia del segundo Bush cuando los ataques constantes de los medios liberales guiaron a las cifras de las encuestas sobre el Presidente a menos del 30 por ciento. Eso quizás no hubiese sucedido si el Presidente se hubiera molestado en defenderse contra la calumnia de los medios. Sin embargo, nada de lo que suceda en los meses y años venideros puede disminuir el impacto sísmico de todas las cosas buenas que ya se han alcanzado desde que Donald Trump asumió la presidencia en la casa del pueblo.

Aun si el presidente Trump resultara ser un pseudoconservador o un globalista de clóset, como muchos de los "Trump jamás" parecen pensar, eso no va a deshacer los adelantos que ha hecho en la libertad de culto o en el apoyo que su administración les ha dado a los cristianos perseguidos alrededor del mundo. Estos y otros temas en la lista de los logros de Trump durante sus primeros quinientos días en el cargo, los mismos que están incluidos en el apéndice de este libro, revelan sencillamente cuán dramáticos han sido los cambios. Incluso si la guerra contra el terror no logra una victoria tras otra, como lo ha hecho hasta ahora, o si nuestras fronteras del sur siguen permitiendo la infiltración de los ilegales, eso no puede minimizar el cambio sísmico provocado por ISIS perdiendo el 90 por ciento de su califato. La tolerancia por el extremismo islámico y las protestas antiestadounidenses, orquestadas y financiadas por Obama a través de su campaña *Organizing for Action*, pueden ser perjudiciales por un tiempo, pero tales tácticas no pueden durar mucho. La gente tolerará ese comportamiento del expresidente hasta cierto punto.

En la política exterior, las cosas quizá no siempre salgan como Trump espera, y su serie de éxitos diplomáticos podría llegar a su fin, pero eso no trasladará la Embajada de Estados Unidos de Jerusalén ni incitará a Corea del Norte a revertir la misión suicida que ha estado procurando durante los últimos setenta años. Si los republicanos perdieran la Cámara de Representantes y el Senado, sin duda significarían reveses a la agenda conservadora, pero incluso eso no reivindicará el subgobierno ni a los funcionarios del FBI corrupto, del Departamento de Justicia y de la CIA, quienes estaban ayudando a Hillary Clinton y poniendo trampas para Donald Trump durante las elecciones decisivas de 2016.

Si Clinton hubiera sido electa, el mundo nunca habría sabido de los mensajes de texto entre los agentes del FBI Peter Strzok y Lisa Page diciendo que ellos se asegurarían de que Trump nunca fuera electo y si lo fuera, ellos tenían "una póliza de seguro". Lo que sabemos ahora es que el agente del FBI involucrado en la investigación del escándalo de los correos electrónicos de Clinton dio pasos para enterrar el asunto y luego lanzaron una investigación contra Donald Trump y una historia fabricada sobre la conspiración rusa en la elección. Strzok envió un texto a su cómplice diciendo que él no podía pensar en ninguna persona en Estados Unidos que debiera votar por Trump, y que él iba a usar su influencia y autoridad para asegurarse de que Clinton ganara. Esa clase de corrupción puede ser un comportamiento normal en una república bananera del tercer mundo, pero no en Estados Unidos de América. Y ahora que estos y otros hechos han sido expuestos a la luz del día, la gente quiere respuestas. La justicia no puede ser negada, y el genio del subgobierno, una vez expuesto, no puede ser devuelto a la lámpara.

Los demócratas siguen hablando de una gran "ola azul", cuando piensan que el público irá al lado de ellos. Pero eso no ha sucedido. Si bien esto podría cambiar con cualquier elección, creo que es debido a que muchos estadounidenses han concluido que los republicamos sonaban más como gente con sentido común, mientras que los candidatos demócratas parecían y sonaban radicales, siniestros y anárquicos. Fundamentalmente, la política estadounidense se trata de ley y orden, favoreciendo las reglas por encima del caos y la anarquía. George Soros ha gastado miles de millones para activar grupos anarquistas violentos, como Antifa y *Black Lives Matter*, y atacar a los conservadores en todo tipo de sitios, incluyendo sus hogares y lugares de trabajo, pero la gente ve lo que está sucediendo, y una mayoría dice que ya están hartos de la agenda izquierdista.

RESTAURAR LAS INSTITUCIONES CULTURALES

El daño hecho por la agenda liberal durante los últimos cuarenta años ya no puede seguirse negando. En la educación, las facultades y las universidades de Estados Unidos han sido contaminadas por las élites izquierdistas durante generaciones. En lugar de aprender sobre nuestra gran historia, sus tradiciones y valores, los estudiantes son adoctrinados por profesores radicales y se les enseña a avergonzar a cualquiera que no se postre ante su ideología izquierdista. Los estudiantes de las escuelas públicas apenas aprenden historia, habilidades del lenguaje o cualquier otra cosa que realmente les ayude a tener éxito en la vida. Les enseñan detalles escabrosos de la sexualidad humana y son adoctrinados con la propaganda izquierdista. La educación incorrecta de la generación más joven ha continuado durante años, pero se oye decir que los cambios están por llegar.

Trump está haciendo retroceder, y la confirmación de Betsy DeVos como secretaria de Educación es un primer paso importante. Aunque ella está recibiendo ataques y amenazas a diario por parte de los defensores de la agenda liberal, ni ella ni el Presidente van a dar marcha atrás. Ellos están haciendo mejoras dramáticas al sistema para restaurar la integridad de las aulas estadounidenses. Las política nuevas están garantizadas para volver loca a la Izquierda, pero lo padres y los demás a quienes les importa el bienestar de las generaciones futuras de estadounidenses se dan cuenta que hemos sido engañados y que los niños de Estados Unidos han sido abusados intelectual y moralmente. No hay nada de mayor consecuencia a largo plazo que la educación de nuestros hijos, y aquí también el cambio está por llegar.

En el sistema de justicia, el presidente Trump ha asignado un listado largo de jueces conservadores a las cortes federales. Para julio 2018, al menos cuarenta y tres jueces federales, incluyendo un juez asociado de la Corte Suprema de Estados Unidos, han sido confirmados por el Senado. Adicionalmente, veintidós jueces fueron confirmados por la Corte de Apelaciones de Estados Unidos y veinte por Cortes de Distrito de Estados Unidos han sido confirmados por el Senado. Para mediados del año, había ochenta y ocho nominados en espera de confirmación, y las nominaciones están siendo anunciadas a una velocidad récord.

Además de la confirmación del juez Gorsuch, el presidente Trump nominó a Brett Kavanaugh para reemplazar al juez Kennedy, quien se jubiló, y probablemente tendrá al menos una oportunidad más para nominar juristas conservadores para la Corte Suprema antes de dejar el cargo. Estos hombres y mujeres tendrán la oportunidad para restaurar los fundamentos de nuestro sistema legal para las generaciones venideras. Y nada tendrá un impacto mayor del legado del Presidente. La importancia de las cortes federales no puede ser sobreestimado. Mientras que la Corte Suprema dictamina solamente entre ochenta y cien casos por año, las cortes federales manejarán hasta cuatrocientos mil casos, lo que significa que los juicios que pasan a este nivel pueden tener una importancia inmensa y duradera.

Estos son solamente algunos de los cambios que se están llevando a cabo desde la investidura de Trump; triunfos para los conservadores y temblores impresionantes para quienes han estado trabajando durante décadas para transformar este país en una utopía socialista. Sin embargo, el listado de los cambios sísmicos es continuo. Tal como lo hemos visto en los debates que se están llevando a cabo en Europa hoy día, los ciudadanos de esos países están siguiendo el ejemplo de Estados Unidos de implementar soluciones de sentido común a los problemas complejos. En el Reino Unido, Brexit es un símbolo del deseo creciente por la libertad, la autonomía y el deseo de la gente de controlar su propio destino sin inclinarse a los edictos de una potencia Orwelliana.

Ronald Reagan dijo que los hombres y las mujeres de todas partes anhelan libertad, pero hay que pelearla, protegerla y pasarla a la nueva generación, o se perderá. Hoy día, en China, Japón y Corea del Norte, la gente está observando lo que está sucediendo aquí, y ellos quieren lo que nosotros tenemos. Han descubierto que Donald Trump habla en serio. Él quiere crear un campo de juego nivelado para todos los estadounidenses, y ha demostrado que usará el poder de nuestro magnífico ejército si fuera necesario. Bajo la administración Obama, las otras naciones nos hicieron pasar por bobos, y el presidente estadounidense realmente se inclinó ante los tiranos y dictadores. Sin embargo, bajo la administración Trump, el juego ha cambiado. Nuestros aliados y adversarios tendrán que pensar dos veces sus políticas con respecto a Estados Unidos.

Durante los últimos años, la policía ha estado recibiendo malos reportes de parte de los medios y de muchos en la Izquierda. Obama nunca defendió a la policía. Muchas veces estuvo del lado de los criminales y agitadores e inspiró odio por los hombres y mujeres en uniforme, quienes arriesgaban su vida por nuestra seguridad. La administración Obama acusaba rutinariamente a los oficiales de policía de racismo y crueldad. Aun los incidentes menores eran manipulados para dar oportunidad para que los izquierdistas, anarquistas y protestantes violentos atacaran a la policía. Sin embargo, a Donald Trump no le gusta nada de eso. Él asiste a las ceremonias de los policías, elogia a nuestros hombres y mujeres en uniforme, los honra y les tiende una mano siempre que necesitan ayuda. Es muy similar con el ejército. Él ha apartado más de US$700 millones para restructurar y revitalizar las fuerzas armadas. Como graduando de una escuela militar, a él le encanta el ejército. Y, en su mayor parte, nuestros soldados, marineros y aviadores están orgullosos de servir a este presidente. En las ceremonias de graduación en la *US Naval Academy*, en mayo de 2018, Trump permaneció por más de noventa minutos después de dirigir su discurso de graduación para conversar y estrechar las manos de los oficiales navales recién comisionados, y ellos correspondieron su apreciación y admiración por el Presidente.

Liderar desde el frente

Para cuando él entró en la contienda por la presidencia, en mayo de 2015, Trump había estado sacudiendo el mundo de la política. Sus mítines, que han continuado desde ese tiempo, están a menudo llenos a capacidad máxima de multitudes de simpatizantes entusiastas y alegres, a veces veinticinco mil personas o más, y él va a lugares que la mayoría de los políticos republicanos nunca han visitado. La clase trabajadora lo aman, y él se identifica con ellos. Cuando él era joven trabajó al lado de sus hermanos. Él admira a estos trabajadores, comprende cómo se sienten y, a cambio, ellos lo aman a él. Muchos de ellos, incluyendo a los sindicalistas, han abandonado al Partido Demócrata porque creen en el mensaje de Trump.

Si bien los demócratas se han vuelto izquierdistas e ignorado los intereses de los trabajadores estadounidenses, poniendo más atención a las exigencias de los extranjeros ilegales que al éxito y seguridad de nuestros ciudadanos, Trump y sus partidarios están dejando en claro que ellos quieren "hacer a Estados Unidos grande otra vez". Y están ganando amigos y simpatizantes por todo el mundo al no postrarse ante los intereses extranjeros, sino colocando a "Estados Unidos primero". Los votantes en Pennsylvania, Wisconsin, Ohio, Michigan, y Iowa pudieron ver hacia dónde se dirigía este presidente, y por eso lo siguieron en el 2016. Ellos ahora están contentos con las nuevas fábricas, con el crecimiento de nuevos negocios, y con los números bajos del desempleo. Estas personas planean permanecer con Trump. Ya no habrá más "liderazgo desde atrás". Estados Unidos estará liderando desde el frente de ahora en adelante, la única manera de dirigir. Y, como era de esperarse, otras naciones nos están siguiendo.

Muy pocos líderes han demostrado tal fortaleza de carácter frente a la adversidad; Winston Churchill siendo uno de solamente unos cuantos en el último siglo. Pero considerando el mundo al que pudimos haber entrado si Hillary Clinton hubiera ganado las elecciones, somos afortunados de tener un líder con tan fuerte sentido de propósito en este momento crítico de la historia. Él no recibe órdenes de nadie, pero busca la participación de todos, incluso de sus enemigos. El dinero no puede comprarlo; él tiene bastante de eso. Los políticos lo eluden, y él pocas veces sigue la línea del partido. Su firma no está a la venta. Parecido al general George Patton en muchas maneras, él cree en su destino y su deber, y quiere hacer lo más directo y sensible.

El subgobierno es una comunidad adversaria, enorme dentro de la burocracia permanente y le encantaría verlo muerto. Esto incluye un gran número de demócratas, pero también varios miembros de su propio partido, aun así, no pueden hacerlo tambalear. El presidente Trump tiene más logros en este punto de su presidencia que cualquier otro presidente en la historia. El titiritero globalista George Soros, en una entrevista en junio de 2018, en el *Washington Post* se lamentó de que el ascenso de Donald Trump y el movimiento antisistema han sido una interrupción grande en su agenda de fronteras abiertas. "Todo lo que podía salir mal, salió mal", dijo. Admitió que no esperaba que Trump ganara en noviembre y añadió, "Aparentemente, yo estaba viviendo en mi propia burbuja".[1] Espero que él se quede en su burbuja indefinidamente.

Al igual que muchas de las personas con quienes he hablado desde las elecciones de 2016, creo que Donald Trump siente que él está siguiendo su destino. Él ha recibido un mandato divino, y no le importa lo que los demás piensen o digan sobre la manera en que está haciendo su trabajo. Él quiere hacer lo que cree correcto, y verdaderamente quiere hacer a Estados Unidos grande otra vez. Para sorpresa de todos, él ha cumplido sus promesas de campaña, un asunto tras otro. Incluso sus partidarios más apasionados han sido sorprendidos por la cantidad de objetivos, listados al inicio de su campaña, que ya han sido alcanzados. Un vistazo al listado de quinientos logros en el apéndice es revelador, y en los temas donde todavía estamos esperando resultados, tales como inmigración y el muro fronterizo, él está presionando al Congreso para que haga su parte. En casi toda forma, él está agitando las cosas, pero ha sido animante ver que, a pesar de todo lo que sus adversarios y los medios de comunicación principales le han lanzado, este presidente continua en pie. Él es un triunfador, un hombre de fe determinada y un hombre de palabra. Indudablemente, somos afortunados de tener un líder así.

"A Dios le encanta redimir al mundo", declaró el presidente Donald Trump en su saludo en la Pascua judía y el domingo de Resurrección, en 2018. También compartió:

> Mis conciudadanos estadounidenses durante la sagrada celebración de la Pascua, las familias judías en todo el mundo dan gracias a Dios por libertar al pueblo judío de la esclavitud en Egipto y llevarlos a la tierra prometida, Israel. Para los cristianos, recordamos el sufrimiento y la muerte del Hijo unigénito de Dios y su gloriosa resurrección al tercer día. El domingo de Resurrección proclamamos con gozo: "¡Cristo ha resucitado!".
>
> Ambas celebraciones sagradas nos recuerdan que el amor de Dios redime al mundo. Hace casi tres mil años, el profeta Isaías escribió: "La tierra está cubierta de tinieblas; pero sobre ti brilla el Señor, como la aurora; sobre ti se puede contemplar su gloria".
>
> En Estados Unidos, vemos a la luz de Dios para guiar nuestros pasos, confiamos en el poder del Todopoderoso para sabiduría y fortaleza, y alabamos a nuestro Padre celestial por las bendiciones de libertad y el don de la vida eterna.[2]

Si nuestra nación pudiera empezar a confiar verdaderamente en Dios y permitir que su luz guie nuestros pasos, entonces, ese es el mayor impacto de todos.

500 DÍAS DE GRANDEZA ESTADOUNIDENSE DEL PRESIDENTE DONALD J. TRUMP

Nuestras familias progresarán. Nuestro pueblo prosperará. Y nuestro país será por siempre seguro y fuerte y orgulloso y poderoso y libre.
—PRESIDENTE DONALD J. TRUMP

500 días: en sus primeros 500 días en el poder, el presidente Donald J. Trump ha logrado resultados tanto dentro del país como internacionalmente para el pueblo estadounidense.[1]

- Desde que está en el poder, el presidente Trump ha fortalecido el liderazgo, seguridad, prosperidad y responsabilidad de Estados Unidos.

- Después de 500 días, los resultados son claros: la economía de Estados Unidos es más fuerte, los trabajadores estadounidenses están experimentando más oportunidades, se ha elevado la confianza y los negocios están en auge.

- El presidente Trump ha reafirmado al liderazgo de Estados Unidos en el escenario mundial, asegurado las inversiones vitales en nuestro ejército, y se defendió contra las amenazas a nuestra seguridad nacional.

- El presidente Trump ha puesto al pueblo estadounidense primero y ha hecho al gobierno más responsable.

LA ECONOMÍA DE ESTADOS UNIDOS ES MÁS FUERTE: la economía de Estados Unidos es más fuerte hoy y los trabajadores estadounidenses están en mejores circunstancias gracias a la agenda a favor del crecimiento del presidente Trump.

- Casi 3 millones de empleos se crearon desde que el presidente Trump asumió el poder.

  ▷ 304,000 empleos de producción se han creado desde que el presidente Trump asumió el poder, y el empleo en producción permanece como el nivel más alto desde diciembre de 2008.

  ▷ 337,000 empleos en construcción se han creado desde que el presidente Trump asumió el poder y el empleo en construcción permanece en su nivel más alto desde junio de 2008.

- Bajo el presidente Trump, la tasa de desempleo ha caído al 3.8, la tasa más baja desde abril de 2000, y la oferta de empleo ha llegado a 6.6 millones, el nivel más alto registrado.

  ▷ 67 por ciento de los estadounidenses cree que ahora es un buen tiempo para encontrar un empleo de calidad, según Gallup.

  ▷ Solo bajo el presidente Trump, más del 50 por ciento de estadounidenses han creído que es un buen tiempo encontrar un trabajo de calidad desde que Gallup empezó a hacer la pregunta hace 17 años.

- El presidente Trump priorizó la capacitación para el empleo y el desarrollo de la fuerza de laboral para facultar a empleados a evaluar más oportunidades, aprobando una orden ejecutiva para expandir las oportunidades de formación.

- El presidente Trump ha restaurado la credibilidad en la economía de Estados Unidos, con la confianza tanto entre los consumidores como en las empresas alcanzando una máxima histórica.

  ▷ La confianza del consumidor en las condiciones actuales ha alcanzado una máxima en 17 años, según la *Conference Board*.

▷ El optimismo entre los fabricantes ha sostenido máximos históricos bajo el presidente Trump, según la Asociación Nacional de Manufacturas.

▷ El optimismo de la pequeña empresa ha mantenido niveles récord bajo el presidente Trump, según la Federación Nacional de Negocios Independientes.

- El presidente Trump aprobó la histórica ley de recortes de impuestos y empleos, reduciendo los impuestos para las familias estadounidenses y haciendo a los negocios más competitivos.

  ▷ Las familias estadounidenses recibieron US$3.2 mil millones en recortes tributario bruto y vio duplicarse el crédito tributario por los hijos menores.

  ▷ La tasa impositiva corporativa máxima se redujo del 35 al 21 por ciento para que las empresas estadounidenses puedan ser más competitivas.

- El presidente Trump superó las expectativas al reducir los reglamentos innecesarios que acaban con los empleos.

  ▷ En el 2017, el presidente Trump sobrepasó su promesa de eliminar regulaciones en una proporción de dos a uno, emitiendo un total de 22 acciones para desregular.

  ▷ La administración redujo normas y reglamentos que afectaban a los agricultores y productores energéticos tales como *Waters of the United States Rule* y el *Clean Power Plan*.

  ▷ Bancos y cooperativas de crédito regionales y comunitarios sintieron alivio cuando el presidente Trump aprobó una ley que reducía los requisitos dañinos impuestos por la Ley Dodd-Frank.

- Desde que está en el poder, el presidente Trump ha promovido acuerdos comerciales amplios, justos y recíprocos que protegen a los trabajadores estadounidenses, terminando con las décadas de políticas comerciales destructivas.

  ▷ Días después de asumir el cargo, el presidente retiró a Estados Unidos de las negociaciones y el acuerdo de la Asociación Transpacífico.

▷ La administración del presidente Trump está trabajando para defender la propiedad intelectual estadounidense de las prácticas desleales de China a través de una serie de acciones.

▷ El presidente mejoró el acuerdo comercial KORUS con la República de Corea, lo que permitirá más exportaciones de automóviles estadounidenses a Corea del Sur con aranceles más bajos y aumentará el acceso de productos farmacéuticos estadounidenses a Corea del Sur.

▷ La agricultura estadounidense ha ganado acceso a nuevos mercados bajo el presidente Trump.

ESTADOS UNIDOS ESTÁ GANANDO EN EL ESCENARIO MUNDIAL: el presidente Trump ha ratificado el liderazgo norteamericano en el escenario mundial y está logrando resultados para el pueblo de Estados Unidos.

- El presidente Trump siguió adelante con su promesa de trasladar la embajada de Estados Unidos en Israel a Jerusalén.

- El presidente Trump ordenó el fin de la participación de Estados Unidos en el tratado horrible de Irán e inmediatamente empezó el proceso de volver a imponer sanciones que habían sido quitadas o no aplicadas.

  ▷ El presidente ha tomado acción para confrontar la agresión de Irán y sus delegados.

  ▷ El *Department of the Treasury* ha emitido un rango de sanciones dirigidas a actividades y entidades iraníes, incluida la Fuerza de Cuerpos-Qods de la Guardia Revolucionaria Islámica.

- Bajo el presidente Trump, Estados Unidos ha dirigido una campaña global sin precedentes para lograr la desnuclearización pacífica de la península coreana.

- El liderazgo del presidente Trump ha contribuido al retorno de 17 estadounidenses detenidos en el extranjero.

  ▷ Solo en mayo de 2018, Venezuela liberó a un estadounidense y Corea del Norte liberó a tres estadounidenses que regresaron a Estados Unidos.

- El presidente ha asegurado incrementos históricos en el financiamiento de la defensa para reestructurar el ejército de nuestro país con los recursos necesarios, después de años de aislamiento perjudicial.

  ▷ El presidente Trump aprobó una ley para proporcionar US$700 mil millones en gastos de defensa para el año fiscal (AF) 2018 y US$716 mil millones para el AF 2019.

- Estados Unidos ha trabajado con aliados internacionales para diezmar a ISIS.

- El presidente Trump ordenó ataques contra Siria en respuesta al uso de armas químicas por parte del régimen en abril de 2017 y abril de 2018.

- La administración Trump ha impuesto una gama de sanciones en la dictadura de Maduro en Venezuela, incluyendo sanciones que tienen como objetivo a Maduro y a otros funcionarios de gobierno.

LAS COMUNIDADES DE ESTADOS UNIDOS SON MÁS SEGURAS Y MÁS CONFIABLES: El presidente Trump ha trabajado para asegurar nuestras fronteras, reforzar nuestras leyes migratorias y proteger la seguridad de las comunidades estadounidenses.

- A pesar de los recursos limitados y de la obstrucción del Congreso, el presidente Trump ha trabajado para tener el control de nuestras fronteras y hacer cumplir nuestras leyes migratorias.

  ▷ El presidente Trump ha convocado al Congreso para proveer los recursos necesarios para asegurar nuestras fronteras y cerrar los vacíos que impiden que las leyes migratorias sean cumplidas completamente.

- El presidente Trump autorizó el despliegue de la guardia nacional para ayudar a asegurar nuestras fronteras.

- La administración del presidente Trump ha llevado a cabo esfuerzos para la ejecución de las reglas legales de inmigración.

  ▷ Desde el inicio de la administración del presidente Trump hasta el año fiscal de 2017, la *US Immigration and Customs Enforcement (ICE) Enforcement* y

Removal Operations (ERO) hicieron 110,568 arrestos de extranjeros ilegales.

▷ Los arrestos hechos en este marco de tiempo representaron un 42 por ciento de aumento en el mismo marco de tiempo del año fiscal de 2016.

▷ De los 110,568 arrestos que se hicieron, el 92 por ciento tenía condenas por delitos, cargos pendientes por delitos, eran fugitivos ICE, o se les había restablecido una orden final de expulsión.

- El presidente Trump había dejado claro que su administración continuaría combatiendo la amenaza de la MS-13 para proteger a las comunidades de la horrenda violencia que las maras habían difundido.

▷ En el 2017, el Departamento de Justicia trabajó con colaboradores en Centroamérica para presentar cargos penales contra más de 4,000 miembros de la MS-13.

- La administración Trump tomó medidas enérgicas sobre la importación y distribución de drogas ilegales para poder impedir que lleguen a nuestras comunidades y causar más devastación.

▷ Hasta abril de 2018, la patrulla fronteriza de Estados Unidos había incautado 284 libras de fentanilo en el año fiscal de 2018, ya sobrepasando el total de 181 libras incautadas en el año fiscal de 2017.

- El Presidente hizo el lanzamiento del esfuerzo a nivel nacional para luchar contra la crisis de opioides, la cual ha devastado a comunidades en todos Estados Unidos.

▷ La Iniciativa Presidencial contra los Opioides busca reducir la demanda de drogas, detener el flujo de drogas ilícitas y salvar vidas al expandir oportunidades de tratamiento.

- El presidente Trump aprobó un proyecto de ley de gastos diversos, que proporciona casi US$4 mil millones para tratar la epidemia de opioides.

▷ El proyecto de ley incluía US$1 mil millones de subvenciones enfocadas en los estados y tribus más afectadas y proporcionaba fondos para un convenio de investigación pública-privada sobre el dolor y la adicción.

EL GOBIERNO DE LOS ESTADOS UNIDOS ES MÁS RESPONSABLE: desde la toma del poder, el presidente Trump ha trabajado para asegurarse que el gobierno sea más responsable ante el pueblo de Estados Unidos.

- El presidente Trump ha confirmado la mayor cantidad de jueces de tribunal de circuito que cualquier otro presidente en su primer año, y confirmó como presidente a Neil Gorsuch en la Corte Suprema de Justicia de Estados Unidos. También a Brett Kavanaugh.

- El presidente Trump ha aprobado una ley para para brindar más responsabilidad al Departamento de Asuntos de Veteranos y brindar a nuestros veteranos más opciones en la atención que reciben.

  ▷ El presidente Trump firmó la ley del Departamento de los Asuntos de los Veteranos de Estados Unidos y de Protección de Denunciantes de 2017, mejorando los procesos por mala conducta.

  ▷ El presidente Trump firmó la *VA Choice* y *Quality Employment Act* como ley, autorizando US$ 2.1 mil millones de fondos adicionales para el *Veterans Choice Program*.

- El presidente Trump exitosamente eliminó la sanción por el engorroso mandato individual de *Obamacare*.

- La administración del presidente está buscando dar más cobertura de salud más económica y un acceso más amplio de alternativas asequibles en comparación a los planes *Obamacare*.

- El presidente Trump ha publicado un plan para bajar los precios de los medicamentos para los estadounidenses.

- El presidente Trump se ha asegurado de que el gobierno Federal proteja y respete las libertades religiosas y de conciencia de los estadounidenses.

  ▷ El presidente Trump firmó una orden ejecutiva para proteger la libertad de expresión y las libertades religiosas de grupos como las *Little Sisters of the Poor*

  ▷ El Departamento de Justicia emitió una guía para todas las agencias ejecutivas sobre la protección de la libertad de culto en los programas federales.

RECONOCIMIENTOS

U N LIBRO, ASÍ como este, cubriendo un amplio espectro de ideas y temas no puede ser producido sin un gran equipo editorial. Afortunadamente, yo no tuve que buscar una editorial. Como propietario de Charisma Media y de sellos editoriales como *FrontLine* y *Casa Creación*, he podido reunir a un gran equipo, y a través de los años hemos publicado más de tres mil títulos, incluyendo catorce éxitos de ventas del *New York Times*, como el libro innovador de Jonathan Cahn, *El presagio*.

Ahora que he empezado a escribir libros en un momento tardío en mi carrera, ha sido interesante trabajar con el equipo como autor y no solo como el jefe. Me gustaría mencionar a todo el grupo editorial, pero sería una lista muy larga. Sin embargo, quiero expresar mi gratitud y aprecio a quienes han trabajado más de cerca conmigo en este proyecto, incluyendo Marcos Pérez, nuestro editor, y Debbie Marrie, vicepresidente de desarrollo de producto, quien pulió el manuscrito con la ayuda de Kimberly Overcast. Son fantásticos, y dirigen un grupo notablemente talentoso.

En mis cuatro décadas en el mundo editorial, he contratado a muchos editores, escritores y trabajadores autónomos. Conozco a la mayoría de los mejores en la industria, y ninguno es mejor que Dr. Jim Nelson Black. Él ha trabajado con muchos autores famosos y ha escrito varios libros propios. He llegado a conocer a Jim y hemos trabajado juntos en varios libros importantes a lo largo de los años, y le pedí que colaborara conmigo con *God and Donald Trump*. Él hizo un trabajo tan increíble que le pedí de nuevo que me ayudara con esta secuela. Mucha de la investigación que han leído en estas páginas es de él, y sus destrezas de edición son grandemente apreciadas. Muchas gracias Jim.

La columna vertebral del proceso editorial es la composición tipográfica, el diseño de la portada y la calidad de impresión la cual es responsabilidad de Frank Hefeli y su equipo, incluyendo a Justin Evans, nuestro director de diseño, quien capturó el tema "sísmico" de la portada y también la unió con el excelente diseño de la portada de *God and Donald Trump*. Lucy Díaz Kurz, vicepresidente de mercadeo; nuestro director de ventas, Ken Peckett, y nuestro representante de ventas al público en general, Ned Clements, son de primera calidad. Ellos ayudaron para que *God and Donald Trump*, excediera las expectativas y se convirtiera en un éxito de ventas. Ahora lo están haciendo de nuevo.

Debo agradecimiento también a Deb Hamilton de *Hamilton Strategies* y Jenny Henneberry de GuestBooker.com, quienes organizaron las entrevistas en FoxNews, CNN, MSNBC y muchos medios de comunicación cristianos, junto con reseñas de *God and Donald Trump* en lugares pocos probables tales como Politico.com. También quiero agradecer a mi nueva asistente administrativa, Chris Schimbeno, quien me ayudó a mantener las cosas en orden mientras estuve trabajando en el manuscrito. Y por supuesto, quiero reconocer a Joy Strang, mi esposa por cuarenta y seis años, quien me ha apoyado de muchas formas durante este proceso. En su rol como directora financiera y como jefa de operaciones de nuestra empresa, ella ha tenido un excelente liderazgo mientras yo he estado ocupado, así como Ken Hartman, nuestro contralor; y el Dr. Steve Greene, vicepresidente ejecutivo de *Charisma Media Group*.

También quiero expresar mi sincero agradecimiento y alabanza a nuestro Señor, no solo por su dirección en este proyecto, sino por permitir que un modesto reportero de periódicos pudiera crecer y de una pequeña manera tocar al mundo a través de los medios de comunicación. Este libro es un ejemplo más de su gracia y misericordia.

ACERCA DEL AUTOR

S TEPHEN E. STRANG es el director ejecutivo de *Charisma Media* en Lake Mary, Florida, y fundador *Charisma*, la revista pentecostal-carismática más destacada en el mundo. El éxito de *Charisma* ha engendrado otras revistas y ha permitido la publicación de libros y Biblias tanto en inglés como en español. Él ha viajado por el mundo, y entre muchas otras cosas, ha entrevistado a cuatro presidentes de Estados Unidos, incluyendo al presidente Donald Trump. También ha sido invitado a hablar en las Naciones Unidas.

Él ha recibido muchos reconocimientos tanto de organizaciones religiosas como seculares incluyendo el prestigioso reconocimiento William Randolf Hearst. Ha sido nombrado por la revista *Time* en el 2005 como uno de los veinticinco evangélicos más influyentes en Estados Unidos. *Lee University* le otorgó un grado honorífico en 1995. Fue nominado como empresario del año y recibió reconocimientos del estado de Florida por crear trabajos en la industria editorial.

Ahora agrega a su currículo el título de autor de éxitos de ventas, gracias al triunfo de su primer libro, *God and Donald Trump*, el cual también le abrió puertas para aparecer varias veces en Fox News, CNN, y MSNBC, así como en varios medios de comunicación cristianos.

Criado en un hogar cristiano, es hijo y nieto de pastores de las Asambleas de Dios. Él recuerda aceptar a Cristo a la edad de cinco años en su casa y recibió el bautismo en el Espíritu Santo a los doce años en un campamento juvenil. Él fue profundamente impactado por el movimiento de Jesús y el creciente movimiento carismático cuando era estudiante de periodismo en la Universidad de Florida, donde fundó y dirigió un grupo carismático de estudiantes. Esto presagió la fundación de la revista *Charisma* unos años después mientras él trabajaba como reportero del *Orlando Sentinel,* un periódico donde estuvo varios años.

Durante cuarenta y seis años ha estado casado con el amor de su vida, Joy Strang. En 1981 ambos cofundaron la empresa que ahora es conocida como *Charisma Media*. Viven en Longwood, Florida y son orgullosos padres de Cameron y Chandler y abuelos de Cohen.

NOTAS

Introducción — Sacudidos hasta el núcleo

1. Neil Irwin, *"We Ran Out of Words to Describe How Good the Jobs Numbers Are,"* New York Times, 1 de junio, 2018, https://www.nytimes.com/2018/06/01/ upshot/ we-ran-out-of-words-to-describe-how-good-the-jobs-numbers-are.html.

2. *"List of Tax Reform Good News,"* Americans for Tax Reform, 2 de julio, 2018, https:// www.atr.org/sites/default/files/assets/National%20List%20of%20Tax%20 Reform%20 Good%20News.pdf.

3. Michael Goodwin, *"The Left Needs to Face Reality: Trump Is Winning,"* New York Post, 30 de junio, 2018, https://nypost.com/2018/06/30/the-left-needs-to-face- reality -trump-is-winning/.

Capítulo 1 — Psicosis capital

1. Erik Wemple, *"Study: 91 Percent of Recent Network Trump Coverage Has Been Negative,"* Washington Post, 12 de septiembre, 2017, https://www.washingtonpost.com/ blogs/erik-wemple/wp/2017/09/12/study-91-percent-of-recent-network- trump-coverage-has-been-negative/?utm_term=.454b12f1e818.

2. Rich Noyes y Mike Ciandella, *"Study: The Liberal Media's Summer of Pummeling Trump,"* NewsBusters (blog), 12 de septiembre, 2017, https://www.newsbusters.org/ blogs/nb/rich-noyes/2017/09/12/liberal-medias-summer-pummeling-trump.

3. Brent Bozell y Tim Graham, *"Bozell & Graham Column: Trump vs. Our Perpetually Panicked Press,"* NewsBusters (blog), 6 de marzo, 2018, https://www. newsbusters.org/ blogs/nb/tim-graham/2018/03/06/bozell-graham-column- trump-vs-our-perpetually-panicked-press.

4. Bozell y Graham, *"Bozell & Graham Column: Trump vs. Our Perpetually Panicked Press."*

5. Julia Glum, *"The Moment Liberals Knew Trump Won: 24 Horrified Quotes, Pictures and Tweets That Capture Election 2016,"* Newsweek, 8 de noviembre, 2017, http:// www.newsweek.com/trump-election-anniversary-liberal-reactions-clinton- loss-704777.

6. *The Rachel Maddow Show,* NBC Universal, 15 de agosto, 2016, http://www.msnbc. com/transcripts/rachel-maddow-show/2016-08-15.

7. CNN Live Event/Special, *"Election Night in America: Clinton Carries California; Hidden Trump Voters,"* Cable News Network, 8 de noviembre, 2016, http:// transcripts.cnn.com/TRANSCRIPTS/1611/08/se.08.html.

8. Keith Olbermann, The Closer, *"The Terrorists Have Won,"* The Scene, 9 de noviembre, 2016, https://thescene.com/watch/gq/the-closer-with-keith-olbermann-the- terrorists-have-won?mbid=email_cne_thescene_hotsheet.

9. Andrew Sullivan, *"The Republic Repeals Itself,"* New York Media LLC, 9 de noviembre, 2016, http://nymag.com/daily/intelligencer/2016/11/andrew-sullivan-president-trump-and-the-end-of-the-republic.html.

10. Jeff Jarvis (@jeffjarvis), *"I'll say it: This is the victory of the uneducated and uninformed. Now more than ever that looks impossible to fix. They now rule,"* Twitter, 8 de noviembre, 2016, 10:51 p.m., https://twitter.com/jeffjarvis/status/796243909890506752.

11. Michael Moore, *"Morning After To-Do List,"* Facebook, 9 de noviembre, 2016, 10:13 a.m., https://www.facebook.com/mmflint/posts/10153913074756857.

12. Ana Navarro (@ananavarro), *"All pollsters should be tarred and feather. Every single one of them. Next time someone shows me a poll, I'm using it to wrap dead fish,"* Twitter, 9 de noviembre, 2016, 7:13 a.m., https://twitter.com/ananavarro/status/796370050383024128.

13. Joy Behar, The View, 9 de noviembre, 2016, viewed at https://www.dailywire.com/news/10662/lol-joy-behar-meltdown-over-trump-too-good-amanda-prestigiacomo.

14. Gary Abernathy, *"Why Would We Abandon Trump? He's Doing What He Said He Would Do.,"* Washington Post, 8 de diciembre, 2017, https://www.washingtonpost.com/opinions/why-would-we-abandon-trump-hes-doing-what- he-said-he-would-do/2017/12/08/2aae3682-db95-11e7-a841-2066faf731ef_ story.html?utm_term=.274224dbfa52.

15. Abernathy, *"Why Would We Abandon Trump? He's Doing What He Said He Would Do."*

16. Abernathy, *"Why Would We Abandon Trump? He's Doing What He Said He Would Do."*

17. Katty Kay, *"Why Trump's Supporters Will Never Abandon Him,"* BBC, 23 de agosto, 2017, https://www.bbc.com/news/world-us-canada-41028733.

18. Kay, *"Why Trump's Supporters Will Never Abandon Him."*

19. Kay, *"Why Trump's Supporters Will Never Abandon Him."*

20. *"Most Republicans Trust the President More Than They Trust the Media,"* The Economist, 3 de agosto, 2017, https://www.economist.com/news/united- states/21725822 -there-also-broad-support-shutting-down-outlets-perceived- biased-most-republicans.

21. Kathy Frankovic, *"Moral Judgments Often Split Along Party Lines,"* YouGov PLC, 19 de marzo, 2018, https://today.yougov.com/topics/philosophy/articles-reports/2018/03/19/moral-judgments-often-split-along-party-lines.

22. Michael Medved, *"Why Democrats Are Suddenly Unforgiving Moralists,"* MichaelMedved.com y Salem National, 22 de marzo, 2018, http://www.michaelmedved.com/column/why-democrats-are-suddenly-unforgiving- moralists/.

23. Frankovic, *"Moral Judgments Often Split Along Party Lines."*

24. Michael Medved, *"For Dems, Hunting Is Worse Than Abortion,"* MichaelMedved.com y Salem National, March 22, 2018, http://www.michaelmedved.com/ column/for-dems-hunting-is-worse-than-abortion/.

25. Jonathan Wilson-Hartgrove, *"Why Evangelicals Support President Trump, Despite His Immorality,"* Time, 16 de febrero, 2018, http://time.com/5161349/president-trump-white-evangelical-support-slaveholders/.

26. Michael Gerson, "*The Last Temptation,*" The Atlantic, abril 2018, https://www.theatlantic.com/magazine/archive/2018/04/the-last-temptation/554066/.

27. "*Hostility to Religion: The Growing Threat to Religious Liberty in the United States,*" Family Research Council, julio 2014, https://downloads.frc.org/EF/ EF14G25.pdf.

28. Masterpiece Cakeshop, Ltd., et al. v. Colorado Civil Rights Commission et al., 16–111 U.S. (2017), https://www.supremecourt.gov/opinions/17pdf/16-111_j4el. pdf.

29. Hugh Hewitt, "*Why Christians Will Stick With Trump,*" Washington Post, 5 de octubre, 2017, https://www.washingtonpost.com/opinions/why-christians-will-stick-with-trump/2017/10/05/7d7d2bb6-a922-11e7-850e-2bdd1236be5d_story. html?utm_term=.8f935c878477.

30. Hewitt,"*Why Christians Will Stick With Trump.*"

31. James Strock, "*This SOTU, Trump Can Move to Drain the Swamp for Good,*" The Hill, 30 de junio, 2018, http://thehill.com/opinion/white-house/369187-this-sotu-trump-can-move-to-drain-the-swamp-for-good.

32. Brink Lindsey and Steven M. Teles, "*Trump Made the Swamp Worse. Here's How to Drain It,*" New York Times, 26 de octubre, 2017, https://www.nytimes. com/2017/10/26/opinion/trump-made-the-swamp-worse-heres-how-to-drain- it.html.

33. "*President Donald J. Trump Is Delivering on Deregulation,*" White House, December 14, 2017, https://www.whitehouse.gov/briefings-statements/president- donald-j-trump-delivering-deregulation/.

34. Thomas Binion, "*The Incredible Trump Agenda: What Most Americans Don't Know About the War the President Has Waged,*" Fox News Network LLC, 2 de marzo, 2018, http://www.foxnews.com/opinion/2018/03/02/incredible-trump- agenda-what-most-americans-dont-know-about-war-president-has-waged.html.

35. Joseph P. Williams, "*The Battle for the Judiciary,*" U.S. News & World Report, 2 de agosto, 2017, https://www.usnews.com/news/the-report/articles/2017-08-02/democrats-take-aim-at-trumps-judicial-appointments.

36. Allan Smith, "*Trump Is Quietly Moving at a Furious Pace to Secure 'The Single Most Important Legacy' of His Administration,*" Business Insider, 27 de julio, 2017, http:// www.businessinsider.com/trump-judges-attorneys-nominations-2017-7.

37. Donald J. Trump (@realDonaldTrump), "*Hundreds of good people, including very important Ambassadors and Judges, are being blocked and/or slow walked by the Democrats in the Senate …,*" Twitter, 14 de marzo, 2018, 6:02 a.m., https://twitter.com/ realdonaldtrump/status/973907142649397251?lang=en.

38. John Kruzel, "*Why Trump Appointments Have Lagged Behind Other Presidents,*" Poynter Institute, 16 de marzo, 2018, http://www.politifact.com/truth-o-meter/ statements/2018/mar/16/donald-trump/why-trump-appointments-have-lagged-behind-other-pr/.

39. "*Press Briefing by Press Secretary Sarah Sanders,*" White House, 7 de marzo, 2018, https://www.whitehouse.gov/briefings-statements/press-briefing-press-secretary- sarah-sanders-030718/.

40. Saunders, "*Trump, Democrats Create Logjam in Diplomat Confirmations,*" American Spectator, 1 de abril, 2018, https://spectator.org/trump-democrats-create-logjam-in-confirmation-of-diplomats/.

41. Saunders, *"Trump, Democrats Create Logjam in Diplomat Confirmations."*

42. Debra J. Saunders, *"Trump Against the World,"* American Spectator, 3 de diciembre, 2017, https://spectator.org/trump-against-the-world/.

43. Saunders, *"Trump Against the World."*

44. Saunders, *"Trump Against the World."*

45. Kristen Soltis Anderson, *"The Democratic Base Wants Congress to Oppose Trump. That May Not Sell With Independents,"* Washington Examiner, 28 de marzo, 2018, https://www.washingtonexaminer.com/opinion/the-democratic-base-wants-congress-to-oppose-trump-that-may-not-sell-with-independents?_amp=true.

46. Sam Schwarz, *"Support for Donald Trump's Impeachment Is Higher Than His Re-election Chances,"* Newsweek, 20 de diciembre, 2017, http://www.newsweek. com/donald-trump-impeachment-reelection-2020-753546.

47. *"NBC News/Wall Street Journal Survey—Study #17409,"* Dow Jones & Company Inc., octubre 2017, https://www.wsj.com/public/resources/documents/17409N BCWSJOctober2017Poll.pdf.

48. Anderson,*"The Democratic Base Wants Congress to Oppose Trump."*

Capítulo 2 — El punto de inflexión

1. Laura Reston, *"Americans Love an Underdog—Just Not Lincoln Chafee, Jim Webb, or Martin O'Malley,"* New Republic, 14 de octubre, 2015, https://newrepublic. com/article/123116/americans-love-underdog-just-not-chafee-webb-or-omalley.

2. Clyde Wayne Crews Jr., *"Obama's Legacy: Here's a Raft of Executive Actions Trump May Target,"* Forbes, 16 de enero, 2017, https://www.forbes.com/sites/waynecrews/2017/01/16/obamas-legacy-heres-a-raft-of-executive-actions-trump-may-target/#54dfc45c2dce.

3. Crews Jr., *"Obama's Legacy."*

4. Kenneth P. Vogel, *"George Soros Rises Again,"* Politico LLC, 27 de julio, 2016, https://www.politico.com/story/2016/07/george-soros-democratic-convention-226267.

5. *"George Soros: Media Mogul,"* Media Research Center, consultado el 20 de julio, 2018, https://www.mrc.org/special-reports/george-soros-media-mogul.

6. Sebastian Mallaby, *"'Go for the Jugular,'"* The Atlantic, 4 de junio, 2010, https://www.theatlantic.com/business/archive/2010/06/go-for-the-jugular/57696/.

7. David Horowitz and Richard Poe, *The Shadow Party* (Nashville: Nelson Current, 2006), xi.

8. Malcolm Gladwell, *The Tipping Point: How Little Things Can Make a Big Difference* (Boston: Back Bay Books, 2000), 295.

9. Richard G. Lee, *The Coming Revolution* (Nashville: Thomas Nelson, 2012), introduction, https://books.google.com/books?id=q39hk2x6uloC&q.

10. *"Remarks by President Trump to the World Economic Forum,"* White House, 26 de enero, 2018, https://www.whitehouse.gov/briefings-statements/remarks- president-trump-world-economic-forum/.

11. Keith Bradsher, *"Trump, in Davos Speech, Sticks to Script as He Declares America Open for Business,"* New York Times, 26 de enero, 2018, https://www.nytimes.com/2018/01/26/business/davos-world-economic-forum-trump.html.

12. John Lloyd, *"Commentary: Global Takeaways From Trump's Davos Speech,"* Reuters, 26 de enero, 2018, https://www.reuters.com/article/us-lloyd-davos-commentary/commentary-global-takeaways-from-trumps-davos-speech- idUSKBN1FF2C8.

13. *"Remarks by President Trump to the World Economic Forum,"* White House.

14. Bradsher, *"Trump, in Davos Speech, Sticks to Script as He Declares America Open for Business."*

15. Claire Zillman, *"Wilbur Ross Tells Davos: U.S. Is Done 'Being a Patsy' on Trade,"* Fortune, 24 de enero, 2018, http://fortune.com/2018/01/24/davos-2018-trump-wilbur-ross-trade-war-tariff/.

16. *"Remarks by President Trump to the World Economic Forum,"* White House.

17. 68 Bradsher, *"Trump, in Davos Speech, Sticks to Script as He Declares America Open for Business."*

18. *"Stocks Rise as Trump Declares America'Open for Business,'"* CBS Money Watch, 26 de enero, 2018, https://www.cbsnews.com/news/stock-futures-rise-as-trump- declares-america-open-for-business/.

19. Eamon Quinn, *"Stocks Hit New Highs on 'Palatable' Trump Speech at Davos,"* Irish Examiner, 27 de enero, 2018, https://www.irishexaminer.com/breakingnews/business/stocks-hit-new-highs-on-palatable-trump-speech-at-davos-825059. html.

20. *"Remarks by President Trump to the World Economic Forum,"* White House.

21. Andrew Ross Sorkin, *"What Happens to the Markets if Donald Trump Wins?,"* New York Times, 31 de octubre, 2016, https://www.nytimes.com/2016/11/01/business/dealbook/what-happens-to-the-markets-if-donald-trump-wins.html.

22. 73 Paul Krugman, *"What Happened on Election Day,"* New York Times, consultado el 23 de julio, 2018, https://www.nytimes.com/interactive/projects/cp/opinion/election-night-2016/paul-krugman-the-economic-fallout.

23. George Soros, *"Remarks Delivered at the World Economic Forum,"* 25 de enero, 2018, https://www.georgesoros.com/2018/01/25/remarks-delivered-at-the-world-economic-forum/.

24. Soros, *"Remarks Delivered at the World Economic Forum."*

25. Ryan Saavedra, *"Soros Threatens: Trump 'Will Disappear in 2020 or Even Sooner,'"* Daily Wire, 25 de enero, 2018, https://www.dailywire.com/news/26347/soros- snaps-trump-will-disappear-2020-or-even-ryan-saavedra.

26. Soros, *"Remarks Delivered at the World Economic Forum."*

27. Eric Lichtblau, *"George Soros Pledges $10 Million to Fight Hate Crimes,"* New York Times, 22 de noviembre, 2016, https://www.nytimes.com/2016/11/22/us/ politics/george-soros-hate-crimes.html.

28. Thomas E. Mann, *"Admit It, Political Scientists: Politics Really Is More Broken Than Ever,"* The Atlantic, 26 de mayo, 2014, https://www.theatlantic.com/politics/archive/2014/05/dysfunction/371544/.

29. Dennis Prager, *"Will the Second Civil War Turn Violent?"* Dennis Prager.com, 2 de mayo, 2017, http://www.dennisprager.com/will-the-second-civil- war-turn-violent/.

30. *"Political Polarization in the American Public,"* Pew Research Center, 12 de junio, 2014, http://assets.pewresearch.org/wp-content/uploads/sites/5/2014/06/6-12- 2014-Political-Polarization-Release.pdf.

31. Russell Blair, *"The Politics of Anger: Rhetoric, Intolerance Seen as Rising in U.S.,"* Hartford Courant, 18 de junio, 2017, http://www.courant.com/politics/hc-baseball-shooting-political-anger-20170615-story.html.

32. Blair, *"The Politics of Anger."*

33. Charles Hurt, *"This Trap Was Set Well Before Trump Won,"* Washington Times, 18 de marzo, 2018, https://www.washingtontimes.com/news/2018/mar/18/trap- was-set-well-trump-won/.

34. Hurt, *"This Trap Was Set Well Before Trump Won."*

35. James Strock, *"This SOTU, Trump Can Move to Drain the Swamp for Good,"* The Hill, 30 de enero, 2018, http://thehill.com/opinion/white-house/369187-this- sotu-trump-can-move-to-drain-the-swamp-for-good.

36. Strock, *"This SOTU, Trump Can Move to Drain the Swamp for Good."*

37. *"Judicial Watch: State Department Records Show Obama Administration Helped Fund George Soros' Left-Wing Political Activities in Albania,"* Judicial Watch Inc., 4 de abril, 2018, https://www.judicialwatch.org/press-room/press-releases/judicial-watch-doj-records-show-obama-administration-helped-fund-george-soros-left-wing-political-activities-albania/.

38. *"Judicial Watch: State Department Records Show Obama Administration Helped Fund George Soros' Left-Wing Political Activities in Albania,"* Judicial Watch Inc.

39. Alexi McCammond, *"Democrats Don't Want Tom Steyer's Impeachment Guide,"* Axios, 3 de abril, 2018, https://www.axios.com/tom-steyer-impeachment-guide-campaign-2018-election-1d8f9649-08a5-45d8-a1c0-93fcb89d73d7.html.

40. Adelle Nazarian, *"Tom Steyer's 'Need to Impeach' Trump Drive Reveals Division Among Democrats,"* Breitbart.com, 7 de abril, 2018, http://www.breitbart.com/california/2018/04/07/tom-steyers-need-to-impeach-trump-drive-reveals- division-among-democrats/.

41. Susan Davis and Scott Detrow, *"A Year Later, the Shock of Trump's Win Hasn't Totally Worn Off in Either Party,"* NPR Morning Edition, 9 de noviembre, 2017, https://www.npr.org/2017/11/09/562307566/a-year-later-the-shock-of- trumps-win-hasn-t-totally-worn-off-in-either-party.

Capítulo 3 - La agenda de rápido inicio de Trump

1. Dana Milbank, *"Trump Supporters Are Talking About Civil War: Could a Loss Provide the Spark?,"* Washington Post, 18 de octubre, 2016, https://www. washingtonpost.com/opinions/trump-supporters-are-talking-about-civil- war-could-a-loss-provide-the-spark/2016/10/18/f5ce081a-9573-11e6-bb29- bf2701dbe0a3_story.html?.

2. Chris Cillizza (@CillizzaCNN),*"I think this is who she sort of is -- at least in the context of a debate. Hyper aggressive,"* Twitter, 4 de febrero, 2016, 6:57 p.m., https://twitter.com/TheFix/status/695441165974269952.

3. Olga Khazan, *"Would You Really Like Hillary More if She Sounded Different?,"* The Atlantic, 1 de agosto, 2016, https://www.theatlantic.com/science/archive/2016/08/hillarys-voice/493565/.

4. Elspeth Reeve, *"Why Do So Many People Hate the Sound of Hillary Clinton's Voice?,"*

The New Republic, 1 de mayo, 2015, https://newrepublic.com/article/121643/why-do-so-many-people-hate-sound-hillary-clintons-voice.

5. Emily Crockett, "*This Awful Morning Joe Clip Shows How Not to Talk About Hillary Clinton,*" Vox Media Inc., updated 3 de febrero, 2016, https://www.vox.com/2016/2/3/10909354/morning-joe-hillary-clinton-shouts-bob-woodward.

6. Francis Wilkinson,v"*Hillary Clinton's 85 Slogans Explain 2016 Campaign,*" Denver Post, 20 de octubre, 2016, https://www.denverpost.com/2016/10/20/hillary- clintons-85-slogans-explain-2016-campaign/.

7. "*Memorandum for the Heads of Executive Departments and Agencies,*" White House, 20 de enero, 2017, https://www.whitehouse.gov/presidential-actions/memorandum-heads-executive-departments-agencies/.

8. Victor Davis Hanson, "*Hanson: How Trump Is Succeeding by Not Playing by the Rules,*" Mercury News, actualizado el 6 de abril, 2018, https://www.mercurynews.com/2018/04/05/hanson-how-trump-is-succeeding-by-not-playing-by-the- rules/.

9. Hanson, "*Hanson: How Trump Is Succeeding by Not Playing by the Rules.*"

10. "*Alexander the Great,*" History.com, https://www.history.com/topics/ancient-history/alexander-the-great.

11. Victor Davis Hanson, "*Trump Is Cutting Old Gordian Knots,*" National Review, 5 de abril, 2018, https://www.nationalreview.com/2018/04/trump-cuts-gordian- knots-with-unconventional-methods/.

12. Donald J. Trump (@realDonaldTrump), "*North Korean Leader Kim Jong Un just stated that the "Nuclear Button is on his desk at all times,*" Twitter, 2 de enero, 2018, 4:49 p.m., https://twitter.com/realDonaldTrump/status/948355557022420992; Donald J. Trump (@realDonaldTrump), "*The Chinese Envoy, who just returned from North Korea, seems to have had no impact on Little Rocket Man,*" Twitter, 30 de noviembre, 2017, 4:25 a.m., https://twitter.com/realDonaldTrump/status/936209447747190784.

13. Matthew Kazin, "*Trump Tariffs Could Dent Economic Growth; President Should Meet With China's Xi, Kevin Brady Says,*" Fox Business, 15 de julio, 2018, https://www.foxbusiness.com/economy/trump-tariffs-could-dent-economic-growth- president -should-meet-with-chinas-xi-kevin-brady-says.

14. Paul Szoldra and Associated Press, "*Here's Who Is Paying the Agreed-Upon Share to NATO—and Who Isn't,*" Business Insider, 16 de febrero, 2017, http://www.businessinsider.com/nato-share-breakdown-country-2017-2.

15. "*Remarks by President Trump at NATO Unveiling of the Article 5 and Berlin Wall Memorials—Brussels, Belgium,*" White House, 25 de mayo, 2017, https://www.whitehouse.gov/briefings-statements/remarks-president-trump-nato-unveiling- article-5-berlin-wall-memorials-brussels-belgium/.

16. Donald J. Trump (@realDonaldTrump), "*Many NATO countries have agreed to step up payments considerably, as they should,*" Twitter, 27 de mayo, 2017, 3:03 a.m., https://twitter.com/realdonaldtrump/status/868407229380268033?lang=en.

17. Hannity Staff, "*IT'S OVER: Trump 'TERMINATES' NAFTA, Unveils New 'US-Mexico Trade Agreement,'*" Sean Hannity and Hannity.com, 27 de agosto, 2018,

https://www.hannity.com/media-room/its-over-trump-terminates-nafta-unveils- new-us-mexico-trade-agreement/.

18. Tessa Berenson, *"Donald Trump Offers Conservatives a Deal on Supreme Court,"* Time, 21 de marzo, 2016, http://time.com/4266700/donald-trump-supreme-court-nominations/.

19. Debra J. Saunders, *"Trump, Democrats Create Logjam in Diplomat Confirmations,"* American Spectator, 1 de abril, 2018, https://spectator.org/trump-democrats-create-logjam-in-confirmation-of-diplomats/.

20. *"Remarks by President Trump to March for Life Participants and Pro-Life Leaders,"* White House, 19 de enero, 2018, https://www.whitehouse.gov/briefings-statements/remarks-president-trump-march-life-participants-pro-life-leaders/.

21. Kimberlee Shaffir, *"The'Mexico City Policy': Why Does It Matter?,"* CBS Interactive Inc., 27 de enero, 2017, https://www.cbsnews.com/news/the-mexico-city-policy-why-does-it-matter-donald-trump-abortion/.

22. *"Remarks by President Trump to March for Life Participants and Pro-Life Leaders,"* White House.

23. *"Remarks by President Trump to March for Life Participants and Pro-Life Leaders,"* White House.

24. *"Remarks by President Trump in Cabinet Meeting,"* White House, 16 de octubre, 2017, https://www.whitehouse.gov/briefings-statements/remarks-president- trump-cabinet-meeting-4/.

25. *"The Index of Consumer Sentiment,"* University of Michigan, consultado el 6 de junio, 2018, http://www.sca.isr.umich.edu/files/tbmics.pdf.

26. Rex Tillerson, *"Raqqa's Liberation From ISIS,"* US Department of State, 20 de octubre, 2017, https://translations.state.gov/2017/10/20/raqqas-liberation-from-isis/.

27. JMattera, *"Trump on the Somali Pirates: 'I Would Wipe Them Off the Face of the Earth,'"* Human Events, 18 de marzo, 2011, http://humanevents.com/2011/03/18/trump-on-the-somali-pirates-i-would-wipe-them-off-the-face-of-the-earth/.

28. Jenna Johnson and Jose A. DelReal, *"Trump Vows to 'Utterly Destroy ISIS,'"* Washington Post, 24 de septiembre, 2016, https://www.washingtonpost.com/politics/trump-vows-to-utterly- destroy-isis--but-he-wont-say-how/2016/09/24/911c6a74-7ffc-11e6-8d0c-fb6c00c90481_story.html?.

29. Richard Baris, *"Trump's First Year Accomplishments Compiled in Shockingly Long List,"* Rasmussen Reports LLC, 29 de diciembre, 2017, http://www.rasmussenreports.com/public_content/political_commentary/commentary_by_richard_baris/trump_s_first_year_accomplishments_compiled_in_shockingly_long_list.

30. *"Enhancing Public Safety in the Interior of the United States,"* Executive Order 13768, Federal Register, 25 de enero, 2017, https://www.federalregister.gov/documents/2017/01/30/2017-02102/enhancing-public-safety-in-the-interior- of-the-united-states.

31. Mason Weaver, *"Why Trump's Signing of Omnibus Bill Was Sheer Genius,"* WorldNetDaily.com, 29 de marzo, 2018, http://www.wnd.com/2018/03/why- trumps-signing-of-omnibus-bill-was-sheer-genius/.

32. Weaver, *"Why Trump's Signing of Omnibus Bill Was Sheer Genius."*

33. Donald J. Trump (@realDonaldTrump), *"Because of the $700 & $716 Billion Dollars gotten to rebuild our Military, many jobs are created and our Military is again rich,"* Twitter, 25 de marzo, 2018, 3:33 a.m., https://twitter.com/realdonaldtrump/status/977 855968364171264?lang=en.

34. Weaver, *"Why Trump's Signing of Omnibus Bill Was Sheer Genius."*

35. Richard Feloni, *"Here Are the 12 Business Leaders Trump Hosted for His First Big White House Meeting,"* Business Insider, 23 de enero, 2017, http://www.business insider.com/business-leaders-trump-white-house-meeting-2017-1.

36. Rachel Cao, *"Dow Chemical CEO on Trump: This Is the Most Pro-Business Adminis-tration Since the Founding Fathers,"* CNBC, 23 de febrero, 2017, https:// www.cnbc. com/2017/02/23/dow-chemical-ceo-on-trump-this-is-the-most-pro-business-adminis-tration-since-the-founding-fathers.html.

37. *"2018 Second Quarter Manufacturers' Outlook Survey,"* National Association of Manu-facturers, consultado el 7 de julio, 2018, http://www.nam.org/outlook/.

38. Baris, *"Trump's First Year Accomplishments Compiled in Shockingly Long List."*

39. Toby Harnden, *"Barack Obama: Nasa Must Try to Make Muslims 'Feel Good,'"* Tele-graph, 6 de julio, 2010, https://www.telegraph.co.uk/news/science/space/7875584/ Barack-Obama-Nasa-must-try-to-make-Muslims-feel-good.html.

40. *"NASA Acting Administrator Statement on the NASA Authorization Act of 2017,"* NASA, 21 de marzo, 2017, https://www.nasa.gov/press-release/nasa-acting-adminis-trator-statement-on-the-nasa-authorization-act-of-2017.

Capítulo 4 - En el foso de los leones

1. Tim Hains, *"Trump on McCain: 'He Is a War Hero Because He Was Captured… I Like People Who Weren't Captured,'"* RealClearHoldings LLC, 19 de julio, 2015, https://www.realclearpolitics.com/video/2015/07/19/trump_on_mccain_he_is_a_ war_hero_because_he_was_captured_i_like_people_who_werent_ captured.html.

2. Hollie McKay, *"Trump, Mattis Turn Military Loose on ISIS, Leaving Terror Caliphate in Tatters,"* Fox News, 8 de diciembre, 2017, http://www.foxnews.com/ world/2017/12/08/trump-mattis-turn-military-loose-on-isis-leaving-terror- caliphate-intatters.html.

3. New Day, *"Pentagon to Pay for Wall; Citizenship Question on Census; NFL Expands Helmet Rule; Evangelicals Still Support Trump.,"* Cable News Network, 28 de marzo, 2018, http://transcripts.cnn.com/TRANSCRIPTS/1803/28/nday.02.html.

4. Shimon Cohen, *"Half-Shekel Coin Bears Profile of Trump,"* Arutz Sheva, 21 de febrero, 2018, http://www.israelnationalnews.com/News/News.aspx/242249.

5. *"Trump Tweets Regarding Immigration; U.S. and South Korea Kick Off War Games; White Evangelicals Split Over Trump's Personal Life,"* Cable News Network, 1 de abril, 2018, http://transcripts.cnn.com/TRANSCRIPTS/1804/01/cnr.01.html.

6. *"MSNBC Live With Craig Melvin,"* NBC Universal, 30 de narzi, 2018, archived at https://archive.org/details/MSNBCW_20180330_170000_MSNBC_Live_With_ Craig_Melvin/start/2760/end/2820.

7. *"Bill of Rights,"* National Archives, consultado el 8 de julio, 2018, https://www. archives. gov/founding-docs/bill-of-rights-transcript.

8. New Day, *"Pentagon to Pay for Wall; Citizenship Question on Census; NFL Expands Helmet Rule; Evangelicals Still Support Trump,"* Cable News Network, 28 de marzo, 2018, http://transcripts.cnn.com/TRANSCRIPTS/1803/28/nday.02.html.

9. Marc A. Thiessen, *"Why Conservative Christians Stick With Trump,"* Washington Post, 23 de marzo, 2018, https://www.washingtonpost.com/opinions/why-conservative-christians-stick-with-trump/2018/03/23/2766309a-2def-11e8-8688-e053ba58f1e4_story.html?utm_term=.6f60173b6d1a.

CAPÍTULO 5 — EL PÚLPITO INTIMIDANTE DE TRUMP

1. *"NBC: Donald Trump Interviewed by Tom Brokaw on The Today Show—August 21, 1980,"* Factbase, consultado el 9 de julio, 2018, https://factba.se/transcript/donald-trump-interview-today-show-august-21-1980.

2. Conor Friedersdorf, *"When Donald Trump Became a Celebrity,"* The Atlantic, 6 de enero, 2016, https://www.theatlantic.com/politics/archive/2016/01/the- decade-when-donald-trump-became-a-celebrity/422838/.

3. Conor Friedersdorf, *"When Donald Trump Became a Celebrity,"* The Atlantic, 6 de enero, 2016, https://www.theatlantic.com/politics/archive/2016/01/the-decade-when-donald-trump-became-a-celebrity/422838/.

4. Traub, *"Trumpologies."*

5. Traub, *"Trumpologies."*

6. Traub, *"Trumpologies."*

7. Mayhill Fowler, *"Obama: No Surprise That Hard-Pressed Pennsylvanians Turn Bitter,"* HuffPost, actualizado el 25 de mayo, 2011, https://www.huffingtonpost.com/mayhill-fowler/obama-no-surprise-that-ha_b_96188.html.

8. Michael C. Haverluck, "Trump's 50% Approval Trumps Obama's 45%," One News Now, 23 de febrero, 2018, https://www.onenewsnow.com/politics-govt/2018/02/23/trumps-50-approval-trumps-obamas-45.

9. Time staff, *"Here's Donald Trump's Presidential Announcement Speech,"* Time, 16 de junio, 2015, http://time.com/3923128/donald-trump-announcement-speech/.

10. Jose A. DelReal, *"Donald Trump Announces Presidential Bid,"* Washington Post, 16 de junio, 2015, https://www.washingtonpost.com/news/post-politics/wp/2015/06/16/donald-trump-to-announce-his-presidential-plans-today/?utm_term=.98adce22b890.

11. Politico wrote: *"In fact, birtherism, as it's been called, reportedly began with innuendo by serial Illinois political candidate Andy Martin, who painted Obama as a closet Muslim in 2004."* Kyle Cheney, *"No, Clinton Didn't Start the Birther Thing; This Guy Did,"* Politico, 16 de septiembre, 2016, https://www.politico.com/ story/2016/09/birther-movement-founder-trump-clinton-228304.

12. Kori Schulman, *"'The President's Speech' at the White House Correspondents' Dinner,"* White House, 1 de mayo, 2011, https://obamawhitehouse.archives.gov/blog/2011/05/01/president-s-speech-white-house-correspondents-dinner.

13. Donald J. Trump (@realDonaldTrump), *"An 'extremely credible source' has called my office and told me that @BarackObama's birth certificate is a fraud,"* Twitter, 6 de agosto, 2012, 1:23 p.m., https://twitter.com/realDonaldTrump/status/232572505238433794.

14. Donald J. Trump (@realDonaldTrump), *"I am starting to think that there is something seriously wrong with President Obama's mental health,"* Twitter, 16 de octubre, 2014, 1:23 a.m., https://twitter.com/realDonaldTrump/ status/522664117438775296.

15. James Lewis *"What Does Donald Trump Really Believe?,"* American Thinker, 28 de febrero, 2016, http://www.americanthinker.com/articles/2016/02/what_does_donald_trump_really_believe.html.

16. Donald J. Trump (@realDonaldTrump), *"I use Social Media not because I like to, but because it is the only way to fight a VERY dishonest and unfair 'press,' now often referred to as Fake News Media,"* Twitter, 30 de diciembre, 2017, 2:36 p.m., https://twitter.com/realdonaldtrump/status/947235015343202304?lang=en.

17. Mathew Ingram, *"Love and Hate: The Media's Co-Dependent Relationship With Donald Trump,"* Fortune, 1 de marzo, 2016, http://fortune.com/2016/03/01/media-love-hate-trump/.

18. Ingram, *"Love and Hate."*

19. *"President Trump Job Approval,"* RealClearHoldings LLC, consultado el 9 de julio, 2018, https://www.realclearpolitics.com/epolls/other/president_trump_job_approval-6179.html.

20. Douglas Ernst, *"Jim Acosta Says Voters Too Stupid to Grasp Trump 'Act': 'Their Elevator Might Not Hit All Floors,'"* Washington Times, 24 de abril, 2018, https://www.washingtontimes.com/news/2018/apr/24/jim-acosta-says-voters-too-stupid-to-grasp-trump-a/.

21. John Nolte, *"Nolte—Media Fail: Trump's Approval Rating Average Hits Year-Long High,"* Breitbart, 1 de mayo, 2018, http://www.breitbart.com/big-government/2018/05/01/media-fail-trumps-approval-rating-average-hits-year-long-high/.

22. Kimberly Fitch, *"Both Sides of the Aisle Agree: The Media Is a Problem,"* Gallup, 29 de enero, 2018, http://news.gallup.com/opinion/gallup/226472/sides-aisle-agree-media-problem.aspx?.

23. Art Swift, *"Democrats' Confidence in Mass Media Rises Sharply From 2016,"* Gallup, 21 de septiembre, 2017, https://news.gallup.com/poll/219824/democrats-confidence-mass-media-rises-sharply-2016.aspx.

24. Nolte, *"Nolte—Media Fail."*

25. Nolte, *"Nolte—Media Fail."*

26. Alexandra Topping, *"'Sweden, Who Would Believe This?': Trump Cites Non- Existent Terror Attack,"* The Guardian, 19 de febrero, 2017, https://www. theguardian.com/us-news/2017/feb/19/sweden-trump-cites-non-existent- terror-attack.

27. Cheryl Chumley, *"Trump Clarifies 'Sweden' Comment, as Press Goes Bonkers,"* WND.com, 20 de febrero, 2017, http://www.wnd.com/2017/02/trump-clarifies-sweden-comment-as-press-goes-bonkers/.

28. Jon Miller, *"The 9 Most Absurd Lies the Media Told About Trump in 2017,"* CRTV.com, 27 de diciembre, 2017, https://www.crtv.com/video/9-most-absurd- lies-the-media-told-about-trump-in-2017--white-house-brief.

29. Miller, *"The 9 Most Absurd Lies the Media Told About Trump in 2017."*

30. The Lead With Jake Tapper, *" Trump Transition Sought Secret Communications With Russia?; North Korea Test-Fires 3rd Missile in Three Weeks,"* Cable News Network,

29 de mayo, 2017, http://transcripts.cnn.com/TRANSCRIPTS/1705/29/cg.01.html; Donald J. Trump (@realDonaldTrump), *"It is my opinion that many of the leaks coming out of the White House are fabricated lies made up by the #FakeNews media,"* Twitter, 28 de mayo, 2017, 5:33 a.m., https://twitter.com/realdonaldtrump/status/868807327 130025984?lang=en; Donald J. Trump (@realDonaldTrump), *"The Fake News Media works hard at disparaging & demeaning my use of social media because they don't want America to hear the real story!,"* Twitter, 28 de mayo, 2017, 5:20 p.m., https://twitter. com/realdonaldtrump/status/868985285207629825?lang=en.

31. Donald J. Trump (@realDonaldTrump), *"Sorry folks, but if I would have relied on the Fake News of CNN, NBC, ABC, CBS, washpost or nytimes, I would have had ZERO chance winning WH,"* Twitter, 6 de junio, 2017, 5:15 a.m., https://twitter.com/realdonaldtrump/status/872064426568036353?lang=en.

32. Donald J. Trump (@realDonaldTrump), *"The Fake News Media hates when I use what has turned out to be my very powerful Social Media—over 100 million people!,"* Twitter, 16 de junio, 2017, 5:23 a.m., https://twitter.com/realdonaldtrump/status/8756902045 64258816?lang=en.

33. Donald J. Trump (@realDonaldTrump), *"The Fake News Media hates when I use what has turned out to be my very powerful Social Media—over 100 million people!,"* Twitter, 16 de junio, 2017, 5:23 a.m., https://twitter.com/realdonaldtrump/status/8756902045 64258816?lang=en.

34. Total combinado de seguidores de estas cuentas hasta el 26 de julio, 2018: Donald J. Trump (@realDonaldTrump), Twitter, https://twitter.com/realDonaldTrump; President Trump (@POTUS), Twitter, https://twitter.com/potus; Donald J. Trump (@ DonaldTrump), Facebook, https://www.facebook.com/DonaldTrump/; President Donald J. Trump (@POTUS), https://www.facebook.com/POTUS/.

35. Mark Joyella, *"Sean Hannity Unrivaled as Fox News Posts 66th Consecutive Quarter at No. 1,"* 3 de julio, 2018, https://www.forbes.com/sites/markjoyella/2018/07/03/ sean-hannity-unrivaled-as-fox-news-posts-66th-consecutive-quarter-at-numberone/#a933e2d536d2; *"The Most-Followed Twitter Accounts on Earth,"* CBS Interactive Inc., consultado el 26 de julio, 2018, rankedhttps://www.cbsnews.com/pictures/ the-biggest-twitter-accounts-on-earth/14/; *"List of Most-Followed Twitter Accounts,"* Wikipedia, https://en.wikipedia.org/wiki/List_of_most-followed_Twitter_accounts.

36. Donald J. Trump (@realDonaldTrump), *"The Fake News is going crazy making up false stories and using only unnamed sources (who don't exist),"* Twitter, 30 de abril, 2018, 3:49 p.m., https://twitter.com/realdonaldtrump/status/991087278515769 345?lang=en.

37. Donald J. Trump (@realDonaldTrump), *"The White House is running very smoothly despite phony Witch Hunts etc.,"* Twitter, 30 de abril, 2018, 4:02 p.m., https://twitter. com/realdonaldtrump/status/991090373417152515?lang=en.

38. Emily Stewart, *"Wonder What Michelle Wolf Said to Make Everyone So Mad? Read It Here,"* Vox, 30 de abril, 2018, https://www.vox.com/ policy-and-politics/2018/4/30/17301436/michelle-wolf-speech-transcript-white-housecorrespondents-dinner-sarah-huckabee-sanders.

39. Andrea Mitchell (@mitchellreports), *"Apology is owed to @PressSec and others grossly*

insulted [by] Michelle Wolf at White House Correspondents Assoc dinner which started with uplifting heartfelt speech by @margarettalev," Twitter, 29 de abril, 2018, 8:03 a.m., https://twitter.com/mitchellreports/status/9906074471601643 52?lang=en.

40. Reince Priebus (@Reince), *"An R/X rated spectacle that started poorly and ended up in the bottom of the canyon,"* Twitter, 28 de abril, 2018, 8:22 p.m., https://twitter.com/reince/status/990431023992320000?lang=en.

41. Gov. Mike Huckabee (@GovMikeHuckabee), *"Those who think that the taste-less classless bullying at the WHCD was an example of the 1st Amendment should never condemn bullying, bigoted comments, racist bile or hate speech,"* Twitter, 29 de abril, 2018, 7:59 a.m., https://twitter.com/govmikehuckabee/status/990606 414287724550?lang=en.

42. Donald J. Trump (@realDonaldTrump), *"The White House Correspondents' Dinner was a failure last year, but this year was an embarrassment to everyone associated with it,"* Twitter, 29 de abril, 2018, 7:38 p.m., https://twitter.com/ realdonaldtrump/status/9 90782291667488768?lang=en.

43. Donald J. Trump (@realDonaldTrump), *"The White House Correspondents' Dinner is DEAD as we know it,"* Twitter, 30 de abril, 2018, 5:10 a.m., https://twitter. com /realdonaldtrump/status/990926480329859073?lang=en.

44. Kate Samuelson, *"Michelle Wolf's Routine Was 'Not in the Spirit' of Our Mission, Says WHCA President,"* Time, 30 de abril, 2018, http://time.com/5259517/whca-president-michelle-wolf-routine-not-in-spirit-of-mission/.

45. Liz Peek, *"Michelle Wolf Assault Was Perfectly in Tune With How Liberal Media Views the Trump White House,"* Fox News, 30 de abril, 2018, http://www.foxnews.com/opinion/2018/04/30/liz-peek-michelle-wolf-assault-was-perfectly-in-tune- with-how-liberal-media-views-trump-white-house.html.

46. Nic Newman and Richard Fletcher, *"Audience Perspectives on Low Trust in the Media,"* Reuters Institute (University of Oxford), consultado el 25 de julio, 2018, https:// reutersinstitute.politics.ox.ac.uk/our-research/bias-bullshit-and-lies-audience-perspectives-low-trust-media.

47. Rob Wile, *"When It Comes to News, America Is in a State of 'Pure Polarization,' Physicist Says,"* Miami Herald, actualizado el 4 de abril, 2018, http://www.miamiherald.com/news/business/article207841309.html.

48. Wile, *"When It Comes to News, America Is in a State of 'Pure Polarization,' Physicist Says."*

49. Lyman Abbott, citado en The Outlook, 27 de febrero, 1909; citado en the New York Times, 6 de marzo, 1909.

50. Victor Davis Hanson, *"Trump Syndromes,"* National Review, 6 de marzo, 2018, https://www.nationalreview.com/2018/03/president-donald-trump-creates-hysterical-hatred-and-fervent-support/.

51. Hanson, *"Trump Syndromes."*

52. *"Trump Administration Embraces Heritage Foundation Policy Recommendations,"* Heritage Foundation, 23 de enero, 2018, https://www.heritage.org/impact/trump-administration-embraces-heritage-foundation-policy-recommendations.

53. Hanson, *"Trump Syndromes."*

54. *"How New Yorkers See the World: View of the World From 9th Avenue,"* Brilliant Maps, 7 de junio, 2015, https://brilliantmaps.com/new-yorkers-world/.

55. Salena Zito, *"The Media Assault on Trump Could Win Him a Second Term,"* New York Post, 29 de abril, 2017, https://nypost.com/2017/04/29/the-media-assault-on-trump-could-win-him-a-second-term/.

56. Zito, *"The Media Assault on Trump Could Win Him a Second Term."*

57. Aaron Blake, *"Trump Voters Don't Have Buyer's Remorse. But Some Hillary Clinton Voters Do,"* Washington Post, 23 de abril, 2017, https:// www.washingtonpost.com/news/the-fix/wp/2017/04/23/trump-voters-dont-have-buyers-remorse-but-some-hillary-clinton-voters- do/?utm_term=.3bb4836a60ae; *"President Trump Is Least Popular President at 100-Day Mark,"* Washington Post, 27 de abril, 2017, https://www .washingtonpost.com/page/2010-2019/WashingtonPost/2017/04/23/National-Politics/Polling/release_466.xml?tid=a_inl.

58. *"President Trump Is Least Popular President at 100-Day Mark,"* Washington Post.

59. Zito, *"The Media Assault on Trump Could Win Him a Second Term."*

60. Salena Zito, *"Anti-Trump Hysteria Has Only Hardened His Voters' Support,"* New York Post, 14 de abril, 2018, https://nypost.com/2018/04/14/anti-trump-hysteria-has-only-hardened-his-voters-support/.

61. Darrell Delamaide, *"Media Courts Backlash With Constant Assault on Trump,"* MarketWatch, 30 de junio, 2017, https://www.marketwatch.com/story/media-courts-backlash-with-constant-assault-on-trump-2017-06-30.

62. Glenn Greenwald, *"CNNJournalists Resign: Latest Example of Media Recklessness on the Russia Threat,"* The Intercept, 27 de junio 2017, https://theintercept.com/2017/06/27/cnn-journalists-resign-latest-example-of-media-recklessness-on-the-russia-threat/.

63. Delamaide, *"Media Courts Backlash With Constant Assault on Trump."*

64. Delamaide, *"Media Courts Backlash With Constant Assault on Trump."*

CAPÍTULO 6 – DIPLOMACIA MUSCULOSA

1. Stephen Loiaconi, *"Trump: 'I've Been Preparing All My Life' for North Korea Summit,"* Sinclair Broadcast Group, 8 de junio, 2018, https://wjla.com/news/nation-world/trump-ive-been-preparing-all-my-life-for-north-korea-summit.

2. NBC News, *"Flashback: Donald Trump Says He'd 'Negotiate Like Crazy' With North Korea | NBC News,"* YouTube, 9 de agosto, 2017, https://www.youtube.com/watch?v=sQUaQo2j42Y.

3. *"Press Conference by President Trump,"* White House, 12 de junio, 2018, https:// www.whitehouse.gov/briefings-statements/press-conference-president-trump/.

4. *"Press Conference by President Trump,"* White House.

5. *"READ: Full Text of Trump-Kim Signed Statement,"* Cable News Network, 12 de junio, 2018, https://www.cnn.com/2018/06/12/politics/read-full-text-of-trump-kim-signed-statement/index.html; *"Press Conference by President Trump,"* White House.

6. Mark Landler, *"Trump and Kim See New Chapter for Nations After Summit,"* New York Times, 11 de junio, 2018, https://www.nytimes.com/2018/06/11/world/asia/trump-kim-summitmeeting.html.

7. Micah Meadowcroft, *"War, Mission, & Memory: Dr. Somerville's Childhood in South Korea,"* Hillsdale Forum, 31 de marzo, 2016, https://hillsdaleforum.com/2016/03/31/war-mission-memory-dr-somervilles-childhood-in-south-korea/.

8. *"Trump 'Bold' Talk on North Korean Christians,"* Religion News Service, 12 de junio, 2018, https://religionnews.com/2018/06/12/press-release-trump-bold-talk-on-north-korean-christians/.

9. *"Message to South Koreans on Reunification,"* NorthKoreanChristians.com, accessed 24 de julio, 2018, http://www.northkoreanchristians.com/unification-korea.html.

10. Estos paralelos interesantes cautivaron mi atención con Kathie Walters de Macon, Georgia, una amiga de toda la vida quien ministra alrededor del mundo y ha dedicado muchos años investigando avivamientos.

11. Ben Archibald, *"Donald Trump's Scots Aunt Is Dead Ringer for US President,"* Scottish Sun, 20 de octubre, 2017, https://www.thescottishsun.co.uk/news/1729757/donald-trumps-aunt-hairdo-president-scot/; *"Desperate Prayers by Trump's Great Aunts in 'Sanctuary' Cottage Said to Spark Hebrides Revival in Scotland,"* World Tribune, 18 de octubre, 2017, http://www.worldtribune.com/desperate-prayers-by-trumps-aunts-in-sanctuary-cottage-said-to-spark-hebrides-revival-in-scotland/.

12. Chang May Choon, *"Trump-Kim Summit: South Korea's Moon Jae in Hopes for Bold Decisions and Miraculous Result,"* Straits Times, 11 de junio, 2018, https://www.straitstimes.com/asia/east-asia/singapore-summit-south-koreas-moon-hopes-for-bold-decisions-and-miraculous-result.

13. *"History of North Korea,"* Liberty in North Korea, consultado el 26 de julio, 2018, https://www.libertyinnorthkorea.org/learn-north-korea-history/.

14. Carey Lodge, *"Christians'Hung On a Cross Over Fire,' Steamrollered and Crushed to Death in North Korea,"* Christian Today, 23 de septiembre, 2016, https://www.christiantoday.com/article/christians-hung-on-a-cross-over-fire-steamrollered-and-crushed-to-death-in-north-korea/96190.htm.

15. Russell Goldman, *"How Trump's Predecessors Dealt With the North Korean Threat,"* New York Times, 17 de agosto, 2017, https://www.nytimes.com/2017/08/17/world/asia/trump-north-korea-threat.html.

16. Goldman, *"How Trump's Predecessors Dealt With the North Korean Threat."*

17. Peter Baker and Choe Sang-Hun, *" Trump Threatens'Fire and Fury' Against North Korea if It Endangers U.S.,"* New York Times, 8 de agosto, 2017, https://www.nytimes.com/2017/08/08/world/asia/north-korea-un-sanctions-nuclear-missile-united-nations.html.

18. *"Trump Sometimes 'Felt Foolish' Using Harsh Rhetoric Against North Korea,"* The Hill, 12 de junio, 2018, http://thehill.com/homenews/administration/391783-trump-i-felt-foolish-using-harsh-rhetoric-against-north-korea-in-the.

19. *"Press Conference by President Trump,"* White House.

20. CNN Newsroom, *"Trump Speaks on Meeting With Kim Jong-un, IG Report, Immigration,"* Cable News Network, June 15, 2018, http://transcripts.cnn.com/TRANSCRIPTS/1806/15/cnr.01.html.

21. *"North Korea Relief,"* Samaritan's Purse, consultado el 10 de julio, 2018, https://www. samaritanspurse.org/donation-items/north-korea-relief/.

22. Samaritan's Purse, *"Mission of Mercy: Samaritan's Purse Airlifts Emergency Aid to Victims of Devastating Floods in North Korea,"* ReliefWeb, 31 de agosto, 2007, https:// reliefweb.int/report/democratic-peoples-republic-korea/mission-mercy- samaritans-purse-airlifts-emergency-aid.

23. Franklin Graham, *"Thank you, Mr. President, Mike Pompeo, and all of the administration's advisors for being willing to work for peace,"* Facebook, 13 de junio, 2018, 7:08 a.m., https://www.facebook.com/FranklinGraham/ posts/1961344047255100.

24. Jessilyn Justice, *" Trump Confronted Kim Jong Un About Atrocities Against Christians,"* CharismaNews.com, 12 de junio, 2018, https://www.charismanews.com/ politics/71603-trump-confronted-kim-jong-un-about-atrocities-against- christians.

25. Justice, *"Trump Confronted Kim Jong Un About Atrocities Against Christians."*

26. Jessilyn Justice, *"North Korea Crushed Christians Under Steamroller, Hung Them on Crosses Above Fire, New Report Says,"* CharismaNews.com, 28 de septiembre, 2016, https://premium.charismanews.com/article/60218.

27. Open Doors, *"World Watch List 2018,"* Open Doors USA, consultado el 10 de julio, 2018, https://www.opendoorsusa.org/wp-content/uploads/2017/05/WWL2018-Booklet-11518.pdf

28. Justice, *"Trump Confronted Kim Jong Un About Atrocities Against Christians."*

29. Justice, *"Trump Confronted Kim Jong Un About Atrocities Against Christians."*

30. *"Press Conference by President Trump,"* White House.

31. Judson Berger, *"Trump to 'Hannity': Kim Jong Un to Start Denuclearization 'Virtually Immediately,'"* FOX News Network LLC, 12 de junio, 2018, http://www.foxnews.com/ politics/2018/06/12/trump-to-hannity-kim-jong-un-to-start-denuclearization-virtually-immediately.html.

32. J. Lee Grady, *"10 Bizarre Facts About North Korea."* Charisma, 13 de junio, 2018, https://www.charismamag.com/blogs/fire-in-my-bones/37295-10-bizarre-facts-about-north-korea.

33. Grady, *"10 Bizarre Facts About North Korea."*

34. Lucas Tomlinson, *"ISIS Has Lost 98 Percent of Its Territory—Mostly Since Trump Took Office, Officials Say,"* Fox News, 26 de diciembre, 2017, http://www.foxnews.com/ politics/2017/12/26/isis-has-lost-98-percent-its-territory-mostly- since-trump-took-office-officials-say.html.

Capítulo 7 – La economía floreciente de Trump

1. Peter Roff, *"Good News Doesn't Always Travel Fast,"* U.S. News & World Report, 16 de enero, 2018, https://www.usnews.com/opinion/thomas-jefferson-street/ articles/2018-01-16/the-economy-is-booming-under-trump-but-mainstream-media-wont-tell-you-that.

2. Thomas Cooley y Peter Rupert, *"U.S. Economic Snapshot,"* Rupert-Cooley Economic Snapshot, 1 de junio, 2018, https://www.econsnapshot.com/2018/06/.

3. Neil Irwin, *"We Ran Out of Words to Describe How Good the Jobs Numbers Are,"*

New York Times, 1 de junio, 2018, https://www.nytimes.com/2018/06/01/upshot/we-ran-out-of-words-to-describe-how-good-the-jobs-numbers-are.html.

4. Donald J. Trump (@realDonaldTrump), *"In many ways this is the greatest economy in the HISTORY of America and the best time EVER to look for a job!,"* Twitter, 4 de junio, 2018, 1:42 p.m., https://twitter.com/realdonaldtrump/status/100373874 4061603843?lang=en.

5. Bloomberg, *"Trump Says 'This Is the Greatest Economy in the HISTORY of America,'"* Fortune, 7 de junio, 2018, http://fortune.com/2018/06/07/trump-eisenhower-greatest-economy-history-america/

6. Wayne Allyn Root, *"The Trump Miracle,"* Townhall.com, 5 de junio, 2018, https://townhall.com/columnists/wayneallynroot/2018/06/05/the-trump-miracle-n2487181.

7. Roff, *"Good News Doesn't Always Travel Fast."*

8. Roff, *"Good News Doesn't Always Travel Fast."*

9. Roff, *"Good News Doesn't Always Travel Fast."* Patrice Lee Onwuka, *"Black Americans' Record Employment, Tax Cuts and More,"* Independent Women's Forum, 9 de enero, 2018, http://iwf.org/news/2805497/Black-America-Winning-With-Record-Employment,-Tax-Cuts-and-More.

10. Roff, *"Good News Doesn't Always Travel Fast."*

11. Roff, *"Good News Doesn't Always Travel Fast."*

12. Bob Bryan, *"Nancy Pelosi Says Companies' Bonuses to Workers Because of the Tax Bill Are 'Crumbs,'"* Business Insider, 11 de enero, 2018, http://www.businessinsider.com/nancy-pelosi-tax-bill-bonuses-crumbs-2018-1.

13. Naomi Jagoda, *"Trump Compares Pelosi's 'Crumbs' Comments to Clinton's 'Deplorables' Remark,"* The Hill, 1 de febrero, 2018, http://thehill.com/policy/finance/371847 -trump-compares-pelosis-crumbs-comments-to-clintons-deplorables-remark

14. Andy Puzder, *"What Trump-Haters Don't Get About the Incredible Power of American Capitalism,"* Fox News, 23 de abril, 2018, http://www.foxnews. com/opinion/2018/04/23/andy-puzder-what-trump-haters-dont-get-about-incredible-power-american-capitalism.html.

15. Puzder, *"What Trump-Haters Don't Get About the Incredible Power of American Capitalism."*

16. Puzder, *"What Trump-Haters Don't Get About the Incredible Power of American Capitalism."*

17. Puzder, *"What Trump-Haters Don't Get About the Incredible Power of American Capitalism."*

18. Puzder, *"What Trump-Haters Don't Get About the Incredible Power of American Capitalism."*

19. Andy Puzder,"If Democrats Decide to Pivot From Trump and Run on an Economic Message, They're Doomed," Fox News, 25 de mayo, 2018, http://www.foxnews.com/opinion/2018/05/25/andy-puzder-if-democrats-decide-to-pivot-from-trump- and-run-on-economic-message-re-doomed.html.

20. Puzder, "If Democrats Decide to Pivot From Trump and Run on an Economic Message, They're Doomed."

21. Matthew Boyle, *"Donald Trump Jr.: Trump Economy Most Helping 'Forgotten Men'*

in 'Forgotten Land Everywhere Between New York City and Malibu,'" Breitbart.
com, 4 de junio, 2018, http://www.breitbart.com/big-government/2018/06/04/
exclusive-trump-jr-trump-economy-helping-forgotten-men-forgotten-land- everywhere-
new-york-city-malibu.

22. Boyle, *"Donald Trump Jr."*

23. Boyle, *"Donald Trump Jr."*

24. Boyle, *"Donald Trump Jr."*

25. Gregg Re, *"GDP Report Shows Booming 4.1 Percent Growth, as Trump Touts
     'Amazing' Numbers,"* Fox News, 27 de julio, 2018, http://www.foxnews.com/
     politics/2018/07/27/gdp-report-shows-booming-4-1-percent-growth-as-trump-touts-
     terrific-numbers.html.

26. Kimberly Amadeo, *"US Economic Outlook for 2018 and Beyond,"* TheBalance. com,
     actualizado el 11 de julio, 2018, https://www.thebalance.com/us-economic-out-
     look-3305669.

27. *"National Debt,"* US Department of the Treasury, consultado el 30 de julio 2018,
     https:// www.treasury.gov/resource-center/faqs/Markets/Pages/national-debt.aspx.

28. *"National Debt,"* US Department of the Treasury.

29. *"National Debt,"* US Department of the Treasury.

30. Brennan Weiss, *"Here's What a Top Intel Chief Says Is the Biggest Internal Threat to
     US National Security,"* Business Insider, 13 de febrero, 2018, http://www.businessin-
     sider.com/dan-coats-biggest-threat-national-security-national-debt-2018-2.

31. Andy Biggs, *"'The Single, Biggest Threat to National Security,'"* Washington Times,
     8 de mayo, 2018, https://www.washingtontimes.com/news/2018/may/8/the-single-
     biggest-threat-to-national-security-is-/.

32. *"Moody's: US' Economic Strength and Integral Role in Global Capital Markets Counter-
     balance Deteriorating Fiscal Position,"* Moody's Investors Services, 9 de febrero, 2018,
     https://www.moodys.com/research/Moodys-US-economic-strength-and-integral-role-
     in-global-capital--PR_379378.

33. Secretary of Defense James N. Mattis, *"Remarks by Secretary Mattis on the National
     Defense Strategy,"* US Department of Defense, 19 de enero, 2018, https://www.
     defense.gov/News/Transcripts/Transcript-View/Article/1420042/remarks-by-secre-
     tary-mattis-on-the-national-defense-strategy/; Andy Biggs, *"The Threat to National
     Security That Hardly Anyone Is Watching,"* 11 de junio, 2018, https://www.dailysignal
     .com/2018/06/11/the-threat-to-national-security-that-hardly-anyone-is-watching/;
     Biggs, *"'The Single, Biggest Threat to National Security.'"*

34. Biggs, *"'The Single, Biggest Threat to National Security.'"*

35. Kimberly Amadeo, *"U.S. Debt by President: By Dollar and Percent,"* TheBalance.com,
     13 de abril, 2018, https://www.thebalance.com/us-debt-by-president-by- dollar-and-
     percent-3306296.

36. Amadeo, *"U.S. Debt by President."*

37. Amadeo, *"U.S. Debt by President."*

38. Garland S. Tucker III, *"Looming Debt Crisis Isn't Just a Fiscal Crisis—It's a Crisis of
     Morality,"* Investor's Business Daily, 13 de abril, 2018, https://www.investors.com/poli-
     tics/commentary/looming-debt-crisis-isnt-just-a-fiscal-crisis-its-a-crisis-of-morality/.

39. Tucker, *"Looming Debt Crisis Isn't Just a Fiscal Crisis."*

40. Tucker, *"Looming Debt Crisis Isn't Just a Fiscal Crisis"*; Sir Alexander Tytler escribió: "Una democracia solo puede existir hasta que la gente descubre que puede votarse generosamente de la tesorería pública. A partir de ese momento, la mayoría siempre vota por el candidato que promete los más beneficios de la tesorería pública, con el resultado que la democracia siempre colapsa sobre la política fiscal imprecisa. ("Alexander Fraser Tytler Quotes," Goodreads Inc., consultado el 30 de julio, 2018, https://www.goodreads .com/author/quotes/5451872.Alexander_Fraser_Tytler).

41. Tucker, *"Looming Debt Crisis Isn't Just a Fiscal Crisis."*

42. Jesse Hathaway, *"Congress Still Ignoring Country's Dangerously Growing Debt,"* Investor's Business Daily, 14 de mayo, 2018, https://www.investors.com/politics/com- mentary/congress-still-ignoring-countrys-dangerously-growing-debt/.

43. Conor Sen, *"Trump's Economic Gamble Might Just Work,"* Chicago Tribune, 28 de febrero, 2018, http://www.chicagotribune.com/news/opinion/commentary/ct-perspec- economy-trump-deficits-growth-productivity-0301-20180228-story. html.

44. Sen, *"Trump's Economic Gamble Might Just Work."*

45. Saleha Mohsin, *"Mnuchin Urges Markets to Shrug Off Tax Cuts, Debt Worries,"* Bloomberg, actualizado el 23 de febrero, 2018, https://www.bloomberg.com/news/arti- cles/2018-02-23/mnuchin-says-trump-policies-will-raise-wages-without- inflation.

46. Sen, *"Trump's Economic Gamble Might Just Work."*

47. Sen, *"Trump's Economic Gamble Might Just Work."*

Capítulo 8 – Multimillonarios radicales

1. Charles Riley, *"What Happens at Davos?,"* CNN Money, 20 de enero, 2018, http:// money.cnn.com/2018/01/19/news/economy/davos-what-is-wef/index.html.

2. *"Transcript of Donald Trump Interview With the Wall Street Journal,"* Wall Street Journal, actualizado el 14 de enero, 2018, https://www.wsj.com/articles/transcript-of- donald-trump-interview-with-the-wall-street-journal-1515715481.

3. Riley, *"What Happens at Davos?"*

4. *"Remarks by President Trump to the World Economic Forum,"* White House.

5. *"Remarks by President Trump to the World Economic Forum,"* White House.

6. Peter S. Goodman and Keith Bradsher, *"Trump Arrived in Davos as a Party Wrecker. He Leaves Praised as a Pragmatist,"* New York Times, 26 de enero, 2018, https://www. nytimes.com/2018/01/26/business/trump-davos-speech-response. html.

7. Ian Schwartz, *"Trump: I Didn't Realize How 'Vicious,' 'Fake' Press Could Be Until I Became a Politician,"* RealClearPolitics, 26 de enero, 2018, https://www. realclearpolitics.com/video/2018/01/26/trump_in_davos_it_wasnt_until_i_ became_a_politician_that_i_realized_how_vicious_fake_the_press_can_be.html.

8. Victor Davis Hanson, *"Is Trump an Island?,"* National Review, 19 de diciembre, 2017, https://www.nationalreview.com/2017/12/trump-accomplishments-speak-themselves- despite-media-attacks/.

9. *"Soros Clones: 5 Liberal Mega-Donors Nearly as Dangerous as George Soros,"* Media Research Center, consultado el 12 de julio, 2018, https://www.mrc.org/special-reports/

soros-clones-5-liberal-mega-donors-nearly-dangerous-george-soros; "George Soros: Media Mogul," Media Research Center, consultado el 12 de julio, 2018, https://www. mrc.org/special-reports/george-soros-media-mogul.

10. *"About ONO,"* Organization of News Ombudsmen, consultado el 12 de julio, 2018, https://www.newsombudsmen.org/about-ono/.

11. *"George Soros: Media Mogul,"* Media Research Center.

12. *"Soros Clones: 5 Liberal Mega-Donors Nearly as Dangerous as George Soros,"* Media Research Center consultado el 31 de julio, 2018, https://www.mrc.org/special-reports/ soros-clones-5-liberal-mega-donors-nearly-dangerous-george-soros.

13. Neil Maghami, *"True Believers: George Soros and the Religious Left's War on President Trump,"* Capital Research Center, 7 de junio, 2017, https://capitalresearch.org/article/ true-believers-george-soros-and-the-religious-lefts-war-on-president-trump/.

14. Jim VandeHei and Chris Cillizza, *"A New Alliance of Democrats Spreads Funding: But Some in Party Bristle at Secrecy and Liberal Tilt,"* Washington Post, 17 de julio, 2006, http://www.washingtonpost.com/wp-dyn/content/article/2006/07/16/ AR2006071600882_pf.html.

15. VandeHei and Cillizza, *"A New Alliance of Democrats Spreads Funding."*

16. Maghami, *"True Believers."*

17. Dan Gainor, *"Soros Spends Over $48 Million Funding Media Organizations"* [Part 2 of 4], Media Research Center, 26 de agosto, 2014, https://www.mrc.org/commentary/ soros-spends-over-48-million-funding-media-organizations.

18. Asra Q. Nomani, *"Billionaire George Soros Has Ties to More Than 50 'Partners' of the Women's March on Washington,"* Women in the World Media LLC, 20 de enero, 2017, https://womenintheworld.com/2017/01/20/billionaire-george-soros-has-ties-to-more-than-50-partners-of-the-womens-march-on-washington/.

19. VandeHei and Cillizza, *"A New Alliance of Democrats Spreads Funding."*

20. Bloomberg Billionaires Index, 31 de julio, 2018, https://www.bloomberg.com/ billionaires/.

21. Andy Kroll, *"Meet the Megadonor Behind the LGBTQ Rights Movement,"* Rolling Stone, 23 de junio, 2017, https://www.rollingstone.com/politics/politics-features/meet-the-megadonor-behind-the-lgbtq-rights-movement-193996/.

22. Kroll, "Meet the Megadonor Behind the LGBTQ Rights Movement."

23. "AB-2943 Unlawful Business Practices: Sexual Orientation Change Efforts," California Legislature 2017–2018 Regular Session, published May 30, 2018, https://leginfo.legislature.ca.gov/faces/billTextClient.xhtml?bill_id=201720180AB2943.

24. Discpad, "George Soros' Lost 1998 60 Minutes Interview (CC)," YouTube, November 24, 2016, https://www.youtube.com/watch?v=rd39zUvreOU.

25. "Making of the Puppet Master," Glenn Beck, November 12, 2010, http://www. foxnews.com/story/2010/11/12/glenn-beck-making-puppet-master.html.

26. Prashanth Perumal, "The Incredible Life of Billionaire Investing Legend George Soros," Business Insider, January 24, 2017, http://www.businessinsider.com/ george-soros-billionaire-investor-profile-2017-1.

27. "About Us," Open Society Foundations, accessed July 31, 2018, https://www.opensocietyfoundations.org/about.

28. Richard Poe,"George Soros' Coup," Newsmax.com, vol. 6, no. 5 (May 2004).

29. "Organizations Funded by George Soros and His Open Society Foundations," DiscoverTheNetworks.org, accessed July 31, 2018, http://www. discoverthenetworks.org/individualProfile.asp?indid=977.

30. Rebecca Hagelin, "Soros vs. America," Townhall.com, February 16, 2018, https://townhall.com/columnists/rebeccahagelin/2018/02/16/draft-n2449953.

31. Jay Richards,"Soros Funding of Sojourners Is Only the Tip of the Iceberg," National Review, August 25, 2010, https://www.nationalreview.com/corner/soros-funding-sojourners-only-tip-iceberg-jay-richards/.

32. Robert A. Sirico, "Soros' Catholic Useful Idiots: Faith-Based Groups Stray When Accepting Progressive Cash," Washington Times, August 30, 2016, https://www.washingtontimes.com/news/2016/aug/30/george-soros-catholic-useful-idiots/.

33. "Mission Statement," Faith in Public Life, accessed July 31, 2018, https://www.faithinpubliclife.org/mission-statement.

34. Maghami," True Believers."

35. "1500 Interfaith Clergy Call on Republican Lawmakers to Reject Trump's Presidential 'Cabinet of Bigotry,'" Faith in Public Life, November 23, 2016, https://www.faithinpubliclife.org/clergyrejectcabinetofbigotry.

36. John Gehring, *"Prophetic Prayer & Moral Resistance,"* Commonwealth, 1 de febrero, 2017, https://www.commonwealmagazine.org/prophetic-prayer-moral-resistance.

37. *"4,000 Faith Leaders Oppose Trump's Forthcoming Executive Action Targeting Refugees From Muslim-Majority Countries,"* Faith in Public Life, 23 de febrero, 2017, https://www.faithinpubliclife.org/4000-faith-leaders-oppose-muslim-ba.

38. "Faith Leaders Denounce Trump's New Executive Order Targeting Muslim Refugees, Call for Immediate Repeal," Faith in Public Life, 6 de marzo, 2017, https://www.faithinpubliclife.org/ohio-clergy-denounce-new-muslim-ban.

39. Maghami, *"True Believers."*

40. *"Be Not Afraid?,"* Faith in Public Life, junio 2013, https://docs.wixstatic.com/ugd/03e723_528c111e09fd4fef8f6102ba47316187.pdf.

41. Matthew Vadum, *"Left-Wing Radicalism in the Church: The Catholic Campaign for Human Development,"* Capital Research Center, 1 de septiembre, 2009, https://capitalresearch.org/article/left-wing-radicalism-in-the-church-the-catholic-campaign-for-human-development-2/.

42. Maghami, *"True Believers."*

43. *"About PICO,"* PICO National Network, consultado el 13 de julio, 2018, archived at https://web.archive.org/web/20170515134943/piconetwork.org/about.

44. *"Father John Baumann, SJ, Discusses PICO and Community Organizing for Passionate Leaders in Social Entrepreneurship Speaker Series,"* Holy Names University, 31 de octubre, 2014, https://www.hnu.edu/about/news/father-john- baumann-sj-discusses-pico
-and-community-organizing-passionate-leaders-social.

45. David Hogberg, *"The Gamaliel Foundation: Alinsky-Inspired Group Uses Stealth Tactics to Manipulate Church Congregations,"* Foundation Watch, julio 2010, https://capitalresearch.org/article/

the-gamaliel-foundation-alinsky-inspired-group-uses-stealth-tactics-to-manipulate-church-congregations/.

46. *"Full Transcript: Face the Nation on March 11, 2018,"* CBS Interactive Inc., 11 de marzo, 2018, https://www.cbsnews.com/news/full-transcript-face-the-nation-on-march-11-2018-2/.

47. Todd Starnes, *"WaPost Columnist Calls Pro-Trump Evangelicals 'Slimy, Political Operatives,'"* 12 de marzo, 2018, https://www.toddstarnes.com/show/wapost-columnist-calls-pro-trump-evangelicals-slimy-political-operatives/.

48. Starnes, *"WaPost Columnist Calls Pro-Trump Evangelicals 'Slimy, Political Operatives.'"*

49. David Horowitz y Richard Poe, *The Shadow Party* (Nashville: Nelson Current, 2006), 243.

50. Horowitz and Poe, *The Shadow Party.*

51. *"WikiLeaks Reveals How Billionaire 'Progressives' Run the Democratic Party,"* Investor's Business Daily, 2 de noviembre, 2016, https://www.investors.com/politics/editorials/wikileaks-reveals-the-billionaire-progressives-that-run-the-democratic-party/.

52. *"Remarks by President Trump to the World Economic Forum,"* White House.

53. *"Remarks by President Trump to the World Economic Forum,"* White House.

54. *"Remarks by President Trump to the World Economic Forum,"* White House.

55. Kenneth P. Vogel, *"George Soros Rises Again,"* Politico, 27 de julio, 2016, https://www.politico.com/story/2016/07/george-soros-democratic-convention-226267.

Capítulo 9 — El tercer mandato de Obama

1. Dan Alexander, *"How Barack Obama Has Made $20 Million Since Arriving in Washington,"* Forbes, 20 de enero, 2017, https://www.forbes.com/sites/danalexander/2017/01/20/how-barack-obama-has-made-20-million-since-arriving-in-washington/#1006876e5bf0.

2. Alexander, *"How Barack Obama Has Made $20 Million Since Arriving in Washington"*; *"Hillary Clinton: 'We Came Out of the White House Dead Broke,'"* RealClearHoldings LLC, 9 de junio, 2014, https://www.realclearpolitics.com/video/2014/06/09/hillary_clinton_we_came_out_of_the_white_house_dead_broke.html.

3. Peter Schweizer, *Throw Them All Out* (New York: Houghton Mifflin, 2011), xvi.

4. Schweizer, *Throw Them All Out*, 76–77.

5. Schweizer, 77.

6. Schweizer, 80.

7. *"Memorandum for the President, From Carol Browner, Ron Klain, Larry Summers, Subject: Renewable Energy Loan Guarantees and Grants,"* Briefing Memo, White House, 25 de octubre, 2010, 1–8, https://archive.org/stream/gov.gpo.fdsys.CHRG-112hhrg76267/CHRG-112hhrg76267_djvu.txt. Citado en Schweizer, *Throw Them All Out*, 83.

8. *"DOE Loan Programs,"* United States Government Accountability Office, abril 2015, https://www.gao.gov/assets/670/669847.pdf.

9. *"Solar Energy,"* United States Government Accountability Office, agosto 2012, https://www.gao.gov/assets/650/647732.pdf.

10. David Williams, *"Solar Energy Delivers Too Little Bang for Billions Invested,"* Forbes, 25 de febrero, 2015, https://www.forbes.com/sites/realspin/2015/02/25/solar-energy-delivers-too-little-bang-for-billions-invested/#6da216ad49f3.

11. Jason Zengerle ,*"Barack Obama Is Preparing for His Third Term,"* GQ, 17 de enero, 2017, https://www.gq.com/story/barack-obama-preparing-for-third-term.

12. Zengerle, *"Barack Obama Is Preparing for His Third Term."*

13. Zengerle, *"Barack Obama Is Preparing for His Third Term."*

14. Zengerle, *"Barack Obama Is Preparing for His Third Term."*

15. Paul Sperry, *"The Myth of Obama's 'Disappearance,'"* New York Post, 30 de junio, 2018, https://nypost.com/2018/06/30/obamas-disappearance-is-a-myth/.

16. Sperry, *"The Myth of Obama's 'Disappearance.'"*

17. Bill Moyers and Michael Winship, *"Hillary Clinton's Inaugural Address,"* Moyers & Co., 6 de diciembre, 2016, https://billmoyers.com/story/hillary-clintons-inaugural-address/.

18. Conor Friedersdorf, *"Barack Obama Reflects on Leaving the Presidency"* (from a BBC podcast recorded by Prince Harry of Wales), The Atlantic, 27 de diciembre, 2017, https://www.theatlantic.com/politics/archive/2017/12/barack-obama- reflects-on-leaving-the-presidency/549236/.

19. Michael Kranish, *"President Obama Says He Could Have Beaten Trump— Trump Says 'NO WAY!,'"* Washington Post, 26 de diciembre, 2016, https:// www.washingtonpost.com/news/post-politics/wp/2016/12/26/president-obama-says-he-would-have-beaten-trump-if-i-had-run-again/?utm_term=.3a715025b787.

20. Warner Todd Huston, *"Obama: My Netflix Projects Will Help ' Train the Next Generation of Leaders' and Heal Our Political Divide,"* Breitbart, 24 de mayo, 2018, https:// www.breitbart.com/big-hollywood/2018/05/24/obama-wants-netflix- projects-to-ease-americas-political-divide/.

21. Edward-Isaac Dovere, *"Inside Obama's Midterm Campaign Plans,"* Politico, 18 de enero, 2018, https://www.politico.com/story/2018/01/18/obama-midterm- campaign-plans-trump-345491.

22. Donald J. Trump (@realDonaldTrump). *"The 'Intelligence' briefing on so-called 'Russian hacking' was delayed until Friday, perhaps more time needed to build a case,"* Twitter, 3 de enero, 2017, 5:14 p.m., https://twitter.com/realdonaldtrump/status/816452807024 840704?lang=en.

23. *The Rachel Maddow Show*, NBC Universal, January 3, 2017, http://www.msnbc.com/transcripts/rachel-maddow-show/2017-01-03.

24. John Wagner and Greg Miller, *"Trump Alleges Delay in His Briefing on 'So-Called' Russian Hacking; U.S. Official Says There Wasn't One,"* Washington Post, 4 de enero, 2017, https://www.washingtonpost.com/news/post-politics/wp/2017/01/03/ trump-says-a-delay-in-his-briefing-on-so-called-russian-hacking-is-very-strange/?.

25. *"A Report of Investigation of Certain Allegations Relating to Former FBI Deputy Director Andrew McCabe,"* Office of the Inspector General, febrero 2018, https:// static01.nyt.com/files/2018/us/politics/20180413a-doj-oig-mccabe-report.pdf.

26. John O. Brennan (@JohnBrennan), *"When the full extent of your venality, moral turpitude, and political corruption becomes known, you will take your rightful place as a*

disgraced demagogue in the dustbin of history," Twitter, 17 de marzo, 2018, 5:00 a.m., https://twitter.com/johnbrennan/status/974978856997224448?lang=en.

27. Tim Hains, *"Reps. Jim Jordan and Mark Meadows: McCabe Lied Four Times, DOJ Needs to 'Come Clean,'"* RealClearHoldings LLC, 30 de marzo, 2018, https://www. realclearpolitics.com/video/2018/03/30/reps_jim_jordan_and_mark_meadows_ mccabe_lied_four_times_doj_needs_to_come_clean.html.

28. *"The Wrong People Are Criticizing Donald Trump,"* New York Times, 19 de marzo, 2018, https://www.nytimes.com/2018/03/19/opinion/trump-mccabe-republicans.html.

29. Eliza Relman, *"Jeff Sessions Explains Why He Recused Himself From Trump Campaign-Related Investigations,"* Business Insider, 13 de junio, 2017, https://www.businessinsider. com/jeff-sessions-on-recusing-himself-trump-investigation- russia-2017-6.

30. Louie Gohmert, *"Robert Mueller: Unmasked,"* consultado el 2 de agosto, 2018, https://1zwchz1jbsr61f1c4mgf0abl-wpengine.netdna-ssl.com/wp-content/ uploads/2018/04/Gohmert_Mueller_UNMASKED.pdf.

31. Peter Baker, *"Trump Pardons Scooter Libby in a Case That Mirrors His Own,"* New York Times, 13 de abril, 2108, https://www.nytimes.com/2018/04/13/us/politics/ trump-pardon-scooter-libby.html.

32. Gohmert, *"Robert Mueller: Unmasked,"* 19.

33. Rollcall Staff, *"Recalling the Injustice Done to Sen. Ted Stevens,"* CQ Roll Call, 28 de octubre, 2014, https://www.rollcall.com/news/recalling_the_injustice_done_ to_sen_ ted_stevens_commentary-237407-1.html.

34. Gohmert, *"Robert Mueller: Unmasked,"* 20.

35. Gohmert, *"Robert Mueller: Unmasked,"* 10.

36. Gohmert, *"Robert Mueller: Unmasked,"* 11.

37. Victor Davis Hanson, *"The Double Standards of the Mueller Investigation,"* Investor's Business Daily, 30 de abril, 2018, https://www.investors.com/politics/columnists/the-double-standards-of-the-mueller-investigation/.

38. Hanson, *"The Double Standards of the Mueller Investigation."*

39. Jed Babbin, *"Time to Shut Mueller Down,"* American Spectator, 7 de mayo, 2018, https://spectator.org/time-to-shut-mueller-down/.

40. Babbin, *"Time to Shut Mueller Down."*

41. Darren Samuelsohn y Josh Gerstein, *"Mueller's Courtroom Bruises Cheer Trump Team,"* Politico, 7 de mayo, 2018, https://www.politico.com/story/2018/05/07/trump-mueller-russia-probe-judges-573221.

42. Donald J. Trump (@realDonaldTrump), *"The 13 Angry Democrats in charge of the Russian Witch Hunt are starting to find out that there is a Court System in place that actually protects people from injustice,"* Twitter, 7 de mayo, 2018, 4:39 a.m., https:// twitter.com/realdonaldtrump/status/993455375755173892.

43. Samuelsohn y Gerstein, *"Mueller's Courtroom Bruises Cheer Trump Team."*

44. *"Public Troubled by'Deep State,'"* Monmouth University, 19 de marzo, 2018, https:// www.monmouth.edu/polling-institute/documents/monmouthpoll_us_031918.pdf/.

45. *"Public Troubled by 'Deep State,'"* Monmouth University

46. *"Public Troubled by 'Deep State,'"* Monmouth University.

47. Donald J. Trump (@realDonaldTrump), *"Crooked Hillary Clinton's top aid, Huma*

Abedin, has been accused of disregarding basic security protocols," Twitter, 2 de enero, 2018, 4:48 a.m., https://twitter.com/realdonaldtrump/status/9481740338829 27104?lang=en.

48. *"Public Troubled by 'Deep State,'"* Monmouth University.

49. Max Greenwood, *"GOP Rep: Obama Running 'Shadow Government' to Undermine Trump,"* The Hill, 10 de marzo, 2017, http://thehill.com/blogs/blog- briefing-room/news/323457-gop-rep-obama-running-a-shadow-government-to- undermine-trump.

50. Greenwood, *"GOP Rep: Obama Running 'Shadow Government' to Undermine Trump."*

51. Greenwood, *"GOP Rep: Obama Running 'Shadow Government' to Undermine Trump."*

52. WCPO staff, *"Kentucky Congressman Claims'Deep State' Undermining President Trump,"* WCPO actualizado el 17 febrero, 2017, https://www.wcpo.com/news/state/state-kentucky/kentucky-congressman-claims-deep-state-undermining- president-trump.

53. WCPO staff, *"Kentucky Congressman Claims'Deep State' Undermining President Trump."*

54. Sam Schwarz, *"Obama Is Returning to Politics in 2018, and Trump Should Be Worried,"* Newsweek, 17 de enero, 2018, http://www.newsweek.com/barack- obama-trump-returning-politics-783421.

55. *"2018 Shaping Up Big for Democrats,"* Public Policy Polling, 28 de septiembre, 2017, https://www.publicpolicypolling.com/wp-content/uploads/2017/10/PPP_ Release_ National_92817-1.pdf.

CAPÍTULO 10 — ESTADOS UNIDOS EN GUERRA (CONTRA SÍ MISMO)

1. Ginni Thomas, "Poll Shows Nation Divided Between America First and Blame America First [Video]," The Daily Caller, December 17, 2017, http://dailycaller.com/2017/12/16/poll-shows-nation-divided-between-america-first-and-blame- america-first -video/.

2. "A Tale of Two Patriotisms," Ear to the Ground, accessed August 2, 2018, https://www.eartotheground.us/a-tale-of-two-patriotisms.

3. "American Views on Patriotism," American Culture and Faith Institute, October–November 2017, https://www.culturefaith.com/wp-content/uploads/2017/12/Patriotism-Summary.pdf.

4. "American Views on Patriotism," American Culture and Faith Institute.

5. Thomas, "Poll Shows Nation Divided Between America First and Blame America First."

6. Thomas, "Poll Shows Nation Divided Between America First and Blame America First."

7. Thomas, "Poll Shows Nation Divided Between America First and Blame America First."

8. Thomas, "Poll Shows Nation Divided Between America First and Blame America First."

9. Carroll Doherty, "Key Takeaways on Americans' Growing Partisan Divide Over Political Values," Pew Research Center, October 5, 2017, http://www.pewresearch.org/

fact-tank/2017/10/05/takeaways-on-americans-growing-partisan-divide-over-political-values/.

10. Doherty, "Key Takeaways on Americans' Growing Partisan Divide Over Political Values."

11. Doherty, "Key Takeaways on Americans' Growing Partisan Divide Over Political Values."

12. Doherty, "Key Takeaways on Americans' Growing Partisan Divide Over Political Values."

13. Doherty, "Key Takeaways on Americans' Growing Partisan Divide Over Political Values."

14. Michael C. Bender, "Donald Trump's Approval Rating Inches Higher, Buoyed by Republican Support," Wall Street Journal, July 22, 2018, https://www.wsj.com/articles/donald-trumps-approval-rating-inches-higher-buoyed-by-republican-support-1532293201.

15. Julia Manchester, "Poll: Americans Deeply Divided on Cultural and Economic Issues," The Hill, September 6, 2017, http://thehill.com/blogs/blog-briefing-room/news/349378-poll-americans-deeply-divided-on-cultural-and-economic-issues

16. Janet Hook,"Political Divisions in U.S. Are Widening, Long-Lasting, Poll Shows," Wall Street Journal, September 6, 2017, https://www.wsj.com/articles/political-divisions-in-u-s-are-widening-long-lasting-poll-shows-1504670461.

17. John Wagner and Scott Clement, "'It's Just Messed Up': Most Think Political Divisions as Bad as Vietnam Era, New Poll Shows," Washington Post, October 28, 2017, https://www.washingtonpost.com/graphics/2017/national/democracy-poll/.

18. Jose A. DelReal and Scott Clement,"Rural Divide," Washington Post, June 17, 2017, https://www.washingtonpost.com/graphics/2017/national/rural-america/.

19. DelReal and Clement,"Rural Divide."

20. John Hawkins, "7 Forces Driving America Toward Civil War," Townhall.com, April 21, 2018, https://townhall.com/columnists/johnhawkins/2018/04/21/draft-n2473193.

21. Hawkins,"7 Forces Driving America Toward Civil War."

22. Benjamin Franklin, as quoted in Respectfully Quoted: A Dictionary of Quotations, accessed August 2, 2018, https://www.bartleby.com/73/1593.html.

23. Hawkins,"7 Forces Driving America Toward Civil War."

24. Hawkins,"7 Forces Driving America Toward Civil War."

25. George Santayana, The Life of Reason (Massachusetts: Massachusetts Institute of Technology, 2011), 172.

26. "Bill of Rights," National Archives.

27. "Sharp Partisan Divisions in Views of National Institutions," Pew Research Center, July 10, 2017, http://www.people-press.org/2017/07/10/sharp-partisan-divisions-in-views-of-national-institutions/.

28. "Sharp Partisan Divisions in Views of National Institutions," Pew Research Center.

29. "Sharp Partisan Divisions in Views of National Institutions," Pew Research Center.

30. "Sharp Partisan Divisions in Views of National Institutions," Pew Research Center.

31. Bill Bumpas, "Poll: GOP vs. Dems Is Really Religion vs. Anti-Religion,"

American Family News Network, July 14, 2017, https://www.onenewsnow.com/church/2017/07/14/poll-gop-vs-dems-is-really-religion-vs-anti-religion.

32. Bumpas,"Poll: GOP vs. Dems Is Really Religion vs. Anti-Religion."

33. Bumpas,"Poll: GOP vs. Dems Is Really Religion vs. Anti-Religion."

34. S. Michael Craven, "The Latest Pew Survey: Christianity Losing, Secularism Winning," Christian Post, October 15, 2012, https://www.christianpost.com/news/the-latest-pew-survey-christianity-losing-secularism-winning-83325/.

35. "'Nones' on the Rise," Pew Research Center, October 9, 2012, http://assets.pewresearch.org/wp-content/uploads/sites/11/2012/10/NonesOnTheRise-full. pdf.

36. Jeff Diamant and Gregory A. Smith,"Religiously, Nonwhite Democrats Are More Similar to Republicans Than to White Democrats," Pew Research Center, May 23, 2018, http://www.pewresearch.org/fact-tank/2018/05/23/religiously-nonwhite- democrats-are-more-similar-to-republicans-than-to-white-democrats/.

37. Diamant and Smith, "Religiously, Nonwhite Democrats Are More Similar to Republicans Than to White Democrats."

38. "When Americans Say They Believe in God, What Do They Mean?," Pew Research Center, April 25, 2018, http://www.pewforum.org/2018/04/25/when-americans-say-they-believe-in-god-what-do-they-mean/.

39. Diamant and Smith, "Religiously, Nonwhite Democrats Are More Similar to Republicans Than to White Democrats."

40. Diamant and Smith, "Religiously, Nonwhite Democrats Are More Similar to Republicans Than to White Democrats."

41. Diamant and Smith, "Religiously, Nonwhite Democrats Are More Similar to Republicans Than to White Democrats."

42. Diamant and Smith, "Religiously, Nonwhite Democrats Are More Similar to Republicans Than to White Democrats."

43. "The State of Abortion in the United States," National Right to Life Committee Inc., January 2018, https://www.nrlc.org/uploads/communications/ stateofabortion2018.pdf.

44. "The State of Abortion in the United States," National Right to Life Committee Inc.

45. "Abortion Is a Common Experience for U.S. Women, Despite Dramatic Declines in Rates," Guttmacher Institute, October 19, 2017, https://www.guttmacher.org/news-release/2017/abortion-common-experience-us-women-despite-dramatic-declines-rates.

46. "Americans' Opinions on Abortion," Knights of Columbus, January 2018, https://www.kofc.org/un/en/resources/communications/abortion-limits-favored.pdf.

47. "Americans' Opinions on Abortion," Knights of Columbus; Jennifer Harper, "New Poll Reveals Pro-Life Leanings Among Majority of Americans, Including Democrats," Washington Times, January 18, 2018, https://www.washingtontimes.com/news/2018/jan/18/new-poll-reveals-pro-life-leanings-among-majority-/.

48. Harper, "New Poll Reveals Pro-Life Leanings Among Majority of Americans, Including Democrats."

49. Irwin,"We Ran Out of Words to Describe How Good the Jobs Numbers Are."

50. "List of Tax Reform Good News," Americans for Tax Reform, accessed August 2,

2018, https://www.atr.org/sites/default/files/assets/National%20List%20of%20 Tax%20Reform%20Good%20News.pdf.

51. Rich Lowry,"Have Democrats Overplayed Their Trump Hand?," Politico Magazine, February 14, 2018, https://www.politico.com/magazine/story/2018/02/14/democrats-trump-presidency-216999. Statistic updated.

52. Josh Hayward, "Democrats Lose the Future by Trusting Their Demographic Doomsday Clock," Breitbart.com, November 23, 2016, http://www.breitbart.com/big-government/2016/11/23/democratic-demographic-doomsday-clock/.

53. Howard Fineman, "Barack Obama Reelection Signals Rise of New America," Huffington Post, updated November 7, 2012, https://www.huffingtonpost.com/2012/11/06/barack-obama-reelection_n_2085819.html.

54. Fineman,"Barack Obama Reelection Signals Rise of New America."

55. Hayward,"Democrats Lose the Future by Trusting Their Demographic Doomsday Clock."

56. Sean Trende, "The God That Failed," RealClearHoldings LLC, November 16, 2016, https://www.realclearpolitics.com/articles/2016/11/16/the_god_that_failed_132363.html.

57. Hayward, *"Democrats Lose the Future by Trusting Their Demographic Doomsday Clock."*

58. Hayward, *"Democrats Lose the Future by Trusting Their Demographic Doomsday Clock."*

59. Hayward, *"Democrats Lose the Future by Trusting Their Demographic Doomsday Clock."*

60. Graham Vyse, *"Democrats Are Losing Their Most Loyal Voters: Black Women,"* New Republic, octubre 2017, https://newrepublic.com/minutes/144925/democrats-losing-loyal-voters-black-women.

61. *"Surprise! Susan Rice's Son Now Leads Republicans,"* WND.com, 31 de mayo, 2017, http://www.wnd.com/2018/05/surprise-susan-rices-son-now-leads-republicans/.

62. Caleb Parke, *"Susan Rice's Son Is Outspoken Pro-Trump GOP Leader at Stanford,"* Fox News Network LLC, 31 de mayo, 2018, http://www.foxnews.com/us/2018/05/31/susan-rices-son-is-outspoken-pro-trump-gop-leader-at-stanford.html.

63. Saagar Enjeti, *"Report: Susan Rice Told NSC Officials to 'Stand Down' in Response to Russian Meddling Attempts,"* The Daily Caller, 9 de marzo, 2018, http://dailycaller.com/2018/03/09/report-susan-rice-obama-stand-down-russian-election-meddling/.

64. Parke,"Susan Rice's Son Is Outspoken Pro-Trump GOP Leader at Stanford."

65. Benjamin Fearnow, *"Pastor Prays for Trump to Defeat Deep State 'Witchcraft,' Speaks in Tongues,"* Newsweek, 23 de agosto, 2018, https://www.newsweek. com/alabama-pastor-john-kilpatrick-witchcraft-trump-jezebel-speaking-tongues-1087386.

66. Pray Alabama, *"Pray Against Witchcraft Coming Against President Trump,"* Face-book, 20 de agosto, 2018, 2:27 p.m., https://www.facebook.com/116678935084921/videos/241848136380412/.

CAPÍTULO 11 – FE Y CONFIANZA RESUELTAS

1. Josh Katz, *"Who Will Be President?,"* New York Times, updated 8 de noviembre, 2016, https://www.nytimes.com/interactive/2016/upshot/presidential-polls- forecast.html.

2. Victor Davis Hanson, *"Hillary's'Sure' Victory Explains Most Everything,"* National Review, 30 de enero, 2018, https://www.nationalreview.com/2018/01/expected-clinton-victory-explains-federal-employee-wrongdoing/.

3. Pardes Seleh, *"Hillary Was So Sure She Would Win the Presidency That She Bought a $1.16 Million Home for White House Staff,"* IJR.com, 10 de septiembre, 2017, https://ijr.com/the-declaration/2017/09/970572-hillary-sure-win-presidency-bought-1-16-million-home-white-house-staff/.

4. *"President Donald J. Trump Proclaims May 4, 2017, as a National Day of Prayer,"* White House, 4 de mayo, 2017, https://www.whitehouse.gov/presidential-actions/president-donald-j-trump-proclaims-may-4-2017-national-day-prayer/.

5. *"President Donald J. Trump Proclaims May 4, 2017, as a National Day of Prayer,"* White House.

6. Kristi Keck, *"Obama Tones Down National Day of Prayer Observance,"* CNN, 6 de mayo, 2009. http://www.cnn.com/2009/POLITICS/05/06/obama.prayer/.

7. Keck, *"Obama Tones Down National Day of Prayer Observance."*

8. *"Statement From President Donald J. Trump on Eid al-Fitr,"* White House, 24 de junio, 2017, https://www.whitehouse.gov/briefings-statements/statement-president-donald-j-trump-eid-al-fitr/.

9. *"Presidential Message on Ramadan,"* White House, 15 de mayo, 2018, https://www.whitehouse.gov/briefings-statements/presidential-message-ramadan/.

10. *"Federal Law Protections for Religious Liberty,"* Office of the Attorney General, 6 de octubre, 2017, https://www.justice.gov/opa/press-release/file/1001891/ download.

11. Robert Barnes, *" Trump Administration Sides With Colorado Baker Who Refused to Make Wedding Cake for Gay Couple,"* Denver Post, 7 de septiembre, 2017, https://www.denverpost.com/2017/09/07/trump-sides-with-colorado-baker-who-refused-to-make-gay-wedding-cake/.

12. Ciara Nugent, *"Who is Andrew Brunson, the Evangelical Pastor at the Center of Trump's Threat Against Turkey?,"* Time, 27 de julio, 2018, http://time.com/5351025/andrew-brunson-trump-turkey-sanctions/.

13. 475 Mike Pence (@VP), *" To President Erdogan and the Turkish government, I have a message, on behalf of the President of the United States of America,"* Twitter, 26 de julio, 2018, 7:49 a.m., https://twitter.com/vp/status/1022494110735851521?lang=en.

14. Donald J. Trump (@realDonaldTrump), "The United States will impose large sanctions on Turkey for their long time detainment of Pastor Andrew Brunson, a great Christian, family man and wonderful human being," Twitter, July 26, 2018, 8:22 a.m., https://twitter.com/realdonaldtrump/status/1022502465147682817?lang=en.

15. Laurie Goodstein, "Has Support for Moore Stained Evangelicals? Some Are Worried," New York Times, December 14, 2017, https://www.nytimes. com/2017/12/14/us/alabama-evangelical-christians-moore.html.

16. 478 Randall Balmer, "Under Trump, America's Religious Right Is Rewriting Its Code of Ethics," The Guardian, February 18, 2018, https://www.theguardian.com/

commentis
free/2018/feb/18/donald-trump-evangelicals-code-of-ethics.

17. Balmer, "Under Trump, America's Religious Right Is Rewriting Its Code of Ethics."

18. Stephen Strang, "Investing in Liberty," Charisma, July 2018, 26.

19. Oscar Wilde, A Woman of No Importance (London: Theatreprint, 1992).

20. Goodstein, "Has Support for Moore Stained Evangelicals?"

21. Goodstein, "Has Support for Moore Stained Evangelicals?"

22. Goodstein, "Has Support for Moore Stained Evangelicals?"

23. Goodstein, "Has Support for Moore Stained Evangelicals?"

24. Goodstein, "Has Support for Moore Stained Evangelicals?"

25. Goodstein, "Has Support for Moore Stained Evangelicals?"

26. Ronald Reagan, "Address Before a Joint Session of the Tennessee State Legislature in Nashville," The American Presidency Project, March 15, 1982, http://www.presidency.ucsb.edu/ws/?pid=42270.

27. Jessica Taylor, "After 'Choosing Donald Trump,' Is the Evangelical Church in Crisis?," NPR, October 29, 2017, https://www.npr.org/2017/10/29/560097406/after-choosing-donald-trump-is-the-evangelical-church-in-crisis.

28. Ian Schwartz, " Tucker Carlson: Modern Liberalism Is a Religious Movement," RealClearHoldings LLC, May 10, 2018, https://www.realclearpolitics.com/video/2018/05/10/tucker_carlson_modern_liberalism_is_a_religious_movement.html?spotim_referrer=social_rail.

29. Schwartz, "Tucker Carlson: Modern Liberalism Is a Religious Movement."

30. Schwartz, "Tucker Carlson: Modern Liberalism Is a Religious Movement."

31. Schwartz, "Tucker Carlson: Modern Liberalism Is a Religious Movement."

Capítulo 12 — La batalla por Jerusalén

1. "Statement by President Trump on Jerusalem," White House, 6 de diciembre, 2017, https://www.whitehouse.gov/briefings-statements/statement-president-trump-jerusalem/.

2. "Statement by President Trump on Jerusalem," White House.

3. Michael D. Evans, "Dr. Mike Evans: Trump and Netanyahu Have a Lot to Discuss," Charisma News, 10 de febrero, 2017, https://www.charismanews.com/politics/opinion/62923-dr-mike-evans-trump-and-netanyahu-have-a-lot-to-discuss.

4. Evans, "Dr. Mike Evans: Trump and Netanyahu Have a Lot to Discuss."

5. "About Our Founder," ACT for America, accessed August 3, 2018, http://www.actforamerica.org/aboutbrigitte.

6. Evans, "Dr. Mike Evans: Trump and Netanyahu Have a Lot to Discuss."

7. Evans, "Dr. Mike Evans: Trump and Netanyahu Have a Lot to Discuss."

8. i24NEWS, "Christian Zionism and the Jerusalem Embassy Move," YouTube, 25 de mayo, 2018, https://www.youtube.com/watch?v=IT_REC7ntCA.

9. Joel B. Pollak, "Exclusive: Hagee Says Trump, Like Truman, Earned 'Political Immortality' by Moving Embassy to Jerusalem," Breitbart, 11 de mayo, 2018, https://www.breitbart.com/big-government/2018/05/11/john-hagee-trump-jerusalem-mbassy/.

10. "Remarks by President Trump and Prime Minister Netanyahu of Israel Before Bilateral

Meeting," White House, 5 de marzo, 2018, https://www.whitehouse.gov/briefings-statements/remarks-president-trump-prime-minister-netanyahu-israel- bilateral-meeting-2/.

11.   Dov Lieber, "How Much Aid Does the US Give Palestinians, and What's It For?," Times of Israel, January 3, 2018, https://www.timesofisrael.com/how-much-aid-does-the-us-give-palestinians-and-whats-it-for/.

Capítulo 13 – El sacudir de la iglesia

1.   Steve Strang, "What Is God Saying One Year After the Inauguration?," CharismaNews.com, January 19, 2018, https://www.charismanews.com/politics/elections/69204-what-is-god-saying-one-year-after-the-inauguration.

2.   BarackObamadotcom, "10 Questions: Religion in America," YouTube, December 17, 2007, https://www.youtube.com/watch?v=35sGJrWKcmY&feature=related.

3.   Time staff, "Read the Sermon Donald Trump Heard Before Becoming President," Time, January 20, 2017, http://time.com/4641208/donald-trump-robert-jeffress-st-john-episcopal-inauguration/.

4.   Time staff, *"Read the Sermon Donald Trump Heard Before Becoming President."*

5.   Time staff, *"Read the Sermon Donald Trump Heard Before Becoming President."*

6.   Time staff, *"Read the Sermon Donald Trump Heard Before Becoming President."*

7.   *"The National Prayer Service for the Fifty-Eighth Presidential Inaugural,"* Washington National Cathedral, 21 de enero, 2017, https://cathedral.org/wp-content/uploads/2017/01/Inaugural-Prayer-Service-2017.pdf.

8.   "Rev. Graham: Trump 'Defending Christian Faith' More Than Any Recent President," FOX News Network LLC, January 21, 2018, http://insider.foxnews. com/2018/01/21/franklin-graham-donald-trump-defending-christianity-more-any-recent-president.

9.   *"Rev. Graham: Trump 'Defending Christian Faith' More Than Any Recent President,"* FOX News Network LLC.

10.   Tim Chapman, *"Trump Should Move Forward on Religious Liberty Order,"* The Hill, February 16, 2017, http://thehill.com/blogs/pundits-blog/religion/319867- trump -should-move-forward-on-religious-liberty-order.

11. 515   Carol Kuruvilla, *"Why These Evangelical Leaders Are Firmly Against Trump,"* Huffington Post, 22 de julio, 2016, https://www.huffingtonpost.com/entry/why-these-evangelical-leaders-are-firmly-against-trump_us_578d0d14e4b0fa896c3f6fc2.

12.   Kuruvilla,"Why These Evangelical Leaders Are Firmly Against Trump."

13.   Brandon Showalter, *"Russell Moore: Religious Right Has Become the People They Warned Against,"* Christian Post, 25 de octubre, 2016, https://www.christianpost.com/news/russell-moore-religious-right-become-people-they-warned-against- first-things-erasmus-171094/.

14.   Peter Wehner, *"The Theology of Donald Trump,"* New York Times, 5 de julio, 2016, https://www.nytimes.com/2016/07/05/opinion/campaign-stops/the-theology-of-donald-trump.html?mtrref=www.google.com&gwh=CE54134672E08077A3 8160293FDD2181&gwt=pay&assetType=opinion.

15.   Wehner, *"The Theology of Donald Trump."*

16.   Max Lucado, *"Trump Doesn't Pass the Decency Test,"* Washington Post, 26 de febrero, 2016, https://www.washingtonpost.com/posteverything/wp/2016/02/26/

max-lucado-trump-doesnt-pass-the-decency-test/?; Max Lucado, "Decency for President," February 24, 2016, https://maxlucado.com/decency-for-president/.

17. *"Anne Graham Lotz: Her Book, America, and Remembering Billy Graham: Part 2,"* CBN.com, consultado el 3 de agosto, 2018, http://www1.cbn.com/anne-graham-lotz-her-book-america-and-remembering-billy-graham-part-2.

18. *"Anne Graham Lotz: Her Book, America, and Remembering Billy Graham: Part 2,"* CBN.com.

19. *"Anne Graham Lotz: Her Book, America, and Remembering Billy Graham: Part 2,"* CBN.com.

20. *"Honoring the Life of Billy Graham,"* Billy Graham Evangelistic Association, March 2, 2018, https://memorial.billygraham.org/funeral-service-transcript/.

21. *"Honoring the Life of Billy Graham,"* Billy Graham Evangelistic Association.

22. *"Anne Graham Lotz: Her Book, America, and Remembering Billy Graham: Part 2,"* CBN.com.

23. Heather Sells, *"Faith Leaders Pray for Trump in Oval Office, Enjoy 'Open Door' at White House,"* CBN News, 12 de julio, 2017, http://www1.cbn.com/cbnnews/us/2017/july/faith-leaders-enjoy-open-door-at-white-house.

24. Sells, *"Faith Leaders Pray for Trump in Oval Office, Enjoy 'Open Door' at White House."*

25. Sells, *"Faith Leaders Pray for Trump in Oval Office, Enjoy 'Open Door' at White House."*

26. *"Authors Discuss President Trump,"* CSPAN, 17 de diciembre, 2017, archived at https://archive.org/details/CSPAN2_20171217_231500_Authors_Discuss_President_Trump.

27. Lauren Markoe, *"Trump Must Aid Persecuted Christians or His Presidency Will Fail, Says Open Doors,"* Religion News Service, 11 de enero, 2017, https://religionnews.com/2017/01/11/trump-must-aid-persecuted-christians-or-his-presidency-will-fail-says-open-doors/.

28. Markoe, *"Trump Must Aid Persecuted Christians or His Presidency Will Fail, Says Open Doors."*

29. Kate Shellnutt, *"Sam Brownback Finally Confirmed as America's Religious Freedom Ambassador,"* Christianity Today, 24 de enero, 2018, https://www.christianitytoday.com/news/2018/january/sam-brownback-is-ambassador-international-religious-freedom.html.

30. *"President Donald J. Trump Proclaims January 16, 2018, as Religious Freedom Day,"* White House, 16 de enero, 2018, https://www.whitehouse.gov/presidential-actions/president-donald-j-trump-proclaims-january-16-2018-religious-freedom-day/.

31. *"Release of the 2017 Annual Report on International Religious Freedom,"* US Department of State, 29 de mayo, 2018, https://www.state.gov/secretary/remarks/2018/05/282789.htm.

32. *"Release of the 2017 Annual Report on International Religious Freedom,"* US Department of State.

33. Katayoun Kishi, *"Key Findings on the Global Rise in Religious Restrictions,"*

Pew Research Center, 21 de junio, 2018, http://www.pewresearch.org/fact-tank/2018/06/21/key-findings-on-the-global-rise-in-religious-restrictions/.

34. *"Global Uptick in Government Restrictions on Religion in 2016,"* Pew Research Center, 21 de junio, 2018, http://www.pewforum.org/2018/06/21/global-uptick-in-government-restrictions-on-religion-in-2016/.

35. *"Release of the 2017 Annual Report on International Religious Freedom,"* US Department of State.

36. *"Remarks by Vice President Pence at the Southern Baptist Convention Annual Meeting,"* White House, 13 de junio, 2018, https://www.whitehouse.gov/briefings-statements/remarks-vice-president-pence-southern-baptist-convention-annual-meeting/.

Conclusión — Un cambio radical sísmico

1. Michael Kranish, *"'I Must Be Doing Something Right': Billionaire George Soros Faces Renewed Attacks With Defiance,"* Washington Post, 9 de junio, 2018, https://www.washingtonpost.com/politics/i-must-be-doing-something-right-billionaire-george-soros-faces-renewed-attacks-with-defiance/2018/06/09/3ba0e2b0-6825-11e8-9e38-24e693b38637_story.html?noredirect=on&utm_term=.424d6fcb2b0a.

2. Craig Bannister, *"Trump: 'God's Love Redeems the World,'"* CNSNews.com, 2 de abril, 2018, https://www.cnsnews.com/blog/craig-bannister/trump-gods-love-redeems-world.

Apéndice — 500 días de grandeza estadounidense del presidente Donald J. Trump

1. *"President Donald J. Trump's 500 Days of American Greatness,"* White House, 4 de junio, 2018, https://www.whitehouse.gov/briefings-statements/president-donald-j-trumps-500-days-american-greatness/.